P

"His huge, _____ ne the genre." —George R. R. Martin, internationally bestselling author of _A Game of Thrones_

"Anyone who's writing epic secondary-world fantasy knows Robert Jordan isn't just a part of the landscape, he's a monolith within the landscape." —Patrick Rothfuss, internationally bestselling author of The Kingkiller Chronicle

"_The Eye of the World_ was a turning point in my life. I read, I enjoyed. (Then continued on to write my larger fantasy novels.)" —Robin Hobb, _New York Times_ bestselling author of The Farseer Trilogy

"Robert Jordan's work has been a formative influence and an inspiration for a generation of fantasy writers." —Brent Weeks, _New York Times_ bestselling author of _The Way of Shadows_

"Jordan has come to dominate the world Tolkien began to reveal." —_The New York Times_

"One of fantasy's most acclaimed series." —_USA Today_

"Robert Jordan was a giant of fiction whose words helped a whole generation of fantasy writers, including myself, find our true voices. I thanked him then, but I didn't thank him enough." —Peter V. Brett, internationally bestselling author of The Demon Cycle

"[Robert Jordan's] impact on the place of fantasy in the culture is colossal. . . . He brought innumerable readers to fantasy. He became the *New York Times* Best Seller List's face of fantasy." —Guy Gavriel Kay, internationally bestselling author of *Tigana*

"Jordan's writing is so amazing! The characterization, the attention to detail!" —Clint McElroy, cocreator of the #1 podcast *The Adventure Zone*

"The Wheel of Time [is] rapidly becoming the definitive American fantasy saga. It is a fantasy tale seldom equaled and still less often surpassed in English."
—*Chicago Sun-Times*

"Hard to put down for even a moment. A fittingly epic conclusion to a fantasy series that many consider one of the best of all time." —*San Francisco Book Review* on *A Memory of Light*

The Wheel of Time®

By Robert Jordan

New Spring: The Novel
The Eye of the World
The Great Hunt
The Dragon Reborn
The Shadow Rising
The Fires of Heaven
Lord of Chaos
A Crown of Swords
The Path of Daggers
Winter's Heart
Crossroads of Twilight
Knife of Dreams

By Robert Jordan and Brandon Sanderson

The Gathering Storm
Towers of Midnight
A Memory of Light

By Robert Jordan and Teresa Patterson

The World of Robert Jordan's The Wheel of Time

By Robert Jordan, Harriet McDougal, Alan Romanczuk, and Maria Simons

The Wheel of Time Companion

THE
DRAGON
REBORN

ROBERT JORDAN

A TOM DOHERTY ASSOCIATES BOOK
NEW YORK

Dedicated to
James Oliver Rigney, Sr.
(1920–1988)

He taught me always to follow the dream,
and when I caught it, to live it.

This is a work of fiction. All of the characters, organizations, and events portrayed in this novel are either products of the author's imagination or are used fictitiously.

THE DRAGON REBORN

Maps by Ellisa Mitchell
Interior illustrations by Matthew C. Nielsen and Ellisa Mitchell

A Tor Book
Published by Tom Doherty Associates
120 Broadway
New York, NY 10271

www.tor-forge.com

Tor® is a registered trademark of Macmillan Publishing Group, LLC.

ISBN 978-1-250-25149-7

Our books may be purchased in bulk for promotional, educational, or business use. Please contact your local bookseller or the Macmillan Corporate and Premium Sales Department at 1-800-221-7945, extension 5442, or by email at MacmillanSpecialMarkets@macmillan.com.

First Edition: November 1991
First Premium Mass Market Edition: November 2019

Printed in the United States of America

0 9 8 7 6

Contents

And his paths shall be many, and who shall know his name, for he shall be born among us many times, in many guises, as he has been and ever will be, time without end. His coming shall be like the sharp edge of the plow, turning our lives in furrows from out of the places where we lie in our silence. The breaker of bonds; the forger of chains. The maker of futures; the unshaper of destiny.

—from *Commentaries
on the Prophecies of the Dragon,*
by Jurith Dorine, Right Hand to the
Queen of Almoren, 742 AB, the Third Age

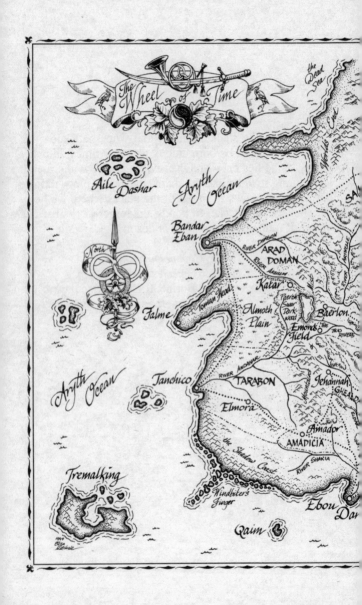

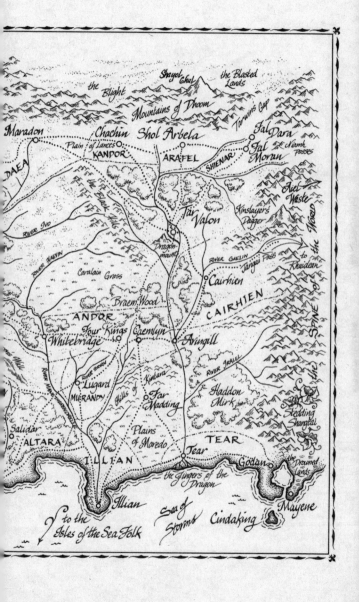

PROLOGUE

Fortress of the Light

Pedron Niall's aged gaze wandered about his private audience chamber, but dark eyes hazed with thought saw nothing. Tattered wall hangings, once battle banners of the enemies of his youth, faded into dark wood paneling laid over stone walls, thick even here in the heart of the Fortress of the Light. The single chair in the room—heavy, high-backed, and almost a throne—was as invisible to him as the few scattered tables that completed the furnishings. Even the white-cloaked man kneeling with barely restrained eagerness on the great sunburst set in the wide planks of the floor had vanished from Niall's mind for the moment, though few would have dismissed him so lightly.

Jaret Byar had been given time to wash before being brought to Niall, but both his helmet and his breastplate were dulled from travel and battered from use. Dark, deep-set eyes shone with a feverish, urgent light in a face that seemed to have had every spare scrap of flesh boiled away. He wore no sword—none was allowed in Niall's presence—but he seemed poised on the edge of violence, like a hound awaiting the loosing of the leash.

Twin fires on long hearths at either end of the room held off the late winter cold. It was a plain, soldier's room, really, everything well made but nothing extravagant—except for the sunburst. Furnishings came to the audience chamber of the Lord Captain Commander of the Children of the Light with the man who rose to the office; the flaring sun of coin gold had been worn smooth by generations of petitioners, replaced and worn smooth again. Gold enough to buy any estate in Amadicia, and the patent of nobility to go with it.

For ten years Niall had walked across that gold and never thought of it twice, any more than he thought of the sun-burst embroidered across the chest of his white tunic. Gold held little interest for Pedron Niall.

Eventually his eyes went back to the table next to him, covered with maps and scattered letters and reports. Three loosely rolled drawings lay among the jumble. He took one up reluctantly. It did not matter which; all depicted the same scene, though by different hands.

Niall's skin was as thin as scraped parchment, drawn tight by age over a body that seemed all bone and sinew, but there was nothing of frailty about him. No man held Niall's office before his hair was white, nor did any man softer than the stones of the Dome of Truth. Still, he was suddenly aware of the tendon-ridged back of the hand holding the drawing, aware of the need for haste. Time was growing short. *His* time was growing short. It had to be enough. He had to make it enough.

He made himself unroll the thick parchment halfway, just enough to see the face that interested him. The chalks were a little smudged from travel in saddlebags, but the face was clear. A gray-eyed youth with reddish hair. He looked tall, but it was hard to say for certain. Aside from the hair and the eyes, he could have been set down in any town without exciting comment.

"This . . . this *boy* has proclaimed himself the Dragon Reborn?" Niall muttered.

The Dragon. The name made him feel the chills of winter and age. The name borne by Lews Therin Telamon when he doomed every man who could channel the One Power, then or ever after, to insanity and death, himself among them. It was more than three thousand years since Aes Sedai pride and the War of the Shadow had brought an end to the Age of Legends. Three thousand years, but prophecy and legend helped men remember—the heart of it, at least, if the details were gone. Lews Therin Kinslayer. The man who had begun the Breaking of the World, when madmen who could tap the power that drove the universe leveled mountains and sank ancient lands beneath the seas, when the whole face of the earth had been changed and all who survived fled like beasts before a wildfire. It had not ended until the last male Aes Sedai lay dead, and a scattered human race could begin trying to rebuild from the rubble—where even rubble remained. It was burned into memory by the stories mothers told children. And prophecy said the Dragon would be born again.

Niall had not really meant it for a question, but Byar took it for one. "Yes, my Lord Captain Commander, he has. It is a worse madness than any false Dragon I've ever heard of. Thousands have declared for him already. Tarabon and Arad Doman are in civil war, as well as at war with each other. There is fighting all across Almoth Plain and Toman Head, Taraboner against Domani against Darkfriends crying for the Dragon—or there was fighting until winter chilled most of it. I've never seen it spread so quickly, my Lord Captain Commander. Like throwing a lantern into a hay barn. The snow may have damped it down, but come spring, the flames will burst out hotter than before."

Niall cut him off with a raised finger. Twice already Niall had let him tell his story through, his voice burning with anger and hate. Parts of it Niall knew from other sources, and in some areas he knew more than Byar, but each time he heard it, it goaded him anew. "Geofram Bornhald and a thousand of the Children dead. And Aes Sedai did it. You have no doubts, Child Byar?"

"None, my Lord Captain Commander. After a skirmish on the way to Falme, I saw two of the Tar Valon witches. They cost us more than fifty dead before we stuck them full of arrows."

"You are *sure*—sure they were Aes Sedai?"

"The ground erupted under our feet." Byar's voice was firm and full of belief. He had little imagination, did Jaret Byar; death was part of a soldier's life, however it came. "Lightnings struck our ranks out of a clear sky. My Lord Captain Commander, what else could they have been?"

Niall nodded grimly. There had been no male Aes Sedai since the Breaking of the World, but the women who still claimed that title were bad enough. They prated of their Three Oaths: to speak no word that was not true, to make no weapon for one man to kill another, to use the One Power as a weapon only against Darkfriends or Shadowspawn. But now they had showed those oaths for the lies

they were. He had always known no one could want the
power they wielded except to challenge the Creator, and
that meant to serve the Dark One.

"And you know nothing of those who took Falme and
killed half of one of my legions?"

"Lord Captain Bornhald said they called themselves
Seanchan, my Lord Captain Commander," Byar said stolidly. "He said they were Darkfriends. And his charge broke
them, even if they killed him." His voice gained intensity.
"There were many refugees from the city. Everyone I spoke
to agreed the strangers had broken and fled. Lord Captain
Bornhald did that."

Niall sighed softly. They were almost the same words
Byar had used the first two times about the army that had
seemingly come out of nowhere to take Falme. *A good soldier*, Niall thought, *so Geofram Bornhald always said, but
not a man to think for himself.*

"My Lord Captain Commander," Byar said suddenly,
"Lord Captain Bornhald *did* command me to stand aside
from the battle. I was to watch, and report to you. And tell
his son, Lord Dain, how he died."

"Yes, yes," Niall said impatiently. For a moment he
studied Byar's hollow-cheeked face, then added, "No one
doubts your honesty or courage. It is exactly the sort of
thing Geofram Bornhald would do, facing a battle in which
he feared his entire command might die." *And not the sort
of thing you have imagination enough to think up.*

There was nothing more to learn from the man. "You
have done well, Child Byar. You have my leave to carry
word of Geofram Bornhald's death to his son. Dain Bornhald is with Eamon Valda—near Tar Valon at last report.
You may join them."

"Thank you, my Lord Captain Commander. Thank you."
Byar rose to his feet and bowed deeply. Yet as he straightened, he hesitated. "My Lord Captain Commander, we
were betrayed." Hatred gave his voice a saw-toothed edge.

"By this one Darkfriend you spoke of, Child Byar?"
He could not keep an edge out of his own voice. A year's
planning lay in ruins amid the corpses of a thousand of the
Children, and Byar wanted to talk only of this one man.
"This young blacksmith you've only seen twice, this Perrin
from the Two Rivers?"

"Yes, my Lord Captain Commander. I do not know how, but I know he is to blame. I know it."

"I will see what can be done about him, Child Byar." Byar opened his mouth again, but Niall raised a thin hand to forestall him. "You may leave me now." The gaunt-faced man had no choice but to bow again and leave.

As the door closed behind him, Niall lowered himself into his high-backed chair. What had brought on Byar's hatred of this Perrin? There were far too many Darkfriends to waste energy on hating any particular one. Too many Darkfriends, high and low, hiding behind glib tongues and open smiles, serving the Dark One. Still, one more name added to the lists would do no harm.

He shifted on the hard chair, trying to find comfort for his old bones. Not for the first time he thought vaguely that perhaps a cushion would not be too much luxury. And not for the first time, he pushed the thought away. The world tumbled toward chaos, and he had no time to give in to age.

He let all the signs that foretold disaster swirl through his mind. War gripped Tarabon and Arad Doman, civil war ripped at Cairhien, and war fever was rising in Tear and Illian, old enemies as they were. Perhaps these wars meant nothing in themselves—men fought wars—but they usually came one at a time. And aside from the false Dragon somewhere on Almoth Plain, another tore at Saldaea, and a third plagued Tear. Three at once. *They must all be false Dragons. They* must *be!*

A dozen small things besides, some perhaps only baseless rumors, but taken together with the rest. . . . Sightings of Aiel reported as far west as Murandy, and Kandor. Only two or three in one place, but one or a thousand, Aiel had come out of the Waste just once in all the years since the Breaking. Only in the Aiel War had they ever left that desolate wilderness. The Atha'an Miere, the Sea Folk, were said to be ignoring trade to seek signs and portents—of what, exactly, they did not say—sailing with ships half full or even empty. Illian had called the Great Hunt of the Horn for the first time in almost four hundred years, had sent out the Hunters to seek the fabled Horn of Valere, which prophecy said would summon dead heroes from the grave to fight in Tarmon Gai'don, the Last Battle against the Shadow. Rumor said the Ogier, always so reclusive that most common people thought them only legend, had called meetings between their far-flung *stedding*.

Most telling of all, to Niall, the Aes Sedai had apparently come into the open. It was said they had sent some of their sisters to Saldaea to confront the false Dragon Mazrim Taim. Rare as it was in men, Taim could channel the One Power. That was a thing to fear and despise in itself, and few thought a man like that could be defeated except with the aid of Aes Sedai. Better to allow Aes Sedai help than to face the inevitable horrors when he went mad, as such men inevitably did. But Tar Valon had apparently sent other Aes Sedai to support the other false Dragon at Falme. Nothing else fit the facts.

The pattern chilled the marrow in his bones. Chaos multiplied; what was unheard of, happening again and again. The whole world seemed to be milling, stirring near the boil. It was clear to him. The Last Battle really was coming.

All his plans were destroyed, the plans that would have secured his name among the Children of the Light for a hundred generations. But turmoil meant opportunity, and he had new plans, with new objectives. If he could keep the strength and will to carry them out. *Light, let me hold on to life long enough.*

A deferential tap on the door brought him out of his dark thoughts. "Come!" he snapped.

A servant in coat and breeches of white-and-gold bowed his way in. Eyes to the floor, he announced that Jaichim Carridin, Anointed of the Light, Inquisitor of the Hand of the Light, came at the command of the Lord Captain Commander. Carridin appeared on the man's heels, not waiting for Niall to speak. Niall gestured the servant to leave.

Before the door was fully closed again, Carridin dropped to one knee with a flourish of his snowy cloak. Behind the sunburst on the cloak's breast lay the scarlet shepherd's crook of the Hand of the Light, called the Questioners by many, though seldom to their faces. "As you have commanded my presence, my Lord Captain Commander," he said in a strong voice, "so have I returned from Tarabon."

Niall examined him for a moment. Carridin was tall, well into his middle years, with a touch of gray in his hair, yet fit and hard. His dark, deep-set eyes had a knowing look about them, as always. And he did not blink under the silent study of the Lord Captain Commander. Few men had consciences so clear or nerves so steady. Carridin knelt there, waiting as calmly as if it were an everyday matter to be ordered curtly to leave his command and return to Amador without delay, no reasons given. But then, it was said Jaichim Carridin could outwait a stone.

"Rise, Child Carridin." As the other man straightened, Niall added, "I have had disturbing news from Falme."

Carridin straightened the folds of his cloak as he answered. His voice rode the edge of suitable respect, almost as if he spoke to an equal rather than to the man he had sworn to obey to the death. "My Lord Captain Commander refers to the news brought by Child Jaret Byar, late second to Lord Captain Bornhald."

The corner of Niall's left eye fluttered, an old presage of anger. Supposedly only three men knew Byar was in Amador, and none besides Niall knew from where he came. "Do not be too clever, Carridin. Your desire to know everything may one day lead you into the hands of your own Questioners."

Carridin showed no reaction beyond a slight tightening of his mouth at the name. "My Lord Captain Commander, the Hand seeks out truth everywhere, to serve the Light."

To serve the Light. Not to serve the Children of the Light. All the Children served the Light, but Pedron Niall often wondered if the Questioners really considered themselves part of the Children at all. "And what truth do you have for me about what occurred in Falme?"

"Darkfriends, my Lord Captain Commander."

"Darkfriends?" Niall's chuckle held no amusement. "A few weeks gone I was receiving reports from you that Geofram Bornhald was a servant of the Dark One because he moved soldiers onto Toman Head against your orders." His voice became dangerously soft. "Do you now mean me to believe that Bornhald, as a Darkfriend, led a thousand of the Children to their deaths fighting other Darkfriends?"

"Whether or not he was a Darkfriend will never be known," Carridin said blandly, "since he died before he could be put to the question. The Shadow's plots are murky, and often seem mad to those who walk in the Light. But that those who seized Falme were Darkfriends, I have no doubt. Darkfriends and Aes Sedai, in support of a false Dragon. It was the One Power that destroyed Bornhald and his men, of that I am sure, my Lord Captain Commander, just as it destroyed the armies that Tarabon and Arad Doman sent against the Darkfriends in Falme."

"And what of the stories that those who took Falme came from across the Aryth Ocean?"

Carridin shook his head. "My Lord Captain Commander, the people are full of rumors. Some claim they were the armies Artur Hawkwing sent across the ocean a thousand years ago, come back to claim the land. Why, some even claim to have seen Hawkwing himself in Falme. And half the heroes of legend besides. The west is boiling from Tarabon to Saldaea, and a hundred new rumors bubble to the surface every day, each more outrageous than the last. These so-called Seanchan were no more than another rabble of Darkfriends gathered to support a false Dragon, only this time with open Aes Sedai support."

"What proof have you?" Niall made his voice sound as if he doubted the point. "You have prisoners?"

"No, my Lord Captain Commander. As Child Byar no doubt told you, Bornhald managed to hurt them badly enough that they dispersed. And certainly no one we've questioned would admit to supporting a false Dragon. As for proof . . . it lies in two parts. If my Lord Captain Commander will permit me?"

Niall gestured impatiently.

"The first part is negative. Few ships have tried to cross the Aryth Ocean, and most never returned. Those that did, turned back before they ran out of food and water. Even the Sea Folk will not cross the Aryth, and they sail wherever there is trade, even to the lands beyond the Aiel Waste. My Lord Captain Commander, if there *are* any lands across the ocean, they are too far to reach, the ocean too wide. To carry an army across it would be as impossible as flying."

"Perhaps," Niall said slowly. "It is certainly indicative. What is your second part?"

"My Lord Captain Commander, many of those we questioned spoke of monsters fighting for the Darkfriends, and held to their claims even under the last degree of the question. What could they be but Trollocs and other Shadowspawn, in some way brought down from the Blight?" Carridin spread his hands as if that were conclusive. "Most people think Trollocs are only travelers' tales and lies, and most of the rest think they were all killed in the Trolloc Wars. What other name would they put to a Trolloc but monster?"

"Yes. Yes, you may be right, Child Carridin. May be, I say." He would not give Carridin the satisfaction of knowing he agreed. *Let him work awhile.* "But what of him?" He indicated the rolled drawings. If he knew Carridin, the Inquisitor had copies in his own chambers. "How dangerous is he? Can he channel the One Power?"

The Inquisitor merely shrugged. "Perhaps he can channel, perhaps not. Aes Sedai could no doubt make people believe a cat could channel, if they wanted to. As to how dangerous he is. . . . Any false Dragon is dangerous until he is put down, and one with Tar Valon openly behind him is ten times dangerous. But he is less dangerous now than he will be in half a year, unchecked. The captives I questioned had never seen him, had no idea where he is now. His forces are fragmented. I doubt there are more than two hundred gathered in any one place. The Taraboners or the Domani, either one, could sweep them away if they weren't so busy fighting each other."

"Even a false Dragon," Niall said dryly, "is not enough to make them forget four hundred years of squabbling over possession of Almoth Plain. As if either of them ever had the strength to hold it." Carridin's face did not change, and Niall wondered how he could keep so calm. *You will not be calm much longer, Questioner.*

"It is of no import, my Lord Captain Commander. Winter keeps them all in their camps, except for scattered skirmishes and raids. When the weather warms enough for troops to move. . . . Bornhald took only half his legion to their deaths on Toman Head. With the other half, I will hunt this false Dragon to his death. A corpse is not dangerous to anyone."

"And if you face what it seems Bornhald faced? Aes Sedai channeling the Power to kill?"

"Their witchery doesn't protect them from arrows, or a knife in the dark. They die as quickly as anyone else." Carridin smiled. "I promise you, I will be successful before summer."

Niall nodded. The man was confident, now. Sure the dangerous questions would already have come, if they were coming. *You should have remembered, Carridin, I was accounted a fine tactician.* "Why," he said quietly, "did you not take your own forces to Falme? With Darkfriends on Toman Head, an army of them holding Falme, why did you try to stop Bornhald?"

Carridin blinked, but his voice remained steady. "At first they were only rumors, my Lord Captain Commander. Rumors so wild, no one could believe. By the time I learned the truth, Bornhald had joined battle. He was dead, and the Darkfriends scattered. Besides, my task was to bring the Light to Almoth Plain. I could not disobey my orders to chase after rumors."

"Your task?" Niall said, his voice rising as he stood. Carridin topped him by a head, but the Inquisitor stepped back. "Your task? Your task was to seize Almoth Plain! An empty bucket that no one holds except by words and claims, and all you had to do was fill it. The nation of Almoth would have lived again, ruled by the Children of the Light, with no need to pay lip service to a fool of a king. Amadicia and Almoth, a vise gripping Tarabon. In five years we would have held sway there as much as here in Amadicia. And you made a dog's dinner of it!"

The smile went at last. "My Lord Captain Commander," Carridin protested. "How could I foresee what happened? Yet another false Dragon. Tarabon and Arad Doman finally going to war after so long merely growling at each other. And Aes Sedai revealing their true selves after three thousand years of dissembling! Even with that, though, all is not lost. I can find and destroy this false Dragon before his followers unite. And once the Taraboners and Domani have weakened themselves, they can be cleared from the plain without—"

"No!" Niall snapped. "Your plans are done with, Carridin. Perhaps I should hand you over to your own Questioners right now. The High Inquisitor would not object. He is gnashing his teeth to find someone to blame for what happened. He would never put forward one of his own, but I doubt he'd quibble if I named you. A few days under the question, and you would confess to anything. Name yourself Darkfriend, even. You would go under the headsman's axe inside a week."

There was sweat beading on Carridin's forehead. "My

Lord Captain Commander. . . ." He stopped to swallow. "My Lord Captain Commander seems to be saying there is another way. If he will but speak it, I am sworn to obey."

Now, Niall thought. *Now to toss the dice.* Prickles ran across his skin, as if he were in battle and had suddenly realized that every man for a hundred paces around him was an enemy. Lord Captain Commanders did not go to the headsman, but more than one had been known to die suddenly and unexpectedly, swiftly mourned and swiftly replaced by men with less dangerous ideas.

"Child Carridin," he said firmly, "you will make certain that this false Dragon does not die. And if any Aes Sedai come to oppose rather than support him, you will make use of your 'knives in the dark.'"

The Inquisitor's jaw dropped. Yet he recovered quickly, eyeing Niall in a speculative fashion. "To kill Aes Sedai is a duty, but. . . . To allow a false Dragon to roam free? That . . . that would be . . . treason. And blasphemy."

Niall drew a deep breath. He could sense the unseen knives waiting in the shadows. But he was committed, now. "It is no treason to do what must be done. And even blasphemy can be tolerated for a cause." Those two sentences alone were enough to kill him. "Do you know how to unite people behind you, Child Carridin? The quickest way? No? Loose a lion—a rabid lion—in the streets. And when panic grips the people, once it has turned their bowels to water, calmly tell them you will deal with it. Then you kill it, and order them to hang the carcass up where everyone can see. Before they have time to think, you give another order, and it will be obeyed. And if you continue to give orders, they will continue to obey, for you will be the one who saved them, and who better to lead?"

Carridin moved his head uncertainly. "Do you mean to . . . take it all, my Lord Captain Commander? Not just Almoth Plain, but Tarabon and Arad Doman as well?"

"What I mean is for me to know. It is for you to obey as you are sworn to do. I expect to hear of messengers on fast horses leaving for the plain by tonight. I am certain you know how to word the orders so no one suspects what they should not. If you must harry someone, let it be the Taraboners and Domani. It would not do to have them kill my lion. No, under the Light, we shall force peace between them."

"As my Lord Captain Commander commands," Carridin
said smoothly. "I hear and obey." Too smoothly.

Niall smiled a cold smile. "In case your oath is not strong
enough, know this. If this false Dragon dies before I command his death, or if he is taken by the Tar Valon witches,
you will be found one morning with a dagger in your heart.
And should any . . . accident . . . befall me—even if I
should die of old age—you will not survive me the month."

"My Lord Captain Commander, I have sworn to obey—"

"So you have." Niall cut him off. "See that you remember
it. Now, go!"

"As my Lord Captain Commander commands." This
time Carridin's voice was not so steady.

The door closed behind the Inquisitor. Niall rubbed his
hands together. He felt cold. The dice were spinning, with
no way of telling what pips would show when they stopped.
The Last Battle truly was coming. Not the Tarmon Gai'don
of legend, with the Dark One breaking free to be faced by
the Dragon Reborn. Not that, he was sure. The Aes Sedai
of the Age of Legends might have made a hole in the Dark
One's prison at Shayol Ghul, but Lews Therin Kinslayer
and his Hundred Companions had sealed it up again. The
counterstroke had tainted the male half of the True Source
forever and driven them mad, and so begun the Breaking,
but one of those ancient Aes Sedai could do what ten of the
Tar Valon witches of today could not. The seals they had
made would hold.

Pedron Niall was a man of cold logic, and he had reasoned out how Tarmon Gai'don would be. Bestial Trolloc
hordes rolling south out of the Great Blight as they had
in the Trolloc Wars, two thousand years before, with the
Myrddraal—the Halfmen—leading, and perhaps even new
human Dreadlords from among the Darkfriends. Humankind, split into nations squabbling among themselves, could
not stand against that. But he, Pedron Niall, would unite humankind behind the banners of the Children of the Light.
There would be new legends, to tell how Pedron Niall had
fought Tarmon Gai'don, and won.

"First," he murmured, "loose a rabid lion in the streets."

"A rabid lion?"

Niall spun on his heel as a bony little man with a huge
beak of a nose slipped from behind one of the hanging ban-

ners. There was just a glimpse of a panel swinging shut as the banner fell back against the wall.

"I showed you that passage, Ordeith," Niall snapped, "so you could come when I summoned you without half the fortress knowing, not so you could listen to my private conversation."

Ordeith made a smooth bow as he crossed the room. "Listen, Great Lord? I would never do such a thing. I only just arrived and could not avoid hearing your final words. No more than that." He wore a half-mocking smile, but it never left his face that Niall had ever seen, even when the fellow had no reason to know anyone was watching.

A month before, in the dead of winter, the gangly little man had arrived in Amadicia, ragged and half-frozen, and somehow managed to talk his way through all the layers of guards to Pedron Niall himself. He seemed to know things about events on Toman Head that were not in Carridin's voluminous if obscure reports, or in Byar's tale, or in any other report or rumor that had come to Niall. His name was a lie, of course. In the Old Tongue, Ordeith meant "wormwood." When Niall challenged him on it, though, all he said was, "Who we were is lost to all men, and life is bitter." But he was clever. It had been he who helped Niall see the pattern emerging in events.

Ordeith moved to the table and took up one of the drawings. As he unrolled it enough to reveal the young man's face, his smile deepened to nearly a grimace.

Niall was still irritated that the man had come unsummoned. "You find a false Dragon funny, Ordeith. Or does he frighten you?"

"A false Dragon?" Ordeith said softly. "Yes. Yes, of course, it must be. Who else could it be." And he barked a shrill laugh that grated on Niall's nerves. Sometimes Niall thought Ordeith was at least half-mad.

But he is clever, mad or not. "What do you mean, Ordeith? You sound as if you know him."

Ordeith gave a start, as though he had forgotten the Lord Captain Commander was there. "Know him? Oh, yes, I know him. His name is Rand al'Thor. He comes from the Two Rivers, in the backcountry of Andor, and he is a Darkfriend so deep in the Shadow it would make your soul cringe to know the half."

"The Two Rivers," Niall mused. "Someone else mentioned another Darkfriend from there, another youth. Strange to think of Darkfriends coming from a place like that. But truly they are everywhere."

"Another, Great Lord?" Ordeith said. "From the Two Rivers? Would that be Matrim Cauthon or Perrin Aybara? They are of an age with him, and close behind in evil."

"His name was given as Perrin," Niall said, frowning. "Three of them, you say? Nothing comes out of the Two Rivers but wool and tabac. I doubt if there is another place men live that is more isolated from the rest of the world."

"In a city, Darkfriends must hide their nature to one extent or another. They must associate with others, with strangers come from other places and leaving to take word of what they have seen. But in quiet villages, cut off from the world, where few outsiders ever go. . . . What better places for all to be Darkfriends?"

"How is it you know the names of three Darkfriends, Ordeith? Three Darkfriends from the far end of forever. You keep too many secrets, Wormwood, and pull more surprises from your sleeve than a gleeman."

"How can any man tell *all* that he knows, Great Lord," the little man said smoothly. "It would be only prattle, until it becomes useful. I will tell you this, Great Lord. This Rand al'Thor, this Dragon, has deep roots in the Two Rivers."

"False Dragon!" Niall said sharply, and the other man bowed.

"Of course, Great Lord. I misspoke myself."

Suddenly Niall became aware of the drawing crumpled and torn in Ordeith's hands. Even while the man's face remained smooth except for that sardonic smile, his hands twitched convulsively around the parchment.

"Stop that!" Niall commanded. He snatched the drawing away from Ordeith and smoothed it as best he could. "I do not have so many likenesses of this man that I can allow them to be destroyed." Much of the drawing was only a smudge, and a rip ran across the young man's breast, but miraculously the face was untouched.

"Forgive me, Great Lord." Ordeith made a deep bow, his smile never slipping. "I hate Darkfriends."

Niall studied the face in chalks. *Rand al'Thor, of the*

Two Rivers. "Perhaps I must make plans for the Two Rivers. When the snows clear. Perhaps."

"As the Great Lord wishes," Ordeith said blandly.

The grimace on Carridin's face as he strode through the halls of the Fortress made other men avoid him, though in truth few sought the company of Questioners. Servants, hurrying about their tasks, tried to fade into the stone walls, and even men with golden knots of rank on their white cloaks took side corridors when they saw his face.

He flung open the door to his rooms and slammed it behind him, feeling none of the usual satisfaction at the fine carpets from Tarabon and Tear in lush reds and golds and blues, the beveled mirrors from Illian, the gold-leaf work on the long, intricately carved table in the middle of the floor. A master craftsman from Lugard had worked nearly a year on that. This time he barely saw it.

"Sharbon!" For once his body servant did not appear. The man was supposed to be readying the rooms. "The Light burn you, Sharbon! Where are you?"

A movement caught the corner of his eye, and he turned ready to shrivel Sharbon with his curses. The curses themselves shriveled as a Myrddraal took another step toward him with the sinuous grace of a serpent.

It was a man in form, no larger than most, but there the resemblance ended. Dead black clothes and cloak, hardly seeming to stir as it moved, made its maggot-white skin appear ever paler. And it had no eyes. That eyeless gaze filled Carridin with fear, as it had filled thousands before.

"Wha. . . ." Carridin stopped to work moisture back into his mouth, to try bringing his voice back down to its normal register. "What are you doing here?" It still sounded shrill.

The Halfman's bloodless lips quirked in a smile. "Where there is shadow, there may I go." Its voice sounded like a snake rustling through dead leaves. "I like to keep a watch on all those who serve me."

"I ser. . . ."

It was no use. With an effort Carridin jerked his eyes away from that smooth expanse of pale, pasty face and turned his back. A shiver ran down his spine, having his back to a Myrddraal. Everything was sharp in the mirror

on the wall in front of him. Everything but the Halfman.
The Myrddraal was an indistinct blur. Hardly soothing to
look at, but better than meeting that stare. A little strength
returned to Carridin's voice.

"I serve the. . . ." He cut off, suddenly aware of where he
was. In the heart of the Fortress of the Light. The rumor
of a whisper of the words he was about to say would have
him given to the Hand of the Light. The lowest of the Children would strike him down on the spot if he heard. He was
alone except for the Myrddraal, and perhaps Sharbon—
Where is that cursed man? It would be good to have someone to share the Halfman's stare, even if the other would
have to be disposed of afterwards—but still he lowered his
voice. "I serve the Great Lord of the Dark, as you do. We
both serve."

"If you wish to see it so." The Myrddraal laughed, a
sound that made Carridin's bones shiver. "Still, I will know
why you are here instead of on Almoth Plain."

"I . . . I was commanded here by word of the Lord Captain Commander."

The Myrddraal grated, "Your Lord Captain Commander's words are dung! You were commanded to find the human called Rand al'Thor and kill him. That before all else.
Above all else! Why are you not obeying?"

Carridin took a deep breath. That gaze on his back felt
like a knife blade grating along his spine. "Things . . . have
changed. Some matters are not as much in my control as
they were." A harsh, scraping noise jerked his head around.

The Myrddraal was drawing a hand across the tabletop,
and thin tendrils of wood curled away from its fingernails.
"Nothing has changed, human. You forswore your oaths to
the Light and swore new oaths, and *those* oaths you will
obey."

Carridin started at the gouges marring the polished
wood and swallowed hard. "I don't understand. Why is it
suddenly so important to kill him? I thought the Great Lord
of the Dark meant to use him."

"You question me? I should take your tongue. It is not
your part to question. Or to understand. It is your part to
obey! You will give dogs lessons in obedience. Do you understand *that*? Heel, dog, and obey your master."

Anger wormed its way through the fear, and Carridin's

hand groped at his side, but his sword was not there. It lay in the next room now, where he had left it on going to attend Pedron Niall.

The Myrddraal moved faster than a striking viper. Carridin opened his mouth to scream as its hand closed on his wrist in a crushing grip; bones grated together, sending jolts of agony up his arm. The scream never left his mouth, though, for the Halfman's other hand gripped his chin and forced his jaws shut. His heels rose up, and then his toes left the floor. Grunting and gurgling, he dangled in the Myrddraal's grasp.

"Hear me, human. You will find this youth and kill him as quickly as possible. Do not think you can dissemble. There are others of your *children* who will tell me if you turn aside in your purpose. But I will give you this to encourage you. If this Rand al'Thor is not dead in a month, I will take one of your blood. A son, a daughter, a sister, an uncle. You will not know who until the chosen has died screaming. If he lives another month, I will take another. And then another, and another. And when there is no one of your blood living except yourself, if he still lives, I will take you to Shayol Ghul itself." It smiled. "You will be years in the dying, human. Do you understand me, now?"

Carridin made a sound, half groan, half whimper. He thought his neck was going to break.

With a snarl, the Myrddraal hurled him across the room. Carridin slammed against the far wall and slid to the rug, stunned. Facedown, he lay fighting for breath.

"Do you understand me, human?"

"I . . . I hear and obey," Carridin managed into the carpet. There was no answer.

He turned his head, wincing at the pain in his neck. The room was empty except for him. Halfmen rode shadows like horses, so the legends said, and when they turned sideways, they disappeared. No wall could keep them out. Carridin wanted to weep. He levered himself up, cursing the jolt of pain from his wrist.

The door opened, and Sharbon hurried in, a plump man with a basket in his arms. He stopped to stare at Carridin. "Master, are you all right? Forgive me for not being here, master, but I went to buy fruits for your—"

With his good hand Carridin struck the basket from

Sharbon's hands, sending withered winter apples rolling across the carpets, and backhanded the man across the face.

"Forgive me, master," Sharbon whispered.

"Fetch me paper and pen and ink," Carridin snarled. "Hurry, fool! I must send orders." *But which? Which?* As Sharbon scurried to obey, Carridin stared at the gouges in the tabletop and shivered.

CHAPTER
I

Waiting

The Wheel of Time turns, and Ages come and pass, leaving memories that become legend. Legend fades to myth, and even myth is long forgotten when the Age that gave it birth comes again. In one Age, called the Third Age by some, an Age yet to come, an Age long past, a wind rose in the Mountains of Mist. The wind was not the beginning. There are neither beginnings nor endings to the turning of the Wheel of Time. But it was *a* beginning.

Down long valleys the wind swept, valleys blue with morning mist hanging in the air, some forested with evergreens, some bare where grasses and wildflowers would soon spring up. It howled across half-buried ruins and broken monuments, all as forgotten as those who had built them. It moaned in the passes, weatherworn cuts between peaks capped with snow that never melted. Thick clouds clung to the mountaintops so that snow and white billows seemed one.

In the lowlands winter was going or gone, yet here in the heights it held awhile, quilting the mountainsides with broad, white patches. Only evergreens clung to leaf or needle; all other branches stood bare, brown or gray against the rock and not yet quickened ground. There was no sound but the crisp rush of wind over snow and stone. The land seemed to be waiting. Waiting for something to burst.

Sitting his horse just inside a thicket of leatherleaf and pine, Perrin Aybara shivered and tugged his fur-lined cloak closer, as close as he could with a longbow in one hand and a great, half-moon axe at his belt. It was a good axe of cold steel; Perrin had pumped the bellows the day master Luhhan had made it. The wind jerked at his cloak, pulling the hood back from his shaggy curls, and cut through his coat; he wiggled his toes in his boots for warmth and shifted on his high-cantled saddle, but his mind was not really on the cold. Eyeing his five companions, he wondered if they, too, felt it. Not the waiting they had been sent there for, but something more.

Stepper, his horse, shifted and tossed his head. He had named the dun stallion for his quick feet, but now Stepper seemed to feel his rider's irritation and impatience. *I am tired of all this waiting, all this sitting while Moiraine holds us as tight as tongs. Burn the Aes Sedai! When will it end?*

He sniffed the wind without thinking. The smell of horse predominated, and of men and men's sweat. A rabbit had gone through those trees not long since, fear powering its run, but the fox on its trail had not killed there. He realized what he was doing, and stopped it. *You'd think I would get a stuffed nose with all this wind.* He almost wished he did have one. *And I wouldn't let Moiraine do anything about it, either.*

Something tickled the back of his mind. He refused to acknowledge it. He did not mention his feeling to his companions.

The other five men sat their saddles, short horsebows at the ready, eyes searching the sky above as well as the thinly treed slopes below. They seemed unperturbed by the wind flaring their cloaks out like banners. A two-handed sword hilt stuck up above each man's shoulder through a slit in his cloak. The sight of their bare heads, shaven except for topknots, made Perrin feel colder. For them, this weather was already well into spring. All softness had been hammered out of them at a harder forge than he had ever known. They were Shienarans, from the Borderlands up along the Great Blight, where Trolloc raids could come in any night, and even a merchant or a farmer might well have to take up sword or bow. And these men were no farmers, but soldiers almost from birth.

He sometimes wondered at the way they deferred to him and followed his lead. It was as if they thought he had some special right, some knowledge hidden from them. *Or maybe it's just my friends*, he thought wryly. They were not as tall as he, nor as big—years as a blacksmith's apprentice had given him arms and shoulders to make two of most men's—but he had begun shaving every day to stop their jokes about his youth. Friendly jokes, but still jokes. He would not have them start again because he spoke of a feeling.

With a start, Perrin reminded himself that he was supposed to be keeping watch, too. Checking the arrow nocked to his longbow, he peered down the valley running off to the west, widening as it fell away, the ground streaked with broad, twisted ribbons of snow, remnants of winter. Most of the scattered trees down there still clawed the sky with stark winter branches, but enough evergreens—pine and leatherleaf, fir and mountain holly, even a few towering greenwoods—stood on the slopes and the valley floor to give cover for anyone who knew how to use it. But no one would be there without a special purpose. The mines were all far to the south or even further north; most people thought there was ill luck in the Mountains of Mist, and few entered them who could avoid it. Perrin's eyes glittered like burnished gold.

The tickling became an itch. *No!*

He could push the itch aside, but the expectation would not go. As if he teetered on a brink. As if everything teetered. He wondered whether something unpleasant lay in the mountains around them. There was a way to know, perhaps. In places like this, where men seldom came, there were almost always wolves. He crushed the thought before it had a chance to firm. *Better to wonder. Better than that.* Their numbers were not many, but they had scouts. If there was anything out there, the outriders would find it. *This is my forge; I'll tend it, and let them tend theirs.*

He could see further than the others, so he was first to spot the rider coming from the direction of Tarabon. Even to him the rider was only a spot of bright colors on horseback winding its way through the trees in the distance, now seen, now hidden. A piebald horse, he thought. *And not before time!* He opened his mouth to announce her—it would be a woman; each rider before had been—when Masema suddenly muttered, "Raven!" like a curse.

Perrin jerked his head up. A big black bird was quartering over the treetops no more than a hundred paces away.

Its quarry might have been carrion dead in the snow or some small animal, yet Perrin could not take the chance. It did not seem to have seen them, but the oncoming rider would soon be in its sight. Even as he spotted the raven, his bow came up, and he drew—fletchings to cheek, to ear— and loosed, all in one smooth motion. He was dimly aware of the slap of bowstrings beside him, but his attention was all on the black bird.

Of a sudden it cartwheeled in a shower of midnight feathers as his arrow found it, and tumbled from the sky as two more arrows streaked through the place where it had been. Bows half-drawn, the other Shienarans searched the sky to see if it had a companion.

"Does it have to report," Perrin asked softly, "or does . . . *he* . . . see what it sees?" He had not meant anyone to hear, but Ragan, the youngest of the Shienarans, less than ten years his elder, answered as he fitted another arrow to his short bow.

"It has to report. To a Halfman, usually." In the Borderlands there was a bounty on ravens; no one there ever dared assume any raven was just a bird. "Light, if Heartsbane saw what the ravens saw, we would all have been dead before we reached the mountains." Ragan's voice was easy; it was a matter of every day to a Shienaran soldier.

Perrin shivered, not from the cold, and in the back of his head something snarled a challenge to the death. Heartsbane. Different names in different lands—Soulsbane and Heartfang, Lord of the Grave and Lord of the Twilight— and everywhere Father of Lies and the Dark One, all to avoid giving him his true name and drawing his attention. The Dark One often used ravens and crows, rats in the cities. Perrin drew another broadhead arrow from the quiver on his hip that balanced the axe on the other side.

"That may be as big as a club," Ragan said admiringly, with a glance at Perrin's bow, "but it can shoot. I would hate to see what it could do to a man in armor." The Shienarans wore only light mail, now, under their plain coats, but usually they fought in armor, man and horse alike.

"Too long for horseback," Masema sneered. The triangular scar on his dark cheek twisted his contemptuous grin even more. "A good breastplate will stop even a pile arrow except at close range, and if your first shot fails, the man you're shooting at will carve your guts out."

"That is just it, Masema." Ragan relaxed a bit as the sky remained empty. The raven must have been alone. "With this Two Rivers bow, I'll wager you don't have to be so close." Masema opened his mouth.

"You two stop flapping your bloody tongues!" Uno snapped. With a long scar down the left side of his face and that eye gone, his features were hard, even for a Shienaran. He had acquired a painted eyepatch on their way into the mountains during the autumn; a permanently frowning eye in a fiery red did nothing to make his stare easier to face. "If you can't keep your bloody minds on the bloody task at hand, I'll see if extra flaming guard duty tonight will bloody settle you." Ragan and Masema subsided under his stare. He gave them a last scowl that faded as he turned to Perrin. "Do you see anything yet?" His tone was a little gruffer than he might have used with a commander put over him by the King of Shienar, or the Lord of Fal Dara, yet there was something in it of readiness to do whatever Perrin suggested.

The Shienarans knew how far he could see, but they seemed to take it as a matter of course, that and the color of his eyes, as well. They did not know everything, not by half, but they accepted him as he was. As they thought he was. They seemed to accept everything and anything. The world was changing, they said. Everything spun on the wheels of chance and change. If a man had eyes a color no man's eyes had ever been, what did it matter, now?

"She's coming," Perrin said. "You should just see her now. There." He pointed, and Uno strained forward, his one real eye squinting, then finally nodded doubtfully.

"There's bloody something moving down there." Some of the others nodded and murmured, too. Uno glared at them, and they went back to studying the sky and the mountains.

Suddenly Perrin realized what the bright colors on the distant rider meant. A vivid green skirt peeking out beneath a bright red cloak. "She's one of the Traveling People," he said, startled. No one else he had ever heard of dressed in such brilliant colors and odd combinations, not by choice.

The women they had sometimes met and guided even deeper into the mountains included every sort: a beggar woman in rags struggling afoot through a snowstorm; a merchant by herself leading a string of laden packhorses; a lady in silks and fine furs, with red-tasseled reins on her palfrey and gold worked on her saddle. The beggar departed with a purse of silver—more than Perrin thought they could afford to give, until the lady left an even fatter purse of gold. Women from every station in life, all alone, from Tarabon, and Ghealdan, and even Amadicia. But he had never expected to see one of the Tuatha'an.

"A bloody Tinker?" Uno exclaimed. The others echoed his surprise.

Ragan's topknot waved as he shook his head. "A Tinker wouldn't be mixed in this. Either she's not a Tinker, or she is not the one we are supposed to meet."

"Tinkers," Masema growled. "Useless cowards."

Uno's eye narrowed until it looked like the pritchel hole of an anvil; with the red painted eye on his patch, it gave him a villainous look. "Cowards, Masema?" he said softly. "If you were a woman, would you have the flaming nerve to ride up here, alone and bloody unarmed?" There was no doubt she would be unarmed if she was of the Tuatha'an. Masema kept his mouth shut, but the scar on his cheek stood out tight and pale.

"Burn me, if I would," Ragan said. "And burn me if you would either, Masema." Masema hitched at his cloak and ostentatiously searched the sky.

Uno snorted. "The Light send that flaming carrion eater was flaming alone," he muttered.

Slowly the shaggy brown-and-white mare meandered closer, picking a way along the clear ground between broad snowbanks. Once the brightly clad woman stopped to peer at something on the ground, then tugged the cowl of her cloak further over her head and heeled her mount forward in a slow walk. *The raven*, Perrin thought. *Stop looking at that bird and come on, woman. Maybe you've brought the word that finally takes us out of here. If Moiraine means to let us leave before spring. Burn her!* For a moment he was not sure whether he meant the Aes Sedai, or the Tinker woman who seemed to be taking her own time.

If she kept on as she was, the woman would pass a good

thirty paces to one side of the thicket. With her eyes fixed on where her piebald stepped, she gave no sign that she had seen them among the trees.

Perrin nudged the stallion's flanks with his heels, and the dun leaped ahead, sending up sprays of snow with his hooves. Behind him, Uno quietly gave the command, "Forward!"

Stepper was halfway to her before she seemed to become aware of them, and then she jerked her mare to a halt with a start. She watched as they formed an arc centered on her. Embroidery of eye-wrenching blue, in the pattern called a Tairen maze, made her red cloak even more garish. She was not young—gray showed thick in her hair where it was not hidden by her cowl—but her face had few lines, other than the disapproving frown she ran over their weapons. If she was alarmed at meeting armed men in the heart of mountain wilderness, though, she gave no sign. Her hands rested easily on the high pommel of her worn but well-kept saddle. And she did not smell afraid.

Stop that! Perrin told himself. He made his voice soft so as not to frighten her. "My name is Perrin, good mistress. If you need help, I will do what I can. If not, go with the Light. But unless the Tuatha'an have changed their ways, you are far from your wagons."

She studied them a moment more before speaking. There was a gentleness in her dark eyes, not surprising in one of the Traveling People. "I seek an . . . a woman."

The skip was small, but it was there. She sought not any woman, but an Aes Sedai. "Does she have a name, good mistress?" Perrin asked. He had done this too many times in the last few months to need her reply, but iron was spoiled for want of care.

"She is called. . . . Sometimes, she is called Moiraine. My name is Leya."

Perrin nodded. "We will take you to her, Mistress Leya. We have warm fires, and with luck something hot to eat." But he did not lift his reins immediately. "How did you find us?" He had asked before, each time Moiraine sent him out to wait at a spot she named, for a woman she knew would come. The answer would be the same as it always was, but he had to ask.

Leya shrugged and answered hesitantly. "I . . . knew that

if I came this way, someone would find me and take me to her. I . . . just . . . knew. I have news for her."

Perrin did not ask what news. The women gave the information they brought only to Moiraine.

And the Aes Sedai tells us what she chooses. He thought. Aes Sedai never lied, but it was said that the truth an Aes Sedai told you was not always the truth you thought it was. *Too late for qualms, now. Isn't it?*

"This way, Mistress Leya," he said, gesturing up the mountain. The Shienarans, with Uno at their head, fell in behind Perrin and Leya as they began to climb. The Borderlanders still studied the sky as much as the land, and the last two kept a special watch on their backtrail.

For a time they rode in silence except for the sounds the horses' hooves made, sometimes crunching through old snowcrust, sometimes sending rocks clattering as they crossed bare stretches. Now and again Leya cast glances at Perrin, at his bow, his axe, his face, but she did not speak. He shifted uncomfortably under the scrutiny, and avoided looking at her. He always tried to give strangers as little chance to notice his eyes as he could manage.

Finally he said, "I was surprised to see one of the Traveling People, believing as you do."

"It is possible to oppose evil without doing violence." Her voice held the simplicity of someone stating an obvious truth.

Perrin grunted sourly, then immediately muttered an apology. "Would it were as you say, Mistress Leya."

"Violence harms the doer as much as the victim," Leya said placidly. "That is why we flee those who harm us, to save them from harm to themselves as much for our own safety. If we do violence to oppose evil, soon we would be no different from what we struggle against. It is with the strength of our belief that we fight the Shadow."

Perrin could not help snorting. "Mistress, I hope you never have to face Trollocs with the strength of your belief. The strength of their swords will cut you down where you stand."

"It is better to die than to—" she began, but anger made him speak right over her. Anger that she just would not see. Anger that she really would die rather than harm anyone, no matter how evil.

"If you run, they will hunt you, and kill you, and eat your corpse. Or they might not wait till it *is* a corpse. Either way, you are dead, and it's evil that has won. And there are men just as cruel. Darkfriends and others. More others than I would have believed even a year ago. Let the Whitecloaks decide you Tinkers don't walk in the Light and see how many of you the strength of your belief can keep alive."

She gave him a penetrating look. "And yet you are not happy with your weapons."

How did she know that? He shook his head irritably, shaggy hair swaying. "The Creator made the world," he muttered, "not I. I must live the best I can in the world the way it is."

"So sad for one so young," she said softly. "Why so sad?"

"I should be watching, not talking," he said curtly. "You won't thank me if I get you lost." He heeled Stepper forward enough to cut off any further conversation, but he could feel her looking at him. *Sad? I'm not sad, just. . . . Light, I don't know. There ought to be a better way, that's all.* The itching tickle came again at the back of his head, but absorbed in ignoring Leya's eyes on his back, he ignored that, too.

Over the slope of the mountain and down they rode, across a forested valley with a broad stream running cold along its bottom, knee-deep on the horses. In the distance, the side of a mountain had been carved into the semblance of two towering forms. A man and a woman, Perrin thought they might be, though wind and rain had long since made that uncertain. Even Moiraine claimed to be unsure who they were supposed to be, or when the granite had been cut.

Pricklebacks and small trout darted away from the horses' hooves, silver flashes in the clear water. A deer raised its head from browsing, hesitated as the party rode up out of the stream, then bounded off into the trees, and a large mountain cat, gray striped and spotted with black, seemed to rise out of the ground, frustrated in its stalk. It eyed the horses a moment, and with a lash of its tail vanished after the deer. But there was little life visible in the mountains yet. Only a handful of birds perched on limbs or pecked at the ground where the snow had melted. More would return to the heights in a few weeks, but not yet. They saw no other ravens.

It was late afternoon by the time Perrin led them between

two steep-sloped mountains, snowy peaks as ever wrapped in cloud, and turned up a smaller stream that splashed downward over gray stones in a series of tiny waterfalls. A bird called in the trees, and another answered it from ahead.

Perrin smiled. Bluefinch calls. A Borderland bird. No one rode this way without being seen. He rubbed his nose, and did not look at the tree the first "bird" had called from.

Their path narrowed as they rode up through scrubby leatherleaf and a few gnarled mountain oaks. The ground level enough to ride beside the stream became barely wider than a man on horseback, and the stream itself no more than a tall man could step across.

Perrin heard Leya behind him, murmuring to herself. When he looked over his shoulder, she was casting worried glances up the steep slopes to either side. Scattered trees perched precariously above them. It appeared impossible they would not fall. The Shienarans rode easily, at last beginning to relax.

Abruptly a deep, oval bowl between the mountains opened out before them, its sides steep but not nearly so precipitous as the narrow passage. The stream rose from a small spring at its far end. Perrin's sharp eyes picked out a man with the topknot of a Shienaran, up in the limbs of an oak to his left. Had a redwinged jay called instead of a bluefinch, he would not have been alone, and the way in would not have been so easy. A handful of men could hold that passage against an army. If an army came, a handful would have to.

Among the trees around the bowl stood log huts, not readily visible, so that those gathered around the cook fires at the bottom of the bowl seemed at first to be without shelter. There were fewer than a dozen in sight. And not many more out of sight, Perrin knew. Most of them looked around at the sound of horses, and some waved. The bowl seemed filled with the smells of men and horses, of cooking and burning wood. A long white banner hung limply from a tall pole near them. One form, at least half again as tall as anyone else, sat on a log engrossed in a book that was small in his huge hands. That one's attention never wavered, even when the only other person without a topknot shouted, "So you found her, did you? I thought you'd be gone the night, this time." It was a young woman's voice, but she wore a boy's coat and breeches and had her hair cut short.

A burst of wind swirled into the bowl, making cloaks flap and rippling the banner out to its full length. For a moment the creature on it seemed to ride the wind. A four-legged serpent scaled in gold and scarlet, golden maned like a lion, and its feet each tipped with five golden claws. A banner of legend. A banner most men would not know if they saw it, but would fear when they learned its name.

Perrin waved a hand that took it all in as he led the way down into the bowl. "Welcome to the camp of the Dragon Reborn, Leya."

CHAPTER
2

Saidin

F ace expressionless, the Tuatha'an woman stared at the banner as it drooped again, then turned her attention to those around the fire. Especially the one reading, the one half again as tall as Perrin and twice as big. "You have an Ogier with you. I would not have thought. . . ." She shook her head. "Where is Moiraine Sedai?" It seemed the Dragon banner might as well not exist as far as she was concerned.

Perrin gestured toward the rough hut that stood furthest up the slope, at the far end of the bowl. With walls and sloping roof of unpeeled logs, it was the largest, though not very big at that. Perhaps just barely large enough to be called a cabin rather than a hut. "That one is hers. Hers and Lan's. He is her Warder. When you have had something hot to drink—"

"No. I must speak to Moiraine."

He was not surprised. All the women who came insisted on speaking to Moiraine immediately, and alone. The news that Moiraine chose to share with the rest of them did not always seem very important, but the women held the intensity of a hunter stalking the last rabbit in the world for his starving family. The half-frozen old beggar woman had refused blankets and a plate of hot stew and tramped up to Moiraine's hut, barefoot in still-falling snow.

Leya slid from her saddle and handed the reins up to Perrin. "Will you see that she is fed?" She patted the piebald mare's nose. "Piesa is not used to carrying me over such rugged country."

"Fodder is scarce, still," Perrin told her, "but she'll have what we can give her."

Leya nodded, and went hurrying away up the slope without another word, holding her bright green skirts up, the blue-embroidered red cloak swaying behind her.

Perrin swung down from his saddle, exchanging a few words with the men who came from the fires to take the horses. He gave his bow to the one who took Stepper. No, except for one raven, they had seen nothing but the mountains and the Tuatha'an woman. Yes, the raven was dead. No, she had told them nothing of what was happening outside the mountains. No, he had no idea whether they would be leaving soon.

Or ever, he added to himself. Moiraine had kept them there all winter. The Shienarans did not think she gave the orders, not here, but Perrin knew that Aes Sedai somehow always seemed to get their way. Especially Moiraine.

Once the horses were led away to the rude log stable, the riders went to warm themselves. Perrin tossed his cloak back over his shoulders and held his hands out to the flames gratefully. The big kettle, Baerlon work by the look of it, gave off smells that had been making his mouth water for some time already. Someone had been lucky hunting today, it seemed, and lumpy roots circled another fire close by, giving off an aroma faintly like turnips as they roasted. He wrinkled his nose and concentrated on the stew. More and more he wanted meat above anything else.

The woman in men's clothes was peering toward Leya, who was just disappearing into Moiraine's hut.

"What do you see, Min?" he asked.

She came to stand beside him, her dark eyes troubled. He did not understand why she insisted on breeches instead of skirts. Perhaps it was because he knew her, but he could not see how anyone could look at her and see a too-handsome youth instead of a pretty young woman.

"The Tinker woman is going to die," she said softly, eyeing the others near the fires. None was close enough to hear.

He was still, thinking of Leya's gentle face. *Ah, Light! Tinkers never harm anyone!* He felt cold despite the warmth of the fire. *Burn me, I wish I'd never asked.* Even the few

Aes Sedai who knew of it did not understand what Min did. Sometimes she saw images and auras surrounding people, and sometimes she even knew what they meant.

Masuto came to stir the stew with a long wood spoon. The Shienaran eyed them, then laid a finger alongside his long nose and grinned widely before he left.

"Blood and ashes!" Min muttered. "He's probably decided we are sweethearts murmuring to each other by the fire."

"Are you sure?" Perrin asked. She raised her eyebrows at him, and he hastily added, "About Leya."

"Is that her name? I wish I didn't know. It always makes it worse, knowing and not being able to. . . . Perrin, I saw her own face floating over her shoulder, covered in blood, eyes staring. It's never any clearer than that." She shivered and rubbed her hands together briskly. "Light, but I wish I saw more happy things. All the happy things seem to have gone away."

He opened his mouth to suggest warning Leya, then closed it again. There was never any doubt about what Min saw and knew, for good or bad. If she was certain, it happened.

"Blood on her face," he muttered. "Does that mean she'll die by violence?" He winced that he said it so easily. *But what can I do? If I tell Leya, if I make her believe somehow, she'll live her last days in fear, and it will change nothing.*

Min gave a short nod.

If she's going to die by violence, it could mean an attack on the camp. But there were scouts out every day, and guards set day and night. And Moiraine had the camp warded, so she said; no creature of the Dark One would see it unless he walked right into it. He thought of the wolves. *No!* The scouts would find anyone or anything trying to approach the camp. "It's a long way back to her people," he said half to himself. "Tinkers wouldn't have brought their wagons any further than the foothills. Anything could happen between here and there."

Min nodded sadly. "And there aren't enough of us to spare even one guard for her. Even if it would do any good."

She had told him; she had tried warning people about bad things when, at six or seven, she had first realized not everyone could see what she saw. She would not say more, but he had the impression that her warnings had only made matters worse, when they were believed at all. It took some doing to believe in Min's viewings until you had proof.

"When?" he said. The word was cold in his ears, and hard as tool steel. *I can't do anything about Leya, but maybe I can figure out whether we're going to be attacked.*

As soon as the word was out of his mouth, she threw up her hands. She kept her voice down, though. "It isn't like that. I can never tell *when* something is going to happen. I only know it will, if I even know what I see means. You don't understand. The seeing doesn't come when I want it to, and neither does knowing. It just happens, and sometimes I know. Something. A little bit. It just happens." He tried to get a soothing word in, but she was letting it all out in a flood he could not stem. "I can see things around a man one day and not the next, or the other way 'round. Most of the time, I don't see anything around anyone. Aes Sedai always have images around them, of course, and Warders, though it's always harder to say what it means with them than with anyone else." She gave Perrin a searching look, half squinting. "A few others always do, too."

"Don't tell me what you see when you look at me," he said harshly, then shrugged his heavy shoulders. Even as a child he had been bigger than most of the others, and he had quickly learned how easy it was to hurt people by accident when you were bigger than they. It had made him cautious and careful, and regretful of his anger when he let it show. "I am sorry, Min. I shouldn't have snapped at you. I did not mean to hurt you."

She gave him a surprised look. "You didn't hurt me. Blessed few people *want* to know what I see. The Light knows, I would not, if it were someone else who could do it." Even the Aes Sedai had never heard of anyone else who had her gift. "Gift" was how they saw it, even if she did not.

"It's just that I wish there were something I could do about Leya. I couldn't stand it the way you do, knowing and not able to do anything."

"Strange," she said softly, "how you seem to care so much about the Tuatha'an. They are utterly peaceful, and I always see violence around—"

He turned his head away, and she cut off abruptly.

"Tuatha'an?" came a rumbling voice, like a huge bumble-bee. "What about the Tuatha'an?" The Ogier came to join them at the fire, marking his place in his book with a finger the size of a large sausage. A thin streamer of tabac smoke rose from the pipe in his other hand. His high-necked coat of dark brown wool buttoned up to the neck, and flared at the knee over turned-down boot tops. Perrin stood hardly as high as his chest.

Loial's face had frightened more than one person, with his nose broad enough almost to be called a snout and his too-wide mouth. His eyes were the size of saucers, with thick eyebrows that dangled like mustaches almost to his cheeks, and his ears poked up through long hair in tufted points. Some who had never seen an Ogier took him for a Trolloc, though Trollocs were as much legend to most of them as Ogier.

Loial's wide smile wavered and his eyes blinked as he became aware of having interrupted them. Perrin wondered how anyone could be frightened of the Ogier for long. *Yet some of the old stories call them fierce, and implacable as enemies.* He could not believe it. Ogier were enemies to no one.

Min told Loial of Leya's arrival, but not of what she had seen. She was usually closemouthed about those seeings, especially when they were bad. Instead, she added, "You should know how I feel, Loial, suddenly caught up by Aes Sedai and these Two Rivers folk."

Loial made a noncommittal sound, but Min seemed to take it for agreement.

"Yes," she said emphatically. "There I was, living my life in Baerlon as I liked it, when suddenly I was grabbed up by the scruff of the neck and jerked off to the Light knows where. Well, I might as well have been. My life has not been my own since I met Moiraine. And these Two Rivers farmboys." She rolled her eyes at Perrin, a wry twist to her mouth. "All I wanted was to live as I pleased, fall in love with a man I chose. . . ." Her cheeks reddened suddenly, and she cleared her throat. "I mean to say, what is wrong with wanting to live your life without all this up-heaval?"

"*Ta'veren,*" Loial began. Perrin waved at him to stop,

but the Ogier could seldom be slowed, much less stopped, when one of his enthusiasms had him in its grip. He was accounted extremely hasty, by the Ogier way of looking at things. Loial pushed his book into a coat pocket and went on, gesturing with his pipe. "All of us, all of our lives, affect the lives of others, Min. As the Wheel of Time weaves us into the Pattern, the life-thread of each of us pulls and tugs at the life-threads around us. *Ta'veren* are the same, only much, much more so. They tug at the entire Pattern— for a time, at least—forcing it to shape around them. The closer you are to them, the more you are affected personally. It's said that if you were in the same room with Artur Hawkwing, you could feel the Pattern rearranging itself. I don't know how true that is, but I've read that it was. But it doesn't only work one way. *Ta'veren* themselves are woven to a tighter line than the rest of us, with fewer choices."

Perrin grimaced. *Bloody few of the ones that matter.*

Min tossed her head. "I just wish they didn't have to be so . . . so bloody *ta'veren* all the time. *Ta'veren* tugging on one side, and Aes Sedai meddling on the other. What chance does a woman have?"

Loial shrugged. "Very little, I suppose, as long as she stays close to *ta'veren.*"

"As if I had a choice," Min growled.

"It was your good fortune—or misfortune, if you see it that way—to fall in with not one, but three *ta'veren*. Rand, Mat, and Perrin. I myself count it very good fortune, and would even if they weren't my friends. I think I might even. . . ." The Ogier looked at them, suddenly shy, his ears twitching. "Promise you will not laugh? I think I might write a book about it. I have been taking notes."

Min smiled, a friendly smile, and Loial's ears pricked back up again. "That's wonderful," she told him. "But some of us feel as if we're being danced about like puppets by these *ta'veren.*"

"I didn't ask for it," Perrin burst out. "I did not ask for it."

She ignored him. "Is that what happened to you, Loial? Is that why you travel with Moiraine? I know you Ogier almost never leave your *stedding.* Did one of these *ta'veren* tug you along with him?"

Loial became engrossed in a study of his pipe. "I just

wanted to see the groves the Ogier planted," he muttered. "Just to see the groves." He glanced at Perrin as if asking for help, but Perrin only grinned.

Let's see how the shoe nails onto your hoof. He did not know all of it, but he did know Loial had run away. He was ninety years old, but not yet old enough by Ogier standards to leave the *stedding*—going Outside, they called it—without the permission of the Elders. Ogier lived a very long time, as humans saw things. Loial said the Elders would not be best pleased when they put their hands on him again. He seemed intent on putting that moment off as long as possible.

There was a stir among the Shienarans, men getting to their feet. Rand was coming out of Moiraine's hut.

Even at that distance Perrin could make him out clearly, a young man with reddish hair and gray eyes. He was of an age with Perrin, and would stand half a head taller if they were side by side, though Rand was more slender, if still broad across the shoulders. Embroidered golden thorns ran up the sleeves of his high-collared, red coat, and on the breast of his dark cloak stood the same creature as on the banner, the four-legged serpent with the golden mane. Rand and he had grown up together as friends. *Are we still friends? Can we be? Now?*

The Shienarans bowed as one, heads held up but hands to knees. "Lord Dragon," Uno called, "we stand ready. Honor to serve."

Uno, who could hardly say a sentence without a curse, spoke now with the deepest respect. The others echoed him. "Honor to serve." Masema, who saw ill in everything, and whose eyes now shone with utter devotion; Ragan; all of them, awaiting a command if it were Rand's pleasure to give one.

From the slope Rand stared down at them a moment, then turned and disappeared into the trees.

"He has been arguing with Moiraine again," Min said quietly. "All day, this time."

Perrin was not surprised, yet he still felt a small shock. Arguing with an Aes Sedai. All the childhood tales came back to him. Aes Sedai, who made thrones and nations dance to their hidden strings. Aes Sedai, whose gift always had a hook in it, whose price was always smaller than you could believe, yet always turned out to be greater than you could imagine. Aes Sedai, whose anger could break the ground and summon lightning. Some of the stories were untrue, he knew now. And at the same time, they did not tell the half.

"I had better go to him," he said. "After they argue, he always needs someone to talk to." And aside from Moiraine and Lan, there were only the three of them—Min, Loial, and him—who did not stare at Rand as if he stood above kings. And of the three only Perrin knew him from before.

He strode up the slope, pausing only to glance at the closed door of Moiraine's hut. Leya would be in there, and Lan. The Warder seldom let himself get far from the Aes Sedai's side.

Rand's much smaller hut was a little lower down, well hidden in the trees, away from all the rest. He had tried living down among the other men, but their constant awe drove him off. He kept to himself, now. Too much to himself, to Perrin's thinking. But he knew Rand was not headed to his hut now.

Perrin hurried on to where one side of the bowl-shaped valley suddenly became sheer cliff, fifty paces high and smooth except for tough brush clinging tenaciously here and there. He knew exactly where a crack in the gray rock wall lay, an opening hardly wider than his shoulders. With only a ribbon of late-afternoon light overhead, it was like walking down a tunnel.

Half a mile the crack ran, abruptly opening out into a narrow vale, less than a mile long, its floor covered with rocks and boulders, and even the steep slopes were thickly forested with tall leatherleaf and pine and fir. Long shadows stretched away from the sun sitting on the mountaintops. The walls of this place were unbroken save for the crack, and as steep as if a giant axe had buried itself in the mountains. It could be even more easily defended by a few than the bowl, but it had neither stream nor spring. No one went there. Except Rand, after he argued with Moiraine.

Rand stood not far from the entrance, leaning against the rough trunk of a leatherleaf, staring at the palms of his hands. Perrin knew that on each there was a heron, branded into the flesh. Rand did not move when Perrin's boot scraped on stone.

Suddenly Rand began to recite softly, never looking up from his hands.

> Twice and twice shall he be marked,
> twice to live, and twice to die.
> Once the heron, to set his path.
> Twice the heron, to name him true.
> Once the Dragon, for remembrance lost.
> Twice the Dragon, for the price he must pay.

With a shudder he tucked his hands under his arms. "But no Dragons, yet." He chuckled roughly. "Not yet."

For a moment Perrin simply looked at him. A man who could channel the One Power. A man doomed to go mad from the taint on *saidin*, the male half of the True Source, and certain to destroy everything around him in his madness. A man—a thing!—everyone was taught to loathe and fear from childhood. Only . . . it was hard to stop seeing the boy he had grown up with. *How do you just* stop *being somebody's friend?* Perrin chose a small boulder with a flat top, and sat, waiting.

After a while Rand turned his head to look at him. "Do you think Mat is all right? He looked so sick, the last I saw him."

"He must be all right by now." *He should be in Tar Valon, by now. They'll Heal him, there. And Nynaeve and Egwene will keep him out of trouble.* Egwene and Nynaeve, Rand and Mat and Perrin. All five from Emond's Field in the Two Rivers. Few people had come into the Two Rivers from outside, except for occasional peddlers, and merchants once a year to buy wool and tabac. Almost no one had ever left. Until the Wheel chose out its *ta'veren*, and five simple country folk could stay where they were no longer. Could be what they had been no longer.

Rand nodded and was silent.

"Lately," Perrin said, "I find myself wishing I was still a blacksmith. Do you. . . . Do you wish you were still just a shepherd?"

"Duty," Rand muttered. "Death is lighter than a feather, duty heavier than a mountain. That's what they say in Shienar. 'The Dark One is stirring. The Last Battle is coming. And the Dragon Reborn has to face the Dark One in the Last Battle, or the Shadow will cover everything. The Wheel of Time broken. Every Age remade in the Dark One's image.' There's only me." He began to laugh mirthlessly, his shoulders shaking. "I have the duty, because there isn't anybody else, now is there?"

Perrin shifted uneasily. The laughter had a raw edge that made his skin crawl. "I understand you were arguing with Moiraine again. The same thing?"

Rand drew a deep, ragged breath. "Don't we always argue about the same thing? They're down there, on Almoth Plain, and the Light alone knows where else. Hundreds of them. Thousands. They declared for the Dragon Reborn because I raised that banner. Because I let myself be called the Dragon. Because I could see no other choice. And they're dying. Fighting, searching, and praying for the man who is supposed to lead them. Dying. And I sit here safe in the mountains all winter. I . . . I owe them . . . something."

"You think I like it?" Perrin swung his head in irritation.

"You take whatever she says to you," Rand grated. "You never stand up to her."

"Much good it has done you, standing up to her. You have argued all winter, and we have sat here like lumps all winter."

"Because she is right." Rand laughed again, that chilling laugh. "The Light burn me, she is right. They are all split up into little groups all over the plain, all across Tarabon and Arad Doman. If I join any one of them, the Whitecloaks and the Domani army and the Taraboners will be on top of them like a duck on a beetle."

Perrin almost laughed himself, in confusion. "If you agree with her, why in the Light do you argue all the time?"

"Because I have to do something. Or I'll . . . I'll—burst like a rotted melon!"

"Do what? If you listen to what she says—"

Rand gave him no chance to say they would sit there forever. "Moiraine says! Moiraine says!" Rand jerked erect, squeezing his head between his hands. "Moiraine has something to say about everything! Moiraine says I mustn't go to the men who are dying in my name. Moiraine says I'll know what to do next because the Pattern will force me to it. Moiraine says! But she never says how I'll know. Oh, no! She doesn't know that." His hands fell to his sides, and he turned toward Perrin, head tilted and eyes narrowed. "Sometimes I feel as if Moiraine is putting me through my paces like a fancy Tairen stallion doing his steps. Do you ever feel that?"

Perrin scrubbed a hand through his shaggy hair. "I. . . . Whatever is pushing us, or pulling us, I know who the enemy is, Rand."

"Ba'alzamon," Rand said softly. An ancient name for the Dark One. In the Trolloc tongue, it meant Heart of the Dark. "And I must face him, Perrin." His eyes closed in a grimace, half smile, half pain. "Light help me, half the time I want it to happen now, to be over and done with, and the other half. . . . How many times can I manage to. . . . Light, it pulls at me so. What if I can't. . . . What if I. . . ." The ground trembled.

"Rand?" Perrin said worriedly.

Rand shivered; despite the chill, there was sweat on his face. His eyes were still shut tight. "Oh, Light," he groaned, "it pulls so."

Suddenly the ground heaved beneath Perrin, and the valley echoed with a vast rumble. It seemed as if the ground was jerked out from under his feet. He fell—or the earth leaped up to meet him. The valley shook as though a vast hand had reached down from the sky to wrench it out of the land. He clung to the ground while it tried to bounce him like a ball. Pebbles in front of his eyes leaped and tumbled, and dust rose in waves.

"Rand!" His bellow was lost in the grumbling roar.

Rand stood with his head thrown back, his eyes still shut tight. He did not seem to feel the thrashing of the ground that had him now at one angle, now at another. His balance never shifted, no matter how he was tossed. Perrin could not be certain, being shaken as he was, but he thought Rand wore a sad smile. The trees flailed about, and the leather-leaf suddenly cracked in two, the greater part of its trunk crashing down not three paces from Rand. He noticed it no more than he noticed any of the rest.

Perrin struggled to fill his lungs. "Rand! For the love of the Light, Rand! Stop it!"

As abruptly as it had begun, it was done. A weakened branch cracked off of a stunted oak with a loud snap. Perrin got to his feet slowly, coughing. Dust hung in the air, sparkling motes in the rays of the setting sun.

Rand was staring at nothing, now, chest heaving as if he had run ten miles. This had never happened before, nor anything remotely like it.

"Rand," Perrin said carefully, "what—?"

Rand still seemed to be looking into a far distance. "It is always there. Calling to me. Pulling at me. *Saidin*. The male half of the True Source. Sometimes I can't stop myself from reaching out for it." He made a motion of plucking something out of the air, and transferred his stare to his closed fist. "I can feel the taint even before I touch it. The Dark One's taint, like a thin coat of vileness trying to hide the Light. It turns my stomach, but I cannot help myself. I cannot! Only sometimes, I reach out, and it's like trying to catch air." His empty hand sprang open, and he gave a bitter laugh. "What if that happens when the Last Battle comes? What if I reach out and catch nothing?"

"Well, you caught something that time," Perrin said hoarsely. "What were you doing?"

Rand looked around as if seeing things for the first time. The fallen leatherleaf, and the broken branches. There was, Perrin realized, surprisingly little damage. He had expected gaping rents in the earth. The wall of trees looked almost whole.

"I did not mean to do this. It was as if I tried to open a tap, and instead pulled the whole tap out of the barrel. It . . . filled me. I had to send it somewhere before it burned me up, but I . . . I did not mean this."

Perrin shook his head. *What use to tell him to try not to do it again? He barely knows more about what he's doing than I do.* He contented himself with, "There are enough who want you dead—and the rest of us—without you doing the job for them." Rand did not seem to be listening. "We had best get on back to the camp. It will be dark soon, and I don't know about you, but I am hungry."

"What? Oh. You go on, Perrin. I will be along. I want to be alone again a while."

Perrin hesitated, then turned reluctantly toward the crack in the valley wall. He stopped when Rand spoke again.

"Do you have dreams when you sleep? Good dreams?"

"Sometimes," Perrin said warily. "I don't remember much of what I dream." He had learned to set guards on his dreaming.

"They're always there, dreams," Rand said, so softly Perrin barely heard. "Maybe they tell us things. True things." He fell silent, brooding.

"Supper's waiting," Perrin said, but Rand was deep in his own thoughts. Finally Perrin turned and left him standing there.

CHAPTER
3

News from the Plain

D arkness shrouded part of the crack, for in one place the tremors had collapsed a part of the wall against the other side, high up. He stared up at the blackness warily before hurrying underneath, but the slab of stone seemed to be solidly wedged in place. The itch had returned to the back of his head, stronger than before. *No, burn me! No!* It went away.

When he came out above the camp, the bowl was filled with odd shadows from the sinking sun. Moiraine was standing outside her hut, peering up at the crack. He stopped short. She was a slender, dark-haired woman no taller than his shoulder, and pretty, with the ageless quality of all Aes Sedai who had worked with the One Power for a time. He could not put any age at all to her, with her face too smooth for many years and her dark eyes too wise for youth. Her dress of deep blue silk was disarrayed and dusty, and wisps stuck out in her usually well-ordered hair. A smudge of dust lay across her face.

He dropped his eyes. She knew about him—she and Lan alone, of those in the camp—and he did not like the knowing in her face when she looked into his eyes. Yellow eyes. Someday, perhaps, he could bring himself to ask her what she knew. An Aes Sedai must know more of it than he did. But this was not the time. There never seemed to be a time. "He. . . . He didn't mean. . . . It was an accident."

"An accident," she said in a flat voice, then shook her head and vanished back inside the hut. The door banged shut a little loudly.

Perrin drew a deep breath and continued on down toward

the cook fires. There would be another argument between Rand and the Aes Sedai, in the morning if not tonight.

Half a dozen trees lay toppled on the slopes of the bowl, roots ripped out of the earth in arcs of soil. A trail of scrapes and churned ground led down to the streamside and a boulder that had not been there before. One of the huts up the opposite slope had collapsed in the tremors, and most of the Shienarans were gathered around it, rebuilding it. Loial was with them. The Ogier could pick up a log it would take four men to lift. Uno's curses occasionally drifted down.

Min stood by the fires, stirring a kettle with a disgruntled expression. There was a small bruise on her cheek, and a faint smell of burned stew hung in the air. "I hate cooking," she announced, and peered doubtfully into the kettle. "If something goes wrong with it, it isn't my fault. Rand spilled half of it on the fire with his. . . . What right does he have to bounce us around like sacks of grain?" She rubbed the seat of her breeches and winced. "When I get my hands on him, I'll thump him so he never forgets." She waved the wooden spoon at Perrin as if she intended to start the thumping with him.

"Was anyone hurt?"

"Only if you count bruises," Min said grimly. "They were upset, all right, at first. Then they saw Moiraine staring off toward Rand's hidey-hole, and decided it was his work. If the *Dragon* wants to shake the mountain down on our heads, then the *Dragon* must have a good reason for it. If he decided to make them take off their skins and dance in their bones, they would think it all right." She snorted and rapped the spoon on the edge of the kettle.

He looked back toward Moiraine's hut. If Leya had been hurt—if she were dead—the Aes Sedai would not simply have gone back inside. The sense of waiting was still there. *Whatever it is, it hasn't happened yet.* "Min, maybe you had better go. First thing in the morning. I have some silver I can let you have, and I'm sure Moiraine would give you enough to take passage with a merchant's train out of Ghealdan. You could be back in Baerlon before you know it."

She looked at him until he began to wonder if he had said something wrong. Finally, she said, "That is very sweet of you, Perrin. But, no."

"I thought you wanted to go. You're always carrying on about having to stay here."

"I knew an old Illianer woman, once," she said slowly. "When she was young, her mother arranged a marriage for her with a man she had never even met. They do that down in Illian, sometimes. She said she spent the first five years raging against him, and the next five scheming to make his life miserable without his knowing who was to blame. It was only years later, she said, when he died, that she realized he really had been the love of her life."

"I don't see what that has to do with this."

Her look said he obviously was not trying to understand, and her voice became overly patient. "Just because fate has chosen something for you instead of you choosing it for yourself doesn't mean it has to be bad. Even if it's something you are sure you would never have chosen in a hundred years. 'Better ten days of love than years of regretting,'" she quoted.

"I understand that even less," he told her. "You don't have to stay if you don't want to."

She hung the spoon on a tall forked stick stuck in the ground, then surprised him by rising on tiptoe to kiss his cheek. "You are a very nice man, Perrin Aybara. Even if you don't understand anything."

Perrin blinked at her uncertainly. He wished that he could be certain Rand was in his right mind, or that Mat were there. He was never sure of his ground with girls, but Rand always seemed to know his way. So did Mat; most of the girls back home in Emond's Field had sniffed that Mat would never grow up, but he had seemed to have a way with them.

"What about you, Perrin? Don't you ever want to go home?"

"All the time," he said fervently. "But I . . . I do not think I can. Not yet." He looked off toward Rand's vale. *We are tied together, it seems, aren't we, Rand?* "Maybe not ever." He thought he had said that too softly for her to hear, but the look she gave him was full of sympathy. And agreement.

His ears caught faint footsteps behind him, and he looked back up toward Moiraine's hut. Two shapes were making their way down through the deepening twilight, one a woman, slender and graceful even on the rough, slanting ground. The man, head and shoulders taller than his companion, turned off toward where the Shienarans were working. Even to Perrin's eyes he was indistinct, sometimes seeming to vanish altogether, then reappear in midstride, parts of him fading into the night and fading back as the wind gusted. Only a Warder's shifting cloak could do that, which made the larger figure Lan, just as the smaller was certainly Moiraine.

Well behind them, another shape, even dimmer, slipped between the trees. *Rand*, Perrin thought, *going back to his hut. Another night when he won't eat because he can't stand the way everybody looks at him.*

"You must have eyes in the back of your head," Min said, frowning toward the approaching woman. "Or else the sharpest ears I have ever heard of. Is that Moiraine?"

Careless. He had grown so used to the Shienarans knowing how well he could see—in daylight at least; they did not know about the night—that he was beginning to slip about other things. *Carelessness might kill me yet.*

"Is the Tuatha'an woman all right?" Min asked as Moiraine came to the fire.

"She is resting." The Aes Sedai's low voice had its usual musical quality, as if speaking were halfway to singing, and her hair and clothes were back in perfect order again. She rubbed her hands over the fire. There was a golden ring on her left hand, a serpent biting its own tail. The Great Serpent, an even older symbol for eternity than the Wheel of Time. Every woman trained in Tar Valon wore such a ring.

For a moment Moiraine's gaze rested on Perrin, and seemed to penetrate too deeply. "She fell and split her scalp when Rand. . . ." Her mouth tightened, but in the next instant her face was utter calm again. "I Healed her, and she is sleeping. There is always a good deal of blood with even a minor scalp wound, but it was not serious. Did you see anything about her, Min?"

Min looked uncertain. "I saw. . . . I thought I saw her death. Her own face, all over blood. I was sure I knew what it meant, but if she split her scalp. . . . Are you sure she is all right?" It was a measure of her discomfort that she asked. An Aes Sedai did not Heal and leave anything wrong that could be Healed. And Moiraine's Talents were particularly strong in that area.

Min sounded so troubled that Perrin was surprised for

a moment. Then he nodded to himself. She did not really like doing what she did, but it was a part of her; she thought she knew how it worked, or some of it, at least. If she was wrong, it would almost be like finding out she did not know how to use her own hands.

Moiraine considered her for a moment, serene and dispassionate. "You have never been wrong in any reading for me, not one about which I had any way of knowing. Perhaps this is the first time."

"When I know, I know," Min whispered obstinately. "Light help me, I do."

"Or perhaps it is yet to come. She has a long way yet to travel, to return to her wagons, and she must ride through unsettled lands."

The Aes Sedai's voice was a cool song, uncaring. Perrin made an involuntary sound in his throat. *Light, did I sound like that? I won't let a death matter that little to me.*

As if he had spoken aloud, Moiraine looked at him. "The Wheel weaves as the Wheel wills, Perrin. I told you long ago that we were in a war. We cannot stop just because some of us may die. Any of us may die before it is done. Leya's weapons may not be the same as yours, but she knew that when she became part of it."

Perrin dropped his eyes. *That's as may be, Aes Sedai, but I will never accept it the way you do.*

Lan joined them across the fire, with Uno and Loial. The flames cast flickering shadows across the Warder's face, making it seem more carved from stone even than it normally did, all hard planes and angles. His cloak was not much easier to look at in the firelight. Sometimes it seemed only a dark gray cloak, or black, but the gray and black appeared to crawl and change if you looked too closely, shades and shadows sliding across it, soaking into it. Other times, it looked as if Lan had somehow made a hole in the night and pulled darkness 'round his shoulders. Not at all an easy thing to watch, and not made any easier by the man who wore it.

Lan was tall and hard, broad-shouldered, with blue eyes like frozen mountain lakes, and he moved with a deadly grace that made the sword on his hip seem a part of him. It was not that he seemed merely capable of violence and death; this man had tamed violence and death and kept them in his pocket, ready to be loosed in a heartbeat, or embraced, should Moiraine give the word. Beside Lan, even Uno appeared less dangerous. There was a touch of gray in the Warder's long hair, held back by a woven leather cord around his forehead, but younger men stepped back from confronting Lan—if they were wise.

"Mistress Leya has the usual news from Almoth Plain," Moiraine said. "Everyone fighting everyone else. Villages burned. People fleeing in every direction. And Hunters have appeared on the plain, searching for the Horn of Valere." Perrin shifted—the Horn was where no Hunter on Almoth Plain would find it; where he hoped no Hunter ever would find it—and she gave him a cool look before continuing. She did not like any of them to speak of the Horn. Except when she chose to, of course.

"She brought different news, as well. The Whitecloaks have perhaps five thousand men on Almoth Plain."

Uno grunted. "That's flamin'—uh, pardon, Aes Sedai. That must be half their strength. They've never committed so much to one place before."

"Then I suppose all those who declared for Rand are dead or scattered," Perrin muttered. "Or they soon will be. You were right, Moiraine." He did not like the thought of Whitecloaks. He did not like the Children of the Light at all.

"That is what is odd," Moiraine said. "Or the first part of it. The Children have announced that their purpose is to bring peace, which is not unusual for them. What *is* unusual is that while they are trying to force the Taraboners and the Domani back across their respective borders, they have not moved in any force against those who have declared for the Dragon."

Min gave an exclamation of surprise. "Is she certain? That does not sound like any Whitecloaks I ever heard of."

"There can't be many blood—uh—many Tinkers left on the plain," Uno said. His voice creaked from the strain of watching his language in front of an Aes Sedai. His real eye matched the frown of the painted one. "They don't like to stay where there's any kind of trouble, especially fighting. There can't be enough of them to see everywhere."

"There are enough for my purposes," Moiraine said firmly. "Most have gone, but some few remained because I asked them to. And Leya is quite certain. Oh, the Children have snapped up some of the Dragonsworn, where there were only a handful gathered. But though they proclaim they will bring down this *false* Dragon, though they have a thousand men supposedly doing nothing but hunting him, they avoid contact with any party of as many as fifty Dragonsworn. Not openly, you understand, but there is always some delay, something that allows those they chase to slip away."

"Then Rand can go down to them as he wants." Loial blinked uncertainly at the Aes Sedai. The whole camp knew of her arguments with Rand. "The Wheel weaves a way for him."

Uno and Lan opened their mouths at the same time, but the Shienaran gave way with a small bow. "More likely," the Warder said, "it is some Whitecloak plot, though the Light burn me if I can see what it is. But when the Whitecloaks give me a gift, I search for the poisoned needle hidden in it." Uno nodded grimly. "Besides which," Lan added, "the Domani and the Taraboners are still trying as hard to kill the Dragonsworn as they are to kill each other."

"And there is another thing," Moiraine said. "Three young men have died in villages Mistress Leya's wagons passed near." Perrin noticed a flicker of Lan's eyelid; for the Warder, it was as much a sign of surprise as a shout from another man. Lan had not expected her to tell this. Moiraine went on. "One died by poison, two by the knife. Each in circumstances where no one should have been able to come close unseen, but that is how it happened." She peered into the flames. "All three young men were taller than most, and had light-colored eyes. Light eyes are uncommon on Almoth Plain, but I think it is very unlucky right now to be a tall young man with light eyes there."

"How?" Perrin asked. "How could they be killed if no one could get close to them?"

"The Dark One has killers you don't notice until it is too late," Lan said quietly.

Uno gave a shiver. "The Soulless. I never heard of one south of the Borderlands before."

"Enough of such talk," Moiraine said firmly.

Perrin had questions—*What in the Light are the Soulless? Are they like a Trolloc, or a Fade? What?*—but he left them unasked. When Moiraine decided enough had been said about something, she would not talk of it anymore.

And when she shut her mouth, you could not pry Lan's open with an iron bar. The Shienarans followed her lead, too. No one wanted to anger an Aes Sedai.

"Light!" Min muttered, uneasily eyeing the deepening darkness around them. "You don't *notice* them? Light!"

"So nothing has changed," Perrin said glumly. "Not really. We cannot go down to the plain, and the Dark One wants us dead."

"Everything changes," Moiraine said calmly, "and the Pattern takes it all in. We must ride on the Pattern, not on the changes of a moment." She looked at them each in turn, then said, "Uno, are you certain your scouts missed nothing suspicious? Even something small?"

"The Lord Dragon's Rebirth has loosed the bonds of certainty, Moiraine Sedai, and there is never certainty if you fight Myrddraal, but I will stake my life that the scouts did as good a job as any Warder." It was one of the longest speeches Perrin had ever heard out of Uno without any curses. There was sweat on the man's forehead from the effort.

"We all may," Moiraine said. "What Rand did might as well have been a fire on the mountaintop for any Myrddraal within ten miles."

"Maybe . . ." Min began hesitantly. "Maybe you ought to set wards that will keep them out." Lan gave her a hard stare. He sometimes questioned Moiraine's decisions himself, though he seldom did so where anyone could overhear, but he did not approve of others doing the same. Min frowned right back at him. "Well, Myrddraal and Trollocs are bad enough, but at least I can see them. I don't like the idea that one of these . . . these Soulless might sneak in here and slit my throat before I even noticed him."

"The wards I set will hide us from the Soulless as well as from any other Shadowspawn," Moiraine said. "When you are weak, as we are, the best choice is often to hide. If there *is* a Halfman close enough to have. . . . Well, to set wards that would kill them if they tried to enter camp is beyond my abilities, and even if I could, such a warding would only pen us here. Since it is not possible to set two kinds of warding at once, I leave the scouts and the guards—and Lan—to defend us, and use the one warding that may do some good."

"I could make a circuit around the camp," Lan said. "If

there is anything out there that the scouts missed, I will find it." It was not a boast, just a statement of fact. Uno even nodded agreement.

Moiraine shook her head. "If you are needed tonight, my Gaidin, it will be here." Her gaze rose toward the dark mountains around them. "There is a feeling in the air."

"Waiting." The word left Perrin's tongue before he could stop it. When Moiraine looked at him—into him—he wished he had it back.

"Yes," she said. "Waiting. Make sure your guards are especially alert tonight, Uno." There was no need to suggest that the men sleep with their weapons close at hand; Shienarans always did that. "Sleep well," she added to them all, as if there were any chance of that now, and started back for her hut. Lan stayed long enough to spoon up three dishes of stew, then hurried after her, quickly swallowed by the night.

Perrin's eyes shone golden as they followed the Warder through the darkness. "Sleep well," he muttered. The smell of cooked meat suddenly made him queasy. "I have the third watch, Uno?" The Shienaran nodded. "Then I will try to take her advice." Others were coming to the fires, and murmurs of conversation followed him up the slope.

He had a hut to himself, a small thing of logs barely tall enough to stand in, the chinks filled with dried mud. A rough bed, padded with pine boughs beneath a blanket, took up nearly half of it. Whoever had unsaddled his horse had also propped his bow just inside the door. He hung up his belt, with axe and quiver, on a peg, then stripped down to his smallclothes, shivering. The nights were cold still, but cold kept him from sleeping too deeply. In deep sleep, dreams came that he could not shake off.

For a time, with a single blanket over him, he lay staring at the log roof, shivering. Then sleep came, and with it, dreams.

CHAPTER
4

Shadows Sleeping

Cold filled the common room of the inn despite the
fire blazing on the long, stone hearth. Perrin rubbed
his hands before the flames, but he could get no
warmth in them. There was an odd comfort in the cold,
though, as if it were a shield. A shield against what, he
could not think. Something murmured in the back of his
mind, a dim sound only vaguely heard, scratching to get in.

"So you will give it up, then. It is the best thing for you.
Come. Sit, and we will talk."

Perrin turned to look at the speaker. The round tables
scattered about the room were empty except for the lone
man seated in a corner, in the shadows. The rest of the room
seemed in some way hazy, almost an impression rather than
a place, especially anything he was not looking at directly.
He glanced back at the fire; it burned on a brick hearth,
now. Somehow, none of it bothered him. *It should.* But he
could not have said why.

The man beckoned, and Perrin walked closer to his table. A square table. The tables were square. Frowning, he
reached out to finger the tabletop, but pulled his hand back.
There were no lamps in that corner of the room, and despite
the light elsewhere, the man and his table were almost hidden, nearly blended with the dimness.

Perrin had a feeling that he knew the man, but it was
as vague as what he saw out of the corner of his eye. The
fellow was in his middle years, handsome and too well
dressed for a country inn, in dark, nearly black, velvets with
white lace falls at his collar and cuffs. He sat stiffly, sometimes pressing a hand to his chest, as if moving hurt him.

His dark eyes were fixed on Perrin's face; they appeared like glistening points in the shadows.

"Give up what?" Perrin asked.

"That, of course." The man nodded to the axe at Perrin's waist. He sounded surprised, as if it were a conversation they had had before, an old argument taken up again.

Perrin had not realized the axe was there, had not felt the weight of it pulling at his belt. He ran a hand over the half-moon blade and the thick spike that balanced it. The steel felt—solid. More solid than anything else there. Maybe even more solid than he was himself. He kept his hand there, to hold onto something real.

"I have thought of it," he said, "but I do not think I can. Not yet." *Not yet?* The inn seemed to flicker, and the murmur sounded again in his head. *No!* The murmur faded.

"No?" The man smiled, a cold smile. "You are a blacksmith, boy. And a good one, from what I hear. Your hands were made for a hammer, not an axe. Made to make things, not to kill. Go back to that before it is too late."

Perrin found himself nodding. "Yes. But I'm *ta'veren*." He had never said that out loud before. *But he knows it already.* He was sure of that, though he could not say why.

For an instant the man's smile became a grimace, but then it returned in more strength than before. A cold strength. "There are ways to change things, boy. Ways to avoid even fate. Sit, and we will talk of them." The shadows appeared to shift and thicken, to reach out.

Perrin took a step back, keeping well in the light. "I don't think so."

"At least have a drink with me. To years past and years to come. Here, you will see things more clearly after." The cup the man pushed across the table had not been there a moment before. It shone bright silver, and dark, blood-red wine filled it to the brim.

Perrin peered at the man's face. Even to his sharp eyes, the shadows seemed to shroud the other man's features like a Warder's cloak. Darkness molded the man like a caress. There was something about the man's eyes, something he thought he could remember if he tried hard enough. The murmur returned.

"No," he said. He spoke to the soft sound inside his head, but when the man's mouth tightened in anger, a flash of rage suppressed as soon as begun, he decided it would do for the wine as well. "I am not thirsty."

He turned and started for the door. The fireplace was rounded river stones; a few long tables lined by benches filled the room. He suddenly wanted to be outside, anywhere away from this man.

"You will not have many chances," the man said behind him in a hard voice. "Three threads woven together share one another's doom. When one is cut, all are. Fate can kill you, if it does not do worse."

Perrin felt a sudden heat against his back, rising then fading just as quickly, as if the doors of a huge smelting furnace had swung open and closed again. Startled, he turned back to the room. It was empty.

Only a dream, he thought, shivering from the cold, and with that everything shifted.

He stared into the mirror, a part of him not comprehending what he saw, another part accepting. A gilded helmet, worked like a lion's head, sat on his head as if it belonged there. Gold leaf covered his ornately hammered breastplate, and gold-work embellished the plate and mail on his arms and legs. Only the axe at his side was plain. A voice—his own—whispered in his mind that he would take it over any other weapon, had carried it a thousand times, in a hundred battles. *No!* He wanted to take it off, throw it away. *I can't!* There was a sound in his head, louder than a murmur, almost at the level of understanding.

"A man destined for glory."

He spun away from the mirror and found himself staring at the most beautiful woman he had ever seen. He noticed nothing else about the room, cared to see nothing but her. Her eyes were pools of midnight, her skin creamy pale and surely softer, more smooth than her dress of white silk. When she moved toward him, his mouth went dry. He realized that every other woman he had ever seen was clumsy and ill-shaped. He shivered, and wondered why he felt cold.

"A man should grasp his destiny with both hands," she said, smiling. It was almost enough to warm him, that smile. She was tall, less than a hand short of being able to look him in the eyes. Silver combs held hair darker than a raven's wing. A broad belt of silver links banded a waist he could have encircled with his hands.

"Yes," he whispered. Inside him, startlement fought with acceptance. He had no use for glory. But when she said it, he wanted nothing else. "I mean. . . ." The murmuring sound dug at his skull. "No!" It was gone, and for a moment, so was acceptance. Almost. He put a hand to his head, touched the golden helmet, took it off. "I . . . I don't think I want this. It is not mine."

"Don't want it?" She laughed. "What man with blood in his veins would not want glory? As much glory as if you had sounded the Horn of Valere."

"I don't," he said, though a piece of him shouted that he lied. The Horn of Valere. *The Horn rang out, and the wild charge began. Death rode at his shoulder, and yet she waited ahead, too. His lover. His destroyer.* "No! I am a blacksmith."

Her smile was pitying. "Such a little thing to want. You must not listen to those who would try to turn you from your destiny. They would demean you, debase you. Destroy you. Fighting fate can only bring pain. Why choose pain, when you can have glory? When your name can be remembered alongside all the heroes of legend?"

"I am no hero."

"You don't know the half of what you are. Of what you can be. Come, share a cup with me, to destiny and glory." There was a shining silver cup in her hand, filled with blood-red wine. "Drink."

He stared at the cup, frowning. There was something . . . familiar about it. A growling chewed at his brain. "No!" He fought away from it, refusing to listen. "No!"

She held out the golden cup to him. "Drink."

Golden? I thought the cup was. . . . It was. . . . The rest of the thought would not come. But in his confusion the sound came again, inside, gnawing, demanding to be heard. "No," he said. "No!" He looked at the golden helmet in his hands and threw it aside. "I am a blacksmith. I am. . . ." The sound within his head fought him, struggling toward being heard. He wrapped his arms around his head to shut it out, and only shut it in. "I—am—a—man!" he shouted.

Darkness enfolded him, but her voice followed, whispering. "The night is always there, and dreams come to all men. Especially you, my wildling. And I will always be in your dreams."

Stillness.

He lowered his arms. He was back in his own coat and breeches again, sturdy and well made, if plain. Suitable garb for a blacksmith, or any country man. Yet he barely noticed them.

He stood on a low-railed bridge of stone, arching from one wide, flat-topped stone spire to another, spires that rose from depths too far for even his eyes to penetrate. The light would have been dim to any other eyes, and he could not make out from where it came. It just was. Everywhere he looked, left and right, up or down, were more bridges, more spires, and railless ramps. There seemed no end to them, no pattern. Worse, some of those ramps climbed to spire tops that had to be directly above the ones they had left. Splashing water echoed, the sound seeming to come from everywhere at once. He shivered with cold.

Suddenly, from the corner of his eye, he caught a motion, and without thinking, he crouched behind the stone railing. There was danger in being seen. He did not know why, but he knew it was true. He just knew.

Cautiously peering over the top of the rail, he sought what he had seen moving. A flash of white flickered on a distant ramp. A woman, he was sure, though he could not quite make her out. A woman in a white dress, hurrying somewhere.

On a bridge slightly below him, and much closer than the ramp where the woman had been, a man suddenly appeared, tall and dark and slender, the silver in his black hair giving him a distinguished look, his dark green coat thickly embroidered with golden leaves. Gold-work covered his belt and pouch, and gems sparkled on his dagger sheath, and golden fringe encircled his boot tops. Where had he come from?

Another man started across the bridge from the other side, his appearance as sudden as the first man's. Black stripes ran down the puffy sleeves of his red coat, and pale lace hung thick at his collar and cuffs. His boots were so worked with silver that it was hard to see the leather. He was shorter than the man he went to meet, more stocky, with close-cropped hair as white as his lace. Age did not make him frail, though. He strode with the same arrogant strength the other man showed.

The two of them approached each other warily. *Like two horse traders who know the other fellow has a spavined mare to sell*, Perrin thought.

The men began to talk. Perrin strained his ears, but he could not hear so much as a murmur above the splashing echoes. Frowns, and glares, and sharp motions as if half on the point of striking. They did not trust one another. He thought they might even hate each other.

He glanced up, searching for the woman, but she was gone. When he looked back down, another man had joined the first two. And somehow, from somewhere, Perrin knew him with the vagueness of an old memory. A handsome man in his middle years, wearing nearly black velvet and white lace. *An inn*, Perrin thought. *And something before that. Something. . . .* Something a long time ago, it seemed. But the memory would not come.

The first two men stood side by side, now, made uncomfortable allies by the presence of the newcomer. He shouted at them and shook his fist, while they shifted uneasily, refusing to meet his glares. If the two hated each other, they feared him more.

His eyes, Perrin thought. *What is strange about his eyes?*

The tall, dark man began to argue back, slowly at first, then with increasing fervor. The white-haired man joined in, and suddenly their temporary alliance broke. All three shouted at once, each at both of the others in turn. Abruptly the man in dark velvets threw his arms wide, as if demanding an end to it. And an expanding ball of fire enveloped them, hid them, spreading out and out.

Perrin threw his arms around his head and dropped behind the stone railing, huddling there as wind buffeted him and tore at his clothes, a wind as hot as fire. A wind that was fire. Even with his eyes shut, he could see it, flame billowing across everything, flame blowing through everything. The fiery gale roared through him, too; he could feel it, burning, tugging, trying to consume him and scatter the ashes. He yelled, trying to hang onto himself, knowing it was not enough.

And between one heartbeat and the next, the wind was gone. There was no diminishing. One instant a storm of flame pummeled him; the next, utter stillness. The echoes of falling water were the only sound.

Slowly, Perrin sat up, examining himself. His clothes were unsinged and whole, his exposed skin unburned. Only the memory of heat made him believe it had happened. A memory in the mind alone; his body felt no memory of it.

Cautiously he peeked over the railing. Only a few paces of half-melted footing at either end remained of the bridge where the men had been standing. Of them, there was no sign.

A prickling in the hair on the back of his neck made him look up. On a ramp above him and to the right, a shaggy gray wolf stood looking at him.

"No!" He scrambled to his feet and ran. "This is a dream! A nightmare! I want to wake up!" He ran, and his vision blurred. The blurs shifted. A buzzing filled his ears, then faded, and as it went, the shimmering in his eyes steadied.

He shivered with the cold and knew this for a dream, certain and sure, from the first moment. He was dimly aware of some shadowy memory of dreams preceding this, but this one he knew. He had been in this place before, on previous nights, and if he understood nothing of it, he still knew it for a dream. For once, knowing changed nothing.

Huge columns of polished redstone surrounded the open space where he stood, beneath a domed ceiling fifty paces or more above his head. He and another man as big could not have encircled one of those columns with their arms. The floor was paved with great slabs of pale gray stone, hard yet worn by countless generations of feet.

And centered beneath the dome was the reason why all those feet had come to this chamber. A sword, hanging hilt down in the air, apparently without support, seemingly where anyone could reach out and take it. It revolved slowly, as if some breath of air caught it. Yet it was not really a sword. It seemed made of glass, or perhaps crystal, blade and hilt and crossguard, catching such light as there was and shattering it into a thousand glitters and flashes.

He walked toward it and put out his hand, as he had done each time before. He clearly remembered doing it. The hilt hung there in front of his face, within easy reach. A foot from the shining sword, his hand splayed out against empty air as if it had touched stone. As he had known it would. He pushed harder, but he might as well have been shoving against a wall. The sword turned and sparkled, a foot away and as far out of reach as if on the other side of an ocean.

Callandor. He was not certain whether the whisper came inside his head or out; it seemed to echo 'round the columns, as soft as the wind, everywhere at once, insistent. *Callandor. Who wields me wields destiny. Take me, and begin the final journey.*

He took a step back, suddenly frightened. That whisper had never come before. Four times before he had had this dream—he could remember that even now; four nights, one after the other—and this was the first time anything had changed in it.

The Twisted Ones come.

It was a different whisper, from a source he knew, and he jumped as if a Myrddraal had touched him. A wolf stood there among the columns, a mountain wolf, almost waist-high and shaggy white and gray. It stared at him intently with eyes as yellow as his own.

The Twisted Ones come.

"No," Perrin rasped. "No! I will not let you in! I—will—not!"

He clawed his way awake and sat up in his hut, shaking with fear and cold and anger. "I will not," he whispered hoarsely.

The Twisted Ones come.

The thought was clear in his head, but the thought was not his own.

The Twisted Ones come, brother.

CHAPTER
5

Nightmares Walking

Leaping from his bed, Perrin snatched his axe and ran outside, barefoot and wearing nothing but thin linen, heedless of the cold. The moon bathed the clouds with pale white. More than enough light for his eyes, more than enough to see the shapes slipping through the trees from all sides, shapes almost as big as Loial, but with faces distorted by muzzles and beaks, half-human heads wearing horns and feathered crests, stealthy forms stalking on hooves or paws as often as booted feet.

He opened his mouth to shout warning, and suddenly the door of Moiraine's hut burst open and Lan dashed out, sword in hand and shouting, "Trollocs! Wake, for your lives! Trollocs!" Shouts answered him as men began to tumble from their huts, garbed for sleep, which for most meant not at all, but with swords ready. With a bestial roar, the Trollocs rushed forward to be met with steel and cries of "Shienar!" and "The Dragon Reborn!"

Lan was fully clothed—Perrin would have bet the Warder had not slept—and he flung himself among the Trollocs as if his wool were armor. He seemed to dance from one to another, man and sword flowing like water or wind, and where the Warder danced, Trollocs screamed and died.

Moiraine was out in the night as well, dancing her own dance among the Trollocs. Her only apparent weapon was a switch, but where she slashed a Trolloc, a line of flame grew on its flesh. Her free hand threw fiery balls summoned from thin air, and Trollocs howled as flames consumed them, thrashing on the ground.

An entire tree burst into flame from root to crown, then

another, and another. Trollocs shrieked at the sudden light, but they did not stop swinging their spiked axes and swords curved like scythes.

Abruptly Perrin saw Leya step hesitantly out of Moiraine's cabin, halfway around the bowl from him, and all thought of anything else left him. The Tuatha'an woman pressed her back against the log wall, a hand to her throat. The light from the burning trees showed him the pain and horror, the loathing on her face as she watched the carnage. "Hide!" Perrin shouted at her. "Get back inside and hide!" The swelling roar of fighting and dying swallowed his words. He ran toward her. "Hide, Leya! For the love of the Light, hide!"

A Trolloc loomed up over him, a cruelly hooked beak where its mouth and nose should have been. Black mail and spikes covered it from shoulders to knees, and it moved on a hawk's talons as it swung one of those strangely curved swords. It smelled of sweat and dirt and blood.

Perrin crouched under the slash, shouting wordlessly as he struck out with his axe. He knew he should have been afraid, but urgency suppressed fear. All that mattered was that he had to reach Leya, had to get her to safety, and the Trolloc was in the way.

The Trolloc fell, roaring and kicking; Perrin did not know where he had hit it, or if it were dying or merely hurt. He leaped over it, where it lay thrashing, and ran scrambling up the slope.

Burning trees cast lurid shadows across the small valley. A flickering shadow beside Moiraine's hut suddenly resolved into a Trolloc, goat-snouted and horned. Gripping a wildly spiked axe with both hands, it seemed on the point of rushing down into the fray when its eyes fell on Leya.

"No!" Perrin shouted. "Light, no!" Rocks skittered away under his bare feet; he did not feel the bruises. The Trolloc's axe rose. "Leyaaaaaaaa!"

At the last instant the Trolloc spun, axe flashing toward Perrin. He threw himself down, yelling as steel scored his back. Desperately he flung out a hand, caught a goat hoof, and pulled with all his strength. The Trolloc's feet came out from under it, and it fell with a crash, but as it slid down the slope, it seized Perrin in hands big enough to make two of his, pulling him along to roll over and over. The stink of it filled his nostrils, goat-stench and sour man-sweat. Massive arms snaked around his chest, squeezing the air out; his ribs creaked on the point of breaking. The Trolloc's axe was gone in the fall, but blunt goat-teeth sank into Perrin's shoulder, powerful jaws chewing. He groaned as pain jolted down his left arm. His lungs labored for breath, and blackness crept in on the edges of his vision, but dimly he was aware that his other arm was free, that somehow he had held on to his own axe. He held it short on the handle, like a hammer, with the spike foremost. With a roar that took the last of his air, he drove the spike into the Trolloc's temple. Soundlessly it convulsed, limbs flinging wide, hurling him away. By instinct alone his hand tightened on the axe, ripping it loose as the Trolloc slid further down the slope, still twitching.

For a moment Perrin lay there, fighting for breath. The gash across his back burned, and he felt the wetness of blood. His shoulder protested as he pushed himself up. "Leya?"

She was still there, huddled in front of the hut, not more than ten paces upslope. And watching him with such a look on her face that he could barely meet her eyes.

"Don't pity me!" he growled at her. "Don't you—!"

The Myrddraal's leap from the roof of the hut seemed to take too long, and its dead black cloak hung during the slow fall as if the Halfman were standing on the ground already. Its eyeless gaze was fixed on Perrin. It smelled like death.

Cold seeped through Perrin's arms and legs as the Myrddraal stared at him. His chest felt like a lump of ice. "Leya," he whispered. It was all he could do not to run. "Leya, please hide. Please."

The Halfman started toward him, slowly, confident that fear held him in a snare. It moved like a snake, unlimbering a sword so black only the burning trees made it visible. "Cut one leg of the tripod," it said softly, "and all fall down." Its voice sounded like dry-rotted leather crumbling.

Suddenly Leya moved, throwing herself forward, attempting to wrap her arms around the Myrddraal's legs. It gave an almost casual backwards swing of its dark sword, never even looking around, and she crumpled.

Tears started in the corners of Perrin's eyes. *I should have helped her . . . saved her. I should have done . . .*

something! But so long as the Myrddraal stared at him with its eyeless gaze, it was an effort even to think.

We come, brother. We come, Young Bull.

The words inside his mind made his head ring like a struck bell; the reverberations shivered through him. With the words came the wolves, scores of them, flooding into his mind as he was aware of them flooding into the bowl-shaped valley. Mountain wolves almost as tall as a man's waist, all white and gray, coming out of the night at the run, aware of the two-legs' surprise as they darted in to take on the Twisted Ones. Wolves filled him till he could barely remember being a man. His eyes gathered the light, shining golden yellow. And the Halfman stopped its advance as if suddenly uncertain.

"Fade," Perrin said roughly, but then a different name came to him, from the wolves. Trollocs, the Twisted Ones, made during the War of the Shadow from melding men and animals, were bad enough, but the Myrddraal—. "Neverborn!" Young Bull spat. Lip curling back in a snarl, he threw himself at the Myrddraal.

It moved like a viper, sinuous and deadly, black sword quick as lightning, but he was Young Bull. That was what the wolves called him. Young Bull, with horns of steel that he wielded with his hands. He was one with the wolves. He was a wolf, and any wolf would die a hundred times over to see one of the Neverborn go down. The Fade fell back before him, its darting blade now trying to deflect his slashes.

Hamstring and throat, that was how wolves killed. Young Bull suddenly threw himself to one side and dropped to a knee, axe slicing across the back of the Halfman's knee. It screamed—a bone-burrowing sound to raise his hair at any other time—and fell, catching itself with one hand. The Halfman—the Neverborn—still held its sword firmly, but before it could set itself, Young Bull's axe struck again. Half severed, the Myrddraal's head flopped over to hang down its back; yet still leaning there on one hand, the Neverborn slashed wildly with its sword. Neverborn were always long in dying.

From the wolves as much as his own eyes Young Bull received impressions of Trollocs thrashing on the ground, shrieking, untouched by wolf or man. Those would have been linked to this Myrddraal, and would die when it did—if no one killed them first.

The urge to rush down the slope and join his brothers, join in killing the Twisted Ones, in hunting the remaining Neverborn, was strong, but a buried fragment that was still man remembered. *Leya.*

He dropped his axe and turned her over gently. Blood covered her face, and her eyes stared up at him, glazed with death. An accusing stare, it seemed to him. "I tried," he told her. "I tried to save you." Her stare did not change. "What else could I have done? It would have killed you if I hadn't killed it!"

Come, Young Bull. Come kill the Twisted Ones.

Wolf rolled over him, enveloped him. Letting Leya back down, Perrin took up his axe, blade gleaming wetly. His eyes shone as he raced down the rocky slope. He was Young Bull.

Trees scattered around the bowl-shaped valley burned like torches; a tall pine flared into flame as Young Bull joined the battle. The night air flashed actinic blue, like sheet lightning, as Lan engaged another Myrddraal, ancient Aes Sedai–made steel meeting black steel wrought in Thakan'dar, in the shadow of Shayol Ghul. Loial wielded a quarterstaff the size of a fence rail, the whirling timber marking a space no Trolloc entered without falling. Men fought desperately in the dancing shadows, but Young Bull—Perrin—noted in a distant way that too many of the Shienaran two-legs were down.

The brothers and sisters fought in small packs of three or four, dodging scythe-like swords and spiked axes, darting in with slashing teeth to sever hamstrings, lunging to bite out throats as their prey fell. There was no honor in the way they fought, no glory, no mercy. They had not come for battle, but to kill. Young Bull joined one of the small packs, the blade of his axe serving for teeth.

He no longer thought of the greater battle. There was only the Trolloc he and the wolves—the brothers—cut off from the rest and brought down. Then there would be another, and another, and another, until none were left. None here, none anywhere. He felt the urge to hurl the axe aside and use his teeth, to run on all fours as his brothers did. Run through the high mountain passes. Run belly-deep in powdery snow pursuing deer. Run, with the cold wind ruffling his fur. He snarled with his brothers, and Trollocs howled with fear at his yellow-eyed gaze even more than they did at the other wolves.

Abruptly he realized there were no more Trollocs standing anywhere in the bowl, though he could feel his brothers pursuing others as they fled. A pack of seven had a different prey, somewhere out there in the darkness. One of the Neverborn ran for its hard-footed four-legs—its horse, a distant part of him said—and his brothers followed, noses filled with its scent, its essence of death. Inside his head, he was with them, seeing with their eyes. As they closed in, the Neverborn turned, cursing, black blade and black-clad Neverborn like part of the night. But night was where his brothers and sisters hunted.

Young Bull snarled as the first brother died, its death pain lancing him, yet the others closed in and more brothers and sisters died, but snapping jaws dragged the Neverborn down. It fought back with its own teeth now, ripping out throats, slashing with fingernails that sliced skin and flesh like the hard claws the two-legs carried, but brothers savaged it even as they died. Finally a lone sister heaved herself out of the still-twitching pile and staggered to one side. Morning Mist, she was called, but as with all their names, it was more than that: a frosty morning with the bite of snows yet to come already in the air, and the mist curling thick across the valley, swirling with the sharp breeze that carried the promise of good hunting. Raising her head, Morning Mist howled to the cloud-hidden moon, mourning her dead.

Young Bull threw back his head and howled with her, mourned with her.

When he lowered his head, Min was staring at him. "Are you all right, Perrin?" she asked hesitantly. There was a bruise on her cheek, and a sleeve half torn from her coat. She had a cudgel in one hand and a dagger in the other, and there was blood and hair on both.

They were all staring at him, he saw, all those who were still on their feet. Loial, leaning wearily on his tall staff. Shienarans, who had been carrying their fallen down to where Moiraine crouched over one of their number with Lan standing at her side. Even the Aes Sedai was looking his way. The burning trees, like huge torches, cast a wavering light.

Dead Trollocs lay everywhere. There were more Shienarans down than standing, and the bodies of his brothers were scattered among them. So many. . . .

Perrin realized he wanted to howl again. Frantically he walled himself off from contact with the wolves. Images seeped through, emotions, as he tried to stop them. Finally, though, he could no longer feel them, feel their pain, or their anger, or the desire to hunt the Twisted Ones, or to run. . . . He gave himself a shake. The wound on his back burned like fire, and his torn shoulder felt as if it had been hammered on an anvil. His bare feet, scraped and bruised, throbbed with his pain. The smell of blood was everywhere. The smell of Trollocs, and death.

"I. . . . I'm all right, Min."

"You fought well, blacksmith," Lan said. The Warder raised his still-bloody sword above his head. *"Tai'shar Manetheren! Tai'shar Andor!"* True Blood of Manetheren. True Blood of Andor.

The Shienarans still standing—so few—lifted their blades and joined him. *"Tai'shar Manetheren! Tai'shar Andor!"*

Loial nodded. *"Ta'veren,"* he added.

Perrin lowered his eyes in embarrassment. Lan had saved him from the questions he did not want to answer, but had given him an honor he did not deserve. The others did not understand. He wondered what they would say if they knew the truth. Min moved closer, and he muttered, "Leya's dead. I couldn't. . . . I almost reached her in time."

"It wouldn't have made any difference," she said softly. "You know that." She leaned to look at his back, and winced. "Moiraine will take care of that for you. She's Healing those she can."

Perrin nodded. His back felt sticky with drying blood all the way to his waist, but despite the pain he hardly noticed it. *Light, I almost didn't come back that time. I can't let that happen again. I won't. Never again!*

But when he was with the wolves, it was all so different. He did not have to worry about strangers being afraid of him just because he was big, then. There was no one thinking he was slow-witted just because he tried to be careful. Wolves knew each other even if they had never met before, and with them he was just another wolf.

No! His hands tightened on the haft of his axe. *No!* He gave a start as Masema suddenly spoke up.

"It was a sign," the Shienaran said, turning in a circle to address everyone. There was blood on his arms and his chest—he had fought in nothing but his breeches—and he moved with a limp, but the light in his eyes was as fervent as it had ever been. More fervent. "A sign to confirm our faith. Even wolves came to fight for the Dragon Reborn. In the Last Battle, the Lord Dragon will summon even the beasts of the forest to fight at our sides. It is a sign for us to go forth. Only Darkfriends will fail to join us." Two of the Shienarans nodded.

"You shut your bloody mouth, Masema!" Uno snapped. He seemed untouched, but then Uno had been fighting Trollocs since before Perrin was born. Yet he sagged with weariness; only the painted eye on his eyepatch seemed fresh. "We'll flaming go forth when the Lord Dragon bloody well tells us, and not before! You sheep-headed farmers flaming remember that!" The one-eyed man looked at the growing row of men being tended by Moiraine—few were able to as much as sit up, even after she was done with them—and shook his head. "At least we'll have plenty of flaming wolf hides to keep the wounded warm."

"No!" The Shienarans seemed surprised at the vehemence in Perrin's voice. "They fought for us, and we'll bury them with our dead."

Uno frowned, and opened his mouth as if to argue, but Perrin fixed him with a steady, yellow-eyed stare. It was the Shienaran who dropped his gaze first, and nodded.

Perrin cleared his throat, embarrassed all over again as Uno gave orders for the Shienarans who were fit to gather the dead wolves. Min was squinting at him the way she did when she saw things. "Where's Rand?" he asked her.

"Out there in the dark," she said, nodding upslope without taking her eyes off him. "He will not talk to anyone. He just sits there, snapping at anyone who comes near him."

"He will talk to me," Perrin said. She followed him, protesting all the while that he ought to wait until Moiraine had seen to his injuries. *Light, what does she see when she looks at me? I don't want to know.*

Rand was seated on the ground just beyond the light

of the burning trees, with his back against the trunk of a stunted oak. Staring at nothing, he had his arms wrapped around himself, hands under his red coat, as if feeling the cold. He did not appear to notice their approach. Min sat down beside him, but he did not move even when she laid a hand on his arm. Even here Perrin smelled blood, and not only his own.

"Rand," Perrin began, but Rand cut him off.

"Do you know what I did during the fight?" Still staring into the distance, Rand addressed the night. "Nothing! Nothing useful. At first, when I reached out for the True Source, I couldn't touch it, couldn't grasp it. It kept sliding away. Then, when I finally had hold of it, I was going to burn them all, burn all the Trollocs and Fades. And all I could do was set fire to some trees." He shook with silent laughter, then stopped with a pained grimace. "*Saidin* filled me till I thought I'd explode like fireworks. I had to channel it somewhere, get rid of it before it burned me up, and I found myself thinking about pulling the mountain down and burying the Trollocs. I almost tried. That was my fight. Not against the Trollocs. Against myself. To keep from burying us all under the mountain."

Min gave Perrin a pained look, as if asking for help.

"We . . . dealt with them, Rand," Perrin said. He shivered, thinking of all the wounded men down below. And the dead. *Better that than the mountain down on top of us.* "We didn't need you."

Rand's head fell back against the tree and his eyes closed. "I felt them coming," he said, nearly whispering. "I didn't know what it was, though. They feel like the taint on *saidin*. And *saidin* is always there, calling to me, singing to me. By the time I knew the difference, Lan was already shouting his warning. If I could only control it, I could have given warning before they were even close. But half the time when I actually manage to touch *saidin*, I don't know what I am doing at all. The flow of it just sweeps me along. I could have given warning, though."

Perrin shifted his bruised feet uncomfortably. "We had warning enough." He knew he sounded as if he were trying to convince himself. *I could have given warning, too, if I'd talked with the wolves. They knew there were Trollocs and Fades in the mountains. They were trying to tell me.* But he wondered: If he did not keep the wolves out of his mind, might he not be running with them now? There had been a man, Elyas Machera, who also could talk to wolves. Elyas ran with the wolves all the time, yet seemed able to remember he was a man. But he had never told Perrin how he did it, and Perrin had not seen him in a long time.

The crunch of boots on rock announced two people coming, and a swirl of air carried their scents to Perrin. He was careful not to speak names, though, until Lan and Moiraine were close enough for even ordinary eyes to make them out.

The Warder had a hand under the Aes Sedai's arm, as if trying to support her without letting her know it. Moiraine's eyes were haggard, and she carried a small, age-dark ivory carving of a woman in one hand. Perrin knew it for an *angreal*, a remnant from the Age of Legends that allowed an Aes Sedai to safely channel more of the Power than she could alone. It was a measure of her tiredness that she was using it for Healing.

Min got to her feet to help Moiraine, but the Aes Sedai motioned her away. "Everyone else is seen to," she told Min. "When I am done here, I can rest." She shook off Lan as well, and a look of concentration appeared on her face as she traced a cool hand across Perrin's bleeding shoulder, then along the wound on his back. Her touch made his skin tingle. "This is not too bad," she said. "The bruising of your shoulder goes deep, but the gashes are shallow. Brace yourself. This will not hurt, but. . . ."

He had never found it easy being near someone he knew was channeling the One Power, and still less if it actually involved him. Yet there had been one or two of those times, and he thought he had some idea what the channeling entailed, but those Healings had been minor, simply washing away tiredness when Moiraine could not afford to have him weary. They had been nothing like this.

The Aes Sedai's eyes suddenly seemed to be seeing inside him, seeing through him. He gasped and almost dropped his axe. He could feel the skin on his back crawling, muscles writhing as they knit back together. His shoulder quivered uncontrollably, and everything blurred. Cold seared him to the bone, then deeper still. He had the impression of moving, falling, flying; he could not tell which, but he felt as if he were rushing—somewhere, somehow—at great speed, forever. After an eternity the world came into focus again. Moiraine was stepping back, half staggering until Lan caught her arm.

Gaping, Perrin looked down at his shoulder. The gashes and bruises were gone; not so much as a twinge remained. He twisted carefully, but the pain in his back had vanished as well. And his feet no longer hurt; he did not need to look to know all the bruises and scrapes were gone. His stomach rumbled loudly.

"You should eat as soon as you can," Moiraine told him. "A good bit of the strength for that came from you. You need to replace it."

Hunger—and images of food—were already filling Perrin's head. Blood rare beef, and venison, and mutton, and. . . . With an effort he made himself stop thinking of meat. He would find some of those roots that smelled like turnips when they were roasted. His stomach growled in protest.

"There's barely even a scar, blacksmith," Lan said behind him.

"Most of the wolves who were hurt made their own way to the forest," Moiraine said, knuckling her back and stretching, "but I Healed those I could find." Perrin gave her a sharp look, yet she seemed to be just making conversation. "Perhaps they came for their own reasons, yet we would likely all be dead without them." Perrin shifted uneasily and dropped his eyes.

The Aes Sedai reached toward the bruise on Min's cheek, but Min stepped back, saying, "I'm not really hurt, and you're tired. I've had worse falling over my own feet."

Moiraine smiled and let her hand fall. Lan took her arm; she swayed in his grip. "Very well. And what of you, Rand? Did you take any hurt? Even a nick from a Myrddraal's blade can be deadly, and some Trolloc blades are almost as bad."

Perrin noticed something for the first time. "Rand, your coat is wet."

Rand pulled his right hand from under his coat, a hand covered in blood. "Not a Myrddraal," he said absently, peering at his hand. "Not even a Trolloc. The wound I took at Falme broke open."

Moiraine hissed and jerked her arm free from Lan, half fell to her knees beside Rand. Pulling back the side of his coat, she studied his wound. Perrin could not see it, for her head was in the way, but the smell of blood was stronger, now. Moiraine's hands moved, and Rand grimaced in pain. "'The blood of the Dragon Reborn on the rocks of Shayol Ghul will free mankind from the Shadow.' Isn't that what the Prophecies of the Dragon say?"

"Who told you that?" Moiraine said sharply.

"If you could get me to Shayol Ghul now," Rand said drowsily, "by Waygate or Portal Stone, there could be an end to it. No more dying. No more dreams. No more."

"If it were as simple as that," Moiraine said grimly, "I would, one way or another, but not all in *The Karaethon Cycle* can be taken at its face. For every thing it says straight out, there are ten that could mean a hundred different things. Do not think you know anything at all of what *must* be, even if someone has told you the whole of the Prophecies." She paused, as if gathering strength. Her grip tightened on the *angreal*, and her free hand slid along Rand's side as if it were not covered in blood. "Brace yourself."

Suddenly Rand's eyes opened wide, and he sat straight up, gasping and staring and shivering. Perrin had thought, when she Healed him, that it went on forever, but in moments she was easing Rand back against the oak.

"I have . . . done as much as I can," she said faintly. "As much as I can. You must be careful. It could break open again if. . . ." As her voice trailed off, she fell.

Rand caught her, but Lan was there in an instant to scoop her up. As the Warder did so, a look passed across his face, a look as close to tenderness as Perrin ever expected to see from Lan.

"Exhausted," the Warder said. "She has cared for everyone else, but there's no one to take her fatigue. I will put her to bed."

"There's Rand," Min said slowly, but the Warder shook his head.

"It isn't that I do not think you would try, sheepherder," he said, "but you know so little you might as soon kill her as help her."

"That's right," Rand said bitterly. "I'm not to be trusted. Lews Therin Kinslayer killed everyone close to him. Maybe I'll do the same before I am done."

"Pull yourself together, sheepherder," Lan said harshly. "The whole world rides on your shoulders. Remember you're a man, and do what needs to be done."

Rand looked up at the Warder, and surprisingly, all of his bitterness seemed to be gone. "I will fight the best I can," he said. "Because there's no one else, and it has to be done, and the duty is mine. I'll fight, but I do not have to like what I've become." He closed his eyes as if going to sleep. "I will fight. Dreams. . . ."

Lan stared down at him a moment, then nodded. He raised his head to look across Moiraine at Perrin and Min. "Get him to his bed, then see to some sleep yourselves. We have plans to make, and the Light alone knows what happens next."

CHAPTER
6

The Hunt Begins

P errin did not expect to sleep, but a stomach stuffed with cold stew—his resolve about the roots had lasted until the smells of supper's leftovers hit his nose—and bone weariness pulled him down on his bed. If he dreamed, he did not remember. He awoke to Lan shaking his shoulders, dawn through the open door turning the Warder to a shadow haloed with light.

"Rand is gone," was all Lan said before he left at a run, but it was more than enough.

Perrin dragged himself up yawning and dressed quickly in the early chill. Outside, only a handful of Shienarans were in sight, using their horses to drag Trolloc bodies into the woods, and most of those moved as if they should be in a sickbed. A body took time to build back the strength that being Healed took.

Perrin's stomach muttered at him, and his nose tested the breeze in the hope that someone had already started cooking. He was ready to eat those turnip-like roots, raw if need be. There were only the lingering stench of slain Myrddraal, the smells of dead Trollocs and men, alive and dead, of horses and the trees. And dead wolves.

Moiraine's hut, high on the other side of the bowl, seemed a center of activity. Min hurried inside, and moments later Masema came out, then Uno. At a trot the one-eyed man vanished into the trees, toward the sheer rock wall beyond the hut, while the other Shienaran limped down the slope.

Perrin started toward the hut. As he splashed across the shallow stream, he met Masema. The Shienaran's face was haggard, the scar on his cheek prominent, and his eyes even more sunken than usual. In the middle of the stream, he raised his head suddenly and caught Perrin's coat sleeve.

"You're from his village," Masema said hoarsely. "You must know. Why did the Lord Dragon abandon us? What sin did we commit?"

"Sin? What are you talking about? Whyever Rand went, it was nothing you did or didn't do." Masema did not appear satisfied; he kept his grip on Perrin's sleeve, peering into his face as if there were answers there. Icy water began to seep into Perrin's left boot. "Masema," he said carefully, "whatever the Lord Dragon did, it was according to his plan. The Lord Dragon would not abandon us." *Or would he? If I were in his place, would I?*

Masema nodded slowly. "Yes. Yes, I see that, now. He has gone out alone to spread the word of his coming. We must spread the word, too. Yes." He limped on across the stream, muttering to himself.

Squelching at every other step, Perrin climbed to Moiraine's hut and knocked. There was no answer. He hesitated a moment, then went in.

The outer room, where Lan slept, was as stark and simple as Perrin's own hut, with a rough bed built against one wall, a few pegs for hanging possessions, and a single shelf. Not much light entered through the open door, and the only other illumination came from crude lamps on the shelf, slivers of oily fat-wood wedged into cracks in pieces of rock. They gave off thin streamers of smoke that made a layer of haze under the roof. Perrin's nose wrinkled at the smell.

The low roof was only a little higher than his head. Loial's head actually brushed it, even seated as he was on one end of Lan's bed, with his knees drawn up to make himself small. The Ogier's tufted ears twitched uneasily. Min sat cross-legged on the dirt floor beside the door that led to Moiraine's room, while the Aes Sedai paced back and forth in thought. Dark thoughts, they must have been. Three paces each way was all she had, but she made vigorous use of the space, the calm on her face belied by the quickness of her step.

"I think Masema is going crazy," Perrin said.

Min sniffed. "With him, how can you tell?"

Moiraine rounded on him, a tightness to her mouth. Her

voice was soft. Too soft. "Is Masema the most important thing in your mind this morning, Perrin Aybara?"

"No. I'd like to know when Rand left, and why. Did anyone see him go? Does anyone know where he went?" He made himself meet her look with one just as level and firm. It was not easy. He loomed over her, but she was Aes Sedai. "Is this of your making, Moiraine? Did you rein him in until he was so impatient he'd go anywhere, do anything, just to stop sitting still?" Loial's ears went stiff, and he motioned a surreptitious warning with one thick-fingered hand.

Moiraine studied Perrin with her head tilted to one side, and it was all he could do not to drop his eyes. "This is none of my doing," she said. "He left sometime during the night. When and how and why, I yet hope to learn."

Loial's shoulders heaved in a quiet sigh of relief. Quiet for an Ogier, it sounded like steam rushing out from quenching red-hot iron. "Never anger an Aes Sedai," he said in a whisper obviously meant just for himself, but audible to everyone. "'Better to embrace the sun than to anger an Aes Sedai.'"

Min reached up enough to hand Perrin a folded piece of paper. "Loial went to see him after we got him to bed last night, and Rand asked to borrow pen and paper and ink."

The Ogier's ears jerked, and he frowned worriedly until his long eyebrows hung down on his cheeks. "I did not know what he was planning. I didn't."

"We know that," Min said. "No one is accusing you of anything, Loial."

Moiraine frowned at the paper, but she did not try to stop Perrin from reading. It was in Rand's hand.

What I do, I do because there is no other way. He is hunting me again, and this time one of us has to die, I think. There is no need for those around me to die, also. Too many have died for me already. I do not want to die either, and will not, if I can manage it. There are lies in dreams, and death, but dreams hold truth, too.

That was all, with no signature. There was no need for Perrin to wonder who Rand meant by "he." For Rand, for all of them, there could be only one. Ba'alzamon.

"He left that tucked under the door there," Min said in a tight voice. "He took some old clothes the Shienarans had hanging out to dry, and his flute, and a horse. Nothing else but a little food, as far as we can tell. None of the guards saw him go, and last night they would have seen a mouse creeping."

"And would it have done any good if they had?" Moiraine said calmly. "Would any of them have stopped the *Lord Dragon*, or even challenged him? Some of them—Masema for one—would slit their own throats if the *Lord Dragon* told them to."

It was Perrin's turn to study her. "Did you expect anything else? They swore to follow him. Light, Moiraine, he'd never have named himself Dragon if not for you. What did you expect of them?" She did not speak, and he went on more quietly. "Do you believe, Moiraine? That he's really the Dragon Reborn? Or do you just think he's someone you can use before the One Power kills him or drives him mad?"

"Go easy, Perrin," Loial said. "Not so angry."

"I'll go easy when she answers me. Well, Moiraine?"

"He is what he is," she said sharply.

"You said the Pattern would force him to the right path eventually. Is that what this is, or is he just trying to get away from you?" For a moment he thought he had gone too far—her dark eyes sparkled with anger—but he refused to back down. "Well?"

Moiraine took a deep breath. "This may well be what the Pattern has chosen, yet I did not mean for him to go off alone. For all his power, he is as defenseless as a babe in many ways, and as ignorant of the world. He channels, but he has no control over whether or not the One Power comes when he reaches for it and almost as little over what he does with it if it does come. The power itself will kill him before he has a chance to go mad if he does not learn that control. There is so much he must learn, yet. He wants to run before he has learned to walk."

"You split hairs and lay false trails, Moiraine." Perrin snorted. "If he is what you say he is, did it never occur to you that he might know what he has to do better than you?"

"He is what he is," she repeated firmly, "but I must keep him alive if he is to do anything. He will fulfill no prophecies dead, and even if he manages to avoid Darkfriends and Shadowspawn, there are a thousand other hands ready to slay him. All it will take is a hint of the hundredth part of what he is. Yet if that were all he might face, I would not worry half so much as I do. There are the Forsaken to be accounted for."

Perrin gave a start; from the corner, Loial moaned. "'The Dark One and all the Forsaken are bound in Shayol Ghul,'" Perrin began by rote, but she gave him no time to finish.

"The seals are weakening, Perrin. Some are broken, though the world does not know that. Must not know that. The Father of Lies is not free. Yet. But as the seals weaken, more and more, which of the Forsaken may be loosed already? Lanfear? Sammael? Asmodean, or Be'lal, or Ravhin? Ishamael himself, the Betrayer of Hope? They were thirteen altogether, Perrin, and bound in the sealing, not in the prison that holds the Dark One. Thirteen of the most powerful Aes Sedai of the Age of Legends, the weakest of them stronger than the ten strongest Aes Sedai living today, the most ignorant with all the knowledge of the Age of Legends. And every man and woman of them gave up the Light and dedicated their souls to the Shadow. What if they are free, and out there waiting for him? I will not let them have him."

Perrin shivered, partly from the icy iron in her last words, and partly from thought of the Forsaken. He did not want to think of even one of the Forsaken loose in the world. His mother had frightened him with those names when he was little. *Ishamael comes for boys who do not tell their mothers the truth. Lanfear waits in the night for boys who do not go to bed when they are supposed to.* Being older did not help, not when he knew now they were all real. Not when Moiraine said they might be free.

"Bound in Shayol Ghul," he whispered, and wished he still believed it. Troubled, he studied Rand's letter again. "Dreams. He was talking about dreams yesterday, too."

Moiraine stepped closer, and peered up into his face. "Dreams?" Lan and Uno came in, but she waved them to silence. The small room was more than crowded now, with five people in it besides the Ogier. "What dreams have *you* had the last few days, Perrin?" She ignored his protest that there was nothing wrong with his dreams. "Tell me," she insisted. "What dream have you had that was not ordinary? Tell me." Her gaze seized him like smithy tongs, willing him to speak.

He looked at the others—they were all watching him fixedly, even Min—then hesitantly told of the one dream that seemed unusual to him, the dream that came every night. The dream of the sword he could not touch. He did not mention the wolf that had appeared in the last.

"Callandor," Lan breathed when he was done. Rock-hard face or no, he looked stunned.

"Yes," Moiraine said, "but we must be absolutely certain. Speak to the others." As Lan hurried out, she turned to Uno. "And what of your dreams? Did you dream of a sword, too?"

The Shienaran shifted his feet. The red eye painted on his patch stared straight at Moiraine, but his real eye blinked and wavered. "I dream about flam—uh, about swords all the time, Moiraine Sedai," he said stiffly. "I suppose I've dreamed about a sword the last few nights. I don't remember my dreams the way Lord Perrin here does."

Moiraine said, "Loial?"

"My dreams are always the same, Moiraine Sedai. The groves, and the Great Trees, and the *stedding.* We Ogier always dream of the *stedding* when we are away from them."

The Aes Sedai turned back to Perrin.

"It was just a dream," he said. "Nothing but a dream."

"I doubt it," she said. "You describe the hall called the Heart of the Stone, in the fortress called the Stone of Tear, as if you had stood in it. And the shining sword is *Callandor,* the Sword That Is Not a Sword, the Sword That Cannot Be Touched."

Loial sat up straight, bumping his head on the roof. He did not seem to notice. "The Prophecies of the Dragon say the Stone of Tear will never fall till *Callandor* is wielded by the Dragon's hand. The fall of the Stone of Tear will be one of the greatest signs of the Dragon's Rebirth. If Rand holds *Callandor,* the whole world must acknowledge him as the Dragon."

"Perhaps." The word floated from the Aes Sedai's lips like a shard of ice on still water.

"Perhaps?" Perrin said. "Perhaps? I thought that was the final sign, the last thing to fulfill your Prophecies."

"Neither the first nor the last," Moiraine said. "*Callandor* will be but one fulfillment of *The Karaethon Cycle*, as his birth on the slopes of Dragonmount was the first. He has yet to break the nations, or shatter the world. Even scholars who have studied the Prophecies for their entire lives do not know how to interpret them all. What does it mean that he 'shall slay his people with the sword of peace, and destroy them with the leaf'? What does it meant that he 'shall bind the nine moons to serve him'? Yet these are given equal weight with *Callandor* in the *Cycle*. There are others. What 'wounds of madness and cutting of hope' has he healed? What chains has he broken, and who put into chains? And some are so obscure that he may already have fulfilled them, although I am not aware of it. But, no. *Callandor* is far from the end of it."

Perrin shrugged uneasily. He knew only bits and pieces of the Prophecies; he had liked hearing them even less since Rand had let Moiraine put that banner in his hands. No, it had been before that, even. Since a journey by Portal Stone had convinced him his life was bound to Rand's.

Moiraine was continuing. "If you think he has simply to put out his hand, Loial son of Arent son of Halan, you are a fool, as is he if he thinks it. Even if he lives to reach Tear, he may never attain the Stone.

"Tairens have no love for the One Power, and less for any man claiming to be the Dragon. Channeling is outlawed, and Aes Sedai are tolerated at best, so long as they do not channel. Telling the Prophecies of the Dragon, or even possessing a copy of them, is enough to put you in prison, in Tear. And no one enters the Stone of Tear without permission of the High Lords; none but the High Lords themselves enter the Heart of the Stone. He is not ready for this. Not ready."

Perrin grunted softly. *The Stone would never fall till the Dragon Reborn held Callandor. How in the Light is he supposed to reach it—inside a bloody fortress!—before the fortress falls? It is madness!*

"Why are we just sitting here?" Min burst out. "If Rand is going to Tear, why aren't we following him? He could be killed, or . . . or. . . . Why are we sitting here?"

Moiraine put a hand on Min's head. "Because I must be sure," she said gently. "It is not comfortable being chosen

by the Wheel, to be great or to be near greatness. The chosen of the Wheel can only take what comes."

"I am tired of taking what comes." Min scrubbed a hand
across her eyes. Perrin thought he saw tears. "Rand could
be dying while we wait." Moiraine smoothed Min's hair;
there was a look almost of pity on the Aes Sedai's face.

Perrin sat down on the end of Lan's bed opposite Loial.
The smell of people was thick in the room—people and
worry and fear; Loial smelled of books and trees as well
as worry. It felt like a trap, with the walls around them, and
all so close. The burning slivers stank. "How can my dream
tell where Rand is going?" he asked. "It was my dream."

"Those who can channel the One Power," Moiraine
said quietly, "those who are particularly strong in Spirit,
can sometimes force their dreams on others." She did not
stop her soothing of Min. "Especially on those who are—
susceptible. I do not believe Rand did it on purpose, but the
dreams of those touching the True Source can be powerful.
For one as strong as he, they could possibly seize an entire
village, or perhaps even a city. He knows little of what he
does, and even less of how to control it."

"Then why didn't you have it, too?" he demanded. "Or
Lan." Uno stared straight ahead, looking as if he would
rather be anywhere else, and Loial's ears wilted. Perrin was
too tired and too hungry to care whether he showed proper
respect for an Aes Sedai. And too angry, as well, he realized. "Why?"

Moiraine answered calmly. "Aes Sedai learn to shield
their dreams. I do it without thinking, when I sleep. Warders are given something much the same in the bonding. The
Gaidin could not do what they must if the Shadow could
steal into their dreams. We are all vulnerable when we
sleep, and the Shadow is strong in the night."

"There's always something new from you," Perrin growled.
"Can't you tell us what to expect once in a while, instead of
explaining after it happens?" Uno looked as though he was
trying to think of a reason to leave.

Moiraine gave Perrin a flat look. "You want me to share
a lifetime of knowledge with you in a single afternoon? Or
even a single year? I will tell you this. Be wary of dreams,
Perrin Aybara. Be very wary of dreams."

He pulled his eyes away from hers. "I am," he murmured. "I am."

After that, silence, and no one seemed to want to break it. Min sat staring at her crossed ankles, but apparently taking some comfort from Moiraine's presence. Uno stood against the wall, not looking at anyone. Loial forgot himself enough to pull a book from his coat pocket and try to read in the dim light. The wait was long, and far from easy for Perrin. *It's not the Shadow in my dreams I'm afraid of. It's wolves. I will not let them in. I won't!*

Lan returned, and Moiraine straightened eagerly. The Warder answered the question in her eyes. "Half of them remember dreaming of swords the last four nights running. Some remember a place with great columns, and five say the sword was crystal, or glass. Masema says he saw Rand holding it last night."

"That one would," Moiraine said. She rubbed her hands together briskly; she seemed suddenly full of energy. "Now I *am* certain. Though I still wish I knew how he left here unseen. If he has rediscovered some Talent from the Age of Legends. . . ."

Lan looked at Uno, and the one-eyed man shrugged in dismay. "I bloody forgot, with all this flaming talk about bloo—" He cleared his throat, shooting a glance at Moiraine. She looked back expectantly, and he went on. "I mean . . . uh . . . that is, I followed the Lord Dragon's tracks. There's another way into that closed valley, now. The . . . the earthquake brought down the far wall. It's a hard climb, but you can get a horse up it. I found more tracks at the top, and there's an easy way from there around the mountain." He let out a long breath when he was done.

"Good," Moiraine said. "At least he has not rediscovered how to fly, or make himself invisible, or something else out of legend. We must follow him without delay. Uno, I will give you enough gold to take you and the others as far as Jehannah, and the name of someone there who will see that you get more. The Ghealdanin are wary of strangers, but if you keep to yourselves, they should not trouble you. Wait there until I send word."

"But we will go with you," he protested. "We have all sworn to follow the Dragon Reborn. I do not see how the

few of us can take a fortress that has never fallen, but with
the Lord Dragon's aid, we will do what must be done."

"So we are 'the People of the Dragon,' now." Perrin
laughed mirthlessly. "'The Stone of Tear will never fall till
the People of the Dragon come.' Have you given us a new
name, Moiraine?"

"Watch your tongue, blacksmith," Lan growled, all ice
and stone.

Moiraine gave them both sharp looks, and they fell silent.
"Forgive me, Uno," she said, "but we must travel quickly if
we are to have a hope of overtaking him. You are the only
Shienaran fit enough for a hard ride, and we cannot afford
the days the others will need to regain full strength. I will
send for you when I can."

Uno grimaced, but he bowed in acquiescence. At her dismissal, he squared his shoulders and left to tell the others.

"Well, I am going along, whatever you say," Min put in
firmly.

"You are going to Tar Valon," Moiraine told her.

"I am no such thing!"

The Aes Sedai went on smoothly as if the other woman
had not spoken. "The Amyrlin Seat must be told what has
happened, and I cannot count on finding one I can trust who
has messenger pigeons. Or that the Amyrlin will see any
message I send by pigeon. It is a long journey, and hard. I
would not send you alone if there were anyone to send with
you, but I will see you have money, and letters to those who
might help you on your way. You must ride quickly, though.
When your horse tires, buy another—or steal one, if you
must—but ride quickly."

"Let Uno take your message. He's fit; you said so. I am
going after Rand."

"Uno has his duties, Min. And do you think a man could
simply walk up to the gates of the White Tower and demand
an audience with the Amyrlin Seat? Even a king would be
made to wait days if he arrived unannounced, and I fear
any of the Shienarans would be left kicking their heels for
weeks, if not forever. Not to mention that something so
unusual would be known to everyone in Tar Valon before
the first sunset. Few women seek audiences with the Amyrlin herself, but it does happen, and it should occasion no
great comment. No one must learn even as much as that the

Amyrlin Seat has received a message from me. Her life—
and ours—could depend on it. You are the one who must go."

Min sat there opening and closing her mouth, obviously searching for another argument, but Moiraine had
already gone on. "Lan, I very much fear we will find more
evidence of his passing than I would like, but I will rely on
your tracking." The Warder nodded. "Perrin? Loial? Will
you come with me after Rand?" From her place against the
wall, Min gave an indignant squawk, but the Aes Sedai ignored it.

"I will come," Loial said quickly. "Rand is my friend.
And I will admit it; I would not miss anything. For my
book, you see."

Perrin was slower to answer. Rand was his friend, whatever he had become in the forging. And there was that near
certainty of their futures being linked, though he would
have avoided that part of it if he could. "It has to be done,
doesn't it?" he said finally. "I will come."

"Good." Moiraine rubbed her hands together again, with
the air of someone settling to work. "You must all ready
yourselves at once. Rand has hours on us. I mean to be well
along his trail before midday."

Slender as she was, the force of her presence herded all
of them but Lan toward the door, Loial walking stooped
over until he was through the doorway. Perrin thought of a
goodwife herding geese.

Once outside, Min hung back for a moment to address
Lan with a too-sweet smile. "And is there any message you
want carried? To Nynaeve, perhaps?"

The Warder blinked as if caught off guard, like a horse
on three legs. "Does everyone know—?" He regained his
balance almost immediately. "If there is anything else she
needs to hear from me, I will tell her myself." He closed the
door nearly in her face.

"Men!" Min muttered at the door. "Too blind to see what
a stone could see, and too stubborn to be trusted to think for
themselves."

Perrin inhaled deeply. Faint smells of death still hung in
the valley air, but it was better than the closeness inside.
Some better.

"Clean air," Loial sighed. "The smoke was beginning to
bother me a little."

They started down the slope together. Beside the stream below, the Shienarans who could stand were gathered around Uno. From his gestures the one-eyed man was making up for lost time with his cursing.

"How did you two become privileged?" Min demanded abruptly. "She *asked* you. She didn't do me the courtesy of asking."

Loial shook his head. "I think she asked because she knew what we would answer, Min. Moiraine seems able to read Perrin and me; she knows what we'll do. But you are a closed book to her."

Min appeared only a little mollified. She looked up at them, Perrin head and shoulders taller on one side and Loial towering even higher on the other. "Much good it does me. I am still going where she wants as easily as you two little lambs. You were doing well for a while, Perrin. Standing up to her like she'd sold you a coat and the seams were popping open."

"I did stand up to her, didn't I," Perrin said wonderingly. He had not really realized he had done that. "It was not so bad as I'd have thought it would be."

"You were lucky," Loial rumbled. "'To anger an Aes Sedai is to put your head in a hornet's nest.'"

"Loial," Min said, "I need to speak to Perrin. Alone. Would you mind?"

"Oh. Of course not." He lengthened his stride to its normal span and quickly moved ahead of them, pulling his pipe and tabac pouch from a coat pocket.

Perrin eyed her warily. She was biting her lip, as if considering what to say. "Do you ever see things about him?" he asked, nodding after the Ogier.

She shook her head. "I think it only works with humans. But I've seen things around you that you ought to know about."

"I've told you—"

"Don't be more thickheaded than you have to be, Perrin. Back there, right after you said you'd go. They were not there before. They must have to do with this journey. Or at least with you deciding to go."

After a moment he said reluctantly, "What did you see?"

"An Aielman in a cage," she said promptly. "A Tuatha'an with a sword. A falcon and a hawk, perching on your shoulders. Both female, I think. And all the rest, of course. What is always there. Darkness swirling 'round you, and—"

"None of that!" he said quickly. When he was sure she had stopped, he scratched his head, thinking. None of it made any sense to him. "Do you have any idea what it all means? The new things, I mean."

"No, but they're important. The things I see always are. Turning points in people's lives, or what's fated. It's always important." She hesitated for a moment, glancing at him. "One more thing," she said slowly. "If you meet a woman— the most beautiful woman you've ever seen—run!"

Perrin blinked. "You saw a beautiful woman? Why should I run from a beautiful woman?"

"Can't you just take advice?" she said irritably. She kicked at a stone and watched it roll down the slope.

Perrin did not like jumping to conclusions—it was one of the reasons some people thought him slow-witted—but he totaled up a number of things Min had said in the last few days and came to a startling conclusion. He stopped dead, hunting for words. "Uh . . . Min, you know I like you. I like you, but. . . . Uh . . . you sort of remind me of my sisters. I mean, you. . . ." The flow stumbled to a halt as she raised her head to look at him, eyebrows arched. She wore a small smile.

"Why, Perrin, you must know that I love you." She stood there, watching his mouth work, then spoke slowly and carefully. "Like a brother, you great wooden-headed lummox! The arrogance of men never ceases to amaze me. You all think everything has to do with you, and every woman has to desire you."

Perrin felt his face growing hot. "I never. . . . I didn't. . . ." He cleared his throat. "What did you see about a woman?"

"Just take my advice," she said, and started down toward the stream again, walking fast. "If you forget all the rest," she called over her shoulder, "heed that!"

He frowned after her—for once his thoughts seemed to arrange themselves quickly—then caught up in two strides. "It's Rand, isn't it?"

She made a sound in her throat and gave him a sidelong look. She did not slow down, though. "Maybe you aren't so boneheaded after all," she muttered. After a moment she added, as if to herself, "I'm bound to him as surely as a stave is bound to the barrel. But I can't see if he'll ever love me in return. And I am not the only one."

"Does Egwene know?" he asked. Rand and Egwene had been all but promised since childhood. Everything but kneeling in front of the Women's Circle of the village to speak the betrothal. He was not sure how far they had drifted from that, if at all.

"She knows," Min said curtly. "Much good it does either of us."

"What about Rand? Does he know?"

"Oh, of course," she said bitterly. "I told him, didn't I? 'Rand, I did a viewing of you, and it seems I have to fall in love with you. I have to share you, too, and I don't much like that, but there it is.' You're a wooden-headed wonder after all, Perrin Aybara." She dashed a hand across her eyes angrily. "If I could be with him, I know I could help. Somehow. Light, if he dies, I don't know if I can stand it."

Perrin shrugged uncomfortably. "Listen, Min. I'll do what I can to help him." *However much that is.* "I promise you that. It really is best for you to go to Tar Valon. You'll be safe there."

"Safe?" She tasted the word as if wondering what it meant. "You think Tar Valon is safe?"

"If there's no safety in Tar Valon, there's no safety anywhere."

She sniffed loudly, and in silence they went to join those preparing to leave.

CHAPTER

7

The Way Out of the Mountains

The way down out of the mountains was hard, but the lower they went, the less Perrin needed his fur-lined cloak. Hour by hour, they rode out of the tailings of winter and into the first days of spring. The last remnants of snow vanished, and grasses and wildflowers—white maiden's hope and pink jump up—began to cover the high meadows they crossed. Trees appeared more often, with more leaves, and grasslarks and robins sang in the branches. And there were wolves. Never in sight—not even Lan mentioned seeing one—but Perrin knew. He kept his mind firmly closed to them, yet now and again a featherlight tickle at the back of his mind reminded him they were there.

Lan spent most of his time scouting their path on his black warhorse, Mandarb, following Rand's tracks as the rest of them followed the signs the Warder left for them. An arrow of stones laid out on the ground, or one lightly scratched in the rock wall of a forking pass. Turn this way. Cross that saddlepass. Take this switchback, this deer trail, this way through the trees and down along a narrow stream, even though there is nothing to indicate anyone has ever gone that way before. Nothing but Lan's signs. A tuft of grass or weeds tied one way to say bear left, another for bear right. A bent branch. A pile of pebbles for a rough climb ahead, two leaves caught on a thorn for a steep descent. The Warder had a hundred signs, it seemed to Perrin, and Moiraine knew them all. Lan rarely came back except when they made camp, to confer with Moiraine quietly, away from the fire. When the sun rose, most often he was hours gone already.

Moiraine was always first into the saddle after him, while the eastern sky was just turning pink. The Aes Sedai would not have climbed down from Aldieb, her white mare, until full dark or later, except that Lan refused to track further once the light began to fail.

"We'll go even slower if a horse breaks a leg," the Warder would tell Moiraine when she complained.

Her reply was always very much the same. "If you cannot move any faster than this, perhaps I should send you off to Myrelle before you get any older. Well, perhaps that can wait, but you must move us faster."

She half sounded as if the threat were irritated truth, half as if she were making a joke. There was something of a threat in it, or maybe a warning, Perrin was sure, from the way Lan's mouth tightened even when she smiled afterwards and reached up to pat his shoulder soothingly.

"Who is Myrelle?" Perrin asked suspiciously, the first time it happened. Loial shook his head, murmuring something about unpleasant things happening to those who pried into Aes Sedai affairs. The Ogier's hairy-fetlocked horse was as tall and heavy as a Dhurran stallion, but with Loial's long legs dangling to either side, the animal looked undersized, like a large pony.

Moiraine gave an amused, secretive smile. "Just a Green sister. Someone to whom Lan must one day deliver a package for safekeeping."

"No day soon," Lan said, and surprisingly, there was open anger in his voice. "Never, if I can help it. You will outlive me long, Moiraine Aes Sedai!"

She has too many secrets, Perrin thought, but asked no more about a subject that could crack the Warder's iron self-control.

The Aes Sedai had a blanket-wrapped bundle tied behind her saddle: the Dragon banner. Perrin was uneasy about having it with them, but Moiraine had neither asked his opinion nor listened when he offered it. Not that anyone was likely to recognize it if he saw it, yet he hoped she was as good at keeping secrets from other people as she was at keeping them from him.

In the beginning, at least, it was a boring journey. One

cloud-capped mountain was very much like another, one pass little different from the next. Supper was usually rabbit, dropped by stones from Perrin's sling. He did not have so many arrows as to risk shooting at rabbits in that rocky country. Breakfast was cold rabbit, more often than not, and the midday meal the same, eaten in the saddle.

Sometimes when they camped near a stream and there was still light enough to see, he and Loial caught mountain trout, lying on their bellies, hands elbow-deep in the cold water, tickling the green-backed fish out from under the rock ledges where they hid. Loial's fingers, big as they were, were even more deft at it than Perrin's.

Once, three days after setting out, Moiraine joined them, stretching herself out on the streamside and undoing rows of pearl buttons to roll up her sleeves as she asked how the thing was done. Perrin exchanged surprised looks with Loial. The Ogier shrugged.

"It is not that hard, really," Perrin told her. "Just bring your hand up from behind the fish, and underneath, as if you're trying to tickle its belly. Then you pull it out. It takes practice, though. You might not catch anything the first few times you try."

"I tried for days before I ever caught anything," Loial added. He was already easing his huge hands into the water, careful to keep his shadow from scaring the fish.

"As difficult as that?" Moiraine murmured. Her hands slipped into the water—and a moment later came out with a splash, holding a fat trout that thrashed the surface. She laughed with delight as she tossed it up onto the bank.

Perrin blinked at the big fish flopping in the fading sunlight. It must have weighed at least five pounds. "You were very lucky," he said. "Trout that size don't often shelter under a ledge this small. We'll have to move upstream a bit. It will be dark before any of them settle under this ledge again."

"Is that so?" Moiraine said. "You two go ahead. I think I will just try here again."

Perrin hesitated a moment before moving up the bank to another overhang. She was up to something, but he could not imagine what. That troubled him. Belly down, and careful not to let his shadow fall on the water, he peered over the edge. Half a dozen slender shapes hung suspended in the water, barely moving a fin to hold their places. All of them together would not weigh as much as Moiraine's fish, he decided with a sigh. If they were lucky, he and Loial might take two apiece, but the shadows of trees on the far bank already stretched across the water. Whatever they caught now would be it, and Loial's appetite was big enough by itself to swallow those four and most of the bigger fish, too. Loial's hands were already easing up behind one of the trout.

Before Perrin could even slide his hands into the water, Moiraine gave a shout. "Three should be enough, I think. The last two are bigger than the first."

Perrin gave Loial a startled look. "She can't have!"

The Ogier straightened, sending the small trout scattering. "She is Aes Sedai," he said simply.

Sure enough, when they returned to Moiraine, three big trout lay on the bank. She was already buttoning her sleeves up again.

Perrin thought about reminding her that whoever took the fish was supposed to clean them, too, but just at that moment she caught his eye. There was no particular expression on her smooth face, but her dark eyes did not waver, and they appeared to know what he was going to say, and to have dismissed it out of hand already. When she turned away, it seemed somehow too late to say anything.

Muttering to himself, Perrin pulled out his beltknife and set to the gutting and heading. "All of a sudden she's forgotten about sharing the chores, it seems. I suppose she'll want us to do the cooking, as well, and the cleaning up after."

"No doubt she will," Loial said without pausing over the fish he was working on. "She is Aes Sedai."

"I seem to remember hearing that somewhere." Perrin's knife ripped into the fish. "The Shienarans might have been willing to run around fetching and carrying for her, but there are only four of us now. We should keep on turn and turn about. It's only fair."

Loial gave a great snort of laughter. "I doubt she sees it that way. First she had to put up with Rand arguing with her all the time, and now you're ready to take over for him. As a rule, Aes Sedai do not let anyone argue with them. I expect she means to have us back in the habit of doing what she says by the time we reach the first village."

"A good habit to be in," Lan said, throwing back his cloak. In the fading light he had appeared out of nowhere.

Perrin nearly fell over from surprise, and Loial's ears went stiff with shock. Neither of them had heard the Warder's step.

"A habit you should never have lost," Lan added, then strode off toward Moiraine and the horses. His boots barely made a sound, even on that rocky ground, and once he was a few paces away the cloak hanging down his back gave him the uneasy appearance of a disembodied head and arms drifting up from the stream.

"We need her to find Rand," Perrin said softly, "but I am not going to let her shape my life anymore." He went back to his cleaning vigorously.

He meant to keep that promise—he really did—but during the days that followed, in some way he did not quite understand, he found that he and Loial were doing the cooking, and the cleaning up, and any other little chore that Moiraine thought of. He even discovered that somehow or other he had taken over tending Aldieb every night, unsaddling the mare and rubbing her down while Moiraine settled herself, apparently deep in thought.

Loial gave in to it as inevitable, but not Perrin. He tried refusing, resisting, but it was hard to resist when she made a reasonable suggestion, and a small one at that. Only there was always another suggestion behind it, as reasonable and small as the first, and then another. The simple force of her presence, the strength of her gaze, made it difficult to protest. Her dark eyes would catch his at the moment he opened his mouth. A lift of her eyebrow to suggest he was being rude, a surprised widening of her eyes that he could object to so small a request, a level stare that held in it everything that was Aes Sedai, all these things could make him hesitate, and once he hesitated there was never any recovering lost ground. He accused her of using the One Power on him, though he did not really think that was it, and she told him not to be a fool. He began to feel like a piece of iron trying to stop a smith from hammering it into a scythe.

The Mountains of Mist gave way abruptly to the forested foothills of Ghealdan, to land that seemed all up and down, but never very high. Deer, which in the mountains had often watched them warily, as if uncertain what a man was, began to bound away, white tails flickering, at the first sight of the horses. Even Perrin now caught only the faintest glimpses of the gray-striped mountain cats that seemed to fade away like smoke. They were coming into the lands of men.

Lan stopped wearing his color-shifting cloak and began riding back to the rest of them more often, telling them what lay ahead. In many places the trees had all been cut down. Soon, fields encircled by rough stone walls and farmers plowing 'round the sides of hills were common sights, if not exactly frequent, along with lines of people moving across the plowed ground, sowing seed from sacks slung from their shoulders. Scattered farmhouses and barns of gray stone sat on hilltops and ridges.

The wolves should not have been there. Wolves avoided places where men were, but Perrin could still sense them, an unseen screen and escort ringing the mounted party. Impatience filled him; impatience to reach a village or a town, any place where there were enough men to make the wolves go away.

A day after sighting the first field, just as the sun touched the horizon behind them, they came to the village of Jarra, not far north of the border with Amadicia.

CHAPTER
8

Jarra

Gray stone houses with slate roofs lay clustered along the few narrow streets of Jarra, clinging to a hillside above a little stream spanned by a low wooden bridge. The muddy streets were empty, and so was the sloping village green, except for one man sweeping the steps of the village's only inn, standing beside its stone stable; but it looked as if there had been a good many people on the green not long before. Half a dozen arches, woven of green branches and dotted with such few flowers as could be found this early in the year, stood in a circle in the middle of the grass. The ground had a trampled look, and there were other signs of a gathering; a woman's red scarf lying tangled at the foot of one of the arches, a child's knitted cap, a pewter pitcher tumbled on its side, a few half-eaten scraps of food.

The aromas of sweet wine and spiced cakes clung about the green, mixed in with smoke from dozens of chimneys and evening meals cooking. For an instant Perrin's nose caught another odor, one he could not identify, a faint trail that raised the hair on the back of his neck with its vileness. Then it was gone. But he was sure something had passed that way, something—wrong. He scrubbed at his nose as if to rub away the memory of it. *That can't be Rand. Light, even if he has gone mad, that can't be him. Can it?*

A painted sign hung above the inn door, a man standing on one foot with his arms thrown in the air: Harilin's Leap. As they drew rein in front of the square stone building, the sweeper straightened, yawning fiercely. He gave a start at Perrin's eyes, but his own already protruding eyes went wide when they fell on Loial. With his wide mouth and no chin to speak of, he looked something like a frog. There was an old smell of sour wine about him—to Perrin, at least. The fellow had certainly been part of the celebration.

The man gave himself a shake, and turned it into a bow with one hand resting on the double row of wooden buttons running down his coat. His eyes flickered from one to another of them, popping even more every time they rested on Loial. "Welcome, good mistress, and the Light illumine your way. Welcome, good masters. You wish food, rooms, baths? All to be had, here at the Leap. Master Harod, the innkeeper, keeps a good house. I am called Simion. If you wish anything, ask for Simion, and he will get it for you." He yawned again, covering his mouth in embarrassment and bowing to hide it. "I beg your pardon, good mistress. You have come far? Have you word of the Great Hunt? The Hunt for the Horn of Valere? Or the false Dragon? It's said there's a false Dragon in Tarabon. Or maybe Arad Doman."

"We have not come that far," Lan said, swinging down from his saddle. "No doubt you know more than I." They all began dismounting.

"You have had a wedding here?" Moiraine said.

"A wedding, good mistress? Why, we've had a lifetime of weddings. A plague of them. All in the last two days. There isn't a woman old enough to speak the betrothal remains unmarried, not in the whole village, not for a mile in any direction. Why, even Widow Jorath dragged old Banas through the arches, and they'd both sworn they'd never marry again. It was like a whirlwind just snatched everybody up. Rilith, the weaver's daughter, she started it, asking Jon the blacksmith to marry her, and him old enough to be her father and more. The old fool just took off his apron and said yes, and she demanded the arches be put up right then and there. Wouldn't hear of a proper wait, and all the other women sided with her. Since then we've had marriages day and night. Why, nobody's had any sleep at all hardly."

"That's very interesting," Perrin said when Simion paused to yawn again, "but have you seen a young—"

"It is very interesting," Moiraine said, cutting him off, "and I would hear more of it later, perhaps. For now, we would like rooms, and a meal." Lan made a small gesture toward Perrin, down low, as if telling him to hold his tongue.

"Of course, good mistress. A meal. Rooms." Simion hesitated, eyeing Loial. "We'll have to push two beds together for—" He leaned closer to Moiraine and dropped his voice. "Pardon, good mistress, but—uh—what exactly—is he? Meaning no disrespect," he added hastily.

He had not spoken softly enough, for Loial's ears twitched irritably. "I am an Ogier! What did you think I was? A Trolloc?"

Simion took a step back at the booming voice. "Trolloc, good—uh—master? Why, I'm a grown man. I don't believe in children's tales. Uh, did you say Ogier? Why, Ogier are childr—I mean . . . that is. . . ." In desperation, he turned to bellow toward the stable next to the inn. "Nico! Patrim! Visitors! Come see to their horses!" After a moment two boys with hay in their hair tumbled out of the stable, yawning and rubbing their eyes. Simion gestured to the steps, bowing, as the boys gathered reins.

Perrin slung his saddlebags and blanketroll over his shoulder and carried his bow as he followed Moiraine and Lan inside, with Simion bowing and bobbing ahead of them. Loial had to duck low under the lintel, and the ceiling inside only cleared his head by a foot. He kept rumbling to himself about not understanding why so few humans remembered the Ogier. His voice was like distant thunder. Even Perrin, right in front of him, could only understand half of his words.

The inn smelled of ale and wine, cheese and weariness, and the aroma of roasting mutton drifted from somewhere in the back. The few men in the common room sagged over their mugs as if they would really like to lie down on the benches and go to sleep. One plump serving woman was drawing a mug of ale from one of the barrels at the end of the room. The innkeeper himself, in a long white apron, sat on a tall stool in the corner, leaning against the wall. As the newcomers entered, he lifted his head, bleary-eyed. His jaw dropped at the sight of Loial.

"Visitors, Master Harod," Simion announced. "They want rooms. Master Harod? He's an Ogier, Master Harod." The serving woman turned and saw Loial, and dropped the mug with a clatter. None of the weary men at the tables even looked up. One had put his head down on the table and was snoring.

Loial's ears twitched violently.

Master Harod got to his feet slowly, eyes fastened on Loial, smoothing his apron all the while. "At least he isn't a Whitecloak," he said at last, then gave a start as if surprised he had spoken aloud. "That is to say, welcome, good mistress. Good masters. Forgive my lack of manners. I can only plead tiredness, good mistress." He darted another glance at Loial, and mouthed "Ogier?" with a look of disbelief.

Loial opened his mouth, but Moiraine forestalled him. "As your man said, good innkeeper, I wish rooms for my party for the night, and a meal."

"Oh! Of course, good mistress. Of course. Simion, show these good people to my best rooms, so they can put down their belongings. I'll have a fine meal laid out for you when you return, good mistress. A fine meal."

"If it pleases you to follow me, good mistress," Simion said. "Good masters." He bowed the way to stairs at one side of the common room.

Behind them, one of the men at the tables suddenly exclaimed, "What in the name of the Light is that?" Master Harod began explaining about Ogier, making it sound as if he were quite familiar with them. Most of what Perrin heard before they left the voices behind was wrong. Loial's ears twitched without stop.

On the second floor, the Ogier's head came near to brushing along the ceiling. The narrow corridor was growing dark, with only the sharp light of sunset through a window next to the door at the far end.

"Candles in the rooms, good mistress," Simion said. "I should have brought a lamp, but my head is still spinning from all those weddings. I'll send someone up to light the fire, if you wish. And you'll want wash water, of course." He pushed open a door. "Our best room, good mistress. We don't have many—not many strangers, you see—but this is our best."

"I'll take the one next to it," Lan said. He had Moiraine's blanketroll and saddlebags on his shoulder as well as his own, and the bundle containing the Dragon banner, too.

"Oh, good master, that's not a very good room at all. Narrow bed. Cramped. Meant for a servant, I suspect, as if we'd ever have anybody here who had a servant. Begging your pardon, good mistress."

"I will take it anyway," Lan said firmly.

"Simion," Moiraine said, "does Master Harod dislike the Children of the Light?"

"Well, he does, good mistress. He didn't, but he does. It isn't good policy, disliking the Children, not so close to the border as we are. They come through Jarra all the time, like there wasn't any border at all. But there was trouble, yesterday. A fistful of trouble. And with the weddings going on, and all."

"What happened, Simion?"

The man looked at her sharply before answering. Perrin did not think anyone else saw how sharply, in the dimness. "There was about twenty of them, come day before yesterday. No trouble then. But yesterday. . . . Why, three of them up and announced they weren't Children of the Light anymore. They took off their cloaks and just rode away."

Lan grunted. "Whitecloaks swear for life. What did their commander do?"

"Why, he would have done something, you can be sure, good master, but another of them announced he was off to find the Horn of Valere. Anyway, still another said they should be hunting the Dragon. That one said he was going to Almoth Plain when he left. Then some of them started saying things to women in the streets, things they shouldn't have, and grabbing at them. The women were screaming, and Children yelling at the ones bothering the women. I never saw such commotion."

"Didn't any of you try to stop them?" Perrin said.

"Good master, you carry that axe like you know how to use it, but it isn't so easy to face up to men with swords and armor and all, when all you know how to use is a broom or a hoe. The rest of the Whitecloaks, those as hadn't gone off, put an end to it. Almost came to drawing swords. And that wasn't the worst. Two more just went mad—if the others weren't. Those two started raving that Jarra was full of Darkfriends. They tried to burn the village down—said they would!—beginning with the Leap. You can see the burn marks out back, where they got it started. Fought the other Whitecloaks when they tried to stop them. The Whitecloaks that were left, they helped us put it out, tied those two up tight, and rode out of here, back toward Amadicia. Good riddance, I say, and if they never come back, it'll be too soon."

"Rough behavior," Lan said, "even for Whitecloaks."

Simion bobbed his head in agreement. "As you say, good master. They never acted like that before. Swagger around, yes. Look at you like you were dirt, and poke their noses in where they hadn't any business. But they never caused trouble before. Not like that, anyway."

"They are gone now," Moiraine said, "and troubles with them. I am sure we will pass a quiet night."

Perrin kept his mouth shut, but he was not quiet inside. *All these weddings and Whitecloaks are all very well, but I'd sooner know if Rand stopped here, and which way he went when he left. That smell couldn't have been him.*

He let Simion guide him on down the hall to another room, with two beds and a washstand, a pair of stools and not much else. Loial stooped to put his head through the doorway. Only a little light came in by the narrow windows. The beds were big enough, with blankets and comforters folded at the foot, but the mattresses looked lumpy. Simion fumbled on the mantel above the fireplace until he found a candle, and a tinderbox to get it alight.

"I'll see about getting some beds put together for you, good—uh—Ogier. Yes, just a moment, now." He showed no sign of hurry to be about it, though, fussing with the candlestick as if he had to place it just right. Perrin thought he looked uneasy.

Well, I'd be more than uneasy if Whitecloaks had been acting like that in Emond's Field. "Simion, has another stranger passed through here in the last day or two? A young man, tall, with gray eyes and reddish hair? He might have played the flute for a meal or a bed."

"I remember him, good master," Simion said, still shifting the candlestick. "Came yesterday morning, early. Looked hungry, he did. He played the flute for all the weddings, yesterday. Good-looking young fellow. Some of the women eyed him, at first, but. . . ." He paused, looking at Perrin sideways. "Is he a friend of yours, good master?"

"I know him," Perrin said. "Why?"

Simion hesitated. "No reason, good master. He was an odd fellow, that's all. He talked to himself, sometimes, and sometimes he laughed when nobody had said anything. Slept in this very room, last night, or part of it. Woke us all in the middle of the night, yelling. It was just a nightmare, but he wouldn't stay any longer. Master Harod didn't make much effort to talk him into it, after all that noise." Simion paused again. "He said something strange when he left."

"What?" Perrin demanded.

"He said somebody was after him. He said. . . ." The chinless man swallowed and went on more slowly. "Said they'd kill him if he didn't go. 'One of us has to die, and I mean it to be him.' His very words."

"He did not mean us," Loial rumbled. "We are his friends."

"Of course, good—uh—good Ogier. Of course, he didn't mean you. I—uh—I don't mean to say anything about a friend of yours, but I—uh—I think he's sick. In the head, you know."

"We will take care of him," Perrin said. "That's why we're following him. Which way did he go?"

"I knew it," Simion said, bouncing on his toes. "I knew she could help as soon as I saw you. Which way? East, good master. East, like the Dark One himself was on his heels. Do you think she'll help me? Help my brother, that is? Noam's bad sick, and Mother Roon says she can't do anything."

Perrin kept his face expressionless, and bought a little time to think by propping his bow in the corner and setting his blanketroll and saddlebags on one of the beds. The problem was that thinking did not help much. He looked at Loial, but found no help there; consternation had the Ogier's ears drooping and his long eyebrows hanging down on his cheeks. "What makes you think she can help your brother?" *Stupid question! The right question is, what does he mean to do about it?*

"Why, I traveled to Jehannah, once, good master, and I saw two . . . two women like her. I couldn't mistake her after that." His voice dropped to a whisper. "It's said *they* can raise the dead, good master."

"Who else knows this?" Perrin asked sharply, and at the same time Loial said, "If your brother is dead, there is nothing anyone can do."

The frog-faced man looked from one to the other of them anxiously, and his words came in a babble. "No one knows but me, good master. Noam isn't dead, good Ogier, only sick. I swear nobody else could recognize her. Even Master Harod's never been more than twenty miles from here in his life. He's so bad sick. I'd ask her myself, only my knees'd be shaking so hard she couldn't hear me talk. What if she took offense and called down lightning on me? And what if I'd been wrong? It isn't the kind of thing you accuse a woman of without. . . . I mean . . . uh. . . ." He raised his hands, half in pleading, half as if to defend himself.

"I can make no promises," Perrin said, "but I'll speak to her. Loial, why don't you keep Simion company till I've spoken to Moiraine?"

"Of course," the Ogier boomed. Simion gave a start when Loial's hand swallowed his shoulder. "He will show me my room, and we will talk. Tell me, Simion, what do you know of trees?"

"T-t-trees, g-good Ogier?"

Perrin did not wait any longer. He hurried back down the dark hall and knocked on Moiraine's door, barely waiting for her peremptory "Come!" before pushing in.

Half a dozen candles showed that the Leap's best room was none too good, though the one bed had four tall posts supporting a canopy, and the mattress looked less full of lumps than Perrin's. There was a scrap of carpet on the floor, and two cushioned chairs instead of stools. Other than that, it looked no different from his room. Moiraine and Lan stood in front of the cold hearth as if they had been discussing something, and the Aes Sedai did not look pleased at being interrupted. The Warder's face was as imperturbable as a carving.

"Rand's been here, all right," Perrin started off. "That fellow Simion remembers him." Moiraine hissed through her teeth.

"You were told to keep your mouth shut," Lan growled.

Perrin squared his feet to face the Warder. That was easier than facing Moiraine's glare. "How could we find out whether he had been here without asking questions? Tell me that. He left last night, if you are interested, heading east. And he was carrying on about somebody following him, trying to kill him."

"East." Moiraine nodded. The utter calm of her voice

was at odds with her disapproving eyes. "That is good to know, though it had to be so if he is going to Tear. But I was fairly certain he had been here even before I heard about the Whitecloaks, and they made it a certainty. Rand is almost surely right about one thing, Perrin. I cannot believe we are the only ones trying to find him. And if they find out about us, they may well try to stop us. We have enough to contend with trying to catch up to Rand without that. You must learn to hold your tongue until I tell you to speak."

"The Whitecloaks?" Perrin said incredulously. *Hold my tongue? Burn me, if I will!* "How could they tell you—? Rand's madness. It is *catching*?"

"Not his madness," Moiraine said, "if he is far enough gone yet to be called mad. Perrin, he is more strongly *ta'veren* than anyone since the Age of Legends. Yesterday, in this village, the Pattern . . . moved, shaped itself around him like clay shaped on a mold. The weddings, the Whitecloaks, these were enough to say Rand had been here, for anyone who knew to listen."

Perrin drew a long breath. "And this is what we'll find everywhere he's been? Light, if there are Shadowspawn after him, they can track him as easily as we can."

"Perhaps," Moiraine said. "Perhaps not. No one knows anything about *ta'veren* as strong as Rand." For just a moment she sounded vexed at not knowing. "Artur Hawkwing was the most strongly *ta'veren* of whom any writings remain. And Hawkwing was in no way as strong as Rand."

"It is said," Lan put in, "that there were times when people in the same room with Hawkwing spoke truth when they meant to lie, made decisions they had not even known they were contemplating. Times when every toss of the dice, every turn of the cards, went his way. But only times."

"You mean you don't know," Perrin said. "He could leave a trail of weddings and Whitecloaks gone mad all the way to Tear."

"I mean I know as much as there is to know," Moiraine said sharply. Her dark-eyed gaze chastised Perrin like a whip. "The Pattern weaves finely around *ta'veren*, and others can follow the shape of those threads if they know where to look. Be careful your tongue does not unravel more than you can know."

In spite of himself Perrin hunched his shoulders as if she were delivering real blows. "Well, you had better be glad I opened my mouth this time. Simion knows you're Aes Sedai. He wants you to Heal his brother Noam of some sickness. If I hadn't talked to him, he would never have worked up nerve enough to ask, but he might have started talking among his friends."

Lan caught Moiraine's eye, and for a moment they stared at one another. The Warder had the air about him of a wolf about to leap. Finally, Moiraine shook her head. "No," she said.

"As you wish. It is your decision." Lan sounded as if he thought she had made the wrong one, but the tension left him.

Perrin stared at them. "You were thinking of. . . . Simion couldn't tell anyone if he were dead, could he?"

"He will not die by my actions," Moiraine said. "But I cannot, and will not, promise that it will always be so. We must find Rand, and I will not fail in that. Is that spoken plainly enough for you?" Caught in her gaze, Perrin could make no answer. She nodded as if his silence were answer enough. "Now take me to Simion."

The door to Loial's room stood open, spilling a pool of candlelight into the hall. The two beds inside had been pushed together, and Loial and Simion were seated on the edge of one. The chinless man was staring up at Loial with his mouth open and an expression of wonder on his face.

"Oh, yes, the *stedding* are wonderful," Loial was saying. "There is such peace there, under the Great Trees. You humans may have your wars and strife, but nothing ever troubles the *stedding*. We tend the trees and live in harmony. . . ." He trailed off when he saw Moiraine, with Lan and Perrin behind her.

Simion scrambled to his feet, bowing and backing away until he came up against the far wall. "Uh . . . good mistress. . . . Uh . . . uh. . . ." Even then, he continued bobbing like a toy on a string.

"Show me to your brother," Moiraine commanded, "and I will do what I can. Perrin, you will come, too, since this good man spoke to you first." Lan lifted an eyebrow, and she shook her head. "If we all go, we might attract attention. Perrin can give me what protection I need."

Lan nodded reluctantly, then gave Perrin a hard look. "See that you do, blacksmith. If any harm befalls her. . . ." His cold blue eyes finished the promise.

Simion snatched one of the candles and scurried into the hallway, still bowing so the candlelight made their shadows dance. "This way—uh—good mistress. This way."

Beyond the door at the end of the hall, outside stairs led down to a cramped alleyway, between inn and stable. Night shrank the candle to a flickering pinpoint. The half moon was up in a star-flecked sky, giving more than enough light for Perrin's eyes. He wondered when Moiraine would tell Simion he did not have to keep bowing, but she never did. The Aes Sedai glided along, clutching her skirts to keep them out of the mud, as though the dark passage were a palace hall and she a queen. The air was already cooling; nights still carried echoes of winter.

"This way." Simion led them back to a small shed behind the stable and hurriedly unbarred the door. "This way." Simion pointed. "There, good mistress. There. My brother. Noam."

The far end of the shed had been barred off with slats of wood; hastily, by the rough look of it. A stout iron lock in a hasp held shut a crude door of wooden slats. Behind those bars, a man lay sprawled on his stomach on the straw-covered floor. He was barefoot, his shirt and breeches ripped as if he had torn at them without knowing how to take them off. There was an odor of unwashed flesh that Perrin thought even Simion and Moiraine must smell.

Noam lifted his head and stared at them silently, without expression. There was nothing at all about him to suggest he was Simion's brother—he had a chin, for one thing, and he was a big man, with heavy shoulders—but that was not what staggered Perrin. Noam stared at them with burnished golden eyes.

"He'd been talking crazy almost a year, good mistress, saying he could . . . could talk with wolves. And his eyes. . . ." Simion darted a glance at Perrin. "Well, he'd talk about it when he'd drunk too much. Everybody laughed at him. Then a month or so ago, he didn't come to town. I went out to see what was the matter, and I found him—like this."

Cautiously, unwillingly, Perrin reached out toward Noam

as he would have toward a wolf. *Running through the woods with the cold wind in his nose. Quick dash from cover, teeth snapping at hamstrings. Taste of blood, rich on the tongue. Kill.* Perrin jerked back as he would have from a fire, sealed himself off. They were not thoughts at all, really, just a chaotic jumble of desires and images, part memory, part yearning. But there was more wolf there than anything else. He put a hand to the wall to steady himself; his knees felt weak. *Light help me!*

Moiraine put a hand on the lock.

"Master Harod has the key, good mistress. I don't know if he'll—"

She gave a tug, and the lock sprang open. Simion gaped at her. She lifted the lock free of the hasp, and the chinless man turned to Perrin.

"Is that safe, good master? He's my brother, but he bit Mother Roon when she tried to help, and he . . . he killed a cow. With his teeth," he finished faintly.

"Moiraine," Perrin said, "the man is dangerous."

"All men are dangerous," she replied in a cool voice. "Now be quiet." She opened the door and went in. Perrin held his breath.

At her first step, Noam's lips peeled back from his teeth, and he began to growl, a rumble that deepened till his whole body quivered. Moiraine ignored it. Still growling, Noam wriggled backwards in the straw as she came closer to him, until he had backed himself into a corner. Or she had backed him.

Slowly, calmly, the Aes Sedai knelt and took his head between her hands. Noam's growl heightened to a snarl, then tailed off in a whimper before Perrin could move. For a long moment Moiraine held Noam's head, then just as calmly released it and rose. Perrin's throat tightened as she turned her back on Noam and walked out of the cage, but the man only stared after her. She pushed the slatted door to, slipped the lock back through the hasp, not bothering to snap it shut— and Noam hurled himself snarling against the wooden bars. He bit at them, and battered them with his shoulders, tried to force his head between them, all the while snarling and snapping.

Moiraine brushed straw from her skirt with a steady hand and no expression.

"You do take chances," Perrin breathed. She looked at him—a steady, knowing gaze—and he dropped his eyes. His yellow eyes.

Simion was staring at his brother. "Can you help him, good mistress?" he asked hoarsely.

"I am sorry, Simion," she said.

"Can't you do anything, good mistress? Something? One of those"—his voice fell to a whisper—"Aes Sedai things?"

"Healing is not a simple matter, Simion, and it comes from within as much as from the Healer. There is nothing here that remembers being Noam, nothing that remembers being a man. There are no maps remaining to show him the path back, and nothing left to take that path. Noam is gone, Simion."

"He—he just used to talk funny, good mistress, when he'd had too much to drink. He just. . . ." Simion scrubbed a hand across his eyes and blinked. "Thank you, good mistress. I know you'd have done something if you could." She put a hand on his shoulder, murmured comforting words, and then she was gone from the shed.

Perrin knew he should follow her, but the man—what had once been a man—snapping at the wooden bars, held him. He took a quick step and surprised himself by removing the dangling lock from the hasp. The lock was a good one, the work of a master smith.

"Good master?"

Perrin stared at the lock in his hand, at the man behind in the cage. Noam had stopped biting at the slats; he stared back at Perrin warily, panting. Some of his teeth had broken off jaggedly.

"You can leave him in here forever," Perrin said, "but I—I don't think he'll ever get any better."

"If he gets out, good master, he'll die!"

"He will die in here or out there, Simion. Out there, at least he'll be free, and as happy as he can be. He is not your brother anymore, but you're the one who has to decide. You can leave him in here for people to stare at, leave him to stare at the bars of his cage until he pines away. You cannot cage a wolf, Simion, not and expect it to be happy. Or live long."

"Yes," Simion said slowly. "Yes, I see." He hesitated, then nodded, and jerked his head toward the shed door.

That was all the answer Perrin needed. He swung back the slatted door and stood aside.

For a moment Noam stared at the opening. Abruptly he darted out of the cage, running on all fours, but with surprising agility. Out of the cage, out of the shed, and into the night. *The Light help us both*, Perrin thought.

"I suppose it's better for him to be free." Simion gave himself a shake. "But I don't know what Master Harod will say when he finds that door standing open and Noam gone."

Perrin shut the cage door; the big lock made a sharp click as he refastened it. "Let him puzzle that out."

Simion barked a quick laugh, abruptly cut off. "He'll make something out of it. They all will. Some of them say Noam turned into a wolf—fur and all!—when he bit Mother Roon. It's not true, but they say it."

Shivering, Perrin leaned his head against the cage door. *He may not have fur, but he's a wolf. He's wolf, not man. Light, help me.*

"We didn't keep him here always," Simion said suddenly. "He was at Mother Roon's house, but she and I got Master Harod to move him here after the Whitecloaks came. They always have a list of names, Darkfriends they're looking for. It was Noam's eyes, you see. One of the names the Whitecloaks had was a fellow named Perrin Aybara, a blacksmith. They said he has yellow eyes, and runs with wolves. You can see why I didn't want them to know about Noam."

Perrin turned his head enough to look at Simion over his shoulder. "Do you think this Perrin Aybara is a Darkfriend?"

"A Darkfriend wouldn't care if my brother died in a cage. I suppose she found you soon after it happened. In time to help. I wish she'd come to Jarra a few months ago."

Perrin was ashamed that he had ever compared the man to a frog. "And I wish she could have done something for him." *Burn me, I wish she could.* Suddenly it burst on him that the whole village must know about Noam. About his eyes. "Simion, would you bring me something to eat in my room?" Master Harod and the rest might have been too taken with staring at Loial to notice his eyes before, but they surely would if he ate in the common room.

"Of course. And in the morning, too. You don't have to come down until you are ready to get on your horse."

"You are a good man, Simion. A good man." Simion looked so pleased that Perrin felt ashamed all over again.

CHAPTER
9

Wolf Dreams

P errin returned to his room by the back way, and after a time Simion came up with a covered tray. The
cloth did not hold in the smells of roasted mutton,
sweetbeans, turnips, and freshly baked bread, but Perrin
lay on his bed, staring at the whitewashed ceiling, until the
aromas grew cold. Images of Noam ran through his head
over and over again. Noam chewing at the wooden slats.
Noam running off into the darkness. He tried to think of
lock-making, of the careful quenching and shaping of the
steel, but it did not work.

Ignoring the tray, he rose and made his way down the
hall to Moiraine's room. She answered his rap on the door
with, "Come in, Perrin."

For an instant all the old stories about Aes Sedai stirred
again, but he pushed them aside and opened the door.

Moiraine was alone—for which he was grateful—sitting
with an ink bottle balanced on her knee, writing in a small,
leather-bound book. She corked the bottle and wiped the
steel nib of her pen on a small scrap of parchment without
looking at him. There was a fire in the fireplace.

"I have been expecting you for some time," she said. "I
have not spoken about this before because it was obvious
you did not want me to. After tonight, though. . . . What do
you want to know?"

"Is that what I can expect?" he asked. "To end like that?"

"Perhaps."

He waited for more, but she only put pen and ink away
in their small case of polished rosewood and blew on her
writing to dry it. "Is that all? Moiraine, don't give me slip-

pery Aes Sedai answers. If you know something, tell me. Please."

"I know very little, Perrin. While searching for other answers among the books and manuscripts two friends keep for their researches, I found a copied fragment of a book from the Age of Legends. It spoke of . . . situations like yours. That may be the only copy anywhere in the world, and it did not tell me much."

"What *did* it tell you? Anything at all is more than I know now. Burn me, I've been worrying about Rand going mad, but I never thought I had to worry about myself!"

"Perrin, even in the Age of Legends, they knew little of this. Whoever wrote it seemed uncertain whether it was truth or legend. And I only saw a fragment, remember. She said that some who talked to wolves lost themselves, that what was human was swallowed up by wolf. Some. Whether she meant one in ten, or five, or nine, I do not know."

"I can shut them out. I don't know how I do it, but I can refuse to listen to them. I can refuse to hear them. Will that help?"

"It may." She studied him, seeming to choose her words carefully. "Mostly, she wrote of dreams. Dreams can be dangerous for you, Perrin."

"You said that once before. What do you mean?"

"According to her, wolves live partly in this world, and partly in a world of dreams."

"A world of dreams?" he said disbelievingly.

Moiraine gave him a sharp look. "That is what I said, and that is what she wrote. The way wolves talk to one another, the way they talk to you, is in some way connected to this world of dreams. I do not claim to understand how." She paused, frowning slightly. "From what I have read of Aes Sedai who had the Talent called Dreaming, Dreamers sometimes spoke of encountering wolves in their dreams, even wolves that acted as guides. I fear you must learn to be as careful sleeping as waking, if you intend to avoid wolves. If that is what you decide to do."

"If that is what I decide? Moiraine, I will not end up like Noam. I won't!"

She eyed him quizzically, shaking her head slowly. "You speak as if you can make all your own choices, Perrin. You are *ta'veren*, remember." He turned his back on her, staring at the night-dark windows, but she continued: "Perhaps, knowing what Rand is, knowing how strongly *ta'veren* he is, I have paid too little attention to the other two *ta'veren* I found with him. Three *ta'veren* in the same village, all born within weeks of one another? That is unheard of. Perhaps you—and Mat—have larger purposes in the Pattern than you, or I, thought."

"I do not want any *purpose* in the Pattern," Perrin muttered. "I surely can't have one if I forget I am a man. Will you help me, Moiraine?" It was hard to say that. *What if it means her using the One Power? Would I rather forget I'm a man?* "Help me keep from—losing myself?"

"If I can keep you whole, I will. I promise you that, Perrin. But I will not endanger the struggle against the Shadow. You must know that, too."

When he turned to look at her, she was regarding him unblinkingly. *And if your struggle means putting me in my grave tomorrow, will you do that, too?* He was icily sure that she would. "What have you not told me?"

"Do not presume too far, Perrin," she said coldly. "Do not press me further than I think proper."

He hesitated before asking the next question. "Can you do for me what you did for Lan? Can you shield my dreams?"

"I already have a Warder, Perrin." Her lips quirked almost into a smile. "And one is all I will have. I am of the Blue Ajah, not the Green."

"You know what I mean. I don't want to be a Warder." *Light, bound to an Aes Sedai the rest of my life? That's as bad as the wolves.*

"It would not aid you, Perrin. The shielding is for dreams from the outside. The danger in your dreams is within you." She opened the small book again. "You should sleep," she said in dismissal. "Be wary of your dreams, but you must sleep sometime." She turned a page, and he left.

Back in his own room, he eased the hold he kept on himself, eased it just a trifle, let his senses spread. The wolves were out there still, beyond the edges of the village, ringing Jarra. Almost immediately he snapped back to rigid self-control. "What I need is a city," he muttered. That would keep them at bay. *After I find Rand. After I finish whatever has to be finished with him.* He was not sure how sorry he was that Moiraine could not shield him. The One Power or the wolves; that was a choice no man should have to make.

He left the fire laid on the hearthstone unlit, and threw open both windows. Cold night air rushed in. Tossing blankets and comforter on the floor, he lay down fully clothed on the lumpy bed, not bothering to try to find a comfortable position. His last thought before sleep came was that if anything would keep him from deep sleep and dangerous dreams, that mattress would.

He was in a long hallway, its high stone ceiling and walls glistening with damp and streaked by odd shadows. They lay in contorted strips, stopping as abruptly as they began, too dark for the light between them. He had no idea where the light came from.

"No," he said, then louder, "No! This is a dream. I need to wake up. Wake up!"

The hallway did not change.

Danger. It was a wolf's thought, faint and distant.

"I will wake up. I will!" He pounded a fist against the wall. It hurt, but he did not wake. He thought one of the sinuous shadows shifted away from his blow.

Run, brother. Run.

"Hopper?" he said wonderingly. He was sure he knew the wolf whose thoughts he heard. Hopper, who had envied the eagles. "Hopper is dead!"

Run!

Perrin lurched into a run, one hand holding his axe to keep the haft from banging against his leg. He had no idea where he was running, or why, but the urgency of Hopper's sending could not be ignored. *Hopper's dead*, he thought. *He's dead!* But Perrin ran.

Other hallways crossed the one he ran along, at odd angles, sometimes descending, sometimes climbing. None looked any different from the passage he was in, though. Damp stone walls unbroken by doors, and strips of darkness.

As he came on one of those crossing halls, he skidded to a halt. A man stood there, blinking at him uncertainly, in strangely cut coat and breeches, the coat flaring over his hips as the bottoms of the breeches flared over his boots.

Both were bright yellow, and his boots were only a little paler.

"This is more than I can stand," the man said, to himself, not Perrin. He had an odd accent, quick and sharp. "Not only do I dream of peasants, now, but foreign peasants, from those clothes. Begone from my dreams, fellow!"

"Who are you?" Perrin asked. The man's eyebrows rose as if he were offended.

The strips of shadow around them writhed. One detached from the ceiling at one end and drifted down to touch the strange man's head. It appeared to tangle in his hair. The man's eyes widened, and everything seemed to happen at once. The shadow jerked back to the ceiling, ten feet overhead, trailing something pale. Wet drops splattered Perrin's face. A bone-rattling shriek shattered the air.

Frozen, Perrin stared at the bloody shape wearing the man's clothes, screaming and thrashing on the floor. Unbidden, his eyes rose to the pale thing like an empty sack that dangled from the ceiling. Part of it was already absorbed by the black strip, but he had no trouble recognizing a human skin, apparently whole and unbroken.

The shadows around him danced in agitation, and Perrin ran, pursued by dying screams. Ripples ran along the shadow strips, pacing him.

"Change, burn you!" he shouted. "I know it's a dream! Light burn you, change!"

Colorful tapestries hung along the walls between tall golden stands holding dozens of candles that illuminated white floor tiles and a ceiling painted with fluffy clouds and fanciful birds in flight. Nothing moved but the flickering candle flames along the length of that hall, stretching as far as he could see, or in the pointed arches of white stone that occasionally broke the walls.

Danger. The sending was even fainter than before. And more urgent, if that were possible.

Axe in hand, Perrin started warily down the hall, muttering to himself. "Wake up. Wake up, Perrin. If you know it's a dream, it changes or you wake up. Wake up, burn you!" The hallway stayed as solid as any he had ever walked.

He came abreast of the first of the pointed white archways. It let into a huge room, apparently windowless, but furnished as ornately as any palace, the furniture all carved and gilded and inlaid with ivory. A woman stood in the middle of the room, frowning at a tattered manuscript lying open on a table. A black-haired, black-eyed, beautiful woman clothed in white and silver.

Even as he recognized her, she lifted her head and looked straight at him. Her eyes widened, in shock, in anger. "You! What are you doing here? How did you—? You'll ruin things you could not begin to imagine!"

Abruptly the space seemed to flatten, as if he were suddenly staring at a picture of a room. The flat image appeared to turn sideways, become only a bright vertical line down the middle of blackness. The line flashed white, and was gone, leaving only the dark, blacker than black.

Just in front of Perrin's boots, the floor tiles came to an abrupt end. As he watched, the white edges dissolved into the black like sand washed away by water. He stepped back hastily.

Run.

Perrin turned, and Hopper was there, a big gray wolf, grizzled and scarred. "You are dead. I saw you die. I *felt* you die!" A sending flooded Perrin's mind.

Run now! You must not be here now. Danger. Great danger. Worse than all the Neverborn. You must go. Go now! Now!

"How?" Perrin shouted. "I want to go, but how?"

Go! Teeth bared, Hopper leaped for Perrin's throat.

With a strangled cry, Perrin sat up on the bed, hands going to his throat to hold in lifeblood. They met unbroken skin. He swallowed with relief, but the next moment his fingers touched a damp spot.

Almost falling in his haste, he scrambled off the bed, stumbled to the washstand and seized the pitcher, splashed water everywhere as he filled the basin. The water turned pink as he washed his face. Pink with the blood of that strangely dressed man.

More dark spots dotted his coat and breeches. He tore them off and tossed them into the furthest corner. He meant to leave them there. Simion could burn them.

A gust of wind whipped in the open window. Shivering in shirt and smallclothes, he sat on the floor and leaned back

against the bed. *This should be uncomfortable enough.*
Sourness tinged his thoughts, and worry, and fear. And determination. *I won't give in to this. I won't!*

He was still shivering when sleep finally came, a shallow
half sleep filled with vague awareness of the room around
him and thoughts of the cold. But the bad dreams that came
were better than some others.

Rand huddled under the trees in the night, watching the
heavy-shouldered black dog come nearer his hiding place.
His side ached, the wound Moiraine could not quite Heal,
but he ignored it. The moon gave barely enough light for
him to make out the dog, waist-high, with its thick neck and
massive head, and its teeth that seemed to shine like wet
silver in the night. It sniffed the air and trotted toward him.

Closer, he thought. *Come closer. No warning for your
master this time. Closer. That's it.* The dog was only ten
paces away, now, a deep growl rumbling in its chest as it
suddenly bounded forward. Straight at Rand.

The Power filled him. Something leaped from his outstretched hands; he was not sure what it was. A bar of white
light, solid as steel. Liquid fire. For an instant, in the middle
of that something, the dog seemed to become transparent,
and then it was gone.

The white light faded except for the afterimage burned
across Rand's vision. He sagged against the nearest tree
trunk, the bark rough on his face. Relief and silent laughter
shook him. *It worked. Light save me, it worked this time.* It
had not always. There had been other dogs this night.

The One Power pulsed in him, and his stomach twisted
with the Dark One's taint on *saidin,* wanted to empty itself.
Sweat beaded on his face despite the cold night wind, and
his mouth tasted full of sickness. He wanted to lie down
and die. He wanted Nynaeve to give him some of her medicines, or Moiraine to Heal him, or. . . . Something, anything, to stop the sick feeling that was suffocating him.

But *saidin* flooded him with life, too, life and energy and
awareness larded through the illness. Life without *saidin*
was a pale copy. Anything else was a wan imitation.

*But they can find me if I hold on. Track me, find me. I
have to reach Tear. I'll find out there. If I am the Dragon,*

there'll be an end to it. And if I am not. . . . If it's all a lie, there will be an end to that, too. An end.

Reluctantly, with infinite slowness, he severed contact with *saidin*, gave up its embrace as if giving up life's breath. The night seemed drab. The shadows lost their infinite sharp shadings and washed together.

In the distance, to the west, a dog howled, a shivering cry in the silent night.

Rand's head came up. He peered in that direction as though he could see the dog if he tried hard enough.

A second dog answered the first, then another, and two more together, all spread out somewhere west of him.

"Hunt me," Rand snarled. "Hunt me if you will. I'm no easy meat. No more!"

Pushing himself away from the tree, he waded a shallow, icy stream, then settled into a steady trot eastward. Cold water filled his boots, and his side hurt, but he ignored both. The night was quiet again behind him, but he ignored that, too. *Hunt me. I can hunt, too. I am no easy meat.*

CHAPTER

10

Secrets

Ignoring her companions for a moment, Egwene al'Vere stood in her stirrups hoping for a glimpse of Tar Valon in the distance, but all she could see was something indistinct, gleaming white in the morning sunlight. It had to be the city on the island, though. The lone, broken-topped mountain called Dragonmount, rising out of the rolling plain, had first appeared on the horizon late the afternoon before, and that lay just this side of the River Erinin from Tar Valon. It was a landmark, that mountain—one jagged fang sticking up out of rolling flatlands—easily seen for many miles, easy to avoid, as all did, even those who went to Tar Valon.

Dragonmount was where Lews Therin Kinslayer had died, so it was said; and other words had been spoken of the mountain, prophecy and warning. Rich reasons to stay away from its black slopes.

She had reason not to stay away, and more than one. Only in Tar Valon could she find the training she needed, the training she had to have. *I will never be collared again!* She pushed the thought away, but it came back turned end about. *I will never lose my freedom again!* In Tar Valon, Anaiya would resume testing her dreams; the Aes Sedai would have to, though she had found no real evidence that Egwene was a Dreamer, as Anaiya suspected. Egwene's dreams had been troubling since leaving Almoth Plain. Aside from dreams of the Seanchan—and those still made her wake sweating—she dreamed more and more of Rand. Rand running. Running toward something, but running away from something, too.

She peered harder toward Tar Valon. Anaiya would be there. *And Galad, too, perhaps.* She blushed in spite of herself, and banished him from her mind entirely. *Think about the weather. Think about anything else. Light, but it feels warm.*

This early in the year, with winter only yesterday's memory, white still capped Dragonmount, but here below, the snows were melted. Early shoots poked through the matted brown of last year's grasses, and where trees topped a low hill here and there, the first red of new growth was showing. After a winter spent traveling, sometimes trapped in village or camp for days by storms, sometimes covering less ground between sunrise and sunset, with snowdrifts belly-deep on the horses, than she could have walked by noon in better weather, it was good to see signs of spring.

Sweeping her thick wool cloak back out of her way, Egwene let herself drop down in the high-cantled saddle, and smoothed her skirts in a gesture of impatience. Her dark eyes filled with distaste. She had worn the dress, divided for riding by her own skill with a needle, for far too long, but the only other she had was even more grubby. And the same color, the dark gray of the Leashed Ones. The choice all those weeks ago, on beginning their ride to Tar Valon, had been dark gray or nothing.

"I swear I will never wear gray again, Bela," she told her shaggy mount, patting the mare's neck. *Not that I'll have much choice once we're back in the White Tower,* she thought. In the Tower, all novices wore white.

"Are you talking to yourself again?" Nynaeve asked, pulling her bay gelding closer. The two women were of a height as well as dressed alike, but the difference in their horses put the former Wisdom of Emond's Field a head taller. Nynaeve frowned now, and tugged at the thick braid of dark hair hanging over her shoulder, the way she did when worried or troubled, or sometimes when she was preparing to be particularly stubborn even for her. A Great Serpent ring on her finger marked her as one of the Accepted, not yet Aes Sedai, but a long step closer than Egwene. "Better you should be keeping watch."

Egwene held her tongue on the retort that she had been watching for Tar Valon. *Did she think I was standing in my stirrups because I do not like my saddle?* Nynaeve seemed to forget too often that she was not the Wisdom of Emond's Field any longer, and Egwene was no longer a child. *But she wears the ring and I do not—yet!—and for her, that means nothing has changed!*

"Do you wonder how Moiraine is treating Lan?" she asked sweetly, and had a moment of pleasure at the sharp jerk Nynaeve gave her braid. The pleasure faded quickly, though. Wounding remarks did not come naturally to her, and she knew Nynaeve's emotions concerning the Warder were like skeins of yarn after a kitten had gotten into the knitting basket. But Lan was no kitten, and Nynaeve would have to do something about the man before his stubborn-stupid nobility made her mad enough to kill him.

They were six altogether, all plainly dressed enough not to stand out in the villages and small towns they had encountered, yet perhaps as odd a party as had crossed the Caralain Grass anytime recently, four of them women, and one of the men in a litter slung between two horses. The litter horses carried light packs, as well, with supplies for the long stretches between villages the way they had come.

Six people, Egwene thought, *and how many secrets?* They all shared more than one, secrets that would have to be kept, perhaps, even in the White Tower. *Life was simpler back home.*

"Nynaeve, do you think Rand is all right? And Perrin?" she added hastily. She could not afford to pretend any longer that one day she would marry Rand; pretending would be all it was, now. She did not like that—she was not entirely reconciled to it—but she knew it.

"Your dreams? Have they been troubling you again?" Nynaeve sounded concerned, but Egwene was in no mood to accept sympathy.

She made her voice sound as everyday as she could manage. "From the rumors we heard, I can't tell what might be going on. They have everything I know about so twisted, so wrong."

"Everything has been wrong since Moiraine came into our lives," Nynaeve said brusquely. "Perrin and Rand. . . ." She hesitated, grimacing. Egwene thought Nynaeve believed everything that Rand had become was Moiraine's doing. "They will have to take care of themselves for now.

I'm afraid we have something to worry about ourselves. Something is not right. I can . . . feel it."

"Do you know what?" Egwene asked.

"It feels almost like a storm." Nynaeve's dark eyes studied the morning sky, clear and blue, with only a few scattered white clouds, and she shook her head again. "Like a storm coming." Nynaeve had always been able to foretell the weather. Listening to the wind, it was called, and the Wisdom of every village was expected to do it, though many really could not. Yet since leaving Emond's Field, Nynaeve's ability had grown, or changed. The storms she felt sometimes had to do with men rather than wind, now.

Egwene bit her underlip, thinking. They could not afford to be stopped or slowed, not after coming so far, not so close to Tar Valon. For Mat's sake, and for reasons that her mind might tell her were more important than the life of one village youth, one childhood friend, but that her heart could not rate so high. She looked at the others, wondering if any of them had noticed something.

Verin Sedai, short and plump and all in shades of brown, rode apparently lost in thought, the hood of her cloak pulled forward till it all but hid her face, in the lead but letting her horse amble at its own pace. She was of the Brown Ajah, and the Brown sisters usually cared more for seeking out knowledge than for anything in the world around them. Egwene was not so sure of Verin's detachment, though. Verin had put herself hip-deep in the affairs of the world by being with them.

Elayne, of an age with Egwene and also a novice, but golden-haired and blue-eyed where Egwene was dark, rode back beside the litter where Mat lay unconscious. In the same gray as Egwene and Nynaeve, she was watching him with the worry they all felt. Mat had not roused in three days, now. The lean, long-haired man riding on the other side of the litter seemed to be trying to look everywhere without anyone noticing, and the lines of his face had deepened in concentration.

"Hurin," Egwene said, and Nynaeve nodded. They slowed to let the litter catch up to them. Verin ambled on ahead.

"Do you sense something, Hurin?" Nynaeve asked. Elayne lifted her eyes, suddenly intent, from Mat's litter.

With the three of them looking at him, the lean man

shifted in his saddle and rubbed the side of his long nose. "Trouble," he said, curt and reluctant at the same time. "I think maybe . . . trouble."

A thief-taker for the King of Shienar, he did not wear a Shienaran warrior's topknot, yet the short sword and notched sword-breaker at his belt were worn with use. Years of experience seemed to have given him some talent at sniffing out wrongdoers, especially those who had done violence.

Twice on the journey he had advised them to leave a village after being there less than an hour. The first time, they had all refused, saying they were too tired, but before the night was done the innkeeper and two other men of the village had tried to murder them in their beds. They were only simple thieves, not Darkfriends, just greedy for the horses and whatever they had in their saddlebags and bundles. But the rest of the village knew of it, and apparently considered strangers fair gleanings. They had been forced to flee a mob waving axe handles and pitchforks. The second time, Verin ordered them to ride on as soon as Hurin spoke.

But the thief-taker was always wary when talking to any of his companions. Except Mat, back when Mat could talk; the two of them had joked and played at dice, when the women were not too close at hand. Egwene thought he might be uneasy at being alone, for all practical purposes, with an Aes Sedai and three women in training for sisterhood. Some men found facing a fight easier than facing Aes Sedai.

"What kind of trouble?" Elayne said.

She spoke easily, but with such a clear note of expecting to be answered, immediately and in detail, that Hurin opened his mouth. "I smell—" He cut himself short and blinked as if surprised, eyes darting from one woman to another. "Just a feeling," he said finally. "A . . . a hunch. I've seen some tracks, yesterday, and today. A lot of horses. Twenty or thirty going this way, twenty or thirty that. It makes me wonder. That's all. A feeling. But I say it's trouble."

Tracks? Egwene had not noticed them. Nynaeve said sharply, "I did not see anything worrisome in them." Nynaeve prided herself on being as good a tracker as any man. "They were days old. What makes you think they are trouble?"

"I just think they are," Hurin said slowly, as if he wanted to say more. He dropped his eyes, rubbing at his nose and inhaling deeply. "It's been a long time since we saw a village," he muttered. "Who knows what news from Falme has come before us? We might not find so good a welcome as we expect. I'm thinking these men could be brigands, killers. We should be wary, I'm thinking. If Mat was on his feet, I'd scout ahead, but maybe it's best I don't leave you alone."

Nynaeve's eyebrows lifted. "Do you believe we cannot look after ourselves?"

"The One Power won't do you much good if somebody kills you before you can use it," Hurin said, addressing the tall pommel of his saddle. "Begging your pardon, but I think I. . . . I'll just ride up with Verin Sedai for a time." He dug in his heels and galloped forward before any of them could speak again.

"Now that is a surprise," Elayne said as Hurin slowed a little distance from the Brown sister. Verin did not seem to notice him any more than she noticed anything else, and he appeared content to leave it so. "He has been staying as far from Verin as he could ever since we left Toman Head. He always looks at her as if he's afraid of what she might say."

"Respecting Aes Sedai doesn't mean he is not afraid of them," Nynaeve said, then added, reluctantly, "Of us."

"If he thinks there might be trouble, we ought to send him out scouting." Egwene took a deep breath and gave the other two women as level a look as she could manage. "If there is trouble, we can defend ourselves better than he could with a hundred soldiers to help him."

"He doesn't know that," Nynaeve said flatly, "and I am not about to tell him. Or anyone else."

"I can imagine what Verin would have to say about it." Elayne sounded anxious. "I wish I had some idea how much she does know. Egwene, I don't know if my mother could help me if the Amyrlin found out, much less help the pair of you. Or even whether she would try." Elayne's mother was Queen of Andor. "She was only able to learn a little of the Power before she left the White Tower, for all she has lived as if she had been raised to full sister."

"We cannot hope to rely on Morgase," Nynaeve said. "She is in Caemlyn, and we will be in Tar Valon. No, we may be in enough trouble already for going off as we did, no matter what we've brought back. It will be best if we stay low, behave humbly, and do nothing to attract more attention than we already have."

Another time, Egwene would have laughed at the idea of Nynaeve pretending to be humble. Even Elayne managed a better job of it. But at present she did not feel like laughing. "And if Hurin is right? If we are attacked? He cannot defend us against twenty or thirty men, and we might be dead if we wait for Verin to do something. You said you sense a storm, Nynaeve."

"You do?" Elayne said. Red-gold curls swung as she shook her head. "Verin will not like it if we. . . ." She trailed off. "Whatever Verin likes or doesn't like, we may have to."

"I will do what must be done," Nynaeve said sharply, "if there is anything to be done, and you two will run, if need be. The White Tower may be all abuzz with your potential, but don't think they will not still you both if the Amyrlin Seat or the Hall of the Tower decides it is necessary."

Elayne swallowed hard. "If they would still us for it," she said in a faint voice, "they would still you, too. We should all run together; or act together. Hurin has been right before. If we want to live to be in trouble in the Tower, we may have to . . . to do what we must."

Egwene shivered. Stilled. Cut off from *saidar*, the female half of the True Source. Few Aes Sedai had ever incurred that penalty, yet there were deeds for which the Tower demanded stilling. Novices were required to learn the names of every Aes Sedai who had ever been stilled, and their crimes.

She could always feel the Source there, now, just out of sight, like the sun at noon over her shoulder. If she often caught nothing when she tried to touch *saidar*, she still wanted to touch it. The more she touched it, the more she wanted to, all the time, no matter what Sheriam Sedai, the Mistress of Novices, said about the dangers of growing too fond of the feel of the One Power. To be cut off from it; still able to sense *saidar*, but never to touch it again. . . .

Neither of the others seemed to want to talk, either.

To cover her shaking, she bent from her saddle to the gently swaying litter. Mat's blankets had become disarrayed, exposing a curved dagger in a golden sheath clutched in one hand, a ruby the size of a pigeon's egg capping the hilt. Careful not to touch the dagger, she eased the blankets back over his hand. He was only a few years older than she, but gaunt cheeks and sallow skin had aged him. His chest barely moved as he breathed hoarsely. A lumpy leather sack lay at his feet. She shifted the blanket to cover that, too. *We have to get Mat to the Tower*, she thought. *And the sack.*

Nynaeve leaned down as well, and felt Mat's forehead. "His fever is worse." She sounded worried. "If only I had some worrynot root or feverbane."

"Perhaps if Verin tried Healing again," Elayne said.

Nynaeve shook her head. She smoothed Mat's hair back and sighed, then straightened before speaking. "She says it is all she can do to keep him alive, now, and I believe her. I—I tried Healing last night myself, but nothing happened."

Elayne gasped. "Sheriam Sedai says we mustn't try to Heal until we've been guided step by step a hundred times."

"You could have killed him," Egwene said sharply.

Nynaeve sniffed loudly. "I was Healing before I ever thought of going to Tar Valon, even if I didn't know I was. But it seems I need my medicines to make it work for me. If I only had some feverbane. I do not think he has much time left. Hours, maybe."

Egwene thought she sounded almost as unhappy about knowing, about how she knew, as she did about Mat. She wondered again why Nynaeve had chosen to go to Tar Valon for training at all. She had learned to channel unknowingly, even if she could not always control the act, and had passed the crisis that killed three out of four women who learned without Aes Sedai guidance. Nynaeve said she wanted to learn more, but often she was as reluctant about it as a child being dosed with sheepstongue root.

"We will have him in the White Tower soon," Egwene said. "They can Heal him there. The Amyrlin will take care of him. She will take care of everything." She did not look at where Mat's blanket covered the sack at his feet. The other two women were studiously not looking at it, either. There were some secrets they would all be relieved to shed.

"Riders," Nynaeve said suddenly, but Egwene had already seen them. Two dozen men appearing over a low rise ahead, white cloaks flapping as they galloped, angling toward them.

"Children of the Light," Elayne said, like a curse. "I think we have found your storm, and Hurin's trouble."

Verin had pulled up, a hand on Hurin's arm to stop him drawing his sword. Egwene touched the lead litter horse to stop it just behind the plump Aes Sedai.

"Let me do all the talking, children," the Aes Sedai said placidly, pushing her cowl back to reveal gray in her hair. Egwene was not sure how old Verin was; she thought old enough to be a grandmother, but the gray streaks were the Aes Sedai's only signs of age. "And whatever you do, do not allow them to make you angry."

Verin's face was as calm as her voice, but Egwene thought she saw the Aes Sedai measuring the distance to Tar Valon. The tops of the towers were visible now, and a high bridge arching over the river to the island, tall enough for the trading ships that plied the river to sail beneath.

Close enough to see, Egwene thought, *but too far to do any good*.

For a moment she was sure the oncoming Whitecloaks meant to charge them, but their leader raised a hand and they abruptly drew rein a scant forty paces off, scattering dust and dirt ahead of them.

Nynaeve muttered angrily under her breath, and Elayne sat straight and full of pride, appearing likely to berate the Whitecloaks for ill manners. Hurin still had a grip on his sword hilt; he looked ready to put himself between the women and the Whitecloaks no matter what Verin said. Verin mildly waved a hand in front of her face to dispel the dust. The white-cloaked riders spread out in an arc, blocking the way firmly.

Their breastplates and conical helmets shone from polishing, and even the mail on their arms gleamed brightly. Each man had the flaring, golden sun on his breast. Some fitted arrows to bows, which they did not raise, but held ready. Their leader was a young man, yet he wore two golden knots of rank beneath the sunburst on his cloak.

"Two Tar Valon witches, unless I miss my guess, yes?" he said with a tight smile that pinched his narrow face. Arrogance brightened his eyes, as if he knew some truth others were too stupid to see. "And two nits, and a pair of lapdogs, one sick and one old." Hurin bristled, but Verin's hand restrained him. "Where do you come from?" the Whitecloak demanded.

"We come from the west," Verin said placidly. "Move out of our way, and let us continue. The Children of the Light have no authority here."

"The Children have authority wherever the Light is, witch, and where the Light is not, we bring it. Answer my questions! Or must I take you to our camp and let the Questioners ask?"

Mat could not afford any more delay in reaching help in the White Tower. And more importantly—Egwene winced to think of it that way—more importantly, they could not let the contents of that sack fall into Whitecloak hands.

"I have answered you," Verin said, still calm, "and more politely than you deserve. Do you really believe you can stop us?" Some of the Whitecloaks raised their bows as if she had uttered a threat, but she went on, her voice never rising. "In some lands you may hold sway by your threats, but not here, in sight of Tar Valon. Can you truly believe that in this place, you will be allowed to carry off Aes Sedai?"

The officer shifted uneasily in his saddle, as though suddenly doubting whether he could back up his words. Then he glanced back at his men—either to remind himself of their support or because he had remembered they were watching—and with that he took himself in hand. "I have no fear of your Darkfriend ways, witch. Answer me, or answer the Questioners." He did not sound as forceful as he had.

Verin opened her mouth as if for idle conversation, but before she could speak, Elayne jumped in, voice ringing with command. "I am Elayne, Daughter-Heir of Andor. If you do not move aside at once, you will have Queen Morgase to answer to, Whitecloak!" Verin hissed with vexation.

The Whitecloak looked taken aback for an instant, but then he laughed. "You think it so, yes? Perhaps you will discover Morgase no longer has so much love for witches, girl. If I take you from them and return you to her side, she will thank me for it. Lord Captain Eamon Valda would like very much to speak to you, Daughter-Heir of Andor." He raised a hand, whether to gesture or signal his men, Egwene could not say. Some of the Whitecloaks gathered their reins.

There's no more time to wait, Egwene thought. *I will not be chained again!* She opened herself to the One Power. It was a simple exercise, and after long practice, it went much more swiftly than the first time she had tried. In a heartbeat her mind emptied of everything, everything but a single rosebud, floating in emptiness. She was the rosebud, opening to the light, opening to *saidar,* the female half of the True Source. The Power flooded her, threatening to sweep her away. It was like being filled with light, with the Light, like being one with the Light, a glorious ecstasy. She fought to keep from being overwhelmed, and focused on the ground in front of the Whitecloak officer's horse. A small patch of ground; she did not want to kill anyone. *You will not take me!*

The man's hand was still going up. With a roar the ground in front of him erupted in a narrow fountain of dirt and rocks higher than his head. Screaming, his horse reared, and he rolled out of his saddle like a sack.

Before he hit the ground, Egwene shifted her focus closer to the other Whitecloaks, and the ground threw up another small explosion. Bela danced sideways, but she controlled the mare with reins and knees without even thinking of it. Wrapped inside emptiness, she was still surprised at a third eruption, not of her making, and a fourth. Distantly, she was aware of Nynaeve and Elayne, both enveloped in the glow that said they, too, had embraced *saidar*, had been embraced by it. That aura would not be visible to any but another woman who could channel, but the results were visible to all. Explosions harried the Whitecloaks on every side, showering them with dirt, shaking them with noise, sending their horses plunging wildly.

Hurin stared around him, mouth open and obviously as frightened as the Whitecloaks, as he tried to keep the litter horses and his own mount from bolting. Verin was wide-eyed with astonishment and anger. Her mouth worked furiously, but whatever she might be saying was lost in the thunder.

And then the Whitecloaks were running away, some dropping their bows in panic, galloping as if the Dark One himself were at their backs. All but the young officer, who was picking himself up off the ground. Shoulders hunched, he stared at Verin, the whites of his eyes showing all the way 'round. Dust stained his fine white cloak, and his face, but he did not seem to notice. "Kill me, then, witch," he said shakily. "Go ahead. Kill me, as you killed my father!"

The Aes Sedai ignored him. Her attention was all on her companions. As if they, too, had forgotten their officer, the fleeing Whitecloaks vanished over the same rise where they had first appeared, all in a body and none looking back. The officer's horse ran with them.

Under Verin's furious gaze, Egwene let go of *saidar*, slowly, unwillingly. It was always hard, letting go. Even more slowly, the glow around Nynaeve vanished. Nynaeve was frowning hard at the pinch-faced Whitecloak before them, as if he might still be capable of some sort of trickery. Elayne looked shocked by what she had done.

"What you have done," Verin began, then stopped to take a deep breath. Her stare took in all three of the younger women. "What you have done is an abomination. An abomination! An Aes Sedai does not use the Power as a weapon except against Shadowspawn, or in the last extreme to defend her life. The Three Oaths—"

"They were ready to kill us," Nynaeve broke in heatedly. "Kill us, or carry us off to be tortured. He was giving the order."

"It . . . it was not really using the Power as a weapon, Verin Sedai." Elayne held her chin high, but her voice shook. "We did not hurt anyone, or even try to hurt anyone. Surely—"

"Do not split hairs with me!" Verin snapped. "When you become full Aes Sedai—if you ever become full Aes Sedai!—you will be bound to obey the Three Oaths, but even novices are expected to do their best to live as if already bound."

"What about him?" Nynaeve gestured to the Whitecloak officer, still standing there and looking stunned. Her face was as tight as a drum; she seemed almost as angry as the Aes Sedai. "He was about to take us prisoner. Mat will die if he doesn't reach the Tower soon, and . . . and. . . ."

Egwene knew what Nynaeve was struggling not to say aloud. *And we can't let that sack fall into any hands but the Amyrlin's.*

Verin regarded the Whitecloak wearily. "He was only trying to bully us, child. He knew very well he could not make us go where we did not want, not without more trouble than he was willing to accept. Not here, not in sight of Tar Valon. I could have talked us past him, with a little time and a little patience. Oh, he might well have tried to kill us if he could have done it from hiding, but no Whitecloak with the brains of a goat will try harming an Aes Sedai who knows he is there. See what you have done! What stories will those men tell, and what harm will it do?"

The officer's face had reddened when she mentioned hiding. "It is no cowardice not to charge the powers that Broke the World," he burst out. "You witches want to Break the World again, in the service of the Dark One!" Verin shook her head in tired disbelief.

Egwene wished she could mend some of the damage she had done. "I am very sorry for what I did," she told the officer. She was glad she was not bound to speak no word that was not true, as full Aes Sedai were, because what she had said was only half true at best. "I should not have, and I apologize. I am sure Verin Sedai will Heal your bruises." He stepped back as if she had offered to have him skinned alive, and Verin sniffed loudly. "We have come a long way," Egwene went on, "all the way from Toman Head, and if I weren't so tired, I would never have—"

"Be quiet, girl!" Verin shouted at the same time the Whitecloak snarled, "Toman Head? Falme! You were at Falme!" He stumbled back another step and half drew his sword. From the look on his face, Egwene did not know whether he meant to attack, or to defend himself. Hurin moved his horse closer to the Whitecloak, a hand on his sword-breaker, but the narrow-faced man went on in a rant, spittle flying with his fury. "My father died at Falme! Byar told me! You witches killed him for your false Dragon! I'll see you dead for it! I will see you burn!"

"Impetuous children," Verin sighed. "Almost as bad as boys for letting your mouths run away with you. Go with the Light, my son," she told the Whitecloak.

Without another word, she guided them around the man, but his shouts followed after. "My name is Dain Bornhald! Remember it, Darkfriends! I will make you fear my name! Remember my name!"

As Bornhald's shouts faded behind them, they rode in

silence for a time. Finally, Egwene said to no one in particular, "I was only trying to make things better."

"Better!" Verin muttered. "You must learn there is a time
to speak all of the truth, and a time to govern your tongue.
The least of the lessons you must learn, but important, if
you mean to live long enough to wear the shawl of a full
sister. Did it never occur to you that word of Falme might
have come ahead of us?"

"Why should it have occurred to her?" Nynaeve asked.
"No one we've met before this had heard more than rumors,
if that, and we have outrun even rumor in the last month."

"And all word has to come along the same roads we
used?" Verin replied. "We have moved slowly. Rumor takes
wing along a hundred paths. Always plan for the worst,
child; that way, all your surprises will be pleasant ones."

"What did he mean about my mother?" Elayne said suddenly. "He must have been lying. She would never turn
against Tar Valon."

"The Queens of Andor have always been friends to Tar
Valon, but all things change." Verin's face was calm again,
yet there was a tightness in her voice. She turned in her saddle to look over them, the three young women, Hurin, Mat
in the litter. "The world is strange, and all things change."
They capped the ridge; a village was in sight ahead of them
now, yellow tile roofs clustered around the great bridge that
led to Tar Valon. "Now you must truly be on your guard,"
Verin told them. "Now the real danger begins."

CHAPTER
II

Tar Valon

The small village of Darein had lain beside the River Erinin almost as long as Tar Valon had occupied its island. Darein's small, red and brown brick houses and shops, its stone-paved streets, gave a feel of permanence, but the village had been burned in the Trolloc Wars, sacked when Artur Hawkwing's armies besieged Tar Valon, looted more than once during the War of the Hundred Years, and put to the torch again in the Aiel War, not quite twenty years before. An unquiet history for a little village, but Darein's place, at the foot of one of the bridges leading out to Tar Valon, ensured it would always be rebuilt, however many times it was destroyed. So long as Tar Valon stood, at least.

At first it seemed to Egwene that Darein was expecting war again. A square of pikemen marched along the streets, ranks and files bristling like a carding comb, followed by bowmen in flat, rimmed helmets, with filled quivers riding at their hips and bows slanted across their chests. A squadron of armored horsemen, faces hidden behind the steel bars of their helmets, gave way to Verin and her party at a wave of their officer's gauntleted hand. All wore the White Flame of Tar Valon, like a snowy teardrop, on their breasts.

Yet townspeople went about their business with apparent unconcern, the market throng dividing around the soldiers as if marching men were obstructions they were long used to. A few men and women carrying trays of fruit kept pace with the soldiers, trying to interest them in wrinkled apples and pears pulled from winter cellars, but aside from

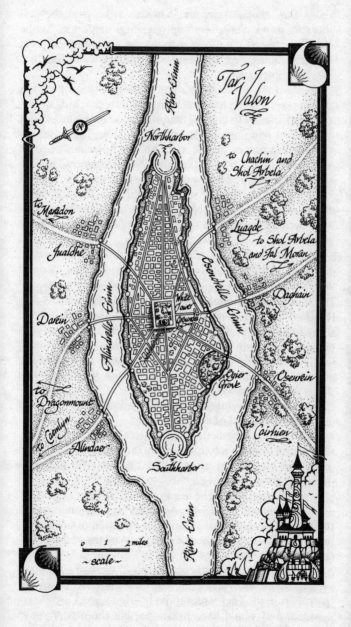

those few, shopkeepers and hawkers alike paid the soldiers no mind. Verin seemingly ignored them, too, as she led Egwene and the others through the village to the great bridge, arching over half a mile or more of water like lace woven from stone.

At the foot of the bridge more soldiers stood guard, a dozen pikemen and half that many archers, checking everyone who wanted to cross. Their officer, a balding man with his helmet hanging on his sword hilt, looked harassed by the waiting line of people afoot and on horseback, people with carts drawn by oxen or horses or the owner. The line was only a hundred paces long, but every time one was let onto the bridge, another joined the far end. Just the same, the balding man seemed to be taking his time about making sure each one had a right to enter Tar Valon before he let them go.

He opened his mouth angrily when Verin led her party to the head of the line, then caught a good look at her face and hurriedly stuffed his helmet onto his head. No one who really knew them needed a Great Serpent ring to identify Aes Sedai. "Good morrow to you, Aes Sedai," he said, bowing with a hand to his heart. "Good morrow. Go right across, if it please you."

Verin reined in beside him. A murmur rose from the waiting line, but no one voiced a complaint aloud. "Trouble from the Whitecloaks, guardsman?"

Why are we stopping? Egwene wondered urgently. "Has she forgotten about Mat?"

"Not really, Aes Sedai," the officer said. "No fighting. They tried to move into Eldone Market, the other side of the river, but we showed them better. The Amyrlin means to make sure they don't try again."

"Verin Sedai," Egwene began carefully, "Mat—"

"In a moment, child," the Aes Sedai said, sounding only halfway absentminded. "I have not forgotten him." Her attention went right back to the officer. "And the outlying villages?"

The man shrugged uncomfortably. "We can't keep the Whitecloaks out, Aes Sedai, but they move off when our patrols ride in. They seem to be trying to goad us." Verin nodded, and would have ridden on, but the officer spoke again. "Pardon, Aes Sedai, but you've obviously come from a distance. Have you any news? Fresh rumors come up-river with every trading vessel. They say there's a new false Dragon out west somewhere. Why, they even say he has Artur Hawkwing's armies, back from the dead, following him, and that he killed a lot of Whitecloaks and destroyed a city—Falme, they call it—in Tarabon, some say."

"They say Aes Sedai helped him!" a man's voice shouted from the waiting line. Hurin breathed deeply, and shifted himself as if he expected violence.

Egwene looked 'round, but there was no sign of who-ever had shouted. Everyone appeared to be concerned only with waiting, patiently or impatiently, for his turn to cross. Things had changed, and not for the better. When she had left Tar Valon, any man who spoke against Aes Sedai would have been lucky to escape with a punch in the nose from whoever overheard. Red in the face, the officer was glaring down the line.

"Rumors are seldom true," Verin told him. "I can tell you that Falme still stands. It isn't even in Tarabon, guardsman. Listen less to rumor, and more to the Amyrlin Seat. The Light shine on you." She lifted her reins, and he bowed as she led the others past him.

The bridge struck Egwene with wonder, as the bridges of Tar Valon always did. The openwork walls looked intricate enough to tax the best craftswoman at her lace-frame. It hardly seemed that such could have been done with stone, or that it could stand even its own weight. The river rolled, strong and steady, fifty paces or more below, and for all that half mile the bridge flowed unsupported from riverbank to island.

Even more wondrous, in its own way, was the feeling that the bridge was taking her home. More wondrous, and shocking. *Emond's Field is my home.* But it was in Tar Valon that she would learn what she must to keep her alive, to keep her free. It was in Tar Valon that she would learn—must learn—why her dreams disturbed her so, and why they sometimes seemed to have meanings she could not puzzle out. Tar Valon was where her life was tied, now. If she ever returned to Emond's Field—the "if" hurt, but she had to be honest—if she returned, it would be to visit, to see her parents. She had already gone beyond being an inn-keeper's daughter. Those bonds would not hold her again,

either, not because she hated them, but because she had out-
grown them.

The bridge was only the beginning. It arched straight to
the walls that surrounded the island, high walls of gleaming white, silver-streaked stone, whose tops looked down
on the bridge's height. At intervals, guard towers interrupted the walls, of the same white stone, their massive foot-
ings washed by the river. But above the walls and beyond
rose the true towers of Tar Valon, the towers of story, pointed
spires and flutes and spirals, some connected by airy bridges
a good hundred paces or more above the ground. And still
only the beginning.

There were no guards on the bronze-clad gates, and they
stood wide enough for twenty abreast to ride through, opening onto one of the broad avenues that crisscrossed the island. Spring might barely have come, but the air already
smelled of flowers and perfumes and spices.

The city took Egwene's breath as if she had never seen it
before. Every square and street crossing had its fountain, or
its monument or statue, some atop great columns as high as
towers, but it was the city itself that dazzled the eye. What
was plain in form might have so many ornaments and carvings that it seemed an ornament itself, or, lacking decoration, used its form alone for grandeur. Great buildings and
small, in stone of every color, looking like shells, or waves,
or wind-sculpted cliffs, flowing and fanciful, captured from
nature or the flights of men's minds. The dwellings, the
inns, the very stables—even the most insignificant buildings in Tar Valon had been made for beauty. Ogier stonemasons had built most of the city in the long years after
the Breaking of the World, and they maintained it had been
their finest work.

Men and women of every nation thronged the streets.
They were dark of skin, and pale, and everything in between, their garments in bright colors and patterns, or drab,
but decked with fringes and braids and shining buttons, or
stark and severe; showing more skin than Egwene thought
proper, or revealing nothing but eyes and fingertips. Sedan
chairs and litters wove through the crowds, the trotting
bearers crying "Give way!" Closed carriages inched along,
liveried coachmen shouting "Hiya!" and "Ho!" as if they
believed they might achieve more than a walk. Street musi-

cians played flute or harp or pipes, sometimes accompanying a juggler or an acrobat, always with a cap set out for coins. Wandering hawkers cried their wares, and shopkeepers standing in front of their shops shouted the excellence of their goods. A hum filled the city like the song of a thing alive.

Verin had pulled her cowl back up, hiding her face. No one seemed to be paying them any mind in these crowds, Egwene thought. Not even Mat in his horse litter drew a second glance, though some folk did edge away from it as they hurried past. People sometimes brought their sick to the White Tower for Healing, and whatever he had might be catching.

Egwene rode up beside Verin and leaned close. "Do you really expect trouble now? We are in the city. We are almost there." The White Tower stood in plain sight now, the great building gleaming broad and tall above the rooftops.

"I always expect trouble," Verin replied placidly, "and so should you. In the Tower most of all. You must all of you be more careful than ever, now. Your . . . tricks"—her mouth tightened for an instant before serenity returned—"frightened away the Whitecloaks, but inside the Tower they may well bring you death or stilling."

"I would not do that in the Tower," Egwene protested. "None of us would." Nynaeve and Elayne had joined them, leaving Hurin to mind the litter horses. They nodded, Elayne fervently, and Nynaeve, it seemed to Egwene, as if she had reservations.

"You should not do it ever again, child. You must not! Ever!" Verin eyed them sideways 'round the edge of her cowl, and shook her head. "And I truly hope you have learned the folly of speaking when you should be silent." Elayne's face went crimson, and Egwene's cheeks grew hot. "Once we enter the Tower grounds, hold your tongues and accept whatever happens. *Whatever* happens! You know nothing of what awaits us in the Tower, and if you did, you would not know how to handle it. So be silent."

"I will do as you say, Verin Sedai," Egwene said, and Elayne echoed her. Nynaeve sniffed. The Aes Sedai stared at her, and she nodded reluctantly.

The street opened into a vast square, centered in the city, and in the middle of the square stood the White Tower, shining in the sun, rising until it seemed to touch the sky from a palace of domes and delicate spires and other shapes surrounded by the Tower grounds. There were surprisingly few people in the square. No one intruded on the Tower unless he had business there, Egwene reminded herself uneasily.

Hurin led the horse litter forward as they entered the square. "Verin Sedai, I must leave you now." He eyed the Tower once, then managed not to look at it again, though it was hard to look at anything else. Hurin came from a land where Aes Sedai were respected, but it was one thing to respect them and quite another to be surrounded by them.

"You have been a great help on our journey, Hurin," Verin told him, "and a long journey it has been. There will be a place in the Tower for you to rest before you travel on."

Hurin shook his head emphatically. "I cannot waste a day, Verin Sedai. Not another hour. I must return to Shienar, to tell King Easar, and Lord Agelmar, the truth of what happened at Falme. I must tell them about—" He cut off abruptly and looked around. There was no one close enough to overhear, but he still lowered his voice and said only, "About Rand. That the Dragon is Reborn. There must be trading ships heading upriver, and I mean to be on the next to sail."

"Go in the Light, then, Hurin of Shienar," Verin said.

"The Light illumine all of you," he replied, gathering his reins. Yet he hesitated a moment, then added, "If you need me—ever—send word to Fal Dara, and I'll find a way to come." Clearing his throat as if embarrassed, he turned his horse and trotted away, heading beyond the Tower. All too soon he was lost to sight.

Nynaeve gave an exasperated shake of her head. "Men! They always say to send for them if you need them, but when you do need one, you need him right then."

"No man can help where we are going now," Verin said dryly. "Remember. Be silent."

Egwene felt a sense of loss with Hurin's going. He would barely talk to any of them, except Mat, and Verin was right. He was only a man, and helpless as a babe when it came to facing whatever might await them in the Tower. Yet his leaving made their number one less, and she could never help thinking that a man with a sword was useful to have around. And he had been a link to Rand, and Perrin. *I have my own troubles to worry about.* Rand and Perrin would have to make do with Moiraine to look after them. *And Min will certainly look after Rand,* she thought with a flash of jealousy that she tried to suppress. She almost succeeded.

With a sigh, she took up the lead of the horse litter. Mat lay bundled to his chin; his breathing was a dry rasp. *Soon,* she thought. *You'll be Healed soon, now. And we'll find out what's waiting for us.* She wished Verin would stop trying to frighten them. She wished she did not think Verin had reason to frighten them.

Verin took them around the Tower grounds to a small side gate that stood open, with two guards. Pausing, the Aes Sedai pushed back her cowl and leaned from her saddle to speak softly to one of the men. He gave a start, and a surprised look at Egwene and the others. With a quick, "As you command, Aes Sedai," he took off into the grounds at a run. Verin was already riding through the gates as he spoke. She rode as if there were no hurry.

Egwene followed with the litter, exchanging glances with Nynaeve and Elayne, wondering what Verin had told the man.

A gray stone guardhouse stood just inside the gate, shaped like a six-pointed star lying on its side. A small knot of guards lounged in the doorway; they left off talking and bowed as Verin rode past.

This part of the Tower grounds could have been some lord's park, with trees and pruned shrubs and wide graveled paths. Other buildings were visible through the trees, and the Tower itself loomed over everything.

The path led them to a stableyard among the trees, where grooms in leather vests came running to take their horses. At the Aes Sedai's direction, some of the grooms unfastened the litter and set it gently off to one side. As the horses were led away into the stable, Verin took the leather sack from Mat's feet and tucked it carelessly under one arm.

Nynaeve paused in knuckling her back and frowned at the Aes Sedai. "You said he has hours, perhaps. Are you just going to—"

Verin held up a hand, but whether it was the gesture that stopped Nynaeve or the crunch of feet approaching on gravel, Egwene could not say.

In a moment Sheriam Sedai appeared, followed by three of the Accepted, their white dresses ringed at the hem with the colors of all seven Ajahs from Blue to Red, and two husky men in rough, laborer's coats. The Mistress of Novices was a slightly plump woman, with the high cheekbones that were common in Saldaea. Flame-red hair and clear, tilted green eyes made her smooth Aes Sedai features striking. She eyed Egwene and the others calmly, but her mouth was tight.

"So you have brought back our three runaways, Verin. With everything that happened, I could almost wish you had not."

"We did not—" Egwene began, but Verin cut her off with a sharp, "BE SILENT!" Verin stared at her—at each of the three of them—as if the intensity of her look could hold their mouths shut.

Egwene was sure that, for her part, it could. She had never seen Verin angry before. Nynaeve crossed her arms beneath her breasts and muttered under her breath, but she said nothing. The three Accepted behind Sheriam kept their silence, of course, but Egwene thought she could see their ears grow from listening.

When she was certain Egwene and the others would remain still, Verin turned back to Sheriam. "The boy must be taken somewhere away from everyone. He is ill, dangerously so. Dangerous to others as well as to himself."

"I was told you had a litter to be carried." Sheriam motioned the two men to the litter, spoke a quiet word to one, and as quickly as that Mat was whisked away.

Egwene opened her mouth to say he needed help now, but at Verin's stare, quick and furious, she closed it again. Nynaeve was tugging her braid nearly hard enough to pull it out of her head.

"I suppose," Verin said, "that the whole Tower knows we have returned by now?"

"Those who do not know," Sheriam told her, "will know before much longer. Comings and goings have become the first topic of conversation and gossip. Even before Falme, and far ahead of the war in Cairhien. Did you think to keep it secret?"

Verin gathered the leather sack in both arms. "I must see the Amyrlin. Immediately."

"And what of these three?"

Verin considered Egwene and her friends, frowning. "They must be closely held until the Amyrlin wishes to see them. If she does wish to. Closely held, mind. Their own rooms will do, I think. No need for cells. Not a word to anyone."

Verin was still speaking to Sheriam, but Egwene knew the last had been meant as a reminder to her and the others. Nynaeve's brows were drawn down, and she jerked at her braid as if she wanted to hit something. Elayne's blue eyes were open wide, and her face was even paler than usual. Egwene was not sure which feelings she shared, anger or fear or worry. Some of all three, she thought.

With a last, searching glance at her three traveling companions, Verin hurried off, clutching the sack to her chest, cloak flapping behind her. Sheriam put her fists on her hips and studied Egwene and the other two. For a moment Egwene felt a lessening of tension. The Mistress of Novices always kept a steady temper and a sympathetic sense of humor even when she was giving you extra chores for breaking the rules.

But Sheriam's voice was grim when she spoke. "Not a word, Verin Sedai said, and not a word shall it be. If one of you speaks—except to answer an Aes Sedai, of course— I'll make you wish you had nothing but a switching and a few hours scrubbing floors to worry about. Do you understand me?"

"Yes, Aes Sedai," Egwene said, and heard the other two say the same, although Nynaeve pronounced the words like a challenge.

Sheriam made a disgusted sound in her throat, almost a growl. "Fewer girls now come to the Tower to be trained than once did, but they still come. Most leave never having learned to sense the True Source, much less touch it. A few learn enough not to harm themselves before they go. A bare handful can aspire to be raised to the Accepted, and fewer still to wear the shawl. It is a hard life, a hard discipline, yet every novice fights to hold on, to attain the ring and the shawl. Even when they are so afraid they cry themselves to sleep every night, they struggle to hold on. And you three, who have more ability born in you than I ever hoped to see in my lifetime, left the Tower without permission, ran away not even half-trained, like irresponsible children, stayed away for months. And now you ride back in as if nothing has happened, as if you can take up your training again on the morrow." She let out a long breath as if she might explode otherwise. "Faolain!"

The three Accepted jumped as if they had been caught eavesdropping, and one, a dark, curly-haired woman, stepped forward. They were all young women, but still older than Nynaeve. Nynaeve's rapid Acceptance had been extraordinary. In the normal course of things, it took years as a novice to earn the Great Serpent rings they wore, and would take years more before they could hope to be raised to full Aes Sedai.

"Take them to their rooms," Sheriam commanded, "and keep them there. They may have bread, cold broth, and water until the Amyrlin Seat says otherwise. And if one of them speaks even a word, you may take her to the kitchens and set her to scrubbing pots." She whirled and stalked away, even her back expressing anger.

Faolain eyed Egwene and the others with almost a hopeful air, especially Nynaeve, who wore a glower like a mask. Faolain's round face held no love for those who broke the rules so extravagantly, and less for one like Nynaeve, a wilder who had earned her ring without ever being a novice, who had channeled power before she ever entered Tar Valon. When it became obvious that Nynaeve meant to keep her anger to herself, Faolain shrugged. "When the Amyrlin sends for you, you'll probably be stilled."

"Give over, Faolain," another of the Accepted said. The oldest of the three, she had a willowy neck and coppery skin, and a graceful way of moving. "I will take you," she told Nynaeve. "I am called Theodrin, and I, too, am a wilder. I will hold you to Sheriam Sedai's order, but I will not bait you. Come."

Nynaeve gave Egwene and Elayne a worried look, then sighed and let Theodrin lead her away.

"Wilders," Faolain muttered. On her tongue, it sounded like a curse. She turned her stare to Egwene.

The third Accepted, a pretty, apple-cheeked young woman, stationed herself beside Elayne. Her mouth was turned up at the corners as if she liked to smile, but the

stern look she gave Elayne said she would brook no nonsense now.

Egwene returned Faolain's stare with as much calm
as she could manage, and, she hoped, a measure of the
haughty, silent contempt that Elayne had adopted. *Red
Ajah*, she thought. *This one will definitely choose the Reds.*
But it was hard not to think of her own troubles. *Light, what
are they going to do to us?* She meant the Aes Sedai, the
Tower, not these women.

"Well, come along," Faolain snapped. "It's bad enough I
have to stand guard on your door without standing here all
day. Come along."

Taking a deep breath, Egwene gripped Elayne's hand and
followed. *Light, let them be Healing Mat.*

CHAPTER

12

The Amyrlin Seat

S iuan Sanche paced the length of her study, pausing
now and again to glance, with a blue-eyed gaze that
had made rulers stammer, at a carved nightwood box
on a long table centered in the room. She hoped she would
not have to use any of the carefully drawn documents
within it. They had been prepared and sealed in secret, by
her own hand, to cover a dozen possible eventualities. She
had laid a warding on the box so that if any hand but hers
opened it, the contents would flash to ash in an instant; very
likely the box itself would burst into flame.

"And burn the thieving fisher-bird, whoever she might
be, so she never forgets it, I hope," she muttered. For the
hundredth time since being told that Verin had returned,
she readjusted her stole on her shoulders without realizing
what she was doing. It hung below her waist, broad and
striped with the colors of the seven Ajahs. The Amyrlin
Seat was of all Ajahs and of none, no matter from which
she had been raised.

The room was ornate, for it had belonged to generations
of women who had worn the stole. The tall fireplace and
broad, cold hearth were all carved golden marble from Kandor, and the diamond-shaped floor tiles, polished redstone
from the Mountains of Mist. The walls were panels of some
pale striped wood, hard as iron and carved in fantastic beasts
and birds of unbelievable plumage, panels brought from the
lands beyond the Aiel Waste by the Sea Folk before Artur
Hawkwing was born. Tall, arched windows, open now to let
in the new, green smells, let onto a balcony overlooking her
small private garden, where she seldom had time to walk.

All that grandeur was in stark contrast to the furnishings Siuan Sanche had brought to the room. The one table and the stout chair behind it were plain, if well polished with age and beeswax, as was the only other chair in the room. That stood off to one side, close enough to be drawn up if she wished a visitor to sit. A small Tairen rug lay in front of the table, woven in simple patterns of blue and brown and gold. A single drawing, tiny fishing boats among reeds, hung above the fireplace. Half a dozen stands held open books about the floor. That was all. Even the lamps would not have been out of place in a farmer's house.

Siuan Sanche had been born poor in Tear, and had worked on her father's fishing boat, one just like the boats in the drawing, in the delta called the Fingers of the Dragon, before ever she dreamed of coming to Tar Valon. Even the nearly ten years since she had been raised to the Seat had not made her comfortable with too much luxury. Her bedchamber was more simple still.

Ten years with the stole, she thought. *Nearly twenty since I decided to sail these dangerous waters. And if I slip now, I'll wish I were back hauling nets.*

She spun at a sound. Another Aes Sedai had slipped into the room, a copper-skinned woman with dark hair cut short. She caught herself in time to keep her voice steady and say only what was expected. "Yes, Leane?"

The Keeper of the Chronicles bowed, just as deeply as she would had others been present. The tall Aes Sedai, as tall as most men, was second only to the Amyrlin in the White Tower, and though Siuan had known her since they were novices together, sometimes Leane's insistence on upholding the dignity of the Amyrlin Seat was enough to make Siuan want to scream.

"Verin is here, Mother, asking leave to speak with you. I have told her you are busy, but she asks—"

"Not too busy to speak to her," Siuan said. Too quickly, she knew, but she did not care. "Send her in. There's no need for you to remain, Leane. I will speak to her alone."

A twitch of her eyebrows was the Keeper's only sign of surprise. The Amyrlin seldom saw anyone, even a queen, without the Keeper present. But the Amyrlin was the Amyrlin. Leane bowed her way out, and in moments Verin took her place, kneeling to kiss the Great Serpent ring on

Siuan's finger. The Brown sister had a good-sized leather sack under her arm.

"Thank you for seeing me, Mother," Verin said as she straightened. "I have urgent news from Falme. And more. I scarcely know where to begin."

"Begin where you will," Siuan said. "These rooms are warded, in case anyone thinks to use childhood tricks of eavesdropping." Verin's eyebrows lifted in surprise, and the Amyrlin added, "Much has changed since you left. Speak."

"Most importantly, then, Rand al'Thor has proclaimed himself the Dragon Reborn."

Siuan felt a tightness loosen in her chest. "I hoped it was he," she said softly. "I have had reports from women who could only tell what they had heard, and rumors by the score come with every trader's boat and merchant's wagon, but I could not be sure." She took a deep breath. "Yet I think I can name the day it happened. Did you know the two false Dragons no longer trouble the world?"

"I had not heard, Mother. That is good news."

"Yes. Mazrim Taim is in the hands of our sisters in Saldaea, and the poor fellow in Haddon Mirk, the Light have pity on his soul, was taken by the Tairens and executed on the spot. No one even seems to know what his name was. Both were taken on the same day and, according to rumor, under the same circumstances. They were in battle, and winning, when suddenly a great light flashed in the sky, and a vision appeared, just for an instant. There are a dozen different versions of what it was, but in both cases the result was exactly the same. The false Dragon's horse reared up and threw him. He was knocked unconscious, and his followers cried out that he was dead, and fled the field, and he was taken. Some of my reports speak of visions in the sky at Falme. I'll wager a gold mark to a week-old delta perch that was the instant Rand al'Thor proclaimed himself."

"The true Dragon has been Reborn," Verin said almost to herself, "and so the Pattern has no room for false Dragons anymore. We have loosed the Dragon Reborn on the world. The Light have mercy on us."

The Amyrlin shook her head irritably. "We have done what must be done." *And if even the newest novice learns of it, I will be stilled before the next sunrise, if I'm not torn to pieces first. Me, and Moiraine, and Verin, and likely any-*

one thought to be a friend of ours, as well. It was not easy to carry on so great a conspiracy when only three women knew of it, when even a close friend would betray them and consider it a duty well done. *Light, but I wish I could be sure they would not be right to do it.* "At least he is safely in Moiraine's hands. She will guide him, and do what must be done. What else have you to tell me, Daughter?"

For answer, Verin placed the leather sack on the table and took out a curled, gold horn, with silver script inlaid around its flaring bell mouth. She laid the horn on the table, then looked to the Amyrlin with quiet expectation.

Siuan did not have to be close enough to read the script to know what it said. *Tia mi aven Moridin isainde vadin.* "The grave is no bar to my call." "The Horn of Valere?" she gasped. "You brought that all the way here, across hundreds of leagues, with the Hunters looking everywhere for it? Light, woman, it was to be left with Rand al'Thor."

"I know, Mother," Verin said calmly, "but the Hunters all expect to find the Horn in some great adventure, not in a sack with four women escorting a sick youth. And it would do Rand no good."

"What do you mean? He is to fight Tarmon Gai'don. The Horn is to summon dead heroes from the grave to fight in the Last Battle. Has Moiraine once again made some new plan without consulting me?"

"This is none of Moiraine's doing, Mother. We plan, but the Wheel weaves the Pattern as it wills. Rand was not first to sound the Horn. Matrim Cauthon did that. And Mat now lies below, dying of his ties to the Shadar Logoth dagger. Unless he can be Healed here."

Siuan shivered. Shadar Logoth, that dead city so tainted that even Trollocs feared to enter, and with reason. By chance, a dagger from that place had come into young Mat's hands, twisting and tainting him with the evil that had killed the city long ago. Killing him. *By chance? Or by the Pattern? He is* ta'veren, *too, after all. But . . .* Mat *sounded the Horn.* Then—

"So long as Mat lives," Verin went on, "the Horn of Valere is no more than a horn to anyone else. If he dies, of course, another can sound it and forge a new link between man and Horn." Her gaze was steady and untroubled by what she seemed to be suggesting.

"Many will die before we are done, Daughter." *And who else could I use to sound it again? I'll not take the risk of trying to return it to Moiraine, now. One of the Gaidin, perhaps. Perhaps.* "The Pattern has yet to make his fate clear."

"Yes, Mother. And the Horn?"

"For the moment," the Amyrlin said finally, "we will find some place to hide this where no one but we two know. I will consider what to do after that."

Verin nodded. "As you say, Mother. Of course, a few hours will make one decision for you."

"Is that all you have for me?" Siuan snapped. "If it is, I have those three runaways to deal with."

"There is the matter of the Seanchan, Mother."

"What of them? All my reports say they have fled back across the ocean, or to wherever they came from."

"It seems so, Mother. But I fear we may have to deal with them again." Verin pulled a small leather notebook from behind her belt and began leafing through it. "They spoke of themselves as the Forerunners, or Those Who Come Before, and talked of the Return, and of reclaiming this land as theirs. I've taken notes on everything I heard of them. Only from those who actually saw them, of course, or had dealings with them."

"Verin, you are worrying about a lionfish out in the Sea of Storms, while here and now the silverpike are chewing our nets to shreds."

The Brown sister continued turning pages. "An apt metaphor, Mother, the lionfish. Once I saw a large shark that a lionfish had chased into the shallows, where it died." She tapped one page with a finger. "Yes. This is the worst. Mother, the Seanchan use the One Power in battle. They use it as a weapon."

Siuan clasped her hands tightly at her waist. The reports the pigeons had brought spoke of that, too. Most had only secondhand knowledge, but a few women wrote of seeing for themselves. The Power used as a weapon. Even dry ink on paper carried an edge of hysteria when they wrote of that. "That is already causing us trouble, Verin, and will cause more as the stories spread, and grow with the spreading. But I can do nothing about that. I am told these people are gone, Daughter. Do you have any evidence otherwise?"

"Well, no, Mother, but—"

"Until you do, let us deal with getting the silverpike out of our nets before they start chewing holes in the boat, too."

With reluctance, Verin closed the notebook and tucked it back behind her belt. "As you say, Mother. If I might ask, what do you intend to do to Nynaeve and the other two girls?"

The Amyrlin hesitated, considering. "Before I am done with them, they will wish they could go down to the river and sell themselves for fishbait." It was the simple truth, but it could be taken in more than one way. "Now. Seat yourself, and tell me everything those three have said and done in the time they were with you. Everything."

CHAPTER
13

Punishments

Lying on her narrow bed, Egwene frowned up at the flickering shadows cast on the ceiling by her single lamp. She wished she could form some plan of action, or reason out what to expect next. Nothing came. The shadows had more pattern than her thoughts. She could hardly even make herself worry about Mat, yet the shame she felt at that was small, crushed by the walls around her.

It was a stark, windowless room, like all those in the novices' quarters, small and square and painted white, with pegs on one wall for hanging her belongings, the bed built against a second, and a tiny shelf on a third, where in other days she had kept a few books borrowed from the Tower library. A washstand and a three-legged stool completed the furnishings. The floorboards were almost white from scrubbing. She had done that task, on hands and knees, every day she had lived there, in addition to her other chores and lessons. Novices lived simply, whether they were innkeepers' daughters or the Daughter-Heir of Andor.

She wore the plain white dress of a novice again—even her belt and pouch were white—but she felt no joy at having rid herself of the hated gray. Her room had become too much of a prison cell. *What if they mean to keep me here. In this room. Like a cell. Like a collar and. . . .*

She glanced at the door—the dark Accepted would still be standing guard on the other side, she knew—and rolled close to the white plastered wall. Just above the mattress was a small hole, almost invisible unless you knew where to look, drilled through into the next room by novices long ago. Egwene kept her voice to a whisper.

"Elayne?" There was no answer. "Elayne? Are you asleep?"

"How could I sleep?" came Elayne's reply, a reedy whisper through the hole. "I thought we might be in some trouble, but I did not expect this. Egwene, what are they going to do to us?"

Egwene had no answer, and her guesses were not of the sort she wanted to voice aloud. She did not even want to think of them. "I actually thought we might be heroes, Elayne. We brought back the Horn of Valere safely. We discovered Liandrin is Black Ajah." Her voice skipped on that. Aes Sedai had always denied the existence of a Black Ajah, an Ajah that served the Dark One, and were known to become angry with anyone who even suggested it was real. *But we know it's real.* "We should be heroes, Elayne."

"'Should and would build no bridges,'" Elayne said. "Light, I used to hate it when Mother said that to me, but it's true. Verin said we mustn't speak of the Horn, or Liandrin, to anyone but her or the Amyrlin Seat. I do not think any of this will work out the way we thought. It is not fair. We've been through so much; you've been through so much. It just is not fair."

"Verin says. Moiraine says. I know why people think Aes Sedai are puppetmasters. I can almost feel the strings on my arms and legs. Whatever they do, it will be what they decide is good for the White Tower, not what is good or fair for us."

"But you still want to be Aes Sedai. Don't you?"

Egwene hesitated, but there was never any real question as to her answer. "Yes," she said. "I still do. It is the only way we will ever be safe. But I will tell you this. I'll not let myself be stilled." That was a new thought, voiced as soon as it came to her, but she realized she did not want to take it back. *Give up touching the True Source?* She could sense it there, even now, the glow just over her shoulder, the shining just out of sight. She resisted the desire to reach out to it. *Give up being filled with the One Power, feeling more alive than I ever have before? I won't!* "Not without a fight."

There was a long silence from the other side of the wall. "How could you stop it? You may be as strong as any of them, now, but neither one of us knows enough yet to stop

even one Aes Sedai from shielding us from the Source, and
there are dozens of them here."

Egwene considered. Finally she said, "I could run away.
Really run away, this time."

"They would come after us, Egwene. I'm sure they
would. Once you show any ability at all, they don't let you
go until you've learned enough not to kill yourself. Or just
die from it."

"I am not a simple village girl anymore. I have seen
something of the world. I can keep out of Aes Sedai hands
if I want to." She was trying to convince herself as much
as Elayne. *And what if I don't know enough, yet? Enough
about the world, enough about the Power? What if just
channeling can still kill me?* She refused to think of that. *So
much I have to learn yet. I won't let them stop me.*

"My mother might protect us," Elayne said, "if what that
Whitecloak said is true. I never thought I would hope something like that was the truth. But if it isn't, Mother is just
as likely to send us both back in chains. Will you teach me
how to live in a village?"

Egwene blinked at the wall. "You will come with me? If
it comes to that, I mean?"

There was another long silence, then a faint whisper. "I
do not want to be stilled, Egwene. I will not be. I will not
be!"

The door swung open, crashing against the wall, and
Egwene sat up with a start. She heard the bang of a door
from the other side of the wall. Faolain stepped into
Egwene's room, smiling as her eyes went to the tiny hole.
Similar holes joined most of the novice rooms; any woman
who had been a novice knew of them.

"Whispering with your friend, eh?" the curly-haired Accepted said with surprising warmth. "Well, it grows lonely,
waiting by yourself. Did you have a nice chat?"

Egwene opened her mouth, then closed it again hastily.
She could answer Aes Sedai, Sheriam had said. No one
else. She regarded the Accepted with a level expression and
waited.

The false sympathy slid off Faolain's face like water running off a roof. "On your feet. The Amyrlin's not to be kept
waiting by the likes of you. You are lucky I did not come in
in time to hear you. Move!"

Novices were supposed to obey the Accepted almost as quickly as they obeyed Aes Sedai, but Egwene got to her feet slowly, and took as much time as she dared in smoothing her dress. She gave Faolain a small curtsy and a tiny smile. The scowl that rolled across the Accepted's face made Egwene's smile grow before she remembered to rein it in; there was no point in pushing Faolain too far. Holding herself straight, pretending her knees were not shaking, she preceded the Accepted out of the room.

Elayne was already waiting outside with the apple-cheeked Accepted, looking fiercely determined to be brave. Somehow, she managed to give the impression that the Accepted was a handmaid carrying her gloves. Egwene hoped that she herself was doing half so well.

The railed galleries of the novices' quarters rose tier on tier above, in a hollow column, and fell as many below, to the Novices' Court. There were no other women in sight. Even if every novice in the Tower had been there, though, less than a quarter of the rooms would have been filled. The four of them walked 'round the empty galleries and down the spiraling ramps in silence; none could bear to have the sounds of voices emphasize the emptiness.

Egwene had never before been into the part of the Tower where the Amyrlin had her rooms. The corridors there were wide enough for a wagon to pass down easily, and taller than they were wide. Colorful tapestries hung on the walls, tapestries in a dozen styles, of floral designs and forest scenes, of heroic deeds and intricate patterns, some so old they looked as if they might break if handled. Their shoes made loud clicks on diamond-shaped floor tiles that repeated the colors of the seven Ajahs.

There were few other women in evidence—an Aes Sedai now and then, sweeping majestically along with no time to notice Accepted or novices; five or six Accepted hurrying self-importantly about their tasks or studies; a sprinkling of serving women with trays, or mops, or armfuls of sheets or towels; a few novices moving on errands even more quickly than the servants.

Nynaeve and her slim-necked escort, Theodrin, joined them. Neither spoke. Nynaeve wore an Accepted's dress, now, white with the seven colored bands at the hem, but her belt and pouch were her own. She gave Egwene and Elayne each a reassuring smile and a hug—Egwene was so relieved to see another friendly face that she returned the hug with barely a thought that Nynaeve was behaving as if she were comforting children—but as they walked on, Nynaeve gave her thick braid a sharp tug from time to time, too.

Very few men came into that part of the Tower, and Egwene saw only two: Warders walking side by side in conversation, one with his sword on his hip, the other with his on his back. One was short and slender, even slight, the other almost as wide as he was tall, yet both moved with a dangerous grace. The color-shifting Warder cloaks made them queasy-making to watch for long, parts of them sometimes seeming to fade into the walls beyond. She saw Nynaeve looking at them, and shook her head. *She has to do something about Lan. If any of us can do anything about anyone after today.*

The antechamber of the Amyrlin Seat's study was grand enough for any palace, though the chairs scattered about for those who might wait were plain, but Egwene had eyes only for Leane Sedai. The Keeper wore her narrow stole of office, blue to show she had been raised from the Blue Ajah, and her face could have been carved from smooth, brownish stone. There was no one else there.

"Did they give any trouble?" The Keeper's clipped way of talking gave no hint now of either anger or sympathy.

"No, Aes Sedai," Theodrin and the apple-cheeked Accepted said together.

"This one had to be pulled by the scruff of her neck, Aes Sedai," Faolain said, indicating Egwene. The Accepted sounded indignant. "She balks as if she has forgotten what the discipline of the White Tower is."

"To lead," Leane said, "is neither to push nor to pull. Go to Marris Sedai, Faolain, and ask her to allow you to contemplate on this while raking the paths in the Spring Garden." She dismissed Faolain and the other two Accepted, and they dropped deep curtsies. From the depth of hers, Faolain shot a furious look at Egwene.

The Keeper paid no attention to the Accepted's leaving. Instead, she studied the remaining women, tapping a forefinger against her lips, till Egwene had the feeling they had all been measured to the inch and weighed to the ounce.

Nynaeve's eyes took on a dangerous sparkle, and she had a tight grip on her braid.

Finally Leane raised a hand toward the doors to the Amyrlin's study. The Great Serpent bit its own tail, a pace across, on the dark wood of each. "Enter," she said.

Nynaeve stepped forward promptly and opened one of the doors. That was enough to get Egwene moving. Elayne held her hand tightly, and she gripped Elayne's just as hard. Leane followed them in and took a place to one side, halfway between the three of them and the table in the center of the room.

The Amyrlin Seat sat behind the table, examining papers. She did not look up. Once Nynaeve opened her mouth, but closed it again, at a sharp look from the Keeper. The three of them stood in a line in front of the Amyrlin's table and waited. Egwene tried not to fidget. Long minutes went by—it seemed like hours—before the Amyrlin raised her head, but when those blue eyes fixed them each in turn, Egwene decided she could have waited longer. The Amyrlin's gaze was like two icicles boring into her heart. The room was cool, but a trickle of sweat began to run down her back.

"So!" the Amyrlin said finally. "Our runaways return."

"We did not run away, Mother." Nynaeve was obviously straining for calm, but her voice shook with emotion. Anger, Egwene knew. That strong will was all too often accompanied by anger. "Liandrin told us we were to go with her, and—" The loud crack of the Amyrlin's hand slapping the table cut her off.

"Do not invoke Liandrin's name here, child!" the Amyrlin snapped. Leane watched them with a stern serenity.

"Mother, Liandrin is Black Ajah," Elayne burst out.

"That is known, child. Suspected, at least, and as good as known. Liandrin left the Tower some months ago, and twelve other—*women*—went with her. None has been seen since. Before they left, they tried to break into the storeroom where the *angreal* and *sa'angreal* are kept, and did manage to enter that where the smaller *ter'angreal* are stored. They stole a number of those, including several we do not know the use of."

Nynaeve stared at the Amyrlin in horror, and Elayne suddenly rubbed her arms as if she were cold. Egwene knew she was shivering, too. Many times she had imagined returning to confront Liandrin and accuse her, to see her condemned to some punishment—except that she had never managed to imagine any punishment strong enough to suit that doll-faced Aes Sedai's crimes. She had even pictured returning to find Liandrin already fled— in terror of her return, it was usually. But she had never imagined anything like this. If Liandrin and the others—she had not really wanted to believe there were others—had stolen those remnants of the Age of Legends, there was no telling what they could do with them. *Thank the Light they did not get any sa'angreal*, she thought. The other was bad enough.

Sa'angreal were like *angreal*, allowing an Aes Sedai to channel more of the Power than she safely could unaided, but far more powerful than *angreal*, and rare. *Ter'angreal* were something different. Existing in greater numbers than either *angreal* or *sa'angreal*, though still not common, they used the One Power rather than helping to channel it, and no one truly understood them. Many would work only for someone who could channel, needing the actual channeling of the Power, while others did what they did for anyone. Where all the *angreal* and *sa'angreal* Egwene had ever heard of were small, *ter'angreal* could seemingly be any size. Each had apparently been made for a specific purpose by those Aes Sedai of three thousand years ago, to do a certain thing, and Aes Sedai since had died trying to learn what; died, or had the ability to channel burned out of them. There were sisters of the Brown Ajah who had made *ter'angreal* their life's study.

Some were in use, if likely not for the purposes they had been made. The stout white rod that the Accepted held while taking the Three Oaths on being raised to Aes Sedai was a *ter'angreal*, binding them to the oaths as surely as if they had been bred in the bone. Another *ter'angreal* was the site of the final test before a novice was raised to the Accepted. There were others, including many no one could make work at all, and many others that seemed to have no practical use.

Why did they take things no one knows how to use? Egwene wondered. *Or maybe the Black Ajah does know.* That possibility made her stomach churn. That might be as bad as *sa'angreal* in Darkfriend hands.

"Theft," the Amyrlin went on in tones as cold as her eyes, "was the least of what they did. Three sisters died that night, as well as two Warders, seven guards, and nine of the servants. Murder, done to hide their thieving and their flight. It may not be proof that they were—*Black Ajah*"—the words grated from her mouth—"but I cannot believe otherwise. When there are fish heads and blood in the water, you don't need to see the silverpike to know they are there."

"Then why are we being treated as criminals?" Nynaeve demanded. "We were tricked by a woman of the—of the Black Ajah. That should be enough to clear us of any wrongdoing."

The Amyrlin barked a mirthless laugh. "You think so, do you, child? It may be your salvation that no one in the Tower but Verin, Leane, and I even suspects you had anything to do with Liandrin. If that were known, much less the little demonstration you put on for the Whitecloaks—no need to look so surprised; Verin told me everything—if it were known you had gone off with Liandrin, the Hall might very well vote for stilling the three of you before you could take a breath."

"That is not fair!" Nynaeve said. Leane stirred, but Nynaeve went on. "It is not right! It—!"

The Amyrlin stood up. That was all, but it cut Nynaeve short.

Egwene thought she was wise to keep quiet. She had always believed Nynaeve was as strong, as strong-willed, as anyone could be. Until she met the woman wearing the striped stole. *Please keep your temper, Nynaeve. We might as well be children—babes—facing our mother, and this Mother can do far worse than beat us.*

It seemed to her a way out was being offered in what the Amyrlin had said, but she was not sure what way. "Mother, forgive me for speaking, but what do you intend to do to us?"

"Do to you, child? I intend to punish you and Elayne for leaving the Tower without permission, and Nynaeve for leaving the city without permission. First, you will each be called to Sheriam Sedai's study, where I've told her to switch you till you wish you had a cushion to sit on for the next week. I have already had this announced to the novices and the Accepted."

Egwene blinked in surprise. Elayne gave an audible grunt, stiffened her back, and muttered something under her breath. Nynaeve was the only one who seemed to take it without shock. Punishment, whether extra labors or something else, was always between the Mistress of Novices and whoever was called to her. Those were usually novices, but included the Accepted who stepped far enough beyond the bounds. *Sheriam always keeps it between you and her,* Egwene thought bleakly. *She can't have told everyone. But better than being imprisoned. Better than being stilled.*

"The announcement is part of the punishment, of course," the Amyrlin went on, as if she had read Egwene's mind. "I have also had it announced that you are all three assigned to the kitchens, to work with the scullions, until further notice. And I have let it be whispered about that 'further notice' might just mean the rest of your natural lives. Do I hear objections to any of this?"

"No, Mother," Egwene said quickly. Nynaeve would hate scrubbing pots even more than the other. *It could be worse, Nynaeve. Light, it could be so much worse.* Nynaeve's nostrils had flared, but she gave her head a tight shake.

"And you, Elayne?" the Amyrlin said. "The Daughter-Heir of Andor is used to gentler treatment."

"I want to be Aes Sedai, Mother," Elayne said in a firm voice.

The Amyrlin fingered a paper in front of her on the table and seemed to study it for a moment. When she raised her head, her smile was not at all pleasant. "If any of you had been silly enough to answer otherwise, I had something to add to your tally that would have had you cursing your mother for ever letting your father steal that first kiss. Letting yourselves be winkled out of the Tower like thoughtless children. Even an infant would never have fallen into that trap. I will teach you to think before you act, or else I'll use you to chink cracks in the water gates!"

Egwene found herself offering silent thanks. A prickle ran over her skin as the Amyrlin continued.

"Now, as to what else I intend to do with you. It seems you have all increased your ability to channel remarkably since you left the Tower. You have learned much. Including some things," she added sharply, "that I intend to see you unlearn!"

Nynaeve surprised Egwene by saying, "I know we have done . . . things . . . we should not have, Mother. I assure you, we will do our best to live as if we had taken the Three Oaths."

The Amyrlin grunted. "See that you do," she said dryly. "If I could, I'd put the Oath Rod in your hands tonight, but as that is reserved for being raised to Aes Sedai, I must trust to your good sense—if you have any—to keep you whole. As it is, you, Egwene, and you, Elayne, are to be raised to the Accepted."

Elayne gasped, and Egwene stammered a shocked, "Thank you, Mother." Leane shifted where she stood. Egwene did not think the Keeper looked best pleased. Not surprised—she had obviously known it was coming—but not pleased, either.

"Do not thank me. Your abilities have gone too far for you to remain novices. Some will think you should not have the ring, not after what you've done, but the sight of you up to your elbows in greasy pots should mute the criticism. And lest *you* start thinking it's some sort of reward, remember that the first few weeks as one of the Accepted are used to pick the rotting fish out of the basket of good ones. Your worst day as a novice will seem a fond dream compared to the least of your studies over the next weeks. I suspect that some of the sisters who teach you will make your trials even worse than they strictly must be, but I don't believe you will complain. Will you?"

I can learn, Egwene thought. *Choose my own studies. I can learn about the dreams, learn now to . . .*

The Amyrlin's smile cut off her train of thought. That smile said nothing the sisters could do to them would be worse than it needed to be, if it left them alive. Nynaeve's face was a mixture of deep sympathy and horrified remembrance of her own first weeks as one of the Accepted. The combination was enough to make Egwene swallow hard. "No, Mother," she said faintly. Elayne's reply was a hoarse whisper.

"Then that's done. Your mother was not at all pleased by your disappearance, Elayne."

"She knows?" Elayne squeaked.

Leane sniffed, and the Amyrlin arched an eyebrow, saying, "I could hardly keep it from her. You missed her by less than a month, which may be as well for you. You might not have survived that meeting. She was mad enough to chew through an oar, at you, at me, at the White Tower."

"I can imagine, Mother," Elayne said faintly.

"I don't think you can, child. You may have ended a tradition that began before there *was* an Andor. A custom stronger than most laws. Morgase refused to take Elaida back with her. For the first time ever, the Queen of Andor does not have an Aes Sedai advisor. She demanded your immediate return to Caemlyn as soon as you were found. I convinced her it would be safer for you to train here a little longer. She was ready to remove your two brothers from their training with the Warders, too. They talked their way out of that themselves. I still do not know how."

Elayne seemed to be looking inward, perhaps seeing Morgase in all her anger. She shivered. "Gawyn is my brother," she said absently. "Galad is not."

"Do not be childish," the Amyrlin told her. "Sharing the same father makes Galad your brother, too, whether or not you like him. I will not allow childishness out of you, girl. A measure of stupidity can be tolerated in a novice; it is not allowed in one of the Accepted."

"Yes, Mother," Elayne said glumly.

"The Queen left a letter for you with Sheriam. Aside from giving you the rough side of her tongue, I believe she states her intention of bringing you home as soon as it is safe for you. She is sure that in a few more months at most you will be able to channel without risking killing yourself."

"But I want to learn, Mother." The iron had returned to Elayne's voice. "I want to be Aes Sedai."

The Amyrlin's smile was even grimmer than her last. "As well that you do, child, because I have no intention of letting Morgase have you. You have the potential to be stronger than any Aes Sedai in a thousand years, and I will not let you go until you achieve the shawl as well as the ring. Not if I have to grind you into sausage to do it. *I will not let you go.* Do I make myself clear?"

"Yes, Mother." Elayne sounded uneasy, and Egwene did not blame her. Caught between Morgase and the White Tower like a towel between two dogs, caught between the Queen of Andor and the Amyrlin Seat. If Egwene had ever envied Elayne her wealth and the throne she would one day occupy, at that moment she surely did not.

The Amyrlin said briskly, "Leane, take Elayne down to Sheriam's study. I have a few words yet to say to these other two. Words I do not think they will enjoy hearing."

Egwene exchanged startled looks with Nynaeve; for a moment, worry dissolved the tension between them. *What does she have to say to us and not to Elayne?* she wondered. *I do not care, so long as she does not try to stop me learning. But why not Elayne, too?*

Elayne grimaced at the mention of the Mistress of Novices's study, but she drew herself up as Leane came to her side. "As you command, Mother," she said formally, lowering herself in a perfect curtsy, skirts sweeping wide, "so shall I obey." She followed Leane out with her head held high.

CHAPTER
14

The Bite of the Thorns

The Amyrlin Seat did not speak at once—she walked to the tall, arched windows and looked out across the balcony at the garden below, hands clasped tightly behind her. Minutes went by before she spoke, still with her back to the two of them.

"I have kept the worst of it from getting out, but how long will that last? The servants do not know of the stolen *ter'angreal*, and they do not connect the deaths with Liandrin and the others leaving. It was not easy to manage that, gossip being what it is. They believe the deaths were the work of Darkfriends. And so they were. Rumors are reaching the city, too. That Darkfriends got into the Tower, that they did murder. There was no way to stop that. It does our reputation no good, but at least it is better than the truth. At least none outside the Tower, and few inside, know Aes Sedai were killed. Darkfriends in the White Tower. Faugh! I've spent my life denying that. I will not let them be here. I will hook them, and gut them, and hang them out in the sun to dry."

Nynaeve gave Egwene an uncertain look—half as uncertain as Egwene felt—then took a deep breath. "Mother, are we to be punished more? Beyond what you've already sentenced us to?"

The Amyrlin looked over her shoulder at them; her eyes were lost in shadow. "Punished more? You might well say that. Some will say I've given you a gift, raising you. Now feel the real bite of that rose's thorns." She strode briskly back to her chair and sat down, then seemed to lose her urgency again. Or to gain uncertainty.

To see the Amyrlin look uncertain made Egwene's stomach clench. The Amyrlin Seat was always sure, always serenely centered on her path. The Amyrlin was strength personified. For all her own raw power, the woman on the other side of the table had the knowledge and experience to wind her around a spindle. To see her suddenly wavering—like a girl who knew she had to dive head first into a pond without any idea of how deep it was or whether there were rocks or mud on the bottom—to see that, chilled Egwene right to her core. *What does she mean, the real bite of the thorns? Light, what does she mean to do to us?*

Fingering a carved black box on the table in front of her, the Amyrlin peered at it as if looking at something beyond. "It is a question of who I can trust," she said softly. "I should be able to trust Leane and Sheriam, at least. But do I dare? Verin?" Her shoulders shook with a quick, silent laugh. "I already trust Verin with more than my life, but how far can I take it? Moiraine?" She was silent for a moment. "I have always believed I could trust Moiraine."

Egwene shifted uneasily. How much did the Amyrlin know? It was not the kind of thing she could ask, not of the Amyrlin Seat. *Do you know that a young man from my village, a man I used to think I'd marry one day, is the Dragon Reborn? Do you know two of your Aes Sedai are helping him?* At least she was sure the Amyrlin did not know she had dreamed of him last night, running from Moiraine. She thought she was sure. She kept silent.

"What are you talking about?" Nynaeve demanded. The Amyrlin looked up at her, and she moderated her tone as she added, "Forgive me, Mother, but are we to be punished more? I do not understand this talk of trust. If you want my opinion, Moiraine is not to be trusted."

"That is your opinion, is it?" the Amyrlin said. "A year out of your village, and you think you know enough of the world to choose which Aes Sedai to trust, and which not? A master sailor who's barely learned to hoist a sail!"

"She did not mean anything, Mother," Egwene said, but she knew Nynaeve meant exactly what she had said. She shot a warning glance at Nynaeve. Nynaeve gave her braid a sharp tug, but she kept her mouth shut.

"Well, who is to say," the Amyrlin mused. "Trust is as slippery as a basket of eels, sometimes. The point is, you

two are what I have to work with, thin reeds though you
may be."

Nynaeve's mouth tightened, though her voice stayed
level. "Thin reeds, Mother?"

The Amyrlin went on as if she had not spoken. "Liandrin
tried to stuff you headfirst into a weir, and it may well be
she left because she learned you were returning, and could
unmask her, so I have to believe you aren't—Black Ajah. I
would rather eat scales and entrails," she muttered, "but I
suppose I'll have to get used to saying that name."

Egwene gaped in shock—*Black Ajah? Us? Light!*—but
Nynaeve barked, "We certainly are not! How dare you say
such a thing? How dare you even suggest it?"

"If you doubt me, child, go ahead!" the Amyrlin said in
a hard voice. "You may have an Aes Sedai's power sometimes, but you are not yet Aes Sedai, not by miles. Well?
Speak, if you have more to say. I promise to leave you
weeping for forgiveness! 'Thin reed'? I'll break you like a
reed! I've no patience left."

Nynaeve's mouth worked. Finally, though, she gave herself a shake, and drew a calming breath. When she spoke
her voice still had an edge, but a small one. "Forgive me,
Mother. But you should not—We are not—We would not
do such a thing."

With a compressed smile, the Amyrlin leaned back in
her chair. "So you can keep your temper, when you want
to. I had to know that." Egwene wondered how much of it
had been a test; there was a tightness around the Amyrlin's
eyes that suggested her patience might well be exhausted.
"I wish I could have found a way to raise you to the shawl,
Daughter. Verin says you are already as strong as any
woman in the Tower."

"The shawl!" Nynaeve gasped. "Aes Sedai? Me?"

The Amyrlin gestured slightly as if tossing something
away, but she looked regretful to lose it. "No point wishing for what can't be. I could hardly raise you to full sister
and send you to scrub pots at the same time. And Verin
also says you still cannot channel consciously unless you
are furious. I was ready to sever you from the True Source
if you even looked like embracing *saidar*. The final tests for
the shawl require you to channel while maintaining utter

calm under pressure. Extreme pressure. Even I cannot—and would not—set that requirement aside."

Nynaeve seemed stunned. She was staring at the Amyrlin with her mouth hanging open.

"I don't understand, Mother," Egwene said after a moment.

"I suppose you don't, at that. You are the only two in the Tower I can be absolutely sure are not Black Ajah." The Amyrlin's mouth still twisted around those words. "Liandrin and her twelve went, but did all of them go? Or did they leave some of their number behind, like a stub in shallow water that you don't see till it puts a hole in your boat? It may be I'll not find that out until it is too late, but I will not let Liandrin and the others get away with what they did. Not the theft, and especially not the murders. No one kills my people and walks away unscathed. And I'll not let thirteen trained Aes Sedai serve the Shadow. I mean to find them, and still them!"

"I don't see what that has to do with us," Nynaeve said slowly. She did not look as if she liked what she was thinking.

"Just this, child. You two are to be my hounds, hunting the Black Ajah. No one will believe it of you, not a pair of half-trained Accepted I humiliated publicly."

"That is crazy!" Nynaeve's eyes had opened wide by the time the Amyrlin reached the words "Black Ajah," and her knuckles were white from her grip on her braid. She bit her words off and spat them: "They are all full Aes Sedai. Egwene hasn't even been raised to Accepted yet, and you know I cannot channel enough to light a candle unless I am angry, not of my own free will. What chance would we have?"

Egwene nodded agreement. Her tongue had stuck to the roof of her mouth. *Hunt the Black Ajah? I'd rather hunt a bear with a switch! She's just trying to scare us, to punish us more. She has to be!* If that was what the Amyrlin was trying, she was succeeding all too well.

The Amyrlin was nodding, too. "Every word you say is true. But each of you is more than a match for Liandrin in sheer power, and she is the strongest of them. Yet they are trained, and you are not, and you, Nynaeve, do have limitations, as yet. But when you don't have an oar, child, any plank will do to paddle the boat ashore."

"But I would be useless," Egwene blurted. Her voice came out as a squeak, but she was too afraid to be ashamed. *She means it! Oh, Light, she means it! Liandrin gave me to the Seanchan, and now she wants me to hunt thirteen like her?* "My studies, my lessons, working in the kitchens. Anaiya Sedai will surely want to continue testing me to see if I am a Dreamer. I'll barely have time left over to sleep and eat. How can I hunt anything?"

"You will have to find the time," the Amyrlin said, cool and serene once more, as if hunting the Black Ajah were no more than sweeping a floor. "As one of the Accepted, you choose your own studies, within limits, and the times for them. And the rules are a little easier for Accepted. A little easier. They must be found, child."

Egwene looked to Nynaeve, but what Nynaeve said was, "Why is Elayne not part of this? It can't be because you think she is Black Ajah. Is it because she is Daughter-Heir of Andor?"

"A full net on the first cast, child. I would make her one of you if I could, but at the moment Morgase gives me enough problems as it is. When I have her combed and curried and prodded back on the proper path, perhaps Elayne will join you. Perhaps then."

"Then leave Egwene out, too," Nynaeve said. "She is barely old enough to be a woman. I will do your hunting for you." Egwene made a sound of protest—*I am a woman!*—but the Amyrlin spoke before her.

"I am not setting you out as bait, child. If I had a hundred of you, I would still not be happy, but there are only you two, so two I will have."

"Nynaeve," Egwene said, "I do not understand you. Do you mean you want to do this?"

"It isn't that I want to," Nynaeve said wearily, "but I'd rather hunt them than sit wondering if the Aes Sedai teaching me is really a Darkfriend. And whatever they are up to, I do not want to wait until they're ready to find out what it is."

The decision Egwene came to twisted her stomach. "Then I will do it, too. I don't want to sit wondering and waiting any more than you do." Nynaeve opened her mouth, and Egwene felt a flash of anger; it was such a relief after fear. "And don't you dare say I'm too young again. At least I can channel when I want to. Most of the time. I am not a little girl anymore, Nynaeve."

Nynaeve stood there, jerking on her braid and not saying a word. Finally the stiffness drained out of her. "You are not, are you? I have said myself you are a woman, but I suppose I did not really believe it, inside. Girl, I—No, woman. Woman, I hope you realize you've climbed into a pickling cauldron with me, and the fire may be lit."

"I know it." Egwene was proud that her voice hardly shook at all.

The Amyrlin smiled as if pleased, but there was something in her blue eyes that made Egwene suspect she had known what their decisions would be all along. For an instant, she felt those puppeteer's strings on her arms and legs again.

"Verin. . . ." The Amyrlin hesitated, then muttered half to herself. "If I must trust someone, it might as well be her. She knows as much as I already, and maybe more." Her voice strengthened. "Verin will give you all that is known of Liandrin and the others, and also a list of the *ter'angreal* that were taken, and what they will do. Those that we know. As for any of the Black Ajah still in the Tower. . . . Listen, watch, and be careful of your questions. Be like mice. If you have even a suspicion, report it to me. I will keep an eye on you myself. No one will think that strange, given what you're being punished for. You can make your reports when I look in on you. Remember, they have killed before. They could easily kill again."

"That's all very well," Nynaeve said, "but we will still be Accepted, and it is Aes Sedai we're after. Any full sister can tell us to go about our business, or send us off to do her laundry, and we will have no choice but to obey. There are places Accepted are not supposed to go, things we're not supposed to do. Light, if we were sure a sister was Black Ajah, she could tell the guards to lock us in our rooms and keep us there, and they would do it. They certainly would not take the word of an Accepted over that of an Aes Sedai."

"For the most part," the Amyrlin said, "you must work within the limitations of the Accepted. The idea is for no one to suspect you. But. . . ." She opened the black box on her table, hesitated and looked at the other two women as if still unsure she wanted to do this, then took out a number of stiff, folded papers. Sorting through them carefully, she hesitated again, then chose out two. The remainder she shoved back into the box, and handed those two to Egwene and Nynaeve. "Keep these well hidden. They are for an emergency only."

Egwene unfolded her thick paper. It held writing in a neat, round hand, and was sealed at the bottom with the White Flame of Tar Valon.

What the bearer does is done at my order and by my authority. Obey, and keep silent, at my command.

> Siuan Sanche
> Watcher of the Seals
> Flame of Tar Valon
> The Amyrlin Seat

"I could do anything with this," Nynaeve said in a wondering voice. "Order the guards to march. Command the Warders." She gave a little laugh. "I could make a Warder dance, with this."

"Until I found out about it," the Amyrlin agreed dryly. "Unless you had a very convincing reason, I'd make you wish Liandrin had caught you."

"I didn't mean to do any of that," Nynaeve said hastily. "I just meant that it gives more authority than I had imagined."

"You may need every shred of it. But just you remember, child. A Darkfriend won't heed that any more than a Whitecloak would. They would both likely kill you just for having it. If that paper is a shield . . . well, paper shields are flimsy, and this one may have a target painted on it."

"Yes, Mother," Egwene and Nynaeve said together. Egwene folded her paper up and tucked it into her belt pouch, resolving not to take it out again unless she absolutely had to. *And how will I know when that is?*

"What about Mat?" Nynaeve asked. "He's very sick, Mother, and he does not have much time left."

"I will send word to you," the Amyrlin said curtly.

"But, Mother—"

"I will send word to you! Now, off with you, children. The hope of the Tower rests in your hands. Go to your rooms and get some rest. Remember, you have appointments with Sheriam, and with the pots."

CHAPTER
15

The Gray Man

Outside the Amyrlin Seat's study, Egwene and Nynaeve found the corridors empty except for an occasional serving woman, hurrying about her duties on soft-slippered feet. Egwene was grateful for their presence. The halls suddenly seemed like caverns, for all the tapestries and stonework. Dangerous caverns.

Nynaeve strode along purposefully, tugging at her braid fitfully again, and Egwene hurried to keep up. She did not want to be left alone.

"If the Black Ajah *is* still here, Nynaeve, and if they even suspect what we're doing. . . . I hope you didn't mean what you said about acting as if we are already bound by the Three Oaths. I don't intend to let them kill me, not if I can stop it by channeling."

"If any of them are still here, Egwene, they will know what we are doing as soon as they see us." Despite what she was saying, Nynaeve sounded preoccupied. "Or at least they will see us as a threat, and that's much the same thing as far as what they will do."

"How will they see us as a threat? Nobody is threatened by someone they can order about. Nobody is threatened by someone who has to scrub pots and turn the spits three times a day. That's why the Amyrlin is putting us to work in the kitchens. Part of the reason, anyway."

"Perhaps the Amyrlin did not think it through," Nynaeve said absently. "Or perhaps she did, and means something different for us than what she claims. Think, Egwene. Liandrin would not have tried to put us out of the way unless she thought we were a threat to her. I can't imagine how, or to what, but I cannot see how it could have changed, either. If there are any Black Ajah still here, they will surely see us the same way, whether they suspect what we're doing or not."

Egwene swallowed. "I hadn't thought of that. Light, I wish I were invisible. Nynaeve, if they are still after us, I will risk being stilled before I let Darkfriends kill me, or maybe worse. And I won't believe you will let them take you, either, no matter what you told the Amyrlin."

"I meant it." For a moment Nynaeve seemed to rouse from her thoughts. Her steps slowed. A pale-haired novice carrying a tray rushed past. "I meant every word, Egwene." Nynaeve went on when the novice was out of hearing. "There are other ways to defend ourselves. If there were not, Aes Sedai would be killed every time they left the Tower. We just have to reason those ways out, and use them."

"I know several ways already, and so do you."

"They are dangerous." Egwene opened her mouth to say they were only dangerous to whoever attacked her, but Nynaeve plowed on over her. "You can come to like them too much. When I let out all my anger at those Whitecloaks this morning. . . . It felt too good. It is too dangerous." She shivered and quickened her pace again, and Egwene had to step lively to catch up.

"You sound like Sheriam. You never have before. You have pushed every limit they've put on you. Why would you accept limits now, when we might have to ignore them to stay alive?"

"What good if it ends with us being put out of the Tower? Stilled or not, what good then?" Nynaeve's voice dropped as if she were speaking to herself. "I can do it. I must, if I'm to stay here long enough to learn, and I must learn if I'm to—" Suddenly she seemed to realize she was speaking aloud. She shot a hard look at Egwene, and her voice firmed. "Let me think. Please, be quiet and let me think."

Egwene held her tongue, but inside she bubbled with unasked questions. What special reason did Nynaeve have for wanting to learn more of what the White Tower could teach? What was it she wanted to do? Why was Nynaeve keeping it secret from her? *Secrets. We've learned to keep too many secrets since coming to the Tower. The Amyrlin is keeping secrets from us, too. Light, what is she going to do about Mat?*

Nynaeve accompanied her all the way back to the novices' quarters, not turning aside to the Accepted's quarters. The galleries were still empty, and they met no one as they climbed the spiraling ramps.

As they came up on Elayne's room, Nynaeve stopped, knocked once, and immediately opened the door and put her head inside. Then she was letting the white door swing shut and striding toward the next, Egwene's room. "She isn't here yet," she said. "I need to talk to both of you."

Egwene caught her shoulders and pulled her to an abrupt halt. "What—?" Something tugged at her hair, stung her ear. A black blur streaked in front of her face to clang against the wall, and in the next breath Nynaeve was bearing her to the gallery floor, behind the railing.

Wide-eyed and sprawling, Egwene stared at what lay on the stone in front of her door, where it had fallen. A bolt from a crossbow. A few dark strands from her hair were tangled in the four heavy prongs, meant for punching through armor. She raised a trembling hand to touch her ear, to touch the tiniest nick, damp with a bead of blood. *If I had not stopped just then. . . . If I hadn't. . . .* The quarrel would have gone right through her head, and would probably have killed Nynaeve, too. "Blood and ashes!" she gasped. "Blood and bloody ashes!"

"Watch your language," Nynaeve admonished, but her heart was not in it. She lay peering between the white stone balusters toward the far side of the galleries. A glow surrounded her, to Egwene's eyes. She had embraced *saidar.*

Hastily, Egwene tried to reach out for the One Power, too, but at first haste defeated her. Haste, and images that kept intruding on the emptiness, images of her head being ripped apart like a rotten melon by a heavy quarrel that went on to bury itself in Nynaeve. She took a deep breath and tried again, and finally the rose floated in nothingness, opened to the True Source, and the Power filled her.

She rolled onto her stomach to peer through the railing beside Nynaeve. "Do you see anything? Do you see him? I'll put a lightning bolt through him!" She could feel it building, pressing on her to loose it. "It *is* a man, isn't it?" She could not imagine a man coming into the novices' quarters, but it was impossible to picture a woman carrying a crossbow through the Tower.

"I don't know." Quiet anger filled Nynaeve's voice; her anger was always at its worst when she grew quiet with it. "I thought I saw—Yes! There!" Egwene felt the Power pulse in the other woman, and then Nynaeve was unhurriedly getting to her feet, brushing at her dress as if there were nothing more to worry about.

Egwene stared at her. "What? What did you do? Nynaeve?"

"'Of the Five Powers,'" Nynaeve said in a lecturing tone, faintly mocking, "'Air, sometimes called Wind, is thought by many to be of the least use. This is far from true.'" She finished with a tight laugh. "I told you there were other ways to defend ourselves. I used Air, to hold him with air. If it is a he; I could not see him clearly. A trick the Amyrlin showed me once, though I doubt she expected me to see how it was done. Well, are you going to lie there all day?"

Egwene scrambled up to hurry after her around the gallery. Before long a man did come into sight around the curve, dressed in plain brown breeches and coat. He stood facing the other way, balanced on the ball of one foot, with the other hanging in midair as if he had been caught in the middle of running. The man would feel as if he were buried in thick jelly, yet it was nothing but air stiffened around him. Egwene remembered the Amyrlin's trick, too, but she did not think she could duplicate it. Nynaeve only had to see a thing done once to know how to do it herself. When she could manage to channel at all, of course.

They came closer, and Egwene's melding with the Power vanished in shock. The hilt of a dagger stood out from the man's chest. His face sagged, and death had already filmed his half-closed eyes. He crumpled to the gallery floor as Nynaeve loosed the trap that had held him.

He was an average-appearing man, of average height and average build, with features so ordinary Egwene did not think she would have noticed him in a group of three. She only studied him a moment, though, before realizing that something was missing. A crossbow.

She gave a start and looked about wildly. "There had to be another one, Nynaeve. Somebody took the crossbow. And somebody stabbed him. He could be out there ready to shoot at us again."

"Calm yourself," Nynaeve said, but she peered both ways along the gallery, jerking at her braid. "Just be calm, and we will figure out what to—" Her words cut off at the sound of steps on the ramp leading up to their level.

Egwene's heart pounded, seemingly in her throat. Eyes fastened on the head of the ramp, she desperately strove to touch *saidar* again, but for her that required calm, and her heartbeats shattered calm.

Sheriam Sedai stopped at the top of the ramp, frowning at what she saw. "What in the name of the Light has happened here?" She hurried forward, her serenity gone for once.

"We found him," Nynaeve said as the Mistress of Novices knelt beside the corpse.

Sheriam put a hand to the man's chest, and jerked it back twice as fast, hissing. Steeling herself visibly, she touched him again, and maintained the Touch longer. "Dead," she muttered. "As dead as it is possible to be, and more." When she straightened, she pulled a handkerchief from her sleeve and wiped her fingers. "You found him? Here? Like this?"

Egwene nodded, sure that if she spoke, Sheriam would hear the lie in her voice.

"We did," Nynaeve said firmly.

Sheriam shook her head. "A man—a dead man, at that!—in the novices' quarters would be scandal enough, but this . . . !"

"What makes him different?" Nynaeve asked. "And how could he be *more* than dead?"

Sheriam took a deep breath, and gave them each a searching look. "He is one of the Soulless. A Gray Man." Absently, she wiped her fingers again, her eyes going back to the body. Worried eyes.

"The Soulless?" Egwene said, a tremor in her voice, at the same time that Nynaeve said, "A Gray Man?"

Sheriam glanced at them, a look as penetrating as it was brief. "Not a part of your studies, yet, but you seem to have gone beyond the rules in a great many ways. And considering you found this. . . ." She gestured to the corpse. "The Soulless, the Gray Men, give up their souls to serve the Dark One as assassins. They are not really alive, after that. Not quite dead, but not truly alive. And despite the name, some Gray Men are women. A very few. Even among Darkfriends, only a handful of women are stupid enough to make that sacrifice. You can look right at them and hardly notice them, until it is too late. He was as much as dead while he walked. Now, only my eyes tell me that what is lying there ever lived at all." She gave them another long look. "No Gray Man has dared enter Tar Valon since the Trolloc Wars."

"What will you do?" Egwene asked. Sheriam's brows rose, and she quickly added, "If I may ask, Sheriam Sedai."

The Aes Sedai hesitated. "I suppose you may, since you had the bad luck to find him. It will be up to the Amyrlin Seat, but with everything that has happened, I believe she will want to keep this as quiet as is possible. We do not need more rumors. You will speak of this to none but me, or to the Amyrlin, should she mention it first."

"Yes, Aes Sedai," Egwene said fervently. Nynaeve's voice was cooler.

Sheriam appeared to take their obedience for granted. She gave no sign of having heard them. Her attention was all on the dead man. The Gray Man. The Soulless. "There will be no hiding the fact that a man was killed here." The glow of the One Power suddenly surrounded her, and just as abruptly, a long, low dome covered the body on the floor, grayish and so opaque that it was hard to see there was a body under it. "But this will keep anyone else from touching him who can discover his nature. I must have this removed before the novices come back."

Her tilted green eyes regarded them as if she had just remembered their presence. "You two go, now. To your room, I think, Nynaeve. Considering what you are already facing, if it became known you were involved in this, even on the edge of it. . . . Go."

Egwene curtsied, and tugged at Nynaeve's sleeve, but Nynaeve said, "Why did you come up here, Sheriam Sedai?"

For a moment Sheriam looked startled, but on the instant she frowned. Fists on her hips, she regarded Nynaeve with all the firmness of her office. "Does the Mistress of Novices now need an excuse for coming to the novices' quarters, Accepted?" she said softly. "Do Accepted now question Aes Sedai? The Amyrlin means to make something of you two, but whether she does or not, I will teach you manners,

at least. Now, the pair of you, go, before I haul you both
down to my study, and not for the appointment the Amyrlin
Seat has already set for you."

A sudden thought came to Egwene. "Forgive me, Sheriam Sedai," she said quickly, "but I must fetch my cloak. I
feel cold." She rushed away, around the gallery before the
Aes Sedai could speak.

If Sheriam found that crossbow bolt in front of her door,
there would be too many questions. No pretending they had
only found the man, that he had no connection to her, then.
But when she reached the door to her room, the heavy bolt
was gone. Only the jagged chip in the stone beside the door
said it had ever been there.

Egwene's skin crawled. *How could anyone take it without one of us seeing. . . . Another Gray Man!* She had embraced *saidar* before she knew it, only the sweet flow of the
Power inside her telling her what she had done. Even so, it
was one of the hardest things she had ever done, opening
that door and going into her room. There was no one there.
She snatched the white cloak off its peg and ran out, anyway, and she did not release *saidar* until she was halfway
back to the others.

Something more had passed between the women while
she was gone. Nynaeve was attempting to appear meek,
and succeeding only in looking as if she had a sour stomach. Sheriam had her fists on her hips and was tapping her
foot irritably, and the stare she was giving Nynaeve, like
green millstones ready to start grinding barley flour, took
in Egwene equally.

"Forgive me, Sheriam Sedai," she said hastily, dropping
a curtsy and settling her cloak on her shoulders at the same
time. "This . . . finding a dead man—a . . . a Gray Man!—it
made me cold. If we may go now?"

At Sheriam's tight nod of dismissal, Nynaeve made a
bare curtsy. Egwene seized her arm and hustled her away.

"Are you trying to *make* more trouble for us?" she demanded when they were two levels down. And safely out of
earshot of Sheriam, she hoped. "What else did you say to
her, to make her glare like that? More questions, I suppose?
I hope you learned something worth making her mad at us."

"She would not say anything," Nynaeve muttered. "We
must ask questions if we are to do any good, Egwene. We

will have to take a few chances, or we'll never learn anything."

Egwene sighed. "Well, be a little more circumspect." From the set of Nynaeve's face, the other woman had no intention of going easy or avoiding risks. Egwene sighed again. "The crossbow bolt was gone, Nynaeve. It must have been another Gray Man who took it."

"So that is why you. . . . Light!" Nynaeve frowned and gave a sharp tug to her braid.

After a time Egwene said, "What was that she did to cover the . . . the body?" She did not want to think of it as a Gray Man; that reminded her there was another one out there. She did not want to think of anything at all, right then.

"Air," Nynaeve replied. "She used Air. A neat trick, and I think I see how to make something useful with it."

The use of the One Power was divided into the Five Powers: Earth, Air, Fire, Water, and Spirit. Different Talents required different combinations of the Five Powers. "I don't understand some of the ways the Five Powers are combined. Take Healing. I can see why it requires Spirit, and maybe Air, but why Water?"

Nynaeve rounded on her. "What are you babbling about? Have you forgotten what we're doing?" She looked around. They had reached the Accepted's quarters, a stack of galleries lower than the novices' quarters, surrounding a garden rather than a court. There was no one in sight except for another Accepted, hurrying along on another level, but she lowered her voice. "Have you forgotten the Black Ajah?"

"I am trying to forget it," Egwene said fiercely. "For a little while, anyway. I am trying to forget that we just left a dead man. I'm trying to forget that he almost killed me, and that he has a companion who might try it again." She touched her ear; the drop of blood had dried, but the nick still hurt. "We are lucky we aren't both dead right now."

Nynaeve's face softened, but when she spoke her voice held something of the time when she had been the Wisdom of Emond's Field, saying words that had to be said for someone's own good. "Remember that body, Egwene. Remember that he tried to kill you. Kill us. Remember the Black Ajah. Remember them all the time. Because if you forget, just once, the next time, it may be you lying dead."

"I know," Egwene sighed. "But I do not have to like it."

"Did you notice what Sheriam did not mention?"

"No. What?"

"She never wondered who stabbed him. Now, come on. My room is just down here, and you can put your feet up while we talk."

CHAPTER
16

Hunters Three

Nynaeve's room was considerably larger than the novice rooms. She had a real bed, not one built into the wall, two ladder-back armchairs instead of a stool, and a wardrobe for her clothes. The furnishings were all plain, suitable for a middling successful farmer's house, but compared to the novices, the Accepted lived in luxury. There was even a small rug, woven with scrolls of yellow and red on blue. The room was not empty when Egwene and Nynaeve entered.

Elayne stood in front of the fireplace, arms crossed beneath her breasts and eyes red at least partly from anger. Two tall young men sprawled in the chairs, all arms and legs. One, with his dark green coat undone to show a snowy shirt, shared Elayne's blue eyes and red-gold hair, and his grinning face marked him plainly as her brother. The other, Nynaeve's age and with his gray coat neatly buttoned, was slender and dark of hair and eye. He rose, all sure confidence and lithely muscled grace, when Egwene and Nynaeve came in. He was, Egwene thought not for the first time, the most handsome man she had ever seen. His name was Galad.

"It is good to see you again," he said, taking her hand. "I have worried much over you. We have worried much."

Her pulse quickened, and she took back her hand before he should feel it. "Thank you, Galad," she murmured. *Light, but he's beautiful.* She told herself to stop thinking that way. It was not easy. She found herself smoothing her dress, wishing he were seeing her in silk instead of this plain white wool, perhaps even one of those Domani dresses Min had told her of, the ones that clung and seemed so thin you thought they must be transparent even though they were not. She flushed furiously and banished the image from her mind, willed him to look away from her face. It did not help that half the women in the Tower, from scullery maids to Aes Sedai themselves, looked at him as if they had the same thoughts. It did not help that his smile seemed for her alone. In fact, his smile made it worse. *Light, if he even suspected what I was thinking, I'd die!*

The golden-haired young man leaned forward in his chair. "The question is, where have you been? Elayne dodges my questions as if she has a pocket full of figs and doesn't want me to have any."

"I have told you, Gawyn," Elayne said in a tight voice, "it is none of your affair. I came here," she added to Nynaeve, "because I did not want to be alone. They saw me, and followed. They would not take no for an answer."

"Wouldn't they," Nynaeve said flatly.

"But it is our affair, sister," Galad said. "Your safety is very much our affair." He looked at Egwene, and she felt her heart jump. "The safety of all of you is very important to me. To us."

"I am not your sister," Elayne snapped.

"If you want company," Gawyn told Elayne with a smile, "we can do as well as any. And after what we went through just to be here, we deserve some explanation of where you've been. I would rather let Galad thump me all over the practice yard all day than face Mother again for a single minute. I'd rather have Coulin mad at me." Coulin was Master of Arms, and kept a tight discipline among the young men who came to train at the White Tower whether they aspired to become Warders or just to learn from them.

"Deny the connection if you will," Galad told Elayne gravely, "but it is still there. And Mother put your safety in our hands."

Gawyn grimaced. "She'll have our hides, Elayne, if anything happens to you. We had to talk fast, or she'd have hauled us back home with her. I have never heard of a queen sending her own sons to the headsman, but Mother sounded ready to make an exception if we don't bring you home safely."

"I am sure," Elayne said, "that your fast talk was all for

me. None of it was meant to let you stay here studying with the Warders." Gawyn's face reddened.

"Your safety was our first concern." Galad sounded as if he meant it, and Egwene was sure he did. "We managed to convince Mother that if you did return here, you would need someone to look after you."

"Look after me!" Elayne exclaimed, but Galad went on smoothly.

"The White Tower has become a dangerous place. There have been deaths—murders—with no real explanations. Even some Aes Sedai have been killed, though they have tried to keep that quiet. And I have heard rumors of the Black Ajah, spoken in the Tower itself. By Mother's command, when it is safe for you to leave your training, we are to return you to Caemlyn."

For answer, Elayne lifted her chin and half turned away from him.

Gawyn ran a hand through his hair in frustration. "Light, Nynaeve, Galad and I are not villains. All we want to do is help. We would do it anyway, but Mother commanded it, so there's no chance of you talking us out of it."

"Morgase's commands carry no weight in Tar Valon," Nynaeve said in a level voice. "As for your offer of help, I will remember it. Should we need help, you will be among the first to hear of it. For now, I wish you to leave." She gestured pointedly to the door, but he ignored her.

"That is all very well, but Mother will want to know Elayne has come back. And why she ran off without a word, and what she was doing these months. Light, Elayne! The whole Tower was in a turmoil. Mother was half-crazed with fear. I thought she'd tear the Tower down with her bare hands." Elayne's face took on a measure of guilt, and Gawyn pressed his advantage. "You owe her that much, Elayne. You owe me that much. Burn me, you're being as stubborn as stone. You've been gone for months, and all I know about it is that you've run afoul of Sheriam. And the only reasons I know that much are because you've been crying and you won't sit down." Elayne's indignant stare said he had squandered whatever momentary advantage he might have had.

"Enough," Nynaeve said. Galad and Gawyn opened their mouths. She raised her voice. "I said enough!" She glared at them until it was clear their silence would hold, then went on. "Elayne *owes* the two of you nothing. Since she chooses to tell you nothing, that is that. Now, this is my room, not the common room of an inn, and I want you out of it."

"But, Elayne——" Gawyn began at the same time that Galad said, "We only want——"

Nynaeve spoke loudly enough to drown them out. "I doubt you asked permission to enter the Accepted's quarters." They stared at her, looking surprised. "I thought not. You will be out of my room, out of my sight, before I count three, or I will write a note to the Master of Arms about this. Coulin Gaidin has a much stronger arm than Sheriam Sedai, and you may be assured that I will be there to see he makes a proper job of it."

"Nynaeve, you wouldn't——" Gawyn began worriedly, but Galad motioned him to silence and stepped closer to Nynaeve.

Her face kept its stern expression, but she unconsciously smoothed the front of her dress as he smiled down at her. Egwene was not surprised. She did not think she had met a woman outside the Red Ajah who would not be affected by Galad's smile.

"I apologize, Nynaeve, for our forcing ourselves on you unwanted," he said smoothly. "We will go, of course. But remember that we are here if you need us. And whatever caused you to run away, we can help with that, as well."

Nynaeve returned his smile. "One," she said.

Galad blinked, his smile fading. Calmly, he turned to Egwene. Gawyn got up and started for the door. "Egwene," Galad said, "you know that you, especially, can call on me at any time, for anything. I hope you know that."

"Two," Nynaeve said.

Galad gave her an irritated look. "We will talk again," he told Egwene, bowing over her hand. With a last smile, he took an unhurried step toward the door.

"Thrrrrrrrrr"—Gawyn darted through the door, and even Galad's graceful stride quickened markedly—"ree," Nynaeve finished as the door banged shut behind them.

Elayne clapped her hands delightedly. "Oh, well done," she said. "Very well done. I did not even know men were forbidden the Accepted's quarters, too."

"They aren't," Nynaeve said dryly, "but those louts did

not know it, either." Elayne clapped her hands again and laughed. "I'd have let them just leave," Nynaeve added, "if Galad had not made such a show of taking his time about it. That young man has too fair a face for his own good." Egwene almost laughed at that; Galad was no more than a year younger that Nynaeve, if that, and Nynaeve was straightening her dress again.

"Galad!" Elayne sniffed. "He'll bother us again, and I do not know whether your trick will work more than once. He does what he sees as right no matter who it hurts, even himself."

"Then I will think of something else," Nynaeve said. "We can't afford to have them looking over our shoulders all the time. Elayne, if you wish, I can make a salve that will soothe you."

Elayne shook her head, then lay down across the bed with her chin in her hands. "If Sheriam found out, we would no doubt both have yet another visit to her study to look forward to. You have not said very much, Egwene. Cat caught your tongue?" Her expression became grimmer. "Or perhaps Galad has?"

Egwene blushed in spite of herself. "I simply did not choose to argue with them," she said in as dignified a tone as she could manage.

"Of course," Elayne said grudgingly. "I will admit that Galad is good-looking. But he is horrid, too. He *always* does right, as he sees it I know that does not sound horrid, but it is. He has never disobeyed Mother, not in the smallest thing that I know of. He will not tell a lie, even a small one, or break a rule. If he turns you in for breaking one, there isn't the slightest spite in it—he seems sad you could not live up to his standards, if anything—but that doesn't change the fact that he *will* turn you in."

"That sounds—uncomfortable," Egwene said carefully, "but not horrid. I cannot imagine Galad doing anything horrid."

Elayne shook her head, as if in disbelief that Egwene found it so hard to see what was clear to her. "If you want to pay attention to someone, try Gawyn. He is nice enough—most of the time—and he's besotted with you."

"Gawyn! He has never looked at me twice."

"Of course not, you fool, the way you stare at Galad

until your eyes look ready to fall out of your face."
Egwene's cheeks felt hot, but she was afraid it might well
be true. "Galad saved his life when Gawyn was a child,"
Elayne went on. "Gawyn will never admit he is interested
in a woman if Galad is interested in her, but I have heard
him talk about you, and I know. He never could hide things
from me."

"That is nice to know," Egwene said, then laughed at
Elayne's grin. "Perhaps I can get him to say some of those
things to me instead of you."

"You could choose Green Ajah, you know. Green sisters
sometimes marry. Gawyn truly is besotted, and you would
be good for him. Besides, I would like to have you for a
sister."

"If you two are finished with girlish chatter," Nynaeve
cut in, "there are important matters to talk about."

"Yes," Elayne said, "such as what the Amyrlin Seat had
to say to you after I left."

"I would rather not talk about that," Egwene said awkwardly. She did not like lying to Elayne. "She did not say
anything that was pleasant."

Elayne gave a sniff of disbelief. "Most people think I get
off easier than the others because I am Daughter-Heir of
Andor. The truth is that if anything, I catch it harder than
the rest because I'm Daughter-Heir. Neither of you did anything I did not, and if the Amyrlin had harsh words for you,
she would have twice as harsh for me. Now, what did she
say?"

"You must keep this just between us three," Nynaeve
said. "The Black Ajah—"

"Nynaeve!" Egwene exclaimed. "The Amyrlin said
Elayne was to be left out of it!"

"The Black Ajah!" Elayne almost shouted, scrambling
up to kneel in the middle of the bed. "You cannot leave me
out after telling me this much. I won't be left out."

"I never meant for you to be," Nynaeve assured her.
Egwene could only stare at her in amazement. "Egwene, it
was you and I who Liandrin saw as a threat. It was you and
I who were just nearly killed—"

"Nearly killed?" Elayne whispered.

"—perhaps because we are still a threat, and perhaps because they already know that we were closeted alone with

the Amyrlin, and even what she told us. We need someone with us who they do not know about, and if she isn't known to the Amyrlin, either, so much the better. I am not sure we can trust the Amyrlin much further than the Black Ajah. She means to use us for her own ends. I mean to see she doesn't use us up. Can you understand that?"

Egwene nodded reluctantly. Just the same, she said, "It will be dangerous, Elayne, as dangerous as anything we faced in Falme. Maybe more so. You do not have to be part of it, this time."

"I know that," Elayne said quietly. She paused, then went on. "When Andor goes to war, the First Prince of the Sword commands the army, but the Queen rides with them, too. Seven hundred years ago, at the Battle of Cuallin Dhen, the Andormen were being routed when Queen Modrellein rode, alone and unarmed, carrying the Lion banner into the midst of the Tairen army. The Andormen rallied and attacked once more, to save her, and won the battle. That is the kind of courage expected of the Queen of Andor. If I have not learned to control my fear yet, I must before I take my mother's place on the Lion Throne." Suddenly her somber mood vanished in a giggle. "Besides, do you think I would pass up an adventure so I could scrub pots?"

"You will do that anyway," Nynaeve told her, "and hope that everyone thinks that is all you are doing. Now listen carefully."

Elayne listened, and her mouth slowly dropped open as Nynaeve unfolded what the Amyrlin Seat had told them, and the task she had laid on them, and the attempt on their lives. She shivered over the Gray Man, and read the document the Amyrlin had given Nynaeve with a look of wonder, then returned it, murmuring, "I wish I could have that when I face Mother next." By the time Nynaeve finished, though, her face was a picture of indignation.

"Why, that's like being told to go up in the hills and find lions, only you do not know whether there are any lions, but if there are, they may be hunting you, and they may be disguised as bushes. Oh, and if you find any lions, try not to let them eat you before you can tell where they are."

"If you are afraid," Nynaeve said, "you can still stand aside. It will be too late, once you've begun."

Elayne tossed her head back. "Of course I am afraid. I am

not a fool. But not afraid enough to quit before I have even started."

"There is something else, too," Nynaeve said. "I am afraid the Amyrlin may mean to let Mat die."

"But an Aes Sedai is supposed to Heal anyone who asks." The Daughter-Heir seemed caught between indignation and disbelief. "Why would she let Mat die? I cannot believe it! I will not!"

"Nor can I!" Egwene gasped. *She could not have meant that! The Amyrlin* couldn't *let him die!* "All the way here Verin said that the Amyrlin would see he was Healed."

Nynaeve shook her head. "Verin said the Amyrlin would 'see to him.' That is not the same thing. And the Amyrlin avoided saying yes or no when I asked her. Maybe she has not made her mind up."

"But *why*?" Elayne asked.

"Because the White Tower does what it does for its own reasons." Nynaeve's voice made Egwene shiver. "I do not know why. Whether they help Mat live or let him die depends on what serves their ends. None of the Three Oaths says they have to Heal him. Mat is just a tool, in the Amyrlin's eyes. So are we. She will use us to hunt the Black Ajah, but if you break a tool so it cannot be fixed, you don't weep over it. You just get another one. Both of you had best remember that."

"What are we going to do about him?" Egwene asked. "What can we do?"

Nynaeve went to her wardrobe and rummaged in the back of it. When she came out, she had a striped cloth bag of herbs. "With my medicines—and luck—perhaps I can Heal him myself."

"Verin could not," Elayne said. "Moiraine and Verin together could not, and Moiraine had an *angreal*. Nynaeve, if you draw too much of the One Power, you could burn yourself to a cinder. Or just still yourself, if you are lucky. If you can call that luck."

Nynaeve shrugged. "They keep telling me I have the potential to be the most powerful Aes Sedai in a thousand years. Perhaps it is time to find out whether they are right." She gave a tug to her braid.

It was plain that however brave Nynaeve's words, she was afraid. *But she won't let Mat die even if it means risking death herself.* "They keep saying we're all three so powerful—or will be. Maybe, if we all try together, we can divide the flow among us."

"We have never tried working together," Nynaeve said slowly. "I am not sure I know how to combine our abilities. Trying could be almost as dangerous as drawing too much of the Power."

"Oh, if we are going to do it," Elayne said, climbing off the bed, "let's do it. The longer we talk of it, the more frightened I will become. Mat is in the guest rooms. I do not know which one, but Sheriam told me that much."

As if to put period to her words, the door banged open, and an Aes Sedai entered as though it were her room, and they the interlopers.

Egwene made her curtsy deep, to hide the dismay on her face.

CHAPTER
17

The Red Sister

Elaida was a handsome woman rather than beautiful,
and the sternness on her face added maturity to her
ageless Aes Sedai features. She did not look old, yet
Egwene could never imagine Elaida as having been young.
Except for the most formal occasions, few Aes Sedai wore
the vine-embroidered shawl with the white teardrop Flame
of Tar Valon large on the wearer's back, but Elaida wore
hers, the long red fringe announcing her Ajah. Red slashed
her dress of cream-colored silk, too, and red slippers peeked
under the edge of her skirts as she moved into the room. Her
dark eyes watched them as a bird's eyes watched worms.

"So all of you are together. Somehow, that does not surprise me." Her voice made no more pretense than her bearing did; she was a woman of power, and ready to wield it
if she decided it was necessary, a woman who knew more
than those she spoke to. It was much the same for a queen
as for a novice.

"Forgive me, Elaida Sedai," Nynaeve said, dropping another curtsy, "but I was about to go out. I have much to
catch up in my studies. If you will forgive—"

"Your studies can wait," Elaida said. "They have waited
long enough already, after all." She plucked the cloth bag
out of Nynaeve's hands and undid the strings, but after one
glance inside she tossed it on the floor. "Herbs. You are not
a village Wisdom any longer, child. Trying to hold on to the
past will only hold you back."

"Elaida Sedai," Elayne said, "I—"

"Be silent, novice." Elaida's voice was cold and soft, as
silk wrapped around steel is soft. "You may have broken

a bond between Tar Valon and Caemlyn that has lasted a
thousand years. You will speak when spoken to." Elayne's
eyes examined the floor in front of her toes. Spots of color
burned in her cheeks. Guilt, or anger? Egwene was not
sure.

Ignoring them all, Elaida sat down in one of the chairs,
carefully arranging her skirts. She made no gesture for the
rest of them to sit. Nynaeve's face tightened, and she began giving sharp little tugs to her braid. Egwene hoped she
would keep her temper well enough not to take the other
chair without permission.

When Elaida had settled herself to her own satisfaction,
she studied them for a time in silence, her face unreadable.
At last she said, "Did you know that we have the Black Ajah
among us?"

Egwene exchanged startled glances with Nynaeve and
Elayne.

"We were told," Nynaeve said cautiously. "Elaida Sedai,"
she added after a pause.

Elaida arched an eyebrow. "Yes. I thought that you might
know of it." Egwene gave a start at her tone, implying so
much more than it said, and Nynaeve opened her mouth angrily, but the Aes Sedai's flat stare stilled tongues. "The two
of you," Elaida went on in a casual tone, "vanish, taking
with you the Daughter-Heir of Andor—the girl who *may*
become Queen of Andor one day, if I do not strip off her
hide and sell it to a glove maker—vanish without permission, without a word, without a trace."

"I was not carried off," Elayne said to the floor. "I went
of my own will."

"Will you obey me, child?" A glow surrounded Elaida.
The Aes Sedai's glare was fixed on Elayne. "Must I teach
you, here and now?"

Elayne raised her head, and there was no mistaking what
was in her face. Anger. For a long moment she met Elaida's
stare.

Egwene's fingernails dug into her palms. It was madden-
ing. She, or Elayne, or Nynaeve, could destroy Elaida where
she sat. If they caught Elaida by surprise, at least; she was
fully trained, after all. *And if we do anything but take whatever she wants to feed us, we throw away everything. Don't
throw it away now, Elayne.*

Elayne's head dropped. "Forgive me, Elaida Sedai," she mumbled. "I—forgot myself."

The glow winked out of existence, and Elaida sniffed audibly. "You have learned bad habits, wherever these two took you. You cannot afford bad habits, child. You will be the first Queen of Andor ever to be Aes Sedai. The first queen anywhere to be Aes Sedai in over a thousand years. You will be one of the strongest of us since the Breaking of the World, perhaps strong enough to be the first ruler since the Breaking to openly tell the world she is Aes Sedai. Do not risk all of that, child, because you can still lose it all. I have invested too much time to see that. Do you understand me?"

"I think so, Elaida Sedai," Elayne said. She sounded as if she did not understand at all. No more did Egwene.

Elaida abandoned the subject. "You may be in grave danger. All three of you. You disappear and return, and in the interval, Liandrin and her . . . companions leave us. There will inevitably be comparisons. We are sure Liandrin and those who went with her are Darkfriends. Black Ajah. I would not see the same charge leveled at Elayne, and to protect her, it seems I must protect all of you. Tell me why you ran away, and what you have been doing these months, and I will do what I can for you." Her eyes fastened on Egwene like grappling hooks.

Egwene floundered for an answer that the Aes Sedai would accept. It was said that Elaida could hear a lie, sometimes. "It . . . it was Mat. He is very sick." She tried to choose her words carefully, to say nothing that was not true, yet give an impression far from truth. *Aes Sedai do it all the time.* "We went to. . . . We brought him back to be Healed. If we hadn't, he would die. The Amyrlin is going to Heal him." *I hope.* She made herself continue to meet the Red Aes Sedai's gaze, willed herself not to shift her feet guiltily. From Elaida's face, there was no way to tell whether she believed a word.

"That is enough, Egwene," Nynaeve said. Elaida's penetrating look shifted to her, but she gave no sign of being affected by it. She met the Aes Sedai's eyes without blinking. "Forgive me for interrupting, Elaida Sedai," she said smoothly, "but the Amyrlin Seat said our transgressions were to be put behind us and forgotten. As part of making a new beginning, we are not even to speak of them. The Amyrlin said it should be as if they never happened."

"She said that, did she?" Still nothing in Elaida's voice or on her face told whether she believed or not. "Interesting. You can hardly forget entirely when your punishment has been announced to the entire Tower. Unprecedented, that. Unheard of, for less than stilling. I can see why you are eager to put it all behind you. I understand you are to be raised to the Accepted, Elayne. And Egwene. That is hardly punishment."

Elayne glanced at the Aes Sedai as though for permission to speak. "The Mother said we were ready," she said. A touch of defiance entered her voice. "I have learned, Elaida Sedai, and grown. She would not have named me to be raised if I had not."

"Learned," Elaida said musingly. "And grown. Perhaps you have." There was no hint in her tone whether she thought this was good. Her gaze shifted back to Egwene and Nynaeve, searching. "You returned with this Mat, a youth from your village. There was another young man from your village. Rand al'Thor."

Egwene felt as if an icy hand had suddenly gripped her stomach.

"I hope he is well," Nynaeve said levelly, but her hand was a fist gripping her braid. "We have not seen him in some time."

"An interesting young man." Elaida studied them as she spoke. "I met him only once, but I found him—most interesting. I believe he must be *ta'veren*. Yes. The answers to many questions may rest in him. This Emond's Field of yours must be an unusual place to produce the two of you. And Rand al'Thor."

"It is just a village," Nynaeve said. "Just a village like any other."

"Yes. Of course." Elaida smiled, a cold quirk of her lips that twisted Egwene's stomach. "Tell me about him. The Amyrlin has not commanded you to be silent about him also, has she?"

Nynaeve gave her braid a tug. Elayne studied the carpet as if something important were hidden in it, and Egwene racked her brain for an answer. *She can hear lies, they say. Light, if she can really hear a lie.* . . . The moment stretched on, until finally Nynaeve opened her mouth.

At that instant the door opened again. Sheriam regarded the room with a measure of surprise. "It is well I find you here, Elayne. I want all three of you. I had not expected you, Elaida."

Elaida stood, arranging her shawl. "We are all curious about these girls. Why they ran away. What adventures they had while gone. They say the Mother has commanded them not to speak of it."

"As well not to," Sheriam said. "They are to be punished, and that should be an end to it. I have always felt that when punishment is done, the fault that caused it should be erased."

For a long moment the two Aes Sedai stood looking at each other, no expression on either smooth face. Then Elaida said, "Of course. Perhaps I will speak to them another time. About other matters." The look she gave to the three women in white seemed to Egwene to carry a warning, and then she was slipping past Sheriam.

Holding the door open, the Mistress of Novices watched the other Aes Sedai go down the gallery. Her face was still unreadable.

Egwene let out a long breath, and heard echoes from Nynaeve and Elayne.

"She threatened me," Elayne said incredulously, and half to herself. "She threatened me with stilling, if I don't stop being—*willful!*"

"You mistook her," Sheriam said. "If being willful were a stilling offense, the list of the stilled would have more names on it than you could learn. Few meek women ever achieve the ring and the shawl. That is not to say, of course, that you must not learn to act meekly when it is required."

"Yes, Sheriam Sedai," they all three said almost as one, and Sheriam smiled.

"You see? You can give the appearance of meekness, at least. And you will have plenty of opportunity to practice before you earn your way back into the Amyrlin's good graces. And mine. Mine will be harder to achieve."

"Yes, Sheriam Sedai," Egwene said, but this time only Elayne spoke with her.

Nynaeve said, "What of . . . the body, Sheriam Sedai? The . . . the Soulless? Have you discovered who killed him? Or why he entered the Tower?"

Sheriam's mouth tightened. "You take one step forward, Nynaeve, and then a step back. Since from Elayne's lack of surprise, you have obviously told her of it—*after I told you not to speak of the matter!*—then there are exactly seven people in the Tower who know a man was killed today in the novices' quarters, and two of them are men who know no more than that. Except that they are to keep their mouths shut. If an order from the Mistress of Novices carries no weight with you—and if that is so, I will correct you— perhaps you will obey one from the Amyrlin Seat. You are to speak of this to no one except the Mother or me. The Amyrlin will not have more rumors piled on those we must already contend with. Do I make myself clear?"

The firmness of her voice produced a chorus of "Yes, Sheriam Sedai"—but Nynaeve refused to stop at that. "Seven, you said, Sheriam Sedai. Plus whoever killed him. And maybe they had help getting into the Tower."

"That is no concern of yours." Sheriam's level gaze included them all. "I will ask whatever questions must be asked about this man. You will forget you know anything at all about a dead man. If I discover you are doing anything else. . . . Well, there are worse things than scrubbing pots to occupy your attention. And I will not accept any excuses. Do I hear any more questions?"

"No, Sheriam Sedai." This time, Nynaeve joined in, to Egwene's relief. Not that she felt very much relief. Sheriam's watchful eye would make it doubly hard to carry out a search for the Black Ajah. For a moment she felt like laughing hysterically. *If the Black Ajah doesn't catch us, Sheriam will.* The urge to laugh vanished. *If Sheriam isn't Black Ajah herself.* She wished she could make that thought go away.

Sheriam nodded. "Very well, then. You will come with me."

"To where?" Nynaeve asked, and added, "Sheriam Sedai," only an instant before the Aes Sedai's eyes narrowed.

"Have you forgotten," Sheriam said in a tight voice, "that in the Tower, Healing is always done in the presence of those who bring their sick to us?"

Egwene thought that the Mistress of Novices's stock of patience with them was about used up, but before she could stop herself, she burst out, "Then she *is* going to Heal him!"

"The Amyrlin Seat herself, among others, will see to him." Sheriam's face held no more expression than her voice. "Did you have reason to doubt it?" Egwene could only shake her head. "Then you waste your friend's life standing here. The Amyrlin Seat is not to be kept waiting." Yet despite her words, Egwene had the feeling the Aes Sedai was in no hurry at all.

CHAPTER
18

Healing

Lamps on iron wall brackets lit the passages deep
beneath the Tower, where Sheriam took them. The
few doors they passed were shut tight, some locked,
some so cunningly worked that they remained unseen until
Egwene was right on top of them. Dark openings marked
most of the crossing hallways, while down others she could
only see the dim glow of distant lights spaced far apart.
She saw no other people. These were not places even Aes
Sedai often came. The air was neither cool nor warm, but
she shivered anyway, and at the same time felt sweat trickling down her back.

It was down here, in the depths of the White Tower, that
novices went through their last test before being raised to
Accepted. Or put out of the Tower, if they failed. Down here,
Accepted took the Three Oaths after passing their final test.
No one, she realized, had ever told her what happened to
an Accepted who failed. Down here, somewhere, was the
room where the Tower's few *angreal* and *sa'angreal* were
kept, and the places where the *ter'angreal* were stored. The
Black Ajah had struck at those storerooms. And if some
of the Black Ajah were lying in wait in one of those dark
side corridors, if Sheriam were leading them not to Mat,
but to. . . .

She gave a squeak when the Aes Sedai stopped suddenly,
then colored when the others looked at her curiously. "I was
thinking about the Black Ajah," she said weakly.

"Do not think of it," Sheriam said, and for once she
sounded like the Sheriam of old, kindly if firm. "The Black

Ajah will not be your worry for years to come. You have
what the rest of us do not: time before you must deal with
it. Much time, yet. When we enter, stay against the wall
and keep silent. You are allowed here as a benevolence, to
attend, not to distract or interfere." She opened a door covered in gray metal worked to look like stone.

The square room within was spacious, its pale stone
walls bare. The only furnishing was a long stone table
draped with a white cloth, in the middle of the room. Mat
lay on that table, fully clothed save for coat and boots, eyes
closed and face so gaunt that Egwene wanted to cry. His labored breathing made a hoarse whistle. The Shadar Logoth
dagger hung sheathed at his belt, the ruby capping its hilt
seeming to gather light, so it glowed like some fierce red
eye despite the illumination of a dozen lamps, magnified by
the pale walls and white-tiled floor.

The Amyrlin Seat stood at Mat's head, and Leane at
his feet. Four Aes Sedai stood down one side of the table,
and three down the other. Sheriam joined the three. One
of them was Verin. Egwene recognized Serafelle, another
Brown sister, and Alanna Mosvani, of the Green Ajah, and
Anaiya, of the Blue, which was Moiraine's Ajah.

Alanna and Anaiya had each taught her some of her lessons in opening herself to the True Source, in how to surrender to *saidar* in order to control it. And between her first
arrival in the White Tower and her departure, Anaiya must
have tested her fifty times to see if she was a Dreamer. The
tests had shown nothing one way or the other, but plain-
faced, kindly Anaiya, with that warm smile that was her
only beauty, had kept calling her back for more tests, as
implacable as a boulder rolling downhill.

The rest were unknown to her, except for one cool-eyed
woman she thought was a White. The Amyrlin and the
Keeper wore their stoles, of course, but none of the others
had anything to mark them out except Great Serpent rings
and ageless Aes Sedai faces. None of them acknowledged
the presence of Egwene and the other two by so much as a
glance.

Despite the outward calm of the women around the table,
Egwene thought she saw signs of uncertainty. A tightness to
Anaiya's mouth. A slight frown on Alanna's darkly beau-
tiful face. The cool-eyed woman kept smoothing her pale

blue dress over her thighs without seeming to realize what she was doing.

An Aes Sedai Egwene did not know set a plain, polished wooden box, long and narrow, on the table and opened it. From its nest in the red silk lining, the Amyrlin took out a white, fluted wand the length of her forearm. It could have been bone, or ivory, but was neither. No one alive knew what it was made of.

Egwene had never seen the wand before, but she recognized it from a lecture Anaiya had given the novices. One of the few *sa'angreal*, and perhaps the most powerful, that the Tower possessed. *Sa'angreal* had no power of their own, of course—they were merely devices for focusing and magnifying what an Aes Sedai could channel—but with that wand, a strong Aes Sedai might be able to crumple the walls of Tar Valon.

Egwene clutched Nynaeve's hand on one side and Elayne's on the other. *Light! They're not sure they can Heal him, even with a* sa'angreal—*with that* sa'angreal! *What chance would* we *have had? We'd probably have killed him, and ourselves, too. Light!*

"I will meld the flows," the Amyrlin said. "Be careful. The Power needed to break the bond with the dagger and Heal its damage is very close to what could kill him. I will focus. Attend." She held the wand straight out in front of her in both hands, above Mat's face. Still unconscious, he shook his head and tightened a fist on the dagger's hilt, muttering something that sounded like a denial.

A glow appeared around each Aes Sedai, that soft, white light that only a woman who could channel could see. Slowly the lights spread, until that which seemed to emanate from one woman touched that which came from the woman beside her, merged with it, till there was only one light, a light that, to Egwene's eyes, diminished the lamps to nothing. And in that brightness was a stronger light still. A bar of bone-white fire. The *sa'angreal*.

Egwene fought the urge to open herself to *saidar* and add her flow to the tide. It was a pull so strong she was about to be jerked off her feet. Elayne tightened her hold on her hand. Nynaeve took a step toward the table, then stopped with an angry shake of her head. *Light*, Egwene thought, *I could do it*. But she did not know what it was she could do.

Light, it's so strong. It's so—wonderful. Elayne's hand was trembling.

On the table, Mat thrashed in the middle of the glow, jerking this way, then that, muttering incomprehensibly. But he did not loosen his hold on the dagger, and his eyes remained closed. Slowly, ever so slowly, he began to arch his back, muscles straining till he shook. Still he fought and bucked, until finally only his heels and his shoulders touched the table. His hand on the dagger sprang open and, quivering, crept back from the hilt; was forced, fighting, from the hilt. His lips skinned away from his teeth in a snarl, a grimace of pain, and his breath came in forced grunts.

"They are killing him," Egwene whispered. "The Amyrlin is killing him! We have to do something."

Just as softly, Nynaeve said, "If we stop them—if we could stop them—he'll die. I do not think I could handle half that much of the Power." She paused as if she had just heard her own words—that she could channel half of what ten full Aes Sedai did with a *sa'angreal*—and her voice grew even fainter. "Light help me, I want to."

She fell silent abruptly. Did she mean that she wanted to help Mat, or that she wanted to channel that flow of Power? Egwene could feel that urge in herself, like a song that compelled her to dance.

"We must trust them," Nynaeve said in an intense whisper, finally. "He has no other chance."

Suddenly Mat shouted, loud and strong. *"Muad'drin tia dar allende caba'drin rhadiem!"* Arched and struggling, eyes squeezed shut, he bellowed the words clearly. *"Los Valdar Cuebiyari! Los! Carai an Caldazar! Al Caldazar!"*

Egwene frowned. She had learned enough to recognize the Old Tongue, if not to understand more than a few words. *Carai an Caldazar! Al Caldazar!* "For the honor of the Red Eagle! For the Red Eagle!" Ancient battle cries of Manetheren, a nation that had vanished during the Trolloc Wars. A nation that had stood where the Two Rivers was now. That much, she knew; but in some way it seemed for a moment that she should understand the rest, too, as if the meaning were just out of sight, and all she had to do was turn her head to know.

With a loud pop of tearing leather, the golden-sheathed dagger rose from Mat's belt, hung a foot above his straining body. The ruby glittered, seemed to send off crimson sparks, as if it, too, fought the Healing.

Mat's eyes opened, and he glared at the women standing around him. *"Mia ayende, Aes Sedai! Caballein misain ye! Inde muagdhe Aes Sedai misain ye! Mia ayende!"* And he began to scream, a roar of rage that went on and on, till Egwene wondered that he had breath left in him.

Hurriedly Anaiya bent to lift a dark metal box from under the table, moving as if it were heavy. When she set it beside Mat and opened the lid, only a small space was revealed within sides at least two inches thick. Anaiya bent again for a set of tongs such as a goodwife might use in her kitchen, and grasped the floating dagger in them as carefully as if it were a poisonous snake.

Mat's scream grew frantic. The ruby shone furiously, flashing blood-red.

The Aes Sedai thrust the dagger into the box and snapped the lid down, letting out a loud sigh as it clicked shut. "A filthy thing," she said.

As soon as the dagger was hidden, Mat's shriek cut off, and he collapsed as if muscle and bone had turned to water. An instant later the glow surrounding Aes Sedai and table winked out.

"Done," the Amyrlin said hoarsely, as if she had been the one screaming. "It is done."

Some of the Aes Sedai sagged visibly, and sweat beaded on more than one brow. Anaiya pulled a plain linen handkerchief from her sleeve and wiped her face openly. The cool-eyed White dabbed almost surreptitiously at her cheeks with a bit of Lugard lace.

"Fascinating," Verin said. "That the Old Blood could flow so strongly in anyone today." She and Serafelle put their heads together, talking softly, but with many gestures.

"Is he Healed?" Nynaeve said. "Will he . . . live?"

Mat lay as if sleeping, but his face still had that hollow-cheeked gauntness. Egwene had never heard of a Healing that did not cure *everything. Unless just separating him from the dagger took* all *of the Power they used. Light!*

"Brendas," the Amyrlin said, "will you see that he is taken back to his room?"

"As you command, Mother," the cool-eyed woman said, her curtsy as emotionless as she herself seemed. When she left to summon bearers, several of the other Aes Sedai left, too, including Anaiya. Verin and Serafelle followed, still talking to one another too quietly for Egwene to make out what they said.

"Is Mat all right?" Nynaeve demanded. Sheriam raised her eyebrows.

The Amyrlin Seat turned toward them. "He is as well as he can be," she said coldly. "Only time will tell. Carrying something with Shadar Logoth's taint for so long . . . who knows what effect it will have on him? Perhaps none, perhaps much. We will see. But the bond with the dagger is broken. Now he needs rest, and as much food as can be gotten into him. He should live."

"What was that he was shouting, Mother?" Elayne asked, then hastily added, "If I may ask."

"He was ordering soldiers." The Amyrlin gave the young man lying on the table a quizzical look. He had not moved since collapsing, but Egwene thought his breathing seemed easier, the rise and fall of his chest more rhythmic. "In a battle two thousand years gone, I would say. The Old Blood comes again."

"It was not all about a battle," Nynaeve said. "I heard him say Aes Sedai. That was no battle. Mother," she added belatedly.

For a moment the Amyrlin seemed to consider, perhaps what to say, perhaps whether to say anything. "For a time," she said finally, "I believe the past and the present were one. He was there, and he was here, and he knew who we were. He commanded us to release him." She paused again. "'I am a free man, Aes Sedai. I am no Aes Sedai meat.' That is what he said."

Leane sniffed loudly, and some of the other Aes Sedai muttered angrily under their breath.

"But, Mother," Egwene said, "he could not have meant it as it sounds. Manetheren was allied with Tar Valon."

"Manetheren was an ally, child," the Amyrlin told her, "but who can know the heart of a man? Not even he himself, I suspect. A man is the easiest animal to put on a leash, and the hardest to keep leashed. Even when he chooses it himself."

"Mother," Sheriam said, "it is late. The cooks will be waiting for these helpers."

"Mother," Egwene asked anxiously, "could we not stay with Mat? If he may still die. . . ."

The Amyrlin's look was level, her face without expression. "You have chores to do, child."

It was not scrubbing pots she meant. Egwene was sure of that. "Yes, Mother." She curtsied, her skirts brushing Nynaeve's and Elayne's as they made theirs. One last time she looked at Mat, then followed Sheriam out. Mat had still not moved.

CHAPTER
19

Awakening

Mat opened his eyes slowly and stared up at the white plaster ceiling, wondering where he was and how he had come there. An intricate fringe of gilded leaves bordered the ceiling, and the mattress under his back felt plumped full of feathers. Somewhere rich, then. Somewhere with money. But his head was empty of the where and the how, and a lot more besides.

He had been dreaming, and bits of those dreams still tumbled together with memories in his head. He could not separate one from the other. Wild flights and fights, strange people from across the ocean, Ways and Portal Stones and pieces of other lives, things right out of a gleeman's tales, these had to be dreams. At least, he thought they must be. But Loial was no dream, and he was an Ogier. Chunks of conversations drifted around in his thoughts, talks with his father, with friends, with Moiraine, and a beautiful woman, and a ship captain, and a well-dressed man who spoke to him like a father giving sage advice. Those were probably real. But it was all bits and fragments. Drifting.

"Muad'drin tia dar allende caba'drin rhadiem," he murmured. The words were only sounds, yet they sparked—something.

The packed lines of spearmen stretched a mile or more to either side below him, dotted with the pennants and banners of towns and cities and minor Houses. The river secured his flank on the left, the bogs and mires on the right. From the hillside he watched the spearmen struggle against the mass of Trollocs trying to break through, ten times the humans' number. Spears pierced black Trolloc mail, and spiked axes carved bloody gaps in the human ranks. Screams and bellows harried the air. The sun burned hot overhead in a cloudless sky, and shimmers of heat rose above the battle line. Arrows still rained down from the enemy, slaying Trolloc and human alike. He had called his archers back, but the Dreadlords did not care so long as they broke his line. On the ridge behind him, the Heart Guard awaited his command, horses stamping impatiently. Armor on men and horses alike shone silver in the sunlight; neither men nor animals could stand the heat much longer.

They must win here or die. He was known as a gambler; it was time to toss the dice. In a voice that carried over the tumult below, he gave the order as he swung up into his saddle. "Footmen prepare to pass cavalry forward!" His bannerman rode close beside him, the Red Eagle banner flapping over his head, as the command was repeated up and down the line.

Below, the spearmen suddenly moved, sidestepping with good discipline, narrowing their formations, opening wide gaps between. Gaps into which the Trollocs poured, roaring bestial cries, like a black, oozing tide of death.

He drew his sword, raised it high. "Forward the Heart Guard!" He dug his heels in, and his mount leaped down the slope. Behind him, hooves thundered in the charge. "Forward!" He was first to strike into the Trollocs, his sword rising and falling, his bannerman close behind. "For the honor of the Red Eagle!" The Heart Guard pounded into the gaps between the spearmen, smashing the tide, hurling it back. "The Red Eagle!" Half-human faces snarled at him, oddly curved swords sought him, but he cut his way ever deeper. Win or die. "Manetheren!"

Mat's hand trembled as he raised it to his forehead. *"Los Valdar Cuebiyari,"* he muttered. He was almost sure he knew what it meant—"Forward the Heart Guard," or maybe "The Heart Guard will advance"—but that could not be. Moiraine had told him a few words of the Old Tongue, and those were all he knew of it. The rest might as well be magpie chatter.

"Crazy," he said roughly. "It probably isn't even the Old Tongue at all. Just gibberish. That Aes Sedai is crazy. It was only a dream."

Aes Sedai. Moiraine. He suddenly became aware of his too-thin wrist and bony hand, and looked at them. He had

been sick. Something to do with a dagger. A dagger with
a ruby in the hilt, and a long-dead, tainted city called Shadar Logoth. It was all foggy and distant, and made no real
sense, but he knew it was no dream. Egwene and Nynaeve
had been taking him to Tar Valon to be Healed. He remembered that much.

He tried to sit up, and fell back, as weak as a newborn
lamb. Laboriously, he pulled himself up and shoved the
single woolen blanket aside. His clothes were gone, perhaps
into the vine-carved wardrobe standing against the wall.
For the moment he did not care about clothes. He struggled
to his feet, tottered across the flowered carpet to cling to
a high-backed armchair, and lurched from the chair to the
table, gilded scrolls on its legs and edges.

Beeswax candles, four to each tall stand and small mirrors behind the flames, lit the room brightly. A larger mirror on the wall above the highly polished washstand threw
his reflection back at him, gaunt and wasted, cheeks hollow
and dark eyes sunken, hair sweat-matted, bent like an old
man and wavering like pasture grass in a breeze. He made
himself stand straight, but it was not much improvement.

A large, covered tray sat on the table in front of his hands,
and his nose caught the smells of food. He twitched aside
the cloth, revealing two large silver pitchers and dishes of
thin green porcelain. He had heard that the Sea Folk charged
its weight in silver for that porcelain. He had expected beef
tea, or sweetbreads, the kinds of things invalids had pushed
on them. Instead, one plate held slices of a beef roast piled
thickly, with brown mustard and horseradish. On others there
were roasted potatoes, sweetbeans with onions, cabbage, and
butterpeas. Pickles, and a wedge of yellow cheese. Thick
slices of crusty bread, and a dish of butter. One pitcher was
filled with milk and still beaded with condensation on the
outside, the other with what smelled like spiced wine. There
was enough of everything for four men. His mouth watered,
and his stomach growled at him.

First I find out where I am. But he rolled up a slice of
beef and dipped it in the mustard before pushing himself
away from the table toward the three tall, narrow windows.

Wooden shutters carved in lacy patterns covered them,
but through the holes he could see that it was night outside.
Lights from other windows made dots in the blackness. For

a moment he sagged against the white stone windowsill in frustration, but then he began to think.

You can turn the worst that comes to your advantage if you only think, his father always said, and certainly Abell Cauthon was the best horse trader in the Two Rivers. When it seemed somebody had taken advantage of Mat's father, it always turned out they had gotten the greasy end of the stick. Not that Abell Cauthon ever did anything dishonest, but even Taren Ferry folk never got the best of him, and everybody knew how close to the bone they cut. All because he thought about things from every side that there was.

Tar Valon. It had to be Tar Valon. This room belonged in a palace. The flowered Domani carpet alone probably cost as much as a farm. More, he did not think he was sick any longer, and from what he had been told, Tar Valon was his only chance to get well. He had never actually felt sick, not that he remembered, not even when Verin—another name swam out of the haze—had told someone nearby that he was dying. Now he felt weak as a babe and hungry as a starving wolf, but somehow, he was sure the Healing had been done. *I feel—whole and well, that's all. I've been Healed.* He grimaced at the shutters.

Healed. That meant they had used the One Power on him. The notion sent goose bumps marching across his skin, but he had known it would be done. "Better than dying," he told himself. Some of the stories he had heard about Aes Sedai came back. "It has to be better than dying. Even Nynaeve thought I was going to die. Anyway, it's done, and worrying about it now won't help anything." He realized he had finished the slice of beef and was licking its juice from his fingers.

Unsteadily, he made his way back to the table. There was a stool underneath. He pulled it out and sat down. Not bothering with knife or fork, he made another roll of beef. How could he turn being in Tar Valon—*In the White Tower. It has to be*—to his advantage?

Tar Valon meant Aes Sedai. That was certainly no reason to stay even an hour. Exactly the opposite. What he remembered of his time with Moiraine, and later with Verin, was not much to go on. He could not recall either of them doing anything really terrible, but then he could not recall a great deal of that time at all. Anyway, whatever Aes Sedai did, they did for their own reasons.

"And those aren't always the reasons you think they are," he mumbled around a mouthful of potato, then swallowed. "An Aes Sedai never lies, but the truth an Aes Sedai tells you isn't always the truth you think it is. That's one thing I have to remember: I can't be sure about them even when I think I know." It was not a cheering conclusion. He filled his mouth with butterpeas.

Thinking about Aes Sedai made him remember a little about them. The seven Ajahs: Blue, Red, Brown, Green, Yellow, White, and Gray. The Reds were the worst. *Except for that Black Ajah they all claim doesn't exist.* But the Red Ajah should be no threat to him. They were only interested in men who could channel.

Rand. Burn me, how could I forget that? Where is he? Is he all right? He sighed regretfully, and spread butter on a piece of still-warm bread. *I wonder if he's gone mad yet.*

Even if he knew the answers, he could do nothing to help Rand. He was not sure he would if he could. Rand could channel, and Mat had grown up with stories of men channeling, stories to frighten children. Stories that frightened adults, too, because some of them were all too true. Discovering what Rand could do had been like finding out his best friend tortured small animals and killed babies. Once you finally made yourself believe it, it was hard to call him a friend any longer.

"I have to look out for myself," he said angrily. He up-ended the wine pitcher over his silver cup and was surprised to find it empty. He filled the cup with milk, instead. "Egwene and Nynaeve want to be Aes Sedai." He had not really remembered that until he said it aloud. "Rand is following Moiraine around and calling himself the Dragon Reborn. The Light knows what Perrin is up to. He's been acting crazy ever since his eyes turned funny. I have to look out for myself." *Burn me, I have to! I'm the last one of us who's still sane. There's only me.*

Tar Valon. Well, it was supposed to be the wealthiest city in the world, and it was the center of trade between the Borderlands and the south, the center of Aes Sedai power. He did not think he could get an Aes Sedai to gamble with him. Or trust the fall of the dice or the turn of the cards if he did. But there had to be merchants, and others with silver and gold. The city itself would be worth a few days. He knew he had traveled far since leaving the Two Rivers, but aside from a few vague memories of Caemlyn and Cairhien, he could remember nothing of any great cities. He had always wanted to see a great city.

"But not one full of Aes Sedai," he muttered sourly, scraping up the last of the butterpeas. He gulped them down and went back for another helping of beef.

Idly, he wondered if the Aes Sedai might let him have the ruby from the Shadar Logoth dagger. He remembered the dagger in only the fuzziest way, but even that was like remembering a terrible injury. His insides knotted up, and sharp pain dug at his temples. Yet the ruby was clear in his mind, as big as his thumbnail, dark as a drop of blood, glittering like some crimson eye. Surely he had more claim to it than they did, and it had to be worth as much as a dozen farms back home.

They'll probably say it is tainted, too. And likely it was. Still he spun a little fancy of trading the ruby to some of the Coplins for their best land. Most of that family—troublemakers from the cradle, where they were not thieves and liars as well—deserved whatever happened to them and more. But he really did not believe the Aes Sedai would give it back to him, did not relish the notion of carrying it as far as Emond's Field if they did. And the thought of owning the largest farm in the Two Rivers was no longer as exciting as it once had been. Once that had been his biggest ambition, that, and to be known as his father's equal as a horse trader. Now it seemed such a small thing to want. A cramped thing, with the whole wide world just waiting out there.

First off, he decided, he would find Egwene and Nynaeve. *Maybe they've come to their senses. Maybe they've given up this foolishness about becoming Aes Sedai.* He did not think they would have, but he could not go without seeing them. He would go; that was sure. A visit with them, a day to see the city, perhaps a game with the dice to pad out his purse, and then he would be off for somewhere where there were no Aes Sedai. Before he returned home—*I will go home one day. One day, I will*—he meant to see something of the world, and without any Aes Sedai making him dance to her tune.

Rummaging around the tray for something more to eat, he was shocked to realize nothing was left but smears and a few crumbs of bread and cheese. The pitchers were both empty. He squinted down at his stomach in wonder. He should have been stuffed to the ears with all that in him, but he felt as if he had hardly eaten at all. He scraped the last bits of cheese together between thumb and forefinger. Halfway to his mouth, his hand froze..

I blew the Horn of Valere. Softly he whistled a bit of tune, then cut it short when the words came to him:

> I'm down at the bottom of the well.
> It's night, and the rain is coming down.
> The sides are falling in,
> and there's no rope to climb.
> I'm down at the bottom of the well.

"There had better be a bloody rope to climb," he whispered. He let the cheese crumbs fall on the tray. For the moment he felt sick again. Determinedly he tried to think, tried to penetrate the fog that shrouded everything in his head.

Verin had been bringing the Horn to Tar Valon, but he could not remember if she knew he was the one who had blown it. She had never said anything to make him think so. He was sure of that. He thought he was. *So what if she does know? What if they all do? Unless Verin did something with it I don't know about, they have the Horn. They don't need me.* But who could say what Aes Sedai thought they needed?

"If they ask," he said grimly, "I never even touched it. If they know. . . . If they know, I'll . . . I'll handle that when it comes. Burn me, they can't want anything from me. They can't!"

A soft knock on the door brought him swaying to his feet, ready to run. If there had been any place to run to, and if he could have managed more than three steps. But there was not, and he could not.

The door opened.

CHAPTER
20

Visitations

The woman who came in, dressed all in white silk and silver, shut the door behind her and leaned back against it to study him with the darkest eyes Mat had ever seen. She was so beautiful he almost forgot to breathe, with hair as black as night held by a finely woven silver band, and as graceful in repose as another woman would be dancing. He halfway thought that he knew her, but he rejected the idea out of hand. No man could ever forget a woman like her.

"You may be passable, I suppose, once you fill out again," she said, "but for now, perhaps you could put on something."

For an instant Mat continued to stare at her; then suddenly he realized he was standing there naked. Face scarlet, he shambled to the bed, pulled the blanket around himself like a cloak, and more fell than sat down on the edge of the mattress. "I'm sorry for . . . I mean, I . . . that is, I didn't expect . . . I . . . I . . ." He drew a deep breath. "I apologize for your finding me this way."

He could still feel the heat in his cheeks. For a moment he wished that Rand, whatever he had become, or even Perrin were there to advise him. They always seemed to get on well with women. Even girls who knew that Rand was all but promised to Egwene used to stare at him, and they seemed to think Perrin's slow ways were gentle and attractive. However hard he tried, he always managed to make a fool of himself in front of girls. As he had just done.

"I would not have visited you in this way, Mat, except that I was here in the . . . in the White Tower—" She smiled as if the name amused her—"for another purpose, and I

wanted to see all of you." Mat's face reddened again, and he
tugged the blanket around him tighter, but she seemed not
to have been teasing him. More graceful than a swan, she
glided to the table. "You are hungry. That's to be expected,
the way they do things. Make sure you eat all they give you.
You will be surprised at how quickly you put weight back
and regain strength."

"Pardon," Mat said diffidently, "but do I know you?
Meaning no offense, but you seem . . . familiar." She looked
at him until he began to shift uneasily. A woman like her
would expect to be remembered.

"You may have seen me," she said finally. "Somewhere.
Call me Selene." Her head tilted slightly; she appeared to
be waiting for him to recognize the name.

It tugged at the edges of memory. He thought he must
have heard it before, but he could not say when or where.
"Are you an Aes Sedai, Selene?"

"No." The word was soft but surprisingly emphatic.

For the first time, he studied her, able now to see more
than her beauty. She was almost as tall as he was, slender
and, he suspected from the way she moved, strong. He was
not sure of her age—a year or two older than he, or maybe
as much as ten—but her cheeks were smooth. Her necklace
of smooth white stones and woven silver matched her wide
belt, but she did not wear a Great Serpent ring. The absence
should not have surprised him—no Aes Sedai would ever
say right out that she was not—yet it did. There was an air
about her—a self-confidence, a surety in her own power to
match any queen's, and something more—that he associated with Aes Sedai.

"You aren't by any chance a novice, are you?" He had
heard that novices wore white, but he could not really believe it of her. *She makes Elayne look like a cringer.* Elayne.
Another name drifting into his head.

"Hardly that," Selene said with a wry twist to her mouth.
"Let us just say that I am someone whose interests coincide
with yours. These . . . Aes Sedai mean to use you, but you
will like it, in the main, I think. And accept it. There is no
need to convince you to seek out glory."

"Use me?" The memory returned to him of thinking that,
but about Rand, that the Aes Sedai meant to use Rand, not
him. *They've no bloody use for me. Light, they can't have!*

"What do you mean? I'm no one important. I am no use to anyone but myself. What kind of glory?"

"I knew that would pull you. You, above all."

Her smile made his head spin. He scrubbed a hand through his hair. The blanket slipped, and he caught it hastily before it could fall. "Now listen, they are not interested in me." *What about me sounding the Horn?* "I am just a farmer." *Maybe they think I'm tied to Rand in some way. No, Verin said. . . .* He was not sure what Verin had said, or Moiraine, but he thought most Aes Sedai knew nothing at all about Rand. He wanted to keep it that way, at least until he was a long way gone. "Just a simple country man. I only want to see a little of the world and go back to my da's farm." *What does she mean, glory?*

Selene shook her head as if she had heard his thoughts. "You are more important than you yet know. Certainly more important than these so-called Aes Sedai know. You *can* have glory, if you know enough not to trust them."

"You certainly sound as if you don't trust them." *Socalled?* A thought came to him, but he could not manage to say it. "Are you a . . . ? Are you . . . ?" It was not the kind of thing you accused someone of.

"A Darkfriend?" Selene said mockingly. She sounded amused, not angered. She sounded contemptuous. "One of those pathetic followers of Ba'alzamon who think he will give them immortality and power? I follow no one. There is one man I could stand beside, but I do not follow."

Mat laughed nervously. "Of course not." *Blood and ashes, a Darkfriend wouldn't name herself Darkfriend. Probably has a poisoned knife, if she is.* He had a vague memory of a woman dressed as one nobly born, a Darkfriend with a deadly dagger in her slender hand. "That wasn't what I meant at all. You look. . . . You look like a queen. That's what I meant. Are you a Lady?"

"Mat, Mat, you must learn to trust me. Oh, I will use you, too—you have too suspicious a nature, especially since carrying that dagger, for me to deny it—but my use will gain you wealth, and power, and glory. I will not compel you. I have always believed men perform better if convinced rather than forced. These Aes Sedai do not even realize how important you are, and he will try to dissuade or kill you, but I can give you what you desire."

"He?" Mat said sharply. *Kill me? Light, it's Rand they were after, not me. How does she know about the dagger? I suppose the whole Tower knows.* "Who wants to kill me?"

Selene's mouth tightened as if she had said too much. "You know what you want, Mat, and I know it every bit as well as you. You must choose who you will trust to gain it for you. I admit I will use you. These Aes Sedai will never do that. I will lead you to wealth and glory. They will keep you tied to a leash until you die."

"You say a lot," Mat said, "but how do I know any of it is true? How do I know I can trust you any more than I can them?"

"By listening to what they tell you, and what they do not. Will they tell you your father came to Tar Valon?"

"My da was here?"

"A man named Abell Cauthon, and another named Tam al'Thor. They made nuisances of themselves until they gained an audience, I have heard, wanting to know where you and your friends were. And Siuan Sanche sent them back to the Two Rivers with empty hands, not even letting them know you were alive. Will they tell you that, unless you ask? Perhaps not even then, for you might try to run away back home."

"My da thinks I am dead?" Mat said slowly.

"He can be told you live. I can see to it. Think on who to trust, Mat Cauthon. Will they tell you that even now Rand al'Thor is trying to escape, and the one called Moiraine is hunting him? Will they tell you that the Black Ajah infests their precious White Tower? Will they even tell you how they mean to use you?"

"Rand is trying to escape? But—" Maybe she knew Rand had proclaimed himself the Dragon Reborn, and maybe she did not, but he would not tell her. *The Black Ajah! Blood and bloody ashes!* "Who are you, Selene? If you're not Aes Sedai, what are you?"

Her smile hid secrets. "Just remember that there is another choice. You need not be a puppet for the White Tower or prey for Ba'alzamon's Darkfriends. The world is more complex than you can imagine. Do as these Aes Sedai wish for the present, but remember your choices. Will you do that?"

"I don't see that I have much choice at all," he said glumly. "I suppose I will."

Selene's look sharpened. Friendliness sloughed off her voice like an old snake skin. "Suppose? I did not come to you like this, talk in this way, for suppose, Matrim Cauthon." She stretched out a slim hand.

Her hand was empty, and she stood halfway across the room, but he leaned back, away from her hand, as if she were right on top of him with a dagger. He did not know why, really, except that there was a threat in her eyes, and he was sure it was real. His skin began to tingle, and his headache returned.

Suddenly tingle and pain vanished together, and Selene's head whipped around as if listening to something beyond the walls. A tiny frown appeared on her face, and she lowered her hand. The frown vanished. "We will talk again, Mat. I have much to say to you. Remember your choices. Remember that there are many hands that would kill you. I alone guarantee you life, and all you seek, if you do as I say." She slipped out of the door as silently and gracefully as she had entered.

Mat let out a long breath. Sweat ran down his face. *Who in the Light is she?* A Darkfriend, perhaps. Except that she had sounded as contemptuous of Ba'alzamon as she was of Aes Sedai. Darkfriends spoke of Ba'alzamon the way anyone else might speak of the Creator. And she had not asked him to conceal her visit from the Aes Sedai.

Right, he thought sourly. *Pardon me, Aes Sedai, but this woman came to see me. She wasn't Aes Sedai, but I think maybe she started to use the One Power on me, and she said she wasn't a Darkfriend, but she did say you mean to use me, and the Black Ajah's in your Tower. Oh, and she said I'm important. I don't know how. You don't mind if I leave now, do you?*

Going was beginning to be a better idea by the minute. He slid awkwardly off the bed and made his way unsteadily to the wardrobe, still clutching his blanket around him. His boots were on the floor inside, and his cloak hung from a peg, under his belt, with pouch and sheathed belt knife. It was just a country knife, with a stout blade, but it could do as much as any fine dagger. The rest of his clothes— two sturdy wool coats, three pairs of breeches, half a dozen linen shirts and smallclothes—had been brushed or washed as required, and neatly folded on the shelves that took up one side of the wardrobe. He felt the pouch hanging from the belt, but it was empty. Its contents lay jumbled on a shelf with what had been emptied from his pockets.

He brushed aside a redhawk's feather, a smooth, striped rock he had liked the colors of, his razor, and his bone-handled pocketknife, and freed his wash-leather purse from some coils of spare bowstring. When he tugged it open, he found his memory had been all too good in this instance.

"Two silver marks and a handful of copper," he muttered. "I won't get far on that." Once it would have seemed a small fortune to him, but that had been before he left Emond's Field.

He stooped to peer back into the shelf. *Where are they?* He began to be afraid the Aes Sedai might have thrown them out, the way his mother would if she had ever found them. *Where . . . ?* He felt a surge of relief. Way in the back, behind his tinderbox and ball of twine for snares and the like, were his two leather dice cups.

They rattled as he pulled them out, but he still popped off the tight-fitting round caps. Everything was as it should be. Five dice carved with symbols, for crowns, and five marked with spots. The spotted dice would do for a number of games, but more men seemed to play crowns than anything else. With these, his two marks would become enough to take him far away from Tar Valon. *Away from Aes Sedai and Selene, both.*

A peremptory knock was followed immediately by the door opening. He whirled around. The Amyrlin Seat and the Keeper of the Chronicles were entering. He would have recognized them even without the Amyrlin's broad, striped stole, and the Keeper's narrower blue stole. He had seen them once and only once, a long way from Tar Valon, but he could not forget the two most powerful women among the Aes Sedai.

The Amyrlin's eyebrows rose at the sight of him standing there with the blanket hanging from his shoulders and his purse and dice cups in his hands. "I don't think you will need those for a while yet, my son," she said dryly. "Put them up and get back to bed before you fall on your face."

He hesitated, his back stiffening, but his knees chose that moment to wobble, and the two Aes Sedai were looking at him, dark eyes and blue alike appearing to read his every rebellious thought. He did as he was told, holding the blanket around him with both hands. He lay down straight as a board, not sure what else he could do.

"How are you feeling?" the Amyrlin asked briskly as she put a hand on his head. Goose bumps covered his skin. Had she done something with the One Power, or was it being touched by an Aes Sedai that made him feel a chill?

"I'm fine," he told her. "Why, I am ready to be on my way. Just let me say goodbye to Egwene and Nynaeve, and I'll be out of your hair. I mean, I will go . . . uh, Mother." Moiraine and Verin had not seemed to care much how he talked, but this was the Amyrlin Seat, after all.

"Nonsense," the Amyrlin said. She pulled the high-backed chair around, closer to the bed, and sat, addressing Leane. "Men always seem to refuse to admit they are sick until they're sick enough to make twice as much work for women. Then they claim they're well too soon, with the same result."

The Keeper glanced at Mat and nodded. "Yes, Mother, yet this one cannot claim he is well when he can barely stand up. At least he has eaten everything on his tray."

"I'd be surprised if he had left enough crumbs to interest a finch. And still hungry, unless I miss my guess."

"I could have someone bring him a pie, Mother. Or some cakes."

"No, I think he has had as much as he can hold for now. If he brings it all back up, it won't do him any good."

Mat scowled. It seemed to him that when you got sick, you became invisible to women unless they were actually talking to you. And then they took at least ten years off your age. Nynaeve, his mother, his sisters, the Amyrlin Seat, they all did it.

"I'm not hungry at all," he announced. "I am fine. If you will let me put my clothes on, I'll show you how well I am. I will be out of here before you know it." They were both looking at him, now. He cleared his throat. "Uh . . . Mother."

The Amyrlin snorted. "You've eaten a meal for five, and you will eat three or four like it every day for days yet, or else you will starve to death. You've just been Healed from a link to the evil that killed every man, woman, and child in Aridhol, and no less strong for near two thousand years waiting for you to pick it up. It was killing you just as surely as it killed them. That is not like having a fish spine stuck in your thumb, boy. We very nearly killed you ourselves trying to save you."

"I am not hungry," he maintained. His stomach growled loudly to give him the lie.

"I read you aright the first time I saw you," the Amyrlin said. "I knew right then you'd bolt like a startled fisher-bird if you ever thought someone was trying to hold you. As well I took precautions."

He eyed them warily. "Precautions?" They looked back, all serenity. He felt as if their eyes were pinning him to the bed.

"Your name and description are on their way to the bridge guards," the Amyrlin said, "and the dockmasters. I'll not try to hold you inside the Tower, but you will not leave Tar Valon until you are well. Should you try to hide in the city, hunger will drive you back here eventually, or if it doesn't, we will find you before you starve."

"Why do you want to keep me here so badly?" he demanded. He heard Selene's voice. *They want to use you.* "Why should you care whether I starve or not? I can feed myself."

The Amyrlin gave a small laugh with little amusement in it. "With two silver marks and a handful of copper, my son? Your dice would need to be very lucky indeed to buy all the food you'll need in the next few days. We do not Heal people, then let them waste our efforts by dying while they still need care. In addition to which, you may yet need more Healing."

"More? You said you had Healed me. Why should I need more?"

"My son, you carried that dagger for months. I believe we dug every trace of it out of you, but if we missed even the smallest speck, it could still be fatal. And who knows what effect your having it in your possession so long may have? Half a year from now, a year, and you may wish you had an Aes Sedai to hand to Heal you again."

"You want me to stay here a year?" he said incredulously, and loudly. Leane shifted her feet and eyed him sharply, but the Amyrlin's calm features were unruffled.

"Perhaps not so long as that, my son. Long enough to be

certain, though. Surely you want as much. Would you set
sail in a boat when you didn't know whether the caulking
would hold, or whether a plank might be rotten?"

"I never had much to do with boats," Mat muttered. It
might be true. Aes Sedai never lied, but there were too
many mights and mays in it for him. "I've been gone from
home a long time, Mother. My da and my mother probably
think I am dead."

"If you wish to write a letter to them, I will see that it is
carried to Emond's Field."

Mat waited for more, but no more came. "Thank you,
Mother." He essayed a small laugh. "I'm half surprised my
da did not come looking for me. He's the kind of man who
would." He was not sure, but he thought there was a small
hesitation before the Amyrlin answered.

"He did come. Leane spoke to him."

The Keeper took it up immediately. "We did not know
where you were then, Mat. I told him so, and he left before
the heavy snows. I gave him some gold to make the journey
home easier."

"No doubt," the Amyrlin said, "he will be pleased to hear
from you. And your mother will, certainly. Give me the letter when you have written it, and I will see to it."

They had told him, but he had had to ask. *And they
didn't mention Rand's da. Maybe because they didn't think
I would care, and maybe because. . . . Burn me, I don't
know. Who can tell with Aes Sedai?* "I was traveling with a
friend, Mother. Rand al'Thor. You remember him. Do you
know if he is all right? I'll bet his da is worried, too."

"As far as I know," the Amyrlin said smoothly, "the boy
is well enough, but who can say? I have seen him only once,
the time I saw you, in Fal Dara." She turned to the Keeper.
"Perhaps he could do with a small piece of pie, Leane. And
something for his throat, if he is going to do all this talking.
Will you see that it is brought to him?"

The tall Aes Sedai left with a murmured, "As you command, Mother."

When the Amyrlin turned back to Mat, she was smiling,
but her eyes were blue ice. "There are things it would be
dangerous for you to talk about, perhaps even in front of
Leane. A flapping tongue has killed more men than sudden
storms ever did."

"Dangerous, Mother?" His mouth felt suddenly parched, but he resisted the urge to lick his lips. *Light, how much does she know about Rand? If only Moiraine didn't keep so many secrets.* "Mother, I don't know anything dangerous. I can hardly remember half of what I do know."

"Do you remember the Horn?"

"What horn is that, Mother?"

She was on her feet and looming over him so fast he hardly saw her move. "You play games with me, boy, and I will make you weep for your mother to come running. I have no time for games, and neither do you. Now, do—you—remember?"

Clutching the blanket tightly around him, he had to swallow before he could say, "I remember, Mother."

She seemed to relax, just a little, and Mat shrugged his shoulders queasily. He felt as if he had just been allowed to lift them off a chopping block.

"Good. That is good, Mat." She sat back down slowly, studying him. "Do you know that you are linked to the Horn?" He mouthed the word "linked" silently, shocked, and she nodded. "I did not think you knew. You were first to blow the Horn of Valere after it was found. For you, it will summon dead heroes back from the grave. For anyone else, it is only a horn—so long as you live."

He took a deep breath. "So long as I live," he said in a dull voice, and the Amyrlin nodded. "You could have let me die." She nodded again. "Then you could have had anyone you want blow it, and it would have worked for them." Another nod. "Blood and ashes! You mean me to blow it for you. When the Last Battle comes, you mean me to call heroes back from the grave to fight the Dark One for you. Blood and bloody ashes!"

She put an elbow on the arm of the chair and propped her chin on her hand. Her eyes never left him. "Would you prefer the alternative?"

He frowned, then remembered what the alternative was. If someone else had to sound the Horn. . . . "You want me to blow the Horn? Then I'll blow the Horn. I never said I would not, did I?"

The Amyrlin gave an exasperated sigh. "You remind me of my uncle Huan. No one could ever pin him down. He liked to gamble, too, and he'd much rather have fun than work. He died pulling children out of a burning house. He wouldn't stop going back as long as there was one left inside. Are you like him, Mat? Will you be there when the flames are high?"

He could not meet her eyes. He studied his fingers as they plucked irritably at his blanket. "I'm no hero. I do what I have to do, but I am no hero."

"Most of those we call heroes only did what they had to do. I suppose it will have to be enough. For now. You must not speak to anyone but me of the Horn, my son. Or of your link to it."

For now? he thought. *It's all you are going to bloody get, now or ever.* "I don't mean to bloody tell everybo—" She arched an eyebrow, and he made his voice smooth again. "I do not want to tell anyone. I wish nobody knew. Why do you want to keep it such a secret? Don't you trust your Aes Sedai?"

For a long moment he thought he had gone too far. Her face hardened, and her look could have carved axe handles.

"If I could make it so that only you and I knew," she said coldly, "I would. The more people know a thing, the more the knowledge spreads, even with the best will. Most of the world believes the Horn of Valere is only legend, and those who know better believe one of the Hunters has yet to find it. But Shayol Ghul knows it has been found, and that means at least some Darkfriends know. But they do not know where it is, and, if the Light shines on us, they do not know you sounded it. Do you really want Darkfriends coming after you? Halfmen, or other Shadowspawn? They want the Horn. You must know that. It will work as well for the Shadow as for the Light. But if it is to work for them, they must take you, or kill you. Do you want to risk that?"

Mat wished he had another blanket, and maybe a goose-down comforter. The room suddenly felt very cold. "Are you telling me Darkfriends could come after me here? I thought the White Tower could keep Darkfriends out." He remembered what Selene had said about the Black Ajah, and wondered what the Amyrlin would say to that.

"A good reason to stay, wouldn't you say?" She got to her feet, smoothing her skirts. "Rest, my son. Soon you will feel much better. Rest." She closed the door softly behind her.

For a long time Mat lay staring up at the ceiling. He barely noticed when a serving woman came with his piece of pie and another pitcher of milk, taking the tray of empty dishes when she went. His stomach rumbled loudly at the warm smell of apples and spices, but he paid that no mind, either. The Amyrlin thought she held him like a sheep in a pen. And Selene. . . . *Who in the Light is she? What does she want?* Selene had been right about some things; but the Amyrlin had told him she meant to use him, and how. In a way. There were too many holes in what she had said to suit him, too many holes she could slip something deadly through. The Amyrlin wanted something, and Selene wanted something, and he was the rope they were tugging between them. He thought he would rather face Trollocs than be caught between those two.

There had to be a way out of Tar Valon, a way out of both their grasps. Once he was beyond the river, he could keep out of Aes Sedai hands, and Selene's, and Darkfriends', too. He was sure of it. There had to be a way. All he had to do was think about it from every angle.

The pie grew cold on the table.

CHAPTER
21

A World of Dreams

E gwene scrubbed her hands with a hand towel as she
hurried down the dimly lit corridor. She had washed
them twice, but they still felt greasy. She had not
thought there could be so many pots in the world. And
today had been bake day, so buckets of ashes had had to
be hauled from the ovens. And the hearths cleaned. And
the tables rubbed bone-white with fine sand, and the floors
scrubbed on hands and knees. Ash and grease stained her
white dress. Her back ached, and she wanted to be in her
bed, but Verin had come to the kitchens, supposedly for a
meal to eat in her rooms, and whispered a summons to her
in passing.

Verin had her quarters above the library, in corridors
used only by a few other Brown sisters. There was a dusty
air to the halls there, as if the women who lived along
them were too busy with other things to bother having the
servants clean very often, and the passages took odd turns
and twists, sometimes dipping or rising unexpectedly. The
tapestries were few, their colorful weavings dulled, apparently cleaned as seldom as everything else here. Many of
the lamps were unlit, plunging much of the hall into gloom.
Egwene thought she had it to herself, except for a flash of
white ahead, perhaps a novice or a servant scurrying about
some task. Her shoes, clicking on bare black and white
floor tiles, made echoes. It was not a comforting place for
one thinking of the Black Ajah.

She found what Verin had told her to look for. A dark
paneled door at the top of a rise, beside a dusty tapestry

of a king on horseback receiving the surrender of another king. Verin had named the pair of them—men dead hundreds of years before Artur Hawkwing was born; Verin always seemed to know such things—but Egwene could not remember their names, or the long-vanished countries they had ruled. It was the only wall hanging she had seen that matched Verin's description, though.

Minus the sound of her own footsteps, the hallway seemed even emptier than before, and more threatening. She rapped on the door, and entered hurriedly on the heels of an absentminded "Who is it? Come in."

One step into the room, she stopped and stared. Shelves lined the walls, except for one door that must lead to inner rooms and except for where maps hung, often in layers, and what seemed to be charts of the night sky. She recognized the names of some constellations—the Plowman and the Haywain, the Archer and the Five Sisters—but others were unfamiliar. Books and papers and scrolls covered nearly every flat surface, with all sorts of odd things interspersed among the piles, and sometimes on top of them. Strange shapes of glass or metal, spheres and tubes interlinked, and circles held inside circles, stood among bones and skulls of every shape and description. What appeared to be a stuffed brown owl, not much bigger than Egwene's hand, stood on what seemed to be a bleached white lizard's skull, but could not be, for the skull was longer than her arm and had crooked teeth as big as her fingers. Candlesticks had been stuck about in a haphazard fashion, giving good light here and shadows there, although seeming in danger of setting fire to papers in some places. The owl blinked at her, and she jumped.

"Ah, yes," Verin said. She was seated behind a table as cluttered as everything else in the room, a torn page held carefully in her hands. "It is you. Yes." She noticed Egwene's sideways glance at the owl, and said absently, "He keeps down mice. They chew paper." Her gesture took in the entire room, and reminded her of the page she held. "Fascinating, this. Rosel of Essam claimed more than a hundred pages survived the Breaking, and she should have known, since she wrote barely two hundred years afterwards, but only this one piece still exists, so far as I know. Perhaps only this very copy.

Rosel wrote that it held secrets the world could not face, and she would not speak of them plainly. I have read this page a thousand times, trying to decipher what she meant."

The tiny owl blinked at Egwene again. She tried not to look at it. "What does it say, Verin Sedai?"

Verin blinked, very much as the owl had. "What does it say? It is a direct translation, mind, and reads almost like a bard reciting in High Chant. Listen. 'Heart of the Dark. Ba'alzamon. Name hidden within name shrouded by name. Secret buried within secret cloaked by secret. Betrayer of Hope. Ishamael betrays all hope. Truth burns and sears. Hope fails before truth. A lie is our shield. Who can stand against the Heart of the Dark? Who can face the Betrayer of Hope? Soul of shadow, Soul of the Shadow, he is—'" She stopped with a sigh. "It ends there. What do you make of it?"

"I don't know," Egwene said. "I do not like it."

"Well, why should you, child? Like it, or understand it? I have studied it nearly forty years, and I do neither." Verin carefully placed the page inside a silk-lined folder of stiff leather, then casually stuffed the folder into a stack of papers. "But you did not come for that." She rummaged across the table, muttering to herself, several times barely catching a pile of books or manuscripts before it toppled. Finally she came up with a handful of pages covered in a thin, spidery hand and tied with nubby string. "Here, child. Everything that is known about Liandrin and the women who went with her. Names, ages, Ajahs, where they were born. Everything I could find in the records. Even how they performed in their studies. What we know of the *ter'angreal* they took, too, which isn't much. Only descriptions, for the most part. I do not know whether any of this will help. I saw nothing of any use in this."

"Perhaps one of us will see something." A sudden wave of suspicion took Egwene by surprise. *If she didn't leave something out.* The Amyrlin seemed to trust Verin only because she had to. What if Verin was Black Ajah herself? She gave herself a shake. She had traveled all the way from Toman Head to Tar Valon with Verin, and she refused to believe this plump scholar could be a Darkfriend. "I trust you, Verin Sedai." *Can I, really?*

The Aes Sedai blinked at her again, then dismissed whatever thought had come to her with a shake of her head. "That list I gave you may be important, or it may be so much waste of paper, but it isn't the only reason I summoned you." She started moving things on the table, making some shaky stacks taller to clear a space. "I understand from Anaiya that you might become a Dreamer. The last was Corianin Nedeal, four hundred and seventy-three years ago, and from what I can make of the records, she barely deserved the name. It would be quite interesting, if you do."

"She tested me, Verin Sedai, but she couldn't be sure that any of my dreams foretold the future."

"That is only part of what a Dreamer does, child. Perhaps the least part. Anaiya believes in bringing girls along too slowly, in my opinion. Look here." With one finger, Verin drew a number of parallel lines across the area she had cleared, lines clear in dust atop the old beeswax. "Let these represent worlds that might exist if different choices had been made, if major turning points in the Pattern had gone another way."

"The worlds reached by the Portal Stones," Egwene said, to show she had listened to Verin's lectures on the journey from Toman Head. What could this possibly have to do with whether or not she was a Dreamer?

"Very good. But the Pattern may be even more complex than that, child. The Wheel weaves our lives to make the Pattern of an Age, but the Ages themselves are woven into the Age Lace, the Great Pattern. Who can know if this is even the tenth part of the weaving, though? Some in the Age of Legends apparently believe that there were still other worlds—even harder to reach than the worlds of the Portal Stones, if that can be believed—lying like this." She drew more lines, cross-hatching the first set. For a moment she stared at them. "The warp and the woof of the weave. Perhaps the Wheel of Time weaves a still greater Pattern from worlds." Straightening, she dusted her hands. "Well, that is neither here nor there. In all of these worlds, whatever their other variations, a few things are constant. One is that the Dark One is imprisoned in all of them."

In spite of herself, Egwene stepped closer to peer at the lines Verin had drawn. "In all of them? How can that be?

Are you saying there is a Father of Lies for each world?"
The thought of so many Dark Ones made her shiver.

"No, child. There is one Creator, who exists everywhere
at once for all of these worlds. In the same way, there is
only one Dark One, who also exists in all of these worlds at
once. If he is freed from the prison the Creator made in one
world, he is freed on all. So long as he is kept prisoner in
one, he remains imprisoned on all."

"That does not seem to make sense," Egwene protested.

"Paradox, child. The Dark One is the embodiment of
paradox and chaos, the destroyer of reason and logic, the
breaker of balance, the unmaker of order."

The owl suddenly took flight on silent wings, landing
atop a large white skull on a shelf behind the Aes Sedai.
It peered down at the two women, blinking. Egwene had
noticed the skull when she came in, with its curled horns
and snout, and vaguely wondered what sort of ram had so
big a head. Now she took in the roundness of it, the high
forehead. Not a ram's skull. A Trolloc.

She drew a shuddering breath. "Verin Sedai, what does
this have to do with being a Dreamer? The Dark One is
bound in Shayol Ghul, and I do not want to even think of
him escaping." *But the seals on his prison are weakening.
Even novices know that, now.*

"Do with being a Dreamer? Why, nothing, child. Except that we must all confront the Dark One in one way or
another. He is prisoned now, but the Pattern did not bring
Rand al'Thor into the world for no purpose. The Dragon
Reborn will face the Lord of the Grave; that much is sure.
If Rand survives that long, of course. The Dark One will try
to distort the Pattern, if he can. Well, we have gone rather
far afield, haven't we?"

"Forgive me, Verin Sedai, but if this"—Egwene indicated the lines drawn in the dust—"has nothing to do with
being a Dreamer, why are you telling me about it?"

Verin stared at her as if she were deliberately being dense.
"Nothing? Of course it has something to do with it, child.
The point is that there is a third constant besides the Creator
and the Dark One. There is a world that lies *within* each of
these others, inside all of them at the same time. Or perhaps
surrounding them. Writers in the Age of Legends called

it *Tel'aran'rhiod*, "the Unseen World." Perhaps "the World of Dreams" is a better translation. Many people—ordinary folk who could not think of channeling—sometimes glimpse *Tel'aran'rhiod* in their dreams, and even catch glimmers of these other worlds through it. Think of some of the peculiar things you have seen in your dreams. But a Dreamer, child—a true Dreamer—can enter *Tel'aran'rhiod*."

Egwene tried to swallow, but a lump in her throat stopped her. *Enter it?* "I . . . I don't think I am a Dreamer, Verin Sedai. Anaiya Sedai's tests—"

Verin cut her off. "—prove nothing one way or the other. And Anaiya still believes that you may very well be one."

"I suppose I will learn whether I am or not eventually," Egwene mumbled. *Light, I want to be, don't I? I want to learn! I want it all.*

"You have no time to wait, child. The Amyrlin has entrusted a great task to you and Nynaeve. You must reach out for any tool you might be able to use." Verin dug a red wooden box from under the welter on her table. The box was large enough to hold sheets of paper, but when the Aes Sedai opened the lid a crack, all she pulled out was a ring carved from stone, all flecks and stripes of blue and brown and red, and too large to be a finger ring. "Here, child."

Egwene shifted the papers to take it, and her eyes widened in surprise. The ring certainly looked like stone, but it felt harder than steel and heavier than lead. And the circle of it was twisted. If she ran a finger along one edge, it would go around twice, inside as well as out; it only had one edge. She moved her finger along that edge twice, just to convince herself.

"Corianin Nedeal," Verin said, "had that *ter'angreal* in her possession for most of her life. You will keep it, now."

Egwene almost dropped the ring. *A ter'angreal? I am to keep a* ter'angreal?

Verin seemed not to notice her shock. "According to her, it eases the passage to *Tel'aran'rhiod*. She claimed it would work for those without Talent as well as for Aes Sedai, so long as you are touching it when you sleep. There are dangers, of course. *Tel'aran'rhiod* is not like other dreams. What happens there is real; you are actually there instead of just glimpsing it." She pushed back the sleeve of her dress, revealing a faded scar the length of her forearm. "I tried it myself, once, some years ago. Anaiya's Healing did not work as well as it should have. Remember that." The Aes Sedai let her sleeve cover the scar again.

"I will be careful, Verin Sedai." *Real? My dreams are bad enough as they are. I want no dreams that leave scars! I'll put it in a sack and stick it in a dark corner and leave it there. I'll*—But she wanted to learn. She wanted to be Aes Sedai, and no Aes Sedai had been a Dreamer in nearly five hundred years. "I'll be very careful." She slipped the ring into her pouch and tugged the drawstrings tight, then picked up the papers Verin had given her.

"Remember to keep it hidden, child. No novice, or even an Accepted, should have a thing like that in her possession. But it may prove useful to you. Keep it hidden."

"Yes, Verin Sedai." Remembering Verin's scar, she almost wished another Aes Sedai would come along and take it from her right then.

"Good, child. Now, off with you. It grows late, and you must be up early to help with breakfast. Sleep well."

Verin sat looking at the door for a time after it closed behind Egwene. The owl hooted softly behind her. Pulling the red box to her, she opened the lid all the way and frowned at what nearly filled the space.

Page upon page, covered with a precise hand, the black ink barely faded after nearly five hundred years. Corianin Nedeal's notes, everything she had learned in fifty years of studying that peculiar *ter'angreal*. A secretive woman, Corianin. She had kept by far the greater part of her knowledge from everyone, trusting it only to these pages. Only chance and a habit of rummaging through old papers in the library had led Verin to them. As far as she could discover, no Aes Sedai besides herself knew of the *ter'angreal*; Corianin had managed to erase its existence from the records.

Once again she considered burning the manuscript, just as she had considered giving it to Egwene. But destroying knowledge, any knowledge, was anathema to her. And for the other. . . . *No. It is best by far to leave things as they are. What will happen, will happen.* She let the lid drop shut. *Now where did I put that page?*

Frowning, she began to search the stacks of books and papers for the leather folder. Egwene was already out of her mind.

CHAPTER
22

The Price of the Ring

Egwene had only gone a short distance from Verin's rooms when Sheriam met her. The Mistress of Novices wore a preoccupied frown.

"If someone hadn't remembered Verin speaking to you, I might not have found you." The Aes Sedai sounded mildly irritated. "Come along, child. You are holding everything up! What are those papers?"

Egwene clutched them a little tighter. She tried to make her voice both meek and respectful. "Verin Sedai thinks I should study them, Aes Sedai." What would she do if Sheriam asked to see them? What excuse could she give for refusing, what explanation for pages telling all about thirteen women of the Black Ajah and the *ter'angreal* they had stolen?

But Sheriam seemed to have dismissed the papers from her mind as soon as she asked. "Never mind that. You are wanted, and everyone is waiting." She took Egwene's arm and forced her to walk faster.

"Wanted, Sheriam Sedai? Waiting for what?"

Sheriam shook her head with exasperation. "Did you forget that you are to be raised to the Accepted? When you come to my study tomorrow, you will be wearing the ring, though I doubt it will soothe you very much."

Egwene tried to stop short, but the Aes Sedai hurried her on, taking a narrow set of stairs that curled down through the library walls. "Tonight? Already? But I am half-asleep, Aes Sedai, and dirty, and. . . . I thought I would have days yet. To get ready. To prepare."

"The hour waits on no woman," Sheriam said. "The

Wheel weaves as the Wheel wills, *when* the Wheel wills.
Besides, how would you prepare? You already know the
things you must. More than your friend Nynaeve did." She
pushed Egwene through a tiny door at the foot of the stairs
and hurried her across another hall to a ramp curving down
and down.

"I listened to the lectures," Egwene protested, "and I
remember them, but . . . can't I have a night's sleep first?"
The winding ramp seemed to have no end.

"The Amyrlin Seat decided there was no point in waiting." Sheriam gave Egwene a sidelong smile. "Her exact words were, 'Once you decide to gut a fish, there's no
use waiting till it rots.' Elayne has already been through
the arches by this time, and the Amyrlin means you to go
through tonight as well. Not that I can see the point of such
a hurry," she added, half to herself, "but when the Amyrlin
commands, we obey."

Egwene let herself be pulled down the ramp in silence, a
knot forming in her belly. Nynaeve had been far from forthcoming about what had happened when she was raised to
the Accepted. She would not speak of it at all, except for a
grimaced 'I hate Aes Sedai!' Egwene was trembling by the
time the ramp finally ended at a broad hallway, far below
the Tower in the rock of the island.

The hall was plain and undecorated, the pale rock
through which it had been hewn smoothed but left otherwise untouched, and there was only one set of dark wooden
doors, as tall and wide as fortress gates and as plain, although of smoothly finished and finely fitted planks, at the
very end. Those great doors were so well balanced, though,
that Sheriam easily pushed one open, and pulled Egwene
through after her, into a great, domed chamber.

"Not before time!" Elaida snapped. She stood to one side
in her red-fringed shawl, beside a table on which sat three
large silver chalices.

Lamps on tall stands illuminated the chamber, and what
sat centered under the dome. Three rounded, silver arches,
just tall enough to walk under, sitting on a thick silver ring
with their ends touching where they joined it. An Aes Sedai
sat cross-legged on the bare rock before each of the spots
where arches joined ring, all three wearing their shawls.

Alanna was the sister of the Green Ajah, but she did not know the Yellow sister, or the White.

Surrounded by the glow of *saidar* embraced, the three Aes Sedai stared fixedly at the arches, and within the silver structure an answering glow flickered and grew. That structure was a *ter'angreal*, and whatever it had been made for in the Age of Legends, now novices passed through it to become Accepted. Inside it, Egwene would have to face her fears. Three times. The white light within the arches no longer flickered; it stayed within them as if confined, but it filled the space, made it opaque.

"Be easy, Elaida," Sheriam said calmly. "We will be done soon." She turned to Egwene. "Novices are given three chances at this. You may refuse twice to enter, but at the third refusal, you are sent away from the Tower forever. That is how it is done usually, and you certainly have the right to refuse, but I do not think the Amyrlin Seat will be pleased with you if you do."

"She should not be given this chance." There was iron in Elaida's voice, and her face was scarcely softer. "I do not care what her potential is. She should be put out of the Tower. Or failing that, set to scrubbing floors for the next ten years."

Sheriam gave the Red sister a sharp look. "You were not so adamant about Elayne. You demanded to be part of this, Elaida—perhaps because of Elayne—and you will do your part for this girl as well, as you are supposed to, or you will leave and I will find another."

The two Aes Sedai stared at one another until Egwene would not have been surprised to see the glow of the One Power surround them. Finally Elaida gave a toss of her head and sniffed loudly.

"If it must be done, let us do it. Give the miserable girl her chance to refuse and be done with it. It is late."

"I won't refuse." Egwene's voice quavered, but she steadied it and held her head high. "I want to go on."

"Good," Sheriam said. "Good. Now I will tell you two things no woman hears until she stands where you do. Once you begin, you must go on to the end. Refuse at any point, and you will be put out of the Tower just as if you had refused to begin for the third time. Second. To seek, to

strive, is to know danger." She sounded as if she had said
this many times. There was a light of sympathy in her eyes,
but her face was almost as stern as Elaida's. The sympathy
frightened Egwene more than the sternness. "Some women
have entered, and never come out. When the *ter'angreal*
was allowed to grow quiet, they—were—not—there. And
they were never seen again. If you will survive, you must
be steadfast. Falter, fail, and. . . ." Sheriam's face drove the
unspoken words home; Egwene shivered. "This is your last
chance. Refuse now, and it counts only as the first. You may
still try twice more. If you accept now, there is no turning
back. It is no shame to refuse. I could not do it, my first
time. Choose."

They never came out? Egwene swallowed hard. *I want
to be Aes Sedai. And first I have to become Accepted.* "I
accept."

Sheriam nodded. "Then ready yourself."

Egwene blinked, then remembered. She had to enter
unclothed. She bent to set down the tied bundle of papers
Verin had given her—and hesitated. If she left them there,
Sheriam or Elaida either one could go through them while
she was inside the *ter'angreal*. They could find that smaller
ter'angreal in her pouch. If she refused to go on, she could
hide them away, perhaps leave them with Nynaeve. Her
breath caught. *I cannot refuse now. I've already begun.*

"Have you already chosen to refuse, child?" Sheriam
asked, frowning. "Knowing what that will mean, now?"

"No, Aes Sedai," Egwene said quickly. Hastily she undressed and folded her clothes, then set them on top of the
pouch and the papers. It would have to do.

Beside the *ter'angreal*, Alanna suddenly spoke. "There
is some sort of—resonance." She never took her eyes from
the arches. "An echo, almost. I do not know from where."

"Is there a problem?" Sheriam asked sharply. She sounded
surprised, too. "I will not send a woman in there if there is
any problem."

Egwene looked yearningly at her piled clothes. *Please,
yes, Light, a problem. Something that will let me hide those
papers without refusing to enter.*

"No," Alanna said. "It is like having a biteme buzz 'round
your head when you're trying to think, but it does not interfere. I would not have mentioned it, only it has never hap-

pened before that I ever heard." She shook her head. "It is gone now."

"Perhaps," Elaida said dryly, "others thought such a small thing was not worth mentioning."

"Let us go on." Sheriam's tone would not put up with any more distractions. "Come."

With a last glance at her clothes and the hidden papers, Egwene followed her toward the arches. The stone felt like ice under her bare feet.

"Whom do you bring with you, Sister?" Elaida intoned.

Continuing her measured pace, Sheriam replied, "One who comes as a candidate for Acceptance, Sister." The three Aes Sedai around the *ter'angreal* did not move.

"Is she ready?"

"She is ready to leave behind what she was, and, passing through her fears, gain Acceptance."

"Does she know her fears?"

"She has never faced them, but now is willing."

"Then let her face what she fears." Even in its formality, there was a note of satisfaction in Elaida's voice.

"The first time," Sheriam said, "is for what was. The way back will come but once. Be steadfast."

Egwene took a deep breath and stepped forward, through the arch and into the glow. Light swallowed her whole.

"Jaim Dawtry dropped by. There's odd news down from Baerlon with the peddler."

Egwene raised her head from the cradle she was rocking. Rand was standing in the doorway. For an instant her head spun. She looked from Rand—*my husband*—to the child in the cradle—*my daughter*—and back again, in wonder.

The way back will come but once. Be steadfast.

It was not her own thought, but a disembodied voice that could have been inside her head or out, male or female, yet emotionless and unknowable. Somehow, it did not seem strange to her.

The moment of wonder passed, and the only thing to wonder about was why she had thought anything seemed out of round. Of course Rand was her husband—her handsome, loving husband—and Joiya was her daughter—the most beautiful, sweetest little girl in the Two Rivers. Tam,

Rand's father, was out with the sheep, supposedly so Rand could work on the barn but really so he could have more time to play with Joiya. This afternoon Egwene's mother and father would come out from the village. And probably Nynaeve, to see if motherhood was interfering with Egwene's studies to replace Nynaeve as Wisdom one day.

"What kind of news?" she asked. She took up rocking the cradle again, and Rand came over to grin down at the tiny child wrapped in swaddling clothes. Egwene laughed softly to herself. He was so taken with his daughter that he did not hear what people said to him half the time. "Rand? What kind of news? Rand?"

"What?" His grin faded. "Strange news. War. There's some big war, taking up most of the world, so Jaim claims." That was strange news; word of wars seldom reached the Two Rivers till the wars were long done. "He says everybody is fighting some folk called the Shawkin, or the Sanchan, or something like that. I never heard of them."

Egwene knew—she thought she knew—Whatever it was, was gone.

"Are you all right?" he asked. "It's nothing to upset us here, my heart. Wars never touch the Two Rivers. We are too far from everywhere for anyone to care."

"I'm not upset. Did Jaim say anything else?"

"Nothing you can believe. He sounded like a Coplin. He said the peddler told him these people use Aes Sedai in battle, but then he claimed they offer a thousand gold marks to anyone who turns an Aes Sedai over to them. And they kill anybody who hides one. It makes no sense. Well, it's nothing to trouble us. It is all a long way from here."

Aes Sedai. Egwene touched her head. *The way back comes but once. Be steadfast.*

She noticed Rand had a hand to his own head. "The headaches?" she asked.

He nodded, his eyes suddenly tight. "That powder Nynaeve gave me doesn't seem to be working the last few days."

She hesitated. These headaches of his worried her. They grew worse every time they came, now. And worst of all was something she had not noticed at first, something she almost wished she never had noticed. When Rand's head hurt, strange things happened soon after. Lightning out of a clear sky, smashing to bits that huge oak stump he had been working two days to root out where he and Tam were clearing new field. Storms that Nynaeve did not hear coming when she listened to the wind. Wildfires in the forest. And the deeper his pain grew, the worse what followed. No one else had connected these things to Rand, not even Nynaeve, and Egwene was grateful for that. She did not want to think about what it might mean.

That is plain stupid foolish, she told herself. *I must know if I am going to help him.* Because she had a secret of her own, one that frightened her even as she tried to puzzle out what it meant. Nynaeve was teaching her the herbs, teaching Egwene to follow her as Wisdom, one day. Nynaeve's cures often worked in near miraculous fashion, wounds healed with barely a scar, sick folk brought back from the edge of the grave. But three times now, Egwene had cured someone Nynaeve had given up for dead. Three times she had sat to hold a hand through the last hour, and seen the person get up from a deathbed. Nynaeve had questioned her closely on what she had done, what herbs she had used, in what blending. Thus far, she had not found the courage to admit that she had done nothing. *I must have done something. Once might be chance, but three times. . . . I have to figure it out. I have to learn.* That set off a buzz in her head, as though the words were echoing inside her skull. *If I could do something for them, I can help my husband.*

"Let me try, Rand," she said. And as she stood, through the open door, she saw a silver arch standing in front of the house, an arch filled with white light. *The way back will come but once. Be steadfast.* She took two steps toward the door before she could stop herself.

She halted, looked back at Joiya gurgling in her cradle, at Rand still pressing hand to his head and looking at her as if wondering where she was going. "No," she said. "No, this is what I want. This is what I want! Why can't I have this, too?" She did not understand her own words. Of course, this was what she wanted, and she had it.

"What is it you want, Egwene?" Rand asked. "If it's anything I can get, you know I will. If I can't get it, I'll make it."

The way back will come but once. Be steadfast.

She took another step, into the doorway. The silver arch

beckoned her. Something waited on the other side. Something she wanted more than anything else in the world. Something she had to do.

"Egwene, I—"

There was a thump behind her. She looked over her shoulder to see Rand on his knees, bowed and head cradled in his hands. The pain had never hit him so hard. *What will come after this?*

"Ah, Light!" he panted. "Light! Hurts! Light, it hurts worse than ever! Egwene?"

Be steadfast.

It was waiting. Something she had to do. Had to. She took a step. It was hard, harder than anything she had ever done in her life. Outside, toward the arch. Behind her, Joiya was laughing.

"Egwene? Egwene, I can't—" He cut off with a loud groan.

Steadfast.

She stiffened her back and kept walking, but she could not keep the tears from rolling down her cheeks. Rand's groans built to a scream, drowning Joiya's laughter. From the corner of her eye, Egwene saw Tam coming, running as hard as he could.

He can't help, she thought, and tears became wracking sobs. *There is nothing he can do. But I could. I could.*

She stepped into the light, and was consumed.

Trembling and sobbing, Egwene stepped out of the arch, the same by which she had entered, memory cascading back with Sheriam's face confronting her. Cold clear water washed away her tears as Elaida slowly emptied a silver chalice over her head. Her weeping went on; she did not think it would ever end.

"You are washed clean," Elaida pronounced, "of what sin you may have done, and of those done against you. You are washed clean of what crime you may have committed, and of those committed against you. You come to us washed clean and pure, in heart and soul."

Light, Egwene thought as the water ran down her body, *let it be so. Can water wash away what I did?* "Her name was Joiya," she told Sheriam between sobs. "Joiya. Nothing can be worth what I just . . . what I. . . ."

"There is a price to become Aes Sedai," Sheriam replied, but the sympathy was back in her eyes, stronger than before. "There is always a price."

"Was it real? Did I dream it?" Weeping swallowed what she wanted to say. *Did I leave him to die? Did I leave my baby?*

Sheriam put an arm around her shoulders, began guiding her around the circle of arches. "Every woman I have ever watched come out of there has asked that question. The answer is, no one knows. It has been speculated that perhaps some of those who do not come back chose to stay because they found a happier place, and lived out their lives there." Her voice hardened. "If it is real, and they stayed from choice, then I hope the lives they live are far from happy. I have no sympathy for any who run from their responsibilities." The edge on her tone softened slightly. "Myself, I believe it is not real. But the danger is. Remember that." She stopped in front of the next glow-filled arch. "Are you ready?"

Shifting her feet, Egwene nodded, and Sheriam took her arm away.

"The second time is for what is. The way back will come but once. Be steadfast."

Egwene trembled. *Whatever happens, it cannot be worse than the last. It cannot be.* She stepped into the glow.

She stared down at her dress, blue silk sewn with pearls, all dusty and torn. Her head came up, and she took in the ruins of a great palace around her. The Royal Palace of Andor, in Caemlyn. She knew that, and wanted to scream.

The way back will come but once. Be steadfast.

The world was not the way she wanted it, no way that she could think of without wanting to cry, but all her tears had been cried away long ago, and the world was as it was. Ruin was what she expected to see.

Careless of making more rips in her dress but as careful of sound as a mouse, she climbed one of the piles of rubble and peered into the curving streets of the Inner City. As far as she could see in every direction lay ruin and desolation, buildings that looked as if they had been torn apart by madmen, thick plumes of smoke rising from the fires still burning. There were people in the streets, bands of armed men prowling, searching. And Trollocs. The men shied away from the Trollocs, and the Trollocs snarled at them and laughed, harsh guttural laughter. But they knew each other, worked together.

A Myrddraal came striding down the street, its black cloak swaying gently with its steps even when the wind gusted to drive dust and rubbish past it. Men and Trollocs alike cowered under its eyeless stare. "Hunt!" Its voice sounded like something long dead crumbling. "Do not stand there shivering! Find him!"

Egwene slipped back down the pile of jumbled stones as silently as she could.

The way back will come but once. Be steadfast.

She stopped, afraid the whisper had come from Shadowspawn. In some way, though, she was sure it had not. Glancing back over her shoulder, half fearful of seeing the Myrddraal standing where she had just been, she hurried onward and into the ruined palace, climbing over fallen timbers, squeezing between heavy blocks of collapsed masonry as she made her way. Once she stepped on a woman's arm, sticking out from under a mound of plaster and bricks that had been an interior wall and perhaps part of the floor above. She noticed the arm as little as she noticed the Great Serpent ring on one finger. She had trained herself not to see the dead buried in the refuse heap Trollocs and Darkfriends had made of Caemlyn. She could do nothing for the dead.

Forcing her way through a narrow gap where part of the ceiling had fallen, she found herself in a room half buried under what had stood above it. Rand lay with a heavy beam pinning him across the waist, his legs hidden beneath the stone blocks that filled half the room. Dust and sweat coated his face. He opened his eyes when she came near him.

"You came back." He forced the words out in a hoarse rasp. "I was afraid—No matter. You have to help me."

She sank wearily to the floor. "I could lift that beam easily with Air, but as soon as it moves, everything else will come down on top of you. On top of both of us. I cannot manage all of it, Rand."

His laugh was bitter and painful, and cut off almost as soon as it began. Fresh sweat glistened on his face, and he spoke with an effort. "I could shift the beam myself. You know that. I could shift that and the stones above, all of them. But I have to let go of myself to do it, and I can't trust that. I cannot trust—" He stopped, wheezing for breath.

"I do not understand," she said slowly. "Let go of yourself? What can't you trust?" *The way back will come but once. Be steadfast.* She rubbed her hands roughly over her ears.

"The madness, Egwene. I am—actually—holding it—at bay." His gasping laugh made her skin prickle. "But it takes everything I have just to do that. If I let go, even a little, even for an instant, the madness will have me. I won't care what I do then. You have to help me."

"How, Rand! I've tried everything I know. Tell me how, and I will do it."

His hand flopped out, fell just short of a dagger lying in the dust bare-bladed. "The dagger," he whispered. His hand made a painful journey back to his chest. "Here. In the heart. Kill me."

She stared at him, at the dagger, as if they were both poisonous serpents. "No! Rand, I will not. I cannot! How could you ask such a thing?"

Slowly his hand crept back toward the dagger. His fingers came short again. He strained, moaning, brushed it with a fingertip. Before he could try again, she kicked it away from him. He collapsed with a sob.

"Tell me why," she demanded. "Why would you ask me to—to murder you? I will Heal you, I will do anything to get you out of there, but I cannot kill you. Why?"

"They can turn me, Egwene." His breathing was so tortured, she wished she could weep. "If they take me—the Myrddraal—the Dreadlords—they can turn me to the Shadow. If madness has me, I cannot fight them. I won't know what they are doing till it is too late. If there is even a spark of life left when they find me, they can still do it. Please, Egwene. For the love of the Light. Kill me."

"I—I can't, Rand. Light help me, I cannot!"

The way back will come but once. Be steadfast.

She looked over her shoulder, and a silver arch filled with white light took up most of the open space among the rubble.

"Egwene, help me."

Be steadfast.

She stood and took a step toward the arch. It was right there in front of her. One more step, and. . . .

"Please, Egwene. Help me. I can't reach it. For the love of the Light, Egwene, help me!"

"I cannot kill you," she whispered. "I can't. Forgive me." She stepped forward.

"HELP ME, EGWENE!"

Light burned her to ash.

Staggering, she stepped out of the arch, neither noticing her nakedness nor caring. A shudder ran through her, and she covered her mouth with both hands. "I couldn't, Rand," she whispered. "I couldn't. Please forgive me." *Light help him. Please, Light help Rand.*

Cold water poured over her head.

"You are washed clean of false pride," Elaida intoned. "You are washed clean of false ambition. You come to us washed clean, in heart and soul."

As the Red sister turned away, Sheriam gently took Egwene's shoulders and guided her toward the last arch. "One more, child. One more, and it is done."

"He said they could turn him to the Shadow," Egwene mumbled. "He said the Myrddraal and the Dreadlords could force him."

Sheriam missed a step, and looked around quickly. Elaida was almost back to the table. The Aes Sedai surrounding the *ter'angreal* stared at it, seeming lost to anything else. "An unpleasant thing to talk of, child," Sheriam said finally, and softly. "Come. One more."

"Can they?" Egwene insisted.

"Custom," Sheriam said, "is not to speak of what happens within the *ter'angreal*. A woman's fears are her own."

"Can they?"

Sheriam sighed, glanced at the other Aes Sedai again, then dropped her voice to a whisper and spoke swiftly. "This is something known only to a few, child, even in the Tower.

You should not learn it now, if ever, but I will tell you. There is—a weakness in being able to channel. That we learn to open ourselves to the True Source means that we can be—opened to other things." Egwene shuddered. "Calm yourself, child. It is not so easily done. It is a thing not done, so far as I know—Light send it has not been done!—since the Trolloc Wars. It took thirteen Dreadlords—Darkfriends who could channel—weaving the flows through thirteen Myrddraal. You see? Not easily done. There are no Dreadlords today. This is a secret of the Tower, child. If others knew, we could never convince them they were safe. Only one who can channel can be turned in this way. The weakness of our strength. Everyone else is as safe as a fortress; only their own deeds and will can turn them to the Shadow."

"Thirteen," Egwene said in a tiny voice. "The same number who left the Tower. Liandrin, and twelve more."

Sheriam's face hardened. "That is nothing for you to dwell on. You will forget it." Her voice climbed to a normal volume. "The third time is for what will be. The way back will come but once. Be steadfast."

Egwene stared at the glowing arch, stared at some far distance beyond it. *Liandrin and twelve others. Thirteen Darkfriends who can channel. Light help us all.* She stepped into the light. It filled her. It shone through her. It burned her to the bone, seared her to the soul. She flashed incandescent in the light. *Light help me!* There was nothing but the light. And the pain.

Egwene stared into the standing mirror, and was not sure whether she was more surprised by the ageless smoothness of her face or the striped stole that hung around her neck. The stole of the Amyrlin Seat.

The way back will come but once. Be steadfast.
Thirteen.

She swayed, caught at the mirror and almost toppled it and herself to the blue-tiled floor of her dressing chamber. *Something is wrong,* she thought. The wrongness had nothing to do with her sudden dizziness, or at least that was not what felt wrong. It was something else. But she had no idea what.

There was an Aes Sedai at her elbow, a woman with

Sheriam's high cheekbones but dark hair and concerned brown eyes, and the hand-wide stole of the Keeper on her shoulders. Not Sheriam, though. Egwene had never seen her before; she was sure she knew her as well as she knew herself. Haltingly, she put a name to the woman. Beldeine.

"Are you ill, Mother?"

Her stole is green. That means she was raised from the Green Ajah. The Keeper always comes from the same Ajah as the Amyrlin she serves. Which means if I'm the Amyrlin—if?—then I was Green Ajah, too. That thought shook her. Not that she had been Green Ajah, but that she had to reason it out. *Light, something is wrong with me.*

The way back will come bu. . . . The voice in her head trailed away to finish in a buzz.

Thirteen Darkfriends.

"I am well, Beldeine," Egwene said. The name felt strange on her tongue; it felt as if she had been saying it for years. "We mustn't keep them waiting." *Keep who waiting?* She did not know, except that she felt infinitely sad about ending that wait, endlessly reluctant.

"They will be growing impatient, Mother." There was a hesitation in Beldeine's voice, as if she felt the same reluctance as Egwene, but for a different reason. Unless Egwene missed her guess, behind that outer calm, Beldeine was terrified.

"In that case, we had best be about it."

Beldeine nodded, then took a deep breath before crossing the carpet to where her staff of office, topped with the snowdrop White Flame of Tar Valon, stood propped beside the door. "I suppose we must, Mother." She took up the staff and opened the door for Egwene, then hurried ahead so that they made a procession of two, Keeper of the Chronicles leading the Amyrlin Seat.

Egwene noticed little of the corridors they took. All her attention was directed inward. *What is the matter with me? Why can't I remember? Why is so much of what I . . . almost remember wrong?* She touched the seven-striped stole on her shoulders. *Why am I half sure I'm still a novice?*

The way back will come but on—This time it ended abruptly.

Thirteen of the Black Ajah.

She stumbled at that. It was a frightening thought, but it

chilled her to the marrow beyond fear. It felt—personal. She wanted to scream, to run and hide. She felt as if they were after her. *Nonsense. The Black Ajah has been destroyed.* That seemed an odd thought, too. Part of her remembered something called the Great Purge. Part of her was sure no such thing had happened.

Eyes fixed ahead, Beldeine had not noticed her stumble. Egwene had to lengthen her stride to catch up. *This woman is scared to her toenails. What in the Light is she taking me to?*

Beldeine stopped before tall, paired doors, their dark wood each inlaid with a large silver Flame of Tar Valon. She wiped her hands on her dress, as if they were suddenly sweaty, before opening one door and leading Egwene up a straight ramp of the same silver-streaked white stone that made Tar Valon's walls. Even here it seemed to shine.

The ramp let into a large, circular room under a domed ceiling at least thirty paces high. A raised platform ran around the outer edge of the room, fronted by steps except where this ramp and two others came out, spaced equally around the circle. The Flame of Tar Valon lay centered in the floor, surrounded by widening spirals of color, the colors of the seven Ajahs. At the opposite side of the room from where the ramp entered, a high-backed chair stood, heavy and ornately carved in vines and leaves, painted in the colors of all the Ajahs.

Beldeine rapped her staff sharply on the floor. There was a tremor in her voice. "She comes. The Watcher of the Seals. The Flame of Tar Valon. The Amyrlin Seat. She comes."

With a rustle of skirts, shawled women on the platform got up from their chairs. Twenty-one chairs in groupings of three, each triad painted and cushioned in the same color as the fringe on the shawls of the women who stood before them.

The Hall of the Tower, Egwene thought as she crossed the floor to her chair. The Amyrlin Seat's chair. *That's all it is. The Hall of the Tower, and the Sitters for the Ajahs. I've been here thousands of times.* But she could not remember one of them. *What am I doing in the Hall of the Tower? Light, they'll skin me alive when they see. . . .* She was not sure what it was they would see, only that she prayed they did not.

The way back will come but—
The way back will—
The way—
The Black Ajah waits. That, at least, was whole. It came from everywhere. Why did no one else seem to hear it?

Settling in the chair of the Amyrlin Seat—the chair that was also the Amyrlin Seat—she realized she had no idea what to do next. The other Aes Sedai had seated themselves when she did, all but Beldeine, who stood beside her with the staff, swallowing nervously. They all seemed to be waiting on her.

"Begin," she said finally.

It seemed to be enough. One of the Red Sitters stood. Egwene was shocked to recognize Elaida. At the same time she knew that Elaida was foremost of the Sitters for the Red, and her own bitterest enemy. The look on Elaida's face as she stared across the chamber made Egwene shiver inside. It was stern and cold—and triumphant. It promised things best not thought of.

"Bring him in," Elaida said loudly.

From one of the ramps—not the one Egwene had entered by—came the crunch of boots on stone. People appeared. A dozen Aes Sedai surrounding three men, two of them burly guards with the white teardrops of the Flame of Tar Valon on their chests, tugging the chains in which the third stumbled as if dazed.

Egwene jerked forward in her chair. The chained man was Rand. Eyes half-closed, head sagging, he seemed nearly asleep, moving only as the chains directed.

"This man," Elaida proclaimed, "has named himself the Dragon Reborn." There was a buzz of distaste, not as if the listeners were surprised, but as though it were not something they wanted to hear. "This man has channeled the One Power." The buzz was louder now, disgusted and tinged with fear. "There is only one penalty for this, known and recognized in every nation, but pronounced only here, in Tar Valon, in the Hall of the Tower. I call on the Amyrlin Seat to pronounce the sentence of gentling on this man."

Elaida's eyes glittered at Egwene. *Rand. What do I do? Light, what do I do?*

"Why do you hesitate?" Elaida demanded. "The sentence

has been set down for three thousand years. Why do you hesitate, Egwene al'Vere?"

One of the Green Sitters was on her feet, anger bright through her calm. "Shame, Elaida! Show respect for the Amyrlin Seat! Show respect for the Mother!"

"Respect," Elaida answered coldly, "can be lost as well as won. Well, Egwene? Can it be you show your weakness, your unfitness for your office, at last? Can it be you will not pronounce sentence on this man?"

Rand tried to lift his head and failed.

Egwene struggled to her feet, head spinning, trying to remember she was the Amyrlin Seat with the power to command all these women, screaming that she was a novice, that she did not belong here, that something was dreadfully wrong. "No," she said shakily. "No, I cannot! I will not—"

"She betrays herself!" Elaida's shout drowned out Egwene's attempt to speak. "She condemns herself out of her own mouth! Take her!"

As Egwene opened her mouth, Beldeine moved beside her. Then the Keeper's staff struck her head.

Blackness.

First there was pain in her head. There was something hard under her back, and cold. Next came the voices. Murmurs.

"Is she still unconscious?" It was a rasp, a file on bone.

"Do not worry," a woman said from far, far away. She sounded uneasy, afraid, and trying not to show either. "She will be dealt with before she knows what is happening to her. Then she is ours, to do with as we will. Perhaps we will give her to you for sport."

"After you make your own use of her."

"Of course."

The distant voices moved further away.

Her hand brushed against her leg, touched bare, pebbly flesh. She opened her eyes a crack. She was naked, bruised, lying on a rough wooden table, in what seemed to be a disused storeroom. Splinters stuck her back. There was a metallic taste of blood in her mouth.

A cluster of Aes Sedai stood to one side of the room, talking among themselves, voices low yet urgent. The pain

in her head made thinking difficult, but it seemed important to count them. Thirteen.

Another group, black-cloaked and hooded men, joined
the Aes Sedai, who seemed caught between cowering and
trying to dominate with their presence. One of the men
turned his head to look toward the table. The dead white
face within the hood had no eyes.

Egwene had no need to count the Myrddraal. She knew.
Thirteen Myrddraal, and thirteen Aes Sedai. Without another thought, she screamed in pure terror. Yet even in the
midst of fear that tried to split her bones, she reached out
for the True Source, clawed desperately for *saidar*.

"She's awake!"

"She cannot be! Not yet!"

"Shield her! Quickly! Quickly! Cut her off from the
Source!"

"It's too late! She is too strong!"

"Seize her! Hurry!"

Hands reached for her arms and legs. Pasty pale hands
like slugs under rocks, ordered by minds behind pale, eyeless faces. If those hands touched her flesh, she knew she
would go mad. The Power filled her.

Flames burst from Myrddraal skin, ripping through
black cloth as if they were solid daggers of fire. Shrieking Halfmen crisped and burned like oiled paper. Fist-
sized chunks of stone tore themselves free of the walls and
whizzed across the room, producing shrieks and grunts as
they thudded into flesh. The air stirred, shifted, howled into
a whirlwind.

Slowly, painfully, Egwene pushed herself off the table.
The wind whipped her hair and made her stagger, but she
continued to drive it as she stumbled toward the door. An
Aes Sedai loomed in front of her, a woman bruised and
bleeding, surrounded by the glow of the Power. A woman
with death in her dark eyes.

Egwene's mind put a name to the face. Gyldan. Elaida's
closest confidante, always whispering together in corners,
closeting themselves in the night. Egwene's mouth tightened. Disdaining stones and wind, she balled up her fist and
punched Gyldan between the eyes as hard as she could. The
Red sister—the *Black* sister—crumpled as if her bones had
melted.

Rubbing her knuckles, Egwene staggered out into the hall. *Thank you, Perrin,* she thought, *for showing me how to do that. But you didn't tell me how much it hurts when you do.*

Shoving the door shut against the wind, she channeled. Stones around the doorway shivered, cracked, settled against the wood. It would not hold them for long, but anything that slowed pursuit for even a minute was worth doing. Minutes might mean life. Gathering her strength, she forced herself to break into a run. It wobbled, but at least it was a run.

She must find some clothes, she decided. A woman clothed had more authority than the same woman naked, and she was going to need every bit of authority. They would look for her first in her rooms, but she had a spare dress and shoes in her study—and another stole—and that lay not far off.

It was unnerving, trotting through empty hallways. The White Tower no longer held the numbers it once had, but there was usually someone about. The loudest sound was the slap of her bare soles on the tiles.

She hurried through the antechamber of her study to the inner room, and at last she found someone. Beldeine was sitting on the floor, head in her hands, weeping.

Egwene stopped warily, as Beldeine raised reddened eyes to meet hers. No glow of *saidar* surrounded the Keeper, but Egwene was still cautious. And confident. She could not see her own glow, of course, but the power—the Power—surging through her was enough. Especially when added to her secret.

Beldeine scrubbed a hand across tearstained cheeks. "I had to. You must understand. I had to. They. . . . They. . . ." She took a deep, shuddering breath; it all came out in a rush. "Three nights ago they took me while I slept and stilled me." Her voice rose to a near shriek. "They *stilled* me! I cannot channel any longer!"

"Light," Egwene breathed. The rush of *saidar* cushioned her against the shock. "The Light help and comfort you, my daughter. Why didn't you tell me? I would have. . . ." She let it trail away, knowing there was nothing she could do.

"What would you have done? What? Nothing! There's nothing you can do. But they said they could give it back to

me, with the power of . . . the power of the Dark One." Her
eyes squeezed shut, leaking tears. "They hurt me, Mother,
and they made me. . . . Oh, Light, they hurt me! Elaida told
me they would make me whole again, make me able to
channel again, if I obeyed. That's why I. . . . I had to!"

"So Elaida *is* Black Ajah," Egwene said grimly. A narrow wardrobe stood against the wall, and in it hung a green
silk dress, kept for when she had no time to return to her
rooms. A striped stole hung beside the dress. She began to
dress herself, quickly. "What have they done with Rand?
Where have they taken him? Answer me, Beldeine! Where
is Rand al'Thor?"

Beldeine huddled, lips trembling, eyes turned bleakly
inward, but finally she roused herself enough to say, "The
Traitor's Court, Mother. They took him to the Traitor's
Court."

Shivers assaulted Egwene. Shivers of fear. Shivers of
rage. Elaida had not waited, not even an hour. The Traitor's
Court was used for only three purposes: executions, the
stilling of an Aes Sedai, or the gentling of a man who could
channel. But all of the three took an order from the Amyrlin Seat. *So who wears the stole out there?* Elaida, she was
sure. *But how could she make them accept her so quickly,
with me not tried, not sentenced? There cannot be another
Amyrlin until I've been stripped of stole and staff. And
they'll not find that easy to do. Light! Rand!* She started for
the door.

"What can you do, Mother?" Beldeine cried. "What can
you do?" It was not clear whether she meant for Rand or for
herself.

"More than anyone suspects," Egwene said. "I never held
the Oath Rod, Beldeine." Beldeine's gasp followed her from
the room.

Egwene's memory still played hide-and-seek with her.
She knew no woman could achieve the shawl and the ring
without pledging the Three Oaths with the Oath Rod firmly
in hand, the *ter'angreal* sealing her to keep those oaths as
if they had been engraved on her bones at birth. No woman
became Aes Sedai without being bound to them. Yet she
knew that somehow, in some fashion she could not begin to
dredge up, she had done just that.

Her shoes clicked swiftly as she ran. At least she knew

now why the halls were empty. Every Aes Sedai, except perhaps those she had left in the storeroom, every Accepted, every novice, even all the servants, would be gathered in the Traitor's Court, according to custom, to watch the will of Tar Valon made fact.

And the Warders would be ringing the courtyard against the possibility that someone might try to free the man to be gentled. The remnants of Guaire Amalasan's armies had attempted it, at the end of what some called the War of the Second Dragon, just before Artur Hawkwing's rise had given Tar Valon other things to worry it, and so had Raolin Darksbane's followers, long years earlier. Whether Rand had any followers or not, she could not remember, but Warders remembered such things, and guarded against them.

If Elaida, or another, truly did wear the stole of the Amyrlin, the Warders might well not admit her to the Traitor's Court. She knew she could force a way in. It would need to be done quickly; there was no point if Rand was gentled while she was still wrapping Warders in Air. Even Warders would break if she loosed the lightnings on them, and balefire, and broke the ground under their feet. *Balefire?* she wondered. But it would also do no good if she broke Tar Valon's power to save Rand. She had to save both.

Well short of the ways that led to the Traitor's Court, she turned aside and climbed, up stairs and ramps that grew narrower and tighter the higher she went, until she thrust open a trapdoor and climbed out onto a sloping tower top, a roof of nearly white tiles. From there, she could see across other roofs, past other towers, into the broad open well of the Traitor's Court.

The court was crowded except for a cleared space in the middle. People filled the windows overlooking it, crowded the balconies and even the rooftops, but she could make out the lone man, small at that distance, swaying in his chains in the center of the cleared space. Rand. Twelve Aes Sedai surrounded him, and another—who Egwene knew had to be wearing a seven-striped stole, even though she could not distinguish it—stood before Rand. *Elaida.* The words she must be saying crept into Egwene's head.

This man, abandoned of the Light, has touched saidin, *the male half of the True Source. Thus do we hold him.*

*Most abominably has this man channeled the One Power,
knowing that* saidin *is tainted by the Dark One, tainted for
men's pride, tainted for men's sin. Thus do we chain him.*

Forcefully, Egwene pushed the rest of it out of her
thoughts. *Thirteen Aes Sedai. Twelve sisters and the Amyrlin, the traditional number for gentling. The same number
as for. . . .* She rid herself of that, too. She had no time for
anything but what she was there to do. If she could only
manage to reason out how.

At that distance, she thought she could manage to lift
him with Air. Pick him right out of the circle of Aes Sedai
and float him straight to her. Maybe. Even if she could find
the strength, even if she did not drop him to his death halfway, it would be a slow process, with him a helpless target
for archers, and the glow of *saidar* pointing out her own
position for any Aes Sedai who looked. Any Myrddraal, for
that matter.

"Light," she muttered, "there's no other way short of
starting a war inside the White Tower. And I may do that
anyway." She gathered the Power, separated skeins, directed flows.

The way back will come but once. Be steadfast.

It had been so long since she last heard those words that
she gave a start, slipped on the smooth tiles, barely caught
herself short of the edge. The ground lay a hundred paces
down. She looked over her shoulder.

There on the tower top, tilted to sit flat against the sloping tiles, was a silver arch filled with a glowing light. The
arch flickered and wavered; streaks of angry red and yellow
darted through the white light.

The way back will come but once. Be steadfast.

The archway thinned to transparency, grew solid again.

Frantic, Egwene gazed toward the Traitor's Court. There
had to be time. There had to be. All she needed was a few
minutes, perhaps ten, and luck.

Voices bored into her head, not the disembodied, unknowable voice that warned her to be steadfast, but women's
voices she almost believed she knew.

*—can't hold much longer. If she does not come out
now—*

Hold! Hold, burn you, or I'll gut you all like sturgeons!

—going wild, Mother! We can't—

The voices faded to a drone, the drone to silence, but the unknowable spoke again.

The way back will come but once. Be steadfast.

There is a price to be Aes Sedai.

The Black Ajah waits.

With a scream of rage, of loss, Egwene threw herself at the arch as it shimmered like a heat haze. She almost wished she would miss and plunge to her death.

Light plucked her apart fiber by fiber, sliced the fibers to hairs, split the hairs to wisps of nothing. All drifted apart on the light. Forever.

CHAPTER
23

Sealed

Light pulled her apart fiber by fiber, sliced the fibers to hairs that drifted apart, burning. Drifting and burning, forever. Forever.

Egwene stepped out of the silver arch cold and stiff with anger. She wanted the iciness of anger to counter the searing of memory. Her body remembered burning, but other memories scored and scorched more deeply. Anger cold as death.

"Is that all there is for me?" she demanded. "To abandon him again and again. To betray him, fail him, again and again? Is that what there is for me?"

Suddenly she realized that all was not as it should be. The Amyrlin was there now, as Egwene had been taught she would be, and a shawled sister from each Ajah, but they all stared at her worriedly. Two Aes Sedai now sat at each place around the *ter'angreal*, sweat running down their faces. The *ter'angreal* hummed, almost vibrated, and violent streaks of color tore the white light inside the arches.

The glow of *saidar* briefly enveloped Sheriam as she put a hand on Egwene's head, sending a new chill through her. "She is well." The Mistress of Novices sounded relieved. "She is unharmed." As if she had not expected it.

Tension seemed to go out of the other Aes Sedai facing Egwene. Elaida let out a long breath, then hurried away for the last chalice. Only the Aes Sedai around the *ter'angreal* did not relax. The hum had lessened, and the light began the flickering that signaled the *ter'angreal* was settling toward quiescence, but those Aes Sedai looked as if they were fighting it every inch of the way.

"What . . . ? What happened?" Egwene asked.

"Be silent," Sheriam said, but gently. "For now, be silent. You are well—that is the main thing—and we must complete the ceremony." Elaida came, close to running, and handed the final silver chalice to the Amyrlin.

Egwene hesitated only a moment before kneeling. *What happened?*

The Amyrlin emptied the chalice slowly over Egwene's head. "You are washed clean of Egwene al'Vere from Emond's Field. You are washed clean of all ties that bind you to the world. You come to us washed clean, in heart and soul. You are Egwene al'Vere, Accepted of the White Tower." The last drop splashed onto Egwene's hair. "You are sealed to us, now."

The last words seemed to have a special meaning, just between Egwene and the Amyrlin. The Amyrlin thrust the chalice at one of the other Aes Sedai and produced a gold ring in the shape of a serpent biting its own tail. Despite herself, Egwene trembled as she raised her left hand, trembled again as the Amyrlin slipped the Great Serpent ring onto the third finger. When she became Aes Sedai, she could wear the ring on the finger she chose, or not at all if it was necessary to hide who she was, but the Accepted wore it there.

Unsmiling, the Amyrlin pulled her to her feet. "Welcome, Daughter," she said, kissing her cheek. Egwene was surprised to feel a thrill. Not child, but daughter. Always before she had been child. The Amyrlin kissed her other cheek. "Welcome."

Stepping back, the Amyrlin regarded her critically, but spoke to Sheriam. "Get her dry and into some clothes, then be certain she is well. Certain, you understand."

"I am certain, Mother." Sheriam sounded surprised. "You saw me delve her."

The Amyrlin grunted, and her eyes shifted to the *ter'angreal*. "I mean to know what went wrong tonight." She strode away in the direction of her glare, skirts swaying purposefully. Most of the other Aes Sedai joined her around the *ter'angreal*, now only a silver structure of arches on a ring.

"The Mother is worried about you," Sheriam said as she

drew Egwene to one side, to where there was a thick towel for her hair, and another for the rest of her.

"How much reason did she have?" Egwene asked. *The Amyrlin wants nothing to happen to her hound till the deer is pulled down.*

Sheriam did not answer. She merely frowned slightly, then waited until Egwene was dry before handing her a white dress banded at the bottom with seven rings.

She slipped into that dress with a flash of disappointment. She was one of the Accepted, with the ring on her finger and the bands on her dress. *Why don't I feel any different?*

Elaida came over, her arms filled with Egwene's novice dress and shoes, her belt and pouch. And the papers Verin had given her. In Elaida's hands.

Egwene made herself wait for the Aes Sedai to hand the bundle to her rather than snatch them away. "Thank you, Aes Sedai." She tried to eye the papers surreptitiously; she could not tell if they had been disturbed. The string was still tied. *How would I know if she's read all of them?* Squeezing her pouch under cover of the novice dress, she felt the peculiar ring, the *ter'angreal,* inside. *At least that's still here. Light, she could have taken that, and I don't know that I would have minded. Yes, I would. I think I would.*

Elaida's face was as cold as her voice. "I did not want you to be brought forward tonight. Not because I feared what happened; no one could foresee that. But because of what you are. A wilder." Egwene tried to protest, but Elaida kept on, as implacable as a mountain glacier. "Oh, I know you learned to channel under Aes Sedai teaching, but you are still a wilder. A wilder in spirit, a wilder in ways. You have vast potential, else you would never have survived in there tonight, but potential changes nothing. I do not believe you will ever be part of the White Tower, not in the way the rest of us are, no matter on which finger you wear your ring. It would have been better for you had you settled for learning enough to stay alive, and gone back to your sleepy village. Far better." Turning on her heel, she stalked away, out of the chamber.

If she isn't Black Ajah, Egwene thought sourly, *she's the next thing to it.* Aloud, she muttered to Sheriam, "You could have said something. You could have helped me."

"I would have helped a novice, child," Sheriam replied calmly, and Egwene winced. She was back to "child" again.

"I try to protect novices where they need it, since they cannot protect themselves. You are Accepted, now. It is time for you to learn to protect yourself."

Egwene studied Sheriam's eyes, wondering if she had imagined an emphasis on that last sentence. Sheriam had had as much opportunity as Elaida to read the list of names, to decide that Egwene was mixed in with the Black Ajah. *Light, you're becoming suspicious of everybody. Better that than dead, or captured by thirteen of them and. . . .* Hastily, she stopped that line of thought; she did not want it in her head. "Sheriam, what did happen tonight?" she asked. "And don't put me off." Sheriam's eyebrows rose almost to her scalp, it seemed, and she hastily amended her question. "Sheriam Sedai, I mean. Forgive me, Sheriam Sedai."

"Remember you aren't Aes Sedai yet, child." Despite the steel in her voice, a smile touched Sheriam's lips, yet it vanished as she went on. "I do not know what happened. Except that I very much fear you almost died."

"Who knows what happens to those who do not come out of a *ter'angreal*?" Alanna said as she joined them. The Green sister was known for her temper and her sense of humor, and some said she could flash from one to the other and back again before you could blink, but the look she gave Egwene was almost diffident. "Child, I should have stopped this when I had the chance, when I first noticed that—reverberation. It came back. That is what happened. It came back a thousandfold. Ten thousand. The *ter'angreal* almost seemed to be trying to shut off the flow from *saidar*—or melt itself through the floor. You have my apologies, though words are not enough. Not for what almost happened to you. I say this, and by the First Oath you know it is true. To show my feelings, I will ask the Mother to let me share your time in the kitchens. And, yes, your visit to Sheriam, too. Had I done as I should, you would not have been in danger of your life, and I will atone for it."

Sheriam's laugh was scandalized. "She will never allow that, Alanna. A sister in the kitchens, much less. . . . It is unheard of. It's impossible! You did what you believed right. There is no fault to you."

"It was not your fault, Alanna Sedai," Egwene said. *Why is Alanna doing this? Unless maybe to convince me she* didn't *have anything to do with whatever went wrong. And maybe so she can keep an eye on me all the time.* It was that image, a proud Aes Sedai up to her elbows in greasy pots three times a day just to watch someone, that convinced her she was letting her imagination run away with her. But it was also unthinkable that Alanna should do as she said she would. In any case, the Green sister certainly had had no chance to see the list of names while tending the *ter'angreal*. But if Nynaeve is *right, she wouldn't need to see those names to want to kill me if she is Black Ajah. Stop that!* "Really, it wasn't."

"Had I done as I should," Alanna maintained, "it would never have happened. The only time I have ever seen anything like it was once years ago when we tried to use a *ter'angreal* in the same room with another that may have been in some way related to it. It is extremely rare to find two such as that. The pair of them melted, and every sister within a hundred paces had such a headache for a week that she couldn't channel a spark. What's the matter, child?"

Egwene's hand had tightened around her pouch till the twisted stone ring impressed itself on her palm through the thick cloth. Was it warm? *Light, I did it myself.* "Nothing, Alanna Sedai. Aes Sedai, you did nothing wrong. You have no reason to share my punishments. None at all. None!"

"A bit vehement," Sheriam observed, "but true." Alanna only shook her head.

"Aes Sedai," Egwene said slowly, "what does it mean to be Green Ajah?" Sheriam's eyes opened wider with amusement, and Alanna grinned openly.

"Just with the ring on your finger," the Green sister said, "and already trying to decide which Ajah to choose? First, you must love men. I don't mean be in love with them, but love them. Not like a Blue, who merely likes men, so long as they share her causes and do not get in her way. And certainly not like a Red, who despises them as if every one of them were responsible for the Breaking." Alviarin, the White sister who had come with the Amyrlin, gave them a cool look and moved on. "And not like a White," Alanna said with a laugh, "who has no room in her life for any passions at all."

"That was not what I meant, Alanna Sedai. I want to know what it *means* to be a Green sister." She was not sure Alanna would understand, because she was not certain she herself understood what she wanted to know, but Alanna nodded slowly as if she did.

"Browns seek knowledge, Blues meddle in causes, and Whites consider the questions of truth with implacable logic. We all do some of it all, of course. But to be a Green means to stand ready." A note of pride entered Alanna's voice. "In the Trolloc Wars, we were often called the Battle Ajah. All Aes Sedai helped where and when they could, but the Green Ajah alone was always with the armies, in almost every battle. We were the counter to the Dreadlords. The Battle Ajah. And now we stand ready, for the Trollocs to come south again, for Tarmon Gai'don, the Last Battle. We will be there. That is what it means to be a Green."

"Thank you, Aes Sedai," Egwene said. *That is what I was? Or what I will be? Light, I wish I knew if it was real, if it had anything at all to do with here and now.*

The Amyrlin joined them, and they swept deep curtsies to her. "Are you well, Daughter?" she asked Egwene. Her eyes flicked to the corner of the papers sticking out from under the novice dress in Egwene's hands, then back to Egwene's face immediately. "I will know the why of what occurred tonight before I am done."

Egwene's cheeks reddened. "I am well, Mother."

Alanna surprised her by asking the Amyrlin just what she had said she would.

"I never heard of such a thing," the Amyrlin barked. "The owner doesn't muck out with the bilge boys even if he has run the boat on a mudflat." She glanced at Egwene, and worry tightened her eyes. And anger. "I share your concern, Alanna. Whatever this child has done, it did not deserve that. Very well. If it will assuage your feelings, you may visit Sheriam. But it is to be strictly between you two. I'll not have Aes Sedai held up to ridicule, even inside the Tower."

Egwene opened her mouth to confess all and let them take the ring—*I don't want the bloody thing, really*—but Alanna forestalled her.

"And the other, Mother?"

"Do not be ridiculous, Daughter." The Amyrlin was angry, and sounded more so by the word. "You'd be a laughingstock inside the day, except for those who decided you were mad. And don't think it would not follow you. Tales like that have a way of traveling. You would find stories told of the *scullion Aes Sedai* from Tear to Maradon. And that would reflect on every sister. No. If you need to rid yourself of some feeling of guilt and cannot handle it as a grown woman would, very well. I have told you that you may visit Sheriam. Accompany her tonight when you leave here. That will give you the rest of the night to decide if it was of any help. And tomorrow you can start finding out what went wrong here tonight!"

"Yes, Mother." Alanna's voice was perfectly neutral.

The desire to confess had died in Egwene. Alanna had shown only one brief flash of disappointment, when she realized the Amyrlin would not allow her to join Egwene in the kitchens. *She doesn't want to be punished any more than any sensible person does. She did want an excuse to be in my company. Light, she couldn't have deliberately caused the* ter'angreal *to go wild; I did that. Can she be Black Ajah?*

Wrapped in thought, Egwene heard a throat cleared, then again, more roughly. Her eyes focused. The Amyrlin was staring right into her, and when she spoke, she bit off each word.

"Since you seem to be asleep standing up, child, I suggest you go to bed." For one instant her glance flashed to the nearly concealed papers in Egwene's hands. "You have much work to do tomorrow, and for many days thereafter." Her eyes held Egwene's a moment longer, and then she was striding away before any of them could curtsy.

Sheriam rounded on Alanna as soon as the Amyrlin was out of earshot. The Green Aes Sedai glowered and took it in silence. "You *are* mad, Alanna! A fool, and doubly a fool if you think I will go lightly on you just because we were novices together. Are you taken by the Dragon, to—?" Suddenly Sheriam became aware of Egwene, and the target of her anger shifted. "Did I not hear the Amyrlin Seat order you to your bed, Accepted? If you breathe a word of this, you will wish I had buried you in a field to manure the ground. And I will see you in my study in the morning, when the bell rings First and not one breath later. Now, go!"

Egwene went, her head spinning. *Is there anybody I can trust? The Amyrlin? She sent us off chasing thirteen of the Black Ajah and forgot to mention that thirteen is just the number needed to turn a woman who can channel to the Shadow against her will. Who can I trust?*

She did not want to be alone, could not stand the thought of it, and so she hurried to the Accepted's quarters, thinking that tomorrow she would be moving there herself, and immediately after knocking pushed open Nynaeve's door. She could trust her with anything. Her and Elayne.

But Nynaeve was seated in one of the two chairs, with Elayne's head buried in her lap. Elayne's shoulders shook to the sound of weeping, the softer weeping that comes after no energy is left for deeper sobs but the emotion still burns. Dampness shone on Nynaeve's cheeks, too. The Great Serpent gleaming on her hand, smoothing Elayne's hair, matched the ring on the hand Elayne used to clutch at Nynaeve's skirt.

Elayne lifted a face red and swollen from long crying, sniffing through her sobs when she saw Egwene. "I could not be that awful, Egwene. I just couldn't!"

The accident with the *ter'angreal*, Egwene's fear that someone might have read the papers Verin had given her, her suspicions of everyone in that chamber, all these had been terrible, but they had buffered her in a rough, ungentle way from what had happened inside the *ter'angreal*. They had come from outside; the other was inside. Elayne's words stripped the buffer away, and what was inside hit Egwene as if the ceiling had collapsed. Rand her husband, and Joiya her baby. Rand pinned and begging her to kill him. Rand chained to be gentled.

Before she was aware of moving, she was on her knees beside Elayne, all the tears that should have fallen earlier coming out in a flood. "I couldn't help him, Nynaeve," she sobbed. "I just left him there."

Nynaeve flinched as if struck, but the next moment her arms were around both Egwene and Elayne, hugging them, rocking them. "Hush," she crooned softly. "It eases with time. It eases, a little. One day we will make them pay our price. Hush. Hush."

CHAPTER

24

Scouting and Discoveries

S unlight through the carved shutters, creeping across
the bed, woke Mat. For a moment, he only lay there,
frowning. He had not reasoned out any plan for escaping from Tar Valon before sleep had overtaken him, but
neither had he given up. Too much memory still lay covered
with fog, but he would not give up.

Two serving women came bustling with hot water and a
tray heavy with food, laughing and telling him how much
better he looked already, and how soon he would be back on
his feet if he did what the Aes Sedai told him. He answered
them curtly, trying not to sound bitter. *Let them think I
mean to go along.* His stomach rumbled at the smells from
the tray.

When they left, he tossed aside his blanket and hopped
out of bed, pausing only to stuff half a slice of ham into his
mouth before pouring out water to wash and shave. Staring
into the mirror above the washstand, he paused in lathering
his face. He did look better.

His cheeks were still hollow, but not quite as hollow as
they had been. The dark circles had vanished from under
his eyes, which no longer seemed set so deep in his head. It
was as if every bite he had eaten the night before had gone
into putting meat on his bones. He even felt stronger.

"At this rate," he muttered, "I will be gone before they
know it." But he was still surprised when, after shaving,
he sat down and consumed every scrap of ham, turnip, and
pear on the tray.

He was sure they expected him to climb back into bed
once he had eaten, but instead, he dressed. Stamping his

feet to settle them in his boots, he eyed his spare clothes
and decided to leave them, for now. *I have to know what
I'm doing, first. And if I have to leave them. . . .* He tucked
the dice cups into his pouch. With those, he could get all the
clothes he needed.

Opening the door, he peeked out. More doors paneled in
pale, golden wood lined the hall, with colorful tapestries
between, and a runner of blue carpet ran down the white-
tiled floor. But there was no one out there. No guard. He
tossed his cloak over one shoulder and hurried out. Now to
find a way outside.

It took some little wandering, down stairs and along
corridors and across open courts, before he found what he
wanted, a doorway to the outside, and he saw people before then: serving women and white-clad novices hurrying
about their chores, the novices running even harder than the
servants; a handful of roughly dressed male servants carrying large chests and other heavy loads; Accepted in their
banded dresses. Even a few Aes Sedai.

The Aes Sedai did not seem to notice him as they strode
along, intent on whatever purpose, or else they gave him no
more than a passing glance. His were country clothes, but
well made; he did not look a vagabond, and the serving men
showed that men were allowed in this part of the Tower. He
suspected they might take him for another servant, and that
was just as well with him, so long as no one asked him to
lift anything.

He did feel some regret that none of the women he saw
was Egwene or Nynaeve, or even Elayne. *She's a pretty
one, even if she does have her nose in the air half the time.
And she could tell me how to find Egwene and the Wisdom.
I cannot go without saying goodbye. Light, I don't suppose
one of them would turn me in, just because they are becoming Aes Sedai themselves? Burn me, for a fool! They'd
never do that. Anyway, I will risk it.*

But once out-of-doors, under a bright morning sky with
only a few drifting white clouds, he put the women from
his mind for the time. He was looking across a wide, flagstoned yard with a plain stone fountain in the middle and
a barracks on the other side that was made of gray stone.
It looked almost like a huge boulder among the few trees
growing out of rimmed holes in the flagstones close by.

Guardsmen in their shirtsleeves sat in front of the long, low building, tending weapons and armor and harness. Guardsmen were what he wanted, now.

He sauntered across the yard and watched the soldiers as if he had nothing better to do. As they worked they talked and laughed among themselves like men after the harvest. Now and again one of them looked curiously at Mat as he strolled among them, but none challenged his right to be there. From time to time he asked a casual question. And finally he got the answer he sought.

"Bridge guard?" said a stocky, dark-haired man no more than five years older than Mat. His words had a heavy Illianer accent. Young he might have been, but a thin white scar crossed his left cheek, and the hands oiling his sword moved with familiarity and competence. He squinted up at Mat before returning to his task. "I do be on the bridge guard, and back there again this even. Why do you ask?"

"I was just wondering what conditions were like on the other side of the river." *I might as well find that out, too.* "Good for traveling? It can't be muddy, unless you have had more rain than I know about."

"Which side of the river?" the guardsman asked placidly. His eyes did not lift from the oiled rag he was running along his blade.

"Uh . . . east. The east side."

"No mud. Whitecloaks." The man leaned to one side to spit, but his voice did not change. "Whitecloaks do be poking their noses into every village for ten miles. They have no hurt anyone yet, but them just being there do upset the folk. Fortune prick me if I do no think they wish to provoke us, for they do look as if they would attack if they could. No good for anyone who do want to travel."

"What about west, then?"

"The same." The guardsman raised his eyes to Mat's. "But you will no be crossing, lad, east or west. Your name do be Matrim Cauthon, or Fortune abandon me. Last night a sister, herself in person, did come to the bridge where I did stand guard. She did drill your features at us till each could speak them back to her. A guest, she did say, and no to be harmed. But no to be allowed out of the city, either, if you must be tied hand and foot to keep you from it." His eyes narrowed. "Is it that you did steal something from them?" he asked doubtfully. "You do no have the look of those the sisters do guest."

"I didn't steal anything!" Mat said indignantly. *Burn me, I didn't even get a chance to work around to it easy. They must all know me.* "I'm no thief!"

"No, it is no that I do see in your face. No thievery. But you do have the look of the fellow who did try to sell me the Horn of Valere three days gone. So he did claim it did be, all bent and battered as it did be. Do you have a Horn of Valere to sell? Or mayhap it do be the Dragon's sword?"

Mat gave a jump at the mention of the Horn, but he managed to keep his voice level. "I was sick." Others of the guardsmen were looking at him now. *Light, they'll all know I am not supposed to leave, now.* He forced a laugh. "The sisters Healed me." Some of the guardsmen frowned at him. Perhaps they thought other men should show more respect than to call the Aes Sedai sisters. "I guess the Aes Sedai don't want me to go before I have all my strength back." He tried willing the men, all of those watching him now, to accept that. *Just a man who was Healed. Nothing more. No reason to trouble yourself about him any further.*

The Illianer nodded. "You do have the look of sickness in your face, too. Perhaps that do be the reason. But never did I hear of so much effort to keep one sick man in the city."

"That's the reason," Mat said firmly. They were all still looking at him. "Well, I need to be going. They said I have to take walks. Lots of long walks. To build up strength, you know."

He felt their eyes following him as he left, and he scowled. He had simply meant to find out how well his description had been passed around. If only the officers among the bridge guards had had it, he might have been able to slip by. He had always been good at slipping into places unseen. And out. It was a talent you developed when your mother always suspected you were up to some mischief and you had two sisters to tell on you. *And now I've made sure half a barracks full of guardsmen will know me. Blood and bloody ashes!*

Much of the Tower grounds were gardens full of trees, leatherleaf and paperbark and elms, and he soon found himself walking along a wide, twisting graveled path. It could have led through countryside, if not for the towers visible over the treetops. And the white bulk of the Tower itself, behind him but pressing on him as if he carried it on his shoulders. If there were ways out of the Tower grounds that were not watched, this seemed the place to find them. If they existed.

A girl in novice white appeared ahead on the path, striding purposefully toward him. Wrapped in her own thoughts, she did not see him at first. When she came close enough for him to make out her big, dark eyes and the way her hair was braided, he grinned suddenly. He knew this girl—memory drifting up from shrouded depths—though he would never have expected to find her here. He had never expected to see her again at all. He grinned to himself. *Good luck to balance bad.* As he remembered, she had quite an eye for the boys.

"Else," he called to her. "Else Grinwell. You remember me, don't you? Mat Cauthon. A friend and I visited your father's farm. Remember? Have you decided to become Aes Sedai, then?"

She stopped short, staring at him. "What are you doing up and out?" she said coldly.

"You know about that, do you?" He moved closer to her, but she stepped back, keeping her distance. He stopped. "It's not catching. I was Healed, Else." Those large, dark eyes seemed more knowing than he remembered, and not nearly so warm, but he supposed studying to be an Aes Sedai could do that. "What is the matter, Else? You look like you don't know me."

"I know you," she said. Her manner was not as he remembered, either; he thought she could give Elayne lessons now. "I have . . . work to be about. Let me by."

He grimaced. The path was broad enough for six to walk abreast without crowding. "I told you it isn't catching."

"Let me by!"

Muttering to himself, he stepped to one edge of the gravel. She went past him along the other side, watching to make sure he did not come closer. Once by, she quickened her steps, glancing over her shoulder at him until she was out of sight around a bend.

Wanted to make sure I didn't follow her, he thought sourly. *First the guardsmen, and now Else. My luck is not in, today.*

He started off again, and soon heard a ferocious clatter from one side ahead, like dozens of sticks being beat together. Curious, he turned off toward it, into the trees.

A little way brought him to a large expanse of bare ground, the earth beaten hard, at least fifty paces across and nearly twice as long. At intervals around it under the trees stood wooden stands holding quarterstaffs, and practice swords made of strips of wood bound loosely together, and a few real swords and axes and spears.

Spaced across the open ground, pairs of men, most stripped to the waist, flailed at each other with more practice swords. Some moved so smoothly it almost seemed they danced with one another, flowing from stance to stance, stroke to counterstroke in continuous motion. There was nothing quickly apparent aside from skill to mark them from the others, but Mat was sure he was watching Warders.

Those who did not move so smoothly were all younger, each pair under the watchful eyes of an older man who seemed to radiate a dangerous grace even standing still. *Warders and students*, Mat decided.

He was not the only audience. Not ten paces from him, half a dozen women with ageless Aes Sedai faces and as many more in the banded white dresses of the Accepted stood watching one pair of students, bare to the waist and slick with sweat, under the guidance of a Warder shaped much like a block of stone. The Warder used a short-stemmed pipe in one hand, trailing tabac smoke, to direct his pupils.

Sitting down cross-legged under a leatherleaf, Mat rooted three large pebbles out of the ground and began to juggle them idly. He did not feel weak, exactly, but it was good to sit. If there was a way out of the Tower grounds, it would not go away while he took a short rest.

Before he had been there five minutes he knew who it was the Aes Sedai and Accepted were watching. One of the blocky Warder's pupils was a tall, lithe young man who moved like a cat. *And almost as pretty as a girl*, Mat thought wryly. Every woman was staring at the tall fellow with sparkling eyes, even the Aes Sedai.

The tall man handled his practice sword almost as deftly as the Warders, now and then earning an approving gravelly

comment from his teacher. It was not that his opponent, a
youth more Mat's age, with red-gold hair, was unskilled.
Far from it, as much as Mat could see, though he had never
claimed to know anything about swords. The golden-haired
man met every lightning attack, turning it away before the
bound strips could strike him, and even launched an occasional attack of his own. But the handsome fellow coun-
tered those attacks and flowed back into his own in the
space of a heartbeat.

Mat shifted the pebbles to one hand, but kept them spinning in the air. He did not think he would care to face either
of them. Certainly not with a sword.

"Break!" The Warder's voice sounded like rocks emptying out of a bucket. Chests heaving, the two men let their
practice swords fall to their sides. Sweat matted their hair.
"You can rest till I finish my pipe. But rest fast; I am almost
in the dottle."

Now that they had stopped dancing about, Mat got a good
look at the youth with the red-gold hair and let the pebbles
drop. *Burn me, I'll bet my whole purse that's Elayne's
brother. And the other one's Galad, or I'll eat my boots.*
On the journey from Toman Head it had seemed half of
Elayne's conversation had been of Gawyn's virtues and
Galad's vices. Oh, Gawyn had some vices according to
Elayne, but they were small; to Mat they sounded like the
sort of things no one but a sister would consider vices at all.
As for Galad, once Elayne was pinned down, he sounded
like what every mother said she wanted her son to be. Mat
did not think he wanted to spend much time in Galad's
company. Egwene blushed whenever Galad was mentioned,
though she seemed to think no one noticed.

A ripple seemed to pass through the watching women
when Gawyn and Galad stopped, and they appeared on
the point of stepping forward almost as one. But Gawyn
caught sight of Mat, said something quietly to Galad, and
the two of them walked by the women. The Aes Sedai and
Accepted turned to follow with their eyes. Mat scrambled
to his feet as the pair approached.

"You are Mat Cauthon, are you not?" Gawyn said with a
grin. "I was sure I recognized you from Egwene's description. And Elayne's. I understand you were sick. Are you
better now?"

"I'm fine," Mat said. He wondered if he was supposed to call Gawyn "my Lord" or something of the sort. He had refused to call Elayne "my Lady"—not that she had demanded it, actually—and he decided he would not do her brother better.

"Did you come to the practice yard to learn the sword?" Galad asked.

Mat shook his head. "I was only out walking. I don't know much about swords. I think I'll put my trust in a good bow, or a good quarterstaff. I know how to use those."

"If you spend much time around Nynaeve," Galad said, "you'll need bow, quarterstaff, *and* sword to protect yourself. And I don't know whether that would be enough."

Gawyn looked at him wonderingly. "Galad, you just very nearly made a joke."

"I do have a sense of humor, Gawyn," Galad said with a frown. "You only think I do not because I do not care to mock people."

With a shake of his head, Gawyn turned back to Mat. "You should learn something of the sword. Everyone can do with that sort of knowledge these days. Your friend— Rand al'Thor—carried a most unusual sword. What do you hear of him?"

"I haven't seen Rand in a long time," Mat said quickly. Just for a moment, when he had mentioned Rand, Gawyn's look had gained intensity. *Light, does* he *know about Rand? He couldn't. If he did, he'd be denouncing me for a Darkfriend just for being Rand's friend. But he knows something.* "Swords aren't the be-all and end-all, you know. I could do fairly well against either of you, I think, if you had a sword and I had my quarterstaff."

Gawyn's cough was obviously meant to swallow a laugh. Much too politely, he said, "You must be very good." Galad's face was frankly disbelieving.

Perhaps it was that they both clearly thought he was making a wild boast. Perhaps it was because he had mishandled questioning the guardsman. Perhaps it was because Else, who had such an eye for the boys, wanted nothing to do with him, and all those women were staring at Galad like cats watching a jug of cream. Aes Sedai and Accepted or not, they were still women. All these explanations ran through Mat's head, but he rejected them angrily, especially the last. He was going to do it because it would be fun. And it might earn some coin. His luck would not even have to be back.

"I will wager," he said, "two silver marks to two from each of you that I can beat both of you at once, just the way I said. You can't have fairer odds than that. There are two of you, and one of me, so two to one are fair odds." He almost laughed aloud at the consternation on their faces.

"Mat," Gawyn said, "there's no need to make wagers. You have been sick. Perhaps we will try this some time when you are stronger."

"It would be far from a fair wager," Galad said. "I'll not take your wager, now or later. You are from the same village as Egwene, are you not? I . . . I would not have her angry with me."

"What does she have to do with it? Thump me once with one of your swords, and I will hand over a silver mark to each of you. If I thump you till you quit, you give me two each. Don't you think you can do it?"

"This is ridiculous," Galad said. "You would have no chance against one trained swordsman, let alone two. I'll not take such advantage."

"Do you think that?" asked a gravel voice. The blocky Warder joined them, thick black eyebrows pulled down in a scowl. "You think you two are good enough with your swords to take a boy with a stick?"

"It would not be fair, Hammar Gaidin," Galad said.

"He has been sick," Gawyn added. "There is no need for this."

"To the yard," Hammar grated with a jerk of his head back over his shoulder. Galad and Gawyn gave Mat regretful looks, then obeyed. The Warder eyed Mat up and down doubtfully. "Are you sure you're up to this, lad? Now I take a close look at you, you ought to be in a sickbed."

"I am already out of one," Mat said, "and I'm up to it. I have to be. I don't want to lose my two marks."

Hammar's heavy brows rose in surprise. "You mean to hold to that wager, lad?"

"I need the money." Mat laughed.

His laughter cut off abruptly as he turned toward the nearest stand that held quarterstaffs and his knees almost buckled. He stiffened them so quickly he thought anyone who noticed would think he had just stumbled. At the stand he took his time choosing out a staff, nearly two inches thick and almost a foot taller than he was. *I have to win this. I opened my fool mouth, and now I have to win. I can't afford to lose those two marks. Without those to build on, it will take forever to win the money I need.*

When he turned back, the quarterstaff in both hands before him, Gawyn and Galad were already waiting out where they had been practicing. *I have to win.* "Luck," he muttered. "Time to toss the dice."

Hammar gave him an odd look. "You speak the Old Tongue, lad?"

Mat stared back at him for a moment, not speaking. He felt cold to the bone. With an effort, he made his feet start out onto the practice yard. "Remember the wager," he said loudly. "Two silver marks from each of you against two from me."

A buzz rose from the Accepted as they realized what was happening. The Aes Sedai watched in silence. Disapproving silence.

Gawyn and Galad split apart, one to either side of him, keeping their distance, neither with his sword more than half-raised.

"No wager," Gawyn said. "There's no wager."

At the same time, Galad said, "I'll not take your money like this."

"I mean to take yours," Mat said.

"Done!" Hammar roared. "If they have not the nerve to cover your wager, lad, I'll pay the score myself."

"Very well," Gawyn said. "If you insist on it—done!"

Galad hesitated a moment more before growling, "Done, then. Let us put an end to this farce."

The moment's warning was all Mat needed. As Galad rushed at him, he slid his hands along the quarterstaff and pivoted. The end of the staff thudded into the tall man's ribs, bringing a grunt and a stumble. Mat let the staff bounce off Galad and spun, carrying it on around just as Gawyn came within range. The staff dipped, darted under Gawyn's practice sword, and clipped his ankle out from under him. As Gawyn fell, Mat completed the spin in time to catch Galad across his upraised wrist, sending his practice sword flying. As if his wrist did not pain him at all, Galad threw himself into a smooth, rolling dive and came up with his sword in both hands.

Ignoring him for the moment, Mat half turned, twisting his wrists to whip the length of the staff back beside him. Gawyn, just starting to rise, took the blow on the side of his head with a loud thump only partly softened by the padding of hair. He went down in a heap.

Mat was only vaguely aware of an Aes Sedai rushing out to tend Elayne's fallen brother. *I hope he's all right. He should be. I've hit myself harder than that falling off a fence.* He still had Galad to deal with, and from the way Galad was poised on the balls of his feet, sword raised precisely, he had begun to take Mat seriously.

Mat's legs chose that moment to tremble. *Light, I can't weaken now.* But he could feel it creeping back in, the wobbly feeling, the hunger as if he had not eaten for days. *If I wait for him to come to me, I'll fall on my face.* It was hard to keep his knees straight as he started forward. *Luck, stay with me.*

From the first blow, he knew that luck, or skill, or whatever had brought him this far, was still there. Galad managed to turn that one with a sharp clack, and the next, and the next, and the next, but strain stiffened his face. That smooth swordsman, almost as good as the Warders, fought with every ounce of his skill to keep Mat's staff from him. He did not attack; it was all he could do to defend. He moved continually to the side, trying not to be forced back, and Mat pressed him, staff a blur. And Galad stepped back, stepped back again, wooden blade a thin shield against the quarterstaff.

Hunger gnawed at Mat as if he had swallowed weasels. Sweat rolled down into his eyes, and his strength began to fade as if it leached out with the sweat. *Not yet. I can't fall yet. I have to win. Now.* With a roar, he threw all his reserves into one last surge.

The quarterstaff flickered past Galad's sword and in quick succession struck knee, wrist, and ribs and finally thrust into Galad's stomach like a spear. With a groan, Galad folded over, fighting not to fall. The staff quivered in Mat's hands, on the point of a final crushing thrust to the throat. Galad sank to the ground.

Mat almost dropped the quarterstaff when he realized

what he had been about to do. *Win, not kill. Light, what was I thinking?* Reflexively he grounded the butt of the staff, and as soon he did, he had to clutch at it to hold himself erect. Hunger hollowed him like a knife reaming marrow from a bone. Suddenly he realized that not only the Aes Sedai and Accepted were watching. All practice, all learning, had stopped. Warders and students alike stood watching him.

Hammar moved to stand beside Galad, still groaning on the ground and trying to push himself up. The Warder raised his voice to shout, "Who was the greatest blademaster of all time?"

From the throats of dozens of students came a massed bellow. "Jearom, Gaidin!"

"Yes!" Hammar shouted, turning to make sure all heard. "During his lifetime, Jearom fought over ten thousand times, in battle and single combat. He was defeated once. By a farmer with a quarterstaff! Remember that. Remember what you just saw." He lowered his eyes to Galad, and lowered his voice as well. "If you cannot get up by now, lad, it is finished." He raised a hand, and the Aes Sedai and Accepted rushed to surround Galad.

Mat slid down the staff to his knees. None of the Aes Sedai even glanced his way. One of the Accepted did, a plump girl he might have liked to ask for a dance if she were not going to be an Aes Sedai. She frowned at him, sniffed, and turned back to peering at what the Aes Sedai were doing around Galad.

Gawyn was on his feet, Mat noted with relief. He pulled himself up as Gawyn came over. *Mustn't let them know. I'll never get out of here if they decide to nurse me from sunup to sunup.* Blood darkened the red-gold hair on the side of Gawyn's head, but there was neither cut nor bruise apparent.

He pushed two silver marks into Mat's hand with a dry "I think I will listen next time." He noticed Mat's glance, touched his head. "They Healed it, but it was not bad. Elayne has given me worse more than once. You are good with that."

"Not as good as my da. He's won the quarterstaff at Bel Tine every year as long as I can remember, except once or twice when Rand's da did." That interested look came back into Gawyn's eyes, and Mat wished he had never mentioned Tam al'Thor. The Aes Sedai and the Accepted were all still clustered around Galad. "I . . . I must have hurt him badly. I did not mean to do that."

Gawyn glanced that way—there was nothing to be seen but two rings of women's backs, Accepted's white dresses making the outer ring as they peered over the shoulders of crouching Aes Sedai—and laughed. "You did not kill him—I heard him groaning—so he should be on his feet by now, but they are not going to let this chance pass, now they have their hands on him. Light, four of them are Green Ajah!" Mat gave him a confused look—*Green Ajah? What does that have to do with anything?*—and Gawyn shook his head. "It doesn't matter. Just rest assured that the worst Galad has to worry about is finding himself Warder to a Green Aes Sedai before his head clears." He laughed. "No, they would not do that. But I will wager you those two marks of mine in your hand that some of them wish they could."

"Not your marks," Mat said, shoving them in his coat pocket, "mine." The explanation had made little sense to him. Except that Galad was well. All he knew of what passed between Warders and Aes Sedai were the pieces he remembered of Lan and Moiraine, and there was nothing there like what Gawyn seemed to be suggesting. "Do you think they'd mind if I collected my wager from him?"

"They very likely would," Hammar said dryly as he joined them. "You are not very popular with those particular Aes Sedai right now." He snorted. "You'd think even Green Aes Sedai would be better than girls just loose from their mother's apron strings. He isn't *that* good-looking."

"He is not," Mat agreed.

Gawyn grinned at both of them, until Hammar glared at him. "Here," the Warder said, pushing two more silver coins into Mat's hand. "I will collect from Galad later. Where are you from, lad?"

"Manetheren." Mat froze when he heard the name come out of his mouth. "I mean, I'm from the Two Rivers. I have heard too many old stories." They just looked at him without saying anything. "I. . . . I think I will go back and see if I can find something to eat." Not even the Midmorning bell had rung yet, but they nodded as if it made sense.

He kept the quarterstaff—no one had told him to put it back—and walked slowly until the trees hid him from the practice yard. When they did, he leaned on the staff as though it were the only thing holding him up. He was not sure it was not.

He thought that if he parted his coat, he would see a hole where his stomach should have been, a hole growing larger as it pulled the rest of him in. But he hardly thought of hunger. He kept hearing voices in his head. *You speak the Old Tongue, lad? Manetheren.* It made him shiver. *Light help me, I keep digging myself deeper. I have to get out of here. But how?* He hobbled back toward the Tower proper like an old, old man. *How?*

CHAPTER
25

Questions

E gwene lay across Nynaeve's bed, chin in her hands,
watching Nynaeve pace back and forth. Elayne
sprawled in front of the fireplace, which was still full
of the ashes of last night's fire. Yet again Elayne was studying the list of names Verin had produced, patiently reading every word one more time. The other pages, the list of
ter'angreal, sat on the table; after one shocked reading they
had not discussed that one further, though they had talked
of everything else. And argued, too.

Egwene stifled a yawn. It was only the middle of the
morning, but none of them had gotten much sleep. They
had had to be up early. For the kitchens, and breakfast. For
other things that she refused to think about. The little sleep
she herself had managed had been filled with unpleasant
dreams. *Maybe Anaiya could help me understand them,
those that need understanding, but. . . . But what if she is
Black Ajah?* After staring at every woman in that chamber
last night, wondering which was Black Ajah, she was finding trust for anyone but her two companions hard to come
by. But she did wish she had some way of interpreting those
dreams.

The nightmares about what had happened inside the
ter'angreal last night were easy enough to understand, though
they had made her wake up weeping. She had dreamed of
the Seanchan, too, of women in dresses with lightning bolts
woven on their breasts, collaring a long line of women who
wore Great Serpent rings, forcing them to call lightning
against the White Tower. That had started her awake in a
cold sweat, but that had to be just a nightmare, too. And

the dream about Whitecloaks binding her father's hands. A nightmare brought on by homesickness, she supposed. But the others. . . .

She glanced at the other two women again. Elayne was still reading. Nynaeve still paced with that steady tread.

There had been a dream of Rand, reaching for a sword that seemed to be made of crystal, never seeing the fine net dropping over him. And one of him kneeling in a chamber where a parched wind blew dust across the floor, and creatures like the one on the Dragon banner, but much smaller, floated on that wind, and settled into his skin. There had been a dream of him walking down into a great hole in a black mountain, a hole filled with a reddish glare as from vast fires below, and even a dream of him confronting Seanchan.

About that last, she was uncertain, but she knew the others had to mean something. Back when she had been sure she could trust Anaiya, back before she had left the Tower, before she learned the reality of the Black Ajah, a little cautious questioning of the Aes Sedai—done, oh, so carefully, so Anaiya would think it no more than the curiosity she showed about other things—had revealed that a Dreamer's dreams about *ta'veren* were almost always significant, and the more strongly *ta'veren*, the more "almost always" became "certainly."

But Mat and Perrin were *ta'veren*, too, and she had also dreamed of them. Odd dreams, even more difficult to understand than the dreams of Rand. Perrin with a falcon on his shoulder, and Perrin with a hawk. Only the hawk held a leash in her talons—Egwene was somehow convinced both hawk and falcon were female—and the hawk was trying to fasten it around Perrin's neck. That made her shiver even now; she did not like dreams about leashes. And that dream of Perrin—with a beard!—leading a huge pack of wolves that stretched as far as the eye could see. Those about Mat had been even nastier. Mat, placing his own left eye on a balance scale. Mat, hanging by his neck from a tree limb. There had been a dream of Mat and Seanchan, too, but she was willing to dismiss that as a nightmare. It had to have been just a nightmare. Just like the one about Mat speaking the Old Tongue. That had to come from what she had heard during his Healing.

She sighed, and the sigh turned into another yawn. She and the others had gone to his room after breakfast to see how he was, but he had not been there.

He is probably well enough to go dancing. Light, now I will probably dream about him dancing with Seanchan! No more dreams, she told herself firmly. *Not now. I will think about them when I am not so tired.* She thought of the kitchens, of the midday meal soon to come, and then supper, and breakfast again tomorrow, and pots and cleaning and scrubbing going on forever. *If I am ever not tired again.* Shifting her position on the bed, she looked at her friends again. Elayne still had her eyes on the list of names. Nynaeve's steps had slowed. *Any moment now, Nynaeve will say it again. Any moment.*

Nynaeve came to a halt, staring down at Elayne. "Put those away. We have been over them twenty times, and there isn't a word that helps. Verin gave us rubbish. The question is, was it all she had, or did she give us rubbish on purpose?"

As expected. Maybe half an hour till she says it again. Egwene frowned down at her hands, glad she could not see them clearly. The Great Serpent ring looked—out of place—on hands all wrinkled from long immersion in hot, soapy water.

"Knowing their names helps," Elayne said, still reading. "Knowing what they look like helps."

"You know very well what I mean," Nynaeve snapped.

Egwene sighed and folded her arms in front of her, rested her chin on them. When she had come out of Sheriam's study that morning, with the sun still not even a glint on the horizon, Nynaeve had been waiting with a candle in the cold, dark hall. She had not been seeing very clearly, but she was sure Nynaeve had looked ready to chew stone. And knowing chewing stones would not change anything in the next few minutes. That was why she was so irritable. *She's as touchy about her pride as any man I ever met. But she should not take it out on Elayne and me. Light, if Elayne can stand it, she should be able to. She isn't the Wisdom anymore.*

Elayne hardly appeared to notice whether Nynaeve was irritable or not. She frowned into the distance thoughtfully. "Liandrin was the only Red. All the other Ajahs lost two each."

"Oh, do be quiet, child," Nynaeve said.

Elayne wiggled her left hand to display her Great Serpent ring, gave Nynaeve a meaningful look, and went right on. "No two were born in the same city, and no more than two in any one country. Amico Nagoyin was the youngest, some fifteen years older than Egwene and I. Joiya Byir could be our great-grandmother's great-grandmother."

Egwene did not like it that one of the Black Ajah shared her daughter's name. *Fool girl! People sometimes have the same name, and you never had a daughter. It wasn't real!*

"And what does that tell us?" Nynaeve's voice was too calm; she was ready to explode like a wagon full of fireworks. "What secrets have you found in it that I missed? I am getting old and blind, after all!"

"It tells us it is all too neat," Elayne said calmly. "What chance that thirteen women chosen solely because they were Darkfriends would be so neatly arrayed across age, across nations, across Ajahs? Shouldn't there be perhaps three Reds, or four born in Cairhien, or just two the same age, if it was all chance? They had women to choose from or they could not have chosen so random a pattern. There are still Black Ajah in the Tower, or elsewhere we don't know about. It must mean that."

Nynaeve gave her braid one ferocious tug. "Light! I think you may be right. You did find secrets I couldn't. Light, I was hoping they all went with Liandrin."

"We do not even know that she is their leader," Elayne said. "She could have been ordered to . . . to *dispose* of us." Her mouth twisted. "I am afraid I can only think of one reason for them to go to such lengths to spread everything out so, to avoid any pattern except a lack of pattern. I think it means there *is* a pattern of some kind to the Black Ajah."

"If there's a pattern," Nynaeve said firmly, "we will find it. Elayne, if watching your mother run her court taught you to think like this, I'm glad you watched closely." Elayne's answering smile made a dimple in her cheek.

Egwene eyed the older woman carefully. It seemed Nynaeve was finally ready to stop being a bear with a sore tooth. She raised her head. "Unless they want us to think they're hiding a pattern, so we will waste our time hunting for it when there isn't one. I am not saying there isn't; I am only saying we do not know yet. Let's look for it, but I think we ought to look at other things, too, don't you?"

"So you finally decided to rouse," Nynaeve said. "I thought you had gone to sleep." But she was still smiling.

"She is right," Elayne said disgustedly. "I have built a bridge out of straw. Worse than straw. Wishes. Maybe you are right, too, Nynaeve. What use is this—this rubbish?" She snatched one paper out of the stack in front of her. "Rianna has black hair with a white streak above her left ear. If I am close enough to see that, it's closer than I want to be." She grabbed another page. "Chesmal Emry is one of the most talented Healers anyone has seen in years. Light, could you imagine being Healed by one of the Black Ajah?" A third sheet. "Marillin Gemalphin is fond of cats and goes out of her way to help injured animals. Cats! Paah!" She scrabbled all the pages together, crumpling them in her fists. "It *is* useless rubbish."

Nynaeve knelt beside her and gently pried her hands from around the papers. "Perhaps, and perhaps not." She smoothed the pages carefully on her breast. "You found in them something for us to look for. Perhaps we will find more, if we are persistent. And there is the other list." Both her eyes and Elayne's darted to Egwene, brown and blue alike frowning worriedly.

Egwene avoided looking at the table where the other sheets lay. She did not want to think about them, but she could not avoid it. The list of *ter'angreal* had etched itself into her mind.

Item. A rod of clear crystal, smooth and perfectly clear, one foot long and one inch in diameter. Use unknown. Last study made by Corianin Nedeal. Item. A figurine of an unclothed woman in alabaster, one hand tall. Use unknown. Last study made by Corianin Nedeal. Item. A disc, apparently of simple iron yet untouched by rust, three inches in diameter, finely engraved on both sides with a tight spiral. Use unknown. Last study made by Corianin Nedeal. Item. Too many items, and more than half the "use unknowns" last studied by Corianin Nedeal. Thirteen of them, to be exact.

Egwene shivered. *It's getting so I do not even like to think of that number.*

The knowns on the list were fewer, not all of any apparent real use, but hardly more comforting, as she saw it. A wooden carving of a hedgehog, no bigger than the last joint of a man's thumb. Such a simple thing, and surely harmless. Any woman who tried to channel through it went to sleep. Half a day of peaceful, dreamless sleep, but it was too close not to make her skin crawl. Three more had to do with sleep in some way. It was almost a relief to read of a fluted rod of black stone, a full pace in length, that produced balefire, with the notation DANGEROUS AND ALMOST IMPOSSIBLE TO CONTROL writ so strong in Verin's hand that it tore the paper in two places. Egwene still had no idea what balefire was, but though it surely sounded dangerous if anything ever did, it just as surely had nothing to do Corianin Nedeal or dreams.

Nynaeve carried the smoothed-out pages to the table and set them down. She hesitated before spreading the others out and running her finger down one page, then the next. "Here's one Mat would enjoy," she said in a voice much too light and airy. "Item. A carved cluster of six spotted dice, joined at the corners, less than two inches across. Use unknown, save that channeling through it seems to suspend chance in some way, or twist it." She began to read aloud. "'Tossed coins presented the same face every time, and in one test landed balanced on edge one hundred times in a row. One thousand tosses of the dice produced five crowns one thousand times.'" She gave a forced laugh. "Mat would love that."

Egwene sighed and got to her feet, walked stiffly to the fireplace. Elayne scrambled up, watching as silently as Nynaeve. Pushing her sleeve as far up her arm as it would go, Egwene reached carefully up the chimney. Her fingers touched wool on the smoke shelf, and she pulled out a wadded, singed stocking with a hard lump in the toe. She brushed a smear of soot from her arm, then took the stocking to the table and shook it out. The twisted ring of striped, flecked stone spun across the tabletop and fell flat atop a page of the *ter'angreal* list. For a few moments they just stared at it.

"Perhaps," Nynaeve said finally, "Verin simply missed the fact that so many of them were last studied by Corianin." She did not sound as if she really believed it.

Elayne nodded, but doubtfully. "I saw her walking in the

rain once, soaking wet, and took a cloak to her. She was so wrapped up in whatever she was thinking, I do not believe she knew it was raining until I put the cloak around her shoulders. She could have missed it."

"Maybe," Egwene said. "If she did not, she had to know I'd notice as soon as I read the list. I do not know. Sometimes I think Verin notices more than she lets on. I just do not know."

"So there's Verin to suspect," Elayne sighed. "If she is Black Ajah, then they know exactly what we are doing. And Alanna." She gave Egwene an uncertain, sidelong look.

Egwene had told them everything. Except what happened inside the *ter'angreal* during her testing; she could not bring herself to talk about that, any more than Nynaeve or Elayne could tell of their testings. Everything that happened in the testing chamber, what Sheriam had said about the terrible weakness conferred by the ability to channel, every word Verin had said, whether it seemed important or not. The one part they had had trouble accepting was Alanna; Aes Sedai just did not do things like that. No one in her right mind did anything like that, but Aes Sedai least of all.

Egwene glowered at them, almost hearing them say it. "Aes Sedai are not supposed to lie, either, but Verin and the Mother seem awfully close with what they tell us. There are not *supposed* to be Black Ajah."

"I like Alanna." Nynaeve tugged her braid, then shrugged. "Oh, very well. Perha—That is, she did behave oddly."

"Thank you," Egwene said, and Nynaeve gave her an acknowledging nod as if she had heard no sarcasm.

"In any case, the Amyrlin knows of it, and she can keep an eye on Alanna far more easily than we can."

"What about Elaida and Sheriam?" Egwene asked.

"I have never been able to like Elaida," Elayne said, "but I cannot truly believe she is Black Ajah. And Sheriam? It's impossible."

Nynaeve snorted. "It should be impossible for any of them. When we do find them, there is nothing says they'll all be women we do not like. But I don't mean to put suspicion— not this kind of suspicion!—on any woman. We need more to go on than that they might have seen something they shouldn't." Egwene nodded agreement as quickly as Elayne, and Nynaeve went on: "We will tell the Amyrlin that much, and put no more weight to it than it deserves. If she ever looks in on us as she said she would. If you are with us when she comes, Elayne, remember she does not know about you."

"I am not likely to forget it," Elayne said fervently. "But we should have some other way to get word to her. My mother would have planned it better."

"Not if she could not trust her messengers," Nynaeve said. "We will wait. Unless you two think one of us should have a talk with Verin? No one would think that remarkable."

Elayne hesitated, then gave her head a small shake. Egwene was quicker and more vigorous with hers; slip of the mind or not, Verin had left out too much to be trusted.

"Good." Nynaeve sounded more than satisfied. "I am just as pleased we cannot talk to the Amyrlin when we choose. This way we make our own decisions, act when and as we decide, without her directing our every step." Her hand ran down the pages listing stolen *ter'angreal* as if she were reading it again, then closed on the striped stone ring. "And the first decision concerns this. It's the first thing we have seen that has any real connection to Liandrin and the others." She frowned at the ring, then took a deep breath. "I am going to sleep with it tonight."

Egwene did not hesitate before taking the ring out of Nynaeve's hand. She wanted to hesitate—she wanted to keep her hands by her sides—but she did not, and she was pleased. "I am the one they say might be a Dreamer. I do not know whether that gives me any advantage, but Verin said it's dangerous using this. Whichever of us uses it, she needs any advantage she can find."

Nynaeve gripped her braid and opened her mouth as if to protest. When she finally spoke, though, it was to say, "Are you sure, Egwene? We do not even know if you *are* a Dreamer, and I can channel more strongly than you. I still think I—" Egwene cut her off.

"You can channel more strongly if you are angry. Can you be sure you'll be angry in a dream? Will you have time to become angry before you need to channel? Light, we don't even know that anyone can channel in a dream.

If one of us has to do it—and you are right; it is the only
connection we have—it should be me. Maybe I really am a
Dreamer. Besides, Verin did give it to me."

Nynaeve looked as if she wanted to argue, but at last she
gave a grudging nod. "Very well. But Elayne and I will be
there. I do not know what we can do, but if anything goes
wrong, perhaps we can wake you up, or. . . . We will be
there." Elayne nodded, too.

Now that she had their agreement, Egwene felt a queasiness in the pit of her stomach. *I talked them into it. I wish I
did not want them to talk me out of it.* She became aware of
a woman standing in the doorway, a woman in novice white,
with her hair in long braids.

"Did no one ever teach you to knock, Else?" Nynaeve
said.

Egwene hid the stone ring inside her fist. She had the
strangest feeling that Else had been staring at it.

"I have a message for you," Else said calmly. Her eyes
studied the table, with all the papers scattered on it, then the
three women around it. "From the Amyrlin."

Egwene exchanged wondering looks with Nynaeve and
Elayne.

"Well, what is it?" Nynaeve demanded.

Else arched an eyebrow in amusement. "The belongings
left behind by Liandrin and the others were put in the third
storeroom on the right from the main stairs in the second
basement under the library." She glanced at the papers on
the table again and left, neither hurrying nor moving slowly.

Egwene felt as if she could not breathe. *We're afraid to
trust anybody, and the Amyrlin decides to trust Else Grinwell of all women?*

"That fool girl cannot be trusted not to blab to anyone
who'll listen!" Nynaeve started for the door.

Egwene grabbed up her skirts and darted past her at a
run. Her shoes skidded on the tiles of the gallery, but she
caught a glimpse of white vanishing down the nearest ramp
and dashed after it. *She must be running, too, to be so far
ahead already. Why is she running?* The flash of white
was already disappearing down another ramp. Egwene followed.

A woman turned to face her at the foot of the ramp, and
Egwene stopped in confusion. Whoever she was, this was

certainly not Else. All in silver and white silk, she sparked feelings Egwene had never had before. She was taller, more beautiful by far, and the look in her black eyes made Egwene feel small, scrawny, and none too clean. *She can probably channel more of the Power than I can, too. Light, she is probably smarter than all three of us put together on top of it. It isn't fair for one woman to*—Abruptly she realized the way her thoughts were going. Her cheeks reddened, and she gave herself a shake. She had never felt—less—than any other woman before, and she was not about to start now.

"Bold," the woman said. "You are bold to go running about so, alone, where so many murders have been done." She sounded almost pleased.

Egwene drew herself up and straightened her dress hurriedly, hoping the other woman would not notice, knowing she did, wishing the woman had not seen her running like a child. *Stop that!* "Pardon, but I am looking for a novice who came this way, I think. She has large, dark eyes and dark hair in braids. She's plump, and pretty in a way. Did you see which way she went?"

The tall woman looked her up and down in an amused way. Egwene could not be sure, but she thought the woman might have glanced a moment at the clenched fist by her side, where she still held the stone ring. "I do not think you will catch up to her. I saw her, and she was running quite fast. I suspect she is far away from here by now."

"Aes Sedai," Egwene began, but she was given no chance to ask which way Else had gone. Something that might have been anger, or annoyance, flashed through those black eyes.

"I have taken up enough time with you for now. I have more important matters to see to. Leave me." She gestured back the way Egwene had come.

So strong was the command in her voice that Egwene turned and was three steps up the ramp before she realized what she was doing. Bristling, she spun back. *Aes Sedai or no, I*—

The gallery was empty.

Frowning, she dismissed the nearest doors—no one lived in those rooms, except possibly mice—and ran down the ramp, peered both ways, followed the curve of the gallery with her eyes all the way around. She even peered over the rail, down into the small Garden of the Accepted, and studied the other galleries, higher as well as lower. She saw two Accepted in their banded dresses, one Faolain and the other a woman she knew by sight if not name. But there was no woman in silver and white anywhere.

CHAPTER
26

Behind a Lock

S haking her head, Egwene walked back to the doors
she had dismissed. *She had to go somewhere.* Inside
the first, the few furnishings were shapeless mounds
under dusty cloths, and the air seemed stale, as if the door
had not been opened in some time. She grimaced; there
were mouse tracks in the dust on the floor. But no others.
Two more doors, opened hastily, showed the same thing. It
was no surprise. There were many more empty rooms than
occupied in the Accepted's galleries.

When she pulled her head out of the third room, Nynaeve
and Elayne were coming down the ramp behind her with no
particular haste.

"Is she hiding?" Nynaeve asked in surprise. "In there?"

"I lost her." Egwene peered both ways along the curving
gallery again. *Where did she go?* She did not mean Else.

"If I had thought Else could outrun you," Elayne said
with a smile, "I'd have chased her, too, but she has always
looked too plump for running to me." Her smile was worried, though.

"We will have to find her later," Nynaeve said, "and
make sure she knows to keep her mouth shut. How could
the Amyrlin trust that girl?"

"I thought I was right on top of her," Egwene said slowly,
"but it was someone else. Nynaeve, I turned my back for
a moment, and she was gone. Not Else—I never even saw
her!—the woman I thought was Else at first. She was just—
gone, and I don't know where."

Elayne's breath caught. "One of the Soulless?" She

looked around hastily, but the gallery was still empty except for the three of them.

"Not her," Egwene said firmly. "She—" *I am not going to tell them she made me feel six years old, with a torn dress, a dirty face, and a runny nose.* "She was no Gray Man. She was tall and striking, with black eyes and black hair. You'd notice her in a crowd of a thousand. I have never seen her before, but I think she is Aes Sedai. She must be."

Nynaeve waited, as though for more, then said impatiently, "If you see her again, point her out to me. If you think there's cause. We've no time to stand here talking. I mean to see what is in that storeroom before Else has a chance to tell the wrong person about it. Maybe they were careless. Let's not give them a chance to correct it, if they were."

As she fell in beside Nynaeve, with Elayne on the other side, Egwene realized she still had the stone ring—*Corianin Nedeal's* ter'angreal—clutched in her fist. Reluctantly, she tucked it into her pouch and pulled the drawstrings tight. *As long as I don't go to sleep with the bloody—But that's what I am planning, isn't it?*

But that was for tonight, and no use worrying about it now. As they made their way through the Tower, she kept an eye out for the woman in silver and white. She was not sure why she was relieved not to see her. *I am a grown woman, and quite capable, thank you.* Still, she was just as glad that no one they encountered looked even remotely like her. The more she thought of the woman, the more she felt there was something—wrong—about her. *Light, I am starting to see the Black Ajah under my bed. Only, maybe they* are *under the bed.*

The library stood a little apart from the tall, thick shaft of the White Tower proper, its pale stone heavily streaked with blue, and it looked much like crashing waves frozen at their climax. Those waves loomed as large as a palace in the morning light, and Egwene knew they certainly contained as many rooms as one, but all those rooms—those below the odd corridors in the upper levels, where Verin had her chambers—were filled with shelves, and the shelves filled with books, manuscripts, papers, scrolls, maps, and charts, collected from every nation over the course of three thousand years. Not even the great libraries in Tear and Cairhien held so many.

The librarians—Brown sisters all—guarded those shelves, and guarded the doors as closely, to make sure not a scrap of paper left unless they knew who took it and why. But it was not to one of the guarded entrances that Nynaeve led Egwene and Elayne.

Around the foundations of the library, lying flat to the ground in the shade of tall pecan trees, were other doors, both large and small. Laborers sometimes needed access to the storerooms beneath, and the librarians did not approve of sweating men tracking through their preserve. Nynaeve pulled up one of those, no bigger than the front door of a farmhouse, and motioned the others down a steep flight of stairs descending into darkness. When she let it down behind them, all light vanished.

Egwene opened herself to *saidar*—it came so smoothly that she barely realized what she was doing—and channeled a trickle of the Power that flooded through her. For a moment the mere feel of that rush surging within her threatened to overwhelm other sensations. A small ball of bluish-white light appeared, balanced in the air above her hand. She took a deep breath and reminded herself of why she was walking stiffly. It was a link to the rest of the world. The feel of her linen shift against her skin returned, of woolen stockings, and her dress. With a small pang of regret, she banished the desire to pull in more, to let *saidar* absorb her.

Elayne made a glowing sphere for herself at the same time, and the pair provided more light than two lanterns would have. "It feels so—wonderful, doesn't it?" she murmured.

"Be careful," Egwene said.

"I am." Elayne sighed. "It just feels. . . . I will be careful."

"This way," Nynaeve told them sharply and brushed by to lead them down. She did not go too far ahead. She was not angry, and had to use the light the other two provided.

The dusty side corridor by which they had entered, lined with wooden doors set in gray stone walls, took nearly a hundred paces to reach the much wider main hall that ran the length of the library. Their lights showed footprints overlaying footprints in the dust, most from the large boots men would wear and most themselves faded by dust. The ceiling was higher here, and some of the doors nearly large enough for a barn. The main stairs at the end, half the width of the hall, were where large things were brought down. Another flight beside them led deeper. Nynaeve took it without a pause.

Egwene followed quickly. The bluish light washed out Elayne's face, but Egwene thought it still looked paler than it should. *We could scream our lungs out down here, and no one would hear a whimper.*

She felt a lightning bolt form, or the potential for one, and nearly stumbled. She had never before channeled two flows at once; it did not seem difficult at all.

The main hall of the second basement was much like the first level, wide and dusty but with a lower ceiling. Nynaeve hurried to the third door on the right and stopped.

The door was not large, but its rough wooden planks somehow gave an impression of thickness. A round iron lock hung from a length of stout chain that was drawn tight through two thick staples, one in the door, the other cemented into the wall. Lock and chain alike had the look of newness; there was almost no dust on them.

"A lock!" Nynaeve jerked at it; the chain had no give, and neither did the lock. "Did either of you see a lock anywhere else?" She pulled it again, then flung it against the door hard enough to bounce. The bang echoed down the hall. "I did not see one other locked door!" She pounded a fist on the rough wood. "Not one!"

"Calm yourself," Elayne said. "There is no need to throw a tantrum. I could open the lock myself, if I could see how the inside of it works. We will open it some way."

"I do not want to calm myself," Nynaeve snapped. "I want to be furious! I want . . . !"

Letting the rest of the tirade fade from her awareness, Egwene touched the chain. She had learned more things than how to make lightning bolts since leaving Tar Valon. One was an affinity for metal. That came from Earth, one of the Five Powers few women had much strength in—the other was Fire—but she had it, and she could feel the chain, feel *inside* the chain, feel the tiniest bits of the cold metal, the patterns they made. The Power within her quivered in time to the vibrations of those patterns.

"Move out of my way, Egwene."

She looked around and saw Nynaeve wrapped in the glow of *saidar* and holding a prybar so close in color to the blue-white of the light that it was nearly invisible. Nynaeve frowned at the chain, muttered something about leverage, and the prybar was suddenly twice as long.

"Move, Egwene."

Egwene moved.

Thrusting the end of the prybar through the chain, Nynaeve braced it, then heaved with all her strength. The chain snapped like thread, Nynaeve gasped and stumbled halfway across the hall in surprise, and the prybar clattered to the floor. Straightening, Nynaeve stared from the bar to the chain in amazement. The prybar vanished.

"I think I did something to the chain," Egwene said. *And I wish I knew what.*

"You could have said something," Nynaeve muttered. She pulled the rest of the chain from the staples and threw open the door. "Well? Are you going to stand there all day?"

The dusty room inside was perhaps ten paces square, but it held only a heap of large bags made of heavy brown cloth, each stuffed full, tagged, and sealed with the Flame of Tar Valon. Egwene did not have to count them to know there were thirteen.

She moved her ball of light to the wall and fastened it there; she was not certain how she did it, but when she took her hand away, the light remained. *I keep learning how to do things without knowing what they are*, she thought nervously.

Elayne frowned at her as if considering, then hung her light on the wall, too. Watching, Egwene thought she saw what it was she had done. *She learned it from me, but I just learned it from her.* She shivered.

Nynaeve went straight to tumbling the bags apart and reading the tags. "Rianna. Joiya Byir. These are what we are after." She examined the seal on one bag, then broke the wax and unwound the binding cords. "At least we know no one's been here before us."

Egwene chose a bag and broke the seal without reading the name on the tag. She did not really want to know whose possessions she was searching. When she upended them onto the dusty floor, they proved to be mainly old clothes and shoes, with a few ripped and crumpled papers of the sort that might hide under the wardrobe of a woman who was not too assiduous in seeing her rooms cleaned. "I don't see anything useful here. A cloak that would not do for rags. A torn half of a map of some city. Tear, it says in the corner. Three stockings that need darning." She stuck her finger through the hole in a velvet slipper that had no mate and waggled it at the others. "This one left no clues behind."

"Amico did not leave anything, either," Elayne said glumly, tossing clothes aside with both hands. "It might as well be rags. Wait, here's a book. Whoever bundled these up must have been in a hurry to toss in a book. *Customs and Ceremonies of the Tairen Court.* The cover is torn off, but the librarians will want it anyway." The librarians certainly would. No one threw away books, no matter how badly damaged.

"Tear," Nynaeve said in a flat voice. Kneeling amid the clutter from the bag she was searching, she retrieved a scrap of paper she had already thrown away. "A list of trading ships on the Erinin, with the dates they sailed from Tar Valon and the dates they were expected to arrive in Tear."

"It could be coincidence," Egwene said slowly.

"Perhaps," Nynaeve said. She folded the paper and tucked it up her sleeve, then broke the seal on another bag.

When they finally finished, every bag searched twice and discarded rubbish heaped around the edges of the room, Egwene sat down on one of the empty bags, so engrossed that she barely noticed her own wince. Drawing up her knees, she studied the little collection they had made, all laid in a row.

"It is too much," Elayne said. "There is too much of it."

"Too much," Nynaeve agreed.

There was a second book, a tattered, leather-bound volume entitled *Observations on a Visit to Tear*, with half its pages falling out. Caught in the lining of a badly torn cloak in Chesmal Emry's bag, where it might have slipped through a rip in one of the pockets of the cloak, had been another list of trading vessels. It said no more than the names, but they were all on the other list, too, and according to that, those vessels all had sailed in the early morning after the night Liandrin and the others left the Tower. There was a hastily sketched plan of some large building, with one room faintly noted as "Heart of the Stone," and a page with the names of five inns, the word "Tear" heading the page badly smudged but barely readable. There was. . . .

"There's something from everyone," Egwene muttered. "Every one of them left something pointing to a journey to Tear. How could anyone miss seeing it, if they looked? Why did the Amyrlin say nothing of this?"

"The Amyrlin," Nynaeve said bitterly, "keeps her own counsel, and what matter if we burn for it!" She drew a deep breath, and sneezed from the dust they had stirred up. "What worries me is that I am looking at bait."

"Bait?" Egwene said. But she saw it as soon as she spoke.

Nynaeve nodded. "Bait. A trap. Or maybe a diversion. But trap or diversion, it's so obvious no one could be taken in by it."

"Unless they do not care whether whoever found this saw the trap or not." Uncertainty tinged Elayne's voice. "Or perhaps they meant it to be so obvious that whoever found it would dismiss Tear immediately."

Egwene wished she could not believe that the Black Ajah could be as sure of themselves as that. She realized she was gripping her pouch in her fingers, running her thumb along the twisted curve of the stone ring inside. "Perhaps they meant to taunt whoever found it," she said softly. "Perhaps they thought whoever found this would rush headlong after them, in anger and pride." *Did they know* we *would find it? Do they see us that way?*

"Burn me!" Nynaeve growled. It was a shock; Nynaeve never used such language.

For a time they simply stared in silence at the array.

"What do we do now?" Elayne asked finally.

Egwene squeezed the ring hard. Dreaming was closely linked to Foretelling; the future, and events in other places, could appear in a Dreamer's dreams. "Maybe we will know after tonight."

Nynaeve looked at her, silent and expressionless, then chose out a dark skirt that seemed not to have too many holes and rips, and began bundling in it the things they had found. "For now," she said, "we will take this back to my room and hide it. I think we just have time, if we don't want to be late to the kitchens."

Late, Egwene thought. The longer she held the ring through her pouch, the greater the urgency she felt. *We're already a step behind, but maybe we won't be too late.*

CHAPTER

27

Tel'aran'rhiod

The room Egwene had been given, on the same gallery with Nynaeve and Elayne, was little different from Nynaeve's. Her bed was a trifle wider, her table a little smaller. Her bit of rug had flowers instead of scrolls. That was all. After the novices' quarters, it seemed like a room in a palace, but when the three of them gathered there late that night, Egwene wished she were back on the novice galleries, with no ring on her finger and no bands on her dress. The others looked as nervous as she felt.

They had worked in the kitchens for two more meals, and in between tried to puzzle out the meaning of what they had found in the storeroom. Was it a trap, or an attempt to divert the search? Did the Amyrlin know of the things, and if she did, why had she not mentioned them? Talking provided no answers, and the Amyrlin never appeared so they could ask her.

Verin had come into the kitchens after the midday meal, blinking as if she were not sure why she was there. When she saw Egwene and the other two on their knees among the cauldrons and kettles, she looked surprised for a moment, then walked over and asked, loud enough for anyone to hear, "Have you found anything?"

Elayne, with her head and shoulders inside a huge soup kettle, banged her head on the rim backing out. Her blue eyes seemed to take up her entire face.

"Nothing but grease and sweat, Aes Sedai," Nynaeve said. The tug she gave her braid left a smear of greasy soap suds on her dark hair, and she grimaced.

Verin nodded as if that were the answer she had been seeking. "Well, keep looking." She peered around the kitchen again, frowning as though puzzled to find herself there, and left.

Alanna came to the kitchens after midday, too, collecting a bowl of big green gooseberries and a pitcher of wine, and Elaida, then Sheriam, appeared after supper, and Anaiya, too.

Alanna had asked Egwene if she wanted to know more of the Green Ajah, inquired when they were going to get on with their studies. Just because the Accepted chose their own lessons and pace did not mean they were not supposed to do any at all. The first few weeks would be bad, of course, but they had to choose, or the choosing would be done for them.

Elaida merely stood for a time, stern-faced and staring at them, hands on her hips, and Sheriam did the same in almost the identical pose. Anaiya stood the same way, but her look was more concerned. Until she saw them glancing at her. Then her face became a match for Elaida's and Sheriam's before her.

None of those visits meant anything that Egwene could see. The Mistress of Novices certainly had reason to check on them, as well as on the novices working in the kitchens, and Elaida had reason to keep an eye on the Daughter-Heir of Andor. Egwene tried not to think of the Aes Sedai's interest in Rand. As for Alanna, she was not the only Aes Sedai who came for a tray to take back to her rooms rather than eat with the others. Half the sisters in the Tower were too busy for meals, too busy to take the time to summon a servant to fetch a tray. And Anaiya . . . ? Anaiya could well be concerned for her Dreamer. Not that she would do anything to ease a punishment set by the Amyrlin Seat herself. That could have been Anaiya's reason for coming. It could have been.

Hanging her dress in the wardrobe, Egwene told herself once again that even Verin's slip could have been perfectly ordinary; the Brown sister was often absentminded. *If it was a slip.* Sitting on the edge of her bed, she pulled up her shift and began rolling down her stockings. She was almost beginning to dislike white as much as she did gray.

Nynaeve stood in front of the fireplace with Egwene's

pouch in one hand, tugging her braid. Elayne sat by the table, making nervous conversation.

"Green Ajah," the golden-haired woman said for what Egwene thought must be the twentieth time since midday. "I might choose Green Ajah myself, Egwene. Then I can have three or four Warders, perhaps marry one of them. Who better for Prince Consort of Andor than a Warder? Unless it is. . . ." She trailed off, blushing.

Egwene felt a pang of jealousy she thought she had put down long ago, and sympathy mixed with it. *Light, how can I be jealous when I cannot look at Galad without shivering and feeling as if I am melting, both at the same time? Rand was mine, but no more. I wish I could give him to you, Elayne, but he is not for either of us, I think. It may be all well and good for the Daughter-Heir to marry a commoner, as long as he's an Andorman, but not to marry the Dragon Reborn.* She let the stockings fall on the floor, telling herself there were more important things to worry about tonight than neatness. "I am ready, Nynaeve."

Nynaeve handed her the pouch, and a long, thin strip of leather. "Perhaps it will work for more than one at once. I could . . . go with you, perhaps."

Emptying the stone ring onto her palm, Egwene threaded the leather strip through it, then tied it around her neck. The stripes and flecks of blue and brown and red seemed more vivid against the white of her shift. "And leave Elayne to watch over the both of us alone? When the Black Ajah may know us?"

"I can do it," Elayne said stoutly. "Or let me go with you, and Nynaeve can keep guard. She is the strongest of us, when she's angry, and if there is need for a guard, you can be sure she will be."

Egwene shook her head. "What if it won't work for two? What if two of us trying makes it not work at all? We would not even know till we woke up, and then we've wasted the night. We cannot waste even one if we are to catch up. We're too far behind them already." They were valid reasons, and she believed them, but there was another, closer to her heart. "Besides, I'll feel better knowing both of you are watching over me, in case. . . ."

She did not want to say it. In case someone came while she was asleep. The Gray Men. The Black Ajah. Any one of the things that had turned the White Tower from a place of safety to a dark woods full of pits and snares. Something coming in while she lay there helpless. Their faces showed they understood.

As she stretched herself out on the bed and plumped a feather pillow behind her head, Elayne moved the chairs, one to either side of the bed. Nynaeve snuffed the candles one by one, then, in the dark, sat in one of the chairs. Elayne took the other.

Egwene closed her eyes and tried to think sleepy thoughts, but she was too conscious of the thing lying between her breasts. Far more conscious than of any soreness remaining from her visit to Sheriam's study. The ring seemed to weigh as much as a brick, now, and thoughts of home and quiet pools of water all slid apart with remembrance of it. Of *Tel'aran'rhiod.* The Unseen World. The World of Dreams. Waiting just the other side of sleep.

Nynaeve began to hum softly. Egwene recognized a nameless, wordless tune her mother used to hum to her when she was little. When she was lying in bed, in her own room, with a fluffy pillow, and warm blankets, and the mingled smells of rose oil and baking from her mother, and. . . . *Rand, are you all right? Perrin? Who was she?* Sleep came.

She stood among rolling hills quilted with wildflowers and dotted with small thickets of leafy trees in the hollows and on the crests. Butterflies floated above the blossoms, wings flashing yellow and blue and green, and two larks sang to each other nearby. Just enough fluffy white clouds drifted in a soft blue sky, and the breeze held that delicate balance between cool and warm that came only a few special days in spring. It was a day too perfect to be anything but a dream.

She looked at her dress, and laughed delightedly. Exactly her favorite shade of sky-blue silk, slashed with white in the skirt—that changed to green as she frowned momentarily—sewn with rows of tiny pearls down the sleeves and across the bosom. She stuck out a foot just to peek at the toe of a velvet slipper. The only jarring note was the twisted ring of multicolored stone hanging around her neck on a leather cord.

She took the ring in her hand and gasped. It felt as light

as a feather. If she tossed it up, she was sure it would drift away like thistledown. Somehow, she did not feel afraid of it any longer. She tucked it inside the neck of her dress to get it out of the way.

"So this is Verin's *Tel'aran'rhiod*," she said. "Corianin Nedeal's World of Dreams. It does not look dangerous to me." But Verin had said it was. Black Ajah or not, Egwene did not see how any Aes Sedai could tell a lie right out. *She could be mistaken.* But she did not believe Verin was.

Just to see if she could, she opened herself to the One Power. *Saidar* filled her. Even here, it was present. She channeled the flow lightly, delicately, directed it into the breeze, swirling butterflies into fluttering spirals of color, into circles linked with circles.

Abruptly she let it go. The butterflies settled back, unconcerned by their brief adventure. Myrddraal and some other Shadowspawn could sense someone channeling. Looking around, she could not imagine such things in that place, but just because she could not imagine them did not mean they were not there. And the Black Ajah had all those *ter'angreal* studied by Corianin Nedeal. It was a sickening reminder of why she was there.

"At least I know I can channel," she muttered. "I'm not learning anything standing here. Perhaps if I look around. . . ." She took a step . . .

. . . and was standing in the dank, dark hallway of an inn. She was an innkeeper's daughter; she was sure it was an inn. There was not a sound, and all the doors along the hall were shut tight. Just as she wondered who was behind the plain wooden door in front of her, it swung silently open.

The room within was bare, and cold wind moaned through open windows, stirring old ash on the hearth. A big dog lay curled up on the floor, shaggy tail across its nose, between the door and a thick pillar of rough-cut, black stone that stood in the middle of the floor. A large, shaggy-haired young man sat leaning back against the pillar in only his smallclothes, head lolling as if asleep. A massive black chain ran around the pillar and across his chest, the ends gripped in his clenched hands. Asleep or not, his heavy muscles strained to hold that chain tight, to prison himself against the pillar.

"Perrin?" she said wonderingly. She stepped into the room. "Perrin, what's the matter with you? Perrin!" The dog uncurled itself and stood.

It was not a dog, but a wolf, all black and gray, lips curling back from glistening white teeth, yellow eyes regarding her as they might have a mouse. A mouse it meant to eat.

Egwene stepped back hastily into the hall in spite of herself. "Perrin! Wake up! There's a wolf!" Verin had said what happened here was real, and showed the scar to prove it. The wolf's teeth looked as big as knives. "Perrin, wake up! Tell it I'm a friend!" She embraced *saidar*. The wolf stalked nearer.

Perrin's head came up; his eyes opened drowsily. Two sets of yellow eyes regarded her. The wolf gathered himself. "Hopper," Perrin shouted, "no! Egwene!"

The door swung shut before her face, and total darkness enveloped her.

She could not see, but she felt sweat beading on her forehead. Not from heat. *Light, where am I? I don't like this place. I want to wake up!*

A whirring sound, and she jumped before she recognized a cricket. A frog gave a bass croak in the darkness, and a chorus answered it. As her eyes adapted, she dimly made out trees all around her. Clouds blanketed the stars, and the moon was a thin sliver.

Off to her right through the woods was another glow, flickering. A campfire.

She considered a moment before moving. Wanting to wake up had not been enough to take her way from *Tel'aran'rhiod*, and she still had not found out anything useful. And she had not been hurt in any way. *So far*, she thought, shivering. But she had no idea who—or what—was at that campfire. *It could be Myrddraal. Besides, I'm not dressed for running around in the forest.* It was the last thought that decided her; she prided herself on knowing when she was being foolish.

Taking a deep breath, she gathered up her silken skirts and crept closer. She might not have Nynaeve's skill at woodcraft, but she knew enough to avoid stepping on dead twigs. At last she peered carefully around the trunk of an old oak at the campfire.

The only one there was a tall young man, sitting and staring into the flames. Rand. Those flames did not burn wood. They did not burn anything that she could see. The fire danced above a bare patch of ground. She did not think they even scorched the soil.

Before she could move, Rand raised his head. She was surprised to see he was smoking a pipe, a thin ribbon of tabac smoke lifting from the bowl. He looked tired, so very tired.

"Who's out there?" he demanded loudly. "You've rustled enough leaves to wake the dead, so you might as well show yourself."

Egwene's lips compressed, but she stepped out. *I did not!* "It's me, Rand. Do not be afraid. It is a dream. I must be in your dreams."

He was on his feet so suddenly that she stopped dead. He seemed in some way larger than she remembered. And a touch dangerous. Perhaps more than a touch. His blue-gray eyes seemed to burn like frozen fire.

"Do you think I don't know it is a dream?" he sneered. "I know that makes it no less real." He stared angrily out into the darkness as if looking for someone. "How long will you try?" he shouted at the night. "How many faces will you send? My mother, my father, now her! Pretty girls won't tempt me with a kiss, not even one I know! I deny you, Father of Lies! I deny you!"

"Rand," she said uncertainly. "It's Egwene. I am Egwene."

There was a sword in his hands, suddenly, out of nowhere. Its blade was worked out of a single flame, slightly curved and graven with a heron. "My mother gave me honeycake," he said in a tight voice, "with the smell of poison rank on it. My father had a knife for my ribs. She—she offered kisses, and more." Sweat slicked his face; his stare seemed enough to set her afire. "What do you bring?"

"You are going to listen to me, Rand al'Thor, if I have to sit on you." She gathered *saidar*, channeled the flows to make the air hold him in a net.

The sword spun in his hands, roaring like an open furnace.

She grunted and staggered; it felt as if a rope stretched too tight had broken and snapped back into her.

Rand laughed. "I learn, you see. When it works. . . ." He grimaced and started toward her. "I could stand any face but that one. Not her face, burn you!" The sword flashed out.

Egwene fled.

She was not sure what it was she did, or how, but she found herself back among the rolling hills under a sunny sky, with larks singing and butterflies playing. She drew a deep, shuddering breath.

I've learned. . . . What? That the Dark One is still after Rand? I knew that already. That maybe the Dark One wants to kill him? That's different. Unless maybe he's gone mad already, and does not know what he is saying. Light, why couldn't I help him? Oh, Light, Rand!

She took another long breath to calm herself. "The only way to help him is to gentle him," she muttered. "As well go ahead and kill him." Her stomach twisted and knotted. "I'll never do that. Never!"

A redbird had perched on a cloudberry bush nearby, crest lifting as it tilted its head to watch her cautiously. She addressed the bird. "Well, I am not helping anything standing here talking to myself, am I? Or talking to you, either."

The redbird took wing as she stepped toward the bush. It was still a flash of crimson as she took the next step, vanished into a thicket as she took a third.

She stopped and fished the stone ring on its cord out of the front of her dress. Why was it not changing? Everything had changed so fast up till now that she could hardly catch her breath. Why not now? Unless there was some answer right here? She looked around uncertainly. The wildflowers taunted her, and the larksong mocked her. This place seemed too much of her own making.

Determined, she tightened her hand around the *ter'angreal*. "Take me where I need to be." She shut her eyes and concentrated on the ring. It was stone, after all; Earth should give her some feeling for it. "Do it. Take me where I need to be." Once again she embraced *saidar*, fed a trickle of the One Power into the ring. She knew it did not need any flow of Power directed at it to work, and she did not try to do anything to it. Only to give it more of the Power to use. "Take me to where I can find an answer. I need to know what the Black Ajah wants. Take me to the answer."

"Well, you've found your way at last, child. All sorts of answers here."

Egwene's eyes snapped open. She stood in a great hall, its vast domed ceiling supported by a forest of massive red-stone columns. And hanging in midair was a sword of crystal, gleaming and sparkling as it slowly revolved. She was not certain, but she thought it might be the sword Rand had been reaching for in that dream. That other dream. This all felt so real, she had to keep reminding herself it was a dream, too.

An old woman stepped out of the shadows of the column, bent and hobbling with a stick. Ugly did not begin to describe her. She had a bony, pointed chin, an even bonier, sharper nose, and it seemed there were more warts growing hairs on her face than there was face.

"Who are you?" Egwene said. The only people she had seen so far in *Tel'aran'rhiod* were those she already knew, but she did not think she could have forgotten this poor old woman.

"Just poor old Silvie, my Lady," the old woman cackled. At the same time she managed a stoop that might have been meant for a curtsy, or possibly a cringe. "You know poor old Silvie, my Lady. Served your family faithfully all these years. Does this old face still frighten you? Don't let it, my Lady. It serves me, when I need it, as good as a prettier."

"Of course, it does," Egwene said. "It's a strong face. A good face." She hoped the woman believed it. Whoever this Silvie was, she seemed to think she knew Egwene. Perhaps she knew answers, too. "Silvie, you said something about finding answers here."

"Oh, you've come to the right place for answers, my Lady. The Heart of the Stone is full of answers. And secrets. The High Lords would not be pleased to see us here, my Lady. Oh, no. None but the High Lords enter here. And servants, of course." She gave a sly, screeching laugh. "The High Lords don't sweep and mop. But who sees a servant?"

"What kind of secrets?"

But Silvie was hobbling toward the crystal sword. "Plots," she said as if to herself. "All of them pretending to serve the Great Lord, and all the while plotting and planning to regain what they lost. Each one thinking he or she is the only one plotting. Ishamael is a fool!"

"What?" Egwene said sharply. "What did you say about Ishamael?"

The old woman turned to present a crooked, ingratiating smile. "Just a thing poor folks say, my Lady. It turns the Forsaken's power, calling them fools. Makes you feel good, and safe. Even the Shadow can't take being called a fool. Try it, my Lady. Say, Ba'alzamon is a fool!"

Egwene's lips twitched on the edge of a smile. "Ba'alzamon is a fool! You are right, Silvie." It actually did feel good, laughing at the Dark One. The old woman chuckled. The sword revolved just beyond her shoulder. "Silvie, what is that?"

"*Callandor*, my Lady. You know that, don't you? The Sword That Cannot Be Touched." Abruptly she swung her stick behind her; a foot from the sword, the stick stopped with a dull *thwack* and bounded back. Silvie grinned wider. "The Sword That Is Not a Sword, though there's precious few knows what it is. But none can touch it save one. They saw to that, who put it here. The Dragon Reborn will hold *Callandor* one day, and prove to the world he's the Dragon by doing it. The first proof, anyway. Lews Therin come back for all the world to see, and grovel before. Ah, the High Lords don't like having it here. They like nothing to do with the Power. They'd rid themselves of it, if they could. If they could. I suppose there's others would take it, if they could. What wouldn't one of the Forsaken give, to hold *Callandor*?"

Egwene stared at the sparkling sword. If the Prophecies of the Dragon were true, if Rand was the Dragon as Moiraine claimed, he would wield it one day, though from the rest of what she knew of the Prophecies concerning *Callandor*, she could not see how it could ever come to be. *But if there's a way to take it, maybe the Black Ajah knows how. If they know it, I can figure it out.*

Cautiously, she reached out with the Power, probing at whatever held and shielded the sword. Her probe touched— something—and stopped. She could sense which of the Five Powers had been used here. Air, and Fire, and Spirit. She could trace the intricate weave made by *saidar*, set with a strength that amazed her. There were gaps in that weave, spaces where her probe should slide through. When she tried, it was like fighting the strongest part of the weave head on. It hit her then, what she was trying to force a way through, and she let her probe vanish. Half that wall had been woven using *saidar*; the other half, the part she could not sense or touch, had been made with *saidin*. That was not it, exactly—the wall was all of one piece—but it was close enough. *A stone wall stops a blind woman as surely as one who can see it.*

Footsteps echoed in the distance. Boots.

Egwene could not tell how many there were, or from which direction they were coming, but Silvie gave a start and immediately stared off among the columns. "He's coming to stare at it again," she muttered. "Awake or asleep, he wants. . . ." She seemed to remember Egwene, and put on a worried smile. "You must leave, now, my Lady. He mustn't find you here, or even know you've been."

Egwene was already backing in among the columns, and Silvie followed, flapping her hands and waving her stick. "I am going, Silvie. I just have to remember the way." She fingered the stone ring. "Take me back to the hills." Nothing happened. She channeled a hairlike flow to the ring. "Take me back to the hills." The redstone columns still surrounded her. The boots were closer, close enough not to be swallowed in their own echoes anymore.

"You don't know the way out," Sylvie said flatly, then went on in a near whisper, ingratiating and mocking at once, an old retainer who felt she could take liberties. "Oh, my Lady, this is a dangerous place to come into, if you don't know the way out. Come, let poor old Silvie take you out. Poor old Silvie will tuck you safe in your bed, my Lady." She wrapped both arms around Egwene, urging her further from the sword. Not that Egwene needed much urging. The boots had stopped; he—whoever he was—was probably gazing at *Callandor*.

"Just show me the way," Egwene whispered back. "Or tell me. There's no need to push." The old woman's fingers had somehow gotten tangled around the stone ring. "Don't touch that, Silvie."

"Safe in your bed."

Pain annihilated the world.

With a throat-wrenching shriek, Egwene sat up in the dark, sweat rolling down her face. For a moment she had no idea where she was, and did not care. "Oh, Light," she moaned, "that hurt. Oh, Light, that hurt!" She ran her hands over herself, sure her skin must be scored or wealed to make such a burning, but she could not find a mark.

"We are here," Nynaeve's voice said from the darkness. "We're here, Egwene."

Egwene threw herself toward the voice and wrapped her arms around Nynaeve's neck in sheer relief. "Oh, Light, I'm back. Light, I'm back."

"Elayne," Nynaeve said.

In a few moments one of the candles was giving a small light. Elayne paused with the candle in hand and the spill she had lit with flint and steel in the other. Then she smiled, and every candle in the room burst into flame. She stopped at the washstand and came back to the bed with a cool, damp cloth to wash Egwene's face.

"Was it bad?" she asked worriedly. "You never stirred. You never mumbled. We did not know whether to wake you or not."

Hurriedly, Egwene fumbled the leather cord from around her neck and hurled it and the stone ring across the room. "Next time," she panted, "we decide on a time, and you wake me after it. Wake me if you have to stick my head in a basin of water!" She had not realized that she had decided there would be a next time. *Would you put your head in a bear's mouth just to show you weren't afraid? Would you do it twice just because you'd done it once and didn't die?*

Yet it was more than a matter of proving to herself that she was not afraid. She was afraid, and knew it. But so long as the Black Ajah had those *ter'angreal* Corianin had studied, she would have to keep going back. She was sure the answer to why they wanted them lay in *Tel'aran'rhiod*. If she could find answers about the Black Ajah there—perhaps other answers, too, if half what she had been told about Dreaming were true—she had to go back. "But not tonight," she said softly. "Not yet."

"What happened?" Nynaeve asked. "What did you . . . dream?"

Egwene lay back on the bed and told them. Of it all, the only thing she left out was about Perrin talking to the wolf. She left the wolf out altogether. She felt a little guilty about keeping secrets from Elayne and Nynaeve, but it was Perrin's secret to tell, when and if he chose, not hers. The rest she gave them word for word, describing everything. When she was done, she felt emptied.

"Aside from being tired," Elayne said, "did he look hurt? Egwene, I cannot believe he would ever hurt you. I cannot believe he would."

"Rand," Nynaeve said dryly, "will have to look after himself awhile longer." Elayne blushed; she looked pretty doing it. Egwene realized that Elayne looked pretty doing anything, even crying, or scrubbing pots. *"Callandor,"* Nynaeve continued. "The Heart of the Stone. That was marked on the plan. I think we know where the Black Ajah is."

Elayne had regained her poise. "It does not change the trap," she said. "If it is not a diversion, it is a trap."

Nynaeve smiled grimly. "The best way to catch whoever set a trap is to spring it and wait for him to come. Or her, in this instance."

"You mean go to Tear?" Egwene said, and Nynaeve nodded.

"The Amyrlin has cut us loose, it seems. We make our own decisions, remember? At least we know the Black Ajah is in Tear, and we know who to look for there. Here, all we can do is sit and stew in our own suspicions of everybody, wonder if there is another Gray Man out there. I would rather be the hound than the rabbit."

"I have to write to my mother," Elayne said. When she saw the looks they gave her, her voice became defensive. "I have already vanished once without her knowing where I was. If I do it again. . . . You do not know Mother's temper. She could send Gareth Bryne and the whole army against Tar Valon. Or hunting after us."

"You could stay here," Egwene said.

"No. I will not let you two go alone. And I won't stay here wondering if the sister teaching me is a Darkfriend, or if the next Gray Man will come after me." She gave a small laugh. "I will not work in the kitchens while you two are off adventuring, either. I just have to tell my mother than I am out of the Tower on the Amyrlin's orders, so she won't become furious if she hears rumors. I do not have to tell her where we are going, or why."

"You surely had better not," Nynaeve said. "She very likely would come after you if she knew about the Black Ajah. For that matter, you can't know how many hands your letter will pass through before it reaches her, or what eyes might read it. Best not to say anything you don't mind anyone knowing."

"That's another thing." Elayne sighed. "The Amyrlin does not know I am one of you. I have to find some way to send it with no chance of her seeing it."

"I will have to think on that." Nynaeve's brows furrowed. "Perhaps once we're on our way. You could leave it at Aringill on the way downriver, if we have time to find someone there going to Caemlyn. A sight of one of those papers the Amyrlin gave us might convince somebody. We will have to hope they work on ship captains, too, unless one of you has more coin than I have." Elayne shook her head dolefully.

Egwene did not even bother. What money they had possessed had all gone on the journey from Toman Head, except for a few coppers each. "When. . . ." She had to stop and clear her throat. "When do we leave? Tonight?"

Nynaeve looked as if she were considering it for a moment, but then she shook her head. "You need sleep, after. . . ." Her gesture took in the stone ring lying where it had bounced off the wall. "We will give the Amyrlin one more chance to seek us out. When we finish with breakfast, you both pack what you want to take, but keep it light. We have to leave the Tower without anyone noticing, remember. If the Amyrlin doesn't reach us by midday, I mean to be on a trading ship, shoving that paper down the captain's throat if need be, before Prime sounds. How does that sound to you two?"

"It sounds excellent," Elayne said firmly, and Egwene said, "Tonight or tomorrow, the sooner the better, as far as I can see." She wished she sounded as confident as Elayne.

"Then we had best get some sleep."

"Nynaeve," Egwene said in a small voice, "I. . . . I don't want to be alone tonight." It pained her to make that admission.

"I don't, either," Elayne said. "I keep thinking about the Soulless. I do not know why, but they frighten me even more than the Black Ajah."

"I suppose," Nynaeve said slowly, "I don't really want to be alone, myself." She eyed the bed where Egwene lay.

"That looks big enough for three, if everybody keeps her elbows to herself."

Later, when they were shifting about trying to find a way to lie that did not feel so crowded, Nynaeve suddenly laughed.

"What is it?" Egwene asked. "You are not that ticklish."

"I just thought of someone who'd be happy to carry Elayne's letter for her. Happy to leave Tar Valon, too. In fact, I'd bet on it."

CHAPTER
28

A Way Out

Clad only in his breeches, Mat was just finishing a snack after breakfast—some ham, three apples, bread, and butter—when the door of his room opened, and Nynaeve, Egwene, and Elayne filed in, all smiling at him brightly. He got up for a shirt, then stubbornly sat down again. They could at least have knocked. In any case, it was good to see their faces. At first, it was.

"Well, you do look better," Egwene said.

"As if you had had a month of good food and rest," Elayne said.

Nynaeve pressed a hand to his forehead. He flinched before he recalled that she had done much the same for at least five years, back home. *She was just the Wisdom then*, he thought. *She wasn't wearing that ring.*

She had noticed his flinch. She gave him a tight smile. "You look ready to be up and about, to me. Are you tired of being cooped up, yet? You never could stand two days in a row indoors."

He eyed the last apple core reluctantly, then dropped it back on the plate. Almost, he started to lick the juice off his fingers, but they were all three looking at him. And still smiling. He realized he was trying to decide which of them was prettiest, and could not. Had they been anybody but who—and what—they were, he would have asked any and all of them to dance a jig or a reel. He had danced with Egwene often enough, back home, and even once with Nynaeve, but that seemed a long time ago.

"'One pretty woman means fun at the dance. Two pretty women mean trouble in the house. Three pretty women mean run for the hills.'" He gave Nynaeve an even tighter smile than her own. "My da used to say that. You're up to something, Nynaeve. You are all smiling like cats staring at a finch caught in a thornbush, and I think I am the finch."

The smiles flickered and vanished. He noticed their hands and wondered why they all looked as if they had been washing dishes. The Daughter-Heir of Andor surely never washed a dish, and he had as hard a time imagining Nynaeve at it, even knowing she had done her own back in Emond's Field. They all three wore Great Serpent rings, now. That was new. And not a particularly pleasant surprise. *Light, it had to happen sometime. It's none of my business, and that is all there is to it. None of my business. It just isn't.*

Egwene shook her head, but it seemed as much for the other two women as for him. "I told you we should ask him straight out. He's stubborn as any mule when he wants to be, and tricksome as a cat. You are, Mat. You know it, so stop frowning."

He put his grin back quickly.

"Hush, Egwene," Nynaeve said. "Mat, just because we want to ask you a favor does not mean we don't care how you feel. We do care, and you know that, unless you're being even more wool-headed than usual. Are you well? You look remarkably well compared to how I last saw you. It really does look more like a month than two days."

"I'm ready to run ten miles and dance a jig at the end of it." His stomach growled, reminding him how long it was to midday yet, but he ignored it, and hoped they had not noticed. He almost did feel as if he had had a month of rest and food. And had had one meal in the last day. "What favor?" he asked suspiciously. Nynaeve did not ask favors, in his recollection; Nynaeve told people what to do and expected to see it done.

"I want you to carry a letter for me," Elayne said before Nynaeve could speak. "To my mother, in Caemlyn." She smiled, making a dimple in her cheek. "I would appreciate it so very much, Mat." The morning light through the windows seemed to pick out highlights in her hair.

I wonder if she likes to dance. He pushed the thought right out of his head. "That does not sound too very hard, but it's a long trip. What do I get out of it?" From the look on her face, he did not think that dimple had failed her very often.

She drew herself up, slim and proud. He could almost see a

throne behind her. "Are you a loyal subject of Andor? Do you not wish to serve the Lion Throne, and your Daughter-Heir?"

Mat snickered.

"I told you that would not work either," Egwene said. "Not with him."

Elayne had a wry twist to her mouth. "I thought it worth a try. It always works on the Guards, in Caemlyn. You said if I smiled—" She cut off short, very obviously not looking at him.

What did you say, Egwene, he thought, furious. *That I'm a fool for any girl who smiles at me?* He kept his outward calm, though, and managed to maintain his grin.

"I wish asking were enough," Egwene said, "but you do not do favors, do you, Mat? Have you ever done anything without being coaxed, wheedled, or bullied?"

He only smiled at her. "I will dance with both of you, Egwene, but I won't run errands." For an instant he thought she was going to stick out her tongue at him.

"If we can go back to what we planned in the first place," Nynaeve said in a too-calm voice. The other two nodded, and she turned her attentions on him. For the first time since coming in, she looked like the Wisdom of old, with a stare that could pin you in your tracks and her braid ready to lash like a cat's tail.

"You are even ruder than I remembered, Matrim Cauthon. With you sick so long—and Egwene, and Elayne, and I taking care of you like a babe in swaddling—I had almost forgotten. Even so, I would think you'd have a little gratitude in you. You've talked about seeing the world, seeing great cities. Well, what better city than Caemlyn? Do what you want, show your gratitude, and help someone all at the same time." She produced a folded parchment from inside her cloak and set it on the table. It was sealed with a lily, in golden yellow wax. "You cannot ask for more than that."

He eyed the paper regretfully. He barely remembered passing through Caemlyn, once, with Rand. It was a shame to stop them now, but he thought it best. *If you want the fun of the jig, you have to pay the harper sooner or later.* And the way Nynaeve was now, the longer he kept from paying, the worse it would be. "Nynaeve, I can't."

"What do you mean, you cannot? Are you a fly on the wall, or a man? A chance to do a favor for the Daughter-

Heir of Andor, to see Caemlyn, to meet Queen Morgase herself in all probability, and you cannot? I really do not know what more you could possibly want. Don't you skitter away like grease on a griddle this time, Matrim Cauthon! Or has your heart changed so you like seeing these all around you?" She waved her left hand in his face, practically hitting him in the nose with her ring.

"Please, Mat?" Elayne said, and Egwene was staring at him as if he had grown horns like a Trolloc.

He squirmed on his chair. "It is not that I don't want to. I cannot! The Amyrlin's made it so I can't get off the bloo— the island. Change that, and I will carry your letter in my teeth, Elayne."

Looks passed between them. He sometimes wondered if women could read each other's minds. They certainly seemed to read his when he least wanted it. But this time, whatever they had decided silently among themselves, they had not read his thoughts.

"Explain," Nynaeve said curtly. "Why would the Amyrlin want to keep you here?"

He shrugged, and looked her straight in the eye, and gave her his best rueful grin. "It's because I was sick. Because it went on so long. She said she would not let me go until she was sure I wouldn't go off somewhere and die. Not that I'm going to, of course. Die, I mean."

Nynaeve frowned, and jerked her braid, and suddenly took his head between her hands; a chill ran through him. *Light, the Power!* Before the thought was done, she had released him.

"What . . . ? What did you do to me, Nynaeve?"

"Not a tenth part of what you deserve, in all likelihood," she said. "You are as healthy as a bull. Weaker than you look, but healthy."

"I told you I was," he said uneasily. He tried to get his grin back. "Nynaeve, she looked like you. The Amyrlin, I mean. Managing to loom even if she is a foot too short for it, and bullying. . . ." The way her eyebrows climbed, he decided that was not a road to go down any further. As long as he kept them away from the Horn. He wondered if they knew. "Well. Anyway, I think they want to keep me here because of that dagger. I mean, until they figure out exactly how it did what it did. You know how Aes Sedai are." He gave a small laugh. They all just looked at him. *Maybe I shouldn't have said that. Burn me! They want to be bloody Aes Sedai. Burn me, I'm going on too long. I wish Nynaeve would stop staring at me like that. Keep it short.* "The Amyrlin made it so I cannot cross a bridge or board a ship without an order from her. You see? It's not that I do not want to help. I just can't."

"But you will if we can get you out of Tar Valon?" Nynaeve said intently.

"You get me out of Tar Valon, and I'll carry Elayne to her mother on my back."

Elayne's eyebrows went up, this time, and Egwene shook her head, mouthing his name with a sharp look in her eyes. Women had no sense of humor, sometimes.

Nynaeve motioned the two of them to follow her to the windows, where they turned their backs to him and talked so softly he could catch only a murmur. He thought he heard Egwene say something about only needing one if they stayed together. Watching, he wondered if they really thought they could get around the Amyrlin's order. *If they can do that, I will carry their bloody letter. I really will carry it in my teeth.*

Without thinking, he picked up an apple core and bit off the end. One chew, and he hastily spit the mouthful of bitter seeds back onto the plate.

When they came back to the table, Egwene handed him a thick, folded paper. He eyed them suspiciously before opening it out. As he read, he began humming to himself without knowing it.

What the bearer does is done at my order and by my authority. Obey, and keep silent, at my command.

> Siuan Sanche
> Watcher of the Seals
> Flame of Tar Valon
> The Amyrlin Seat

And sealed at the bottom with the Flame of Tar Valon in a circle of white wax as hard as stone.

He realized he was humming "A Pocket Full of Gold" and stopped. "Is this real? You didn't . . . ? How did you get this?"

"She did not forge it, if that is what you mean," Elayne said.

"Never you mind how we got it," Nynaeve said. "It is real. That is all that need concern you. I would not show it around, were I you, or the Amyrlin will take it back, but it will get you past the guards and onto a ship. You said you'd take the letter, if we did that."

"You can consider it in Morgase's hands right now." He did not want to stop reading the paper, but he folded it back up anyway, and laid it on top of Elayne's letter. "You wouldn't happen to have a little coin to go with this, would you? Some silver? A gold mark or two? I have almost enough for my passage, but I hear things are growing expensive downriver."

Nynaeve shook her head. "Don't you have money? You gambled with Hurin almost every night until you grew too sick to hold the dice. Why should things be more expensive downriver?"

"We gambled for coppers, Nynaeve, and he would not even do that after a while. It doesn't matter. I will manage. Don't you listen to what people say? There's civil war in Cairhien, and I hear it is bad in Tear, too. I've heard a room at an inn in Aringill costs more than a good horse back home."

"We have been busy," she said sharply, and exchanged worried looks with Egwene and Elayne that set him wondering again.

"It doesn't matter. I can make out." There had to be gaming in the inns near the docks. A night with the dice would put him aboard a ship in the morning with a full purse.

"Just you deliver that letter to Queen Morgase, Mat," Nynaeve said. "And do not let anyone know you have it."

"I'll take it to her. I said I would, didn't I? You would think I didn't keep my promises." The looks he got from Nynaeve and Egwene reminded him of a few he had not kept. "I will do it. Blood and—I will do it!"

They stayed awhile longer, talking of home for the most part. Egwene and Elayne sat on the bed, and Nynaeve took the armchair, while he kept his stool. Talk of Emond's Field made him homesick, and it seemed to make Nynaeve and Egwene sad, as if they were speaking of something they would never see again. He was sure their eyes moistened, but when he tried to change the subject, they brought it back again, to people they knew, to the festivals of Bel Tine and Sunday, to harvest dances and picnic gatherings for the shearing.

Elayne talked to him of Caemlyn, of what to expect at the Royal Palace and who to speak to, and a little of the city. Sometimes she held herself in a way that made him all but see a crown on her head. A man would have to be a fool to let himself get involved with a woman like her. When they rose to leave, he was sorry to see them go.

He stood, suddenly feeling awkward. "Look, you have done me a favor here." He touched the Amyrlin's paper, on the table. "A big favor. I know you're all going to be Aes Sedai"—he stumbled a little on that—"and you will be a queen one day, Elayne, but if you ever need help, if there is ever anything I can do, I will come. You can count on it. Did I say something funny?"

Elayne had a hand over her mouth, and Egwene was struggling openly with a laugh. "No, Mat," Nynaeve said smoothly, but her lips twitched. "Just something I have observed about men."

"You would have to be a woman to understand," Elayne said.

"Journey well and safely, Mat," Egwene said. "And remember, if a woman does need a hero, she needs him today, not tomorrow." The laughter bubbled out of her.

He stared at the door closing behind them. Women, he decided for at least the hundredth time, were odd.

Then his eye fell on Elayne's letter, and the folded paper lying atop it. The Amyrlin's blessed, not-to-be-understood, but welcome-as-a-fire-in-winter paper. He danced a little caper in the middle of the flowered carpet. Caemlyn to see, and a queen to meet. *Your own words will free me of you, Amyrlin. And get me away from Selene, too.*

"You'll never catch me," he laughed, and meant it for both of them. "You'll never catch Mat Cauthon."

CHAPTER
29

A Trap to Spring

I n a corner the spit dog was lying at its ease. Glaring at it, Nynaeve mopped sweat from her forehead with her hand and leaned her back into doing the work he should have done. *I'd not have put it past them to shove me in his wicker wheel instead of letting me turn this Light-forsaken handle! Aes Sedai! Burn them all!* It was a measure of her upset that she used such language, and another that she did not even notice she had done it. She did not think the fire in the long, gray stone fireplace would seem any hotter if she crawled into it. She was sure the brindle dog was grinning at her.

Elayne was skimming grease out of the dripping pan under the roasts with a long-handled wooden spoon, while Egwene used its twin to baste the meat. The great kitchen went on about its midday routine around them. Even the novices had grown so used to seeing Accepted there that they hardly even glanced at the three women. Not that the cooks allowed the novices to dawdle for gawking. Work built character, so the Aes Sedai said, and the cooks saw to it that the novices built strong character. And the three Accepted, too.

Laras, the Mistress of the Kitchens—she was really the chief cook, but so many had used the other for so long that it might as well have been her title—came over to examine the roasts. And the women sweating over them. She was more than merely stout, with layers of chins, and a spotless white apron that could have made three novice dresses. She carried her own long-handled wooden spoon like a scepter. It was not for stirring, that spoon. It was for directing

those under her, and smacking those who were not building character quickly enough to suit her. She studied the
roasts, sniffed disparagingly, and turned her frown on the
three Accepted.

Nynaeve met Laras' look with a level look of her own
and kept turning the spit. The massive woman's face never
altered. Nynaeve had tried smiling, but that did nothing to
change Laras' expression. Stopping work to speak to her,
quite civilly, had been a disaster. It was bad enough being
bullied and chivied by Aes Sedai. She had to put up with
that, however much it rankled and burned, if she was to
learn how to use her abilities. Not that she liked what she
could do—it was one thing to know Aes Sedai were not
Darkfriends for channeling the Power, but quite another to
know she herself could channel—yet she had to learn if she
was to get back at Moiraine; hating Moiraine for what she
had done to Egwene and the other Emond's Fielders, pulling their lives apart and manipulating them all for Aes Sedai purposes, was nearly all that kept her going. But to be
treated as a lazy, none-too-bright child by this Laras, to be
forced to curtsy and scurry for this woman she could have
put in her place with a few well-chosen words back home—
that made her grind her teeth almost as much as did the
thought of Moiraine. *Maybe if I just do not look at her. . . .
No! I will be burned if I'll drop my eyes before this . . . this
cow!*

Laras sniffed more loudly and walked away. She rolled
from side to side as she crossed the freshly mopped gray
tiles.

Still bending with spoon and greasepot, Elayne glowered
after her. "If that woman strikes me but once more, I shall
have Gareth Bryne arrest her and—"

"Be quiet," Egwene whispered. She did not stop basting
the roasts, and she never looked at Elayne. "She has ears
like a—"

Laras turned back as if she had indeed heard, her frown
deepening, and her mouth opened wide. Before a sound
emerged, the Amyrlin Seat entered the kitchen like a whirlwind. Even the striped stole on her shoulders seemed to
bristle. For once, Leane was nowhere to be seen.

At last, Nynaeve thought grimly. *And not beforetime, either!*

But the Amyrlin did not glance her way. The Amyrlin did not say a word to anyone. Running her hand across a tabletop scrubbed bone-white, she looked at her fingers and grimaced as if at filth. Laras was at her side in an instant, all smiles, but the Amyrlin's flat stare made her swallow them in silence.

The Amyrlin stalked about the kitchen. She stared at the women slicing oatcake. She glared at the women peeling vegetables. She sneered into the soup kettles, then at the women tending them; the women became engrossed in studying the surface of the soup. Her frown set the girls carrying plates and bowls out to the dining hall to a run. Her glower put the novices darting like mice sighting a cat. By the time she had made her way half around the kitchen, every woman there was working twice as fast as she had been. By the time she completed her circuit, Laras was the only one even daring to glance at her.

The Amyrlin stopped in front of the roasting spit, fists on her hips, and looked at Laras. She only looked, expression-less, blue eyes cold and hard.

The large woman gulped, and her chins wobbled as she smoothed her apron. The Amyrlin did not blink. Laras' eyes dropped, and she shifted heavily from foot to foot. "If the Mother will pardon me," she said in a faint voice. Making something that might have been meant for a curtsy, she rushed away, so forgetting herself that she joined the women at one of the soup kettles and began stirring with her own spoon.

Nynaeve smiled, keeping her head down to hide it. Egwene and Elayne kept working, too, but they also kept glancing at the Amyrlin, standing with her back to them not two paces away.

The Amyrlin was spreading her stare across the entire kitchen from where she stood. "If they are this easily cowed," she muttered softly, "perhaps they really have been getting away with too much for too long."

Easily cowed indeed, Nynaeve thought. *Pitiful excuses for women. All she did was look at them!* The Amyrlin glanced over a stole-covered shoulder, caught her eye for an instant. Suddenly Nynaeve realized she was turning the spit faster. She told herself she had to pretend to be cowed like everyone else.

The Amyrlin's gaze fell on Elayne, and abruptly she spoke, nearly loud enough to rattle the copper pots and pans hanging on the walls. "There are some words I will not tolerate in a young woman's mouth, Elayne of House Trakand. If you let them in, I will see them scrubbed out!" Everyone in the kitchen jumped.

Elayne looked confused, and indignation crept across Egwene's face.

Nynaeve shook her head, small frantic shakes. *No, girl! Hold your tongue! Don't you see what she is doing?*

But Egwene did open her mouth, with a respectful if determined, "Mother, she did not—"

"Silence!" The Amyrlin's roar produced another ripple of jumps. "Laras! Can you find something to teach two girls to speak when they should and say what they should, *Mistress* of the Kitchens? Can you manage that?"

Laras came waddling faster than Nynaeve had ever seen the woman move before, darting at Elayne and Egwene to seize an ear of each, all the while repeating, "Yes, Mother. Immediately, Mother. As you command, Mother." She hurried the two young women out of the kitchen as if eager to escape the Amyrlin's stare.

The Amyrlin was now close enough to Nynaeve to touch her, but still looking over the kitchen. A young cook, turning with a mixing bowl in her hands, chanced to catch the Amyrlin's eye. She gave a great squeak as she scuttled away across the floor.

"I did not mean for Egwene to be caught in that." The Amyrlin barely moved her lips. It looked as if she were muttering to herself, and from the expression on her face, no one in the kitchen wanted to hear what she was saying. Nynaeve could just make out the words. "But perhaps it will teach her to think before she speaks."

Nynaeve turned the spit and kept her head down, trying to look as if she were also muttering under her breath if anyone looked. "I thought you were going to keep a close eye on us, Mother. So we could report what we find."

"If I come stare at you every day, Daughter, some would grow suspicious." The Amyrlin kept up her study of the kitchen. Most of the women seemed to be avoiding even looking in her direction for fear of incurring her wrath. "I planned to have you brought to my study after the midday meal. To scold you for not choosing your studies, so I implied to Leane. But there is news that could not wait. Sheriam found another Gray Man. A woman. Dead as last week's fish, and not a mark on her. She was laid out as if resting, right in the middle of Sheriam's bed. Not very pleasant for Sheriam."

Nynaeve stiffened, and the spit halted for a moment before she put it back to revolving. "Sheriam had a chance to see the lists Verin gave to Egwene. So did Elaida. I make no accusations, but they had the chance. And Egwene said Alanna . . . behaved oddly, too."

"She told you of that, did she? Alanna is Arafellin. They have strange ideas about honor and debts in Arafel." She shrugged dismissively, but said, "I suppose I can keep an eye on her. Have you learned anything useful yet, child?"

"Some," Nynaeve muttered grimly. *What about keeping an eye on Sheriam? Maybe she didn't just find that Gray Man. The Amyrlin could watch Elaida, too, for that matter. So Alanna really did. . . .* "I do not understand why you trust Else Grinwell, but your message was helpful."

In short, quick sentences, Nynaeve told of the things they had found in the storeroom under the library, making it seem only she and Egwene had gone, and added the conclusions they had reached concerning them. She did not mention Egwene's dream—or whatever it had been; Egwene insisted it had been real—of *Tel'aran'rhiod*. Nor did she speak of the *ter'angreal* Verin had given Egwene. She could not make herself entirely trust the woman wearing the seven-striped stole—or any woman who could wear the shawl, for that matter—and it seemed best to keep some things in reserve.

When she was done, the Amyrlin was silent so long that Nynaeve began to think the woman had not heard. She was about to repeat herself, a little louder, when the Amyrlin finally spoke, still hardly moving her lips.

"I sent no message, Daughter. The things Liandrin and the others left were searched thoroughly, and burned after nothing was found. No one would use Black Ajah leavings. As for Else Grinwell. . . . I remember the girl. She could have learned, had she applied herself, but all she wanted was to smile at the men at the Warders' practice yard. Else

Grinwell was put on a trading vessel and sent back to her mother ten days ago."

Nynaeve tried to swallow the lump that had formed in her throat. The Amyrlin's words made her think of bullies taunting smaller children. The bullies were always so contemptuous of the littler children, always so sure the small ones were too stupid to realize what was happening, that they made little effort to disguise their snares. That the Black Ajah was so contemptuous of her made her blood boil. That they could set this snare filled her stomach with ice. *Light, if Else was sent away. . . . Light, anybody I talk to could be Liandrin, or any of the others. Light!*

The spit had stopped. Hastily she started it turning once more. No one seemed to have noticed, though. They were all still doing their best not to look at the Amyrlin.

"And what do you mean to do about this . . . so-obvious trap?" the Amyrlin said softly, still staring over the kitchen, away from Nynaeve. "Do you mean to fall into this one, too?"

Nynaeve's face reddened. "I know this trap for a trap, Mother. And the best way to catch whoever set a trap is to spring it and wait for him—or her—to come." It sounded weaker than it had when she had said it to Egwene and Elayne, after what the Amyrlin had just told her, but she still meant it.

"Perhaps so, child. Perhaps it is the way to find them. If they do not come and find you held tightly in their net." She gave a vexed sigh. "I will put gold in your room for the journey. And I will let it be whispered about that I have sent you out to a farm to hoe cabbages. Will Elayne be going with you?"

Nynaeve forgot herself enough to stare at the Amyrlin, then hurriedly put her eyes back on her hands. Her knuckles were white on the spit handle. "You scheming old. . . . Why all the pretense, if you knew? Your sly plots have had us squirming nearly as much as the Black Ajah has. Why?" The Amyrlin's face had tightened, enough to make her force a more respectful tone. "If I may ask, Mother."

The Amyrlin snorted. "Putting Morgase back on the proper path whether she wants to go or not will be hard enough without her thinking I've sent her daughter to sea in a leaky skiff. This way I can say straight out that it was none of my doing. It may be a bit hard on Elayne, when she finally has to face her mother, but I have three hounds, now, not two. I told you I'd have a hundred if I could." She adjusted her stole on her shoulders. "This has gone on long enough. If I stay this close to you, it may be noticed. Have you anything more to tell me? Or to ask? Make it quick, Daughter."

"What is *Callandor*, Mother?" Nynaeve asked.

This time it was the Amyrlin who forgot herself, half turning toward Nynaeve before jerking herself back. "They cannot be allowed to have that." Her whisper was barely audible, as if meant for her own ears alone. "They cannot possibly take it, but. . . ." She took a deep breath, and her soft words firmed enough to be clear to Nynaeve, if to no one two paces further away. "No more than a dozen women in the Tower know what *Callandor* is, and perhaps as many outside. The High Lords of Tear know, but they never speak of it except when a Lord of the Land is told on being raised. The Sword That Cannot Be Touched is a *sa'angreal*, girl. Only two more powerful were ever made, and thank the Light, neither of those was ever used. With *Callandor* in your hands, child, you could level a city at one blow. If you die keeping that out of the Black Ajah's hands—you, and Egwene, and Elayne, all three—you'll have done a service to the whole world, and cheap at the price."

"How could they take it?" Nynaeve asked. "I thought only the Dragon Reborn could touch *Callandor*."

The Amyrlin gave her a sideways look sharp enough to carve the roasts on the spit. "They could be after something else," she said after a moment. "They stole *ter'angreal* here. The Stone of Tear holds nearly as many *ter'angreal* as the Tower."

"I thought the High Lords hated anything to do with the One Power," Nynaeve whispered incredulously.

"Oh, they do hate it, child. Hate it, and fear it. When they find a Tairen girl who can channel, they bundle her onto a ship for Tar Valon before the day is done, with hardly time to speak goodbyes to her family." The Amyrlin's murmur was bitter with memory. "Yet they hold one of the most powerful focuses of the Power the world has ever seen, inside their precious Stone. It is my belief that is why they have collected so many *ter'angreal*—and indeed, anything to do with the Power—over the years, as if by doing so they can diminish the existence of the thing they cannot rid themselves of, the thing that reminds them of their own doom every time they enter the Heart of the Stone. Their fortress that has broken a hundred armies will fall as one of the signs the Dragon is Reborn. Not even the only sign; just one. How that must rankle their proud hearts. Their downfall will not even be the one great sign of the world's change. They cannot even ignore it by staying out of the Heart. That is where Lords of the Land are raised to High Lords, and where they must perform what they call the Rite of the Guarding four times a year, claiming that they guard the whole world against the Dragon by holding *Callandor*. It must bite at their souls like a bellyful of live silverpike, and no more than they deserve." She gave herself a shake, as if realizing she had said far more than she had intended. "Is that all, child?"

"Yes, Mother," Nynaeve said. *Light, it always comes back to Rand, doesn't it? Always back to the Dragon Reborn.* It was still an effort to think of him that way. "That's all."

The Amyrlin shifted her stole again, frowning at the frenzied scurry in the kitchen. "I'll have to set this aright. I needed to speak to you without delay, but Laras is a good woman, and she manages the kitchen and the larders well."

Nynaeve sniffed, and addressed her hands on the spit handle. "Laras is a sour lump of lard, and too handy with that spoon by half." She thought she had muttered it under her breath, but she heard the Amyrlin chuckle wryly.

"You are a fine judge of character, child. You must have done well as the Wisdom of your village. It was Laras who went to Sheriam and demanded to know how long you three are to be kept to the dirtiest and hardest work, without a turn at lighter. She said she would not be a party to breaking any woman's health or spirit, no matter what I said. A fine judge of character, child."

Laras came back into the kitchen doorway then, hesitating to enter her own domain. The Amyrlin went to meet her, smiles replacing her frowns and stares.

"It all looks very well to me, Laras." The Amyrlin's words came loud enough for the entire kitchen to hear. "I see nothing out of place, and everything as it should be.

You are to be commended. I think I will make Mistress of
the Kitchens a formal title."

The stout woman's face fluttered from uneasiness to
shock to beaming pleasure. By the time the Amyrlin swept
out of the kitchen, Laras was all smiles. Her frown returned, though, as she looked from the Amyrlin's departing
back to her workers. The kitchen seemed to leap into motion. Laras' grim stare settled on Nynaeve.

Turning the spit again, Nynaeve tried smiling at the big
woman.

Laras' frown deepened, and she began tapping her spoon
on her thigh, apparently forgetting that for once it had been
used for its intended purpose. It left smears of soup on the
white of her apron.

I will smile at her if it kills me, Nynaeve thought, though
she had to grit her teeth to do it.

Egwene and Elayne appeared, twisting their faces and
scrubbing their mouths with their sleeves. At a stare from
Laras, they dashed to the spit and resumed their labors.

"Soap," Elayne muttered thickly, "tastes horrid!"

Egwene trembled as she spooned juice from the dripping
pan over the roasts. "Nynaeve, if you tell me the Amyrlin
told us to stay here, I will scream. I might run away for
real."

"We leave after the washing up is done," she told them,
"just as quickly as we can fetch our belongings from our
rooms." She wished she could share the eagerness that
flashed in their eyes. *Light send we aren't walking into a
trap we can't get out of. Light send it so.*

CHAPTER
30

The First Toss

After Nynaeve and the others left him, Mat spent most of the day in his room, except for one brief excursion. He was planning. And eating. He ate nearly everything the serving women brought him, and asked for more. They were more than happy to oblige. It was bread and cheese and fruit he asked for, and he piled winter-wrinkled apples and pears, wedges of cheese and loaves of bread inside the wardrobe, leaving empty trays for them to take away.

At midday he had to endure a visit from an Aes Sedai—Anaiya, he seemed to remember her name was. She put her hands on his head and sent cold chills through him. It was the One Power, he decided, not simply being touched by an Aes Sedai. She was a plain woman despite her smooth cheeks and Aes Sedai serenity.

"You seem much better," she told him, smiling. Her smile made him think of his mother. "Even hungrier than I expected, so I hear, but better. I am informed you are trying to eat the larders bare. Believe me when I say we will see you have all the food you need. You do not have to worry that we'll let you miss a meal before you are fully well again."

He gave the grin he used on his mother when he especially wanted her to believe him. "I know you won't. And I do feel better. I thought I might see some of the city this afternoon. If you have no objections, of course. Maybe visit an inn tonight. There's nothing like a night of common-room talk to pick one's spirits up."

He thought her lips twitched on the edge of a bigger smile. "No one will try to stop you, Mat. But do not try to leave the city. It will only upset the guards, and bring you nothing but a trip back here under escort."

"I would not do that, Aes Sedai. The Amyrlin Seat said I'd starve to death in a few days if I left."

She nodded as if she did not believe a word he said. "Of course." As she turned from him, her eyes fell on the quarterstaff he had brought from the practice yard, propped in the corner of the room. "You do not need to protect yourself from us, Mat. You are as safe here as you could be anywhere. Almost certainly safer."

"Oh, I know that, Aes Sedai. I do." After she left he frowned at the door, wondering if he had managed to convince her of anything.

It was more evening than afternoon when he left the room for what he hoped was the final time. The sky was purpling, and the setting sun painted clouds to the west in shades of red. Once he had his cloak around him, and the big leather scrip he had found on his one earlier foray dangling from his shoulder and bulging with the bread and cheese and fruit he had squirreled away, one look in the mirror told him there was no hiding what he intended. He tied the rest of his clothes up in a roll with the blanket from the bed and slung that across his shoulders, too. The quarterstaff did for a walking staff. He left nothing behind. His coat pockets held all his smaller belongings, and his belt pouch held the most important. The Amyrlin Seat's paper. Elayne's letter. And his dice cups.

He saw Aes Sedai as he made his way out of the Tower, and some of them noticed him, though most merely flickered an eyebrow, and none spoke to him. Anaiya was one. She gave him an amused smile and a rueful shake of her head. He returned a shrug and the guiltiest grin he could manage, and she went silently on, still shaking her head. The guards at the Tower gates simply looked at him.

It was not until he was across the big square and into the streets of the city that relief finally surged up in him. And triumph. *If you can't hide what you are going to do, do it so everybody thinks you are a fool. Then they stand around waiting to see you fall on your face. Those Aes Sedai will be waiting for the guards to bring me back. When I do not return by morning, then they'll start a search. Not too frantic at first, because they'll think I have gone to ground*

*somewhere in the city. By the time they realize I haven't,
this rabbit will be a long way downriver from the hounds.*

With as light a heart as he could remember having in
years, or so it seemed, he began to hum "We're Over the
Border Again," heading toward the harbor where vessels
would be sailing down to Tear and all the villages along the
Erinin between. He would not be going so far as that, of
course. Aringill, where he would take to land again for the
rest of the trip to Caemlyn, was only halfway downriver.

*I'll deliver your bloody letter. The nerve of her, thinking
I'd say I would, then not. I will deliver the bloody thing if
it kills me.*

Twilight was beginning to cover Tar Valon, but there
was still enough light to grace the fantastical buildings, and
the oddly shaped towers connected by high bridges spanning open air over hundred-pace drops. People yet filled
the streets, in so many different kinds of clothing that he
thought every nation must be represented. Along the major avenues, pairs of lamplighters used their ladders to light
lanterns atop tall poles. But in the part of Tar Valon he
sought, the only light was what spilled from windows.

Ogier had built the great buildings and towers of Tar
Valon, but other, newer parts had grown under the hands
of men. Newer meaning two thousand years in some cases.
Down near Southharbor, men's hands had tried to match,
if not duplicate, the fanciful Ogier work. Inns where ships'
crews caroused bore enough stonework for palaces. Statues in niches and cupolas on rooftops, ornately worked
cornices and intricately carved friezes, all decorated chan-
dlers' shops and merchant houses. Bridges arched across
the streets here, too, but the streets were cobblestone, not
great paving blocks, and many of the bridges were wood
instead of stone, sometimes as low as the second stories of
the buildings they joined, and never higher than four.

The dark streets hummed with as much life as any in Tar
Valon. Traders off their vessels and those who bought what
the vessels carried, people who traveled the River Erinin and
people who worked it, all filled the taverns and the common rooms of the inns, in company with those who sought
the money such folk carried, by fair means or murky. Raucous music filled the streets from bittern and flute, harp and
hammered dulcimer. The first inn Mat entered had three

dice games in progress, men crouched in circles near the common-room walls and shouting the wins and losses.

He only meant to gamble an hour or so before finding a ship, just long enough to add a few coins to his purse, but he won. He had always won more than he lost, as far as he could remember, and there had been times with Hurin, and in Shienar, when six or eight tosses in a row won for him. Tonight, every toss won. Every toss.

From the looks some of the men gave him, he was glad he had left his own dice in his pouch. Those looks made him decide to move on. With surprise he realized that he had nearly thirty silver marks in his purse now, but he had not won so much from any one man that they would not all be glad to see him go.

Except for one dark sailor with tight curls—one of the Sea Folk, someone had said, though Mat wondered what one of the Atha'an Miere was doing so far from the sea—who followed him down the darkened street, arguing for a chance to make good his losses. He wanted to reach the docks—thirty silver marks was more than enough—but the sailor argued on, and he had only used half his hour, so he gave in, and with the man entered the next tavern they passed.

He won again, and it was as if a fever gripped him. He won every throw. From tavern to inn to tavern he went, never staying long enough to anger anyone with the amount of his winnings. And he still won every toss. He exchanged silver for gold with a money changer. He played at crowns, and fives, and maiden's ruin. He played games with five dice, and with four, and three, and even only two. He played games he did not know before he squatted in the circle, or took a place at the table. And he won. Somewhere during the night, the dark sailor—Raab, he had said his name was—staggered away, exhausted but with a full purse; he had decided to put his wagers on Mat. Mat visited another money changer—or perhaps two; the fever seemed to cloud his brain as badly as his memories of the past were clouded—and made his way to another game. Winning.

And so he found himself, he did not know how many hours later, in a tavern filled with tabac smoke—The Tremalking Splice, he thought it was called—staring down at five dice, each showing a deeply carved crown. Most of the patrons here seemed interested only in drinking as much as they could, but the rattle of dice and shouts of players from another game in the far corner were almost submerged by a woman singing to a quick tune from a hammered dulcimer.

> I'll dance with a girl with eyes of brown,
> or a girl with eyes of green,
> I'll dance with a girl with any color eyes,
> but yours are the prettiest I've seen.
> I'll kiss a girl with hair of black,
> or a girl with hair of gold,
> I'll kiss a girl with any color hair,
> but it's you I want to hold.

The singer had named the song as "What He Said to Me." Mat remembered the tune as "Will You Dance With Me," with different words, but at that moment all he could think of were those dice.

"The king again," one of the men squatting with Mat muttered. It was the fifth time in a row Mat had thrown the king.

He had won the bet of a gold mark, not even caring by this time that his Andoran mark outweighed the other man's Illianer coin, but he scooped the dice into the leather cup, rattled it hard, and spun them across the floor again. Five crowns. *Light, it can't be. Nobody ever threw the king six times running. Nobody.*

"The Dark One's own luck," another man growled. He was a bulky fellow, his dark hair tied at the nape of his neck with a black ribbon, with heavy shoulders, scars on his face, and a nose that had been broken more than once.

Mat was scarcely aware of moving before he had the bulky man by the collar, hauling him to his feet, slamming him back against the wall. "Don't you say that!" he snarled. "Don't you ever say that!" The man blinked down at him in astonishment; he was a full head taller than Mat.

"Just a saying," somebody behind him was muttering. "Light, it's just a saying."

Mat released his grip on the scar-faced man's coat and backed away. "I. . . . I . . . I don't like anybody saying things like that about me. I'm no Darkfriend!" *Burn me, not the Dark One's luck. Not that! Oh, Light, did that bloody dagger really do something to me?*

"Nobody said you was," the broken-nosed man muttered. He seemed to be getting over his surprise, and trying to decide whether to be angry.

Gathering his belongings from where he had piled them behind him, Mat walked out of the tavern, leaving the coins where they lay. It was not that he was afraid of the big man. He had forgotten the man, and the coins, too. All he wanted was to be outside, in fresh air, where he could think.

In the street, he leaned against the wall of the tavern not far from the door, breathing the coolness in. The dark streets of Southharbor were all but empty, now. Music and laughter still floated from the inns and taverns, but few people made their way through the night. Holding the quarterstaff upright in front of him with both hands, he lowered his head to his fists and tried to think at the puzzle from every side.

He knew he was lucky. He could remember always being lucky. But somehow, his memories from Emond's Field did not show him as lucky as he had been since leaving. Certainly he had gotten away with a great deal, but he could remember also being caught in pranks he had been sure would succeed. His mother had always seemed to know what he was up to, and Nynaeve able to see through whatever defenses he put up. But it was not just since leaving the Two Rivers that he had become lucky. The luck had come once he took the dagger from Shadar Logoth. He remembered playing at dice back home with a sharp-eyed, skinny man who worked for a merchant come down from Baerlon to buy tabac. He remembered the strapping his father had given him, too, on learning Mat owed the man a silver mark and four pence.

"But I'm free of the bloody dagger," he mumbled. "Those bloody Aes Sedai said I was." He wondered how much he had won tonight.

When he dug into his coat pockets, he found them filled with loose coins, crowns and marks, both silver and gold that glittered and glinted in the light from nearby windows. He had two purses now, it seemed, and both fat. He undid the strings, and found more gold. And still more stuffed into his belt pouch between and around and on top of his dice cups, crumpling Elayne's letter and the Amyrlin's paper. He had a memory of tossing silver pence to serving girls because they had pretty smiles or pretty eyes or pretty ankles, and because silver pence were not worth keeping.

Not worth keeping? Maybe they weren't. Light, I'm rich! I am bloody rich! Maybe it was something the Aes Sedai did. Something they did Healing me. By accident, maybe. That could be it. Better that the other. Those bloody Aes Sedai must have done it to me.

A big man moved out from the tavern, the door already swinging shut to cut off the light that might have shown his face.

Mat pressed his back close against the wall, stuffed the purses back into his coat, and firmed his grip on the quarterstaff. Wherever his luck tonight had come from, he did not mean to lose all that gold to a footpad.

The man turned toward him, peered, then gave a start. "C-cool night," he said drunkenly. He staggered closer, and Mat saw that most of his size was fat. "I have to. . . . I have to. . . ." Stumbling, the fat man moved on up the street, talking to himself disjointedly.

"Fool!" Mat muttered, but he was not sure whether he meant it for the fat man or for himself. "Time to find a ship to take me away from here." He squinted at the black sky, trying to estimate how long till dawn. Two, maybe three hours, he thought. "Past time." His stomach growled at him; he dimly recalled eating in some of the inns, but he did not remember what. The fever of the dice had had him by the throat. A hand pushed into the scrip found only crumbs. "Way past time. Or one of them will come pick me up with her fingers and stick me in her pouch." He pushed away from the wall and started for the docks, where the ships would be.

At first he thought the faint sounds behind him were echoes of his boots on the cobblestones. Then he realized someone was following him. And trying to be stealthy. *Well, these are footpads, for sure.*

Hefting the quarterstaff, he briefly considered turning to confront them. But it was dark, and the footing on cobblestones uncertain, and he had no idea how many there were. *Just because you did well against Gawyn and Galad doesn't make you a bloody hero out of a story.*

He turned down a narrower, twisting side street, trying to walk on tiptoe and move quickly at the same time. Every

window was dark here, and most shuttered. He was almost
to the end when he saw movement ahead, two men peering
into the side street from where it let out onto another. And
he heard slow footsteps behind him, soft scrapes of boot
leather on stone.

In an instant he ducked into the shadowy corner where
one building stuck out further than the next. It seemed the
best he could do for the moment. Gripping the quarterstaff
nervously, he waited.

A man appeared from back the way he had come, crouching as he eased himself ahead one slow step at a time, and
then another man. Each carried a knife in his hand and
moved as if stalking.

Mat tensed. If they came just a few steps closer before
they noticed him hiding in the deeper shadows of the corner, he could take them by surprise. He wished his stomach would stop fluttering. Those knives were a great deal
shorter than the practice swords, but they were steel, not
wood.

One of the men squinted toward the far end of the narrow
street and suddenly straightened, shouting, "Didn't he come
your way, then?"

"I have seen nothing but the shadows," came the answer
in a heavy accent. "I wish to be out of this. There are the
strange things moving this night." ·

Not four paces from Mat, the two men exchanged looks,
sheathed their knives, and trotted back the way they had
come.

He let out a long, slow breath. *Luck. Burn me if it's not
good for more than dice.*

He could no longer see the men at the mouth of the street,
but he knew they were still out on the next street somewhere. And more behind him the other way.

One of the buildings he was crouched against stood only
a single story high here, and the roof looked flat enough.
And a white stone frieze carved in huge grape leaves ran up
the joining of the two buildings.

Easing his quarterstaff up till one end rested on the edge
of the roof, he gave it a hard shove. It landed with a clatter
on the roof tiles. Not waiting to see if anyone had heard, he
scrambled up the frieze, the big leaves giving easy toeholds
even for a man in boots. In seconds he had the staff back

in hand and was trotting across the roof, trusting to luck for his footing.

Three more times he climbed, each time gaining one story. The slightly sloping, tiled roofs ran some distance at that level, and there was a breeze at that height, prickling the hair on the back of his neck with its chill and almost making him think he was being followed. *Stop that, fool! They're three streets away by now, looking for somebody else with a fat purse, and bad luck to them.*

His boots slipped on the tiles, and he decided it might be a good idea to think about getting back down into the street himself. Cautiously, he moved to the edge of the roof and peered down. An empty street lay a good forty feet or more below him, with three taverns and an inn spilling light and music onto the cobblestones. But off to his right was a stone bridge running from the top floor of his building to the one on the other side.

The bridge looked awfully narrow, running through darkness untouched by the tavern lights, arcing over a long fall to hard cobblestones, but he tossed the quarterstaff down and made himself follow before he could think about it too much. His boots thumped onto the bridge, and he let himself roll the way he had as a boy falling out of a tree. He fetched up against the waist-high railing.

"Bad habits pay off in the long run," he told himself as he got to his feet and picked up the staff.

The window at the other end of the bridge was tightly shuttered and lightless. He did not think whoever lived in there would appreciate a stranger appearing in the middle of the night. He could see lots of stonework, but if there was as much as a fingerhold in reach of the bridge, the night hid it. *Well, stranger or no stranger, inside I go.*

He turned from the railing and suddenly became aware of a man sharing the bridge with him. A man with a dagger in his hand.

Mat grabbed at the hand as the knife darted toward his throat. He barely caught the fellow's wrist with his fingers, and then the quarterstaff between them tangled itself in his legs, tripping him to fall back against the railing, to fall half over it pulling the other man on top of him. Balanced there on the small of his back, teetering with his assailant's bared teeth in his face, he was as aware of the long drop under

his head as he was of the blade catching faint moonlight
as it edged toward his throat. His finger grip on the man's
wrist was slipping, and his other hand was caught with the
quarterstaff between their bodies. Only seconds had passed
since he first saw the man, and in seconds more, he was going to die with a knife in his throat.

"Time to toss the dice," he said. He thought the other
man looked confused for an instant, but an instant was all
he had. With a heave of his legs, Mat flipped them both off
into the empty air.

For a stretched-out moment he seemed to have no weight.
Air whistled past his ears and ruffled his hair. He thought
he heard the other man scream, or start to. The impact
knocked all the air out of his lungs and made silver-black
flecks dance across his blurring vision.

When he could breathe again—and see—he realized
he was lying on top of the man who had attacked him, his
fall cushioned by the other's body. "Luck," he whispered.
Slowly he climbed to his feet, cursing the bruise the quarterstaff had put across his ribs.

He expected the other man to be dead—not many could
survive a thirty-foot fall to cobblestones with another's
weight on top of him—but what he had not expected was
to see the fellow's dagger driven to the hilt into his own
heart. Such an ordinary-looking man to have tried to kill
him. Mat did not think he would even have noticed him in
a crowded room.

"You had bad luck, fellow," he told the corpse shakily.

Suddenly, everything that had happened rushed back in
on him. The footpads in the twisting street. The scramble
over the rooftops. This fellow. The fall. His eyes rose to
the bridge overhead, and a fit of trembling hit him. *I must
have been crazy. A little adventure is one thing, but Rogosh
Eagle-eye wouldn't ask for this.*

He realized he was standing over a dead man with a dagger in his chest, just waiting for someone to come along and
run shouting for city guards with the Flame of Tar Valon on
their chests. The Amyrlin's paper might get him away from
them, but maybe not before she found out. He could still
end up back in the White Tower, without that paper, and
possibly not even allowed outside the Tower grounds.

He knew he should be on his way to the docks right then,

and on the first vessel sailing if it was a rotten tub full of old fish, but his knees were shaking hard enough in reaction that he could hardly walk. What he wanted was to sit down for just a minute. Just a minute to steady his knees, and then he was headed for the docks.

The taverns were closer, but he started toward the inn. The common room of an inn was a friendly place, where a man could rest a minute and not worry about who might be sneaking up behind him. Enough light came out through the windows for him to make out the sign. A woman with her hair in braids, holding what he thought was an olive branch, and the words "The Woman of Tanchico."

CHAPTER
31

The Woman of Tanchico

The common room of the inn was brightly lit, the tables not near a quarter full so late. A few white-aproned serving women with mugs of ale or wine passed among the men, and a low murmur of talk ran under the sound of a harp being strummed and plucked. The patrons, some with pipes clenched in their teeth and one pair hunched over a stones board, had the look of ship's officers and minor merchants from the smaller houses, their coats well cut and of fine wool, but with none of the gold or silver or embroidery that richer men might have had. And for once there was no clack and rattle of dice to be heard. Fires blazed on the long hearths at the ends of the room, but even without those there would have been a warm feeling about the place.

The harper stood on a tabletop, reciting "Mara and the Three Foolish Kings," to the music of his harp. His instrument, all worked in gold and silver, was fit for a palace. Mat knew him. He had saved Mat's life, once.

The harper was a lean man who would have been tall except for a stoop, and he moved with a limp when he shifted his footing on the tabletop. Even here inside, he wore his cloak, all covered with fluttering patches in a hundred colors. He always wanted everyone to know he was a gleeman. His long mustaches and bushy eyebrows were as snow-white as the thick hair on his head, and his blue eyes held a look of sorrow as he recited. The look was as unexpected as the man. Mat had never known Thom Merrilin to be a sorrowful man.

He took a table, setting his things on the floor by his stool, and ordered two mugs. The pretty young serving girl's big brown eyes twinkled at him.

"Two, young master? You do not look such a hard-drinking man as that." Her voice held a mischievous edge of laughter.

After rummaging a bit, he brought out two silver pennies from his pocket. One more than paid for the wine, but he slipped her another for her eyes. "My friend will be joining me."

He knew Thom had seen him. The old gleeman had nearly stopped the story dead when Mat came in. That was new, too. Few things startled Thom enough for him to let it show, and nothing short of Trollocs had ever made him stop a story in the middle that Mat knew. When the girl brought the wine and his coppers in change, he let the pewter mugs sit and listened to the end of the story.

"'It was as we have said it should be,' said King Madel, trying to untangle a fish from his long beard." Thom's voice seemed almost to echo inside a great hall, not an ordinary common room. His plucked harp sounded the three kings' final foolishness. "'It was as we said it would be,' announced Orander. And, feet slipping in the mud, he sat down with a great splash. 'It was as we said it must be,' proclaimed Kadar as he searched, up to his elbows in the river, for his crown. 'The woman knows not whereof she speaks. She is the fool!' Madel and Orander agreed with him loudly. And with that, Mara had had enough. 'I've given them all the chances they deserve and more,' she murmured to herself. Slipping Kadar's crown into her bag with the first two, she climbed back onto her cart, clucked to her mare, and drove straight back to her village. And when Mara had told them all that happened, the people of Heape would have no king at all." He strummed the major theme of the kings' foolishness once more, this time sliding to a crescendo that sounded even more like laughter, made a sweeping bow, and nearly fell off the table.

Men laughed and stamped their feet, though likely every one of them had heard the story many times before, and called for more. The story of Mara was always well received, except perhaps by kings.

Thom nearly fell again climbing down from the table, and he was more unsteady in his walk than a somewhat stiff

leg could account for as he came to where Mat was sitting.
Casually putting his harp on the table, he dropped onto a
stool in front of the second mug and gave Mat a flat stare.
His eyes had always been sharp as awls, but they seemed to
be having trouble focusing.

"Common," he muttered. His voice was still deep, but
it no longer seemed to reverberate. "The tale is a hundred
times better in Plain Chant, and a thousand in High, but
they want Common." Without another word, he buried his
face in his wine.

Mat could not recall ever seeing Thom finish playing that
harp without immediately putting it away in its hard leather
case. He had never seen him the worse for drink. It was a
relief to hear the gleeman complaining about his listeners;
Thom never thought their standards were as high as his. At
least something of him had not changed.

The serving girl was back, with no twinkle in her eyes.
"Oh, Thom," she said softly, then rounded on Mat. "If I'd
known he was the friend you awaited, I'd not have brought
you wine for him if you gave a hundred silver pence."

"I did not know he was drunk," Mat protested.

But her attention was back on Thom, her voice gentle
again. "Thom, you need some rest. They'll keep you telling
stories all night and all day, if you let them."

Another woman appeared on Thom's other side, lifting
her apron off over her head. She was older than the first, but
no less pretty. The two might have been sisters. "A beautiful
story, I've always thought, Thom, and you tell it beautifully.
Come, I've slipped a warming pan into your bed, and you
can tell me all about the court in Caemlyn."

Thom peered into the mug as if surprised to find it
empty, then blew out his long mustaches and looked from
one woman to the other. "Pretty Mada. Pretty Saal. Did I
ever tell you that two pretty women have loved me in my
life? That is more than most men can claim."

"You've told us all about it, Thom," the older woman said
sadly. The younger glared at Mat as if this were all his fault.

"Two," Thom murmured. "Morgase had a temper, but I
thought I could ignore that, so it ended with her wanting to
kill me. Dena, I killed. As good as. Not much difference.
Two chances I've had, more than most, and I threw them
both away."

"I will take care of him," Mat said. Mada and Saal were both glaring at him, now. He gave them his best smile, but it did not work. His stomach muttered loudly. "Don't I smell chicken roasting? Bring me three or four." The two women blinked and exchanged startled looks when he added, "Do you want something to eat, too, Thom?"

"I could do with more of this fine Andoran wine." The gleeman raised his cup hopefully.

"No more wine for you tonight, Thom." The older woman would have taken his cup if he had let her.

Almost on top of the first woman, the younger said, in a mixture of firmness and pleading, "You'll have some chicken, Thom. It is very good."

Neither would leave until the gleeman agreed to eat something, and when they did go, they gave Mat such a combination of stares and sniffs that he could only shake his head. *Burn me, you would think I was encouraging him to drink more! Women! But pretty eyes on the pair of them.*

"Rand said you were alive," he told Thom when Mada and Saal were out of hearing. "Moiraine always said she thought you were. But I heard you were in Cairhien, and meaning to go on to Tear."

"Rand is still well, then?" Thom's eyes sharpened to almost the keenness Mat remembered. "I am not sure I expected that. Moiraine is still with him, is she? A fine-looking woman. A fine woman, if she were not Aes Sedai. Meddle with that sort, and you get more than your fingers burned."

"Why wouldn't you expect Rand to be all right?" Mat asked carefully. "Do you know of something that could harm him?"

"Know? I don't know anything, boy. I suspect more than is healthy for me, but I know nothing."

Mat abandoned that line of talk. *No use firming his suspicions. No use letting him know I know more than's healthy myself.*

The older woman—Thom called her Mada—came back with three chickens with crisp, brown skins, giving the white-haired man a worried look, and Mat a warning one, before she left. Mat ripped off a leg and set to as he talked. Thom frowned into his cup and never looked at the birds.

"Why are you here in Tar Valon, Thom? It's the last place

I'd have expected to see you, the way you feel about Aes Sedai. I heard you were coining money in Cairhien."

"Cairhien," the old gleeman muttered, the sharpness fading from his eyes again. "Such trouble it causes killing a man, even when he deserves killing." He made a flourish with one hand and was holding a knife. Thom always had knives secreted about him. Drunk he might have been, but he held the blade steady enough. "Kill a man who needs killing, and sometimes others pay for it. The question is, was it worth doing anyway? There's always a balance, you know. Good and evil. Light and Shadow. We would not be human if there wasn't a balance."

"Put that away," Mat growled around a mouthful. "I don't want to talk about killing." *Light, that fellow is still lying right out there in the street. Burn me, I ought to be on a ship by now.* "I just asked why you're in Tar Valon. If you had to leave Cairhien because you killed someone, I do not want to know about it. Blood and ashes, if you can't pull your wits out of the wine enough to talk straight, I'll leave now."

With a sour look, Thom made the knife disappear. "Why am I in Tar Valon? I'm here because it is the worst place I could be, except maybe Caemlyn. It's what I deserve, boy. Some of the Red Ajah still remember me. I saw Elaida in the street the other day. If she knew I was here, she would peel my hide off in strips, and then she would stop being pleasant."

"I never knew you to feel sorry for yourself," Mat said disgustedly. "Do you mean to drown yourself in wine?"

"What do you know of it, boy?" Thom snarled. "Put a few years on you, see something of life, maybe love a woman or two, and then you'll know. Perhaps you will, if you have the brains to learn. Aaaah! You want to know why I'm in Tar Valon? Why are you in Tar Valon? I remember you shivering when you found out Moiraine was Aes Sedai. You nearly soiled yourself every time anybody even mentioned the Power. What are you doing in Tar Valon, with Aes Sedai on every side?"

"I am leaving Tar Valon. That's what I am doing here. Leaving!" Mat grimaced. The gleeman had saved his life, and maybe more. A Fade had been involved. That was why Thom's right leg did not work as well as it should. *There*

could not be enough wine on a ship to keep him this drunk.
"I am going to Caemlyn, Thom. If you need to risk your
fool life for some reason, why not come with me?"

"Caemlyn?" Thom said musingly.

"Caemlyn, Thom. Elaida will likely be going back there
sooner or later, so you'd have her to worry about. And from
what I remember, if Morgase puts her hands on you, you
will wish Elaida had you."

"Caemlyn. Yes. Caemlyn would fit my mood like a
glove." The gleeman glanced at the chicken platter and gave
a start. "What did you do, boy? Stuff them up your sleeve?"
There was nothing left of the three birds but bones and carcasses with only a few strips of flesh remaining.

"Sometimes I get hungry," Mat muttered. It was an effort
not to lick his fingers. "Are you coming with me, or not?"

"Oh, I will come, boy." As Thom pushed himself to his
feet, he did not seem as unsteady as he had been. "You wait
here—and try not to eat the table—while I get my things
and say some goodbyes." He limped away, not staggering
once.

Mat drank a little of his wine and stripped off a few
shreds that were left on the chicken carcasses, wondering if
he had time to order another, but Thom was back quickly.
His harp and flute in their dark leather cases hung on his
back with a tied blanketroll. He carried a plain walking
staff as tall as he was. The two serving women followed
on either side. Mat decided they were sisters. Identical big
brown eyes looked up at the gleeman with identical expressions. Thom was kissing first Saal, then Mada, and patting
cheeks as he headed for the door, jerking his head for Mat
to follow. He was outside before Mat could finish collecting
his own belongings and pick up his quarterstaff.

The younger of the two women, Saal, stopped Mat as he
reached the door. "Whatever you said to him, I forgive you
for the wine, even if it is taking him away. I've not seen him
this alive in weeks." She pressed something into his hand,
and when he glanced at it, his eyes widened in confusion.
She had given him a silver Tar Valon mark. "For whatever it
was you said. Besides, whoever is feeding you is not doing
a good job of it, but you still have pretty eyes." She laughed
at the expression on his face.

Mat was laughing, too, in spite of himself, as he went out

into the street, rolling the silver coin across the backs of his fingers. *So I have pretty eyes, do I?* His laughter shut off like the last drip from a wine barrel: Thom was there, but not the corpse. The windows of the taverns down the street put enough light across the cobblestones for him to be sure of it. The city guard would not have carried a dead man away without asking questions, at those taverns and at The Woman of Tanchico, too.

"What are you staring at, boy?" Thom asked. "No Trollocs in those shadows."

"Footpads," Mat muttered. "I was thinking about footpads."

"No street thieves or strong-arms in Tar Valon, either, boy. When the guards take a footpad—not that many try that game here; the word spreads—but when they do, they haul him to the Tower, and whatever it is the Aes Sedai do to him, the fellow leaves Tar Valon the next day as wide-eyed as a goosed girl. I understand they're even harder on women caught thieving. No, the only way you'll have your money stolen here is somebody selling you polished brass for gold or using shaved dice. There are no footpads."

Mat turned on his heel and strode past Thom, heading toward the docks, quarterstaff thumping off the cobblestones as if he could push himself ahead faster. "We're going to be on the first ship sailing, whatever it is. The first, Thom."

Thom's stick clicked hurriedly after him. "Slow down, boy. What's your hurry? There are plenty of ships, sailing day and night. Slow down. There aren't any footpads."

"The first bloody ship, Thom! If it's sinking, we'll be on it!" *If they weren't footpads, what were they? They had to be thieves. What else could they be?*

CHAPTER
32

The First Ship

Southharbor itself, the great Ogier-made basin, was huge and round, surrounded by high walls of the same silver-streaked white stone as the rest of Tar Valon. One long wharf, most of it roofed, ran all the way around, except where the wide water gates stood open to give access to the river. Vessels of every size lined the wharf, most moored by the stern, and despite the hour dockmen in coarse, sleeveless shirts hurried about loading and unloading bales and chests, crates and barrels, with ropes and booms, or on their backs. Lamps hanging from the roof beams lit the wharfs and made a band of light around the black water in the middle of the harbor. Small open boats scuttled through the darkness, the square lanterns atop their tall sternposts making it seem as if fireflies skittered across the harbor. They were small only compared to the ships, though; some had as many as six pairs of long oars.

When Mat led a still-muttering Thom under an arch of polished redstone and down broad steps to the wharf, crewmen on one three-masted ship were unfastening the mooring lines not twenty paces away. The vessel was larger than most Mat could see, between fifteen and twenty spans from sharp bow to squared stern, with a flat, railed deck almost level with the wharf. The important thing was that it was casting off. *The first ship that sails.*

A gray-haired man came up the wharf: three lines of hemp rope sewn down the sleeves of his dark coat marked him as a dockmaster. His wide shoulders suggested that he might have begun as a dockman hauling rope instead of wearing it. He glanced casually in Mat's direction, and stopped, surprise on his leathery face. "Your bundles say what you're planning, lad, but you might as well forget it. The sister showed me a drawing of you. You'll board no ship in Southharbor, lad. Go back up those stairs so I don't have to tell a man off to watch you."

"What under the Light . . . ?" Thom murmured.

"That's all changed," Mat said firmly. The ship was casting off the last mooring line; the furled triangular sails still made thick, pale bundles on the long, slanted booms, but men were readying the sweeps. He pulled the Amyrlin's paper out of his pouch and thrust it in the dockmaster's face. "As you can see, I'm on the business of the Tower, at the order of the Amyrlin Seat herself. And I have to leave on that very vessel there."

The dockmaster read the words, then read them again. "I never saw such a thing in my life. Why would the Tower say you couldn't go, then give you . . . *that*?"

"Ask the Amyrlin, if you want," Mat told him in a weary voice that said he did not think anyone could possibly be stupid enough to do that, "but she'll have my hide, and yours, if I do not sail on that ship."

"You'll never make it," the dockmaster said, but he was already cupping his hands to his mouth. "Aboard the *Gray Gull* there! Stop! The Light burn you, stop!"

The shirtless fellow at the tiller looked back, then spoke to a tall companion in a dark coat with puffy sleeves. The tall man never took his eyes off the crewmen just dipping the sweeps into the water. "Give way together," he called, and sweepblades curled up froth.

"I'll make it," Mat snapped. *The first ship I said, and the first ship I meant!* "Come on, Thom!"

Without waiting to see if the gleeman followed, he ran down the wharf, dodging around men and barrows stacked with cargo. The gap between the *Gray Gull*'s stern and the wharf widened as the sweeps bit deeper. Hefting his quarterstaff, he hurled it ahead of him toward the ship like a spear, took one more step, and jumped as hard as he could.

The dark water passing beneath his feet looked icy, but in a heartbeat he had cleared the ship's rail and was rolling across the deck. As he scrambled to his feet, he heard a grunt and a curse behind him.

Thom Merrilin hoisted himself up on the railing with another curse, and climbed over onto the deck. "I lost my stick," he muttered. "I'll want another." Rubbing his right leg, he peered down at the still widening strip of water behind the vessel and shivered. "I had a bath today already." The shirtless steersman stared wide-eyed from him to Mat and back again, clutching the tiller as if wondering whether he could use it to defend himself from madmen.

The tall man seemed nearly as stunned. His pale blue eyes bulged, and his mouth worked soundlessly for a moment. His dark beard, cut to a point, seemed to quiver with rage, and his narrow face grew purple. "By the Stone!" he bellowed finally. "What is the meaning of this? I've no room on this vessel for as much as a ship's cat, and I'd not take vagabonds who leap onto my decks if I did. Sanor! Vasa! Heave this rubbish over the side!" Two extremely large men, barefoot and stripped to the waist, straightened from coiling lines and started toward the stern. The men at the sweeps continued their work, bending to lift the blades, taking three long steps along the deck, then straightening and walking backwards, hauling the ship ahead on their blades.

Mat waved the Amyrlin's paper toward the bearded man—the captain, he supposed—with one hand, and fished a gold crown out of his pouch with the other, taking care even in his haste that the fellow saw there were more where that came from. Tossing the heavy coin to the man, he spoke quickly, still waving the paper. "For the inconvenience of our boarding as we did, Captain. More to come for passage. On business of the White Tower. Personal command of the Amyrlin Seat. Imperative we sail immediately. To Aringill, in Andor. Utmost urgency. The blessings of the White Tower on all who aid us; the Tower's wrath on any who impede us."

Certain the man had seen the Flame of Tar Valon seal by that time—and little more, Mat hoped—he folded the paper again and thrust it back out of sight. Eyeing the two big men uneasily as they came up on either side of the captain—*Burn me, they both have arms like Perrin's!*—he wished he had his quarterstaff in hand. He could see it lying where it had landed, further down the deck. He tried to look sure and confident, the sort of man others had better not trifle with, a man with the power of the White Tower behind him. *A long way behind me, I hope.*

The captain looked at Mat doubtfully, and even more so at Thom in his gleeman's cloak and none too steady afoot, but he motioned Sanor and Vasa to stop where they were. "I would not anger the Tower. Burn my soul, for the time being the river trade takes me from Tear to this den of. . . . I come too often to anger . . . anyone." A tight smile appeared on his face. "But I spoke the truth. By the Stone, I did! Six cabins I have for passengers, and all full. You can sleep on deck and eat with the crew for another gold crown. Each."

"That is ridiculous!" Thom snapped. "I don't care what the war has done downriver, that is ridiculous!" The two large sailors shifted their bare feet.

"It is the price," the captain said firmly. "I do not want to anger anyone, but I'd as soon not have any business you can be on aboard my vessel. Like letting a man pay you so he can coat you with hot tar, mixing in *that* business. You pay the price, or you go over the side, and the Amyrlin Seat herself can dry you off. And I'll keep this for the trouble you've given me, thank you." He stuffed the gold crown Mat has tossed him into a pocket of his puffy-sleeved coat.

"How much for one of the cabins?" Mat asked. "To ourselves. You can put whoever is in it now with someone else." He did not want to sleep out in the cold night. *And if you don't overwhelm a fellow like this, he'll steal your breeches and say he is doing you a favor.* His stomach rumbled loudly. "And we eat what you eat, not with the crew. And plenty of it!"

"Mat," Thom said, "I'm the one who is supposed to be drunk here." He turned to the captain, flourishing his patch-covered cloak as well as he could with blanketroll and instrument cases hung about him. "As you may have noticed, Captain, I am a gleeman." Even in the open air, his voice suddenly seemed to echo. "For the price of our passages, I would be more than glad to entertain your passengers and your crew—"

"My crew is aboard to work, gleeman, not be entertained." The captain stroked his pointed beard; his pale eyes priced Mat's plain coat to the copper. "So you want a cabin, do you?" He barked a laugh. "And my meals? Well, you can

344 THE DRAGON REBORN

have my cabin and my meals. For five gold crowns from each of you! Andoran weight!" Those were the heaviest. He began to laugh so hard his words came out in wheezes. Flanking him, Sanor and Vasa grinned wide grins. "For ten crowns, you can take my cabin, and my meals, and I'll move in with the passengers and eat with the crew. Burn my soul, I will! By the Stone, I swear it! For ten gold crowns. . . ." Laughter choked off anything else.

He was still laughing and gasping for breath and wiping tears from his eyes when Mat pulled out one of his two purses, but laughter stopped by the time Mat had counted five crowns into his hands. The captain blinked in disbelief; the two big crewmen looked poleaxed.

"Andoran weight, you said?" Mat asked. It was hard to judge without scales, but he laid seven more on the pile. Two actually were Andoran, and he thought the others made up the weight. *Close enough, for this fellow.* After a moment, he added another two gold Tairen crowns. "For whoever you'll be pushing out of the cabin they paid for." He did not think the passengers would see a copper of it, but it sometimes paid to appear generous. "Unless you mean to share with them? No, of course not. They ought to have something for having to crowd in with others. There's no need for you to eat with your crew, Captain. You are welcome to share Thom's meals and mine in your cabin." Thom stared at him as hard as the others did.

"Are you . . . ?" The bearded man's voice was a hoarse whisper. "Are you . . . by any chance . . . a young lord in disguise?"

"I am no lord." Mat laughed. He had reason to laugh. The *Gray Gull* was well out into the darkness of the harbor, now, with the wharf a band of light pointing up the black gap, not far ahead now, where the water gates let out onto the river. The sweeps drove the vessel toward that gap quickly. Men were already swinging the long, slanting booms around preparatory to unlashing the sails. And with gold in his hands, the captain no longer seemed ready to throw anyone overboard. "If you don't mind, Captain, could we see our cabin? Your cabin, I mean. It's late, and I for one want a few hours' sleep." His stomach spoke to him. "And supper!"

As the vessel put its bow into the blackness, the bearded man himself led the way down a ladder to a short, narrow passage lined with doors set close together. While the captain cleared his things from his cabin—it ran the width of the stern, with its bed and all of its furnishings built into the walls except two chairs and a few chests—and saw that Mat and Thom were settled, Mat learned a great deal, beginning with the fact that the man would not be pushing any passengers out of their quarters. He had too much respect for the coin they had paid, if not for them, to allow that. The captain would take his first's cabin, and that officer would take the second's bed, pushing each lower man down till the deckmaster would end sleeping up in the bow with the crew.

Mat did not think that information could be very useful, but he listened to everything the man said. It was always best to know not only where you were going, but who you were dealing with, or they might just take your coat and boots and leave you to walk home through the rain in bare feet.

The captain was a Tairen named Huan Mallia, and he spoke with great volubility once he had worked out Mat and Thom to his own satisfaction. He was not nobly born, he said, not him, but he would not have anyone think he was a fool. A young man with more gold than any young man should have by right might be a thief, if everyone did not know thieves never escaped Tar Valon with their haul. A young man dressed like a farmboy but with the air and confidence of the lord he denied being—"By the Stone, I'll not say you are, if you say you are not." Mallia winked and chuckled and tugged the point of his beard. A young man carrying a paper bearing the Amyrlin Seat's seal and bound for Andor. There was no secret that Queen Morgase had visited Tar Valon, though her reason certainly was. It was obvious to Mallia something was afoot between Caemlyn and Tar Valon. And Mat and Thom were messengers—for Morgase, he thought, by Mat's accent. Anything he could do to help in so great an enterprise would be his pleasure, not that he meant to poke where he was not wanted.

Mat exchanged startled looks with Thom, who was stowing his instrument cases under a table built out from one wall. The room had two small windows on either side, and a pair of lamps in jointed brackets for light. "That's nonsense," Mat said.

"Of course," Mallia replied. He straightened from pulling clothes out of a chest at the foot of the bed and smiled. "Of course." A cupboard in the wall seemed to hold charts of the river he would need. "I'll say no more."

But he did mean to poke, though he attempted to disguise it, and he rambled while he tried to pry. Mat listened, and answered the questions with grunts or shrugs or a word or two, while Thom said less than that. The gleeman kept shaking his head while unburdening himself of his possessions.

Mallia had been a river man all his life, though he dreamed of sailing on the sea. He hardly spoke of a country beside Tear without contempt; Andor was the only one to escape, and the praise he finally managed was grudging despite his obvious efforts. "Good horses in Andor, I've heard. Not bad. Not as good as Tairen stock, but good enough. You make good steel, and iron goods, bronze and copper—I've traded for them often enough, though you charge a weighty price—but then you have those mines in the Mountains of Mist. Gold mines, too. We have to earn our gold, in Tear."

Mayene received his greatest contempt. "Even less a country than Murandy is. One city and a few leagues of land. They underprice the oil from our good Tairen olives just because their ships know how to find the oilfish shoals. They've no right to be a country at all."

He hated Illian. "One day we'll loot Illian bare, tear down every town and village, and sow their filthy ground with salt." Mallia's beard almost bristled with outrage at how filthy the Illian land was. "Even their olives are putrid! One day we'll carry every last Illianer pig off in chains! That is what the High Lord Samon says."

Mat wondered what the man thought Tear would do with all those people if they actually fulfilled this scheme. The Illianers would have to be fed, and they would surely do no work in chains. It made no sense to him, but Mallia's eyes shone when he spoke of it.

Only fools let themselves be ruled by a king or a queen, by one man or woman. "Except Queen Morgase, of course," he put in hastily. "She is a fine woman, so I've heard. Beautiful, I'm told." All those fools bowing to one fool. The High Lords ruled Tear together, reaching decisions in concert, and that was how things should be. The High Lords knew

what was right and good and true. Especially the High Lord
Samon. No man could go wrong obeying the High Lords.
Especially the High Lord Samon.

Beyond kings and queens, beyond even Illian, lay a bigger hatred Mallia attempted to keep hidden, but he talked
so much in trying to find out what they were up to, and
grew so carried away by the sound of his own voice, that he
let more slip than he intended.

They must travel a great deal, serving a great Queen like
Morgase. They must have seen many lands. He dreamed of
the sea because then he could see lands he had only heard
of, because then he could find the Mayener oilfish shoals,
could out-trade the Sea Folk and the filthy Illianers. And
the sea was far from Tar Valon. They must understand that,
forced as they were to travel among odd places and people,
places and people they could not have stomached if they
were not serving Queen Morgase.

"I never liked docking there, never knowing who might
be using the Power." He almost spat the last word. Since he
had heard the High Lord Samon speak, though. . . . "Burn
my soul, it makes me feel like hullworms are burrowing
into my belly just looking at their White Tower, now, knowing what they plan."

The High Lord Samon said the Aes Sedai meant to rule
the world. Samon said they meant to crush every nation, put
their foot on every man's throat. Samon said Tear could no
longer hold the Power out of its own lands and believe that
was enough. Samon said Tear had its rightful day of glory
coming, but Tar Valon stood between Tear and glory.

"There's no hope for it. Sooner or later they will have to
be hunted down and killed, every last Aes Sedai. The High
Lord Samon says the others might be saved—the young
ones, the novices, the Accepted—if they're brought to the
Stone, but the rest must be eradicated. That's what the High
Lord Samon says. The White Tower must be destroyed."

For a moment Mallia stood in the middle of his cabin,
arms full of clothes and books and rolled charts, hair almost brushing the deck beams overhead, staring at nothing
with pale blue eyes while the White Tower tumbled into
ruin. Then he gave a start as if realizing what he had just
said. His pointed beard waggled uncertainly.

"That is . . . that's what he says. I . . . I think that may be going too far, myself. The High Lord Samon. . . . He speaks so that he carries a man beyond his own beliefs. If Caemlyn can make covenants with the Tower, why, so can Tear." He shivered and did not seem to know it. "That is what I say."

"As you say," Mat told him, and felt mischief bubble inside. "I think your suggestion is the right one, Captain. But don't stop with a few Accepted, though. Ask a dozen Aes Sedai to come, or two. Think what the Stone of Tear would be like with two dozen Aes Sedai in it."

Mallia shuddered. "I will send a man for my money chest," he said stiffly, and stalked out.

Mat frowned at the closed door. "I think I shouldn't have said that."

"I don't know why you might think that," Thom said dryly. "Next you could try telling the Lord Captain Commander of the Whitecloaks he should marry the Amyrlin Seat." His brows drew down, like white caterpillars. "High Lord Samon. I never heard of any High Lord Samon."

It was Mat's turn to be dry. "Well, even you cannot know everything about all the kings and queens and nobles there are, Thom. One or two might just have escaped your notice."

"I know the names of the kings and queens, boy, and the names of all the High Lords of Tear, too. I suppose they could have raised a Lord of the Land, but I'd think I would have heard of the old High Lord dying. If you had settled for booting some poor fellows out of their cabin instead of taking the captain's, we'd each have a bed to ourselves, narrow and hard as it might be. Now we have to share Mallia's. I hope you don't snore, boy. I cannot abide snoring."

Mat ground his teeth. As he recalled, Thom had a snore like a woodrasp working on an oak knot. He had forgotten that.

It was one of the two large men—Sanor or Vasa; he did not give his name—who came to pull the captain's ironbound money chest from under the bed. He never said a word, only made sketchy bows, and frowned at them when he thought they were not looking, and left.

Mat was beginning to wonder if the luck that had been with him all night had deserted him at last. He was going to have to put up with Thom's snoring, and truth to tell, it might not have been the best luck in the world to jump onto this particular ship waving a paper signed by the Amyrlin Seat and sealed with the Flame of Tar Valon. On impulse he pulled out one of his cylindrical leather dice cups, popped off the tight-fitting lid, and upended the dice onto the table.

They were spotted dice, and five single pips stared up at him. The Dark One's Eyes, that was called in some games. It was a losing toss in those, a winning in other games. *But what game am I playing?* He scooped the dice up, tossed them again. Five pips. Another toss, and again the Dark One's Eyes winked at him.

"If you used those dice to win all that gold," Thom said quietly, "no wonder you had to leave by the first ship sailing." He had stripped down to his shirt, and had that half over his head when he spoke. His knees were knobby and his legs seemed all sinew and stringy muscle, the right a little shrunken. "Boy, a twelve-year-old girl would cut your heart out if she knew you were using dice like that against her."

"It isn't the dice," Mat muttered. "It's the luck." *Aes Sedai luck? Or the Dark One's luck?* He pushed the dice back into the cup and capped it.

"I suppose," Thom said, climbing into the bed, "you aren't going to tell me where all that gold came from, then."

"I won it. Tonight. With their dice."

"Uh-huh. And I suppose you're not going to explain that paper you were waving around—I saw the seal, boy!—or all that talk about White Tower business, or why the dock-master had your description from an Aes Sedai, either."

"I am carrying a letter to Morgase for Elayne, Thom," Mat said a good deal more patiently than he felt. "Nynaeve gave me the paper. I don't know where she got it."

"Well, if you are not going to tell me, I am going to sleep. Blow out the lamps, will you?" Thom rolled on his side and pulled a pillow over his head.

Even after Mat had stripped off down to his smallclothes and crawled under the blankets—after blowing out the lamps—he could not sleep, though Mallia had done well by himself with a good feather mattress. He had been right about Thom's snoring, and that pillow muffled nothing. It sounded as if Thom were cutting wood cross-grain with a rusty saw. And he could not stop thinking. How *had* Nynaeve and Egwene, and Elayne, gotten that paper

from the Amyrlin? They had to be involved with the Amyrlin Seat herself—in some plot, one of those White Tower
machinations—but now that he thought about it, they had
to be holding something back from the Amyrlin, too.

"'Please carry a letter to my mother, Mat,'" he said
softly, in a high-pitched, mocking voice. "Fool! The Amyrlin would have sent a Warder with any letter from the
Daughter-Heir to the Queen. Blind fool, wanting to get out
of the Tower so bad I couldn't see it." Thom's snore seemed
to trumpet agreement.

Most of all, though, he thought about luck, and footpads.

The first bump of something against the stern barely registered on him. He paid no attention to a thump and scuffle
from the deck overhead, or the tread of boots. The vessel
itself made enough noises, and there had to be someone on
deck for the ship to make its way downriver. But stealthy
footsteps in the passageway leading to his door merged
with thoughts of footpads and made his ears prick up.

He nudged Thom in the ribs with an elbow. "Wake up,"
he said softly. "There's somebody outside in the hall." He
was already easing himself off the bed, hoping the cabin
floor—*Deck, floor, whatever it bloody is!*—would not
creak under his feet. Thom grunted, smacked his lips, and
resumed snoring.

There was no time to worry about Thom. The footsteps
were right outside. Taking up his quarterstaff, Mat placed
himself in front of the door and waited.

The door swung open slowly, and two cloaked men, one
behind the other, were faintly outlined by dim moonlight
through the hatch at the top of the ladder they had crept
down. The moonlight was enough to glint off bare knife
blades. Both men gasped; they obviously had not expected
to find anyone waiting for them.

Mat thrust with the quarterstaff, catching the first man
hard right under where his ribs joined together. He heard
his father's voice as he struck. *It's a killing blow, Mat.
Don't ever use it unless it's your life.* But those knives made
it for his life; there was no room in the cabin for swinging
a staff.

Even as the man made a choking sound and folded
toward the deck, fighting vainly for breath, Mat stepped forward and drove the end of the quarterstaff over him into

the second man's throat with a loud crunch. That fellow dropped his knife to clutch at his throat, and fell on top of his companion, both of them scraping their boots across the deck, death rattles already sounding in their throats.

Mat stood there, staring down at them. *Two men. No, burn me, three! I don't think I ever hurt another human being before, and now I've killed three men in one night. Light!*

Silence filled the dark passageway, and he heard the thump of boots on the deck overhead. The crewmen all went barefoot.

Trying not to think about what he was doing, Mat ripped the cloak from one of the dead men and settled it around his shoulders, hiding the pale linen of his smallclothes. On bare feet he padded down the passage and climbed the ladder, barely sticking his eyes above the hatch coping.

Pale moonlight reflected off the taut sails, but night still covered the deck with shadows, and there was no sound except the rush of water along the vessel's sides. Only one man at the tiller, the hood of his cloak pulled up against the chill, seemed to be on deck. The man shifted, and boot leather scuffed on the deck planks.

Holding the quarterstaff low and hoping it would not be noticed, Mat climbed on up. "He's dead," he muttered in a low, rough whisper.

"I hope he squealed when you cut his throat." The heavily accented voice was one Mat remembered calling from the mouth of a twisting street in Tar Valon. "This boy, he causes us too much of the trouble. Wait! Who are you?"

Mat swung the staff with all his strength. The thick wood smashed into the man's head, the hood of his cloak only partly muffling a sound like a melon hitting the floor.

The man fell across the tiller, shoving it over, and the vessel lurched, staggering Mat. Out of the corner of his eye he saw a shape rising out of the shadows by the railing, and the gleam of a blade, and he knew he would never get his staff around before it struck home. Something else that shone streaked through the night and merged with the dim shape with a dull *thunk*. The rising motion became a fall, and a man sprawled almost at Mat's feet.

A babble of voices rose belowdecks as the ship swung again, the tiller shifting with the first man's weight.

Thom limped from the hatch in cloak and smallclothes, raising the shutter on a bull's-eye lantern. "You were lucky, boy. One of those below had this lantern. Could have set the ship on fire, lying there." The light showed a knife hilt sticking up from the chest of a man with dead, staring eyes. Mat had never seen him before; he was sure he would have remembered someone with that many scars on his face. Thom kicked a dagger away from the dead man's outflung hand, then bent to retrieve his own knife, wiping the blade on the corpse's cloak. "Very lucky, boy. Very lucky indeed."

There was a rope tied to the stern rail. Thom stepped over to it, shining the light down astern, and Mat joined him. At the other end of the rope was one of the small boats from Southharbor, its square lantern extinguished. Two more men stood among the pulled-in oars.

"The Great Lord take me, it's him!" one of them gasped. The other darted forward to work frantically at the knot holding the rope.

"You want to kill these two as well?" Thom asked, his voice booming as it did when he performed.

"No, Thom," Mat said quietly. "No."

The men in the boat must have heard the question and not the answer, for they abandoned the attempt to free their boat and leaped over the side with great splashes. The sound of them thrashing away across the river was loud.

"Fools," Thom muttered. "The river narrows somewhat after Tar Valon, but it must still be half a mile or more wide here. They'll never make it in the dark."

"By the Stone!" came a shout from the hatch. "What happens here? There are dead men in the passageway! What's Vasa doing lying on the tiller? He'll run us onto a mudbank!" Naked save for linen underbreeches, Mallia dashed to the tiller, hauling the dead man off roughly as he pulled the long lever to put the course straight again. "That isn't Vasa! Burn my soul, who are all these dead men?" Others were clambering on deck now, barefoot crewmen and frightened passengers wrapped in cloaks and blankets.

Shielding his actions with his body, Thom slipped his knife under the rope and severed it in one stroke. The small boat began falling back into the darkness. "River brigands, Captain," he said. "Young Mat and I have saved your vessel from river brigands. They might have cut everyone's throat if not for us. Perhaps you should reconsider your passage fee."

"Brigands!" Mallia exclaimed. "There are plenty of those down around Cairhien, but I never heard of it this far north!" The huddled passengers began to mutter about brigands and having their throats cut.

Mat walked stiffly to the hatch. Behind him, he heard Mallia. "He's a cold one. I never heard that Andor employed assassins, but burn my soul, he is a cold one."

Mat stumbled down the ladder, stepped over the two bodies in the passage, and slammed the door of the captain's cabin behind him. He made it halfway to the bed before the shaking hit him, and then all he could do was sink down on his knees. *Light, what game am I playing in? I have to know the game if I'm going to win. Light, what game?*

Playing "Rose of the Morning" softly on his flute, Rand peered into his campfire, where a rabbit was roasting on a stick slanting over the flames. A night wind made the flames flicker; he barely noticed the smell of the rabbit, though a vagrant thought did come that he needed to find more salt in the next village or town. "Rose of the Morning" was one of the tunes he had played at those weddings.

How many days ago was that? Were there really so many, or did I imagine it? Every woman in the village deciding to marry at once? What was its name? Am I going mad already?

Sweat beaded on his face, but he played on, barely loud enough to be heard, staring into the fire. Moiraine had told him he was *ta'veren.* Everyone said he was *ta'veren.* Maybe he really was. People like that—changed—things around them. A *ta'veren* might have *caused* all those weddings. But that was too close to something he did not want to think about.

They say I'm the Dragon Reborn, too. They all say it. The living say it, and the dead. That doesn't make it true. I had to let them proclaim me. Duty. I had no choice, but that does not make it true.

He could not seem to stop playing that one tune. It made him think of Egwene. He had thought once that he would marry Egwene. A long time ago, that seemed. That was gone, now. She had come in his dreams, though. *It might have been her. Her face. It was her face.*

Only, there had been so many faces, faces he knew. Tam, and his mother, and Mat, and Perrin. All trying to kill him. It had not really been them, of course. Only their faces, on Shadowspawn. He thought it had not really been them. Even in his dreams it seemed the Shadowspawn walked. Were they only dreams? Some dreams were real, he knew. And others were only dreams, nightmares, or hopes. But how to tell the difference? Min had walked his dreams one night— and tried to plant a knife in his back. He was still surprised at how much that had pained him. He had been careless, let her come close, let down his guard. Around Min, he had not felt any need to be on his guard in so long, despite the things she saw when she looked at him. Being with her had been like having balm soothed into his wounds.

And then she tried to kill me! The music rose to a discordant screech, but he pulled it back to softness. *Not her. Shadowspawn with her face. Least of them all would Min hurt me.* He could not understand why he thought that, but he was sure it was true.

So many faces in his dreams. Selene had come, cool and mysterious and so lovely his mouth went dry just thinking of her, offering him glory as she had—so long ago, it seemed—but now it was the sword she said he had to take. And with the sword would come Selene. *Callandor.* That was always in his dreams. Always. And taunting faces. Hands, pushing Egwene, and Nynaeve, and Elayne into cages, snaring them in nets, hurting them. Why should he weep more for Elayne than for the other two?

His head spun. His head hurt as much as his side, and sweat rolled down his face, and he softly played "Rose of the Morning" through the night, fearing to sleep. Fearing to dream.

CHAPTER
33

Within the Weave

From his saddle, Perrin frowned down at the flat stone half hidden in weeds by the roadside. This road of hard-packed dirt, already called the Lugard Road now they were near the Manetherendrelle and the border of Murandy, had been paved once, long in the past, so Moiraine had said two days earlier, and bits of paving stone still worked their way to the surface from time to time. This one had an odd marking on it.

If dogs had been able to make footprints on stone, he would have said it was the print of a large hound. There were no hound's footprints in any of the bare ground he could see, where softer dirt on the verge might take one, and no smell of any dog's trail. Just a faint trace in the air of something burned, almost the sulphurous smell left by setting off fireworks. There was a town ahead, where the road struck the river; maybe some children had sneaked out here with some of the Illuminators' handiwork.

A long way yet for children to sneak. But he had seen farms. It could have been farm children. *Whatever it is, it has nothing to do with that marking. Horses don't fly, and dogs don't make footprints on stone. I'm getting too tired to think straight.*

Yawning, he dug his heels into Stepper's ribs, and the dun broke into a gallop after the others. Moiraine had been pushing them hard since leaving Jarra, and there was no waiting for anyone who stopped for even a moment. When the Aes Sedai put her mind on something, she was as hard as cold hammered iron. Loial had given up reading as he rode six days earlier, after looking up to find himself left a mile behind and everyone else almost out of sight over the next hill.

Perrin slowed Stepper alongside the Ogier's big horse, behind Moiraine's white mare, and yawned again. Lan was up ahead somewhere, scouting. The sun behind them stood no more than an hour above the treetops, but the Warder had said they would reach a town called Remen, on the Manetherendrelle, before dark. Perrin was not sure he wanted to see what awaited them there. He did not know what it might be, but the days since Jarra had made him wary.

"I don't see why you can't sleep," Loial told him. "I am so tired by the time she lets us halt for the night, I fall asleep before I can lie down."

Perrin only shook his head. There was no way to explain to Loial that he did not dare sleep soundly, that even his lightest sleep was full of troubled dreams. Like that odd one with Egwene and Hopper in it. *Well, no wonder I dream about her. Light, I wonder how she is. Safe in the Tower by now, and learning how to be Aes Sedai. Verin will look after her, and after Mat, too.* He did not think anyone needed to look after Nynaeve; around Nynaeve, to his mind, other people needed someone to look after them.

He did not want to think about Hopper. He was succeeding in keeping live wolves out of his head, although at the price of feeling as if he had been hammered-and-drawn by a hasty hand; he did not want to think a dead wolf might be creeping in. He shook himself and forced his eyes wide open. Not even Hopper.

There had been more reasons than bad dreams not to sleep well. They had found other signs left by Rand's passage. Between Jarra and the River Boern there had been none Perrin could see, but when they crossed the Boern by a stone bridge arching from one fifty-foot river cliff to another, they had left behind a town called Sidon all in ashes. Every building. Only a few stone walls and chimneys still stood among the ruins.

Bedraggled townspeople said a lantern dropped in a barn had started it, and then the fire seemed to run wild, and everything went wrong. Half the buckets that could be found had holes in them. Every last burning wall had fallen outward instead of in, setting houses to either side alight. Flaming timbers from the inn had somehow tumbled as far as the main well in the square, so no one could draw more water from it to fight the fires, and houses had fallen right on top of three other wells. Even the wind had seemed to shift, fanning the flames in every direction.

There had been no need to ask Moiraine if Rand's presence had caused it; her face, like cold iron, was answer enough. The Pattern shaped itself around Rand, and chance ran wild.

Beyond Sidon they had ridden through four small towns where only Lan's tracking told them Rand was still ahead. Rand was afoot, now, and had been for some time. They had found his horse back beyond Jarra, dead, looking as if it had been mauled by wolves, or dogs run wild. It had been hard for Perrin not to reach out, then, especially when Moiraine looked up from the horse to frown at him. Luckily, Lan had found the tracks of Rand's boots, running from where the dead horse lay. One boot heel had a three-cornered gouge from a rock; it made his prints plain. But afoot or mounted, he seemed to be staying ahead of them.

In the four villages after Sidon, the biggest excitement anyone could remember was seeing Loial ride in, and discovering that he was an Ogier, for real and for true. They were so caught up with that, that they barely even noticed Perrin's eyes, and when they did. . . . Well, if Ogier were real, then men could very well have any color eyes at all.

But after those came a little place named Willar, and it was celebrating. The spring on the village common was flowing again, after a year of hauling water a mile from a stream when all efforts at digging wells had failed and half the people had moved away. Willar would not die after all. Three more untouched villages had been followed in quick succession, all in one day, by Samaha, where every well in town had gone dry just the night before, and people were muttering about the Dark One; then Tallan, where all the old arguments the village had ever known had bubbled to the surface like overflowing cesspits a morning earlier, and it had taken three murders to shock everyone back to his senses; and finally Fyall, where the crops this spring looked to be the poorest anyone could remember, but the Mayor, digging a new privy behind his house, had found rotted leather sacks full of gold, so none would go hungry. No one in Fyall recognized the fat coins, with a woman's face on one side and an eagle on the other; Moiraine said they had been minted in Manetheren.

Perrin had finally asked her about it, as they sat around their campfire one night. "After Jarra, I thought.... They were all so happy, with their weddings. Even the White-cloaks were only made to look like fools. Fyall was all right—Rand couldn't have had anything to do with their crops; they were failing before he ever came, and that gold was surely good, with their need—but all this other.... That town burning, and the wells failing, and.... That is evil, Moiraine. I can't believe Rand is evil. The Pattern may be shaping itself around him, but how can the Pattern be that evil? It makes no sense, and things have to make sense. If you make a tool with no sense to it, it's wasted metal. The Pattern wouldn't make waste."

Lan gave him a wry look, and vanished into the darkness to make a circuit around their campsite. Loial, already stretched out in his blankets, lifted his head to listen, ears pricking forward.

Moiraine was silent for a time, warming her hands. Finally she spoke while staring into the flames. "The Creator is good, Perrin. The Father of Lies is evil. The Pattern of Age, the Age Lace itself, is neither. The Pattern is what is. The Wheel of Time weaves all lives into the Pattern, all actions. A pattern that is all one color is no pattern. For the Pattern of an Age, good and ill are the warp and the woof."

Even riding through late-afternoon sunshine three days later, Perrin felt the chill he had had on first hearing her say those words. He wanted to believe the Pattern was good. He wanted to believe that when men did evil things, they were going against the Pattern, distorting it. To him the Pattern was a fine and intricate creation made by a master smith. That it mixed pot metal and worse in with good steel with never a care was a cold thought.

"I care," he muttered softly. "Light, I do care." Moiraine glanced back at him, and he fell silent. He was not sure what the Aes Sedai cared about, beyond Rand.

A few minutes later Lan appeared from ahead and swung his black warhorse in beside Moiraine's mare. "Remen lies just over the next hill," he said. "They have had an eventful day or two, it seems."

Loial's ears twitched once. "Rand?"

The Warder shook his head. "I do not know. Perhaps Moiraine can say, when she sees." The Aes Sedai gave him a searching look, then heeled her white mare to a quicker step.

They topped the hill, and Remen lay spread out below them, hard against the river. The Manetherendrelle stretched more than half a mile wide here, and there was no bridge, though two crowded, bargelike ferries crept across, propelled by long oars, and one nearly empty was returning. Three more shared long stone docks with nearly a dozen river traders' vessels, some with one mast, some with two. A few bulky gray stone warehouses separated the docks from the town itself, where the buildings seemed mostly of stone, as well, though roofed in tiles of every color from yellow to red to purple, and the streets ran every which way around a central square.

Moiraine pulled up the deep hood of her cloak to hide her face before they rode down.

As usual, the people in the streets stared at Loial, but this time Perrin heard awed murmurs of "Ogier." Loial sat straighter in his saddle than he had in some time, and his ears stood straight, and a smile just curled the ends of his wide mouth. He was obviously trying not to let on that he was pleased, but he looked like a cat having its ears scratched.

Remen looked like any of a dozen towns to Perrin—it was full of man-made aromas and man smell; with a strong smell of the river, of course—and he was wondering what Lan could have meant when the hair on the back of his neck stirred as he scented something—wrong. As soon as his nose took it in, it was gone like a horsehair dropped onto hot coals, but he remembered it. He had smelled the same smell at Jarra, and it had vanished the same way, then. It was not a Twisted One or a Neverborn—*Trolloc, burn me, not a Twisted One! Not a Neverborn! A Myrddraal, a Fade, a Halfman, anything but a Neverborn!*—not a Trolloc or a Fade, yet the stench had been every bit as sharp, every bit as vile. But whatever gave off that scent left no lasting trail, it seemed.

They rode into the town square. One of the big paving blocks had been pried up, right in the middle of the square, so a gibbet could be erected. A single thick timber rose out of the dirt, supporting a braced crosspiece from which hung an iron cage, the bottom of it four paces high. A tall man dressed all in grays and browns sat in the cage, holding his knees under his chin. He had no room to do otherwise. Three small boys were pitching stones at him. The man looked straight ahead, not flinching when a stone made it between the bars. More than one trickle of blood stained his face. The townspeople walking by paid no more mind to what the boys were doing than the man did, though every last one of them looked at the cage, most of them with approval, and some with fear.

Moiraine made a sound in her throat that might have been disgust.

"There is more," Lan said. "Come. I've already arranged rooms at an inn. I think you will find it interesting."

Perrin looked back over his shoulder at the caged man as he rode after them. There was something familiar about the man, but he could not place it.

"They shouldn't do that." Loial's rumble sounded half-way to a snarl. "The children, I mean. The grown-ups should stop them."

"They should," Perrin agreed, barely paying attention. *Why is he familiar?*

The sign over the door of the inn Lan led them to, nearer the river, read Wayland's Forge, which Perrin took for a good omen, though there seemed to be nothing of the smithy about the place except the leather-aproned man with a hammer painted on the sign. It was a large, purple-roofed, three-story building of squared and polished gray stones, with large windows and scroll-carved doors, and it had a prosperous look. Stablemen came running to take the horses, bowing even more deeply after Lan tossed them coins.

Inside, Perrin stared at the people. The men and women at the tables were all dressed in their feastday clothes, it seemed to him, with more embroidered coats, more lace on dresses, more colored ribbons and fringed scarves, than he had seen in a long time. Only four men sitting at one table wore plain coats, and they were the only ones who did not look up expectantly when Perrin and the others walked in. The four men kept on talking softly. He could make out a little of what they were saying, about the virtues of ice peppers over furs as cargo and what the troubles in Saldaea might have done to prices. Captains of trading ships, he decided. The others seemed to be local folk. Even the serving women appeared to be wearing their best, their long aprons covering embroidered dresses with bits of lace at the neck.

The kitchen was working heavily; he could smell mutton, lamb, chicken, and beef, as well as some sort of vegetables. And a spicy cake that made him forget meat for a moment.

The innkeeper himself met them just inside, a plump, bald-headed man with shining brown eyes in a smooth pink face, bowing and dry-washing his hands. If he had not come to them, Perrin would never have taken him for the landlord, for instead of the expected white apron, he wore a coat like everyone else, all white-and-green embroidery on stout blue wool that had the man sweating with its weight.

Why are they all wearing clothes for festival? Perrin wondered.

"Ah, Master Andra," the innkeeper said, addressing Lan. "And an Ogier, just as you said. Not that I doubted, of course. Not with all that's happened, and never your word, master. Why not an Ogier? Ah, friend Ogier, to be having you in the house gives me more pleasure than you can be knowing. 'Tis a fine thing, and a fitting cap to it all. Ah, and mistress. . . ." His eyes took in the deep blue silk of her dress and the rich wool of her cloak, dusty from travel but still fine. "Forgive me, Lady, please." His bow bent him like a horseshoe. "Master Andra did not make your station clear, Lady. I meant no disrespect. You are even more welcome than friend Ogier here, of course, Lady. Please, take no offense at Gainor Furlan's poor tongue."

"I take none." Moiraine's voice calmly accepted the title Furlan gave her. It was far from the first time the Aes Sedai had gone under another name, or pretended to be something she was not. It was not the first Perrin had heard Lan name himself Andra, either. The deep hood still hid Moiraine's smooth Aes Sedai features, and she held her cloak around her with one hand as if taken with a chill. Not the hand on which she wore her Great Serpent ring. "You have had strange occurrences in the town, innkeeper, so I understand. Nothing to trouble travelers, I trust."

"Ah, Lady, you might be calling them strange indeed. Your own radiant presence is more than enough to honor this humble house, Lady, and bringing an Ogier with you, but we have Hunters in Remen, too. Right here in Wayland's Forge, they are. Hunters for the Horn of Valere, set out from Illian for adventure. And adventure they found, Lady, here in Remen, or just a mile or two upriver, fighting wild Aielmen, of all things. Can you imagine black-veiled Aiel savages in Altara, Lady?"

Aiel. Now Perrin knew what was familiar about the man in the cage. He had seen an Aiel, once, one of those fierce, nearly legendary denizens of the harsh land called the Waste. The man had looked a good deal like Rand, taller than most, with gray eyes and reddish hair, and he had been dressed like the man in the cage, all in browns and grays that would fade into rock or brush, with soft boots laced to his knees. Perrin could almost hear Min's voice again. *An Aielman in a cage. A turning point in your life, or something important that will happen.*

"Why do you have . . . ?" He stopped to clear his throat so he would not sound so hoarse. "How did an Aiel come to be caged in your town square?"

"Ah, young master, that is a story to. . . ." Furlan trailed off, eyeing him up and down, taking in his plain country clothes and the longbow in his hands, pausing over the axe at his belt opposite his quiver. The plump man gave a start when his study reached Perrin's face, as if, with a Lady and an Ogier present, he had just now noticed Perrin's yellow eyes. "He would be your servant, Master Andra?" he asked cautiously.

"Answer him," was all Lan said.

"Ah. Ah, of course, Master Andra. But here's who can tell it better than myself. 'Tis Lord Orban, himself. 'Tis he we have gathered to hear."

A dark-haired, youngish man in a red coat, with a bandage wound around his temples, was making his way down the stairs at the side of the common room using padded crutches, the left leg of his breeches cut away so more bandages could strap his calf from ankle to knee. The townspeople murmured as if seeing something wondrous. The ship captains went on with their quiet talking; they had come 'round to furs.

Furlan might have thought the man in the red coat could tell the story better, but he went ahead himself. "Lord Orban and Lord Gann faced twenty wild Aielmen with only ten retainers. Ah, fierce was the fighting and hard, with many wounds given and received. Six good retainers died, and every man took hurts, Lord Orban and Lord Gann worst of all, but every Aiel they slew, save those who fled, and one they took prisoner. 'Tis that one you see out there in the square, where he'll not be troubling the countryside anymore with his savage ways, no more than the dead ones will."

"You have had trouble from Aiel in this district?" Moiraine asked.

Perrin was wondering the same thing, with no little consternation. If some people still occasionally used "black-veiled Aiel" as a term for someone violent, it was testimony to the impression the Aiel War had left, but that was twenty years in the past, now, and the Aiel had never come out of the Waste before or since. *But I saw one this side of the Spine of the World, and now I've seen two.*

The innkeeper rubbed at his bald head. "Ah. Ah, no, Lady, not exactly. But we would have had, you can be sure, with twenty savages loose. Why, everyone remembers how they killed and looted and burned their way across Cairhien. Men from this very village marched to the Battle of the Shining Walls, when the nations gathered to throw them back. I myself suffered from a twisted back at the time and so could not go, but I remember well, as we all do. How they came here, so far from their own land, or why, I do not know, but Lord Orban and Lord Gann saved us from them." There was a murmur of agreement from the folk in feastday clothes.

Orban himself came stumping across the common room, not seeming to see anyone but the innkeeper. Perrin could smell stale wine before he was even close. "Where's that old woman taken herself off to with her herbs, Furlan?" Orban demanded roughly. "Gann's wounds are paining him, and my head feels about to split open."

Furlan almost bent his head to the floor. "Ah, Mother Leich will be back in the morning, Lord Orban. A birthing, Lord. But she said she'd stitched and poulticed your wounds, and Lord Gann's, so there'd be no worrying. Ah, Lord Orban, I'm sure she'll be seeing to you first thing on the morrow."

The bandaged man muttered something under his breath—under his breath to any ears but Perrin's—about waiting on a farmwife "throwing her litter" and something else about being "sewn up like a sack of meal." He shifted sullen, angry eyes, and for the first time appeared to see the newcomers. Perrin, he dismissed immediately, which did not surprise Perrin at all. His eyes widened a little at Loial—*He's seen Ogier*, Perrin thought, *but he never thought to see one here*—narrowed a bit at Lan—*He knows a fighting man when he sees one, and he does not like seeing one*—and brightened as he stooped to peer inside Moiraine's hood, though he was not close enough to see her face.

Perrin decided not to think anything at all about that, not concerning an Aes Sedai, and he hoped neither Moiraine nor Lan thought anything of it, either. A light in the Warder's eyes told him he had missed on that hope, at least.

"Twelve of you fought twenty Aiel?" Lan asked in a flat voice.

Orban straightened, wincing. In an elaborately casual tone, he said, "Aye, you must expect things such as that when you seek the Horn of Valere. It was not the first such encounter for Gann and me, nor will it be the last before we find the Horn. If the Light shines on us." He sounded as if the Light could not possibly do anything else. "Not all our fights have been with Aiel, of course, but there are always those who would stop Hunters, if they could. Gann and I, we do not stop easily." Another approving murmur came from the townspeople. Orban stood a little straighter.

"You lost six, and took one prisoner." From Lan's voice, it was not clear if that was a good exchange or a poor one.

"Aye," Orban said, "we slew the rest, save those who ran. No doubt they're hiding their dead now; I've heard they do that. The Whitecloaks are out searching for them, but they'll never find them."

"There are Whitecloaks here?" Perrin asked sharply.

Orban glanced at him, and dismissed him once more. The man addressed Lan again. "Whitecloaks always put their noses in where they are not wanted or needed. Incompetent louts, all of them. Aye, they'll ride all over the countryside for days, but I doubt they'll find as much as their own shadows."

"I suppose they won't," Lan said.

The bandaged man frowned as if unsure exactly what Lan meant, then rounded on the innkeeper again. "You find that old woman, hear! My head is splitting." With a last glance at Lan, he hobbled away, climbing back up the stairs one at a time, followed by murmurs of admiration for a Hunter of the Horn who had slain Aielmen.

"This is an eventful town." Loial's deep voice drew every eye to him. Except for the ship captains, who seemed to be discussing rope, as near as Perrin could make out. "Everywhere I go, you humans are doing things, hurrying and scurrying, having things happen to you. How can you stand so much excitement?"

"Ah, friend Ogier," Furlan said, "'tis the way of us humans to want excitement. How much I regret not being able to march to the Shining Walls. Why, let me tell you—"

"Our rooms." Moiraine did not raise her voice, but her words cut the innkeeper short like a sharp knife. "Andra did arrange rooms, did he not?"

"Ah, Lady, forgive me. Yes, Master Andra did indeed hire rooms. Forgive me, please. 'Tis all the excitement, makes my head empty itself. Please forgive me, Lady. This way, if you please. If you'll please to follow me." Bowing and scraping, apologizing and babbling without pause, Furlan led them up the stairs.

At the top, Perrin paused to look back. He heard the murmurs of "Lady" and "Ogier" down there, could feel all those eyes, but it seemed to him that he felt one pair of eyes in particular, someone staring not at Moiraine and Loial, but at him.

He picked her out immediately. For one thing, she stood apart from the others, and for another she was the only woman in the room not wearing at least a little lace. Her dark gray, almost black, dress was as plain as the ship captains' clothes, with wide sleeves and narrow skirts, and never a frill or stitch of fancy-work. The dress was divided for riding, he saw when she moved, and she wore soft boots that peeked out under the hem. She was young—no older than he was, perhaps—and tall for a woman, with black hair to her shoulders. A nose that just missed being too large and too bold, a generous mouth, high cheekbones, and dark, slightly tilted eyes. He could not quite decide whether she was beautiful or not.

As soon as he looked down, she turned to address one of the serving women and did not glance at the stairs again, but he was sure he had been right. She had been staring at him.

CHAPTER
34

A Different Dance

Furlan burbled on as he showed them to their rooms, though Perrin did not really listen. He was too busy wondering if the black-haired girl knew what yellow eyes meant. *Burn me, she* was *looking at me.* Then he heard the innkeeper say the words "proclaiming the Dragon in Ghealdan," and he thought his ears would go to sharp points like Loial's.

Moiraine stopped dead in the doorway to her room. "There is another false Dragon, innkeeper? In Ghealdan?" The hood of her cloak still hid her face, but she sounded shaken to her toes. Even listening for the man's reply, Perrin could not help staring at her; he smelled something close to fear.

"Ah, Lady, never you fear. 'Tis a hundred leagues to Ghealdan, and none will trouble you here, not with Master Andra about, and Lord Orban and Lord Gann. Why—"

"Answer her!" Lan said harshly. "Is there a false Dragon in Ghealdan?"

"Ah. Ah, no, Master Andra, not precisely. I said there's a man proclaiming the Dragon in Ghealdan, so we heard a few days gone. Preaching his coming, you might say. Talking about that fellow over in Tarabon we've heard about. Though some do say 'tis Arad Doman, not Tarabon. A long way from here, in any case. Why, any other day, I expect we'd talk more of that than anything else, except maybe the wild tales about Hawkwing's army come back—" Lan's cold eyes might as well have been knife blades from the way Furlan swallowed and scrubbed his hands faster. "I

only know what I hear, Master Andra. 'Tis said the fellow
has a stare can pin you where you stand, and he talks all
sorts of rubbish about the Dragon coming to save us, and
we all have to follow, and even the beasts will fight for the
Dragon. I don't know whether they've arrested him yet or
not. 'Tis likely; the Ghealdanin would not put up long with
that kind of talk."

Masema, Perrin thought wonderingly. *It's bloody
Masema.*

"You are right, innkeeper," Lan said. "This fellow isn't
likely to trouble us here. I knew a fellow once who liked to
make wild speeches. You remember him, Lady Alys, don't
you? Masema?"

Moiraine gave a start. "Masema. Yes. Of course. I had
put him out of my mind." Her voice firmed. "When next I
see Masema, he will wish someone had peeled his hide to
make boots." She slammed the door behind her so hard that
the crash echoed down the hallway.

"Keep a quiet!" came a muffled shout from the far end.
"My head is splitting!"

"Ah." Furlan washed his hands in one direction, then
rubbed them in the other. "Ah. Forgive me, Master Andra,
but Lady Alys is a fierce-sounding woman."

"Only with those who displease her," Lan said blandly.
"Her bite is far worse than her bark."

"Ah. Ah. Ah. Your rooms are this way. Ah, friend Ogier,
when Master Andra told me you were coming, I had an old
Ogier bed brought from the attic where it has been gathering dust these three hundred years or more. Why, 'tis. . . ."

Perrin let the words wash over him, hearing them no
more than a river rock hears the water. The black-haired
young woman worried him. And the caged Aiel.

Once in his own room—a small one in the back; Lan
had done nothing to disabuse the innkeeper of the notion
that Perrin was a servant—he moved mechanically, still
wrapped in thought. He unstrung his bow and propped it
in the corner—keeping it strung too long ruined bow and
string alike—set down his blanketroll and saddlebags beside the washstand and threw his cloak across them. He
hung his belts with quiver and axe from pegs on the wall,
and nearly lay down on the bed before a jaw-cracking yawn
reminded him how dangerous that might be. The bed was

narrow, and the mattress appeared to be all lumps; it looked more inviting than any bed he could remember. He sat on the three-legged stool, instead, and thought. Always he liked to think things through.

After a time, Loial rapped on the door and put his head in. The Ogier's ears practically quivered with excitement, and his grin very nearly split his broad face in two. "Perrin, you will not believe it! My bed is sung wood! Why, it must be well over a thousand years old. No Treesinger has sung a piece so large in at least that long. I myself would not care to try it, and I have the talent more strongly than most, now. Well, to be truthful, there are not many of us with the talent at all, anymore. But I *am* among the best of those who can sing wood."

"That is very interesting," Perrin said. *An Aiel in a cage. That is what Min said. Why was that girl staring at me?*

"I thought it was." Loial sounded a little put out that he did not share the Ogier's excitement, but all Perrin wanted to do was think. "Supper is ready below, Perrin. They have prepared their finest in case the Hunters want anything, but we can have some."

"You go on, Loial. I'm not hungry." The smells of cooking meat floating up from the kitchen did not interest him. He hardly noticed Loial going.

Hands on his knees, yawning now and again, he tried to work it out. It seemed like one of those puzzles Master Luhhan made, the metal pieces appearing to be linked inextricably. But there was always a trick to make the iron loops and whirls come apart, and there had to be here, too.

The girl had been looking at him. His eyes might explain that, except that the innkeeper had ignored them, and no one else had even noticed. They had an Ogier to look at, and Hunters of the Horn in the house, and a Lady visiting, and an Aiel caged in the square. Nothing as small as the color of a man's eyes could seize their attention; nothing about a servant could compete with the rest. *So why did she pick me to stare at?*

And the Aiel in the cage. What Min saw was always important. But how? What was he supposed to do? *I could have stopped those children throwing rocks. I should have.* It was no use telling himself the adults would certainly have told him to go on about his business, that he was a stranger in Remen and the Aiel was none of his concern. *I should have tried.*

No answers came to him, so he went back to the beginning and patiently worked through it once more, then again, and again. Still he found nothing except regret for what he had not done.

It came to him after a time that night had finally fallen. The room was dark except for a little moonlight through the lone window. He thought about the tallow candle and the tinderbox he had seen on the mantel over the narrow fireplace, but there was more than enough light for his eyes. *I have to do something, don't I?*

He buckled on his axe, then paused. He had done it without thinking; wearing the thing had become as natural as breathing. He did not like that. But he left the belt around his waist, and went out.

Light from the stairs made the hallway seem almost bright after his room. Talk and laughter drifted up from the common room, and cooking smells from the kitchen. He strode toward the front of the inn, to Moiraine's room, knocked once, and went in. And stopped, his face burning.

Moiraine pulled the pale blue robe that hung from her shoulders around herself. "You wish something?" she asked coolly. She had a silver-backed hairbrush in one hand, and her dark hair, spilling down her neck in dark waves, glistened as if she had been brushing it. Her room was far finer than his, with polished wooden paneling on the walls and silver-chased lamps and a warm fire on the wide brick hearth. The air smelled of rose-scented soap.

"I. . . . I thought Lan was here," he managed to get out. "You two always have your heads together, and I thought he'd. . . . I thought. . . ."

"What do you want, Perrin?"

He took a deep breath. "Is this Rand's doing? I know Lan followed him here, and it all seems odd—the Hunters, and Aiel—but did he do it?"

"I do not think so. I will know more when Lan tells me what he discovers tonight. With luck, what he finds will help with the choice I must make."

"A choice?"

"Rand could have crossed the river and be on his way to Tear cross-country. Or he could have taken ship downriver to Illian, meaning to board another there for Tear. The journey is leagues longer that way, but days faster."

"I don't think we are going to catch him, Moiraine. I don't know how he's doing it, but even afoot he is staying ahead of us. If Lan is right, he is still half a day ahead."

"I could almost suspect he had learned to Travel," Moiraine said with a small frown, "except that if he had, he would have gone straight to Tear. No, he has the blood of long walkers and strong runners in him. But we may take the river anyway. If I cannot catch him, I will be in Tear close behind him. Or waiting for him."

Perrin shifted his feet uneasily; there was cold promise in her voice. "You told me once that you could sense a Darkfriend, one who was far gone into the Shadow, at least. Lan, too. Have you sensed anything like that here?"

She gave a loud sniff and turned back to a tall standing mirror with finely made silver-work set in the legs. Holding her robe closed with one hand, she ran the brush through her hair with the other. "Very few humans are so far gone as that, Perrin, even among the worst Darkfriends." The brush halted in midstroke. "Why do you ask?"

"There was a girl down in the common room staring at me. Not at you and Loial, like everybody else. At me."

The brush resumed motion, and a smile briefly touched Moiraine's lips. "You sometimes forget, Perrin, that you are a good-looking young man. Some girls admire a pair of shoulders." He grunted and shuffled his feet. "Was there something else, Perrin?"

"Uh . . . no." She could not help with Min's viewing, not beyond telling him what he already knew, that it was important. And he did not want to tell her what Min had seen. Or that Min had seen anything, for that matter.

Back out in the hall with the door closed, he leaned against the wall for a moment. *Light, just walking in on her like that, and her. . . .* She was a pretty woman. *And likely old enough to be my mother, or more.* He thought Mat would probably have asked her down to the common room to dance. *No, he wouldn't. Even Mat isn't fool enough to try charming an Aes Sedai.* Moiraine did dance. He had danced with her once himself. And nearly fallen over his own feet with every other step. *Stop thinking about her like a village girl just because you saw. . . . She's bloody Aes*

Sedai! You have that Aiel to worry about. He gave himself
a shake and went downstairs.

The common room was full as it could be, with every
chair taken, and stools and benches brought in, and those
who had nowhere to sit standing along the walls. He did
not see the black-haired girl, and no one else looked at him
twice as he hurriedly crossed the room.

Orban occupied a table to himself, his bandaged leg
propped up on a chair with a cushion, with a soft slipper
on that foot, a silver goblet in his hand, the serving women
keeping it filled with wine. "Aye," he was saying to the
whole room, "we knew the Aiel for fierce fighters, Gann
and I, but there was no time to hesitate. I drew my sword,
and dug my heels into Lion's ribs. . . ."

Perrin gave a start before he realized the man meant his
horse was named Lion. *Wouldn't put it past him to say he
was riding a lion.* He felt a little ashamed; just because he
did not like the man was no reason to suppose the Hunter
would take his boasting that far. He hurried on outside
without looking back.

The street in front of the inn was as crowded as inside,
with people who could not find a place in the common
room peering in through the windows, and twice as many
huddling around the doors to listen to Orban's tale. No one
glanced at Perrin twice, though his passage brought muttered complaints from those jostled a little further from the
door.

Everyone who was out in the night must have been at the
inn, for he saw no one as he walked to the square. Sometimes the shadow of a person moved across a lighted window, but that was all. He had the feel of being watched,
though, and looked around uneasily. Nothing but night-
cloaked streets dotted with glowing windows. Around the
square, most of the windows were dark except a few on upper floors.

The gibbet stood as he remembered, the man—the
Aiel—still in the cage, hanging higher than he could reach.
The Aiel seemed to be awake—at least his head was up—
but he never looked down at Perrin. The stones the children
had been throwing were scattered beneath the cage.

The cage hung from a thick rope tied to a ring on one of
the upper bars and running through a heavy pulley on the

crosspiece down to a pair of stubs, waist-high from the bottom of the upright on either side. The excess rope lay in a careless tangle of coils at the foot of the gibbet.

Perrin looked around again, searching the dark square. He still had the feel of being watched, but he still saw nothing. He listened, and heard nothing. He smelled chimney smoke and cooking from the houses, and man-sweat and old blood from the man in the cage. There was no fear scent from him.

His weight, and then there's the cage, he thought as he moved closer to the gibbet. He did not know when he had decided to do this, or even if he really had decided, but he knew he was going to do it.

Hooking a leg around the heavy upright, he heaved on the rope, hoisting the cage enough to gain a little slack. The way the rope jerked told him the man in the cage had finally moved, but he was in too much of a hurry to stop and tell him what he was doing. The slack let him unwind the rope from around the stubs. Still bracing himself with his leg around the upright, he quickly lowered the cage hand over hand to the paving blocks.

The Aiel was looking at him now, studying him silently. Perrin said nothing. When he got a good look at the cage, his mouth tightened. If a thing was made, even a thing like this, it should be made well. The entire front of the cage was a door, on rude hinges made by a hasty hand, held by a good iron lock on a chain as badly wrought as the cage. He fumbled the chain around until he found the worst link, then jammed the thick spike on his axe through it. A sharp twist of his wrist forced the link open. In seconds he separated the chain, rattled it free, and swung open the front of the cage.

The Aiel sat there, knees yet under his chin, staring at him.

"Well?" Perrin whispered hoarsely. "I opened it, but I'm not going to bloody carry you." He looked hastily around the night-dark square. Still nothing moved, but he still had the feel of eyes watching.

"You are strong, wetlander." The Aiel did not move beyond working his shoulders. "It took three men to hoist me up there. And now you bring me down. Why?"

"I don't like seeing people in cages," Perrin whispered.

He wanted to go. The cage was open, and those eyes were watching. But the Aiel was not moving. *If you do a thing, do it right.* "Will you get out of there before somebody comes?"

The Aiel grasped the frontmost overhead bar of the cage, heaved himself out and to his feet in one motion, then half hung there, supporting himself with his grip on the bar. He would have been nearly a head taller than Perrin, standing straight. He glanced at Perrin's eyes—Perrin knew how they must shine, burnished gold in the moonlight—but he did not mention them. "I have been in there since yesterday, wetlander." He sounded like Lan. Not that their voices or accents were anything alike, but the Aiel had that same unruffled coolness, that same calm sureness. "It will take a moment for my legs to work. I am Gaul, of the Imran sept of the Shaarad Aiel, wetlander. I am *Shae'en M'taal*, a Stone Dog. My water is yours."

"Well, I am Perrin Aybara. Of the Two Rivers. I'm a blacksmith." The man was out of the cage; he could go now. Only, if anyone came along before Gaul could walk, he would be right back into the cage unless they killed him, and either way would waste Perrin's work. "If I had thought, I'd have brought a waterbottle, or a skin. Why do you call me 'wetlander'?"

Gaul gestured toward the river; even Perrin's eyes could not be sure in the moonlight, but he thought the Aiel looked uneasy for the first time. "Three days ago, I watched a girl sporting in a huge pool of water. It must have been twenty paces across. She . . . pulled herself out into it." He made an awkward swimming gesture with one hand. "A brave girl. Crossing these . . . rivers . . . has nearly unmanned me. I never thought there could be such a thing as too much water, but I never thought there was so much water in the world as you wetlanders have."

Perrin shook his head. He knew the Aiel Waste held little water—it was one of the few things he knew about the Waste or the Aiel—but he had not thought it could be scarce enough to cause this reaction. "You're a long way from home, Gaul. Why are you here?"

"We search," Gaul said slowly. "We look for He Who Comes With the Dawn."

Perrin had heard that name before, under circumstances

that made him sure who it meant. *Light, it always comes back to Rand. I am tied to him like a mean horse for shoeing.* "You are looking in the wrong direction, Gaul. I'm looking for him, too, and he is on his way to Tear."

"Tear?" The Aiel sounded surprised. "Why . . . ? But it must be. Prophecy says when the Stone of Tear falls, we will leave the Three-fold Land at last." That was the Aiel name for the Waste. "It says we will be changed, and find again what was ours, and was lost."

"That may be. I don't know your prophecies, Gaul. Are you about ready to leave? Somebody could come any minute."

"It is too late to run," Gaul said, and a deep voice shouted, "The savage is loose!" Ten or a dozen white-cloaked men came running across the square, drawing swords, their conical helmets shining in the moonlight. Children of the Light.

As if he had all the time in the world, Gaul calmly lifted a dark cloth from his shoulders and wrapped it around his head, finishing with a thick black veil that hid his face except for his eyes. "Do you like to dance, Perrin Aybara?" he asked. With that, he darted away from the cage. Straight at the oncoming Whitecloaks.

For an instant they were caught by surprise, but an instant was apparently all the Aiel needed. He kicked the sword out of the grip of the first to reach him, then his stiffened hand struck like a dagger at the Whitecloak's throat, and he slid around the soldier as he fell. The next man's arm made a loud snap as Gaul broke it. He pushed that man under the feet of a third, and kicked a fourth in the face. It *was* like a dance, from one to the next without stopping or slowing, though the tripped fellow was climbing back to his feet, and the one with the broken arm had shifted his sword. Gaul danced on in the midst of them.

Perrin had only an amazed moment himself, for not all the Whitecloaks had put their attentions on the Aiel. Barely in time, he gripped the axe haft with both hands to block a sword thrust, swung . . . and wanted to cry out as the half-moon blade tore the man's throat. But he had no time for crying out, none for regrets; more Whitecloaks followed before the first fell. He hated the gaping wounds the axe made, hated the way it chopped through mail to rend flesh beneath, split helmet and skull with almost equal ease. He hated it all. But he did not want to die.

Time seemed to compress and stretch out, both at once. His body felt as if he fought for hours, and breath rasped raw in his throat. Men seemed to move as though floating through jelly. They seemed to leap in an instant from where they started to where they fell. Sweat rolled down his face, yet he felt as cold as quenching water. He fought for his life, and he could not have said whether it lasted seconds or all night.

When he finally stood, panting and nearly stunned, looking at a dozen white-cloaked men lying on the paving blocks of the square, the moon appeared not to have moved at all. Some of the men groaned; others lay silent and still. Gaul stood among them, still veiled, still empty-handed. Most of the men down were his work. Perrin wished they all were, and felt ashamed. The smell of blood and death was sharp and bitter.

"You do not dance the spears badly, Perrin Aybara."

Head spinning, Perrin muttered, "I don't see how twelve men fought twenty of you and won, even if two of them are Hunters."

"Is that what they say?" Gaul laughed softly. "Sarien and I were careless, being so long in these soft lands, and the wind was from the wrong direction, so we smelled nothing. We walked into them before we knew it. Well, Sarien is dead, and I was caged like a fool, so perhaps we paid enough. It is time for running now, wetlander. Tear; I will remember it." At last he lowered the black veil. "May you always find water and shade, Perrin Aybara." Turning, he ran into the night.

Perrin started to run, too, then realized he had a bloody axe in his hands. Hastily he wiped the curved blade on a dead man's cloak. *He's dead, burn me, and there's blood on it already.* He made himself put the haft back through the loop on his belt before he broke into a trot.

At his second step he saw her, a slim shape at the edge of the square, in dark, narrow skirts. She turned to run; he could see they were divided for riding. She darted back into the street and vanished.

Lan met him before he reached the place where she had been standing. The Warder took in the cage sitting empty beneath the gibbet, the shadowed white mounds that caught the moonlight, and he tossed his head as if he were about to erupt. In a voice as tight and hard as a new wheel rim, he said, "Is this your work, blacksmith? The Light burn me! Is there anyone who can connect it to you?"

"A girl," Perrin said. "I think she saw. I don't want you to hurt her, Lan! Plenty of others could have seen, too. There are lighted windows all around."

The Warder grabbed Perrin's coat sleeve and gave him a push toward the inn. "I saw a girl running, but I thought. . . . No matter. You dig the Ogier out and haul him down to the stable. After this, we need to get our horses to the docks as quickly as possible. The Light alone knows if there is a ship sailing tonight, or what I'll have to pay to hire one if there isn't. Don't ask questions, blacksmith! Do it! Run!"

CHAPTER
35

The Falcon

T he Warder's long legs outdistanced Perrin's, and by
the time he pushed through the throng outside the
inn doors, Lan was already striding up the stairs,
not seeming in any particular hurry. Perrin made himself
walk as slowly. From the doorway behind him came grumbles about people pushing ahead of other people.

"Again?" Orban was saying, holding his silver cup up to
be refilled. "Aye, very well. They lay in ambush close beside the road we traveled, and an ambush I did not expect
so close to Remen. Screaming, they rushed upon us from
the crowding brush. In a breath they were in our midst,
their spears stabbing, slaying two of my best men and one
of Gann's immediately. Aye, I knew Aiel when I saw them,
and. . . ."

Perrin hurried up the stairs. *Well, Orban knows them
now.*

Voices came from behind Moiraine's door. He did not
want to hear what she had to say about this. He hurried past
to stick his head into Loial's room.

The Ogier bed was a low, massive thing, twice as long
and half as wide as any human bed Perrin had ever seen.
It took up much of the room, and that was as large and as
fine as Moiraine's. Perrin vaguely remembered Loial saying something about it being sung wood, and at any other
time he might have stopped to admire those flowing curves
that made it seem as if the bed had somehow grown where
it stood. Ogier really must have stopped in Remen at some
time in the past, for the innkeeper had also found a wooden

armchair that fit Loial, and filled it with cushions. The Ogier was comfortably sitting on them in his shirt and breeches, idly scratching a bare ankle with a toenail as he wrote in a large, cloth-bound book on an arm of the chair.

"We're leaving!" Perrin said.

Loial gave a jump, nearly upsetting his ink bottle and almost dropping the book. "Leaving? We only just arrived," he rumbled.

"Yes, leaving. Meet us at the stable as quickly as you can. And don't let anyone see you go. I think there's a back stair that runs down by the kitchen." The smell of food at his end of the hall had been too strong for there not to be.

The Ogier gave one regretful look at the bed, then started tugging on his high boots. "But why?"

"The Whitecloaks," Perrin said. "I'll tell you more later." He ducked back out before Loial could ask any more.

He had not unpacked. Once he had belted on his quiver, slung his cloak around him, tossed blanketroll and saddlebags on his shoulder, and picked up his bow, there was no sign he had ever been there. Not a wrinkle in the folded blankets at the foot of the bed, not a splash of water in the cracked basin on the washstand. Even the tallow candle still had a fresh wick, he realized. *I must have known I would not be staying. I don't seem to leave any mark behind me, of late.*

As he had suspected, a narrow stair at the back led down to a hall that ran out past the kitchen. He peered cautiously into the kitchen. A spit dog trotted in his big wicker wheel, turning a long spit that held a haunch of lamb, a large piece of beef, five chickens, and a goose. Fragrant steam rose from a soup cauldron hanging from a sturdy crane over a second hearth. But there was not a cook to be seen, nor any living soul except the dog. Thankful for Orban's lies, he hurried on into the night.

The stable was a large structure of the same stone as the inn, though only the stone faces around the big doors had been polished. A single lantern hanging from a stall-post gave a dim light. Stepper and the other horses stood in stalls near the doors; Loial's big mount nearly filled his. The smell of hay and horses was familiar and comforting. Perrin was the first to arrive.

There was only one stableman on duty, a narrow-faced fellow in a dirty shirt, with lanky gray hair, who demanded to know who Perrin was to order four horses saddled, and who was his master, and what he was doing all bundled up to travel in the middle of the night, and did Master Furlan know he was sneaking off like this, and what did he have hidden in those saddlebags, and what was wrong with his eyes, was he sick?

A coin flipped through the air from behind Perrin, glinting gold in the lantern light. The stableman snagged it with one hand and bit it.

"Saddle them," Lan said. His voice was soft, as cold iron is soft, and the stableman bobbed a bow and scurried to make the horses ready.

Moiraine and Loial came into the stable just as they could take up their reins, and then they were all leading their horses behind Lan, off down a street that ran behind the stable toward the river. The soft clop of the horses' hooves on the paving blocks attracted only a slat-ribbed dog that barked once and ran away as they went by.

"This brings back memories, doesn't it, Perrin?" Loial said, quietly for him.

"Keep your voice down," Perrin whispered. "What memories?"

"Why, it is like old times." The Ogier had managed to mute his voice; he sounded like a bumblebee only the size of a dog instead of a horse. "Sneaking away in the night, with enemies behind us, and maybe enemies ahead, and danger in the air, and the cold tang of adventure."

Perrin frowned at Loial over Stepper's saddle. It was easy enough; his eyes cleared the saddle, and Loial stood head and shoulders and chest above it on the other side. "What are you talking about? I believe you are coming to like danger! Loial, you must be crazy!"

"I am only fixing the mood in my head," Loial said, sounding formal. Or perhaps defensive. "For my book. I have to put it all in. I believe I am coming to like it. Adventuring. Of course, I am." His ears gave two violent twitches. "I have to like it if I wish to write of it."

Perrin shook his head.

At the stone wharves the bargelike ferries lay snugged

for the night, still and dark, as did most of the ships. Lantern lights and people moved around on the dock alongside a two-masted vessel, though, and on the deck as well. The main smells were tar and rope, with strong hints of fish, though something back in the nearest warehouse gave off sharp, spicy aromas that the others nearly submerged.

Lan located the captain, a short, slight man with an odd way of holding his head tilted to one side while he listened. The bargaining was over soon enough, and booms and sling rigged to hoist the horses aboard. Perrin kept a close eye on the horses, talking to them; horses had little tolerance for the unusual, such as being lifted into the air, but even the Warder's stallion seemed soothed by his murmurs.

Lan gave gold to the captain, and silver to two sailors who ran barefoot to a warehouse for sacks of oats. More crewmen tethered the horses between the masts in a sort of small pen made of rope, all the while muttering about the mess they would have to clean. Perrin did not think anyone was supposed to overhear, but his ears caught the words. The men were just not used to horses.

In short order the *Snow Goose* was ready to sail, only a little ahead of what the captain—his name was Jaim Adarra—had intended. Lan led Moiraine below as the lines were cast off, and Loial followed yawning. Perrin stayed at the railing near the bow, though the Ogier's every yawn had summoned one of his own. He wondered if the *Snow Goose* could outrun wolves down the river, outrun dreams. Men began readying the sweeps to push the vessel away from the wharf.

As the last line was tossed ashore and seized by a dockman, a girl in narrow, divided skirts burst out of the shadows between two warehouses, a bundle in her arms and a dark cloak streaming behind her. She leaped onto the deck just as the men at the sweeps began pushing off.

Adarra bustled from his place by the tiller, but she calmly set down her bundle and said briskly, "I will take passage downriver . . . oh . . . say, as far as he is going." She nodded toward Perrin without looking at him. "I've no objections to sleeping on deck. Cold and wet do not bother me."

A few minutes of bargaining followed. She passed over three silver marks, frowned at the coppers she got back, then stuffed them into her purse and came forward to stand beside Perrin.

She had an herbal scent to her, light and fresh and clean. Those dark, tilted eyes regarded him over high cheekbones, then turned to look back toward shore. She was about his own age, he decided; he could not decide if her nose fit her face, or dominated it. *You* are *a fool, Perrin Aybara. Why care what she looks like?*

The gap to the wharf was a good twenty paces, now; the sweeps dug in, cutting white furrows in black water. For a moment he considered tossing her over the side.

"Well," she said after a moment, "I never expected my travels to take me back to Illian so soon as this." Her voice was high, and she had a flat way of speaking, but it was not unpleasant. "You *are* going to Illian, are you not?" He tightened his mouth. "Don't sulk," she said. "You left quite a mess back there, you and that Aielman between you. The uproar was just beginning when I left."

"You did not tell them?" he said in surprise.

"The townsfolk think the Aielman chewed through the chain, or broke it with his bare hands. They had not decided which when I left." She made a sound suspiciously like a giggle. "Orban was quite loud in his disgust that his wounds would keep him from hunting down the Aielman personally."

Perrin snorted. "If he ever sees an Aiel again, he'll bloody soil himself." He cleared his throat and muttered, "Sorry."

"I do not know about that," she said, as if his remark had been nothing out of the way. "I saw him in Jehannah during the winter. He fought four men together, killed two and made the other two yield. Of course, he started the fight, so that takes something away from it, but they knew what they were doing. He did not pick a fight with men who could not defend themselves. Still, he is a fool. He has these peculiar ideas about the Great Blackwood. What some call the Forest of Shadows. Have you ever heard of it?"

He eyed her sideways. She spoke of fighting and killing as calmly as another woman might speak of baking. He had never heard of any Great Blackwood, but the Forest of Shadows lay just south of the Two Rivers. "Are you following me? You were staring at me, back at the inn. Why? And why didn't you tell them what you saw?"

"An Ogier," she said, staring at the river, "is obviously an Ogier, and the others were not much more difficult to figure out. I managed a much better look inside *Lady Alys*'s hood than Orban did, and her face makes that stone-faced fellow a Warder. The Light burn me if I'd want that one angry with me. Does he always look like that, or did he eat a rock for his last meal? Anyway, that left only you. I do not like things I cannot account for."

Once again he considered tossing her over the side. Seriously, this time. But Remen was now only a blotch of light well behind them in the darkness, and no telling how far it was to shore.

She seemed to take his silence as an urging to go on. "So there I have an"—she looked around, then dropped her voice, though the closest crewman was working a sweep ten feet away—"an Aes Sedai, a Warder, an Ogier—and you. A countryman, by first look at you." Her tilted eyes rose to study his yellow ones intently—he refused to look away—and she smiled. "Only you free a caged Aielman, hold a long talk with him, then help him chop a dozen White-cloaks into sausage. I assume you do this regularly; you certainly looked as if it were nothing out of the ordinary for you. I scent something strange in a party of travelers such as yours, and strange trails are what Hunters look for."

He blinked; there was no mistaking that emphasis. "A Hunter? You? You cannot be a Hunter. You're a girl."

Her smile became so innocent that he almost walked away from her. She stepped back, made a flourish with each hand, and was holding two knives as neatly as old Thom Merrilin could have done it. One of the men at the sweeps made a choking sound, and two others stumbled; sweeps thrashed and tangled, and the *Snow Goose* lurched a little before the captain's shouts set things right. By that time, the black-haired girl had made the knives disappear again.

"Nimble fingers and nimble wits will take you a good deal further than a sword and muscles. Sharp eyes help, as well, but fortunately, I have these things."

"And modesty, as well," Perrin murmured. She did not seem to notice.

"I took the oath and received the blessing in the Great Square of Tammaz, in Illian. Perhaps I *was* the youngest, but in that crowd, with all the trumpets and drums and cymbals and shouting. . . . A six-year-old could have taken the oath, and none would have noticed. There were over a thousand of us, perhaps two, and every one with an idea of where to find the Horn of Valere. I have mine—it still may be the right one—but no Hunter can afford to pass up a strange trail. The Horn will certainly lie at the end of a strange trail, and I have never seen one any stranger than the trail you four make. Where are you bound? Illian? Somewhere else?"

"What was your idea?" he asked. "About where the Horn is?" *Safe in Tar Valon, I hope, and the Light send I never see it again.* "You think it's in Ghealdan?"

She frowned at him—he had the feeling she did not give up a scent once she had raised it, but he was ready to offer her as many side trails as she would take—then said, "Have you ever heard of Manetheren?"

He nearly choked. "I have heard of it," he said cautiously.

"Every queen of Manetheren was an Aes Sedai, and the king the Warder bound to her. I can't imagine a place like that, but that is what the books say. It was a large land—most of Andor and Ghealdan and more besides—but the capital, the city itself, was in the Mountains of Mist. That is where I think the Horn is. Unless you four lead me to it."

His hackles stirred. She was lecturing him as if he were an untaught village lout. "You'll not find the Horn or Manetheren. The city was destroyed during the Trolloc Wars, when the last queen drew too much of the One Power to destroy the Dreadlords who had killed her husband." Moiraine had told him the names of that king and queen, but he did not remember them.

"Not in Manetheren, farmboy," she said calmly, "though a land such as that would make a good hiding place. But there were other nations, other cities, in the Mountains of Mist, so old that not even Aes Sedai remember them. And think of all those stories about it being bad luck to enter the mountains. What better place for the Horn to be hidden than in one of those forgotten cities."

"I have heard stories of something being hidden in the mountains." *Would she believe him?* He had never been good at lying. "The stories did not say what, but it's supposed to be the greatest treasure in the world, so maybe it

is the Horn. But the Mountains of Mist stretch for hundreds
of leagues. If you are going to find it, you should not waste
time following us. You'll need it all to find the Horn before
Orban and Gann."

"I told you, those two have some strange idea the Horn
is hidden in the Great Blackwood." She smiled up at him.
Her mouth was not too big at all, when she smiled. "And I
told you a Hunter has to follow strange trails. You are lucky
Orban and Gann were injured fighting all those Aielmen,
or they might well be aboard, too. At least I will not get
in your way, or try to take over, or pick a fight with the
Warder."

He growled disgustedly. "We are just travelers on our
way to Illian, girl. What is your name? If I have to share
this ship with you for days yet, I can't keep calling you girl."

"I call myself Mandarb." He could not stop the guffaw
that burst out of him. Those tilted eyes regarded him with
heat. "I will teach you something, farmboy." Her voice remained level. Barely. "In the Old Tongue, Mandarb means
'blade.' It is a name worthy of a Hunter of the Horn!"

He managed to get his laughter under control, and hardly
wheezed at all as he pointed to the rope pen between the
masts. "You see that black stallion? His name is Mandarb."

The heat went out of her eyes, and spots of color bloomed
on her cheeks. "Oh. I was born Zarine Bashere, but Zarine
is no name for a Hunter. In the stories, Hunters have names
like Rogosh Eagle-eye."

She looked so crestfallen that he hastened to say, "I like
the name Zarine. It suits you." The heat flashed back into
her eyes, and for a moment he thought she was about to
produce one of her knives again. "It is late, Zarine. I want
some sleep."

He turned his back to start for the hatch that led be-
lowdeck, prickles running across his shoulders. Crewmen
still padded up the deck and back, working the sweeps.
*Fool. A girl would not stick a knife in me. Not with all these
people watching. Would she?* Just as he reached the hatch,
she called to him.

"Farmboy! Perhaps I will call myself Faile. My father
used to call me that, when I was little. It means 'falcon.'"

He stiffened and almost missed the first step of the ladder. *Coincidence.* He made himself go down without looking

back toward her. *It has to be.* The passageway was dark, but enough moonlight filtered down behind him for him to make his way. Someone was snoring loudly in one of the cabins. *Min, why did you have to go seeing things?*

CHAPTER
36

Daughter of the Night

Realizing that he had no way of knowing which cabin was supposed to be his, he put his head into several. They were dark, and all of them had two men asleep in the narrow beds built against each side, all but one, which held Loial, sitting on the floor between the beds—and barely fitting—scribbling in his cloth-bound book of notes by the light of a gimballed lantern. The Ogier wanted to talk about the events of the day, but Perrin, jaws creaking with the effort of holding his yawns in, thought the ship must have run far enough downriver by now to make it safe to sleep. Safe to dream. Even if they tried, wolves could not long keep pace with the sweeps and the current.

Finally he found a windowless cabin with no one in it at all, which suited him as well. He wanted to be alone. *A coincidence in the name, that's all*, he thought as he lit the lantern mounted on the wall. *Anyway, her real name is Zarine.* But the girl with the high cheekbones and dark, tilted eyes was not uppermost in his thoughts. He put his bow and other belongings on one cramped bed, tossed his cloak over them, and sat on the other to tug off his boots.

Elyas Machera had found a way to live with what he was, a man somehow linked with wolves, and he had not gone mad. Thinking back, Perrin was sure Elyas had been living that way for years before he ever met the man. *He wants to be that way. He accepts it, anyway.* That was no solution. Perrin did not want to live that way, did not want to accept. *But if you have the bar stock to make a knife, you accept it and make a knife, even if you'd like a woodaxe. No! My life is more than iron to be hammered into shape.*

Cautiously, he reached out with his mind, feeling for wolves, and found—nothing. Oh, there was a dim impression of wolves somewhere in the distance, but it faded even as he touched it. For the first time in so long, he was alone. Blessedly alone.

Blowing out the lantern, he lay down, for the first time in days. *How in the Light will Loial manage in one of these?* Those all but sleepless nights rolled over him, exhaustion slacking his muscles. It came to him that he had managed to put the Aiel out of his head. And the Whitecloaks. *Light-forsaken axe! Burn me, I wish I had never seen it,* was his last thought before sleep.

Thick gray fog surrounded him, dense enough low down that he could not see his own boots, and so heavy on every side that he could not make out anything ten paces away. There was surely nothing nearer. Anything at all might lie within it. The mist did not feel right; there was no dampness to it. He put a hand to his belt, seeking the comfort of knowing he could defend himself, and gave a start. His axe was not there.

Something moved in the fog, a swirling in the grayness. Something coming his way.

He tensed, wondering if it was better to run or stand and fight with his bare hands, wondering if there was anything to fight.

The billowing furrow boring through the fog resolved itself into a wolf, its shaggy form almost one with the heavy mist.

Hopper?

The wolf hesitated, then came to stand beside him. It was Hopper—he was certain—but something about the wolf's stance, something in the yellow eyes that looked up briefly to meet his, demanded silence, in mind as well as body. Those eyes demanded that he follow, too.

He laid a hand on the wolf's back, and as he did, Hopper started forward. He let himself be led. The fur under his hand was thick and shaggy. It felt real.

The fog began to thicken, until only his hand told him Hopper was still there, until a glance down did not even show him his own chest. Just gray mist. He might as well have been wrapped in new-sheared wool for all he could see. It struck him that he had heard nothing, either. Not even the sound of his own footsteps. He wiggled his toes, and was relieved to feel the boots on his feet.

The gray became darker, and he and the wolf walked through pitch-blackness. He could not see his hand when he touched his nose. He could not see his nose, for that matter. He tried closing his eyes for a moment, and could not tell any difference. There was still no sound. His hand felt the rough hair of Hopper's back, but he was not sure he could feel anything under his boots.

Suddenly Hopper stopped, forcing him to halt, too. He looked around . . . and snapped his eyes shut. He could tell a difference, now. And feel something, too, a queasy twisting of his stomach. He made himself open his eyes and look down.

What he saw could not have been there, not unless he and Hopper were standing in midair. He could see nothing of the wolf or himself, as if neither had bodies at all—that thought nearly tied his stomach into knots—but below him, as clear as if lit by a thousand lamps, stretched a vast array of mirrors, seemingly hanging in blackness though as level as if they stood on a vast floor. They stretched as far as he could see in every direction, but right beneath his feet, there was a clear space. And people in it. Suddenly he could hear their voices as well as if he had been standing among them.

"Great Lord," one of the men muttered, "where is this place?" He looked around once, flinching at his image cast back at him many thousandfold, and held his eyes forward after that. The others huddled around him seemed even more afraid. "I was asleep in Tar Valon, Great Lord. I *am* asleep in Tar Valon! Where is this place? Have I gone mad?"

Some of the men around him wore ornate coats full of embroidery, others plainer garb, while some seemed to be naked, or in their smallclothes.

"I, too, sleep," a naked man nearly screamed. "In Tear. I remember lying down with my wife!"

"And I do sleep in Illian," a man in red and gold said, sounding shaken. "I know that I do sleep, but that cannot be. I know that I do dream, but that does be impossible. Where does this be, Great Lord? Are you really come to me?"

The dark-haired man who faced them was garbed in black, with silver lace at his throat and wrists. Now and again he put a hand to his chest, as if it hurt him. There was light everywhere down there, coming from nowhere, but this man below Perrin seemed cloaked in shadow. Darkness rolled around him, caressed him.

"Silence!" The black-clothed man did not speak loudly, but he had no need to. For the space of that word, he had raised his head; his eyes and mouth were holes boring into a raging forge-fire, all flame and fiery glow.

Perrin knew him, then. Ba'alzamon. He was staring down at Ba'alzamon himself. Fear struck through him like hammered spikes. He would have run, but he could not feel his feet.

Hopper shifted. He felt the thick fur under his hand and gripped it hard. Something real. Something more real, he hoped, than what he saw. But he knew that both were real.

The men huddling together cowered.

"You have been given tasks," Ba'alzamon said. "Some of these tasks you have carried out. At others, you have failed." Now and again his eyes and mouth vanished in flame again, and the mirrors flashed with reflected fire. "Those who have been marked for death must die. Those who have been marked for taking must bow to me. To fail the Great Lord of the Dark cannot be forgiven." Fire shone through his eyes, and the darkness around him roiled and spun. "You." His finger pointed out the man who had spoken of Tar Valon, a fellow dressed like a merchant, in plainly cut clothes of the finest cloth. The others shied away from him as if he had blackbile fever, leaving him to cower alone. "You allowed the boy to escape Tar Valon."

The man screamed, and began to quiver like a file struck against an anvil. He seemed to become less solid, and his scream thinned with him.

"You all dream," Ba'alzamon said, "but what happens in this dream is real." The shrieking man was only a bundle of mist shaped like a man, his scream far distant, and then even the mist was gone. "I fear he will never wake." He laughed, and his mouth roared flame. "The rest of you will not fail me again. Begone! Wake, and obey!" The other men vanished.

For a moment Ba'alzamon stood alone, then suddenly there was a woman with him, clad all in white and silver.

Shock hit Perrin. He could never forget a woman so beautiful. She was the woman from his dream, the one who had urged him to glory.

An ornate silver throne appeared behind her, and she sat, carefully arranging her silken skirts. "You make free use of my domain," she said.

"Your domain?" Ba'alzamon said. "You claim it yours, then? Do you no longer serve the Great Lord of the Dark?" The darkness around him thickened for an instant, seemed to boil.

"I serve," she said quickly. "I have served the Lord of the Twilight long. Long did I lie imprisoned for my service, in an endless, dreamless sleep. Only Gray Men and Myrddraal are denied dreams. Even Trollocs can dream. Dreams were always mine, to use and walk. Now I am free again, and I will use what is mine."

"What is yours," Ba'alzamon said. The blackness swirling 'round him seemed mirthful. "You always thought yourself greater than you were, Lanfear."

The name cut at Perrin like a newly honed knife. One of the Forsaken had been in his dreams. Moiraine had been right. Some of them were free.

The woman in white was on her feet, the throne gone. "I am as great as I am. What have your plans come to? Three thousand years and more of whispering in ears and pulling the strings of throned puppets like an Aes Sedai!" Her voice invested the name with all scorn. "Three thousand years, and yet Lews Therin walks the world again, and these Aes Sedai all but have him leashed. Can you control him? Can you turn him? He was mine before ever that straw-haired chit Ilyena saw him! He will be mine again!"

"Do you serve yourself now, Lanfear?" Ba'alzamon's voice was soft, but flame raged continuously in his eyes and mouth. "Have you abandoned your oaths to the Great Lord of the Dark?" For an instant the darkness nearly obliterated him, only the glowing fires showing through. "They are not so easily broken as the oaths to the Light you forsook, proclaiming your new master in the very Hall of the Servants. Your master claims you forever, Lanfear. Will you serve, or do you choose an eternity of pain, of endless dying without release?"

"I serve." Despite her words, she stood tall and defiant. "I serve the Great Lord of the Dark and none other. Forever!"

The vast array of mirror began to vanish as if black waves rolled in over it, ever closer to the center. The tide rolled over Ba'alzamon and Lanfear. There was only blackness.

Perrin felt Hopper move, and he was more than glad to follow, guided only by the feel of fur under his hand. It was not until he was moving that he realized he could. He tried to puzzle out what he had seen, without any success. Ba'alzamon and Lanfear. His tongue stuck to the roof of his mouth. For some reason, Lanfear frightened him more than Ba'alzamon did. Perhaps because she had been in his dreams in the mountains. *Light! One of the Forsaken in my dreams! Light!* And unless he had missed something, she had defied the Dark One. He had been told and taught that the Shadow could have no power over you if you denied it; but how could a Darkfriend—not just a Darkfriend; one of the Forsaken!—defy the Shadow? *I must be mad, like Simion's brother. These dreams have driven me mad!*

Slowly the blackness became fog again, and the fog gradually thinned until he walked out of it with Hopper onto a grassy hillside bright with daylight. Birds began to sing from a thicket at the foot of the hill. He looked back. A hilly plain dotted with clumps of trees stretched to the horizon. There was no sign of fog anywhere. The big, grizzled wolf stood watching him.

"What was that?" he demanded, struggling in his mind to turn the question to thoughts the wolf could understand. "Why did you show it to me? What was it?"

Emotions and images flooded his thoughts, and his mind put words to them. *What you must see. Be careful, Young Bull. This place is dangerous. Be wary as a cub hunting porcupine.* That came as something closer to Small Thorny Back, but his mind named the animal the way he knew it as a man. *You are too young, too new.*

"Was it real?"

All is real, what is seen, and what is not seen. That seemed to be all the answer Hopper was going to give.

"Hopper, how are you here? I saw you die. I felt you die!"

All are here. All brothers and sisters that are, all that

were, all that will be. Perrin knew that wolves did not smile, not the way humans did, but for an instant he had the impression that Hopper was grinning. *Here, I soar like the eagle.* The wolf gathered himself and leaped, up into the air. Up and up it carried him, until he dwindled to a speck in the sky, and a last thought came. *To soar.*

Perrin stared after him with his mouth hanging open. *He did it.* His eyes burned suddenly, and he cleared his throat and scrubbed at his nose. *I will be crying like a girl, next.* Without thinking, he looked around to see if anyone had seen him, and that quickly everything changed.

He was standing on a rise, with shadowy, indistinct dips and swells all around him. They seemed to fade into the distance too soon. Rand stood below him. Rand, and a ragged circle of Myrddraal and men and women his eyes seemed to slide right past. Dogs howled somewhere in the distance, and Perrin knew they were hunting something. Myrddraal scent and the stink of burned sulphur filled the air. Perrin's hackles rose.

The circle of Myrddraal and people came closer to Rand, all walking as if asleep. And Rand began to kill them. Balls of fire flew from his hands and consumed two. Lightning flashed from above to shrivel others. Bars of light like white-hot steel flew from his fists to more. And the survivors continued to walk slowly closer, as if none of them saw what was happening. One by one they died, until none were left, and Rand sank down on his knees, panting. Perrin was not sure whether he was laughing or crying; it seemed to be some of each.

Shapes appeared over the rises, more people coming, more Myrddraal, all intent on Rand.

Perrin cupped his hands to his mouth. "Rand! Rand, there are more coming!"

Rand looked up at him from his crouch, snarling, sweat slicking his face.

"Rand, they're—!"

"Burn you!" Rand howled.

Light burned Perrin's eyes, and pain seared everything.

Groaning, he rolled into a ball on the narrow bed, the light still burning behind his eyelids. His chest hurt. He raised a hand to it and winced when he felt a burn under his shirt, a spot no bigger than a silver penny.

Bit by bit he forced his knotted muscles to let him straighten his legs and lie flat in the dark cabin. *Moiraine. I have to tell Moiraine this time. Just have to wait till the pain goes away.*

But as the pain began to fade, exhaustion took him. He barely had a thought that he must get up before sleep pulled him down again.

When he opened his eyes again, he lay staring at the beams overhead. Light at the top and bottom of the door told him morning had come. He put a hand to his chest to convince himself he had imagined it, imagined it so well that he had actually felt a burn. . . .

His fingers found the burn. *I didn't imagine it, then.* He had dim memories of a few other dreams, fading even as he recalled them. Ordinary dreams. He even felt as if he had had a good night's sleep. *And could use another one right now.* But it meant he could sleep. *As long as there are no wolves around, anyway.*

He remembered making a decision in that brief waking after the dream with Hopper, and after a moment he decided it had been a good one.

It took knocking on five doors and being cursed at twice—the inhabitants of two cabins had gone on deck— before he found Moiraine. She was fully dressed, but sitting on one of the narrow beds cross-legged, reading in her book of notes by lantern light. Back near the beginning, he saw, notes that must have been made even before she had come to Emond's Field. Lan's things were neatly placed on the other bed.

"I had a dream," he told her, and proceeded to tell her of it. All of it. He even pulled up his shirt to show her the small circle on his chest, red, with wavy red lines radiating from it. He had kept things from her before, and he suspected he would again, but this might be too important to hold back. The pin was the smallest part of a pair of scissors, and the easiest made, but without it, the scissors cut no cloth. When he was done, he stood there waiting.

She had watched him without expression, except that those dark eyes had examined every word as it came out of his mouth, weighed it, measured it, held it up to the light.

Now she sat the same way, only it was he who was examined, weighed, and held up to the light.

"Well, is it important?" he demanded finally. "I think it was one of those wolf dreams you told me about—I'm sure it was; it must have been!—but that doesn't make what I saw real. Only, you said maybe some of the Forsaken are free, and he called her Lanfear, and. . . . Is it important, or am I standing here making a fool out of myself?"

"There are women," she said slowly, "who would do their best to gentle you if they heard what I just did." His lungs seemed to freeze; he could not breathe. "I am not accusing you of being able to channel," she went on, and the ice inside him melted, "or even of being able to learn. An attempt at gentling would not harm you, beyond the rough treatment the Red Ajah would give you before they realized their error. Such men are so rare, even the Reds with all their hunting have not found more than three in the last ten years. Before the outbreak of false Dragons, at least. What I am trying to make clear to you is that I do not think you will suddenly begin wielding the Power. You do not have to be afraid of that."

"Well, thank you very much for that," he said bitterly. "You did not have to scare me to death just so you could tell me there was no need to be frightened!"

"Oh, you do have reason to be frightened. Or at least careful, as the wolf suggested. Red sisters, or others, might kill you before they discovered there was nothing to gentle in you."

"Light! Light burn me!" He stared at her with a frown. "You're trying to lead me around by the nose, Moiraine, but I am no calf, and there's no ring in my nose. The Red Ajah or any other would not think of gentling unless there was something real in what I dreamed. Does it mean the Forsaken are loose?"

"I told you before that they might be. Some of them. Your . . . dreams are nothing I expected, Perrin. Dreamers have written of wolves, but I did not expect this."

"Well, I think it was real. I think I saw something that really happened, something I wasn't supposed to see." *What you must see.* "I think Lanfear is loose at the very least. What are you going to do?"

"I am going to Illian. And then I will go to Tear, and

hope to reach it before Rand. We had need to leave Remen too quickly for Lan to learn whether he crossed the river or went down it. We should know before we reach Illian, though. We will find sign if he has gone this way." She glanced at her book as if she wanted to resume her reading.

"Is that all you are going to do? With Lanfear loose, and the Light alone knows how many of the others?"

"Do not question me," she said coldly. "You do not know which questions to ask, and you would comprehend less than half the answers if I gave them. Which I will not."

He shifted his feet under her gaze until it became clear she would say no more on the matter. His shirt rubbed painfully at the burn on his chest. It did not seem a bad hurt— *Not for being struck by lightning it doesn't!*—but how he had come by it was another matter. "Uh. . . . Will you Heal this?"

"Are you no longer uneasy about the One Power being used on you, then, Perrin? No, I will not Heal it. It is not serious, and it will remind you of the need to be careful." Careful about pressing her, he knew, as well as about dreams or letting others know of them. "If there is nothing else, Perrin?"

He started for the door, then stopped. "There is one thing. If you knew a woman's name was Zarine, would you think it meant anything about her?"

"Why under the Light do you ask this question?"

"A girl," he said awkwardly. "A young woman. I met her last night. She's one of the other passengers." He would let her discover for herself that Zarine knew she was Aes Sedai. And seemed to think following them would lead her to the Horn of Valere. He would not keep back anything he thought was important, but if Moiraine could be secretive, so could he.

"Zarine. It is a Saldaean name. No woman would name her daughter that unless she expected her to be a great beauty. And a heartbreaker. One to lie on cushions in palaces, surrounded by servants and suitors." She smiled, briefly but with great amusement. "Perhaps you have another reason to be careful, Perrin, if there is a Zarine as a passenger with us."

"I intend to be careful," he told her. At least he knew why

Zarine did not like her name. Hardly fitting for a Hunter of the Horn. *As long as she doesn't call herself "falcon."*

When he went on deck, Lan was there, looking over Mandarb. And Zarine was sitting on a coil of rope near the railing, sharpening one of her knives and watching him. The big, triangular sails were set and taut, and the *Snow Goose* flew downriver.

Zarine's eyes followed Perrin as he walked by her to stand in the bow. The water curled to either side of the prow like earth turning around a good plow. He wondered about dreams and Aielmen, Min's viewings and falcons. His chest hurt. Life had *never* been as tangled as this.

Rand sat up out of his exhausted sleep, gasping, the cloak he had used as a blanket falling away. His side ached, the old wound from Falme throbbing. His fire had burned down to coals with only a few wavering flames, but it was still enough to make the shadows move. *That was Perrin. It was! It was* him, *not a dream. Somehow. I almost killed him! Light, I have to be careful!*

Shivering, he picked up a length of oak branch and started to shove it into the coals. The trees were scattered in these Murandian hills, still close to the Manetherendrelle, but he had found just enough fallen branches for his fire, the wood just old enough to be properly cured but not rotten. Before the wood touched the coals, he stopped. There were horses coming, ten or a dozen of them, walking slowly. *I have to be careful. I cannot make another mistake.*

The horses swung toward his failing fire, entered the dim light, and stopped. The shadows obscured their riders, but most seemed to be rough-faced men wearing round helmets and long leather jerkins sewn all over with metal discs like fish scales. One was a woman with graying hair and a no-nonsense look on her face. Her dark dress was plain wool, but the finest weave, and adorned with a silver pin in the shape of a lion. A merchant, she seemed to him; he had seen her sort among those who came to buy tabac and wool in the Two Rivers. A merchant and her guards.

I have to be careful, he thought as he stood. *No mistakes.*

"You have chosen a good campsite, young man," she said. "I have often used it on my way to Remen. There is a small spring nearby. I trust you have no objection to my sharing it?" Her guards were already dismounting, hitching at their sword belts and loosening saddle girths.

"None," Rand told her. *Careful.* Two steps brought him close enough, and he leaped into the air, spinning— Thistledown Floats on the Whirlwind—heron-mark blade carved from fire coming into his hands to take her head off before surprise could even form on her face. *She was the most dangerous.*

He alighted as the woman's head rolled from the crupper of her horse. The guards yelled and clawed for their swords, screamed as they realized his blade burned. He danced among them in the forms Lan had taught him, and knew he could have killed all ten with ordinary steel, but the blade he wielded was part of him. The last man fell, and it had been so like practicing the forms that he had already begun the sheathing called Folding the Fan before he remembered he wore no scabbard and this blade would have turned it to ash at a touch if he had.

Letting the sword vanish, he turned to examine the horses. Most had run away, but some not far, and the woman's tall gelding stood with rolling eyes, whickering uneasily. Her headless corpse, lying on the ground, had maintained its grip on the reins, and held the animal's head down.

Rand pulled them free, pausing only to gather his few belongings before swinging into the saddle. *I have to be careful*, he thought as he looked over the dead. *No mistakes.*

The Power still filled him, the flow from *saidin* sweeter than honey, ranker than rotted meat. Abruptly he channeled—not really understanding what it was he did, or how, only that it seemed right; and it worked, lifting the corpses. He set them in a line, facing him, kneeling, faces in the dirt. For those who had faces left. Kneeling to him.

"If I *am* the Dragon Reborn," he told them, "that is the way it is supposed to be, isn't it?" Letting go of *saidin* was hard, but he did it. *If I hold it too much, how will I keep the madness away?* He laughed bitterly. *Or is it too late for that?*

Frowning, he peered at the line. He had been sure there were only ten men, but eleven men knelt in that line, one of them without armor of any sort but with a dagger still gripped in his hand.

"You chose the wrong company," Rand told that man.

Wheeling the gelding, he dug in his heels and set the animal to a dead gallop into the night. It was a long way to Tear, yet, but he meant to get there by the straightest way, if he had to kill horses or steal them. *I will put an end to it. The taunting. The baiting. I will end it! Callandor.* It called to him.

CHAPTER
37

Fires in Cairhien

Egwene returned a graceful nod to the respectful bow
of the ship's crewman who padded past her, barefoot, on his way to pull a rope that already seemed
taut, possibly shifting a trifle the way one of the big square
sails set. As he trotted back toward where the round-faced
captain stood by the tillerman, he bowed again, and she
nodded once more before returning her attentions to the
forested Cairhien shore, separated from the *Blue Crane* by
less than twenty spans of water.

A village was sliding past, or what had been a village
once. Half the houses were only smoldering piles of rubble with chimneys sticking starkly out of the ruins. On
the other houses, doors swung with the wind, and pieces
of furniture, bits of clothing and houseware littered the dirt
street, tumbled about as if thrown. Nothing living moved
in the village except for one half-starved dog that ignored the passing ship as it trotted out of sight behind the
toppled walls of what appeared to have been an inn. She
could never see such a sight without a queasiness settling
in her belly, but she tried to maintain the dispassionate
serenity she thought an Aes Sedai might have. It did not
help much. Beyond the village, a thick plume of smoke
was rising into the sky. Three or four miles off, she estimated.

This was not the first such plume of smoke she had seen
since the Erinin began to flow along the border of Cairhien,
nor the first such village. At least this time there were no
bodies in sight. Captain Ellisor sometimes had to sail close

to the Cairhienin shore because of mudflats—he said they shifted in this part of the river—but however close he came, she had not seen a single living person.

The village and the smoke plume slipped away behind the ship, but already another column of smoke was coming into view ahead, further from the river. The forest was thinning, ash and leatherleaf and black elder giving way to willow and whitewood and wateroak, and some she did not recognize.

The wind caught her cloak, but she let it stream, feeling the cold cleanness of the air, feeling the freedom of wearing brown instead of any sort of white, though it had not been her first choice. Yet dress and cloak were of the best wool, well cut and well sewn.

Another sailor trotted by, bowing as he went. She vowed to learn at least some of what it was they were doing; she did not like feeling ignorant. Wearing her Great Serpent ring on her right hand made for a good deal of bowing with a captain and crew born mainly in Tar Valon.

She had won that argument with Nynaeve, though Nynaeve had been sure she herself was the only one of the three of them old enough for people to believe she was Aes Sedai. But Nynaeve had been wrong. Egwene was ready to admit that both she and Elayne had received startled looks on boarding the *Blue Crane* that afternoon at Southharbor, and Captain Ellisor's eyebrows had climbed almost to where his hair would have begun had he had any, but he had been all smiles and bows.

"An honor, Aes Sedai. Three Aes Sedai to travel on my vessel? An honor indeed. I promise you a quick journey as far as you wish. And no trouble with Cairhienin brigands. I no longer put in on that side of the river. Unless you wish it, of course, Aes Sedai. Andoran soldiers do hold a few towns on the Cairhienin side. An honor, Aes Sedai."

His eyebrows had shot up again when they asked for just one cabin among them—not even Nynaeve wanted to be alone at night if she did not have to be. Each could have a cabin to herself at no extra charge, he told them; he had no other passengers, his cargo was aboard, and if Aes Sedai had urgent business downriver, he would not wait even an hour for anyone else who might want passage. They said again that one cabin would be sufficient.

He was startled, and it had been plain from his face that he did not understand, but Chin Ellisor, born and bred in Tar Valon, was not one to question Aes Sedai once they made their intentions clear. If two of them seemed very young, well, some Aes Sedai were young.

The abandoned ruins vanished behind Egwene. The column of smoke drew closer, and there was a hint of another much further still from the riverbank. The forest was turning to low, grassy hills dotted with thickets. Trees that made flowers in the spring had them, tiny white blossoms on snowberry and bright red sugarberry. One tree she did not know was covered in round white flowers bigger than her two hands together. Occasionally a climbing wild-rose put swaths of yellow or white through branches thick with the green of leaves and the red of new growth. It was all too sharp a contrast to the ashes and rubble to be entirely pleasant.

Egwene wished she had an Aes Sedai to question herself right then. One she could trust. Brushing her pouch with her fingers, she could barely feel the twisted stone ring of the *ter'angreal* inside.

She had tried it every night but two since leaving Tar Valon, and it had not worked the same way twice. Oh, she always found herself in *Tel'aran'rhiod*, but the only thing she saw that might have been any use was the Heart of the Stone again, each time without Silvie to tell her things. There was certainly nothing about the Black Ajah.

Her own dreams, without the *ter'angreal*, had been filled with images that seemed almost like glimpses of the Unseen World. Rand holding a sword that blazed like the sun, till she could hardly see that it was a sword, could hardly make out that it was him at all. Rand threatened in a dozen ways, none of them the least bit real. In one dream he had been on a huge stones board, the black and white stones as big as boulders, and him dodging the monstrous hands that moved them and seemed to try to crush him under them. It could have meant something. It very probably did, but beyond the fact that Rand was in danger from someone, or two someones—she thought that much was clear—beyond that, she simply did not know.

*I cannot help him, now. I have my own duty. I don't even
know where he is, except that it is probably five hundred
leagues from here.*

She had dreamed of Perrin with a wolf, and with a falcon, and a hawk—and the falcon and the hawk fighting—of
Perrin running from someone deadly, and Perrin stepping willingly over the edge of a towering cliff while saying, "It must be done. I must learn to fly before I reach
the bottom." There had been one dream of an Aiel, and
she thought that had to do with Perrin, too, but she was
not sure. And a dream of Min, springing a steel trap but
somehow walking through it without so much as seeing
it. There had been dreams of Mat, too. Of Mat with dice
spinning 'round him—she felt she knew where that one
came from—of Mat being followed by a man who was not
there—she still did not understand that; there was a man
following, or maybe more than one, but in some way there
was no one there—of Mat riding desperately toward something unseen in the distance that he had to reach, and Mat
with a woman who seemed to be tossing fireworks about.
An Illuminator, she assumed, but that made no more sense
than anything else.

She had had so many dreams that she was beginning
to doubt them all. Maybe it had to do with using the
ter'angreal so often, or maybe with just carrying it.
Maybe she was finally learning what a Dreamer did. Frantic dreams, hectic dreams. Men and women breaking out
of a cage, then putting on crowns. A woman playing with
puppets, and another dream where the strings on puppets
led to the hands of larger puppets, and their strings led
to still greater puppets, on and on until the last strings
vanished into unimaginable heights. Kings dying, queens
weeping, battles raging. Whitecloaks ravaging the Two
Rivers. She had even dreamed of the Seanchan again.
More than once. Those she shut away in a dark corner;
she would not let herself think of them. Her mother and
father, every night.

She was certain what that meant, at least, or thought
she was. *It means I'm off hunting the Black Ajah, and I do
not know what my dreams mean or how to make the fool*
ter'angreal *do what it should, and I'm frightened, and. . . .
And homesick.* For an instant she thought how good it

would be to have her mother send her up to bed knowing everything would be better in the morning. *Only mother can't solve my problems for me anymore, and father can't promise to chase away monsters and make me believe it. I have to do it myself now.*

How far in the past all that was, now. She did not want it back, not really, but it had been a warm time, and it seemed so long ago. It would be wonderful just to see them again, to hear their voices. *When I wear this ring on the finger I choose by right.*

She had finally let Nynaeve and Elayne each try sleeping one night with the stone ring—surprised at how reluctant she had been to let it out of her own hands—and they had awakened to speak of what was surely *Tel'aran'rhiod*, but neither had seen more than a glimpse of the Heart of the Stone, nothing that was of any use.

The thick column of smoke now lay abreast of the *Blue Crane*. Perhaps five or six miles from the river, she thought. The other was only a smudge on the horizon. It could almost have been a cloud, but she was sure it was not. Small thickets grew tight along the riverbank in some places, and between them the grass came right down to the water except where an undercut bank had fallen in.

Elayne came on deck and joined her at the rail, the wind whipping her dark cloak as well. She wore sturdy wool, too. That had been one argument Nynaeve won. Their clothes. Egwene had maintained that Aes Sedai always wore the best, even when they traveled—she had been thinking of the silks she wore in *Tel'aran'rhiod*—but Nynaeve pointed out that even with as much gold as the Amyrlin had left in the back of her wardrobe, and it was a fat purse, they still had no idea how much things would cost downriver. The servants said Mat had been right about the civil war in Cairhien, and what it had done to prices. To Egwene's surprise, Elayne had pointed out that Brown sisters wore wool more often than silk. Elayne had been so eager to be away from the kitchen, Egwene thought, she would have worn rags.

I wonder how Mat is doing? No doubt trying to dice with the captain for whatever ship he's traveling on.

"Terrible," Elayne murmured. "It is so terrible."

"What is?" Egwene said absently. *I hope he isn't showing that paper we gave him around too freely.*

Elayne gave her a startled look, and then a frown. "That!" She gestured toward the distant smoke. "How can you ignore it?"

"I can ignore it because I do not want to think of what the people are going through, because I cannot do anything about it, and because we have to reach Tear. Because what we're hunting is in Tear." She was surprised at her own vehemence. *I can't do anything about it. And the Black Ajah is in Tear.*

The more she thought of it, the more certain she became that they would have to find a way into the Heart of the Stone. Perhaps no one but the High Lords of Tear were allowed into it, but she was becoming convinced that the key to springing the Black Ajah's trap and thwarting them lay in the Heart of the Stone.

"I know all of that, Egwene, but it does not stop me feeling for the Cairhienin."

"I have heard lectures about the wars Andor fought with Cairhien," Egwene said dryly. "Bennae Sedai says you and Cairhien have fought more often than any two nations except Tear and Illian."

The other woman gave her a sidelong look. Elayne had never gotten used to Egwene's refusal to admit she was Andoran herself. At least, lines on maps said the Two Rivers was part of Andor, and Elayne believed the maps.

"We have fought wars against them, Egwene, but since the damage they suffered in the Aiel War, Andor has sold them nearly as much grain as Tear has. The trade has stopped, now. With every Cairhienin House fighting every other for the Sun Throne, who would buy the grain, or see it distributed to the people? If the fighting is as bad as what we've seen on the banks. . . . Well. You cannot feed a people for twenty years and feel nothing for them when they must be starving."

"A Gray Man," Egwene said, and Elayne jumped, trying to look in every direction at once. The glow of *saidar* surrounded her.

"Where?"

Egwene took a slower look around the decks, but to make

sure no one was close enough to overhear. Captain Ellisor
still stood in the stern, by the shirtless man holding the long
tiller. Another sailor was up in the very bow, scanning the
waters ahead for signs of submerged mudbanks, and two
more padded about the deck, now and again adjusting a
rope to the sails. The rest of the crew were all below. One
of the pair stopped to check the lashings on the rowboat
tied upside down on the deck; she waited for him to go on
before speaking.

"Fool!" she muttered softly. "Me, Elayne, not you, so
don't glower at me like that." She continued in a whisper.
"A Gray Man is after Mat, Elayne. That must be what that
dream meant, but I never saw it. I *am* a fool!"

The glow around Elayne vanished. "Do not be so hard on
yourself," she whispered back. "Perhaps it does mean that,
but I did not see it, and neither did Nynaeve." She paused;
red-gold curls swung as she shook her head. "But it doesn't
make sense, Egwene. Why would a Gray Man be after Mat?
There is nothing in my letter to my mother that could harm
us in the slightest."

"I do not know why." Egwene frowned. "There has to be
a reason. I am sure that is what that dream means."

"Even if you are right, Egwene, there is nothing you can
do about it."

"I know that," Egwene said bitterly. She did not even
know whether he was ahead of them or behind. Ahead, she
suspected; Mat would have left without any delay. "Either
way," she muttered to herself, "it does no good. I finally
know what one of my dreams means, and it doesn't help a
hemstitch worth!"

"But if you know one meaning," Elayne told her, "perhaps now you will know others. If we sit down and talk
them over, perhaps—"

The *Blue Crane* gave a shuddering lurch, throwing
Elayne to the deck and Egwene on top of her. When Egwene
struggled to her feet, the shoreline no longer slid by. The
vessel had halted, with the bow raised and the deck canted
to one side. The sails flapped noisily in the wind.

Chin Ellisor pushed himself to his feet and ran for the
bow, leaving the tillerman to rise on his own. "You blind
worm of a farmer!" he roared toward the man in the bow,

who was clinging to the rail to keep from falling the rest of the way over. "You dirt-grubbing get of a goat! Haven't you been on the river long enough yet to recognize how the water ruffles over a mudflat?" He seized the man on the rail by the shoulders and pulled him back onto the deck, but only to shove him out of the way so he could peer down over the bow himself. "If you've put a hole in my hull, I will use your guts for caulking!"

The other crewmen were clambering to their feet, now, and more came scrambling up from below. They all ran to cluster around the captain.

Nynaeve appeared at the head of the ladder that led down to the passenger cabins, still straightening her skirts. With a sharp tug at her braid, she frowned at the knot of men in the bow, then strode to Egwene and Elayne. "He ran us onto something, did he? After all his talk of knowing the river as well as he knows his wife. The woman probably never receives as much as a smile from him." She jerked the thick braid again and went forward, pushing her way through the sailors to reach the captain. They were all intent on the water below.

There was no point in joining her. *He will have us off faster if he's left to it.* Nynaeve was probably telling him how to do the work. Elayne seemed to feel the same way, from the rueful shake of the head she gave as she watched the captain and crewmen all turn their attention respectfully from whatever was under the bow to Nynaeve.

A ripple of agitation ran through the men, and grew stronger. For a moment the captain's hands could be seen, waving in protest over the other men's heads, and then Nynaeve was striding away from them—they made way, bowing now—with Ellisor hurrying beside her and mopping his round face with a large red handkerchief. His anxious voice became audible as they drew near.

". . . a good fifteen miles to the next village on the Andor side, Aes Sedai, and at least five or six miles downriver on the Cairhien side! Andoran soldiers hold it, it is true, but they do not hold the miles from here to there!" He wiped at his face as if he were dripping sweat.

"A sunken ship," Nynaeve told the other two women. "The work of river brigands, the captain thinks. He means to try backing off it with the sweeps, but he does not seem to think that will work."

"We were running fast when we hit, Aes Sedai. I wanted to make good speed for you." Ellisor rubbed even harder at his face. He was afraid the Aes Sedai would blame him, Egwene realized. "We are stuck hard. But I do not think we are taking water, Aes Sedai. There is no need to worry. Another ship will be along. Two sets of sweeps will surely get us free. There is no need for you to be put ashore, Aes Sedai. I do swear it, by the Light."

"You were thinking of leaving the ship?" Egwene asked. "Do you think that is wise?"

"Of course, it's—!" Nynaeve stopped and frowned at her. Egwene returned the frown with a level stare. Nynaeve went on in a calmer tone, if still a tight one. "The captain says it may be an hour before another ship comes along. One with enough sweeps to make a difference. Or a day. Or two, maybe. I do not think we can afford to waste a day or two waiting. We can be in this village—what did you call it, Captain? Jurene?—we can walk to Jurene in two hours or less. If Captain Ellisor frees his vessel as quickly as he hopes, we can reboard then. He says he will stop to see if we are there. If he does not get free, though, we can take ship from Jurene. We may even find a vessel waiting. The captain says traders do stop there, because of the Andoran soldiers." She drew a deep breath, but her voice grew tighter. "Have I explained my reasoning fully enough? Do you need more?"

"It is clear to me," Elayne put in quickly before Egwene could speak. "And it sounds a good idea. You think it is a good idea, too, don't you, Egwene?"

Egwene gave a grudging nod. "I suppose it is."

"But, Aes Sedai," Ellisor protested, "at least go to the Andor bank. The war, Aes Sedai. Brigands, and every sort of ruffian, and the soldiers not much better. The very wreck under our bow shows the sort of men they are."

"We have not seen a living soul on the Cairhien side," Nynaeve said, "and in any case, we are far from defenseless, Captain. And I will not walk fifteen miles when I can walk six."

"Of course, Aes Sedai." Ellisor really was sweating, now. "I did not mean to suggest. . . . Of course you are not defenseless, Aes Sedai. I did not mean to suggest it." He wiped his face furiously, but it still glistened.

Nynaeve opened her mouth, glanced at Egwene, and seemed to change what she had intended to say. "I am going below for my things," she told the air halfway between Egwene and Elayne, then turned on Ellisor. "Captain, make your rowboat ready." He bowed and scurried away even before she turned for the hatch, and was shouting for men to put the boat over the side before she was below.

"If one of you says 'up,'" Elayne murmured, "the other says 'down.' If you do not stop it, we may not reach Tear."

"We will reach Tear," Egwene said. "And sooner once Nynaeve realizes she is not the Wisdom any longer. We are all"—she did not say Accepted; there were too many men hurrying about—"on the same level, now." Elayne sighed.

In short order the rowboat had ferried them ashore, and they were standing on the bank with walking staffs in hand, their belongings in bundles on their backs, and hung about them in pouches and scripts. Rolling grassland and scattered copses surrounded them, though the hills were forested a few miles in from the river. The sweeps on the *Blue Crane* were cutting up froth, but failing to budge the vessel. Egwene turned and started south without another glance. And before Nynaeve could take the lead.

When the others caught up to her, Elayne gave her a reproving look. Nynaeve walked staring straight ahead. Elayne told Nynaeve what Egwene had said about Mat and a Gray Man, but the older woman listened in silence and only said, "He'll have to look after himself," without pausing in her stride. After a time, the Daughter-Heir gave up trying to make the other two talk, and they all walked in silence.

Clumps of trees close along the riverbank soon hid the *Blue Crane*, thick growths of wateroak and willow. They did not go through the copses, small as they were, for anything at all might be hiding in the shadows under their branches. A few low bushes grew scattered between the thickets here close to the river, but they were too sparse to hide a child much less a brigand, and they were widely spaced.

"If we do see brigands," Egwene announced, "I am going to defend myself. There is no Amyrlin looking over our shoulders here."

Nynaeve's mouth thinned. "If need be," she told the air in front of her, "we can frighten off any brigands the way we did those Whitecloaks. If we can find no other way."

"I wish you would not talk of brigands," Elayne said. "I would like to reach this village without—"

A figure in brown and gray rose from behind a bush standing by itself almost in front of them.

CHAPTER
38

Maidens of the Spear

E gwene embraced *saidar* before the scream was
well out of her mouth, and she saw the glow around
Elayne, too. For an instant she wondered if Ellisor
had heard their screams and would send help; the *Blue
Crane* could not be more than a mile upriver. Then she was
dismissing the need for help, already weaving flows of Air
and Fire into lightning. She could almost still hear their
yelling.

Nynaeve was simply standing there with her arms crossed
beneath her breasts and a firm expression on her face, but
Egwene was not sure whether that was because she was not
angry enough to touch the True Source, or because she had
already seen what Egwene was just now seeing. The person
facing them was a woman no older than Egwene herself, if
somewhat taller.

She did not let go of *saidar.* Men were sometimes silly
enough to think a woman was harmless merely because she
was a woman; Egwene had no such illusions. In a corner of
her mind she noted that Elayne was no longer surrounded
by the glow. The Daughter-Heir must still harbor foolish
notions. *She was never a Seanchan prisoner.*

Egwene did not think many men would be stupid enough
to think the woman in front of them was not dangerous,
even though her hands were empty and she wore no visible weapon. Blue-green eyes and reddish hair cut short except for a narrow tail that hung to her shoulders; soft, laced
knee-boots and close-fitting coat and breeches all in the
shades of earth and rock. Such coloring and clothing had
been described to her once; this woman was Aiel.

Looking at her, Egwene felt a sudden odd affinity for the woman. She could not understand it. *She looks like Rand's cousin, that's why.* Yet even that feeling—almost of kinship—could not stifle her curiosity. *What under the Light are Aiel doing here? They never leave the Waste; not since the Aiel War.* She had heard all of her life how deadly Aiel were—these Maidens of the Spear no less than the members of the male warrior societies—but she felt no particular fear and, indeed, some irritation at having been afraid. With *saidar* feeding the One Power into her, she had no need to fear anyone. *Except maybe a fully trained sister,* she admitted. *But certainly not one woman, even if she is Aiel.*

"My name is Aviendha," the Aiel woman said, "of the Nine Valleys sept of the Taardad Aiel." Her face was as flat and expressionless as her voice. "I am *Far Dareis Mai*, a Maiden of the Spear." She paused a moment, studying them. "You have not the look in your faces, but we saw the rings. In your lands, you have women much like our Wise Ones, the women called Aes Sedai. Are you women of the White Tower, or not?"

For a moment Egwene did feel unease. *We?* She looked around them carefully, but saw no one behind any bush within twenty paces.

If there were others, they had to be in the next thicket, more than two hundred paces ahead, or in the last one, twice that distance behind. Too far to threaten. *Unless they have bows.* But they would have to be good with them. Back home, in the competitions at Bel Tine and Sunday, only the best bowmen shot at any distance much beyond two hundred paces.

But she still felt better knowing she could hurl a lightning bolt at anyone who tried such a shot.

"We are women of the White Tower," Nynaeve said calmly. She was very obvious in not looking around for other Aiel. Even Elayne was peering about. "Whether you would consider any of us wise is another matter," Nynaeve went on. "What do you want of us?"

Aviendha smiled. She was really quite lovely, Egwene realized; the grim expression had masked it. "You talk as the Wise Ones do. To the point, and small suffering of fools." Her smile faded, but her voice remained calm. "One of us lies gravely hurt, perhaps dying. The Wise Ones often heal those who would surely die without them, and I have heard Aes Sedai can do more. Will you aid her?"

Egwene almost shook her head in confusion. *A friend of hers is dying? She sounds as if she is asking if we'll lend her a cup of barley flour!*

"I will help her if I can," Nynaeve said slowly. "I cannot make promises, Aviendha. She may die despite anything I can do."

"Death comes for us all," the Aiel said. "We can only choose how to face it when it comes. I will take you to her."

Two women in Aiel garb stood up no more than ten paces away, one out of a little fold in the ground that Egwene would not have supposed could hide a dog, and the other in grass that reached only halfway to her knees. They lowered their black veils as they stood—that gave her another jolt; she was sure Elayne had told her the Aiel only hid their faces when they might have to do killing—and settled the cloth that had wrapped their heads about their shoulders. One had the same reddish hair as Aviendha, with gray eyes, the other dark blue eyes and hair like fire. Neither was any older than Egwene or Elayne, and both looked ready to use the short spears in their hands.

The woman with fiery hair handed Aviendha weapons; a long, heavy-bladed knife to belt at her waist, and a bristling quiver for the other side; a dark, curved bow that had the dull shine of horn, in a case to fasten on her back; and four short spears with long points to grip in her left hand along with a small, round hide buckler. Aviendha wore them as naturally as a woman in Emond's Field would wear a scarf, just as her companions did. "Come," she said, and started for the thicket they had already passed.

Egwene finally released *saidar.* She suspected all three of the Aiel could stab her with those spears before she could do anything about it, if that was what they wanted, but though they were wary, she did not think they would. *And what if Nynaeve can't Heal their friend? I wish she would ask before she makes these decisions that involve all of us!*

As they headed for the trees, the Aiel scanned the land around them as if they expected the empty landscape to hold enemies as adept at hiding as themselves. Aviendha strode ahead, and Nynaeve kept up with her.

"I am Elayne of House Trakand," Egwene's friend said as if making conversation, "Daughter-Heir to Morgase, Queen of Andor."

Egwene stumbled. *Light, is she mad? I know Andor fought them in the Aiel War. It might be twenty years, but they say Aiel have long memories.*

But the flame-haired Aiel closest to her only said, "I am Bain, of the Black Rock sept of the Shaarad Aiel."

"I am Chiad," the shorter, blonder woman on her other side said, "of the Stones River sept of the Goshien Aiel."

Bain and Chiad glanced at Egwene; their expressions did not change, but she had the feeling they thought she was showing bad manners.

"I am Egwene al'Vere," she told them. They seemed to expect more, so she added, "Daughter of Marin al'Vere, of Emond's Field, in the Two Rivers." That seemed to satisfy them, in a way, but she would have bet they understood it no more than she did all these septs and clans. *It must mean families, in some way.*

"You are first-sisters?" Bain seemed to be taking in all three of them.

Egwene thought they must mean sisters as it was used for Aes Sedai, and said "Yes," just as Elayne said "No."

Chiad and Bain exchanged a very quick look that suggested they were talking to women who might not be completely whole in their minds.

"First-sister," Elayne told Egwene as if she were lecturing, "means women who have the same mother. Second-sister means their mothers are sisters." She turned her words to the Aiel. "We neither of us know a great deal of your people. I ask you to excuse our ignorance. I sometimes think of Egwene as a first-sister, but we are not blood kin."

"Then why do you not speak the words before your Wise Ones?" Chiad asked. "Bain and I became first-sisters."

Egwene blinked. "How can you *become* first-sisters? Either you have the same mother, or you do not. I do not mean to offend. Most of what I know about the Maidens of the Spear comes from the little Elayne has told me. I know you fight in battle and don't care for men, but no more than that." Elayne nodded; the way she had described the Maidens to Egwene had sounded much like a cross between female Warders and the Red Ajah.

That look flashed back across the Aiel's faces, as if they were not certain how much sense Egwene and Elayne had.

"We do not care for men?" Chiad murmured as if puzzled.

Bain knotted her brow in thought. "What you say comes near truth, yet misses it completely. When we wed the spear, we pledge to be bound to no man or child. Some do give up the spear, for a man or a child"—her expression said she herself did not understand this—"but once given up, the spear cannot be taken back."

"Or if she is chosen to go to Rhuidean," Chiad put in. "A Wise One cannot be wedded to the spear."

Bain looked at her as if she had announced the sky was blue, or that rain fell from clouds. The glance she gave Egwene and Elayne said perhaps they did not know these things. "Yes, that is true. Though some try to struggle against it."

"Yes, they do." Chiad sounded as though she and Bain were sharing something between them.

"But I have gone far from the trail of my explanation," Bain went on. "The Maidens do not dance the spears with one another even when our clans do, but the Shaarad Aiel and the Goshien Aiel have held blood feud between them over four hundred years, so Chiad and I felt our wedding pledge was not enough. We went to speak the words before the Wise Ones of our clans—she risking her life in my hold, and I in hers—to bond us as first-sisters. As is proper for first-sisters who are Maidens, we guard each other's backs, and neither will let a man come to her without the other. I would not say we do not care for men." Chiad nodded, with just the hint of a smile. "Have I made the truth clear to you, Egwene?"

"Yes," Egwene said faintly. She glanced at Elayne and saw the bewilderment in her blue eyes she knew must be in her own. *Not Red Ajah. Green, maybe. A cross between Warders and Green Ajah, and I do not understand another thing out of that.* "The truth is quite clear to me, now, Bain. Thank you."

"If the two of you feel you are first-sisters," Chiad said, "you should go to your Wise Ones and speak the words. But you are Wise Ones, though young. I do not know how it would be done in that case."

Egwene did not know whether to laugh or blush. She kept having an image of her and Elayne sharing the same man. *No, that is only for first-sisters who are Maidens of the Spear. Isn't it?* Elayne did have spots of color in her cheeks, and Egwene was sure she was thinking of Rand. *But we do not share him, Elayne. We can neither of us have him.*

Elayne cleared her throat. "I do not think there is a need for that, Chiad. Egwene and I already guard each other's backs."

"How can that be?" Chiad asked slowly. "You are not wedded to the spear. And you are Wise Ones. Who would lift a hand against a Wise One? This confuses me. What need have you for guarding of backs?"

Egwene was spared having to come up with an answer by their arrival at the copse. There were two more Aiel under the trees, deep into the thicket, but next to the river. Jolien, of the Salt Flat sept of the Nakai Aiel, a blue-eyed woman with red-gold hair nearly the color of Elayne's, was watching over Dailin, of Aviendha's sept and clan. Sweat matted Dailin's hair, making it a darker red, and she only opened her gray eyes once, when they first came near, then closed them again. Her coat and shirt lay beside her, and red stained the bandages wrapped around her middle.

"She took a sword," Aviendha said. "Some of those fools that the oath-breaking treekillers call soldiers thought we were another handful of the bandits who infest this land. We had to kill them to convince them otherwise, but Dailin. . . . Can you heal her, Aes Sedai?"

Nynaeve went to her knees beside the injured woman and lifted the bandages enough to peer under them. She winced at what she saw. "Have you moved her since she was hurt? There is scabbing, but it has been broken."

"She wanted to die near water," Aviendha said. She glanced once at the river, then quickly away again. Egwene thought she might have shivered, too.

"Fools!" Nynaeve began rummaging in her pouch of herbs. "You could have killed her moving her with an injury like that. She wanted to die near water!" she said disgustedly. "Just because you carry weapons like men doesn't mean you have to think like them." She pulled a deep wooden cup out of the bag and pushed it at Chiad. "Fill that. I need water to mix these so she can drink them."

Chiad and Bain stepped to the river's edge and returned together. Their faces never changed, but Egwene thought they had almost expected the river to reach up and grab them.

"If we had not brought her here to the . . . river, Aes Sedai," Aviendha said, "we would never have found you, and she would have died anyway."

Nynaeve snorted and began sifting powdered herbs into the cup of water, muttering to herself. "Corenroot helps make blood, and dogwort for knitting flesh, and healall, of course, and. . . ." Her mutters trailed off into whispers too low to hear. Aviendha was frowning at her.

"The Wise Ones use herbs, Aes Sedai, but I had not heard that Aes Sedai used them."

"I use what I use!" Nynaeve snapped and went back to sorting through her powders and whispering to herself.

"She truly does sound like a Wise One," Chiad told Bain softly, and the other woman gave a tight nod.

Dailin was the only Aiel without her weapons in hand, and they all looked ready to use them in a heartbeat. *Nynaeve surely isn't soothing anyone,* Egwene thought. *Get them talking about something. Anything. Nobody feels like fighting if they're talking of something peaceful.*

"Do not be offended," she said carefully, "but I notice you are all uneasy about the river. It does not grow violent unless there is a storm. You could swim in it if you wanted, though the current is strong away from the banks." Elayne shook her head.

The Aiel looked blank; Aviendha said, "I saw a man—a Shienaran—do this swimming . . . once."

"I don't understand," Egwene said. "I know there isn't much water in the Waste, but you said you were 'Stones River sept,' Jolien. Surely you have swum in the Stones River?" Elayne looked at her as if she were mad.

"Swim," Jolien said awkwardly. "It means . . . to get in the water? All that water? With nothing to hold on to." She shuddered. "Aes Sedai, before I crossed the Dragonwall, I had never seen flowing water I could not step across. The Stones River. . . . Some claim it had water in it once, but that is only boasting. There are only the stones. The oldest records of the Wise Ones and the clan chief say there was never anything but stones since the first day our sept broke

off from the High Plain sept and claimed that land. Swim!"
She gripped her spears as if to fight the very word. Chiad
and Bain moved a pace further from the riverbank.

Egwene sighed. And colored when she met Elayne's eye.
*Well, I am not a Daughter-Heir, to know all these things. I
will learn them, though.* As she looked around at the Aiel
women, she realized that far from soothing them, she had
put them even more on edge. *If they try anything, I will hold
them with Air.* She had no idea whether she could seize four
people at once, but she opened herself to *saidar,* wove the
flows in Air and held them ready. The Power pulsed in her
with eagerness to be used. No glow surrounded Elayne, and
she wondered why. Elayne looked right at her and shook
her head.

"I would never harm an Aes Sedai," Aviendha said
abruptly. "I would have you know that. Whether Dailin
lives or dies, it makes no difference in that. I would never
use this"—she lifted one short spear a trifle—"against any
woman. And you are Aes Sedai." Egwene had the sudden
feeling that the woman was trying to soothe *them.*

"I knew that," Elayne said, as if talking to Aviendha,
but her eyes told Egwene the words were for her. "No one
knows much of your people, but I was taught that Aiel
never harm women unless they are—what did you call it?—
wedded to the spear."

Bain seemed to think Elayne was failing to see truth
clearly again. "That is not exactly the way of it, Elayne. If a
woman not wedded came at me with weapons, I would drub
her until she knew better of it. A man. . . . A man might
think a woman of your lands was wedded if she bore weapons; I do not know. Men can be strange."

"Of course," Elayne said. "But so long as we do not attack you with weapons, you will not try to harm us." All
four Aiel looked shocked, and she gave Egwene a quick significant look.

Egwene held on to *saidar* anyway. Just because Elayne had
been taught something did not mean it was true, even if the
Aiel said the same thing. And *saidar* felt . . . good in her.

Nynaeve lifted up Dailin's head and began pouring her
mixture into the woman's mouth. "Drink," she said firmly.
"I know it tastes bad, but drink it all." Dailin swallowed,
choked, and swallowed again.

"Not even then, Aes Sedai," Aviendha told Elayne. She kept her eyes on Dailin and Nynaeve, though. "It is said that once, before the Breaking of the World, we served the Aes Sedai, though no story says how. We failed in that service. Perhaps that is the sin that sent us to the Three-fold Land; I do not know. No one knows what the sin was, except maybe the Wise Ones, or the clan chiefs, and they do not say. It is said if we fail the Aes Sedai again, they will destroy us."

"Drink it all," Nynaeve muttered. "Swords! Swords and muscles and no brains!"

"*We* are not going to destroy you," Elayne said firmly, and Aviendha nodded.

"As you say, Aes Sedai. But the old stories are all clear on one point. We must never fight Aes Sedai. If you bring your lightnings and your balefire against me, I will dance with them, but I will not harm you."

"Stabbing people," Nynaeve growled. She lowered Dailin's head, and laid a hand on the woman's brow. Dailin's eyes had closed again. "Stabbing women!" Aviendha shifted her feet and frowned again, and she was not alone among the Aiel.

"Balefire," Egwene said. "Aviendha, what is balefire?"

The Aiel woman turned her frown on her. "Do you not know, Aes Sedai? In the old stories, Aes Sedai wielded it. The stories make it a fearsome thing, but I know no more. It is said we have forgotten much that we once knew."

"Perhaps the White Tower has forgotten much, too," Egwene said. *I knew of it in that . . . dream, or whatever it was. It was as real as* Tel'aran'rhiod. *I'd gamble with Mat on that.*

"No right!" Nynaeve snapped. "No one has a right to tear bodies so! It is not right!"

"Is she angry?" Aviendha asked uneasily. Chiad and Bain and Jolien exchanged worried looks.

"It is all right," Elayne said.

"It is better than all right," Egwene added. "She *is* getting angry, and it is much better than all right."

The glow of *saidar* surrounded Nynaeve suddenly— Egwene leaned forward, trying to see, and so did Elayne— and Dailin started up with a scream, eyes wide open. In an instant, Nynaeve was easing her back down, and the glow faded. Dailin's eyes slid shut, and she lay there panting.

I saw it, Egwene thought. *I . . . think I did.* She was not sure she had even been able to make out all the many flows, much less the way Nynaeve had woven them together. What Nynaeve had done in those few seconds had seemed like weaving four carpets at once while blindfolded.

Nynaeve used the bloody bandages to wipe Dailin's stomach, smearing away bright red new blood and black crusts of dried old. There was no wound, no scar, only healthy skin considerably paler than Dailin's face.

With a grimace, Nynaeve took the bloody cloths, stood up, and threw them into the river. "Wash the rest of that off of her," she said, "and put some clothes back on her. She's cold. And be ready to feed her. She will be hungry." She knelt by the water to wash her hands.

CHAPTER
39

Threads in the Pattern

Jolien put an unsteady hand to where the wound had been in Dailin's middle; when she touched smooth skin, she gasped as if she had not believed her own eyes.

Nynaeve straightened, drying her hands on her cloak. Egwene had to admit that good wool did better for a towel than silk or velvet. "I said wash her and get some clothes on her," Nynaeve snapped.

"Yes, Wise One," Jolien said quickly, and she, Chiad, and Bain all leaped to obey.

A short laugh burst from Aviendha, a laugh almost at the edge of tears. "I have heard that a Wise One in the Jagged Spire sept is said to be able to do this, and one in the Four Holes sept, but I always thought it was boasting." She drew a deep breath, regaining her composure. "Aes Sedai, I owe you a debt. My water is yours, and the shade of my septhold will welcome you. Dailin is my second-sister." She saw Nynaeve's uncomprehending look and added, "She is my mother's sister's daughter. Close blood, Aes Sedai. I owe a blood debt."

"If I have any blood to spill," Nynaeve said dryly, "I will spill it myself. If you wish to repay me, tell me if there is a ship at Jurene. The next village south of here?"

"The village where the soldiers fly the White Lion banner?" Aviendha said. "There was a ship there when I scouted yesterday. The old stories mention ships, but it was strange to see one."

"The Light send it is still there." Nynaeve began putting away her folded papers of powdered herbs. "I have done what I can for the girl, Aviendha, and we must go on. All that she needs now is food and rest. And try not to let people stick swords in her."

"What comes, comes, Aes Sedai," the Aiel woman replied.

"Aviendha," Egwene said, "feeling as you do about rivers, how do you cross them? I am sure there is at least one river nearly as big as the Erinin between here and the Waste."

"The Alguenya," Elayne said. "Unless you went around it."

"You have many rivers, but some have things called bridges where we had need to cross, and others we could wade. For the rest, Jolien remembered that wood floats." She slapped the trunk of a tall whitewood. "These are big, but they float as well as a branch. We found dead ones and made ourselves a . . . ship . . . a little ship, of two or three lashed together to cross the big river." She said it matter-of-factly.

Egwene stared in wonder. If she were as afraid of something as the Aiel obviously were of rivers, could she make herself face it the way they did? She did not think so. *What about the Black Ajah*, a small voice asked. *Have you stopped being afraid of them? That is different*, she told it. *There's no bravery in that. I either hunt them, or else I sit like a rabbit waiting for a hawk.* She quoted the old saying to herself. *"It is better to be the hammer than the nail."*

"We had best be on our way," Nynaeve said.

"In a moment," Elayne told her. "Aviendha, why have you come all this way and put up with such hardship?"

Aviendha shook her head disgustedly. "We have not come far at all; we were among the last to set out. The Wise Ones nipped at me like wild dogs circling a calf, saying I had other duties." Suddenly she grinned, gesturing to the other Aiel. "These stayed back to taunt me in my misery, so they said, but I do not think the Wise Ones would have let me go if they had not been there to companion me."

"We seek the one foretold," Bain said. She was holding a sleeping Dailin so Chiad could slip a shirt of brown linen onto her. "He Who Comes With the Dawn."

"He will lead us out of the Three-fold Land," Chiad added. "The prophecies say he was born of *Far Dareis Mai*."

Elayne looked startled. "I thought you said the Maidens of the Spear were not allowed to have children. I am sure I was taught that." Bain and Chiad exchanged those looks again, as if Elayne had come near truth and yet missed it once more.

"If a Maiden bears a child," Aviendha explained carefully, "she gives the child to the Wise Ones of her sept, and they pass the child to another woman in such a way that none knows whose child it is." She, too, sounded as if she were explaining that stone is hard. "Every woman wants to foster such a child in the hope she may raise He Who Comes With the Dawn."

"Or she may give up the spear and wed the man," Chiad said, and Bain added, "There are sometimes reasons one must give up the spear."

Aviendha gave them a level look, but continued as if they had not spoken. "Except that now the Wise Ones say he is to be found here, beyond the Dragonwall. 'Blood of our blood mixed with the old blood, raised by an ancient blood not ours.' I do not understand it, but the Wise Ones spoke in such a way as to leave no doubts." She paused, obviously choosing her words. "You have asked many questions, Aes Sedai. I wish to ask one. You must understand that we look for omens and signs. Why do three Aes Sedai walk a land where the only hand without a knife in it is a hand too weak with hunger to grasp the hilt? Where do you go?"

"Tear," Nynaeve said briskly, "unless we stay here talking until the Heart of the Stone crumbles to dust." Elayne began adjusting the cord of her bundle and the strap of her scrip for walking, and after a moment Egwene did the same.

The Aiel women were looking at one another, Jolien frozen in the act of closing Dailin's gray-brown coat. "Tear?" Aviendha said in a cautious tone. "Three Aes Sedai walking through a troubled land on their way to Tear. This is a strange thing. Why do you go to Tear, Aes Sedai?"

Egwene glanced at Nynaeve. *Light, a moment ago they were laughing, and now they're as tense as they ever were.*

"We hunt some evil women," Nynaeve said carefully. "Darkfriends."

"Shadowrunners." Jolien twisted her mouth around the word as if she had bitten into a rotten apple.

"Shadowrunners in Tear," Bain said, and as if part of the same sentence Chiad added, "And three Aes Sedai seeking the Heart of the Stone."

"I did not say we were going to the Heart of the Stone," Nynaeve said sharply. "I merely said I did not want to stay here till it falls to dust. Egwene, Elayne, are you ready?" She started out of the thicket without waiting for an answer, walking staff thumping the ground and long strides carrying her south.

Egwene and Elayne made hasty goodbyes before following after her. The four Aiel on their feet stood watching them go.

When the two of them were a little way beyond the trees, Egwene said, "My heart almost stopped when you named yourself. Weren't you afraid they might try to kill you, or to take you prisoner? The Aiel War was not *that* long ago, and whatever they said about not harming women who don't carry spears, they looked ready enough to use those spears on anything, to me."

Elayne shook her head ruefully. "I have just learned how much I do not know about the Aiel, but I was taught that they do not think of the Aiel War as a war at all. From the way they behaved toward me, I think maybe that much of what I learned is truth. Or maybe it was because they think I am Aes Sedai."

"I know they are strange, Elayne, but *no* one can call three years of battles anything but a war. I do not care how much they fight among themselves, a war is a war."

"Not to them. Thousands of Aiel crossed the Spine of the World, but apparently they saw themselves more like thief-takers, or headsmen, come after King Laman of Cairhien for the crime of cutting down *Avendoraldera*. To the Aiel, it was not a war; it was an execution."

Avendoraldera, according to one of Verin's lectures, had been an offshoot of the Tree of Life itself, brought to Cairhien some five hundred years ago as an unprecedented offer of peace from the Aiel, given along with the right to cross the Waste, a right otherwise given to none but peddlers, gleemen, and the Tuatha'an. Much of Cairhien's wealth had been built on the trade in ivory and perfumes and spices and, most of all, silk, from the lands beyond the Waste. Not

even Verin had any idea of how the Aiel had come by a sapling of *Avendesora*—for one thing, the old books were clear
that it made no seed; for another, no one knew where the
Tree of Life was, except for a few stories that were clearly
wrong, but surely the Tree of Life could have nothing to do
with the Aiel—or of why the Aiel had called the Cairhienin
the Watersharers, or insisted their trains of merchant wagons fly a banner bearing the trefoil leaf of *Avendesora*.

Egwene supposed, grudgingly, that she could understand why they had started a war—even if they did not
think it was one—after King Laman cut down their gift
to make a throne unlike any other in the world. Laman's
Sin, she had heard it called. According to Verin, not only
had Cairhien's trade across the Waste ended with the war,
but those Cairhienin who ventured into the Waste now vanished. Verin claimed they were said to be "sold as animals"
in the lands beyond the Waste, but not even she understood
how a man or a woman could be sold.

"Egwene," Elayne said, "you know who He Who Comes
With the Dawn must be, don't you?"

Staring at Nynaeve's back still well ahead of them, Egwene
shook her head—*Does she mean to race us to Jurene?*—
then almost stopped walking. "You do not mean—?"

Elayne nodded. "I think so. I do not know much of the
Prophecies of the Dragon, but I have heard a few lines. One
I remember is, 'On the slopes of Dragonmount shall he be
born, born of a maiden wedded to no man.' Egwene, Rand
does look like an Aiel. Well, he looks like the pictures I
have seen of Tigraine, too, but she vanished before he was
born, and I hardly think she could have been his mother
anyway. I think Rand's mother was a Maiden of the Spear."

Egwene frowned in thought as she hurried along, running everything she knew of Rand's birth through her head.
He had been raised by Tam al'Thor after Kari al'Thor died,
but if what Moiraine said was true, they could not be his
real mother and father. Nynaeve had sometimes seemed
to know some secret about Rand's birth. *But I will bet I
couldn't pry it out of her with a fork!*

They caught up to Nynaeve, Egwene glowering as she
thought, Nynaeve staring straight ahead toward Jurene and
that ship, and Elayne frowning at the pair of them as if they

were two children sulking over who should have the larger piece of cake.

After a time of silent strides, Elayne said, "You handled that very well, Nynaeve. The Healing, and the rest, too. I do not think they ever doubted you were Aes Sedai. Or that we all were, because of the way you bore yourself."

"You did do a good job," Egwene said after a minute. "That was the first time I have ever really watched what is done during a Healing. It makes making lightning look like mixing oatcake."

A surprised smile appeared on Nynaeve's face. "Thank you," she murmured, and reached over to give Egwene's hair a little tug the way she had when Egwene was a little girl.

I am not a little girl any longer. The moment passed as quickly as it had come, and they went on in silence once more. Elayne sighed loudly.

They covered another mile, or a little more, swiftly, despite swinging in from the river to go around the thickets along the bank. Nynaeve insisted on staying well clear of the trees. Egwene thought it was silly to think more Aiel would be hiding in the copses, but the swing inland did not add much distance to what they had to cover; none of the growths were very big.

Elayne watched the trees, though, and she was the one who suddenly screamed, "Look out!"

Egwene jerked her head around; men were stepping out from among the trees, slings whirling 'round their heads. She reached for *saidar*, and something struck her head, and darkness drank everything.

Egwene could feel herself swaying, feel something moving under her. Her head seemed to be nothing but pain. She tried to raise a hand to her temples, but something dug into her wrists, and her hands did not move.

"—better than lying there all day waiting for dark," a man's rough voice said. "Who knows if another ship would come by close in? And I don't trust that boat. It leaks."

"You do better hope Adden does believe you did see those rings before you did decide," another man said. "He does want fat cargoes, not women, I think." the first man muttered something coarse about what Adden could do with his leaky boat, and the cargoes, too.

Her eyes opened. Silver-flecked spots danced across her vision; she thought she might be going to throw up on the ground swaying past under her head. She was tied across the back of a horse, her wrists and ankles joined by a rope running under its belly, her hair hanging down.

It was still daylight. She craned her neck to look around. So many rough-dressed men on horses surrounded her that she could not see whether Nynaeve and Elayne had been captured, as well. Some of the men wore bits of armor—a battered helmet, or a dented breastplate, or a jerkin sewn all over with metal scales—but most wore only coats that had not been cleaned in months, if ever. From the smell, the men had not cleaned themselves in months, either. They all wore swords, at their waists or on their backs.

Rage hit her, and fear, but most of all white-hot anger. *I won't be a prisoner. I won't be bound! I won't!* She reached for *saidar* and the pain nearly lifted the top of her head; she barely stifled a moan.

The horse paused for a moment of shouts and the creak of rusty hinges, then went ahead a little further, and the men began to dismount. As they moved apart, she could see something of where they were. A log palisade surrounded them, built atop a large, round earthen mound, and men with bows stood guard on a wooden walk built just high enough for them to see over the rough-hewn ends of the logs. One low, windowless log house seemed to be built into the mounded dirt under the wall. There was no other structure beyond a few lean-to sheds. Aside from the men and horses that had just entered, the rest of the open space was filled with cook fires, and tethered horses, and more unwashed men. There must have been at least a hundred. Caged goats and pigs and chickens filled the air with squeals and grunts and clucks that blended with coarse shouts and laughter to make a din that pierced her head.

Her eyes found Nynaeve and Elayne, bound head down across saddleless horses as she was. Neither seemed to be stirring; the very end of Nynaeve's braid dragged across the dirt as her horse stirred. A small hope faded; that one of them might be free, to help whoever was held escape. *Light, I cannot stand to be a prisoner again. Not again.* Gingerly, she tried reaching for *saidar* again. The pain was not so bad this time—merely as if someone had dropped a rock on her head—but it shattered the emptiness before she could even think of a rose.

"One of them's awake!" a man's panicked voice shouted.

Egwene tried to hang limp and look unthreatening. *How in the Light could I look threatening tied up like a sack of meal! Burn me, I have to buy time. I have to!* "I will not harm you," she told the sweaty-faced fellow who came running toward her. Or she tried to tell him. She was not sure how much she had actually said before something crashed into her head again and darkness rolled over her in a wave of nausea.

Waking was easier the next time. Her head still hurt, but not as much as it had, though her thoughts did seem to spin dizzily. *At least my stomach isn't. . . . Light, I'd better not think of that.* There was a taste of sour wine and something bitter in her mouth. Strips of lamplight showed through horizontal cracks in a crudely made wall, but she lay in darkness, on her back. On dirt, she thought. The door did not seem to fit well either, but it looked all too sturdy.

She pushed herself to her hands and knees, and was surprised to find she was not tied in any way. Except for that one wall of unpeeled logs, the others all seemed to be of rough stone. The light through the cracks was enough to show her Nynaeve and Elayne lying sprawled on the dirt. There was blood on the Daughter-Heir's face. Neither of them moved except for the rise and fall of their chests as they breathed. Egwene hesitated between trying to wake them immediately and seeing what lay on the other side of that wall. *Just a peek*, she told herself. *I might as well see what we have guarding us before I wake them.*

She told herself it was not because she was afraid she might be unable to waken them. As she put her eye to one of the cracks near the door, she thought of the blood on Elayne's face and tried to remember exactly what it was Nynaeve had done for Dailin.

The next room was large—it had to be all the rest of the log building she had seen—and windowless, but brightly lit with gold and silver lamps hanging from spikes driven into the walls and the logs that made the high ceiling. There was no fireplace. On the packed dirt floor farmhouse tables and chairs mingled with chests covered in gilt-work and inlaid with ivory. A carpet woven in peacocks lay beside a huge canopied bed, piled deep with filthy blankets and comforters, with elaborately carved and gilded posts.

A dozen men stood or sat around the room, but all eyes were on one large, fair-haired man who might have been handsome if his face were cleaner. He stood staring down at the top of a table with fluted legs and gilded scrollwork, one hand on his sword hilt, a finger of the other pushing something she could not make out in small circles on the tabletop.

The outer door opened, revealing night outside, and a lanky man with his left ear gone came in. "He has no come, yet," he said roughly. He was missing two fingers on his left hand, too. "I do no like dealing with that kind."

The big, fair-haired man paid him no mind, only kept moving whatever it was on the table. "Three Aes Sedai," he murmured, then laughed. "Good prices for Aes Sedai, if you have the belly to deal with the right buyer. If you're ready to risk having your belly ripped out through your mouth should you try selling him a pig in a sack. Not so safe as slitting the crew's throats on a trader's ship, eh, Coke? Not so easy, wouldn't you say?"

There was a nervous stir among the other men, and the one addressed, a stocky fellow with shifty eyes, leaned forward anxiously. "They *are* Aes Sedai, Adden." She recognized that voice; the man who had made the coarse suggestions. "They must be, Adden. The rings prove it, I tell you!" Adden picked up something from the table, a small circle that glinted gold in the lamplight.

Egwene gasped and felt at her fingers. *They took my ring!*

"I do no like it," muttered the lanky man with the missing ear. "Aes Sedai. Any one of them could kill us all. Fortune prick me! You do be a stone-carved fool, Coke, and I ought to carve your throat. What if one of them do wake before he does come?"

"They'll not wake for hours." That was a fat man with a hoarse voice and a gap-toothed sneer. "My granny taught me of that stuff we fed them. They'll sleep till sunrise, and he'll come long afore then."

Egwene worked her mouth around the sour wine taste and the bitterness. *Whatever it was, your granny lied to you. She should have strangled you in your cradle!* Before this "he" came, this man who thought he could buy Aes Sedai—*like a bloody Seanchan!*—she would have Nynaeve and Elayne on their feet. She crawled to Nynaeve.

As near as she could tell, Nynaeve seemed to be sleeping, so she began with the simple expedient of shaking her. To her surprise, Nynaeve's eyes shot open.

"Wha—?"

She got a hand over Nynaeve's mouth in time to stop the word. "We are being held prisoner," she whispered. "There are a dozen men on the other side of that wall, and more outside. A great many more. They gave us something to make us sleep, but it wasn't very successful. Do you remember, yet?"

Nynaeve pulled Egwene's hand aside. "I remember." Her voice was soft and grim. She grimaced and twisted her mouth, then suddenly barked a nearly silent laugh. "Sleepwell root. The fools gave us sleepwell root mixed in wine. Wine near gone to vinegar, it tastes like. Quick, do you remember anything of what I taught you? What does sleepwell root do?"

"It clears headaches so you can sleep," Egwene said just as softly. And nearly as grimly, until she heard what she was saying. "It makes you a little drowsy, but that is all." The fat man had not listened well to what his granny told him. "All they did was help clear the pain of being hit in the head."

"Exactly," Nynaeve said. "And once we wake Elayne, we'll give them a thanking they won't forget." She rose, only to crouch beside the golden-haired woman.

"I think I saw more than a hundred of them outside when they brought us in," Egwene whispered to Nynaeve's back. "I am sure you won't mind if I use the Power as a weapon this time. And someone is apparently coming to *buy* us. I mean to do something to that fellow that will make him walk in the Light till the day he dies!" Nynaeve was still crouched over Elayne, but neither of them was moving. "What is the matter?"

"She is hurt badly, Egwene. I think her skull is broken, and she is barely breathing. Egwene, she is dying as surely as Dailin was."

"Can't you do something?" Egwene tried to remember all the flows Nynaeve had woven to Heal the Aiel woman, but she could recall no more than every third thread. "You have to!"

"They took my herbs," Nynaeve muttered fiercely, her voice trembling. "I can't! Not without the herbs!" Egwene was shocked to realize Nynaeve was on the point of tears. "Burn them all, I can't do it without—!" Suddenly she seized Elayne's shoulders as if she meant to lift the unconscious woman and shake her. "Burn you, girl," she rasped, "I did not bring you all this way to die! I should have left you scrubbing pots! I should have tied you up in a sack for Mat to carry to your mother! I will not let you die on me! Do you hear me? I won't allow it!" *Saidar* suddenly shone around her, and Elayne's eyes and mouth opened wide together.

Egwene got her hands over Elayne's mouth just in time to muffle any sound, she thought, but as she touched her, the eddies of Nynaeve's Healing caught her like a straw on the edge of a whirlpool. Cold froze her to the bone, meeting heat that seared outward as if it meant to crisp her flesh; the world vanished in a sensation of rushing, falling, flying, spinning.

When it finally ended, she was breathing hard and staring down at Elayne, who stared back over the hands she still had pressed over her mouth. The last of Egwene's headache was gone. Even the backwash of what Nynaeve had done had apparently been enough for that. The murmur of voices from the other room was no louder; if Elayne had made any noise—or if she had—Adden and the others had not noticed.

Nynaeve was on her hands and knees, head down and shaking. "Light!" she muttered. "Doing it that way . . . was like peeling off . . . my own skin. Oh, Light!" She peered at Elayne. "How do you feel, girl?" Egwene pulled her hands away.

"Tired," Elayne murmured. "And hungry. Where are we? There were some men with slings. . . ."

Hastily Egwene told her what had happened. Elayne's face began to darken a long way before she was done.

"And now," Nynaeve added in a voice like iron, "we are going to show these louts what it means to meddle with us." *Saidar* shone around her once more.

Elayne was unsteady getting to her feet, but the glow surrounded her, as well. Egwene reached out to the True Source almost gleefully.

When they looked through the cracks again, to see exactly what they had to deal with, there were three Myrddraal in the room.

Dead-black garb hanging unnaturally still, they stood by the table, and every man but Adden had moved as far from them as he could, till they all had their backs against the walls and their eyes on the dirt floor. Across the table from the Myrddraal, Adden faced those eyeless stares, but sweat made runnels in the dirt on his face.

The Fade picked up a ring from the table. Egwene saw now that it was a much heavier circle of gold than the Great Serpent rings.

Face pressed against the crack between two logs, Nynaeve gasped softly and fumbled at the neck of her dress.

"Three *Aes Sedai*," the Halfman hissed, its amusement sounding like dead things powdering to dust, "and one carried this." The ring made a heavy thud as the Myrddraal tossed it back on the table.

"They are the ones I seek," another of them rasped. "You will be well rewarded, human."

"We must take them by surprise," Nynaeve said softly. "What kind of lock holds this door?"

Egwene could just see the lock on the outside of the door, an iron thing on a chain heavy enough to hold an enraged bull. "Be ready," she said.

She thinned one flow of Earth to finer than a hair, hoping the Halfmen could not sense so small a channeling, and wove it into the iron chain, into the tiniest bits of it.

One of the Myrddraal lifted its head. Another leaned across the table toward Adden. "I itch, human. Are you sure they sleep?" Adden swallowed hard and nodded his head.

The third Myrddraal turned to stare at the door to the room where Egwene and the others crouched.

The chain fell to the floor, the Myrddraal staring at it snarled, and the outer door swung open, black-veiled death flowing in from the night.

The room erupted in screams and shouts as men clawed for their swords to fight stabbing Aiel spears. The Myrddraal drew blades blacker than their garb and fought for their lives, too. Egwene had once seen six cats all fighting each other; this was that a hundredfold. And yet in seconds, silence reigned. Or almost silence.

Every human not wearing a black veil lay dead with a spear through him; one pinned Adden to the wall. Two Aiel lay still, as well, amid the jumble of overturned furniture and dead. The three Myrddraal stood back-to-back in the center of the room, black swords in their hands. One was clutching his side as if wounded, though he gave no other sign of it. Another had a long gash down its pale face; it did not bleed. Around them circled the five veiled Aiel still alive, crouching. From outside came screams and clashes of metal that said more Aiel still fought in the night, but in the room was a softer sound.

As they circled, the Aiel drummed their spears against their small hide bucklers. *Thrum-thrum-THRUM-thrum . . . thrum-thrum-THRUM-thrum . . . thrum-thrum-THRUM-thrum.* The Myrddraal turned with them, and their eyeless faces seemed uncertain, uneasy that the fear their gaze struck into every human heart did not seem to touch these.

"Dance with me, Shadowman," one of the Aiel called suddenly, tauntingly. He sounded like a young man.

"Dance with me, Eyeless." That was a woman.

"Dance with me."

"Dance with me."

"I think," Nynaeve said, straightening, "that it is time." She threw open the door, and the three women wrapped in the glow of *saidar* stepped out.

It seemed as though, for the Myrddraal, the Aiel had ceased to exist, and for the Aiel, the Myrddraal. The Aiel stared at Egwene and the others above their veils as if not quite sure what they were seeing; she heard one of the women gasp loudly. The Myrddraal's eyeless stare was different. Egwene could almost feel the Halfmen's knowledge of their own deaths in it; Halfmen knew women embracing the True

Source when they saw them. She was sure she could feel a desire for her death, too, if theirs could buy hers, and an even stronger desire to strip the soul out of her flesh and make both playthings for the Shadow, a desire to. . . .

She had just stepped into the room, yet it seemed she had been meeting that stare for hours. "I'll take no more of this," she growled, and unleashed a flow of Fire.

Flames burst out of all three Myrddraal, sprouting in every direction, and they shrieked like splintered bones jamming a meat-grinder. Yet she had forgotten she was not alone, that Elayne and Nynaeve were with her. Even as the flames consumed the Halfmen, the very air seemed suddenly to push them together in midair, crushing them into a ball of fire and blackness that grew smaller and smaller. Their screams dug at Egwene's spine, and *something* shot out from Nynaeve's hands—a thin bar of white light that made noonday sun seem dark, a bar of fire that made molten metal seem cold, connecting her hands to the Myrddraal. And they ceased to exist as if they had never been. Nynaeve gave a startled jump, and the glow around her vanished.

"What . . . what was that?" Elayne asked.

Nynaeve shook her head; she looked as stunned as Elayne sounded. "I don't know. I . . . I was so angry, so afraid, at what they wanted to. . . . I do not know what it was."

Balefire, Egwene thought. She did not know how she knew, but she was certain of it. Reluctantly, she made herself release *saidar*; made it release her. She did not know which was harder. *And I did not see a thing of what she did!*

The Aiel unveiled themselves, then. A trifle hastily, Egwene thought, as if to tell her and the other two they were no longer ready to fight. Three of the Aiel were male, one an older man with more than touches of gray in his dark red hair. They were tall, these Aielmen, and young or old, they had that calm sureness in their eyes, that dangerous grace of motion Egwene associated with Warders; death rode on their shoulders, and they knew it was there and were not afraid. One of the women was Aviendha. The screams and shouts outside were dying away.

Nynaeve started toward the fallen Aiel.

"There is no need, Aes Sedai," the older man said. "They took Shadowman steel."

Nynaeve still bent to check each, pulling their veils away so she could peel back eyelids and feel throats for a pulse. When she straightened from the second, her face was white. It was Dailin. "Burn you! Burn you!" It was not clear whether she meant Dailin, or the man with gray in his hair, or Aviendha, or all Aiel. "I did not Heal her so she could die like this!"

"Death comes to us all," Aviendha began, but when Nynaeve rounded on her, she fell silent. The Aiel exchanged glances, as if not certain whether Nynaeve might do to them what had been done to the Myrddraal. It was not fear in their eyes, only awareness.

"Shadowman steel kills," Aviendha said, "it does not wound." The older man looked at her, a slight surprise in his eyes—Egwene decided that, like Lan, for this man that flicker of the eyelids was the equivalent of another man's open astonishment—and Aviendha said, "They know little of some things, Rhuarc."

"I am sorry," Elayne said in a clear voice, "that we interrupted your . . . dance. Perhaps we should not have interfered."

Egwene gave her a startled look, then saw what she was doing. *Put them at ease, and give Nynaeve a chance to cool down.* "You were handling things quite well," she said. "Perhaps we offended by putting our noses in."

The graying man—Rhuarc—gave a deep chuckle. "Aes Sedai, I for one am glad of . . . whatever it was you did." For a moment he looked not entirely sure of that, but in the next he had his good temper back. He had a good smile, and a strong, square face; he was handsome, if a little old. "We could have killed them, but three Shadowmen. . . . They would have killed two or three of us, certainly, perhaps all, and I cannot say we would have finished them all. For the young, death is an enemy they wish to try their strength against. For those of us a little older, she is an old friend, an old lover, but one we are not eager to meet again soon."

Nynaeve seemed to relax with his speech, as if meeting an Aiel who did not seem anxious to die had leached the tension out of her. "I should thank you," she said, "and I do. I will admit I am surprised to see you, though. Aviendha, did you expect to find us here? How?"

"I followed you." The Aiel woman seemed unembarrassed. "To see what you would do. I saw the men take you, but I was too far back to help. I was sure you must see me if I came too close, so I stayed a hundred paces behind. By the time I saw you could not help yourselves, it was too late to try alone."

"I am sure you did what you could," Egwene said faintly. *She was just a hundred paces behind us? Light, the brigands never saw anything.*

Aviendha took her words as urging to tell more. "I knew where Coram must be, and he knew where Dhael and Luaine were, and they knew. . . ." She paused, frowning at the older man. "I did not expect to find any clan chief, much less my own, among those who came. Who leads the Taardad Aiel, Rhuarc, with you here?"

Rhuarc shrugged as if it were of no account. "The sept chiefs will take their turns, and try to decide if they truly wish to go to Rhuidean when I die. I would not have come, except that Amys and Bair and Melaine and Seana stalked me like ridgecats after a wild goat. The dreams said I must go. They asked if I truly wanted to die old and fat in a bed."

Aviendha laughed as if at a great joke. "I have heard it said that a man caught between his wife and a Wise One often wishes for a dozen old enemies to fight instead. A man caught between a wife and three Wise Ones, and the wife a Wise One herself, must consider trying to slay Sightblinder."

"The thought came to me." He frowned down at something on the floor; three Great Serpent rings, Egwene saw, and a much heavier golden ring made for a man's large finger. "It still does. All things must change, but I would not be a part of that change if I could set myself aside from it. Three Aes Sedai, traveling to Tear." The other Aiel glanced at one another as if they did not want Egwene and her companions to notice.

"You spoke of dreams," Egwene said. "Do your Wise Ones know what their dreams mean?"

"Some do. If you would know more than that, you must speak to them. Perhaps they will tell an Aes Sedai. They do not tell men, except what the dreams say we must do." He sounded tired, suddenly. "And that is usually what we would avoid, if we could."

He stooped to pick up the man's ring. On it, a crane flew above a lance and crown; Egwene knew it now. She had seen it often before, dangling about Nynaeve's neck on a leather cord. Nynaeve stepped on the other rings to snatch it out of his hand; her face was flushed, with anger and too many other emotions for Egwene to read. Rhuarc made no move to take it back, but went on in the same weary tone.

"And one of them carries a ring I have heard of as a boy. The ring of Malkieri kings. They rode with the Shienarans against the Aiel in my father's time. They were good in the dance of the spears. But Malkier fell to the Blight. It is said only a child king survived, and he courts the death that took his land as other men court beautiful women. Truly, this is a strange thing, Aes Sedai. Of all the strange sights I thought I might see when Melaine harried me out of my own hold and over the Dragonwall, none has been so strange as this. The path you set me is one I never thought my feet would follow."

"I set no paths for you," Nynaeve said sharply. "All I want is to continue my journey. These men had horses. We will take three of them and be on our way."

"In the night, Aes Sedai?" Rhuarc said. "Is your journey so urgent that you would travel these dangerous lands in the dark?"

Nynaeve struggled visibly before saying, "No." In a firmer tone she added, "But I mean to leave with the sunrise."

The Aiel carried the dead outside the palisade, but neither Egwene nor her companions wanted to use the filthy bed Adden had slept in. They picked up their rings and slept under the sky in their cloaks and the blankets the Aiel gave them.

When dawn pearled the sky to the east, the Aiel produced a breakfast of tough, dried meat—Egwene hesitated over that until Aviendha told her it was goat—flatbread that was almost as difficult to chew as the stringy meat, and a blue-veined white cheese that had a tart taste and was hard enough to make Elayne murmur that the Aiel must practice by chewing rocks. But the Daughter-Heir ate as much as

Egwene and Nynaeve together. The Aiel turned the horses loose—they did not ride unless they had to, Aviendha explained, sounding as if she herself would as soon run on blistered feet—after choosing out the three best for Egwene and the others. They were all tall and nearly as big as warhorses, with proud necks and fierce eyes. A black stallion for Nynaeve, a roan mare for Elayne, and a gray mare for Egwene.

She chose to call the gray Mist, in the hope that a gentle name might soothe her, and indeed, Mist did seem to step lightly as they rode south, just as the sun lifted a red rim above the horizon.

The Aiel accompanied them afoot, all those who had survived the fight. Three more had died aside from the two the Myrddraal killed. They were nineteen, altogether, now. They loped along easily alongside the horses. At first, Egwene tried holding Mist to a slow walk, but the Aiel thought this very funny.

"I will race you ten miles," Aviendha said, "and we shall see who wins, your horse or I."

"I will race you twenty!" Rhuarc called, laughing.

Egwene thought they might actually be serious, and when she and the others let their horses walk at a quicker pace, the Aiel certainly showed no sign of falling back.

When the thatched rooftops of Jurene came in sight, Rhuarc said, "Fare you well, Aes Sedai. May you always find water and shade. Perhaps we will meet again before the change comes." He sounded grim. As the Aiel curved away to the south, Aviendha and Chiad and Bain each raised a hand in farewell. They did not seem to be slowing down now that they no longer ran with the horses; if anything, they ran a little faster. Egwene had a suspicion they meant to maintain that pace until they reached wherever it was they were going.

"What did he mean by that?" she asked. "'Perhaps we will meet again before the change'?" Elayne shook her head.

"It does not matter what he meant," Nynaeve said. "I am just as glad they came last night, but I am glad to have them gone, too. I hope there is a ship here."

Jurene itself was a small place, all wooden houses and none more than a single story, but the White Lion banner of Andor flew over it on a tall staff, and fifty of the Queen's Guards held it, in red coats with long white collars beneath shining breastplates. They had been placed there, their captain said, to make a safe haven for refugees who wished to flee to Andor, but fewer such came every day. Most went to villages further downriver, now, nearer Aringill. It was a good thing the three women had come when they did, as he expected to receive orders returning his company to Andor any day. The few inhabitants of Jurene would likely go with them, leaving what remained for brigands and the Cairhienin soldiers of warring Houses.

Elayne kept her face hidden in the hood of her sturdy wool cloak, but none of the soldiers seemed to associate the girl with red-gold hair with their Daughter-Heir. Some asked her to stay; Egwene was not sure whether Elayne was pleased or shocked. She herself told the men who asked her that she had no time for them. It was nice, in an odd way, to be asked; she certainly had no wish to kiss any of these fellows, but it was pleasant to be reminded that some men, at least, thought she was as pretty as Elayne. Nynaeve slapped one man's face. That almost made Egwene laugh, and Elayne smiled openly; Egwene thought Nynaeve had been pinched, and despite the glare on her face, she did not look entirely displeased, either.

They were not wearing their rings. It had not taken much effort on Nynaeve's part to convince them that one place they did not want to be taken for Aes Sedai was Tear, especially if the Black Ajah was there. Egwene had hers in her pouch with the stone *ter'angreal*; she touched it often to remind herself they were still there. Nynaeve wore hers on the cord that held Lan's heavy ring between her breasts.

There was a ship in Jurene, tied to the single stone dock sticking into the Erinin. Not the ship Aviendha had seen, it seemed, but still a ship. Egwene was dismayed when she saw it. Twice as wide as the *Blue Crane*, the *Darter* belied its name with a bluff bow as round as its captain.

That worthy fellow blinked at Nynaeve and scratched his ear when she asked if his vessel was fast. "Fast? I am full of fancy wood from Shienar and rugs from Kandor. What need to be fast with a cargo like that? Prices only go up. Yes, I suppose there are faster ships behind me, but they'll not put in here. I would not have stopped myself if I hadn't found worms in the meat. Fool notion that they'd have meat to sell in Cairhien. The *Blue Crane*? Aye, I saw Ellisor hung up on something upriver this morning. He'll not get off soon, I'm thinking. That's what a fast ship brings you."

Nynaeve paid their fares—and twice as much again for the horses—with such a look on her face that neither Egwene nor Elayne spoke to her until long after the *Darter* had wallowed away from Jurene.

CHAPTER
40

A Hero in the Night

L eaning on the rail, Mat watched the walled town of
Aringill come closer as the sweeps worked the *Gray
Gull* in toward the long, tarred-timber docks. Protected by high stone wing-walls that thrust out into the river,
those docks swarmed with people, and more were leaving the ships of various sizes that lay tied all along them.
Some of the people pushed barrows, or pulled sledges or
tall-wheeled carts, all piled high with furniture and chests
lashed in place, but most carried bundles on their backs, if
that. Not everyone bustled. Many men and women huddled
together uncertainly, and children clung crying to their
legs. Soldiers in red coats and shiny breastplates kept trying
to make them move off the docks into the town, but most
seemed too frightened to move.

Mat turned and shaded his eyes to peer at the river they
were leaving. The Erinin was busier here than he had seen
it south of Tar Valon, with nearly a dozen vessels under way
in sight, ranging from a long, sharp-prowed splinter darting
upriver against the current, pushed by two triangular sails,
to a wide, bluff-bowed ship with square sails, still wallow-
ing along well to the north.

Nearly half the ships he could see had nothing to do with
the river trade, though. Two broad-beamed craft with empty
decks were lumbering across the river, toward a smaller
town on the far bank, while three others labored back
toward Aringill, their decks packed with people like barrels
of fish. The setting sun, still its own height above the horizon, shadowed a banner flying over that other town. That
shore was Cairhien, but he did not need to see the banner to

know it was the White Lion of Andor. There had been talk enough in the few Andoran villages where the *Gray Gull* had stopped briefly.

He shook his head. Politics did not interest him. *As long as they don't try telling me again I'm an Andorman just because of some map. Burn me, they might even try to make me fight in their bloody army, if this Cairhien business spreads. Following orders. Light!* With a shiver, he turned back to Aringill. Barefoot men on the *Gray Gull* were readying ropes to toss to others on the docks.

Captain Mallia was eyeing him from back by the tiller. The fellow had never given up his efforts to ingratiate himself with them, his attempts to learn what their important mission was. Mat had finally shown him the sealed letter and told him that he was carrying it from the Daughter-Heir to the Queen. A personal message from a daughter to her mother; no more. Mallia had only seemed to hear the words "Queen Morgase."

Mat grinned to himself. A deep coat pocket held two purses fatter than when he had boarded the vessel; he had enough loose coin to more than fill another two. His luck had not been quite so good as on that first, strange night when the dice and everything else had seemed to go crazy, but still it was good enough. After the third night, Mallia had given up trying to show his friendliness by gambling, but his money chest was already lighter by then. It would be lighter still after Aringill. Mallia had need to restock his food—Mat glanced at the people milling on the docks—if he could, here, at any price.

The grin faded as his thoughts went back to the letter. A little work with a hot knife blade, and the golden lily seal had been lifted. He had found nothing: Elayne was studying hard and making progress and eager to learn. She was a dutiful daughter, and the Amyrlin Seat had punished her for running away and told her never to speak of it again, so her mother would understand why she could not say more. She said she had been raised to the Accepted, and was that not wonderful, so soon, and she was being trusted with greater duties now, and would have to leave Tar Valon for just a short time on the service of the Amyrlin herself. Her mother was not to worry.

It was all very well for her to tell Morgase not to worry. It was him she had landed in the soup kettle. This silly letter had to be the reason those men had come after him, but even Thom had been able to make nothing of it, though he muttered about "ciphers" and "codes" and "the Game of Houses."

Mat had the letter safe in the lining of his coat, now, its seal replaced, and he was willing to bet no one would ever know. If someone wanted it badly enough to kill him for it, they might try again. *I told you I'd deliver it, Nynaeve, and I bloody will, no matter who tries to stop me.* Even so, he would have words to say the next time he saw those three irritating women—*If I ever do. Light, I never thought of that*—words he did not think they would enjoy hearing.

As the crewmen hurled their lines onto the dock, Thom came on deck, his instrument cases on his back and his bundle in one hand. Even with a limp he strutted to the rail, giving the tail of his cloak little flourishes to make the colored patches flutter, and blowing out his long, white mustaches importantly.

"Nobody is watching, Thom," Mat said. "I don't think they would even see a gleeman unless he had food in his hands."

Thom stared at the docks. "Light! I had heard it was bad, but I did not expect this! Poor fools. Half of them look as if they are starving. It may cost us one of your purses for a room tonight. And the other for a meal, if you intend to keep on the way you've been going. Nearly made me ill to watch you. You try eating that way where those people down there can see you, and you may have your brains battered out."

Mat only smiled at him.

Mallia came stumping down the deck, tugging the point of his beard, as the *Gray Gull* was warped into her berth. Crewmen ran to set a gangplank, and Sanor stood guard on it, heavy arms folded across his chest, in case the throng on the docks tried to board. None of them did.

"So you will be leaving me here," Mallia told Mat. The captain's smile was not as ready as it might have been. "Are you certain there is nothing I can do to help further? Burn my soul, I never saw such a rabble! Those soldiers ought to clear the docks—with the sword, if need be!—so decent traders can do business. Perhaps Sanor can make a path through this scum to your inn for you."

So you'll know where we are staying? Not bloody likely. "I had thought of eating before I went ashore, and maybe a game of dice to pass the time." Mallia's face went white. "But I think I would like a steady floor under me for my next meal. So we will leave you now, Captain. It has been an enjoyable voyage."

While relief still battled consternation on the captain's face, Mat picked up his things from the deck and, using the quarterstaff as a walking stick, made his way to the gangplank with Thom. Mallia followed as far as the head of the plank, murmuring regrets at their departure that jumped from real to insincere and back again. Mat was certain the man hated losing a chance to ingratiate himself with his High Lord Samon by learning details of a pact between Andor and Tar Valon.

As Mat and the gleeman pushed through the crowds, Thom muttered, "I know the man is far from likable, but why do you have to keep taunting him? Wasn't it enough that you ate every scrap of what he thought would feed him all the way to Tear?"

"I have not been eating it all for nearly two days." The hunger had simply been gone one morning, to his great relief. It had been as if Tar Valon had loosed its last hold on him. "I've been throwing most of it over the side, and a hard job it was making sure nobody saw." Among these drawn faces, many of them children's, it did not seem so funny anymore. "Mallia deserved taunting. What about that ship, yesterday? The one that was stuck on a mudbank or something. He could have stopped to help, but he would not go near it however much they shouted." There was a woman with long, dark hair ahead who might have been pretty if she had not looked so bone weary, peering into the face of every man who passed her as if looking for someone; a boy little taller than her waist and two girls shorter clung to her, all crying. "All that talk about river brigands and traps. It didn't look like any trap to me."

Thom dodged around a high-wheeled cart—a cage holding two squealing pigs was lashed atop the canvas-covered mound—and nearly tripped over a sledge being pulled, by a man and a woman. "And you go out of your way to help people, do you? Strange how that has escaped my eye."

"I'll help anyone who can pay," Mat said firmly. "Only fools in stories do something for nothing."

The two girls sobbed into their mother's skirts while the boy fought his tears. The woman's deep-set eyes rested on Mat for a moment, studying his face, before drifting on; they looked as if she wished she could weep, too. On impulse he dug a fistful of loose coins out of his pocket without looking to see what they were and pressed them into her hand. She gave a start of surprise, stared at the gold and silver in her hand with incomprehension that quickly turned to a smile, and opened her mouth, tears of gratitude filling her eyes.

"Buy them something to eat," he said quickly, and hurried on before she could speak. He noticed Thom looking at him. "What are you gawking at? Coin comes easily as long as I can find somebody who likes to dice." Thom nodded slowly, but Mat was not sure he had gotten his point across. *Bloody children's crying was getting on my nerves, that's all. Fool gleeman will probably expect me to give gold away to every waif that comes along, now. Fool!* For an uncomfortable moment, he was not certain whether the last had been meant for Thom or himself.

Taking himself in hand, he avoided looking at any face long enough to really see it until he found the one he wanted, at the foot of the dock. The helmetless soldier in red coat and breastplate, urging people into the town, had the grizzled look of a squadman, an experienced leader of ten or so. Squinting into the setting sun, he reminded Mat of Uno, though he had both his eyes. He looked almost as tired as the people he was chivying. "Move along," he was shouting in a hoarse voice. "You can't bloody stay here. Move along. Into the town with you."

Mat stationed himself squarely in front of the soldier and put on a smile. "Your pardon, Captain, but can you tell me where I might find a decent inn? And a stable with good horses to sell. We have a long way to go, come morning."

The soldier eyed him up and down, examined Thom and his gleeman's cloak, then shifted back to Mat. "Captain, is it? Well, boy, you'll have the Dark One's own luck if you find a stable to sleep in. Most of this lot are sleeping under hedges. And if you find a horse that hasn't been slaughtered for cooking, you'll likely have to fight the man who owns it to make him sell."

"Eating horse!" Thom muttered disgustedly. "Has it really become that bad on this side of the river? Isn't the Queen sending food?"

"It is bad, gleeman." The soldier looked as if he wanted to spit. "They're crossing over faster than the mills can grind flour, or wagons carry foodstuffs from the farms. Well, it will not last much longer. The order has come down. To-morrow, we stop letting anyone across, and if they try, we send them back." He scowled at the people milling on the dock as if it were all their fault, then brought the same hard look to bear on Mat. "You are taking up space, traveler. Move along." His voice rose to a shout again, directed at everyone within hearing. "Move along! You cannot bloody stay here! Move along!"

Mat and Thom joined the thin stream of people, carts, and sledges flowing toward the gates in the town wall, and into Aringill.

The main streets were paved with flat gray stones, but they were crowded with so many people that it was difficult to see the stones under your own boots. Most appeared to be moving aimlessly, with nowhere to go, and those who had given up squatted dejectedly along the sides of the street, the lucky ones with bundled belongings in front of them or some cherished possession clutched in their arms. Mat saw three men holding clocks, and a dozen or more with silver goblets or platters. The women held children to their breasts, mainly. A babble filled the air, a low, wordless hum of worry. He pushed through the crowd with a frown on his face, searching for the sign that would mark an inn. The buildings were every sort, wood and brick and stone all cheek by jowl, with roofs of tile, or slate, or thatch.

"It does not sound like Morgase," Thom said after a time, half to himself. His bushy eyebrows were pulled down like a white arrow pointing to his nose.

"What does not sound like her?" Mat asked absently.

"Stopping the crossings. Sending people back. She always had a temper like lightning, but she always had a soft heart, too, for anyone poor or hungry." He shook his head.

Mat saw a sign, then—The Riverman, it said, and showed

a barefoot, shirtless fellow doing a jig—and turned that way, forcing an angle across the flow with the quarterstaff. "Well, it had to be her. Who else could it be? Forget Morgase, Thom. We've a long way to Caemlyn, yet. First let us see how much gold it takes to buy a bed for the night."

The common room of The Riverman looked as crowded as the street outside, and when the innkeeper heard what Mat wanted, he laughed till his chins shook. "I am sleeping four to a bed, now. If my own mother came to me, I could not give her a blanket by the fire."

"As you must have noticed," Thom said, his voice taking on that echoing quality, "I am a gleeman. Surely you can find at least pallets in a corner in return for me entertaining your patrons with stories and juggling, eating of fire, and sleight of hand." The innkeeper laughed in his face.

As Mat pulled him back into the street, Thom growled in his normal voice, "You never gave me a chance to ask after his stable. Surely I could have gotten us a place in the hayloft, at least."

"I have slept in enough stables and barns since leaving Emond's Field," Mat told him, "and under enough bushes, too. I want a bed."

But at the next four inns he found, the innkeeper gave him the same answer as the first; the last two almost threw him out bodily when he offered to dice for a bed. And when the owner of the fifth told him he could not give a pallet to the Queen herself—this at a place called The Good Queen—he sighed and asked, "What about your stable, then? Surely we can bed down in the hayloft for a price."

"My stable is for horses," the round-faced man said, "not that many are left in the city." He had been polishing a silver cup; now he opened one door of a shallow cupboard standing on top of a deep, drawered chest and placed it inside with others; none of them matched. A tooled-leather dice cup sat atop the chest, just beyond the arc of the cupboard's doors. "I do not put people in there to frighten the horses, and perhaps make off with them. Those who pay me for stabling their animals want them well tended, and I've two of my own in there, besides. There are no beds in my stable for you."

Mat eyed the dice cup thoughtfully. He pulled a gold Andoran crown out of his pocket and set it atop the chest. The next coin was a silver Tar Valon mark, then a gold one, and a gold Tairen crown. The innkeeper looked at the coins and licked his plump lips. Mat added two silver Illianer marks and another gold Andoran crown, and looked at the round-faced man. The innkeeper hesitated. Mat reached for the coins. The innkeeper's hand reached them first.

"Perhaps just the two of you would not disturb the horses too greatly."

Mat smiled at him. "Speaking of horses, what price for those two of yours? With saddles and bridles, of course."

"I will not sell my horses," the man said, clutching the coins to his chest.

Mat picked up the dice cup and rattled it. "Twice as much again against the horses, saddles, and bridles." He shook his coat pocket to make the loose coins rattle, too, to show he had more to cover the wager. "My one toss against the best of your two." He almost laughed as greed lit the inn-keeper's entire face.

When Mat walked into the stable, the first thing he did was check along the half-dozen stalls with horses in them for a pair of brown geldings. They were nondescript ani-mals, but they were his. They needed currying badly, but otherwise they seemed in good condition, especially con-sidering that all the stablemen but one had run off. The inn-keeper had been extremely disparaging of their complaints that they could no longer live on what he paid them, and he seemed to think it a crime that the one man who remained had actually had the audacity to say he was going home to bed just because he was tired from doing three men's work.

"Five sixes," Thom muttered behind him. The looks he cast around the stable did not seem as enthralled as they might, seeing that he had suggested it in the first place. Dust motes shone in the last light of the setting sun coming through the big doors, and the ropes used to hoist hay bales hung like vines from pulleys in the roof beams. The hayloft was dim in the gloom above. "When he threw four sixes and a five on his second toss, he thought you'd lost for sure, and so did I. You have not been winning every toss of late."

"I win enough." Mat was just as relieved not to be win-ning every throw. Luck was one thing, but remembering that night still sent shivers down his back. Still, for one mo-ment as he shook that dice cup, he had all but known what the pips would be. As he tossed the quarterstaff up into the loft, thunder crashed in the sky. He scrambled up the ladder, calling back to Thom. "This was a good idea. I'd think you would be happy to be in out of the rain tonight."

Most of the hay was in bales stacked against the outer walls, but there was more than enough loose for him to make a bed with his cloak over it. Thom appeared at the top of the ladder as he was pulling two loaves of bread and a wedge of green-veined cheese from his leather scrip. The innkeeper—his name was Jeral Florry—had parted with the food for merely enough coin to have bought one of those horses in more peaceful days. They ate while rain began drumming on the roof, washing the food down with water from their waterbottles—Florry had had no wine at any price—and when they were done, Thom dug out his tinder-box and thumbed his long-stemmed pipe full of tabac and settled back for a smoke.

Mat was lying on his back, staring at the shadowed roof and wondering if the rain would break before morning—he wanted that letter out of his hands as quickly as possible—when he heard an axle creak into the stable. Rolling to the edge of the loft, he peered down. There was enough dusk left for him to see.

A slender woman was straightening from the shafts of the high-wheeled cart she had just dragged in out of the rain, pulling off her cloak and muttering to herself as she shook the wet from it. Her hair was plaited in a multitude of small braids, and her silk dress—he thought it was a pale green—was elaborately embroidered across her breasts. The dress had been fine, once, but now it was tattered and stained. She knuckled her back, still talking to herself in a low voice, and hurried to the stable doors to peer out into the rain. Just as hurriedly, she ducked out to pull the big doors shut, enclosing the stable in darkness. There was a rustling below, a clink and a slosh, and suddenly a small flare of light bloomed into a lantern in her hands. She looked around, found a hook on a stall post, hung the lantern, and went to dig under the roped canvas covering her cart.

"She did that quickly," Thom said softly around his pipe. "She could have set fire to the stable striking flint and steel in the dark like that."

The woman came out with the end of a loaf of bread,

which she gnawed as if it were hard and her hunger did not care.

"Is there any of that cheese left?" Mat whispered. Thom shook his head.

The woman began sniffing at the air, and Mat realized she probably smelled Thom's tabac smoke. He was about to stand and announce their presence when one of the stable doors opened again.

The woman crouched, ready to run, as four men walked in out of the rain, doffing their wet cloaks to reveal pale coats with wide sleeves and embroidery across the chest, and baggy breeches embroidered down the legs. Their clothes might be fancy, but they were all big men, and their faces were grim.

"So, Aludra," a man in a yellow coat said, "you did not run so fast as you thought to, eh?" He had a strange accent, to Mat's ear.

"Tammuz," the woman said as if it were a curse. "It is not enough that you cause me to be cast out of the Guild with your blundering, you great ox-brain you, but now you chase after me as well." She had the same odd way of speaking as the man. "Do you think that I am glad to see you?"

The one called Tammuz laughed. "You are a very large fool, Aludra, which I always knew. Had you merely gone away, you could have lived a long life in some quiet place. But you could not forget the secrets in your head, eh? Did you believe we would not hear that you try to earn your way making what it is the right of the Guild alone to make?" Suddenly there was a knife in his hand. "It will be a great pleasure to cut your throat, Aludra."

Mat was not even aware that he had stood up until one of the doubled ropes dangling from the ceiling was in his hands and he had launched himself out of the loft. *Burn me for a bloody fool!*

He only had time for that one frantic thought, and then he was plowing through the cloaked men, sending them toppling like pins in a game of bowls. The ropes slipped through his hands, and he fell, tumbling across the straw-covered floor himself, coins spilling from his pockets, to end up against a stall. When he scrambled to his feet, the four men were already rising, too. And they all had knives in their hands, now. *Light-blind fool! Burn me! Burn me!*

"Mat!"

He looked up, and Thom tossed his quarterstaff down to him. He snagged it out of the air just in time to knock the blade out of Tammuz's fist and thump him a sharp crack on the side of the head. The man crumpled, but the other three were right behind, and for a hectic moment Mat had all he could do with a whirling staff to keep knife blades away from him, rapping knees and ankles and ribs until he could land a good blow on a head. When the last man fell, he stared at them a moment, then raised his glare to the woman. "Did you have to choose this stable to be murdered in?"

She slipped a slim-bladed dagger back into a sheath at her belt. "I would have helped you, but I feared that you might mistake me for one of these great buffoons if I came near with steel in my hand. And I chose this stable because the rain is wet and so am I, and no one was watching this place."

She was older than he had thought, at least ten or fifteen years older than he, but pretty still, with large, dark eyes and a small, full mouth that seemed on the point of a pout. *Or getting ready for a kiss.* He gave a small laugh and leaned on his staff. "Well, what is done is done. I suppose you were not trying to bring us trouble."

Thom was climbing down from the loft, awkwardly because of his leg, and Aludra looked from him to Mat. The gleeman had put his cloak back on; he seldom let anyone see him without it, especially for the first time. "This is like a story," she said. "I am rescued by a gleeman and a young hero"—she frowned at the men sprawled on the stable floor—"from these whose mothers were pigs!"

"Why did they want to kill you?" Mat asked. "He said something about secrets."

"The secrets," Thom said in very nearly his performing voice, "of making fireworks, unless I miss my guess. You are an Illuminator, are you not?" He made a courtly bow with an elaborate swirl of his cloak. "I am Thom Merrilin, a gleeman, as you have seen." Almost as an afterthought, he added, "And this is Mat, a young man with a knack for finding trouble."

"I was an Illuminator," Aludra said stiffly, "but this great pig Tammuz, he ruined a performance for the King of

Cairhien, and nearly he destroyed the chapter house, too. But me, I was Mistress of the Chapter House, so it was me that the Guild held responsible." Her voice became defensive. "I do not tell the secrets of the Guild, no matter what that Tammuz says, but I will not let myself starve while I can make fireworks. I am no more in the Guild, so the laws of the Guild, they do not apply to me now."

"Galldrian," Thom said, sounding almost as wooden as she had. "Well, he is a dead king now, and he'll see no more fireworks."

"The Guild," she said, sounding tired, "they all but blame me for this war in Cairhien, as if that one night of disaster, it made Galldrian die." Thom grimaced. "It seems I can no longer remain here," she went on. "Tammuz and these other oxen, they will wake soon. Perhaps this time they will tell the soldiers that I stole what I have made." She eyed Thom and then Mat, frowning in thought, and seemed to reach a decision. "I must reward you, but I have no money. However, I have something that is perhaps as good as gold. Maybe better. We shall see what you think."

Mat exchanged glances with Thom as she went to root under the canvas covering her cart. *I'll help anyone who can pay.* He thought a speculative light had appeared in Thom's blue eyes.

Aludra separated one bundle from a number like it, a short roll of heavy, oiled cloth almost as fat as her arms would go around. Setting it down on the straw, she undid the binding cords and unrolled the cloth across the floor. Four rows of pockets ran along the length of it, the pockets in each row larger than those in the one before. Each pocket held a wax-coated cylinder of paper just large enough for its end, trailing a dark cord, to stick out.

"Fireworks," Thom said. "I knew it. Aludra, you must not do this. You can sell those for enough to live ten days or more at a good inn, and eat well every day. Well, anywhere but here in Aringill."

Kneeling beside the long strip of oiled cloth, she sniffed at him. "Be quiet, you old one you." She made it sound not unkindly. "I am not allowed to show gratitude? You think I would give you this if I had no more for selling? Attend me closely."

Mat squatted beside her, fascinated. He had seen fireworks

twice in his life. Peddlers had brought them to Emond's Field, at great expense to the Village Council. When he was ten, he had tried to cut one open to see what was inside, and had caused an uproar. Bran al'Vere, the Mayor, had cuffed him; Doral Barran, who had been the Wisdom then, had switched him; and his father had strapped him when he got home. Nobody in the village would talk to him for a month, except for Rand and Perrin, and they mostly told him what a fool he had been. He reached out to touch one of the cylinders. Aludra slapped his hand away.

"Attend me first, I say! These smallest, they will make a loud bang, but no more." They were the size of his little finger. "These next, they make a bang and a bright light. The next, they make the bang, and the light, and many sparkles. The last"—these were fatter than his thumb—"make all of those things, but the sparkles, they are many colors. Almost like a nightflower, but not up in the sky."

Nightflower? Mat thought.

"You must be especially careful of these. You see, the fuse, it is very long." She saw his blank look, and waggled one of the long, dark cords at him. "This, this!"

"Where you put the fire," he muttered. "I know that." Thom made a sound in his throat and stroked his mustaches with a knuckle as if covering a smile.

Aludra grunted. "Where you put the fire. Yes. Do not stay close to any of them, but these largest, you run away from when you light the fuse. You comprehend me?" She briskly rolled up the long cloth. "You may sell these if you wish, or use them. Remember, you must never put this close to fire. Fire will make them all explode. So many as this at once, it could destroy a house, maybe." She hesitated over retying the cords, then added, "And there is one last thing, which you may have heard. Do not cut open any of these, as some great fools do to see what is inside. Sometimes when what is inside touches air, it will explode without the need of fire. You can lose fingers, or even a hand."

"I've heard that," Mat said dryly.

She frowned at him as if wondering whether he meant to do it anyway, then finally pushed the rolled bundle toward him. "Here. I must go now, before these sons of goats awaken." Glancing at the still open door, and the rain falling in the night beyond, she sighed. "Perhaps I will find somewhere else dry. I think I will go toward Lugard, to-morrow. These pigs, they will expect me to go to Caemlyn, yes?"

It was even further to Lugard than to Caemlyn, and Mat suddenly remembered that hard end of bread. And she had said she had no money. The fireworks would buy no meals until she found someone who could afford them. She had never even looked at the gold and silver that had spilled from his pockets when he fell; it glittered and sparkled among the straw in the lantern light. *Ah, Light, I cannot let her go hungry, I suppose.* He scooped up as much as he could reach quickly.

"Uh . . . Aludra? I have plenty, you can see. I thought perhaps. . . ." He held out the coins toward her. "I can always win more."

She paused with her cloak half around her shoulders, then smiled at Thom as she swept it the rest of the way on. "He is young yet, eh?"

"He is young," Thom agreed. "And not half so bad as he would like to think himself. Sometimes he is not."

Mat glowered at both of them and lowered his hand.

Lifting the shafts of her cart, Aludra got it turned around and started for the door, giving Tammuz a kick in the ribs as she passed. He groaned groggily.

"I would like to know something, Aludra," Thom said. "How did you light that lantern so quickly in the dark?"

Stopping short of the door, she smiled over her shoulder at him. "You wish me to tell you all of my secrets? I am grateful, but I am not in love. That secret, not even the Guild knows, for it is my discovery alone. I will tell you this much. When I know how to make it work properly, and work only when I want it to, sticks will make my fortune for me." Throwing her weight against the shafts, she pulled the cart into the rain, and the night swallowed her.

"Sticks?" Mat said. He wondered if she might not be a little strange in the head.

Tammuz groaned again.

"Best we do the same as she, boy," Thom said. "Else it's a choice between slitting four throats and maybe spending the next few days explaining ourselves to the Queen's Guards. These look the sort who'd set them on us out of spite. And they have enough to be spiteful for, I suppose."

One of Tammuz's companions twitched as if coming to, and muttered something incomprehensible.

By the time they had gathered everything and saddled the horses, Tammuz was up on his hands and knees with his head hanging, and the others were stirring and groaning, too.

Swinging into his saddle, Mat stared at the rain outside the open door, falling harder than ever. "A bloody hero," he said. "Thom, if I ever look like acting the hero again, you kick me."

"And what would you have done differently?"

Mat scowled at him, then pulled up his hood and spread the tail of his cloak over the fat roll tied behind the high cantle of his saddle. Even with oiled cloth, a little more protection from the rain could not hurt. "Just kick me!" He booted his horse in the ribs and galloped into the rainy night.

CHAPTER
41

A Hunter's Oath

As the *Snow Goose* moved toward the long stone docks of Illian, sails furled and propelled by its sweeps, Perrin stood near the stern watching great numbers of long-legged birds wading in the tall marsh grass that all but encircled the great harbor. He recognized the small white cranes, and could guess at their much larger blue brothers, but many of the crested birds—red-feathered or rosy, some with flat bills broader than a duck's—he did not know at all. A dozen sorts of gulls swooped and soared above the harbor itself, and a black bird with a long, sharp beak skimmed just above the water, its underbeak cutting a furrow. Ships three and four times as long as the *Snow Goose* lay anchored across the expanse of the harbor, waiting their turns at the docks, or for the tides to shift so they could sail beyond the long breakwater. Small fishing boats worked close to the marsh, and in the creeks winding through it, two or three men in each dragging nets on long poles swung out from either side of the boat.

The wind carried a sharp scent of salt, and did little to break the heat. The sun stood well over halfway down to the horizon, but it seemed like noon. The air felt damp; it was the only way he could think of it. Damp. His nose caught the smell of fresh fish from the boats, of old fish and mud from the marsh, and the sour stink of a large tanning yard that lay on a treeless island in the marsh grass.

Captain Adarra muttered something softly behind him, the tiller creaked, and the *Snow Goose* changed its course a trifle. Barefoot men at the sweeps moved as if not wanting to make a sound. Perrin did not glance at them beyond a flicker of his eye.

He peered at the tannery, instead, watching men scrape hides stretched on rows of wooden frames, and other men lift hides out of huge, sunken vats with long sticks. Sometimes they stacked the hides on barrows, wheeling them into the long, low building at the edge of the yard; sometimes the hides went back into the vats, with an addition of liquids poured from large stone crocks. They probably made more leather in a day than was made in Emond's Field in months, and he could see another tannery on another island beyond the first.

It was not that he had any real interest in ships or fishing boats or tanning yards, or even very much in the birds—though he did wonder what those pale red ones could be fishing for with their flat bills, and some of them looked good to eat unless he watched himself—but anything at all was better than watching the scene behind him on the deck of the *Snow Goose*. The axe at his belt was no defense against that. *A stone wall wouldn't be defense enough*, he thought.

Moiraine had been neither pleased nor displeased to discover that Zarine—*I'll not call her Faile, whatever she wants to name herself! She is no falcon!*—knew she was Aes Sedai, though she had been perhaps a little upset with him for not telling her. *A little upset. She called me a fool, but that was all. Then.* Moiraine did not seem to care one way or another about Zarine being a Hunter of the Horn. But once she learned the girl thought they would lead her to the Horn of Valere, once she learned he had known that, too, and not told her—Zarine had been more than forthcoming about both subjects with Moiraine, to his mind—then her cold dark stare had taken on a quality that made him feel as if he had been packed in a barrel of snow in the dead of winter. The Aes Sedai said nothing, but she stared too often and too hard for any comfort.

He looked over his shoulder and quickly returned to studying the shoreline. Zarine was sitting cross-legged on the deck near the horses tethered between the masts, her bundle and dark cloak beside her, her narrow, divided skirts neatly arrayed, pretending to study the rooftops and towers of the oncoming city. Moiraine was studying Illian, too, from just ahead of the men working the sweeps, but now and then she shot a hard look at the girl from under the deep hood of her fine gray wool cloak. *How can she stand wearing that?* His own coat was unbuttoned and his shirt unlaced at the neck.

Zarine met each Aes Sedai look with a smile, but every time Moiraine turned away, she swallowed and wiped her forehead.

Perrin rather admired her for managing that smile when Moiraine was watching. It was a good deal more than he could do. He had never seen the Aes Sedai truly lose her temper, but he himself was at the point of wishing she would shout, or rage, or anything but stare at him. *Light, maybe not* anything*!* Maybe the stare was bearable.

Lan sat further toward the bow than Moiraine—his color-shifting cloak was still in the saddlebags at his feet—outwardly absorbed in examining his sword blade, but making little effort to hide his amusement. Sometimes his lips appeared to quirk very close to a smile. Perrin was not certain; at times he thought it was only a shadow. Shadows could make a hammer seem to smile. Each woman obviously thought she was the object of that amusement, but the Warder did not appear to mind the tight-lipped frowns he received from both of them.

A few days earlier Perrin had heard Moiraine ask Lan, in a voice like ice, whether he saw something to laugh at. "I would never laugh at you, Moiraine Sedai," he had replied calmly, "but if you truly intend to send me to Myrelle, I must become used to smiling. I hear that Myrelle tells her Warders jokes. Gaidin must smile at their bondholder's quips; you have often given me quips to laugh at, have you not? Perhaps you would rather I stay with you after all." She had given him a look that would have nailed any other man to the mast, but the Warder never blinked. Lan made cold steel seem like tin.

The crew had taken to padding about their work in utter silence when Moiraine and Zarine were on deck together. Captain Adarra held his head tilted, and looked as if he were listening for something he did not want to hear. He passed his orders in whispers, instead of the shouts he had used at first. Everyone knew Moiraine was Aes Sedai, now, and everyone knew she was displeased. Perrin had let himself get into one shouting match with Zarine, and he was not sure which of them had said the words "Aes Sedai," but the whole crew knew. *Bloody woman!* He was uncertain whether he meant Moiraine or Zarine. *If she is the falcon, what is the hawk supposed to be? Am I going to be stuck with* two *women like her? Light! No! She is not a falcon, and that is an end to it!* The only good thing he could find in all this was that with an angry Aes Sedai to worry about, none of the crew looked twice at his eyes.

Loial was nowhere in sight, at the moment. The Ogier stayed in his stifling cabin whenever Moiraine and Zarine were topside together—working on his notes, he said. He only came on deck at night, to smoke his pipe. Perrin did not see how he could take the heat; even Moiraine and Zarine were better than being belowdecks.

He sighed and kept his eyes on Illian. The city the ship was approaching was large—as big as Cairhien or Caemlyn, the only two great cities he had ever seen—and it reared out of a huge marsh that stretched for miles like a plain of waving grass. Illian had no walls at all, but it seemed to be all towers and palaces. The buildings were all pale stone, except for some that appeared covered with white plaster, but the stone was white and gray and reddish and even faint shades of green. Rooftops of tile sparkled under the sun with a hundred different hues. The long docks held many ships, most dwarfing the *Snow Goose*, and bustled with the loading and unloading of cargo. There were shipyards at the far end of the city, where great ships stood in every stage from skeletons of thick wooden ribs to nearly ready to slide into the harbor.

Perhaps Illian was large enough to keep wolves at bay. They surely would not hunt in those marshes. The *Snow Goose* had outrun the wolves that had followed him from the mountains. He reached out for them gingerly, now, and felt—nothing. A curiously empty feeling, given that it was what he wanted. His dreams had been his own—for the most part—since that first night. Moiraine had asked about them in a cold voice, and he had told the truth. Twice he had found himself in that odd sort of wolf dream, and both times Hopper had appeared, chasing him away, telling him he was too young yet, too new. What Moiraine made of that, he had no idea; she told him nothing, except to say he had best be wary.

"That's as well by me," he growled. He was almost becoming used to Hopper being dead but not dead, in the wolf dreams, at least. Behind him, he heard Captain Adarra scuff his boots on the deck and mutter something, startled that anyone would speak aloud.

Lines were hurled ashore from the ship. While they were still being made fast to stone posts along the docks, the slightly built captain leaped into motion, whispering fiercely to his crew. He had booms rigged to lift the horses onto the wharf almost as quickly as the gangplank was laid in place. Lan's black warhorse kicked and nearly broke the boom hoisting him. Loial's huge, hairy-fetlocked mount needed two.

"An honor," Adarra whispered to Moiraine with a bow as she stepped onto the wide plank leading to the dock. "An honor to have served you, Aes Sedai." She strode ashore without looking at him, her face hidden in her deep hood.

Loial did not appear until everyone else was on the dock, and the horses, too. The Ogier came thumping up the gangplank trying to don his long coat while carrying his big saddlebags and striped blanketroll, and his cloak over one arm. "I did not know we had arrived," he rumbled breathlessly. "I was rereading my. . . ." He trailed off with a glance at Moiraine. She appeared to be absorbed in watching Lan saddle Aldieb, but the Ogier's ears flickered like a nervous cat's.

His notes, Perrin thought. *One of these days I have to see what he is saying about all this.* Something tickled the back of his neck, and he jumped a foot before he realized he was smelling a clean, herbal scent through the spices and tar and stinks of the docks.

Zarine wiggled her fingers, smiling at them. "If I can do that with just a brush of my fingers, farmboy, I wonder how high you would jump if I—?"

He was growing a little tired of considering looks from those dark, tilted eyes. *She may be pretty, but she looks at me the way I'd look at a tool I'd never seen before, trying to puzzle out how it was made, and what it is supposed to be used for.*

"Zarine." Moiraine's voice was cool but unruffled.

"I am called Faile," Zarine said firmly, and for a moment, with her bold nose, she did look like a falcon.

"Zarine," Moiraine said firmly, "it is time for our ways to part. You will find better Hunting elsewhere, and safer."

"I think not," Zarine said just as firmly. "A Hunter must follow the trail she sees, and no Hunter would ignore the trail you four leave. And I am Faile." She spoiled it a bit by swallowing, but she did not blink as she met Moiraine's eyes.

"Are you certain?" Moiraine said softly. "Are you sure you will not change your mind . . . Falcon?"

"I will not. There is nothing you or your stone-faced Warder can do to stop me." Zarine hesitated, then added slowly, as if she had decided to be entirely truthful, "At least, there is nothing that you will do that can stop me. I know a little of Aes Sedai; I know, for all the stories, that there are things you will not do. And I do not believe stone-face would do what he must to make me give over."

"Are you sure enough of that to risk it?" Lan spoke quietly, and his face did not change, but Zarine swallowed again.

"There is no need to threaten her, Lan," Perrin said. He was surprised to realize he was glaring at the Warder.

Moiraine's glance silenced him and the Warder both. "You believe you know what an Aes Sedai will not do, do you?" she said more softly than before. Her smile was not pleasant. "If you wish to go with us, this is what you must do." Lan's eyelids flickered in surprise; the two women stared at each other like falcon and mouse, but Zarine was not the falcon, now. "You will swear by your Hunter's oath to do as I say, to heed me, and not to leave us. Once you know more than you should of what we do, I will not allow you to fall into the wrong hands. Know that for truth, girl. You will swear to act as one of us, and do nothing that will endanger our purpose. You will ask no questions of where we go or why: you will be satisfied with what I choose to tell you. All of this you will swear, or you will remain here in Illian. And you will not leave this marsh until I return to release you, if it takes the rest of your life. That *I* swear."

Zarine turned her head uneasily, watching Moiraine out of one eye. "I may accompany you if I swear?" The Aes Sedai nodded. "I will be one of you, the same as Loial or stone-face. But I can ask no questions. Are they allowed to ask questions?" Moiraine's face lost a little of its patience. Zarine stood up straighter and held her head high. "Very well, then. I swear, by the oath I took as a Hunter. If I break one, I will have broken both. I swear it!"

"Done," Moiraine said, touching the younger woman's forehead; Zarine shivered. "Since you brought her to us, Perrin, she is your responsibility."

"Mine!" he yelped.

"I am no one's responsibility but my own!" Zarine nearly shouted.

The Aes Sedai went serenely on as if they had never opened their mouths. "It seems you have found Min's falcon, *ta'veren*. I have tried to discourage her, but it appears she will perch on your shoulder whatever I do. The Pattern weaves a future for you, it seems. Yet remember this. If I must, I will snip your thread from the Pattern. And if the girl endangers what must be, you will share her fate."

"I did not ask for her to come along!" Perrin protested. Moiraine calmly mounted Aldieb, adjusting her cloak over the white mare's saddle. "I did not ask for her!" Loial shrugged at him and silently mouthed something. No doubt a saying about the dangers of angering Aes Sedai.

"You are *ta'veren*?" Zarine said disbelievingly. Her gaze ran over his sturdy country clothes and settled on his yellow eyes. "Well, perhaps. Whatever you are, she threatens you as easily as she does me. Who is Min? What does she mean, I will perch on your shoulder?" Her face tightened. "If you try making me your responsibility, I will carve your ears. Do you hear me?"

Grimacing, he slipped his unstrung bow under the saddle girths along Stepper's flank, and climbed into the saddle. Restive after days on the ship, the dun lived up to his name until Perrin calmed him with a firm hand on the reins and pats to his neck.

"None of that deserves an answer," he growled. *Min bloody told her! Burn you, Min! Burn you, too, Moiraine! And Zarine!* He could never remember Rand or Mat being bullied by women on every side. Or himself, before leaving Emond's Field. Nynaeve had been the only one. And Mistress Luhhan, of course; she ran him and Master Luhhan both, everywhere but in the smithy. And Egwene had had a way about her, though mostly with Rand. Mistress al'Vere, Egwene's mother, always had a smile, but things seemed to end up being done as she wanted, too. And the Women's Circle had looked over everybody's shoulder.

Grumbling to himself, he reached down and took Zarine by an arm; she gave a squawk and nearly dropped her bundle as he hoisted her up behind his saddle. Those divided skirts of hers made it easy for her to straddle Stepper. "Moiraine will have to buy you a horse," he muttered. "You cannot walk the whole way."

"You are strong, blacksmith," Zarine said, rubbing her arm, "but I am not a piece of iron." She shifted around, stuffing her bundle and her cloak between them. "I can buy my own horse, if I need one. The whole way where?"

Lan was already riding off the dock into the city, with Moiraine and Loial behind him. The Ogier looked back at Perrin.

"No questions, remember? And my name is Perrin, Zarine. Not 'big man,' or 'blacksmith,' or anything else. Perrin. Perrin Aybara."

"And mine is Faile, shaggy-hair."

With something close to a snarl, he booted Stepper after the others. Zarine had to throw her arms around his waist to keep from being tossed over the dun's crupper. He thought she was laughing.

CHAPTER

42

Easing the Badger

The hubbub of the city quickly submerged Zarine's laughter—if that was what it was—beneath all the clamor that Perrin remembered from Caemlyn and Cairhien. The sounds were different here, slower, and pitched differently, but they were the same, too. Boots and wheels and hooves on rough, uneven paving stones, cart and wagon axles squealing, music and song and laughter drifting from inns and taverns. Voices. A hum of voices like putting his head into a giant beehive. A great city, living.

From down a side street he heard the clang of hammer on anvil, and shifted his shoulders unconsciously. He missed the hammer and tongs in his hands, the white-hot metal giving off sparks as his blows shaped it. The smithy sounds faded behind, buried under the rumble of carts and wagons, and the babble of shopkeepers and people in the streets. Under all the smells of people and horses, cooking and baking, and a hundred scents he had found peculiar to cities lay the smell of marsh and salt water.

He was surprised the first time they came to a bridge inside the city—a low arch of stone over a waterway no more than thirty paces across—but by the third such bridge, he realized that Illian was crisscrossed by as many canals as streets, with men poling laden barges as often as plying whips to move heavy wagons. Sedan chairs wove through the crowds in the streets, and occasionally the lacquered coach of some wealthy merchant or a noble, with crest or House sign painted large on the doors. Many of the men wore peculiar beards that left their upper lip bare, while the women seemed to favor hats with wide brims and attached scarves that they wound around their necks.

Once they crossed a great square, many hides in extent, surrounded by huge columns of white marble at least fifteen spans tall and two spans thick, supporting nothing but a wreath of carved olive branches at the top of each. A huge, white palace stood at either end of the square, each all columned walks and airy balconies, slender towers and purple roofs. Each reflected the other exactly, at first glance, but then Perrin realized that one was just a fraction smaller in each dimension, its towers perhaps less than a pace shorter.

"The King's Palace," Zarine said against his back, "and the Great Hall of the Council. It is said the first King of Illian said the Council of Nine could have any palace they wished, just as long as they did not try to build one larger than his. So the Council copied the King's palace exactly, but two feet smaller in every measurement. That has been the way of Illian ever since. The King and the Council of Nine duel with each other, and the Assemblage struggles with both, and so while they carry on their battles, the people live much as they wish, with none to look over their shoulders too much. It is not a bad way to live, if you must be tied to one city. You would also like to know, I think, blacksmith, that this is the Square of Tammaz, where I took the Hunter's Oath. I think I will end up teaching you so much, no one will notice the hay in your hair."

Perrin held his tongue with an effort, resolving not to stare so openly again.

No one seemed to take Loial as anything much out of the ordinary. A few people looked at him twice, and some small children scampered along in their wake for a time, but it appeared that Ogier were not unknown in Illian. None of the folk seemed to notice the heat or the damp, either.

For once, Loial did not appear pleased with the people's acceptance. His long eyebrows drooped down on his cheeks, and his ears had wilted, though Perrin was not sure that was not just the air. His own shirt clung to him with a mixture of sweat and the damp air.

"Are you afraid you'll find other Ogier here, Loial?" he asked. He felt Zarine stir against his back and cursed his tongue. He meant to let the woman know even less than Moiraine apparently meant to tell her. That way, perhaps, she would grow bored enough to leave. *If Moiraine will let her go, now. Burn me, I don't want any bloody falcon perched on my shoulder, even if she is pretty.*

Loial nodded. "Our stonemasons sometimes come here." He spoke in a whisper not only for an Ogier, but for anyone. Even Perrin could barely hear. "From Stedding Shangtai, I mean. It was masons from our *stedding* who built part of Illian—the Palace of the Assemblage, the Great Hall of the Council, some of the others—and they always send to us when repairs need to be done. Perrin, if there are Ogier here, they will make me go back to the *stedding*. I should have thought of it before now. This place makes me uneasy, Perrin." His ears shifted nervously.

Perrin moved Stepper closer and reached up to pat Loial's shoulder. It was a long reach, above his head. Conscious of Zarine at his back, he chose his words carefully. "Loial, I do not believe Moiraine would let them take you. You have been with us a long time, and she seems to want you with us. She will not let them take you, Loial." *Why not?* he wondered suddenly. *She keeps me because she thinks I may be important to Rand, and maybe because she doesn't want me telling what I know to anyone. Maybe that's why she wants him to stay.*

"Of course, she would not," Loial said in a slightly stronger voice, and his ears perked up. "I am very useful, after all. She may need to travel the Ways again, and she could not without me." Zarine shifted against Perrin's back, and he shook his head, trying to catch Loial's eye. But Loial was not looking. He seemed to have just heard what he had said, and the tufts on his ears had fallen a little. "I do hope it's not that, Perrin." The Ogier looked at the city around them, and his ears went all the way back down. "I do not like this place, Perrin."

Moiraine rode closer to Lan and spoke softly, but Perrin managed to catch her words. "Something is wrong in this city." The Warder nodded.

Perrin felt an itch between his shoulders. The Aes Sedai had sounded grim. *First Loial, and now her. What don't I see?* The sun shone down on the sparkling roof tiles, made reflections from pale stone walls. Those buildings looked as if they might be cool, inside. The buildings were clean and bright, and so were the people. The people.

At first he saw nothing out of the ordinary. Men and women moving about their business, purposeful, but slower than he was used to further north. He thought it might be the heat, and the bright sun. Then he spotted a baker's lad trotting down the street with a big tray of fresh loaves balanced on his head; the young fellow wore a grimace on his face that was nearly a snarl. A woman in front of a weaver's shop looked as if she might bite the man holding up the bright-colored bolts for her inspection. A juggler on a corner ground his teeth and stared at the folk who tossed coins into the cap lying in front of him as if he hated them. Not everyone looked so, but it seemed to him that at least one face in five wore anger and hatred. And he did not think they were even aware of it.

"What is the matter?" Zarine asked. "You are tensing. It is like holding on to a rock."

"Something is wrong," he told her. "I do not know what, but something is wrong." Loial nodded sadly, and murmured about how they would make him go back.

The buildings around them began to change as they rode, crossing more bridges as they crossed Illian to its other side. The pale stone was as often undressed as polished, now. The towers and palaces vanished, to be replaced by inns and warehouses. Many of the men in the streets, and some of the women, had an oddly rolling gait; they all had the bare feet he associated with sailors. The smells of pitch and hemp were strong in the air, and the scent of wood, both freshly cut and cured, with sour mud overlying both. The canals' odors changed, too, making his nose wrinkle. *Chamber pots*, he thought. *Chamber pots and old privies.* It made him feel queasy.

"The Bridge of Flowers," Lan announced as they crossed yet another low bridge. He inhaled deeply. "And now we are in the Perfumed Quarter. The Illianers are a poetic people."

Zarine stifled a laugh against Perrin's back.

As if he were suddenly impatient with the slow pace of Illian, the Warder led them quickly through the streets to an inn, two stories of rough, green-veined stone topped with pale green tiles. Evening was coming on, the light growing softer as the sun settled. It gave a little relief from the heat,

but not much. Boys seated on mounting blocks in front of
the inn hopped up to take their horses. One black-haired lad
about ten asked Loial if he were an Ogier, and when Loial
said he was, the boy said, "I did think you did be," with a
self-satisfied nod. He led Loial's big horse away, tossing the
copper Loial had given him into the air and catching it.

Perrin frowned up at the inn sign for a moment before
following the others in. A white-striped badger danced on
its hind legs with a man carrying what seemed to be a silver
shovel. Easing the Badger, it read. *It must be some story I
never heard.*

The common room had sawdust on the floor, and tabac
smoke filled the air. It also smelled of wine, and fish cooking in the kitchen, and a heavy, flowered perfume. The
exposed beams of the high ceiling were rough-hewn and
age-dark. This early in the evening, no more than a quarter
of the stools and benches were filled, by men in workmen's
plain coats and vests, some with the bare feet of sailors. All
of them sat clustered as close as they could manage around
one table where a pretty, dark-eyed girl, the wearer of the
perfume, sang to the strumming of a twelve-string bittern
and danced on the tabletop with swirls of her skirt. Her
loose, white blouse had an extremely low neck. Perrin recognized the tune—"The Dancing Lass"—but the words the
girl sang were different from what he knew.

> A Lugard girl, she came to town, to see what
>   she could see.
> With a wink of her eye, and a smile on her lip,
>   she snagged a boy or three, or three.
> With an ankle slim, and skin so pale,
>   she caught the owner of a ship, a ship.
> With a soft little sigh, and a gay little laugh,
>   she made her way so free. So free.

She launched into another verse, and when Perrin realized what she was singing, his face grew hot. He had
thought nothing could shock him after seeing Tinker girls
dance, but that had only hinted at things. This girl was singing them right out.

Zarine was nodding in time to the music and grinning.
Her grin widened when she looked at him. "Why, farmboy,

I do not think I ever knew a man your age who could still blush."

He glared at her and barely stopped himself from saying something he knew would be stupid. *This bloody woman has me jumping before I can think. Light, I'll wager she thinks I never even kissed a girl!* He tried not to listen to any more of what the girl was singing. If he could not get the red out of his face, Zarine was sure to make more of it.

A flash of startlement had passed across the face of the proprietress when they entered. A large, round woman with her hair in a thick roll at the back of her neck and a smell of strong soap about her, she suppressed her surprise quickly, though, and hurried to Moiraine.

"Mistress Mari," she said, "I did never think to see you here today." She hesitated, eyeing Perrin and Zarine, glanced once at Loial, but not in the searching way she looked at them. Her eyes actually brightened at the sight of the Ogier, but her real attention was all on "Mistress Mari." She lowered her voice, "Have my pigeons no arrived safely?" Lan, she seemed to accept as a part of Moiraine.

"I am sure they have, Nieda," Moiraine said. "I have been away, but I am sure Adine has noted down everything you reported." She eyed the girl singing on the table with no outward disapproval, nor any other expression. "The Badger was considerably quieter when last I was here."

"Aye, Mistress Mari, it did be that. But the louts have no gotten over the winter yet, it does seem. I have no had a fight in the Badger in ten years, till the tail of this winter gone." She nodded toward the one man not sitting near the singer, a fellow even bigger than Perrin, standing against the wall with his thick arms folded, tapping his foot to the music. "Even Bili did have a hard time keeping them down, so I did hire the girl to take their minds from anger. From some place in Altara, she does come." She tilted her head, listening for a moment. "A fair voice, but I did sing it better—aye, and dance better, too—when I did be her age."

Perrin gaped at the thought of this huge woman capering on a table, singing that song—a bit of it came through; "I'll wear no shift at all. At all"—until Zarine fisted him hard in the short ribs. He grunted.

Nieda looked his way. "I'll mix you some honey and sulphur, lad, for that throat. You'll no want to take a chill before the weather warms, no with a pretty girl like that one on your arm."

Moiraine gave him a look that said he was interfering with her. "Strange that you should suffer fights," she said. "I well remember how your nephew stops such. Has something occurred to make people more irritable?"

Nieda mused for a moment. "Perhaps. It do be hard to say. The young lordlings do always come down to the docks for the wenching and carousing they can no get away with where the air does smell fresher. Perhaps they do come more often, now, since the hard of the winter. Perhaps. And others do snap at each other more, too. It did be a hard winter. That does make men angrier, and women as well. All that rain, and cold. Why, I did wake two mornings to find ice in my washbasin. No so hard as the last winter, of course, but that did be a winter for a thousand years. Almost enough to make me believe those travelers' tales of frozen water falling from the sky." She giggled to show how little she believed that. It was an odd sound from such a large woman.

Perrin shook his head. *She doesn't believe in snow?* But if he thought this weather was cool, he could believe it of her.

Moiraine bent her head in thought, her hood shadowing her face.

The girl on the table was beginning a new verse, and Perrin found himself listening in spite of himself. He had never heard of any woman doing anything remotely like what the girl was singing about, but it did sound interesting. He noticed Zarine watching him listen, and tried to pretend he had not been.

"What has occurred out of the ordinary in Illian of late?" Moiraine said finally.

"I do suppose you could call Lord Brend's ascension to the Council of Nine unusual," Nieda said. "Fortune prick me, I can no remember ever hearing his name before the winter, but he did come to the city—from somewhere near the Murandian border, it be rumored—and did be raised inside a week. It do be said he be a good man, and strongest of the Nine—they all do follow his lead, it be said, though he be newest and unknown—but sometimes I do have strange dreams of him."

Moiraine had opened her mouth—to tell Nieda she had meant in the last few nights, Perrin was sure—but she hesitated, and instead said, "What sort of strange dreams, Nieda?"

"Oh, foolishness, Mistress Mari. Just foolishness. You do truly wish to hear it? Dreams of Lord Brend in strange places, and walking bridges hanging in air. All fogged, these dreams do be, but near every night they do come. Did you ever hear of such? Foolishness, Fortune prick me! Yet, it do be odd. Bili does say he does dream the same dreams. I do think he does hear my dreams and copy them. Bili do be none too bright, sometimes, I do think."

"You may do him an injustice," Moiraine breathed.

Perrin stared at her dark hood. She had sounded shaken, even more shaken than when she thought a new false Dragon had risen in Ghealdan. He could not smell fear, but. . . . Moiraine was frightened. It was a far more terrifying thought than Moiraine angry. He could imagine her angry; he could not begin to conceive of her afraid.

"How I do maunder on," Nieda said, patting the rolled hair at the back of her neck. "As if my foolish dreams do be important." She giggled again. A quick giggle; this was not as foolish as believing in snow. "You do sound tired, Mistress Mari. I will show you to your rooms. And then a good meal of fresh-caught red-stripe."

Red-stripe? A fish, he thought it must be; he could smell fish cooking.

"Rooms," Moiraine said. "Yes. We will take rooms. The meal can wait. Ships. Nieda, what ships sail for Tear? Early on the morrow. I have that which I must do tonight." Lan glanced at her, frowning.

"For Tear, Mistress Mari?" Nieda laughed. "Why, none for Tear. The Nine did forbid any ship to sail for Tear a month gone now, nor any from Tear to call here, though I do think the Sea Folk pay it no mind. But there do be no Sea Folk ship in the harbor. It do be odd, that. The order of the Nine, I do mean, and the King silent on it, when he does always raise his voice if they but take a step without his lead. Or perhaps it be no that, exactly. All talk do be of war with Tear, but the boatmen and wagoneers who do carry supplies to the army do say the soldiers do all look north, to Murandy."

"The paths of the Shadow are tangled," Moiraine said in a tight voice. "We will do what we must. The rooms, Nieda. And then we will eat that meal."

Perrin's room was more comfortable than he expected, given the look of the rest of the Badger. The bed was wide, the mattress soft. The door was made of tilted slats, and when he opened the windows, a breeze crossed the room carrying the smells of the harbor. And something of the canals, too, but at least it was cooling. He hung his cloak on a peg along with his quiver and axe, and propped his bow in the corner. Everything else he left in the saddlebags and blanketroll. The night might not be restful.

If Moiraine had sounded afraid before, it had been nothing to when she said that something must be done tonight. For an instant then, fear scent had steamed from her as from a woman announcing that she was going to stick her hand in a hornets' nest and crush them with her bare fingers. *What in the Light is she up to? If Moiraine is frightened, I should be terrified.*

He was not, he realized. Not terrified, or even frightened. He felt . . . excited. Ready for something to happen, almost eager. Determined. He recognized the feelings. They were what wolves felt just before they fought. *Burn me, I'd rather be afraid!*

He was first back down to the common except for Loial. Nieda had arranged a large table for them, with ladder-back chairs instead of benches. She had even found a chair big enough for Loial. The girl across the room was singing a song about a rich merchant who, having just lost his team of horses in an improbable way, had for some reason decided to pull his carriage himself. The men listening around her roared with laughter. The windows showed darkness coming on more quickly than he had expected; the air smelled as if it might be making up to rain.

"This inn has an Ogier room," Loial said as Perrin sat down. "Apparently, every inn in Illian has one, in hopes of gaining Ogier custom when the stonemasons come. Nieda claims it is lucky, having an Ogier under the roof. I cannot think they get many. The masons always stay together when they go Outside to work. Humans are so hasty, and the Elders are always afraid tempers will flare and someone will put a long handle on his axe." He eyed the men around the

singer as if he suspected them of it. His ears were drooping
again.

The rich merchant was in the process of losing his carriage, to more laughter. "Did you find out whether any
Ogier from Stedding Shangtai are in Illian?"

"There were, but Nieda said they left during the winter.
She said they had not finished their work. I do not understand it. The masons would not have left work undone unless they were not paid, and Nieda said it was not that. One
morning, they were just gone, though someone saw them
walking down the Maredo Causeway in the night. Perrin, I
do not like this city. I do not know why, but it makes me . . .
uneasy."

"Ogier," Moiraine said, "are sensitive to some things."
She still had her face hidden, but Nieda had apparently sent
someone to buy her a light cloak of dark blue linen. The
fear smell was gone from her, but her voice sounded under
tight control. Lan held her chair for her; his eyes looked
worried.

Zarine was the last down, running her fingers through
just-washed hair. The herbal scent was stronger around her
than before. She stared at the platter Nieda placed on the
table and muttered under her breath. "I hate fish."

The stout woman had brought all the food on a small cart
with shelves; it was dusty in places, as if it had been hastily
brought out from the storeroom in Moiraine's honor. The
dishes were Sea Folk porcelain, too, if chipped.

"Eat," Moiraine said, looking straight at Zarine. "Remember that any meal can be your last. You chose to travel
with us, so tonight you will eat fish. Tomorrow, you may
die."

Perrin did not recognize the nearly round white fish with
red stripes, but they smelled good. He lifted two onto his
plate with the serving fork, and grinned at Zarine around
a mouthful. They tasted good, too, lightly spiced. *Eat your
nasty fish, falcon*, he thought. He also thought that Zarine
looked as if she might bite him.

"Do you wish me to stop the girl singing, Mistress Mari?"
Nieda asked. She was setting bowls of peas and some sort
of stiff yellow mush on the table. "So you can eat in quiet?"

Staring at her plate, Moiraine did not seem to hear.

Lan listened a moment—the merchant had already lost,

in succession, his carriage, his cloak, his boots, his gold, and the rest of his clothes, and was now reduced to wrestling a pig for its dinner—and shook his head. "She will not bother us." He looked close to smiling for a moment, before he glanced at Moiraine. Then the worry returned to his eyes.

"What is wrong?" Zarine said. She was ignoring the fish. "I know something is. I have not see that much expression on you, stone-face, since I met you."

"No questions!" Moiraine said sharply. "You will know what I tell you and no more!"

"What *will* you tell me?" Zarine demanded.

The Aes Sedai smiled. "Eat your fish."

The meal went on in near silence after that, except for the songs drifting across the room. There was one about a rich man whose wife and daughters made a fool of him time and again without ever deflating his self-importance, another that concerned a young woman who decided to take a walk without any clothes, and one that told of a blacksmith who managed to shoe himself instead of the horse. Zarine nearly choked laughing at that one, forgot herself enough to take a bite of fish, and suddenly grimaced as if she had put mud in her mouth.

I won't laugh at her, Perrin told himself. *However foolish she looks, I'll show her what manners are.* "They taste good, don't they," he said. Zarine gave him a bitter look, and Moiraine a frown for interrupting her thoughts, and that was all the talk there was.

Nieda was clearing away the dishes and setting an array of cheeses on the table when a stink of something vile lifted the hackles on the back of Perrin's neck. It was a smell of something that should not be, and he had smelled it twice before. He peered about the common room uneasily.

The girl still sang to the knot of listeners, some men were strolling across the floor from the door, and Bili still leaned on the wall tapping his foot to the sounds of the bittern. Nieda patted her rolled hair, gave the room a quick glance, and turned to push the cart away.

He looked at his companions. Loial, unsurprisingly, had pulled a book from his coat pocket and seemed to have forgotten where he was. Zarine, absently rolling a piece of white cheese into a ball, was eyeing first Perrin, then Moiraine, then him again, while trying to pretend she was not.

It was Lan and Moiraine he was really interested in, though. They could sense a Myrddraal, or a Trolloc, or any Shadow-spawn, before it came closer than a few hundred paces, but the Aes Sedai was staring distantly at the table in front of her, and the Warder was cutting a chunk of yellow cheese and watching her. Yet the smell of wrongness was there, as at Jarra and the edge of Remen, and this time it was not going away. It seemed to be coming from something within the common room.

He studied the room again. Bili against the wall, some men crossing the floor, the girl singing on the table, all the laughing men sitting around her. *Men crossing the floor?* He frowned at them. Six men with ordinary faces, walk-ing toward where he was sitting. Very ordinary faces. He was just starting to reinspect the men listening to the girl when suddenly it came to him that the stink of wrongness was rolling from the six. Abruptly they had daggers in their hands, as if they had realized he had seen them.

"They have knives!" he roared, and threw the cheese platter at them.

The common erupted into confusion, men shouting, the singer screaming, Nieda shouting for Bili, everything hap-pening at once. Lan leaped to his feet, and a ball of fire darted from Moiraine's hand, and Loial snatched up his chair like a club, and Zarine danced to one side, cursing. She had a knife in her hand, too, but Perrin was too busy to notice much of what anyone else did. Those men seemed to be looking straight at him, and his axe was hanging from a peg up in his room.

Seizing a chair, he ripped off a thick chair leg that ran up to make one side of the ladder-back, hurled the rest of the chair at the men, and set about him with his long bludgeon. They were trying to reach him with their naked steel, as if Lan and the others were only obstacles in their way. It was a tight tangle where all he could manage was to knock blades away from him, and his wilder swings threatened Lan and Loial and Zarine as much as any of his six attackers. From the corner of his eye he saw Moiraine standing to one side, frustration on her face; they were all so mixed together that she could do nothing without endangering friend as well as foe. None of the knife wielders as much as glanced at her; she was not between them and Perrin.

Panting, he managed to crack one of the ordinary-looking men across the head so hard that he heard bone splinter, and abruptly realized they were all down. It all seemed to him to have gone on for a quarter of an hour or more, but he saw that Bili was just halting, his large hands working as he stared at the six men sprawled dead on the floor. Bili had not even had time to reach the fight before it was done.

Lan wore a face even grimmer than usual; he began searching the bodies, thoroughly, but with a quickness that spoke of distaste. Loial still had his chair raised to swing; he gave a start and set it down with an embarrassed grin. Moiraine was staring at Perrin, and so was Zarine as she retrieved her knife from the chest of one of the dead men. That stench of wrongness was gone, as if it had died with them.

"Gray Men," the Aes Sedai said softly, "and after you."

"Gray Men?" Nieda laughed, both loud and nervously. "Why, Mistress Mari, next you'll say you do believe in boggles and bugbears and Fetches, and Old Grim riding with the black dogs in the Wild Hunt." Some of the men who had been listening to the songs laughed, too, though they looked as uneasily at Moiraine as at the dead men. The singer stared at Moiraine, as well, her eyes wide. Perrin remembered that one ball of fire, before everything grew too jumbled. One of the Gray Men had a somewhat charred look about him, and gave off a sickly sweet burned smell.

Moiraine turned from Perrin to the stout woman. "A man may walk in the Shadow," the Aes Sedai said calmly, "without being Shadowspawn."

"Oh, aye, Darkfriends." Nieda put her hands on generous hips and frowned at the corpses. Lan had finished his searching; he glanced at Moiraine and shook his head as if he had not really expected to find anything. "More likely thieves, though I did never hear of thieves bold enough to come right into an inn. I did never have even one killing in the Badger before. Bili! Clear these out, into a canal, and put down fresh sawdust. The back way, mind. I do no want the Watch putting their long noses into the Badger." Bili nodded as if eager to be useful after failing to take a hand earlier. He grabbed a dead man by the belt in either hand and carried them back toward the kitchen.

"Aes Sedai?" the dark-eyed singer said. "I did not mean to offend with my common songs." She was covering the exposed part of her bosom, which was most of it, with her hands. "I can sing others, if you would so like."

"Sing whatever you wish, girl," Moiraine told her. "The White Tower is not so isolated from the world as you seem to think, and I have heard rougher songs than you would sing." Even so, she did not look pleased that the common now knew she was Aes Sedai. She glanced at Lan, gathered the linen cloak around her, and started for the door.

The Warder moved quickly to intercept her, and they spoke quietly in front of the door, but Perrin could hear as well as if they whispered right next to him.

"Do you mean to go without me?" Lan said. "I pledged to keep you whole, Moiraine, when I took your bond."

"You have always known there were some dangers you are not equipped to handle, my Gaidin. I must go alone."

"Moiraine—"

She cut him off. "Heed me, Lan. Should I fail, you will know it, and you will be compelled to return to the White Tower. I would not change that even if I had time. I do not mean you to die in a vain attempt to avenge me. Take Perrin with you. It seems the Shadow has made his importance in the Pattern known to me, if not clear. I was a fool. Rand is so strongly *ta'veren* that I ignored what it must mean that he had two others close by him. With Perrin and Mat, the Amyrlin may still be able to affect the course of events. With Rand loose, she will have to. Tell her what has happened, my Gaidin."

"You speak as if you are already dead," Lan said roughly.

"The Wheel weaves as the Wheel wills, and the Shadow darkens the world. Heed me, Lan, and obey, as you swore to." With that, she was gone.

CHAPTER
43

Shadowbrothers

The dark-eyed girl climbed back on her table and started singing again, in an unsteady voice. The tune was one Perrin knew as "Mistress Aynora's Rooster," and though the words were different once more, to his disappointment—and embarrassment that he was disappointed—it actually was about a rooster. Mistress Luhhan herself would not have disapproved. *Light, I'm getting as bad as Mat.*

None of the listeners complained; some of the men did look a bit disgruntled, but they seemed to be as anxious about what Moiraine might approve as the singer was. No one wished to offend an Aes Sedai, even with her gone. Bili came back and hoisted two more Gray Men; a few of the men listening to the song glanced at the corpses and shook their heads. One of them spat on the sawdust.

Lan came to stand in front of Perrin. "How did you know them, blacksmith?" he asked quietly. "Their taint of evil is not strong enough for Moiraine or me to sense. Gray Men have walked past a hundred guards without being noticed, and Warders among them."

Very conscious of Zarine's eyes on him, Perrin tried to make his voice even softer than Lan's. "I . . . I smelled them. I've smelled them before, at Jarra and at Remen, but it always vanished. They were gone before we got there, both times." He was not sure whether Zarine had overheard or not; she was leaning forward trying to listen, and trying to appear not to at the same time.

"Following Rand, then. Following you, now, blacksmith." The Warder gave no visible sign of surprise. He raised his voice to a more normal level. "I am going to look around outside, blacksmith. Your eyes might see something I miss." Perrin nodded; it was a measure of the Warder's worry that he asked for help. "Ogier, your folk see better than most, too."

"Oh, ah," Loial said. "Well, I suppose I could take a look, too." His big, round eyes rolled sideways toward the two Gray Men still on the floor. "I would not think any more of them were out there. Would you?"

"What are we looking for, stone-face?" Zarine said.

Lan eyed her a moment, then shook his head as if he had decided not to say something. "Whatever we find, girl. I will know it when I see it."

Perrin thought about going upstairs for his axe, but the Warder made for the door, and he was not wearing his sword. *He hardly needs it*, Perrin thought grumpily. *He is almost as dangerous without it as with.* He held on to the chair leg as he followed. It was a relief to see that Zarine still had her knife in her hand.

Thick black clouds were roiling overhead. The street was as dark as late twilight, and empty of people who had apparently not waited to be caught in the rain. One fellow was running across a bridge down the street; he was the only person Perrin saw in any direction. The wind was picking up, blowing a rag along the uneven paving stones; another, caught under the edge of one of the mounting blocks, flapped with a small snapping sound. Thunder grumbled and rolled.

Perrin wrinkled his nose. There was a smell of fireworks on that wind. *No, not fireworks, exactly.* It was a burned sulphur sort of smell. Almost.

Zarine tapped the chair leg in his hands with her knife blade. "You really are strong, big man. You tore that chair apart as if it were made of twigs."

Perrin grunted. He realized he was standing straighter, and deliberately made himself slouch. *Fool girl!* Zarine laughed softly, and suddenly he did not know whether to straighten or stay as he was. *Fool!* This time he meant it for himself. *You're supposed to be looking. For what?* He did not see anything but the street, did not smell anything but the almost burned sulphur scent. And Zarine, of course.

Loial appeared to be wondering what it was he was looking

for, too. He scratched a tufted ear, peered one way down the street, then the other, then scratched the other ear. Then he stared up at the roof of the inn.

Lan appeared from the alleyway beside the inn and moved out into the street, eyes studying the darker shadows along the buildings.

"Maybe he missed seeing something," Perrin muttered, though he found it hard to believe, and turned toward the alley. *I am supposed to be looking, so I'll look. Maybe he did miss something.*

Lan had stopped a little way down the street, staring at the paving stones in front of his feet. The Warder started back toward the inn, walking quickly, but peering at the street ahead of him as if following something. Whatever it was led straight to one of the mounting blocks, almost beside the inn door. He stopped there, staring at the top of the gray stone block.

Perrin decided to abandon going down the alley—it stank as much as the canals in this part of Illian, for one thing—and walked over to Lan, instead. He saw what the Warder was staring at right away. Pressed into the top of the stone mounting block were two prints, as if a huge hound had rested its forepaws there. The smell that was almost burned sulphur was strongest here. *Dogs don't make footprints in stone. Light, they don't!* He could make out the trail Lan had followed, too. The hound had trotted up the street as far as the mounting block, then turned and gone back the way it had come. Leaving tracks in the stone as if they had been a plowed field. *They just don't!*

"Darkhound," Lan said, and Zarine gasped. Loial moaned softly. For an Ogier. "A Darkhound leaves no mark on dirt, blacksmith, not even on mud, but stone is another matter. There hasn't been a Darkhound seen south of the Mountains of Dhoom since the Trolloc Wars. This one was hunting for something, I'd say. And now that it has found it, it has gone to tell its master."

Me? Perrin thought. *Gray Men and Darkhounds hunting me? This is crazy!*

"Are you telling me Nieda was right?" Zarine demanded in a shaky voice. "Old Grim is really riding with the Wild Hunt? Light! I always thought it was just a story."

"Don't be a complete fool, girl," Lan said harshly. "If the

Dark One were free, we'd all be worse than dead by now."
He peered off down the street, the way the tracks went.
"But Darkhounds are real enough. Almost as dangerous as
Myrddraal, and harder to kill."

"Now you bring Fetches into it," Zarine muttered. "Gray
Men. Fetches. Darkhounds. You had better lead me to the
Horn of Valere, farmboy. What other surprises do you have
waiting for me?"

"No questions," Lan told her. "You still know little
enough that Moiraine will release you from your oath, if
you swear not to follow. I'll take that oath myself, and you
can go now. You would be wise to give it."

"You will not frighten me away, stone-face," Zarine said.
"I do not frighten easily." But she sounded frightened. And
smelled it, too.

"I have a question," Perrin said, "and I want an answer.
You didn't sense this Darkhound, Lan, and neither did Moiraine. Why not?"

The Warder was silent for a time. "The answer to that,
blacksmith," he said grimly at last, "may be more than you
or I, either one, want to know. I hope the answer does not
kill us all. You three get what sleep you can. I doubt we
will stay the night in Illian, and I fear we have hard riding
ahead."

"What are you going to do?" Perrin asked.

"I am going after Moiraine. To tell her about the Darkhound. She can't be angry with me for following for that,
not when she would not know it was there until it took her
throat."

The first big drops of rain splatted on the paving stones
as they went back inside. Bili had removed the last of the
dead Gray Men and was sweeping up the sawdust where
they had bled. The dark-eyed girl was singing a sad song
about a boy leaving his love. Mistress Luhhan would have
enjoyed it greatly.

Lan ran ahead of them, across the common room and up
the stairs, and by the time Perrin reached the second floor,
the Warder was already starting back down, buckling his
sword belt on, color-shifting cloak hanging over his arm as
if he hardly cared who saw it.

"If he is wearing that in a city. . . ." Loial's shaggy hair
almost brushed the ceiling as he shook his head. "I do not

know if I can sleep, but I will try. Dreams will be more
pleasant than staying awake."

Not always, Loial, Perrin thought as the Ogier went on
down the hall.

Zarine seemed to want to stay with him, but he told her
to go to sleep and firmly shut the slatted door in her face.
He stared at his own bed reluctantly as he stripped down to
his underbreeches.

"I have to find out," he sighed, and crawled onto the bed.
Rain drummed down outside, and thunder boomed. The
breeze across his bed carried some of the rain's coolness,
but he did not think he would need any of the blankets at the
foot of the mattress. His last thought before sleep claimed
him was that he had forgotten to light a candle again,
though the room was dark. *Careless. Mustn't be careless.
Carelessness ruins the work.*

Dreams tumbled through his head. Darkhounds chasing
him; he never saw them, but he could hear their howling.
Fades, and Gray Men. A tall, slender man flashed into them
again and again, in richly embroidered coat and boots with
gold fringe; most of the time he held what seemed to be
a sword, shining like the sun, and laughed triumphantly.
Sometimes the man sat on a throne, and kings and queens
groveled before him. These felt strange, as if they were not
really his dreams at all.

Then the dreams changed, and he knew he was in the
wolf dream he sought. This time he had hoped for it.

He stood atop a high, flat-topped stone spire, the wind
ruffling his hair, bringing a thousand dry scents and a faint
hint of water hidden in the far distance. For an instant he
thought he had the form of a wolf, and fumbled at his own
body to make sure what he saw was really him. He wore his
own coat and breeches and boots; he held his bow, and his
quiver hung at his side. The axe was not there.

"Hopper! Hopper, where are you?" The wolf did not come.

Rugged mountains surrounded him, and other tall spires
separated by arid flats and jumbled ridges, and sometimes a
large plateau rising with sheer sides. Things grew, but nothing lush. Tough, short grass. Bushes wiry and covered with
thorn, and other things that even seemed to have thorns

on their fat leaves. Scattered, stunted trees, twisted by the wind. Yet wolves could find hunting even in this land.

As he peered at this rough land, a circle of darkness suddenly blanked out a part of the mountains; he could not have said whether the darkness was right in front of his face or halfway to the mountains, but he seemed to be seeing through it, and beyond. Mat, rattling a dice cup. His opponent stared at Mat with eyes of fire. Mat did not seem to see the man, but Perrin knew him.

"Mat!" he shouted. "It's Ba'alzamon! Light, Mat, you're dicing with Ba'alzamon!"

Mat made his toss, and as the dice spun, the vision faded, and the dark place was dry mountains again.

"Hopper!" Perrin turned slowly, looking in every direction. He even looked up in the sky—*He can fly, now*—where clouds promised a rain the ground far below the spire top would drink up as soon as it fell. "Hopper!"

A darkness formed among the clouds, a hole into somewhere else. Egwene and Nynaeve and Elayne stood looking at a huge metal cage, with a raised door held on a heavy spring. They stepped in and reached up together to loose the catch. The barred door snapped down behind them. A woman with her hair all in braids laughed at them, and another woman all in white laughed at her. The hole in the sky closed, and there were only clouds.

"Hopper, where are you?" he called. "I need you! Hopper!"

And the grizzled wolf was there, alighting on the spire top as if he had leaped from somewhere higher.

Dangerous. You have been warned, Young Bull. Too young. Too new yet.

"I need to know, Hopper. You said there were things I must see. I need to see more, know more." He hesitated, thinking of Mat, of Egwene and Nynaeve and Elayne. "The strange things I see here. Are they real?" Hopper's sending seemed slow, as if it were so simple the wolf could not understand the need to explain it, or how to. Finally, though, something came.

What is real is not real. What is not real is real. Flesh is a dream, and dreams have flesh.

"That doesn't tell me anything, Hopper. I do not understand." The wolf looked at him, as if he had said he did not understand that water was wet. "You said I had to see something, and you showed me Ba'alzamon, and Lanfear."

Heartfang. Moonhunter.

"Why did you show me, Hopper? Why did I have to see them?"

The Last Hunt comes. Sadness filled the sending, and a sense of inevitability. *What will be must be.*

"I do not understand! The Last Hunt? What Last Hunt? Hopper, Gray Men came to kill me tonight."

The Notdead hunt you?

"Yes! Gray Men! After me! And a Darkhound was right outside the inn! I want to know why they're after me."

Shadowbrothers! Hopper crouched, looking to either side as if he almost expected an attack. *Long since we have seen the Shadowbrothers. You must go, Young Bull. Great danger! Flee the Shadowbrothers!*

"Why are they after me, Hopper? You do know. I know you do!"

Flee, Young Bull. Hopper leaped, forepaws hitting Perrin's chest, knocking him back, over the edge. *Flee the Shadowbrothers.*

The wind rushed in his ears as he fell. Hopper and the edge of the spire top dwindled above him. "Why, Hopper?" he shouted. "I have to know why!"

The Last Hunt comes.

He was going to hit. He knew it. The ground below rushed up at him, and he tensed against the crushing impact that. . . .

He started awake, staring at the candle flickering on the small table beside the bed. Lightning flashes lit the window, and thunder rattled it. "What did he mean, the Last Hunt?" he mumbled. *I did not light any candle.*

"You talk to yourself. And thrash in your sleep."

He jumped, and cursed himself for not having noticed the herbal scent in the air. Zarine sat on a stool at the edge of the candlelight, elbow on her knee, chin on her fist, watching him.

"You are *ta'veren*," she said as if ticking off a point. "Stone-face thinks those odd eyes of yours can see things he can't. Gray Men want to kill you. You travel with an Aes

Sedai, a Warder, and an Ogier. You free caged Aiel and kill Whitecloaks. Who are you, farmboy, the Dragon Reborn?" Her voice said that was the most ridiculous thing she could think of, but he still shifted uneasily. "Whoever you are, big man," she added, "you could do with a little more hair on your chest."

He twisted around, cursing, and scrabbled one of the blankets over him to his neck. *Light, she keeps making me jump like a frog on a hot rock.* Zarine's face was at the edge of shadows. He could not see her clearly except when lightning shone through the window, the harsh illumination casting its own shadows across her strong nose and high cheekbones. Suddenly he remembered Min saying he should run from a beautiful woman. Once he had recognized Lanfear in that wolf dream, he had thought Min must mean her—he did not think it was possible for a woman to be any more beautiful than Lanfear—but she was just in a dream. Zarine was sitting there staring at him with those dark, tilted eyes, considering, weighing.

"What are you doing here?" he demanded. "What do you want? Who are you?"

She threw back her head and laughed. "I am Faile, farmboy, a Hunter of the Horn. Who do you think I am, the woman of your dreams? Why did you jump that way? You would think I had goosed you."

Before he could find words, the door crashed back against the wall, and Moiraine stood in the doorway, her face as pale and grim as death. "Your wolf dreams tell as truly as a Dreamer's, Perrin. The Forsaken *are* loose, and one of them rules in Illian."

CHAPTER
44

Hunted

Perrin climbed off the bed and started dressing, not caring whether Zarine was watching or not. He knew what he intended to do, but he asked Moiraine anyway. "Do we leave?"

"Unless you want to make closer acquaintance with Sammael," she said dryly. Thunder crashed overhead as if to punctuate her sentence, and lightning flashed. The Aes Sedai barely glanced at Zarine.

Stuffing his shirttail into his breeches, he suddenly wished he had his coat and cloak on. Naming which one of the Forsaken it was made the room seem cold. *Ba'alzamon isn't bad enough; we have to have the Forsaken loose, too. Light, does it even matter if we find Rand, now? Is it too late?* But he kept dressing, stamping his feet into his boots. It was that or give up, and Two Rivers folk were not known for giving up.

"Sammael?" Zarine said faintly. "One of the Forsaken rules . . . ? Light!"

"Do you still wish to follow?" Moiraine said softly. "I would not make you stay here, not now, but I will give you one last chance to swear to go another way than I."

Zarine hesitated, and Perrin paused with his coat half on. Surely no one would choose to go with people who had incurred the wrath of one of the Forsaken. Not now that she knew something of what they faced. *Not unless she has a very good reason.* For that matter, anyone who heard one of the Forsaken was loose should already be running for a Sea Folk ship and asking passage to the other side of the Aiel Waste, not sitting there thinking.

"No," Zarine said finally, and he began to relax. "No, I will not swear to go another way. Whether you lead me to the Horn of Valere or not, not even whoever does find the Horn will have a story such as this. I think this story will be told for the ages, Aes Sedai, and I will be part of it."

"No!" Perrin snapped. "That is not good enough. What do you want?"

"I have no time for this bickering," Moiraine broke in. "Any moment *Lord Brend* may learn that one of his Dark-hounds is dead. You can be sure he will know that means a Warder, and he will come looking for the Gaidin's Aes Sedai. Do you mean to sit here until he discovers where you are? Move, you foolish children! Move!" She vanished down the hall before he could open his mouth.

Zarine did not wait, either, running from the room without her candle. Perrin hastily gathered his things and dashed for the back stairs still buckling his axe belt around his waist. He caught up to Loial going down, the Ogier trying to stuff a wood-bound book into his saddlebags and put on his cloak at the same time. Perrin gave him a hand with the cloak while they both ran down the stairs, and Zarine caught the pair of them before they could dash out into the pouring rain.

Perrin hunched his shoulders against the wet and ran for the stable across the storm-darkened yard without waiting to pull up the hood of his cloak. *She has to have a reason. Being in a bloody story isn't reason enough for any but a madwoman!* The rain soaked his shaggy curls, laying them flat around his head, before he darted through the stable door.

Moiraine was there before them, in an oiled cloak still beaded with rain, and Nieda holding a lantern for Lan to finish saddling the horses. There was an extra, a bay gelding with an even stronger nose than Zarine's.

"I will send pigeons every day," the stout woman was saying. "No one will suspect me. Fortune prick me! Even Whitecloaks do speak well of me."

"Listen to me, woman!" Moiraine snapped. "This is not a Whitecloak or a Darkfriend I speak of. You will flee this city, and make anyone you care for flee with you. For a dozen years you have obeyed me. Obey me now!" Nieda nodded, but reluctantly, and Moiraine growled with exasperation.

"The bay is yours, girl," Lan said to Zarine. "Get on his back. If you do not know how to ride, you must learn by doing, or take my offer."

Putting one hand on the high pommel, she vaulted easily into the saddle. "I was on a horse once, stone-face, now that I think of it." She twisted around to tie her bundle behind her.

"What did you mean, Moiraine?" Perrin demanded as he tossed his saddlebag across Stepper's back. "You said he would find out where I am. He knows. The Gray Men!" Nieda giggled, and he wondered irritably how much she really knew or believed among the things she said she did not believe in.

"Sammael did not send the Gray Men." Moiraine mounted Aldieb with a cool, straight-backed precision, almost as if there were no hurry. "The Darkhound was his, however. I believe it followed my trail. He would not have sent both. Someone wants you, but I do not think Sammael even knows you exist. Yet." Perrin stopped with one foot in the stirrup, staring at her, but she seemed more concerned with patting her mare's arching neck than with the questions on his face.

"As well I went after you," Lan said, and the Aes Sedai sniffed loudly.

"I could wish you were a woman, Gaidin. I would send you to the Tower as a novice to learn to obey!" He raised an eyebrow and touched the hilt of his sword, then swung into his saddle, and she sighed. "Perhaps it is as well you are disobedient. Sometimes it is well. Besides, I do not think Sheriam and Siuan Sanche together could teach you obedience."

"I do not understand," Perrin said. *I seem to be saying that a great deal, and I'm tired of it. I want some answers I can understand.* He pulled himself the rest of the way up so Moiraine would not be looking down at him; she had enough advantage without that. "If he did not send the Gray Men, who did? If a Myrddraal, or another Forsaken. . . ." He stopped to swallow. *ANOTHER Forsaken! Light!* "If somebody else sent them, why did they not tell him? They're all Darkfriends, aren't they? And why me, Moiraine? Why me? Rand is the bloody Dragon Reborn!"

He heard the gasps from Zarine and Nieda, and only then

realized what he had said. Moiraine's stare seemed to skin him like the sharpest steel. *Hasty bloody tongue. When did I stop thinking before I speak?* It seemed to him it had happened when he first felt Zarine's eyes watching him. She was watching him now, with her mouth hanging open.

"You are sealed to us, now," Moiraine told the bold-faced woman. "There is no turning back for you. Ever." Zarine looked as if she wanted to say something and was afraid to, but the Aes Sedai had already turned her attention elsewhere. "Nieda, flee Illian tonight. In this hour! And hold your tongue even better than you have held it all these years. There are those who would cut it out for what you could say, before I could even find you." Her hard tone left doubts as to exactly how she meant that, and Nieda nodded vigorously as if she had heard it both ways.

"As for you, Perrin." The white mare moved closer, and he leaned back from the Aes Sedai despite all he could do. "There are many threads woven in the Pattern, and some are as black as the Shadow itself. Take care one of them does not strangle you." Her heels touched Aldieb's flanks, and the mare darted into the rain, Mandarb following close behind.

Burn you, Moiraine, Perrin thought as he rode after them. *Sometimes I do not know which side you are on.* He glanced at Zarine, riding beside him as if she had been born in a saddle. *And whose side are you on?*

Rain kept people off the streets and canals, so no visible eyes watched them go, but it made the footing uncertain for the horses on the uneven paving stones. By the time they reached the Maredo Causeway, a wide road of packed dirt stretching north through the marsh, the downpour had begun to slacken. Thunder still boomed, but the lightning flashed far behind them, perhaps out to sea.

Perrin felt a bit of luck was coming their way. The rain had stayed long enough to hide their departure, but now it seemed they would have a clear night for riding. He said as much, but Lan shook his head.

"Darkhounds like clear, moonlit nights best, blacksmith, rain the least. A good thunderstorm can keep them away completely." As if his words had bidden it, the rain faded to a faint drizzle. Perrin heard Loial groan behind him.

Causeway and marsh ended together, some two miles

or so from the city, but the road kept on, slowly bearing a little eastward. Cloud-dark evening faded into night, and the misting rain continued. Moiraine and Lan kept a steady, ground-eating pace. The horses' hooves splashed through puddles on the hard-packed dirt. The moon shone through gaps in the clouds. Low hills began to rise around them, and trees to appear more and more often. Perrin thought there must be forest ahead, but he was not sure how he liked the idea. Woods could hide them from pursuit; woods could let pursuit come close before they saw.

A thin howl rose far behind them. For a moment he thought it was a wolf; he surprised himself by nearly reaching out to the wolf before he could stop. The cry came again, and he knew it was no wolf. Others answered it, all miles behind, eerie wails holding blood and death, cries that spoke of nightmares. To his surprise, Lan and Moiraine slowed, the Aes Sedai studying the hills around them in the night.

"They are a long way," he said. "They'll not catch us if we keep on."

"The Darkhounds?" Zarine muttered. "Those are the Darkhounds? Are you sure it isn't the Wild Hunt, Aes Sedai?"

"But it is," Moiraine replied. "It is."

"You can never outrun the Darkhounds, blacksmith," Lan said, "not on the fastest horse. Always, you must face them and defeat them, or they will pull you down."

"I could have stayed in the *stedding*, you know," Loial said. "My mother would have had me married by now, but it would not have been a bad life. Plenty of books. I did not have to come Outside."

"There," Moiraine said, pointing to a tall, treeless mound well off to their right. There were no trees that Perrin could see for two hundred paces or more around it, either, and they were still sparse beyond that. "We must see them coming to have a chance."

The Darkhounds' dire cries rose again, closer, yet still far.

Lan quickened Mandarb's pace a little, now that Moiraine had chosen their ground. As they climbed, the horses' hooves clattered on rocks half-buried in the dirt and slicked by the drizzle. To Perrin's eyes, most of them had too many squared corners to be natural. At the top, they dismounted around what seemed to be a low, rounded boulder. The moon appeared through a gap in the clouds, and he found himself looking at a weathered stone face two paces long. A woman's face, he thought from the length of the hair. The rain made her seem to be weeping.

Moiraine dismounted and stood looking off in the direction of the howls. She was a shadowed, hooded shape, rain catching moonlight as it rolled down her oiled cloak.

Loial led his horse over to peer at the carving, then bent closer and felt the features. "I think she was an Ogier," he said at last. "But this is not an old *stedding*; I would feel it. We all would. And we would be safe from Shadowspawn."

"What are you two staring at?" Zarine squinted at the rock. "What is it? Her? Who?"

"Many nations have risen and fallen since the Breaking," Moiraine said without turning, "some leaving no more than names on a yellowed page, or lines on a tattered map. Will we leave as much behind?" The blood-drenched howls rose again, still closer. Perrin tried to calculate their pace, and thought Lan had been right; the horses could not have outrun them, after all. They would not have long to wait.

"Ogier," Lan said, "you and the girl hold the horses." Zarine protested, but he rode straight over to her. "Your knives will not do much good here, girl." His sword blade gleamed in the moonlight as he drew it. "Even this is a last resort. It sounds like ten out there, not one. Your work is to keep the horses from running when they smell the Darkhounds. Even Mandarb does not like that smell."

If the Warder's sword was no good, then neither was the axe. Perrin felt something near to relief at that, even if they were Shadowspawn; he would not have to use the axe. He drew the length of his unstrung bow from under Stepper's saddle girths. "Maybe this will do some good."

"Try if you wish, blacksmith," Lan said. "They do not die easily. Perhaps you will kill one."

Perrin drew a fresh bowstring from his pouch, trying to shield it from the soft rain. The beeswax coating was thin, and not much protection against prolonged damp. Setting the bow slantwise between his legs, he bent it easily, fixing the loops of the bowstring into the horn nocks at the ends of the bow. When he straightened, he could see the Darkhounds.

They ran like horses at a gallop, and as he caught sight of them, they gathered speed. They were only ten large shapes running in the night, sweeping through the scattered trees, yet he pulled a broadhead arrow from his quiver, nocked it but did not draw. He had been far from the best bowman in Emond's Field, but among the younger men, only Rand had been better.

At three hundred paces he would shoot, he decided. *Fool! You'd have a hard time hitting a target standing still at that distance. But if I wait, the way they are moving. . . .* Stepping up beside Moiraine, he raised his bow—*I just have to imagine that moving shadow is a big dog*—drew the goosefeather fletchings to his ear, and loosed. He was sure the shaft merged with the nearest shadow, but the only result was a snarl. *It is not going to work. They're coming too fast!* He was already drawing another arrow. *Why aren't you doing something, Moiraine?* He could see their eyes, shining like silver, their teeth gleaming like burnished steel. Black as the night itself and as big as small ponies, they sped toward him, silent now, seeking the kill. The wind carried a stink near to burned sulphur; the horses whickered fearfully, even Lan's warhorse. *Burn you, Aes Sedai, do something!* He loosed again; the frontmost Darkhound faltered and came on. *They can die!* He shot once more, and the lead Darkhound tumbled, staggered to its feet, then fell, yet even as it did he knew a moment of despair. One down, and the other nine had covered two thirds of the distance already; they seemed to be running even faster, like shadows flowing across the ground. *One more arrow. Time for one more, maybe, and then it's the axe. Burn you, Aes Sedai!* He drew again.

"Now," Moiraine said as his arrow left the bow. The air between her hands caught fire and streaked toward the Darkhounds, vanquishing night. The horses squealed and leaped against being held.

Perrin threw an arm across his eyes to shield them from a white-hot glare like burning, heat like a forge cracking open; sudden noon flared in the darkness, and was gone. When he uncovered his eyes, spots flickered across his vision, and the faint, fading image of that line of fire. Where the Darkhounds had been was nothing but night-covered ground and the soft rain; the only shadows that moved were cast by clouds crossing the moon.

I thought she'd throw fire at them, or call lightning, but this. . . . "What was that?" he asked hoarsely.

Moiraine was peering off toward Illian again, as if she could see through all those miles of darkness. "Perhaps he did not see," she said, almost to herself. "It is far, and if he was not watching, perhaps he did not notice."

"Who?" Zarine demanded. "Sammael?" Her voice shook a little. "You said he was in Illian. How could he see anything here? What did you do?"

"Something forbidden," Moiraine said coolly. "Forbidden by vows almost as strong as the Three Oaths." She took Aldieb's reins from the girl, and patted the mare's neck, calming her. "Something not used in nearly two thousand years. Something I might be stilled just for knowing."

"Perhaps . . . ?" Loial's voice was a faint boom. "Perhaps we should be going? There could be more."

"I think not," the Aes Sedai said, mounting. "He would not loose two packs at once, even if he has two; they would turn on each other instead of their prey. And I think we are not his main quarry, or he would have come himself. We were . . . an annoyance, I think"—her tone was calm, but it was clear she did not like being regarded so lightly—"and perhaps a little something extra to slip into his gamebag, if we were not too much trouble. Still, there is small good in remaining any nearer him than we must."

"Rand?" Perrin asked. He could almost feel Zarine leaning forward to listen. "If we are not what he hunts, is it Rand?"

"Perhaps," Moiraine said. "Or perhaps Mat. Remember that he is *ta'veren* also, and he blew the Horn of Valere."

Zarine made a strangled sound. "He *blew* it? Someone has *found* it already?"

The Aes Sedai ignored her, leaning out of her saddle to stare closely into Perrin's eyes, dark gleaming into burnished gold. "Once again events outpace me. I do not like that. And neither should you. If events outrun me, they may well trample you, and the rest of the world with you."

"We have many leagues to Tear yet," Lan said. "The

Ogier's suggestion is a good one." He was already in his saddle.

After a moment Moiraine straightened and touched the mare's ribs with her heels. She was halfway down the side of the mound before he could get his bow unstrung and take Stepper's reins from Loial. *Burn you, Moiraine! I'll find some answers somewhere!*

Leaning back against a fallen log, Mat enjoyed the warmth of the campfire—the rains had drifted south three days earlier, but he still felt damp—yet right at that moment, he was hardly aware of the dancing flames. He peered thoughtfully at the small, wax-covered cylinder in his hand. Thom was engrossed in tuning his harp, muttering to himself of rain and wet, never glancing Mat's way. Crickets chirped in the dark thicket around them. Caught between villages by sunset, they had chosen this copse away from the road. Two nights they had tried to buy a room for the night; twice a farmer had loosed his dogs on them.

Mat unsheathed his belt knife, and hesitated. *Luck. It only explodes sometimes, she said. Luck.* As carefully as he could, he slit along the length of the tube. It *was* a tube, and of paper, as he had thought—he had found bits of paper on the ground after fireworks were set off, back home— layers of paper, but all that filled the inside was something that looked like dirt, or maybe tiny gray-black pebbles and dust. He stirred them on his palm with one finger. *How in the Light could pebbles explode?*

"The Light burn me!" Thom roared. He thrust his harp into its case as if to protect it from what was in Mat's hand. "Are you trying to kill us, boy? Haven't you ever heard those things explode ten times as hard for air as for fire? Fireworks are the next thing to Aes Sedai work, boy."

"Maybe," Mat said, "but Aludra did not look like any Aes Sedai to me. I used to think that about Master al'Vere's clock—that it had to be Aes Sedai work—but once I got the back of the cabinet open, I saw it was full of little pieces of metal." He shifted uncomfortably at the memory. Mistress al'Vere had been the first to reach him that time, with the Wisdom and his father and the Mayor all right behind her, and none believing he just meant to look. *I could have put them all back together.* "I think Perrin could make one, if he saw those little wheels and springs and I don't know what all."

"You would be surprised, boy," Thom said dryly. "Even a bad clockmaker is a fairly rich man, and they earn it. But a clock does not explode in your face!"

"Neither did this. Well, it is useless, now." He tossed the handful of paper and little pebbles into the fire to a screech from Thom; the pebbles sparked and made tiny flashes, and there was a smell of acrid smoke.

"You *are* trying to kill us." Thom's voice was unsteady, and it rose in intensity and pitch as he spoke. "If I decide I want to die, I will go to the Royal Palace when we reach Caemlyn, and I'll pinch Morgase!" His long mustaches flailed. "Do not do that again!"

"It did not explode," Mat said, frowning at the fire. He fished into the oiled-cloth roll on the other side of the log and pulled out a firework of the next larger size. "I wonder why there was no bang."

"I do not care why there was no bang! Do not do it again!"

Mat glanced at him and laughed. "Stop shaking, Thom. There's no need to be afraid. I know what is inside them, now. At least, I know what it looks like, but. . . . Don't say it. I will not be cutting any more open, Thom. It is more fun to set them off, anyway."

"I am not afraid, you mud-footed swineherd," Thom said with elaborate dignity. "I am shaking with rage because I'm traveling with a goat-brained lout who might kill the pair of us because he cannot think past his own—"

"Ho, the fire!"

Mat exchanged glances with Thom as horses' hooves approached. It was late for anyone honest to be traveling. But the Queen's Guards kept the roads safe this close to Caemlyn, and the four who rode into the firelight certainly did not look like robbers. One was a woman. The men all wore long cloaks and seemed to be her retainers, while she was pretty and blue-eyed, in gold necklace and a gray silk dress and a velvet cloak with a wide hood. The men dismounted. One held her reins and another her stirrup, and she smiled at Mat, doffing her gloves as she came near the fire.

"I fear we are caught out late, young master," she said, "and I would trouble you for directions to an inn, if you know one."

He grinned and started to rise. He had made it as far as a crouch when he heard one of the men mutter something, and another produced a crossbow from under his cloak, already drawn, with a clip holding the bolt.

"Kill him, fool!" the woman shouted, and Mat tossed the firework into the flames and threw himself toward his quarterstaff. There was a loud bang and a flash of light— "Aes Sedai!" a man cried. "Fireworks, fool!" the woman shouted—and he rolled to his feet with the staff in his hand to see the crossbow bolt sticking out of the fallen log almost where he had been sitting, and the crossbowman falling with the hilt of one of Thom's knives adorning his chest.

It was all he had time to see, for the other two men darted past the fire at him, drawing swords. One of them suddenly stumbled to his knees, dropping his sword to claw at the knife in his back as he fell facedown. The last man did not see his companion fall; he obviously expected to be one of a pair, dividing their opponent's attention, as he thrust his blade at Mat's middle. Feeling almost contemptuous, Mat cracked the fellow's wrist with one end of his staff, sending the sword flying, and cracked his forehead with the other. The man's eyes rolled up in his head as he collapsed.

From the corner of his eye, Mat saw the woman walking toward him, and he stuck a finger at her like a knife. "Fine clothes you wear for a thief, woman! You sit down till I decide what to do with you, or I'll—"

She looked as surprised as Mat at the knife that suddenly bloomed in her throat, a red flower of spreading blood. He took a half step as if to catch her as she fell, knowing it was no good. Her long cloak settled over her, covering everything but her face, and the hilt of Thom's knife.

"Burn you," Mat muttered. "Burn you, Thom Merrilin! A woman! Light, we could have tied her up, given her to the Queen's Guards tomorrow in Caemlyn. Light, I might even have let her go. She'd rob nobody without these three, and the only one that lives will be days before he can see straight and months before he can hold a sword. Burn you, Thom, there was no need to kill her!"

The gleeman limped to where the woman lay, and kicked

back her cloak. The dagger had half fallen from her hand, its blade as wide as Mat's thumb and two hands long. "Would you rather I had waited till she nested that in your ribs, boy?" He retrieved his own knife, wiping the blade on her cloak.

Mat realized he was humming "She Wore a Mask That Hid Her Face," and stopped it. He bent down and hid hers with the hood of her cloak. "Best we move on," he said quietly. "I do not want to have to explain this if a patrol of the Guards happens by."

"With her in those clothes?" Thom said. "I should say not! They must have robbed a merchant's wife, or some noblewoman's carriage." His voice became gentler. "If we're going, boy, you had best see to saddling your horse."

Mat gave a start and pulled his eyes from the dead woman. "Yes, I had better, hadn't I?" He did not look at her again.

He had no such compunction about the men. As far as he was concerned, a man who decided to rob and kill deserved what he got when he lost the game. He did not dwell on them, but neither did he jerk his eyes away if they fell on one of the robbers. It was after he had saddled his gelding and tied his things on behind, while he was kicking dirt onto the fire, that he found himself looking at the man who had shot the crossbow. There was something familiar about those features, about the way the smothering fire made shadows across them. *Luck*, he told himself. *Always the luck*.

"The crossbowman was a good swimmer, Thom," he said as he climbed into the saddle.

"What foolery are you talking, now?" The gleeman was on his horse, too, and far more concerned with how his instrument cases rode behind his saddle than he was with the dead. "How could you know whether he could even swim at all?"

"He made it ashore from a small boat in the middle of the Erinin in the middle of the night. I guess that used up all his luck." He checked the lashings on the roll of fireworks again. *If that fool thought one of these was Aes Sedai, I wonder what he'd have thought if they all went off.*

"Are you sure, boy? The chances of it being the same man. . . . Why, even you wouldn't lay a wager against those odds."

"I am sure, Thom." *Elayne, I will wring your neck when I put my hands on you. And Egwene's and Nynaeve's, too.* "And I am sure I intend to have this bloody letter out of my hands an hour after we reach Caemlyn."

"I tell you, there is nothing in that letter, boy. I played *Daes Dae'mar* when I was younger than you, and I can recognize a code or a cipher even when I don't know what it says."

"Well, I never played your Great Game, Thom, your bloody Game of Houses, but I know when someone is chasing me, and they'd not be chasing this hard or this far for the gold in my pockets, not for less than a chest full of gold. It has to be the letter." *Burn me, pretty girls always get me in trouble.* "Do you feel like sleeping tonight, after this?"

"With the sleep of an innocent babe, boy. But if you want to ride, I'll ride."

The face of a pretty woman floated into Mat's head, with a dagger in her throat. *You had no luck, pretty woman.* "Then let's ride!" he said savagely.

CHAPTER
45

Caemlyn

Mat had vague memories of Caemlyn, but when they approached it in the early hours after sunrise, it seemed as if he had never been there before. They had not been alone on the road since first light, and other riders surrounded them now, and trains of merchants' wagons and folk afoot, all streaming toward the great city.

Built on rising hills, it was surely as large as Tar Valon, and outside the huge walls—a fifty-foot height of pale, grayish stone streaked with white and silver sparkling in the sun, spaced with tall, round towers with the Lion Banner of Andor waving atop them, white on red—outside those walls, it seemed as if another great city had been placed, wrapping around the walled city, all red brick and gray stone and white plastered walls, inns pushed in on houses of three and four stories so fine they must belong to wealthy merchants, shops with goods displayed on tables under awnings crowding against wide, windowless warehouses. Open markets under red and purple roof tiles lined the road on both sides, men and women already crying their wares, bargaining at the top of their voices, while penned calves and sheep and goats and pigs, caged geese and chickens and ducks, added to the din. He seemed to remember thinking Caemlyn was too noisy when he was here before; now it sounded like a heartbeat, pumping wealth.

The road led to arched gates twenty feet high, standing open under the watchful eye of red-coated Queen's Guards in their shining breastplates—they eyed Thom and him no more than anyone else, not even the quarterstaff slanted across his saddle in front of him; all they cared was that people keep moving, it seemed—and then they were within. Slender towers here rose even taller than those along the walls, and gleaming domes shone white and gold above streets teeming with people. Just inside the gates the road split into two parallel streets, separated by a wide strip of grass and trees. The hills of the city rose like steps toward a peak, which was surrounded by another wall, shining as white as Tar Valon's, with still more domes and towers within. That was the Inner City, Mat recalled, and atop those highest hills stood the Royal Palace.

"No point waiting," he told Thom. "I'll take the letter straight on." He looked at the sedan chairs and carriages making their way through the crowds, the shops with all their goods displayed. "A man could earn some gold in this city, Thom, once he found a game of dice, or cards." He was not quite so lucky at cards as at dice, but few except nobles and the wealthy played those games anyway. *Now that's who I should find a game with.*

Thom yawned at him and hitched at his gleeman's cloak as if it were a blanket. "We have ridden all night, boy. Let's at least find something to eat, first. The Queen's Blessing has good meals." He yawned again. "And good beds."

"I remember that," Mat said slowly. He did, in a way. The innkeeper was a fat man with graying hair, Master Gill. Moiraine had caught up to Rand and him there, when he had thought they were finally free of her. *She's off playing her game with Rand, now. Nothing to do with me. Not anymore.* "I will meet you there, Thom. I said I'd have this letter out of my hands an hour after I arrived, and I mean to. You go on."

Thom nodded and turned his horse aside, calling over his shoulder through a yawn. "Do not become lost, boy. It's a big city, Caemlyn."

And a rich one. Mat heeled his mount on up the crowded street. *Lost! I can find my bloody way.* The sickness appeared to have erased parts of his memory. He could look at an inn, its upper floors sticking out over the ground floor all the way around and its sign creaking in the breeze, and remember seeing it before, yet not recall another thing he could see from that spot. A hundred paces of street might abruptly spark in his memory, while the parts before and after remained as mysterious as dice still in the cup.

Even with the holes in his memory he was sure he had

never been to the Inner City or the Royal Palace—*I couldn't forget that!*—yet he did not need to remember the way. The streets of the New City—he remembered that name suddenly; it was the part of Caemlyn less than two thousand years old—ran every which way, but the main boulevards all led to the Inner City. The Guards at the gates made no effort to stop anyone.

Within those white walls were buildings that could almost have fit in Tar Valon. The curving streets topped hills to reveal thin towers, their tiled walls sparkling with a hundred colors in the sunlight, or to look down on parks laid out in patterns made to be viewed from above, or to show sweeping vistas across the entire city to the rolling plains and forests beyond. It did not really matter which streets he took here. They all spiraled in on what he sought, the Royal Palace of Andor.

In no time, he found himself crossing the huge oval plaza before the Palace, riding toward its tall, gilded gates. The pure white Palace of Andor would certainly not have been out of place among Tar Valon's wonders, with its slender towers and golden domes shining in the sun, its high balconies and intricate stonework. The gold leaf on one of those domes could have kept him in luxury for a year.

There were fewer people in the plaza than elsewhere, as if it were reserved for great occasions. A dozen of the Guards stood before the closed gates, bows slanted, all at exactly the same angle, across their gleaming breastplates, faces hidden by the steel bars of their burnished helmets' faceguards. A heavyset officer, with his red cloak thrown back to reveal a knot of gold braid on his shoulder, was walking up and down the line, eyeing each man as if he thought he might find rust or dust.

Mat drew rein and put on a smile. "Good morning to you, Captain."

The officer turned, staring at him through the bars of his face-guard with deep, beady eyes, like a pudgy rat in a cage. The man was older than he had expected—surely old enough to have more than one knot of rank—and fat rather than stocky. "What do you want, farmer?" he demanded roughly.

Mat drew a breath. *Make it good. Impress this fool so he doesn't keep me waiting all day. I don't want to have to flash the Amyrlin's paper around to keep from kicking my heels.* "I come from Tar Valon, from the White Tower, bearing a letter from—"

"*You* come from Tar Valon, farmer?" The fat officer's stomach shook as he laughed, but then his laughter cut off as if severed with a knife, and he glared. "We want no letters from Tar Valon, rogue, *if* you have such a thing! Our good Queen—may the Light illumine her!—will take no word from the White Tower until the Daughter-Heir is returned to her. I never heard of any messenger from the Tower wearing a countryman's coat and breeches. It is plain to me you are up to some trick, perhaps thinking you'll find a few coins if you come claiming to carry letters, but you will be lucky if you don't end in a prison cell! If you do come from Tar Valon, go back and tell the Tower to return the Daughter-Heir before we come and take her! If you're a trickster after silver, get out of my sight before I have you beaten within an inch of your life! Either way, you half-wit looby, be gone!"

Mat had been trying to edge a word in from the beginning of the man's speech. He said quickly, "The letter is from her, man. It is from—"

"Did I not tell you to be gone, ruffian?" the fat man bellowed. His face was growing nearly as red as his coat. "Take yourself out of my sight, you gutter scum! If you are not gone by the time I count ten, I will arrest you for littering the plaza with your presence! One! Two!"

"Can you count so high, you fat fool?" Mat snapped. "I tell you, Elayne sent—"

"Guards!" The officer's face was purple now. "Seize this man for a Darkfriend!"

Mat hesitated a moment, sure no one could take such a charge seriously, but the red-coated Guards dashed toward him, all dozen men in breastplates and helmets, and he wheeled his horse and galloped ahead of them, followed by the fat man's shouts. The gelding was no racer, but it outdistanced men afoot easily enough. People dodged out of his way along the curving streets, shaking fists after him and shouting as many curses as the officer had.

Fool, he thought, meaning the fat officer, then added another for himself. *All I had to do was say her bloody name in the beginning. "Elayne, the Daughter-Heir of Andor, sends this letter to her mother, Queen Morgase." Light, who could have thought they'd think that way about Tar Valon.* From what he remembered of his last visit, Aes Sedai and the White Tower had been close behind Queen Morgase in the Guards' affections. *Burn her, Elayne could have told me.* Reluctantly, he added, *I could have asked questions, too.*

Before he reached the arched gates that let out into the New City, he slowed to a walk. He did not think the Guards from the Palace could still be chasing him, and there was no point in attracting the eyes of those at the gate by galloping through, but they looked at him no more now than when he had first entered.

As he rode under the broad arch, he smiled and almost turned back. He had suddenly remembered something, and had an idea that appealed to him a good deal more than walking through the Palace gates. Even if that fat officer had not been watching the gates, he thought he would like it better.

He became lost twice while searching for The Queen's Blessing, but at last he found the sign with a man kneeling before a woman with red-gold hair and a crown of golden roses, her hand on his head. It was a broad stone building of three stories, with tall windows even up under the red roof tiles. He rode around back to the stableyard, where a horse-faced fellow, in a leather vest that could hardly be any tougher than his skin, took his horse's reins. He thought he remembered the fellow. *Yes. Ramey.*

"It has been a long time, Ramey." Mat tossed him a silver mark. "You remember me, don't you?"

"Can't say as I . . ." Ramey began, then caught the shine of silver where he had expected copper; he coughed, and his short nod turned into something that combined a knuckled forehead with a jerky bow. "Why, of course I do, young master. Forgive me. Slipped my mind. Mind no good for people. Good for horses. I know horses, I do. A fine animal, young master. I'll take good care of him, you can be sure." He delivered it all quickly, with no room for Mat to say a word, then hurried the gelding into the stable before he might have to come up with Mat's name.

With a sour grimace, Mat put the fat roll of fireworks under his arm and shouldered the rest of his belongings. *Fellow couldn't tell me from Hawkwing's toenails.* A bulky,

muscular man was sitting on an upturned barrel beside the
door to the kitchen, gently scratching the ear of a black-and-
white cat crouched on his knee. The man studied Mat with
heavy-lidded eyes, especially the quarterstaff across his
shoulder, but he never stopped his scratching. Mat thought
he remembered him, but he could not bring up a name. He
said nothing as he went through the door, and neither did
the man. *No reason they should remember me. Probably
have bloody Aes Sedai coming for people every day.*

In the kitchen, two undercooks and three scullions were
darting between stoves and roasting spits under the direction of a round woman with her hair in a bun and a long
wooden spoon that she used to point out what she wanted
done. Mat was sure he remembered the round woman. *Coline, and what a name for a woman that wide, but everybody called her Cook.*

"Well, Cook," he announced, "I am back, and not a year
since I left."

She peered at him a moment, then nodded. "I remember
you." He began to grin. "You were with that young prince,
weren't you?" she went on. "The one who looked so like
Tigraine, the Light illumine her memory. You're his serving man, aren't you? Is he coming back, then, the young
prince?"

"No," he said curtly. *A prince! Light!* "I do not think he
will be anytime soon, and I don't think you would like it if
he did." She protested, saying what a fine, handsome young
man the prince was—*Burn me, is there a woman anywhere
who doesn't moon over Rand and make calf-eyes if you
mention his bloody name? She'd bloody scream if she knew
what he is doing now*—but he refused to let her get it out.
"Is Master Gill about? And Thom Merrilin?"

"In the library," she said with a tight sniff. "You tell
Basel Gill when you see him that I said those drains need
cleaning. Today, mind." She caught sight of something one
of the undercooks was doing to a beef roast and waddled
over to her. "Not so much, child. You will make the meat
too sweet if you put so much arrath on it." She seemed to
have forgotten Mat already.

He shook his head as he went in search of this library he
could not remember. He could not remember that Coline
was married to Master Gill, either, but if he had ever heard

a goodwife send instructions to her husband, that had been it. A pretty serving girl with big eyes giggled and directed him down a hall beside the common room.

When he stepped into the library, he stopped and stared. There had to be more than three hundred books on the shelves built on the walls, and more lying on the tables; he had never seen so many books in one place in his life. He noticed a leather-bound copy of *The Travels of Jain Farstrider* on a table near the door. He had always meant to read that—Rand and Perrin had always been telling him things out of it—but he never did seem to get around to reading the books he meant to read.

Pink-faced Basel Gill and Thom Merrilin were seated at one of the tables, facing each other across a stones board, pipes in their teeth trailing thin blue streamers of tabac smoke. A calico cat sat on the table beside a wooden dice cup, her tail curled over her feet, watching them play. The gleeman's cloak was nowhere in sight, so Mat supposed he had already gotten a room.

"You're done sooner than I expected, boy," Thom said around his pipestem. He tugged one long, white mustache as he considered where to place his next stone on the board's cross-hatchings. "Basel, you remember Mat Cauthon."

"I remember," the fat innkeeper said, peering at the board. "Sickly, the last time you were here, I recall. I hope you are better now, lad."

"I am better," Mat said. "Is that all you remember? That I was sick?"

Master Gill winced at Thom's move and took his pipe out of his mouth. "Considering who you left with, lad, and considering the way things are now, maybe it's best I remember no more than that."

"Aes Sedai not in such good odor now, are they?" Mat set his things in one big armchair, the quarterstaff propped against the back, and himself in another with one leg swinging over the arm. "The Guards at the Palace seemed to think the White Tower had stolen Elayne." Thom eyed the roll of fireworks uneasily, looked at his smoking pipe, and muttered to himself before going back to his study of the board.

"Hardly that," Gill said, "but the whole city knows she disappeared from the Tower. Thom says she's returned, but we've heard none of that here. Perhaps Morgase knows, but everyone down to a stableboy is stepping lightly so she doesn't snap off his head. Lord Gaebril has kept her from actually sending anyone to the headsman, but I'd not say she would not do it. And he has certainly not soothed her temper toward Tar Valon. If anything, I think he has made it worse."

"Morgase has a new advisor," Thom said in a dry voice. "Gareth Bryne did not like him, so Bryne has been retired to his estate to watch his sheep grow wool. Basel, are you going to place a stone or not?"

"In a moment, Thom. In a moment. I want to set it right." Gill clamped his teeth around his pipestem and frowned at the board, puffing up smoke.

"So the Queen has an advisor who doesn't like Tar Valon," Mat said. "Well, that explains the way the Guards acted when I said I came from there."

"If you told them that," Gill said, "you might be lucky you escaped without any broken bones. If it was any of the new men, at least. Gaebril has replaced half the Guards in Caemlyn with men of his choosing, and that is no mean feat considering how short a time he has been here. Some say Morgase may marry him." He started to put a stone on the board, then took it back with a shake of his head. "Times change. People change. Too much change for me. I suppose I am growing old."

"You seem to mean us both to grow old before you place a stone," Thom muttered. The cat stretched and slinked across the table for him to stroke her back. "Talking all day will not let you find a good move. Why don't you just admit defeat, Basel?"

"I never admit defeat," Gill said stoutly. "I'll beat you yet, Thom." He set a white stone on the intersection of two lines. "You will see." Thom snorted.

From what Mat could see of the board, he did not think Gill had much chance. "I will just have to avoid the Guards and put Elayne's letter right into Morgase's hands." *Especially if they're all like that fat fool. Light, I wonder if he's told them all I'm a Darkfriend?*

"You did not deliver it?" Thom barked. "I thought you were anxious to be rid of the thing."

"You have a letter from the Daughter-Heir?" Gill exclaimed. "Thom, why did you not tell me?"

"I am sorry, Basel," the gleeman muttered. He glared at Mat from under those bushy eyebrows and blew out his mustaches. "The boy thinks someone is out to kill him over it, so I thought I'd let him say what he wanted and no more. Seems he does not care any longer."

"What kind of letter?" Gill asked. "Is she coming home? And Lord Gawyn? I hope they are. I've actually heard talk of war with Tar Valon, as if anyone could be fool enough to go to war with Aes Sedai. If you ask me, it is all one with those mad rumors we've heard about Aes Sedai supporting a false Dragon somewhere in the west, and using the Power as a weapon. Not that I can see why that would make anyone want to go to war with them; just the opposite."

"Are you married to Coline?" Mat asked, and Master Gill gave a start.

"The Light preserve me from that! You would think the inn was hers now. If she was my wife . . . ! What does that have to do with the Daughter-Heir's letter?"

"Nothing," Mat said, "but you went on so long, I thought you must have forgotten your own questions." Gill made a choking sound, and Thom barked a laugh. Mat hurried on before the innkeeper could speak. "The letter is sealed; Elayne did not tell me what it says." Thom was eyeing him sideways and stroking his mustaches. *Does he think I'll admit we opened the thing?* "But I don't think she is coming home. She means to be Aes Sedai, if you ask me." He told them about his attempt to deliver the letter, smoothing over a few edges they had no need to know about.

"The new men," Gill said. "That officer sounds it, at least. I'll wager on it. No better than brigands, most of them, except the ones with a sly eye. You wait until this afternoon, lad, when the Guards on the gate will have changed. Say the Daughter-Heir's name right out, and just in case the new fellow is one of Gaebril's men, too, duck your head a little. A knuckle to your forehead, and you'll have no trouble."

"Burn me if I will. I pull wool and scratch gravel for nobody. Not to Morgase herself. This time, I'll not go near the Guards at all." *I would just as soon not know what word that fat fellow has spread.* They stared at him as if he were mad.

"How under the Light," Gill said, "do you mean to enter the Royal Palace without passing the Guards?" His eyes widened as if he were remembering something. "Light, you don't mean to. . . . Lad, you'd need the Dark One's own luck to escape with your life!"

"What are you going on about now, Basel? Mat, what fool thing do you intend to try?"

"I am lucky, Master Gill," Mat said. "You just have a good meal waiting when I come back." As he stood, he picked up the dice cup and spun the dice out beside the stones board for luck. The calico cat leaped down, hissing at him with her back arched. The five spotted dice came to rest, each showing a single pip. *The Dark One's Eyes*.

"That's the best toss or the worst," Gill said. "It depends on the game you are playing, doesn't it. Lad, I think you mean to play a dangerous game. Why don't you take that cup out into the common room and lose a few coppers? You look to me like a fellow who might like a little gamble. I will see the letter gets to the Palace safely."

"Coline wants you to clean the drains," Mat told him, and turned to Thom while the innkeeper was still blinking and muttering to himself. "It doesn't seem to make any odds whether I get an arrow in me trying to deliver that letter or a knife in my back waiting. It's six up, and a half dozen down. Just you have that meal waiting, Thom." He tossed a gold mark on the table in front of Gill. "Have my things put in a room, innkeeper. If it takes more coin, you will have it. Be careful of the big roll; it frightens Thom something awful."

As he stalked out, he heard Gill say to Thom, "I always thought that lad was a rascal. How does he come by gold?"

I always win, that's how, he thought grimly. *I just have to win once more, and I'm done with Elayne, and that's the last of the White Tower for me. Just once more.*

CHAPTER
46

A Message Out of the Shadow

E ven as he returned to the Inner City on foot, Mat was far from certain that what he intended would actually work. It would, if what he had been told was true, but it was the truth of that he was not sure of. He avoided the oval plaza in front of the Palace, but wandered around the sides of the huge structure and its grounds, along streets that curved with the contours of the hills. The golden domes of the Palace glittered, mockingly out of reach. He had made his way almost all the way around, nearly back to the plaza, when he saw it. A steep slope thick with low flowers, rising from the street to a white wall of rough stone. Several leafy tree limbs stuck over the top of the wall, and he could see the tops of others beyond, in a garden of the Royal Palace.

A wall made to look like a cliff, he thought, *and a garden on the other side. Maybe Rand was telling the truth.*

A casual look both ways showed him he had the curving street to himself for the moment. He would have to hurry; the curves did not allow him to see very far; someone could come along any moment. He scrambled up the slope on all fours, careless of how his boots ripped holes in the banks of red and white blossoms. The rough stone of the wall gave plenty of fingerholds, and ridges and knobs provided toeholds even for a man in boots.

Careless of them to make it so easy, he thought as he climbed. For a moment the climbing took him back home with Rand and Perrin, to a journey they had made beyond the Sand Hills, into the edge of the Mountains of Mist. When they returned to Emond's Field, they had all caught

the fury from everyone who could lay hands on them—him
worst of all; everyone assumed it had been his idea—but for
three days they had climbed the cliffs, and slept under the
sky, and eaten eggs filched from redcrests' nests, and plump,
gray-winged grouse fetched with an arrow, or a stone from
a sling, and rabbits caught with snares, all the while laughing about how they were not afraid of the mountains' bad
luck and how they might find a treasure. He had brought
home an odd rock from that expedition, with the skull of a
good-sized fish somehow pressed into it, and a long, white
tail feather dropped by a snow eagle, and a piece of white
stone as big as his hand that looked almost as if it had been
carved into a man's ear. He thought it looked like an ear,
even if Rand and Perrin did not, and Tam al'Thor had said
it might be.

His fingers slipped out of a shallow groove, his balance
shifted and he lost the toehold under his left foot. With a
gasp, he barely caught hold of the top of the wall, and pulled
himself up the rest of the way. For a moment he lay there,
breathing hard. It would not have been that long a fall, but
enough to break his head. *Fool, letting my mind wander
like that. Nearly killed myself on those cliffs that way. That
was all a long time ago.* His mother had likely thrown all
those things out already, anyway. With one last look each
way to make sure no one had seen him—the curving length
of street below was still empty—he dropped inside the Palace grounds.

It was a large garden, with flagstoned walks through expanses of grass among the trees, and grapevines thick on
arbors over the walks. And everywhere, flowers. White
blossoms covering the pear trees, and white and pink dotting the apple trees. Roses in every color, and bright golden
sunburst, and purple Emond's Glory, and many he could
not identify. Some he was not sure could be real. One had
odd blossoms in scarlet and gold that looked almost like
birds, and another seemed no different from a sunflower except that its yellow flowers were two feet and more across
and stood on stalks as tall as an Ogier.

Boots crunched on flagstone, and he crouched low behind a bush against the wall as two guardsmen marched
past, their long, white collars hanging over their breastplates. They never glanced his way, and he grinned to him-

self. *Luck. With just a little luck, they'll never see me till I hand the bloody thing to Morgase.*

He slipped through the garden like a shadow, as if stalking rabbits, freezing by a bush or hard against a tree trunk when he heard boots. Two more pairs of soldiers strode by along the paths, the second close enough for him to have taken two steps and goosed them. As they vanished among the flowers and trees, he plucked a deep red starblaze and stuck the wavy-petaled flower in his hair with a grin. This was as much fun as stealing applecakes at Sunday, and easier. Women always kept a sharp watch on their baking; the fool soldiers never took their eyes off the flagstones.

It was not long before he found himself against the white wall of the Palace itself, and began sliding along it behind a row of flowering white roses on slatted frames, searching for a door. There were plenty of wide, arched windows just over his head, but he thought it might be a bit harder to explain being found climbing in through a window than walking down a hall. Two more soldiers appeared, and he froze; they would pass within three paces of him. He could hear voices from the window over his head, two men, just loud enough for him to make out the words.

"—on their way to Tear, Great Master." The man sounded frightened and obsequious.

"Let them ruin his plans, if they can." This voice was deeper and stronger, a man used to command. "It will serve him right if three untrained girls can foil him. He was always a fool, and he is still a fool. Is there any word of the boy? He is the one who can destroy us all."

"No, Great Master. He has vanished. But, Great Master, one of the girls is Morgase's nit."

Mat half turned, then caught himself. The soldiers were coming closer; they did not appear to have seen his start through the thickly woven rose stems. *Move, you fools! Get by so I can see who this man bloody is!* He had lost some of the conversation.

"—has been far too impatient since regaining his freedom," the deep voice was saying. "He never realized the best plans take time to mature. He wants the world in a day, and *Callandor* besides. The Great Lord take him! He may seize the girl and try to make some use of her. And that might strain my own plans."

"As you say, Great Master. Shall I order her brought out of Tear?"

"No. The fool would take it as a move against him, if he knew. And who can say what he chooses to watch aside from the sword? See that she dies quietly, Comar. Let her death attract no notice at all." His laughter was a rich rumble. "Those ignorant slatterns in their Tower will have a difficult time producing her after this disappearance. This may all be just as well. Let it be done quickly. Quickly, before he has time to take her himself."

The two soldiers were almost abreast of him; Mat tried to will their feet to move faster.

"Great Master," the other man said uncertainly, "that may be difficult. We know she is on her way to Tear, but the vessel she traveled on was found at Aringill, and all three of them had left it earlier. We do not know whether she has taken another ship, or is riding south. And it may not be easy to find her once she reaches Tear, Great Master. Perhaps if you—"

"Are there none but fools in the world, now?" the deep voice said harshly. "Do you think I could move in Tear without him knowing? I do not mean to fight him, not now, not yet. Bring me the girl's head, Comar. Bring me all three heads, or you will pray for me to take yours!"

"Yes, Great Master. It shall be as you say. Yes. Yes."

The soldiers crunched past, never looking to either side. Mat only waited for their backs to pass before leaping up to catch the broad stone windowsill and pull himself high enough to see through the window.

He barely noticed the fringed Tarabon carpet on the floor, worth a fat purse of silver. One of the broad, carved doors was swinging shut. A tall man, with wide shoulders and a deep chest straining the green silk of his silver-embroidered coat, was staring at the door with dark blue eyes. His black beard was close cut, with a streak of white over his chin. All in all, he looked a hard man, and one used to giving orders.

"Yes, Great Master," he said suddenly, and Mat almost lost his grip on the sill. He had thought this must be the man with the deep voice, but it was the cringing voice he heard. Not cringing now, but still the same. "It shall be as you say, Great Master," the man said bitterly. "I will cut the three wenches' heads off myself. As soon as I can find them!" He strode through the door, and Mat let himself back down.

For a moment he crouched there behind the rose frames. Someone in the Palace wanted Elayne dead, and had thrown in Egwene and Nynaeve as afterthoughts. *What under the Light are they doing, going to Tear?* It had to be them.

He pulled the Daughter-Heir's letter out of the lining of his coat and frowned at it. Maybe, with this in his hand, Morgase would believe him. He could describe one of the men. But the time for skulking was past; the big fellow could be off to Tear before he even found Morgase, and whatever she did then, there was no guarantee it could stop him.

Taking a deep breath, Mat wiggled between two of the rose frames at the cost of only a few pricks and snags from the thorns, and started down the flagstone path after the soldiers. He held Elayne's letter out in front of him so the golden lily seal was plainly visible, and went over in his mind exactly what he meant to say. When he had been sneaking about, guardsmen kept popping up like mushrooms after rain, but now he walked almost the length of the garden without seeing even one. He passed several doors. It would not be so good to enter the Palace without permission—the Guards might do nasty things first and listen after—but he was beginning to think about going through a door when it opened and a helmetless young officer with one golden knot on his shoulder strode out.

The man's hand immediately went to his sword hilt, and he had a foot of steel bared before Mat could push the letter toward him. "Elayne, the Daughter-Heir, sends this letter to her mother, Queen Morgase, Captain." He held the letter so the lily seal was prominent.

The officer's dark eyes flickered to either side, as if searching for other people, without really ever leaving Mat. "How did you come into this garden?" He did not draw his sword further, but he did not sheath it, either. "Elber is on the main gates. He's a fool, but he would never let anyone wander loose into the Palace."

"A fat man with eyes like a rat?" Mat cursed his tongue, but the officer gave a sharp nod; he almost smiled, too, but it did not seem to lessen his vigilance, or his suspicion. "He grew angry when he learned I had come from Tar Valon, and he wouldn't even give me a chance to show the letter or mention the Daughter-Heir's name. He said he would arrest me if I did not go, so I climbed the wall. I promised I would deliver this to Queen Morgase herself, you see, Captain. I promised it, and I always keep my promises. You see the seal?"

"That bloody garden wall again," the officer muttered. "It should be built three times so high." He eyed Mat. "Guardsman-lieutenant, not captain. I am Guardsman-lieutenant Tallanvor. I recognize the Daughter-Heir's seal." His sword finally slid all the way back into the sheath. He stretched out a hand; not his sword hand. "Give me the letter, and I will take it to the Queen. After I show you out. Some would not be so gentle at finding you walking about loose."

"I promised to put it in her hands myself," Mat said. *Light, I never thought they might not let me give it to her.* "I did promise. To the Daughter-Heir."

Mat hardly realized Tallanvor's hand was moving before the officer's sword was resting against his neck. "I will take you to the Queen, countryman," Tallanvor said softly. "But know that I can take your head before you blink if you so much as think of harming her."

Mat put on his best grin. That slightly curved blade felt sharp on the side of his neck. "I am a loyal Andorman," he said, "and a faithful subject of the Queen, the Light illumine her. Why, if I had been here during the winter, I'd have followed Lord Gaebril for sure."

Tallanvor gave him a tight-mouthed stare, then finally took his sword away. Mat swallowed and stopped himself from touching his throat to see if he had been cut.

"Take the flower out of your hair," Tallanvor said as he sheathed his blade. "Do you think you came here courting?"

Mat snatched the starblaze blossom out of his hair and followed the officer. *Bloody fool, putting a flower in my hair. I have to stop playing the fool, now.*

It was not so much following, really, for Tallanvor kept an eye on him even while he led the way. The result was an odd sort of procession, with the officer to one side of him and ahead, but half turned in case Mat tried anything. For his part, Mat attempted to look as innocent as a babe splashing in his bathwater.

The colorful tapestries on the walls had earned their weavers silver, and so had the rugs on the white tile floors, even here in the halls. Gold and silver stood everywhere, plates and platters, bowls and cups, on chests and low cabinets of polished wood, as fine as anything he had seen in the Tower. Servants darted everywhere, in red livery with white collars and cuffs and the White Lion of Andor on their breasts. He found himself wondering if Morgase played at dice. *Wool-headed thought. Queens don't toss dice. But when I give her this letter and tell her somebody in her Palace means to kill Elayne, I'll wager she gives me a fat purse.* He indulged himself in a small fancy of being made a lord; surely the man who revealed a plot to murder the Daughter-Heir could expect some such reward.

Tallanvor led him down so many corridors and across so many courtyards that he was beginning to wonder if he could find his way out again without help, when suddenly one of the courts had more than servants in it. A columned walk surrounded the court, with a round pool in the middle with white and yellow fish swimming beneath lily pads and floating white water lilies. Men in colorful coats embroidered in gold or silver, women with wide dresses worked even more elaborately, stood attendance on a woman with red-gold hair who sat on the raised rim of the pool, trailing her fingers in the water and staring sadly at the fish that rose to her fingertips in hopes of food. A Great Serpent ring encircled the third finger of her left hand. A tall, dark man stood at her shoulder, the red silk of his coat almost hidden by the gold leaves and scrolls worked on it, but it was the woman who held Mat's eye.

He did not need the wreath of finely made golden roses in her hair, or the stole hanging over her dress of white slashed with red, the red length of the stole embroidered with the Lions of Andor, to know he was looking at Morgase, by the Grace of the Light, Queen of Andor, Defender of the Realm, Protector of the People, High Seat of House Trakand. She had Elayne's face and beauty, but it was what Elayne would have when she had ripened. Every other woman in the courtyard faded into the background by her very presence.

I'd dance a jig with her, and steal a kiss in the moonlight, too, no matter how old she is. He shook himself. *Remember exactly who she is!*

Tallanvor went to one knee, a fist pressed to the white stone of the courtyard. "My Queen, I bring a messenger who bears a letter from the Lady Elayne."

Mat eyed the man's posture, then contented himself with a deep bow. "From the Daughter-Heir . . . uh . . . my Queen." He held out the letter as he bowed, so the golden yellow wax of the seal was visible. *Once she reads it, and knows Elayne is all right, I will tell her.* Morgase turned her deep blue eyes on him. *Light! As soon as she's in a good mood.*

"You bring a letter from my scapegrace child?" Her voice was cold, but with an edge that spoke of heat ready to rise. "That must mean she is alive, at least! Where is she?"

"In Tar Valon, my Queen," he managed to get out. *Light, wouldn't I like to see a staring match between her and the Amyrlin.* On second thought, he decided he would rather not. "At least, she was when I left."

Morgase waved a hand impatiently, and Tallanvor rose to take the letter from Mat and hand it to her. For a moment she frowned at the lily seal, then broke it with a sharp twist of her wrists. She murmured to herself as she read, shaking her head at every other line. "She can say no more, can she?" she muttered. "We shall see whether she holds to that. . . ." Abruptly her face brightened. "Gaebril, she has been raised to the Accepted. Less than a year in the Tower, and raised already." The smile went as suddenly as it had come, and her mouth tightened. "When I put my hands on the wretched child, she will wish she were still a novice."

Light, Mat thought, *will nothing put her in a good mood?* He decided he was just going to have to say it out, but he wished she did not look as if she meant to cut someone's head off. "My Queen, by chance I overheard—"

"Be silent, boy," the dark man in the gold-encrusted coat said calmly. He was a handsome man, almost as good-looking as Galad and nearly as youthful-seeming, despite the white streaking his temples, but built on a bigger scale, with more than Rand's height and very nearly Perrin's shoulders. "We will hear what you have to say in a moment." He reached over Morgase's shoulder and plucked the letter out of her hand. Her glare turned on him—Mat could see her temper heating—but the dark man laid a strong hand on her shoulder, never taking his eyes off what he was reading, and Morgase's anger melted. "It seems she has left the Tower again," he said. "On the service of the Amyrlin Seat. The woman oversteps herself again, Morgase."

Mat had no trouble holding his tongue. *Luck*. It was stuck to the roof of his mouth. *Sometimes I don't know if it's good or bad*. The dark man was the owner of the deep voice, the "Great Master" who wanted Elayne's head. *She called him Gaebril. Her advisor wants to murder Elayne? Light!* And Morgase was staring up at him like an adoring dog with her master's hand on her shoulder.

Gaebril turned nearly black eyes on Mat. The man had a forceful gaze, and a look of knowing. "What can you tell us of this, boy?"

"Nothing . . . uh . . . my Lord." Mat cleared his throat; the man's stare was worse than the Amyrlin's. "I went to Tar Valon to see my sister. She's a novice. Else Grinwell. I'm Thom Grinwell, my Lord. The Lady Elayne learned I was meaning to see Caemlyn on my way back home—I'm from Comfrey, my Lord; a little village north of Baerlon; I'd never seen any place bigger than Baerlon before I went to Tar Valon—and she—the Lady Elayne, I mean—gave me that letter to bring." He thought Morgase had glanced at him when he said he came from north of Baerlon, but he knew there was a village called Comfrey there; he remembered hearing it mentioned.

Gaebril nodded, but he said, "Do you know where Elayne was going, boy? Or on what business? Speak the truth, and you have nothing to fear. Lie, and you will be put to the question."

Mat did not have to pretend a worried frown. "My Lord, I only saw the Daughter-Heir the once. She gave me the letter—and a gold mark!—and told me to bring it to the Queen. I know no more of what is in it than I've heard here." Gaebril appeared to consider it, with no sign on that dark face of whether he believed a word or not.

"No, Gaebril," Morgase said suddenly. "Too many have been put to the question. I can see the need as you have shown it to me, but not for this. Not a boy who only brought a letter whose contents he does not know."

"As my Queen commands, so shall it be," the dark man said. The tone was respectful, but he touched her cheek in a way that made color come to her face and her lips part as if she expected a kiss.

Morgase drew an unsteady breath. "Tell me, Thom Grinwell, did my daughter look well when you saw her?"

"Yes, my Queen. She smiled, and laughed, and showed a saucy tongue—I mean. . . ."

Morgase laughed softly at the look on his face. "Do not be afraid, young man. Elayne does have a saucy tongue, far too often for her own good. I am happy she is well." Those blue eyes studied him deeply. "A young man who has left his small village often finds it difficult to return to it. I think you will travel far before you see Comfrey again. Perhaps you will even return to Tar Valon. If you do, and if you see my daughter, tell her that what is said in anger is often repented. I will not remove her from the White Tower before time. Tell her that I often think of my own time there, and miss the quiet talks with Sheriam in her study. Tell her that I said that, Thom Grinwell."

Mat shrugged uncomfortably. "Yes, my Queen. But . . . uh . . . I do not mean to go to Tar Valon again. Once in any man's life is enough. My da needs me to help work the farm. My sisters will be stuck with the milking, with me gone."

Gaebril laughed, a deep rumble of amusement. "Are you anxious then to milk cows, boy? Perhaps you should see something of the world before it changes. Here!" He produced a purse and tossed it; Mat felt coins through the wash-leather when he caught it. "If Elayne can give you a gold mark for carrying her letter, I will give you ten for bringing it safely. See the world before you go back to your cows."

"Yes, my Lord." Mat lifted the purse and managed a weak grin. "Thank you, my Lord."

But the dark man had already waved him away and turned to Morgase with his fists on his hips. "I think the time has come, Morgase, to lance that festering sore on the border of Andor. By your marriage to Taringail Damodred, you have a claim to the Sun Throne. The Queen's Guards can make that claim as strong as any. Perhaps I can even aid them, in some small way. Hear me."

Tallanvor touched Mat on the arm, and they backed away, bowing. Mat did not think anyone noticed. Gaebril was still speaking, and every lord and lady seemed to hang on his words. Morgase was frowning as she listened, yet she nodded as much as any other.

CHAPTER
47

To Race the Shadow

From the small courtyard with its pool of fish, Tallanvor led Mat swiftly to the great court at the front of the Palace, behind the tall, gilded gates gleaming in the sun. It would be midday, soon. Mat felt an urge to be gone, a need to hurry. It was hard keeping his pace to the young officer's. Someone might wonder, if he started running, and maybe—just maybe—things had really been the way they seemed back there. Maybe Gaebril really did not suspect that he knew. *Maybe.* He remembered those nearly black eyes, seizing and holding like a pair of pitchfork tines through his head. *Light, maybe.* He forced himself to walk as if he had all the time in the world—*Just a haybrain country lout staring at the rugs and the gold. Just a mudfoot who'd never think anyone might put a knife in his back*—until Tallanvor let him through a sallyport in one of the gates, and followed him out.

The fat officer with the rat's eyes was still there with the Guards, and when he saw Mat his face went red again. Before he could open his mouth, though, Tallanvor spoke. "He has delivered a letter to the Queen from the Daughter-Heir. Be glad, Elber, that neither Morgase nor Gaebril knows you tried to keep it from them. Lord Gaebril was most interested in the Lady Elayne's missive."

Elber's face went from red to as white as his collar. He glared once at Mat, and scuttled back along the line of guardsmen, his beady eyes peering through the bars of their face-guards as if to determine whether any of them had seen his fear.

"Thank you," Mat told Tallanvor, and meant it. He had

forgotten all about the fat man until he was staring him in the face again. "Fare you well, Tallanvor."

He started across the oval plaza, trying not to walk too fast, and was surprised when Tallanvor walked along. *Light, is he Gaebril's man, or Morgase's?* He was just beginning to feel an itch between his shoulder blades, as if a knife might be about to go in—*He doesn't know, burn me! Gaebril doesn't suspect I know!*—when the young officer finally spoke.

"Did you spend long in Tar Valon? In the White Tower? Long enough to learn anything of it?"

"I was only there three days," Mat said cautiously. He would have made the time less—if he could have delivered the letter without admitting ever being in Tar Valon, he would have—but he did not think the man would believe he had gone all that way to see his sister and left the same day. *What under the Light is he after?* "I learned what I saw in that time. Nothing of any importance. They did not guide me around and tell me things. I was only there to see Else."

"You must have heard something, man. Who is Sheriam? Does talking to her in her study mean anything?"

Mat shook his head vigorously to keep relief from showing on his face. "I don't know who she is," he said truthfully. Perhaps he had heard Egwene, or perhaps Nynaeve, mention the name. An Aes Sedai, maybe? "Why should it mean anything?"

"I do not know," Tallanvor said softly. "There is too much I do not know. Sometimes I think she is trying to say something. . . ." He gave Mat a sharp look. "*Are* you a loyal Andorman, Thom Grinwell?"

"Of course I am." *Light, if I say that much more often, I may start believing it.* "What about you? Do you serve Morgase and Gaebril loyally?"

Tallanvor gave him a look as hard as the dice's mercy. "I serve Morgase, Thom Grinwell. Her, I serve to the death. Fare you well!" He turned and strode back toward the Palace with a hand gripping his sword hilt.

Watching him go, Mat muttered to himself. "I will wager this"—he gave Gaebril's wash-leather purse a toss—"that Gaebril says the same." Whatever games they played in the Palace, he wanted no place in any of them. And he meant to make sure Egwene and the others were out of them, too.

Fool women! Now I have to keep their bacon from burning instead of looking after my own! He did not start to run until the streets hid him from the Palace.

When he came dashing into The Queen's Blessing, nothing very much had changed in the library. Thom and the innkeeper still sat over the stones board—a different game, he saw from the positions of the stones, but no better for Gill—and the calico cat was back on the table, washing herself. A tray holding their unlit pipes and the remains of a meal for two sat near the cat, and his belongings were gone from the armchair. Each man had a wine cup at his elbow.

"I will be leaving, Master Gill," he said. "You can keep the coin and take a meal out of it. I'll stay long enough to eat, but then I am on the road to Tear."

"What is your hurry, boy?" Thom seemed to be watching the cat more than the board. "We only just arrived here."

"You delivered the Lady Elayne's letter, then?" the innkeeper said eagerly. "And kept your skin whole, it seems. Did you really climb over that wall like the other young man? No, that does not matter. Did the letter soothe Morgase? Do we still have to keep tiptoeing on eggs, man?"

"I suppose it soothed her," Mat said. "I think it did." He hesitated a moment, bouncing Gaebril's purse on his hand. It made a clinking sound. He had not looked to see if it really held ten gold marks; the weight was about right. "Master Gill, what can you tell me of Gaebril? Aside from the fact that he does not like Aes-Sedai. You said he had not been in Caemlyn long?"

"Why do you want to know about him?" Thom asked. "Basel, are you going to place a stone or not?" The innkeeper sighed and stuck a black stone on the board, and the gleeman shook his head.

"Well, lad," Gill said, "there is not much to tell. He came out of the west during the winter. Somewhere out your way, I think. Maybe it was the Two Rivers. I've heard the mountains mentioned."

"We have no lords in the Two Rivers," Mat said. "Maybe there are some up around Baerlon. I do not know."

"That could be it, lad. I had never even heard of him before, but I do not keep up with the country lords. Came while Morgase was still in Tar Valon, he did, and half the city was afraid the Tower was going to make her disappear, too. The other half did not want her back. The riots started up again, the way they did last year at the tail of winter."

Mat shook his head. "I do not care about politics, Master Gill. It's Gaebril I want to know about." Thom frowned at him, and began cleaning the dottle from his long-stemmed pipe with a straw.

"It is Gaebril I am telling you about, lad," Gill said. "During the riots, he made himself leader of the faction supporting Morgase—got himself wounded in the fighting, I hear—and by the time she returned, he had it all suppressed. Gareth Bryne didn't like Gaebril's methods—he can be a very hard man—but Morgase was so pleased to find order restored that she named him to the post Elaida used to hold."

The innkeeper stopped. Mat waited for him to go on, but he did not. Thom thumbed his pipe full of tabac and walked over to light a spill at a small lamp kept for the purpose on the mantel above the fireplace.

"What else?" Mat asked. "The man has to have a reason for what he does. If he marries Morgase, would he be king when she dies? If Elayne were dead, too, I mean?"

Thom choked lighting his pipe, and Gill laughed. "Andor has a queen, lad. Always a queen. If Morgase and Elayne both died—the Light send it not so!—then Morgase's nearest female relative would take the throne. At least there's no question of who that is this time—a cousin, the Lady Dyelin—not like the Succession, after Tigraine vanished. It took two years before Morgase sat on the Lion Throne, then. Dyelin could keep Gaebril as her advisor, or marry him to cement the line—though she would not likely do that unless Morgase had had a child by him—but he would be the Prince Consort even then. No more than that. Thank the Light, Morgase is a young woman, yet. And Elayne is healthy. Light! The letter did not say she is ill, did it?"

"She is well." *For now, at least.* "Isn't there anything else you can tell me about him? You do not seem to like him. Why?"

The innkeeper frowned in thought, and scratched his chin, and shook his head. "I suppose I would not like him marrying Morgase, but I do not truly know why. He's said to be a fine man; the nobles all look to him. I do not like most of the men he's brought into the Guards. Too much has changed since he came, but I cannot lay it all at his door. There just seem to be too many people muttering in corners since he came. You would think we were all Cairhienin, the way they were before this civil war, all plotting and trying to find advantage. I keep having bad dreams since Gaebril came, and I am not the only one. Fool thing to worry about, dreams. It is probably only worry about Elayne, and what Morgase means to do concerning the White Tower, and people acting like Cairhienin. I just do not know. Why are you asking all these questions about Lord Gaebril?"

"Because he wants to kill Elayne," Mat said, "and Egwene and Nynaeve with her." There was nothing useful in what Gill had told him that he could see. *Burn me, I don't have to know why he wants them dead. I just have to stop it.* Both men were staring at him again. As if he were mad. Again.

"Are you coming down sick again?" Gill said suspiciously. "I remember you staring crossways at everyone the last time. It's either that, or else you think this is some sort of prank. You have the look of a prankster to me. If that is it, it's a nasty one!"

Mat grimaced. "It is no bloody prank. I overheard him telling some man called Comar to cut Elayne's head off. And Egwene's and Nynaeve's while he was about it. A big man, with a white stripe in his beard."

"That does sound like Lord Comar," Gill said slowly. "He was a fine soldier, but it is said he left the Guard over some matter of weighted dice. Not that anyone says it to his face; Comar was one of the best blades in the Guards. You really mean it, don't you?"

"I think he does, Basel," Thom said. "I very much think he does."

"The Light shine on us! What did Morgase say? You did tell her, didn't you? The Light burn you, you did tell her!"

"Of course, I did," Mat said bitterly. "With Gaebril standing right there, and her gazing at him like a lovesick lapdog! I said, 'I may be a simple village man who just climbed over your wall half an hour past, but I already happen to know your trusted advisor there, the one you seem to be in love with, intends to murder your daughter.' Light, man, she'd have cut *my* head off!"

"She might have at that." Thom stared into the elaborate carvings on the bowl of his pipe and tugged one mustache.

"Her temper was ever as sudden as lightning, and twice as dangerous."

"You know it better than most, Thom," Gill said absently. Staring at nothing, he scrubbed both hands through his graying hair. "There has to be something I can do. I haven't held a sword since the Aiel War, but. . . . Well, that would do no good. Get myself killed and do nothing by it. But I must do something!"

"Rumor." Thom rubbed the side of his nose; he seemed to be studying the stones board and talking to himself. "No one can keep rumors from reaching Morgase's ears, and if she hears it strongly enough, she will start to wonder. Rumor is the voice of the people, and the voice of the people often speaks truth. Morgase knows that. There is not a man alive I would back against her in the Game. Love or no love, once Morgase starts examining Gaebril closely, he'll not be able to hide as much as his childhood scars from her. And if she learns he means harm to Elayne"—he placed a stone on the board; it seemed an odd placement at first glance, but Mat saw that in three more moves, a third of Gill's stones would be trapped—"Lord Gaebril will have a most elaborate funeral."

"You and your Game of Houses," Gill muttered. "Still, it might work." A sudden smile appeared on his face. "I even know who to tell to start it. All I need do is mention to Gilda that I dreamed it, and in three days she'll have told serving girls in half the New City that it is a fact. She is the greatest gossip the Creator ever made."

"Just be certain it cannot be traced back to you, Basel."

"No fear of that, Thom. Why a week ago, a man told me one of my own bad dreams as a thing he'd heard from somebody who'd had it from someone else. Gilda must have eavesdropped on me telling it to Coline, but when I asked, he gave me a string of names that led all the way to the other side of Caemlyn and vanished. Why, I actually went over there and found the last man, just out of curiosity to see how many mouths had passed it, and he claimed it was his very own dream. No fear, Thom."

Mat did not really care what they did with their rumors—no rumors would help Egwene or the others—but one thing puzzled him. "Thom, you seem to be taking this all very calmly. I thought Morgase was the great love of your life."

The gleeman stared into the bowl of his pipe again. "Mat, a very wise woman once told me that time would heal my wounds, that time smoothed everything over. I didn't believe her. Only she was right."

"You mean you do not love Morgase anymore."

"Boy, it has been fifteen years since I left Caemlyn a half step ahead of the headsman's axe, with the ink of Morgase's signature still wet on the warrant. Sitting here listening to Basel natter on"—Gill protested, and Thom raised his voice—"natter on, I say, about Morgase and Gaebril, and how they might marry, I realized the passion faded a long time gone. Oh, I suppose I am still fond of her, perhaps I even love her a little, but it is not a grand passion anymore."

"And here I half thought you'd go running up to the Palace to warn her." He laughed, and was surprised when Thom joined him.

"I am not so big a fool as that, boy. Any fool knows men and women think differently at times, but the biggest difference is this. Men forget, but never forgive; women forgive, but never forget. Morgase might kiss my cheek and give me a cup of wine and say how she has missed me. And then she might just let the Guards haul me off to prison and the headsman. No. Morgase is one of the most capable women I've ever known, and that is saying something. I could almost pity Gaebril once she learns what he is up to. Tear, you say? Is there any chance of you waiting until tomorrow to leave? I could use a night's sleep."

"I mean to be as far toward Tear as I can before nightfall." Mat blinked. "Do you mean to come with me? I thought you meant to stay here."

"Did you not just hear me say I had decided *not* to have my head cut off? Tear sounds a safer place to me than Caemlyn, and suddenly that does not seem so bad. Besides, I like those girls." A knife appeared in his hand and was as suddenly gone again. "I'd not like anything to happen to them. But if you mean to reach Tear quickly, it's Aringill you want. A fast boat will have us there days sooner than horses, even if we rode them to death. And I don't say it just because my bottom has already taken on the shape of a saddle."

"Aringill, then. As long as it's fast."

"Well," Gill said, "I suppose if you are leaving, lad, I had better see about getting you that meal." He pushed back his chair and started for the door.

"Hold this for me, Master Gill," Mat said, and tossed him the wash-leather purse.

"What's this, lad? Coin?"

"Stakes. Gaebril doesn't know it, but he and I have a wager." The cat jumped down as Mat picked up the wooden dice cup and spun the dice out on the table. Five sixes. "And I always win."

CHAPTER
48

Following the Craft

As the *Darter* wallowed toward the docks of Tear, on the west bank of the River Erinin, Egwene did not see anything of the oncoming city. Slumped head down at the rail, she stared down at the waters of the Erinin rolling past the ship's fat hull, and the frontmost sweep on her side as it swung into her vision and back again, cutting white furrows in the river. It made her queasy, but she knew raising her head would only make the sickness worse. Looking at the shore would only make the slow, corkscrew motion of the *Darter* more apparent.

The vessel had moved in that twisting roll ever since Jurene. She did not care how it had sailed before then; she found herself wishing the *Darter* had sunk before reaching Jurene. She wished they had made the captain put in at Aringill so they could find another ship. She wished they had never gone near a ship. She wished a great many things, most of them just to take her mind off where she was.

The twisting was less now, under sweeps, than it had been under sail, but it had gone on too many days now for the change to make much difference to her. Her stomach seemed to be sloshing about inside her like milk in a stone jug. She gulped and tried to forget that image.

They had not done much in the way of planning on the *Darter*, she and Elayne and Nynaeve. Nynaeve could seldom go ten minutes without vomiting, and seeing that always made Egwene lose whatever food she had managed to get down. The increasing warmth as they went further downriver did not help. Nynaeve was below now, no doubt with Elayne holding a basin for her again.

Oh, Light, no! Don't think about that! Green fields. Meadows. Light, meadows do not heave like that. Hummingbirds. No, not hummingbirds! Larks. Larks singing.

"Mistress Joslyn? Mistress Joslyn!"

It took her a moment to recognize the name she had chosen to give Captain Canin, and the captain's voice. She raised her head slowly and fixed her eyes on his long face.

"We are docking, Mistress Joslyn. You've kept saying how eager you were to be ashore. Well, we're there." His voice did not hide his eagerness to be rid of his three passengers, two of whom did little more than sick up, as he called it, and moan all night.

Barefoot, shirtless sailors were tossing lines to men on the stone dock that thrust out into the river; the dockmen seemed to be wearing long leather vests in place of shirts. The sweeps had already been drawn in, except for a pair fending the ship off from coming against the dock too hard. The flat stones of the dock were wet; the air had a feel of rain not long gone, and that was a little soothing. The twisting motion had ceased some time since, she realized, but her stomach remembered. The sun was falling toward the west. She tried not to think of supper.

"Very good, Captain Canin," she said with all the dignity she could summon. *He'd not sound like that if I were wearing my ring, not even if I were sick on his boots.* She shuddered at the picture in her mind.

Her Great Serpent ring and the twisted ring of the *ter'angreal* hung on a leather cord about her neck, now. The stone ring felt cool against her skin—almost enough to counteract the damp warmth of the air—but aside from that, she had found that the more she used the *ter'angreal*, the more she wanted to touch it, without pouch or cloth between it and her.

Tel'aran'rhiod still showed her little of immediate use. Sometimes there had been glimpses of Rand, or Mat, or Perrin, and more in her own dreams without the *ter'angreal*, but nothing of which she could make any sense. The Seanchan, who she refused to think about. Nightmares of a Whitecloak putting Master Luhhan in the middle of a huge, toothed trap for bait. Why should Perrin have a falcon on his shoulder, and what was important about him choosing between that axe he wore now and a blacksmith's hammer?

What did it mean that Mat was dicing with the Dark One, and why did he keep shouting, "I am coming!" and why did she think in the dream that he was shouting at her? And Rand. He had been sneaking through utter darkness toward *Callandor*, while all around him six men and five women walked, some hunting him and some ignoring him, some trying to guide him toward the shining crystal sword and some trying to stop him from reaching it, appearing not to know where he was, or only to see him in flashes. One of the men had eyes of flame, and he wanted Rand dead with a desperation she could nearly taste. She thought she knew him. Ba'alzamon. But who were the others? Rand in that dry, dusty chamber again, with those small creatures settling into his skin. Rand confronting a horde of Seanchan. Rand confronting her, and the women with her, and one of *them* was a Seanchan. It was all too confusing. She had to stop thinking about Rand and the others and put her mind to what was right ahead of her. *What is the Black Ajah up to? Why don't I dream something about them? Light, why can't I learn to make it do what I want?*

"Have the horses put ashore, Captain," she told Canin. "I will tell Mistress Maryim and Mistress Caryla." That was Nynaeve—Maryim—and Elayne—Caryla.

"I have sent a man to tell them, Mistress Joslyn. And your animals will be on the dock as soon as my men can rig a boom."

He sounded very pleased to be rid of them. She thought about telling him not to hurry, but rejected it immediately. The *Darter*'s corkscrewing might have stopped, but she wanted dry land under her feet again. Now. Still, she stopped to pat Mist's nose and let the gray mare nuzzle her palm, to let Canin see she was in no great rush.

Nynaeve and Elayne appeared at the ladder from the cabins, laden with their bundles and saddlebags, and Elayne almost as laden with Nynaeve. When Nynaeve saw Egwene watching, she pushed herself away from the Daughter-Heir and walked unaided the rest of the way to where men were setting a narrow gangplank to the dock. Two crewmen came to fasten a wide canvas sling under Mist's belly, and Egwene hurried below for her own things. When she came back up, her mare was already on the dock and Elayne's roan dangled in the canvas sling halfway there.

For a moment after her feet were on the dock, all she felt was relief. This would not pitch and roll. Then she began to look at this city whose reaching had caused them such pains.

Stone warehouses backed the long docks themselves, and there seemed to be a great many ships, large and small, alongside the docks or anchored in the river. Hastily she avoided looking at the ships. Tear had been built on flat land, with barely a bump. Down muddy dirt streets between the warehouses, she could see houses and inns and taverns of wood and stone. Their roofs of slate or tile had oddly sharp corners, and some rose to a point. Beyond these, she could make out a high wall of dark gray stone, and behind it the tops of towers with balconies high around them and white-domed palaces. The domes had a squared shape to them, and the tower tops looked pointed, like some of the roofs outside the wall. All in all, Tear was easily as big as Caemlyn or Tar Valon, and if not so beautiful as either, it was still one of the great cities. Yet she found it hard to look at anything but the Stone of Tear.

She had heard of it in stories, heard that it was the greatest fortress in the world and the oldest, the first built after the Breaking of the World, yet nothing had prepared her for this sight. At first she thought it was a huge, gray stone hill or a small, barren mountain covering hundreds of hides, its length stretching from the Erinin west through the wall and into the city. Even after she saw the huge banner flapping from its greatest height—three white crescent moons slanting across a field half red, half gold; a banner waving at least three hundred paces above the river, yet large enough to be clearly seen at that height—even after she made out battlements and towers, it was difficult to believe the Stone of Tear had been built rather than carved out of a mountain already there.

"Made with the Power," Elayne murmured. She was staring at the Stone, too. "Flows of Earth woven to draw stone from the ground, Air to bring it from every corner of the world, and Earth and Fire to make it all in one piece, without seam or joint or mortar. Atuan Sedai says the Tower could not do it, today. Strange, given how the High Lords feel concerning the Power now."

"I think," Nynaeve said softly, eyeing the dockmen

moving around them, "that given that very thing, we should not mention certain other things aloud." Elayne appeared torn between indignation—she had spoken very softly—and agreement; the Daughter-Heir agreed with Nynaeve too often and too readily to suit Egwene.

Only when Nynaeve is right, she admitted to herself grudgingly. A woman who wore the ring, or was even associated with Tar Valon, would be watched here. The barefoot, leather-vested dockmen were not paying the three of them any mind as they hurried about, carrying bales or crates on their backs as often as on barrows. A strong odor of fish hung in the air; the next three docks had dozens of small fishing boats clustered around them, just like those in the drawing in the Amyrlin's study. Shirtless men and barefoot women were hoisting baskets of fish out of the boats, mounds of silver and bronze and green, and colors she had never suspected fish might be, such as bright red, and deep blue, and brilliant yellow, some with stripes or splotches of white and other colors.

She lowered her voice for Elayne's ear alone. "She is right, Caryla. Remember why you are Caryla." She did not want Nynaeve to hear such admissions. Her face did not change when she heard, but Egwene could feel satisfaction radiating from her like heat from a cook stove.

Nynaeve's black stallion was just being lowered to the dock; sailors had already carried their tack off the ship and simply dumped it on the wet stones of the dock. Nynaeve glanced at the horses and opened her mouth—Egwene was sure it was to tell them to saddle their animals—then closed it again, tight-lipped, as if it had cost her an effort. She gave her braid one hard tug. Before the sling was well out of the way, Nynaeve tossed the blue-striped saddle blanket across the black's back and hoisted her high-cantled saddle atop it. She did not even look at the other two women.

Egwene was not anxious to ride at that moment—the motion of a horse might be too close to the motion of the *Darter* for her stomach—but another look at those muddy streets convinced her. Her shoes were sturdy, but she would not enjoy having to clean mud off them, or having to hold her skirts up as she walked, either. She saddled Mist quickly and climbed onto her back, settling her skirts, before she could decide the mud might not be so bad after all.

A little needlework on the *Darter*—Elayne had done it all, this time; the Daughter-Heir sewed a very fine stitch—had divided all their dresses nicely for riding astride.

Nynaeve's face paled for a moment when she swung into her saddle and the stallion decided to frisk. She kept a tight-mouthed grip on herself and a firm hand on her reins and soon had him under control. By the time they had ridden slowly past the warehouses, she could speak. "We need to locate Liandrin and the others without them learning we are asking after them. They surely know we are coming—that someone is, at least—but I would like them not to know we are here until it is too late for them." She drew a deep breath. "I confess I have not thought of any way to do this. Yet. Do either of you have any suggestions?"

"A thief-taker," Elayne said without hesitation. Nynaeve frowned at her.

"You mean like Hurin?" Egwene said. "But Hurin was in the service of his king. Wouldn't any thief-taker here serve the High Lords?"

Elayne nodded, and for a moment Egwene envied the Daughter-Heir her stomach. "Yes, they would. But thief-takers are not like the Queen's Guards, or the Tairen Defenders of the Stone. They serve the ruler, but people who have been robbed sometimes pay them to retrieve what was stolen. And they also sometimes take money to find people. At least, they do in Caemlyn. I cannot think it is different here in Tear."

"Then we take rooms at an inn," Egwene said, "and ask the innkeeper to find us a thief-taker."

"Not an inn," Nynaeve said as firmly as she guided the stallion; she never seemed to let the animal get out of her control. After a moment she moderated her tone a little. "Liandrin, at least, knows us, and we have to assume the others do, too. They will surely be watching the inns for whoever followed the trail they sprinkled behind them. I mean to spring their trap in their faces, but not with us inside. We'll not stay at an inn."

Egwene refused to give her the satisfaction of asking.

"Where then?" Elayne's brow furrowed. "If I made myself known—and could make anyone believe it, in these clothes and with no escort—we would be welcomed by most of the noble Houses, and very likely in the Stone itself—there

are good relations between Caemlyn and Tear—but there
would be no keeping it quiet. The entire city would know
before nightfall. I cannot think of anywhere else except an
inn, Nynaeve. Unless you mean to go out to a farm in the
country, but we will never find them from the country."

Nynaeve glanced at Egwene. "I will know when I see it.
Let me look."

Elayne's frown swept from Nynaeve to Egwene and back
again. "'Do not cut off your ears because you do not like
your earrings,'" she muttered.

Egwene put her attention firmly on the street they were
riding along. *I will be burned if I'll let her think I am even
wondering!*

There were not a great many people out, not compared to
the streets of Tar Valon. Perhaps the thick mud in the street
discouraged them. Carts and wagons lurched past, most
pulled by oxen with wide horns, the carter or wagoneer
walking alongside with a long goad of some pale, ridged
wood. No carriages or sedan chairs used these streets. The
odor of fish hung in the air here, too, and no few of the
men who hurried past carried huge baskets full of fish on
their backs. The shops did not look prosperous; none displayed wares outside, and Egwene seldom saw anyone go in.
The shops had signs—the tailor's needle and bolt of cloth,
the cutler's knife and scissors, the weaver's loom, and the
like—but the paint on most of them was peeling. The few
inns had signs in as bad a state, and looked no busier. The
small houses crowded between inns and shops often had
tiles or slates missing from their roofs. This part of Tear, at
least, was poor. And from what she saw on the faces, few of
the people here cared to try any longer. They were moving,
working, but most of them had given up. Few as much as
glanced at three women riding where everyone else walked.

The men wore baggy breeches, usually tied at the ankle. Only a handful wore coats, long, dark garments that fit
arms and chest tightly, then became looser below the waist.
There were more men in low shoes than in boots, but most
went barefoot in the mud. A good many wore no coat or
shirt at all, and had their breeches held up by a broad sash,
sometimes colored and often dirty. Some had wide, conical
straw hats on their heads, and a few, cloth caps that sagged
down one side of the face. The women's dresses had high

necks, right up to their chins, and hems that stopped at the ankle. Many had short aprons in pale colors, sometimes two or three, each smaller than the one beneath it, and most wore the same straw hats as the men, but dyed to complement the aprons.

It was on a woman that she first saw how those who wore shoes dealt with the mud. The woman had small wooden platforms tied to the soles of her shoes, lifting them two hands out of the mud; she walked along as if her feet were planted firmly on the ground. Egwene saw others wearing the platforms after that, men as well as women. Some of the women went barefoot, but not as many as the men.

She was wondering which shop might sell those platforms, when Nynaeve suddenly turned her black down an alleyway between a long, narrow two-story house and a stone-walled potter's shop. Egwene exchanged glances with Elayne—the Daughter-Heir shrugged—and then they followed. Egwene did not know where Nynaeve was going or why—and she meant to have words with her about it—but she did not mean to become separated, either.

The alley suddenly let into a small yard behind the house, fenced in by the buildings around it. Nynaeve had already dismounted and tied her reins to a fig tree, where the stallion could not reach the green things sprouting in a vegetable patch that took up half the yard. A line of stones had been laid to make a path to the back door. Nynaeve strode to the door and knocked.

"What is it?" Egwene demanded in spite of herself. "Why are we stopping here?"

"Did you not see the herbs in the front windows?" Nynaeve knocked again.

"Herbs?" Elayne said.

"A Wisdom," Egwene told her as she got down from her saddle and tied Mist alongside the black. *Gaidin is no good name for a horse. Does she think I don't know who she means it for?* "Nynaeve has found herself a Wisdom, or Seeker, or whatever they call her here."

A woman opened the door just enough to look out suspiciously. At first Egwene thought she was stout, but then the woman opened the door the rest of the way. She was certainly well padded, but the way she moved spoke of muscle underneath. She looked as strong as Mistress Luhhan, and some in Emond's Field claimed Alsbet Luhhan was almost as strong as her husband. It was not true, but it was not far wrong.

"How can I help you?" the woman said in an accent like the Amyrlin's. Her gray hair was arranged in thick curls that hung down the sides of her head, and her three aprons were in shades of green, each slightly darker than the one below, but even the topmost pale. "Which one of you needs me?"

"I do," Nynaeve said. "I need something for a queasy stomach. And perhaps one of my companions does, too. That is, if we've come to the right place?"

"You're not Tairen," the woman said. "I should have known that by your clothes, before you spoke. I'm called Mother Guenna. I am called a Wise Woman, too, but I'm old enough not to trust that to caulk a seam. You come, and I will give you something for your stomach."

It was a neat kitchen, though not large, with copper pots hanging on the wall, and dried herbs and sausages from the ceiling. Several tall cupboards of pale wood had doors carved with some sort of tall grass. The table had been scrubbed almost white, and the backs of the chairs were carved with flowers. A pot of fishy-smelling soup was simmering atop the stone stove, and a kettle with a spout, just beginning to steam. There was no fire on the stone hearth, for which Egwene was more than grateful; the stove added enough to the heat, though Mother Guenna seemed not to notice it at all. Dishes lined the mantel, and more were stacked neatly on shelves to either side. The floor looked as if it had just been swept.

Mother Guenna closed the door after them, and as she was crossing the kitchen to her cupboards, Nynaeve said, "Which tea will you give me? Chainleaf? Or bluewort?"

"I would if I had any of either." Mother Guenna rooted in the shelves a moment and came out with a stone jar. "Since I've had no time to glean of late, I will give you a brew of marshwhite leaves."

"I am not familiar with that," Nynaeve said slowly.

"It works as well as chainleaf, but it has a bite to the taste some don't care for." The big woman sprinkled dried and broken leaves into a blue teapot and carried it over to the fireplace to add hot water. "Do you follow the craft, then?

Sit." She gestured to the table with a hand holding two blue-glazed cups she had taken from the mantel. "Sit, and we'll talk. Which one of you has the other stomach?"

"I am fine," Egwene said casually as she took a chair. "Are you queasy, Caryla?" The Daughter-Heir shook her head with perhaps a touch of exasperation.

"No matter." The gray-haired woman poured out a cup of dark liquid for Nynaeve, then sat across the table from her. "I made enough for two, but marshwhite tea keeps longer than salted fish. It works better the longer it sits, too, but it also grows more bitter. Makes a race between how much you need your stomach settled and what your tongue can stand. Drink, girl." After a moment, she filled the second cup and took a sip. "You see? It will not hurt you."

Nynaeve raised her own cup, making a small sound of displeasure at the first taste. When she lowered the cup again, though, her face was smooth. "It is just a little bitter perhaps. Tell me, Mother Guenna, will we have to put up with this rain and mud much longer?"

The older woman frowned, parceling displeasure among the three of them before she settled on Nynaeve. "I am not a Sea Folk Windfinder, girl," she said quietly. "If I could tell the weather, I'd sooner stick live silverpike down my dress than admit it. The Defenders take that sort of thing for next to Aes Sedai work. Now, do you follow the craft or not? You look as if you have been traveling. What is good for fatigue?" she barked suddenly.

"Flatwort tea," Nynaeve said calmly, "or andilay root. Since you ask questions, what would you do to ease birthing?"

Mother Guenna snorted. "Apply warm towels, child, and perhaps give her a little whitefennel if it was an especially hard birth. A woman needs no more than that, and a soothing hand. Can't you think of a question any country farmwife could not answer? What do you give for pains in the heart? The killing kind."

"Powdered gheandin blossom on the tongue," Nynaeve said crisply. "If a woman has biting pains in her belly and spits up blood, what do you do?"

They settled down as if testing each other, tossing questions and answers back and forth faster and faster. Sometimes the questioning lagged a moment when one spoke of a plant the other knew only by another name, but they picked up speed again, arguing the merits of tinctures against teas, salves against poultices, and when one was better than another. Slowly, all the quick questions began shifting toward the herbs and roots one knew that the other did not, digging for knowledge. Egwene began to grow irritable listening.

"After you give him the boneknit," Mother Guenna was saying, "you wrap the broken limb in toweling soaked in water where you've boiled blue goatflowers—only the blue, mind!"—Nynaeve nodded impatiently—"and as hot as he can stand it. One part blue goatflowers to ten of water, no weaker. Replace the towels as soon as they stop steaming, and keep it up all day. The bone will knit twice as fast as with boneknit alone, and twice as strong."

"I will remember that," Nynaeve said. "You mentioned using sheepstongue root for eye pain. I've never heard—"

Egwene could stand it no longer. "Maryim," she broke in, "do you really believe you'll ever need to know these things again? You are not a Wisdom any longer, or have you forgotten?"

"I have not forgotten anything," Nynaeve said sharply. "I remember a time when you were as eager to learn new things as I am."

"Mother Guenna," Elayne said blandly, "what do you do for two women who cannot stop arguing?"

The gray-haired woman pursed her lips and frowned at the table. "Usually, men or women, I tell them to stay away from each other. That is the best thing, and the easiest."

"Usually?" Elayne said. "What if there is a reason they cannot stay apart. Say they are sisters."

"I do have a way to make an arguer stop," the big woman said slowly. "It is not something I urge anyone to try, but some do come to me." Egwene thought there was a suspicion of a smile at the corners of her mouth. "I charge a silver mark each for women. Two for men, because men make more fuss. There are some will buy anything, if it costs enough."

"But what is the cure?" Elayne asked.

"I tell them they have to bring the other one here with them, the one they argue with. Both expect me to quiet the other's tongue." Despite herself, Egwene was listening. She noticed Nynaeve seemed to be paying sharp attention, as

well. "When they have paid me," Mother Guenna continued, flexing one hefty arm, "I take them out back and stick
their heads in my rain barrel till they agree to stop their
arguing."

Elayne burst out laughing.

"I think I may have done something very like that my-
self," Nynaeve said in a voice that was much too light.
Egwene hoped her own expression looked nothing like
Nynaeve's.

"I'd not be surprised if you have." Mother Guenna was
grinning openly now. "I tell them the next time I hear
they've been arguing, I will do it for free, but I'll use the
river. It is remarkable how often the cure works, for men
especially. And it is remarkable what it has done for my
reputation. For some reason, none of the people I cure this
way ever tells anyone else the details, so someone asks for
the cure every few months. If you've been fool enough to
eat mudfish, you do not go around telling people. I trust
none of you have any wish to spend a silver mark."

"I think not," Egwene said, and glared at Elayne when
she went off in peals of laughter again.

"Good," the gray-haired woman said. "Those I cure of
arguing have a tendency to avoid me like stingweed caught
in their nets, unless they actually take sick, and I am enjoying your company. Most of those who come at present
want something to take away bad dreams, and they grow
sour when I have nothing to give them." For a moment she
slipped into a frown, rubbing her temples. "It is good to see
three faces that do not look as if there is nothing left but
to jump over the side and drown. If you are staying long
in Tear, you must come see me again. The girl called you
Maryim? I am Ailhuin. The next time, we'll talk over some
good Sea Folk tea instead of something that curdles your
tongue. Light, but I hate the taste of marshwhite; mudfish
would taste sweeter. In fact, if you have time to stay now,
I'll brew a pot of Tremalking black. Not long till supper,
either. It's just bread and soup and cheese, but you are welcome."

"That would be very nice, Ailhuin," Nynaeve said. "Actually. . . . Ailhuin, if you have a spare bedroom, I'd like to
hire it for the three of us."

The big woman looked at each of them without saying

anything. Getting to her feet, she tucked the pot of marsh-white tea away in the herb cupboard, then fetched a red tea-pot and a pouch from another. Only when she had brewed a pot of Tremalking black, put four clean cups and a bowl of honeycomb on the table along with pewter spoons, and reclaimed her chair did she speak.

"I've three empty bedrooms upstairs, now my daughters are all married. My husband, the Light shine on him, was lost in a storm in the Fingers of the Dragon near twenty years ago. There need be no talk of hiring, if I decide to let you have the rooms. If, Maryim." Stirring honey into her tea, she studied them again.

"What will make you decide?" Nynaeve asked quietly.

Ailhuin continued to stir, as if she had forgotten to drink. "Three young women, riding fine horses. I don't know much about horses, but those look as fine as what the lords and ladies ride, to me. You, Maryim, know enough of the craft that you ought to have hung herbs in your window al-ready, or should be choosing where to do it. I've never heard of a woman practicing the craft too far from where she was born, but by your tongue, you are a long way." She glanced at Elayne. "Not many places with hair that color. Andor, I'd say, by your speech. Fool men are always talking about finding a yellow-haired Andor girl. What I want to know is why? Running away from something? Or running after something? Only, you don't look like thieves to me, and I never heard of three women chasing after a man together. So tell me why, and if I like it, the rooms are yours. If you want to pay something, you buy a bit of meat now and then. Meat is dear since the trade up to Cairhien fell away. But first the why, Maryim."

"We are chasing after something, Ailhuin," Nynaeve said. "Or rather, after some people." Egwene schooled her-self to stillness and hoped she was doing as well as Elayne, who was sipping her tea as if she were listening to talk about dresses. Egwene did not believe Ailhuin Guenna's dark eyes missed a great deal. "They stole some things, Ailhuin," Nynaeve went on. "From my mother. And they did murder. We are here to see justice done."

"Burn my soul," the large woman said, "have you no menfolk? Men are not good for much beyond heavy hauling and getting in the way, most of the time—and kissing and such—but if there's a battle to be fought or a thief to catch, I say let them do it. Andor is as civilized as Tear. You are not Aiel."

"There was no one else but us," Nynaeve said. "Those who might have come in our place were killed."

The three murdered Aes Sedai, Egwene thought. *They could not have been Black Ajah. But if they had not been killed, the Amyrlin would not have been able to trust them. She's trying to keep to the bloody Three Oaths, but she is skirting it close.*

"Aaah," Ailhuin said sadly. "They killed your men? Brothers, or husbands, or fathers?" Spots of color bloomed in Nynaeve's cheeks, and the older woman mistook the emotion. "No, don't tell me, girl. I'll not pull up old grief. Let it lie on the bottom till it melts away. There, there, you calm yourself." It was an effort for Egwene not to growl with disgust.

"I must tell you this," Nynaeve said in a stiff voice. The red still colored her face. "These murderers and thieves are Darkfriends. They are women, but they are as dangerous as any swordsman, Ailhuin. If you wondered why we did not seek an inn, that is why. They may know we follow, and they may be watching for us."

Ailhuin waved it all away with a sniff. "Of the four most dangerous folk I know, two are women who never carry as much as a knife, and only one of the men is a swordsman. As for Darkfriends. . . . Maryim, when you are as old as I, you'll learn that false Dragons are dangerous, lionfish are dangerous, sharks are dangerous, and sudden storms out of the south; but Darkfriends are fools. Filthy fools, but fools. The Dark One is locked up where the Creator put him, and no Fetches or fangfish to scare children will get him out. Fools don't frighten me unless they're working the boat I'm riding. I suppose you don't have any proof you could take to the Defenders of the Stone? It would be just your word against theirs?"

What is a "Fetch"? Egwene wondered. *Or a "fangfish," for that matter.*

"We will have proof when we find them," Nynaeve said. "They will have the things they stole, and we can describe them. They are old things, and of little value to anyone but us, and our friends."

"You would be surprised what old things can be worth," Ailhuin said dryly. "Old Leuese Mulan pulled up three heartstone bowls and a cup in his nets last year, down in the Fingers of the Dragon. Now, instead of a fishing smack, he owns a ship trading up the river. Old fool did not even know what he had till I told him. Very likely there's more right where those came from, but Leuese couldn't even remember the exact spot. I do not know how he ever managed to get a fish into his net. Half the fishing boats in Tear were down there for months afterwards, dragging for *cuendillar*, not grunts or flatfish, and some had lords saying where to pull the nets. That's what old things can be worth, if they are old enough. Now, I've decided you do need a man in this, and I know just the one."

"Who?" Nynaeve said quickly. "If you mean a lord, one of the High Lords, remember we have no proof to offer till we find them."

Ailhuin laughed until she wheezed. "Girl, nobody from the Maule knows a High Lord, or any kind of lord. Mudfish don't school with silversides. I will bring you the dangerous man I know who isn't a swordsman, and the more dangerous of the two, at that. Juilin Sandar is a thief-catcher. The best of them. I do not know how it is in Andor, but here a thief-catcher will work for you or me as soon as for a lord or a merchant, and charge less at that. Juilin can find these women for you if they *can* be found, and bring your things back without you having to go near these Darkfriends."

Nynaeve agreed as if she were still not entirely sure, and Ailhuin tied those platforms to her shoes—clogs, she called them—and hurried out. Egwene watched her go, through one of the kitchen windows, past the horses and around the corner up the alley.

"You are learning how to be Aes Sedai, *Maryim*," she said as she turned from the window. "You manipulate people as well as Moiraine." Nynaeve's face went white.

Elayne stalked across the floor and slapped Egwene's face. Egwene was so shocked she could only stare. "You go too far," the golden-haired woman said sharply. "Too far. We must live together, or we will surely die together! Did you give Ailhuin your true name? Nynaeve told her what we could, that we seek Darkfriends, and that was risk enough, linking us with Darkfriends. She told her they were dangerous, murderers. Would you have had her say they are Black Ajah? In Tear? Would you risk everything on whether Ailhuin would keep *that* to herself?"

Egwene rubbed her cheek gingerly. Elayne had a strong arm. "I do not have to like doing it."

"I know," Elayne sighed. "Neither do I. But we *do* have to."

Egwene turned back to peering through the window at the horses. *I know we do. But I do not have to like it.*

CHAPTER
49

A Storm in Tear

Egwene finally returned to the table and her tea. She thought perhaps Elayne was right, that she had gone too far, but she could not bring herself to apologize, and they sat in silence.

When Ailhuin returned, she had a man with her, a lean fellow in his middle years who looked as if he had been carved from aged wood. Juilin Sandar took off his clogs by the door and hung his flat, conical straw hat on a peg. A sword-breaker, much like Hurin's but with short slots to either side of the long one, hung from a belt over his brown coat, and he carried a staff exactly as tall as he was, but not much thicker than his thumb and made of that pale wood, like ridged joints, that the ox-drivers used for their goads. His short-cut black hair lay flat on his head, and his quick, dark eyes seemed to note and record every detail of the room. And of everyone in it. Egwene would have bet he examined Nynaeve twice, and to her, at least, Nynaeve's lack of reaction was blatant; it was obvious she knew it, too.

Ailhuin motioned him to a place at the table, where he turned back the cuffs of his coat sleeves, bowed to each of them in turn, and sat with his staff propped against his shoulder, not speaking until the gray-haired woman had made a fresh pot of tea and everyone had sipped from their cups.

"Mother Guenna has told me of your problem," he said quietly as he set his cup down. "I will help you if I can, but the High Lords may have their own business to put me to, soon."

The big woman snorted. "Juilin, when did you begin

haggling like a shopkeeper trying to charge silk prices for linen? Do not claim you know when the High Lords will summon you before they do."

"I won't claim it," Sandar told her with a smile, "but I know when I've seen men on the rooftops in the night. Just out of the corner of my eye—they can hide like pipefish in reeds—but I have seen the movement. No one has reported a theft yet, but there are thieves working inside the walls, and you can buy your supper with that. Mark me. Before another week, I'll be summoned to the Stone because a band of thieves is breaking into merchants' houses, or even lords' manors. The Defenders may guard the streets, but when thieves need tracking they send for a thief-catcher, and me before any other. I am not trying to drive up my price, but whatever I do for these pretty women, I must do soon."

"I believe he speaks the truth," Ailhuin said reluctantly. "He'll tell you the moon is green and water white if he thinks it will bring him a kiss, but he lies less than most men about other things. He may be the most honest man ever born in the Maule." Elayne put a hand over her mouth, and Egwene struggled not to laugh. Nynaeve sat unmoved and obviously impatient.

Sandar grimaced at the gray-haired woman, then apparently decided to ignore what she had said. He smiled at Nynaeve. "I will admit that I'm curious about these thieves. I've known women thieves, and bands of thieves, but I never heard of a band of women thieves before. And I owe Mother Guenna favors." His eyes seemed to record Nynaeve all over again.

"What do you charge?" she asked sharply.

"To recover stolen goods," he said briskly, "I ask the tenth part of the value of what I recover. For finding someone, I ask a silver mark for each person. Mother Guenna says the things stolen have little value except to you, mistress, so I suggest you take that choice." He smiled again; he had very white teeth. "I would not take money from you at all, except that the brotherhood would frown on it, but I will take as little as I can. A copper or two, no more."

"I know a thief-taker," Elayne told him. "From Shienar. A very *respectful* man. He carries a sword as well as a sword-breaker. Why do you not?"

Sandar looked startled for a moment, and then upset with himself for being startled. He had not caught her hint, or else had decided to ignore it. "You are not Tairen. I have heard of Shienar, mistress, tales of Trollocs, and every man a warrior." His smile said these were tales for children.

"True stories," Egwene said. "Or true enough. I have been to Shienar."

He blinked at her, and went on. "I am not a lord, nor a wealthy merchant, nor even a soldier. The Defenders do not trouble foreigners much for carrying swords—unless they mean to stay long, of course—but I would be thrust into a cell under the Stone. There are laws, mistress." His hand rubbed along his staff, as if unconsciously. "I do as well as may be, without a sword." He focused his smile on Nynaeve once more. "Now, if you will describe these things—"

He stopped as she set her purse on the edge of the table and counted out thirteen silver marks. Egwene thought she had chosen the lightest coins; most were Tairen, only one Andoran. The Amyrlin had given them a great deal of gold, but even that would not last forever.

Nynaeve looked into the purse thoughtfully before tightening the strings and putting it back into her pouch. "There are thirteen women for you to find, Master Sandar, with as much silver again when you do. Find them, and we will recover our property ourselves."

"I will do that myself for less than this," he protested. "And there's no need for extra rewards. I charge what I charge. Have no fear I'll take a bribe."

"There is no fear of that," Ailhuin agreed. "I said he is honest. Just do not believe him if he says he loves you." Sandar glared at her.

"I pay the coin, Master Sandar," Nynaeve said firmly, "so I choose what I am buying. Will you find these women, and no more?" She waited for him to nod, reluctantly, before going on. "They may be together, or not. The first is a Taraboner. She is a little taller than I, with dark eyes and pale, honey-colored hair that she wears in many small braids after the Tarabon fashion. Some men might think her pretty, but she would not consider it a compliment. She has a mean, sulky mouth. The second is Kandori. She has long black hair with a white streak above her left ear, and. . . ."

She gave no names, and Sandar asked for none. Names

were so easily changed. His smile was gone now that the business was at hand. Thirteen women she described as he listened intently, and when she was done, Egwene was sure he could have recited them back word for word.

"Mother Guenna may have told you this," Nynaeve finished, "but I will repeat it. These women are more dangerous than you can believe. Over a dozen have died at their hands already, that I know of, and I would not be surprised if that was only a drop of the blood on their hands." Sandar and Ailhuin both blinked at that. "If they discover you are asking after them, you will die. If they take you, they will make you tell where we are, and Mother Guenna will probably die with us." The gray-haired woman looked disbelieving. "Believe it!" Nynaeve's stare demanded agreement. "Believe it, or I'll take back the silver and find another with more brains!"

"When I was young," Sandar said, voice serious, "a cutpurse put her knife in my ribs because I thought a pretty young girl wouldn't be as quick to stab as a man. I do not make that mistake anymore. I will behave as if these women are all Aes Sedai, and Black Ajah." Egwene almost choked, and he gave her a rueful grin as he scooped the coins into his own purse and stuck it behind his sash. "I did not mean to frighten you, mistress. There are no Aes Sedai in Tear. It may take a few days, unless they are together. Thirteen women together will be easy to find; apart, they will be harder. But either way, I will find them. And I will not frighten them away before you learn where they are."

When he had donned his straw hat and clogs and departed by the back door, Elayne said, "I hope he is not overconfident. Ailhuin, I heard what he said but. . . . He does understand that they are dangerous, does he not?"

"He has never been a fool except for a pair of eyes or a pretty ankle," the gray-haired woman said, "and that is a failing of every man. He is the best thief-catcher in Tear. Have no worry. He will find these Darkfriends of yours."

"It will rain again before morning." Nynaeve shivered, despite the warmth of the room. "I feel a storm gathering." Ailhuin only shook her head and set about filling bowls with fish soup for supper.

After they ate and cleaned up, Nynaeve and Ailhuin sat at the table talking of herbs and cures. Elayne worked on a small patch of embroidery she had begun on the shoulder of her cloak, tiny blue and white flowers, then read in a copy of *The Essays of Willim of Maneches* that Ailhuin had on her small shelf of books. Egwene tried reading, but neither the essays, nor *The Travels of Jain Farstrider*, nor the humorous tales of Aleria Elffin could hold her interest for more than a few pages. She fingered the stone *ter'angreal* through the bosom of her dress. *Where are they? What do they want in the Heart? None but the Dragon—none but Rand—can touch* Callandor, *so what do they want? What? What?*

As night deepened, Ailhuin showed them each to a bedroom on the second floor, but after she had gone to her own, they gathered in Egwene's by the light of a single lamp. Egwene had already undressed to her shift; the cord hung 'round her neck with the two rings. The striped stone felt far heavier than the gold. This was what they had done every night since leaving Tar Valon, with the sole exception of that night with the Aiel.

"Wake me after an hour," she told them.

Elayne frowned. "So short, this time?"

"Do you feel uneasy?" Nynaeve said. "Perhaps you are using it too often."

"We would still be in Tar Valon scrubbing pots and hoping to find a Black sister before a Gray Man found us if I had not," Egwene said sharply. *Light, Elayne's right. I am snapping like a sulky child.* She took a deep breath. "Perhaps I *am* uneasy. Maybe it is because we are so close to the Heart of the Stone, now. So close to *Callandor.* So close to the trap, whatever it is."

"Be careful," Elayne said, and Nynaeve said, more quietly, "Be very careful, Egwene. Please." She was tugging her braid in short jerks.

As Egwene lay down on the low-posted bed, with them on stools to either side, thunder rolled across the sky. Sleep came slowly.

It was the rolling hills again, as always at first, flowers and butterflies under spring sunshine, soft breezes and birds singing. She wore green silk, this time, with golden birds embroidered over her breasts, and green velvet slippers.

The *ter'angreal* seemed light enough to drift up out of her dress except for the weight of the Great Serpent ring holding it down.

By simple trial and error she had learned a little of the rules of *Tel'aran'rhiod*—even this World of Dreams, this Unseen World, had its rules, if odd ones; she was sure she did not know a tenth of them—and one way to make herself go where she wanted. Closing her eyes, she emptied her mind as she would have to embrace *saidar*. It was not as easy, because the rosebud kept trying to form, and she kept sensing the True Source, kept aching to embrace it, but she had to fill the emptiness with something else. She pictured the Heart of the Stone, as she had seen it in these dreams, formed it in every detail, perfect within the void. The huge, polished redstone columns. The age-worn stones of the floor. The dome, far overhead. The crystal sword, untouchable, slowly revolving hilt-down in mid-air. When it was so real she was sure she could reach out and touch it, she opened her eyes, and she was there, in the Heart of the Stone. Or the Heart of the Stone as it existed in *Tel'aran'rhiod*.

The columns were there, and *Callandor*. And around the sparkling sword, almost as dim and insubstantial as shadows, thirteen women sat cross-legged, staring at *Callandor* as it revolved. Honey-haired Liandrin turned her head, looking straight at Egwene with those big, dark eyes, and her rosebud mouth smiled.

Gasping, Egwene sat up in bed so fast she almost fell off the side.

"What is the matter?" Elayne demanded. "What happened? You look frightened."

"You only just closed your eyes," Nynaeve said softly. "This is the first time since the very beginning that you've come back without us waking you. Something did happen, didn't it?" She tugged her braid sharply. "Are you all right?"

How did I get back? Egwene wondered. *Light, I do not even know what I did.* She knew she was only trying to put off what she had to say. Unfastening the cord around her neck, she held the Great Serpent ring and the larger, twisted *ter'angreal* on her palm. "They are waiting for us," she said finally. There was no need to say who. "And I think they know we are in Tear."

Outside, the storm broke over the city.

Rain drumming on the deck over his head, Mat stared at the stones board on the table between him and Thom, but he could not really concentrate on the game, even with an Andoran silver mark riding on the outcome. Thunder crashed, and lightning flashed in the small windows. Four lamps lit the captain's cabin of the *Swift*. *Bloody ship may be as sleek as the bird, but it's still taking too bloody long.* The vessel gave a small jolt, then another; the motion seemed to change. *He had better not run us into the bloody mud! If he is not making the best time he can wring out of this buttertub, I will stuff that gold down his throat!* Yawning—he had not slept well since leaving Caemlyn; he could not stop worrying enough to sleep well—yawning, he set a white stone on the intersection of two lines; in three moves, he would capture nearly a fifth of Thom's black stones.

"You could be a good player, boy," the gleeman said around his pipe, placing his next stone, "if you put your mind to it." His tabac smelled like leaves and nuts.

Mat reached for another stone from the pile at his elbow, then blinked and let it lie. In the same three moves, Thom's stones would surround over a third of his. He had not seen it coming, and he could see no escape. "Do you ever lose a game? Have you ever lost a game?"

Thom removed his pipe and knuckled his mustaches. "Not in a long while. Morgase used to beat me about half the time. It is said good commanders of soldiers and good players of the Great Game are good at stones, as well. She is the one, and I've no doubt she could command a battle, too."

"Wouldn't you rather dice some more? Stones take too much time."

"I like a chance to win more than one toss in nine or ten," the white-haired man said dryly.

Mat bounded to his feet as the door banged open to admit Captain Derne. The square-faced man whipped his cloak from his shoulders, shaking the rain off and muttering curses to himself. "The Light sear my bones, I do not know why I ever let you hire *Swift*. You, demanding more flaming speed in the blackest night or the heaviest rain. More speed. Always more bloody speed! Could have run on a bloody mudflat a hundred times over by now!"

"You wanted the gold," Mat said harshly. "You said this heap of old boards was fast, Derne. When do we reach Tear?"

The captain smiled a tight smile. "We are tying off to the dock, now. And burn me for a bloody farmer if I carry anything that can flaming talk ever again! Now, where is the rest of my gold?"

Mat hurried to one of the small windows and peered out. In the harsh glare of lightning flashes he could see a wet stone dock, if not much else. He fished the second purse of gold from his pocket and tossed it to Derne. *Whoever heard of a riverman who didn't dice!* "About time," he growled. *Light send I'm not too late.*

He had stuffed all of his spare clothes and his blankets into the leather scrip, and he hung that on one side of him and the roll of fireworks on the other, from the cord he tied to it. His cloak covered it all, but gapped a little in the front. Better he got wet than the fireworks. He could dry out and be as good as new; a test with a bucket had shown fireworks could not. *I guess Rand's da was right.* Mat had always thought the Village Council would not set them off in the rain because they made a better show on clear nights.

"Aren't you about ready to sell those things?" Thom was settling his gleeman's cloak on his shoulders. It covered his leather-cased harp and flute, but his bundle of clothes and blankets he slung on his back outside the patch-covered cloak.

"Not until I figure out how they work, Thom. Besides, think what fun it will be when I set them all off."

The gleeman shuddered. "As long as you don't do it all at once, boy. As long as you don't throw them in the fireplace at supper. I'd not put it past you, the way you've been behaving with them. You're lucky the captain here did not throw us off the ship two days ago."

"He wouldn't." Mat laughed. "Not while that purse was in the offing. Eh, Derne?"

Derne was tossing the purse of gold in his hand. "I have not asked before this, but you've given me the gold, now, and you'll not take it back. What is this all about? All this flaming speed."

"A wager, Derne." Yawning, Mat picked up his quarterstaff, ready to go. "A wager."

"A wager!" Derne stared at the heavy purse. The other just like it was locked in his money chest. "There must be a flaming kingdom riding on it!"

"More than that," Mat said.

Rain bucketed down on the deck so hard that he could not see the gangplank except when lightning crackled above the city; the roar of the downpour barely let him hear himself think. He could see lights in windows up a street, though. There would be inns, up there. The captain had not come on deck to see them ashore, and none of the crew had stayed out in the rain, either. Mat and Thom made their way to the stone dock alone.

Mat cursed when his boots sank into the mud of the street, but there was nothing for it, so he kept on, striding along as fast as he could with his boots and the butt of his staff sticking at every step. The air smelled of fish, rank even with the rain. "We'll find an inn," he said, loudly, so he could be heard, "and then I will go out looking."

"In this weather?" Thom shouted back. Rain was rolling down his face, but he was more interested in keeping his instruments covered than his face.

"Comar could have left Caemlyn before us. If he had a good horse instead of the crowbaits we were riding, he could have set out downriver from Aringill maybe a full day ahead of us, and I don't know how much of that we caught up with that idiot Derne."

"It was a quick passage," Thom allowed. "*Swift* deserves its name."

"Be that as it may, Thom, rain or no rain, I have to find him before he finds Egwene and Nynaeve, and Elayne."

"A few more hours won't make much difference, boy. There are hundreds of inns in a city the size of Tear. There may be hundreds more outside the walls, some of them little places with no more than a dozen rooms to let, so tiny you could walk right by them and never know they were there." The gleeman hitched the hood of his cloak up more, muttering to himself. "It will take weeks to search them all.

But it will take Comar the same weeks. We can spend the night in out of the rain. You can wager whatever coin you have left that Comar won't be out in it."

Mat shook his head. *A tiny inn with a dozen rooms.* Before he left Emond's Field, the biggest building he had ever seen was the Winespring Inn. He doubted if Bran al'Vere had any more than a dozen rooms to let. Egwene had lived with her parents and her sisters in the rooms at the front of the second floor. *Burn me, sometimes I think we should never any of us have left Emond's Field.* But Rand surely had had to, and Egwene would probably have died if she had not gone to Tar Valon. *Now she might die because she did go.* He did not think he could settle for the farm again; the cows and the sheep certainly would not play dice. But Perrin still had a chance to go home. *Go home, Perrin,* he found himself thinking. *Go home while you still can.* He gave himself a shake. *Fool! Why would he want to?* He thought of bed, but pushed it away. *Not yet.*

Lightning streaked across the sky, three jagged bolts together, casting a stark light over a narrow house that seemed to have bunches of herbs hanging in the windows, and a shop, shut up tight, but a potter's from the sign with its bowls and plates. Yawning, he hunched his shoulders against the driving rain and tried to pull his boots out of the clinging mud more quickly.

"I think I can forget about this part of the city, Thom," he shouted. "All this mud, and that stink of fish. Can you see Nynaeve or Egwene—or Elayne!—choosing to stay here? Women like things neat and tidy, Thom, and smelling good."

"May be, boy," Thom muttered, then coughed. "You would be surprised what women will put up with. But it may be."

Holding his cloak to keep the roll of fireworks covered, Mat lengthened his stride. "Come on, Thom. I want to find Comar or the girls tonight, one or the other."

Thom limped after him, coughing now and again.

They strode through the wide gates in the city—unguarded, in the rain—and Mat was relieved to feel paving stones under his feet again. And not more than fifty paces up the street was an inn, the windows of the common room spilling light onto the street, music drifting out into the night. Even Thom covered that last fifty paces through the rain quickly, limp or no limp.

The White Crescent had a landlord whose girth made his long blue coat fit snugly below the waist as well as above, unlike those of most of the men in the low-backed chairs at the tables. Mat thought the landlord's baggy breeches, tied at the ankle above low shoes, had to be big enough for two ordinary men to fit inside, one in each leg. The serving women wore dark, high-necked dresses and short white aprons. There was a fellow playing a hammered dulcimer between the two stone fireplaces. Thom eyed the fellow critically and shook his head.

The rotund innkeeper, Cavan Lopar by name, was more than glad to give them rooms. He frowned at their muddy boots, but silver from Mat's pocket—the gold was running low—and Thom's patch-covered cloak smoothed his fat forehead. When Thom said he would perform for a small fee some nights, Lopar's chins waggled with pleasure. Of a big man with a white streak in his beard, he knew nothing, nor of three women meeting the descriptions Mat gave. Mat left everything but his cloak and his quarterstaff in his room, barely looking to see that it had a bed—sleep was enticing, but he refused to let himself think of it—then wolfed down a spicy fish stew and rushed back out into the rain. He was surprised that Thom came with him.

"I thought you wanted to be in where it's dry, Thom."

The gleeman patted the flute case he still had under his cloak. The rest of his things were up in his room. "People talk to a gleeman, boy. I may learn something you would not. I'd not like to see those girls harmed any more than you."

There was another inn a hundred paces down the rain-filled street on the other side, and another two hundred beyond that, and then more. Mat took them as he came to them, ducking in long enough for Thom to flourish his cloak and tell a story, then let someone buy him a cup of wine afterwards while Mat asked around after a tall man with a white streak in his close-cut black beard and three women. He won a few coins at dice, but he learned nothing, and neither did Thom. He was just glad the gleeman seemed to be taking only a few sips of wine at each inn; Thom had been close to abstemious on the boat, but Mat had not been certain he would not dive back into the wine once they reached Tear. By the time they had visited two dozen common rooms, Mat felt as if his eyelids had weights. The rain had lessened a bit, but it still fell steadily in big drops, and as the rain fell off the wind had freshened. The sky had the dark gray look of coming dawn.

"Boy," Thom muttered, "if we don't go back to The White Crescent, I am going to go to sleep here in the rain." He stopped to cough. "Do you realize you've marched right past three inns? Light, I am so tired I can't think. Do you have a scheme of where to go that you have not told me?"

Mat stared blearily up the street at a tall man in a cloak hurrying around a corner. *Light, I am tired. Rand is five hundred leagues from here, playing at being the bloody Dragon.* "What? Three inns?" They were standing almost in front of another, The Golden Cup according to the sign creaking in the wind. It looked nothing like a dice cup, but he decided to give it a try anyway. "One more, Thom. If we don't find them here, we'll go back and go to bed." Bed sounded better than a dice game with a hundred gold marks riding on the toss, but he made himself go in.

Two steps into the common room Mat saw him. The big man wore a green coat with blue stripes down puffy sleeves, but it was Comar, close-cut black beard with a white streak over his chin and all. He sat in one of the strangely low-backed chairs, at a table on the far side of the room, rattling a leather dice cup and smiling at the man across from him. That fellow wore a long coat and baggy breeches, and he was not smiling. He stared at the coins on the table as if wishing he had them back in his purse. Another dice cup sat at Comar's elbow.

Comar upended the leather cup in his hand, and began laughing almost before the dice stopped spinning. "Who is next?" he called loudly, pulling the wager to his side of the table. There was already a considerable pile of silver in front of him. He scooped the dice into the cup and rattled them. "Surely someone else wants to try his luck?" It seemed that no one did, but he kept rattling the cup and laughing.

The innkeeper was easy to pick out, though they did not seem to wear aprons in Tear. His coat was the same shade of deep blue as that of every other innkeeper Mat had spoken to. A plump man, though little more than half the size of Lopar and with half that fellow's number of chins, he was sitting at a table by himself, polishing a pewter mug furiously and glaring across the room toward Comar, though not when Comar was looking. Some of the other men gave the bearded man sidelong frowns, too. But not when he was looking.

Mat suppressed his first urge, which was to rush over to Comar, drub him over the head with his quarterstaff, and demand to know where Egwene and the others were. Something was wrong here. Comar was the first man he had seen wearing a sword, but the way the men looked at him was more than fear of a swordsman. Even the serving woman who brought Comar a fresh cup of wine—and was pinched for her trouble—had a nervous laugh for him.

Look at it from every side, Mat thought wearily. *Half the trouble I get into is from not doing that. I have to think.* Tiredness seemed to have stuffed his head with wool. He motioned to Thom, and they strolled over to the innkeeper, who eyed them suspiciously when they sat down. "Who is the man with the stripe in his beard?" Mat asked.

"Not from the city, are you?" the innkeeper said. "He is a foreigner, too. I've never seen him before tonight, but I know what he is. Some outlander who has come here and made his fortune in trade. A merchant rich enough to wear a sword. That is no reason for him to treat us like this."

"If you have never seen him before," Mat said, "how do you know he is a merchant?"

The innkeeper looked at him as if he were stupid. "His coat, man, and his sword. He cannot be a lord or a soldier if he's from off, so he has to be a rich merchant." He shook his head for the stupidity of foreigners. "They come to our places, to look down their noses at us, and fondle the girls under our very eyes, but he has no call to do this. If I go to the Maule, I don't gamble for some fisherman's coins. If I go to the Tavar, I do not dice with the farmers come to sell their crops." His polishing gained in ferocity. "Such luck, the man has. It must be how he made his fortune."

"He wins, does he?" Yawning, Mat wondered how he would do dicing with another man who had luck.

"Sometimes he loses," the innkeeper muttered, "when the stake is a few silver pennies. Sometimes. But let it reach a silver mark. . . . No less than a dozen times tonight, I have seen him win at Crowns with three crowns and two roses. And half again as often, at Top, it has been three sixes and two fives. He tosses nothing but sixes at Threes, and three sixes and a five every throw at Compass. If he has such luck, I say the Light shine on him, and well to him, but let him use it with other merchants, as is proper. How can a man have such luck?"

"Weighted dice," Thom said, then coughed. "When he wants to be sure of winning, he uses dice that always show the same face. He is smart enough not to have made it the highest toss—folk become suspicious if you always throw the king"—he raised an eyebrow at Mat—"just one that's all but impossible to beat, but he cannot change that they always show the same face."

"I have heard of such," the innkeeper said slowly. "Illian-ers use them, I hear." Then he shook his head. "But both men use the same cup and dice. It cannot be."

"Bring me two dice cups," Thom said, "and two sets of dice. Crowns or spots, it makes no difference, so long as they are the same."

The innkeeper frowned at him, but left—prudently tak-ing the pewter cup with him—and came back with two leather cups. Thom rolled the five bone cubes from one onto the table in front of Mat. Whether with spots or symbols, every set of dice Mat had ever seen had been either bone or wood. These had spots. He picked them up, frowning at Thom. "Am I supposed to see something?"

Thom dumped the dice from the other cup into his hand, then, almost too quickly to follow, dropped them back in and twisted the cup over to rest upside down on the table before the dice could fall out. He kept his hand on top of the cup. "Put a mark on each of them, boy. Something small, but something you'll know for your mark."

Mat found himself exchanging puzzled glances with the innkeeper. Then they both looked at the cup upside down under Thom's hand. He knew Thom was up to something tricky—gleemen were always doing things that were im-possible, like eating fire and pulling silk out of the air—but he did not see how Thom could do anything with him watching close. He unsheathed his belt knife and made a small scratch on each die, right across the circle of six spots.

"All right," he said, setting them back on the table. "Show me your trick."

Thom reached over and picked up the dice, then set them down again a foot away. "Look for your marks, boy."

Mat frowned. Thom's hand was still on the upended leather cup; the gleeman had not moved it or taken Mat's dice anywhere near it. He picked up the dice . . . and blinked. There was not a scratch on them. The innkeeper gasped.

Thom turned his free hand over, revealing five dice. "Your marks are on these. That is what Comar is doing. It is a child's trick, simple, though I'd never have thought he had the fingers for it."

"I do not think I want to play dice with you after all," Mat said slowly. The innkeeper was staring at the dice, but not as if he saw any solution. "Call the Watch, or whatever you call it here," Mat told him. "Have him arrested." *He'll kill nobody in a prison cell. Yet what if they are already dead?* He tried not to listen, but the thought persisted. *Then I'll see him dead, and Gaebril, whatever it takes! But they aren't, burn me! They can't be!*

The innkeeper was shaking his head. "Me? Me, denounce a merchant to the Defenders? They would not even look at his dice. He could say one word, and I would be in chains working the channeldredges in the Fingers of the Dragon. He could cut me down where I stood, and the Defenders would say I had earned it. Perhaps he will go away after a while."

Mat gave him a wry grimace. "If I expose him, will that be good enough? Will you call the Watch, or the Defenders or whoever, then?"

"You do not understand. You are a foreigner. Even if he is from off, he is a wealthy man, important."

"Wait here," Mat told Thom. "I do not mean to let him reach Egwene and the others, whatever it takes." He yawned as he scraped back his chair.

"Wait, boy," Thom called after him, soft yet urgent. The gleeman pushed himself up out of his chair. "Burn you, you don't know what you're putting your foot into!"

Mat waved for him to stay there and walked over to Comar. No one else had taken up the bearded man's challenge, and he eyed Mat with interest as Mat leaned his quarterstaff against the table and sat down.

Comar studied Mat's coat and grinned nastily. "You want to wager coppers, farmer? I do not waste my time with—" He cut off as Mat set an Andoran gold crown on the table and yawned at him, making no effort to cover his mouth. "You say little, farmer, though your manners could use improving, but gold has a voice of its own and no need of manners." He shook the leather cup in his hand and spilled the dice out. He was chuckling before they came to rest, showing three crowns and two roses. "You'll not beat that, farmer. Perhaps you have more gold hidden in those rags that you want to lose? What did you do? Rob your master?"

He reached for the dice, but Mat scooped them up ahead of him. Comar glared, but let him have the cup. If both tosses were the same, they would throw again until one man won. Mat smiled as he rattled the dice. He did not mean to give Comar a chance to change them. If they threw the same toss three or four times in a row—exactly the same, every time—even these Defenders would listen. The whole common room would see; they would have to back his word.

He spilled the dice onto the tabletop. They bounced oddly. He felt—something—shifting. It was as if his luck had gone wild. The room seemed to be writhing around him, tugging at the dice with threads. For some reason he wanted to look at the door, but he kept his eyes on the dice. They came to rest. Five crowns. Comar's eyes looked ready to pop out of his head.

"You lose," Mat said softly. If his luck was in to this extent, perhaps it was time to push it. A voice in the back of his head told him to think, but he was too tired to listen. "I think your luck is about used up, Comar. If you've harmed those girls, it's all gone."

"I have not even found . . ." Comar began, still staring at the dice, then jerked his head up. His face had gone white. "How do you know my name?"

He had not found them, yet. *Luck, sweet luck, stay with me.* "Go back to Caemlyn, Comar. Tell Gaebril you could not find them. Tell him they are dead. Tell him anything, but leave Tear tonight. If I see you again, I'll kill you."

"Who are you?" the big man said unsteadily. "Who—?" The next instant his sword was out and he was on his feet.

Mat shoved the table at him, overturning it, and grabbed for his quarterstaff. He had forgotten how big Comar was. The bearded man pushed the table right back at him. Mat fell over with his chair, holding a bare grasp on his staff, as Comar heaved the table out of the way and stabbed at him. Mat threw his feet against the man's middle to stop his rush, swung the staff awkwardly, just enough to deflect the sword. But the blow knocked the staff from his fingers, and he found himself gripping Comar's wrist, instead, with the man's blade a hand from his face. With a grunt he rolled backwards, heaving as hard as he could with his legs. Comar's eyes widened as he sailed over Mat to crash onto a table, face up. Mat scrambled for his staff, but when he had it, Comar had not moved.

The big man lay with his hips and legs sprawled across the top of the table, the rest of him hanging down with his head on the floor. The men who had been sitting at the table were on their feet a safe distance away, wringing their hands and eyeing each other nervously. A low, worried buzz filled the common room, not the noise Mat expected.

Comar's sword lay within easy reach of his hand. But he did not move. He stared at Mat, though, as Mat kicked the sword away and went to one knee beside him. *Light! I think his back is broken!* "I told you you should have gone, Comar. Your luck is all used up."

"Fool," the big man breathed. "Do you . . . think I . . . was the only . . . one hunting them? They won't . . . live till. . . ." His eyes stared at Mat, and his mouth was open, but he said no more. Nor ever would again.

Mat met the glazing stare, trying to will more words out of the dead man. *Who else, burn you? Who? Where are they? My luck. Burn me, what happened to my luck?* He became aware of the innkeeper pulling frantically at his arm.

"You must go. You must. Before the Defenders come. I will show them the dice. I will tell them it was an outlander, but a tall man. With red-colored hair, and gray eyes. No one will suffer. A man I dreamed of last night. No one real. No one will contradict me. He took coin from everyone with his dice. But you must go. You must!" Everyone else in the room was studiously looking another way.

Mat let himself be hauled away from the dead man and pushed outside. Thom was already waiting in the rain. He seized Mat's arm and limped down the street hurriedly, pulling Mat stumbling behind him. Mat's hood hung down his back; the rain soaked his hair and poured down his face, down his neck, but he did not notice. The gleeman kept looking over his shoulder, searching the street beyond Mat.

"Are you asleep, boy? You did not look asleep back there. Come on, boy. The Defenders will arrest any outlander within two streets, no matter what description that innkeeper gives."

"It's the luck," Mat mumbled. "I've figured it out. The dice. My luck works best when things are . . . random. Like dice. Not much good for cards. No good at stones. Too much pattern. It has to be random. Even finding Comar. I'd stopped visiting every inn. I walked into that one by chance. Thom, if I am going to find Egwene and the others in time, I have to look without any pattern."

"What are you talking about? The man is dead. If he already killed them. . . . Well, you've avenged them. If he hasn't, you saved them. Now will you bloody walk faster? The Defenders won't be long coming, and they are not so gentle as the Queen's Guards."

Mat shook his arm free and picked up his pace unsteadily, dragging the quarterstaff. "He let it slip that he hadn't located them, yet. But he said he was not the only one. Thom, I believe him. I was looking him in the eye, and he was telling the truth. I still have to find them, Thom. And now I don't even know who is after them. I have to find them."

Stifling a huge yawn with his fist, Thom pulled Mat's hood up against the rain. "Not tonight, boy. I need sleep, and so do you."

Wet. My hair's dripping in my face. His head seemed fuzzy. With a need for sleep, he realized after a moment. And he realized how tired he was, if he had to think just to know it. "All right, Thom. But I am going to look again as soon as it's light." Thom nodded and coughed, and they made their way back to The White Crescent through the rain.

Dawn was not long in coming, but Mat rousted himself out of bed, and he and Thom set off trying to search every inn inside the walls of Tear. Mat let himself wander wherever the mood and the next turning took him, not looking for inns at all, and tossing a coin to decide whether to go in. For three days and nights he did this, and for three days and nights it rained without stopping, sometimes thundering, sometimes quiet, but always pouring down.

Thom's cough grew worse, so he had to stop playing the flute and telling stories, and he would not carry his harp out in that weather; he insisted on going along, however, and men still talked to a gleeman. Mat's luck with the dice seemed even better since he had begun this random wander, though he never stayed in one inn or tavern long enough to win more than a few coins. Neither of them heard anything useful. Rumors of war with Illian. Rumors of invading Mayene. Rumors of invasion from Andor, of the Sea Folk shutting off trade, of Artur Hawkwing's armies returning from the dead. Rumors the Dragon was coming. The men Mat gambled with were as gloomy about one rumor as the next; they seemed to him to hunt for the darkest rumors they could find and half believe them all. But he heard not a whisper that might lead him to Egwene and the others. Not one innkeeper had seen women matching their descriptions.

He began to have bad dreams, no doubt from all his worrying. Egwene and Nynaeve and Elayne, and some fellow with close-cropped white hair, wearing a coat with puffy, striped sleeves like Comar's, laughing and weaving a net around them. Only sometimes it was Moiraine he was weaving the net for, and sometimes he held a crystal sword instead, a sword that blazed like the sun as soon as he touched it. Sometimes it was Rand who held the sword. For some reason, he dreamed of Rand a good deal.

Mat was sure it was all because he was not getting enough sleep, not eating except when he happened to remember, but he would not stop. He had a wager to win, he told himself, and he meant to win this one if it killed him.

CHAPTER
50

The Hammer

The afternoon sun was hot as the ferry docked in Tear; puddles stood on the steaming stones of the dock, and the air seemed almost as damp to Perrin as Illian's had. The air smelled of pitch and wood and rope—he could see shipyards further south along the river—of spices and iron and barley, of perfumes and wines and a hundred different aromas he could not single out from the melange, most coming from the warehouses behind the docks. When the wind swirled momentarily out of the north, he caught the scents of fish, too, but those faded as the wind swung back. No smells of anything to hunt. His mind reached out to feel for wolves before he realized what he was doing and snapped his guards shut. He had done that too often of late. There had been no wolves, of course. Not in a city like this. He wished it did not feel so—alone.

As soon as the ramp at the end of the barge was lowered, he led Stepper up to the dock after Moiraine and Lan. The huge shape of the Stone of Tear lay off to their left, shadowed so that it looked like a mountain despite the great banner at its highest point. He did not want to look at the Stone, but it seemed impossible to look at the city without seeing it. *Is he here yet? Light, if he has already tried to get into* that, *he could be dead already.* And then it would all be for nothing.

"What are we meant to find here?" Zarine asked behind him. She had not stopped asking questions; she just did not ask them of the Aes Sedai or the Warder. "Illian showed us Gray Men and the Wild Hunt. What does Tear hold that—that someone wants to keep you from so badly?"

Perrin glanced around; none of the dockmen shuttling cargo about seemed to have heard. He was sure he would have smelled fear if they had. He bit back the sharp remark that hung on the end of his tongue. She had a quicker tongue, and a sharper.

"I wish you did not sound so eager," Loial rumbled. "You seem to think it will all be as easy as Illian, Faile."

"Easy?" Zarine muttered. "Easy! Loial, we were nearly killed twice in one night. Illian was enough for a Hunter's song in itself. What makes you call it easy?"

Perrin grimaced. He wished Loial had not decided to call Zarine by that name she had chosen; it was a constant reminder that Moiraine thought she was Min's falcon. And it did nothing to stop Perrin wondering if she was the beautiful woman Min had warned him against, too. *At least I've not run up against the hawk. Or a Tuatha'an with a sword! Now that would be the strangest of all, or I am a wool merchant!*

"Stop asking questions, Zarine," he said as he swung up into Stepper's saddle. "You will find out why we are here when Moiraine decides to tell you." He tried not to look at the Stone.

She turned those dark, tilted eyes on him. "I do not think you know why, blacksmith. I think that is why you will not tell me, because you cannot. Admit it, farmboy."

With a small sigh, he rode off the docks after Moiraine and Lan. Zarine did not dig at Loial in that cutting way when the Ogier refused to answer her questions. He thought she must be trying to browbeat him into using that name. He would not.

Moiraine had tied the oiled cloak behind her saddle, atop the innocuous-looking bundle that held the Dragon banner, and despite the heat had donned the blue linen cloak from Illian. Its deep, wide hood hid her face. Her Great Serpent ring was on a cord around her neck. Tear, she had said, did not forbid the presence of Aes Sedai, only channeling, but the Defenders of the Stone kept a close eye on any woman who wore the ring. She did not want to be watched on this visit to Tear.

Lan had stuffed his color-shifting cloak into his saddlebags two days earlier, when it had become apparent that whoever had sent the Darkhounds—*Sammael*, Perrin thought with a shiver, and tried not to think of the name at all—whoever had sent them had not sent any more pursuit. The Warder had made no concessions to the heat of Illian, and he made none to the lesser heat of Tear. His gray-green coat was buttoned up all the way.

Perrin wore his coat half undone, and the neck of his shirt untied. Tear might be a little cooler than Illian, but it was still as hot as summer in the Two Rivers, and as always after rain, the dampness of the air made the heat seem worse. His axe belt hung looped around the tall pommel of his saddle. It was handy there, if he needed it, and he felt better not wearing it.

He was surprised at the mud in the first streets they rode along. Only villages and smaller towns had dirt streets, that he had seen, and Tear was one of the great cities. But the people did not seem to mind, many going barefoot. A woman walking on little wooden platforms caught his attention for a time, and he wondered why they did not all wear them. Those baggy breeches on the men looked as if they might be cooler than the snug ones he wore, but he was sure he would feel a fool if he tried them. He made a picture in his head of himself wearing those breeches and one of those round straw hats, and chuckled at it.

"What do you find funny, Perrin?" Loial asked. His ears were drooping till their tufts were hidden in his hair, and he looked at the people in the street worriedly. "These folk look . . . defeated, Perrin. They did not look this way when I was here last. Even people who let their grove be cut down do not deserve to look like this."

As Perrin began to study faces instead of just looking at everything at once, he saw that Loial was right. Something had gone out of too many of those faces. Hope, maybe. Curiosity. They barely glanced at the party riding by, except to get out of the way of the horses. The Ogier, mounted on an animal as big as a draft horse, might as well have been Lan, or Perrin.

The streets changed, gaining wide stone paving, after they passed inside the gates of the high, gray city wall, past the hard, dark eyes of soldiers in breastplates over red coats with wide sleeves ending in narrow white cuffs, and rimmed, round helmets with a ridge over the top. Instead of the baggy breeches other men wore, theirs were tight, and tucked into knee-high boots. The soldiers frowned at Lan's sword and fingered their own, stared sharply at Perrin's axe and his bow, but in a way, despite their frowns and sharp looks, there was something beaten in their faces, too, as if nothing were really worth the effort any longer.

The buildings were larger and taller inside the walls, though most were made no differently from those outside. The roofs looked a bit odd to Perrin, especially those that came to points, but he had seen so many different kinds of roof since leaving home that he only wondered what kind of nails they used with their tiles. In some places, the people did not use nails on their roof tiles at all.

Palaces and great buildings stood among the smaller and more ordinary, seemingly placed haphazardly; a structure of towers and squarish, white domes, surrounded on all sides by wide streets, might have shops and inns and houses on the other sides of those streets. A huge hall fronted by squared columns of marble four paces on a side, with fifty steps to climb to reach bronze doors five spans high, had a bakery one side and a tailor on the other.

More men wore coats and breeches like the soldiers' here, though in brighter colors and without armor, and some even wore swords. None of them went barefoot, not even those in baggy breeches. The women's dresses were often longer, their necklines lower to bare shoulders and even bosom, the cloth as likely to be silk as wool. The Sea Folk traded a good deal of silk through Tear. As many sedan chairs and carriages drawn by teams of horses moved through the streets as ox-carts and wagons. Yet too many of the faces had that same look of having given up.

The inn Lan chose, the Star, had a weaver's shop on one side and a smithy on the other, with narrow alleyways between. The smithy was of undressed gray stone, the weaver's and the inn of wood, though the Star stood four stories tall and had small windows in its roof as well. The rattle of looms was hard-pressed to compete with the clang of the smith's hammer. They handed their horses over to stablemen, to be taken around back, and went inside the inn. There were fish smells from the kitchen, baking and perhaps stewing, and the scent of roast mutton. The men in the common room all wore the tight coats and loose breeches; Perrin did not think richer men—somehow he was sure the men in colorful coats with puffy sleeves and the bare-shouldered women in bright silk were all rich, or nobles—those folk would not put up with the noise. Perhaps that was why Lan had chosen it.

"How are we supposed to sleep with this racketing?" Zarine muttered.

"No questions?" he said with a smile. For a moment he thought she was going to stick out her tongue at him.

The innkeeper was a round-faced, balding man in a long, deep blue coat and those loose breeches, who bowed over hands clasped across his stout belly. His face had that look, a weary resignation. "The Light shine on you, mistresses, and welcome," he sighed. "The Light shine on you, masters, and welcome." He gave a small start at Perrin's yellow eyes, then passed wearily on to Loial. "The Light shine on you, friend Ogier, and welcome. It is a year or more since I have seen one of your kind in Tear. Some work or other at the Stone. They stayed in the Stone, of course, but I saw them in the street one day." He finished with another sigh, seemingly unable to summon any curiosity as to why another Ogier had come to Tear, or why any of them had come, for that matter.

The balding man, whose name was Jurah Haret, showed them to their rooms himself. Apparently Moiraine's silk dress and the way she kept her face hidden, taken with Lan's hard face and sword, made them a lady and her guard in his eyes, and so worthy of his personal attention. Perrin he obviously took as some kind of retainer, and Zarine he was plainly unsure of—to her visible disgust—and Loial was, after all, an Ogier. He called men to push beds together for Loial, and offered Moiraine a private room for her meals if she wished. She accepted graciously.

They kept together through it all, making a small procession through the upper halls until Haret bowed and sighed his way out of their presence, leaving them all where they had begun, outside Moiraine's room. The walls were white plaster, and Loial's head brushed the hall ceiling.

"Odious fellow," Zarine muttered, brushing furiously at the dust on her narrow skirts with both hands. "I believe he took me for your handmaid, Aes Sedai. I will not stand for that!"

"Watch your tongue," Lan said softly. "If you use that

name where folk can hear, you will regret it, girl." She
looked as if she were going to argue, but his icy blue eyes
stilled her tongue this time, if it did not cool her glare.

Moiraine ignored them. Staring off at nothing, she
worked her cloak in her hands almost as if wiping them.
Unaware what she was doing, in Perrin's opinion.

"How do we go about finding Rand?" he asked, but she
did not appear to hear him. "Moiraine?"

"Remain close to the inn," she said after a moment. "Tear
can be a dangerous city for those who do not know its ways.
The Pattern can be torn, here." That last was soft, as if to
herself. In a stronger voice she said, "Lan, let us see what
we can discover without attracting attention. The rest of
you, stay close to the inn!"

"'Stay close to the inn,'" Zarine mimicked as the Aes
Sedai and the Warder disappeared down the stairs. But she
said it quietly enough that they would not hear. "This Rand.
He is the one you called the. . . ." If she looked like a falcon
right then, it was a very uneasy falcon. "And we are in Tear,
where the Heart of the Stone holds. . . . And the Prophecies
say. . . . The Light burn me, *ta'veren*, is this a story I want
to be in?"

"It is not a story, Zarine." For a moment Perrin felt almost as hopeless as the innkeeper had sounded. "The
Wheel weaves us into the Pattern. You chose to tangle your
thread with ours; it's too late to untangle it, now."

"Light!" she growled. "Now you sound like *her*!"

He left her there with Loial and went to put his things
in his room—it had a low bed, comfortable but small, as
city people seemed to think befitted a servant, a washstand,
a stool, and a few pegs on the cracked plaster wall—and
when he came out, they were both gone. The ring of hammer on anvil called to him.

So much in Tear looked odd that it was a relief to walk
into the smithy. The ground floor was all one large room
with no back wall except for two long doors that stood open
on a yard for shoeing horses and oxen, complete with an ox
sling. Hammers stood in their stands, tongs of various kinds
and sizes hung on the exposed joists of the walls, buttresses
and hoof knives and other farrier's tools lay neatly arranged
on wooden benches with chisels and beak irons and swages
and all the implements of the blacksmith's craft. Bins held

lengths of iron and steel in various thicknesses. Five grinding wheels of different roughness stood about the hard dirt floor, six anvils, and three stone-sided forges with their bellows, though only one held glowing coals. Quenching barrels stood ready to hand.

The smith was plying his hammer on yellow-hot iron gripped in heavy tongs. He wore baggy breeches and had pale blue eyes, but the long leather vest over his bare chest and apron were not much different from those Perrin and Master Luhhan had worn back in Emond's Field, and his thick arms and shoulders spoke of years working metal. His dark hair had almost the same amount of gray that Perrin remembered in Master Luhhan's. More vests and aprons hung on the wall, as if the man had apprentices, but they were not in evidence now. The forge-fire smelled like home. The hot iron smelled like home.

The smith turned to thrust the piece he was working back into the coals, and Perrin stepped over to work the bellows for him. The man glanced at him, but said nothing. Perrin pulled the bellows handle up and down with slow, steady, even strokes, keeping the coals at the right heat. The smith went back to working the hot iron, on the rounded horn of the anvil, this time. Perrin thought he might be making a barrel scrape. The hammer rang with sharp, quick blows.

The man spoke without looking up from his work. "Apprentice?" was all he said.

"Yes," Perrin replied just as simply.

The smith worked on for a time. It *was* a barrel scrape, for cleaning the insides of wooden barrels. Now and again he eyed Perrin consideringly. Setting his hammer down, just for a moment, the smith picked up a short length of thick, square stock and pushed it into Perrin's hand, then picked up his hammer again and resumed work. "See what you can do with that," he said.

Without even thinking about it, Perrin stepped over to an anvil on the other side of the forge and tapped the stock against its edge. It made a nice ring. The steel had not been left long enough in the slowfurnace to pick up a great deal of carbon from the coal. He pushed it into the hot coals for almost its entire length, tasted the two water barrels to see which had been salted—the third was olive oil—then took off his coat and shirt and chose a leather vest that would fit his chest. Most of these Tairen fellows were not as large as he, but he found one that would do. Finding an apron was easier.

When he turned around, he saw the smith, still with his head down over his work, nodding and smiling to himself. But just because he knew his way around a smithy did not mean he had any skill at smithing. That was yet to be shown.

When he came back to the anvil with two hammers, a set of long-handled flat-tongs, and a sharp-topped hardy, the steel bar had heated to a dark red except for a small bit of what he had left out of the coals. He worked the bellows, watching the color of the metal lighten, until it reached a yellow just short of white. Then he pulled it out with the tongs, laid it on the anvil, and picked up the heavier of the two hammers. About ten pounds, he estimated, and with a longer handle than most people, who did not know metal working, thought was necessary. He held it near the end; hot metal gave off sparks, sometimes, and he had seen the scars on the hands of the smith from up at Roundhill, a careless fellow.

He did not want to make anything elaborate or fancy. Simple things seemed best at the moment. He began by rounding the edges of the bar, then hammered the middle out into a broad blade, almost as thick as the original at the butt, but a good hand and a half long. From time to time he returned the metal to the coals, to keep it at the pale yellow, and after a time he shifted to the lighter hammer, half the weight of the first. The piece beyond the blade, he thinned down, then bent it over the anvil horn in a curve down beside the blade. A wooden handle could be fixed onto that, eventually. Setting the sharp-chisel hardy in the anvil's hardy-hole, he laid the glowing metal atop it. One sharp blow of the hammer cut off the tool he had made. Or almost made. It would be a chamfer knife, for smoothing and leveling the tops of barrel staves after they were hopped together, among other things. When he was done. The other man's barrel scrape had made him think of it.

As soon as he had made the hot-cut, he tossed the glowing metal into the salted quenching barrel. Unsalted gave a harder quench, for the hardest metal, while the oil gave the softest, for good knives. And swords, he had heard, but he had never had any part in making anything like that.

When the metal had cooled enough, to a dull gray, he removed it from the water and took it to the grinding wheels. A little slow work with the footpedals ground a polish onto the blade. Carefully, he heated the blade portion again. This time the colors deepened, to straw, to bronze. When the bronze color began to run up the blade in waves, he set it aside to cool. The final edge could be sharpened then. Quenching again would destroy the tempering he had just done.

"A very neat bit of work," the smith said. "No wasted motion. You looking for work? My apprentices just walked away, all three of them, the worthless fools, and I've plenty you could do."

Perrin shook his head. "I do not know how long I will be in Tear. I'd like to work a little longer, if you do not mind. It has been a long time, and I miss it. Maybe I could do some of the work your apprentices would have done."

The smith snorted loudly. "You're a deal better than any of those louts, moping around and staring, muttering about their nightmares. As if everyone doesn't have nightmares, sometimes. Yes, you can work here, as long as you want. Light, I've orders for a dozen drawknives and three cooper's adzes, and a carpenter down the street needs a mortise hammer, and. . . . Too much to list it. Start with the drawknives, and we will see how far we get before night."

Perrin lost himself in the work, for a time forgetting everything but the heat of the metal, the ring of his hammer, and the smell of the forge, but there came a time when he looked up and found the smith—Dermid Ajala, he had said his name was—taking off his vest, and the shoeing yard dark. All the light came from the forge and a pair of lamps. And Zarine was sitting on an anvil by one of the cold forges, watching him.

"So you really are a blacksmith, blacksmith," she said.

"He is that, mistress," Ajala said. "Apprentice, he says, but the work he did today amounts to his master's piece as far as I am concerned. Fine stroking, and better than steady." Perrin shifted his feet at the compliments, and the smith grinned at him. Zarine stared at both of them with a lack of comprehension.

Perrin went to replace the vest and apron on their peg, but once he had them off, he was suddenly conscious of Zarine's eyes on his back. It was if she were touching him; for a moment, the herbal scent of her seemed overwhelming.

He quickly pulled his shirt over his head, stuffed it raggedly into his breeches, and jerked on his coat. When he turned around, Zarine wore one of those small, secretive smiles that had always made him nervous.

"Is this what you mean to do, then?" she asked. "Did you come all this way to be a blacksmith again?" Ajala paused in the act of pulling the yard doors closed and listened.

Perrin picked up the heavy hammer he had used, a ten-pound head with a handle as long as his forearm. It felt good in his hands. It felt right. The smith had glanced at his eyes once and never even blinked; it was the work that was important, the skill with metal, not the color of a man's eyes. "No," he said sadly. "One day, I hope. But not yet." He started to hang the hammer back on the wall.

"Take it." Ajala cleared his throat. "I do not usually give away good hammers, but. . . . The work you've done today is worth more than the price of that hammer by far, and maybe it will help you to that 'one day.' Man, if I have ever seen anyone made to hold a smith's hammer, it is you. So take it. Keep it."

Perrin closed his hand around the haft. It did feel right. "Thank you," he said. "I cannot say what this means to me."

"Just remember the 'one day,' man. Just you remember it."

As they left, Zarine looked up at him and said, "Do you have any idea how strange men are, blacksmith? No. I did not think you did." She darted ahead, leaving him holding the hammer in one hand and scratching his head with the other.

No one in the common room looked at him twice, a golden-eyed man carrying a smith's hammer. He went up to his room, remembering for once to light a tallow candle. His quiver and the axe hung from the same peg on the plaster wall. He hefted the axe in one hand, the hammer in the other. By weight of metal, the axe, with its half-moon blade and thick spike, was a good five or six pounds lighter than the hammer, but it felt ten times heavier. Replacing the axe in the loop on its belt, he set the hammer on the floor beneath the peg, handle against the wall. Axe haft and hammer haft almost touched, two pieces of wood equally thick. Two pieces of metal, near enough the same weight. For a long time he sat on the stool staring at them. He was still staring when Lan put his head into the room.

"Come, blacksmith. We have things to talk over."

"I *am* a blacksmith," Perrin said, and the Warder frowned at him.

"Don't go winter-crazy on me now, blacksmith. If you cannot carry your weight any longer, you may drag us all down the mountain."

"I'll carry my weight," Perrin growled. "I will do what has to be done. What do you want?"

"You, blacksmith. Don't you listen? Come on, farmboy."

That name that Zarine so often called him pulled him to his feet angrily, now, but Lan was already turning away. Perrin hurried into the hall and followed him toward the front of the inn, meaning to tell the Warder he had had enough of this "blacksmith" and "farmboy," his name was Perrin Aybara. The Warder ducked into the inn's only private dining room, overlooking the street.

Perrin followed him. "Now listen, *Warder*, I—"

"You listen, Perrin," Moiraine said. "Be quiet and listen." Her face was smooth, but her eyes looked as grim as her voice sounded.

Perrin had not realized anyone was in the room except for himself and the Warder, standing with one arm up on the mantel of the unlit fireplace. Moiraine sat at the table in the middle of the floor, a simple piece, of black oak. None of the other chairs with their high, carved backs were occupied. Zarine was leaning against the wall at the other end of the room from Lan, scowling, and Loial had chosen to sit on the floor since none of the chairs really fit him.

"I'm glad you decided to join us, farmboy," Zarine said sarcastically. "Moiraine would not say anything till you came. She just looks at us as if she is deciding which of us is going to die. I—"

"Be quiet," Moiraine told her sharply. "One of the Forsaken is in Tear. The High Lord Samon is Be'lal." Perrin shivered.

Loial squeezed his eyes shut and groaned. "I could have remained in the *stedding*. I would probably have been very happy, married, whoever my mother chose. She is a fine woman, my mother, and she would not give me to a bad wife." His ears seemed to have hidden themselves completely in his shaggy hair.

"You can go back to Stedding Shangtai," Moiraine said. "Leave now, if you wish. I will not stop you."

Loial opened one eye. "I can go?"

"If you wish," she said.

"Oh." He opened the other eye, and scratched his cheek with blunt fingers the size of sausages. "I suppose. . . . I suppose . . . if I have a choice . . . that I will stay with all of you. I have taken a great many notes, but not nearly enough to complete my book, and I would not like to leave Perrin, and Rand—"

Moiraine cut him off in a cold voice. "Good, Loial. I am glad that you are staying. I will be glad to use any knowledge you have. But until this is done, I have no time to listen to your complaints!"

"I suppose," Zarine said in an unsteady voice, "that there is no chance of me leaving?" She looked at Moiraine, and shivered. "I thought not. Blacksmith, if I live through this, I will make you pay."

Perrin stared at her. *Me! The fool woman thinks it my fault? Did I ask her to come?* He opened his mouth, saw the look in Moiraine's eyes, and closed it again quickly. After a moment he said, "Is he after Rand? To stop him, or kill him?"

"I think not," she said quietly. Her voice was like cold steel. "I fear he means to let Rand enter the Heart of the Stone and take *Callandor*, then take it away from him. I fear he means to kill the Dragon Reborn with the very weapon that is meant to herald him."

"Do we run again?" Zarine said. "Like Illian? I never thought to run, but I never thought to find the Forsaken when I took the Hunter's oath."

"This time," Moiraine said, "we do not run. We dare not run. Worlds and time rest on Rand, on the Dragon Reborn. This time, we fight."

Perrin took a chair uneasily. "Moiraine, you are saying a lot of things right out that you told us we must not even think about. You *do* have this room warded against listening, don't you?" When she shook her head, he gripped the edge of the table hard enough to make the dark oak creak.

"I do not speak of a Myrddraal, Perrin. No one knows the strength of the Forsaken, except that Ishamael and Lanfear were the strongest, but the weakest of them could sense any warding I might set from a mile or more away. And rip all of us to shreds in seconds. Possibly without stirring from where he stood."

"You're saying he can tie you in knots," Perrin muttered. "Light! What are we supposed to do? How can we do anything?"

"Even the Forsaken cannot stand up to balefire," she said. He wondered if that was what she had used on the Darkhounds; it still made him uneasy, what he had seen, and what she had said then. "I have learned things in the last year, Perrin. I am . . . more dangerous than when I came to Emond's Field. If I can come close enough to Be'lal, I can destroy him. But if he sees me first, he can destroy us all, long before I have a chance." She turned her attention to Loial. "What can you tell me of Be'lal?"

Perrin blinked in confusion. *Loial?*

"Why are you asking him?" Zarine burst out angrily. "First you tell the blacksmith you mean us to fight one of the Forsaken!—who can kill us all before we can even think!— and now you ask Loial about him?" Loial murmured urgently, that name she used—"Faile! Faile!"—but she did not even slow. "I thought Aes Sedai knew everything. Light, at least I am smart enough not to say I will fight someone unless I know everything I can of him! You. . . ." She trailed off under Moiraine's stare, muttering.

"Ogier," the Aes Sedai said coolly, "have long memories, girl. It has been well over a hundred generations since the Breaking for humans, but less than thirty for Ogier. We still learn things from their stories that we did not know. Now tell me, Loial. What do you know of Be'lal. And briefly, for once. I want your long memory, not your long wind."

Loial cleared his throat, a sound much like firewood tumbling down a chute. "Be'lal." His ears flickered out of his hair like hummingbird wings, then snapped down again. "I do not know what can be in the stories about him you do not already know. He is not much mentioned, except in the razing of the Hall of the Servants just before Lews Therin Kinslayer and the Hundred Companions sealed him up with the Dark One. Jalanda son of Aried son of Coiam wrote that he was called the Envious, that he forsook the Light because he envied Lews Therin, and that he envied Ishamael and Lanfear, too. In *A Study of the War of the*

Shadow, Moilin daughter of Hamada daughter of Juendan called Be'lal the Netweaver, but I do not know why. She mentioned him playing a game of stones with Lews Therin and winning, and that he always boasted of it." He glanced at Moiraine and rumbled, "I am trying to be brief. I do not know anything important about him. Several writers say Be'lal and Sammael were both leaders in the fight against the Dark One before they forsook the Light, and both were masters of the sword. That is truly all I know. He may be mentioned in other books, other stories, but I have not read them. Be'lal is just not spoken of very often. I am sorry I could not tell you anything useful."

"Perhaps you have," Moiraine told him. "I did not know of the name, the Netweaver. Or that he envied the Dragon as well as his companions in the Shadow. That strengthens my belief that he wants *Callandor*. That must be the reason he has chosen to make himself a High Lord of Tear. And the Netweaver—a name for a schemer, a patient and cunning planner. You have done well, Loial." For a moment the Ogier's wide mouth curved up in a pleased smile, but then it curved down again.

"I will not pretend I am not afraid," Zarine said suddenly. "Only a fool would not be afraid of the Forsaken. But I swore I would be one of you, and I will. That is all that I wanted to say."

Perrin shook his head. *She* must *be crazy. I could wish I were not one of this party. I could wish I were back home working Master Luhhan's forge.* Aloud, he said, "If he is inside the Stone, if he is waiting there for Rand, we must go inside to reach him. How do we do that? Everyone keeps saying no one enters the Stone without the permission of the High Lords, and looking at it, I don't see any way but through the gates."

"You do not go in," Lan said. "Moiraine and I will be the only ones to enter. The more who go, the harder it will be. Whatever way in I find, I cannot believe it will be easy even for only two."

"Gaidin," Moiraine began in a firm voice, but the Warder cut her off with one just as firm.

"We go together, Moiraine. I will not stand aside this time." After a moment she nodded. Perrin thought he saw Lan relax. "The rest of you had better get some sleep," the

Warder went on. "I have to be out studying the Stone." He paused. "There is a thing that your news drove out of my head, Moiraine. A small thing, and I cannot see what it might mean. There are Aiel in Tear."

"Aiel!" Loial exclaimed. "Impossible! The entire city would be in a panic if one Aiel came through the gates."

"I did not say they were walking the streets, Ogier. The rooftops and chimneys of the city make as good hiding as the Waste. I saw no less than three, though apparently no one else in Tear has seen any of them. And if I saw three, you can be sure there are many times that I did not see."

"It means nothing to me," Moiraine said slowly. "Perrin, why are you frowning in that way?"

He had not known that he was frowning. "I was thinking about that Aiel in Remen. He said that when the Stone falls, the Aiel will leave the Three-fold Land. That's the Waste, isn't it? He said it was a prophecy."

"I have read every word of the Prophecies of the Dragon," Moiraine said softly, "in every translation, and there is no mention of the Aiel. We stagger blindly while Be'lal weaves his nets, and the Wheel weaves the Pattern around us. But are the Aiel the Wheel's weaving, or Be'lal's? Lan, you must find me the way into the Stone quickly. Us. Find us a way in quickly."

"As you command, Aes Sedai," he said, but his tone was more warm than formal. He vanished through the door. Moiraine frowned at the table, eyes clouded in thought.

Zarine came over to look down at Perrin, her head tilted to one side. "And what are you going to do, blacksmith? It seems they mean us to wait and watch while they go adventuring. Not that I will complain."

He doubted that last. "First," he told her, "I am going to have something to eat. And then I am going to think about a hammer." *And try to puzzle out how I feel about you. Falcon.*

CHAPTER
51

Bait for the Net

From the corner of her eye, Nynaeve thought she glimpsed a tall man with reddish hair, in a swirling brown cloak, well down the sunlit street, but as she turned to peer from under the wide brim of the blue straw hat Ailhuin had given her, an ox-drawn wagon was already lumbering between them. When it lurched on, the man was nowhere to be seen. She was almost certain that had been a wooden flute case on his back, and his clothes were certainly not Tairen. *It couldn't be Rand. Just because I keep dreaming about him does not mean he is going to come all the way from Almoth Plain.*

One of the barefoot men hurrying past, with the sickle-shaped tails of a dozen large fish sticking up from the basket on his back, suddenly tripped, catapulting silver-scaled fish over his head as he fell. He landed on hands and knees in the mud, staring at the fish that had come out of his basket. Every one of the long, sleek shapes stood upright, stuck nose down in the mud, forming a neat circle. Even a few passersby gaped at that. Slowly the man got to his feet, apparently unaware of the mud on him. Unslinging his basket, he began gathering the fish back into it, shaking his head and muttering to himself.

Nynaeve blinked, but her business was with this cow-faced brigand, facing her in the doorway of his shop with bloody cuts of meat hanging from hooks behind him. She gave her braid a tug and fixed the fellow with her eye.

"Very well," she said sharply, "I will take it, but if this is what you charge for so poor a cut, you'll not have more business from me."

He shrugged placidly as he took her coins, then wrapped the fatty mutton roast in a cloth she produced from the basket on her arm. She glared at him as she put the wrapped meat into the basket, but that did not affect him.

She whirled to stalk away—and nearly fell. She was still not used to these clogs; they kept sticking in the mud, and she could not see how the folk who wore them managed. She hoped this sunshine dried the ground soon, but she had a feeling that the mud was more or less permanent in the Maule.

Stepping gingerly, she started back toward Ailhuin's house, muttering under her breath. The prices were outrageous for everything, the quality inevitably poor, and almost no one seemed to care, not the people buying or those selling. It was a relief to pass a woman shouting at a shopkeeper, waving a bruised reddish-yellow fruit—Nynaeve did not know what; they had a good many fruits and vegetables she had never heard of, here—in each hand and calling for everyone to see what refuse the man sold, but the shopkeeper only stared at her wearily, not even bothering to argue back.

There was some excuse for the prices, she knew—Elayne had explained all about the grain being eaten by rats in the granaries because no one in Cairhien could buy, and how big the Cairhienin grain trade had become since the Aiel War—but nothing excused the way everyone seemed ready to lie down and die. She had seen hail ruin food crops in the Two Rivers, and grasshoppers eat them and blacktongue kill the sheep and redspot wither the tabac so there was nothing to sell when the merchants came down from Baerlon. She could remember two years in a row when there had been little to eat except turnip soup and old barley, and hunters had been lucky to bring home a scrawny rabbit, but Two Rivers folk picked themselves up when they were knocked down and went back to work. These people had had only one bad year, and their fisheries and their other trade seemed to be flourishing. She had no patience with them. The trouble was, she knew she should have a little patience. They were odd people with odd ways, and things she took for cringing, they seemed to see as a matter of course, even Ailhuin and Sandar. She should be able to summon up just a little patience.

If for them, why not for Egwene? She put that aside. The child behaved wretchedly, snapping at the most obvious suggestions, objecting to the most sensible things. Even when it was plain what they should do, Egwene wanted to be convinced. Nynaeve was not used to having to convince people, especially not people she had changed swaddling clothes for. The fact that she was only a matter of seven years older than Egwene was of no account.

It is all those bad dreams, she told herself. *I cannot understand what they mean, and now Elayne and I are having them, too, and I do not know what that means either, and Sandar won't say anything except that he is still looking, and I am so frustrated I . . . I could just spit!* She jerked her braid so hard it hurt. At least she had been able to convince Egwene not to use the *ter'angreal* again, to put the thing back in her pouch instead of wearing it next to her skin always. If the Black Ajah was in *Tel'aran'rhiod*. . . . She did not want to think about that possibility. *We* will *find them!*

"I will bring them down," she muttered. "Trying to sell me like a sheep! Hunting me like an animal! I am the hunter this time, not the rabbit! That Moiraine! If she had never come to Emond's Field, I could have taught Egwene enough. And Rand. . . . I could have . . . I could have done something." That she knew neither was true did not help; it made it worse. She hated Moiraine almost as much as she hated Liandrin and the Black Ajah, maybe as much as she hated the Seanchan.

She rounded a corner, and Juilin Sandar had to leap out of her way to keep from being trampled. Even used to them as he was, he nearly tripped over his own clogs, only his staff saving him from falling on his face in the mud. That pale, ridged wood was called bamboo, she had learned, and it was stronger than it looked.

"Mistress—uh—Mistress Maryim," Sandar said, regaining his balance. "I was . . . looking for you." He flashed her a nervous smile. "Are you angry? Why are you frowning at me that way?"

She smoothed her forehead. "I was not frowning at you, Master Sandar. The butcher. . . . It does not matter. Why are you looking for me?" Her breath caught. "Have you found them?"

He looked around as if he suspected the passersby of trying to listen. "Yes. Yes, you must come back with me. The others are waiting. The others. And Mother Guenna."

"Why are you so nervous? You did not let them discover your interest?" she said sharply. "What has frightened you?"

"No! No, mistress. I—I did not reveal myself." His eyes darted again, and he stepped closer, his voice dropping to a breathy, urgent whisper. "These women you seek, they are in the Stone! Guests of a High Lord! The High Lord Samon! Why did you call them thieves? The High Lord Samon!" he almost squeaked. There was sweat on his face.

Inside the Stone! With a High Lord! Light, how do we reach them now? She suppressed her impatience with an effort. "Be easy," she said soothingly. "Be at ease, Master Sandar. We can explain everything to your satisfaction." *I hope we can. Light, if he goes running to the Stone to tell this High Lord we are searching for them. . . .* "Come with me to Mother Guenna's house. Joslyn, Caryla, and I will explain it all to you. Truly. Come."

He gave a short, uneasy nod, and walked alongside her, keeping his pace to what she could manage with the clogs. He looked as if he wanted to run.

At the Wise Woman's house, she hurried around to the back. No one ever used the front door, that she had seen, not even Mother Guenna herself. The horses were tied to a bamboo hitching rail, now—well away from Ailhuin's new figs as well as her vegetables—with their saddles and bridles stored inside. For once she did not stop to pat Gaidin's nose and tell him he was a good boy, and more sensible than his namesake. Sandar halted to scrape mud from his clogs with the butt of his staff, but she hurried inside.

Ailhuin Guenna was sitting in one of her high-backed chairs pulled out into the room, her arms at her sides. The gray-haired woman's eyes were bulging with anger and fear, and she struggled furiously without moving a muscle. Nynaeve did not need to sense the subtle weaving of Air to know what had happened. *Light, they've found us! Burn you, Sandar!*

Rage flooded her, washed away the walls inside that usually kept her from the Power, and as the basket fell from her hands, she was a white blossom on a blackthorn bush, opening to embrace *saidar*, opening. . . . It was as if she had run into another wall, a wall of clear glass; she could feel the True Source, but the wall stopped everything except the ache to be filled with the One Power.

The basket hit the floor, and as it bounced, the door behind her opened and Liandrin stepped in, followed by a black-haired woman with a white streak above her left ear. They wore long, colorful silk dresses cut to bare their shoulders, and the glow of *saidar* surrounded them.

Liandrin smoothed her red dress and smiled with that pouting rosebud mouth. Her doll's face was filled with amusement. "You see, do you not, wilder," she began, "you have no—"

Nynaeve hit her in the mouth as hard as she could. *Light, I have to get away.* She backhanded Rianna so hard the black-haired woman fell on her silk-covered rump with a grunt. *They must have the others, but if I can make it out the door, if I can get far enough away they can't shield me, I can do something.* She pushed Liandrin hard, shoving her away from the door. *Just let me escape their shielding, and I'll. . . .*

Blows hit her from every side, like fists and sticks, pummeling her. Neither Liandrin, blood trickling from a corner of her now-grim mouth, nor Rianna, her hair as disarrayed as her green dress, lifted a hand. Nynaeve could feel the flows of Air weaving about her as well as she could feel the blows themselves. She still struggled to reach the door, but she realized that she was on her knees, now, and the unseen blows would not stop, invisible sticks and fists striking at her back and her stomach, her head and her hips, her shoulders, her breasts, her legs, her head. Groaning, she fell onto her side and curled into a ball, trying to protect herself. *Oh, Light, I tried. Egwene! Elayne! I tried! I will not cry out! Burn you, you can beat me to death, but I won't cry!*

The blows stopped, but Nynaeve could not stop quivering. She felt bruised and battered from crown to toe.

Liandrin crouched beside her, arms around her knees, silk rustling against silk. She had wiped the blood away from her mouth. Her dark eyes were hard, and there was no amusement on her face now. "Perhaps you are too stupid to know when you are defeated, wilder. You fought almost as wildly as that other foolish girl, that Egwene. She almost went mad. You must all learn to submit. You *will* learn to submit."

Nynaeve shivered and reached for *saidar* again. It was not that she had any real hope, but she had to do something. Forcing through her pain, she reached out . . . and struck that invisible shield. Liandrin did have amusement back in her eyes, now, the grim mirth of a nasty child who pulls the wings off flies.

"We have no use for this one, at least," Rianna said, standing beside Ailhuin. "I will stop her heart." Ailhuin's eyes nearly came out of her head.

"No!" Liandrin's short, honey-colored braids swung as her head snapped around. "Always you kill too quickly, and only the Great Lord can make use of the dead." She smiled at the woman held to the chair by invisible bonds. "You saw the soldiers who came with us, old woman. You know who waits for us in the Stone. The High Lord Samon, he will not be pleased if you speak of what happened inside your house today. If you hold your tongue, you will live, perhaps to serve him again one day. If you speak, you will serve only the Great Lord of the Dark, from beyond the grave. Which do you choose?"

Suddenly Ailhuin could move her head. She shook her gray curls, working her mouth. "I. . . . I will hold my tongue," she said dejectedly, then gave Nynaeve an embarrassed, shamed look. "If I speak, what good will it do? A High Lord could have my head by raising an eyebrow. What good can I do you, girl? What good?"

"It is all right," Nynaeve said wearily. *Who could she tell? All she could do is die.* "I know you would help if you could." Rianna threw back her head and laughed. Ailhuin slumped, released completely, but she only sat there, staring at her hands in her lap.

Between them, Liandrin and Rianna pulled Nynaeve to her feet and pushed her toward the front of the house. "You give us any trouble," the black-haired woman said in a hard voice, "and I will make you peel off your own skin and dance in your bones."

Nynaeve almost laughed. *What trouble could I give?* She was shielded from the True Source. Her bruises ached so much she could barely stand. Anything she might do, they could handle like a child's tantrum. *But my bruises will heal, burn you, and you'll make a slip yet! And when you do. . . .*

There were others in the front room of the house. Two big soldiers in rimmed, round helmets and shiny breastplates over those puffy-sleeved red coats. The two men had sweat on their faces, and their dark eyes rolled as if they were as afraid as she. Amico Nagoyin was there, slender and pretty with her long neck and pale skin, looking as innocent as a girl gathering flowers. Joiya Byir had a friendly face despite that smooth-cheeked calm of a woman who had worked long with the Power, almost a grandmother's face in its welcoming appearance, though her age had put no touch of gray in her dark hair, any more than it had wrinkled her skin. Her gray eyes looked more like those of the step-mother in the stories, the one who murdered the children of her husband's first wife. Both women shone with the Power.

Elayne stood between the two Black sisters, with a bruised eye and a swollen cheek and a split lip, one sleeve of her dress torn halfway off. "I am sorry, Nynaeve," she said thickly, as if her jaw hurt. "We never saw them until it was too late."

Egwene lay in a crumpled heap on the floor, her face swollen with bruises, almost unrecognizable. As Nynaeve and her escort came in, one of the big soldiers hoisted Egwene over his shoulder. She dangled there as limply as a half-empty barley sack.

"What did you do to her?" Nynaeve demanded. "Burn you, what—!" Something unseen struck her across the mouth hard enough to make her eyes go blank for a moment.

"Now, now," Joiya Byir said with a smile that her eyes belied. "I will not stand for demands, or bad language." She sounded like a grandmother, too. "You speak when you are spoken to."

"I told you the girl, she would not stop fighting, yes?" Liandrin said. "Let it be a lesson to you. If you try to cause any trouble, you will be treated no more gently."

Nynaeve ached to do something for Egwene, but she let herself be pushed out into the street. She made them push her; it was a small way of fighting back, refusing to cooperate, but it was all she had at the moment.

There were few people in the muddy street, as if everyone

had decided it was much better to be somewhere else, and those few scurried by on the other side without a glance at the shiny, black-lacquered coach standing behind a team of six matched whites with tall white plumes on their bridles. A coachman dressed like the soldiers, but without armor or sword, sat on the seat, and another opened the door as they appeared from the house. Before he did, Nynaeve saw the sigil painted there. A silver-gauntleted fist clutching jagged lightning bolts.

She supposed it was High Lord Samon's sign—*A Darkfriend, he must be, if he deals with the Black Ajah. The Light burn him!*—but she was more interested in the man who dropped to his knees in the mud at their appearance. "Burn you, Sandar, why—?" She jumped as something that felt like a stick of wood struck her across the shoulders.

Joiya Byir smiled chidingly and waggled a finger. "You will be respectful, child. Or you might lose that tongue."

Liandrin laughed. Tangling a hand in Sandar's black hair, she wrenched his head back. He stared up at her with the eyes of a faithful hound—or of a cur expecting a kick. "Do not be too hard on this man." She even made "man" sound like "dog." "He had to be . . . persuaded . . . to serve. But I am very good at persuading, no?" She laughed again.

Sandar turned a confused stare on Nynaeve. "I had to do it, Mistress Maryim. I . . . had to." Liandrin twisted his hair, and his eyes went back to her, the anxious hound's once more.

Light! Nynaeve thought. *What did they do to him? What are they going to do to us?*

She and Elayne were bundled roughly into the coach, with Egwene slumped between them, her head lolling, and Liandrin and Rianna climbed in and took the seat facing forward. The glow of *saidar* still surrounded them. Where the others went, Nynaeve did not much care at that moment. She wanted to reach Egwene, to touch her, to comfort her hurts, but she could not move a muscle below her neck except to writhe. Flows of Air bound the three of them like layers of tightly wrapped blankets. The coach lurched into motion, swaying hard in the mud despite its leather springs.

"If you have hurt her. . . ." *Light, I can see they've hurt her. Why don't I say what I mean?* But it was almost as hard to force the words out as it would have been to lift a hand.

"If you have killed her, I won't rest till you are all hunted down like wild dogs."

Rianna glared, but Liandrin only sniffed. "Do not be a complete fool, wilder. You are wanted alive. Dead bait will catch nothing."

Bait? For what? For who? "You are the fool, Liandrin! Do you think we are here alone? Only three of us, and not even full Aes Sedai? We are bait, Liandrin. And you have walked into the trap like a fat grouse."

"Do not tell her that!" Elayne said sharply, and Nynaeve blinked before she realized Elayne was helping her fabrication. "If you let your anger get the best of you, you will tell them what they must not hear. They must take us inside the Stone. They must—"

"Be quiet!" Nynaeve snapped. "You are letting *your* tongue run away with you!" Elayne managed to look abashed behind her bruises. *Let them chew on that*, Nynaeve thought.

But Liandrin only smiled. "Once your time as bait is done, you will tell us everything. You will want to. They say you will be very strong one day, but I will make sure you will always obey me, even before the Great Master Be'lal works his plans for you. He is sending for Myrddraal. Thirteen of them." Those rosebud lips laughed the final words.

Nynaeve felt her stomach twist. One of the Forsaken! Her brain numbed with shock. *The Dark One and all the Forsaken are bound in Shayol Ghul, bound by the Creator in the moment of creation.* But the catechism did not help; she knew too well how much of it was false. Then the rest of it came home to her. Thirteen Myrddraal. And thirteen sisters of the Black Ajah. She heard Elayne screaming before she realized she was screaming herself, jerking uselessly in those invisible bonds of Air. It was impossible to say which was louder, their despairing screams, or the laughter from Liandrin and Rianna.

CHAPTER
52

In Search of a Remedy

Slumped on the stool in the gleeman's room, Mat grimaced as Thom coughed again. *How are we going to keep looking if he's so bloody sick he can't walk?* He was ashamed as soon as he thought it. Thom had been as assiduous in searching as he had, pushing himself day and night, when he had to know he was coming down sick. Mat had been so absorbed in his hunt that he had paid too little attention to Thom's coughing. The change from constant rain to steamy heat had not helped it.

"Come on, Thom," he said. "Lopar says there's a Wise Woman not far. That is what they call a Wisdom here—a Wise Woman. Wouldn't Nynaeve like that!"

"I do not need . . . any foul-tasting . . . concoctions . . . poured down my throat, boy." Thom stuffed a fist through his mustaches in a vain attempt to stop his hacking. "You go ahead looking. Just give me . . . a few hours : . . on my bed . . . and I'll join you." The wracking wheezes doubled him over till his head was almost on his knees.

"So I am supposed to do all the work while you take your ease?" Mat said lightly. "How can I find anything without you? You learn most of what we hear." That was not exactly true; men talked as freely over dice as they did while buying a gleeman a cup of wine. More freely than they did with a gleeman hacking so hard they feared contagion. But he was beginning to think that Thom's cough was not going to go away by itself. *If the old goat dies on me, who will I play stones with?* he told himself roughly. "Anyway, your bloody coughing keeps me awake even in the next room."

Ignoring the white-haired man's protests, he pulled Thom

to his feet. He was shocked at how much of the gleeman's weight he had to support. Despite the damp heat, Thom insisted on his patch-covered cloak. Mat had his own coat unbuttoned completely and all three ties of his shirt undone, but he let the old goat have his way. No one in the common room even looked up as he half carried Thom out into the muggy afternoon.

The innkeeper had given simple directions, but when they reached the gate, and faced the mud of the Maule, Mat almost turned back to ask after another Wise Woman. There had to be more than one in a city this size. Thom's wheezing decided him. With a grimace Mat stepped off into the mud, half carrying the gleeman.

He had thought from the directions that they must have passed the Wise Woman's house on their way up from the dock that first night, and when he saw the long, narrow house with bunches of herbs hanging in the windows, right next to a potter's shop, he remembered it. Lopar had said something about going to the back door, but he had had enough of mud.

And the stink of fish, he thought, frowning at the barefoot men squelching by with their baskets on their backs. There were tracks of horses in the street, too, just beginning to be obliterated by feet and ox-carts. Horses pulling a wagon, or maybe a carriage. He had seen nothing but oxen drawing carts or wagons either one in Tear—the nobles and the merchants were proud of their fine stock, and never let one be put to anything like work—but he had not seen any carriages since leaving the walled city, either.

Dismissing horses and wheel tracks from his mind, he took Thom to the front door and knocked. After a time he knocked again. Then again.

He was on the point of giving up and returning to The White Crescent despite Thom coughing on his shoulder when he heard shuffling footsteps inside.

The door opened barely more than a crack, and a stout, gray-haired woman peered out. "What do you want?" she asked in a tired voice.

Mat put on his best grin. *Light, but I am getting sick myself at all these people who sound like there's no bloody hope.* "Mother Guenna? My name is Mat Cauthon. Cavan

Lopar told me you might do something for my friend's cough. I can pay well."

She studied them a moment, seemed to listen to Thom's wheezes, then sighed. "I suppose I can still do that, at least. You might as well come in." She swung the door open and was already plodding toward the back of the house before Mat moved.

Her accent sounded so much like the Amyrlin's that he shivered, but he followed, all but carrying Thom.

"I don't . . . need this," the gleeman wheezed. "Bloody mixtures . . . always taste like . . . dung!"

"Shut up, Thom."

Leading them all the way to the kitchen, the stout woman rummaged in one of the cupboards, taking out small stone pots and packets of herbs while muttering to herself.

Mat sat Thom down in one of the high-backed chairs, and glanced through the nearest window. There were three good horses tied out back; he was surprised the Wise Woman had more than one, or any for that matter. He had not seen anyone in Tear riding except nobles and the wealthy, and these animals looked as if they had cost more than a little silver. *Horses again. I don't care about bloody horses now!*

Mother Guenna brewed some sort of strong tea with a rank smell and forced it down Thom's throat, holding his nose when he tried to complain. Mat decided she had less fat on her than he had thought, from the way she held the gleeman's head steady in the crook of one arm while she poured the black liquid into him no matter how hard he tried to stop her.

When she took the cup away, Thom coughed and scrubbed at his mouth with equal vigor. "Gaaah! Woman . . . I don't know . . . whether you . . . mean to drown me . . . or kill me . . . with the taste! You ought . . . to be a bloody . . . blacksmith!"

"You will take the same twice a day till that hacking is gone," she said firmly. "And I have a salve that you'll rub on your chest every night." Some of the weariness left her voice as she confronted the gleeman, fists on her broad hips. "That salve stinks as bad as this tea tastes, but you will rub it on—thoroughly!—or I'll drag you upstairs like a scrawny carp in a net and tie you to a bed with that cloak of yours! I never had a gleeman come to me before, and I'll not let the first one that does cough himself to death."

Thom glowered and blew out his mustaches with a cough, but he seemed to take her threat seriously. At least, he did not say anything, but he looked as if he meant to throw her tea and her salve right back at her.

The more this Mother Guenna talked, the more she sounded like the Amyrlin to Mat. From the sour look on Thom's face, and the steady stare on hers, he decided he had better smooth matters over a little before the gleeman refused to take her medicines. And she decided to make him. "I knew a woman once who talked like you," he said. "All fish and nets and things. Sounded like you, too. The same accent, I mean. I suppose she's Tairen."

"Perhaps." The gray-haired woman suddenly sounded tired again, and she kept staring at the floor. "I knew some girls with the sound of your speech on their tongues, too. Two of them had it, anyway." She sighed heavily.

Mat felt his scalp prickle. *My luck can't be this good.* But he would not bet a copper on two other women with Two Rivers accents just happening to be in Tear. "Three girls? Young women? Named Egwene, and Nynaeve, and Elayne? That one has hair like the sun, and blue eyes."

She frowned at him. "Those were not the names they gave," she said slowly, "yet I suspected they did not give me their true names. But they had their reasons, I thought. One of them was a pretty girl with bright blue eyes and red-gold hair to her shoulders." She described Nynaeve with her braid to her waist and Egwene with her big, dark eyes and ready smile, too. Three pretty women as different from one another as they could be. "I see they are the ones you know," she finished. "I am sorry, boy."

"Why are you sorry? I have been trying to find them for days!" *Light, I walked right past this place the first night! Right past them! I wanted random. What could be more random than where a ship docks on a rainy night, and where you happen to look in a bloody lightning flash? Burn me! Burn me!* "Tell me where they are, Mother Guenna."

The gray-haired woman stared wearily at the stove where her spouted kettle was steaming. Her mouth worked, but she said nothing.

"Where are they?" Mat demanded. "It is important! They are in danger if I don't find them."

"You do not understand," she said softly. "You are an outlander. The High Lords. . . ."

"I do not care about any—" Mat blinked, and looked at Thom. The gleeman seemed to be frowning, but he was coughing so hard, Mat could not be sure. "What do the High Lords have to do with my friends?"

"You just do not—"

"Don't tell me I do not understand! I will pay for the information!"

Mother Guenna glared at him. "I do not take money for . . . !" She grimaced fiercely. "You ask me to tell you things I have been told not to speak of. Do you know what will happen to me if I do and you breathe my name? I will lose my tongue, to begin. Then I will lose other parts before the High Lords have what is left of me hung up to scream its last hours as a reminder to others to obey. And it will do those young women no good, not my telling or my dying!"

"I promise I will never mention your name to anyone. I swear it." *And I'll keep that oath, old woman, if you only tell me where they bloody are!* "Please? They are in danger."

She studied him for a long time; before she was done he had the feeling she knew every detail of him. "On that oath, I will tell you. I . . . liked them. But you can do nothing. You are too late, Matrim Cauthon. Too late by nearly three hours. They have been taken to the Stone. The High Lord Samon sent for them." She shook her head in worried puzzlement. "He sent . . . women who . . . could channel. I hold nothing against Aes Sedai myself, but that is against the law. The law the High Lords made. If they break every other law, they would not break that one. Why would a High Lord send Aes Sedai on his errands? Why would he want those girls at all?"

Mat almost burst out laughing. "Aes Sedai? Mother Guenna, you had my heart in my throat, and maybe my liver, too. If Aes Sedai came for them, there is nothing to worry about. All three of them are going to be Aes Sedai themselves. Not that I like it much, but that's what they—" His grin faded at the heavy way she shook her head.

"Boy, those girls fought like lionfish in a net. Whether they mean to be Aes Sedai or not, those who took them treated them like bilge pumpings. Friends do not give bruises like that."

He felt his face twisting. *Aes Sedai hurt them? What in the Light? The bloody Stone. It makes the Palace in Caemlyn look like walking into a barnyard! Burn me! I stood right out there in the rain and stared at this house! Burn me for a bloody Light-blinded fool!*

"If you break your hand," Mother Guenna said, "I will splint and poultice it, but if you damage my wall, I will strip your hide like a redfish!"

He blinked, then looked at his fist, at scraped knuckles. He did not even remember punching the wall.

The broad woman took his hand in a strong grip, but the fingers she used to probe were surprisingly gentle. "Nothing broken," she grunted after a while. Her eyes were just as gentle as she studied his face. "It seems you care for them. One of them, at least, I suppose it is. I am sorry, Mat Cauthon."

"Don't be," he told her. "At least I know where they are, now. All I have to do is get them out." He fished out his last two Andoran gold crowns and pressed them into her hand. "For Thom's medicines, and for letting me know about the girls." On impulse, he gave her a quick kiss on the cheek and a grin. "And that's for me."

Startled, she touched her cheek, not seeming to know whether to look at the coins or at him. "Get them out, you say. Just like that. Out of the Stone." Abruptly she stabbed him in the ribs with a finger as hard as a tree stub. "You remind me of my husband, Mat Cauthon. He was a headstrong fool who would sail into the teeth of a gale and laugh, too. I could almost think you'll manage it." Suddenly she saw his muddy boots, apparently for the first time. "It took me six months to teach him not to track mud into my house. If you do get those girls out, whichever of them you have your eye on will have a hard time training you to make you fit to be let inside."

"You are the only woman who could do that," he said with a grin that broadened at her glare. *Get them out. That's all I have to do. Bring them right out of the Stone of bloody Tear.* Thom coughed again. *He isn't going into the Stone like that. Only, how do I stop him?* "Mother Guenna, can I leave my friend here? I think he is too sick to go back to the inn."

"What?" Thom barked. He tried to push himself out of the chair, coughing so he could hardly speak. "I am no . . . such thing, boy! You think . . . walking into the Stone . . . will be like . . . walking into your mother's kitchen? You think you . . . would make it . . . as far as the gates . . . without me?" He hung on the back of the chair, his wheezing and hacking keeping him from rising more than halfway to his feet.

Mother Guenna put a hand on his shoulder and pushed him back down as easily as a child. The gleeman gave her a startled look. "I will take care of him, Mat Cauthon," she said.

"No!" Thom shouted. "You cannot . . . do this to me! You can't . . . leave me . . . with this old. . . ." Only her hand on his shoulder kept him from doubling over.

Mat grinned at the white-haired man. "I have enjoyed knowing you, Thom."

As he hurried out into the street, he found himself wondering why he had said that. *He isn't going to bloody die. That woman will keep him alive if she has to drag him kicking and screaming out of his grave by his mustaches. Yes, but who is going to keep me alive?*

Ahead of him, the Stone of Tear loomed over the city, impregnable, a fortress besieged a hundred times, a stone on which a hundred armies had broken their teeth. And he had to get inside, somehow. And bring out three women. Somehow.

With a laugh that made even the sullen folk in the street look at him, he headed back for The White Crescent, uncaring of mud or the damp heat. He could feel the dice tumbling inside his head.

CHAPTER

53

A Flow of the Spirit

Perrin shrugged into his coat as he walked back toward the Star through the evening shadows. A good tiredness soaked through his arms and shoulders; along with more common work, Master Ajala had had him make a large piece of ornamental work, all elaborate curves and scrolls, to go on some country lord's new gate. He had enjoyed making something so pretty.

"I thought his eyes would come out of his face, blacksmith, when you said you would not make that thing if it was for a High Lord."

He glanced sideways at Zarine, walking beside him, the shadows masking her face. Even for his eyes, the shadows were there, just fainter than they would have been for another's. They emphasized her high cheekbones, softened the strong curve of her nose. He just could not make up his mind about her. Even if Moiraine and Lan still insisted they stay close to the inn, he wished she could find something else to do besides watch him work. For some reason, he had found himself growing awkward whenever he thought of her tilted eyes on him. More than once he had fumbled with his hammer till Master Ajala frowned at him wonderingly. Girls had always been able to make him feel awkward especially when they smiled at him, but Zarine did not have to smile. Only look. He wondered again if she was the beautiful woman Min had warned him against. *Better if she is the falcon.* That thought surprised him so much that he stumbled.

"I did not want anything I make to get into the hands of one of the Forsaken." His eyes glowed golden as he looked at her. "If it was for a High Lord, how could I tell where it might end?" She shivered. "I did not mean to frighten you, Fai— Zarine."

She smiled broadly, no doubt thinking he could not see her. "You will fall yet, farmboy. Have you ever thought of wearing a beard?"

It is bad enough she's always mocking me, but half the time I do not even understand her!

As they reached the front door of the inn, Moiraine and Lan met them, coming the other way. Moiraine wore that linen cloak with the wide, deep hood that hid her face. Light from the common-room windows made yellow pools on the paving stones. Two or three carriages rumbled past, and there were perhaps a dozen people in sight, hurrying home for their suppers, but for the most part, shadows populated the street. The weaver's shop was closed tight. The silence was deafening.

"Rand is in Tear." The Aes Sedai's cool voice issued from the depths of her hood as from a cavern.

"Are you sure?" Perrin asked. "I have not heard of anything strange happening. No weddings, or wells drying up." He saw Zarine frown in confusion. Moiraine had not been forthcoming with her, and neither had he. Keeping Loial's tongue silent had been more difficult.

"Don't you listen to rumors, blacksmith?" the Warder said. "There have been marriages, as many in the last four days as in half a year before. And as many murders as in a whole year. A child fell from a tower balcony today. A hundred paces onto stone paving. She got up and ran to her mother without a bruise. The First of Mayene, a 'guest' in the Stone since before the winter, announced today that she will submit to the will of the High Lords, after saying yesterday she would see Mayene and all its ships burn before one Tairen country lord set foot in the city. They had not brought themselves to torture her, and that young woman has a will like iron, so you tell me if you think it might be Rand's doing. Blacksmith, from top to bottom, Tear bubbles like a cauldron."

"These things were not needed to tell me," Moiraine said. "Perrin, did you dream of Rand last night?"

"Yes," he admitted. "He was in the Heart of the Stone, holding that sword"—he felt Zarine shift beside him—"but

I have been worrying about that so much it is no wonder I dream of it. I had nothing but nightmares last night."

"A tall man?" Zarine said. "With reddish hair and gray eyes? Holding something that shines so brightly it hurts your eyes? In a place that is all great redstone columns? Blacksmith, tell me that was not your dream."

"You see," Moiraine said. "I have heard this dream spoken of a hundred times today. They all speak of nightmares—Be'lal apparently does not care to shield his dreams—but that one above all else." She laughed suddenly, like low, cool chimes. "People say he is the Dragon Reborn. They say he is coming. They whisper it fearfully in corners, but they say it."

"And what of Be'lal?" Perrin asked.

Moiraine's reply was cold-drawn steel. "I will deal with him tonight." There was no fear scent from her.

"*We* will deal with him tonight," Lan told her.

"Yes, my Gaidin. We will deal with him."

"And what do we do? Sit here and wait? I had enough waiting to last me a lifetime in the mountains, Moiraine."

"You and Loial—and Zarine—will go to Tar Valon," she told him. "Until this is done. It will be the safest place for you."

"Where is the Ogier?" Lan said. "I want all three of you on your way north as soon as possible."

"Upstairs, I suppose," Perrin said. "In his room, or maybe the dining room. There are lights in the windows up there. He is always working on those notes of his. I suppose he will have plenty to say in his book about us running away." He was surprised at the bitterness in his voice. *Light, fool, do you want to face one of the Forsaken? No. No, but I am tired of running. I remember not running, once. I remember fighting back, and it was better. Even if I thought I was going to die, it was better.*

"I will find him," Zarine announced. "I have no shame in admitting I will be glad enough to run from this fight. Men fight when they should run, and fools fight when they should run. But I had no need to say it twice." She strode ahead of them, her narrow, divided skirts making small whisking noises as they entered the inn.

Perrin glanced around the common room as they followed her toward the stairs in the back. There were fewer men at the tables than he expected. Some sat alone, with dull eyes, but where two or three sat together they talked in frightened whispers his ears could barely catch. Even so, he heard "Dragon" three times.

As he reached the top of the stairs, he heard another soft sound, a thump as of something falling in the private dining room. He peered that way along the hall. "Zarine?" There was no answer. He felt the hair on the back of his neck shift, and padded that way. "Zarine?" He pushed open the door. "Faile!"

She was lying on the floor near the table. As he started to rush into the room, Moiraine's commanding shout halted him.

"Stop, you fool! Stop, for your life!" She came along the hallway slowly, head turning as if she were listening for something, or searching for something. Lan followed with his hand on his sword—and a look in his eye as if he already knew steel would do no good. She came abreast of the door and stopped. "Move back, Perrin. Move back!"

In agony he stared at Zarine. At Faile. She lay there as if lifeless. Finally he made himself step back from the door, leaving it open, standing where he could see her. She looked as if she were dead. He could not see her chest stir. He wanted to howl. Frowning, he worked his hand, the one he had used to push the door into the room, opening and closing his fingers. It tingled sharply, as if he had struck his elbow. "Aren't you going to do anything, Moiraine? If you will not, I am going to her."

"Stand still or you will go nowhere," she said calmly. "What is that by her right hand? As if it dropped from her grip when she fell. I cannot make it out."

He glared at her, then peered into the room. "A hedgehog. It looks like a hedgehog carved out of wood. Moiraine, tell me what is going on! What has happened? Tell me!"

"A hedgehog," she murmured. "A hedgehog. Be silent, Perrin. I must think. I felt it trigger. I can sense the residues of the flows woven to set it. Spirit. Pure Spirit, and nothing else. Almost nothing uses pure flows of Spirit! Why does that hedgehog make me think of Spirit?"

"You felt what trigger, Moiraine? What was set? A trap?"

"Yes, a trap," she said, irritation making tiny cracks in her cool serenity. "A trap meant for me. I would have been

first into that room if Zarine had not rushed ahead. Lan and
I would surely have gone there to plan and wait for supper.
I will not wait on supper now. Be quiet, if you wish me
to help the girl at all. Lan! Bring me that innkeeper!" The
Warder flowed away down the stairs.

Moiraine paced up and down in the hall, sometimes stopping to peer through the door from the depths of her hood.
Perrin could see no sign that Zarine lived. Her breast did
not stir. He tried listening for her heartbeat, but even for his
ears it was impossible.

When Lan returned, shoving a frightened Jurah Haret
ahead of him by the scruff of his fat neck, the Aes Sedai
rounded on the balding man. "You promised to keep this
room for me, Master Haret." Her voice was as hard, as
precise, as a skinning knife. "To allow not even a serving
woman to enter to clean unless I was present. Who did you
let enter it, Master Haret? Tell me!"

Haret shook like a bowl of pudding. "O-only the t-two
Ladies, mistress. T-they w-wished to leave a surprise for
you. I swear, mistress. T-they showed it t-to me. A little
h-hedgehog. T-they said you w-would be surprised."

"I was surprised, innkeeper," she said softly. "Leave me!
And if you whisper a word of this, even in your sleep, I will
pull this inn down and leave only a hole in the ground."

"Y-yes, mistress," he whispered. "I swear it! I do swear!
"Go!"

The innkeeper fell to his knees in his haste to reach the
stairs, and went scrambling down with thumps that suggested he fell more than once as he ran.

"He knows I am here," Moiraine told the Warder, "and
he has found someone of the Black Ajah to set his trap, yet
perhaps he thinks I am caught in it. It was a tiny flash of the
Power, but perhaps he is strong enough to have sensed it."

"Then he will not suspect we are coming," Lan said quietly. He almost smiled.

Perrin stared at them, his teeth bared. "What about her?"
he demanded. "What was done to her, Moiraine? Is she
alive? I cannot see her breathe!"

"She is alive," Moiraine said slowly. "I cannot, I dare not,
go close enough to her to tell much beyond that, but she
is alive. She . . . sleeps, in a way. As a bear sleeps in the
winter. Her heart beats so slowly you could count minutes

between. Her breathing is the same. She sleeps." Even from within that hood, he could feel her eyes on him. "I fear she is not there, Perrin. Not in her body any longer."

"What do you mean she is not in her body? Light! You don't mean they . . . took her soul. Like the Gray Men!" Moiraine shook her head, and he drew a relieved breath. His chest hurt as if he had not breathed since she last spoke. "Then where is she, Moiraine?"

"I do not know," she said. "I have a suspicion, but I do not know."

"A suspicion, a hint, anything! Burn me, where?" Lan shifted at the roughness in his voice, but he knew he would try to break the Warder like iron over a hardy if the man tried to stop him. "Where?"

"I know very little, Perrin." Moiraine's voice was like cold, unfeeling music. "I have remembered the little I know of what connects a carved hedgehog with Spirit. The carving is a *ter'angreal* last studied by Corianin Nedeal, the last Dreamer the Tower had. The Talent called Dreaming is a thing of Spirit, Perrin. It is not a thing I have ever studied; my Talents lie in other ways. I believe that Zarine has been trapped inside a dream, perhaps even the World of Dreams, *Tel'aran'rhiod*. All that is her is inside that dream. All. A Dreamer sends only a part of herself. If Zarine does not return soon, her body will die. Perhaps she will live on in the dream. I do not know."

"There is too much you don't know," Perrin muttered. He peered into the room and wanted to cry. Zarine looked so small, lying there, so helpless. *Faile. I swear I will only call you Faile, ever again.* "Why don't you do something!"

"The trap has been sprung, Perrin, but it is a trap that will still catch anyone who steps into that room. I would not reach her side before it took me. And I have work I must do tonight."

"Burn you, Aes Sedai! Burn your work! This World of Dreams? Is it like the wolf dreams? You said these Dreamers sometimes saw wolves."

"I have told you what I can," she said sharply. "It is time for you to go. Lan and I must be on our way to the Stone. There can be no waiting, now."

"No." He said it quietly, but when Moiraine opened her mouth, he raised his voice. "No! I will not leave her!"

The Aes Sedai took a deep breath. "Very well, Perrin." Her voice was ice; calm, smooth, cold. "Remain if you wish. Perhaps you will survive this night. Lan!"

She and the Warder strode down the hall to their rooms. In moments they returned, Lan wearing his color-changing cloak, and vanished down the stairs without another word to him.

He stared through the open door at Faile. *I have to do something. If it is like the wolf dreams. . . .*

"Perrin," came Loial's deep rumble, "what is this about Faile?" The Ogier came striding down the hall in his shirt-sleeves, ink on his fingers and a pen in his hand. "Lan told me I had to go, and then he said something about Faile, in a trap. What did he mean?"

Distractedly, Perrin told him what Moiraine had said. *It might work. It might. It has to!* He was surprised when Loial growled.

"No! Perrin, it is not right! Faile was so free. It is not right to trap her!"

Perrin peered up at Loial's face, and suddenly remembered the old stories that claimed Ogier were implacable enemies. Loial's ears had laid back along the sides of his head, and his broad face was as hard as an anvil.

"Loial, I am going to try to help Faile. But I will be helpless myself while I do. Will you guard my back?"

Loial raised those huge hands that held books so carefully, and his thick fingers curled as if to crush stone. "None will pass me while I live, Perrin. Not Myrddraal or the Dark One himself." He said it like a simple statement of fact.

Perrin nodded, and looked through the door again. *It has to work. I don't care if Min warned me against her or not!* With a snarl he leaped toward Faile, stretching out his hand. He thought he touched her ankle before he was gone.

Whether this dream of the trap was *Tel'aran'rhiod* or not, Perrin did not know, but he knew it for the wolf dream. Rolling, grassy hills surrounded him, and scattered thickets. He saw deer browsing at the edges of the trees, and a herd of some sort of running animal bounding across the grass, like brown-striped deer, but with long, straight horns. The smells on the wind told him they were good to eat, and other scents spoke of more good hunting all around him. This was the wolf dream.

He was wearing the blacksmith's long leather vest, he realized, with his arms bare. And there was a weight at his side. He touched the axe belt, but it was not the axe hanging from its loop. He ran his fingers over the head of the heavy smith's hammer. It felt right.

Hopper alighted in front of him.

Again you come, like a fool. The sending was of a cub sticking its nose into a hollow tree trunk to lap honey despite the bees stinging its muzzle and eyes. *The danger is greater than ever, Young Bull. Evil things walk the dream. The brothers and sisters avoid the mountains of stone the two-legs pile up, and almost fear to dream to one another. You must go!*

"No," Perrin said. "Faile is here, somewhere, trapped. I have to find her, Hopper. I have to!" He felt a shifting inside him, something changing. He looked down at his curly-haired legs, his wide paws. He was an even larger wolf than Hopper.

You are here too strongly! Every sending carried shock. *You will die, Young Bull!*

If I do not free the falcon, I do not care, brother.

Then we hunt, brother.

Noses to the wind, the two wolves ran across the plain, seeking the falcon.

CHAPTER
54

Into the Stone

The rooftops of Tear were no place for a sensible man to be in the night, Mat decided as he peered into the moon shadows. A little more than fifty paces of broad street, or perhaps narrow plaza, separated the Stone from his tiled roof, itself three stories above the paving stones. *But when was I ever sensible? The only people I ever met who were sensible all the time were so boring that watching them could put you to sleep.* Whether the thing was a street or a plaza, he had followed it all the way around the Stone since nightfall; the only place it did not go was on the river side, where the Erinin ran right along the foot of the fortress, and nothing interrupted it except the city wall. That wall was only two houses to his right. So far, the top of the wall seemed the best path to the Stone, but not one he would be overjoyed to take.

Picking up his quarterstaff and a small, wire-handled tin box, he moved carefully to a brick chimney a little nearer the wall. The roll of fireworks—what had been the roll of fireworks before he worked on it back in his room—shifted on his back. It was more of a bundle, now, all jammed together as tight as he could make it, but still too big for carrying around rooftops in the dark. Earlier, a slip of his foot because of the thing had sent a roof tile skittering over the edge, and roused the man sleeping in a room below to bellow "thief!" and send him running. He hitched the bundle back into position without thinking about it, and crouched in the shadows of the chimney. After a moment he set the tin box down; the wire handle was beginning to grow uncomfortably warm.

It felt a little safer, studying the Stone from the shadows, but not much more encouraging. The city wall was not nearly as thick as those he had seen in other places, in Caemlyn or Tar Valon, no more than a pace wide, supported by great stone buttresses cloaked in darkness, now. A pace was more than sufficient width for walking, of course, except that the fall to either side was nearly ten spans. Through the dark, to hard pavement. *But some of these bloody houses back right up against it, I can make it to the top easily enough, and it bloody runs straight to the bloody Stone!*

It did that, but that was no particular comfort. The sides of the Stone looked like cliffs. Eyeing the height again, he told himself he should be able to climb it. *Of course, I can. Just like those cliffs in the Mountains of Mist.* Over a hundred paces straight up before there was a battlement. There must be arrowslits lower down, but he could not make them out in the night. And he could not squeeze through an arrowslit. *A hundred bloody paces. Maybe a hundred and twenty. Burn me, even Rand would not try to climb that.* But it was the one way in he had found. Every gate he had seen had been shut tight and looked strong enough to stop a herd of bulls, not to mention the dozen or so soldiers guarding very nearly every last one, in helmets and breastplates, and swords at their belts.

Suddenly he blinked, and squinted at the side of the Stone. There *was* some fool climbing it, just visible as a moving shadow in the moonlight, and over halfway up already, with a drop of seventy paces to the pavement under his feet. *Fool, is he? Well, I'm as big a one, because I am going up, too. Burn me, he'll probably raise an alarm in there and get me caught.* He could not see the climber anymore. *Who in the Light is he? What does it matter who he is? Burn me, but this is a bloody way to win a wager. I'm going to want a kiss from all of them, even Nynaeve!*

He shifted to peer toward the wall, trying to choose his spot to climb, and suddenly there was steel across his throat. Without thinking, he knocked it away and swept the man's feet out from under him with his staff. Someone else kicked his own feet away and he fell almost on top of the man he had knocked down. He rolled off onto the roof tiles, loosing the bundle of fireworks—*If that falls into the street, I'll break their necks!*—staff whirling; he felt it strike flesh, and a second time, heard grunts. Then there were two blades at his throat.

He froze, arms outflung. The points of short spears, dull so they hardly caught the faint light of the moon at all, pressed into his flesh just short of bringing blood. His eyes followed them up to the faces of whoever was holding them, but their heads were shrouded, their faces veiled in black except for their eyes, staring at him. *Burn me, I have to run into real thieves! What happened to my luck?*

He put on a grin, with plenty of teeth so they could see it in the moonlight. "I do not mean to trouble you in your work, so if you let me go my way, I'll let you go yours and say nothing." The veiled men did not move, and neither did their spears. "I want no more outcry than you. I'll not betray you." They stood like statues, staring down at him. *Burn me, I do not have time for this. Time to toss the dice.* For a chilling moment he thought the words in his head had been strange. He tightened his grip on the quarterstaff, lying out to one side of him—and almost cried out when someone stepped hard on his wrist.

He rolled his eyes to see who. *Burn me for a fool, I forgot the one I fell on.* But he saw another shape moving behind the one standing on his wrist, and decided maybe it was as well he had not managed to bring the staff into use after all.

It was a soft boot, laced to the knee, that rested on his arm. It tugged at his memory. Something about a man met in mountains. He eyed the night-cloaked shape the rest of the way up, trying to make out the cut and colors of his clothes—they seemed all shadow, colors that blended with the darkness too well to see them clearly—past a long-bladed knife at the fellow's waist, right up to the dark veil across his face. A black-veiled face. Black-veiled.

Aiel! Burn me, what are bloody Aiel doing here! He had a sinking feeling in his stomach as he remembered hearing that Aiel veiled themselves when they killed.

"Yes," said a man's voice, "we are Aiel." Mat gave a start; he had not realized he had spoken aloud.

"You dance well for one caught by surprise," a young woman's voice said. He thought she was the one standing on his wrist. "Perhaps another day I will have time to dance with you properly."

He started to smile—*If she wants to dance, they can't*

be going to kill me, at least!—then frowned instead. He seemed to remember Aiel sometimes meant something different when they said that.

The spears were pulled back, and hands hauled him to his feet. He shook them away and brushed himself off as if he were standing in a common room instead of on a night-cloaked rooftop with four Aiel. It always paid to let the other man know you had a steady nerve. The Aiel had quivers at their waists as well as knives, and more of those short spears on their backs with cased bows, the long spear points sticking up above their shoulders. He heard himself humming "I'm Down at the Bottom of the Well," and stopped it.

"What do you do here?" the man's voice asked. With the veils, Mat was not entirely sure which one had spoken; the voice sounded older, confident, used to command. He thought he could pick out the woman, at least; she was the only one shorter than he, and that not by much. The others all stood a head taller than he or more. *Bloody Aiel*, he thought. "We have watched you for some little time," the older man went on, "watched you watch the Stone. You have studied it from every side. Why?"

"I could ask the same of all of you," another voice said. Mat was the only one who gave a start as a man in baggy breeches stepped out of the shadows. The fellow appeared to be shoeless, for better footing on the tiles. "I expected to find thieves, not Aiel," the man went on, "but do not think your numbers frighten me." A slim staff no taller than his head made a blur and a hum as he whirled it. "My name is Juilin Sandar, and I am a thief-catcher, and I would know why you are on the rooftops, staring at the Stone."

Mat shook his head. *How many bloody people are on the roofs tonight?* All that was needed was for Thom to appear and play his harp, or someone to come looking for an inn. *A bloody thief-taker!* He wondered why the Aiel were just standing there.

"You stalk well, for a city man," the older man's voice said. "But why do you follow us? We have stolen nothing. Why have you looked so often at the Stone tonight yourself?"

Even in the moonlight this Sandar's surprise was evident. He gave a start, opened his mouth—and closed it again as four more Aiel rose out of the dimness behind him. With a sigh, he leaned on his slender staff. "It seems I am caught myself," he muttered. "It seems *I* must answer *your* questions." He peered toward the Stone, then shook his head. "I . . . did a thing today that . . . troubles me." He sounded almost as though he were talking to himself, trying to puzzle it out. "Part of me says it was right, what I did, that I must obey. Surely, it seemed right when I did it. But a small voice tells me I . . . betrayed something. I am certain this voice is wrong, and it is very small, but it will not stop." He stopped then himself, shaking his head again.

One of the Aiel nodded, and spoke with the older man's voice. "I am Rhuarc, of the Nine Valleys sept of the Taardad Aiel, and once I was *Aethan Dor*, a Red Shield. Sometimes the Red Shields do as your thief-catchers do. I say this so you will understand that I know what it is you do, and the kind of man you must be. I mean no harm to you, Juilin Sandar of the thief-catchers, nor to the people of your city, but you will not be suffered to raise the armcry. If you will keep silence, you will live; if not, not."

"You mean no harm to the city," Sandar said slowly. "Why are you here, then?"

"The Stone." Rhuarc's tone made it plain that was all he meant to say.

After a moment Sandar nodded, and muttered, "I could almost wish you had the power to harm the Stone, Rhuarc. I will hold my tongue."

Rhuarc turned his veiled face to Mat. "And you, nameless youngling? Will you tell me now why you watch the Stone so closely?"

"I just wanted a walk in the moonlight," Mat said lightly. The young woman put her spearpoint to his throat again; he tried not to swallow. *Well, maybe I can tell them something of it.* He must not let them know he was shaken; if you let the other fellow know that, you lost whatever edge you might have. Very carefully, with two fingers, he moved her steel away from him. It seemed to him that she laughed softly. "Some friends of mine are inside the Stone," he said, trying to sound casual. "Prisoners. I mean to bring them out."

"Alone, nameless one?" Rhuarc said.

"Well, there doesn't seem to be anyone else," Mat said

dryly. "Unless you care to help? You seem interested in the Stone yourself. If you mean to go into it, perhaps we could go together. It is a tight roll of the dice any way you look at it, but my luck runs good." *So far, anyway. I've run into black-veiled Aiel and they have not cut my throat; luck cannot get much better than that. Burn me, it would not be bad to have a few Aiel along with me in there.* "You could do worse than betting on my luck."

"We are not here for prisoners, gambler," Rhuarc said.

"It is time, Rhuarc." Mat could not tell from which of the Aiel that came, but Rhuarc nodded.

"Yes, Gaul." He looked from Mat to Sandar and back. "Do not give the armcry." He turned away, and in two steps he had blended into the night.

Mat gave a start. The other Aiel were gone, too, leaving him alone with the thief-taker. *Unless they left somebody to watch us. Burn me, how could I tell if they did?* "I hope you don't mean to try stopping me, either," he told Sandar as he slung the bundle of fireworks on his back again and picked up his quarterstaff. "I mean to go inside, by you or through you, one way or the other." He went over to the chimney to pick up the tin box; the wire handle was more than warm, now.

"These friends of yours," Sandar said. "They are three women?"

Mat frowned at him, wishing there was enough light to show the man's face clearly. The fellow's voice sounded odd. "What do you know of them?"

"I know they are inside the Stone. And I know a small gate near the river where a thief-catcher can gain entrance with a prisoner, to take him to the cells. The cells where they must be. If you will trust me, gambler, I can take us that far. What happens after that is up to chance. Perhaps your luck will bring us out again alive."

"I have always been lucky," Mat said slowly. *Do I feel lucky enough to trust him?* He did not much like the idea of pretending to be a prisoner; it seemed too easy for pretense to become reality. But it seemed no bigger risk than trying to climb three hundred feet or more straight up in the dark.

He glanced toward the city wall, and stared. Shadows flowed along it; dim shapes trotting. Aiel, he was sure. There must have been over a hundred. They vanished, but now he could make out shadows moving on the cliff face that was the sheer side of the Stone of Tear. So much for going up that way. That one fellow earlier might have made it inside without raising an alarm—Rhuarc's armcry—but a hundred or more Aiel would have to be like sounding bells. They might make a diversion, though. If they caused a commotion somewhere up there, inside the Stone, then whoever was guarding the cells might not pay as much attention to a thief-taker bringing a thief.

I might as well add a little to the confusion. I worked hard enough on it. "Very well, thief-taker. Just don't decide I am a real prisoner at the last minute. We can start for your gate as soon as I stir the anthill a bit." He thought Sandar frowned, but he did not mean to tell the man more than he had to.

Sandar followed him across the rooftops, climbing to higher levels as easily as he did. The last roof was only a little lower than the top of the wall and ran right up to it, a matter of pulling himself up rather than climbing.

"What are you doing?" Sandar whispered.

"Wait here for me."

With the tin box dangling from one hand by its wire handle and his quarterstaff held horizontally in front of him, Mat took a deep breath and started toward the Stone. He tried not to think of how far it was to the pavement below. *Light, the bloody thing is three feet wide! I could walk it with a bloody blindfold, in my sleep!* Three feet wide, in the dark, and better than fifty feet to the pavement. He tried not to think about Sandar not being there when he came back, either. He was all but committed to this fool notion of pretending to be a thief caught by the man, but it seemed all too probable that he would return to the roof to find Sandar gone, maybe bringing more men to make him a prisoner in truth. *Don't think about it. Just do the job at hand. At least I'll finally see what it is like.*

As he had suspected, there was an arrowslit in the wall of the Stone right at the end of the wall, a deep wedge cut into the rock holding a tall, narrow opening for an archer to shoot through. If the Stone were attacked, the soldiers inside would want some way to stop any trying to follow this path. The slit was dark, now. There did not appear to be anyone watching. That was something he had tried not to think about, too.

Quickly he set down the tin box at his feet, balanced his quarterstaff across the wall right against the side of the Stone, and unslung the bundle from his back. Hurriedly he wedged it into the slit, forcing it in as far as he could; he wanted as much of the noise to be inside as he could manage. Pulling aside a corner of the oiled cloth cover revealed knotted fuses. After a little thinking, back in his room, he had cut the longer fuses to match the shortest, using the pieces to help tie all the fuses together. It seemed they should all go off at once, and a bang-and-flash like that should be enough to pull everyone who was not completely deaf.

The lid of the tin box was hot enough that he had to blow on his fingers twice before he could pry it off—he wished he had whatever Aludra's trick had been, lighting that lantern so easily—to expose the dark bit of charcoal inside, lying on a bed of sand. The wire handle came off to make tongs, and a little blowing had the coal glowing red again. He touched the hot coal to the knotted fuses, let tongs and coal fall over the side of the wall as the fuses hissed into flame, snatched up his quarterstaff and darted back along the wall.

This is crazy, he thought as he ran. *I don't care how big a bang it makes. I could break my fool neck doing thi—!*

The roar behind him was louder than anything he had ever heard in his life; a monstrous fist punched him in the back, knocking all the wind out of him even before he landed, sprawled on his belly on the wall top, barely holding on to his staff as it swung over the edge. For a moment he lay there, trying to make his lungs work again, trying not to think how he *must* have used up all his luck this time by not falling off the wall. His ears rang like all the bells in Tar Valon.

Pushing himself up carefully, he looked back toward the Stone. A cloud of smoke hung around the arrowslit. Behind the smoke, the shadowed shape of the arrowslit itself seemed different. Larger. He did not understand how or why, but it did seem larger.

He only thought for a moment. At one end of the wall

Sandar might be waiting, might be intending to take him
into the Stone as a pretend prisoner—or might be hurrying
back with soldiers. At the other end of the wall, there might
be a way inside without any chance of Sandar betraying
him. He darted back the way he had just come, no longer
worrying about the darkness or the drop to either side.

The arrowslit *was* larger, most of the thinner stone at the
middle simply gone, leaving a rough hole as if someone
had hammered at it with a sledge for hours. A hole just big
enough for a man. *How in the Light?* There was no time for
wondering.

He pushed through the jagged opening, coughing at
the acrid smoke, jumped to the floor inside, and had run a
dozen steps before Defenders of the Stone appeared, at least
ten of them, all shouting in confusion. Most wore only their
shirts, and none had helmet or breastplate. Some carried
lanterns. Some held bared swords.

Fool! he shouted inside his head. *This is why you set the
bloody things off in the first place! Light-blinded fool!*

He had no time to make it back out onto the wall. Quarterstaff spinning, he threw himself at the soldiers before they
had a chance to do more than see he was there, hurled himself into them, smashing at heads, swords, knees, whatever he
could reach, knowing they were too many for him to handle
alone, knowing that his fool toss of the dice had cost Egwene
and the others whatever chance he might have had.

Suddenly Sandar was there beside him, in the light of
lanterns dropped by men clawing for their swords, his
slender staff whirling even faster than Mat's quarterstaff.
Caught between two staffmen, taken by surprise, the soldiers went down like pins in a game of bowls.

Sandar stared at the fallen men, shaking his head. "Defenders of the Stone. I have attacked Defenders! They will
have my head for—! What was it that you did, gambler?
That flash of light, and thunder, breaking stone. Did you
call lightning?" His voice fell to a whisper. "Have I joined
myself to a man who can channel?"

"Fireworks," Mat said curtly. His ears were still ringing,
but he could hear more boots coming, running boots thudding on stone. "The cells, man! Show me the way to the
cells before any more get here!"

Sandar shook himself. "This way!" He dashed down a

side hall, away from the oncoming boots. "We must hurry! They will kill us if they find us!" Somewhere above, gongs began to sound an alarm, and more thundered echoes through the Stone.

I'm coming, Mat thought as he ran after the thief-taker. *I'll get you out or die! I promise it!*

The alarm gongs sent echoes crashing through the Stone, but Rand paid no more attention to them than he had to the roar that had come before, like muffled thunder from somewhere below. His side ached; the old wound burned, strained almost to tearing by the climb up the side of the fortress. He gave the pain no heed, either. A crooked smile was fixed on his face, a smile of anticipation and dread he could not have wiped away if he had wanted to. It was close, now. What he had dreamed of. *Callandor.*

I will finish it at last. One way or another, it will be done with. The dreams, finished. The baiting, and the taunting, and the hunting. I'll finish it all!

Laughing to himself, he hurried through the dark corridors of the Stone of Tear.

Egwene put a hand to her face, wincing. Her mouth had a bitter taste, and she was thirsty. *Rand? What? Why was I dreaming about Mat again, all mixed with Rand, and shouting that he was coming? What?*

She opened her eyes, stared at the gray stone walls, one smoky rush torch casting flickering shadows, and screamed as she remembered it all. "No! I will not be chained again! I won't be collared! No!"

Nynaeve and Elayne were beside her in an instant, their bruised faces too worried and fearful for the soothing sounds they made to be believed. But just the fact that they were there was enough to still her screams. She was not alone. A prisoner, but not alone. And not collared.

She tried to sit up, and they helped her. They had to help her; she ached in every muscle. She could remember every unseen blow during the frenzy that had all but driven her mad when she realized. . . . *I will not think about that. I have to think about how we are to escape.* She slid backwards

until she could lean against a wall. Her pains fought with
weariness; that struggle when she had refused to give in
had taken every last scrap of her strength, and the bruises
seemed to sap even more.

The cell was absolutely empty except for the three of
them and the torch. The floor was bare, and cold, and hard.
The door of rough planks, splintered as if countless futile
fingers had clawed at it, was the only break in the walls.
Messages had been scratched in the stone, most by unsteady
hands. The Light have mercy and let me die, one read. She
blanked that out of her head.

"Are we still shielded?" she mumbled. Even talking hurt.
Even as Elayne nodded, she realized she had not had to ask.
The swollen cheek on the golden-haired woman, her split
lip and black eye, were answer enough, even if her own
pains had not been. If Nynaeve had been able to reach the
True Source, they surely would have been Healed.

"I have tried," Nynaeve said despairingly. "I have tried,
and tried, and tried." She gave her braid a sharp tug, anger
seeping through despite the hopeless fear in her voice. "One
of them is sitting outside. Amico, that milk-faced chit, if
they have not changed since we were thrown in here. I suppose one is enough to maintain the shielding once it has
been woven." She barked a bitter laugh. "For all the pains
they took—and gave!—to take us, you would think we
were of no importance at all. It has been hours since they
slammed that door behind us, and no one has come to ask
a question, or look, or even bring a drop of water. Perhaps
they mean to leave us here until we die of thirst."

"Bait." Elayne's voice quavered, though she was obviously trying to sound unafraid. And failing miserably. "Liandrin said we are bait."

"Bait for what?" Nynaeve asked shakily. "Bait for who?
If I am bait, I'd like to shove myself down their throats till
they choke on me!"

"Rand." Egwene stopped to swallow; even a drop of water
would be welcome. "I dreamed about Rand, and *Callandor*.
I think he is coming here." *But why did I dream of Mat?
And Perrin? It was a wolf, but I am sure it was him.* "Do
not be so afraid," she said, trying to sound confident. "We
will escape them somehow. If we could better the Seanchan,
we can best Liandrin."

Nynaeve and Elayne exchanged looks over her. Nynaeve said, "Liandrin said thirteen Myrddraal are coming, Egwene."

She found herself staring at that message scratched on the stone wall again: The Light have mercy and let me die. Her hands clenched into fists. Her jaws cramped with the effort of not screaming those words. *Better to die. Better death than being turned to the Shadow, made to serve the Dark One!*

She realized that one of her hands had tightened around the pouch at her belt. She could feel the two rings inside, the small circle of the Great Serpent and the larger, twisted stone ring.

"They did not take the *ter'angreal*," she said wonderingly. She fumbled it out of her pouch. It lay heavily on her palm, all stripes and flecks of color, a ring with only one edge.

"We were not even important enough to search," Elayne sighed. "Egwene, are you certain Rand is coming here? I would much rather free myself than wait for the chance of him, but if there is anyone who can defeat Liandrin and the rest of them, it must be him. The Dragon Reborn is meant to wield *Callandor*. He *must* be able to defeat them."

"Not if we pull him into a cage after us," Nynaeve muttered. "Not if they have a trap set he does not see. Why are you staring at that ring, Egwene? *Tel'aran'rhiod* will not help us now. Not unless you can dream a way out of here."

"Perhaps I can," she said slowly. "I could channel in *Tel'aran'rhiod*. Their shielding won't stop me reaching it. All I need do is sleep, not channel. And I am surely weary enough to sleep."

Elayne frowned, wincing as it pulled her bruises. "I will take any chance, but how can you channel even in a dream, cut off from the True Source? And if you can, how can it help us here?"

"I do not know, Elayne. Just because I am shielded here does not mean I am shielded in the World of Dreams. It is at least worth a try."

"Perhaps," Nynaeve said worriedly. "I will take any chance, too, but you saw Liandrin and the others the last time you used that ring. And you said they saw you, too. What if they are there again?"

"I hope they are," Egwene said grimly. "I hope they are."

Clutching the *ter'angreal* in her hand, she closed her eyes. She could feel Elayne smoothing her hair, hear her murmuring softly. Nynaeve began to hum that wordless lullaby from her childhood; for once, she felt no anger at it at all. The soft sounds and touches soothed her, let her surrender to her weariness, let sleep come.

She wore blue silk this time, but she barely noticed more than that. Soft breezes caressed her unbruised face, and sent the butterflies swirling above the wildflowers. Her thirst was gone, her aches. She reached out to embrace *saidar* and was filled with the One Power. Even the triumph she felt at succeeding was small beside the surging of the Power through her.

Reluctantly she made herself release it, closed her eyes, and filled the emptiness with a perfect image of the Heart of the Stone. That was the one place in the Stone she could picture aside from her cell, and how to distinguish one featureless cubicle from another? When she opened her eyes, she was there. But she was not alone.

The form of Joiya Byir stood before *Callandor*, her shape so insubstantial that the surging light of the sword shone through her. The crystal sword no longer merely glittered with refracted light. In pulses it glowed, as if some light inside it were being uncovered, then covered and uncovered again. The Black sister started with surprise and spun to face Egwene. "How? You are shielded! Your Dreaming is at an end!"

Before the first words were out of the woman's mouth, Egwene reached for *saidar* again, wove the complicated flow of Spirit as she remembered it being used against her, and cut Joiya Byir off from the Source. The Darkfriend's eyes widened, those cruel eyes so incongruous in that beautiful, kindly face, but Egwene was already weaving Air. The other woman's form might seem like mist, but the bonds held it. It seemed to Egwene that there was no effort involved in holding both flows in their weaving. There was sweat on Joiya Byir's forehead as she walked closer.

"You have a *ter'angreal*!" Fear was plain on the woman's face, but her voice fought to hide it. "That must be it. A *ter'angreal* that escaped us, and one that does not require channeling. Do you think it will do you any good, girl? Whatever you do here, it cannot affect what happens in the real world. *Tel'aran'rhiod* is a dream! When I wake, I will take your *ter'angreal* from you myself. Be careful what you do, lest I have reason to be angry when I come to your cell."

Egwene smiled at her. "Are you certain you will wake, Darkfriend? If your *ter'angreal* requires channeling, why did you not wake as soon as I shielded you? Perhaps you cannot wake so long as you are shielded here." Her smile faded away; the effort of smiling at this woman was more than she could bear. "A woman once showed me a scar she received in *Tel'aran'rhiod*, Darkfriend. What happens here *is* still real when you wake."

The sweat rolled down the Black sister's smooth, ageless face, now. Egwene wondered if she thought she was about to die. She almost wished she were cruel enough to do that. Most of the unseen blows she had received had come from this woman, like a pounding of fists, for no reason more than that she had kept trying to crawl away, no reason more than that she had refused to give up.

"A woman who can give such beatings," she said, "should have no objections to a milder one." She wove another flow of Air quickly; Joiya Byir's dark eyes bulged in disbelief as the first blow landed across her hips. Egwene saw how to adjust the weaving so she did not have to maintain it. "You will remember this, and feel it, when you waken. When I allow you to waken. Remember this, too. If you ever even try to beat me again, I will return you here and leave you for the rest of your life!" The Black sister's eyes stared hate at her, but there was a suggestion of tears in them, too.

Egwene felt a moment of shame. Not at what she was doing to Joiya—the woman deserved every blow, if not for her own beating, then for the deaths in the Tower—not that, not really, but because she had spent time on her own revenge while Nynaeve and Elayne were sitting in a cell hoping against hope that she might be able to rescue them.

She tied off and set the flows of her weavings before she knew she had done it, then paused to study what she had done. Three separate weavings, and not only had it been no trouble to hold them all at once, but now she had done something so they would maintain themselves. She thought she could remember how, too. And it might be useful.

After a moment, she unraveled one of the weavings, and the Darkfriend sobbed as much from relief as from pain. "I am not like you," Egwene said. "This is the second time I have done something like this, and I do not like it. I am going to have to learn to cut throats instead." From the Black sister's face, she thought Egwene meant to start learning with her.

Making a disgusted sound, Egwene left her standing there, trapped and shielded, and hurried into the forest of polished redstone columns. There had to be a way down to the cells somewhere.

The stone corridor fell silent as the final dying scream was cut off by Young Bull's jaws closing on the two-legs's throat, crushing it. The blood was bitter on his tongue.

He knew this was the Stone of Tear, though he could not say how he knew. The two-legs lying around him, one kicking his last with Hopper's teeth buried in his throat, had smelled rank with fear as they fought. They had smelled confused. He did not think they had known where they were—they certainly did not belong in the wolf dream—but they had been set to keep him from that tall door ahead, with its iron lock. To guard it, at least. They had seemed startled to see wolves. He thought they had been startled at being there themselves.

He wiped his mouth, then stared at his hand with a momentary lack of comprehension. He was a man again. He was Perrin. Back in his own body, in the blacksmith's vest, with the heavy hammer at his side.

We must hurry, Young Bull. There is something evil near.

Perrin pulled the hammer from his belt as he strode to the door. "Faile must be here." One sharp blow shattered the lock. He kicked open the door.

The room was empty except for a long stone block in the middle of the floor. Faile lay on that block as if sleeping, her black hair spread out like a fan, her body so wrapped in chains that it took him a moment to realize she was unclothed. Every chain was held to the stone by a thick bolt.

He was hardly aware of crossing the space until his hand touched her face, tracing her cheekbone with a finger.

She opened her eyes and smiled up at him. "I kept dreaming you would come, blacksmith."

"I will have you free in a moment, Faile." He raised his hammer, smashed one of the bolts as if it were wood.

"I was sure of it. Perrin."

As his name faded from her tongue, she faded, too. With a clatter, the chains dropped to the stone where she had been.

"No!" he cried. "I found her!"

The dream is not like the world of flesh, Young Bull. Here, the same hunt can have many endings.

He did not turn to look at Hopper. He knew his teeth were bared in a snarl. Again he raised the hammer, brought it down with all his strength against the chains that had held Faile. The stone block cracked in two under his blow; the Stone itself rang like a struck bell.

"Then I will hunt again," he growled.

Hammer in hand, Perrin strode out of the room with Hopper beside him. The Stone was a place of men. And men, he knew, were crueler hunters than ever wolves were.

Alarm gongs somewhere above sent sonorous clangs down the corridor, not quite drowning out the ring of metal on metal and the shouts of fighting men rather closer. The Aiel and the Defenders, Mat suspected. Tall, golden lamp stands, each with four golden lamps, lined the hall where Mat was, and silk tapestries of battle scenes hung on the polished stone walls. There were even silk carpets on the floor, dark red on dark blue, woven in the Tairen maze. For once, Mat was too busy to put a price on anything.

This bloody fellow is good, he thought as he managed to sweep a sword thrust away from him, but the blow he aimed at the man's head with the other end of the staff had to turn into another block of that darting blade. *I wonder if he is one of these bloody High Lords?* He almost managed a solid blow at a knee, but his opponent sprang back, his straight blade raised on guard.

The blue-eyed man certainly wore the puffy-sleeved coat, yellow with thread-of-gold stripes, but it was all undone, his shirt only half tucked into his breeches, and his feet bare. His short-cropped, dark hair was tousled, like that of a man roused hastily from sleep, but he did not fight like it. Five minutes ago he had come darting out from one of the tall, carved doors that lined this hall, a scabbardless sword in his hands, and Mat was only grateful the fellow had appeared in front of them and not behind. He was not the first man dressed so that Mat had faced already, but he was surely the best.

"Can you make it past me, thief-catcher?" Mat called, careful not to take his eyes off the man waiting for him with blade poised to strike. Sandar had insisted irritably on "thief-catcher," not "thief-taker," though Mat could not see any difference.

"I cannot," Sandar called from behind him. "If you move to let me by, you will lose room to swing that oar you call a staff, and he will spit you like a grunt."

Like a what? "Well, think of something, Tairen. This ragamuffin is grating my nerves."

The man in the gold-striped coat sneered. "You will be honored to die on the blade of the High Lord Darlin, peasant, if I allow it so." It was the first time he had deigned to speak. "Instead, I think I will have the pair of you hung by the heels, and watch while the skin is stripped from your bodies—"

"I do not think I'd like that," Mat said.

The High Lord's face reddened with indignation at being interrupted, but Mat gave him no time for any outraged comment. Quarterstaff whirling in a tight double-loop weave, so quick the staff blurred at the ends, he leaped forward. It was all a snarling Darlin could do to keep the staff from him. For the moment. Mat knew he could not keep this up very long, and if he was lucky then, it would all go back to the strike and counterstrike. If he was lucky. But he had no intention of counting on luck this time. As soon as the High Lord had a moment to set himself in a pattern of defense, Mat altered his attack in midwhirl. The end of the staff Darlin had been expecting at his head dipped instead to sweep his legs out from under him. The other end did strike at his head then, as he fell, a sharp crack that rolled his eyes back up in his head.

Panting, Mat leaned on his staff over the unconscious High Lord. *Burn me, if I have to fight one or two more like this, I'll bloody well fall over from exhaustion! The stories do not tell you being a hero is such hard work! Nynaeve always did find a way to make me work.*

Sandar came to stand beside him, frowning down at the

crumpled High Lord. "He does not look so mighty lying there," he said wonderingly. "He does not look so much greater than me."

Mat gave a start and peered down the hall, where a man had just gone trotting across along a joining corridor. *Burn me, if I did not know it was crazy, I would swear that was Rand!*

"Sandar, you find that—" he began, swinging his staff up onto his shoulder, and cut off when it thudded into something.

Spinning, he found himself facing another half-dressed High Lord, this one with his sword on the floor, his knees buckling, and both hands to his head where Mat's staff had split his scalp. Hastily, Mat poked him hard in the stomach with the butt of the staff to bring his hands down, then gave him another thump on the head to put him down in a heap on top of his sword.

"Luck, Sandar," he muttered. "You cannot beat bloody luck. Now, why don't you find this bloody private way the High Lords take down to the cells?" Sandar had insisted there was such a stairway, and using it would avoid having to run through most of the Stone. Mat did not think he liked men so eager to watch people put to the question that they wanted a quick route to the prisoners from their apartments.

"Just be glad you *were* so lucky," Sandar said unsteadily, "or this one would have killed us both before we saw him. I know the door is here somewhere. Are you coming? Or do you mean to wait for another High Lord to appear?"

"Lead on." Mat stepped over the unconscious High Lord. "I am no bloody hero."

Trotting, he followed the thief-catcher, who peered at the tall doors they passed, muttering that he knew it was here somewhere.

CHAPTER
55

What Is Written in Prophecy

Rand entered the chamber slowly, walking among the great polished redstone columns he remembered from his dreams. Silence filled the shadows, yet something called to him. And something flashed ahead, a momentary light throwing back shadow, a beacon. He stepped out beneath a great dome, and saw what he sought. *Callandor*, hanging hilt down in midair, waiting for no hand but that of the Dragon Reborn. As it revolved, it broke what little light there was into splinters, and now and then it flared as if with a light of its own. Calling him. Waiting for him.

If I am the Dragon Reborn. If I am not just some half-mad man cursed with the ability to channel, a puppet dancing for Moiraine and the White Tower.

"Take it, Lews Therin. Take it, Kinslayer."

He spun to face the voice. The tall man with close-cropped white hair who stepped from the shadows among the columns was familiar to him. Rand had no idea who he was, this fellow in a red silk coat with black stripes down its puffy sleeves and black breeches tucked into elaborately silver-worked boots. He did not know the man, but he had seen him in his dreams. "You put them in a cage," he said. "Egwene, and Nynaeve, and Elayne. In my dreams. You kept putting them in a cage, and hurting them."

The man made a dismissive gesture of his hand. "They are less than nothing. Perhaps one day, when they have been trained, but not now. I confess surprise that you cared enough to make them useful. But you were ever a fool, ever ready to follow your heart before power. You came too soon, Lews Therin. Now you must do what you are not yet ready for, or else die. Die, knowing you have left these women you care for in my hands." He seemed to be waiting for something, expectant. "I mean to use them more, Kinslayer. They will serve me, serve my power. And that will hurt them far more than anything they have suffered before."

Behind Rand, *Callandor* flashed, throwing one pulse of warmth against his back. "Who are you?"

"You do not remember me, do you?" The white-haired man laughed suddenly. "I do not remember you, either, looking this way. A country lad with a flute case on his back. Did Ishamael speak the truth? He was ever one to lie when it gained him an inch or a second. Do you remember nothing, Lews Therin?"

"A name!" Rand demanded. "What is your name?"

"Call me Be'lal." The Forsaken scowled when Rand did not react to the name. "Take it!" Be'lal snapped, throwing a hand toward the sword behind Rand. "Once we rode to war side by side, and for that I give you a chance. A bare chance, but a chance to save yourself, a chance to save those three I mean to make my pets. Take the sword, *countryman*. Perhaps it will be enough to help you survive me."

Rand laughed. "Do you believe you can frighten me so easily, Forsaken? Ba'alzamon himself has hunted me. Do you think I will cower now for you? Grovel before a Forsaken when I have denied the Dark One to his face?"

"Is that what you think?" Be'lal said softly. "Truly, you know nothing." Suddenly there was a sword in his hands, a sword with a blade carved from black fire. "Take it! Take *Callandor*! Three thousand years, while I lay imprisoned, it has waited there. For you. One of the most powerful *sa'angreal* we ever made. Take it, and defend yourself, if you can!"

He moved toward Rand as if to drive him back toward *Callandor*, but Rand raised his own hands—*saidin* filled him; sweet rushing flow of the Power; stomach-wrenching vileness of the taint—and he held a sword wrought from red flame, a sword with a heron-mark on its fiery blade. He stepped into the forms Lan had taught him till he flowed from one to the next as if in a dance. Parting the Silk. Water Flows Downhill. Wind and Rain. Blade of black fire met blade of red in showers of sparks, roars like white-hot metal shattering.

Rand came back smoothly into a guard stance, trying not to let his sudden uncertainty show. A heron stood on the black blade, too, a bird so dark as to be nearly invisible. Once he had faced a man with a heron-mark blade of steel, and barely survived. He knew that he himself had no real right to the blademaster's mark; it had been on the sword his father had given him, and when he thought of a sword in his hands, he thought of that sword. Once he had embraced death, as the Warder had taught, but this time, he knew, his death would be final. Be'lal was better than he with the sword. Stronger. Faster. A true blademaster.

The Forsaken laughed, amused, swinging his blade in quick flourishes to either side of him; the black fire roared as if swift passage through the air quickened it. "You were a greater swordsman, once, Lews Therin," he said mockingly. "Do you remember when we took that tame sport called swords and learned to kill with it, as the old volumes said men once had? Do you remember even one of those desperate battles, even one of our dire defeats? Of course not. You remember nothing, do you? This time you have not learned enough. This time, Lews Therin, I will kill you." Be'lal's mockery deepened. "Perhaps if you take *Callandor*, you might extend your life a little longer. A little longer."

He came forward slowly, almost as if to give Rand time to do just that, turn and race to *Callandor*, to the Sword That Cannot Be Touched, to take it. But the doubts were still strong in Rand. *Callandor* could only be touched by the Dragon Reborn. He had allowed them to proclaim him so for a hundred reasons that seemed to leave him no choice at the time. But was he truly the Dragon Reborn? If he raced to touch *Callandor* in truth, not in a dream, would his hand meet an invisible wall while Be'lal cut him down from behind?

He met the Forsaken with the sword he knew, the blade of fire wrought with *saidin*. And was driven back. The Falling Leaf met Watered Silk. The Cat Dances on the Wall met the Boar Rushes Downhill. The River Undercuts the Bank nearly lost him his head, and he had to throw himself inelegantly to one side with black flame brushing his hair, rolling to his feet to confront the Stone Falls From the Mountain. Methodically, deliberately, Be'lal drove him back in a spiral that slowly tightened on *Callandor.*

Shouts echoed among the columns, screams, the clash of steel, but Rand barely heard. He and Be'lal were no longer alone in the Heart of the Stone. Men in breastplates and rimmed helmets fought with swords against shadowy, veiled shapes that darted among the columns with short spears stabbing. Some of the soldiers formed a rank; arrows flashing out of the dimness took them in the throat, the face, and they died in their line. Rand hardly noticed the fighting, even when men fell dead within paces of him. His own fight was too desperate; it took all of his concentration. Wet warmth trickled down his side. The old wound was breaking open.

He stumbled suddenly, not seeing the dead man at his feet until he was lying on his back atop his flute case on the stone floor.

Be'lal raised his blade of black fire, snarling. "Take it! Take *Callandor* and defend yourself! Take it, or I will kill you now! If you will not take it, I will slay you!"

"No!"

Even Be'lal gave a start at the command in that woman's voice. The Forsaken stepped back out of the arc of Rand's sword and turned his head to frown at Moiraine as she came striding through the battle, her eyes fixed on him, ignoring the screaming deaths around her. "I thought you were neatly out of the way, woman. No matter. You are only an annoyance. A stinging fly. A biteme. I will cage you with the others, and teach you to serve the Shadow with your puny powers," he finished with a contemptuous laugh, and raised his free hand.

Moiraine had not stopped or slowed while he spoke. She was no more than thirty paces from him when he moved his hand, and she raised both of hers as well.

There was an instant of surprise on the Forsaken's face, and he had time to scream "No!" Then a bar of white fire hotter than the sun shot from the Aes Sedai's hands, a glaring rod that banished all shadows. Before it, Be'lal became a shape of shimmering motes, specks dancing in the light for less than a heartbeat, flecks consumed before his cry faded.

There was silence in the chamber as that bar of light

vanished, silence except for the moans of the wounded. The
fighting had stopped dead, veiled men and men in breastplates alike standing as if stunned.

"He was right concerning one thing," Moiraine said, as
coolly serene as if she were standing in a meadow. "You
must take *Callandor*. He meant to slay you for it, but it is
your birthright. Better by far that you knew more before
your hand held that hilt, yet you have come to the point now,
and there is no further time for learning. Take it, Rand."

Whips of black lightning curled around her; she screamed
as they lifted her, hurled her to slide along the floor like a
sack until she came up against one of the columns.

Rand stared up at where the lightning had come from.
There was a deeper shadow up there, near the top of the
columns, a blackness that made all other shadows look like
noonday, and from it, two eyes of fire stared back at him.

Slowly the shadow descended, resolving into Ba'alzamon,
clothed in dead black, like a Myrddraal's black. Yet even
that was not so dark as the shadow that clung to him. He
hung in the air, two spans above the floor, glaring at Rand
with a rage as fierce as his eyes. "Twice in this life I have
offered you the chance to serve me living." Flames leaped
in his mouth as he spoke, and every word roared like a furnace. "Twice you have refused, and wounded me. Now you
will serve the Lord of the Grave in death. Die, Lews Therin
Kinslayer. Die, Rand al'Thor. It is time for you to die! I take
your soul!"

As Ba'alzamon put forth his hand, Rand pushed himself
up, threw himself desperately toward *Callandor*, still glittering and flashing in midair. He did not know whether he
could reach it, or touch it if he did, but he was sure it was
his only chance.

Ba'alzamon's blow struck him as he leapt, struck inside
him, a ripping and crumpling, tearing something loose, trying to pull a part of him away. Rand screamed. He felt as if
he were collapsing like an empty sack, as if he were being
turned inside out. The pain in his side, the wound taken
at Falme, was almost welcome, something to hang on to,
a reminder of life. His hand closed convulsively. On *Callandor*'s hilt.

The One Power surged through him, a torrent greater
than he could believe, from *saidin* into the sword. The crys-

tal blade shone brighter than even Moiraine's fire had. It was impossible to look at, impossible any longer to see that it was a sword, only that light blazed in his fist. He fought the flow, wrestled with the implacable tide that threatened to carry him, all that was really him, into the sword with it. For a heartbeat that took centuries he hung, wavering, balanced on the brink of being scoured away like sand before a flash flood. With infinite slowness the balance firmed. It was still as though he stood barefoot on a razor's edge above a bottomless drop, yet something told him this was the best that could be expected. To channel this much of the Power, he must dance on that sharpness as he had danced the forms of the sword.

He turned to face Ba'alzamon. The tearing within him had ceased as soon as his hand touched *Callandor.* Only an instant had passed, yet it seemed to have lasted forever. "You will not take my soul," he shouted. "This time, I mean to finish it once and for all! I mean to finish it now!"

Ba'alzamon fled, man and shadow vanishing.

For a moment Rand stared, frowning. There had been a sense of—folding—as Ba'alzamon left. A twisting, as if Ba'alzamon had in some way *bent* what was. Ignoring the men staring at him, ignoring Moiraine crumpled at the column base, Rand reached out, through *Callandor,* and twisted reality to make a door to somewhere else. He did not know to where, except that it was where Ba'alzamon had gone.

"I am the hunter now," he said, and stepped through.

The stone shook under Egwene's feet. The Stone shook; it rang. She caught her balance and stopped, listening. There was no more sound, no other tremor. Whatever had happened, it was over. She hurried on. A door of iron bars stood in her way, with a lock as big as her head. She channeled Earth before she reached it, and when she pushed against the bars, the lock tore in half.

She walked quickly across the chamber beyond it, trying not to look at the things hanging on the walls. Whips and iron pincers were the most innocuous. With a small shudder she pushed open a smaller iron gate and entered a corridor lined with rough wooden doors, rush torches burning at intervals in iron brackets; she felt almost as much relief at leaving those things behind as she did at finding what she sought. *But which cell?*

The wooden doors opened easily. Some were unlocked, and the locks on the others lasted no longer than that larger lock had earlier. But every cell was empty. *Of course. No one would dream themselves in this place. Any prisoner who managed to reach Tel'aran'rhiod would dream of a pleasanter place.*

For a moment she felt something close to despair. She had wanted to believe that finding the right cell would make a difference. Even finding it could be impossible, though. This first corridor stretched on and on, and others joined it.

Suddenly she saw something flicker just ahead of her. A shape even less substantial than Joiya Byir had been. It had been a woman, though. She was sure of that. A woman seated on a bench beside one of the cell doors. The image flickered into being again, and was gone. There was no mistaking that slender neck and the pale, innocent-appearing face with its eyelids fluttering on the edge of sleep. Amico Nagoyin was drifting toward sleep, dreaming of her guard duties. And apparently toying drowsily with one of the stolen *ter'angreal*. Egwene could understand that; it had been a great effort to stop using the one Verin had given her, even for a few days.

She knew it was possible to cut a woman off from the True Source even if she had already embraced *saidar*, but severing a weave already established had to be much harder than damming the flow before it began. She set the patterns of the weaving, readied them, making the threads of Spirit much stronger, this time, thicker and heavier, a denser weave with a cutting edge like a knife.

The wavering shape of the Darkfriend appeared again, and Egwene struck out with the flows of Air and Spirit. For an instant something seemed to resist the weaving of Spirit, and she forced it with all of her might. It slid into place.

Amico Nagoyin screamed. It was a thin sound, barely heard, as faint as she herself was, and she seemed almost like a shadow of what Joiya Byir had been. Yet the bonds woven of Air held her; she did not vanish again. Terror twisted the Darkfriend's lovely face; she seemed to be babbling, but her shouts were whispers too soft for Egwene to understand.

Tying and setting the weaves around the Black sister, Egwene turned her attentions to the cell door. Impatiently, she let Earth flood into the iron lock. It fell away in black dust, in a mist that dissolved completely before it struck the floor. She swung open the door, and was not surprised to find the cell empty except for one burning rush torch.

But Amico is bound, and the door is open.

For a moment she thought of what to do next. Then she stepped out of the dream . . .

. . . and woke to all her bruises and aches and thirst, to the wall of the cell against her back, staring at the tightly shut cell door. *Of course. What happens to living things there is real when they wake. What I did to stone or iron or wood has no effect in the waking world.*

Nynaeve and Elayne were still kneeling beside her.

"Whoever is out there," Nynaeve said, "screamed a few moments ago, but nothing else has happened. Did you find a way out?"

"We should be able to walk out," Egwene said. "Help me to my feet, and I will get rid of the lock. Amico will not trouble us. That scream was her."

Elayne shook her head. "I have been trying to embrace *saidar* ever since you left. It is different, now, but I am still cut off."

Egwene formed the emptiness inside her, became the rosebud opening to *saidar*. The invisible wall was still there. It shimmered now. There were moments when she almost thought she could feel the True Source beginning to fill her with the Power. Almost. The shield wavered in and out of existence too fast for her to detect. It might as well have still been solid.

She stared at the other two women. "I bound her. I shielded her. She is a living thing, not lifeless iron. She *must* be shielded still."

"*Some*thing has happened to the shield set on us," Elayne said, "but Amico is still managing to hold it."

Egwene let her head sag back against the wall. "I will have to try again."

"Are you strong enough?" Elayne grimaced. "To be blunt, you sound even weaker than you did before. This try took something out of you, Egwene."

"I am strong enough there." She did feel more weary, less strong, but it was their only chance that she could see. She said as much, and their faces said they agreed with her, however reluctantly.

"Can you go to sleep again so soon?" Nynaeve asked finally.

"Sing to me." Egwene managed a smile. "Like when I was a little girl. Please?" Holding Nynaeve's hand with one of hers, the stone ring clasped in the other, she closed her eyes and tried to find sleep in the wordless humming tune.

The wide door of iron bars stood open, and the room beyond seemed empty of life, but Mat entered cautiously. Sandar was still out in the hall, trying to peer both ways at once, certain that a High Lord, or maybe a hundred Defenders or so, would appear at any moment.

There were no men in the room now—and by the looks of the half-eaten meals on a long table, they had left hurriedly; no doubt because of the fighting above—and from the looks of the things on the walls, he was just as glad he did not have to meet any of them. Whips in different sizes and lengths, different thicknesses, with different numbers of tails. Pincers, and tongs, and clamps, and irons. Things that looked like metal boots, and gauntlets, and helmets, with great screws all over them as if to tighten them down. Things he could not even begin to guess the use of. If he had met the men who used these things, he thought he would surely have checked that *they* were dead before he walked away.

"Sandar!" he hissed. "Are you going to stay out there all bloody night!" He hurried to the inner door—barred like the outer, but smaller—without waiting for an answer, and went through.

The hall beyond was lined by rough wooden doors, and lit by the same rush torches as the room he had just left. No more than twenty paces from him, a woman sat on a bench beside one of the doors, leaning back against the wall in a curiously stiff fashion. She turned her head slowly toward him at the sound of his boots grating on the stone. A pretty young woman. He wondered why she did not move more than her head, and why even that moved as if she were half-asleep.

Was she a prisoner? *Out in the hall? But nobody with a face like that could be one of the people who uses the things on those walls.* She did look almost asleep, with her eyes only partly open. And the suffering on that lovely face surely made her one of the tortured, not a torturer.

"Stop!" Sandar shouted behind him. "She is Aes Sedai! She is one of those who took the women you seek!"

Mat froze in the middle of a step, staring at the woman. He remembered Moiraine hurling balls of fire. He wondered if he could deflect a ball of fire with his quarterstaff. He wondered if his luck extended to outrunning Aes Sedai.

"Help me," she said faintly. Her eyes still looked nearly asleep, but the pleading in her voice was fully awake. "Help me. Please!"

Mat blinked. She still had not moved a muscle below her neck. Cautiously, he stepped closer, waving to Sandar to stop his groaning about her being Aes Sedai. She moved her head to follow him. No more than that.

A large iron key hung at her belt. For a moment he hesitated. Aes Sedai, Sandar said. *Why doesn't she move?* Swallowing, he eased the key free as carefully as if he were trying to take a piece of meat from a wolf's jaws. She rolled her eyes toward the door beside her and made a sound like a cat that had just seen a huge dog come snarling into the room and knew there was no way out.

He did not understand it, but as long as she did not try to stop him opening that door, he did not care why she just sat there like a stuffed scarecrow. On the other hand, he wondered if there was something on the other side worth being afraid of. *If she is one of those who took Egwene and the others, it stands to reason she's guarding them.* Tears leaked from the woman's eyes. *Only she looks like it's a bloody Halfman in there.* But there was only one way to find out. Propping his staff against the wall, he turned the key in the lock and flung open the door, ready to run if need be.

Nynaeve and Elayne were kneeling on the floor with Egwene apparently asleep between them. He gasped at the sight of Egwene's swollen face, and changed his mind about her sleeping. The other two women turned toward him as he opened the door—they were almost as battered as Egwene; *Burn me! Burn me!*—looked at him, and gaped.

"Matrim Cauthon," Nynaeve said, sounding shocked, "what under the Light are *you* doing here?"

"I came to bloody rescue you," he said. "Burn me if I expected to be greeted as if I had come to steal a pie. You can tell me why you look as if you'd been fighting bears later, if you want. If Egwene cannot walk, I'll carry her on my back. There are Aiel all over the Stone, or near enough, and either they are killing the bloody Defenders or the bloody Defenders are killing them, but whichever way it is, we had better get out of here while we bloody well can. *If* we can!"

"Mind your language," Nynaeve told him, and Elayne gave him one of those disapproving stares women were so good at. Neither one seemed to have her full attention in it, though. They began shaking Egwene as if she were not covered with more bruises than he had ever seen in his life.

Egwene's eyelids fluttered open, and she groaned. "Why did you wake me? I must understand it. If I loose the bonds on her, she will wake and I'll never catch her again. But if I do not, she cannot go all the way to sleep, and—" Her eyes fell on him and widened. "Matrim Cauthon, what under the Light are *you* doing here?"

"You tell her," he told Nynaeve. "I am too busy trying to rescue you to watch my langu—" They were all staring beyond him, glaring as if they wished they had knives in their hands.

He spun, but all he saw was Juilin Sandar, looking as if he had swallowed a rotten plum whole.

"They have cause," he told Mat. "I. . . . I betrayed them. But I had to." That was addressed past Mat to the women. "The one with many honey-colored braids spoke to me, and I. . . . I had to do it." For a long moment the three continued to stare.

"Liandrin has vile tricks, Master Sandar," Nynaeve said finally. "Perhaps you are not entirely to blame. We can apportion guilt later."

"If that is all cleared up," Mat said, "could we go now?" It was as clear as mud to him, but he was more interested in leaving right then.

The three women limped after him into the hall, but they stopped around the woman on the bench. She rolled her eyes at them and whimpered. "Please. I will come back to the Light. I will swear to obey you. With the Oath Rod in my hands I will swear. Please do not—"

Mat jumped as Nynaeve suddenly reared back and swung a fist, knocking the woman completely off the bench. She lay there, her eyes closed all the way finally, but even lying on her side she was still in exactly the same position she had been in on the bench.

"It is gone," Elayne said excitedly.

Egwene bent to rummage in the unconscious woman's pouch, transferring something Mat could not make out to her own. "Yes. It feels wonderful. Something changed about her when you hit her, Nynaeve. I do not know what, but I felt it."

Elayne nodded. "I felt it, too."

"I would like to change every last thing about her," Nynaeve said grimly. She took Egwene's head in her hands; Egwene rose onto her toes, gasping. When Nynaeve took her hands away to put them on Elayne, Egwene's bruises were gone. Elayne's vanished as quickly.

"Blood and bloody ashes!" Mat growled. "What do you mean hitting a woman who was just sitting there? I don't think she could even move!" They all three turned to look at him, and he made a strangled sound as the air seemed to turn to thick jelly around him. He lifted into the air, until his boots dangled a good pace above the floor. *Oh, burn me, the Power! Here I was afraid that Aes Sedai would use the bloody Power on me, and now the bloody women I'm rescuing do it! Burn me!*

"You do not understand anything, Matrim Cauthon," Egwene said in a tight voice.

"Until you do understand," Nynaeve said in an even tighter, "I suggest you keep your opinions to yourself."

Elayne contented herself with a glare that made him think of his mother going out to cut a switch.

For some reason he found himself giving them the grin that had so often sent his mother after that switch. *Burn me, if they can do this, I don't see how anybody ever locked them in that cell in the first place!* "What I understand is that I got you out of something you couldn't get yourselves

out of, and you all have as much gratitude as a bloody Taren
Ferry man with a toothache!"

"You are right," Nynaeve said, and his boots suddenly hit
the floor so hard his teeth jarred. But he could move again.
"As much as it pains me to say it, Mat, you are right."

He was tempted to answer something sarcastic, but there
was barely enough apology in her voice as it was. "Now can
we go? With the fighting going on, Sandar thinks he and I
can take you out by a small gate near the river."

"I am not leaving just yet, Mat," Nynaeve said.

"I mean to find Liandrin and skin her," Egwene said,
sounding almost as if she meant it literally.

"All I want to do," Elayne said, "is pound Joiya Byir till
she squeals, but I will settle for any of them."

"Are you all deaf?" he growled. "There is a battle going
on out there! I came here to rescue you, and I mean to rescue you." Egwene patted his cheek as she walked by him,
and so did Elayne. Nynaeve merely sniffed. He stared after
them with his mouth hanging open. "Why didn't you say
something?" he growled at the thief-catcher.

"I saw what speaking earned you," Sandar said simply.
"I am no fool."

"Well, I am not staying in the middle of a battle!" he
shouted at the women. They were just disappearing through
the small, barred door. "I am leaving, do you hear?" They
did not even look back. *Probably get themselves killed out
there! Somebody will stick a sword in them while they're
looking the other way!* With a snarl, he put his quarterstaff
across his shoulder and started after. "Are you going to
stand there?" he called to the thief-catcher. "I did not come
this far to let them die now!"

Sandar caught up to him in the room with the whips.
The three women were already gone, but Mat had a feeling
they would not be too hard to find. *Just find the men bloody
hanging in midair! Bloody women!* He quickened his pace
to a trot.

Perrin strode down the halls of the Stone grimly, searching
for some sign of Faile. He had rescued her twice more, now,
breaking her out of an iron cage once, much like the one
that had held the Aiel in Remen, and once breaking open a

steel chest with a falcon worked on its side. Both times she had melted into air after saying his name. Hopper trotted by his side, sniffing the air. As sharp as Perrin's nose was, the wolf's was sharper; it had been Hopper who led them to the chest.

Perrin wondered whether he was ever going to free her in truth. There had not been any sign in a long time, it seemed. The halls of the Stone were empty, lamps burning, tapestries and weapons hanging on the walls, but nothing moved except himself and Hopper. *Except I think that was Rand.* It had only been a glimpse, a man running as if chasing someone. *It could not be him. It couldn't, but I think it was.*

Hopper quickened his steps suddenly, heading for another set of tall doors, these clad in bronze. Perrin tried to match the pace, stumbled, and fell to his knees, throwing out a hand to catch himself short of dropping on his face. Weakness washed through him as if all his muscles had gone to water. Even after the feeling receded, it took some of his strength with it. It was an effort to struggle to his feet. Hopper had turned to look at him.

You are here too strongly, Young Bull. The flesh weakens. You do not care to hold on to it enough. Soon flesh and dream will die together.

"Find her," Perrin said. "That is all I ask. Find Faile."

Yellow eyes met yellow eyes. The wolf turned and trotted to the doors. *Beyond here, Young Bull.*

Perrin reached the doors and pushed. They did not budge. There seemed to be no way to open them, no handles, nothing to grip. There was a tiny pattern worked into the metal, so fine his eyes almost did not see it. Falcons. Thousands of tiny falcons.

She has to be here. I do not think I can last much longer. With a shout, he swung his hammer against the bronze. It rang like a great gong. Again he struck, and the peal deepened. A third blow, and the bronze doors shattered like glass.

Within, a hundred paces from the broken doors, a circle of light surrounded a falcon chained to a perch. Darkness filled all the rest of that vast chamber, darkness and faint rustlings as of hundreds of wings.

He took a step into the room, and a falcon stooped out of the murk, talons scoring his face as it passed. He threw an

arm across his eyes—talons tore at his forearm—and staggered toward the perch. Again and again the birds came,
falcons diving, striking him, tearing him, but he lumbered
on with blood pouring down his arms and shoulders, that
one arm protecting the eyes he had fixed on the falcon on
the perch. He had lost the hammer; he did not know where,
but he knew that if he went back to search, he would die
before he found it.

As he reached the perch, the slicing talons drove him
to his knees. He peered up under his arm at the falcon on
the perch, and she stared back with dark, unblinking eyes.
The chain that held her leg was fastened to the perch with a
tiny lock shaped like a hedgehog. He seized the chain with
both hands, careless of the other falcons that now became
a whirlwind of cutting talons around him, and with his last
strength snapped it. Pain and the falcons brought darkness.

He opened his eyes to stinging agony, as if his face and
arms and shoulders had been sliced with a thousand knives.
It did not matter. Faile was kneeling over him, those dark,
tilted eyes filled with worry, wiping his face with a cloth
already soaked in his blood.

"My poor Perrin," she said softly. "My poor blacksmith.
You are hurt so badly."

With an effort that cost more pain, he turned his head.
This was the private dining room in the Star, and near one
leg of the table lay a wooden carving of a hedgehog, broken
in half. "Faile," he whispered to her. "My falcon."

Rand was still in the Heart of the Stone, but it was different. There were no men fighting here, no dead men, no one
at all but himself. Abruptly the sound of a great gong rang
through the Stone, then again, and the very stones beneath
his feet resonated. A third time the booming came, but cut
off abruptly, as if the gong had shattered. All was still.

Where is this place? he wondered. *More important,
where is Ba'alzamon?*

As if to answer him, a blazing shaft like the one Moiraine had made shot out of the shadows among the columns, straight toward his chest. His wrist twisted the sword

instinctively; it was instinct as much as anything else that made him loose flows from *saidin* into *Callandor*, a flood of the Power that made the sword blaze brighter even than that bar streaking at him. His uncertain balance between existence and destruction wavered. Surely that torrent would consume him.

The shaft of light struck the blade of *Callandor*—and parted on its edge, forking to stream past on either side. He felt his coat singe from its near passage, smelled the wool beginning to burn. Behind him, the two prongs of frozen fire, of liquid light, struck huge redstone columns; where they struck, stone ceased to exist, and the burning bars bored through to other columns, severing those instantaneously as well. The Heart of the Stone rumbled as columns fell and shattered in clouds of dust, sprays of stone fragments. What fell into the light, however, simply—was not, anymore.

A snarl of rage came from the shadows, and the blazing shaft of pure white heat vanished.

Rand swung *Callandor* as if he were striking at something in front of him. The white light obscuring the blade extended, blazed ahead, and sheared through the redstone column that hid the snarl. The polished stone sliced like silk. The severed column trembled; part of it tore loose and dropped from the ceiling, smashing into huge, jagged chunks on the floor. As the rumbling faded, he heard beyond it the sound of boots on stone. Running.

Callandor at the ready, Rand hurried after Ba'alzamon.

The tall archway leading out of the Heart collapsed as he reached it, the entire wall falling in clouds of dust and rock as if to bury him, but he threw the Power at it, and all became dust floating in the air. He ran on. He was not sure what he had done, or how, but he had no time to think on it. He ran after Ba'alzamon's retreating footsteps, echoing down the halls of the Stone.

Myrddraal and Trollocs leaped out of thin air, huge bestial shapes and eyeless faces distorted with a rage to kill, in hundreds, so they jammed the hall before him and behind, scythelike swords and blades of deadly black steel seeking his blood. Without knowing how, he turned them to vapor that parted before him—and vanished. The air around him suddenly became choking soot, clogging his nostrils, shutting off breath, but he made it fresh air again, a cool mist. Flames leaped from the floor beneath his feet, spurted from the walls, the ceiling, furious jets that flashed tapestries and rugs, tables and chests to wisps of ash, flung ornaments and lamps ahead of them as drops of molten, burning gold; he smashed the fires flat, hardened them into a red glaze on the rock.

The stones around him faded almost to mist; the Stone faded. Reality trembled; he could feel it unraveling, feel himself unraveling. He was being pushed out of the here, into some other place where nothing existed at all. *Callandor* blazed in his hands like the sun till he thought it would melt. He thought he himself would melt from the surge of the One Power through him, the flood that he somehow directed into sealing up the hole that had opened around him, into holding himself on the side of existence. The Stone became solid again.

He could not even begin to imagine what it was that he did. The One Power raged inside him till he barely knew himself, till he barely was himself, till what was himself almost did not exist. His precarious stability teetered. To either side lay the endless fall, obliteration by the Power that coursed through him into the sword. Only in the dance along the razor's sharp edge was there even an uncertain safety. *Callandor* shone in his fist until it seemed he carried the sun. Dimly within him, fluttering like a candle flame in a storm, was the surety that holding *Callandor*, he could do anything. Anything.

Through endless corridors he ran, dancing along the razor, chasing the one who would slay him, the one he must slay. There could be no other end, this time. This time one of them *must* die! That Ba'alzamon knew it as well was clear. Always he fled, always staying ahead of sight so that only the sounds of his flight drew Rand on, but even fleeing he turned this Stone of Tear that was not the Stone of Tear against Rand, and Rand fought back with instinct and guesses and chance, fought and ran down that knife edge in perfect balance with the Power, the tool and weapon that would consume him utterly if he faltered.

Water filled the halls from top to bottom, thick and black as the bottom of the sea, choking off breath. He made it air again, unknowingly, and ran on, and suddenly the air gained weight until it seemed every inch of his skin supported a mountain, squeezing in from all directions. In the instant before he was crushed to nothingness he chose tides out of the flood of Power raging through him—he did not know how or which or why; it was too fast for thought or knowing—and the pressure vanished. He pursued Ba'alzamon, and the very air was abruptly solid rock encasing him, then molten stone, then nothing at all to fill his lungs. The ground beneath his boots pulled at him as if every pound suddenly weighed a thousand, then all weight vanished so that a step left him spinning in midair. Unseen maws gaped to rip his mind from his body, to tear away his soul. He sprang each trap and ran on; what Ba'alzamon twisted to destroy him, he made right without being aware of how. Vaguely he knew that in some way he had brought things back into natural balance, forced them into line with his own dance down that impossibly thin divide between existence and nothingness, but that knowledge was distant. All his awareness lay in the pursuit, the hunt, the death that must end it.

And then he was in the Heart of the Stone again, stalking through the rubbled gap that had been a wall. Some of the columns hung like broken teeth, now. And Ba'alzamon backed away from him, eyes burning, shadow cloaking him. Black lines like steel wires seemed to run off from Ba'alzamon into the darkness mounding around him, vanishing into unimaginable heights and distances within that blackness.

"I will not be undone!" Ba'alzamon cried. His mouth was fire; his shriek echoed among the columns. "I cannot be defeated! Aid me!" Some of the darkness shrouding him drifted into his hands, formed into a ball so black it seemed to soak up even the light of *Callandor*. Sudden triumph blazed in the flames of his eyes.

"You are destroyed!" Rand shouted. *Callandor* spun in his hands. Its light roiled the darkness, severed the steel-black lines around Ba'alzamon, and Ba'alzamon convulsed. As if there were two of him he seemed to dwindle and grow larger at the same time. "You are undone!" Rand plunged the shining blade into Ba'alzamon's chest.

Ba'alzamon screamed, and the fires of his face flared wildly. "Fool!" he howled. "The Great Lord of the Dark can never be defeated!"

Rand pulled *Callandor*'s blade free as Ba'alzamon's body sagged and began to fall, the shadow around him vanishing.

And suddenly Rand was in another Heart of the Stone, surrounded by columns still whole, and fighting men screaming and dying, veiled men and men in breastplates and helmets. Moiraine still lay crumpled at the base of a redstone column. And at Rand's feet lay the body of a man, sprawled on its back with a hole burned through the chest. He might have been a handsome man in his middle years, except that where his eyes and mouth should have been were only pits from which rose tendrils of black smoke.

I have done it, he thought. *I have killed Ba'alzamon, killed Shai'tan! I have won the Last Battle! Light, I AM the Dragon Reborn! The breaker of nations, the Breaker of the World. No! I will END the breaking, end the killing! I will MAKE it end!*

He raised *Callandor* above his head. Silver lightning crackled from the blade, jagged streaks arching toward the great dome above. "Stop!" he shouted. The fighting ceased; men stared at him in wonder, over black veils, from beneath the rims of round helmets. "I am Rand al'Thor!" he called, so his voice rang through the chamber. "I am the Dragon Reborn!" *Callandor* shone in his grasp.

One by one, veiled men and helmeted, they knelt to him, crying, "The Dragon is Reborn! The Dragon is Reborn!"

CHAPTER
56

People of the Dragon

Throughout the city of Tear people woke with the dawn, speaking of the dreams they had had, dreams of the Dragon battling Ba'alzamon in the Heart of the Stone, and when their eyes rose to the great fortress of the Stone, they beheld a banner waving from its greatest height. Across a field of white flowed a sinuous form like a great serpent scaled in scarlet and gold, but with a golden lion's mane and four legs, each tipped with five golden claws. Men came, stunned and frightened, from the Stone to speak in hushed tones of what had happened in the night, and men and women thronged the streets, weeping as they shouted the fulfillment of Prophecy.

"The Dragon!" they shouted. "Al'Thor! The Dragon! Al'Thor!"

Peering through an arrowslit high on the side of the Stone, Mat shook his head as he listened to the chorus rising out of the city in waves. *Well, maybe he is.* He was still having a hard enough time coming to grips with Rand really being there.

Everyone in the Stone seemed to agree with the people below, or if they did not, they were not letting on. He had seen Rand just once since the night before, striding along a hall with *Callandor* in his hand, surrounded by a dozen veiled Aiel and trailing a cloud of Tairens, a knot of Defenders of the Stone and most of the few surviving High Lords. The High Lords, at least, seemed to think Rand would need them to help him rule the world; the Aiel kept everyone back with sharp looks, though, and spears if need be. They surely believed Rand was the Dragon, though they called him He Who Comes With the Dawn. There were nearly two hundred Aiel in the Stone. They had lost a third of their numbers in the fight, but they had killed or captured ten times as many Defenders.

As he turned from the arrowslit, his eyes brushed across Rhuarc. There was a tall stand at one end of the room, carved and polished upright wheels of some pale, dark-striped wood with shelves slung between them so all of the shelves would stay flat as the wheels were revolved. Each shelf held a large book, bound in gold, covers set with sparkling gems. The Aiel had one of the books open and was reading. Some sort of essays, Mat thought. *Who would have thought an Aiel would read books? Who'd have thought an Aiel could bloody read?*

Rhuarc glanced in his direction, all cold blue eyes and level stare. Mat looked away hastily, before the Aiel could read his thoughts on his face. *At least he is not veiled, thank the Light! Burn me, that Aviendha nearly took my head off when I asked her if she could do any dances without spears.* Bain and Chiad presented another problem. They were certainly pretty and more than friendly, but he could not manage to talk to one without the other. The male Aiel seemed to think his efforts to get one of them alone were funny, and for that matter, so did Bain and Chiad. *Women are odd, but Aiel women make odd seem normal!*

The great table in the middle of the room, ornately carved and gilded on edges and thick legs, had been meant for gatherings of the High Lords. Moiraine sat in one of the thronelike chairs, with the Crescent Banner of Tear worked into its towering back in gilt and polished carnelian and pearlshell. Egwene, Nynaeve, and Elayne sat close by her.

"I still cannot believe Perrin is here in Tear," Nynaeve was saying. "Are you sure he is all right?"

Mat shook his head. He would have expected Perrin to have been up in the Stone last night; the blacksmith had always been braver than anyone with good sense.

"He was well when I left him." Moiraine's voice was serene. "Whether he still is, I do not know. His . . . companion is in some considerable danger, and he may have put himself into it, also."

"His companion?" Egwene said sharply. "Wha— Who is Perrin's companion?"

"What sort of danger?" Nynaeve demanded.

"Nothing that need concern you," the Aes Sedai said calmly. "I will go and see to her as I may, shortly. I have delayed only to show you this, which I found among the *ter'angreal* and other things of the Power the High Lords collected over the years." She took something from her pouch and laid it on the table before her. It was a disc the size of a man's hand, seemingly made of two teardrops fitted together, one black as pitch, the other white as snow.

Mat seemed to remember seeing others like it. Ancient, like this one, but broken, where this was whole. Three of them, he had seen; not all together, but all in pieces. But that could not be; he remembered that they were made of *cuendillar*, unbreakable by any power, even the One Power.

"One of the seven seals Lews Therin Kinslayer and the Hundred Companions put on the Dark One's prison when they resealed it," Elayne said, nodding as if confirming her own memory.

"More precisely," Moiraine told her, "a focus point for one of the seals. But in essence, you are correct. During the Breaking of the World they were scattered and hidden for safety; since the Trolloc Wars they have been lost in truth." She sniffed. "I begin to sound like Verin."

Egwene shook her head. "I suppose I should have expected to find that here. Twice before Rand faced Ba'alzamon, and both times at least one of the seals was present."

"And this time unbroken," Nynaeve said. "For the first time, the seal is unbroken. As if that mattered, now."

"You think it does not?" Moiraine's voice was dangerous in its quiet, and the other women frowned at her.

Mat rolled his eyes. They kept talking about unimportant things. He did not much like standing not twenty feet from that disc now that he knew what it was, no matter the value of *cuendillar*, but. . . . "Your pardon?" he said.

They all turned to stare at him as if he were interrupting something important. *Burn me! Break them out of a prison cell, save their lives half a dozen times between them before the night is done, and they glower as hard as the bloody Aes Sedai! Well, they did not thank me then, either, did they? You'd have thought I was sticking my nose in where it wasn't wanted then, too, instead of keeping some bloody Defender from putting a sword through one of them.* Aloud, he said mildly, "You do not mind if I ask a question, do you? You have all been talking this Aes Sedai . . . uh . . . business, and no one has bothered to tell me anything."

"Mat?" Nynaeve said warningly, tugging her braid, but Moiraine said, in a calm only just touched with impatience, "What is it that you wish to know?"

"I want to know how all of this can be." He meant to keep his tone soft, but despite himself he picked up intensity as he went along. "The Stone of Tear has fallen! The Prophecies said that would never happen till the People of the Dragon came. Does that mean *we* are the bloody People of the Dragon? You, me, Lan, and a few hundred bloody Aiel?" He had seen the Warder during the night; there had not seemed to be much edge between Lan and the Aiel as to who was the more deadly. As Rhuarc straightened to stare at him, he hastily added, "Uh, sorry, Rhuarc. Slip of the tongue."

"Perhaps," Moiraine said slowly. "I came to stop Be'lal from killing Rand. I did not expect to see the Stone of Tear fall. Perhaps we are. Prophecies are fulfilled as they are meant to be, not as we think they should be."

Be'lal. Mat shivered. He had heard that name last night, and he did not like it any more in daylight. If he had known one of the Forsaken was loose—and inside the Stone—he would never have gone near the place. He glanced at Egwene, and Nynaeve, and Elayne. *Well, I'd have come in like a bloody mouse, anyway, not thumping people left and right!* Sandar had gone scurrying out of the Stone at daybreak; to take the news to Mother Guenna, he claimed, but Mat thought it was just to escape those stares from the three women, who looked as if they had not yet quite decided what to do about him.

Rhuarc cleared his throat. "When a man wishes to become a clan chief, he must go to Rhuidean, in the lands of the Jenn Aiel, the clan that is not." He spoke slowly and frowned often at the red-fringed silk carpet under his soft boots, a man trying to explain what he did not want to explain at all. "Women who wish to become Wise Ones also make this journey, but their marking, if they *are* marked, is kept secret among themselves. The men who are chosen at Rhuidean, those who survive, return marked on the left arm. So."

He pushed back the sleeves of his coat and shirt together to reveal his left forearm, the skin much paler than that of his hands and face. Etched into the skin as if part of it, wrapped twice around, marched the same gold-and-scarlet form as rippled on the banner above the Stone.

The Aiel let his sleeve fall with a sigh. "It is a name not spoken except among the clan chiefs and the Wise Ones. We are. . . ." He cleared his throat again, unable to say it here.

"The Aiel are the People of the Dragon." Moiraine spoke quietly, but she sounded as close to startlement as Mat could remember ever hearing her. "That I did not know."

"Then it really is all done," Mat said, "just as the Prophecies said. We can all go on our way with no more worries." *The Amyrlin won't need me to blow that bloody Horn now!*

"How can you say that?" Egwene demanded. "Don't you understand the Forsaken are loose?"

"Not to mention the Black Ajah," Nynaeve added grimly. "We took only Amico and Joiya here. Eleven escaped— and I would like to know how!—and the Light alone knows how many others there are we do not know."

"Yes," Elayne said in a tone just as hard. "I may not be up to facing one of the Forsaken, but I mean to take pieces out of Liandrin's hide!"

"Of course," Mat said smoothly. "Of course." *Are they crazy? They want to chase after the Black Ajah* and *the Forsaken?* "I only meant the hardest part is done. The Stone has fallen to the People of the Dragon, Rand has *Callandor*, and Shai'tan is dead." Moiraine's stare was so hard that he thought the Stone shook for a moment.

"Be quiet, you fool!" the Aes Sedai said in a voice like a knife. "Do you want to call his attention to you, naming the Dark One?"

"But he's dead!" Mat protested. "Rand killed him. I saw the body!" *And a fine stink that was, too. I never thought anything could rot that fast.*

"You saw 'the body,'" Moiraine said with a twist to her mouth. "A man's body. Not the Dark One, Mat."

He looked at Egwene and the other two women; they appeared as confused as he. Rhuarc looked to be thinking of a battle he had thought was won and now learned had not even been fought. "Then who was it?" Mat demanded. "Moiraine, my memory has holes big enough for a wagon and team, but I remember Ba'alzamon being in my dreams. I remember! Burn me, I do not see how I can ever forget! And I recognized what was left of that face."

"You recognized Ba'alzamon," Moiraine said. "Or rather, the man who called himself Ba'alzamon. The Dark One yet lives, imprisoned at Shayol Ghul, and the Shadow yet lies across the Pattern."

"The Light illumine and protect us," Elayne murmured in a faint voice. "I thought. . . . I thought the Forsaken were the worst we had to worry about, now."

"Are you sure, Moiraine?" Nynaeve said. "Rand was certain—*is* certain—that he killed the Dark One. You seem to be saying Ba'alzamon was not the Dark One at all. I don't understand! How can you be so sure? And if he was not the Dark One, who was he?"

"I can be sure for the simplest of reasons, Nynaeve. However fast decay took it, that was a man's body. Can you believe that if the Dark One were killed he would leave a human body? The man Rand killed *was* a man. Perhaps he was the first of the Forsaken freed, or perhaps he was never entirely bound. We may never know which."

"I . . . may know who he was." Egwene paused with an uncertain frown. "At least, I may have a clue. Verin showed me a page from an old book that mentioned Ba'alzamon and Ishamael together. It was almost High Chant and very nearly incomprehensible, but I remember something about 'a name hidden behind a name.' Maybe Ba'alzamon was Ishamael."

"Perhaps," Moiraine said. "Perhaps it was Ishamael. But if it was, at least nine of the thirteen still live. Lanfear, and Sammael, and Ravhin, and. . . . Paah! Even knowing that some of those nine at least are free is not the most important thing." She laid a hand atop the black-and-white disc on the table. "Three of the seals are broken. Only four still hold. Only those four seals stand between the Dark One and the world, and it may be that even with those whole he can touch the world after a fashion. Whatever battle we won here—battle or skirmish—it is far from the last."

Mat watched their faces firm—Egwene's and Nynaeve's

and Elayne's; slowly, reluctantly, but determinedly, too—and shook his head. *Bloody women! They're all ready to go on with this, go on chasing the Black Ajah, trying to fight the Forsaken and the bloody Dark One. Well, they needn't think I am going to come pull them out of the soup pot again. They just needn't think it, that's all!*

One of the tall, paired doors pushed open while he was trying to think of something to say, and a tall young woman of regal bearing entered the room, wearing a coronet with a golden hawk in flight above her brows. Her black hair swept to pale shoulders, and her dress of the finest red silk left those shoulders bare, along with a considerable expanse of what Mat noted as an admirable bosom. For a moment she studied Rhuarc interestedly with large, dark eyes; then she turned them on the women at the table, coolly imperious. Mat she appeared to ignore completely.

"I am not used to being given messages to carry," she announced, flourishing a folded parchment in one slim hand.

"And who are you, child?" Moiraine asked.

The young woman drew herself up even more, which Mat would have thought was impossible. "I am Berelain, First of Mayene." She tossed the parchment down on the table in front of Moiraine with a haughty gesture and turned back to the door.

"A moment, child," Moiraine said, unfolding the parchment. "Who gave this to you? And why did you bring it, if you are so unused to carrying messages?"

"I . . . do not know." Berelain stood facing the door; she sounded puzzled. "She was . . . impressive." She gave herself a shake and seemed to recover her opinion of herself. For a moment she studied Rhuarc with a small smile. "You are the leader of these Aielmen? Your fighting disturbed my sleep. Perhaps I will ask you to dine with me. One day quite soon." She looked over her shoulder at Moiraine. "I am told the Dragon Reborn has taken the Stone. Inform the Lord Dragon that the First of Mayene will dine with him tonight." And she marched out of the room; Mat could think of no other way to describe that stately, one-woman procession.

"I would like to have *her* in the Tower as novice." Egwene and Elayne said it almost like echoes, then shared a tight smile.

"Listen to this," Moiraine said. "'Lews Therin was mine, he is mine, and he will be mine, forever. I give him into your charge, to keep for me until I come.' It is signed 'Lanfear.'" The Aes Sedai turned that cool gaze on Mat. "And you thought it was done? You are *ta'veren*, Mat, a thread more crucial to the Pattern than most, and the sounder of the Horn of Valere. Nothing is done for you, yet."

They were all looking at him. Nynaeve sadly, Egwene as though she had never seen him before, Elayne as if she expected him to change into someone else. Rhuarc had a certain respect in his eyes, though Mat would just as soon have done without it, all things considered.

"Well, of course," he told them. *Burn me!* "I understand." *I wonder how soon Thom will be fit to travel? Time to run. Maybe Perrin will come with us.* "You can count on me."

From outside, the cries still rose, unceasing. "The Dragon! Al'Thor! The Dragon! Al'Thor! The Dragon! Al'Thor! The Dragon!"

And it was written that no hand but his should wield the Sword held in the Stone, but he did draw it out, like fire in his hand, and his glory did burn the world. Thus did it begin. Thus do we sing his Rebirth. Thus do we sing the beginning.

—from *Do'in Toldara te, Songs of the Last Age*,
Quarto Nine: The Legend of the Dragon.
Composed by Boanne, Songmistress
at Taralan, the Fourth Age.

The End

of the Third Book of

The Wheel of Time

GLOSSARY

A Note on Dates in This Glossary. Three systems of recording dates have been in general use since the Breaking of the World. The first recorded years After the Breaking (AB). Since the years of the Breaking and immediately after were years of almost total chaos, and since this calendar was adopted a good hundred years after the end of the Breaking, its starting point was arbitrarily assigned. At the end of the Trolloc Wars many records had been lost, so much so that there was argument about the exact year under the old system. A new calendar was therefore established, dating from the end of the Wars and celebrating the supposed freedom of the world from the Trolloc threat. This second calendar recorded each year as Free Year (FY). After the disruption, death, and destruction caused by the War of the Hundred Years, a third calendar came into being. This calendar, of the New Era (NE), is currently in use.

Accepted, the: Young women in training to be Aes Sedai who have reached a certain level of power and passed certain tests. It normally takes five to ten years to be raised from novice to the Accepted. Accepted are somewhat less confined by rules than novices, and are allowed to choose their own areas of study, within limits. An Accepted has the right to wear a Great Serpent ring, but only on the third finger of her left hand. When an Accepted is raised to Aes Sedai, she chooses her Ajah, gains the right to wear the shawl, and may wear the ring on any finger or not at all if circumstances warrant.

Aes Sedai (EYEZ seh-DEYE): Wielders of the One Power.

Since the Time of Madness, all surviving Aes Sedai are women. Widely distrusted and feared, even hated, they are blamed by many for the Breaking of the World, and are thought to meddle in the affairs of nations. At the same time, few rulers will be without an Aes Sedai advisor, even in lands where the existence of such a connection must be kept secret. After some years of channeling the One Power, Aes Sedai take on an ageless quality, so that an Aes Sedai who is old enough to be a grandmother may show no signs of age except perhaps a few gray hairs. *See also* Ajah; Amyrlin Seat; Time of Madness.

Age of Legends: The Age ended by the War of the Shadow and the Breaking of the World. A time when Aes Sedai performed wonders now only dreamed of. *See also* Wheel of Time; Breaking of the World; War of the Shadow.

Aiel (eye-EEL): The people of the Aiel Waste. Fierce and hardy. Also called Aielmen. They veil their faces before they kill, giving rise to the saying "acting like a black-veiled Aiel" to describe someone who is being violent. Deadly warriors with any weapon or with nothing but their bare hands, they will not touch a sword. Their pipers play them into battle with the music of dances, and Aielmen call battle "the dance," and "the dance of spears." *See also* Aiel warrior societies; Aiel Waste.

Aiel War, the: (976–78 NE) When King Laman of Cairhien cut down Avendoraldera, several clans of the Aiel crossed the Spine of the World. They looted and burned the capital city of Cairhien as well as many other cities and towns, and the conflict extended into Andor and Tear. The conventional view is that the Aiel were finally defeated at the Battle of the Shining Walls, before Tar Valon, but in fact, Laman was killed in that battle, and having done what they had come for, the Aiel recrossed the Spine. *See also Avendoraldera*; Cairhien.

Aiel warrior societies: Aiel warriors are all members of one of the warrior societies, such as the Stone Dogs (*Shae'en M'taal*), the Red Shields (*Aethan Dor*), or the Maidens of the Spear (*Far Dareis Mai*). Each society has its own customs, and sometimes specific duties. For example, Red Shields act as police. Stone Dogs often vow not to retreat once battle has been joined, and will die to the last man if necessary to fulfill this vow. The clans of the Aiel—among them the Goshien, Reyn, Shaarad, and Taardad Aiel—frequently fight among themselves, but members of the same society will not fight each other even if their clans are doing so. In this way, there are always lines of contact between the clans even when they are in open warfare. *See also* Aiel; Aiel Waste; *Far Dareis Mai*.

Aiel Waste: The harsh, rugged, and all-but-waterless land east of the Spine of the World. Called the Three-fold Land by the Aiel. Few outsiders go there, not only because water is almost impossible to find for one not born there, but because the Aiel consider themselves at war with all other peoples and do not welcome strangers. Only peddlers, gleemen, and the Tuatha'an are allowed safe entry, and contact even with them is limited. No maps of the Waste itself are known to exist.

Ajah (AH-jah): Societies among the Aes Sedai to which all Aes Sedai except the Amyrlin Seat belong. They are designated by colors: Blue, Red, White, Green, Brown, Yellow, and Gray. Each follows a specific philosophy of the use of the One Power and the purposes of the Aes Sedai. For example, the Red Ajah bends all its energies to finding men who are attempting to wield the Power, and to gentling them. The Brown Ajah, on the other hand, forsakes involvement with the mundane world and dedicates itself to seeking knowledge, while the White Ajah, largely eschewing both the world and the value of worldly knowledge, devotes itself to questions of philosophy and truth. The Green Ajah (called the Battle Ajah during the Trolloc Wars) holds itself ready to counter any new Dreadlords when Tarmon Gai'don comes. There are rumors of a Black Ajah, dedicated to serving the Dark One.

Alanna Mosvani (ah-LAN-nah mos-VANH-nie): An Aes Sedai of the Green Ajah.

al'Meara, Nynaeve (al-MEER-ah, NIGH-neev): A woman once the Wisdom of Emond's Field, in the Two Rivers district of Andor (AN-door). Now one of the Accepted.

al'Thor, Rand (al-THOR, RAND): A young man from Emond's Field who is *ta'veren*. Once a shepherd. Now proclaimed as the Dragon Reborn.

al'Vere, Egwene (ahl-VEER, eh-GWAIN): A young woman from Emond's Field. Now in training to be Aes Sedai.

Amalasan, Guaire (ahm-ah-LAH-sin, Gware): *See* War of the Second Dragon.

Amyrlin Seat (AHM-ehr-lin SEAT): (1) Leader of the Aes Sedai. Elected for life by the Hall of the Tower, the highest council of the Aes Sedai, which consists of three representatives (called Sitters, as in "a Sitter for the Green") from each of the seven Ajahs. The Amyrlin Seat has, theoretically at least, almost supreme authority among the Aes Sedai, and ranks socially as the equal of a king or queen. A slightly less formal usage is simply the Amyrlin. (2) The throne on which the leader of the Aes Sedai sits.

Anaiya (ah-NYE-yah): An Aes Sedai of the Blue Ajah.

angreal (anh-gree-AHL): Remnants of the Age of Legends that allow anyone capable of channeling the One Power to handle a greater amount of the Power than could safely be channeled unaided. Their making is no longer known. Few remain in existence. *See also sa'angreal; ter'angreal.*

Artur Hawkwing: *See* Hawkwing, Artur.

Assemblage, the: A body in Illian, chosen by and from the merchants and shipowners, that is supposed to advise both the King and the Council of Nine, but historically has contended with them for power.

Atha'an Miere (ah-thah-AHN mee-EHR): *See* Sea Folk.

Avendesora (AH-vehn-deh-SO-rah): In the Old Tongue, "the Tree of Life." Mentioned in many stories and legends.

Avendoraldera (AH-ven-doh-ral-DEH-rah): A tree grown in the city of Cairhien from a sapling of *Avendesora*. This sapling was a gift from the Aiel in 566 NE, despite the fact that no record shows any connection whatsoever between the Aiel and *Avendesora. See also* Aiel War.

Aviendha (Ah-vee-EHN-dah): A woman of the Nine Valleys sept of the Taardad Aiel; a *Far Dareis Mai*, a Maiden of the Spear.

Aybara, Perrin (ay-BAHR-ah, PEHR-rihn): A young man from Emond's Field, formerly a blacksmith's apprentice.

Ba'alzamon (bah-AHL-zah-mon): In the Trolloc tongue,

"Heart of the Dark." Believed to be the Trolloc name for the Dark One. *See also* Dark One; Trollocs.

Bashere, Zarine (bah-SHEER, zah-REEN): A young woman from Saldaea who is a Hunter of the Horn. She wishes to be called Faile (fah-EEL), which, in the Old Tongue, means "falcon."

Be'lal (beh-LAAL): One of the Forsaken.

Bel Tine (BEHL TINE): Spring festival celebrating the end of winter, the first sprouting of crops, and the birth of the first lambs.

Betrayer of Hope: *See* Ishamael.

biteme (BITE-me): A small, almost invisible biting insect.

bittern (BIHT-tehrn): A musical instrument that may have six, nine, or twelve strings, and is held flat on the knees and played by plucking or strumming.

Blight, the: *See* Great Blight, the.

Borderlands, the: The nations bordering the Great Blight: Saldaea, Arafel, Kandor, and Shienar.

Bornhald, Dain (BOHRN-hahld, DAY-ihn): An officer of the Children of the Light, son of Lord Captain Geofraim Bornhald, who died at Falme, on Toman Head.

Breaking of the World, the: During the Time of Madness, male Aes Sedai who had gone insane, and who could wield the One Power to a degree now unknown, changed the face of the earth. They caused great earthquakes, leveled old mountain ranges and raised new mountains, lifted dry land where seas had been and made the ocean rush in where dry land had been. Many parts of the world were completely depopulated, and the survivors were scattered like dust on the wind. This destruction is remembered in stories, legends, and history as the Breaking of the World. *See also* Time of Madness; Hundred Companions, the.

Byar, Jaret (BY-ahr, JAH-ret): An officer of the Children of the Light.

Caemlyn (KAYM-lihn): The capital city of Andor.

Cairhien (KEYE-ree-EHN): Both a nation along the Spine of the World and the capital city of that nation. The city was burned and looted during the Aiel War, as were many other towns and villages. The consequent abandonment of farmland near the Spine of the World made necessary the importation of great quantities of grain. The assassination of King Galldrian (998 NE) has resulted in a civil war among the noble Houses for succession to the Sun Throne, in the disruption of grain shipments, and in famine. The sign of Cairhien is a many-rayed golden sun rising from the bottom of a field of sky blue.

Callandor (CAH-lahn-DOOR): The Sword That Is Not a Sword, the Sword That Cannot Be Touched. A crystal sword held in the Stone of Tear, in the chamber called the Heart of the Stone. No hand can touch it except that of the Dragon Reborn. According to the Prophecies of the Dragon, one of the major signs of the Dragon's Rebirth and the approach of Tarmon Gai'don will be that the Dragon Reborn has taken *Callandor*.

Cauthon, Mat (CAW-thon, MAT): A young man from Emond's Field in the Two Rivers. Full name: Matrim (MAT-trim) Cauthon.

channel: (verb) To control the flow of the One Power. *See also* One Power.

Children of the Light: A society holding strict ascetic beliefs, dedicated to the defeat of the Dark One and the destruction of all Darkfriends. Founded during the War of the Hundred Years by Lothair Mantelar (LOH-thayr MAHN-tee-LAHR) to proselytize against an increase in the numbers of Darkfriends, they evolved during the war into a completely military organization. They are extremely rigid in their beliefs, and certain that only they know the truth and the right. They hate Aes Sedai, considering them, and any who support or befriend them, Darkfriends. They are known disparagingly as Whitecloaks. Their sign is a golden sunburst on a field of white. *See also* Questioners.

Chronicles, Keeper of the: Second in authority to the Amyrlin Seat among the Aes Sedai, she also acts as secretary to the Amyrlin. Chosen for life by the Hall of the Tower, and usually of the same Ajah as the Amyrlin. *See also* Amyrlin Seat; Ajah.

Council of Nine: In Illian, a council of nine Lords who are supposed to advise the King, but who historically contend with him for power. Both the King and the Nine often must contend with the Assemblage, as well.

cuendillar (CWAIN-deh-yar): *See* heartstone.

Daes Dae'mar (DAH-ess day-MAR): The Great Game, also known as the Game of Houses. Name given the scheming, plots, and manipulations for advantage by the noble Houses. Great value is given to subtlety, to aiming at one thing while seeming to aim at another, and to achieving ends with the least visible effort.

Damodred, Lord Galadedrid (DAHM-oh-drehd, gah-LAHD-eh-drihd): Half brother to Elayne and Gawyn. His sign is a winged silver sword, point down.

Darkfriends: Those who follow the Dark One and believe they will gain great power and rewards, and even immortality, when he is freed from his prison.

Darkhounds: *See* Wild Hunt.

Dark One: Most common name, used in every land, for Shai'tan. The source of evil, antithesis of the Creator. Imprisoned by the Creator in Shayol Ghul at the moment of Creation. The attempt to free him from that prison brought about the War of the Shadow, the tainting of *saidin*, the Breaking of the World, and the end of the Age of Legends.

Dark One, naming the: Saying the true name of the Dark One (Shai'tan) draws his attention, inevitably bringing ill fortune at best, disaster at worst. For that reason, many euphemisms are used, among them the Dark One, Father of Lies, Sightblinder, Lord of the Grave, Shepherd of the Night, Hearstbane, Soulsbane, Heartfang, Old Grim, Grassburner, and Leafblighter. Darkfriends call him the Great Lord of the Dark. Someone who seems to be inviting ill fortune is often said to be "naming the Dark One."

Daughter-Heir: Title of the heir to the throne of Andor. The eldest daughter of the Queen succeeds her mother on the throne. Without a surviving daughter, the throne goes to the nearest female blood relation of the Queen.

Daughter of the Night: *See* Lanfear.

Dragon, false: Occasionally men claim to be the Dragon Reborn, and sometimes one of these men gains following enough to require an army to put it down. Some have begun wars that involved many nations. Over the centuries most of these have been men unable to channel the One Power, but a few could do so. All, however, either disappeared or were captured or killed without fulfilling any of the Prophecies concerning the Rebirth of the Dragon.

These men are called false Dragons. Among those who could channel, the most powerful were Raolin Darksbane (335–36 AB), Yurian Stonebow (circa 1300–1308 AB), Davian (FY 351), Guaire Amalasan (FY 939–43), and Logain (997 NE). *See also* Dragon Reborn.

Dragon, Prophecies of the: Little known and seldom spoken of, the Prophecies, given in *The Karaethon Cycle*, foretell that the Dark One will be freed again to touch the world. And that Lews Therin Telamon, the Dragon, Breaker of the World, will be reborn to fight Tarmon Gai'don, the Last Battle against the Shadow. *See also* Dragon, the.

Dragon, the: The name by which Lews Therin Telamon was known during the War of the Shadow. In the madness that overtook all male Aes Sedai, Lews Therin killed every living person who carried any of his blood, as well as everyone he loved, thus earning the name Kinslayer. *See also* Dragon Reborn; Dragon, Prophecies of the.

Dragon Reborn: According to prophecy and legend the Dragon will be born again at mankind's greatest hour of need to save the world. This is not something people look forward to, both because the Prophecies say the Dragon Reborn will bring a new Breaking to the world and because Lews Therin Kinslayer, the Dragon, is a name to make men shudder, even more than three thousand years after his death. *See also* Dragon, the; Dragon, false; Dragon, Prophecies of the.

Dreadlords: Men and women able to channel the One Power, who went over to the Shadow during the Trolloc Wars, acting as commanders of the Trolloc forces. Occasionally confused with the Forsaken by the less well educated.

Dreamer: *See* Talents.

Elaida (eh-LY-da): An Aes Sedai of the Red Ajah. Former advisor to Queen Morgase of Andor. She sometimes has the Foretelling.

Elayne of House Trakand (trah-KAND): Queen Morgase's daughter, the Daughter-Heir to the throne of Andor. Now in training to be Aes Sedai. Her sign is a golden lily.

Far Dareis Mai (FAHR DAH-rize MY): Literally "Maidens of the Spear." A warrior society of the Aiel, which, unlike any of the others, admits women and only women. A Maiden may not marry and remain in the society, nor may she fight while carrying a child. Any child born to a Maiden is given to another woman to raise, in such a way that no one knows who the child's mother was. ("You may belong to no man, nor may any man belong to you, nor any child. The spear is your lover, your child, and your life.") These children are treasured, for it is prophesied that a child born of a Maiden will unite the clans and return the Aiel to the greatness they knew during the Age of Legends. *See also* Aiel; Aiel warrior societies.

Fetches: *See* Myrddraal.

Five Powers, the: There are threads to the One Power, and anyone who can channel can usually grasp some threads better than others. These threads are named according to the sorts of things that can be done using them—Earth, Air (sometimes called Wind), Fire, Water, and Spirit—and are called the Five Powers. Any wielder of the Power will have a greater degree of strength with one, or possibly two, of these, and lesser strength in the others. Some few may have great strength with three, but since the Age of Legends no one has had great strength with all five. Even then this was extremely rare. The degree of strength can vary greatly between individuals. Performing certain acts with the One Power requires the ability to weave flows in one or more of the Five Powers. For example, starting or controlling a fire requires Fire, and affecting the weather requires Air and Water, while Healing requires Air, Water and Spirit. While Spirit was found equally in men and in women, great ability with Earth and/or Fire was found much more often among men; with Water and/or Air among women. There were exceptions, but it was so often so that Earth and Fire came to be regarded as male Powers, Air and Water as female. Generally, no ability is considered stronger than any other, though there is a saying among Aes Sedai: "There is no rock so strong that water and wind cannot wear it away, no fire so fierce that water cannot quench it or wind snuff it out." It should be noted that any equivalent saying among male Aes Sedai is long lost.

Flame of Tar Valon: Symbol of Tar Valon, the Amyrlin

Seat, and the Aes Sedai. A stylized representation of a flame; a white teardrop with the point upward.

Forsaken, the: Name given to thirteen of the most powerful Aes Sedai of the Age of Legends, which made them among the most powerful ever known, who went over to the Dark One during the War of the Shadow in return for the promise of immortality. According to both legend and fragmentary records, they were imprisoned along with the Dark One when his prison was resealed. Their names—among them Lanfear, Be'lal, Sammael, Asmodean, Rahvin, and Ishamael—are still used to frighten children.

Fortress of the Light: The great fortress of the Children of the Light, located in Amador (AH-mah-door), the capital of Amadicia (AH-mah-DEE-cee-ah). There is a King of Amadicia, but the Children rule in all but name. *See also* Children of the Light.

Gaidin (GYE-deen): Literally "Brother to Battles." A title used by Aes Sedai for the Warders. *See also* Warder.

Galad (gah-LAHD): *See* Damodred, Lord Galadedrid.

Game of Houses, the: *See Daes Dae'mar.*

Gaul (GAHWL): An Aiel of the Imran sept of the Shaarad, a *Shae'en M'taal*, a Stone Dog.

Gawyn (GAH-wihn) **of House Trakand** (trah-KAND): Queen Morgase's son, and Elayne's brother, who will be First Prince of the Sword when Elayne ascends to the throne. His sign is a white boar.

gentling: The act, performed by Aes Sedai, of shutting off a male who can channel from the One Power. This is necessary because any man who learns to channel will go insane from the taint on *saidin* and will almost certainly do horrible things with the Power in his madness. A man who has been gentled can still sense the True Source, but he cannot touch it. Whatever madness has come before gentling is arrested by the act of gentling, but not cured by it, and if it is done soon enough death can be averted. *See also* One Power, the; stilling.

gleeman: A traveling storyteller, musician, juggler, tumbler, and all-around entertainer. Known by their trademark cloaks of many-colored patches, gleemen perform mainly in the villages and smaller towns.

Gray Man: Someone who has voluntarily surrendered his or her soul in order to become an assassin serving the Shadow. Gray Men are so ordinary in appearance that the eye can slide right past without noticing them. The vast majority of Gray Men are indeed men, but a small number are women.

Great Blight, the: A region in the far north, entirely corrupted by the Dark One. A haunt of Trollocs, Myrddraal, and other creatures of the Shadow.

Great Game, the: *See Daes Dae'mar.*

Great Hunt of the Horn, The: A cycle of stories concerning the legendary search for the Horn of Valere, in the years between the end of the Trolloc Wars and the beginning of the War of the Hundred Years. If told in its entirety, the cycle would take many days. *See also* Horn of Valere.

Great Lord of the Dark: The name by which Darkfriends refer to the Dark One, claiming that to use his true name would be blasphemous.

Great Serpent: A symbol for time and eternity, ancient before the Age of Legends began, consisting of a serpent eating its own tail. A ring in the shape of the Great Serpent is awarded to women who have been raised to the Accepted among the Aes Sedai.

Grim, Old: *See* Dark One; Wild Hunt.

Halfman: *See* Myrddraal.

Hawkwing, Artur: A legendary king (ruled FY 943–94) who united all the lands west of the Spine of the World. He even sent armies across the Aryth Ocean (FY 992), but all contact with these was lost at his death, which set off the War of the Hundred Years. His sign was a golden hawk in flight. *See also* War of the Hundred Years.

Heart of the Stone: *See Callandor.*

heartstone: An indestructible substance created during the Age of Legends. Any force used in an attempt to break it is absorbed, making heartstone stronger. Another name for *cuendillar.*

hide: A unit of area for measuring land, equal to 100 paces by 100 paces.

High Lords of Tear: Acting as a council, the High Lords are the rulers of the nation of Tear, which has neither king nor queen. Their numbers are not fixed, and have varied over the years from as many as twenty to as few as six. Not to be confused with the Lords of the Land, who are lesser Tairen lords.

Hopper: A wolf.

Horn of Valere (vah-LEER): The legendary object of the Great Hunt of the Horn. The Horn supposedly can call back dead heroes from the grave to fight against the Shadow.

Hundred Companions, the: One hundred male Aes Sedai, among the most powerful of the Age of Legends, who, led by Lews Therin Telamon, launched the final stroke that ended the War of the Shadow by sealing the Dark One back into his prison. The Dark One's counter-stroke tainted *saidin*; the Hundred Companions went mad and began the Breaking of the World. *See also* Time of Madness; Breaking of the World; True Source; One Power.

Illian (IHL-lee-an): A great port on the Sea of Storms, capital city of the nation of the same name.

Illuminators, Guild of: A society that holds the secret of making fireworks. It guards this secret very closely, even to murder. The Guild gains its name from the grand displays, called Illuminations, that it provides for rulers and sometimes for great lords. Lesser fireworks are sold for use by others, but with dire warnings of the disaster that can result from attempting to learn what is inside them. The Guild chapter house is in Tanchico, the capital of Tarabon. The Guild established one other chapter house in Cairhien, but it is no longer active.

Ishamael (ih-SHAH-may-EHL): In the Old Tongue, "Betrayer of Hope." One of the Forsaken. Name given to the leader of the Aes Sedai who went over to the Dark One in the War of the Shadow. It is said that even he forgot his true name. *See also* Forsaken.

Karaethon Cycle, The (ka-REE-ah-thon): *See* Dragon, Prophecies of the.

Laman (LAY-mahn): A king of Cairhien, of House Damodred, who lost his throne in the Aiel War. *See also* Aiel War; *Avendoraldera*.

Lan (LAN); al'Lan Mandragoran (AHL-LAN man-DRAG-

or-an): A Warder, bonded to Moiraine. Uncrowned King of Malkier, Dai Shan, and the last surviving Malkieri lord. *See also* Warder; Moiraine; Malkier.

Lanfear (LAN-fear): In the Old Tongue, "Daughter of the Night." One of the Forsaken, perhaps the most powerful next to Ishamael. Unlike the other Forsaken, she chose this name herself. She is said to have been in love with Lews Therin Telamon, and to have hated his wife, Ilyena. *See also* Forsaken; Dragon, the.

league: *See* length, units of.

Leane (lee-AHN-eh): An Aes Sedai of the Blue Ajah, and Keeper of the Chronicles. *See also* Ajah; Chronicles, Keeper of the.

length, units of: 10 inches = 1 foot; 3 feet = 1 pace; 2 paces = 1 span; 1000 spans = 1 mile; 4 miles = 1 league.

Lews Therin Telamon; Lews Therin Kinslayer: *See* Dragon, the.

Liandrin (lee-AHN-drihn): An Aes Sedai formerly of the Red Ajah, from Tarabon. Now known to be of the Black Ajah.

Light, Children of the: *See* Children of the Light.

Loial (LOY-ahl) **son of Arent son of Halan:** An Ogier from Stedding Shangtai.

Malkier (mahl-KEER): A nation, once one of the Borderlands, now consumed by the Blight. The sign of Malkier was a golden crane in flight.

Manetheren (mahn-EHTH-ehr-ehn): One of the Ten Nations that made the Second Covenant. Also the capital city of that nation. Both city and nation were utterly destroyed in the Trolloc Wars.

Masema (mah-SEE-mah): A Shienaran soldier who hates Aiel.

Mayene (may-EHN): City-state on the Sea of Storms that derives its wealth and its independence from knowledge of where to find the oilfish shoals, which rival in economic importance the olive groves of Tear, Illian, and Tarabon. Oilfish and olives provide nearly all lamp oil. The current ruler of Mayene is Berelain, the First of Mayene. The Rulers of Mayene claim to be descendants of Artur Hawkwing. The sign of Mayene is a golden hawk in flight.

Merrilin, Thom (MER-rih-lihn, TOM): A gleeman, and once the lover of Queen Morgase.

mile: *See* length, units of.

Min (MIN): A young woman with the ability to read things about people in the auras and images she sometimes sees surrounding them.

Moiraine (mwah-RAIN): An Aes Sedai of the Blue Ajah. Born in House Damodred, though not in line of succession to the throne, she was raised in the Royal Palace in Cairhien.

Morgase (moor-GAYZ): By the Grace of the Light, Queen of Andor, Defender of the Realm, Protector of the People, High Seat of House Trakand. Her sign is three golden keys. The sign of House Trakand is a silver keystone.

Myrddraal (MUHRD-draal): Creatures of the Dark One, commanders of the Trollocs. Twisted offspring of Trollocs in which the human stock used to create the Trollocs has resurfaced, but tainted by the evil that made the Trollocs. They have no eyes, but can see like eagles in light or dark. They have certain powers stemming from the Dark One, including the ability to cause paralyzing fear with a look and the ability to vanish wherever there are shadows. They have few known weaknesses, but one of these is that they are reluctant to cross running water. In different lands they are known by many names, among them Halfman, the Eyeless, Shadowman, Lurk, Fetch, and Fade.

Nedeal, Corianin: *See* Talents.

Niall, Pedron (NEYE-awl, PAY-drohn): Lord Captain Commander of the Children of the Light. *See also* Children of the Light.

Oaths, Three: The oaths taken by an Accepted who is being raised to Aes Sedai. Spoken while holding the Oath Rod, a *ter'angreal* that makes oaths binding. They are: (1) To speak no word that is not true. (2) To make no weapon with which one man may kill another. (3) Never to use the One Power as a weapon except against Shadowspawn, or in the last extreme of defense of her own life, or that of her Warder or another Aes Sedai. These oaths were not always required, but various events before and since the Breaking caused them to be necessary. The second oath was the first adopted, in reaction to the War of the Power. The first oath, while held to the letter, is often circumvented by careful speaking. It is believed that the last two are inviolable.

Ogier (OH-gehr): (1) A non-human race, characterized by great height (ten feet is average for adult males), broad, almost snoutlike noses, and long, tufted ears. They live in areas called *stedding.* Their separation from these *stedding* after the Breaking of the World (a time called the Exile by Ogier) resulted in what is called the Longing; an Ogier who is too long out of the *stedding*, sickens and dies. Widely known as wondrous stonemasons who built the great human cities after the Breaking, they consider stonework simply something learned during the Exile and not as important as tending the trees of the *stedding*, especially the towering Great Trees. Except for stonework, they rarely leave their *stedding* and typically have little contact with humankind. Knowledge of them among humans is sparse, and many believe Ogier to be only legends. Although believed to be a pacific people and extremely slow to anger, some old stories say they fought alongside humans in the Trolloc Wars, and call them implacable enemies. By and large, they are extremely fond of knowledge, and their books and stories often contain information lost to humans. A typical Ogier life-span is at least three to four times that of a human. (2) Any individual of that non-human race. *See also* Breaking of the World; *stedding;* Treesinger.

Old Grim: *See Dark One.*

Old Tongue: The language spoken during the Age of Legends. It is generally expected that nobles and the educated will have learned to speak this, but most know only a few words.

One Power, the: The power drawn from the True Source. The vast majority of people are completely unable to learn to channel the One Power. A very small number can be taught to channel, and an even tinier number have the ability inborn. For these few there is no need to be taught; they will touch the True Source and channel the Power whether they want to or not, perhaps without even realizing what they are doing. This inborn ability usually manifests itself in late adolescence or early adulthood. If control is not taught, or self-learned (extremely difficult, with a success rate of only one in four), death is certain. Since the Time of Madness, no man has been able to channel the Power without eventually going completely, horribly mad, and then, even if he has learned some control, dying from a wasting sickness that causes the sufferer to rot alive, a sickness caused, as is the madness, by the Dark One's taint on *saidin*. For a woman the death that comes without control of the Power is less horrible, but it is death just the same. Aes Sedai search for girls with the inborn ability as much to save their lives as to increase Aes Sedai numbers, and for men with it in order to stop the terrible things they inevitably do with the Power in their madness. *See also* Aes Sedai; channel; Five Powers; Time of Madness; True Source.

Ordeith (OHR-deeth): In the Old Tongue, "Wormwood." Name taken by a man who advises the Lord Captain Commander of the Children of the Light.

Pattern of an Age: The Wheel of Time weaves the threads of human lives into the Pattern of an Age, often called simply the Pattern, which forms the substance of reality for that Age. *See also ta'veren.*

Powers, the Five: *See* Five Powers, the.

Questioners, the: An order within the Children of the Light. Their avowed purposes are to discover the truth in disputations and uncover Darkfriends. In the search for truth and the Light, their normal method of inquiry is torture; their normal manner that they know the truth already and must only make their victim confess to it. The Questioners refer to themselves as the Hand of the Light, the Hand that digs out truth, and at times act as if they were entirely separate from the Children and the Council of the Anointed, which commands the Children. The head of the Questioners is the High Inquisitor, who sits on the Council of the Anointed. Their sign is a blood-red shepherd's crook.

Red Shields: *See* Aiel warrior societies.

Rhuarc (RHOURK): An Aiel, clan chief of the Taardad Aiel.

Rogosh Eagle-eye: A legendary hero mentioned in a number of old stories.

sa'angreal (SAH-ahn-GREE-ahl): Any one of a number of objects that allow an individual to channel much more of the One Power than would otherwise be possible or safe. A *sa'angreal* is like unto, but much more powerful than, an *angreal*. The amount of the Power that can be wielded with a *sa'angreal* compares to the amount of the Power that can be handled with an *angreal* as the power wielded with the aid of an *angreal* does to the amount of the Power that can be handled unaided. Remnants of the Age of Legends, their making is no longer known. Only a handful remain, far fewer even than *angreal*.

saidar (sah-ih-DAHR); *saidin* (sah-ih-DEEN): *See* True Source.

Sea Folk: More properly, the Atha'an Miere (ah-thah-AHN mee-AIR), the People of the Sea. Inhabitants of islands in the Aryth (AH-rihth) Ocean and the Sea of Storms, they spend little time on those islands, living most of their lives on their ships. Most seaborne trade is carried by the Sea Folk's ships.

Seanchan (SHAWN-CHAN): (1) Descendants of the armies Artur Hawkwing sent across the Aryth Ocean. (2) The land from which the Seanchan come.

Selene (seh-LEEN): A name used by the Forsaken called Lanfear.

Servants, Hall of the: In the Age of Legends, the great meeting hall of the Aes Sedai.

Shadar Logoth (SHAH-dahr LOH-goth): A city abandoned and shunned since the Trolloc Wars. It is tainted ground, and not a pebble of it is safe.

Shai'tan (SHAY-ih-TAN): *See* Dark One.

Shayol Ghul (SHAY-ol GHOOL): A mountain in the Blasted Lands, the site of the Dark One's prison.

Sheriam (SHEER-ee-ahm): An Aes Sedai of the Blue Ajah. The Mistress of Novices in the White Tower.

Siuan Sanche (SWAHN SAHN-chay): The daughter of a Tairen fisherman, she was, according to Tairen law, put on a ship to Tar Valon before the second sunset after it was discovered that she had the potential to channel. Formerly of the Blue Ajah. Raised to the Amyrlin Seat in 988 NE.

Soulless: *See* Gray Man.

span: *See* length, units of.

Spine of the World, the: A towering mountain range, with
  only a few passes, which separates the Aiel Waste from
  the lands to the west.

stedding (STEHD-ding): An Ogier (OH-geer) homeland.
  Many *stedding* have been abandoned since the Breaking
  of the World. They are shielded in some way, no longer
  understood, so that within them no Aes Sedai can channel the One Power, nor even sense that the True Source
  exists. Attempts to wield the One Power from outside a
  stedding have no effect inside a *stedding* boundary. No
  Trolloc will enter a *stedding* unless driven, and even a
  Myrddraal will do so only at the greatest need and then
  with the greatest reluctance and distaste. Even Darkfriends, if truly dedicated, feel uncomfortable within a
  stedding.

stilling: The act, performed by Aes Sedai, of shutting off a
  woman who can channel from the One Power. A woman
  who has been stilled can sense the True Source, but she
  cannot touch it. So seldom has it been done that novices
  are required to learn the names and crimes of all women
  who have suffered it.

Stone Dogs: *See* Aiel warrior societies.

Stone of Tear: A great fortress in the city of Tear, said to
  have been made soon after the Breaking of the World,
  and to have been made using the One Power. It has been
  besieged or attacked countless times, but never success-
  fully. The Stone is mentioned twice in the Prophecies
  of the Dragon. Once they say the Stone will never fall
  until the People of the Dragon come. In another place,
  they say the Stone will never fall until the Dragon's
  hand wields the Sword That Cannot Be Touched, *Callandor.* Some believe that these Prophecies account for
  the antipathy of the High Lords to the One Power, and
  for the Tairen law that forbids channeling. Despite this
  antipathy, the Stone contains a collection of *an'greal* and
  ter'angreal rivaling that of the White Tower, a collection
  which was gathered, some say, in an attempt to diminish
  the glare of possessing *Callandor.*

Sunday: A feastday and festival in midsummer, widely celebrated in many parts of the world.

sung wood: *See* Treesinger.

Talents: Abilities in the use of the One Power in specific areas. The best known of these, of course, is Healing. Some, such as Traveling, the ability to shift oneself from one place to another without crossing the intervening space, have been lost. Others such as Foretelling (the ability to foretell future events, but in a general way) are now found only rarely if at all. Another Talent long thought lost is Dreaming, which involves, among other things, interpreting the Dreamer's dreams to foretell future events in more specific fashion than Foretelling does. Some Dreamers had the ability to enter *Tel'aran'rhiod*, the World of Dreams, and (it is said) even other people's dreams. The last known Dreamer was Corianin Nedeal, who died in 526 NE.

ta'maral'ailen (tah-MAHR-ahl-EYE-lehn): In the Old Tongue, "Web of Destiny." A great change in the Pattern of an Age, centered around one or more people who are *ta'veren*. *See also* Pattern of an Age; *ta'veren*.

Tanreall, Artur Paendrag (tahn-REE-ahl, AHR-tuhr PAY-ehn-DRAG): *See* Hawkwing, Artur.

Tarmon Gai'don (TAHR-mohn GAY-dohn)**:** The Last Battle. *See also* Dragon, Prophecies of the; Horn of Valere.

ta'veren (tah-VEER-ehn): A person around whom the Wheel of Time weaves all surrounding life-threads, perhaps ALL life-threads, to form a Web of Destiny. *See also* Pattern of an Age.

Tear (TEER): A nation on the Sea of Storms. Also the capital city of that nation, a great seaport. The banner of Tear is three white crescent moons slanting across a field half red, half gold. *See also* Stone of Tear.

Telamon, Lews Therin (TEHL-ah-mon, LOOZ THEH-rihn): *See* Dragon, the.

Tel'aran'rhiod (tel-AYE-rahn-rhee-ODD): In the Old Tongue, "the Unseen World," or "the World of Dreams." A world glimpsed in dreams which was believed by the ancients to permeate and surround all other possible worlds. Unlike other dreams, what happens to living things in the World of Dreams is real; a wound taken there will still be there on awakening, and one who dies there does not wake at all.

ter'angreal (TEER-ahn-GREE-ahl): Any one of a number of remnants of the Age of Legends that use the One Power. Unlike *angreal* and *sa'angreal*, each *ter'angreal* was made to do a particular thing. For example, one makes oaths taken with it binding. Some *ter'angreal* are used by Aes Sedai, but the original purposes of many others are largely unknown. Some will kill or destroy the ability to channel of any woman who uses them. *See also angreal; sa'angreal.*

Tigraine (tee-GRAIN): As Daughter-Heir of Andor, she married Taringail Damodred and bore his son Galadedrid. Her disappearance in 972 NE, shortly after her brother Luc vanished in the Blight, led to the struggle in Andor called the Succession, and caused the events in Cairhien that eventually brought on the Aiel War. Her sign was a woman's hand gripping a thorny rose stem with a white blossom.

Time of Madness: The years after the Dark One's counterstroke tainted the male half of the True Source, when male Aes Sedai went mad and Broke the world. The exact duration of this period is unknown, but it is believed to have lasted nearly one hundred years. It ended completely only with the death of the last male Aes Sedai. *See also* Hundred Companions; True Source; One Power.

Traveling People: *See* Tuatha'an.

Travels of Jain Farstrider, The: A very well-known book of travel stories and observations by a noted Malkieri writer and traveler. The book was first printed in 968 NE and has been reprinted continuously ever since. Jain Farstrider disappeared shortly after the Aiel War and is generally believed to be dead.

Treekillers: An Aiel name for the Cairhienin, always said in tones of horror and disgust.

Treesinger: An Ogier who has the ability to sing to trees (called "treesong"), either healing them, or helping them to grow and flower, or making things from the wood without damaging the tree. Objects made in this manner are called "sung wood" and are highly prized. Few Ogier remain who are Treesingers; the ability seems to be dying out.

Trollocs (TRAHL-lohks): Creatures of the Dark One, created during the War of the Shadow. Huge of stature, they are a twisted blend of animal and human stock. They are divided into tribelike bands, among them the Dha'vol, the Ko'bal, and the Dhai'mon. Vicious by nature, they kill for the pure pleasure of killing. Deceitful in the extreme, they cannot be trusted unless coerced by fear.

Trolloc Wars: A series of wars, beginning about 1000 AB and lasting more than three hundred years, during which Trolloc armies ravaged the world. Eventually the Trollocs were driven back into the Great Blight, but some nations ceased to exist, and others that survived were almost depopulated. All records of the time are fragmentary.

True Source: The driving force of the universe, which turns the Wheel of Time. It is divided into a male half (*saidin*) and a female half (*saidar*), which work at the same time with and against each other. Only a man can draw on *saidin*, only a woman on *saidar*. Since the beginning of the Time of Madness, *saidin* has been tainted by the Dark One's touch. *See also* One Power.

Tuatha'an (too-AH-thah-AHN): A wandering folk, also known as the Tinkers and as the Traveling People, who live in brightly painted wagons and follow a totally pacifist philosophy called the Way of the Leaf. Things mended by Tinkers are often better than new. They are among the few who can cross the Aiel Waste unmolested, for the Aiel strictly avoid all contact with them.

Verin Mathwin (VEHR-ihn MAH-thwihn): An Aes Sedai of the Brown Ajah.

Warder: A warrior bonded to an Aes Sedai. The bonding is a thing of the One Power, and by it he gains such gifts as quick healing, the ability to go long periods without food, water, or rest, and the ability to sense the taint of the Dark One at a distance. So long as a Warder lives, the Aes Sedai to whom he is bonded knows he is alive however far away he is, and when he dies she will know the moment and manner of his death. While most Ajahs believe an Aes Sedai may have one Warder bonded to her at a time, the Red Ajah refuse to bond any Warders at all, while the Green Ajah believe an Aes Sedai may bond as many Warders as she wishes. Ethically the Warder must accede to the bonding voluntarily, but it has been known

to be done against the Warder's will. What the Aes Sedai
gain from the bonding is a closely held secret. *See also*
Aes Sedai.

War of Power: *See* War of the Shadow.

War of the Hundred Years: A series of overlapping wars
among constantly shifting alliances, precipitated by the
death of Artur Hawkwing and the resulting struggle for his
empire. It lasted from FY 994 to FY 1117. The War of the
Hundred Years depopulated large parts of the lands between the Aryth Ocean and the Aiel Waste, from the Sea
of Storms to the Great Blight. So great was the destruction
that only fragmentary records of the time remain. The
empire of Artur Hawkwing was pulled apart in the wars,
and the nations of the present day were formed. *See also*
Hawkwing, Artur.

War of the Second Dragon: The war fought (FY 939–
43) against the false Dragon Guaire Amalasan. During
this war a young king named Artur Tanreall Paendrag,
later known as Artur Hawkwing, rose to overwhelming
prominence.

War of the Shadow: Also known as the War of Power,
this war ended the Age of Legends. It began shortly after
the attempt to free the Dark One, and soon involved the
whole world. In a world where war had been forgotten,
even the memory of it, every facet of war was rediscovered, often twisted by the Dark One's touch on the world,
and the One Power was used as a weapon. The war was
ended by the resealing of the Dark One into his prison.
See also Hundred Companions, the; Dragon, the.

weight, units of: 10 ounces = 41 pound; 10 pounds = 1
stone; 10 stone = 1 hundredweight; 10 hundredweight = 1
ton.

Wheel of Time, the: Time is a wheel with seven spokes,
each spoke an Age. As the Wheel turns, the Ages come
and go, each leaving memories that fade to legend, then
to myth, and are forgotten by the time that Age comes
again. The Pattern of an Age is slightly different each
time an Age comes, and each time it is subject to greater
change.

Whitecloaks: *See* Children of the Light.

wilder: A woman who has learned to channel the One
Power on her own, surviving the crisis as only one in

four does. Such women usually build barriers against knowing what it is they are doing, but if these can be broken down, wilders are among the most powerful of channelers. The term is often used in derogatory fashion.

Wild Hunt: It is believed by many that the Dark One (often called Grim, or Old Grim, in Tear, Illian, Murandy, Altara, and Ghealdan) rides out in the night with the "black dogs," or the Darkhounds, hunting souls. This is the Wild Hunt. Rain can keep the Darkhounds out of the night, but once they are on the trail, they must be confronted and defeated or the victim's death is inevitable. It is believed that merely seeing the Wild Hunt pass means imminent death, either for the viewer or for someone dear to the viewer.

Wisdom: In villages, a woman chosen by the Women's Circle for her knowledge of such things as healing, and foretelling the weather, as well as for common good sense. A position of great responsibility and authority, both actual and implied. She is generally considered the equal of the Mayor, and in some villages his superior. Unlike the Mayor, she is chosen for life, and it is very rare for a Wisdom to be removed from office before her death. Almost traditionally in conflict with the Mayor. Depending on the land, she may instead have another title, such as Guide, Healer, Wise Woman, Seeker, or Wise One.

CHAPTER

I

A preview of
The Shadow Rising

Book Four of
The Wheel of Time

Seeds of Shadow

The Wheel of Time turns, and Ages come and pass, leaving memories that become legend. Legend fades to myth, and even myth is long forgotten when the Age that gave it birth comes again. In one Age, called the Third Age by some, an Age yet to come, an Age long past, a wind rose on the great plain called the Caralain Grass. The wind was not the beginning. There are neither beginnings nor endings to the turning of the Wheel of Time. But it was *a* beginning.

North and east the wind blew beneath early morning sun, over endless miles of rolling grass and far-scattered thickets, across the swift-flowing River Luan, past the broken-topped fang of Dragonmount, mountain of legend towering above the slow swells of the rolling plain, looming so high that clouds wreathed it less than halfway to the smoking peak. Dragonmount, where the Dragon had died—and with him, some said, the Age of Legends—where prophecy said he would be born again. Or had been. North and east, across the villages of Jualdhe and Darein and Alindaer, where bridges like stone lacework arched out to the Shining

Walls, the great white walls of what many called the greatest city in the world. Tar Valon. A city just touched by the
reaching shadow of Dragonmount each evening.

Within those walls Ogier-made buildings well over two
thousand years old seemed to grow out of the ground rather
than having been built, or to be the work of wind and water
rather than that of even the fabled hands of Ogier stonemasons. Some suggested birds taking flight, or huge shells
from distant seas. Soaring towers, flared or fluted or spiraled,
stood connected by bridges hundreds of feet in the air, often
without rails. Only those long in Tar Valon could avoid gaping like country folk who had never been off the farm.

Greatest of those towers, the White Tower dominated the
city, gleaming like polished bone in the sun. *The Wheel of
Time turns around Tar Valon*, so people said in the city, *and
Tar Valon turns around the Tower*. The first sight travelers had of Tar Valon, before their horses came in view of
the bridges, before their river boat captains sighted the island, was the Tower reflecting the sun like a beacon. Small
wonder then that the great square surrounding the walled
Tower grounds seemed smaller than it was under the massive
Tower's gaze, the people in it dwindling to insects. Yet
the White Tower could have been the smallest in Tar Valon,
the fact that it was the heart of Aes Sedai power would still
have overawed the island city.

Despite their numbers, the crowd did not come close to
filling the square. Along the edges people jostled each other
in a milling mass, all going about their day's business, but
closer to the Tower grounds there were ever fewer people,
until a band of bare paving stones at least fifty paces wide
bordered the tall white walls. Aes Sedai were respected and
more in Tar Valon, of course, and the Amyrlin Seat ruled
the city as she ruled the Aes Sedai, but few wanted to be
closer to Aes Sedai power than they had to. There was a difference between being proud of a grand fireplace in your hall
and walking into the flames.

A very few did go closer, to the broad stairs that led up to
the Tower itself, to the intricately carved doors wide enough
for a dozen people abreast. Those doors stood open, welcoming. There were always some people in need of aid or an answer they thought only Aes Sedai could give, and they came
from far as often as near, from Arafel and Ghealdan, from

Saldaea and Illian. Many would find help or guidance inside, though often not what they had expected or hoped for.

Min kept the wide hood of her cloak pulled up, shadowing her face in its depths. In spite of the warmth of the day, the garment was light enough not to attract comment, not on a woman so obviously shy. And a good many people were shy when they went to the Tower. There was nothing about her to attract notice. Her dark hair was longer than when she was last in the Tower, though still not quite to her shoulders, and her dress, plain blue except for narrow bands of white Jaerecruz lace at neck and wrists, would have suited the daughter of a well-to-do farmer, wearing her feastday best to the Tower just like the other women approaching the wide stairs. Min hoped she looked the same, at least. She had to stop herself from staring at them to see if they walked or held themselves differently. *I can do it*, she told herself.

She had certainly not come all this way to turn back now. The dress was a good disguise. Those who remembered her in the Tower remembered a young woman with close-cropped hair, always in a boy's coat and breeches, never in a dress. It had to be a good disguise. She had no choice about what she was doing. Not really.

Her stomach fluttered the closer she came to the Tower, and she tightened her grip on the bundle clutched to her breast. Her usual clothes were in there, and her good boots, and all her possessions except the horse she had left at an inn not far from the square. With luck, she would be back on the gelding in a few hours, riding for the Ostrein Bridge and the road south.

She was not really looking forward to climbing onto a horse again so soon, not after weeks in the saddle with never a day's pause, but she longed to leave this place. She had never seen the White Tower as hospitable, and right now it seemed nearly as awful as the Dark One's prison at Shayol Ghul. Shivering, she wished she had not thought of the Dark One. *I wonder if Moiraine thinks I came just because she asked me? The Light help me, acting like a fool girl. Doing fool things because of a fool man!*

She mounted the stairs uneasily—each was deep enough to take two strides for her to reach the next—and unlike most of the others, she did not pause for an awed stare up the pale height of the Tower. She wanted this over.

Inside, archways almost surrounded the large, round entry hall, but the petitioners huddled in the middle of the chamber, shuffling together beneath a flat-domed ceiling. The pale stone floor had been worn and polished by countless nervous feet over the centuries. No one thought of anything except where they were, and why. A farmer and his wife in rough woolens, clutching each other's callused hands, rubbed shoulders with a merchant in velvet-slashed silks, a maid at her heels clutching a small worked-silver casket, no doubt her mistress's gift for the Tower. Elsewhere, the merchant would have stared down her nose at farm folk who brushed so close, and they might well have knuckled their foreheads and backed away apologizing. Not now. Not here.

There were few men among the petitioners, which was no surprise to Min. Most men were nervous around Aes Sedai. Everyone knew it had been male Aes Sedai, when there still had been male Aes Sedai, who were responsible for the Breaking of the World. Three thousand years had not dimmed that memory, even if time had altered many of the details. Children were still frightened by tales of men who could channel the One Power, men doomed to go mad from the Dark One's taint on *saidin*, the male half of the True Source. Worst was the story of Lews Therin Telamon, the Dragon, Lews Therin Kinslayer, who had begun the Breaking. For that matter, the stories frightened adults, too. Prophecy said the Dragon would be born again in mankind's greatest hour of need, to fight the Dark One in Tarmon Gai'don, the Last Battle, but that made little difference in how most people looked at any connection between men and the Power. Any Aes Sedai would hunt down a man who could channel, now; of the seven Ajahs, the Red did little else.

Of course, none of that had anything to do with seeking help from Aes Sedai, yet few men felt easy about being linked in any way to Aes Sedai and the Power. Few, that is, except Warders, but each Warder was bonded to an Aes Sedai; Warders could hardly be taken for the general run of men. There was a saying: "A man will cut off his own hand to get rid of a splinter before asking help from Aes Sedai." Women meant it as a comment on men's stubborn foolishness, but Min had heard some men say the loss of a hand might be the better decision.

She wondered what these people would do if they knew what she knew. Run screaming, perhaps. And if they knew her reason for being here, she might not survive to be taken up by the Tower guards and thrown into a cell. She did have friends in the Tower, but none with power or influence. If her purpose was discovered, it was much less likely that they could help her than that she would pull them to the gallows or the headsman behind her. That was saying she lived to be tried, of course; more likely her mouth would be stopped permanently long before a trial.

She told herself to stop thinking like that. *I'll make it in, and I'll make it out. The Light burn Rand al'Thor for getting me into this!*

Three or four Accepted, women Min's age or perhaps a little older, were circulating through the round room, speaking softly to the petitioners. Their white dresses had no decoration except for seven bands of color at the hem, one band for each Ajah. Now and again a novice, a still younger woman or girl all in white, came to lead someone deeper into the Tower. The petitioners always followed the novices with an odd mix of excited eagerness and foot-dragging reluctance.

Min's grip tightened on her bundle as one of the Accepted stopped in front of her. "The Light illumine you," the curly-haired woman said perfunctorily. "I am called Faolain. How may the Tower help you?"

Faolain's dark, round face held the patience of someone doing a tedious job when she would rather be doing something else. Studying, probably, from what Min knew of the Accepted. Learning to be Aes Sedai. Most important, however, was the lack of recognition in the Accepted's eyes; the two of them had met when Min was in the Tower before, though only briefly.

Just the same, Min lowered her face in assumed diffidence. It was not unnatural; a good many country folk did not really understand the great step up from Accepted to full Aes Sedai. Shielding her features behind the edge of her cloak, she looked away from Faolain.

"I have a question I must ask the Amyrlin Seat," she began, then cut off abruptly as three Aes Sedai stopped to look into the entry hall, two from one archway and one from another.

Accepted and novices curtsied when their rounds took them close to one of the Aes Sedai, but otherwise went on about their tasks, perhaps a trifle more briskly. That was all. Not so for the petitioners. They seemed to catch their breaths all together. Away from the White Tower, away from Tar Valon, they might simply have thought the Aes Sedai three women whose ages they could not guess, three women in the flush of their prime, yet with more maturity than their smooth cheeks suggested. In the Tower, though, there was no question. A woman who had worked very long with the One Power was not touched by time in the same way as other women. In the Tower, no one needed to see a golden Great Serpent ring to know an Aes Sedai.

A ripple of curtsies spread through the huddle, and jerky bows from the few men. Two or three people even fell to their knees. The rich merchant looked frightened; the farm couple at her side stared at legends come to life. How to deal with Aes Sedai was a matter of hearsay for most; it was unlikely that any here, except those who actually lived in Tar Valon, had seen an Aes Sedai before, and probably not even the Tar Valoners had been this close.

But it was not the Aes Sedai themselves that halted Min's tongue. Sometimes, not often, she saw things when she looked at people, images and auras that usually flared and were gone in moments. Occasionally she knew what they meant. It happened rarely, the knowing—much more rarely than the seeing, even—but when she knew, she was always right.

Unlike most others, Aes Sedai—and their Warders— always had images and auras, sometimes so many dancing and shifting that they made Min dizzy. The numbers made no difference in interpreting them, though; she knew what they meant for Aes Sedai as seldom as for anyone else. But this time she knew more than she wanted to, and it made her shiver.

A slender woman with black hair falling to her waist, the only one of the three she recognized—her name was Ananda; she was Yellow Ajah—wore a sickly brown halo, shriveled and split by rotting fissures that fell in and widened as they decayed. The small, fair-haired Aes Sedai beside Ananda was Green Ajah, by her green-fringed shawl. The White Flame of Tar Valon on it showed for a moment when she turned her back. And on her shoulder, as if nestled among the grape vines and flowering apple branches worked on her shawl, sat a human skull. A small woman's skull, picked clean and sun-bleached. The third, a plumply pretty woman halfway around the room, wore no shawl; most Aes Sedai did not except for ceremony. The lift of her chin and the set of her shoulders spoke of strength and pride. She seemed to be casting cool blue eyes on the petitioners through a tattered curtain of blood, crimson streamers running down her face.

Blood and skull and halo faded away in the dance of images around the three, came and faded again. The petitioners stared in awe, seeing only three women who could touch the True Source and channel the One Power. No one but Min saw the rest. No one but Min knew those three women were going to die. All on the same day.

"The Amyrlin cannot see everyone," Faolain said with poorly hidden impatience. "Her next public audience is not for ten days. Tell me what you want, and I will arrange for you to see the sister who can best help you."

Min's eye flew to the bundle in her arms and stayed there, partly so she would not have to see again what she had already seen. *All* three *of them! Light!* What chance was there that three Aes Sedai would die on the same day? But she knew. She knew.

"I have the right to speak to the Amyrlin Seat. In person." It was a right seldom demanded—who would dare?—but it existed. "Any woman has that right, and I ask it."

"Do you think the Amyrlin Seat herself can see everyone who comes to the White Tower? Surely another Aes Sedai can help you." Faolain gave heavy weight to the titles as if to overpower Min. "Now tell me what your question is about. And give me your name, so the novice will know who to come for."

"My name is . . . Elmindreda." Min winced in spite of herself. She had always hated the name, but the Amyrlin was one of the few people living who had ever heard it. If only she remembered. "I have the right to speak to the Amyrlin. And my question is for her alone. I have the right."

The Accepted arched an eyebrow. "Elmindreda?" Her mouth twitched toward an amused smile. "And you claim your rights. Very well. I will send word to the Keeper of the

Chronicles that you wish to see the Amyrlin Seat personally, Elmindreda."

Min wanted to slap the woman for the way she emphasized "Elmindreda," but instead she forced out a murmured "Thank you."

"Do not thank me yet. No doubt it will be hours before the Keeper finds time to reply, and it will certainly be that you can ask your question at the Mother's next public audience. Wait with patience. Elmindreda." She gave Min a tight smile, almost a smirk, as she turned away.

Grinding her teeth, Min took her bundle to stand against the wall between two of the archways, where she tried to blend into the pale stonework. *Trust no one, and avoid notice until you reach the Amyrlin*, Moiraine had told her. Moiraine was one Aes Sedai she did trust. Most of the time. It was good advice in any case. All she had to do was reach the Amyrlin, and it would be over. She could don her own clothes again, see her friends, and leave. No more need for hiding.

She was relieved to see that the Aes Sedai had gone. Three Aes Sedai dying on one day. It was impossible; that was the only word. Yet it was going to happen. Nothing she said or did could change it—when she knew what an image meant, it happened—but she had to tell the Amyrlin about this. It might even be as important as the news she brought from Moiraine, though that was hard to believe.

Another Accepted came to replace one already there, and to Min's eyes bars floated in front of her apple-cheeked face, like a cage. Sheriam, the Mistress of Novices, looked into the hall—after one glance, Min kept her gaze on the stone under her feet; Sheriam knew her all too well— and the red-haired Aes Sedai's face seemed battered and bruised. It was only the viewing, of course, but Min still had to bite her lip to stifle a gasp. Sheriam, with her calm authority and sureness, was as indestructible as the Tower. Surely nothing could harm Sheriam. But something was going to.

An Aes Sedai unknown to Min, wearing the shawl of the Brown Ajah, accompanied a stout woman in finely woven red wool to the doors. The stout woman walked as lightly as a girl, face shining, almost laughing with pleasure. The Brown sister was smiling, too, but her aura faded like a guttering candle flame.

Death. Wounds, captivity, and death. To Min it might as well have been printed on a page.

She set her eyes on her feet. She did not want to see any more. *Let her remember*, she thought. She had not felt desperation at any time on her long ride from the Mountains of Mist, not even on the two occasions when someone tried to steal her horse, but she felt it now. *Light, let her remember that bloody name.*

"Mistress Elmindreda?"

Min gave a start. The black-haired novice who stood before her was barely old enough to be away from home, perhaps fifteen or sixteen, though she made a great effort at dignity. "Yes? I am. . . . That is my name."

"I am Sahra. If you will come with me"—Sahra's piping voice took on a note of wonder—"the Amyrlin Seat will see you in her study now."

Min gave a sigh of relief and followed eagerly.

Her cloak's deep hood still hid her face, but it did not stop her seeing, and the more she saw, the more she grew eager to reach the Amyrlin. Few people walked the broad corridors that spiraled upward with their brightly colored floor tiles, and their wall hangings and golden lampstands—the Tower had been built to hold far greater numbers than it did now—but nearly everyone she saw as she climbed higher wore an image or aura that spoke to her of violence and danger.

Warders hurried by with barely a glance for the two women, men who moved like hunting wolves, their swords only an afterthought to their deadliness, but they seemed to have bloody faces, or gaping wounds. Swords and spears danced about their heads, threatening. Their auras flashed wildly, flickered on the knife edge of death. She saw dead men walking, knew they would die on the same day as the Aes Sedai in the entry hall, or at most a day later. Even some of the servants, men and women with the Flame of Tar Valon on their breasts, hurrying about their work, bore signs of violence. An Aes Sedai glimpsed down a side hallway appeared to have chains in the air around her, and another, crossing the corridor ahead of Min and her guide, seemed for most of those few strides to wear a silver collar around her neck. Min's breath caught at that; she wanted to scream.

"It can all be overwhelming to someone who's never seen

it before," Sahra said, trying and failing to sound as if the Tower were as ordinary to her now as her home village. "But you are safe here. The Amyrlin Seat will make things right." Her voice squeaked when she mentioned the Amyrlin.

"Light, let her do just that," Min muttered. The novice gave her a smile that was meant to be soothing.

By the time they reached the hall outside the Amyrlin's study, Min's stomach was churning and she was treading almost on Sahra's heels. Only the need to pretend that she was a stranger had kept her from running ahead long since.

One of the doors to the Amyrlin's chambers opened, and a young man with red-gold hair came stalking out, nearly striding into Min and her escort. Tall and straight and strong in his blue coat thickly embroidered with gold on sleeves and collar, Gawyn of House Trakand, son of Queen Morgase of Andor, looked every inch the proud young lord. A furious young lord. There was no time to drop her head; he was staring down into her hood, right into her face.

His eyes widened in surprise, then narrowed to slits of blue ice. "So you are back. Do you know where my sister and Egwene have gone?"

"They are not here?" Min forgot everything in a rising flood of panic. Before she knew what she was doing she had seized his sleeves, peering up at him urgently, and forced him back a step. "Gawyn, they started for the Tower months ago! Elayne and Egwene, and Nynaeve, too. With Verin Sedai and. . . . Gawyn, I . . . I. . . ."

"Calm yourself," he said, gently undoing her grip on his coat. "Light! I didn't mean to frighten you so. They arrived safely. And would not say a word of where they had been, or why. Not to me. I suppose there's scant hope you will?" She thought she kept her face straight, but he took one look and said, "I thought not. This place has more secrets than. . . . They've vanished again. And Nynaeve, too." Nynaeve was almost an offhand addition; she might be one of Min's friends, but she meant nothing to him. His voice began to roughen once more, growing tighter by the second. "Again without a word. Not a word! Supposedly they're on a farm somewhere as penance for running away, but I cannot find out where. The Amyrlin won't give me a straight answer."

Min flinched; for a moment, streaks of dried blood had made his face a grim mask. It was like a double hammer blow. Her friends were gone—it had eased her coming to the Tower, knowing they were here—and Gawyn was going to be wounded on the day the Aes Sedai died.

Despite all she had seen since entering the Tower, despite her fear, none of it had really touched her personally until now. Disaster striking the Tower would spread far from Tar Valon, yet she was not of the Tower and never could be. But Gawyn was someone she knew, someone she liked, and he was going to be hurt more than the blood told, hurt somehow deeper than wounds to his flesh. It hit her that if catastrophe seized the Tower, not only distant Aes Sedai would be harmed, women she could never feel close to, but her friends as well. They *were* of the Tower.

In a way she was glad Egwene and the others were not there, glad she could not look at them and perhaps see signs of death. Yet she wanted to look, to be sure, to look at her friends and see nothing, or see that they would live. Where in the Light were they? Why had they gone? Knowing those three, she thought it possible that if Gawyn did not know where they were, it was because they did not want him to know. It could be that.

Suddenly she remembered where she was and why, and that she was not alone with Gawyn. Sahra seemed to have forgotten she was taking Min to the Amyrlin; she seemed to have forgotten everything but the young lord, making calf-eyes that he was not noticing. Even so, there was no use pretending any longer to be a stranger to the Tower. She was at the Amyrlin's door; nothing could stop her now.

"Gawyn, I don't know where they are, but if they are doing penance on a farm, they're probably all sweat, and mud to their hips, and you are the last one they will want to see them." She was not much easier about their absence than Gawyn was, in truth. Too much had happened, too much was happening, too much with ties to them, and to her. But it was not impossible they had been sent off for punishment. "You won't help them by making the Amyrlin angry."

"I don't know that they *are* on a farm. Or even alive. Why all this hiding and sidestepping if they're just pulling weeds? If anything happens to my sister. . . . Or to Egwene. . . ." He frowned at the toes of his boots. "I am supposed to look after Elayne. How can I protect her when I don't know where she is?"

Min sighed. "Do you think she needs looking after? Either of them?" But if the Amyrlin had sent them somewhere, maybe they did. The Amyrlin was capable of sending a woman into a bear's den with nothing but a switch if it suited her purposes. And she would expect the woman to come back with a bearskin, or the bear on a leash, as instructed. But telling Gawyn that would only inflame his temper and his worries. "Gawyn, they have pledged to the Tower. They won't thank you for meddling."

"I know Elayne isn't a child," he said patiently, "even if she does bounce back and forth between running off like one and playing at being Aes Sedai. But she *is* my sister, and beyond that, she is Daughter-Heir of Andor. She'll be queen, after Mother. Andor needs her whole and safe to take the throne, not another Succession."

Playing at being Aes Sedai? Apparently he did not realize the extent of his sister's talent. The Daughter-Heirs of Andor had been sent to the Tower to train for as long as there had been an Andor, but Elayne was the first to have enough talent to be raised to Aes Sedai, and a powerful Aes Sedai at that. Very likely he also did not know Egwene was just as strong.

"So you will protect her whether she wants it or not?" She said it in a flat voice meant to let him know he was making a mistake, but he missed the warning and nodded agreement.

"That has been my duty since the day she was born. My blood shed before hers; my life given before hers. I took that oath when I could barely see over the side of her cradle; Gareth Bryne had to explain to me what it meant. I won't break it now. Andor needs her more than it needs me."

He spoke with a calm certainty, an acceptance of something natural and right, that sent chills through her. She had always thought of him as boyish, laughing and teasing, but now he was something alien. She thought the Creator must have been tired when it came time to make men; sometimes they hardly seemed human. "And Egwene? What oath did you take about her?"

His face did not change, but he shifted his feet warily. "I'm concerned about Egwene, of course. And Nynaeve. What happens to Elayne's companions might happen to Elayne. I assume they're still together; when they *were* here, I seldom saw one without the others."

"My mother always told me to marry a poor liar, and you qualify. Except that I think someone else has first claim."

"Some things are meant to be," he said quietly, "and some never can. Galad is heartsick because Egwene is gone." Galad was his half-brother, the pair of them sent to Tar Valon to train under the Warders. That was another Andoran tradition. Galadedrid Damodred was a man who took doing the right thing to the point of a fault, as Min saw it, but Gawyn could see no wrong in him. And he would not speak his feelings for a woman Galad had set his heart on.

She wanted to shake him, shake some sense into him, but there was no time now. Not with the Amyrlin waiting, not with what she had to tell the Amyrlin waiting. Certainly not with Sahra standing there, calf-eyes or no calf-eyes. "Gawyn, I am summoned to the Amyrlin. Where can I find you, when she is done with me?"

"I will be in the practice yard. The only time I can stop worrying is when I am working the sword with Hammar." Hammar was a blademaster, and the Warder who taught the sword. "Most days I'm there until the sun sets."

"Good, then. I will come as soon as I can. And try to watch what you say. If you make the Amyrlin angry with you, Elayne and Egwene might share in it."

"That I cannot promise," he said firmly. "Something is wrong in the world. Civil war in Cairhien. The same and worse in Tarabon and Arad Doman. False Dragons. Troubles and rumors of troubles everywhere. I don't say the Tower is behind it, but even here things are not what they should be. Or what they seem. Elayne and Egwene vanishing isn't the whole of it. Still, they are the part that concerns me. I *will* find out where they are. And if they have been hurt. . . . If they are dead. . . ."

He scowled, and for an instant his face was that bloody mask again. More: a sword floated above his head, and a banner waved behind it. The long-hilted sword, like those most Warders used, had a heron engraved on its slightly curved blade, symbol of a blademaster, and Min could not say whether it belonged to Gawyn or threatened him. The banner bore Gawyn's sigil of the charging White Boar, but on a field of green rather than the red of Andor. Both sword and banner faded with the blood.

"Be careful, Gawyn." She meant it two ways. Careful of what he said, and careful in a way she could not explain, even to herself. "You must be very careful."

His eyes searched her face as if he had heard some of her deeper meaning. "I . . . will try," he said finally. He put on a grin, almost the grin she remembered, but the effort was plain. "I suppose I had better get myself back to the practice yard if I expect to keep up with Galad. I managed two out of five against Hammar this morning, but Galad actually won three, the last time he bothered to come to the yard." Suddenly he appeared to really see her for the first time, and his grin became genuine. "You ought to wear dresses more often. It's pretty on you. Remember, I will be there till sunset."

As he strode away with something very close to the dangerous grace of a Warder, Min realized she was smoothing the dress over her hip and stopped immediately. *The Light burn all men!*

Sahra exhaled as if she had been holding her breath. "He is very good-looking, isn't he?" she said dreamily. "Not as good-looking as Lord Galad, of course. And you really know him." It was half a question, but only half.

Min echoed the novice's sigh. The girl would talk with her friends in the novices' quarters. The son of a queen was a natural topic, especially when he was handsome and had an air about him like the hero in a gleeman's tale. A strange woman only made for more interesting speculation. Still, there was nothing to be done about it. At any rate, it could hardly cause any harm now.

"The Amyrlin Seat must be wondering why we haven't come," she said.

Sahra came to herself with a wide-eyed start and a loud gulp. Seizing Min's sleeve with one hand, she jumped to open one of the doors, pulling Min behind her. The moment they were inside, the novice curtsied hastily and burst out in panic, "I've brought her, Leane Sedai. Mistress Elmindreda? The Amyrlin Seat wants to see her?"

The tall, coppery-skinned woman in the anteroom wore the hand-wide stole of the Keeper of the Chronicles, blue to show she had been raised from the Blue Ajah. Fists on hips, she waited for the girl to finish, then dismissed her with a clipped "Took you long enough, child. Back to your chores, now." Sahra bobbed another curtsy and scurried out as quickly as she had entered.

Min stood with her eyes on the floor, her hood still pulled up around her face. Blundering in front of Sahra had been bad enough—though at least the novice did not know her name—but Leane knew her better than anyone in the Tower except the Amyrlin. Min was sure it could make no difference now, but after what had happened in the hallway, she meant to hold to Moiraine's instructions until she was alone with the Amyrlin.

This time her precautions did no good. Leane took two steps, pushed back the hood, and grunted as if she had been poked in the stomach. Min raised her head and stared back defiantly, trying to pretend she had not been attempting to sneak past. Straight, dark hair only a little longer than her own framed the Keeper's face; the Aes Sedai's expression was a blend of surprise and displeasure at being surprised.

"So you are Elmindreda, are you?" Leane said briskly. She was always brisk. "I must say you look it more in that dress than in your usual . . . garb."

"Just Min, Leane Sedai, if you please." Min managed to keep her face straight, but it was difficult not to glare. The Keeper's voice had held too much amusement. If her mother had had to name her after someone in a story, why did it have to be a woman who seemed to spend most of her time sighing at men, when she was not inspiring them to compose songs about her eyes, or her smile?

"Very well. Min. I'll not ask where you've been, nor why you've come back in a dress, apparently wanting to ask a question of the Amyrlin. Not now, at least." Her face said she meant to ask later, though, and get answers. "I suppose the Mother knows who Elmindreda is? Of course. I should have known that when she said to send you straight in, and alone. The Light alone knows why she puts up with you." She broke off with a concerned frown. "What is the matter, girl? Are you ill?"

Min carefully blanked her face. "No. No, I am all right." For a moment the Keeper had been looking through a transparent mask of her own face, a screaming mask. "May I go in now, Leane Sedai?"

Leane studied her a moment longer, then jerked her head toward the inner chamber. "In with you." Min's leap to obey would have satisfied the hardest taskmistress.

The Amyrlin Seat's study had been occupied by many grand and powerful women over the centuries, and reminders of the fact filled the room, from the tall fireplace all of golden marble from Kandor, cold now, to the paneled walls of pale, oddly striped wood, iron hard yet carved in wondrous beasts and wildly feathered birds. Those panels had been brought from the mysterious lands beyond the Aiel Waste well over a thousand years ago, and the fireplace was more than twice as old. The polished red-stone of the floor had come from the Mountains of Mist. High arched windows let onto a balcony. The iridescent stone framing the windows shone like pearls, and had been salvaged from the remains of a city sunk into the Sea of Storms by the Breaking of the World; no one had ever seen its like.

The current occupant, Siuan Sanche, had been born a fisherman's daughter in Tear, though, and the furnishings she had chosen were simple, if well made and well polished. She sat in a stout chair behind a large table plain enough to have served a farmhouse. The only other chair in the room, just as plain and usually set off to one side, now stood in front of the table atop a small Tairen rug, simple in blue and brown and gold. Half a dozen books rested open on tall reading stands about the floor. That was all of it. A drawing hung above the fireplace: tiny fishing boats working among reeds in the Fingers of the Dragon, just as her father's boat had.

At first glance, despite her smooth Aes Sedai features, Siuan Sanche herself looked as simple as her furnishings. She herself was sturdy, and handsome rather than beautiful, and the only bit of ostentation in her clothing was the broad stole of the Amyrlin Seat she wore, with one colored stripe for each of the seven Ajahs. Her age was indeterminate, as with any Aes Sedai; not even a hint of gray showed in her dark hair. But her sharp blue eyes brooked no nonsense, and her firm jaw spoke of the determination of the youngest woman ever to be chosen Amyrlin Seat. For over ten years Siuan Sanche had been able to summon rulers, and the powerful, and they had come, even if they hated the White Tower and feared Aes Sedai.

As the Amyrlin strode around in front of the table, Min

set down her bundle and began an awkward curtsy, muttering irritably under her breath at having to do so. Not that she wanted to be disrespectful—that did not even occur to one facing a woman like Siuan Sanche—but the bow she usually would have made seemed foolish in a dress, and she had only a rough idea of how to curtsy.

Halfway down, with her skirts already spread, she froze like a crouching toad. Siuan Sanche was standing there as regal as any queen, and for a moment she was also lying on the floor, naked. Aside from her being in only her skin, there was something odd about the image, but it vanished before Min could say what. It was as strong a viewing as she had ever seen, and she had no idea what it meant.

"Seeing things again, are you?" the Amyrlin said. "Well, I can certainly make use of that ability of yours. I could have used it all the months you were gone. But we'll not talk of that. What's done is done. The Wheel weaves as the Wheel wills." She smiled a tight smile. "But if you do it again, I'll have your hide for gloves. Stand up, girl. Leane forces enough ceremony on me in a month to last any sensible woman a year. I don't have time for it. Not these days. Now, what did you just see?"

Min straightened slowly. It was a relief to be back with someone who knew of her talent, even if it was the Amyrlin Seat herself. She did not have to hide what she saw from the Amyrlin. Far from it. "You were. . . . You weren't wearing any clothes. I . . . I don't know what it means, Mother."

Siuan barked a short, mirthless laugh. "No doubt that I'll take a lover. But I have no time for that, either. There's no time for winking at the men when you're busy bailing the boat."

"Maybe," Min said slowly. It could have meant that, though she doubted it. "I just do not know. But, Mother, I've been seeing things ever since I walked into the Tower. Something bad is going to happen, something terrible."

She started with the Aes Sedai in the entry hall and told everything she had seen, as well as what everything meant, when she was sure. She held back what Gawyn had said, though, or most of it; it was no use telling him not to anger the Amyrlin if she did it for him. The rest she laid out as starkly as she had seen it. Some of her fear came out as she dredged it all up, seeing it all again; her voice shook before she was done.

The Amyrlin's expression never changed. "So you spoke with young Gawyn," she said when Min finished. "Well, I think I can convince him to keep quiet. And if I remember Sahra correctly, the girl could do with some time working in the country. She'll spread no gossip hoeing a vegetable patch."

"I don't understand," Min said. "Why should Gawyn keep quiet? About what? I told him nothing. And Sahra . . . ? Mother, perhaps I didn't make myself clear. Aes Sedai and Warders are going to die. It has to mean a battle. And unless you send a lot of Aes Sedai and Warders off somewhere—and servants, too; I saw servants dead and injured, too—unless you do that, that battle will be here! In Tar Valon!"

About the Author

Robert Jordan was born in 1948 in Charleston, South Carolina. He taught himself to read when he was four with the incidental aid of a twelve-years-older brother, and was tackling Mark Twain and Jules Verne by five. He was a graduate of the Citadel, the Military College of South Carolina, with a degree in physics. He served two tours in Vietnam with the U.S. Army; among his decorations are the Distinguished Flying Cross with bronze oak leaf cluster, the Bronze Star with "V" and bronze oak leaf cluster, and two Vietnamese Gallantry Crosses with Palm. A history buff, he also wrote dance and theater criticism. He enjoyed the outdoor sports of hunting, fishing, and sailing, and the indoor sports of poker, chess, pool, and pipe collecting. He began writing in 1977 and continued until his death on September 16, 2007.

Praise for
Robert Jordan and
The Wheel of Time®

"His huge, ambitious Wheel of Time series helped redefine the genre." —George R. R. Martin, internationally bestselling author of *A Game of Thrones*

"Anyone who's writing epic secondary world fantasy knows Robert Jordan isn't just a part of the landscape, he's a monolith within the landscape." —Patrick Rothfuss, internationally bestselling author of The Kingkiller Chronicle

"*The Eye of the World* was a turning point in my life. I read, I enjoyed. (Then continued on to write my larger fantasy novels.)" —Robin Hobb, *New York Times* bestselling author of The Farseer Trilogy

"Robert Jordan's work has been a formative influence and an inspiration for a generation of fantasy writers." —Brent Weeks, *New York Times* bestselling author of *The Way of Shadows*

"Jordan has come to dominate the world Tolkien began to reveal." —*The New York Times*

"One of fantasy's most acclaimed series." —*USA Today*

"Robert Jordan was a giant of fiction whose words helped a whole generation of fantasy writers, including myself, find our true voices. I thanked him then, but I didn't thank him enough." —Peter V. Brett, internationally bestselling author of The Demon Cycle

The Wheel of Time®

By Robert Jordan

By Robert Jordan and Brandon Sanderson

By Robert Jordan and Teresa Patterson

By Robert Jordan, Harriet McDougal, Alan Romanczuk, and Maria Simons

THE EYE OF THE WORLD

ROBERT JORDAN

A TOM DOHERTY ASSOCIATES BOOK
NEW YORK

This is a work of fiction. All of the characters, organizations, and events portrayed in this novel are either products of the author's imagination or are used fictitiously.

THE EYE OF THE WORLD

Maps by Ellisa Mitchell and Thomas Canty
Interior illustrations by Matthew C. Nielsen

A Tor Book
Published by Tom Doherty Associates
120 Broadway
New York, NY 10271

www.tor-forge.com

Tor® is a registered trademark of Macmillan Publishing Group, LLC.

ISBN 978-1-250-25146-6

Our books may be purchased in bulk for promotional, educational, or business use. Please contact your local bookseller or the Macmillan Corporate and Premium Sales Department at 1-800-221-7945, extension 5442, or by email at MacmillanSpecialMarkets@macmillan.com.

First Edition: February 1990
First Premium Mass Market Edition: November 2019

Printed in the United States of America

0 9 8 7 6

To Harriet
Heart of my heart,
Light of my life,
Forever.

CONTENTS

THE EYE
OF THE
WORLD

EARLIER

Ravens

T his far below Emond's Field, halfway to the Waterwood, trees lined the banks of the Winespring Water. Mostly willows, their leafy branches made a shady canopy over the water near the bank. Summer was not far off, and the sun was climbing toward midday, yet here in the shadows a soft breeze made Egwene's sweat feel cool on her skin. Tying the skirts of her brown wool dress up above her knees, she waded a little way into the river to fill her wooden bucket. The boys just waded in, not caring whether their snug breeches got wet. Some of the girls and boys filling buckets laughed and used their wooden dippers to fling water at one another, but Egwene settled for enjoying the stir of the current on her bare legs, and her toes wriggling on the sandy bottom as she climbed back out. She was not here to play. At nine, she was carrying water for the first time, but she was going to be the best water-carrier ever.

Pausing on the bank, she set down her bucket to unfasten her skirts and let them fall to her ankles. And to retie the dark green kerchief that gathered her hair at the nape of her neck. She wished she could cut it at her shoulders, or even shorter, like the boys. She would not need to have long hair for years yet, after all. Why did you have to keep doing something just because it had always been done that way? But she knew her mother, and she knew her hair was going to stay long.

Close to a hundred paces further down the river, men stood knee-deep in the water, washing the black-faced sheep that would later be sheared. They took great care getting the bleating animals into the river and back out safely. The

Winespring Water did not flow as swiftly here as it did in Emond's Field, yet it was not slow. A sheep that got swept away might drown before it could struggle ashore.

A large raven flew across the river to perch high in the branches of a whitewood near where the men were washing sheep. Almost immediately a redcrest began diving at the raven, a flash of scarlet that chattered noisily. The redcrest must have a nest nearby. Instead of taking flight and maybe attacking the smaller bird, though, the raven just shuffled sideways on the limb to where a few smaller branches sheltered it a little. It peered down toward the working men.

Ravens sometimes bothered the sheep, but ignoring the redcrest's attempts to frighten it away was more than unusual. More than that, she had the strange feeling that the black bird was watching the men, not the sheep. Which was silly, except . . . She had heard people say that ravens and crows were the Dark One's eyes. That thought made goosebumps break out all down her arms and even on her back. It *was* a silly idea. What would the Dark One want to see in the Two Rivers? Nothing ever happened in the Two Rivers.

"What are you up to, Egwene?" Kenley Ahan demanded, stopping beside her. "You can't play with the children today." Two years older than she, he carried himself very straight, stretching to seem taller than he was. This was his last year carrying water at the shearing, and he behaved as if that cloaked him with some sort of authority.

She gave him a level look, but it did not work as well as she hoped.

His square face twisted up in a frown. "If you're turning sick, go see the Wisdom. If not . . . well . . . get on about your work." With a quick nod, as if he had solved a problem, he hurried off making a great show of holding his bucket with one hand, well away from his side. *He won't keep that up long once he's out of my sight,* she thought sourly. She was going to have to work on that look. She had seen it work for older girls.

The dipper's handle slid on the rim of her bucket as she picked it up with both hands. It was heavy, and she was not big for her age, but she followed Kenley as quickly as she could. Not because of anything he had said, certainly. She *did* have work to do, and she *was* going to be the best water-carrier ever. Her face set with determination. The mulch of last year's leaves rustled under her feet as she walked through the river's shadowy fringe of trees, out into the sunlight. The heat was not too bad, but a few small white clouds high in the sky seemed to emphasize the brightness of the morning.

Widow Aynal's Meadow—it had been called that as long as anyone could remember, though no one knew which Aynal widow it had been named after—the tree-ringed meadow stood empty most of the year, but now people and sheep crowded the whole long length of it, a good many more sheep than people. Large stones stuck out of the ground here and there, a few almost as tall as a man, but they did not interfere with the activity in the meadow. Farmers came from all around Emond's Field for this, and village folk came out to help relatives. Everyone in the village had kith or kin of some sort on the farms. Shearing would be going on all across the Two Rivers, down at Deven Ride and up to Watch Hill. Not at Taren Ferry, of course. Many of the women wore shawls draped loosely over their arms and flowers in their hair, for the formality, and so did some of the older girls, though their hair was not in the long braid the women had. A few even wore dresses with embroidery around the neck, as if this really were a feastday. In contrast, most of the men and boys went coatless, and some even had their shirts unlaced. Egwene did not understand why they were allowed to do that. The women's work was no cooler than the men's.

Big, wooden-railed pens at the far end of the meadow held sheep already sheared, and others held those waiting to be washed, all watched by boys of twelve and up. The sheepdogs sprawled around the pens were no good for this work. Groups of those older boys were using wooden staffs to herd sheep to the river for washing, then to keep them from lying down and getting dirty again until they were dry for the men at this end of the meadow who were doing the shearing. Once the sheep were shorn, the boys herded them back to the pens while men carried the fleece to the slatted tables where women sorted the wool and folded it for baling. They kept a tally, and had to be careful that no one's wool was mixed with anyone else's. Along the trees to Egwene's left, other women were beginning to set out food for the midday meal on long trestle tables. If she was good enough at carrying water, maybe they would let her help with the food or the wool next year, instead of two years later. If she did the best job ever, no one would ever be able to call her a baby again.

She began making her way through the crowd, sometimes carrying the bucket in both hands, sometimes shifting it from one to the other, pausing whenever someone motioned for a dipper of water. Soon she began to perspire again, sweating dark patches on her woolen dress. Maybe the boys with their shirts unlaced were not just being foolish. She ignored the younger children, running around rolling hoops and tossing balls and playing keep-away.

There were only five times each year when so many gathered: at Bel Tine, which was past; at shearing; when the merchants came to buy the wool, still a month or more off; when the merchants came for the cured tabac, after Sunday; and at Foolday, in the fall. There were other feastdays, of course, but none where *everyone* got together. Her eyes kept moving, searching the crowd. Among all these people, it would be all too easy to walk up on one of her four sisters. She always avoided them as much as possible. Berowyn, the eldest, was worst. She had been widowed by the breakbone fever last fall and moved back home in the spring. It was hard not to feel for Berowyn, but she *fussed* so, wanting to dress Egwene and brush her hair. Sometimes she wept and told Egwene how lucky she felt that the fever had not taken her *baby* sister, too. Feeling for Berowyn would have been easier if Egwene could stop thinking that sometimes Berowyn saw her as the infant she had lost along with her husband. Maybe all the time. She was just watching for Berowyn. Or one of the other three. That was all.

Near the sheep-pens, she stopped to wipe the sweat from her forehead. Her bucket was lighter, now, and no trouble to hold with one hand. She eyed the nearest dog cautiously. Standing in front of one of the pens, it was a large animal with a close, curly gray coat and intelligent eyes that seemed to know she was no danger to the sheep. Still, it was very big, almost waist-high to a grown man. Mainly the dogs helped protect the flocks when they were in pasture, guarding against wolves and bears and the big mountain cats. She edged away from the dog. Three boys passed her, herding a few dozen sheep toward the river. All five or six years older than she, the boys barely gave her a glance, their full

attention on the animals. The herding was easy enough—
she could have done it, she was sure—but they had to make
sure none of the sheep had a chance to crop grass. A sheep
that ate before being sheared could get the gasping and die.
A quick look around told her that none of the other boys in
sight was anyone she wanted to speak to. Not that she was
looking for a particular boy to speak to, of course. She was
just looking. Anyway, her bucket would need refilling soon.
It was time to start back toward the Winespring Water.

This time she decided to go by way of the row of trestle
tables. The smells were tantalizing, as good as any feastday, everything from roast goose to honeycakes. The spicy
aroma of the honeycakes filled her nose more than all the
rest. Every woman who cooked would have done her very
best for the shearing. As she made her way down the tables,
she offered water to the women setting out food, but they just
smiled at her and shook their heads. She kept on, though,
and not just because of the smells. They had tea water boiling on fires behind the tables, but some of them might want
cool water from the river. Well, not so cool, now, but still . . .

Ahead of her Kenley was slouching along beside the
tables, no longer trying for every inch of height. If anything,
he seemed to be trying for shorter. He still carried his bucket
in one hand, but from the way it swung, it must have been
empty, so he could not be offering water to anyone. Egwene frowned. Furtive was the only word to describe him.
Now, what was he . . . ? Abruptly his hand darted out and
snatched a honeycake from the table. Egwene's mouth fell
open indignantly. And he had the nerve to talk to her about
children? He was as bad as Ewin Finngar!

Before Kenley could take a second step, Mistress Ayellin
descended on him like a stooping falcon, seizing his ear
with one hand and the honeycake with the other. They were
her honeycakes. A slim woman with a thick gray braid that
hung below her hips, Corin Ayellin baked the best sweets in
Emond's Field. *Except for mother,* Egwene added loyally.
But even her mother said Mistress Ayellin was better. With
sweets, anyway. Mistress Ayellin handed out crusty cakes
and slices of pie with a free hand, so long as it was not
near mealtime or your mother had not asked her not to, but
she could deal heavily with boys who tried to filch behind
her back. Or with anyone else. Stealing, she called it, and

Mistress Ayellin did not abide stealing. She still had Kenley by his ear and was shaking a finger at him, talking in a low voice. Kenley's face was all twisted up as if he was about to cry, and he shrank in on himself till he appeared shorter than Egwene. She gave a satisfied nod. She did not think he would try to give orders to anyone any time soon.

She moved further from the tables as she walked on by Mistress Ayellin and Kenley, so no one would suspect *her* of trying to filch sweets. The thought had never entered her head. Not really, anyway, not so it counted.

Suddenly she leaned forward, peering between the people moving back and forth in front of her. Yes. That was Perrin Aybara, a stocky boy taller than most his age. And he was a friend of Rand. She darted through the crowd without noticing whether anyone motioned for water and did not stop until she was only a few paces from Perrin.

He was with his parents, and his mother had the baby, Paetram, on her hip, and little Deselle clinging to her skirt with one hand, though Perrin's little sister was looking around with interest at all the people and even sheep being herded past. Adora, his other sister, stood with her arms folded across her chest and a sullen expression that she was trying to hide from her mother. Adora would not have to carry water until next year, and she probably was anxious to be off playing with her friends. The last person in the little group was Master Luhhan. The tallest man in Emond's Field, with arms like tree trunks and a chest that strained his white shirt, he made Master Aybara look slight instead of just slender. He was talking with Mistress Aybara and Master Aybara both. That puzzled Egwene. Master Luhhan was the blacksmith in Emond's Field, but neither Master Aybara nor Mistress Aybara would bring the whole family to ask after smithing. He was on the Village Council, too, but the same thing applied. Besides, Mistress Aybara would no sooner open her mouth about Council business than Master Aybara would about Women's Circle business. Egwene might only be nine, but she knew that much. Whatever they were talking about, they were almost done, and that was good. She did not *care* what they were talking about.

"He's a good lad, Joslyn," Master Luhhan said. "A good lad, Con. He'll do just fine."

Mistress Aybara smiled fondly. Joslyn Aybara was a pretty

woman, and when she smiled, it seemed the sun might hide its head in defeat. Perrin's father laughed softly and ruffled Perrin's curly hair. Perrin blushed very red and said nothing. But then, he was shy, and he seldom said very much.

"Make me fly, Perrin," Deselle said, lifting up her hands to him. "Make me fly."

Perrin barely waited to sketch a polite bow to the grownups before turning to take his sister's hands. They moved a few steps from the others, and then Perrin begin to spin around and around, faster and faster, until Deselle's feet left the ground. Round and round he spun her, higher and higher in great swoops, while she laughed and laughed in delight.

After a few minutes, Mistress Aybara said, "That's enough, Perrin. Put her down before she sicks up." But she said it kindly, with a smile.

Once Deselle's feet were back on the ground, she clung to one of Perrin's hands with both of hers, staggering a little, and maybe not too far from sicking up. But she kept laughing and demanding he make her fly some more. Shaking his head, he bent to talk to her. He was always so serious. He did not laugh very often.

Abruptly Egwene realized that someone else was watching Perrin. Cilia Cole, a pink-cheeked girl a couple of years older than she, stood only a few feet away with a silly smile on her face, making calf eyes at him. All he needed to do was turn his head to *see* her! Egwene grimaced in disgust. *She* would never be fool enough to make big eyes at a boy like some kind of woolhead. Anyway, Perrin was not even a whole year older than Cilia. Three or four years older was best. Egwene's sisters might have no time to talk to her, but she listened to other girls old enough to know. Some said more, but most thought three or four. Perrin glanced toward Egwene and Cilia and went back to talking quietly to Deselle. Egwene shook her head. Maybe Cilia was a ninny, but he ought to at least *notice*.

Movement in the limbs of a big wateroak beyond Cilia caught her eye, and she gave a start. The raven was up there, and it still seemed to be watching. And there was a raven in that tall pine tree, too, and one in the next, and in that hickory, and . . . Nine or ten ravens that she could see, and they all seemed to be watching. It had to be her imagination. Just her—

"Why were you staring at him?"

Startled, Egwene jumped and spun around so fast that she banged herself on the knee with her bucket. A good thing it was nearly empty, or she could have hurt herself. She shifted her feet, wishing she could rub her knee. Adora stood looking up at her with a perplexed expression on her face, but she could not be more puzzled than Egwene.

"What are you talking about, Adora?"

"Perrin, of course. Why were you staring at him? Everybody says you'll marry Rand al'Thor. When you're older, I mean, and have your hair in a braid."

"What do you mean, *everybody* says?" Egwene said dangerously, but Adora just giggled. It was exasperating. Nothing was working the way it should today.

"Perrin *is* pretty, of course. At least, I've heard lots of girls say so. And lots of girls look at him, just like you and Cilia."

Egwene blinked and managed to put that last out of her head. She had not been looking at him anything at *all* the way Cilia had! But, Perrin, pretty? Perrin? She looked over her shoulder to see whether she could find pretty in him. He was gone! His father was still there, and his mother, with Paetram and Deselle, but Perrin was nowhere to be seen. Drat! She had meant to follow him.

"Aren't you lonely without your dolls, Adora?" she said sweetly. "I didn't think you ever left your house without at least two."

Adora's open-mouth stare of outrage was quite satisfying.

"Excuse me," Egwene said, brushing past her. "Some of us are old enough to have work to do." She managed not to limp as she made her way back to the river.

This time she did not pause to look at the men washing sheep, and she very carefully did not look for a raven. She did examine her knee, but it was not even bruised. Carrying her filled bucket back out to the meadow, she refused to limp. It had just been a little bump.

She kept watching cautiously for her sisters as she carried water, pausing only to let someone take the dipper. And for Perrin. Mat would be as good as Perrin, but she did not see him, either. Drat Adora! She had no right to say things like that!

Walking in among the tables where women were sorting the wool, Egwene came to a dead stop, staring at her youngest sister. She froze, hoping Loise would look the other way, just for an instant. That was what she got for trying to watch for Perrin and Mat as well as her sisters. Loise was only fifteen, but she had a sour expression on her face and her hands on her hips as she confronted Dag Coplin. Egwene could never make herself call him Master Coplin except aloud, to be polite; her mother said you had to be polite, even to someone like Dag Coplin.

Dag was a wrinkled old man with gray hair that he did not wash very often. Or maybe not at all. The tag hanging from the table by a string was inked to match the ear-notches on his sheep. "That's good wool you're setting aside," he growled at Loise. "I won't be cheated on my clip, girl. Step aside and I'll show you what goes where my own self."

Loise did not move an inch. "Wool from bellies, hindquarters, and tails has to be washed again, Master Coplin." She put just a bit of emphasis on 'Master.' She *was* feeling snippish. "You know as well as I, if the merchants find twice-washed wool in just one bale, everyone will get less for their clip. Maybe my father can explain it to you better than I can."

Dag drew in his chin and grumbled something under his breath. He knew better than to try this with Egwene's father.

"I'm sure my mother could explain it so you'd understand," Loise said relentlessly.

Dag's cheek twitched, and he put on a sickly grin. Muttering that he trusted Loise to do what was right, he backed away, then hurried off little short of running. He was not foolish enough to bring himself to the attention of the Women's Circle if he could help it. Loise watched him go with a definite look of satisfaction.

Egwene took the opportunity to dart away, breathing a sigh of relief when Loise did not shout after her. Loise might prefer sorting wool to helping with the cooking, but she would much rather be climbing trees or swimming in the Waterwood, even if most girls had abandoned that sort of thing by her age. And she would take her chore out on Egwene, given half a chance. Egwene would have liked to go swimming with her, but Loise plainly considered her

company a nuisance, and Egwene was too proud to ask.
She scowled. All of her sisters treated her like a baby. Even
Alene, when Alene noticed her at all. Most of the time, Alene
had her nose in a book, reading and re-reading their father's
library. He had almost *forty* books! Egwene's favorite was
The Travels of Jain Farstrider. She dreamed of seeing all
those strange lands he wrote about. But if she was reading a
book and Alene wanted it, she always said it was much too
'complex' for Egwene and just took it! Drat all *four* of them!

She saw some of the water-carriers taking breaks to sit in
the shade or trade jokes, but she kept moving, although her
arms did ache. Egwene al'Vere was not going to slack off.
She kept watching for her sisters, too. And for Perrin. And
Mat. Drat Adora, anyway! Drat *all* of them!

She did pause when she neared the Wisdom. Doral Barran
was the oldest woman in Emond's Field, maybe in the whole
Two Rivers, white-haired and frail, but still clear-eyed and
not stooped at all. The Wisdom's apprentice, Nynaeve, was
on her knees with her back to Egwene, tending Bili Congar,
wrapping a bandage around his leg. His breeches had been
cut away short. Bili, sitting on a log, was another grownup
who Egwene found it hard to show the proper respect. He
was always doing silly things and getting himself hurt. He
was the same age as Master Luhhan, but he looked at
least ten years older, his face hollow-cheeked and his eyes
sunken.

"You've played the fool often enough in the past, Bili
Congar," Mistress Barran said sternly, "but drinking while
handling wool-shears is worse than playing the fool." Oddly,
she was not looking down at him, but at Nynaeve.

"I only had a little ale, Wisdom," he whined. "Because of
the heat. Just a swallow."

The Wisdom sniffed in disbelief, but she continued to
watch Nynaeve like a hawk. That was surprising. Mistress
Barran often praised Nynaeve publicly for being such a
quick learner. She had apprenticed Nynaeve three years earlier, after her then-apprentice died of some sickness even
Mistress Barran could not cure. Nynaeve had been a recent
orphan, and a lot of people said the Wisdom should have
sent her to her relatives in the country after her mother
died, and taken on someone years older. Egwene's mother
did not say so, but Egwene knew she thought it.

Nynaeve straightened on her knees, done with fastening the bandage, and gave a satisfied nod. And to Egwene's surprise, Mistress Barran knelt down and undid it again, even lifting the bread-poultice to peer at the gash in Bili's thigh before beginning to wrap the cloth back around his leg. She actually looked . . . disappointed. But why? Nynaeve began fiddling with her braid, tugging at it the way she did when she was nervous, or trying to bring attention to the fact that she was a grown woman, now.

When is she going to outgrow that? Egwene thought. It was nearly a year since the Women's Circle had let Nynaeve braid her hair.

A flutter of motion in the air caught Egwene's eye, and she stared. More ravens dotted the trees around the meadow now. Dozens and dozens of them, and all watching. She knew they were. Not one made a try to steal anything from the tables of food. That was just unnatural. Come to think of it, the birds were not looking at the trestle tables at all. Or at the tables where women were working with the wool. They were watching the boys herding sheep. And the men shearing sheep and carrying wool. And the boys carrying water, too. Not the girls, or the women, just the men and boys. She would have bet on it, even if her mother did say she should not bet. She opened her mouth to ask the Wisdom what it meant.

"Don't you have work to do, Egwene?" Nynaeve said without turning around.

Egwene jumped in spite of herself. Nynaeve had been doing that ever since last fall, knowing that Egwene was there without looking, and Egwene wished she would stop.

Nynaeve turned her head then, and looked at her over one shoulder. It was a level look, the sort Egwene had been trying on Kenley. She did not have to hop for Nynaeve the way she would for the Wisdom. Nynaeve was just trying to make up for Mistress Barran doubting her work. Egwene thought about telling her that Mistress Ayellin wanted to talk to her about a pie. Studying Nynaeve's face, she decided that might not be a good notion. Anyway, she had been doing what she had vowed not to, slacking off, standing around watching Nynaeve and the Wisdom. Making as much of a curtsey as she could while holding her bucket—to the Wisdom, not Nynaeve—she turned away. She was not hopping, and not because Nynaeve looked at her. Certainly not. And not hurrying, either. Just walking—quickly—to get back to her work.

Still, she walked quickly enough that before she realized it, she was back among the tables where the women were working wool. And face to face across one of the tables with her sister Elisa. Elisa was folding fleece for baling, and making a bad job of it. She seemed distracted, barely even noticing Egwene, and Egwene knew why. Elisa was eighteen, but her waist-length hair was still tied with a blue kerchief. Not that she was thinking about getting married— most girls waited at least a few years—but she was a year older than Nynaeve. Elisa often worried aloud about why the Women's Circle still thought she was too young. It was hard not to feel sympathy. Especially since Egwene had been thinking about Elisa's predicament for weeks, now. Well, not about Elisa's problem, exactly, but it had set her thinking.

Off to one side of the tables, Calle Coplin was talking with some young men from the farms, giggling and twisting her skirts. She was always talking to some man or other, but she was *supposed* to be folding fleece. That was not why she caught Egwene's eye, though.

"Elisa, you shouldn't worry so," she said gently. "Maybe Berowyn and Alene got their hair braided at sixteen . . ." *Most girls did,* she thought. She was not *all* sympathy. Elisa had a habit of offering sayings. "The hour wasted won't be found again," or "A smile makes the work lighter," till your teeth started to ache from them. Egwene knew for a fact that a smile would not make her bucket lighter by one dipper-full. ". . . but Calle's twenty, with her nameday coming in a few months now. Her hair's not braided, and you don't see her moping."

Elisa's hands went still on the fleece on the table in front of her. For some reason, the women on either side of her put their hands over their mouths, trying to hide laughter. For some reason, Elisa's face turned bright red. Very bright red.

"Children should not . . ." Elisa spluttered. Her face might be burning like the sun, but for all her spluttering her voice was cold as mid-winter snow. "A child who talks when . . . Children who . . ." Jillie Lewin, a year younger than Elisa and her black hair in a thick braid that hung below her waist, sank to her knees, she was laughing into her hand so hard. "Go away, child!" Elisa snapped. "Grownups are trying to work here!"

With an indignant glare, Egwene turned and stalked away from the folding tables, the bucket thumping her leg at every step. Try to help someone, try to buck up her spirits, and see what you got? *I should have told her she* isn't *a grownup,* she thought fiercely. *Not until the Circle lets her braid her hair, she isn't. That's what I should have said.*

The fierce mood stayed with her until her bucket was empty again, and when she filled it once more, she squared her shoulders. If you were going to do a thing, then you had to *do* it. Heading straight for the sheep-pens, she walked as fast as she could and ignored anyone who motioned for water. It was not slacking off. The boys would need water, too.

At the pens, the dozen or so boys waiting to move sheep gave her surprised looks when she offered the dipper, and some said they could get water when they went to the river, but she kept on. And she always asked the same question. "Have you seen Perrin? Or Mat? Where can I find them?"

Some told her Perrin and Mat were herding sheep to the river, and others that they had seen the pair of them watching sheep that had already been shorn, but she did not mean to go chasing off just to find them already gone. Finally, a big-eyed boy named Wil al'Seen, from one of the farms south of Emond's Field, gave her a suspicious look and said, "Why do you want them?" Some girls said Wil was pretty, but Egwene thought his ears looked funny.

She started to give him a level look, then thought better of it. "I . . . need to ask them something," she said. It was only a small lie. She really did hope one of them would lead her to some answers. He said nothing for a long time, studying her, and she waited. "Patience is always repaid," Elisa often said. Too often. She wished she could forget Elisa's sayings. She tried to forget. But kicking Wil's shins would not get what she wanted from him. Even if he did deserve it.

"They're over behind that far pen," he said finally, jerking his head toward the east side of the meadow. "The one with the sheep that have Paet al'Caar's ear-marks." The boys herding sheep had to talk that way, even if it was not really proper, or no one would know whether they were talking about Paet al'Caar's sheep or Jac al'Caar's or sheep belonging to one of a dozen other al'Caars. "They're just taking a rest, mind. Now, don't you go getting them in hot water by telling anybody different."

"Thank you, Wil," she said, just to show that she could be polite even to a woolhead. As if she would run carrying tales! He looked startled, and she thought about kicking his shins anyway.

The large pen holding Paet al'Caar's shorn sheep was almost to the trees on the Waterwood side of the meadow. Master al'Caar's big black sheep-dog raised her head from where she was lying in front of the pen and watched Egwene approach for a moment before settling back down. Egwene eyed the sheep-dog warily. She did not like dogs very much, and they did not seem to care for her, either. The dog went out of her head completely, though, once she was close enough to see clearly. The split wooden railings of the pen gave little concealment, and she could see a group of boys behind the pen. She could not really make out who they were, though.

Setting her bucket down carefully, she walked along the side of the sheep-pen. Not sneaking. She just did not want to make too much noise, in case . . . In case noise might startle the sheep; that was it. At the corner of the pen, she peeked around the cornerpost.

Perrin was there, and Mat Cauthon, just as Wil had said, and some other boys about the same age, all with their shirts unlaced and sweaty. There was Dav Ayellin and Lem Thane, Ban Crawe and Elam Dowtry. And Rand, a skinny boy, almost as tall as Perrin, with hands and feet that were too big for his size. He could always be found with Mat or Perrin sooner or later. Rand, who everybody said she would marry one day. They were talking and laughing and punching one another on the shoulder. Why did boys do that?

Glowering, she pulled back from the cornerpost and leaned back against the railings. One of the sheep inside the pen snuffled at her back, but she ignored it. She had heard women say that about her and Rand, but she had not known that *everybody* said it. Drat Elisa! If Elisa had not started sighing and moaning over her hair, Egwene would never have started thinking about husbands. She expected she would marry one day—most women in the Two Rivers did—but she was not like those scatterbrains she heard going on about how they could hardly wait. Most women waited at least a few years after their hair was braided, and she . . . She wanted to see those lands that Jain Farstrider had written about. How would a husband feel about that? About his wife going off to see strange lands. Nobody ever left the Two Rivers, as far as she knew.

I *will*, she vowed silently.

Even if she did marry, would Rand make a good husband? She was not sure what made a good husband. Someone like her father, brave and kind and wise. She thought Rand was kind. He had carved her a whistle once, and a horse, and he had given her an eagle's black-tipped feather when she said it was pretty, though she still suspected he had wanted to keep it for himself. And he watched his father's sheep in pasture, so he had to be brave. The sheep-dog would help, if wolves came, or a bear, but the boy watching had to be ready with his sling, or a bow if he was old enough. Only . . . She saw him every time he and his father came in from their farm, but she did not really know him. She hardly knew anything *about* him. Now was as good a time as any to start learning. She eased back to the cornerpost and peeked around it again.

"I'd like to a be a king," Rand was saying. "That's what I'd like to be." He flourished his arm and made an awkward bow, laughing to show that he was joking. A good thing, too. Egwene grimaced. A king! She studied his face. No, he was not pretty. Well, perhaps he was. Maybe it did not matter. But it might be nice to have a husband she liked to look at. His eyes were blue. No, gray. They seemed to change while you watched. Nobody else in the Two Rivers had blue eyes. Sometimes his eyes looked sad. His mother had died when he was little, and Egwene thought he envied boys who had mothers. She could not imagine losing her mother. She did not even want to try.

"A king of sheep!" Mat hooted. He was smaller than the others, always bouncing on his toes. One glance at his face, and you knew he was looking for mischief. He *always* looked for mischief. And usually found it. "Rand al'Thor, King of the Sheep." Lem snickered. Ban punched him on the shoulder, and Lem punched Ban back, and then they both snickered. Egwene shook her head.

"It's better than saying you want to run off and never have to work," Rand said mildly. He never seemed to get angry. Not that she had seen, anyway. "How could you live without working, Mat?"

"Sheep aren't so bad," Elam said, rubbing at his long nose. His hair was cut short, and he had a cowlick that stood up at the back. He looked a little like a sheep.

"I'll rescue an Aes Sedai, and she'll reward me," Mat shot back. "Anyway, I don't go around looking for work when there's more than work enough without looking." He grinned and poked Perrin's shoulder.

Perrin rubbed his nose, abashed. "Sometimes you have to be sensible, Mat," he said slowly. "Sometimes you have to think ahead." Perrin always talked slowly, when he talked at all. And he moved carefully, as if he was afraid he might break something. Rand spoke before he thought, sometimes, and he always looked as though he was ready to start haring off and not stop until he caught the horizon.

"'Sensible' says I'll work in my da's mill," Lem sighed. "Inherit it one day, I expect. Not too soon, I hope. I'd like to have an adventure first, though, wouldn't you, Rand?"

"Of course." Rand laughed. "But where do I find an adventure in the Two Rivers?"

"There has to be a way," Ban muttered. "Maybe there's gold up in the mountains. Or Trollocs?" He suddenly sounded as if he was not so certain about going up in the mountains. Did he really believe in *Trollocs?*

"I want to have more sheep than anybody in the whole Two Rivers," Elam said stoutly. Mat rolled his eyes in exasperation.

Dav had been sitting back on his heels listening, and now he shook his head. "You *look* like a sheep, Elam," he muttered. At least *she* had not said it aloud. Dav was taller than Mat, and stockier, but his eyes had that same light. His clothes were always rumpled from something he should not have been doing. "Listen, I just got a great idea."

"I just got a better one," Mat put in quickly. "Come on. I'll show you." He and Dav glared at one another.

Elam and Ban and Lem looked ready to follow either one, or both, if they could figure out how. Rand put a hand on Mat's shoulder, though. "Hold on. Let's hear these great ideas, first." Perrin nodded thoughtfully.

Egwene sighed. Dav and Mat seemed to *compete* to see who could get into the most trouble. And Rand might sound sensible, but when he was around the village, they often managed to pull him along, too. And Perrin, as well. The other three would fall in with anything at all Mat or Dav suggested.

It seemed time for her to leave. She would not be able to follow them to see what they were getting up to, not without them seeing her. She would die before she let Rand suspect that she had been watching him like some goosebrain. *And I didn't even learn anything.*

As she walked back along the sheep-pen to where she had left her bucket, Dannil Lewin passed her, heading toward the back of the pen. At thirteen, he was even skinnier than Rand, with a thrusting nose. She hesitated over the bucket, listening. At first, she heard nothing but murmurs. Then . . .

"The Mayor wants me?" Mat exclaimed. "He can't want me! I haven't done anything!"

"He wants *all* of you, and double quick," Dannil said. "I'd get over to him now, if it was me."

Quickly picking up the bucket, Egwene walked slowly away from the sheep-pen, back toward the river. Rand and the others soon passed her, trotting in the same direction. Egwene smiled, a small smile. When her father sent for people, they came. Even the Women's Circle knew Brandelwyn al'Vere was no man to trifle with. Egwene was not supposed to know that, but she had overheard Mistress Luhhan and Mistress Ayellin and some of the others talking to her mother about her father being stubborn and how her mother had to do something about it. She let the boys get a little ahead—just a little—then increased her pace to keep up.

"I don't understand it," Mat grumbled as they came near the line of men shearing. "Sometimes the Mayor knows what I'm doing as soon as I do it. My mother does it, too. But how?"

"The Women's Circle probably tells your mother," Dav muttered. "They see everything. And the Mayor's the Mayor." The other boys nodded glumly.

Ahead of them Egwene saw her father, a round man with thinning gray hair, his shirtsleeves rolled up past his elbows, a pipe in his teeth, and a set of shears in his hand. And ten paces off from the sheep shearers, watching

the boys approach, stood Mistress Cauthon, Mat's mother,
flanked by her two daughters, Bodewhin and Eldrin. Natti
Cauthon was a calm, collected woman, as she would have to
be with a son like Mat, and at the moment she wore a contented smile. Bodewhin and Eldrin wore almost identical
smiles, and they watched Mat twice as hard as his mother
did. Bode was not quite old enough to carry water, yet, and
it would be two years before Eldrin could. *Rand and the
others must be blind!* Egwene thought. Anyone with eyes
could see how Mistress Cauthon always knew.

Mistress Cauthon and her daughters slipped away into
the crowd as the boys approached Egwene's father. None of
the boys appeared to notice her. They all had eyes for no
one but Egwene's father. All but Mat looked wary; he wore
a big grin that made him look guilty of something, for sure.
Rand's father glanced up from the sheep he was bent over,
and caught Rand's eye with a smile that made Rand, at
least, seem less like a heron ready to take flight.

Egwene began offering water to the men shearing with
her father, all of them on the Village Council. Well, Master Cole appeared to be taking a nap with his back against
a waist-high stone thrusting out of the ground. He was as
old as the Wisdom, maybe older, though he still had all of
his hair, white as it was. But the others were shearing, the
fleece falling away from the sheep in thick white sheets.
Master Buie, the thatcher, a gnarled man but spry, muttered
under his breath as he worked, and the others did two sheep
to his one, but everyone else seemed caught up in the work.
When a man was done, he let the sheep go to be gathered up by waiting boys and herded away while another was
brought to him. Egwene went slowly, to have an excuse to
linger. She was not really slacking; she just wanted to know
what was going to happen.

Her father studied the boys for a moment, pursing his
lips, then said, "Well, lads, I know you've been working
hard." Mat gave Rand a startled look, and Perrin shrugged
his shoulders uncomfortably. Rand just nodded, but uncertainly. "So I thought it might be time for that story I promised
you," her father finished. Egwene grinned. Her father told the
best stories.

Mat straightened up. "I want a story with adventures." The
look he shot at Rand this time was defiant.

"I want Aes Sedai and Warders," Dav said hurriedly.

"I want Trollocs," Mat added, "and . . . and . . . and a false Dragon!"

Dav opened his mouth, and closed it again without saying anything. He glared at Mat, though. There was no way for him to top a false Dragon, and he knew it.

Egwene's father chuckled. "I'm no gleeman, lads. I don't know any stories like that. Tam? Would you like to give it a try?" Egwene blinked. Why would Rand's father know stories like that if her father did not? Master al'Thor had been chosen to the Council to speak for the farmers around Emond's Field, but as far she knew, all he had ever done was farm sheep and tabac like anyone else.

Master al'Thor looked troubled, and Egwene began to hope he did not know any stories like that. She did not want anyone to show up her father. Of course, she liked Rand's father, so she did not want him embarrassed, either. He was a sturdy man with gray flecks in his hair, a quiet man, and just about everybody liked him.

Master al'Thor finished shearing his sheep, and as he was brought another, he exchanged smiles with Rand. "As it happens," he said, "I do know a story something like that. I'll tell you about the real Dragon, not a false one."

Master Buie straightened from his half-shorn sheep so fast that the animal nearly got away from him. His eyes narrowed, though they were always pretty narrow. "We'll have none of that, Tam al'Thor," he growled in his scratchy voice. "That's nothing fit for decent ears to hear."

"Be easy, Cenn," Egwene's father said soothingly. "It's only a story." But he glanced toward Rand's father, and plainly he was not quite as certain as he sounded.

"Some stories shouldn't be told," Master Buie insisted. "Some stories shouldn't be known! It isn't decent, I say. I don't like it. If they need to hear about wars, give them something about the War of the Hundred Years, or Trolloc Wars. That'll give them Aes Sedai and Trollocs, if you have to talk about such things. Or the Aiel War." For a moment, Egwene thought Master al'Thor's face changed. For an instant he seemed harder. Hard enough to make the merchants' guards look soft. She was imagining a lot of things, today. She did not usually allow her imagination to run away with her this way.

Master Cole's eyes popped open. "It's just a *story* he'll be telling them, Cenn. Just a story, man." His eyes drifted shut again. You could never tell when Master Cole was really napping.

"You never heard, smelled, or saw anything you did like, Cenn," Master al'Dai said. He was Bili's grandfather, a lean man with wispy white hair, and as old as Master Cole, if not older. He had to walk with a stick most of the time, but his eyes were clear and sharp, and so was his mind. He was almost as quick with the wool-shears as Master al'Thor. "My advice to you, Cenn, is chew on your liver in silence and let Tam get on with it."

Master Buie subsided with a bad grace, muttering under his breath. Scowling at Rand's father, he bent back to his sheep. Egwene shook her head in surprise. She had often heard Master Buie telling people how important he was on the Council, and how all the other men always listened to him.

The boys moved closer to Master al'Thor and squatted on their heels in a semicircle. Any story that caused an argument on the Council was sure to be of interest. Master al'Thor carried on with his shearing, but at a slower pace. He would not want to risk cutting the sheep with his attention divided.

"This is just a story," he said, ignoring Master Buie's scowls, "because no one knows everything that happened. But it really did happen. You've heard of the Age of Legends?"

Some of the boys nodded, doubtfully. Egwene nodded, too, in spite of herself. She had heard grownups say, "Maybe in the Age of Legends," when they did not believe something had really happened or doubted a thing could be done. It was just another way of saying, "When pigs had wings," though. At least, she had thought it was.

"Three thousand years ago and more, it was," Rand's father went on. "There were great cities full of buildings taller that the White Tower, and that's taller than anything but a mountain. Machines that used the One Power carried people across the ground faster than a horse can run, and some say machines carried people through the air, too. There was no sickness anywhere. No hunger. No war. And then the Dark One touched the World."

The boys jumped, and Elam actually fell over. He scrambled back up, blushing and trying to pretend he had not toppled at all. Egwene held her breath. The Dark One. Maybe it was because she had been thinking about him earlier, but he seemed particularly frightening now. She hoped that Master al'Thor would not actually name him. *He wouldn't* name *the Dark One,* she thought, but that did not stop her being afraid that he might.

Master al'Thor smiled at the boys to soften the shock of what he had said, but he went on. "The Age of Legends hadn't so much as the memory of war, so they say, but once the Dark One touched the world, they learned fast enough. This wasn't a war like those you hear about when the merchants come for wool and tabac, between two nations. This war covered the whole world. The War of the Shadow, it came to be called. Those who stood for the Light faced as many who stood for the Shadow, and besides Darkfriends beyond counting, there were armies of Myrddraal and Trollocs greater than anything the Blight spewed up during the Trolloc Wars. Aes Sedai went over to the Shadow, too. They were called the Forsaken."

Egwene shivered, and was glad to see some of the boys wrapping their arms around themselves. Mothers used the Forsaken to frighten their children when they were bad. *If you keep lying, Semirhage will come and get you. Lanfear waits for children who steal.* Egwene was glad her mother did not do that. Wait. The Forsaken had been Aes Sedai? She hoped Master al'Thor did not say that too freely, or the Women's Circle would come calling on him. Anyway, some of the Forsaken were men, so he had to be wrong.

"You'll be expecting me to tell you about the glories of battle, but I won't." For a moment, he sounded grim, but only for a moment. "No one knows anything about those battles, except that they were huge. Maybe the Aes Sedai have some records, but if they do, they don't let anyone see them except other Aes Sedai. You've heard about the great battles during Artur Hawkwing's rise, and during the War of the Hundred Years? A hundred thousand men on each side?" Eager nods answered him. From Egwene, too, though hers was not eager. All those men trying to kill one another did not excite her the way it did the boys. "Well," Master al'Thor went on, "those battles would have been counted small in the War of the Shadow. Whole cities were destroyed, razed to the ground. The countryside outside the cities fared as badly. Wherever a battle was fought, it left only devastation and ruin behind. The war went on for years and years, all over the world. And slowly the Shadow began to win. The Light was pushed back and back, until it appeared certain the Shadow would conquer everything. Hope faded away like mist in the sun. But the Light had a leader who would never give up, a man called Lews Therin Telamon. The Dragon."

One of the boys gasped in surprise. Egwene was too busy goggling to see who. She forgot even to pretend that she was offering water. The Dragon was the man who had destroyed everything! She did not know much about the Breaking of the World—well, almost nothing, in truth—but everybody knew that much. Surely he had fought for the Shadow!

"Lews Therin gathered men around him, the Hundred Companions, and a small army. Small as they counted such things then. Ten thousand men. Not a small army now, would you say?" The words seemed an invitation to laugh, but there was no laughter in Master al'Thor's quiet voice. He sounded almost as though he had been there. Egwene certainly did not laugh, and none of the boys did, either. She listened, and tried to remember to breathe. "With only a forlorn hope, Lews Therin attacked the valley of Thakan'dar, the heart of the Shadow itself. Trollocs in the hundreds of thousands fell on them, Trollocs and Myrddraal. Trollocs live to kill. A Trolloc can rip a man to pieces with its bare hands. Myrddraal *are* death. Aes Sedai fighting for the Shadow rained fire and lightning on Lews Therin and his men. The men following the Dragon did not die one by one, but ten at a time, or twenty, or fifty. Beneath a twisted sky, in a place where nothing grew or ever would again, they fought and died. But they did not retreat or give up. All the way to Shayol Ghul they fought, and if Thakan'dar is the heart of the Shadow, then Shayol Ghul is the heart of the heart. Every man in that army died, and most of the Hundred Companions, but at Shayol Ghul they sealed the Dark One back into the prison the Creator made for him, and the Forsaken with him. And the world was saved from the Dark One."

Silence fell. The boys stared at Master al'Thor with wide eyes. Shining eyes, as if they could see it all, the Trollocs and the Myrddraal and Shayol Ghul. Egwene shivered again. *The Dark One and all the Forsaken are bound at Shayol Ghul, bound away from the world of men,* she recited to herself. She could not remember the rest, but it helped. Only, if the Dragon had saved the world, how had he destroyed it?

Cenn Buie spat. He spat! Just like some merchant's smelly guard! She did not believe she would think of him as Master Buie again after today.

That broke the boys out of their reverie, of course. They tried to look anywhere but at the gnarled man.

Perrin scatched at his head. "Master al'Thor," he said slowly, "what does 'the Dragon' mean? If somebody's called the Lion, it means he's supposed to be like a lion. But what's a dragon?" Egwene stared at him. She had never thought of that. Maybe Perrin was not as slow as he appeared.

"I don't know," Rand's father answered simply. "I don't think anyone does. Maybe not even the Aes Sedai." He let the sheep go that he been shearing, and motioned for another to be brought. Egwene realized that he had been done with it for some time. He must not have wanted to interrupt his story.

Master Cole opened his eyes and grinned. "The Dragon. It surely sounds fierce, though, now doesn't it?" he said before letting his eyes drift shut again.

"I suppose it does at that," her father said. "But it all happened long ago and far away, and it doesn't have anything to do with us. Well, you've had your story, lads. Back to work with you." As the boys began standing up reluctantly, he added, "There are plenty of lads here from the farms I don't think any of you know, yet. It's always good to know your neighbors, so you should acquaint yourselves with them. I don't want any of you working together today; you already know one another. Now, off with you."

The boys exchanged startled glances. Had they really thought he would let them go back to whatever mischief they had been planning? Mat and Dav looked especially glum as they walked away exchanging glances. She thought about following, but they were already splitting up, and she would have to trail after Rand to learn anything more. She grimaced. If he noticed, he might think she was goose-brained like Cilia Cole. Besides, there were those far-off lands. She did intend to see them.

Abruptly she became aware of ravens, many more than there had been before, flapping out of the trees, flying away west, toward the Mountains of Mist. She shifted her shoulders. She felt as if someone were staring at her back. Someone, or . . .

She did not want to turn around, but she did, raising her eyes to the trees behind the men shearing. Midway up a tall pine, a solitary raven stood on a branch. Staring at her. Right at her! She felt cold right down to her middle. The only thing she wanted to do was run. Instead, she made herself stare back, trying to copy Nynaeve's level look. After a moment the raven gave a harsh cry and threw itself off the branch, black wings carrying it west after the others.

Maybe I'm starting to get that look right, she thought, and then felt silly. She had to stop letting her imagination get the better of her. It was just a bird. And she had important things to do, like being the best water-carrier ever. The best water-carrier ever would not be frightened of birds or anything else. Squaring her shoulders, she set out through the crowd again, watching for Berowyn. But this time, it was so she could offer Berowyn the dipper. If she could face down a raven, she could face down her sister. She hoped.

Egwene had to carry water again the next year, which was a great disappointment to her, but once again she tried to be the best. If you were going to do a thing, you might as well do the best you could. It must have worked, because the year after that she was allowed to help with the food, a year early! She set herself a new goal, then: to be allowed to braid her hair younger than anybody ever. She did not really think the Women's Circle would allow it, but a goal that was easy was no goal at all.

She stopped wanting to hear stories from the grownups, though she would have liked to hear a gleeman, but she still liked to read of distant lands with strange ways, and dreamed of seeing them. The boys stopped wanting stories, too. She did not think they even read very much. They all grew older, thinking their world would never change, and many of those stories faded to fond memories while others were forgotten, or half so. And if they learned that some of those stories really had been more than stories, well . . . The War of the Shadow? The Breaking of the World? Lews Therin Telamon? How could it matter now? And what *had* really happened back then, anyway?

PROLOGUE

Dragonmount

The palace still shook occasionally as the earth rumbled in memory, groaned as if it would deny what had happened. Bars of sunlight cast through rents in the walls made motes of dust glitter where they yet hung in the air. Scorch-marks marred the walls, the floors, the ceilings. Broad black smears crossed the blistered paints and gilt of once-bright murals, soot overlaying crumbling friezes of men and animals which seemed to have attempted to walk before the madness grew quiet. The dead lay everywhere, men and women and children, struck down in attempted flight by the lightnings that had flashed down every corridor, or seized by the fires that had stalked them, or sunken into stone of the palace, the stones that had flowed and sought, almost alive, before stillness came again. In odd counterpoint, colorful tapestries and paintings, masterworks all, hung undisturbed except where bulging walls had pushed them awry. Finely carved furnishings, inlaid with ivory and gold, stood untouched except where rippling floors had toppled them. The mind-twisting had struck at the core, ignoring peripheral things.

Lews Therin Telamon wandered the palace, deftly keeping his balance when the earth heaved. "Ilyena! My love, where are you?" The edge of his pale gray cloak trailed through blood as he stepped across the body of a woman, her golden-haired beauty marred by the horror of her last moments, her still-open eyes frozen in disbelief. "Where are you, my wife? Where is everyone hiding?"

His eyes caught his own reflection in a mirror hanging askew from bubbled marble. His clothes had been regal once, in gray and scarlet and gold; now the finely-woven cloth, brought by merchants from across the World Sea, was torn and dirty, thick with the same dust that covered his hair and skin. For a moment he fingered the symbol on his cloak, a circle half white and half black, the colors separated by a sinuous line. It meant something, that symbol. But the embroidered circle could not hold his attention long. He gazed at his own image with as much wonder. A tall man just into his middle years, handsome once, but now with hair already more white than brown and a face lined by strain and worry, dark eyes that had seen too much. Lews Therin began to chuckle, then threw back his head; his laughter echoed down the lifeless halls.

"Ilyena, my love! Come to me, my wife. You must see this."

Behind him the air rippled, shimmered, solidified into a man who looked around, his mouth twisting briefly with distaste. Not so tall as Lews Therin, he was clothed all in black, save for the snow-white lace at his throat and the silverwork on the turned-down tops of his thigh-high boots. He stepped carefully, handling his cloak fastidiously to avoid brushing the dead. The floor trembled with after-shocks, but his attention was fixed on the man staring into the mirror and laughing.

"Lord of the Morning," he said, "I have come for you."

The laughter cut off as if it had never been, and Lews Therin turned, seeming unsurprised. "Ah, a guest. Have you the Voice, stranger? It will soon be time for the Singing, and here all are welcome to take part. Ilyena, my love, we have a guest. Ilyena, where are you?"

The black-clad man's eyes widened, darted to the body of the golden-haired woman, then back to Lews Therin. "Shai'tan take you, does the taint already have you so far in its grip?"

"That name. Shai—" Lews Therin shuddered and raised a hand as though to ward off something. "You mustn't say that name. It is dangerous."

"So you remember that much, at least. Dangerous for you, fool, not for me. What else do you remember? Remember, you Light-blinded idiot! I will not let it end with you swaddled in unawareness! Remember!"

For a moment Lews Therin stared at his raised hand, fascinated by the patterns of grime. Then he wiped his hand on his even dirtier coat and turned his attention back to the other man. "Who are you? What do you want?"

The black-clad man drew himself up arrogantly. "Once I was called Elan Morin Tedronai, but now—"

"Betrayer of Hope." It was a whisper from Lews Therin. Memory stirred, but he turned his head, shying away from it.

"So you do remember some things. Yes, Betrayer of Hope. So have men named me, just as they named you Dragon, but unlike you I embrace the name. They gave me the name to revile me, but I will yet make them kneel and worship it. What will you do with your name? After this day, men will call you Kinslayer. What will you do with that?"

Lews Therin frowned down the ruined hall. "Ilyena should be here to offer a guest welcome," he murmured absently, then raised his voice. "Ilyena, where are you?" The floor shook; the golden-haired woman's body shifted as if in answer to his call. His eyes did not see her.

Elan Morin grimaced. "Look at you," he said scornfully. "Once you stood first among the Servants. Once you wore the Ring of Tamyrlin, and sat in the High Seat. Once you summoned the Nine Rods of Dominion. Now look at you! A pitiful, shattered wretch. But it is not enough. You humbled me in the Hall of Servants. You defeated me at the Gates of Paaran Disen. But I am the greater, now. I will not let you die without knowing that. When you die, your last thought will be the full knowledge of your defeat, of how complete and utter it is. If I let you die at all."

"I cannot imagine what is keeping Ilyena. She will give me the rough side of her tongue if she thinks I have been hiding a guest from her. I hope you enjoy conversation, for she surely does. Be forewarned. Ilyena will ask you so many questions you may end up telling her everything you know."

Tossing back his black cloak, Elan Morin flexed his hands. "A pity for you," he mused, "that one of your Sisters is not here. I was never very skilled at Healing, and I follow a different power now. But even one of them could only give you a few lucid minutes, if you did not destroy her first. What I can do will serve as well, for my purposes." His sudden smile was cruel. "But I fear Shai'tan's healing is different from the sort you know. Be healed, Lews Therin!" He extended his hands, and the light dimmed as if a shadow had been laid across the sun.

Pain blazed in Lews Therin, and he screamed, a scream that came from his depths, a scream he could not stop. Fire seared his marrow; acid rushed along his veins. He toppled backwards, crashing to the marble floor; his head struck the stone and rebounded. His heart pounded, trying to beat its way out of his chest, and every pulse gushed new flame through him. Helplessly he convulsed, thrashing, his skull a sphere of purest agony on the point of bursting. His hoarse screams reverberated through the palace.

Slowly, ever so slowly, the pain receded. The outflowing seemed to take a thousand years and left him twitching weakly, sucking breath through a raw throat. Another thousand years seemed to pass before he could manage to heave himself over, muscles like jellyfish, and shakily push himself up on hands and knees. His eyes fell on the golden-haired woman, and the scream that was ripped out of him dwarfed every sound he had made before. Tottering, almost falling, he scrabbled brokenly across the floor to her. It took every bit of his strength to pull her up into his arms. His hands shook as he smoothed her hair back from her staring face.

"Ilyena! Light help me, Ilyena!" His body curved around hers protectively, his sobs the full-throated cries of a man who had nothing left to live for. "Ilyena, no! *No!*"

"You can have her back, Kinslayer. The Great Lord of the Dark can make her live again, if you will serve him. If you will serve me."

Lews Therin raised his head, and the black-clad man took an involuntary step back from that gaze. "Ten years, Betrayer," Lews Therin said softly, the soft sound of steel being bared. "Ten years your foul master has wracked the world. And now this. I will. . . ."

"Ten years! You pitiful fool! This war has not lasted ten years, but since the beginning of time. You and I have fought a thousand battles with the turning of the Wheel, a thousand times a thousand, and we will fight until time dies and the Shadow is triumphant!" He finished in a shout, with a raised fist, and it was Lews Therin's turn to pull back, breath catching at the glow in the Betrayer's eyes.

Carefully Lews Therin laid Ilyena down, fingers gently brushing her hair. Tears blurred his vision as he stood, but his voice was iced iron. "For what else you have done, there can be no forgiveness, Betrayer, but for Ilyena's death I will destroy you beyond anything your master can repair. Prepare to—"

"Remember, you fool! Remember your futile attack on the Great Lord of the Dark! Remember his counterstroke! Remember! Even now the Hundred Companions are tearing the world apart, and every day a hundred men more join them. What hand slew Ilyena Sunhair, Kinslayer? Not mine. Not mine. What hand struck down every life that bore a drop of your blood, everyone who loved you, everyone you loved? Not mine, Kinslayer. Not mine. Remember, and know the price of opposing Shai'tan!"

Sudden sweat made tracks down Lews Therin's face through the dust and dirt. He remembered, a cloudy memory like a dream of a dream, but he knew it true.

His howl beat at the walls, the howl of a man who had discovered his soul damned by his own hand, and he clawed at his face as if to tear away the sight of what he had done. Everywhere he looked his eyes found the dead. Torn they were, or broken or burned, or half-consumed by stone. Everywhere lay lifeless faces he knew, faces he loved. Old servants and friends of his childhood, faithful companions through the long years of battle. And his children. His own sons and daughters, sprawled like broken dolls, play stilled forever. All slain by his hand. His children's faces accused him, blank eyes asking why, and his tears were no answer. The Betrayer's laughter flogged him, drowned out his howls. He could not bear the faces, the pain. He could not bear to remain any longer. Desperately he reached out to the True Source, to tainted *saidin*, and he Traveled.

The land around him was flat and empty. A river flowed nearby, straight and broad, but he could sense there were no people within a hundred leagues. He was alone, as alone as a man could be while still alive, yet he could not escape memory. The eyes pursued him through the endless caverns of his mind. He could not hide from them. His children's eyes. Ilyena's eyes. Tears glistened on his cheeks as he turned his face to the sky.

"Light, forgive me!" He did not believe it could come, forgiveness. Not for what he had done. But he shouted to the sky anyway, begged for what he could not believe he could receive. "Light, forgive me!"

He was still touching *saidin,* the male half of the power that drove the universe, that turned the Wheel of Time, and he could feel the oily taint fouling its surface, the taint of the Shadow's counterstroke, the taint that doomed the world. Because of him. Because in his pride he had believed that men could match the Creator, could mend what the Creator had made and they had broken. In his pride he had believed.

He drew on the True Source deeply, and still more deeply, like a man dying of thirst. Quickly he had drawn more of the One Power than he could channel unaided; his skin felt as if it were aflame. Straining, he forced himself to draw more, tried to draw it all.

"Light, forgive me! Ilyena!"

The air turned to fire, the fire to light liquefied. The bolt that struck from the heavens would have seared and blinded any eye that glimpsed it, even for an instant. From the heavens it came, blazed through Lews Therin Telamon, bored into the bowels of the earth. Stone turned to vapor at its touch. The earth thrashed and quivered like a living thing in agony. Only a heartbeat did the shining bar exist, connecting ground and sky, but even after it vanished the earth yet heaved like the sea in a storm. Molten rock fountained five hundred feet into the air, and the groaning ground rose, thrusting the burning spray ever upward, ever higher. From north and south, from east and west, the wind howled in, snapping trees like twigs, shrieking and blowing as if to aid the growing mountain ever skyward. Ever skyward.

At last the wind died, the earth stilled to trembling mutters. Of Lews Therin Telamon, no sign remained. Where he had stood a mountain now rose miles into the sky, molten lava still gushing from its broken peak. The broad, straight river had been pushed into a curve away from the mountain, and there it split to form a long island in its midst. The shadow of the mountain almost reached the island; it lay dark across the land like the ominous hand of prophecy. For a time the dull, protesting rumbles of the earth were the only sound.

On the island, the air shimmered and coalesced. The black-clad man stood staring at the fiery mountain rising out of the plain. His face twisted in rage and contempt.

"You cannot escape so easily, Dragon. It is not done between us. It will not be done until the end of time."

Then he was gone, and the mountain and the island stood alone. Waiting.

And the Shadow fell upon the Land, and the World was riven stone from stone. The oceans fled, and the mountains were swallowed up, and the nations were scattered to the eight corners of the World. The moon was as blood, and the sun was as ashes. The seas boiled, and the living envied the dead. All was shattered, and all but memory lost, and one memory above all others, of him who brought the Shadow and the Breaking of the World. And him they named Dragon.

> (From *Aleth nin Taerin alta Camora,*
> *The Breaking of the World.*
> Author unknown, the Fourth Age)

And it came to pass in those days, as it had come before and would come again, that the Dark lay heavy on the land and weighed down the hearts of men, and the green things failed, and hope died. And men cried out to the Creator, saying, O Light of the Heavens, Light of the World, let the Promised One be born of the mountain, according to the prophecies, as he was in ages past and will be in ages to come. Let the Prince of the Morning sing to the land that green things will grow and the valleys give forth lambs. Let the arm of the Lord of the Dawn shelter us from the Dark, and the great sword of justice defend us. Let the Dragon ride again on the winds of time.

> (From *Charal Drianaan te Calamon,*
> *The Cycle of the Dragon.*
> Author unknown, the Fourth Age)

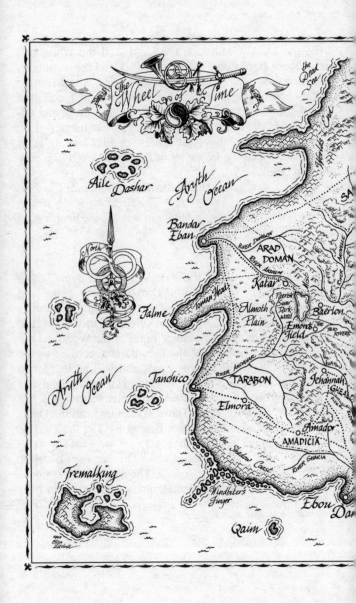

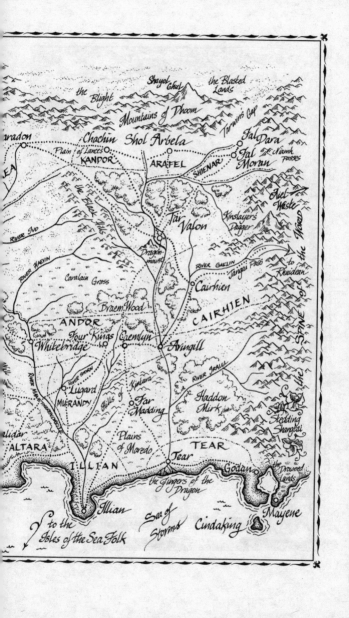

CHAPTER
I

An Empty Road

The Wheel of Time turns, and Ages come and pass, leaving memories that become legend. Legend fades to myth, and even myth is long forgotten when the Age that gave it birth comes again. In one Age, called the Third Age by some, an Age yet to come, an Age long past, a wind rose in the Mountains of Mist. The wind was not the beginning. There are neither beginnings nor endings to the turning of the Wheel of Time. But it was *a* beginning.

Born below the ever cloud-capped peaks that gave the mountains their name, the wind blew east, out across the Sand Hills, once the shore of a great ocean, before the Breaking of the World. Down it flailed into the Two Rivers, into the tangled forest called the Westwood, and beat at two men walking with a cart and horse down the rock-strewn track called the Quarry Road. For all that spring should have come a good month since, the wind carried an icy chill as if it would rather bear snow.

Gusts plastered Rand al'Thor's cloak to his back, whipped the earth-colored wool around his legs, then streamed it out behind him. He wished his coat were heavier, or that he had worn an extra shirt. Half the time when he tried to tug the cloak back around him it caught on the quiver swinging at his hip. Trying to hold the cloak one-handed did not do much good anyway; he had his bow in the other, an arrow nocked and ready to draw.

As a particularly strong blast tugged the cloak out of his hand, he glanced at his father over the back of the shaggy brown mare. He felt a little foolish about wanting to reassure himself that Tam was still there, but it was that kind

of day. The wind howled when it rose, but aside from that,
quiet lay heavy on the land. The soft creak of the axle
sounded loud by comparison. No birds sang in the forest,
no squirrels chittered from a branch. Not that he expected
them, really; not this spring.

Only trees that kept leaf or needle through the winter had
any green about them. Snarls of last year's bramble spread
brown webs over stone outcrops under the trees. Nettles
numbered most among the few weeds; the rest were the
sorts with sharp burrs or thorns, or stinkweed, which left
a rank smell on the unwary boot that crushed it. Scattered
white patches of snow still dotted the ground where tight
clumps of trees kept deep shade. Where sunlight did reach,
it held neither strength nor warmth. The pale sun sat above
the trees to the east, but its light was crisply dark, as if
mixed with shadow. It was an awkward morning, made for
unpleasant thoughts.

Without thinking he touched the nock of the arrow; it
was ready to draw to his cheek in one smooth movement,
the way Tam had taught him. Winter had been bad enough
on the farms, worse than even the oldest folk remembered,
but it must have been harsher still in the mountains, if the
number of wolves driven down into the Two Rivers was any
guide. Wolves raided the sheep pens and chewed their way
into barns to get the cattle and horses. Bears had been after
the sheep, too, where a bear had not been seen in years. It
was no longer safe to be out after dark. Men were the prey
as often as sheep, and the sun did not always have to be
down.

Tam was taking steady strides on the other side of Bela,
using his spear as a walking staff, ignoring the wind that
made his brown cloak flap like a banner. Now and again
he touched the mare's flank lightly, to remind her to keep
moving. With his thick chest and broad face, he was a pillar of reality in that morning, like a stone in the middle of
a drifting dream. His sun-roughened cheeks might be lined
and his hair have only a sprinkling of black among the gray,
but there was a solidness to him, as though a flood could
wash around him without uprooting his feet. He stumped
down the road now impassively. Wolves and bears were all
very well, his manner said, things that any man who kept

sheep must be aware of, but they had best not try to stop
Tam al'Thor getting to Emond's Field.

With a guilty start Rand returned to watching his side
of the road, Tam's matter-of-factness reminding him of his
task. He was a head taller than his father, taller than anyone
else in the district, and had little of Tam in him physically,
except perhaps for a breadth of shoulder. Gray eyes and the
reddish tinge to his hair came from his mother, so Tam said.
She had been an outlander, and Rand remembered little of
her aside from a smiling face, though he did put flowers on
her grave every year, at Bel Tine, in the spring, and at Sunday, in the summer.

Two small casks of Tam's apple brandy rested in the lurching cart, and eight larger barrels of apple cider, only slightly
hard after a winter's curing. Tam delivered the same every
year to the Winespring Inn for use during Bel Tine, and he
had declared that it would take more than wolves or a cold
wind to stop him this spring. Even so they had not been to
the village for weeks. Not even Tam traveled much these
days. But Tam had given his word about the brandy and cider, even if he had waited to make delivery until the day before Festival. Keeping his word was important to Tam. Rand
was just glad to get away from the farm, almost as glad as
about the coming of Bel Tine.

As Rand watched his side of the road, the feeling grew
in him that he was being watched. For a while he tried to
shrug it off. Nothing moved or made a sound among the
trees, except the wind. But the feeling not only persisted, it
grew stronger. The hairs on his arms stirred; his skin prickled as if it itched on the inside.

He shifted his bow irritably to rub at his arms, and told
himself to stop letting fancies take him. There was nothing in
the woods on his side of the road, and Tam would have spoken if there had been anything on the other. He glanced over
his shoulder . . . and blinked. Not more than twenty spans
back down the road a cloaked figure on horseback followed
them, horse and rider alike black, dull and ungleaming.

It was more habit than anything else that kept him walking backward alongside the cart even while he looked.

The rider's cloak covered him to his boot tops, the cowl
tugged well forward so no part of him showed. Vaguely

Rand thought there was something odd about the horseman, but it was the shadowed opening of the hood that fascinated him. He could see only the vaguest outlines of a face, but he had the feeling he was looking right into the rider's eyes. And he could not look away. Queasiness settled in his stomach. There was only shadow to see in the hood, but he felt hatred as sharply as if he could see a snarling face, hatred for everything that lived. Hatred for him most of all, for him above all things.

Abruptly a stone caught his heel and he stumbled, breaking his eyes away from the dark horseman. His bow dropped to the road, and only an outthrust hand grabbing Bela's harness saved him from falling flat on his back. With a startled snort the mare stopped, twisting her head to see what had caught her.

Tam frowned over Bela's back at him. "Are you all right, lad?"

"A rider," Rand said breathlessly, pulling himself upright. "A stranger, following us."

"Where?" The older man lifted his broad-bladed spear and peered back warily.

"There, down the. . . ." Rand's words trailed off as he turned to point. The road behind was empty. Disbelieving, he stared into the forest on both sides of the road. Bare-branched trees offered no hiding place, but there was not a glimmer of horse or horseman. He met his father's questioning gaze. "He was there. A man in a black cloak, on a black horse."

"I wouldn't doubt your word, lad, but where has he gone?"

"I don't know. But he was there." He snatched up the fallen bow and arrow, hastily checked the fletching before renocking, and half drew before letting the bowstring relax. There was nothing to aim at. "He was."

Tam shook his grizzled head. "If you say so, lad. Come on, then. A horse leaves hoofprints, even on this ground." He started toward the rear of the cart, his cloak whipping in the wind. "If we find them, we'll know for a fact he was there. If not . . . well, these are days to make a man think he's seeing things."

Abruptly Rand realized what had been odd about the horseman, aside from his being there at all. The wind that beat at Tam and him had not so much as shifted a fold of that black cloak. His mouth was suddenly dry. He must have imagined it. His father was right; this was a morning to prickle a man's imagination. But he did not believe it. Only, how did he tell his father that the man who had apparently vanished into air wore a cloak the wind did not touch?

With a worried frown he peered into the woods around them; it looked different than it ever had before. Almost since he was old enough to walk, he had run loose in the forest. The ponds and streams of the Waterwood, beyond the last farms east of Emond's Field, were where he had learned to swim. He had explored into the Sand Hills—which many in the Two Rivers said was bad luck—and once he had even gone to the very foot of the Mountains of Mist, him and his closest friends, Mat Cauthon and Perrin Aybara. That was a lot further afield than most people in Emond's Field ever went; to them a journey to the next village, up to Watch Hill or down to Deven Ride, was a big event. Nowhere in all of that had he found a place that made him afraid. Today, though, the Westwood was not the place he remembered. A man who could disappear so suddenly could reappear just as suddenly, maybe even right beside them.

"No, father, there's no need." When Tam stopped in surprise, Rand covered his flush by tugging at the hood of his cloak. "You're probably right. No point looking for what isn't there, not when we can use the time getting on to the village and out of this wind."

"I could do with a pipe," Tam said slowly, "and a mug of ale where it's warm." Abruptly he gave a broad grin. "And I expect you're eager to see Egwene."

Rand managed a weak smile. Of all things he might want to think about right then, the Mayor's daughter was far down the list. He did not need any more confusion. For the past year she had been making him increasingly jittery whenever they were together. Worse, she did not even seem to be aware of it. No, he certainly did not want to add Egwene to his thoughts.

He was hoping his father had not noticed he was afraid when Tam said, "Remember the flame, lad, and the void."

It was an odd thing Tam had taught him. Concentrate on a single flame and feed all your passions into it—fear, hate, anger—until your mind became empty. Become one with the void, Tam said, and you could do anything. Nobody else in Emond's Field talked that way. But Tam won the archery competition at Bel Tine every year with his flame and his void. Rand thought he might have a chance at placing this year himself, if he could manage to hold onto the void. For Tam to bring it up now meant he *had* noticed, but he said nothing more about it.

Tam clucked Bela into motion once more, and they resumed their journey, the older man striding along as if nothing untoward had happened and nothing untoward could. Rand wished he could imitate him. He tried forming the emptiness in his mind, but it kept slipping away into images of the black-cloaked horseman.

He wanted to believe that Tam was right, that the rider had just been his imagination, but he could remember that feeling of hatred too well. There *had* been someone. And that someone had meant him harm. He did not stop looking back until the high-peaked, thatched roofs of Emond's Field surrounded him.

The village lay close onto the Westwood, the forest gradually thinning until the last few trees stood actually among the stout frame houses. The land sloped gently down to the east. Though not without patches of woods, farms and hedge-bordered fields and pastures quilted the land beyond the village all the way to the Waterwood and its tangle of streams and ponds. The land to the west was just as fertile, and the pastures there lush in most years, but only a handful of farms could be found in the Westwood. Even those few dwindled to none miles short of the Sand Hills, not to mention the Mountains of Mist, which rose above the Westwood treetops, distant but in plain sight from Emond's Field. Some said the land was too rocky, as if there were not rocks everywhere in the Two Rivers, and others said it was hard-luck land. A few muttered that there was no point getting any closer to the mountains than needs be. Whatever the reasons, only the hardiest men farmed in the Westwood.

Small children and dogs dodged around the cart in whooping swarms once it passed the first row of houses. Bela plodded on patiently, ignoring the yelling youngsters who tumbled under her nose, playing tag and rolling hoops. In the last months there had been little of play or laughter from the children; even when the weather had slackened enough to let children out, fear of wolves kept them in. It seemed the approach of Bel Tine had taught them how to play again.

Festival had affected the adults as well. Broad shutters were thrown back, and in almost every house the goodwife stood in a window, apron tied about her and long-braided hair done up in a kerchief, shaking sheets or hanging mattresses over the windowsills. Whether or not leaves had appeared on the trees, no woman would let Bel Tine come before her spring cleaning was done. In every yard rugs hung from stretched lines, and children who had not been quick enough to run free in the streets instead vented their frustration on the carpets with wicker beaters. On roof after roof the goodman of the house clambered about, checking the thatch to see if the winter's damage meant calling on old Cenn Buie, the thatcher.

Several times Tam paused to engage one man or another in brief conversation. Since he and Rand had not been off the farm for weeks, everyone wanted to catch up on how things were out that way. Few Westwood men had been in. Tam spoke of damage from winter storms, each one worse than the one before, and stillborn lambs, of brown fields where crops should be sprouting and pastures greening, of ravens flocking in where songbirds had come in years before. Grim talk, with preparations for Bel Tine going on all around them, and much shaking of heads. It was the same on all sides.

Most of the men rolled their shoulders and said, "Well, we'll survive, the Light willing." Some grinned and added, "And if the Light doesn't will, we'll still survive."

That was the way of most Two Rivers people. People who had to watch the hail beat their crops or the wolves take their lambs, and start over, no matter how many years it happened, did not give up easily. Most of those who did were long since gone.

Tam would not have stopped for Wit Congar if the man had not come out into the street so they had to halt or let Bela run over him. The Congars—and the Coplins; the two families were so intermarried no one really knew where one family let off and the other began—were known from Watch Hill to Deven Ride, and maybe as far as Taren Ferry, as complainers and troublemakers.

"I have to get this to Bran al'Vere, Wit," Tam said, nodding to the barrels in the cart, but the scrawny man held his ground with a sour expression on his face. He had been sprawled on his front steps, not up on his roof, though the thatch looked as if it badly needed Master Buie's attention. He never seemed ready to start over, or to finish what he started the first time. Most of the Coplins and Congars were like that, those who were not worse.

"What are we going to do about Nynaeve, al'Thor?" Congar demanded. "We can't have a Wisdom like that for Emond's Field."

Tam sighed heavily. "It's not our place, Wit. The Wisdom is women's business."

"Well, we'd better do something, al'Thor. She said we'd have a mild winter. And a good harvest. Now you ask her what she hears on the wind, and she just scowls at you and stomps off."

"If you asked her the way you usually do, Wit," Tam said patiently, "you're lucky she didn't thump you with that stick she carries. Now if you don't mind, this brandy—"

"Nynaeve al'Meara is just too young to be Wisdom, al'Thor. If the Women's Circle won't do something, then the Village Council has to."

"What business of yours is the Wisdom, Wit Congar?" roared a woman's voice. Wit flinched as his wife marched out of the house. Daise Congar was twice as wide as Wit, a hard-faced woman without an ounce of fat on her. She glared at him with her fists on her hips. "You try meddling in Women's Circle business, and see how you like eating your own cooking. Which you won't do in my kitchen. And washing your own clothes and making your own bed. Which won't be under my roof."

"But, Daise," Wit whined, "I was just. . . ."

"If you'll pardon me, Daise," Tam said. "Wit. The Light shine on you both." He got Bela moving again, leading her around the scrawny fellow. Daise was concentrating on her husband now, but any minute she could realize whom it was Wit had been talking to.

That was why they had not accepted any of the invitations to stop for a bite to eat or something hot to drink. When they saw Tam, the goodwives of Emond's Field went on point like hounds spotting a rabbit. There was not a one of them who did not know just the perfect wife for a widower with a good farm, even if it was in the Westwood.

Rand stepped along just as quickly as Tam, perhaps even more so. He was sometimes cornered when Tam was not around, with no way to escape outside of rudeness. Herded onto a stool by the kitchen fire, he would be fed pastries or honeycakes or meatpies. And always the goodwife's eyes weighed and measured him as neatly as any merchant's scales and tapes while she told him that what he was eating was not nearly so good as her widowed sister's cooking, or her next-to-eldest cousin's. Tam was certainly not getting any younger, she would say. It was good that he had loved his wife so—it boded well for the next woman in his life—but he had mourned long enough. Tam needed a good woman. It was a simple fact, she would say, or something very close, that a man just could not do without a woman to take care of him and keep him out of trouble. Worst of all were those who paused thoughtfully at about that point, then asked with elaborate casualness exactly how old *he* was now.

Like most Two Rivers folk, Rand had a strong stubborn streak. Outsiders sometimes said it was the prime trait of people in the Two Rivers, that they could give mules lessons and teach stones. The goodwives were fine and kindly women for the most part, but he hated being pushed into anything, and they made him feel as if he were being prodded with sticks. So he walked fast, and wished Tam would hurry Bela along.

Soon the street opened onto the Green, a broad expanse in the middle of the village. Usually covered with thick grass, the Green this spring showed only a few fresh patches among the yellowish brown of dead grass and the black of bare earth. A double handful of geese waddled about, beadily eyeing the ground but not finding anything worth pecking, and someone had tethered a milkcow to crop the sparse growth.

Toward the west end of the Green, the Winespring itself gushed out of a low stone outcrop in a flow that never failed, a flow strong enough to knock a man down and sweet enough to justify its name a dozen times over. From the spring the rapidly widening Winespring Water ran swiftly off to the east, willows dotting its banks all the way to Master Thane's mill and beyond, until it split into dozens of streams in the swampy depths of the Waterwood. Two low, railed footbridges crossed the clear stream at the Green, and one bridge wider than the others and stout enough to bear wagons. The Wagon Bridge marked where the North Road, coming down from Taren Ferry and Watch Hill, became the Old Road, leading to Deven Ride. Outsiders sometimes found it funny that the road had one name to the north and another to the south, but that was the way it had always been, as far as anyone in Emond's Field knew, and that was that. It was a good enough reason for Two Rivers people.

On the far side of the bridges, the mounds were already building for the Bel Tine fires, three careful stacks of logs almost as big as houses. They had to be on cleared dirt, of course, not on the Green, even sparse as it was. What of Festival did not take place around the fires would happen on the Green.

Near the Winespring a score of older women sang softly as they erected the Spring Pole. Shorn of its branches, the straight, slender trunk of a fir tree stood ten feet high even in the hole they had dug for it. A knot of girls too young to wear their hair braided sat cross-legged and watched enviously, occasionally singing snatches of the song the women sang.

Tam clucked at Bela as if to make her speed her pace, though she ignored it, and Rand studiously kept his eyes from what the women were doing. In the morning the men would pretend to be surprised to find the Pole, then at noon the unmarried women would dance the Pole, entwining it with long, colored ribbons while the unmarried men sang. No one knew when the custom began or why—it was another thing that was the way it had always been—but it was an excuse to sing and dance, and nobody in the Two Rivers needed much excuse for that.

The whole day of Bel Tine would be taken up with singing and dancing and feasting, with time out for footraces, and contests in almost everything. Prizes would be given not only in archery, but for the best with the sling, and the quarterstaff. There would be contests at solving riddles and puzzles, at the rope tug, and lifting and tossing weights, prizes for the best singer, the best dancer and the best fiddle player, for the quickest to shear a sheep, even the best at bowls, and at darts.

Bel Tine was supposed to come when spring had well and truly arrived, the first lambs born and the first crop up. Even with the cold hanging on, though, no one had any idea of putting it off. Everyone could use a little singing and dancing. And to top everything, if the rumors could be believed, a grand display of fireworks was planned for the Green—if the first peddler of the year appeared in time, of course. That had been causing considerable talk; it was ten years since the last such display, and that was still talked about.

The Winespring Inn stood at the east end of the Green, hard beside the Wagon Bridge. The first floor of the inn was river rock, though the foundation was of older stone some said came from the mountains. The whitewashed second story—where Brandelwyn al'Vere, the innkeeper and Mayor of Emond's Field for the past twenty years, lived in the back with his wife and daughters—jutted out over the lower floor all the way around. Red roof tile, the only such roof in the village, glittered in the weak sunlight, and smoke drifted from three of the inn's dozen tall chimneys.

At the south end of the inn, away from the stream, stretched the remains of a much larger stone foundation, once part of the inn—or so it was said. A huge oak grew in the middle of it now, with a bole thirty paces around and spreading branches as thick as a man. In the summer, Bran al'Vere set tables and benches under those branches, shady with leaves then, where people could enjoy a cup and a cooling breeze while they talked or perhaps set out a board for a game of stones.

"Here we are, lad." Tam reached for Bela's harness, but she stopped in front of the inn before his hand touched leather. "Knows the way better than I do," he chuckled.

As the last creak of the axle faded, Bran al'Vere appeared from the inn, seeming as always to step too lightly for a man of his girth, nearly double that of anyone else in the village. A smile split his round face, which was topped by a sparse fringe of gray hair. The innkeeper was in his shirt-sleeves despite the chill, with a spotless white apron wrapped around him. A silver medallion in the form of a set of balance scales hung on his chest.

The medallion, along with the full-size set of scales used to weigh the coins of the merchants who came down from Baerlon for wool or tabac, was the symbol of the Mayor's office. Bran only wore it for dealing with the merchants and for festival feastdays, and weddings. He had it on a day early now, but that night was Winternight, the night before

Bel Tine, when every one would visit back and forth almost the whole night long exchanging small gifts, having a bite to eat and a touch to drink at every house. *After the winter,* Rand thought, *he probably considers Winternight excuse enough not to wait until tomorrow.*

"Tam," the Mayor shouted as he hurried toward them. "The Light shine on me, it's good to see you at last. And you, Rand. How are you, my boy?"

"Fine, Master al'Vere," Rand said. "And you, sir?" But Bran's attention was already back on Tam.

"I was almost beginning to think you wouldn't be bringing your brandy this year. You've never waited so late before."

"I've no liking for leaving the farm these days, Bran," Tam replied. "Not with the wolves the way they are. And the weather."

Bran harrumphed. "I could wish somebody wanted to talk about something besides the weather. Everyone complains about it, and folk who should know better expect me to set it right. I've just spent twenty minutes explaining to Mistress al'Donel that I can do nothing about the storks. Though what she expected me to do. . . ." He shook his head.

"An ill omen," a scratchy voice announced, "no storks nesting on the rooftops at Bel Tine." Cenn Buie, as gnarled and dark as an old root, marched up to Tam and Bran and leaned on his walking staff, near as tall as he was and just as gnarled. He tried to fix both men at once with a beady eye. "There's worse to come, you mark my words."

"Have you become a soothsayer, then, interpreting omens?" Tam asked dryly. "Or do you listen to the wind, like a Wisdom? There's certainly enough of it. Some originating not far from here."

"Mock if you will," Cenn muttered, "but if it doesn't warm enough for crops to sprout soon, more than one root cellar will come up empty before there's a harvest. By next winter there may be nothing left alive in the Two Rivers but wolves and ravens. If it is next winter at all. Maybe it will still be this winter."

"Now what is that supposed to mean?" Bran said sharply.

Cenn gave them a sour look. "I've not much good to say about Nynaeve al'Meara. You know that. For one thing, she's too young to— No matter. The Women's Circle seems to object to the Village Council even talking about their business, though they interfere in ours whenever they want to, which is most of the time, or so it seems to—"

"Cenn," Tam broke in, "is there a point to this?"

"This is the point, al'Thor. Ask the Wisdom when the winter will end, and she walks away. Maybe she doesn't want to tell us what she hears on the wind. Maybe what she hears is that the winter won't end. Maybe it's just going to go on being winter until the Wheel turns and the Age ends. There's your point."

"Maybe sheep will fly," Tam retorted, and Bran threw up his hands.

"The Light protect me from fools. You sitting on the Village Council, Cenn, and now you're spreading that Coplin talk. Well, you listen to me. We have enough problems without. . . ."

A quick tug at Rand's sleeve and a voice pitched low, for his ear alone, distracted him from the older men's talk. "Come on, Rand, while they're arguing. Before they put you to work."

Rand glanced down, and had to grin. Mat Cauthon crouched beside the cart so Tam and Bran and Cenn could not see him, his wiry body contorted like a stork trying to bend itself double.

Mat's brown eyes twinkled with mischief, as usual. "Dav and I caught a big old badger, all grouchy at being pulled out of his den. We're going to let it loose on the Green and watch the girls run."

Rand's smile broadened; it did not sound as much like fun to him as it would have a year or two back, but Mat never seemed to grow up. He took a quick look at his father—the men had their heads together still, all three talking at once—then lowered his own voice. "I promised to unload the cider. I can meet you later, though."

Mat rolled his eyes skyward. "Toting barrels! Burn me, I'd rather play stones with my baby sister. Well, I know of better things than a badger. We have strangers in the Two Rivers. Last evening—"

For an instant Rand stopped breathing. "A man on horseback?" he asked intently. "A man in a black cloak, on a black horse? And his cloak doesn't move in the wind?"

Mat swallowed his grin, and his voice dropped to an even

hoarser whisper. "You saw him, too? I thought I was the only one. Don't laugh, Rand, but he scared me."

"I'm not laughing. He scared me, too. I could swear he hated me, that he wanted to kill me." Rand shivered. Until that day he had never thought of anyone wanting to kill him, really wanting to kill him. That sort of thing just did not happen in the Two Rivers. A fistfight, maybe, or a wrestling match, but not killing.

"I don't know about hating, Rand, but he was scary enough anyway. All he did was sit on his horse looking at me, just outside the village, but I've never been so frightened in my life. Well, I looked away, just for a moment—it wasn't easy, mind you—then when I looked back he'd vanished. Blood and ashes! Three days, it's been, and I can hardly stop thinking about him. I keep looking over my shoulder." Mat attempted a laugh that came out as a croak. "Funny how being scared takes you. You think strange things. I actually thought—just for a minute, mind—it might be the Dark One." He tried another laugh, but no sound at all came out this time.

Rand took a deep breath. As much to remind himself as for any other reason, he said by rote, "The Dark One and all of the Forsaken are bound in Shayol Ghul, beyond the Great Blight, bound by the Creator at the moment of Creation, bound until the end of time. The hand of the Creator shelters the world, and the Light shines on us all." He drew another breath and went on. "Besides, if he was free, what would the Shepherd of the Night be doing in the Two Rivers watching farmboys?"

"I don't know. But I do know that rider was . . . evil. Don't laugh. I'll take oath on it. Maybe it was the Dragon."

"You're just full of cheerful thoughts, aren't you?" Rand muttered. "You sound worse than Cenn."

"My mother always said the Forsaken would come for me if I didn't mend my ways. If I ever saw anybody who looked like Ishamael, or Aginor, it was him."

"Everybody's mother scared them with the Forsaken," Rand said dryly, "but most grow out of it. Why not the Shadowman, while you're about it?"

Mat glared at him. "I haven't been so scared since. . . . No, I've never been that scared, and I don't mind admitting it."

"Me, either. My father thinks I was jumping at shadows under the trees."

Mat nodded glumly and leaned back against the cart wheel. "So does my da. I told Dav, and Elam Dowtry. They've been watching like hawks ever since, but they haven't seen anything. Now Elam thinks I was trying to trick him. Dav thinks he's down from Taren Ferry—a sheepstealer, or a chickenthief. A chickenthief!" He lapsed into affronted silence.

"It's probably all foolishness anyway," Rand said finally. "Maybe he is just a sheepstealer." He tried to picture it, but it was like picturing a wolf taking the cat's place in front of a mouse hole.

"Well, I didn't like the way he looked at me. And neither did you, not if how you jumped at me is any guide. We ought to tell someone."

"We already have, Mat, both of us, and we weren't believed. Can you imagine trying to convince Master al'Vere about this fellow, without him seeing him? He'd send us off to Nynaeve to see if we were sick."

"There are two of us, now. Nobody could believe we both imagined it."

Rand rubbed the top of his head briskly, wondering what to say. Mat was something of a byword around the village. Few people had escaped his pranks. Now his name came up whenever a washline dropped the laundry in the dirt or a loose saddle girth deposited a farmer in the road. Mat did not even have to be anywhere around. His support might be worse than none.

After a moment Rand said, "Your father would believe you put me up to it, and mine. . . ." He looked over the cart to where Tam and Bran and Cenn had been talking, and found himself staring his father in the eyes. The Mayor was still lecturing Cenn, who took it now in sullen silence.

"Good morning, Matrim," Tam said brightly, hefting one of the brandy casks up onto the side of the cart. "I see you've come to help Rand unload the cider. Good lad."

Mat leaped to his feet at the first word and began backing away. "Good morning to you, Master al'Thor. And to you, Master al'Vere. Master Buie. May the Light shine on you. My da sent me to—"

"No doubt he did," Tam said. "And no doubt, since you are

a lad who does his chores right off, you've finished the task already. Well, the quicker you lads get the cider into Master al'Vere's cellar, the quicker you can see the gleeman."

"Gleeman!" Mat exclaimed, stopping dead in his footsteps, at the same instant that Rand asked, "When will he get here?"

Rand could remember only two gleemen coming into the Two Rivers in his whole life, and for one of those he had been young enough to sit on Tam's shoulders to watch. To have one there actually during Bel Tine, with his harp and his flute and his stories and all. . . . Emond's Field would still be talking about this Festival ten years off, even if there were not any fireworks.

"Foolishness," Cenn grumbled, but fell silent at a look from Bran that had all the weight of the Mayor's office in it.

Tam leaned against the side of the cart, using the brandy cask as a prop for his arm. "Yes, a gleeman, and already here. According to Master al'Vere, he's in a room in the inn right now."

"Arrived in the dead of night, he did." The innkeeper shook his head in disapproval. "Pounded on the front door till he woke the whole family. If not for Festival, I'd have told him to stable his own horse and sleep in the stall with it, gleeman or not. Imagine coming in the dark like that."

Rand stared wonderingly. No one traveled beyond the village by night, not these days, certainly not alone. The thatcher grumbled under his breath again, too low this time for Rand to understand more than a word or two. "Madman" and "unnatural."

"He doesn't wear a black cloak, does he?" Mat asked suddenly.

Bran's belly shook with his chuckle. "Black! His cloak is like every gleeman's cloak I've ever seen. More patches than cloak, and more colors than you can think of."

Rand startled himself by laughing out loud, a laugh of pure relief. The menacing black-clad rider as a gleeman was a ridiculous notion, but. . . . He clapped a hand over his mouth in embarrassment.

"You see, Tam," Bran said. "There's been little enough laughter in this village since winter came. Now even the gleeman's cloak brings a laugh. That alone is worth the expense of bringing him down from Baerlon."

"Say what you will," Cenn spoke up suddenly. "I still say it's a foolish waste of money. And those fireworks you all insisted on sending off for."

"So there are fireworks," Mat said, but Cenn went right on.

"They should have been here a month ago with the first peddler of the year, but there hasn't been a peddler, has there? If he doesn't come by tomorrow, what are we going to do with them? Hold another Festival just to set them off? That's if he even brings them, of course."

"Cenn"—Tam sighed—"you've as much trust as a Taren Ferry man."

"Where is he, then? Tell me that, al'Thor."

"Why didn't you tell us?" Mat demanded in an aggrieved voice. "The whole village would have had as much fun with the waiting as with the gleeman. Or almost, anyway. You can see how everybody's been over just a rumor of fireworks."

"I can see," Bran replied with a sidelong look at the thatcher. "And if I knew for sure how that rumor started . . . if I thought, for instance, that somebody had been complaining about how much things cost where people could hear him when the things are supposed to be secret. . . ."

Cenn cleared his throat. "My bones are too old for this wind. If you don't mind, I'll just see if Mistress al'Vere won't fix me some mulled wine to take the chill off. Mayor. Al'Thor." He was headed for the inn before he finished, and as the door swung shut behind him, Bran sighed.

"Sometimes I think Nynaeve is right about. . . . Well, that's not important now. You young fellows think for a minute. Everyone's excited about the fireworks, true, and that's only at a rumor. Think how they'll be if the peddler doesn't get here in time, after all their anticipating. And with the weather the way it is, who knows when he will come. They'd be fifty times as excited about a gleeman."

"And feel fifty times as bad if he hadn't come," Rand said slowly. "Even Bel Tine might not do much for people's spirits after that."

"You have a head on your shoulders when you choose to use it," Bran said. "He'll follow you on the Village Council one day, Tam. Mark my words. He couldn't do much worse right now than someone I could name."

"None of this is unloading the cart," Tam said briskly,

handing the first cask of brandy to the Mayor. "I want a warm fire, my pipe, and a mug of your good ale." He hoisted the second brandy cask onto his shoulder. "I'm sure Rand will thank you for your help, Matrim. Remember, the sooner the cider is in the cellar. . . ."

As Tam and Bran disappeared into the inn, Rand looked at his friend. "You don't have to help. Dav won't keep that badger long."

"Oh, why not?" Mat said resignedly. "Like your da said, the quicker it's in the cellar. . . ." Picking up one of the casks of cider in both arms, he hurried toward the inn in a half trot. "Maybe Egwene is around. Watching you stare at her like a poleaxed ox will be as good as a badger any day."

Rand paused in the act of putting his bow and quiver in the back of the cart. He really had managed to put Egwene out of his mind. That was unusual in itself. But she would likely be around the inn somewhere. There was not much chance he could avoid her. Of course, it had been weeks since he saw her last.

"Well?" Mat called from the front of the inn. "I didn't say I would do it by myself. You aren't on the Village Council yet."

With a start, Rand took up a cask and followed. Perhaps she would not be there after all. Oddly, that possibility did not make him feel any better.

CHAPTER
2

Strangers

When Rand and Mat carried the first barrels through the common room, Master al'Vere was already filling a pair of mugs with his best brown ale, his own make, from one of the casks racked against one wall. Scratch, the inn's yellow cat, crouched atop it with his eyes closed and his tail wrapped around his feet. Tam stood in front of the big fireplace of river rock, thumbing a long-stemmed pipe full of tabac from a polished canister the innkeeper always kept on the plain stone mantel. The fireplace stretched half the length of the big, square room, with a lintel as high as a man's shoulder, and the crackling blaze on the hearth vanquished the chill outside.

At that time of the busy day before Festival, Rand expected to find the common room empty except for Bran and his father and the cat, but four more members of the Village Council, including Cenn, sat in high-backed chairs in front of the fire, mugs in hand and blue-gray pipesmoke wreathing their heads. For once none of the stones boards were in use, and all of Bran's books stood idle on the shelf opposite the fireplace. The men did not even talk, peering silently into their ale or tapping pipestems against their teeth in impatience, as they waited for Tam and Bran to join them.

Worry was not uncommon for the Village Council these days, not in Emond's Field, and likely not in Watch Hill, or Deven Ride. Or even Taren Ferry, though who knew what Taren Ferry folk really thought about anything?

Only two of the men before the fire, Haral Luhhan, the blacksmith, and Jon Thane, the miller, so much as glanced at the boys as they entered. Master Luhhan, though, made it more than a glance. The blacksmith's arms were as big as most men's legs, roped with heavy muscle, and he still wore his long leather apron as if he had hurried to the meeting straight from the forge. His frown took them both in, then he straightened around in his chair deliberately, turning his attention back to an over-studious tamping of his pipe with a thick thumb.

Curious, Rand slowed, then barely bit back a yelp as Mat kicked his ankle. His friend nodded insistently toward the doorway at the back of the common room and hurried on without waiting. Limping slightly, Rand followed less quickly.

"What was that about?" he demanded as soon as he was in the hall that led to the kitchen. "You almost broke my—"

"It's old Luhhan," Mat said, peering past Rand's shoulder into the common room. "I think he suspects I was the one who—" He cut off abruptly as Mistress al'Vere bustled out of the kitchen, the aroma of fresh-baked bread wafting ahead of her.

The tray in her hands carried some of the crusty loaves for which she was famous around Emond's Field, as well as plates of pickles and cheese. The food reminded Rand abruptly that he had eaten only an end of bread before leaving the farm that morning. His stomach gave an embarrassing rumble.

A slender woman, with her thick braid of graying hair pulled over one shoulder, Mistress al'Vere smiled in a motherly fashion that took in both of them. "There is more of this in the kitchen, if you two are hungry, and I never knew boys your age who weren't. Or any other age, for that matter. If you prefer, I'm baking honeycakes this morning."

She was one of the few married women in the area who never tried to play matchmaker with Tam. Toward Rand her motherliness extended to warm smiles and a quick snack whenever he came by the inn, but she did as much for every young man in the area. If she occasionally looked at him as if she wanted to do more, at least she took it no further than looks, for which he was deeply grateful.

Without waiting for a reply she swept on into the common room. Immediately there was the sound of chairs scraping on the floor as the men got to their feet, and exclaimings over the smell of the bread. She was easily the best cook in

Emond's Field, and not a man for miles around but eagerly leaped at a chance to put his feet under her table.

"Honeycakes," Mat said, smacking his lips.

"After," Rand told him firmly, "or we'll never get done."

A lamp hung over the cellar stairs, just beside the kitchen door, and another made a bright pool in the stone-walled room beneath the inn, banishing all but a little dimness in the furthest corners. Wooden racks along the walls and across the floor held casks of brandy and cider, and larger barrels of ale and wine, some with taps driven in. Many of the wine barrels were marked with chalk in Bran al'Vere's hand, giving the year they had been bought, what peddler had brought them, and in which city they had been made, but all of the ale and brandy was the make of Two Rivers farmers or of Bran himself. Peddlers, and even merchants, sometimes brought brandy or ale from outside, but it was never as good and cost the earth, besides, and nobody ever drank it more than once.

"Now," Rand said, as they set their casks in the racks, "what did you do that you have to avoid Master Luhhan?"

Mat shrugged. "Nothing, really. I told Adan al'Caar and some of his snot-nosed friends—Ewin Finngar and Dag Coplin—that some farmers had seen ghost hounds, breathing fire and running through the woods. They ate it up like clotted cream."

"And Master Luhhan is mad at you for that?" Rand said doubtfully.

"Not exactly." Mat paused, then shook his head. "You see, I covered two of his dogs with flour, so they were all white. Then I let them loose near Dag's house. How was I to know they'd run straight home? It really isn't my fault. If Mistress Luhhan hadn't left the door open they couldn't have gotten inside. It isn't like I intended to get flour all over her house." He gave a bark of laughter. "I hear she chased old Luhhan and the dogs, all three, out of the house with a broom."

Rand winced and laughed at the same time. "If I were you, I'd worry more about Alsbet Luhhan than about the blacksmith. She's almost as strong, and her temper is a lot worse. No matter, though. If you walk fast, maybe he won't notice you." Mat's expression said he did not think Rand was funny.

When they went back through the common room, though, there was no need for Mat to hurry. The six men had their chairs in a tight knot before the fireplace. With his back to the fire, Tam was speaking in a low voice, and the others were leaning forward to listen, so intent on his words they would likely not have noticed if a flock of sheep had been driven through. Rand wanted to move closer, to hear what they were talking about, but Mat plucked at his sleeve and gave him an agonized look. With a sigh he followed Mat out to the cart.

On their return to the hallway they found a tray by the top of the steps, and hot honeycakes filling the hall with their sweet aroma. There were two mugs, as well, and a pitcher of steaming mulled cider. Despite his own admonition about waiting until later Rand found himself making the last two trips between cart and cellar while trying to juggle a cask and a piping honeycake.

Setting his final cask in the racks, he wiped crumbs from his mouth while Mat was unburdening himself, then said, "Now for the glee—"

Feet clattered on the stairs, and Ewin Finngar half fell into the cellar in his haste, his pudgy face shining with eagerness to impart his news. "There are strangers in the village." He caught his breath and gave Mat a wry look. "I haven't seen any ghost hounds, but I hear somebody floured Master Luhhan's dogs. I hear Mistress Luhhan has ideas who to look for, too."

The years separating Rand and Mat from Ewin, only fourteen, were usually more than enough for them to give short shrift to anything he had to say. This time they exchanged one startled glance, then both were talking at once.

"In the village?" Rand asked. "Not in the woods?"

Right on top of him Mat added, "Was his cloak black? Could you see his face?"

Ewin looked uncertainly from one of them to the other, then spoke quickly when Mat took a threatening step. "Of course I could see his face. And his cloak is green. Or maybe gray. It changes. It seems to fade into wherever he's standing. Sometimes you don't see him even when you look right at him, not unless he moves. And hers is blue, like the sky, and ten times fancier than any feastday clothes I ever saw. She's ten times prettier than anybody I ever saw, too. She's a high-born lady, like in the stories. She must be."

"Her?" Rand said. "Who are you talking about?" He stared at Mat, who had put both hands on top of his head and squeezed his eyes shut.

"They're the ones I meant to tell you about," Mat muttered, "before you got me off onto—" He cut off, opening his eyes for a sharp glance at Ewin. "They arrived last evening," Mat went on after a moment, "and took rooms here at the inn. I saw them ride in. Their horses, Rand. I never saw horses so tall, or so sleek. They look like they could run forever. I think he works for her."

"In service," Ewin broke in. "They call it being in service, in the stories."

Mat continued as if Ewin had not spoken. "Anyway, he defers to her, does what she says. Only he isn't like a hired man. A soldier, maybe. The way he wears his sword, it's part of him, like his hand or his foot. He makes the merchants' guards look like cur dogs. And her, Rand. I never even imagined anyone like her. She's out of a gleeman's story. She's like . . . like. . . ." He paused to give Ewin a sour look. ". . . Like a high-born lady," he finished with a sigh.

"But who are they?" Rand asked. Except for merchants, once a year to buy tabac and wool, and the peddlers, outsiders never came into the Two Rivers, or as good as never. Maybe at Taren Ferry, but not this far south. Most of the merchants and peddlers had been coming for years, too, so they did not really count as strangers. Just outsiders. It was a good five years since the last time a real stranger appeared in Emond's Field, and he had been trying to hide from some sort of trouble up in Baerlon that nobody in the village understood. He had not stayed long. "What do they want?"

"What do they want?" Mat exclaimed. "I don't care what they want. Strangers, Rand, and strangers like you never even dreamed of. Think of it!"

Rand opened his mouth, then closed it without speaking. The black-cloaked rider had him as nervous as a cat in a dog run. It just seemed like an awful coincidence, three strangers around the village at the same time. Three if this fellow's cloak that changed colors never changed to black.

"Her name is Moiraine," Ewin said into the momentary

silence. "I heard him say it. Moiraine, he called her. The Lady Moiraine. His name is Lan. The Wisdom may not like her, but I do."

"What makes you think Nynaeve dislikes her?" Rand said.

"She asked the Wisdom for directions this morning," Ewin said, "and called her 'child.'" Rand and Mat both whistled softly through their teeth, and Ewin tripped over his tongue in his haste to explain. "The Lady Moiraine didn't know she was the Wisdom. She apologized when she found out. She did. And asked some questions about herbs, and about who is who around Emond's Field, just as respectfully as any woman in the village—more so than some. She's always asking questions, about how old people are, and how long they've lived where they live, and . . . oh, I don't know what all. Anyway, Nynaeve answered like she'd bitten a green sweetberry. Then, when the Lady Moiraine walked away, Nynaeve stared after her like, like . . . well, it wasn't friendly, I can tell you that."

"Is that all?" Rand said. "You know Nynaeve's temper. When Cenn Buie called her a child last year, she thumped him on the head with her stick, and he's on the Village Council, and old enough to be her grandfather, besides. She flares up at anything, and never stays angry past turning around."

"That's too long for me," Ewin muttered.

"I don't care who Nynaeve thumps"—Mat chortled—"so long as it isn't me. This is going to be the best Bel Tine ever. A gleeman, a lady—who could ask for more? Who needs fireworks?"

"A gleeman?" Ewin said, his voice rising sharply.

"Come on, Rand," Mat went on, ignoring the younger boy. "We're done here. You have to see this fellow."

He bounded up the stairs, with Ewin scrambling behind him calling, "Is there really a gleeman, Mat? This isn't like the ghost hounds, is it? Or the frogs?"

Rand paused long enough to turn down the lamp, then hurried after them.

In the common room Rowan Hum and Samel Crawe had joined the others in front of the fire, so that the entire Village Council was there. Bran al'Vere spoke now, his normally bluff voice pitched so low that only a rumbling murmur traveled beyond the close-gathered chairs. The Mayor emphasized his words by tapping a thick forefinger into the palm of his other hand, and eyed each man in turn. They all nodded in agreement with whatever he was saying, though Cenn more reluctantly than the rest.

The way the men all but huddled together spoke more plainly than a painted sign. Whatever they were talking about, it was for the Village Council alone, at least for now. They would not appreciate Rand trying to listen in. Reluctantly he pulled himself away. There was still the gleeman. And these strangers.

Outside, Bela and the cart were gone, taken away by Hu or Tad, the inn's stablemen. Mat and Ewin stood glaring at one another a few paces from the front door of the inn, their cloaks whipping in the wind.

"For the last time," Mat barked, "I am *not* playing a trick on you. There *is* a gleeman. Now go away. Rand, will you tell this woolhead I am telling the truth so he'll leave me alone?"

Pulling his cloak together, Rand stepped forward to support Mat, but words died as the hairs stirred on the back of his neck. He was being watched again. It was far from the feeling the hooded rider had given him, but neither was it pleasant, especially so soon after that encounter.

A quick look about the Green showed him only what he had seen before—children playing, people preparing for Festival, and no one more than glancing in his direction. The Spring Pole stood alone, now, waiting. Bustle and childish shouts filled the side streets. All was as it should be. Except that he was being watched.

Then something led him to turn around, to raise his eyes. On the edge of the inn's tile roof perched a large raven, swaying a little in the gusting wind from the mountains. Its head was cocked to one side, and one beady, black eye was focused . . . on him, he thought. He swallowed, and suddenly anger flickered in him, hot and sharp.

"Filthy carrion eater," he muttered.

"I am tired of being stared at," Mat growled, and Rand realized his friend had stepped up beside him and was frowning at the raven, too.

They exchanged a glance, then as one their hands darted for rocks.

The two stones flew true . . . and the raven stepped aside; the stones whistled through the space where it had been. Fluffing its wings once, it cocked its head again, fixing them with a dead black eye, unafraid, giving no sign that anything had happened.

Rand stared at the bird in consternation. "Did you ever see a raven do that?" he asked quietly.

Mat shook his head without looking away from the raven. "Never. Nor any other bird, either."

"A vile bird," came a woman's voice from behind them, melodious despite echoes of distaste, "to be mistrusted in the best of times."

With a shrill cry the raven launched itself into the air so violently that two black feathers drifted down from the roof's edge.

Startled, Rand and Mat twisted to follow the bird's swift flight, over the Green and toward the cloud-tipped Mountains of Mist, tall beyond the Westwood, until it dwindled to a speck in the west, then vanished from view.

Rand's gaze fell to the woman who had spoken. She, too, had been watching the flight of the raven, but now she turned back, and her eyes met his. He could only stare. This had to be the Lady Moiraine, and she was everything that Mat and Ewin had said, everything and more.

When he had heard she called Nynaeve child, he had pictured her as old, but she was not. At least, he could not put any age to her at all. At first he thought she was as young as Nynaeve, but the longer he looked the more he thought she was older than that. There was a maturity about her large, dark eyes, a hint of knowing that no one could have gotten young. For an instant he thought those eyes were deep pools about to swallow him up. It was plain why Mat and Ewin named her a lady from a gleeman's tale, too. She held herself with a grace and air of command that made him feel awkward and stumble-footed. She was barely tall enough to come up to his chest, but her presence was such that her height seemed the proper one, and he felt ungainly in his tallness.

Altogether she was like no one he had ever seen before. The wide hood of her cloak framed her face and dark hair, hanging in soft ringlets. He had never seen a grown woman with her hair unbraided; every girl in the Two Rivers waited eagerly for the Women's Circle of her village to say she was old enough to wear a braid. Her clothes were just as strange. Her cloak was sky-blue velvet, with thick silver embroidery, leaves and vines and flowers, all along the edges. Her dress gleamed faintly as she moved, a darker blue than the cloak, and slashed with cream. A necklace of heavy gold links hung around her neck, while another gold chain, delicate and fastened in her hair, supported a small, sparkling blue stone in the middle of her forehead. A wide belt of woven gold encircled her waist, and on the second finger of her left hand was a gold ring in the shape of a serpent biting its own tail. He had certainly never seen a ring like that, though he recognized the Great Serpent, an even older symbol for eternity than the Wheel of Time.

Fancier than any feastday clothes, Ewin had said, and he was right. No one ever dressed like that in the Two Rivers. Not ever.

"Good morning, Mistress . . . ah . . . Lady Moiraine," Rand said. His face grew hot at his tongue's fumbling.

"Good morning, Lady Moiraine," Mat echoed somewhat more smoothly, but only a little.

She smiled, and Rand found himself wondering if there was anything he might do for her, something that would give him an excuse to stay near her. He knew she was smiling at all of them, but it seemed meant for him alone. It really was just like seeing a gleeman's tale come to life. Mat had a foolish grin on his face.

"You know my name," she said, sounding delighted. As if her presence, however brief, would not be the talk of the village for a year! "But you must call me Moiraine, not lady. And what are your names?"

Ewin leaped forward before either of the others could speak. "My name is Ewin Finngar, my lady. I told them your name; that's how they know. I heard Lan say it, but I wasn't eavesdropping. No one like you has ever come to Emond's Field, before. There's a gleeman in the village for Bel Tine, too. And tonight is Winternight. Will you come to my house? My mother has apple cakes."

"I shall have to see," she replied, putting a hand on Ewin's shoulder. Her eyes twinkled with amusement, though she gave no other sign of it. "I do not know how well I could compete against a gleeman, Ewin. But you must all call me Moiraine." She looked expectantly at Rand and Mat.

"I'm Matrim Cauthon, La . . . ah . . . Moiraine," Mat said. He made a stiff, jerking bow, then went red in the face as he straightened.

Rand had been wondering if he should do something of the sort, the way men did in stories, but with Mat's example, he merely spoke his name. At least he did not stumble over his own tongue this time.

Moiraine looked from him to Mat and back again. Rand thought her smile, a bare curve of the corners of her mouth, was now the sort Egwene wore when she had a secret. "I may have some small tasks to be done from time to time while I am in Emond's Field," she said. "Perhaps you would be willing to assist me?" She laughed as their assents tumbled over one another. "Here," she said, and Rand was surprised when she pressed a coin into his palm, closing his hand tightly around it with both of hers.

"There's no need," he began, but she waved aside his protest as she gave Ewin a coin as well, then pressed Mat's hand around one the same way she had Rand's.

"Of course, there is," she said. "You cannot be expected to work for nothing. Consider this a token, and keep it with you, so you will remember that you have agreed to come to me when I ask it. There is a bond between us now."

"I'll never forget," Ewin piped up.

"Later we must talk," she said, "and you must tell me all about yourselves."

"Lady . . . I mean, Moiraine?" Rand asked hesitantly as she turned away. She stopped and looked back over her shoulder, and he had to swallow before going on. "Why have you come to Emond's Field?" Her expression was unchanged, but suddenly he wished he had not asked, though he could not have said why. He rushed to explain himself, anyway. "I don't mean to be rude. I'm sorry. It's just that no one comes into the Two Rivers except the merchants, and peddlers when the snow isn't too deep to get down from Baerlon. Almost no one. Certainly no one like you. The merchants' guards sometimes say this is the back end of forever, and I suppose it must seem that way to anyone from outside. I just wondered."

Her smile did fade then, slowly, as if something had been recalled to her. For a moment she merely looked at him. "I am a student of history," she said at last, "a collector of old stories. This place you call the Two Rivers has always interested me. Sometimes I study the stories of what happened here long ago, here and at other places."

"Stories?" Rand said. "What ever happened in the Two Rivers to interest someone like—I mean, what could have happened here?"

"And what else would you call it beside the Two Rivers?" Mat added. "That's what it has always been called."

"As the Wheel of Time turns," Moiraine said, half to herself and with a distant look in her eyes, "places wear many names. Men wear many names, many faces. Different faces, but always the same man. Yet no one knows the Great Pattern the Wheel weaves, or even the Pattern of an Age. We can only watch, and study, and hope."

Rand stared at her, unable to say a word, even to ask what she meant. He was not sure she had meant for them to hear. The other two were just as tongue-tied, he noticed. Ewin's mouth hung open.

Moiraine focused on them again, and all three gave a little shake as if waking up. "Later we will talk," she said. None of them said a word. "Later." She moved on toward the Wagon Bridge, appearing to glide over the ground rather than walk, her cloak spreading on either side of her like wings.

As she left, a tall man Rand had not noticed before moved away from the front of the inn and followed her, one hand resting on the long hilt of a sword. His clothes were a dark grayish green that would have faded into leaf or shadow, and his cloak swirled through shades of gray and green and brown as it shifted in the wind. It almost seemed to disappear at times, that cloak, fading into whatever lay beyond it. His hair was long, and gray at the temples, held back from his face by a narrow leather headband. That face was made from stony planes and angles, weathered but unlined despite the gray in his hair. When he moved, Rand could think of nothing but a wolf.

In passing the three youths his gaze ran over them, eyes as cold and blue as a midwinter dawn. It was as if he were weighing them in his mind, and there was no sign on his face of what the scales told him. He quickened his pace until he caught up to Moiraine, then slowed to walk by her shoulder, bending to speak to her. Rand let out a breath he had not realized he had been holding.

"That was Lan," Ewin said throatily, as if he, too, had been holding his breath. It had been that kind of look. "I'll bet he's a Warder."

"Don't be a fool." Mat laughed, but it was a shaky laugh. "Warders are just in stories. Anyway, Warders have swords and armor covered in gold and jewels, and spend all their time up north, in the Great Blight, fighting evil and Trollocs and such."

"He *could* be a Warder," Ewin insisted.

"Did you see any gold or jewels on him?" Mat scoffed. "Do we have Trollocs in the Two Rivers? We have sheep. I wonder what could ever have happened here to interest someone like her."

"Something could have," Rand answered slowly. "They say the inn's been here for a thousand years, maybe more."

"A thousand years of sheep," Mat said.

"A silver penny!" Ewin burst out. "She gave me a whole silver penny! Think what I can buy when the peddler comes."

Rand opened his hand to look at the coin she had given him, and almost dropped it in surprise. He did not recognize the fat silver coin with the raised image of a woman balancing a single flame on her upturned hand, but he had watched while Bran al'Vere weighed out the coins merchants brought from a dozen lands, and he had an idea of its value. That much silver would buy a good horse anywhere in the Two Rivers, with some left over.

He looked at Mat and saw the same stunned expression he knew must be on his own face. Tilting his hand so Mat could see the coin but not Ewin, he raised a questioning eyebrow. Mat nodded, and for a minute they stared at one another in perplexed wonder.

"What kind of chores does she have?" Rand asked finally.

"I don't know," Mat said firmly, "and I don't care. I won't spend it, either. Even when the peddler comes." With that he thrust his coin into his coat pocket.

Nodding, Rand slowly did the same with his. He was not sure why, but somehow what Mat said seemed right. The coin should not be spent. Not when it came from her. He could not think of anything else silver was good for, but. . . .

"Do you think I should keep mine, too?" Anguished indecision painted Ewin's face.

"Not unless you want to," Mat said.

"I think she gave it to you to spend," Rand said.

Ewin looked at his coin, then shook his head and stuffed the silver penny into his pocket. "I'll keep it," he said mournfully.

"There's still the gleeman," Rand said, and the younger boy brightened.

"If he ever wakes up," Mat added.

"Rand," Ewin asked, "*is* there a gleeman?"

"You'll see," Rand answered with a laugh. It was clear Ewin would not believe until he set eyes on the gleeman. "He has to come down sooner or later."

Shouting drifted across the Wagon Bridge, and when Rand looked to see what was causing it, his laughter became wholehearted. A milling crowd of villagers, from gray-haired oldsters to toddlers barely able to walk, escorted a tall wagon toward the bridge, a huge wagon drawn by eight horses, the outside of its rounded canvas cover hung about with bundles like bunches of grapes. The peddler had come at last. Strangers and a gleeman, fireworks and a peddler. It was going to be the best Bel Tine ever.

CHAPTER
3

The Peddler

C lusters of pots clattered and banged as the peddler's wagon rumbled over the heavy timbers of the Wagon Bridge. Still surrounded by a cloud of villagers and farmers come for Festival, the peddler reined his horses to a stop in front of the inn. From every direction people streamed to swell the numbers around the great wagon, its wheels taller than any of the people with their eyes fastened to the peddler above them on the wagon seat.

The man on the wagon was Padan Fain, a pale, skinny fellow with gangly arms and a massive beak of a nose. Fain, always smiling and laughing as if he knew a joke that no one else knew, had driven his wagon and team into Emond's Field every spring for as long as Rand could remember.

The door of the inn flew open even as the team halted in a jangle of harness, and the Village Council appeared, led by Master al'Vere and Tam. They marched out deliberately, even Cenn Buie, amid all the excited shouting of the others for pins or lace or books or a dozen other things. Reluctantly the crowd parted to let them to the fore, everyone closing in quickly behind and never stopping their calling to the peddler. Most of all, the villagers called for news.

In the eyes of the villagers, needles and tea and the like were no more than half the freight in a peddler's wagon. Every bit as important was word of outside, news of the world beyond the Two Rivers. Some peddlers simply told what they knew, throwing it out in a heap, a pile of rubbish with which they could not be bothered. Others had to have every word dragged out of them, speaking grudgingly, with a bad grace. Fain, however, spoke freely if often teasingly, and spun out the telling, making a show to rival a gleeman. He enjoyed being the center of attention, strutting around like an under-sized rooster, with every eye on him. It occurred to Rand that Fain might not be best pleased to find a real gleeman in Emond's Field.

The peddler gave the Council and villagers alike exactly the same attention as he fussed with tying his reins off just so, which was to say hardly any attention at all. He nodded casually at no one in particular. He smiled without speaking, and waved absently to people with whom he was particularly friendly, though his friendliness had always been of a peculiarly distant kind, backslapping without ever getting close.

The demands for him to speak grew louder, but Fain waited, fiddling with small tasks about the driver's seat, for the crowd and the anticipation to reach the size he wanted. The Council alone kept silent. They maintained the dignity befitting their position, but increasing clouds of pipesmoke rising above their heads showed the effort of it.

Rand and Mat edged into the crowd, getting as close to the wagon as they could. Rand would have stopped halfway, but Mat wriggled through the press, pulling Rand behind him, until they were right behind the Council.

"I had been thinking you were going to stay out on the farm through the whole Festival," Perrin Aybara shouted at Rand over the clamor. Half a head shorter than Rand, the curly-haired blacksmith's apprentice was so stocky as to seem a man and a half wide, with arms and shoulders thick enough to rival those of Master Luhhan himself. He could easily have pushed through the throng, but that was not his way. He picked his path carefully, offering apologies to people who had only half a mind to notice anything but the peddler. He made the apologies anyway, and tried not to jostle anyone as he worked through the crowd to Rand and Mat. "Imagine it," he said when he finally reached them. "Bel Tine and a peddler, both together. I'll bet there really are fireworks."

"You don't know a quarter of it." Mat laughed.

Perrin eyed him suspiciously, then looked a question at Rand.

"It's true," Rand shouted, then gestured at the growing mass of people, all giving voice. "Later. I'll explain later. Later, I said!"

At that moment Padan Fain stood up on the wagon seat, and the crowd quieted in an instant. Rand's last words exploded into utter silence, catching the peddler with an arm raised dramatically and his mouth open. Everybody turned to stare at Rand. The bony little man on the wagon, prepared to have everyone hanging on his first words, gave Rand a sharp, searching look.

Rand's face reddened, and he wished he were Ewin's size so he did not stand out so clearly. His friends shifted uncomfortably, too. It had only been the year before that Fain had taken notice of them for the first time, acknowledging them as men. Fain did not usually have time for anyone too young to buy a good deal of things off his wagon. Rand hoped he had not been relegated to a child again in the peddler's eyes.

With a loud harrumph, Fain tugged at his heavy cloak. "No, not later," the peddler declaimed, once more throwing up a hand grandly. "I will be telling you now." As he spoke he made broad gestures, casting his words over the crowd. "You are thinking you have had troubles in the Two Rivers, are you? Well, all the world has troubles, from the Great Blight south to the Sea of Storms, from the Aryth Ocean in the west to the Aiel Waste in the east. And even beyond. The winter was harsher than you've ever seen before, cold enough to jell your blood and crack your bones? Ahhh! Winter was cold and harsh everywhere. In the Borderlands they'd be calling your winter spring. But spring does not come, you say? Wolves have killed your sheep? Perhaps wolves have attacked men? Is that the way of it? Well, now. Spring is late everywhere. There are wolves everywhere, all hungry for any flesh they can sink a tooth into, be it sheep or cow or man. But there are things worse than wolves or winter. There are those who would be glad to have only your little troubles." He paused expectantly.

"What could be worse than wolves killing sheep, and men?" Cenn Buie demanded. Others muttered in support.

"Men killing men." The peddler's reply, in portentous tones, brought shocked murmurs that increased as he went on. "It is war I mean. There is war in Ghealdan, war and madness. The snows of the Dhallin Forest are red with the blood of men. Ravens and the cries of ravens fill the air. Armies march to Ghealdan. Nations, great houses and great men, send their soldiers to fight."

"War?" Master al'Vere's mouth fit awkwardly around the unfamiliar word. No one in the Two Rivers had ever had anything to do with a war. "Why are they having a war?"

Fain grinned, and Rand had the feeling he was mocking the villagers' isolation from the world, and their ignorance. The peddler leaned forward as if he were about to impart a secret to the Mayor, but his whisper was meant to carry and did. "The standard of the Dragon has been raised, and men flock to oppose. And to support."

One long gasp left every throat together, and Rand shivered in spite of himself.

"The Dragon!" someone moaned. "The Dark One's loose in Ghealdan!"

"Not the Dark One," Haral Luhhan growled. "The Dragon's not the Dark One. And this is a false Dragon, anyway."

"Let's hear what Master Fain has to say," the Mayor said, but no one would be quieted that easily. People cried out from every side, men and women shouting over one another.

"Just as bad as the Dark One!"

"The Dragon broke the world, didn't he?"

"He started it! He caused the Time of Madness!"

"You know the prophecies! When the Dragon is reborn, your worst nightmares will seem like your fondest dreams!"

"He's just another false Dragon. He must be!"

"What difference does that make? You remember the last false Dragon. He started a war, too. Thousands died, isn't that right, Fain? He laid siege to Illian."

"It's evil times! No one claiming to be the Dragon Reborn for twenty years, and now three in the last five years. Evil times! Look at the weather!"

Rand exchanged looks with Mat and Perrin. Mat's eyes shone with excitement, but Perrin wore a worried frown. Rand could remember every tale he had heard about the men who named themselves the Dragon Reborn, and if they had all proven themselves false Dragons by dying or disappearing without fulfilling any of the prophecies, what they had done was bad enough. Whole nations torn by battle, and cities and towns put to the torch. The dead fell like autumn leaves, and refugees clogged the roads like sheep in a pen. So the peddlers said, and the merchants, and no one in the Two Rivers with any sense doubted it. The world would end, so some said, when the real Dragon was born again.

"Stop this!" the Mayor shouted. "Be quiet! Stop working yourselves to a lather out of your own imaginations. Let Master Fain tell us about this false Dragon." The people began to quieten, but Cenn Buie refused to be silent.

"*Is* this a false Dragon?" the thatcher asked sourly.

Master al'Vere blinked as if taken by surprise, then snapped, "Don't be an old fool, Cenn!" But Cenn had kindled the crowd again.

"He can't be the Dragon Reborn! Light help us, he can't be!"

"You old fool, Buie! You *want* bad luck, don't you?"

"Be naming the Dark One, next! You're taken by the Dragon, Cenn Buie! Trying to bring us all harm!"

Cenn looked around defiantly, trying to stare down the glowers, and raised his voice. "I didn't hear Fain say this was a false Dragon. Did you? Use your eyes! Where are the crops that should be knee high or better? Why is it still winter when spring should be here a month?" There were angry shouts for Cenn to hold his tongue. "I will not be silent! I've no liking for this talk, either, but I won't hide my head under a basket till a Taren Ferry man comes to cut my throat. And I won't dangle on Fain's pleasure, not this time. Speak it out plain, peddler. What have you heard? Eh? Is this man a false Dragon?"

If Fain was perturbed by the news he brought or the upset he had caused, he gave no sign of it. He merely shrugged and laid a skinny finger alongside his nose. "As to that, now, who can say until it is over and done?" He paused with one of his secretive grins, running his eyes over the crowd as if imagining how they would react and finding it funny. "I do know," he said, too casually, "that he can wield the One Power. The others couldn't. But he can channel. The ground opens beneath his enemies' feet, and strong walls crumble at his shout. Lightning comes when he calls and strikes where he points. That I've heard, and from men I believe."

A stunned silence fell. Rand looked at his friends. Perrin seemed to be seeing things he did not like, but Mat *still* looked excited.

Tam, his face only a little less composed than usual, drew the Mayor close, but before he could speak Ewin Finngar burst out.

"He'll go mad and die! In the stories, men who channel the Power always go mad, and then waste away and die. Only women can touch it. Doesn't he know that?" He ducked under a cuff from Master Buie.

"Enough of that from you, boy." Cenn shook a gnarled fist in Ewin's face. "Show a proper respect and leave this to your elders. Get away with you!"

"Hold steady, Cenn," Tam growled. "The boy is just curious. There's no need of this foolishness from you."

"Act your age," Bran added. "And for once remember you're a member of the Council."

Cenn's wrinkled face grew darker with every word from Tam and the Mayor, until it was almost purple. "You know what kind of women he's talking about. Stop frowning at me, Luhhan, and you, too, Crawe. This is a decent village of decent folk, and it's bad enough to have Fain here talking about false Dragons using the Power without this Dragon-possessed fool of a boy bringing Aes Sedai into it. Some things just shouldn't be talked about, and I don't care if you will be letting that fool gleeman tell any kind of tale he wants. It isn't right or decent."

"I never saw or heard or smelled anything that couldn't be talked about," Tam said, but Fain was not finished.

"The Aes Sedai are already into it," the peddler spoke up. "A party of them has ridden south from Tar Valon. Since he can wield the Power, none but Aes Sedai can defeat him, for all the battles they fight, or deal with him once he's defeated. If he is defeated."

Someone in the crowd moaned aloud, and even Tam and Bran exchanged uneasy frowns. Huddles of villagers clumped together, and some pulled their cloaks tighter around themselves, though the wind had actually lessened.

"Of course, he'll be defeated," someone shouted.

"They're always beaten in the end, false Dragons."

"He has to be defeated, doesn't he?"

"What if he isn't?"

Tam had finally managed to speak quietly into the Mayor's ear, and Bran, nodding from time to time and ignoring the hubbub around them, waited until he was finished before raising his own voice.

"All of you listen. Be quiet and listen!" The shouting died to a murmur again. "This goes beyond mere news from outside. It must be discussed by the Village Council. Master Fain, if you will join us inside the inn, we have questions to ask."

"A good mug of hot mulled wine would not go far amiss with me just now," the peddler replied with a chuckle. He jumped down from the wagon, dusted his hands on his coat, and cheerfully righted his cloak. "Will you be looking after my horses, if you please?"

"I want to hear what he has to say!" More than one voice was raised in protest.

"You can't take him off! My wife sent me to buy pins!" That was Wit Congar; he hunched his shoulders at the stares some of the others gave him, but he held his ground.

"We've a right to ask questions, too," somebody back in the crowd shouted. "I—"

"Be silent!" the Mayor roared, producing a startled hush. "When the Council has asked its questions, Master Fain will be back to tell you all his news. And to sell you his pots and pins. Hu! Tad! Stable Master Fain's horses."

Tam and Bran moved in on either side of the peddler, the rest of the Council gathered behind them, and the whole cluster swept into the Winespring Inn, firmly shutting the door in the faces of those who tried to crowd inside after them. Pounding on the door brought only a single shout from the Mayor.

"Go home!"

People milled around in front of the inn muttering about what the peddler had said, and what it meant, and what questions the Council was asking, and why they should be allowed to listen and ask questions of their own. Some peered in through the front windows of the inn, and a few even questioned Hu and Tad, though it was far from clear what they were supposed to know. The two stolid stablemen just grunted in reply and went on methodically removing the team's harness. One by one they led Fain's horses away and, when the last was gone, did not return.

Rand ignored the crowd. He took a seat on the edge of the old stone foundation, gathered his cloak around him, and stared at the inn door. Ghealdan. Tar Valon. The very names were strange and exciting. They were places he knew only from peddlers' news, and tales told by merchants' guards. Aes Sedai and wars and false Dragons: those were the stuff of stories told late at night in front of the fireplace, with one candle making strange shapes on the wall and the wind howling against the shutters. On the whole, he believed he would rather have blizzards and wolves. Still, it must be different out there, beyond the Two Rivers, like living in the middle of a gleeman's tale. An adventure. One long adventure. A whole lifetime of it.

Slowly the villagers dispersed, still muttering and shaking their heads. Wit Congar paused to stare into the now-abandoned wagon as though he might find another peddler hidden inside. Finally only a few of the younger folk were left. Mat and Perrin drifted over to where Rand sat.

"I don't see how the gleeman could beat this," Mat said excitedly. "I wonder if we might get to see this false Dragon?"

Perrin shook his shaggy head. "I don't want to see him. Somewhere else, maybe, but not in the Two Rivers. Not if it means war."

"Not if it means Aes Sedai here, either," Rand added. "Or have you forgotten who caused the Breaking? The Dragon may have started it, but it was Aes Sedai who actually broke the world."

"I heard a story once," Mat said slowly, "from a wool-buyer's guard. He said the Dragon would be reborn in mankind's greatest hour of need, and save us all."

"Well, he was a fool if he believed that," Perrin said firmly. "And you were a fool to listen." He did not sound angry; he was slow to anger. But he sometimes got exasperated with Mat's quicksilver fancies, and there was a touch of that in his voice. "I suppose he claimed we'd all live in a new Age of Legends afterwards, too."

"I didn't say I believed it," Mat protested. "I just heard it. Nynaeve did, too, and I thought she was going to skin me and the guard both. He said—the guard did—that a lot of people do believe, only they're afraid to say so, afraid of the Aes Sedai or the Children of the Light. He wouldn't say any more after Nynaeve lit into us. She told the merchant, and he said it was the guard's last trip with him."

"A good thing, too," Perrin said. "The Dragon going to save us? Sounds like Coplin talk to me."

"What kind of need would be great enough that we'd want the Dragon to save us from it?" Rand mused. "As well ask for help from the Dark One."

"He didn't say," Mat replied uncomfortably. "And he didn't mention any new Age of Legends. He said the world would be torn apart by the Dragon's coming."

"That would surely save us," Perrin said dryly. "Another Breaking."

"Burn me!" Mat growled. "I'm only telling you what the guard said."

Perrin shook his head. "I just hope the Aes Sedai and this Dragon, false or not, stay where they are. Maybe that way the Two Rivers will be spared."

"You think they're really Darkfriends?" Mat was frowning thoughtfully.

"Who?" Rand asked.

"Aes Sedai."

Rand glanced at Perrin, who shrugged. "The stories," he began slowly, but Mat cut him off.

"Not all the stories say they serve the Dark One, Rand."

"Light, Mat," Rand said, "they caused the Breaking. What more do you want?"

"I suppose." Mat sighed, but the next moment he was grinning again. "Old Bili Congar says they don't exist. Aes Sedai. Darkfriends. Says they're just stories. He says he doesn't believe in the Dark One, either."

Perrin snorted. "Coplin talk from a Congar. What else can you expect?"

"Old Bili named the Dark One. I'll bet you didn't know that."

"Light!" Rand breathed.

Mat's grin broadened. "It was last spring, just before the cutworm got into his fields and nobody else's. Right before everybody in his house came down with yelloweye fever. I heard him do it. He still says he doesn't believe, but whenever I ask him to name the Dark One now, he throws something at me."

"You are just stupid enough to do that, aren't you, Matrim

Cauthon?" Nynaeve al'Meara stepped into their huddle, the dark braid pulled over her shoulder almost bristling with anger. Rand scrambled to his feet. Slender and barely taller than Mat's shoulder, at the moment the Wisdom seemed taller than any of them, and it did not matter that she was young and pretty. "I suspected something of the sort about Bili Congar at the time, but I thought you at least had more sense than to try taunting him into such a thing. You may be old enough to be married, Matrim Cauthon, but in truth you shouldn't be off your mother's apron strings. The next thing, you'll be naming the Dark One yourself."

"No, Wisdom," Mat protested, looking as if he would rather be anywhere else than there. "It was old Bil—I mean, Master Congar, not me! Blood and ashes, I—"

"Watch your tongue, Matrim!"

Rand stood up straighter, though her glare was not directed at him. Perrin looked equally abashed. Later one or another of them would almost certainly complain about being scolded by a woman not all that much older than themselves—someone always did after one of Nynaeve's scoldings, if never in her hearing—but the gap in ages always seemed more than wide enough when face-to-face with her. Especially if she was angry. The stick in her hand was thick at one end and a slender switch at the other, and she was liable to give a flail to anybody she thought was acting the fool—head or hands or legs—no matter their age or position.

The Wisdom so held his attention that at first Rand failed to see she was not alone. When he realized his mistake, he began to think about leaving no matter what Nynaeve would say or do later.

Egwene stood a few paces behind the Wisdom, watching intently. Of a height with Nynaeve, and with the same dark coloring, she could at that moment have been a reflection of Nynaeve's mood, arms crossed beneath her breasts, mouth tight with disapproval. The hood of her soft gray cloak shaded her face, and her big brown eyes held no laughter now.

If there was any fairness, he thought that being two years older than her should give him some advantage, but that was not the way of it. At the best of times he was never very nimble with his tongue when talking to any of the village girls, not like Perrin, but whenever Egwene gave him that intent look, with her eyes as wide as they would go, as if every last ounce of her attention was on him, he just could not seem to make the words go where he wanted. Perhaps he could get away as soon as Nynaeve finished. But he knew he would not, even if he did not understand why.

"If you are done staring like a moonstruck lamb, Rand al'Thor," Nynaeve said, "perhaps you can tell me why you were talking about something even you three great bullcalves ought to have sense enough to keep out of your mouths."

Rand gave a start and pulled his eyes away from Egwene; she had grown a disconcerting smile when the Wisdom began speaking. Nynaeve's voice was tart, but she had the beginnings of a knowing smile on her face, too—until Mat laughed aloud. The Wisdom's smile vanished, and the look she gave Mat cut his laughter off in a strangled croak.

"Well, Rand?" Nynaeve said.

Out of the corner of his eye he saw Egwene still smiling. *What does she think is so funny?* "It was natural enough to talk of it, Wisdom," he said hurriedly. "The peddler—Padan Fain . . . ah . . . Master Fain—brought news of a false Dragon in Ghealdan, and a war, and Aes Sedai. The Council thought it was important enough to talk to him. What else would we be talking about?"

Nynaeve shook her head. "So that's why the peddler's wagon stands abandoned. I heard people rushing to meet it, but I couldn't leave Mistress Ayellin till her fever broke. The Council is questioning the peddler about what's happening in Ghealdan, are they? If I know them, they're asking all the wrong questions and none of the right ones. It will take the Women's Circle to find out anything useful." Settling her cloak firmly on her shoulders she disappeared into the inn.

Egwene did not follow the Wisdom. As the inn door closed behind Nynaeve, the younger woman came to stand in front of Rand. The frowns were gone from her face, but her unblinking stare made him uneasy. He looked to his friends, but they moved away, grinning broadly as they abandoned him.

"You shouldn't let Mat get you mixed up in his foolishness, Rand," Egwene said, as solemn as a Wisdom herself, then abruptly she giggled. "I haven't seen you look like that since Cenn Buie caught you and Mat up in his apple trees when you were ten."

He shifted his feet and glanced at his friends. They stood not far away, Mat gesturing excitedly as he talked.

"Will you dance with me tomorrow?" That was not what he had meant to say. He did want to dance with her, but at the same time he wanted nothing so little as the uncomfortable way he was sure to feel while he was with her. The way he felt right then.

The corners of her mouth quirked up in a small smile. "In the afternoon," she said. "I will be busy in the morning."

From the others came Perrin's exclamation. "A gleeman!"

Egwene turned toward them, but Rand put a hand on her arm. "Busy? How?"

Despite the chill she pushed back the hood of her cloak and with apparent casualness pulled her hair forward over her shoulder. The last time he had seen her, her hair had hung in dark waves below her shoulders, with only a red ribbon keeping it back from her face; now it was worked into a long braid.

He stared at that braid as if it were a viper, then stole a glance at the Spring Pole, standing alone on the Green now, ready for tomorrow. In the morning unmarried women of marriageable age would dance the Pole. He swallowed hard. Somehow, it had never occurred to him that she would reach marriageable age at the same time that he did.

"Just because someone is old enough to marry," he muttered, "doesn't mean they should. Not right away."

"Of course not. Or ever, for that matter."

Rand blinked. "Ever?"

"A Wisdom almost never marries. Nynaeve has been teaching me, you know. She says I have a talent, that I can learn to listen to the wind. Nynaeve says not all Wisdoms can, even if they say they do."

"Wisdom!" he hooted. He failed to notice the dangerous glint in her eye. "Nynaeve will be Wisdom here for another fifty years at least. Probably more. Are you going to spend the rest of your life as her apprentice?"

"There are other villages," she replied heatedly. "Nynaeve says the villages north of the Taren always choose a Wisdom from away. They think it stops her from having favorites among the village folk."

His amusement melted as fast as it had come. "Outside the Two Rivers? I'd never see you again."

"And you wouldn't like that? You have not given any sign lately that you'd care one way or another."

"No one ever leaves the Two Rivers," he went on. "Maybe somebody from Taren Ferry, but they're all strange anyway. Hardly like Two Rivers folk at all."

Egwene gave an exasperated sigh. "Well, maybe I'm strange, too. Maybe I want to see some of the places I hear about in the stories. Have you ever thought of that?"

"Of course I have. I daydream sometimes, but I know the difference between daydreams and what's real."

"And I do not?" she said furiously, and promptly turned her back on him.

"That wasn't what I meant. I was talking about me. Egwene?"

She jerked her cloak around her, a wall to shut him off, and stiffly walked a few paces away. He rubbed his head in frustration. How to explain? This was not the first time she had squeezed meanings from his words that he never knew were in them. In her present mood, a misstep would only make matters worse, and he was fairly sure that nearly anything he said would be a misstep.

Mat and Perrin came back then. Egwene ignored their coming. They looked at her hesitantly, then crowded close to Rand.

"Moiraine gave Perrin a coin, too," Mat said. "Just like ours." He paused before adding, "And he saw the rider."

"Where?" Rand demanded. "When? Did anybody else see him? Did you tell anyone?"

Perrin raised broad hands in a slowing gesture. "One question at a time. I saw him on the edge of the village, watching the smithy, just at twilight yesterday. Gave me the shivers, he did. I told Master Luhhan, only nobody was there when he looked. He said I was seeing shadows. But he carried his biggest hammer around with him while we were banking the forge-fire and putting the tools up. He's never done that before."

"So he believed you," Rand said, but Perrin shrugged.

"I don't know. I asked him why he was carrying the hammer if all I saw was shadows, and he said something about wolves getting bold enough to come into the village. Maybe he thought that's what I saw, but he ought to know I can tell the difference between a wolf and a man on horseback, even at dusk. I know what I saw, and nobody is going to make me believe different."

"I believe you," Rand said. "Remember, I saw him, too." Perrin gave a satisfied grunt, as if he had not been sure of that.

"What *are* you talking about?" Egwene demanded suddenly.

Rand suddenly wished he had spoken more quietly. He would have if he had realized she was listening. Mat and Perrin, grinning like fools, fell all over themselves telling her of their encounters with the black-cloaked rider, but Rand kept silent. He was sure he knew what she would say when they were done.

"Nynaeve was right," Egwene announced to the sky when the two youths fell silent. "None of you is ready to be off leading strings. People do ride horses, you know. That doesn't make them monsters out of a gleeman's tale." Rand nodded to himself; it was just as he had thought. She rounded on him. "And you've been spreading these tales. Sometimes you have no sense, Rand al'Thor. The winter has been frightening enough without you going about scaring the children."

Rand gave a sour grimace. "I haven't spread anything, Egwene. But I saw what I saw, and it was no farmer out looking for a strayed cow."

Egwene drew a deep breath and opened her mouth, but whatever she had been going to say vanished as the door of the inn opened and a man with shaggy white hair came hurrying out as if pursued.

CHAPTER
4

The Gleeman

The door of the inn banged shut behind the white-haired man, and he spun around to glare at it. Lean, he would have been tall if not for a stoop to his shoulders, but he moved in a spry fashion that belied his apparent age. His cloak seemed a mass of patches, in odd shapes and sizes, fluttering with every breath of air, patches in a hundred colors. It was really quite thick, Rand saw, despite what Master al'Vere had said, with the patches merely sewn on like decorations.

"The gleeman!" Egwene whispered excitedly.

The white-haired man whirled, cloak flaring. His long coat had odd, baggy sleeves and big pockets. Thick mustaches, as snowy as the hair on his head, quivered around his mouth, and his face was gnarled like a tree that had seen hard times. He gestured imperiously at Rand and the others with a long-stemmed pipe, ornately carved, that trailed a wisp of smoke. Blue eyes peered out from under bushy white brows, drilling into whatever he looked at.

Rand stared at the man's eyes almost as much as at the rest of him. Everybody in the Two Rivers had dark eyes, and so did most of the merchants, and their guards, and everyone else he had ever seen. The Congars and the Coplins had made fun of him for his gray eyes, until the day he finally punched Ewal Coplin in the nose; the Wisdom had surely gotten onto him for that. He wondered if there was a place where nobody had dark eyes. *Maybe Lan comes from there, too.*

"What sort of place is this?" the gleeman demanded in a deep voice that sounded in some way larger than that of an

ordinary man. Even in the open air it seemed to fill a great
room and resonate from the walls. "The yokels in that village on the hill tell me I can get here before dark, neglecting to say that that was only if I left well before noon. When
I finally do arrive, chilled to the bone and ready for a warm
bed, your innkeeper grumbles about the hour as if I were
a wandering swineherd and your Village Council hadn't
begged me to display my art at this festival of yours. And
he never even told me he was the Mayor." He slowed for a
breath, taking them all in with a glare, but he was off again
on the instant. "When I came downstairs to smoke my pipe
before the fire and have a mug of ale, every man in the common room stares at me as if I were his least favorite brother-
in-law seeking to borrow money. One old grandfather starts
ranting at me about the kind of stories I should or should
not tell, then a girl-child shouts at me to get out, and threatens me with a great club when I don't move quickly enough
for her. Who ever heard of treating a gleeman so?"

Egwene's face was a study, her goggle-eyed amaze at a
gleeman in the flesh marred by a desire to defend Nynaeve.

"Your pardon, Master Gleeman," Rand said. He knew he
was grinning foolishly, himself. "That was our Wisdom,
and—"

"That pretty little slip of a girl?" the gleeman exclaimed.
"A village Wisdom? Why, at her age she should better be
flirting with the young men than foretelling the weather and
curing the sick."

Rand shifted uncomfortably. He hoped Nynaeve never
overheard the man's opinion. At least, not until he had done
with his performing. Perrin winced at the gleeman's words,
and Mat whistled soundlessly, as if both had had the same
thought as he had.

"The men were the Village Council," Rand went on. "I'm
sure they intended no discourtesy. You see, we just learned
there's a war in Ghealdan, and a man claiming to be the
Dragon Reborn. A false Dragon. Aes Sedai are riding there
from Tar Valon. The Council is trying to decide if we might
be in danger here."

"Old news, even in Baerlon," the gleeman said dismissively, "and that is the last place in the world to hear
anything." He paused, looking around the village, and dryly
added, "Almost the last place." Then his eyes fell on the

wagon in front of the inn, standing alone now, with its shafts
on the ground. "So. I thought I recognized Padan Fain in
there." His voice was still deep, but the resonance had gone,
replaced by scorn. "Fain was always one to carry bad news
quickly, and the worse, the faster. There's more raven in
him than man."

"Master Fain has come often to Emond's Field, Master
Gleeman," Egwene said, a hint of disapproval finally breaking through her delight. "He is always full of laughter, and
he brings much more good news than bad."

The gleeman eyed her for a moment, then smiled broadly.
"Now you're a lovely lass. You should have rose buds in
your hair. Unfortunately, I cannot pull roses from the air,
not this year, but how would you like to stand beside me
tomorrow for a part of my performance? Hand me my flute
when I want it, and certain other apparatus. I always choose
the prettiest girl I can find as my assistant."

Perrin snickered, and Mat, who had been snickering,
laughed out loud. Rand blinked in surprise; Egwene was
glaring at him, and he had not even smiled. She straightened around and spoke in a too-calm voice.

"Thank you, Master Gleeman. I would be happy to assist
you."

"Thom Merrilin," the gleeman said. They stared. "My
name is Thom Merrilin, not Master Gleeman." He hitched
the multihued cloak up on his shoulders, and abruptly his
voice once more seemed to reverberate in a great hall.
"Once a Courtbard, I am now indeed risen to the exalted
rank of Master Gleeman, yet my name is plain Thom Merrilin, and gleeman is the simple title in which I glory." And
he swept a bow so elaborate with flourishes of his cloak that
Mat clapped and Egwene murmured appreciatively.

"Master . . . ah . . . Master Merrilin," Mat said, unsure exactly what form of address to take out of what Thom Merrilin
had said, "what *is* happening in Ghealdan? Do you know
anything about this false Dragon? Or the Aes Sedai?"

"Do I look like a peddler, boy?" the gleeman grumbled,
tapping out his pipe on the heel of his palm. He made the pipe
disappear somewhere inside his cloak, or his coat; Rand
was not sure where it had gone or how. "I am a gleeman,
not a newsmonger. And I make a point of never knowing
anything about Aes Sedai. Much safer that way."

"But the war," Mat began eagerly, only to be cut off by Master Merrilin.

"In wars, boy, fools kill other fools for foolish causes. That's enough for anyone to know. I am here for my art." Suddenly he thrust a finger at Rand. "You, lad. You're a tall one. Not with your full growth on you yet, but I doubt there's another man in the district with your height. Not many in the village with eyes that color, either, I'll wager. The point is, you're an axe handle across the shoulders and as tall as an Aielman. What's your name, lad?"

Rand gave it hesitantly, not sure whether or not the man was making fun of him, but the gleeman had already turned his attention to Perrin. "And you have almost the size of an Ogier. Close enough. How are you called?"

"Not unless I stand on my own shoulders." Perrin laughed. "I'm afraid Rand and I are just ordinary folk, Master Merrilin, not made-up creatures from your stories. I'm Perrin Aybara."

Thom Merrilin tugged at one of his mustaches. "Well, now. Made-up creatures from my stories. Is that what they are? You lads are widely traveled, then, it seems."

Rand kept his mouth shut, certain they were the butt of a joke, now, but Perrin spoke up.

"We've all of us been as far as Watch Hill, and Deven Ride. Not many around here have gone as far." He was not boasting; Perrin seldom did. He was just telling the truth.

"We've all seen the Mire, too," Mat added, and he did sound boastful. "That's the swamp at the far end of the Water-wood. Nobody at all goes there—it's full of quicksands and bogs—except us. And nobody goes to the Mountains of Mist, either, but we did, once. To the foot of them, anyway."

"As far as that?" the gleeman murmured, brushing at his mustaches now continually. Rand thought he was hiding a smile, and he saw that Perrin was frowning.

"It's bad luck to enter the mountains," Mat said, as if he had to defend himself for not going further. "Everybody knows that."

"That's just foolishness, Matrim Cauthon," Egwene cut in angrily. "Nynaeve says. . . ." She broke off, her cheeks turning pink, and the look she gave Thom Merrilin was not as friendly as it had been. "It is not right to make. . . . It isn't. . . ." Her face went redder, and she fell silent. Mat blinked, as if he was just getting a suspicion of what had been going on.

"You're right, child," the gleeman said contritely. "I apologize humbly. I am here to entertain. Aah, my tongue has always gotten me into trouble."

"Maybe we haven't traveled as far as you," Perrin said flatly, "but what does how tall Rand is have to do with anything?"

"Just this, lad. A little later I will let you try to pick me up, but you won't be able to lift my feet from the ground. Not you, nor your tall friend there—Rand, is it?—nor any other man. Now what do you think of that?"

Perrin snorted a laugh. "I think I can lift you right now." But when he stepped forward Thom Merrilin motioned him back.

"Later, lad, later. When there are more folk to watch. An artist needs an audience."

A score of folk had gathered on the Green since the gleeman appeared from the inn, young men and women down to children who peeked, wide-eyed and silent, from behind the older onlookers. All looked as if they were waiting for miraculous things from the gleeman. The white-haired man looked them over—he appeared to be counting them—then gave a slight shake of his head and sighed.

"I suppose I had better give you a small sample. So you can run tell the others. Eh? Just a taste of what you'll see tomorrow at your festival."

He took a step back, and suddenly leaped into the air, twisting and somersaulting to land facing them atop the old stone foundation. More than that, three balls—red, white, and black—began dancing between his hands even as he landed.

A soft sound came from the watchers, half astonishment, half satisfaction. Even Rand forgot his irritation. He flashed Egwene a grin and got a delighted one in return, then both turned to stare unabashedly at the gleeman.

"You want stories?" Thom Merrilin declaimed. "I have stories, and I will give them to you. I will make them come alive before your eyes." A blue ball joined the others from somewhere, then a green one, and a yellow. "Tales of great wars and great heroes, for the men and boys. For the women and girls, the entire *Aptarigine Cycle*. Tales of Artur Paendrag

Tanreall, Artur Hawkwing, Artur the High King, who once ruled all the lands from the Aiel Waste to the Aryth Ocean, and even beyond. Wondrous stories of strange people and strange lands, of the Green Man, of Warders and Trollocs, of Ogier and Aiel. *The Thousand Tales of Anla, the Wise Counselor.* 'Jaem the Giant-Slayer.' *How Susa Tamed Jain Farstrider.* 'Mara and the Three Foolish Kings.'"

"Tell us about Lenn," Egwene called. "How he flew to the moon in the belly of an eagle made of fire. Tell about his daughter Salya walking among the stars."

Rand looked at her out of the corner of his eye, but she seemed intent on the gleeman. She had never liked stories about adventures and long journeys. Her favorites were always the funny ones, or stories about women outwitting people who were supposed to be smarter than everyone else. He was sure she had asked for tales about Lenn and Salya to put a burr under his shirt. Surely she could see the world outside was no place for Two Rivers folk. Listening to tales of adventures, even dreaming about them, was one thing; having them take place around you would be something else again.

"Old stories, those," Thom Merrilin said, and abruptly he was juggling three colored balls with each hand. "Stories from the Age before the Age of Legends, some say. Perhaps even older. But I have *all* stories, mind you now, of Ages that were and will be. Ages when men ruled the heavens and the stars, and Ages when man roamed as brother to the animals. Ages of wonder, and Ages of horror. Ages ended by fire raining from the skies, and Ages doomed by snow and ice covering land and sea. I have all stories, and I will tell all stories. Tales of Mosk the Giant, with his Lance of fire that could reach around the world, and his wars with Elsbet, the Queen of All. Tales of Materese the Healer, Mother of the Wondrous Ind."

The balls now danced between Thom's hands in two intertwining circles. His voice was almost a chant, and he turned slowly as he spoke, as if surveying the onlookers to gauge his effect. "I will tell you of the end of the Age of Legends, of the Dragon, and his attempt to free the Dark One into the world of men. I will tell of the Time of Madness, when Aes Sedai shattered the world; of the Trolloc Wars, when men battled Trollocs for rule of the earth; of the War of the Hundred Years, when men battled men and the nations of our day were wrought. I will tell the adventures of men and women, rich and poor, great and small, proud and humble. *The Siege of the Pillars of the Sky.* 'How Goodwife Karil Cured Her Husband of Snoring.' *King Darith and the Fall of the House of—*"

Abruptly the flow of words and the juggling alike stopped. Thom simply snatched the balls from the air and stopped talking. Unnoticed by Rand, Moiraine had joined the listeners. Lan was at her shoulder, though he had to look twice to see the man. For a moment Thom looked at Moiraine sideways, his face and body still except for making the balls disappear into his capacious coat sleeves. Then he bowed to her, holding his cloak wide. "Your pardon, but you are surely not from this district?"

"Lady!" Ewin hissed fiercely. "The Lady Moiraine."

Thom blinked, then bowed again, more deeply. "Your pardon again . . . ah, Lady. I meant no disrespect."

Moiraine made a small waving-away gesture. "None was perceived, Master Bard. And my name is simply Moiraine. I am indeed a stranger here, a traveler like yourself, far from home and alone. The world can be a dangerous place when one is a stranger."

"The Lady Moiraine collects stories," Ewin put in. "Stories about things that happened in the Two Rivers. Though I don't know what ever happened here to make a story of."

"I trust you will like my stories, as well . . . Moiraine." Thom watched her with obvious wariness. He looked not best pleased to find her there. Suddenly Rand wondered what sort of entertainment a lady like her might be offered in a city like Baerlon, or Caemlyn. Surely it could not be anything better than a gleeman.

"That is a matter of taste, Master Bard," Moiraine replied. "Some stories I like, and some I do not."

Thom's bow was his deepest yet, bending his long body parallel to the ground. "I assure you, none of my stories will displease. All will please and entertain. And you do me too much honor. I am a simple gleeman; that and nothing more."

Moiraine answered his bow with a gracious nod. For an instant she seemed even more the lady Ewin had named her, accepting an offering from one of her subjects. Then she turned away, and Lan followed, a wolf heeling a gliding swan. Thom stared after them, bushy brows drawn down, stroking his long mustaches with a knuckle, until they were halfway up the Green. *He's not pleased at all,* Rand thought.

"Are you going to juggle some more, now?" Ewin demanded.

"Eat fire," Mat shouted. "I want to see you eat fire."

"The harp!" a voice cried from the crowd. "Play the harp!" Someone else called for the flute.

At that moment the door of the inn opened and the Village Council trundled out, Nynaeve in their midst. Padan Fain was not with them, Rand saw; apparently the peddler had decided to remain in the warm common room with his mulled wine.

Muttering about "a strong brandy," Thom Merrilin abruptly jumped down from the old foundation. He ignored the cries of those who had been watching him, pressing inside past the Councilors before they were well out of the doorway.

"Is he supposed to be a gleeman or a king?" Cenn Buie asked in annoyed tones. "A waste of good money, if you ask me."

Bran al'Vere half turned after the gleeman, then shook his head. "That man may be more trouble than he's worth."

Nynaeve, busy gathering her cloak around her, sniffed loudly. "Worry about the gleeman if you want, Brandelwyn al'Vere. At least he is in Emond's Field, which is more than you can say for this false Dragon. But as long as you are worrying, there are others here who *should* excite your worry."

"If you please, Wisdom," Bran said stiffly, "kindly leave who should worry me to my deciding. Mistress Moiraine and Master Lan are guests in my inn, and decent, respectable folk, so I say. Neither of *them* has called me a fool in front of the whole Council. Neither of *them* has told the Council it hasn't a full set of wits among them."

"It seems my estimate was too high by half," Nynaeve retorted. She strode away without a backward glance, leaving Bran's jaw working as he searched for a reply.

Egwene looked at Rand as if she were going to speak, then darted after the Wisdom instead. Rand knew there must be some way to stop her from leaving the Two Rivers, but the only way he could think of was not one he was prepared to take, even if she was willing. And she had as much as said she was not willing at all, which made him feel even worse.

"That young woman wants a husband," Cenn Buie growled, bouncing on his toes. His face was purple, and getting darker. "She lacks proper respect. We're the Village Council, not boys raking her yard, and—"

The Mayor breathed heavily through his nose, and suddenly rounded on the old thatcher. "Be quiet, Cenn! Stop acting like a black-veiled Aiel!" The skinny man froze on his toes in astonishment. The Mayor never let his temper get the best of him. Bran glared. "Burn me, but we have better things to be about than this foolishness. Or do you intend to prove Nynaeve right?" With that he stumped back into the inn and slammed the door behind him.

The Council members glanced at Cenn, then moved off in their separate directions. All but Haral Luhhan, who accompanied the stony-visaged thatcher, talking quietly. The blacksmith was the only one who could ever get Cenn to see reason.

Rand went to meet his father, and his friends trailed after him.

"I've never seen Master al'Vere so mad," was the first thing Rand said, getting him a disgusted look from Mat.

"The Mayor and the Wisdom seldom agree," Tam said, "and they agreed less than usual today. That's all. It's the same in every village."

"What about the false Dragon?" Mat asked, and Perrin added eager murmurs. "What about the Aes Sedai?"

Tam shook his head slowly. "Master Fain knew little more than he had already told. At least, little of interest to us. Battles won or lost. Cities taken and retaken. All in Ghealdan, thank the Light. It hasn't spread, or had not the last Master Fain knew."

"Battles interest me," Mat said, and Perrin added, "What did he say about them?"

"Battles don't interest me, Matrim," Tam said. "But I'm sure he will be glad to tell you all about them later. What does interest me is that we shouldn't have to worry about them here, as far as the Council can tell. We can see no reason for Aes Sedai to come here on their way south. And as for the return journey, they aren't likely to want to cross the Forest of Shadows and swim the White River."

Rand and the others chuckled at the idea. There were three reasons why no one came into the Two Rivers except from the north, by way of Taren Ferry. The Mountains of Mist, in the west, were the first, of course, and the Mire blocked the east just as effectively. To the south was the White River, which got its name from the way rocks and boulders churned its swift waters to froth. And beyond the White lay the Forest of Shadows. Few Two Rivers folk had ever crossed the White, and fewer still returned if they did. It was generally agreed, though, that the Forest of Shadows stretched south for a hundred miles or more without a road or a village, but with plenty of wolves and bears.

"So that's an end to it for us," Mat said. He sounded at least a little disappointed.

"Not quite," Tam said. "Day after tomorrow we will send men to Deven Ride and Watch Hill, and Taren Ferry, too, to arrange for a watch to be kept. Riders along the White and the Taren, both, and patrols between. It should be done today, but only the Mayor agrees with me. The rest can't see asking anyone to spend Bel Tine off riding across the Two Rivers."

"But I thought you said we didn't have to worry," Perrin said, and Tam shook his head.

"I said should not, boy, not did not. I've seen men die because they were sure that what should not happen, would not. Besides, the fighting will stir up all sorts of people. Most will just be trying to find safety, but others will be looking for a way to profit from the confusion. We'll offer any of the first a helping hand, but we must be ready to send the second type on their way."

Abruptly Mat spoke up. "Can we be part of it? I want to, anyway. You know I can ride as well as anyone in the village."

"You want a few weeks of cold, boredom, and sleeping rough?" Tam chuckled. "Likely that's all there will be to it. I hope that's all. We're well out of the way even for refugees. But you can speak to Master al'Vere if your mind is made up. Rand, it's time for us to be getting back to the farm."

Rand blinked in surprise. "I thought we were staying for Winternight."

"Things need seeing to at the farm, and I need you with me."

"Even so, we don't have to leave for hours yet. And I want to volunteer for the patrols, too."

"We are going now," his father replied in a tone that brooked no argument. In a softer voice he added, "We'll be back tomorrow in plenty of time for you to speak to the Mayor. And plenty of time for Festival, too. Five minutes, now, then meet me in the stable."

"Are you going to join Rand and me on the watch?" Mat asked Perrin as Tam left. "I'll bet there's nothing like this ever happened in the Two Rivers before. Why, if we get up to the Taren, we might even see soldiers, or who knows what. Even Tinkers."

"I expect I will," Perrin said slowly, "if Master Luhhan doesn't need me, that is."

"The war is in Ghealdan," Rand snapped. With an effort he lowered his voice. "The war is in Ghealdan, and the Aes Sedai are the Light knows where, but none of it is here. The man in the black cloak is, or have you forgotten him already?" The others exchanged embarrassed looks.

"Sorry, Rand," Mat muttered. "But a chance to do something besides milk my da's cows doesn't come along very often." He straightened under their startled stares. "Well, I do milk them, and every day, too."

"The black rider," Rand reminded them. "What if he hurts somebody?"

"Maybe he's a refugee from the war," Perrin said doubtfully.

"Whatever he is," Mat said, "the watch will find him."

"Maybe," Rand said, "but he seems to disappear when he wants to. It might be better if they knew to look for him."

"We'll tell Master al'Vere when we volunteer for the patrols," Mat said, "he'll tell the Council, and they'll tell the watch."

"The Council!" Perrin said incredulously. "We'd be lucky if the Mayor didn't laugh out loud. Master Luhhan and Rand's father already think the two of us are jumping at shadows."

Rand sighed. "If we're going to do it, we might as well do it now. He won't laugh any louder today than he will tomorrow."

"Maybe," Perrin said with a sidelong glance at Mat, "we

should try finding some others who've seen him. We'll see just about everybody in the village tonight." Mat's scowl deepened, but he still did not say anything. All of them understood that Perrin meant they should find witnesses who were more reliable than Mat. "He won't laugh any louder tomorrow," Perrin added when Rand hesitated. "And I'd just as soon have somebody else with us when we go to him. Half the village would suit me fine."

Rand nodded slowly. He could already hear Master al'Vere laughing. More witnesses certainly could not hurt. And if three of them had seen the fellow, others had to have, too. They must have. "Tomorrow, then. You two find whoever you can tonight, and tomorrow we go to the Mayor. After that. . . ." They looked at him silently, no one raising the question of what happened if they could not find anyone else who had seen the black-cloaked man. The question was clear in their eyes, though, and he had no answer. He sighed heavily. "I'd better go, now. My father will be wondering if I fell into a hole."

Followed by their goodbyes, he trotted around to the stableyard where the high-wheeled cart stood propped on its shafts.

The stable was a long, narrow building, topped by a high-peaked, thatched roof. Stalls, their floors covered with straw, filled both sides of the dim interior, lit only by the open double doors at either end. The peddler's team munched their oats in eight stalls, and Master al'Vere's massive Dhurrans, the team he hired out when farmers had hauling beyond the abilities of their own horses, filled six more, but only three others were occupied. Rand thought he could match up horse and rider with no trouble. The tall, deep-chested black stallion that swung up his head fiercely had to be Lan's. The sleek white mare with an arched neck, her quick steps as graceful as a girl dancing, even in the stall, could only belong to Moiraine. And the third unfamiliar horse, a rangy, slab-sided gelding of a dusty brown, fit Thom Merrilin perfectly.

Tam stood in the rear of the stable, holding Bela by a lead rope and speaking quietly to Hu and Tad. Before Rand had taken two steps into the stable his father nodded to the stablemen and brought Bela out, wordlessly gathering up Rand as he went.

They harnessed the shaggy mare in silence. Tam appeared

so deep in thought that Rand held his tongue. He did not really look forward to trying to convince his father about the black-cloaked rider, much less the Mayor. Tomorrow would have to be time enough, when Mat and the rest had found others who had seen the man. If they found others.

As the cart lurched into motion, Rand took his bow and quiver from the back, awkwardly belting the quiver at his waist as he half trotted alongside. When they reached the last row of houses in the village, he nocked an arrow, carrying it half raised and partly drawn. There was nothing to see except mostly leafless trees, but his shoulders tightened. The black rider could be on them before either of them knew it. There might not be time to draw the bow if he was not already halfway to it.

He knew he could not keep up the tension on the bowstring for long. He had made the bow himself, and Tam was one of the few others in the district who could even draw it all the way to the cheek. He cast around for something to take his mind off thinking about the dark rider. Surrounded by the forest, their cloaks flapping in the wind, it was not easy.

"Father," he said finally, "I don't understand why the Council had to question Padan Fain." With an effort he took his eyes off the woods and looked across Bela at Tam. "It seems to me, the decision you reached could have been made right on the spot. The Mayor frightened everybody half out of their wits, talking about Aes Sedai and the false Dragon here in the Two Rivers."

"People are funny, Rand. The best of them are. Take Haral Luhhan. Master Luhhan is a strong man, and a brave one, but he can't bear to see butchering done. Turns pale as a sheet."

"What does that have to do with anything? Everybody knows Master Luhhan can't stand the sight of blood, and nobody but the Coplins and the Congars thinks anything of it."

"Just this, lad. People don't always think or behave the way you might believe they would. Those folk back there . . . let the hail beat their crops into the mud, and the wind take off every roof in the district, and the wolves kill half their livestock, and they'll roll up their sleeves and start from scratch. They'll grumble, but they won't waste any time with it. But you give them just the thought of Aes Sedai and a false Dragon in Ghealdan, and soon enough they'll start thinking that Ghealdan is not that far the other side of the Forest of Shadows, and a straight line from Tar Valon to Ghealdan wouldn't pass that much to the east of us. As if the Aes Sedai wouldn't take the road through Caemlyn and Lugard instead of traveling cross-country! By tomorrow morning half the village would have been sure the entire war was about to descend on us. It would take weeks to undo. A fine Bel Tine that would make. So Bran gave them the idea before they could get it for themselves.

"They've seen the Council take the problem under consideration, and by now they'll be hearing what we decided. They chose us for the Village Council because they trust we can reason things out in the best way for everybody. They trust our opinions. Even Cenn's, which doesn't say much for the rest of us, I suppose. At any rate, they will hear there isn't anything to worry about, and they'll believe it. It is not that they couldn't reach the same conclusion, or would not, eventually, but this way we won't have Festival ruined, and nobody has to spend weeks worrying about something that isn't likely to happen. If it does, against all odds . . . well, the patrols will give us enough warning to do what we can. I truly don't think it will come to that, though."

Rand puffed out his cheeks. Apparently, being on the Council was more complicated than he had believed. The cart rumbled on along the Quarry Road.

"Did anyone besides Perrin see this strange rider?" Tam asked.

"Mat did, but—" Rand blinked, then stared across Bela's back at his father. "You believe me? I have to go back. I have to tell them." Tam's shout halted him as he turned to run back to the village.

"Hold, lad, hold! Do you think I waited this long to speak for no reason?"

Reluctantly Rand kept on beside the cart, still creaking along behind patient Bela. "What made you change your mind? Why can't I tell the others?"

"They'll know soon enough. At least, Perrin will. Mat, I'm not sure of. Word must be gotten to the farms as best it can, but in another hour there won't be anyone in Emond's Field above sixteen, those who can be responsible about it, at least, who doesn't know a stranger is skulking around and likely not the sort you would invite to Festival. The winter has been bad enough without this to scare the young ones."

"Festival?" Rand said. "If you had seen him you wouldn't want him closer than ten miles. A hundred, maybe."

"Perhaps so," Tam said placidly. "He could be just a refugee from the troubles in Ghealdan, or more likely a thief who thinks the pickings will be easier here than in Baerlon or Taren Ferry. Even so, no one around here has so much they can afford to have it stolen. If the man is trying to escape the war . . . well, that's still no excuse for scaring people. Once the watch is mounted, it should either find him or frighten him off."

"I hope it frightens him off. But why do you believe me now, when you didn't this morning?"

"I had to believe my own eyes then, lad, and I saw nothing." Tam shook his grizzled head. "Only young men see this fellow, it seems. When Haral Luhhan mentioned Perrin jumping at shadows, though, it all came out. Jon Thane's oldest son saw him, too, and so did Samel Crawe's boy, Bandry. Well, when four of you say you've seen a thing—and solid lads, all—we start thinking maybe it's there whether we can see it or not. All except Cenn, of course. Anyway, that's why we're going home. With both of us away, this stranger could be up to any kind of mischief there. If not for Festival, I wouldn't come back tomorrow, either. But we can't make ourselves prisoners in our own homes just because this fellow is lurking about."

"I didn't know about Ban or Lem," Rand said. "The rest of us were going to the Mayor tomorrow, but we were worried he wouldn't believe us, either."

"Gray hairs don't mean our brains have curdled," Tam said dryly. "So you keep a sharp eye. Maybe I'll catch sight of him, too, if he shows up again."

Rand settled down to do just that. He was surprised to realize that his step felt lighter. The knots were gone from his shoulders. He was still scared, but it was not so bad as it had been. Tam and he were just as alone on the Quarry Road as they had been that morning, but in some way he felt as if the entire village were with them. That others knew and believed made all the difference. There was nothing the black-cloaked horseman could do that the people of Emond's Field could not handle together.

CHAPTER
5

Winternight

The sun stood halfway down from its noonday high by the time the cart reached the farmhouse. It was not a big house, not nearly so large as some of the sprawling farmhouses to the east, dwellings that had grown over the years to hold entire families. In the Two Rivers that often included three or four generations under one roof, including aunts, uncles, cousins, and nephews. Tam and Rand were considered out of the ordinary as much for being two men living alone as for farming in the Westwood.

Here most of the rooms were on one floor, a neat rectangle with no wings or additions. Two bedrooms and an attic storeroom fitted up under the steeply sloped thatch. If the whitewash was all but gone from the stout wooden walls after the winter storms, the house was still in a tidy state of repair, the thatch tightly mended and the doors and shutters well-hung and snug-fitting.

House, barn, and stone sheep pen formed the points of a triangle around the farmyard, where a few chickens had ventured out to scratch at the cold ground. An open shearing shed and a stone dipping trough stood next to the sheep pen. Hard by the fields between the farmyard and the trees loomed the tall cone of a tight-walled curing shed. Few farmers in the Two Rivers could make do without both wool and tabac to sell when the merchants came.

When Rand took a look in the stone pen, the heavy-horned herd ram looked back at him, but most of the black-faced flock remained placidly where they lay, or stood with their heads in the feed trough. Their coats were thick and curly, but it was still too cold for shearing.

"I don't think the black-cloaked man came here," Rand called to his father, who was walking slowly around the farmhouse, spear held at the ready, examining the ground intently. "The sheep wouldn't be so settled if that one had been around."

Tam nodded but did not stop. When he had made a complete circuit of the house, he did the same around the barn and the sheep pen, still studying the ground. He even checked the smokehouse and the curing shed. Drawing a bucket of water from the well, he filled a cupped hand, sniffed the water, and gingerly touched it with the tip of his tongue. Abruptly he barked a laugh, then drank it down in a quick gulp.

"I suppose he didn't," he told Rand, wiping his hand on his coat front. "All this about men and horses I can't see or hear just makes me look crossways at everything." He emptied the well water into another bucket and started for the house, the bucket in one hand and his spear in the other. "I'll start some stew for supper. And as long as we're here, we might as well get caught up on a few chores."

Rand grimaced, regretting Winternight in Emond's Field. But Tam was right. Around a farm the work never really got done; as soon as one thing was finished two more always needed doing. He hesitated about it, but kept his bow and quiver close at hand. If the dark rider did appear, he had no intention of facing him with nothing but a hoe.

First was stabling Bela. Once he had unharnessed her and put her into a stall in the barn next to their cow, he set his cloak aside and rubbed the mare down with handfuls of dry straw, then curried her with a pair of brushes. Climbing the narrow ladder to the loft, he pitched down hay for her feed. He fetched a scoopful of oats for her as well, though there was little enough left and might be no more for a long while unless the weather warmed soon. The cow had been milked that morning before first light, giving a quarter of her usual yield; she seemed to be drying up as the winter hung on.

Enough feed had been left to see the sheep for two days—they should have been in the pasture by now, but there was none worth calling it so—but he topped off their water. Whatever eggs had been laid needed to be gathered, too. There were only three. The hens seemed to be getting cleverer at hiding them.

He was taking a hoe to the vegetable garden behind the house when Tam came out and settled on a bench in front of the barn to mend harness, propping his spear beside him. It made Rand feel better about the bow lying on his cloak a pace from where he stood.

Few weeds had pushed above ground, but more weeds than anything else. The cabbages were stunted, barely a sprout of the beans or peas showed, and there was not a sign of a beet. Not everything had been planted, of course; only part, in hopes the cold might break in time to make a crop of some kind before the cellar was empty. It did not take long to finish hoeing, which would have suited him just fine in years past, but now he wondered what they would do if nothing came up this year. Not a pleasant thought. And there was still firewood to split.

It seemed to Rand like years since there had *not* been firewood to split. But complaining would not keep the house warm, so he fetched the axe, propped up bow and quiver beside the chopping block, and got to work. Pine for a quick, hot flame, and oak for long burning. Before long he was warm enough to put his coat aside. When the pile of split wood grew big enough, he stacked it against the side of the house, beside other stacks already there. Most reached all the way to the eaves. Usually by this time of year the woodpiles were small and few, but not this year. Chop and stack, chop and stack, he lost himself in the rhythm of the axe and the motions of stacking wood. Tam's hand on his shoulder brought him back to where he was, and for a moment he blinked in surprise.

Gray twilight had come on while he worked, and already it was fading quickly toward night. The full moon stood well above the treetops, shimmering pale and bulging as if about to fall on their heads. The wind had grown colder without his noticing, too, and tattered clouds scudded across the darkling sky.

"Let's wash up, lad, and see about some supper. I've already carried in water for hot baths before sleep."

"Anything hot sounds good to me," Rand said, snatching up his cloak and tossing it round his shoulders. Sweat soaked his shirt, and the wind, forgotten in the heat of swinging the axe, seemed to be trying to freeze it now that he had stopped work. He stifled a yawn, shivering as he gathered the rest of his things. "And sleep, too, for that. I might just sleep right through Festival."

"Would you care to make a small wager about that?" Tam smiled, and Rand had to grin back. He would not miss Bel Tine if he had had no sleep in a week. No one would.

Tam had been extravagant with the candles, and a fire crackled in the big stone fireplace, so that the main room had a warm, cheerful feel to it. A broad oaken table was the main feature of the room other than the fireplace, a table long enough to seat a dozen or more, though there had seldom been so many around it since Rand's mother died. A few cabinets and chests, most of them skillfully made by Tam himself, lined the walls, and high-backed chairs stood around the table. The cushioned chair that Tam called his reading chair sat angled before the flames. Rand preferred to do his reading stretched out on the rug in front of the fire. The shelf of books by the door was not nearly as long as the one at the Winespring Inn, but books were hard to come by. Few peddlers carried more than a handful, and those had to be stretched out among everyone who wanted them.

If the room did not look quite so freshly scrubbed as most farm wives kept their homes—Tam's piperack and *The Travels of Jain Farstrider* sat on the table, while another wood-bound book rested on the cushion of his reading chair; a bit of harness to be mended lay on the bench by the fireplace, and some shirts to be darned made a heap on a chair—if not quite so spotless, it was still clean and neat enough, with a lived-in look that was almost as warming and comforting as the fire. Here, it was possible to forget the chill beyond the walls. There was no false Dragon here. No wars or Aes Sedai. No men in black cloaks. The aroma from the stewpot hanging over the fire permeated the room, and filled Rand with ravenous hunger.

His father stirred the stewpot with a long-handled wooden spoon, then took a taste. "A little while longer."

Rand hurried to wash his face and hands; there was a pitcher and basin on the washstand by the door. A hot bath was what he wanted, to take away the sweat and soak the chill out, but that would come when there had been time to heat the big kettle in the back room.

Tam rooted around in a cabinet and came up with a key as long as his hand. He twisted it in the big iron lock on the door. At Rand's questioning look he said, "Best to be safe. Maybe I'm taking a fancy, or maybe the weather is blacking my mood, but. . . ." He sighed and bounced the key on his palm. "I'll see to the back door," he said, and disappeared toward the back of the house.

Rand could not remember either door ever being locked. No one in the Two Rivers locked doors. There was no need. Until now, at least.

From overhead, from Tam's bedroom, came a scraping, as of something being dragged across the floor. Rand frowned. Unless Tam had suddenly decided to move the furniture around, he could only be pulling out the old chest he kept under his bed. Another thing that had never been done in Rand's memory.

He filled a small kettle with water for tea and hung it from a hook over the fire, then set the table. He had carved the bowls and spoons himself. The front shutters had not yet been closed, and from time to time he peered out, but full night had come and all he could see were moon shadows. The dark rider could be out there easily enough, but he tried not to think about that.

When Tam came back, Rand stared in surprise. A thick belt slanted around Tam's waist, and from the belt hung a sword, with a bronze heron on the black scabbard and another on the long hilt. The only men Rand had ever seen wearing swords were the merchants' guards. And Lan, of course. That his father might own one had never even occurred to him. Except for the herons, the sword looked a good deal like Lan's sword.

"Where did that come from?" he asked. "Did you get it from a peddler? How much did it cost?"

Slowly Tam drew the weapon; firelight played along the gleaming length. It was nothing at all like the plain, rough blades Rand had seen in the hands of merchants' guards. No gems or gold adorned it, but it seemed grand to him, nonetheless. The blade, very slightly curved and sharp on only one edge, bore another heron etched into the steel. Short quillons, worked to look like braid, flanked the hilt. It seemed almost fragile compared with the swords of the merchants' guards; most of those were double-edged, and thick enough to chop down a tree.

"I got it a long time ago," Tam said, "a long way from

here. And I paid entirely too much; two coppers is too much for one of these. Your mother didn't approve, but she was always wiser than I. I was young then, and it seemed worth the price at the time. She always wanted me to get rid of it, and more than once I've thought she was right, that I should just give it away."

Reflected fire made the blade seem aflame. Rand started. He had often daydreamed about owning a sword. "Give it away? How could you give a sword like that away?"

Tam snorted. "Not much use in herding sheep, now is it? Can't plow a field or harvest a crop with it." For a long minute he stared at the sword as if wondering what he was doing with such a thing. At last he let out a heavy sigh. "But if I am not just taken by a black fancy, if our luck runs sour, maybe in the next few days we'll be glad I tucked it in that old chest, instead." He slid the sword smoothly back into its sheath and wiped his hand on his shirt with a grimace. "The stew should be ready. I'll dish it out while you fix the tea."

Rand nodded and got the tea canister, but he wanted to know everything. Why would Tam have bought a sword? He could not imagine. And where had Tam come by it? How far away? No one ever left the Two Rivers; or very few, at least. He had always vaguely supposed his father must have gone outside—his mother had been an outlander—but a sword . . . ? He had a lot of questions to ask once they had settled at the table.

The tea water was boiling fiercely, and he had to wrap a cloth around the kettle's handle to lift it off the hook. Heat soaked through immediately. As he straightened from the fire, a heavy thump at the door rattled the lock. All thoughts of the sword, or the hot kettle in his hand, flew away.

"One of the neighbors," he said uncertainly. "Master Dautry wanting to borrow. . . ." But the Dautry farm, their nearest neighbor, was an hour away even in the daylight, and Oren Dautry, shameless borrower that he was, was still not likely to leave his house by dark.

Tam softly placed the stew-filled bowls on the table. Slowly he moved away from the table. Both of his hands rested on his sword hilt. "I don't think—" he began, and the door burst open, pieces of the iron lock spinning across the floor.

A figure filled the doorway, bigger than any man Rand had ever seen, a figure in black mail that hung to his knees, with spikes at wrists and elbows and shoulders. One hand clutched a heavy, scythe-like sword; the other hand was flung up before his eyes as if to shield them from the light.

Rand felt the beginnings of an odd sort of relief. Whoever this was, it was not the black-cloaked rider. Then he saw the curled ram's horns on the head that brushed the top of the doorway, and where mouth and nose should have been was a hairy muzzle. He took in all of it in the space of one deep breath that he let out in a terrified yell as, without thinking, he hurled the hot kettle at that half-human head.

The creature roared, part scream of pain, part animal snarl, as boiling water splashed over its face. Even as the kettle struck, Tam's sword flashed. The roar abruptly became a gurgle, and the huge shape toppled back. Before it finished falling, another was trying to claw its way past. Rand glimpsed a misshapen head topped by spike-like horns before Tam struck again, and two huge bodies blocked the door. He realized his father was shouting at him.

"Run, lad! Hide in the woods!" The bodies in the doorway jerked as others outside tried to pull them clear. Tam thrust a shoulder under the massive table; with a grunt he heaved it over atop the tangle. "There are too many to hold! Out the back! Go! Go! I'll follow!"

Even as Rand turned away, shame filled him that he obeyed so quickly. He wanted to stay and help his father, though he could not imagine how, but fear had him by the throat, and his legs moved on their own. He dashed from the room, toward the back of the house, as fast as he had ever run in his life. Crashes and shouts from the front door pursued him.

He had his hands on the bar across the back door when his eye fell on the iron lock that was never locked. Except that Tam had done just that tonight. Letting the bar stay where it was, he darted to a side window, flung up the sash and threw back the shutters. Night had replaced twilight completely. The full moon and drifting clouds made dappled shadows chase one another across the farmyard.

Shadows, he told himself. Only shadows. The back door creaked as someone outside, or something, tried to push it open. His mouth went dry. A crash shook the door in its frame and lent him speed; he slipped through the window like a hare going to ground, and cowered against the side of the house. Inside the room, wood splintered like thunder.

He forced himself up to a crouch, made himself peer inside, just with one eye, just at the corner of the window. In the dark he could not make out much, but more than he really wanted to see. The door hung askew, and shadowed shapes moved cautiously into the room, talking in low, guttural voices. Rand understood none of what was said; the language sounded harsh, unsuited to a human tongue. Axes and spears and spiked things dully reflected stray glimmers of moonlight. Boots scraped on the floor, and there was a rhythmic click, as of hooves, as well.

He tried to work moisture back into his mouth. Drawing a deep, ragged breath, he shouted as loudly as he could. "They're coming in the back!" The words came out in a croak, but at least they came out. He had not been sure they would. "I'm outside! Run, father!" With the last word he was sprinting away from the farmhouse.

Coarse-voiced shouts in the strange tongue raged from the back room. Glass shattered, loud and sharp, and something thudded heavily to the ground behind him. He guessed one of them had broken through the window rather than try to squeeze through the opening, but he did not look back to see if he was right. Like a fox running from hounds he darted into the nearest moon-cast shadows as if headed for the woods, then dropped to his belly and slithered back to the barn and its larger, deeper shadows. Something fell across his shoulders, and he thrashed about, not sure if he was trying to fight or escape, until he realized he was grappling with the new hoe handle Tam had been shaping.

Idiot! For a moment he lay there, trying to stop panting. *Coplin fool idiot!* At last he crawled on along the back of the barn, dragging the hoe handle with him. It was not much, but it was better than nothing. Cautiously he looked around the corner at the farmyard and the house.

Of the creature that had jumped out after him there was no sign. It could be anywhere. Hunting him, surely. Even creeping up on him at that very moment.

Frightened bleats filled the sheep pen to his left; the flock milled as if trying to find an escape. Shadowed shapes flickered in the lighted front windows of the house, and the clash of steel on steel rang through the darkness. Suddenly one of the windows burst outward in a shower of glass and wood as Tam leaped through it, sword still in hand. He landed on his feet, but instead of running away from the house he dashed toward the back of it, ignoring the monstrous things scrambling after him through the broken window and the doorway.

Rand stared in disbelief. Why was he not trying to get away? Then he understood. Tam had last heard his voice from the rear of the house. "Father!" he shouted. "I'm over here!"

In mid-stride Tam whirled, not running toward Rand, but at an angle away from him. "Run, lad!" he shouted, gesturing with the sword as if to someone ahead of him. "Hide!" A dozen huge forms streamed after him, harsh shouts and shrill howls shivering the air.

Rand pulled back into the shadows behind the barn. There he could not be seen from the house, in case any of the creatures were still inside. He was safe; for the moment, at least. But not Tam. Tam, who was trying to lead those things away from him. His hands tightened on the hoe handle, and he had to clench his teeth to stop a sudden laugh. A hoe handle. Facing one of those creatures with a hoe handle would not be much like playing at quarterstaffs with Perrin. But he could not let Tam face what was chasing him alone.

"If I move like I was stalking a rabbit," he whispered to himself, "they'll never hear me, or see me." The eerie cries echoed in the darkness, and he tried to swallow. "More like a pack of starving wolves." Soundlessly he slipped away from the barn, toward the forest, gripping the hoe handle so hard that his hands hurt.

At first, when the trees surrounded him, he took comfort from them. They helped hide him from whatever the creatures were that had attacked the farm. As he crept through the woods, though, moon shadows shifted, and it began to seem as if the darkness of the forest changed and moved, too. Trees loomed malevolently; branches writhed toward him. But were they just trees and branches? He could almost hear the growling chuckles stifled in their throats while they waited for him. The howls of Tam's pursuers no longer filled the night, but in the silence that replaced them he flinched every time the wind scraped one limb against another. Lower and lower he crouched, and moved more and more slowly. He hardly dared to breathe for fear he might be heard.

Suddenly a hand closed over his mouth from behind, and an iron grip seized his wrist. Frantically he clawed over his shoulder with his free hand for some hold on the attacker.

"Don't break my neck, lad," came Tam's hoarse whisper.

Relief flooded him, turning his muscles to water. When his father released him he fell to his hands and knees, gasping as if he had run for miles. Tam dropped down beside him, leaning on one elbow.

"I wouldn't have tried that if I had thought how much you've grown in the last few years," Tam said softly. His eyes shifted constantly as he spoke, keeping a sharp watch on the darkness. "But I had to make sure you didn't speak out. Some Trollocs can hear like a dog. Maybe better."

"But Trollocs are just. . . ." Rand let the words trail off. Not just a story, not after tonight. Those things could be Trollocs or the Dark One himself for all he knew. "Are you sure?" he whispered. "I mean . . . Trollocs?"

"I'm sure. Though what brought them to the Two Rivers. . . . I never saw one before tonight, but I've talked with men who have, so I know a little. Maybe enough to keep us alive. Listen closely. A Trolloc can see better than a man in the dark, but bright lights blind them, for a time at least. That may be the only reason we got away from so many. Some can track by scent or sound, but they're said to be lazy. If we can keep out of their hands long enough, they should give up."

That made Rand feel only a little better. "In the stories they hate men, and serve the Dark One."

"If anything belongs in the Shepherd of the Night's flocks, lad, it is Trollocs. They kill for the pleasure of killing, so I've been told. But that's the end of my knowledge, except that they cannot be trusted unless they're afraid of you, and then not far."

Rand shivered. He did not think he would want to meet anyone a Trolloc was afraid of. "Do you think they're still hunting for us?"

"Maybe, maybe not. They don't seem very smart. Once we got into the forest, I sent the ones after me off toward the mountains without much trouble." Tam fumbled at his right side, then put his hand close to his face. "Best act as if they are, though."

"You're hurt."

"Keep your voice down. It's just a scratch, and there is nothing to be done about it now, anyway. At least the weather seems to be warming." He lay back with a heavy sigh. "Perhaps it won't be too bad spending the night out."

In the back of his mind Rand had just been thinking fond thoughts of his coat and cloak. The trees cut the worst of the wind, but what gusted through still sliced like a frozen knife. Hesitantly he touched Tam's face, and winced. "You're on fire. I have to get you to Nynaeve."

"In a bit, lad."

"We don't have any time to waste. It's a long way in the dark." He scrambled to his feet and tried to pull his father up. A groan barely stifled by Tam's clenched teeth made Rand hastily ease him back down.

"Let me rest a while, boy. I'm tired."

Rand pounded his fist on his thigh. Snug in the farmhouse, with a fire and blankets, plenty of water and willowbark, he might have been willing to wait for daybreak before hitching Bela and taking Tam into the village. Here was no fire, no blankets, no cart, and no Bela. But those things were still back at the house. If he could not carry Tam to them, perhaps he could bring some of them, at least, to Tam. If the Trollocs were gone. They had to go sooner or later.

He looked at the hoe handle, then dropped it. Instead he drew Tam's sword. The blade gleamed dully in the pale moonlight. The long hilt felt odd in his hand; the weight and heft were strange. He slashed at the air a few times before stopping with a sigh. Slashing at air was easy. If he had to do it against a Trolloc he was surely just as likely to run instead, or freeze stiff so he could not move at all until the Trolloc swung one of those odd swords and. . . . *Stop it! It's not helping anything!*

As he started to rise, Tam caught his arm. "Where are you going?"

"We need the cart," he said gently. "And blankets." He was shocked at how easily he pulled his father's hand from his sleeve. "Rest, and I'll be back."

"Careful," Tam breathed.

He could not see Tam's face in the moonlight, but he could feel his eyes on him. "I will be." *As careful as a mouse exploring a hawk's nest,* he thought.

As silently as another shadow, he slid into the darkness. He thought of all the times he had played tag in the woods with his friends as children, stalking one another, straining not to be heard until he put a hand on someone's shoulder. Somehow he could not make this seem the same.

Creeping from tree to tree, he tried to make a plan, but by the time he reached the edge of the woods he had made and discarded ten. Everything depended on whether or not the Trollocs were still there. If they were gone, he could simply walk up to the house and take what he needed. If they were still there. . . . In that case, there was nothing for it but go back to Tam. He did not like it, but he could do Tam no good by getting killed.

He peered toward the farm buildings. The barn and the sheep pen were only dark shapes in the moonlight. Light spilled from the front windows of the house, though, and through the open front door. *Just the candles father lit, or are there Trollocs waiting?*

He jumped convulsively at a nighthawk's reedy cry, then sagged against a tree, shaking. This was getting him nowhere. Dropping to his belly, he began to crawl, holding the sword awkwardly before him. He kept his chin in the dirt all the way to the back of the sheep pen.

Crouched against the stone wall, he listened. Not a sound disturbed the night. Carefully he eased up enough to look over the wall. Nothing moved in the farmyard. No shadows flickered against the lit windows of the house, or in the doorway. *Bela and the cart first, or the blankets and other things.* It was the light that decided him. The barn was dark. Anything could be waiting inside, and he would have no way of knowing until it was too late. At least he would be able to see what was inside the house.

As he started to lower himself again, he stopped suddenly. There was *no* sound. Most of the sheep might have settled down already and gone back to sleep, though it was not likely, but a few were always awake even in the middle of the night, rustling about, bleating now and again. He could barely make out the shadowy mounds of sheep on the ground. One lay almost beneath him.

Trying to make no noise, he hoisted himself onto the wall until he could stretch out a hand to the dim shape. His fingers touched curly wool, then wetness; the sheep did not move. Breath left him in a rush as he pushed back, almost dropping the sword as he fell to the ground outside the pen. *They kill for fun.* Shakily he scrubbed the wetness from his hand in the dirt.

Fiercely he told himself that nothing had changed. The Trollocs had done their butchery and gone. Repeating that in his mind, he crawled on across the farmyard, keeping as low as he could, but trying to watch every direction, too. He had never thought he would envy an earthworm.

At the front of the house he lay close beside the wall, beneath the broken window, and listened. The dull thudding of blood in his ears was the loudest sound he heard. Slowly he reared up and peered inside.

The stewpot lay upside down in the ashes on the hearth. Splintered, broken wood littered the room; not a single piece of furniture remained whole. Even the table rested at an angle, two legs hacked to rough stubs. Every drawer had been pulled out and smashed; every cupboard and cabinet stood open, many doors hanging by one hinge. Their contents were strewn over the wreckage, and everything was dusted with white. Flour and salt, to judge from the slashed sacks tossed down by the fireplace. Four twisted bodies made a tangle in the remnants of the furnishings. Trollocs.

Rand recognized one by its ram's horns. The others were much the same, even in their differences, a repulsive melange of human faces distorted by muzzles, horns, feathers, and fur. Their hands, almost human, only made it worse. Two wore boots; the others had hooves. He watched without blinking until his eyes burned. None of the Trollocs moved. They had to be dead. And Tam was waiting.

He ran in through the front door and stopped, gagging at the stench. A stable that had not been mucked out in months was the only thing he could think of that might come close to matching it. Vile smears defiled the walls. Trying to breathe through his mouth, he hurriedly began poking through the mess on the floor. There had been a waterbag in one of the cupboards.

A scraping sound behind him sent a chill to his marrow, and he spun, almost falling over the remains of the table.

He caught himself, and moaned behind teeth that would have chattered had he not had them clenched until his jaw ached.

One of the Trollocs was getting to its feet. A wolf's muzzle jutted out below sunken eyes. Flat, emotionless eyes, and all too human. Hairy, pointed ears twitched incessantly. It stepped over one of its dead companions on sharp goat hooves. The same black mail the others wore rasped against leather trousers, and one of the huge, scythe-curved swords swung at its side.

It muttered something, guttural and sharp, then said, "Others go away. Narg stay. Narg smart." The words were distorted and hard to understand, coming from a mouth never meant for human speech. Its tone was meant to be soothing, he thought, but he could not take his eyes off the stained teeth, long and sharp, that flashed every time the creature spoke. "Narg know some come back sometime. Narg wait. You no need sword. Put sword down."

Until the Trolloc spoke Rand had not realized that he held Tam's sword wavering before him in both hands, its point aimed at the huge creature. It towered head and shoulders above him, with a chest and arms to dwarf Master Luhhan.

"Narg no hurt." It took a step closer, gesturing. "You put sword down." The dark hair on the backs of its hands was thick, like fur.

"Stay back," Rand said, wishing his voice were steadier. "Why did you do this? Why?"

"Vlja daeg roghda!" The snarl quickly became a toothy smile. "Put sword down. Narg no hurt. Myrddraal want talk you." A flash of emotion crossed the distorted face. Fear. "Others come back, you talk Myrddraal." It took another step, one big hand coming to rest on its own sword hilt. "You put sword down."

Rand wet his lips. Myrddraal! The worst of the stories was walking tonight. If a Fade was coming, it made a Trolloc pale by comparison. He had to get away. But if the Trolloc drew that massive blade he would not have a chance. He forced his lips into a shaky smile. "All right." Grip tightening on the sword, he let both hands drop to his sides. "I'll talk."

The wolf-smile became a snarl, and the Trolloc lunged for him. Rand had not thought anything that big could move so fast. Desperately he brought his sword up. The monstrous body crashed into him, slamming him against the wall. Breath left his lungs in one gasp. He fought for air as they fell to the floor together, the Trolloc on top. Frantically he struggled beneath the crushing weight, trying to avoid thick hands groping for him, and snapping jaws.

Abruptly the Trolloc spasmed and was still. Battered and bruised, half suffocated by the bulk on top of him, for a moment Rand could only lie there in disbelief. Quickly he came to his senses, though, enough to writhe out from under the body, at least. And body it was. The bloodied blade of Tam's sword stood out from the center of the Trolloc's back. He had gotten it up in time after all. Blood covered Rand's hands, as well, and made a blackish smear across the front of his shirt. His stomach churned, and he swallowed hard to keep from being sick. He shook as hard as he had in the worst of his fear, but this time in relief at still being alive.

Others come back, the Trolloc had said. The other Trollocs would be returning to the farmhouse. And a Myrddraal, a Fade. The stories said Fades were twenty feet tall, with eyes of fire, and they rode shadows like horses. When a Fade turned sideways, it disappeared, and no wall could stop them. He had to do what he had come for, and get away quickly.

Grunting with the effort he heaved the Trolloc's body over to get to the sword—and almost ran when open eyes stared at him. It took him a minute to realize they were staring through the glaze of death.

He wiped his hands on a tattered rag—it had been one of Tam's shirts only that morning—and tugged the blade free. Cleaning the sword, he reluctantly dropped the rag on the floor. There was no time for neatness, he thought with a laugh that he had to clamp his teeth shut to stop. He did not see how they could ever clean the house well enough for it to be lived in again. The horrible stench had probably already soaked right into the timbers. But there was no time to think of that. *No time for neatness. No time for anything, maybe.*

He was sure he was forgetting any number of things they would need, but Tam was waiting, and the Trollocs were coming back. He gathered what he could think of on the run. Blankets from the bedrooms upstairs, and clean cloths to bandage Tam's wound. Their cloaks and coats. A water-bag that he carried when he took the sheep to pasture. A clean shirt. He did not know when he would have time to change, but he wanted to get out of his blood-smeared shirt at the first opportunity. The small bags of willowbark and their other medicines were part of a dark, muddy-looking pile he could not bring himself to touch.

One bucket of the water Tam had brought in still stood by the fireplace, miraculously unspilled and untouched. He filled the waterbag from it, gave his hands a hasty wash in the rest, and made one more quick search for anything he might have forgotten. He found his bow among the wreckage, broken cleanly in two at the thickest point. He shuddered as he let the pieces fall. What he had gathered already would have to do, he decided. Quickly he piled everything outside the door.

The last thing before leaving the house, he dug a shuttered lantern from the mess on the floor. It still held oil. Lighting it from one of the candles, he closed the shutters—partly against the wind, but mostly to keep from drawing attention—and hurried outside with the lantern in one hand and the sword in the other. He was not sure what he would find in the barn. The sheep pen kept him from hoping too much. But he needed the cart to get Tam to Emond's Field, and for the cart he needed Bela. Necessity made him hope a little.

The barn doors stood open, one creaking on its hinges as it shifted in the wind. The interior looked as it always had, at first. Then his eyes fell on empty stalls, the stall doors ripped from their hinges. Bela and the cow were gone. Quickly he went to the back of the barn. The cart lay on its side, half the spokes broken out of its wheels. One shaft was only a foot-long stump.

The despair he had been holding at bay filled him. He was not sure he could carry Tam as far as the village even if his father could bear to be carried. The pain of it might kill Tam more quickly than the fever. Still, it was the only chance left. He had done all he could do here. As he turned to go, his eyes fell on the hacked-off cart shaft lying on the straw-strewn floor. Suddenly he smiled.

Hurriedly he set the lantern and the sword on the straw-covered floor, and in the next instant he was wrestling with the cart, tipping it back over to fall upright with a snap of more breaking spokes, then throwing his shoulder into it to heave it over on the other side. The undamaged shaft stood straight out. Snatching up the sword he hacked at the well-seasoned ash. To his pleased surprise great chips flew with his strokes, and he cut through as quickly as he could have with a good axe.

When the shaft fell free, he looked at the sword blade in wonder. Even the best-sharpened axe would have dulled chopping through that hard, aged wood, but the sword looked as brightly sharp as ever. He touched the edge with his thumb, then hastily stuck it in his mouth. The blade was still razor-sharp.

But he had no time for wonder. Blowing out the lantern—there was no need to have the barn burn down on top of everything else—he gathered up the shafts and ran back to get what he had left at the house.

Altogether it made an awkward burden. Not a heavy one, but hard to balance and manage, the cart shafts shifting and twisting in his arms as he stumbled across the plowed field. Once back in the forest they were even worse, catching on trees and knocking him half off his feet. They would have been easier to drag, but that would leave a clear trail behind him. He intended to wait as long as possible before doing that.

Tam was right where he had left him, seemingly asleep. He hoped it was sleep. Suddenly fearful, he dropped his burdens and put a hand to his father's face. Tam still breathed, but the fever was worse.

The touch roused Tam, but only into a hazy wakefulness. "Is that you, boy?" he breathed. "Worried about you. Dreams of days gone. Nightmares." Murmuring softly, he drifted off again.

"Don't worry," Rand said. He lay Tam's coat and cloak over him to keep off the wind. "I'll get you to Nynaeve just as quick as I can." As he went on, as much to reassure himself as for Tam's benefit, he peeled off his bloodstained shirt, hardly even noticing the cold in his haste to be rid of it, and hurriedly pulled on the clean one. Throwing his old shirt away made him feel as if he had just had a bath. "We'll be safe in the village in no time, and the Wisdom will set everything right. You'll see. Everything's going to be all right."

That thought was like a beacon as he pulled on his coat and bent to tend Tam's wound. They would be safe once they reached the village, and Nynaeve would cure Tam. He just had to get him there.

CHAPTER
6

The Westwood

In the moonlight Rand could not really see what he was doing, but Tam's wound seemed to be only a shallow gash along the ribs, no longer than the palm of his hand. He shook his head in disbelief. He had seen his father take more of an injury than that and not even stop work except to wash it off. Hastily he searched Tam from head to foot for something bad enough to account for the fever, but the one cut was all he could find.

Small as it was, that lone cut was still grave enough; the flesh around it burned to the touch. It was even hotter than the rest of Tam's body, and the rest of him was hot enough to make Rand's jaws clench. A scalding fever like that could kill, or leave a man a husk of what he had once been. He soaked a cloth with water from the skin and laid it across Tam's forehead.

He tried to be gentle about washing and bandaging the gash on his father's ribs, but soft groans still interrupted Tam's low muttering. Stark branches loomed around them, threatening as they shifted as in the wind. Surely the Trollocs would go on their way when they failed to find Tam and him, when they came back to the farmhouse and found it still empty. He tried to make himself believe it, but the wanton destruction at the house, the senselessness of it, left little room for belief of that sort. Believing they would give up short of killing everyone and everything they could find was dangerous, a foolish chance he could not afford to take.

Trollocs. Light above, Trollocs! Creatures out of a gleeman's tale coming out of the night to bash in the door. And a Fade. Light shine on me, a Fade!

Abruptly he realized he was holding the untied ends of the bandage in motionless hands. *Frozen like a rabbit that's seen a hawk's shadow,* he thought scornfully. With an angry shake of his head he finished tying the bandage around Tam's chest.

Knowing what he had to do, even getting on with it, did not stop him being afraid. When the Trollocs came back they would surely begin searching the forest around the farm for some trace of the people who had escaped them. The body of the one he had killed would tell them those people were not far off. Who knew what a Fade would do, or could do? On top of that, his father's comment about Trollocs' hearing was as loud in his mind as if Tam had just said it. He found himself resisting the urge to put a hand over Tam's mouth, to still his groans and murmurs. *Some track by scent. What can I do about that? Nothing.* He could not waste time worrying over problems he could do nothing about.

"You have to keep quiet," he whispered in his father's ear. "The Trollocs will be back."

Tam spoke in hushed, hoarse tones. "You're still lovely, Kari. Still lovely as a girl."

Rand grimaced. His mother had been dead fifteen years. If Tam believed she was still alive, then the fever was even worse than Rand had thought. How could he be kept from speaking, now that silence might mean life?

"Mother wants you to be quiet," Rand whispered. He paused to clear his throat of a sudden tightness. She had had gentle hands; he remembered that much. "Kari wants you to be quiet. Here. Drink."

Tam gulped thirstily from the waterskin, but after a few swallows he turned his head aside and began murmuring softly again, too low for Rand to understand. He hoped it was too low to be heard by hunting Trollocs, too.

Hastily he got on with what was needed. Three of the blankets he wove around and between the shafts cut from the cart, contriving a makeshift litter. He would only be able to carry one end, letting the other drag on the ground, but it would have to do. From the last blanket he cut a long strip with his belt knife, then tied one end of the strip to each of the shafts.

As gently as he could, he lifted Tam onto the litter, wincing with every moan. His father had always seemed indestructible. Nothing could harm him; nothing could stop him, or even slow him down. For him to be in this condition almost robbed Rand of what courage he had managed to gather. But he had to keep on. That was all that kept him moving. He had to.

When Tam finally lay on the litter, Rand hesitated, then took the sword belt from his father's waist. When he fastened it around himself, it felt odd there; it made him feel odd. Belt and sheath and sword together only weighed a few pounds, but when he sheathed the blade it seemed to drag at him like a great weight.

Angrily he berated himself. This was no time or place for foolish fancies. It was only a big knife. How many times had he daydreamed about wearing a sword and having adventures? If he could kill one Trolloc with it, he could surely fight off any others as well. Only, he knew all too well that what had happened in the farmhouse had been the purest luck. And his daydream adventures had never included his teeth chattering, or running for his life through the night, or his father at the point of death.

Hastily he tucked the last blanket around Tam, and laid the waterskin and the rest of the cloths beside his father on the litter. With a deep breath he knelt between the shafts and lifted the strip of blanket over his head. It settled across his shoulders and under his arms. When he gripped the shafts and straightened, most of the weight was on his shoulders. It did not seem like very much. Trying to keep a smooth pace, he set out for Emond's Field, the litter scraping along behind him.

He had already decided to make his way to the Quarry Road and follow that to the village. The danger would almost certainly be greater along the road, but Tam would receive no help at all if he got them lost trying to find his way through the woods and the dark.

In the darkness he was almost out onto the Quarry Road before he knew it. When he realized where he was, his throat tightened like a fist. Hurriedly he turned the litter around and dragged it back into the trees a way, then stopped to catch his breath and let his heart stop pounding. Still panting, he turned east, toward Emond's Field.

Traveling through the trees was more difficult than taking Tam down the road, and the night surely did not help, but going out onto the road itself would be madness. The idea was to reach the village *without* meeting any Trollocs; without even seeing any, if he had his wish. He had to assume the Trollocs were still hunting them, and sooner or later they would realize the two had set off for the village. That was the most likely place to go, and the Quarry Road the most likely route. In truth, he found himself closer to the road than he liked. The night and the shadows under the trees seemed awfully bare cover in which to hide from the eyes of anyone traveling along it.

Moonlight filtering through bare branches gave only enough illumination to fool his eyes into thinking they saw what was underfoot. Roots threatened to trip him at every step, old brambles snagged his legs, and sudden dips or rises in the ground had him half falling as his foot met nothing but air where he expected firm earth, or stumbling when his toe struck dirt while still moving forward. Tam's mutterings broke into a sharp groan whenever one of the shafts bumped too quickly over root or rock.

Uncertainty made him peer into the darkness until his eyes burned, listen as he had never listened before. Every scrape of branch against branch, every rustle of pine needles, brought him to a halt, ears straining, hardly daring to breathe for fear he might not hear some warning sound, for fear he might hear that sound. Only when he was sure it was just the wind would he go on.

Slowly weariness crept into his arms and legs, driven home by a night wind that mocked his cloak and coat. The weight of the litter, so little at the start, now tried to pull him to the ground. His stumbles were no longer all from tripping. The almost constant struggle not to fall took as much out of him as did the actual work of pulling the litter. He had been up before dawn to begin his chores, and even with the trip to Emond's Field he had done almost a full day's work. On any normal night he would be resting before the fireplace, reading one of Tam's small collection of books before going to bed. The sharp chill soaked into his bones, and his stomach reminded him that he had had nothing to eat since Mistress al'Vere's honeycakes.

He muttered to himself, angry at not taking some food at the farm. A few minutes more could not have made any difference. A few minutes to find some bread and cheese. The Trollocs would not have come back in just a few minutes more. Or just the bread. Of course, Mistress al'Vere would insist on putting a hot meal in front of him once they reached the inn. A steaming plate of her thick lamb stew, probably. And some of that bread she had been baking. And lots of hot tea.

"They came over the Dragonwall like a flood," Tam said suddenly, in a strong, angry voice, "and washed the land with blood. How many died for Laman's sin?"

Rand almost fell from surprise. Wearily he lowered the litter to the ground and untangled himself. The strip of blanket left a burning groove in his shoulders. Shrugging to work the knots out, he knelt beside Tam. Fumbling for the waterbag, he peered through the trees, trying vainly in the dim moonlight to see up and down the road, not twenty paces away. Nothing moved there but shadows. Nothing but shadows.

"There isn't any flood of Trollocs, father. Not now, anyway. We'll be safe in Emond's Field soon. Drink a little water."

Tam brushed aside the waterbag with an arm that seemed to have regained all of its strength. He seized Rand's collar, pulling him close enough to feel the heat of his father's fever in his own cheek. "They called them savages," Tam said urgently. "The fools said they could be swept aside like rubbish. How many battles lost, how many cities burned, before they faced the truth? Before the nations stood together against them?" He loosed his hold on Rand, and sadness filled his voice. "The field at Marath carpeted with the dead, and no sound but the cries of ravens and the buzzing of flies. The topless towers of Cairhien burning in the night like torches. All the way to the Shining Walls they burned and slew before they were turned back. All the way to—"

Rand clamped a hand over his father's mouth. The sound came again, a rhythmic thudding, directionless in the trees, fading then growing stronger again as the wind shifted. Frowning, he turned his head slowly, trying to decide from where it came. A flicker of motion caught the corner of his eye, and in an instant he was crouched over Tam. He was startled to feel the hilt of the sword clutched tight in his hand, but most of him concentrated on the Quarry Road as if the road were the only real thing in the entire world.

Wavering shadows to the east slowly resolved themselves into a horse and rider followed up the road by tall, bulky shapes trotting to keep up with the animal. The pale light of the moon glittered from spearheads and axe blades. Rand never even considered that they might be villagers coming to help. He knew what they were. He could feel it, like grit scraping his bones, even before they drew close enough for moonlight to reveal the hooded cloak swathing the horseman, a cloak that hung undisturbed by the wind. All of the shapes appeared black in the night, and the horse's hooves made the same sounds that any other's would, but Rand knew this horse from any other.

Behind the dark rider came nightmare forms with horns and muzzles and beaks, Trollocs in a double file, all in steps, boots and hooves striking the ground at the same instant as if obeying a single mind. Rand counted twenty as they ran past. He wondered what kind of man would dare turn his back on so many Trollocs. Or on one, for that matter.

The trotting column disappeared westward, thumping footfalls fading into the darkness, but Rand remained where he was, not moving a muscle except to breathe. Something told him to be certain, absolutely certain, they were gone before he moved. At long last he drew a deep breath and began to straighten.

This time the horse made no sound at all. In eerie silence the dark rider returned, his shadowy mount stopping every few steps as it walked slowly back down the road. The wind gusted higher, moaning through the trees; the horseman's cloak lay still as death. Whenever the horse halted, that hooded head swung from side to side as the rider peered into the forest, searching. Exactly opposite Rand the horse stopped again, the shadowed opening of the hood turning toward where he crouched above his father.

Rand's hand tightened convulsively on the sword hilt. He felt the gaze, just as he had that morning, and shivered again from the hatred even if he could not see it. That shrouded man hated everyone and everything, everything that lived. Despite the cold wind, sweat beaded on Rand's face.

Then the horse was moving on, a few soundless steps and stop, until all Rand could see was a barely distinguishable blur in the night far down the road. It could have been anything, but he had not taken his eyes off it for a second. If he lost it, he was afraid the next time he saw the black-cloaked rider might be when that silent horse was on top of him.

Abruptly the shadow was rushing back, passing him in a silent gallop. The rider looked only ahead of him as he sped westward into the night, toward the Mountains of Mist. Toward the farm.

Rand sagged, gulping air and scrubbing cold sweat off his face with his sleeve. He did not care any more about why the Trollocs had come. If he never found out why, that would be fine, just as long as it was all ended.

With a shake he gathered himself, hastily checking his father. Tam was still murmuring, but so softly Rand could not make out the words. He tried to give him a drink, but the water spilled over his father's chin. Tam coughed and choked on the trickle that made it into his mouth, then began muttering again as if there had not been any interruption.

Rand splashed a little more water on the cloth on Tam's forehead, pushed the waterbag back on the litter, and scrambled between the shafts again.

He started out as if he had had a good night's sleep, but the new strength did not last long. Fear masked his tiredness in the beginning, but though the fear remained, the mask melted away quickly. Soon he was back to stumbling forward, trying to ignore hunger and aching muscles. He concentrated on putting one foot in front of the other without tripping.

In his mind he pictured Emond's Field, shutters thrown back and the houses lit for Winternight, people shouting greetings as they passed back and forth on their visits, fiddles filling the streets with "Jaem's Folly" and "Heron on the Wing." Haral Luhhan would have one too many brandies and start singing "The Wind in the Barley" in a voice like a bullfrog—he always did—until his wife managed to shush him, and Cenn Buie would decide to prove he could still dance as well as ever, and Mat would have something planned that would not quite happen the way he intended, and everybody would know he was responsible even if no one could prove it. He could almost smile thinking about how it would be.

After a time Tam spoke up again.

"*Avendesora*. It's said it makes no seed, but they brought a cutting to Cairhien, a sapling. A royal gift of wonder for the king." Though he sounded angry, he was barely loud enough for Rand to understand. Anyone who could hear him would be able to hear the litter scraping across the ground, too. Rand kept on, only half listening. "They never make peace. Never. But they brought a sapling, as a sign of peace. Five hundred years it grew. Five hundred years of peace with those who make no peace with strangers. Why did he cut it down? Why? Blood was the price for *Avendoraldera*. Blood the price for Laman's pride." He faded off into muttering once more.

Tiredly Rand wondered what fever-dream Tam could be having now. *Avendesora*. The Tree of Life was supposed to have all sorts of miraculous qualities, but none of the stories mentioned any sapling, or any "they." There was only the one, and that belonged to the Green Man.

Only that morning he might have felt foolish at musing over the Green Man and the Tree of Life. They were only stories. *Are they? Trollocs were just stories this morning.* Maybe all the stories were as real as the news the peddlers and merchants brought all the gleeman's tales and all the stories told at night in front of the fireplace. Next he might actually meet the Green Man, or an Ogier giant, or a wild, black-veiled Aielman.

Tam was talking again, he realized, sometimes only murmuring, sometimes loud enough to understand. From time to time he stopped to pant for breath, then went on as if he thought he had been speaking the whole time.

". . . battles are always hot, even in the snow. Sweat heat. Blood heat. Only death is cool. Slope of the mountain . . . only place didn't stink of death. Had to get away from smell of it . . . sight of it. . . . heard a baby cry. Their women fight alongside the men, sometimes, but why they had let her come, I don't . . . gave birth there alone, before she died of her wounds. . . . covered the child with her cloak, but the wind . . . blown the cloak away. . . . child, blue with the cold. Should have been dead, too. . . . crying there. Crying in the snow. I couldn't just leave a child. . . . no children of our own. . . . always knew you wanted children. I knew you'd take it to your heart, Kari. Yes, lass. Rand is a good name. A good name."

Suddenly Rand's legs lost the little strength they had. Stumbling, he fell to his knees. Tam moaned with the jolt,

and the strip of blanket cut into Rand's shoulders, but he
was not aware of either. If a Trolloc had leaped up in front
of him right then, he would just have stared at it. He looked
over his shoulder at Tam, who had sunk back into wordless
murmurs. *Fever-dreams,* he thought dully. Fevers always
brought bad dreams, and this was a night for nightmares
even without a fever.

"You are my father," he said aloud, stretching back a hand
to touch Tam, "and I am—" The fever was worse. Much
worse.

Grimly he struggled to his feet. Tam murmured something, but Rand refused to listen to any more. Throwing his
weight against the improvised harness he tried to put all
of his mind into taking one leaden step after another, into
reaching the safety of Emond's Field. But he could not stop
the echo in the back of his mind. *He's my father. It was just
a fever-dream. He's my father. It was just a fever-dream.
Light, who am I?*

CHAPTER
7

Out of the Woods

G ray first light came while Rand still trudged through
the forest. At first he did not really see. When he
finally did, he stared at the fading darkness in surprise. No matter what his eyes told him, he could hardly
believe he had spent all night trying to travel the distance
from the farm to Emond's Field. Of course, the Quarry
Road by day, rocks and all, was a far cry from the woods by
night. On the other hand, it seemed days since he had seen
the black-cloaked rider on the road, weeks since he and
Tam had gone in for their supper. He no longer felt the strip
of cloth digging into his shoulders, but then he felt nothing
in his shoulders except numbness, nor in his feet, for that
matter. In between, it was another matter. His breath came
in labored pants that had long since set his throat and lungs
to burning, and hunger twisted his stomach into queasy
sickness.

Tam had fallen silent some time before. Rand was not
sure how long it had been since the murmurs ceased, but
he did not dare halt now to check on Tam. If he stopped he
would never be able to force himself to start out again. Anyway, whatever Tam's condition, he could do nothing beyond
what he was doing. The only hope lay ahead, in the village.
He tried wearily to increase his pace, but his wooden legs
continued their slow plod. He barely even noticed the cold,
or the wind.

Vaguely he caught the smell of woodsmoke. At least he
was almost there if he could smell the village chimneys.
A tired smile had only begun on his face, though, when it
turned to a frown. Smoke lay heavy in the air—too heavy.

With the weather, a fire might well be blazing on every hearth in the village, but the smoke was still too strong. In his mind he saw again the Trollocs on the road. Trollocs coming from the east, from the direction of Emond's Field. He peered ahead, trying to make out the first houses, and ready to shout for help at the first sight of anyone, even Cenn Buie or one of the Coplins. A small voice in the back of his head told him to hope someone there could still give help.

Suddenly a house became visible through the last bare-branched trees, and it was all he could do to keep his feet moving. Hope turning to sharp despair, he staggered into the village.

Charred piles of rubble stood in the places of half the houses of Emond's Field. Soot-coated brick chimneys thrust like dirty fingers from heaps of blackened timbers. Thin wisps of smoke still rose from the ruins. Grimy-faced villagers, some yet in their night clothes, poked through the ashes, here pulling free a cookpot, there simply prodding forlornly at the wreckage with a stick. What little had been rescued from the flames dotted the streets; tall mirrors and polished sideboards and highchests stood in the dust among chairs and tables buried under bedding, cooking utensils, and meager piles of clothing and personal belongings.

The destruction seemed scattered at random through the village. Five houses marched untouched in one row, while in another place a lone survivor stood surrounded by desolation.

On the far side of the Winespring Water, the three huge Bel Tine bonfires roared, tended by a cluster of men. Thick columns of black smoke bent northward with the wind, flecked by careless sparks. One of Master al'Vere's Dhurran stallions was dragging something Rand could not make out over the ground toward the Wagon Bridge, and the flames.

Before he was well out of the trees, a sooty-faced Haral Luhhan hurried to him, clutching a woodsman's axe in one thick-fingered hand. The burly blacksmith's ash-smeared nightshirt hung to his boots, the angry red welt of a burn across his chest showing through a ragged tear. He dropped to one knee beside the litter. Tam's eyes were closed, and his breathing came low and hard.

"Trollocs, boy?" Master Luhhan asked in a smoke-hoarse voice. "Here, too. Here, too. Well, we may have been luckier than anyone has a right to be, if you can credit it. He needs the Wisdom. Now where in the Light is she? Egwene!"

Egwene, running by with her arms full of bedsheets torn into bandages, looked around at them without slowing. Her eyes stared at something in the far distance; dark circles made them appear even larger than they actually were. Then she saw Rand and stopped, drawing a shuddering breath. "Oh, no, Rand, not your father? Is he . . . ? Come, I'll take you to Nynaeve."

Rand was too tired, too stunned, to speak. All through the night Emond's Field had been a haven, where he and Tam would be safe. Now all he could seem to do was stare in dismay at her smoke-stained dress. He noticed odd details as if they were very important. The buttons down the back of her dress were done up crookedly. And her hands were clean. He wondered why her hands were clean when smudges of soot marked her cheeks.

Master Luhhan seemed to understand what had come over him. Laying his axe across the shafts, the blacksmith picked up the rear of the litter and gave it a gentle push, prodding him to follow Egwene. He stumbled after her as if walking in his sleep. Briefly he wondered how Master Luhhan knew the creatures were Trollocs, but it was a fleeting thought. If Tam could recognize them, there was no reason why Haral Luhhan could not.

"All the stories are real," he muttered.

"So it seems, lad," the blacksmith said. "So it seems."

Rand only half heard. He was concentrating on following Egwene's slender shape. He had pulled himself together just enough to wish she would hurry, though in truth she was keeping her pace to what the two men could manage with their burden. She led them halfway down the Green, to the Calder house. Char blackened the edges of its thatch, and smut stained the whitewashed walls. Of the houses on either side only the foundation stones were left, and two piles of ash and burned timbers. One had been the house of Berin Thane, one of the miller's brothers. The other had been Abell Cauthon's. Mat's father. Even the chimneys had toppled.

"Wait here," Egwene said, and gave them a look as if expecting an answer. When they only stood there, she muttered something under her breath, then dashed inside.

"Mat," Rand said. "Is he . . . ?"

"He's alive," the blacksmith said. He set down his end of the litter and straightened slowly. "I saw him a little while ago. It's a wonder any of us are alive. The way they came after my house, and the forge, you'd have thought I had gold and jewels in there. Alsbet cracked one's skull with a frying pan. She took one look at the ashes of our house this morning and set out hunting around the village with the biggest hammer she could dig out of what's left of the forge, just in case any of them hid instead of running away. I could almost pity the thing if she finds one." He nodded to the Calder house. "Mistress Calder and a few others took in some of those who were hurt, the ones with no home of their own still standing. When the Wisdom's seen Tam, we'll find him a bed. The inn, maybe. The Mayor offered it already, but Nynaeve said the hurt folk would heal better if there weren't so many of them together."

Rand sank to his knees. Shrugging out of his blanket harness, he wearily busied himself with checking Tam's covers. Tam never moved or made a sound, even when Rand's wooden hands jostled him. But he was still breathing, at least. *My father. The other was just the fever talking.* "What if they come back?" he said dully.

"The Wheel weaves as the Wheel wills," Master Luhhan said uneasily. "If they come back. . . . Well, they're gone, now. So we pick up the pieces, build up what's been torn down." He sighed, his face going slack as he knuckled the small of his back. For the first time Rand realized that the heavyset man was as tired as he was himself, if not more so. The blacksmith looked at the village, shaking his head. "I don't suppose today will be much of a Bel Tine. But we'll make it through. We always have." Abruptly he took up his axe, and his face firmed. "There's work waiting for me. Don't you worry, lad. The Wisdom will take good care of him, and the Light will take care of us all. And if the Light doesn't, well, we'll just take care of ourselves. Remember, we're Two Rivers folk."

Still on his knees, Rand looked at the village as the blacksmith walked away, really looked for the first time. Master Luhhan was right, he thought, and was surprised that he was not surprised by what he saw. People still dug in the ruins of their homes, but even in the short time he had been there more of them had begun to move with a sense of purpose. He could almost feel the growing determination. But he wondered. They had seen Trollocs; had they seen the black-cloaked rider? Had they felt his hatred?

Nynaeve and Egwene appeared from the Calder house, and he sprang to his feet. Or rather, he tried to spring to his feet; it was more of a stumbling lurch that almost put him on his face in the dust.

The Wisdom dropped to her knees beside the litter without giving him so much as a glance. Her face and dress were even dirtier than Egwene's, and the same dark circles lined her eyes, though her hands, too, were clean. She felt Tam's face and thumbed open his eyelids. With a frown she pulled down the coverings and eased the bandage aside to look at the wound. Before Rand could see what lay underneath she had replaced the wadded cloth. Sighing, she smoothed the blanket and cloak back up to Tam's neck with a gentle touch, as if tucking a child in for the night.

"There's nothing I can do," she said. She had to put her hands on her knees to straighten up. "I'm sorry, Rand."

For a moment he stood, not understanding, as she started back to the house, then he scrambled after her and pulled her around to face him. "He's dying," he cried.

"I know," she said simply, and he sagged with the matter-of-factness of it.

"You have to do something. You have to. You're the Wisdom."

Pain twisted her face, but only for an instant, then she was all hollow-eyed resolve again, her voice emotionless and firm. "Yes, I am. I know what I can do with my medicines, and I know when it's too late. Don't you think I would do something if I could? But I can't. I can't, Rand. And there are others who need me. People I *can* help."

"I brought him to you as quickly as I could," he mumbled. Even with the village in ruins, there had been the Wisdom for hope. With that gone, he was empty.

"I know you did," she said gently. She touched his cheek with her hand. "It isn't your fault. You did the best anyone could. I am sorry, Rand, but I have others to tend to. Our troubles are just beginning, I'm afraid."

Vacantly he stared after her until the door of the house closed behind her. He could not make any thought come except that she would not help.

Suddenly he was knocked back a step as Egwene cannoned into him, throwing her arms around him. Her hug was hard enough to bring a grunt from him any other time; now he only looked silently at the door behind which his hopes had vanished.

"I'm so sorry, Rand," she said against his chest. "Light, I wish there was something I could do."

Numbly he put his arms around her. "I know. I . . . I have to do something, Egwene. I don't know what, but I can't just let him. . . ." His voice broke, and she hugged him harder.

"Egwene!" At Nynaeve's shout from the house, Egwene jumped. "Egwene, I need you! And wash your hands again!"

She pushed herself free from Rand's arms. "She needs my help, Rand."

"Egwene!"

He thought he heard a sob as she spun away from him. Then she was gone, and he was left alone beside the litter. For a moment he looked down at Tam, feeling nothing but hollow helplessness. Suddenly his face hardened. "The Mayor will know what to do," he said, lifting the shafts once more. "The Mayor will know." Bran al'Vere always knew what to do. With weary obstinacy he set out for the Winespring Inn.

Another of the Dhurran stallions passed him, its harness straps tied around the ankles of a big shape draped with a dirty blanket. Arms covered with coarse hair dragged in the dirt behind the blanket, and one corner was pushed up to reveal a goat's horn. The Two Rivers was no place for stories to become horribly real. If Trollocs belonged anywhere it was in the world outside, for places where they had Aes Sedai and false Dragons and the Light alone knew what else come to life out of the tales of gleemen. Not the Two Rivers. Not Emond's Field.

As he made his way down the Green, people called to him, some from the ruins of their homes, asking if they could help. He heard them only as murmurs in the background, even when they walked alongside him for a distance as they spoke. Without really thinking about it he managed words that said he needed no help, that everything was being taken care of. When they left him, with worried looks, and sometimes a comment about sending Nynaeve to him, he noticed that just as little. All he let himself be aware of was the purpose he had fixed in his head. Bran al'Vere could do something to help Tam. What that could be he tried not to dwell on. But the Mayor would be able to do something, to think of something.

The inn had almost completely escaped the destruction that had taken half the village. A few scorch marks marred its walls, but the red roof tiles glittered in the sunlight as brightly as ever. All that was left of the peddler's wagon, though, were blackened iron wheel-rims leaning against the charred wagon box, now on the ground. The big round hoops that had held up the canvas cover slanted crazily, each at a different angle.

Thom Merrilin sat cross-legged on the old foundation stones, carefully snipping singed edges from the patches on his cloak with a pair of small scissors. He set down cloak and scissors when Rand drew near. Without asking if Rand needed or wanted help, he hopped down and picked up the back of the litter.

"Inside? Of course, of course. Don't you worry, boy. Your Wisdom will take care of him. I've watched her work, since last night, and she has a deft touch and a sure skill. It could be a lot worse. Some died last night. Not many, perhaps, but any at all are too many for me. Old Fain just disappeared, and that's the worst of all. Trollocs will eat anything. You should thank the Light your father's still here, and alive for the Wisdom to heal."

Rand blotted out the words—*He is my father!*—reducing the voice to meaningless sound that he noticed no more than a fly's buzzing. He could not bear any more sympathy, any more attempts to boost his spirits. Not now. Not until Bran al'Vere told him how to help Tam.

Suddenly he found himself facing something scrawled on the inn door, a curving line scratched with a charred stick, a charcoal teardrop balanced on its point. So much had happened that it hardly surprised him to find the Dragon's Fang marked on the door of the Winespring Inn. Why anyone would want to accuse the innkeeper or his family of evil, or bring the inn bad luck, was beyond him, but the night had convinced him of one thing. Anything was possible. Anything at all.

At a push from the gleeman he lifted the latch, and went in.

The common room was empty except for Bran al'Vere, and cold, too, for no one had found time to lay a fire. The Mayor sat at one of the tables, dipping his pen in an ink-well with a frown of concentration on his face and his gray-fringed head bent over a sheet of parchment. Nightshirt tucked hastily into his trousers and bagging around his considerable waist, he absently scratched at one bare foot with the toes of the other. His feet were dirty, as if he had been outside more than once without bothering about boots, despite the cold. "What's your trouble?" he demanded without looking up. "Be quick with it. I have two dozen things to do right this minute, and more that should have been done an hour ago. So I have little time or patience. Well? Out with it!"

"Master al'Vere?" Rand said. "It's my father."

The Mayor's head jerked up. "Rand? Tam!" He threw down the pen and knocked over his chair as he leaped up. "Perhaps the Light hasn't abandoned us altogether. I was afraid you were both dead. Bela galloped into the village an hour after the Trollocs left, lathered and blowing as if she'd run all the way from the farm, and I thought. . . . No time for that, now. We'll take him upstairs." He seized the rear of the litter, shouldering the gleeman out of the way. "You go get the Wisdom, Master Merrilin. And tell her I said hurry, or I'll know the reason why! Rest easy, Tam. We'll soon have you in a good, soft bed. Go, gleeman, go!"

Thom Merrilin vanished through the doorway before Rand could speak. "Nynaeve wouldn't do anything. She said she couldn't help him. I knew . . . I hoped you'd think of something."

Master al'Vere looked at Tam more sharply, then shook his head. "We will see, boy. We will see." But he no longer sounded confident. "Let's get him into a bed. He can rest easy, at least."

Rand let himself be prodded toward the stairs at the back of the common room. He tried hard to keep his certainty that somehow Tam would be all right, but it had been thin to begin with, he realized, and the sudden doubt in the Mayor's voice shook him.

On the second floor of the inn, at the front, were half a dozen snug, well-appointed rooms with windows overlooking the Green. Mostly they were used by the peddlers, or people down from Watch Hill or up from Deven Ride, but the merchants who came each year were often surprised to find such comfortable rooms. Three of them were taken now, and the Mayor hurried Rand to one of the unused ones.

Quickly the down comforter and blankets were stripped back on the wide bed, and Tam was transferred to the thick feather mattress, with goose-down pillows tucked under his head. He made no sound beyond hoarse breathing as he was moved, not even a groan, but the Mayor brushed away Rand's concern, telling him to set a fire to take the chill off the room. While Rand dug wood and kindling from the woodbox next to the fireplace, Bran threw back the curtains on the window, letting in the morning light, then began to gently wash Tam's face. By the time the gleeman returned, the blaze on the hearth was warming the room.

"She will not come," Thom Merrilin announced as he stalked into the room. He glared at Rand, his bushy white brows drawing down sharply. "You didn't tell me she had seen him already. She almost took my head off."

"I thought . . . I don't know . . . maybe the Mayor could do something, could make her see. . . ." Hands clenched in anxious fists, Rand turned from the fireplace to Bran. "Master al'Vere, what can I do?" The rotund man shook his head helplessly. He laid a freshly dampened cloth on Tam's forehead and avoided meeting Rand's eye. "I can't just watch him die, Master al'Vere. I have to do something." The gleeman shifted as if to speak. Rand rounded on him eagerly. "Do you have an idea? I'll try anything."

"I was just wondering," Thom said, tamping his long-stemmed pipe with his thumb, "if the Mayor knew who scrawled the Dragon's Fang on his door." He peered into the bowl, then looked at Tam and replaced the unlit pipe between his teeth with a sigh. "Someone seems not to like him anymore. Or maybe it's his guests they don't like."

Rand gave him a disgusted look and turned away to stare into the fire. His thoughts danced like the flames, and like the flames they concentrated fixedly on one thing. He would not give up. He could not just stand there and watch Tam die. *My father,* he thought fiercely. *My father.* Once the fever was gone, that could be cleared up as well. But the fever first. Only, how?

Bran al'Vere's mouth tightened as he looked at Rand's back, and the glare he directed at the gleeman would have given a bear pause, but Thom just waited expectantly as if he had not noticed it.

"It's probably the work of one of the Congars, or a Coplin," the Mayor said finally, "though the Light alone knows which. They're a large brood, and if there's ill to be said of someone, or even if there isn't, they'll say it. They make Cenn Buie sound honey-tongued."

"That wagonload who came in just before dawn?" the gleeman asked. "They hadn't so much as smelled a Trolloc, and all they wanted to know was when Festival was going to start, as if they couldn't see half the village in ashes."

Master al'Vere nodded grimly. "One branch of the family. But none of them are very different. That fool Darl Coplin spent half the night demanding I put Mistress Moiraine and Master Lan out of the inn, out of the village, as if there would be any village at all left without them."

Rand had only half listened to the conversation, but this last tugged him to speak. "What did they do?"

"Why, she called ball lightning out of a clear night sky," Master al'Vere replied. "Sent it darting straight at the Trollocs. You've seen trees shattered by it. The Trollocs stood it no better."

"Moiraine?" Rand said incredulously, and the Mayor nodded.

"Mistress Moiraine. And Master Lan was a whirlwind with that sword of his. His sword? The man himself is a weapon, and in ten places at once, or so it seemed. Burn me, but I still wouldn't believe it if I couldn't step outside and see. . . ." He rubbed a hand over his bald head. "Winternight visits just beginning, our hands full of presents and honeycakes and our heads full of wine, then the dogs snarling, and suddenly the two of them burst out of the inn, running through the village, shouting about Trollocs. I thought they'd had too much wine. After all . . . Trollocs? Then, before anyone knew what was happening, those . . . those things were right in the streets with us, slashing at people with their swords, torching houses, howling to freeze a man's blood." He made a sound of disgust in his throat.

"We just ran like chickens with a fox in the henyard till Master Lan put some backbone into us."

"No need to be so hard," Thom said. "You did as well as anyone could. Not every Trolloc lying out there fell to the two of them."

"Umm . . . yes, well." Master al'Vere gave himself a shake. "It's still almost too much to believe. An Aes Sedai in Emond's Field. And Master Lan is a Warder."

"An Aes Sedai?" Rand whispered. "She can't be. I talked to her. She isn't. . . . She doesn't. . . ."

"Did you think they wore signs?" the Mayor said wryly. "'Aes Sedai' painted across their backs, and maybe, 'Danger, stay away'?" Suddenly he slapped his forehead. "Aes Sedai. I'm an old fool, and losing my wits. There's a chance, Rand, if you're willing to take it. I can't tell you to do it, and I don't know if I'd have the nerve, if it were me."

"A chance?" Rand said. "I'll take any chance, if it'll help."

"Aes Sedai can heal, Rand. Burn me, lad, you've heard the stories. They can cure where medicines fail. Gleeman, you should have remembered that better than I. Gleemen's tales are full of Aes Sedai. Why didn't you speak up, instead of letting me flail around?"

"I'm a stranger here," Thom said, looking longingly at his unlit pipe, "and Goodman Coplin isn't the only one who wants nothing to do with Aes Sedai. Best the idea came from you."

"An Aes Sedai," Rand muttered, trying to make the woman who had smiled at him fit the stories. Help from an Aes Sedai was sometimes worse than no help at all, so the stories said, like poison in a pie, and their gifts always had a hook in them, like fishbait. Suddenly the coin in his pocket, the coin Moiraine had given him, seemed like a burning coal. It was all he could do not to rip it out of his coat and throw it out the window.

"Nobody wants to get involved with Aes Sedai, lad," the Mayor said slowly. "It is the only chance I can see, but it's still no small decision. I cannot make it for you, but I have seen nothing but good from Mistress Moiraine . . . Moiraine Sedai, I should call her, I suppose. Sometimes"—he gave a meaningful look at Tam—"you have to take a chance, even if it's a poor one."

"Some of the stories are exaggerated, in a way," Thom added, as if the words were being dragged from him. "Some of them. Besides, boy, what choice do you have?"

"None," Rand sighed. Tam still had not moved a muscle; his eyes were sunken as if he had been sick a week. "I'll . . . I'll go find her."

"The other side of the bridges," the gleeman said, "where they are . . . disposing of the dead Trollocs. But be careful, boy. Aes Sedai do what they do for reasons of their own, and they aren't always the reasons others think."

The last was a shout that followed Rand through the door. He had to hold onto the sword hilt to keep the scabbard from tangling in his legs as he ran, but he would not take the time to remove it. He clattered down the stairs and dashed out of the inn, tiredness forgotten for the moment. A chance for Tam, however small, was enough to overcome a night without sleep, for a time at least. That the chance came from an Aes Sedai, or what the price of it might be, he did not want to consider. And as for actually facing an Aes Sedai. . . . He took a deep breath and tried to move faster.

The bonfires stood well beyond the last houses to the north, on the Westwood side of the road to Watch Hill. The wind still carried the oily black columns of smoke away from the village, but even so a sickly sweet stink filled the air, like a roast left hours too long on the spit. Rand gagged at the smell, then swallowed hard when he realized its source. A fine thing to do with Bel Tine fires. The men tending the fires had cloths tied over their noses and mouths, but their grimaces made it plain the vinegar dampening the cloths was not enough. Even if it did kill the stench, they still knew the stench was there, and they still knew what they were doing.

Two of the men were untying the harness straps of one of the big Dhurrans from a Trolloc's ankles. Lan, squatting beside the body, had tossed back the blanket enough to reveal the Trolloc's shoulders and goat-snouted head. As Rand trotted up the Warder unfastened a metal badge, a blood-red enameled trident, from one spiked shoulder of the Trolloc's shirt of black mail.

"Ko'bal," he announced. He bounced the badge on his palm and snatched it out of the air with a growl. "That makes seven bands so far."

Moiraine, seated cross-legged on the ground a short distance off, shook her head tiredly. A walking staff, covered from end to end in carved vines and flowers, lay across her knees, and her dress had the rumpled look of having been worn too long. "Seven bands. Seven! That many have not acted together since the Trolloc Wars. Bad news piles on bad news. I am afraid, Lan. I thought we had gained a march, but we may be further behind than ever."

Rand stared at her, unable to speak. An Aes Sedai. He had been trying to convince himself that she would not look any different now that he knew who . . . what he was looking at, and to his surprise she did not. She was no longer quite so pristine, not with wisps of her hair sticking out in all directions and a faint streak of soot across her nose, yet not really different, either. Surely there must be something about an Aes Sedai to mark her for what she was. On the other hand, if outward appearance reflected what was inside, and if the stories were true, then she should look closer to a Trolloc than to a more than handsome woman whose dignity was not dented by sitting in the dirt. And she could help Tam. Whatever the cost, there was that before anything else.

He took a deep breath. "Mistress Moiraine . . . I mean, Moiraine Sedai." Both turned to look at him, and he froze under her gaze. Not the calm, smiling gaze he remembered from the Green. Her face was tired, but her dark eyes were a hawk's eyes. Aes Sedai. Breakers of the world. Puppeteers who pulled strings and made thrones and nations dance in designs only the women from Tar Valon knew.

"A little more light in the darkness," the Aes Sedai murmured. She raised her voice. "How are your dreams, Rand al'Thor?"

He stared at her. "My dreams?"

"A night like that can give a man bad dreams, Rand. If you have nightmares, you must tell me of it. I can help with bad dreams, sometimes."

"There's nothing wrong with my. . . . It's my father. He's hurt. It's not much more than a scratch, but the fever is burning him up. The Wisdom won't help. She says she can't. But the stories—" She raised an eyebrow, and he stopped and swallowed hard. *Light, is there a story with an Aes Sedai where she isn't a villain?* He looked at the Warder, but Lan appeared more interested in the dead Trolloc than in anything Rand might say. Fumbling his way under her eyes, he went on. "I . . . ah . . . it's said Aes Sedai can heal. If you can help him . . . anything you can do for him . . . whatever the cost. . . . I mean. . . ." He took a deep breath and finished up in a rush. "I'll pay any price in my power if you help him. Anything."

"Any price," Moiraine mused, half to herself. "We will speak of prices later, Rand, if at all. I can make no promises. Your Wisdom knows what she is about. I will do what I can, but it is beyond my power to stop the Wheel from turning."

"Death comes sooner or later to everyone," the Warder said grimly, "unless they serve the Dark One, and only fools are willing to pay that price."

Moiraine made a clucking sound. "Do not be so gloomy, Lan. We have some reason to celebrate. A small one, but a reason." She used the staff to pull herself to her feet. "Take me to your father, Rand. I will help him as much as I am able. Too many here have refused to let me help at all. They have heard the stories, too," she added dryly.

"He's at the inn," Rand said. "This way. And thank you. Thank you!"

They followed, but his pace took him quickly ahead. He slowed impatiently for them to catch up, then darted ahead again and had to wait again.

"Please hurry," he urged, so caught up in actually getting help for Tam that he never considered the temerity of prodding an Aes Sedai. "The fever is burning him up."

Lan glared at him. "Can't you see she's tired? Even with an *angreal,* what she did last night was like running around the village with a sack of stones on her back. I don't know that you are worth it, sheepherder, no matter what she says."

Rand blinked and held his tongue.

"Gently, my friend," Moiraine said. Without slowing her pace, she reached up to pat the Warder's shoulder. He towered over her protectively, as if he could give her strength just by being close. "You think only of taking care of me. Why should he not think the same of his father?" Lan scowled, but fell silent. "I am coming as quickly as I can, Rand, I promise you."

The fierceness of her eyes, or the calm of her voice—

not gentle, exactly; more firmly in command—Rand did not
know which to believe. Or perhaps they did go together.
Aes Sedai. He was committed, now. He matched his stride
to theirs, and tried not to think of what the price might be
that they would talk about later.

CHAPTER
8

A Place of Safety

While he was still coming through the door Rand's eyes went to his father—his father no matter what *anyone* said. Tam had not moved an inch; his eyes were still shut, and his breath came in labored gasps, low and rasping. The white-haired gleeman cut off a conversation with the Mayor—who was bent over the bed again, tending Tam—and gave Moiraine an uneasy look. The Aes Sedai ignored him. Indeed, she ignored everyone except for Tam, but at him she stared with an intent frown.

Thom stuck his unlit pipe between his teeth, then snatched it out again and glowered at it. "Man cannot even smoke in peace," he muttered. "I had better make sure some farmer doesn't steal my cloak to keep his cow warm. At least I can have my pipe out there." He hurried out of the room.

Lan stared after him, his angular face as expressionless as a rock. "I do not like that man. There is something about him I don't trust. I did not see a hair of him last night."

"He was there," Bran said, watching Moiraine uncertainly. "He must have been. His cloak did not get singed in front of the fireplace."

Rand did not care if the gleeman had spent the night hiding in the stable. "My father?" he said to Moiraine pleadingly.

Bran opened his mouth, but before he could speak Moiraine said, "Leave me with him, Master al'Vere. There is nothing you can do here now except get in my way."

For a minute Bran hesitated, torn between dislike of being ordered about in his own inn and reluctance to disobey an Aes Sedai. Finally, he straightened to clap Rand on the shoulder. "Come along, boy. Let us leave Moiraine Sedai to her . . . ah . . . her. . . . There's plenty you can give me a hand with downstairs. Before you know it Tam will be shouting for his pipe and a mug of ale."

"Can I stay?" Rand spoke to Moiraine, though she did not really seem to be aware of anyone besides Tam. Bran's hand tightened, but Rand ignored him. "Please? I'll keep out of your way. You won't even know I am here. He's my father," he added with a fierceness that startled him and widened the Mayor's eyes in surprise. Rand hoped the others put it down to tiredness, or the strain of dealing with an Aes Sedai.

"Yes, yes," Moiraine said impatiently. She had tossed her cloak and staff carelessly across the only chair in the room, and now she pushed up the sleeves of her gown, baring her arms to her elbows. Her attention never really left Tam, even while she spoke. "Sit over there. And you, too, Lan." She gestured vaguely in the direction of a long bench against the wall. Her eyes traveled slowly from Tam's feet to his head, but Rand had the prickly feeling that she was looking *beyond* him in some fashion. "You may talk if you wish," she went on absently, "but do it quietly. Now, you go, Master al'Vere. This is a sickroom, not a gathering hall. See that I am not disturbed."

The Mayor grumbled under his breath, though not loudly enough to catch her attention, of course, squeezed Rand's shoulder again, then obediently, if reluctantly, closed the door behind him.

Muttering to herself, the Aes Sedai knelt beside the bed and rested her hands lightly on Tam's chest. She closed her eyes, and for a long time she neither moved nor made a sound.

In the stories Aes Sedai wonders were always accompanied by flashes and thunderclaps, or other signs to indicate mighty works and great powers. *The* Power. The One Power, drawn from the True Source that drove the Wheel of Time. That was not something Rand wanted to think about, the Power involved with Tam, himself in the same room where the Power might be used. In the same village was bad enough. For all he could tell, though, Moiraine might just as well have gone to sleep. But he thought Tam's breathing sounded easier. She must be doing something. So intent was he that he jumped when Lan spoke softly.

"That is a fine weapon you wear. Is there by chance a heron on the blade, as well?"

For a moment Rand stared at the Warder, not grasping what it was he was talking about. He had completely forgotten Tam's sword in the lather of dealing with an Aes Sedai. It did not seem so heavy anymore. "Yes, there is. What is she doing?"

"I'd not have thought to find a heron-mark sword in a place like this," Lan said.

"It belongs to my father." He glanced at Lan's sword, the hilt just visible at the edge of his cloak; the two swords did look a good deal alike, except that no herons showed on the Warder's. He swung his eyes back to the bed. Tam's breathing did sound easier; the rasp was gone. He was sure of it. "He bought it a long time ago."

"Strange thing for a sheepherder to buy."

Rand spared a sidelong look for Lan. For a stranger to wonder about the sword was prying. For a Warder to do it. . . . Still, he felt he had to say something. "He never had any use for it, that I know of. He said it *had* no use. Until last night, anyway. I didn't even know he had it till then."

"He called it useless, did he? He must not always have thought so." Lan touched the scabbard at Rand's waist briefly with one finger. "There are places where the heron is a symbol of the master swordsman. That blade must have traveled a strange road to end up with a sheepherder in the Two Rivers."

Rand ignored the unspoken question. Moiraine still had not moved. *Was* the Aes Sedai doing anything? He shivered and rubbed his arms, not sure he really wanted to know what she was doing. An Aes Sedai.

A question of his own popped into his head then, one he did not want to ask, one he needed an answer to. "The Mayor—" He cleared his throat, and took a deep breath. "The Mayor said the only reason there's anything left of the village is because of you and her." He made himself look at the Warder. "If you had been told about a man in the woods . . . a man who made people afraid just by looking at them . . . would that have warned you? A man whose horse doesn't make any noise? And the wind doesn't touch his cloak? Would you have known what was going to happen? Could you and Moiraine Sedai have stopped it if you'd known about him?"

"Not without half a dozen of my sisters," Moiraine said, and Rand started. She still knelt by the bed, but she had taken her hands from Tam and half turned to face the two of them on the bench. Her voice never raised, but her eyes pinned Rand to the wall. "Had I known when I left Tar Valon that I would find Trollocs and Myrddraal here, I would have brought half a dozen of them, a dozen, if I had to drag them by the scruffs of their necks. By myself, a month's warning would have made little difference. Perhaps none. There is only so much one person can do, even calling on the One Power, and there were probably well over a hundred Trollocs scattered around this district last night. An entire fist."

"It would still have been good to know," Lan said sharply, the sharpness directed at Rand. "When did you see him, exactly, and where?"

"That's of no consequence now," Moiraine said. "I will not have the boy thinking he is to blame for something when he is not. I am as much to blame. That accursed raven yesterday, the way it behaved, should have warned me. And you, too, my old friend." Her tongue clicked angrily. "I was overconfident to the point of arrogance, sure that the Dark One's touch could not have spread so far. Nor so heavily, not yet. So sure."

Rand blinked. "The raven? I don't understand."

"Carrion eaters." Lan's mouth twisted in distaste. "The Dark One's minions often find spies among creatures that feed on death. Ravens and crows, mainly. Rats, in the cities, sometimes."

A quick shiver ran through Rand. Ravens and crows as spies of the Dark One? There were ravens and crows everywhere now. The Dark One's touch, Moiraine had said. The Dark One was always there—he knew that—but if you tried to walk in the Light, tried to live a good life, and did not name him, he could not harm you. That was what everybody believed, what everybody learned with his mother's milk. But Moiraine seemed to be saying. . . .

His glance fell on Tam, and everything else was pushed right out of his head. His father's face was noticeably less flushed than it had been, and his breathing sounded almost normal. Rand would have leaped up if Lan had not caught his arm. "You've done it."

Moiraine shook her head and sighed. "Not yet. I hope it is only not yet. Trolloc weapons are made at forges in the valley called Thakan'dar, on the very slopes of Shayol Ghul itself. Some of them take a taint from that place, a stain of evil in the metal. Those tainted blades make wounds that will not heal unaided, or cause deadly fevers, strange sicknesses that medicines cannot touch. I have soothed your father's pain, but the mark, the taint, is still in him. Left alone, it will grow again, and consume him."

"But you won't leave it alone." Rand's words were half plea, half command. He was shocked to realize he had spoken to an Aes Sedai like that, but she seemed not to notice his tone.

"I will not," she agreed simply. "I am very tired, Rand, and I have had no chance to rest since last night. Ordinarily it would not matter, but for this kind of hurt. . . . This"— she took a small bundle of white silk from her pouch—"is an *angreal.*" She saw his expression. "You know of *angreal,* then. Good."

Unconsciously he leaned back, further away from her and what she held. A few stories mentioned *angreal,* those relics of the Age of Legends that Aes Sedai used to perform their greatest wonders. He was startled to see her unwrap a smooth ivory figurine, age-darkened to deep brown. No longer than her hand, it was a woman in flowing robes, with long hair falling about her shoulders.

"We have lost the making of these," she said. "So much is lost, perhaps never to be found again. So few remain, the Amyrlin Seat almost did not allow me to take this one. It is well for Emond's Field, and for your father, that she did give her permission. But you must not hope too much. Now, even with it, I can do little more than I could have without it yesterday, and the taint is strong. It has had time to fester."

"You can help him," Rand said fervently. "I know you can."

Moiraine smiled, a bare curving of her lips. "We shall see." Then she turned back to Tam. One hand she laid on his forehead; the other cupped the ivory figure. Eyes closed, her face took on a look of concentration. She scarcely seemed to breathe.

"That rider you spoke of," Lan said quietly, "the one who made you afraid—that was surely a Myrddraal."

"A Myrddraal!" Rand exclaimed. "But Fades are twenty feet tall and. . . ." The words faded away under the Warder's mirthless grin.

"Sometimes, sheepherder, stories make things larger than truth. Believe me, the truth is big enough with a Halfman. Halfman, Lurk, Fade, Shadowman; the name depends on the land you're in, but they all mean Myrddraal. Fades are Trolloc spawn, throwbacks almost to the human stock the Dreadlords used to make the Trollocs. Almost. But if the human strain is made stronger, so is the taint that twists the Trollocs. Halfmen have powers of a kind, the sort that stem from the Dark One. Only the weakest Aes Sedai would fail to be a match for a Fade, one against one, but many a good man and true has fallen to them. Since the wars that ended the Age of Legends, since the Forsaken were bound, they have been the brain that tells the Trolloc fists where to strike. In the days of the Trolloc Wars, Halfmen led the Trollocs in battle, under the Dreadlords."

"He scared me," Rand said faintly. "He just looked at me, and. . . ." He shivered.

"No need for shame, sheepherder. They scare me, too. I've seen men who have been soldiers all their lives freeze like a bird facing a snake when they confronted a Halfman. In the north, in the Borderlands along the Great Blight, there is a saying. The look of the Eyeless is fear."

"The Eyeless?" Rand said, and Lan nodded.

"Myrddraal see like eagles, in darkness or in light, but they have no eyes. I can think of few things more dangerous than facing a Myrddraal. Moiraine Sedai and I both tried to kill the one that was here last night, and we failed every time. Halfmen have the Dark One's own luck."

Rand swallowed. "A Trolloc said the Myrddraal wanted to talk to me. I didn't know what it meant."

Lan's head jerked up; his eyes were blue stones. "You *talked* to a Trolloc?"

"Not exactly," Rand stammered. The Warder's gaze held him like a trap. "It talked to me. It said it wouldn't hurt me, that the Myrddraal wanted to talk to me. Then it tried to kill me." He licked his lips and rubbed his hand along the nobby leather of the sword hilt. In short, choppy sentences he explained about returning to the farmhouse. "I killed it, instead," he finished. "By accident, really. It jumped at me, and I had the sword in my hand."

Lan's face softened slightly, if rock could be said to soften. "Even so, that is something to speak of, sheepherder. Until last night there were few men south of the Borderlands who could say they had seen a Trolloc, much less killed one."

"And fewer still who have slain a Trolloc alone and un-aided," Moiraine said wearily. "It is done, Rand. Lan, help me up."

The Warder sprang to her side, but he was no quicker than Rand darting to the bed. Tam's skin was cool to the touch, though his face had a pale, washed-out look, as if he had spent far too long out of the sun. His eyes were still closed, but he drew the deep breaths of normal sleep.

"He will be all right now?" Rand asked anxiously.

"With rest, yes," Moiraine said. "A few weeks in bed, and he will be as good as ever." She walked unsteadily, despite holding Lan's arm. He swept her cloak and staff from the chair cushion for her to sit, and she eased herself down with a sigh. With a slow care she rewrapped the *angreal* and returned it to her pouch.

Rand's shoulders shook; he bit his lip to keep from laughing. At the same time he had to scrub a hand across his eyes to clear away tears. "Thank you."

"In the Age of Legends," Moiraine went on, "some Aes Sedai could fan life and health to flame if only the smallest spark remained. Those days are gone, though—perhaps forever. So much was lost; not just the making of *angreal*. So much that could be done which we dare not even dream of, if we remember it at all. There are far fewer of us now. Some talents are all but gone, and many that remain seem weaker. Now there must be both will and strength for the body to draw on, or even the strongest of us can do nothing in the way of Healing. It is fortunate that your father is a strong man, both in body and spirit. As it is, he used up much of his strength in the fight for life, but all that is left now is for him to recuperate. That will take time, but the taint is gone."

"I can never repay you," he told her without taking his eyes from Tam, "but anything I can do for you, I will. Anything at all." He remembered the talk of prices, then, and his promise. Kneeling beside Tam he meant it even more than before, but it still was not easy to look at her. "Anything. As long as it does not hurt the village, or my friends."

Moiraine raised a hand dismissively. "If you think it is necessary. I would like to talk with you, anyway. You will no doubt leave at the same time we do, and we can speak at length then."

"Leave!" he exclaimed, scrambling to his feet. "Is it really that bad? Everyone looked to me as if they were ready to start rebuilding. We are pretty settled folk in the Two Rivers. Nobody ever leaves."

"Rand—"

"And where would we go? Padan Fain said the weather is just as bad everywhere else. He's . . . he was . . . the peddler. The Trollocs. . . ." Rand swallowed, wishing Thom Merrilin had not told him what Trollocs ate. "The best I can see to do is stay right here where we belong, in the Two Rivers, and put things back together. We have crops in the ground, and it has to warm enough for the shearing, soon. I don't know who started this talk about leaving—one of the Coplins, I'll bet—but whoever it was—"

"Sheepherder," Lan broke in, "you talk when you should be listening."

He blinked at both of them. He had been half babbling, he realized, and he had rambled on while she tried to talk. While an Aes Sedai tried to talk. He wondered what to say, how to apologize, but Moiraine smiled while he was still thinking.

"I understand how you feel, Rand," she said, and he had the uncomfortable feeling that she really did. "Think no more of it." Her mouth tightened, and she shook her head. "I have handled this badly, I see. I should have rested, first, I suppose. It is you who will be leaving, Rand. You who must leave, for the sake of your village."

"Me?" He cleared his throat and tried again. "Me?" It sounded a little better this time. "Why do I have to go? I don't understand any of this. I don't want to go anywhere."

Moiraine looked at Lan, and the Warder unfolded his arms. He looked at Rand from under his leather headband,

and Rand had the feeling of being weighed on invisible scales again. "Did you know," Lan said suddenly, "that some homes were not attacked?"

"Half the village is in ashes," he protested, but the Warder waved it away.

"Some houses were only torched to create confusion. The Trollocs ignored them afterwards, and the people who fled from them as well, unless they actually got in the way of the true attack. Most of the people who've come in from the outlying farms never saw a hair of a Trolloc, and that only at a distance. Most never knew there was any trouble until they saw the village."

"I did hear about Darl Coplin," Rand said slowly. "I suppose it just didn't sink in."

"Two farms were attacked," Lan went on. "Yours and one other. Because of Bel Tine everyone who lived at the second farm was already in the village. Many people were saved because the Myrddraal was ignorant of Two Rivers customs. Festival and Winternight made its task all but impossible, but it did not know that."

Rand looked at Moiraine, leaning back in the chair, but she said nothing, only watched him, a finger laid across her lips. "Our farm, and who else's?" he asked finally.

"The Aybara farm," Lan replied. "Here in Emond's Field, they struck first at the forge, and the blacksmith's house, and Master Cauthon's house."

Rand's mouth was suddenly dry. "That's crazy," he managed to get out, then jumped as Moiraine straightened.

"Not crazy, Rand," she said. "Purposeful. The Trollocs did not come to Emond's Field by happenstance, and they did not do what they did for the pleasure of killing and burning, however much that delighted them. They knew what, or rather who, they were after. The Trollocs came to kill or capture young men of a certain age who live near Emond's Field."

"My age?" Rand's voice shook, and he did not care. "Light! Mat. What about Perrin?"

"Alive and well," Moiraine assured him, "if a trifle sooty."

"Ban Crawe and Lem Thane?"

"Were never in any danger," Lan said. "At least, no more than anyone else."

"But they saw the rider, the Fade, too, and they're the same age as I am."

"Master Crawe's house was not even damaged," Moiraine said, "and the miller and his family slept through half the attack before the noise woke them. Ban is ten months older than you, and Lem eight months younger." She smiled dryly at his surprise. "I told you I asked questions. And I also said young men of a *certain* age. You and your two friends are within weeks of one another. It was you three the Myrddraal sought, and none others."

Rand shifted uneasily, wishing she would not look at him like that, as if her eyes could pierce his brain and read what lay in every corner of it. "What would they want with us? We're just farmers, shepherds."

"That is a question that has no answer in the Two Rivers," Moiraine said quietly, "but the answer is important. Trollocs where they have not been seen in almost two thousand years tells us that much."

"Lots of stories tell about Trolloc raids," Rand said stubbornly. "We just never had one here before. Warders fight Trollocs all the time."

Lan snorted. "Boy, I expect to fight Trollocs along the Great Blight, but not here, nearly six hundred leagues to the south. That was as hot a raid last night as I'd expect to see in Shienar, or any of the Borderlands."

"In one of you," Moiraine said, "or all three, there is something the Dark One fears."

"That . . . that's impossible." Rand stumbled to the window and stared out at the village, at the people working among the ruins. "I don't care what's happened, that is just impossible." Something on the Green caught his eye. He stared, then realized it was the blackened stump of the Spring Pole. A fine Bel Tine, with a peddler, and a gleeman, and strangers. He shivered, and shook his head violently. "No. No, I'm a shepherd. The Dark One can't be interested in me."

"It took a great deal of effort," Lan said grimly, "to bring so many Trollocs so far without raising a hue and cry from the Borderlands to Caemlyn and beyond. I wish I knew how they did it. Do you really believe they went to all that bother just to burn a few houses?"

"They will be back," Moiraine added.

Rand had his mouth open to argue with Lan, but that brought him up short. He spun to face her. "Back? Can't you stop them? You did last night, and you were surprised, then. Now you know they are here."

"Perhaps," Moiraine replied. "I could send to Tar Valon for some of my sisters; they might have time to make the journey before we need them. The Myrddraal knows *I* am here, too, and it probably will not attack—not openly, at least—lacking reinforcements, more Myrddraal and more Trollocs. With enough Aes Sedai and enough Warders, the Trollocs can be beaten off, though I cannot say how many battles it will take."

A vision danced in his head, of Emond's Field all in ashes. All the farms burned. And Watch Hill, and Deven Ride, and Taren Ferry. All ashes and blood. "No," he said, and felt a wrenching inside as if he had lost his grip on something. "That's why I have to leave, isn't it? The Trollocs won't come back if I am not here." A last trace of obstinacy made him add, "If they really are after me."

Moiraine's eyebrows raised as if she were surprised that he was not convinced, but Lan said, "Are you willing to bet your village on it, sheepherder? Your whole Two Rivers?"

Rand's stubbornness faded. "No," he said again, and felt that emptiness inside again, too. "Perrin and Mat have to go, too, don't they?" Leaving the Two Rivers. Leaving his home and his father. At least Tam would get better. At least he would be able to hear him say all that on the Quarry Road had been nonsense. "We could go to Baerlon, I suppose, or even Caemlyn. I've heard there are more people in Caemlyn than in the whole Two Rivers. We'd be safe there." He tried out a laugh that sounded hollow. "I used to daydream about seeing Caemlyn. I never thought it would come about like this."

There was a long silence, then Lan said, "I would not count on Caemlyn for safety. If the Myrddraal want you badly enough, they will find a way. Walls are a poor bar to a Halfman. And you would be a fool not to believe they want you very badly indeed."

Rand thought his spirits had sunk as low as they possibly could, but at that they slid deeper.

"There is a place of safety," Moiraine said softly, and Rand's ears pricked up to listen. "In Tar Valon you would be among Aes Sedai and Warders. Even during the Trolloc Wars the forces of the Dark One feared to attack the Shining Walls. The one attempt was their greatest defeat until the very end. And Tar Valon holds all the knowledge we Aes Sedai have gathered since the Time of Madness. Some fragments even date from the Age of Legends. In Tar Valon, if anywhere, you will be able to learn why the Myrddraal want you. Why the Father of Lies wants you. That I can promise."

A journey all the way to Tar Valon was almost beyond thinking. A journey to a place where he would be surrounded by Aes Sedai. Of course, Moiraine had healed Tam—or it looked as if she had, at least—but there were all those stories. It was uncomfortable enough to be in a room with one Aes Sedai, but to be in a city full of them. . . . And she still had not demanded her price. There was always a price, so the stories said.

"How long will my father sleep?" he asked at last. "I . . . I have to tell him. He shouldn't just wake and find me gone." He thought he heard Lan give a sigh of relief. He looked at the Warder curiously, but Lan's face was as expressionless as ever.

"It is unlikely he will wake before we depart," Moiraine said. "I mean to go soon after full dark. Even a single day of delay could be fatal. It will be best if you leave him a note."

"In the night?" Rand said doubtfully, and Lan nodded.

"The Halfman will discover we are gone soon enough. There is no need to make things any easier for it than we must."

Rand fussed with his father's blankets. It was a very long way to Tar Valon. "In that case. . . . In that case, I had better go find Mat and Perrin."

"I will attend to that." Moiraine got to her feet briskly and donned her cloak with suddenly restored vigor. She put a hand on his shoulder, and he tried very hard not to flinch. She did not press hard, but it was an iron grip that held him as surely as a forked stick held a snake. "It will be best if we keep all of this just among us. Do you understand? The same ones who put the Dragon's Fang on the inn door might make trouble if they knew."

"I understand." He drew a relieved breath when she took her hand away.

"I will have Mistress al'Vere bring you something to eat," she went on just as if she had not noticed his reaction. "Then you need to sleep. It will be a hard journey tonight even if you are rested."

The door closed behind them, and Rand stood looking down at Tam—looking at Tam, but seeing nothing. Not until that very minute had he realized that Emond's Field was a part of him as much as he was a part of it. He realized it now because he knew that was what he had felt tearing loose. He was apart from the village, now. The Shepherd of the Night wanted him. It was impossible—he was only a farmer—but the Trollocs had come, and Lan was right about one thing. He could not risk the village on the chance Moiraine was wrong. He could not even tell anyone; the Coplins really would make trouble about something like that. He had to trust an Aes Sedai.

"Don't wake him, now," Mistress al'Vere said, as the Mayor shut the door behind his wife and himself. The cloth-covered tray she carried gave off delicious, warm smells. She set it on the chest against the wall, then firmly moved Rand away from the bed.

"Mistress Moiraine told me what he needs," she said softly, "and it does not include you falling on top of him from exhaustion. I've brought you a bite to eat. Don't let it get cold, now."

"I wish you wouldn't call her that," Bran said peevishly. "Moiraine Sedai is proper. She might get mad."

Mistress al'Vere gave him a pat on the cheek. "You just leave me to worry about that. She and I had a long talk. And keep your voice down. If you wake Tam, you'll have to answer to me *and* Moiraine Sedai." She put an emphasis on Moiraine's title that made Bran's insistence seem foolish. "The two of you keep out of my way." With a fond smile for her husband, she turned to the bed and Tam.

Master al'Vere gave Rand a frustrated look. "She's an Aes Sedai. Half the women in the village act as if she sits in the Women's Circle, and the rest as if she were a Trolloc. Not a one of them seems to realize you have to be careful around Aes Sedai. The men may keep looking at her sideways, but at least they aren't doing anything that might provoke her."

Careful, Rand thought. It was not too late to start being

careful. "Master al'Vere," he said slowly, "do you know how many farms were attacked?"

"Only two that I've heard of so far, including your place." The Mayor paused, frowning, then shrugged. "It doesn't seem enough, with what happened here. I should be glad of it, but. . . . Well, we'll probably hear of more before the day is out."

Rand sighed. No need to ask which farms. "Here in the village, did they. . . . I mean, was there anything to show what they were after?"

"After, boy? I don't know that they were after anything, except maybe killing us all. It was just the way I said. The dogs barking, and Moiraine Sedai and Lan running through the streets, then somebody shouted that Master Luhhan's house and the forge were on fire. Abell Cauthon's house flared up—odd that; it's nearly in the middle of the village. Anyway, the next thing the Trollocs were all among us. No, I don't think they were *after* anything." He gave an abrupt bark of a laugh, and cut it short with a wary look at his wife. She did not look around from Tam. "To tell the truth," he went on more quietly, "they seemed almost as confused as we were. I doubt they expected to find an Aes Sedai here, or a Warder."

"I suppose not," Rand said, grimacing.

If Moiraine had told the truth about that, she probably had told the truth about the rest, too. For a moment he thought about asking the Mayor's advice, but Master al'Vere obviously knew little more about Aes Sedai than anyone else in the village. Besides, he was reluctant to tell even the Mayor what was going on—what Moiraine said was going on. He was not sure if he was more afraid of being laughed at or being believed. He rubbed a thumb against the hilt of Tam's sword. His father had been out into the world; he must know more about Aes Sedai than the Mayor did. But if Tam really had been out of the Two Rivers, then maybe what he had said in the Westwood. . . . He scrubbed both hands through his hair, scattering that line of thought.

"You need sleep, lad," the Mayor said.

"Yes, you do," Mistress al'Vere added. "You're almost falling down where you stand."

Rand blinked at her in surprise. He had not even realized

she had left his father. He did need sleep; just the thought set off a yawn.

"You can take the bed in the next room," the Mayor said. "There's already a fire laid."

Rand looked at his father; Tam was still deep in sleep, and that made him yawn again. "I'd rather stay in here, if you don't mind. For when he wakes up."

Sickroom matters were in Mistress al'Vere's province, and the Mayor left it to her. She hesitated only a moment before nodding. "But you let him wake on his own. If you bother his sleep. . . ." He tried to say he would do as she ordered, but the words got tangled in yet another yawn. She shook her head with a smile. "You will be asleep yourself in no time at all. If you must stay, curl up next to the fire. And drink a little of that beef broth before you doze off."

"I will," Rand said. He would have agreed to anything that kept him in that room. "And I won't wake him."

"See that you do not," Mistress al'Vere told him firmly, but not in an unkindly way. "I'll bring you up a pillow and some blankets."

When the door finally closed behind them, Rand dragged the lone chair in the room over beside the bed and sat down where he could watch Tam. It was all very well for Mistress al'Vere to talk about sleep—his jaws cracked as he stifled a yawn—but he could not sleep yet. Tam might wake at any time, and maybe only stay awake a short while. Rand had to be waiting when he did.

He grimaced and twisted in the chair, absently shifting the sword hilt out of his ribs. He still felt backward about telling anyone what Moiraine had said, but this was Tam, after all. This was. . . . Without realizing it he set his jaw determinedly. *My father. I can tell my father anything.*

He twisted a little more in the chair and put his head against the chairback. Tam was his father, and nobody could tell him what to say or not say to his father. He just had to stay awake until Tam woke up. He just had to. . . .

CHAPTER
9

Tellings of the Wheel

Rand's heart pounded as he ran, and he stared in dismay at the barren hills surrounding him. This was not just a place where spring was late in coming; spring had never come here, and never would come. Nothing grew in the cold soil that crunched under his boots, not so much as a bit of lichen. He scrambled past boulders, twice as tall as he was; dust coated the stone as if never a drop of rain had touched it. The sun was a swollen, blood-red ball, more fiery than on the hottest day of summer and bright enough to sear his eyes, but it stood stark against a leaden cauldron of a sky where clouds of sharp black and silver roiled and boiled on every horizon. For all the swirling clouds, though, no breath of breeze stirred across the land, and despite the sullen sun the air burned cold like the depths of winter.

Rand looked over his shoulder often as he ran, but he could not see his pursuers. Only desolate hills and jagged black mountains, many topped by tall plumes of dark smoke rising to join the milling clouds. If he could not see his hunters, though, he could hear them, howling behind him, guttural voices shouting with the glee of the chase, howling with the joy of blood to come. Trollocs. Coming closer, and his strength was almost gone.

With desperate haste he scrambled to the top of a knife-edged ridge, then dropped to his knees with a groan. Below him a sheer rock wall fell away, a thousand-foot cliff plummeting into a vast canyon. Steamy mists covered the canyon floor, their thick gray surface rolling in grim waves, rolling and breaking against the cliff beneath him, but more slowly than any ocean wave had ever moved. Patches of fog glowed red for an instant as if great fires had suddenly flared beneath, then died. Thunder rumbled in the depths of the valley, and lightning crackled through the gray, sometimes striking up at the sky.

It was not the valley itself that sapped his strength and filled the empty spaces left with helplessness. From the center of the furious vapors a mountain thrust upward, a mountain taller than any he had ever seen in the Mountains of Mist, a mountain as black as the loss of all hope. That bleak stone spire, a dagger stabbing at the heavens, was the source of his desolation. He had never seen it before, but he knew it. The memory of it flashed away like quicksilver when he tried to touch it, but the memory was there. He knew it was there.

Unseen fingers touched him, pulled at his arms and legs, trying to draw him to the mountain. His body twitched, ready to obey. His arms and legs stiffened as if he thought he could dig his fingers and toes into the stone. Ghostly strings entwined around his heart, pulling him calling him to the spire mountain. Tears ran down his face, and he sagged to the ground. He felt his will draining away like water out of a holed bucket. Just a little longer, and he would go where he was called. He would obey, do as he was told. Abruptly he discovered another emotion: anger. Push him, pull him, he was not a sheep to be prodded into a pen. The anger squeezed itself into one hard knot, and he clung to it as he would have clung to a raft in a flood.

Serve me, a voice whispered in the stillness of his mind. A familiar voice. If he listened hard enough he was sure he would know it. *Serve me.* He shook his head to try to get it out of his head. *Serve me!* He shook his fist at the black mountain. "The Light consume you, Shai'tan!"

Abruptly the smell of death lay thick around him. A figure loomed over him, in a cloak the color of dried blood, a figure with a face. . . . He did not want to see the face that looked down at him. He did not want to think of that face. It hurt to think of it, turned his mind to embers. A hand reached toward him. Not caring if he fell over the edge, he threw himself away. He had to get away. Far away. He fell, flailing at the air, wanting to scream, finding no breath for screaming, no breath at all.

Abruptly he was no longer in the barren land, no longer falling. Winter-brown grass flattened under his boots; it seemed like flowers. He almost laughed to see scattered trees and bushes, leafless as they were, dotting the gently rolling plain that now surrounded him. In the distance reared a single mountain, its peak broken and split, but this mountain brought no fear or despair. It was just a mountain, though oddly out of place there, with no other in sight.

A broad river flowed by the mountain, and on an island in the middle of that river was a city such as might live in a gleeman's tale, a city surrounded by high walls gleaming white and silver beneath the warm sun. With mingled relief and joy he started for the walls, for the safety and serenity he somehow knew he would find behind them.

As he came closer he made out soaring towers, many joined by wondrous walkways that spanned the open air. High bridges arched from both banks of the river to the island city. Even at a distance he could see lacy stonework on those spans, seemingly too delicate to withstand the swift waters that rushed beneath them. Beyond those bridges lay safety. Sanctuary.

Of a sudden a chill ran along his bones; an icy clamminess settled on his skin, and the air around him turned fetid and dank. Without looking back he ran, ran from the pursuer whose freezing fingers brushed his back and tugged at his cloak, ran from the light-eating figure with the face that. . . . He could not remember the face, except as terror. He did not want to remember the face. He ran, and the ground passed beneath his feet, rolling hills and flat plain . . . and he wanted to howl like a dog gone mad. The city was receding before him. The harder he ran, the further away drifted the white shining walls and haven. They grew smaller, and smaller, until only a pale speck remained on the horizon. The cold hand of his pursuer clutched at his collar. If those fingers touched him he knew he would go mad. Or worse. Much worse. Even as that surety came to him he tripped and fell . . .

"Noooo!" he screamed.

. . . and grunted as paving stones smacked the breath out of him. Wonderingly he got to his feet. He stood on the approaches to one of the marvelous bridges he had seen rearing over the river. Smiling people walked by on either side of him, people dressed in so many colors they made him think of a field of wildflowers. Some of them spoke to him, but he could not understand, though the words sounded as if he should. But the faces were friendly, and the people gestured him onward, over the bridge with its intricate stonework, onward toward the shining, silver-streaked walls and the towers beyond. Toward the safety he knew waited there.

He joined the throng streaming across the bridge and into the city through massive gates set in tall, pristine walls. Within was a wonderland where the meanest structure seemed a palace. It was as though the builders had been told to take stone and brick and tile and create beauty to take the breath of mortal men. There was no building, no monument that did not make him stare with goggling eyes. Music drifted down the streets, a hundred different songs, but all blending with the clamor of the crowds to make one grand, joyous harmony. The scents of sweet perfumes and sharp spices, of wondrous foods and myriad flowers, all floated in the air, as if every good smell in the world were gathered there.

The street by which he entered the city, broad and paved with smooth, gray stone, stretched straight before him toward the center of the city. At its end loomed a tower larger and taller than any other in the city, a tower as white as fresh-fallen snow. That tower was where safety lay, and the knowledge he sought. But the city was such as he had never dreamed of seeing. Surely it would not matter if he delayed just a short time in going to the tower? He turned aside onto a narrower street, where jugglers strolled among hawkers of strange fruits.

Ahead of him down the street was a snow-white tower. The same tower. In just a little while, he thought, and rounded another corner. At the far end of this street, too, lay the white tower. Stubbornly he turned another corner, and another, and each time the alabaster tower met his eyes. He spun to run away from it . . . and skidded to a halt. Before him, the white tower. He was afraid to look over his shoulder, afraid it would be there, too.

The faces around him were still friendly, but shattered hope filled them now, hope he had broken. Still the people gestured him forward, pleading gestures. Toward the tower.

Their eyes shone with desperate need, and only he could fulfill it, only he could save them.

Very well, he thought. The tower was, after all, where he wanted to go.

Even as he took his first step forward disappointment faded from those about him, and smiles wreathed every face. They moved with him, and small children strewed his path with flower petals. He looked over his shoulder in confusion, wondering who the flowers were meant for, but behind him were only more smiling people gesturing him on. *They must be for me,* he thought, and wondered why that suddenly did not seem strange at all. But wonderment lasted only a moment before melting away; all was as it should be.

First one, then another of the people began to sing, until every voice was lifted in a glorious anthem. He still could not understand the words, but a dozen interweaving harmonies shouted joy and salvation. Musicians capered through the on-flowing crowd, adding flutes and harps and drums in a dozen sizes to the hymn, and all the songs he had heard before blended in without seam. Girls danced around him, laying garlands of sweet-smelling blossoms across his shoulders, twining them about his neck. They smiled at him, their delight growing with every step he took. He could not help but smile back. His feet itched to join in their dance, and even as he thought of it he was dancing, his steps fitting as if he had known it all from birth. He threw back his head and laughed; his feet were lighter than they had ever been, dancing with. . . . He could not remember the name, but it did not seem important.

It is your destiny, a voice whispered in his head, and the whisper was a thread in the paean.

Carrying him like a twig on the crest of a wave, the crowd flowed into a huge square in the middle of the city, and for the first time he saw that the white tower rose from a great palace of pale marble, sculpted rather than built, curving walls and swelling domes and delicate spires fingering the sky. The whole of it made him gasp in awe. Broad stairs of pristine stone led up from the square, and at the foot of those stairs the people halted, but their song rose ever higher. The swelling voices buoyed his feet. *Your destiny,* the voice whispered, insistent now, eager.

He no longer danced, but neither did he stop. He mounted the stairs without hesitation. This was where he belonged.

Scrollwork covered the massive doors at the top of the stairs, carvings so intricate and delicate that he could not imagine a knife blade fine enough to fit. The portals swung open, and he went in. They closed behind him with an echoing crash like thunder.

"We have been waiting for you," the Myrddraal hissed.

Rand sat bolt upright, gasping for breath and shivering, staring. Tam was still asleep on the bed. Slowly his breathing slowed. Half-consumed logs blazed in the fireplace with a good bed of coals built up around the fire-irons; someone had been there to tend it while he slept. A blanket lay at his feet, where it had fallen when he woke. The makeshift litter was gone, too, and his and Tam's cloaks had been hung by the door.

He wiped cold sweat from his face with a hand that was none too steady and wondered if naming the Dark One in a dream brought his attention the same way that naming him aloud did.

Twilight darkened the window; the moon was well up, round and fat, and evening stars sparkled above the Mountains of Mist. He had slept the day away. He rubbed a sore spot on his side. Apparently he had slept with the sword hilt jabbing him in the ribs. Between that and an empty stomach and the night before, it was no wonder he had had nightmares.

His belly rumbled, and he got up stiffly and made his way to the table where Mistress al'Vere had left the tray. He twitched aside the white napkin. Despite the time he had slept, the beef broth was still warm, and so was the crusty bread. Mistress al'Vere's hand was plain; the tray had been replaced. Once she decided you needed a hot meal, she did not give up till it was inside you.

He gulped down some broth, and it was all he could do to put some meat and cheese between two pieces of bread before stuffing it in his mouth. Taking big bites, he went back to the bed.

Mistress al'Vere had apparently seen to Tam, as well. Tam had been undressed, his clothes now clean and neatly folded on the bedside table, and a blanket was drawn up under his chin. When Rand touched his father's forehead, Tam opened his eyes.

"There you are, boy. Marin said you were here, but I couldn't even sit up to see. She said you were too tired for her to wake just so I could look at you. Even Bran can't get around her when she has her mind set."

Tam's voice was weak, but his gaze was clear and steady. *The Aes Sedai was right,* Rand thought. With rest he would be as good as ever.

"Can I get you something to eat? Mistress al'Vere left a tray."

"She fed me already . . . if you can call it that. Wouldn't let me have anything but broth. How can a man avoid bad dreams with nothing but broth in his. . . ." Tam fumbled a hand from under the cover and touched the sword at Rand's waist. "Then it wasn't a dream. When Marin told me I was sick, I thought I had been. . . . But you're all right. That is all that matters. What of the farm?"

Rand took a deep breath. "The Trollocs killed the sheep. I think they took the cow, too, and the house needs a good cleaning." He managed a weak smile. "We were luckier than some. They burned half the village."

He told Tam everything that had happened, or at least most of it. Tam listened closely, and asked sharp questions, so he found himself having to tell about returning to the farmhouse from the woods, and that brought in the Trolloc he had killed. He had to tell how Nynaeve had said Tam was dying to explain why the Aes Sedai had tended him instead of the Wisdom. Tam's eyes widened at that, an Aes Sedai in Emond's Field. But Rand could see no need to go over every step of the journey from the farm, or his fears, or the Myrddraal on the road. Certainly not his nightmares as he slept by the bed. Especially he saw no reason to mention Tam's ramblings under the fever. Not yet. Moiraine's story, though: there was no avoiding that.

"Now that's a tale to make a gleeman proud," Tam muttered when he was done. "What would Trollocs want with you boys? Or the Dark One, Light help us?"

"You think she was lying? Master al'Vere said she was telling the truth about only two farms being attacked. And about Master Luhhan's house, and Master Cauthon's."

For a moment Tam lay silent before saying, "Tell me what she said. Her exact words, mind, just as she said them."

Rand struggled. Who ever remembered the *exact* words they heard? He chewed at his lip and scratched his head, and bit by bit he brought it out, as nearly as he could remember. "I can't think of anything else," he finished. "Some of it I'm not too sure she didn't say a little differently, but it's close, anyway."

"It's good enough. It has to be, doesn't it? You see, lad, Aes Sedai are tricksome. They don't lie, not right out, but the truth an Aes Sedai tells you is not always the truth you think it is. You take care around her."

"I've heard the stories," Rand retorted. "I'm not a child."

"So you're not, so you're not." Tam sighed heavily, then shrugged in annoyance. "I should be going along with you, just the same. The world outside the Two Rivers is nothing like Emond's Field."

That was an opening to ask about Tam going outside and all the rest of it, but Rand did not take it. His mouth fell open, instead. "Just like that? I thought you would try to talk me out of it. I thought you'd have a hundred reasons I should not go." He realized he had been hoping Tam would have a hundred reasons, and good ones.

"Maybe not a hundred," Tam said with a snort, "but a few did come to mind. Only they don't count for much. If Trollocs are after you, you will be safer in Tar Valon than you could ever be here. Just remember to be wary. Aes Sedai do things for their own reasons, and those are not always the reasons you think."

"The gleeman said something like that," Rand said slowly.

"Then he knows what he's talking about. You listen sharp, think deep, and guard your tongue. That's good advice for any dealings beyond the Two Rivers, but most especially with Aes Sedai. And with Warders. Tell Lan something, and you've as good as told Moiraine. If he's a Warder, then he's bonded to her as sure as the sun rose this morning, and he won't keep many secrets from her, if any."

Rand knew little about the bonding between Aes Sedai and Warders, though it played a big part in every story about Warders he had ever heard. It was something to do with the Power, a gift to the Warder, or maybe some sort of exchange. The Warders got all sorts of benefits, according to the stories. They healed more quickly than other men, and could go longer without food or water or sleep. Supposedly they could sense Trollocs, if they were close enough, and other creatures of the Dark One, too, which explained how Lan and Moiraine had tried to warn the village before the attack. As to what the Aes Sedai got out of it, the stories were silent, but he was not about to believe they did not get something.

"I'll be careful," Rand said. "I just wish I knew why. It doesn't make any sense. Why me? Why us?"

"I wish I knew, too, boy. Blood and ashes, I wish I knew." Tam sighed heavily. "Well, no use trying to put a broken egg back in the shell, I suppose. How soon do you have to go? I'll be back on my feet in a day or two, and we can see about starting a new flock. Oren Dautry has some good stock he might be willing to part with, with the pastures all gone, and so does Jon Thane."

"Moiraine . . . the Aes Sedai said you had to stay in bed. She said weeks." Tam opened his mouth, but Rand went on. "And she talked to Mistress al'Vere."

"Oh. Well, maybe I can talk Marin around." Tam did not sound hopeful of it, though. He gave Rand a sharp look. "The way you avoided answering means you have to leave soon. Tomorrow? Or tonight?"

"Tonight," Rand said quietly, and Tam nodded sadly.

"Yes. Well, if it must be done, best not to delay. But we will see about this 'weeks' business." He plucked at his blankets with more irritation than strength. "Perhaps I'll follow in a few days anyway. Catch you up on the road. We will see if Marin can keep me in bed when I want to get up."

There was a tap at the door, and Lan stuck his head into the room. "Say your goodbyes quickly, sheepherder, and come. There may be trouble."

"Trouble?" Rand said, and the Warder growled at him impatiently.

"Just hurry!"

Hastily Rand snatched up his cloak. He started to undo the sword belt, but Tam spoke up.

"Keep it. You will probably have more need of it than I, though, the Light willing, neither of us will. Take care, lad. You hear?"

Ignoring Lan's continued growls, Rand bent to grab Tam in a hug. "I will come back. I promise you that."

"Of course you will." Tam laughed. He returned the hug weakly, and ended by patting Rand on the back. "I know that. And I'll have twice as many sheep for you to tend when you return. Now go, before that fellow does himself an injury."

Rand tried to hang back, tried to find the words for the question he did not want to ask, but Lan entered the room to catch him by the arm and pull him into the hall. The Warder had donned a dull gray-green tunic of overlapping metal scales. His voice rasped with irritation.

"We have to hurry. Don't you understand the word *trouble*?"

Outside the room Mat waited, cloaked and coated and carrying his bow. A quiver hung at his waist. He was rocking anxiously on his heels, and he kept glancing off toward the stairs with what seemed to be equal parts impatience and fear. "This isn't much like the stories, Rand, is it?" he said hoarsely.

"What kind of trouble?" Rand demanded, but the Warder ran ahead of him instead of answering, taking the steps down two at a time. Mat dashed after him with quick gestures for Rand to follow.

Shrugging into his cloak, he caught up to them downstairs. Only a feeble light filled the common room; half the candles had burned out and most of the rest were guttering. It was empty except for the three of them. Mat stood next to one of the front windows, peeping out as if trying not to be seen. Lan held the door open a crack and peered into the inn yard.

Wondering what they could be watching, Rand went to join him. The Warder muttered at him to take a care, but he did open the door a trifle wider to make room for Rand to look, too.

At first he was not sure exactly what he was seeing. A crowd of village men, some three dozen or so, clustered near the burned-out husk of the peddler's wagon, night pushed back by the torches some of them carried. Moiraine faced them, her back to the inn, leaning with seeming casualness on her walking staff. Hari Coplin stood in the front of the crowd with his brother, Darl, and Bili Congar. Cenn Buie was there, as well, looking uncomfortable. Rand was startled to see Hari shake his fist at Moiraine.

"Leave Emond's Field!" the sour-faced farmer shouted. A few voices in the crowd echoed him, but hesitantly, and no one pushed forward. They might be willing to confront an Aes Sedai from within a crowd, but none of them wanted to be singled out. Not by an Aes Sedai who had every reason to take offense.

"You brought those monsters!" Darl roared. He waved a torch over his head, and there were shouts of, "You brought them!" and "It's your fault!" led by his cousin Bili.

Hari elbowed Cenn Buie, and the old thatcher pursed his lips and gave him a sidelong glare. "Those things . . . those Trollocs didn't appear until after you came," Cenn muttered, barely loud enough to be heard. He swung his head from side to side dourly as if wishing he were somewhere else and looking for a way to get there. "You're an Aes Sedai. We want none of your sort in the Two Rivers. Aes Sedai bring trouble on their backs. If you stay, you will only bring more."

His speech brought no response from the gathered villagers, and Hari scowled in frustration. Abruptly he snatched Darl's torch and shook it in her direction. "Get out!" he shouted. "Or we'll burn you out!"

Dead silence fell, except for the shuffling of a few feet as men drew back. Two Rivers folk could fight back if they were attacked, but violence was far from common, and threatening people was foreign to them, beyond the occasional shaking of a fist. Cenn Buie, Bili Congar, and the Coplins were left out front alone. Bili looked as if he wanted to back away, too.

Hari gave an uneasy start at the lack of support, but he recovered quickly. "Get out!" he shouted again, echoed by Darl and, more weakly, by Bili. Hari glared at the others. Most of the crowd failed to meet his eye.

Suddenly Bran al'Vere and Haral Luhhan moved out of the shadows, stopping apart from both the Aes Sedai and the crowd. In one hand the Mayor casually carried the big wooden maul he used to drive spigots into casks. "Did someone suggest burning my inn?" he asked softly.

The two Coplins took a step back, and Cenn Buie edged away from them. Bili Congar dived into the crowd. "Not that," Darl said quickly. "We never said that, Bran . . . ah, Mayor."

Bran nodded. "Then perhaps I heard you threatening to harm guests in my inn?"

"She's an Aes Sedai," Hari began angrily, but his words cut off as Haral Luhhan moved.

The blacksmith simply stretched, thrusting thick arms over his head, tightening massive fists until his knuckles cracked, but Hari looked at the burly man as if one of those fists had been shaken under his nose. Haral folded his arms across his chest. "Your pardon, Hari. I did not mean to cut you off. You were saying?"

But Hari, shoulders hunched as though he were trying to draw into himself and disappear, seemed to have nothing more to say.

"I'm surprised at you people," Bran rumbled. "Paet al'Caar, your boy's leg was broken last night, but I saw him walking on it today—because of her. Eward Candwin, you were lying on your belly with a gash down your back like a fish for cleaning, till she laid hands on you. Now it looks as if it happened a month ago, and unless I misdoubt there'll barely be a scar. And you, Cenn." The thatcher started to fade back into the crowd, but stopped, held uncomfortably by Bran's gaze. "I'd be shocked to see any man on the Village Council here, Cenn, but you most of all. Your arm would still be hanging useless at your side, a mass of burns and bruises, if not for her. If you have no gratitude, have you no shame?"

Cenn half lifted his right hand, then looked away from it angrily. "I cannot deny what she did," he muttered, and he did sound ashamed. "She helped me, and others," he went on in a pleading tone, "but she's an Aes Sedai, Bran. If those Trollocs didn't come because of her, why did they come? We want no part of Aes Sedai in the Two Rivers. Let them keep their troubles away from us."

A few men, safely back in the crowd, shouted then. "We want no Aes Sedai troubles!" "Send her away!" "Drive her out!" "Why did they come if not because of her?"

A scowl grew on Bran's face, but before he could speak Moiraine suddenly whirled her vine-carved staff above her head, spinning it with both hands. Rand's gasp echoed that of the villagers, for a hissing white flame flared from each end of the staff, standing straight out like spearpoints despite the rod's whirling. Even Bran and Haral edged away from her. She snapped her arms down straight out before her, the staff parallel to the ground, but the pale fire still jetted out, brighter than the torches. Men shied away, held up hands to shield their eyes from the pain of that brilliance.

"Is this what Aemon's blood has come to?" The Aes Sedai's voice was not loud, but it overwhelmed every other sound. "Little people squabbling for the right to hide like rabbits? You have forgotten who you were, forgotten what you were, but I had hoped some small part was left, some memory in blood and bone. Some shred to steel you for the long night coming."

No one spoke. The two Coplins looked as if they never wanted to open their mouths again.

Bran said, "Forgotten who we were? We are who we always have been. Honest farmers and shepherds and craftsmen. Two Rivers folk."

"To the south," Moiraine said, "lies the river you call the White River, but far to the east of here men call it still by its rightful name. Manetherendrelle. In the Old Tongue, Waters of the Mountain Home. Sparkling waters that once coursed through a land of bravery and beauty. Two thousand years ago Manetherendrelle flowed by the walls of a mountain city so lovely to behold that Ogier stonemasons came to stare in wonder. Farms and villages covered this region, and that you call the Forest of Shadows, as well, and beyond. But all of those folk thought of themselves as the people of the Mountain Home, the people of Manetheren.

"Their King was Aemon al Caar al Thorin, Aemon son of Caar son of Thorin, and Eldrene ay Ellan ay Carlan was his Queen. Aemon, a man so fearless that the greatest compliment for courage any could give, even among his enemies, was to say a man had Aemon's heart. Eldrene, so beautiful that it was said the flowers bloomed to make her smile. Bravery and beauty and wisdom and a love that death could not sunder. Weep, if you have a heart, for the loss of them, for the loss of even their memory. Weep, for the loss of their blood."

She fell silent then, but no one spoke. Rand was as bound as the others in the spell she had created. When she spoke again, he drank it in, and so did the rest.

"For nearly two centuries the Trolloc Wars had ravaged the length and breadth of the world, and wherever battles raged, the Red Eagle banner of Manetheren was in the forefront. The men of Manetheren were a thorn to the Dark One's foot and a bramble to his hand. Sing of Manetheren, that would never bend knee to the Shadow. Sing of Manetheren, the sword that could not be broken.

"They were far away, the men of Manetheren, on the Field of Bekkar, called the Field of Blood, when news came that a Trolloc army was moving against their home. Too far to do else but wait to hear of their land's death, for the forces of the Dark One meant to make an end of them. Kill the mighty oak by hacking away its roots. Too far to do else but mourn. But they were the men of the Mountain Home.

"Without hesitation, without thought for the distance they must travel, they marched from the very field of victory, still covered in dust and sweat and blood. Day and night they marched, for they had seen the horror a Trolloc army left behind it, and no man of them could sleep while such a danger threatened Manetheren. They moved as if their feet had wings, marching further and faster than friends hoped or enemies feared they could. At any other day that march alone would have inspired songs. When the Dark One's armies swooped down upon the lands of Manetheren, the men of the Mountain Home stood before it, with their backs to the Tarendrelle."

Some villager raised a small cheer then, but Moiraine kept on as if she had not heard. "The host that faced the men of Manetheren was enough to daunt the bravest heart. Ravens blackened the sky; Trollocs blackened the land. Trollocs and their human allies. Trollocs and Darkfriends in tens of tens of thousands, and Dreadlords to command. At night their cook-fires outnumbered the stars, and dawn revealed the banner of Ba'alzamon at their head. Ba'alzamon, Heart of the Dark. An ancient name for the Father of Lies. The Dark One could not have been free of his prison at Shayol Ghul, for if he had been, not all the forces of humankind together could have stood against him, but there was power there. Dreadlords, and some evil that made that light-destroying banner seem no more than right and sent a chill into the souls of the men who faced it.

"Yet, they knew what they must do. Their homeland lay just across the river. They must keep that host, and the power with it, from the Mountain Home. Aemon had sent out messengers. Aid was promised if they could hold for but three days at the Tarendrelle. Hold for three days against odds that should overwhelm them in the first hour. Yet somehow, through bloody assault and desperate defense, they held through an hour, and the second hour, and the third. For three days they fought, and though the land became a butcher's yard, no crossing of the Tarendrelle did they yield. By the third night no help had come, and no messengers, and they fought on alone. For six days. For nine. And on the tenth day Aemon knew the bitter taste of betrayal. No help was coming, and they could hold the river crossings no more."

"What did they do?" Hari demanded. Torchfires flickered in the chill night breeze, but no one made a move to draw a cloak tighter.

"Aemon crossed the Tarendrelle," Moiraine told them, "destroying the bridges behind him. And he sent word throughout his land for the people to flee, for he knew the powers with the Trolloc horde would find a way to bring it across the river. Even as the word went out, the Trolloc crossing began, and the soldiers of Manetheren took up the fight again, to buy with their lives what hours they could for their people to escape. From the city of Manetheren, Eldrene organized the flight of her people into the deepest forests and the fastness of the mountains.

"But some did not flee. First in a trickle, then a river, then a flood, men went, not to safety, but to join the army fighting for their land. Shepherds with bows, and farmers with pitchforks, and woodsmen with axes. Women went, too, shouldering what weapons they could find and marching side by side with their men. No one made that journey who did not know they would never return. But it was their land. It had been their fathers', and it would be their children's, and they went to pay the price of it. Not a step of ground was given up until it was soaked in blood, but at the last the army of Manetheren was driven back, back to here, to this place you now call Emond's Field. And here the Trolloc hordes surrounded them."

Her voice held the sound of cold tears. "Trolloc dead and

the corpses of human renegades piled up in mounds, but always more scrambled over those charnel heaps in waves of death that had no end. There could be but one finish. No man or woman who had stood beneath the banner of the Red Eagle at that day's dawning still lived when night fell. The sword that could not be broken was shattered.

"In the Mountains of Mist, alone in the emptied city of Manetheren, Eldrene felt Aemon die, and her heart died with him. And where her heart had been was left only a thirst for vengeance, vengeance for her love, vengeance for her people and her land. Driven by grief she reached out to the True Source, and hurled the One Power at the Trolloc army. And there the Dreadlords died wherever they stood, whether in their secret councils or exhorting their soldiers. In the passing of a breath the Dreadlords and the generals of the Dark One's host burst into flame. Fire consumed their bodies, and terror consumed their just-victorious army.

"Now they ran like beasts before a wildfire in the forest, with no thought for anything but escape. North and south they fled. Thousands drowned attempting to cross the Tarendrelle without the aid of the Dreadlords, and at the Manetherendrelle they tore down the bridges in their fright at what might be following them. Where they found people, they slew and burned, but to flee was the need that gripped them. Until, at last, no one of them remained in the lands of Manetheren. They were dispersed like dust before the whirlwind. The final vengeance came more slowly, but it came, when they were hunted down by other peoples, by other armies in other lands. None was left alive of those who did murder at Aemon's Field.

"But the price was high for Manetheren. Eldrene had drawn to herself more of the One Power than any human could ever hope to wield unaided. As the enemy generals died, so did she die, and the fires that consumed her consumed the empty city of Manetheren, even the stones of it, down to the living rock of the mountains. Yet the people had been saved.

"Nothing was left of their farms, their villages, or their great city. Some would say there was nothing left for them, nothing but to flee to other lands, where they could begin anew. They did not say so. They had paid such a price in blood and hope for their land as had never been paid before, and now they were bound to that soil by ties stronger than steel. Other wars would wrack them in years to come, until at last their corner of the world was forgotten and at last they had forgotten wars and the ways of war. Never again did Manetheren rise. Its soaring spires and splashing fountains became as a dream that slowly faded from the minds of its people. But they, and their children, and their children's children, held the land that was theirs. They held it when the long centuries had washed the why of it from their memories. They held it until, today, there is you. Weep for Manetheren. Weep for what is lost forever."

The fires on Moiraine's staff winked out, and she lowered it to her side as if it weighed a hundred pounds. For a long moment the moan of the wind was the only sound. Then Paet al'Caar shouldered past the Coplins.

"I don't know about your story," the long-jawed farmer said. "I'm no thorn to the Dark One's foot, nor ever likely to be, neither. But my Wil is walking because of you, and for that I am ashamed to be here. I don't know if you can forgive me, but whether you will or no, I'll be going. And for me, you can stay in Emond's Field as long as you like."

With a quick duck of his head, almost a bow, he pushed back through the crowd. Others began to mutter then, offering shamefaced penitence before they, too, slipped away one by one. The Coplins, sour-mouthed and scowling once more, looked at the faces around them and vanished into the night without a word. Bili Congar had disappeared even before his cousins.

Lan pulled Rand back and shut the door. "Let's go, boy." The Warder started for the back of the inn. "Come along, both of you. Quickly!"

Rand hesitated, exchanging a wondering glance with Mat. While Moiraine had been telling the story, Master al'Vere's Dhurrans could not have dragged him away, but now something else held his feet. This was the real beginning, leaving the inn and following the Warder into the night. . . . He shook himself, and tried to firm his resolve. He had no choice but to go, but he would come back to Emond's Field, however far or long this journey was.

"What are you waiting for?" Lan asked from the door

that led out of the back of the common room. With a start
Mat hurried to him.

Trying to convince himself that he was beginning a
grand adventure, Rand followed them through the darkened
kitchen and out into the stableyard.

CHAPTER
10

Leavetaking

A single lantern, its shutters half closed, hung from a nail on a stall post, casting a dim light. Deep shadows swallowed most of the stalls. As Rand came through the doors from the stableyard, hard on the heels of Mat and the Warder, Perrin leaped up in a rustle of straw from where he had been sitting with his back against a stall door. A heavy cloak swathed him.

Lan barely paused to demand, "Did you look the way I told you, blacksmith?"

"I looked," Perrin replied. "There's nobody here but us. Why would anybody hide—"

"Care and a long life go together, blacksmith." The Warder ran a quick eye around the shadowed stable and the deeper shadows of the hayloft above, then shook his head. "No time," he muttered, half to himself. "Hurry, she says."

As if to suit his words, he strode quickly to where the five horses stood tethered, bridled and saddled at the back of the pool of light. Two were the black stallion and white mare that Rand had seen before. The others, if not quite so tall or so sleek, certainly appeared to be among the best the Two Rivers had to offer. With hasty care Lan began examining cinches and girth straps, and the leather ties that held saddlebags, water-skins, and blanketrolls behind the saddles.

Rand exchanged shaky smiles with his friends, trying hard to look as if he really was eager to be off.

For the first time Mat noticed the sword at Rand's waist, and pointed to it. "You becoming a Warder?" He laughed, then swallowed it with a quick glance at Lan. The Warder apparently took no notice. "Or at least a merchant's guard,"

Mat went on with a grin that seemed only a little forced. He hefted his bow. "An honest man's weapon isn't good enough for him."

Rand thought about flourishing the sword, but Lan being there stopped him. The Warder was not even looking in his direction, but he was sure the man was aware of everything that went on around him. Instead he said with exaggerated casualness, "It might be useful," as if wearing a sword were nothing out of the ordinary.

Perrin moved, trying to hide something under his cloak. Rand glimpsed a wide leather belt encircling the apprentice blacksmith's waist, with the handle of an axe thrust through a loop on the belt.

"What do you have there?" he asked.

"Merchant's guard, indeed," Mat hooted.

The shaggy-haired youth gave Mat a frown that suggested he had already had more than his fair share of joking, then sighed heavily and tossed back his cloak to uncover the axe. It was no common woodsman's tool. A broad half-moon blade on one side of the head and a curved spike on the other made it every bit as strange for the Two Rivers as Rand's sword. Perrin's hand rested on it with a sense of familiarity, though.

"Master Luhhan made it about two years ago, for a wool-buyer's guard. But when it was done the fellow wouldn't pay what he had agreed, and Master Luhhan would not take less. He gave it to me when"—he cleared his throat, then shot Rand the same warning frown he'd given Mat—"when he found me practicing with it. He said I might as well have it since he couldn't make anything useful from it."

"Practicing," Mat snickered, but held up his hands soothingly when Perrin raised his head. "As you say. It's just as well one of us knows how to use a real weapon."

"That bow is a real weapon," Lan said suddenly. He propped an arm across the saddle of his tall black and regarded them gravely. "So are the slings I've seen you village boys with. Just because you never used them for anything but hunting rabbits or chasing a wolf away from the sheep makes no difference. Anything can be a weapon, if the man or woman who holds it has the nerve and will to make it so. Trollocs aside, you had better have that clear in your minds before we leave the Two Rivers, before we leave Emond's Field, if you want to reach Tar Valon alive."

His face and voice, cold as death and hard as a rough-hewn gravestone, stifled their smiles and their tongues. Perrin grimaced and pulled his cloak back over the axe. Mat stared at his feet and stirred the straw on the stable floor with his toe. The Warder grunted and went back to his checking, and the silence lengthened.

"It isn't much like the stories," Mat said, finally.

"I don't know," Perrin said sourly. "Trollocs, a Warder, an Aes Sedai. What more could you ask?"

"Aes Sedai," Mat whispered, sounding as if he were suddenly cold.

"Do you believe her, Rand?" Perrin asked. "I mean, what would Trollocs want with us?"

As one, they glanced at the Warder. Lan appeared absorbed in the white mare's saddle girth, but the three of them moved back toward the stable door, away from Lan. Even so, they huddled together and spoke softly.

Rand shook his head. "I don't know, but she had it right about our farms being the only ones attacked. And they attacked Master Luhhan's house and the forge first, here in the village. I asked the Mayor. It's as easy to believe they are after us as anything else I can think of." Suddenly he realized they were both staring at him.

"You asked the Mayor?" Mat said incredulously. "She said not to tell anybody."

"I didn't tell him why I was asking," Rand protested. "Do you mean you didn't talk to anybody at all? You didn't let anybody know you're going?"

Perrin shrugged defensively. "Moiraine Sedai said not anybody."

"We left notes," Mat said. "For our families. They'll find them in the morning. Rand, my mother thinks Tar Valon is the next thing to Shayol Ghul." He gave a little laugh to show he did not share her opinion. It was not very convincing. "She'd try to lock me in the cellar if she believed I was even thinking of going there."

"Master Luhhan is stubborn as stone," Perrin added, "and Mistress Luhhan is worse. If you'd seen her digging through what's left of the house, saying she hoped the Trollocs did come back so she could get her hands on them. . . ."

"Burn me, Rand," Mat said, "I know she's an Aes Sedai and all, but the Trollocs were really here. She said not to tell anybody. If an Aes Sedai doesn't know what to do about something like this, who does?"

"I don't know." Rand rubbed at his forehead. His head hurt; he could not get that dream out of his mind. "My father believes her. At least, he agreed that we had to go."

Suddenly Moiraine was in the doorway. "You talked to your father about this journey?" She was clothed in dark gray from head to foot, with a skirt divided for riding astride, and the serpent ring was the only gold she wore now.

Rand eyed her walking staff; despite the flames he had seen, there was no sign of charring, or even soot. "I couldn't go off without letting him know."

She eyed him for a moment with pursed lips before turning to the others. "And did you also decide that a note was not enough?" Mat and Perrin talked on top of each other, assuring her they had only left notes, the way she had said. Nodding, she waved them to silence, and gave Rand a sharp look. "What is done is already woven in the Pattern. Lan?"

"The horses are ready," the Warder said, "and we have enough provisions to reach Baerlon with some to spare. We can leave at any time. I suggest now."

"Not without me." Egwene slipped into the stable, a shawl-wrapped bundle in her arms. Rand nearly fell over his own feet.

Lan's sword had come half out of its sheath; when he saw who it was he shoved the blade back, his eyes suddenly flat. Perrin and Mat began babbling to convince Moiraine they had not told Egwene about leaving. The Aes Sedai ignored them; she simply looked at Egwene, tapping her lips thoughtfully with one finger.

The hood of Egwene's dark brown cloak was pulled up, but not enough to hide the defiant way she faced Moiraine. "I have everything I need here. Including food. And I will not be left behind. I'll probably never get another chance to see the world outside the Two Rivers."

"This isn't a picnic trip into the Waterwood, Egwene," Mat growled. He stepped back when she looked at him from under lowered brows.

"Thank you, Mat. I wouldn't have known. Do you think you three are the only ones who want to see what's outside? I've dreamed about it as long as you have, and I don't intend to miss this chance."

"How did you find out we were leaving?" Rand demanded. "Anyway, you can't go with us. We aren't leaving for the fun of it. The Trollocs are after us." She gave him a tolerant look, and he flushed and stiffened indignantly.

"First," she told him patiently, "I saw Mat creeping about, trying hard not to be noticed. Then I saw Perrin attempting to hide that absurd great axe under his cloak. I knew Lan had bought a horse, and it suddenly occurred to me to wonder why he needed another. And if he could buy one, he could buy others. Putting that with Mat and Perrin sneaking about like bull calves pretending to be foxes . . . well, I could see only one answer. I don't know if I'm surprised or not to find you here, Rand, after all your talk about daydreams. With Mat and Perrin involved, I suppose I should have known you would be in it, too."

"I have to go, Egwene," Rand said. "All of us do, or the Trollocs will come back."

"The Trollocs!" Egwene laughed incredulously. "Rand, if you've decided to see some of the world, well and good, but please spare me any of your nonsensical tales."

"It's true," Perrin said as Mat began, "The Trollocs—"

"Enough," Moiraine said quietly, but it cut their talk as sharply as a knife. "Did anyone else notice all of this?" Her voice was soft, but Egwene swallowed and drew herself up before answering.

"After last night, all they can think about is rebuilding, that and what to do if it happens again. They couldn't see anything else unless it was pushed under their noses. And I told no one what I suspected. No one."

"Very well," Moiraine said after a moment. "You may come with us."

A startled expression darted across Lan's face. It was gone in an instant, leaving him outwardly calm, but furious words erupted from him. "No, Moiraine!"

"It is part of the Pattern, now, Lan."

"It is ridiculous!" he retorted. "There's no reason for her to come along, and every reason for her not to."

"There *is* a reason for it," Moiraine said calmly. "A part of the Pattern, Lan." The Warder's stony face showed nothing, but he nodded slowly.

"But, Egwene," Rand said, "the Trollocs will be chasing us. We won't be safe until we get to Tar Valon."

"Don't try to frighten me off," she said. "I am going."

Rand knew that tone of voice. He had not heard it since she decided that climbing the tallest trees was for children, but he remembered it well. "If you think being chased by Trollocs will be fun," he began, but Moiraine interrupted.

"We have no time for this. We must be as far away as possible by daybreak. If she is left behind, Rand, she could rouse the village before we have gone a mile, and that would surely warn the Myrddraal."

"I would not do that," Egwene protested.

"She can ride the gleeman's horse," the Warder said. "I'll leave him enough to buy another."

"That will not be possible," came Thom Merrilin's resonant voice from the hayloft. Lan's sword left its sheath this time, and he did not put it back as he stared up at the gleeman.

Thom tossed down a blanketroll, then slung his cased flute and harp across his back and shouldered bulging saddlebags. "This village has no use for me, now, while on the other hand, I have never performed in Tar Valon. And though I usually journey alone, after last night I have no objections at all to traveling in company."

The Warder gave Perrin a hard look, and Perrin shifted uncomfortably. "I didn't think of looking in the loft," he muttered.

As the long-limbed gleeman scrambled down the ladder from the loft, Lan spoke, stiffly formal. "Is this part of the Pattern, too, Moiraine Sedai?"

"Everything is a part of the Pattern, my old friend," Moiraine replied softly. "We cannot pick and choose. But we shall see."

Thom put his feet on the stable floor and turned from the ladder, brushing straw from his patch-covered cloak. "In fact," he said in more normal tones, "you might say that I insist on traveling in company. I have given many hours over many mugs of ale to thinking of how I might end my days. A Trolloc's cookpot was not one of the thoughts." He looked askance at the Warder's sword. "There's no need for that. I am not a cheese for slicing."

"Master Merrilin," Moiraine said, "we must go quickly, and almost certainly in great danger. The Trollocs are still out there, and we go by night. Are you sure that you want to travel with us?"

Thom eyed the lot of them with a quizzical smile. "If it is not too dangerous for the girl, it can't be too dangerous for me. Besides, what gleeman would not face a little danger to perform in Tar Valon?"

Moiraine nodded, and Lan scabbarded his sword. Rand suddenly wondered what would have happened if Thom had changed his mind, or if Moiraine had not nodded. The gleeman began saddling his horse as if similar thoughts had never crossed his mind, but Rand noticed that he eyed Lan's sword more than once.

"Now," Moiraine said. "What horse for Egwene?"

"The peddler's horses are as bad as the Dhurrans," the Warder replied sourly. "Strong, but slow plodders."

"Bela," Rand said, getting a look from Lan that made him wish he had kept silent. But he knew he could not dissuade Egwene; the only thing left was to help. "Bela may not be as fast as the others, but she's strong. I ride her sometimes. She can keep up."

Lan looked into Bela's stall, muttering under his breath. "She might be a little better than the others," he said finally. "I don't suppose there is any other choice."

"Then she will have to do," Moiraine said. "Rand, find a saddle for Bela. Quickly, now! We have tarried too long already."

Rand hurriedly chose a saddle and blanket in the tack room, then fetched Bela from her stall. The mare looked back at him in sleepy surprise when he put the saddle on her back. When he rode her, it was barebacked; she was not used to a saddle. He made soothing noises while he tightened the girth strap, and she accepted the oddity with no more than a shake of her mane.

Taking Egwene's bundle from her, he tied it on behind the saddle while she mounted and adjusted her skirts. They were not divided for riding astride, so her wool stockings were bared to the knee. She wore the same soft leather shoes as all the other village girls. They were not at all suited for journeying to Watch Hill, much less Tar Valon.

"I still think you shouldn't come," he said. "I wasn't making it up about the Trollocs. But I promise I will take care of you."

"Perhaps I'll take care of you," she replied lightly. At his exasperated look she smiled and bent down to smooth his hair. "I know you'll look after me, Rand. We will look after each other. But now you had better look after getting on your horse."

All of the others were already mounted and waiting for him, he realized. The only horse left riderless was Cloud, a tall gray with a black mane and tail that belonged to Jon Thane, or had. He scrambled into the saddle, though not without difficulty as the gray tossed his head and pranced sideways as Rand put his foot in the stirrup, and his scabbard caught in his legs. It was not chance that his friends had not chosen Cloud. Master Thane often raced the spirited gray against merchants' horses, and Rand had never known him to lose, but he had never known Cloud to give anyone an easy ride, either. Lan must have given a huge price to make the miller sell. As he settled in the saddle Cloud's dancing increased, as if the gray were eager to run. Rand gripped the reins firmly and tried to think that he would have no trouble. Perhaps if he convinced himself, he could convince the horse, too.

An owl hooted in the night outside, and the village people jumped before they realized what it was. They laughed nervously and exchanged shamefaced looks.

"Next thing, field mice will chase us up a tree," Egwene said with an unsteady chuckle.

Lan shook his head. "Better if it had been wolves."

"Wolves!" Perrin exclaimed, and the Warder favored him with a flat stare.

"Wolves don't like Trollocs, blacksmith, and Trollocs don't like wolves, or dogs, either. If I heard wolves I would be sure there were no Trollocs waiting out there for us." He moved into the moonlit night, walking his tall black slowly.

Moiraine rode after him without a moment's hesitation, and Egwene kept hard to the Aes Sedai's side. Rand and the gleeman brought up the rear, following Mat and Perrin.

The back of the inn was dark and silent, and dappled moon shadows filled the stableyard. The soft thuds of the hooves faded quickly, swallowed by the night. In the darkness the Warder's cloak made him a shadow, too. Only the need to let him lead the way kept the others from clustering around him. Getting out of the village without being seen was going to be no easy task, Rand decided as he neared the gate. At least, without being seen by villagers. Many windows in the village emitted pale yellow light, and although those glows seemed very small in the night now, shapes moved frequently within them, the shapes of villagers watching to see what this night brought. No one wanted to be caught by surprise again.

In the deep shadows beside the inn, just on the point of leaving the stableyard, Lan abruptly halted, motioning sharply for silence.

Boots rattled on the Wagon Bridge, and here and there on the bridge moonlight glinted off metal. The boots clattered across the bridge, grated on gravel, and approached the inn. No sound at all came from those in the shadow. Rand suspected his friends, at least, were too frightened to make a noise. Like him.

The footsteps halted before the inn in the grayness just beyond the dim light from the common-room windows. It was not until Jon Thane stepped forward, a spear propped on his stout shoulder, an old jerkin sewn all over with steel disks straining across his chest, that Rand saw them for what they were. A dozen men from the village and the surrounding farms, some in helmets or pieces of armor that had lain dust-covered in attics for generations, all with a spear or a woodaxe or a rusty bill.

The miller peered into a common-room window, then turned with a curt, "It looks right here." The others formed in two ragged ranks behind him, and the patrol marched into the night as if stepping to three different drums.

"Two Dha'vol Trollocs would have them all for breakfast," Lan muttered when the sound of their boots had faded, "but they have eyes and ears." He turned his stallion back. "Come."

Slowly, quietly, the Warder took them back across the stableyard, down the bank through the willows and into the Winespring Water. So close to the Winespring itself the cold, swift water, gleaming as it swirled around the horses' legs, was deep enough to lap against the soles of the riders' boots.

Climbing out on the far bank, the line of horses wound its way under the Warder's deft direction, keeping away from any of the village houses. From time to time Lan stopped, signing them all to be quiet, though no one else heard or saw anything. Each time he did, however, another patrol of villagers and farmers soon passed. Slowly they moved toward the north edge of the village.

Rand peered at the high-peaked houses in the dark, trying to impress them on his memory. *A fine adventurer I am,* he thought. He was not even out of the village yet, and already he was homesick. But he did not stop looking.

They passed beyond the last farmhouses on the outskirts of the village and into the countryside, paralleling the North Road that led to Taren Ferry. Rand thought that surely no night sky elsewhere could be as beautiful as the Two Rivers sky. The clear black seemed to reach to forever, and myriad stars gleamed like points of light scattered through crystal. The moon, only a thin slice less than full, appeared almost close enough to touch, if he stretched, and. . . .

A black shape flew slowly across the silvery ball of the moon. Rand's involuntary jerk on the reins halted the gray. A bat, he thought weakly, but he knew it was not. Bats were a common sight of an evening, darting after flies and bitemes in the twilight. The wings that carried this creature might have the same shape, but they moved with the slow, powerful sweep of a bird of prey. And it was hunting. The way it cast back and forth in long arcs left no doubt of that. Worst of all was the size. For a bat to seem so large against the moon it would have had to be almost within arm's reach. He tried to judge in his mind how far away it must be, and how big. The body of it had to be as large as a man, and the wings. . . . It crossed the face of the moon again, wheeling suddenly downward to be engulfed by the night.

He did not realize that Lan had ridden back to him until the Warder caught his arm. "What are you sitting here and staring at, boy? We have to keep moving." The others waited behind Lan.

Half expecting to be told he was letting fear of the Trollocs overcome his sense, Rand told what he had seen. He hoped that Lan would dismiss it as a bat, or a trick of his eyes.

Lan growled a word, sounding as if it left a bad taste in his mouth. "Draghkar." Egwene and the other Two Rivers folk stared at the sky nervously in all directions, but the gleeman groaned softly.

"Yes," Moiraine said. "It is too much to hope otherwise. And if the Myrddraal has a Draghkar at his command, then he will soon know where we are, if he does not already. We must move more quickly than we can cross-country. We may still reach Taren Ferry ahead of the Myrddraal, and he and his Trollocs will not cross as easily as we."

"A Draghkar?" Egwene said. "What is it?"

It was Thom Merrilin who answered her hoarsely. "In the war that ended the Age of Legends, worse than Trollocs and Halfmen were created."

Moiraine's head jerked toward him as he spoke. Not even the dark could hide the sharpness of her look.

Before anyone could ask the gleeman for more, Lan began giving directions. "We take to the North Road, now. For your lives, follow my lead, keep up and keep together."

He wheeled his horse about, and the others galloped wordlessly after him.

CHAPTER

II

The Road to Taren Ferry

On the hard-packed dirt of the North Road the horses stretched out, manes and tails streaming back in the moonlight as they raced northward, hooves pounding a steady rhythm. Lan led the way, black horse and shadow-clad rider all but invisible in the cold night. Moiraine's white mare, matching the stallion stride for stride, was a pale dart speeding through the dark. The rest followed in a tight line, as if they were all tied to a rope with one end in the Warder's hands.

Rand galloped last in line, with Thom Merrilin just ahead and the others less distinct beyond. The gleeman never turned his head, reserving his eyes for where they ran, not what they ran from. If Trollocs appeared behind, or the Fade on its silent horse, or that flying creature, the Draghkar, it would be up to Rand to sound an alarm.

Every few minutes he craned his neck to peer behind while he clung to Cloud's mane and reins. The Draghkar. . . . Worse than Trollocs and Fades, Thom had said. But the sky was empty, and only darkness and shadows met his eyes on the ground. Shadows that could hide an army.

Now that the gray had been let loose to run, the animal sped through the night like a ghost, easily keeping pace with Lan's stallion. And Cloud wanted to go faster. He wanted to catch the black, strained to catch the black. Rand had to keep a firm hand on the reins to hold him back. Cloud lunged against his restraint as if the gray thought this were a race, fighting him for mastery with every stride. Rand clung to saddle and reins with every muscle taut. Fervently he hoped his mount did not detect how uneasy he was. If Cloud did, he would lose the one real edge he held, however precariously.

Lying low on Cloud's neck, Rand kept a worried eye on Bela and on her rider. When he had said the shaggy mare could stay with the others, he had not meant on the run. She kept up now only by running as he had not thought she could. Lan had not wanted Egwene in their number. Would he slow for her if Bela began to flag? Or would he try to leave her behind? The Aes Sedai and the Warder thought Rand and his friends were important in some way, but for all of Moiraine's talk of the Pattern, he did not think they included Egwene in that importance.

If Bela fell back, he would fall back, too, whatever Moiraine and Lan had to say about it. Back where the Fade and the Trollocs were. Back where the Draghkar was. With all his heart and desperation he silently shouted at Bela to run like the wind, silently tried to will strength into her. *Run!* His skin prickled, and his bones felt as if they were freezing, ready to split open. *The Light help her, run!* And Bela ran.

On and on they sped, northward into the night, time fading into an indistinct blur. Now and again the lights of farmhouses flashed into sight, then disappeared as quickly as imagination. Dogs' sharp challenges faded swiftly behind, or cut off abruptly as the dogs decided they had been chased away. They raced through darkness relieved only by watery pale moonlight, a darkness where trees along the road loomed up without warning, then were gone. For the rest, murk surrounded them, and only a solitary night-bird's cry, lonely and mournful, disturbed the steady pounding of hooves.

Abruptly Lan slowed, then brought the file of horses to a stop. Rand was not sure how long they had been moving, but a soft ache filled his legs from gripping the saddle. Ahead of them in the night, lights sparkled, as if a tall swarm of fireflies held one place among the trees.

Rand frowned at the lights in puzzlement, then suddenly gasped with surprise. The fireflies were windows, the windows of houses covering the sides and top of a hill. It was Watch Hill. He could hardly believe they had come so far. They had probably made the journey as fast as it had ever been traveled. Following Lan's example, Rand and Thom

Merrilin dismounted. Cloud stood head down, sides heaving. Lather, almost indistinguishable from the horse's smoky sides, flecked the gray's neck and shoulders. Rand thought that Cloud would not be carrying anyone further that night.

"Much as I would like to put all these villages behind me," Thom announced, "a few hours rest would not go amiss right now. Surely we have enough of a lead to allow that?"

Rand stretched, knuckling the small of his back. "If we're stopping the rest of the night in Watch Hill, we may as well go on up."

A vagrant gust of wind brought a fragment of song from the village, and smells of cooking that made his mouth water. They were still celebrating in Watch Hill. There had been no Trollocs to disturb their Bel Tine. He looked for Egwene. She was leaning against Bela, slumped with weariness. The others were climbing down as well, with many a sigh and much stretching of aching muscles. Only the Warder and the Aes Sedai showed no visible sign of fatigue.

"I could do with some singing," Mat put in tiredly. "And maybe a hot mutton pie at the White Boar." Pausing, he added, "I've never been further than Watch Hill. The White Boar's not nearly as good as the Winespring Inn."

"The White Boar isn't so bad," Perrin said. "A mutton pie for me, too. And lots of hot tea to take the chill off my bones."

"We cannot stop until we are across the Taren," Lan said sharply. "Not for more than a few minutes."

"But the horses," Rand protested. "We'll run them to death if we try to go any further tonight. Moiraine Sedai, surely you—"

He had vaguely noticed her moving among the horses, but he had not paid any real attention to what she did. Now she brushed past him to lay her hands on Cloud's neck. Rand fell silent. Suddenly the horse tossed his head with a soft whicker, nearly pulling the reins from Rand's hands. The gray danced a step sideways, as restive as if he had spent a week in a stable. Without a word Moiraine went to Bela.

"I did not know she could do that," Rand said softly to Lan, his cheeks hot.

"You, of all people, should have suspected it," the Warder

replied. "You watched her with your father. She will wash all the fatigue away. First from the horses, then from the rest of you."

"The rest of us. Not you?"

"Not me, sheepherder. I don't need it, not yet. And not her. What she can do for others, she cannot do for herself. Only one of us will ride tired. You had better hope she does not grow too tired before we reach Tar Valon."

"Too tired for what?" Rand asked the Warder.

"You were right about your Bela, Rand," Moiraine said from where she stood by the mare. "She has a good heart, and as much stubbornness as the rest of you Two Rivers folk. Strange as it seems, she may be the least weary of all."

A scream ripped the darkness, a sound like a man dying under sharp knives, and wings swooped low above the party. The night deepened in the shadow that swept over them. With panicked cries the horses reared wildly.

The wind of the Draghkar's wings beat at Rand with a feel like the touch of slime, like chittering in the dank dimness of a nightmare. He had no time even to feel the fear of it, for Cloud exploded into the air with a scream of his own, twisting desperately as if attempting to shake off some clinging thing. Rand, hanging onto the reins, was jerked off his feet and dragged across the ground, Cloud screaming as though the big gray felt wolves tearing at his hocks.

Somehow he maintained his grip on the reins; using the other hand as much as his legs he scrambled onto his feet, taking leaping, staggering steps to keep from being pulled down again. His breath came in ragged pants of desperation. He could not let Cloud get away. He threw out a frantic hand, barely catching the bridle. Cloud reared, lifting him into the air; Rand clung helplessly, hoping against hope that the horse would quieten.

The shock of landing jarred Rand to his teeth, but suddenly the gray was still, nostrils flaring and eyes rolling, stiff-legged and trembling. Rand was trembling as well, and all but hanging from the bridle. *That jolt must have shaken the fool animal, too,* he thought. He took three or four deep, shaky breaths. Only then could he look around and see what had happened to the others.

Chaos reigned among the party. They clutched reins against jerking heads, trying with little success to calm the rearing horses that dragged them about in a milling mass. Only two seemingly had no trouble at all with their mounts. Moiraine sat straight in her saddle, the white mare stepping delicately away from the confusion as if nothing at all out of the ordinary had happened. On foot, Lan scanned the sky, sword in one hand and reins in the other; the sleek black stallion stood quietly beside him.

Sounds of merrymaking no longer came from Watch Hill. Those in the village must have heard the cry, too. Rand knew they would listen awhile, and perhaps watch for what had caused it, then return to their jollity. They would soon forget the incident, its memory submerged by song and food and dance and fun. Perhaps when they heard the news of what had happened in Emond's Field some would remember, and wonder. A fiddle began to play, and after a moment a flute joined in. The village was resuming its celebration.

"Mount!" Lan commanded curtly. Sheathing his sword, he leaped onto the stallion. "The Draghkar would not have showed itself unless it had already reported our whereabouts to the Myrddraal." Another strident shriek drifted down from far above, fainter but no less harsh. The music from Watch Hill silenced raggedly once more. "It tracks us now, marking us for the Halfman. He won't be far."

The horses, fresh now as well as fear-struck, pranced and backed away from those trying to mount. A cursing Thom Merrilin was the first into his saddle, but the others were up soon after. All but one.

"Hurry, Rand!" Egwene shouted. The Draghkar gave shrill voice once more, and Bela ran a few steps before she could rein the mare in. "Hurry!"

With a start Rand realized that instead of trying to mount Cloud he had been standing there staring at the sky in a vain attempt to locate the source of those vile shrieks. More, all unaware, he had drawn Tam's sword as if to fight the flying thing.

His face reddened, making him glad for the night to hide him. Awkwardly, with one hand occupied by the reins, he re-sheathed the blade, glancing hastily at the others. Moiraine, Lan, and Egwene all were looking at him, though he could not be sure how much they could see in the moonlight. The rest seemed too absorbed with keeping their horses under control to pay him any mind. He put a hand on the pommel and reached the saddle in one leap, as if he had been doing the like all his life. If any of his friends had noticed the sword, he would surely hear about it later. There would be time enough to worry about it then.

As soon as he was in the saddle they were all off at a gallop again, up the road and by the dome-like hill. Dogs barked in the village; their passage was not entirely unnoticed. *Or maybe the dogs smelled Trollocs,* Rand thought. The barking and the village lights alike vanished quickly behind them.

They galloped in a knot, horses all but jostling together as they ran. Lan ordered them to spread out again, but no one wanted to be even a little alone in the night. A scream came from high overhead. The Warder gave up and let them run clustered.

Rand was close behind Moiraine and Lan, the gray straining in an effort to force himself between the Warder's black and the Aes Sedai's trim mare. Egwene and the gleeman raced on either flank of him, while Rand's friends crowded in behind. Cloud, spurred by the Draghkar's cries, ran beyond anything Rand could do to slow him even had he wished to, yet the gray could not gain so much as a step on the other two horses.

The Draghkar's shriek challenged the night.

Stout Bela ran with neck outstretched and tail and mane streaming in the wind of her running, matching the larger horses' every stride. *The Aes Sedai must have done something more than simply ridding her of fatigue.*

Egwene's face in the moonlight was smiling in excited delight. Her braid streamed behind like the horses' manes, and the gleam in her eyes was not all from the moon, Rand was sure. His mouth dropped open in surprise, until a swallowed biteme set him off into a fit of coughing.

Lan must have asked a question, for Moiraine suddenly shouted over the wind and the pounding of hooves. "I cannot! Most especially not from the back of a galloping horse. They are not easily killed, even when they can be seen. We must run, and hope."

They galloped through a tatter of fog, thin and no higher than the horses' knees. Cloud sped through it in two strides, and Rand blinked, wondering if he had imagined it. Surely the night was too cold for fog. Another patch of ragged gray whisked by them to one side, larger than the first. It had been growing, as if the mist oozed from the ground. Above them, the Draghkar screamed in rage. Fog enveloped the riders for a brief moment and was gone, came again and vanished behind. The icy mist left a chill dampness on Rand's face and hands. Then a wall of pale gray loomed before them, and they were suddenly enshrouded. The thickness of it muffled the sound of their hooves to dullness, and the cries from overhead seemed to come through a wall. Rand could only just make out the shapes of Egwene and Thom Merrilin on either side of him.

Lan did not slow their pace. "There is still only one place we can be going," he called, his voice sounding hollow and directionless.

"Myrddraal are sly," Moiraine replied. "I will use its own slyness against it." They galloped on silently.

Slaty mist obscured both sky and ground, so that the riders, themselves turned to shadow, appeared to float through night clouds. Even the legs of their own horses seemed to have vanished.

Rand shifted in his saddle, shrinking away from the icy fog. Knowing that Moiraine could do things, even seeing her do them, was one thing; having those things leave his skin damp was something else again. He realized he was holding his breath, too, and called himself nine kinds of idiot. He could not ride all the way to Taren Ferry without breathing. She had used the One Power on Tam, and he seemed all right. Still, he had to make himself let that breath go and inhale. The air was heavy, but if colder it was otherwise no different than that on any other foggy night. He told himself that, but he was not sure he believed it.

Lan encouraged them to keep close, now, to stay where each could see the outlines of others in that damp, frosty grayness. Yet the Warder still did not slacken his stallion's dead run. Side by side, Lan and Moiraine led the way through the fog as if they could see clearly what lay ahead. The rest could only trust and follow. And hope.

The shrill cries that had hounded them faded as they galloped, and then were gone, but that gave small comfort. Forest and farmhouses, moon and road were shrouded and hidden. Dogs still barked, hollow and distant in the gray haze, when they passed farms, but there was no other sound save the dull drumming of their horses' hooves. Nothing in that featureless ashen fog changed. Nothing gave any hint of the passage of time except the growing ache in thigh and back.

It had to have been hours, Rand was sure. His hands had clutched his reins until he was not sure he could release them, and he wondered if he would ever walk properly again. He glanced back only once. Shadows in the fog raced behind him, but he could not even be certain of their number. Or even that they really were his friends. The chill and damp soaked through his cloak and coat and shirt, soaked into his bones, so it seemed. Only the rush of air past his face and the gather and stretch of the horse beneath him told him he was moving at all. It must have been hours.

"Slow," Lan called suddenly. "Draw rein."

Rand was so startled that Cloud forced between Lan and Moiraine, forging ahead for half a dozen strides before he could pull the big gray to a halt and stare.

Houses loomed in the fog on all sides, houses strangely tall to Rand's eye. He had never seen this place before, but he had often heard descriptions. That tallness came from high redstone foundations, necessary when the spring melt in the Mountains of Mist made the Taren overflow its banks. They had reached Taren Ferry.

Lan trotted the black warhorse past him. "Don't be so eager, sheepherder."

Discomfited, Rand fell into place without explaining as the party moved deeper into the village. His face was hot, and for the moment the fog was welcome.

A lone dog, unseen in the cold mist, barked at them furiously, then ran away. Here and there a light appeared in a window as some early-riser stirred. Other than the dog, no sound save the muted clops of their horses' hooves disturbed the last hour of the night.

Rand had met few people from Taren Ferry. He tried to recall what little he knew about them. They seldom ventured down into what they called "the lower villages," with their noses up as if they smelled something bad. The few he had met bore strange names, like Hilltop and Stoneboat. One and all, Taren Ferry folk had a reputation for slyness and trickery. If you shook hands with a Taren Ferry man, people said, you counted your fingers afterwards.

Lan and Moiraine stopped before a tall, dark house that looked exactly like any other in the village. Fog swirled around the Warder like smoke as he leaped from his saddle and mounted the stairs that rose to the front door, as high above the street as their heads. At the top of the stairs Lan hammered with his fist on the door.

"I thought he wanted quiet," Mat muttered.

Lan's pounding went on. A light appeared in the window of the next house, and someone shouted angrily, but the Warder kept on with his drumming.

Abruptly the door was flung back by a man in a nightshirt that flapped about his bare ankles. An oil lamp in one hand illumined a narrow face with pointed features. He opened his mouth angrily, then let it stay open as his head swiveled to take in the fog, eyes bulging. "What's this?" he said. "What's this?" Chill gray tendrils curled into the doorway, and he hurriedly stepped back away from them.

"Master Hightower," Lan said. "Just the man I need. We want to cross over on your ferry."

"He never even saw a high tower," Mat snickered. Rand made shushing motions at his friend. The sharp-faced fellow raised his lamp higher and peered down at them suspiciously.

After a minute Master Hightower said crossly, "The ferry goes over in daylight. Not in the night. Not ever. And not in this fog, neither. Come back when the sun's up and the fog's gone."

He started to turn away, but Lan caught his wrist. The ferryman opened his mouth angrily. Gold glinted in the lamplight as the Warder counted out coins one by one into the other's palm. Hightower licked his lips as the coins clinked, and by inches his head moved closer to his hand, as if he could not believe what he was seeing.

"And as much again," Lan said, "when we are safely on the other side. But we leave now."

"Now?" Chewing his lower lip, the ferrety man shifted his feet and peered out at the mist-laden night, then nodded abruptly. "Now it is. Well, let loose my wrist. I have to rouse my haulers. You don't think I pull the ferry across myself, do you?"

"I will wait at the ferry," Lan said flatly. "For a little while."
He released his hold on the ferryman.

Master Hightower jerked the handful of coins to his chest
and, nodding agreement, hastily shoved the door closed
with his hip.

CHAPTER
12

Across the Taren

Lan came down the stairs, telling the company to dismount and lead their horses after him through the fog. Again they had to trust that the Warder knew where he was going. The fog swirled around Rand's knees, hiding his feet, obscuring everything more than a yard away. The fog was not as heavy as it had been outside the town, but he could barely make out his companions.

Still no human stirred in the night except for them. A few more windows than before showed a light, but the thick mist turned most of them to dim patches, and as often as not that hazy glow, hanging in the gray, was all that was visible. Other houses, revealing a little more, seemed to float on a sea of cloud or to thrust abruptly out of the mist while their neighbors remained hidden, so that they could have stood alone for miles around.

Rand moved stiffly from the ache of the long ride, wondering if there was any way he could walk the rest of the way to Tar Valon. Not that walking was much better than riding at that moment, of course, but even so his feet were almost the only part of him that was not sore. At least he was used to walking.

Only once did anyone speak loudly enough for Rand to hear clearly. "You must handle it," Moiraine said in answer to something unheard from Lan. "He will remember too much as it is, and no help for it. If I stand out in his thoughts. . . ."

Rand grumpily shifted his now-sodden cloak on his shoulders, keeping close with the others. Mat and Perrin grumbled to themselves, muttering under their breaths, with bitten-off exclamations whenever one stubbed a toe on something unseen. Thom Merrilin grumbled, too, words like "hot meal" and "fire" and "mulled wine" reaching Rand, but neither the Warder nor the Aes Sedai took notice. Egwene marched along without a word, her back straight and her head high. It was a somewhat painfully hesitant march, to be sure, for she was as unused to riding as the rest.

She was getting her adventure, he thought glumly, and as long as it lasted he doubted if she would notice little things like fog or damp or cold. There must be a difference in what you saw, it seemed to him, depending on whether you sought adventure or had it forced on you. The stories could no doubt make galloping through a cold fog, with a Draghkar and the Light alone knew what else chasing you, sound thrilling. Egwene might be feeling a thrill; he only felt cold and damp and glad to have a village around him again, even if it was Taren Ferry.

Abruptly he walked into something large and warm in the murk: Lan's stallion. The Warder and Moiraine had stopped, and the rest of the party did the same, patting their mounts as much to comfort themselves as the animals. The fog was a little thinner here, enough for them to see one another more clearly than they had in a long while, but not enough to make out much more. Their feet were still hidden by low billows like gray floodwater. The houses seemed to have all been swallowed.

Cautiously Rand led Cloud forward a little way and was surprised to hear his boots scrape on wooden planks. The ferry landing. He backed up carefully, making the gray back as well. He had heard what the Taren Ferry landing was like—a bridge that led nowhere except to the ferryboat. The Taren was supposed to be wide and deep, with treacherous currents that could pull under the strongest swimmer. Much wider than the Winespring Water, he supposed. With the fog added in. . . . It was a relief when he felt dirt under his feet again.

A fierce "Hsst!" from Lan, as sharp as the fog. The Warder gestured at them as he dashed to Perrin's side and threw back the stocky youth's cloak, exposing the great axe. Obediently, if still not understanding, Rand tossed his own cloak over his shoulder to show his sword. As Lan moved swiftly back to his horse, bobbing lights appeared in the mist, and muffled footsteps approached.

Six stolid-faced men in rough clothes followed Master Hightower. The torches they carried burned away a patch of fog around them. When they stopped, all of the party from Emond's Field could be plainly seen, the lot of them surrounded by a gray wall that seemed thicker for the torch-light reflected from it. The ferryman examined them, his narrow head tilted, nose twitching like a weasel sniffing the breeze for a trap.

Lan leaned against his saddle with apparent casualness, but one hand rested ostentatiously on the long hilt of his sword. There was an air about him of a metal spring, compressed, waiting.

Rand hurriedly copied the Warder's pose—at least insofar as putting his hand on his sword. He did not think he could achieve that deadly-seeming slouch. *They'd probably laugh if I tried.*

Perrin eased his axe in its leather loop and planted his feet deliberately. Mat put a hand to his quiver, though Rand was not sure what condition his bowstring was in after being out in all this damp. Thom Merrilin stepped forward grandly and held up one empty hand, turning it slowly. Suddenly he gestured with a flourish, and a dagger twirled between his fingers. The hilt slapped into his palm, and, abruptly nonchalant, he began trimming his fingernails.

A low, delighted laugh floated from Moiraine. Egwene clapped as if watching a performance at Festival, then stopped and looked abashed, though her mouth twitched with a smile just the same.

Hightower seemed far from amused. He stared at Thom, then cleared his throat loudly. "There was mention made of more gold for the crossing." He looked around at them again, a sullen, sly look. "What you gave me before is in a safe place now, hear? It's none of it where you can get at it."

"The rest of the gold," Lan told him, "goes into your hand when we are on the other side." The leather purse hanging at his waist clinked as he gave it a little shake.

For a moment the ferryman's eyes darted, but at last he nodded. "Let's be about it, then," he muttered, and stalked out onto the landing followed by his six helpers. The fog burned away around them as they moved; gray tendrils closed in behind, quickly filling where they had been. Rand hurried to keep up.

The ferry itself was a wooden barge with high sides, boarded by a ramp that could be raised to block off the end. Ropes as thick as a man's wrist ran along each side of it, ropes fastened to massive posts at the end of the landing and disappearing into the night over the river. The ferryman's helpers stuck their torches in iron brackets on the ferry's sides, waited while everyone led their horses aboard, then pulled up the ramp. The deck creaked beneath hooves and shuffling feet, and the ferry shifted with the weight.

Hightower muttered half under his breath, growling for them to keep the horses still and stay to the center, out of the haulers' way. He shouted at his helpers, chivvying them as they readied the ferry to cross, but the men moved at the same reluctant speed whatever he said, and he was half-hearted about it, often cutting off in mid-shout to hold his torch high and peer into the fog. Finally he stopped shouting altogether and went to the bow, where he stood staring into the mist that covered the river. He did not move until one of the haulers touched his arm; then he jumped, glaring.

"What? Oh. You, is it? Ready? About time. Well, man, what are you waiting for?" He waved his arms, heedless of the torch and the way the horses whickered and tried to move back. "Cast off! Give way! Move!" The man slouched off to comply, and Hightower peered once more into the fog ahead, rubbing his free hand uneasily on his coat front.

The ferry lurched as its moorings were loosed and the strong current caught it, then lurched again as the guide-ropes held it. The haulers, three to a side, grabbed hold of the ropes at the front of the ferry and laboriously began walking toward the back, muttering uneasily as they edged out onto the gray-cloaked river.

The landing disappeared as mist surrounded them, tenuous streamers drifting across the ferry between the flickering torches. The barge rocked slowly in the current. Nothing except the steady tread of the haulers, forward to take hold of the ropes and back down again pulling, gave a hint of any other movement. No one spoke. The villagers kept as close to the center of the ferry as they could. They had heard the Taren was far wider than the streams they were used to; the fog made it infinitely vaster in their minds.

After a time Rand moved closer to Lan. Rivers a man could not wade or swim or even see across were nervous-making to someone who had never seen anything broader or deeper than a Waterwood pond. "Would they really have tried to rob us?" he asked quietly. "He acted more as if he were afraid we would rob him."

The Warder eyed the ferryman and his helpers—none appeared to be listening—before answering just as softly. "With the fog to hide them . . . well, when what they do is hidden, men sometimes deal with strangers in ways they wouldn't if there were other eyes to see. And the quickest to harm a stranger are the soonest to think a stranger will harm them. This fellow . . . I believe he might sell his mother to Trollocs for stew meat if the price was right. I'm a little surprised you ask. I heard the way people in Emond's Field speak of those from Taren Ferry."

"Yes, but. . . . Well, everyone says they. . . . But I never thought they would actually. . . ." Rand decided he had better stop thinking that he knew anything at all of what people were like beyond his own village. "He might tell the Fade we crossed on the ferry," he said at last. "Maybe he'll bring the Trollocs over after us."

Lan chuckled dryly. "Robbing a stranger is one thing, dealing with a Halfman something else again. Can you really see him ferrying Trollocs over, especially in this fog, no matter how much gold was offered? Or even talking to a Myrddraal, if he had any choice? Just the thought of it would keep him running for a month. I don't think we have to worry very much about Darkfriends in Taren Ferry. Not here. We are safe . . . for a time, at least. From this lot, anyway. Watch yourself."

Hightower had turned from peering into the fog ahead. Pointed face pushed forward and torch held high, he stared at Lan and Rand as if seeing them clearly for the first time. Deck-planks creaked under the haulers' feet and the occasional stamp of a hoof. Abruptly the ferryman twitched as he realized they were watching him watching them. With a leap he spun back to looking for the far bank, or whatever it was he sought in the fog.

"Say no more." Lan said, so softly Rand almost could not understand. "These are bad days to speak of Trollocs, or Darkfriends, or the Father of Lies, with strange ears to hear. Such talk can bring worse than the Dragon's Fang scrawled on your door."

Rand felt no desire to go on with his questions. Gloom settled on him even more than it had before. Darkfriends! As if Fades and Trollocs and Draghkar were not enough to worry about. At least you could tell a Trolloc at sight.

Abruptly pilings loomed shadowy in the mist before them. The ferry thudded against the far bank, and then the haulers were hurrying to lash the craft fast and let down the ramp at that end with a thump, while Mat and Perrin announced loudly that the Taren was not half as wide as they had heard. Lan led his stallion down the ramp, followed by Moiraine and the others. As Rand, the last, took Cloud down behind Bela, Master Hightower called out angrily.

"Here, now! Here! Where's my gold?"

"It shall be paid." Moiraine's voice came from somewhere in the mist. Rand's boots clumped from the ramp to a wooden landing. "And a silver mark for each of your men," the Aes Sedai added, "for the quick crossing."

The ferryman hesitated, face pushed forward as if he smelled danger, but at the mention of silver the haulers roused themselves. Some paused to seize a torch, but they all thumped down the ramp before Hightower could open his mouth. With a sullen grimace, the ferryman followed his crew.

Cloud's hooves clumped hollowly in the fog as Rand made his way carefully along the landing. The gray mist was as thick here as over the river. At the foot of the landing, the Warder was handing out coins, surrounded by the torches of Hightower and his fellows. Everyone else except Moiraine waited just beyond in an anxious cluster. The Aes Sedai stood looking at the river, though what she could see was beyond Rand. With a shiver he hitched up his cloak, sodden as it was. He was really out of the Two Rivers, now, and it seemed much farther away than the width of a river.

"There," Lan said, handing a last coin to Hightower. "As agreed." He did not put up his purse, and the ferrety-faced man eyed it greedily.

With a loud creak, the landing shivered. Hightower jerked upright, head swiveling back toward the mist-cloaked ferry. The torches remaining on board were a pair of dim, fuzzy points of light. The landing groaned, and with a thunderous crack of snapping wood, the twin glows lurched, then began to revolve. Egwene cried out wordlessly, and Thom cursed.

"It's loose!" Hightower screamed. Grabbing his haulers, he pushed them toward the end of the landing. "The ferry's loose, you fools! Get it! Get it!"

The haulers stumbled a few steps under Hightower's shoves, then stopped. The faint lights on the ferry spun faster, then faster still. The fog above them swirled, sucked into a spiral. The landing trembled. The cracking and splintering of wood filled the air as the ferry began breaking apart.

"Whirlpool," one of the haulers said, his voice filled with awe.

"No whirlpools on the Taren." Hightower sounded empty. "Never been a whirlpool. . . ."

"An unfortunate occurrence." Moiraine's voice was hollow in the fog that made her a shadow as she turned from the river.

"Unfortunate," Lan agreed in a flat tone. "It seems you'll be carrying no one else across the river for a time. An ill thing that you lost your craft in our service." He delved again into his purse, ready in his hand. "This should repay you."

For a moment Hightower stared at the gold, glinting in Lan's hand in the torchlight, then his shoulders hunched and his eyes darted to the others he had carried across. Made indistinct by the fog, the Emond's Fielders stood silently. With a frightened, inarticulate cry, the ferryman snatched the coins from Lan, whirled, and ran into the mist. His haulers were only half a step behind him, their torches quickly swallowed as they vanished upriver.

"There is nothing further to hold us here," the Aes Sedai said as if nothing out of the ordinary had happened. Leading her white mare, she started away from the landing, up the bank.

Rand stood staring at the hidden river. *It could have been happenstance. No whirlpools, he said, but it. . . .* Abruptly he realized everyone else had gone. Hurriedly he scrambled up the gently sloping bank.

In the space of three paces the heavy mist faded away to nothing. He stopped dead and stared back. Along a line running down the shore thick gray hung on one side, on the other shone a clear night sky, still dark though the sharpness of the moon hinted at dawn not far off.

The Warder and the Aes Sedai stood conferring beside

their horses a short distance beyond the border of the fog. The others huddled a little apart; even in the moonlit darkness their nervousness was palpable. All eyes were on Lan and Moiraine, and all but Egwene were leaning back as if torn between losing the pair and getting too close. Rand trotted the last few spans to Egwene's side, leading Cloud, and she grinned at him. He did not think the shine in her eyes was all from moonlight.

"It follows the river as if drawn with a pen," Moiraine was saying in satisfied tones. "There are not ten women in Tar Valon who could do that unaided. Not to mention from the back of a galloping horse."

"I don't mean to complain, Moiraine Sedai," Thom said, sounding oddly diffident for him, "but would it not have been better to cover us a little further? Say to Baerlon? If that Draghkar looks on this side of the river, we'll lose everything we have gained."

"Draghkar are not very smart, Master Merrilin," the Aes Sedai said dryly. "Fearsome and deadly dangerous, and with sharp eyes, but little intelligence. It will tell the Myrddraal that this side of the river is clear, but the river itself is cloaked for miles in both directions. The Myrddraal will know the extra effort that cost me. He will have to consider that we may be escaping down the river, and that will slow him. He will have to divide his efforts. The fog should hold long enough that he will never be sure that we did not travel at least partway by boat. I could have extended the fog a little way toward Baerlon, instead, but then the Draghkar could search the river in a matter of hours, and the Myrddraal would know exactly where we were headed."

Thom made a puffing sound and shook his head. "I apologize, Aes Sedai. I hope I did not offend."

"Ah, Moi . . . ah, Aes Sedai." Mat stopped to swallow audibly. "The ferry . . . ah . . . did you . . . I mean . . . I don't understand why. . . ." He trailed off weakly, and there was a silence so deep that the loudest sound Rand heard was his own breathing.

Finally Moiraine spoke, and her voice filled the empty silence with sharpness. "You all want explanations, but if I explained my every action to you, I would have no time for anything else." In the moonlight, the Aes Sedai seemed taller, somehow, almost looming over them. "Know this. I intend to see you safely in Tar Valon. That is the one thing you need to know."

"If we keep standing here," Lan put in, "the Draghkar will not need to search the river. If I remember correctly. . . ." He led his horse on up the riverbank.

As if the Warder's movement had loosened something in his chest, Rand drew a deep breath. He heard others doing the same, even Thom, and remembered an old saying. Better to spit in a wolf's eye than to cross an Aes Sedai. Yet the tension had lessened. Moiraine was not looming over anyone; she barely reached his chest.

"I don't suppose we could rest a bit," Perrin said hopefully, ending with a yawn. Egwene, slumped against Bela, sighed tiredly.

It was the first sound even approaching a complaint that Rand had heard from her. *Maybe now she realizes this isn't some grand adventure after all.* Then he guiltily remembered that, unlike him, she had not slept the day away. "We do need to rest, Moiraine Sedai," he said. "After all, we have ridden all night."

"Then I suggest we see what Lan has for us," Moiraine said. "Come."

She led them on up the bank, into the woods beyond the river. Bare branches thickened the shadows. A good hundred spans from the Taren they came to a dark mound beside a clearing. Here a long-ago flood had undermined and toppled an entire stand of leatherleafs, washing them together into a great, thick tangle, an apparently solid mass of trunks and branches and roots. Moiraine stopped, and suddenly a light appeared low to the ground, coming from under the heap of trees.

Thrusting a stub of a torch ahead of him, Lan crawled out from under the mound and straightened. "No unwelcome visitors," he told Moiraine. "And the wood I left is still dry, so I started a small fire. We will rest warm."

"You expected us to stop here?" Egwene said in surprise.

"It seemed a likely place," Lan replied. "I like to be prepared, just in case."

Moiraine took the torch from him. "Will you see to the horses? When you are done I will do what I can about everyone's tiredness. Right now I want to talk to Egwene. Egwene?"

Rand watched the two women crouch down and disappear under the great pile of tree trunks. There was a low opening, barely big enough to crawl into. The light of the torch vanished.

Lan had included feedbags and a small quantity of oats in the supplies, but he stopped the others from unsaddling their horses. Instead he produced the hobbles he had also packed. "They would rest easier without the saddles, but if we must leave quickly, there may be no time to replace them."

"They don't look to me like they need any rest," Perrin said as he attempted to slip a feedbag over his mount's muzzle. The horse tossed its head before allowing him to put the straps in place. Rand was having difficulties with Cloud, too, taking three tries before he could get the canvas bag over the gray's nose.

"They do," Lan told them. He straightened from hobbling his stallion. "Oh, they can still run. They will run at their fastest, if we let them, right up to the second they drop dead from exhaustion they never even felt. I would rather Moiraine Sedai had not had to do what she did, but it was necessary." He patted the stallion's neck, and the horse bobbed his head as if acknowledging the Warder's touch. "We must go slowly with them for the next few days, until they recover. More slowly than I would like. But with luck it will be enough."

"Is that . . . ?" Mat swallowed audibly. "Is that what she meant? About our tiredness?"

Rand patted Cloud's neck and stared at nothing. Despite what she had done for Tam, he had no desire for the Aes Sedai to use the Power on him. *Light, she as much as admitted sinking the ferry.*

"Something like it." Lan chuckled wryly. "But you will not have to worry about running yourself to death. Not unless things get a lot worse than they are. Just think of it as an extra night's sleep."

The shrill scream of the Draghkar suddenly echoed from above the fog-covered river. Even the horses froze. Again it came, closer now, and again, piercing Rand's skull like needles. Then the cries were fading, until they had faded away entirely.

"Luck," Lan breathed. "It searches the river for us." He

gave a quick shrug and abruptly sounded matter-of-fact. "Let's get inside. I could do with some hot tea and something to fill my belly."

Rand was the first to crawl on hands and knees through the opening in the tangle of trees and down a short tunnel. At the end of it, he stopped, still crouching. Ahead was an irregularly shaped space, a woody cave easily large enough to hold them all. The roof of tree trunks and branches came too low to allow any but the women to stand. Smoke from a small fire on a bed of river stones drifted up and through; the draft was enough to keep the space free of smoke, but the interweaving was too thick to let out even a glimmer of the flames. Moiraine and Egwene, their cloaks thrown aside, sat cross-legged, facing one another beside the fire.

"The One Power," Moiraine was saying, "comes from the True Source, the driving force of Creation, the force the Creator made to turn the Wheel of Time." She put her hands together in front of her and pushed them against each other. "*Saidin,* the male half of the True Source, and *saidar,* the female half, work against each other and at the same time together to provide that force. *Saidin*"—she lifted one hand, then let it drop—"is fouled by the touch of the Dark One, like water with a thin slick of rancid oil floating on top. The water is still pure, but it cannot be touched without touching the foulness. Only *saidar* is still safe to be used." Egwene's back was to Rand. He could not see her face, but she was leaning forward eagerly.

Mat poked Rand from behind and muttered something, and he moved on into the tree cavern. Moiraine and Egwene ignored his entry. The other men crowded in behind him, tossing off damp cloaks, settling around the fire, and holding hands out to the warmth. Lan, the last to enter, pulled waterbags and leather sacks from a nook in the wall, took out a kettle, and began to prepare tea. He paid no attention to what the women were saying, but Rand's friends began to stop toasting their hands and stare openly. Thom pretended that all of his interest was engaged in loading his thickly carved pipe, but the way he leaned toward the women gave him away. Moiraine and Egwene acted as if they were alone.

"No," Moiraine said in answer to a question Rand had missed, "the True Source cannot be used up, any more than the river can be used up by the wheel of a mill. The Source is the river; the Aes Sedai, the waterwheel."

"And you really think I can learn?" Egwene asked. Her face shone with eagerness. Rand had never seen her look so beautiful, or so far away from him. "I can become an Aes Sedai?"

Rand jumped up, cracking his head against the low roof of logs. Thom Merrilin grabbed his arm, yanking him back down.

"Don't be a fool," the gleeman murmured. He eyed the women—neither seemed to have noticed—and the look he gave Rand was sympathetic. "It's beyond you now, boy."

"Child," Moiraine said gently, "only a very few can learn to touch the True Source and use the One Power. Some of those can learn to a greater degree, some to a lesser. You are one of the bare handful for whom there is no need to learn. At least, touching the Source will come to you whether you want it or not. Without the teaching you can receive in Tar Valon, though, you will never learn to channel it fully, and you may not survive. Men who have the ability to touch *saidin* born in them die, of course, if the Red Ajah does not find them and gentle them. . . ."

Thom growled deep in his throat, and Rand shifted uncomfortably. Men like those of whom the Aes Sedai spoke were rare—he had only heard of three in his whole life, and thank the Light never in the Two Rivers—but the damage they did before the Aes Sedai found them was always bad enough for the news to carry, like the news of wars, or earthquakes that destroyed cities. He had never really understood what the Ajahs did. According to the stories they were societies among the Aes Sedai that seemed to plot and squabble among themselves more than anything else, but the stories were clear on one point. The Red Ajah held its prime duty to be the prevention of another Breaking of the World, and they did it by hunting down every man who even dreamed of wielding the One Power. Mat and Perrin looked as if they suddenly wished they were back home in their beds.

". . . but some of the women die, too. It is hard to learn without a guide. The women we do not find, those who live, often become . . . well, in this part of the world they might become Wisdoms of their villages." The Aes Sedai paused thoughtfully. "The old blood is strong in Emond's Field, and the old blood sings. I knew you for what you were the moment I saw you. No Aes Sedai can stand in the presence of a woman who can channel, or who is close to her change, and not feel it." She rummaged in the pouch at her belt and produced the small blue gem on a gold chain that she had earlier worn in her hair. "You are very close to your change, your first touching. It will be better if I guide you through it. That way you will avoid the . . . unpleasant effects that come to those who must find their own way."

Egwene's eyes widened as she looked at the stone, and she wet her lips repeatedly. "Is . . . does that have the Power?"

"Of course not," Moiraine snapped. "*Things* do not have the Power, child. Even an *angreal* is only a tool. This is just a pretty blue stone. But it can give off light. Here."

Egwene's hands trembled as Moiraine laid the stone on her fingertips. She started to pull back, but the Aes Sedai held both her hands in one of hers and gently touched the other to the side of Egwene's head.

"Look at the stone," the Aes Sedai said softly. "It is better this way than fumbling alone. Clear your mind of everything but the stone. Clear your mind, and let yourself drift. There is only the stone and emptiness. I will begin it. Drift, and let me guide you. No thoughts. Drift."

Rand's fingers dug into his knees; his jaws clenched until they hurt. *She has to fail. She has to.*

Light bloomed in the stone, just one flash of blue and then gone, no brighter than a firefly, but he flinched as if it had been blinding. Egwene and Moiraine stared into the stone, faces empty. Another flash came, and another, until the azure light pulsed like the beating of a heart. *It's the Aes Sedai,* he thought desperately. *Moiraine's doing it. Not Egwene.*

One last, feeble flicker, and the stone was merely a bauble again. Rand held his breath.

For a moment Egwene continued to stare at the small stone, then she looked up at Moiraine. "I . . . I thought I felt . . . something, but. . . . Perhaps you're mistaken about me. I am sorry I wasted your time."

"I have wasted nothing, child." A small smile of satisfaction flitted across Moiraine's lips. "That last light was yours alone."

"It was?" Egwene exclaimed, then slid immediately back into glumness. "But it was barely there at all."

"Now you are behaving like a foolish village girl. Most who come to Tar Valon must study for many months before they can do what you just did. You may go far. Perhaps even the Amyrlin Seat, one day, if you study hard and work hard."

"You mean . . . ?" With a cry of delight Egwene threw her arms around the Aes Sedai. "Oh, thank you. Rand, did you hear? I'm going to be an Aes Sedai!"

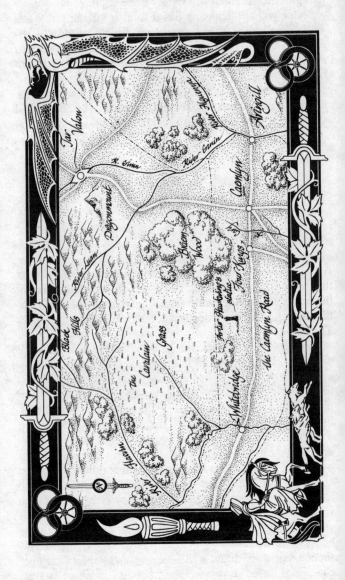

CHAPTER

13

Choices

Before they went to sleep Moiraine knelt by each in turn and laid her hands on their heads. Lan grumbled that he had no need and she should not waste her strength, but he did not try to stop her. Egwene was eager for the experience, Mat and Perrin clearly frightened of it, and frightened to say no. Thom jerked away from the Aes Sedai's hands, but she seized his gray head with a look that allowed no nonsense. The gleeman scowled through the entire thing. She smiled mockingly once she took her hands away. His frown deepened, but he did look refreshed. They all did.

Rand had drawn back into a niche in the uneven wall where he hoped he would be overlooked. His eyes wanted to slide closed once he leaned back against the timber jumble, but he forced himself to watch. He pushed a fist against his mouth to stifle a yawn. A little sleep, an hour or two, and he would be just fine. Moiraine did not forget him, though.

He flinched at the coolness of her fingers on his face, and said, "I don't—" His eyes widened in wonder. Tiredness drained out of him like water running downhill; aches and soreness ebbed to dim memories and vanished. He stared at her with his mouth hanging open. She only smiled and withdrew her hands.

"It is done," she said, and as she stood with a weary sigh he was reminded that she could not do the same for herself. Indeed, she only drank a little tea, refusing the bread and cheese Lan tried to press on her, before curling up beside the fire. She seemed to fall asleep the instant she wrapped her cloak around her.

The others, all save Lan, were dropping asleep wherever they could find a space to stretch out, but Rand could not imagine why. He felt as if he had already had a full night in a good bed. No sooner did he lean back against the log wall, though, than sleep rolled him under. When Lan poked him awake an hour later he felt as though he had had three days rest.

The Warder awakened them all, except Moiraine, and he sternly hushed any sound that might disturb her. Even so, he allowed them only a short stay in the snug cave of trees. Before the sun was twice its own height above the horizon, all traces that anyone had ever stopped there had been cleared away and they were all mounted and moving north toward Baerlon, riding slowly to conserve the horses. The Aes Sedai's eyes were shadowed, but she sat her saddle upright and steady.

Fog still hung thick over the river behind them, a gray wall resisting the efforts of the feeble sun to burn it away and hiding the Two Rivers from view. Rand watched over his shoulder as he rode, hoping for one last glimpse, even of Taren Ferry, until the fogbank was lost to sight.

"I never thought I'd ever be this far from home," he said when the trees at last hid both the fog and the river. "Remember when Watch Hill seemed a long way?" *Two days ago, that was. It seems like forever.*

"In a month or two, we'll be back," Perrin said in a strained voice. "Think what we'll have to tell."

"Even Trollocs can't chase us forever," Mat said. "Burn me, they can't." He straightened around with a heavy sigh, slumping in his saddle as if he did not believe a word that had been said.

"Men!" Egwene snorted. "You get the adventure you're always prating about, and already you're talking about home." She held her head high, yet Rand noticed a tremor to her voice, now that nothing more was to be seen of the Two Rivers.

Neither Moiraine nor Lan made any attempt to reassure them, not a word to say that of course they would come back. He tried not to think on what that might mean. Even rested, he was full enough of doubts without searching out more. Hunching in his saddle he began a waking dream of tending the sheep alongside Tam in a pasture with deep, lush grass and larks singing of a spring morning. And a trip into Emond's Field, and Bel Tine the way it had been, dancing on the Green with never a care beyond whether he might stumble in the steps. He managed to lose himself in it for a long time.

The journey to Baerlon took almost a week. Lan muttered about the laggardness of their travel, but it was he who set the pace and forced the rest to keep it. With himself and his stallion, Mandarb—he said it meant "Blade" in the Old Tongue—he was not so sparing. The Warder covered twice as much ground as they did, galloping ahead, his color-shifting cloak swirling in the wind, to scout what lay before them, or dropping behind to examine their backtrail. Any others who tried to move at more than a walk, though, got cutting words on taking care of their animals, biting words on how well they would do afoot if the Trollocs did appear. Not even Moiraine was proof against his tongue if she let the white mare pick up her step. Aldieb, the mare was called; in the Old Tongue, "Westwind," the wind that brought the spring rains.

The Warder's scouting never turned up any sign of pursuit, or ambush. He spoke only to Moiraine of what he saw, and that quietly, so it could not be overheard, and the Aes Sedai informed the rest of them of what she thought they needed to know. In the beginning, Rand looked over his shoulder as much as he did ahead. He was not the only one. Perrin fingered his axe often, and Mat rode with an arrow nocked to his bow, in the beginning. But the land behind remained empty of Trollocs or figures in black cloaks, the sky remained empty of Draghkar. Slowly, Rand began to think perhaps they really had escaped.

No very great cover was to be had, even in the thickest parts of the woods. Winter clung as hard north of the Taren as it did in the Two Rivers. Stands of pine or fir or leatherleaf, and here and there a few spicewoods or laurels, dotted a forest of otherwise bare, gray branches. Not even the elders showed a leaf. Only scattered green sprigs of new growth stood out against brown meadows beaten flat by the winter's snows. Here, too, much of what did grow was stinging nettles and coarse thistle and stinkweed. On the bare dirt of the forest floor some of the last snow still hung on, in shady patches and in drifts beneath the low branches of evergreens. Everyone kept their cloaks drawn well about them, for the thin sunlight had no warmth to it and the night cold pierced deep. No more birds flew here than in the Two Rivers, not even ravens.

There was nothing leisurely about the slowness of their movement. The North Road—Rand continued to think of it that way, though he suspected it might have a different name here, north of the Taren—still ran almost due north, but at Lan's insistence their path snaked this way and that through the forest as often as it ran along the hard-packed dirt road. A village, or a farm, or any sign of men or civilization sent them circling for miles to avoid it, though there were few enough of any of those. The whole first day Rand saw no evidence aside from the road that men had ever been in that woods. It came to him that even when he had gone to the foot of the Mountains of Mist he might not have been as far from a human habitation as he was that day.

The first farm he saw—a large frame house and tall barn with high-peaked, thatched roofs, a curl of smoke rising from a stone chimney—was a shock.

"It's no different from back home," Perrin said, frowning at the distant buildings, barely visible through the trees. People moved around the farmyard, as yet unaware of the travelers.

"Of course it is," Mat said. "We're just not close enough to see."

"I tell you, it's no different," Perrin insisted.

"It must be. We're north of the Taren, after all."

"Quiet, you two," Lan growled. "We don't want to be seen, remember? This way." He turned west, to circle the farm through the trees.

Looking back, Rand thought Perrin was right. The farm looked much the same as any around Emond's Field. There was a small boy toting water from the well, and older boys tending sheep behind a rail fence. It even had a curing shed, for tabac. But Mat was right, too. *We're north of the Taren. It must be different.*

Always they halted while light still clung to the sky, to choose a spot sloped for drainage and sheltered from the wind that seldom died completely, only changed direction. Their fire was always small and hidden from only a few yards off, and once tea was brewed, the flames were doused and the coals buried.

At their first stop, before the sun sank, Lan began teaching the boys what to do with the weapons they carried. He started with the bow. After watching Mat put three arrows into a knot the size of a man's head, on the fissured trunk of a dead leatherleaf, at a hundred paces, he told the others to take their turns. Perrin duplicated Mat's feat, and Rand, summoning the flame and the void, the empty calm that let the bow become a part of him, or him of it, clustered his three where the points almost touched one another. Mat gave him a congratulatory clap on the shoulder.

"Now if you all had bows," the Warder said dryly when they started grinning, "and if the Trollocs agreed not to come so close you couldn't use them. . . ." The grins faded abruptly. "Let me see what I can teach you in case they do come that close."

He showed Perrin a bit of how to use that great-bladed axe; raising an axe to someone, or something, that had a weapon was not at all like chopping wood or flailing around in pretend. Setting the big apprentice blacksmith to a series of exercises, block, parry, and strike, he did the same for Rand and his sword. Not the wild leaping about and slashing that Rand had in mind whenever he thought about using it, but smooth motions, one flowing into another, almost a dance.

"Moving the blade is not enough," Lan said, "though some think it is. The mind is part of it, most of it. Blank your mind, sheepherder. Empty it of hate or fear, of everything. Burn them away. You others listen to this, too. You can use it with the axe or the bow, with a spear, or a quarterstaff, or even your bare hands."

Rand stared at him. "The flame and the void," he said wonderingly. "That's what you mean, isn't it? My father taught me about that."

The Warder gave him an unreadable look in return. "Hold the sword as I showed you, sheepherder. I cannot make a mud-footed villager into a blademaster in an hour, but perhaps I can keep you from slicing off your own foot."

Rand sighed and held the sword upright before him in both hands. Moiraine watched without expression, but the next evening she told Lan to continue the lessons.

The meal at evening was always the same as at midday and breakfast, flatbread and cheese and dried meat, except

that evenings they had hot tea to wash it down instead of
water. Thom entertained them, evenings. Lan would not
let the gleeman play harp or flute—no need to rouse the
countryside, the Warder said—but Thom juggled and told
stories. "Mara and the Three Foolish Kings," or one of the
hundreds about Anla the Wise Counselor, or something
filled with glory and adventure, like *The Great Hunt of the
Horn,* but always with a happy ending and a joyous home-
coming.

Yet if the land was peaceful around them, if no Trollocs
appeared among the trees, no Draghkar among the clouds,
it seemed to Rand that they managed to raise their tension
themselves, whenever it was in danger of vanishing.

There was the morning that Egwene awoke and began
unbraiding her hair. Rand watched her from the corner of
his eye as he made up his blanketroll. Every night when the
fire was doused, everyone took to their blankets except for
Egwene and the Aes Sedai. The two women always went
aside from the others and talked for an hour or two, returning when the others were asleep. Egwene combed her hair
out—one hundred strokes; he counted—while he was saddling Cloud, tying his saddlebags and blanket behind the
saddle. Then she tucked the comb away, swept her loose
hair over her shoulder, and pulled up the hood of her cloak.

Startled, he asked, "What are you doing?" She gave him
a sidelong look without answering. It was the first time he
had spoken to her in two days, he realized, since the night
in the log shelter on the bank of the Taren, but he did not let
that stop him. "All your life you've waited to wear your hair
in a braid, and now you're giving it up? Why? Because she
doesn't braid hers?"

"Aes Sedai don't braid their hair," she said simply. "At
least, not unless they want to."

"You aren't an Aes Sedai. You're Egwene al'Vere from
Emond's Field, and the Women's Circle would have a fit if
they could see you now."

"Women's Circle business is none of yours, Rand al'Thor.
And I *will* be an Aes Sedai. Just as soon as I reach Tar Valon."

He snorted. "As soon as you reach Tar Valon. Why?
Light, tell me that. You're no Darkfriend."

"Do you think Moiraine Sedai is a Darkfriend? Do you?"
She squared around to face him with her fists clenched,

and he almost thought she was going to hit him. "After she saved the village? After she saved your father?"

"I don't know what she is, but whatever she is, it doesn't say anything about the rest of them. The stories—"

"Grow up, Rand! Forget the stories and use your eyes."

"My eyes saw her sink the ferry! Deny that! Once you get an idea in your head, you won't budge even if somebody points out you're trying to stand on water. If you weren't such a Light-blinded fool, you'd see—!"

"Fool, am I? Let me tell you a thing or two, Rand al'Thor! You are the muliest, most wool-headed—!"

"You two trying to wake everybody inside ten miles?" the Warder asked.

Standing there with his mouth open, trying to get a word in edgewise, Rand suddenly realized he had been shouting. They both had.

Egwene's face went scarlet to her eyebrows, and she spun away with a muttered, "Men!" that seemed as much for the Warder as for him.

Warily, Rand looked around the camp. Everybody was looking at him, not just the Warder. Mat and Perrin, with their faces white. Thom, tensed as if ready to run or fight. Moiraine. The Aes Sedai's face was expressionless, but her eyes seemed to bore into his head. Desperately, he tried to recall exactly what he had said, about Aes Sedai and Dark-friends.

"It is time to be going," Moiraine said. She turned to Al-dieb, and Rand shivered as if he had been let out of a trap. He wondered if he had been.

Two nights later, with the fire burning low, Mat licked the last crumbs of cheese from his fingers and said, "You know, I think we've lost them for good." Lan was off in the night, taking a last look around. Moiraine and Egwene had gone aside for one of their conversations. Thom was half dozing over his pipe, and the young men had the fire to themselves.

Perrin, idly poking the embers with a stick, answered. "If we've lost them, why does Lan keep scouting?" Nearly asleep, Rand rolled over, his back to the fire.

"We lost them back at Taren Ferry." Mat lay back with his fingers laced behind his head, staring at the moon-filled sky. "If they were even really after us."

"You think that Draghkar was chasing us because it liked us?" Perrin asked.

"I say, stop worrying about Trollocs and such," Mat went on as if Perrin had not spoken, "and start thinking about seeing the world. We're out where the stories come from. What do you think a real city is like?"

"We're going to Baerlon," Rand said sleepily, but Mat snorted.

"Baerlon's all very well, but I've seen that old map Master al'Vere has. If we turn south once we reach Caemlyn, the road leads all the way to Illian, and beyond."

"What's so special about Illian?" Perrin said, yawning.

"For one thing," Mat replied, "Illian isn't full of Aes Se—"

A silence fell, and Rand was suddenly wide awake. Moiraine had come back early. Egwene was with her, but it was the Aes Sedai, standing at the edge of the firelight, who held their attention. Mat lay there on his back, his mouth still open, staring at her. Moiraine's eyes caught the light like dark, polished stones. Abruptly Rand wondered how long she had been standing there.

"The lads were just—" Thom began, but Moiraine spoke right over the top of him.

"A few days respite, and you are ready to give up." Her calm, level voice contrasted sharply with her eyes. "A day or two of quiet, and already you have forgotten Winternight."

"We haven't forgotten," Perrin said. "It's just—" Still not raising her voice, the Aes Sedai treated him as she had the gleeman.

"Is that the way you all feel? You are all eager to run off to Illian and forget about Trollocs, and Halfmen, and Draghkar?" She ran her eyes over them—that stony glint playing against the everyday tone of voice made Rand uneasy—but she gave no one a chance to speak. "The Dark One is after you three, one or all, and if I let you go running off wherever you want to go, he will take you. Whatever the Dark One wants, I oppose, so hear this and know it true. Before I let the Dark One have you, I will destroy you myself."

It was her voice, so matter-of-fact, that convinced Rand. The Aes Sedai would do exactly what she said, if she thought it was necessary. He had a hard time sleeping that night, and he was not the only one. Even the gleeman did not begin snoring till long after the last coals died. For once, Moiraine offered no help.

Those nightly talks between Egwene and the Aes Sedai were a sore point for Rand. Whenever they disappeared into the darkness, aside from the rest for privacy, he wondered what they were saying, what they were doing. What was the Aes Sedai doing to Egwene?

One night, he waited until the other men had all settled down, Thom snoring like a saw cutting an oak knot. Then he slipped away, clutching his blanket around him. Using every bit of skill he had gained stalking rabbits, he moved with the moon shadows until he was crouched at the base of a tall leatherleaf tree, thick with tough, broad leaves, close enough to hear Moiraine and Egwene, where they sat on a fallen log with a small lantern for light.

"Ask," Moiraine was saying, "and if I can tell you now, I will. Understand, there is much for which you are not yet ready, things you cannot learn until you have learned other things which require still others to be learned before them. But ask what you will."

"The Five Powers," Egwene said slowly. "Earth, Wind, Fire, Water, and Spirit. It doesn't seem fair that men should have been strongest in wielding Earth and Fire. Why should they have had the strongest Powers?"

Moiraine laughed. "Is that what you think, child? Is there a rock so hard that wind and water cannot wear it away, a fire so strong that water cannot quench it or wind snuff it out?"

Egwene was silent for a time, digging her toe into the forest floor. "They . . . they were the ones who . . . who tried to free the Dark One and the Forsaken, weren't they? The male Aes Sedai?" She took a deep breath and picked up speed. "The women were not part of it. It was the men who went mad and broke the world."

"You are afraid," Moiraine said grimly. "If you had remained in Emond's Field, you would have become Wisdom, in time. That was Nynaeve's plan, was it not? Or, you would have sat in the Women's Circle and managed the affairs of Emond's Field while the Village Council thought it was doing so. But you did the unthinkable. You left Emond's Field, left the Two Rivers, seeking adventure. You wanted to do it, and at the same time you are afraid of it. And you are stubbornly refusing to let your fear best you. You would not have asked me how a woman becomes an Aes Sedai, otherwise. You would not have thrown custom and convention over the fence, otherwise."

"No," Egwene protested. "I'm not afraid. I do want to become an Aes Sedai."

"Better for you if you were afraid, but I hope you hold to that conviction. Few women these days have the ability to become initiates, much less have the wish to." Moiraine's voice sounded as if she had begun musing to herself. "Surely never before two in one village. The old blood is indeed still strong in the Two Rivers."

In the shadows, Rand shifted. A twig snapped under his foot. He froze instantly, sweating and holding his breath, but neither of the women looked around.

"Two?" Egwene exclaimed. "Who else? Is it Kari? Kari Thane? Lara Ayellan?"

Moiraine gave an exasperated click of her tongue, then said sternly, "You must forget I said that. Her road lies another way, I fear. Concern yourself with your own circumstances. It is not an easy road you have chosen."

"I will not turn back," Egwene said.

"Be that as it may. But you still want reassurance, and I cannot give it to you, not in the way you want."

"I don't understand."

"You want to know that Aes Sedai are good and pure, that it was those wicked men of the legends who caused the Breaking of the World, not the women. Well, it was the men, but they were no more wicked than any men. They were insane, not evil. The Aes Sedai you will find in Tar Valon are human, no different from any other women except for the ability that sets us apart. They are brave and cowardly, strong and weak, kind and cruel, warm-hearted and cold. Becoming an Aes Sedai will not change you from what you are."

Egwene drew a heavy breath. "I suppose I was afraid of that, that I'd be changed by the Power. That and the Trollocs. And the Fade. And. . . . Moiraine Sedai, in the name of the Light, why did the Trollocs come to Emond's Field?"

The Aes Sedai's head swung, and she looked straight at

Rand's hiding place. His breath seized in his throat; her eyes were as hard as when she had threatened them, and he had the feeling they could penetrate the leatherleaf's thick branches. *Light, what will she do if she finds me listening?*

He tried to melt back into the deeper shadows. With his eyes on the women, a root snagged his foot, and he barely caught himself from tumbling into dead brush that would have pointed him out with a crackle of snapping branches like fireworks. Panting, he scrambled away on all fours, keeping silent as much by luck as by anything he did. His heart pounded so hard he thought that might give him away itself. *Fool! Eavesdropping on an Aes Sedai!*

Back where the others were sleeping, he managed to slip in among them silently. Lan moved as he dropped to the ground and jerked his blanket up, but the Warder settled back with a sigh. He had only been rolling over in his sleep. Rand let out a long, silent breath.

A moment later Moiraine appeared out of the night, stopping where she could study the slumbering shapes. Moonlight made a nimbus around her. Rand closed his eyes and breathed evenly, all the while listening hard for footsteps coming closer. None did. When he opened his eyes again, she was gone.

When finally sleep came, it was fitful and filled with sweaty dreams where all the men in Emond's Field claimed to be the Dragon Reborn and all the women had blue stones in their hair like the one Moiraine wore. He did not try to overhear Moiraine and Egwene again.

On into the sixth day the slow journey stretched. The warmthless sun slid slowly toward the treetops, while a handful of thin clouds drifted high to the north. The wind gusted higher for a moment, and Rand pulled his cloak back up onto his shoulders, muttering to himself. He wondered if they would ever get to Baerlon. The distance they had traveled from the river already was more than enough to take him from Taren Ferry to the White River, but Lan always said it was just a short journey whenever he was asked, hardly worth calling a journey at all. It made him feel lost.

Lan appeared ahead of them in the woods, returning from one of his forays. He reined in and rode beside Moiraine, his head bent close to hers.

Rand grimaced, but he did not ask any questions. Lan simply refused to acknowledge all such questions aimed at him.

Only Egwene, among the others, even appeared to notice Lan's return, so used to this arrangement had they become, and she kept back, too. The Aes Sedai might have begun acting as if Egwene were in charge of the Emond's Fielders, but that gave her no say when the Warder made his reports. Perrin was carrying Mat's bow, wrapped in the thoughtful silence that seemed to take them all more and more as they got further from the Two Rivers. The horses' slow walk allowed Mat to practice juggling three small stones under Thom Merrilin's watchful eye. The gleeman had given lessons each night, too, as well as Lan.

Lan finished whatever he had been telling Moiraine, and she twisted in her saddle to look back at the others. Rand tried not to stiffen when her eyes moved across him. Did they linger on him a moment longer than on anyone else? He had the queasy feeling that she knew who had been listening in the darkness that night.

"Hey, Rand," Mat called, "I can juggle four!" Rand waved in reply without looking around. "I told you I'd get to four before you. I—Look!"

They had topped a low hill, and below them, a scant mile away through the stark trees and the stretching shadows of evening, lay Baerlon. Rand gasped, trying to smile and gape at the same time.

A log wall, nearly twenty feet tall, surrounded the town, with wooden watchtowers scattered along its length. Within, rooftops of slate and tile glinted with the sinking sun, and feathers of smoke drifted upward from chimneys. Hundreds of chimneys. There was not a thatched roof to be seen. A broad road ran east from the town, and another west, each with at least a dozen wagons and twice as many ox-carts trudging toward the palisade. Farms lay scattered about the town, thickest to the north while only a few broke the forest to the south, but they might as well not have existed so far as Rand was concerned. *It's bigger than Emond's Field and Watch Hill and Deven Ride all put together! And maybe Taren Ferry, too.*

"So that's a city," Mat breathed, leaning forward across his horse's neck to stare.

Perrin could only shake his head. "How can so many people live in one place?"

Egwene simply stared.

Thom Merrilin glanced at Mat, then rolled his eyes and blew out his mustaches. "City!" he snorted.

"And you, Rand?" Moiraine said. "What do you think of your first sight of Baerlon?"

"I think it's a long way from home," he said slowly, bringing a sharp laugh from Mat.

"You have further to go yet," Moiraine said. "Much further. But there is no other choice, except to run and hide and run again for the rest of your lives. And short lives they would be. You must remember that, when the journey becomes hard. You have no choice."

Rand exchanged glances with Mat and Perrin. By their faces, they were thinking the same thing he was. How could she talk as if they had any choice after what she had said? *The Aes Sedai's made our choices.*

Moiraine went on as if their thoughts were not plain. "The danger begins again here. Watch what you say within those walls. Above all, do not mention Trollocs, or Halfmen, or any such. You must not even think of the Dark One. Some in Baerlon have even less love for Aes Sedai than do the people of Emond's Field, and there may even be Darkfriends." Egwene gasped, and Perrin muttered under his breath. Mat's face paled, but Moiraine went on calmly. "We must attract as little attention as possible." Lan was exchanging his cloak of shifting grays and greens for one of dark brown, more ordinary, though of fine cut and weave. His color-changing cloak made a large bulge in one of his saddlebags. "We do not go by our own names here," Moiraine continued. "Here I am known as Alys, and Lan is Andra. Remember that. Good. Let us be within the walls before night catches us. The gates of Baerlon are closed from sundown to sunrise."

Lan led the way down the hill and through the woods toward the log wall. The road passed half a dozen farms—none lay close, and none of the people finishing their chores seemed to notice the travelers—ending at heavy wooden gates bound with wide straps of black iron. They were closed tight, even if the sun was not down yet.

Lan rode close to the wall and gave a tug to a frayed rope

hanging down beside the gates. A bell clanged on the other side of the wall. Abruptly a wizened face under a battered cloth cap peered down suspiciously from atop the wall, glaring between the cut-off ends of two of the logs, a good three spans over their heads.

"What's all this, eh? It's too late in the day to be opening this gate. Too late, I say. Go around to the Whitebridge Gate if you want to—" Moiraine's mare moved out to where the man atop the wall had a clear view of her. Suddenly his wrinkles deepened in a gap-toothed smile, and he seemed to quiver between speaking and doing his duty. "I didn't know it was you, mistress. Wait. I'll be right down. Just wait. I'm coming. I'm coming."

The head dipped out of sight, but Rand could still hear muffled shouts for them to stay where they were, that he was coming. With great creaks of disuse, the right-hand gate slowly swung outward. It stopped when open just wide enough for one horse to pass through at a time, and the gatekeeper poked his head into the gap, flashed his half-toothless smile at them again and darted back out of the way. Moiraine followed Lan through, with Egwene right behind her.

Rand trotted Cloud after Bela and found himself in a narrow street fronted by high wooden fences and warehouses, tall and windowless, broad doors closed up tight. Moiraine and Lan were already on foot, speaking to the wrinkle-faced gatekeeper, so Rand dismounted, too.

The little man, in a much-mended cloak and coat, held his cloth cap crumpled in one hand and ducked his head whenever he spoke. He peered at those dismounting behind Lan and Moiraine, and shook his head. "Downcountry folk." He grinned. "Why, Mistress Alys, you taken up collecting downcountry folk with hay in their hair?" His look took in Thom Merrilin, then. "You ain't a sheepfarmer. I remember letting you go through some days back, I do. Didn't like your tricks downcountry, eh, gleeman?"

"I hope you remembered to forget letting us through, Master Avin," Lan said, pressing a coin into the man's free hand. "And letting us back in, too."

"No need for that, Master Andra. No need for that. You give me plenty when you went out. Plenty." Just the same, Avin made the coin disappear as deftly as if he were a gleeman, too. "I ain't told nobody, and I won't, neither. Especially not them Whitecloaks," he finished with a scowl. He pursed up his lips to spit, then glanced at Moiraine and swallowed, instead.

Rand blinked, but kept his mouth shut. The others did, too, though it appeared to be an effort for Mat. *Children of the Light,* Rand thought wonderingly. Stories told about the Children by peddlers and merchants and merchants' guards varied from admiration to hatred, but all agreed the Children hated Aes Sedai as much as they did Darkfriends. He wondered if this was more trouble already.

"The Children are in Baerlon?" Lan demanded.

"They surely are." The gatekeeper bobbed his head. "Came the same day you left, as I recall. Ain't nobody here likes them at all. Most don't let on, of course."

"Have they said why they are here?" Moiraine asked intently.

"Why they're here, mistress?" Avin was so astonished he forgot to duck his head. "Of course, they said why—Oh, I forgot. You been downcountry. Likely you ain't heard nothing but sheep bleating. They say they're here because of what's going on down in Ghealdan. The Dragon, you know—well, him as calls himself Dragon. They say the fellow's stirring up evil—which I expect he is—and they're here to stamp it out, only he's down there in Ghealdan, not here. Just an excuse to meddle in other people's business, is what I figure. There's already been the Dragon's Fang on some people's doors." This time he did spit.

"Have they caused much trouble, then?" Lan said, and Avin shook his head vigorously.

"Not that they don't want to, I expect, only the Governor don't trust them no more than I do. He won't let but maybe ten or so inside the walls at one time, and ain't they mad about that. The rest have a camp a little ways north, I hear. Bet they got the farmers looking over their shoulders. The ones that do come in, they just stalk around in those white cloaks, looking down their noses at honest folk. Walk in the Light, they say, and it's an order. Near come to blows more than once with the wagoneers and miners and smelters and all, and even the Watch, but the Governor wants it all peaceful, and that's how it's been so far. If they're hunting evil, I say why aren't they up in Saldaea? There's some kind of trouble up there, I hear. Or down in Ghealdan? There's been a big battle down there, they say. Real big."

Moiraine drew a soft breath. "I had heard that Aes Sedai were going to Ghealdan."

"Yes, they did, mistress." Avin's head started bobbing again. "They went to Ghealdan, all right, and that's what started this battle, or so I hear. They say some of those Aes Sedai are dead. Maybe all of them. I know some folks don't hold with Aes Sedai, but I say, who else is going to stop a false Dragon? Eh? And those damned fools who think they can be men Aes Sedai or some such. What about them? Course, some say—not the Whitecloaks, mind, and not me, but some folks—that maybe this fellow really is the Dragon Reborn. He can do things, I hear. Use the One Power. There's thousands following him."

"Don't be a fool," Lan snapped, and Avin's face folded into a hurt look.

"I'm only saying what I heard, ain't I? Just what I heard, Master Andra. They say, some do, that he's moving his army east and south, toward Tear." His voice became heavy with meaning. "They say he's named them the People of the Dragon."

"Names mean little," Moiraine said calmly. If anything she had heard disturbed her, she gave no outward sign of it now. "You could call your mule People of the Dragon, if you wanted."

"Not likely, mistress." Avin chuckled. "Not with the Whitecloaks around, for sure. I don't expect anybody else would look kindly on a name like that, neither. I see what you mean, but . . . oh, no, mistress. Not *my* mule."

"No doubt a wise decision," Moiraine said. "Now we must be off."

"And don't you worry, mistress," Avin said, with a deep bob of his head, "I ain't seen nobody." He darted to the gate and began tugging it closed with quick jerks. "Ain't seen nobody, and ain't seen nothing." The gate thudded shut, and he pulled down the locking bar with a rope. "In fact, mistress, this gate ain't been open in days."

"The Light illumine you, Avin," Moiraine said.

She led them away from the gate, then. Rand looked back, once, and Avin was still standing in front of the gate.

He seemed to be polishing a coin with an edge of his cloak and chuckling.

The way led through dirt streets barely the width of two wagons, empty of people, all lined with warehouses and occasional high, wooden fences. Rand walked a time beside the gleeman. "Thom, what was all that about Tear, and the People of the Dragon? Tear is a city all the way down on the Sea of Storms, isn't it?"

"*The Karaethon Cycle,*" Thom said curtly.

Rand blinked. *The Prophecies of the Dragon.* "Nobody tells the . . . those stories in the Two Rivers. Not in Emond's Field, anyway. The Wisdom would skin them alive, if they did."

"I suppose she would, at that," Thom said dryly. He glanced at Moiraine up ahead with Lan, saw she could not overhear, and went on. "Tear is the greatest port on the Sea of Storms, and the Stone of Tear is the fortress that guards it. The Stone is said to be the first fortress built after the Breaking of the World, and in all this time it has never fallen, though more than one army has tried. One of the Prophecies says that the Stone of Tear will never fall until the People of the Dragon come to the Stone. Another says the Stone will never fall till the Sword That Cannot Be Touched is wielded by the Dragon's hand." Thom grimaced. "The fall of the Stone will be one of the major proofs that the Dragon has been reborn. May the Stone stand till I am dust."

"The sword that cannot be touched?"

"That's what it says. I don't know whether it is a sword. Whatever it is, it lies in the Heart of the Stone, the central citadel of the fortress. None but the High Lords of Tear can enter there, and they never speak of what lies inside. Certainly not to gleemen, anyway."

Rand frowned. "The Stone cannot fall until the Dragon wields the sword, but how can he, unless the Stone has already fallen? Is the Dragon supposed to be a High Lord of Tear?"

"Not much chance of that," the gleeman said dryly. "Tear hates anything to do with the Power even more than Amador, and Amador is the stronghold of the Children of the Light."

"Then how can the Prophecy be fulfilled?" Rand asked. "I'd like it well enough if the Dragon was never reborn, but a prophecy that cannot be fulfilled doesn't make much sense. It sounds like a story meant to make people think the Dragon never will be reborn. Is that it?"

"You ask an awful lot of questions, boy," Thom said. "A prophecy that was easily fulfilled would not be worth much, now would it?" Suddenly his voice brightened. "Well, we're here. Wherever here is."

Lan had stopped by a section of head-high wooden fence that looked no different from any other they had passed. He was working the blade of his dagger between two of the boards. Abruptly he gave a grunt of satisfaction, pulled, and a length of the fence swung out like a gate. In fact it was a gate, Rand saw, though one meant to be opened only from the other side. The metal latch that Lan had lifted with his dagger showed that.

Moiraine went through immediately, drawing Aldieb behind her. Lan motioned the others to follow, and brought up the rear, closing the gate behind him.

On the other side of the fence Rand found himself in the stableyard of an inn. A loud bustle and clatter came from the building's kitchen, but what struck him was its size: it covered more than twice as much ground as the Winespring Inn, and was four stories high besides. Well over half the windows were aglow in the deepening twilight. He wondered at this city, that could have so many strangers in it.

No sooner had they come well into the stableyard than three men in dirty canvas aprons appeared at the huge stable's broad, arched doors. One, a wiry fellow and the only one without a manure fork in his hands, came forward waving his arms.

"Here! Here! You can't come in that way! You'll have to go round the front!"

Lan's hand went to his purse again, but even as it did another man, as big around as Master al'Vere, came hurrying out of the inn. Puffs of hair stuck out above his ears, and his sparkling white apron was as good as a sign proclaiming him the innkeeper.

"It's all right, Mutch," the newcomer said. "It's all right. These folk are expected guests. Take care of their horses, now. Good care."

Mutch sullenly knuckled his forehead, then motioned his two companions to come help. Rand and the others hurriedly got their saddlebags and blanketrolls down while the innkeeper turned to Moiraine. He gave her a deep bow, and spoke with a genuine smile.

"Welcome, Mistress Alys. Welcome. It's good to be seeing you, you and Master Andra, both. Very good. Your fine conversation has been missed. Yes, it has. I must say I worried, you going downcountry and all. Well, I mean, at a time like this, with the weather all crazy and wolves howling right up to the walls in the night." Abruptly he slapped both hands against his round belly and shook his head. "Here I go on like this, chattering away, instead of taking you inside. Come. Come. Hot meals and warm beds, that's what you'll be wanting. And the best in Baerlon are right here. The very best."

"And hot baths, too, I trust, Master Fitch?" Moiraine said, and Egwene echoed her fervently. "Oh, yes."

"Baths?" the innkeeper said. "Why, just the best and the hottest in Baerlon. Come. Welcome to the Stag and Lion. Welcome to Baerlon."

CHAPTER
14

The Stag and Lion

I nside, the inn was every bit as busy as the sounds coming from it had indicated and more. The party from
Emond's Field followed Master Fitch through the back
door, soon weaving around and between a constant stream
of men and women in long aprons, platters of food and trays
of drink held high. The bearers murmured quick apologies
when they got in anyone's way, but they never slowed by a
step. One of the men took hurried orders from Master Fitch
and disappeared at a run.

"The inn is near full, I'm afraid," the innkeeper told
Moiraine. "Almost to the rafters. Every inn in the town is
the same. With the winter we just had . . . well, as soon as
it cleared enough for them to get down out of the mountains we were inundated—yes, that's the word—inundated
by men from the mines and smelters, all telling the most
horrible tales. Wolves, and worse. The kind of tales men
tell when they've been cooped up all winter. I can't think
there's anyone left up there at all, we have that many here.
But never fear. Things may be a little crowded, but I'll do
my best by you and Master Andra. And your friends, too,
of course." He glanced curiously once or twice at Rand and
the others; except for Thom their clothes named them country folk, and Thom's gleeman's cloak made him a strange
traveling companion as well for "Mistress Alys" and "Master Andra." "I will do my best, you may rest assured."

Rand stared at the bustle around them and tried to avoid
being stepped on, though none of the help really seemed to
be in any danger of that. He kept thinking of how Master

al'Vere and his wife tended the Winespring Inn with sometimes a little assistance from their daughters.

Mat and Perrin craned their necks in interest toward the
common room, from which rolled a wave of laughter and
singing and jovial shouting whenever the wide door at the
end of the hall swung open. Muttering about finding out the
news, the Warder grimly disappeared through that swinging door, swallowed by a wave of merriment.

Rand wanted to follow him, but he wanted a bath even
more. He could have done with people and laughing right
then, but the common room would appreciate his presence
more when he was clean. Mat and Perrin apparently felt the
same; Mat was scratching surreptitiously.

"Master Fitch," Moiraine said, "I understand there are
Children of the Light in Baerlon. Is there likely to be trouble?"

"Oh, never you worry about them, Mistress Alys. They're
up to their usual tricks. Claim there's an Aes Sedai in the
town." Moiraine lifted an eyebrow, and the innkeeper spread
his plump hands. "Don't you worry. They've tried it before.
There's no Aes Sedai in Baerlon, and the Governor knows
it. The Whitecloaks think if they show an Aes Sedai, some
woman they claim is an Aes Sedai, people will let all of them
inside the walls. Well, I suppose some would. Some would.
But most people know what the Whitecloaks are up to,
and they support the Governor. No one wants to see some
harmless old woman hurt just so the Children can have an
excuse for whipping up a frenzy."

"I am glad to hear it," Moiraine said dryly. She put a
hand on the innkeeper's arm. "Is Min still here? I wish to
talk with her, if she is."

Master Fitch's answer was lost to Rand in the arrival of
attendants to lead them to the baths. Moiraine and Egwene
vanished behind a plump woman with a ready smile and an
armload of towels. The gleeman and Rand and his friends
found themselves following a slight, dark-haired fellow,
Ara by name.

Rand tried asking Ara about Baerlon, but the man barely
said two words together except to say Rand had a funny accent, and then the first sight of the bath chamber drove all
thoughts of talk right out of Rand's head. A dozen tall, copper

bathtubs sat in a circle on the tiled floor, which sloped down slightly to a drain in the center of the big stone-walled room. A thick towel, neatly folded, and a large cake of yellow soap sat on a stool behind each tub, and big black iron cauldrons of water stood heating over fires along one wall. On the opposite wall logs blazing in a deep fireplace added to the general warmth.

"Almost as good as the Winespring Inn back home," Perrin said loyally, if not exactly with a great attention to truth.

Thom barked a laugh, and Mat sniggered, "Sounds like we brought a Coplin with us and didn't know it."

Rand shrugged out of his cloak and stripped off his clothes while Ara filled four of the copper tubs. None of the others was far behind Rand in choosing a bathtub. Once their clothes were all in piles on the stools, Ara brought them each a large bucket of hot water and a dipper. That done, he sat on a stool by the door, leaning back against the wall with his arms crossed, apparently lost in his own thoughts.

There was little in the way of conversation while they lathered and sluiced away a week of grime with dippers of steaming water. Then it was into the tubs for a long soak; Ara had made the water hot enough that settling in was a slow process of luxuriant sighs. The air in the room went from warm to misty and hot. For a long time there was no sound except the occasional long, relaxing exhalation as tight muscles loosened and a chill that they had come to think permanent was drawn out of their bones.

"Need anything else?" Ara asked suddenly. He did not have much room to talk about people's accents; he and Master Fitch both sounded as if they had a mouth full of mush. "More towels? More hot water?"

"Nothing," Thom said in his reverberant voice. Eyes closed, he gave an indolent wave of his hand. "Go and enjoy the evening. At a later time I will see that you receive more than adequate recompense for your services." He settled lower in the tub, until the water covered everything but his eyes and nose.

Ara's eyes went to the stools behind the tubs, where their clothes and belongings were stacked. He glanced at the bow, but lingered longest over Rand's sword and Perrin's axe. "Is there trouble downcountry, too?" he said abruptly. "In the Rivers, or whatever you call it?"

"The Two Rivers," Mat said, pronouncing each separate word distinctly. "It's the Two Rivers. As for trouble, why—"

"What do you mean, too?" Rand asked. "Is there some kind of trouble here?"

Perrin, enjoying his soak, murmured, "Good! Good!" Thom raised himself back up a little, and opened his eyes.

"Here?" Ara snorted. "Trouble? Miners having fistfights in the streets in the dark of the morning aren't trouble. Or. . . ." He stopped and eyed them a moment. "I meant the Ghealdan kind of trouble," he said finally. "No, I suppose not. Nothing but sheep downcountry, is there? No offense. I just meant it's quiet down there. Still, it's been a strange winter. Strange things in the mountains. I heard the other day there were Trollocs up in Saldaea. But that's the Borderlands then, isn't it?" He finished with his mouth still open, then snapped it shut, appearing surprised that he had said so much.

Rand had tensed at the word *Trollocs,* and tried to hide it by wringing his washcloth out over his head. As the fellow went on he relaxed, but not everyone kept his mouth shut.

"Trollocs?" Mat chortled. Rand splashed water at him, but Mat just wiped it off of his face with a grin. "You just let me tell you about Trollocs."

For the first time since climbing into his tub, Thom spoke. "Why don't you not? I am a little tired of hearing my own stories back from you."

"He's a gleeman," Perrin said, and Ara gave him a scornful look.

"I saw the cloak. You going to perform?"

"Just a minute," Mat protested. "What's this about me telling Thom's stories? Are you all—?"

"You just don't tell them as well as Thom," Rand cut him off hastily, and Perrin hopped in. "You keep adding in things, trying to make it better, and they never do."

"And you get it all mixed up, too," Rand added. "Best leave it to Thom."

They were all talking so fast that Ara stared at them with his mouth hanging open. Mat stared, too, as if everyone else had suddenly gone crazy. Rand wondered how to shut him up short of jumping on him.

The door banged open to admit Lan, brown cloak slung over one shoulder, along with a gust of cooler air that momentarily thinned the mist.

"Well," the Warder said, rubbing his hands, "this is what I have been waiting for." Ara picked up a bucket, but Lan waved it away. "No, I will see to myself." Dropping his cloak on one of the stools, he bundled the bath attendant out of the room, despite the fellow's protests, and shut the door firmly after him. He waited there a moment, his head cocked to listen, and when he turned back to the rest of them his voice was stony and his eyes stabbed at Mat. "It's a good thing I got back when I did, farmboy. Don't you listen to what you are told?"

"I didn't do anything," Mat protested. "I was just going to tell him about the Trollocs, not about. . . ." He stopped, and leaned back from the Warder's eyes, flat against the back of the tub.

"Don't talk about Trollocs," Lan said grimly. "Don't even think about Trollocs." With an angry snort he began filling himself a bathtub. "Blood and ashes, you had better remember, the Dark One has eyes and ears where you least expect. And if the Children of the Light heard Trollocs were after you, they'd be burning to get their hands on you. To them, it would be as much as naming you Darkfriend. It may not be what you are used to, but until we get where we are going, keep your trust small unless Mistress Alys or I tell you differently." At his emphasis on the name Moiraine was using, Mat flinched.

"There was something that fellow wouldn't tell us," Rand said. "Something he thought was trouble, but he wouldn't say what it was."

"Probably the Children," Lan said, pouring more hot water into his tub. "Most people consider them trouble. Some don't, though, and he did not know you well enough to risk it. You might have gone running to the Whitecloaks, for all he knew."

Rand shook his head; this place already sounded worse than Taren Ferry could possibly be.

"He said there were Trollocs in . . . in Saldaea, wasn't it?" Perrin said.

Lan hurled his empty bucket to the floor with a crash. "You will talk about it, won't you? There are always Trollocs in the Borderlands, blacksmith. Just you put it in the front of your mind that we want no more attention than mice in a field. Concentrate on that. Moiraine wants to get you all to Tar Valon alive, and I will do it if it can be done, but if you bring any harm to her. . . ."

The rest of their bathing was done in silence, and dressing afterwards, too.

When they left the bath chamber, Moiraine was standing at the end of the hall with a slender girl not much taller than herself. At least, Rand thought it was a girl, though her dark hair was cut short and she wore a man's shirt and trousers. Moiraine said something, and the girl looked at the men sharply, then nodded to Moiraine and hurried away.

"Well, now," Moiraine said as they drew closer, "I am sure a bath has given you all an appetite. Master Fitch has given us a private dining room." She talked on inconsequentially as she turned to lead the way, about their rooms and the crowding in the town, and how the innkeeper hoped Thom would favor the common room with some music and a story or two. She never mentioned the girl, if girl it had been.

The private dining room had a polished oak table with a dozen chairs around it, and a thick rug on the floor. As they entered, Egwene, freshly gleaming hair combed out around her shoulders, turned from warming her hands at the fire crackling on the hearth. Rand had had plenty of time for thought during the long silence in the bath chamber. Lan's constant admonitions not to trust anyone, and especially Ara being afraid to trust them, had made him think of just how alone they really were. It seemed they could not trust anyone but themselves, and he was still not too sure how far they could trust Moiraine, or Lan. Just themselves. And Egwene was still Egwene. Moiraine said it would have happened to her anyway, this touching the True Source. She had no control over it, and that meant it was not her fault. And she was still Egwene.

He opened his mouth to apologize, but Egwene stiffened and turned her back before he could get a word out. Staring sullenly at her back, he swallowed what he had been going to say. *All right, then. If she wants to be like that, there's nothing I can do.*

Master Fitch bustled in then, followed by four women in white aprons as long as his, with a platter holding three roast chickens and others bearing silver, and pottery dishes, and covered bowls. The women began setting the table immediately, while the innkeeper bowed to Moiraine.

"My apologies, Mistress Alys, for making you wait like this, but with so many people in the inn, it's a wonder anybody gets served at all. I am afraid the food isn't what it should be, either. Just the chickens, and some turnips and henpeas, with a little cheese for after. No, it just isn't what it should be. I truly do apologize."

"A feast." Moiraine smiled. "For these troubled times, a feast indeed, Master Fitch."

The innkeeper bowed again. His wispy hair, sticking out in all directions as if he constantly ran his hands through it, made the bow comical, but his grin was so pleasant that anyone who laughed would be laughing with him, not at him. "My thanks, Mistress Alys. My thanks." As he straightened he frowned and wiped an imagined bit of dust from the table with a corner of his apron. "It isn't what I would have laid before you a year ago, of course. Not nearly. The winter. Yes. The winter. My cellars are emptying out, and the market is all but bare. And who can blame the farm folk? Who? There's certainly no telling when they'll harvest another crop. No telling at all. It's the wolves get the mutton and beef that should go on people's tables, and. . . ."

Abruptly he seemed to realize that this was hardly the conversation to settle his guests to a comfortable meal. "How I do run on. Full of old wind, that's me. Old wind. Mari, Cinda, let these good people eat in peace." He made shooing gestures at the women and, as they scurried from the room, swung back to bow to Moiraine yet again. "I hope you enjoy your meal, Mistress Alys. If there's anything else you need, just speak it, and I will fetch it. Just you speak it. It is a pleasure serving you and Master Andra. A pleasure." He gave one more deep bow and was gone, closing the door softly behind him.

Lan had slouched against the wall through all of this as if half asleep. Now he leaped up and was at the door in two long strides. Pressing an ear to a door panel, he listened intently for a slow count of thirty, then snatched open the door and stuck his head into the hall. "They're gone," he said at last, closing the door. "We can talk safely."

"I know you say not to trust anyone," Egwene said, "but if you suspect the innkeeper, why stay here?"

"I suspect him no more than anyone else," Lan replied.

"But then, until we reach Tar Valon, I suspect everyone. There, I'll suspect only half."

Rand started to smile, thinking the Warder was making a joke. Then he realized there was not a trace of humor on Lan's face. He really would suspect people in Tar Valon. Was anywhere safe?

"He exaggerates," Moiraine told them soothingly. "Master Fitch is a good man, honest and trustworthy. But he does like to talk, and with the best will in the world he might let something slip to the wrong ear. And I have never yet stopped at an inn where half the maids did not listen at doors and spend more time gossiping than making beds. Come, let us be seated before our meal gets cold."

They took places around the table, with Moiraine at the head and Lan at the foot, and for a while everyone was too busy filling their plates for talk. It might not have been a feast, but after close to a week of flatbread and dried meat, it tasted like one.

After a time, Moiraine asked, "What did you learn in the common room?" Knives and forks stilled, suspended in midair, and all eyes turned to the Warder.

"Little that's good," Lan replied. "Avin was right, at least as far as talk has it. There was a battle in Ghealdan, and Logain was the victor. A dozen different stories are floating about, but they all agree on that."

Logain? That must be the false Dragon. It was the first time Rand had heard a name put to the man. Lan sounded almost as if he knew him.

"The Aes Sedai?" Moiraine asked quietly, and Lan shook his head.

"I don't know. Some say they were all killed, some say none." He snorted. "Some even say they went over to Logain. There's nothing reliable, and I did not care to show too much interest."

"Yes," Moiraine said. "Little that is good." With a deep breath she brought her attention back to the table. "And what of our own circumstances?"

"There, the news is better. No odd happenings, no strangers around who might be Myrddraal, certainly no Trollocs. And the Whitecloaks are busy trying to make trouble for Governor Adan because he won't cooperate with them. They will not even notice us unless we advertise ourselves."

"Good," Moiraine said. "That agrees with what the bath maid said. Gossip does have its points. Now," she addressed the entire company, "we have a long journey still ahead of us, but the last week has not been easy, either, so I propose to remain here tonight and tomorrow night, and leave early the following morning." All the younger folk grinned; a city for the first time. Moiraine smiled, but she still said, "What does Master Andra say to that?"

Lan eyed the grinning faces flatly. "Well enough, if they remember what I've told them for a change."

Thom snorted through his mustaches. "These country folk loose in a . . . a city." He snorted again and shook his head.

With the crowding at the inn there were only three rooms to be had, one for Moiraine and Egwene, and two to take the men. Rand found himself sharing with Lan and Thom, on the fourth floor at the back, close up under the overhanging eaves, with a single small window that overlooked the stableyard. Full night had fallen, and light from the inn made a pool outside. It was a small room to begin, and an extra bed set up for Thom made it smaller, though all three were narrow. And hard, Rand found when he threw himself down on his. Definitely not the best room.

Thom stayed only long enough to uncase his flute and harp, then left already practicing grand poses. Lan went with him.

It was strange, Rand thought as he shifted uncomfortably on the bed. A week ago he would have been downstairs like a falling rock for just the chance he might see a gleeman perform, for just the rumor of it. But he had heard Thom tell his stories every night for a week, and Thom would be there tomorrow night, and the next, and the hot bath had loosened kinks in muscles that he had thought would be there forever, and his first hot meal in a week oozed lethargy into him. Sleepily he wondered if Lan really did know the false Dragon, Logain. A muffled shout came from belowstairs, the common room greeting Thom's arrival, but Rand was already asleep.

The stone hallway was dim and shadowy, and empty except for Rand. He could not tell where the light came from, what little there was of it; the gray walls were bare of candles or lamps, nothing at all to account for the faint glow that seemed to just be there. The air was still and dank, and somewhere in the distance water dripped with a steady, hollow plonk. Wherever this was, it was not the inn. Frowning, he rubbed at his forehead. Inn? His head hurt, and thoughts were hard to hold on to. There had been something about . . . an inn? It was gone, whatever it was.

He licked his lips and wished he had something to drink. He was awfully thirsty, dry-as-dust thirsty. It was the dripping sound that decided him. With nothing to choose by except his thirst, he started toward that steady *plonk—plonk—plonk*.

The hallway stretched on, without any crossing corridor and without the slightest change in appearance. The only features at all were the rough doors set at regular intervals in pairs, one on either side of the hall, the wood splintered and dry despite the damp in the air. The shadows receded ahead of him, staying the same, and the dripping never came any closer. After a long time he decided to try one of those doors. It opened easily, and he stepped through into a grim, stone-walled chamber.

One wall opened in a series of arches onto a gray stone balcony, and beyond that was a sky such as he had never seen. Striated clouds in blacks and grays, reds and oranges, streamed by as if storm winds drove them, weaving and interweaving endlessly. *No one* could ever have seen a sky like that; it could not exist.

He pulled his eyes away from the balcony, but the rest of the room was no better. Odd curves and peculiar angles, as if the chamber had been melted almost haphazardly out of the stone, and columns that seemed to grow out of the gray floor. Flames roared on the hearth like a forge-fire with the bellows pumping, but gave no heat. Strange oval stones made the fireplace; they just looked like stones, wet-slick despite the fire, when he looked straight at them, but when he glimpsed them from the corner of his eye they seemed to be faces instead, the faces of men and women writhing in anguish, screaming silently. The high-backed chairs and the polished table in the middle of the room were perfectly ordinary, but that in itself emphasized the rest. A single mirror hung on the wall, but that was not ordinary at all. When he looked at it he saw only a blur where his reflection should have been. Everything else in the room was shown true, but not him.

A man stood in front of the fireplace. He had not noticed the man when he first came in. If he had not known it was impossible, he would have said no one had been there until he actually looked at the man. Dressed in dark clothes of a fine cut, he seemed in the prime of his maturity, and Rand supposed women would have found him good-looking.

"Once more we meet face-to-face," the man said and, just for an instant, his mouth and eyes became openings into endless caverns of flame.

With a yell Rand hurled himself backwards out of the room, so hard that he stumbled across the hall and banged into the door there, knocking it open. He twisted and grabbed at the doorhandle to keep from falling to the floor—and found himself staring wide-eyed into a stone room with an impossible sky through the arches leading to a balcony, and a fireplace. . . .

"You cannot get away from me that easily," the man said.

Rand twisted, scrambling back out of the room, trying to regain his feet without slowing down. This time there was no corridor. He froze half crouched not far from the polished table, and looked at the man by the fireplace. It was better than looking at the fireplace stones, or at the sky.

"This is a dream," he said as he straightened. Behind him he heard the click of the door closing. "It's some kind of nightmare." He shut his eyes, thinking about waking up. When he was a child the Wisdom had said if you could do that in a nightmare, it would go away. *The . . . Wisdom? What?* If only his thoughts would stop sliding away. If only his head would stop hurting, then he could think straight.

He opened his eyes again. The room was still as it had been, the balcony, the sky. The man by the fireplace.

"Is it a dream?" the man said. "Does it matter?" Once again, for a moment, his mouth and eyes became peepholes into a furnace that seemed to stretch forever. His voice did not change; he did not seem to notice it happening at all.

Rand jumped a little this time, but he managed to keep from yelling. *This is a dream. It has to be.* All the same, he stepped backwards all the way to the door, never taking his eyes off the fellow by the fire, and tried the handle. It did not move; the door was locked.

"You seem thirsty," the man by the fire said. "Drink."

On the table was a goblet, shining gold and ornamented

with rubies and amethysts. It had not been there before. He
wished he could stop jumping. It was only a dream. His
mouth felt like dust.

"I am, a little," he said, picking up the goblet. The man
leaned forward intently, one hand on the back of a chair,
watching him. The smell of spiced wine drove home to Rand
just how thirsty he was, as if he had had nothing to drink in
days. *Have I?*

With the wine halfway to his mouth, he stopped. Whispers of smoke were rising from the chairback between the
man's fingers. And those eyes watched him so sharply,
flickering rapidly in and out of flames.

Rand licked his lips and put the wine back on the table,
untasted. "I'm not as thirsty as I thought." The man straightened abruptly, his face without expression. His disappointment could not have been more plain if he had cursed. Rand
wondered what was in the wine. But that was a stupid question, of course. This was all a dream. *Then why won't it
stop?* "What do you want?" he demanded. "Who are you?"

Flames rose in the man's eyes and mouth; Rand thought
he could hear them roar. "Some call me Ba'alzamon."

Rand found himself facing the door, jerking frantically at
the handle. All thought of dreams had vanished. The Dark
One. The doorhandle would not budge, but he kept twisting.

"Are you the one?" Ba'alzamon said suddenly. "You cannot hide it from me forever. You cannot even hide yourself from me, not on the highest mountain or in the deepest
cave. I know you down to the smallest hair."

Rand turned to face the man—to face Ba'alzamon. He
swallowed hard. A nightmare. He reached back to give the
door-handle one last pull, then stood up straighter.

"Are you expecting glory?" Ba'alzamon said. "Power?
Did they tell you the Eye of the World would serve you?
What glory or power is there for a puppet? The strings that
move you have been centuries weaving. Your father was
chosen by the White Tower, like a stallion roped and led to
his business. Your mother was no more than a brood mare
to their plans. And those plans lead to your death."

Rand's hands knotted in fists. "My father is a good man,
and my mother was a good woman. Don't you talk about
them!"

The flames laughed. "So there is some spirit in you after

all. Perhaps you *are* the one. Little good it will do you. The Amyrlin Seat will use you until you are consumed, just as Davian was used, and Yurian Stonebow, and Guaire Amalasan, and Raolin Darksbane. Just as Logain is being used. Used until there is nothing left of you."

"I don't know. . . ." Rand swung his head from side to side. That one moment of clear thinking, born in anger, was gone. Even as he groped for it again he could not remember how he had reached it the first time. His thoughts spun around and around. He seized one like a raft in the whirlpool. He forced the words out, his voice strengthening the further he went. "You . . . are bound . . . in Shayol Ghul. You and all the Forsaken . . . bound by the Creator until the end of time."

"The end of time?" Ba'alzamon mocked. "You live like a beetle under a rock, and you think your slime is the universe. The death of time will bring me power such as you could not dream of, worm."

"You are bound—"

"Fool, I have never been bound!" The fires of his face roared so hot that Rand stepped back, sheltering behind his hands. The sweat on his palms dried from the heat. "I stood at Lews Therin Kinslayer's shoulder when he did the deed that named him. It was I who told him to kill his wife, and his children, and all his blood, and every living person who loved him or whom he loved. It was I who gave him the moment of sanity to know what he had done. Have you ever heard a man scream his soul away, worm? He could have struck at me, then. He could not have won, but he could have tried. Instead he called down his precious One Power upon himself, so much that the earth split open and reared up Dragonmount to mark his tomb.

"A thousand years later I sent the Trollocs ravening south, and for three centuries they savaged the world. Those blind fools in Tar Valon said I was beaten in the end, but the Second Covenant, the Covenant of the Ten Nations, was shattered beyond remaking, and who was left to oppose me then? I whispered in Artur Hawkwing's ear, and the length and breadth of the land Aes Sedai died. I whispered again, and the High King sent his armies across the Aryth Ocean, across the World Sea, and sealed two dooms. The doom of his dream of one land and one people, and a doom yet to come. At his deathbed I was there when his councilors told him only Aes Sedai could save his life. I spoke, and he ordered his councilors to the stake. I spoke, and the High King's last words were to cry that Tar Valon must be destroyed.

"When men such as these could not stand against me, what chance do you have, a toad crouching beside a forest puddle. You will serve me, or you will dance on Aes Sedai strings until you die. And then you *will* be mine. The dead belong to me!"

"No," Rand muttered, "this is a dream. It is a dream!"

"Do you think you are safe from me in your dreams? Look!" Ba'alzamon pointed commandingly, and Rand's head turned to follow, although he did not turn it; he did not want to turn.

The goblet was gone from the table. Where it had been, crouched a large rat, blinking at the light, sniffing the air warily. Ba'alzamon crooked his finger, and with a squeak the rat arched its back, forepaws lifting into the air while it balanced awkwardly on its hind feet. The finger curved more, and the rat toppled over, scrabbling frantically, pawing at nothing, squealing shrilly, its back bending, bending, bending. With a sharp snap like the breaking of a twig, the rat trembled violently and was still, lying bent almost double.

Rand swallowed. "Anything can happen in a dream," he mumbled. Without looking he swung his fist back against the door again. His hand hurt, but he still did not wake up.

"Then go to the Aes Sedai. Go to the White Tower and tell them. Tell the Amyrlin Seat of this . . . dream." The man laughed; Rand felt the heat of the flames on his face. "That is one way to escape them. They will not use you, then. No, not when they know that I know. But will they let you live, to spread the tale of what they do? Are you a big enough fool to believe they will? The ashes of many like you are scattered on the slopes of Dragonmount."

"This is a dream," Rand said, panting. "It's a dream, and I am going to wake up."

"Will you?" Out of the corner of his eye he saw the man's finger move to point at him. "Will you, indeed?" The finger crooked, and Rand screamed as he arched backwards, every muscle in his body forcing him further. "Will you ever wake again?"

Convulsively Rand jerked up in the darkness, his hands tightening on cloth. A blanket. Pale moonlight shone through the single window. The shadowed shapes of the other two beds. A snore from one of them, like canvas ripping: Thom Merrilin. A few coals gleamed among the ashes on the hearth.

It had been a dream, then, like that nightmare in the Winespring Inn the day of Bel Tine, everything that he had heard and done all jumbled in together with old tales and nonsense from nowhere. He pulled the blanket up around his shoulders, but it was not cold that made him shake. His head hurt, too. Perhaps Moiraine could do something to stop these dreams. *She said she could help with nightmares.*

With a snort he lay back. Were the dreams really bad enough for him to ask the help of an Aes Sedai? On the other hand, could anything he did now get him in any deeper? He had left the Two Rivers, come away with an Aes Sedai. But there had not been any choice, of course. So did he have any choice but to trust her? An Aes Sedai? It was as bad as the dreams, thinking about it. He huddled under his blanket, trying to find the calmness of the void the way Tam had taught him, but sleep was a long time returning.

CHAPTER
15

Strangers and Friends

Sunlight streaming across his narrow bed finally woke
Rand out of a deep but restless sleep. He pulled a pillow over his head, but it did not really shut out the
light, and he did not really want to go back to sleep. There
had been more dreams after the first. He could not remember any but the first, but he knew he wanted no more.

With a sigh he tossed the pillow aside and sat up, wincing
as he stretched. All the aches he thought had soaked out in
the bath were back. And his head still hurt, too. It did not
surprise him. A dream like that was enough to give anybody
a headache. The others had already faded, but not that one.

The other beds were empty. Light poured in through the
window at a steep angle; the sun stood well above the horizon. By this hour back on the farm he would have already
fixed something to eat and been well into his chores. He
scrambled out of bed, muttering angrily to himself. A city to
see, and they did not even wake him. At least someone had
seen that there was water in the pitcher, and still warm, too.

He washed and dressed quickly, hesitating a moment over
Tam's sword. Lan and Thom had left their saddlebags and
blanketrolls behind in the room, of course, but the Warder's
sword was nowhere to be seen. Lan had worn his sword in
Emond's Field even before there was any hint of trouble. He
thought he would take the older man's lead. Telling himself
it was not because he had often daydreamed about walking
the streets of a real city wearing a sword, he belted it on and
tossed his cloak over his shoulder like a sack.

Taking the stairs two at a time, he hurried down to the
kitchen. That was surely the quickest place to get a bite,

and on his only day in Baerlon he did not want to waste any more time than he already had. *Blood and ashes, but they could have waked me.*

Master Fitch was in the kitchen, confronting a plump woman whose arms were covered in flour to her elbows, obviously the cook. Rather, she was confronting him, shaking her finger under his nose. Serving maids and scullions, potboys and spitboys, hurried about their tasks, elaborately ignoring what was going on in front of them.

". . . my Cirri is a good cat," the cook was saying sharply, "and I won't hear a word otherwise, do you hear? Complaining about him doing his job too well, that's what you're doing, if you ask me."

"I have had complaints," Master Fitch managed to get in. "Complaints, mistress. Half the guests—"

"I won't hear of it. I just won't hear of it. If they want to complain about my cat, let *them* do the cooking. My poor old cat, who's just doing his job, and me, we'll go somewhere where we're appreciated, see if we don't." She untied her apron and started to lift it over her head.

"No!" Master Fitch yelped, and leaped to stop her. They danced in a circle with the cook trying to take her apron off and the innkeeper trying to put it back on her. "No, Sara," he panted. "There's no need for this. No need, I say! What would I do without you? Cirri's a fine cat. An excellent cat. He's the best cat in Baerlon. If anyone else complains, I'll tell them to be thankful the cat is doing his job. Yes, thankful. You mustn't go. Sara? Sara!"

The cook stopped their circling and managed to snatch her apron free of him. "All right, then. All right." Clutching the apron in both hands, she still did not retie it. "But if you expect me to have anything ready for midday, you'd best get out of here and let me get to it. This may be your inn, but it's my kitchen. Unless you want to do the cooking?" She made as if to hand the apron to him.

Master Fitch stepped back with his hands spread wide. He opened his mouth, then stopped, looking around for the first time. The kitchen help still studiously ignored the cook and the innkeeper, and Rand began an intensive search of his coat pockets, though except for the coin Moiraine had given him there was nothing in them but a few coppers and a handful of odds and ends. His pocket knife and sharpening stone. Two spare bowstrings and a piece of string he had thought might be useful.

"I am sure, Sara," Master Fitch said carefully, "that everything will be up to your usual excellence." With that he took one last suspicious look at the kitchen help, then left with as much dignity as he could manage.

Sara waited until he was gone before briskly tying her apron strings again, then fastened her eye on Rand. "I suppose you want something to eat, eh? Well, come on in." She gave him a quick grin. "I don't bite, I don't, no matter what you may have seen as you shouldn't've. Ciel, get the lad some bread and cheese and milk. That's all there is right now. Sit yourself, lad. Your friends have all gone out, except one lad I understand wasn't feeling well, and I expect you'll be wanting to do the same."

One of the serving maids brought a tray while Rand took a stool at the table. He began eating as the cook went back to kneading her bread dough, but she was not finished talking.

"You mustn't take any mind of what you saw, now. Master Fitch is a good enough man, though the best of you aren't any bargains. It's the folk complaining as has him on edge, and what do they have to complain about? Would they rather find live rats than dead ones? Though it isn't like Cirri to leave his handiwork behind. And over a dozen? Cirri wouldn't let so many get into the inn, he wouldn't. It's a clean place, too, and not one to be so troubled. And all with backs broken." She shook her head at the strangeness of it all.

The bread and cheese turned to ashes in Rand's mouth. "Their backs were broken?"

The cook waved a floury hand. "Think on happier things, that's my way of looking. There's a gleeman, you know. In the common room right this minute. But then, you came with him, didn't you? You are one of those as came with Mistress Alys last evening, aren't you? I thought you were. I won't get much chance to see this gleeman myself, I'm thinking, not with the inn as full as it is, and most of them riffraff down from the mines." She gave the dough an especially heavy thump. "Not the sort we'd let in most times, only the whole town is filled up with them. Better than some they could be, though, I suppose. Why, I haven't seen a gleeman since before the winter, and. . . ."

Rand ate mechanically, not tasting anything, not listening to what the cook said. Dead rats, with their backs broken. He finished his breakfast hastily, stammered his thanks, and hurried out. He had to talk to someone.

The common room of the Stag and Lion shared little except its purpose with the same room at the Winespring Inn. It was twice as wide and three times as long, and colorful pictures of ornate buildings with gardens of tall trees and bright flowers were painted high on the walls. Instead of one huge fireplace, a hearth blazed on each wall, and scores of tables filled the floor, with almost every chair, bench, or stool taken.

Every man among the crowd of patrons with pipes in their teeth and mugs in their fists leaned forward with his attention on one thing: Thom, standing atop a table in the middle of the room, his many-colored cloak tossed over a nearby chair. Even Master Fitch held a silver tankard and a polishing cloth in motionless hands.

". . . prancing, silver hooves and proud, arched necks," Thom proclaimed, while somehow seeming not only to be riding a horse, but to be one of a long procession of riders. "Silken manes flutter with tossed heads. A thousand streaming banners whip rainbows against an endless sky. A hundred brazen-throated trumpets shiver the air, and drums rattle like thunder. Wave on wave, cheers roll from watchers in their thousands, roll across the rooftops and towers of Illian, crash and break unheard around the thousand ears of riders whose eyes and hearts shine with their sacred quest. The Great Hunt of the Horn rides forth, rides to seek the Horn of Valere that will summon the heroes of the Ages back from the grave to battle for the Light. . . ."

It was what the gleeman had called Plain Chant, those nights beside the fire on the ride north. Stories, he said, were told in three voices, High Chant, Plain Chant, and Common, which meant simply telling it the way you might tell your neighbor about your crop. Thom told stories in Common, but he did not bother to hide his contempt for the voice.

Rand closed the door without going in and slumped against the wall. He would get no advice from Thom. Moiraine—what *would* she do if she knew?

He became aware of people staring at him as they passed, and realized he was muttering under his breath. Smoothing his coat, he straightened. He had to talk to somebody. The cook had said one of the others had not gone out. It was an effort not to run.

When he rapped on the door of the room where the other boys had slept and poked his head in, only Perrin was there, lying on his bed and still not dressed. He twisted his head on the pillow to look at Rand, then closed his eyes again. Mat's bow and quiver were propped in the corner.

"I heard you weren't feeling well," Rand said. He came in and sat on the next bed. "I just wanted to talk. I. . . ." He did not know how to bring it up, he realized. "If you're sick," he said, half standing, "maybe you ought to sleep. I can go."

"I don't know if I'll ever sleep again." Perrin sighed. "I had a bad dream, if you must know, and couldn't get back to sleep. Mat will be quick enough to tell you. He laughed this morning, when I told them why I was too tired to go out with him, but he dreamed, too. I listened to him for most of the night, tossing and muttering, and you can't tell me he got a good night's sleep." He threw a thick arm across his eyes. "Light, but I'm tired. Maybe if I just stay here for an hour or two, I'll feel like getting up. Mat will never let me hear the end of it if I miss seeing Baerlon because of a dream."

Rand slowly lowered himself to the bed again. He licked his lips, then said quickly, "Did he kill a rat?"

Perrin lowered his arm and stared at him. "You, too?" he said finally. When Rand nodded, he said, "I wish I was back home. He told me . . . he said. . . . What are we going to do? Have you told Moiraine?"

"No. Not yet. Maybe I won't. I don't know. What about you?"

"He said. . . . Blood and ashes, Rand, I don't know." Perrin raised up on his elbow abruptly. "Do you think Mat had the same dream? He laughed, but it sounded forced, and he looked funny when I said I couldn't sleep because of a dream."

"Maybe he did," Rand said. Guiltily, he felt relieved he was not the only one. "I was going to ask Thom for advice. He's seen a lot of the world. You . . . you don't think we should tell Moiraine, do you?"

Perrin fell back on his pillow. "You've heard the stories about Aes Sedai. Do you think we can trust Thom? If we can trust anybody. Rand, if we get out of this alive, if we ever get back home, and you hear me say anything about leaving Emond's Field, even to go as far as Watch Hill, you kick me. All right?"

"That's no way to talk," Rand said. He put on a smile, as cheerful as he could make it. "Of course we'll get home. Come on, get up. We're in a city, and we have a whole day to see it. Where are your clothes?"

"You go. I just want to lie here awhile." Perrin put his arm back across his eyes. "You go ahead. I'll catch you up in an hour or two."

"It's your loss," Rand said as he got up. "Think of what you might miss." He stopped at the door. "Baerlon. How many times have we talked about seeing Baerlon one day?" Perrin lay there with his eyes covered and did not say a word. After a minute Rand stepped out and closed the door behind him.

In the hallway he leaned against the wall, his smile fading. His head still hurt; it was worse, not better. He could not work up much enthusiasm for Baerlon, either, not now. He could not summon enthusiasm about anything.

A chambermaid came by, her arms full of sheets, and gave him a concerned look. Before she could speak he moved off down the hall, shrugging into his cloak. Thom would not be finished in the common room for hours yet. He might as well see what he could. Perhaps he could find Mat, and see if Ba'alzamon had been in his dreams, too. He went downstairs more slowly this time, rubbing his temple.

The stairs ended near the kitchen, so he took that way out, nodding to Sara but hurrying on when she seemed about to take up where she had left off. The stableyard was empty except for Mutch, standing in the stable door, and one of the other ostlers carrying a sack on his shoulder into the stable. Rand nodded to Mutch, too, but the stableman gave him a truculent look and went inside. He hoped the rest of the city was more like Sara and less like Mutch. Ready to see what a city was like, he picked up his step.

At the open stableyard gates, he stopped and stared. People packed the street like sheep in a pen, people swathed to the eyes in cloaks and coats, hats pulled down against the cold, weaving in and out at a quick step as though the wind whistling over the rooftops blew them along, elbowing past one another with barely a word or a glance. *All strangers,* he thought. *None of them know each other.*

The smells were strange, too, sharp and sour and sweet all mixed in a hodgepodge that had him rubbing his nose. Even at the height of Festival he had never seen so many people so jammed together. Not even half so many. And this was only one street. Master Fitch and the cook said the whole city was full. The whole city . . . like this?

He backed slowly away from the gate, away from the street full of people. It really was not right to go off and leave Perrin sick in bed. And what if Thom finished his storytelling while Rand was off in the city? The gleeman might go out himself, and Rand needed to talk to someone. Much better to wait a bit. He breathed a sigh of relief as he turned his back on the swarming street.

Going back inside the inn did not appeal to him, though, not with his headache. He sat on an upended barrel against the back of the inn and hoped the cold air might help his head.

Mutch came to the stable door from time to time to stare at him, and even across the stableyard he could make out the fellow's disapproving scowl. Was it country people the man did not like? Or had he been embarrassed by Master Fitch greeting them after he had tried to chase them off for coming in the back way? *Maybe he's a Darkfriend,* he thought, expecting to chuckle at the idea, but it was not a funny thought. He rubbed his hand along the hilt of Tam's sword. There was not much left that was funny at all.

"A shepherd with a heron-mark sword," said a low, woman's voice. "That's almost enough to make me believe anything. What trouble are you in, downcountry boy?"

Startled, Rand jumped to his feet. It was the crop-haired young woman who had been with Moiraine when he came out of the bath chamber, still dressed in a boy's coat and breeches. She was a little older than he was, he thought, with dark eyes even bigger than Egwene's, and oddly intent.

"You are Rand, aren't you?" she went on. "My name is Min."

"I'm not in trouble," he said. He did not know what Moiraine had told her, but he remembered Lan's admonition not to attract any notice. "What makes you think I'm in trouble? The Two Rivers is a quiet place, and we're all quiet people. No place for trouble, unless it has to do with crops, or sheep."

"Quiet?" Min said with a faint smile. "I've heard men talk about you Two Rivers folk. I've heard the jokes about wooden-headed sheepherders, and then there are men who have actually been downcountry."

"Wooden-headed?" Rand said, frowning. "What jokes?"

"The ones who know," she went on as if he had not spoken, "say you walk around all smiles and politeness, just as meek and soft as butter. On the surface, anyway. Underneath, they say, you're all as tough as old oak roots. Prod too hard, they say, and you dig up stone. But the stone isn't buried very deep in you, or in your friends. It's as if a storm has scoured away almost all the covering. Moiraine didn't tell me everything, but I see what I see."

Old oak roots? Stone? It hardly sounded like the sort of thing the merchants or their people would say. That last made him jump, though.

He looked around quickly; the stableyard was empty, and the nearest windows were closed. "I don't know anybody named—what was it again?"

"Mistress Alys, then, if you prefer," Min said with an amused look that made his cheeks color. "There's no one close enough to hear."

"What makes you think Mistress Alys has another name?"

"Because she told me," Min said, so patiently that he blushed again. "Not that she had a choice, I suppose. I saw she was . . . different . . . right away. When she stopped here before, on her way downcountry. She knew about me. I've talked to . . . others like her before."

"'Saw'?" Rand said.

"Well, I don't suppose you'll go running to the Children. Not considering who your traveling companions are. The Whitecloaks wouldn't like what I do any more than they like what she does."

"I don't understand."

"She says I see pieces of the Pattern." Min gave a little laugh and shook her head. "Sounds too grand, to me. I just see things when I look at people, and sometimes I know what they mean. I look at a man and a woman who've never even talked to one another, and I know they'll marry. And they do. That sort of thing. She wanted me to look at you. All of you together."

Rand shivered. "And what did you see?"

"When you're all in a group? Sparks swirling around you, thousands of them, and a big shadow, darker than midnight. It's so strong, I almost wonder why everybody can't see it. The sparks are trying to fill the shadow, and the shadow is trying to swallow the sparks." She shrugged. "You are all tied together in something dangerous, but I can't make any more of it."

"All of us?" Rand muttered. "Egwene, too? But they weren't after—I mean—"

Min did not seem to notice his slip. "The girl? She's part of it. And the gleeman. All of you. You're in love with her." He stared at her. "I can tell that even without seeing any images. She loves you, too, but she's not for you, or you for her. Not the way you both want."

"What's that supposed to mean?"

"When I look at her, I see the same as when I look at . . . Mistress Alys. Other things, things I don't understand, too, but I know what *that* means. She won't refuse it."

"This is all foolishness," Rand said uncomfortably. His headache was fading to numbness; his head felt packed with wool. He wanted to get away from this girl and the things she saw. And yet. . . . "What do you see when you look at . . . the rest of us?"

"All sorts of things," Min said, with a grin as if she knew what he really wanted to ask. "The War . . . ah . . . Master Andra has seven ruined towers around his head, and a babe in a cradle holding a sword, and. . . ." She shook her head. "Men like him—you understand?—always have so many images they crowd one another. The strongest images around the gleeman are a man—not him—juggling fire, and the White Tower, and that doesn't make any sense at all for a man. The strongest things I see about the big, curly-haired fellow are a wolf, and a broken crown, and trees flowering all around him. And the other one—a red eagle, an eye on a balance scale, a dagger with a ruby, a horn, and a laughing face. There are other things, but you see what I mean. This time I can't make up or down out of any of it." She waited then, still grinning, until he finally cleared his throat and asked.

"What about me?"

Her grin stopped just short of outright laughter. "The same kind of things as the rest. A sword that isn't a sword, a golden crown of laurel leaves, a beggar's staff, you pouring water on sand, a bloody hand and a white-hot iron, three women standing over a funeral bier with you on it, black rock wet with blood—"

"All right," he broke in uneasily. "You don't have to list it all."

"Most of all, I see lightning around you, some striking at you, some coming out of you. I don't know what any of it means, except for one thing. You and I will meet again." She gave him a quizzical look, as if she did not understand that either.

"Why shouldn't we?" he said. "I'll be coming back this way on my way home."

"I suppose you will, at that." Suddenly her grin was back, wry and mysterious, and she patted his cheek. "But if I told you everything I saw, you'd be as curly-haired as your friend with the shoulders."

He jerked back from her hand as if it were red-hot. "What do you mean? Do you see anything about rats? Or dreams?"

"Rats! No, no rats. As for dreams, maybe it's your idea of a dream, but I never thought it was mine."

He wondered if she was crazy, grinning like that. "I have to go," he said, edging around her. "I . . . I have to meet my friends."

"Go, then. But you won't escape."

He didn't exactly break into a run, but every step he took was quicker than the step before.

"Run, if you want," she called after him. "You can't escape from me."

Her laughter sped him across the stableyard and out into the street, into the hubbub of people. Her last words were too close to what Ba'alzamon had said. He blundered into people as he hurried through the crowd, earning hard looks and hard words, but he did not slow down until he was several streets away from the inn.

After a time he began to pay attention again to where he was. His head felt like a balloon, but he stared and enjoyed anyway. He thought Baerlon was a grand city, if not exactly in the same way as cities in Thom's stories. He wandered up broad streets, most paved with flagstone, and down narrow, twisting lanes, wherever chance and the shifting of the crowd took him. It had rained during the night, and the streets that were unpaved had already been churned to mud by the crowds, but muddy streets were nothing new to him. None of the streets in Emond's Field was paved.

There certainly were no palaces, and only a few houses were very much bigger than those back home, but every house had a roof of slate or tile as fine as the roof of the Winespring Inn. He supposed there would be a palace or two in Caemlyn. As for inns, he counted nine, not one smaller than the Winespring and most as large as the Stag and Lion, and there were plenty of streets he had not seen yet.

Shops dotted every street, with awnings out front sheltering tables covered with goods, everything from cloth to books to pots to boots. It was as if a hundred peddlers' wagons had spilled out their contents. He stared so much that more than once he had to hurry on at the suspicious look of a shopkeeper. He had not understood the first shopkeeper's stare. When he did understand, he started to get angry until he remembered that here he was the stranger. He could not have bought much, anyway. He gasped when he saw how many coppers were exchanged for a dozen discolored apples or a handful of shriveled turnips, the sort that would be fed to the horses in the Two Rivers, but people seemed eager to pay.

There were certainly more than enough people, to his estimation. For a while the sheer number of them almost overwhelmed him. Some wore clothes of finer cut than anyone in the Two Rivers—almost as fine as Moiraine's—and quite a few had long, fur-lined coats that flapped around their ankles. The miners everybody at the inn kept talking about, they had the hunched look of men who grubbed underground. But most of the people did not look any different from those he had grown up with, not in dress or in face. He had expected they would, somehow. Indeed, some of them had so much the look of the Two Rivers in their faces that he could imagine they belonged to one family or another that he knew around Emond's Field. A toothless, gray-haired fellow with ears like jug handles, sitting on a bench outside one of the inns and peering mournfully into an empty tankard, could easily have been Bili Congar's close cousin. The lantern-jawed tailor sewing in front of his shop might have been Jon Thane's brother, even to the same bald spot on the back of his head. A near mirror image of Samel Crawe pushed past Rand as he turned a corner, and. . . .

In disbelief he stared at a bony little man with long arms and a big nose, shoving hurriedly through the crowd in clothes that looked like a bundle of rags. The man's eyes were sunken and his dirty face gaunt, as if he had not eaten or slept in days, but Rand could swear. . . . The ragged man saw him then, and froze in mid-step, heedless of people who all but stumbled over him. The last doubt in Rand's mind vanished.

"Master Fain!" he shouted. "We all thought you were—"

As quick as a blink the peddler darted away, but Rand dodged after him, calling apologies over his shoulder to the people he bumped. Through the crowd he just caught sight of Fain dashing into an alleyway, and he turned after.

A few steps into the alleyway the peddler had stopped in his tracks. A tall fence made it into a dead end. As Rand skidded to a halt, Fain rounded on him, crouching warily and backing away. He flapped grimy hands at Rand to stay back. More than one rip showed in his coat, and his cloak was worn and tattered as if it had seen much harder use than it was meant for.

"Master Fain?" Rand said hesitantly. "What is the matter? It's me, Rand al'Thor, from Emond's Field. We all thought the Trollocs had taken you."

Fain gestured sharply and, still in a crouch, ran a few crabbed steps toward the open end of the alley. He did not try to pass Rand, or even come close to him. "Don't!" he rasped. His head shifted constantly as he tried to see everything in the street beyond Rand. "Don't mention"—his voice dropped to a hoarse whisper, and he turned his head away, watching Rand with quick, sidelong glances—"*them*. There be Whitecloaks in the town."

"They have no reason to bother us," Rand said. "Come back to the Stag and Lion with me. I'm staying there with friends. You know most of them. They'll be glad to see you. We all thought you were dead."

"Dead?" the peddler snapped indignantly. "Not Padan Fain. Padan Fain knows which way to jump and where to land." He straightened his rags as if they were feastday clothes. "Always have, and always will. I'll live a long time. Longer than—" Abruptly his face tightened and his hands clutched hold of his coat front. "They burned my wagon, and all my goods. Had no cause to be doing that, did they? I couldn't get to my horses. *My* horses, but that fat old inn-keeper had them locked up in his stable. I had to step quick not to get my throat slit, and what did it get me? All that I've got left is what I stand up in. Now, is that fair? Is it, now?"

"Your horses are safe in Master al'Vere's stable. You can get them anytime. If you come to the inn with me, I'm sure Moiraine will help you get back to the Two Rivers."

"Aaaaah! She's . . . she's the Aes Sedai, is she?" A guarded look came over Fain's face. "Maybe, though. . . ." He paused, licking his lips nervously. "How long will you be at this— What was it? What did you call it?—the Stag and Lion?"

"We leave tomorrow," Rand said. "But what does that have to do with—?"

"You just don't know," Fain whined, "standing there with a full belly and a good night's sleep in a soft bed. I've hardly slept a wink since that night. My boots are all worn out with running, and as for what I've had to eat. . . ." His face twisted. "I don't want to be within miles of an Aes Sedai," he spat the last words, "not miles and miles, but I may have to. I've no choice, have I? The thought of her eyes on me, of her even knowing where I am. . . ." He reached toward Rand as if he wanted to grab his coat, but his hands stopped short, fluttering, and he actually took a step back. "Promise me you won't tell her. She frightens me. There's no need to be telling her, no reason for an Aes Sedai to even be knowing I'm alive. You have to promise. You have to!"

"I promise," Rand said soothingly. "But there's no reason for you to be afraid of her. Come with me. The least you'll get is a hot meal."

"Maybe. Maybe." Fain rubbed his chin pensively. "To-morrow, you say? In that time. . . . You won't forget your promise? You won't be letting her . . . ?"

"I won't let her hurt you," Rand said, wondering how he could stop an Aes Sedai, whatever she wanted to do.

"She won't hurt me," Fain said. "No, she won't. I won't be letting her." Like a flash he hared past Rand into the crowd.

"Master Fain!" Rand called. "Wait!"

He dashed out of the alley just in time to catch sight of a

ragged coat disappearing around the next corner. Still calling, he ran after it, darted around the corner. He only had time to see a man's back before he crashed into it and they both went down in a heap in the mud.

"Can't you watch where you're going?" came a mutter from under him, and Rand scrambled up in surprise.

"Mat?"

Mat sat up with a baleful glare and began scraping mud off his cloak with his hands. "You must really be turning into a city man. Sleep all morning and run right over people." Climbing to his feet, he stared at his muddy hands, then muttered and wiped them off on his cloak. "Listen, you'll never guess who I thought I just saw."

"Padan Fain," Rand said.

"Padan Fa— How did you know?"

"I was talking to him, but he ran off."

"So the Tro—" Mat stopped to look around warily, but the crowd was passing them by with never a glance. Rand was glad he had learned a little caution. "So they didn't get him. I wonder why he left Emond's Field, without a word like that? Probably started running then, too, and didn't stop until he got here. But why was he running just now?"

Rand shook his head and wished he had not. It felt as though it might fall off. "I don't know, except that he's afraid of M . . . Mistress Alys." All this watching what you said was not easy. "He doesn't want her to know he's here. He made me promise I wouldn't tell her."

"Well, his secret is safe with me," Mat said. "I wish she didn't know where I was, either."

"Mat?" People still streamed by without paying them any heed, but Rand lowered his voice anyway, and leaned closer. "Mat, did you have a nightmare last night? About a man who killed a rat?"

Mat stared at him without blinking. "You, too?" he said finally. "And Perrin, I suppose. I almost asked him this morning, but. . . . He must have. Blood and ashes! Now somebody's making us dream things. Rand, I wish *nobody* knew where I was."

"There were dead rats all over the inn this morning." He did not feel as afraid at saying it as he would have earlier. He did not feel much of anything. "Their backs were broken." His voice rang in his own ears. If he was getting sick, he might have to go to Moiraine. He was surprised that even the thought of the One Power being used on him did not bother him.

Mat took a deep breath, hitching his cloak, and looked around as if searching for somewhere to go. "What's happening to us, Rand? What?"

"I don't know. I'm going to ask Thom for advice. About whether to tell . . . anyone else."

"No! Not her. Maybe him, but not her."

The sharpness of it took Rand by surprise. "Then you believed him?" He did not need to say which "him" he meant; the grimace on Mat's face said he understood.

"No," Mat said slowly. "It's the chances, that's all. If we tell her, and he was lying, then maybe nothing happens. Maybe. But maybe just him being in our dreams is enough for. . . . I don't know." He stopped to swallow. "If we don't tell her, maybe we'll have some more dreams. Rats or no rats, dreams are better than. . . . Remember the ferry? I say we keep quiet."

"All right." Rand remembered the ferry—and Moiraine's threat, too—but somehow it seemed a long time ago. "All right."

"Perrin won't say anything, will he?" Mat went on, bouncing on his toes. "We have to get back to him. If he tells her, she'll figure it out about all of us. You can bet on it. Come on." He started off briskly through the crowd.

Rand stood there looking after him until Mat came back and grabbed him. At the touch on his arm he blinked, then followed his friend.

"What's the matter with you?" Mat asked. "You going to sleep again?"

"I think I have a cold," Rand said. His head was as tight as a drum, and almost as empty.

"You can get some chicken soup when we get back to the inn," Mat said. He kept up a constant chatter as they hunted through the packed streets. Rand made an effort to listen, and even to say something now and then, but it *was* an effort. He was not tired; he did not want to sleep. He just felt as if he were drifting. After a while he found himself telling Mat about Min.

"A dagger with a ruby, eh?" Mat said. "I like that. I don't know about the eye, though. Are you sure she wasn't making it up? It seems to me she would know what it all means if she really is a soothsayer."

"She didn't say she's a soothsayer," Rand said. "I believe she does see things. Remember, Moiraine was talking to her when we finished our baths. And she knows who Moiraine is."

Mat frowned at him. "I thought we weren't supposed to use that name."

"No," Rand muttered. He rubbed his head with both hands. It was so hard to concentrate on anything.

"I think maybe you really are sick," Mat said, still frowning. Suddenly he pulled Rand to a stop by his coat sleeve. "Look at them."

Three men in breastplates and conical steel caps, burnished till they shone like silver, were making their way down the street toward Rand and Mat. Even the mail on their arms gleamed. Their long cloaks, pristine white and embroidered on the left breast with a golden sunburst, just cleared the mud and puddles of the street. Their hands rested on their sword hilts, and they looked around them as if looking at things that had wriggled out from under a rotting log. Nobody looked back, though. Nobody even seemed to notice them. Just the same, the three did not have to push through the crowd; the bustle parted to either side of the white-cloaked men as if by happenstance, leaving them to walk in a clear space that moved with them.

"Do you suppose they're Children of the Light?" Mat asked in a loud voice. A passerby looked hard at Mat, then quickened his pace.

Rand nodded. Children of the Light. Whitecloaks. Men who hated Aes Sedai. Men who told people how to live, causing trouble for those who refused to obey. If burned farms and worse could be called as mild as trouble. *I should be afraid,* he thought. *Or curious.* Something, at any rate. Instead he stared at them passively.

"They don't look like so much to me," Mat said. "Full of themselves, though, aren't they?"

"They don't matter," Rand said. "The inn. We have to talk to Perrin."

"Like Eward Congar. He always has his nose in the air, too." Suddenly Mat grinned, a twinkle in his eye. "Remember when he fell off the Wagon Bridge and had to tramp home dripping wet? That took him down a peg for a month."

"What does that have to do with Perrin?"

"See that?" Mat pointed to a cart resting on its shafts in an alleyway just ahead of the Children. A single stake held a dozen stacked barrels in place on the flat bed. "Watch." Laughing, he darted into a cutler's shop to their left.

Rand stared after him, knowing he should do something. That look in Mat's eyes always meant one of his tricks. But oddly, he found himself looking forward to whatever Mat was going to do. Something told him that feeling was wrong, that it was dangerous, but he smiled in anticipation anyway.

In a minute Mat appeared above him, climbing half out of an attic window onto the tile roof of the shop. His sling was in his hands, already beginning to whirl. Rand's eyes went back to the cart. Almost immediately there was a sharp crack, and the stake holding the barrels broke just as the Whitecloaks came abreast of the alley. People jumped out of the way as the barrels rolled down the cart shafts with an empty rumble and jounced into the street, splashing mud and muddy water in every direction. The three Children jumped no less quickly than anyone else, their superior looks replaced by surprise. Some passersby fell down, making more splashes, but the three moved agilely, avoiding the barrels with ease. They could not avoid the flying mud that splattered their white cloaks, though.

A bearded man in a long apron hurried out of the alley, waving his arms and shouting angrily, but one look at the three trying vainly to shake the mud from their cloaks and he vanished back into the alley even faster than he had come out. Rand glanced up at the shop roof; Mat was gone. It had been an easy shot for any Two Rivers lad, but the effect was certainly all that could be hoped for. He could not help laughing; the humor seemed to be wrapped in wool, but it was still funny. When he turned back to the street, the three Whitecloaks were staring straight at him.

"You find something funny, yes?" The one who spoke stood a little in front of the others. He wore an arrogant, unblinking look, with a light in his eyes as if he knew something important, something no one else knew.

Rand's laughter cut off short. He and the Children were

alone with the mud and the barrels. The crowd that had been all around them had found urgent business up or down the street.

"Does fear of the Light hold your tongue?" Anger made the Whitecloak's narrow face seem even more pinched. He glanced dismissively at the sword hilt sticking out from Rand's cloak. "Perhaps you are responsible for this, yes?" Unlike the others he had a golden knot beneath the sunburst on his cloak.

Rand moved to cover the sword, but instead swept his cloak back over his shoulder. In the back of his head was a frantic wonder at what he was doing, but it was a distant thought. "Accidents happen," he said. "Even to the Children of the Light."

The narrow-faced man raised an eyebrow. "You are that dangerous, youngling?" He was not much older than Rand.

"Heron-mark, Lord Bornhald," one of the others said warningly.

The narrow-faced man glanced at Rand's sword hilt again—the bronze heron was plain—and his eyes widened momentarily. Then his gaze rose to Rand's face, and he sniffed dismissively. "He is too young. You are not from this place, yes?" he said coldly to Rand. "You come from where?"

"I just arrived in Baerlon." A tingling thrill ran along Rand's arms and legs. He felt flushed, almost warm. "You wouldn't know of a good inn, would you?"

"You avoid my questions," Bornhald snapped. "What evil is in you that you do not answer me?" His companions moved up to either side of him, faces hard and expressionless. Despite the mudstains on their cloaks, there was nothing funny about them now.

The tingling filled Rand; the heat had grown to a fever. He wanted to laugh, it felt so good. A small voice in his head shouted that something was wrong, but all he could think of was how full of energy he felt, nearly bursting with it. Smiling, he rocked on his heels and waited for what was going to happen. Vaguely, distantly, he wondered what it would be.

The leader's face darkened. One of the others drew his sword enough for an inch of steel to show and spoke in a voice quivering with anger. "When the Children of the Light ask questions, you gray-eyed bumpkin, we expect answers, or—" He cut off as the narrow-faced man threw an arm across his chest. Bornhald jerked his head up the street.

The Town Watch had arrived, a dozen men in round steel caps and studded leather jerkins, carrying quarterstaffs as if they knew how to use them. They stood watching, silently, from ten paces off.

"This town has lost the Light," growled the man who had half drawn his sword. He raised his voice to shout at the Watch. "Baerlon stands in the Shadow of the Dark One!" At a gesture from Bornhald he slammed his blade back into its scabbard.

Bornhald turned his attention back to Rand. The light of knowing burned in his eyes. "Darkfriends do not escape us, youngling, even in a town that stands in the Shadow. We will meet again. You may be sure of it!"

He spun on his heel and strode away, his two companions close behind, as if Rand had ceased to exist. For the moment, at least. When they reached the crowded part of the street, the same seemingly accidental pocket as before opened around them. The Watchmen hesitated, eyeing Rand, then shouldered their quarterstaffs and followed the white-cloaked three. They had to push their way into the crowd, shouting, "Make way for the Watch!" Few did make way, except grudgingly.

Rand still rocked on his heels, waiting. The tingle was so strong that he almost quivered; he felt as if he were burning up.

Mat came out of the shop, staring at him. "You aren't sick," he said finally. "You are crazy!"

Rand drew a deep breath, and abruptly it was all gone like a pricked bubble. He staggered as it vanished, the realization of what he had just done flooding in on him. Licking his lips, he met Mat's stare. "I think we had better go back to the inn, now," he said unsteadily.

"Yes," Mat said. "Yes. I think we better had."

The street had begun to fill up again, and more than one passerby stared at the two boys and murmured something to a companion. Rand was sure the story would spread. A crazy man had tried to start a fight with three Children of the Light. That was something to talk about. *Maybe the dreams are driving me crazy.*

The two lost their way several times in the haphazard

streets, but after a while they fell in with Thom Merrilin, making a grand procession all by himself through the throng. The gleeman said he was out to stretch his legs and for a bit of fresh air, but whenever anyone looked twice at his colorful cloak he would announce in a resounding voice, "I am at the Stag and Lion, tonight only."

It was Mat who began disjointedly telling Thom about the dream and their worry over whether or not to tell Moiraine, but Rand joined in, for there were differences in exactly how they remembered it. *Or maybe each dream was a little different,* he thought. The major part of the dreams was the same, though.

They had not gone far in the telling before Thom started paying full attention. When Rand mentioned Ba'alzamon, the gleeman grabbed them each by a shoulder with a command to hold their tongues, raised on tiptoe to look over the heads of the crowd, then hustled them out of the press to a dead-end alley that was empty except for a few crates and a slat-ribbed, yellow dog huddled out of the cold.

Thom stared out at the crowd, looking for anyone stopping to listen, before turning his attention to Rand and Mat. His blue eyes bored into theirs, between flickering away to watch the mouth of the alley. "Don't ever say that name where strangers can hear." His voice was low, but urgent. "Not even where a stranger *might* hear. It is a very dangerous name, even where Children of the Light are not wandering the streets."

Mat snorted. "I could tell you about Children of the Light," he said with a wry look at Rand.

Thom ignored him. "If only one of you had had this dream. . . ." He tugged at his mustache furiously. "Tell me everything you can remember about it. Every detail." He kept up his wary watch while he listened.

". . . he named the men he said had been used," Rand said finally. He thought he had told everything else. "Guaire Amalasan. Raolin Darksbane."

"Davian," Mat added before he could go on. "And Yurian Stonebow."

"And Logain," Rand finished.

"Dangerous names," Thom muttered. His eyes seemed to drill at them even more intently than before. "Nearly as dangerous as that other, one way and another. All dead, now, except for Logain. Some long dead. Raolin Darksbane nearly two thousand years. But dangerous just the same. Best you don't say them aloud even when you're alone. Most people wouldn't recognize a one of them, but if the wrong person overhears. . . ."

"But who were they?" Rand said.

"Men," Thom murmured. "Men who shook the pillars of heaven and rocked the world on its foundations." He shook his head. "It doesn't matter. Forget about them. They are dust now."

"Did the . . . were they used, like he said?" Mat asked. "And killed?"

"You might say the White Tower killed them. You might say that." Thom's mouth tightened momentarily, then he shook his head again. "But used . . . ? No, I cannot see that. The Light knows the Amyrlin Seat has enough plots going, but I can't see that."

Mat shivered. "He said so many things. Crazy things. All that about Lews Therin Kinslayer, and Artur Hawkwing. And the Eye of the World. What in the Light is that supposed to be?"

"A legend," the gleeman said slowly. "Maybe. As big a legend as the Horn of Valere, at least in the Borderlands. Up there, young men go hunting the Eye of the World the way young men from Illian hunt the Horn. Maybe a legend."

"What do we do, Thom?" Rand said. "Do we tell her? I don't want any more dreams like that. Maybe she could do something."

"Maybe we wouldn't like what she did," Mat growled.

Thom studied them, considering and stroking his mustache with a knuckle. "I say hold your peace," he said finally. "Don't tell anyone, for the time, at least. You can always change your mind, if you have to, but once you tell, it's done, and you're tied up worse than ever with . . . with her." Suddenly he straightened, his stoop almost disappearing. "The other lad! You say he had the same dream? Does he have sense enough to keep his mouth shut?"

"I think so," Rand said at the same time that Mat said, "We were going back to the inn to warn him."

"The Light send we're not too late!" Cloak flapping around

his ankles, patches fluttering in the wind, Thom strode out of the alley, looking back over his shoulder without stopping. "Well? Are your feet pegged to the ground?"

Rand and Mat hurried after him, but he did not wait for them to catch up. This time he did not pause for people who looked at his cloak, or those who hailed him as a gleeman, either. He clove through the crowded streets as if they were empty, Rand and Mat half running to follow in his wake. In much less time than Rand expected they were hurrying up to the Stag and Lion.

As they started in, Perrin came speeding out, trying to throw his cloak around his shoulders as he ran. He nearly fell in his effort not to carom into them. "I was coming looking for you two," he panted when he had caught his balance.

Rand grabbed him by the arm. "Did you tell anyone about the dream?"

"Say that you didn't," Mat demanded.

"It's very important," Thom said.

Perrin looked at them in confusion. "No, I haven't. I didn't even get out of bed until less than an hour ago." His shoulders slumped. "I've given myself a headache trying not to think about it, much less talk about it. Why did you tell him?" He nodded at the gleeman.

"We had to talk to somebody or go crazy," Rand said.

"I will explain later," Thom added with a significant look at the people passing in and out of the Stag and Lion.

"All right," Perrin replied slowly, still looking confused. Suddenly he slapped his head. "You almost made me forget why I was looking for you, not that I don't wish I could. Nynaeve is inside."

"Blood and ashes!" Mat yelped. "How did she get here? Moiraine. . . . The ferry. . . ."

Perrin snorted. "You think a little thing like a sunken ferry could stop her? She rooted Hightower out—I don't know how he got back over the river, but she said he was hiding in his bedroom and didn't want to go near the river—anyway, she bullied him into finding a boat big enough for her and her horse and rowing her across. Himself. She only gave him time to find one of his haulers to work another set of oars."

"Light!" Mat breathed.

"What is she doing here?" Rand wanted to know. Mat and Perrin both gave him a scornful look.

"She came after us," Perrin said. "She's with . . . with Mistress Alys right now, and it's cold enough in there to snow."

"Couldn't we just go somewhere else for a while?" Mat asked. "My da says, only a fool puts his hand in a hornet nest until he absolutely has to."

Rand cut in. "She can't make us go back. Winternight should have been enough to make her see that. If she doesn't, we will have to make her."

Mat's eyebrows lifted higher with every word, and when Rand finished he let out a low whistle. "You ever try to make Nynaeve see something she doesn't want to see? I have. I say we stay away till night, and sneak in then."

"From my observation of the young woman," Thom said, "I don't think she will stop until she has had her say. If she is not allowed to have it soon, she might keep on until she attracts attention none of us wants."

That brought them all up short. They exchanged glances, drew deep breaths, and marched inside as if to face Trollocs.

CHAPTER
16

The Wisdom

Perrin led the way into the depths of the inn. Rand was so intent on what he intended to say to Nynaeve that he did not see Min until she seized his arm and pulled him to one side. The others kept on a few steps down the hall before realizing he had stopped, then they halted, too, half impatient to go on, half reluctant to do so.

"We don't have time for that, boy," Thom said gruffly.

Min gave the white-haired gleeman a sharp look. "Go juggle something," she snapped, drawing Rand further away from the others.

"I really don't have time," Rand told her. "Certainly not for any more fool talk about escaping and the like." He tried to get his arm loose, but every time he pulled free, she grabbed it again.

"And I don't have time for your foolishness, either. Will you be still!" She gave the others a quick look, then moved closer, lowering her voice. "A woman arrived a little while ago—shorter than I, young, with dark eyes and dark hair in a braid down to her waist. She's part of it, right along with the rest of you."

For a minute Rand just stared at her. *Nynaeve? How can she be involved? Light, how can I be involved?* "That's . . . impossible."

"You know her?" Min whispered.

"Yes, and she can't be mixed in . . . in whatever it is you. . . ."

"The sparks, Rand. She met Mistress Alys coming in, and there were sparks, with just the two of them. Yesterday I couldn't see sparks without at least three or four of you together, but today it's all sharper, and more furious." She looked at Rand's friends, waiting impatiently, and shivered before turning back to him. "It's almost a wonder the inn doesn't catch fire. You're all in more danger today than yesterday. Since she came."

Rand glanced at his friends. Thom, his brows drawn down in a bushy V, was leaning forward on the point of taking some action to hurry him along. "She won't do anything to hurt us," he told Min. "I have to go, now." He succeeded in getting his arm back, this time.

Ignoring her squawk, he joined the others, and they started off again down the corridor. Rand looked back once. Min shook her fist at him and stamped her foot.

"What did she have to say?" Mat asked.

"Nynaeve is part of it," Rand said without thinking, then shot Mat a hard look that caught him with his mouth open. Then understanding slowly spread across Mat's face.

"Part of what?" Thom said softly. "Does that girl know something?"

While Rand was still trying to gather in his head what to say, Mat spoke up. "Of course she's part of it," he said grumpily. "Part of the same bad luck we've been having since Winternight. Maybe having the Wisdom show up is no great affair to you, but I'd as soon have the Whitecloaks here, myself."

"She saw Nynaeve arrive," Rand said. "Saw her talking to Mistress Alys, and thought she might have something to do with us." Thom gave him a sidelong look and ruffled his mustaches with a snort, but the others seemed to accept Rand's explanation. He did not like keeping secrets from his friends, but Min's secret could be as dangerous for her as any of theirs was for them.

Perrin stopped suddenly in front of a door, and despite his size he seemed oddly hesitant. He drew a deep breath, looked at his companions, took another breath, then slowly opened the door and went in. One by one the rest of them followed. Rand was the last, and he closed the door behind him with the utmost reluctance.

It was the room where they had eaten the night before. A blaze crackled on the hearth, and a polished silver tray sat in the middle of the table holding a gleaming silver pitcher and cups. Moiraine and Nynaeve sat at opposite ends of the table, neither taking her eyes from the other. All the other chairs were empty. Moiraine's hands rested on the table, as still as her face. Nynaeve's braid was thrown over her shoulder, the end gripped in one fist; she kept giving it little tugs the way she did when she was being even more stubborn than usual with the Village Council. *Perrin was right.* Despite the fire it seemed freezing cold, and all coming from the two women at the table.

Lan was leaning against the mantel, staring into the flames and rubbing his hands for warmth. Egwene, her back flat against the wall, had her cloak on with the hood pulled up. Thom, Mat, and Perrin stopped uncertainly in front of the door.

Shrugging uncomfortably, Rand walked to the table. *Sometimes you have to grab the wolf by the ears*, he reminded himself. But he remembered another old saying, too. *When you have a wolf by the ears, it's as hard to let go as to hold on.* He felt Moiraine's eyes on him, and Nynaeve's, and his face became hot, but he sat down anyway, halfway between the two.

For a minute the room was as still as a carving, then Egwene and Perrin, and finally Mat, made their reluctant way to the table and took seats—toward the middle, with Rand. Egwene tugged her hood further forward, enough to half hide her face, and they all avoided looking at anyone.

"Well," Thom snorted, from his place beside the door. "At least that much is done."

"Since everyone is here," Lan said, leaving the fireplace and filling one of the silver cups with wine, "perhaps you will finally take this." He proffered the cup to Nynaeve; she looked at it suspiciously. "There is no need to be afraid," he said patiently. "You saw the innkeeper bring the wine, and neither of us has had a chance to put anything in it. It is quite safe."

The Wisdom's mouth tightened angrily at the word *afraid*, but she took the cup with a murmured, "Thank you."

"I am interested," he said, "in how you found us."

"So am I." Moiraine leaned forward intently. "Perhaps you are willing to speak now that Egwene and the boys have been brought to you?"

Nynaeve sipped the wine before answering the Aes Sedai. "There was nowhere for you to go except Baerlon. To be safe, though, I followed your trail. You certainly cut back and forth enough. But then, I suppose you would not care to risk meeting decent people."

"You . . . followed our trail?" Lan said, truly surprised for the first time that Rand could remember. "I must be getting careless."

"You left very little trace, but I can track as well as any man in the Two Rivers, except perhaps Tam al'Thor." She hesitated, then added, "Until my father died, he took me hunting with him, and taught me what he would have taught the sons he never had." She looked at Lan challengingly, but he only nodded with approval.

"If you can follow a trail I have tried to hide, he taught you well. Few can do that, even in the Borderlands."

Abruptly Nynaeve buried her face in her cup. Rand's eyes widened. She was blushing. Nynaeve never showed herself even the least bit disconcerted. Angry, yes; outraged, often; but never out of countenance. But she was certainly red-cheeked now, and trying to hide in the wine.

"Perhaps now," Moiraine said quietly, "you will answer a few of my questions. I have answered yours freely enough."

"With a great sackful of gleeman's tales," Nynaeve retorted. "The only *facts* I can see are that four young people have been carried off, for the Light alone knows what reason, by an Aes Sedai."

"You have been told that isn't known here," Lan said sharply. "You must learn to guard your tongue."

"Why should I?" Nynaeve demanded. "Why should I help hide you, or what you are? I've come to take Egwene and the boys back to Emond's Field, not help you spirit them away."

Thom broke in, in a scornful voice. "If you want them to see their village again—or you, either—you had better be more careful. There are those in Baerlon who would kill her"—he jerked his head toward Moiraine—"for what she is. Him, too." He indicated Lan, then abruptly moved forward to put his fists on the table. He loomed over Nynaeve, and his long mustaches and thick eyebrows suddenly seemed threatening.

Her eyes widened, and she started to lean back, away from him; then her back stiffened defiantly. Thom did not appear to notice; he went right on in an ominously soft voice. "They'd swarm over this inn like murderous ants on a rumor, a whisper. Their hate is that strong, their desire to kill or take any like these two. And the girl? The boys? You? You are all associated with them, enough for the Whitecloaks, anyway. You wouldn't like the way they ask questions, especially when the White Tower is involved. Whitecloak Questioners assume you're guilty before they start, and they have only one sentence for that kind of guilt. They don't care about finding the truth; they think they know that already. All they go after with their hot irons and pincers is a confession. Best you remember some secrets are too dangerous for saying aloud, even when you think you know who hears." He straightened with a muttered, "I seem to tell that to people often of late."

"Well put, gleeman," Lan said. The Warder had that weighing look in his eyes again. "I'm surprised to find you so concerned."

Thom shrugged. "It's known I arrived with you, too. I don't care for the thought of a Questioner with a hot iron telling me to repent my sins and walk in the Light."

"That," Nynaeve put in sharply, "is just one more reason for them to come home with me in the morning. Or this afternoon, for that matter. The sooner we're away from you and on our way back to Emond's Field, the better."

"We can't," Rand said, and was glad that his friends all spoke up at the same time. That way Nynaeve's glare had to be spread around; she spared no one as it was. But he had spoken first, and they all fell silent, looking at him. Even Moiraine sat back in her chair, watching him over steepled fingers. It was an effort for him to meet the Wisdom's eyes. "If we go back to Emond's Field, the Trollocs will come back, too. They're . . . hunting us. I don't know why, but they are. Maybe we can find out why in Tar Valon. Maybe we can find out how to stop it. It's the only way."

Nynaeve threw up her hands. "You sound just like Tam. He had himself carried to the village meeting and tried to convince everybody. He'd already tried with the Village Council. The Light knows how your . . . Mistress Alys"— she invested the name with a wagonload of scorn—"managed to make him believe; he has a mite of sense, usually, more than most men. In any case, the Council is a pack of fools most of the time, but not foolish enough for that, and neither was anyone else. They agreed you had to be found.

Then Tam wanted to be the one to come after you, and him not able to stand by himself. Foolishness must run in your family."

Mat cleared his throat, then mumbled, "What about my da? What did he say?"

"He's afraid you'll try your tricks with outlanders and get your head thumped. He seemed more afraid of that than of . . . Mistress Alys, here. But then, he was never much brighter than you."

Mat seemed unsure how to take what she had said, or how to reply, or even whether to reply.

"I expect," Perrin began hesitantly. "I mean, I suppose Master Luhhan was not too pleased about my leaving, either."

"Did you expect him to be?" Nynaeve shook her head disgustedly and looked at Egwene. "Maybe I should not be surprised at this harebrained idiocy from you three, but I thought others had more judgment."

Egwene sat back so she was shielded by Perrin. "I left a note," she said faintly. She tugged at the hood of her cloak as if she was afraid her unbound hair showed. "I explained everything." Nynaeve's face darkened.

Rand sighed. The Wisdom was on the point of one of her tongue-lashings, and it looked as if it might be a first-rate one. If she took a position in the heat of anger—if she said she intended to see them back in Emond's Field no matter what anybody said, for instance—she would be nearly impossible to budge. He opened his mouth.

"A note!" Nynaeve began, just as Moiraine said, "You and I must still talk, Wisdom."

If Rand could have stopped himself, he would have, but the words poured out as if it were a floodgate he had opened instead of his mouth. "All this is very well, but it doesn't change anything. We can't go back. We have to go on." He spoke more slowly toward the end, and his voice sank, so he finished in a whisper, with the Wisdom and the Aes Sedai both looking at him. It was the sort of look he received if he came on women talking Women's Circle business, the sort that said he had stepped in where he did not belong. He sat back, wishing he was somewhere else.

"Wisdom," Moiraine said, "you must believe that they are safer with me than they would be back in the Two Rivers."

"Safer!" Nynaeve tossed her head dismissively. "You are

the one who brought them here, where the Whitecloaks are. The same Whitecloaks who, if the gleeman tells the truth, may harm them because of *you*. Tell me how they are safer, Aes Sedai."

"There are many dangers from which I cannot protect them," Moiraine agreed, "any more than you can protect them from being struck by lightning if they go home. But it is not lightning of which they must be afraid, nor even Whitecloaks. It is the Dark One, and minions of the Dark One. From those things I *can* protect. Touching the True Source, touching *saidar*, gives me that protection, as it does to every Aes Sedai." Nynaeve's mouth tightened skeptically. Moiraine's grew tighter, too, with anger, but she went on, her voice hard on the edge of patience. "Even those poor men who find themselves wielding the Power for a short time gain that much, though sometimes touching *saidin* protects, and sometimes the taint makes them more vulnerable. But I, or any Aes Sedai, can extend my protection to those close by me. No Fade can harm them as long as they are as close to me as they are right now. No Trolloc can come within a quarter of a mile without Lan knowing it, feeling the evil of it. Can you offer them half as much if they return to Emond's Field with you?"

"You stand up straw men," Nynaeve said. "We have a saying in the Two Rivers. 'Whether the bear beats the wolf or the wolf beats the bear, the rabbit always loses.' Take your contest somewhere else and leave Emond's Field folk out of it."

"Egwene," Moiraine said after a moment, "take the others and leave the Wisdom alone with me for a while." Her face was impassive; Nynaeve squared herself at the table as if getting ready for an all-in wrestling match.

Egwene bounced to her feet, her desire to be dignified obviously warring with her desire to avoid a confrontation with the Wisdom over her unbraided hair. She had no difficulty gathering up everyone by eye, though. Mat and Perrin scraped back their chairs hurriedly, making polite murmurs while trying not to actually run on their way out. Even Lan started for the door at a signal from Moiraine, drawing Thom with him.

Rand followed, and the Warder shut the door behind them, then took up guard across the hallway. Under Lan's

eyes the others moved on down the hall a short distance;
they were not to be allowed even the slightest chance of
eavesdropping. When they had gone far enough to suit him,
Lan leaned back against the wall. Even without his color-
shifting cloak, he was so still that it would be easy not to
notice him until you were right on him.

The gleeman muttered something about better things to
do with his time and left with a stern, "Remember what I
said," over his shoulder to the boys. No one else seemed
inclined to leave.

"What did he mean?" Egwene asked absently, her eyes
on the door that hid Moiraine and Nynaeve. She kept fiddling with her hair as if torn between continuing to hide the
fact that it was no longer braided and pushing back the hood
of her cloak.

"He gave us some advice," Mat said.

Perrin gave him a sharp look. "He said not to open our
mouths until we were sure what we were going to say."

"That sounds like good advice," Egwene said, but clearly
she was not really interested.

Rand was engrossed in his own thoughts. How could
Nynaeve possibly be part of it? How could any of them
be involved with Trollocs, and Fades, and Ba'alzamon appearing in their dreams? It was crazy. He wondered if Min
had told Moiraine about Nynaeve. *What are they saying in
there??*

He had no idea how long he had been standing there when
the door finally opened. Nynaeve stepped out, and gave a
start when she saw Lan. The Warder murmured something
that made her toss her head angrily, then he slipped past her
through the door.

She turned toward Rand, and for the first time he realized
the others had all quietly disappeared. He did not want to
face the Wisdom alone, but he could not get away now that
he had met Nynaeve's eye. *A particularly searching eye*, he
thought, puzzled. *What did they say?* He drew himself up
as she came closer.

She indicated Tam's sword. "That seems to fit you, now,
though I would like it better if it did not. You've grown,
Rand."

"In a week?" He laughed, but it sounded forced, and she

shook her head as if he did not understand. "Did she convince you?" he asked. "It really is the only way." He paused, thinking of Min's sparks. "Are you coming with us?"

Nynaeve's eyes opened wide. "Coming with you! Why would I do that? Mavra Mallen came up from Deven Ride to see to things till I return, but she'll be wanting to get back as soon as she can. I still hope to make you see sense and come home with me."

"We can't." He thought he saw something move at the still-open door, but they were alone in the hallway.

"You told me that, and she did, too." Nynaeve frowned. "If *she* wasn't mixed up in it. . . . Aes Sedai are not to be trusted, Rand."

"You sound as if you really do believe us," he said slowly. "What happened at the village meeting?"

Nynaeve looked back at the doorway before answering; there was no movement there now. "It was a shambles, but there is no need for her to know we can't handle our affairs any better than that. And I believe only one thing: you are all in danger as long as you are with her."

"Something happened," he insisted. "Why do you want us to go back if you think there's even a chance we are right? And why you, at all? As soon send the Mayor himself as the Wisdom."

"You *have* grown." She smiled, and for a moment her amusement had him shifting his feet. "I can think of a time when you would not have questioned where I chose to go or what I chose to do, wherever or whatever it was. A time just a week ago."

He cleared his throat and pressed on stubbornly. "It doesn't make sense. Why are you really here?"

She half glanced at the still-empty doorway, then took his arm. "Let's walk while we talk." He let himself be led away, and when they were far enough from the door not to be overheard, she began again. "As I said, the meeting was a shambles. Everybody agreed someone had to be sent after you, but the village split into two groups. One wanted you rescued, though there was considerable argument over how that was to be done considering that you were with a . . . the likes of *her*."

He was glad she was remembering to watch what she said. "The others believed Tam?" he said.

"Not exactly, but they thought you shouldn't be among

strangers, either, especially not with someone like *her*. Either way, though, almost every man wanted to be one of the party. Tam, and Bran al'Vere, with the scales of office around his neck, and Haral Luhhan, till Alsbet made him sit down. Even Cenn Buie. The Light save me from men who think with the hair on their chests. Though I don't know as there are any other kind." She gave a hearty sniff, and looked up at him, an accusing glance. "At any rate, I could see it would be another day, perhaps more, before they came to any decision, and somehow . . . somehow I was sure we did not dare wait that long. So I called the Women's Circle together and told them what had to be done. I cannot say they liked it, but they saw the right of it. And that is why I am here; because the men around Emond's Field are stubborn wool-heads. They're probably still arguing about who to send, though I left word I would take care of it."

Nynaeve's story explained her presence, but it did nothing to reassure him. She was still determined to bring them back with her.

"What did she say to you in there?" he asked. Moiraine would surely have covered every argument, but if there was one she had missed, he would make it.

"More of the same," Nynaeve replied. "And she wanted to know about you boys. To see if she could reason out why you . . . have attracted the kind of attention you have . . . she *said*." She paused, watching him out of the corner of her eye. "She tried to disguise it, but most of all she wanted to know if any of you was born outside the Two Rivers."

His face was suddenly as taut as a drumhead. He managed a hoarse chuckle. "She does think of some odd things. I hope you assured her we're all Emond's Field born."

"Of course," she replied. There had only been a heartbeat's pause before she spoke, so brief he would have missed it if he had not been watching for it.

He tried to think of something to say, but his tongue felt like a piece of leather. *She knows.* She was the Wisdom, after all, and the Wisdom was supposed to know everything about everyone. *If she knows, it was no fever-dream. Oh, Light help me, father!*

"Are you all right?" Nynaeve asked.

"He said . . . said I . . . wasn't his son. When he was delirious . . . with the fever. He said he found me. I thought it was just. . . ." His throat began to burn, and he had to stop.

"Oh, Rand." She stopped and took his face in both hands. She had to reach up to do it. "People say strange things in a fever. Twisted things. Things that are not true, or real. Listen to me. Tam al'Thor ran away seeking adventure when he was a boy no older than you. I can just remember when he came back to Emond's Field, a grown man with a red-haired, outlander wife and a babe in swaddling clothes. I remember Kari al'Thor cradling that child in her arms with as much love given and delight taken as I have ever seen from any woman with a babe. Her child, Rand. You. Now you straighten up and stop this foolishness."

"Of course," he said. *I was born outside the Two Rivers.* "Of course." Maybe Tam had been having a fever-dream, and maybe he had found a baby after a battle. "Why didn't you tell her?"

"It is none of any outlander's business."

"Were any of the others born outside?" As soon as the question was out, he shook his head. "No, don't answer. It's none of my business, either." But it would be nice to know if Moiraine had some special interest in him, over and above what she had in the whole lot of them. *Would it?*

"No, it isn't your business," Nynaeve agreed. "It might not mean anything. She could just be searching blindly for a reason, any reason, why those things are after you. After *all* of you."

Rand managed a grin. "Then you do believe they're chasing us."

Nynaeve shook her head wryly. "You've certainly learned how to twist words since you met her."

"What are you going to do?" he asked.

She studied him; he met her eyes steadily. "Today, I am going to have a bath. For the rest, we will have to see, won't we?"

CHAPTER
17

Watchers and Hunters

After the Wisdom left him, Rand made his way to the common room. He needed to hear people laughing, to forget what Nynaeve had said and the trouble she might cause alike.

The room was crowded indeed, but no one was laughing, though every chair and bench was filled and people lined the walls. Thom was performing again, standing on a table against the far wall, his gestures grand enough to fill the big room. It was *The Great Hunt of the Horn* again, but no one complained, of course. There were so many tales to be told about each of the Hunters, and so many Hunters to tell of, that no two tellings were ever the same. The whole of it in one telling would have taken a week or more. The only sound competing with the gleeman's voice and harp was the crackling of the fires in the fireplaces.

". . . To the eight corners of the world, the Hunters ride, to the eight pillars of heaven, where the winds of time blow and fate seizes the mighty and the small alike by the forelock. Now, the greatest of the Hunters is Rogosh of Talmour, Rogosh Eagle-eye, famed at the court of the High King, feared on the slopes of Shayol Ghul. . . ." The Hunters were always mighty heroes, all of them.

Rand spotted his two friends and squeezed onto a place Perrin made for him on the end of their bench. Kitchen smells drifting into the room reminded him that he was hungry, but even the people who had food in front of them gave it little attention. The maids who should have been serving stood entranced, clutching their aprons and looking at the gleeman, and nobody seemed to mind at all. Listening was better than eating, no matter how good the food.

". . . since the day of her birth has the Dark One marked Blaes as his own, but not of this mind is she—no Darkfriend, Blaes of Matuchin! Strong as the ash she stands, lithe as the willow branch, beautiful as the rose. Goldenhaired Blaes. Ready to die before she yields. But hark! Echoing from the towers of the city, trumpets blare, brazen and bold. Her heralds proclaim the arrival of a hero at her court. Drums thunder and cymbals sing! Rogosh Eagle-eye comes to do homage . . ."

"The Bargain of Rogosh Eagle-eye" wound its way to an end, but Thom paused only to wet his throat from a mug of ale before launching into "Lian's Stand." In turn that was followed by "The Fall of Aleth-Loriel," and "Gaidal Cain's Sword," and "The Last Ride of Buad of Albhain." The pauses grew longer as the evening wore on, and when Thom exchanged the harp for his flute, everyone knew it was the end of storytelling for the night. Two men joined Thom, with a drum and a hammered dulcimer, but sitting beside the table while he remained atop it.

The three young men from Emond's Field began clapping their hands with the first note of "The Wind That Shakes the Willow," and they were not the only ones. It was a favorite in the Two Rivers, and in Baerlon, too, it seemed. Here and there voices even took up the words, not so off-key as for anyone to hush them.

> My love is gone, carried away
> by the wind that shakes the willow,
> and all the land is beaten hard
> by the wind that shakes the willow.
> But I will hold her close to me
> in heart and dearest memory,
> and with her strength to steel my soul,
> her love to warm my heart-strings,
> I will stand where we once sang,
> though cold wind shakes the willow.

The second song was not so sad. In fact, "Only One Bucket of Water" seemed even more merry than usual by comparison, which might have been the gleeman's intent.

People rushed to clear tables from the floor to make room for dancing, and began kicking up their heels until the walls shook from the stomping and whirling. The first dance ended with laughing dancers leaving the floor holding their sides, and new people taking their places.

Thom played the opening notes of "Wild Geese on the Wing," then paused for people to take their places for the reel.

"I think I'll try a few steps," Rand said, getting to his feet. Perrin popped up right behind him. Mat was the last to move, and so found himself staying behind to guard the cloaks, along with Rand's sword and Perrin's axe.

"Remember I want a turn, too," Mat called after them.

The dancers formed two long lines facing each other, men in one, women in the other. First the drum and then the dulcimer took up the beat, and all the dancers began bending their knees in time. The girl across from Rand, her dark hair in braids that made him think of home, gave him a shy smile, and then a wink that was not shy at all. Thom's flute leaped into the tune, and Rand moved forward to meet the dark-haired girl; she threw back her head and laughed as he spun her around and passed her on to the next man in line.

Everyone in the room was laughing, he thought as he danced around his next partner, one of the serving maids with her apron flapping wildly. The only unsmiling face he saw was on a man huddled by one of the fireplaces, and that fellow had a scar that crossed his whole face from one temple to the opposite jaw, giving his nose a slant and drawing the corner of his mouth down. The man met his gaze and grimaced, and Rand looked away in embarrassment. Maybe with that scar the fellow could not smile.

He caught his next partner as she spun, and whirled her in a circle before passing her on. Three more women danced with him as the music gained speed, then he was back with the first dark-haired girl for a fast promenade that changed the lines about completely. She was still laughing, and she gave him another wink.

The scar-faced man was scowling at him. His step faltered and his cheeks grew hot. He had not meant to embarrass the fellow; he really did not think he had stared. He turned to meet his next partner and forgot all about the man. The next woman to dance into his arms was Nynaeve.

He stumbled through the steps, almost tripping over his own feet, nearly stepping on hers. She danced gracefully enough to make up for his clumsiness, smiling the while.

"I thought you were a better dancer," she laughed as they changed partners.

He had only a moment to gather himself before they changed again, and he found himself dancing with Moiraine. If he had thought he was stumble-footed with the Wisdom, it was nothing to how he felt with the Aes Sedai. She glided across the floor smoothly, her gown swirling about her; he almost fell twice. She gave him a sympathetic smile, which made it worse rather than helping. It was a relief to go to his next partner in the pattern, even if it was Egwene.

He regained some of his poise. After all, he had danced with her for years. Her hair still hung unbraided, but she had gathered it back with a red ribbon. *Probably couldn't decide whether to please Moiraine or Nynaeve,* he thought sourly. Her lips were parted, and she looked as if she wanted to say something, but she never spoke, and he was not about to speak first. Not after the way she had cut off his earlier attempt in the private dining room. They stared at one another soberly and danced apart without a word.

He was glad enough to return to the bench when the reel was done. The music for another dance, a jig, began while he was sitting down. Mat hurried to join in, and Perrin slid onto the bench as he was leaving.

"Did you see her?" Perrin began before he was even seated. "Did you?"

"Which one?" Rand asked. "The Wisdom, or Mistress Alys? I danced with both of them."

"The Ae . . . Mistress Alys, too?" Perrin exclaimed. "I danced with Nynaeve. I didn't even know she danced. She never does at any of the dances back home."

"I wonder," Rand said thoughtfully, "what the Women's Circle would say about the Wisdom dancing? Maybe that's why."

Then the music and the clapping and the singing were too loud for any further talk. Rand and Perrin joined in the clapping as the dancers circled the floor. Several times he became aware of the scar-faced man staring at him. The man had a right to be touchy, with that scar, but Rand did not see anything he could do now that would not make matters worse. He concentrated on the music and avoided looking at the fellow.

The dancing and singing went on into the night. The maids finally did remember their duties; Rand was glad to wolf down some hot stew and bread. Everyone ate where they sat or stood. Rand joined in three more dances, and he managed his steps better when he found himself dancing with Nynaeve again, and with Moiraine, as well. This time they both complimented him on his dancing, which made him stammer. He danced with Egwene again, too; she stared at him, dark-eyed and always seeming on the point of speaking, but never saying a word. He was just as silent as she, but he was sure he did not scowl at her, no matter what Mat said when he returned to the bench.

Toward midnight Moiraine left. Egwene, after one harried look from the Aes Sedai to Nynaeve, hurried after her. The Wisdom watched them with an unreadable expression, then deliberately joined in another dance before she left, too, with a look as if she had gained a point on the Aes Sedai.

Soon Thom was putting his flute into its case and arguing good-naturedly with those who wanted him to stay longer. Lan came by to gather up Rand and the others.

"We have to make an early start," the Warder said, leaning close to be heard over the noise, "and we will need all the rest we can get."

"There's a fellow been staring at me," Mat said. "A man with a scar across his face. You don't think he could be a . . . one of the *friends* you warned us about?"

"Like this?" Rand said, drawing a finger across his nose to the corner of his mouth. "He stared at me, too." He looked around the room. People were drifting away, and most of those still left clustered around Thom. "He's not here, now."

"I saw the man," Lan said. "According to Master Fitch, he's a spy for the Whitecloaks. He's no worry to us." Maybe he was not, but Rand could see something was bothering the Warder.

Rand glanced at Mat, who had the stiff expression on his face that always meant he was hiding something. *A Whitecloak spy. Could Bornhald want to get back at us that much?* "We're leaving early?" he said. "Really early?" Maybe they could be gone before anything came of it.

"At first light," the Warder replied.

As they left the common room, Mat singing snatches of song under his breath, and Perrin stopping now and again to try out a new step he had learned, Thom joined them in high spirits. Lan's face was expressionless as they headed for the stairs.

"Where is Nynaeve sleeping?" Mat asked. "Master Fitch said we got the last rooms."

"She has a bed," Thom said dryly, "in with Mistress Alys and the girl."

Perrin whistled between his teeth, and Mat muttered, "Blood and ashes! I wouldn't be in Egwene's shoes for all the gold in Caemlyn!"

Not for the first time, Rand wished Mat could think seriously about something for more than two minutes. Their own shoes were not very comfortable right then. "I'm going to get some milk," he said. Maybe it would help him sleep. *Maybe I won't dream tonight.*

Lan looked at him sharply. "There's something wrong tonight. Don't wander far. And remember, we leave whether you are awake enough to sit your saddle or have to be tied on."

The Warder started up the stairs; the others followed him, their jollity subdued. Rand stood in the hall alone. After having so many people around, it was lonely indeed.

He hurried to the kitchen, where a scullery maid was still on duty. She poured a mug of milk from a big stone crock for him.

As he came out of the kitchen, drinking, a shape in dull black started toward him down the length of the hall, raising pale hands to toss back the dark cowl that had hidden the face beneath. The cloak hung motionless as the figure moved, and the face. . . . A man's face, but pasty white, like a slug under a rock, and eyeless. From oily black hair to puffy cheeks was as smooth as an eggshell. Rand choked, spraying milk.

"You are one of them, boy," the Fade said, a hoarse whisper like a file softly drawn across bone.

Dropping the mug, Rand backed away. He wanted to run, but it was all he could do to make his feet take one halting step at a time. He could not break free of that eyeless face; his gaze was held, and his stomach curdled. He tried to shout for help, to scream; his throat was like stone. Every ragged breath hurt.

The Fade glided closer, in no hurry. Its strides had a sinuous, deadly grace, like a viper, the resemblance emphasized by the overlapping black plates of armor down its chest. Thin, bloodless lips curved in a cruel smile, made more mocking by the smooth, pale skin where eyes should have been. The voice made Bornhald's seem warm and soft. "Where are the others? I know they are here. Speak, boy, and I will let you live."

Rand's back struck wood, a wall or a door—he could not make himself look around to see which. Now that his feet had stopped, he could not make them start again. He shivered, watching the Myrddraal slither nearer. His shaking grew harder with every slow stride.

"Speak, I say, or—"

From above came a quick clatter of boots, from the stairs up the hall, and the Myrddraal cut off, whirling. The cloak hung still. For an instant the Fade's head tilted, as if that eyeless gaze could pierce the wooden wall. A sword appeared in a dead-white hand, blade as black as the cloak. The light in the hall seemed to grow dimmer in the presence of that blade. The pounding of boots grew louder, and the Fade spun back to Rand, an almost boneless movement. The black blade rose; narrow lips peeled back in a rictus snarl.

Trembling, Rand knew he was going to die. Midnight steel flashed at his head . . . and stopped.

"You belong to the Great Lord of the Dark." The breathy grating of that voice sounded like fingernails scratched across a slate. "You are his."

Spinning in a black blur, the Fade darted down the hall away from Rand. The shadows at the end of the hall reached out and embraced it, and it was gone.

Lan leaped down the last stairs, landing with a crash, sword in hand.

Rand struggled to find his voice. "Fade," he gasped. "It was. . . ." Abruptly he remembered his sword. With the Myrddraal facing him he had never thought of it. He fumbled the heron-mark blade out now, not caring if it was too late. "It ran that way!"

Lan nodded absently; he seemed to be listening to something else. "Yes. It's going; fading. No time to pursue it, now. We're leaving, sheepherder."

More boots stumbled down the stairs; Mat and Perrin and Thom, hung about with blankets and saddlebags. Mat was still buckling his bedroll, with his bow awkward under his arm.

"Leaving?" Rand said. Sheathing his sword, he took his things from Thom. "Now? In the night?"

"You want to wait for the Halfman to come back, sheepherder?" the Warder said impatiently. "For half a dozen of them? It knows where we are, now."

"I will ride with you again," Thom told the Warder, "if you have no great objections. Too many people remember that I arrived with you. I fear that before tomorrow this will be a bad place to be known as your friend."

"You can ride with us, or ride to Shayol Ghul, gleeman." Lan's scabbard rattled from the force with which he rammed his sword home.

A stableman came darting past them from the rear door, and then Moiraine appeared with Master Fitch, and behind them Egwene, with her bundled shawl in her arms. And Nynaeve. Egwene looked frightened almost to tears, but the Wisdom's face was a mask of cool anger.

"You must take this seriously," Moiraine was telling the innkeeper. "You will certainly have trouble here by morning. Darkfriends, perhaps; perhaps worse. When it comes, quickly make it clear that we are gone. Offer no resistance. Just let whoever it is know that we left in the night, and they should bother you no further. It is us they are after."

"Never you worry about trouble," Master Fitch replied jovially. "Never a bit. If any come around my inn trying to make trouble for my guests . . . well, they'll get short shrift from the lads and I. Short shrift. And they'll hear not a word about where you've gone or when, or even if you were ever here. I've no use for that kind. Not a word will be spoken about you by any here. Not a word!"

"But—"

"Mistress Alys, I really must see to your horses if you're going to leave in good order." He pulled loose from her grip on his sleeve and trotted in the direction of the stables.

Moiraine sighed vexedly. "Stubborn, stubborn man. He will not listen."

"You think Trollocs might come here hunting for us?" Mat asked.

"Trollocs!" Moiraine snapped. "Of course not! There are other things to fear, not the least of which is how we were found." Ignoring Mat's bristle, she went right on. "The Fade cannot believe we will remain here, now that we know it has found us, but Master Fitch takes Darkfriends too lightly. He thinks of them as wretches hiding in the shadows, but Darkfriends can be found in the shops and streets of every city, and in the highest councils, too. The Myrddraal may send them to see if he can learn of our plans." She turned on her heel and left, Lan close behind her.

As they started for the stableyard, Rand fell in beside Nynaeve. She had her saddlebags and blankets, too. "So you're coming after all," he said. *Min was right.*

"*Was* there something down here?" she asked quietly. "*She* said it was—" She stopped abruptly and looked at him.

"A Fade," he answered. He was amazed that he could say it so calmly. "It was in the hall with me, and then Lan came."

Nynaeve shrugged her cloak against the wind as they left the inn. "Perhaps there is something after you. But I came to see you safely back in Emond's Field, all of you, and I will not leave till that is done. I won't leave you alone with *her* sort." Lights moved in the stables where the ostlers were saddling the horses.

"Mutch!" the innkeeper shouted from the stable door where he stood with Moiraine. "Stir your bones!" He turned back to her, appearing to attempt to soothe her rather than really listening when she spoke, though he did it deferentially, with bows interspersed among the orders called to the stablemen.

The horses were led out, the stablemen grumbling softly about the hurry and the lateness. Rand held Egwene's bundle, handing it up to her when she was on Bela's back. She looked back at him with wide, fear-filled eyes. *At least she doesn't think it's an adventure anymore.*

He was ashamed as soon as he thought it. She was in danger because of him and the others. Even riding back to Emond's Field alone would be safer than going on. "Egwene, I. . . ."

The words died in his mouth. She was too stubborn to just turn back, not after saying she was going all the way to Tar Valon. *What about what Min saw? She's part of it. Light, part of what?*

"Egwene," he said, "I'm sorry. I can't seem to think straight anymore."

She leaned down to grip his hand hard. In the light from the stable he could see her face clearly. She did not look as frightened as she had.

Once they were all mounted, Master Fitch insisted on leading them to the gates, the stablemen lighting the way with their lamps. The round-bellied innkeeper bowed them on their way with assurances that he would keep their secrets, and invitations to come again. Mutch watched them leave as sourly as he had watched them arrive.

There was one, Rand thought, who would not give short shrift to anyone, or any kind of shrift. Mutch would tell the first person who asked him when they had gone and everything else he could think of concerning them. A little distance down the street, he looked back. One figure stood, lamp raised high, peering after them. He did not need to see the face to know it was Mutch.

The streets of Baerlon were abandoned at that hour of the night; only a few faint glimmers here and there escaped tightly closed shutters, and the light of the moon in its last quarter waxed and waned with the wind-driven clouds. Now and again a dog barked as they passed an alleyway, but no other sound disturbed the night except their horses' hooves and the wind whistling across the rooftops. The riders held an even deeper silence, huddled in their cloaks and their own thoughts.

The Warder led the way, as usual, with Moiraine and Egwene close behind. Nynaeve kept near the girl, and the others brought up the rear in a tight cluster. Lan kept the horses moving at a brisk walk.

Rand watched the streets around them warily, and he noticed his friends doing the same. Shifting moon shadows recalled the shadows at the end of the hall, the way they had seemed to reach out to the Fade. An occasional noise in the distance, like a barrel toppling, or another dog barking, jerked every head around. Slowly, bit by bit as they made their way through the town, they all bunched their horses closer to Lan's black stallion and Moiraine's white mare.

At the Caemlyn Gate Lan dismounted and hammered with his fist on the door of a small square stone building squatting against the wall. A weary Watchman appeared, rubbing sleepily at his face. As Lan spoke, his sleepiness vanished, and he stared past the Warder to the others.

"You want to leave?" he exclaimed. "Now? In the night? You must be mad!"

"Unless there is some order from the Governor that prohibits our leaving," Moiraine said. She had dismounted as well, but she stayed back from the door, out of the light that spilled into the dark street.

"Not exactly, mistress." The Watchman peered at her, frowning as he tried to make out her face. "But the gates stay shut from sundown to sunup. No one to come in except in daylight. That's the order. Anyway, there're wolves out there. Killed a dozen cows in the last week. Could kill a man just as easy."

"No one to come in, but nothing about leaving," Moiraine said as if that settled the matter. "You see? We are not asking you to disobey the Governor."

Lan pressed something into the Watchman's hand. "For your trouble," he murmured.

"I suppose," the Watchman said slowly. He glanced at his hand; gold glinted before he hastily stuffed it in his pocket. "I suppose leaving wasn't mentioned at that. Just a minute." He stuck his head back inside. "Arin! Dar! Get out here and help me open the gate. There's people want to leave. Don't argue. Just do it."

Two more of the Watch appeared from inside, stopping to stare in sleepy surprise at the party of eight waiting to leave. Under the first Watchman's urgings they shuffled over to heave at the big wheel that raised the thick bar across the gates, then turned their efforts to cranking the gates open. The crank-and-ratchet made a rapid clicking sound, but the well-oiled gates swung outward silently. Before they were even a quarter open, though, a cold voice spoke out of the darkness.

"What is this? Are these gates not ordered closed until sunrise?"

Five white-cloaked men walked into the light from the guardhouse door. Their cowls were drawn up to hide their faces, but each man rested his hand on his sword, and the golden suns on their left breasts were a plain announcement of who they were. Mat muttered under his breath. The Watchmen stopped their cranking and exchanged uneasy looks.

"This is none of your affair," the first Watchman said belligerently. Five white hoods turned to regard him, and he finished in a weaker tone. "The Children hold no sway here. The Governor—"

"The Children of the Light," the white-cloaked man who had first spoken said softly, "hold sway wherever men walk in the Light. Only where the Shadow of the Dark One reigns are the Children denied, yes?" He swung his hood from the Watchman to Lan, then suddenly gave the Warder a second, more wary, look.

The Warder had not moved; in fact, he seemed completely at ease. But not many people could look at the Children so uncaringly. Lan's stony face could as well have been looking at a bootblack. When the Whitecloak spoke again, he sounded suspicious.

"What kind of people want to leave town walls in the night during times like these? With wolves stalking the darkness, and the Dark One's handiwork seen flying over the town?" He eyed the braided leather band that crossed Lan's forehead and held his long hair back. "A northerner, yes?"

Rand hunched lower in his saddle. A Draghkar. It had to be that, unless the man just named anything he did not understand as the Dark One's handiwork. With a Fade at the Stag and Lion, he should have expected a Draghkar, but at the moment he was hardly thinking about it. He thought he recognized the Whitecloak's voice.

"Travelers," Lan replied calmly. "Of no interest to you or yours."

"Everyone is of interest to the Children of the Light."

Lan shook his head slightly. "Are you really after more trouble with the Governor? He has limited your numbers in the town, even had you followed. What will he do when he discovers you're harassing honest citizens at his gates?" He turned to the Watchmen. "Why have you stopped?" They hesitated, put their hands back on the crank, then hesitated again when the Whitecloak spoke.

"The Governor does not know what happens under his nose. There is evil he does not see, or smell. But the Children of the Light see." The Watchmen looked at one another; their hands opened and closed as if regretting the spears left inside the guardhouse. "The Children of the Light smell the evil." The Whitecloak's eyes turned to the people on horseback. "We smell it, and root it out. Wherever it is found."

Rand tried to make himself even smaller, but the movement drew the man's attention.

"What have we here? Someone who does not wish to be seen? What do you—? Ah!" The man brushed back the hood of his white cloak, and Rand was looking at the face he had known would be there. Bornhald nodded with obvious satisfaction. "Clearly, Watchman, I have saved you from a great disaster. These are Darkfriends you were about to help escape from the Light. You should be reported to your Governor for discipline, or perhaps given to the Questioners to discover your true intent this night." He paused, eyeing the Watchman's fear; it seemed to have no effect on him. "You would not wish that, no? Instead, I will take these ruffians to our camp, that they may be questioned in the Light—instead of you, yes?"

"You will take me to your camp, Whitecloak?" Moiraine's voice came suddenly from every direction at once. She had moved back into the night at the Children's approach, and shadows clumped around her. "You will question me?" Darkness wreathed her as she took a step forward; it made her seem taller. "You will bar my way?"

Another step, and Rand gasped. She *was* taller, her head level with his where he sat on the gray's back. Shadows clung about her face like thunderclouds.

"Aes Sedai!" Bornhald shouted, and five swords flashed from their sheaths. "Die!" The other four hesitated, but he slashed at her in the same motion that cleared his sword.

Rand cried out as Moiraine's staff rose to intercept the blade. That delicately carved wood could not possibly stop hard-swung steel. Sword met staff, and sparks sprayed in a fountain, a hissing roar hurling Bornhald back into his white-cloaked companions. All five went down in a heap.

Tendrils of smoke rose from Bornhald's sword, on the ground beside him, blade bent at a right angle where it had been melted almost in two.

"You dare attack me!" Moiraine's voice roared like a whirlwind. Shadow spun in on her, draped her like a hooded cloak; she loomed as high as the town wall. Her eyes glared down, a giant staring at insects.

"Go!" Lan shouted. In one lightning move he snatched the reins of Moiraine's mare and leaped into his own saddle. "Now!" he commanded. His shoulders brushed either gate as his stallion tore through the narrow opening like a flung stone.

For a moment Rand remained frozen, staring. Moiraine's head and shoulders stood above the wall, now. Watchmen and Children alike cowered away from her, huddling with their backs against the front of the guardhouse. The Aes Sedai's face was lost in the night, but her eyes, as big as full moons, shone with impatience as well as anger when they touched him. Swallowing hard, he booted Cloud in the ribs and galloped after the others.

Fifty paces from the wall, Lan drew them up, and Rand looked back. Moiraine's shadowed shape towered high over the log palisade, head and shoulders a deeper darkness against the night sky, surrounded by a silver nimbus from the hidden moon. As he watched, mouth hanging open, the Aes Sedai stepped over the wall. The gates began swinging shut frantically. As soon as her feet were on the ground outside, she was suddenly her normal size again.

"Hold the gates!" an unsteady voice shouted inside the wall. Rand thought it was Bornhald. "We must pursue them, and take them!" But the Watchmen did not slow the pace of closing. The gates slammed shut, and moments later the bar crashed into place, sealing them. *Maybe some of those other Whitecloaks aren't as eager to confront an Aes Sedai as Bornhald.*

Moiraine hurried to Aldieb, stroking the white mare's nose once before she tucked her staff under the girth strap. Rand did not need to look this time to know there was not even a nick in the staff.

"You were taller than a giant," Egwene said breathlessly, shifting on Bela's back. No one else spoke, though Mat and Perrin edged their horses away from the Aes Sedai.

"Was I?" Moiraine said absently as she swung into her saddle.

"I saw you," Egwene protested.

"The mind plays tricks in the night; the eye sees what is not there."

"This is no time for games," Nynaeve began angrily, but Moiraine cut her off.

"No time for games indeed. What we gained at the Stag and Lion we may have lost here." She looked back at the gate and shook her head. "If only I could believe the Draghkar was on the ground." With a self-deprecatory sniff she added, "Or if only the Myrddraal were truly blind. If I am wishing, I might as well wish for the truly impossible. No matter. They know the way we must go, but with luck we will stay a step ahead of them. Lan!"

The Warder moved off eastward down the Caemlyn Road, and the rest followed close behind, hooves thudding rhythmically on the hard-packed earth.

They kept to an easy pace, a fast walk the horses could maintain for hours without any Aes Sedai help. Before they had been even one hour on their way, though, Mat cried out, pointing back the way they had come.

"Look there!"

They all drew rein and stared.

Flames lit the night over Baerlon as if someone had built a house-size bonfire, tinting the undersides of the cloud with red. Sparks whipped into the sky on the wind.

"I warned him," Moiraine said, "but he would not take it seriously." Aldieb danced sideways, an echo of the Aes Sedai's frustration. "He would not take it seriously."

"The inn?" Perrin said. "That's the Stag and Lion? How can you be sure?"

"How far do you want to stretch coincidence?" Thom asked. "It could be the Governor's house, but it isn't. And it isn't a warehouse, or somebody's kitchen stove, or your grandmother's haystack."

"Perhaps the Light shines on us a little this night," Lan said, and Egwene rounded on him angrily.

"How can you say that? Poor Master Fitch's inn is burning! People may be hurt!"

"If they have attacked the inn," Moiraine said, "perhaps our exit from the town and my . . . display went unnoticed."

"Unless that's what the Myrddraal wants us to think," Lan added.

Moiraine nodded in the darkness. "Perhaps. In any case, we must press on. There will be little rest for anyone tonight."

"You say that so easily, Moiraine," Nynaeve exclaimed. "What about the people at the inn? People must be hurt, and the innkeeper has lost his livelihood, because of you! For all your talk about walking in the Light you're ready to go on without sparing a thought for him. His trouble is because of you!"

"Because of those three," Lan said angrily. "The fire, the injured, the going on—all because of those three. The fact that the price must be paid is proof that it is worth paying. The Dark One wants those boys of yours, and anything he wants this badly, he must be kept from. Or would you rather let the Fade have them?"

"Be at ease, Lan," Moiraine said. "Be at ease. Wisdom, you think I can help Master Fitch and the people at the inn? Well, you are right." Nynaeve started to say something, but Moiraine waved it away and went on. "I can go back by myself and give some help. Not too much, of course. That would draw attention to those I helped, attention they would not thank me for, especially with the Children of the Light in the town. And that would leave only Lan to protect the rest of you. He is very good, but it will take more than him if a Myrddraal and a fist of Trollocs find you. Of course, we could all return, though I doubt I can get all of us back into Baerlon unnoticed. And that would expose all of you to whomever set that fire, not to mention the Whitecloaks. Which alternative would you choose, Wisdom, if you were I?"

"I would do something," Nynaeve muttered unwillingly.

"And in all probability hand the Dark One his victory," Moiraine replied. "Remember what—who—it is that he wants. We are in a war, as surely as anyone in Ghealdan, though thousands fight there and only eight of us here. I will have gold sent to Master Fitch, enough to rebuild the Stag and Lion, gold that cannot be traced to Tar Valon. And help for any who were hurt, as well. Any more than that will only endanger them. It is far from simple, you see. Lan." The Warder turned his horse and took up the road again.

From time to time Rand looked back. Eventually all he could see was the glow on the clouds, and then even that was lost in the darkness. He hoped Min was all right.

All was still pitch-dark when the Warder finally led them off the packed dirt of the road and dismounted. Rand estimated there were no more than a couple of hours till dawn. They hobbled the horses, still saddled, and made a cold camp.

"One hour," Lan warned as everyone except him was wrapping up in their blankets. He would stand guard while they slept. "One hour, and we must be on our way." Silence settled over them.

After a few minutes Mat spoke in a whisper that barely reached Rand. "I wonder what Dav did with that badger." Rand shook his head silently, and Mat hesitated. Finally he said, "I thought we were safe, you know, Rand. Not a sign of anything since we crossed the Taren, and there we were in a city, with walls around us. I thought we were safe. And then that dream. And a Fade. Are we ever going to be safe again?"

"Not until we get to Tar Valon," Rand said. "That's what she told us."

"Will we be safe then?" Perrin asked softly, and all three of them looked to the shadowy mound that was the Aes Sedai. Lan had melded into the darkness; he could have been anywhere.

Rand yawned suddenly. The others twitched nervously at the sound. "I think we'd better get some sleep," he said. "Staying awake won't answer anything."

Perrin spoke quietly. "She should have done something." No one answered.

Rand squirmed onto his side to avoid a root, tried his back, then rolled off of a stone onto his belly and another root. It was not a good campsite they had stopped at, not like the spots the Warder had chosen on the way north from the Taren. He fell asleep wondering if the roots digging into his ribs would make him dream, and woke at Lan's touch on his shoulder, ribs aching, and grateful that if any dreams had come he did not remember them.

It was still the dark just before dawn, but once the blankets were rolled and strapped behind their saddles Lan had them riding east again. As the sun rose they made a bleary-eyed breakfast on bread and cheese and water, eating while they rode, huddled in their cloaks against the wind. All except Lan, that is. He ate, but he was not bleary-eyed, and he did not huddle. He had changed back into his shifting cloak, and it whipped around him, fluttering through grays and greens, and the only mind he paid it was to keep it clear of his sword-arm. His face remained without expression, but his eyes searched constantly, as if he expected an ambush any moment.

CHAPTER
18

The Caemlyn Road

T he Caemlyn Road was not very different from the
North Road through the Two Rivers. It was considerably wider, of course, and showed the wear
of much more use, but it was still hard-packed dirt, lined
on either side by trees that would not have been at all out
of place in the Two Rivers, especially since only the evergreens carried a leaf.

The land itself was different, though, for by midday the
road entered low hills. For two days the road ran through
the hills—cut right through them, sometimes, if they were
wide enough to have made the road go much out of its way
and not so big as to have made digging through too difficult.
As the angle of the sun shifted each day it became apparent
that the road, for all it appeared straight to the eye, curved
slowly southward as it ran east. Rand had daydreamed over
Master al'Vere's old map—half the boys in Emond's Field
had daydreamed over it—and as he remembered, the road
curved around something called the Hills of Absher until it
reached Whitebridge.

From time to time Lan had them dismount atop one of
the hills, where he could get a good view of the road both
ahead and behind, and the surrounding countryside as well.
The Warder would study the view while the others stretched
their legs or sat under the trees and ate.

"I used to like cheese," Egwene said on the third day after leaving Baerlon. She sat with her back to the bole of a
tree, grimacing over a dinner that was once again the same
as breakfast, as supper would be. "Not a chance of tea. Nice

hot tea." She pulled her cloak tighter and shifted around the tree in a vain effort to avoid the swirling wind.

"Flatwort tea and andilay root," Nynaeve was saying to Moiraine, "are best for fatigue. They clear the head and dim the burn in tired muscles."

"I am sure they do," the Aes Sedai murmured, giving Nynaeve a sidelong glance.

Nynaeve's jaw tightened, but she continued in the same tone. "Now, if you must go without sleep. . . ."

"No tea!" Lan said sharply to Egwene. "No fire! We can't see them yet, but they are back there, somewhere, a Fade or two and their Trollocs, and they know we are taking this road. No need to tell them exactly where we are."

"I wasn't asking," Egwene muttered into her cloak. "Just regretting."

"If they know we're on the road," Perrin asked, "why don't we go straight across to Whitebridge?"

"Even Lan cannot travel as fast cross-country as by road," Moiraine said, interrupting Nynaeve, "especially not through the Hills of Absher." The Wisdom gave an exasperated sigh. Rand wondered what she was up to; after ignoring the Aes Sedai completely for the first day, Nynaeve had spent the last two trying to talk to her about herbs. Moiraine moved away from the Wisdom as she went on. "Why do you think the road curves to avoid them? And we would have to come back to this road eventually. We might find them ahead of us instead of following."

Rand looked doubtful, and Mat muttered something about "the long way round."

"Have you seen a farm this morning?" Lan asked. "Or even the smoke from a chimney? You haven't, because it's all wilderness from Baerlon to Whitebridge, and Whitebridge is where we must cross the Arinelle. That is the only bridge spanning the Arinelle south of Maradon, in Saldaea."

Thom snorted and blew out his mustaches. "What is to stop them from having someone, something, at Whitebridge already?"

From the west came the keening wail of a horn. Lan's head whipped around to stare back down the road behind them. Rand felt a chill. A part of him remained calm enough to think, ten miles, no more.

"Nothing stops them, gleeman," the Warder said. "We

trust to the Light and luck. But now we know for certain there are Trollocs behind us."

Moiraine dusted her hands. "It is time for us to move on." The Aes Sedai mounted her white mare.

That set off a scramble for the horses, speeded by a second winding of the horn. This time others answered, the thin sounds floating out of the west like a dirge. Rand made ready to put Cloud to a gallop right away, and everyone else settled their reins with the same urgency. Everyone except Lan and Moiraine. The Warder and the Aes Sedai exchanged a long look.

"Keep them moving, Moiraine Sedai," Lan said finally. "I will return as soon as I am able. You will know if I fail." Putting a hand on Mandarb's saddle, he vaulted to the back of the black stallion and galloped down the hill. Heading west. The horns sounded again.

"The Light go with you, last Lord of the Seven Towers," Moiraine said almost too softly for Rand to hear. Drawing a deep breath, she turned Aldieb to the east. "We must go on," she said, and started off at a slow, steady trot. The others followed her in a tight file.

Rand twisted once in his saddle to look for Lan, but the Warder was already lost to sight among the low hills and leafless trees. Last Lord of the Seven Towers, she had called him. He wondered what that meant. He had not thought anyone besides himself had heard, but Thom was chewing the ends of his mustaches, and he had a speculative frown on his face. The gleeman seemed to know a great many things.

The horns called and answered once more behind them. Rand shifted in his saddle. They were closer this time; he was sure of it. Eight miles. Maybe seven. Mat and Egwene looked over their shoulders, and Perrin hunched as if he expected something to hit him in the back. Nynaeve rode up to speak to Moiraine.

"Can't we go any faster?" she asked. "Those horns are getting closer."

The Aes Sedai shook her head. "And why do they let us know they are there? Perhaps so we will hurry on without thinking of what might be ahead."

They kept on at the same steady pace. At intervals the horns gave cry behind them, and each time the sound was closer. Rand tried to stop thinking of how close, but the thought came unbidden at every brazen wail. Five miles, he was thinking anxiously, when Lan suddenly burst around the hill behind them at a gallop.

He came abreast of Moiraine, reining in the stallion. "At least three fists of Trollocs, each led by a Halfman. Maybe five."

"If you were close enough to see them," Egwene said worriedly, "they could have seen you. They could be right on your heels."

"He was not seen." Nynaeve drew herself up as everyone looked at her. "I have followed his trail, remember."

"Hush," Moiraine commanded. "Lan is telling us there are perhaps five hundred Trollocs behind us." A stunned silence followed, then Lan spoke again.

"And they are closing the gap. They will be on us in an hour or less."

Half to herself, the Aes Sedai said, "If they had that many before, why were they not used at Emond's Field? If they did not, how did they come here since?"

"They are spread out to drive us before them," Lan said, "with scouts quartering ahead of the main parties."

"Driving us toward what?" Moiraine mused. As if to answer her a horn sounded in the distance to the west, a long moan that was answered this time by others, all ahead of them. Moiraine stopped Aldieb; the others followed her lead, Thom and the Emond's Field folk looking around fearfully. Horns cried out before them, and behind. Rand thought they held a note of triumph.

"What do we do now?" Nynaeve demanded angrily. "Where do we go?"

"All that is left is north or south," Moiraine said, more thinking aloud than answering the Wisdom. "To the south are the Hills of Absher, barren and dead, and the Taren, with no way to cross, and no traffic by boat. To the north, we can reach the Arinelle before nightfall, and there will be a chance of a trader's boat. If the ice has broken at Maradon."

"There is a place the Trollocs will not go," Lan said, but Moiraine's head whipped around sharply.

"No!" She motioned to the Warder, and he put his head close to hers so their talk could not be overheard.

The horns winded, and Rand's horse danced nervously.

"They're trying to frighten us," Thom growled, attempting to steady his mount. He sounded half angry and half as if the Trollocs were succeeding. "They're trying to scare us until we panic and run. They'll have us, then."

Egwene's head swung with every blast of a horn, staring first ahead of them, then behind, as if looking for the first Trollocs. Rand wanted to do the same thing, but he tried to hide it. He moved Cloud closer to her.

"We go north," Moiraine announced.

The horns keened shrilly as they left the road and trotted into the surrounding hills.

The hills were low, but the way was all up and down, with never a flat stretch, beneath bare-branched trees and through dead undergrowth. The horses climbed laboriously up one slope only to canter down the other. Lan set a hard pace, faster than they had used on the road.

Branches lashed Rand across the face and chest. Old creepers and vines caught his arms, and sometimes snagged his foot right out of the stirrup. The keening horns came ever closer, and ever more frequently.

As hard as Lan pushed them, they were not getting farther on very quickly. They traveled two feet up or down for every one forward, and every foot was a scrambling effort. And the horns were coming nearer. *Two miles,* he thought. *Maybe less.*

After a time Lan began peering first one way then another, the hard planes of his face as close to worry as Rand had seen them. Once the Warder stood in his stirrups to stare back the way they had come. All Rand could see were trees. Lan settled back into his saddle and unconsciously pushed back his cloak to clear his sword as he resumed searching the forest.

Rand met Mat's eye questioningly, but Mat only grimaced at the Warder's back and shrugged helplessly.

Lan spoke, then, over his shoulder. "There are Trollocs nearby." They topped a hill and started down the other side. "Some of the scouts, sent ahead of the rest. Probably. If we come on them, stay with me at all costs, and do as I do. We must keep on the way we are going."

"Blood and ashes!" Thom muttered. Nynaeve motioned to Egwene to keep close.

Scattered stands of evergreens provided the only real

cover, but Rand tried to peer in every direction at once, his imagination turning gray tree trunks caught out of the corner of his eye into Trollocs. The horns were closer, too. And directly behind them. He was sure of it. Behind and coming closer.

They topped another hill.

Below them, just starting up the slope, marched Trollocs carrying poles tipped with great loops of rope or long hooks. Many Trollocs. The line stretched far to either side, the ends out of sight, but at its center, directly in front of Lan, a Fade rode.

The Myrddraal seemed to hesitate as the humans appeared atop the hill, but in the next instant it produced a sword with the black blade Rand remembered so queasily, and waved it over its head. The line of Trollocs scrambled forward.

Even before the Myrddraal moved, Lan's sword was in his hand. "Stay with me!" he cried, and Mandarb plunged down the slope toward the Trollocs. "For the Seven Towers!" he shouted.

Rand gulped and booted the gray forward; the whole group of them streamed after the Warder. He was surprised to find Tam's sword in his fist. Caught up by Lan's cry, he found his own. "Manetheren! Manetheren!"

Perrin took it up. "Manetheren! Manetheren!"

But Mat shouted, *"Carai an Caldazar! Carai an Ellisande! Al Ellisande!"*

The Fade's head turned from the Trollocs to the riders charging toward him. The black sword froze over its head, and the opening of its cowl swiveled, searching among the oncoming horsemen.

Then Lan was on the Myrddraal, as the human folk fell on the Trolloc line. Warder's blade met black steel from the forges at Thakan'dar with a clang like a great bell, the toll echoing in the hollow, a flash of blue light filling the air like sheet lightning.

Beast-muzzled almost-men swarmed around each of the humans, catchpoles and hooks flailing. Only Lan and the Myrddraal did they avoid; those two fought in a clear circle, black horses matching step for step, swords matching stroke for stroke. The air flashed and pealed.

Cloud rolled his eyes and screamed, rearing and lashing

out with his hooves at the snarling, sharp-toothed faces surrounding him. Heavy bodies crowded shoulder-to-shoulder around him. Digging his heels in ruthlessly, Rand forced the gray on regardless, swinging his sword with little of the skill Lan had tried to impart, hacking as if hewing wood. *Egwene!* Desperately he searched for her as he kicked the gray onward, slashing a path through the hairy bodies as though chopping undergrowth.

Moiraine's white mare dashed and cut at the slightest touch of the Aes Sedai's hand on the reins. Her face was as hard as Lan's as her staff lashed out. Flame enveloped Trollocs, then burst with a roar that left misshapen forms unmoving on the ground. Nynaeve and Egwene rode close to the Aes Sedai with frantic urgency, teeth bared almost as fiercely as the Trollocs', belt knives in hand. Those short blades would be no use at all if a Trolloc came close. Rand tried to turn Cloud toward them, but the gray had the bit in his teeth. Screaming and kicking, Cloud struggled forward however hard Rand tugged at the reins.

Around the three women a space opened as Trollocs tried to flee from Moiraine's staff, but as they attempted to avoid her, she sought them out. Fires roared, and the Trollocs howled in rage and fury. Above roar and howl crashed the tolling of the Warder's sword against the Myrddraal's; the air flared blue around them, flared again. Again.

A noose on the end of a pole swept at Rand's head. With an awkward slash, he cut the catchpole in two, then hacked the goat-faced Trolloc that held it. A hook caught his shoulder from behind and tangled in his cloak, jerking him backwards. Frantically, almost losing his sword, he clutched the pommel of his saddle to keep his seat. Cloud twisted, shrieking. Rand hung onto saddle and reins desperately; he could feel himself slipping, inch by inch, falling to the hook. Cloud swung around; for an instant Rand saw Perrin, half out of his saddle, struggling to wrest his axe away from three Trollocs. They had him by one arm and both legs. Cloud plunged, and only Trollocs filled Rand's eyes.

A Trolloc dashed in and seized Rand's leg, forcing his foot free of the stirrup. Panting, he let go of the saddle to stab it. Instantly the hook pulled him out of the saddle, to Cloud's hindquarters; his death-grip on the reins was all that kept him from the ground. Cloud reared and shrieked.

And in that same moment the pulling vanished. The Trolloc at his leg threw up its hands and screamed. All of the Trollocs screamed, a howl like all the dogs in the world gone mad.

Around the humans Trollocs fell writhing to the ground, tearing at their hair, clawing their own faces. All of the Trollocs. Biting at the ground, snapping at nothing, howling, howling, howling.

Then Rand saw the Myrddraal. Still upright in the saddle of its madly dancing horse, black sword still flailing, it had no head.

"It won't die until nightfall," Thom had to shout, between heavy breaths, over the unrelenting screams. "Not completely. That is what I've heard, anyway."

"Ride!" Lan shouted angrily. The Warder had already gathered Moiraine and the other two women and had them halfway up the next hill. "This is not all of them!" Indeed, the horns dirged again, above the shrieks of the Trollocs on the ground, to east and west and south.

For a wonder, Mat was the only one who had been unhorsed. Rand trotted toward him, but Mat tossed a noose away from him with a shudder, gathered his bow, and scrambled into his saddle unaided, though rubbing at his throat.

The horns bayed like hounds with the scent of a deer. Hounds closing in. If Lan had set a hard pace before, he doubled it now, till the horses scrabbled uphill faster than they had gone down before, then nearly threw themselves at the other side. But still the horns came ever nearer, until the guttural shouts of pursuit were heard whenever the horns paused, until eventually the humans reached a hilltop just as Trollocs appeared on the next hill behind them. The hilltop blackened with Trollocs, snouted, distorted faces howling, and three Myrddraal overawed them all. Only a hundred spans separated the two parties.

Rand's heart shriveled like an old grape. *Three!*

The Myrddraal's black swords rose as one; Trollocs boiled down the slope, thick, triumphant cries rising, catchpoles bobbing above as they ran.

Moiraine climbed down from Aldieb's back. Calmly she removed something from her pouch, unwrapped it. Rand glimpsed dark ivory. The *angreal*. With *angreal* in one hand and staff in the other, the Aes Sedai set her feet, facing the onrushing Trollocs and the Fades' black swords, raised her staff high, and stabbed it down into the earth.

The ground rang like an iron kettle struck by a mallet. The hollow clang dwindled, faded away. For an instant then, it was silent. Everything was silent. The wind died. The Trolloc cries stilled; even their charge forward slowed and stopped. For a heartbeat, everything waited. Slowly the dull ringing returned, changing to a low rumble, growing until the earth moaned.

The ground trembled beneath Cloud's hooves. This was Aes Sedai work like the stories told about; Rand wished he were a hundred miles away. The tremble became a shaking that set the trees around them quivering. The gray stumbled and nearly fell. Even Mandarb and riderless Aldieb staggered as if drunk, and those who rode had to cling to reins and manes, to anything, to keep their seats.

The Aes Sedai still stood as she had begun, holding the *angreal* and her upright staff thrust into the hilltop, and neither she nor the staff moved an inch, for all that the ground shook and shivered around her. Now the ground rippled, springing out from in front of her staff, lapping toward the Trollocs like ripples on a pond, ripples that grew as they ran, toppling old bushes, flinging dead leaves into the air, growing, becoming waves of earth, rolling toward the Trollocs. Trees in the hollow lashed like switches in the hands of small boys. On the far slope Trollocs fell in heaps, tumbled over and over by the raging earth.

Yet as if the ground were not rearing all around them, the Myrddraal moved forward in a line, their dead-black horses never missing a step, every hoof in unison. Trollocs rolled on the ground all about the black steeds, howling and grabbing at the hillside that heaved them up, but the Myrddraal came slowly on.

Moiraine lifted her staff, and the earth stilled, but she was not done. She pointed to the hollow between the hills, and flame gouted from the ground, a fountain twenty feet high. She flung her arms wide, and the fire raced to left and right as far as the eye could see, spreading into a wall separating humans and Trollocs. The heat made Rand put his hands in front of his face, even on the hilltop. The Myrddraal's black mounts, whatever strange powers they had, screamed at the fire, reared and fought their riders as the

Myrddraal beat at them, trying to force them through the flames.

"Blood and ashes," Mat said faintly. Rand nodded numbly.

Abruptly Moiraine wavered and would have fallen had Lan not leaped from his horse to catch her. "Go on," he told the others. The harshness of his voice was at odds with the gentle way he lifted the Aes Sedai to her saddle. "That fire won't burn forever. Hurry! Every minute counts!"

The wall of flame roared as if it would indeed burn forever, but Rand did not argue. They galloped northward as fast as they could make their horses go. The horns in the distance shrilled out disappointment, as if they already knew what had happened, then fell silent.

Lan and Moiraine soon caught up with the others, though Lan led Aldieb by the reins while the Aes Sedai swayed and held the pommel of her saddle with both hands. "I will be all right soon," she said to their worried looks. She sounded tired yet confident, and her gaze was as compelling as ever. "I am not at my strongest when working with Earth and Fire. A small thing."

The two of them moved into the lead again at a fast walk. Rand did not think Moiraine could stay in the saddle at any faster pace. Nynaeve rode foward beside the Aes Sedai, steadying her with a hand. For a time as the party went on across the hills the two women whispered, then the Wisdom delved into her cloak and handed a small packet to Moiraine. Moiraine unfolded it and swallowed the contents. Nynaeve said something more, then fell back with the others, ignoring their questioning looks. Despite their circumstances, Rand thought she had a slight look of satisfaction.

He did not really care what the Wisdom was up to. He rubbed the hilt of his sword continually, and whenever he realized what he was doing, he stared down at it in wonder. *So that's what a battle is like.* He could not remember much of it, not any particular part. Everything ran together in his head, a melted mass of hairy faces and fear. Fear and heat. It had seemed as hot as a midsummer noon while it was going on. He could not understand that. The icy wind was trying to freeze beads of perspiration all over his face and body.

He glanced at his two friends. Mat was scrubbing sweat

off his face with the edge of his cloak. Perrin, staring at something in the distance and not liking what he was seeing, appeared unaware of the beads glistening on his forehead.

The hills grew smaller, and the land began to level out, but instead of pressing on, Lan stopped. Nynaeve moved as if to rejoin Moiraine, but the Warder's look kept her away. He and the Aes Sedai rode ahead and put their heads together, and from Moiraine's gestures it became apparent they were arguing. Nynaeve and Thom stared at them, the Wisdom frowning worriedly, the gleeman muttering under his breath and pausing to stare back the way they had come, but everyone else avoided looking at them altogether. Who knew what might come out of an argument between an Aes Sedai and a Warder?

After a few minutes Egwene spoke to Rand quietly, casting an uneasy eye at the still-arguing pair. "Those things you were shouting at the Trollocs." She stopped as if unsure how to proceed.

"What about them?" Rand asked. He felt a little awkward—warcries were all right for Warders; Two Rivers folk did not do things like that, whatever Moiraine said— but if she made fun of him over it. . . . "Mat must have repeated that story ten times."

"And badly," Thom put in. Mat grunted in protest.

"However he told it," Rand said, "we've all heard it any number of times. Besides, we had to shout something. I mean, that's what you do at a time like that. You heard Lan."

"And we have a right," Perrin added thoughtfully. "Moiraine says we're all descended from those Manetheren people. They fought the Dark One, and we're fighting the Dark One. That gives us a right."

Egwene sniffed as if to show what she thought of that. "I wasn't talking about that. What . . . what was it you were shouting, Mat?"

Mat shrugged uncomfortably. "I don't remember." He stared at them defensively. "Well, I don't. It's all foggy. I don't know what it was, or where it came from, or what it means." He gave a self-deprecating laugh. "I don't suppose it means anything."

"I . . . I think it does," Egwene said slowly. "When you shouted, I thought—just for a minute—I thought I understood you. But it's all gone, now." She sighed and shook her head. "Perhaps you're right. Strange what you can imagine at a time like that, isn't it?"

"Carai an Caldazar," Moiraine said. They all twisted to stare at her. *"Carai an Ellisande. Al Ellisande.* For the honor of the Red Eagle. For the honor of the Rose of the Sun. The Rose of the Sun. The ancient warcry of Manetheren, and the warcry of its last king. Eldrene was called the Rose of the Sun." Moiraine's smile took in Egwene and Mat both, though her gaze may have rested a moment longer on him than on her. "The blood of Aemon's line is still strong in the Two Rivers. The old blood still sings."

Mat and Egwene looked at each other, while everyone else looked at them both. Egwene's eyes were wide, and her mouth kept quirking into a smile that she bit back every time it began, as if she was not sure just how to take this talk of the old blood. Mat was sure, from the scowling frown on his face.

Rand thought he knew what Mat was thinking. The same thing he was thinking. If Mat was a descendant of the ancient kings of Manetheren, maybe the Trollocs were really after him and not all three of them. The thought made him ashamed. His cheeks colored, and when he caught a guilty grimace on Perrin's face, he knew Perrin had been having the same thought.

"I can't say that I have ever heard the like of this," Thom said after a minute. He shook himself and became brusque. "Another time I might even make a story out of it, but right now. . . . Do you intend to remain here for the rest of the day, Aes Sedai?"

"No," Moiraine replied, gathering her reins.

A Trolloc horn keened from the south as if to emphasize her word. More horns answered, east and west. The horses whickered and sidled about nervously.

"They have passed the fire," Lan said calmly. He turned to Moiraine. "You are not strong enough for what you intend, not yet, not without rest. And neither Myrddraal nor Trolloc will enter that place."

Moiraine raised a hand as if to cut him off, then sighed and let it fall instead. "Very well," she said irritably. "You are right, I suppose, but I would rather there was any other choice." She pulled her staff from under the girth strap of her saddle. "Gather in around me, all of you. As close as you can. Closer."

Rand urged Cloud nearer the Aes Sedai's mare. At Moiraine's insistence they kept on crowding closer in a circle around her until every horse had its head stretched over the croup or withers of another. Only then was the Aes Sedai satisfied. Then, without speaking, she stood in the stirrups and swung her staff over their heads, stretching to make certain it covered everyone.

Rand flinched each time the staff passed over him. A tingle ran through him with every pass. He could have followed the staff without seeing it, just by following the shivers as it moved over people. It was no surprise to him that Lan was the only one not affected.

Abruptly Moiraine thrust the staff out to the west. Dead leaves whirled into the air and branches whipped as if a dust-devil ran along the line she pointed to. As the invisible whirlwind vanished from sight she settled back into her saddle with a sigh.

"To the Trollocs," she said, "our scents and our tracks will seem to follow that. The Myrddraal will see through it in time, but by then. . . ."

"By then," Lan said, "we will have lost ourselves."

"Your staff is very powerful," Egwene said, earning a sniff from Nynaeve.

Moiraine made a clicking sound. "I have told you, child, things do not have power. The One Power comes from the True Source, and only a living mind can wield it. This is not even an *angreal,* merely an aid to concentration." Wearily she slid the staff back under her girth strap. "Lan?"

"Follow me," the Warder said, "and keep quiet. It will ruin everything if the Trollocs hear us."

He led the way north again, not at the crashing pace they had been making, but rather in the quick walk with which they had traveled the Caemlyn Road. The land continued to flatten, though the forest remained as thick.

Their path was no longer straight, as it had been before, for Lan chose out a route that meandered over hard ground and rocky outcrops, and he no longer let them force their way through tangles of brush, instead taking the time to make their way around. Now and again he dropped to the rear, intently studying the trail they made. If anyone so much as coughed, it drew a sharp grunt from him.

Nynaeve rode beside the Aes Sedai, concern battling dislike on her face. And there was a hint of something more, Rand thought, almost as if the Wisdom saw some goal in sight. Moiraine's shoulders were slumped, and she held her reins and the saddle with both hands, swaying with every step Aldieb took. It was plain that laying the false trail, small as that might have seemed beside producing an earthquake and a wall of flame, had taken a great deal out of her, strength she no longer had to lose.

Rand almost wished the horns would start again. At least they were a way of telling how far back the Trollocs were. And the Fades.

He kept looking behind them, and so was not the first to see what lay ahead. When he did, he stared, perplexed. A great, irregular mass stretched off to either side out of sight, in most places as high as the trees that grew right up to it, with even taller spires here and there. Leafless vines and creepers covered it all in thick layers. A cliff? *The vines will make climbing easy, but we'll never get the horses up.*

Suddenly, as they rode a little closer, he saw a tower. It was clearly a tower, not some kind of rock formation, with an odd, pointed dome on the top. "A city!" he said. And a city wall, and the spires were guard towers on the wall. His jaw dropped. It had to be ten times as big as Baerlon. Fifty times as big.

Mat nodded. "A city," he agreed. "But what's a city doing in the middle of a forest like this?"

"And without any people," Perrin said. When they looked at him, he pointed to the wall. "Would people let vines grow over everything like that? You know how creepers can tear down a wall. Look how it's fallen."

What Rand saw adjusted itself in his mind again. It was as Perrin said. Under almost every low place in the wall was a brush-covered hill; rubble from the collapsed wall above. No two of the guard towers were the same height.

"I wonder what city it was," Egwene mused. "I wonder what happened to it. I don't remember anything from papa's map."

"It was called Aridhol," Moiraine said. "In the days of the Trolloc Wars, it was an ally of Manetheren." Staring at the massive walls, she seemed almost unaware of the others, even of Nynaeve, who supported her in the saddle with a hand on her arm. "Later Aridhol died, and this place was called by another name."

"What name?" Mat asked.

"Here," Lan said. He stopped Mandarb in front of what had once been a gate wide enough for fifty men to march through abreast. Only the broken, vine-encrusted watch-towers remained; of the gates there was no sign. "We enter here." Trolloc horns shrieked in the distance. Lan peered in the direction of the sound, then looked at the sun, half-way down toward the treetops in the west. "They have dis-covered it's a false trail. Come, we must find shelter before dark."

"What name?" Mat asked again.

Moiraine answered as they rode into the city. "Shadar Logoth," she said. "It is called Shadar Logoth."

CHAPTER
19

Shadow's Waiting

Broken paving stones crunched under the horses' hooves as Lan led the way into the city. The entire city was broken, what Rand could see of it, and as abandoned as Perrin had said. Not so much as a pigeon moved, and weeds, mainly old and dead, sprouted from cracks in walls as well as pavement. More buildings had roofs fallen in than had them whole. Tumbled walls spilled fans of brick and stone into the streets. Towers stopped, abrupt and jagged, like broken sticks. Uneven rubble hills with a few stunted trees growing on their slopes could have been the remains of palaces or of entire blocks of the city.

Yet what was left standing was enough to take Rand's breath. The largest building in Baerlon would have vanished in the shadows of almost anything here. Pale marble palaces topped with huge domes met him wherever he looked. Every building appeared to have at least one dome; some had four or five, and each one shaped differently. Long walks lined by columns ran hundreds of paces to towers that seemed to reach the sky. At every intersection stood a bronze fountain, or the alabaster spire of a monument, or a statue on a pedestal. If the fountains were dry, most of the spires toppled, and many of the statues broken, what remained was so great that he could only marvel.

And I thought Baerlon was a city! Burn me, but Thom must have been laughing up his sleeve. Moiraine and Lan, too.

He was so caught up in staring that he was taken by surprise when Lan suddenly stopped in front of a white stone building that had once been twice as big as the Stag and Lion in Baerlon. There was nothing to say what it had been when

the city lived and was great, perhaps even an inn. Only a
hollow shell remained of the upper floors—the afternoon
sky was visible through empty window frames, glass and
wood alike long since gone—but the ground floor seemed
sound enough.

Moiraine, hands still on the pommel, studied the building intently before nodding. "This will do."

Lan leaped from his saddle and lifted the Aes Sedai down
in his arms. "Bring the horses inside," he commanded. "Find
a room in the back to use for a stable. Move, farmboys. This
isn't the village green." He vanished inside carrying the Aes
Sedai.

Nynaeve scrambled down and hurried after him, clutching her bag of herbs and ointments. Egwene was right behind her. They left their mounts standing.

"'Bring the horses inside,'" Thom muttered wryly, and
puffed out his mustaches. He climbed down, stiff and slow,
knuckled his back, and gave a long sigh, then took Aldieb's
reins. "Well?" he said, lifting an eyebrow at Rand and his
friends.

They hurried to dismount, and gathered up the rest of
the horses. The doorway, without anything to say there had
ever been a door in it, was more than big enough to get the
animals through, even two abreast.

Inside was a huge room, as wide as the building, with
a dirty tile floor and a few ragged wall hangings, faded to
a dull brown, that looked as if they would fall apart at a
touch. Nothing else. Lan had made a place in the nearest
corner for Moiraine with his cloak and hers. Nynaeve, muttering about the dust, knelt beside the Aes Sedai, digging in
her bag, which Egwene held open.

"I may not like her, it is true," Nynaeve was saying to the
Warder as Rand, leading Bela and Cloud, came in behind
Thom, "but I help anyone who needs my help, whether I
like them or not."

"I made no accusation, Wisdom. I only said, have a care
with your herbs."

She gave him a look from the corner of her eye. "The fact
is, she needs my herbs, and so do you." Her voice was acer-
bic to start, and grew more tart as she spoke. "The fact is,
she can only do so much, even with her One Power, and she
has done about as much as she can without collapsing. The

fact is, your sword cannot help her now, Lord of the Seven Towers, but my herbs can."

Moiraine laid a hand on Lan's arm. "Be at ease, Lan. She means no harm. She simply does not know." The Warder snorted derisively.

Nynaeve stopped digging in her bag and looked at him, frowning, but it was to Moiraine she spoke. "There are many things I don't know. What thing is this?"

"For one," Moiraine replied, "all I truly need is a little rest. For another, I agree with you. Your skills and knowledge will be more useful than I thought. Now, if you have something that will help me sleep for an hour and not leave me groggy—?"

"A weak tea of foxtail, marisin, and—"

Rand missed the last of it as he followed Thom into a room behind the first, a chamber just as big and even emptier. Here was only the dust, thick and undisturbed until they came. Not even the tracks of birds or small animals marked the floor.

Rand began to unsaddle Bela and Cloud, and Thom, Aldieb and his gelding, and Perrin, his horse and Mandarb. All but Mat. He dropped his reins in the middle of the room. There were two doorways from the room besides the one by which they had entered.

"Alley," Mat announced, drawing his head back in from the first. They could all see that much from where they were. The second doorway was only a black rectangle in the rear wall. Mat went through slowly, and came out much faster, vigorously brushing old cobwebs out of his hair. "Nothing in there," he said, giving the alleyway another look.

"You going to take care of your horse?" Perrin said. He had already finished his own and was lifting the saddle from Mandarb. Strangely, the fierce-eyed stallion gave him no trouble at all, though he did watch Perrin. "Nobody is going to do it for you."

Mat gave the alley one last look and went to his horse with a sigh.

As Rand laid Bela's saddle on the floor, he noticed that Mat had taken on a glum stare. His eyes seemed a thousand miles away, and he was moving by rote.

"Are you all right, Mat?" Rand said. Mat lifted the saddle from his horse, and stood holding it. "Mat? Mat!"

Mat gave a start and almost dropped the saddle. "What? Oh. I . . . I was just thinking."

"Thinking?" Perrin hooted from where he was replacing Mandarb's bridle with a hackamore. "You were asleep."

Mat scowled. "I was thinking about . . . about what happened back there. About those words I. . . ." Everybody turned to look at him then, not just Rand, and he shifted uneasily. "Well, you heard what Moiraine said. It's as if some dead man was speaking with my mouth. I don't like it." His scowl grew deeper when Perrin chuckled.

"Aemon's warcry, she said—right? Maybe you're Aemon come back again. The way you go on about how dull Emond's Field is, I'd think you would like that—being a king and hero reborn."

"Don't say that!" Thom drew a deep breath; everybody stared at him now. "That is dangerous talk, stupid talk. The dead can be reborn, or take a living body, and it is not something to speak of lightly." He took another breath to calm himself before going on. "The old blood, she said. The blood, not a dead man. I've heard that it can happen, sometimes. Heard, though I never really thought. . . . It was your roots, boy. A line running from you to your father to your grandfather, right on back to Manetheren, and maybe beyond. Well, now you know your family is old. You ought to let it go at that and be glad. Most people don't know much more than that they had a father."

Some of us can't even be sure of that, Rand thought bitterly. *Maybe the Wisdom was right. Light, I hope she was.*

Mat nodded at what the gleeman said. "I suppose I should. Only . . . do you think it has anything to do with what's happened to us? The Trollocs and all? I mean . . . oh, I don't know what I mean."

"I think you ought to forget about it, and concentrate on getting out of here safely." Thom produced his long-stemmed pipe from inside his cloak. "And I think I am going to have a smoke." With a waggle of the pipe in their direction, he disappeared into the front room.

"We are all in this together, not just one of us," Rand told Mat.

Mat gave himself a shake, and laughed, a short bark. "Right. Well, speaking of being in things together, now that we're done with the horses, why don't we go see a little more of this city. A real city, and no crowds to jostle your elbow and poke you in the ribs. Nobody looking down their long noses at us. There's still an hour, maybe two, of daylight left."

"Aren't you forgetting the Trollocs?" Perrin said.

Mat shook his head scornfully. "Lan said they wouldn't come in here, remember? You need to listen to what people say."

"I remember," Perrin said. "And I do listen. This city—Aridhol?—was an ally of Manetheren. See? I listen."

"Aridhol must have been the greatest city in the Trolloc Wars," Rand said, "for the Trollocs to still be afraid of it. They weren't afraid to come into the Two Rivers, and Moiraine said Manetheren was—how did she put it?—a thorn to the Dark One's foot."

Perrin raised his hands. "Don't mention the Shepherd of the Night. Please?"

"What do you say?" Mat laughed. "Let's go."

"We should ask Moiraine," Perrin said, and Mat threw up his hands.

"Ask Moiraine? You think she'll let us out of her sight? And what about Nynaeve? Blood and ashes, Perrin, why not ask Mistress Luhhan while you're about it?"

Perrin nodded reluctant agreement, and Mat turned to Rand with a grin. "What about you? A real city? With palaces!" He gave a sly laugh. "And no Whitecloaks to stare at us."

Rand gave him a dirty look, but he hesitated only a minute. Those palaces were like a gleeman's tale. "All right."

Stepping softly so as not to be heard in the front room, they left by the alley, following it away from the front of the building to a street on the other side. They walked quickly, and when they were a block away from the white stone building Mat suddenly broke into a capering dance.

"Free." He laughed. "Free!" He slowed until he was turning a circle, staring at everything and still laughing. The afternoon shadows stretched long and jagged, and the sinking sun made the ruined city golden. "Did you ever even dream of a place like this? Did you?"

Perrin laughed, too, but Rand shrugged uncomfortably. This was nothing like the city in his first dream, but just the same. . . . "If we're going to see anything," he said, "we had better get on with it. There isn't much daylight left."

Mat wanted to see everything, it seemed, and he pulled the others along with his enthusiasm. They climbed over dusty fountains with basins wide enough to hold everybody in Emond's Field and wandered in and out of structures chosen at random, but always the biggest they could find. Some they understood, and some not. A palace was plainly a palace, but what was a huge building that was one round, white dome as big as a hill outside and one monstrous room inside? And a walled place, open to the sky and big enough to have held all of Emond's Field, surrounded by row on row on row of stone benches?

Mat grew impatient when they found nothing but dust, or rubble, or colorless rags of wall hangings that crumbled at a touch. Once some wooden chairs stood stacked against a wall; they all fell to bits when Perrin tried to pick one up.

The palaces, with their huge, empty chambers, some of which could have held the Winespring Inn with room to spare on every side and above as well, made Rand think too much of the people who had once filled them. He thought everybody in the Two Rivers could have stood under that round dome, and as for the place with the stone benches. . . . He could almost imagine he could see the people in the shadows, staring in disapproval at the three intruders disturbing their rest.

Finally even Mat tired, grand as the buildings were, and remembered that he had had only an hour's sleep the night before. Everyone began to remember that. Yawning, they sat on the steps of a tall building fronted by row on row of tall stone columns and argued about what to do next.

"Go back," Rand said, "and get some sleep." He put the back of his hand against his mouth. When he could talk again, he said, "Sleep. That's all I want."

"You can sleep anytime," Mat said determinedly. "Look at where we are. A ruined city. Treasure."

"Treasure?" Perrin's jaws cracked. "There isn't any treasure here. There isn't anything but dust."

Rand shaded his eyes against the sun, a red ball sitting close to the rooftops. "It's getting late, Mat. It'll be dark soon."

"There could be treasure," Mat maintained stoutly. "Anyway, I want to climb one of the towers. Look at that one over there. It's whole. I'll bet you could see for miles from up there. What do you say?"

"The towers are not safe," said a man's voice behind them.

Rand leaped to his feet and spun around clutching his sword hilt, and the others were just as quick.

A man stood in the shadows among the columns at the top of the stairs. He took half a step forward, raised his hand to shield his eyes, and stepped back again. "Forgive me," he said smoothly. "I have been quite a long time in the dark inside. My eyes are not yet used to the light."

"Who are you?" Rand thought the man's accent sounded odd, even after Baerlon; some words he pronounced strangely, so Rand could barely understand them. "What are you doing here? We thought the city was empty."

"I am Mordeth." He paused as if expecting them to recognize the name. When none of them gave any sign of doing so, he muttered something under his breath and went on. "I could ask the same questions of you. There has been no one in Aridhol for a long time. A long, long time. I would not have thought to find three young men wandering its streets."

"We're on our way to Caemlyn," Rand said. "We stopped to take shelter for the night."

"Caemlyn," Mordeth said slowly, rolling the name around his tongue, then shook his head. "Shelter for the night, you say? Perhaps you will join me."

"You still haven't said what you're doing here," Perrin said.

"Why, I am a treasure hunter, of course."

"Have you found any?" Mat demanded excitedly.

Rand thought Mordeth smiled, but in the shadows he could not be sure. "I have," the man said. "More than I expected. Much more. More than I can carry away. I never expected to find three strong, healthy young men. If you will help me move what I *can* take to where my horses are, you may each have a share of the rest. As much as you can carry. Whatever I leave will be gone, carried off by some other treasure hunter, before I can return for it."

"I told you there must be treasure in a place like this," Mat exclaimed. He darted up the stairs. "We'll help you carry it. Just take us to it." He and Mordeth moved deeper into the shadows among the columns.

Rand looked at Perrin. "We can't leave him." Perrin glanced at the sinking sun, and nodded.

They went up the stairs warily, Perrin easing his axe in its belt loop. Rand's hand tightened on his sword. But Mat and Mordeth were waiting among the columns, Mordeth with arms folded, Mat peering impatiently into the interior.

"Come," Mordeth said. "I will show you the treasure." He slipped inside, and Mat followed. There was nothing for the others to do but go on.

The hall inside was shadowy, but almost immediately Mordeth turned aside and took some narrow steps that wound around and down through deeper and deeper dark until they fumbled their way in pitch-blackness. Rand felt along the wall with one hand, unsure there would be a step below until his foot met it. Even Mat began to feel uneasy, judging by his voice when he said, "It's awfully dark down here."

"Yes, yes," Mordeth replied. The man seemed to be having no trouble at all with the dark. "There are lights below. Come."

Indeed the winding stairs abruptly gave way to a corridor dimly lit by scattered, smoky torches set in iron sconces on the walls. The flickering flames and shadows gave Rand his first good look at Mordeth, who hurried on without pausing, motioning them to follow.

There was something odd about him, Rand thought, but he could not pick out what it was, exactly. Mordeth was a sleek, somewhat overfed man, with drooping eyelids that made him seem to be hiding behind something and staring. Short, and completely bald, he walked as if he were taller than any of them. His clothes were certainly like nothing Rand had ever seen before, either. Tight black breeches and soft red boots with the tops turned down at his ankles. A long, red vest thickly embroidered in gold, and a snowy white shirt with wide sleeves, the points of his cuffs hanging almost to his knees. Certainly not the kind of clothes in which to hunt through a ruined city in search of treasure. But it was not that which made him seem strange, either.

Then the corridor ended in a tile-walled room, and he forgot about any oddities Mordeth might have. His gasp was an echo of his friends'. Here, too, light came from a few torches staining the ceiling with their smoke and giving everyone more than one shadow, but that light was reflected a thousand times by the gems and gold piled on the floor, mounds of coins and jewelry, goblets and plates and platters, gilded, gem-encrusted swords and daggers, all heaped together carelessly in waist-high mounds.

With a cry Mat ran forward and fell to his knees in front of one of the piles. "Sacks," he said breathlessly, pawing through the gold. "We'll need sacks to carry all of this."

"We can't carry it all," Rand said. He looked around helplessly; all the gold the merchants brought to Emond's Field in a year would not have made the thousandth part of just one of those mounds. "Not now. It's almost dark."

Perrin pulled an axe free, carelessly tossing back the gold chains that had been tangled around it. Jewels glittered along its shiny black handle, and delicate gold scrollwork covered the twin blades. "Tomorrow, then," he said, hefting the axe with a grin. "Moiraine and Lan will understand when we show them this."

"You are not alone?" Mordeth said. He had let them rush past him into the treasure room, but now he followed. "Who else is with you?"

Mat, wrist deep in the riches before him, answered absently. "Moiraine and Lan. And then there's Nynaeve, and Egwene, and Thom. He's a gleeman. We're going to Tar Valon."

Rand caught his breath. Then the silence from Mordeth made him look at the man.

Rage twisted Mordeth's face, and fear, too. His lips pulled back from his teeth. "Tar Valon!" He shook clenched fists at them. "Tar Valon! You said you were going to this . . . this . . . Caemlyn! You lied to me!"

"If you still want," Perrin said to Mordeth, "we'll come back tomorrow and help you." Carefully he set the axe back on the heap of gem-encrusted chalices and jewelry. "If you want."

"No. That is. . . ." Panting, Mordeth shook his head as if he could not decide. "Take what you want. Except. . . . Except. . . ."

Suddenly Rand realized what had been nagging at him about the man. The scattered torches in the hallway had given each of them a ring of shadows, just as the torches in the treasure room did. Only. . . . He was so shocked he said it out loud. "You don't have a shadow."

A goblet fell from Mat's hand with a crash.

Mordeth nodded, and for the first time his fleshy eyelids opened all the way. His sleek face suddenly appeared pinched and hungry. "So." He stood straighter, seeming taller. "It is decided." Abruptly there was no seeming to it. Like a balloon Mordeth swelled, distorted, head pressed against the ceiling, shoulders butting the walls, filling the end of the room, cutting off escape. Hollow-cheeked, teeth bared in a rictus snarl, he reached out with hands big enough to engulf a man's head.

With a yell Rand leaped back. His feet tangled in a gold chain, and he crashed to the floor, the wind knocked out of him. Struggling for breath, he struggled at the same time for his sword, fighting his cloak, which had become wrapped around the hilt. The yells of his friends filled the room, and the clash of gold platters and goblets clattering across the floor. Suddenly an agonized scream shivered in Rand's ears.

Almost sobbing, he managed to inhale at last, just as he got the sword out of its sheath. Cautiously, he got to his feet, wondering which of his friends had given that scream. Perrin looked back at him wide-eyed from across the room, crouched and holding his axe back as if about to chop down a tree. Mat peered around the side of a treasure pile, clutching a dagger snatched from the trove.

Something moved in the deepest part of the shadows left by the torches, and they all jumped. It was Mordeth, clutching his knees to his chest and huddled as deep into the furthest corner as he could get.

"He tricked us," Mat panted. "It was some kind of trick."

Mordeth threw back his head and wailed; dust sifted down as the walls trembled. "You are all dead!" he cried. "All dead!" And he leaped up, diving across the room.

Rand's jaw dropped, and he almost dropped the sword as well. As Mordeth dove through the air, he stretched out and thinned, like a tendril of smoke. As thin as a finger he struck a crack in the wall tiles and vanished into it. A last cry hung in the room as he vanished, fading slowly away after he was gone.

"You are all dead!"

"Let's get out of here," Perrin said faintly, firming his grip on his axe while he tried to face every direction at once. Gold ornaments and gems scattered unnoticed under his feet.

"But the treasure," Mat protested. "We *can't* just leave it now."

"I don't want anything of his," Perrin said, still turning

one way after another. He raised his voice and shouted at the walls. "It's your treasure, you hear? We are not taking any of it!"

Rand stared angrily at Mat. "Do you want him coming after us? Or are you going to wait here stuffing your pockets until he comes back with ten more like him?"

Mat just gestured to all the gold and jewels. Before he could say anything, though, Rand seized one of his arms and Perrin grabbed the other. They hustled him out of the room, Mat struggling and shouting about the treasure.

Before they had gone ten steps down the hall, the already dim light behind them began to fail. The torches in the treasure room were going out. Mat stopped shouting. They hastened their steps. The first torch outside the room winked out, then the next. By the time they reached the winding stairs there was no need to drag Mat any longer. They were all running, with the dark closing in behind them. Even the pitch-black of the stairs only made them hesitate an instant, then they sped upwards, shouting at the top of their lungs. Shouting to scare anything that might be waiting; shouting to remind themselves they were still alive.

They burst out into the hall above, sliding and falling on the dusty marble, scrambling out through the columns, to tumble down the stairs and land in a bruised heap in the street.

Rand untangled himself and picked Tam's sword up from the pavement, looking around uneasily. Less than half of the sun still showed above the rooftops. Shadows reached out like dark hands, made blacker by the remaining light, nearly filling the street. He shivered. The shadows looked like Mordeth, reaching.

"At least we're out of it." Mat got up from the bottom of the pile, dusting himself off in a shaky imitation of his usual manner. "And at least I—"

"Are we?" Perrin said.

Rand knew it was not his imagination this time. The back of his neck prickled. Something was watching them from the darkness in the columns. He spun around, staring at the buildings across the way. He could feel eyes on him from there, too. His grip tightened on his sword hilt, though he wondered what good it would be. Watching eyes seemed to be everywhere. The others looked around warily; he knew they could feel it, too.

"We stay in the middle of the street," he said hoarsely. They met his eyes; they looked as frightened as he felt. He swallowed hard. "We stay in the middle of the street, keep out of shadows as much as we can, and walk fast."

"Walk very fast," Mat agreed fervently.

The watchers followed them. Or else there were lots of watchers, lots of eyes staring out of almost every building. Rand could not see anything move, hard as he tried, but he could feel the eyes, eager, hungry. He did not know which would be worse. Thousands of eyes, or just a few, following them.

In the stretches where the sun still reached them, they slowed, just a little, squinting nervously into the darkness that always seemed to lay ahead. None of them was eager to enter the shadows; no one was really sure something might not be waiting. The watchers' anticipation was a palpable thing whenever shadows stretched across the street, barring their way. They ran through those dark places shouting. Rand thought he could hear dry, rustling laughter.

At last, with twilight falling, they came in sight of the white stone building they had left what seemed like days ago. Suddenly the watching eyes departed. Between one step and the next, they vanished in a blink. Without a word Rand broke into a trot, followed by his friends, then a full run that only ended when they hared through the doorway and collapsed, panting.

A small fire burned in the middle of the tile floor, the smoke vanishing through a hole in the ceiling in a way that reminded Rand unpleasantly of Mordeth. Everyone except Lan was there, gathered around the flames, and their reactions varied considerably. Egwene, warming her hands at the fire, gave a start as the three burst into the room, clutching her hands to her throat; when she saw who it was, a relieved sigh spoiled her attempt at a withering look. Thom merely muttered something around his pipestem, but Rand caught the word "fools" before the gleeman went back to poking the flames with a stick.

"You wool-headed witlings!" the Wisdom snapped. She bristled from head to foot; her eyes glittered, and bright spots of red burned on her cheeks. "Why under the Light did you run off like that? Are you all right? Have you no sense at all? Lan is out looking for you now, and you'll be luckier than you deserve if he does not pound some sense into the lot of you when he gets back."

The Aes Sedai's face betrayed no agitation at all, but her hands had loosed a white-knuckled grip on her dress at the sight of them. Whatever Nynaeve had given her must have helped, for she was on her feet. "You should not have done what you did," she said in a voice as clear and serene as a Waterwood pond. "We will speak of it later. Something happened out there, or you would not be falling all over one another like this. Tell me."

"You said it was safe," Mat complained, scrambling to his feet. "You said Aridhol was an ally of Manetheren, and Trollocs wouldn't come into the city, and—"

Moiraine stepped forward so suddenly that Mat cut off with his mouth open, and Rand and Perrin paused in getting up, halfway crouched or on their knees. "Trollocs? Did you see Trollocs inside the walls?"

Rand swallowed. "Not Trollocs," he said, and all three began talking excitedly, all at the same time.

Everyone began in a different place. Mat started with finding the treasure, sounding almost as if he had done it alone, while Perrin began explaining why they had gone off in the first place without telling anyone. Rand jumped right to what he thought was important, meeting the stranger among the columns. But they were all so excited that nobody told anything in the order it happened; whenever one of them thought of something, he blurted it out with no regard for what came before or after, or for who was saying what. The watchers. They all babbled about the watchers.

It made the whole tale close to incoherent, but their fear came through. Egwene began casting uneasy glances at the empty windows fronting the street. Out there the last remnants of twilight were fading; the fire seemed very small and dim. Thom took his pipe from between his teeth and listened with his head cocked, frowning. Moiraine's eyes showed concern, but not an undue amount. Until. . . .

Suddenly the Aes Sedai hissed, and grabbed Rand's elbow in a tight grip. "Mordeth! Are you sure of that name? Be very sure, all of you. Mordeth?"

They murmured a chorused "Yes," taken aback by the Aes Sedai's intensity.

"Did he touch you?" she asked them all. "Did he give you anything, or did you do anything for him? I must know."

"No," Rand said. "None of us. None of those things."

Perrin nodded agreement, and added, "All he did was try to kill us. Isn't that enough? He swelled up until he filled half the room, shouted that we were all dead men, then vanished." He moved his hand to demonstrate. "Like smoke." Egwene gave a squeak.

Mat twisted away petulantly. "Safe, you said! All that talk about Trollocs not coming here. What were we supposed to think?"

"Apparently you did not think at all," she said, coolly composed once more. "Anyone who thinks would be wary of a place that Trollocs are afraid to enter."

"Mat's doing," Nynaeve said, certainty in her voice. "He's always talking some mischief or other, and the others lose the little wits they were born with when they're around him."

Moiraine nodded briefly, but her eyes remained on Rand and his two friends. "Late in the Trolloc Wars, an army camped within these ruins—Trollocs, Darkfriends, Myrddraal, Dreadlords, thousands in all. When they did not come out, scouts were sent inside the walls. The scouts found weapons, bits of armor, and blood splattered everywhere. And messages scratched on walls in the Trolloc tongue, calling on the Dark One to aid them in their last hour. Men who came later found no trace of the blood or the messages. They had been scoured away. Halfmen and Trollocs remember still. That is what keeps them outside this place."

"And this is where you picked for us to hide?" Rand said in disbelief. "We'd be safer out there trying to outrun them."

"If you had not gone running off," Moiraine said patiently, "you would know that I set wards around this building. A Myrddraal would not even know these wards were there, for it is a different kind of evil they are meant to stop, but what resides in Shadar Logoth will not cross them, or even come too near. In the morning it will be safe for us to go; these things cannot stand the light of the sun. They will be hiding deep in the earth."

"Shadar Logoth?" Egwene said uncertainly. "I thought you said this city was called Aridhol."

"Once it was called Aridhol," Moiraine replied, "and

was one of the Ten Nations, the lands that made the Second Covenant, the lands that stood against the Dark One from the first days after the Breaking of the World. In the days when Thorin al'Toren al Ban was King of Manetheren, the King of Aridhol was Balwen Mayel, Balwen Ironhand. In a twilight of despair during the Trolloc Wars, when it seemed the Father of Lies must surely conquer, the man called Mordeth came to Balwen's court."

"The same man?" Rand exclaimed, and Mat said, "It couldn't be!" A glance from Moiraine silenced them. Stillness filled the room except for the Aes Sedai's voice.

"Before Mordeth had been long in the city he had Balwen's ear, and soon he was second only to the King. Mordeth whispered poison in Balwen's ear, and Aridhol began to change. Aridhol drew in on itself, hardened. It was said that some would rather see Trollocs come than the men of Aridhol. The victory of the Light is all. That was the battlecry Mordeth gave them, and the men of Aridhol shouted it while their deeds abandoned the Light.

"The story is too long to tell in full, and too grim, and only fragments are known, even in Tar Valon. How Thorin's son, Caar, came to win Aridhol back to the Second Covenant, and Balwen sat his throne, a withered shell with the light of madness in his eyes, laughing while Mordeth smiled at his side and ordered the deaths of Caar and the embassy as Friends of the Dark. How Prince Caar came to be called Caar One-Hand. How he escaped the dungeons of Aridhol and fled alone to the Borderlands with Mordeth's unnatural assassins at his heels. How there he met Rhea, who did not know who he was, and married her, and set the skein in the Pattern that led to his death at her hands, and hers by her own hand before his tomb, and the fall of Aleth-Loriel. How the armies of Manetheren came to avenge Caar and found the gates of Aridhol torn down, no living thing inside the walls, but something worse than death. No enemy had come to Aridhol but Aridhol. Suspicion and hate had given birth to something that fed on that which created it, something locked in the bedrock on which the city stood. Mashadar waits still, hungering. Men spoke of Aridhol no more. They named it Shadar Logoth, the Place Where the Shadow Waits, or more simply, Shadow's Waiting.

"Mordeth alone was not consumed by Mashadar, but he

was snared by it, and he, too, has waited within these walls through the long centuries. Others have seen him. Some he has influenced through gifts that twist the mind and taint the spirit, the taint waxing and waning until it rules . . . or kills. If ever he convinces someone to accompany him to the walls, to the boundary of Mashadar's power, he will be able to consume the soul of that person. Mordeth will leave, wearing the body of the one he worse than killed, to wreak his evil on the world again."

"The treasure," Perrin mumbled when she stopped. "He wanted us to help carry the treasure to his horses." His face was haggard. "I'll bet they were supposed to be outside the city somewhere." Rand shivered.

"But we are safe, now, aren't we?" Mat asked. "He didn't give us anything, and he didn't touch us. We're safe, aren't we, with the wards you set?"

"We are safe," Moiraine agreed. "He cannot cross the ward lines, nor can any other denizen of this place. And they must hide from the sunlight, so we can leave safely once it is day. Now, try to sleep. The wards will protect us until Lan returns."

"He has been gone a long time." Nynaeve looked worriedly at the night outside. Full dark had fallen, as black as pitch.

"Lan will be well," Moiraine said soothingly, and spread her blankets beside the fire while she spoke. "He was pledged to fight the Dark One before he left the cradle, a sword placed in his infant hands. Besides, I would know the minute of his death and the way of it, just as he would know mine. Rest, Nynaeve. All will be well." But as she was rolling herself into her blankets, she paused, staring at the street as if she, too, would have liked to know what kept the Warder.

Rand's arms and legs felt like lead and his eyes wanted to slide shut on their own, yet sleep did not come quickly, and once it did, he dreamed, muttering and kicking off his blankets. When he woke, it was suddenly, and he looked around for a moment before he remembered where he was.

The moon was up, the last thin sliver before the new moon, its faint light defeated by the night. Everyone else was still asleep, though not all soundly. Egwene and his two friends twisted and murmured inaudibly. Thom's snores, soft for once, were broken from time to time by half-formed words. There was still no sign of Lan.

Suddenly he felt as if the wards were no protection at all.

Anything at all could be out there in the dark. Telling himself he was being foolish, he added wood to the last coals of the fire. The blaze was too small to give much warmth, but it gave more light.

He had no idea what had awakened him from his unpleasant dream. He had been a little boy again, carrying Tam's sword and with a cradle strapped to his back, running through empty streets, pursued by Mordeth, who shouted that he only wanted his hand. And there had been an old man who watched them and cackled with mad laughter the whole time.

He gathered his blankets and lay back, staring at the ceiling. He wanted very much to sleep, even if he had more dreams like the last one, but he could not make his eyes close.

Suddenly the Warder trotted silently out of the darkness into the room. Moiraine came awake and sat up as if he had rung a bell. Lan opened his hand; three small objects fell to the tiles in front of her with the clink of iron. Three blood-red badges in the shape of horned skulls.

"There are Trollocs inside the walls," Lan said. "They will be here in little more than an hour. And the Dha'vol are the worst of them." He began waking the others.

Moiraine smoothly began folding her blankets. "How many? Do they know we are here?" She sounded as if there were no urgency at all.

"I don't think they do," Lan replied. "There are well over a hundred, frightened enough to kill anything that moves, including one another. The Halfmen are having to drive them—four just to handle one fist—and even the Myrddraal seem to want nothing more than to pass through the city and out as quickly as possible. They are not going out of their way to search, and they're so slipshod that if they were not heading nearly straight for us I would say we had nothing to worry about." He hesitated.

"There is something else?"

"Only this," Lan said slowly. "The Myrddraal forced the Trollocs into the city. What forced the Myrddraal?"

Everyone had been listening in silence. Now Thom cursed under his breath, and Egwene breathed a question. "The Dark One?"

"Don't be a fool, girl," Nynaeve snapped. "The Dark One is bound in Shayol Ghul by the Creator."

"For the time being, at least," Moiraine agreed. "No, the Father of Lies is not out there, but we must leave in any case."

Nynaeve eyed her narrowly. "Leave the protection of the wards, and cross Shadar Logoth in the night."

"Or stay here and face the Trollocs," Moiraine said. "To hold them off here would require the One Power. It would destroy the wards and attract the very thing the wards are meant to protect against. Besides, as well build a signal fire atop one of those towers for every Halfman within twenty miles. To leave is not what I would choose to do, but we are the hare, and it is the hounds who dictate the chase."

"What if there are more outside the walls?" Mat asked. "What are we going to do?"

"We will use my original plan," Moiraine said. Lan looked at her. She held up a hand and added, "Which I was too tired to carry out before. But I am rested, now, thanks to the Wisdom. We will make for the river. There, with our backs guarded by the water, I can raise a smaller ward that will hold the Trollocs and Halfmen back until we can make rafts and cross over. Or better yet, we may even be able to hail a trader's boat coming down from Saldaea."

The faces of the Emond's Fielders looked blank. Lan noticed.

"Trollocs and Myrddraal loathe deep water. Trollocs are terrified of it. Neither can swim. A Halfman will not wade anything more than waist deep, especially if it's moving. Trollocs won't do even that if they can find any way to avoid it."

"So once we get across the river we're safe," Rand said, and the Warder nodded.

"The Myrddraal will find it almost as hard to make the Trollocs build rafts as it was to drive them into Shadar Logoth, and if they try to make them cross the Arinelle that way, half will run away and the rest probably drown."

"Get to your horses," Moiraine said. "We are not across the river yet."

CHAPTER
20

Dust on the Wind

As they left the white stone building on their nervously shifting horses, the icy wind came in gusts, moaning across the rooftops, whipping cloaks like banners, driving thin clouds across the thin sliver of the moon. With a quiet command to stay close, Lan led off down the street. The horses danced and tugged at the reins, eager to be away.

Rand looked up warily at the buildings they passed, looming now in the night with their empty windows like eye sockets. Shadows seemed to move. Occasionally there was a clatter—rubble toppled by the wind. *At least the eyes are gone.* His relief was momentary. Why *are they gone?*

Thom and the Emond's Fielders made a cluster with him, all keeping close enough to touch one another. Egwene's shoulders were hunched, as if she were trying to ease Bela's hooves to the pavement. Rand did not even want to breathe. Sound might attract attention.

Abruptly he realized that a distance had opened ahead of them, separating them from the Warder and the Aes Sedai. The two were indistinct shapes a good thirty paces ahead.

"We're falling behind," he murmured, and booted Cloud to a quicker step. A thin tendril of silver-gray fog drifted low across the street ahead of him.

"Stop!" It was a strangled shout from Moiraine, sharp and urgent, but pitched not to carry far.

Uncertain, he pulled up short. The splinter of fog lay completely across the street now, slowly fattening as if more were oozing out of the buildings on either side of the street. It was as thick as a man's arm now. Cloud whickered and tried to back further away as Egwene and Thom and the others came up on him. Their horses, too, tossed their heads and bridled against coming too near the fog.

Lan and Moiraine rode slowly toward the fog, grown to as big around as a leg, stopping on the other side, well back. The Aes Sedai studied the branch of mist that separated them. Rand shrugged at a sudden itch of fear between his shoulder blades. A faint light accompanied the fog, growing as the foggy tentacle became fatter, but still only a little more than the moonlight. The horses shifted uneasily, even Aldieb and Mandarb.

"What is it?" Nynaeve asked.

"The evil of Shadar Logoth," Moiraine replied. "Mashadar. Unseeing, unthinking, moving through the city as aimlessly as a worm burrows through the earth. If it touches you, you will die." Rand and the others let their horses dance a few quick steps back, but not too far. As much as Rand would have given to be free of the Aes Sedai, she was as safe as home compared to what lay around them.

"Then how do we join you?" Egwene said. "Can you kill it . . . clear a way?"

Moiraine's laugh was bitter and short. "Mashadar is vast, girl, as vast as Shadar Logoth itself. The whole White Tower could not kill it. If I damaged it enough to let you pass, drawing that much of the One Power would pull the Halfmen like a trumpet call. And Mashadar would rush in to heal whatever harm I did, rush in and perhaps catch us in its net."

Rand exchanged looks with Egwene, then asked her question again. Moiraine sighed before answering.

"I do not like it, but what must be done, must be done. This thing will not be above ground everywhere. Other streets will be clear. See that star?" She twisted in her saddle to point to a red star low in the eastern sky. "Keep on toward that star, and it will bring you to the river. Whatever happens, keep moving toward the river. Go as quickly as you can, but above all make no noise. There are still the Trollocs, remember. And four Halfmen."

"But how will we find you again?" Egwene protested.

"I will find you," Moiraine said. "Be assured, I can find you. Now be off. This thing is utterly mindless, but it can sense food." Indeed, ropes of silver-gray had lifted from the larger body. They drifted, wavering, like the tentacles of a hundredarms on the bottom of a Waterwood pond.

When Rand looked up from the thick trunk of opaque mist, the Warder and the Aes Sedai were gone. He licked his lips and met his companions' eyes. They were as nervous as he was. And something worse: they all seemed to be waiting for someone else to move first. Night and ruins surrounded them. The Fades were out there, somewhere, and the Trollocs, maybe around the next corner. The tentacles of fog drifted nearer, halfway to them now, and no longer wavering. They had chosen their intended prey. Suddenly he missed Moiraine very much.

Everyone was still staring, wondering which way to go. He turned Cloud, and the gray broke into a half trot, tugging against the reins to go faster. As if moving first had made him the leader, everyone followed.

With Moiraine gone, there was no one to protect them should Mordeth appear. And the Trollocs. And. . . . Rand forced himself to stop thinking. He would follow the red star. He could hold onto that thought.

Three times they had to backtrack from a street blocked from side to side by a hill of stone and brick the horses could never have crossed. Rand could hear the others breathing, short and sharp, just shy of panic. He gritted his teeth to stop his own panting. *You have to at least make them think you're not afraid. You're doing a good job, wool-head! You'll get everybody out safely.*

They rounded the next corner. A wall of fog bathed the broken pavement with a light as bright as a full moon. Streamers as thick as their horses broke off toward them. Nobody waited. Wheeling, they galloped away in a tight knot with no heed for the clatter of hooves they raised.

Two Trollocs stepped into the street before them, not ten spans away.

For an instant the humans and the Trollocs just stared at one another, each more surprised than the other. Another pair of Trollocs appeared, and another, and another, colliding with the ones in front, folding into a shocked mass at the sight of the humans. Only for an instant did they remain frozen, though. Guttural howls echoed from the buildings, and the Trollocs bounded forward. The humans scattered like quail.

Rand's gray reached full gallop in three strides. "This way!" he shouted, but he heard the same cry from five throats. A hasty glance over his shoulder showed him his companions disappearing in as many directions, Trollocs pursuing them all.

Three Trollocs ran at his own heels, catchpoles waving in the air. His skin crawled as he realized they were matching Cloud stride for stride. He dropped low on Cloud's neck and urged the gray on, chased by thick cries.

The street narrowed ahead, broken-topped buildings leaning out drunkenly. Slowly the empty windows filled with a silvery glow, a dense mist bulging outward. Mashadar.

Rand risked a glance over his shoulder. The Trollocs still ran less than fifty paces back; the light from the fog was enough to see them clearly. A Fade rode behind them now, and they seemed to flee the Halfman as much as to pursue Rand. Ahead of Rand, half a dozen gray tendrils wavered from the windows, a dozen, feeling the air. Cloud tossed his head and screamed, but Rand dug his heels in brutally, and the horse lunged forward wildly.

The tendrils stiffened as Rand galloped between them, but he crouched low on Cloud's back and refused to look at them. The way beyond was clear. *If one of them touches me. . . . Light!* He booted Cloud harder, and the horse leaped forward into the welcome shadows. With Cloud still running, he looked back as soon as the glow of Mashadar began to lessen.

The waving gray tentacles of Mashadar blocked half the street, and the Trollocs were balking, but the Fade snatched a whip from its saddlebow, cracking it over the heads of the Trollocs with a sound like a lightning bolt, popping sparks in the air. Crouching, the Trollocs lurched after Rand. The Halfman hesitated, black cowl studying Mashadar's reaching arms, before it, too, spurred forward.

The thickening tentacles of fog swung uncertainly for a moment, then struck like vipers. At least two latched to each Trolloc, bathing them in gray light; muzzled heads went back to scream, but fog rolled over open mouths, and in, eating the howls. Four leg-thick tentacles whipped around the Fade, and the Halfman and its black horse twitched as if dancing, till the cowl fell back, baring that pale, eyeless face. The Fade shrieked.

There was no sound from that cry, any more than from the Trollocs, but something came through, a piercing whine just beyond hearing, like all the hornets in the world, digging into Rand's ears with all the fear that could exist. Cloud convulsed, as if he, too, heard, and ran harder than ever. Rand hung on, panting, his throat as dry as sand.

After a time he realized he could no longer hear the silent shriek of the Fade dying, and suddenly the clatter of his gallop seemed as loud as shouts. He reined Cloud hard, stopping beside a jagged wall, right where two streets met. A nameless monument reared in the darkness before him.

Slumped in the saddle, he listened, but there was nothing to hear except the blood pounding in his ears. Cold sweat beaded on his face, and he shivered as the wind flailed his cloak.

Finally he straightened. Stars spangled the sky where the clouds did not hide them, but the red star low in the east was easy to mark. *Is anybody else alive to see it?* Were they free, or in the Trollocs' hands? *Egwene, Light blind me, why didn't you follow me?* If they were alive and free, they would be following that star. If not. . . . The ruins were vast; he could search for days without finding anyone, if he could keep away from the Trollocs. And the Fades, and Mordeth, and Mashadar. Reluctantly he decided to make for the river.

He gathered the reins. On the crossing street, one stone fell against another with a sharp click. He froze, not even breathing. He was hidden in the shadows, one step from the corner. Frantically he thought of backing up. What was behind him? What would make a noise and give him away? He could not remember, and he was afraid to take his eyes from the corner of the building.

Darkness bulked at that corner, with the longer darkness of a shaft sticking out of it. Catchpole! Even as the thought flashed into Rand's head, he dug his heels into Cloud's ribs and his sword flew from the scabbard; a wordless shout accompanied his charge, and he swung the sword with all of his might. Only a desperate effort stopped the blade short. With a yelp Mat tumbled back, half falling off his horse and nearly dropping his bow.

Rand drew a deep breath and lowered his sword. His arm shook. "Have you seen anybody else?" he managed.

Mat swallowed hard before pulling himself awkwardly back into his saddle. "I . . . I . . . . Just Trollocs." He put a hand to his throat, and licked his lips. "Just Trollocs. You?"

Rand shook his head. "They must be trying to reach the river. We better do the same." Mat nodded silently, still feeling his throat, and they started toward the red star.

Before they had covered a hundred spans the keening cry of a Trolloc horn rose behind them in the depths of the city. Another answered, from outside the walls.

Rand shivered, but he kept to his slow pace, watching the darkest places and avoiding them when he could. After one jerk at his reins as if he might gallop off, Mat did the same. Neither horn sounded again, and it was in silence that they came to an opening in the vine-shrouded wall where a gate had once been. Only the towers remained, standing broken-topped against the black sky.

Mat hesitated at the gateway, but Rand said softly, "Is it any safer in here than out there?" He did not slow the gray, and after a moment Mat followed him out of Shadar Logoth, trying to look every way at once. Rand let out a slow breath; his mouth was dry. *We're going to make it. Light, we're going to make it!*

The walls vanished behind, swallowed by the night and the forest. Listening for the slightest sound, Rand kept the red star dead ahead.

Suddenly Thom galloped by from behind, slowing only long enough to shout, "Ride, you fools!" A moment later hunting cries and crashes in the brush behind him announced the presence of Trollocs on his trail.

Rand dug in his heels, and Cloud sprang after the glee-man's gelding. *What happens when we get to the river without Moiraine? Light, Egwene!*

Perrin sat his horse in the shadows, watching the open gate-way, some little distance off yet, and absently ran his thumb along the blade of his axe. It seemed to be a clear way out of the ruined city, but he had sat there for five minutes study-ing it. The wind tossed his shaggy curls and tried to carry his cloak away, but he pulled the cloak back around him without really noticing what he was doing.

He knew that Mat, and almost everyone else in Emond's

Field, considered him slow of thought. It was partly because he was big and usually moved carefully—he had always been afraid he might accidentally break something or hurt somebody, since he was so much bigger than the boys he grew up with—but he really did prefer to think things all the way through if he could. Quick thinking, careless thinking, had put Mat into hot water one time after another, and Mat's quick thinking usually managed to get Rand, or him, or both, in the cookpot alongside Mat, too.

His throat tightened. *Light, don't think about being in a cookpot.* He tried to order his thoughts again. Careful thought was the way.

There had been some sort of square in front of the gate once, with a huge fountain in its middle. Part of the fountain was still there, a cluster of broken statues standing in a big, round basin, and so was the open space around it. To reach the gate he would have to ride nearly a hundred spans with only the night to shield him from searching eyes. That was not a pleasant thought, either. He remembered those unseen watchers too well.

He considered the horns he had heard in the city a little while earlier. He had almost turned back, thinking some of the others might have been taken, before realizing that he could not do anything alone if they had been captured. *Not against—what did Lan say—a hundred Trollocs and four Fades. Moiraine Sedai said get to the river.*

He went back to consideration of the gate. Careful thought had not given him much, but he had made his decision. He rode out of the deeper shadow into the lesser darkness.

As he did, another horse appeared from the far side of the square and stopped. He stopped, too, and felt for his axe; it gave him no great sense of comfort. If that dark shape was a Fade. . . .

"Rand?" came a soft, hesitant call.

He let out a long, relieved breath. "It's Perrin, Egwene," he called back, just as softly. It still sounded too loud in the darkness.

The horses came together near the fountain.

"Have you seen anybody else?" they both asked at the same time, and both answered by shaking their heads.

"They'll be all right," Egwene muttered, patting Bela's neck. "Won't they?"

"Moiraine Sedai and Lan will look after them," Perrin replied. "They will look after all of us once we get to the river." He hoped it was so.

He felt a great relief once they were beyond the gate, even if there *were* Trollocs in the forest. Or Fades. He stopped that line of thought. The bare branches were not enough to keep him from guiding on the red star, and they were beyond Mordeth's reach now. That one had frightened him worse than the Trollocs ever had.

Soon they would reach the river and meet Moiraine, and she would put them beyond the Trollocs' reach as well. He believed it because he needed to believe. The wind scraped branches together and rustled the leaves and needles on the evergreens. A nighthawk's lonely cry drifted in the dark, and he and Egwene moved their horses closer together as though they were huddling for warmth. They were very much alone.

A Trolloc horn sounded somewhere behind them, quick, wailing blasts, urging the hunters to hurry, hurry. Then thick, half-human howls rose on their trail, spurred on by the horn. Howls that grew sharper as they caught the human scent.

Perrin put his horse to a gallop, shouting, "Come on!" Egwene came, both of them booting their horses, heedless of noise, heedless of the branches that slapped at them.

As they raced through the trees, guided as much by instinct as by the dim moonlight, Bela fell behind. Perrin looked back. Egwene kicked the mare and flailed her with the reins, but it was doing no good. By their sounds, the Trollocs were coming closer. He drew in enough not to leave her behind.

"Hurry!" he shouted. He could make out the Trollocs now, huge dark shapes bounding through the trees, bellowing and snarling to chill the blood. He gripped the haft of his axe, hanging at his belt, until his knuckles hurt. "Hurry, Egwene! Hurry!"

Suddenly his horse screamed, and he was falling, tumbling out of the saddle as the horse dropped away beneath him. He flung out his hands to brace himself and splashed headfirst into icy water. He had ridden right off the edge of a sheer bluff into the Arinelle.

The shock of freezing water ripped a gasp from him, and he swallowed more than a little before he managed to fight his way to the surface. He felt more than heard another splash, and thought that Egwene must have come right after him. Panting and blowing, he treaded water. It was not easy to keep afloat; his coat and cloak were already sodden, and his boots had filled. He looked around for Egwene, but saw only the glint of moonlight on the black water, ruffled by the wind.

"Egwene? Egwene!"

A spear flashed right in front of his eyes and threw water in his face. Others splashed into the river around him, too. Guttural voices raised in argument on the riverbank, and the Trolloc spears stopped coming, but he gave up on calling for the time being.

The current washed him downriver, but the thick shouts and snarls followed along the bank, keeping pace. Undoing his cloak, he let the river take it. A little less weight to drag him down. Doggedly, he set out swimming for the far bank. There were no Trollocs there. He hoped.

He swam the way they did back home, in the ponds in the Waterwood, stroking with both hands, kicking with both feet, keeping his head out of the water. At least, he tried to keep his head out of the water; it was not easy. Even without the cloak, his coat and boots each seemed to weigh as much as he did. And the axe dragged at his waist, threatening to roll him over if it did not pull him under. He thought about letting the river have that, too; he thought about it more than once. It would be easy, much easier than struggling out of his boots, for instance. But every time he thought of it, he thought of crawling out on the far bank to find Trollocs waiting. The axe would not do him much good against half a dozen Trollocs—or even against one, maybe—but it was better than his bare hands.

After a while he was not even certain he would be able to lift the axe if Trollocs were there. His arms and legs became leaden; it was an effort to move them, and his face no longer came as far out of the river with each stroke. He coughed from water that went up his nose. *A day at the forge has no odds on this,* he thought wearily, and just then his kicking foot struck something. It was not until he kicked it again that he realized what it was. The bottom. He was in the shallows. He was across the river.

Sucking air through his mouth, he got to his feet, splashing about as his legs almost gave way. He fumbled his axe out of its loop as he floundered ashore, shivering in the wind. He did not see any Trollocs. He did not see Egwene, either. Just a few scattered trees along the riverbank, and a moonlight ribbon on the water.

When he had his breath again, he called their names again and again. Faint shouts from the far side answered him; even at that distance he could make out the harsh voices of Trollocs. His friends did not answer, though.

The wind surged, its moan drowning out the Trollocs, and he shivered. It was not cold enough to freeze the water soaking his clothes, but it felt as if it was; it sliced to the bone with an icy blade. Hugging himself was only a gesture that did not stop the shivering. Alone, he climbed tiredly up the riverbank to find shelter against the wind.

Rand patted Cloud's neck, soothing the gray with whispers. The horse tossed his head and danced on quick feet. The Trollocs had been left behind—or so it seemed—but Cloud had the smell of them thick in his nostrils. Mat rode with an arrow nocked, watching for surprises out of the night, while Rand and Thom peered through the branches, searching for the red star that was their guide. Keeping it in view had been easy enough, even with all the branches overhead, so long as they were riding straight toward it. But then more Trollocs had appeared, ahead, and they went galloping off to the side with both packs howling after them. The Trollocs could keep up with a horse, but only for a hundred paces or so, and finally they left the pursuit and the howls behind. But with all the twists and turns, they had lost the guiding star.

"I still say it's over there," Mat said, gesturing off to his right. "We were going north at the end, and that means east is that way."

"There it is," Thom said abruptly. He pointed through the tangled branches to their left, straight at the red star. Mat mumbled something under his breath.

Out of the corner of his eye Rand caught the movement as a Trolloc leaped out from behind a tree without a sound, swinging its catchpole. Rand dug his heels in, and the gray bounded forward just as two more plunged from the shadows after the first. A noose brushed the back of Rand's neck, sending a shiver down his spine.

An arrow took one of the bestial faces in the eye, then Mat swung in beside him as their horses pounded through the trees. They were running toward the river, he realized, but he was not sure it was going to do any good. The Trollocs sped after them, almost close enough to reach out and grab the streaming tails of their horses. Half a step gained, and the catchpoles could drag them both out of their saddles.

He leaned low on the gray's neck to put that much more distance between his own neck and the nooses. Mat's face was nearly buried in his horse's mane. But Rand wondered where Thom was. Had the gleeman decided he was better off on his own, since all three Trollocs had fastened on the boys?

Suddenly Thom's gelding galloped out of the night, hard behind the Trollocs. The Trollocs had only time enough to look back in surprise before the gleeman's hands whipped back and then forward. Moonlight flashed off steel. One Trolloc tumbled forward, rolling over and over before landing in a heap, while a second dropped to its knees with a scream, clawing at its back with both hands. The third snarled, baring a muzzleful of sharp teeth, but as its companions toppled it whirled away into the darkness. Thom's hand made the whip-like motion again, and the Trolloc shrieked, but the shrieks faded into the distance as it ran.

Rand and Mat pulled up and stared at the gleeman.

"My second-best knives," Thom muttered, but he made no effort to get down and retrieve them. "That one will bring others. I hope the river isn't too far. I hope. . . ." Instead of saying what else he hoped, he shook his head and set off at a quick canter. Rand and Mat fell in behind him.

Soon they reached a low bank where trees grew right to the edge of the night-black water, its moon-streaked surface riffled by the wind. Rand could not see the far side at all. He did not like the idea of crossing on a raft in the dark, but he liked the idea of staying on this side even less. *I'll swim if I have to.*

Somewhere away from the river a Trolloc horn brayed, sharp, quick, and urgent in the darkness. It was the first sound from the horns since they had left the ruins. Rand wondered if it meant some of the others had been captured.

"No use staying here all night," Thom said. "Pick a direction. Upriver, or down?"

"But Moiraine and the others could be anywhere," Mat protested. "Any way we choose could just take us further away."

"So it could." Clucking to his gelding, Thom turned downriver, heading along the bank. "So it could." Rand looked at Mat, who shrugged, and they turned after him.

For a time nothing changed. The bank was higher in some places, lower in others, the trees grew thicker, or thinned out in small clearings, but the night and the river and the wind were all the same, cold and black. And no Trollocs. That was one change Rand was glad to forgo.

Then he saw a light ahead, just a single point. As they drew closer he could see that the light was well above the river, as if it were in a tree. Thom quickened the pace and began to hum under his breath.

Finally they could make out the source of the light, a lantern hoisted atop one of the masts of a large trader's boat, tied up for the night beside a small clearing in the trees. The boat, a good eighty feet long, shifted slightly with the current, tugging against the mooring ropes tied to trees. The rigging hummed and creaked in the wind. The lantern doubled the moonlight on the deck, but no one was in sight.

"Now that," Thom said as he dismounted, "is better than an Aes Sedai's raft, isn't it?" He stood with his hands on his hips, and even in the dark his smugness was apparent. "It doesn't look as if this vessel is made to carry horses, but considering the danger he's in, which we are going to warn him of, the captain may be reasonable. Just let me do all the talking. And bring your blankets and saddlebags, just in case."

Rand climbed down and began untying the things behind his saddle. "You don't mean to leave without the others, do you?"

Thom had no chance to say what he meant to do. Into the clearing burst two Trollocs, howling and waving their catchpoles, with four more right behind. The horses reared

and whinnied. Shouts in the distance said more Trollocs
were on the way.

"Onto the boat!" Thom shouted. "Quick! Leave all that!
Run!" Suiting his own words, he ran for the boat, patches
flapping and instrument cases on his back banging together.
"You on the boat!" he shouted. "Wake up, you fools! Trollocs!"

Rand jerked his blanketroll and saddlebags free of the
last thong and was right on the gleeman's heels. Tossing
his burdens over the rail, he vaulted after them. He just had
time to see a man curled up on the deck, beginning to sit
up as if he had only that moment awakened, when his feet
came down right on top of the fellow. The man grunted
loudly, Rand stumbled, and a hooked catchpole slammed
into the railing just where he had come over. Shouts rose all
over the boat, and feet pounded along the deck.

Hairy hands caught the railing beside the catchpole, and
a goat-horned head lifted above it. Off balance, stumbling,
Rand still managed to draw his sword and swing. With a
scream the Trolloc dropped away.

Men ran everywhere on the boat, shouting, hacking
mooring lines with axes. The boat lurched and swung as if
eager to be off. Up in the bow three men struggled with a
Trolloc. Someone thrust over the side with a spear, though
Rand could not see what he was stabbing at. A bowstring
snapped, and snapped again. The man Rand had stepped on
scrabbled away from him on hands and knees, then flung up
his hands when he saw Rand looking at him.

"Spare me!" he cried. "Take whatever you want, take the
boat, take everything, but spare me!"

Suddenly something slammed across Rand's back,
smashing him to the deck. His sword skittered away from
his outstretched hand. Openmouthed, gasping for a breath
that would not come, he tried to reach the sword. His muscles responded with agonized slowness; he writhed like a
slug. The fellow who wanted to be spared gave one frightened, covetous look at the sword, then vanished into the
shadows.

Painfully Rand managed to look over his shoulder, and
knew his luck had run out. A wolf-muzzled Trolloc stood
balanced on the railing, staring down at him and holding the splintered end of the catchpole that had knocked

the wind out of him. Rand struggled to reach the sword,
to move, to get away, but his arms and legs moved jerk-
ily, and only half as he wanted. They wobbled and went in
odd directions. His chest felt as if it were strapped with iron
bands; silver spots swam in his eyes. Frantically he hunted
for some way to escape. Time seemed to slow as the Trolloc
raised the jagged pole as if to spear him with it. To Rand
the creature appeared to be moving as if in a dream. He
watched the thick arm go back; he could already feel the
broken haft ripping through his spine, feel the pain of it
tearing him open. He thought his lungs would burst. *I'm
going to die! Light help me, I'm going to . . . !* The Trolloc's
arm started forward, driving the splintered shaft, and Rand
found the breath for one yell. "No!"

Suddenly the ship lurched, and a boom swung out of the
shadows to catch the Trolloc across the chest with a crunch
of breaking bones, sweeping it over the side.

For a moment Rand lay panting and staring up at the
boom swinging back and forth above him. *That has to have
used up my luck,* he thought. *There can't be any more after
that.*

Shakily he got to his feet and picked up his sword, for
once holding it in both hands the way Lan had taught him,
but there was nothing left on which to use it. The gap of
black water between the boat and the bank was widening
quickly; the cries of the Trollocs were fading behind in the
night.

As he sheathed his sword and slumped against the railing, a stocky man in a coat that hung to his knees strode
up the deck to glare at him. Long hair that fell to his thick
shoulders and a beard that left his upper lip bare framed a
round face. Round but not soft. The boom swung out again,
and the bearded man spared part of his glare for that as he
caught it; it made a crisp *splat* against his broad palm.

"Gelb!" he bellowed. "Fortune! Where do you be, Gelb?"
He spoke so fast, with all the words running together, that
Rand could barely understand him. "You can no hide from
me on my own ship! Get Floran Gelb out here!"

A crewman appeared with a bull's-eye lantern, and two
more pushed a narrow-faced man into the circle of light it cast.
Rand recognized the fellow who had offered him the boat.
The man's eyes shifted from side to side, never meeting those

of the stocky man. The captain, Rand thought. A bruise was coming up on Gelb's forehead where one of Rand's boots had caught him.

"Were you no supposed to secure this boom, Gelb?" the captain asked with surprising calm, though just as fast as before.

Gelb looked truly surprised. "But I did. Tied it down tight. I admit I'm a little slow about things now and then, Captain Domon, but I get them done."

"So you be slow, do you? No so slow at sleeping. Sleeping when you should be standing watch. We could be murdered to a man, for all of you."

"No, Captain, no. It was him." Gelb pointed straight at Rand. "I was on guard, just like I was supposed to be, when he sneaked up and hit me with a club." He touched the bruise on his head, winced, and glared at Rand. "I fought him, but then the Trollocs came. He's in league with them, Captain. A Darkfriend. In league with the Trollocs."

"In league with my aged grandmother!" Captain Domon roared. "Did I no warn you the last time, Gelb? At Whitebridge, off you do go! Get out of my sight before I put you off now." Gelb darted out of the lantern light, and Domon stood opening and closing his hands while he stared at nothing. "These Trollocs do be following me. Why will they no leave me be? Why?"

Rand looked over the rail and was shocked to find the riverbank no longer in sight. Two men manned the long steering oar that stuck out over the stern, and there were six sweeps working to a side now, pulling the ship like a waterbug further out into the river.

"Captain," Rand said, "we have friends back there. If you go back and pick them up, I am sure they'll reward you."

The captain's round face swung toward Rand, and when Thom and Mat appeared he included them in his expressionless stare as well.

"Captain," Thom began with a bow, "allow me to—"

"You come below," Captain Domon said, "where I can see what manner of thing be hauled up on my deck. Come. Fortune desert me, somebody secure this horn-cursed boom!" As crewmen rushed to take the boom, he stumped off toward the stern of the boat. Rand and his two companions followed.

Captain Domon had a tidy cabin in the stern, reached by

climbing down a short ladder, where everything gave the impression of being in its proper place, right down to the coats and cloaks hanging from pegs on the back of the door. The cabin stretched the width of the ship, with a broad bed built against one side and a heavy table built out from the other. There was only one chair, with a high back and sturdy arms, and the captain took that himself, motioning the others to find places on various chests and benches that were the only other furnishings. A loud harrumph stopped Mat from sitting on the bed.

"Now," said the captain when they were all seated. "My name be Bayle Domon, captain and owner of the *Spray,* which be this ship. Now who be you, and where be you going out here in the middle of nowhere, and why should I no throw you over the side for the trouble you've brought me?"

Rand still had as much trouble as before in following Domon's rapid speech. When he worked out the last part of what the captain had said he blinked in surprise. *Throw us over the side?*

Mat hurriedly said, "We didn't mean to cause you any trouble. We're on our way to Caemlyn, and then to—"

"And then where the wind takes us," Thom interrupted smoothly. "That's how gleemen travel, like dust on the wind. I am a gleeman, you understand, Thom Merrilin by name." He shifted his cloak so the multihued patches stirred, as if the captain could have missed them. "These two country louts want to become my apprentices, though I am not yet sure I want them." Rand looked at Mat, who grinned.

"That be all very well, man," Captain Domon said placidly, "but it tells me nothing. Less. Fortune prick me, that place be on no road to Caemlyn from anywhere I ever heard tell of."

"Now that is a story," Thom said, and he straightaway began to unfold it.

According to Thom, he had been trapped by the winter snows in a mining town in the Mountains of Mist beyond Baerlon. While there he heard legends of a treasure dating from the Trolloc Wars, in the lost ruin of a city called Aridhol. Now it just so happened that he had earlier learned the location of Aridhol from a map given him many years ago by a dying friend in Illian whose life he had once saved, a man who expired breathing that the map would make

Thom rich, which Thom never believed until he heard the legends. When the snows melted enough, he set out with a few companions, including his two would-be apprentices, and after a journey of many hardships they actually found the ruined city. But it turned out the treasure had belonged to one of the Dreadlords themselves, and Trollocs had been sent to fetch it back to Shayol Ghul. Almost every danger they really had faced—Trollocs, Myrddraal, Draghkar, Mordeth, Mashadar—assailed them at one point or another of the story, though the way Thom told it they all seemed to be aimed at him personally, and to have been handled by him with the greatest adroitness. With much derring-do, mostly by Thom, they escaped, pursued by Trollocs, though they became separated in the night, until finally Thom and his two companions sought refuge on the last place left to them, Captain Domon's most welcome ship.

As the gleeman finished up, Rand realized his mouth had been hanging open for some time and shut it with a click. When he looked at Mat, his friend was staring wide-eyed at the gleeman.

Captain Domon drummed his fingers on the arm of his chair. "That be a tale many folk would no believe. Of course, I did see the Trollocs, did I no."

"Every word true," Thom said blandly, "from one who lived it."

"Happen you have some of this treasure with you?"

Thom spread his hands regretfully. "Alas, what little we managed to carry away was with our horses, which bolted when those last Trollocs appeared. All I have left are my flute and my harp, a few coppers, and the clothes on my back. But believe me, you want no part of that treasure. It has the taint of the Dark One. Best to leave it to the ruins and the Trollocs."

"So you've no money to pay your passage. I'd no let my own brother sail with me if he could no pay his passage, especially if he brought Trollocs behind him to hack up my railings and cut up my rigging. Why should I no let you swim back where you came from, and be rid of you?"

"You wouldn't just put us ashore?" Mat said. "Not with Trollocs there?"

"Who said anything about shore?" Domon replied dryly. He studied them a moment, then spread his hands flat on the table. "Bayle Domon be a reasonable man. I'd no toss you over the side if there be a way out of it. Now, I see one of your apprentices has a sword. I need a good sword, and fine fellow that I be, I'll let you have passage far as White-bridge for it."

Thom opened his mouth, and Rand spoke up quickly, "No!" Tam had not given it to him to trade away. He ran his hand down the hilt, feeling the bronze heron. As long as he had it, it was as if Tam were with him.

Domon shook his head. "Well, if it be no, it be no. But Bayle Domon no give free passage, not to his own mother."

Reluctantly Rand emptied his pocket. There was not much, a few coppers and the silver coin Moiraine had given him. He held it out to the captain. After a second, Mat sighed and did the same. Thom glared, but a smile replaced it so quickly that Rand was not sure it had been there at all.

Captain Domon deftly plucked the two fat silver coins out of the boys' hands and produced a small set of scales and a clinking bag from a brass-bound chest behind his chair. After careful weighing, he dropped the coins in the bag and returned them each some smaller silver and copper. Mostly copper. "As far as Whitebridge," he said, making a neat entry in a leather-bound ledger.

"That's a dear passage just to Whitebridge," Thom grumbled.

"Plus damages to my vessel," the captain answered placidly. He put the scales and the bag back in the chest and closed it in a satisfied way. "Plus a bit for bringing Trollocs down on me so I must run downriver in the night when there be shallows aplenty to pile me up."

"What about the others?" Rand asked. "Will you take them, too? They should have reached the river by now, or they soon will, and they'll see that lantern on your mast."

Captain Domon's eyebrows rose in surprise. "Happen you think we be standing still, man? Fortune prick me, we be three, four miles downriver from where you came aboard. Trollocs make those fellows put their backs into the oars—they know Trollocs better than they like—and the current helps, too. But it makes no nevermind. I'd no put in again tonight if my old grandmother was on the riverbank. I may no put in again at all until I reach Whitebridge. I've had my fill of Trollocs dogging my heels long before tonight, and I'll have no more can I help it."

Thom leaned forward interestedly. "You have had encounters with Trollocs before? Lately?"

Domon hesitated, eyeing Thom narrowly, but when he spoke he merely sounded disgusted. "I wintered in Saldaea, man. Not my choice, but the river froze early and the ice broke up late. They say you can see the Blight from the highest towers in Maradon, but I've no mind for that. I've been there before, and there always be talk of Trollocs attacking a farm or the like. This winter past, though, there be farms burning every night. Aye, and whole villages, too, betimes. They even came right up to the city walls. And if that no be bad enough, the people be all saying it meant the Dark One be stirring, that the Last Days be come." He gave a shiver, and scratched at his head as if the thought made his scalp itch. "I can no wait to get back where people think Trollocs be just tales, the stories I tell be traveler's lies."

Rand stopped listening. He stared at the opposite wall and thought about Egwene and the others. It hardly seemed right for him to be safe on the *Spray* while they were still back there in the night somewhere. The captain's cabin did not seem so comfortable as before.

He was surprised when Thom pulled him to his feet. The gleeman pushed Mat and him toward the ladder with apologies over his shoulder to Captain Domon for the country louts. Rand climbed up without a word.

Once they were on deck Thom looked around quickly to make sure he would not be overheard, then growled, "I could have gotten us passage for a few songs and stories if you two hadn't been so quick to show silver."

"I'm not so sure," Mat said. "He sounded serious about throwing us in the river to me."

Rand walked slowly to the rail and leaned against it, staring back up the night-shrouded river. He could not see anything but black, not even the riverbank. After a minute Thom put a hand on his shoulder, but he did not move.

"There isn't anything you can do, lad. Besides, they're likely safe with the . . . with Moiraine and Lan by this time. Can you think of any better than those two for getting the lot of them clear?"

"I tried to talk her out of coming," Rand said.

"You did what you could, lad. No one could ask more."

"I told her I'd take care of her. I should have tried harder." The creak of the sweeps and the hum of the rigging in the wind made a mournful tune. "I should have tried harder," he whispered.

CHAPTER
21

Listen to the Wind

S unrise creeping across the River Arinelle found its way into the hollow not far from the riverbank where Nynaeve sat with her back against the trunk of a young oak, breathing the deep breath of sleep. Her horse slept, too, head down and legs spraddled in the manner of horses. The reins were wrapped around her wrist. As sunlight fell on the horse's eyelids, the animal opened its eyes and raised its head, jerking the reins. Nynaeve came awake with a start.

For a moment she stared, wondering where she was, then stared around even more wildly when she remembered. But there were only the trees, and her horse, and a carpet of old, dry leaves across the bottom of the hollow. In the deepest dimness, some of last year's shadowshand mushrooms made rings on a fallen log.

"The Light preserve you, woman," she murmured, sagging back, "if you can't stay awake one night." She untied the reins and massaged her wrist as she stood. "You could have awakened in a Trolloc cookpot."

The dead leaves rustled as she climbed to the lip of the hollow and peeped over. No more than a handful of ash trees stood between her and the river. Their fissured bark and bare branches made them seem dead. Beyond, the wide blue-green water flowed by. Empty. Empty of anything. Scattered clumps of evergreens, willows and firs, dotted the far bank, and there seemed to be fewer trees altogether than on her side. If Moiraine or any of the younglings were over there, they were well hidden. Of course, there was no reason they had to have crossed, or tried to cross, in sight of

where she was. They could be anywhere ten miles upriver
or down. *If they're alive at all, after last night.*

Angry with herself for thinking of the possibility, she
slid back down into the hollow. Not even Winternight, or
the battle before Shadar Logoth, had prepared her for last
night, for that thing, Mashadar. All that frantic galloping,
wondering if anyone else was still alive, wondering when
she was going to come face-to-face with a Fade, or Trollocs. She had heard Trollocs growling and shouting in the
distance, and the quivering shrieks of Trolloc horns had
chilled her deeper than the wind ever could, but aside from
that first encounter in the ruins she saw Trollocs only once,
and that once she was outside. Ten or so of them seemed
to spring out of the ground not thirty spans in front of her,
bounding toward her on the instant, howling and shouting,
brandishing hooked catchpoles. Yet as she pulled her horse
around, they fell silent, lifting muzzles to sniff at the air.
She watched, too astonished to run, as they turned their
backs and vanished into the night. And that had been the
most frightening of all.

"They know the smell of who they want," she told her
horse, standing in the hollow, "and it is not me. The Aes
Sedai is right, it seems, the Shepherd of the Night swallow
her up."

Reaching a decision, she set out downriver, leading her
horse. She moved slowly, keeping a wary watch on the forest around her; just because the Trollocs had not wanted
her last night did not mean they would let her go if she
stumbled on them again. As much attention as she gave the
woods, she gave even more to the ground in front of her.
If the others had crossed below her during the night, she
should see some signs of them, signs she might miss from
horseback. She might even come on them all still on this
side. If she found neither, the river would take her to Whitebridge eventually, and there was a road from Whitebridge
to Caemlyn, and all the way to Tar Valon if need be.

The prospect was almost enough to daunt her. Before
this she had been no further from Emond's Field than had
the boys. Taren Ferry had seemed strange to her; Baerlon
would have had her staring in wonder if she had not been so
set on finding Egwene and the others. But she allowed none

of that to weaken her resolve. Sooner or later she would find Egwene and the boys. Or find a way to make the Aes Sedai answer for whatever had happened to them. One or the other, she vowed.

At intervals she found tracks, plenty of them, but usually her best efforts could not say whether those who made them had been searching or chasing or pursued. Some had been made by boots that could have belonged to humans or Trollocs either one. Others were hoofprints, like goats or oxen; those were Trollocs for sure. But never a clear sign that she could definitely say came from any of those she sought.

She had covered perhaps four miles when the wind brought her a whiff of woodsmoke. It came from further downriver, and not too far, she thought. She hesitated only a moment before tying her horse to a fir tree, well back from the river in a small, thick stand of evergreens that should keep the animal hidden. The smoke could mean Trollocs, but the only way to find out was to look. She tried not to think about the use Trollocs might be making of a fire.

Crouching, she slipped from tree to tree, mentally cursing the skirts she had to hold up out of the way. Dresses were not made for stalking. The sound of a horse slowed her, and when she finally peered cautiously around the trunk of an ash, the Warder was dismounting from his black warhorse in a small clearing on the bank. The Aes Sedai sat on a log beside a small fire where a kettle of water was just coming to a boil. Her white mare browsed behind her among sparse weeds. Nynaeve remained where she was.

"They are all gone," Lan announced grimly. "Four Halfmen started south about two hours before dawn, as near as I can tell—they don't leave much trace behind—but the Trollocs have vanished. Even the corpses, and Trollocs are not known for carrying off their dead. Unless they're hungry."

Moiraine tossed a handful of something into the boiling water and moved the kettle from the fire. "One could always hope they had gone back into Shadar Logoth and been consumed by it, but that would be too much to wish for."

The delicious odor of tea drifted to Nynaeve. *Light, don't let my stomach grumble.*

"There was no clear sign of the boys, or any of the others. The tracks are too muddled to tell anything." In her concealment, Nynaeve smiled; the Warder's failure was a slight vindication of her own. "But this other is important, Moiraine," Lan went on, frowning. He waved away the Aes Sedai's offer of tea and began marching up and down in front of the fire, one hand on his sword hilt and his cloak changing colors as he turned. "I could accept Trollocs in the Two Rivers, even a hundred Trollocs. But this? There must have been almost a thousand in the hunt for us yesterday."

"We were very lucky that not all stayed to search Shadar Logoth. The Myrddraal must have doubted we would hide there, but they also feared to return to Shayol Ghul leaving even the slightest chance uncovered. The Dark One was never a lenient master."

"Don't try to evade it. You know what I am saying. If those thousand were here to be sent into the Two Rivers, why were they not? There is only one answer. They were sent only after we crossed the Taren, when it was known that one Myrddraal and a hundred Trollocs were no longer enough. How? How were they sent? If a thousand Trollocs can be brought so far south from the Blight, so quickly, unseen—not to mention being taken off the same way—can ten thousand be sent into the heart of Saldaea, or Arafel, or Shienar? The Borderlands could be overrun in a year."

"The whole world will be overrun in five if we do not find those boys," Moiraine said simply. "The question worries me, also, but I have no answers. The Ways are closed, and there has not been an Aes Sedai powerful enough to Travel since the Time of Madness. Unless one of the Forsaken is loose—the Light send it is not so, yet or ever—there is still no one who can. In any case, I do not think all the Forsaken together could move a thousand Trollocs. Let us deal with the problems that face us here and now; everything else must wait."

"The boys." It was not a question.

"I have not been idle while you were away. One is across the river, and alive. As for the others, there was a faint trace downriver, but it faded away as I found it. The bond had been broken for hours before I began my search."

Crouched behind her tree, Nynaeve frowned in puzzlement.

Lan stopped his pacing. "You think the Halfmen heading south have them?"

"Perhaps." Moiraine poured herself a cup of tea before

going on. "But I will not admit the possibility of them being dead. I cannot. I dare not. You know how much is at stake. I must have those young men. That Shayol Ghul will hunt them, I expect. Opposition from within the White Tower, even from the Amyrlin Seat, I accept. There are always Aes Sedai who will accept only one solution. But. . . ." Suddenly she put her cup down and sat up straight, grimacing. "If you watch the wolf too hard," she muttered, "a mouse will bite you on the ankle." And she looked right at the tree behind which Nynaeve was hiding. "Mistress al'Meara, you may come out now, if you wish."

Nynaeve scrambled to her feet, hastily dusting dead leaves from her dress. Lan had spun to face the tree as soon as Moiraine's eyes moved; his sword was in his hand before she finished speaking Nynaeve's name. Now he sheathed it again with more force than was strictly necessary. His face was almost as expressionless as ever, but Nynaeve thought there was a touch of chagrin about the set of his mouth. She felt a stab of satisfaction; the Warder had not known she was there, at least.

Satisfaction lasted only a moment, though. She fastened her eyes on Moiraine and walked toward her purposefully. She wanted to remain cold and calm, but her voice quivered with anger. "What have you meshed Egwene and the boys in? What filthy Aes Sedai plots are you planning to use them in?"

The Aes Sedai picked up her cup and calmly sipped her tea. When Nynaeve was close, though, Lan put out an arm to bar her way. She tried to brush the obstruction aside, and was surprised when the Warder's arm moved no more than an oak branch would have. She was not frail, but his muscles were like iron.

"Tea?" Moiraine offered.

"No, I don't want any tea. I would not drink your tea if I was dying of thirst. You won't use any Emond's Field folk in your dirty Aes Sedai schemes."

"You have very little room to talk, Wisdom." Moiraine showed more interest in her hot tea than in anything she was saying. "You can wield the One Power yourself, after a fashion."

Nynaeve pushed at Lan's arm again; it still did not move,

and she decided to ignore it. "Why don't you try claiming I am a Trolloc?"

Moiraine's smile was so knowing that Nynaeve wanted to hit her. "Do you think I can stand face-to-face with a woman who can touch the True Source and channel the One Power, even if only now and then, without knowing what she is? Just as you sensed the potential in Egwene. How do you think I knew you were behind that tree? If I had not been distracted, I would have known the moment you came close. You certainly are not a Trolloc, for me to feel the evil of the Dark One. So what did I sense, Nynaeve al'Meara, Wisdom of Emond's Field and unknowing wielder of the One Power?"

Lan was looking down at Nynaeve in a way she did not like; surprised and speculative, it seemed to her, though nothing had changed about his face but his eyes. Egwene *was* special; she had always known that. Egwene would make a fine Wisdom. *They're working together,* she thought, *trying to put me off balance.* "I won't listen to any more of this. You—"

"You must listen," Moiraine said firmly. "I had my suspicions in Emond's Field even before I met you. People told me how upset the Wisdom was that she had not predicted the hard winter and the lateness of spring. They told me how good she was at foretelling weather, at telling the crops. They told me how wonderful her cures were, how she sometimes healed injuries, that should have been crippling, so well there was barely a scar, and not a limp or a twinge. The only ill word I heard about you was from a few who thought you too young for the responsibility, and that only strengthened my suspicions. So much skill so young."

"Mistress Barran taught me well." She tried looking at Lan, but his eyes still made her uncomfortable, so she settled for staring over the Aes Sedai's head at the river. *How dare the village gossip in front of an outlander!* "Who said I was too young?" she demanded.

Moiraine smiled, refusing to be diverted. "Unlike most women who claim to listen to the wind, you actually can, sometimes. Oh, it has nothing to do with the wind, of course. It is of Air and Water. It is not something you needed to be taught; it was born into you, just as it was born into

Egwene. But you have learned to handle it, which she still has to learn. Two minutes after I came face-to-face with you, I knew. Do you remember how I suddenly asked you if you were the Wisdom? Why, do you think? There was nothing to distinguish you from any other pretty young woman getting ready for Festival. Even looking for a young Wisdom I expected someone half again your age."

Nynaeve remembered that meeting all too well; this woman, more self-possessed than anyone in the Women's Circle, in a dress more beautiful than any she had ever seen, addressing her as a child. Then Moiraine had suddenly blinked as if surprised and out of a clear sky asked. . . .

She licked lips gone abruptly dry. They were both looking at her, the Warder's face as unreadable as a stone, the Aes Sedai's sympathetic yet intent. Nynaeve shook her head. "No! No, it's impossible. I would know. You are just trying to trick me, and it will not work."

"Of course you do not know," Moiraine said soothingly. "Why should you even suspect? All of your life you have heard about listening to the wind. In any case, you would as soon announce to all of Emond's Field that you were a Darkfriend as admit to yourself, even in the deepest recesses of your mind, that you have anything to do with the One Power, or the dreaded Aes Sedai." Amusement flitted across Moiraine's face. "But I can tell you how it began."

"I don't want to hear any more of your lies," she said, but the Aes Sedai went right on.

"Perhaps as much as eight or ten years ago—the age varies, but always comes young—there was something you wanted more than anything else in the world, something you needed. And you got it. A branch suddenly falling where you could pull yourself out of a pond instead of drowning. A friend, or a pet, getting well when everyone thought they would die.

"You felt nothing special at the time, but a week or ten days later you had your first reaction to touching the True Source. Perhaps fever and chills that came on suddenly and put you to bed, then disappeared after only a few hours. None of the reactions, and they vary, lasts more than a few hours. Headaches and numbness and exhilaration all mixed together, and you taking foolish chances or acting giddy. A spell of dizziness, when you tripped and stumbled whenever you tried to move, when you could not say a sentence without your tongue mangling half the words. There are others. Do you remember?"

Nynaeve sat down hard on the ground; her legs would not hold her up. She remembered, but she shook her head anyway. It had to be coincidence. Or else Moiraine had asked more questions in Emond's Field than she had thought. The Aes Sedai had asked a great many questions. It had to be that. Lan offered a hand, but she did not even see it.

"I will go further," Moiraine said when Nynaeve kept silent. "You used the Power to Heal either Perrin or Egwene at some time. An affinity develops. You can sense the presence of someone you have Healed. In Baerlon you came straight to the Stag and Lion, though it was not the nearest inn to any gate by which you could have entered. Of the people from Emond's Field, only Perrin and Egwene were at the inn when you arrived. Was it Perrin, or Egwene? Or both?"

"Egwene," Nynaeve mumbled. She had always taken it for granted that she could sometimes tell who was approaching her even when she could not see them; not until now had she realized that it was always someone on whom her cures had worked almost miraculously well. And she had always known when the medicine would work beyond expectations, always felt the certainty when she said the crops would be especially good, or that the rains would come early or late. That was the way she thought it was supposed to be. Not all Wisdoms could listen to the wind, but the best could. That was what Mistress Barran always said, just as she said Nynaeve would be one of the best.

"She had breakbone fever." She kept her head down and spoke to the ground. "I was still apprentice to Mistress Barran, and she set me to watch Egwene. I was young, and I didn't know the Wisdom had everything well in hand. It's terrible to watch, breakbone fever. The child was soaked with sweat, groaning and twisting until I could not understand why I didn't hear her bones snapping. Mistress Barran had told me the fever would break in another day, two at the most, but I thought she was doing me a kindness. I thought Egwene was dying. I used to look after her sometimes when she was a toddler—when her mother was busy—and I started crying because I was going to have to watch her die.

When Mistress Barran came back an hour later, the fever had broken. She was surprised, but she made over me more than Egwene. I always thought she believed I had given the child something and was too frightened to admit it. I always thought she was trying to comfort me, to make sure I knew I hadn't hurt Egwene. A week later I fell on the floor in her sitting room, shaking and burning up by turns. She bundled me into bed, but by suppertime it was gone."

She dropped her head in her hands as she finished speaking. *The Aes Sedai chose a good example,* she thought, *Light burn her! Using the Power like an Aes Sedai. A filthy, Darkfriend Aes Sedai!*

"You were very lucky," Moiraine said, and Nynaeve sat erect. Lan stepped back as if what they talked about was none of his business, and busied himself with Mandarb's saddle, not even glancing at them.

"Lucky!"

"You have managed a crude control over the Power, even if touching the True Source still comes at random. If you had not, it would have killed you eventually. As it will, in all probability, kill Egwene if you manage to stop her from going to Tar Valon."

"If I learned to control it. . . ." Nynaeve swallowed hard. It was like admitting all over again that she could do what the Aes Sedai said. "If I learned to control it, so can she. There is no need for her to go to Tar Valon, and get mixed up in your intrigues."

Moiraine shook her head slowly. "Aes Sedai search for girls who can touch the True Source unguided just as assiduously as we search for men who can do so. It is not a desire to increase our numbers—or at least, not only that—nor is it a fear that those women will misuse the Power. The rough control of the Power they may gain, if the Light shines on them, is rarely enough to do any great damage, especially since the actual touching of the Source is beyond their control without a teacher, and comes only randomly. And, of course, they do not suffer the madness that drives men to evil or twisted things. We want to save their lives. The lives of those who never do manage any control at all."

"The fever and chills I had couldn't kill anyone," Nynaeve insisted. "Not in three or four hours. I had the other things, too, and they couldn't kill anybody, either. And they stopped after a few months. What about that?"

"Those were only reactions," Moiraine said patiently. "Each time, the reaction comes closer to the actual touching of the Source, until the two happen almost together. After that there are no more reactions that can be seen, but it is as if a clock has begun ticking. A year. Two years. I know one woman who lasted five years. Of four who have the inborn ability that you and Egwene have, three die if we do not find them and train them. It is not as horrible a death as the men die, but neither is it pretty, if any death can be called so. Convulsions. Screaming. It takes days, and once it begins there is nothing that can be done to stop it, not by all the Aes Sedai in Tar Valon together."

"You're lying. All those questions you asked in Emond's Field. You found out about Egwene's fever breaking, about my fever and chills, all of it. You made all of this up."

"You know I did not," Moiraine said gently.

Reluctantly, more reluctantly than she had ever done anything in her life, Nynaeve nodded. It had been a last stubborn effort to deny what was plain, and there was never any good in that, however unpleasant it might be. Mistress Barran's first apprentice had died the way the Aes Sedai said when Nynaeve was still playing with dolls, and there had been a young woman in Deven Ride only a few years ago. She had been a Wisdom's apprentice, too, one who could listen to the wind.

"You have great potential, I think," Moiraine continued. "With training you might become even more powerful than Egwene, and I believe she can become one of the most powerful Aes Sedai we have seen in centuries."

Nynaeve pushed herself back from the Aes Sedai as she would have from a viper. "No! I'll have nothing to do with—" *With what? Myself?* She slumped, and her voice became hesitant. "I would ask you not to tell anyone about this. Please?" The word nearly stuck in her throat. She would rather Trollocs had appeared than she had been forced to say please to this woman. But Moiraine only nodded assent, and some of her spirit returned. "None of this explains what you want with Rand, and Mat, and Perrin."

"The Dark One wants them," Moiraine replied. "If the

Dark One wants a thing, I oppose it. Can there be a simpler reason, or a better?" She finished her tea, watching Nynaeve over the rim of her cup. "Lan, we must be going. South, I think. I fear the Wisdom will not be accompanying us."

Nynaeve's mouth tightened at the way the Aes Sedai said "Wisdom"; it seemed to suggest she was turning her back on great things in favor of something petty. *She doesn't want me along. She's trying to put my back up so I'll go back home and leave them alone with her.* "Oh, yes, I will be going with you. You cannot keep me from it."

"No one will try to keep you from it," Lan said as he rejoined them. He emptied the tea kettle over the fire and stirred the ashes with a stick. "A part of the Pattern?" he said to Moiraine.

"Perhaps so," she replied thoughtfully. "I should have spoken to Min again."

"You see, Nynaeve, you are welcome to come." There was a hesitation in the way Lan said her name, a hint of an unspoken "Sedai" after it.

Nynaeve bristled, taking it for mockery, and bristled, too, at the way they spoke of things in front of her—things she knew nothing about—without the courtesy of an explanation, but she would not give them the satisfaction of asking.

The Warder went on preparing for departure, his economical motions so sure and swift that he was quickly done, saddlebags, blankets, and all fastened behind the saddles of Mandarb and Aldieb.

"I will fetch your horse," he told Nynaeve as he finished with the last saddle tie.

He started up the riverbank, and she allowed herself a small smile. After the way she had watched him undiscovered, he was going to try to find her horse unaided. He would learn that she left little in the way of tracks when she was stalking. It would be a pleasure when he came back empty-handed.

"Why south?" she asked Moiraine. "I heard you say one of the boys is across the river. And how do you know?"

"I gave each of the boys a token. It created a bond of sorts between them and me. So long as they are alive and have those coins in their possession, I will be able to find them." Nynaeve's eyes turned in the direction the Warder had gone, and Moiraine shook her head. "Not like that. It only allows me to discover if they still live, and find them should we become separated. Prudent, do you not think, under the circumstances?"

"I don't like anything that connects you with anyone from Emond's Field," Nynaeve said stubbornly. "But if it will help us find them. . . ."

"It will. I would gather the young man across the river first, if I could." For a moment frustration tinged the Aes Sedai's voice. "He is only a few miles from us. But I cannot afford to take the time. He should make his way down to Whitebridge safely now that the Trollocs have gone. The two who went downriver may need me more. They have lost their coins, and Myrddraal are either pursuing them or else trying to intercept us all at Whitebridge." She sighed. "I must take care of the greatest need first."

"The Myrddraal could have . . . could have killed them," Nynaeve said.

Moiraine shook her head slightly, denying the suggestion as if it were too trivial to be considered. Nynaeve's mouth tightened. "Where is Egwene, then? You haven't even mentioned her."

"I do not know," Moiraine admitted, "but I hope that she is safe."

"You don't know? You hope? All that talk about saving her life by taking her to Tar Valon, and she could be dead for all you know!"

"I could look for her and allow the Myrddraal more time before I arrive to help the two young men who went south. It is them the Dark One wants, not her. They would not bother with Egwene, so long as their true quarry remains uncaught."

Nynaeve remembered her own encounter, but she refused to admit the sense of what Moiraine said. "So the best you have to offer is that she may be alive, if she was lucky. Alive, maybe alone, frightened, even hurt, days from the nearest village or help except for us. And you intend to leave her."

"She may just as easily be safe with the boy across the river. Or on her way to Whitebridge with the other two. In any case, there are no longer Trollocs here to threaten her, and she is strong, intelligent, and quite capable of finding her way to Whitebridge alone, if need be. Would you rather stay on the chance that she may need help, or do you want to try to help those we know are in need? Would you have me search for her and let the boys—and the Myrddraal who are surely pursuing them—go? As much as I hope for Egwene's safety, Nynaeve, I fight against the Dark One, and for now that sets my path."

Moiraine's calm never slipped while she laid out the horrible alternatives; Nynaeve wanted to scream at her. Blinking back tears, she turned her face so the Aes Sedai could not see. *Light, a Wisdom is supposed to look after* all *of her people. Why do I have to choose like this?*

"Here is Lan," Moiraine said, rising and settling her cloak about her shoulders.

To Nynaeve it was only a tiny blow as the Warder led her horse out of the trees. Still, her lips thinned when he handed her the reins. It would have been a small boost to her spirits if there had been even a trace of gloating on his face instead of that insufferable stony calm. His eyes widened when he saw her face, and she turned her back on him to wipe tears from her cheeks. *How dare he mock my crying!*

"Are you coming, Wisdom?" Moiraine asked coolly.

She took one last, slow look at the forest, wondering if Egwene was out there, before sadly mounting her horse. Lan and Moiraine were already in their saddles, turning their horses south. She followed, stiff-backed, refusing to let herself look back; instead she kept her eyes on Moiraine. The Aes Sedai was so confident in her power and her plans, she thought, but if they did not find Egwene and the boys, all of them, alive and unharmed, not all of her power would protect her. Not all her Power. *I can use it, woman! You told me so yourself. I can use it against you!*

CHAPTER
22

A Path Chosen

In a small copse of trees, beneath a pile of cedar branches roughly cut in the dark, Perrin slept long after sunrise. It was the cedar needles, pricking him through his still-damp clothes, that finally pricked through his exhaustion as well. Deep in a dream of Emond's Field, of working at Master Luhhan's forge, he opened his eyes and stared, uncomprehending, at the sweet-smelling branches interwoven over his face, sunlight trickling through.

Most of the branches fell away as he sat up in surprise, but some hung haphazardly from his shoulders, and even his head, making him appear something like a tree himself. Emond's Field faded as memory rushed back, so vivid that for a moment the night before seemed more real than anything around him now.

Panting, frantic, he scrabbled his axe out of the pile. He clutched it in both hands and peered around cautiously, holding his breath. Nothing moved. The morning was cold and still. If there were Trollocs on the east bank of the Arinelle, they were not moving, at least not close to him. Taking a deep, calming breath, he lowered the axe to his knees, and waited a moment for his heart to stop pounding.

The small stand of evergreens surrounding him was the first shelter he had found last night. It was sparse enough to give little protection against watching eyes if he stood up. Plucking branches from his head and shoulders, he pushed aside the rest of his prickly blanket, then crawled on hands and knees to the edge of the copse. There he lay studying the riverbank and scratching where the needles had stabbed him.

The cutting wind of the night before had faded to a silent breeze that barely rippled the surface of the water. The river ran by, calm and empty. And wide. Surely too wide and too deep for Fades to cross. The far bank appeared a solid mass of trees as far as he could see upriver and down. Certainly nothing moved in his view over there.

He was not sure how he felt about that. Fades and Trollocs he could do without quite easily, even on the other side of the river, but a whole list of worries would have vanished with the appearance of the Aes Sedai, or the Warder, or, even better, any of his friends. *If wishes were wings, sheep would fly.* That was what Mistress Luhhan always said.

He had not seen a sign of his horse since riding over the bluff—he hoped it had swum out of the river safely—but he was more used to walking than riding anyway, and his boots were stout and well soled. He had nothing to eat, but his sling was still wrapped around his waist, and that or the snarelines in his pocket ought to yield a rabbit in a little time. Everything for making a fire was gone with his saddlebags, but the cedar trees would yield tinder and a firebow with a bit of work.

He shivered as the breeze gusted into his hiding place. His cloak was somewhere in the river, and his coat and everything else he wore were still clammy cold from the soaking in the river. He had been too tired for the cold and damp to bother him last night, but now he was wide awake to every chill. Just the same, he decided against hanging his clothes on the branches to dry. If the day was not precisely cold, it was not even close to warm.

Time was the problem, he thought with a sigh. Dry clothes, with a little time. A rabbit to roast and a fire to roast it over, with a little time. His stomach rumbled, and he tried to forget about eating altogether. There were more important uses for that time. One thing at a time, and the most important first. That was his way.

His eyes followed the strong flow of the Arinelle downriver. He was a stronger swimmer than Egwene. If she had made it across. . . . No, not *if.* The place where she *had* made it across would be downriver. He drummed on the ground with his fingers, weighing, considering.

His decision made, he wasted no time in picking up his axe and setting off down the river.

This side of the Arinelle lacked the thick forest of the west bank. Clumps of trees spotted across what would be grassland if spring ever came. Some were big enough to be called thickets, with swathes of evergreens among the barren ash and alder and hardgum. Down by the river the stands were smaller and not so tight. They gave poor cover, but they were all the cover there was.

He dashed from growth to growth in a crouch, throwing himself down when he was among the trees to study the riverbanks, the far side as well as his. The Warder said the river would be a barrier to Fades and Trollocs, but would it? Seeing him might be enough to overcome their reluctance to cross deep water. So he watched carefully from behind the trees and ran from one hiding place to the next, fast and low.

He covered several miles that way, in spurts, until suddenly, halfway to the beckoning shelter of a growth of willows, he grunted and stopped dead, staring at the ground. Patches of bare earth spotted the matted brown of last year's grass, and in the middle of one of those patches, right under his nose, was a clear hoofprint. A slow smile spread across his face. Some Trollocs had hooves, but he doubted if any wore horseshoes, especially horseshoes with the double crossbar Master Luhhan added for strength.

Forgetting possible eyes on the other side of the river, he cast about for more tracks. The plaited carpet of dead grass did not take impressions well, but his sharp eyes found them anyway. The scanty trail led him straight away from the river to a dense stand of trees, thick with leatherleaf and cedar that made a wall against wind or prying eyes. The spreading branches of a lone hemlock towered in the middle of it all.

Still grinning, he pushed his way through the interwoven branches, not caring how much noise he made. Abruptly he stepped into a little clearing under the hemlock—and stopped. Behind a small fire, Egwene crouched, her face grim, with a thick branch held like a club and her back against Bela's flank.

"I guess I should have called out," he said with an abashed shrug.

Tossing her club down, she ran to throw her arms around him. "I thought you had drowned. You're still wet. Here, sit by the fire and warm yourself. You lost your horse, didn't you?"

He let her push him to a place by the fire and rubbed his hands over the flames, grateful for the warmth. She produced an oiled paper packet from her saddlebags and gave him some bread and cheese. The package had been so tightly wrapped that even after its dunking the food was dry. *Here you were worrying about her, and she's done better than you did.*

"Bela got me across," Egwene said, patting the shaggy mare. "She headed away from the Trollocs and just towed me along." She paused. "I haven't seen anybody else, Perrin."

He heard the unspoken question. Regretfully eyeing the packet that she was rewrapping, he licked the last crumbs from his fingers before speaking. "I've seen no one but you since last night. No Fades or Trollocs, either; there's that."

"Rand has to be all right," Egwene said, quickly adding, "they all do. They have to. They're probably looking for us right now. They might find us anytime now. Moiraine is an Aes Sedai, after all."

"I keep being reminded of that," he said. "Burn me, I wish I could forget."

"I did not hear you complaining when she stopped the Trollocs from catching us," Egwene said tartly.

"I just wish we could do without her." He shrugged uncomfortably under her steady gaze. "I suppose we can't, though. I've been thinking." Her eyebrows rose, but he was used to surprise whenever he claimed an idea. Even when his ideas were as good as theirs, they always remembered how deliberate he was in thinking of them. "We can wait for Lan and Moiraine to find us."

"Of course," she cut in. "Moiraine Sedai said she would find us if we were separated."

He let her finish, then went on. "Or the Trollocs could find us, first. Moiraine could be dead, too. All of them could be. No, Egwene. I'm sorry, but they could be. I hope they are all safe. I hope they'll walk up to this fire any minute. But hope is like a piece of string when you're drowning; it just isn't enough to get you out by itself."

Egwene closed her mouth and stared at him with her jaw set. Finally, she said, "You want to go downriver to Whitebridge? If Moiraine Sedai doesn't find us here, that's where she will look next."

"I suppose," he said slowly, "that Whitebridge is where we *should* go. But the Fades probably know that, too. That's where they'll be looking, and this time we don't have an Aes Sedai or a Warder to protect us."

"I suppose you're going to suggest running off somewhere, the way Mat wanted to? Hiding somewhere the Fades and Trollocs won't find us? Or Moiraine Sedai, either?"

"Don't think I haven't considered it," he said quietly. "But every time we think we are free, Fades and Trollocs find us again. I don't know if there *is* anyplace we could hide from them. I don't like it much, but we need Moiraine."

"I don't understand then, Perrin. Where do we go?"

He blinked in surprise. She was waiting for his answer. Waiting for *him* to tell her what to do. It had never occurred to him that she would look to him to take the lead. Egwene never liked doing what someone else had planned out, and she never let anybody tell her what to do. Except maybe the Wisdom, and he thought sometimes she balked at that. He smoothed the dirt in front of him with his hand and cleared his throat roughly.

"If this is where we are now, and that is Whitebridge," he stabbed the ground twice with his finger, "then Caemlyn should be somewhere around here." He made a third mark, off to the side.

He paused, looking at the three dots in the dirt. His entire plan was based on what he remembered of her father's old map. Master al'Vere said it was not too accurate, and, anyway, he had never mooned over it as much as Rand and Mat. But Egwene said nothing. When he looked up, she was still watching him with her hands in her lap.

"Caemlyn?" She sounded stunned.

"Caemlyn." He drew a line in the dirt between two of the dots. "Away from the river, and straight across. Nobody would expect that. We'll wait for them in Caemlyn." He dusted his hands and waited. He thought it was a good plan, but surely she would have objections now. He expected she would take charge—she was always bullying him into something—and that was all right with him.

To his surprise, she nodded. "There must be villages. We can ask directions."

"What worries me," Perrin said, "is what we do if the Aes Sedai *doesn't* find us there. Light, who'd ever have thought I'd worry about something like that? What if she doesn't come to Caemlyn? Maybe she thinks we're dead. Maybe she'll take Rand and Mat straight to Tar Valon."

"Moiraine Sedai said she could find us," Egwene said firmly. "If she can find us here, she can find us in Caemlyn, and she will."

Perrin nodded slowly. "If you say so, but if she doesn't appear in Caemlyn in a few days, we go on to Tar Valon and put our case before the Amyrlin Seat." He took a deep breath. *Two weeks ago you'd never even seen an Aes Sedai, and now you're talking about the Amyrlin Seat. Light!* "According to Lan, there's a good road from Caemlyn." He looked at the oiled paper packet beside Egwene and cleared his throat. "What chance of a little more bread and cheese?"

"This might have to last a long time," she said, "unless you have better luck with snares than I did last night. At least the fire was easy." She laughed softly as if she had made a joke, tucking the packet back into her saddlebags.

Apparently there were limits to how much leadership she was willing to accept. His stomach rumbled. "In that case," he said, standing, "we might as well start now."

"But you're still wet," she protested.

"I'll walk myself dry," he said firmly, and began kicking dirt over the fire. If he was the leader, it was time to start leading. The wind from the river was picking up.

CHAPTER
23

Wolfbrother

From the start Perrin knew the journey to Caemlyn was going to be far from comfortable, beginning with Egwene's insistence that they take turns riding Bela. They did not know how far it was, she said, but it was too far for her to be the only one who rode. Her jaw firmed, and her eyes stared at him unblinking.

"I'm too big to ride Bela," he said. "I'm used to walking, and I'd rather."

"And I am not used to walking?" Egwene said sharply.

"That isn't what I—"

"I'm the only one who's supposed to get saddlesore, is that it? And when you walk till your feet are ready to fall off, you'll expect me to look after you."

"Let it be," he breathed when she looked like going on. "Anyway, you'll take the first turn." Her face turned even more stubborn, but he refused to let her get a word in edgewise. "If you won't get in the saddle by yourself, I'll put you there."

She gave him a startled look, and a small smile curved her lips. "In that case. . . ." She sounded as if she were about to laugh, but she climbed up.

He grumbled to himself as he turned away from the river. Leaders in stories never had to put up with this sort of thing.

Egwene did insist on him taking his turns, and whenever he tried to avoid it, she bullied him into the saddle. Blacksmithing did not lend itself to a slender build, and Bela was not very large as horses went. Every time he put his foot in the stirrup the shaggy mare looked at him with what he was sure was reproach. Small things, perhaps, but they irritated.

Soon he flinched whenever Egwene announced, "It's your turn, Perrin."

In stories leaders seldom flinched, and they were never bullied. But, he reflected, they never had to deal with Egwene, either.

There were only short rations of bread and cheese to begin with, and what there was gave out by the end of the first day. Perrin set snares along likely rabbit runs—they looked old, but it was worth a chance—while Egwene began laying a fire. When he was done, he decided to try his hand with his sling before the light failed altogether. They had not seen a sign of anything at all alive, but. . . . To his surprise, he jumped a scrawny rabbit almost at once. He was so surprised when it burst from under a bush right beneath his feet that it almost got away, but he fetched it at forty paces, just as it was darting around a tree.

When he came back to the camp with the rabbit, Egwene had broken limbs all laid for the fire, but she was kneeling beside the pile with her eyes closed. "What are you doing? You can't wish a fire."

Egwene gave a jump at his first words, and twisted around to stare at him with a hand to her throat. "You . . . you startled me."

"I was lucky," he said, holding up the rabbit. "Get your flint and steel. We eat well tonight, at least."

"I don't have a flint," she said slowly. "It was in my pocket, and I lost it in the river."

"Then how . . . ?"

"It was so easy back there on the riverbank, Perrin. Just the way Moiraine Sedai showed me. I just reached out, and. . . ." She gestured as if grasping for something, then let her hand fall with a sigh. "I can't find it, now."

Perrin licked his lips uneasily. "The . . . the Power?" She nodded, and he stared at her. "Are you crazy? I mean . . . the One Power! You can't just play around with something like that."

"It was so easy, Perrin. I can do it. I can channel the Power."

He took a deep breath. "I'll make a firebow, Egwene. Promise you won't try this . . . this . . . *thing* again."

"I will not." Her jaw firmed in a way that made him sigh. "Would you give up that axe of yours, Perrin Aybara?

Would you walk around with one hand tied behind your back? I won't do it!"

"I'll make the firebow," he said wearily. "At least, don't try it again tonight? Please?"

She acquiesced grudgingly, and even after the rabbit was roasting on a spit over the flames, he had the feeling she felt she could have done it better. She would not give up trying, either, every night, though the best she ever did was a trickle of smoke that vanished almost immediately. Her eyes dared him to say a word, and he wisely kept his mouth shut.

After that one hot meal, they subsisted on coarse wild tubers and a few young shoots. With still no sign of spring, none of it was plentiful, and none of it tasty, either. Neither complained, but not a meal passed without one or the other sighing regretfully, and they both knew it was for the tang of a bit of cheese, or even the smell of bread. A find of mushrooms—Queen's Crowns, the best—one afternoon in a shady part of the forest was enough to seem a great treat. They gobbled them down, laughing and telling stories from back in Emond's Field, stories that began, "Do you remember when—" but the mushrooms did not last long, and neither did the laughter. There was little mirth in hunger.

Whichever was walking carried a sling, ready to let fly at the sight of a rabbit or squirrel, but the only time either hurled a stone was in frustration. The snares they set so carefully each evening yielded nothing at dawn, and they did not dare stay a day in one place to leave the snares out. Neither of them knew how far it was to Caemlyn, and neither would feel safe until they got there, if then. Perrin began to wonder if his stomach could shrink enough to make a hole all the way through his middle.

They made good time, as he saw it, but as they got farther and farther from the Arinelle without seeing a village, or even a farmhouse where they could ask directions, his doubts about his own plan grew. Egwene continued to appear outwardly as confident as when they set out, but he was sure that sooner or later she would say it would have been better to risk the Trollocs than to wander around lost for the rest of their lives. She never did, but he kept expecting it.

Two days from the river the land changed to thickly

forested hills, as gripped by the tail end of winter as everywhere else, and a day after that the hills flattened out again, the dense forest broken by glades, often a mile or more across. Snow still lay in hidden hollows, and the air was brisk of a morning, and the wind cold always. Nowhere did they see a road, or a plowed field, or chimney smoke in the distance, or any other sign of human habitation—at least, none where men still dwelt.

Once the remains of tall stone ramparts encircled a hilltop. Parts of roofless stone houses stood inside the fallen circle. The forest had long swallowed it; trees grew right through everything, and spiderwebs of old creeper enveloped the big stone blocks. Another time they came on a stone tower, broken-topped and brown with old moss, leaning on the huge oak whose thick roots were slowly toppling it. But they found no place where men had breathed in living remembrance. Memories of Shadar Logoth kept them away from the ruins and hurried their footsteps until they were once more deep in places that seemed never to have known a human footstep.

Dreams plagued Perrin's sleep, fearful dreams. Ba'alzamon was in them, chasing him through mazes, hunting him, but Perrin never met him face-to-face, so far as he remembered. And their journey had been enough to bring a few bad dreams. Egwene complained of nightmares about Shadar Logoth, especially the two nights after they found the ruined fort and the abandoned tower. Perrin kept his own counsel even when he woke sweating and shaking in the dark. She was looking to him to lead them safely to Caemlyn, not share worries about which they could do nothing.

He was walking at Bela's head, wondering if they would find anything to eat this evening, when he first caught the smell. The mare flared her nostrils and swung her head in the next moment. He seized her bridle before she could whicker.

"That's smoke," Egwene said excitedly. She leaned forward in the saddle, drew a deep breath. "A cookfire. Somebody is roasting dinner. Rabbit."

"Maybe," Perrin said cautiously, and her eager smile faded. He exchanged his sling for the wicked half-moon of the axe. His hands opened and closed uncertainly on the thick haft. It was a weapon, but neither his hidden practice behind the forge nor Lan's teachings had really prepared him to use it as one. Even the battle before Shadar Logoth was too vague in his mind to give him any confidence. He could never quite manage that void that Rand and the Warder talked about, either.

Sunlight slanted through the trees behind them, and the forest was a still mass of dappled shadows. The faint smell of woodsmoke drifted around them, tinged with the aroma of cooking meat. *It could be rabbit,* he thought, and his stomach grumbled. And it could be something else, he reminded himself. He looked at Egwene; she was watching him. There were responsibilities to being leader.

"Wait here," he said softly. She frowned, but he cut her off as she opened her mouth. "And be quiet! We don't know who it is, yet." She nodded. Reluctantly, but she did it. Perrin wondered why that did not work when he was trying to make her take his turn riding. Drawing a deep breath, he started for the source of the smoke.

He had not spent as much time in the forests around Emond's Field as Rand or Mat, but still he had done his share of hunting rabbits. He crept from tree to tree without so much as snapping a twig. It was not long before he was peering around the bole of a tall oak with spreading, serpentine limbs that bent to touch the ground then rose again. Beyond lay a campfire, and a lean, sun-browned man was leaning against one of the limbs not far from the flames.

At least he was not a Trolloc, but he was the strangest fellow Perrin had ever seen. For one thing, his clothes all seemed to be made from animal skins, with the fur still on, even his boots and the odd, flat-topped round cap on his head. His cloak was a crazy quilt of rabbit and squirrel; his trousers appeared to be made from the long-haired hide of a brown and white goat. Gathered at the back of his neck with a cord, his graying brown hair hung to his waist. A thick beard fanned across half his chest. A long knife hung at his belt, almost a sword, and a bow and quiver stood propped against a limb close to hand.

The man leaned back with his eyes closed, apparently asleep, but Perrin did not stir from his concealment. Six sticks slanted over the fellow's fire, and on each stick a rabbit was skewered, roasted brown and now and then dripping juice that hissed in the flames. The smell of them, so close, made his mouth water.

"You done drooling?" The man opened one eye and cocked it at Perrin's hiding place. "You and your friend might as well sit and have a bite. I haven't seen you eat much the last couple of days."

Perrin hesitated, then stood slowly, still gripping his axe tightly. "You've been watching me for two days?"

The man chuckled deep in his throat. "Yes, I been watching you. And that pretty girl. Pushes you around like a bantam rooster, doesn't she? Heard you, mostly. The horse is the only one of you doesn't trample around loud enough to be heard five miles off. You going to ask her in, or are you intending to eat all the rabbit yourself?"

Perrin bristled; he knew he did not make much noise. You could not get close enough to a rabbit in the Waterwood to fetch it with a sling if you made noise. But the smell of rabbit made him remember that Egwene was hungry, too, not to mention waiting to discover if it was a Trolloc fire they had smelled.

He slipped the haft of his axe through the belt loop and raised his voice. "Egwene! It's all right! It *is* rabbit!" Offering his hand, he added in a more normal tone, "My name is Perrin. Perrin Aybara."

The man considered his hand before taking it awkwardly, as if unused to shaking hands. "I'm called Elyas," he said, looking up. "Elyas Machera."

Perrin gasped, and nearly dropped Elyas's hand. The man's eyes were yellow, like bright, polished gold. Some memory tickled at the back of Perrin's mind, then fled. All he could think of right then was that all of the Trollocs' eyes he had seen had been almost black.

Egwene appeared, cautiously leading Bela. She tied the mare's reins to one of the smaller branches of the oak, and made polite sounds when Perrin introduced her to Elyas, but her eyes kept drifting to the rabbits. She did not seem to notice the man's eyes. When Elyas motioned them to the food, she fell to with a will. Perrin hesitated only a minute longer before joining her.

Elyas waited silently while they ate. Perrin was so hungry he tore off pieces of meat so hot he had to juggle them from hand to hand before he could hold them in his mouth. Even Egwene showed little of her usual neatness; greasy juice ran down her chin. Day faded into twilight before they began to slow down, moonless darkness closing in around the fire, and then Elyas spoke.

"What are you doing out here? There isn't a house inside fifty miles in any direction."

"We're going to Caemlyn," Egwene said. "Perhaps you could—" Her eyebrows lifted coolly as Elyas threw back his head and roared with laughter. Perrin stared at him, a rabbit leg half raised to his mouth.

"Caemlyn?" Elyas wheezed when he could talk again. "The path you're following, the line you've taken the last two days, you'll pass a hundred miles or more north of Caemlyn."

"We were going to ask directions," Egwene said defensively. "We just haven't found any villages or farms, yet."

"And none you will," Elyas said, chuckling. "The way you're going, you can travel all the way to the Spine of the World without seeing another human. Of course, if you managed to climb the Spine—it can be done, some places—you could find people in the Aiel Waste, but you wouldn't like it there. You'd broil by day, and freeze by night, and die of thirst anytime. It takes an Aielman to find water in the Waste, and they don't like strangers much. No, not much, I'd say." He set off into another, more furious, burst of laughter, this time actually rolling on the ground. "Not much at all," he managed.

Perrin shifted uneasily. *Are we eating with a madman?*

Egwene frowned, but she waited until Elyas's mirth faded a little, then said, "Perhaps you could show us the way. You seem to know a good deal more about where places are than we do."

Elyas stopped laughing. Raising his head, he replaced his round fur cap, which had fallen off while he was rolling about, and stared at her from under lowered brows. "I don't much like people," he said in a flat voice. "Cities are full of people. I don't go near villages, or even farms, very often. Villagers, farmers, they don't like my friends. I wouldn't even have helped you if you hadn't been stumbling around as helpless and innocent as newborn cubs."

"But at least you can tell us which way to go," she insisted. "If you direct us to the nearest village, even if it's fifty miles away, surely they'll give us directions to Caemlyn."

"Be still," Elyas said. "My friends are coming."

Bela suddenly whinnied in fear, and began jerking to

pull her reins free. Perrin half rose as shapes appeared all around them in the darkening forest. Bela reared and twisted, screaming.

"Quiet the mare," Elyas said. "They won't hurt her. Or you, if you're still."

Four wolves stepped into the firelight, shaggy, waist-high forms with jaws that could break a man's leg. As if the people were not there they walked up to the fire and lay down between the humans. In the darkness among the trees firelight reflected off the eyes of more wolves, on all sides.

Yellow eyes, Perrin thought. Like Elyas's eyes. That was what he had been trying to remember. Carefully watching the wolves among them, he reached for his axe.

"I would not do that," Elyas said. "If they think you mean harm, they'll stop being friendly."

They were staring at him, those four wolves, Perrin saw. He had the feeling that all the wolves, those in the trees, as well, were staring at him. It made his skin itch. Cautiously he moved his hands away from the axe. He imagined he could feel the tension ease among the wolves. Slowly he sat back down; his hands shook until he gripped his knees to stop them. Egwene was so stiff she almost quivered. One wolf, close to black with a lighter gray patch on his face, lay nearly touching her.

Bela had ceased her screaming and rearing. Instead she stood trembling and shifting in an attempt to keep all of the wolves in view, kicking occasionally to show the wolves that she could, intending to sell her life dearly. The wolves seemed to ignore her and everyone else. Tongues lolling out of their mouths, they waited at their ease.

"There," Elyas said. "That's better."

"Are they tame?" Egwene asked faintly, and hopefully, too. "They're . . . pets?"

Elyas snorted. "Wolves don't tame, girl, not even as well as men. They're my friends. We keep each other company, hunt together, converse, after a fashion. Just like any friends. Isn't that right, Dapple?" A wolf with fur that faded through a dozen shades of gray, dark and light, turned her head to look at him.

"You talk to them?" Perrin marveled.

"It isn't exactly talking," Elyas replied slowly. "The words don't matter, and they aren't exactly right, either.

Her name isn't Dapple. It's something that means the way
shadows play on a forest pool at a midwinter dawn, with the
breeze rippling the surface, and the tang of ice when the
water touches the tongue, and a hint of snow before nightfall in the air. But that isn't quite it, either. You can't say it
in words. It's more of a feeling. That's the way wolves talk.
The others are Burn, Hopper, and Wind." Burn had an old
scar on his shoulder that might explain his name, but there
was nothing about the other two wolves to give any indication of what their names might mean.

For all the man's gruffness, Perrin thought Elyas was
pleased to have the chance to talk to another human. He
seemed eager enough to do it, at least. Perrin eyed the
wolves' teeth glistening in the firelight and thought it might
be a good idea to keep him talking. "How . . . how did you
learn to talk to wolves, Elyas?"

"They found out," Elyas replied, "I didn't. Not at first.
That's always the way of it, I understand. The wolves find
you, not you them. Some people thought me touched by
the Dark One, because wolves started appearing wherever
I went. I suppose I thought so, too, sometimes. Most decent
folk began to avoid me, and the ones who sought me out
weren't the kind I wanted to know, one way or another. Then
I noticed there were times when the wolves seemed to know
what I was thinking, to respond to what was in my head. That
was the real beginning. They were curious about me. Wolves
can sense people, usually, but not like this. They were glad to
find me. They say it's been a long time since they hunted with
men, and when they say a long time, the feeling I get is like a
cold wind howling all the way down from the First Day."

"I never heard of men hunting with wolves," Egwene
said. Her voice was not entirely steady, but the fact that the
wolves were just lying there seemed to give her heart.

If Elyas heard her, he gave no sign. "Wolves remember
things differently from the way people do," he said. His
strange eyes took on a faraway look, as if he were drifting
off on the flow of memory himself. "Every wolf remembers the history of all wolves, or at least the shape of it. Like
I said, it can't be put into words very well. They remember running down prey side-by-side with men, but it was so
long ago that it's more like the shadow of a shadow than a
memory."

"That's very interesting," Egwene said, and Elyas looked at her sharply. "No, I mean it. It is." She wet her lips. "Could . . . ah . . . could you teach us to talk to them?"

Elyas snorted again. "It can't be taught. Some can do it, some can't. They say he can." He pointed at Perrin.

Perrin looked at Elyas's finger as if it were a knife. *He really is a madman.* The wolves were staring at him again. He shifted uncomfortably.

"You say you're going to Caemlyn," Elyas said, "but that still doesn't explain what you're doing out here, days from anywhere." He tossed back his fur-patch cloak and lay down on his side, propped on one elbow and waiting expectantly.

Perrin glanced at Egwene. Early on they had concocted a story for when they found people, to explain where they were going without bringing them any trouble. Without letting anyone know where they were really from, or where they were really going, eventually. Who knew what careless word might reach a Fade's ear? They had worked on it every day, patching it together, honing out flaws. And they had decided Egwene was the one to tell it. She was better with words than he was, and she claimed she could always tell when he was lying by his face.

Egwene began at once, smoothly. They were from the north, from Saldaea, from farms outside a tiny village. Neither of them had been more than twenty miles from home in their whole lives before this. But they had heard gleemen's stories, and merchants' tales, and they wanted to see some of the world. Caemlyn, and Illian. The Sea of Storms, and maybe even the fabled islands of the Sea Folk.

Perrin listened with satisfaction. Not even Thom Merrilin could have made a better tale from the little they knew of the world outside the Two Rivers, or one better suited to their needs.

"From Saldaea, eh?" Elyas said when she was done.

Perrin nodded. "That's right. We thought about seeing Maradon first. I'd surely like to see the King. But the capital city would be the first place our fathers would look."

That was his part of it, to make it plain they had never been to Maradon. That way no one would expect them to know anything about the city, just in case they ran into someone who really had been there. It was all a long way from Emond's Field and the events of Winternight. Nobody hearing the tale would have any reason to think of Tar Valon, or Aes Sedai.

"Quite a story." Elyas nodded. "Yes, quite a story. There's a few things wrong with it, but the main thing is Dapple says it's all a lump of lies. Every last word."

"Lies!" Egwene exclaimed. "Why would we lie?"

The four wolves had not moved, but they no longer seemed to be just lying there around the fire; they crouched, instead, and their yellow eyes watched the Emond's Fielders without blinking.

Perrin did not say anything, but his hand strayed to the axe at his waist. The four wolves rose to their feet in one quick movement, and his hand froze. They made no sound, but the thick hackles on their necks stood erect. One of the wolves back under the trees raised a growling howl into the night. Others answered, five, ten, twenty, till the darkness rippled with them. Abruptly they, too, were still. Cold sweat trickled down Perrin's face.

"If you think. . . ." Egwene stopped to swallow. Despite the chill in the air there was sweat on her face, too. "If you think we are lying, then you'll probably prefer that we make our own camp for the night, away from yours."

"Ordinarily I would, girl. But right now I want to know about the Trollocs. And the Halfmen." Perrin struggled to keep his face impassive, and hoped he was doing better at it than Egwene. Elyas went on in a conversational tone. "Dapple says she smelled Halfmen and Trollocs in your minds while you were telling that fool story. They all did. You're mixed up with Trollocs, somehow, and the Eyeless. Wolves hate Trollocs and Halfmen worse than wildfire, worse than anything, and so do I.

"Burn wants to be done with you. It was Trollocs gave him that mark when he was a yearling. He says game is scarce, and you're fatter than any deer he's seen in months, and we should be done with you. But Burn is always impatient. Why don't you tell me about it? I hope you're not Darkfriends. I don't like killing people after I've fed them. Just remember, they'll know if you lie, and even Dapple is already near as upset as Burn." His eyes, as yellow as the wolves' eyes, blinked no more than theirs did. *They* are *a wolf's eyes,* Perrin thought.

Egwene was looking at him, he realized, waiting for

him to decide what they should do. *Light, suddenly I'm the leader again.* They had decided from the first that they could not risk telling the real story to anyone, but he saw no chance for them to get away even if he managed to get his axe out before. . . .

Dapple growled deep in her throat, and the sound was taken up by the other three around the fire, then by the wolves in the darkness. The menacing rumble filled the night.

"All right," Perrin said quickly. "All right!" The growling cut off, sharp and sudden. Egwene unclenched her hands and nodded. "It all started a few days before Winternight," Perrin began, "when our friend Mat saw a man in a black cloak. . . ."

Elyas never changed his expression or the way he lay on his side, but there was something about the tilt of his head that spoke of ears pricking up. The four wolves sat down as Perrin went on; he had the impression they were listening, too. The story was a long one, and he told almost all of it. The dream he and the others had had in Baerlon, though, he kept to himself. He waited for the wolves to make some sign they had caught the omission, but they only watched. Dapple seemed friendly, Burn angry. He was hoarse by the time he finished.

". . . and if she doesn't find us in Caemlyn, we'll go on to Tar Valon. We don't have any choice except to get help from the Aes Sedai."

"Trollocs and Halfmen this far south," Elyas mused. "Now that's something to consider." He rooted behind him and tossed Perrin a hide waterbag, not really looking at him. He appeared to be thinking. He waited until Perrin had drunk and replaced the plug before he spoke again. "I don't hold with Aes Sedai. The Red Ajah, those that like hunting for men who mess with the One Power, they wanted to gentle me, once. I told them to their faces they were Black Ajah; served the Dark One, I said, and they didn't like that at all. They couldn't catch me, though, once I got into the forest, but they did try. Yes, they did. Come to that, I doubt any Aes Sedai would take kindly to me, after that. I had to kill a couple of Warders. Bad business, that, killing Warders. Don't like it."

"This talking to wolves," Perrin said uneasily. "It . . . it has to do with the Power?"

"Of course not," Elyas growled. "Wouldn't have worked on me, gentling, but it made me mad, them wanting to try. This is an old thing, boy. Older than Aes Sedai. Older than anybody using the One Power. Old as humankind. Old as wolves. They don't like that either, Aes Sedai. Old things coming again. I'm not the only one. There are other things, other folk. Makes Aes Sedai nervous, makes them mutter about ancient barriers weakening. Things are breaking apart, they say. They're afraid the Dark One will get loose, is what. You'd think I was to blame, the way some of them looked at me. Red Ajah, anyway, but some others, too. The Amyrlin Seat. . . . Aaaah! I keep clear of them, mostly, and clear of friends of Aes Sedai, as well. You will, too, if you're smart."

"I'd like nothing better than to stay away from Aes Sedai," Perrin said.

Egwene gave him a sharp look. He hoped she would not burst out that she wanted to be an Aes Sedai. But she said nothing, though her mouth tightened, and Perrin went on.

"It isn't as if we have a choice. We've had Trollocs chasing us, and Fades, and Draghkar. Everything but Darkfriends. We can't hide, and we can't fight back alone. So who is going to help us? Who else is strong enough, except Aes Sedai?"

Elyas was silent for a time, looking at the wolves, most often at Dapple or Burn. Perrin shifted nervously and tried not to watch. When he watched he had the feeling that he could almost hear what Elyas and the wolves were saying to one another. Even if it had nothing to do with the Power, he wanted no part of it. *He* had *to be making some crazy joke. I can't talk to wolves.* One of the wolves—Hopper, he thought—looked at him and seemed to grin. He wondered how he had put a name to him.

"You could stay with me," Elyas said finally. "With us." Egwene's eyebrows shot up, and Perrin's mouth dropped open. "Well, what could be safer?" Elyas challenged. "Trollocs will take any chance they get to kill a wolf by itself, but they'll go miles out of their way to avoid a pack. And you won't have to worry about Aes Sedai, either. They don't often come into these woods."

"I don't know." Perrin avoided looking at the wolves to either side of him. One was Dapple, and he could feel her eyes on him. "For one thing, it isn't just the Trollocs."

Elyas chuckled coldly. "I've seen a pack pull down one of the Eyeless, too. Lost half the pack, but they wouldn't give up once they had its scent. Trollocs, Myrddraal, it's all one to the wolves. It's you they really want, boy. They've heard of other men who can talk to wolves, but you're the first they've ever met besides me. They'll accept your friend, too, though, and you'll all be safer here than in any city. There's Darkfriends in cities."

"Listen," Perrin said urgently, "I wish you'd stop saying that. I can't—do that . . . what you do, what you're saying."

"As you wish, boy. Play the goat, if you've a mind to. Don't you want to be safe?"

"I'm not deceiving myself. There's nothing to deceive myself about. All we want—"

"We are going to Caemlyn," Egwene spoke up firmly. "And then to Tar Valon."

Closing his mouth, Perrin met her angry look with one of his own. He knew that she followed his lead when she wanted to and not when she did not, but she could at least let him answer for himself. "What about you, Perrin?" he said, and answered himself. "Me? Well, let me think. Yes. Yes, I think I'll go on." He turned a mild smile on her. "Well, Egwene, that makes both of us. I guess I'm going with you, at that. Good to talk these things out before making a decision, isn't it?" She blushed, but the set of her jaw never lessened.

Elyas grunted. "Dapple said that's what you'd decide. She said the girl's planted firmly in the human world, while you"—he nodded at Perrin—"stand halfway between. Under the circumstances, I suppose we'd better go south with you. Otherwise, you'll probably starve to death, or get lost, or—"

Abruptly Burn stood up, and Elyas turned his head to regard the big wolf. After a moment Dapple rose, too. She moved closer to Elyas, so that she also was meeting Burn's stare. The tableau was frozen for long minutes, then Burn whirled and vanished into the night. Dapple shook herself, then resumed her place, flopping down as if nothing had happened.

Elyas met Perrin's questioning eyes. "Dapple runs this pack," he explained. "Some of the males could best her if they challenged, but she's smarter than any of them, and they all know it. She's saved the pack more than once. But Burn thinks the pack is wasting time with you three. Hating Trollocs is about all there is to him, and if there are Trollocs this far south he wants to be off killing them."

"We quite understand," Egwene said, sounding relieved. "We really can find our own way . . . with some directions, of course, if you'll give them."

Elyas waved a hand. "I said Dapple leads this pack, didn't I? In the morning, I'll start south with you, and so will they." Egwene looked as if that was not the best news she could have heard.

Perrin sat wrapped in his own silence. He could *feel* Burn leaving. And the scarred male was not the only one; a dozen others, all young males, loped after him. He wanted to believe it was all Elyas playing on his imagination, but he could not. Just before the departing wolves faded from his mind, he felt a thought he knew came from Burn, as sharp and clear as if it were his own thought. Hatred. Hatred and the taste of blood.

CHAPTER
24

Flight Down the Arinelle

Water dripped in the distance, hollow splashes echoing and reechoing, losing their source forever. There were stone bridges and railless ramps everywhere, all sprouting off from broad, flat-topped stone spires, all polished and smooth and streaked with red and gold. Level on level, the maze stretched up and down through the murk, without any apparent beginning or end. Every bridge led to a spire, every ramp to another spire, other bridges. Whatever direction Rand looked, as far as his eye could make out in the dimness it was the same, above as well as below. There was not enough light to see clearly, and he was almost glad of it. Some of those ramps led to platforms that had to be directly above the ones below. He could not see the base of any of them. He pressed, seeking freedom, knowing it was an illusion. Everything was illusion.

He knew the illusion; he had followed it too many times not to know. However far he went, up or down or in any direction, there was only the shiny stone. Stone, but the dankness of deep, fresh-turned earth permeated the air, and the sickly sweetness of decay. The smell of a grave opened out of its time. He tried not to breathe, but the smell filled his nostrils. It clung to his skin like oil.

A flicker of motion caught his eye, and he froze where he was, half crouched against the polished guardwall around one of the spire tops. It was no hiding place. From a thousand places a watcher could have seen him. Shadow filled the air, but there were no deeper shadows in which to hide. The light did not come from lamps, or lanterns, or torches; it was simply there, such as it was, as if it seeped out of the air. Enough by which to see, after a fashion; enough by which to be seen. But stillness gave a little protection.

The movement came again, and now it was clear. A man striding up a distant ramp, careless of the lack of railings and the drop to nothing below. The man's cloak rippled with his stately haste, and his head turned, searching, searching. The distance was too far for Rand to see more than the shape in the murk, but he did not need to be closer to know the cloak was the red of fresh blood, that the searching eyes blazed like two furnaces.

He tried tracing the maze with his eyes, to see how many connections Ba'alzamon needed before reaching him, then gave it up as useless. Distances were deceiving here, another lesson he had learned. What seemed far away might be reached by turning a corner; what appeared close could be out of reach altogether. The only thing to do, as it had been from the beginning, was to keep moving. Keep moving, and not think. Thinking was dangerous, he knew.

Yet, as he turned away from Ba'alzamon's distant form, he could not help wondering about Mat. Was Mat somewhere in this maze? *Or are there two mazes, two Ba'alzamons?* His mind skittered away from that; it was too dreadful to dwell on. *Is this like Baerlon? Then why can't he find me?* That was a little better. A small comfort. *Comfort? Blood and ashes, where's the comfort in it?*

There had been two or three close brushes, though he could not remember them clearly, but for a long, long time— how long?—he had run while Ba'alzamon vainly pursued. Was this like Baerlon, or was it only a nightmare, only a dream like other men's dreams?

For an instant, then—just for the length of time it took to take a breath—he knew why it was dangerous to think, what it was dangerous to think about. As it had before, every time he allowed himself to think of what surrounded him as a dream, the air shimmered, clouding his eyes. It turned to jell, holding him. Just for an instant.

The gritty heat prickled his skin, and his throat had long since gone dry as he trotted down the thorn-hedge maze. How long had it been now? His sweat evaporated before it had a chance to bead, and his eyes burned. Overhead—and not too far overhead, at that—boiled furious, steely clouds streaked with black, but not a breath of air stirred in the maze. For a moment he thought it had been different, but the thought evaporated in the heat. He had been here a long time. It was dangerous to think, he knew that.

Smooth stones, pale and rounded, made a sketchy pavement, half buried in the bone-dry dust that rose in puffs at even his lightest step. It tickled his nose, threatening a sneeze that might give him away; when he tried to breathe through his mouth, dust clogged his throat until he choked.

This was a dangerous place; he knew that, too. Ahead of him he could see three openings in the high wall of thorns, then the way curved out of sight. Ba'alzamon could be approaching any one of those corners at that very moment. There had been two or three encounters already, though he could not remember much beyond that they had happened and he had escaped . . . somehow. Dangerous to think too much.

Panting in the heat, he stopped to examine the maze wall. Thickly woven thorn bushes, brown and dead-looking, with cruel black thorns like inch-long hooks. Too tall to see over, too dense to see through. Gingerly he touched the wall, and gasped. Despite all his care, a thorn pierced his finger, burning like a hot needle. He stumbled back, his heels catching on the stones, shaking his hand and scattering thick drops of blood. The burn began to subside, but his whole hand throbbed.

Abruptly he forgot the pain. His heel had overturned one of the smooth stones, kicked it out of the dry ground. He stared at it, and empty eye sockets stared back. A skull. A human skull. He looked along the pathway at all the smooth, pale stones, all exactly alike. He shifted his feet hastily, but he could not move without walking on them, and he could not stay still without standing on them. A stray thought took vague shape, that things might not be what they seemed, but he pushed it down ruthlessly. Thinking was dangerous here.

He took a shaky hold on himself. Staying in one place was dangerous, too. That was one of the things he knew dimly but with certainty. The flow of blood from his finger had dwindled to a slow drip, and the throb was almost gone. Sucking his fingertip, he started down the path in the direction he happened to be facing. One way was as good as another in here.

Now he remembered hearing once that you could get out of a maze by always turning in the same direction. At the first opening in the wall of thorns he turned right, then right again at the next. And found himself face-to-face with Ba'alzamon.

Surprise flitted across Ba'alzamon's face, and his blood-red cloak settled as he stopped short. Flames soared in his eyes, but in the heat of the maze Rand barely felt them.

"How long do you think you can evade me, boy? How long do you think you can evade your fate? You are mine!"

Stumbling back, Rand wondered why he was fumbling at his belt, as if for a sword. "Light help me," he muttered. "Light help me." He could not remember what it meant.

"The Light will not help you, boy, and the Eye of the World will not serve you. You are my hound, and if you will not course at my command, I will strangle you with the corpse of the Great Serpent!"

Ba'alzamon stretched out his hand, and suddenly Rand knew a way to escape, a misty, half-formed memory that screamed danger, but nothing to the danger of being touched by the Dark One.

"A dream!" Rand shouted. "This is a dream!"

Ba'alzamon's eyes began to widen, in surprise or anger or both, then the air shimmered, and his features blurred, and faded.

Rand turned about in one spot, staring. Staring at his own image thrown back at him a thousandfold. Ten thousandfold. Above was blackness, and blackness below, but all around him stood mirrors, mirrors set at every angle, mirrors as far as he could see, all showing him, crouched and turning, staring wide-eyed and frightened.

A red blur drifted across the mirrors. He spun, trying to catch it, but in every mirror it drifted behind his own image and vanished. Then it was back again, but not as a blur. Ba'alzamon strode across the mirrors, ten thousand Ba'alzamons, searching, crossing and recrossing the silvery mirrors.

He found himself staring at the reflection of his own face, pale and shivering in the knife-edge cold. Ba'alzamon's image grew behind his, staring at him; not seeing, but staring still. In every mirror, the flames of Ba'alzamon's face raged behind him, enveloping, consuming, merging. He wanted

THE EYE OF THE WORLD

to scream, but his throat was frozen. There was only one
face in those endless mirrors. His own face. Ba'alzamon's
face. One face.

Rand jerked, and opened his eyes. Darkness, lessened only
slightly by a pale light. Barely breathing, he moved nothing except his eyes. A rough wool blanket covered him to
his shoulders, and his head was cradled on his arms. He
could feel smooth wooden planks under his hands. Deck
planks. Rigging creaked in the night. He let out a long
breath. He was on the *Spray*. It was over . . . for another
night, at least.

Without thinking he put his finger in his mouth. At the
taste of blood, he stopped breathing. Slowly he put his hand
close to his face, to where he could see in the dim moonlight, to where he could watch the bead of blood form on
his fingertip. Blood from the prick of a thorn.

The *Spray* made haste slowly down the Arinelle. The wind
came strong, but from directions that made the sails useless. With all Captain Domon's demand for speed, the vessel crept along. By night a man in the bows cast a tallowed
lead by lantern light, calling back the depth to the steersman, while the current carried her downriver against the
wind with the sweeps pulled in. There were no rocks to fear
in the Arinelle, but shallows and shoals there were aplenty,
where a boat could go hard aground to remain, bows and
more dug into the mud, until help came. If it was help that
came first. By day the sweeps worked from sunrise to sunset, but the wind fought them as if it wanted to push the
boat back upriver.

They did not put in to shore, neither by day nor by night.
Bayle Domon drove boat and crew alike hard, railing at the
contrary winds, cursing the slow pace. He blistered the crew
for sluggards at the oars and flayed them with his tongue for
every mishandled line, his low, hard voice painting Trollocs ten feet tall among them on the deck, ripping out their
throats. For two days that was enough to send every man
leaping. Then the shock of the Trolloc attack began to fade,
and men began to mutter about an hour to stretch their legs

ashore, and about the dangers of running downriver in the dark.

The crew kept their grumbles quiet, watching out of the corners of their eyes to make sure Captain Domon was not close enough to hear, but he seemed to hear everything said on his boat. Each time the grumblings began, he silently brought out the long, scythe-like sword and cruelly hooked axe that had been found on the deck after the attack. He would hang them on the mast for an hour, and those who had been wounded would finger their bandages, and the mutterings quieted for a day or so, at least, until one or another of the crew began thinking once more that surely they had left the Trollocs far behind by now, and the cycle began yet again.

Rand noticed that Thom Merrilin stayed clear of the crew when they began whispering together and frowning, though usually he was slapping backs and telling jokes and exchanging banter in a way that put a grin on even the hardest-working man. Thom watched those secretive mutters with a wary eye while appearing to be absorbed in lighting his long-stemmed pipe, or tuning his harp, or almost anything except paying any mind at all to the crew. Rand did not understand why. It was not the three who had come aboard chased by Trollocs whom the crew seemed to blame, but rather Floran Gelb.

For the first day or two Gelb's wiry figure could almost always be found addressing any crewman he could corner, telling his version of the night Rand and the others came on board. Gelb's manner slid from bluster to whines and back again, and his lip always curled when he pointed to Thom or Mat, or especially Rand, trying to lay the blame on them.

"They're strangers," Gelb pleaded, quietly and with an eye out for the captain. "What do we know of them? The Trollocs came with them, that's what we know. They're in league."

"Fortune, Gelb, stow it," growled a man with his hair in a pigtail and a small blue star tattooed on his cheek. He did not look at Gelb as he coiled a line on deck, working it in with his bare toes. All the sailors went barefoot despite the cold; boots could slip on a wet deck. "You'd call your mother Darkfriend if it'd let you slack. Get away from me!" He spat on Gelb's foot and went back to the line.

All the crew remembered the watch Gelb had not kept, and the pigtailed man's was the politest response he got. No one even wanted to work with him. Gelb found himself relegated to solitary tasks, all of them filthy, such as scrubbing the galley's greasy pots, or crawling into the bilges on his belly to search for leaks among years of slime. Soon he stopped talking to anyone. His shoulders took on a defensive hunch, and injured silence became his stance—the more people watching, the more injured, though it earned him no more than a grunt. When Gelb's eyes fell on Rand, however, or on Mat or Thom, murder flashed across his long-nosed face.

When Rand mentioned to Mat that Gelb would cause them trouble sooner or later, Mat looked around the boat, saying, "Can we trust any of them? Any at all?" Then he went off to find a place where he could be alone, or as alone as he could get on a boat less than thirty paces from its raised bow to the sternpost where the steering oars were mounted. Mat had spent too much time alone since the night at Shadar Logoth; brooding, as Rand saw it.

Thom said, "Trouble won't come from Gelb, boy, if it comes. Not yet, at least. None of the crew will back him, and he hasn't the nerve to try anything alone. But the others, now . . . ? Domon almost seems to think the Trollocs are chasing him, personally, but the rest are beginning to think the danger is past. They might just decide they have had enough. They're on the edge of it, as it is." He hitched his patch-covered cloak, and Rand had the feeling he was checking his hidden knives—his second-best set. "If they mutiny, boy, they won't leave passengers behind to tell the tale. The Queen's Writ might not have much force this far from Caemlyn, but even a village mayor will do something about that." That was when Rand, too, began trying not to be noticed when he watched the crewmen.

Thom did his part in diverting the crew from thoughts of mutiny. He told stories, with all the flourishes, every morning and every night, and in between he played any song they requested. To support the notion that Rand and Mat wanted to be apprentice gleemen, he set aside a time each day for lessons, and that was an entertainment for the crew, as well. He would not let either of them touch his harp, of course, and their sessions with the flute produced pained winces, in the beginning, at least, and laughter from the crew even while they were covering their ears.

He taught the boys some of the easier stories, a little simple tumbling, and, of course, juggling. Mat complained about what Thom demanded of them, but Thom blew out his mustaches and glared right back.

"I don't know how to play at teaching, boy. I either teach a thing, or I don't. Now! Even a country bumpkin ought to be able to do a simple handstand. Up you go."

Crewmen who were not working always gathered, squatting in a circle around the three. Some even tried their hand at the lessons Thom taught, laughing at their own fumblings. Gelb stood alone and watched it all darkly, hating them all.

A good part of each day Rand spent leaning on the railing, staring at the shore. It was not that he really expected to see Egwene or any of the others suddenly appear on the riverbank, but the boat traveled so slowly that he sometimes hoped for it. They could catch up without riding too hard. If they had escaped. If they were still alive.

The river rolled on without any sign of life, nor any boat to be seen except the *Spray*. But that was not to say there was nothing to see, and wonder at. In the middle of the first day, the Arinelle ran between high bluffs that stretched for half a mile on either side. For that whole length the stone had been cut into figures, men and women a hundred feet tall, with crowns proclaiming them kings and queens. No two were alike in that royal procession, and long years separated the first from the last. Wind and rain had worn those at the north end smooth and almost featureless, with faces and details becoming more distinct as they went south. The river lapped around the statues' feet, feet washed to smooth nubs, those that were not gone completely. *How long have they stood there,* Rand wondered. *How long for the river to wear away so much stone?* None of the crew so much as looked up from their work, they had seen the ancient carvings so many times before.

Another time, when the eastward shore had become flat grassland again, broken only occasionally by thickets; the sun glinted off something in the distance. "What can that be?" Rand wondered aloud. "It looks like metal."

Captain Domon was walking by, and he paused, squinting

toward the glint. "It do be metal," he said. His words still
ran together, but Rand had come to understand without having to puzzle it out. "A tower of metal. I have seen it close
up, and I know. River traders use it as a marker. We be ten
days from Whitebridge at the rate we go."

"A metal tower?" Rand said, and Mat, sitting cross-legged
with his back against a barrel, roused from his brooding to
listen.

The captain nodded. "Aye. Shining steel, by the look and
feel of it, but no a spot of rust. Two hundred feet high, it be,
as big around as a house, with no a mark on it and never an
opening to be found."

"I'll bet there's treasure inside," Mat said. He stood up
and stared toward the far tower as the river carried the
Spray beyond it. "A thing like that must have been made to
protect something valuable."

"Mayhap, lad," the captain rumbled. "There be stranger
things in the world than this, though. On Tremalking, one
of the Sea Folk's isles, there be a stone hand fifty feet high
sticking out of a hill, clutching a crystal sphere as big as
this vessel. There be treasure under that hill if there be treasure anywhere, but the island people want no part of digging
there, and the Sea Folk care for naught but sailing their ships
and searching for the Coramoor, their Chosen One."

"I'd dig," Mat said. "How far is this . . . Tremalking?"
A clump of trees slid in front of the shining tower, but he
stared as if he could see it yet.

Captain Domon shook his head. "No, lad, it no be the
treasure that makes for seeing the world. If you find yourself a fistful of gold, or some dead king's jewels, all well
and good, but it be the strangeness you see that pulls you to
the next horizon. In Tanchico—that be a port on the Aryth
Ocean—part of the Panarch's Palace were built in the Age
of Legends, or so it be said. There be a wall there with a frieze
showing animals no man living has ever seen."

"Any child can draw an animal nobody's ever seen,"
Rand said, and the captain chuckled.

"Aye, lad, so they can. But can a child make the bones of
those animals? In Tanchico they have them, all fastened together like the animal was. They stand in a part of the Panarch's Palace where any can enter and see. The Breaking
left a thousand wonders behind, and there been half a dozen

FLIGHT DOWN THE ARINELLE

empires or more since, some rivaling Artur Hawkwing's, every one leaving things to see and find. Lightsticks and razorlace and heartstone. A crystal lattice covering an island, and it hums when the moon is up. A mountain hollowed into a bowl, and in its center, a silver spike a hundred spans high, and any who comes within a mile of it, dies. Rusted ruins, and broken bits, and things found on the bottom of the sea, things not even the oldest books know the meaning of I've gathered a few, myself. Things you never dreamed of, in more places than you can see in ten lifetimes. That be the strangeness that will draw you on."

"We used to dig up bones in the Sand Hills," Rand said slowly. "Strange bones. There was part of a fish—I think it was a fish—as big as this boat, once. Some said it was bad luck, digging in the hills."

The captain eyed him shrewdly. "You thinking about home already, lad, and you just set out in the world? The world will put a hook in your mouth. You'll set off chasing the sunset, you wait and see . . . and if you ever go back, your village'll no be big enough to hold you."

"No!" He gave a start. How long had it been since he had thought of home, of Emond's Field? And what of Tam? It had to be days. It felt like months. "I will go home, one day, when I can. I'll raise sheep, like . . . like my father, and if I never leave again it will be too soon. Isn't that right, Mat? As soon as we can we're going home and forget all this even exists."

With a visible effort Mat pulled away from staring upriver after the vanished tower. "What? Oh. Yes, of course. We'll go home. Of course." As he turned to go, Rand heard him muttering under his breath. "I'll bet he just doesn't want anybody else going after the treasure." He did not seem to realize he had spoken aloud.

Four days into their trip downriver found Rand atop the mast, sitting on the blunt end with his legs wrapped in the stays. The *Spray* rolled gently on the river, but fifty feet above the water that easy roll made the top of the mast sway back and forth through wide arcs. He threw back his head and laughed into the wind that blew in his face.

The oars were out, and from here the boat looked like some twelve-legged spider creeping down the Arinelle. He had been as high as this before, in trees back in the Two

Rivers, but this time there were no branches to block his view. Everything on deck, the sailors at the sweeps, men on their knees scrubbing the deck with smoothstones, men doing things with lines and hatchcovers, looked so odd when seen from right overhead, all squat and foreshortened, that he had spent an hour just staring at them and chuckling.

He still chuckled whenever he looked down at them, but now he was staring at the riverbanks flowing by. That was the way it seemed, as if he were still—except for the swaying back and forth, of course—and the banks slid slowly by, trees and hills marching along to either side. He was still, and the whole world moved past him.

On sudden impulse he unwrapped his legs from the stays bracing the mast and held his arms and legs out to either side, balancing against the sway. For three complete arcs he kept his balance like that, then suddenly it was gone. Arms and legs windmilling, he toppled forward and grabbed the forestay. Legs splayed to either side of the mast, nothing holding him to his precarious perch but his two hands on the stay, he laughed. Gulping huge breaths of the fresh, cold wind, he laughed with the exhilaration of it.

"Lad," came Thom's hoarse voice. "Lad, if you're trying to break your fool neck, don't do it by falling on me."

Rand looked down. Thom clung to the ratlines just below him, staring up the last few feet grimly. Like Rand, the gleeman had left his cloak below. "Thom," he said delightedly. "Thom, when did you come up here?"

"When you wouldn't pay any attention to people shouting at you. Burn me, boy, you've got everybody thinking you've gone mad."

He looked down and was surprised to see all the faces staring up at him. Only Mat, sitting cross-legged up in the bows with his back to the mast, was not looking at him. Even the men at the oars had their eyes raised, letting their stroke go ragged. And no one was berating them for it. Rand twisted his head around to look under his arm at the stern. Captain Domon stood by the steering oar, ham-like fists on his hips, glaring at him atop the mast. He turned back to grin at Thom. "You want me to come down, then?"

Thom nodded vigorously. "I would appreciate it greatly."

"All right." Shifting his grip on the forestay, he sprang forward off the mast top. He heard Thom bite off an oath as his fall was cut short and he dangled from the forestay by his hands. The gleeman scowled at him, one hand half stretched out to catch him. He grinned at Thom again. "I'm going down now."

Swinging his legs up, he hooked one knee over the thick line that ran from the mast to the bow, then caught it in the crook of his elbow and let go with his hands. Slowly, then with increasing speed, he slid down. Just short of the bow he dropped to his feet on the deck right in front of Mat, took one step to catch his balance, and turned to face the boat with arms spread wide, the way Thom did after a tumbling trick.

Scattered clapping rose from the crew, but he was looking down at Mat in surprise, and at what Mat held, hidden from everyone else by his body. A curved dagger with a gold scabbard worked in strange symbols. Fine gold wire wrapped the hilt, which was capped by a ruby as big as Rand's thumbnail, and the quillons were golden-scaled serpents baring their fangs.

Mat continued to slide the dagger in and out of its sheath for a moment. Still playing with the dagger he raised his head slowly; his eyes had a faraway look. Suddenly they focused on Rand, and he gave a start and stuffed the dagger under his coat.

Rand squatted on his heels, with his arms crossed on his knees. "Where did you get that?" Mat said nothing, looking quickly to see if anyone else was close by. They were alone, for a wonder. "You didn't take it from Shadar Logoth, did you?"

Mat stared at him. "It's your fault. Yours and Perrin's. The two of you pulled me away from the treasure, and I had it in my hand. Mordeth didn't give it to me. I took it, so Moiraine's warnings about his gifts don't count. You won't tell anybody, Rand. They might try to steal it."

"I won't tell anybody," Rand said. "I think Captain Domon is honest, but I wouldn't put anything past the rest of them, especially Gelb."

"Not anybody," Mat insisted. "Not Domon, not Thom, not anybody. We're the only two left from Emond's Field, Rand. We can't afford to trust anybody else."

"They're alive, Mat. Egwene, and Perrin. I know they're alive." Mat looked ashamed. "I'll keep your secret, though.

Just the two of us. At least we don't have to worry about money now. We can sell it for enough to travel to Tar Valon like kings."

"Of course," Mat said after a minute. "If we have to. Just don't tell anybody until I say so."

"I said I wouldn't. Listen, have you had any more dreams since we came on the boat? Like in Baerlon? This is the first chance I've had to ask without six people listening."

Mat turned his head away, giving him a sidelong look. "Maybe."

"What do you mean, maybe? Either you have or you haven't."

"All right, all right, I have. I don't want to talk about it. I don't even want to think about it. It doesn't do any good."

Before either of them could say more Thom came striding up the deck, his cloak over his arm. The wind whipped his white hair about, and his long mustaches seemed to bristle. "I managed to convince the captain you aren't crazy," he announced, "that it was part of your training." He caught hold of the forestay and shook it. "That fool stunt of yours, sliding down the rope, helped, but you are lucky you didn't break your fool neck."

Rand's eyes went to the forestay and followed it up to the top of the mast, and as they did his mouth dropped open. He *had* slid down that. And he had been sitting on top of. . . .

Suddenly he could see himself up there, arms and legs spread wide. He sat down hard, and barely caught himself short of ending up flat on his back. Thom was looking at him thoughtfully.

"I didn't know you had such a good head for heights, lad. We might be able to play in Illian, or Ebou Dar, or even Tear. People in the big cities in the south like tightrope walkers and slackwire artists."

"We're going to—" At the last minute Rand remembered to look around for anyone close enough to overhear. Several of the crew were watching them, including Gelb, glaring as usual, but none could hear what he was saying. "To Tar Valon," he finished. Mat shrugged as if it were all the same to him where they went.

"At the moment, lad," Thom said, settling down beside them, "but tomorrow . . . who knows? That's the way with a gleeman's life." He took a handful of colored balls from one of his wide sleeves. "Since I have you down out of the air, we'll work on the triple crossover."

Rand's gaze drifted to the top of the mast, and he shivered. *What's happening to me? Light, what?* He had to find out. He had to get to Tar Valon before he really did go mad.

CHAPTER
25

The Traveling People

Bela walked along placidly under the weak sun as if the three wolves trotting not far off were only village dogs, but the way she rolled her eyes at them from time to time, showing white all the way around, indicated she felt nothing of the sort. Egwene, on the mare's back, was just as bad. She watched the wolves constantly from the corner of her eye, and sometimes she twisted in the saddle to look around. Perrin was sure she was hunting for the rest of the pack, though she denied it angrily when he suggested as much, denied being afraid of the wolves that paced them, denied worrying about the rest of the pack or what it was up to. She denied, and went right on looking, tight-eyed and wetting her lips uneasily.

The rest of the pack was far distant; he could have told her that. *What good, even if she believed me? Especially if she did.* He was of no mind to open that basket of snakes until he had to. He did not want to think about *how* he knew. The fur-clad man loped ahead of them, sometimes looking almost like a wolf himself, and he never looked around when Dapple, Hopper, and Wind appeared, but he knew, too.

The Emond's Fielders had wakened at dawn that first morning to find Elyas cooking more rabbit and watching them over his full beard without much expression. Except for Dapple, Hopper, and Wind, no wolves were to be seen. In the pale, early daylight, deep shade still lingered under the big oak, and the bare trees beyond looked like fingers stripped to the bone.

"They're around," Elyas answered when Egwene asked where the rest of the pack had gone. "Close enough to help, if need be. Far enough off to avoid any human trouble we get into. Sooner or later there's always trouble when there's two humans together. If we need them, they'll be there."

Something tickled the back of Perrin's mind as he ripped free a bite of roast rabbit. A direction, vaguely sensed. *Of course! That's where they. . . .* The hot juices in his mouth abruptly lost all taste. He picked at the tubers Elyas had cooked in the coals—they tasted something like turnips— but his appetite was gone.

When they had started out Egwene insisted that everyone take a turn riding, and Perrin did not even bother to argue.

"First turn is yours," he told her.

She nodded. "And then you, Elyas."

"My own legs are good enough for me," Elyas said. He looked at Bela, and the mare rolled her eyes as if he were one of the wolves. "Besides, I don't think she wants me riding her."

"That's nonsense," Egwene replied firmly. "There is no point in being stubborn about it. The sensible thing is for everybody to ride sometimes. According to you we have a long way still to go."

"I said no, girl."

She took a deep breath, and Perrin was wondering if she would succeed in bullying Elyas the way she did him, when he realized she was standing there with her mouth open, not saying a word. Elyas was looking at her, just looking, with those yellow wolf's eyes. Egwene stepped back from the raw-boned man, and licked her lips, and stepped back again. Before Elyas turned away, she had backed all the way to Bela and scrambled up onto the mare's back. As the man turned to lead them south, Perrin thought his grin was a good deal like a wolf's, too.

For three days they traveled in that manner, walking and riding south and east all day, stopping only when twilight thickened. Elyas seemed to scorn the haste of city men, but he did not believe in wasting time when there was some- where to go.

The three wolves were seldom seen. Each night they came to the fire for a time, and sometimes in the day they showed themselves briefly, appearing close at hand when least ex- pected and vanishing in the same manner. Perrin knew they were out there, though, and where. He knew when they were scouting the path ahead and when they were watching the backtrail. He knew when they left the pack's usual hunting grounds, and Dapple sent the pack back to wait for her. Sometimes the three that remained faded from his mind, but long before they were close enough to see again, he was aware of them returning. Even when the trees dwindled to wide-scattered groves separated by great swathes of winter-dead grass, they were as ghosts when they did not want to be seen, but he could have pointed a finger straight at them at any time. He did not know how he knew, and he tried to convince himself that it was just his imagination playing tricks, but it did no good. Just as Elyas knew, he knew.

He tried not thinking about wolves, but they crept into his thoughts all the same. He had not dreamed about Ba'alzamon since meeting Elyas and the wolves. His dreams, as much as he remembered of them on waking, were of everyday things, just as he might have dreamed at home . . . before Baerlon . . . before Winternight. Normal dreams—with one addition. In every dream he remembered there was a point where he straightened from Master Luhhan's forge to wipe the sweat from his face, or turned from dancing with the village girls on the Green, or lifted his head from a book in front of the fireplace, and whether he was outside or under a roof, there was a wolf close to hand. Always the wolf's back was to him, and always he knew—in the dreams it seemed the normal course of things, even at Alsbet Luhhan's dinner table—that the wolf's yellow eyes were watching for what might come, guarding against what might come. Only when he was awake did the dreams seem strange.

Three days they journeyed, with Dapple, Hopper, and Wind bringing them rabbits and squirrels, and Elyas pointing out plants, few of which Perrin recognized, as good to eat. Once a rabbit burst out almost from under Bela's hooves; before Perrin could get a stone in his sling, Elyas skewered it with his long knife at twenty paces. Another time Elyas brought down a fat pheasant, on the wing, with his bow. They ate far better than they had when on their own, but Perrin would as soon have gone back on short rations if it had meant different company. He was not sure how Egwene felt, but he would have been willing to go hungry if he could do it without the wolves. Three days, into the afternoon.

A stand of trees lay ahead, larger than most they had

seen, a good four miles across. The sun sat low in the western sky, pushing slanted shadows off to their right, and the wind was picking up. Perrin felt the wolves give over quartering behind them and start forward, not hurrying. They had smelled and seen nothing dangerous. Egwene was taking her turn on Bela. It was time to start looking for a camp for the night, and the big copse would serve the purpose well.

As they came close to the trees, three mastiffs burst from cover, broad-muzzled dogs as tall as the wolves and even heavier, teeth bared in loud, rumbling snarls. They stopped short as soon as they were in the open, but no more than thirty feet separated them from the three people, and their dark eyes kindled with a killing light.

Bela, already on edge from the wolves, whinnied and almost unseated Egwene, but Perrin had his sling whirling around his head in an instant. No need to use the axe on dogs; a stone in the ribs would send the worst dog running.

Elyas waved a hand at him without taking his eyes from the stiff-legged dogs. "Hssst! None of that now!"

Perrin gave him a puzzled frown, but let the sling slow its spin and finally fall to his side. Egwene managed to get Bela under control; she and the mare both watched the dogs warily.

The mastiffs' hackles stood stiff, and their ears were laid back, and their growls sounded like earthquakes. Abruptly Elyas raised one finger shoulder high and whistled, a long, shrill whistle that rose higher and higher and did not end. The growls cut off raggedly. The dogs stepped back, whining and turning their heads as if they wanted to go but were held. Their eyes remained locked to Elyas's finger.

Slowly Elyas lowered his hand, and the pitch of his whistle lowered with it. The dogs followed, until they lay flat on the ground, tongues lolling from their mouths. Three tails wagged.

"See," Elyas said, walking to the dogs. "There's no need for weapons." The mastiffs licked his hands, and he scratched their broad heads and fondled their ears. "They look meaner than they are. They meant to frighten us off, and they wouldn't have bitten unless we tried to go into the trees. Anyway, there's no worry of that, now. We can make the next thicket before full dark."

When Perrin looked at Egwene, her mouth was hanging open. He shut his own mouth with a click of teeth.

Still patting the dogs, Elyas studied the stand of trees. "There'll be Tuatha'an here. The Traveling People." They stared at him blankly, and he added, "Tinkers."

"Tinkers?" Perrin exclaimed. "I've always wanted to see the Tinkers. They camp across the river from Taren Ferry sometimes, but they don't come down into the Two Rivers, as far as I know. I don't know why not."

Egwene sniffed. "Probably because the Taren Ferry folk are as great thieves as the Tinkers. They'd no doubt end up stealing each other blind. Master Elyas, if there really are Tinkers close by, shouldn't we go on? We don't want Bela stolen, and . . . well, we do not have much else, but everybody knows Tinkers will steal anything."

"Including infants?" Elyas asked dryly. "Kidnap children, and all that?" He spat, and she blushed. Those stories about babies were told sometimes, but most often by Cenn Buie or one of the Coplins or Congars. The other tales, everybody knew. "The Tinkers make me sick sometimes, but they don't steal any more than most folks. A good bit less than some I know."

"It will be getting dark soon, Elyas," Perrin said. "We have to camp somewhere. Why not with them, if they'll have us?" Mistress Luhhan had a Tinker-mended pot that she claimed was better than new. Master Luhhan was not too happy about his wife's praise of the Tinker work, but Perrin wanted to see how it was done. Yet there was a reluctance about Elyas that he did not understand. "Is there some reason we shouldn't?"

Elyas shook his head, but the reluctance was still there, in the set of his shoulders and the tightness of his mouth. "May as well. Just don't pay any mind to what they say. Lot of foolishness. Most times the Traveling People do things any which way, but there's times they set a store by formality, so you do what I do. And keep your secrets. No need to tell the world everything."

The dogs trailed along beside them, wagging their tails, as Elyas led the way into the trees. Perrin felt the wolves slow, and knew they would not enter. They were not afraid of the dogs—they were contemptuous of dogs, who had given up freedom to sleep by a fire—but people they avoided.

Elyas walked surely, as if he knew the way, and near the center of the stand the Tinkers' wagons appeared, scattered among the oak and ash.

Like everyone else in Emond's Field, Perrin had heard a good deal about the Tinkers even if he had never seen any, and the camp was just what he expected. Their wagons were small houses on wheels, tall wooden boxes lacquered and painted in bright colors, reds and blues and yellows and greens and some hues to which he could not put a name. The Traveling People were going about work that was disappointingly everyday, cooking, sewing, tending children, mending harness, but their clothes were even more colorful than the wagons—and seemingly chosen at random; sometimes coat and breeches, or dress and shawl, went together in a way that hurt his eyes. They looked like butterflies in a field of wildflowers.

Four or five men in different places around the camp played fiddles and flutes, and a few people danced like rainbow-hued hummingbirds. Children and dogs ran playing among the cookfires. The dogs were mastiffs just like those that had confronted the travelers, but the children tugged at their ears and tails and climbed on their backs, and the massive dogs accepted it all placidly. The three with Elyas, tongues hanging out, looked up at the bearded man as if he were their best friend. Perrin shook his head. They were still big enough to reach a man's throat while barely getting their front feet off the ground.

Abruptly the music stopped, and he realized all the Tinkers were looking at him and his companions. Even the children and dogs stood still and watched, warily, as if on the point of flight.

For a moment there was no sound at all, then a wiry man, gray-haired and short, stepped forward and bowed gravely to Elyas. He wore a high-collared red coat, and baggy, bright green trousers tucked into knee boots. "You are welcome to our fires. Do you know the song?"

Elyas bowed in the same way, both hands pressed to his chest. "Your welcome warms my spirit, Mahdi, as your fires warm the flesh, but I do not know the song."

"Then we seek still," the gray-haired man intoned. "As it was, so shall it be, if we but remember, seek, and find." He swept an arm toward the fires with a smile, and his voice took on a cheerful lightness. "The meal is almost ready. Join us, please."

As if that had been a signal the music sprang up again, and the children took up their laughter and ran with the dogs. Everyone in the camp went back to what they had been doing just as though the newcomers were long-accepted friends.

The gray-haired man hesitated, though, and looked at Elyas. "Your . . . other friends? They will stay away? They frighten the poor dogs so."

"They'll stay away, Raen." Elyas's headshake had a touch of scorn. "You should know that by now."

The gray-haired man spread his hands as if to say nothing was ever certain. As he turned to lead them into the camp, Egwene dismounted and moved close to Elyas. "You two are friends?" A smiling Tinker appeared to take Bela; Egwene gave the reins up reluctantly, after a wry snort from Elyas.

"We know each other," the fur-clad man replied curtly.

"His name is Mahdi?" Perrin said.

Elyas growled something under his breath. "His name's Raen. Mahdi's his title. Seeker. He's the leader of this band. You can call him Seeker if the other sounds odd. He won't mind."

"What was that about a song?" Egwene asked.

"That's why they travel," Elyas said, "or so they say. They're looking for a song. That's what the Mahdi seeks. They say they lost it during the Breaking of the World, and if they can find it again, the paradise of the Age of Legends will return." He ran his eye around the camp and snorted. "They don't even know what the song is; they claim they'll know it when they find it. They don't know how it's supposed to bring paradise, either, but they've been looking near to three thousand years, ever since the Breaking. I expect they'll be looking until the Wheel stops turning."

They reached Raen's fire, then, in the middle of the camp. The Seeker's wagon was yellow trimmed in red, and the spokes of its tall, red-rimmed wheels alternated red and yellow. A plump woman, as gray as Raen but smooth-cheeked still, came out of the wagon and paused on the steps at its back end, straightening a blue-fringed shawl on her shoulders. Her blouse was yellow and her skirt red, both bright.

The combination made Perrin blink, and Egwene made a strangled sound.

When she saw the people following Raen, the woman came down with a welcoming smile. She was Ila, Raen's wife, a head taller than her husband, and she soon made Perrin forget about the colors of her clothes. She had a motherliness that reminded him of Mistress al'Vere and had him feeling welcome from her first smile.

Ila greeted Elyas as an old acquaintance, but with a distance that seemed to pain Raen. Elyas gave her a dry grin and a nod. Perrin and Egwene introduced themselves, and she clasped their hands in both of hers with much more warmth than she had shown Elyas, even hugging Egwene.

"Why, you're lovely, child," she said, cupping Egwene's chin and smiling. "And chilled to the bone, too, I expect. You sit close to the fire, Egwene. All of you sit. Supper is almost ready."

Fallen logs had been pulled around the fire for sitting. Elyas refused even that concession to civilization. He lounged on the ground, instead. Iron tripods held two small kettles over the flames, and an oven rested in the edge of the coals. Ila tended them.

As Perrin and the others were taking their places, a slender young man wearing green stripes strolled up to the fire. He gave Raen a hug and Ila a kiss, and ran a cool eye over Elyas and the Emond's Fielders. He was about the same age as Perrin, and he moved as if he were about to begin dancing with his next step.

"Well, Aram"—Ila smiled fondly—"you have decided to eat with your old grandparents for a change, have you?" Her smile slid over to Egwene as she bent to stir a kettle hanging over the cookfire. "I wonder why?"

Aram settled to an easy crouch with his arms crossed on his knees, across the fire from Egwene. "I am Aram," he told her in a low, confident voice. He no longer seemed aware that anyone was there except her. "I have waited for the first rose of spring, and now I find it at my grandfather's fire."

Perrin waited for Egwene to snicker, then saw that she was staring back at Aram. He looked at the young Tinker again. Aram had more than his share of good looks, he admitted. After a minute Perrin knew who the fellow reminded him of. Wil al'Seen, who had all the girls staring and whispering behind his back whenever he came up from Deven Ride to Emond's Field. Wil courted every girl in sight, and managed to convince every one of them that he was just being polite to all the others.

"Those dogs of yours," Perrin said loudly, and Egwene gave a start, "look as big as bears. I'm surprised you let the children play with them."

Aram's smile slipped, but when he looked at Perrin it came back again, even more sure than before. "They will not harm you. They make a show to frighten away danger, and warn us, but they are trained according to the Way of the Leaf."

"The Way of the Leaf?" Egwene said. "What is that?"

Aram gestured to the trees, his eyes fastened intently on hers. "The leaf lives its appointed time, and does not struggle against the wind that carries it away. The leaf does no harm, and finally falls to nourish new leaves. So it should be with all men. And women." Egwene stared back at him, a faint blush rising in her cheeks.

"But what does that mean?" Perrin said. Aram gave him an irritated glance, but it was Raen who answered.

"It means that no man should harm another for any reason whatsoever." The Seeker's eyes flickered to Elyas. "There is no excuse for violence. None. Not ever."

"What if somebody attacks you?" Perrin insisted. "What if somebody hits you, or tries to rob you, or kill you?"

Raen sighed, a patient sigh, as if Perrin was just not seeing what was so clear to him. "If a man hit me, I would ask him why he wanted to do such a thing. If he still wanted to hit me, I would run away, as I would if he wanted to rob or kill me. Much better that I let him take what he wanted, even my life, than that I should do violence. And I would hope that he was not harmed too greatly."

"But you said you wouldn't hurt him," Perrin said.

"I would not, but violence harms the one who does it as much as the one who receives it." Perrin looked doubtful. "You could cut down a tree with your axe," Raen said. "The axe does violence to the tree, and escapes unharmed. Is that how you see it? Wood is soft compared to steel, but the sharp steel is dulled as it chops, and the sap of the tree will rust and pit it. The mighty axe does violence to the helpless tree, and is harmed by it. So it is with men, though the harm is in the spirit."

"But—"

"Enough," Elyas growled, cutting Perrin off. "Raen, it's bad enough you trying to convert village younglings to that nonsense—it gets you in trouble almost everywhere you go, doesn't it?—but I didn't bring this lot here for you to work on them. Leave over."

"And leave them to you?" Ila said, grinding herbs between her palms and letting them trickle into one of the kettles. Her voice was calm, but her hands rubbed the herbs furiously. "Will you teach them your way, to kill or die? Will you lead them to the fate you seek for yourself, dying alone with only the ravens and your . . . your friends to squabble over your body?"

"Be at peace, Ila," Raen said gently, as if he had heard this all and more a hundred times. "He has been welcomed to our fire, my wife."

Ila subsided, but Perrin noticed that she made no apology. Instead she looked at Elyas and shook her head sadly, then dusted her hands and began taking spoons and pottery bowls from a red chest on the side of the wagon.

Raen turned back to Elyas. "My old friend, how many times must I tell you that we do not try to convert anyone. When village people are curious about our ways, we answer their questions. It is most often the young who ask, true, and sometimes one of them will come with us when we journey on, but it is of their own free will."

"You try telling that to some farm wife who's just found out her son or daughter has run off with you Tinkers," Elyas said wryly. "That's why the bigger towns won't even let you camp nearby. Villages put up with you for your mending things, but the cities don't need it, and they don't like you talking their young folks into running off."

"I would not know what the cities allow." Raen's patience seemed inexhaustible. He certainly did not appear to be getting angry at all. "There are always violent men in cities. In any case, I do not think the song could be found in a city."

"I don't mean to offend you, Seeker," Perrin said slowly, "but. . . . Well, I don't look for violence. I don't think I've even wrestled anybody in years, except for feastday games. But if somebody hit me, I'd hit him back. If I didn't, I would just be encouraging him to think he could hit me whenever he wanted to. Some people think they can take advantage of others, and if you don't let them know they can't, they'll just go around bullying anybody weaker than they are."

"Some people," Aram said with a heavy sadness, "can never overcome their baser instincts." He said it with a look at Perrin that made it clear he was not talking about the bullies Perrin spoke of.

"I'll bet you get to run away a lot," Perrin said, and the young Tinker's face tightened in a way that had nothing to do with the Way of the Leaf.

"I think it is interesting," Egwene said, glaring at Perrin, "to meet someone who doesn't believe his muscles can solve every problem."

Aram's good spirits returned, and he stood, offering her his hands with a smile. "Let me show you our camp. There is dancing."

"I would like that." She smiled back.

Ila straightened from taking loaves of bread from the small iron oven. "But supper is ready, Aram."

"I'll eat with mother," Aram said over his shoulder as he drew Egwene away from the wagon by her hand. "We will both eat with mother." He flashed a triumphant smile at Perrin. Egwene was laughing as they ran.

Perrin got to his feet, then stopped. It was not as if she could come to any harm, not if the camp followed this Way of the Leaf as Raen said. Looking at Raen and Ila, both staring dejectedly after their grandson, he said, "I'm sorry. I am a guest, and I shouldn't have—"

"Don't be foolish," Ila said soothingly. "It was his fault, not yours. Sit down and eat."

"Aram is a troubled young man," Raen added sadly. "He is a good boy, but sometimes I think he finds the Way of the Leaf a hard way. Some do, I fear. Please. My fire is yours. Please?"

Perrin sat back down slowly, still feeling awkward. "What happens to somebody who can't follow the Way?" he asked. "A Tinker, I mean."

Raen and Ila exchanged a worried look, and Raen said, "They leave us. The Lost go to live in the villages."

Ila stared in the direction her grandson had gone. "The

Lost cannot be happy." She sighed, but her face was placid again when she handed out the bowls and spoons.

Perrin stared at the ground, wishing he had not asked, and there was no more talk while Ila filled their bowls with a thick vegetable stew and handed out thick slices of her crusty bread, nor while they ate. The stew was delicious, and Perrin finished three bowls before he stopped. Elyas, he noted with a grin, emptied four.

After the meal Raen filled his pipe, and Elyas produced his own and stuffed it from Raen's oilskin pouch. When the lighting and tamping and relighting were done, they settled back in silence. Ila took out a bundle of knitting. The sun was only a blaze of red above the treetops to the west. The camp had settled in for the night, but the bustle did not slow, only changed. The musicians who had been playing when they entered the camp had been replaced by others, and even more people than before danced in the light of the fires, their shadows leaping against the wagons. Somewhere in the camp a chorus of male voices rose. Perrin slid down in front of the log and soon felt himself dozing.

After a time Raen said, "Have you visited any of the Tuatha'an, Elyas, since you were with us last spring?"

Perrin's eyes drifted open and half shut again.

"No," Elyas replied around his pipestem. "I don't like being around too many people at once."

Raen chuckled. "Especially people who live in a way so opposite to your own, eh? No, my old friend, don't worry. I gave up years ago hoping you would come to the Way. But I have heard a story since last we met, and if you have not heard it yet, it might interest you. It interests me, and I have heard it again and again, every time we meet others of the People."

"I'll listen."

"It begins in the spring two years ago, with a band of the People who were crossing the Waste by the northern route."

Perrin's eyes shot open. "The Waste? The Aiel Waste? They were crossing the Aiel Waste?"

"Some people can enter the Waste without being both-ered," Elyas said. "Gleemen. Peddlers, if they're honest. The Tuatha'an cross the Waste all the time. Merchants from Cairhien used to, before the Tree, and the Aiel War."

"The Aielmen avoid us," Raen said sadly, "though many of us have tried to speak with them. They watch us from a distance, but they will not come near us, nor let us come near them. Sometimes I worry that they might know the song, though I suppose it isn't likely. Among Aiel, men do not sing, you know. Isn't that strange? From the time an Aiel boy becomes a man he will not sing anything but battle chants, or their dirge for the slain. I have heard them singing over their dead, and over those they have killed. That song is one to make the stones weep." Ila, listening, nodded agreement over her knitting.

Perrin did some quick rethinking. He had thought the Tinkers must be afraid all the time, with all this talk of running away, but no one who was afraid would even think of crossing the Aiel Waste. From what he had heard, no one who was sane would try crossing the Waste.

"If this is some story about a song," Elyas began, but Raen shook his head.

"No, my old friend, not a song. I am not sure I know what it is about." He turned his attention to Perrin. "Young Aiel often travel into the Blight. Some of the young men go alone, thinking for some reason that they have been called to kill the Dark One. Most go in small groups. To hunt Trollocs." Raen shook his head sadly, and when he went on his voice was heavy. "Two years ago a band of the People crossing the Waste about a hundred miles south of the Blight found one of these groups."

"Young women," Ila put in, as sorrowful as her husband. "Little more than girls."

Perrin made a surprised sound, and Elyas grinned at him wryly.

"Aiel girls don't have to tend house and cook if they don't want to, boy. The ones who want to be warriors, instead, join one of the warrior societies, *Far Dareis Mai,* the Maidens of the Spear, and fight right alongside the men."

Perrin shook his head. Elyas chuckled at his expression.

Raen took up the story again, distaste and perplexity mingled in his voice. "The young women were all dead except one, and she was dying. She crawled to the wagons. It was clear she knew they were Tuatha'an. Her loathing outweighed her pain, but she had a message so important to her that she must pass it on to someone, even us, before she died.

Men went to see if they could help any of the others—there was a trail of her blood to follow—but all were dead, and so were three times their number in Trollocs."

Elyas sat up, his pipe almost falling from between his teeth. "A hundred miles into the Waste? Impossible! *Djevik K'Shar,* that's what Trollocs call the Waste. The Dying Ground. They wouldn't go a hundred miles into the Waste if all the Myrddraal in the Blight were driving them."

"You know an awful lot about Trollocs, Elyas," Perrin said.

"Go on with your story," Elyas told Raen gruffly.

"From trophies the Aiel carried, it was obvious they were coming back from the Blight. The Trollocs had followed, but by the tracks only a few lived to return after killing the Aiel. As for the girl, she would not let anyone touch her, even to tend her wounds. But she seized the Seeker of that band by his coat, and this is what she said, word for word. 'Leafblighter means to blind the Eye of the World, Lost One. He means to slay the Great Serpent. Warn the People, Lost One. Sightburner comes. Tell them to stand ready for He Who Comes With the Dawn. Tell them. . . .' And then she died. Leafblighter and Sightburner," Raen added to Perrin, "are Aiel names for the Dark One, but I don't understand another word of it. Yet she thought it important enough to approach those she obviously despised, to pass it on with her last breath. But to who? We are ourselves, the People, but I hardly think she meant it for us. The Aiel? They would not let us tell them if we tried." He sighed heavily. "She called *us* the Lost. I never knew before how much they loathe us." Ila set her knitting in her lap and touched his head gently.

"Something they learned in the Blight," Elyas mused. "But none of it makes sense. Slay the Great Serpent? Kill time itself? And blind the Eye of the World? As well say he's going to starve a rock. Maybe she was babbling, Raen. Wounded, dying, she could have lost her grip on what was real. Maybe she didn't even know who those Tuatha'an were."

"She knew what she was saying, and to whom she was saying it. Something more important to her than her own life, and we cannot even understand it. When I saw you walking into our camp, I thought perhaps we would find the answer at last, since you were"—Elyas made a quick

motion with his hand, and Raen changed what he had
been going to say—"are a friend, and know many strange
things."

"Not about this," Elyas said in a tone that put an end
to talk. The silence around the campfire was broken only
by the music and laughter drifting from other parts of the
night-shrouded camp.

Lying with his shoulders propped on one of the logs
around the fire, Perrin tried puzzling out the Aiel woman's
message, but it made no more sense to him than it had to
Raen or Elyas. The Eye of the World. That had been in his
dreams, more than once, but he did not want to think about
those dreams. Elyas, now. There was a question there he
would like answered. What had Raen been about to say
about the bearded man, and why had Elyas cut him off? He
had no luck with that, either. He was trying to imagine what
Aiel girls were like—going into the Blight, where only
Warders went that he had ever heard; fighting Trollocs—
when he heard Egwene coming back, singing to herself.

Scrambling to his feet, he went to meet her at the edge
of the firelight. She stopped short, looking at him with her
head tilted to one side. In the dark he could not read her
expression.

"You've been gone a long time," he said. "Did you have
fun?"

"We ate with his mother," she answered. "And then we
danced . . . and laughed. It seems like forever since I danced."

"He reminds me of Wil al'Seen. You always had sense
enough not to let Wil put you in his pocket."

"Aram is a gentle boy who is fun to be with," she said in
a tight voice. "He makes me laugh."

Perrin sighed. "I'm sorry. I'm glad you had fun dancing."

Abruptly she flung her arms around him, weeping on
his shirt. Awkwardly he patted her hair. *Rand would know
what to do,* he thought. Rand had an easy way with girls.
Not like him, who never knew what to do or say. "I told you
I'm sorry, Egwene. I really am glad you had fun dancing.
Really."

"Tell me they're alive," she mumbled into his chest.

"What?"

She pushed back to arm's length, her hands on his arms,

and looked up at him in the darkness. "Rand and Mat. The others. Tell me they are alive."

He took a deep breath and looked around uncertainly. "They are alive," he said finally.

"Good." She scrubbed at her cheeks with quick fingers. "That is what I wanted to hear. Good night, Perrin. Sleep well." Standing on tiptoe, she brushed a kiss across his cheek and hurried past him before he could speak.

He turned to watch her. Ila rose to meet her, and the two women went into the wagon talking quietly. *Rand might understand it,* he thought, *but I don't.*

In the distant night the wolves howled the first thin sliver of the new moon toward the horizon, and he shivered. Tomorrow would be time enough to worry about the wolves again. He was wrong. They were waiting to greet him in his dreams.

CHAPTER
26

Whitebridge

T he last unsteady note of what had been barely recognizable as "The Wind That Shakes the Willow"
faded mercifully away, and Mat lowered Thom's
gold-and-silver-chased flute. Rand took his hands from his
ears. A sailor coiling a line on the deck nearby heaved a
loud sigh of relief. For a moment the only sounds were the
water slapping against the hull, the rhythmic creak of the
oars, and now and again the hum of rigging strummed by
the wind. The wind blew dead on to the *Spray*'s bow, and
the useless sails were furled.

"I suppose I should thank you," Thom Merrilin muttered
finally, "for teaching me how true the old saying is. Teach
him how you will, a pig will never play the flute." The sailor
burst out laughing, and Mat raised the flute as if to throw
it at him. Deftly, Thom snagged the instrument from Mat's
fist and fitted it into its hard leather case. "I thought all you
shepherds whiled away the time with the flock playing the
pipes or the flute. That will show me to trust what I don't
know firsthand."

"Rand's the shepherd," Mat grumbled. "He plays the pipes,
not me."

"Yes, well, he does have a little aptitude. Perhaps we had
better work on juggling, boy. At least you show some talent
for that."

"Thom," Rand said, "I don't know why you're trying so
hard." He glanced at the sailor and lowered his voice. "After
all, we aren't really trying to become gleemen. It's only something to hide behind until we find Moiraine and the others."

Thom tugged at an end of his mustache and seemed to be

studying the smooth, dark brown leather of the flute case on his knees. "What if you don't find them, boy? There's nothing to say they're even still alive."

"They're alive," Rand said firmly. He turned to Mat for support, but Mat's eyebrows were pinched down on his nose, and his mouth was a thin line, and his eyes were fixed on the deck. "Well, speak up," Rand told him. "You can't be that mad over not being able to play the flute. I can't either, not very well. You never wanted to play the flute before."

Mat looked up, still frowning. "What if they are dead?" he said softly. "We have to accept facts, right?"

At that moment the lookout in the bow sang out, "Whitebridge! Whitebridge ahead!"

For a long minute, unwilling to believe that Mat could say something like that so casually, Rand held his friend's gaze amid the scramble of sailors preparing to put in. Mat glowered at him with his head pulled down between his shoulders. There was so much Rand wanted to say, but he could not manage to get it all into words. They had to believe the others were alive. They had to. *Why?* nagged a voice in the back of his head. *So it will all turn out like one of Thom's stories? The heroes find the treasure and defeat the villain and live happily ever after? Some of his stories don't end that way. Sometimes even heroes die. Are you a hero, Rand al'Thor? Are you a hero, sheepherder?*

Abruptly Mat flushed and pulled his eyes away. Freed from his thoughts, Rand jumped up to move through the hurly-burly to the rail. Mat came after him slowly, not even making an effort to dodge the sailors who ran across his path.

Men dashed about the boat, bare feet thumping the deck, hauling on ropes, tying off some lines and untying others. Some brought up big oilskin bags stuffed almost to bursting with wool, while others readied cables as thick as Rand's wrist. Despite their haste, they moved with the assurance of men who had done it all a thousand times before, but Captain Domon stumped up and down the deck shouting orders and cursing those who did not move fast enough to suit him.

Rand's attention was all for what lay ahead, coming plainly into sight as they rounded a slight bend of the Arinelle. He had heard of it, in song and story and peddlers' tales, but now he would actually see the legend.

The White Bridge arched high over the wide waters, twice as high as the *Spray*'s mast and more, and from end to end it gleamed milky white in the sunlight, gathering the light until it seemed to glow. Spidery piers of the same stuff plunged into the strong currents, appearing too frail to support the weight and width of the bridge. It looked all of one piece, as if it had been carved from a single stone or molded by a giant's hand, broad and tall, leaping the river with an airy grace that almost made the eye forget its size. All in all it dwarfed the town that sprawled about its foot on the east bank, though Whitebridge was larger by far than Emond's Field, with houses of stone and brick as tall as those in Taren Ferry and wooden docks like thin fingers sticking out into the river. Small boats dotted the Arinelle thickly, fishermen hauling their nets. And over it all the White Bridge towered and shone.

"It looks like glass," Rand said to no one in particular.

Captain Domon paused behind him and tucked his thumbs behind his broad belt. "Nay, lad. Whatever it be, it no be glass. Never so hard the rains come, it no be slippery, and the best chisel and the strongest arm no make a mark on it."

"A remnant from the Age of Legends," Thom said. "I have always thought it must be."

The captain gave a dour grunt. "Mayhap. But still useful despite. Could be someone else built it. Does no *have* to be Aes Sedai work, Fortune prick me. It no has to be so old as all that. Put your back into it, you bloody fool!" He hurried off down the deck.

Rand stared even more wonderingly. *From the Age of Legends.* Made by Aes Sedai, then. That was why Captain Domon felt the way he did, for all his talk about the wonder and strangeness of the world. Aes Sedai work. One thing to hear about it, another to see it, and touch it. *You know that, don't you?* For an instant it seemed to Rand that a shadow rippled through the milk-white structure. He pulled his eyes away, to the docks coming nearer, but the bridge still loomed in the corner of his vision.

"We made it, Thom," he said, then forced a laugh. "And no mutiny."

The gleeman only harrumphed and blew out his mustaches, but two sailors readying a cable nearby gave Rand a sharp glance, then bent quickly back to their work. He stopped laughing and tried not to look at the two for the rest of the approach to Whitebridge.

The *Spray* curved smoothly in beside the first dock, thick timbers sitting on heavy, tar-coated pilings, and stopped with a backing of oars that swirled the water to froth around the blades. As the oars were drawn in, sailors tossed cables to men on the dock, who fastened them off with a flourish, while other crewmen slung the bags of wool over the side to protect the hull from the dock pilings.

Before the boat was even pulled snug against the dock, carriages appeared at the end of the dock, tall and lacquered shiny black, each one with a name painted on the door in large letters, gold or scarlet. The carriages' passengers hurried up the gangplank as soon as it dropped in place, smooth-faced men in long velvet coats and silk-lined cloaks and cloth slippers, each followed by a plainly dressed servant carrying his iron-bound moneybox.

They approached Captain Domon with painted smiles that slipped when he abruptly roared in their faces. "You!" He thrust a thick finger past them, stopping Floran Gelb in his tracks at the length of the boat. The bruise on Gelb's forehead from Rand's boot had faded away, but he still fingered the spot from time to time as if to remind himself. "You've slept on watch for the last time on my vessel! Or on any vessel, if I have my way of it. Choose your own side— the dock or the river—but off my vessel *now*!"

Gelb hunched his shoulders, and his eyes glittered hate at Rand and his friends, at Rand especially, a poisonous glare. The wiry man looked around the deck for support, but there was little hope in that look. One by one, every man in the crew straightened from what he was doing and stared back coldly. Gelb wilted visibly, but then his glare returned, twice as strong as it had been. With a muttered curse he darted below to the crew's quarters. Domon sent two men after him to see he did no mischief and dismissed him with a grunt. When the captain turned back to them, the merchants took up their smiles and bows as if they had never been interrupted.

At a word from Thom, Mat and Rand began gathering their things together. There was not much aside from the clothes on their backs, not for any of them. Rand had his blanketroll and saddlebags, and his father's sword. He held the sword for a minute, and homesickness rolled over him so strongly that his eyes stung. He wondered if he would ever see Tam again. Or home? Home. *Going to spend the rest of your life running, running and afraid of your own dreams.* With a shuddering sigh he slipped the belt around his waist over his coat.

Gelb came back on deck, followed by his twin shadows. He looked straight ahead, but Rand could still feel hatred coming off him in waves. Back rigid and face dark, Gelb walked stiff-legged down the gangplank and pushed roughly into the thin crowd on the dock. In a minute he was gone from sight, vanished beyond the merchants' carriages.

There were not a great many people on the dock, and those were a plainly dressed mix of workmen, fishermen mending nets, and a few townspeople who had come out to see the first boat of the year to come downriver from Saldaea. None of the girls was Egwene and no one looked the least bit like Moiraine, or Lan, or anyone else Rand was hoping to see.

"Maybe they didn't come down to the dock," he said.

"Maybe," Thom replied curtly. He settled his instrument cases on his back with care. "You two keep an eye out for Gelb. He will make trouble if he can. We want to pass through Whitebridge so softly that nobody remembers we were here five minutes after we're gone."

Their cloaks flapped in the wind as they walked to the gangplank. Mat carried his bow crossed in front on his chest. Even after all their days on the boat, it still got a few looks from the crewmen; their bows were short affairs.

Captain Domon left the merchants to intercept Thom at the gangplank.

"You be leaving me now, gleeman? Can I no talk you into continuing on? I be going all the way down to Illian, where folk have a proper regard for gleemen. There be no finer place in the world for your art. I'd get you there in good time for the Feast of Sefan. The competitions, you know. A hundred gold marks for the best telling of *The Great Hunt of the Horn*."

"A great prize, Captain," Thom replied with an elaborate bow and a flourish of his cloak that set the patches to fluttering, "and great competitions, which rightly draw gleemen from the whole world over. But," he added dryly, "I fear we could not afford the fare at the rates you charge."

"Aye, well, as to that. . . ." The captain produced a leather purse from his coat pocket and tossed it to Thom. It clinked when Thom caught it. "Your fares back, and a bit more besides. The damage was no so bad as I thought, and you've worked your way and more with your tales and your harp. I could maybe manage as much again if you stay aboard to the Sea of Storms. And I would set you ashore in Illian. A good gleeman can make his fortune there, even aside from the competitions."

Thom hesitated, weighing the purse on his palm, but Rand spoke up. "We're meeting friends here, Captain, and going on to Caemlyn together. We'll have to see Illian another time."

Thom's mouth twisted wryly, then he blew out his long mustaches and tucked the purse into his pocket. "Perhaps if the people we are to meet are not here, Captain."

"Aye," Domon said sourly. "You think on it. Too bad I can no keep Gelb aboard to take the others' anger, but I do what I say I will do. I suppose I must ease up now, even if it means taking three times as long to reach Illian as I should. Well, mayhap those Trollocs *were* after you three."

Rand blinked but kept silent, but Mat was not so cautious.

"Why do you think they weren't?" he demanded. "They were after the same treasure we were hunting."

"Mayhap," the captain grunted, sounding unconvinced. He combed thick fingers through his beard, then pointed at the pocket where Thom had put the purse. "Twice that if you come back to keep the men's minds off how hard I work them. Think on it. I sail with the first light on the morrow." He turned on his heel and strode back to the merchants, arms spreading wide as he began an apology for keeping them waiting.

Thom still hesitated, but Rand hustled him down the gangplank without giving him a chance to argue, and the gleeman let himself be herded. A murmur passed through the people on the dock as they saw Thom's patch-covered cloak, and some called out to discover where he would be performing. *So much for not being noticed,* Rand thought, dismayed. By sundown it would be all over Whitebridge that there was a gleeman in town. He hurried Thom along, though, and Thom, wrapped in sulky silence, did not even try to slow down enough to preen under the attention.

The carriage drivers looked down at Thom with interest from their high perches, but apparently the dignity of their positions forbade shouting. With no idea of where to go exactly, Rand turned up the street that ran along the river and under the bridge.

"We need to find Moiraine and the others," he said. "And fast. We should have thought of changing Thom's cloak."

Thom suddenly shook himself and stopped dead. "An innkeeper will be able to tell us if they're here, or if they've passed through. The right innkeeper. Innkeepers have all the news and gossip. If they aren't here. . . ." He looked back and forth from Rand to Mat. "We have to talk, we three." Cloak swirling around his ankles, he set off into the town, away from the river. Rand and Mat had to step quickly to keep up.

The broad, milk-white arch that gave the town its name dominated Whitebridge as much close up as it did from afar, but once Rand was in the streets he realized that the town was every bit as big as Baerlon, though not so crowded with people. A few carts moved in the streets, pulled by horse or ox or donkey or man, but no carriages. Those most likely all belonged to the merchants and were clustered down at the dock.

Shops of every description lined the streets, and many of the tradesmen worked in front of their establishments, under the signs swinging in the wind. They passed a man mending pots, and a tailor holding folds of cloth up to the light for a customer. A shoemaker, sitting in his doorway, tapped his hammer on the heel of a boot. Hawkers cried their services at sharpening knives and scissors, or tried to interest the passersby in their skimpy trays of fruit or vegetables, but none was getting much interest. Shops selling food had the same pitiful displays of produce Rand remembered from Baerlon. Even the fishmongers displayed only small piles of small fish, for all the boats on the river. Times were not really hard yet, but everyone could see what was coming if the weather did not change soon, and those faces that were not fixed into worried frowns seemed to stare at something unseen, something unpleasant.

Where the White Bridge came down in the center of the town was a big square, paved with stones worn by generations of feet and wagon wheels. Inns surrounded the square, and shops, and tall, red brick houses with signs out front bearing the same names Rand had seen on the carriages at the dock. It was into one of those inns, seemingly chosen at random, that Thom ducked. The sign over the door, swinging in the wind, had a striding man with a bundle on his back on one side and the same man with his head on a pillow on the other, and proclaimed The Wayfarers' Rest.

The common room stood empty except for the fat innkeeper drawing ale from a barrel and two men in rough workman's clothes staring glumly into their mugs at a table in the back. Only the innkeeper looked up when they came in. A shoulder-high wall split the room in two from front to back, with tables and a blazing fireplace on each side. Rand wondered idly if all innkeepers were fat and losing their hair.

Rubbing his hands together briskly, Thom commented to the innkeeper on the late cold and ordered hot spiced wine, then added quietly, "Is there somewhere my friends and I could talk without being disturbed?"

The innkeeper nodded to the low wall. "The other side that's as best I've got unless you want to take a room. For when sailors come up from the river. Seems like half the crews got grudges against the other half. I won't have my place broke up by fights, so I keep them apart." He had been eyeing Thom's cloak the whole while, and now he cocked his head to one side, a sly look in his eyes. "You staying? Haven't had a gleeman here in some time. Folks would pay real good for something as would take their minds off things. I'd even take some off on your room and meals."

Unnoticed, Rand thought glumly.

"You are too generous," Thom said with a smooth bow. "Perhaps I will take up your offer. But for now, a little privacy."

"I'll bring your wine. Good money here for a gleeman."

The tables on the far side of the wall were all empty, but Thom chose one right in the middle of the space. "So no one can listen without us knowing," he explained. "Did you hear that fellow? He'll take some off. Why, I'd double his custom just by sitting here. Any honest innkeeper gives a gleeman room and board and a good bit besides."

The bare table was none too clean, and the floor had not been swept in days if not weeks. Rand looked around and grimaced. Master al'Vere would not have let his inn get that dirty if he had had to climb out of a sickbed to see to it. "We're only after information. Remember?"

"Why here?" Mat demanded. "We passed other inns that looked cleaner."

"Straight on from the bridge," Thom said, "is the road to Caemlyn. Anyone passing through Whitebridge comes through this square, unless they're going by river, and we know your friends aren't doing that. If there is no word of them here, it doesn't exist. Let me do the talking. This has to be done carefully."

Just then the innkeeper appeared, three battered pewter mugs gripped in one fist by the handles. The fat man flicked at the table with a towel, set the mugs down, and took Thom's money. "If you stay, you won't have to pay for your drinks. Good wine, here."

Thom's smile touched only his mouth. "I will think on it, innkeeper. What news is there? We have been away from hearing things."

"Big news, that's what. Big news."

The innkeeper draped the towel over his shoulder and pulled up a chair. He crossed his arms on the table, took root with a long sigh, saying what a comfort it was to get off his feet. His name was Bartim, and he went on about his feet in detail, about corns and bunions and how much time he spent standing and what he soaked them in, until Thom mentioned the news, again, and then he shifted over with hardly a pause.

The news was just as big as he said it was. Logain, the false Dragon, had been captured after a big battle near Lugard while he was trying to move his army from Ghealdan to Tear. The Prophecies, they understood? Thom nodded, and Bartim went on. The roads in the south were packed with people, the lucky ones with what they could carry on their backs. Thousands fleeing in all directions.

"None"—Bartim chuckled wryly—"supported Logain, of course. Oh, no, you won't find many to admit to that, not now. Just refugees trying to find a safe place during the troubles."

Aes Sedai had been involved in taking Logain, of course.

Bartim spat on the floor when he said that, and again when he said they were taking the false Dragon north to Tar Valon. Bartim was a decent man, he said, a respectable man, and Aes Sedai could all go back to the Blight where they came from and take Tar Valon with them, as far as he was concerned. He would get no closer to an Aes Sedai than a thousand miles, if he had his way. Of course, they were stopping at every village and town on the way north to display Logain, so he had heard. To show people that the false Dragon had been taken and the world was safe again. He would have liked to see that, even if it did mean getting close to Aes Sedai. He was halfway tempted to go to Caemlyn.

"They'll be taking him there to show to Queen Morgase." The innkeeper touched his forehead respectfully. "I've never seen the Queen. Man ought to see his own Queen, don't you think?"

Logain could do "things," and the way Bartim's eyes shifted and his tongue darted across his lips made it clear what he meant. He had seen the last false Dragon, two years ago, when he was paraded through the countryside, but that was just some fellow who thought he could make himself a king. There had been no need for Aes Sedai, that time. Soldiers had had him chained up on a wagon. A sullen-looking fellow who moaned in the middle of the wagonbed, covering his head with his arms whenever people threw stones or poked him with sticks. There had been a lot of that, and the soldiers had done nothing to stop it, as long as they did not kill the fellow. Best to let the people see he was nothing special after all. He could not do "things." This Logain would be something to see, though. Something for Bartim to tell his grandchildren about. If only the inn would let him get away.

Rand listened with an interest that did not have to be faked. When Padan Fain had brought word to Emond's Field of a false Dragon, a man actually wielding the Power, it had been the biggest news to come into the Two Rivers in years. What had happened since had pushed it to the back of his mind, but it was still the sort of thing people would be talking about for years, and telling their grandchildren about, too. Bartim would probably tell his that he had seen Logain whether he did or not. Nobody would ever think what happened to some village folk from the Two Rivers was worth talking about, not unless they were Two Rivers people themselves.

"That," Thom said, "would be something to make a story of, a story they'd tell for a thousand years. I wish I had been there." He sounded as if it was the simple truth, and Rand thought it really was. "I might try to see him anyway. You didn't say what route they were taking. Perhaps there are some other travelers around? They might have heard the route."

Bartim waved a grubby hand dismissively. "North, that's all anybody knows around here. You want to see him, go to Caemlyn. That's all I know, and if there's anything to know in Whitebridge, I know it."

"No doubt you do," Thom said smoothly. "I expect a lot of strangers passing through stop here. Your sign caught my eye from the foot of the White Bridge."

"Not just from the west, I'll have you know. Two days ago there was a fellow in here, an Illianer, with a proclamation all done up with seals and ribbons. Read it right out there in the square. Said he's taking it all the way to the Mountains of Mist, maybe even to the Aryth Ocean, if the passes are open. Said they've sent men to read it in every land in the world." The innkeeper shook his head. "The Mountains of Mist. I hear they're covered with fog all the year round, and there's things in the fog will strip the flesh off your bones before you can run." Mat snickered, earning a sharp look from Bartim.

Thom leaned forward intently. "What did the proclamation say?"

"Why, the hunt for the Horn, of course," Bartim exclaimed. "Didn't I say that? The Illianers are calling on everybody as will swear their lives to the hunt to gather in Illian. Can you imagine that? Swearing your life to a legend? I suppose they'll find some fools. There's always fools around. This fellow claimed the end of the world is coming. The last battle with the Dark One." He chuckled, but it had a hollow sound, a man laughing to convince himself something really was worth laughing at. "Guess they think the Horn of Valere has to be found before it happens. Now what do you think of that?" He chewed a knuckle pensively for a minute. "Course, I don't know as I could argue with them after this winter. The winter, and this fellow Logain, and those other two before, as well. Why all these fellows the last few years claiming to be the Dragon? And the winter. Must mean something. What do you think?"

Thom did not seem to hear him. In a soft voice the gleeman began to recite to himself.

> In the last, lorn fight
> 'gainst the fall of long night,
> the mountains stand guard,
> and the dead shall be ward,
> for the grave is no bar to my call.

"That's it." Bartim grinned as if he could already see the crowds handing him their money while they listened to Thom. "That's it. *The Great Hunt of the Horn*. You tell that one, and they'll be hanging from the rafters in here. Everybody's heard about the proclamation."

Thom still seemed to be a thousand miles away, so Rand said, "We're looking for some friends who were coming this way. From the west. Have there been many strangers passing through in the last week or two?"

"Some," Bartim said slowly. "There's always some, from east and west both." He looked at each of them in turn, suddenly wary. "What do they look like, these friends of yours?"

Rand opened his mouth, but Thom, abruptly back from wherever he had been, gave him a sharp, silencing look. With an exasperated sigh the gleeman turned to the innkeeper. "Two men and three women," he said reluctantly. "They may be together, or maybe not." He gave thumbnail sketches, painting each one in just a few words, enough for anyone who had seen them to recognize without giving away anything about who they were.

Bartim rubbed one hand over his head, disarranging his thinning hair, and stood up slowly. "Forget about performing here, gleeman. In fact, I'd appreciate it if you drank your wine and left. Leave Whitebridge, if you're smart."

"Someone else has been asking after them?" Thom took a drink, as if the answer were the least important thing in the world, and raised an eyebrow at the innkeeper. "Who would that be?"

Bartim scrubbed his hand through his hair again and

shifted his feet on the point of walking away, then nodded to himself. "About a week ago, as near as I can say, a weasely fellow came over the bridge. Crazy, everybody thought. Always talking to himself, never stopped moving even when he was standing still. Asked about the same people . . . some of them. He asked like it was important, then acted like he didn't care what the answer was. Half the time he was saying as he had to wait here for them, and the other half as he had to go on, he was in a hurry. One minute he was whining and begging, the next making demands like a king. Near got himself a thrashing a time or two, crazy or not. The Watch almost took him in custody for his own safety. He went off toward Caemlyn that same day, talking to himself and crying. Crazy, like I said."

Rand looked at Thom and Mat questioningly, and they both shook their heads. If this weasely fellow was looking for them, he was still nobody they recognized.

"Are you sure it was the same people he wanted?" Rand asked.

"Some of them. The fighting man, and the woman in silk. But it wasn't them as he cared about. It was three country boys." His eyes slid across Rand and Mat and away again so fast that Rand was not sure if he had really seen the look or imagined it. "He was desperate to find them. But crazy, like I said."

Rand shivered, and wondered who the crazy man could be, and why he was looking for them. *A Darkfriend? Would Ba'alzamon use a madman?*

"He was crazy, but the other one. . . ." Bartim's eyes shifted uneasily, and his tongue ran over his lips as if he could not find enough spit to moisten them. "Next day . . . next day the other one came for the first time." He fell silent.

"The other one?" Thom prompted finally.

Bartim looked around, although their side of the divided room was still empty except for them. He even raised up on his toes and looked over the low wall. When he finally spoke, it was in a whispered rush.

"All in black he is. Keeps the hood of his cloak pulled up so you can't see his face, but you can feel him looking at you, feel it like an icicle shoved into your spine. He . . . he spoke to me." He flinched and stopped to chew at his lip before going on. "Sounded like a snake crawling through dead leaves. Fair turned my stomach to ice. Every time as he comes back, he asks the same questions. Same questions the crazy man asked. Nobody ever sees him coming—he's just there all of a sudden, day or night, freezing you where you stand. People are starting to look over their shoulders. Worst of it is, the gatetenders claim as he's never passed through any of the gates, coming or going."

Rand worked at keeping his face blank; he clenched his jaw until his teeth ached. Mat scowled, and Thom studied his wine. The word none of them wanted to say hung in the air between them. Myrddraal.

"I think I'd remember if I ever met anyone like that," Thom said after a minute.

Bartim's head bobbed furiously. "Burn me, but you would. Light's truth, you would. He . . . he wants the same lot as the crazy man, only he says as there's a girl with them. And"—he glanced sideways at Thom—"and a white-haired gleeman."

Thom's eyebrows shot up in what Rand was sure was unfeigned surprise. "A white-haired gleeman? Well, I'm hardly the only gleeman in the world with a little age on him. I assure you, I don't know this fellow, and he can have no reason to be looking for me."

"That's as may be," Bartim said glumly. "He didn't say it in so many words, but I got the impression as he would be very displeased with anyone as tried to help these people, or tried to hide them from him. Anyway, I'll tell you what I told him. I haven't seen any of them, nor heard tell of them, and that's the truth. Not any of them," he finished pointedly. Abruptly he slapped Thom's money down on the table. "Just finish your wine and go. All right? All right?" And he trundled away as fast as he could, looking over his shoulder.

"A Fade," Mat breathed when the innkeeper was gone. "I should have known they'd be looking for us here."

"And he'll be back," Thom said, leaning across the table and lowering his voice. "I say we sneak back to the boat and take Captain Domon up on his offer. The hunt will center on the road to Caemlyn while we're on our way to Illian, a thousand miles from where the Myrddraal expect us."

"No," Rand said firmly. "We wait for Moiraine and the others in Whitebridge, or we go on to Caemlyn. One or the other, Thom. That's what we decided."

"That's crazed, boy. Things have changed. You listen to

me. No matter what this innkeeper says, when a Myrddraal stares at him, he'll tell all about us down to what we had to drink and how much dust we had on our boots." Rand shivered, remembering the Fade's eyeless stare. "As for Caemlyn. . . . You think the Halfmen don't know you want to get to Tar Valon? It's a good time to be on a boat headed south."

"No, Thom." Rand had to force the words out, thinking of being a thousand miles from where the Fades were looking, but he took a deep breath and managed to firm his voice. "No."

"Think, boy. Illian! There isn't a grander city on the face of the earth. And the Great Hunt of the Horn! There hasn't been a Hunt of the Horn in near four hundred years. A whole new cycle of stories waiting to be made. Just think. You never dreamed of anything like it. By the time the Myrddraal figure out where you've gone to, you'll be old and gray and so tired of watching your grandchildren you won't care if they do find you."

Rand's face took on a stubborn set. "How many times do I have to say no? They'll find us wherever we go. There'd be Fades waiting in Illian, too. And how do we escape the dreams? I want to know what's happening to me, Thom, and why. I'm going to Tar Valon. With Moiraine if I can; without her if I have to. Alone, if I have to. I need to know."

"But Illian, boy! And a safe way out, downriver while they're looking for you in another direction. Blood and ashes, a dream can't hurt you."

Rand kept silent. *A dream can't hurt? Do dream thorns draw real blood?* He almost wished he had told Thom about that dream, too. *Do you dare tell anybody? Ba'alzamon is in your dreams, but what's between dreaming and waking, now? Who do you dare to tell that the Dark One is touching you?*

Thom seemed to understand. The gleeman's face softened. "Even *those* dreams, lad. They are still just dreams, aren't they? For the Light's sake, Mat, talk to him. I know you don't want to go to Tar Valon, at least."

Mat's face reddened, half embarrassment and half anger. He avoided looking at Rand and scowled at Thom instead. "Why are you going to all this fuss and bother? You want to go back to the boat? Go back to the boat. We'll take care of ourselves."

The gleeman's thin shoulders shook with silent laughter, but his voice was anger tight. "You think you know enough about Myrddraal to escape by yourself, do you? You're ready to walk into Tar Valon alone and hand yourself over to the Amyrlin Seat? Can you even tell one Ajah from another? The Light burn me, boy, if you think you can even get to Tar Valon alone, you tell me to go."

"Go," Mat growled, sliding a hand under his cloak. Rand realized with a shock that he was gripping the dagger from Shadar Logoth, maybe even ready to use it.

Raucous laughter broke out on the other side of the low wall dividing the room, and a scornful voice spoke up loudly.

"Trollocs? Put on a gleeman's cloak, man! You're drunk! Trollocs! Borderland fables!"

The words doused anger like a pot of cold water. Even Mat half turned to the wall, eyes widening.

Rand stood just enough to see over the wall, then ducked back down again with a sinking feeling in his stomach. Floran Gelb sat on the other side of the wall, at the table in the back with the two men who had been there when they came in. They were laughing at him, but they were listening. Bartim was wiping a table that badly needed it, not looking at Gelb and the two men, but he was listening, too, scrubbing one spot over and over with his towel and leaning toward them until he seemed almost ready to fall over.

"Gelb," Rand whispered as he dropped back into his chair, and the others tensed. Thom swiftly studied their side of the room.

On the other side of the wall the second man's voice chimed in. "No, no, there used to be Trollocs. But they killed them all in the Trolloc Wars."

"Borderland fables!" the first man repeated.

"It's true, I tell you," Gelb protested loudly. "I've been in the Borderlands. I've seen Trollocs, and these were Trollocs as sure as I'm sitting here. Those three claimed the Trollocs were chasing them, but I know better. That's why I wouldn't stay on the *Spray*. I've had my suspicions about Bayle Domon for some time, but those three are Darkfriends for sure. I tell you. . . ." Laughter and coarse jokes drowned out the rest of what Gelb had to say.

How long, Rand wondered, before the innkeeper heard a description of "those three"? If he had not already. If he did not just leap to the three strangers he had already seen. The only door from their half of the common room would take them right past Gelb's table.

"Maybe the boat isn't such a bad idea," Mat muttered, but Thom shook his head.

"Not anymore." The gleeman spoke softly and fast. He pulled out the leather purse Captain Domon had given him and hastily divided the money into three piles. "That story will be all through the town in an hour, whether anybody believes it or not, and the Halfman could hear any time. Domon isn't sailing until tomorrow morning. At best he'll have Trollocs chasing him all the way to Illian. Well, he's half expecting it for some reason, but that won't do us any good. There's nothing for it but to run, and run hard."

Mat quickly stuffed the coins Thom shoved in front of him into his pocket. Rand picked his pile up more slowly. The coin Moiraine had given him was not among them. Domon had given an equal weight of silver, but Rand, for some reason he could not fathom, wished he had the Aes Sedai's coin instead. Stuffing the money in his pocket, he looked a question at the gleeman.

"In case we're separated," Thom explained. "We probably won't be, but if it does happen . . . well, you two will make out all right by yourselves. You're good lads. Just keep clear of Aes Sedai, for your lives."

"I thought you were staying with us," Rand said.

"I am, boy. I am. But they're getting close, now, and the Light only knows. Well, no matter. It isn't likely anything will happen." Thom paused, looking at Mat. "I hope you no longer mind me staying with you," he said dryly.

Mat shrugged. He eyed each of them, then shrugged again. "I'm just on edge. I can't seem to get rid of it. Every time we stop for a breath, they're there, hunting us. I feel like somebody's staring at the back of my head all the time. What are we going to do?"

The laughter erupted on the other side of the wall, broken again by Gelb, trying loudly to convince the two men that he was telling the truth. How much longer, Rand wondered. Sooner or later Bartim had to put together Gelb's three and the three of them.

Thom eased his chair and rose, but kept his height crouched. No one looking casually toward the wall from the other side could see him. He motioned for them to follow, whispering, "Be very quiet."

The windows on either side of the fireplace on their side of the wall looked out into an alleyway. Thom studied one of the windows carefully before drawing it up just enough for them to squeeze through. It barely made a sound, nothing that could have been heard three feet away over the laughing argument on the other side of the low wall.

Once in the alley, Mat started for the street right away, but Thom caught his arm. "Not so fast," the gleeman told him. "Not till we know what we're doing." Thom lowered the window again as much as he could from outside, and turned to study the alley.

Rand followed Thom's eyes. Except for half a dozen rain barrels against the inn and the next building, a tailor shop, the alley was empty, the hard-packed dirt dry and dusty.

"Why are you doing this?" Mat demanded again. "You'd be safer if you left us. Why are you staying with us?"

Thom stared at him for a long moment. "I had a nephew, Owyn," he said wearily, shrugging out of his cloak. He made a pile with his blanket-roll as he talked, carefully setting his cased instruments on top. "My brother's only son, my only living kin. He got in trouble with the Aes Sedai, but I was too busy with . . . other things. I don't know what I could have done, but when I finally tried, it was too late. Owyn died a few years later. You could say Aes Sedai killed him." He straightened up, not looking at them. His voice was still level, but Rand glimpsed tears in his eyes as he turned his head away. "If I can keep you two free of Tar Valon, maybe I can stop thinking about Owyn. Wait here." Still avoiding their eyes, he hurried to the mouth of the alley, slowing before he reached it. After one quick look around, he strolled casually into the street and out of sight.

Mat half rose to follow, then settled back. "He won't leave these," he said, touching the leather instrument cases. "You believe that story?"

Rand squatted patiently beside the rain barrels. "What's the matter with you, Mat? You aren't like this. I haven't heard you laugh in days."

"I don't like being hunted like a rabbit," Mat snapped. He sighed, letting his head fall back against the brick wall of the inn. Even like that he seemed tense. His eyes shifted warily. "Sorry. It's the running, and all these strangers, and . . . and just everything. It makes me jumpy. I look at somebody, and I can't help wondering if he's going to tell the Fades about us, or cheat us, or rob us, or. . . . Light, Rand, doesn't it make you nervous?"

Rand laughed, a quick bark in the back of his throat. "I'm too scared to be nervous."

"What do you think the Aes Sedai did to his nephew?"

"I don't know," Rand said uneasily. There was only one kind of trouble that he knew of for a man to get into with Aes Sedai. "Not like us, I guess."

"No. Not like us."

For a time they leaned against the wall, not talking. Rand was not sure how long they waited. A few minutes, probably, but it felt like an hour, waiting for Thom to come back, waiting for Bartim and Gelb to open the window and denounce them for Darkfriends. Then a man turned in at the mouth of the alley, a tall man with the hood of his cloak pulled up to hide his face, a cloak black as night against the light of the street.

Rand scrambled to his feet, one hand wrapped around the hilt of Tam's sword so hard that his knuckles hurt. His mouth went dry, and no amount of swallowing helped. Mat rose to a crouch with one hand under his cloak.

The man came closer, and Rand's throat grew tighter with every step. Abruptly the man stopped and tossed back his cowl. Rand's knees almost gave way. It was Thom.

"Well, if you don't recognize me"—the gleeman grinned— "I guess it's a good enough disguise for the gates."

Thom pushed past them and began transferring things from his patch-covered cloak to his new one so nimbly that Rand could not make out any of them. The new cloak was dark brown, Rand saw now. He drew a deep, ragged breath; his throat still felt as if it were clutched in a fist. Brown, not black. Mat still had his hand under his cloak, and he stared at Thom's back as if he were thinking of using the hidden dagger.

Thom glanced up at them, then gave them a sharper look. "This is no time to get skittish." Deftly he began folding his old cloak into a bundle around his instrument cases, inside out so the patches were hidden. "We'll walk out of here one at a time, just close enough to keep each other in sight. Shouldn't be remembered especially, that way. Can't you slouch?" he added to Rand. "That height of yours is as bad as a banner." He slung the bundle across his back and stood, drawing his hood back up. He looked nothing like a white-haired gleeman. He was just another traveler, a man too poor to afford a horse, much less a carriage. "Let's go. We've wasted too much time already."

Rand agreed fervently, but even so he hesitated before stepping out of the alley into the square. None of the sparse scattering of people gave them a second look—most did not look at them at all—but his shoulders knotted, waiting for the cry of Darkfriend that could turn ordinary people into a mob bent on murder. He ran his eyes across the open area, over people moving about on their daily business, and when he brought them back a Myrddraal was halfway across the square.

Where the Fade had come from, he could not begin to guess, but it strode toward the three of them with a slow deadliness, a predator with the prey under its gaze. People shied away from the black-cloaked shape, avoided looking at it. The square began to empty out as people decided they were needed elsewhere.

The black cowl froze Rand where he stood. He tried to summon up the void, but it was like fumbling after smoke. The Fade's hidden gaze knifed to his bones and turned his marrow to icicles.

"Don't look at its face," Thom muttered. His voice shook and cracked, and it sounded as if he were forcing the words out. "The Light burn you, don't look at its face!"

Rand tore his eyes away—he almost groaned; it felt like tearing a leech off of his face—but even staring at the stones of the square he could still see the Myrddraal coming, a cat playing with mice, amused at their feeble efforts to escape, until finally the jaws snapped shut. The Fade had halved the distance. "Are we just going to stand here?" he mumbled. "We have to run . . . get away." But he could not make his feet move.

Mat had the ruby-hilted dagger out at last, in a trembling hand. His lips were drawn back from his teeth, a snarl and a rictus of fear.

"Think. . . ." Thom stopped to swallow, and went on hoarsely. "Think you can outrun it, do you, boy?" He began to mutter to himself; the only word Rand could make out was "Owyn." Abruptly Thom growled, "I never should have gotten mixed up with you boys. Should never have." He shrugged the bundled gleeman's cloak off of his back and thrust it into Rand's arms. "Take care of that. When I say run, you run and don't stop until you get to Caemlyn. The Queen's Blessing. An inn. Remember that, in case. . . . Just remember it."

"I don't understand," Rand said. The Myrddraal was not twenty paces away, now. His feet felt like lead weights.

"Just remember it!" Thom snarled. "The Queen's Blessing. Now. RUN!"

He gave them a push, one hand on the shoulder of each of them, to get them started, and Rand stumbled away in a lurching run with Mat at his side.

"RUN!" Thom sprang into motion, too, with a long, wordless roar. Not after them, but toward the Myrddraal. His hands flourished as if he were performing at his best, and daggers appeared. Rand stopped, but Mat pulled him along.

The Fade was just as startled. Its leisurely pace faltered in mid-stride. Its hand swept toward the hilt of the black sword hanging at its waist, but the gleeman's long legs covered the distance quickly. Thom crashed into the Myrddraal before the black blade was half drawn, and both went down in a thrashing heap. The few people still in the square fled.

"RUN!" The air in the square flashed an eye-searing blue, and Thom began to scream, but even in the middle of the scream he managed a word. *"RUN!"*

Rand obeyed. The gleeman's screams pursued him.

Clutching Thom's bundle to his chest, he ran as hard as he could. Panic spread from the square out through the town as Rand and Mat fled on the crest of a wave of fear. Shopkeepers abandoned their goods as the boys passed. Shutters banged down over storefronts, and frightened faces appeared in the windows of houses, then vanished. People who had not been close enough to see ran through the streets wildly, paying no heed. They bumped into one another, and those who were knocked down scrambled to their feet or were trampled. Whitebridge roiled like a kicked anthill.

As he and Mat pounded toward the gates, Rand abruptly remembered what Thom had said about his height. Without slowing down, he crouched as best he could without look-

ing as if he was crouching. But the gates themselves, thick
wood bound with black iron straps, stood open. The two
gatetenders, in steel caps and mail tunics worn over cheap-
looking red coats with white collars, fingered their halberds
and stared uneasily into the town. One of them glanced at
Rand and Mat, but they were not the only ones running
out of the gates. A steady stream boiled through, panting
men clutching wives, weeping women carrying babes and
dragging crying children, pale-faced craftsmen still in their
aprons, still heedlessly gripping their tools.

There would be no one who could tell which way they
had gone, Rand thought as he ran, dazed. *Thom. Oh, Light
save me, Thom.*

Mat staggered beside him, caught his balance, and they
ran until the last of the fleeing people had fallen away, ran
until the town and the White Bridge were far out of sight
behind them.

Finally Rand fell to his knees in the dust, pulling air raggedly into his raw throat with great gulps. The road behind
stretched empty until it was lost to sight among bare trees.
Mat plucked at him.

"Come on. Come on." Mat panted the words. Sweat and
dust streaked his face, and he looked ready to collapse. "We
have to keep going."

"Thom," Rand said. He tightened his arms around the
bundle of Thom's cloak; the instrument cases were hard
lumps inside. "Thom."

"He's dead. You saw. You heard. Light, Rand, he's dead!"

"You think Egwene and Moiraine and the rest are dead,
too. If they're dead, why are the Myrddraal still hunting
them? Answer me that?"

Mat dropped to his knees in the dust beside him. "All
right. Maybe they are alive. But Thom—You saw! Blood and
ashes, Rand, the same thing can happen to us."

Rand nodded slowly. The road behind them was still
empty. He had been halfway expecting—hoping, at least—to
see Thom appear, striding along, blowing out his mustaches
to tell them how much trouble they were. The Queen's Blessing in Caemlyn. He struggled to his feet and slung Thom's
bundle on his back alongside his blanketroll. Mat stared up at
him, narrow-eyed and wary.

"Let's go," Rand said, and started down the road toward

Caemlyn. He heard Mat muttering, and after a moment he caught up to Rand.

They trudged along the dusty road, heads down and not talking. The wind spawned dustdevils that whirled across their path. Sometimes Rand looked back, but the road behind was always empty.

CHAPTER
27

Shelter From the Storm

Perrin fretted over the days spent with the Tuatha'an, traveling south and east in a leisurely fashion. The Traveling People saw no need to hurry; they never did. The colorful wagons did not roll out of a morning until the sun was well above the horizon, and they stopped as early as midafternoon if they came across a congenial spot. The dogs trotted easily alongside the wagons, and often the children did, too. They had no difficulty in keeping up. Any suggestion that they might go further, or more quickly, was met with laughter, or perhaps, "Ah, but would you make the poor horses work so hard?"

He was surprised that Elyas did not share his feelings. Elyas would not ride on the wagons—he preferred to walk, sometimes loping along at the head of the column—but he never suggested leaving, or pressing on ahead.

The strange bearded man in his strange skin clothes was so different from the gentle Tuatha'an that he stood out wherever he went among the wagons. Even from across the camp there was no mistaking Elyas for one of the People, and not just because of clothes. Elyas moved with the lazy grace of a wolf, only emphasized by his skins and his fur hat, radiating danger as naturally as a fire radiated heat, and the contrast with the Traveling People was sharp. Young and old, the People were joyful on their feet. There was no danger in their grace, only delight. Their children darted about filled with the pure zest of moving, of course, but among the Tuatha'an, graybeards and grandmothers, too, still stepped lightly, their walk a stately dance no less exuberant for its dignity. All the People seemed on the point of dancing, even when standing still, even during the rare times when there was no music in the camp. Fiddles and flutes, dulcimers and zithers and drums spun harmony and counterpoint around the wagons at almost any hour, in camp or on the move. Joyous songs, merry songs, laughing songs, sad songs; if someone was awake in the camp there was usually music.

Elyas met friendly nods and smiles at every wagon he passed, and a cheerful word at any fire where he paused. This must be the face the People always showed to outsiders— open, smiling faces. But Perrin had learned that hidden beneath the surface was the wariness of a half-tame deer. Something deep lay behind the smiles directed at the Emond's Fielders, something that wondered if they were safe, something that faded only slightly over the days. With Elyas the wariness was strong, like deep summer heat shimmering in the air, and it did not fade. When he was not looking they watched him openly as if unsure what he was going to do. When he walked across the camp, feet ready for dancing seemed ready for flight, as well.

Elyas was certainly no more comfortable with their Way of the Leaf than they were with him. His mouth wore a permanent twist when he was around the Tuatha'an. It was not quite condescension and certainly not contempt, but looked as though he would rather be elsewhere than where he was, almost anywhere else. Yet whenever Perrin brought up leaving, Elyas made soothing noises about resting, just for a few days.

"You had hard days before you met me," Elyas said, the third or fourth time he asked, "and you'll have harder still ahead, with Trollocs and Halfmen after you, and Aes Sedai for friends." He grinned around a mouthful of Ila's dried-apple pie. Perrin still found his yellow-eyed gaze disconcerting, even when he was smiling. Perhaps even more when he was smiling; smiles seldom touched those hunter's eyes. Elyas lounged beside Raen's fire, as usual refusing to sit on the logs drawn up for the purpose. "Don't be in such a bloody hurry to put yourself in Aes Sedai hands."

"What if the Fades find us? What's to keep them from it if we just sit here, waiting? Three wolves can't hold them off, and the Traveling People won't be any help. They won't even defend themselves. The Trollocs will butcher them, and it will be our fault. Anyway, we have to leave them sooner or later. It might as well be sooner."

"Something tells me to wait. Just a few days."

"Something!"

"Relax, lad. Take life as it comes. Run when you have to, fight when you must, rest when you can."

"What are you talking about, something?"

"Have some of this pie. Ila doesn't like me, but she surely feeds me well when I visit. Always good food in the People's camps."

"What 'something'?" Perrin demanded. "If you know something you aren't telling the rest of us. . . ."

Elyas frowned at the piece of pie in his hand, then set it down and dusted his hands together. "Something," he said finally, with a shrug of his shoulders as if he did not understand it completely himself. "Something tells me it's important to wait. A few more days. I don't get feelings like this often, but when I do, I've learned to trust them. They've saved my life in the past. This time it's different, somehow, but it's important. That's clear. You want to run on, then run on. Not me."

That was all he would say, no matter how many times Perrin asked. He lay about, talking with Raen, eating, napping with his hat over his eyes, and refused to discuss leaving. Something told him to wait. Something told him it was important. He would know when it was time to go. Have some pie, lad. Don't lather yourself. Try some of this stew. Relax.

Perrin could not make himself relax. At night he wandered among the rainbow wagons worrying, as much because no one else seemed to see anything to worry about as for any other reason. The Tuatha'an sang and danced, cooked and ate around their campfires—fruits and nuts, berries and vegetables; they ate no meat—and went about a myriad domestic chores as if they had not a care in the world. The children ran and played everywhere, hide-and-seek among the wagons, climbing in the trees around the camp, laughing and rolling on the ground with the dogs. Not a care in the world, for anyone.

Watching them, he itched to get away. *Go, before we bring the hunters down on them. They took us in, and we repay their kindness by endangering them. At least they*

have reason to be lighthearted. Nothing is hunting them.
But the rest of us. . . .

It was hard to get a word with Egwene. Either she was
talking with Ila, their heads together in a way that said no
men were welcome, or she was dancing with Aram, swinging
round and round to the flutes and fiddles and drums, to tunes
the Tuatha'an had gathered from all over the world, or to the
sharp, trilling songs of the Traveling People themselves, sharp
whether they were quick or slow. They knew many songs,
some he recognized from home, though often under different
names than they were called in the Two Rivers. "Three Girls
in the Meadow," for instance, the Tinkers named "Pretty
Maids Dancing," and they said "The Wind From the North"
was called "Hard Rain Falling" in some lands and "Berin's
Retreat" in others. When he asked, not thinking, for "The
Tinker Has My Pots," they fell all over themselves laughing.
They knew it, but as "Toss the Feathers."

He could understand wanting to dance to the People's
songs. Back in Emond's Field no one considered him more
than an adequate dancer, but these songs tugged at his feet,
and he thought he had never danced so long, or so hard, or
so well in his life. Hypnotic, they made his blood pound in
rhythm to the drums.

It was the second evening when for the first time Perrin saw women dance to some of the slow songs. The fires
burned low, and the night hung close around the wagons, and
fingers tapped a slow rhythm on the drums. First one drum,
then another, until every drum in the camp kept the same
low, insistent beat. There was silence except for the drums. A
girl in a red dress swayed into the light, loosening her shawl.
Strings of beads hung in her hair, and she had kicked off her
shoes. A flute began the melody, wailing softly, and the girl
danced. Outstretched arms spread her shawl behind her; her
hips undulated as her bare feet shuffled to the beat of the
drums. The girl's dark eyes fastened on Perrin, and her smile
was as slow as her dance. She turned in small circles, smiling
over her shoulder at him.

He swallowed hard. The heat in his face was not from
the fire. A second girl joined the first, the fringe on their
shawls shaking in time to the drums and the slow rotation
of their hips. They smiled at him, and he cleared his throat
hoarsely. He was afraid to look around; his face was as red

as a beet, and anyone who was not watching the dancers was probably laughing at him. He was sure of it.

As casually as he could manage, he slid off the log as if he were just getting comfortable, but he carefully ended up looking away from the fire, away from the dancers. There was nothing like that in Emond's Field. Dancing with the girls on the Green on a feastday did not even come close. For once he wished that the wind would pick up, to cool him off.

The girls danced into his field of view again, only now they were three. One gave him a sly wink. His eyes darted frantically. *Light,* he thought. *What do I do now? What would Rand do? He knows about girls.*

The dancing girls laughed softly; beads clicked as they tossed their long hair on their shoulders, and he thought his face would burn up. Then a slightly older woman joined the girls, to show them how it was done. With a groan, he gave up altogether and shut his eyes. Even behind his eyelids their laughter taunted and tickled. Even behind his eyelids he could still see them. Sweat beaded on his forehead, and he wished for the wind.

According to Raen the girls did not dance that dance often, and the women rarely did, and according to Elyas it was thanks to Perrin's blushes that they did so every night thereafter.

"I have to thank you," Elyas told him, his tone sober and solemn. "It's different with you young fellows, but at my age it takes more than a fire to warm my bones." Perrin scowled. There was something about Elyas's back as he walked away that said even if nothing showed, he was laughing inside.

Perrin soon learned better than to look away from the dancing women and girls, though the winks and smiles still made him wish he could. One would have been all right, maybe—but five or six, with everyone watching. . . . He never did entirely conquer his blushes.

Then Egwene began learning the dance. Two of the girls who had danced that first night taught her, clapping the rhythm while she repeated the shuffling steps with a borrowed shawl swaying behind her. Perrin started to say something, then decided it was wiser not to crack his teeth. When the girls added the hip movements Egwene started laughing, and the three girls fell giggling into one another's arms. But Egwene persevered, with her eyes glistening and bright spots of color in her cheeks.

Aram watched her dancing with a hot, hungry gaze. The handsome young Tuatha'an had given her a string of blue beads that she wore all the time. Worried frowns now replaced the smiles Ila had worn when she first noticed her grandson's interest in Egwene. Perrin resolved to keep a close eye on young Master Aram.

Once he managed to get Egwene alone, beside a wagon painted in green and yellow. "Enjoying yourself, aren't you?" he said.

"Why shouldn't I?" She fingered the blue beads around her neck, smiling at them. "We don't all have to work at being miserable, the way you do. Don't we deserve a little chance to enjoy ourselves?"

Aram stood not far off—he never got far from Egwene—with his arms folded across his chest, a little smile on his face, half smugness and half challenge. Perrin lowered his voice. "I thought you wanted to get to Tar Valon. You won't learn to be an Aes Sedai here."

Egwene tossed her head. "And I thought you didn't like me wanting to become an Aes Sedai," she said, too sweetly.

"Blood and ashes, do you believe we're safe here? Are these people safe with us here? A Fade could find us anytime."

Her hand trembled on the beads. She lowered it and took a deep breath. "Whatever is going to happen will happen whether we leave today or next week. That's what I believe now. Enjoy yourself, Perrin. It might be the last chance we have."

She brushed his cheek sadly with her fingers. Then Aram held out his hand to her, and she darted to him, already laughing again. As they ran away to where fiddles sang, Aram flashed a triumphant grin over his shoulder at Perrin as if to say, she is not yours, but she will be mine.

They were all falling too much under the spell of the People, Perrin thought. *Elyas is right. They don't have to try to convert you to the Way of the Leaf. It seeps into you.*

Ila had taken one look at him huddling out of the wind, then produced a thick wool cloak out of her wagon; a dark green cloak, he was pleased to see, after all the reds and yellows. As he swung it round his shoulders, thinking what a wonder it was that the cloak was big enough for him, Ila said primly, "It could fit better." She glanced at the axe at his belt, and when she looked up at him her eyes were sad above her smile. "It could fit much better."

All the Tinkers did that. Their smiles never slipped, there was never any hesitation in their invitations to join them for a drink or to listen to the music, but their eyes always touched the axe, and he could feel what they thought. A tool of violence. There is never any excuse for violence to another human being. The Way of the Leaf.

Sometimes he wanted to shout at them. There were Trollocs in the world, and Fades. There were those who would cut down every leaf. The Dark One was out there, and the Way of the Leaf would burn in Ba'alzamon's eyes. Stubbornly he continued to wear the axe. He took to keeping his cloak thrown back, even when it was windy, so the half-moon blade was never hidden. Now and again Elyas looked quizzically at the weapon hanging heavy at his side and grinned at him, those yellow eyes seeming to read his mind. That almost made him cover the axe. Almost.

If the Tuatha'an camp was a source of constant irritation, at least his dreams were normal there. Sometimes he woke up sweating from a dream of Trollocs and Fades storming into the camp, rainbow-colored wagons turning to bonfires from hurled torches, people falling in pools of blood, men and women and children who ran and screamed and died but made no effort to defend themselves against slashing scythe-like swords. Night after night he bolted upright in the dark, panting and reaching for his axe before he realized the wagons were not in flames, that no bloody-muzzled shapes snarled over torn and twisted bodies littering the ground. But those were ordinary nightmares, and oddly comforting in their way. If there was ever a place for the Dark One to be in his dreams, it was in those, but he was not. No Ba'alzamon. Just ordinary nightmares.

He was aware of the wolves, though, when he was awake. They kept their distance from the camps, and from the caravan on the move, but he always knew where they were. He could feel their contempt for the dogs guarding the Tuatha'an. Noisy beasts who had forgotten what their jaws were for, had forgotten the taste of warm blood; they might frighten humans, but they would slink away on their bellies if the pack ever came. Each day his awareness was sharper, more clear.

Dapple grew more impatient with every sunset. That Elyas wanted to do this thing of taking the humans south made it worth doing, but if it must be done, then let it be done. Let this slow travel end. Wolves were meant to roam, and she did not like being away from the pack so long. Impatience burned in Wind, too. Hunting was worse than poor here, and he despised living on field mice, something for cubs to stalk while learning to hunt, fit food for the old, no longer able to pull down a deer or hamstring a wild ox. Sometimes Wind thought that Burn had been right; leave human troubles to humans. But he was wary of such thoughts when Dapple was around, and even more so around Hopper. Hopper was a scarred and grizzled fighter, impassive with the knowledge of years, with guile that more than made up for anything of which age might have robbed him. For humans he cared nothing, but Dapple wished this thing done, and Hopper would wait as she waited and run as she ran. Wolf or man, bull or bear, whatever challenged Dapple would find Hopper's jaws waiting to send him to the long sleep. That was the whole of life for Hopper, and that kept Wind cautious, and Dapple seemed to ignore the thoughts of both.

All of it was clear in Perrin's mind. Fervently he wished for Caemlyn, for Moiraine and Tar Valon. Even if there were no answers, there could be an end to it. Elyas looked at him, and he was sure the yellow-eyed man knew. *Please, let there be an end.*

The dream began more pleasantly than most he had of late. He was at Alsbet Luhhan's kitchen table, sharpening his axe with a stone. Mistress Luhhan never allowed forge work, or anything that smacked of it, to be brought into the house. Master Luhhan even had to take her knives outside to sharpen them. But she tended her cooking and never said a word about the axe. She did not even say anything when a wolf entered from deeper in the house and curled up between Perrin and the door to the yard. Perrin went on sharpening; it would be time to use it, soon.

Abruptly the wolf rose, rumbling deep in its throat, the thick ruff of fur on its neck rising. Ba'alzamon stepped into the kitchen from the yard. Mistress Luhhan went on with her cooking.

Perrin scrambled to his feet, raising the axe, but Ba'alzamon ignored the weapon, concentrating on the wolf, instead. Flames danced where his eyes should be. "Is this what you have to protect you? Well, I have faced this before. Many times before."

He crooked a finger, and the wolf howled as fire burst out of its eyes and ears and mouth, out of its skin. The stench of burning meat and hair filled the kitchen. Alsbet Luhhan lifted the lid on a pot and stirred with a wooden spoon.

Perrin dropped the axe and jumped forward, trying to beat out the flames with his hands. The wolf crumpled to black ash between his palms. Staring at the shapeless pile of char on Mistress Luhhan's clean-swept floor, he backed away. He wished he could wipe the greasy soot from his hands, but the thought of scrubbing it off on his clothes turned his stomach. He snatched up the axe, gripping the haft until his knuckles cracked.

"Leave me alone!" he shouted. Mistress Luhhan tapped the spoon on the rim of the pot and replaced the lid, humming to herself.

"You cannot run from me," Ba'alzamon said. "You cannot hide from me. If you are the one, you are mine." The heat from the fires of his face forced Perrin across the kitchen until his back came up against the wall. Mistress Luhhan opened the oven to check her bread. "The Eye of the World will consume you," Ba'alzamon said. "I mark you mine!" He flung out his clenched hand as if throwing something; when his fingers opened, a raven streaked at Perrin's face.

Perrin screamed as the black beak pierced his left eye . . .

. . . and sat up, clutching his face, surrounded by the sleeping wagons of the Traveling People. Slowly he lowered his hands. There was no pain, no blood. But he could remember it, remember the stabbing agony.

He shuddered, and suddenly Elyas was squatting beside him in the predawn, one hand outstretched as if to shake him awake. Beyond the trees where the wagons lay, the wolves howled, one sharp cry from three throats. He shared their sensations. *Fire. Pain. Fire. Hate. Hate! Kill!*

"Yes," Elyas said softly. "It is time. Get up, boy. It's time for us to go."

Perrin scrambled out of his blankets. While he was still bundling his blanketroll, Raen came out of his wagon, rubbing sleep from his eyes. The Seeker glanced at the sky and froze halfway down the steps, his hands still raised to his face. Only his eyes moved as he studied the sky intently, though Perrin could not understand what he was looking at. A few clouds hung in the east, undersides streaked with pink from the sun yet to rise, but there was nothing else to see. Raen seemed to listen, as well, and smell the air, but there was no sound except the wind in the trees and no smell but the faint smoky remnant of last night's campfires.

Elyas returned with his own scanty belongings, and Raen came the rest of the way down. "We must change the direction we travel, my old friend." The Seeker looked uneasily at the sky again. "We go another way this day. Will you be coming with us?" Elyas shook his head, and Raen nodded as if he had known all along. "Well, take care, my old friend. There is something about today. . . ." He started to look up once more, but pulled his eyes back down before they rose above the wagon tops. "I think the wagons will go east. Perhaps all the way to the Spine of the World. Perhaps we'll find a *stedding,* and stay there awhile."

"Trouble never enters the *stedding,*" Elyas agreed. "But the Ogier are none too open to strangers."

"Everyone is open to the Traveling People," Raen said, and grinned. "Besides, even Ogier have pots and things to mend. Come, let us have some breakfast, and we'll talk about it."

"No time," Elyas said. "We move on today, too. As soon as possible. It's a day for moving, it seems."

Raen tried to convince him to at least stay long enough for food, and when Ila appeared from the wagon with Egwene, she added her arguments, though not as strenuously as her husband. She said all of the right words, but her politeness was stiff, and it was plain she would be glad to see Elyas's back, if not Egwene's.

Egwene did not notice the regretful, sidelong looks Ila gave her. She asked what was going on, and Perrin prepared himself for her to say she wanted to stay with the Tuatha'an, but when Elyas explained she only nodded thoughtfully and hurried back into the wagon to gather her things.

Finally Raen threw up his hands. "All right. I don't know

that I have ever let a visitor leave this camp without a farewell feast, but. . . ." Uncertainly, his eyes raised toward the sky again. "Well, we need an early start ourselves, I think. Perhaps we will eat as we journey. But at least let everyone say goodbye."

Elyas started to protest, but Raen was already hurrying from wagon to wagon, pounding on the doors where there was no one awake. By the time a Tinker came, leading Bela, the whole camp had turned out in their finest and brightest, a mass of color that made Raen and Ila's red-and-yellow wagon seem almost plain. The big dogs strolled through the crowd with their tongues lolling out of their mouths, looking for someone to scratch their ears, while Perrin and the others endured handshake after handshake and hug after hug. The girls who had danced every night would not be content with shaking hands, and their hugs made Perrin suddenly wish he was not leaving after all—until he remembered how many others were watching, and then his face almost matched the Seeker's wagon.

Aram drew Egwene a little aside. Perrin could not hear what he had to say to her over the noise of goodbyes, but she kept shaking her head, slowly at first, then more firmly as he began to gesture pleadingly. His face shifted from pleading to arguing, but she continued to shake her head stubbornly until Ila rescued her with a few sharp words to her grandson. Scowling, Aram pushed away through the crowd, abandoning the rest of the farewell. Ila watched him go, hesitating on the point of calling him back. *She's relieved, too,* Perrin thought. *Relieved he doesn't want to go with us—with Egwene.*

When he had shaken every hand in the camp at least once and hugged every girl at least twice, the crowd moved back, opening a little space around Raen and Ila, and the three visitors.

"You came in peace," Raen intoned, bowing formally, hands on his chest. "Depart now in peace. Always will our fires welcome you, in peace. The Way of the Leaf is peace."

"Peace be on you always," Elyas replied, "and on all the People." He hesitated, then added, "I will find the song, or another will find the song, but the song will be sung, this year or in a year to come. As it once was, so shall it be again, world without end."

Raen blinked in surprise, and Ila looked completely flabbergasted, but all the other Tuatha'an murmured in reply, "World without end. World and time without end." Raen and his wife hurriedly said the same after everyone else.

Then it really was time to go. A few last farewells, a few last admonitions to take care, a few last smiles and winks, and they were making their way out of the camp. Raen accompanied them as far as the edge of the trees, a pair of the dogs cavorting by his side.

"Truly, my old friend, you must take great care. This day. . . . There is wickedness loose in the world, I fear, and whatever you pretend, you are not so wicked that it will not gobble you up."

"Peace be on you," Elyas said.

"And on you," Raen said sadly.

When Raen was gone, Elyas scowled at finding the other two looking at him. "So I don't believe in their fool song," he growled. "No need to make them feel bad by messing up their ceremony, was there? I told you they set a store by ceremony sometimes."

"Of course," Egwene said gently. "No need at all." Elyas turned away muttering to himself.

Dapple, Wind, and Hopper came to greet Elyas, not frolicking as the dogs had done, but a dignified meeting of equals. Perrin caught what passed between them. *Fire eyes. Pain. Heartfang. Death. Heartfang.* Perrin knew what they meant. The Dark One. They were telling about his dream. Their dream.

He shivered as the wolves ranged out ahead, scouting the way. It was Egwene's turn to ride Bela, and he walked beside her. Elyas led, as usual, a steady, ground-eating pace.

Perrin did not want to think about his dream. He had thought that the wolves made them safe. *Not complete. Accept. Full heart. Full mind. You still struggle. Only complete when you accept.*

He forced the wolves out of his head, and blinked in surprise. He had not known he could do that. He determined not to let them back in again. *Even in dreams?* He was not sure if the thought was his or theirs.

Egwene still wore the string of blue beads Aram had given her, and a little sprig of something with tiny, bright red leaves in her hair, another gift from the young Tuatha'an.

That Aram had tried to talk her into staying with the Traveling People, Perrin was sure. He was glad she had not given in, but he wished she did not finger the beads so fondly.

Finally he said, "What did you spend so much time talking about with Ila? If you weren't dancing with that long-legged fellow, you were talking to her like it was some kind of secret."

"Ila was giving me advice on being a woman," Egwene replied absently. He began laughing, and she gave him a hooded, dangerous look that he failed to see.

"Advice! Nobody tells us how to be men. We just are."

"That," Egwene said, "is probably why you make such a bad job of it." Up ahead, Elyas cackled loudly.

CHAPTER
28

Footprints in Air

Nynaeve stared in wonder at what lay ahead down
the river, the White Bridge gleaming in the sun
with a milky glow. *Another legend*, she thought,
glancing at the Warder and the Aes Sedai, riding just ahead
of her. *Another legend, and they don't even seem to notice*. She resolved not to stare where they could see. *They'll
laugh if they see me gaping like a country bumpkin*. The
three rode on silently toward the fabled White Bridge.

Since that morning after Shadar Logoth, when she had
found Moiraine and Lan on the bank of the Arinelle, there
had been little in the way of real conversation between her
and the Aes Sedai. There had been talk, of course, but nothing of substance as Nynaeve saw it. Moiraine's attempts to
talk her into going to Tar Valon, for instance. Tar Valon.
She would go there, if need be, and take their training, but
not for the reasons the Aes Sedai thought. If Moiraine had
brought harm to Egwene and the boys. . . .

Sometimes, against her will, Nynaeve had found herself
thinking of what a Wisdom could do with the One Power, of
what she could do. Whenever she realized what was in her
head, though, a flash of anger burned it out. The Power was a
filthy thing. She would have nothing to do with it. Unless she
had to.

The cursed woman only wanted to talk about taking her
to Tar Valon for training. Moiraine would not tell her anything! It was not as if she wanted to know so much.

"How do you mean to find them?" she remembered demanding.

"As I have told you," Moiraine replied without bothering

to look back at her, "I will know when I am close to the two who have lost their coins." It was not the first time Nynaeve had asked, but the Aes Sedai's voice was like a still pond that refused to ripple no matter how many stones Nynaeve threw; it made the Wisdom's blood boil every time she was exposed to it. Moiraine went on as if she could not feel Nynaeve's eyes on her back; Nynaeve knew she must be able to, she was staring so hard. "The longer it takes, the closer I must come, but I will know. As for the one who still has his token, so long as he has it in his possession I can follow him across half the world, if need be."

"And then? What do you plan when you've found them, Aes Sedai?" She did not for a minute believe the Aes Sedai would be so intent on finding them if she did not have plans.

"Tar Valon, Wisdom."

"Tar Valon, Tar Valon. That's all you ever say, and I am becoming—"

"Part of the training you will receive in Tar Valon, Wisdom, will teach you to control your temper. You can do nothing with the One Power when emotion rules your mind." Nynaeve opened her mouth, but the Aes Sedai went right on. "Lan, I must speak with you a moment."

The two put their heads together, and Nynaeve was left with a sullen glower that she hated every time she realized it was on her face. It came too often as the Aes Sedai deftly turned her questions off onto another subject, slid easily by her conversational traps, or ignored her shouts until they ended in silence. The scowl made her feel like a girl who had been caught acting the fool by someone in the Women's Circle. That was a feeling Nynaeve was not used to, and the calm smile on Moiraine's face only made it worse.

If only there was some way to get rid of the woman. Lan would be better by himself—a Warder should be able to handle what was needed, she told herself hastily, feeling a sudden flush; no other reason—but one meant the other.

And yet, Lan made her even more furious than Moiraine. She could not understand how he managed to get under her skin so easily. He rarely said anything—sometimes not a dozen words in a day—and he never took part in any of the . . . discussions with Moiraine. He was often apart from the two women, scouting the land, but even when he was there he kept a little to one side, watching them as if watching a duel.

Nynaeve wished he would stop. If it was a duel, she had not managed to score once, and Moiraine did not even seem to realize she was in a fight. Nynaeve could have done without his cool blue eyes, without even a silent audience.

That had been the way of their journey, for the most part. Quiet, except when her temper got the best of her, and sometimes when she shouted the sound of her voice seemed to crash in the silence like breaking glass. The land itself was quiet, as if the world were pausing to catch its breath. The wind moaned in the trees, but all else was still. The wind seemed distant, too, even when it was cutting through the cloak on her back.

At first the stillness was restful after everything that had happened. It seemed as if she had not known a moment of quiet since before Winternight. By the end of the first day alone with the Aes Sedai and the Warder, though, she was looking over her shoulder and fidgeting in her saddle as if she had an itch in the middle of her back where she could not reach. The silence seemed like crystal doomed to shatter, and waiting for the first crack put her teeth on edge.

It weighed on Moiraine and Lan, too, as outwardly unperturbable as they were. She soon realized that, beneath their calm surfaces, hour by hour they wound tighter and tighter, like clocksprings being forced to the breaking point. Moiraine seemed to listen to things that were not there, and what she heard put a crease in her forehead. Lan watched the forest and the river as if the leafless trees and wide, slow water carried the signs of traps and ambushes waiting ahead.

Part of her was glad that she was not the only one who apprehended that poised-on-the-brink feel to the world, but if it affected them, it was real, and another part of her wanted nothing so much as for it to be just her imagination. Something of it tickled the corners of her mind, as when she listened to the wind, but now she knew that that had to do with the One Power, and she could not bring herself to embrace those ripples at the edge of thought.

"It is nothing," Lan said quietly when she asked. He did not look at her while he spoke; his eyes never ceased their scanning. Then, contradicting what he had just said, he added, "You should go back to your Two Rivers when we reach Whitebridge, and the Caemlyn Road. It's too danger-

ous here. Nothing will try to stop you going back, though."
It was the longest speech he made all that day.

"She is part of the Pattern, Lan," Moiraine said chidingly. Her gaze was elsewhere, too. "It is the Dark One, Nynaeve. The storm has left us . . . for a time, at least." She raised one hand as though feeling the air, then scrubbed it on her dress unconsciously, as if she had touched filth. "He is still watching, however"—she sighed—"and his gaze is stronger. Not on us, but on the world. How much longer before he is strong enough to. . . ."

Nynaeve hunched her shoulders; suddenly she could almost feel someone staring at her back. It was one explanation she would just as soon the Aes Sedai had not given her.

Lan scouted their path down the river, but where before he had chosen the way, now Moiraine did so, as surely as if she followed some unseen track, footprints in air, the scent of memory. Lan only checked the route she intended, to see that it was safe. Nynaeve had the feeling that even if he said it was not, Moiraine would insist on it anyway. And he would go, she was sure. Straight down the river to. . . .

With a start, Nynaeve pulled out of her thoughts. They were at the foot of the White Bridge. The pale arch shone in the sunlight, a milky spiderweb too delicate to stand, sweeping across the Arinelle. The weight of a man would bring it crashing down, much less that of a horse. Surely it would collapse under its own weight any minute.

Lan and Moiraine rode unconcernedly ahead, up the gleaming white approach and onto the bridge, hooves ringing, not like steel on glass, but like steel on steel. The surface of the bridge certainly looked as slick as glass, wet glass, but it gave the horses a firm, sure footing.

Nynaeve made herself follow, but from the first step she half waited for the entire structure to shatter under them. *If lace were made of glass,* she thought, *it would look like this.*

It was not until they were almost all the way across that she noticed the tarry smell of char thickening the air. In a moment she saw.

Around the square at the foot of the White Bridge piles of blackened timbers, still leaking smoky threads, replaced half a dozen buildings. Men in poorly fitting red uniforms and tarnished armor patrolled the streets, but they marched

quickly, as if afraid of finding anything, and they looked
over their shoulders as they went. Townspeople—the few
who were out—almost ran, shoulders hunched, as though
something were chasing them.

Lan looked grim, even for him, and people walked wide
of the three of them, even the soldiers. The Warder sniffed
the air and grimaced, growling under his breath. It was no
wonder to Nynaeve, with the stink of burn so strong.

"The Wheel weaves as the Wheel wills," Moiraine mumbled. "No eye can see the Pattern until it is woven."

In the next moment she was down off Aldieb and speaking to townsfolk. She did not ask questions; she gave sympathy, and to Nynaeve's surprise it appeared genuine. People
who shied away from Lan, ready to hurry from any stranger,
stopped to speak with Moiraine. They appeared startled
themselves at what they were doing, but they opened up, after a fashion, under Moiraine's clear gaze and soothing voice.
The Aes Sedai's eyes seemed to share the people's hurt, to
empathize with their confusion, and tongues loosened.

They still lied, though. Most of them. Some denied there
had been any trouble at all. Nothing at all. Moiraine mentioned the burned buildings all around the square. Everything was fine, they insisted, staring past what they did not
want to see.

One fat fellow spoke with a hollow heartiness, but his
cheek twitched at every noise behind him. With a grin that
kept slipping, he claimed an overturned lamp had started
a fire that spread with the wind before anything could be
done. One glance showed Nynaeve that no burned structure
stood alongside another.

There were almost as many different stories as there
were people. Several women lowered their voices conspira-
torially. The truth of the matter was there was a man somewhere in the town meddling with the One Power. It was
time to have the Aes Sedai in; past time, was the way they
saw it, no matter what the men said about Tar Valon. Let the
Red Ajah settle matters.

One man claimed it had been an attack by bandits, and
another said a riot by Darkfriends. "Those ones going to see
the false Dragon, you know," he confided darkly. "They're
all over the place. Darkfriends, every one."

Still others spoke of some kind of trouble—they were

vague about exactly what kind—that had come downriver on a boat.

"We showed them," a narrow-faced man muttered, scrubbing his hand together nervously. "Let them keep that kind of thing in the Borderlands, where it belongs. We went down to the docks and—" He cut off so abruptly his teeth clicked. Without another word he scurried off, peering back over his shoulder at them as if he thought they might chase him down.

The boat had gotten away—that much was clear, eventually, from others—cutting its moorings and fleeing downriver only the day before while a mob poured onto the docks. Nynaeve wondered if Egwene and the boys had been on board. One woman said that a gleeman had been on the boat. If that had been Thom Merrilin. . . .

She tried her opinion on Moiraine, that some of the Emond's Fielders might have fled on the boat. The Aes Sedai listened patiently, nodding, until she was done.

"Perhaps," Moiraine said then, but she sounded doubtful.

An inn still stood in the square, the common room divided in two by a shoulder-high wall. Moiraine paused as she stepped into the inn, feeling the air with her hand. She smiled at whatever it was she felt, but she would say nothing of it, then.

Their meal was consumed in silence, silence not only at their table, but throughout the common room. The handful of people eating there concentrated on their own plates and their own thoughts. The innkeeper, dusting tables with a corner of his apron, muttered to himself continually, but always too low to be heard. Nynaeve thought it would not be pleasant sleeping there; even the air was heavy with fear.

About the time they pushed their plates away, wiped clean with the last scraps of bread, one of the red-uniformed soldiers appeared in the doorway. He seemed resplendent to Nynaeve, in his peaked helmet and burnished breastplate, until he took a pose just inside the door, with a hand resting on the hilt of his sword and a stern look on his face, and used a finger to ease his too-tight collar. It made her think of Cenn Buie trying to act the way a Village Councilor should.

Lan spared him one glance and snorted. "Militia. Useless."

The soldier looked over the room, letting his eyes come to rest on them. He hesitated, then took a deep breath before stomping over to demand, all in a rush, who they were, what their business was in Whitebridge, and how long they intended to stay.

"We are leaving as soon as I finish my ale," Lan said. He took another slow swallow before looking up at the soldier. "The Light illumine good Queen Morgase."

The red-uniformed man opened his mouth, then took a good look at Lan's eyes and stepped back. He caught himself immediately, with a glance at Moiraine and her. She thought for a moment that he was going to do something foolish to keep from looking the coward in front of two women. In her experience, men were often idiots that way. But too much had happened in Whitebridge; too much uncertainty had escaped from the cellars of men's minds. The militiaman looked back at Lan and reconsidered once more. The Warder's hard-planed face was expressionless, but there were those cold blue eyes. So cold.

The militiaman settled on a brisk nod. "See that you do. Too many strangers around these days for the good of the Queen's peace." Turning on his heel he stomped out again, practicing his stern look on the way. None of the locals in the inn seemed to notice.

"Where are we going?" Nynaeve demanded of the Warder. The mood in the room was such that she kept her voice low, but she made sure it was firm, too. "After the boat?"

Lan looked at Moiraine, who shook her head slightly and said, "First I must find the one I can be sure of finding, and at present he is somewhere to the north of us. I do not think the other two went with the boat in any case." A small, satisfied smile touched her lips. "They were in this room, perhaps a day ago, no more than two. Afraid, but they left alive. The trace would not have lasted without that strong emotion."

"Which two?" Nynaeve leaned over the table intently. "Do you know?" The Aes Sedai shook her head, the slightest of motions, and Nynaeve settled back. "If they're only a day or two ahead, why don't we go after them first?"

"I know they were here," Moiraine said in that insufferably calm voice, "but beyond that I cannot say if they went east or north or south. I trust they are smart enough to have gone east, toward Caemlyn, but I do not know, and lacking their tokens, I will not know where they are until I am perhaps within half a mile. In two days they could have gone twenty miles, or forty, in any direction, if fear urged them, and they were certainly afraid when they left here."

"But—"

"Wisdom, however fearful they were, in whatever direction they ran, eventually they will remember Caemlyn, and it is there I will find them. But I will help the one I can find now, first."

Nynaeve opened her mouth again, but Lan cut her off in a soft voice. "They had reason to be afraid." He looked around, then lowered his voice. "There was a Halfman here." He grimaced, the way he had in the square. "I can still smell him everywhere."

Moiraine sighed. "I will keep hope until I know it is gone. I refuse to believe the Dark One can win so easily. I will find all three of them alive and well. I must believe it."

"I want to find the boys, too," Nynaeve said, "but what about Egwene? You never even mention her, and you ignore me when I ask. I thought you were going to take her off to"—she glanced at the other tables, and lowered her voice—"to Tar Valon."

The Aes Sedai studied the tabletop for a moment before raising her eyes to Nynaeve's, and when she did, Nynaeve started back from a flash of anger that almost seemed to make Moiraine's eyes glow. Then her back stiffened, her own anger rising, but before she could say a word, the Aes Sedai spoke coldly.

"I hope to find Egwene alive and well, too. I do not easily give up young women with that much ability once I have found them. But it will be as the Wheel weaves."

Nynaeve felt a cold ball in the pit of her stomach. *Am I one of those young women you won't give up? We'll see about that, Aes Sedai. The Light burn you, we'll see about that!*

The meal was finished in silence, and it was a silent three who rode through the gates and down the Caemlyn Road. Moiraine's eyes searched the horizon to the northeast. Behind them, the smoke-stained town of Whitebridge cowered.

CHAPTER
29

Eyes Without Pity

Elyas pushed for speed across the brown grass flatland as if trying to make up for the time spent with the Traveling People, setting a pace southward that had even Bela grateful to stop when twilight deepened. Despite his desire for haste, though, he took precautions he had not taken before. At night they had a fire only if there was dead wood already on the ground. He would not let them break so much as a twig off of a standing tree. The fires he made were small, and always hidden in a pit carefully dug where he had cut away a plug of sod. As soon as their meal was prepared, he buried the coals and replaced the plug. Before they set out again in the gray false dawn, he went over the campsite inch by inch to make sure there was no sign that anyone had ever been there. He even righted overturned rocks and straightened bent-down weeds. He did it quickly, never taking more than a few minutes, but they did not leave until he was satisfied.

Perrin did not think the precautions were much good against dreams, but when he began to think of what they might be good against, he wished it were only the dreams. The first time, Egwene asked anxiously if the Trollocs were back, but Elyas only shook his head and urged them on. Perrin said nothing. He knew there were no Trollocs close; the wolves scented only grass and trees and small animals. It was not fear of Trollocs that drove Elyas, but that something else of which even Elyas was not sure. The wolves knew nothing of what it was, but they sensed Elyas's urgent wariness, and they began to scout as if danger ran at their heels or waited in ambush over the next rise.

The land became long, rolling crests, too low to be called hills, rising across their path. A carpet of tough grass, still winter sere and dotted with rank weeds, spread before them, rippled by an east wind that had nothing to cut it for a hundred miles. The groves of trees grew more scattered. The sun rose reluctantly, without warmth.

Among the squat ridges Elyas followed the contours of the land as much as possible, and he avoided topping the rises whenever possible. He seldom talked, and when he did. . . .

"You know how long this is taking, going around every bloody little hill like this? Blood and ashes! I'll be till summer getting you off my hands. No, we can't just go in a straight line! How many times do I have to tell you? You have any idea, even the faintest, how a man stands out on a ridgeline in country like this? Burn me, but we're going back and forth as much as forward. Wiggling like a snake. I could move faster with my feet tied. Well, you going to stare at me, or you going to walk?"

Perrin exchanged glances with Egwene. She stuck her tongue out at Elyas's back. Neither of them said anything. The one time Egwene had protested that Elyas was the one who wanted to go around the hills and he should not blame them, it got her a lecture on how sound carried, delivered in a growl that could have been heard a mile off. He gave the lecture over his shoulder, and he never even slowed to give it.

Whether he was talking or not, Elyas's eyes searched all around them, sometimes staring as if there were something to see except the same coarse grass that was under their feet. If he did see anything, Perrin could not, and neither could the wolves. Elyas's forehead grew extra furrows, but he would not explain, not why they had to hurry, not what he was afraid was hunting them.

Sometimes a longer ridge than usual lay across their path, stretching miles and miles to east and west. Even Elyas had to agree that going around those would take them too far out of their way. He did not let them simply cross over, though. Leaving them at the base of the slope, he would creep up to the crest on his belly, peering over as cautiously as though the wolves had not scouted there ten minutes before. Waiting at the bottom of the ridge, minutes passed like hours,

and the not knowing pressed on them. Egwene chewed her
lip and unconsciously clicked the beads Aram had given
her through her fingers. Perrin waited doggedly. His stomach twisted up in a sick knot, but he managed to keep his
face calm, managed to keep the turmoil hidden inside.

*The wolves will warn if there's danger. It would be wonder-
ful if they went away, if they just vanished, but right now . . .
right now, they'll give warning. What is he looking for? What?*

After a long search with only his eyes above the rise,
Elyas always motioned them to come ahead. Every time
the way ahead was clear—until the next time they found
a ridge they could not go around. At the third such ridge,
Perrin's stomach lurched. Sour fumes rose in his throat, and
he knew if he had to wait even five minutes he would vomit.
"I. . . ." He swallowed. "I'm coming, too."

"Keep low," was all Elyas said.

As soon as he spoke Egwene jumped down from Bela.

The fur-clad man pushed his round hat forward and peered
at her from under the edge. "You expecting to make that
mare crawl?" he said dryly.

Her mouth worked, but no sound came out. Finally she
shrugged, and Elyas turned away without another word and
began climbing the easy slope. Perrin hurried after him.

Well short of the crest Elyas made a downward motion
and a moment later flattened himself on the ground, wriggling forward the last few yards. Perrin flopped on his belly.

At the top, Elyas took off his hat before raising his head
ever so slowly. Peering through a clump of thorny weeds,
Perrin saw only the same rolling plain that lay behind them.
The down-slope was bare, though a clump of trees a hundred paces across grew in the hollow, perhaps half a mile
south from the ridge. The wolves had already been through
it, smelling no trace of Trollocs or Myrddraal.

East and west the land was the same as far as Perrin
could see, rolling grassland and wide-scattered thickets.
Nothing moved. The wolves were more than a mile ahead,
out of sight; at that distance he could barely feel them. They
had seen nothing when they covered this ground. *What is
he looking for? There's nothing there.*

"We're wasting time," he said, starting to stand, and a
flock of ravens burst out of the trees below, fifty, a hundred
black birds, spiraling into the sky. He froze in a crouch as

they milled over the trees. *The Dark One's Eyes. Did they see me?* Sweat trickled down his face.

As if one thought had suddenly sparked in a hundred tiny minds, every raven broke sharply in the same direction. South. The flock disappeared over the next rise, already descending. To the east another thicket disgorged more ravens. The black mass wheeled twice and headed south.

Shaking, he lowered himself to the ground slowly. He tried to speak, but his mouth was too dry. After a minute he managed to work up some spit. "Was that what you were afraid of? Why didn't you say something? Why didn't the wolves see them?"

"Wolves don't look up in trees much," Elyas growled. "And no, I wasn't looking for this. I told you, I didn't know what. . . ." Far to the west a black cloud rose over yet another grove and winged southward. They were too far off to make out individual birds. "It isn't a big hunt, thank the Light. They don't know. Even after. . . ." He turned to stare back the way they had come.

Perrin swallowed. Even after the dream, Elyas had meant. "Not big?" he said. "Back home you won't see that many ravens in a whole year."

Elyas shook his head. "In the Borderlands I've seen sweeps with a thousand ravens to the flock. Not too often—there's a bounty on ravens there—but it has happened." He was still looking north. "Hush, now."

Perrin felt it, then; the effort of reaching out to the distant wolves. Elyas wanted Dapple and her companions to quit scouting ahead, to hurry back and check their backtrail. His already gaunt face tightened and thinned under the strain. The wolves were so far away Perrin could not even feel them. *Hurry. Watch the sky. Hurry.*

Faintly Perrin caught the reply from far to the south. *We come.* An image flashed in his mind—wolves running, muzzles pointing into the wind of their haste, running as if wildfire raced behind, running—flashed and was gone in an instant.

Elyas slumped and drew a deep breath. Frowning, he peered over the ridge, then back to the north, and muttered under his breath.

"You think there are more ravens behind us?" Perrin asked.

"Could be," Elyas said vaguely. "They do it that way, sometimes. I know a place, if we can reach it by dark. We have to keep moving until full dark anyway, even if we don't get there, but we can't go as fast as I would like. Can't afford to get too close to the ravens ahead of us. But if they're behind us, too. . . ."

"Why dark?" Perrin said. "What place? Somewhere safe from the ravens?"

"Safe from ravens," Elyas said, "but too many people know. . . . Ravens roost for the night. We don't have to worry about them finding us in the dark. The Light send ravens are all we have to worry about then." With one more look over the crest, he rose and waved to Egwene to bring Bela up. "But dark is a long way off. We have to get moving." He started down the far slope in a shambling run, each stride barely catching him on the edge of falling. "Move, burn you!"

Perrin moved, half running, half sliding, after him.

Egwene topped the rise behind them, kicking Bela to a trot. A grin of relief bloomed on her face when she saw them. "What's going on?" she called, urging the shaggy mare to catch up. "When you disappeared like that, I thought. . . . What happened?"

Perrin saved his breath for running until she reached them. He explained about the ravens and Elyas's safe place, but it was a disjointed story. After a strangled, "Ravens!" she kept interrupting with questions for which, as often as not, he had no answers. Between them, he did not finish until they reached the next ridge.

Ordinarily—if anything about the journey could be called ordinary—they would have gone around this one rather than over, but Elyas insisted on scouting anyway.

"You want to just saunter right into the middle of them, boy?" was his sour comment.

Egwene stared at the crest of the ridge, licking her lips, as if she wanted to go with Elyas this time and wanted to stay where she was, too. Elyas was the only one who showed no hesitation.

Perrin wondered if the ravens ever doubled back. It would be a fine thing to reach the crest at the same time as a flock of ravens.

At the top he inched his head up until he could just see,

and heaved a sigh of relief when all he saw was a copse of trees a little to the west. There were no ravens to be seen. Abruptly a fox burst out of the trees, running hard. Ravens poured from the branches after it. The beat of their wings almost drowned out a desperate whining from the fox. A black whirlwind dove and swirled around it. The fox's jaws snapped at them, but they darted in, and darted away untouched, black beaks glistening wetly. The fox turned back toward the trees, seeking the safety of its den. It ran awkwardly now, head low, fur dark and bloody, and the ravens flapped around it, more and more of them at once, the fluttering mass thickening until it hid the fox completely. As suddenly as they had descended the ravens rose, wheeled, and vanished over the next rise to the south. A misshapen lump of torn fur marked what had been the fox.

Perrin swallowed hard. *Light! They could do that to us. A hundred ravens. They could—*

"Move," Elyas growled, jumping up. He waved to Egwene to come on, and without waiting set off at a trot toward the trees. "Move, burn you!" he called over his shoulder. "Move!"

Egwene galloped Bela over the rise and caught them before they reached the bottom of the slope. There was no time for explanations, but her eyes picked out the fox right away. Her face went as white as snow.

Elyas reached the trees and turned there, at the edge of the copse, waving vigorously for them to hurry. Perrin tried to run faster and stumbled. Arms windmilling, he barely caught himself short of going flat on his face. *Blood and ashes! I'm running as fast as I can!*

A lone raven winged out of the copse. It tilted toward them, screamed, and spun toward the south. Knowing he was already too late, Perrin fumbled his sling from around his waist. He was still trying to get a stone from his pocket to the sling when the raven abruptly folded up in mid-air and plummeted to the ground. His mouth dropped open, and then he saw the sling hanging from Egwene's hand. She grinned at him unsteadily.

"Don't stand there counting your toes!" Elyas called.

With a start Perrin hurried into the trees, then jumped out of the way to avoid being trampled by Egwene and Bela.

Far to the west, almost out of sight, what seemed like a

dark mist rose into the air. Perrin felt the wolves passing in that direction, heading north. He felt them notice ravens, to the left and right of them, without slowing. The dark mist swirled northward as if pursuing the wolves, then abruptly broke off and flashed to the south.

"Do you think they saw us?" Egwene asked. "We were already in the trees, weren't we? They couldn't see us at that distance. Could they? Not that far off."

"We saw them at that distance," Elyas said dryly. Perrin shifted uneasily, and Egwene drew a frightened breath. "If they had seen us," Elyas growled, "they'd have been down on us like they were on that fox. Think, if you want to stay alive. Fear will kill you if you don't control it." His penetrating stare held on each of them for a moment. Finally he nodded. "They're gone, now, and we should be, too. Keep those slings handy. Might be useful again."

As they moved out of the copse, Elyas angled them westward from the line of march they had been following. Perrin's breath snagged in his throat; it was as if they were chasing after the last ravens they had seen. Elyas kept on tirelessly, and there was nothing for them to do but follow. After all, Elyas knew a safe place. Somewhere. So he said.

They ran to the next hill, waited till the ravens moved on, then ran again, waited, ran. The steady progress they had been keeping had been tiring enough, but all except Elyas quickly began to flag under this jerky pace. Perrin's chest heaved, and he gulped air when he had a few minutes to lie on a hilltop, leaving the search to Elyas. Bela stood head down, nostrils flaring, at every stop. Fear lashed them on, and Perrin did not know if it was controlled or not. He only wished the wolves would tell them what was behind them, if anything was, whatever it was.

Ahead were more ravens than Perrin ever hoped to see again. To the left and right the black birds billowed up, and to the south. A dozen times they reached the hiding place of a grove or the scant shelter of a slope only moments before ravens swept into the sky. Once, with the sun beginning to slide from its midday height, they stood in the open, frozen as still as statues, half a mile from the nearest cover, while a hundred of the Dark One's feathered spies flashed by a bare mile to the east. Sweat rolled down Perrin's face despite the wind, until the last black shape dwindled to a dot and vanished. He lost count of the stragglers they brought down with their slings.

He saw more than enough evidence lying in the path the ravens had covered to justify his fear. He had stared with a queasy fascination at a rabbit that had been torn to pieces. The eyeless head stood upright, with the other bits—legs, entrails—scattered in a rough circle around it. Birds, too, stabbed to shapeless masses of feathers. And two more foxes.

He remembered something Lan had said. All the Dark One's creatures delight in killing. The Dark One's power is death. And if the ravens found them? Pitiless eyes shining like black beads. Stabbing beaks swirling around them. Needle-sharp beaks drawing blood. A hundred of them. *Or can they call more of their kind? Maybe all of them in the hunt?* A sickening image built up in his mind. A pile of ravens as big as a hill, seething like maggots, fighting over a few bloody shreds.

Suddenly the image was swept away by others, each one clear for an instant, then spinning and fading into another. The wolves had found ravens to the north. Screaming birds dove and whirled and dove again, beaks drawing blood with every swoop. Snarling wolves dodged and leaped, twisting in the air, jaws snapping. Again and again Perrin tasted feathers and the foul taste of fluttering ravens crushed alive, felt the pain of oozing gashes all over his body, knew with a despair that never touched on giving up that all his effort was not enough. Suddenly the ravens broke away, wheeling overhead for one last shriek of rage at the wolves. Wolves did not die as easily as foxes, and they had a mission. A flap of black wings, and they were gone, a few black feathers drifting down on their dead. Wind licked at a puncture on his left foreleg. There was something wrong with one of Hopper's eyes. Ignoring her own hurts, Dapple gathered them and they settled into a painful lope in the direction the ravens had gone. Blood matted their fur. *We come. Danger comes before us.*

Moving in a stumbling trot, Perrin exchanged a glance with Elyas. The man's yellow eyes were expressionless, but he knew. He said nothing, just watched Perrin and waited, all the while maintaining that effortless lope.

Waiting for me. Waiting for me to admit I feel the wolves.

"Ravens," Perrin panted reluctantly. "Behind us."

"He was right," Egwene breathed. "You can talk to them."

Perrin's feet felt like lumps of iron on the ends of wooden posts, but he tried to make them move faster. If he could outrun their eyes, outrun the ravens, outrun the wolves, but above all Egwene's eyes, that knew him now for what he was. *What are you? Tainted, the Light blind me! Cursed!*

His throat burned as it never had from breathing the smoke and heat of Master Luhhan's forge. He staggered and hung on to Egwene's stirrup until she climbed down and all but pushed him into the saddle despite his protests that he could keep going. It was not long, though, before she was clutching the stirrup as she ran, holding up her skirts with her other hand, and only a little while after that until he dismounted, his knees still wobbling. He had to pick her up to make her take his place, but she was too tired to fight him.

Elyas would not slow down. He urged them, and taunted them, and kept them so close behind the searching ravens to the south that Perrin thought all it would take would be for one bird to look back. "Keep moving, burn you! Think you'll do any better than that fox did, if they catch us? The one with its insides piled on its head?" Egwene swayed out of the saddle and vomited noisily. "I knew you'd remember. Just keep going a little more. That's all. Just a little more. Burn you, I thought farm youngsters had endurance. Work all day and dance all night. Sleep all day and sleep all night, looks like to me. Move your bloody feet!"

They began coming down off the hills as soon as the last raven vanished over the next one, then while the last trailers still flapped above the hilltop. *One bird looking back.* To east and west the ravens searched while they hurried across the open spaces between. *One bird is all it will take.*

The ravens behind were coming fast. Dapple and the other wolves worked their way around them and were coming on without stopping to lick their wounds, but they had learned all the lessons they needed about watching the sky. *How close? How long?* The wolves had no notions of time the way men did, no reasons to divide a day into hours. The seasons were time enough for them, and the light and the dark. No need for more. Finally Perrin worked out an image of where the sun would stand in the sky when the ravens overran them from behind. He glanced over his shoulder at the setting sun, and licked his lips with a dry tongue. In an hour the ravens would be on them, maybe less. An hour, and it was a good two hours to sunset, at least two to full dark.

We'll die with the setting sun, he thought, staggering as he ran. Slaughtered like the fox. He fingered his axe, then moved to his sling. That would be more use. Not enough, though. Not against a hundred ravens, a hundred darting targets, a hundred stabbing beaks.

"It's your turn to ride, Perrin," Egwene said tiredly.

"In a bit," he panted. "I'm good for miles, yet." She nodded, and stayed in the saddle. *She* is *tired. Tell her? Or let her think we still have a chance to escape? An hour of hope, even if it is desperate, or an hour of despair?*

Elyas was watching him again, saying nothing. He must know, but he did not speak. Perrin looked at Egwene again and blinked away hot tears. He touched his axe and wondered if he had the courage. In the last minutes, when the ravens descended on them, when all hope was gone, would he have the courage to spare her the death the fox had died? *Light make me strong!*

The ravens ahead of them suddenly seemed to vanish. Perrin could still make out dark, misty clouds, far to the east and west, but ahead . . . nothing. *Where did they go? Light, if we've overrun them. . . .*

Abruptly a chill ran through him, one cold, clean tingle as if he had jumped into the Winespring Water in midwinter. It rippled through him and seemed to carry away some of his fatigue, a little of the ache in his legs and the burning of his lungs. It left behind . . . something. He could not say what, only he felt different. He stumbled to a halt and looked around, afraid.

Elyas watched him, watched them all, with a gleam behind his eyes. He knew what it was, Perrin was sure of it, but he only watched them.

Egwene reined in Bela and looked around uncertainly, half wondering and half fearful. "It's . . . strange," she whispered. "I feel as if I lost something." Even the mare had her head up expectantly, nostrils flaring as if they detected a faint odor of new-mown hay.

"What . . . what was that?" Perrin asked.

Elyas cackled suddenly. He bent over, shoulders shaking, to

rest his hands on his knees. "Safety, that's what. We made it, you bloody fools. No raven will cross that line . . . not one that carries the Dark One's eyes, anyways. A Trolloc would have to be driven across, and there'd need to be something fierce pushing the Myrddraal to make him do the driving. No Aes Sedai, either. The One Power won't work here; they can't touch the True Source. Can't even feel the Source, like it vanished. Makes them itch inside, that does. Gives them the shakes like a seven-day drunk. It's safety."

At first, to Perrin's eyes, the land was unchanged from the rolling hills and ridges they had crossed the whole day. Then he noticed green shoots among the grass; not many, and they were struggling, but more than he had seen anywhere else. There were fewer weeds in the grass, too. He could not imagine what it was, but there was . . . something about this place. And something in what Elyas said tickled his memory.

"What is it?" Egwene asked. "I feel. . . . What is this place? I don't think I like it."

"A *stedding*," Elyas roared. "You never listen to stories? Of course, there hasn't been an Ogier here in three thousand odd years, not since the Breaking of the World, but it's the *stedding* makes the Ogier, not the Ogier make the *stedding*."

"Just a legend," Perrin stammered. In the stories, the *stedding* were always havens, places to hide, whether it was from Aes Sedai or from creatures of the Father of Lies.

Elyas straightened; if not exactly fresh, he gave no sign that he had spent most of a day running. "Come on. We'd better get deeper into this legend. The ravens can't follow, but they can still see us this close to the edge, and there could be enough of them to watch the whole border of it. Let them keep hunting right on by it."

Perrin wanted to stay right there, now that he was stopped; his legs trembled and told him to lie down for a week. Whatever refreshment he had felt had been momentary; all the weariness and aches were back. He forced himself to take one step, then another. It did not get easier, but he kept at it. Egwene flapped the reins to get Bela moving again. Elyas settled into an effortless lope, only slowing to a walk when it became apparent the others could not keep up. A fast walk.

"Why don't—we stay here?" Perrin panted. He was breathing through his mouth, and he forced the words out between deep, wracking breaths. "If it's really—a *stedding*. We'd be safe. No Trollocs. No Aes Sedai. Why don't we— just stay here—until it's all over?" *Maybe the wolves won't come here, either.*

"How long will that be?" Elyas looked over his shoulder with one eyebrow raised. "What would you eat? Grass, like the horse? Besides, there's others know about this place, and nothing keeps men out, not even the worst of them. And there is only one place where there's still water to be found." Frowning uneasily, he turned in a complete circle, scanning the land. When he was done, he shook his head and muttered to himself. Perrin felt him calling to the wolves. *Hurry. Hurry.* "We take our chances on a choice of evils, and the ravens are sure. Come on. It's only another mile or two."

Perrin would have groaned if he had been willing to spare the breath.

Huge boulders began to dot the low hills, irregular lumps of gray, lichen-coated stone half buried in the ground, some as big as a house. Brambles webbed them, and low brush half hid most. Here and there amid the desiccated brown of brambles and brush a lone green shoot announced that this was a special place. Whatever wounded the land beyond its borders hurt it, too, but here the wound did not go quite as deep.

Eventually they straggled over one more rise, and at the base of this hill lay a pool of water. Any of them could have waded across it in two strides, but it was clear and clean enough to show the sandy bottom like a sheet of glass. Even Elyas hurried eagerly down the slope.

Perrin threw himself full length on the ground when he reached the pool and plunged his head in. An instant later he was spluttering from the cold of water that had welled up from the depths of the earth. He shook his head, his long hair spraying a rain of drops. Egwene grinned and splashed back at him. Perrin's eyes grew sober. She frowned and opened her mouth, but he stuck his face back in the water. *No questions. Not now. No explanations. Not ever.* But a small voice taunted him. *But you would have done it, wouldn't you?*

Eventually Elyas called them away from the pool. "Anybody wants to eat, I want some help."

Egwene worked cheerfully, laughing and joking as they prepared their scanty meal. There was nothing left but cheese and dried meat; there had been no chance to hunt. At least there was still tea. Perrin did his share, but silently. He felt Egwene's eyes on him, saw growing worry on her face, but he avoided meeting her eyes as much as he could. Her laughter faded, and the jokes came further apart, each one more strained than the last. Elyas watched, saying nothing. A somber mood descended, and they began their meal in silence. The sun grew red in the west, and their shadows stretched out long and thin.

Not quite an hour till dark. If not for the stedding, *all of you would be dead now. Would you have saved her? Would you have cut her down like so many bushes? Bushes don't bleed, do they? Or scream, and look in your eyes and ask, why?*

Perrin drew in on himself more. He could feel something laughing at him, deep in the back of his mind. Something cruel. Not the Dark One. He almost wished it was. Not the Dark One; himself.

For once Elyas had broken his rule about fires. There were no trees, but he had snapped dead branches from the brush and built his fire against a huge chunk of rock sticking out of the hillside. From the layers of soot staining the stone, Perrin thought the site must have been used by generation after generation of travelers.

What showed above ground of the big rock was rounded somewhat, with a sharp break on one side where moss, old and brown, covered the ragged surface. The grooves and hollows eroded in the rounded part looked odd to Perrin, but he was too absorbed in gloom to wonder about it. Egwene, though, studied it as she ate.

"That," she said finally, "looks like an eye." Perrin blinked; it *did* look like an eye, under all that soot.

"It is," Elyas said. He sat with his back to the fire and the rock, studying the land around them while he chewed a strip of dried meat almost as tough as leather. "Artur Hawkwing's eye. The eye of the High King himself. This is what his power and glory came to, in the end." He said it ab-

sently. Even his chewing was absentminded; his eyes and
his attention were on the hills.

"Artur Hawkwing!" Egwene exclaimed. "You're joking
with me. It isn't an eye at all. Why would somebody carve
Artur Hawkwing's eye on a rock out here?"

Elyas glanced over his shoulder at her, muttering, "What
do they teach you village whelps?" He snorted and straightened back to his watching, but he went on talking. "Artur
Paendrag Tanreall, Artur Hawkwing, the High King, united
all the lands from the Great Blight to the Sea of Storms,
from the Aryth Ocean to the Aiel Waste, and even some
beyond the Waste. He even sent armies the other side of the
Aryth Ocean. The stories say he ruled the whole world, but
what he really did rule was enough for any man outside of a
story. And he brought peace and justice to the land."

"All stood equal before the law," Egwene said, "and no
man raised his hand against another."

"So you've heard the stories, at least." Elyas chuckled, a
dry sound. "Artur Hawkwing brought peace and justice, but
he did it with fire and sword. A child could ride alone with a
bag of gold from the Aryth Ocean to the Spine of the World
and never have a moment's fear, but the High King's justice
was as hard as that rock there for anyone who challenged
his power, even if it was just by being who they were, or by
people thinking they were a challenge. The common folk
had peace, and justice, and full bellies, but he laid a twenty-
year siege to Tar Valon and put a price of a thousand gold
crowns on the head of every Aes Sedai."

"I thought you didn't like Aes Sedai," Egwene said.

Elyas gave a wry smile. "Doesn't matter what I like, girl.
Artur Hawkwing was a proud fool. An Aes Sedai healer
could have saved him when he took sick—or was poisoned,
as some say—but every Aes Sedai still alive was penned
up behind the Shining Walls, using all their Power to hold
off an army that lit up the night with their campfires. He
wouldn't have let one near him, anyway. He hated Aes Sedai as much as he hated the Dark One."

Egwene's mouth tightened, but when she spoke, all she
said was, "What does all that have to do with whether that's
Artur Hawkwing's eye?"

"Just this, girl. With peace except for what was going on

across the ocean, with the people cheering him wherever he went—they really loved him, you see; he was a harsh man, but never with the common folk—well, with all of that, he decided it was time to build himself a capital. A new city, not connected in any man's mind with any old cause or faction or rivalry. Here, he'd build it, at the very center of the land bordered by the seas and the Waste and the Blight. Here, where no Aes Sedai would ever come willing or could use the Power if they did. A capital from which, one day, the whole world would receive peace and justice. When they heard the proclamation, the common people subscribed enough money to build a monument to him. Most of them looked on him as only a step below the Creator. A short step. It took five years to carve and build. A statue of Hawkwing, himself, a hundred times bigger than the man. They raised it right here, and the city was to rise around it."

"There was never any city here," Egwene scoffed. "There would have to be something left if there was. Something."

Elyas nodded, still keeping his watch. "Indeed there was not. Artur Hawkwing died the very day the statue was finished, and his sons and the rest of his blood fought over who would sit on Hawkwing's throne. The statue stood alone in the midst of these hills. The sons and the nephews and the cousins died, and the last of the Hawkwing's blood vanished from the earth—except maybe for some of those who went over the Aryth Ocean. There were those who would have erased even the memory of him, if they could. Books were burned just because they mentioned his name. In the end there was nothing left of him but the stories, and most of them wrong. That's what his glory came to.

"The fighting didn't stop, of course, just because the Hawkwing and his kin were dead. There was still a throne to be won, and every lord and lady who could muster fighting men wanted it. It was the beginning of the War of the Hundred Years. Lasted a hundred and twenty-three, really, and most of the history of that time is lost in the smoke of burning towns. Many got a part of the land, but none got the whole, and sometime during those years the statue was pulled down. Maybe they couldn't stand measuring themselves against it any longer."

"First you sound as if you despise him," Egwene said,

"and now you sound as if you admire him." She shook her head.

Elyas turned to look at her, a flat, unblinking stare. "Get some more tea now, if you want any. I want the fire out before dark."

Perrin could make out the eye clearly now, despite the failing light. It was bigger than a man's head, and the shadows falling across it made it seem like a raven's eye, hard and black and without pity. He wished they were sleeping somewhere else.

CHAPTER

30

Children of Shadow

E gwene sat by the fire, staring up at the fragment of
statue, but Perrin went down by the pool to be alone.
Day was fading, and the night wind was already
rising out of the east, ruffling the surface of the water. He
took the axe from the loop on his belt and turned it over in
his hands. The ashwood haft was as long as his arm, and
smooth and cool to the touch. He hated it. He was ashamed
of how proud he had been of the axe back in Emond's Field.
Before he knew what he might be willing to do with it.

"You hate her that much?" Elyas said behind him.

Startled, he jumped and half raised the axe before he saw
who it was. "Can . . . ? Can you read my mind, too? Like
the wolves?"

Elyas cocked his head to one side and eyed him quizzically. "A blind man could read your face, boy. Well, speak
up. Do you hate the girl? Despise her? That's it. You were
ready to kill her because you despise her, always dragging
her feet, holding you back with her womanish ways."

"Egwene never dragged her feet in her life," he protested.
"She always does her share. I don't despise her, I love her."
He glared at Elyas, daring him to laugh. "Not like that. I
mean, she isn't like a sister, but she and Rand. . . . Blood
and ashes! If the ravens caught us. . . . If. . . . I don't know."

"Yes, you do. If she had to choose her way of dying,
which do you think she'd pick? One clean blow of your axe,
or the way the animals we saw today died? I know which
I'd take."

"I don't have any right to choose for her. You won't tell
her, will you? About. . . ." His hands tightened on the axe

haft; the muscles in his arms corded, heavy muscles for his age, built by long hours swinging the hammer at Master Luhhan's forge. For an instant he thought the thick wooden shaft would snap. "I hate this bloody thing," he growled. "I don't know what I'm doing with it, strutting around like some kind of fool. I couldn't have done it, you know. When it was all pretend and maybe, I could swagger, and play as if I. . . ." He sighed, his voice fading. "It's different, now. I don't ever want to use it again."

"You'll use it."

Perrin raised the axe to throw it in the pool, but Elyas caught his wrist.

"You'll use it, boy, and as long as you hate using it, you will use it more wisely than most men would. Wait. If ever you don't hate it any longer, then will be the time to throw it as far as you can and run the other way."

Perrin hefted the axe in his hands, still tempted to leave it in the pool. *Easy for him to say wait. What if I wait and then* can't *throw it away?*

He opened his mouth to ask Elyas, but no words came out. A sending from the wolves, so urgent that his eyes glazed over. For an instant he forgot what he had been going to say, forgot he had been going to say anything, forgot even how to speak, how to breathe. Elyas's face sagged, too, and his eyes seemed to peer inward and far away. Then it was gone, as quickly as it had come. It had only lasted a heartbeat, but that was enough.

Perrin shook himself and filled his lungs deeply. Elyas did not pause; as soon as the veil lifted from his eyes, he sped toward the fire without any hesitation. Perrin ran wordlessly behind him.

"Douse the fire!" Elyas called hoarsely to Egwene. He gestured urgently, and he seemed to be trying to shout in a whisper. "Get it out!"

She rose to her feet, staring at him uncertainly, then stepped closer to the fire, but slowly, clearly not understanding what was happening.

Elyas pushed roughly past her and snatched up the tea kettle, cursing when it burned him. Juggling the hot pot, he upended it over the fire just the same. A step behind him, Perrin arrived in time to start kicking dirt over the hissing coals as the last of the tea splashed into the fire, hissing and rising in tendrils of steam. He did not stop until the last vestige of the fire was buried.

Elyas tossed the kettle to Perrin, who immediately let it fall with a choked-off yell. Perrin blew on his hands, frowning at Elyas, but the fur-clad man was too busy giving their campsite a hasty look to pay any attention.

"No chance to hide that somebody's been here," Elyas said. "We'll just have to hurry and hope. Maybe they won't bother. Blood and ashes, but I was sure it was the ravens."

Hurriedly Perrin tossed the saddle on Bela, propping the axe against his thigh while he bent to tighten the girth.

"What is it?" Egwene asked. Her voice shook. "Trollocs? A Fade?"

"Go east or west," Elyas told Perrin. "Find a place to hide, and I'll join you as soon as I can. If they see a wolf. . . ." He darted away, crouching almost as if he intended to go to all fours, and vanished into the lengthening shadows of evening.

Egwene hastily gathered her few belongings, but she still demanded an explanation from Perrin. Her voice was insistent and growing more frightened by the minute as he kept silent. He was frightened, too, but fear made them move faster. He waited until they were headed toward the setting sun. Trotting ahead of Bela and holding the axe across his chest in both hands, he told what he knew over his shoulder in snatches while hunting for a place to go to ground and wait for Elyas.

"There are a lot of men coming, on horses. They came up behind the wolves, but the men didn't see them. They're heading toward the pool. Probably they don't have anything to do with us; it's the only water for miles. But Dapple says. . . ." He glanced over his shoulder. The evening sun painted odd shadows on her face, shadows that hid her expression. *What is she thinking? Is she looking at you as if she doesn't know you anymore? Does she know you?* "Dapple says they smell wrong. It's . . . sort of the way a rabid dog smells wrong." The pool was lost to sight behind them. He could still pick out boulders—fragments of Artur Hawkwing's statue—in the deepening twilight, but not to tell which was the stone where the fire had been. "We'll stay away from them, find a place to wait for Elyas."

"Why should they bother us?" she demanded. "We're

supposed to be safe here. It's supposed to be safe. Light, there has to be someplace safe."

Perrin began looking harder for somewhere to hide. They could not be very far from the pool, but the twilight was thickening. Soon it would be too dark to travel. Faint light still bathed the crests. From the hollows between, where there was barely enough to see, it seemed bright by contrast. Off to the left a dark shape stood sharp against the sky, a large, flat stone slanting out of a hillside, cloaking the slope beneath in darkness.

"This way," he said.

He trotted toward the hill, glancing over his shoulder for any sign of the men who were coming. There was nothing—yet. More than once he had to stop and wait while the others stumbled after him. Egwene was crouched over Bela's neck, and the mare was picking her way carefully over the uneven ground. Perrin thought they both must be more tired than he had believed. *This had better be a good hiding place. I don't think we can hunt for another.*

At the base of the hill he studied the massive, flat rock outlined against the sky, jutting out the slope almost at the crest. There was an odd familiarity to the way the top of the huge slab seemed to form irregular steps, three up and one down. He climbed the short distance and felt across the stone, walking along it. Despite the weathering of centuries he could still feel four joined columns. He glanced up at the step-like top of the stone, towering over his head like a huge lean-to. Fingers. *We'll shelter in Artur Hawkwing's hand. Maybe some of his justice is left here.*

He motioned for Egwene to join him. She did not move, so he slid back down to the base of the hill and told her what he had found.

Egwene peered up the hill with her head pushed forward. "How can you see anything?" she asked.

Perrin opened his mouth, then shut it. He licked his lips as he looked around, for the first time really aware of what he was seeing. The sun was down. All the way down, now, and clouds hid the full moon, but it still seemed like the deep purple fringes of twilight to him. "I felt the rock," he said finally. "That's what it has to be. They won't be able to pick us out against the shadow of it even if they come this far." He took Bela's bridle to lead her to the shelter of the hand. He could feel Egwene's eyes on his back.

As he was helping her down from the saddle, the night broke out in shouts back toward the pool. She laid a hand on Perrin's arm, and he heard her unspoken question.

"The men saw Wind," he said reluctantly. It was difficult to pick out the meaning of the wolves' thoughts. Something about fire. "They have torches." He pressed her down at the base of the fingers and crouched beside her. "They're breaking up into parties to search. So many of them, and the wolves are all hurt." He tried to make his voice heartier. "But Dapple and the others should be able to keep out of their way, even injured, and they don't expect us. People don't see what they don't expect. They'll give up soon enough and make camp." Elyas was with the wolves, and would not leave them while they were hunted. *So many riders. So persistent. Why so persistent?*

He saw Egwene nod, but in the dark she did not realize it. "We'll be all right, Perrin."

Light, he thought wonderingly, she's *trying to comfort* me.

The shouts went on and on. Small knots of torches moved in the distance, flickering points of light in the darkness.

"Perrin," Egwene said softly, "will you dance with me at Sunday? If we're home by then?"

His shoulders shook. He made no sound, and he did not know if he was laughing or crying. "I will. I promise." Against his will his hands tightened on the axe, reminding him that he still held it. His voice dropped to a whisper. "I promise," he said again, and hoped.

Groups of torch-carrying men now rode through the hills, bunches of ten or twelve. Perrin could not tell how many groups there were. Sometimes three or four were in sight at once, quartering back and forth. They continued to shout to one another, and sometimes there were screams in the night, the screams of horses, the screams of men.

He saw it all from more than one vantage. He crouched on the hillside with Egwene, watching the torches move through the darkness like fireflies, and in his mind he ran in the night with Dapple, and Wind, and Hopper. The wolves had been too hurt by the ravens to run far or fast, so they intended to drive the men out of the darkness, drive them to the shelter of their fires. Men always sought the safety of fires in the end, when wolves roamed the night. Some of the mounted men led strings of horses without riders; they whinnied and reared with wide, rolling eyes when the gray shapes darted among them, screaming and pulling their lead ropes from the hands of the men who held them, scattering in all directions as fast as they could run. Horses with men on their backs screamed, too, when gray shadows flashed out of the dark with hamstringing fangs, and sometimes their riders screamed as well, just before jaws tore out their throats. Elyas was out there, also, more dimly sensed, stalking the night with his long knife, a two-legged wolf with one sharp steel tooth. The shouts became curses more often than not, but the searchers refused to give up.

Abruptly Perrin realized that the men with torches were following a pattern. Each time some of the parties came in view, one of them, at least, was closer to the hillside where he and Egwene were hiding. Elyas had said to hide, but. . . . *What if we run? Maybe we could hide in the dark, if we keep moving. Maybe. It has to be dark enough for that.*

He turned to Egwene, but as he did the decision was taken away from him. Bunched torches, a dozen of them, came around the base of the hill, wavering with the trot of the horses. Lanceheads gleamed in the torchlight. He froze, holding his breath, hands tightening on his axe haft.

The horsemen rode past the hill, but one of the men shouted, and the torches swung back. He thought desperately, seeking for a way to go. But as soon as they moved they would be seen, if they had not already been, and once they were marked they would have no chance, not even with the darkness to help.

The horsemen drew up at the foot of the hill, each man holding a torch in one hand and a long lance in the other, guiding his horse by the pressure of his knees. By the light of the torches Perrin could see the white cloaks of the Children of the Light. They held the torches high and leaned forward in their saddles, peering up at the deep shadows under Artur Hawkwing's fingers.

"There *is* something up there," one of them said. His voice was too loud, as if he was afraid of what lay outside the light of his torch. "I told you somebody could hide in that. Isn't that a horse?"

Egwene laid a hand on Perrin's arm; her eyes were big

in the dark. Her silent question plain despite the shadow hiding her features. What to do? Elyas and the wolves still hunted through the night. The horses below shifted their feet nervously. *If we run now, they'll chase us down.*

One of the Whitecloaks stepped his horse forward and shouted up the hill. "If you can understand human speech, come down and surrender. You'll not be harmed if you walk in the Light. If you don't surrender, you will all be killed. You have one minute." The lances lowered, long steel heads bright with torchlight.

"Perrin," Egwene whispered, "we can't outrun them. If we don't give up, they'll kill us. Perrin?"

Elyas and the wolves were still free. Another distant, bubbling scream marked a Whitecloak who had hunted Dapple too closely. *If we run. . . .* Egwene was looking at him, waiting for him to tell her what to do. *If we run. . . .* He shook his head wearily and stood up like a man in a trance, stumbling down the hill toward the Children of the Light. He heard Egwene sigh and follow him, her feet dragging reluctantly. *Why are the Whitecloaks so persistent, as if they hate wolves with a passion? Why do they smell wrong?* He almost thought he could smell the wrongness himself, when the wind gusted from the riders.

"Drop that axe," the leader barked.

Perrin stumbled toward him, wrinkling his nose to get rid of the smell he thought he smelt.

"Drop it, bumpkin!" The leader's lance shifted toward Perrin's chest.

For a moment he stared at the lancehead, enough sharp steel to go completely through him, and abruptly he shouted, "No!" It was not at the horseman he shouted.

Out of the night Hopper came, and Perrin was one with the wolf. Hopper, the cub who had watched the eagles soar, and wanted so badly to fly through the sky as the eagles did. The cub who hopped and jumped and leaped until he could leap higher than any other wolf, and who never lost the cub's yearning to soar through the sky. Out of the night Hopper came and left the ground in a leap, soaring like the eagles. The Whitecloaks had only a moment to begin cursing before Hopper's jaws closed on the throat of the man with his lance leveled at Perrin. The big wolf's momentum carried them both off the other side of the horse. Perrin felt the throat crushing, tasted the blood.

Hopper landed lightly, already apart from the man he had killed. Blood matted his fur, his own blood and that of others. A gash down his face crossed the empty socket where his left eye had been. His good eye met Perrin's two for just an instant. *Run, brother!* He whirled to leap again, to soar one last time, and a lance pinned him to the earth. A second length of steel thrust through his ribs, driving into the ground under him. Kicking, he snapped at the shafts that held him. *To soar.*

Pain filled Perrin, and he screamed, a wordless scream that had something of a wolf's cry in it. Without thinking he leaped forward, still screaming. All thought was gone. The horsemen had bunched too much to be able to use their lances, and the axe was a feather in his hands, one huge wolf's tooth of steel. Something crashed into his head, and as he fell, he did not know if it was Hopper or himself who died.

". . . soar like the eagles."

Mumbling, Perrin opened his eyes woozily. His head hurt, and he could not remember why. Blinking against the light, he looked around. Egwene was kneeling and watching him where he lay. They were in a square tent as big as a medium-sized room in a farmhouse, with a ground cloth for a floor. Oil lamps on tall stands, one in each corner, gave a bright light.

"Thank the Light, Perrin," she breathed. "I was afraid they had killed you."

Instead of answering, he stared at the gray-haired man seated in the lone chair in the tent. A dark-eyed, grandfatherly face looked back at him, a face at odds in his mind with the white-and-gold tabard the man wore, and the burnished armor strapped over his pure-white undercoat. It seemed a kindly face, bluff and dignified, and something about it fit the elegant austerity of the tent's furnishings. A table and a folding bed, a washstand with a plain white basin and pitcher, a single wooden chest inlaid in simple geometric patterns. Where there was wood, it was polished to a soft glow, and the metal gleamed, but not too brightly,

and nothing was showy. Everything in the tent had the look
of craftsmanship, but only someone who had watched the
work of craftsmen—like Master Luhhan, or Master Aydaer,
the cabinetmaker—would see it.

Frowning, the man stirred two small piles of objects on
the table with a blunt finger. Perrin recognized the contents
of his pockets in one of those piles, and his belt knife. The
silver coin Moiraine had given him toppled out, and the
man pushed it back thoughtfully. Pursing his lips, he left
the piles and lifted Perrin's axe from the table, hefting it.
His attention came back to the Emond's Fielders.

Perrin tried to get up. Sharp pain stabbing along his arms
and legs turned the movement into a flop. For the first time
he realized that he was tied, hand and foot. His eyes went
to Egwene. She shrugged ruefully, and twisted so that he
could see her back. Half a dozen lashings wrapped her
wrists and ankles, the cords making ridges in her flesh. A
length of rope ran between the bonds around ankles and
wrists, short enough to stop her from straightening to more
than a crouch if she got to her feet.

Perrin stared. That they were tied was shock enough, but
they wore enough ropes to hold horses. *What do they think
we are?*

The gray-haired man watched them, curious and thoughtful, like Master al'Vere puzzling out a problem. He held the
axe as if he had forgotten it.

The tent flap shifted aside, and a tall man stepped into
the tent. His face was long and gaunt, with eyes so deeply
set they seemed to look out from caves. There was no excess flesh on him, no fat at all; his skin was pulled tight over
the muscle and bone beneath.

Perrin had a glimpse of night outside, and campfires, and
two white-cloaked guards at the entrance of the tent, then
the flap fell back into place. As soon as the newcomer was
into the tent, he stopped, standing as rigid as an iron rod,
staring straight ahead of him at the far wall of the tent. His
plate-and-mail armor gleamed like silver against his snowy
cloak and undercoat.

"My Lord Captain." His voice was as hard as his posture,
and grating, but somehow flat, without expression.

The gray-haired man made a casual gesture. "Be at your

ease, Child Byar. You have tallied our costs for this . . . encounter?"

The tall man moved his feet apart, but other than that Perrin did not see anything ease about his stance. "Nine men dead, my Lord Captain, and twenty-three injured, seven seriously. All can ride, though. Thirty horses had to be put down. They were hamstrung!" He emphasized that in his emotionless voice, as if what had happened to the horses were worse than the deaths and injuries to men. "Many of the remounts are scattered. We may find some at daybreak, my Lord Captain, but with wolves to send them on their way, it will take days to gather them all. The men who were supposed to be watching them have been assigned to night guard until we reach Caemlyn."

"We do not have days, Child Byar," the gray-haired man said mildly. "We ride at dawn. Nothing can change that. We must be in Caemlyn in time, yes?"

"As you command, my Lord Captain."

The gray-haired man glanced at Perrin and Egwene, then away again. "And what have we to show for it, aside from these two younglings?"

Byar drew a deep breath and hesitated. "I have had the wolf that was with this lot skinned, my Lord Captain. The hide should make a fine rug for my Lord Captain's tent."

Hopper! Not even realizing what he was doing, Perrin growled and struggled against his bonds. The ropes dug into his skin—his wrists became slippery with blood—but they did not give.

For the first time Byar looked at the prisoners. Egwene started back from him. His face was as expressionless as his voice, but a cruel light burned in his sunken eyes, as surely as flames burned in Ba'alzamon's. Byar hated them as if they were enemies of long years instead of people never seen before tonight.

Perrin stared back defiantly. His mouth curled into a tight smile at the thought of his teeth meeting in the man's throat.

Abruptly his smile faded, and he shook himself. *My teeth? I'm a man, not a wolf! Light, there has to be an end to this!* But he still met Byar's glare, hate for hate.

"I do not care about wolf-hide rugs, Child Byar." The rebuke in the Lord Captain's voice was gentle, but Byar's back snapped rigid again, his eyes locking to the wall of the tent. "You were reporting on what we achieved this night, no? If we achieved anything."

"I would estimate the pack that attacked us at fifty beasts or more, my Lord Captain. Of that, we killed at least twenty, perhaps thirty. I did not consider it worth the risk of losing more horses to have the carcasses brought in tonight. In the morning I will have them gathered and burned, those that aren't dragged off in the dark. Besides these two, there were at least a dozen other men. I believe we disposed of four or five, but it is unlikely we will find any bodies, given the Darkfriends' propensity for carrying away their dead to hide their losses. This seems to have been a coordinated ambush, but that raises the question of. . . ."

Perrin's throat tightened as the gaunt man went on. Elyas? Cautiously, reluctantly, he felt for Elyas, for the wolves . . . and found nothing. It was as if he had never been able to feel a wolf's mind. *Either they're dead, or they've abandoned you.* He wanted to laugh, a bitter laugh. At last he had what he had been wishing for, but the price was high.

The gray-haired man did laugh, just then, a rich, wry chuckle that made a red spot bloom on each of Byar's cheeks. "So, Child Byar, it is your considered estimate that we were attacked in a planned ambush by upwards of fifty wolves and better than half a score of Darkfriends? Yes? Perhaps when you've seen a few more actions. . . ."

"But, my Lord Captain Bornhald. . . ."

"I would say six or eight wolves, Child Byar, and perhaps no other humans than these two. You have the true zeal, but no experience outside the cities. It is a different thing, bringing the Light, when streets and houses are far distant. Wolves have a way of seeming more than they are, in the night—and men, also. Six or eight at most, I think." Byar's flush deepened slowly. "I also suspect they were here for the same reason we are: the only easy water for at least a day in any direction. A much simpler explanation than spies or traitors within the Children, and the simplest explanation is usually the truest. You will learn, with experience."

Byar's face went deathly white as the grandfatherly man spoke; by contrast, the two spots in his hollow cheeks deepened from red to purple. He cut his eyes toward the two prisoners for an instant.

He hates us even more, now, Perrin thought, *for hearing this. But why did he hate us in the first place?*

"What do you think of this?" the Lord Captain said, holding up Perrin's axe.

Byar looked a question at his commander and waited for an answering nod before he broke his rigid stance to take the weapon. He hefted the axe and gave a surprised grunt, then whirled it in a tight arc above his head that barely missed the top of the tent. He handled it as surely as if he had been born with an axe in his hands. A look of grudging admiration flickered across his face, but by the time he lowered the axe he was expressionless once more.

"Excellently balanced, my Lord Captain. Plainly made, but by a very good weaponsmith, perhaps even a master." His eyes burned darkly at the prisoners. "Not a villager's weapon, my Lord Captain. Nor a farmer's."

"No." The gray-haired man turned toward Perrin and Egwene with a weary, slightly chiding smile, a kindly grandfather who knew his grandchildren had been up to some mischief. "My name is Geofram Bornhald," he told them. "You are Perrin, I understand. But you, young woman, what is your name?"

Perrin glowered at him, but Egwene shook her head. "Don't be silly, Perrin. I'm Egwene."

"Just Perrin, and just Egwene," Bornhald murmured. "But I suppose if you truly are Darkfriends, you wish to hide your identities as much as possible."

Perrin heaved himself up to his knees; he could rise no further because of the way he was bound. "We aren't Darkfriends," he protested angrily.

The words were not completely out of his mouth before Byar reached him. The man moved like a snake. He saw the handle of his own axe swinging toward him and tried to duck, but the thick haft caught him over the ear. Only the fact that he was moving away from the blow kept his skull from being split. Even so, lights flashed in his eyes. Breath left him as he struck the ground. His head rung, and blood ran down his cheek.

"You have no right," Egwene began, and screamed as the axe handle whipped toward her. She threw herself aside, and the blow whistled through empty air as she tumbled to the ground cloth.

"You will keep a civil tongue," Byar said, "when speaking to an Anointed of the Light, or you will have no tongue." The worst of it was his voice still had no emotion at all. Cutting out their tongues would give him no pleasure and no regret; it was just something he would do.

"Go easy, Child Byar." Bornhald looked at the captives again. "I expect you do not know much about the Anointed, or about Lords Captain of the Children of the Light, do you? No, I thought not. Well, for Child Byar's sake, at least, try not to argue or shout, yes? I want no more than that you should walk in the Light, and letting anger get the better of you won't help any of us."

Perrin looked up at the gaunt-faced man standing over them. *For Child Byar's sake?* He noticed that the Lord Captain did not tell Byar to leave them alone. Byar met his eyes and smiled; the smile touched only his mouth, but the skin of his face drew tighter, until it looked like a skull. Perrin shivered.

"I have heard of this thing of men running with wolves," Bornhald said musingly, "though I have not seen it before. Men supposedly talking with wolves, and with other creatures of the Dark One. A filthy business. It makes me fear the Last Battle is indeed coming soon."

"Wolves aren't—" Perrin cut off as Byar's boot drew back. Taking a deep breath, he went on in a milder tone. Byar lowered his foot with a disappointed grimace. "Wolves aren't creatures of the Dark One. They hate the Dark One. At least, they hate Trollocs, and Fades." He was surprised to see the gaunt-faced man nod as if to himself.

Bornhald raised an eyebrow. "Who told you that?"

"A Warder," Egwene said. She scrunched away from Byar's heated eyes. "He said wolves hate Trollocs, and Trollocs are afraid of wolves." Perrin was glad she had not mentioned Elyas.

"A Warder," the gray-haired man sighed. "A creature of the Tar Valon witches. What else would that sort tell you, when he is a Darkfriend himself, and a servant of Darkfriends? Do you not know Trollocs have wolves' muzzles and teeth, and wolves' fur?"

Perrin blinked, trying to clear his head. His brain still felt like jellied pain, but there was something wrong here. He could not get his thoughts straight enough to puzzle it out.

"Not all of them," Egwene muttered. Perrin gave Byar a wary look, but the gaunt man only watched her. "Some of them have horns, like rams or goats, or hawks' beaks, or . . . or . . . all sorts of things."

Bornhald shook his head sadly. "I give you every chance, and you dig yourself deeper with every word." He held up one finger. "You run with wolves, creatures of the Dark One." A second finger. "You admit to being acquainted with a Warder, another creature of the Dark One. I doubt he would have told you what he did if it was only in passing." A third finger. "You, boy, carry a Tar Valon mark in your pocket. Most men outside Tar Valon get rid of those as fast as they can. Unless they serve the Tar Valon witches." A fourth. "You carry a fighting man's weapon while you dress like a farmboy. A skulker, then." The thumb rose. "You know Trollocs, and Myrddraal. This far south, only a few scholars and those who have traveled in the Borderlands believe they are anything but stories. Perhaps you have been to the Borderlands? If so, tell me where? I have traveled a good deal in the Borderlands; I know them well. No? Ah, well, then." He looked at his spread hand, then dropped it hard on the table. The grandfatherly expression said the grandchildren had been up to some very serious mischief indeed. "Why do you not tell me the truth of how you came to be running in the night with wolves?"

Egwene opened her mouth, but Perrin saw the stubborn set of her jaw and knew right away she was going to tell one of the stories they had worked out. That would not do. Not now, not here. His head ached, and he wished he had time to think it out, but there was no time. Who could tell where this Bornhald had traveled, with what lands and cities he was familiar? If he caught them in a lie, there would be no going back to the truth. Bornhald would be convinced they were Darkfriends, then.

"We're from the Two Rivers," he said quickly.

Egwene stared at him openly before she caught herself, but he pressed on with the truth—or a version of it. The two of them had left the Two Rivers to see Caemlyn. On the way they had heard of the ruins of a great city, but when they found Shadar Logoth, there were Trollocs there. The two of them managed to escape across the River Arinelle, but by that time they were completely lost. Then they fell

in with a man who offered to guide them to Caemlyn. He
had said his name was none of their business, and he hardly
seemed friendly, but they needed a guide. The first either of
them had seen of wolves had been after the Children of the
Light appeared. All they had been trying to do was hide so
they would not get eaten by wolves or killed by the men on
horses.

". . . If we'd known you were Children of the Light," he
finished, "we'd have gone to you for help."

Byar snorted with disbelief. Perrin did not care overmuch; if the Lord Captain was convinced, Byar could not
harm them. It was plain that Byar would stop breathing if
Lord Captain Bornhald told him to.

"There is no Warder in that," the gray-haired man said
after a moment.

Perrin's invention failed him; he knew he should have
taken time to think it out. Egwene leaped into the breach.
"We met him in Baerlon. The city was crowded with men
who had come down from the mines after the winter, and
we were put at the same table in an inn. We only talked to
him for the length of a meal."

Perrin breathed again. *Thank you, Egwene.*

"Give them back their belongings, Child Byar. Not the
weapons, of course." When Byar looked at him in surprise, Bornhald added, "Or are you one of those who have
taken to looting the unenlightened, Child Byar? It is a bad
business, that, yes? No man can be a thief and walk in the
Light." Byar seemed to struggle with disbelief at the suggestion.

"Then you're letting us go?" Egwene sounded surprised.
Perrin lifted his head to stare at the Lord Captain.

"Of course not, child," Bornhald said sadly. "You may
be telling the truth about being from the Two Rivers,
since you know about Baerlon, and the mines. But Shadar
Logoth . . . ? That is a name very, very few know, most of
them Darkfriends, and anyone who knows enough to know
the name, knows enough not to go there. I suggest you think
of a better story on the journey to Amador. You will have
time, since we must pause in Caemlyn. Preferably the truth,
child. There is freedom in truth and the Light."

Byar forgot some of his diffidence toward the gray-
haired man. He spun from the prisoners, and there was an

outraged snap to his words. "You can't! It is not allowed!" Bornhald raised one eyebrow quizzically, and Byar pulled himself up short, swallowing. "Forgive me, my Lord Captain. I forgot myself, and I humbly beg pardon and submit myself for penance, but as my Lord Captain himself has pointed out, we must reach Caemlyn in time, and with most of our remounts gone, we will be hard pressed enough without carrying prisoners along."

"And what would you suggest?" Bornhald asked calmly.

"The penalty for Darkfriends is death." The flat voice made it all the more jarring. He might have been suggesting stepping on a bug. "There is no truce with the Shadow. There is no mercy for Darkfriends."

"Zeal is to be applauded, Child Byar, but, as I must often tell my son, Dain, overzealousness can be a grievous fault. Remember that the Tenets also say, 'No man is so lost that he cannot be brought to the Light.' These two are young. They cannot yet be deep in the Shadow. They can yet be led to the Light, if they will only allow the Shadow to be lifted from their eyes. We must give them that chance."

For a moment Perrin almost felt affection for the grandfatherly man who stood between them and Byar. Then Bornhald turned his grandfather's smile on Egwene.

"If you refuse to come to the Light by the time we reach Amador, I will be forced to turn you over to the Questioners, and beside them Byar's zeal is but a candle beside the sun." The gray-haired man sounded like a man who regretted what he must do, but who had no intention of ever doing anything but his duty as he saw it. "Repent, renounce the Dark One, come to the Light, confess your sins and tell what you know of this vileness with wolves, and you will be spared that. You will walk free, in the Light." His gaze centered on Perrin, and he sighed sadly. Ice filled Perrin's spine. "But you, just Perrin from the Two Rivers. You killed two of the Children." He touched the axe that Byar still held. "For you, I fear, a gibbet waits in Amador."

CHAPTER
31

Play for Your Supper

R and narrowed his eyes, watching the dust-tail that rose ahead, three or four bends of the road away. Mat was already headed toward the wild hedgerow alongside the roadway. Its evergreen leaves and densely intermeshed branches would hide them as well as a stone wall, if they could find a way through to the other side. The other side of the road was marked by the sparse brown skeletons of head-high bushes, and beyond was an open field for half a mile to the woods. It might have been part of a farm not too long abandoned, but it offered no quick hiding place. He tried to judge the speed of the dust-tail, and the wind.

A sudden gust swirled road dust up around him, obscuring everything. He blinked and adjusted the plain, dark scarf across his nose and mouth. None too clean now, it made his face itch, but it kept him from inhaling dust with every breath. A farmer had given it to him, a long-faced man with grooves in his cheeks from worry.

"I don't know what you're running from," he had said with an anxious frown, "and I don't want to. You understand? My family." Abruptly the farmer had dug two long scarves out of his coat pocket and pushed the tangle of wool at them. "It's not much, but here. Belong to my boys. They have others. You don't know me, understand? It's hard times."

Rand treasured the scarf. The list of kindnesses he had made in his mind in the days since Whitebridge was a short one, and he did not believe it would get much longer.

Mat, all but his eyes hidden by the scarf wrapped around his head, hunted swiftly along the tall hedgerow, pulling at the leafy branches. Rand touched the heron-marked hilt at his belt, but let his hand fall away. Once already, cutting a hole through a hedge had almost given them away. The dust-tail was moving toward them, and staying together too long. Not the wind. At least it was not raining. Rain settled the dust. No matter how hard it fell, it never turned the hard-packed road to mud, but when it rained there was no dust. Dust was the only warning they had before whoever it was came close enough to hear. Sometimes that was too late.

"Here," Mat called softly. He seemed to step right through the hedge.

Rand hurried to the spot. Someone had cut a hole there, once. It was partly grown over, and from three feet away it looked as solid as the rest, but close up there was only a thin screen of branches. As he pushed through, he heard horses coming. Not the wind.

He crouched behind the barely covered opening, clutch-ing the hilt of his sword as the horsemen rode by. Five . . . six . . . seven of them. Plainly dressed men, but swords and spears said they were not villagers. Some wore leather tu-nics with metal studs, and two had round steel caps. Mer-chants' guards, perhaps, between hirings. Perhaps.

One of them casually swung his eyes toward the hedge as he went by the opening, and Rand bared an inch of his sword. Mat snarled silently like a cornered badger, squint-ing above his scarf. His hand was under his coat; he always clutched the dagger from Shadar Logoth when there was danger. Rand was no longer sure if it was to protect himself or to protect the ruby-hilted dagger. Of late Mat seemed to forget he had a bow, sometimes.

The riders passed at a slow trot, going somewhere with a purpose but not too great a haste. Dust sifted through the hedge.

Rand waited until the clop of the hooves faded before he stuck his head cautiously back through the hole. The dust-tail was well down the road, going the way they had come. Eastward the sky was clear. He climbed out onto the road-way, watching the column of dust move west.

"Not after us," he said, halfway between a statement and a question.

Mat scrambled out after him, looking warily in both di-rections. "Maybe," he said. "Maybe."

Rand had no idea which way he meant it, but he nodded. Maybe. It had not begun like this, their journey down the Caemlyn Road.

For a long time after leaving Whitebridge, Rand would suddenly find himself staring back down the road behind them. Sometimes he would see someone who made his breath catch, a tall, skinny man hurrying up the road, or a lanky, white-haired fellow up beside the driver on a wagon, but it was always a pack-peddler, or farmers making their way to market, never Thom Merrilin. Hope faded as the days passed.

There was considerable traffic on the road, wagons and carts, people on horses and people afoot. They came singly and in groups, a train of merchants' wagons or a dozen horsemen together. They did not jam the road, and often there was nothing in sight except the all but leafless trees lining the hard-packed roadbed, but there were certainly more people traveling than Rand had ever seen in the Two Rivers.

Most traveled in the same direction that they did, eastward toward Caemlyn. Sometimes they got a ride in a farmer's wagon for a little distance, a mile, or five, but more often they walked. Men on horseback they avoided; when they spotted even one rider in the distance they scrambled off the road and hid until he was past. None ever wore a black cloak, and Rand did not really think a Fade would let them see him coming, but there was no point in taking chances. In the beginning it was just the Halfmen they feared.

The first village after Whitebridge looked so much like Emond's Field that Rand's steps dragged when he saw it. Thatched roofs with high peaks, and goodwives in their aprons gossiping over the fences between their houses, and children playing on a village green. The women's hair hung unbraided around their shoulders, and other small things were different, too, but the whole together was like home. Cows cropped on the green, and geese waddled self-importantly across the road. The children tumbled, laughing, in the dust where the grass was gone altogether. They did not even look around when Rand and Mat went by. That was another thing that was different. Strangers were no oddity there; two more did not draw so much as a second glance. Village dogs only raised their heads to sniff as he and Mat passed; none stirred themselves.

It was coming on evening as they went through the village, and he felt a pang of homesickness as lights appeared in the windows. *No matter what it looks like,* a small voice whispered in his mind, *it isn't really home. Even if you go into one of those houses Tam won't be there. If he was, could you look him in the face? You know, now, don't you? Except for little things like where you come from and who you are. No fever-dreams.* He hunched his shoulders against taunting laughter inside his head. *You might as well stop,* the voice snickered. *One place is as good as another when you aren't from anywhere, and the Dark One has you marked.*

Mat tugged at his sleeve, but he pulled loose and stared at the houses. He did not want to stop, but he did want to look and remember. *So much like home, but you'll never see that again, will you?*

Mat yanked at him again. His face was taut, the skin around his mouth and eyes white. "Come on," Mat muttered. "Come on." He looked at the village as if he suspected something of hiding there. "Come on. We can't stop yet."

Rand turned in a complete circle, taking in the whole village, and sighed. They were not very far from Whitebridge. If the Myrddraal could get past Whitebridge's wall without being seen, it would have no trouble at all searching this small village. He let himself be drawn on into the countryside beyond, until the thatch-roofed houses were left behind.

Night fell before they found a spot by moonlight, under some bushes still bearing their dead leaves. They filled their bellies with cold water from a shallow rivulet not far away and curled up on the ground, wrapped in their cloaks, without a fire. A fire could be seen; better to be cold.

Uneasy with his memories, Rand woke often, and every time he could hear Mat muttering and tossing in his sleep. He did not dream, that he could remember, but he did not sleep well. *You'll never see home again.*

That was not the only night they spent with just their cloaks to protect them from the wind, and sometimes the rain, cold and soaking. It was not the only meal they made from nothing but cold water. Between them they had enough coins for a few meals at an inn, but a bed for the night would take too much. Things cost more outside the Two Rivers, more this side of the Arinelle than in Baerlon. What money they had left had to be saved for an emergency.

One afternoon Rand mentioned the dagger with the ruby in its hilt, while they were trudging down the road with bellies too empty to rumble, and the sun low and weak, and nothing in view for the coming night but more bushes. Dark clouds built up overhead for rain during the night. He hoped they were lucky; maybe no more than an icy drizzle.

He went on a few steps before he realized that Mat had stopped. He stopped, too, wriggling his toes in his boots. At least his feet felt warm. He eased the straps across his shoulders. His blanketroll and Thom's bundled cloak were not heavy, but even a few pounds weighed heavy after miles on an empty stomach. "What's the matter, Mat?" he said.

"Why are you so anxious to sell it?" Mat demanded angrily. "I found it, after all. You ever think I might like to keep it? For a while, anyway. If you want to sell something, sell that bloody sword!"

Rand rubbed his hand along the heron-marked hilt. "My father gave this sword to me. It was his. I wouldn't ask you to sell something your father gave you. Blood and ashes, Mat, do you like going hungry? Anyway, even if I could find somebody to buy it, how much would a sword bring? What would a farmer want with a sword? That ruby would fetch enough to take us all the way to Caemlyn in a carriage. Maybe all the way to Tar Valon. And we'd eat every meal in an inn, and sleep every night in a bed. Maybe you like the idea of walking halfway across the world and sleeping on the ground?" He glared at Mat, and his friend glared back.

They stood like that in the middle of the road until Mat suddenly gave an uncomfortable shrug, and dropped his eyes to the road. "Who would I sell it to, Rand? A farmer would have to pay in chickens; we couldn't buy a carriage with chickens. And if I even showed it in any village we've been through, they'd probably think we stole it. The Light knows what would happen then."

After a minute Rand nodded reluctantly. "You're right. I know it. I'm sorry; I didn't mean to snap at you. It's only that I'm hungry and my feet hurt."

"Mine, too." They started down the road again, walking even more wearily than before. The wind gusted up, blowing dust in their faces. "Mine, too." Mat coughed.

Farms did provide some meals and a few nights out of the cold. A haystack was nearly as warm as a room with a fire, at least compared to lying under the bushes, and a haystack, even one without a tarp over it, kept all but the heaviest rain off, if you dug yourself in deeply enough. Sometimes Mat tried his hand at stealing eggs, and once he attempted to milk a cow left unattended, staked out on a long rope to crop in a field. Most farms had dogs, though, and farm dogs were watchful. A two-mile run with baying hounds at their heels was too high a price for two or three eggs as Rand saw it, especially when the dogs sometimes took hours to go away and let them down out of the tree where they had taken shelter. The hours were what he regretted.

He did not really like doing it, but Rand preferred to approach a farmhouse openly in broad daylight. Now and again they had the dogs set on them anyway, without a word being said, for the rumors and the times made everyone who lived apart from other people nervous about strangers, but often an hour or so chopping wood or hauling water would earn a meal and a bed, even if the bed was a pile of straw in the barn. But an hour or two doing chores was an hour or two of daylight when they were standing still, an hour or two for the Myrddraal to catch up. Sometimes he wondered how many miles a Fade could cover in an hour. He begrudged every minute of it—though admittedly not so much when he was wolfing down a goodwife's hot soup. And when they had no food, knowing they had spent every possible minute moving toward Caemlyn did not do much to soothe an empty belly. Rand could not make up his mind if it was worse to lose time or go hungry, but Mat went beyond worrying about his belly or pursuit.

"What do we know about them, anyway?" Mat demanded one afternoon while they were mucking out stalls on a small farm.

"Light, Mat, what do they know about us?" Rand sneezed. They were working stripped to the waist, and sweat and straw covered them both liberally, and motes of straw-dust hung in the air. "What I know is they'll give us some roast lamb and a real bed to sleep in."

Mat dug his hayfork into the straw and manure and gave a sidelong frown at the farmer, coming from the back of the barn with a bucket in one hand and his milking stool in the other. A stooped old man with skin like leather and thin, gray hair, the farmer slowed when he saw Mat looking at him, then looked away quickly and hurried on out of the barn, slopping milk over the rim of the bucket in his haste.

"He's up to something, I tell you," Mat said. "See the way he wouldn't meet my eye? Why are they so friendly to a couple of wanderers they never laid eyes on before? Tell me that."

"His wife says we remind her of their grandsons. Will you stop worrying about them? What we have to worry about is behind us. I hope."

"He's up to something," Mat muttered.

When they finished, they washed up at the trough in front of the barn, their shadows stretching long with the sinking sun. Rand toweled off with his shirt as they walked to the farmhouse. The farmer met them at the door; he leaned on a quarterstaff in a too-casual manner. Behind him his wife clutched her apron and peered past his shoulder, chewing her lip. Rand sighed; he did not think he and Mat reminded them of their grandsons any longer.

"Our sons are coming to visit tonight," the old man said. "All four of them. I forgot. They're all four coming. Big lads. Strong. Be here any time, now. I'm afraid we don't have the bed we promised you."

His wife thrust a small bundle wrapped in a napkin past him. "Here. It's bread, and cheese, and pickles, and lamb. Enough for two meals, maybe. Here." Her wrinkled face asked them to please take it and go.

Rand took the bundle. "Thank you. I understand. Come on, Mat."

Mat followed him, grumbling while he pulled his shirt over his head. Rand thought it best to cover as many miles as they could before stopping to eat. The old farmer had a dog.

It could have been worse, he thought. Three days earlier, while they were still working, they'd had the dogs set on them. The dogs, and the farmer, and his two sons waving cudgels chased them out to the Caemlyn Road and half a mile down it before giving up. They had barely had time to snatch up their belongings and run. The farmer had carried a bow with a broad-head arrow nocked.

"Don't come back, hear!" he had shouted after them.

"I don't know what you're up to, but don't let me see your shifty eyes again!"

Mat had started to turn back, fumbling at his quiver, but Rand pulled him on. "Are you crazy?" Mat gave him a sullen look, but at least he kept running.

Rand sometimes wondered if it was worthwhile stopping at farms. The further they went, the more suspicious of strangers Mat became, and the less he was able to hide it. Or bothered to. The meals got skimpier for the same work, and sometimes not even the barn was offered as a place to sleep. But then a solution to all their problems came to Rand, or so it seemed, and it came at Grinwell's farm.

Master Grinwell and his wife had nine children, the eldest a daughter not more than a year younger than Rand and Mat. Master Grinwell was a sturdy man, and with his children he probably had no need of any more help, but he looked them up and down, taking in their travel-stained clothes and dusty boots, and allowed as how he could always find work for more hands. Mistress Grinwell said that if they were going to eat at her table, they would not do it in those filthy things. She was about to do laundry, and some of her husband's old clothes would fit them well enough for working. She smiled when she said it, and for a minute she looked to Rand just like Mistress al'Vere, though her hair was yellow; he had never seen hair that color before. Even Mat seemed to lose some of his tension when her smile touched him. The eldest daughter was another matter.

Dark-haired, big-eyed, and pretty, Else grinned impudently at them whenever her parents were not looking. While they worked, moving barrels and sacks of grain in the barn, she hung over a stall door, humming to herself and chewing the end of one long pigtail, watching them. Rand she watched especially. He tried to ignore her, but after a few minutes he put on the shirt Master Grinwell had loaned him. It was tight across the shoulders and too short, but it was better than nothing. Else laughed out loud when he tugged it on. He began to think that this time it would not be Mat's fault when they were chased off.

Perrin would know how to handle this, he thought. *He'd make some offhand comment, and pretty soon she'd be laughing at his jokes instead of mooning around where her father can see.* Only he could not think of any offhand comment, or any jokes, either. Whenever he looked in her direction, she smiled at him in a way that would have her father loosing the dogs on them if he saw. Once she told him she liked tall men. All the boys on the farms around there were short. Mat gave a nasty snicker. Wishing he could think of a joke, Rand tried to concentrate on his hayfork.

The younger children, at least, were a blessing in Rand's eyes. Mat's wariness always eased a little when there were children around. After supper they all settled in front of the fireplace, with Master Grinwell in his favorite chair thumbing his pipe full of tabac and Mistress Grinwell fussing with her sewing box and the shirts she had washed for him and Mat. Mat dug out Thom's colored balls and began to juggle. He never did that unless there were children. The children laughed when he pretended to be dropping the balls, snatching them at the last minute, and they clapped for fountains and figure-eights and a six-ball circle that he really did almost drop. But they took it in good part, Master Grinwell and his wife applauding as hard as their children. When Mat was done, bowing around the room with as many flourishes as Thom might have made, Rand took Thom's flute from its case.

He could never handle the instrument without a pang of sadness. Touching its gold-and-silver scrollwork was like touching Thom's memory. He never handled the harp except to see that it was safe and dry—Thom had always said the harp was beyond a farmboy's clumsy hands—but whenever a farmer allowed them to stay, he always played one tune on the flute after supper. It was just a little something extra to pay the farmer, and maybe a way of keeping Thom's memory fresh.

With a laughing mood already set by Mat's juggling, he played "Three Girls in the Meadow." Master and Mistress Grinwell clapped along, and the smaller children danced around the floor, even the smallest boy, who could barely walk, stomping his feet in time. He knew he would win no prizes at Bel Tine, but after Thom's teaching he would not be embarrassed to enter.

Else was sitting cross-legged in front of the fire, and as he lowered the flute after the last note, she leaned forward with a long sigh and smiled at him. "You play so beautifully. I never heard anything so beautiful."

Mistress Grinwell suddenly paused in her sewing and raised an eyebrow at her daughter, then gave Rand a long, appraising look.

He had picked up the leather case to put the flute away, but under her stare he dropped the case and almost the flute, too. If she accused him of trifling with her daughter. . . . In desperation he put the flute back to his lips and played another song, then another, and another. Mistress Grinwell kept watching him. He played "The Wind That Shakes the Willow," and "Coming Home From Tarwin's Gap," and "Mistress Aynora's Rooster," and "The Old Black Bear." He played every song he could think of, but she never took her eyes off him. She never said anything, either, but she watched, and weighed.

It was late when Master Grinwell finally stood up, chuckling and rubbing his hands together. "Well, this has been rare fun, but it's way past our bedtime. You traveling lads make your own hours, but morning comes early on a farm. I'll tell you lads, I have paid good money at an inn for no better entertainment than I've had this night. For worse."

"I think they should have a reward, father," Mistress Grinwell said as she picked up her youngest boy, who had long since fallen asleep in front of the fire. "The barn is no fit place to sleep. They can sleep in Else's room tonight, and she will sleep with me."

Else grimaced. She was careful to keep her head down, but Rand saw it. He thought her mother did, too.

Master Grinwell nodded. "Yes, yes, much better than the barn. If you don't mind sleeping two to a bed, that is." Rand flushed; Mistress Grinwell was still looking at him. "I do wish I could hear more of that flute. And your juggling, too. I like that. You know, there's a little task you could help with tomorrow, and—"

"They'll be wanting an early start, father," Mistress Grinwell cut in. "Arien is the next village the way they're going, and if they intend to try their luck at the inn there, they'll have to walk all day to get there before dark."

"Yes, mistress," Rand said, "we will. And thank you."

She gave him a tight-lipped smile as if she knew very well that his thanks were for more than her advice, or even supper and a warm bed.

The whole next day Mat twitted him about Else as they

made their way down the road. He kept trying to change the subject, and what the Grinwells had suggested about performing at inns was the easiest thing to mind. In the morning, with Else pouting as he left, and Mistress Grinwell watching with a sharp-eyed look of good-riddance and soonest-mended, it was just something to keep Mat from talking. By the time they did reach the next village, it was something else again.

With dusk descending, they entered the only inn in Arien, and Rand spoke to the innkeeper. He played "Ferry O'er the River"—which the plump innkeeper called "Darling Sara"—and part of "The Road to Dun Aren," and Mat did a little juggling, and the upshot was that they slept in a bed that night and ate roasted potatoes and hot beef. It was the smallest room in the inn, to be sure, up under the eaves in the back, and the meal came in the middle of a long night of playing and juggling, but it was still a bed beneath a roof. Even better, to Rand, every daylight hour had been spent traveling. And the inn's patrons did not seem to care if Mat stared at them suspiciously. Some of them even looked askance at one another. The times made suspicion of strangers a commonplace, and there were always strangers at an inn.

Rand slept better than he had since leaving Whitebridge, despite sharing a bed with Mat and his nocturnal muttering. In the morning the innkeeper tried to talk them into staying another day or two, but when he could not, he called over a bleary-eyed farmer who had drunk too much to drive his cart home the night before. An hour later they were five miles further east, sprawling on their backs on the straw in the back of Eazil Forney's cart.

That became the way of their traveling. With a little luck, and maybe a ride or two, they could almost always reach the next village by dark. If there was more than one inn in a village, the innkeepers would bid for them once they heard Rand's flute and saw Mat juggle. Together they still did not come close to a gleeman, but they were more than most villages saw in a year. Two or three inns in a town meant a better room, with two beds, and more generous portions of a better cut of meat, and sometimes even a few coppers in their pockets when they left besides. In the mornings there was almost always someone to offer a ride, another farmer who had stayed too late and drunk too much, or a merchant who had liked their entertainment enough not to mind if they hopped up on the back of one of his wagons. Rand began to think their problems were over till they reached Caemlyn. But then they came to Four Kings.

CHAPTER
32

Four Kings in Shadow

T he village was bigger than most, but still a scruffy
town to bear a name like Four Kings. As usual,
the Caemlyn Road ran straight through the center
of the town, but another heavily traveled highway came in
from the south, too. Most villages were markets and gathering places for the farmers of the area, but there were few
farmers to be seen here. Four Kings survived as a stopover
for merchants' wagon trains on their way to Caemlyn and
to the mining towns in the Mountains of Mist beyond Baerlon, as well as the villages between. The southern road carried Lugard's trade with the mines in the west; Lugarder
merchants going to Caemlyn had a more direct route. The
surrounding country held few farms, barely enough to feed
themselves and the town, and everything in the village
centered on the merchants and their wagons, the men who
drove them and the laborers who loaded the goods.

Plots of bare earth, ground to dust, lay scattered through
Four Kings, filled with wagons parked wheel to wheel
and abandoned except for a few bored guards. Stables and
horse-lots lined the streets, all of which were wide enough
to allow wagons to pass and deeply rutted from too many
wheels. There was no village green, and the children played
in the ruts, dodging wagons and the curses of wagon drivers. Village women, their heads covered with scarves, kept
their eyes down and walked quickly, sometimes followed
by wagoneers' comments that made Rand blush; even Mat
gave a start at some of them. No woman stood gossiping over the fence with a neighbor. Drab wooden houses
stood cheek by jowl, with only narrow alleys between and

whitewash—where anyone had bothered to whitewash the weathered boards—faded as if it had not been freshened in years. Heavy shutters on the houses had not been open in so long that the hinges were solid lumps of rust. Noise hung over everything, clanging from blacksmiths, shouts from the wagon drivers, raucous laughter from the town's inns.

Rand swung down from the back of a merchant's canvas-topped wagon as they came abreast of a garishly painted inn, all greens and yellows that caught the eye from afar among the leaden houses. The line of wagons kept moving. None of the drivers even seemed to notice that he and Mat had gone; dusk was falling, and they all had their eyes on unhitching the horses and reaching the inns. Rand stumbled in a rut, then leaped quickly to avoid a heavy-laden wagon clattering the other way. The driver shouted a curse at him as the wagon rolled by. A village woman stepped around him and hurried on without ever meeting his eye.

"I don't know about this place," he said. He thought he could hear music mixed in the din, but he could not tell from where it was coming. From the inn, maybe, but it was hard to be sure. "I don't like it. Maybe we'd better go on this time."

Mat gave him a scornful look, then rolled his eyes at the sky. Dark clouds thickened overhead. "And sleep under a hedge tonight? In that? I'm used to a bed again." He cocked his head to listen, then grunted. "Maybe one of these places doesn't have musicians. Anyway, I'll bet they don't have a juggler." He slung his bow across his shoulders and started for the bright yellow door, studying everything through narrowed eyes. Rand followed doubtfully.

There were musicians inside, their zither and drum almost drowned in coarse laughter and drunken shouting. Rand did not bother to find the landlord. The next two inns had musicians as well, and the same deafening cacophony. Roughly dressed men filled the tables and stumbled across the floor, waving mugs and trying to fondle serving maids who dodged with fixed, long-suffering smiles. The buildings shook with the racket, and the smell was sour, a stench of old wine and unwashed bodies. Of the merchants, in their silk and velvet and lace, there was no sign; private dining rooms abovestairs protected their ears and noses. He and Mat only put their heads in the doors before leaving.

He was beginning to think they would have no choice but to move on.

The fourth inn, The Dancing Cartman, stood silent.

It was as gaudy as the other inns, yellow trimmed in bright red and bilious, eye-wrenching green, though here the paint was cracked and peeling. Rand and Mat stepped inside.

Only half a dozen men sat at the tables that filled the common room, hunched over their mugs, each one glumly alone with his thoughts. Business was definitely not good, but it had been better once. Exactly as many serving maids as there were patrons busied themselves around the room. There was plenty for them to do—dirt crusted the floor and cobwebs filled the corners of the ceiling—but most were not doing anything really useful, only moving so they would not be seen standing still.

A bony man with long, stringy hair to his shoulders turned to scowl at them as they came through the door. The first slow peal of thunder rumbled across Four Kings. "What do you want?" He was rubbing his hands on a greasy apron that hung to his ankles. Rand wondered if more grime was coming off on the apron or on the man's hands. He was the first skinny innkeeper Rand had seen. "Well? Speak up, buy a drink, or get out! Do I look like a raree show?"

Flushing, Rand launched into the spiel he had perfected at inns before this. "I play the flute, and my friend juggles, and you'll not see two better in a year. For a good room and a good meal, we'll fill this common room of yours." He remembered the filled common rooms he had already seen that evening, especially the man who had vomited right in front of him at the last one. He had had to step lively to keep his boots untouched. He faltered, but caught himself and went on. "We'll fill your inn with men who will repay the little we cost twenty times over with the food and drink they buy. Why should—"

"I've got a man plays the dulcimer," the innkeeper said sourly.

"You have a drunk, Saml Hake," one of the serving maids said. She was passing him with a tray and two mugs, and she paused to give Rand and Mat a plump smile. "Most times, he can't see well enough to find the common room," she confided in a loud whisper. "Haven't even seen him in two days."

Without taking his eyes off Rand and Mat, Hake casually backhanded her across the face. She gave a surprised grunt and fell heavily to the unwashed floor; one of the mugs broke, and the spilled wine washed rivulets in the dirt. "You're docked for the wine and breakage. Get 'em fresh drinks. And hurry. Men don't pay to wait while you laze around." His tone was as offhand as the blow. None of the patrons looked up from their wine, and the other serving maids kept their eyes averted.

The plump woman rubbed her cheek and stared pure murder at Hake, but she gathered the empty mug and the broken pieces on her tray and went off without a word.

Hake sucked his teeth thoughtfully, eyeing Rand and Mat. His gaze clung to the heron-mark sword before he pulled it away. "Tell you what," he said finally. "You can have a couple of pallets in an empty storeroom in the back. Rooms are too expensive to give away. You eat when everybody's gone. There ought to be something left."

Rand wished there was an inn in Four Kings they had not yet tried. Since leaving Whitebridge he had met coolness, indifference, and outright hostility, but nothing that gave him the sense of unease that this man and this village did. He told himself it was just the dirt and squalor and noise, but the misgivings did not go away. Mat was watching Hake as if he suspected some trap, but he gave no sign of wanting to give up The Dancing Cartman for a bed under a hedge. Thunder rattled the windows. Rand sighed.

"The pallets will do if they're clean, and if there are enough clean blankets. But we eat two hours after full dark, no later, and the best you have. Here. We'll show you what we can do." He reached for the flute case, but Hake shook his head.

"Don't matter. This lot'll be satisfied with any kind of screeching so long as it sounds something like music." His eyes touched Rand's sword again; his thin smile touched nothing but his lips. "Eat when you want, but if you don't bring the crowd in, out you go in the street." He nodded over his shoulder at two hard-faced men sitting against the wall. They were not drinking, and their arms were thick enough for legs. When Hake nodded at them, their eyes shifted to Rand and Mat, flat and expressionless.

Rand put one hand on his sword hilt, hoping the twisting in his stomach did not show on his face. "As long as we get what's agreed on," he said in a level tone.

Hake blinked, and for a moment he seemed uneasy himself. Abruptly he nodded. "What I said, isn't it? Well, get started. You won't bring anybody in just standing there." He stalked off, scowling and shouting at the serving maids as if there were fifty customers they were neglecting.

There was a small, raised platform at the far end of the room, near the door to the back. Rand lifted a bench up on it, and settled his cloak, blanketroll, and Thom's bundled cloak behind the bench with the sword lying atop them.

He wondered if he had been wise to keep wearing the sword openly. Swords were common enough, but the heron-mark attracted attention and speculation. Not from everybody, but any notice at all made him uncomfortable. He could be leaving a clear trail for the Myrddraal—if Fades needed that kind of trail. They did not seem to. In any case, he was reluctant to stop wearing it. Tam had given it to him. His father. As long as he wore the sword, there was still some connection between Tam and him, a thread that gave him the right to still call Tam father. *Too late now,* he thought. He was not sure what he meant, but he was sure it was true. *Too late.*

At the first note of "Cock o' the North" the half-dozen patrons in the common room lifted their heads out of their wine. Even the two bouncers sat forward a little. They all applauded when he finished, including the two toughs, and once more when Mat sent a shower of colored balls spinning through his hands. Outside, the sky muttered again. The rain was holding off, but the pressure of it was palpable; the longer it waited, the harder it would fall.

Word spread, and by the time it was dark outside the inn was packed full with men laughing and talking so loud that Rand could barely hear what he was playing. Only the thunder overpowered the noise in the common room. Lightning flashed in the windows, and in the momentary lulls he could faintly hear rain drumming on the roof. Men who came in now dripped trails across the floor.

Whenever he paused, voices shouted the names of tunes

through the din. A good many names he did not recognize, though when he got someone to hum a bit of it, he often found he did know the song. It had been that way other places, before. "Jolly Jaim" was "Rhea's Fling" here, and had been "Colors of the Sun" at an earlier stop. Some names stayed the same; others changed with ten miles' distance, and he had learned new songs, too. "The Drunken Peddler" was a new one, though sometimes it was called "Tinker in the Kitchen." "Two Kings Came Hunting" was "Two Horses Running" and several other names besides. He played the ones he knew, and men pounded the tables for more.

Others called for Mat to juggle again. Sometimes fights broke out between those wanting music and those who fancied juggling. Once a knife flashed, and a woman screamed, and a man reeled back from a table with blood streaming down his face, but Jak and Strom, the two bouncers, closed in swiftly and with complete impartiality threw everyone involved into the street with lumps on their heads. That was their tactic with any trouble. The talk and the laughing went on as if nothing had occurred. Nobody even looked around except those the bouncers jostled on their way to the door.

The patrons were free with their hands, too, when one of the serving maids let herself grow unwary. More than once Jak or Strom had to rescue one of the women, though they were none too quick about it. The way Hake carried on, screaming and shaking the woman involved, he always considered it her fault, and the teary eyes and stammered apologies said she was willing to accept his opinion. The women jumped whenever Hake frowned, even if he was looking somewhere else. Rand wondered why any of them put up with it.

Hake smiled when he looked at Rand and Mat. After a while Rand realized Hake was not smiling at them; the smiles came when his eyes slid behind them, to where the heron-mark sword lay. Once, when Rand set the gold-and-silver-chased flute down beside his stool, the flute got a smile, too.

The next time he changed places with Mat at the front of the dais, he leaned over to speak in Mat's ear. Even that close he had to speak loudly, but with all the noise he doubted if anyone else could hear. "Hake's going to try to rob us."

Mat nodded as if it was nothing he had not expected. "We'll have to bar our door tonight."

"Bar our door? Jak and Strom could break down a door with their fists. Let's get out of here."

"Wait till after we eat, at least. I'm hungry. They can't do anything here," Mat added. The packed common room shouted impatiently for them to get on with it. Hake was glaring at them. "Anyway, you want to sleep outside tonight?" An especially strong crack of lightning drowned out everything else, and for an instant the light through the windows was stronger than the lamps.

"I just want to get out without my head being broken," Rand said, but Mat was already slouching back to take his rest on the stool. Rand sighed and launched into "The Road to Dun Aren." A lot of them seemed to like that one; he had already played it four times, and they still shouted for it.

The trouble was that Mat was right, as far as he went. He was hungry, too. And he could not see how Hake could give them any trouble while the common room was full, and getting fuller. For every man who left or was thrown out by Jak and Strom, two came in from the street. They shouted for the juggling or for a particular tune, but mostly they were interested in drinking and fondling the serving maids. One man was different, though.

He stood out in every way among the crowd in The Dancing Cartman. Merchants apparently had no use for the run-down inn; there were not even any private dining rooms for them, as far as he could make out. The patrons were all rough-dressed, with the tough skin of men who labored in the sun and wind. This man was sleekly fleshy, with a soft look to his hands, and a velvet coat, and a dark green velvet cloak lined with blue silk was slung around his shoulders. All of his clothes had an expensive cut to them. His shoes—soft velvet slippers, not boots—were not made for the rutted streets of Four Kings, or for any streets at all, for that matter.

He came in well after dark, shaking the rain off his cloak as he looked around, a twist of distaste on his mouth. He scanned the room once, already turning to go, then suddenly gave a start at nothing Rand could see and sat down at a table Jak and Strom had just emptied. A serving maid stopped at his table, then brought him a mug of wine which he pushed to one side and never touched again. She seemed in a hurry to leave his table both times, though he did not try to touch her or even look at her. Whatever it was about him that made her uneasy, others who came close to him noticed it, too. For all of his soft look, whenever some callus-handed wagon driver decided to share his table, one glance was all it took to send the man looking elsewhere. He sat as if there were no one else in the room but him— and Rand and Mat. Them he watched over steepled hands that glittered with a ring on each finger. He watched them with a smile of satisfied recognition.

Rand murmured to Mat as they were changing places again, and Mat nodded. "I saw him," he muttered. "Who *is* he? I keep thinking I know him."

The same thought had occurred to Rand, tickling the back of his memory, but he could not bring it forward. Yet he was sure that face was one he had never seen before.

When they had been performing for two hours, as near as Rand could estimate, he slipped the flute into its case and he and Mat gathered up their belongings. As they were stepping down from the low platform, Hake came bustling up, anger twisting his narrow face.

"It's time to eat," Rand said to forestall him, "and we don't want our things stolen. You want to tell the cook?" Hake hesitated, still angry, trying unsuccessfully to keep his eyes off what Rand held in his arms. Casually Rand shifted his bundles so he could rest one hand on the sword. "Or you can *try* throwing us out." He made the emphasis deliberately, then added, "There's a lot of night left for us to play, yet. We have to keep our strength up if we're going to perform well enough to keep this crowd spending money. How long do you think this room will stay full if we fall over from hunger?"

Hake's eyes twitched over the room full of men putting money in his pocket, then he turned and stuck his head through the door to the rear of the inn. "Feed 'em!" he shouted. Rounding on Rand and Mat, he snarled, "Don't be all night about it. I expect you up there till the last man's gone."

Some of the patrons were shouting for the musician and the juggler, and Hake turned to soothe them. The man in the velvet cloak was one of the anxious ones. Rand motioned Mat to follow him.

A stout door separated the kitchen from the front of the

inn, and, except when it opened to let a serving maid through, the rain pounding the roof was louder in the kitchen than the shouts from the common room. It was a big room, hot and steamy from stoves and ovens, with a huge table covered with half-prepared food and dishes ready to be served. Some of the serving maids sat clustered on a bench near the rear door, rubbing their feet and chattering away all at once with the fat cook, who talked back at the same time and waved a big spoon to emphasize her points. They all glanced up as Rand and Mat came in, but it did not slow their conversation or stop their foot rubbing.

"We ought to get out of here while we have the chance," Rand said softly, but Mat shook his head, his eyes fixed on the two plates the cook was filling with beef and potatoes and peas. She hardly looked at the two of them, keeping up her talk with the other women while she pushed things aside on the table with her elbows and set the plates down, adding forks.

"After we eat is time enough." Mat slid onto a bench and began using his fork as if it were a shovel.

Rand sighed, but he was right behind Mat. He had had only a butt-end of bread to eat since the night before. His belly felt as empty as a beggar's purse, and the cooking smells that filled the kitchen did not help. He quickly had his mouth full, though Mat was getting his plate refilled by the cook before he had finished half of his.

He did not mean to eavesdrop on the women's talk, but some of the words reached out and grabbed him.

"Sounds crazy to me."

"Crazy or not, it's what I hear. He went to half the inns in town before he came here. Just walked in, looked around, and walked out without saying one word, even at the Royal Inn. Like it wasn't raining at all."

"Maybe he thought here was the most comfortable." That brought gales of laughter.

"What I hear is he didn't even get to Four Kings till after nightfall, and his horses blowing like they'd been pushed hard."

"Where'd he come from, to get caught out after dark? Nobody but a fool or a madman travels anywhere and plans it that badly."

"Well, maybe he's a fool, but he's a rich one. I hear he

even has another carriage for his servants and baggage. There's money there, mark my words. Did you see that cloak of his? I wouldn't mind having that my ownself."

"He's a little plump for my taste, but I always say a man can't be too fat if enough gold comes with it." They all doubled over giggling, and the cook threw back her head and roared with laughter.

Rand dropped his fork on his plate. A thought he did not like bubbled in his head. "I'll be back in a minute," he said. Mat barely nodded, stuffing a piece of potato into his mouth.

Rand picked up his sword belt along with his cloak as he stood, and buckled it around his waist on the way to the back door. No one paid him any mind.

The rain was bucketing down. He swung his cloak around his shoulders and pulled the hood over his head, holding the cloak closed as he trotted across the stableyard. A curtain of water hid everything except when lightning flashed, but he found what he was hunting. The horses had been taken into the stable, but the two black-lacquered carriages glistened wetly outside. Thunder grumbled, and a bolt of lightning streaked above the inn. In the brief burst of light he made out a name in gold script on the coach doors. Howal Gode.

Unmindful of the rain beating at him, he stood staring at the name he could no longer see. He remembered where he had last seen black-lacquered coaches with their owners' names on the door, and sleek, overfed men in silk-lined velvet cloaks and velvet slippers. Whitebridge. A Whitebridge merchant could have a perfectly legitimate reason to be on his way to Caemlyn. *A reason that sends him to half the inns in town before he chooses the one where you are? A reason that makes him look at you as if he's found what he's searching for?*

Rand shivered, and suddenly he was aware of rain trickling down his back. His cloak was tightly woven, but it had never been meant to stand up to this kind of downpour. He hurried back to the inn, splashing through deepening puddles. Jak blocked the door as he started through.

"Well, well, well. Out here alone in the dark. Dark's dangerous, boy."

Rain slicked Rand's hair down across his forehead. The stableyard was empty except for them. He wondered if Hake had decided he wanted the sword and the flute badly enough to forgo keeping the crowd in the common room.

Brushing water out of his eyes with one hand, he put the other on his sword. Even wet, the nobby leather made a sure grip for his fingers. "Has Hake decided all those men will stay just for his ale, instead of going where there's entertainment, too? If he has, we'll call the meal even for what we've done so far and be on our way."

Dry in the doorway, the big man looked out at the rain and snorted. "In this?" His eyes slid down to Rand's hand on the sword. "You know, me and Strom got a bet. He figures you stole that from your old grandmother. Me, I figure your grandmother'd kick you round the pigpen and hang you out to dry." He grinned. His teeth were crooked and yellow, and the grin made him look even meaner. "Night's long yet, boy."

Rand brushed past him, and Jak let him by with an ugly chuckle.

Inside, he tossed off his cloak and dropped on the bench at the table he had left only minutes before. Mat was done with his second plate and working on a third, eating more slowly now, but intently, as if he planned to finish every bite if it killed him. Jak took up a place by the door to the stable-yard, leaning against the wall and watching them. Even the cook seemed to feel no urge to talk with him there.

"He's from Whitebridge," Rand said softly. There was no need to say who "he" was. Mat's head swiveled toward him, a piece of beef on the end of the fork suspended halfway to his mouth. Conscious of Jak watching, Rand stirred the food on his plate. He could not have gotten a mouthful down if he had been starving, but he tried to pretend an interest in the peas as he told Mat about the carriages, and what the women had said, in case Mat had not been listening.

Obviously he had not been. Mat blinked in surprise and whistled between his teeth, then frowned at the meat on his fork and grunted as he tossed the fork onto his plate. Rand wished he would make at least an effort to be circumspect.

"After us," Mat said when he finished. The creases in Mat's forehead deepened. "A Darkfriend?"

"Maybe. I don't know." Rand glanced at Jak and the big man stretched elaborately, shrugging shoulders as big as any blacksmith's. "Do you think we can get past him?"

"Not without him making enough noise to bring Hake and the other one. I knew we should never have stopped here."

Rand gaped, but before he could say anything Hake pushed through the door from the common room. Strom bulked large over his shoulder. Jak stepped in front of the back door. "You going to eat all night?" Hake barked. "I didn't feed you so you could lie around out here."

Rand looked at his friend. Later, Mat mouthed, and they gathered their things under the watchful eyes of Hake, Strom, and Jak.

In the common room, cries for juggling and the names of tunes burst through the clamor as soon as Rand and Mat appeared. The man in the velvet cloak—Howal Gode—still appeared to ignore everyone around him, but he was nonetheless seated on the edge of his chair. At the sight of them he leaned back, the satisfied smile returning to his lips.

Rand took the first turn at the front of the dais, playing "Drawing Water From the Well" with only half his mind on it. No one seemed to notice the few wrong notes. He tried to think of how they were going to get away, and tried to avoid looking at Gode, too. If he was after them, there was no point in letting him know they knew it. As for getting away. . . .

He had never realized before what a good trap an inn made. Hake, Jak, and Strom did not even have to keep a close eye on them; the crowd would let them know if he or Mat left the dais. As long as the common room was full of people, Hake could not send Jak and Strom after them, but as long as the common room was full of people they could not get away without Hake knowing. And Gode was watching their every move, too. It was so funny he would have laughed if he had not been on the point of throwing up. They would just have to be wary and wait their chance.

When he changed places with Mat, Rand groaned to himself. Mat glared at Hake, at Strom, at Jak, without a care to whether they noticed or wondered why. When he was not actually handling the balls, his hand rested under his coat. Rand hissed at him, but he paid no attention. If Hake saw that ruby, he might not wait until they were alone. If the men in the common room saw it, half of them might join in with Hake.

Worst of all, Mat stared at the Whitebridge merchant—

the Darkfriend?—twice as hard as at anyone else, and Gode
noticed. There was no way he could avoid noticing. But it
did not disturb his aplomb in the least. His smile deepened,
if anything, and he nodded to Mat as if to an old acquaintance, then looked at Rand and raised a questioning eyebrow. Rand did not want to know what the question was.
He tried to avoid looking at the man, but he knew it was too
late for that. *Too late. Too late again.*

Only one thing seemed to shake the velvet-cloaked man's
equilibrium. Rand's sword. He had left it on. Two or three
men staggered up to ask if he thought his playing was so
bad that he needed protection, but none of them had noticed the heron on the hilt. Gode noticed. His pale hands
clenched, and he frowned at the sword for a long time before his smile came back. When it did, it was not as sure as
before.

One good thing, at least, Rand thought. *If he believes I
can live up to the heron-mark, maybe he'll leave us alone.
Then all we have to worry about is Hake and his bullies.* It
was hardly a comforting thought, and, sword or no sword,
Gode kept watching. And smiling.

To Rand the night seemed to last a year. All those eyes
looking at him: Hake and Jak and Strom like vultures watching a sheep caught in a bog, Gode waiting like something
even worse. He began to think that everybody in the room
was watching with some hidden motive. Sour wine fumes
and the stench of dirty, sweating bodies made his head swim,
and the din of voices beat at him till his eyes blurred and
even the sound of his own flute scratched at his ears. The
crash of the thunder seemed to be inside his skull. Weariness
hung on him like an iron weight.

Eventually the need to be up with the dawn began to pull
men reluctantly out into the dark. A farmer had only himself to answer to, but merchants were notoriously unfeeling
about hangovers when they were paying drivers' wages. In
the small hours the common room slowly emptied as even
those who had rooms abovestairs staggered off to find their
beds.

Gode was the last patron. When Rand reached for the
leather flute case, yawning, Gode stood up and slung his
cloak over his arm. The serving maids were cleaning up,
muttering among themselves about the mess of spilled wine

and broken crockery. Hake was locking the front door with a big key. Gode cornered Hake for a moment, and Hake called one of the women to show him to a room. The velvet-cloaked man gave Mat and Rand a knowing smile before he disappeared upstairs.

Hake was looking at Rand and Mat. Jak and Strom stood at his shoulders.

Rand hastily finished hanging his things from his shoulders, holding them all awkwardly behind him with his left hand so he could reach his sword. He made no move toward it, but he wanted to know it was ready. He suppressed a yawn; how tired he was was something they should not know.

Mat shouldered his bow and his few other belongings awkwardly, but he put his hand under his coat as he watched Hake and his toughs approach.

Hake was carrying an oil lamp, and to Rand's surprise he gave a little bow and gestured to a side door with it. "Your pallets are this way." Only a slight twist of his lips spoiled his act.

Mat thrust his chin out at Jak and Strom. "You need those two to show us our beds?"

"I'm a man of property," Hake said, smoothing the front of his soiled apron, "and men of property can't be too careful." A crash of thunder rattled the windows, and he glanced significantly at the ceiling, then gave them a toothy grin. "You want to see your beds or not?"

Rand wondered what would happen if he said they wanted to leave. *If you really did know more about using a sword than the few exercises Lan showed you. . . .* "Lead the way," he said, trying to make his voice hard. "I don't like having anybody behind me."

Strom snickered, but Hake nodded placidly and turned toward the side door, and the two big men swaggered after him. Taking a deep breath, Rand gave a wishful glance at the door to the kitchen. If Hake had already locked the back door, running now would only begin what he was hoping to avoid. He followed the innkeeper glumly.

At the side door he hesitated, and Mat crowded into his back. The reason for Hake's lamp was apparent. The door let into a hall as black as pitch. Only the lamp Hake carried, silhouetting Jak and Strom, gave him the courage to keep on. If they turned, he would know it. *And do what?* The floor creaked under his boots.

The hall ended in a rough, unpainted door. He had not seen if there were any other doors along the way. Hake and his bullies went through, and he followed quickly, before they could have a chance to set a trap, but Hake merely lifted the lamp high and gestured at the room.

"Here it is."

An old storeroom, he had called it, and by the look of it not used in some time. Weathered barrels and broken crates filled half the floor. Steady drips fell from more than one place on the ceiling, and a broken pane in the filthy window let the rain blow in freely. Unidentifiable odds and ends littered the shelves, and thick dust covered almost everything. The presence of the promised pallets was a surprise.

The sword makes him nervous. He won't try anything until we're sound asleep. Rand had no intention of sleeping under Hake's roof. As soon as the innkeeper left, he intended to be out the window. "It'll do," he said. He kept his eyes on Hake, wary for a signal to the two grinning men at the innkeeper's side. It was an effort not to wet his lips. "Leave the lamp."

Hake grunted, but pushed the lamp onto a shelf. He hesitated, looking at them, and Rand was sure he was about to give the word for Jak and Strom to jump them, but his eyes went to Rand's sword with a calculating frown, and he jerked his head at the two big men. Surprise flashed across their broad faces, but they followed him out of the room without a backward glance.

Rand waited for the *creak-creak-creak* of their footsteps to fade away, then counted to fifty before sticking his head into the hall. The blackness was broken only by a rectangle of light that seemed as distant as the moon: the door to the common room. As he pulled his head in, something big moved in the darkness near the far door. Jak or Strom, standing guard.

A quick examination of the door told him all he needed to know, little of it good. The boards were thick and stout, but there was no lock, and no bar on the inside. It did open into the room, though.

"I thought they were going for us," Mat said. "What are they waiting for?" He had the dagger out, gripped in a white-knuckled fist. Lamplight flickered on the blade. His bow and quiver lay forgotten on the floor.

"For us to go to sleep." Rand started rummaging through the barrels and crates. "Help me find something to block the door."

"Why? You don't really intend to sleep here, do you? Let's get out the window and gone. I'd rather be wet than dead."

"One of them is at the end of the hall. We make any noise, and they'll be down on us before we can blink. I think Hake would rather face us awake than risk letting us get away."

Muttering, Mat joined his search, but there was nothing useful in any of the litter on the floor. The barrels were empty, the crates splintered, and the whole lot of them piled in front of the door would not stop anyone from opening it. Then something familiar on a shelf caught Rand's eye. Two splitting wedges, covered with rust and dust. He took them down with a grin.

Hastily he shoved them under the door and, when the next roll of thunder rattled the inn, drove them in with two quick kicks of his heel. The thunder faded, and he held his breath, listening. All he heard was the rain pounding on the roof. No floorboards creaking under running feet.

"The window," he said.

It had not been opened in years, from the dirt crusted around it. They strained together, pushing up with all their might. Rand's knees wobbled before the sash budged; it groaned with each reluctant inch. When the opening was wide enough for them to slip through, he crouched, then stopped.

"Blood and ashes!" Mat growled. "No wonder Hake wasn't worried about us slipping out."

Iron bars in an iron frame glistened wetly in the light from the lamp. Rand pushed at them; they were as solid as a boulder.

"I saw something," Mat said. He pawed hurriedly through the litter on the shelves and came back with a rusty crowbar. He rammed the end of it under the iron frame on one side, and Rand winced.

"Remember the noise, Mat."

Mat grimaced and muttered under his breath, but he waited. Rand put his hands on the crowbar and tried to find good footing in the growing puddle of water under the window. Thunder rolled and they heaved. With a tortured squeal of nails that made the hairs lift on Rand's neck, the frame shifted—a quarter of an inch, if that. Timing themselves to peals of thunder and lightning cracks, they heaved on the crowbar again and again. Nothing. A quarter of an inch. Nothing. A hairsbreadth. Nothing. Nothing.

Suddenly Rand's feet slipped in the water, and they crashed to the floor. The crowbar clattered against the bars like a gong. He lay in a puddle holding his breath and listening. Silence but for the rain.

Mat nursed bruised knuckles and glared at him. "We'll never get out at this rate." The iron frame was pushed out from the window not quite far enough to get two fingers under it. Dozens of thick nails crossed the narrow opening.

"We just have to keep trying," Rand said, getting up. But as he set the crowbar under the edge of the frame, the door creaked as someone tried to open it. The splitting wedges held it shut. He exchanged a worried look with Mat. Mat pulled the dagger out again. The door gave another screak.

Rand took a deep breath and tried to make his voice steady. "Go away, Hake. We're trying to sleep."

"I fear you mistake me." The voice was so sleek and full of itself that it named its owner. Howal Gode. "Master Hake and his . . . minions will not trouble us. They sleep soundly, and in the morning they will only be able to wonder where you vanished to. Let me in, my young friends. We must talk."

"We don't have anything to talk to you about," Mat said. "Go away and let us sleep."

Gode's chuckle was nasty. "Of course we have things to talk about. You know that as well as I. I saw it in your eyes. I know what you are, perhaps better than you do. I can feel it coming from you in waves. Already you halfway belong to my master. Stop running and accept it. Things will be so much easier for you. If the Tar Valon hags find you, you'll wish you could cut your own throat before they are done, but you won't be able to. Only my master can protect you from them."

Rand swallowed hard. "We don't know what you're talking about. Leave us alone." The floorboards in the hall squeaked.

Gode was not alone. How many men could he have brought in two carriages?

"Stop being foolish, my young friends. You know. You know very well. The Great Lord of the Dark has marked you for his own. It is written that when he awakes, the new Dreadlords will be there to praise him. You must be two of them, else I would not have been sent to find you. Think of it. Life everlasting, and power beyond dreams." His voice was thick with hunger for that power himself.

Rand glanced back at the window just as lightning split the sky, and he almost groaned. The brief flash of light showed men outside, men ignoring the rain that drenched them as they stood watching the window.

"I tire of this," Gode announced. "You will submit to my master—to your master—or you will be made to submit. That would not be pleasant for you. The Great Lord of the Dark rules death, and he can give life in death or death in life as he chooses. Open this door. One way or another, your running is at an end. Open it, I say!"

He must have said something else, too, for suddenly a heavy body thudded against the door. It shivered, and the wedges slid a fraction of an inch with a grate of rust rubbing off on wood. Again and again the door trembled as bodies hurled themselves at it. Sometimes the wedges held; sometimes they slid another tiny bit, and bit by tiny bit the door crept inexorably inward.

"Submit," Gode demanded from the hall, "or spend eternity wishing that you had!"

"If we don't have any choice—" Mat licked his lips under Rand's stare. His eyes darted like the eyes of a badger in a trap; his face was pale, and he panted as he spoke. "We could say yes, and then get away later. Blood and ashes, Rand, there's no way out!"

The words seemed to drift to Rand through wool stuffed in his ears. *No way out.* Thunder muttered overhead, and was drowned in a slash of lightning. *Have to find a way out.* Gode called to them, demanding, appealing; the door slid another inch toward being open. *A way out!*

Light filled the room, flooding vision; the air roared and burned. Rand felt himself picked up and dashed against the wall. He slid down in a heap, ears ringing and every hair on his body trying to stand on end. Dazed, he staggered to his feet. His knees wobbled, and he put a hand against the wall to steady himself. He looked around in amazement.

The lamp, lying on its side on the edge of one of the few shelves still clinging to the walls, still burned and gave light. All the barrels and crates, some blackened and smoldering, lay toppled where they had been hurled. The window, bars and all, and most of the wall, too, had vanished, leaving a splintered hole. The roof sagged, and tendrils of smoke fought the rain around the jagged edges of the opening. The door hung off its hinges, jammed in the doorframe at an angle slanting into the hall.

With a feeling of woozy unreality he stood the lamp up. It seemed the most important thing in the world was making sure it did not break.

A pile of crates suddenly heaved apart, and Mat stood up in the middle of it. He weaved on his feet, blinking and fumbling at himself as if wondering if everything was still attached. He peered toward Rand. "Rand? Is that you? You're alive. I thought we were both—" He broke off, biting his lip and shaking. It took Rand a moment to realize he was laughing, and on the edge of hysteria.

"What happened, Mat? Mat? Mat! What happened?"

One last shiver wracked Mat, and then he was still. "Lightning, Rand. I was looking right at the window when it hit the bars. Lightning. I can't see worth—" He broke off, squinting at the aslant door, and his voice went sharp. "Where's Gode?"

Nothing moved in the dark corridor beyond the door. Of Gode and his companions there was neither sign nor sound, though anything could have lain in the blackness. Rand found himself hoping they were dead, but he would not have put his head into the hall to find out for sure if he had been offered a crown. Nothing moved out in the night beyond where the wall had been, either, but others were up and about. Confused shouts came from abovestairs in the inn, and the pounding of running feet.

"Let's go while we can," Rand said.

Hastily helping separate their belongings from the rubble, he grabbed Mat's arm and half pulled, half guided his friend through the gaping hole into the night. Mat clutched his arm, stumbling beside him with his head pushed forward in an effort to see.

As the first rain hit Rand's face, lightning forked above the inn, and he came to a convulsive stop. Gode's men were still there, lying with their feet toward the opening. Pelted by the rain, their open eyes stared at the sky.

"What is it?" Mat asked. "Blood and ashes! I can hardly see my own bloody hand!"

"Nothing," Rand said. *Luck. The Light's own. . . . Is it?* Shivering, he carefully guided Mat around the bodies. "Just the lightning."

There was no light save the lightning, and he stumbled in the ruts as they ran staggering away from the inn. With Mat almost hanging on him, every stumble almost pulled them both down, but tottering, panting, they ran.

Once he looked back. Once, before the rain thickened to a deafening curtain that blotted The Dancing Cartman from sight. Lightning silhouetted the figure of a man at the back of the inn, a man shaking his fist at them, or at the sky. Gode or Hake, he did not know, but either one was as bad as the other. The rain came in a deluge, isolating them in a wall of water. He hurried through the night, listening through the roar of the storm for the sound of pursuit.

CHAPTER
33

The Dark Waits

Under a leaden sky the high-wheeled cart bumped east along the Caemlyn Road. Rand pulled himself out of the straw in back to look over the side. It was easier than it had been an hour earlier. His arms felt as if they might stretch instead of drawing him up, and for a minute his head wanted to keep on going and float away, but it was easier. He hooked his elbows over the low slats and watched the land roll past. The sun, still hidden by dull clouds, yet stood high overhead, but the cart was clattering into another village of vine-covered, red brick houses. Towns had been getting closer together since Four Kings.

Some of the people waved or called a greeting to Hyam Kinch, the farmer whose cart it was. Master Kinch, leathery-faced and taciturn, shouted back a few words each time, around the pipe in his teeth. The clenched teeth made what he said all but unintelligible, but it sounded jovial and seemed to satisfy; they went back to what they were doing without another glance at the cart. No one appeared to pay any mind to the farmer's two passengers.

The village inn moved through Rand's field of vision. It was whitewashed, with a gray slate roof. People bustled in and out, nodding casually and waving to one another. Some of them stopped to speak. They knew one another. Villagers, mostly, by their clothes—boots and trousers and coats not much different from what he wore himself, though with an inordinate fondness for colorful stripes. The women wore deep bonnets that hid their faces and white aprons with stripes. Maybe they were all townsmen and local farmfolk. *Does that make any difference?*

He dropped back on the straw, watching the village dwindle between his feet. Fenced fields and trimmed hedges lined the road, and small farmhouses with smoke rising from red brick chimneys. The only woods near the road were coppices, well tended for firewood, tame as a farmyard. But the branches stood leafless against the sky, as stark as in the wild woods to the west.

A line of wagons heading the other way rumbled down the center of the road, crowding the cart over onto the verge. Master Kinch shifted his pipe to the corner of his mouth and spat between his teeth. With one eye on his off-side wheel, to make sure it did not tangle in the hedge, he kept the cart moving. His mouth tightened as he glanced at the merchants' train.

None of the wagon drivers cracking their long whips in the air above eight-horse teams, none of the hard-faced guards slouching in their saddles alongside the wagons, looked at the cart. Rand watched them go, his chest tight. His hand was under his cloak, gripping his sword hilt, until the last wagon lurched by.

As that final wagon rattled away toward the village they had just left, Mat turned on the seat beside the farmer and leaned back until he found Rand's eyes. The scarf that did duty for dust, when need be, shaded his own eyes, folded over thickly and tied low around his forehead. Even so he squinted in the gray daylight. "You see anything back there?" he asked quietly. "What about the wagons?"

Rand shook his head, and Mat nodded. He had seen nothing either.

Master Kinch glanced at them out of the corner of his eye, then shifted his pipe again, and flapped the reins. That was all, but he had noticed. The horse picked up the pace a step.

"Your eyes still hurt?" Rand asked.

Mat touched the scarf around his head. "No. Not much. Not unless I look almost right at the sun, anyway. What about you? Are you feeling any better?"

"Some." He really was feeling better, he realized. It was a wonder to get over being sick so fast. More than that, it was a gift of the Light. *It has to be the Light. It has to be.*

Suddenly a body of horsemen was passing the cart, heading west like the merchants' wagons. Long white collars hung down over their mail and plate, and their cloaks and undercoats were red, like the gatetenders' uniforms in Whitebridge, but better made and better fitting. Each man's conical helmet shone like silver. They sat their horses with straight backs. Thin red streamers fluttered beneath the heads of their lances, every lance held at the same angle.

Some of them glanced into the cart as they passed in two columns. A cage of steel bars masked each face. Rand was glad his cloak covered his sword. A few nodded to Master Kinch, not as if they knew him, but in a neutral greeting. Master Kinch nodded back in much the same way, but despite his unchanging expression there was a hint of approval in his nod.

Their horses were at a walk, but with the speed of the cart added, they went by quickly. With a part of his mind Rand counted them. Ten . . . twenty . . . thirty . . . thirty-two. He raised his head to watch the columns move on down the Caemlyn Road.

"Who were they?" Mat asked, half wondering, half suspicious.

"Queen's Guards," Master Kinch said around his pipe. He kept his eyes on the road ahead. "Won't go much further than Breen's Spring, 'less they're called for. Not like the old days." He sucked on his pipe, then added, "I suppose, these days, there's parts of the Realm don't see the Guards in a year or more. Not like the old days."

"What are they doing?" Rand asked.

The farmer gave him a look. "Keeping the Queen's peace and upholding the Queen's law." He nodded to himself as if he liked the sound of that, and added, "Searching out malefactors and seeing them before a magistrate. Mmmph!" He let out a long streamer of smoke. "You two must be from pretty far off not to recognize the Queen's Guard. Where you from?"

"Far off," Mat said at the same instant that Rand said, "The Two Rivers." He wished he could take it back as soon as he said it. He still was not thinking clearly. Trying to hide, and mentioning a name a Fade would hear like a bell.

Master Kinch glanced at Mat out of the corner of his eye, and puffed his pipe in silence for a while. "That's far off, all right," he said finally. "Almost to the border of the Realm. But things must be worse than I thought if there's places in the Realm where people don't even *recognize* the Queen's Guards. Not like the old days at all."

Rand wondered what Master al'Vere would say if someone told him the Two Rivers was part of some Queen's Realm. The Queen of Andor, he supposed. Perhaps the Mayor did know—he knew a lot of things that surprised Rand—and maybe others did, too, but he had never heard anyone mention it. The Two Rivers was the Two Rivers. Each village handled its own problems, and if some difficulty involved more than one village the Mayors, and maybe the Village Councils, solved it between them.

Master Kinch pulled on the reins, drawing the cart to a halt. "Far as I go." A narrow cart path led off to the north; several farmhouses were visible in that direction across open fields, plowed but still bare of crops. "Two days will see you in Caemlyn. Least, it would if your friend had his legs under him."

Mat hopped down and retrieved his bow and other things, then helped Rand climb off the tail of the cart. Rand's bundles weighed on him, and his legs wobbled, but he shrugged off his friend's hand and tried a few steps on his own. He still felt unsteady, but his legs held him up. They even seemed to grow stronger as he used them.

The farmer did not start his horse up again right away. He studied them for a minute, sucking on his pipe. "You can rest up a day or two at my place, if you want. Won't miss anything in that time, I suppose. Whatever sickness you're getting over, young fellow . . . well, the old woman and me, we already had about every sickness you can think of before you were born, and nursed our younglings through 'em, too. I expect you're past the catching stage, anyway."

Mat's eyes narrowed, and Rand caught himself frowning. *Not everyone is part of it. It can't be everybody.*

"Thank you," he said, "but I'm all right. Really. How far to the next village?"

"Carysford? You can reach it before dark, walking." Master Kinch took his pipe from between his teeth and pursed his lips thoughtfully before going on. "First off, I reckoned you for runaway 'prentices, but now I expect it's something more serious you're running from. Don't know what. Don't care. I'm a good enough judge to say you're not Darkfriends, and not likely to rob or hurt anybody. Not like some on the road these days. I got in trouble a time or two myself when I was your age. You need a place to keep out of sight a few days, my farm is five miles that way"—he jerked his head toward the cart track—"and don't nobody ever come out there. Whatever's chasing you, won't likely find you there." He cleared his throat as if embarrassed by speaking so many words together.

"How would you know what Darkfriends look like?" Mat demanded. He backed away from the cart, and his hand went under his coat. "What do you know about Dark-friends?"

Master Kinch's face tightened. "Suit yourselves," he said, and clucked to his horse. The cart rolled off down the narrow path, and he never looked back.

Mat looked at Rand, and his scowl faded. "Sorry, Rand. You need a place to rest. Maybe if we go after him. . . ." He shrugged. "I just can't get over the feeling that everybody's after us. Light, I wish I knew why they were. I wish it was over. I wish. . . ." He trailed off miserably.

"There are still some good people," Rand said. Mat started toward the cart path, jaw clenched as if it were the last thing he wanted to do, but Rand stopped him. "We can't afford to stop just to rest, Mat. Besides, I don't think there is anywhere to hide."

Mat nodded, his relief evident. He tried to take some of Rand's burdens, the saddlebags and Thom's cloak wrapped around the cased harp, but Rand held onto them. His legs really did feel stronger. *Whatever's chasing us?* he thought as they started off down the road. *Not chasing. Waiting.*

The rain had continued through the night they staggered away from The Dancing Cartman, hammering at them as hard as the thunder out of a black sky split by lightning. Their clothes became sodden in minutes; in an hour Rand's skin felt sodden, too, but they had left Four Kings behind them. Mat was all but blind in the dark, squinting painfully at the sharp flashes that made trees stand out starkly for an instant. Rand led him by the hand, but Mat still felt out each step uncertainly. Worry creased Rand's forehead. If Mat did not regain his sight, they would be slowed to a crawl. They would never get away.

Mat seemed to sense his thought. Despite the hood of his cloak, the rain had plastered Mat's hair across his face. "Rand," he said, "you won't leave me, will you? If I can't keep up?" His voice quavered.

"I won't leave you." Rand tightened his grip on his friend's hand. "I won't leave you no matter what." *Light help us!* Thunder crashed overhead, and Mat stumbled, almost falling, almost pulling him down, too. "We have to stop, Mat. If we keep going, you'll break a leg."

"Gode." Lightning split the dark right above them as Mat spoke, and the thunder crack pounded every other sound into the ground, but in the flash Rand could make out the name on Mat's lips.

"He's dead." *He has to be. Light, let him be dead.*

He led Mat to some bushes the lightning flash had showed him. They had leaves enough to give a little shelter from the driving rain. Not as much as a good tree might, but he did not want to risk another lightning strike. They might not be so lucky, next time.

Huddled together beneath the bushes, they tried to arrange their cloaks to make a little tent over the branches. It was far too late to think of staying dry, but just stopping the incessant pelting of the raindrops would be something. They crouched against each other to share what little body warmth was left to them. Dripping wet as they were, and more drips coming through the cloaks, they shivered themselves into sleep.

Rand knew right away it was a dream. He was back in Four Kings, but the town was empty except for him. The wagons were there, but no people, no horses, no dogs. Nothing alive. He knew someone was waiting for him, though.

As he walked down the rutted street, the buildings seemed to blur as they slid behind him. When he turned his head, they were all there, solid, but the indistinctness remained at the corners of his vision. It was as if only what he saw really existed, and then just while he was seeing. He was sure if he turned quickly enough he would see. . . . He was not sure what, but it made him uneasy, thinking about it.

The Dancing Cartman appeared in front of him. Somehow its garish paint seemed gray and lifeless. He went in. Gode was there, at a table.

He only recognized the man from his clothes, his silk

and dark velvets. Gode's skin was red, burned and cracked and oozing. His face was almost a skull, his lips shriveled to bare teeth and gums. As Gode turned his head, some of his hair cracked off, powdering to soot when it hit his shoulder. His lidless eyes stared at Rand.

"So you are dead," Rand said. He was surprised that he was not afraid. Perhaps it was knowing that it was a dream this time.

"Yes," said Ba'alzamon's voice, "but he did find you for me. That deserves some reward, don't you think?"

Rand turned, and discovered he could be afraid, even knowing it was a dream. Ba'alzamon's clothes were the color of dried blood, and rage and hate and triumph battled on his face.

"You see, youngling, you cannot hide from me forever. One way or another I find you. What protects you also makes you vulnerable. One time you hide, the next you light a signal fire. Come to me, youngling." He held out his hand to Rand. "If my hounds must pull you down, they may not be gentle. They are jealous of what you will be, once you have knelt at my feet. It is your destiny. You belong to me." Gode's burned tongue made an angry, eager garble of sound.

Rand tried to wet his lips, but he had no spit in his mouth. "No," he managed, and then the words came more easily. "I belong to myself. Not you. Not ever. Myself. If your Dark-friends kill me, you'll never have me."

The fires in Ba'alzamon's face heated the room till the air swam. "Alive or dead, youngling, you are mine. The grave belongs to me. Easier dead, but better alive. Better for you, youngling. The living have more power in most things." Gode made a gabbling sound again. "Yes, my good hound. Here is your reward."

Rand looked at Gode just in time to see the man's body crumble to dust. For an instant the burned face held a look of sublime joy that turned to horror in the final moment, as if he had seen something waiting he did not expect. Gode's empty velvet garments settled on the chair and the floor among the ash.

When he turned back, Ba'alzamon's outstretched hand had become a fist. "You are mine, youngling, alive or dead. The Eye of the World will never serve you. I mark you as mine." His fist opened, and a ball of flame shot out. It struck Rand in the face, exploding, searing.

Rand lurched awake in the dark, water dripping through the cloaks onto his face. His hand trembled as he touched his cheeks. The skin felt tender, as if sunburned.

Suddenly he realized Mat was twisting and moaning in his sleep. He shook him, and Mat came awake with a whimper.

"My eyes! Oh, Light, my eyes! He took my eyes!"

Rand held him close, cradling him against his chest as if he were a baby. "You're all right, Mat. You're all right. He can't hurt us. We won't let him." He could feel Mat shaking, sobbing into his coat. "He can't hurt us," he whispered, and wished he believed it. *What protects you makes you vulnerable. I* am *going mad.*

Just before first light the downpour dwindled, the last drizzle fading as dawn came. The clouds remained, threatening until well into the morning. The wind came up, then, driving the clouds off to the south, baring a warmthless sun and slicing through their dripping wet clothes. They had not slept again, but groggily they donned their cloaks and set off eastward, Rand leading Mat by the hand. After a while Mat even felt well enough to complain about what the rain had done to his bowstring. Rand would not let him stop to exchange it for a dry string from his pocket, though; not yet.

They came on another village shortly after midday. Rand shivered harder at the sight of snug brick houses and smoke rising from chimneys, but he kept clear, leading Mat through the woods and fields to the south. A lone farmer working with a spading fork in a muddy field was the only person he saw, and he took care that the man did not see them, crouching through the trees. The farmer's attention was all on his work, but Rand kept one eye on him till he was lost to sight. If any of Gode's men were alive, perhaps they would believe he and Mat had taken the southern road out of Four Kings when they could not find anyone who had seen them in this village. They came back to the road out of sight of the town, and walked their clothes, if not dry, at least to just damp.

An hour beyond the town a farmer gave them a ride in his half-empty haywain. Rand had been taken by surprise while lost in worry about Mat. Mat shielded his eyes from the sun with his hand, weak as the afternoon light was, squinting through slitted lids even so, and he muttered continually about how bright the sun was. When Rand heard the rumble of the haywain, it was too late already. The sodden road deadened sound, and the wagon with its two-horse hitch was only fifty yards behind them, the driver already peering at them.

To Rand's surprise he drew up and offered them a lift. Rand hesitated, but it was too late to avoid being seen, and refusing a ride might fix them in the man's mind. He helped Mat up to the seat beside the farmer, then climbed up behind him.

Alpert Mull was a stolid man, with a square face and square hands, both worn and grooved from hard work and worry, and he wanted someone to talk to. His cows had gone dry, his chickens had stopped laying, and there was no pasture worth the name. For the first time in memory he had had to buy hay, and half a wagon was all "old Bain" would let him have. He wondered whether there was any chance of getting hay on his own land this year, or any kind of crop.

"The Queen should do something, the Light illumine her," he muttered, knuckling his forehead respectfully but absentmindedly.

He hardly looked at Rand or Mat, but when he let them down by the narrow, rail-lined track that led off to his farm, he hesitated, then said, almost as if to himself, "I don't know what you're running from, and I don't want to. I have a wife and children. You understand? My family. It's hard times for helping strangers."

Mat tried to stick his hand under his coat, but Rand had his wrist and he held on. He stood in the road, looking at the man without speaking.

"If I was a good man," Mull said, "I'd offer a couple of lads soaked to the skin a place to dry out and get warm in front of my fire. But it's hard times, and strangers. . . . I don't know what you're running from, and I don't want to. You understand? My family." Suddenly he pulled two long, woolen scarves, dark and thick, out of his coat pocket. "It's not much, but here. Belong to my boys. They have others. You don't know me, understand? It's hard times."

"We never even saw you," Rand agreed as he took the scarves. "You *are* a good man. The best we've met in days."

The farmer looked surprised, then grateful. Gathering his reins, he turned his horses down the narrow lane. Before he completed the turn Rand was leading Mat on down the Caemlyn Road.

The wind stiffened as dusk closed in. Mat began to ask querulously when they were going to stop, but Rand kept moving, pulling Mat behind him, searching for more shelter than a spot under a hedge. With their clothes still clammy and the wind getting colder by the minute, he was not sure they could survive another night in the open. Night fell without him spotting anything useful. The wind grew icy, beating his cloak. Then, through the darkness ahead, he saw lights. A village.

His hand slid into his pocket, feeling the coins there. More than enough for a meal and a room for the two of them. A room out of the cold night. If they stayed in the open, in the wind and cold in damp clothes, anyone who found them would likely as not find only two corpses. They just had to keep from attracting any more notice than they could help. No playing the flute, and with his eyes, Mat certainly could not juggle. He grasped Mat's hand again and set out toward the beckoning lights.

"When are we going to stop?" Mat asked again. The way he peered ahead, with his head stuck forward, Rand was not sure if Mat could see him, much less the village lights.

"When we're somewhere warm," he replied.

Pools of light from house windows lit the streets of the town, and people walked them unconcerned with what might be out in the dark. The only inn was a sprawling building, all on one floor, with the look of having had rooms added in bunches over the years without any particular plan. The front door opened to let someone out, and a wave of laughter rolled out after him.

Rand froze in the street, the drunken laughter at The Dancing Cartman echoing in his head. He watched the man go down the street with a none-too-steady stride, then took a deep breath and pushed the door open. He took care that his cloak covered his sword. Laughter swept over him.

Lamps hanging from the high ceiling made the room bright, and right away he could see and feel the difference from Saml Hake's inn. There was no drunkenness here, for one thing. The room was filled with people who looked to be farmers and townsmen, if not entirely sober, not too far from it. The laughter was real, if a bit forced around the edges. People laughing to forget their troubles, but with true mirth in it, too. The common room itself was neat and clean, and warm from a fire roaring in a big fireplace at the far end. The serving maids' smiles were as warm as the fire, and when they laughed Rand could tell it was because they wanted to.

The innkeeper was as clean as his inn, with a gleaming white apron around his bulk. Rand was glad to see he was a stout man; he doubted if he would ever again trust a skinny innkeeper. His name was Rulan Allwine—a good omen, Rand thought, with so much of the sound of Emond's Field to it—and he eyed them up and down, then politely mentioned paying in advance.

"Not suggesting you're the sort, understand, but there's some on the road these days aren't too particular about paying up come morning. Seems to be a lot of young folks headed for Caemlyn."

Rand was not offended, not as damp and bedraggled as he was. When Master Allwine mentioned the price, though, his eyes widened, and Mat made a sound as if he had choked on something.

The innkeeper's jowls swung as he shook his head regretfully, but he seemed to be used to it. "Times are hard," he said in a resigned voice. "There isn't much, and what there is costs five times what it used to. It'll be more next month, I'll lay oath on it."

Rand dug his money out and looked at Mat. Mat's mouth tightened stubbornly. "You want to sleep under a hedge?" Rand asked. Mat sighed and reluctantly emptied his pocket. When the reckoning was paid, Rand grimaced at the little that remained to divide with Mat.

But ten minutes later they were eating stew at a table in a corner near the fireplace, pushing it onto their spoons with chunks of bread. The portions were not as large as Rand could have wished, but they were hot, and filling. Warmth from the hearth seeped into him slowly. He pretended to keep his eyes on his plate, but he watched the door intently. Those who came in or went out all looked like farmers, but it was not enough to quiet his fear.

Mat ate slowly, savoring each bite, though he muttered about the light from the lamps. After a time he dug out the scarf Alpert Mull had given him and wound it around his forehead, pulling it down until his eyes were almost hidden. That got them some looks Rand wished they could have avoided. He cleaned his plate hurriedly, urging Mat to do the same, then asked Master Allwine for their room.

The innkeeper seemed surprised that they were retiring so early, but he made no comment. He got a candle and showed them through a jumble of corridors to a small room, with two narrow beds, back in a far corner of the inn. When he left, Rand dropped his bundles beside his bed, tossed his cloak over a chair, and fell on the coverlet fully dressed. All of his clothes were still damp and uncomfortable, but if they had to run, he wanted to be ready. He left the sword belt on, too, and slept with his hand on the hilt.

A rooster crowing jerked him awake in the morning. He lay there, watching dawn lighten the window, and wondered if he dared sleep a little longer. Sleep during daylight, when they could be moving. A yawn made his jaws crack.

"Hey," Mat exclaimed, "I can see!" He sat up on his bed, squinting around the room. "Some, anyway. Your face is still a little blurry, but I can tell who you are. I knew I'd be all right. By tonight I'll see better than you do. Again."

Rand sprang out of bed, scratching as he scooped up his cloak. His clothes were wrinkled from drying on him while he slept, and they itched. "We're wasting daylight," he said. Mat scrambled up as fast as he had; he was scratching, too.

Rand did feel good. They were a day away from Four Kings, and none of Gode's men had showed up. A day closer to Caemlyn, where Moiraine would be waiting for them. She would. No more worrying about Darkfriends once they were back with the Aes Sedai and the Warder. It was strange to be looking forward so much to being with an Aes Sedai. *Light, when I see Moiraine again, I'll kiss her!* He laughed at the thought. He felt good enough to invest some of their dwindling stock of coins in breakfast—a big loaf of bread and a pitcher of milk, cold from the springhouse.

They were eating in the back of the common room when a young man came in, a village youth by the look of him, with a cocky spring to his walk and twirling a cloth cap, with a feather in it, on one finger. The only other person in the room was an old man sweeping out; he never looked up from his broom. The young man's eyes swept jauntily around the room, but when they lit on Rand and Mat, the cap fell off his finger. He stared at them for a full minute before snatching the cap from the floor, then stared some more, running his fingers through his thick head of dark curls. Finally he came over to their table, his feet dragging.

He was older than Rand, but he stood looking down at them diffidently. "Mind if I sit down?" he asked, and immediately swallowed hard as if he might have said the wrong thing.

Rand thought he might be hoping to share their breakfast, though he looked able to buy his own. His blue-striped shirt was embroidered around the collar, and his dark blue cloak all around the hem. His leather boots had never been near any work that scuffed them, that Rand could see. He nodded to a chair.

Mat stared at the fellow as he drew the chair to the table. Rand could not tell if he was glaring or just trying to see clearly. In any case, Mat's frown had an effect. The young man froze halfway to sitting, and did not lower himself all the way until Rand nodded again.

"What's your name?" Rand asked.

"My name? My name. Ah . . . call me Paitr." His eyes shifted nervously. "Ah . . . this is not my idea, you understand. I have to do it. I didn't want to, but they made me. You have to understand that. I don't—"

Rand was beginning to tense when Mat growled, "Darkfriend."

Paitr gave a jerk and half lifted out of his chair, staring wildly around the room as if there were fifty people to overhear. The old man's head was still bent over the broom, his attention on the floor. Paitr sat back down and looked from Rand to Mat and back uncertainly. Sweat beaded on his upper lip. It was accusation enough to make anyone sweat, but he said not a word against it.

Rand shook his head slowly. After Gode, he knew that Darkfriends did not necessarily have the Dragon's Fang on their foreheads, but except for his clothes this Paitr could have fit right in Emond's Field. Nothing about him hinted at murder and worse. Nobody would have remarked him twice. At least Gode had been . . . different.

"Leave us alone," Rand said. "And tell your friends to

leave us alone. We want nothing from them, and they'll get nothing from us."

"If you don't," Mat added fiercely, "I'll name you for what you are. See what your village friends think of that."

Rand hoped he did not really mean it. That could cause as much trouble for the two of them as it did for Paitr.

Paitr seemed to take the threat seriously. His face grew pale. "I . . . I heard what happened at Four Kings. Some of it, anyway. Word travels. We have ways of hearing things. But there's nobody here to trap you. I'm alone, and . . . and I just want to talk."

"About what?" Mat asked at the same time that Rand said, "We're not interested." They looked at each other, and Mat shrugged. "We're not interested," he said.

Rand gulped the last of the milk and stuffed the heel of his half of the bread into his pocket. With their money almost gone, it might be their next meal.

How to leave the inn? If Paitr discovered that Mat was almost blind, he would tell others . . . other Darkfriends. Once Rand had seen a wolf separate a crippled sheep from the flock; there were other wolves around, and he could neither leave the flock nor get a clear shot with his bow. As soon as the sheep was alone, bleating with terror, hobbling frantically on three legs, the one wolf chasing it became ten as if by magic. The memory of it turned his stomach. They could not stay there, either. Even if Paitr was telling the truth about being alone, how long would he stay that way?

"Time to go, Mat," he said, and held his breath. As Mat started to stand, he pulled Paitr's eyes to himself by leaning forward and saying, "Leave us alone, Darkfriend. I won't tell you again. Leave—us—alone."

Paitr swallowed hard and pressed back in his chair; there was no blood left in his face at all. It made Rand think of a Myrddraal.

By the time he looked back at Mat, Mat was on his feet, his awkwardness unseen. Rand hastily hung his own saddlebags and other bundles around him, trying to keep his cloak over the sword as he did. Maybe Paitr already knew about it; maybe Gode had told Ba'alzamon, and Ba'alzamon had told Paitr; but he did not think so. He thought Paitr had only the vaguest idea of what had happened in Four Kings. That was why he was so frightened.

The comparatively bright outline of the door helped Mat make a beeline for it, if not quickly, then not slow enough to seem unnatural, either. Rand followed closely, praying for him not to stumble. He was thankful Mat had a clear, straight path, with no tables or chairs in the way.

Behind him Paitr suddenly leaped to his feet. "Wait," he said desperately. "You have to wait."

"Leave us alone," Rand said without looking back. They were almost to the door, and Mat had not put a foot wrong yet.

"Just listen to me," Paitr said, and put his hand on Rand's shoulder to stop him.

Images spun in his head. The Trolloc, Narg, leaping at him in his own home. The Myrddraal threatening at the Stag and Lion in Baerlon. Halfmen everywhere, Fades chasing them to Shadar Logoth, coming for them in White-bridge. Darkfriends everywhere. He whirled, his hand balling up. "I said, leave us alone!" His fist took Paitr flush on the nose.

The Darkfriend fell on his bottom and sat there on the floor staring at Rand. Blood trickled from his nose. "You won't get away," he spat angrily. "No matter how strong you are, the Great Lord of the Dark is stronger. The Shadow will swallow you!"

There was a gasp from further into the common room, and the clatter of a broom handle hitting the floor. The old man with the broom had finally heard. He stood staring wide-eyed at Paitr. The blood drained from his wrinkled face and his mouth worked, but no sound came out. Paitr stared back for an instant, then gave a wild curse and sprang to his feet, darting out of the inn and down the street as if starving wolves were at his heels. The old man shifted his attention to Rand and Mat, looking not a whit less frightened.

Rand hustled Mat out of the inn and out of the village as fast as he could, listening all the while for a hue and cry that never came but was no less loud in his ears for that.

"Blood and ashes," Mat growled, "they're always there, always right on our heels. We'll never get away."

"No they're not," Rand said. "If Ba'alzamon knew we were here, do you think he'd have left it to that fellow? There'd have been another Gode, and twenty or thirty bully-boys. They're still hunting, but they won't know until Paitr tells them, and maybe he really is alone. He might have to go all the way to Four Kings, for all we know."

"But he said—"

"I don't care." He was unsure which "he" Mat meant, but it changed nothing. "We're not going to lie down and let them take us."

They got six rides, short ones, during the day. A farmer told them that a crazy old man at the inn in Market Sheran was claiming there were Darkfriends in the village. The farmer could hardly talk for laughing; he kept wiping tears off his cheeks. Darkfriends in Market Sheran! It was the best story he had heard since Ackley Farren got drunk and spent the night on the inn roof.

Another man, a round-faced wagonwright with tools hanging from the sides of his cart and two wagon wheels in the back, told a different story. Twenty Darkfriends had held a gathering in Market Sheran. Men with twisted bodies, and the women worse, all dirty and in rags. They could make your knees grow weak and your stomach heave just by looking at you, and when they laughed, the filthy cackles rang in your ears for hours and your head felt as if it were splitting open. He had seen them himself, just at a distance, far enough off to be safe. If the Queen would not do something, then somebody ought to ask the Children of the Light for help. Somebody should do something.

It was a relief when the wagonwright let them down.

With the sun low behind them they walked into a small village, much like Market Sheran. The Caemlyn Road split the town neatly in two, but on both sides of the wide road stood rows of small brick houses with thatched roofs. Webs of vine covered the bricks, though only a few leaves hung on them. The village had one inn, a small place no bigger than the Winespring Inn, with a sign on a bracket out front, creaking back and forth in the wind. The Queen's Man.

Strange, to think of the Winespring Inn as small. Rand could remember when he thought it was about as big as a building could be. Anything bigger would be a palace. But he had seen a few things, now, and suddenly he realized that nothing would look the same to him when he got back home. *If you ever do.*

He hesitated in front of the inn, but even if prices at The Queen's Man were not as high as in Market Sheran, they could not afford a meal or a room, either one.

Mat saw where he was looking and patted the pocket where he kept Thom's colored balls. "I can see well enough, as long as I don't try to get too fancy." His eyes had been getting better, though he still wore the scarf around his forehead, and had squinted whenever he looked at the sky during the day. When Rand said nothing, Mat went on. "There can't be Darkfriends at every inn between here and Caemlyn. Besides, I don't want to sleep under a bush if I can sleep in a bed." He made no move toward the inn, though, just stood waiting for Rand.

After a moment Rand nodded. He felt as tired as he had at any time since leaving home. Just thinking of a night in the open made his bones ache. *It's all catching up. All the running, all the looking over your shoulder.*

"They can't be everywhere," he agreed.

With the first step he took into the common room, he wondered if he had made a mistake. It was a clean place, but crowded. Every table was filled, and some men leaned against the walls because there was nowhere for them to sit. From the way the serving maids scurried between the tables with harried looks—and the landlord, too—it was a larger crowd than they were used to. Too many for this small village. It was easy to pick out the people who did not belong there. They were dressed no differently from the rest, but they kept their eyes on their food and drink. The locals watched the strangers as much as anything else.

A drone of conversation hung in the air, enough that the innkeeper took them into the kitchen when Rand made him understand that they needed to talk to him. The noise was almost as bad there, with the cook and his helpers banging pots and darting about.

The innkeeper mopped his face with a large handkerchief. "I suppose you're on your way to Caemlyn to see the false Dragon like every other fool in the Realm. Well, it's six to a room and two or three to a bed, and if that doesn't suit, I've nothing for you."

Rand gave his spiel with a feeling of queasiness. With so many people on the road, every other one could be a Darkfriend, and there was no way to pick them out from the rest.

Mat demonstrated his juggling—he kept it to three balls, and was careful even then—and Rand took out Thom's flute. After only a dozen notes of "The Old Black Bear," the innkeeper nodded impatiently.

"You'll do. I need something to take those idiots' minds off this Logain. There's been three fights already over whether or not he's really the Dragon. Stow your things in the corner, and I'll go clear a space for you. If there's any room to. Fools. The world's full of fools who don't know enough to stay where they belong. That's what's causing all the trouble. People who won't stay where they belong." Mopping his face again, he hurried out of the kitchen, muttering under his breath.

The cook and his helpers ignored Rand and Mat. Mat kept adjusting the scarf around his head, pushing it up, then blinking at the light and tugging it back down again. Rand wondered if he could see well enough to do anything more complicated than juggle three balls. As for himself. . . .

The queasiness in his stomach grew thicker. He dropped on a low stool, holding his head in his hands. The kitchen felt cold. He shivered. Steam filled the air; stoves and ovens crackled with heat. His shivers became stronger, his teeth chattering. He wrapped his arms around himself, but it did no good. His bones felt as if they were freezing.

Dimly he was aware of Mat asking him something, shaking his shoulder, and of someone cursing and running out of the room. Then the innkeeper was there, with the cook frowning at his side, and Mat was arguing loudly with them both. He could not make out any of what they said; the words were a buzz in his ears, and he could not seem to think at all.

Suddenly Mat took his arm, pulling him to his feet. All of their things—saddlebags, blanketrolls, Thom's bundled cloak and instrument cases—hung from Mat's shoulders with his bow. The innkeeper was watching them, wiping his face anxiously. Weaving, more than half supported by Mat, Rand let his friend steer him toward the back door.

"S-s-sorry, M-m-mat," he managed. He could not stop his teeth from chattering. "M-m-must have . . . b-been t-the . . . rain. O-one m-more . . . night out . . . w-won't h-hurt . . . I guess." Twilight darkened the sky, spotted by a handful of stars.

"Not a bit of it," Mat said. He was trying to sound cheerful, but Rand could hear the hidden worry. "He was scared the other folk would find out there was somebody sick in his inn. I told him if he kicked us out, I'd take you into the common room. That'd empty half his rooms in ten minutes. For all his talk about fools, he doesn't want that."

"Then w-where?"

"Here," Mat said, pulling open the stable door with a loud creak of hinges.

It was darker inside than out, and the air smelled of hay and grain and horses, with a strong undersmell of manure. When Mat lowered him to the straw-covered floor, he folded over with his chest on his knees, still hugging himself and shaking from head to toe. All of his strength seemed to go for the shaking. He heard Mat stumble and curse and stumble again, then a clatter of metal. Suddenly light blossomed. Mat held up a battered old lantern.

If the inn was full, so was its stable. Every stall had a horse, some raising their heads and blinking at the light. Mat eyed the ladder to the hayloft, then looked at Rand, crouched on the floor, and shook his head.

"Never get you up there," Mat muttered. Hanging the lantern on a nail, he scrambled up the ladder and began tossing down armloads of hay. Hurriedly climbing back down, he made a bed at the back of the stable and got Rand onto it. Mat covered him with both their cloaks, but Rand pushed them off almost immediately.

"Hot," he murmured. Vaguely he knew that he had been cold only a moment before, but now he felt as if he were in an oven. He tugged at his collar, tossing his head. "Hot." He felt Mat's hand on his forehead.

"I'll be right back," Mat said, and disappeared.

He twisted fitfully on the hay, how long he was not sure, until Mat returned with a heaped plate in one hand, a pitcher in the other, and two white cups dangling from fingers by their handles.

"There's no Wisdom here," he said, dropping to his knees beside Rand. He filled one of the cups and held it to Rand's mouth. Rand gulped the water down as if he had had nothing to drink in days; that was how he felt. "They don't even know what a Wisdom is. What they do have is somebody called Mother Brune, but she's off somewhere birthing a baby, and nobody knows when she'll be back. I did get some bread, and cheese, and sausage. Good Master Inlow will give us anything as long as we stay out of sight of his guests. Here, try some."

Rand turned his head away from the food. The sight of it, the thought of it, made his stomach heave. After a minute Mat sighed and settled down to eat himself. Rand kept his eyes averted, and tried not to listen.

The chills came once more, and then the fever, to be replaced by the chills, and the fever again. Mat covered him when he shook, and fed him water when he complained of thirst. The night deepened, and the stable shifted in the flickering lantern light. Shadows took shape and moved on their own. Then he saw Ba'alzamon striding down the stable, eyes burning, a Myrddraal at either side with faces hidden in the depths of their black cowls.

Fingers scrabbling for his sword hilt, he tried to get to his feet, yelling, "Mat! Mat, they're here! Light, they're here!"

Mat jerked awake where he sat cross-legged against the wall. "What? Darkfriends? Where?"

Wavering on his knees, Rand pointed frantically down the stable . . . and gaped. Shadows stirred, and a horse stamped in its sleep. Nothing more. He fell back on the straw.

"There's nobody but us," Mat said. "Here, let me take that." He reached for Rand's sword belt, but Rand tightened his grip on the hilt.

"No. No. I have to keep it. He's my father. You understand? He's m-my f-father!" The shivering swept over him once more, but he clung to the sword as if to a lifeline. "M-my f-father!" Mat gave up trying to take it and pulled the cloaks back over him.

There were other visitations in the night, while Mat dozed. Rand was never sure if they were really there or not. Sometimes he looked at Mat, with his head on his chest, wondering if he would see them, too, if he woke.

Egwene stepped out of the shadows, her hair in a long, dark braid as it had been in Emond's Field, her face pained and mournful. "Why did you leave us?" she asked. "We're dead because you left us."

Rand shook his head weakly on the hay. "No, Egwene. I didn't want to leave you. Please."

"We're all dead," she said sadly, "and death is the king-dom of the Dark One. The Dark One has us, because you abandoned us."

"No. I had no choice, Egwene. Please. Egwene, don't go. Come back, Egwene!"

But she turned into the shadows, and was shadow.

Moiraine's expression was serene, but her face was blood-less and pale. Her cloak might as well have been a shroud, and her voice was a lash. "That is right, Rand al'Thor. You have no choice. You must go to Tar Valon, or the Dark One will take you for his own. Eternity chained in the Shadow. Only Aes Sedai can save you, now. Only Aes Sedai."

Thom grinned at him sardonically. The gleeman's clothes hung in charred rags that made him see the flashes of light as Thom wrestled with the Fade to give them time to run. The flesh under the rags was blackened and burned. "Trust Aes Sedai, boy, and you'll wish you were dead. Remember, the price of Aes Sedai help is always smaller than you can believe, always greater than you can imagine. And what Ajah will find you first, eh? Red? Maybe Black. Best to run, boy. Run."

Lan's stare was as hard as granite, and blood covered his face. "Strange to see a heron-mark blade in the hands of a sheepherder. Are you worthy of it? You had better be. You're alone, now. Nothing to hold to behind you, and noth-ing before, and anyone can be a Darkfriend." He smiled a wolf's smile, and blood poured but of his mouth. "Anyone."

Perrin came, accusing, pleading for help. Mistress al'Vere, weeping for her daughter, and Bayle Domon, cursing him for bringing Fades down on his vessel, and Master Fitch, wringing his hands over the ashes of his inn, and Min, screaming in a Trolloc's clutches, people he knew, people he had only met. But the worst was Tam. Tam stood over him, frowning and shaking his head, and said not a word.

"You have to tell me," Rand begged him. "Who am I? Tell me, please. Who am I? *Who am I?*" he shouted.

"Easy, Rand."

For a moment he thought it was Tam answering, but then he saw that Tam was gone. Mat bent over him, holding a cup of water to his lips.

"Just rest easy. You're Rand al'Thor, that's who you are,

with the ugliest face and the thickest head in the Two Rivers. Hey, you're sweating! The fever's broken."

"Rand al'Thor?" Rand whispered. Mat nodded, and there was something so comforting in it that Rand drifted off to sleep without even touching the water.

It was a sleep untroubled by dreams—at least by any he remembered—but light enough that his eyes drifted open whenever Mat checked on him. Once he wondered if Mat was getting any sleep at all, but he fell back asleep himself before the thought got very far.

The squeal of the door hinges roused him fully, but for a moment he only lay there in the hay wishing he was still asleep. Asleep he would not be aware of his body. His muscles ached like wrung-out rags, and had about as much strength. Weakly he tried to raise his head; he made it on the second try.

Mat sat in his accustomed place against the wall, within arm's reach of Rand. His chin rested on his chest, which rose and fell in the easy rhythm of deep sleep. The scarf had slipped down over his eyes.

Rand looked toward the door.

A woman stood there holding it open with one hand. For a moment she was only a dark shape in a dress, outlined by the faint light of early morning, then she stepped inside, letting the door swing shut behind her. In the lantern light he could see her more clearly. She was about the same age as Nynaeve, he thought, but she was no village woman. The pale green silk of her dress shimmered as she moved. Her cloak was a rich, soft gray, and a frothy net of lace caught up her hair. She fingered a heavy gold necklace as she looked thoughtfully at Mat and him.

"Mat," Rand said, then louder, "Mat!"

Mat snorted and almost fell over as he came awake. Scrubbing sleep from his eyes, he stared at the woman.

"I came to look at my horse," she said, gesturing vaguely at the stalls. She never took her eyes away from the two of them, though. "Are you ill?"

"He's all right," Mat said stiffly. "He just caught a chill in the rain, that's all."

"Perhaps I should look at him," she said. "I have some knowledge. . . ."

Rand wondered if she were Aes Sedai. Even more than her clothes, her self-assured manner, the way she held her head as if on the point of giving a command, did not belong here. *And if she is Aes Sedai, of what Ajah?*

"I'm fine, now," he told her. "Really, there's no need."

But she came down the length of the stable, holding her skirt up and placing her gray slippers gingerly. With a grimace for the straw, she knelt beside him and felt his forehead.

"No fever," she said, studying him with a frown. She was pretty, in a sharp-featured fashion, but there was no warmth in her face. It was not cold, either; it just seemed to lack any feeling whatsoever. "You *were* sick, though. Yes. Yes. And still weak as a day-old kitten. I think. . . ." She reached under her cloak, and suddenly things were happening too fast for Rand to do more than give a strangled shout.

Her hand flashed from under her cloak; something glittered as she lunged across Rand toward Mat. Mat toppled sideways in a flurry of motion, and there was a solid *tchunk* of metal driven into wood. It all took just an instant, and then everything was still.

Mat lay half on his back, one hand gripping her wrist just above the dagger she had driven into the wall where his chest had been, his other hand holding the blade from Shadar Logoth to her throat.

Moving nothing but her eyes, she tried to look down at the dagger Mat held. Eyes widening, she drew a ragged breath and tried to pull back from it, but he kept the edge against her skin. After that, she was as still as a stone.

Licking his lips, Rand stared at the tableau above him. Even if he had not been so weak, he did not believe he could have moved. Then his eyes fell on her dagger, and his mouth went dry. The wood around the blade was blackening; thin tendrils of smoke rose from the char.

"Mat! Mat, her dagger!"

Mat flicked a glance at the dagger, then back to the woman, but she had not moved. She was licking *her* lips nervously. Roughly Mat pried her hand off the hilt and gave her a push; she toppled back, sprawling away from them and catching herself with her hands behind her, still watching the blade in his hand. "Don't move," he said. "I'll use this if you move. Believe me, I will." She nodded slowly; her eyes never left Mat's dagger. "Watch her, Rand."

Rand was not sure what he was supposed to do if she tried anything—shout, maybe; he certainly could not run after her if she tried to flee—but she sat there without twitching while Mat yanked her dagger free of the wall. The black spot stopped growing, though a faint wisp of smoke still trailed up from it.

Mat looked around for somewhere to put the dagger, then thrust it toward Rand. He took it gingerly, as if it were a live adder. It looked ordinary, if ornate, with a pale ivory hilt and a narrow, gleaming blade no longer than the palm of his hand. Just a dagger. Only he had seen what it could do. The hilt was not even warm, but his hand began to sweat. He hoped he did not drop it in the hay.

The woman did not move from her sprawl as she watched Mat slowly turn toward her. She watched him as if wondering what he would do next, but Rand saw the sudden tightening of Mat's eyes, the tightening of his hand on the dagger. "Mat, no!"

"She tried to kill me, Rand. She'd have killed you, too. She's a Darkfriend." Mat spat the word.

"But we're not," Rand said. The woman gasped as if she had just realized what Mat had intended. "We are not, Mat."

For a moment Mat remained frozen, the blade in his fist catching the lantern light. Then he nodded. "Move over there," he told the woman, gesturing with the dagger toward the door to the tack room.

She got to her feet slowly, pausing to brush the straw from her dress. Even when she started in the direction Mat indicated, she moved as if there were no reason to hurry. But Rand noticed that she kept a wary eye on the ruby-hilted dagger in Mat's hand. "You really should stop struggling," she said. "It would be for the best, in the end. You will see."

"The best?" Mat said wryly, rubbing his chest where her blade would have gone if he had not moved. "Get over there."

She gave a casual shrug as she obeyed. "A mistake. There has been considerable . . . confusion since what happened with that egotistical fool Gode. Not to mention whoever the idiot was who started the panic in Market Sheran. No one is sure what happened there, or how. That makes it more dangerous for you, don't you see? You will have honored places if you come to the Great Lord of your own free will, but as long as you run, there will be pursuit, and who can tell what will happen then?"

Rand felt a chill. *My hounds are jealous, and may not be gentle.*

"So you're having trouble with a couple of farmboys." Mat's laugh was grim. "Maybe you Darkfriends aren't as dangerous as I've always heard." He flung open the door of the tack room and stepped back.

She paused just through the doorway, looking at him over her shoulder. Her gaze was ice, and her voice colder still. "You will find out how dangerous we are. When the Myrddraal gets here—"

Whatever else she had to say was cut off as Mat slammed the door and pulled the bar down into its brackets. When he turned, his eyes were worried. "Fade," he said in a tight voice, tucking the dagger back under his coat. "Coming here, she says. How are your legs?"

"I can't dance," Rand muttered, "but if you'll help me get on my feet, I can walk." He looked at the blade in his hand and shuddered. "Blood and ashes, I'll run."

Hurriedly hanging himself about with their possessions, Mat pulled Rand to his feet. Rand's legs wobbled, and he had to lean on his friend to stay upright, but he tried not to slow Mat down. He held the woman's dagger well away from himself. Outside the door was a bucket of water. He tossed the dagger into it as they passed. The blade entered the water with a hiss; steam rose from the surface. Grimacing, he tried to take faster steps.

With light come, there were plenty of people in the streets, even so early. They were about their own business, though, and no one had any attention to spare for two young men walking out of the village, not with so many strangers about. Just the same, Rand stiffened every muscle, trying to stand straight. With each step he wondered if any of the folk hurrying by were Darkfriends. *Are any of them waiting for the woman with the dagger? For the Fade?*

A mile outside the village his strength gave out. One minute he was panting along, hanging on Mat; the next they were both on the ground. Mat tugged him over to the side of the road.

"We have to keep going," Mat said. He scrubbed his hand through his hair, then tugged the scarf down above his eyes.

"Sooner or later, somebody will let her out, and they'll be after us again."

"I know," Rand panted. "I know. Give me a hand."

Mat pulled him up again, but he wavered there, knowing it was no good. The first time he tried to take a step, he would be flat on his face again.

Holding him upright, Mat waited impatiently for a horse-cart, approaching from the village, to pass them. Mat gave a grunt of surprise when the cart slowed to a stop before them. A leathery-faced man looked down from the driver's seat.

"Something wrong with him?" the man asked around his pipe.

"He's just tired," Mat said.

Rand could see that was not going to do, not leaning on Mat the way he was. He let go of Mat and took a step away from him. His legs quivered, but he willed himself to stay erect. "I haven't slept in two days," he said. "Ate something that made me sick. I'm better, now, but I haven't slept."

The man blew a streamer of smoke from the corner of his mouth. "Going to Caemlyn, are you? Was your age, I expect I might be off to see this false Dragon myself."

"Yes." Mat nodded. "That's right. We're going to see the false Dragon."

"Well, climb on up, then. Your friend in the back. If he's sick again, best it's on the straw, not up here. Name's Hyam Kinch."

CHAPTER
34

The Last Village

It was after dark when they reached Carysford, longer than Rand had thought it would take from what Master Kinch said when he let them down. He wondered if his whole sense of time was getting skewed. Only three nights since Howal Gode and Four Kings, two since Paitr had surprised them in Market Sheran. Just a bare day since the nameless Darkfriend woman tried to kill them in the stable of The Queen's Man, but even that seemed a year ago, or a lifetime.

Whatever was happening to time, Carysford appeared normal enough, on the surface, at least. Neat, vine-covered brick houses and narrow lanes, except for the Caemlyn Road itself, quiet and outwardly peaceful. *But what's underneath?* he wondered. Market Sheran had been peaceful to look at, and so had the village where the woman. . . . He had never learned the name of that one, and he did not want to think about it.

Light spilled from the windows of the houses into streets all but empty of people. That suited Rand. Slinking from corner to corner, he avoided the few people abroad. Mat stuck to his shoulder, freezing when the crunch of gravel announced the approach of a villager, dodging from shadow to shadow when the dim shape had gone past.

The River Cary was a bare thirty paces wide there, and the black water moved sluggishly, but the ford had long since been bridged over. Centuries of rain and wind had worn the stone abutments until they seemed almost like natural formations. Years of freight wagons and merchant trains had ground at the thick wooden planks, too. Loose boards rattled under their boots, sounding as loud as drums. Until long after they were through the village and into the countryside beyond, Rand waited for a voice to demand to know who they were. Or worse, knowing who they were.

The countryside had been filling up the further they went, becoming more and more settled. There were always the lights of farmhouses in sight. Hedges and rail fences lined the road and the fields beyond. Always the fields were there, and never a stretch of woods close to the road. It seemed as if they were always on the outskirts of a village, even when they were hours from the nearest town. Neat and peaceful. And with never an indication that Darkfriends or worse might be lurking.

Abruptly Mat sat down in the road. He had pushed the scarf up on top of his head, now that the only light came from the moon. "Two paces to the span," he muttered. "A thousand spans to the mile, four miles to the league. . . . I'm not walking another ten paces unless there's a place to sleep at the end of it. Something to eat wouldn't be amiss, either. You haven't been hiding anything in your pockets, have you? An apple, maybe? I won't hold it against you if you have. You could at least look."

Rand peered down the road both ways. They were the only things moving in the night. Or they had been. He glanced at Mat, who had pulled off one boot and was rubbing his foot. His own feet hurt, too. A tremor ran up his legs as if to tell him he had not yet regained as much strength as he thought.

Dark mounds stood in a field just ahead of them. Haystacks, diminished by winter feeding, but still haystacks.

He nudged Mat with his toe. "We'll sleep there."

"Haystacks again." Mat sighed, but he tugged on his boot and got up.

The wind was rising, the night chill growing deeper. They climbed over the smooth poles of the fence and quickly were burrowing into the hay. The tarp that kept the rain off the hay cut the wind, too.

Rand twisted around in the hollow he had made until he found a comfortable position. Hay still managed to poke at him through his clothes, but he had learned to put up with that. He tried counting the haystacks he had slept in since Whitebridge. Heroes in the stories never had to sleep in haystacks, or under hedges. But it was not easy to pretend, anymore, that he was a hero in a story, even for a little while. With a sigh, he pulled his collar up in the hopes of keeping hay from getting down his back.

"Rand?" Mat said softly. "Rand, do you think we'll make it?"

"Tar Valon? It's a long way yet, but—"

"Caemlyn. Do you think we'll make it to Caemlyn?"

Rand raised his head, but it was dark in their burrow; the only thing that told him where Mat was was his voice. "Master Kinch said two days. Day after tomorrow, the next day, we'll get there."

"If there aren't a hundred Darkfriends waiting for us down the road, or a Fade or two." There was silence for a moment, then Mat said, "I think we're the last ones left, Rand." He sounded frightened. "Whatever it's all about, it's just us two, now. Just us."

Rand shook his head. He knew Mat could not see in the darkness, but it was more for himself than Mat, anyway. "Go to sleep, Mat," he said tiredly. But he lay awake a long time himself, before sleep came. *Just us.*

A cock's crow woke him, and he scrambled out into the false dawn, brushing hay off his clothes. Despite his precautions some had worked its way down his back; the straws clung between his shoulder blades, itching. He took off his coat and pulled his shirt out of his breeches to get to it. It was while he had one hand down the back of his neck and the other twisted up behind him that he became aware of the people.

The sun was not yet truly up, but already a steady trickle moved down the road in ones and twos, trudging toward Caemlyn, some with packs or bundles on their backs, others with nothing but a walking staff, if that. Most were young men, but here and there was a girl, or someone older. One and all they had the travel-stained look of having walked a long way. Some had their eyes on their feet and a weary slump to their shoulders, early as it was; others had their gaze fixed on something out of sight ahead, something toward the dawn.

Mat rolled out of the haystack, scratching vigorously. He only paused long enough to wrap the scarf around his head;

it shaded his eyes a little less this morning. "You think we might get something to eat today?"

Rand's stomach rumbled in sympathy. "We can think about that when we're on the road," he said. Hastily arranging his clothes, he dug his share of their bundles out of the haystack.

By the time they reached the fence, Mat had noticed the people, too. He frowned, stopping in the field while Rand climbed over. A young man, not much older than they, glanced at them as he passed. His clothes were dusty, and so was the blanketroll strapped across his back.

"Where are you bound?" Mat called.

"Why, Caemlyn, for to see the Dragon," the fellow shouted back without stopping. He raised an eyebrow at the blankets and saddlebags hanging from their shoulders, and added, "Just like you." With a laugh he went on, his eyes already seeking eagerly ahead.

Mat asked the same question several times during the day, and the only people who did not give much the same answer were local folk. If those answered at all, it was by spitting and turning away in disgust. They turned away, but they kept a watchful eye, too. They looked at all the travelers the same way, out of the corners of their eyes. Their faces said strangers might get up to anything if not watched.

People who lived in the area were not only wary of the strangers, they seemed more than a little put out. Just enough people were on the road, scattered out just enough, that when farmers' carts and wagons appeared with the sun peeking over the horizon, even their usually slow pace was halved. None of them was in any mood to give a ride. A sour grimace, and maybe a curse for the work they were missing, were more likely.

The merchants' wagons rolled by with little hindrance beyond shaken fists, whether they were going toward Caemlyn or away from it. When the first merchants' train appeared, early on in the morning, coming at a stiff trot with the sun barely above the horizon behind the wagons, Rand stepped out of the road. They gave no sign of slowing for anything, and he saw other folk scrambling out of the way. He moved all the way over onto the verge, but kept walking.

A flicker of motion as the first wagon rumbled close was

all the warning he had. He went sprawling on the ground as the wagon driver's whip cracked in the air where his head had been. From where he lay he met the driver's eyes as the wagon rolled by. Hard eyes above a mouth in a tight grimace. Not a care that he might have drawn blood, or taken an eye.

"Light blind you!" Mat shouted after the wagon. "You can't—" A mounted guard caught him on the shoulder with the butt of his spear, knocking him down atop Rand.

"Out of the way, you dirty Darkfriend!" the guard growled without slowing.

After that, they kept their distance from the wagons. There were certainly enough of them. The rattle and clatter of one hardly faded before another could be heard coming. Guards and drivers, they all stared at the travelers heading for Caemlyn as if seeing dirt walk.

Once Rand misjudged a driver's whip, just by the length of the tip. Clapping his hand to the shallow gash over his eyebrow, he swallowed hard to keep from vomiting at how close it had come to his eye. The driver smirked at him. With his other hand he grabbed Mat, to stop him nocking an arrow.

"Let it go," he said. He jerked his head at the guards riding alongside the wagons. Some of them were laughing; others gave Mat's bow a hard eye. "If we're lucky, they'd just beat us with their spears. If we're lucky."

Mat grunted sourly, but he let Rand pull him on down the road.

Twice squadrons of the Queen's Guards came trotting down the road, streamers on their lances fluttering in the wind. Some of the farmers hailed them, wanting something done about the strangers, and the Guards always paused patiently to listen. Near midday Rand stopped to listen to one such conversation.

Behind the bars of his helmet, the Guard captain's mouth was a tight line. "If one of them steals something, or trespasses on your land," he growled at the lanky farmer frowning beside his stirrup, "I'll haul him before a magistrate, but they break no Queen's Law by walking on the Queen's Highway."

"But they're all over the place," the farmer protested. "Who knows who they are, or what they are. All this talk about the Dragon. . . ."

"Light, man! You only have a handful here. Caemlyn's walls are bulging with them, and more coming every day." The captain's scowl deepened as he caught sight of Rand and Mat, standing in the road nearby. He gestured down the road with a steel-backed gauntlet. "Get on with you, or I'll have you in for blocking traffic."

His voice was no rougher with them than with the farmer, but they moved on. The captain's eyes followed them for a time; Rand could feel them on his back. He suspected the Guards had little patience left with the wanderers, and no sympathy for a hungry thief. He decided to stop Mat if he suggested stealing eggs again.

Still, there was a good side to all the wagons and people on the road, especially all the young men heading for Caemlyn. For any Darkfriends hunting them, it would be like trying to pick out two particular pigeons in a flock. If the Myrddraal on Winternight had not known exactly who it was after, maybe its fellow would do no better here.

His stomach rumbled frequently, reminding him that they had next to no money left, certainly not enough for a meal at the prices charged this close to Caemlyn. He realized once he had a hand on the flute case, and firmly pushed it around to his back. Gode had known all about the flute, and the juggling. There was no telling how much Ba'alzamon had learned from him before the end—if what Rand had seen had *been* the end—or how much had been passed to other Darkfriends.

He looked regretfully at a farm they were passing. A man patrolled the fences with a pair of dogs, growling and tugging at their leashes. The man looked as if he wanted nothing more than an excuse to let them loose. Not every farm had the dogs out, but no one was offering jobs to travelers.

Before the sun went down, he and Mat walked through two more villages. The village folk stood in knots, talking among themselves and watching the steady stream pass by. Their faces were no friendlier than the faces of the farmers, or the wagon drivers, or the Queen's Guards. All these strangers going to see the false Dragon. Fools who did not know enough to stay where they belonged. Maybe followers of the false Dragon. Maybe even Darkfriends. If there was any difference between the two.

With evening coming, the stream began to thin at the

second town. The few who had money disappeared into the
inn, though there seemed to be some argument about letting them inside; others began hunting for handy hedges or
fields with no dogs. By dusk he and Mat had the Caemlyn
Road to themselves. Mat began talking about finding another haystack, but Rand insisted on keeping on.

"As long as we can see the road," he said. "The further
we go before stopping, the further ahead we are." *If they
are chasing you. Why should they chase now, when they've
been waiting for you to come to them so far?*

It was argument enough for Mat. With frequent glances
over his shoulder, he quickened his step. Rand had to hurry
to keep up.

The night thickened, relieved only a bit by scant moonlight. Mat's burst of energy faded, and his complaints
started up again. Aching knots formed in Rand's calves. He
told himself he had walked further in a hard day working
on the farm with Tam, but repeat it as often as he would,
he could not make himself believe it. Gritting his teeth, he
ignored the aches and pains and would not stop.

With Mat complaining and him concentrating on the
next step, they were almost on the village before he saw the
lights. He tottered to a stop, suddenly aware of a burning
that ran from his feet right up his legs. He thought he had a
blister on his right foot.

At the sight of the village lights, Mat sagged to his knees
with a groan. "Can we stop now?" he panted. "Or do you
want to find an inn and hang out a sign for the Darkfriends?
Or a Fade."

"The other side of the town," Rand answered, staring
at the lights. From this distance, in the dark, it could have
been Emond's Field. *What's waiting there?* "Another mile,
that's all."

"All! I'm not walking another span!"

Rand's legs felt like fire, but he made himself take a step,
and then another. It did not get any easier, but he kept on,
one step at a time. Before he had gone ten paces he heard
Mat staggering after him, muttering under his breath. He
thought it was just as well he could not make out what Mat
was saying.

It was late enough for the streets of the village to be empty,
though most houses had a light in at least one window. The

inn in the middle of town was brightly lit, surrounded by a golden pool that pushed back the darkness. Music and laughter, dimmed by thick walls, drifted from the building. The sign over the door creaked in the wind. At the near end of the inn, a cart and horse stood in the Caemlyn Road with a man checking the harness. Two men stood at the far end of the building, on the very edge of the light.

Rand stopped in the shadows beside a house that stood dark. He was too tired to hunt through the lanes for a way around. A minute resting could not hurt. Just a minute. Just until the men went away. Mat slumped against the wall with a grateful sigh, leaning back as if he meant to go to sleep right there.

Something about the two men at the rim of the shadows made Rand uneasy. He could not put a finger on anything, at first, but he realized the man at the cart felt the same way about them. He reached the end of the strap he was checking, adjusted the bit in the horse's mouth, then went back and started over from the beginning again. He kept his head down the whole while, his eyes on what he was doing and away from the other men. It could have been that he simply was not aware of them, though they were less than fifty feet off, except for the stiff way he moved and the way he sometimes turned awkwardly in what he was doing so he would not be looking toward them.

One of the men in the shadows was only a black shape, but the other stood more into the light, with his back to Rand. Even so it was plain he was not overjoyed at the conversation he was having. He wrung his hands and kept his eyes on the ground, jerking his head in a nod now and then at something the other had said. Rand could not hear anything, but he got the impression that the man in the shadows was doing all the talking; the nervous man just listened, and nodded, and wrung his hands anxiously.

Eventually the one who was wrapped in darkness turned away, and the nervous fellow started back into the light. Despite the chill he was mopping his face with the long apron he wore, as if he were drenched in sweat.

Skin prickling, Rand watched the shape moving off in the night. He did not know why, but his uneasiness seemed to follow that one, a vague tingling in the back of his neck and the hair stirring on his arms as if he had suddenly

realized something was sneaking up on him. With a quick
shake of his head, he rubbed his arms briskly. *Getting as
foolish as Mat, aren't you?*

At that moment the form slipped by the edge of the light
from a window—just on the brink of it—and Rand's skin
crawled. The inn's sign went *scree-scree-scree* in the wind,
but the dark cloak never stirred.

"Fade," he whispered, and Mat jerked to his feet as if he
had shouted.

"What—?"

He clamped a hand over Mat's mouth. "Softly." The dark
shape was lost in the darkness. *Where?* "It's gone, now. I
think. I hope." He took his hand away; the only sound Mat
made was a long, indrawn breath.

The nervous man was almost to the inn door. He stopped
and smoothed down his apron, visibly composing himself
before he went inside.

"Strange friends you've got, Raimun Holdwin," the man by
the cart said suddenly. It was an old man's voice, but strong.
The speaker straightened, shaking his head. "Strange friends
in the dark for an innkeeper."

The nervous man jumped when the other spoke, looking
around as if he had not seen the cart and the other man until right then. He drew a deep breath and gathered himself,
then asked sharply, "And what do you mean by that, Almen
Bunt?"

"Just what I said, Holdwin. Strange friends. He's not from
around here, is he? Lot of odd folk coming through the last
few weeks. Awful lot of odd folk."

"You're a fine one to talk." Holdwin cocked an eye at
the man by the cart. "I know a lot of men, even men from
Caemlyn. Not like you, cooped up alone out on that farm of
yours." He paused, then went on as if he thought he had to
explain further. "He's from Four Kings. Looking for a couple of thieves. Young men. They stole a heron-mark sword
from him."

Rand's breath had caught at the mention of Four Kings;
at the mention of the sword he glanced at Mat. His friend
had his back pressed hard against the wall and was staring
into the darkness with eyes so wide they seemed to be all
whites. Rand wanted to stare into the night, too—the Half-

man could be anywhere—but his eyes went back to the two men in front of the inn.

"A heron-mark sword!" Bunt exclaimed. "No wonder he wants it back."

Holdwin nodded. "Yes, and them, too. My friend's a rich man, a . . . a merchant, and they've been stirring up trouble with the men who work for him. Telling wild stories and getting people upset. They're Darkfriends, and followers of Logain, too."

"Darkfriends *and* followers of the false Dragon? And telling wild stories, too? Getting up to a lot for young fellows. You did say they were young?" There was a sudden note of amusement in Bunt's voice, but the innkeeper did not seem to notice.

"Yes. Not yet twenty. There's a reward—a hundred crowns in gold—for the two of them." Holdwin hesitated, then added, "They've sly tongues, these two. The Light knows what kind of tales they'll tell, trying to turn people against one another. And dangerous, too, even if they don't look it. Vicious. Best you stay clear if you think you see them. Two young men, one with a sword, and both looking over their shoulders. If they're the right ones, my . . . my friend will pick them up once they're located."

"You sound almost as if you know them to look at."

"I'll know them when I see them," Holdwin said confidently. "Just don't try to take them yourself. No need for anyone to get hurt. Come tell me if you see them. My . . . friend will deal with them. A hundred crowns for the two, but he wants the pair."

"A hundred crowns for the two," Bunt mused. "How much for this sword he wants so bad?"

Abruptly Holdwin appeared to realize the other man was making fun of him. "I don't know why I'm telling you," he snapped. "You're still fixed on that fool plan of yours, I see."

"Not such a fool plan," Bunt replied placidly. "There might not be another false Dragon to see before I die—Light send it so!—and I'm too old to eat some merchant's dust all the way to Caemlyn. I'll have the road to myself, and I'll be in Caemlyn bright and early tomorrow."

"To yourself?" The innkeeper's voice had a nasty quiver.

"You can never tell what might be out in the night, Almen Bunt. All alone on the road, in the dark. Even if somebody hears you scream, there's no one will unbar a door to help. Not these days, Bunt. Not your nearest neighbor."

None of that seemed to ruffle the old farmer at all; he answered as calmly as before. "If the Queen's Guards can't keep the road safe this close to Caemlyn, then we're none of us safe even in our own beds. If you ask me, one thing the Guards could do to make sure the roads are safe would be clap that friend of yours in irons. Sneaking around in the dark, afraid to let anybody get a look at him. Can't tell me he's not up to no good."

"Afraid!" Holdwin exclaimed. "You old fool, if you knew—" His teeth clicked shut abruptly, and he gave himself a shake. "I don't know why I'm wasting time on you. Get off with you! Stop cluttering up the front of my place of business." The door of the inn boomed shut behind him.

Muttering to himself, Bunt took hold of the edge of the cart seat and set his foot on the wheelhub.

Rand hesitated only a moment. Mat caught his arm as he started forward.

"Are you crazy, Rand? He'll recognize us for sure!"

"You'd rather stay here? With a Fade around? How far do you think we'll get on foot before it finds us?" He tried not to think of how far they would get in a cart if it found them. He shook free of Mat and trotted up the road. He carefully held his cloak shut so the sword was hidden; the wind and the cold were excuse enough for that.

"I couldn't help overhearing you're going to Caemlyn," he said.

Bunt gave a start, jerking a quarterstaff out of the cart. His leathery face was a mass of wrinkles and half his teeth were gone, but his gnarled hands held the staff steady. After a minute he lowered one end of the staff to the ground and leaned on it. "So you two are going to Caemlyn. To see the Dragon, eh?"

Rand had not realized that Mat had followed him. Mat was keeping well back, though, out of the light, watching the inn and the old farmer with as much suspicion as he was the night.

"The false Dragon," Rand said with emphasis.

Bunt nodded. "Of course. Of course." He threw a sideways look at the inn, then abruptly shoved his staff back under the cart seat. "Well, if you want a ride, get in. I've wasted enough time." He was already climbing to the seat.

Rand clambered over the back as the farmer flicked the reins. Mat ran to catch up as the cart started off. Rand caught his arms and pulled him aboard.

The village faded quickly into the night at the pace Bunt set. Rand lay back on the bare boards, fighting the lulling creak of the wheels. Mat stifled his yawns with a fist, warily staring into the countryside. Darkness weighed heavily on the fields and farms, dotted with the lights of farmhouses. The lights seemed distant, seemed to struggle vainly against the night. An owl called, a mourner's cry, and the wind moaned like lost souls in the Shadow.

It could be out there anywhere, Rand thought.

Bunt seemed to feel the oppression of the night, too, for he suddenly spoke up. "You two ever been to Caemlyn before?" He gave a little chuckle. "Don't suppose you have. Well, wait till you see it. The greatest city in the world. Oh, I've heard all about Illian and Ebou Dar and Tear and all— there's always some fool thinks a thing is bigger and better just because it's off somewheres over the horizon—but for my money, Caemlyn is the grandest there is. Couldn't be grander. No, it couldn't. Unless maybe Queen Morgase, the Light illumine her, got rid of that witch from Tar Valon."

Rand was lying back with his head pillowed on his blanketroll atop the bundle of Thom's cloak, watching the night drift by, letting the farmer's words wash by him. A human voice kept the darkness at bay and muted the mournful wind. He twisted around to look up at the dark mass of Bunt's back. "You mean an Aes Sedai?"

"What else would I mean? Sitting there in the Palace like a spider. I'm a good Queen's man—never say I'm not— but it just isn't right. I'm not one of those saying Elaida's got too much influence over the Queen. Not me. And as for the fools who claim Elaida's really the queen in all but name. . . ." He spat into the night. "That for them. Morgase is no puppet to dance for any Tar Valon witch."

Another Aes Sedai. If . . . when Moiraine got to Caemlyn, she might well go to a sister Aes Sedai. If the worst happened, this Elaida might help them reach Tar Valon. He looked at Mat, and just as if he had spoken aloud Mat shook his head. He could not see Mat's face, but he knew it was fixed in denial.

Bunt went right on talking, flicking the reins whenever his horse slowed but otherwise letting his hands rest on his knees. "I'm a good Queen's man, like I said, but even fools say something worthwhile now and again. Even a blind pig finds an acorn sometimes. There's got to be some changes. This weather, the crops failing, cows drying up, calves and lambs born dead, or with two heads. Bloody ravens don't even wait for things to die. People are scared. They want somebody to blame. Dragon's Fang turning up on people's doors. Things creeping about in the night. Barns getting burned. Fellows around like that friend of Holdwin, scaring people. The Queen's got to do something before it's too late. You see that, don't you?" Rand made a noncommittal sound. It sounded as if they had been even luckier than he had thought to find this old man and his cart. They might not have gotten further than that last village if they had waited for daylight. Things creeping about in the night. He lifted up to look over the side of the cart at the darkness. Shadows and shapes seemed to writhe in the black. He dropped back before his imagination convinced him there was something there.

Bunt took it for agreement. "Right. I'm a good Queen's man, and I'll stand against any who try to harm her, but I'm right. You take the Lady Elayne and the Lord Gawyn, now. There's a change wouldn't harm anything, and might do some good. Sure, I know we've always done it that way in Andor. Send the Daughter-Heir off to Tar Valon to study with the Aes Sedai, and the eldest son off to study with the Warders. I believe in tradition, I do, but look what it got us last time. Luc dead in the Blight before he was ever anointed First Prince of the Sword, and Tigraine vanished—run off or dead—when it came time for her to take the throne. Still troubling us, that.

"There's some saying she's still alive, you know, that Morgase isn't the rightful Queen. Bloody fools. I remember what happened. Remember like it was yesterday. No Daughter-Heir to take the throne when the old Queen died, and every House in Andor scheming and fighting for the right. And Taringail Damodred. You wouldn't have thought he'd lost his wife, him hot to figure which House would win so he could marry again and become Prince Consort after all. Well, he managed it, though why Morgase chose . . . ah, no man knows the mind of a woman, and a queen is twice a woman, wed to a man, wed to the land. He got what he wanted, anyway, if not the way he wanted it.

"Brought Cairhien into the plotting before he was done, and you know how that ended. The Tree chopped down, and black-veiled Aiel coming over the Dragonwall. Well, he got himself decently killed after he'd fathered Elayne and Gawyn, so there's an end to it, I suppose. But why send them to Tar Valon? It's time men didn't think of the throne of Andor and Aes Sedai in the same thought anymore. If they've got to go some place else to learn what they need, well, Illian's got libraries as good as Tar Valon, and they'll teach the Lady Elayne as much about ruling and scheming as ever the witches could. Nobody knows more about scheming than an Illianer. And if the Guards can't teach the Lord Gawyn enough about soldiering, well, they've soldiers in Illian, too. And in Shienar, and Tear, for that matter. I'm a good Queen's man, but I say let's stop all this truck with Tar Valon. Three thousand years is long enough. Too long. Queen Morgase can lead us and put things right without help from the White Tower. I tell you, there's a woman makes a man proud to kneel for her blessing. Why, once. . . ."

Rand fought the sleep his body cried out for, but the rhythmic creak and sway of the cart lulled him and he floated off on the drone of Bunt's voice. He dreamed of Tam. At first they were at the big oak table in the farmhouse, drinking tea while Tam told him about Prince Consorts, and Daughter-Heirs, and the Dragonwall, and black-veiled Aielmen. The heron-mark sword lay on the table between them, but neither of them looked at it. Suddenly he was in the Westwood, pulling the makeshift litter through the moon-bright night. When he looked over his shoulder, it was Thom on the litter, not his father, sitting cross-legged and juggling in the moonlight.

"The Queen is wed to the land," Thom said as brightly colored balls danced in a circle, "but the Dragon . . . the Dragon is one with the land, and the land is one with the Dragon."

Further back Rand saw a Fade coming, black cloak undisturbed by the wind, horse ghosting silently through the trees. Two severed heads hung at the Myrddraal's saddle-bow, dripping blood that ran in darker streams down its mount's coal-black shoulder. Lan and Moiraine, faces distorted in grimaces of pain. The Fade pulled on a fistful of tethers as it rode. Each tether ran back to the bound wrists of one of those who ran behind the soundless hooves, their faces blank with despair. Mat and Perrin. And Egwene.

"Not her!" Rand shouted. "The Light blast you, it's me you want, not her!"

The Halfman gestured, and flames consumed Egwene, flesh crisping to ash, bone blacking and crumbling.

"The Dragon is one with the land," Thom said, still juggling unconcernedly, "and the land is one with the Dragon."

Rand screamed . . . and opened his eyes.

The cart creaked along the Caemlyn Road, filled with night and the sweetness of long-vanished hay and the faint smell of horse. A shape blacker than the night rested on his chest, and eyes blacker than death looked into his.

"You are mine," the raven said, and the sharp beak stabbed into his eye. He screamed as it plucked his eyeball out of his head.

With a throat-ripping shriek, he sat up, clapping both hands to his face.

Early morning daylight bathed the cart. Dazed, he stared at his hands. No blood. No pain. The rest of the dream was already fading, but that. . . . Gingerly he felt his face and shuddered.

"At least. . . ." Mat yawned, cracking his jaws. "At least you got some sleep." There was little sympathy in his bleary eyes. He was huddled under his cloak, with his blanketroll doubled up beneath his head. "He talked all bloody night."

"You all the way awake?" Bunt said from the driver's seat. "Gave me a start, you did, yelling like that. Well, we're there." He swept a hand out in front of them in a grand gesture. "Caemlyn, the grandest city in the world."

CHAPTER
35

Caemlyn

Rand twisted up to kneel behind the driver's seat. He could not help laughing with relief. "We made it, Mat! I told you we'd. . . ."

Words died in his mouth as his eyes fell on Caemlyn. After Baerlon, even more after the ruins of Shadar Logoth, he had thought he knew what a great city would look like, but this . . . this was more than he would have believed.

Outside the great wall, buildings clustered as if every town he had passed through had been gathered and set down there, side-by-side and all pushed together. Inns thrust their upper stories above the tile roofs of houses, and squat warehouses, broad and windowless, shouldered against them all. Red brick and gray stone and plastered white, jumbled and mixed together, they spread as far as the eye could see. Baerlon could have vanished into it without being noticed, and Whitebridge swallowed up twenty times over with hardly a ripple.

And the wall itself. The sheer, fifty-foot height of pale gray stone, streaked with silver and white, swept out in a great circle, curving to north and south till he wondered how far it must run. All along its length towers rose, round and standing high above the wall's own height, red-and-white banners whipping in the wind atop each one. From inside the wall other towers peeked out, slender towers even taller than those at the walls, and domes gleaming white and gold in the sun. A thousand stories had painted cities in his mind, the great cities of kings and queens, of thrones and powers and legends, and Caemlyn fit into those mind-deep pictures as water fits into a jug.

The cart creaked down the wide road toward the city, toward tower-flanked gates. The wagons of a merchants' train rolled out of those gates, under a vaulting archway in the stone that could have let a giant through, or ten giants abreast. Unwalled markets lined the road on both sides, roof tiles glistening red and purple, with stalls and pens in the spaces between. Calves bawled, cattle lowed, geese honked, chickens clucked, goats bleated, sheep baaed, and people bargained at the top of their lungs. A wall of noise funneled them toward the gates of Caemlyn.

"What did I tell you?" Bunt had to raise his voice to near a shout in order to be heard. "The grandest city in the world. Built by Ogier, you know. Least, the Inner City and the Palace were. It's that old, Caemlyn is. Caemlyn, where good Queen Morgase, the Light illumine her, makes the law and holds the peace for Andor. The greatest city on earth."

Rand was ready to agree. His mouth hung open, and he wanted to put his hands over his ears to shut out the din. People crowded the road, as thick as folk in Emond's Field crowded the Green at Bel Tine. He remembered thinking there were too many people in Baerlon to be believed, and almost laughed. He looked at Mat and grinned. Mat did have his hands over his ears, and his shoulders were hunched up as if he wanted to cover them with those, too.

"How are we going to hide in this?" he demanded loudly when he saw Rand looking. "How can we tell who to trust with so many? So bloody many. Light, the noise!"

Rand looked at Bunt before answering. The farmer was caught up in staring at the city; with the noise, he might not have heard anyway. Still, Rand put his mouth close to Mat's ear. "How can they find us among so many? Can't you see it, you wool-headed idiot? We're safe, if you ever learn to watch your bloody tongue!" He flung out a hand to take in everything, the markets, the city walls still ahead. "Look at it, Mat! Anything could happen here. Anything! We might even find Moiraine waiting for us, and Egwene, and all the rest."

"If they're alive. If you ask me, they're as dead as the gleeman."

The grin faded from Rand's face, and he turned to watch the gates come nearer. Anything could happen in a city like Caemlyn. He held that thought stubbornly.

The horse could not move any faster, flap the reins as Bunt would; the closer to the gates they came, the thicker the crowd grew, jostling together shoulder to shoulder, pressing against the carts and wagons heading in. Rand was glad to see a good many were dusty young men afoot with little in the way of belongings. Whatever their ages, a lot of the crowd pushing toward the gates had a travel-worn look, rickety carts and tired horses, clothes wrinkled from many nights of sleeping rough, dragging steps and weary eyes. But weary or not, those eyes were fixed on the gates as if getting inside the walls would strip away all their fatigue.

Half a dozen of the Queen's Guards stood at the gates, their clean red-and-white tabards and burnished plate-and-mail a sharp contrast to most of the people streaming under the stone arch. Backs rigid and heads straight, they eyed the incomers with disdainful wariness. It was plain they would just as soon have turned away most of those coming in. Aside from keeping a way clear for traffic leaving the city, though, and having a hard word with those who tried to push too fast, they did not hinder anyone.

"Keep your places. Don't push. Don't push, the Light blind you! There's room for everybody, the Light help us. Keep your places."

Bunt's cart rolled past the gates with the slow tide of the throng, into Caemlyn.

The city rose on low hills, like steps climbing to a center. Another wall encircled that center, shining pure white and running over the hills. Inside that were even more towers and domes, white and gold and purple, their elevation atop the hills making them seem to look down on the rest of Caemlyn. Rand thought that must be the Inner City of which Bunt had spoken.

The Caemlyn Road itself changed as soon as it was inside the city, becoming a wide boulevard, split down the middle by broad strips of grass and trees. The grass was brown and the tree branches bare, but people hurried by as if they saw nothing unusual, laughing, talking, arguing, doing all the things that people do. Just as if they had no idea that there had been no spring yet this year and might be none. They did not see, Rand realized, could not or would not. Their eyes slid away from leafless branches, and they walked across the dead and dying grass without once looking down. What they did not see, they could ignore; what they did not see was not really there.

Gaping at the city and the people, Rand was taken by surprise when the cart turned down a side street, narrower than the boulevard, but still twice as wide as any street in Emond's Field. Bunt drew the horse to a halt and turned to look back at them hesitantly. The traffic was a bit lighter here; the crowd split around the cart without breaking stride.

"What you're hiding under your cloak, is it really what Holdwin says?"

Rand was in the act of tossing his saddlebags over his shoulder. He did not even twitch. "What do you mean?" His voice was steady, too. His stomach was a sour knot, but his voice was steady.

Mat stifled a yawn with one hand, but he shoved the other under his coat—clutching the dagger from Shadar Logoth, Rand knew—and his eyes had a hard, hunted look under the scarf around his head. Bunt avoided looking at Mat, as if he knew there was a weapon in that hidden hand.

"Don't mean nothing, I suppose. Look, now, if you heard I was coming to Caemlyn, you were there long enough to hear the rest. Was I after a reward, I'd have made some excuse to go in the Goose and Crown, speak to Holdwin. Only I don't much like Holdwin, and I don't like that friend of his, not at all. Seems like he wants you two more than he wants . . . anything else."

"I don't know what he wants," Rand said. "We've never seen him before." It might even be the truth; he could not tell one Fade from another.

"Uh-huh. Well, like I say, I don't know nothing, and I guess I don't want to. There's enough trouble around for everybody without I go looking for more."

Mat was slow in gathering his things, and Rand was already in the street before he started climbing down. Rand waited impatiently. Mat turned stiffly from the cart, hugging bow and quiver and blanketroll to his chest, muttering under his breath. Heavy shadows darkened the undersides of his eyes.

Rand's stomach rumbled, and he grimaced. Hunger combined with a sour twisting in his gut made him afraid he was going to vomit. Mat was staring at him now, expectantly. *Which way to go? What to do now?*

Bunt leaned over and beckoned him closer. He went, hoping for advice about Caemlyn.

"I'd hide that. . . ." The old farmer paused and looked around warily. People pushed by on both sides of the cart, but except for a few passing curses about blocking the way, no one paid them any attention. "Stop wearing it," he said, "hide it, sell it. Give it away. That's my advice. Thing like that's going to draw attention, and I guess you don't want any of that."

Abruptly he straightened, clucking to his horse, and drove slowly on down the crowded street without another word or a backward glance. A wagon loaded with barrels rumbled toward them. Rand jumped out of the way, staggered, and when he looked again Bunt and his cart were lost to sight.

"What do we do now?" Mat demanded. He licked his lips, staring wide-eyed at all the people pushing by and the buildings towering as much as six stories above the street. "We're in Caemlyn, but what do we do?" He had uncovered his ears, but his hands twitched as if he wanted to put them back. A hum lay on the city, the low, steady drone of hundreds of shops working, thousands of people talking. To Rand it was like being inside a giant beehive, constantly buzzing. "Even if they are here, Rand, how could we find them in all of this?"

"Moiraine will find us," Rand said slowly. The immensity of the city was a weight on his shoulders; he wanted to get away, to hide from all the people and noise. The void eluded him despite Tam's teachings; his eyes drew the city into it. He concentrated instead on what was right around him, ignoring everything that lay beyond. Just looking at that one street, it almost seemed like Baerlon. Baerlon, the last place they had all thought they were safe. *Nobody's safe anymore. Maybe they* are *all dead. What do you do then?*

"They're alive! Egwene's alive!" he said fiercely. Several passersby looked at him oddly.

"Maybe," Mat said. "Maybe. What if Moiraine doesn't find us? What if nobody does but the . . . the. . . ." He shuddered, unable to say it.

"We'll think about that when it happens," he told Mat firmly. "If it happens." The worst meant seeking out Elaida, the Aes Sedai in the Palace. He would go on to Tar Valon, first. He did not know if Mat remembered what Thom had said about the Red Ajah—and the Black—but he surely did. His stomach twisted again. "Thom said to find an inn called The Queen's Blessing. We'll go there first."

"How? We can't afford one meal between the two of us."

"At least it's a place to start. Thom thought we could find help there."

"I can't. . . . Rand, they're everywhere." Mat dropped his eyes to the paving stones and seemed to shrink in on himself, trying to pull away from the people that were all around them. "Wherever we go, they're right behind us, or they're waiting for us. They'll be at The Queen's Blessing, too. I can't. . . . I. . . . Nothing's going to stop a Fade."

Rand grabbed Mat's collar in a fist that he was trying hard to keep from trembling. He needed Mat. Maybe the others were alive—*Light, please!*—but right then and there, it was just Mat and him. The thought of going on alone. . . . He swallowed hard, tasting bile.

He looked around quickly. No one seemed to have heard Mat mention the Fade; the crowd pressed past lost in its own worries. He put his face close to Mat's. "We've made it this far, haven't we?" he asked in a hoarse whisper. "They haven't caught us yet. We can make it all the way, if we just don't quit. I won't just quit and wait for them like a sheep for slaughter. I won't! Well? Are you going to stand here till you starve to death? Or until they come pick you up in a sack?"

He let go of Mat and turned away. His fingernails dug into his palms, but his hands still trembled. Suddenly Mat was walking alongside him, his eyes still down, and Rand let out a long breath.

"I'm sorry, Rand," Mat mumbled.

"Forget it," Rand said.

Mat barely looked up enough to keep from walking into people while the words poured out in a lifeless voice. "I can't stop thinking I'll never see home again. I want to go home. Laugh if you want; I don't care. What I wouldn't give to have my mother blessing me out for something right now. It's like weights on my brain; hot weights. Strangers all around, and no way to tell who to trust, if I can trust anybody. Light, the Two Rivers is so far away it might as well be on the other side of the world. We're alone, and we'll never get home. We're going to die, Rand."

"Not yet, we won't," Rand retorted. "Everybody dies. The Wheel turns. I'm not going to curl up and wait for it to happen, though."

"You sound like Master al'Vere," Mat grumbled, but his voice had a little spirit in it.

"Good," Rand said. "Good." *Light, let the others be all right. Please don't let us be alone.*

He began asking directions to The Queen's Blessing. The responses varied widely, a curse for all those who did not stay where they belonged or a shrug and a blank look being the most common. Some stalked on by with no more than a glance, if that.

A broad-faced man, nearly as big as Perrin, cocked his head and said, "The Queen's Blessing, eh? You country boys Queen's men?" He wore a white cockade on his wide-brimmed hat, and a white armband on his long coat. "Well, you've come too late."

He went off roaring with laughter, leaving Rand and Mat to stare at one another in puzzlement. Rand shrugged; there were plenty of odd folk in Caemlyn, people like he had never seen before.

Some of them stood out in the crowd, skins too dark or too pale, coats of strange cut or bright colors, hats with pointed peaks or long feathers. There were women with veils across their faces, women in stiff dresses as wide as the wearer was tall, women in dresses that left more skin bare than any tavernmaid he had seen. Occasionally a carriage, all vivid paint and gilt, squeezed through the thronged streets behind a four-or six-horse team with plumes on their harness. Sedan chairs were everywhere, the polemen pushing along with never a care for who they shoved aside.

Rand saw one fight start that way, a brawling heap of men swinging their fists while a pale-skinned man in a red-striped coat climbed out of the sedan chair lying on its side. Two roughly dressed men, who seemed to have been just passing by up till then, jumped on him before he was clear. The crowd that had stopped to watch began to turn ugly, muttering and shaking fists. Rand pulled at Mat's sleeve and hurried on. Mat needed no second urging. The roar of a small riot followed them down the street.

Several times men approached the two of them instead of the other way around. Their dusty clothes marked them as newcomers, and seemed to act like a magnet on some types. Furtive fellows who offered relics of Logain for sale with darting eyes and feet set to run. Rand calculated he was offered enough scraps of the false Dragon's cloak and fragments of his sword to make two swords and half a dozen cloaks. Mat's face brightened with interest, the first time at least, but Rand gave them all a curt no, and they took it with a bob of the head and a quick, "Light illumine the Queen, good master," and vanished. Most of the shops had plates and cups painted with fanciful scenes purporting to show the false Dragon being displayed before the Queen in chains. And there were Whitecloaks in the streets. Each walked in an open space that moved with him, just as in Baerlon.

Staying unnoticed was something Rand thought about a great deal. He kept his cloak over his sword, but that would not be good enough for very long. Sooner or later someone would wonder what he was hiding. He would not—could not—take Bunt's advice to stop wearing it, not his link to Tam. To his father.

Many others among the throng wore swords, but none with the heron-mark to pull the eye. All the Caemlyn men, though, and some of the strangers, had their swords wound in strips of cloth, sheath and hilt, red bound with white cord, or white bound with red. A hundred heron-marks could be hidden under those wrappings and no one would see. Besides, following local fashion would make them seem to fit in more.

A good many shops were fronted with tables displaying the cloth and cord, and Rand stopped at one. The red cloth was cheaper than the white, though he could see no difference apart from the color, so he bought that and the white cord to go with it, despite Mat's complaints about how little money they had left. The tight-lipped shopkeeper eyed them up and down with a twist to his mouth while he took Rand's coppers, and cursed them when Rand asked for a place inside to wrap his sword.

"We didn't come to see Logain," Rand said patiently. "We just came to see Caemlyn." He remembered Bunt, and added, "The grandest city in the world." The shopkeeper's grimace remained in place. "The Light illumine good Queen Morgase," Rand said hopefully.

"You make any trouble," the man said sourly, "and there's a hundred men in sound of my voice will take care of you even if the Guards won't." He paused to spit, just missing Rand's foot. "Get on about your filthy business."

Rand nodded as if the man had bid him a cheerful farewell, and pulled Mat away. Mat kept looking back over his shoulder toward the shop, growling to himself, until Rand tugged him into an empty alleyway. With their backs to the street no passerby could see what they were doing. Rand pulled off the sword belt and set to wrapping the sheath and hilt.

"I'll bet he charged you double for that bloody cloth," Mat said. "Triple."

It was not as easy as it looked, fastening the strips of cloth and the cord so the whole thing would not fall off.

"They'll all be trying to cheat us, Rand. They think we've come to see the false Dragon, like everybody else. We'll be lucky if somebody doesn't hit us on the head while we sleep. This is no place to be. There are too many people. Let's leave for Tar Valon now. Or south, to Illian. I wouldn't mind seeing them gather for the Hunt of the Horn. If we can't go home, let's just go."

"I'm staying," Rand said. "If they're not here already, they'll come here sooner or later, looking for us."

He was not sure if he had the wrappings done the way everyone else did, but the herons on scabbard and hilt were hidden and he thought it was secure. As he went back out on the street, he was sure that he had one less thing to worry about causing trouble. Mat trailed along beside him as reluctantly as if he were being pulled on a leash.

Bit by bit Rand did get the directions he wanted. At first they were vague, on the order of "somewhere in that direction" and "over that way." The nearer they came, though, the clearer the instructions, until at last they stood before a broad stone building with a sign over the door creaking in the wind. A man kneeling before a woman with red-gold hair and a crown, one of her hands resting on his bowed head. The Queen's Blessing.

"Are you sure about this?" Mat asked.

"Of course," Rand said. He took a deep breath and pushed open the door.

The common room was large and paneled with dark wood, and fires on two hearths warmed it. A serving maid was sweeping the floor, though it was clean, and another was polishing candlesticks in the corner. Each smiled at the two newcomers before going back to her work.

Only a few tables had people at them, but a dozen men was a crowd for so early in the day, and if none looked exactly happy to see him and Mat, at least they looked clean and sober. The smells of roasting beef and baking bread drifted from the kitchen, making Rand's mouth water.

The innkeeper was fat, he was pleased to see, a pink-faced man in a starched white apron, with graying hair combed back over a bald spot that it did not quite cover. His sharp eye took them in from head to toe, dusty clothes and bundles and worn boots, but he had a ready, pleasant smile, too. Basel Gill was his name.

"Master Gill," Rand said, "a friend of ours told us to come here. Thom Merrilin. He—" The innkeeper's smile slipped. Rand looked at Mat, but he was too busy sniffing the aromas coming from the kitchen to notice anything else. "Is something wrong? You do know him?"

"I know him," Gill said curtly. He seemed more interested in the flute case at Rand's side now, than in anything else. "Come with me." He jerked his head toward the back. Rand gave Mat a jerk to get him started, then followed, wondering what was going on.

In the kitchen, Master Gill paused to speak to the cook, a round woman with her hair in a bun at the back of her head who almost matched the innkeeper pound for pound. She kept stirring her pots while Master Gill talked. The smells were so good—two days' hunger made a fine sauce for anything, but this smelled as good as Mistress al'Vere's kitchen—that Rand's stomach growled. Mat was leaning toward the pots, nose first. Rand nudged him; Mat hastily wiped his chin where he had begun drooling.

Then the innkeeper was hurrying them out the back door. In the stableyard he looked around to make sure no one was close, then rounded on them. On Rand. "What's in the case, lad?"

"Thom's flute," Rand said slowly. He opened the case,

as if showing the gold-and-silver-chased flute would help. Mat's hand crept under his coat.

Master Gill did not take his eyes off Rand. "Aye, I recognize it. I saw him play it often enough, and there's not likely two like that outside a royal court." The pleasant smiles were gone, and his sharp eyes were suddenly as sharp as a knife. "How did you come by it? Thom would part with his arm as soon as that flute."

"He gave it to me." Rand took Thom's bundled cloak from his back and set it on the ground, unfolding enough to show the colored patches, as well as the end of the harp case. "Thom's dead, Master Gill. If he was your friend, I'm sorry. He was mine, too."

"Dead, you say. How?"

"A . . . a man tried to kill us. Thom pushed this at me and told us to run." The patches fluttered in the wind like butterflies. Rand's throat caught; he folded the cloak carefully back up again. "We'd have been killed if it hadn't been for him. We were on our way to Caemlyn together. He told us to come here, to your inn."

"I'll believe he's dead," the innkeeper said slowly, "when I see his corpse." He nudged the bundled cloak with his toe and cleared his throat roughly. "Nay, nay, I believe you saw whatever it was you saw; I just don't believe he's dead. He's a harder man to kill than you might believe, is old Thom Merrilin."

Rand put a hand on Mat's shoulder. "It's all right, Mat. He's a friend."

Master Gill glanced at Mat, and sighed. "I suppose I am at that."

Mat straightened up slowly, folding his arms over his chest. He was still watching the innkeeper warily, though, and a muscle in his cheek twitched.

"Coming to Caemlyn, you say?" The innkeeper shook his head. "This is the last place on earth I'd expect Thom to come, excepting maybe it was Tar Valon." He waited for a stableman to pass, leading a horse, and even then he lowered his voice. "You've trouble with the Aes Sedai, I take it."

"Yes," Mat grumbled at the same time that Rand said, "What makes you think that?"

Master Gill chuckled dryly. "I know the man, that's

what. He'd jump into that kind of trouble, especially to help a couple of lads about the age of you. . . ." The reminiscence in his eyes flickered out, and he stood up straight with a chary look. "Now . . . ah . . . I'm not making any accusations, mind, but . . . ah . . . I take it neither of you can . . . ah . . . what I'm getting at is . . . ah . . . what exactly is the nature of your trouble with Tar Valon, if you don't mind my asking?"

Rand's skin prickled as he realized what the man was suggesting. The One Power. "No, no, nothing like that. I swear. There was even an Aes Sedai helping us. Moiraine was. . . ." He bit his tongue, but the innkeeper's expression never changed.

"Glad to hear it. Not that I've all that much love for Aes Sedai, but better them than . . . that other thing." He shook his head slowly. "Too much talk of that kind of thing, with Logain being brought here. No offense meant, you understand, but . . . well, I had to know, didn't I?"

"No offense," Rand said. Mat's murmur could have been anything, but the innkeeper appeared to take it for the same as Rand had said.

"You two look the right sort, and I do believe you were—are—friends of Thom, but it's hard times and stony days. I don't suppose you can pay? No, I didn't think so. There's not enough of anything, and what there is costs the earth, so I'll give you beds—not the best, but warm and dry—and something to eat, and I cannot promise more, however much I'd like."

"Thank you," Rand said with a quizzical glance at Mat. "It's more than I expected." What was the right sort, and why *should* he promise more?

"Well, Thom's a good friend. An old friend. Hotheaded and liable to say the worst possible thing to the one person he shouldn't, but a good friend all the same. If he doesn't show up . . . well, we'll figure something out then. Best you don't talk any more talk about Aes Sedai helping you. I'm a good Queen's man, but there are too many in Caemlyn right now who'd take it wrong, and I don't mean just the Whitecloaks."

Mat snorted. "For all I care, the ravens can take every Aes Sedai straight to Shayol Ghul!"

"Watch your tongue," Master Gill snapped. "I said I don't

love them; I didn't say I'm a fool thinks they're behind everything that's wrong. The Queen supports Elaida, and the Guards stand for the Queen. The Light send things don't go so bad that changes. Anyway, lately some Guards have forgotten themselves enough to be a little rough with folks they overhear speaking against Aes Sedai. Not on duty, thank the Light, but it's happened, just the same. I don't need off-duty Guards breaking up my common room to teach you a lesson, and I don't need Whitecloaks egging somebody on to paint the Dragon's Fang on my door, so if you want any help out of me, you just keep thoughts about Aes Sedai to yourself, good or bad." He paused thoughtfully, then added, "Maybe it's best you don't mention Thom's name, either, where anyone but me can hear. Some of the Guards have long memories, and so does the Queen. No need taking chances."

"Thom had trouble with the Queen?" Rand said incredulously, and the innkeeper laughed.

"So he didn't tell you everything. Don't know why he should. On the other hand, I don't know why you shouldn't know, either. Not like it's a secret, exactly. Do you think every gleeman thinks as much of himself as Thom does? Well, come to think of it, I guess they do, but it always seemed to me Thom had an extra helping of thinking a lot of himself. He wasn't always a gleeman, you know, wandering from village to village and sleeping under a hedge as often as not. There was a time Thom Merrilin was Court-bard right here in Caemlyn, and known in every royal court from Tear to Maradon."

"Thom?" Mat said.

Rand nodded slowly. He could picture Thom at a Queen's court, with his stately manner and grand gestures.

"That he was," Master Gill said. "It was not long after Taringail Damodred died that the . . . trouble about his nephew cropped up. There were some said Thom was, shall we say, closer to the Queen than was proper. But Morgase was a young widow, and Thom was in his prime, then, and the Queen can do as she wishes is the way I look at it. Only she's always had a temper, has our good Morgase, and he took off without a word when he learned what kind of trouble his nephew was in. The Queen didn't much like that. Didn't like him meddling in Aes Sedai matters, either. Can't say I think it was right, either, nephew or no. Anyway, when he came back, he said some words, all right. Words you don't say to a Queen. Words you don't say to any woman with Morgase's spirit. Elaida was set against him because of his trying to mix in the business with his nephew, and between the Queen's temper and Elaida's animosity, Thom left Caemlyn half a step ahead of a trip to prison, if not the headsman's axe. As far as I know, the writ still stands."

"If it was a long time ago," Rand said, "maybe nobody remembers."

Master Gill shook his head. "Gareth Bryne is Captain-General of the Queen's Guards. He personally commanded the Guardsmen Morgase sent to bring Thom back in chains, and I misdoubt he'll ever forget returning empty-handed to find Thom had already been back to the Palace and left again. And the Queen never forgets *anything*. You ever know a woman who did? My, but Morgase was in a taking. I'll swear the whole city walked soft and whispered for a month. Plenty of other Guardsmen old enough to remember, too. No, best you keep Thom as close a secret as you keep that Aes Sedai of yours. Come, I'll get you something to eat. You look as if your bellies are gnawing at your backbones."

CHAPTER
36

Web of the Pattern

Master Gill took them to a corner table in the common room and had one of the serving maids bring them food. Rand shook his head when he saw the plates, with a few thin slices of gravy-covered beef, a spoonful of mustard greens, and two potatoes on each. It was a rueful, resigned headshake, though, not angry. Not enough of anything, the innkeeper had said. Picking up his knife and fork, Rand wondered what would happen when there was nothing left. It made his half-covered plate seem like a feast. It made him shiver.

Master Gill had chosen a table well away from anyone else, and he sat with his back to the corner, where he could watch the room. Nobody could get close enough to overhear what they said without him seeing. When the maid left, he said softly, "Now, why don't you tell me about this trouble of yours? If I'm going to help, I'd best know what I'm getting into."

Rand looked at Mat, but Mat was frowning at his plate as if he were mad at the potato he was cutting. Rand took a deep breath. "I don't really understand it myself," he began.

He kept the story simple, and he kept Trollocs and Fades out of it. When somebody offered help, it would not do to tell them it was all about fables. But he did not think it was fair to understate the danger, either, not fair to pull someone in when they had no idea what they were getting into. Some men were after him and Mat, and a couple of friends of theirs, too. They appeared where they were least expected, these men, and they were deadly dangerous and set on killing him and his friends, or worse. Moiraine said some of them were

Darkfriends. Thom did not trust Moiraine completely, but he stayed on with them, he said, because of his nephew. They had been separated during an attack while trying to reach Whitebridge, and then, in Whitebridge, Thom died saving them from another attack. And there had been other tries. He knew there were holes in it, but it was the best he could do on short notice without telling more than was safe.

"We just kept on till we reached Caemlyn," he explained. "That was the plan, originally. Caemlyn, and then Tar Valon." He shifted uncomfortably on the edge of his chair. After keeping everything secret for so long, it felt odd to be telling somebody even as much as he was. "If we stay on that route, the others will be able to find us, sooner or later."

"If they're alive," Mat muttered at his plate.

Rand did not even glance at Mat. Something compelled him to add, "It could bring you trouble, helping us."

Master Gill waved it off with a plump hand. "Can't say as I want trouble, but it wouldn't be the first I've seen. No bloody Darkfriend will make me turn my back on Thom's friends. This friend of yours from up north, now—if she comes to Caemlyn, I'll hear. There are people keep their eyes on comings and goings like that around here, and word spreads."

Rand hesitated, then asked, "What about Elaida?"

The innkeeper hesitated, too, and finally shook his head. "I don't think so. Maybe if you didn't have a connection to Thom. She'd winkle it out, and then where would you be? No telling. Maybe in a cell. Maybe worse. They say she has a way of feeling things, what's happened, what's going to happen. They say she can cut right through to what a man wants to hide. I don't know, but I wouldn't risk it. If it wasn't for Thom, you could go to the Guards. They'd take care of any Darkfriends quick enough. But even if you could keep Thom quiet from the Guards, word would reach Elaida as soon as you mentioned Darkfriends, and then you're back where we started."

"No Guards," Rand agreed. Mat nodded vigorously while stuffing a fork into his mouth and got gravy on his chin.

"Trouble is, you're caught up in the fringes of politics, lad, even if it's none of your doing, and politics is a foggy mire full of snakes."

"What about—" Rand began, but the innkeeper grimaced

suddenly, his chair creaking under his bulk as he sat up straight.

The cook was standing in the doorway to the kitchen, wiping her hands with her apron. When she saw the innkeeper looking she motioned for him to come, then vanished back into the kitchen.

"Might as well be married to her." Master Gill sighed. "Finds things that need fixing before I know there's anything wrong. If it's not the drains stopped up, or the downspouts clogged, it's rats. I keep a clean place, you understand, but with so many people in the city, rats are everywhere. Crowd people together and you get rats, and Caemlyn has a plague of them all of a sudden. You wouldn't believe what a good cat, a prime ratter, fetches these days. Your room is in the attic. I'll tell the girls which; any of them can show you to it. And don't worry about Darkfriends. I can't say much good about the Whitecloaks, but between them and the Guards, that sort won't dare show their filthy faces in Caemlyn." His chair squeaked again as he pushed it back and stood. "I hope it isn't the drains again."

Rand went back to his food, but he saw that Mat had stopped eating. "I thought you were hungry," he said. Mat kept staring at his plate, pushing one piece of potato in a circle with his fork. "You have to eat, Mat. We need to keep up our strength if we're going to reach Tar Valon."

Mat let out a low, bitter laugh. "Tar Valon! All this time it's been Caemlyn. Moiraine would be waiting for us in Caemlyn. We'd find Perrin and Egwene in Caemlyn. Everything would be all right if we only got to Caemlyn. Well, here we are, and nothing's right. No Moiraine, no Perrin, no anybody. Now it's everything will be all right if we only get to Tar Valon."

"We're alive," Rand said, more sharply than he had intended. He took a deep breath and tried to moderate his tone. "We are alive. That much is all right. And I intend to stay alive. I intend to find out why we're so important. I won't give up."

"All these people, and any of them could be Darkfriends. Master Gill promised to help us awfully quick. What kind of man just shrugs off Aes Sedai and Darkfriends? It isn't natural. Any decent person would tell us to get out, or . . . or . . . or something."

"Eat," Rand said gently, and watched until Mat began chewing a piece of beef.

He left his own hands resting beside his plate for a minute, pressing them against the table to keep them from
shaking. He was scared. Not about Master Gill, of course,
but there was enough without that. Those tall city walls
would not stop a Fade. Maybe he should tell the innkeeper
about that. But even if Gill believed, would he be as willing
to help if he thought a Fade might show up at The Queen's
Blessing? And the rats. Maybe rats did thrive where there
were a lot of people, but he remembered the dream that was
not a dream in Baerlon, and a small spine snapping. *Sometimes the Dark One uses carrion eaters as his eyes,* Lan
had said. *Ravens, crows, rats. . . .*

He ate, but when he was done he could not remember
tasting a single bite.

A serving maid, the one who had been polishing candlesticks when they came in, showed them up to the attic room.
A dormer window pierced the slanting outer wall, with a
bed on either side of it and pegs beside the door for hanging
their belongings. The dark-eyed girl had a tendency to twist
her skirt and giggle whenever she looked at Rand. She was
pretty, but he knew if he said anything to her he would just
make a fool of himself. She made him wish he had Perrin's
way with girls; he was glad when she left.

He expected some comment from Mat, but as soon as she
was gone, Mat threw himself on one of the beds, still in his
cloak and boots, and turned his face to the wall.

Rand hung his things up, watching Mat's back. He
thought Mat had his hand under his coat, clutching that
dagger again.

"You just going to lie up here hiding?" he said finally.

"I'm tired," Mat mumbled.

"We have questions to ask Master Gill, yet. He might
even be able to tell us how to find Egwene, and Perrin. They
could be in Caemlyn already if they managed to hang onto
their horses."

"They're dead," Mat said to the wall.

Rand hesitated, then gave up. He closed the door softly
behind him, hoping Mat really would sleep.

Downstairs, however, Master Gill was nowhere to be
found, though the sharp look in the cook's eye said she was
looking for him, too. For a while Rand sat in the common
room, but he found himself eyeing every patron who came

in, every stranger who could be anyone—or anything—especially in the moment when he was first silhouetted as a cloaked black shape in the doorway. A Fade in the room would be like a fox in a chicken coop.

A Guardsman entered from the street. The red-uniformed man stopped just inside the door, running a cool eye over those in the room who were obviously from outside the city. Rand studied the tabletop when the Guardsman's eyes fell on him; when he looked up again, the man was gone.

The dark-eyed maid was passing with her arms full of towels. "They do that sometimes," she said in a confiding tone as she went by. "Just to see there's no trouble. They look after good Queen's folk, they do. Nothing for you to worry about." She giggled.

Rand shook his head. Nothing for him to worry about. It was not as if the Guardsman would have come over and demanded to know if he knew Thom Merrilin. He was getting as bad as Mat. He scraped back his chair.

Another maid was checking the oil in the lamps along the wall.

"Is there another room where I could sit?" he asked her. He did not want to go back upstairs and shut himself up with Mat's sullen withdrawal. "Maybe a private dining room that's not being used?"

"There's the library." She pointed to a door. "Through there, to your right, at the end of the hall. Might be empty, this hour."

"Thank you. If you see Master Gill, would you tell him Rand al'Thor needs to talk to him if he can spare a minute?"

"I'll tell him," she said, then grinned. "Cook wants to talk to him, too."

The innkeeper was probably hiding, he thought as he turned away from her.

When he stepped into the room to which she had directed him, he stopped and stared. The shelves must have held three or four hundred books, more than he had ever seen in one place before. Clothbound, leatherbound with gilded spines. Only a few had wooden covers. His eyes gobbled up the titles, picking out old favorites. *The Travels of Jain Farstrider. The Essays of Willim of Maneches.* His breath caught at the sight of a leatherbound copy of *Voyages Among the Sea Folk.* Tam had always wanted to read that.

Picturing Tam, turning the book over in his hands with a smile, getting the feel of it before settling down before the fireplace with his pipe to read, his own hand tightened on his sword hilt with a sense of loss and emptiness that dampened all his pleasure in the books.

A throat cleared behind him, and he suddenly realized he was not alone. Ready to apologize for his rudeness, he turned. He was used to being taller than almost everyone he met, but this time his eyes traveled up and up and up, and his mouth fell open. Then he came to the head almost reaching the ten-foot ceiling. A nose as broad as the face, so wide it was more a snout than a nose. Eyebrows that hung down like tails, framing pale eyes as big as teacups. Ears that poked up to tufted points through a shaggy, black mane. *Trolloc!* He let out a yell and tried to back up and draw his sword. His feet got tangled, and he sat down hard, instead.

"I wish you humans wouldn't do that," rumbled a voice as deep as a drum. The tufted ears twitched violently, and the voice became sad. "So few of you remember us. It's our own fault, I suppose. Not many of us have gone out among men since the Shadow fell on the Ways. That's . . . oh, six generations, now. Right after the War of the Hundred Years, it was." The shaggy head shook and let out a sigh that would have done credit to a bull. "Too long, too long, and so few to travel and see, it might as well have been none."

Rand sat there for a minute with his mouth hanging open, staring up at the apparition in wide-toed, knee-high boots and a dark blue coat that buttoned from the neck to the waist, then flared out to his boot tops like a kilt over baggy trousers. In one hand was a book, seeming tiny by comparison, with a finger broad enough for three marking the place.

"I thought you were—" he began, then caught himself. "What are—?" That was not any better. Getting to his feet, he gingerly offered his hand. "My name is Rand al'Thor."

A hand as big as a ham engulfed his; it was accompanied by a formal bow. "Loial, son of Arent son of Halan. Your name sings in my ears, Rand al'Thor."

That sounded like a ritual greeting to Rand. He returned the bow. "Your name sings in my ears, Loial, son of Arent . . . ah . . . son of Halan."

It was all a little unreal. He still did not know *what* Loial was. The grip of Loial's huge fingers was surprisingly gentle, but he was still relieved to get his hand back in one piece.

"You humans are very excitable," Loial said in that bass rumble. "I had heard all the stories, and read the books, of course, but I didn't realize. My first day in Caemlyn, I could not believe the uproar. Children cried, and women screamed, and a mob chased me all the way across the city, waving clubs and knives and torches, and shouting, 'Trolloc!' I'm afraid I was almost beginning to get a little upset. There's no telling what would have happened if a party of the Queen's Guards hadn't come along."

"A lucky thing," Rand said faintly.

"Yes, but even the Guardsmen seemed almost as afraid of me as the others. Four days in Caemlyn now, and I haven't been able to put my nose outside this inn. Good Master Gill even asked me not to use the common room." His ears twitched. "Not that he hasn't been very hospitable, you understand. But there was a bit of trouble that first night. All the humans seemed to want to leave at once. Such screaming and shouting, everyone trying to get through the door at the same time. Some of them could have been hurt."

Rand stared in fascination at those twitching ears.

"I'll tell you, it was not for this I left the *stedding*."

"You're an Ogier!" Rand exclaimed. "Wait! Six generations? You said the War of the Hundred Years! How old are you?" He knew it was rude as soon as he said it, but Loial became defensive rather than offended.

"Ninety years," the Ogier said stiffly. "In only ten more I'll be able to address the Stump. I think the Elders should have let me speak, since they were deciding whether I could leave or not. But then they always worry about anyone of any age going Outside. You humans are so hasty, so erratic." He blinked and gave a short bow. "Please forgive me. I shouldn't have said that. But you do fight all the time, even when there's no need to."

"That's all right," Rand said. He was still trying to take in Loial's age. Older than old Cenn Buie, and still not old enough to. . . . He sat down in one of the high-backed chairs. Loial took another, made to hold two; he filled it. Sitting, he was as tall as most men standing. "At least they did let you go."

Loial looked at the floor, wrinkling his nose and rubbing at it with one thick finger. "Well, as to that, now. You see, the Stump had not been meeting very long, not even a year, but I could tell from what I heard that by the time they reached a decision I would be old enough to go without their permission. I am afraid they'll say I put a long handle on my axe, but I just . . . left. The Elders always said I was too hotheaded, and I fear I've proven them right. I wonder if they have realized I'm gone, yet? But I had to go."

Rand bit his lip to keep from laughing. If Loial was a hotheaded Ogier, he could imagine what most Ogier were like. Had not been meeting very long, not even a year? Master al'Vere would just shake his head in wonder; a Village Council meeting that lasted half a day would have everybody jumping up and down, even Haral Luhhan. A wave of homesickness swept over him, making it hard to breathe for memories of Tam, and Egwene, and the Winespring Inn, and Bel Tine on the Green in happier days. He forced them away.

"If you don't mind my asking," he said, clearing his throat, "why did you want to go . . . ah, Outside, so much? I wish I'd never left my home, myself."

"Why, to see," Loial said as if it were the most obvious thing in the world. "I read the books, all the travelers' accounts, and it began to burn in me that I had to see, not just read." His pale eyes brightened, and his ears stiffened. "I studied every scrap I could find about traveling, about the Ways, and customs in human lands, and the cities we built for you humans after the Breaking of the World. And the more I read, the more I knew that I had to go Outside, go to those places we had been, and see the groves for myself."

Rand blinked. "Groves?"

"Yes, the groves. The trees. Only a few of the Great Trees, of course, towering to the sky to keep memories of the *stedding* fresh." His chair groaned as he shifted forward, gesturing with his hands, one of which still held the book. His eyes were brighter than ever, and his ears almost quivered. "Mostly they used the trees of the land and the place. You cannot make the land go against itself. Not for long; the land will rebel. You must shape the vision to the land, not the land to the vision. In every grove was planted every tree that would grow and thrive in that place, each balanced against the next, each placed to complement the others, for the best growing, of course, but also so that the balance would sing in the eye and the heart. Ah, the books spoke of groves to make Elders weep and laugh at the same time, groves to remain green in memory forever."

"What about the cities?" Rand asked. Loial gave him a puzzled look. "The cities. The cities the Ogier built. Here, for instance. Caemlyn. Ogier built Caemlyn, didn't you? The stories say so."

"Working with stone. . . ." His shoulders gave a massive shrug. "That was just something learned in the years after the Breaking, during the Exile, when we were still trying to find the *stedding* again. It is a fine thing, I suppose, but not the true thing. Try as you will—and I have read that the Ogier who built those cities truly did try—you cannot make stone live. A few still do work with stone, but only because you humans damage the buildings so often with your wars. There were a handful of Ogier in . . . ah . . . Cairhien, it's called now . . . when I passed through. They were from another *stedding,* luckily, so they didn't know about me, but they were still suspicious that I was Outside alone so young. I suppose it's just as well there was no reason for me to linger there. In any case, you see, working with stone is just something that was thrust on us by the weaving of the Pattern; the groves came from the heart."

Rand shook his head. Half the stories he had grown up with had just been stood on their heads. "I didn't know Ogier believed in the Pattern, Loial."

"Of course, we believe. The Wheel of Time weaves the Pattern of the Ages, and lives are the threads it weaves. No one can tell how the thread of his own life will be woven into the Pattern, or how the thread of a people will be woven. It gave us the Breaking of the World, and the Exile, and Stone, and the Longing, and eventually it gave us back the *stedding* before we all died. Sometimes I think the reason you humans are the way you are is because your threads are so short. They must jump around in the weaving. Oh, there, I've done it again. The Elders say you humans don't like to be reminded of how short a time you live. I hope I didn't hurt your feelings."

Rand laughed and shook his head. "Not at all. I suppose it'd be fun to live as long as you do, but I never really thought about it. I guess if I live as long as old Cenn Buie, that'll be long enough for anybody."

"He is a very old man?"

Rand just nodded. He was not about to explain that old Cenn Buie was not quite as old as Loial.

"Well," Loial said, "perhaps you humans do have short lives, but you do so much with them, always jumping around, always so hasty. And you have the whole world to do it in. We Ogier are bound to our *stedding*."

"You're Outside."

"For a time, Rand. But I must go back, eventually. This world is yours, yours and your kind's. The *stedding* are mine. There's too much hurly-burly Outside. And so much is changed from what I read about."

"Well, things do change over the years. Some, anyway."

"Some? Half the cities I read about aren't even there any longer, and most of the rest are known by different names. You take Cairhien. The city's proper name is Al'cair'rahienallen, Hill of the Golden Dawn. They don't even remember, for all of the sunrise on their banners. And the grove there. I doubt if it has been tended since the Trolloc Wars. It's just another forest, now, where they cut firewood. The Great Trees are all gone, and no one remembers them. And here? Caemlyn is still Caemlyn, but they let the city grow right over the grove. We're not a quarter of a mile from the center of it right where we sit—from where the center of it should be. Not a tree of it left. I've been to Tear and Illian, too. Different names, and no memories. There's only pasture for their horses where the grove was at Tear, and at Illian the grove is the King's park, where he hunts his deer, and none allowed inside without his permission. It has all changed, Rand. I fear very much that I will find the same everywhere I go. All the groves gone, all the memories gone, all the dreams dead."

"You can't give up, Loial. You can't ever give up. If you give up, you might as well be dead." Rand sank back in his chair as far as he could go, his face turning red. He expected the Ogier to laugh at him, but Loial nodded gravely instead.

"Yes, that's the way of your kind, isn't it?" The Ogier's voice changed, as if he were quoting something. "Till shade is gone, till water is gone, into the Shadow with teeth bared, screaming defiance with the last breath, to spit in Sightblinder's eye on the Last Day." Loial cocked his shaggy head expectantly, but Rand had no idea what it was he expected.

A minute went by with Loial waiting, then another, and his long eyebrows began to draw down in puzzlement. But he still waited, the silence growing uncomfortable for Rand.

"The Great Trees," Rand said finally, just for something to break that silence. "Are they like *Avendesora*?"

Loial sat up sharply; his chair squealed and cracked so loudly Rand thought it was going to come apart. "You know better than that. You, of all people."

"Me? How would I know?"

"Are you playing a joke on me? Sometimes you Aielmen think the oddest things are funny."

"What? I'm not an Aielman! I'm from the Two Rivers. I never even saw an Aielman!"

Loial shook his head, and the tufts on his ears drooped outward. "You see? Everything is changed, and half of what I know is useless. I hope I did not offend you. I'm sure your Two Rivers is a very fine place, wherever it is."

"Somebody told me," Rand said, "that it was once called Manetheren. I'd never heard it, but maybe you. . . ."

The Ogier's ears had perked up happily. "Ah! Yes. Manetheren." The tufts went down again. "There was a very fine grove there. Your pain sings in my heart, Rand al'Thor. We could not come in time."

Loial bowed where he sat, and Rand bowed back. He suspected Loial would be hurt if he did not, would think he was rude at the least. He wondered if Loial thought he had the same sort of memories the Ogier seemed to. The corners of Loial's mouth and eyes were certainly turned down as if he were sharing the pain of Rand's loss, just as if the destruction of Manetheren were not something that happened two thousand years ago, near enough, something that Rand only knew about because of Moiraine's story.

After a time Loial sighed. "The Wheel turns," he said, "and no one knows its turning. But you have come almost as far from your home as I have. A very considerable distance, as things are now. When the Ways were freely open, of course—but that is long past. Tell me, what brings you so far? Is there something you want to see, too?"

Rand opened his mouth to say that they had come to see the false Dragon—and he could not say it. Perhaps it was because Loial acted as if he were no older than Rand, ninety years old or no ninety years old. Maybe for an Ogier ninety years was not any older than he was. It had been a long time since he had been able to really talk to anyone about what was happening. Always the fear that they might be Darkfriends, or think he was. Mat was so drawn in on himself, feeding his fears on his own suspicions, that he was no good for talking. Rand found himself telling Loial about Winternight. Not a vague story about Darkfriends; the truth about Trollocs breaking in the door, and a Fade on the Quarry Road.

Part of him was horrified at what he was doing, but it was almost as if he were two people, one trying to hold his tongue while the other only felt the relief at being able to tell it all finally. The result was that he stumbled and stuttered and jumped around in the story. Shadar Logoth and losing his friends in the night, not knowing if they were alive or dead. The Fade in Whitebridge, and Thom dying so they could escape. The Fade in Baerlon. Darkfriends later, Howal Gode, and the boy who was afraid of them, and the woman who tried to kill Mat. The Halfman outside the Goose and Crown.

When he started babbling about dreams, even the part of him that wanted to talk felt the hackles rising on the back of his neck. He bit his tongue clamping his teeth shut. Breathing heavily through his nose, he watched the Ogier warily, hoping he thought he had meant nightmares. The Light knew it all sounded like a nightmare, or enough to give anyone nightmares. Maybe Loial would just think he was going mad. Maybe. . . .

"*Ta'veren,*" Loial said.

Rand blinked. "What?"

"*Ta'veren.*" Loial rubbed behind a pointed ear with one blunt finger and gave a little shrug. "Elder Haman always said I never listened, but sometimes I did. Sometimes, I listened. You know how the Pattern is woven, of course?"

"I never really thought about it," he said slowly. "It just is."

"Um, yes, well. Not exactly. You see, the Wheel of Time weaves the Pattern of the Ages, and the threads it uses are lives. It is not fixed, the Pattern, not always. If a man tries to change the direction of his life and the Pattern has room for it, the Wheel just weaves on and takes it in. There is always room for small changes, but sometimes the Pattern simply won't accept a big change, no matter how hard you try. You understand?"

Rand nodded. "I could live on the farm or in Emond's Field, and that would be a small change. If I wanted to be a king, though. . . ." He laughed, and Loial gave a grin that almost split his face in two. His teeth were white, and as broad as chisels.

"Yes, that's it. But sometimes the change chooses you, or the Wheel chooses it for you. And sometimes the Wheel bends a life-thread, or several threads, in such a way that all the surrounding threads are forced to swirl around it, and those force other threads, and those still others, and on and on. That first bending to make the Web, that is *ta'veren,* and there is nothing you can do to change it, not until the Pattern itself changes. The Web—*ta'maral'ailen,* it's called—can last for weeks, or for years. It can take in a town, or even the whole Pattern. Artur Hawkwing was *ta'veren.* So was Lews Therin Kinslayer, for that matter, I suppose." He let out a booming chuckle. "Elder Haman would be proud of me. He always droned on, and the books about traveling were much more interesting, but I did listen sometimes."

"That's all very well," Rand said, "but I don't see what it has to do with me. I'm a shepherd, not another Artur Hawkwing. And neither is Mat, or Perrin. It's just . . . ridiculous."

"I didn't say you were, but I could almost feel the Pattern swirl just listening to you tell your tale, and I have no Talent there. You are *ta'veren,* all right. You, and maybe your friends, too." The Ogier paused, rubbing the bridge of his broad nose thoughtfully. Finally he nodded to himself as if he had reached a decision. "I wish to travel with you, Rand."

For a minute Rand stared, wondering if he had heard correctly. "With me?" he exclaimed when he could speak. "Didn't you hear what I said about . . . ?" He eyed the door suddenly. It was shut tight, and thick enough that anyone trying to listen on the other side would hear only a murmur, even with his ear pressed against the wooden panels. Just the same he went on in a lower voice. "About who's chasing me? Anyway, I thought you wanted to go see your trees."

"There is a very fine grove at Tar Valon, and I have been

told the Aes Sedai keep it well tended. Besides, it is not just
the groves I want to see. Perhaps you are not another Artur
Hawkwing, but for a time, at least, part of the world will
shape itself around you, perhaps is even now shaping itself
around you. Even Elder Haman would want to see that."

Rand hesitated. It would be good to have someone else
along. The way Mat was behaving, being with him was almost like being alone. The Ogier was a comforting presence. Maybe he was young as Ogier reckoned age, but he
seemed as unflappable as a rock, just like Tam. And Loial
had been all of those places, and knew about others. He
looked at the Ogier, sitting there with his broad face a picture of patience. Sitting there, and taller sitting than most
men standing. *How do you hide somebody almost ten feet
tall?* He sighed and shook his head.

"I don't think that is a good idea, Loial. Even if Moiraine
finds us here, we'll be in danger all the way to Tar Valon.
If she does not. . . ." *If she doesn't, then she's dead and so
is everyone else. Oh, Egwene.* He gave himself a shake.
Egwene was not dead, and Moiraine would find them.

Loial looked at him sympathetically and touched his
shoulder. "I am sure your friends are well, Rand."

Rand nodded his thanks. His throat was too tight to speak.

"Will you at least talk with me sometimes?" Loial sighed,
a bass rumble. "And perhaps play a game of stones? I have
not had anyone to talk to in days, except good Master Gill,
and he is busy most of the time. The cook seems to run him
unmercifully. Perhaps she really owns the inn?"

"Of course, I will." His voice was hoarse. He cleared his
throat and tried to grin. "And if we meet in Tar Valon, you
can show me the grove there." *They have to be all right.
Light send they're all right.*

CHAPTER
37

The Long Chase

Nynaeve gripped the reins of the three horses and peered into the night as if she could somehow pierce the darkness and find the Aes Sedai and the Warder. Skeletal trees surrounded her, stark and black in the dim moonlight. The trees and the night made an effective screen for whatever Moiraine and Lan were doing, not that either of them had paused to let her know what that was. A low "Keep the horses quiet," from Lan, and they were gone, leaving her standing like a stableboy. She glanced at the horses and sighed with exasperation.

Mandarb blended into the night almost as well as his master's cloak. The only reason the battle-trained stallion was letting her get this close was because Lan had handed her the reins himself. He seemed calm enough now, but she remembered all too well the lips drawing back silently when she reached for his bridle without waiting for Lan's approval. The silence had made the bared teeth seem that much more dangerous. With a last wary look at the stallion, she turned to peer in the direction the other two had gone, idly stroking her own horse. She gave a startled jump when Aldieb pushed a pale muzzle under her hand, but after a minute she gave the white mare a pat, too.

"No need to take it out on you, I suppose," she whispered, "just because your mistress is a cold-faced—" She strained at the darkness again. *What were they doing?*

After leaving Whitebridge they had ridden through villages that seemed unreal in their normality, ordinary market villages that seemed to Nynaeve unconnected to a world that had Fades and Trollocs and Aes Sedai. They had followed the Caemlyn Road, until at last Moiraine sat forward in Aldieb's saddle, peering eastward as if she could see the whole length of the great highway, all the many miles to Caemlyn, and see, too, what waited there.

Eventually the Aes Sedai let out a long breath and settled back. "The Wheel weaves as the Wheel wills," she murmured, "but I cannot believe it weaves an end to hope. I must first take care of that of which I can be certain. It will be as the Wheel weaves." And she turned her mare north, off the road into the forest. One of the boys was in that direction with the coin Moiraine had given him. Lan followed.

Nynaeve gave a long last look at the Caemlyn Road. Few people shared the roadway with them there, a couple of high-wheeled carts and one empty wagon in the distance, a handful of folk afoot with their belongings on their backs or piled on pushcarts. Some of those were willing to admit they were on their way to Caemlyn to see the false Dragon, but most denied it vehemently, especially those who had come through Whitebridge. At Whitebridge she had begun to believe Moiraine. Somewhat. More, at any rate. And there was no comfort in that.

The Warder and the Aes Sedai were almost out of sight through the trees before she started after them. She hurried to catch up. Lan looked back at her frequently, and waved for her to come on, but he kept at Moiraine's shoulder, and the Aes Sedai had her eyes fixed ahead.

One evening after they left the road, the invisible trail failed. Moiraine, the unflappable Moiraine, suddenly stood up beside the small fire where the tea kettle was boiling, her eyes widening. "It is gone," she whispered at the night.

"He is . . . ?" Nynaeve could not finish the question. *Light, I don't even know which one it is!*

"He did not die," the Aes Sedai said slowly, "but he no longer has the token." She sat down, her voice level and her hands steady as she took the kettle off the flames and tossed in a handful of tea. "In the morning we will keep on as we've been going. When I get close enough, I can find him without the coin."

As the fire burned down to coals, Lan rolled himself in his cloak and went to sleep. Nynaeve could not sleep. She watched the Aes Sedai. Moiraine had her eyes closed, but she sat upright, and Nynaeve knew she was awake.

Long after the last glow had faded from the coals, Moiraine opened her eyes and looked at her. She could feel the Aes Sedai's smile even in the dark. "He has regained the coin, Wisdom. All will be well." She lay down on her blankets with a sigh and almost at once was breathing deep in slumber.

Nynaeve had a hard time joining her, tired as she was. Her mind conjured up the worst no matter how she tried to stop it. *All will be well.* After Whitebridge, she could no longer make herself believe that so easily.

Abruptly Nynaeve was jerked from memory back to the night; there really was a hand on her arm. Stifling the cry that rose in her throat, she fumbled for the knife at her belt, her hand closing on the hilt before she realized that the hand was Lan's.

The Warder's hood was thrown back, but his chameleon-like cloak blended so well with the night that the dim blur of his face seemed to hang suspended in the night. The hand on her arm appeared to come out of thin air.

She drew a shuddering breath. She expected him to comment on how easily he had come on her unaware, but instead he turned to dig into his saddlebags. "You are needed," he said, and knelt to fasten hobbles on the horses.

As soon as the horses were secured, he straightened, grasped her hand, and headed off into the night again. His dark hair fit into the night almost as well as his cloak, and he made even less noise than she did. Grudgingly she had to admit that she could never have followed him through the darkness without his grip as a guide. She was not certain she could pull loose if he did not want to release her, anyway; he had very strong hands.

As they came up on a small rise, barely enough to be called a hill, he sank to one knee, pulling her down beside him. It took her a moment to see that Moiraine was there, too. Unmoving, the Aes Sedai could have passed for a shadow in her dark cloak. Lan gestured down the hillside to a large clearing in the trees.

Nynaeve frowned in the dim moonlight, then suddenly smiled in understanding. Those pale blurs were tents in regular rows, a darkened encampment.

"Whitecloaks," Lan whispered, "two hundred of them, maybe more. There's good water down there. And the lad we're after."

"In the camp?" She felt, more than saw, Lan nod.

"In the middle of it. Moiraine can point right to him. I went close enough to see he's under guard."

"A prisoner?" Nynaeve said. "Why?"

"I don't know. The Children should not be interested in a village boy, not unless there was something to make them suspicious. The Light knows it doesn't take much to make Whitecloaks suspicious, but it still worries me."

"How are you going to free him?" It was not until he glanced at her that she realized how much assurance there had been in her that he could march into the middle of two hundred men and come back with the boy. *Well, he* is *a Warder. Some of the stories must be true.*

She wondered if he was laughing at her, but his voice was flat and businesslike. "I can bring him out, but he'll likely be in no shape for stealth. If we're seen, we may find two hundred Whitecloaks on our heels, and us riding double. Unless they are too busy to chase us. Are you willing to take a chance?"

"To help an Emond's Fielder? Of course! What kind of chance?"

He pointed into the darkness again, beyond the tents. This time she could make out nothing but shadows. "Their horse-lines. If the picket-ropes are cut, not all the way through, but enough so they'll break when Moiraine creates a diversion, the Whitecloaks will be too busy chasing their own horses to come after us. There are two guards on that side of the camp, beyond the picket-lines, but if you are half as good as I think you are, they'll never see you."

She swallowed hard. Stalking rabbits was one thing; guards, though, with spears and swords. . . . *So he thinks I'm good, does he?* "I'll do it."

Lan nodded again, as if he had expected no less. "One other thing. There are wolves about, tonight. I saw two, and if I saw that many, there are probably more." He paused, and though his voice did not change she had the feeling he was puzzled. "It was almost as if they wanted me to see them. Anyway, they shouldn't bother you. Wolves usually stay away from people."

"I wouldn't have known that," she said sweetly. "I only grew up around shepherds." He grunted, and she smiled into the darkness.

"We'll do it now, then," he said.

Her smile faded as she peered down at the camp full of armed men. Two hundred men with spears and swords and. . . . Before she could reconsider, she eased her knife in its sheath and started to slip away. Moiraine caught her arm in a grip almost as strong as Lan's.

"Take care," the Aes Sedai said softly. "Once you cut the ropes, return as quickly as you can. You are a part of the Pattern, too, and I would not risk you, any more than any of the others, if the whole world was not at risk in these days."

Nynaeve rubbed her arm surreptitiously when Moiraine released it. She was not about to let the Aes Sedai know the grip had hurt. But Moiraine turned back to watching the camp below as soon as she let go. And the Warder was gone, Nynaeve realized with a start. She had not heard him leave. *Light blind the bloody man!* Quickly she tied her skirts up to give her legs freedom, and hurried into the night.

After that first rush, with fallen branches cracking under her feet, she slowed down, glad there was no one there to see her blush. The idea was to be quiet, and she was not in any kind of competition with the Warder. *Oh, no?*

She shook off the thought and concentrated on making her way through the dark woods. It was not hard in and of itself; the faint light of the waning moon was more than enough for anyone who had been taught by her father, and the ground had a slow, easy roll. But the trees, bare and stark against the night sky, constantly reminded her that this was no childhood game, and the keening wind sounded all too much like Trolloc horns. Now that she was alone in the darkness, she remembered that the wolves that usually ran away from people had been behaving differently in the Two Rivers this winter.

Relief flooded through her like warmth when she finally caught the smell of horses. Almost holding her breath, she got down on her stomach and crawled upwind, toward the smell.

She was nearly on the guards before she saw them, marching toward her out of the night, white cloaks flapping in the wind and almost shining in the moonlight. They might as well have carried torches; torchlight could not have made them much more visible. She froze, trying to make herself a part of the ground. Nearly in front of her, not ten paces away, they marched to a halt with a stomp of feet, facing each other, spears shouldered. Just beyond them she could make out shadows that had to be the horses. The stable smell, horse and manure, was strong.

"All is well with the night," one white-cloaked shape announced. "The Light illumine us, and protect us from the Shadow."

"All is well with the night," the other replied. "The Light illumine us, and protect us from the Shadow."

With that they turned and marched off into the darkness again.

Nynaeve waited, counting to herself while they made their circuit twice. Each time they took exactly the same count, and each time they rigidly repeated the same formula, not a word more or less. Neither so much as glanced to one side; they stared straight ahead as they marched up, then marched away. She wondered if they would have noticed her even if she had been standing up.

Before the night swallowed the pale swirls of their cloaks a third time, she was already on her feet, running in a crouch toward the horses. As she came close, she slowed so as not to startle the animals. The Whitecloak guards might not see what was not shoved under their noses, but they would certainly investigate if the horses suddenly began whickering.

The horses along the picket-lines—there was more than one row—were barely realized masses in the darkness, heads down. Occasionally one snorted or stamped a foot in its sleep. In the dim moonlight she was nearly on the endpost of the picket-line before she saw it. She reached for the picket-line, and froze when the nearest horse raised its head and looked at her. Its single lead-rein was tied in a big loop around the thumb-thick line that ended at the post. *One whinny.* Her heart tried to pound its way out of her chest, sounding loud enough to bring the guards.

Never taking her eyes off the horse, she sliced at the picket-rope, feeling in front of her blade to see how far she had cut. The horse tossed its head, and her breath went cold. *Just one whinny.*

Only a few thin strands of hemp remained whole under her fingers. Slowly she headed toward the next line, watching the horse until she could no longer see if it was looking at her or not, then drew a ragged breath. If they were all like that, she did not think she would last.

At the next picket-rope, though, and the next, and the next, the horses remained asleep, even when she cut her thumb and bit off a yelp. Sucking the cut, she looked warily back the way she had come. Upwind as she was, she could no longer hear the guards make their exchange, but they might have heard her if they were in the right place. If they were coming to see what the noise had been, the wind would keep her from hearing them until they were right on top of her. *Time to go. With four horses out of five running loose, they won't be chasing anyone.*

But she did not move. She could imagine Lan's eyes when he heard what she had done. There would be no accusation in them; her reasoning was sound, and he would not expect any more of her. She was a Wisdom, not a bloody great invincible Warder who could make himself all but invisible. Jaw set, she moved to the last picket-line. The first horse on it was Bela.

There was no mistaking that squat, shaggy shape; for there to be another horse like that, here and now, was too big a coincidence. Suddenly she was so glad that she had not left off this last line that she was shaking. Her arms and legs trembled so that she was afraid to touch the picket-rope, but her mind was as clear as the Winespring Water. Whichever of the boys was in the camp, Egwene was there, too. And if they left riding double, some of the Children would catch them no matter how well the horses were scattered, and some of them would die. She was as certain as if she were listening to the wind. That stuck a spike of fear into her belly, fear of *how* she was certain. This had nothing to do with weather or crops or sickness. *Why did Moiraine tell me I can use the Power? Why couldn't she leave me alone?*

Strangely, the fear stilled her trembling. With hands as steady as if she were grinding herbs in her own house she slit the picket-rope as she had the others. Thrusting the dagger back into its sheath, she untied Bela's lead-rein. The shaggy mare woke with a start, tossing her head, but

Nynaeve stroked her nose and spoke comforting words softly in her ear. Bela gave a low snort and seemed content.

Other horses along that line were awake, too, and looking at her. Remembering Mandarb, she reached hesitantly to the next lead-rein, but that horse gave no objection to a strange hand. Indeed, it seemed to want some of the muzzle-stroking that Bela had received. She gripped Bela's rein tightly and wrapped the other around her other wrist, all the while watching the camp nervously. The pale tents were only thirty yards off, and she could see men moving among them. If they noticed the horses stirring and came to see what caused it. . . .

Desperately she wished for Moiraine not to wait on her return. Whatever the Aes Sedai was going to do, let her do it now. *Light, make her do it now, before.* . . .

Abruptly lightning shattered the night overhead, for a moment obliterating darkness. Thunder smote her ears, so hard she thought her knees would buckle, as a jagged trident stabbed the ground just beyond the horses, splashing dirt and rocks like a fountain. The crash of riven earth fought the thunderstroke. The horses went mad, screaming and rearing; the picket-ropes snapped like thread where she had cut them. Another lightning bolt sliced down before the image of the first faded.

Nynaeve was too busy to exult. At the first clash Bela jerked one way while the other horse reared away in the opposite direction. She thought her arms were being pulled out of their sockets. For an endless minute she hung suspended between the horses, her feet off the ground, her scream flattened by the second crash. Again the lightning struck, and again, and again, in one continuous, raging roar from the heavens. Balked in the way they wanted to go, the horses surged back, letting her drop. She wanted to crouch on the ground and soothe her tortured shoulders, but there was no time. Bela and the other horse buffeted her, eyes rolling wildly till only whites showed, threatening to knock her down and trample her. Somehow she made her arms lift, clutched her hands in Bela's mane, pulled herself onto the heaving mare's back. The other rein was still around her wrist, pulled tight into the flesh.

Her jaw dropped as a long, gray shadow snarled past, seeming to ignore her and the horses with her, but teeth snapping at the crazed animals now darting in every direction. A second shadow of death followed close behind. Nynaeve wanted to scream again, but nothing came out. *Wolves! Light help us! What is Moiraine doing?*

The heels she dug into Bela's sides were not needed. The mare ran, and the other was more than happy to follow. Anywhere, so long as they could run, so long as they could escape the fire from the sky that killed the night.

CHAPTER
38

Rescue

Perrin shifted as best he could with his wrists bound behind him and finally gave up with a sigh. Every rock he avoided brought him two more. Awkwardly he tried to work his cloak back over him. The night was cold, and the ground seemed to draw all the heat out of him, as it had every night since the Whitecloaks took them. The Children did not think prisoners needed blankets, or shelter. Especially not dangerous Darkfriends.

Egwene lay huddled against his back for warmth, sleeping the deep sleep of exhaustion. She never even murmured at his shifting. The sun was long hours below the horizon, and he ached from head to foot after a day walking behind a horse with a halter around his neck, but sleep would not come for him.

The column did not move that fast. With most of their remounts lost to the wolves in the *stedding,* the Whitecloaks could not push on as hard as they wanted; the delay was another thing they held against the Emond's Fielders. The sinuous double line did move steadily, though—Lord Bornhald meant to reach Caemlyn in time for whatever it was—and always in the back of Perrin's mind was the fear that if he fell the Whitecloak holding his leash would not stop, no matter Lord Captain Bornhald's orders to keep them alive for the Questioners in Amador. He knew he could not save himself if that happened; the only times they freed his hands were when he was fed and for visits to the latrine pit. The halter made every step momentous, every rock underfoot potentially fatal. He walked with muscles tense, scanning the ground with anxious eyes. Whenever he glanced at

Egwene, she was doing the same. When she met his eyes, her face was tight and frightened. Neither of them dared take their eyes off the ground long enough for more than a glance.

Usually he collapsed like a wrung-out rag as soon as the Whitecloaks let him stop, but tonight his mind was racing. His skin crawled with dread that had been building for days. If he closed his eyes, he would see only the things Byar promised for them once they reached Amador.

He was sure Egwene still did not believe what Byar told them in that flat voice. If she did, she would not be able to sleep no matter how tired she was. In the beginning he had not believed Byar either. He still did not want to; people just did not do things like that to other people. But Byar did not really threaten; as if he were talking about getting a drink of water he talked about hot irons and pincers, about knives slicing away skin and needles piercing. He did not appear to be trying to frighten them. There was never even a touch of gloating in his eyes. He just did not care if they were frightened or not, if they were tortured or not, if they were alive or not. That was what brought cold sweat to Perrin's face once it got through to him. That was what finally convinced him Byar was telling the simple truth.

The two guards' cloaks gleamed grayly in the faint moonlight. He could not make out their faces, but he knew they were watching. As if they could try something, tied hand and foot the way they were. From when there had still been light enough to see, he remembered the disgust in their eyes and the pinched looks on their faces, as though they had been set to guard filth-soaked monsters, stinking and repellent to look at. All the Whitecloaks looked at them that way. It never changed. *Light, how do I make them believe we aren't Darkfriends when they're already convinced we are?* His stomach twisted sickeningly. In the end, he would probably confess to anything just to make the Questioners stop.

Someone was coming, a Whitecloak carrying a lantern. The man stopped to speak with the guards, who answered respectfully. Perrin could not hear what was said, but he recognized the tall, gaunt shape.

He squinted as the lantern was held close to his face. Byar had Perrin's axe in his other hand; he had appropriated the weapon as his own. At least, Perrin never saw him without it.

"Wake up," Byar said emotionlessly, as if he thought Perrin slept with his head raised. He accompanied the words with a heavy kick in the ribs.

Perrin gave a grunt through gritted teeth. His sides were a mass of bruises already from Byar's boots.

"I said, wake up." The foot went back again, and Perrin spoke quickly.

"I'm awake." You had to acknowledge what Byar said, or he found ways to get your attention.

Byar set the lantern on the ground and bent to check his bonds. The man jerked roughly at his wrist, twisting his arms in their sockets. Finding those knots still as tight as he had left them, Byar pulled at his ankle rope, scraping him across the rocky ground. The man looked too skeletal to have any strength, but Perrin might as well have been a child. It was a nightly routine.

As Byar straightened, Perrin saw that Egwene was still asleep. "Wake up!" he shouted. "Egwene! Wake up!"

"Wha . . . ? What?" Egwene's voice was frightened and still thick with sleep. She lifted her head, blinking in the lantern light.

Byar gave no sign of disappointment at not being able to kick her awake; he never did. He just jerked at her ropes the same way he had Perrin's, ignoring her groans. Causing pain was another of those things that seemed not to affect him one way or another; Perrin was the only one he really went out of his way to hurt. Even if Perrin could not remember it, Byar remembered that he had killed two of the Children.

"Why should Darkfriends sleep," Byar said dispassionately, "when decent men must stay awake to guard them?"

"For the hundredth time," Egwene said wearily, "we aren't Darkfriends."

Perrin tensed. Sometimes such a denial brought a lecture delivered in a grating near monotone, on confession and repentance, leading into a description of the Questioners' methods of obtaining them. Sometimes it brought the lecture and a kick. To his surprise, this time Byar ignored it.

Instead the man squatted in front of him, all angles and sunken hollows, with the axe across his knees. The golden sun on his cloak's left breast, and the two golden stars beneath it, glittered in the lantern light. Taking off his helmet, he set it beside the lantern. For a change there was something besides disdain or hatred on his face, something intent and unreadable. He rested his arms on the axehandle and studied Perrin silently. Perrin tried not to shift under that hollow-eyed stare.

"You are slowing us down, Darkfriend, you and your wolves. The Council of the Anointed has heard reports of such things, and they want to know more, so you must be taken to Amador and given to the Questioners, but you are slowing us down. I had hoped we could move fast enough, even without the remounts, but I was wrong." He fell silent, frowning at them.

Perrin waited; Byar would tell him when he was ready.

"The Lord Captain is caught in the cleft of a dilemma," Byar said finally. "Because of the wolves he must take you to the Council, but he must reach Caemlyn, too. We have no spare horses to carry you, but if we continue to let you walk, we will not reach Caemlyn by the appointed time. The Lord Captain sees his duties with a single-minded vision, and he intends to see you before the Council."

Egwene made a sound. Byar was staring at Perrin, and he stared back, almost afraid to blink. "I don't understand," he said slowly.

"There is nothing to understand," Byar replied. "Nothing but idle speculation. If you escaped, we would not have time to track you down. We don't have an hour to spare if we are to reach Caemlyn in time. If you frayed your ropes on a sharp rock, say, and vanished into the night, the Lord Captain's problem would be solved." Never taking his gaze from Perrin, he reached under his cloak and tossed something on the ground.

Automatically Perrin's eyes followed it. When he realized what it was, he gasped. A rock. A split rock with a sharp edge.

"Just idle speculation," Byar said. "Your guards tonight also speculate."

Perrin's mouth was suddenly dry. *Think it through! Light help me, think it through and don't make any mistakes!*

Could it be true? Could the Whitecloaks' need to get to Caemlyn quickly be important enough for this? Letting suspected Darkfriends escape? There was no use trying that way; he did not know enough. Byar was the only Whitecloak who would talk to them, aside from Lord Captain Bornhald, and neither was exactly free with information. Another way. If Byar wanted them to escape, why not simply cut their bonds? If Byar wanted them to escape? Byar, who was convinced to his marrow that they were Darkfriends. Byar, who hated Darkfriends worse than he did the Dark One himself. Byar, who looked for any excuse to cause him pain because he had killed two Whitecloaks. *Byar* wanted them to escape?

If he had thought his mind was racing before, now it sped like an avalanche. Despite the cold, sweat ran down his face in rivulets. He glanced at the guards. They were only shadows of pale gray, but it seemed to him that they were poised, waiting. If he and Egwene were killed trying to escape, and their ropes had been cut on a rock that could have been lying there by chance. . . . The Lord Captain's dilemma would be solved, all right. And Byar would have them dead, the way he wanted them.

The gaunt man picked up his helmet from beside the lantern and started to stand.

"Wait," Perrin said hoarsely. His thoughts tumbled over and over as he searched in vain for some way out. "Wait, I want to talk. I—"

Help comes!

The thought blossomed in his mind, a clear burst of light in the midst of chaos, so startling that for a moment he forgot everything else, even where he was. Dapple was alive. *Elyas,* he thought at the wolf, demanding without words to know if the man was alive. An image came back. Elyas, lying on a bed of evergreen branches beside a small fire in a cave, tending a wound in his side. It all took only an instant. He gaped at Byar, and his face broke into a foolish grin. Elyas was alive. Dapple was alive. Help was coming.

Byar paused, risen only to a crouch, looking at him. "Some thought has come to you, Perrin of the Two Rivers, and I would know what it is."

For a moment Perrin thought he meant the thought from Dapple. Panic fled across his face, followed by relief. Byar could not possibly know.

Byar watched his changes of expression, and for the first

time the Whitecloak's eyes went to the rock he had tossed
on the ground.

He was reconsidering, Perrin realized. If he changed
his mind about the rock, would he dare risk leaving them
alive to talk? Ropes could be frayed after the people wearing them were dead, even if it made for risk of discovery.
He looked into Byar's eyes—the shadowed hollows of the
man's eye sockets made them appear to stare at him from
dark caves—and he saw death decided.

Byar opened his mouth, and as Perrin waited for sentence to be pronounced, things began to happen too fast for
thought.

Suddenly one of the guards vanished. One minute there
were two dim shapes, the next the night swallowed one of
them. The second guard turned, the beginning of a cry on
his lips, but before the first syllable was uttered there was a
solid *tchunk* and he toppled over like a felled tree.

Byar spun, swift as a striking viper, the axe whirling in
his hands so fast that it hummed. Perrin's eyes bulged as
the night seemed to flow into the lantern light. His mouth
opened to yell, but his throat locked tight with fear. For an
instant he even forgot that Byar wanted to kill them. The
Whitecloak was another human being, and the night had
come alive to take them all.

Then the darkness invading the light became Lan, cloak
swirling through shades of gray and black as he moved.
The axe in Byar's hands lashed out like lightning . . . and
Lan seemed to lean casually aside, letting the blade pass
so close he must have felt the wind of it. Byar's eyes widened as the force of his blow carried him off balance, as the
Warder struck with hands and feet in rapid succession, so
quick that Perrin was not sure what he had just seen. What
he was sure of was Byar collapsing like a puppet. Before
the falling Whitecloak had finished settling to the ground,
the Warder was on his knees extinguishing the lantern.

In the sudden return to darkness, Perrin stared blindly.
Lan seemed to have vanished again.

"Is it really . . . ?" Egwene gave a stifled sob. "We thought
you were dead. We thought you were all dead."

"Not yet." The Warder's deep whisper was tinged with
amusement.

Hands touched Perrin, found his bonds. A knife sliced

through the ropes with barely a tug, and he was free. Aching muscles protested as he sat up. Rubbing his wrists, he peered at the graying mound that marked Byar. "Did you . . . ? Is he . . . ?"

"No," Lan's voice answered quietly from the darkness. "I do not kill unless I mean to. But he won't bother anyone for a while. Stop asking questions and get a pair of their cloaks. We do not have much time."

Perrin crawled to where Byar lay. It took an effort to touch the man, and when he felt the Whitecloak's chest rising and falling he almost jerked his hands away. His skin crawled as he made himself unfasten the white cloak and pull it off. Despite what Lan said, he could imagine the skull-faced man suddenly rearing up. Hastily he fumbled around till he found his axe, then crawled to another guard. It seemed strange, at first, that he felt no reluctance to touch this unconscious man, but the reason came to him. All the Whitecloaks hated him, but that was a human emotion. Byar felt nothing beyond that he should die; there was no hate in it, no emotion at all.

Gathering the two cloaks in his arms, he turned—and panic grabbed him. In the darkness he suddenly had no sense of direction, of how to find his way back to Lan and the others. His feet rooted to the ground, afraid to move. Even Byar was hidden by the night without his white cloak. There was nothing by which to orient himself. Any way he went might be out into the camp.

"Here."

He stumbled toward Lan's whisper until hands stopped him. Egwene was a dim shadow, and Lan's face was a blur; the rest of the Warder seemed not to be there at all. He could feel their eyes on him, and he wondered if he should explain.

"Put on the cloaks," Lan said softly. "Quickly. Bundle your own. And make no sound. You aren't safe yet."

Hurriedly Perrin passed one of the cloaks to Egwene, relieved at being saved from having to tell of his fear. He made his own cloak into a bundle to carry, and swung the white cloak around his shoulders in its place. He felt a prickle as it settled around his shoulders, a stab of worry between his shoulder blades. Was it Byar's cloak he had ended up with? He almost thought he could smell the gaunt man on it.

Lan directed them to hold hands, and Perrin gripped his axe in one hand and Egwene's hand with the other, wishing the Warder would get on with their escape so he could stop his imagination from running wild. But they just stood there, surrounded by the tents of the Children, two shapes in white cloaks and one that was sensed but not seen.

"Soon," Lan whispered. "Very soon."

Lightning broke the night above the camp, so close that Perrin felt the hair on his arms, his head, lifting as the bolt charged the air. Just beyond the tents the earth erupted from the blow, the explosion on the ground merging with that in the sky. Before the light faded Lan was leading them forward.

At their first step another strike sliced open the blackness. Lightning came like hail, so that the night flickered as if the darkness were coming in momentary flashes. Thunder drummed wildly, one roar rumbling into the next, one continuous, rippling peal. Fear-stricken horses screamed, their whinnies drowned except for moments when the thunder faded. Men tumbled out of their tents, some in their white cloaks, some only half clothed, some dashing to and fro, some standing as if stunned.

Through the middle of it Lan pulled them at a trot, Perrin bringing up the rear. Whitecloaks looked at them, wild-eyed, as they passed. A few shouted at them, the shouts lost in the pounding from the heavens, but with their white cloaks gathered around them no one tried to stop them. Through the tents, out of the camp and into the night, and no one raised a hand against them.

The ground turned uneven under Perrin's feet, and brush slapped at him as he let himself be drawn along. The lightning flickered fitfully and was gone. Echoes of thunder rolled across the sky before they, too, faded away. Perrin looked over his shoulder. A handful of fires burned back there, among the tents. Some of the lightning must have struck home, or perhaps men had knocked over lamps in their panic. Men still shouted, voices tiny in the night, trying to restore order, to find out what had happened. The land began to slope upwards, and tents and fires and shouting were left behind.

Suddenly he almost trod on Egwene's heels as Lan stopped. Ahead in the moonlight stood three horses.

A shadow stirred, and Moiraine's voice came, weighted with irritation. "Nynaeve has not returned. I fear that young woman has done something foolish." Lan spun on his heel as if to return the way they had come, but a single whip-crack word from Moiraine halted him. "No!" He stood looking at her sideways, only his face and hands truly visible, and they but dimly shadowed blurs. She went on in a gentler tone; gentler but no less firm. "Some things are more important than others. You know that." The Warder did not move, and her voice hardened again. "Remember your oaths, al'Lan Mandragoran, Lord of the Seven Towers! What of the oath of a Diademed Battle Lord of the Malkieri?"

Perrin blinked. Lan was all of that? Egwene was murmuring, but he could not take his eyes off the tableau in front of him, Lan standing like a wolf from Dapple's pack, a wolf at bay before the diminutive Aes Sedai and vainly seeking escape from doom.

The frozen scene was broken by a crash of breaking branches in the woods. In two long strides Lan was between Moiraine and the sound, the pale moonlight rippling along his sword. To the crackle and snap of underbrush a pair of horses burst from the trees, one with a rider.

"Bela!" Egwene exclaimed at the same time that Nynaeve said from the shaggy mare's back, "I almost didn't find you again. Egwene! Thank the Light you're alive!"

She slid down off Bela, but as she started toward the Emond's Fielders Lan caught her arm and she stopped short, staring up at him.

"We must go, Lan," Moiraine said, once more sounding unruffled, and the Warder released his grip.

Nynaeve rubbed her arm as she hurried to hug Egwene, but Perrin thought he heard her give a low laugh, too. It puzzled him because he did not think it had anything to do with her happiness at seeing them again.

"Where are Rand and Mat?" he asked.

"Elsewhere," Moiraine replied, and Nynaeve muttered something in a sharp tone that made Egwene gasp. Perrin blinked; he had caught the edge of a wagoneer's oath, and a coarse one. "The Light send they are well," the Aes Sedai went on as if she had not noticed.

"We will none of us be well," Lan said, "if the White-cloaks find us. Change your cloaks, and get mounted."

Perrin scrambled up onto the horse Nynaeve had brought behind Bela. The lack of a saddle did not hamper him; he did not ride often at home, but when he did it was more likely bareback than not. He still carried the white cloak, now rolled up and tied to his belt. The Warder said they must leave no more traces for the Children to find than they could help. He still thought he could smell Byar on it.

As they started out, the Warder leading on his tall black stallion, Perrin felt Dapple's touch on his mind once more. *One day again.* More a feeling than words, it sighed with the promise of a meeting foreordained, with anticipation of what was to come, with resignation to what was to come, all streaked in layers. He tried to ask when and why, fumbling in haste and sudden fear. The trace of the wolves grew fainter, fading. His frantic questions brought only the same heavy-laden answer. *One day again.* It hung haunting in his mind long after awareness of the wolves winked out.

Lan pressed southward slowly but steadily. The night-draped wilderness, all rolling ground and underbrush hidden until it was underfoot, shadowed trees thick against the sky, allowed no great speed in any case. Twice the Warder left them, riding back toward the slivered moon, he and Mandarb becoming one with the night behind. Both times he returned to report no sign of pursuit.

Egwene stayed close beside Nynaeve. Soft-spoken scraps of excited talk floated back to Perrin. Those two were as buoyed up as if they had found home again. He hung back at the tail of their little column. Sometimes the Wisdom turned in her saddle to look back at him, and each time he gave her a wave, as if to say that he was all right, and stayed where he was. He had a lot to think about, though he could not get any of it straight in his head. *What was to come. What* was *to come?*

Perrin thought it could not be much short of dawn when Moiraine finally called a halt. Lan found a gully where he could build a fire hidden within a hollow in one of the banks.

Finally they were allowed to rid themselves of the white cloaks, burying them in a hole dug near the fire. As he was about to toss in the cloak he had used, the embroidered golden sun on the breast caught his eye, and the two golden stars beneath. He dropped the cloak as if it stung and walked away, scrubbing his hands on his coat, to sit alone.

"Now," Egwene said, once Lan was shoveling dirt into the hole, "will somebody tell me where Rand and Mat are?"

"I believe they are in Caemlyn," Moiraine said carefully, "or on their way there." Nynaeve gave a loud, disparaging grunt, but the Aes Sedai went on as if she had not been interrupted. "If they are not, I will yet find them. That I promise."

They made a quiet meal on bread and cheese and hot tea. Even Egwene's enthusiasm succumbed to weariness. The Wisdom produced an ointment from her bag for the weals the ropes had left on Egwene's wrists, and a different one for her other bruises. When she came to where Perrin sat on the edge of the firelight, he did not look up.

She stood looking at him silently for a time, then squatted with her bag beside her, saying briskly, "Take your coat and shirt off, Perrin. They tell me one of the Whitecloaks took a dislike to you."

He complied slowly, still half lost in Dapple's message, until Nynaeve gasped. Startled, he stared at her, then at his own bare chest. It was a mass of color, the newer, purple blotches overlaying older ones faded into shades of brown and yellow. Only thick slabs of muscle earned by hours at Master Luhhan's forge had saved him from broken ribs. With his mind filled by the wolves, he had managed to forget the pain, but he was reminded of it now, and it came back gladly. Involuntarily he took a deep breath, and clamped his lips on a groan.

"How could he have disliked you so much?" Nynaeve asked wonderingly.

I killed *two men.* Aloud, he said, "I don't know."

She rummaged in her bag, and he flinched when she began spreading a greasy ointment over his bruises. "Ground ivy, five-finger, and sunburst root," she said.

It was hot and cold at the same time, making him shiver while he broke into a sweat, but he did not protest. He had had experience of Nynaeve's ointments and poultices before. As her fingers gently rubbed the mixture in, the heat and cold vanished, taking the pain with them. The purple splotches faded to brown, and the brown and yellow paled, some disappearing altogether. Experimentally, he took a deep breath; there was barely a twinge.

"You look surprised," Nynaeve said. She looked a little surprised herself, and strangely frightened. "Next time, you can go to *her*."

"Not surprised," he said soothingly, "just glad." Sometimes Nynaeve's ointments worked fast and sometimes slow, but they always worked. "What . . . what happened to Rand and Mat?"

Nynaeve began stuffing her vials and pots back into her bag, jamming each one in as if she were thrusting it through a barrier. "*She* says they're all right. *She* says we'll find them. In Caemlyn, *she* says. *She* says it's too important for us not to, whatever *that* means. *She* says a great many things."

Perrin grinned in spite of himself. Whatever else had changed, the Wisdom was still herself, and she and the Aes Sedai were still far from fast friends.

Abruptly Nynaeve stiffened, staring at his face. Dropping her bag, she pressed the backs of her hands to his cheeks and forehead. He tried to pull back, but she caught his head in both hands and thumbed back his eyelids, peering into his eyes and muttering to herself. Despite her small size she held his face easily; it was never easy to get away from Nynaeve when she did not want you to.

"I don't understand," she said finally, releasing him and settling back to sit on her heels. "If it was yelloweye fever, you wouldn't be able to stand. But you don't have any fever, and the whites of your eyes aren't yellowed, just the irises."

"Yellow?" Moiraine said, and Perrin and Nynaeve both jumped where they sat. The Aes Sedai's approach had been utterly silent. Egwene was asleep by the fire, wrapped in her cloaks, Perrin saw. His own eyelids wanted to slide closed.

"It isn't anything," he said, but Moiraine put a hand under his chin and turned his face up so she could peer into his eyes the way Nynaeve had. He jerked away, prickling. The two women were handling him as if he were a child. "I said it isn't anything."

"There was no foretelling this." Moiraine spoke as if to herself. Her eyes seemed to look at something beyond him. "Something ordained to be woven, or a change in the

Pattern? If a change, by what hand? The Wheel weaves as the Wheel wills. It must be that."

"Do you know what it is?" Nynaeve asked reluctantly, then hesitated. "Can you do something for him? Your Healing?" The request for aid, the admission that she could do nothing, came out of her as if dragged.

Perrin glared at both the women. "If you're going to talk about me, talk to me. I'm sitting right here." Neither looked at him.

"Healing?" Moiraine smiled. "Healing can do nothing about this. It is not an illness, and it will not. . . ." She hesitated briefly. She did glance at Perrin, then, a quick look that regretted many things. The look did not include him, though, and he muttered sourly as she turned back to Nynaeve. "I was going to say it will not harm him, but who can say what the end will be? At least I can say it will not harm him directly."

Nynaeve stood, dusting off her knees, and confronted the Aes Sedai eye to eye. "That's not good enough. If there's something wrong with—"

"What is, is. What is woven already is past changing." Moiraine turned away abruptly. "We must sleep while we can and leave at first light. If the Dark One's hand grows too strong. . . . We must reach Caemlyn quickly."

Angrily, Nynaeve snatched up her bag and stalked off before Perrin could speak. He started to growl an oath, but a thought hit him like a blow and he sat there gaping silently. Moiraine knew. The Aes Sedai knew about the wolves. And she thought it could be the Dark One's doing. A shiver ran through him. Hastily he shrugged back into his shirt, tucking it in awkwardly, and pulled his coat and cloak back on. The clothing did not help very much; he felt chilled right down to his bones, his marrow like frozen jelly.

Lan dropped to the ground cross-legged, tossing back his cloak. Perrin was glad of that. It was unpleasant, looking at the Warder and having his eyes slide past.

For a long moment they simply stared at one another. The hard planes of the Warder's face were unreadable, but in his eyes Perrin thought he saw . . . something. Sympathy? Curiosity? Both?

"You know?" he said, and Lan nodded.

"I know some, not all. Did it just come to you, or did you meet a guide, an intermediary?"

"There was a man," Perrin said slowly. *He knows, but does he think the same as Moiraine?* "He said his name was Elyas. Elyas Machera." Lan drew a deep breath, and Perrin looked at him sharply. "You know him?"

"I knew him. He taught me much, about the Blight, and about this." Lan touched his sword hilt. "He was a Warder, before . . . before what happened. The Red Ajah. . . ." He glanced to where Moiraine was, lying before the fire.

It was the first time Perrin could remember any uncertainty in the Warder. At Shadar Logoth Lan had been sure and strong, and when he was facing Fades and Trollocs. He was not afraid now—Perrin was convinced of that—but he was wary, as if he might say too much. As if what he said could be dangerous.

"I've heard of the Red Ajah," he told Lan.

"And most of what you've heard is wrong, no doubt. You must understand, there are . . . factions within Tar Valon. Some would fight the Dark One one way, some another. The goal is the same, but the differences . . . the differences can mean lives changed, or ended. The lives of men or nations. He is well, Elyas?"

"I think so. The Whitecloaks said they killed him, but Dapple—" Perrin glanced at the Warder uncomfortably. "I don't know." Lan seemed to accept that he did not, reluctantly, and it emboldened him to go on. "This communicating with the wolves. Moiraine seems to think it's something the . . . something the Dark One did. It isn't, is it?" He would not believe Elyas was a Darkfriend.

But Lan hesitated, and sweat started on Perrin's face, chill beads made colder by the night. They were sliding down his cheeks by the time the Warder spoke.

"Not in itself, no. Some believe it is, but they are wrong; it was old and lost long before the Dark One was found. But what of the chance involved, blacksmith? Sometimes the Pattern has a randomness to it—to our eyes, at least— but what chance that you should meet a man who could guide you in this thing, and you one who could follow the guiding? The Pattern is forming a Great Web, what some call the Lace of Ages, and you lads are central to it. I don't

think there is much chance left in your lives, now. Have you
been chosen out, then? And if so, by the Light, or by the
Shadow?"

"The Dark One can't touch us unless we name him." Immediately Perrin thought of the dreams of Ba'alzamon, the
dreams that were more than dreams. He scrubbed the sweat
off his face. "He can't."

"Rock-hard stubborn," the Warder mused. "Maybe stubborn enough to save yourself, in the end. Remember the
times we live in, blacksmith. Remember what Moiraine Sedai told you. In these times many things are dissolving, and
breaking apart. Old barriers weaken, old walls crumble.
The barriers between what is and what was, between what
is and what will be." His voice turned grim. "The walls of
the Dark One's prison. This may be the end of an Age. We
may see a new Age born before we die. Or perhaps it is the
end of Ages, the end of time itself. The end of the world."
Suddenly he grinned, but his grin was as dark as a scowl;
his eyes sparkled merrily, laughing at the foot of the gallows. "But that's not for us to worry about, eh, blacksmith?
We'll fight the Shadow as long as we have breath, and if it
overruns us, we'll go under biting and clawing. You Two
Rivers folk are too stubborn to surrender. Don't you worry
whether the Dark One has stirred in your life. You are back
among friends, now. Remember, the Wheel weaves as the
Wheel wills, and even the Dark One cannot change that,
not with Moiraine to watch over you. But we had better find
your friends soon."

"What do you mean?"

"They have no Aes Sedai touching the True Source to
protect them. Blacksmith, perhaps the walls have weakened
enough for the Dark One himself to touch events. Not with
a free hand, or we'd be done already, but maybe tiny shift-
ings in the threads. A chance turning of one corner instead
of another, a chance meeting, a chance word, or what seems
like chance, and they could be so far under the Shadow not
even Moiraine could bring them back."

"We have to find them," Perrin said, and the Warder gave
a grunt of a laugh.

"What have I been saying? Get some sleep, blacksmith."
Lan's cloak swung back around him as he stood. In the faint
light from fire and moon he seemed almost part of the shad-

ows beyond. "We have a hard few days to Caemlyn. Just you pray we find them there."

"But Moiraine . . . she can find them anywhere, can't she? She says she can."

"But can she find them in time? If the Dark One is strong enough to take a hand himself, time is running out. You pray we find them in Caemlyn, blacksmith, or we may all be lost."

CHAPTER
39

Weaving of the Web

Rand looked down on the crowds from the high window of his room in The Queen's Blessing. They ran shouting along the street, all streaming in the same direction, waving pennants and banners, the white lion standing guard on a thousand fields of red. Caemlyners and outlanders, they ran together, and for a change no one appeared to want to bash anyone else's head. Today, maybe, there was only one faction.

He turned from the window grinning. Next to the day when Egwene and Perrin walked in, alive and laughing over what they had seen, this was the day he had been waiting for most.

"Are you coming?" he asked again.

Mat glowered from where he lay curled up in a ball on his bed. "Take that Trolloc you're so friendly with."

"Blood and ashes, Mat, he's not a Trolloc. You're just being stubborn stupid. How many times do you want to have this argument? Light, it's not as if you'd never heard of Ogier before."

"I never heard they looked like Trollocs." Mat pushed his face into his pillow and curled himself tighter.

"Stubborn stupid," Rand muttered. "How long are you going to hide up here? I'm not going to keep bringing you your meals up all those stairs forever. You could do with a bath, too." Mat shrugged around on the bed as if he were trying to burrow deeper into it. Rand sighed, then went to the door. "Last chance to go together, Mat. I'm leaving now." He closed the door slowly, hoping that Mat would change his mind, but his friend did not stir. The door clicked shut.

In the hallway, he leaned against the doorframe. Master Gill said there was an old woman two streets over, Mother Grubb, who sold herbs and poultices, besides birthing babies, tending the sick, and telling fortunes. She sounded a little like a Wisdom. Nynaeve was who Mat needed, or maybe Moiraine, but Mother Grubb was who he had. Bringing her to The Queen's Blessing might bring the wrong kind of attention as well, though, if she would even come. For her as well as for Mat and him.

Herbalists and hedge-doctors were lying low in Caemlyn right now; there was talk against anyone who did any kind of healing, or fortunetelling. Every night the Dragon's Fang was scrawled on doors with a free hand, sometimes even in the daylight, and people might forget who had cured their fevers and poulticed their toothaches when the cry of Darkfriend went up. That was the temper in the city.

It was not as if Mat were really sick. He ate everything Rand carried up from the kitchen—he would take nothing from anyone else's hand, though—and never complained about aches or fever. He just refused to leave the room. But Rand had been sure today would bring him out.

He settled his cloak on his shoulders and hitched his sword belt around so the sword, and the red cloth wrapped around it, was covered more.

At the foot of the stairs he met Master Gill just starting up. "There's someone been asking after you in the city," the innkeeper said around his pipe. Rand felt a surge of hope. "Asking after you and those friends of yours, by name. You younglings, anyway. Seems to want you three lads most."

Anxiety replaced hope. "Who?" Rand asked. He still could not help glancing up and down the hall. Except for they two, it was empty, from the exit into the alley to the common room door.

"Don't know his name. Just heard about him. I hear most things in Caemlyn, eventually. Beggar." The innkeeper grunted. "Half mad, I hear. Even so, he could take the Queen's Bounty at the Palace, even with things as hard as they are. On High Days, the Queen gives it out with her own hands, and there's never anyone turned away for any reason. No one needs to beg in Caemlyn. Even a man under warrant can't be arrested while he's taking the Queen's Bounty."

"A Darkfriend?" Rand said reluctantly. *If the Dark-friends know our names. . . .*

"You've got Darkfriends on the brain, young fellow. They're around, certainly, but just because the Whitecloaks have everybody stirred up is no reason for you to think the city's full of them. Do you know what rumor those idiots have started now? 'Strange shapes.' Can you believe it? Strange shapes creeping around outside the city in the night." The innkeeper chuckled till his belly shook.

Rand did not feel like laughing. Hyam Kinch had talked about strange shapes, and there had surely enough been a Fade back there. "What kind of shapes?"

"What kind? I don't know what kind. Strange shapes. Trollocs, probably. The Shadowman. Lews Therin Kinslayer himself, come back fifty feet high. What kind of shapes do you *think* people will imagine now the idea's in their heads? It's none of our worry." Master Gill eyed him for a moment. "Going out, are you? Well, I can't say I care for it, myself, even today, but there's hardly anybody left here but me. Not your friend?"

"Mat's not feeling very well. Maybe later."

"Well, be that as it may. You watch yourself, now. Even today good Queen's men will be outnumbered out there, Light burn the day I ever thought to see it so. Best you leave by the alleyway. There's two of those blood-be-damned traitors sitting across the street watching my front door. They know where I stand, by the Light!"

Rand stuck his head out and looked both ways before slipping into the alley. A bulky man Master Gill had hired stood at the head of the alley, leaning on a spear and watching the people run past with an apparent lack of interest. It was only apparent, Rand knew. The fellow—his name was Lamgwin—saw everything through those heavy-lidded eyes, and for all his bullish bulk he could move like a cat. He also thought Queen Morgase was the Light made flesh, or near enough. There were a dozen like him scattered around The Queen's Blessing.

Lamgwin's ear twitched when Rand reached the mouth of the alley, but he never took his disinterest off the street. Rand knew the man had heard him coming.

"Watch your back today, man." Lamgwin's voice sounded like gravel in a pan. "When the trouble starts, you'll be a handy one to have here, not somewhere with a knife in your back."

Rand glanced at the blocky man, but his surprise was muted. He always tried to keep the sword out of sight, but this was not the first time one of Master Gill's men had assumed he would know his way in a fight. Lamgwin did not look back at him. The man's job was guarding the inn, and he did it.

Pushing his sword back a little further under his cloak, Rand joined the flow of people. He saw the two men the innkeeper had mentioned, standing on upturned barrels across the street from the inn so they could see over the crowd. He did not think they noticed him coming out of the alley. They made no secret of their allegiance. Not only were their swords wrapped in white tied with red, they wore white armbands and white cockades on their hats.

He had not been in Caemlyn long before learning that red wrappings on a sword, or a red armband or cockade, meant support for Queen Morgase. White said the Queen and her involvement with Aes Sedai and Tar Valon were to blame for everything that had gone wrong. For the weather, and the failed crops. Maybe even for the false Dragon.

He did not want to get involved in Caemlyn politics. Only, it was too late, now. It was not just that he had already chosen—by accident, but there it was. Matters in the city had gone beyond letting anyone stay neutral. Even outlanders wore cockades and armbands, or wrapped their swords, and more wore the white than the red. Maybe some of them did not think that way, but they were far from home and that was the way sentiment was running in Caemlyn. Men who supported the Queen went about in groups for their own protection, when they went out at all.

Today, though, it was different. On the surface, at least. Today, Caemlyn celebrated a victory of the Light over the Shadow. Today the false Dragon was being brought into the city, to be displayed before the Queen before he was taken north to Tar Valon.

No one talked about that part of it. No one but the Aes Sedai could deal with a man who could actually wield the One Power, of course, but no one wanted to talk about it. The Light had defeated the Shadow, and soldiers from Andor had been in the forefront of the battle. For today, that

was all that was important. For today, everything else could
be forgotten.

Or could it, Rand wondered. The crowd ran, singing and
waving banners, laughing, but men displaying the red kept
together in knots of ten or twenty, and there were no women
or children with them. He thought there were at least ten
men showing white for every one proclaiming allegiance
to the Queen. Not for the first time, he wished white cloth
had been the cheaper. *But would Master Gill have helped if
you'd been showing the white?*

The crowd was so thick that jostling was inevitable.
Even Whitecloaks did not enjoy their little open spaces in
the throng today. As Rand let the crowd carry him toward
the Inner City, he realized that not all animosities were being reined in. He saw one of the Children of the Light, one
of three, bumped so hard he almost fell. The Whitecloak
barely caught himself and started an angry oath at the man
who had bumped him when another man staggered him
with a deliberate, aimed shoulder. Before matters could go
any further the Whitecloak's companions pulled him over to
the side of the street to where they could shelter in a doorway. The three seemed caught between their normal glaring
stare and disbelief. The crowd streamed on by as if none had
noticed, and perhaps none had.

No one would have dared do such a thing two days
earlier. More, Rand realized, the men who had done the
bumping wore white cockades on their hats. It was widely
believed the Whitecloaks supported those who opposed the
Queen and her Aes Sedai advisor, but that made no difference. Men were doing things of which they had never
before thought. Jostling a Whitecloak, today. Tomorrow,
perhaps pulling down a Queen? Suddenly he wished there
were a few more men close to him showing red; jostled by
white cockades and armbands, he abruptly felt very alone.

The Whitecloaks noticed him looking at them and stared
back as if meeting a challenge. He let a singing swirl in the
crowd sweep him out of their sight, and joined in their song.

> Forward the Lion,
> forward the Lion,
> the White Lion takes the field.
> Roar defiance at the Shadow.

Forward the Lion,
forward, Andor triumphant.

The route that would bring the false Dragon into Caemlyn was well known. Those streets themselves were kept clear by solid lines of the Queen's Guards and red-cloaked pikemen, but people packed the edges of them shoulder to shoulder, even the windows and the rooftops. Rand worked his way into the Inner City, trying to get closer to the Palace. He had some thought of actually seeing Logain displayed before the Queen. To see the false Dragon and a Queen, both . . . that was something he had never dreamed of back home.

The Inner City was built on hills, and much of what the Ogier had made still remained. Where streets in the New City mostly ran every which way in a crazy-quilt, here they followed the curves of the hills as if they were a natural part of the earth. Sweeping rises and dips presented new and surprising vistas at every turn. Parks seen from different angles, even from above, where their walks and monuments made patterns pleasing to the eye though barely touched with green. Towers suddenly revealed, tile-covered walls glittering in the sunlight with a hundred changing colors. Sudden rises where the gaze was thrown out across the entire city to the rolling plains and forests beyond. All in all, it would have been something to see if not for the crowd that hurried him along before he had a chance to really take it in. And all those curving streets made it impossible to see very far ahead.

Abruptly he was swept around a bend, and there was the Palace. The streets, even following the natural contours of the land, had been laid out to spiral in on this—this glee-man's tale of pale spires and golden domes and intricate stonework traceries, with the banner of Andor waving from every prominence, a centerpiece for which all the other vistas had been designed. It seemed more sculpted by an artist than simply built like ordinary buildings.

That glimpse showed him he would get no nearer. No one was being allowed close to the Palace. Queen's Guards made scarlet ranks ten deep flanking the Palace gates. Along the tops of the white walls, on high balconies and towers, more Guards stood rigidly straight, bows precisely slanted across breastplated chests. They, too, looked like something out of a gleeman's tale, a guard of honor, but Rand did not believe that was why they were there. The clamoring crowd lining the streets was almost solid with white-wrapped swords, white armbands, and white cockades. Only here and there was the white wall broken by a knot of red. The red-uniformed guards seemed a thin barrier against all that white.

Giving up on making his way closer to the Palace, he sought a place where he could use his height to advantage. He did not have to be in the front row to see everything. The crowd shifted constantly, people shoving to get nearer the front, people hurrying off to what they thought was a better vantage point. In one of those shifts he found himself only three people from the open street, and all in front of him were shorter than he, including the pikemen. Almost everyone was. People crowded against him from both sides, sweating from the press of so many bodies. Those behind him muttered about not being able to see, and tried to wriggle past. He stood his ground, making an impervious wall with those to either side. He was content. When the false Dragon passed by, he would be close enough to see the man's face clearly.

Across the street and down toward the gates to the New City, a ripple passed through the tight-packed crowd; around the curve, an eddy of people was drawing back to let something go by. It was not like the clear space that followed Whitecloaks on any day but today. These people jerked themselves back with startled glances that became grimaces of distaste. Pressing themselves out of the way, they turned their faces from whatever it was, but watched out of the corners of their eyes until it was past.

Other eyes around him noted the disturbance, too. Keyed for the coming of the Dragon but with nothing to do now but wait, the crowd found anything at all worthy of comment. He heard speculation ranging from an Aes Sedai to Logain himself, and a few coarser suggestions that brought rough laughter from the men and disdainful sniffs from the women.

The ripple meandered through the crowd, drawing closer to the edge of the street as it came. No one seemed to hesitate in letting it go where it wanted, even if that meant losing a good spot for viewing as the crowd flowed back in on itself behind the passing. Finally, directly across from Rand, the crowd bulged into the street, pushing aside red-cloaked pikemen who struggled to shove them back, and broke open. The stooped shape that shuffled hesitantly out into the open looked more like a pile of filthy rags than a man. Rand heard murmurs of disgust around him.

The ragged man paused on the far edge of the street. His cowl, torn and stiff with dirt, swung back and forth as if searching for something, or listening. Abruptly he gave a wordless cry and flung out a dirty claw of a hand, pointing straight at Rand. Immediately he began to scuttle across the street like a bug.

The beggar. Whatever ill chance had led the man to find him like this, Rand was suddenly sure that, Darkfriend or not, he did not want to meet him face-to-face. He could feel the beggar's eyes, like greasy water on his skin. Especially he did not want the man close to him here, surrounded by people balanced on the brink of violence. The same voices that had laughed before now cursed him as he pushed his way back, away from the street.

He hurried, knowing the densely packed mass through which he had to shove and wriggle would give way before the filthy man. Struggling to force a path through the crowd, he staggered and almost fell when he abruptly broke free. Flailing his arms to keep his balance he turned the stagger into a run. People pointed at him; he was the only one not pressing the other way, and running at that. Shouts followed him. His cloak flapped behind him, exposing his red-clad sword. When he realized that, he ran faster. A lone supporter of the Queen, running, could well spark a white-cockaded mob to pursuit, even today. He ran, letting his long legs eat paving stones. Not until the shouts were left far behind did he allow himself to collapse against a wall, panting.

He did not know where he was, except that he was still within the Inner City. He could not remember how many twists and turns he had taken along those curving streets. Poised to run again, he looked back the way he had come. Only one person moved on the street, a woman walking placidly along with her shopping basket. Almost everyone in the city was gathered for a glimpse of the false Dragon. *He can't have followed me. I must have left him behind.*

The beggar would not give up; he was sure of it, though he could not say why. That ragged shape would be working its way through the crowds at that very minute, searching, and if Rand returned to see Logain he ran the risk of a meeting. For a moment he considered going back to The Queen's Blessing, but he was sure he would never get another chance to see a Queen, and he hoped he would never have another to see a false Dragon. There seemed to be something cowardly in letting a bent beggar, even a Darkfriend, chase him into hiding.

He looked around, considering. The way the Inner City was laid out, buildings were kept low, if there were buildings at all, so that someone standing at a particular spot would have nothing to interrupt the planned view. There had to be places from where he could see the procession pass with the false Dragon. Even if he could not see the Queen, he could see Logain. Suddenly determined, he set off.

In the next hour he found several such places, every last one already packed cheek-to-cheek with people avoiding the crush along the procession route. They were a solid front of white cockades and armbands. No red at all. Thinking what the sight of his sword might do in a crowd like that, he slipped away carefully, and quickly.

Shouting floated up from the New City, cries and the blaring of trumpets, the martial beat of drums. Logain and his escort were already in Caemlyn, already on their way to the Palace.

Dispirited, he wandered the all but empty streets, still halfheartedly hoping to find some way to see Logain. His eyes fell on the slope, bare of buildings, rising above the street where he was walking. In a normal spring the slope would be an expanse of flowers and grass, but now it was brown all the way to the high wall along its crest, a wall over which the tops of trees were visible.

This part of the street had not been designed for any grand view, but just ahead, over the rooftops, he could see some of the Palace spires, topped by White Lion banners fluttering in the wind. He was not sure exactly where the curve of the street ran after it rounded the hill beyond his sight, but he suddenly had a thought about that hilltop wall.

The drums and trumpets were drawing nearer, the shouting growing louder. Anxiously he scrambled up the slope.

It was not meant to be climbed, but he dug his boots into the dead sod and pulled himself up using leafless shrubs as handholds. Panting as much with desire as effort, he scrambled the last yards to the wall. It reared above him, easily twice his height and more. The air thundered with the drumbeat, rang with trumpet blasts.

The face of the wall had been left much in the natural state of the stone, the huge blocks fitted together so well that the joins were nearly invisible, the roughness making it seem almost a natural cliff. Rand grinned. The cliffs just beyond the Sand Hills were higher, and even Perrin had climbed those. His hands sought rocky knobs, his booted feet found ridges. The drums raced him as he climbed. He refused to let them win. He would reach the top before they reached the Palace. In his haste, the stone tore his hands and scraped his knees through his breeches, but he flung his arms over the top and heaved himself up with a sense of victory.

Hastily he twisted himself around to a seat on the flat, narrow top of the wall. The leafy branches of a towering tree stuck out over his head, but he had no thought for that. He looked across tiled rooftops, but from the wall his line of sight was clear. He leaned out, just a little, and could see the Palace gate, and the Queen's Guards drawn up there, and the expectant crowd. Expectant. Their shouts drowned out by the thunder of drums and trumpets, but waiting still. He grinned. *I won.*

Even as he settled in place, the first part of the procession rounded the final curve before the Palace. Twenty ranks of trumpeters came first, splitting the air with peal after triumphant peal, a fanfare of victory. Behind them, as many drummers thundered. Then came the banners of Caemlyn, white lions on red, borne by mounted men, followed by the soldiers of Caemlyn, rank on rank on rank of horsemen, armor gleaming, lances proudly held, crimson pennants fluttering. Treble rows of pikemen and archers flanked them, and came on and on after the horsemen began passing between the waiting Guards and through the Palace gates.

The last of the foot soldiers rounded the curve, and behind them was a massive wagon. Sixteen horses pulled it in hitches of four. In the center of its flat bed was a large cage of iron bars, and on each corner of the wagonbed sat two women, watching the cage as intently as if the procession and the crowd did not exist. Aes Sedai, he was certain. Between the wagon and the footmen, and to either side, rode a dozen Warders, their cloaks swirling and tangling the eye. If the Aes Sedai ignored the crowd, the Warders scanned it as if there were no other guards but they.

With all of that, it was the man in the cage who caught and held Rand's eyes. He was not close enough to see Logain's face, as he had wanted to, but suddenly he thought he was as close as he cared for. The false Dragon was a tall man, with long, dark hair curling around his broad shoulders. He held himself upright against the sway of the wagon with one hand on the bars over his head. His clothes seemed ordinary, a cloak and coat and breeches that would not have caused comment in any farming village. But the way he wore them. The way he held himself. Logain was a king in every inch of him. The cage might as well not have been there. He held himself erect, head high, and looked over the crowd as if they had come to do him honor. And wherever his gaze swept, there the people fell silent, staring back in awe. When Logain's eyes left them, they screamed with redoubled fury as if to make up for their silence, but it made no difference in the way the man stood, or in the silence that passed along with him. As the wagon rolled through the Palace gates, he turned to look back at the assembled masses. They howled at him, beyond words, a wave of sheer animal hate and fear, and Logain threw back his head and laughed as the Palace swallowed him.

Other contingents followed behind the wagons, with banners representing more who had fought and defeated the false Dragon. The Golden Bees of Illian, the three White Crescents of Tear, the Rising Sun of Cairhien, others, many others, of nations and of cities, and of great men with their own trumpets, their own drums to thunder their grandeur. It was anticlimactic after Logain.

Rand leaned out a bit further to try to catch one last sight of the caged man. *He* was *defeated, wasn't he? Light, he wouldn't be in a bloody cage if he wasn't defeated.*

Overbalanced, he slipped and grabbed at the top of the wall, pulled himself back to a somewhat safer seat. With Logain gone, he became aware of the burning in his hands, where the stone had scraped his palms and fingers. Yet he could not shake free of the images. The cage and the Aes

Sedai. Logain, undefeated. No matter the cage, that had not been a defeated man. He shivered and rubbed his stinging hands on his thighs.

"Why were the Aes Sedai watching him?" he wondered aloud.

"They're keeping him from touching the True Source, silly."

He jerked to look up, toward the girl's voice, and suddenly his precarious seat was gone. He had only time to realize that he was toppling backward, falling, when something struck his head and a laughing Logain chased him into spinning darkness.

CHAPTER
40

The Web Tightens

It seemed to Rand that he was sitting at table with Logain and Moiraine. The Aes Sedai and the false Dragon sat watching him silently, as if neither knew the other was there. Abruptly he realized the walls of the room were becoming indistinct, fading off into gray. A sense of urgency built in him. Everything was going, blurring away. When he looked back to the table, Moiraine and Logain had vanished, and Ba'alzamon sat there instead. Rand's whole body vibrated with urgency; it hummed inside his head, louder and louder. The hum became the pounding of blood in his ears.

With a jerk he sat up, and immediately groaned and clutched his head, swaying. His whole skull hurt; his left hand found sticky dampness in his hair. He was sitting on the ground, on green grass. That troubled him, vaguely, but his head spun and everything he looked at lurched, and all he could think of was lying down until it stopped.

The wall! The girl's voice!

Steadying himself with one hand flat on the grass, he looked around slowly. He had to do it slowly; when he tried to turn his head quickly everything started whirling again. He was in a garden, or a park; a slate-paved walk meandered by through flowering bushes not six feet away, with a white stone bench beside it and a leafy arbor over the bench for shade. He *had* fallen inside the wall. *And the girl?*

He found the tree, close behind his back, and found her, too—climbing down out of it. She reached the ground and turned to face him, and he blinked and groaned again. A deep blue velvet cloak lined with pale fur rested on her shoulders, its hood hanging down behind to her waist with a cluster of silver bells at the peak. They jingled when she moved. A silver filigree circlet held her long, red-gold curls, and delicate silver rings hung at her ears, while a necklace of heavy silver links and dark green stones he thought were emeralds lay around her throat. Her pale blue dress was smudged with bark stains from her tree climbing, but it was still silk, and embroidered with painstakingly intricate designs, the skirt slashed with inserts the color of rich cream. A wide belt of woven silver encircled her waist, and velvet slippers peeked from under the hem of her dress.

He had only ever seen two women dressed in this fashion, Moiraine and the Darkfriend who had tried to kill Mat and him. He could not begin to imagine who would choose to climb trees in clothes like that, but he was sure she had to be someone important. The way she was looking at him redoubled the impression. She did not seem in the least troubled at having a stranger tumble into her garden. There was a self-possession about her that made him think of Nynaeve, or Moiraine.

He was so enmeshed in worrying whether or not he had gotten himself into trouble, whether or not she was someone who could and would call the Queen's Guards even on a day when they had other things to occupy them, that it took him a few moments to see past the elaborate clothes and lofty attitude to the girl herself. She was perhaps two or three years younger than he, tall for a girl, and beautiful, her face a perfect oval framed by that mass of sunburst curls, her lips full and red, her eyes bluer than he could believe. She was completely different from Egwene in height and face and body, but every bit as beautiful. He felt a twinge of guilt, but told himself that denying what his eyes saw would not bring Egwene safely to Caemlyn one whit faster.

A scrabbling sound came from up in the tree and bits of bark fell, followed by a boy dropping lightly to the ground behind her. He was a head taller than she and a little older, but his face and hair marked him as her close kin. His coat and cloak were red and white and gold, embroidered and brocaded, and for a male even more ornate than hers. That increased Rand's anxiety. Only on a feastday would any ordinary man dress in anything like that, and never with that much grandeur. This was no public park. Perhaps the Guards were too busy to bother with trespassers.

The boy studied Rand over the girl's shoulder, fingering the dagger at his waist. It seemed more a nervous habit than any thought that he might use it. Not completely, though. The boy had the same self-possession as the girl, and they both looked at him as if he were a puzzle to be solved. He had the odd feeling that the girl, at least, was cataloguing everything about him from the condition of his boots to the state of his cloak.

"We will never hear the end of this, Elayne, if mother finds out," the boy said suddenly. "She told us to stay in our rooms, but you just had to get a look at Logain, didn't you? Now look what it has got us."

"Be quiet, Gawyn." She was clearly the younger of the two, but she spoke as though she took it for granted that he would obey. The boy's face struggled as if he had more to say, but to Rand's surprise he held his peace. "Are you all right?" she said suddenly.

It took Rand a minute to realize she was speaking to him. When he did, he tried to struggle to his feet. "I'm fine. I just—" He tottered, and his legs gave way. He sat back down hard. His head swam. "I'll just climb back over the wall," he muttered. He attempted to stand again, but she put a hand on his shoulder, pressing him down. He was so dizzy the slight pressure was enough to hold him in place.

"You *are* hurt." Gracefully she knelt beside him. Her fingers gently parted the blood-matted hair on the left side of his head. "You must have struck a branch coming down. You will be lucky if you didn't break anything more than your scalp. I don't think I ever saw anyone as skillful at climbing as you, but you don't do so well falling."

"You'll get blood on your hands," he said, drawing back.

Firmly she pulled his head back to where she could get at it. "Hold still." She did not speak sharply, but again there was that note in her voice as if she expected to be obeyed. "It does not look *too* bad, thank the Light." From pockets on the inside of her cloak she began taking out an array of tiny vials and twisted packets of paper, finishing with a handful of wadded bandage.

He stared at the collection in amazement. It was the sort of thing he would have expected a Wisdom to carry, not someone dressed as she was. She had gotten blood on her fingers, he saw, but it did not seem to bother her.

"Give me your water flask, Gawyn," she said. "I need to wash this."

The boy she called Gawyn unfastened a leather bottle from his belt and handed it to her, then squatted easily at Rand's feet with his arms folded on his knees. Elayne went about what she was doing in a very workmanlike manner. He did not flinch at the sting of cold water when she washed the cut in his scalp, but she held the top of his head with one hand as if she expected him to try to pull away again and would have none of it. The ointment she smoothed on after, from one of her small vials, soothed almost as much as one of Nynaeve's preparations would have.

Gawyn smiled at him as she worked, a calming smile, as if he, too, expected Rand to jerk away and maybe even run. "She's always finding stray cats and birds with broken wings. You are the first human being she has had to work on." He hesitated, then added, "Do not be offended. I am not calling you a stray." It was not an apology, just a statement of fact.

"No offense taken," Rand said stiffly. But the pair were acting as if he were a skittish horse.

"She does know what she is doing," Gawyn said. "She has had the best teachers. So do not fear, you are in good hands."

Elayne pressed some of the bandaging against his temple and pulled a silk scarf from her belt, blue and cream and gold. For any girl in Emond's Field it would have been a treasured feastday cloth. Elayne deftly began winding it around his head to hold the wad of bandage in place.

"You can't use that," he protested.

She went on winding. "I told you to hold still," she said calmly.

Rand looked at Gawyn. "Does she always expect everybody to do what she tells them?"

A flash of surprise crossed the young man's face, and his mouth tightened with amusement. "Most of the time she does. And most of the time they do."

"Hold this," Elayne said. "Put your hand there while I tie—" She exclaimed at the sight of his hands. "You did not do that falling. Climbing where you should not have been climbing is more like it." Quickly finishing her knot, she turned his hands palms upward in front of him, muttering to herself about how little water was left. The washing made the lacerations burn, but her touch was surprisingly delicate. "Hold still, this time."

The vial of ointment was produced again. She spread it thinly along the scrapes, all of her attention apparently on rubbing it in without hurting him. A coolness spread through his hands, as if she were rubbing the torn places away.

"Most of the time they do exactly what she says," Gawyn went on with an affectionate grin at the top of her head. "Most people. Not Mother, of course. Or Elaida. And not Lini. Lini was her nurse. You can't give orders to someone who switched you for stealing figs when you were little. And even not so little." Elayne raised her head long enough to give him a dangerous look. He cleared his throat and carefully blanked his expression before hurrying on. "And Gareth, of course. No one gives orders to Gareth."

"Not even Mother," Elayne said, bending her head back over Rand's hands. "She makes suggestions, and he always does what she suggests, but I've never heard her give him a command." She shook her head.

"I don't know why that always surprises you," Gawyn answered her. "Even you don't try telling Gareth what to do. He's served three Queens and been Captain-General, and First Prince Regent, for two. I daresay there are some think he's more a symbol of the Throne of Andor than the Queen is."

"Mother should go ahead and marry him," she said absently. Her attention was on Rand's hands. "She wants to; she can't hide it from me. And it would solve so many problems."

Gawyn shook his head. "One of them must bend first. Mother cannot, and Gareth will not."

"If she commanded him. . . ."

"He would obey. I think. But she won't. You know she won't."

Abruptly they turned to stare at Rand. He had the feeling they had forgotten he was there. "Who . . . ?" He had to stop to wet his lips. "Who is your mother?"

Elayne's eyes widened in surprise, but Gawyn spoke in an ordinary tone that made his words all the more jarring. "Morgase, by the Grace of the Light, Queen of Andor, Defender of the Realm, Protector of the People, High Seat of the House Trakand."

"The Queen," Rand muttered, shock spreading through him in waves of numbness. For a minute he thought his head was going to begin spinning again. *Don't attract any attention. Just fall into the Queen's garden and let the Daughter-Heir tend your cuts like a hedge-doctor.* He wanted to laugh, and knew it for the fringes of panic.

Drawing a deep breath, he scrambled hastily to his feet. He held himself tightly in rein against the urge to run, but the need to get away filled him, to get away before anyone else discovered him there.

Elayne and Gawyn watched him calmly, and when he leaped up they rose gracefully, not hurried in the least. He put up a hand to pull the scarf from his head, and Elayne seized his elbow. "Stop that. You will start the bleeding again." Her voice was still calm, still sure that he would do as he was told.

"I have to go," Rand said. "I'll just climb back over the wall and—"

"You really didn't know." For the first time she seemed as startled as he was. "Do you mean you climbed up on that wall to see Logain without even knowing where you were? You could have gotten a much better view down in the streets."

"I . . . I don't like crowds," he mumbled. He sketched a bow to each of them. "If you'll pardon me, ah . . . my Lady." In the stories, royal courts were full of people all calling one another Lord and Lady and Royal Highness and Majesty, but if he had ever heard the correct form of address for the Daughter-Heir, he could not think clearly enough to remember. He could not think clearly about anything beyond the need to be far away. "If you will pardon me, I'll just leave now. Ah . . . thank you for the. . . ." He touched the scarf around his head. "Thank you."

"Without even telling us your name?" Gawyn said. "A poor payment for Elayne's care. I've been wondering about you. You sound like an Andorman, though not a Caemlyner, certainly, but you look like. . . . Well, you know our names. Courtesy would suggest you give us yours."

Looking longingly at the wall, Rand gave his right name before he thought what he was doing, and even added, "From Emond's Field, in the Two Rivers."

"From the west," Gawyn murmured. "Very far to the west."

Rand looked around at him sharply. There had been a

note of surprise in the young man's voice, and Rand caught some of it still on his face when he turned. Gawyn replaced it with a pleasant smile so quickly, though, that he almost doubted what he had seen.

"Tabac and wool," Gawyn said. "I have to know the principal products of every part of the Realm. Of every land, for that matter. Part of my training. Principal products and crafts, and what the people are like. Their customs, their strengths and weaknesses. It's said Two Rivers people are stubborn. They can be led, if they think you are worthy, but the harder you try to push them, the harder they dig in. Elayne ought to choose her husband from there. It'll take a man with a will like stone to keep from being trampled by her."

Rand stared at him. Elayne was staring, too. Gawyn looked as much under control as ever, but he was babbling. *Why?*

"What's this?"

All three of them jumped at the sudden voice, and spun to face it.

The young man who stood there was the handsomest man Rand had ever seen, almost too handsome for masculinity. He was tall and slender, but his movements spoke of whipcord strength and a sure confidence. Dark of hair and eye, he wore his clothes, only a little less elaborate in red and white than Gawyn's, as if they were of no importance. One hand rested on his sword hilt, and his eyes were steady on Rand.

"Stand away from him, Elayne," the man said. "You, too, Gawyn."

Elayne stepped in front of Rand, between him and the newcomer, head high and as confident as ever. "He is a loyal subject of our mother, and a good Queen's man. And he is under my protection, Galad."

Rand tried to remember what he had heard from Master Kinch, and since from Master Gill. Galadedrid Damodred was Elayne's half-brother, Elayne's and Gawyn's, if he remembered correctly; the three shared the same father. Master Kinch might not have liked Taringail Damodred too well—neither did anyone else that he had heard—but the son was well thought of by wearers of the red and the white alike, if talk in the city was any guide.

"I am aware of your fondness for strays, Elayne," the

slender man said reasonably, "but the fellow is armed, and he hardly looks reputable. In these days, we cannot be too careful. If he's a loyal Queen's man, what is he doing here where he does not belong? It is easy enough to change the wrappings on a sword, Elayne."

"He is here as my guest, Galad, and I vouch for him. Or have you appointed yourself my nurse, to decide whom I may talk to, and when?"

Her voice was rich with scorn, but Galad seemed unmoved. "You know I make no claims for control over your actions, Elayne, but this . . . guest of yours is not proper, and you know that as well as I. Gawyn, help me convince her. Our mother would—"

"Enough!" Elayne snapped. "You are right that you have no say over my actions, nor have you any right to judge them. You may leave me. Now!"

Galad gave Gawyn a rueful look; at one and the same time it seemed to ask for help while saying that Elayne was too headstrong to be helped. Elayne's face darkened, but just as she opened her mouth again, he bowed, in all formality yet with the grace of a cat, took a step back, then turned and strode down the paved path, his long legs carrying him quickly out of sight beyond the arbor.

"I hate him," Elayne breathed. "He is vile and full of envy."

"There you go too far, Elayne," Gawyn said. "Galad does not know the meaning of envy. Twice he has saved my life, with none to know if he held his hand. If he had not, he would be your First Prince of the Sword in my place."

"Never, Gawyn. I would choose anyone before Galad. Anyone. The lowest stableboy." Suddenly she smiled and gave her brother a mock-stern look. "You say I am fond of giving orders. Well, I command you to let nothing happen to you. I command you to be my First Prince of the Sword when I take the throne—the light send that day is far off!—and to lead the armies of Andor with the sort of honor Galad cannot dream of."

"As you command, my Lady." Gawyn laughed, his bow a parody of Galad's.

Elayne gave Rand a thoughtful frown. "Now we must get you out of here quickly."

"Galad always does the right thing," Gawyn explained,

"even when he should not. In this case, finding a stranger in the gardens, the right thing is to notify the Palace guards. Which I suspect he is on his way to do right this minute."

"Then it's time I was back over the wall," Rand said. *A fine day for going unnoticed! I might as well carry a sign!* He turned to the wall, but Elayne caught his arm.

"Not after the trouble I went to with your hands. You'll only make fresh scrapes and then let some back-alley crone put the Light knows what on them. There is a small gate on the other side of the garden. It's overgrown, and no one but me even remembers it's there."

Suddenly Rand heard boots pounding toward them over the slate paving stones.

"Too late," Gawyn muttered. "He must have started running as soon as he was out of eyeshot."

Elayne growled an oath, and Rand's eyebrows shot up. He had heard that one from the stablemen at The Queen's Blessing and had been shocked then. The next moment she was in cool self-possession once more.

Gawyn and Elayne appeared content to remain where they were, but he could not make himself stay for the Queen's Guards with such equanimity. He started once more for the wall, knowing he would be no more than halfway up before the guards arrived, but unable to stand still.

Before he had taken three steps red-uniformed men burst into sight, breastplates catching the sun as they dashed up the path. Others came like breaking waves of scarlet and polished steel, seemingly from every direction. Some held drawn swords; others only waited to set their boots before raising bows and nocking feathered shafts. Behind the barred faceguards every eye was grim, and every broadhead arrow was pointed unwaveringly at him.

Elayne and Gawyn leaped as one, putting themselves between him and the arrows, their arms spread to cover him. He stood very still and kept his hands in plain sight, away from his sword.

While the thud of boots and the creak of bowstrings still hung in the air, one of the soldiers, with the golden knot of an officer on his shoulder, shouted, "My Lady, my Lord, down, quickly!"

Despite her outstretched arms Elayne drew herself up regally. "You dare to bring bare steel into my presence, Tal-

lanvor? Gareth Bryne will have you mucking stables with
the meanest trooper for this, if you are lucky!"

The soldiers exchanged puzzled glances, and some of
the bowmen uneasily half lowered their bows. Only then
did Elayne let her arms down, as if she had only held them
up because she wished to. Gawyn hesitated, then followed
her example. Rand could count the bows that had not been
lowered. The muscles of his stomach tensed as though they
could stop a broadhead shaft at twenty paces.

The man with the officer's knot seemed the most perplexed of all. "My Lady, forgive me, but Lord Galadedrid
reported a dirty peasant skulking in the gardens, armed and
endangering my Lady Elayne and my Lord Gawyn." His
eyes went to Rand, and his voice firmed. "If my Lady and
my Lord will please to step aside, I will take the villain into
custody. There is too much riff-raff in the city these days."

"I doubt very much if Galad reported anything of the
kind," Elayne said. "Galad does not lie."

"Sometimes I wish he would," Gawyn said softly, for
Rand's ear. "Just once. It might make living with him easier."

"This man is my guest," Elayne continued, "and here under my protection. You may withdraw, Tallanvor."

"I regret that will not be possible, my Lady. As my Lady
knows, the Queen, your lady mother, has given orders regarding anyone on Palace grounds without Her Majesty's permission, and word has been sent to Her Majesty of this intruder."
There was more than a hint of satisfaction in Tallanvor's voice.
Rand suspected the officer had had to accept other commands
from Elayne that he did not think proper; this time the man
was not about to, not when he had a perfect excuse.

Elayne stared back at Tallanvor; for once she seemed at
a loss.

Rand looked a question at Gawyn, and Gawyn understood. "Prison," he murmured. Rand's face went white, and
the young man added quickly, "Only for a few days, and
you will not be harmed. You'll be questioned by Gareth
Bryne, the Captain-General, personally, but you will be set
free once it's clear you meant no harm." He paused, hidden thoughts in his eyes. "I hope you were telling the truth,
Rand al'Thor from the Two Rivers."

"You will conduct all three of us to my mother," Elayne
announced suddenly. A grin bloomed on Gawyn's face.

Behind the steel bars across his face, Tallanvor appeared taken aback. "My Lady, I—"

"Or else conduct all three of us to a cell," Elayne said. "We will remain together. Or will you give orders for hands to be laid upon my person?" Her smile was victorious, and the way Tallanvor looked around as if he expected to find help in the trees said he, too, thought she had won.

Won what? How?

"Mother is viewing Logain," Gawyn said softly, as if he had read Rand's thoughts, "and even if she was not busy, Tallanvor would not dare troop into her presence with Elayne and me, as if *we* were under guard. Mother has a bit of a temper, sometimes."

Rand remembered what Master Gill had said about Queen Morgase. *A bit of a temper?*

Another red-uniformed soldier came running down the path, skidding to a halt to salute with an arm across his chest. He spoke softly to Tallanvor, and his words brought satisfaction back to Tallanvor's face.

"The Queen, your lady mother," Tallanvor announced, "commands me to bring the intruder to her immediately. It is also the Queen's command that my Lady Elayne and my Lord Gawyn attend her. Also immediately."

Gawyn winced, and Elayne swallowed hard. Her face composed, she still began industriously brushing at the stains on her dress. Aside from dislodging a few pieces of bark, her effort did little good.

"If my Lady pleases?" Tallanvor said smugly. "My Lord?"

The soldiers formed around them in a hollow box that started along the slate path with Tallanvor leading. Gawyn and Elayne walked on either side of Rand, both appearing lost in unpleasant thoughts. The soldiers had sheathed their swords and returned arrows to quivers, but they were no less on guard than when they had had weapons in hand. They watched Rand as if they expected him at any moment to snatch his sword and try to cut his way to freedom.

Try anything? I won't try anything. *Unnoticed! Hah!*

Watching the soldiers watching him, he suddenly became aware of the garden. One thing had happened after another, each new shock coming before the last had a chance to fade, and his surroundings had been a blur, except for the wall and his devout wish to be back on the other side of it. Now he *saw* the green grass that had only tickled the back of his mind before. *Green!* A hundred shades of green. Trees and bushes green and thriving, thick with leaves and fruit. Lush vines covering arbors over the path. Flowers everywhere. So many flowers, spraying the garden with color. Some he knew—bright golden sunburst and tiny pink tallowend, crimson starblaze and purple Emond's Glory, roses in every color from purest white to deep, deep red—but others were strange, so fanciful in shape and hue he wondered if they could be real.

"It's green," he whispered. "Green." The soldiers muttered to themselves; Tallanvor gave them a sharp look over his shoulder and they fell silent.

"Elaida's work," Gawyn said absently.

"It is not right," Elayne said. "She asked if I wanted to pick out the one farm she could do the same for, while all around it the crops still failed, but it still isn't right for us to have flowers when there are people who do not have enough to eat." She drew a deep breath, and refilled her self-possession. "Remember yourself," she told Rand briskly. "Speak up clearly when you are spoken to, and keep silent otherwise. And follow my lead. All will be well."

Rand wished he could share her confidence. It would have helped if Gawyn had seemed to have it as well. As Tallanvor led them into the Palace, he looked back at the garden, at all the green streaked with blossoms, colors wrought for a Queen by an Aes Sedai's hand. He was in deep water, and there was no bank in sight.

Palace servants filled the halls, in red liveries with collars and cuffs of white, the White Lion on the left breast of their tunics, scurrying about intent on tasks that were not readily apparent. When the soldiers trooped by with Elayne and Gawyn, and Rand, in their midst, they stopped dead in their tracks to stare openmouthed.

Through the middle of all the consternation a gray-striped tomcat wandered unconcernedly down the hall, weaving between the goggling servants. Suddenly the cat struck Rand as odd. He had been in Baerlon long enough to know that even the meanest shop had cats lurking in every corner. Since entering the Palace, the tom was the only cat he had seen.

"You don't have rats?" he said in disbelief. *Every* place had rats.

"Elaida doesn't like rats," Gawyn muttered vaguely. He was frowning worriedly down the hall, apparently already seeing the coming meeting with the Queen. "We never have rats."

"Both of you be quiet." Elayne's voice was sharp, but as absent as her brother's. "I am trying to think."

Rand watched the cat over his shoulder until the guards took him round a corner, hiding the tom from sight. A lot of cats would have made him feel better; it would have been nice if there was one thing normal about the Palace, even if it was rats.

The path Tallanvor took turned so many times that Rand lost his sense of direction. Finally the young officer stopped before tall double doors of dark wood with a rich glow, not so grand as some they had passed, but still carved all over with rows of lions, finely wrought in detail. A liveried servant stood to either side.

"At least it isn't the Grand Hall." Gawyn laughed unsteadily. "I never heard that Mother commanded anyone's head cut off from here." He sounded as if he thought she might set a precedent.

Tallanvor reached for Rand's sword, but Elayne moved to cut him off. "He is my guest, and by custom and law, guests of the royal family may go armed even in Mother's presence. Or will you deny my word that he is my guest?"

Tallanvor hesitated, locking eyes with her, then nodded. "Very well, my Lady." She smiled at Rand as Tallanvor stepped back, but it lasted only a moment. "First rank to accompany me," Tallanvor commanded. "Announce the Lady Elayne and the Lord Gawyn to Her Majesty," he told the doorkeepers. "Also Guardsman-Lieutenant Tallanvor, at Her Majesty's command, with the intruder under guard."

Elayne scowled at Tallanvor, but the doors were already swinging open. A sonorous voice sounded, announcing those who came.

Grandly Elayne swept through the doors, spoiling her regal entrance only a little by motioning for Rand to keep close behind her. Gawyn squared his shoulders and strode in flanking her, one measured pace to her rear. Rand followed, uncertainly keeping level with Gawyn on her other side. Tallanvor stayed close to Rand, and ten soldiers came with him. The doors closed silently behind them.

Suddenly Elayne dropped into a deep curtsy, simultane-
ously bowing from the waist, and stayed there, holding her
skirt wide. Rand gave a start, then hastily emulated Gawyn
and the other men, shifting awkwardly until he had it right.
Down on his right knee, head bowed, bending forward to
press the knuckles of his right hand against the marble tiles,
his left hand resting on the end of his sword hilt. Gawyn,
without a sword, put his hand on his dagger the same way.

Rand was just congratulating himself on getting it right
when he noticed Tallanvor, his head still bent, glaring sideways at him from behind his face-guard. *Was I supposed to
do something else?* He was suddenly angry that Tallanvor
expected him to know what to do when no one had told
him. And angry over being afraid of the guards. He had
done nothing to be fearful for. He knew his fear was not
Tallanvor's fault, but he was angry at him anyway.

Everyone held their positions, frozen as if waiting for the
spring thaw. He did not know what they were waiting for,
but he took the opportunity to study the place to which he
had been brought. He kept his head down, just turning it
enough to see. Tallanvor's scowl deepened, but he ignored it.

The square chamber was about the size of the common
room at The Queen's Blessing, its walls presenting hunting
scenes carved in relief in stone of the purest white. The tapestries between the carvings were gentle images of bright
flowers and brilliantly plumaged hummingbirds, except for
the two at the far end of the room, where the White Lion
of Andor stood taller than a man on scarlet fields. Those
two hangings flanked a dais, and on the dais a carved and
gilded throne where sat the Queen.

A bluff, blocky man stood bareheaded by the Queen's
right hand in the red of the Queen's Guards, with four
golden knots on the shoulder of his cloak and wide golden
bands breaking the white of his cuffs. His temples were
heavy with gray, but he looked as strong and immovable as
a rock. That had to be the Captain-General, Gareth Bryne.
Behind the throne and to the other side a woman in deep
green silk sat on a low stool, knitting something out of dark,
almost black, wool. At first the knitting made Rand think
she was old, but at second glance he could not put an age to
her at all. Young, old, he did not know. Her attention seemed
to be entirely on her needles and yarn, just as if there were

not a Queen within arm's reach of her. She was a handsome woman, outwardly placid, yet there was something terrible in her concentration. There was no sound in the room except for the click of her needles.

He tried to look at everything, yet his eyes kept going back to the woman with the gleaming wreath of finely wrought roses on her brow, the Rose Crown of Andor. A long red stole, the Lion of Andor marching along its length, hung over her silken dress of red and white pleats, and when she touched the Captain-General's arm with her left hand, a ring in the shape of the Great Serpent, eating its own tail, glittered. Yet it was not the grandeur of clothes or jewelry or even crown that drew Rand's eyes again and again: it was the woman who wore them.

Morgase had her daughter's beauty, matured and ripened. Her face and figure, her presence, filled the room like a light that dimmed the other two with her. If she had been a widow in Emond's Field, she would have had a line of suitors outside her door even if she was the worst cook and most slovenly housekeeper in the Two Rivers. He saw her studying him and ducked his head, afraid she might be able to tell his thoughts from his face. *Light, thinking about the Queen like she was a village woman! You fool!*

"You may rise," Morgase said in a rich, warm voice that held Elayne's assurance of obedience a hundred times over.

Rand stood with the rest.

"Mother—" Elayne began, but Morgase cut her off.

"You have been climbing trees, it seems, daughter." Elayne plucked a stray fragment of bark from her dress and, finding there was no place to put it, held it clenched in her hand. "In fact," Morgase went on calmly, "it would seem that despite my orders to the contrary you have contrived to take your look at this Logain. Gawyn, I have thought better of you. You must learn not only to obey your sister, but at the same time to be counterweight for her against disaster." The Queen's eyes swung to the blocky man beside her, then quickly away again. Bryne remained impassive, as if he had not noticed, but Rand thought those eyes noticed everything. "That, Gawyn, is as much the duty of the First Prince as is leading the armies of Andor. Perhaps if your training is intensified, you will find less time for letting your sister lead you into trouble. I will ask the Captain-General to see that you do not lack for things to do on the journey north."

Gawyn shifted his feet as if about to protest, then bowed his head instead. "As you command, mother."

Elayne grimaced. "Mother, Gawyn cannot keep me out of trouble if he is not with me. It was for that reason alone he left his rooms. Mother, surely there could be no harm in just looking at Logain. Almost everyone in the city was closer to him than we."

"Everyone in the city is not the Daughter-Heir." Sharpness underlay the Queen's voice. "I have seen this fellow Logain from close, and he is dangerous, child. Caged, with Aes Sedai to guard him every minute, he is still as dangerous as a wolf. I wish he had never been brought near Caemlyn."

"He will be dealt with in Tar Valon." The woman on the stool did not take her eyes from her knitting as she spoke. "What is important is that the people see that the Light has once again vanquished the Dark. And that they see you are part of that victory, Morgase."

Morgase waved a dismissive hand. "I would still rather he had never come near Caemlyn. Elayne, I know your mind."

"Mother," Elayne protested, "I do mean to obey you. Truly I do."

"You do?" Morgase asked in mock surprise, then chuckled. "Yes, you do try to be a dutiful daughter. But you constantly test how far you may go. Well, I did the same with my mother. That spirit will stand you in good stead when you ascend to the throne, but you are not Queen yet, child. You have disobeyed me and had your look at Logain. Be satisfied with that. On the journey north you will not be allowed within one hundred paces of him, neither you nor Gawyn. If I did not know just how hard your lessons will be in Tar Valon, I would send Lini along to see that you obey. She, at least, seems able to make you do as you must."

Elayne bowed her head sullenly.

The woman behind the throne seemed occupied with counting her stitches. "In one week," she said suddenly, "you will be wanting to come home to your mother. In a month you will be wanting to run away with the Traveling People. But my sisters will keep you away from the unbeliever. That sort of thing is not for you, not yet." Abruptly she turned on

the stool to look intently at Elayne, all her placidity gone as
if it had never been. "You have it in you to be the greatest
Queen that Andor has ever seen, that any land has seen in
more than a thousand years. It is for that we will shape you,
if you have the strength for it."

Rand stared at her. She had to be Elaida, the Aes Sedai.
Suddenly he was glad he had not come to her for help, no
matter what her Ajah. A sternness far beyond Moiraine's
radiated from her. He had sometimes thought of Moiraine
as steel covered with velvet; with Elaida the velvet was only
an illusion.

"Enough, Elaida," Morgase said, frowning uneasily.
"She has heard that more than enough. The Wheel weaves
as the Wheel wills." For a moment she was silent, looking
at her daughter. "Now there is the problem of this young
man"—she gestured to Rand without taking her eyes off
Elayne's face—"and how and why he came here, and why
you claimed guest-right for him to your brother."

"May I speak, mother?" When Morgase nodded her assent, Elayne told of events simply, from the time she first
saw Rand climbing up the slope to the wall. He expected
her to finish by proclaiming the innocence of what he had
done, but instead she said, "Mother, often you tell me I
must know our people, from the highest to the lowest, but
whenever I meet any of them it is with a dozen attendants.
How can I come to know anything real or true under such
circumstances? In speaking with this young man I have
already learned more about the people of the Two Rivers,
what kind of people they are, than I ever could from books.
It says something that he has come so far and has put on
the red, when so many incomers wear the white from fear.
Mother, I beg you not to misuse a loyal subject, and one
who has taught me much about the people you rule."

"A loyal subject from the Two Rivers." Morgase sighed.
"My child, you should pay more heed to those books. The
Two Rivers has not seen a tax collector in six generations,
nor the Queen's Guards in seven. I daresay they seldom
even think to remember they are part of the Realm." Rand
shrugged uncomfortably, recalling his surprise when he
was told the Two Rivers was part of the Realm of Andor.
The Queen saw him, and smiled ruefully at her daughter.
"You see, child?"

Elaida had put down her knitting, Rand realized, and was studying him. She rose from her stool and slowly came down from the dais to stand before him. "From the Two Rivers?" she said. She reached a hand toward his head; he pulled away from her touch, and she let her hand drop. "With that red in his hair, and gray eyes? Two Rivers people are dark of hair and eye, and they seldom have such height." Her hand darted out to push back his coat sleeve, exposing lighter skin the sun had not reached so often. "Or such skin."

It was an effort not to clench his fists. "I was born in Emond's Field," he said stiffly. "My mother was an outlander; that's where my eyes come from. My father is Tam al'Thor, a shepherd and farmer, as I am."

Elaida nodded slowly, never taking her eyes from his face. He met her gaze with a levelness that belied the sour feeling in his stomach. He saw her note the steadiness of his look. Still meeting him eye to eye, she moved her hand slowly toward him again. He resolved not to flinch this time.

It was his sword she touched, not him, her hand closing around the hilt at the very top. Her fingers tightened and her eyes opened wide with surprise. "A shepherd from the Two Rivers," she said softly, a whisper meant to be heard by all, "with a heron-mark sword."

Those last few words acted on the chamber as if she had announced the Dark One. Leather and metal creaked behind Rand, boots scuffling on the marble tiles. From the corner of his eye he could see Tallanvor and another of the guardsmen backing away from him to gain room, hands on their swords, prepared to draw and, from their faces, prepared to die. In two quick strides Gareth Bryne was at the front of the dais, between Rand and the Queen. Even Gawyn put himself in front of Elayne, a worried look on his face and a hand on his dagger. Elayne herself looked at him as if she were seeing him for the first time. Morgase did not change expression, but her hands tightened on the gilded arms of her throne.

Only Elaida showed less reaction than the Queen. The Aes Sedai gave no sign that she had said anything out of the ordinary. She took her hand from the sword, causing the soldiers to tense even more. Her eyes stayed on his, unruffled and calculating.

"Surely," Morgase said, her voice level, "he is too young to have earned a heron-mark blade. He cannot be any older than Gawyn."

"It belongs with him," Gareth Bryne said.

The Queen looked at him in surprise. "How can that be?"

"I do not know, Morgase," Bryne said slowly. "He *is* too young, yet still it belongs with him, and he with it. Look at his eyes. Look how he stands, how the sword fits him, and he it. He is too young, but the sword is his."

When the Captain-General fell silent, Elaida said, "How did you come by this blade, Rand al'Thor from the Two Rivers?" She said it as if she doubted his name as much as she did where he was from.

"My father gave it to me," Rand said. "It was his. He thought I'd need a sword, out in the world."

"Yet *another* shepherd from the Two Rivers with a heron-mark blade." Elaida's smile made his mouth go dry. "When did you arrive in Caemlyn?"

He had had enough of telling this woman the truth. She made him as afraid as any Darkfriend had. It was time to start hiding again. "Today," he said. "This morning."

"Just in time," she murmured. "Where are you staying? Don't say you have not found a room somewhere. You look a little tattered, but you have had a chance to freshen. Where?"

"The Crown and Lion." He remembered passing The Crown and Lion while looking for The Queen's Blessing. It was on the other side of the New City from Master Gill's inn. "I have a bed there. In the attic." He had the feeling that she knew he was lying, but she only nodded.

"What chance this?" she said. "Today the unbeliever is brought into Caemlyn. In two days he will be taken north to Tar Valon, and with him goes the Daughter-Heir for her training. And at just this juncture a young man appears in the Palace gardens, claiming to be a loyal subject from the Two Rivers . . ."

"I *am* from the Two Rivers." They were all looking at him, but all ignored him. All but Tallanvor and the guards; those eyes never blinked.

". . . with a story calculated to entice Elayne and bearing a heron-mark blade. He does not wear an armband or a cockade to proclaim his allegiance, but wrappings that carefully conceal the heron from inquisitive eyes. What chance this, Morgase?"

The Queen motioned the Captain-General to stand aside, and when he did she studied Rand with a troubled look. It was to Elaida that she spoke, though. "What are you naming him? Darkfriend? One of Logain's followers?"

"The Dark One stirs in Shayol Ghul," the Aes Sedai replied. "The Shadow lies across the Pattern, and the future is balanced on the point of a pin. This one is dangerous."

Suddenly Elayne moved, throwing herself onto her knees before the throne. "Mother, I beg you not to harm him. He would have left immediately had I not stopped him. He wanted to go. It was I who made him stay. I cannot believe he is a Darkfriend."

Morgase made a soothing gesture toward her daughter, but her eyes remained on Rand. "Is this a Foretelling, Elaida? Are you reading the Pattern? You say it comes on you when you least expect it and goes as suddenly as it comes. If this is a Foretelling, Elaida, I command you to speak the truth clearly, without your usual habit of wrapping it in so much mystery that no one can tell if you have said yes or no. Speak. What do you see?"

"This I Foretell," Elaida replied, "and swear under the Light that I can say no clearer. From this day Andor marches toward pain and division. The Shadow has yet to darken to its blackest, and I cannot see if the Light will come after. Where the world has wept one tear, it will weep thousands. This I Foretell."

A pall of silence clung to the room, broken only by Morgase expelling her breath as if it were her last.

Elaida continued to stare into Rand's eyes. She spoke again, barely moving her lips, so softly that he could barely hear her less than an arm's length away. "This, too, I Foretell. Pain and division come to the whole world, and this man stands at the heart of it. I obey the Queen," she whispered, "and speak it clearly."

Rand felt as if his feet had become rooted in the marble floor. The cold and stiffness of the stone crept up his legs and sent a shiver up his spine. No one else could have heard. But she was still looking at him, and he had heard.

"I'm a shepherd," he said for the entire room. "From the Two Rivers. A shepherd."

"The Wheel weaves as the Wheel wills," Elaida said aloud, and he could not tell if there was a touch of mockery in her tone or not.

"Lord Gareth," Morgase said, "I need the advice of my Captain-General."

The blocky man shook his head. "Elaida Sedai says the lad is dangerous, my Queen, and if she could tell more I would say summon the headsman. But all she says is what any of us can see with our own eyes. There's not a farmer in the countryside won't say things will get worse, without any Foretelling. Myself, I believe the boy is here through mere happenstance, though an ill one for him. To be safe, my Queen, I say clap him in a cell till the Lady Elayne and the Lord Gawyn are well on their way, then let him go. Unless, Aes Sedai, you have more to Foretell concerning him?"

"I have said all that I have read in the Pattern, Captain-General," Elaida said. She flashed a hard smile at Rand, a smile that barely bent her lips, mocking his inability to say that she was not telling the truth. "A few weeks imprisoned will not harm him, and it may give me a chance to learn more." Hunger filled her eyes, deepening his chill. "Perhaps another Foretelling will come."

For a time Morgase considered, chin on her fist and elbow on the arm of her throne. Rand would have shifted under her frowning gaze if he could have moved at all, but Elaida's eyes froze him solid. Finally the Queen spoke.

"Suspicion is smothering Caemlyn, perhaps all of Andor. Fear and black suspicion. Women denounce their neighbors for Darkfriends. Men scrawl the Dragon's Fang on the doors of people they have known for years. I will not become part of it."

"Morgase—" Elaida began, but the Queen cut her off.

"I will not become part of it. When I took the throne I swore to uphold justice for the high and the low, and I will uphold it even if I am the last in Andor to remember justice. Rand al'Thor, do you swear under the Light that your father, a shepherd in the Two Rivers, gave you this heron-mark blade?"

Rand worked his mouth to get enough moisture to speak. "I do." Abruptly remembering to whom he was speaking he hastily added, "My Queen." Lord Gareth raised a heavy eyebrow, but Morgase did not seem to mind.

"And you climbed the garden wall simply to gain a look at the false Dragon?"

"Yes, my Queen."

"Do you mean harm to the throne of Andor, or to my daughter, or my son?" Her tone said the last two would gain him even shorter shrift than the first.

"I mean no harm to anyone, my Queen. To you and yours least of all."

"I will give you justice then, Rand al'Thor," she said. "First, because I have the advantage of Elaida and Gareth in having heard Two Rivers speech when I was young. You have not the look, but if a dim memory can serve me you have the Two Rivers on your tongue. Second, no one with your hair and eyes would claim that he is a Two Rivers shepherd unless it was true. And that your father gave you a heron-mark blade is too preposterous to be a lie. And third, the voice that whispers to me that the best lie is often one too ridiculous to be taken for a lie . . . that voice is not proof. I will uphold the laws I have made. I give you your freedom, Rand al'Thor, but I suggest you take a care where you trespass in the future. If you are found on the Palace grounds again, it will not go so easily with you."

"Thank you, my Queen," he said hoarsely. He could feel Elaida's displeasure like a heat on his face.

"Tallanvor," Morgase said, "escort this . . . escort my daughter's guest from the Palace, and show him every courtesy. The rest of you go as well. No, Elaida, you stay. And if you will too, please, Lord Gareth. I must decide what to do about these Whitecloaks in the city."

Tallanvor and the guardsmen sheathed their swords reluctantly, ready to draw again in an instant. Still Rand was glad to let the soldiers form a hollow box around him and to follow Tallanvor. Elaida was only half attending what the Queen was saying; he could feel her eyes on his back. *What would have happened if Morgase had not kept the Aes Sedai with her?* The thought made him wish the soldiers would walk faster.

To his surprise, Elayne and Gawyn exchanged a few words outside the door, then fell in beside him. Tallanvor was surprised, too. The young officer looked from them back to the doors, closing now.

"My mother," Elayne said, "ordered him to be escorted

from the Palace, Tallanvor. With every courtesy. What are you waiting for?"

Tallanvor scowled at the doors, behind which the Queen was conferring with her advisors. "Nothing, my Lady," he said sourly, and needlessly ordered the escort forward.

The wonders of the Palace slid by Rand unseen. He was befuddled, snatches of thought spinning by too fast to grasp. *You have not the look. This man stands at the heart of it.*

The escort stopped. He blinked, startled to find himself in the great court at the front of the Palace, standing at the tall, gilded gates, gleaming in the sun. Those gates would not be opened for a single man, certainly not for a trespasser, even if the Daughter-Heir did claim guest-right for him. Wordlessly Tallanvor unbarred a sally-port, a small door set within one gate.

"It is the custom," Elayne said, "to escort guests as far as the gates, but not to watch them go. It is the pleasure of a guest's company that should be remembered, not the sadness of parting."

"Thank you, my Lady," Rand said. He touched the scarf bandaging his head. "For everything. Custom in the Two Rivers is for a guest to bring a small gift. I'm afraid I have nothing. Although," he added dryly, "apparently I did teach you something of the Two Rivers folk."

"If I had told Mother I think you are handsome, she certainly would have had you locked in a cell." Elayne favored him with a dazzling smile. "Fare you well, Rand al'Thor."

Gaping, he watched her go, a younger version of Morgase's beauty and majesty.

"Do not try to bandy words with her." Gawyn laughed. "She will win every time."

Rand nodded absently. *Handsome? Light, the Daughter-Heir to the throne of Andor!* He gave himself a shake to clear his head.

Gawyn seemed to be waiting for something. Rand looked at him for a moment.

"My Lord, when I told you I was from the Two Rivers you were surprised. And everybody else, your mother, Lord Gareth, Elaida Sedai"—a shiver ran down his back—"none of them. . . ." He could not finish it; he was not even sure why he started. *I am Tam al'Thor's son, even if I was not born in the Two Rivers.*

Gawyn nodded as if it was for this he had been waiting. Still he hesitated. Rand opened his mouth to take back
the unspoken question, and Gawyn said, "Wrap a *shoufa*
around your head, Rand, and you would be the image of an
Aielman. Odd, since Mother seems to think you *sound* like
a Two Rivers man, at least. I wish we could have come to
know one another, Rand al'Thor. Fare you well."

An Aielman.

Rand stood watching Gawyn's retreating back until an
impatient cough from Tallanvor reminded him where he
was. He ducked through the sally-port, barely clearing his
heels before Tallanvor slammed it behind him. The bars inside were jammed into place loudly.

The oval plaza in front of the Palace was empty, now. All
the soldiers gone, all the crowds, trumpets, and drums vanished in silence. Nothing left but a scattering of litter blowing across the pavement and a few people hurrying about
their business now that the excitement was done. He could
not make out if they showed the red or the white.

Aielman.

With a start he realized he was standing right in front of
the Palace gates, right where Elaida could find him easily
once she finished with the Queen. Pulling his cloak close,
he broke into a trot, across the plaza and into the streets of
the Inner City. He looked back frequently to see if anyone
was following him, but the sweeping curves kept him from
seeing very far. He could remember Elaida's eyes all too
well, though, and imagined them watching. By the time he
reached the gates to the New City, he was running.

CHAPTER
41

Old Friends and New Threats

Back at The Queen's Blessing, Rand threw himself against the front doorframe, panting. He had run all the way, not caring if anyone saw that he wore the red, or even if they took his running as an excuse to chase him. He did not think even a Fade could have caught him.

Lamgwin was sitting on a bench by the door, a brindle cat in his arms, when he came running up. The man stood to look for trouble the way Rand had come, still calmly scratching behind the cat's ears. Seeing nothing, he sat back down again, careful not to disturb the animal. "Fools tried to steal some of the cats a while back," he said. He examined his knuckles before going back to his scratching. "Good money in cats these days."

The two men showing the white were still across the way, Rand saw, one with a black eye and a swollen jaw. That one wore a sour scowl and rubbed his sword hilt with a sullen eagerness as he watched the inn.

"Where's Master Gill?" Rand asked.

"Library," Lamgwin replied. The cat began purring, and he grinned. "Nothing bothers a cat for long, not even somebody trying to stick him in a sack."

Rand hurried inside, through the common room, now with its usual complement of men wearing the red and talking over their ale. About the false Dragon, and whether the Whitecloaks would make trouble when he was taken north. No one cared what happened to Logain, but they all knew the Daughter-Heir and Lord Gawyn would be traveling in the party, and no man there would countenance any risk to them.

He found Master Gill in the library, playing stones with Loial. A plump tabby sat on the table, feet tucked under her, watching their hands move over the cross-hatched board.

The Ogier placed another stone with a touch oddly delicate for his thick fingers. Shaking his head, Master Gill took the excuse of Rand's appearance to turn from the table. Loial almost always won at stones. "I was beginning to worry where you were, lad. Thought you might have had trouble with some of those white-flashing traitors, or run into that beggar or something."

For a minute Rand stood there with his mouth open. He had forgotten all about that bundle-of-rags of a man. "I saw him," he said finally, "but that's nothing. I saw the Queen, too, and Elaida; that's where the trouble is."

Master Gill snorted a laugh. "The Queen, eh? You don't say. We had Gareth Bryne out in the common room an hour or so ago, arm-wrestling the Lord Captain-Commander of the Children, but the Queen, now . . . that's something."

"Blood and ashes," Rand growled, "everybody thinks I'm lying today." He tossed his cloak across the back of a chair and threw himself onto another. He was too wound up to sit back. He perched on the front edge, mopping his face with a handkerchief. "I saw the beggar, and he saw me, and I thought. . . . That's not important. I climbed up on a wall around a garden, where I could see the plaza in front of the Palace, where they took Logain in. And I fell off, on the inside."

"I almost believe you aren't making fun," the innkeeper said slowly.

"Ta'veren," Loial murmured.

"Oh, it happened," Rand said. "Light help me, it did."

Master Gill's skepticism melted slowly as he went on, turning to quiet alarm. The innkeeper leaned more and more forward until he was perched on the edge of his chair the same as Rand was. Loial listened impassively, except that every so often he rubbed his broad nose and the tufts on his ears gave a little twitch.

Rand told everything that had happened, everything except what Elaida had whispered to him. And what Gawyn had said at the Palace gate. One he did not want to think about; the other had nothing to do with anything. *I'm Tam*

*al'Thor's son, even if I wasn't born in the Two Rivers. I am!
I'm Two Rivers blood, and Tam is my father.*

Abruptly he realized he had stopped talking, caught up in his thoughts, and they were looking at him. For one panicky moment he wondered if he had said too much.

"Well," Master Gill said, "there's no more waiting for your friends for you. You will have to leave the city, and fast. Two days at the most. Can you get Mat on his feet in that time, or should I send for Mother Grubb?"

Rand gave him a perplexed look. "Two days?"

"Elaida is Queen Morgase's advisor, right next to Captain-General Gareth Bryne himself. Maybe ahead of him. If she sets the Queen's Guards looking for you—Lord Gareth won't stop her unless she interferes with their other duties—well, the Guards can search every inn in Caemlyn in two days. And that's saying some ill chance doesn't bring them here the first day, or the first hour. Maybe there's a little time if they start over at the Crown and Lion, but none for dawdling."

Rand nodded slowly. "If I can't get Mat out of that bed, you send for Mother Grubb. I have a little money left. Maybe enough."

"I'll take care of Mother Grubb," the innkeeper said gruffly. "And I suppose I can lend you a couple of horses. You try walking to Tar Valon and you'll wear through what's left of your boots halfway there."

"You're a good friend," Rand said. "It seems like we've brought you nothing but trouble, but you're still willing to help. A good friend."

Master Gill seemed embarrassed. He shrugged his shoulders and cleared his throat and looked down. That brought his eyes to the stones board, and he jerked them away again. Loial was definitely winning. "Aye, well, Thom's always been a good friend to me. If he's willing to go out of his way for you, I can do a little bit, too."

"I would like to go with you when you leave, Rand," Loial said suddenly.

"I thought that was settled, Loial." He hesitated—Master Gill still did not know the whole of the danger—then added, "You know what waits for Mat and me, what's chasing us."

"Darkfriends," the Ogier replied in a placid rumble, "and Aes Sedai, and the Light knows what else. Or the Dark One. You are going to Tar Valon, and there is a very fine grove there, which I have heard the Aes Sedai tend well. In any case, there is more to see in the world than the groves. You truly are *ta'veren,* Rand. The Pattern weaves itself around you, and you stand in the heart of it."

This man stands at the heart of it. Rand felt a chill. "I don't stand at the heart of anything," he said harshly.

Master Gill blinked, and even Loial seemed taken aback at his anger. The innkeeper and the Ogier looked at each other, and then at the floor. Rand forced his expression smooth, drawing deep breaths. For a wonder he found the void that had eluded him so often of late, and calmness. They did not deserve his anger.

"You can come, Loial," he said. "I don't know why you would want to, but I'd be grateful for the company. You . . . you know how Mat is."

"I know," Loial said. "I still cannot go into the streets without raising a mob shouting 'Trolloc' after me. But Mat, at least, only uses words. He has not tried to kill me."

"Of course not," Rand said. "Not Mat." *He wouldn't go that far. Not Mat.*

A tap came at the door, and one of the serving maids, Gilda, stuck her head into the room. Her mouth was tight, and her eyes worried. "Master Gill, come quickly, please. There's Whitecloaks in the common room."

Master Gill leaped up with an oath, sending the cat jumping from the table to stalk out of the room, tail stiff and offended. "I'll come. Run tell them I'm coming, then stay out of their way. You hear me, girl? Keep away from them." Gilda bobbed her head and vanished. "You had best stay here," he told Loial.

The Ogier snorted, a sound like sheets ripping. "I have no desire for any more meetings with the Children of the Light."

Master Gill's eye fell on the stones board and his mood seemed to lighten. "It looks as if we'll have to start the game over later."

"No need for that." Loial stretched an arm to the shelves and took down a book; his hands dwarfed the clothbound volume. "We can take up from where the board lies. It is your turn."

Master Gill grimaced. "If it isn't one thing, it's another," he muttered as he hurried from the room.

Rand followed him, but slowly. He had no more desire than Loial to become involved with the Children. *This man stands at the heart of it.* He stopped at the door to the common room, where he could see what went on, but far enough back that he hoped he would not be noticed.

Dead silence filled the room. Five Whitecloaks stood in the middle of the floor, studiously being ignored by the folk at the tables. One of them had the silver lightning-flash of an under-officer beneath the sunburst on his cloak. Lamgwin was lounging against the wall by the front door, intently cleaning his fingernails with a splinter. Four more of the guards Master Gill had hired were spaced across the wall from him, all industriously paying no attention at all to the Whitecloaks. If the Children of the Light noticed anything, they gave no sign. Only the under-officer showed any emotion at all, impatiently tapping his steel-backed gauntlets against his palm as he waited for the innkeeper.

Master Gill crossed the room to him quickly, a cautiously neutral look on his face. "The Light illumine you," he said with a careful bow, not too deep, but not slight enough to actually be insulting, either, "and our good Queen Morgase. How may I help—"

"I've no time for your drivel, innkeeper," the under-officer snapped. "I've been to twenty inns already today, each a worse pigsty than the last, and I'll see twenty more before the sun sets. I'm looking for Darkfriends, a boy from the Two Rivers—"

Master Gill's face grew darker with every word. He puffed up as if he would explode, and finally he did, cutting the Whitecloak off in turn. "There are no Darkfriends in my establishment! Every man here is a good Queen's man!"

"Yes, and we all know where Morgase stands," the under-officer twisted the Queen's name into a sneer, "and her Tar Valon witch, don't we?"

The scrape of chair legs was loud. Suddenly every man in the room was on his feet. They stood still as statues, but every one staring grimly at the Whitecloaks. The under-officer did not appear to notice, but the four behind him looked around uneasily.

"It will go easier with you, innkeeper," the under-officer said, "if you cooperate. The temper of the times goes hard with those who shelter Darkfriends. I wouldn't think an inn with the Dragon's Fang on its door would get much custom. Might have trouble with fire, with that on your door."

"You get out of here now," Master Gill said quietly, "or I'll send for the Queen's Guards to cart what's left of you to the middens."

Lamgwin's sword rasped out of its sheath, and the coarse scrape of steel on leather was repeated throughout the room as swords and daggers filled hands. Serving maids scurried for the doors.

The under-officer looked around in scornful disbelief. "The Dragon's Fang—"

"Won't help you five," Master Gill finished for him. He held up a clenched fist and raised his forefinger. "One."

"You must be mad, innkeeper, threatening the Children of the Light."

"Whitecloaks hold no writ in Caemlyn. Two."

"Can you really believe this will end here?"

"Three."

"We'll be back," the under-officer snapped, and then he was hastily turning his men around, trying to pretend he was leaving in good order and in his own time. He was hampered in this by the eagerness his men showed for the door, not running, but not making secret that they wanted to be outside.

Lamgwin stood across the door with his sword, only giving way in response to Master Gill's frantic waves. When the Whitecloaks were gone, the innkeeper dropped heavily onto a chair. He rubbed a hand across his forehead, then stared at it as if surprised that it was not covered with sweat. All over the room men seated themselves again, laughing over what they had done. Some went over to clap Master Gill on the shoulder.

When he saw Rand, the innkeeper tottered off the chair and over to him. "Who would have thought I had it in me to be a hero?" he said wonderingly. "The Light illumine me." Abruptly he gave himself a shake, and his voice regained almost its normal tone. "You'll have to stay out of sight until I can get you out of the city." With a careful look back into the common room, he pushed Rand deeper into the hall. "That lot will be back, or else a few spies wearing red for the day. After that little show I put on, I doubt they'll care whether you're here or not, but they'll act as though you are."

"That's crazy," Rand protested. At the innkeeper's gesture he lowered his voice. "The Whitecloaks don't have any reason to be after me."

"I don't know about reasons, lad, but they're after you and Mat for certain sure. What *have* you been up to? Elaida *and* the Whitecloaks."

Rand raised his hands in protest, then let them fall. It made no sense, but he had heard the Whitecloak. "What about you? The Whitecloaks will make trouble for you even when they don't find us."

"No worries about that, lad. The Queen's Guards still uphold the law, even if they do let traitors strut around showing white. As for the night . . . well, Lamgwin and his friends might not get much sleep, but I could almost pity anybody who tries to put a mark on my door."

Gilda appeared beside them, dropping a curtsy to Master Gill. "Sir, there's . . . there's a lady. In the kitchens." She sounded scandalized at the combination. "She's asking for Master Rand, sir, and Master Mat, by name."

Rand exchanged a puzzled look with the innkeeper.

"Lad," Master Gill said, "if you've actually managed to bring the Lady Elayne down from the Palace to my inn, we'll all end up facing the headsman." Gilda squeaked at the mention of the Daughter-Heir and gave Rand a round-eyed stare. "Off with you, girl," the innkeeper said sharply. "And keep quiet about what you've heard. It's nobody's business." Gilda bobbed again and darted down the hallway, flashing glances over her shoulder at Rand as she went. "In five minutes"—Master Gill sighed—"she will be telling the other women you're a prince in disguise. By nightfall it will be all over the New City."

"Master Gill," Rand said, "I never mentioned Mat to Elayne. It can't be—" Suddenly a huge smile lit up his face, and he ran for the kitchens.

"Wait!" the innkeeper called behind him. "Wait until you know. Wait, you fool!"

Rand threw open the door to the kitchens, and there they were. Moiraine rested her serene eyes on him, unsurprised. Nynaeve and Egwene ran laughing to throw their arms around him, with Perrin crowding in behind them, all three patting his shoulders as if they had to be convinced that he was really there. In the doorway leading to the stableyard Lan lounged with one boot up on the doorframe, dividing his attention between the kitchen and the yard outside.

Rand tried to hug the two women and shake Perrin's hand, all at the same time, and it was a tangle of arms and laughter complicated by Nynaeve trying to feel his face for fever. They looked somewhat the worse for wear—bruises on Perrin's face, and he had a way of keeping his eyes downcast that he had never had before—but they were alive, and together again. His throat was so tight he could barely talk. "I was afraid I'd never see you again," he managed finally. "I was afraid you were all. . . ."

"I knew you were alive," Egwene said against his chest. "I always knew it. Always."

"I did not," Nynaeve said. Her voice was sharp for just that moment, but it softened in the next, and she smiled up at him. "You look well, Rand. Not overfed by any means, but well, thank the Light."

"Well," Master Gill said behind him, "I guess you know these people after all. Those friends you were looking for?"

Rand nodded. "Yes, my friends." He made introductions all around; it still felt odd to be giving Lan and Moiraine their right names. They both eyed him sharply when he did.

The innkeeper greeted everyone with an open smile, but he was properly impressed at meeting a Warder, and especially at Moiraine. At her he gaped openly—it was one thing knowing an Aes Sedai had been helping the boys, quite something else having her appear in the kitchen—then bowed deeply. "You are welcome to The Queen's Blessing, Aes Sedai, as my guest. Though I suppose you will be staying at the Palace with Elaida Sedai, and the Aes Sedai who came with the false Dragon." Bowing again, he gave Rand a quick, worried look. It was all very well to say he did not speak ill of Aes Sedai, but that was not the same as saying he wanted one sleeping under his roof.

Rand nodded encouragingly, trying to tell him silently that it was all right. Moiraine was not like Elaida, with a threat hidden behind every glance, under every word. *Are you sure? Even now, are you sure?*

"I believe I will stay here," Moiraine said, "for the short time I remain in Caemlyn. And you must allow me to pay."

A calico cat sauntered in from the hallway to strop the innkeeper's ankles. No sooner had the calico begun than a fuzzy gray sprang from under the table, arching its back and hissing. The calico crouched with a threatening growl, and the gray streaked past Lan into the stableyard.

Master Gill began apologizing for the cats at the same time he protested that Moiraine would honor him by being his guest, and was she sure she would not prefer the Palace, which he would quite understand, but he hoped she would accept his best room as a gift. It made a jumble to which Moiraine seemed to pay no attention at all. Instead she bent down to scratch the orange-and-white cat; it promptly left Master Gill's ankles for hers.

"I've seen four other cats here, so far," she said. "You have a problem with mice? Rats?"

"Rats, Moiraine Sedai." The innkeeper sighed. "A terrible problem. Not that I don't keep a clean place, you understand. It's all the people. The whole city is full of people and rats. But my cats take care of it. You'll not be troubled, I promise."

Rand exchanged a fleeting look with Perrin, who put his eyes down again right away. There was something odd about Perrin's eyes. And he was so silent; Perrin was almost always slow to speak, but now he was saying nothing at all. "It could be all the people," he said.

"With your permission, Master Gill," Moiraine said, as if she took it for granted. "It is a simple matter to keep rats away from this street. With luck, the rats will not even realize they are being kept away."

Master Gill frowned at that last, but he bowed, accepting her offer. "If you are sure you don't want to stay at the Palace, Aes Sedai."

"Where is Mat?" Nynaeve said suddenly. "*She* said he was here, too."

"Upstairs," Rand said. "He's . . . not feeling well."

Nynaeve's head came up. "He's sick? I'll leave the rats to *her*, and I'll attend to him. Take me to him now, Rand."

"All of you go up," Moiraine said. "I will join you in a few minutes. We are crowding Master Gill's kitchen, and it would be best if we could all be somewhere quiet for a time." There was an undercurrent in her voice. *Stay out of sight. The hiding is not done yet.*

"Come on," Rand said. "We'll go up the back way."

The Emond's Field folk crowded after him to the back staircase, leaving the Aes Sedai and the Warder in the kitchen with Master Gill. He could not get over being back together. It was nearly as if he were home again. He could not stop grinning.

The same relief, almost joyous, seemed to be affecting the others. They chuckled to themselves, and kept reaching out to grip his arm. Perrin's voice seemed subdued, and he still kept his head down, but he began to talk as they climbed.

"Moiraine said she could find you and Mat, and she did. When we rode into the city, the rest of us couldn't stop staring—well, all except Lan, of course—all the people, the buildings, everything." His thick curls swung as he shook his head in disbelief. "It's all so big. And so many people. Some of them kept staring at us, too, shouting 'Red or white?' like it made some kind of sense."

Egwene touched Rand's sword, fingering the red wrappings. "What does it mean?"

"Nothing," he said. "Nothing important. We're leaving for Tar Valon, remember?"

Egwene gave him a look, but she removed her hand from the sword and took up where Perrin had left off. "Moiraine didn't look at anything any more than Lan did. She led us back and forth through all those streets so many times, like a dog hunting a scent, that I thought you couldn't be here. Then, all of a sudden, she took off down a street, and the next thing I knew we were handing the horses to the stablemen and marching into the kitchen. She never even asked if you were here. Just told a woman who was mixing batter to go tell Rand al'Thor and Mat Cauthon that someone wanted to see them. And there you were"—she grinned—"like a ball popping into the gleeman's hand out of nowhere."

"Where is the gleeman?" Perrin asked. "Is he with you?"

Rand's stomach lurched and the good feeling of having friends around him dimmed. "Thom's dead. I think he's dead. There was a Fade. . . ." He could not say any more. Nynaeve shook her head, muttering under her breath.

The silence thickened around them, stifling the little chuckles, flattening the joy, until they reached the head of the stairs.

"Mat's not sick, exactly," he said then. "It's. . . . You'll see." He flung open the door to the room he shared with Mat. "Look who's here, Mat."

Mat was still curled up in a ball on the bed, just as Rand had left him. He raised his head to stare at them. "How do you know they're really who they look like?" he said hoarsely. His face was flushed, the skin tight and slick with sweat. "How do I know you're who you look like?"

"Not sick?" Nynaeve gave Rand a disdainful look as she pushed past him, already unslinging her bag from her shoulder.

"Everybody changes," Mat rasped. "How can I be sure? Perrin? Is that you? You've changed, haven't you?" His laugh sounded more like a cough. "Oh, yes, you've changed."

To Rand's surprise Perrin dropped onto the edge of the other bed with his head in hands, staring at the floor. Mat's hacking laughter seemed to pierce him.

Nynaeve knelt beside Mat's bed and put a hand to his face, pushing up his headcloth. He jerked back from her with a scornful look. His eyes were bright and glazed. "You're burning," she said, "but you should not be sweating with this much fever." She could not keep the worry out of her voice. "Rand, you and Perrin fetch some clean cloths and as much cool water as you can carry. I'll bring your temperature down first, Mat, and—"

"Pretty Nynaeve," Mat spat. "A Wisdom isn't supposed to think of herself as a woman, is she? Not a pretty woman. But you do, don't you? Now. You can't make yourself forget that you're a pretty woman, now, and it frightens you. Everybody changes." Nynaeve's face paled as he spoke—whether with anger or something else, Rand could not tell. Mat gave a sly laugh, and his feverish eyes slid to Egwene. "Pretty Egwene," he croaked. "Pretty as Nynaeve. And you share other things now, don't you? Other dreams. What do you dream about now?" Egwene took a step back from the bed.

"We are safe from the Dark One's eyes for the time being," Moiraine announced as she walked into the room with Lan at her heels. Her eyes fell on Mat as she stepped through the doorway, and she hissed as if she had touched a hot stove. "Get away from him!"

Nynaeve did not move except for turning to stare at the Aes Sedai in surprise. In two quick steps Moiraine seized the Wisdom by the shoulders, hauling her across the floor like a sack of grain. Nynaeve struggled and protested, but Moiraine did not release her until she was well away from the bed. The Wisdom continued her protests as she got to her feet, angrily straightening her clothes, but Moiraine ignored her completely. The Aes Sedai watched Mat to the exclusion of everything else, eyeing him the way she would a viper.

"All of you stay away from him," she said. "And be quiet."

Mat stared back as intently as she. He bared his teeth in a silent, snarling rictus, and pulled himself into an ever tighter knot, but he never took his eyes from hers. Slowly she put one hand on him, lightly, on a knee drawn up to his chest. A convulsion shook him at her touch, a shudder of revulsion spasming through his entire body, and abruptly he pulled one hand out, slashing at her face with the ruby-hilted dagger.

One minute Lan was in the doorway, the next he was at the bedside, as if he had not bothered with the intervening space. His hand caught Mat's wrist, stopping the slash as if it had struck stone. Still Mat held himself in that tight ball. Only the hand with the dagger tried to move, straining against the Warder's implacable grip. Mat's eyes never left Moiraine, and they burned with hate.

Moiraine also did not move. She did not flinch from the blade only inches from her face, as she had not when he first struck. "How did he come by this?" she asked in a steel voice. "I asked if Mordeth had given you anything. I asked, and I warned you, and you said he had not."

"He didn't," Rand said. "He. . . . Mat took it from the treasure room." Moiraine looked at him, her eyes seeming to burn as much as Mat's. He almost stepped back before she turned away again, back to the bed. "I didn't know until after we were separated. I didn't know."

"You did not know." Moiraine studied Mat. He still lay with his knees pulled up to his chest, still snarled soundlessly at her, and his hand yet fought Lan to reach her with the dagger. "It is a wonder you got this far, carrying this. I felt the evil of it when I laid eyes on him, the touch of Mashadar, but a Fade could sense it for miles. Even though he would not know exactly where, he would know it was near, and Mashadar would draw his spirit while his bones remembered that this same evil swallowed an army—Dreadlords, Fades, Trollocs, and all. Some Darkfriends could probably feel it, too. Those who have truly given away their souls. There could not help but be those who would wonder at suddenly feeling this, as if the very air around them itched. They would be compelled to seek it. It should have drawn them to it as a magnet draws iron filings."

"There were Darkfriends," Rand said, "more than once, but we got away from them. And a Fade, the night before we reached Caemlyn, but he never saw us." He cleared his throat. "There are rumors of strange things in the night outside the city. It could be Trollocs."

"Oh, it's Trollocs, sheepherder," Lan said wryly. "And where Trollocs are, there are Fades." Tendons stood out on the back of his hand from the effort of holding Mat's wrist, but there was no strain in his voice. "They've tried to hide their passage, but I have seen sign for two days. And heard farmers and villagers mutter about things in the night. The Myrddraal managed to strike into the Two Rivers unseen, somehow, but every day they come closer to those who can send soldiers to hunt them down. Even so, they won't stop now, sheepherder."

"But we're in Caemlyn," Egwene said. "They can't get to us as long as—"

"They can't?" the Warder cut her off. "The Fades are building their numbers in the countryside. That's plain enough from the sign, if you know what to look for. Already there are more Trollocs than they need just to watch all the ways out of the city, a dozen fists, at least. There can only be one reason; when the Fades have enough numbers, they will come into the city after you. That act may send half the armies of the south marching to the Borderlands, but the evidence is that they're willing to take that risk. You three have escaped them too long. It looks as if you've brought a new Trolloc War to Caemlyn, sheepherder."

Egwene gave a gasping sob, and Perrin shook his head as though to deny it. Rand felt a sickness in his stomach at the thought of Trollocs in the streets of Caemlyn. All those people at one another's throats, never realizing the real threat waiting to come over the walls. What would they do when they suddenly found Trollocs and Fades in their midst, killing them? He could see the towers burning, flames breaking through the domes, Trollocs pillaging through the curving streets and vistas of the Inner City. The Palace itself in flames. Elayne, and Gawyn, and Morgase . . . dead.

"Not yet," Moiraine said absently. She was still intent on Mat. "If we can find a way out of Caemlyn, the Halfmen will have no more interest here. If. So many if's."

"Better we were all dead," Perrin said suddenly, and Rand jumped at the echo of his own thoughts. Perrin still sat staring at the floor—glaring at it now—and his voice was bitter. "Everywhere we go, we bring pain and suffering on our backs. It would be better for everyone if we were dead."

Nynaeve rounded on him, her face half fury and half worried fear, but Moiraine forestalled her.

"What do you think to gain, for yourself or anyone else, by dying?" the Aes Sedai asked. Her voice was level, yet sharp. "If the Lord of the Grave has gained as much freedom to touch the Pattern as I fear, he can reach you dead more easily than alive, now. Dead, you can help no one, not the people who have helped you, not your friends and family back in the Two Rivers. The Shadow is falling over the world, and none of you can stop it dead."

Perrin raised his head to look at her, and Rand gave a start. The irises of his friend's eyes were more yellow than brown. With his shaggy hair and the intensity of his gaze, there was something about him. . . . Rand could not grasp it enough to make it out.

Perrin spoke with a soft flatness that gave his words more weight than if he had shouted. "We can't stop it alive, either, now can we?"

"I will have time to argue with you later," Moiraine said, "but your friend needs me now." She stepped aside so they could all see Mat clearly. His eyes still on her with a rage-filled stare, he had not moved or changed his position on the bed. Sweat stood out on his face, and his lips were bloodless in an unchanging snarl. All of his strength seemed to be pouring into the effort to reach Moiraine with the dagger Lan held motionless. "Or had you forgotten?"

Perrin gave an embarrassed shrug and spread his hands wordlessly.

"What's wrong with him?" Egwene asked, and Nynaeve added, "Is it catching? I can still treat him. I don't seem to catch sick, no matter what it is."

"Oh, it is catching," Moiraine said, "and your . . . protection would not save you." She pointed to the ruby-hilted dagger, careful not to let her finger touch it. The blade trembled as Mat strained to reach her with it. "This is from Shadar Logoth. There is not a pebble of that city that is not tainted and dangerous to bring outside the walls, and this is far more than a pebble. The evil that killed Shadar Logoth is in it, and in Mat, too, now. Suspicion and hatred so strong that even those closest are seen as enemies, rooted so deep in the bone that eventually the only thought left is to kill. By carrying the dagger beyond the walls of Shadar Logoth he freed it, this seed of it, from what bound it to that place. It will have waxed and waned in him, what he is in the heart of him fighting what the contagion of Mashadar sought to make him, but now the battle inside him is almost done, and he almost defeated. Soon, if it does not kill him first, he will spread that evil like a plague wherever he goes. Just as one scratch from that blade is enough to infect and destroy, so, soon, a few minutes with Mat will be just as deadly."

Nynaeve's face had gone white. "Can you do anything?" she whispered.

"I hope so." Moiraine sighed. "For the sake of the world, I hope I am not too late." Her hand delved into the pouch at her belt and came out with the silk-shrouded *angreal.* "Leave me. Stay together, and find somewhere you will not be seen, but leave me. I will do what I can for him."

CHAPTER
42

Remembrance of Dreams

I t was a subdued group that Rand led back down the stairs. None of them wanted to talk to him now, or to one another. He did not feel much like talking, either.

The sun was far enough across the sky to dim the back stairwell, but the lamps had not yet been lit. Sunlight and shadow striped the stairs. Perrin's face was as closed as the others, but where worry creased everyone else's brow, his was smooth. Rand thought the look Perrin wore was resignation. He wondered why, and wanted to ask, but whenever Perrin walked through a deeper patch of shadow, his eyes seemed to gather in what little light there was, glowing softly like polished amber.

Rand shivered and tried to concentrate on his surroundings, on the walnut paneled walls and the oak stair railing, on sturdy, everyday things. He wiped his hands on his coat several times, but each time sweat sprang out on his palms anew. *It'll all be all right, now. We're together again, and. . . . Light, Mat.*

He took them to the library by the back way that went by the kitchens, avoiding the common room. Not many travelers used the library; most of those who could read stayed at more elegant inns in the Inner City. Master Gill kept it more for his own enjoyment than for the handful of patrons who wanted a book now and then. Rand did not want to think why Moiraine wanted them to keep out of sight, but he kept remembering the Whitecloak under-officer saying he would be back, and Elaida's eyes when she asked where he was staying. Those were reasons enough, whatever Moiraine wanted.

He took five steps into the library before he realized that everyone else had stopped, crowded together in the doorway, openmouthed and goggling. A brisk blaze crackled in the fireplace, and Loial was sprawled on the long couch, reading, a small black cat with white feet curled and half asleep on his stomach. When they entered he closed the book with a huge finger marking his place and gently set the cat on the floor, then stood to bow formally.

Rand was so used to the Ogier that it took him a minute to realize that Loial was the object of the others' stares. "These are the friends I was waiting for, Loial," he said. "This is Nynaeve, the Wisdom of my village. And Perrin. And this is Egwene."

"Ah, yes," Loial boomed, "Egwene. Rand has spoken of you a great deal. Yes. I am Loial."

"He's an Ogier," Rand explained, and watched their amazement change in kind. Even after Trollocs and Fades in the flesh, it was still astonishing to meet a legend walking and breathing. Remembering his own first reaction to Loial, he grinned ruefully. They were doing better than he had.

Loial took their gaping in his stride. Rand supposed he hardly noticed it compared with a mob shouting "Trolloc." "And the Aes Sedai, Rand?" Loial asked.

"Upstairs with Mat."

The Ogier raised one bushy eyebrow thoughtfully. "Then he *is* ill. I suggest we all be seated. She will be joining us? Yes. Then there's nothing to do but wait."

The act of sitting seemed to loosen some catch inside the Emond's Field folk, as if being in a well-stuffed chair with a fire in the fireplace and a cat now curled up on the hearth made them feel at home. As soon as they were settled they excitedly began asking the Ogier questions. To Rand's surprise, Perrin was the first to speak.

"The *stedding*, Loial. Are they really havens, the way the stories say?" His voice was intent, as if he had a particular reason for asking.

Loial was glad to tell about the *stedding*, and how he came to be at The Queen's Blessing, and what he had seen in his travels. Rand soon leaned back, only partly listening. He had heard it all before, in detail. Loial liked to talk, and talk at length when he had the slightest chance, though he usually seemed to think a story needed two or three hundred years of background to make it understood. His sense of time was very strange; to him three hundred years seemed a reasonable length of time for a story or explanation to cover. He always talked about leaving the *stedding* as if it were just a few months before, but it had finally come out that he had been gone more than three years.

Rand's thoughts drifted to Mat. *A dagger. A bloody knife, and it might kill him just from carrying it. Light, I don't want any more adventure. If she can heal him, we should all go . . . not home. Can't go home. Somewhere. We'll all go somewhere they've never heard of Aes Sedai or the Dark One. Somewhere.*

The door opened, and for a moment Rand thought he was still imagining. Mat stood there, blinking, with his coat buttoned up and the dark scarf wrapped low around his forehead. Then Rand saw Moiraine, with her hand on Mat's shoulder, and Lan behind them. The Aes Sedai was watching Mat carefully, as one watches someone only lately out of a sickbed. As always, Lan was watching everything while appearing to watch nothing.

Mat looked as if he had never been sick a day. His first, hesitant smile included everyone, though it slipped into an openmouthed stare at the sight of Loial, as if he were seeing the Ogier for the first time. With a shrug and a shake, he turned his attention back to his friends. "I . . . ah . . . that is. . . ." He took a deep breath. "It . . . ah . . . it seems I've been acting . . . ah . . . sort of oddly. I don't remember much of it, really." He gave Moiraine an uneasy look. She smiled back confidently, and he went on. "Everything is hazy after Whitebridge. Thom, and the. . . ." He shivered and hurried on. "The further from Whitebridge, the hazier it gets. I don't really remember arriving in Caemlyn at all." He eyed Loial askance. "Not really. Moiraine Sedai says I . . . upstairs, I . . . ah. . . ." He grinned, and suddenly he truly was the old Mat. "You can't hold a man to blame for what he does when he's crazy, can you?"

"You always were crazy," Perrin said, and for a moment he, too, sounded as of old.

"No," Nynaeve said. Tears made her eyes bright, but she was smiling. "None of us blames you."

Rand and Egwene began talking at once then, telling

Mat how happy they were to see him well and how well he looked, with a few laughing comments thrown in about hoping that he was done with tricks now that one so ugly had been played on him. Mat met banter with banter as he found a chair with all of his old swagger. As he sat down, still grinning, he absentmindedly touched his coat as if to make sure that something tucked behind his belt was still there, and Rand's breath caught.

"Yes," Moiraine said quietly, "he still has the dagger." The laughter and talk was still going on among the rest of the Emond's Field folk, but she had noticed his sudden intake of breath and had seen what had caused it. She moved closer to his chair, where she did not have to raise her voice for him to hear clearly. "I cannot take it away from him without killing him. The binding has lasted too long, and grown too strong. That must be unknotted in Tar Valon; it is beyond me, or any lone Aes Sedai, even with an *angreal*."

"But he doesn't look sick anymore." He had a thought and looked up at her. "As long as he has the dagger, the Fades will know where we are. Darkfriends, too, some of them. You said so."

"I have contained that, after a fashion. If they come close enough to sense it now, they will be on top of us anyway. I cleansed the taint from him, Rand, and did what I could to slow its return, but return it will, in time, unless he receives help in Tar Valon."

"A good thing that's where we're going, isn't it?" He thought maybe it was the resignation in his voice, and the hope for something else, that made her give him a sharp look before turning away.

Loial was on his feet, bowing to her. "I am Loial, son of Arent son of Halan, Aes Sedai. The *stedding* offers sanctuary to the Servants of the Light."

"Thank you, Loial, son of Arent," Moiraine answered dryly, "but I would not be too free with that greeting if I were you. There are perhaps twenty Aes Sedai in Caemlyn at this moment, and every one but I of the Red Ajah." Loial nodded sagely, as if he understood. Rand could only shake his head in confusion; he would be Lightblinded if *he* knew what she meant. "It is strange to find you here," the Aes Sedai went on. "Few Ogier leave the *stedding* in recent years."

"The old stories caught me, Aes Sedai. The old books filled my unworthy head with pictures. I want to see the groves. And the cities we built, too. There do not seem to be many of either still standing, but if buildings are a poor substitute for trees, they are still worth seeing. The Elders think I'm odd, wanting to travel. I always have, and they always have. None of them believe there is anything worth seeing outside the *stedding*. Perhaps when I return and tell them what I've seen, they will change their minds. I hope so. In time."

"Perhaps they will," Moiraine said smoothly. "Now, Loial, you must forgive me for being abrupt. It is a failing of humankind, I know. My companions and I have urgent need to plan our journey. If you could excuse us?"

It was Loial's turn to look confused. Rand came to his rescue. "He's coming with us. I promised him he could."

Moiraine stood looking at the Ogier as if she had not heard, but finally she nodded. "The Wheel weaves as the Wheel wills," she murmured. "Lan, see that we are not taken unaware." The Warder vanished from the room, silently but for the click of the door shutting behind him.

Lan's disappearance acted like a signal; all talk was cut off. Moiraine moved to the fireplace, and when she turned back to the room every eye was on her. Slight of build as she was, her presence dominated. "We cannot remain long in Caemlyn, nor are we safe here in The Queen's Blessing. The Dark One's eyes are already in the city. They have not found what they are searching for, or they would not still be looking. That we have to our advantage. I have set wards to keep them away, and by the time the Dark One realizes that there is a part of the city the rats no longer enter, we will be gone. Any ward that will turn a man aside, though, would be as good as a beacon fire for the Myrddraal, and there are Children of the Light in Caemlyn, also, looking for Perrin and Egwene." Rand made a sound, and Moiraine raised an eyebrow at him.

"I thought they were looking for Mat and me," he said.

The explanation made both the Aes Sedai's eyebrows lift. "Why would you think the Whitecloaks were looking for you?"

"I heard one say they were looking for someone from the Two Rivers. Darkfriends, he said. What else was I supposed to think? With everything that's been happening, I'm lucky I can think at all."

"It has been confusing, I know, Rand," Loial put in, "but you can think more clearly than that. The Children hate Aes Sedai. Elaida would not—"

"Elaida?" Moiraine cut in sharply. "What has Elaida Sedai to do with this?"

She was looking at Rand so hard that he wanted to lean back. "She wanted to throw me in prison," he said slowly. "All I wanted was a look at Logain, but she wouldn't believe I was in the Palace gardens with Elayne and Gawyn just by chance." They were all staring at him as if he had suddenly sprouted a third eye, all except Loial. "Queen Morgase let me go. She said there was no proof I meant any harm and she was going to uphold the law no matter what Elaida suspected." He shook his head, the memory of Morgase in all her radiance making him forget for a minute that anyone was looking at him. "Can you imagine me meeting a Queen? She's beautiful, like the queens in stories. So is Elayne. And Gawyn . . . you'd like Gawyn, Perrin. Perrin? Mat?" They were still staring. "Blood and ashes, I just climbed up on the wall for a look at the false Dragon. I didn't do anything wrong."

"That's what I always say," Mat said blandly, though he was suddenly grinning hard, and Egwene asked in a decidedly neutral voice, "Who's Elayne?"

Moiraine muttered something crossly.

"A Queen," Perrin said, shaking his head. "You really have had adventures. All we met were Tinkers and some Whitecloaks." He avoided looking at Moiraine so obviously that Rand saw the avoidance plain. Perrin touched the bruises on his face. "On the whole, singing with the Tinkers was more fun than the Whitecloaks."

"The Traveling People live for their songs," Loial said. "For all songs, for that matter. For the search for them, at least. I met some Tuatha'an a few years back, and they wanted to learn the songs we sing to trees. Actually, the trees won't listen to very many anymore, and so not many Ogier learn the songs. I have a scrap of that Talent, so Elder Arent insisted I learn. I taught the Tuatha'an what they could learn, but the trees never listen to humans. For the Traveling People they were only songs, and just as well received for that, since none was the song they seek. That's what they call the leader of each band, the Seeker. They come to Stedding Shangtai, sometimes. Few humans do."

"If you please, Loial," Moiraine said, but he cleared his throat suddenly and went on in a quick rumble as if afraid she might stop him.

"I've just remembered something, Aes Sedai, something I have always wanted to ask an Aes Sedai if ever I met one, since you know many things and have great libraries in Tar Valon, and now I have, of course, and . . . may I?"

"If you make it brief," she said curtly.

"Brief," he said as though wondering what it meant. "Yes. Well. Brief. There was a man came to Stedding Shangtai a little time back. This was not unusual in itself, at the time, since a great many refugees had come to the Spine of the World fleeing what you humans call the Aiel War." Rand grinned. A little time back; twenty years, near enough. "He was at the point of death, though there was no wound or mark on him. The Elders thought it might be something Aes Sedai had done"—Loial gave Moiraine an apologetic look—"since as soon as he was within the *stedding* he quickly got well. A few months. One night he left without a word to anyone, simply sneaked away when the moon was down." He looked at Moiraine's face and cleared his throat again. "Yes. Brief. Before he left, he told a curious tale which he said he meant to carry to Tar Valon. He said the Dark One intended to blind the Eye of the World, and slay the Great Serpent, kill time itself. The Elders said he was as sound in his mind as in his body, but that was what he said. What I have wanted to ask is, can the Dark One do such a thing? Kill time itself? And the Eye of the World? Can he blind the eye of the Great Serpent? What does it mean?"

Rand expected almost anything from Moiraine except what he saw. Instead of giving Loial an answer, or telling him she had no time for it now, she stood there staring right through the Ogier, frowning in thought.

"That's what the Tinkers told us," Perrin said.

"Yes," Egwene said, "the Aiel story."

Moiraine turned her head slowly. No other part of her moved. "What story?"

It was an expressionless look she gave them, but it made Perrin take a deep breath, though when he spoke he was as deliberate as ever. "Some Tinkers crossing the Waste—they said they could do that unharmed—found Aiel dying after a battle with Trollocs. Before the last Aiel died, she—they were all women, apparently—told the Tinkers what Loial just said. The Dark One—they called him Sightblinder—intends to blind the Eye of the World. This was only three years ago, not twenty. Does it mean something?"

"Perhaps everything," Moiraine said. Her face was still, but Rand had the feeling her mind raced behind those dark eyes.

"Ba'alzamon," Perrin said suddenly. The name cut off all sound in the room. No one appeared to breathe. Perrin looked at Rand, then at Mat, his eyes strangely calm and more yellow than ever. "At the time I wondered where I'd heard that name before . . . the Eye of the World. Now I remember. Don't you?"

"I don't want to remember anything," Mat said stiffly.

"We have to tell her," Perrin continued. "It's important now. We can't keep it secret any longer. You see it, don't you, Rand?"

"Tell me what?" Moiraine's voice was harsh, and she seemed to be bracing for a blow. Her gaze had settled on Rand.

He did not want to answer. He did not want to remember any more than Mat, but he did remember—and he knew Perrin was right. "I've. . . ." He looked at his friends. Mat nodded reluctantly, Perrin decisively, but at least they had done it. He did not have to face her alone. "We have had . . . dreams." He rubbed the spot on his finger where the thorn had stuck him once, remembering the blood when he woke. Queasily remembering the sunburned feel of his face another time. "Except maybe they weren't dreams, exactly. Ba'alzamon was in them." He knew why Perrin had used that name; it was easier than saying the Dark One had been in your dreams, inside your head. "He said . . . he said all sorts of things, but once he said the Eye of the World would never serve me." For a minute his mouth was as dry as dust.

"He told me the same thing," Perrin said, and Mat sighed heavily, then nodded. Rand found he had spit in his mouth again. "You aren't angry with us?" Perrin asked, sounding surprised, and Rand realized that Moiraine did not seem angry. She was studying them, but her eyes were clear and calm, if intent.

"More with myself than you. But I did ask you to tell me if you had strange dreams. In the beginning, I asked." Though her voice remained level, a flash of anger crossed her eyes, and was gone in an instant. "Had I known after the first such, I might have been able to. . . . There has not been a Dreamwalker in Tar Valon for nearly a thousand years, but I could have tried. Now it is too late. Each time the Dark One touches you, he makes the next touching easier for him. Perhaps my presence can still shield you somewhat, but even then. . . . Remember the stories of the Forsaken binding men to them? Strong men, men who had fought the Dark One from the start. Those stories are true, and none of the Forsaken had a tenth of the strength of their master, not Aginor or Lanfear, not Balthamel or Demandred, not even Ishamael, the Betrayer of Hope himself."

Nynaeve and Egwene were looking at him, Rand saw, him and Mat and Perrin all three. The women's faces were a blood-drained blend of fear and horror. *Are they afraid for us, or afraid of us?*

"What can we do?" he asked. "There has to be something."

"Staying close by me," Moiraine replied, "will help. Some. The protection from touching the True Source extends around me a little, remember. But you cannot always remain close to me. You can defend yourself, if you have the strength for it, but you must find the strength and will within yourself. I cannot give it to you."

"I think I've already found my protection," Perrin said, sounding resigned rather than happy.

"Yes," Moiraine said, "I suppose you have." She looked at him until he dropped his eyes, and even then she stood considering. Finally she turned to the others. "There are limits to the Dark One's power inside you. Yield even for an instant and he will have a string tied to your heart, a string you may never be able to cut. Surrender, and you will be his. Deny him, and his power fails. It is not easy when he touches your dreams, but it can be done. He can still send Halfmen against you, and Trollocs, and Draghkar, and other things, but he cannot make you his unless you let him."

"Fades are bad enough," Perrin said.

"I don't want him inside my head again," Mat growled. "Isn't there any way to keep him out?"

Moiraine shook her head. "Loial has nothing to fear, nor Egwene, nor Nynaeve. Out of the mass of humanity, the Dark One can touch an individual only by chance, unless that person seeks it. But for a time, at least, you three are central to the Pattern. A Web of Destiny is being woven, and every thread leads straight to you. What else did the Dark One say to you?"

"I don't remember it all that well," Perrin said. "There was something about one of us being chosen, something like that. I remember him laughing," he finished bleakly, "about who we were chosen by. He said I—we could serve him or die. And then we'd still serve him."

"He said the Amyrlin Seat would try to use us," Mat added, his voice fading as he remembered to whom he was speaking. He swallowed and went on. "He said just like Tar Valon used—he had some names. Davian, I think. I can't remember very well, either."

"Raolin Darksbane," Perrin said.

"Yes," Rand said, frowning. He had tried to forget everything about those dreams. It was unpleasant bringing them back. "Yurian Stonebow was another, and Guaire Amalasan." He stopped suddenly, hoping Moiraine had not noticed how suddenly. "I don't recognize any of them."

But he had recognized one, now that he dredged them from the depths of memory. The name he had barely stopped himself from saying. Logain. The false Dragon. *Light! Thom said they were dangerous names. Is that what Ba'alzamon meant? Moiraine wants to use one of us as a false Dragon? Aes Sedai hunt down false Dragons, they don't use them. Do they? Light help me, do they?*

Moiraine was looking at him, but he could not read her face. "Do you know them?" he asked her. "Do they mean anything?"

"The Father of Lies is a good name for the Dark One," Moiraine replied. "It was always his way to seed the worm of doubt wherever he could. It eats at men's minds like a canker. When you believe the Father of Lies, it is the first step toward surrender. Remember, if you surrender to the Dark One, he will make you his."

An Aes Sedai never lies, but the truth she speaks may not

be the truth you think you hear. That was what Tam had said, and she had not really answered his question. He kept his face expressionless and held his hands still on his knees, trying not to scrub the sweat off them on his breeches.

Egwene was crying softly. Nynaeve had her arms around her, but she looked as if she wanted to cry, too. Rand almost wished he could.

"They are *all ta'veren*," Loial said abruptly. He seemed brightened by the prospect, looking forward to watching from close by as the Pattern wove itself around them. Rand looked at him incredulously, and the Ogier gave an abashed shrug, but it was not enough to dim his eagerness.

"So they are," Moiraine said. "*Three* of them, when I expected one. A great many things have happened that I did not expect. This news concerning the Eye of the World changes much." She paused, frowning. "For a time the Pattern does seem to be swirling around all three of you, just as Loial says, and the swirl will grow greater before it becomes less. Sometimes being *ta'veren* means the Pattern is forced to bend to you, and sometimes it means the Pattern forces you to the needed path. The Web can still be woven many ways, and some of those designs would be disastrous. For you, for the world.

"We cannot remain in Caemlyn, but by any road, Myrddraal and Trollocs will be on us before we have gone ten miles. And just at this point we hear of a threat to the Eye of the World, not from one source, but three, each seeming independent of the others. The Pattern is forcing our path. The Pattern still weaves itself around you three, but what hand now sets the warp, and what hand controls the shuttle? Has the Dark One's prison weakened enough for him to exert that much control?"

"There's no need for that kind of talk!" Nynaeve said sharply. "You'll only frighten them."

"But not you?" Moiraine asked. "It frightens me. Well, perhaps you are right. Fear cannot be allowed to affect our course. Whether this is a trap or a timely warning, we must do what we must, and that is to reach the Eye of the World quickly. The Green Man must know of this threat."

Rand gave a start. *The Green Man?* The others stared, too, all but Loial, whose broad face looked worried.

"I cannot even risk stopping in Tar Valon for help,"

Moiraine continued. "Time traps us. Even if we could ride out of the city unhindered, it would take many weeks to reach the Blight, and I fear we no longer have weeks."

"The Blight!" Rand heard himself echoed in a chorus, but Moiraine ignored them all.

"The Pattern presents a crisis, and at the same time a way to surmount it. If I did not know it was impossible, I could almost believe the Creator is taking a hand. There is a way." She smiled as if at a private joke, and turned to Loial. "There was an Ogier grove here at Caemlyn, and a Waygate. The New City now spreads out over where the grove once stood, so the Waygate must be inside the walls. I know not many Ogier learn the Ways now, but one who has a Talent and learns the old Songs of Growing must be drawn to such knowledge, even if he believes it will never be used. Do you know the Ways, Loial?"

The Ogier shifted his feet uneasily. "I do, Aes Sedai, but—"

"Can you find the path to Fal Dara along the Ways?"

"I've never heard of Fal Dara," Loial said, sounding relieved.

"In the days of the Trolloc Wars it was known as Mafal Dadaranell. Do you know *that* name?"

"I know it," Loial said reluctantly, "but—"

"Then you can find the path for us," Moiraine said. "A curious turn, indeed. When we can neither stay nor leave by any ordinary means, I learn of a threat to the Eye, and in the same place there is one who can take us there in days. Whether it is the Creator, or fate, or even the Dark One, the Pattern has chosen our path for us."

"No!" Loial said, an emphatic rumble like thunder. Everyone turned to look at him and he blinked under the attention, but there was nothing hesitant about his words. "If we enter the Ways, we will all die—or be swallowed by the Shadow."

CHAPTER

43

Decisions and Apparitions

The Aes Sedai appeared to know what Loial meant, but she said nothing. Loial peered at the floor, rubbing under his nose with a thick finger, as if he was abashed by his outburst. No one wanted to speak.

"Why?" Rand asked at last. "Why would we die? What *are* the Ways?"

Loial glanced at Moiraine. She turned away to take a chair in front of the fireplace. The little cat stretched, its claws scratching on the hearthstone, and languidly walked over to butt its head against her ankles. She rubbed behind its ears with one finger. The cat's purring was a strange counterpoint to the Aes Sedai's level voice. "It is your knowledge, Loial. The Ways are the only path to safety for us, the only path to forestalling the Dark One, if only for a time, but the telling is yours."

The Ogier did not appear comforted by her speech. He shifted awkwardly on his chair before beginning. "During the Time of Madness, while the world was still being broken, the earth was in upheaval, and humankind was being scattered like dust on the wind. We Ogier were scattered, too, driven from the *stedding,* into the Exile and the Long Wandering, when the Longing was graven on our hearts." He gave Moiraine another sidelong look. His long eyebrows drew down into two points. "I will try to be brief, but this is not a thing that can be told too briefly. It is of the others I must speak, now, those few Ogier who held in their *stedding* while around them the world was tearing apart. And of the Aes Sedai"—he avoided looking at Moiraine, now—"the male Aes Sedai who were dying even as they destroyed the world in their madness. It was to those Aes Sedai—those who had so far managed to avoid the madness—that the *stedding* first made the offer of sanctuary. Many accepted, for in the *stedding* they were protected from the taint of the Dark One that was killing their kind. But they were cut off from the True Source. It was not just that they could not wield the One Power, or touch the Source; they could no longer even sense that the Source existed. In the end, none could accept that isolation, and one by one they left the *stedding,* hoping that by that time the taint was gone. It never was."

"Some in Tar Valon," Moiraine said quietly, "claim that Ogier sanctuary prolonged the Breaking and made it worse. Others say that if all of those men had been allowed to go mad at once, there would have been nothing left of the world. I am of the Blue Ajah, Loial; unlike the Red Ajah, we hold to the second view. Sanctuary helped to save what could be saved. Continue, please."

Loial nodded gratefully. Relieved of a concern, Rand realized.

"As I was saying," the Ogier went on, "the Aes Sedai, the male Sedai, left. But before they went, they gave a gift to the Ogier in thanks for our sanctuary. The Ways. Enter a Waygate, walk for a day, and you may depart through another Waygate a hundred miles from where you started. Or five hundred. Time and distance are strange in the Ways. Different paths, different bridges, lead to different places, and how long it takes to get there depends on which path you take. It was a marvelous gift, made more so by the times, for the Ways are not part of the world we see around us, nor perhaps of any world outside themselves. Not only did the Ogier so gifted not have to travel through the world, where even after the Breaking men fought like animals to live, in order to reach another *stedding,* but within the Ways there was no Breaking. The land between two *stedding* might split open into deep canyons or rise in mountain ranges, but in the Way between them there was no change.

"When the last Aes Sedai left the *stedding,* they gave to the Elders a key, a talisman, that could be used for growing more. They are a living thing in some fashion, the Ways and the Waygates. I do not understand it; no Ogier ever has, and even the Aes Sedai have forgotten, I am told. Over the years the Exile ended for us. As those Ogier who had been gifted by the Aes Sedai found a *stedding* where Ogier had returned from the Long Wandering, they grew a Way to it. With the stonework we learned during the Exile, we built cities for men, and planted the groves to comfort the Ogier who did the building, so the Longing would not overcome them. To those groves Ways were grown. There was a grove, and a Waygate, at Mafal Dadaranell, but that city was razed during the Trolloc Wars, no stone left standing on another, and the grove was chopped down and burned for Trolloc fires." He left no doubt which had been the greater crime.

"Waygates are all but impossible to destroy," Moiraine said, "and humankind not much less so. There are people at Fal Dara still, though not the great city the Ogier built, and the Waygate yet stands."

"How did they make them?" Egwene asked. Her puzzled look took in Moiraine and Loial both. "The Aes Sedai, the men. If they couldn't use the One Power in a *stedding,* how could they make the Ways? Or did they use the Power at all? Their part of the True Source was tainted. Is tainted. I don't know much about what Aes Sedai can do, yet. Maybe it's a silly question."

Loial explained. "Each *stedding* has a Waygate on its border, but outside. Your question is not silly. You've found the seed of why we do not dare travel the Ways. No Ogier has used the Ways in my lifetime, and before. By edict of the Elders, all the Elders of all the *stedding,* none may, human or Ogier.

"The Ways were made by men wielding Power fouled by the Dark One. About a thousand years ago, during what you humans call the War of the Hundred Years, the Ways began to change. So slowly in the beginning that none really noticed, they grew dank and dim. Then darkness fell along the bridges. Some who went in were never seen again. Travelers spoke of being watched from the dark. The numbers who vanished grew, and some who came out had gone mad, raving about *Machin Shin,* the Black Wind. Aes Sedai Healers could aid some, but even with Aes Sedai help they were never the same. And they never remembered anything of what had occurred. Yet it was as if the darkness had sunken into their bones. They never laughed again, and they feared the sound of the wind."

For a moment there was silence but for the cat purring beside Moiraine's chair, and the snap and crackle of the fire, popping out sparks. Then Nynaeve burst out angrily, "And you expect us to follow you into that? You must be mad!"

"Which would you choose instead?" Moiraine asked quietly. "The Whitecloaks within Caemlyn, or the Trollocs without? Remember that my presence in itself gives some protection from the Dark One's works."

Nynaeve settled back with an exasperated sigh.

"You still have not explained to me," Loial said, "why I should break the edict of the Elders. And I have no desire to enter the Ways. Muddy as they often are, the roads men make have served me well enough since I left Stedding Shangtai."

"Humankind and Ogier, everything that lives, we are at war with the Dark One," Moiraine said. "The greater part of the world does not even know it yet, and most of the few who do fight skirmishes and believe they are battles. While the world refuses to believe, the Dark One may be at the brink of victory. There is enough power in the Eye of the World to undo his prison. If the Dark One has found some way to bend the Eye of the World to his use. . . ."

Rand wished the lamps in the room were lit. Evening was creeping over Caemlyn, and the fire in the fireplace did not give enough light. He wanted no shadows in the room.

"What can we do?" Mat burst out. "Why are we so important? Why do we have to go to the Blight? The Blight!"

Moiraine did not raise her voice, but it filled the room, compelling. Her chair by the fire suddenly seemed like a throne. Suddenly even Morgase would have paled in her presence. "One thing we can do. We can try. What seems like chance is often the Pattern. Three threads have come together here, each giving a warning: the Eye. It cannot be chance; it is the Pattern. You three did not choose; you were chosen by the Pattern. And you are here, where the danger is known. You can step aside, and perhaps doom the world. Running, hiding, will not save you from the weaving of the Pattern. Or you can try. You can go to the Eye of the World, three *ta'veren,* three centerpoints of the Web, placed where the danger lies. Let the Pattern be woven around you there, and you may save the world from the Shadow. The choice is yours. I cannot make you go."

"I'll go," Rand said, trying to sound resolute. However hard he sought the void, images kept flashing through his head. Tam, and the farmhouse, and the flock in the pasture. It had been a good life; he had never really wanted anything more. There was comfort—a small comfort—hearing Perrin and Mat add their agreement to his. They sounded as dry-mouthed as he.

"I suppose there isn't any choice for Egwene or me, either," Nynaeve said.

Moiraine nodded. "You are part of the Pattern, too, both of you, in some fashion. Perhaps not *ta'veren*—perhaps—but strong even so. I have known it since Baerlon. And no doubt by this time the Fades know it, too. And Ba'alzamon. Yet you have as much choice as the young men. You could remain here, proceed to Tar Valon once the rest of us have gone."

"Stay behind!" Egwene exclaimed. "Let the rest of you go off into danger while we hide under the covers? I won't do it!" She caught the Aes Sedai's eye and drew back a little, but not all of her defiance vanished. "I won't do it," she muttered stubbornly.

"I suppose that means both of us will accompany you." Nynaeve sounded resigned, but her eyes flashed when she added, "You still need my herbs, Aes Sedai, unless you've suddenly gained some ability I don't know about." Her voice held a challenge Rand did not understand, but Moiraine merely nodded and turned to the Ogier.

"Well, Loial, son of Arent son of Halan?"

Loial opened his mouth twice, his tufted ears twitching, before he spoke. "Yes, well. The Green Man. The Eye of the World. They're mentioned in the books, of course, but I don't think any Ogier has actually seen them in, oh, quite a long time. I suppose. . . . But must it be the Ways?" Moiraine nodded, and his long eyebrows sagged till the ends brushed his cheeks. "Very well, then. I suppose I must guide you. Elder Haman would say it's no less than I deserve for being so hasty all the time."

"Our choices are made, then," Moiraine said. "And now that they are made, we must decide what to do about them, and how."

Long into the night they planned. Moiraine did most of it, with Loial's advice concerning the Ways, but she listened to questions and suggestions from everyone. Once dark fell Lan joined them, adding his comments in that iron-cored drawl. Nynaeve made a list of what supplies they needed, dipping her pen in the inkwell with a steady hand despite the way she kept muttering under her breath.

Rand wished he could be as matter-of-fact as the Wisdom. He could not stop pacing up and down, as if he had energy to burn or burst from it. He knew his decision was made, knew it was the only one he could make with the knowledge he had, but that did not make him like it. The Blight. Shayol Ghul was somewhere in the Blight, beyond the Blasted Lands.

He could see the same worry in Mat's eyes, the same fear he knew was in his own. Mat sat with his hands clasped, knuckles white. If he let go, Rand thought, he would be clutching the dagger from Shadar Logoth instead.

There was no worry on Perrin's face at all, but what was there was worse: a mask of weary resignation. Perrin looked as though he had fought something until he could fight it no longer and was waiting for it to finish him. Yet sometimes. . . .

"We do what we must, Rand," he said. "The Blight. . . ." For an instant those yellow eyes lit with eagerness, flashing in the fixed tiredness of his face, as if they had a life of their own apart from the big blacksmith's apprentice. "There's good hunting along the Blight," he whispered. Then he shuddered, as if he had just heard what he had said, and once more his face was resigned.

And Egwene. Rand drew her apart at one point, over by the fireplace where those planning around the table could not hear. "Egwene, I. . . ." Her eyes, like big dark pools drawing him in, made him stop and swallow. "It's me the Dark One's after, Egwene. Me, and Mat, and Perrin. I don't care what Moiraine Sedai says. In the morning you and Nynaeve could start for home, or Tar Valon, or anywhere you want to go, and nobody will try to stop you. Not the Trollocs, not the Fades, not anybody. As long as you aren't with us. Go home, Egwene. Or go to Tar Valon. But go."

He waited for her to tell him she had as much right to go where she wanted as he did, that he had no right to tell her what to do. To his surprise, she smiled and touched his cheek.

"Thank you, Rand," she said softly. He blinked, and closed his mouth as she went on. "You know I can't, though. Moiraine Sedai told us what Min saw, in Baerlon. You should have told me who Min was. I thought. . . . Well, Min says I am part of this, too. And Nynaeve. Maybe I'm not *ta'veren*," she stumbled over the word, "but the Pattern sends me to the Eye of the World, too, it seems. Whatever involves you, involves me."

"But, Egwene—"

"Who is Elayne?"

For a minute he stared at her, then told the simple truth. "She's the Daughter-Heir to the throne of Andor."

Her eyes seemed to catch fire. "If you can't be serious for more than a minute, Rand al'Thor, I do not want to talk to you."

Incredulous, he watched her stiff back return to the table, where she leaned on her elbows next to Moiraine to listen to what the Warder was saying. *I need to talk to Perrin,* he thought. *He knows how to deal with women.*

Master Gill entered several times, first to light the lamps, then to bring food with his own hands, and later to report on what was happening outside. Whitecloaks were watching the inn from down the street in both directions. There had been a riot at the gates to the Inner City, with the Queen's Guards arresting white cockades and red alike. Someone had tried to scratch the Dragon's Fang on the front door and been sent on his way by Lamgwin's boot.

If the innkeeper found it odd that Loial was with them, he gave no sign of it. He answered the few questions Moiraine put to him without trying to discover what they were planning, and each time he came he knocked at the door and waited till Lan opened it for him, just as if it were not his inn and his library. On his last visit, Moiraine gave him the sheet of parchment covered in Nynaeve's neat hand.

"It won't be easy this time of night," he said, shaking his head as he perused the list, "but I'll arrange it all."

Moiraine added a small wash-leather bag that clinked as she handed it to him by the drawstrings. "Good. And see that we are wakened before daybreak. The watchers will be at their least alert, then."

"We'll leave them watching an empty box, Aes Sedai." Master Gill grinned.

Rand was yawning by the time he shuffled out of the room with the rest in search of baths and beds. As he scrubbed himself, with a coarse cloth in one hand and a big yellow cake of soap in the other, his eyes drifted to the stool beside Mat's tub. The golden-sheathed tip of the dagger from Shadar Logoth peeked from under the edge of Mat's neatly folded coat. Lan glanced at it from time to time, too. Rand wondered if it was really as safe to have around as Moiraine claimed.

"Do you think my da'll ever believe it?" Mat laughed, scrubbing his back with a long-handled brush. "Me, saving the world? My sisters won't know whether to laugh or cry."

He sounded like the old Mat. Rand wished he could forget the dagger.

It was pitch-black when he and Mat finally got up to their room under the eaves, the stars obscured by clouds. For the first time in a long while Mat undressed before getting into bed, but he casually tucked the dagger under his pillow, too. Rand blew out the candle and crawled into his own bed. He could feel the wrongness from the other bed, not from Mat, but from beneath his pillow. He was still worrying about it when sleep came.

From the first he knew it was a dream, one of those dreams that was not entirely dream. He stood staring at the wooden door, its surface dark and cracked and rough with splinters. The air was cold and dank, thick with the smell of decay. In the distance water dripped, the splashes hollow echoes down stone corridors.

Deny it. Deny him, and his power fails.

He closed his eyes and concentrated on The Queen's Blessing, on his bed, on himself asleep in his bed. When he opened his eyes the door was still there. The echoing splashes came on his heartbeat, as if his pulse counted time for them. He sought the flame and the void, as Tam had taught him, and found inner calm, but nothing outside of him changed. Slowly he opened the door and went in.

Everything was as he remembered it in the room that seemed burned out of the living rock. Tall, arched windows led onto an unrailed balcony, and beyond it the layered clouds streamed like a river in flood. The black metal lamps, their flames too bright to look at, gleamed, black yet somehow as bright as silver. The fire roared but gave no heat in the fearsome fireplace, each stone still vaguely like a face in torment.

All was the same, but one thing was different. On the polished tabletop stood three small figures, the rough, featureless shapes of men, as if the sculptor had been hasty with his clay. Beside one stood a wolf, its clear detail emphasized by the crudeness of the man-shape, and another clutched a tiny dagger, a point of red on the hilt glittering in the light. The last held a sword. The hair stirring on the back of his neck, he moved close enough to see the heron in exquisite detail on that small blade.

His head jerked up in panic, and he stared directly into the lone mirror. His reflection was still a blur, but not so misty as before. He could almost make out his own features. If he imagined he was squinting, he could nearly tell who it was.

"You've hidden from me too long."

He whirled from the table, breath rasping his throat. A moment before he had been alone, but now Ba'alzamon stood before the windows. When he spoke caverns of flame replaced his eyes and mouth.

"Too long, but not much longer."

"I deny you," Rand said hoarsely. "I deny that you hold any power over me. I deny that you are."

Ba'alzamon laughed, a rich sound rolling from fire. "Do you think it is that easy? But then, you always did. Each time we have stood like this, you have thought you could defy me."

"What do mean, each time? I deny you!"

"You always do. In the beginning. This contest between us has taken place countless times before. Each time your face is different, and your name, but each time it is you."

"I deny you." It was a desperate whisper.

"Each time you throw your puny strength against me, and each time, in the end, you know which of us is the master. Age after Age, you kneel to me, or die wishing you still had strength to kneel. Poor fool, you can never win against me."

"Liar!" he shouted. "Father of Lies. Father of Fools if you

can't do better than that. Men found you in the last Age, in the Age of Legends, and bound you back where you belong."

Ba'alzamon laughed again, peal after mocking peal, until Rand wanted to cover his ears to shut it out. He forced his hands to stay at his sides. Void or no, they were trembling when the laughter finally stopped.

"You worm, you know nothing at all. As ignorant as a beetle under a rock, and as easily crushed. This struggle has gone on since the moment of creation. Always men think it a new war, but it is just the same war discovered anew. Only now change blows on the winds of time. Change. This time there will be no drifting back. Those proud Aes Sedai who think to stand you up against me. I will dress them in chains and send them running naked to do my bidding, or stuff their souls into the Pit of Doom to scream for eternity. All but those who already serve me. They will stand but a step beneath me. You can choose to stand with them, with the world groveling at your feet. I offer it one more time, one last time. You can stand above them, above every power and dominion but mine. There have been times when you made that choice, times when you lived long enough to know your power."

Deny him! Rand grabbed hold to what he could deny. "No Aes Sedai serve you. Another lie!"

"Is that what they told you? Two thousand years ago I took my Trollocs across the world, and even among Aes Sedai I found those who knew despair, who knew the world could not stand before Shai'tan. For two thousand years the Black Ajah has dwelt among the others, unseen in the shadows. Perhaps even those who claim to help you."

Rand shook his head, trying to shake away the doubts that came welling up in him, all the doubts he had had about Moiraine, about what the Aes Sedai wanted with him, about what she planned for him. "What do you want from me?" he cried. *Deny him! Light help me deny him!*

"Kneel!" Ba'alzamon pointed to the floor at his feet. "Kneel, and acknowledge me your master! In the end, you will. You will be my creature, or you will die."

The last word echoed through the room, reverberating back on itself, doubling and redoubling, till Rand threw up his arms as if to shield his head from a blow. Staggering back until he thumped into the table, he shouted, trying to drown the sound in his ears. "Nooooooooooooo!"

As he cried out, he spun, sweeping the figures to the floor. Something stabbed his hand, but he ignored it, stomping the clay to shapeless smears underfoot. But when his shout failed, the echo was still there, and growing stronger:

die-die-die-die-die-DIE-DIE-DIE-DIE-DIE-DIE-DIE-DIE-DIE-DIE-DIE-DIE

The sound pulled on him like a whirlpool, drawing him in, ripping the void in his mind to shreds. The light dimmed, and his vision narrowed down to a tunnel with Ba'alzamon standing tall in the last spot of brightness at the end, dwindling until it was the size of his hand, a fingernail, nothing. Around and around the echo whirled him, down into blackness and death.

The thump as he hit the floor woke him, still struggling to swim up out of that darkness. The room was dark, but not so dark as that. Frantically he tried to center on the flame, to shovel fear into it, but the calm of the void eluded him. Tremors ran down his arms and legs, but he held the image of the single flame until the blood stopped pounding in his ears.

Mat was tossing and twisting on his bed, groaning in his sleep. ". . . deny you, deny you, deny you. . . ." It faded off into unintelligible moans.

Rand reached out to shake him awake, and at the first touch Mat sat up with a strangled grunt. For a minute Mat stared around wildly, then drew a long, shuddering breath and dropped his head into his hands. Abruptly he twisted around, digging under his pillow, then sank back clutching the ruby-hilted dagger in both hands on his chest. He turned his head to look at Rand, his face hidden in shadow. "He's back, Rand."

"I know."

Mat nodded. "There were these three figures. . . ."

"I saw them, too."

"He knows who I am, Rand. I picked up the one with the dagger, and he said, 'So that's who you are.' And when I looked again, the figure had my face. My face, Rand! It looked like flesh. It felt like flesh. Light help me, I could feel my own hand gripping me, like I was the figure."

Rand was silent for a moment. "You have to keep denying him, Mat."

"I did, and he laughed. He kept talking about some eternal war, and saying we'd met like that a thousand times before, and. . . . Light, Rand, the Dark One knows me."

"He said the same thing to me. I don't think he does," he added slowly. "I don't think he knows which of us. . . ."

Which of us what?

As he levered himself up, pain stabbed his hand. Making his way to the table, he managed to get the candle lit after three tries, then spread his hand open in the light. Driven into his palm was a thick splinter of dark wood, smooth and polished on one side. He stared at it, not breathing. Abruptly he was panting, plucking at the splinter, fumbling with haste.

"What's the matter?" Mat asked.

"Nothing."

Finally he had it, and a sharp yank pulled it free. With a grunt of disgust he dropped it, but the grunt froze in his throat. As soon as the splinter left his fingers, it vanished.

The wound was still there in his hand, though, bleeding. There was water in the stoneware pitcher. He filled the basin, his hands shaking so that he splashed water onto the table. Hurriedly he washed his hands, kneading his palm till his thumb brought more blood, then washed them again. The thought of the smallest sliver remaining in his flesh terrified him.

"Light," Mat said, "he made me feel dirty, too." But he still lay where he was, holding the dagger in both hands.

"Yes," Rand said. "Dirty." He fumbled a towel from the stack beside the basin. There was a knock at the door, and he jumped. It came again. "Yes?" he said.

Moiraine put her head into the room. "You are awake already. Good. Dress quickly and come down. We must be away before first light."

"Now?" Mat groaned. "We haven't had an hour's sleep yet."

"An hour?" she said. "You have had four. Now hurry, we do not have much time."

Rand shared a confused look with Mat. He could remember every second of the dream clearly. It had begun as soon as he closed his eyes, and lasted only minutes.

Something in that exchange must have communicated itself to Moiraine. She gave them a penetrating look and came all the way in. "What has happened? The dreams?"

"He knows who I am," Mat said. "The Dark One knows my face."

Rand held up his hand wordlessly, palm toward her. Even in the shadowed light from the one candle the blood was plain.

The Aes Sedai stepped forward and grasped his upheld hand, her thumb across his palm covering the wound. Cold pierced him to the bone, so chill that his fingers cramped and he had to fight to keep them open. When she took her fingers away, the chill went, too.

He turned his hand, then, stunned, scrubbed the thin smear of blood away. The wound was gone. Slowly he raised his eyes to meet those of the Aes Sedai.

"Hurry," she said softly. "Time grows very short."

He knew she was not speaking of the time for their leaving anymore.

CHAPTER
44

The Dark Along the Ways

I n the darkness just before dawn Rand followed Moiraine down to the back hall, where Master Gill and the others were waiting, Nynaeve and Egwene as anxiously as Loial, Perrin almost as calm as the Warder. Mat stayed on Rand's heels as if he were afraid to be even a little alone now, even as much as a few feet away. The cook and her helpers straightened, staring as the party passed silently into the kitchen, already brightly lit and hot with preparations for breakfast. It was not usual for patrons of the inn to be up and out at that hour. At Master Gill's soothing words, the cook gave a loud sniff and slapped her dough down hard. They were all back to tending griddles and kneading dough before Rand reached the stableyard door.

Outside, the night was still pitch-black. To Rand, everyone else was only a darker shadow at best. He followed the innkeeper and Lan blindly, blind in truth, hoping Master Gill's knowledge of his own stableyard and the Warder's instincts would get them across it without someone breaking a leg. Loial stumbled more than once.

"I don't see why we can't have just one light," the Ogier grumbled. "We don't go running about in the dark in the *stedding*. I'm an Ogier, not a cat." Rand had a sudden image of Loial's tufted ears twitching irritably.

The stable loomed up suddenly out of the night, a threatening mass until the stable door creaked open, spilling a narrow stream of light into the yard. The innkeeper only opened it wide enough for them to go in one at a time, and hastily pulled it to behind Perrin, almost clipping his heels. Rand blinked in the sudden light inside.

The stablemen were not surprised by their appearance, as the cook had been. Their horses were saddled and waiting. Mandarb stood arrogantly, ignoring everyone but Lan, but Aldieb stretched her nose out to nuzzle Moiraine's hand. There was a packhorse, bulky with wicker panniers, and a huge animal with hairy fetlocks, taller even than the Warder's stallion, for Loial. It looked big enough to pull a loaded haywain by itself, but compared with the Ogier it seemed a pony.

Loial eyed the big horse and muttered doubtfully, "My own feet have always been good enough."

Master Gill motioned to Rand. The innkeeper was lending him a bay almost the color of his own hair, tall and deep of chest, but with none of the fire in his step that Cloud had had, Rand was glad to see. Master Gill said his name was Red.

Egwene went straight to Bela, and Nynaeve to her long-legged mare.

Mat brought his dun-colored horse over by Rand. "Perrin's making me nervous," he muttered. Rand looked at him sharply. "Well, he's acting strange. Don't you see it, too? I swear it's not my imagination, or . . . or. . . ."

Rand nodded. *Not the dagger taking hold of him again, thank the Light.* "He is, Mat, but just be easy. Moiraine knows about . . . whatever it is. Perrin's fine." He wished he could believe it, but it seemed to satisfy Mat, a little at least.

"Of course," Mat said hastily, still watching Perrin out of the corner of his eye. "I never said he wasn't."

Master Gill conferred with the head groom. That leathery-skinned man, with a face like one of the horses, knuckled his forehead and hurried to the back of the stable. The innkeeper turned to Moiraine with a satisfied smile on his round face. "Ramey says the way is clear, Aes Sedai."

The rear wall of the stable appeared solid and stout, lined with heavy racks of tools. Ramey and another stableman cleared away the hayforks, rakes, and shovels, then reached behind the racks to manipulate hidden latches. Abruptly a section of the wall swung inward on hinges so well concealed that Rand was not sure he could find them even with the disguised door standing open. Light from the stable illuminated a brick wall only a few feet away.

"It's only a narrow run between buildings," the innkeeper

said, "but nobody outside this stable knows there's a way into it from here. Whitecloaks or white cockades, there'll not be any watchers to see where you come out."

The Aes Sedai nodded. "Remember, good innkeeper, if you fear any trouble from this, write to Sheriam Sedai, of the Blue Ajah, in Tar Valon, and she will help. I fear my sisters and I have a good deal to put right already for those who have helped me."

Master Gill laughed; not the laugh of a worried man. "Why, Aes Sedai, you've already given me the only inn in all of Caemlyn without any rats. What more could I ask for? I can double my custom on that alone." His grin faded into seriousness. "Whatever you're up to, the Queen holds with Tar Valon, and I hold with the Queen, so I wish you well. The Light illumine you, Aes Sedai. The Light illumine you all."

"The Light illumine you, also, Master Gill," Moiraine replied with a bow of her head. "But if the Light is to shine on any of us, we must be quick." Briskly she turned to Loial. "Are you ready?"

With a wary look at its teeth, the Ogier took the reins of the big horse. Trying to keep that mouth the length of the reins from his hand, he led the animal to the opening at the back of the stable. Ramey hopped from one foot to the other, impatient to close it again. For a moment Loial paused with his head cocked as if feeling a breeze on his cheek. "This way," he said, and turned down the narrow alley.

Moiraine followed right behind Loial's horse, then Rand, and Mat. Rand had the first turn leading the packhorse. Nynaeve and Egwene made the middle of the column, with Perrin behind them, and Lan bringing up the rear. The hidden door swung hastily shut as soon as Mandarb stepped into the dirt alleyway. The *snick-snick* of latches locking, shutting them off, sounded unnaturally loud to Rand.

The run, as Master Gill had called it, was very narrow indeed, and even darker than the stableyard, if that was possible. Tall, blank walls of brick or wood lined both sides, with only a narrow strip of black sky overhead. The big, woven baskets slung on the packhorse scraped the buildings on both sides. The panniers bulged with supplies for

the journey, most of it clay jars filled with oil. A bundle
of poles was lashed lengthwise down the horse's back, and
each had a lantern swinging at the end of it. In the Ways,
Loial said, it was darker than the darkest night.

The partially-filled lanterns sloshed with the motion
of the horse, and clinked against each other with a tinny
sound. It was not a very loud noise, but in the hour before
dawn Caemlyn was quiet. Silent. The dull metallic clinks
sounded as if they could be heard a mile away.

When the run let out into a street, Loial chose his direction without a pause. He seemed to know exactly where
he was going, now, as if the route he needed to follow was
becoming clearer. Rand did not understand how the Ogier
could find the Waygate, and Loial had not been able to explain very well. He just knew, he said; he could feel it. Loial
claimed it was like trying to explain how to breathe.

As they hurried up the street Rand looked back toward
the corner where The Queen's Blessing lay. According to
Lamgwin, there were still half a dozen Whitecloaks not far
down from that corner. Their interest was all on the inn, but
a noise would surely bring them. No one was out at this hour
for a reputable reason. The horseshoes seemed to ring on
the paving stones like bells; the lanterns clattered as if the
packhorse were shaking them deliberately. Not until they
had rounded another corner did he stop looking over his
shoulder. He heard relieved sighs from the other Emond's
Fielders as they came round it, too.

Loial appeared to be following the most direct path to
the Waygate, wherever it took them. Sometimes they trotted down broad avenues, empty save for an occasional dog
skulking in the dark. Sometimes they hurried along alleys
as narrow as the stable run, where things squished under an
unwary step. Nynaeve complained softly about the resulting smells, but no one slowed down.

The darkness began to lessen, fading toward a dark gray.
Faint glimmers of dawn pearled the sky above the eastern
rooftops. A few people appeared on the streets, bundled up
against the early cold, heads down while they yet dreamed
of their beds. Most paid no mind to anyone else. Only a
handful even glanced at the line of people and horses with
Loial at its head, and only one of those truly saw them.

That one man flicked his eyes at them, just like the others,

already sinking back into his own thoughts when suddenly
he stumbled and almost fell, turning himself back around
to stare. There was only light enough to see shapes, but
that was too much. Seen at a distance by himself, the Ogier
could have passed for a tall man leading an ordinary horse,
or for an ordinary man leading an under-sized horse. With
the others in a line behind him to give perspective, Loial
looked exactly as big as he was, half again as tall as any
man should be. The man took one look and, with a strangled cry, set off running, his cloak flapping behind him.

There would be more people in the streets soon—very
soon. Rand eyed a woman hurrying past on the other side
of the street, seeing nothing but the pavement in front of
her feet. More people to notice soon. The eastern sky grew
lighter.

"There," Loial announced at last. "It is under there." It
was a shop he pointed to, still closed for the night. The tables out front were bare, the awnings over them rolled up
tight, the door stoutly shuttered. The windows above, where
the shopkeeper lived, were still dark.

"Under?" Mat exclaimed incredulously. "How in the Light
can we—?"

Moiraine raised a hand that cut him off, and motioned
for them to follow her into the alley beside the shop. Horses
and people together, they crowded the opening between the
two buildings. Shaded by the walls, it was darker there than
on the street, near to full night again.

"There must be a cellar door," Moiraine muttered. "Ah,
yes."

Abruptly light blossomed. A coolly glowing ball the size
of a man's fist hung suspended over the Aes Sedai's palm,
moving as she moved her hand. Rand thought that it was
a measure of what they had been through that everyone
seemed to take it as a matter of course. She put it close to
the doors she had found, slanted almost flat to the ground,
with a hasp held by thick bolts and an iron lock bigger than
Rand's hand and thick with old rust.

Loial gave the lock a tug. "I can pull it off, hasp and all,
but it will make enough noise to wake the whole neighbor-
hood."

"Let us not damage the goodman's property if we can
avoid it." Moiraine studied the lock intently for a moment.

Suddenly she gave the rusty iron a tap with her staff, and the lock fell open neatly.

Hastily Loial undid the lock and swung the doors up, propping them back. Moiraine went down the ramp thus revealed, lighting her way with the glowing ball. Aldieb stepped delicately behind her.

"Light the lanterns and come down," she called softly. "There is plenty of room. Hurry. It will be light out soon."

Rand hurriedly untied the poled lanterns off the pack-horse, but even before the first was lit he realized he could see Mat's features. People would be filling the streets in minutes, and the shopkeeper would be coming down to open up for business, all wondering why the alleyway was crammed full of horses. Mat muttered something nervously about taking horses indoors, but Rand was glad to lead his down the ramp. Mat followed, grumbling but no less quickly.

Rand's lantern swung on the end of its pole, bumping the ceiling if he was not careful, and neither Red nor the pack-horse liked the ramp. Then he was down and getting out of Mat's way. Moiraine let her floating light die, but as the rest joined them, the added lanterns lit the open space.

The cellar was as long and as wide as the building above, much of the space taken up by brick columns, flaring up from narrow bases to five times as big at the ceiling. The place seemed made up from a series of arches. There was plenty of room, but Rand still felt crowded. Loial's head brushed the ceiling. As the rusted lock had foretold, the cellar had not been used in a long time. The floor was bare except for a few broken barrels filled with odds and ends, and a thick layer of dust. Motes, stirred up by so many feet, sparkled in the lantern light.

Lan was last in, and as soon as he had Mandarb down the ramp he climbed back to pull the doors shut.

"Blood and ashes," Mat growled, "why would they build one of these gates in a place like this?"

"It was not always like this," Loial said. His rumbling voice echoed in the cavernous space. "Not always. No!" The Ogier was angry, Rand realized with a shock. "Once trees stood here. Every kind of tree that would grow in this place, every kind of tree that Ogier could coax to grow here. The Great Trees, a hundred spans high. Shade of branch, and

cool breezes to catch the smell of leaf and flower and hold
the memory of the peace of the *stedding*. All that, murdered
for this!" His fist thumped a column.

The column seemed to shake under that blow. Rand was
certain he heard bricks crack. Waterfalls of dry mortar slid
down the column.

"What is already woven cannot be undone," Moiraine
said gently. "It will not make the trees grow again for you
to bring the building down on our heads." Loial's drooping eyebrows made him look more abashed than a human
face could have managed. "With your help, Loial, perhaps
we can keep the groves that still stand from falling under
the Shadow. You have brought us to what we seek."

As she moved to one of the walls, Rand realized that
that wall was different from the others. They were ordinary
brick; this was intricately worked stone, fanciful swirls of
leaves and vines, pale even under its coat of dust. The brick
and mortar were old, but something about the stone said
it had stood there long, long before the brick was fired.
Later builders, themselves centuries gone, had incorporated
what already stood, and still later men had made it part of
a cellar.

One part of the carved stone wall, right in the center,
was more elaborate than the rest. As well done as the rest
was, it appeared a crude copy in comparison. Worked in
hard stone, those leaves seemed soft, caught in one frozen
moment as a gentle summer breeze stirred them. For all of
that, they had the feel of age, as much greater than the rest
of the stone as the rest was older than the brick. That old
and more. Loial looked at them as if he would rather be
anywhere else but there, even out in the streets with another
mob.

"*Avendesora*," Moiraine murmured, resting her hand on
a trefoil leaf in the stonework. Rand scanned the carving;
that was the only leaf of its kind he could find. "The leaf of
the Tree of Life is the key," the Aes Sedai said, and the leaf
came away in her hand.

Rand blinked; from behind him he heard gasps. That
leaf had seemed no less a part of the wall than any other.
Just as simply, the Aes Sedai set it against the pattern a
handspan lower. The three-pointed leaf fit there as if the
space had been intended for it, and once more it was a part

of the whole. As soon as it was in place the entire nature of the central stonework changed.

He was sure now that he could see the leaves ruffled by some unfelt breeze; he almost thought they were verdant under the dust, a tapestry of thick spring greenery there in the lantern-lit cellar. Almost imperceptibly at first, a split opened up in the middle of the ancient carving, widening as the two halves slowly swung into the cellar until they stood straight out. The backs of the gates were worked as the fronts, the same profusion of vines and leaves, almost alive. Behind, where should have been dirt or the cellar of the next building, a dull, reflective shimmering faintly caught their images.

"I have heard," Loial said, half mourning, half fearful, "that once the Waygates shone like mirrors. Once, who entered the Ways walked through the sun and the sky. Once."

"We have no time for waiting," Moiraine said.

Lan went past her, leading Mandarb, poled lantern in hand. His shadowy reflection approached him, leading a shadowy horse. Man and reflection seemed to step into each other at the shimmering surface, and both were gone. For a moment the black stallion balked, an apparently continuous rein connecting him to the dim shape of his own image. The rein tightened, and the warhorse, too, vanished.

For a minute everyone in the cellar stood staring at the Waygate.

"Hurry," Moiraine urged. "I must be the last through. We cannot leave this open for anyone to find by chance. Hurry."

With a heavy sigh Loial strode into the shimmer. Tossing its head, his big horse tried to hold back from the surface and was hauled through. They were gone as completely as the Warder and Mandarb.

Hesitantly, Rand poked his lantern at the Waygate. The lantern sank into its reflection, the two merging until both were gone. He made himself keep on walking forward, watching the pole disappear into itself inch by inch, and then he was stepping into himself, entering the gate. His mouth fell open. Something icy slid along his skin, as if he were passing through a wall of cold water. Time stretched out; the cold enveloped one hair at a time, shivered over his clothes thread by thread.

Abruptly the chill burst like a bubble, and he paused to

catch his breath. He was inside the Ways. Just ahead Lan and Loial waited patiently by their horses. All around them was blackness that seemed to stretch on forever. Their lanterns made a small pool of light around them, too small, as if something pressed back the light, or ate it.

Of a sudden anxious, he jerked at his reins. Red and the packhorse came leaping through, nearly knocking him down. Stumbling, he caught himself and hurried to the Warder and the Ogier, pulling the nervous horses behind him. The animals whickered softly. Even Mandarb appeared to take some comfort from the presence of other horses.

"Go easy when you pass through a Waygate, Rand," Loial cautioned. "Things are . . . different inside the Ways than out. Look."

He looked back the way the Ogier pointed, thinking to see the same dull shimmer. Instead he could see into the cellar, as if through a large piece of smoked glass set in the blackness. Disturbingly the darkness around the window into the cellar gave a sense of depth, as though the opening stood alone with nothing around or behind it but the dark. He said as much with a shaky laugh, but Loial took him seriously.

"You could walk all the way around it, and you would not see a thing from the other side. I would not advise it, though. The books aren't very clear about what lies behind the Waygates. I think you could become lost there, and never find your way out."

Rand shook his head and tried to concentrate on the Waygate itself rather than what lay behind it, but that was just as disturbing in its own fashion. If there had been anything to look at in the darkness besides the Waygate, he would have looked at it. In the cellar, through the smoky dimness, Moiraine and the others were plain enough, but they moved as if in a dream. Every blink of an eye seemed a deliberate, exaggerated gesture. Mat was making his way to the Waygate as though walking through clear jelly, his legs seeming to swim forward.

"The Wheel turns faster in the Ways," Loial explained. He looked at the darkness surrounding them, and his head sunk in between his shoulders. "None alive know more than fragments. I fear what I don't know about the Ways, Rand."

"The Dark One," Lan said, "cannot be defeated without

chancing risks. But we are alive at this moment, and before us is the hope of remaining alive. Do not surrender before you are beaten, Ogier."

"You would not speak so confidently if you had ever been in the Ways." The normal distant thunder of Loial's voice was muted. He stared at the blackness as if he saw things there. "I never have before, either, but I've seen Ogier who have been through a Waygate and come out again. You would not speak so if you had."

Mat stepped through the gate and regained normal speed. For an instant he stared at the seemingly endless darkness, then came running to join them, his lantern bobbing on its pole, his horse leaping behind him, almost sending him sprawling. One by one the others passed through, Perrin and Egwene and Nynaeve, each pausing in shocked silence before hurrying to join the rest. Each lantern enlarged the pool of light, but not as much as it should have. It was as if the dark became denser the more light there was, thickening as it fought against being diminished.

That was not a line of reasoning Rand wanted to follow. It was bad enough just being there without giving the darkness a will of its own. Everyone seemed to feel the oppressiveness, though. There were no wry comments from Mat here, and Egwene looked as if she wished she could rethink her decision to come. They all silently watched the Waygate, that last window into the world they knew.

Finally only Moiraine was left in the cellar, dimly lit by the lantern she had taken. The Aes Sedai still moved in that dreamlike way. Her hand crept as it found the leaf of *Avendesora*. It was located lower in the stonework on this side, Rand saw, just where she had placed it on the other. Plucking it free, she put it back in the original position. He wondered suddenly if the leaf on the other side had moved back, too.

The Aes Sedai came through, leading Aldieb, as the stone gates slowly, slowly began closing behind her. She came to join them, the light of her lantern leaving the gates before they were shut. Blackness swallowed the narrowing view of the cellar. In the constrained light of their lanterns, blackness surrounded them totally.

Suddenly it seemed as if the lanterns were the only light left in the world. Rand realized that he was jammed shoulder-to-shoulder in between Perrin and Egwene. Egwene gave him a wide-eyed look and pressed closer, and Perrin made no move to give him room. There was something comforting about touching another human being when the whole world had just been swallowed up by dark. Even the horses seemed to feel the Ways pushing them into a tighter and tighter knot.

Outwardly unconcerned, Moiraine and Lan swung into their saddles, and the Aes Sedai leaned forward, arms resting on her carved staff across the high pommel of her saddle. "We must be on our way, Loial."

Loial gave a start, and nodded vigorously. "Yes. Yes, Aes Sedai, you are right. Not a minute longer than need be." He pointed to a broad strip of white running under their feet, and Rand stepped away from it hastily. All the Two Rivers folk did. Rand thought the floor had been smooth once, but the smoothness was pitted now, as if the stone had the pox. The white line was broken in several places. "This leads from the Waygate to the first Guiding. From there. . . ." Loial looked around anxiously, then scrambled onto his horse with none of the reluctance he had shown earlier. The horse wore the biggest saddle the head groom had been able to find, but Loial filled it from pommel to cantle. His feet hung down on either side almost to the animal's knees. "Not a minute longer than need be," he muttered. Reluctantly the others mounted.

Moiraine and Lan rode on either side of the Ogier, following the white line through the dark. Everyone else crowded in behind as close as they could get, the lanterns bobbing over their heads. The lanterns should have given enough light to fill a house, but ten feet away from them it stopped. The blackness stopped it as if it had struck a wall. The creak of saddles and click of horseshoes on stone seemed to travel only to the edge of light.

Rand's hand kept drifting to his sword. It was not that he thought there was anything out there against which he could use the sword to defend himself; it did not seem as if there was anywhere for something to be. The bubble of light around them could as well have been a cave surrounded by stone, completely surrounded, with no way out. The horses might have been walking a treadmill for the change around them. He gripped the hilt as if the pressure of his hand there could press away the stone he felt weighing down on him. Touching the sword, he could remember Tam's teaching. For a little while he could find the calm of the void. But the weight always returned, compressing the void until it was only a cavern inside his mind, and he had to start over again, touching Tam's sword to remember.

It was a relief when something did change, even if it was only a tall slab of stone, standing on end, that appeared out of the dark before them, the broad white line stopping at its base. Sinuous curves of metal inlaid the wide surface, graceful lines that vaguely reminded Rand of vines and leaves. Discolored pocks marked stone and metal alike.

"The Guiding," Loial said, and leaned out of his saddle to frown at the cursive metal inlays.

"Ogier script," Moiraine said, "but so broken I can barely make out what it says."

"I hardly can, either," Loial said, "but enough to know we go this way." He turned his horse aside from the Guiding.

The edges of their light caught other stoneworks, what appeared to be stone-walled bridges arcing off into the darkness, and gently sloping ramps, without railings of any kind, leading up and down. Between the bridges and the ramps ran a chest-high balustrade, however, as though falling was a danger there at any rate. Plain white stone made the balustrade, in simple curves and rounds fitted together in complex patterns. Something about all of it seemed almost familiar to Rand, but he knew it had to be his imagination groping for anything familiar where everything was strange.

At the foot of one of the bridges Loial paused to read the single line on the narrow column stone there. Nodding, he rode up onto the bridge. "This is the first bridge of our path," he said over his shoulder.

Rand wondered what held the bridge up. The horses' hooves made a gritty sound, as if bits of stone flaked off at every step. Everything he could see was covered with shallow holes, some tiny pinpricks, others shallow, rough-edged craters a stride across, as if there had been a rain of acid, or the stone was rotting. The guardwall showed cracks and holes, too. In places it was gone altogether for as much as a span. For all he knew the bridge could be solid stone all the way to the center of the earth, but what he saw made him hope it would stand long enough for them to reach the other end. *Wherever that is.*

The bridge did end, eventually, in a place that looked no different from its beginning. All Rand could see was what their little pool of light touched, but he had the impression that it was a large space, like a flat-topped hill, with bridges and ramps leaving all around it. An Island, Loial called it. There was another script-covered Guiding—Rand placed it in the middle of the Island, with no way of knowing if he was right or not. Loial read, then took them up one of the ramps, curving up and up.

After an interminable climb, curving continuously, the ramp let off onto another Island just like the one where it had begun. Rand tried to imagine the curve of the ramp and gave up. *This Island can't be right on top of the other one. It* can't *be.*

Loial consulted yet another slab filled with Ogier script, found another signpost column, led them onto another bridge. Rand no longer had any idea in what direction they were traveling.

In their huddle of light in the dark, one bridge was exactly like another, except that some had breaks in the guard-walls and some did not. Only the degree of damage to the Guidings gave any difference to the Islands. Rand lost track of time; he was not even sure how many bridges they had crossed or how many ramps they had traveled. The Warder must have had a clock in his head, though. Just when Rand felt the first stir of hunger, Lan announced quietly that it was midday and dismounted to parcel out bread and cheese and dried meat from the packhorse. Perrin was leading the animal by that time. They were on an Island, and Loial was busily deciphering the directions on the Guiding.

Mat started to climb down from his saddle, but Moiraine said, "Time is too valuable in the Ways to waste. For us, much too valuable. We will stop when it is time to sleep." Lan was already back on Mandarb.

Rand's appetite slipped at the thought of sleeping in the Ways. It was always night there, but not the kind of night for sleeping. He ate while he rode, though, like everyone else. It was an awkward affair, trying to juggle his food, the lantern pole, and his reins, but for all of his imagined lack of appetite he licked the last crumbs of bread and cheese off his hands when he was done, and thought fondly of more. He even began to think the Ways were not so bad, not nearly as bad as Loial made out. They might have the heavy feel of the hour before a storm, but nothing changed. Nothing happened. The Ways were almost boring.

Then the silence was broken by a startled grunt from Loial. Rand stood in his stirrups to peer past the Ogier, and swallowed hard at what he saw. They were in the middle of a bridge, and only a few feet ahead of Loial the bridge ended in a jagged gap.

CHAPTER
45

What Follows in Shadow

The light of their lanterns stretched just far enough to touch the other side, thrusting out of the dark like a giant's broken teeth. Loial's horse stamped a hoof nervously, and a loose stone fell away into the dead black below. If there was any sound of it striking bottom, Rand never heard it.

He edged Red closer to the gap. As far down as he could thrust his lantern on its pole, there was nothing. Blackness below as blackness above, shearing off the light. If there was a bottom, it could be a thousand feet down. Or never. But on the other side, he could see what was under the bridge, holding it up. Nothing. Less than a span in thickness, and absolutely nothing underneath.

Abruptly the stone under his feet seemed as thin as paper, and the endless drop over the edge pulled at him. The lantern and pole seemed suddenly heavy enough to pull him right out of the saddle. Head spinning, he backed the bay away from the abyss as cautiously as he had approached.

"Is it to this you've brought us, Aes Sedai?" Nynaeve said. "All this just to find out we have to go back to Caemlyn after all?"

"We do not have to go back," Moiraine said. "Not all the way to Caemlyn. There are many paths along the Ways to any place. We need only go back far enough for Loial to find another path that will lead to Fal Dara. Loial? Loial!"

The Ogier pulled himself away from staring at the gap with a visible effort. "What? Oh. Yes, Aes Sedai. I can find another path. I had. . . ." His eyes drifted back to the chasm, and his ears twitched. "I had not dreamed the decay had gone so far. If the bridges themselves are breaking, it may be that I cannot find the path you want. It may be that I cannot find a path back, either. The bridges could be falling behind us even now."

"There has to be a way," Perrin said, his voice flat. His eyes seemed to gather the light, to glow golden. *A wolf at bay,* Rand thought, startled. *That's what he looks like.*

"It will be as the Wheel weaves," Moiraine said, "but I do not believe the decay is as fast as you fear. Look at the stone, Loial. Even I can tell that this is an old break."

"Yes," Loial said slowly. "Yes, Aes Sedai. I can see it. There is no rain or wind here, but that stone has been in the air for ten years, at least." He nodded with a relieved grin, so happy with the discovery that for a moment he seemed to forget his fear. Then he looked around and shrugged uncomfortably. "I could find other paths more easily than Mafal Dadaranell. Tar Valon, for instance? Or Stedding Shangtai. It's only three bridges to Stedding Shangtai from the last Island. I suppose the Elders want to talk to me by this time."

"Fal Dara, Loial," Moiraine said firmly. "The Eye of the World lies beyond Fal Dara, and we must reach the Eye."

"Fal Dara," the Ogier agreed reluctantly.

Back at the Island Loial pored over the script-covered slab intently, drooping eyebrows drawn down as he muttered half to himself. Soon he was talking completely to himself, for he dropped into the Ogier language. That inflected tongue sounded like deep-voiced birds singing. It seemed odd to Rand that a people so big had such a musical language.

Finally the Ogier nodded. As he led them to the chosen bridge, he turned to peer forlornly at the signpost beside another. "Three crossings to Stedding Shangtai." He sighed. But he took them on past without stopping and turned onto the third bridge beyond. He looked back regretfully as they started across, though the bridge to his home was hidden in the dark.

Rand took the bay up beside the Ogier. "When this is over, Loial, you show me your *stedding,* and I'll show you Emond's Field. No Ways, though. We'll walk, or ride, if it takes all summer."

"You believe it will ever be over, Rand?"

He frowned at the Ogier. "You said it would take two days to reach Fal Dara."

"Not the Ways, Rand. All the rest." Loial looked over his shoulder at the Aes Sedai, talking softly with Lan as they rode side-by-side. "What makes you believe it will ever be over?"

The bridges and ramps led up and down and across. Sometimes a white line ran off into the dark from the Guiding, just like the line they had followed from the Waygate in Caemlyn. Rand saw that he was not the only one who eyed those lines curiously, and a little wistfully. Nynaeve, Perrin, Mat, and even Egwene left the lines reluctantly. There was a Waygate at the other end of each of them, a gate back into the world, where there was sky and sun and wind. Even the wind would have been welcome. Leave them they did, under the Aes Sedai's sharp eye. But Rand was not the only one to look back even after dark swallowed Island and Guiding and line.

Rand was yawning by the time Moiraine announced that they would stop for the night on one of the Islands. Mat looked at the blackness all around them and snickered loudly, but he got down as quickly as anyone else. Lan and the boys unsaddled and hobbled the horses while Nynaeve and Egwene set up a small oil stove to make tea. Looking like the base of a lantern, it was what Lan said Warders used in the Blight, where the wood could be dangerous to burn. The Warder produced tripod legs from the baskets they took off the packhorse, so the lantern poles could be set in a circle around their campsite.

Loial examined the Guiding for a moment, then dropped down cross-legged and rubbed a hand across the dusty, pockmarked stone. "Once things grew on the Islands," he said sadly. "All the books tell of it. There was green grass to sleep on, soft as any feather bed. Fruit trees to spice the food you'd brought with an apple or a pear or a bellfruit, sweet and crisp and juicy whatever the time of year outside."

"Nothing to hunt," Perrin growled, then looked surprised that he had spoken.

Egwene handed Loial a cup of tea. He held it without drinking, staring at it as if he could find the fruit trees in its depths.

"Aren't you going to set wards?" Nynaeve asked Moiraine. "Surely there must be worse than rats in this. Even if I haven't seen anything, I can still feel."

The Aes Sedai rubbed her fingers against her palms distastefully. "You feel the taint, the corruption of the Power that made the Ways. I will not use the One Power in the Ways unless I must. The taint is so strong that whatever I tried to do would surely be corrupted."

That made everyone as silent as Loial. Lan settled down to his meal methodically, as if he were stoking a fire, the food less important than fueling his body. Moiraine ate well, too, and as tidily as if they were not squatting on bare stone quite literally in the middle of nowhere, but Rand only picked at his food. The tiny flame of the oil stove gave just enough heat to boil water, but he crouched toward it as if he could soak up warmth. His shoulders brushed Mat and Perrin. They all made a tight circle around the stove. Mat held his bread and meat and cheese forgotten in his hands, and Perrin set his tin plate down after only a few bites. The mood became more and more glum, and everyone looked down, avoiding the dark around them.

Moiraine studied them as she ate. Finally she put her plate aside and patted her lips with a napkin. "I can tell you one cheerful thing. I do not think Thom Merrilin is dead."

Rand looked at her sharply. "But . . . the Fade. . . ."

"Mat told me what happened in Whitebridge," the Aes Sedai said. "People there mentioned a gleeman, but they said nothing of him dying. They would have, I think, if a gleeman had been killed. Whitebridge is not so big as for a gleeman to be a small thing. And Thom is a part of the Pattern that weaves itself around you three. Too important a part, I believe, to be cut off yet."

Too important? Rand thought. *How could Moiraine know . . . ?* "Min? She saw something about Thom?"

"She saw a great deal," Moiraine said wryly. "About all of you. I wish I could understand half of what she saw, but even she does not. Old barriers fail. But whether what Min does is old or new, she sees true. Your fates are bound together. Thom Merrilin's, too."

Nynaeve gave a dismissive sniff and poured herself another cup of tea.

"I don't see how she saw anything about any of us," Mat

said with a grin. "As I remember it, she spent most of her time looking at Rand."

Egwene raised an eyebrow. "Oh? You didn't tell me that, Moiraine Sedai."

Rand glanced at her. She was not looking at him, but her tone had been too carefully neutral. "I talked to her once," he said. "She dresses like a boy, and her hair is as short as mine."

"You talked to her. Once." Egwene nodded slowly. Still not looking at him, she raised her cup to her lips.

"Min was just somebody who worked at the inn in Baerlon," Perrin said. "Not like Aram."

Egwene choked on her tea. "Too hot," she muttered.

"Who's Aram?" Rand asked. Perrin smiled, much like Mat's smile in the old days when he was up to mischief, and hid behind his cup.

"One of the Traveling People," Egwene said casually, but red spots bloomed in her cheeks.

"One of the Traveling People," Perrin said blandly. "He dances. Like a bird. Wasn't that what you said, Egwene? It was like flying with a bird?"

Egwene set her cup down deliberately. "I don't know if anyone else is tired, but I'm going to sleep."

As she rolled herself up in her blankets, Perrin reached over to nudge Rand in the ribs and winked. Rand found himself grinning back. *Burn me, if I didn't come out best for a change. I wish I knew as much about women as Perrin.*

"Maybe, Rand," Mat said slyly, "you ought to tell Egwene about Farmer Grinwell's daughter, Else." Egwene lifted her head to stare first at Mat, then at him.

He hastily got up to fetch his own blankets. "Sleep sounds good to me right now."

All the Emond's Field people began seeking their blankets then, and Loial, too. Moiraine sat sipping her tea. And Lan. The Warder did not look as if he ever intended to sleep, or needed to.

Even rolled up for sleep, no one wanted to get very far from the others. They made a small circle of blanket-covered mounds right around the stove, almost touching one another.

"Rand," Mat whispered, "*was* there anything between

you and Min? I barely got a look at her. She *was* pretty, but she must be nearly as old as Nynaeve."

"What about this Else?" Perrin added from the other side of him. "She pretty?"

"Blood and ashes," he mumbled, "can't I even talk to a girl? You two are as bad as Egwene."

"As the Wisdom would say," Mat chided mockingly, "watch your tongue. Well, if you won't talk about it, I'm going to get some sleep."

"Good," Rand grumbled. "That's the first decent thing you've said."

Sleep was not easily come by, though. The stone was hard, however Rand lay, and he could feel the pits through his blanket. There was no way to imagine he was anywhere but in the Ways, made by the men who had broken the world, tainted by the Dark One. He kept picturing the broken bridge, and the nothing under it.

When he turned one way he found Mat looking at him; looking through him, really. Mocking was forgotten when the dark around them was remembered. He rolled the other way, and Perrin had his eyes open, too. Perrin's face was less afraid than Mat's, but he had his hands on his chest, tapping his thumbs together worriedly.

Moiraine made a circuit of them, kneeling by each person's head and bending down to speak softly. Rand could not hear what she said to Perrin, but it made his thumbs stop. When she bent over Rand, her face almost touching his, she said in a low, comforting voice, "Even here, your destiny protects you. Not even the Dark One can change the Pattern completely. You are safe from him, so long as I am close. Your dreams are safe. For a time, yet, they are safe."

As she passed from him to Mat, he wondered if she thought it was that simple, that she could tell him he was safe and he would believe it. But somehow he did feel safe—safer, at least. Thinking that, he drifted into sleep and did not dream.

Lan woke them. Rand wondered if the Warder had slept; he did not look tired, not even as tired as those who had laid some hours on the hard stone. Moiraine allowed enough time to make tea, but only one cup apiece. They ate breakfast in the saddle, Loial and the Warder leading. It was the same meal as the others, bread and meat and cheese. Rand thought it would be easy to get tired of bread and meat and cheese.

Not long after the last crumb was licked off a finger, Lan said quietly, "Someone is following us. Or something." They were in the middle of a bridge, both ends of it hidden.

Mat jerked an arrow from his quiver and, before anyone could stop him, loosed it in the dark behind them.

"I knew I shouldn't have done this," Loial muttered. "Never deal with an Aes Sedai except in a *stedding*."

Lan pushed the bow down before Mat could nock another. "Stop that, you village idiot. There's no way to tell who it is."

"That's the only place they're safe," the Ogier went on.

"What else would be in a place like this besides something evil?" Mat demanded.

"That's what the Elders say, and I should have listened to them."

"We are, for one," the Warder said dryly.

"Maybe it's another traveler," Egwene said hopefully. "An Ogier, perhaps."

"Ogier have more sense than to use the Ways," Loial growled. "All but Loial, who has no sense at all. Elder Haman always said it, and it's true."

"What do you feel, Lan?" Moiraine asked. "Is it something that serves the Dark One?"

The Warder shook his head slowly. "I don't know," he said as if that surprised him. "I cannot tell. Perhaps it's the Ways, and the taint. It all feels wrong. But whoever it is, or whatever, he's not trying to catch us. He almost caught up at the last Island and scampered back across the bridge so as not to. If I fall behind, I might surprise him though, and see who, or what, he is."

"If you fall behind, Warder," Loial said firmly, "you'll spend the rest of your life in the Ways. Even if you can read Ogier, I have never heard or read of a human who could find his path off the first Island lacking an Ogier guide. *Can* you read Ogier?"

Lan shook his head again, and Moiraine said, "So long as he does not trouble us, we will not trouble him. We have no time. No time."

As they rode off the bridge onto the next Island, Loial said, "If I remember the last Guiding correctly, there is a path from here that leads toward Tar Valon. Half a day's journey at most. Not quite as long as it will take us to reach Mafal Dadaranell. I'm sure that—"

He cut off as the light of their lanterns reached the Guiding. Near the top of the slab, deeply chiseled lines, sharp and angular, made wounds in the stone. Suddenly Lan's alertness was no longer hidden. He remained easily erect in his saddle, but Rand had the sudden impression that the Warder could feel everything around him, even feel the rest of them breathing. Lan began circling his stallion around the Guiding, spiraling outward. He rode as if he were ready to be attacked, or to attack himself.

"This explains much," Moiraine said softly, "and it makes me afraid. So much. I should have guessed. The taint, the decay. I should have guessed."

"Guessed what?" Nynaeve demanded just as Loial asked, "What is it? Who did this? I've never seen or heard of anything like it."

The Aes Sedai faced them calmly. "Trollocs." She ignored their frightened gasps. "Or Fades. Those are Trolloc runes. The Trollocs have discovered how to enter the Ways. That must be how they got to the Two Rivers undiscovered; through the Waygate at Manetheren. There is at least one Waygate in the Blight." She glanced toward Lan before continuing; the Warder was far enough away that only the faint light of his lantern could be seen. "Manetheren was destroyed, but almost nothing can destroy a Waygate. That is how the Fades could gather a small army around Caemlyn without raising an alarm in every nation between the Blight and Andor." Pausing, she touched her lips thoughtfully. "But they cannot know all the paths yet, else they would have been pouring into Caemlyn through the gate we used. Yes."

Rand shivered. Walking through the Waygate to find Trollocs waiting in the dark, hundreds of them, perhaps thousands, twisted giants with half-animal faces snarling as they leaped forward in the blackness to kill. Or worse.

"They don't use the Ways easily," Lan called. His lantern was no more than twenty spans off, but the light of it was only a dim, fuzzy ball that seemed very distant to those around the Guiding. Moiraine led the way to him. Rand wished his stomach were empty when he saw what the Warder had found.

At the foot of one of the bridges the frozen shapes of Trollocs reared, caught flailing about them with hooked axes and scythe-like swords. Gray and pitted like the stone, the huge bodies were half sunken in the swollen, bubbled surface. Some of the bubbles had burst, revealing more snouted faces, forever snarling with fear. Rand heard someone retching behind him, and swallowed hard to keep from joining whoever it was. Even for Trollocs it had been a horrible way to die.

A few feet beyond the Trollocs the bridge ended. The signpost lay shattered into a thousand shards.

Loial got down from his horse gingerly, eyeing the Trollocs, as if he thought they might come back to life. He examined the remains of the signpost hurriedly, picking out the metal script that had been inlaid in the stone, then scrambled back into his saddle. "This was the first bridge of the path from here to Tar Valon," he said.

Mat was scrubbing the back of his hand across his mouth, with his head turned away from the Trollocs. Egwene hid her face in her hands. Rand moved his horse close to Bela and touched her shoulder. She twisted around and clutched him, shuddering. He wanted to shudder, too; her holding him was the only thing that kept him from it.

"As well we are not going to Tar Valon yet," Moiraine said.

Nynaeve rounded on the Aes Sedai. "How can you take it so calmly? The same could happen to us!"

"Perhaps," Moiraine said serenely, and Nynaeve ground her teeth so hard Rand could hear them grate. "It is more likely, though," Moiraine went on, unruffled, "that the men, the Aes Sedai, who made the Ways protected them, building in traps for creatures of the Dark One. It is something they must have feared then, before the Halfmen and Trollocs had been driven into the Blight. In any case, we cannot tarry here, and whatever way we choose, back or ahead, is as likely to have a trap as any other. Loial, do you know the next bridge?"

"Yes. Yes, they did not ruin that part of the Guiding, thank the Light." For the first time Loial seemed as eager to go on as Moiraine did. He had his big horse moving before he finished speaking.

Egwene clung to Rand's arm for two more bridges. He regretted it when she finally let go with a murmured apology and a forced laugh, and not just because it had felt good having her hold onto him that way. It was easier to be brave, he discovered, when someone needed your protection.

Moiraine might not have believed a trap could be set for them, but for all the haste she spoke of, she made them travel more slowly than before, pausing before letting them onto any bridge, or off one onto an Island. She would step Aldieb forward, feeling the air in front of her with an outstretched hand, and not even Loial, or Lan, was allowed to go ahead until she gave permission.

Rand had to trust her judgment about traps, but he peered into the darkness around them as if he could actually see anything more than ten feet away, and strained his ears listening. If Trollocs could use the Ways, then whatever was following them could be another creature of the Dark One. Or more than one. Lan had said he could not tell in the Ways. But as they crossed bridge after bridge, ate a midday meal riding, and crossed still more bridges, all he could hear were their own saddles creaking, and the horses' hooves, and sometimes one of the others coughing, or muttering to himself. Later there was a distant wind, too, off in the black somewhere. He could not say in which direction. At first he thought it was his imagination, but with time he became sure.

It'll be good to feel the wind again, even if it's cold.

Suddenly he blinked. "Loial, didn't you say there isn't any wind in the Ways?"

Loial pulled his horse up just short of the next Island and cocked his head to listen. Slowly his face paled, and he licked his lips. *"Machin Shin,"* he whispered hoarsely. "The Black Wind. The Light illumine and protect us. It's the Black Wind."

"How many more bridges?" Moiraine asked sharply. "Loial, how many more bridges?"

"Two. I think, two."

"Quickly, then," she said, trotting Aldieb onto the Island. "Find it quickly!"

Loial talked to himself, or to anyone who was listening,

while he read the Guiding. "They came out mad, screaming about *Machin Shin*. Light help us! Even those Aes Sedai could heal, they. . . ." He scanned the stone hastily, and galloped toward the chosen bridge with a shouted, "This way!"

This time Moiraine did not wait to check. She urged them on to a gallop, the bridge trembling beneath the horses, lanterns swinging wildly overhead. Loial ran his eyes over the next Guiding and wheeled his big mount around like a racer almost before it had stopped. The sound of the wind became louder. Rand could hear it even over the pounding of hooves on stone. Behind them, and gusting closer.

They did not bother with the last Guiding. As soon as the light of the lanterns caught the white line running from it, they swung in that direction, still galloping. The Island vanished behind, and there was only the pitted, gray stone underfoot and the white line. Rand was breathing so hard he was no longer sure if he could hear the wind.

Out of the darkness the gates appeared, vine-carved and standing alone in the black like a tiny piece of wall in the night. Moiraine leaned out of her saddle, reaching toward the carvings, and suddenly pulled back. "The *Avendesora* leaf is not here!" she said. "The key is gone!"

"Light!" Mat shouted. "Bloody light!" Loial threw back his head and gave a mournful cry, like a howl of dying.

Egwene touched Rand's arm. Her lips trembled, but she only looked at him. He put his hand on top of hers, hoping he did not look more frightened than she did. He felt it. Back toward the Guiding, the wind howled. He almost thought he could hear voices in it, voices screaming vileness that, even half understood, brought bile up in his throat.

Moiraine raised her staff and flame lanced from the end of it. It was not the pure, white flame that Rand remembered from Emond's Field, and the battle before Shadar Logoth. Sickly yellow streaked through the fire, and slow-drifting flecks of black, like soot. A thin, acrid smoke drifted from the flame, setting Loial coughing and the horses dancing nervously, but Moiraine thrust it at the gates. The smoke rasped Rand's throat and burned his nose.

Stone melted like butter, leaf and vine withering in the flame and vanishing. The Aes Sedai moved the fire as fast as she could, but cutting an opening big enough for everyone to get through was no quick task. To Rand, it seemed as if the line of melted stone crept along its arc at a snail's pace. His cloak stirred, as if caught by the edge of a breeze, and his heart froze.

"I can feel it," Mat said, his voice quavering. "Light, I can bloody feel it!"

The flame winked out, and Moiraine lowered her staff. "Done," she said. "Half done."

A thin line ran across the stone carving. Rand thought he could see light—dim, but still light—through the crack. But despite the cutting, the two big, curved wedges of stone still stood there, half an arc out of each door. The opening would be big enough for everyone to ride through, though Loial might have to lie flat on his horse's back. Once the two wedges of stone were gone, it would be big enough. He wondered how much each weighed. A thousand pounds? More? *Maybe if we all get down and push. Maybe we can push one of them over before the wind gets here.* A gust tugged at his cloak. He tried not to listen to what the voices cried.

As Moiraine stepped back, Mandarb leaped forward, straight toward the gates, Lan crouched in the saddle. At the last instant the warhorse twisted to catch the stone with his shoulder, just as he had been taught to catch other horses in battle. With a crash the stone toppled outward, and the Warder and his horse were carried by their momentum through the smoky shimmer of a Waygate. The light that came through was mid-morning light, pale and thin, but it seemed to Rand as if the noonday summer sun blazed in his face.

On the far side of the gate Lan and Mandarb slowed to a crawl, stumbling in slow motion as the Warder reined back around toward the gate. Rand did not wait. Pushing Bela's head toward the opening, he slapped the shaggy mare hard on the croup. Egwene had just enough time to throw a startled look over her shoulder at him before Bela carried her out of the Ways.

"All of you, out!" Moiraine directed. "Quickly! Go!"

As she spoke, the Aes Sedai thrust her staff out at arm's length, pointed back toward the Guiding. Something leaped from the end of the staff, like liquid light rendered to a syrup of fire, a blazing spear of white and red and yellow, streaking into the black, exploding, coruscating like shattered diamonds. The wind shrieked in agony; it screamed in rage. The thousand murmurs that hid in the wind roared like thunder, roars of madness, half-heard voices cackling and howling promises that twisted Rand's stomach as much by the pleasure in them as by what he almost understood them to say.

He booted Red forward, crowding into the opening, squeezing after the others, all forcing through the smoky glistening at once. The icy chill ran through him again, the peculiar sensation of being slowly lowered facedown into a winter pond, the cold water crawling across his skin by infinitesimal increments. Just as before it seemed to go on forever, while his mind raced, wondering if the wind could catch them while they were held like that.

As suddenly as a pricked bubble the chill vanished, and he was outside. His horse, for one abrupt instant moving twice as fast as he had been, stumbled and almost pitched him over his head. He threw both arms around the bay's neck and hung on for dear life. While he got back into the saddle, Red shook himself, then trotted over to join the others as calmly as if nothing at all odd had happened. It was cold, not the chill of the Waygate, but welcome, natural winter-cold that slowly, steadily burrowed into flesh.

He pulled his cloak around him, his eyes on the dull glimmer of the Waygate. Beside him Lan leaned forward in his saddle, one hand on his sword; man and horse were tensed, as if on the point of charging back through if Moiraine did not appear.

The Waygate stood in a jumble of stones at the base of a hill, hidden by bushes except where the falling pieces had broken down the bare, brown branches. Alongside the carvings on the remains of the gates, the brush looked more lifeless than the stone.

Slowly the murky surface bulged like some strange, long bubble rising to the surface of a pond. Moiraine's back broke through the bubble. Inchmeal, the Aes Sedai and her dim reflection backed out of each other. She still held her staff out in front of her, and she kept it there as she drew Aldieb out of the Waygate after her, the white mare dancing with fear, eyes rolling. Still watching the Waygate, Moiraine backed away.

The Waygate darkened. The hazy shimmer became

murkier, sinking through gray to charcoal, then to black as deep as the heart of the Ways. As if from a great distance the wind howled at them, hidden voices filled with an unquenchable thirst for living things, filled with a hunger for pain, filled with frustration.

The voices seemed to whisper in Rand's ears, right at the brink of understanding, and within it. *Flesh so fine, so fine to tear, to gash the skin; skin to strip, to plait, so nice to plait the strips, so nice, so red the drops that fall; blood so red, so red, so sweet; sweet screams, pretty screams, singing screams, scream your song, sing your screams. . . .*

The whispers drifted, the blackness lessened, faded, and the Waygate was again a murky shimmer seen through an arch of carved stone.

Rand let out a long, shuddering breath. He was not the only one; he heard other relieved exhalations. Egwene had Bela alongside Nynaeve's horse, and the two women had their arms around each other, their heads on each other's shoulders. Even Lan seemed relieved, though the hard planes of his face showed nothing; it was more in the way he sat Mandarb, a loosening of the shoulders as he looked at Moiraine, a tilt of the head.

"It could not pass," Moiraine said. "I thought it could not; I hoped it could not. Faugh!" She tossed her staff on the ground and scrubbed her hand on her cloak. Char, thick and black, marked the staff for over half its length. "The taint corrupts everything in that place."

"What was that?" Nynaeve demanded. "What was it?"

Loial appeared confused. "Why, *Machin Shin,* of course. The Black Wind that steals souls."

"But *what* is it?" Nynaeve persisted. "Even with a Trolloc, you can look at it, touch it if you have a strong stomach. But that. . . ." She gave a convulsive shiver.

"Something left from the Time of Madness, perhaps," Moiraine replied. "Or even from the War of the Shadow, the War of Power. Something hiding in the Ways so long it can no longer get out. No one, not even among the Ogier, knows how far the Ways run, or how deep. It could even be something of the Ways themselves. As Loial said, the Ways are living things, and all living things have parasites. Perhaps even a creature of the corruption itself, something born of the decay. Something that hates life and light."

"Stop!" Egwene cried. "I don't want to hear any more. I could hear *it,* saying. . . ." She cut off, shivering.

"There is worse to be faced yet," Moiraine said softly. Rand did not think she meant it to be heard.

The Aes Sedai climbed into her saddle wearily and settled there with a grateful sigh. "This is dangerous," she said, looking at the broken gates. Her charred staff received only a glance. "The thing cannot get out, but anyone could wander in. Agelmar must send men to wall it up, once we reach Fal Dara." She pointed to the north, to towers in the misty distance above the barren treetops.

Chapter
46

Fal Dara

The country around the Waygate was rolling, forested hills, but aside from the gates themselves there was no sign of any Ogier grove. Most of the trees were gray skeletons clawing at the sky. Fewer evergreens than Rand was used to dotted the forest, and of them, dead, brown needles and leaves covered many. Loial made no comment beyond a sad shaking of his head.

"As dead as the Blasted Lands," Nynaeve said, frowning. Egwene pulled her cloak around her and shivered.

"At least we're out," Perrin said, and Mat added, "Out where?"

"Shienar," Lan told them. "We're in the Borderlands." In his hard voice was a note that said home, almost.

Rand gathered his cloak against the cold. The Borderlands. Then the Blight was close by. The Blight. The Eye of the World. And what they had come to do.

"We are close to Fal Dara," Moiraine said. "Only a few miles." Across the treetops, towers rose to the north and east of them, dark against the morning sky. Between the hills and the woods, the towers often vanished as they rode, only to reappear again when they topped a particularly tall rise.

Rand noticed trees split open as if struck by lightning.

"The cold," Lan answered when he asked. "Sometimes the winter is so cold here the sap freezes, and trees burst. There are nights when you can hear them cracking like fireworks, and the air is so sharp you think that might shatter, too. There are more than usual, this winter past."

Rand shook his head. Trees *bursting*? And that was during an ordinary winter. What must this winter have been like? Surely like nothing he could imagine.

"Who says winter's past?" Mat said, his teeth chattering.

"Why this, a fine spring, sheepherder," Lan said. "A fine spring to be alive. But if you want warm, well, it will be warm in the Blight."

Softly Mat muttered, "Blood and ashes. Blood and bloody ashes!" Rand barely heard him, but it sounded heartfelt.

They began to pass farms, but though it was the hour for midday meals to be cooking, no smoke rose from the high stone chimneys. The fields were empty of men and livestock both, though sometimes a plow or a wagon stood abandoned as if the owner meant to be back any minute.

At one farm close by the road a lone chicken scratched in the yard. One barn door swung freely with the wind; the other had broken off the bottom hinge and hung at an angle. The tall house, odd to Rand's Two Rivers eyes, with its sharp-peaked roof of big wooden shingles running almost to the ground, was still and silent. No dog came out to bark at them. A scythe lay in the middle of the barnyard; buckets were overturned in a heap beside the well.

Moiraine frowned at the farmhouse as they rode by. She lifted Aldieb's reins, and the white mare quickened her pace.

The Emond's Fielders were clustered with Loial a little behind the Aes Sedai and the Warder.

Rand shook his head. He could not imagine anything growing there ever. But then he could not really imagine the Ways, either. Even now that he was past them, he could not.

"I don't think she expected this," Nynaeve said quietly, with a gesture that took in all the empty farms they had seen.

"Where did they all go?" Egwene said. "Why? They can't have been gone very long."

"What makes you say that?" Mat asked. "From the look of that barn door, they could have been gone all winter." Nynaeve and Egwene both looked at him as if he were slow-witted.

"The curtains in the windows," Egwene said patiently.

"They look too light for winter curtains, even here. As cold as it is here, no woman would have had those up more than a week or two, maybe less." The Wisdom nodded.

"Curtains." Perrin chuckled. He immediately wiped the smile off his face when the two women raised their eyebrows at him. "Oh, I agree with you. There wasn't enough rust on that scythe for any more than a week in the open. You should have seen that, Mat. Even if you missed the curtains."

Rand glanced sideways at Perrin, trying not to stare. His eyes were sharper than Perrin's—or had been, when they used to hunt rabbits together—but he had not been able to see that scythe-blade well enough to make out any rust.

"I really don't care where they went," Mat grumbled. "I just want to find someplace with a fire. Soon."

"But why did they go?" Rand said under his breath. The Blight was not far off here. The Blight, where all the Fades and Trollocs were, those not down in Andor chasing them. The Blight, where they were going.

He raised his voice enough to be heard by those close to him. "Nynaeve, maybe you and Egwene don't have to go to the Eye with us." The two women looked at him as if he were speaking gibberish, but with the Blight so close he had to make one last try. "Maybe it's enough for you to be close. Moiraine didn't say you have to go. Or you, Loial. You could stay at Fal Dara. Until we come back. Or you could start for Tar Valon. Maybe there'll be a merchant train, or I'll bet Moiraine would even hire a coach. We will meet in Tar Valon, when it's all over."

"*Ta'veren.*" Loial's sigh was a rumble like thunder on the horizon. "You swirl lives around you, Rand al'Thor, you and your friends. Your fate chooses ours." The Ogier shrugged, and suddenly a broad grin split his face. "Besides, it will be something to meet the Green Man. Elder Haman always talks about his meeting with the Green Man, and so does my father, and most of the Elders."

"So many?" Perrin said. "The stories say the Green Man is hard to find, and no one can find him twice."

"Not twice, no," Loial agreed. "But then, I have never met him, and neither have you. He doesn't seem to avoid Ogier quite the way he does you humans. He knows so much about trees. Even the Tree Songs."

Rand said, "The point I was trying to make is—"

The Wisdom cut him off. "*She* says Egwene and I are part of the Pattern, too. All woven in with you three. If she is to be believed, there's something about the way that piece of the Pattern is woven that might stop the Dark One. And I am afraid I do believe her; too much has happened not to. But if Egwene and I go away, what might we change about the Pattern?"

"I was only trying to—"

Again Nynaeve interrupted, sharply. "I know what you were trying to do." She looked at him until he shifted uneasily in his saddle, then her face softened. "I know what you were trying to do, Rand. I have little liking for any Aes Sedai, and this one least of all, I think. I have less for going into the Blight, but least of all is the liking I have for the Father of Lies. If you boys . . . you men, can do what has to be done when you'd rather do almost anything else, why do you think I will do less? Or Egwene?" She did not appear to expect an answer. Gathering her reins, she frowned toward the Aes Sedai up ahead. "I wonder if we're going to reach this Fal Dara place soon, or does she mean us to spend the night out in this?"

As she trotted toward Moiraine, Mat said, "She called us men. It seems like only yesterday she was saying we shouldn't be off leading strings, and now she calls us men."

"You still shouldn't be off your mother's apron strings," Egwene said, but Rand did not think her heart was in it. She moved Bela close to his bay, and lowered her voice so none of the others could hear although Mat, at least, tried. "I only danced with Aram, Rand," she said softly, not looking at him. "You wouldn't hold it against me, dancing with somebody I will never see again, would you?"

"No," he told her. *What had made her bring it up now?* "Of course not." But suddenly he remembered something Min had said in Baerlon, what seemed a hundred years ago. *She's not for you, nor you for her; at least, not in the way you both want.*

The town of Fal Dara was built on hills higher than the surrounding country. It was nowhere near as big as Caemlyn, but the wall around it was as high as Caemlyn's. For a full mile outside that wall in every direction the ground was clear of anything taller than grass, and that cut low. Nothing could come close without being seen from one of the many tall towers topped by wooden hoardings. Where the walls of Caemlyn had a beauty about them, the builders of Fal Dara seemed not to have cared if anyone found their wall beautiful. The gray stone was grimly implacable, proclaiming that it existed for one purpose alone: to hold. Pennants atop the hoardings whipped in the wind, making the stooping Black Hawk of Shienar seem to fly all along the walls.

Lan tossed back the hood of his cloak and, despite the cold, motioned for the others to do the same. Moiraine had already lowered hers. "It's the law in Shienar," the Warder said. "In all the Borderlands. No one may hide his face inside a town's walls."

"Are they all that good-looking?" Mat laughed.

"A Halfman can't hide with his face exposed," the Warder said in a flat voice.

Rand's grin slid off his face. Hastily Mat pushed back his hood.

The gates stood open, tall and covered with dark iron, but a dozen armored men stood guard in golden yellow surcoats bearing the Black Hawk. The hilts of long swords on their backs peeked over their shoulders, and broadsword or mace or axe hung at every waist. Their horses were tethered nearby, made grotesque by the steel bardings covering chests and necks and heads, with lances to stirrup, all ready to ride at an instant. The guards made no move to stop Lan and Moiraine and the others. Indeed, they waved and called out happily.

"Dai Shan!" one cried, shaking steel-gauntleted fists over his head as they rode past. "Dai Shan!"

A number of others shouted, "Glory to the Builders!" and, *"Kiserai ti Wansho!"* Loial looked surprised, then a broad smile split his face and he waved to the guards.

One man ran alongside Lan's horse a little way, unhampered by the armor he wore. "Will the Golden Crane fly again, Dai Shan?"

"Peace, Ragan," was all the Warder said, and the man fell away. He returned the guards' waves, but his face was suddenly even more grim.

As they rode through stone-paved streets crowded with people and wagons, Rand frowned worriedly. Fal Dara was bulging at the seams, but the people were neither the eager crowds of Caemlyn, enjoying the grandeur of the city even as they squabbled, nor the milling throngs of Baerlon. Packed cheek by jowl, these folk watched their party ride by with leaden eyes and faces blanked of emotion. Carts and wagons jammed every alleyway and half the streets, piled high with jumbled household furnishings, and carved chests packed so tight that clothes spilled. On top sat the children. Adults kept the younglings up where they could be seen and did not let them stray even to play. The children were even more silent than their elders, their eyes bigger, more haunting in their stares. The nooks and crannies between the wagons were filled with shaggy cattle and black-spotted pigs in makeshift pens. Crates of chickens and ducks and geese fitfully made up for the silence of the people. He knew now where all the farmers had gone.

Lan led the way to the fortress in the middle of the town, a massive stone pile atop the highest hill. A dry moat, deep and wide, its bottom a forest of sharp steel spikes, razor-edged and as tall as a man, surrounded the towered walls of the keep. A place for a last defense, if the rest of the town fell. From one of the gate towers an armored man called down, "Welcome, Dai Shan." Another shouted to the inside of the fortress, "The Golden Crane! The Golden Crane!"

Their hooves drummed on the heavy timbers of the lowered drawbridge as they crossed the moat and rode under the sharp points of the stout portcullis. Once through the gates, Lan swung down out of his saddle to lead Mandarb, signaling the others to dismount.

The first courtyard was a huge square paved with big stone blocks and surrounded by towers and battlements as fierce as those on the outside of the walls. As big as it was, the courtyard appeared just as crowded as the streets, and as much in turmoil, though there was an order to the crowding here. Everywhere were armored men and armored horses. At half a dozen smithies around the court, hammers clanged, and big bellows, tugged by two leather-aproned men apiece, made the forge-fires roar. A steady stream of boys ran with new-made horseshoes for the farriers. Fletchers sat making arrows, and every time a basket was filled it was whisked away and replaced with an empty one.

Liveried grooms appeared on the run, eager and smiling in black-and-gold. Rand hastily untied his belongings from behind the saddle and gave the bay up to one of the grooms as a man in plate-and-mail and leather bowed formally. He wore a bright yellow cloak edged in red over his armor, with the Black Hawk on the breast, and a yellow surcoat bearing a gray owl. He wore no helmet and was bareheaded, truly, for his hair had all been shaved except for a topknot tied with a leather cord. "It has been long, Moiraine Aes Sedai. It is good to see you, Dai Shan. Very good." He bowed again, to Loial, and murmured, "Glory to the Builders. *Kiserai ti Wansho.*"

"I am unworthy," Loial replied formally, "and the work small. *Tsingu ma choba.*"

"You honor us, Builder," the man said. *"Kiserai ti Wansho."* He turned back to Lan. "Word was sent to Lord Agelmar, Dai Shan, as soon as you were seen coming. He is waiting for you. This way, please."

As they followed him into the fortress, along drafty stone corridors hung with colorful tapestries and long silk screens of hunting scenes and battles, he continued. "I am glad the call reached you, Dai Shan. Will you raise the Golden Crane banner once more?" The halls were stark except for the wall hangings, and even they used the fewest figures made with the fewest lines necessary to convey meaning, though in bright colors.

"Are things really as bad as they appear, Ingtar?" Lan asked quietly. Rand wondered if his own ears were twitching like Loial's.

The man's topknot swayed as he shook his head, but he hesitated before putting on a grin. "Things are never as bad as they appear, Dai Shan. A little worse than usual this year, that is all. The raids continued through the winter, even in the hardest of it. But the raiding was no worse than anywhere else along the Border. They still come in the night, but what else can be expected in the spring, if this can be called spring. Scouts return from the Blight—those who do come back—with news of Trolloc camps. Always fresh news of more camps. But we will meet them at Tarwin's Gap, Dai Shan, and turn them back as we always have."

"Of course," Lan said, but he did not sound certain.

Ingtar's grin slipped, but came back immediately. Silently he showed them into Lord Agelmar's study, then claimed the press of his duties and left.

It was a room as purpose-made as all the rest of the fortress, with arrowslits in the outer wall and a heavy bar for the thick door, which had its own arrowpiercings and was bound by iron straps. Only one tapestry hung here. It covered an entire wall and showed men, armored like the men of Fal Dara, fighting Myrddraal and Trollocs in a mountain pass.

A table, one chest, and a few chairs were the only furnishings except for two racks on the wall, and they caught Rand's eye as much as the tapestry. One held a two-handed sword, taller than a man, a more ordinary broadsword, and below them a studded mace and a long, kite-shaped shield bearing three foxes. From the other hung a suit of armor, complete and arranged as one would wear it. Crested helmet with its barred face-guard over a double-mail camail. Mail hauberk, split for riding, and leather undercoat, polished from wear. Breastplate, steel gauntlets, knee and elbow cops, and half-plate for shoulders and arms and legs. Even here in the heart of the Keep, weapons and armor seemed ready to be donned at any moment. Like the furniture, they were simply and severely decorated with gold.

Agelmar himself rose at their entrance and came around the table, littered with maps and sheafs of paper and pens standing in inkpots. He seemed at first glance too peaceful for the room in his blue velvet coat with its tall, wide collar, and soft leather boots, but a second look showed Rand differently. Like all the fighting men he had seen, Agelmar's head was shaved except for a topknot, and that pure white. His face was as hard as Lan's, the only lines creases at the corners of his eyes, and those eyes like brown stone, though they bore a smile now.

"Peace, but it is good to see you, Dai Shan," the Lord of Fal Dara said. "And you, Moiraine Aes Sedai, perhaps even more. Your presence warms me, Aes Sedai."

"Ninte calichniye no domashita, Agelmar Dai Shan," Moiraine replied formally, but with a note in her voice that said they were old friends. "Your welcome warms me, Lord Agelmar."

"Kodome calichniye ga ni Aes Sedai hei. Here is always a welcome for Aes Sedai." He turned to Loial. "You are far from the *stedding,* Ogier, but you honor Fal Dara. Always glory to the Builders. *Kiserai ti Wansho hei."*

"I am unworthy," Loial said, bowing. "It is you who do me honor." He glanced at the stark stone walls and seemed to struggle with himself. Rand was glad the Ogier managed to refrain from adding further comment.

Servants in black-and-gold appeared on silent, soft-slippered feet. Some brought folded cloths, damp and hot, on silver trays for wiping the dust from faces and hands. Others bore mulled wine and silver bowls of dried plums and apricots. Lord Agelmar gave orders for rooms to be prepared, and baths.

"A long journey from Tar Valon," he said. "You must be tired."

"A short journey the path we came," Lan told him, "but more tiring than the long way."

Agelmar looked puzzled when the Warder said no more, but he merely said, "A few days' rest will put you all in fine fettle."

"I ask one night's shelter, Lord Agelmar," Moiraine said, "for ourselves and our horses. And fresh supplies in the morning, if you can spare them. We must leave you early, I am afraid."

Agelmar frowned. "But I thought. . . . Moiraine Sedai, I have no right to ask it of you, but you would be worth a thousand lances in Tarwin's Gap. And you, Dai Shan. A thousand men *will* come when they hear the Golden Crane flies once more."

"The Seven Towers are broken," Lan said harshly, "and Malkier is dead; the few of her people left, scattered across the face of the earth. I am a Warder, Agelmar, sworn to the Flame of Tar Valon, and I am bound into the Blight."

"Of course, Dai Sh—Lan. Of course. But surely a few days' delay, a few weeks at most, will make no difference. You are needed. You, and Moiraine Sedai."

Moiraine took a silver goblet from one of the servants. "Ingtar seems to believe you will defeat this threat as you have defeated many others across the years."

"Aes Sedai," Agelmar said wryly, "if Ingtar had to ride alone to Tarwin's Gap, he would ride the whole way proclaiming that the Trollocs would be turned back once more. He has almost pride enough to believe he *could* do it alone."

"He is not as confident as you think, this time, Agelmar."

The Warder held a cup, but he did not drink. "How bad is it?"

Agelmar hesitated, pulling a map from the tangle on the table. He stared unseeing at the map for a moment, then tossed it back. "When we ride to the Gap," he said quietly, "the people will be sent south to Fal Moran. Perhaps the capital can hold. Peace, it must. Something must hold."

"That bad?" Lan said, and Agelmar nodded wearily.

Rand exchanged worried looks with Mat and Perrin. It was easy to believe the Trollocs gathering in the Blight were after him, after them. Agelmar went on grimly.

"Kandor, Arafel, Saldaea—the Trollocs raided them all straight through the winter. Nothing like that has happened since the Trolloc Wars; the raids have never been so fierce, or so large, or pressed home so hard. Every king and council is sure a great thrust is coming out of the Blight, and every one of the Borderlands believes it is coming at them. None of their scouts, and none of the Warders, report Trolloc massing above their borders, as we have here, but they believe, and each is afraid to send fighting men elsewhere. People whisper that the world is ending, that the Dark One is loose again. Shienar will ride to Tarwin's Gap alone, and we will be outnumbered at least ten to one. At least. It may be the last Ingathering of the Lances.

"Lan—no!—Dai Shan, for you *are* a Diademed Battle Lord of Malkier whatever you say. Dai Shan, the Golden Crane banner in the van would put heart into men who know they are riding north to die. The word will spread like wildfire, and though their kings have told them to hold where they are, lances will come from Arafel and Kandor, and even from Saldaea. Though they cannot come in time to stand with us in the Gap, they may save Shienar."

Lan peered into his wine. His face did not change, but wine slopped over his hand; the silver goblet crumpled in his grip. A servant took the ruined cup and wiped the Warder's hand with a cloth; a second put a fresh goblet in his hand while the other was whisked away. Lan did not seem to notice. "I cannot!" he whispered hoarsely. When he raised his head his blue eyes burned with a fierce light, but his voice was calm again, and flat. "I am a Warder, Agelmar." His sharp gaze slid across Rand and Mat and Perrin to Moiraine. "At first light I ride to the Blight."

Agelmar sighed heavily. "Moiraine Sedai, will you not come, at least? An Aes Sedai could make the difference."

"I cannot, Lord Agelmar." Moiraine seemed troubled. "There is indeed a battle to be fought, and it is not chance that the Trollocs gather above Shienar, but our battle, the true battle with the Dark One, will take place in the Blight, at the Eye of the World. You must fight your battle, and we ours."

"You cannot be saying he is loose!" Rocklike Agelmar sounded shaken, and Moiraine quickly shook her head.

"Not yet. If we win at the Eye of the World, perhaps not ever again."

"Can you even find the Eye, Aes Sedai? If holding the Dark One depends on that, we might as well be dead. Many have tried and failed."

"I can find it, Lord Agelmar. Hope is not lost yet."

Agelmar studied her, and then the others. He appeared puzzled by Nynaeve and Egwene; their farmclothes contrasted sharply with Moiraine's silk dress, though all were travel-stained. "They are Aes Sedai, too?" he asked doubtfully. When Moiraine shook her head, he seemed even more confused. His gaze ran over the young men from Emond's Field, settling on Rand, brushing the red-wrapped sword at his waist. "A strange guard you take with you, Aes Sedai. Only one fighting man." He glanced at Perrin, and at the axe hanging from his belt. "Perhaps two. But both barely more than lads. Let me send men with you. A hundred lances more or less will make no difference in the Gap, but you will need more than one Warder and three youths. And two women will not help, unless they are Aiel in disguise. The Blight is worse than usual this year. It—stirs."

"A hundred lances would be too many," Lan said, "and a thousand not enough. The larger the party we take into the Blight, the more chance we will attract attention. We must reach the Eye without fighting, if we can. You know the outcome is all but foretold when Trollocs force battle inside the Blight."

Agelmar nodded grimly, but he refused to give up. "Fewer, then. Even ten good men would give you a better chance of escorting Moiraine Sedai and the other two women to the Green Man than will just these young fellows."

Rand abruptly realized the Lord of Fal Dara assumed it

was Nynaeve and Egwene who with Moiraine would fight against the Dark One. It was natural. That sort of struggle meant using the One Power, and that meant women. *That sort of struggle means using the Power.* He tucked his thumbs behind his sword belt and gripped the buckle hard to keep his hands from shaking.

"No men," Moiraine said. Agelmar opened his mouth again, and she went on before he could speak. "It is the nature of the Eye, and the nature of the Green Man. How many from Fal Dara have ever found the Green Man and the Eye?"

"Ever?" Agelmar shrugged. "Since the War of the Hundred Years, you could count them on the fingers of one hand. No more than one in five years from all the Borderlands together."

"No one finds the Eye of the World," Moiraine said, "unless the Green Man wants them to find it. Need is the key, and intention. I know where to go—I have been there before." Rand's head whipped around in surprise; his was not the only one among the Emond's Fielders, but the Aes Sedai did not seem to notice. "But one among us seeking glory, seeking to add his name to those four, and we may never find it though I take us straight to the spot I remember."

"You have seen the Green Man, Moiraine Sedai?" The Lord of Fal Dara sounded impressed, but in the next breath he frowned. "But if you have already met him once. . . ."

"Need is the key," Moiraine said softly, "and there can be no greater need than mine. Than ours. And I have something those other seekers have not."

Her eyes barely stirred from Agelmar's face, but Rand was sure they had drifted toward Loial, just for an instant before the Aes Sedai pulled them back. Rand met the Ogier's eyes, and Loial shrugged.

"Ta'veren," the Ogier said softly.

Agelmar threw up his hands. "It will be as you say, Aes Sedai. Peace, if the real battle is to be at the Eye of the World, I am tempted to take the Black Hawk banner after you instead of to the Gap. I could cut a path for you—"

"That would be disaster, Lord Agelmar. Both at Tarwin's Gap and at the Eye. You have your battle, and we ours."

"Peace! As you say, Aes Sedai."

Having reached a decision, however much he disliked it,

the shaven-headed Lord of Fal Dara seemed to put it out of his mind. He invited them to table with him, all the while making conversation about hawks and horses and dogs, but with never a mention of Trollocs, or Tarwin's Gap, or the Eye of the World.

The chamber where they ate was as stark and plain as Lord Agelmar's study had been, with little more furnishing it than the table and chairs themselves, and they were severe in line and form. Beautiful, but severe. A big fireplace warmed the room, but not so much that a man called out hurriedly would be stunned by the cold outside. Liveried servants brought soup and bread and cheese, and the talk was of books and music until Lord Agelmar realized the Emond's Field folk were not talking. Like a good host he asked gently probing questions designed to bring them out of their quiet.

Rand soon found himself competing to tell about Emond's Field and the Two Rivers. It was an effort not to say too much. He hoped the others were guarding their tongues, Mat especially. Nynaeve alone held herself back, eating and drinking silently.

"There's a song in the Two Rivers," Mat said. "'Coming Home From Tarwin's Gap.'" He finished hesitantly, as if suddenly realizing that he was bringing up what they had been avoiding, but Agelmar handled it smoothly.

"Little wonder. Few lands have not sent men to hold back the Blight over the years."

Rand looked at Mat and Perrin. Mat silently formed the word Manetheren.

Agelmar whispered to one of the servants, and while others cleared the table that man vanished and returned with a canister, and clay pipes for Lan, Loial, and Lord Agelmar. "Two Rivers tabac," the Lord of Fal Dara said as they filled their pipes. "Hard to come by, here, but worth the cost."

When Loial and the two older men were puffing contentedly, Agelmar glanced at the Ogier. "You seem troubled, Builder. Not beset by the Longing, I hope. How long have you been away from the *stedding*?"

"It is not the Longing; I have not been gone such a time as that." Loial shrugged, and the blue-gray streamer rising from his pipe made a spiral above the table as he gestured.

"I expected—hoped—that the grove would still be here. Some remnant of Mafal Dadaranell, at least."

"Kiserai ti Wansho," Agelmar murmured. "The Trolloc Wars left nothing but memories, Loial, son of Arent, and people to build on them. They could not duplicate the Builders' work, any more than could I. Those intricate curves and patterns your people create are beyond human eyes and hands to make. Perhaps we wished to avoid a poor imitation that would only have been an ever-present reminder to us of what we had lost. There is a different beauty in simplicity, in a single line placed just so, a single flower among the rocks. The harshness of the stone makes the flower more precious. We try not to dwell too much on what is gone. The strongest heart will break under that strain."

"The rose petal floats on water," Lan recited softly. "The kingfisher flashes above the pond. Life and beauty swirl in the midst of death."

"Yes," Agelmar said. "Yes. That one has always symbolized the whole of it to me, too." The two men bowed their heads to one another.

Poetry out of Lan? The man was like an onion; every time Rand thought he knew something about the Warder, he discovered another layer underneath.

Loial nodded slowly. "Perhaps I also dwell too much on what is gone. And yet, the groves were beautiful." But he was looking at the stark room as if seeing it anew, and suddenly finding things worth seeing.

Ingtar appeared and bowed to Lord Agelmar. "Your pardon, Lord, but you wanted to know of anything out of the ordinary, however small."

"Yes, what is it?"

"A small thing, Lord. A stranger tried to enter the town. Not of Shienar. By his accent, a Lugarder. Sometimes, at least. When the South Gate guards attempted to question him, he ran away. He was seen to enter the forest, but only a short time later he was found scaling the wall."

"A small thing!" Agelmar's chair scraped across the floor as he stood. "Peace! The tower watch is so negligent a man can reach the walls unseen, and you call it a small thing?"

"He is a madman, Lord." Awe touched Ingtar's voice. "The Light shields madmen. Perhaps the Light cloaked the tower watch's eyes and allowed him to reach the walls. Surely one poor madman can do no harm."

"Has he been brought to the keep yet? Good. Bring him to me here. Now." Ingtar bowed and left, and Agelmar turned to Moiraine. "Your pardon, Aes Sedai, but I must see to this. Perhaps he is only a pitiful wretch with his mind blinded by the Light, but. . . . Two days gone, five of our own people were found in the night trying to saw through the hinges of a horse-gate. Small, but enough to let Trollocs in." He grimaced. "Darkfriends, I suppose, though I hate to think it of any Shienaran. They were torn to pieces by the people before the guards could take them, so I'll never know. If Shienarans can be Darkfriends, I must be especially careful of outlanders in these days. If you wish to withdraw, I will have you shown to your rooms."

"Darkfriends know neither border nor blood," Moiraine said. "They are found in every land, and are *of* none. I, too, am interested in seeing this man. The Pattern is forming a Web, Lord Agelmar, but the final shape of the Web is not yet set. It may yet entangle the world, or unravel and set the Wheel to a new weaving. At this point, even small things can change the shape of the Web. At this point I am wary of small things out of the ordinary."

Agelmar glanced at Nynaeve and Egwene. "As you wish, Aes Sedai."

Ingtar returned, with two guards carrying long bills, and escorting a man who looked like a ragbag turned inside out. Grime layered his face and matted his scraggly, uncut hair and beard. He hunched into the room, sunken eyes darting this way and that. A rancid smell wafted ahead of him.

Rand sat forward intently, trying to see through all the dirt.

"You've no cause to be holding me like this," the filthy man whined. "I'm only a poor destitute, abandoned by the Light and seeking a place, like everyone else, to shelter from the Shadow."

"The Borderlands are a strange place to seek—" Agelmar began, when Mat cut him off.

"The peddler!"

"Padan Fain," Perrin agreed, nodding.

"The beggar," Rand said, suddenly hoarse. He sat back at

the sudden hatred that flared in Fain's eyes. "He's the man who was asking about us in Caemlyn. He has to be."

"So this concerns you after all, Moiraine Sedai," Agelmar said slowly.

Moiraine nodded. "I greatly fear that it does."

"I didn't want to." Fain began to cry. Fat tears cut runnels in the dirt on his cheeks, but they were unable to reach the bottom layer. "He made me! Him and his burning eyes." Rand flinched. Mat had his hand under his coat, no doubt clutching the dagger from Shadar Logoth again. "He made me his hound! His hound, to hunt and follow with never a bit of rest. Only his hound, even after he threw me away."

"It does concern us all," Moiraine said grimly. "Is there a place where I can talk with him alone, Lord Agelmar?" Her mouth tightened with distaste. "And wash him first. I may need to touch him." Agelmar nodded and spoke softly to Ingtar, who bowed and disappeared through the door.

"I will not be compelled!" The voice was Fain's, but he was no longer crying, and an arrogant snap had replaced the whine. He stood upright, not crouching at all. Throwing back his head, he shouted at the ceiling. "Never again! I— will—not!" He faced Agelmar as if the men flanking him were his own bodyguard and the Lord of Fal Dara his equal rather than his captor. His tone became sleek and oily. "There is a misunderstanding here, Great Lord. I am sometimes taken by spells, but that will pass soon. Yes, soon I will be rid of them." Contemptuously he flicked his fingers against the rags he wore. "Do not be misled by these, Great Lord. I have had to disguise myself against those who have tried to stop me, and my journey has been long and hard. But at last I have reached lands where men still know the dangers of Ba'alzamon, where men still fight the Dark One."

Rand stared, goggling. It *was* Fain's voice, but the words did not sound like the peddler at all.

"So you've come here because we fight Trollocs," Agelmar said. "And you are so important that someone wants to stop you. These people say you are a peddler called Padan Fain, and that you are following them."

Fain hesitated. He glanced at Moiraine and hurriedly pulled his eyes away from the Aes Sedai. His gaze ran across the Emond's Fielders, then jerked back to Agelmar. Rand felt the hate in that look, and the fear. When Fain spoke again, though, his voice was unruffled. "Padan Fain is simply one of the many disguises I have been forced to wear over the years. Friends of the Dark pursue me, for I have learned how to defeat the Shadow. I can show you how to defeat him, Great Lord."

"We do as well as men can," Agelmar said dryly. "The Wheel weaves as the Wheel wills, but we have fought the Dark One almost since the Breaking of the World without peddlers to teach us how."

"Great Lord, your might is unquestioned, but can it stand against the Dark One forever? Do you not often find yourself pressed to hold? Forgive my temerity, Great Lord; he will crush you in the end, as you are. I know; believe me, I do. But I can show you how to scour the Shadow from the land, Great Lord." His tone became even more unctuous, though still haughty. "If you but try what I advise, you will see, Great Lord. You will cleanse the land. You, Great Lord, can do it, if you direct your might in the right direction. Avoid letting Tar Valon entangle you in its snares, and you can save the world. Great Lord, you will be the man remembered through history for bringing final victory to the Light." The guards held their places, but their hands shifted on the long shafts of the bills as if they thought they might have to use them.

"He thinks a great deal of himself for a peddler," Agelmar said to Lan over his shoulder. "I think Ingtar is right. He is mad."

Fain's eyes tightened angrily, but his voice remained smooth. "Great Lord, I know my words must appear grandiose, but if you will only—" He cut off abruptly, stepping back, as Moiraine rose and started slowly around the table. Only the guards' lowered bills kept Fain from backing right out of the room.

Stopping behind Mat's chair, Moiraine put a hand on his shoulder and bent to whisper in his ear. Whatever she said, the tension went out of his face, and he took his hand from under his coat. The Aes Sedai went on until she stood beside Agelmar, confronting Fain. As she came to a halt, the peddler sank into a crouch once more.

"I hate him," he whimpered. "I want to be free of him.

I want to walk in the Light again." His shoulders began to shake, and tears streamed down his face even more heavily than before. "He made me do it."

"I am afraid he is more than a peddler, Lord Agelmar," Moiraine said. "Less than human, worse than vile, more dangerous than you can imagine. He can be bathed after I have spoken with him. I dare not waste a minute. Come, Lan."

CHAPTER

47

More Tales of the Wheel

An itchy restlessness had Rand pacing beside the dining table. Twelve strides. The table was exactly twelve strides long no matter how many times he stepped it off. Irritably he made himself stop keeping tally. *Stupid thing to be doing. I don't care how long the bloody table is.* A few minutes later he discovered that he was counting the number of trips he made up the table and back. *What is he saying to Moiraine and Lan? Does he know why the Dark One is after us? Does he know which of us the Dark One wants?*

He glanced at his friends. Perrin had crumbled a piece of bread and was idly pushing the crumbs around on the table with one finger. His yellow eyes stared unblinking at the crumbs, but they seemed to see something far off. Mat slouched in his chair, eyes half closed and the beginnings of a grin on his face. It was a nervous grin, not amusement. Outwardly he looked like the old Mat, but from time to time he unconsciously touched the Shadar Logoth dagger through his coat. *What is Fain telling her? What does he know?*

Loial, at least, did not look worried. The Ogier was studying the walls. First he had stood in the middle of the room and stared, turning slowly in a circle; now he was almost pressing his broad nose against the stone while he gently traced a particular join with fingers thicker than most men's thumbs. Sometimes he closed his eyes, as if the feeling was more important than seeing. His ears gave an occasional twitch, and he muttered to himself in Ogier, appearing to have forgotten anyone else was in the room with him.

Lord Agelmar stood talking quietly with Nynaeve and Egwene in front of the long fireplace at the end of the room. He was a good host, adept at making people forget their troubles; several of his stories had Egwene in giggles. Once even Nynaeve threw back her head and roared with laughter. Rand gave a start at the unexpected sound, and jumped again when Mat's chair crashed to the floor.

"Blood and ashes!" Mat growled, ignoring the way Nynaeve's mouth tightened at his language. "What's taking her so long?" He righted his chair and sat back down without looking at anyone. His hand strayed to his coat.

The Lord of Fal Dara looked at Mat disapprovingly—his gaze took in Rand and Perrin without any improvement—then turned back to the women. Rand's pacing had taken him close to them.

"My Lord," Egwene was saying, as glibly as if she had been using titles all of her life, "I thought he was a Warder, but you call him Dai Shan, and talk about a Golden Crane banner, and so did those other men. Sometimes you sound almost as if he's a king. I remember once Moiraine called him the last Lord of the Seven Towers. Who is he?"

Nynaeve began studying her cup intently, but it was obvious to Rand that abruptly she was listening even more closely than was Egwene. Rand stopped and tried to overhear without seeming to eavesdrop.

"Lord of the Seven Towers," Agelmar said with a frown. "An ancient title, Lady Egwene. Not even the High Lords of Tear have older, though the Queen of Andor comes close." He heaved a sigh, and shook his head. "He will not speak of it, yet the story is well known along the Border. He is a king, or should have been, al'Lan Mandragoran, Lord of the Seven Towers, Lord of the Lakes, crownless King of the Malkieri." His shaven head lifted high, and there was a light in his eye as if he felt a father's pride. His voice grew stronger, filled with the force of his feeling. The whole room could hear without straining. "We of Shienar call ourselves Bordermen, but fewer than fifty years ago, Shienar was not truly of the Borderlands. North of us, and of Arafel, was Malkier. The lances of Shienar rode north, but it was Malkier that held back the Blight. Malkier, Peace favor her memory, and the Light illumine her name."

"Lan is from Malkier," the Wisdom said softly, looking up. She seemed troubled.

It was not a question, but Agelmar nodded. "Yes, Lady Nynaeve, he is the son of al'Akir Mandragoran, last crowned King of the Malkieri. How did he become as he is? The beginning, perhaps, was Lain. On a dare, Lain Mandragoran, the King's brother, led his lances through the Blight to the Blasted Lands, perhaps to Shayol Ghul itself. Lain's wife, Breyan, made that dare for the envy that burned her heart that al'Akir had been raised to the throne instead of Lain. The King and Lain were as close as brothers could be, as close as twins even after the royal 'al' was added to Akir's name, but jealousy wracked Breyan. Lain was acclaimed for his deeds, and rightfully so, but not even he could outshine al'Akir. He was, man and king, such as comes once in a hundred years, if that. Peace favor him, and el'Leanna.

"Lain died in the Blasted Lands with most of those who followed him, men Malkier could ill afford to lose, and Breyan blamed the King, saying that Shayol Ghul itself would have fallen if al'Akir had led the rest of the Malkieri north with her husband. For revenge, she plotted with Cowin Gemallan, called Cowin Fairheart, to seize the throne for her son, Isam. Now Fairheart was a hero almost as well loved as al'Akir himself, and one of the Great Lords, but when the Great Lords had cast the rods for king, only two separated him from Akir, and he never forgot that two men laying a different color on the Crowning Stone would have set him on the throne instead. Between them, Cowin and Breyan moved soldiers back from the Blight to seize the Seven Towers, stripping the Borderforts to bare garrisons.

"But Cowin's jealousy ran deeper." Disgust tinged Agelmar's voice. "Fairheart the hero, whose exploits in the Blight were sung throughout the Borderlands, was a Darkfriend. With the Borderforts weakened, Trollocs poured into Malkier like a flood. King al'Akir and Lain together might have rallied the land; they had done so before. But Lain's doom in the Blasted Lands had shaken the people, and the Trolloc invasion broke men's spirit and their will to resist. Too many men. Overwhelming numbers pushed the Malkieri back into the heartland.

"Breyan fled with her infant son Isam, and was run down

by Trollocs as she rode south with him. No one knows their fate of a certainty, but it can be guessed. I can find pity only for the boy. When Cowin Fairheart's treachery was revealed and he was taken by young Jain Charin—already called Jain Farstrider—when Fairheart was brought to the Seven Towers in chains, the Great Lords called for his head on a pike. But because he had been second only to al'Akir and Lain in the hearts of the people, the King faced him in single combat and slew him. Al'Akir wept when he killed Cowin. Some say he wept for a friend who had given himself to the Shadow, and some say for Malkier." The Lord of Fal Dara shook his head sadly.

"The first peal of the doom of the Seven Towers had been struck. There was no time to gather aid from Shienar or Arafel, and no hope that Malkier could stand alone, with five thousand of her lances dead in the Blasted Lands, her Borderforts overrun.

"Al'Akir and his Queen, el'Leanna, had Lan brought to them in his cradle. Into his infant hands they placed the sword of Malkieri kings, the sword he wears today. A weapon made by Aes Sedai during the War of Power, the War of the Shadow that brought down the Age of Legends. They anointed his head with oil, naming him Dai Shan, a Diademed Battle Lord, and consecrated him as the next King of the Malkieri, and in his name they swore the ancient oath of Malkieri kings and queens." Agelmar's face hardened, and he spoke the words as if he, too, had sworn that oath, or one much similar. "To stand against the Shadow so long as iron is hard and stone abides. To defend the Malkieri while one drop of blood remains. To avenge what cannot be defended." The words rang in the chamber.

"El'Leanna placed a locket around her son's neck, for remembrance, and the infant, wrapped in swaddling clothes by the Queen's own hand, was given over to twenty chosen from the King's Bodyguard, the best swordsmen, the most deadly fighters. Their command: to carry the child to Fal Moran.

"Then did al'Akir and el'Leanna lead the Malkieri out to face the Shadow one last time. There they died, at Herat's Crossing, and the Malkieri died, and the Seven Towers were broken. Shienar, and Arafel, and Kandor, met the Halfmen and the Trollocs at the Stair of Jehaan and threw them back, but not as far as they had been. Most of Malkier remained in Trolloc hands, and year by year, mile by mile, the Blight has swallowed it." Agelmar drew a heavyhearted breath. When he went on, there was a sad pride in his eyes and voice.

"Only five of the Bodyguards reached Fal Moran alive, every man wounded, but they had the child unharmed. From the cradle they taught him all they knew. He learned weapons as other children learn toys, and the Blight as other children their mother's garden. The oath sworn over his cradle is graven in his mind. There is nothing left to defend, but he can avenge. He denies his titles, yet in the Borderlands he is called the Uncrowned, and if ever he raised the Golden Crane of Malkier, an army would come to follow. But he will not lead men to their deaths. In the Blight he courts death as a suitor courts a maiden, but he will not lead others to it.

"If you must enter the Blight, and with only a few, there is no man better to take you there, nor to bring you safely out again. He is the best of the Warders, and that means the best of the best. You might as well leave these boys here, to gain a little seasoning, and put your entire trust in Lan. The Blight is no place for untried boys."

Mat opened his mouth, and shut it again at a look from Rand. *I wish he'd learn to keep it shut.*

Nynaeve had listened just as wide-eyed as Egwene, but now she was staring into her cup again, her face pale. Egwene put a hand on her arm and gave her a sympathetic look.

Moiraine appeared in the doorway, Lan at her heels. Nynaeve turned her back on them.

"What did he say?" Rand demanded. Mat rose, and Perrin, too.

"Country oaf," Agelmar muttered, then raised his voice to a normal tone. "Did you learn anything, Aes Sedai, or is he simply a madman?"

"He is mad," Moiraine said, "or close to it, but there is nothing simple about Padan Fain." One of the black-and-gold-liveried servants bowed his way in with a blue washbasin and pitcher, a bar of yellow soap, and a small towel on a silver tray; he looked anxiously at Agelmar. Moiraine directed him to put them on the table. "Your pardon for commanding your servants, Lord Agelmar," she said. "I took the liberty of asking for this."

Agelmar nodded to the servant, who put the tray on the table and left hurriedly. "My servants are yours to command, Aes Sedai."

The water Moiraine poured into the basin steamed as if only just off the boil. She pushed up her sleeves and began vigorously washing her hands without regard for the heat of the water. "I said he was worse than vile, but I did not come close. I do not believe I have ever met someone so abject and debased, yet at the same time so foul. I feel soiled from touching him, and I do not mean for the filth on his skin. Soiled in here." She touched her breast. "The degradation of his soul almost makes me doubt he has one. There is something worse to him than a Darkfriend."

"He looked so pitiful," Egwene murmured. "I remember him arriving in Emond's Field each spring, always laughing and full of news from outside. Surely there's some hope for him? 'No man can stand in the Shadow so long that he cannot find the Light again,'" she quoted.

The Aes Sedai toweled her hands briskly. "I have always believed it so," she said. "Perhaps Padan Fain can be redeemed. But he has been a Darkfriend more than forty years, and what he has done for that, in blood and pain and death, would freeze your heart to hear. Among the least of these—though not small to you, I suspect—he brought the Trollocs to Emond's Field."

"Yes," Rand said softly. He heard Egwene gasp. *I should have guessed. Burn me, I should have, as soon as I recognized him.*

"Did he bring any here?" Mat asked. He looked at the stone walls around them and shivered. Rand thought he was remembering the Myddraal more than Trollocs; walls had not stopped the Fade at Baerlon, or at Whitebridge.

"If he did"—Agelmar laughed—"they'll break their teeth on the walls of Fal Dara. Many others have before." He was speaking to everyone, but obviously addressing his words to Egwene and Nynaeve, from the glances he gave them. "And do not worry yourself about Halfmen, either." Mat's face reddened. "Every street and alley in Fal Dara is lit by night. And no man may hide his face inside the walls."

"Why would Master Fain do that?" Egwene asked.

"Three years ago. . . ." With a heavy sigh Moiraine sat down, folding up as if what she had done with Fain had drained her. "Three years, this summer. As far back as that. The Light surely favors us, else the Father of Lies would have triumphed while I still sat planning in Tar Valon. Three years, Fain has been hunting you for the Dark One."

"That's crazy!" Rand said. "He's come into the Two Rivers every spring as regular as a clock. Three years? We've been right there in front of him, and he never looked at any of us twice before last year." The Aes Sedai pointed a finger at him, fixing him.

"Fain told me everything, Rand. Or almost everything. I believe he managed to hold back something, something important, despite all I could do, but he said enough. Three years ago, a Halfman came for him in a town in Murandy. Fain was terrified, of course, but it is considered a very great honor among Darkfriends to be so summoned. Fain believed he had been chosen for great things, and he had, though not in the manner he believed. He was brought north to the Blight, to the Blasted Lands. To Shayol Ghul. Where he met a man with eyes of fire, who named himself Ba'alzamon."

Mat shifted uneasily, and Rand swallowed hard. It had to have been that way, of course, but that did not make it any easier to accept. Only Perrin looked at the Aes Sedai as if nothing could surprise him any longer.

"The Light protect us," Agelmar said fervently.

"Fain did not like what was done to him at Shayol Ghul," Moiraine continued calmly. "While we talked, he screamed often of fire and burning. It almost killed him, bringing it all out from where he had it hidden. Even with my Healing he is a shattered ruin. It will take much to make him whole again. I will make the effort, though, if for no other reason than to learn what more he still hides. He had been chosen because of where he did his peddling. No," she said quickly when they stirred, "not the Two Rivers only, not then. The Father of Lies knew roughly where to find what he sought, but not much better than we in Tar Valon.

"Fain said he has been made the Dark One's hound, and in a way he is right. The Father of Lies set Fain to hunt, first changing him so he could carry out that hunt. It is the things done to bring about those changes that Fain fears to remember; he hates his master for them as much as he fears him. So Fain was sent sniffing and hunting through all the villages around Baerlon, and all the way to the Mountains of Mist, and down to the Taren and across into the Two Rivers."

"Three springs ago?" Perrin said slowly. "I remember that spring. Fain came later than usual, but what was strange was that he lingered on. A whole week he remained, idle and gnashing his teeth about laying out money for a room at the Winespring Inn. Fain likes his money."

"I remember, now," Mat said. "Everybody was wondering was he sick, or had he fallen for a local woman? Not that any of them would marry a peddler, of course. As well marry one of the Traveling People." Egwene raised an eyebrow at him, and he shut his mouth.

"After that, Fain was taken to Shayol Ghul again, and his mind was—distilled." Rand's stomach turned over at the tone in the Aes Sedai's voice; it told more of what she meant than the grimace that flashed across her face. "What he had . . . sensed . . . was concentrated and fed back. When he entered the Two Rivers the next year, he was able to choose his targets out more clearly. Indeed, more clearly even than the Dark One had expected. Fain knew for a certainty that the one he sought was one of three in Emond's Field."

Perrin grunted, and Mat began cursing in a soft monotone that even Nynaeve's glare did not stop. Agelmar looked at them curiously. Rand felt only the faintest chill, and wondered at it. Three years the Dark One had been hunting him . . . hunting them. He was sure it should have made his teeth chatter.

Moiraine did not allow Mat to interrupt her. She raised her voice enough to be heard over him. "When Fain returned to Lugard, Ba'alzamon came to him in a dream. Fain abased himself and performed rites that would strike you deaf to hear the half of them, binding himself even more tightly to the Dark One. What is done in dreams can be more dangerous than what is done awake." Rand stirred at the sharp, warning look, but she did not pause. "He was promised great rewards, power over kingdoms after Ba'alzamon's victory, and told that when he returned to Emond's Field he was to mark the three he had found. A Halfman would be there, waiting for him with Trollocs. We know now how the Trollocs came to the Two Rivers. There must have been an Ogier grove and a Waygate at Manetheren."

"The most beautiful of all," Loial said, "except for Tar Valon." He had been listening as intently as everyone else. "Manetheren is remembered fondly by the Ogier." Agelmar formed the name silently, his eyebrows raised in wonder. Manetheren.

"Lord Agelmar," Moiraine said, "I will tell you how to find the Waygate of Mafal Dadaranell. It must be walled up and a guard set, and none allowed near. The Halfmen have not learned all of the Ways yet, but that Waygate is to the south and only hours from Fal Dara."

The Lord of Fal Dara gave himself a shake, as if he were coming out of a trance. "South? Peace! We don't need that, the Light shine on us. It shall be done."

"Did Fain follow us through the Ways?" Perrin asked. "He must have done."

Moiraine nodded. "Fain would follow you three into the grave, because he must. When the Myrddraal failed at Emond's Field, it brought Fain with the Trollocs on our trail. The Fade would not let Fain ride with him; although he thought he should have the best horse in the Two Rivers and ride at the head of the band, the Myrddraal forced him to run with the Trollocs, and the Trollocs to carry him when his feet gave out. They talked so that he could understand, arguing about the best way to cook him when his usefulness was done. Fain claims he turned against the Dark One before they reached the Taren. But sometimes his greed for his promised rewards seeps into the open.

"When we had escaped across the Taren the Myrddraal took the Trollocs back to the closest Waygate, in the Mountains of Mist, and sent Fain across alone. He thought he was free then, but before he reached Baerlon another Fade found him, and that one was not so kind. It made him sleep doubled up on himself in a Trolloc kettle at night, to remind him of the price of failure. That one used him as far as Shadar Logoth. By then Fain was willing to give the Myrddraal his mother if it would free him, but the Dark One never willingly loosens a hold he has gained.

"What I did there, sending an illusion of our tracks and smell off toward the mountains, fooled the Myrddraal, but not Fain. The Halfmen did not believe him; afterward, they dragged him behind them on a leash. Only when we seemed to keep always just ahead, no matter how hard they pressed, did some begin to credit him. Those were the four who returned to Shadar Logoth. Fain claims it was Ba'alzamon himself who drove the Myrddraal."

Agelmar shook his head contemptuously. "The Dark One? Pah! The man's lying or mad. If Heartsbane were loose, we'd all of us be dead by now, or worse."

"Fain spoke the truth as he saw it," Moiraine said. "He could not lie to me, though he hid much. His words. 'Ba'alzamon appeared like a flickering candle flame, vanishing and reappearing, never in the same place twice. His eyes seared the Myrddraal, and the fires of his mouth scourged us.'"

"*Something*," Lan said, "drove four Fades to where they feared to go—a place they fear almost as much as they fear the wrath of the Dark One."

Agelmar grunted as if he had been kicked; he looked sick.

"It was evil against evil in the ruins of Shadar Logoth," Moiraine continued, "foul fighting vile. When Fain spoke of it, his teeth chattered and he whimpered. Many Trollocs were slain, consumed by Mashadar and other things, including the Trolloc that held Fain's leash. He fled the city as if it were the Pit of Doom, at Shayol Ghul.

"Fain believed he was free at last. He intended to run until Ba'alzamon could never find him again, to the ends of the earth if necessary. Imagine his horror when he discovered that the compulsion to hunt did not lessen. Instead, it grew stronger and sharper with every day that passed. He could not eat, except what he could scavenge while he hunted you—beetles and lizards snatched while he ran, half-rotten refuse dug from midden heaps in the dark of night—nor could he stop until exhaustion collapsed him like an empty sack. And as soon as he had strength to stand again, he was driven on. By the time he reached Caemlyn he could *feel* his quarry even when it was a mile away. Here, in the cells below, he would sometimes look up without realizing what he was doing. He was looking in the direction of this room."

Rand had a sudden itch between his shoulder blades; it was as if he could feel Fain's eyes on him then, through the intervening stone. The Aes Sedai noticed his uneasy shrug, but she went on implacably.

"If Fain was half mad by the time he reached Caemlyn, he sank even further when he realized that only two of those he sought were there. He was compelled to find *all* of you, but he could do no other than follow the two who were there, either. He spoke of screaming when the Waygate opened in Caemlyn. The knowledge of how to do it was in his mind; he does not know how it came there; his hands moved of their own accord, burning with the fires of Ba'alzamon when he tried to stop them. The owner of the shop, who came to investigate the noise, Fain murdered. Not because he had to, but out of envy that the man could walk freely out of the cellar while his feet carried him inexorably into the Ways."

"Then Fain was the one you sensed following us," Egwene said. Lan nodded. "How did he escape the . . . the Black Wind?" Her voice shook; she stopped to swallow. "It was right behind us at the Waygate."

"He escaped, and he did not," Moiraine said. "The Black Wind caught him—and he claimed to understand the voices. Some greeted him as like to them; others feared him. No sooner did the Wind envelop Fain than it fled."

"The Light preserve us." Loial's whisper rumbled like a giant bumblebee.

"Pray that it does," Moiraine said. "There is much yet hidden about Padan Fain, much I must learn. The evil goes deeper in him, and stronger, than in any man I have yet seen. It maybe that the Dark One, in doing what he did to Fain, impressed some part of himself on the man, perhaps even, unknowing, some part of his intent. When I mentioned the Eye of the World, Fain clamped his jaws shut, but I felt something knowing behind the silence. If only I had the time now. But we cannot wait."

"If this man knows something," Agelmar said, "I can get it out of him." His face held no mercy for Darkfriends; his voice promised no pity for Fain. "If you can learn even a part of what you will face in the Blight, it's worth an extra day. Battles have been lost for not knowing what the enemy intends."

Moiraine sighed and shook her head ruefully. "My lord, if we did not need at least one good night's sleep before facing the Blight, I would ride within the hour, though it meant the risk of meeting a Trolloc raid in the dark. Consider what I did learn from Fain. Three years ago the Dark One had to have Fain brought to Shayol Ghul to touch him, despite the fact that Fain is a Darkfriend dedicated to his marrow. One year ago, the Dark One could command Fain, the Darkfriend, through his dreams. This year, Ba'alzamon walks in the dreams of those who live in the Light, and actually appears, if with difficulty, at Shadar Logoth. Not in his own body, of course, but even a projection of the Dark One's mind, even a projection that flickers and cannot hold, is more deathly dangerous to the world than all the Trolloc hordes combined. The seals on Shayol Ghul are weakening desperately, Lord Agelmar. There is no time."

Agelmar bowed his head in acquiescence, but when he raised it again there was still a stubborn set to his mouth. "Aes Sedai, I can accept that when I lead the lances to Tarwin's Gap we will be no more than a diversion, or a skirmish on the outskirts of the real battle. Duty takes men where it will as surely as does the Pattern, and neither promises that what we do will have greatness. But our skirmish will be useless, even should we win, if you lose the battle. If you say your party must be small, I say well and good, but I beg you to make every effort to see that you *can* win. Leave these young men here, Aes Sedai. I swear to you that I can find three experienced men with no thought of glory in their heads to replace them, good swordsmen who are almost as handy in the Blight as Lan. Let me ride to the Gap knowing that I have done what I can to help you be victorious."

"I must take them and no others, Lord Agelmar," Moiraine said gently. "They are the ones who will fight the battle at the Eye of the World."

Agelmar's jaw dropped, and he stared at Rand and Mat and Perrin. Suddenly the Lord of Fal Dara took a step back, his hand groping unconsciously for the sword he never wore inside the fortress. "They aren't. . . . You are not Red Ajah, Moiraine Sedai, but surely not even you would. . . ." Sudden sweat glistened on his shaven head.

"They are *ta'veren*," Moiraine said soothingly. "The Pattern weaves itself around them. Already the Dark One has tried to kill each of them more than once. Three *ta'veren* in one place are enough to change the life around them as surely as a whirlpool changes the path of a straw. When the place is the Eye of the World, the Pattern might weave even the Father of Lies into itself, and make him harmless again."

Agelmar stopped trying to find his sword, but he still looked at Rand and the others doubtfully. "Moiraine Sedai, if you say they are, then they are, but I cannot see it. Farmboys. Are you certain, Aes Sedai?"

"The old blood," Moiraine said, "split out like a river breaking into a thousand times a thousand streams, but sometimes streams join together to make a river again. The old blood of Manetheren is strong and pure in almost all these young men. Can you doubt the strength of Manetheren's blood, Lord Agelmar?"

Rand glanced sideways at the Aes Sedai. *Almost all.* He risked a look at Nynaeve; she had turned back to watch as well as listen, though she still avoided looking at Lan. He caught the Wisdom's eye. She shook her head; she had not told the Aes Sedai that he was not Two Rivers born. *What does Moiraine know?*

"Manetheren," Agelmar said slowly, nodding. "I would not doubt that blood." Then, more quickly, "The Wheel brings strange times. Farmboys carry the honor of Manetheren into the Blight, yet if any blood can strike a fell blow at the Dark One, it would be the blood of Manetheren. It shall be done as you wish, Aes Sedai."

"Then let us go to our rooms," Moiraine said. "We must leave with the sun, for time grows short. The young men must sleep close to me. Time is too short before the battle to allow the Dark One another strike at them. Too short."

Rand felt her eyes on him, studying him and his friends, weighing their strength, and he shivered. Too short.

CHAPTER
48

The Blight

T he wind whipped Lan's cloak, sometimes making
him hard to see even in the sunlight, and Ingtar and
the hundred lances Lord Agelmar had sent to escort
them to the Border, in case they met a Trolloc raid, made a
brave display in double column with their armor and their
red pennants and their steel-clad horses led by Ingtar's
Gray Owl banner. They were easily as grand as a hundred
of the Queen's Guards, but it was the towers just in sight
ahead of them that Rand studied. He had had all morning to
watch the Shienaran lances.

Each tower stood tall and solid atop a hill, half a mile
from its neighbor. East and west others rose, and more
beyond those. A broad, walled ramp spiraled around each
stone shaft, winding all the way around by the time it
reached the heavy gates halfway to the crenellated top. A
sortie from the garrison would be protected by the wall until it reached the ground, but enemies striving to reach the
gate would climb under a hail of arrows and stones and hot
oil from the big kettles poised on the outward flaring ramparts above. A large steel mirror, carefully turned down,
away from the sun, now, glittered atop each tower below
the high iron cup where signal fires could be lit when the
sun did not shine. The signal would be flashed, to towers
further from the Border, and by those to still others, and so
relayed to the heartland fortresses, from where the lances
would ride to turn back the raid. Were times normal, they
would.

From the two nearest tower tops men watched them approach. Just a few men on each, peering curiously through

the crenels. In the best of times the towers were only manned enough for self-defense, depending more on stone walls than strong arms to survive, but every man who could be spared, and more, was riding to Tarwin's Gap. The fall of the towers would not matter if the lances failed to hold the Gap.

Rand shivered as they rode between the towers. It was almost as if he had ridden through a wall of colder air. This was the Border. The land beyond looked no different from Shienar, but out there, somewhere beyond the leafless trees, was the Blight.

Ingtar lifted a steel fist to halt the lances short of a plain stone post in sight of the towers. A borderpost, marking the boundary between Shienar and what once was Malkier. "Your pardon, Moiraine Aes Sedai. Pardon, Dai Shan. Pardon, Builder. Lord Agelmar commanded me to go no further." He sounded unhappy about it, disgruntled at life in general.

"That is as we planned, Lord Agelmar and I," Moiraine said.

Ingtar grunted sourly. "Pardon, Aes Sedai," he apologized, not sounding as if he meant it. "To escort you here means we may not reach the Gap before the fighting is done. I am robbed of the chance to stand with the rest, and at the same time I am commanded not to ride one step beyond the borderpost, as if I had never before been in the Blight. And My Lord Agelmar will not tell me why." Behind the bars of his face-guard, his eyes turned the last word into a question to the Aes Sedai. He scorned to look at Rand and the others; he had learned they would accompany Lan into the Blight.

"He can have my place," Mat muttered to Rand. Lan gave them both a sharp look. Mat dropped his eyes, his face turning red.

"Each of us has his part in the Pattern, Ingtar," Moiraine said firmly. "From here we must thread ours alone."

Ingtar's bow was stiffer than his armor made it. "As you wish it, Aes Sedai. I must leave you, now, and ride hard in order to reach Tarwin's Gap. At least I will be . . . *allowed* . . . to face Trollocs there."

"Are you truly that eager?" Nynaeve asked. "To fight Trollocs?"

Ingtar gave her a puzzled look, then glanced at Lan as if

the Warder might explain. "That is what I do, Lady," he said slowly. "That is why I am." He raised a gauntleted hand to Lan, open palm toward the warder. "*Suravye ninto man-shima taishite, Dai Shan.* Peace favor your sword." Pulling his horse around, Ingtar rode east with his bannerman and his hundred lances. They went at a walk, but a steady pace, as fast as armored horses could manage with a far distance yet to go.

"What a strange thing to say," Egwene said. "Why do they use it like that? Peace."

"When you have never known a thing except to dream," Lan replied, heeling Mandarb forward, "it becomes more than a talisman."

As Rand followed the Warder past the stone borderpost, he turned in his saddle to look back, watching Ingtar and the lances disappear behind barren trees, and the border-post vanish, and last of all the towers on their hilltops, looking over the trees. All too soon they were alone, riding north under the leafless canopy of the forest. Rand sank into watchful silence, and for once even Mat had nothing to say.

That morning the gates of Fal Dara had opened with the dawn. Lord Agelmar, armored and helmeted now like his soldiers, rode with the Black Hawk banner and the Three Foxes from the East Gate toward the sun, still only a red sliver above the trees. Like a steel snake undulating to mounted kettledrums, the column wound its way out of the town four abreast, Agelmar at its head hidden in the forest before its tail left Fal Dara keep. There were no cheers in the streets to speed them on their way, only their own drums and their pennants' cracking in the wind, but their eyes looked toward the rising sun with purpose. Eastward they would join other steel serpents, from Fal Moran, behind King Easar himself with his sons at his side, and from Ankor Dail, that held the Eastern Marches and guarded the Spine of the World; from Mos Shirare and Fal Sion and Camron Caan, and all the other fortresses in Shienar, great and small. Joined into a greater serpent, they would turn north to Tarwin's Gap.

Another exodus had begun at the same time, using the King's Gate that led out on the way to Fal Moran. Carts and wagons, people mounted and people afoot, driving their livestock, carrying children on their backs, faces as long as the morning shadows. Reluctance to leave their homes, perhaps forever, slowed their feet, yet fear of what was coming spurred them, so that they went in bursts, feet dragging, then breaking into a run for a dozen paces only to fall back, once more, to shuffling through the dust. A few paused outside the town to watch the soldiers' armored line winding into the forest. Hope blossomed in some eyes, and prayers were muttered, prayers for the soldiers, prayers for themselves, before they turned south again, trudging.

The smallest column went out of the Malkier Gate. Left behind were a few who would remain, soldiers and a sprinkling of older men, their wives dead and their grown children making the slow way south. A last handful so that whatever happened in Tarwin's Gap, Fal Dara would not fall undefended. Ingtar's Gray Owl led the way, but it was Moiraine who took them north. The most important column of all, and the most desperate.

For at least an hour after they passed the borderpost there was no change in land or forest. The Warder kept them at a hard pace, as fast a walk as the horses could maintain, but Rand kept wondering when they would reach the Blight. The hills became a little higher, but the trees, and the creepers, and the underbrush were no different than what he had seen in Shienar, gray and all but leafless. He began to feel warmer, warm enough to sling his cloak across the pommel of his saddle.

"This is the best weather we've seen all year," Egwene said, shrugging out of her own cloak.

Nynaeve shook her head, frowning as if listening to the wind. "It feels wrong."

Rand nodded. He could feel it, too, though he could not say what it was exactly he was feeling. The wrongness went beyond the first warmth he could remember out of doors this year; it was more than the simple fact that it should not be so warm this far north. It must be the Blight, but the land was the same.

The sun climbed high, a red ball that could not give so much warmth despite the cloudless sky. A little while later he unbuttoned his coat. Sweat trickled down his face.

He was not the only one. Mat took his coat off, openly displaying the gold-and-ruby dagger, and wiped his face with the end of his scarf. Blinking, he rewound the scarf into a narrow band low over his eyes. Nynaeve and Egwene fanned themselves; they rode slumped as if they were wilting. Loial undid his high-collared tunic all the way down, and his shirt as well; the Ogier had a narrow strip of hair up the middle of his chest, as thick as fur. He muttered apologies all around.

"You must forgive me. Stedding Shangtai is in the mountains, and cool." His broad nostrils flared, drawing in air that was becoming warmer by the minute. "I don't like this heat, and damp."

It *was* damp, Rand realized. It felt like the Mire in the depths of summer, back in the Two Rivers. In that boggy swamp every breath came as if through a wool blanket soaked in hot water. There was no soggy ground here—only a few ponds and streams, trickles to someone used to the Waterwood—but the air was like that in the Mire. Only Perrin, still in his coat, was breathing easily. Perrin and the Warder.

There were a few leaves now, on trees that were not evergreen. Rand reached out to touch a branch, and stopped with his hand short of the leaves. Sickly yellow mottled the red of the new growth, and black flecks like disease.

"I told you not to touch anything." The Warder's voice was flat. He still wore his shifting cloak, as if heat made no more impression on him than cold; it almost made his angular face seem to float unsupported above Mandarb's back. "Flowers can kill in the Blight, and leaves maim. There's a little thing called a Stick that likes to hide where the leaves are thickest, looking like its name, waiting for something to touch it. When something does, it bites. Not poison. The juice begins to digest the Stick's prey for it. The only thing that can save you is to cut off the arm or leg that was bitten. But a Stick won't bite unless you touch it. Other things in the Blight will."

Rand jerked his hand back, leaves untouched, and wiped it on his pants leg.

"Then we're in the Blight?" Perrin said. Strangely, he did not sound frightened.

"Just the fringe," Lan said grimly. His stallion kept moving forward, and he spoke over his shoulder. "The real Blight still lies ahead. There are things in the Blight that hunt by sound, and some may have wandered this far south. Sometimes they cross the Mountains of Dhoom. Much worse than Sticks. Keep quiet and keep up, if you want to stay alive." He continued to set a hard pace, not waiting for an answer.

Mile by mile the corruption of the Blight became more apparent. Leaves covered the trees in ever greater profusion, but stained and spotted with yellow and black, with livid red streaks like blood poisoning. Every leaf and creeper seemed bloated, ready to burst at a touch. Flowers hung on trees and weeds in a parody of spring, sickly pale and pulpy, waxen things that appeared to be rotting while Rand watched. When he breathed through his nose, the sweet stench of decay, heavy and thick, sickened him; when he tried breathing through his mouth, he almost gagged. The air tasted like a mouthful of spoiled meat. The horses' hooves made a soft squishing as rotten-ripe things broke open under them.

Mat leaned out of his saddle and spewed until his stomach was empty. Rand sought the void, but calmness was little help against the burning bile that kept creeping up his throat. Empty or not, Mat heaved again a mile later, bringing up nothing, and yet again after that. Egwene looked as if she wanted to be sick, too, swallowing constantly, and Nynaeve's face was a white mask of determination, her jaw set and her eyes fixed on Moiraine's back. The Wisdom would not admit to feeling ill unless the Aes Sedai did, first, but Rand did not think she would have to wait long. Moiraine's eyes were tight, and her lips pale.

Despite the heat and damp, Loial wrapped a scarf around his nose and mouth. When he met Rand's gaze, the Ogier's outrage and disgust were plain in his eyes. "I had heard—" he began, his voice muffled by the wool, then stopped to clear his throat with a grimace. "Faugh! It tastes like. . . . Faugh! I had heard and read about the Blight, but nothing could describe. . . ." His gesture somehow took in the smell as well as the eye-sickening growth. "That even the Dark One should do this to trees! Faugh!"

The Warder was not affected, of course, at least not that Rand could see, but to his surprise neither was Perrin. Or rather, not in the way the rest of them were. The big youth glared at the obscene forest through which they rode as he might have at an enemy, or the banner of an enemy. He caressed the axe at his belt as if unaware of what he was doing, and muttered to himself, half growling in a way that made the hair on Rand's neck stir. Even in full sunlight his eyes glowed, golden and fierce.

The heat did not abate as the bloody sun fell toward the horizon. In the distance to the north, mountains rose, higher than the Mountains of Mist, black against the sky. Sometimes an icy wind from the sharp peaks gusted far enough to reach them. The torrid humidity leached away most of the mountain chill, but what remained was winter-cold compared to the swelter it replaced, if just for a moment. The sweat on Rand's face seemed to flash into beads of ice; as the wind died, the beads melted again, running angry lines down his cheeks, and the thick heat returned harder than before by comparison. For the instant the wind surrounded them, it swept away the fetor, yet he would have done without that, too, if he could have. The cold was the chill of the grave, and it carried the dusty must of an old tomb newly opened.

"We cannot reach the mountains by nightfall," Lan said, "and it is dangerous to move at night, even for a Warder alone."

"There is a place not far off," Moiraine said. "It will be a good omen for us to camp there."

The Warder gave her a flat look, then nodded reluctantly. "Yes. We must camp somewhere. It might as well be there."

"The Eye of the World was beyond the high passes when I found it," Moiraine said. "Better to cross the Mountains of Dhoom in full daylight, at noon, when the Dark One's powers in this world are weakest."

"You talk as if the Eye isn't always in the same place." Egwene spoke to the Aes Sedai, but it was Loial who answered.

"No two among the Ogier have found it in exactly the same place. The Green Man seems to be found where he is needed. But it has always been beyond the high passes. They are treacherous, the high passes, and haunted by creatures of the Dark One."

"We must reach the passes before we need worry about them," Lan said. "Tomorrow we will be truly into the Blight."

Rand looked at the forest around him, every leaf and

flower diseased, every creeper decaying as it grew, and he could not repress a shudder. *If this isn't truly the Blight, what is?*

Lan turned them westward, at an angle to the sinking sun. The Warder maintained the pace he had set before, but there was reluctance in the set of his shoulders.

The sun was a sullen red ball just touching the treetops when they crested a hill and the Warder drew rein. Beyond them to the west lay a network of lakes, the waters glittering darkly in the slanting sunlight, like beads of random size on a necklace of many strings. In the distance, circled by the lakes, stood jagged-topped hills, thick in the creeping shadows of evening. For one brief instant the sun's rays caught the shattered tops, and Rand's breath stilled. Not hills. The broken remnants of seven towers. He was not sure if anyone else had seen it; the sight was gone as quickly as it came. The Warder was dismounting, his face as lacking in emotion as a stone.

"Couldn't we camp down by the lakes?" Nynaeve asked, patting her face with her kerchief. "It must be cooler down by the water."

"Light," Mat said, "I'd just like to stick my head in one of them. I might never take it out."

Just then something roiled the waters of the nearest lake, the dark water phosphorescing as a huge body rolled beneath the surface. Length on man-thick length sent ripples spreading, rolling on and on until at last a tail rose, waving a point like a wasp's stinger for an instant in the twilight, at least five spans into the air. All along that length fat tentacles writhed like monstrous worms, as many as a centipede's legs. It slid slowly beneath the surface and was gone, only the fading ripples to say it had ever been.

Rand closed his mouth and exchanged a look with Perrin. Perrin's yellow eyes were as disbelieving as he knew his own must be. Nothing that big could live in a lake that size. *Those couldn't have been* hands *on those tentacles. They couldn't have been.*

"On second thought," Mat said faintly, "I like it right here just fine."

"I will set guarding wards around this hill," Moiraine said. She had already dismounted from Aldieb. "A true barrier would draw the attention we do not want like flies to honey, but if any creation of the Dark One or anything that serves the Shadow comes within a mile of us, I will know."

"I'd be happier with the barrier," Mat said as his boots touched the ground, "just as long as it kept that, that . . . thing on the other side."

"Oh, do be quiet, Mat," Egwene said curtly, at the same time as Nynaeve spoke. "And have them waiting for us when we leave in the morning? You *are* a fool, Matrim Cauthon." Mat glowered at the two women as they climbed down, but he kept his mouth shut.

As he took Bela's reins, Rand shared a grin with Perrin. For a moment it was almost like being home, having Mat saying what he should not at the worst possible time. Then the smile faded from Perrin's face; in the twilight his eyes *did* glow, as if they had a yellow light behind them. Rand's grin slipped away, too. *It isn't like home at all.*

Rand and Mat and Perrin helped Lan unsaddle and hobble the horses while the others began setting up the camp. Loial muttered to himself as he set up the Warder's tiny stove, but his thick fingers moved deftly. Egwene was humming as she filled the tea kettle from a bulging waterbag. Rand no longer wondered why the Warder had insisted on bringing so many full waterskins.

Setting the bay's saddle in line with the others, he unfastened his saddlebags and blanketroll from the cantle, turned, and stopped with a tingle of fear. The Ogier and the women were gone. So was the stove and all the wicker panniers from the packhorse. The hilltop was empty except for evening shadows.

With a numb hand he fumbled for his sword, dimly hearing Mat curse. Perrin had his axe out, his shaggy head swiveling to find the danger.

"Sheepherders," Lan muttered. Unconcernedly the Warder strode across the hilltop, and at his third step, he vanished.

Rand exchanged wide-eyed looks with Mat and Perrin, and then they were all darting for where the Warder had disappeared. Abruptly Rand skidded to a halt, taking another step when Mat ran into his back. Egwene looked up from setting the kettle atop the tiny stove. Nynaeve was closing the mantle on a second lit lantern. They were all there, Moiraine sitting cross-legged, Lan lounging on an elbow, Loial taking a book out of his pack.

Cautiously Rand looked behind him. The hillside was there as it had been, the shadowed trees, the lakes beyond sinking into darkness. He was afraid to step back, afraid they would all disappear again and perhaps this time he would not be able to find them. Edging carefully around him, Perrin let out a long breath.

Moiraine noticed the three of them standing there, gaping. Perrin looked abashed, and slipped his axe back into the heavy belt loop as if he thought no one might notice. A smile touched her lips. "It is a simple thing," she said, "a bending, so any eye looking at us sees around us, instead. We cannot have the eyes that will be out there seeing our lights tonight, and the Blight is no place to be in the dark."

"Moiraine Sedai says I might be able to do it." Egwene's eyes were bright. "She says I can handle enough of the One Power right now."

"Not without training, child," Moiraine cautioned. "The simplest matter concerning the One Power can be dangerous to the untrained, and to those around them." Perrin snorted, and Egwene looked so uncomfortable that Rand wondered if she had already been trying her abilities.

Nynaeve set down the lantern. Together with the tiny flame of the stove, the pair of lanterns gave a generous light. "When you go to Tar Valon, Egwene," she said carefully, "perhaps I'll go with you." The look she gave Moiraine was strangely defensive. "It will do her good to see a familiar face among strangers. She'll need someone to advise her besides Aes Sedai."

"Perhaps that would be for the best, Wisdom," Moiraine said simply.

Egwene laughed and clapped her hands. "Oh, that *will* be wonderful. And you, Rand. You'll come, too, won't you?" He paused in the act of sitting across the stove from her, then slowly lowered himself. He thought her eyes had never been bigger, or brighter, or more like pools that he could lose himself in. Spots of color appeared in her cheeks, and she gave a smaller laugh. "Perrin, Mat, you two will come, won't you? We'll all be together." Mat gave a grunt that could have signified anything, and Perrin only shrugged, but she took it for assent. "You see, Rand. We'll all be together."

Light, but a man could drown in those eyes and be happy

doing it. Embarrassed, he cleared his throat. "Do they have sheep in Tar Valon? That's all I know, herding sheep and growing tabac."

"I believe," Moiraine said, "that I can find something for you to do in Tar Valon. For all of you. Not herding sheep, perhaps, but something you will find interesting."

"There," Egwene said as if it were settled. "I know. I will make you my Warder, when I'm an Aes Sedai. You would like being a Warder, wouldn't you? My Warder?" She sounded sure, but he saw the question in her eyes. She wanted an answer, needed it.

"I'd like being your Warder," he said. *She's not for you, nor you for her. Why did Min have to tell me that?*

Darkness came down heavily, and everyone was tired. Loial was the first to roll over and ready himself for sleep, but others followed soon after. No one used their blankets, except for a pillow. Moiraine had put something in the oil of the lamps that dispelled the stench of the Blight from the hilltop, but nothing diminished the heat. The moon gave a wavering, watery light, but the sun might have been at its zenith for all the cool the night had.

Rand found sleep impossible, even with the Aes Sedai stretched out not a span away to shield his dreams. It was the thick air that kept him awake. Loial's soft snores were a rumble that made Perrin's seem nonexistent, but they did not stop weariness from claiming the others. The Warder was still awake, seated not far from him with his sword across his knees, watching the night. To Rand's surprise, so was Nynaeve.

The Wisdom looked at Lan silently for a long time, then poured a cup of tea and brought it to him. When he reached out with a murmur of thanks, she did not let go right away. "I should have known you would be a king," she said quietly. Her eyes were steady on the Warder's face, but her voice trembled slightly.

Lan looked back at her just as intently. It seemed to Rand that the Warder's face actually softened. "I am not a king, Nynaeve. Just a man. A man without as much to his name as even the meanest farmer's croft."

Nynaeve's voice steadied. "Some women don't ask for land, or gold. Just the man."

"And the man who would ask her to accept so little would

not be worthy of her. You are a remarkable woman, as beautiful as the sunrise, as fierce as a warrior. You are a lioness, Wisdom."

"A Wisdom seldom weds." She paused to take a deep breath, as if steeling herself. "But if I go to Tar Valon, it may be that I will be something other than a Wisdom."

"Aes Sedai marry as seldom as Wisdoms. Few men can live with so much power in a wife, dimming them by her radiance whether she wishes to or not."

"Some men are strong enough. I know one such." If there could have been any doubt, her look left none as to whom she meant.

"All I have is a sword, and a war I cannot win, but can never stop fighting."

"I've told you I care nothing for that. Light, you've made me say more than is proper already. Will you shame me to the point of asking you?"

"I will never shame you." The gentle tone, like a caress, sounded odd to Rand's ears in the Warder's voice, but it made Nynaeve's eyes brighten. "I will hate the man you choose because he is not me, and love him if he makes you smile. No woman deserves the sure knowledge of widow's black as her brideprice, you least of all." He set the untouched cup on the ground and rose. "I must check the horses."

Nynaeve remained there, kneeling, after he had gone.

Sleep or no, Rand closed his eyes. He did not think the Wisdom would like it if he watched her cry.

CHAPTER
49

The Dark One Stirs

D awn woke Rand with a start, the sullen sun pricking his eyelids as it peeked reluctantly over the treetops of the Blight. Even so early, heat covered the spoiled lands in a heavy blanket. He lay on his back with his head pillowed on his blanketroll, staring at the sky. It was still blue, the sky. Even here, that, at least, was untouched.

He was surprised to realize that he had slept. For a minute the dim memory of a conversation overheard seemed like part of some dream. Then he saw Nynaeve's red-rimmed eyes; she had not slept, obviously. Lan's face was harder than ever, as if he had resumed a mask and did not intend to let it slip again.

Egwene went over and crouched beside the Wisdom, her face concerned. He could not make out what they said. Egwene spoke, and Nynaeve shook her head. Egwene said something else, and the Wisdom waved her away dismissively. Instead of going, Egwene bent her head closer, and for a few minutes the two women talked even more softly, with Nynaeve still shaking her head. The Wisdom ended it with a laugh, hugging Egwene and, by her expression, making soothing talk. When Egwene stood, though, she glared at the Warder. Lan did not seem to notice; he did not look in Nynaeve's direction at all.

Shaking his head, Rand gathered his things, and gave his hands and face and teeth a hasty wash with the little water Lan allowed for such things. He wondered if women had a way of reading men's minds. It was an unsettling thought. *All women are Aes Sedai.* Telling himself he was letting the

Blight get to him, he rinsed out his mouth and hurried to get the bay saddled.

It was more than a little disconcerting, having the campsite disappear before he reached the horses, but by the time his saddle girth was tight everything on the hill winked back into view. Everyone was hurrying.

The seven towers stood plain in the morning light, distant broken stumps, like huge, rough hills that merely hinted at grandeur gone. The hundred lakes were a smooth, unruffled blue. Nothing broke the surface this morning. When he looked at the lakes and the ruined towers, he could almost ignore the sickly things growing around the hill. Lan did not seem to be avoiding looking at the towers, any more than he seemed to be avoiding Nynaeve, but somehow he never did as he concentrated on getting them ready to go.

After the wicker panniers were fastened on the packhorse, after every scrap and smudge and track were gone and everyone else was mounted, the Aes Sedai stood in the middle of the hilltop with her eyes closed, not even seeming to breathe. Nothing happened that Rand could see, except that Nynaeve and Egwene shivered despite the heat and rubbed their arms briskly. Egwene's hands suddenly froze on her arms, and she opened her mouth, staring at the Wisdom. Before she could speak, Nynaeve also ceased her rubbing and gave her a sharp look. The two women looked at one another, then Egwene nodded and grinned, and after a moment Nynaeve did, too, though her smile was only half-hearted.

Rand scrubbed his fingers through his hair, already more damp with sweat than with the water he had splashed in his face. He was sure there was something in the silent exchange that he should understand, but that feather-light brush across his mind vanished before he could grasp it.

"What are we waiting for?" Mat demanded, the low band of his scarf across his forehead. He had his bow across the pommel of his saddle with an arrow nocked, and his quiver pulled around on his belt for an easy reach.

Moiraine opened her eyes and started down the hill. "For me to remove the last vestige of what I did here last night. The residues would have dissipated on their own in a day, but I will not take any risk I can avoid now. We are too close, and the Shadow is too strong here. Lan?"

The Warder only waited for her to settle in Aldieb's saddle before he led them north, toward the Mountains of Dhoom, looming in the near distance. Even under the sunrise the peaks rose black and lifeless, like jagged teeth. In a wall they stretched, east and west as far as the eye could see.

"Will we reach the Eye today, Moiraine Sedai?" Egwene asked.

The Aes Sedai gave Loial a sidelong look. "I hope that we will. When I found it before, it was just the other side of the mountains, at the foot of the high passes."

"He says it moves," Mat said, nodding at Loial. "What if it isn't where you expect?"

"Then we will continue to hunt until we do find it. The Green Man senses need, and there can be no need greater than ours. Our need is the hope of the world."

As the mountains drew closer, so did the true Blight. Where a leaf had been spotted black and mottled yellow before, now foliage fell wetly while he watched, breaking apart from the weight of its own corruption. The trees themselves were tortured, crippled things, twisted branches clawing at the sky as if begging mercy from some power that refused to hear. Ooze slid like pus from bark cracked and split. As if nothing truly solid was left to them, the trees seemed to tremble from the passage of the horses over the ground.

"Look as if they want to grab us," Mat said nervously. Nynaeve gave him an exasperated, scornful look, and he added fiercely, "Well, they do look it."

"And some of them do want it," the Aes Sedai said. Her eyes over her shoulder were harder than Lan's for an instant. "But they want no part of what I am, and my presence protects you."

Mat laughed uneasily, as if he thought it a joke on her part.

Rand was not so sure. This *was* the Blight, after all. *But trees don't move. Why would a tree grab a man, even if it could? We're imagining things, and she's just trying to keep us alert.*

Abruptly he stared off to his left, into the forest. That tree, not twenty paces away, *had* trembled, and it was none of his imagination. He could not say what kind it was, or had been, so gnarled and tormented was its shape. As he watched, the tree suddenly whipped back and forth again, then bent down, flailing at the ground. Something screamed, shrill and piercing. The tree sprang back straight; its limbs entwined around a dark mass that writhed and spat and screamed.

He swallowed hard and tried to edge Red away, but trees stood on every side, and trembled. The bay rolled his eyes, whites showing all the way around. Rand found himself in a solid knot of horseflesh as everyone else tried to do the same as he.

"Keep moving," Lan commanded, drawing his sword. The Warder wore steel-backed gauntlets now, and his gray-green scale tunic. "Stay with Moiraine Sedai." He pulled Mandarb around, not toward the tree and its prey, but in the other direction. With his color-shifting cloak, he was swallowed by the Blight before the black stallion was out of sight.

"Close," Moiraine urged. She did not slow her white mare, but she motioned the others to huddle nearer to her. "Stay as close as you can."

A roar sprang up from the direction the Warder had gone. It beat at the air, and the trees quivered from it, and when it faded away, it seemed to echo still. Again the roar came, filled with rage and death.

"Lan," Nynaeve said. "He—"

The awful sound cut her off, but there was a new note in it. Fear. Abruptly it was gone.

"Lan can look after himself," Moiraine said. "Ride, Wisdom."

From out of the trees the Warder appeared, holding his sword well clear of himself and his mount. Black blood stained the blade, and steam rose from it. Carefully, Lan wiped the blade clean with a cloth he took from his saddle-bags, examining the steel to make sure he had gotten every spot. When he dropped the cloth, it fell apart before it reached the ground, even the fragments dissolving.

Silently a massive body leaped out of the trees at them. The Warder spun Mandarb, but even as the warhorse reared, ready to strike with steel-shod hooves, Mat's arrow flashed, piercing the one eye in a head that seemed mostly mouth and teeth. Kicking and screaming, the thing fell, one bound short of them. Rand stared as they hurried past. Stiff hair like long bristles covered it, and it had too many legs, joining a body as big as a bear at odd angles. Some of them at least, those coming out of its back, had to be useless for walking, but the finger-long claws at their ends tore the earth in its death agony.

"Good shooting, sheepherder." Lan's eyes had already forgotten what was dying behind them, and were searching the forest.

Moiraine shook her head. "It should not have been willing to come so close to one who touches the True Source."

"Agelmar said the Blight stirs," Lan said. "Perhaps the Blight also knows a Web is forming in the Pattern."

"Hurry." Moiraine dug her heels into Aldieb's flanks. "We must get over the high passes quickly."

But even as she spoke the Blight rose against them. Trees whipped in, reaching for them, not caring if Moiraine touched the True Source or not.

Rand's sword was in his hand; he did not remember unsheathing it. He struck out again and again, the heron-mark blade slicing through corrupted limbs. Hungry branches jerked back severed, writhing stumps—he almost thought he heard them scream—but always more came, wriggling like snakes, attempting to snare his arms, his waist, his neck. Teeth bared in a rictus snarl, he sought the void, and found it in the stony, stubborn soil of the Two Rivers. "Manetheren!" He screamed back at the trees till his throat ached. The heron-mark steel flashed in the strengthless sunlight. "Manetheren! Manetheren!"

Standing in his stirrups, Mat sent arrow after arrow flashing into the forest, striking at deformed shapes that snarled and gnashed uncounted teeth on the shafts that killed them, bit at the clawed forms fighting to get over them, to reach the mounted figures. Mat, too, was lost to the present. *"Carai an Caldazar!"* he shouted as he drew fletchings to cheek and loosed. *"Carai an Ellisande! Al Ellisande! Mordero daghain pas duente cuebiyar! Al Ellisande!"*

Perrin also stood in his stirrups, silent and grim. He had taken the lead, and his axe hewed a path through forest and foul flesh alike, whichever came before him. Flailing trees and howling things shied from the stocky axeman, shying as much from the fierce golden eyes as from the whistling axe. He forced his horse forward, step by determined step.

Fireballs streaked from Moiraine's hands, and where they struck, a writhing tree became a torch, a toothed shape shrieked and beat with human hands, rent its own flaming flesh with fierce claws until it died.

Again and again the Warder took Mandarb into the trees, his blade and gauntlets dripping with blood that bubbled and steamed. When he came back now, more often than not there were gashes in his armor, bleeding gashes in his flesh, and his warhorse stumbled and bled, too. Each time the Aes Sedai paused to lay her hands on the wounds, and when she took them away, only the blood was left on unmarked flesh.

"I light signal fires for the Halfmen," she said bitterly. "Press on. Press on!" They made their way one slow pace at a time.

If the trees had not struck into the mass of attacking flesh as much as at the humans, if the creatures, no two alike, had not fought the trees and one another as much as to reach them, Rand was sure they would have been overwhelmed. He was not certain it would not happen still. Then a fluting cry arose behind them. Distant and thin, it cut through the snarling from the denizens of the Blight around them.

In an instant the snarling ceased, as if it had been sliced off with a knife. The attacking shapes froze; the trees went still. As suddenly as the things with legs had appeared, they melted away, vanishing into the twisted forest.

The reedy shrill came again, like a cracked shepherd's pipes, and was answered in kind by a chorus. Half a dozen, singing among themselves, far behind.

"Worms," Lan said grimly, bringing a moan from Loial. "They've given us a respite, if we have time to use it." His eyes were measuring the distance yet to the mountains. "Few things in the Blight will face a Worm, can it be avoided." He dug his heels into Mandarb's flanks. "Ride!" The whole party plunged after him, through a Blight that suddenly seemed truly dead, except for the piping behind.

"They were scared off by worms?" Mat said incredulously. He was bouncing in his saddle, trying to sling his bow across his back.

"A Worm"—there was a sharp difference in the way the Warder said it from the way Mat had—"can kill a Fade, if the Fade hasn't the Dark One's own luck with it. We have an entire pack on our trail. Ride! Ride!" The dark peaks

were closer now. An hour, Rand estimated, at the pace the
Warder was setting.

"Won't the Worms follow us into the mountains?" Egwene
asked breathlessly, and Lan gave a sharp laugh.

"They won't. Worms are afraid of what lives in the high
passes." Loial moaned again.

Rand wished the Ogier would stop doing that. He was
well aware that Loial knew more about the Blight than any
of them except Lan, even if it was from reading books in
the safety of a *stedding*. *But why does he have to keep reminding me that there's worse yet than we've seen?*

The Blight flowed past, weeds and grasses splashing
rotten under galloping hooves. Trees of the kinds that had
earlier attacked did not so much as twitch even when they
rode directly under the twisted branches. The Mountains of
Dhoom filled the sky ahead, black and bleak, and almost
near enough to touch, it seemed. The piping came both sharp
and clear, and there were squishing sounds behind them,
louder than the things crushed under hooves. Too loud, as if
half-decayed trees were being crushed by huge bodies slith-
ering over them. Too near. Rand looked over his shoulder.
Back there treetops whipped and went down like grass. The
land began sloping upward, toward the mountains, tilting
enough so that he knew they were climbing.

"We are not going to make it," Lan announced. He did
not slow Mandarb's gallop, but his sword was suddenly in
his hand again. "Watch yourself in the high passes, Moiraine, and you'll get through."

"No, Lan!" Nynaeve called.

"Be quiet, girl! Lan, even you cannot stop a Wormpack. I
will not have it. I will need you for the Eye."

"Arrows," Mat called breathlessly.

"The Worms wouldn't even feel them," the Warder
shouted. "They must be cut to pieces. Don't feel much but
hunger. Sometimes fear."

Clinging to his saddle with a deathgrip, Rand shrugged,
trying to loosen the tightness in his shoulders. His whole
chest felt tight, until he could hardly breathe, and his skin
stung in hot pinpricks. The Blight had turned to foothills.
He could see the route they must climb once they reached
the mountains, the twisting path and the high pass beyond,
like an axe blow cleaving into the black stone. *Light, what's*

*up ahead that can scare what's behind? Light help me, I've
never been so afraid. I don't want to go any further. No further!* Seeking the flame and the void, he railed at himself.
*Fool! You frightened, cowardly fool! You can't stay here,
and you can't go back. Are you going to leave Egwene to
face it alone?* The void eluded him, forming, then shivering
into a thousand points of light, re-forming and shattering
again, each point burning into his bones until he quivered
with the pain and thought he must burst open. *Light help
me, I can't go on. Light help me!*

He was gathering the bay's reins to turn back, to face the
Worms or anything rather than what lay ahead, when the
nature of the land changed. Between one slope of a hill and
the next, between crest and peak, the Blight was gone.

Green leaves covered peacefully spreading branches.
Wildflowers made a carpet of bright patches in grasses
stirred by a sweet spring breeze. Butterflies fluttered from
blossom to blossom, with buzzing bees, and birds trilled
their songs.

Gaping, he galloped on, until he suddenly realized that
Moiraine and Lan and Loial had stopped, the others, too.
Slowly he drew rein, his face frozen in astonishment.
Egwene's eyes were about to come out of her head, and
Nynaeve's jaw had dropped.

"We have reached safety," Moiraine said. "This is the
Green Man's place, and the Eye of the World is here. Nothing of the Blight can enter here."

"I thought it was on the other side of the mountains,"
Rand mumbled. He could still see the peaks filling the
northern horizon, and the high passes. "You said it was always beyond the passes."

"This place," said a deep voice from the trees, "is always
where it is. All that changes is where those who need it are."

A figure stepped out of the foliage, a man-shape as much
bigger than Loial as the Ogier was bigger than Rand. A
man-shape of woven vines and leaves, green and growing. His hair was grass, flowing to his shoulders; his eyes,
huge hazelnuts; his fingernails, acorns. Green leaves made
his tunic and trousers; seamless bark, his boots. Butterflies
swirled around him, lighting on his fingers, his shoulders,
his face. Only one thing spoiled the verdant perfection. A

deep fissure ran up his cheek and temple across the top of his head, and in that the vines were brown and withered.

"The Green Man," Egwene whispered, and the scarred face smiled. For a moment it seemed as if the birds sang louder.

"Of course I am. Who else would be here?" The hazelnut eyes regarded Loial. "It is good to see you, little brother. In the past, many of you came to visit me, but few of recent days."

Loial scrambled down from his big horse and bowed formally. "You honor me, Treebrother. *Tsingu ma choshih, T'ingshen.*"

Smiling, the Green Man put an arm around the Ogier's shoulders. Alongside Loial, he looked like a man beside a boy. "There is no honoring, little brother. We will sing Tree Songs together, and remember the Great Trees, and the *stedding,* and hold the Longing at bay." He studied the others, just now getting down from their horses, and his eyes lit on Perrin. "A Wolfbrother! Do the old times truly walk again then?"

Rand stared at Perrin. For his part, Perrin turned his horse so it was between him and the Green Man, and bent to check the girth. Rand was sure he just wanted to avoid the Green Man's searching gaze. Suddenly the Green Man spoke to Rand.

"Strange clothes you wear, Child of the Dragon. Has the Wheel turned so far? Do the People of the Dragon return to the first Covenant? But you wear a sword. That is neither now nor then."

Rand had to work moisture in his mouth before he could speak. "I don't know what you're talking about. What do you mean?"

The Green Man touched the brown scar across his head. For a moment he seemed confused. "I . . . cannot say. My memories are torn and often fleeting, and much of what remains is like leaves visited by caterpillars. Yet, I am sure. . . . No, it is gone. But you are welcome here. You, Moiraine Sedai, are more than a surprise. When this place was made, it was made so that none could find it twice. How have you come here?"

"Need," Moiraine replied. "My need, the world's need.

Most of all is the world's need. We have come to see the Eye of the World."

The Green Man sighed, the wind sighing through thick-leafed branches. "Then it has come again. That memory remains whole. The Dark One stirs. I have feared it. Every turning of years, the Blight strives harder to come inside, and this turn the struggle to keep it out has been greater than ever since the beginning. Come, I will take you."

CHAPTER
50

Meetings at the Eye

Leading the bay, Rand followed the Green Man with the other Emond's Fielders, all staring as if they could not decide whether to look at the Green Man or the forest. The Green Man was a legend, of course, with stories told about him, and the Tree of Life, in front of every fireplace in the Two Rivers, and not just for the children. But after the Blight, the trees and flowers would have been a wonder of normality even if the rest of the world was not still trapped in winter.

Perrin hung a little to the rear. When Rand glanced back, the big, curly-haired youth looked as if he did not want to hear anything else the Green Man had to say. He could understand that. *Child of the Dragon.* Warily he watched the Green Man, walking ahead with Moiraine and Lan, butterflies surrounding him in a cloud of yellows and reds. *What did he mean? No. I don't want to know.*

Even so, his step felt lighter, his legs springier. The uneasiness still lay in his gut, churning his stomach, but the fear had become so diffuse it might as well be gone. He did not think he could expect more, not with the Blight half a mile away, even if Moiraine was right about nothing from the Blight being able to enter here. The thousands of burning points piercing his bones had winked out; at the very moment he came within the Green Man's domain, he was sure. *It's him that winked them out,* he thought, *the Green Man, and this place.*

Egwene felt it, and Nynaeve, too, the soothing peace, the calm of beauty. He could tell. They wore small, serene smiles, and brushed flowers with their fingers, pausing to smell, and breathing deep.

When the Green Man noticed, he said, "Flowers are meant to adorn. The plants or humans, it is much the same. None mind, so long as you don't take too many." And he began plucking one from this plant and one from that, never more than two from any. Soon Nynaeve and Egwene wore caps of blossoms in their hair, pink wildrose and yellowbell and white morningstar. The Wisdom's braid seemed a garden of pink and white to her waist. Even Moiraine received a pale garland of morningstar on her brow, woven so deftly that the flowers still seemed to be growing.

Rand was not sure they were not growing. The Green Man tended his forest garden as he walked, while he talked softly to Moiraine, taking care of whatever needed care without really thinking about it. His hazelnut eyes caught a crooked limb on a climbing wildrose, forced into an awkward angle by the blossom-covered limb of an apple tree, and he paused, still talking, to run his hand along the bend. Rand was not sure if his eyes were playing tricks, or if thorns actually did bend out of the way so as not to prick those green fingers. When the towering shape of the Green Man moved on, the limb ran straight and true, spreading red petals among the white of apple blossoms. He bent to cup one huge hand around a tiny seed lying on a patch of pebbles, and when he straightened, a small shoot had roots through the rocks to good soil.

"All things must grow where they are, according to the Pattern," he explained over his shoulder, as if apologizing, "and face the turning of the Wheel, but the Creator will not mind if I give just a little help."

Rand led Red around the shoot, careful not to let the bay's hooves crush it. It did not seem right to destroy what the Green Man had done just to avoid an extra step. Egwene smiled at him, one of her secret smiles, and touched his arm. She was so pretty, with her unbound hair full of flowers, that he smiled back at her until she blushed and lowered her eyes. *I will protect you,* he thought. *Whatever else happens, I will see you safe, I swear it.*

Into the heart of the spring forest the Green Man took them, to an arched opening in the side of a hill. It was a simple stone arch, tall and white, and on the keystone was a circle halved by a sinuous line, one half rough, the other smooth. The ancient symbol of Aes Sedai. The opening itself was shadowed.

For a moment everyone simply looked in silence. Then Moiraine removed the garland from her hair and gently hung it on the limb of a sweetberry bush beside the arch. It was as if her movement restored speech.

"It's in there?" Nynaeve asked. "What we've come for?"

"I'd really like to see the Tree of Life," Mat said, not taking his eyes off the halved circle above them. "We can wait that long, can't we?"

The Green Man gave Rand an odd look, then shook his head. "*Avendesora* is not here. I have not rested beneath its ungentle branches in two thousand years."

"The Tree of Life is not why we came," Moiraine said firmly. She gestured to the arch. "In there, is."

"I will not go in with you," the Green Man said. The butterflies around him swirled as if they shared some agitation. "I was set to guard it long, long ago, but it makes me uneasy to come too close. I feel myself being unmade; my end is linked with it, somehow. I remember the making of it. Some of the making. Some." His hazelnut eyes stared, lost in memory, and he fingered his scar. "It was the first days of the Breaking of the World, when the joy of victory over the Dark One turned bitter with the knowledge that all might yet be shattered by the weight of the Shadow. A hundred of them made it, men and women together. The greatest Aes Sedai works were always done so, joining *saidin* and *saidar,* as the True Source is joined. They died, all, to make it pure, while the world was torn around them. Knowing they would die, they charged me to guard it against the need to come. It was not what I was made for, but all was breaking apart, and they were alone, and I was all they had. It was not what I was made for, but I have kept the faith." He looked down at Moiraine, nodding to himself. "I have kept faith, until it was needed. And now it ends."

"You have kept the faith better than most of us who gave you the charge," the Aes Sedai said. "Perhaps it will not come as badly as you fear."

The scarred, leafy head shook slowly from side to side. "I know an ending when it comes, Aes Sedai. I will find another place to make things grow." Nutbrown eyes swept sadly over the green forest. "Another place, perhaps. When you come out, I will see you again, if there is time." With that he strode away, trailing butterflies, becoming one with the forest more completely than Lan's cloak ever could.

"What did he mean?" Mat demanded. "If there's time?"

"Come," Moiraine said. And she stepped through the arch. Lan went at her heels.

Rand was not sure what he expected when he followed. The hair stirred uneasily on his arms, and rose on the back of his neck. But it was only a corridor, its polished walls rounded overhead like the arch, winding gently downward. There was headroom enough and to spare for Loial; there would have been room enough for the Green Man. The smooth floor, slick to the eye like oiled slate, yet somehow gave a sure footing. Seamless, white walls glittered with uncounted flecks in untold colors, giving a low, soft light even after the sunlit archway vanished around a curve behind. He was sure the light was no natural thing, but he sensed it was benign, too. *Then why is your skin still crawling?* Down they went, and down.

"There," Moiraine said at last, pointing. "Ahead."

And the corridor opened into a vast, domed space, the rough, living rock of its ceiling dotted with clumps of glowing crystals. Below it, a pool took up the entire cavern, except for the walkway around it, perhaps five paces wide. In the oval shape of an eye, the pool was lined about its rim with a low, flat edging of crystals that glowed with a duller, yet fiercer, light than those above. Its surface was as smooth as glass and as clear as the Winespring Water. Rand felt as if his eyes could penetrate it forever, but he could not see any bottom to it.

"The Eye of the World," Moiraine said softly beside him.

As he looked around in wonder, he realized that the long years since the making—three thousand of them—had worked their way while no one came. Not all the crystals in the dome glowed with the same intensity. Some were stronger, some weaker; some flickered, and others were only faceted lumps to sparkle in a captured light. Had all shone, the dome would have been as bright as noonday, but they made it only late afternoon, now. Dust coated the walkway, and bits of stone and even crystal. Long years waiting, while the Wheel turned and ground.

"But *what* is it?" Mat asked uneasily. "That doesn't look like any water I ever saw." He kicked a lump of dark stone the size of his fist over the edge. "It—"

The stone struck the glassy surface and slid into the pool without a splash, or so much as a ripple. As it sank, the rock began to swell, growing ever larger, larger and more attenuated, a blob the size of his head that Rand could almost see through, a faint blur as wide as his arm was long. Then it was gone. He thought his skin would creep right off his body.

"What is it?" he demanded, and was shocked at the hoarse harshness of his own voice.

"It might be called the essence of *saidin*." The Aes Sedai's words echoed round the dome. "The essence of the male half of the True Source, the pure essence of the Power wielded by men before the Time of Madness. The Power to mend the seal on the Dark One's prison, or to break it open completely."

"The Light shine on us and protect us," Nynaeve whispered. Egwene clutched her as if she wanted to hide behind the Wisdom. Even Lan stirred uneasily, though there was no surprise in his eyes.

Stone thudded into Rand's shoulders, and he realized he had backed as far as the wall, as far from the Eye of the World as he could get. He would have pushed himself right through the wall, if he could have. Mat, too, was splayed out against the stone as flat as he could make himself. Perrin was staring at the pool with his axe half drawn. His eyes shone, yellow and fierce.

"I always wondered," Loial said uneasily. "When I read about it, I always wondered what it was. Why? Why did they do it? And how?"

"No one living knows." Moiraine no longer looked at the pool. She was watching Rand and his two friends, studying them, her eyes weighing. "Neither the how, nor more of the why than that it would be needed one day, and that that need would be the greatest and most desperate the world had faced to that time. Perhaps ever would face.

"Many in Tar Valon have attempted to find a way to use this Power, but it is as untouchable for any woman as the moon is for a cat. Only a man could channel it, but the last male Aes Sedai is nearly three thousand years gone. Yet the need they saw was a desperate one. They worked through the taint of the Dark One on *saidin* to make it, and make it pure, knowing that doing so would kill them all. Male Aes Sedai and female together. The Green Man spoke true. The greatest wonders of the Age of Legends were done in that way, *saidin* and *saidar* together. All the women in Tar Valon, all the Aes Sedai in all the courts and cities, even with those in the lands beyond the Waste, even counting those who may still live beyond the Aryth Ocean, could not fill a spoon with the Power, lacking men to work with them."

Rand's throat rasped as if he had been screaming. "Why did you bring us here?"

"Because you are *ta'veren*." The Aes Sedai's face was unreadable. Her eyes shimmered, and seemed to pull at him. "Because the Dark One's power will strike here, and because it must be confronted and stopped, or the Shadow will cover the world. There is no need greater than that. Let us go out into the sunlight again, while there is yet time." Without waiting to see if they would follow, she started back up the corridor with Lan, who stepped perhaps a bit more quickly than usual for him. Egwene and Nynaeve hurried behind her.

Rand edged along the wall—he could not make himself get even one step closer to what the pool was—and scrambled into the corridor in a tangle with Mat and Perrin. He would have run if it had not meant trampling Egwene and Nynaeve, Moiraine and Lan. He could not stop shaking even when he was back outside.

"I do not like this, Moiraine," Nynaeve said angrily when the sun shone on them again. "I believe the danger is as great as you say or I would not be here, but this is—"

"I have found you at last."

Rand jerked as if a rope had tightened around his neck. The words, the voice . . . for a moment he believed it was Ba'alzamon. But the two men who walked out of the trees, faces hidden by their cowls, did not wear cloaks the color of dried blood. One cloak was a dark gray, the other almost as dark a green, and they seemed musty even in the open air. And the men were not Fades; the breeze stirred their cloaks.

"Who are you?" Lan's stance was cautious, his hand on

his sword hilt. "How did you come here? If you are seeking the Green Man—"

"He guided us." The hand that pointed to Mat was old and shriveled to scarcely human, lacking a fingernail and with knuckles gnarled like knots in a piece of rope. Mat took a step back, eyes widening. "An old thing, an old friend, an old enemy. But he is not the one we seek," the green-cloaked man finished. The other man stood as if he would never speak.

Moiraine straightened to her full height, no more than shoulder high to any man there, but suddenly seeming as tall as the hills. Her voice rang like a bell, demanding, "Who are you?"

Hands pushed back hoods, and Rand goggled. The old man was older than old; he made Cenn Buie look like a child in the bloom of health. The skin of his face was like crazed parchment drawn tight over a skull, then pulled tighter still. Wispy tufts of brittle hair stood at odd places on his scabrous scalp. His ears were withered bits like scraps of ancient leather; his eyes sunken, peering out of his head as if from the ends of tunnels. Yet the other was worse. A tight, black leather carapace covered that one's head and face completely, but the front of it was worked into a perfect face, a young man's face, laughing wildly, laughing insanely, frozen forever. *What is he hiding if the other shows what he shows?* Then even thought froze in his head, shattered to dust and blew away.

"I am called Aginor," the old one said. "And he is Balthamel. He no longer speaks with his tongue. The Wheel grinds exceedingly fine over three thousand years imprisoned." His sunken eyes slid to the arch; Balthamel leaned forward, his mask's eyes on the white stone opening, as if he wanted to go straight in. "So long without," Aginor said softly. "So long."

"The Light protect—" Loial began, his voice shaking, and cut off abruptly when Aginor looked at him.

"The Forsaken," Mat said hoarsely, "are bound in Shayol Ghul—"

"Were bound." Aginor smiled; his yellowed teeth had the look of fangs. "Some of us are bound no longer. The seals weaken, Aes Sedai. Like Ishamael, we walk the world again, and soon the rest of us will come. I was too close to this world

in my captivity, I and Balthamel, too close to the grinding of
the Wheel, but soon the Great Lord of the Dark will be free,
and give us new flesh, and the world will be ours once more.
You will have no Lews Therin Kinslayer, this time. No Lord
of the Morning to save you. We know the one we seek now,
and there is no more need for the rest of you."

Lan's sword sprang from its scabbard too fast for Rand's
eye to follow. Yet the Warder hesitated, eyes flickering to
Moiraine, to Nynaeve. The two women stood well apart; to
put himself between either of them and the Forsaken would
put him further from the other. Only for a heartbeat the hesitation lasted, but as the Warder's feet moved, Aginor raised
his hand. It was a scornful gesture, a flipping of his gnarled
fingers as if to shoo away a fly. The Warder flew backwards
through the air as though a huge fist had caught him. With
a dull thud Lan struck the stone arch, hanging there for an
instant before dropping in a flaccid heap, his sword lying
near his outstretched hand.

"NO!" Nynaeve screamed.

"Be still!" Moiraine commanded, but before anyone else
could move the Wisdom's knife had left her belt, and she
was running toward the Forsaken, her small blade upraised.

"The Light blind you," she cried, striking at Aginor's
chest.

The other Forsaken moved like a viper. While her blow
still fell, Balthamel's leather-cased hand darted out to seize
her chin, fingers sinking into one cheek while thumb dug
into the other, driving the blood out with their pressure
and raising the flesh in pale ridges. A convulsion wracked
Nynaeve from head to toe, as if she had been cracked like
a whip. Her knife dropped uselessly from dangling fingers
as Balthamel lifted her by his grip, brought her up to where
the leather mask stared into her still-quivering face. Her
toes spasmed a foot above the ground; flowers rained from
her hair.

"I have almost forgotten the pleasures of the flesh." Aginor's tongue crossed his withered lips, sounding like stone
on rough leather. "But Balthamel remembers much." The
laughter of the mask seemed to grow wilder, and the wail
that left Nynaeve burned Rand's ears like despair ripped
from her living heart.

Suddenly Egwene moved, and Rand saw that she was going to help Nynaeve. "Egwene, no!" he shouted, but she did not stop. His hand had gone to his sword at Nynaeve's cry, but now he abandoned it and threw himself at Egwene. He thudded into her before she took her third step, carrying them both to the ground. Egwene landed under him with a gasp, immediately thrashing to get free.

Others were moving, too, he realized. Perrin's axe whirled into his hands, and his eyes glowed golden and fierce. "Wisdom!" Mat howled, the dagger from Shadar Logoth in his fist.

"No!" Rand called. "You can't fight the Forsaken!" But they ran past him as if they had not heard, their eyes on Nynaeve and the two Forsaken.

Aginor glanced at them, unconcernedly . . . and smiled.

Rand felt the air stir above him like the crack of a giant's whip. Mat and Perrin, not even halfway to the Forsaken, stopped as if they had run into a wall, bounced back to sprawl on the ground.

"Good," Aginor said. "A fitting place for you. If you learn to abase yourself properly in worship of us, I might let you live."

Hastily Rand scrambled to his feet. Perhaps he could not fight the Forsaken—no ordinary human could—but he would not let them believe for a minute that he was groveling before them. He tried to help Egwene up, but she slapped his hands away and stood by herself, angrily brushing off her dress. Mat and Perrin had also stubbornly pushed themselves unsteadily erect.

"You will learn," Aginor said, "if you want to live. Now that I have found what I need"—his eyes went to the stone archway—"I may take the time to teach you."

"This shall not be!" The Green Man strode out of the trees with a voice like lightning striking an ancient oak. "You do not belong here!"

Aginor spared him a brief, contemptuous glance. "Begone! Your time is ended, all your kind but you long since dust. Live what life is left to you and be glad you are beneath our notice."

"This is my place," the Green Man said, "and you shall hurt no living thing here."

Balthamel tossed Nynaeve aside like a rag, and like a crumpled rag she fell, eyes staring, limp as if all her bones had melted. One leather-clad hand lifted, and the Green Man roared as smoke rose from the vines that wove him. The wind in the trees echoed his pain.

Aginor turned back to Rand and the others, as if the Green Man had been dealt with, but one long stride and massive, leafy arms wrapped themselves around Balthamel, raising him high, crushing him against a chest of thick creepers, black leather mask laughing into hazelnut eyes dark with anger. Like serpents Balthamel's arms writhed free, his gloved hands grasping the Green Man's head as though he would wrench it off. Flames shot up where those hands touched, vines withering, leaves falling. The Green Man bellowed as thick, dark smoke poured out between the vines of his body. On and on he roared, as if all of him were coming out of his mouth with the smoke that billowed between his lips.

Suddenly Balthamel jerked in the Green Man's grasp. The Forsaken's hands tried to push him away instead of clutching him. One gloved hand flung wide . . . and a tiny creeper burst through the black leather. A fungus, such as rings trees in the deep shadows of the forest, ringed his arm, sprang from nowhere to full-grown, swelling to cover the length of it. Balthamel thrashed, and a shoot of stink-weed ripped open his carapace, lichens dug in their roots and split tiny cracks across the leather of his face, nettles broke the eyes of his mask, deathshead mushrooms tore open the mouth.

The Green Man threw the Forsaken down. Balthamel twisted and jerked as all the things that grew in the dark places, all the things with spores, all the things that loved the dank, swelled and grew, tore cloth and leather and flesh— Was it flesh, seen in that brief moment of verdant rage?—to tattered shreds and covered him until only a mound remained, indistinguishable from many in the shaded depths of the green forest, and the mound moved no more than they.

With a groan like a limb breaking under too great a weight, the Green Man crashed to the ground. Half his head was charred black. Tendrils of smoke still rose from him, like gray creepers. Burned leaves fell from his arm as he painfully stretched out his blackened hand to gently cup an acorn.

The earth rumbled as an oak seedling pushed up between

his fingers. The Green Man's head fell, but the seedling reached for the sun, straining. Roots shot out and thickened, delved beneath the ground and rose again, thickened more as they sank. The trunk broadened and stretched upward, bark turning gray and fissured and ancient. Limbs spread and grew heavy, as big as arms, as big as men, and lifted to caress the sky, thick with green leaves, dense with acorns. The massive web of roots turned the earth like plows as it spread; the already huge trunk shivered, grew wider, round as a house. Stillness came. And an oak that could have stood five hundred years covered the spot where the Green Man had been, marking the tomb of a legend. Nynaeve lay on the gnarled roots, grown curved to her shape, to make a bed for her to rest upon. The wind sighed through the oak's branches; it seemed to murmur farewell.

Even Aginor seemed stunned. Then his head lifted, cavernous eyes burning with hate. "Enough! It is past time to end this!"

"Yes, Forsaken," Moiraine said, her voice as cold as deepwinter ice. "Past time!"

The Aes Sedai's hand rose, and the ground fell away beneath Aginor's feet. Flame roared from the chasm, whipped to a frenzy by wind howling in from every direction, sucking a maelstrom of leaves into the fire, which seemed to solidify into a red-streaked yellow jelly of pure heat. In the middle of it Aginor stood, his feet supported only by air. The Forsaken looked startled, but then he smiled and took a step forward. It was a slow step, as if the fire tried to root him to the spot, but he took it, and then another.

"Run!" Moiraine commanded. Her face was white with strain. "All of you run!" Aginor stepped across the air, toward the edge of the flames.

Rand was aware of others moving, Mat and Perrin dashing away at the edge of his vision, Loial's long legs carrying him into the trees, but all he could really see was Egwene. She stood there rigid, face pale and eyes closed. It was not fear that held her, he realized. She was trying to throw her puny, untrained wielding of the Power against the Forsaken.

Roughly he grabbed her arm and pulled her around to face him. "Run!" he shouted at her. Her eyes opened, staring at him, angry with him for interfering, liquid with hate for Aginor, with fear of the Forsaken. "Run," he said, pushing her toward the trees hard enough to start her. "Run!" Once started, she did run.

But Aginor's withered face turned toward him, toward the running Egwene behind him, as the Forsaken walked through the flames, as if what the Aes Sedai was doing did not concern Aginor at all. Toward Egwene.

"Not her!" Rand shouted. "The Light burn you, not her!" He snatched up a rock and threw it, meaning to draw Aginor's attention. Halfway to the Forsaken's face, the stone turned to a handful of dust.

He hesitated only a moment, long enough to glance over his shoulder and see that Egwene was hidden in the trees. The flames still surrounded Aginor, patches of his cloak smoldering, but he walked as if he had all the time in the world, and the fire's rim was near. Rand turned and ran. Behind him he heard Moiraine begin to scream.

CHAPTER
51

Against the Shadow

The land tended upward the way Rand went, but fear lent his legs strength and they ate ground in long strides, tearing his way through flowering bushes and tangles of wildrose, scattering petals, not caring if thorns ripped his clothes or even his flesh. Moiraine had stopped screaming. It seemed as if the shrieks had gone on forever, each one more throat-wrenching than the last, but he knew they had lasted only moments altogether. Moments before Aginor would be on his trail. He knew it would be him that Aginor followed. He had seen the certainty in the Forsaken's hollow eyes, in that last second before terror whipped his feet to run.

The land grew ever steeper, but he scrambled on, pulling himself forward by handfuls of undergrowth, rocks and dirt and leaves spilling down the slope from under his feet, finally crawling on hands and knees when the slant became too great. Ahead, above, it leveled out a little. Panting, he scrabbled his way the last few spans, got to his feet, and stopped, wanting to howl aloud.

Ten paces in front of him, the hilltop dropped away sharply. He knew what he would see before he reached it, but he took the steps anyway, each heavier than the one before, hoping there might be some track, a goat path, anything. At the edge he looked down a sheer hundred-foot drop, a stone wall as smooth as planed timber.

There has to be some way. I'll go back and find a way around. Go back and—

When he turned, Aginor was there, just reaching the crest. The Forsaken topped the hill without any difficulty, walking up the steep slope as if it were level ground. Deep-sunken eyes burned at him from that drawn parchment face; somehow, it seemed less withered than before, more fleshed, as if Aginor had fed well on something. Those eyes were fixed on him, yet when Aginor spoke, it was almost to himself.

"Ba'alzamon will give rewards beyond mortal dreaming for the one who brings you to Shayol Ghul. Yet my dreams have always been beyond those of other men, and I left mortality behind millennia ago. What difference if you serve the Great Lord of the Dark alive or dead? None, to the spread of the Shadow. Why should I share power with you? Why should I bend knee to you? I, who faced Lews Therin Telamon in the Hall of the Servants itself. I, who threw my might against the Lord of the Morning and met him stroke for stroke. I think not."

Rand's mouth dried like dust; his tongue felt as shriveled as Aginor. The edge of the precipice grated under his heels, stone falling away. He did not dare look back, but he heard the rocks bounding and rebounding from the sheer wall, just as his body would if he moved another inch. It was the first he knew that he had been backing up, away from the Forsaken. His skin crawled until he thought he must see it writhing if he looked, if he could only take his eyes off the Forsaken. *There has to be some way to get away from him. Some way to escape! There has to be! Some way!*

Suddenly he felt something, saw it, though he knew it was not there to see. A glowing rope ran off from Aginor, behind him, white like sunlight seen through the purest cloud, heavier than a blacksmith's arm, lighter than air, connecting the Forsaken to something distant beyond knowing, something within the touch of Rand's hand. The rope pulsed, and with every throb Aginor grew stronger, more fully fleshed, a man as tall and strong as himself, a man harder than the Warder, more deadly than the Blight. Yet beside that shining cord, the Forsaken seemed almost not to exist. The cord was all. It hummed. It sang. It called Rand's soul. One bright finger-strand lifted away, drifted, touched him, and he gasped. Light filled him, and heat that should have burned yet only warmed as if it took the chill of the grave from his bones. The strand thickened. *I have to get away!*

"No!" Aginor shouted. "You shall not have it! It is mine!"

Rand did not move, and neither did the Forsaken, yet

they fought as surely as if they grappled in the dust. Sweat beaded on Aginor's face, no longer withered, no longer old, that of a strong man in his prime. Rand pulsed with the beating in the cord, like the heartbeat of the world. It filled his being. Light filled his mind, till only a corner was left for what was himself. He wrapped the void around that nook; sheltered in emptiness. *Away!*

"Mine!" Aginor cried. "Mine!"

Warmth built in Rand, the warmth of the sun, the radiance of the sun, bursting, the awful radiance of light, of the Light. *Away!*

"Mine!" Flame shot from Aginor's mouth, broke through his eyes like spears of fire, and he screamed.

Away!

And Rand was no longer on the hilltop. He quivered with the Light that suffused him. His mind would not work; light and heat blinded it. The Light. In the midst of the void, the Light blinded his mind, stunned him with awe.

He stood in a broad mountain pass, surrounded by jagged black peaks like the teeth of the Dark One. It was real; he was there. He felt the rocks under his boots, the icy breeze on his face.

Battle surrounded him, or the tail end of battle. Armored men on armored horses, shining steel dusty now, slashed and stabbed at snarling Trollocs wielding spiked axes and scythe-like swords. Some men fought afoot, their horses down, and barded horses galloped through the fight with empty saddles. Fades moved among them all, nightblack cloaks hanging still however their dark mounts galloped, and wherever their light-eating swords swung, men died. Sound beat at Rand, beat at him and bounced from the strangeness that had him by the throat. The clash of steel against steel, the panting and grunting of men and Trollocs striving, the screams of men and Trollocs dying. Over the din, banners waved in dust-filled air. The Black Hawk of Fal Dara, the White Hart of Shienar, others. And Trolloc banners. In just the little space around him he saw the horned skull of the Dha'vol, the blood-red trident of the Ko'bal, the iron fist of the Dhai'mon.

Yet it was indeed the tail end of battle, a pausing, as humans and Trollocs alike fell back to regroup. None seemed to notice Rand as they paid a few last strokes and broke away, galloping, or running in a stagger, to the ends of the pass.

Rand found himself facing the end of the pass where the humans were re-forming, pennants stirring beneath gleaming lancepoints. Wounded men wavered in their saddles. Riderless horses reared and galloped. Plainly they could not stand another meeting, yet just as plainly they readied themselves for one final charge. Some of them saw him now; men stood in their stirrups to point at him. Their shouts came to him as tiny piping.

Staggering, he turned. The forces of the Dark One filled the other end of the pass, bristling black pikes and spearpoints swelling up onto mountain slopes made blacker still by the great mass of Trollocs that dwarfed the army of Shienar. Fades in hundreds rode across the front of the horde, the fierce, muzzled faces of Trollocs turning away in fear as they passed, huge bodies pulling back to make way. Overhead, Draghkar wheeled on leathery pinions, shrieks challenging the wind. Halfmen saw him now, too, pointed, and Draghkar spun and dove. Two. Three. Six of them, crying shrilly as they plummeted toward him.

He stared at them. Heat filled him, the burning heat of the touched sun. He could see the Draghkar clearly, soulless eyes in pale men's faces on winged bodies that had nothing of humanity about them. Terrible heat. Crackling heat.

From the clear sky lightning came, each bolt crisp and sharp, searing his eyes, each bolt striking a winged black shape. Hunting cries became shrieks of death, and charred forms fell to leave the sky clean again.

The heat. The terrible heat of the Light.

He fell to his knees; he thought he could hear his tears sizzling on his cheeks. "No!" He clutched at tufts of wiry grass for some hold on reality; the grass burst in flame. "Please, nooooooo!"

The wind rose with his voice, howled with his voice, roared with his voice down the pass, whipping the flames to a wall of fire that sped away from him and toward the Trolloc host faster than a horse could run. Fire burned into the Trollocs, and the mountains trembled with their screams, screams almost as loud as the wind and his voice.

"It has to end!"

He beat at the ground with his fist, and the earth tolled like a gong. He bruised his hands on stony soil, and the earth trembled. Ripples ran through the ground ahead of him in everris-

ing waves, waves of dirt and rock towering over Trollocs and
Fades, breaking over them as the mountains shattered under
their hooved feet. A boiling mass of flesh and rubble churned
across the Trolloc army. What was left standing was still a
mighty host, but now no more than twice the human army in
numbers, and milling in fright and confusion.

The wind died. The screams died. The earth was still.
Dust and smoke swirled back down the pass to surround him.

"The Light blind you, Ba'alzamon! This has to end!"

IT IS NOT HERE.

It was not Rand's thought, making his skull vibrate.

*I WILL TAKE NO PART. ONLY THE CHOSEN ONE
CAN DO WHAT MUST BE DONE, IF HE WILL.*

"Where?" He did not want to say it, but he could not stop
himself. "Where?"

The haze surrounding him parted, leaving a dome of clear,
clean air ten spans high, walled by billowing smoke and dust.
Steps rose before him, each standing alone and unsupported,
stretching up into the murk that obscured the sun.

NOT HERE.

Through the mist, as from the far end of the earth, came
a cry. "The Light wills it!" The ground rumbled with the
thunder of hooves as the forces of humankind launched
their last charge.

Within the void, his mind knew a moment of panic. The
charging horsemen could not see him in the dust; their
charge would trample right over him. The greater part of
him ignored the shaking ground as a petty thing beneath
concern. Dull anger driving his feet, he mounted the first
steps. *It has to be ended!*

Darkness surrounded him, the utter blackness of total nothing. The steps were still there, hanging in the black, under
his feet and ahead. When he looked back, those behind were
gone, faded away to nothing, into the nothingness around him.
But the cord was yet there, stretching behind him, the glowing line dwindling and vanishing into the distance. It was not
so thick as before, but it still pulsed, pumping strength into
him, pumping life, filling him with the Light. He climbed.

It seemed forever that he climbed. Forever, and minutes.
Time stood still in nothingness. Time ran faster. He climbed
until suddenly a door stood before him, its surface rough
and splintered and old, a door well-remembered. He touched

it, and it burst to fragments. While they still fell, he stepped through, bits of shattered wood falling from his shoulders.

The chamber, too, was as he remembered, the mad, striated sky beyond the balcony, the melted walls, the polished table, the terrible fireplace with its roaring, heatless flames. Some of those faces that made the fireplace, writhing in torment, shrieking in silence, tugged at his memory as if he knew them, but he held the void close, floated within himself in emptiness. He was alone. When he looked at the mirror on the wall, his face was there as clear as if it *was* him. *There is calm in the void.*

"Yes," Ba'alzamon said from in front of the fireplace, "I thought Aginor's greed would overcome him. But it makes no difference in the end. A long search, but ended now. You are here, and I know you."

In the midst of the Light the void drifted, and in the midst of the void floated Rand. He reached for the soil of his home, and felt hard rock, unyielding and dry, stone without pity, where only the strong could survive, only those as hard as the mountains. "I am tired of running." He could not believe his voice was so calm. "Tired of you threatening my friends. I will run no more." Ba'alzamon had a cord, too, he saw. A black cord, thicker by far than his own, so wide it should have dwarfed the human body, yet dwarfed by Ba'alzamon, instead. Each pulse along that black vein ate light.

"You think it makes any difference, whether you run or stay?" The flames of Ba'alzamon's mouth laughed. The faces in the hearth wept at their master's mirth. "You have fled from me many times, and each time I run you down and make you eat your pride with sniveling tears for spice. Many times you have stood and fought, then groveled in defeat, begging mercy. You have this choice, worm, and this choice only: kneel at my feet and serve me well, and I will give you power above thrones; or be Tar Valon's puppet fool and scream while you are ground into the dust of time."

Rand shifted, glancing back through the door as if seeking a way to escape. Let the Dark One think that. Beyond the doorway was still the black of nothing, split by the shining thread that ran from his body. And out there Ba'alzamon's heavier cord ran as well, so black that it stood out in the dark as if against snow. The two cords beat like heartveins in countertime, against each other, the light barely resisting the waves of dark.

"There are other choices," Rand said. "The Wheel weaves the Pattern, not you. Every trap you've laid for me, I have escaped. I've escaped your Fades and Trollocs, escaped your Darkfriends. I tracked you here, and destroyed your army on the way. You do not weave the Pattern."

Ba'alzamon's eyes roared like two furnaces. His lips did not move, but Rand thought he heard a curse screamed at Aginor. Then the fires died, and that ordinary human face smiled at him in a way that chilled even through the warmth of the Light.

"Other armies can be raised, fool. Armies you have not dreamed of will yet come. And you tracked me? You slug under a rock, track me? I began the setting of your path the day you were born, a path to lead you to your grave, or here. Aiel allowed to flee, and one to live, to speak the words that would echo down the years. Jain Farstrider, a hero," he twisted the word to a sneer, "whom I painted like a fool and sent to the Ogier thinking he was free of me. The Black Ajah, wriggling like worms on their bellies across the world to search you out. I pull the strings and the Amyrlin Seat dances and thinks she controls events."

The void trembled; hastily Rand firmed it again. *He knows it all. He could have done. It could be the way he says.* The Light warmed the void. Doubt cried out and was stilled, till only the seed remained. He struggled, not knowing whether he wanted to bury the seed or make it grow. The void steadied, smaller than before, and he floated in calm.

Ba'alzamon seemed to notice nothing. "It matters little if I have you alive or dead, except to you, and to what power you might have. You will serve me, or your soul will. But I would rather have you kneel to me alive than dead. A single fist of Trollocs sent to your village when I could have sent a thousand. One Darkfriend to face you where a hundred could come on you asleep. And you, fool, you don't even know them all, neither those ahead, nor those behind, nor those by your side. You are mine, have always been mine, my dog on a leash, and I brought you here to kneel to your master or die and let your soul kneel."

"I deny you. You have no power over me, and I will not kneel to you, alive or dead."

"Look," Ba'alzamon said. "Look." Unwilling, Rand yet turned his head.

Egwene stood there, and Nynaeve, pale and frightened, with flowers in their hair. And another woman, little older than the Wisdom, gray-eyed and beautiful, clothed in a Two Rivers dress, bright blossoms embroidered round the neck.

"Mother?" he breathed, and she smiled, a hopeless smile. His mother's smile. "No! My mother is dead, and the other two are safe away from here. I deny you!" Egwene and Nynaeve blurred, became wafting mist, dissipated. Kari al'Thor still stood there, her eyes big with fear.

"She, at least," Ba'alzamon said, "is mine to do with as I will."

Rand shook his head. "I deny you." He had to force the words out. "She is dead, and safe from you in the Light."

His mother's lips trembled. Tears trickled down her cheeks; each one burned him like acid. "The Lord of the Grave is stronger than he once was, my son," she said. "His reach is longer. The Father of Lies has a honeyed tongue for unwary souls. My son. My only, darling son. I would spare you if I could, but he is my master, now, his whim, the law of my existence. I can but obey him, and grovel for his favor. Only you can free me. Please, my son. Please help me. Help me. Help me! PLEASE!"

The wail ripped out of her as barefaced Fades, pale and eyeless, closed round. Her clothes ripped away in their blood-less hands, hands that wielded pincers and clamps and things that stung and burned and whipped against her naked flesh. Her scream would not end.

Rand's scream echoed hers. The void boiled in his mind. His sword was in his hand. Not the heron-mark blade, but a blade of light, a blade of the Light. Even as he raised it, a fiery white bolt shot from the point, as if the blade itself had reached out. It touched the nearest Fade, and blinding ca-nescence filled the chamber, shining through the Halfmen like a candle through paper, burning through them, blind-ing his eyes to the scene.

From the midst of the brilliance, he heard a whisper. "Thank you, my son. The Light. The blessed Light."

The flash faded, and he was alone in the chamber with Ba'alzamon. Ba'alzamon's eyes burned like the Pit of Doom, but he shied back from the sword as if it truly were the Light itself. "Fool! You will destroy yourself! You cannot wield it so, not yet! Not until I teach you!"

"It is ended," Rand said, and he swung the sword at Ba'alzamon's black cord.

Ba'alzamon screamed as the sword fell, screamed till the stone walls trembled, and the endless howl redoubled as the blade of Light severed the cord. The cut ends rebounded apart as if they had been under tension. The end stretching into the nothingness outside began to shrivel as it sprang away; the other whipped back into Ba'alzamon, hurling him against the fireplace. There was silent laughter in the soundless shrieks of the tortured faces. The walls shivered and cracked; the floor heaved, and chunks of stone crashed to the floor from the ceiling.

As all broke apart around him, Rand pointed the sword at Ba'alzamon's heart. "It is ended!"

Light lanced from the blade, coruscating in a shower of fiery sparks like droplets of molten, white metal. Wailing, Ba'alzamon threw up his arms in a vain effort to shield himself. Flames shrieked in his eyes, joining with other flames as the stone ignited, the stone of the cracking walls, the stone of the pitching floor, the stone showering from the ceiling. Rand felt the bright thread attached to him thinning, till only the glow itself remained, but he strained harder, not knowing what he did, or how, only that this had to be ended. *It* has *to be ended!*

Fire filled the chamber, a solid flame. He could see Ba'alzamon withering like a leaf, hear him howling, feel the shrieks grating on his bones. The flame became pure, white light, brighter than the sun. Then the last flicker of the thread was gone, and he was falling through endless black and Ba'alzamon's fading howl.

Something struck him with tremendous force, turning him to jelly, and the jelly shook and screamed from the fire raging inside, the hungry cold burning without end.

CHAPTER

52

There Is Neither Beginning Nor End

He became aware of the sun, first, moving across a cloudless sky, filling his unblinking eyes. It seemed to go by fits and starts, standing still for days, then darting ahead in a streak of light, jerking toward the far horizon, day falling with it. Light. *That should mean something.* Thought was a new thing. *I can think. I means me.* Pain came next, the memory of raging fever, the bruises where shaking chills had thrown him around like a rag doll. And a stink. A greasy, burned smell, filling his nostrils, and his head.

With aching muscles, he heaved himself over, pushed up to hands and knees. Uncomprehending, he stared at the oily ashes in which he had been lying, ashes scattered and smeared over the stone of the hilltop. Bits of dark green cloth lay mixed in the char, edge-blackened scraps that had escaped the flames.

Aginor.

His stomach heaved and twisted. Trying to brush black streaks of ash from his clothes, he lurched away from the remains of the Forsaken. His hands flapped feebly, not making much headway. He tried to use both hands and fell forward. A sheer drop loomed under his face, a smooth rock wall spinning in his eyes, depth pulling him. His head swum, and he vomited over the edge of the cliff.

Trembling, he crawled backwards on his belly until there was solid stone under his eyes, then flopped over onto his back, panting for breath. With an effort he fumbled his sword from its scabbard. Only a few ashes remained from the red cloth. His hands shook when he held it up in front of his face; it took both hands. It was a heron-mark blade—

Heron-mark? Yes. Tam. My father—but only steel for that. He needed three wavering tries to sheathe it again. *It had been something else. Or there was another sword.*

"My name," he said after a while, "is Rand al'Thor." More memory crashed back into his head like a lead ball, and he groaned. "The Dark One," he whispered to himself. "The Dark One is dead." There was no more need for caution. "Shai'tan is dead." The world seemed to lurch. He shook in silent mirth until tears poured from his eyes. "Shai'tan is dead!" He laughed at the sky. Other memories. "Egwene!" That name meant something important.

Painfully he got to his feet, wavering like a willow in a high wind, and staggered past Aginor's ashes without looking at them. *Not important anymore.* He fell more than climbed down that first, steep part of the slope, tumbling and sliding from bush to bush. By the time he reached more level ground, his bruises ached twice as much, but he found strength enough to stand, barely. *Egwene.* He broke into a shambling run. Leaves and flower petals showered around him as he blundered through the undergrowth. *Have to find her. Who is she?*

His arms and legs seemed to flail about more like long blades of grass than go as he wanted them to. Tottering, he fell against a tree, slamming against the trunk so hard that he grunted. Foliage rained on his head while he pressed his face to the rough bark, clutching to keep from falling. *Egwene.* He pushed himself away from the tree and hurried on. Almost immediately he tilted again, falling, but he forced his legs to work faster, to run into the fall so that he was staggering along at a good clip, all the while one step from falling flat on his face. Moving made his legs begin to obey him more. Slowly, he found himself running upright, arms pumping, long legs pulling him down the slope in leaps. He bounded into the clearing, half-filled now by the great oak marking the Green Man's grave. There was the white stone arch marked with the ancient symbol of the Aes Sedai, and the blackened, gaping pit where fire and wind had tried to trap Aginor and failed.

"Egwene! Egwene, where are you?" A pretty girl looked up with big eyes from where she knelt beneath the spreading branches, flowers in her hair, and brown oak leaves. She was slender and young, and frightened. *Yes, that's who she is. Of course.* "Egwene, thank the Light you're all right."

There were two other women with her, one with haunted eyes and a long braid, still decorated with a few white morningstars. The other lay outstretched, her head pillowed on folded cloaks, her own sky-blue cloak not quite hiding her tattered dress. Charred spots and tears in the rich cloth showed, and her face was pale, but her eyes were open. *Moiraine. Yes, the Aes Sedai. And the Wisdom, Nynaeve.* All three women looked at him, unblinking and intent.

"You *are* all right, aren't you? Egwene? He didn't harm you." He could walk without stumbling, now—the sight of her made him feel like dancing, bruises and all—but it still felt good to drop down cross-legged beside them.

"I never even saw him after you pushed—" Her eyes were uncertain on his face. "What about you, Rand?"

"I'm fine." He laughed. He touched her cheek, and wondered if he had imagined a slight pulling away. "A little rest, and I'll be newmade. Nynaeve? Moiraine Sedai?" The names felt new in his mouth.

The Wisdom's eyes were old, ancient in her young face, but she shook her head. "A little bruised," she said, still watching him. "Moiraine is the only . . . the only one of us who was really hurt."

"I suffered more injury to my pride than anything else," the Aes Sedai said irritably, plucking at her cloak blanket. She looked as if she had been a long time ill, or hard used, but despite the dark circles under them her eyes were sharp and full of power. "Aginor was surprised and angry that I held him as long as I did, but fortunately, he had no time to spare for me. I am surprised myself that I held him so long. In the Age of Legends, Aginor was close behind the Kinslayer and Ishamael in power."

"'The Dark One and all the Forsaken,'" Egwene quoted in a faint, unsteady voice, "'are bound in Shayol Ghul, bound by the Creator. . . .'" She drew a shuddering breath.

"Aginor and Balthamel must have been trapped near the surface." Moiraine sounded as if she had already explained this, impatient at doing so again. "The patch on the Dark One's prison weakened enough to free them. Let us be thankful no more of the Forsaken were freed. If they had been, we would have seen them."

"It doesn't matter," Rand said. "Aginor and Balthamel are dead, and so is Shai'—"

"The Dark One," the Aes Sedai cut him off. Ill or not, her voice was firm, and her dark eyes commanding. "Best we still call him the Dark One. Or Ba'alzamon, at least."

He shrugged. "As you wish. But he's dead. The Dark One's dead. I killed him. I burned him with. . . ." The rest of memory flooded back then, leaving his mouth hanging open. *The One Power. I wielded the One Power. No man can.* . . . He licked lips that were suddenly dry. A gust of wind swirled fallen and falling leaves around them, but it was no colder than his heart. They were looking at him, the three of them. Watching. Not even blinking. He reached out to Egwene, and there was no imagination in her drawing back this time. "Egwene?" She turned her face away, and he let his hand drop.

Abruptly she flung her arms around him, burying her face in his chest. "I'm sorry, Rand. I'm sorry. I don't care. Truly, I don't." Her shoulders shook. He thought she was crying. Awkwardly patting her hair, he looked at the other two women over the top of her head.

"The Wheel weaves as the Wheel wills," Nynaeve said slowly, "but you are still Rand al'Thor of Emond's Field. But, the Light help me, the Light help us all, you are too dangerous, Rand." He flinched from the Wisdom's eyes, sad, regretting, and already accepting loss.

"What happened?" Moiraine said. "Tell me *everything*!"

And with her eyes on him, compelling, he did. He wanted to turn away, to make it short, leave things out, but the Aes Sedai's eyes drew everything from him. Tears ran down his face when he came to Kari al'Thor. His mother. He emphasized that. "He had my mother. My mother!" There was sympathy and pain on Nynaeve's face, but the Aes Sedai's eyes drove him on, to the sword of Light, to severing the black cord, and the flames consuming Ba'alzamon. Egwene's arms tightened around him as if she would pull him back from what had happened. "But it wasn't me," he finished. "The Light . . . pulled me along. It wasn't really me. Doesn't that make any difference?"

"I had suspicions from the first," Moiraine said. "Suspicions are not proof, though. After I gave you the token, the coin, and made that bonding, you should have been willing to fall in with whatever I wanted, but you resisted, questioned. That told me something, but not enough. Manetheren blood was always stubborn, and more so after Aemon died and Eldrene's heart was shattered. Then there was Bela."

"Bela?" he said. *Nothing makes any difference.*

The Aes Sedai nodded. "At Watch Hill, Bela had no need of me to cleanse her of tiredness; someone had already done it. She could have outrun Mandarb, that night. I should have thought of who Bela carried. With Trollocs on our heels, a Draghkar overhead, and a Halfman the Light alone knew where, how you must have feared that Egwene would be left behind. You needed something more than you had ever needed anything before in your life, and you reached out to the one thing that could give it to you. *Saidin.*"

He shivered. He felt so cold his fingers hurt. "If I never do it again, if I never touch it again, I won't. . . ." He could not say it. Go mad. Turn the land and people around him to madness. Die, rotting while he still lived.

"Perhaps," Moiraine said. "It would be much easier if there was someone to teach you, but it might be done, with a supreme effort of will."

"You can teach me. Surely, you—" He stopped when the Aes Sedai shook her head.

"Can a cat teach a dog to climb trees, Rand? Can a fish teach a bird to swim? I know *saidar,* but I can teach you nothing of *saidin.* Those who could are three thousand years dead. Perhaps you are stubborn enough, though. Perhaps your will is strong enough."

Egwene straightened, wiping reddened eyes with the back of her hand. She looked as if she wanted to say something, but when she opened her mouth, nothing came out. *At least she isn't pulling away. At least she can look at me without screaming.*

"The others?" he said.

"Lan took them into the cavern," Nynaeve said. "The Eye is gone, but there's something in the middle of the pool, a crystal column, and steps to reach it. Mat and Perrin wanted to look for you first—Loial did, too—but Moiraine said. . . ." She glanced at the Aes Sedai, troubled. Moiraine returned her look calmly. "She said we mustn't disturb you while you were. . . ."

His throat constricted until he could hardly breathe. *Will they turn their faces the way Egwene did? Will they scream and run away like I'm a Fade?* Moiraine spoke as if she did not notice the blood draining from his face.

"There was a vast amount of the One Power in the Eye. Even in the Age of Legends, few could have channeled so much unaided without being destroyed. Very few."

"You told them?" he said hoarsely. "If everybody knows. . . ."

"Only Lan," Moiraine said gently. "He must know. And Nynaeve and Egwene, for what they are and what they will become. The others have no need, yet."

"Why not?" The rasp in his throat made his voice harsh. "You will be wanting to gentle me, won't you? Isn't that what Aes Sedai do to men who can wield the Power? Change them so they can't? Make them safe? Thom said men who have been gentled die because they stop wanting to live. Why aren't you talking about taking me to Tar Valon to be gentled?"

"You are *ta'veren,*" Moiraine replied. "Perhaps the Pattern has not finished with you."

Rand sat up straight. "In the dreams Ba'alzamon said Tar Valon and the Amyrlin Seat would try to use me. He named names, and I remember them, now. Raolin Darksbane and Guaire Amalasan. Yurian Stonebow. Davian. Logain." The last was the hardest of all to say. Nynaeve went pale and Egwene gasped, but he pressed on angrily. "Every one a false Dragon. Don't try to deny it. Well, I won't be used. I am not a tool you can throw on the midden heap when it's worn out."

"A tool made for a purpose is not demeaned by being used for that purpose," Moiraine's voice was as harsh as his own, "but a man who believes the Father of Lies demeans himself. You say you will not be used, and then you let the Dark One set your path like a hound sent after a rabbit by his master."

His fists clenched, and he turned his head away. It was too close to the things Ba'alzamon had said. "I am no one's hound. Do you hear me? No one's!"

Loial and the others appeared in the arch, and Rand scrambled to his feet, looking at Moiraine.

"They will not know," the Aes Sedai said, "until the Pattern makes it so."

Then his friends were coming close. Lan led the way,

looking as hard as ever but still somewhat the worse for wear. He had one of Nynaeve's bandages around his temples, and a stiffbacked way of walking. Behind him, Loial carried a large gold chest, ornately worked and chased with silver. No one but an Ogier could have lifted it unaided. Perrin had his arms wrapped around a big bundle of folded white cloth, and Mat was cupping what appeared to be fragments of pottery in his two hands.

"So you're alive after all." Mat laughed. His face darkened, and he jerked his head at Moiraine. "She wouldn't let us look for you. Said we had to find out what the Eye was hiding. I'd have gone anyway, but Nynaeve and Egwene sided with her and almost threw me through the arch."

"You're here, now," Perrin said, "and not too badly beaten about, by the look of you." His eyes did not glow, but the irises were all yellow, now. "That's the important thing. You're here, and we're done with what we came for, whatever it was. Moiraine Sedai says we're done, and we can go. Home, Rand. The Light burn me, but I want to go home."

"Good to see you alive, sheepherder," Lan said gruffly. "I see you hung onto your sword. Maybe you'll learn to use it, now." Rand felt a sudden burst of affection for the Warder; Lan knew, but on the surface at least, nothing had changed. He thought that perhaps, for Lan, nothing had changed inside either.

"I must say," Loial said, setting the chest down, "that traveling with ta'veren has turned out to be even more interesting than I expected." His ears twitched violently. "If it becomes any more interesting, I will go back to Stedding Shangtai immediately, confess everything to Elder Haman, and never leave my books again." Suddenly the Ogier grinned, that wide mouth splitting his face in two. "It is so good to see you, Rand al'Thor. The Warder is the only one of these three who cares much at all for books, and he won't talk. What happened to you? We all ran off and hid in the woods until Moiraine Sedai sent Lan to find us, but she would not let us look for you. Why were you gone so long, Rand?"

"I ran and ran," he said slowly, "until I fell down a hill and hit my head on a rock. I think I hit every rock on the way down." That should explain his bruises. He tried to watch the Aes Sedai, and Nynaeve and Egwene, too, but their faces never changed. "When I came to, I was lost, and finally I stumbled back here. I think Aginor is dead, burned. I found some ashes, and pieces of his cloak."

The lies sounded hollow in his ears. He could not understand why they did not laugh with scorn and demand the truth, but his friends nodded, accepting, and made sympathetic sounds as they gathered around the Aes Sedai to show her what they had found.

"Help me up," Moiraine said. Nynaeve and Egwene lifted her until she was sitting; they had to support her even then.

"How could these things be inside the Eye," Mat asked, "without being destroyed like that rock?"

"They were not put there to be destroyed," the Aes Sedai said curtly, and frowned away their questions while she took the pottery fragments, black and white and shiny, from Mat.

They seemed like rubble to Rand, but she fitted them together deftly on the ground beside her, making a perfect circle the size of a man's hand. The ancient symbol of the Aes Sedai, the Flame of Tar Valon joined with the Dragon's Fang, black siding white. For a moment Moiraine only looked at it, her face unreadable, then she took the knife from her belt and handed it to Lan, nodding to the circle.

The Warder separated out the largest piece, then raised the knife high and brought it down with all his might. A spark flew, the fragment leaped with the force of the blow, and the blade snapped with a sharp crack. He examined the stump left attached to the hilt, then tossed it aside. "The best steel from Tear," he said dryly.

Mat snatched the fragment up and grunted, then showed it around. There was no mark on it.

"*Cuendillar*," Moiraine said. "Heartstone. No one has been able to make it since the Age of Legends, and even then it was made only for the greatest purpose. Once made, nothing can break it. Not the One Power itself wielded by the greatest Aes Sedai who ever lived aided by the most powerful *sa'angreal* ever made. Any power directed against heartstone only makes it stronger."

"Then how . . . ?" Mat's gesture with the piece he held took in the other bits on the ground.

"This was one of the seven seals on the Dark One's prison," Moiraine said. Mat dropped the piece as if it had become white-hot. For a moment, Perrin's eyes seemed to glow again. The Aes Sedai calmly began gathering the fragments.

"It doesn't matter anymore," Rand said. His friends looked at him oddly, and he wished he had kept his mouth shut.

"Of course," Moiraine replied. But she carefully put all the pieces into her pouch. "Bring me the chest." Loial lifted it closer.

The flattened cube of gold and silver appeared to be solid, but the Aes Sedai's fingers felt across the intricate work, pressing, and with a sudden click a top flung back as if on springs. A curled, gold horn nestled within. Despite its gleam, it seemed plain beside the chest that held it. The only markings were a line of silver script inlaid around the mouth of the bell. Moiraine lifted the horn out as if lifting a babe. "This must be carried to Illian," she said softly.

"Illian!" Perrin growled. "That's almost to the Sea of Storms, nearly as far south of home as we are north now."

"Is it . . . ?" Loial stopped to catch his breath. "Can it be . . . ?"

"You can read the Old Tongue?" Moiraine asked, and when he nodded, she handed him the horn.

The Ogier took it as gently as she had, delicately tracing the script with one broad finger. His eyes went wider and wider, and his ears stood up straight. *"Tia mi aven Moridin isainde vadin,"* he whispered. "The grave is no bar to my call."

"The Horn of Valere." For once the Warder appeared truly shaken; there was a touch of awe in his voice.

At the same time Nynaeve said in a shaky voice, "To call the heroes of the Ages back from the dead to fight the Dark One."

"Burn me!" Mat breathed.

Loial reverently laid the horn back in its golden nest.

"I begin to wonder," Moiraine said. "The Eye of the World was made against the greatest need the world would ever face, but was it made for the use to which . . . we . . . put it, or to guard these things? Quickly, the last, show it to me."

After the first two, Rand could understand Perrin's reluctance. Lan and the Ogier took the bundle of white cloth from him when he hesitated, and unfolded it between them. A long, white banner spread out, lifting on the air. Rand could only stare. The whole thing seemed of a piece, neither woven, nor dyed, nor painted. A figure like a serpent,

scaled in scarlet and gold, ran the entire length, but it had
scaled legs, and feet with five long, golden claws on each,
and a great head with a golden mane and eyes like the sun.
The stirring of the banner made it seem to move, scales
glittering like precious metals and gems, alive, and he almost thought he could hear it roar defiance.

"What is it?" he said.

Moiraine answered slowly. "The banner of the Lord of
the Morning when he led the forces of light against the
Shadow. The banner of Lews Therin Telamon. The banner
of the Dragon." Loial almost dropped his end.

"Burn me!" Mat said faintly.

"We will take these things with us when we go," Moiraine
said. "They were not put here by chance, and I must know
more." Her fingers brushed her pouch, where the pieces of
the shattered seal were. "It is too late in the day for starting now. We will rest, and eat, but we will leave early. The
Blight is all around here, not as along the Border, and strong.
Without the Green Man, this place cannot hold long. Let me
down," she told Nynaeve and Egwene. "I must rest."

Rand became aware of what he had been seeing all along,
but not noticing. Dead, brown leaves falling from the great
oak. Dead leaves rustling thick on the ground in the breeze,
brown mixed with petals dropped from thousands of flowers. The Green Man had held back the Blight, but already
the Blight was killing what he had made.

"It is done, isn't it?" he asked Moiraine. "It is finished."

The Aes Sedai turned her head on its pillow of cloaks.
Her eyes seemed as deep as the Eye of the World. "We
have done what we came here to do. From here you may
live your life as the Pattern weaves. Eat, then sleep, Rand
al'Thor. Sleep, and dream of home."

CHAPTER
53

The Wheel Turns

D awn revealed devastation in the Green Man's garden. The ground was thick with fallen leaves, almost knee-deep in places. All the flowers were gone except a few clinging desperately to the edge of the clearing. Little could grow in the soil under an oak, but a thin circle of flowers and grass centered on the thick trunk above the Green Man's grave. The oak itself retained only half its leaves, and that was far more than any other tree had, as if some remnant of the Green Man still fought to hold there. The cool breezes had died, replaced by a growing sticky heat, the butterflies were gone, the birds silent. It was a silent group who prepared to leave.

Rand climbed into the bay's saddle with a sense of loss. *It shouldn't be this way. Blood and ashes, we won!*

"I wish he had found his other place," Egwene said as she mounted Bela. A litter, fashioned by Lan, was slung between the shaggy mare and Aldieb, to carry Moiraine; Nynaeve would ride beside with the white mare's reins. The Wisdom dropped her eyes whenever she saw Lan glance at her, avoiding his gaze; the Warder looked at her whenever her eyes were averted, but he would not speak to her. No one had to ask who Egwene meant.

"It is not right," Loial said, staring at the oak. The Ogier was the only one still not mounted. "It is not right that Treebrother should fall to the Blight." He handed the reins of his big horse to Rand. "Not right."

Lan opened his mouth as the Ogier walked to the great oak. Moiraine, lying on the litter, weakly raised her hand, and the Warder said nothing.

Before the oak, Loial knelt, closing his eyes and stretching out his arms. The tufts on his ears stood straight as he lifted his face to the sky. And he sang.

Rand could not say if there were words, or if it was pure song. In that rumbling voice it was as if the earth sang, yet he was sure he heard the birds trilling again, and spring breezes sighing softly, and the sound of butterfly wings. Lost in the song, he thought it lasted only minutes, but when Loial lowered his arms and opened his eyes, he was surprised to see the sun stood well above the horizon. It had been touching the trees when the Ogier began. The leaves still on the oak seemed greener, and more firmly attached than before. The flowers encircling it stood straighter, the morningstars white and fresh, the loversknots a strong crimson.

Mopping sweat from his broad face, Loial rose and took his reins from Rand. His long eyebrows drooped, abashed, as if they might think he had been showing off. "I've never sung so hard before. I could not have done it if something of Treebrother was not still there. My Tree Songs do not have his power." When he settled himself in his saddle, there was satisfaction in the look he gave the oak and the flowers. "This little space, at least, will not sink into the Blight. The Blight will not have Treebrother."

"You are a good man, Ogier," Lan said.

Loial grinned. "I will take that as a compliment, but I do not know what Elder Haman would say."

They rode in a single file, with Mat behind the Warder where he could use his bow to effect if needed, and Perrin bringing up the rear with his axe across the pommel of his saddle. They crested a hill, and in an eyeblink the Blight was all around them, twisted and rotted in virulent rainbow hues. Rand looked over his shoulder, but the Green Man's garden was nowhere to be seen. Only the Blight stretching behind them as before. Yet he thought, just for a moment, that he saw the towering top of the oak tree, green and lush, before it shimmered and was gone. Then there was only the Blight.

He half expected they would have to fight their way out as they fought their way in, but the Blight was as quiet and still as death. Not a single branch trembled as if to lash at them, nothing screamed or howled, neither nearby nor in the distance. The Blight seemed to crouch, not to pounce, but as if it had been struck a great blow and waited for the next to fall. Even the sun was less red.

When they passed the necklace of lakes, the sun hung not far past its zenith. Lan kept them well away from the lakes and did not even look at them, but Rand thought the seven towers seemed taller than when he first saw them. He was sure the jagged tops were further from the ground, and above them something almost seen, seamless towers gleaming in the sun, and banners with Golden Cranes flying on the wind. He blinked and stared, but the towers refused to vanish completely. They were there at the edge of vision until the Blight hid the lakes once more.

Before sunset the Warder chose a campsite, and Moiraine had Nynaeve and Egwene help her up to set wards. The Aes Sedai whispered in the other women's ears before she began. Nynaeve hesitated, but when Moiraine closed her eyes, all three women did so together.

Rand saw Mat and Perrin staring, and wondered how they could be surprised. *Every woman is an Aes Sedai,* he thought mirthlessly. *The Light help me, so am I.* Bleakness held his tongue.

"Why is it so different?" Perrin asked as Egwene and the Wisdom helped Moiraine to her bed. "It feels. . . ." His thick shoulders shrugged as if he could not find the word.

"We struck a mighty blow at the Dark One," Moiraine replied, settling herself with a sigh. "The Shadow will be a long time recovering."

"How?" Mat demanded. "What did we do?"

"Sleep," Moiraine said. "We are not out of the Blight yet."

But the next morning, still nothing changed that Rand could see. The Blight faded as they rode south, of course. Twisted trees were replaced by straight. The stifling heat diminished. Rotting foliage gave way to the merely diseased. And then not diseased, he realized. The forest around them became red with new growth, thick on the branches. Buds sprouted on the undergrowth, creepers covered the rocks with green, and new wildflowers dotted the grass as thick and bright as where the Green Man walked. It was as if spring, so long held back by winter, now raced to catch up to where it should be.

He was not the only one who stared. "A mighty blow," Moiraine murmured, and would say no more.

Climbing wildrose entwined the stone column marking the Border. Men came out of the watchtowers to greet them. There was a stunned quality to their laughter, and their eyes shone with amaze, as if they could not believe the new grass under their steel-clad feet.

"The Light has conquered the Shadow!"

"A great victory in Tarwin's Gap! We have had the message! Victory!"

"The Light blesses us again!"

"King Easar is strong in the Light," Lan replied to all their shouts.

The watchmen wanted to tend Moiraine, or at least send an escort with them, but she refused it all. Even flat on her back on a litter, the Aes Sedai's presence was such that the armored men fell back, bowing and acceding to her wishes. Their laughter followed as Rand and the others rode on.

In the late afternoon they reached Fal Dara, to find the grim-walled city ringing with celebration. Ringing in truth. Rand doubted if there could be a bell in the city not clanging, from the tiniest silver harness chime to great bronze gongs in their tower tops. The gates stood wide open, and men ran laughing and singing in the streets, flowers stuck in their topknots and the crevices of their armor. The common people of the town had not yet returned from Fal Moran, but the soldiers were newly come from Tarwin's Gap, and their joy was enough to fill the streets.

"Victory in the Gap! We won!"

"A miracle in the Gap! The Age of Legends has come back!"

"Spring!" a grizzled old soldier laughed as he hung a garland of morningstars around Rand's neck. His own topknot was a white cluster of them. "The Light blesses us with spring once more!"

Learning they wanted to go to the keep, a circle of men clad in steel and flowers surrounded them, running to clear a way through the celebration.

Ingtar's was the first face Rand saw that was not smiling. "I was too late," Ingtar told Lan with a sour grimness. "Too late by an hour to see. Peace!" His teeth ground audibly, but then his expression became contrite. "Forgive me. Grief makes me forget my duties. Welcome, Builder. Welcome to you all. It is good to see you safely out of the Blight. I will bring the healer to Moiraine Sedai in her chambers, and inform Lord Agelmar—"

"Take me to Lord Agelmar," Moiraine commanded. "Take us all." Ingtar opened his mouth to protest, and bowed under the force of her eyes.

Agelmar was in his study, with his swords and armor back on their racks, and his was the second face that did not smile. He wore a troubled frown that deepened when he saw Moiraine carried in on her litter by liveried servants. Women in the black-and-gold fluttered over bringing the Aes Sedai to him without a chance to freshen herself or be brought the healer. Loial carried the gold chest. The pieces of the seal were still in Moiraine's pouch; Lews Therin Kinslayer's banner was wrapped in her blanketroll and still tied behind Aldieb's saddle. The groom who had led the white mare away had received the strictest orders to see the blanketroll was placed untouched in the chambers assigned to the Aes Sedai.

"Peace!" the Lord of Fal Dara muttered. "Are you injured, Moiraine Sedai? Ingtar, why have you not seen the Aes Sedai to her bed and brought the healer to her?"

"Be still, Lord Agelmar," Moiraine said. "Ingtar has done as I commanded him. I am not so frail as everyone here seems to think." She motioned two of the women to help her to a chair. For a moment they clasped their hands, exclaiming that she was too weak, that she should be in a warm bed, and the healer brought, and a hot bath. Moiraine's eyebrows lifted; the women shut their mouths abruptly and hurried to aid her into the chair. As soon as she was settled she waved them away irritably. "I would speak with you, Lord Agelmar."

Agelmar nodded, and Ingtar waved the servants from the room. The Lord of Fal Dara eyed those who remained expectantly; especially, Rand thought, Loial and the golden chest.

"We hear," Moiraine said as soon as the door shut behind Ingtar, "that you won a great victory in Tarwin's Gap."

"Yes," Agelmar said slowly, his troubled frown returning. "Yes, Aes Sedai, and no. The Halfmen and their Trollocs were destroyed to the last, but we barely fought. A miracle, my men call it. The earth swallowed them; the mountains buried them. Only a few Draghkar were left, too frightened to do else but fly north as fast as they could."

"A miracle indeed," Moiraine said. "And spring has come again."

"A miracle," Agelmar said, shaking his head, "but. . . . Moiraine Sedai, men say many things about what happened in the Gap. That the Light took on flesh and fought for us. That the Creator walked in the Gap to strike at the Shadow. But I saw a man, Moiraine Sedai. I saw a man, and what he did, cannot be, must not be."

"The Wheel weaves as the Wheel wills, Lord of Fal Dara."

"As you say, Moiraine Sedai."

"And Padan Fain? He is secure? I must speak with him when I am rested."

"He is held as you commanded, Aes Sedai, whining at his guards half the time and trying to command them the rest, but. . . . Peace, Moiraine Sedai, what of you, in the Blight? You found the Green Man? I see his hand in the new things growing."

"We found him," she said flatly. "The Green Man is dead, Lord Agelmar, and the Eye of the World is gone. There will be no more quests by young men seeking glory."

The Lord of Fal Dara frowned, shaking his head in confusion. "Dead? The Green Man? He cannot be. . . . Then you were defeated? But the flowers, and the growing things?"

"We won, Lord Agelmar. We won, and the land freed from winter is the proof, but I fear the last battle has not yet been fought." Rand stirred, but the Aes Sedai gave him a sharp look and he stood still again. "The Blight still stands, and the forges of Thakan'dar still work below Shayol Ghul. There are many Halfmen yet, and countless Trollocs. Never think the need for watchfulness in the Borderlands is gone."

"I did not think it so, Aes Sedai," he said stiffly.

Moiraine motioned for Loial to set the gold chest at her feet, and when he did, she opened it, revealing the horn. "The Horn of Valere," she said, and Agelmar gasped. Rand almost thought the man would kneel.

"With that, Moiraine Sedai, it matters not how many Halfmen or Trollocs remain. With the heroes of old come back from the tomb, we will march to the Blasted Lands and level Shayol Ghul."

"NO!" Agelmar's mouth fell open in surprise, but Moiraine

continued calmly. "I did not show it to you to taunt you, but so that you will know that in whatever battles yet come, our might will be as great as that of the Shadow. Its place is not here. The Horn must be carried to Illian. It is there, if fresh battles threaten, that it must rally the forces of the Light. I will ask an escort of your best men to see that it reaches Illian safely. There are Darkfriends still, as well as Halfmen and Trollocs, and those who come to the horn will follow whoever winds it. It must reach Illian."

"It shall be as you say, Aes Sedai." But when the lid of the chest closed, the Lord of Fal Dara looked like a man being denied his last glimpse of the Light.

Seven days later, bells still rang in Fal Dara. The people had returned from Fal Moran, adding their celebration to that of the soldiers, and shouts and singing blended with the pealing of the bells on the long balcony where Rand stood. The balcony overlooked Agelmar's private gardens, green and flowering, but he did not give them a second look. Despite the sun high in the sky, spring in Shienar was cooler than he was used to, yet sweat glistened on his bare chest and shoulders as he swung the heron-mark blade, each move precise yet distant from where he floated in the void. Even there, he wondered how much joy there would be in the town if they knew of the banner Moiraine still kept hidden.

"Good, sheepherder." Leaning against the railing with his arms folded across his chest, the Warder watched him critically. "You are doing well, but don't push so hard. You can't become a blademaster in a few weeks."

The void vanished like a pricked bubble. "I don't care about being a blademaster."

"It's a blademaster's blade, sheepherder."

"I just want my father to be proud of me." His hand tightened on the rough leather of the hilt. *I just want Tam to be my father.* He slammed the sword into its scabbard. "Anyway, I don't have a few weeks."

"Then you've not changed your mind?"

"Would you?" Lan's expression had not altered; the flat planes of his face looked as if they could not change. "You won't try to stop me? Or Moiraine Sedai?"

"You can do as you will, sheepherder, or as the Pattern

weaves for you." The Warder straightened. "I'll leave you now."

Rand turned to watch Lan go, and found Egwene standing there.

"Changed your mind about what, Rand?"

He snatched up his shirt and coat, suddenly feeling the cool. "I'm going away, Egwene."

"Where?"

"Somewhere. I don't know." He did not want to meet her eyes, but he could not stop looking at her. She wore red wild-roses twined in her hair, flowing about her shoulders. She held her cloak close, dark blue and embroidered along the edge with a thin line of white flowers in the Shienaran fashion, and the blossoms made a line straight up to her face. They were no paler than her cheeks; her eyes seemed so large and dark. "Away."

"I'm sure Moiraine Sedai will not like you just going off. After . . . after what you've done, you deserve some reward."

"Moiraine does not know I am alive. I have done what she wanted, and that's an end to it. She doesn't even speak to me when I go to her. Not that I've tried to stay close to her, but she's avoided me. She won't care if I go, and I don't care if she does."

"Moiraine is still not completely well, Rand." She hesitated. "I have to go to Tar Valon for my training. Nynaeve is coming, too. And Mat still needs to be Healed of whatever binds him to that dagger, and Perrin wants to see Tar Valon before he goes . . . wherever. You could come with us."

"And wait for some Aes Sedai besides Moiraine to find out what I am and gentle me?" His voice was rough, almost a sneer; he could not change it. "Is that what you want?"

"No."

He knew he would never be able to tell her how grateful he was that she had not hesitated before answering.

"Rand, you aren't afraid. . . ." They were alone, but she looked around and still lowered her voice. "Moiraine Sedai says you don't have to touch the True Source. If you don't touch *saidin*, if you don't try to wield the Power, you'll be safe."

"Oh, I won't ever touch it again. Not if I have to cut my hand off, first." *What if I can't stop? I never* tried *to wield it, not even at the Eye. What if I can't stop?*

"Will you go home, Rand? Your father must be dying to see you. Even Mat's father must be dying to see him by now. I'll be coming back to Emond's Field next year. For a little while, at least."

He rubbed his palm over the hilt of his sword, feeling the bronze heron. *My father. Home. Light, how I want to see....* "Not home." *Someplace where there aren't any people to hurt if I can't stop myself. Somewhere alone.* Suddenly it felt as cold as snow on the balcony. "I'm going away, but not home." *Egwene, Egwene, why did you have to be one of those...?* He put his arms around her, and whispered into her hair. "Not ever home."

In Agelmar's private garden, under a thick bower dotted with white blossoms, Moiraine shifted on her bedchair. The fragments of the seal lay on her lap, and the small gem she sometimes wore in her hair spun and glittered on its gold chain from the ends of her fingers. The faint blue glow faded from the stone, and a smile touched her lips. It had no power in itself, the stone, but the first use she had ever learned of the One Power, as a girl, in the Royal Palace in Cairhien, was using the stone to listen to people when they thought they were too far off to be overheard.

"The Prophecies will be fulfilled," the Aes Sedai whispered. "The Dragon is Reborn."

The End

of the First Book of

The Wheel of Time

GLOSSARY

A Note on Dates in This Glossary. The Toman Calendar (devised by Toma dur Ahmid) was adopted approximately two centuries after the death of the last male Aes Sedai and recorded years After the Breaking of the World (AB). Many records were destroyed in the Trolloc Wars, so much so that with the end of the Wars there was argument about the exact year under the old system. A new calendar was proposed by Tiam of Gazar, celebrating the supposed freedom from the Trolloc threat and recording each year as a Free Year (FY). The Gazaran Calendar gained wide acceptance within twenty years after the Wars' end. Artur Hawkwing attempted to establish a new calendar based on the founding of his empire (FF, From the Founding), but this is now known and referred to only by historians. After the widespread destruction, death and disruption of the War of the Hundred Years, a fourth calendar was devised by Uren din Jubai Soaring Gull, a scholar of the Sea Folk, and promulgated by the Panarch Farede of Tarabon. The Farede Calendar, dating from the arbitrarily decided end of the War of the Hundred Years and recording years of the New Era (NE), is currently in use.

Adan, Heran (ay-DAN, HEH-ran): Governor of Baerlon.
Aes Sedai (EYEZ seh-DEYE): Wielders of the One Power. Since the Time of Madness, all surviving Aes Sedai are women. Widely distrusted and feared, even hated, they are blamed by many for the Breaking of the World, and are generally thought to meddle in the affairs of nations. At the same time, few rulers will be without an Aes

Sedai adviser, even in lands where the existence of such a connection must be kept secret. Used as an honorific, so: Sheriam Sedai; and as a high honorific, so: Sheriam Aes Sedai. *See also* Ajah; Amyrlin Seat.

Age Lace: *See* Pattern of an Age.

Age of Legends: The Age ended by the War of the Shadow and the Breaking of the World. A time when Aes Sedai performed wonders now only dreamed of. *See also* Wheel of Time.

Agelmar; Lord Agelmar of House of Jagad (AGH-el-mar; JAH-gad): Lord of Fal Dara. His sign is three running red foxes.

Aiel (eye-EEL): The people of the Aiel Waste. Fierce and hardy. Also called Aielmen. They veil their faces before they kill, giving rise to the saying "acting like a black-veiled Aiel" to describe someone who is being violent. Deadly warriors with weapons or with nothing but their bare hands, they will not touch a sword. Their pipers play them into battle with the music of dances, and Aielmen call battle "the Dance."

Aiel Waste: The harsh, rugged and all-but-waterless land east of the Spine of the World. Few outsiders venture there, not only because water is almost impossible to find for one not born there, but because the Aiel consider themselves at war with all other peoples and do not welcome strangers.

Ajah (AH-jah): Societies among the Aes Sedai, to which all Aes Sedai belong. They are designated by colors: Blue Ajah, Red Ajah, White Ajah, Green Ajah, Brown Ajah, Yellow Ajah, and Gray Ajah. Each follows a specific philosophy of the use of the One Power and purposes of the Aes Sedai. For example, the Red Ajah bends all its energies to finding and gentling men who are attempting to wield the Power. The Brown Ajah, on the other hand, forsakes involvement with the world and dedicates itself to seeking knowledge. There are rumors (hotly denied, and never safely mentioned in front of any Aes Sedai) of a Black Ajah, dedicated to serving the Dark One.

Al Ellisande! (ahlehl-lih-SAHN-dah): In the Old Tongue, "For the Rose of the Sun!"

Aldieb (ahl-DEEB): In the Old Tongue, "West Wind," the wind that brings the spring rains.

al'Meara, Nynaeve (ahl-MEER-ah, NIGH-neev): The Wisdom of Emond's Field.

al'Thor, Rand (ahl-THOR, RAND): A young farmer and sheepherder from the Two Rivers.

al'Vere, Egwene (ahl-VEER, eh-GWAIN): Youngest daughter of the innkeeper in Emond's Field.

Amyrlin Seat (AHM-ehr-lin): (1.) The title of the leader of the Aes Sedai. Elected for life by the Hall of the Tower, the highest council of the Aes Sedai, which consists of three representatives from each of the seven Ajahs. The Amyrlin Seat has, theoretically at least, almost supreme authority among the Aes Sedai. She ranks as the equal of a king or queen. (2.) The throne upon which the leader of the Aes Sedai sits.

Andor (AN-door): The realm within which the Two Rivers lies. The sign of Andor is a rampant white lion on a field of red.

angreal (ahn-gree-AHL): A very rare object which allows anyone capable of channeling the One Power to handle a greater amount of the Power than would be safely possible unaided. Remnants of the Age of Legends, the means of their making is no longer known. *See also sa'angreal.*

Arafel (AH-rah-fehl): One of the Borderlands. The sign of Arafel is three white roses on a field of red, quartered with three red roses on a field of white.

Aram (AY-ram): A young man of the Tuatha'an.

Avendesora (Ah-vehn-deh-SO-rah): In the Old Tongue, "the Tree of Life." Mentioned in many stories and legends.

Aybara, Perrin (ay-BAHR-ah, PEHR-rihn): A young blacksmith's apprentice from Emond's Field.

Ba'alzamon (bah-AHL-zah-mon): In the Trolloc tongue, "Heart of the Dark." Believed to be the Trolloc name for the Dark One.

Baerlon (BAYR-lon): A city in Andor on the road from Caemlyn to the mines in the Mountains of Mist.

Barron, Doral (BAHR-rahn, DOOR-ahl): The Wisdom in Emond's Field prior to Nynaeve al'Meara.

Bel Tine (BEHL TINE): Spring festival in the Two Rivers.

biteme (BITE-me): A small, almost invisible biting insect.

Black Ajah: *See* Ajah.

Blasted Lands: Desolated lands surrounding Shayol Ghul, beyond the Great Blight.

Blight, the: *See* Great Blight, the.

Blue Ajah: *See* Ajah.

Borderlands, the: The nations bordering the Great Blight: Saldaea, Arafel, Kandor, and Shienar.

Bornhald, Dain (BOHRN-hahld, DAY-ihn): An officer of the Children of the Light, son of Lord Captain Geofram Bornhald.

Bornhald, Geofram (BOHRN-hahld, JEHF-rahm): A Lord Captain of the Children of the Light.

Breaking of the World, the: When Lews Therin Telamon and the Hundred Companions resealed the Dark One's prison, the counterstroke tainted *saidin*. Eventually every male Aes Sedai went horribly insane. In their madness these men, who could wield the One Power to a degree now unknown, changed the face of the earth. They caused great earthquakes, leveled mountain ranges, raised new mountains, lifted dry land where seas had been, made the ocean rush in where dry land had been. Many parts of the world were completely depopulated, and the survivors were scattered like dust on the wind. This destruction is remembered in stories, legends and history as the Breaking of the World. *See also* Hundred Companions, the.

Bryne, Gareth (BRIHN, GAH-rehth): Captain-General of the Queen's Guard in Andor. Also serves as Morgase's First Prince of the Sword. His sign is three golden stars, each of five rays.

Byar, Jaret (BY-ahr, JAH-ret): An officer of the Children of the Light.

Caemlyn (KAYM-lihn): The capital city of Andor.

Cairhien (KEYE-ree-EHN): Both a nation along the Spine of the World and the capital city of that nation. The city was burned and looted during the Aiel War (976–978 NE). The sign of Cairhien is a many-rayed golden sun rising from the bottom of a field of sky blue.

Carai an Caldazar! (cah-REYE ahn cahl-dah-ZAHR): In the Old Tongue, "For the honor of the Red Eagle!" The ancient battle cry of Manetheren.

***Carai an Ellisande!*:** In the Old Tongue, "For the honor of the Rose of the Sun!" The battle cry of the last king of Manetheren.

Cauthon, Matrim (Mat) (CAW-thon, MAT-rihm): A young farmer from the Two Rivers.

channel: (1) *(verb)* To control the flow of the One Power. (2) *(noun)* The act of controlling the flow of the One Power.

Charin, Jain (CHAH-rihn, JAY-ihn): *See* Farstrider, Jain.

Children of the Light: A society holding strict ascetic beliefs, dedicated to the defeat of the Dark One and the destruction of all Darkfriends. Founded during the War of the Hundred Years by Lothair Mantelar (LOH-thayr MAHN-tee-LAHR) to proselytize against increasing numbers of Darkfriends, they evolved during the war into a completely military organization, extremely rigid in their beliefs and completely certain that only they know the truth and the right. They hate Aes Sedai, considering them, and any who support or befriend them, Darkfriends. They are known disparagingly as Whitecloaks; their sign is a golden sunburst on a field of white.

Covenant of the Ten Nations: A union formed in the centuries after the Breaking of the World (circa 200 AB). Dedicated to the defeat of the Dark One. Broken apart by the Trolloc Wars.

cuendillar (CWAIN-deh-yar): *See* heartstone.

Damodred, Lord Galadedrid (DAHM-oh-drehd, gah-LAHD-eh-drihd): Only son of Taringail Damodred and Tigraine; half-brother to Elayne and Gawyn. His sign is a winged silver sword, point-down.

Damodred, Prince Taringail (DAHM-oh-drehd, TAH-rihn-gail): A Royal Prince of Cairhien, he married Tigraine and fathered Galadedrid. When Tigraine disappeared and was declared dead, he married Morgase and fathered Elayne and Gawyn. He died in a hunting accident. His sign was a golden, double-bitted battle axe.

Dark One: Most common name, used in every land, for Shai'tan: the source of evil, antithesis of the Creator. Imprisoned by the Creator at the moment of Creation in a prison at Shayol Ghul; an attempt to free him from that prison brought about the War of the Shadow, the tainting of *saidin,* the Breaking of the World, and the end of the Age of Legends.

Dark One, naming the: Saying the true name of the Dark One (Shai'tan) draws his attention, inevitably bringing ill fortune at best, disaster at worst. For that reason many euphemisms are used, among them the Dark One, Father of Lies, Sightblinder, Lord of the Grave, Shepherd of the Night, Heartsbane, Heartfang, Grassburner, and Leafblighter. Someone who seems to be inviting ill fortune is often said to be "naming the Dark One."

Darkfriends: Those who follow the Dark One and believe they will gain great power and rewards when he is freed from his prison.

Daughter-heir: Title of the heir to the throne of Andor. The eldest daughter of the Queen succeeds her mother on the throne. Without a surviving daughter, the throne goes to the nearest female blood-relation of the Queen.

Dha'vol, Dhai'mon (DAH-vohl, DEYE-mon): *See* Trollocs.

Djevik K'Shar (DJEH-vihk KEH-SHAHR): In the Trolloc tongue, "The Dying Ground." The Trolloc name for the Aiel Waste.

Domon, Bayle (DOH-mon, BAIL): The captain of the *Spray.*

Dragon, the: The name by which Lews Therin Telamon was known during the War of the Shadow. In the madness which overtook all male Aes Sedai, Lews Therin killed every living person who carried any of his blood, as well as everyone he loved, thus earning the name Kinslayer. A saying is now used, "taken by the Dragon," or "possessed of the Dragon," to indicate that someone is endangering those around him or threatening them, especially if without cause. *See also* Dragon Reborn.

Dragon, false: Occasionally men claim to be the Dragon Reborn, and sometimes one of them gains following enough to require an army to put it down. Some have begun wars that involved many nations. Over the centuries most have been men unable to channel the One Power, but a few could. All, however, either disappeared, or were captured or killed, without fulfilling any of the Prophecies concerning the Rebirth of the Dragon. These men are called false Dragons. *See also* Dragon Reborn.

Dragon Reborn: According to prophecy and legend the Dragon will be born again at mankind's greatest hour of need to save the world. This is not something people look forward to, both because the prophecies say the Dragon Reborn will bring a new Breaking to the world, and because Lews Therin Kinslayer, the Dragon, is a name to make men shudder, even more than three thousand years after his death. *See also* Dragon, the; Dragon, false.

Dragon's Fang, the: A stylized mark, usually black, in the shape of a teardrop balanced on its point. Scrawled on a door or a house, it is an accusation of evil against the people inside.

Dreadlords: Those men and women who, able to channel the One Power, went over to the Shadow during the Trolloc Wars, acting as commanders of the Trolloc forces.

Easar; King Easar of House Togita (EE-zar; toh-GHEE-tah): King of Shienar. His sigh is a white hart, which according to Shienaran custom is held also to be a sign of Shienar along with the Black Hawk.

Elaida (eh-LY-da): An Aes Sedai who advises Queen Morgase of Andor.

Elayne (ee-LAIN): Queen Morgase's daughter, the Daughter-heir to the Throne of Andor. Her sign is a golden lily.

Else; Else Grinwell (EHLZ GRIHN-wehl): A farmer's daughter met on the Caemlyn Road.

Eyeless, the: *See* Myrddraal.

Fade: *See* Myrddraal.

Fain, Padan (FAIN, PAHD-ahn): A peddler who arrives in Emond's Field just before Winternight.

Far Dareis Mai (FAHR DAH-rize MY): Literally, "Maidens of the Spear." One of a number of warrior societies of the Aiel; unlike any of the others, it admits women and only women. A Maiden may not marry and remain in the society, nor may she fight while carrying a child. Any child born to a Maiden is given to another woman to raise, in such a way that no one knows who the child's mother was. ("You may belong to no man, nor may any man belong to you, nor any child. The spear is your lover, your child, and your life.") These children are treasured, for it is prophesied that a child born of a Maiden will unite the clans and return to the Aiel to the greatness they knew during the Age of Legends.

Farstrider, Jain (JAY-ihn): A hero of the northern lands who journeyed to many lands and had many adventures; the author of several books, as well as being the subject of books and stories. He vanished in 981 NE, after returning from a trip into the Great Blight which some say had taken him all the way to Shayol Ghul.

Father of Lies: *See* Dark One.

First Prince of the Sword: Title normally held by the eldest brother of the Queen of Andor, who has been trained since childhood to command the Queen's armies in time of war and to be her adviser in time of peace. If the Queen has no surviving brother, she will appoint someone to that title.

fist: The basic military unit of the Trollocs, varying in number; always more than one hundred, but never more than two hundred. A fist is usually, but not always, commanded by a Myrddraal.

Five Powers, the: There are threads to the One Power, and each person who can channel the One Power can usually grasp some threads better than others. These threads are named according to the sorts of things that can be done under them—Earth, Air, Fire, Water, and Spirit—and are called the Five Powers. Any wielder of the One Power will have a greater degree of strength with one, or possibly two, of these, and lesser strength in the others. Some few may have great strength with three, but since the Age of Legends no one has had great strength with all five. Even then this was extremely rare. The degree of strength can vary greatly between individuals, so that some who can channel are much stronger than others. Performing certain acts with the One Power requires ability in one or more of the Five Powers. For example, starting or controlling a fire requires Fire, and affecting the weather requires Air and Water, while Healing requires Water and Spirit. While Spirit was found equally in men and in women, great ability with Earth and/or Fire was found much more often among men, with Water and/or Air among women. There were exceptions, but it was so often so that Earth and Fire came to be regarded as male Powers, Air and Water as female. Generally, no ability is considered stronger than any other, though there is a saying among Aes Sedai: "There is no rock so strong that water and wind cannot wear it away, no fire so fierce that water cannot quench it or wind snuff it out." It should be noted this saying came into use long after the last male Aes Sedai was dead. Any equivalent saying among male Aes Sedai is long lost.

Flame of Tar Valon: The symbol of Tar Valon and the Aes Sedai. A stylized representation of a flame; a white teardrop with the point upward.

Forsaken, the: Name given to thirteen of the most powerful Aes Sedai ever known, who went over to the Dark One during the War of the Shadow in return for the promise of immortality. According to both legend and fragmentary records, they were imprisoned along with the Dark One when his prison was reseated. Their names are still used to frighten children.

Galad (gah-LAHD): *See* Damodred, Lord Galadedrid.

Gawyn (GAH-wihn): Queen Morgase's son, Elayne's brother, who will be First Prince of the Sword when Elayne ascends the throne. His sign is a white boar.

gentling: The act, performed by Aes Sedai, of shutting off a male who can channel from the One Power. This is necessary because any man who learns to channel will go insane from the taint upon *saidin* and will almost certainly do horrible things with the Power in his madness. A man who has been gentled can still sense the True Source, but he cannot touch it. Whatever madness has come before gentling is arrested by the act of gentling, but not cured by it, and if it is done soon enough death can be averted.

gleeman: A traveling storyteller, musician, juggler, tumbler and all-around entertainer. Known by their trademark cloaks of many-colored patches, they perform mainly in the villages and smaller towns, since larger towns and cities have other entertainments available.

Great Blight, the: A region in the far north, entirely corrupted by the Dark One. A haunt of Trollocs, Myrddraal, and other creatures of the Dark One.

Great Hunt of the Horn, the: A cycle of stories concerning the legendary search for the Horn of Valere, in the years between the end of the Trolloc Wars and the beginning of the War of the Hundred Years. If told in their entirety, the cycle would take many days.

Great Lord of the Dark: The name by which Darkfriends refer to the Dark One, claiming that to use his true name would be blasphemous.

Great Pattern: The Wheel of Time weaves the Patterns of the Ages into the Great Pattern, which is the whole of existence and reality, past, present and future. Also known as the Lace of Ages. *See also* Pattern of an Age; Wheel of Time.

Great Serpent: A symbol for time and eternity, ancient before the Age of Legends began, consisting of a serpent eating its own tail.

Halfman: *See* Myrddraal.

Hawkwing, Artur: A legendary king who united all the lands west of the Spine of the World, as well as some lands beyond the Aiel Waste. He even sent armies across the Aryth Ocean, but all contact with these was lost at his death, which set off the War of the Hundred Years. His sign was a golden hawk in flight. *See also* War of the Hundred Years.

Heartfang; Heartsbane: *See* Dark One.

heartstone: An indestructible substance created during the Age of Legends. Any known force used in an attempt to break it is absorbed, making heartstone stronger.

Horn of Valere (vah-LEER): The legendary object of the Great Hunt of the Horn. The Horn supposedly can call back dead heroes from the grave to fight against the Shadow.

Hundred Companions, the: One hundred male Aes Sedai, among the most powerful of the Age of Legends, who, led by Lews Therin Telamon, launched the final stroke that ended the War of the Shadow by sealing the Dark One back into his prison. The Dark One's counterstroke tainted *saidin;* the Hundred Companions went mad and began the Breaking of the World.

Illian (IHL-lee-ahn): A great port on the Sea of Storms, capital city of the nation of the same name. The sign of Illian is nine golden bees on a field of dark green.

Ingtar; Lord Ingtar of House Shinowa (IHNG-tahr; shih-NOH-wah): A Shienaran warrior met at Fal Dara.

Kandor (KANH-dohr): One of the Borderlands. The sign of Kandor is a rearing red horse on a field of pale green.

Kinch, Hyam (KIHNCH, HY-ahm): A farmer met on the Caemlyn Road.

Ko'bal (KOH-bahl): *See* Trollocs.

Lace of Ages: *See* Great Pattern, the.

Lan; al'Lan Mandragoran (AHL-LAN man-DRAG-or-an): A warrior from the north; Moiraine's companion.

Leafblighter: *See* Dark One.

league: A measure of distance equal to four miles. *See also* mile.

Luc; Lord Luc of House Mantear (LUKE; MAN-tee-ahr): Tigraine's brother, who would have been her First Prince of the Sword when she ascended the throne. His disappearance in the Great Blight is believed to be in some way connected to Tigraine's later disappearance. His sign was an acorn.

Lurk (LUHRK): *See* Myrddraal.

Machera, Elyas (mah-CHEER-ah, ee-LY-ahs): A man encountered by Perrin and Egwene in the forest.

Mahdi (MAH-dee): In the Old Tongue, "Seeker." Title of the leader of a Tuatha'an carvan.

Malkier (mahl-KEER): A nation, once one of the Borderlands, now consumed by the Blight. The sign of Malkier was a golden crane in flight.

Mandarb (MAHN-dahrb): In the Old Tongue, "Blade."

Manetheren (mahn-EHTH-ehr-ehn): One of the Ten Nations that made the Second Covenant, and also the capital city of that nation. Both city and nation were utterly destroyed in the Trolloc Wars.

Maradon (MAH-rah-don): The capital city of Saldaea.

Merrilin, Thom (MER-rih-lihn, TOM): A gleeman who comes to Emond's Field to perform at Bel Tine.

mile: A measure of distance equal to one thousand spans. Four miles make one league. *See also* span.

Min (MIN): A young woman encountered at the Stag and Lion in Baerlon.

Moiraine (mwah-RAIN): A visitor to Emond's Field who arrives just before Winternight.

Morgase (moor-GAYZ): By the Grace of the Light, Queen

of Andor, High Seat of House Trakand (TRAHK-ahnd). Her sign is three golden keys. The sign of House Trakand is a silver keystone.

Myrddraal (MUHRD-draal): Creatures of the Dark One, commanders of the Trollocs. Twisted offspring of Trollocs in which the human stock used to create the Trollocs has resurfaced, but tainted by the evil that made the Trollocs. Physically they are like men except that they have no eyes, but can see like eagles in light or dark. They have certain powers stemming from the Dark One, including the ability to cause paralyzing fear with a look and the ability to vanish wherever there are shadows. One of their few known weaknesses is that they are reluctant to cross running water. In different lands they are known by many names, among them Halfmen, the Eyeless, Shadowmen, Lurk, and Fade.

One Power, the: The power drawn from the True Source. The vast majority of people are completely unable to learn to channel the One Power. A very small number can be taught to channel, and an even tinier number have the ability inborn. For these few there is no need to be taught; they will touch the True Source and channel the Power whether they want to or not, perhaps without even realizing what they are doing. This inborn ability usually manifests itself in late adolescence or early adulthood. If control is not taught, or self-learned (extremely difficult, with a success rate of only one in four), death is certain. Since the time of Madness, no man has been able to channel the Power without eventually going completely, horribly mad; and then, even if he has learned some control, dying from a wasting sickness which causes the sufferer to rot alive—a sickness caused, as is the madness, by the Dark One's taint on *saidin*. For a woman the death that comes without control of the Power is less horrible, but it is death just the same. Aes Sedai search for girls with the inborn ability as much to save their lives as to increase Aes Sedai numbers, and for men with it in order to stop the terrible things they inevitably do with the Power in their madness. *See also* channel; Time of Madness; True Source.

Pattern of an Age: The Wheel of Time weaves the threads of human lives into the Pattern of an Age, which forms the substance of reality for that Age; also known as Age Lace. *See also ta'veren.*

Questioners, the: An order within the Children of the Light. Their avowed purposes are discovering the truth in disputations and uncovering Darkfriends. In the search for truth and the Light, as they see it, they are even more zealous than the Children of the Light as a whole. Their normal method of inquiry is by torture; their normal attitude that they know the truth already and must only make their victim confess to it. The Questioners refer to themselves as the Hand of the Light, and at times act as if they were entirely separate from the Children and the Council of the Anointed, which commands the Children. The head of the Questioners is the High Inquisitor, who sits on the Council of the Anointed.

Red Ajah: *See* Ajah.

sa'angreal (SAH-ahn-GREE-ahl): An extremely rare object which allows an individual to channel much more of the One Power than would otherwise be possible or safe. A *sa'angreal* is like unto, but much, much more powerful than, an *angreal*. Remnants of the Age of Legends, the means of their making is no longer known.

saidar; saidin (sah-ih-DAHR; sah-ih-DEEN): *See* True Source.

Saldaea (sahl-DAY-ee-ah): One of the Borderlands. The sign of Saldaea is three silver fish on a field of dark blue.

Sea Folk: Inhabitants of islands in the Aryth (AH-rihth) Ocean and the Sea of Storms, they spend little time on those islands, living most of their lives on their ships. Most sea-borne trade is carried by the Sea Folk's ships.

Second Covenant: *See* Covenant of the Ten Nations.

Shadar Logoth (SHAH-dahr LOH-goth): In the Old Tongue, "the Place Where the Shadow Waits." A city abandoned and shunned since the Trolloc Wars. Also called "Shadow's Waiting."

Shadowman: *See* Myrddraal.

Shai'tan (SHAY-ih-TAN): *See* Dark One.

Shayol Ghul (SHAY-ol GHOOL): A mountain in the Blasted Lands, the site of the Dark One's prison.

Shepherd of the Night: *See* Dark One.

Sheriam (SHEER-ee-ahm): An Aes Sedai, of the Blue Ajah.

Shienar (shy-NAHR): One of the Borderlands. The sign of Shienar is a stooping black hawk.

shoufa (SHOO-fah): A garment of the Aiel, a cloth, usually the color of sand or rock, that wraps around the head and neck, leaving only the face bare.

Sightburner: *See* Dark One.

span: A measure of distance equal to two paces. A thousand spans make a mile.

Spine of the World, the: A towering mountain range, with only a few passes, which separates the Aiel Waste from the lands to the west.

stedding (STEHD-ding): An Ogier (OH-geer) homeland. Many *stedding* have been abandoned since the Breaking of the World. They are portrayed in story and legend as havens, and with reason. They are shielded in some way, no longer understood, so that within them no Aes Sedai can channel the One Power, nor even sense that the True Source exists. Attempts to wield the One Power from outside a *stedding* have no effect inside a *stedding* boundary. No Trolloc will enter a *stedding* unless driven, and even a Myrddraal will do so only at the greatest need and then with the greatest reluctance and distaste. Even Darkfriends, if truly dedicated, feel uncomfortable within a *stedding*.

Stone of Tear: The fortress guarding the city of Tear. Said to be the earliest fortress built after the Time of Madness, and said by some to have been built *during* the Time of Madness. *See also* Tear.

Sunday: A feastday and festival in midsummer, widely celebrated.

tabac (tah-BAHK): A weed, widely cultivated. The leaves of it, when dried and cured, are burned in wooden holders called *pipes*, the fumes being inhaled.

Tallanvor, Martyn (TAHL-ahn-vohr, mahr-TEEN): Guardsman-Lieutenant of the Queen's Guard; met in Caemlyn.

ta'maral'ailen (tah-MAHR-ahl-EYE-lehn): In the Old Tongue, "Web of Destiny."

Tanreall, Artur Paendrag (tahn-REE-ahl, AHR-tuhr PAY-ehn-DRAG): *See* Hawkwing, Artur.

Tar Valon (TAHR VAH-lon): A city on an island in the River Erinin. The center of Aes Sedai power, and location of the Amyrlin Seat.

ta'veren (tah-VEER-ehn): A person around whom the Wheel of Time weaves all surrounding life-threads, perhaps *all* life-threads, to form a Web of Destiny. *See also* Pattern of an Age.

Tear (TEER): A great seaport on the Sea of Storms. The sign of Tear is three white crescents on a field of red and gold.

Telamon, Lews Therin (TEHL-ah-mon, LOOZ THEH-rihn): *See also* Dragon, the.

Thakan'dar (thah-kahn-DAHR): An eternally fog-shrouded valley below the slopes of Shayol Ghul.

Tigraine (tee-GRAIN): As Daughter-heir of Andor, she married Taringail Damodred and bore his son Galadedrid. Her disappearance in 972 NE, shortly after her brother Luc vanished in the Blight, led to the struggle in Andor called the Succession, and caused the events in Cairhien which eventually brought on the Aiel War. Her sign was a woman's hand gripping a thorny rose-stem with a white blossom.

Time of Madness: *See* Breaking of the World, the.

Tinkers: *See* Tuatha'an.

Traveling People: *See* Tuatha'an.

Trolloc Wars: A series of wars, beginning about 1000 AB and lasting more than three hundred years, during which Trolloc armies ravaged the world. Eventually the Trollocs were slain or driven back into the Great Blight, but some nations ceased to exist, while others were almost depopulated. All records of the time are fragmentary. *See also* Covenant of the Ten Nations.

Trollocs (TRAHL-lohks): Creatures of the Dark One, created during the War of the Shadow. Huge in stature, vicious in the extreme, they are a twisted blend of animal and human stock, and kill for the pure pleasure of killing. Sly, deceitful and treacherous, they can be trusted only by those they fear. They are omnivorous and will

eat any kind of meat, including human flesh and the flesh
of other Trollocs. Largely of human origin, they are able
to interbreed with humankind, but the offspring are usually stillborn, and those which are not often fail to survive. They are divided into tribe-like bands, chief among
them being the Ahf'frait, Al'ghol, Bhan'sheen, Dha'vol,
Dhai'mon, Dhjin'nen, Ghar'ghael, Ghob'hlin, Gho'hlem,
Ghraem'lan, Ko'bal, and the Kno'mon.

True Source: The driving force of the universe, which
turns the Wheel of Time. It is divided into a male half
(*saidin*) and a female half (*saidar*), which work at the same
time with and against each other. Only a man can draw
on *saidin,* only a woman on *saidar.* Since the beginning
of the Time of Madness, *saidin* has been tainted by the
Dark One's touch. *See also* One Power.

Tuatha'an (too-AH-thah-AHN): A wandering folk, also
known as the Tinkers and as the Traveling People, who
live in brightly painted wagons and follow a totally pacifist philosophy called the Way of the Leaf. Things mended
by Tinkers are often better than new, but the Tuatha'an
are shunned by many villages because of stories that they
steal children and try to convert young people to their
beliefs.

Village Council: In most villages a group of men, elected
by the townsmen and headed by a Mayor, who are responsible for making decisions which affect the village
as a whole and for negotiating with the Councils of other
villages over matters which affect the villages jointly.
They are at odds with the Women's Circle in so many villages that this conflict is seen as almost traditional. *See
also* Women's Circle.

War of the Hundred Years: A series of overlapping wars
among constantly shifting alliances, precipitated by the
death of Artur Hawkwing and the resulting struggle for
his empire. It lasted from FY 994 to FY 1117. The war
depopulated large parts of the lands between the Aryth
Ocean and the Aiel Waste, from the Sea of Storms to
the Great Blight. So great was the destruction that only
fragmentary records of the time remain. The empire of

Artur Hawkwing was pulled apart, and the nations of the present day were formed.

War of the Shadow: Also known as the War of Power, it ended the Age of Legends. It began shortly after the attempt to free the Dark One, and soon involved the whole world. In a world where even the memory of war had been forgotten, every facet of war was rediscovered, often twisted by the Dark One's touch on the World, and the One Power was used as a weapon. The war was ended by the resealing of the Dark One into his prison.

Warder: A warrior bonded to an Aes Sedai. The bonding is a thing of the One Power, and by it he gains such gifts as quick healing, the ability to go long periods without food, water or rest, and the ability to sense the taint of the Dark One at a distance. So long as a Warder lives, the Aes Sedai to whom he is bonded knows he is alive however far away he is, and when he dies she will know the moment and manner of his death. While most Ajahs believe an Aes Sedai may have one Warder bonded to her at a time, the Red Ajah refuses to bond any Warders at all, while the Green Ajah believes an Aes Sedai may bond as many Warders as she wishes. Ethically the Warder must accede to the bonding, but it has been known to be done involuntarily. What the Aes Sedai gain from the bonding is a closely-held secret. *See also* Aes Sedai.

Web of Destiny: A great change in the Pattern of an Age, centered around one or more people who are *ta'veren*.

Wheel of Time, the: Time is a wheel with seven spokes, each spoke an Age. As the Wheel turns, the Ages come and go, each leaving memories that fade to legend, then to myth, and are forgotten by the time that Age comes again. The Pattern of an Age is slightly different each time an Age comes, and each time it is subject to greater change, but each time it is the same Age.

White Ajah: *See* Ajah.

White Tower: The palace of the Amyrlin Seat in Tar Valon.

Whitecloaks: *See* Children of the Light.

Wisdom: In villages, a woman chosen by the Women's Circle to sit in the Circle for her knowledge of such things as healing and foretelling the weather, as well as for common good sense. A position of great responsibility and authority, both actual and implied. She is generally considered the equal of the Mayor, and in some villages his superior. Unlike the Mayor, she is chosen for life, and it is very rare for a Wisdom to be removed from office before her death. Almost traditionally in conflict with the Mayor. *See also* Women's Circle.

Women's Circle: A group of women elected by the women of a village, responsible for deciding such matters as are considered solely women's responsibility (for example, when to plant the crops and when to harvest). Equal in authority to the Village Council, with clearly-delineated lines and areas of responsibility. Often at odds with the Village Council. *See also* Village Council.

PROLOGUE

A preview of
The Great Hunt

Book Two of
The Wheel of Time

In the Shadow

The man who called himself Bors, at least in this place, sneered at the low murmuring that rolled around the vaulted chamber like the soft gabble of geese. His grimace was hidden by the black silk mask that covered his face, though, just like the masks that covered the hundred other faces in the chamber. A hundred black masks, and a hundred pairs of eyes trying to see what lay behind them.

If one did not look too closely, the huge room could have been in a palace, with its tall marble fireplaces and its golden lamps hanging from the domed ceiling, its colorful tapestries and intricately patterned mosaic floor. If one did not look too closely. The fireplaces were cold, for one thing. Flames danced on logs as thick as a man's leg, but gave no heat. The walls behind the tapestries, the ceiling high above the lamps, were undressed stone, almost black. There were no windows, and only two doorways, one at either end of the room. It was as if someone had intended to give the semblance of a palace reception chamber but had not cared enough to bother with more than the outline and a few touches for detail.

Where the chamber was, the man who called himself

.Bors did not know, nor did he think any of the others knew. He did not like to think about where it might be. It was enough that he had been summoned. He did not like to think about that, either, but for such a summons, even he came.

He shifted his cloak, thankful that the fires were cold, else it would have been too hot for the black wool draping him to the floor. All his clothes were black. The bulky folds of the cloak hid the stoop he used to disguise his height, and bred confusion as to whether he was thin or thick. He was not the only one there enveloped in a tailor's span of cloth.

Silently he watched his companions. Patience had marked much of his life. Always, if he waited and watched long enough, someone made a mistake. Most of the men and women here might have had the same philosophy; they watched, and listened silently to those who had to speak. Some people could not bear waiting, or silence, and so gave away more than they knew.

Servants circulated through the guests, slender, golden-haired youths proffering wine with a bow and a wordless smile. Young men and young women alike, they wore tight white breeches and flowing white shirts. And male and female alike, they moved with disturbing grace. Each looked more than a mirror image of the others, the boys as handsome as the girls were beautiful. He doubted he could distinguish one from another, and he had an eye and a memory for faces.

A smiling, white-clad girl offered her tray of crystal goblets to him. He took one with no intention of drinking; it might appear untrusting—or worse, and either could be deadly here—if he refused altogether, but anything could be slipped into a drink. Surely some among his companions would have no objections to seeing the number of their rivals for power dwindle, whomever the unlucky ones happened to be.

Idly he wondered whether the servants would have to be disposed of after this meeting. *Servants hear everything.* As the serving girl straightened from her bow, his eye caught hers above that sweet smile. Blank eyes. Empty eyes. A doll's eyes. Eyes more dead than death.

He shivered as she moved gracefully away, and raised the goblet to his lips before he caught himself. It was not what had been done to the girl that chilled him. Rather, every time he thought he detected a weakness in those he now served, he found himself preceded, the supposed weakness cut out with a ruthless precision that left him amazed. And worried. The first rule of his life had always been to search for weakness, for every weakness was a chink where he could probe and pry and influence. If his current masters, his masters for the moment, had no weakness. . . .

Frowning behind his mask, he studied his companions. At least there was plenty of weakness there. Their nervousness betrayed them, even those who had sense enough to guard their tongues. A stiffness in the way this one held himself, a jerkiness in the way that one handled her skirts.

A good quarter of them, he estimated, had not bothered with disguise beyond the black masks. Their clothes told much. A woman standing before a gold-and-crimson wall hanging, speaking softly to a figure—impossible to say whether it were man or woman—cloaked and hooded in gray. She had obviously chosen the spot because the colors of the tapestry set off her garb. Doubly foolish to draw attention to herself, for her scarlet dress, cut low in the bodice to show too much flesh and high at the hem to display golden slippers, marked her from Illian, and a woman of wealth, perhaps even of noble blood.

Not far beyond the Illianer, another woman stood, alone and admirably silent. With a swan's neck and lustrous black hair falling in waves below her waist, she kept her back to the stone wall, observing everything. No nervousness there, only serene self-possession. Very admirable, that, but her coppery skin and her creamy, high-necked gown—leaving nothing but her hands uncovered, yet clinging and only just barely opaque, so that it hinted at everything and revealed nothing—marked her just as clearly of the first blood of Arad Doman. And unless the man who called himself Bors missed his guess entirely, the wide golden bracelet on her left wrist bore her House symbols. They would be for her own House; no Domani bloodborn would bend her stiff pride enough to wear the sigils of another House. Worse than foolishness.

A man in a high-collared, sky-blue Shienaran coat passed him with a wary, head-to-toe glance through the eyeholes of his mask. The man's carriage named him soldier; the set of his shoulders, the way his gaze never rested in one place for long, and the way his hand seemed ready to dart for a sword that was not there, all proclaimed it. The Shienaran wasted little time on the man who called himself Bors; stooped shoulders and a bent back held no threat.

The man who called himself Bors snorted as the Shienaran moved on, right hand clenching and eyes already studying elsewhere for danger. He could read them all, to class and country. Merchant and warrior, commoner and noble. From Kandor and Cairhien, Saldaea and Ghealdan. From every nation and nearly every people. His nose wrinkled in sudden disgust. Even a Tinker, in bright green breeches and a virulent yellow coat. *We can do without* those *come the Day.*

The disguised ones were no better, many of them, cloaked and shrouded as they were. He caught sight, under the edge of one dark robe, of the silver-worked boots of a High Lord of Tear, and under another a glimpse of golden lion-head spurs, worn only by high officers in the Andoran Queen's Guards. A slender fellow—slender even in a floor-dragging black robe and an anonymous gray cloak caught with a plain silver pin—watched from the shadows of his deep cowl. He could be anyone, from anywhere . . . except for the six-pointed star tattooed on the web between thumb and forefinger of his right hand. One of the Sea Folk then, and a look at his left hand would show the marks of his clan and line. The man who called himself Bors did not bother to try.

Suddenly his eyes narrowed, fixing on a woman enveloped in black till nothing showed but her fingers. On her right hand rested a gold ring in the shape of a serpent eating its own tail. Aes Sedai, or at least a woman trained in Tar Valon by Aes Sedai. None else would wear that ring. Either way made no difference to him. He looked away before she could notice his watching, and almost immediately he spotted another woman swathed from head to toe in black and wearing a Great Serpent ring. The two witches gave no sign that they knew each other. In the White Tower they sat like spiders in the middle of a web, pulling the strings that made kings and queens dance, meddling. *Curse them all to death eternal!* He realized that he was grinding his teeth. If numbers must dwindle—and they must, before the Day—there were some who would be missed even less than Tinkers.

A chime sounded, a single, shivering note that came from everywhere at once and cut off all other sounds like a knife.

The tall doors at the far end of the chamber swung open, and two Trollocs stepped into the room, spikes decorating the black mail that hung to their knees. Everyone shied back. Even the man who called himself Bors.

Head and shoulders taller than the tallest man there, they were a stomach-turning blend of man and animal, human faces twisted and altered. One had a heavy, pointed beak where his mouth and nose should have been, and feathers covered his head instead of hair. The other walked on hooves, his face pushed out in a hairy muzzle, and goat horns stuck up above his ears.

Ignoring the humans, the Trollocs turned back toward the door and bowed, servile and cringing. The feathers on the one lifted in a tight crest.

A Myrddraal stepped between them, and they fell to their knees. It was garbed in black that made the Trollocs' mail and the humans' masks seem bright, garments that hung still, without a ripple, as it moved with a viper's grace.

The man who called himself Bors felt his lips drawing back over his teeth, half snarl and half, he was shamed to admit even to himself, fear. It had its face uncovered. Its pasty pale face, a man's face, but eyeless as an egg, like a maggot in a grave.

The smooth white face swiveled, regarding them all one by one, it seemed. A visible shiver ran through them under that eyeless look. Thin, bloodless lips quirked in what might almost have been a smile as, one by one, the masked ones tried to press back into the crowd, milling to avoid that gaze. The Myrddraal's look shaped them into a semicircle facing the door.

The man who called himself Bors swallowed. *There will come a day, Halfman. When the Great Lord of the Dark comes again, he will choose his new Dreadlords, and you will cower before them. You will cower before men. Before me! Why doesn't it speak? Stop staring at me, and speak!*

"Your Master comes." The Myrddraal's voice rasped like a dry snakeskin crumbling. "To your bellies, worms! Grovel, lest his brilliance blind and burn you!"

Rage filled the man who called himself Bors, at the tone

as much as the words, but then the air above the Half-man shimmered, and the import drove home. *It can't be! It can't . . . !* The Trollocs were already on their bellies, writhing as if they wanted to burrow into the floor.

Without waiting to see if anyone else moved, the man who called himself Bors dropped facedown, grunting as he bruised himself on the stone. Words sprang to his lips like a charm against danger—they were a charm, though a thin reed against what he feared—and he heard a hundred other voices, breathy with fear, speaking the same against the floor.

"The Great Lord of the Dark is my Master, and most heartily do I serve him to the last shred of my very soul." In the back of his mind a voice chattered with fear. *The Dark One and all the Forsaken are bound. . . .* Shivering, he forced it to silence. He had abandoned that voice long since. "Lo, my Master is death's Master. Asking nothing do I serve against the Day of his coming, yet do I serve in the sure and certain hope of life everlasting." *. . . bound in Shayol Ghul, bound by the Creator at the moment of creation. No, I serve a different master now.* "Surely the faithful shall be exalted in the land, exalted above the unbelievers, exalted above thrones, yet do I serve humbly against the Day of his Return." *The hand of the Creator shelters us all, and the Light protects us from the Shadow. No, no! A different master.* "Swift come the Day of Return. Swift come the Great Lord of the Dark to guide us and rule the world forever and ever."

The man who called himself Bors finished the creed panting, as if he had run ten miles. The rasp of breath all around told him he was not the only one.

"Rise. All of you, rise."

The mellifluous voice took him by surprise. Surely none of his companions, lying on their bellies with their masked faces pressed to the mosaic tiles, would have spoken, but it was not the voice he expected from. . . . Cautiously, he raised his head enough to see with one eye.

The figure of a man floated in the air above the Myrddraal, the hem of his blood red robe hanging a span over the Halfman's head. Masked in blood red, too. Would the Great Lord of the Dark appear to them as a man? And masked, besides? Yet the Myrddraal, its very gaze fear, trembled and almost cowered where it stood in the figure's shadow. The man who called himself Bors grasped for an answer his mind could contain without splitting. One of the Forsaken, perhaps.

That thought was only a little less painful. Even so, it meant the Day of the Dark One's return must be close at hand if one of the Forsaken was free. The Forsaken, thirteen of the most powerful wielders of the One Power in an Age filled with powerful wielders, had been sealed up in Shayol Ghul along with the Dark One, sealed away from the world of men by the Dragon and the Hundred Companions. And the backblast of that sealing had tainted the male half of the True Source; and all the male Aes Sedai, those cursed wielders of the Power, went mad and broke the world, tore it apart like a pottery bowl smashed on rocks, ending the Age of Legends before they died, rotting while they still lived. A fitting death for Aes Sedai, to his mind. Too good for them. He regretted only that the women had been spared.

Slowly, painfully, he forced the panic to the back of his mind, confined it and held it tight though it screamed to get out. It was the best he could do. None of those on their bellies had risen, and only a few had even dared raise their heads.

"Rise." There was a snap in the red-masked figure's voice this time. He gestured with both hands. "Stand!"

The man who called himself Bors scrambled up awkwardly, but halfway to his feet, he hesitated. Those gesturing hands were horribly burned, crisscrossed by black fissures, the raw flesh between as red as the figure's robes. *Would the Dark One appear so? Or even one of the Forsaken?* The eyeholes of that blood red mask swept slowly across him, and he straightened hastily. He thought he could feel the heat of an open furnace in that gaze.

The others obeyed the command with no more grace and no less fear in their rising. When all were on their feet, the floating figure spoke.

"I have been known by many names, but the one by which you shall know me is Ba'alzamon."

The man who called himself Bors clamped his teeth to keep them from chattering. Ba'alzamon. In the Trolloc tongue, it meant Heart of the Dark, and even unbelievers knew it was the Trolloc name for the Great Lord of the

Dark. He Whose Name Must Not Be Uttered. Not the True Name, Shai'tan, but still forbidden. Among those gathered here, and others of their kind, to sully either with a human tongue was blasphemy. His breath whistled through his nostrils, and all around him he could hear others panting behind their masks. The servants were gone, and the Trollocs as well, though he had not seen them go.

"The place where you stand lies in the shadow of Shayol Ghul." More than one voice moaned at that; the man who called himself Bors was not sure his own was not among them. A touch of what might almost be called mockery entered Ba'alzamon's voice as he spread his arms wide. "Fear not, for the Day of your Master's rising upon the world is near at hand. The Day of Return draws nigh. Does it not tell you so that I am here, to be seen by you favored few among your brothers and sisters? Soon the Wheel of Time will be broken. Soon the Great Serpent will die, and with the power of that death, the death of Time itself, your Master will remake the world in his own image for this Age and for all Ages to come. And those who serve me, faithful and steadfast, will sit at my feet above the stars in the sky and rule the world of men forever. So have I promised, and so shall it be, without end. You shall live and rule forever."

A murmur of anticipation ran through the listeners, and some even took a step forward, toward the floating, crimson shape, their eyes lifted, rapturous. Even the man who called himself Bors felt the pull of that promise, the promise for which he had dealt away his soul a hundred times over.

"The Day of Return comes closer," Ba'alzamon said. "But there is much yet to do. Much to do."

The air to Ba'alzamon's left shimmered and thickened, and the figure of a young man hung there, a little lower than Ba'alzamon. The man who called himself Bors could not decide whether it was a living being or not. A country lad, by his clothes, with a light of mischief in his brown eyes and the hint of a smile on his lips, as if in memory or anticipation of a prank. The flesh looked warm, but the chest did not move with breath, the eyes did not blink.

The air to Ba'alzamon's right wavered as if with heat, and a second country-clad figure hung suspended a little below Ba'alzamon. A curly-haired youth, as heavily muscled as a blacksmith. And an oddity: a battle-axe hung at his side, a

great, steel half-moon balanced by a thick spike. The man
who called himself Bors suddenly leaned forward, intent on
an even greater strangeness. A youth with yellow eyes.

For the third time air solidified into the shape of a young
man, this time directly under Ba'alzamon's eye, almost at his
feet. A tall fellow, with eyes now gray, now almost blue as
the light took them, and dark, reddish hair. Another villager,
or farmer. The man who called himself Bors gasped. Yet another thing out of the ordinary, though he wondered why he
should expect anything to be ordinary here. A sword swung
from the figure's belt, a sword with a bronze heron on the
scabbard and another inset into the long, two-handed hilt. *A
village boy with a heron-mark blade? Impossible! What can
it mean? And a boy with yellow eyes.* He noticed the Myrddraal looking at the figures, trembling; and unless he misjudged entirely, its trembling was no longer fear, but hatred.

Dead silence had fallen, silence that Ba'alzamon let
deepen before he spoke. "There is now one who walks the
world, one who was and will be, but is not yet, the Dragon."

A startled murmur ran through his listeners.

"The Dragon Reborn! We are to kill him, Great Lord?"
That from the Shienaran, hand grasping eagerly at his side
where his sword would hang.

"Perhaps," Ba'alzamon said simply. "And perhaps not.
Perhaps he can be turned to my use. Sooner or later it will
be so, in this Age or another."

The man who called himself Bors blinked. *In this Age or
another? I thought the Day of Return was near. What matter to me what happens in another Age if I grow old and die
waiting in this one?* But Ba'alzamon was speaking again.

"Already a bend is forming in the Pattern, one of many
points where he who will become the Dragon may be
turned to my service. Must be turned! Better that he serve
me alive than dead, but alive or dead, serve me he must and
will! These three you must know, for each is a thread in the
pattern *I* mean to weave, and it will be up to you to see that
they are placed as I command. Study them well, that you
will know them."

Abruptly all sound was gone. The man who called himself
Bors shifted uneasily, and saw others doing the same. All but
the Illianer woman, he realized. With her hands spread over
her bosom as if to hide the rounded flesh she exposed, eyes

wide, half frightened and half ecstatic, she was nodding eagerly as though to someone face-to-face with her. Sometimes she appeared to give a reply, but the man who called himself Bors heard not a word. Suddenly she arched backwards, trembling and rising on her toes. He could not see why she did not fall, unless something unseen held her. Then, just as abruptly, she settled back to her feet and nodded again, bowing, shivering. Even as she straightened, one of the women wearing a Great Serpent ring gave a start and began nodding.

So each of us hears his own instructions, and none hears another's. The man who called himself Bors muttered in frustration. If he knew what even one other was commanded, he might be able to use the knowledge to advantage, but this way. . . . Impatiently he waited for his turn, forgetting himself enough to stand straight.

One by one the gathering received their orders, each walled in silence yet still giving tantalizing clues, if only he could read them. The man of the Atha'an Miere, the Sea Folk, stiffening with reluctance as he nodded. The Shienaran, his stance bespeaking confusion even while he acquiesced. The second woman of Tar Valon giving a start, as of shock, and the gray-swathed figure whose sex he could not determine shaking its head before falling to its knees and nodding vigorously. Some underwent the same convulsion as the Illianer woman, as if pain itself lifted them to toe tips.

"Bors."

The man who called himself Bors jerked as a red mask filled his eyes. He could still see the room, still see the floating shape of Ba'alzamon and the three figures before him, but at the same time all he could see was the red-masked face. Dizzy, he felt as if his skull were splitting open and his eyes were being pushed out of his head. For a moment he thought he could see flames through the eyeholes of the mask.

"Are you faithful . . . Bors?"

The hint of mocking in the name sent a chill down his backbone. "I am faithful, Great Lord. I cannot hide from you." *I am faithful! I swear it!*

"No, you cannot."

The certainty in Ba'alzamon's voice dried his mouth, but

he forced himself to speak. "Command me, Great Lord, and I obey."

"Firstly, you are to return to Tarabon and continue your *good* works. In fact, I command you to redouble your efforts."

He stared at Ba'alzamon in puzzlement, but then fires flared again behind the mask, and he took the excuse of a bow to pull his eyes away. "As you command, Great Lord, so shall it be."

"Secondly, you will watch for the three young men, and have your followers watch. Be warned; they are dangerous."

The man who called himself Bors glanced at the figures floating in front of Ba'alzamon. *How can I do that? I can see them, but I can't see anything except* his *face.* His head felt about to burst. Sweat slicked his hands under his thin gloves, and his shirt clung to his back. "Dangerous, Great Lord? Farmboys? Is one of them the—"

"A sword is dangerous to the man at the point, but not to the man at the hilt. Unless the man holding the sword is a fool, or careless, or unskilled, in which case it is twice as dangerous to him as to anyone else. It is enough that I have told you to know them. It is enough that you obey me."

"As you command, Great Lord, so shall it be."

"Thirdly, regarding those who have landed at Toman Head, and the Domani. Of this you will speak to no one. When you return to Tarabon. . . ."

The man who called himself Bors realized as he listened that his mouth was sagging open. The instructions made no sense. *If I knew what some of the others were told, perhaps I could piece it together.*

Abruptly, he felt his head grasped as though by a giant hand crushing his temples, felt himself being lifted, and the world blew apart in a thousand starbursts, each flash of light becoming an image that fled across his mind or spun and dwindled into the distance before he could more than barely grasp it. An impossible sky of striated clouds, red and yellow and black, racing as if driven by the mightiest wind the world had ever seen. A woman—a girl?—dressed in white receded into blackness and vanished as soon as she appeared. A raven stared him in the eye, *knowing* him, and was gone. An armored man in a brutal helm, shaped and painted and gilded like some monstrous, poisonous insect, raised a sword and plunged to one side, beyond his view. A horn, curled and golden, came hurtling out of the far distance. One piercing note it sounded as it flashed toward him, tugging his soul. At the last instant it flashed into a blinding, golden ring of light that passed through him, chilling him beyond death. A wolf leaped from the shadows of lost sight and ripped out his throat. He could not scream. The torrent went on, drowning him, burying him. He could barely remember who he was, or what he was. The skies rained fire, and the moon and stars fell; rivers ran in blood, and the dead walked; the earth split open and fountained molten rock. . . .

The man who called himself Bors found himself half crouching in the chamber with the others, most watching him, all silent. Wherever he looked, up or down or in any direction, the masked face of Ba'alzamon overwhelmed his eyes. The images that had flooded into his mind were fading; he was sure many were already gone from memory. Hesitantly, he straightened, Ba'alzamon always before him.

"Great Lord, what—?"

"Some commands are too important to be known even by he who carries them out."

The man who called himself Bors bent almost double in his bow. "As you command, Great Lord," he whispered hoarsely, "so shall it be."

When he straightened, he was alone in silence once more. Another, the Taren High Lord, nodded and bowed to someone none else saw. The man who called himself Bors put an unsteady hand to his brow, trying to hold on to something of what had burst through his mind, though he was not completely certain he wanted to remember. The last remnant flickered out, and suddenly he was wondering what it was that he was trying to recall. *I know there was something, but what? There* was *something! Wasn't there?* He rubbed his hands together, grimacing at the feel of sweat under his gloves, and turned his attention to the three figures hanging suspended before Ba'alzamon's floating form.

The muscular, curly-haired youth; the farmer with the sword; and the lad with the look of mischief on his face. Already, in his mind, the man who called himself Bors had named them the Blacksmith, the Swordsman, and the

Trickster. *What is their place in the puzzle?* They must be important, or Ba'alzamon would not have made them the center of this gathering. But from his orders alone they could all die at any time, and he had to think that some of the others, at least, had orders as deadly for the three. *How important are they?* Blue eyes could mean the nobility of Andor—unlikely in those clothes—and there were Borderlanders with light eyes, as well as some Tareni, not to mention a few from Ghealdan, and, of course. . . . No, no help there. But *yellow* eyes? *Who* are *they?* What *are they?*

He started at a touch on his arm, and looked around to find one of the white-clad servants, a young man, standing by his side. The others were back, too, more than before, one for each of the masked. He blinked. Ba'alzamon was gone. The Myrddraal was gone, too, and only rough stone was where the door it had used had been. The three figures still hung there, though. He felt as if they were staring at him.

"If it please you, my Lord Bors, I will show you to your room."

Avoiding those dead eyes, he glanced once more at the three figures, then followed. Uneasily he wondered how the youth had known what name to use. It was not until the strange carved doors closed behind him and they had walked a dozen paces that he realized he was alone in the corridor with the servant. His brows drew down suspiciously behind his mask, but before he could open his mouth, the servant spoke.

"The others are also being shown to their rooms, my Lord. If you please, my Lord? Time is short, and our Master is impatient."

The man who called himself Bors ground his teeth, both at the lack of information and at the implication of sameness between himself and the servant, but he followed in silence. Only a fool ranted at a servant, and worse, remembering the fellow's eyes, he was not sure it would do any good. *And how did he know what I was going to ask?* The servant smiled.

The man who called himself Bors did not feel at all comfortable until he was back in the room where he had waited on first arriving, and then not much. Even finding the seals on his saddlebags untouched was small comfort.

The servant stood in the hallway, not entering. "You may change to your own garments if you wish, my Lord. None will see you depart here, nor arrive at your destination, but it may be best to arrive already properly clothed. Someone will come soon to show you the way."

Untouched by any visible hand, the door swung shut.

The man who called himself Bors shivered in spite of himself. Hastily he undid the seals and buckles of his saddlebags and pulled out his usual cloak. In the back of his mind a small voice wondered if the promised power, even the immortality, was worth another meeting like this, but he laughed it down immediately. *For that much power, I would praise the Great Lord of the Dark under the Dome of Truth.* Remembering the commands given him by Ba'alzamon, he fingered the golden, flaring sun worked on the breast of the white cloak, and the red shepherd's crook behind the sun, symbol of his office in the world of men, and he almost laughed. There was work, great work, to be done in Tarabon, and on Almoth Plain.

About the Author

Robert Jordan was born in 1948 in Charleston, South Carolina. He taught himself to read when he was four with the incidental aid of a twelve-years-older brother, and was tackling Mark Twain and Jules Verne by five. He was a graduate of the Citadel, the Military College of South Carolina, with a degree in physics. He served two tours in Vietnam with the U.S. Army; among his decorations are the Distinguished Flying Cross with bronze oak leaf cluster, the Bronze Star with "V" and bronze oak leaf cluster, and two Vietnamese Gallantry Crosses with Palm. A history buff, he also wrote dance and theater criticism. He enjoyed the outdoor sports of hunting, fishing, and sailing, and the indoor sports of poker, chess, pool, and pipe collecting. He began writing in 1977 and continued until his death on September 16, 2007.

Praise for Robert Jordan and The Wheel of Time®

"His huge, ambitious Wheel of Time series helped redefine the genre." —George R. R. Martin, internationally bestselling author of *A Game of Thrones*

"Anyone who's writing epic secondary world fantasy knows Robert Jordan isn't just a part of the landscape, he's a monolith within the landscape." —Patrick Rothfuss, internationally bestselling author of The Kingkiller Chronicle

"*The Eye of the World* was a turning point in my life. I read, I enjoyed. (Then continued on to write my larger fantasy novels.)" —Robin Hobb, *New York Times* bestselling author of The Farseer Trilogy

"Robert Jordan's work has been a formative influence and an inspiration for a generation of fantasy writers." —Brent Weeks, *New York Times* bestselling author of *The Way of Shadows*

"Jordan has come to dominate the world Tolkien began to reveal." —*The New York Times*

"One of fantasy's most acclaimed series." —*USA Today*

"Robert Jordan was a giant of fiction whose words helped a whole generation of fantasy writers, including myself, find our true voices. I thanked him then, but I didn't thank him enough." —Peter V. Brett, internationally bestselling author of The Demon Cycle

"[Robert Jordan's] impact on the place of fantasy in the culture is colossal. . . . He brought innumerable readers to fantasy. He became the *New York Times* Best Seller List's face of fantasy." —Guy Gavriel Kay, internationally bestselling author of *Tigana*

"Jordan's writing is so amazing! The characterization, the attention to detail!" —Clint McElroy, cocreator of the #1 podcast *The Adventure Zone*

"The Wheel of Time [is] rapidly becoming the definitive American fantasy saga. It is a fantasy tale seldom equaled and still less often surpassed in English." —*Chicago Sun-Times*

"Hard to put down for even a moment. A fittingly epic conclusion to a fantasy series that many consider one of the best of all time." —*San Francisco Book Review* on *A Memory of Light*

The Wheel of Time®

By Robert Jordan

By Robert Jordan and Brandon Sanderson

By Robert Jordan and Teresa Patterson

By Robert Jordan, Harriet McDougal, Alan Romanczuk, and Maria Simons

THE GREAT HUNT

ROBERT JORDAN

A TOM DOHERTY ASSOCIATES BOOK
NEW YORK

This is a work of fiction. All of the characters, organizations, and events portrayed in this novel are either products of the author's imagination or are used fictitiously.

THE GREAT HUNT

Copyright © 1990 by Bandersnatch Group, Inc.

Excerpt from *The Dragon Reborn* copyright © 1991 by Bandersnatch Group, Inc.

The phrase "The Wheel of Time" and the snake-wheel symbol are trademarks of Bandersnatch Group, Inc.

Maps by Ellisa Mitchell
Interior art by Matthew C. Nielsen and Ellisa Mitchell

A Tor Book
Published by Tom Doherty Associates
120 Broadway
New York, NY 10271

www.tor-forge.com

Tor® is a registered trademark of Macmillan Publishing Group, LLC.

ISBN 978-1-250-25148-0

Our books may be purchased in bulk for promotional, educational, or business use. Please contact your local bookseller or the Macmillan Corporate and Premium Sales Department at 1-800-221-7945, extension 5442, or by email at MacmillanSpecialMarkets@macmillan.com.

First Edition: November 1990
First Premium Mass Market Edition: November 2019

Printed in the United States of America

0   9   8   7   6

This book is dedicated to Lucinda Culpin, Al Dempsey, Tom Doherty, Susan England, Dick Gallen, Cathy Grooms, Marisa Grooms, Wilson and Janet Grooms, John Jarrold, the Johnson City Boys (Mike Leslie, Kenneth Loveless, James D. Lund, Paul R. Robinson), Karl Lundgren, William McDougal, the Montana Gang (Eldon Carter, Ray Grenfell, Ken Miller, Rod Moore, Dick Schmidt, Ray Sessions, Ed Wildey, Mike Wildey, and Sherman Williams), Charlie Moore, Louisa Cheves Popham Raoul, Ted and Sydney Rigney, Robert A. T. Scott, Bryan and Sharon Webb, and Heather Wood.

They came to my aid when God walked across the water and the true Eye of the World passed over my house.

—Robert Jordan
Charleston, SC
February 1990

Contents

And it shall come to pass that what men made shall be shattered, and the Shadow shall lie across the Pattern of the Age, and the Dark One shall once more lay his hand upon the world of man. Women shall weep and men quail as the nations of the earth are rent like rotting cloth. Neither shall anything stand nor abide . . .

Yet one shall be born to face the Shadow, born once more as he was born before and shall be born again, time without end. The Dragon shall be Reborn, and there shall be wailing and gnashing of teeth at his rebirth. In sackcloth and ashes shall he clothe the people, and he shall break the world again by his coming, tearing apart all ties that bind. Like the unfettered dawn shall he blind us, and burn us, yet shall the Dragon Reborn confront the Shadow at the Last Battle, and his blood shall give us the Light. Let tears flow, O ye people of the world. Weep for your salvation.

> —from *The Karaethon Cycle:*
> *The Prophecies of the Dragon,*
> as translated by Ellaine Marise'idin Alshinn,
> Chief Librarian at the Court of Arafel,
> in the Year of Grace 231
> of the New Era, the Third Age

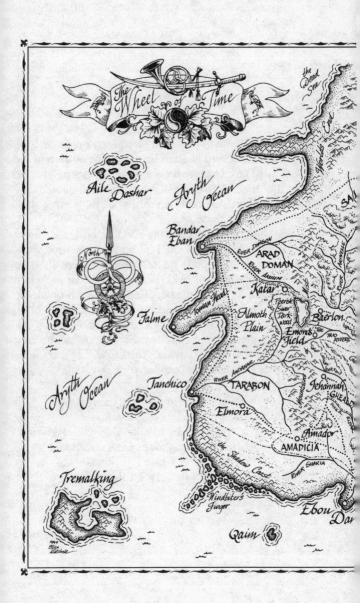

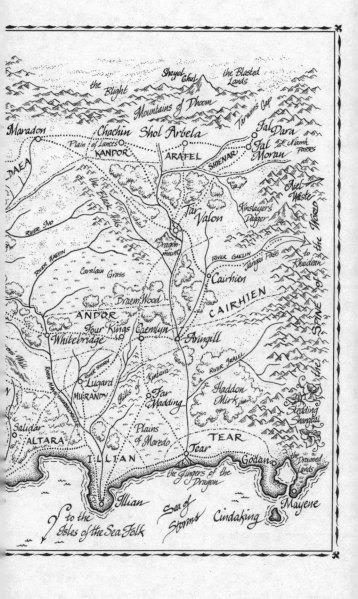

PROLOGUE

In the Shadow

The man who called himself Bors, at least in this place, sneered at the low murmuring that rolled around the vaulted chamber like the soft gabble of geese. His grimace was hidden by the black silk mask that covered his face, though, just like the masks that covered the hundred other faces in the chamber. A hundred black masks, and a hundred pairs of eyes trying to see what lay behind them.

If one did not look too closely, the huge room could have been in a palace, with its tall marble fireplaces and its golden lamps hanging from the domed ceiling, its colorful tapestries and intricately patterned mosaic floor. If one did not look too closely. The fireplaces were cold, for one thing. Flames danced on logs as thick as a man's leg, but gave no heat. The walls behind the tapestries, the ceiling high above the lamps, were undressed stone, almost black. There were no windows, and only two doorways, one at either end of the room. It was as if someone had intended to give the semblance of a palace reception chamber but had not cared enough to bother with more than the outline and a few touches for detail.

Where the chamber was, the man who called himself Bors did not know, nor did he think any of the others knew. He did not like to think about where it might be. It was enough that he had been summoned. He did not like to think about that, either, but for such a summons, even he came.

He shifted his cloak, thankful that the fires were cold, else it would have been too hot for the black wool draping him to the floor. All his clothes were black. The bulky folds of the cloak hid the stoop he used to disguise his height, and bred confusion as to whether he was thin or thick. He was not the only one there enveloped in a tailor's span of cloth.

Silently he watched his companions. Patience had marked much of his life. Always, if he waited and watched long enough, someone made a mistake. Most of the men and women here might have had the same philosophy; they watched, and listened silently to those who had to speak. Some people could not bear waiting, or silence, and so gave away more than they knew.

Servants circulated through the guests, slender, golden-haired youths proffering wine with a bow and a wordless smile. Young men and young women alike, they wore tight white breeches and flowing white shirts. And male and female alike, they moved with disturbing grace. Each looked more than a mirror image of the others, the boys as handsome as the girls were beautiful. He doubted he could distinguish one from another, and he had an eye and a memory for faces.

A smiling, white-clad girl offered her tray of crystal goblets to him. He took one with no intention of drinking; it might appear untrusting—or worse, and either could be deadly here—if he refused altogether, but anything could be slipped into a drink. Surely some among his companions would have no objections to seeing the number of their rivals for power dwindle, whomever the unlucky ones happened to be.

Idly he wondered whether the servants would have to be disposed of after this meeting. *Servants hear everything.* As the serving girl straightened from her bow, his eye caught hers above that sweet smile. Blank eyes. Empty eyes. A doll's eyes. Eyes more dead than death.

He shivered as she moved gracefully away, and raised the goblet to his lips before he caught himself. It was not what had been done to the girl that chilled him. Rather, every time he thought he detected a weakness in those he now served, he found himself preceded, the supposed weakness cut out with a ruthless precision that left him amazed. And worried. The first rule of his life had always been to search for weakness, for every weakness was a chink where he could probe and pry and influence. If his current masters, his masters for the moment, had no weakness. . . .

Frowning behind his mask, he studied his companions. At least there was plenty of weakness there. Their nervousness betrayed them, even those who had sense enough to guard their tongues. A stiffness in the way this one held himself, a jerkiness in the way that one handled her skirts.

A good quarter of them, he estimated, had not bothered with disguise beyond the black masks. Their clothes told much. A woman standing before a gold-and-crimson wall hanging, speaking softly to a figure—impossible to say whether it was man or woman—cloaked and hooded in gray. She had obviously chosen the spot because the colors of the tapestry set off her garb. Doubly foolish to draw attention to herself, for her scarlet dress, cut low in the bodice to show too much flesh and high at the hem to display golden slippers, marked her from Illian, and a woman of wealth, perhaps even of noble blood.

Not far beyond the Illianer, another woman stood, alone and admirably silent. With a swan's neck and lustrous black hair falling in waves below her waist, she kept her back to the stone wall, observing everything. No nervousness there, only serene self-possession. Very admirable, that, but her coppery skin and her creamy, high-necked gown—leaving nothing but her hands uncovered, yet clinging and only just barely opaque, so that it hinted at everything and revealed nothing—marked her just as clearly of the first blood of Arad Doman. And unless the man who called himself Bors missed his guess entirely, the wide golden bracelet on her left wrist bore her House symbols. They would be for her own House; no Domani bloodborn would bend her stiff pride enough to wear the sigils of another House. Worse than foolishness.

A man in a high-collared, sky-blue Shienaran coat passed him with a wary, head-to-toe glance through the eyeholes of his mask. The man's carriage named him soldier; the set of his shoulders, the way his gaze never rested in one place for long, and the way his hand seemed ready to dart for a sword that was not there, all proclaimed it. The Shienaran wasted little time on the man who called himself Bors; stooped shoulders and a bent back held no threat.

The man who called himself Bors snorted as the Shie-naran moved on, right hand clenching and eyes already studying elsewhere for danger. He could read them all, to class and country. Merchant and warrior, commoner and noble. From Kandor and Cairhien, Saldaea and Gheal-dan. From every nation and nearly every people. His nose wrinkled in sudden disgust. Even a Tinker, in bright green breeches and a virulent yellow coat. *We can do without those come the Day.*

The disguised ones were no better, many of them, cloaked and shrouded as they were. He caught sight, under the edge of one dark robe, of the silver-worked boots of a High Lord of Tear, and under another a glimpse of golden lion-head spurs, worn only by high officers in the Andoran Queen's Guards. A slender fellow—slender even in a floor-dragging black robe and an anonymous gray cloak caught with a plain silver pin—watched from the shadows of his deep cowl. He could be anyone, from anywhere . . . except for the six-pointed star tattooed on the web between thumb and forefinger of his right hand. One of the Sea Folk then, and a look at his left hand would show the marks of his clan and line. The man who called himself Bors did not bother to try.

Suddenly his eyes narrowed, fixing on a woman envel-oped in black till nothing showed but her fingers. On her right hand rested a gold ring in the shape of a serpent eating its own tail. Aes Sedai, or at least a woman trained in Tar Valon by Aes Sedai. None else would wear that ring. Either way made no difference to him. He looked away before she could notice his watching, and almost immediately he spot-ted another woman swathed from head to toe in black and wearing a Great Serpent ring. The two witches gave no sign that they knew each other. In the White Tower they sat like spiders in the middle of a web, pulling the strings that made kings and queens dance, meddling. *Curse them all to death eternal!* He realized that he was grinding his teeth. If num-bers must dwindle—and they must, before the Day—there were some who would be missed even less than Tinkers.

A chime sounded, a single, shivering note that came from everywhere at once and cut off all other sounds like a knife.

The tall doors at the far end of the chamber swung open, and two Trollocs stepped into the room, spikes decorating the black mail that hung to their knees. Everyone shied back. Even the man who called himself Bors.

Head and shoulders taller than the tallest man there, they were a stomach-turning blend of man and animal, human faces twisted and altered. One had a heavy, pointed beak where his mouth and nose should have been, and feathers covered his head instead of hair. The other walked on hooves, his face pushed out in a hairy muzzle, and goat horns stuck up above his ears.

Ignoring the humans, the Trollocs turned back toward the door and bowed, servile and cringing. The feathers on the one lifted in a tight crest.

A Myrddraal stepped between them, and they fell to their knees. It was garbed in black that made the Trollocs' mail and the humans' masks seem bright, garments that hung still, without a ripple, as it moved with a viper's grace.

The man who called himself Bors felt his lips drawing back over his teeth, half snarl and half, he was shamed to admit even to himself, fear. It had its face uncovered. Its pasty pale face, a man's face, but eyeless as an egg, like a maggot in a grave.

The smooth white face swiveled, regarding them all one by one, it seemed. A visible shiver ran through them under that eyeless look. Thin, bloodless lips quirked in what might almost have been a smile as, one by one, the masked ones tried to press back into the crowd, milling to avoid that gaze. The Myrddraal's look shaped them into a semicircle facing the door.

The man who called himself Bors swallowed. *There will come a day, Halfman. When the Great Lord of the Dark comes again, he will choose his new Dreadlords, and you will cower before them. You will cower before men. Before me! Why doesn't it speak? Stop staring at me, and speak!*

"Your Master comes." The Myrddraal's voice rasped like a dry snake skin crumbling. "To your bellies, worms! Grovel, lest his brilliance blind and burn you!"

Rage filled the man who called himself Bors, at the tone as much as the words, but then the air above the Halfman shimmered, and the import drove home. *It can't be! It can't . . . !* The Trollocs were already on their bellies, writhing as if they wanted to burrow into the floor.

Without waiting to see if anyone else moved, the man

who called himself Bors dropped facedown, grunting as
he bruised himself on the stone. Words sprang to his lips
like a charm against danger—they were a charm, though a
thin reed against what he feared—and he heard a hundred
other voices, breathy with fear, speaking the same against
the floor.

"The Great Lord of the Dark is my Master, and most
heartily do I serve him to the last shred of my very soul."
In the back of his mind a voice chattered with fear. *The
Dark One and all the Forsaken are bound.* . . . Shivering,
he forced it to silence. He had abandoned that voice long
since. "Lo, my Master is death's Master. Asking nothing do
I serve against the Day of his coming, yet do I serve in the
sure and certain hope of life everlasting." . . . *bound in Shayol
Ghul, bound by the Creator at the moment of creation.
No, I serve a different master now.* "Surely the faithful
shall be exalted in the land, exalted above the unbelievers,
exalted above thrones, yet do I serve humbly against the
Day of his Return." *The hand of the Creator shelters us all,
and the Light protects us from the Shadow. No, no! A different master.* "Swift come the Day of Return. Swift come
the Great Lord of the Dark to guide us and rule the world
forever and ever."

The man who called himself Bors finished the creed
panting, as if he had run ten miles. The rasp of breath all
around told him he was not the only one.

"Rise. All of you, rise."

The mellifluous voice took him by surprise. Surely none
of his companions, lying on their bellies with their masked
faces pressed to the mosaic tiles, would have spoken, but
it was not the voice he expected from. . . . Cautiously, he
raised his head enough to see with one eye.

The figure of a man floated in the air above the Myrddraal, the hem of his blood-red robe hanging a span over
the Halfman's head. Masked in blood-red, too. Would the
Great Lord of the Dark appear to them as a man? And
masked, besides? Yet the Myrddraal, its very gaze fear,
trembled and almost cowered where it stood in the figure's
shadow. The man who called himself Bors grasped for an
answer his mind could contain without splitting. One of the
Forsaken, perhaps.

That thought was only a little less painful. Even so, it

meant the Day of the Dark One's return must be close at hand if one of the Forsaken was free. The Forsaken, thirteen of the most powerful wielders of the One Power in an Age filled with powerful wielders, had been sealed up in Shayol Ghul along with the Dark One, sealed away from the world of men by the Dragon and the Hundred Companions. And the backblast of that sealing had tainted the male half of the True Source; and all the male Aes Sedai, those cursed wielders of the Power, went mad and broke the world, tore it apart like a pottery bowl smashed on rocks, ending the Age of Legends before they died, rotting while they still lived. A fitting death for Aes Sedai, to his mind. Too good for them. He regretted only that the women had been spared.

Slowly, painfully, he forced the panic to the back of his mind, confined it and held it tight though it screamed to get out. It was the best he could do. None of those on their bellies had risen, and only a few had even dared raise their heads.

"Rise." There was a snap in the red-masked figure's voice this time. He gestured with both hands. "Stand!"

The man who called himself Bors scrambled up awkwardly, but halfway to his feet, he hesitated. Those gesturing hands were horribly burned, crisscrossed by black fissures, the raw flesh between as red as the figure's robes. *Would the Dark One appear so? Or even one of the Forsaken?* The eyeholes of that blood-red mask swept slowly across him, and he straightened hastily. He thought he could feel the heat of an open furnace in that gaze.

The others obeyed the command with no more grace and no less fear in their rising. When all were on their feet, the floating figure spoke.

"I have been known by many names, but the one by which you shall know me is Ba'alzamon."

The man who called himself Bors clamped his teeth to keep them from chattering. Ba'alzamon. In the Trolloc tongue, it meant Heart of the Dark, and even unbelievers knew it was the Trolloc name for the Great Lord of the Dark. He Whose Name Must Not Be Uttered. Not the True Name, Shai'tan, but still forbidden. Among those gathered here, and others of their kind, to sully either with a human tongue was blasphemy. His breath whistled through his nostrils, and all around him he could hear others panting behind their masks. The servants were gone, and the Trollocs as well, though he had not seen them go.

"The place where you stand lies in the shadow of Shayol Ghul." More than one voice moaned at that; the man who called himself Bors was not sure his own was not among them. A touch of what might almost be called mockery entered Ba'alzamon's voice as he spread his arms wide. "Fear not, for the Day of your Master's rising upon the world is near at hand. The Day of Return draws nigh. Does it not tell you so that I am here, to be seen by you favored few among your brothers and sisters? Soon the Wheel of Time will be broken. Soon the Great Serpent will die, and with the power of that death, the death of Time itself, your Master will remake the world in his own image for this Age and for all Ages to come. And those who serve me, faithful and steadfast, will sit at my feet above the stars in the sky and rule the world of men forever. So have I promised, and so shall it be, without end. You shall live and rule forever."

A murmur of anticipation ran through the listeners, and some even took a step forward, toward the floating, crimson shape, their eyes lifted, rapturous. Even the man who called himself Bors felt the pull of that promise, the promise for which he had dealt away his soul a hundred times over.

"The Day of Return comes closer," Ba'alzamon said. "But there is much yet to do. Much to do."

The air to Ba'alzamon's left shimmered and thickened, and the figure of a young man hung there, a little lower than Ba'alzamon. The man who called himself Bors could not decide whether it was a living being or not. A country lad, by his clothes, with a light of mischief in his brown eyes and the hint of a smile on his lips, as if in memory or anticipation of a prank. The flesh looked warm, but the chest did not move with breath, the eyes did not blink.

The air to Ba'alzamon's right wavered as if with heat, and a second country-clad figure hung suspended a little below Ba'alzamon. A curly-haired youth, as heavily muscled as a blacksmith. And an oddity: a battle axe hung at his side, a great, steel half-moon balanced by a thick spike. The man who called himself Bors suddenly leaned forward, intent on an even greater strangeness. A youth with yellow eyes.

For the third time air solidified into the shape of a young

man, this time directly under Ba'alzamon's eye, almost at his feet. A tall fellow, with eyes now gray, now almost blue as the light took them, and dark, reddish hair. Another villager, or farmer. The man who called himself Bors gasped. Yet another thing out of the ordinary, though he wondered why he should expect anything to be ordinary here. A sword swung from the figure's belt, a sword with a bronze heron on the scabbard and another inset into the long, two-handed hilt. *A village boy with a heron-mark blade? Impossible! What can it mean? And a boy with yellow eyes.* He noticed the Myrddraal looking at the figures, trembling; and unless he misjudged entirely, its trembling was no longer fear, but hatred.

Dead silence had fallen, silence that Ba'alzamon let deepen before he spoke. "There is now one who walks the world, one who was and will be, but is not yet, the Dragon."

A startled murmur ran through his listeners.

"The Dragon Reborn! We are to kill him, Great Lord?" That from the Shienaran, hand grasping eagerly at his side where his sword would hang.

"Perhaps," Ba'alzamon said simply. "And perhaps not. Perhaps he can be turned to my use. Sooner or later it will be so, in this Age or another."

The man who called himself Bors blinked. *In this Age or another? I thought the Day of Return was near. What matter to me what happens in another Age if I grow old and die waiting in this one?* But Ba'alzamon was speaking again.

"Already a bend is forming in the Pattern, one of many points where he who will become the Dragon may be turned to my service. Must be turned! Better that he serve me alive than dead, but alive or dead, serve me he must and will! These three you must know, for each is a thread in the pattern *I* mean to weave, and it will be up to you to see that they are placed as I command. Study them well, that you will know them."

Abruptly all sound was gone. The man who called himself Bors shifted uneasily, and saw others doing the same. All but the Illianer woman, he realized. With her hands spread over her bosom as if to hide the rounded flesh she exposed, eyes wide, half frightened and half ecstatic, she was nodding eagerly as though to someone face-to-face with her. Sometimes she appeared to give a reply, but the man

who called himself Bors heard not a word. Suddenly she
arched backwards, trembling and rising on her toes. He
could not see why she did not fall, unless something unseen
held her. Then, just as abruptly, she settled back to her feet
and nodded again, bowing, shivering. Even as she straightened, one of the women wearing a Great Serpent ring gave
a start and began nodding.

*So each of us hears his own instructions, and none hears
another's.* The man who called himself Bors muttered
in frustration. If he knew what even one other was commanded, he might be able to use the knowledge to advantage, but this way. . . . Impatiently he waited for his turn,
forgetting himself enough to stand straight.

One by one the gathering received their orders, each
walled in silence yet still giving tantalizing clues, if only
he could read them. The man of the Atha'an Miere, the Sea
Folk, stiffening with reluctance as he nodded. The Shienaran, his stance bespeaking confusion even while he acquiesced. The second woman of Tar Valon giving a start, as of
shock, and the gray-swathed figure whose sex he could not
determine shaking its head before falling to its knees and
nodding vigorously. Some underwent the same convulsion
as the Illianer woman, as if pain itself lifted them to toe
tips.

"Bors."

The man who called himself Bors jerked as a red mask
filled his eyes. He could still see the room, still see the floating shape of Ba'alzamon and the three figures before him,
but at the same time all he could see was the red-masked
face. Dizzy, he felt as if his skull were splitting open and
his eyes were being pushed out of his head. For a moment
he thought he could see flames through the eyeholes of the
mask.

"Are you faithful . . . Bors?"

The hint of mocking in the name sent a chill down his
backbone. "I am faithful, Great Lord. I cannot hide from
you." *I am faithful! I swear it!*

"No, you cannot."

The certainty in Ba'alzamon's voice dried his mouth, but
he forced himself to speak. "Command me, Great Lord,
and I obey."

"Firstly, you are to return to Tarabon and continue your

good works. In fact, I command you to redouble your efforts."

He stared at Ba'alzamon in puzzlement, but then fires flared again behind the mask, and he took the excuse of a bow to pull his eyes away. "As you command, Great Lord, so shall it be."

"Secondly, you will watch for the three young men, and have your followers watch. Be warned; they are dangerous."

The man who called himself Bors glanced at the figures floating in front of Ba'alzamon. *How can I do that? I can see them, but I can't see anything except* his *face.* His head felt about to burst. Sweat slicked his hands under his thin gloves, and his shirt clung to his back. "Dangerous, Great Lord? Farmboys? Is one of them the—"

"A sword is dangerous to the man at the point, but not to the man at the hilt. Unless the man holding the sword is a fool, or careless, or unskilled, in which case it is twice as dangerous to him as to anyone else. It is enough that I have told you to know them. It is enough that you obey me."

"As you command, Great Lord, so shall it be."

"Thirdly, regarding those who have landed at Toman Head, and the Domani. Of this you will speak to no one. When you return to Tarabon. . . ."

The man who called himself Bors realized as he listened that his mouth was sagging open. The instructions made no sense. *If I knew what some of the others were told, perhaps I could piece it together.*

Abruptly he felt his head grasped as though by a giant hand crushing his temples, felt himself being lifted, and the world blew apart in a thousand starbursts, each flash of light becoming an image that fled across his mind or spun and dwindled into the distance before he could more than barely grasp it. An impossible sky of striated clouds, red and yellow and black, racing as if driven by the mightiest wind the world had ever seen. A woman—a girl?—dressed in white receded into blackness and vanished as soon as she appeared. A raven stared him in the eye, *knowing* him, and was gone. An armored man in a brutal helm, shaped and painted and gilded like some monstrous, poisonous insect, raised a sword and plunged to one side, beyond his view. A horn, curled and golden, came hurtling out of the far distance. One piercing note it sounded as it flashed toward him,

tugging his soul. At the last instant it flashed into a blinding, golden ring of light that passed through him, chilling
him beyond death. A wolf leaped from the shadows of lost
sight and ripped out his throat. He could not scream. The
torrent went on, drowning him, burying him. He could
barely remember who he was, or what he was. The skies
rained fire, and the moon and stars fell; rivers ran in blood,
and the dead walked; the earth split open and fountained
molten rock. . . .

The man who called himself Bors found himself half
crouching in the chamber with the others, most watching
him, all silent. Wherever he looked, up or down or in any
direction, the masked face of Ba'alzamon overwhelmed his
eyes. The images that had flooded into his mind were fading; he was sure many were already gone from memory.
Hesitantly, he straightened, Ba'alzamon always before him.

"Great Lord, what—?"

"Some commands are too important to be known even
by he who carries them out."

The man who called himself Bors bent almost double
in his bow. "As you command, Great Lord," he whispered
hoarsely, "so shall it be."

When he straightened, he was alone in silence once
more. Another, the Tairen High Lord, nodded and bowed
to someone none else saw. The man who called himself
Bors put an unsteady hand to his brow, trying to hold on
to something of what had burst through his mind, though
he was not completely certain he wanted to remember. The
last remnant flickered out, and suddenly he was wondering
what it was that he was trying to recall. *I know there was
something, but what? There* was *something! Wasn't there?*
He rubbed his hands together, grimacing at the feel of sweat
under his gloves, and turned his attention to the three figures hanging suspended before Ba'alzamon's floating form.

The muscular, curly-haired youth; the farmer with the
sword; and the lad with the look of mischief on his face.
Already, in his mind, the man who called himself Bors
had named them the Blacksmith, the Swordsman, and the
Trickster. *What is their place in the puzzle?* They must be
important, or Ba'alzamon would not have made them the
center of this gathering. But from his orders alone they
could all die at any time, and he had to think that some of

the others, at least, had orders as deadly for the three. *How important are they?* Blue eyes could mean the nobility of Andor—unlikely in those clothes—and there were Borderlanders with light eyes, as well as some Tairens, not to mention a few from Ghealdan, and, of course. . . . No, no help there. But *yellow* eyes? *Who* are *they?* *What* are *they?*

He started at a touch on his arm, and looked around to find one of the white-clad servants, a young man, standing by his side. The others were back, too, more than before, one for each of the masked. He blinked. Ba'alzamon was gone. The Myrddraal was gone, too, and only rough stone was where the door it had used had been. The three figures still hung there, though. He felt as if they were staring at him.

"If it please you, my Lord Bors, I will show you to your room."

Avoiding those dead eyes, he glanced once more at the three figures, then followed. Uneasily he wondered how the youth had known what name to use. It was not until the strange carved doors closed behind him and they had walked a dozen paces that he realized he was alone in the corridor with the servant. His brows drew down suspiciously behind his mask, but before he could open his mouth, the servant spoke.

"The others are also being shown to their rooms, my Lord. If you please, my Lord? Time is short, and our Master is impatient."

The man who called himself Bors ground his teeth, both at the lack of information and at the implication of sameness between himself and the servant, but he followed in silence. Only a fool ranted at a servant, and worse, remembering the fellow's eyes, he was not sure it would do any good. *And how did he know what I was going to ask?* The servant smiled.

The man who called himself Bors did not feel at all comfortable until he was back in the room where he had waited on first arriving, and then not much. Even finding the seals on his saddlebags untouched was small comfort.

The servant stood in the hallway, not entering. "You may change to your own garments if you wish, my Lord. None will see you depart here, nor arrive at your destination, but it may be best to arrive already properly clothed. Someone will come soon to show you the way."

Untouched by any visible hand, the door swung shut.

The man who called himself Bors shivered in spite of himself. Hastily he undid the seals and buckles of his saddlebags and pulled out his usual cloak. In the back of his mind a small voice wondered if the promised power, even the immortality, was worth another meeting like this, but he laughed it down immediately. *For that much power, I would praise the Great Lord of the Dark under the Dome of Truth.* Remembering the commands given him by Ba'alzamon, he fingered the golden, flaring sun worked on the breast of the white cloak, and the red shepherd's crook behind the sun, symbol of his office in the world of men, and he almost laughed. There was work, great work, to be done in Tarabon, and on Almoth Plain.

CHAPTER
I

The Flame of Tar Valon

The Wheel of Time turns, and Ages come and pass leaving memories that become legend, then fade to myth, and are long forgot when that Age comes again. In one Age, called the Third Age by some, an Age yet to come, an Age long past, a wind rose in the Mountains of Dhoom. The wind was not the beginning. There are neither beginnings nor endings to the turning of the Wheel of Time. But it was a beginning.

Born among black, knife-edged peaks, where death roamed the high passes yet hid from things still more dangerous, the wind blew south across the tangled forest of the Great Blight, a forest tainted and twisted by the touch of the Dark One. The sickly sweet smell of corruption faded by the time the wind crossed that invisible line men called the border of Shienar, where spring flowers hung thick in the trees. It should have been summer by now, but spring had been late in coming, and the land had run wild to catch up. New-come pale green bristled on every bush, and red new growth tipped every tree branch. The wind rippled farmers' fields like verdant ponds, solid with crops that almost seemed to creep upward visibly.

The smell of death was all but gone long before the wind reached the stone-walled town of Fal Dara on its hills, and whipped around a tower of the fortress in the very center of the town, a tower atop which two men seemed to dance. Hard-walled and high, Fal Dara, both keep and town, never taken, never betrayed. The wind moaned across wood-shingled rooftops, around tall stone chimneys and taller towers, moaned like a dirge.

Stripped to the waist, Rand al'Thor shivered at the wind's cold caress, and his fingers flexed on the long hilt of the practice sword he held. The hot sun had slicked his chest, and his dark, reddish hair clung to his head in a sweat-curled mat. A faint odor in the swirl of air made his nose twitch, but he did not connect the smell with the image of an old grave fresh-opened that flashed through his head. He was barely aware of odor or image at all; he strove to keep his mind empty, but the other man sharing the tower top with him kept intruding on the emptiness. Ten paces across, the tower top was, encircled by a chest-high, crenellated wall. Big enough and more not to feel crowded, except when shared with a Warder.

Young as he was, Rand was taller than most men, but Lan stood just as tall and more heavily muscled, if not quite so broad in the shoulders. A narrow band of braided leather held the Warder's long hair back from his face, a face that seemed made from stony planes and angles, a face unlined as if to belie the tinge of gray at his temples. Despite the heat and exertion, only a light coat of sweat glistened on his chest and arms. Rand searched Lan's icy blue eyes, hunting for some hint of what the other man intended. The Warder never seemed to blink, and the practice sword in his hands moved surely and smoothly as he flowed from one stance to another.

With a bundle of thin, loosely bound staves in place of a blade, the practice sword would make a loud clack when it struck anything, and leave a welt where it hit flesh. Rand knew all too well. Three thin red lines stung on his ribs, and another burned his shoulder. It had taken all his efforts not to wear more decorations. Lan bore not a mark.

As he had been taught, Rand formed a single flame in his mind and concentrated on it, tried to feed all emotion and passion into it, to form a void within himself, with even thought outside. Emptiness came. As was too often the case of late it was not a perfect emptiness; the flame still remained, or some sense of light sending ripples through the stillness. But it was enough, barely. The cool peace of the void crept over him, and he was one with the practice sword, with the smooth stones under his boots, even with Lan. All was one, and he moved without thought in a rhythm that matched the Warder's step for step and move for move.

The wind rose again, bringing the ringing of bells from the town. *Somebody's still celebrating that spring has finally come.* The extraneous thought fluttered through the void on waves of light, disturbing the emptiness, and as if the Warder could read Rand's mind, the practice sword whirled in Lan's hands.

For a long minute the swift *clack-clack-clack* of bundled lathes meeting filled the tower top. Rand made no effort to reach the other man; it was all he could do to keep the Warder's strikes from reaching him. Turning Lan's blows at the last possible moment, he was forced back. Lan's expression never changed; the practice sword seemed alive in his hands. Abruptly the Warder's swinging slash changed in mid-motion to a thrust. Caught by surprise, Rand stepped back, already wincing with the blow he knew he could not stop this time.

The wind howled across the tower . . . and trapped him. It was as if the air had suddenly jelled, holding him in a cocoon. Pushing him forward. Time and motion slowed; horrified, he watched Lan's practice sword drift toward his chest. There was nothing slow or soft about the impact. His ribs creaked as if he had been struck with a hammer. He grunted, but the wind would not allow him to give way; it still carried him forward, instead. The lathes of Lan's practice sword flexed and bent—ever so slowly, it seemed to Rand—then shattered, sharp points oozing toward his heart, jagged lathes piercing his skin. Pain lanced through his body; his whole skin felt slashed. He burned as though the sun had flared to crisp him like bacon in a pan.

With a shout, he threw himself stumbling back, falling against the stone wall. Hand trembling, he touched the gashes on his chest and raised bloody fingers before his gray eyes in disbelief.

"And what was that fool move, sheepherder?" Lan grated. "You know better by now, or should unless you have forgotten everything I've tried to teach you. How badly are you—?" He cut off as Rand looked up at him.

"The wind." Rand's mouth was dry. "It—it pushed me! It. . . . It was solid as a wall!"

The Warder stared at him in silence, then offered a hand. Rand took it and let himself be pulled to his feet.

"Strange things can happen this close to the Blight," Lan said finally, but for all the flatness of the words he sounded troubled. That in itself was strange. Warders, those half-legendary warriors who served the Aes Sedai, seldom showed emotion, and Lan showed little even for a Warder. He tossed the shattered lathe sword aside and leaned against the wall where their real swords lay, out of the way of their practice.

"Not like that," Rand protested. He joined the other man, squatting with his back against the stone. That way the top of the wall was higher than his head, protection of a kind from the wind. If it was a wind. No wind had ever felt . . . solid . . . like that. "Peace! Maybe not even *in* the Blight."

"For someone like you. . . ." Lan shrugged as if that explained everything. "How long before you leave, sheepherder? A month since you said you were going, and I thought you'd be two weeks gone by now."

Rand stared up at him in surprise. *He's acting like nothing happened!* Frowning, he set down the practice sword and lifted his real sword to his knees, fingers running along the long, leather-wrapped hilt inset with a bronze heron. Another bronze heron stood on the scabbard, and yet another was scribed on the sheathed blade. It was still a little strange to him that he had a sword. Any sword, much less one with a blademaster's mark. He was a farmer from the Two Rivers, so far away, now. Maybe far away forever, now. He was a shepherd like his father—*I was a shepherd. What am I now?*—and his father had given him a heron-marked sword. *Tam is my father, no matter what anybody says.* He wished his own thoughts did not sound as if he was trying to convince himself.

Again Lan seemed to read his mind. "In the Borderlands, sheepherder, if a man has the raising of a child, that child is his, and none can say different."

Scowling, Rand ignored the Warder's words. It was no one's business but his own. "I want to learn how to use this. I need to." It had caused him problems, carrying a heron-marked sword. Not everybody knew what it meant, or even noticed it, but even so a heron-mark blade, especially in the hands of a youth barely old enough to be called a man, still attracted the wrong sort of attention. "I've been able to bluff sometimes, when I could not run, and I've been lucky, besides. But what happens when I can't run, and I can't bluff, and my luck runs out?"

"You could sell it," Lan said carefully. "That blade is rare even among heron-mark swords. It would fetch a pretty price."

"No!" It was an idea he had thought of more than once, but he rejected it now for the same reason he always had, and more fiercely for coming from someone else. *As long as I keep it, I have the right to call Tam father. He gave it to me, and it gives me the right.* "I thought any heron-mark blade was rare."

Lan gave him a sidelong look. "Tam didn't tell you, then? He must know. Perhaps he didn't believe. Many do not." He snatched up his own sword, almost the twin of Rand's except for the lack of herons, and whipped off the scabbard. The blade, slightly curved and single-edged, glittered silvery in the sunlight.

It was the sword of the kings of Malkier. Lan did not speak of it—he did not even like others to speak of it—but al'Lan Mandragoran was Lord of the Seven Towers, Lord of the Lakes, and uncrowned King of Malkier. The Seven Towers were broken now, and the Thousand Lakes the lair of unclean things. Malkier lay swallowed by the Great Blight, and of all the Malkieri lords, only one still lived.

Some said Lan had become a Warder, bonding himself to an Aes Sedai, so he could seek death in the Blight and join the rest of his blood. Rand had indeed seen Lan put himself in harm's way seemingly without regard for his own safety, but far beyond his own life and safety he held those of Moiraine, the Aes Sedai who held his bond. Rand did not think Lan would truly seek death while Moiraine lived.

Turning his blade in the light, Lan spoke. "In the War of the Shadow, the One Power itself was used as a weapon, and weapons were made with the One Power. Some weapons *used* the One Power, things that could destroy an entire city at one blow, lay waste to the land for leagues. Just as well those were all lost in the Breaking; just as well no one remembers the making of them. But there were simpler weapons, too, for those who would face Myrddraal, and worse things the Dreadlords made, blade to blade.

"With the One Power, Aes Sedai drew iron and other
metals from the earth, smelted them, formed and wrought
them. All with the Power. Swords, and other weapons, too.
Many that survived the Breaking of the World were destroyed by men who feared and hated Aes Sedai work, and
others have vanished with the years. Few remain, and few
men truly know what they are. There have been legends of
them, swollen tales of swords that seemed to have a power
of their own. You've heard the gleemen's tales. The reality
is enough. Blades that will not shatter or break, and never
lose their edge. I've seen men sharpening them—playing
at sharpening, as it were—but only because they could not
believe a sword did not need it after use. All they ever did
was wear away their oilstones.

"Those weapons the Aes Sedai made, and there will
never be others. When it was done, war and Age ended together, with the world shattered, with more dead unburied
than there were alive and those alive fleeing, trying to find
some place, any place, of safety, with every second woman
weeping because she'd never see husband or sons again;
when it was done, the Aes Sedai who still lived swore they
would never again make a weapon for one man to kill another. Every Aes Sedai swore it, and every woman of them
since has kept that oath. Even the Red Ajah, and they care
little what happens to any male.

"One of those swords, a plain soldier's sword"—with
a faint grimace, almost sad, if the Warder could be said
to show emotion, he slid the blade back into its sheath—
"became something more. On the other hand, those made
for lord-generals, with blades so hard no bladesmith could
mark them, yet marked already with a heron, those blades
became sought after."

Rand's hands jerked away from the sword propped on
his knees. It toppled, and instinctively he grabbed it before
it hit the floorstones. "You mean Aes Sedai made this? I
thought you were talking about *your* sword."

"Not all heron-mark blades are Aes Sedai work. Few
men handle a sword with the skill to be named blademaster and be awarded a heron-mark blade, but even so, not
enough Aes Sedai blades remain for more than a handful
to have one. Most come from master bladesmiths; the finest

steel men can make, yet still wrought by a man's hands. But that one, sheepherder . . . that one could tell a tale of three thousand years and more."

"I can't get away from them," Rand said, "can I?" He balanced the sword in front of him on scabbard point; it looked no different than it had before he knew. "Aes Sedai work." *But Tam gave it to me. My* father *gave it to me.* He refused to think of how a Two Rivers shepherd had come by a heron-mark blade. There were dangerous currents in such thoughts, deeps he did not want to explore.

"Do you really want to get away, sheepherder? I'll ask again. Why are you not gone, then? The sword? In five years I could make you worthy of it, make you a blademaster. You have quick wrists, good balance, and you don't make the same mistake twice. But I do not have five years to give over to teaching you, and you do not have five years for learning. You have not even one year, and you know it. As it is, you will not stab yourself in the foot. You hold yourself as if the sword belongs at your waist, sheepherder, and most village bullies will sense it. But you've had that much almost since the day you put it on. So why are you still here?"

"Mat and Perrin are still here," Rand mumbled. "I don't want to leave before they do. I won't ever—I might not see them again for—for years, maybe." His head dropped back against the wall. "Blood and ashes! At least they just think I'm crazy not to go home with them. Half the time Nynaeve looks at me like I'm six years old and I've skinned my knee, and she's going to make it better; the other half she looks like she's seeing a stranger. One she might offend if she looks too closely, at that. She's a Wisdom, and besides that, I don't think she's ever been afraid of anything, but she. . . ." He shook his head. "And Egwene. Burn me! She knows why I have to go, but every time I mention it she looks at me, and I knot up inside and. . . ." He closed his eyes, pressing the sword hilt against his forehead as if he could press what he was thinking out of existence. "I wish. . . . I wish. . . ."

"You wish everything could be the way it was, sheepherder? Or you wish the girl would go with you instead of to Tar Valon? You think she'll give up becoming an Aes

Sedai for a life of wandering? With you? If you put it to her in the right way, she might. Love is an odd thing." Lan sounded suddenly weary. "As odd a thing as there is."

"No." It was what he had been wishing, that she would want to go with him. He opened his eyes and squared his back and made his voice firm. "No, I wouldn't let her come with me if she did ask." He could not do that to her. *But Light, wouldn't it be sweet, just for a minute, if she said she wanted to?* "She gets muley stubborn if she thinks I'm trying to tell her what to do, but I can still protect her from that." He wished she were back home in Emond's Field, but all hope of that had gone the day Moiraine came to the Two Rivers. "Even if it means she does become an Aes Sedai!" The corner of his eye caught Lan's raised eyebrow, and he flushed.

"And that is all the reason? You want to spend as much time as you can with your friends from home before they go? That's why you're dragging your feet? You know what's sniffing at your heels."

Rand surged angrily to his feet. "All right, it's Moiraine! I wouldn't even be here if not for her, and she won't as much as talk to me."

"You'd be dead if not for her, sheepherder," Lan said flatly, but Rand rushed on.

"She tells me . . . tells me horrible things about myself"— his knuckles whitened on the sword. *That I'm going to go mad and die!*—"and then suddenly she won't even say two words to me. She acts as if I'm no different than the day she found me, and that smells wrong, too."

"You want her to treat you like what you are?"

"No! I don't mean that. Burn me, I don't know what I mean half the time. I don't want that, and I'm scared of the other. Now she's gone off somewhere, vanished . . ."

"I told you she needs to be alone sometimes. It isn't for you, or anyone else, to question her actions."

". . . without telling anybody where she was going, or when she'd be back, or even if she would be back. She has to be able to tell me something to help me, Lan. Something. She has to. If she ever comes back."

"She's back, sheepherder. Last night. But I think she has told you all she can. Be satisfied. You've learned what you can from her." With a shake of his head, Lan's voice became brisk. "You certainly aren't learning anything standing there. Time for a little balance work. Go through Parting the Silk, beginning from Heron Wading in the Rushes. Remember that that Heron form is only for practicing balance. Anywhere but doing forms, it leaves you wide open; you can strike home from it, if you wait for the other man to move first, but you'll never avoid his blade."

"She *has* to be able to tell me something, Lan. That wind. It wasn't natural, and I don't care how close to the Blight we are."

"Heron Wading in the Rushes, sheepherder. And mind your wrists."

From the south came a faint peal of trumpets, a rolling fanfare slowly growing louder, accompanied by the steady *thrum-thrum-THRUM-thrum* of drums. For a moment Rand and Lan stared at each other, then the drums drew them to the tower wall to stare southward.

The city stood on high hills, the land around the city walls cleared to ankle height for a full mile in all directions, and the keep covered the highest hill of all. From the tower top, Rand had a clear view across the chimneys and roofs to the forest. The drummers appeared first from the trees, a dozen of them, drums lifting as they stepped to their own beat, mallets whirling. Next came trumpeters, long, shining horns raised, still calling the flourish. At that distance Rand could not make out the huge, square banner whipping in the wind behind them. Lan grunted, though; the Warder had eyes like a snow eagle.

Rand glanced at him, but the Warder said nothing, his eyes intent on the column emerging from the forest. Mounted men in armor rode out of the trees, and women ahorseback, too. Then a palanquin borne by horses, one before and one behind, its curtains down, and more men on horseback. Ranks of men afoot, pikes rising above them like a bristle of long thorns, and archers with their bows held slanted across their chests, all stepping to the drums. The trumpets cried again. Like a singing serpent the column wound its way toward Fal Dara.

The wind flapped the banner, taller than a man, straight out to one side. As big as it was, it was close enough now for Rand to see clearly. A swirl of colors that meant nothing to him, but at the heart of it, a shape like a pure white teardrop. His breath froze in his throat. The Flame of Tar Valon.

"Ingtar's with them." Lan sounded as if his thoughts were elsewhere. "Back from his hunting at last. Been gone long enough. I wonder if he had any luck?"

"Aes Sedai," Rand whispered when he finally could. All those women out there. . . . Moiraine was Aes Sedai, yes, but he had traveled with her, and if he did not entirely trust her, at least he knew her. Or thought he did. But she was only one. So many Aes Sedai together, and coming like this, was something else again. He cleared his throat; when he spoke, his voice grated. "Why so many, Lan? Why any at all? And with drums and trumpets and a banner to announce them."

Aes Sedai were respected in Shienar, at least by most people, and the rest respectfully feared them, but Rand had been in places where it was different, where there was only the fear, and often hate. Where he had grown up, some men, at least, spoke of "Tar Valon witches" as they would speak of the Dark One. He tried to count the women, but they kept no ranks or order, moving their horses around to converse with one another or with whoever was in the palanquin. Goose bumps covered him. He had traveled with Moiraine, and met another Aes Sedai, and he had begun to think of himself as worldly. Nobody ever left the Two Rivers, or almost nobody, but he had. He had seen things no one back in the Two Rivers had ever laid eyes on, done things they had only dreamed of, if they had dreamed so far. He had seen a queen and met the Daughter-Heir of Andor, faced a Myrddraal and traveled the Ways, and none of it had prepared him for this moment.

"Why so many?" he whispered again.

"The Amyrlin Seat's come in person." Lan looked at him, his expression as hard and unreadable as a rock. "Your lessons are done, sheepherder." He paused then, and Rand almost thought there was sympathy on his face. That could not be, of course. "Better for you if you were a week gone." With that the Warder snatched up his shirt and disappeared down the ladder into the tower.

Rand worked his mouth, trying to get a little moisture. He stared at the column approaching Fal Dara as if it really were a snake, a deadly viper. The drums and trumpets

sang, loud in his ears. The Amyrlin Seat, who ordered the
Aes Sedai. *She's come because of me.* He could think of no
other reason.

They knew things, had knowledge that could help him,
he was sure. And he did not dare ask any of them. He
was afraid they had come to gentle him. *And afraid they
haven't, too,* he admitted reluctantly. *Light, I don't know
which scares me more.*

"I didn't mean to channel the Power," he whispered. "It
was an accident! Light, I don't want anything to do with it.
I swear I'll never touch it again! I swear it!"

With a start, he realized that the Aes Sedai party was entering the city gates. The wind swirled up fiercely, chilling
his sweat like droplets of ice, making the trumpets sound
like sly laughter; he thought he could smell an opened
grave, strong in the air. *My grave, if I keep standing here.*

Grabbing his shirt, he scrambled down the ladder and
began to run.

CHAPTER

2

The Welcome

The halls of Fal Dara keep, their smooth stone walls sparsely decorated with elegantly simple tapestries and painted screens, bustled with news of the Amyrlin Seat's imminent arrival. Servants in black-and-gold darted about their tasks, running to prepare rooms or carry orders to the kitchens, moaning that they could not have everything ready for so great a personage when they had had no warning. Dark-eyed warriors, their heads shaven except for a topknot bound with a leather cord, did not run, but haste filled their steps and their faces shone with an excitement normally reserved for battle. Some of the men spoke as Rand hurried past.

"Ah, there you are, Rand al'Thor. Peace favor your sword. On your way to clean up? You'll want to look your best when you are presented to the Amyrlin Seat. She'll want to see you and your two friends as well as the women, you can count on it."

He trotted toward the broad stairs, wide enough for twenty men abreast, that led up to the men's apartments.

"The Amyrlin herself, come with no more warning than a pack peddler. Must be because of Moiraine Sedai and you southerners, eh? What else?"

The wide, iron-bound doors of the men's apartments stood open, and half jammed with top-knotted men buzzing with the Amyrlin's arrival.

"Ho, southlander! The Amyrlin's here. Come for you and your friends, I suppose. Peace, what honor for you! She seldom leaves Tar Valon, and she's never come to the Borderlands in my memory."

He fended them all off with a few words. He had to wash. Find a clean shirt. No time to talk. They thought they understood, and let him go. Not a one of them knew a thing except that he and his friends traveled in company with an Aes Sedai, that two of his friends were women who were going to Tar Valon to train as Aes Sedai, but their words stabbed at him as if they knew everything. *She's come for me.*

He dashed through the men's apartments, darted into the room he shared with Mat and Perrin . . . and froze, his jaw dropping in astonishment. The room was filled with women wearing the black-and-gold, all working purposefully. It was not a big room, and its windows, a pair of tall, narrow arrowslits looking down on one of the inner courtyards, did nothing to make it seem larger. Three beds on black-and-white tiled platforms, each with a chest at the foot, three plain chairs, a washstand by the door, and a tall, wide wardrobe crowded the room. The eight women in there seemed like fish in a basket.

The women barely glanced at him, and went right on clearing his clothes—and Mat's and Perrin's—out of the wardrobe and replacing them with new. Anything found in the pockets was put atop the chests, and the old clothes were bundled up carelessly, like rags.

"What are you doing?" he demanded when he caught his breath. "Those are my clothes!" One of the women sniffed and poked a finger through a tear in the sleeve of his only coat, then added it to the pile on the floor.

Another, a black-haired woman with a big ring of keys at her waist, set her eyes on him. That was Elansu, *shatayan* of the keep. He thought of the sharp-faced woman as a housekeeper, though the house she kept was a fortress and scores of servants did her bidding. "Moiraine Sedai said all of your clothes are worn out, and the Lady Amalisa had new made to give you. Just keep out of our way," she added firmly, "and we will be done the quicker." There were few men the *shatayan* could not bully into doing as she wished—some said even Lord Agelmar—and she plainly did not expect any trouble with one man young enough to be her son.

He swallowed what he had been going to say; there was no time for arguing. The Amyrlin Seat could be sending for him at any minute. "Honor to the Lady Amalisa for her gift," he managed, after the Shienaran way, "and honor to you, Elansu Shatayan. Please, convey my words to the Lady Amalisa, and tell her I said, heart and soul to serve." That ought to satisfy the Shienaran love of ceremony for both women. "But now if you'll pardon me, I want to change."

"That is well," Elansu said comfortably. "Moiraine Sedai said to remove all the old. Every stitch. Smallclothes, too." Several of the women eyed him sideways. None of them made a move toward the door.

He bit his cheek to keep from laughing hysterically. Many ways were different in Shienar from what he was used to, and there were some to which he would never become accustomed if he lived forever. He had taken to bathing in the small hours of the morning, when the big, tiled pools were empty of people, after he discovered that at any other time a woman might well climb into the water with him. It could be a scullion or the Lady Amalisa, Lord Agelmar's sister herself—the baths were one place in Shienar where there was no rank—expecting him to scrub her back in return for the same favor, asking him why his face was so red, had he taken too much sun? They had soon learned to recognize his blushes for what they were, and not a woman in the keep but seemed fascinated by them.

I might be dead or worse in another hour, and they're waiting to see me blush! He cleared his throat. "If you'll wait outside, I will pass the rest out to you. On my honor."

One of the women gave a soft chortle, and even Elansu's lips twitched, but the *shatayan* nodded and directed the other women to gather up the bundles they had made. She was the last to leave, and she paused in the doorway to add, "The boots, too. Moiraine Sedai said everything."

He opened his mouth, then closed it again. His boots, at least, were certainly still good, made by Alwyn al'Van, the cobbler back in Emond's Field, and well broken in and comfortable. But if giving up his boots would make the *shatayan* leave him alone so he could go, he would give her the boots, and anything else she wanted. He had no time. "Yes. Yes, of course. On my honor." He pushed on the door, forcing her out.

Alone, he dropped onto his bed to tug off his boots—they *were* still good, a little worn, the leather cracked here and

there, but still wearable and well broken-in to fit his feet—
then hastily stripped off, piling everything atop the boots,
and washed at the basin just as quickly. The water was cold;
the water was always cold in the men's apartments.

The wardrobe had three wide doors carved in the simple
Shienaran manner, suggesting more than showing a series
of waterfalls and rocky pools. Pulling open the center door,
he stared for a moment at what had replaced the few garments he had brought with him. A dozen high-collared
coats of the finest wool and as well cut as any he had ever
seen on a merchant's back or a lord's, most embroidered
like feastday clothes. A dozen! Three shirts for every coat,
both linen and silk, with wide sleeves and tight cuffs. Two
cloaks. Two, when he had made do with one at a time all
his life. One cloak was plain, stout wool and dark green,
the other deep blue with a stiff-standing collar embroidered
in gold with herons . . . and high on the left breast, where a
lord would wear his sign. . . .

His hand drifted to the cloak of its own accord. As if uncertain what they would feel, his fingers brushed the stitching of a serpent curled almost into a circle, but a serpent
with four legs and a lion's golden mane, scaled in crimson and gold, its feet each tipped with five golden claws.
His hand jerked back as if burned. *Light help me! Was it
Amalisa had this made, or Moiraine? How many saw it?
How many know what it is, what it means? Even one is too
many. Burn me, she's trying to get me killed. Bloody Moiraine won't even talk to me, but now she's given me bloody
fine new clothes to die in!*

A rap at the door sent him leaping half out of his skin.

"Are you done?" came Elansu's voice. "Every stitch, now.
Perhaps I had better. . . ." A creak as if she were trying the
knob.

With a start Rand realized he was still naked. "I'm
done," he shouted. "Peace! Don't come in!" Hurriedly he
gathered up what he had been wearing, boots and all. "I'll
bring them!" Hiding behind the door, he opened it just wide
enough to shove the bundle into the arms of the *shatayan*.
"That's everything."

She tried to peer through the gap. "Are you sure? Moiraine Sedai said everything. Perhaps I had better just
look—"

"It's everything," he growled. "On my honor!" He shouldered the door shut in her face, and heard laughter from the other side.

Muttering under his breath, he dressed hurriedly. He would not put it past any of them to find some excuse to come bulling in anyway. The gray breeches were snugger than he was used to, but still comfortable, and the shirt, with its billowy sleeves, was white enough to satisfy any goodwife in Emond's Field on laundry day. The knee-high boots fit as if he had worn them a year. He hoped it was just a good cobbler, and not more Aes Sedai work.

All of these clothes would make a pack as big as he was. Yet, he had grown used to the comfort of clean shirts again, of not wearing the same breeches day after day until sweat and dirt made them as stiff as his boots, then wearing them still. He took his saddlebags from his chest and stuffed what he could into them, then reluctantly spread the fancy cloak out on the bed and piled a few more shirts and breeches on that. Folded with the dangerous sigil inside and tied with a cord looped so it could be slung on a shoulder, it looked not much different from the packs he had seen carried by other young men on the road.

A peal of trumpets rolled through the arrowslits, trumpets calling the fanfare from outside the walls, trumpets answering from the keep towers.

"I'll pick out the stitching when I get a chance," he muttered. He had seen women picking out embroidery when they had made a mistake or changed their mind on the pattern, and it did not look very hard.

The rest of the clothes—most of them, in fact—he stuffed back into the wardrobe. No need to leave evidence of flight to be found by the first person to poke a head in after he went.

Still frowning, he knelt beside his bed. The tiled platforms on which the beds rested were stoves, where a small fire damped down to burn all night could keep the bed warm through the worst night in a Shienaran winter. The nights were still cooler than he was used to this time of year, but blankets were enough for warmth now. Pulling open the firebox door, he took out a bundle he could not leave behind. He was glad Elansu had not thought anyone would keep clothes in there.

Setting the bundle atop the blankets, he untied one end and partially unfolded it. A gleeman's cloak, turned inside out to hide the hundreds of patches that covered it, patches in every size and color imaginable. The cloak itself was sound enough; the patches were a gleeman's badge. Had been a gleeman's badge.

Inside nestled two hard leather cases. The larger held a harp, which he never touched. *The harp was never meant for a farmer's clumsy fingers, boy.* The other, long and slim, contained the gold-and-silver chased flute he had used to earn his supper and bed more than once since leaving home. Thom Merrilin had taught him to play that flute, before the gleeman died. Rand could never touch it without remembering Thom, with his sharp blue eyes and his long white mustaches, shoving the bundled cloak into his hands and shouting for him to run. And then Thom had run himself, knives appearing magically in his hands as if he were performing, to face the Myrddraal that was coming to kill them.

With a shiver, he redid the bundle. "That's all over with." Thinking of the wind on the tower top, he added, "Strange things happen this close to the Blight." He was not sure he believed it, not the way Lan had apparently meant it. In any case, even without the Amyrlin Seat, it was past time for him to be gone from Fal Dara.

Shrugging into the coat he had kept out—it was a deep, dark green, and made him think of the forests at home, Tam's Westwood farm where he had grown up, and the Waterwood where he had learned to swim—he buckled the heron-mark sword to his waist and hung his quiver, bristling with arrows, on the other side. His unstrung bow stood propped in the corner with Mat's and Perrin's, the stave two hands taller than he was. He had made it himself since coming to Fal Dara, and besides him, only Lan and Perrin could draw it. Stuffing his blanketroll and his new cloak through the loops on his bundles, he slung the pair from his left shoulder, tossed his saddlebags atop the cords, and grabbed the bow. *Leave the sword-arm free,* he thought. *Make them think I'm dangerous. Maybe* somebody *will.*

Cracking the door revealed the hall all but empty; one liveried servant dashed by, but he never so much as glanced at Rand. As soon as the man's rapid footfalls faded, Rand slipped out into the corridor.

He tried to walk naturally, casually, but with saddlebags on his shoulder and bundles on his back, he knew he looked like what he was, a man setting out on a journey and not meaning to come back. The trumpets called again, sounding fainter here inside the keep.

He had a horse, a tall bay stallion, in the north stable, called the Lord's Stable, close by the salley gate that Lord Agelmar used when he went riding. Neither the Lord of Fal Dara nor any of his family would be riding today, though, and the stable might be empty except for the stableboys. There were two ways to reach the Lord's Stable from Rand's room. One would take him all the way around the keep, behind Lord Agelmar's private garden, then down the far side and through the farrier's smithy, likewise certainly empty now, to the stableyard. Time enough that way for orders to be given, for a search to start, before he reached his horse. The other was far shorter; first across the outer courtyard, where even now the Amyrlin Seat was arriving with another dozen or more Aes Sedai.

His skin prickled at the thought; he had had more than enough of Aes Sedai for any sane lifetime. One was too many. All the stories said it, and he knew it for fact. But he was not surprised when his feet took him toward the outer courtyard. He would never see legendary Tar Valon—he could not afford that risk, now or ever—but he might catch a glimpse of the Amyrlin Seat before he left. That would be as much as seeing a queen. *There can't be anything dangerous in just looking, from a distance. I'll keep moving and be gone before she ever knows I was there.*

He opened a heavy, iron-strapped door onto the outer courtyard and stepped out into silence. People forested the guardwalk atop every wall, top-knotted soldiers, and liveried servants, and menials still in their muck, all pressed together cheek by jowl, with children sitting on shoulders to look over their elders' heads or squeezing in to peer around waists and knees. Every archers' balcony was packed like a barrel of apples, and faces even showed in the narrow arrowslits in the walls. A thick mass of people bordered the courtyard like another wall. And all of them watched and waited in silence.

He pushed his way along the wall, in front of the smithies and fletchers' stalls that lined the court—Fal Dara was a fortress, not a palace, despite its size and grim grandeur, and everything about it served that end—apologizing quietly to the people he jostled. Some looked around with a frown, and a few gave a second stare to his saddlebags and bundles, but none broke the silence. Most did not even bother to look at who had bumped past them.

He could easily see over the heads of most of them, enough to make out clearly what was going on in the courtyard. Just inside the main gate, a line of men stood beside their horses, fourteen of them. No two wore the same kind of armor or carried the same sort of sword, and none looked like Lan, but Rand did not doubt they were Warders. Round faces, square faces, long faces, narrow faces, they all had the look, as if they saw things other men did not see, heard things other men did not hear. Standing at their ease, they looked as deadly as a pack of wolves. Only one other thing about them was alike. One and all they wore the color-shifting cloak he had first seen on Lan, the cloak that often seemed to fade into whatever was behind it. It did not make for easy watching or a still stomach, so many men in those cloaks.

A dozen paces in front of the Warders, a row of women stood by their horses' heads, the cowls of their cloaks thrown back. He could count them, now. Fourteen. Fourteen Aes Sedai. They must be. Tall and short, slender and plump, dark and fair, hair cut short or long, hanging loose down their backs or braided, their clothes were as different as the Warders' were, in as many cuts and colors as there were women. Yet they, too, had a sameness, one that was only obvious when they stood together like this. To a woman, they seemed ageless. From this distance he would have called them all young, but closer he knew they would be like Moiraine. Young-seeming yet not, smooth-skinned but with faces too mature for youth, eyes too knowing.

Closer? Fool! I'm too close already! Burn me, I should have gone the long way. He pressed on toward his goal, another iron-bound door at the far end of the court, but he could not stop looking.

Calmly the Aes Sedai ignored the onlookers and kept their attention on the curtained palanquin, now in the center of the courtyard. The horses bearing it held as still as if ostlers stood at their harness, but there was only one tall woman beside the palanquin, her face an Aes Sedai's face, and she paid no mind to the horses. The staff she held upright before her with both hands was as tall as she, the gilded flame capping it standing above her eyes.

Lord Agelmar faced the palanquin from the far end of the court, bluff and square and face unreadable. His high-collared coat of dark blue bore the three running red foxes of the House Jagad as well as the stooping black hawk of Shienar. Beside him stood Ronan, age-withered but still tall; three foxes carved from red avatine topped the tall staff the *shambayan* bore. Ronan was Elansu's equal in ordering the keep, *shambayan* and *shatayan*, but Elansu left little for him except ceremonies and acting as Lord Agelmar's secretary. Both men's topknots were snow-white.

All of them—the Warders, the Aes Sedai, the Lord of Fal Dara, and his *shambayan*—stood as still as stone. The watching crowd seemed to hold its breath. Despite himself, Rand slowed.

Suddenly Ronan rapped his staff loudly three times on the broad paving stones, calling into the silence, "Who comes here? Who comes here? Who comes here?"

The woman beside the palanquin tapped her staff three times in reply. "The Watcher of the Seals. The Flame of Tar Valon. The Amyrlin Seat."

"Why should we watch?" Ronan demanded.

"For the hope of humankind," the tall woman replied.

"Against what do we guard?"

"The shadow at noon."

"How long shall we guard?"

"From rising sun to rising sun, so long as the Wheel of Time turns."

Agelmar bowed, his white topknot stirring in the breeze. "Fal Dara offers bread and salt and welcome. Well come is the Amyrlin Seat to Fal Dara, for here is the watch kept, here is the Pact maintained. Welcome."

The tall woman drew back the curtain of the palanquin, and the Amyrlin Seat stepped out. Dark-haired, ageless as all Aes Sedai were ageless, she ran her eyes over the assembled watchers as she straightened. Rand flinched when her gaze crossed him; he felt as if he had been touched. But her eyes passed on and came to rest on Lord Agelmar. A liver-ied servant knelt at her side with folded towels, steam still rising, on a silver tray. Formally, she wiped her hands and patted her face with a damp cloth. "I offer thanks for your welcome, my son. May the Light illumine House Jagad. May the Light illumine Fal Dara and all her people."

Agelmar bowed again. "You honor us, Mother." It did not sound odd, her calling him son or him calling her Mother, though comparing her smooth cheeks to his craggy face made him seem more like her father, or even grandfather. She had a presence that more than matched his. "House Jagad is yours. Fal Dara is yours."

Cheers rose on every side, crashing against the walls of the keep like breaking waves.

Shivering, Rand hurried toward the door to safety, careless of whom he bumped into now. *Just your bloody imagination. She doesn't even know who you are. Not yet. Blood and ashes, if she did. . . .* He did not want to think of what would have happened if she knew who he was, what he was. What would happen when she finally found out. He wondered if she had had anything to do with the wind atop the tower; Aes Sedai could do things like that. When he pushed through that door and slammed it shut behind him, muting the roar of welcome that still shook the courtyard, he heaved a relieved sigh.

The halls here were as empty as the others had been, and he all but ran. Out across a smaller courtyard, with a fountain splashing in the center, down yet another corridor and out into the flagstoned stableyard. The Lord's Stable itself, built into the wall of the keep, stood tall and long, with big windows here inside the walls, and horses kept on two floors. The smithy across the courtyard stood silent, the farrier and his helpers gone to see the Welcome.

Tema, the leathery-faced head groom, met him at the wide doors with a deep bow, touching his forehead and then his heart. "Spirit and heart to serve, my Lord. How may Tema serve, my Lord?" No warrior's topknot here; Tema's hair sat on his head like an inverted gray bowl.

Rand sighed. "For the hundredth time, Tema, I am not a lord."

"As my Lord wishes." The groom's bow was even lower this time.

It was his name that caused the problem, and a similarity. Rand al'Thor. Al'Lan Mandragoran. For Lan, according to the custom of Malkier, the royal "al" named him King, though he never used it himself. For Rand, "al" was just a part of his name, though he had heard that once, long ago, before the Two Rivers was called the Two Rivers, it had meant "son of." Some of the servants in Fal Dara keep, though, had taken it to mean he was a king, too, or at least a prince. All of his argument to the contrary had only managed to demote him to lord. At least, he thought it had; he had never seen quite so much bowing and scraping, even with Lord Agelmar.

"I need Red saddled, Tema." He knew better than to offer to do it himself; Tema would not let Rand soil his hands. "I thought I'd spend a few days seeing the country around the town." Once he was on the big bay stallion's back, a few days would see him at the River Erinin, or across the border into Arafel. *They'll never find me then.*

The groom bent himself almost double, and stayed bent. "Forgive, my Lord," he whispered hoarsely. "Forgive, but Tema cannot obey."

Flushing with embarrassment, Rand took an anxious look around—there was no one else in sight—then grabbed the man's shoulder and pulled him upright. He might not be able to stop Tema and a few others from acting like this, but he could try to stop anyone else from seeing it. "Why not, Tema? Tema, look at me, please. Why not?"

"It is commanded, my Lord," Tema said, still whispering. He kept dropping his eyes, not afraid, but ashamed that he could not do what Rand asked. Shienarans took shame the way other people took being branded a thief. "No horse may leave this stable until the order is changed. Nor any stable in the keep, my Lord."

Rand had his mouth open to tell the man it was all right, but instead he licked his lips. "No horse from any stable?"

"Yes, my Lord. The order came down only a short time ago. Only moments." Tema's voice picked up strength. "All the gates are closed as well, my Lord. None may enter or leave without permission. Not even the city patrol, so Tema has been told."

Rand swallowed hard, but it did not lessen the feeling of fingers clutching his windpipe. "The order, Tema. It came from Lord Agelmar?"

"Of course, my Lord. Who else? Lord Agelmar did not

speak the command to Tema, of course, nor even to the man who did speak to Tema, but, my Lord, who else could give such a command in Fal Dara?"

Who else? Rand jumped as the biggest bell in the keep bell tower let out a sonorous peal. The other bells joined in, then bells from the town.

"If Tema may be bold," the groom called above the reverberations, "my Lord must be very happy."

Rand had to shout back to be heard. "Happy? Why?"

"The Welcome is finished, my Lord." Tema's gesture took in the bell tower. "The Amyrlin Seat will be sending for my Lord, and my Lord's friends, to come to her, now."

Rand broke into a run. He just had time to see the surprise on Tema's face, and then he was gone. He did not care what Tema thought. *She will be sending for me now.*

CHAPTER
3

Friends and Enemies

Rand did not run far, only as far as the sally gate around the corner from the stable. He slowed to a walk before he got there, trying to appear casual and unhurried.

The arched gate was closed tight. It was barely big enough for two men to ride through abreast, but like all the gates in the outer wall, it was covered with broad strips of black iron, and locked shut with a thick bar. Two guards stood before the gate in plain conical helmets and plate-and-mail armor, with long swords on their backs. Their golden surcoats bore the Black Hawk on the chest. He knew one of them slightly, Ragan. The scar from a Trolloc arrow made a white triangle against Ragan's dark cheek behind the bars of his face-guard. The puckered skin dimpled with a grin when he saw Rand.

"Peace favor you, Rand al'Thor." Ragan almost shouted to be heard over the bells. "Do you intend to go hit rabbits over the head, or do you still insist that club is a bow?" The other guard shifted to stand more in front of the gate.

"Peace favor you, Ragan," Rand said, stopping in front of them. It was an effort to keep his voice calm. "You know it's a bow. You've seen me shoot it."

"No good from a horse," the other guard said sourly. Rand recognized him, now, with his deep-set, almost-black eyes that never seemed to blink. They peered from his helmet like twin caves inside another cave. He supposed there could be worse luck for him than Masema guarding the gate, but he was not sure how, short of a Red Aes Sedai.

"It's too long," Masema added. "I can shoot three arrows with a horsebow while you loose one with that monster."

Rand forced a grin, as if he thought it was a joke. Masema had never made a joke in his hearing, nor laughed at one. Most of the men at Fal Dara accepted Rand; he trained with Lan, and Lord Agelmar had him at table, and most important of all, he had arrived at Fal Dara in company with Moiraine, an Aes Sedai. Some seemed unable to forget his being an outlander, though, barely saying two words to him, and then only if they had to. Masema was the worst of those.

"It's good enough for me," Rand said. "Speaking of rabbits, Ragan, how about letting me out? All this noise and bustle is too much for me. Better to be out hunting rabbits, even if I never see one."

Ragan half turned to look at his companion, and Rand's hopes began to lift. Ragan was an easygoing man, his manner belying his grim scar, and he seemed to like Rand. But Masema was already shaking his head. Ragan sighed. "It cannot be, Rand al'Thor." He gave a tiny nod toward Masema as if to explain. If it were up to him alone. . . . "No one is to leave without a written pass. Too bad you did not ask a few minutes ago. The command just came down to bar the gates."

"But why would Lord Agelmar want to keep *me* in?" Masema was eyeing the bundles on Rand's back, and his saddlebags. Rand tried to ignore him. "I'm his guest," he went on to Ragan. "By my honor, I could have left anytime these past weeks. Why would he mean this order for me? It is Lord Agelmar's order, isn't it?" Masema blinked at that, and his perpetual frown deepened; he almost appeared to forget Rand's packs.

Ragan laughed. "Who else could give such an order, Rand al'Thor? Of course, it was Uno who passed it to me, but whose order could it have been?"

Masema's eyes, fixed on Rand's face, did not blink. "I just want to go out by myself, that's all," Rand said. "I'll try one of the gardens, then. No rabbits, but at least there won't be a crowd. The Light illumine you, and peace favor you."

He walked away without waiting for an answering blessing, resolving not to go near any of the gardens on any account. *Burn me, once the ceremonies are done there could be Aes Sedai in any of them.* Aware of Masema's eyes on his back—he was sure it was Masema—he kept his pace normal.

Suddenly the bells stopped ringing, and he skipped a step. Minutes were passing. A great many of them. Time for the Amyrlin Seat to be shown to her chambers. Time for her to send for him, to start a search when he was not found. As soon as he was out of sight of the sally gate, he began to run again.

Near the barracks' kitchens, the Carters' Gate, where all the foodstuffs for the keep were brought in, stood closed and barred, behind a pair of soldiers. He hurried past, across the kitchen yard, as if he had never meant to stop.

The Dog Gate, at the back of the keep, just high enough and wide enough for one man on foot, had its guards, too. He turned around before they saw him. There were not many gates, even as big as the keep was, but if the Dog Gate was guarded, they all would be.

Perhaps he could find a length of rope. . . . He climbed one of the stairs to the top of the outer wall, to the wide parapet with its crenellated walls. It was not comfortable for him, being so high and exposed if that wind came again, but from there he could see across the tall chimneys and sharp roofs of the town all the way to the city wall. Even after nearly a month, the houses still looked odd to his Two Rivers eyes, eaves reaching almost to the ground as if the houses were all wood-shingled roof, and chimneys angled to let heavy snow slide past. A broad, paved square surrounded the keep, but only a hundred paces from the wall lay streets full of people going about their daily business, aproned shopkeepers out under the awnings in front of their shops, rough-clothed farmers in town to buy and sell, hawkers and tradesmen and townspeople gathered in knots, no doubt to talk about the surprise visit from the Amyrlin Seat. He could see carts and people flowing through one of the gates in the town wall. Apparently the guards there had no orders about stopping anyone.

He looked up at the nearest guardtower; one of the soldiers raised a gauntleted hand to him. With a bitter laugh, he waved back. Not a foot of the wall but was under the eyes of guards. Leaning through an embrasure, he peered down past the slots in the stone for setting hoardings, down the sheer expanse of stone to the drymoat far below. Twenty paces wide and ten deep, faced with stone polished slippery smooth. A low wall, slanted to give no hiding place, surrounded it to keep anyone from falling in by accident, and its bottom was a forest of razor-sharp spikes. Even with a rope to climb down and no guards watching, he could not cross that. What served to keep Trollocs out in the last extreme served just as well to keep him in.

Suddenly he felt weary to the bone, drained. The Amyrlin Seat was there, and there was no way out. No way out, and the Amyrlin Seat there. If she knew he was there, if she had sent the wind that had seized him, then she was already hunting him, hunting with an Aes Sedai's powers. Rabbits had more chance against his bow. He refused to give up, though. There were those who said Two Rivers folk could teach stones and give lessons to mules. When there was nothing else left, Two Rivers people hung on to their stubbornness.

Leaving the wall, he wandered through the keep. He paid no mind to where he went, so long as it was nowhere he would be expected. Not anywhere near his room, nor any of the stables, nor any gate—Masema might risk Uno's tongue to report him trying to leave—nor garden. All he could think of was keeping away from *any* Aes Sedai. Even Moiraine. She *knew* about him. Despite that, she had done nothing against him. *So far. So far as you know. What if she's changed her mind? Maybe she sent for the Amyrlin Seat.*

For a moment, feeling lost, he leaned against the corridor wall, the stone hard under his shoulder. Eyes blank, he stared at a distant nothing and saw things he did not want to see. *Gentled. Would it be so bad, to have it all over? Really over?* He closed his eyes, but he could still see himself, huddling like a rabbit with nowhere left to run, and Aes Sedai closing round him like ravens. *They almost always die soon after, men who've been gentled. They stop wanting to live.* He remembered Thom Merrilin's words too well to face that. With a brisk shake, he hurried on down the hall. No need to stay in one place until he was found. *How long till they find you anyway? You're like a sheep in a pen. How long?* He touched the sword hilt at his side. *No, not a sheep. Not for Aes Sedai or anybody else.* He felt a little foolish, but determined.

People were returning to their tasks. A din of voices and clattering pots filled the kitchen that lay nearest the Great Hall, where the Amyrlin Seat and her party would feast that night. Cooks and scullions and potboys all but ran at their work; the spit dogs trotted in their wicker wheels to turn the spitted meats. He made his way quickly through the heat and steam, through the smells of spices and cooking. No one spared him a second glance; they were all too busy.

The back halls, where the servants lived in small apartments, were stirring like a kicked antheap as men and women scurried to don their best livery. Children did their playing in corners, out of the way. Boys waved wooden swords, and girls played with carved dolls, some announcing that *hers* was the Amyrlin Seat. Most of the doors stood open, doorways blocked only by beaded curtains. Normally, that meant whoever lived there was open to visitors, but today it simply meant the residents were in a hurry. Even those who bowed to him did so with hardly a pause.

Would any of them hear, when they went to serve, that he was being sought, and speak of seeing him? Speak to an Aes Sedai and tell her where to find him? The eyes that he passed suddenly appeared to be studying him slyly, and to be weighing and considering behind his back. Even the children took on sharper looks in his mind's eye. He knew it was just his imagination—he was sure it was; it had to be—but when the servants' apartments were behind him, he felt as if he had escaped before a trap could spring shut.

Some places in the keep were empty of people, the folk who normally worked there released for the sudden holiday. The armorer's forge, with all the fires banked, the anvils silent. Silent. Cold. Lifeless. Yet somehow not empty. His skin prickled, and he spun on his heel. No one there. Just the big square tool chests and the quenching barrels full of oil. The hair on the back of his neck stirred, and he whipped round again. The hammers and tongs hung in their places on the wall. Angrily he stared around the big room. *There's nobody there. It's just my imagination. That wind, and the Amyrlin; that's enough to make me imagine things.*

Outside in the armorer's yard, the wind swirled up around

him momentarily. Despite himself he jumped, thinking it meant to catch him. For a moment he smelled the faint odor of decay again, and heard someone behind him laughing slyly. Just for a moment. Frightened, he edged in a circle, peering warily. The yard, paved with rough stone, was empty except for him. *Just your bloody imagination!* He ran anyway, and behind him he thought he heard the laughter again, this time without the wind.

In the woodyard, the presence returned, the sense of someone there. The feel of eyes peering at him around tall piles of split firewood under the long sheds, darting glances over the stacks of seasoned planks and timbers waiting on the other side of the yard for the carpenter's shop, now closed up tight. He refused to look around, refused to think of how one set of eyes could move from place to place so fast, could cross the open yard from the firewood shed to the lumbershed without even a flicker of movement that he could see. He was sure it was one set of eyes. *Imagination. Or maybe I'm going crazy already.* He shivered. *Not yet. Light, please not yet.* Stiff-backed, he stalked across the woodyard, and the unseen watcher followed.

Down deep corridors lit only by a few rush torches, in storerooms filled with sacks of dried peas or beans, crowded with slatted racks heaped with wrinkled turnips and beets, or stacked with barrels of wine and casks of salted beef and kegs of ale, the eyes were always there, sometimes following him, sometimes waiting when he entered. He never heard a footstep but his own, never heard a door creak except when he opened and closed it, but the eyes were there. *Light, I* am *going crazy.*

Then he opened another storeroom door, and human voices, human laughter, drifted out to fill him with relief. There would be no unseen eye here. He went in.

Half the room was stacked to the ceiling with sacks of grain. In the other half a thick semicircle of men knelt in front of one of the bare walls. They all seemed to wear the leather jerkins and bowl-cut hair of menials. No warriors' topknots, no livery. No one who might betray him accidentally. *What about on purpose?* The rattle of dice came through their soft murmurs, and somebody let out a raucous laugh at the throw.

Loial was watching them dice, rubbing his chin thought-fully with a finger thicker than a big man's thumb, his head almost reaching the rafters nearly two spans up. None of the dicers gave him a glance. Ogier were not exactly common in the Borderlands, or anywhere else, but they were known and accepted here, and Loial had been in Fal Dara long enough to excite little comment. The Ogier's dark, stiff-collared tunic was buttoned up to his neck and flared below the waist over his high boots, and one of the big pockets bulged and sagged with the weight of something. Books, if Rand knew him. Even watching men gamble, Loial would not be far from a book.

In spite of everything, Rand found himself grinning. Loial often had that effect on him. The Ogier knew so much about some things, so little about others, and he seemed to want to know everything. Yet Rand could remember the first time he ever saw Loial, with his tufted ears and his eye-brows that dangled like long mustaches and his nose almost as wide as his face—saw him and thought he was facing a Trolloc. It still shamed him. Ogier and Trollocs. Myrddraal, and things from the dark corners of midnight tales. Things out of stories and legends. That was how he had thought of them before he left Emond's Field. But since leaving home he had seen too many stories walking in the flesh ever to be so sure again. Aes Sedai, and unseen watchers, and a wind that caught and held. His smile faded.

"All the stories are real," he said softly.

Loial's ears twitched, and his head turned toward Rand. When he saw who it was, the Ogier's face split in a grin, and he came over. "Ah, there you are." His voice was a deep bumblebee rumble. "I did not see you at the Welcome. That was something I had not seen before. Two things. The Shienaran Welcome, and the Amyrlin Seat. She looks tired, don't you think? It cannot be easy, being Amyrlin. Worse than being an Elder, I suppose." He paused, with a thought-ful look, but only for a breath. "Tell me, Rand, do you play at dice, too? They play a simpler game here, with only three dice. We use four in the *stedding*. They won't let me play, you know. They just say, 'Glory to the Builders,' and will not bet against me. I don't think that's fair, do you? The dice they use *are* rather small"—he frowned at one of his hands, big enough to cover a human head—"but I still think—"

Rand grabbed his arm and cut him off. *The Builders!* "Loial, Ogier built Fal Dara, didn't they? Do you know any way out except by the gates? A crawl hole. A drain pipe. Anything at all, if it's big enough for a man to wiggle through. Out of the wind would be good, too."

Loial gave a pained grimace, the ends of his eyebrows almost brushing his cheeks. "Rand, Ogier built Mafal Dadaranell, but that city was destroyed in the Trolloc Wars. This"—he touched the stone wall lightly with broad fingertips—"was built by men. I can sketch a plan of Mafal Dadaranell—I saw the maps, once, in an old book in Stedding Shangtai—but of Fal Dara, I know no more than you. It *is* well built, though, isn't it? Stark, but well made."

Rand slumped against the wall, squeezing his eyes shut. "I need a way out," he whispered. "The gates are barred, and they won't let anyone pass, but I need a way out."

"But why, Rand?" Loial said slowly. "No one here will hurt you. Are you all right? Rand?" Suddenly his voice rose. "Mat! Perrin! I think Rand is sick."

Rand opened his eyes to see his friends straightening up out of the knot of dicers. Mat Cauthon, long-limbed as a stork, wearing a half smile as if he saw something funny that no one else saw. Shaggy-haired Perrin Aybara, with heavy shoulders and thick arms from his work as a blacksmith's apprentice. They both still wore their Two Rivers garb, plain and sturdy, but travel-worn.

Mat tossed the dice back into the semicircle as he stepped out, and one of the men called, "Here, southlander, you can't quit while you're winning."

"Better than when I'm losing," Mat said with a laugh. Unconsciously he touched his coat at the waist, and Rand winced. Mat had a dagger with a ruby in its hilt under there, a dagger he was never without, a dagger he could not be without. It was a tainted blade, from the dead city of Shadar Logoth, tainted and twisted by an evil almost as bad as the Dark One, the evil that had killed Shadar Logoth two thousand years before, yet still lived among the abandoned ruins. That taint would kill Mat if he kept the dagger; it would kill him even faster if he put it aside. "You'll have another chance to win it back." Wry snorts from the kneeling men indicated they did not think there was much chance of that.

Perrin kept his eyes down as he followed Mat across to

Rand. Perrin always kept his eyes down these days, and his shoulders sagged as if he carried a weight too heavy even for their width.

"What's the matter, Rand?" Mat asked. "You're as white as your shirt. Hey! Where did you get those clothes? You turning Shienaran? Maybe I'll buy myself a coat like that, and a fine shirt." He shook his coat pocket, producing a clink of coins. "I seem to have luck with the dice. I can hardly touch them without winning."

"You don't have to buy anything," Rand said tiredly. "Moiraine had all our clothes replaced. They're burned already for all I know, all but what you two are wearing. Elansu will probably be around to collect those, too, so I'd change fast if I were you, before she takes them off your back." Perrin still did not look up, but his cheeks turned red; Mat's grin deepened, though it looked forced. They too had had encounters in the baths, and only Mat tried to pretend it did not matter. "And I'm not sick. I just need to get out of here. The Amyrlin Seat is here. Lan said . . . he said with her here, it would have been better for me if I were gone a week. I need to leave, and all the gates are barred."

"He said that?" Mat frowned. "I don't understand. He'd never say *anything* against an Aes Sedai. Why now? Look, Rand, I don't like Aes Sedai any more than you do, but they aren't going to do anything to us." He lowered his voice to say that, and looked over his shoulder to see if any of the gamblers was listening. Feared the Aes Sedai might be, but in the Borderlands, they were far from being hated, and a disrespectful comment about them could land you in a fight, or worse. "Look at Moiraine. She isn't so bad, even if she is Aes Sedai. You're thinking like old Cenn Buie telling his tall tales back home, in the Winespring Inn. I mean, she hasn't hurt us, and they won't. Why would they?"

Perrin's eyes lifted. Yellow eyes, gleaming in the dim light like burnished gold. *Moiraine hasn't hurt us?* Rand thought. Perrin's eyes had been as deep a brown as Mat's when they left the Two Rivers. Rand had no idea how the change had come about—Perrin did not want to talk about it, or about very much of anything since it happened—but it had come at the same time as the slump in his shoulders, and a distance in his manner as if he felt alone even with friends around him. Perrin's eyes and Mat's dagger. Neither would have happened if they had not left Emond's Field, and it was Moiraine who had taken them away. He knew that was not fair. They would probably all be dead at Trollocs' hands, and a good part of Emond's Field as well, if she had not come to their village. But that did not make Perrin laugh the way he used to, or take the dagger from Mat's belt. *And me? If I was home and still alive, would I still be what I am now? At least I wouldn't be worrying about what the Aes Sedai are going to do to me.*

Mat was still looking at him quizzically, and Perrin had raised his head enough to stare from under his eyebrows. Loial waited patiently. Rand could not tell them why he had to stay away from the Amyrlin Seat. They did not know what he was. Lan knew, and Moiraine. And Egwene, and Nynaeve. He wished none of them knew, and most of all he wished Egwene did not, but at least Mat and Perrin—and Loial, too—believed he was still the same. He thought he would rather die than let them know, than see the hesitation and worry he sometimes caught in Egwene's eyes, and Nynaeve's, even when they were trying their best.

"Somebody's . . . watching me," he said finally. "Following me. Only. . . . Only, there's nobody there."

Perrin's head jerked up, and Mat licked his lips and whispered, "A Fade?"

"Of course not," Loial snorted. "How could one of the Eyeless enter Fal Dara, town or keep? By law, no one may hide his face inside the town walls, and the lamplighters are charged with keeping the streets lit at night so there isn't a shadow for a Myrddraal to hide in. It could not happen."

"Walls don't stop a Fade," Mat muttered. "Not when it wants to come in. I don't know as laws and lamps will do any better." He did not sound like someone who had half thought Fades were only gleemen's tales less than half a year before. He had seen too much, too.

"And there was the wind," Rand added. His voice hardly shook as he told what had happened on the tower top. Perrin's fists tightened until his knuckles cracked. "I just want to leave here," Rand finished. "I want to go south. Somewhere away. Just somewhere away."

"But if the gates are barred," Mat said, "how do we get out?"

Rand stared at him. "We?" He had to go alone. It would

be dangerous for anyone near him, eventually. He would be dangerous, and even Moiraine could not tell him how long he had. "Mat, you know you have to go to Tar Valon with Moiraine. She said that's the only place you can be separated from that bloody dagger without dying. And you know what will happen if you keep it."

Mat touched his coat over the dagger, not seeming to realize what he was doing. "'An Aes Sedai's gift is bait for a fish,'" he quoted. "Well, maybe I don't want to put the hook in my mouth. Maybe whatever she wants to do in Tar Valon is worse than if I don't go at all. Maybe she's lying. 'The truth an Aes Sedai tells is never the truth you think it is.'"

"You have any more old sayings you want to rid yourself of?" Rand asked. "'A south wind brings a warm guest, a north wind an empty house'? 'A pig painted gold is still a pig'? What about, 'talk shears no sheep'? 'A fool's words are dust'?"

"Easy, Rand," Perrin said softly. "There is no need to be so rough."

"Isn't there? Maybe I don't want you two going with me, always hanging around, falling into trouble and expecting me to pull you out. You ever think of that? Burn me, did it ever occur to you I might be tired of always having you there whenever I turn around? Always there, and I'm tired of it." The hurt on Perrin's face cut him like a knife, but he pushed on relentlessly. "There are some here think I'm a lord. A lord. Maybe I like that. But look at you, dicing with stablehands. When I go, I go by myself. You two can go to Tar Valon or go hang yourselves, but I leave here alone."

Mat's face had gone stiff, and he clutched the dagger through his coat till his knuckles were white. "If that is how you want it," he said coldly. "I thought we were. . . . However you want it, al'Thor. But if I decide to leave at the same time you do, I'll go, and you can stand clear of me."

"Nobody is going anywhere," Perrin said, "if the gates are barred." He was staring at the floor again. Laughter rolled from the gamblers against the wall as someone lost.

"Go or stay," Loial said, "together or apart, it doesn't matter. You are all three *ta'veren*. Even I can see it, and I don't have that Talent, just by what happens around you. And Moiraine Sedai says it, too."

Mat threw up his hands. "No more, Loial. I don't want to hear about that anymore."

Loial shook his head. "Whether you hear it or not, it is still true. The Wheel of Time weaves the Pattern of the Age, using the lives of men for thread. And you three are *ta'veren*, centerpoints of the weaving."

"No more, Loial."

"For a time, the Wheel will bend the Pattern around you three, whatever you do. And whatever you do is more likely to be chosen by the Wheel than by you. *Ta'veren* pull history along behind them and shape the Pattern just by being, but the Wheel weaves *ta'veren* on a tighter line than other men. Wherever you go and whatever you do, until the Wheel chooses otherwise you will—"

"No more!" Mat shouted. The men dicing looked around, and he glared at them until they bent back to their game.

"I am sorry, Mat," Loial rumbled. "I know I talk too much, but I did not mean—"

"I am not staying here," Mat told the rafters, "with a big-mouthed Ogier and a fool whose head is too big for a hat. You coming, Perrin?" Perrin sighed, and glanced at Rand, then nodded.

Rand watched them go with a stick caught in his threat. *I must go alone. Light help me, I have to.*

Loial was staring after them, too, eyebrows drooping worriedly. "Rand, I really didn't mean to—"

Rand made his voice harsh. "What are you waiting for? Go on with them! I don't see why you're still here. You are no use to me if you don't know a way out. Go on! Go find your trees, and your precious groves, if they haven't all been cut down, and good riddance to them if they have."

Loial's eyes, as big as cups, looked surprised and hurt, at first, but slowly they tightened into what almost might be anger. Rand did not think it could be. Some of the old stories claimed Ogier were fierce, though they never said how, exactly, but Rand had never met anyone as gentle as Loial.

"If you wish it so, Rand al'Thor," Loial said stiffly. He gave a rigid bow and stalked away after Mat and Perrin.

Rand slumped against the stacked sacks of grain. *Well,* a voice in his head taunted, *you did it, didn't you. I had to,* he told it. *I will be dangerous just to be around. Blood*

*and ashes, I'm going to go mad, and. . . . No! No, I won't!
I will not use the Power, and then I won't go mad, and. . . .
But I can't risk it. I can't, don't you see?* But the voice only
laughed at him.

The gamblers were looking at him, he realized. All of
them, still kneeling against the wall, had turned to stare
at him. Shienarans of any class were almost always polite
and correct, even to blood enemies, and Ogier were never
any enemies of Shienar. Shock filled the gamblers' eyes.
Their faces were blank, but their eyes said what he had
done was wrong. Part of him thought they were right, and
that drove their silent accusation deep. They only looked at
him, but he stumbled out of the storeroom as if they were
chasing him.

Numbly he went on through the storerooms, hunting
a place to secrete himself until some traffic was allowed
through the gates again. Then he could hide in the bottom
of a victualer's cart, maybe. If they did not search the carts
on the way out. If they did not search the storerooms, search
the whole keep for him. Stubbornly he refused to think
about that, stubbornly concentrated on finding a safe place.
But every place he found—a hollow in a stack of grain
sacks, a narrow alley along the wall behind some wine barrels, an abandoned storeroom half filled with empty crates
and shadows—he could imagine searchers finding him
there. He could imagine that unseen watcher, whoever it
was—or whatever—finding him there, too. So he hunted
on, thirsty and dusty and with cobwebs in his hair.

And then he came out into a dimly torch-lit corridor,
and Egwene was creeping along it, pausing to peer into the
storerooms she passed. Her dark hair, hanging to her waist,
was caught back with a red ribbon, and she wore a goose-
gray dress in the Shienaran fashion, trimmed in red. At the
sight of her, sadness and loss rolled over him, worse than
when he had chased Mat and Perrin and Loial away. He had
grown up thinking he would marry Egwene one day; they
both had. But now. . . .

She jumped when he popped out right in front of her, and
her breath caught loudly, but what she said was, "So there
you are. Mat and Perrin told me what you did. And Loial.
I know what you're trying to do, Rand, and it is plain foolish." She crossed her arms under her breasts, and her big,

dark eyes fixed him sternly. He always wondered how she managed to seem to be looking down at him—she did it at will—although she was only as tall as his chest, and two years younger besides.

"Good," he said. Her hair suddenly made him angry. He had never seen a grown woman with her hair unbraided until he left the Two Rivers. There, every girl waited eagerly for the Women's Circle of her village to say she was old enough to braid her hair. Egwene certainly had. And here she was with her hair loose except for a ribbon. *I want to go home and can't, and she can't wait to forget Emond's Field.* "You go away and leave me alone, too. You don't want to keep company with a shepherd anymore. There are plenty of Aes Sedai here for you to moon around, now. And don't tell any of them you saw me. They're after me, and I don't need you helping them."

Bright spots of color bloomed in her cheeks. "Do you think I would—"

He turned to walk away, and with a cry she threw herself at him, flung her arms around his legs. They both tumbled to the stone floor, his saddlebags and bundles flying. He grunted when he hit, sword hilt digging into his side, and again when she scrabbled up and plopped herself down on his back as if he were a chair. "My mother," she said firmly, "always told me the best way to learn to deal with a man was to learn to ride a mule. She said they have about equal brains most of the time. Sometimes the mule is smarter."

He raised his head to look over his shoulder at her. "Get off me, Egwene. Get off! Egwene, if you don't get off"—he lowered his voice ominously—"I'll do something to you. You know what I am." He added a glare for good measure.

Egwene sniffed. "You wouldn't, if you could. You would not hurt anybody. But you can't, anyway. I know you cannot channel the One Power whenever you want; it just happens, and you cannot control it. So you are not going to do anything to me or anybody else. I, on the other hand, have been taking lessons with Moiraine, so if you don't listen to some sense, Rand al'Thor, I might just set your breeches on fire. I can manage that much. You keep on as you are and see if I cannot." Suddenly, for just a moment, the torch nearest them on the wall flared up with a roar. She gave a squeak and stared at it, startled.

Twisting around, he grabbed her arm, pulled her off his back, and sat her against the wall. When he sat up himself, she was sitting there across from him, rubbing her arm furiously. "You really would have, wouldn't you?" he said angrily. "You're fooling with things you don't understand. You could have burned both of us to charcoal!"

"Men! When you cannot win an argument, you either run away or resort to force."

"Hold on there! Who tripped who? Who sat on who? And you threatened—tried!—to—" He raised both hands. "No, you don't. You do this to me all the time. Whenever you realize the argument isn't going the way you want, suddenly we are arguing about something else completely. Not this time."

"I am not arguing," she said calmly, "and I am not changing the subject, either. What is hiding except running away? And after you hide, you'll run away for true. And what about hurting Mat, and Perrin, and Loial? And me? I know why. You're afraid you will hurt somebody even worse if you let them stay near you. If you don't do what you shouldn't, then you do not have to worry about hurting anybody. All this running around and striking out, and you don't even know if there's a reason. Why should the Amyrlin, or any Aes Sedai but Moiraine, even know you exist?"

For a moment he stared at her. The longer she spent with Moiraine and Nynaeve, the more she took on their manner, at least when she wanted to. They were much alike at times, the Aes Sedai and the Wisdom, distant and knowing. It was disconcerting coming from Egwene. Finally he told her what Lan had said. "What else could he mean?"

Her hand froze on her arm, and she frowned with concentration. "Moiraine knows about you, and she hasn't done anything, so why should she now? But if Lan. . . ." Still frowning, she met his eyes. "The storerooms are the first place they will look. If they do look. Until we find out if they are looking, we need to put you somewhere they would never think of searching. I know. The dungeon."

He scrambled to his feet. "The dungeon!"

"Not in a cell, silly. I go there some evenings to visit Padan Fain. Nynaeve does, too. No one will think it odd if I go early today. In truth, with everybody looking to the Amyrlin, no one will even notice us."

"But, Moiraine. . . ."

"She doesn't go to the dungeons to question Master Fain. She has him brought to her. And she has not done that very much for weeks. Believe me, you will be safe there."

Still, he hesitated. Padan Fain. "Why do you visit the peddler, anyway? He's a Darkfriend, admitted out of his own mouth, and a bad one. Burn me, Egwene, he brought the Trollocs to Emond's Field! The Dark One's hound, he called himself, and he has been sniffing on my trail since Winternight."

"Well, he is safe behind iron bars now, Rand." It was her turn to hesitate, and she looked at him almost pleading. "Rand, he has brought his wagon into the Two Rivers every spring since before I was born. He knows all the people I know, all the places. It's strange, but the longer he has been locked up, the easier in himself he has become. It's almost as if he is breaking free of the Dark One. He laughs again, and tells funny stories, about Emond's Field folk, and sometimes about places I never heard of before. Sometimes he is almost like his old self. I just like to talk to somebody about home."

Since I've been avoiding you, he thought, *and since Perrin's been avoiding everybody, and Mat's been spending all his time gambling and carousing.* "I shouldn't have kept to myself so much," he muttered, then sighed. "Well, if Moiraine thinks it's safe enough for you, I suppose it is safe enough for me. But there's no need for you to be mixed in it."

Egwene got to her feet and concentrated on brushing off her dress, avoiding his eye.

"Moiraine *has* said it's safe? Egwene?"

"Moiraine Sedai has never told me I could not visit Master Fain," she said carefully.

He stared at her, then burst out, "You never asked her. She doesn't know. Egwene, that's stupid. Padan Fain's a Darkfriend, and as bad as ever a Darkfriend was."

"He is locked in a cage," she said stiffly, "and I do not have to ask Moiraine's permission for everything I do. It is a little late for you to start worrying about doing what an Aes Sedai thinks, isn't it? Now, are you coming?"

"I can find the dungeon without you. They are looking for me, or will be, and it won't do you any good to be found with me."

"Without me," she said dryly, "you'll likely trip over your own feet and fall in the Amyrlin Seat's lap, then confess everything while trying to talk your way out of it."

"Blood and ashes, you ought to be in the Women's Circle back home. If men were all as fumble-footed and helpless as you seem to think, we'd never—"

"Are you going to stand here talking until they do find you? Pick up your things, Rand, and come with me." Not waiting for an answer, she spun around and started off down the hall. Muttering under his breath, he reluctantly obeyed.

There were few people—servants, mainly—in the back ways they took, but Rand had the feeling that they all took special notice of him. Not notice of a man burdened for a journey, but of *him*, Rand al'Thor in particular. He knew it was his imagination—he hoped it was—but even so, he felt no relief when they stopped in a passageway deep beneath the keep, before a tall door with a small iron grill set in it, as thickly strapped with iron as any in the outer wall. A clapper hung below the grill.

Through the grill Rand could see bare walls, and two top-knotted soldiers sitting bareheaded at a table with a lamp on it. One of the men was sharpening a dagger with long, slow strokes of a stone. His strokes never faltered when Egwene rapped with the clapper, a sharp clang of iron on iron. The other man, his face flat and sullen, looked at the door as if considering before he finally rose and came over. He was squat and stocky, barely tall enough to look through the cross-hatched bars.

"What do you want? Oh, it's you again, girl. Come to see your Darkfriend? Who's that?" He made no move to open the door.

"He's a friend of mine, Changu. He wants to see Master Fain, too."

The man studied Rand, his upper lip quivering back to bare teeth. Rand did not think it was supposed to be a smile. "Well," Changu said finally. "Well. Tall, aren't you? Tall. And fancy dressed for your kind. Somebody catch you young in the Eastern Marches and tame you?" He slammed back the bolts and yanked open the door. "Well, come in if you're coming." He took on a mocking tone. "Take care not to bump your head, my Lord."

There was no danger of that; the door was tall enough for Loial. Rand followed Egwene in, frowning and wondering if this Changu meant to make some sort of trouble. He was the first rude Shienaran Rand had met; even Masema was only cold, not really rude. But the fellow just banged the door shut and rammed the heavy bolts home, then went to some shelves beyond the end of the table and took one of the lamps there. The other man never ceased stropping his knife, never even looked up from it. The room was bare except for the table and benches and shelves, with straw on the floor and another iron-bound door leading deeper in.

"You'll want some light, won't you," Changu said, "in there in the dark with your Darkfriend friend." He laughed, coarse and humorless, and lit the lamp. "He's waiting for you." He thrust the lamp at Egwene, and undid the inner door almost eagerly. "Waiting for you. In there, in the dark."

Rand paused uneasily at the blackness beyond, and Changu grinning behind, but Egwene caught his sleeve and pulled him in. The door slammed, almost catching his heel; the latch bars clanged shut. There was only the light of the lamp, a small pool around them in the darkness.

"Are you sure he'll let us out?" he asked. The man had never even looked at his sword or bow, he realized, never asked what was in his bundles. "They aren't very good guards. We could be here to break Fain free for all he knows."

"They know me better than that," she said, but she sounded troubled, and she added, "They seem worse every time I come. All the guards do. Meaner, and more sullen. Changu told jokes the first time I came, and Nidao never even speaks anymore. But I suppose working in a place like this can't give a man a light heart. Maybe it is just me. This place does not do my heart any good, either." Despite her words, she drew him confidently into the black. He kept his free hand on his sword.

The pale lamplight showed a wide hall with flat iron grills to either side, fronting stone-walled cells. Only two of the cells they passed held prisoners. The occupants sat up on their narrow cots as the light struck them, shielding their eyes with their hands, glaring between their fingers. Even with their faces hidden, Rand was sure they were glaring. Their eyes glittered in the lamplight.

"That one likes to drink and fight," Egwene murmured, indicating a burly fellow with sunken knuckles. "This time he wrecked the common room of an inn in the town single-handed, and hurt some men badly." The other prisoner wore a gold-embroidered coat with wide sleeves, and low, gleaming boots. "He tried to leave the city without settling his inn bill"—she sniffed loudly at that; her father was an innkeeper as well as Mayor of Emond's Field—"nor paying half a dozen shopkeepers and merchants what he owed."

The men snarled at them, guttural curses as bad as any Rand had heard from merchants' guards.

"They grow worse every day, too," she said in a tight voice, and quickened her step.

She was enough ahead of him when they reached Padan Fain's cell, at the very end, that Rand was out of the light entirely. He stopped there, in the shadows behind her lamp.

Fain was sitting on his cot, leaning forward expectantly as if waiting, just as Changu had said. He was a bony, sharp-eyed man, with long arms and a big nose, even more gaunt now than Rand remembered. Not gaunt from the dungeon—the food here was the same as the servants ate, and not even the worst prisoner was shorted—but from what he had done before coming to Fal Dara.

The sight of him brought back memories Rand would just as soon have done without. Fain on the seat of his big ped-dler's wagon wheeling across the Wagon Bridge, arriving in Emond's Field the day of Winternight. And on Winternight the Trollocs came, killing and burning, hunting. Hunting three young men, Moiraine had said. *Hunting me, if they only knew it, and using Fain for their trail hound.*

Fain stood at Egwene's approach, not shielding his eyes or even blinking at the light. He smiled at her, a smile that touched only his lips, then raised his eyes above her head. Looking straight at Rand, hidden in the blackness behind the light, he pointed a long finger at him. "I feel you there, hiding, Rand al'Thor," he said, almost crooning. "You can't hide, not from me, and not from them. You thought it was over, did you not? But the battle's never done, al'Thor. They are coming for me, and they're coming for you, and the war goes on. Whether you live or die, it's never over for you. Never." Suddenly he began to chant.

Soon comes the day all shall be free.
Even you, and even me.
Soon comes the day all shall die.
Surely you, but never I.

He let his arm fall, and his eyes rose to stare intently at an angle up into the darkness. A crooked grin twisting his mouth, he chuckled deep in his throat as if whatever he saw was amusing. "Mordeth knows more than all of you. Mordeth knows."

Egwene backed away from the cell until she reached Rand, and only the edge of the light touched the bars of Fain's cell. Darkness hid the peddler, but they could still hear his chuckles. Even unable to see him, Rand was sure Fain was still peering off at nothing.

With a shiver, he pried his fingers off his sword hilt. "Light!" he said hoarsely. "This is what you call being like he used to be?"

"Sometimes he's better, and sometimes worse." Egwene's voice was unsteady. "This is worse—much worse than usual."

"What is he seeing, I wonder. He's mad, staring at a stone ceiling in the dark." *If the stone weren't there, he'd be looking straight at the women's apartments. Where Moiraine is, and the Amyrlin Seat.* He shivered again. "He's mad."

"This was not a good idea, Rand." Looking over her shoulder at the cell, she drew him away from it and lowered her voice as if afraid Fain might overhear. Fain's chuckles followed them. "Even if they don't look here, I cannot stay here with him like this, and I do not think you should, either. There is something about him today that. . . ." She drew a shaky breath. "There is one place even safer from search than here. I did not mention it before because it was easier to get you in here, but they will never look in the women's apartments. Never."

"The women's . . . ! Egwene, Fain may be mad, but you're madder. You can't hide from hornets in a hornets' nest."

"What better place? What is the one part of the keep no man will enter without a woman's invitation, not even Lord Agelmar? What is the one place no one would ever think to look for a man?"

"What is the one place in the keep sure to be full of Aes Sedai? It is crazy, Egwene."

Poking at his bundles, she spoke as if it were all decided. "You must wrap your sword and bow in your cloak, and then it will look as if you are carrying things for me. It should not be too hard to find you a jerkin and a shirt that isn't so pretty. You will have to stoop, though."

"I told you, I won't do it."

"Since you're acting stubborn as a mule, you should take right to playing my beast of burden. Unless you would really rather stay down here with him."

Fain's laughing whisper came through the black shadows. "The battle's never done, al'Thor. Mordeth knows."

"I'd have a better chance jumping off the wall," Rand muttered. But he unslung his bundles and set about wrapping sword and bow and quiver as she had suggested.

In the darkness, Fain laughed. "It's never over, al'Thor. Never."

CHAPTER

4

Summoned

Alone in her rooms in the women's apartments, Moiraine adjusted the shawl, embroidered with curling ivy and grapevines, on her shoulders and studied the effect in the tall frame mirror standing in a corner. Her large, dark eyes could appear as sharp as a hawk's when she was angry. They seemed to pierce the silvered glass, now. It was only happenstance that she had had the shawl in her saddlebags when she came to Fal Dara. With the blazing white Flame of Tar Valon centered on the wearer's back and long fringe colored to show her Ajah—Moiraine's was as blue as a morning sky—the shawls were seldom worn outside Tar Valon, and even there usually only inside the White Tower. Little in Tar Valon besides a meeting of the Hall of the Tower called for the formality of the shawls, and beyond the Shining Walls a sight of the Flame would send too many people running, to hide or perhaps to fetch the Children of the Light. A Whitecloak's arrow was as fatal to an Aes Sedai as to anyone else, and the Children were too wily to let an Aes Sedai see the bowman before the arrow struck, while she still might do something about it. Moiraine had certainly never expected to wear the shawl in Fal Dara. But for an audience with the Amyrlin, there were proprieties to observe.

She was slender and not at all tall, and smooth-cheeked Aes Sedai agelessness often made her appear younger than she was, but Moiraine had a commanding grace and calm presence that could dominate any gathering. A manner ingrained growing up in the Royal Palace of Cairhien had been heightened, not submerged, by still more years as an

Aes Sedai. She knew she might need every bit of it today.
Yet much of the calm was on the surface, today. *There must
be trouble, or she would not have come herself,* she thought
for at least the tenth time. But beyond that lay a thousand
questions more. *What trouble, and who did she choose to
accompany her? Why here? Why now? It cannot be allowed
to go wrong now.*

The Great Serpent ring on her right hand caught the light
dully as she touched the delicate golden chain fastened
in her dark hair, which hung in waves to her shoulders.
A small, clear blue stone dangled from the chain, in the
middle of her forehead. Many in the White Tower knew of
the tricks she could do using that stone as a focus. It was
only a polished bit of blue crystal, just something a young
girl had used in her first learning, with no one to guide her.
That girl had remembered tales of *angreal* and even more
powerful *sa'angreal*—those fabled remnants of the Age of
Legends that allowed Aes Sedai to channel more of the One
Power than any could safely handle unaided—remembered
and thought some such focus was required to channel at all.
Her sisters in the White Tower knew a few of her tricks,
and suspected others, including some that did not exist,
some that had shocked her when she learned of them. The
things she did with the stone were simple and small, if occasionally useful; the kind a child would imagine. But if the
wrong women had accompanied the Amyrlin, the crystal
might put them off balance, because of the tales.

A rapid, insistent knocking came at the chamber door.
No Shienaran would knock that way, not at anyone's door,
but least of all hers. She remained looking into the mirror
until her eyes stared back serenely, all thought hidden in
their dark depths. She checked the soft leather pouch hanging at her belt. *Whatever troubles brought her out of Tar
Valon, she will forget them when I lay this trouble before
her.* A second thumping, even more vigorous than the first,
sounded before she crossed the room and opened the door
with a calm smile for the two women who had come for her.

She recognized them both. Dark-haired Anaiya in her
blue-fringed shawl, and fair-haired Liandrin in her red.
Liandrin, not only young-seeming but young and pretty,
with a doll's face and a small, petulant mouth, had her hand
raised to pound again. Her dark brows and darker eyes were

a sharp contrast to the multitude of pale honey braids brushing her shoulders, but the combination was not uncommon in Tarabon. Both women were taller than Moiraine, though Liandrin by less than a hand.

Anaiya's blunt face broke into a smile as soon as Moiraine opened the door. That smile gave her the only beauty she would ever have, but it was enough; almost everyone felt comforted, safe and special, when Anaiya smiled at them. "The Light shine on you, Moiraine. It's good to see you again. Are you well? It has been so long."

"My heart is lighter for your presence, Anaiya." That was certainly true; it was good to know she had at least one friend among the Aes Sedai who had come to Fal Dara. "The Light illumine you."

Liandrin's mouth tightened, and she gave her shawl a twitch. "The Amyrlin Seat, she requires your presence, Sister." Her voice was petulant, too, and cold-edged. Not for Moiraine's sake, or not solely; Liandrin always sounded dissatisfied with something. Frowning, she tried to look over Moiraine's shoulder into the room. "This chamber, it is warded. We cannot enter. Why do you ward against your sisters?"

"Against all," Moiraine replied smoothly. "Many of the serving women are curious about Aes Sedai, and I do not want them pawing through my rooms when I am not here. There was no need to make a distinction until now." She pulled the door shut behind her, leaving all three of them in the corridor. "Shall we go? We must not keep the Amyrlin waiting."

She started down the hallway with Anaiya chatting at her side. Liandrin stood for a moment staring at the door as if wondering what Moiraine was hiding, then hurried to join the others. She bracketed Moiraine, walking as stiffly as a guard. Anaiya merely walked, keeping company. Their slippered footsteps fell softly on thick-woven carpets with simple patterns.

Liveried women curtsied deeply as they passed, many more deeply than they would have for the Lord of Fal Dara himself. Aes Sedai, three together, and the Amyrlin Seat herself in the keep; it was more honor than any woman of the keep had ever expected in her lifetime. A few women of noble Houses were out in the halls, and they curtsied,

too, which they most certainly would not have done for
Lord Agelmar. Moiraine and Anaiya smiled and bowed
their heads to acknowledge each reverence, from servant or
noble equally. Liandrin ignored them all.

There were only women here, of course, no men. No
Shienaran male above the age of ten would enter the women's
rooms without permission or invitation, although a few
small boys ran and played in the halls here. They knelt on
one knee, awkwardly, when their sisters dropped deep curtsies. Now and then Anaiya smiled and ruffled a small head
as she passed.

"This time, Moiraine," Anaiya said, "you have been
gone from Tar Valon too long. Much too long. Tar Valon
misses you. Your sisters miss you. And you are needed in
the White Tower."

"Some of us must work in the world," Moiraine said gen-
tly. "I will leave the Hall of the Tower to you, Anaiya. Yet in
Tar Valon, you hear more of what occurs in the world than
I. Too often I outrun what happens where I was yesterday.
What news have you?"

"Three more false Dragons." Liandrin bit the words off.
"In Saldaea, Murandy, and Tear false Dragons ravage the
land. The while, you Blues smile and talk of nothing, and
try to hold on to the past." Anaiya raised an eyebrow, and
Liandrin snapped her mouth shut with a sharp sniff.

"Three," Moiraine mused softly. For an instant her eyes
gleamed, but she masked it quickly. "Three in the last two
years, and now three more at once."

"As the others were, these will be dealt with also. This
male vermin and any ragtag rabble who follow their banners."

Moiraine was almost amused by the certainty in Liandrin's
voice. Almost. She was too aware of the realities, too aware
of the possibilities. "Have a few months been enough for
you to forget, Sister? The last false Dragon all but tore
Ghealdan apart before his army, ragtag rabble or not, was
defeated. Yes, Logain is in Tar Valon by now, gentled and
safe, I suppose, but some of our sisters died to overpower
him. Even one sister dead is more loss than we can bear,
but Ghealdan's losses were much worse. The two before
Logain could not channel, yet even so the people of Kandor and Arad Doman remember them well. Villages burned

and men dead in battle. How easily can the world deal with three at one time? How many will flock to their banners? There has never been a shortage of followers for any man claiming to be the Dragon Reborn. How great will the wars be this time?"

"It isn't so grim as that," Anaiya said. "As far as we know, only the one in Saldaea can channel. He has not had time to attract many followers, and sisters should already be there to deal with him. The Tairens are harrying their false Dragon and his followers through Haddon Mirk, while the fellow in Murandy is already in chains." She gave a short, wondering laugh. "To think the Murandians, of all people, would deal with theirs so quickly. Ask, and they do not even call themselves Murandians, but Lugarders, or Inishlinni, or this or that lord's or lady's man. Yet for fear one of their neighbors would take the excuse to invade, the Murandians leaped on their false Dragon almost as soon as he opened his mouth to proclaim himself."

"Still," Moiraine said, "three at the same time cannot be ignored. Has any sister been able to do a Foretelling?" It was a slight chance—few Aes Sedai had manifested any part of that Talent, even the smallest part, in centuries—so she was not surprised when Anaiya shook her head. Not surprised, but a little relieved.

They reached a juncture of hallways at the same time as the Lady Amalisa. She dropped a full curtsy, bowing deep and spreading her pale green skirts wide. "Honor to Tar Valon," she murmured. "Honor to Aes Sedai."

The sister of the Lord of Fal Dara required more than a nod of the head. Moiraine took Amalisa's hands and drew her to her feet. "You honor us, Amalisa. Rise, Sister."

Amalisa straighted gracefully, with a flush on her face. She had never as much as been to Tar Valon, and to be called Sister by an Aes Sedai was heady even for someone of her rank. Short and of middle years, she had a dark, mature beauty, and the color in her cheeks set it off. "You honor me too greatly, Moiraine Sedai."

Moiraine smiled. "How long have we known each other, Amalisa? Must I now call you my Lady Amalisa, as if we had never sat over tea together?"

"Of course not." Amalisa smiled back. The strength evident in her brother's face was in hers, too, and no less for the softer line of cheek and jaw. There were those who said that as hard and renowned a fighter as Agelmar was, he was no better than an even match for his sister. "But with the Amyrlin Seat here. . . . When King Easar visits Fal Dara, in private I call him *Magami,* Little Uncle, as I did when I was a child and he gave me rides on his shoulder, but in public it must be different."

Anaiya *tsked.* "Sometimes formality is necessary, but men often make more of it than they must. Please, call me Anaiya, and I will call you Amalisa, if I may."

From the corner of her eye, Moiraine saw Egwene, far down the side hall, disappearing hurriedly around a corner. A stooped shape in a leather jerkin, head down and arms loaded with bundles, shambled at her heels. Moiraine permitted herself a small smile, quickly masked. *If the girl shows as much initiative in Tar Valon,* she thought wryly, *she will sit in the Amyrlin Seat one day. If she can learn to control that initiative. If there is an Amyrlin Seat left on which to sit.*

When she turned her attention back to the others, Liandrin was speaking.

". . . and I would welcome the chance to learn more of your land." She wore a smile, open and almost girlish, and her voice was friendly.

Moiraine schooled her face to stillness as Amalisa extended an invitation to join her and her ladies in her private garden, and Liandrin accepted warmly. Liandrin made few friends, and none outside the Red Ajah. *Certainly never outside the Aes Sedai. She would sooner make friends with a man, or a Trolloc.* Moiraine was not sure Liandrin saw much difference between men and Trollocs. She was not sure any of the Red Ajah did.

Anaiya explained that just now they must attend the Amyrlin Seat. "Of course," Amalisa said. "The Light illumine her, and the Creator shelter her. But later, then." She stood straight and bowed her head as they left her.

Moiraine studied Liandrin as they walked, never looking at her directly. The honey-haired Aes Sedai was staring straight ahead, rosebud lips pursed thoughtfully. She appeared to have forgotten Moiraine and Anaiya both. *What is she up to?*

Anaiya seemed not to have noticed anything out of the

ordinary, but then she always managed to accept people both as they were and as they wanted to be. It constantly amazed Moiraine that Anaiya dealt as well as she did in the White Tower, but those who were devious always seemed to take her openness and honesty, her acceptance of everyone, as cunning devices. They were always caught completely off balance when she turned out to mean what she said and say what she meant. Too, she had a way of seeing to the heart of things. And of accepting what she saw. Now she blithely resumed speaking of the news.

"The word from Andor is both good and bad. The street riots in Caemlyn died down with the coming of spring, but there is still talk, too much talk, blaming the Queen, and Tar Valon as well, for the long winter. Morgase holds her throne less securely than she did last year, but she holds it still, and will so long as Gareth Bryne is Captain-General of the Queen's Guards. And the Lady Elayne, the Daughter-Heir, and her brother, the Lord Gawyn, have come safely to Tar Valon for their training. There was some fear in the White Tower that the custom would be broken."

"Not while Morgase has breath in her body," Moiraine said.

Liandrin gave a little start, as if she had just awakened. "Pray that she continues to have breath. The Daughter-Heir's party was followed to the River Erinin by the Children of the Light. To the very bridges to Tar Valon. More still camp outside Caemlyn, for the chance of mischief, and inside Caemlyn still are those who listen."

"Perhaps it is time Morgase learned a little caution," Anaiya sighed. "The world is becoming more dangerous every day, even for a queen. Perhaps especially for a queen. She was ever headstrong. I remember when she came to Tar Valon as a girl. She did not have the ability to become a full sister, and it rankled in her. Sometimes I think she pushes her daughter because of that, whatever the girl chooses."

Moiraine sniffed disdainfully. "Elayne was born with the spark in her; it was not a matter of choosing. Morgase would not risk letting the girl die from lack of training if all the Whitecloaks in Amadicia were camped outside Caemlyn. She would command Gareth Bryne and the Queen's Guards to cut a path through them to Tar Valon, and Gareth Bryne would do it if he had to do it alone." *But she still must keep*

the full extent of the girl's potential secret. Would the peo-
ple of Andor knowingly accept Elayne on the Lion Throne
after Morgase if they knew? Not just a queen trained in Tar
Valon according to custom, but a full Aes Sedai? In all of
recorded history there had been only a handful of queens
with the right to be called Aes Sedai, and the few who let it
be known had all lived to regret it. She felt a touch of sadness. But too much was afoot to spare aid, or even worry,
for one land and one throne. "What else, Anaiya?"

"You must know that the Great Hunt of the Horn has
been called in Illian, the first time in four hundred years.
The Illianers say the Last Battle is coming"—Anaiya gave
a little shiver, as well she might, but went on without a
pause—"and the Horn of Valere must be found before the
final battle against the Shadow. Men from every land are
already gathering, all eager to be part of the legend, eager
to find the Horn. Murandy and Altara are on their toes, of
course, thinking it's all a mask for a move against one of
them. That is probably why the Murandians caught their
false Dragon so quickly. In any case, there will be a new lot
of stories for the bards and gleemen to add to the cycle. The
Light send it is only new stories."

"Perhaps not the stories they expect," Moiraine said. Liandrin looked at her sharply, and she kept her face still.

"I suppose not," Anaiya said placidly. "The stories they
least expect will be exactly the ones they will add to the
cycle. Beyond that, I have only rumor to offer. The Sea Folk
are agitated, their ships flying from port to port with barely
a pause. Sisters from the islands say the Coramoor, their
Chosen One, is coming, but they won't say more. You know
how closemouthed the Atha'an Miere are with outsiders
about the Coramoor, and in this our sisters seem to think
more as Sea Folk than Aes Sedai. The Aiel appear to be
stirring, too, but no one knows why. No one ever knows
with the Aiel. At least there is no evidence they mean to
cross the Spine of the World again, thank the Light." She
sighed and shook her head. "What I would not give for even
one sister from among the Aiel. Just one. We know too little
of them."

Moiraine laughed. "Sometimes I think you belong in the
Brown Ajah, Anaiya."

"Almoth Plain," Liandrin said, and looked surprised that she had spoken.

"Now that truly *is* rumor, Sister," Anaiya said. "A few whispers heard as we were leaving Tar Valon. There may be fighting on Almoth Plain, and perhaps Toman Head, as well. I say, may be. The whispers were faint. Rumors of rumors. We left before we could hear more."

"It would have to be Tarabon and Arad Doman," Moiraine said, and shook her head. "They have squabbled over Almoth Plain for nearly three hundred years, but it has never come to open blows." She looked at Liandrin; Aes Sedai were supposed to throw off all their old loyalties to lands and rulers, but few did so completely. It was hard not to care for the land of your birth. "Why would they now—?"

"Enough of idle talk," the honey-haired woman broke in angrily. "For you, Moiraine, the Amyrlin waits." She took three quick strides ahead of the others and threw open one of a pair of tall doors. "For you, the Amyrlin will have no idle talk."

Unconsciously touching the pouch at her waist, Moiraine went past Liandrin through the doorway, with a nod as if the other woman were holding the door for her. She did not even smile at the white flash of anger on Liandrin's face. *What* is *the wretched girl up to?*

Brightly colored carpets covered the anteroom floor in layers, and the room was pleasantly furnished with chairs and cushioned benches and small tables, the wood simply worked or just polished. Brocaded curtains sided the tall arrowslits to make them seem more like windows. No fires burned in the fireplaces; the day was warm, and the Shienaran chill would not come until nightfall.

Fewer than half a dozen of the Aes Sedai who had accompanied the Amyrlin were there. Verin Mathwin and Serafelle, of the Brown Ajah, did not look up at Moiraine's entrance. Serafelle was intently reading an old book with a worn, faded leather cover, handling its tattered pages carefully, while plump Verin, sitting cross-legged beneath an arrowslit, held a small blossom up to the light and made notes and sketches in a precise hand in a book balanced on her knee. She had an open inkpot on the floor beside her, and a small pile of flowers on her lap. The Brown sisters concerned themselves with little beside seeking knowledge. Moiraine sometimes wondered if they were really aware of what was going on in the world, or even immediately around them.

The three other women already in the room turned, but they made no effort to approach Moiraine, only looked at her. One, a slender woman of the Yellow Ajah, she did not know; she spent too little time in Tar Valon to know all the Aes Sedai, although their numbers were no longer very great. She was acquainted with the two remaining, however. Carlinya was as pale of skin and cold of manner as the white fringe on her shawl, the exact opposite in every way of dark, fiery Alanna Mosvani, of the Green, but they both stood and stared at her without speaking, without expression. Alanna sharply snugged her shawl around her, but Carlinya made no move at all. The slender Yellow sister turned away with an air of regret.

"The Light illumine you all, Sisters," Moiraine said. No one answered. She was not sure Serafelle or Verin had even heard. *Where are the others?* There was no need for them all to be there—most would be resting in their rooms, freshing from the journey—but she was on edge now, all the questions she could not ask running through her head. None of it showed on her face.

The inner door opened, and Leane appeared, without her gilt-flamed staff. The Keeper of the Chronicles was as tall as most men, willowy and graceful, still beautiful, with coppery skin and short, dark hair. She wore a blue stole, a hand wide, instead of a shawl, for she sat in the Hall of the Tower, though as Keeper, not to represent her Ajah.

"There you are," she said briskly to Moiraine, and gestured to the door behind her. "Come, Sister. The Amyrlin Seat is waiting." She spoke naturally in a clipped, quick way that never changed, whether she was angry or joyful or excited. As Moiraine followed Leane in, she wondered what emotion the Keeper was feeling now. Leane pulled the door to behind them; it banged shut with something of the sound of a cell door closing.

The Amyrlin Seat herself sat behind a broad table in the middle of the carpet, and on the table rested a flattened cube of gold, the size of a travel chest and ornately worked with silver. The table was heavily built, its legs stout, but it seemed to squat under a weight two strong men would have had trouble lifting.

At the sight of the golden cube Moiraine had difficulty keeping her face unruffled. The last she had seen of it, it had been safely locked in Agelmar's strongroom. On learning of the Amyrlin Seat's arrival she had meant to tell her of it herself. That it was already in the Amyrlin's possession was a trifle, but a worrisome trifle. Events could be outpacing her.

She swept a deep curtsy and said formally, "As you called me, Mother, so have I come." The Amyrlin extended her hand, and Moiraine kissed her Great Serpent ring, no different from that of any other Aes Sedai. Rising, she made her tone more conversational, but not too much so. She was aware of the Keeper standing behind her, beside the door. "I hope you had a pleasant journey, Mother."

The Amyrlin had been born in Tear, of a simple fisherman's family, not a noble House, and her name was Siuan Sanche, though very few had used that name, or even thought of it, in the ten years since she had been raised from the Hall of the Tower. She was the Amyrlin Seat; that was the whole of it. The broad stole on her shoulders was striped in the colors of the seven Ajahs; the Amyrlin was of all Ajahs and of none. She was only of medium height, and handsome rather than beautiful, but her face held a strength that had been there before her elevation, the strength of the girl who had survived the streets of the Maule, Tear's port district, and her clear blue gaze had made kings and queens, and even the Captain Commander of the Children of the Light, drop their eyes. Her own eyes were strained, now, and there was a new tightness to her mouth.

"We called the winds to speed our vessels up the Erinin, Daughter, and even turned the currents to our aid." The Amyrlin's voice was deep, and sad. "I have seen the flooding we caused in villages along the river, and the Light only knows what we have done to the weather. We will not have endeared ourselves by the damage we've done and the crops we may have ruined. All to reach here as quickly as possible." Her eyes strayed to the ornate golden cube, and she half lifted a hand as if to touch it, but when she spoke it was to say, "Elaida is in Tar Valon, Daughter. She came with Elayne and Gawyn."

Moiraine was conscious of Leane standing to one side, quiet as always in the presence of the Amyrlin. But watching, and listening. "I am surprised, Mother," she said carefully. "This is no time for Morgase to be without Aes Sedai counsel." Morgase was one of the few rulers to openly admit to an Aes Sedai councilor; almost all had one, but few admitted it.

"Elaida insisted, Daughter, and queen or not, I doubt Morgase is a match for Elaida in a contest of wills. In any case, perhaps this time she did not wish to be. Elayne has potential. More than I have ever seen before. Already she shows progress. The Red sisters are swollen up like puff-fish with it. I don't think the girl leans to their way of thinking, but she is young, and there is no telling. Even if they don't manage to bend her, it will make little difference. Elayne could well be the most powerful Aes Sedai in a thousand years, and it is the Red Ajah who found her. They have gained much status in the Hall from the girl."

"I have two young women with me in Fal Dara, Mother," Moiraine said. "Both from the Two Rivers, where the blood of Manetheren still runs strong, though they do not even remember there was once a land called Manetheren. The old blood sings, Mother, and it sings loudly in the Two Rivers. Egwene, a village girl, is at least as strong as Elayne. I have seen the Daughter-Heir, and I know. As for the other, Nynaeve was the Wisdom in their village, yet she is little more than a girl herself. It says something of her that the women of her village chose her Wisdom at her age. Once she gains conscious control of what she now does without knowing, she will be as strong as any in Tar Valon. With training, she will shine like a bonfire beside the candles of Elayne and Egwene. And there is no chance these two will choose the Red. They are amused by men, exasperated by them, but they do like them. They will easily counter whatever influence the Red Ajah gains in the White Tower from finding Elayne."

The Amyrlin nodded as if it were all of no consequence. Moiraine's eyebrows lifted in surprise before she caught herself and smoothed her features. Those were the two main concerns in the Hall of the Tower, that fewer girls who could be trained to channel the One Power were found every year, or so it seemed, and that fewer of real power were found. Worse than the fear in those who blamed Aes Sedai for the Breaking of the World, worse than the hatred from the Children of the Light, worse even than the workings of Darkfriends, were the sheer dwindling of numbers and the lessening of abilities. The corridors of the White Tower were sparsely populated where once they had been crowded, and what could once be done easily with the One Power could now be done only with difficulty, or not at all.

"Elaida had another reason for coming to Tar Valon, Daughter. She sent the same message by six different pigeons to make sure I received it—and to whom else in Tar Valon she sent pigeons, I can only guess—then came herself. She told the Hall of the Tower that you are meddling with a young man who is *ta'veren*, and dangerous. He was in Caemlyn, she said, but when she found the inn where he had been staying, she discovered you had spirited him away."

"The people at that inn served us well and faithfully, Mother. If she harmed any of them. . . ." Moiraine could not keep the sharpness out of her voice, and she heard Leane shift. One did not speak to the Amyrlin Seat in that tone; not even a king on his throne did.

"You should know, Daughter," the Amyrlin said dryly, "that Elaida harms no one except those she considers dangerous. Darkfriends, or those poor fool men who try to channel the One Power. Or one who threatens Tar Valon. Everyone else who isn't Aes Sedai might as well be pieces on a stones board as far as she is concerned. Luckily for him, the innkeeper, one Master Gill as I remember, apparently thinks much of Aes Sedai, and so answered her questions to her satisfaction. Elaida actually spoke well of him. But she spoke more of the young man you took away with you. More dangerous than any man since Artur Hawkwing, she said. She has the Foretelling sometimes, you know, and her words carried weight with the Hall."

For Leane's sake, Moiraine made her voice as meek as she could. That was not very meek, but it was the best she could do. "I have three young men with me, Mother, but none of them is a king, and I doubt very much if any of them even dreams of uniting the world under one ruler. No one has dreamed Artur Hawkwing's dream since the War of the Hundred Years."

"Yes, Daughter. Village youths, so Lord Agelmar tells me. But one of them is *ta'veren*." The Amyrlin's eyes strayed to the flattened cube again. "It was put forward in the Hall that you should be sent into retreat for contemplation. This was proposed by one of the Sitters for the Green Ajah, with the other two nodding approval as she spoke."

Leane made a sound of disgust, or perhaps frustration. She always kept in the background when the Amyrlin Seat spoke, but Moiraine could understand the small interruption this time. The Green Ajah had been allied with the Blue for a thousand years; since Artur Hawkwing's time, they had all but spoken with one voice. "I have no desire to hoe vegetables in some remote village, Mother." *Nor will I, whatever the Hall of the Tower says.*

"It was further proposed, also by the Greens, that your care during your retreat should be given to the Red Ajah. The Red Sitters tried to appear surprised, but they looked like fisher-birds who knew the catch was unguarded." The Amyrlin sniffed. "The Reds professed reluctance to take custody of one not of their Ajah, but said they would accede to the wishes of the Hall."

Despite herself, Moiraine shivered. "That would be . . . most unpleasant, Mother." It would be worse than unpleasant, much worse; the Reds were never gentle. She put the thought of it firmly to one side, to deal with later. "Mother, I cannot understand this apparent alliance between the Greens and the Reds. Their beliefs, their attitudes toward men, their views of our very purposes as Aes Sedai, are completely opposite. A Red and a Green cannot even talk to each other without coming to shouts."

"Things change, Daughter. Four of the last five women raised Amyrlin have come from the Blue. Perhaps they feel that is too many, or that the Blue way of thinking no longer suffices in a world full of false Dragons. After a thousand years, many things change." The Amyrlin grimaced and spoke as if to herself. "Old walls weaken, and old barriers fall." She shook herself, and her voice firmed. "There was yet another proposal, one that still smells like week-old fish on the jetty. Since Leane is of the Blue Ajah and I came from the Blue, it was put forward that sending two sisters of the Blue with me on this journey would give the Blue four representatives. Proposed in the Hall, to my face, as if they were discussing repairing the drains. Two of the White Sisters stood against me, and two Green. The Yellow muttered among themselves, then would not speak for or against. One more saying nay, and your sisters Anaiya and Maigan would not be here. There was even some talk, open talk, that I should not leave the White Tower at all."

Moiraine felt a greater shock than on hearing that the Red Ajah wanted her in their hands. Whatever Ajah she came from, the Keeper of the Chronicles spoke only for the Amyrlin, and the Amyrlin spoke for all Aes Sedai and all Ajahs. That was the way it had always been, and no one had ever suggested otherwise, not in the darkest days of the Trolloc Wars, not when Artur Hawkwing's armies had penned every surviving Aes Sedai inside Tar Valon. Above all, the Amyrlin Seat was the Amyrlin Seat. Every Aes Sedai was pledged to obey her. No one could question what she did or where she chose to go. This proposal went against three thousand years of custom and law.

"Who would dare, Mother?"

The Amyrlin Seat's laugh was bitter. "Almost anyone, Daughter. Riots in Caemlyn. The Great Hunt called without any of us having a hint of it until the proclamation. False Dragons popping up like redbells after a rain. Nations fading, and more nobles playing at the Game of Houses than at any time since Artur Hawkwing cut all their plottings short. And worst of all, every one of us knows the Dark One is stirring again. Show me a sister who does not think the White Tower is losing its grip on events, and if she is not Brown Ajah, she is dead. Time may be growing short for all of us, Daughter. Sometimes I think I can almost feel it growing shorter."

"As you say, Mother, things change. But there are still worse perils outside the Shining Walls than within."

For a long moment the Amyrlin met Moiraine's gaze, then nodded slowly. "Leave us, Leane. I would talk to my Daughter Moiraine alone."

There was only a moment's hesitation before Leane said, "As you wish, Mother." Moiraine could feel her surprise. The Amyrlin gave few audiences without the Keeper present, especially not to a sister she had reason to chastise.

The door opened and closed behind Leane. She would not say a word in the anteroom of what had occurred inside, but the news that Moiraine was alone with the Amyrlin would spread through the Aes Sedai in Fal Dara like wildfire through a dry forest, and the speculation would begin.

As soon as the door closed the Amyrlin stood, and Moiraine felt a momentary tingle in her skin as the other woman channeled the One Power. For an instant, the Amyrlin Seat seemed to her to be surrounded by a nimbus of bright light.

"I don't know that any of the others have your old trick," the Amyrlin Seat said, lightly touching the blue stone on Moiraine's forehead with one finger, "but most of us have some small tricks remembered from childhood. In any event, no one can hear what we say now."

Suddenly she threw her arms around Moiraine, a warm hug between old friends; Moiraine hugged back as warmly.

"You are the only one, Moiraine, with whom I can remember who I was. Even Leane always acts as if I had *become* the stole and the staff, even when we are alone, as if we'd never giggled together as novices. Sometimes I wish we still were novices, you and I. Still innocent enough to see it all as a gleeman's tale come true, still innocent enough to think we would find men—they would be princes, remember, handsome and strong and gentle?—who could bear to live with women of an Aes Sedai's power. Still innocent enough to dream of the happy ending to the gleeman's tale, of living our lives as other women do, just with more than they."

"We are Aes Sedai, Siuan. We have our duty. Even if you and I had not been born to channel, would you give it up for a home and a husband, even a prince? I do not believe it. That is a village goodwife's dream. Not even the Greens go so far."

The Amyrlin stepped back. "No, I would not give it up. Most of the time, no. But there have been times I envied that village goodwife. At this moment, I almost do. Moiraine, if anyone, even Leane, discovers what we plan, we will both be stilled. And I can't say they would be wrong to do it."

CHAPTER
5

The Shadow in Shienar

S tilled. The word seemed to quiver in the air, almost
visible. When it was done to a man who could channel the Power, who must be stopped before madness
drove him to the destruction of all around him, it was called
gentling, but for Aes Sedai it was stilling. Stilled. No longer
able to channel the flow of the One Power. Able to sense
saidar, the female half of the True Source, but no longer
having the ability to touch it. Remembering what was gone
forever. So seldom had it been done that every novice was
required to learn the name of each Aes Sedai since the
Breaking of the World who had been stilled, and her crime,
but none could think of it without a shudder. Women bore
being stilled no better than men did being gentled.

Moiraine had known the risk from the first, and she knew
it was necessary. That did not mean it was pleasant to dwell
on. Her eyes narrowed, and only the gleam in them showed
her anger, and her worry. "Leane would follow you to the
slopes of Shayol Ghul, Siuan, and into the Pit of Doom. You
cannot think she would betray you."

"No. But then, would she think it betrayal? Is it betrayal
to betray a traitor? Do you never think of that?"

"Never. What we do, Siuan, is what must be done. We
have both known it for nearly twenty years. The Wheel
weaves as the Wheel wills, and you and I were chosen for
this by the Pattern. We are a part of the Prophecies, and the
Prophecies must be fulfilled. Must!"

"The Prophecies must be fulfilled. We were taught that
they will be, and must be, and yet that fulfillment is treason to everything else we were taught. Some would say

to everything we stand for." Rubbing her arms, the Amyrlin Seat walked over to peer through the narrow arrowslit at the garden below. She touched the curtains. "Here in the women's apartments they hang draperies to soften the rooms, and they plant beautiful gardens, but there is no part of this place not purpose-made for battle, death, and killing." She continued in the same pensive tone. "Only twice since the Breaking of the World has the Amyrlin Seat been stripped of stole and staff."

"Tetsuan, who betrayed Manetheren for jealousy of Ellisande's powers, and Bonwhin, who tried to use Artur Hawkwing for a puppet to control the world and so nearly destroyed Tar Valon."

The Amyrlin continued her study of the garden. "Both of the Red, and both replaced by Amyrlin from the Blue. The reason there has not been an Amyrlin chosen from the Red since Bonwhin, and the reason the Red Ajah will take any pretext to pull down an Amyrlin from the Blue, all wrapped neatly together. I have no wish to be the third to lose the stole and the staff, Moiraine. For you, of course, it would mean being stilled and put outside the Shining Walls."

"Elaida, for one, would never let me off so easily." Moiraine watched her friend's back intently. *Light, what has come over her? She has never been like this before. Where is her strength, her fire?* "But it will not come to that, Siuan."

The other woman went on as if she had not spoken. "For me, it would be different. Even stilled, an Amyrlin who has been pulled down cannot be allowed to wander about loose; she might be seen as a martyr, become a rallying point for opposition. Tetsuan and Bonwhin were kept in the White Tower as servants. Scullery maids, who could be pointed to as cautions as to what can happen to the mightiest. No one can rally around a woman who must scrub floors and pots all day. Pity her, yes, but not rally to her."

Eyes blazing, Moiraine leaned her fists on the table. "Look at me, Siuan. Look at me! Are you saying that you want to give up, after all these years, after all we have done? Give up, and let the world go? And all for fear of a switching for not getting the pots clean enough!" She put into it all the scorn she could summon, and was relieved when her friend spun to face her. The strength was still there, strained but still there. Those clear blue eyes were as hot with anger as her own.

"I remember which of the two of us squealed the loudest when we were switched as novices. You had lived a soft life in Cairhien, Moiraine. Not like working a fishing boat." Abruptly Siuan slapped the table with a loud crack. "No, I am not suggesting giving up, but neither do I propose to watch everything slide out of our hands *while I can do nothing!* Most of my troubles with the Hall stem from you. Even the Greens wonder why I haven't called you to the Tower and taught you a little discipline. Half the sisters with me think you should be handed over to the Reds, and if that happens, you will wish you were a novice again, with nothing worse to look forward to than a switching. Light! If any of them remember we were friends as novices, I'd be there beside you.

"We had a plan! A plan, Moiraine! Locate the boy and bring him to Tar Valon, where we could hide him, keep him safe and guide him. Since you left the Tower, I have had only two messages from you. Two! I feel as if I'm trying to sail the Fingers of the Dragon in the dark. One message to say you were entering the Two Rivers, going to this village, this Emond's Field. Soon, I thought. He's found, and she'll have him in hand soon. Then word from Caemlyn to say you were coming to Shienar, to Fal Dara, not Tar Valon. Fal Dara, with the Blight almost close enough to touch. Fal Dara, where Trollocs raid and Myrddraal ride as near every day as makes no difference. Nearly twenty years of planning and searching, and you toss all our plans practically in the Dark One's face. Are you mad?"

Now that she had stirred life in the other woman, Moiraine returned to outward calm, herself. Calm, but firm insistence, too. "The Pattern pays no heed to human plans, Siuan. With all our scheming, we forgot what we were dealing with. *Ta'veren.* Elaida is wrong. Artur Paendrag Tanreall was never this strongly *ta'veren*. The Wheel will weave the Pattern around this young man as *it* wills, whatever our plans."

The anger left Amyrlin's face, replaced by white-faced shock. "It sounds as if *you* are saying we might as well give up. Do *you* now suggest standing aside and watching the world burn?"

"No, Siuan. Never standing aside." *Yet the world will burn, Siuan, one way or another, whatever we do. You could never see that.* "But we must now realize that our plans are precarious things. We have even less control than we thought. Perhaps only a fingernail's grip. The winds of destiny are blowing, Siuan, and we must ride them where they take us."

The Amyrlin shivered as if she felt those winds icy on the back of her neck. Her hands went to the flattened cube of gold, blunt, capable fingers finding precise points in the complex designs. Cunningly balanced, the top lifted back to reveal a curled, golden horn nestled within a space designed to hold it. She lifted the instrument and traced the flowing silver script, in the Old Tongue, inlaid around the flaring mouth.

" 'The grave is no bar to my call,' " she translated, so softly she seemed to be speaking to herself. "The Horn of Valere, made to call dead heroes back from the grave. And prophecy said it would only be found just in time for the Last Battle." Abruptly she thrust the Horn back into its niche and closed the lid as if she could no longer bear the sight of it. "Agelmar pushed it into my hands as soon as the Welcome was done. He said he was afraid to go into his own strongroom any longer, with it there. The temptation was too great, he said. To sound the Horn himself and lead the host that answered its call north through the Blight to level Shayol Ghul itself and put an end to the Dark One. He burned with the ecstasy of glory, and it was that, he said, that told him it was not to be him, must not be him. He could not wait to be rid of it, yet he wanted it still."

Moiraine nodded. Agelmar was familiar with the Prophecy of the Horn; most who fought the Dark One were. " 'Let whosoever sounds me think not of glory, but only of salvation.' "

"Salvation." The Amyrlin laughed bitterly. "From the look in Agelmar's eyes, he didn't know whether he was giving away salvation or rejecting the condemnation of his own soul. He only knew he had to be rid of it before it burned him up. He has tried to keep it secret, but he says there are rumors in the keep already. I do not feel his temptation, yet the Horn still makes my skin crawl. He will have to take it back into his strongroom until I leave. I could not sleep with it even in the next room." She rubbed frown lines from her forehead and sighed. "And it was not to be found until just before the Last Battle. Can it be that close? I thought, hoped, we would have more time."

"The Karaethon Cycle."

"Yes, Moiraine. You do not have to remind me. I've lived with the Prophecies of the Dragon as long as you." The Amyrlin shook her head. "Never more than one false Dragon in a generation since the Breaking, and now three loose in the world at one time, and three more in the past two years. The Pattern demands a Dragon because the Pattern weaves toward Tarmon Gai'don. Sometimes doubt fills me, Moiraine." She said it musingly, as if wondering at it, and went on in the same tone. "What if Logain was the one? He could channel, before the Reds brought him to the White Tower, and we gentled him. So can Mazrim Taim, the man in Saldaea. What if it is him? There are sisters in Saldaea already; he may be taken by now. What if we have been wrong since the start? What happens if the Dragon Reborn is gentled before the Last Battle even begins? Even prophecy can fail if the one prophesied is slain or gentled. And then we face the Dark One naked to the storm."

"Neither of them is the one, Siuan. The Pattern does not demand *a* Dragon, but the one true Dragon. Until he proclaims himself, the Pattern will continue to throw up false Dragons, but after that there will be no others. If Logain or the other were the one, there would be no others."

" 'For he shall come like the breaking dawn, and shatter the world again with his coming, and make it anew.' Either we go naked in the storm, or cling to a protection that will scourge us. The Light help us all." The Amyrlin shook herself as if to throw off her own words. Her face was set, as though bracing for a blow. "You could never hide what you were thinking from me as you do from everyone else, Moiraine. You have more to tell me, and nothing good."

For answer Moiraine took the leather pouch from her belt and upended it, spilling the contents on the table. It appeared to be only a heap of fragmented pottery, shiny black and white.

The Amyrlin Seat touched one bit curiously, and her breath caught. *"Cuendillar."*

"Heartstone," Moiraine agreed. The making of *cuendillar* had been lost at the Breaking of the World, but what had been made of heartstone had survived the cataclysm. Even those objects swallowed by the earth or sunk in the sea had survived; they must have. No known force could break *cuendillar* once it was complete; even the One Power directed against heartstone only made it stronger. Except that some power *had* broken this.

The Amyrlin hastily assembled the pieces. What they formed was a disk the size of a man's hand, half blacker than pitch and half whiter than snow, the colors meeting along a sinuous line, unfaded by age. The ancient symbol of Aes Sedai, before the world was broken, when men and women wielded the Power together. Half of it was now called the Flame of Tar Valon; the other half was scrawled on doors, the Dragon's Fang, to accuse those within of evil. Only seven like it had been made; everything ever made of heartstone was recorded in the White Tower, and those seven were remembered above all. Siuan Sanche stared at it as she would have at a viper on her pillow.

"One of the seals on the Dark One's prison," she said finally, reluctantly. It was those seven seals over which the Amyrlin Seat was supposed to be Watcher. The secret hidden from the world, if the world ever thought of it, was that no Amyrlin Seat had known where any of the seals were since the Trolloc Wars.

"We know the Dark One is stirring, Siuan. We know his prison cannot stay sealed forever. Human work can never match the Creator's. We knew he has touched the world again, even if, thank the Light, only indirectly. Darkfriends multiply, and what we called evil but ten years ago seems almost caprice compared with what now is done every day."

"If the seals are already breaking. . . . We may have no time at all."

"Little enough. But that little may be enough. It will have to be."

The Amyrlin touched the fractured seal, and her voice grew tight, as if she were forcing herself to speak. "I saw the boy, you know, in the courtyard during the Welcome. It is one of my Talents, seeing *ta'veren*. A rare Talent these days, even more rare than *ta'veren*, and certainly not of much use. A tall boy, a fairly handsome young man. Not much different from any young man you might see in any town." She paused to draw breath. "Moiraine, he blazed like the sun. I've seldom been afraid in my life, but the sight of him made me afraid right down to my toes. I wanted to cower, to howl. I could barely speak. Agelmar thought I was angry with him, I said so little. That young man . . . he's the one we have sought these twenty years."

There was a hint of question in her voice. Moiraine answered it. "He is."

"Are you certain? Can he . . . ? Can he . . . channel the One Power?"

Her mouth strained around the words, and Moiraine felt the tension, too, a twisting inside, a cold clutching at her heart. She kept her face smooth, though. "He can." A man wielding the One Power. That was a thing no Aes Sedai could contemplate without fear. It was a thing the whole world feared. *And I will loose it on the world.* "Rand al'Thor will stand before the world as the Dragon Reborn."

The Amyrlin shuddered. "Rand al'Thor. It does not sound like a name to inspire fear and set the world on fire." She gave another shiver and rubbed her arms briskly, but her eyes suddenly shone with a purposeful light. "If he is the one, then we truly may have time enough. But is he safe here? I have two Red sisters with me, and I can no longer answer for Green or Yellow, either. The Light consume me, I can't answer for any of them, not with this. Even Verin and Serafelle would leap on him the way they would a scarlet adder in a nursery."

"He is safe, for the moment."

The Amyrlin waited for her to say more. The silence stretched, until it was plain she would not. Finally the Amyrlin said, "You say our old plan is useless. What do you suggest now?"

"I have purposely let him think I no longer have any interest in him, that he may go where he pleases for all of me." She raised her hands as the Amyrlin opened her mouth. "It was necessary, Siuan. Rand al'Thor was raised in the Two Rivers, where Manetheren's stubborn blood flows in every vein, and his own blood is like rock beside clay compared to Manetheren's. He must be handled gently, or he will bolt in any direction but the one we want."

"Then we'll handle him like a newborn babe. We'll wrap

him in swaddling clothes and play with his toes, if that's what you think we need. But to what immediate purpose?"

"His two friends, Matrim Cauthon and Perrin Aybara, are ripe to see the world before they sink back into the obscurity of the Two Rivers. If they can sink back; they are *ta'veren*, too, if lesser than he. I will induce them to carry the Horn of Valere to Illian." She hesitated, frowning. "There is . . . a problem with Mat. He carries a dagger from Shadar Logoth."

"Shadar Logoth! Light, why did you ever let them get near that place. Every stone of it is tainted. There isn't a pebble safe to carry away. Light help us, if Mordeth touched the boy. . . ." The Amyrlin sounded as though she were strangling. "If that happened, the world would be doomed."

"But it did not, Siuan. We do what we must from necessity, and it was necessary. I have done enough so that Mat will not infect others, but he had the dagger too long before I knew. The link is still there. I had thought I must take him to Tar Valon to cure it, but with so many sisters present, it might be done here. So long as there are a few you can trust not to see Darkfriends where there are none. You and I and two others will suffice, using my *angreal*."

"Leane will do for one, and I can find another." Suddenly the Amyrlin Seat gave a wry grin. "The Hall wants that *angreal* back, Moiraine. There are not very many of them left, and you are now considered . . . unreliable."

Moiraine smiled, but it did not touch her eyes. "They will think worse of me before I am done. Mat will leap at the chance to be so big a part of the legend of the Horn, and Perrin should not be hard to convince. He needs something to take his mind off his own troubles. Rand knows what he is—some of it, at least; a little—and he is afraid of it, naturally. He wants to go off somewhere alone, where he cannot hurt anyone. He says he will never wield the Power again, but he fears not being able to stop it."

"As well he might. Easier to give up drinking water."

"Exactly. And he wants to be free from Aes Sedai." Moiraine gave a small, mirthless smile. "Offered the chance to leave Aes Sedai behind and still stay with his friends a while longer, he should be as eager as Mat."

"But how is he leaving Aes Sedai behind? Surely you must travel with him. We can't lose him now, Moiraine."

"I cannot travel with him." *It is a long way from Fal Dara to Illian, but he has traveled almost as far already.* "He must be let off the leash for a time. There is no help for it. I have had all of their old clothes burned. There has been too much opportunity for some shred of what they were wearing to have fallen into the wrong hands. I will cleanse them before they leave; they will not even realize it has been done. There will be no chance they can be tracked that way, and the only other threat of that kind is locked away here in the dungeon." The Amyrlin, midway in nodding approval, gave her a questioning look, but she did not pause. "They will travel as safely as I can manage, Siuan. And when Rand needs me in Illian, I will be there, and I will see that it is he who presents the Horn to the Council of Nine and the Assemblage. I will see to everything in Illian. Siuan, the Illianers would follow the Dragon, or Ba'alzamon himself, if he came bearing the Horn of Valere, and so will the greater part of those gathered for the Hunt. The true Dragon Reborn will not need to gather a following before nations move against him. He will begin with a nation around him and an army at his back."

The Amyrlin dropped back into her chair, but immediately leaned forward. She seemed caught between weariness and hope. "But *will* he proclaim himself? If he's afraid. . . . The Light knows he should be, Moiraine, but men who name themselves as the Dragon *want* the power. If he does not. . . ."

"I have the means to see him named Dragon whether he wills it or not. And even if I somehow fail, the Pattern itself will see him named Dragon whether he wills it or not. Remember, he is *ta'veren*, Siuan. He has no more control over his fate than a candle wick has over the flame."

The Amyrlin sighed. "It's risky, Moiraine. Risky. But my father used to say, 'Girl, if you won't take a chance, you'll never win a copper.' We have plans to make. Sit down; this won't be done quickly. I will send for wine and cheese."

Moiraine shook her head. "We have been closeted alone too long already. If any did try listening and found your Warding, they will be wondering already. It is not worth the risk. We can contrive another meeting tomorrow." *Besides, my dearest friend, I cannot tell you everything, and I cannot risk letting you know I am holding anything back.*

"I suppose you are right. But first thing in the morning. There's so much I have to know."

"The morning," Moiraine agreed. The Amyrlin rose, and they hugged again. "In the morning I will tell you everything you need to know."

Leane gave Moiraine a sharp look when she came out into the anteroom, then darted into the Amyrlin's chamber. Moiraine tried to put on a chastened face, as if she had endured one of the Amyrlin's infamous upbraidings—most women, however strong-willed, returned from those big-eyed and weak-kneed—but the expression was foreign to her. She looked more angry than anything else, which served much the same purpose. She was only vaguely aware of the other women in the outer room; she thought some had gone and others come since she went in, but she barely looked at them. The hour was growing late, and there was much to be done before the morning came. Much, before she spoke to the Amyrlin Seat again.

Quickening her step, she moved deeper into the keep.

The column would have made an impressive sight under the waxing moon, moving through the Tarabon night to the jangle of harness, had there been anyone to see it. A full two thousand Children of the Light, well mounted, in white tabards and cloaks, armor burnished, with their train of supply wagons, and farriers, and grooms with the strings of remounts. There were villages in this sparsely forested country, but they had left roads behind, and stayed clear of even farmers' crofts. They were to meet . . . someone . . . at a flyspeck village near the northern border of Tarabon, at the edge of Almoth Plain.

Geofram Bornhald, riding at the head of his men, wondered what it was all about. He remembered too well his interview with Pedron Niall, Lord Captain Commander of the Children of the Light, in Amador, but he had learned little there.

"We are alone, Geofram," the white-haired man had said. *His voice was thin and reedy with age. "I remember giving you the oath . . . what . . . thirty-six years ago, it must be, now."*

Bornhald straightened. *"My Lord Captain Commander,*

*may I ask why I was called back from Caemlyn, and with
such urgency? A push, and Morgase could be toppled.
There are Houses in Andor that see dealing with Tar Valon
as we do, and they were ready to lay claim to the throne.
I left Eamon Valda in charge, but he seemed intent on following the Daughter-Heir to Tar Valon. I would not be surprised to learn the man has kidnapped the girl, or even
attacked Tar Valon." And Dain, Bornhald's son, had arrived just before Bornhald was recalled. Dain was full of
zeal. Too much zeal, sometimes. Enough to fall in blindly
with whatever Valda proposed.*

"Valda walks in the Light, Geofram. But you are the
best battle commander among the Children. You will as-
semble a full legion, the best men you can find, and take
them into Tarabon, avoiding any eyes attached to a tongue
that may speak. Any such tongue must be silenced, if the
eyes see."

Bornhald hesitated. Fifty Children together, or even a
hundred, could enter any land without question, at least
without open question, but an entire legion. . . . "Is it war,
my Lord Captain Commander? There is talk in the streets.
Wild rumors, mainly, about Artur Hawkwing's armies
come back." The old man did not speak. "The King. . . ."

"Does not command the Children, Lord Captain Bornhald." For the first time there was a snap in the Lord
Captain Commander's voice. "I do. Let the King sit in his
palace and do what he does best. Nothing. You will be met
at a village called Alcruna, and there you will receive your
final orders. I expect your legion to ride in three days. Now
go, Geofram. You have work to do."

Bornhald frowned. "Pardon, my Lord Captain Commander, but who will meet me? Why am I risking war with
Tarabon?"

"You will be told what you must know when you reach
Alcruna." The Lord Captain Commander suddenly looked
more than his age. Absently he plucked at his white tunic,
with the golden sunburst of the Children large on the chest.
"There are forces at work beyond what you know, Geofram.
Beyond what even you can know. Choose your men quickly.
Now go. Ask me no more. And the Light ride with you."

Now Bornhald straightened in his saddle, working a knot
out of his back. *I am getting old*, he thought. A day and a

night in the saddle, with two pauses to water the horses, and he felt every gray hair on his head. He would not even have noticed a few years ago. *At least I have not killed any innocents.* He could be as hard on Darkfriends as any man sworn to the Light—Darkfriends must be destroyed before they pulled the whole world under the Shadow—but he wanted to be sure they *were* Darkfriends first. It had been difficult avoiding Taraboner eyes with so many men, even in the backcountry, but he had managed it. No tongues had needed to be silenced.

The scouts he had sent out came riding back, and behind them came more men in white cloaks, some carrying torches to ruin the night vision of everyone at the head of the column. With a muttered curse, Bornhald ordered a halt while he studied those who came to meet him.

Their cloaks bore the same golden sunburst on the breast as his, the same as every Child of the Light, and their leader even had golden knots of rank below it equivalent to Bornhald's. But behind their sunbursts were red shepherd's crooks. Questioners. With hot irons and pinchers and dripping water the Questioners pulled confession and repentance from Darkfriends, but there were those who said they decided guilt before ever they began. Geofram Bornhald was one who said it.

I have been sent here to meet Questioners?

"We have been waiting for you, Lord Captain Bornhald," the leader said in a harsh voice. He was a tall, hook-nosed man with the gleam of certainty in his eyes that every Questioner had. "You could have made better time. I am Einor Saren, second to Jaichim Carridin, who commands the Hand of the Light in Tarabon." The Hand of the Light— the Hand that dug out truth, so they said. They did not like the name Questioners. "There is a bridge at the village. Have your men move across. We will talk in the inn. It is surprisingly comfortable."

"I was told by the Lord Captain Commander himself to avoid all eyes."

"The village has been . . . pacified. Now move your men. *I* command, now. I have orders with the Lord Captain Commander's seal, if you doubt."

Bornhald suppressed the growl that rose in his throat. Pacified. He wondered if the bodies had been piled outside the village, or if they had been thrown into the river. It would be like the Questioners, cold enough to kill an entire village for secrecy and stupid enough to throw the bodies into the river to float downstream and trumpet their deed from Alcruna to Tanchico. "What I doubt is why I am in Tarabon with two thousand men, Questioner."

Saren's face tightened, but his voice remained harsh and demanding. "It is simple, Lord Captain. There are towns and villages across Almoth Plain with none in authority above a mayor or a Town Council. It is past time they were brought to the Light. There will be many Darkfriends in such places."

Bornhald's horse stamped. "Are you saying, Saren, that I've brought an entire legion across most of Tarabon in secrecy to root a few Darkfriends out of some grubby villages?"

"You are here to do as you are told, Bornhald. To do the work of the Light! Or are you sliding from the Light?" Saren's smile was a grimace. "If battle is what you seek, you may have your chance. The strangers have a great force on Toman Head, more than Tarabon and Arad Doman together may be able to hold, even if they can stop their own bickering long enough to work together. If the strangers break through, you will have all the fighting you can handle. The Taraboners claim the strangers are monsters, creatures of the Dark One. Some say they have Aes Sedai to fight for them. If they *are* Darkfriends, these strangers, they will have to be dealt with, too. In their turn."

For a moment, Bornhald stopped breathing. "Then the rumors are true. Artur Hawkwing's armies have returned."

"Strangers," Saren said flatly. He sounded as if he regretted having mentioned them. "Strangers, and probably Darkfriends, from wherever they came. That is all we know, and all you need to know. They do not concern you now. We are wasting time. Move your men across the river, Bornhald. I will give you your orders in the village." He whirled his horse and galloped back the way he had come, his torchbearers riding at his heels.

Bornhald closed his eyes to hasten the return of his night sight. *We are being used like stones on a board.* "Byar!" He opened his eyes as his second appeared at his side, stiffening in his saddle before the Lord Captain. The gaunt-faced man

had almost the Questioner's light in his eyes, but he was a
good soldier despite. "There is a bridge ahead. Move the
legion across the river and make camp. I will join you as
soon as I can."

He gathered his reins and rode in the direction the Questioner had taken. *Stones on a board. But who is moving us?
And why?*

Afternoon shadows gave way to evening as Liandrin made
her way through the women's apartments. Beyond the arrowslits, darkness grew and pressed on the light from the
lamps in the corridor. Twilight was a troubled time for
Liandrin of late, that and dawn. At dawn the day was born,
just as twilight gave birth to night, but at dawn, night died,
and at twilight, day. The Dark One's power was rooted in
death; he gained power from death, and at those times she
thought she could feel his power stirring. Something stirred
in the half dark, at least. Something she almost thought she
could catch if she turned quickly enough, something she
was sure she could see if she looked hard enough.

Serving women in black-and-gold curtsied as she passed,
but she did not respond. She kept her eyes fixed straight
ahead, and did not see them.

At the door she sought, she paused for a quick glance up
and down the hall. The only women in sight were servants;
there were no men, of course. She pushed open the door
and went in without knocking.

The outer room of the Lady Amalisa's chambers was
brightly lit, and a blazing fire on the hearth held back the
chill of the Shienaran night. Amalisa and her ladies sat
about the room, in chairs and on the layered carpets, listening while one of their number, standing, read aloud to them.
It was *The Dance of the Hawk and the Hummingbird,* by
Teven Aerwin, which purported to set forth the proper
conduct of men toward women and women toward men.
Liandrin's mouth tightened; she certainly had not read it,
but she had heard as much as she needed about it. Amalisa
and her ladies greeted each pronouncement with gales of
laughter, falling against each other and drumming their
heels on the carpets like girls.

The reader was the first to become aware of Liandrin's

presence. She cut off with a surprised widening of her eyes. The others turned to see what she was staring at, and silence replaced laughter. All but Amalisa scrambled to their feet, hastily smoothing hair and skirts.

The Lady Amalisa rose gracefully, with a smile. "You honor us with your presence, Liandrin. This is a most pleasant surprise. I did not expect you until tomorrow. I thought you would want to rest after your long jour—"

Liandrin cut her off sharply, addressing the air. "I will speak to the Lady Amalisa alone. All of you will leave. Now."

There was a moment of shocked silence, then the other women made their goodbyes to Amalisa. One by one they curtsied to Liandrin, but she did not acknowledge them. She continued to stare straight ahead at nothing, but she saw them, and heard. Honorifics offered with breathy unease at the Aes Sedai's mood. Eyes falling when she ignored them. They squeezed past her to the door, pressing back awkwardly so their skirts did not disturb hers.

As the door closed behind the last of them, Amalisa said, "Liandrin, I do not underst—"

"Do you walk in the Light, my daughter?" There would be none of that foolishness of calling her sister here. The other woman was older by some years, but the ancient forms would be observed. However long they had been forgotten, it was time they were remembered.

As soon as the question was out of her mouth, though, Liandrin realized she had made a mistake. It was a question guaranteed to cause doubt and anxiety, coming from an Aes Sedai, but Amalisa's back stiffened, and her face hardened.

"That is an insult, Liandrin Sedai. I am Shienaran, of a noble House and the blood of soldiers. My line has fought the Shadow since before there *was* a Shienar, three thousand years without fail or a day's weakness."

Liandrin shifted her point of attack, but she did not retreat. Striding across the room, she took the leather-bound copy of *The Dance of the Hawk and the Hummingbird* from the mantelpiece and hefted it without looking at it. "In Shienar above other lands, my daughter, the Light must be precious, and the Shadow feared." Casually she threw the book into the fire. Flames leaped as if it were a log of fatwood, thundering as they licked up the chimney. In the same instant every lamp in the room flared, hissing, so fiercely did they burn, flooding the chamber with light. "Here above all. Here, so close to the cursed Blight, where corruption waits. Here, even one who thinks he walks in the Light may still be corrupted by the Shadow."

Beads of sweat glistened on Amalisa's forehead. The hand she had raised in protest for her book fell slowly to her side. Her features still held firm, but Liandrin saw her swallow, and her feet shift. "I do not understand, Liandrin Sedai. Is it the book? It is only foolishness."

There was a faint quaver in her voice. *Good.* Glass lamp mantles cracked as the flames leaped higher and hotter, lighting the room as bright as unsheltered noon. Amalisa stood as stiff as a post, her face tight as she tried not to squint.

"It is you who are foolish, my daughter. I care nothing for books. Here, men enter the Blight, and walk in its taint. In the very Shadow. Why wonder you that that taint may seep into them? Whether or not against their will, still it may seep. Why think you the Amyrlin Seat herself has come?"

"No." It was a gasp.

"Of the Red am I, my daughter," Liandrin said relentlessly. "I hunt all men corrupted."

"I don't understand."

"Not only those foul ones who try the One Power. All men corrupted. High and low do I hunt."

"I don't. . . ." Amalisa licked her lips unsteadily and made a visible effort to gather herself. "I do not understand, Liandrin Sedai. Please. . . ."

"High even before low."

"No!" As if some invisible support had vanished, Amalisa fell to her knees, and her head dropped. "Please, Liandrin Sedai, say you do not mean Agelmar. It cannot be him."

In that moment of doubt and confusion, Liandrin struck. She did not move, but lashed out with the One Power. Amalisa gasped and gave a jerk, as if she had been pricked with a needle, and Liandrin's petulant mouth perked in a smile.

This was her own special trick from childhood, the first learned of her abilities. It had been forbidden to her as soon as the Mistress of Novices discovered it, but to Liandrin that only meant one more thing she needed to conceal from those who were jealous of her.

She strode forward and pulled Amalisa's chin up. The metal that had stiffened her was still there, but it was baser metal now, malleable to the right pressures. Tears trickled from the corners of Amalisa's eyes, glistening on her cheeks. Liandrin let the fires die back to normal; there was no longer any need for such. She softened her words, but her voice was as unyielding as steel.

"Daughter, no one wants to see you and Agelmar thrown to the people as Darkfriends. I will help you, but you must help."

"H-help you?" Amalisa put her hands to her temples; she looked confused. "Please, Liandrin Sedai, I don't . . . understand. It is all so. . . . It's all. . . ."

It was not a perfect ability; Liandrin could not force anyone to do what she wanted—though she had tried; oh, how she had tried. But she could open them wide to her arguments, make them want to believe her, want more than anything to be convinced of her rightness.

"Obey, daughter. Obey, and answer my questions truthfully, and I promise that no one will speak of you and Agelmar as Darkfriends. You will not be dragged naked through the streets, to be flogged from the city if the people do not tear you to pieces first. I will not let this happen. You understand?"

"Yes, Liandrin Sedai, yes. I will do as you say and answer you truly."

Liandrin straightened, looking down at the other woman. The Lady Amalisa stayed as she was, kneeling, her face as open as a child's, a child waiting to be comforted and helped by someone wiser and stronger. There was a rightness about it to Liandrin. She had never understood why a simple bow or curtsy was sufficient for Aes Sedai when men and women knelt to kings and queens. *What queen has within her my power?* Her mouth twisted angrily, and Amalisa shivered.

"Be easy in yourself, my daughter. I have come to help you, not to punish. Only those who deserve it will be punished. Truth only, speak to me."

"I will, Liandrin Sedai. I will, I swear it by my House and honor."

"Moiraine came to Fal Dara with a Darkfriend."

Amalisa was too frightened to show surprise. "Oh, no, Liandrin Sedai. No. That man came later. He is in the dungeons now."

"Later, you say. But it is true that she speaks often with him? She is often in company with this Darkfriend? Alone?"

"S-sometimes, Liandrin Sedai. Only sometimes. She wishes to find out why he came here. Moiraine Sedai is—" Liandrin held up her hand sharply, and Amalisa swallowed whatever else she had been going to say.

"By three young men Moiraine was accompanied. This I *know*. Where are they? I have been to their rooms, and they are not to be found."

"I—I do not know, Liandrin Sedai. They seem nice boys. Surely you don't think they are Darkfriends."

"Not Darkfriends, no. Worse. By far more dangerous than Darkfriends, my daughter. The entire world is in danger from them. They must be found. You will command your servants to search the keep, and your ladies, and yourself. Every crack and cranny. To this, you will see personally. Personally! And to no one will you speak of it, save those I name. None else may know. None. From Fal Dara in secrecy these young men must be removed, and to Tar Valon taken. In utter secrecy."

"As you command, Liandrin Sedai. But I do not understand the need for secrecy. No one here will hinder Aes Sedai."

"Of the Black Ajah you have heard?"

Amalisa's eyes bulged, and she leaned back away from Liandrin, raising her hands as though to shield herself from a blow. "A v-vile rumor, Liandrin Sedai. V-vile. There are n-no Aes Sedai who s-serve the Dark One. I do not believe it. You must believe me! Under the Light, I s-swear I do not believe it. By my honor and my House, I swear. . . ."

Coolly Liandrin let her go on, watching the last remaining strength leach out of the other woman with her own silence. Aes Sedai had been known to become angry, very angry, with those who even mentioned the Black Ajah much less those who said they believed in its hidden existence. After this, with her will already weakened by that little childhood trick, Amalisa would be as clay in her hands. After one more blow.

"The Black Ajah is *real*, child. Real, and here within Fal Dara's walls." Amalisa knelt there, her mouth hanging open. The Black Ajah. Aes Sedai who were also Darkfriends. Almost as horrible to learn the Dark One himself walked Fal Dara keep. But Liandrin would not let up now. "Any Aes Sedai in the halls you pass, a Black sister could be. This I swear. I cannot tell you which they are, but my protection you can have. If in the Light you walk and me obey."

"I will," Amalisa whispered hoarsely. "I will. Please, Liandrin Sedai, please say you will protect my brother, and my ladies. . . ."

"Who deserves protection I will protect. Concern yourself with yourself, my daughter. And think only of what I have commanded of you. Only that. The fate of the world rides on this, my daughter. All else you must forget."

"Yes, Liandrin Sedai. Yes. Yes."

Liandrin turned and crossed the room, not looking back until she reached the door. Amalisa was still on her knees, still watching her anxiously. "Rise, my Lady Amalisa." Liandrin made her voice pleasant, with only a hint of the mocking she felt. *Sister, indeed! Not one day as a novice would she last. And power to command she *has*.* "Rise." Amalisa straightened in slow, stiff jerks, as if she had been bound hand and foot for hours. As she finally came upright, Liandrin said, the steel back in full strength, "And if you fail the world, if you fail me, that wretched Darkfriend in the dungeon will be your envy."

From the look on Amalisa's face, Liandrin did not think failure would come from any lack of effort on her part.

Pulling the door shut behind her, Liandrin suddenly felt a prickling across her skin. Breath catching, she whirled about, looking up and down the dimly lit hall. Empty. It was full night beyond the arrowslits. The hall was empty, yet she was sure there had been eyes on her. The vacant corridor, shadowy between the lamps on the walls, mocked her. She shrugged uneasily, then started down the hall determinedly. *Fancies take me. Nothing more.*

Full night already, and there was much to do before dawn. Her orders had been explicit.

Pitch-blackness covered the dungeons whatever the hour, unless someone brought in a lantern, but Padan Fain sat on the edge of his cot, staring into the dark with a smile on his face. He could hear the other two prisoners grumbling in their sleep, muttering in nightmares. Padan Fain was waiting for something, something he had been awaiting for a long time. For too long. But not much longer.

The door to the outer guardroom opened, spilling in a flood of light, darkly outlining a figure in the doorway.

Fain stood. "You! Not who I expected." He stretched with a casualness he did not feel. Blood raced through his veins; he thought he could leap over the keep if he tried. "Surprises for everyone, eh? Well, come on. The night's getting old, and I want some sleep sometime."

As a lamp came into the cell chamber, Fain raised his head, grinning at something, unseen yet felt, beyond the dungeon's stone ceiling. "It isn't over yet," he whispered. "The battle's never over."

CHAPTER
6

Dark Prophecy

The farmhouse door shook under furious blows from outside; the heavy bar across the door jumped in its brackets. Beyond the window next to the door moved the heavy-muzzled silhouette of a Trolloc. There were windows everywhere, and more shadowy shapes outside. Not shadowy enough, though. Rand could still make them out.

The windows, he thought desperately. He backed away from the door, clutching his sword before him in both hands. *Even if the door holds, they can break in the windows. Why aren't they trying the windows?*

With a deafening metallic screech, one of the brackets pulled partly away from the doorframe, hanging loose on nails ripped a finger's width out of the wood. The bar quivered from another blow, and the nails squealed again.

"We have to stop them!" Rand shouted. *Only we can't. We can't stop them.* He looked around for a way to run, but there was only the one door. The room was a box. Only one door, and so many windows. "We have to do something. Something!"

"It's too late," Mat said. "Don't you understand?" His grin looked odd on a bloodless pale face, and the hilt of a dagger stood out from his chest, the ruby that capped it blazing as if it held fire. The gem had more life than his face. "It's too late for us to change anything."

"I've finally gotten rid of them," Perrin said, laughing. Blood streamed down his face like a flood of tears from his empty sockets. He held out red hands, trying to make Rand look at what he held. "I'm free, now. It's over."

"It's never over, al'Thor," Padan Fain cried, capering in the middle of the floor. "The battle's never done."

The door exploded in splinters, and Rand ducked away from the flying shards of wood. Two red-clad Aes Sedai stepped through, bowing their master in. A mask the color of dried blood covered Ba'alzamon's face, but Rand could see the flames of his eyes through the eyeslits; he could hear the roaring fires of Ba'alzamon's mouth.

"It is not yet done between us, al'Thor," Ba'alzamon said, and he and Fain spoke together as one, "For you, the battle is never done."

With a strangled gasp Rand sat up on the floor, clawing his way awake. It seemed he could still hear Fain's voice, as sharp as if the peddler were standing beside him. *It's never over. The battle's never done.*

Bleary-eyed, he looked around to convince himself that he was still hidden away where Egwene had left him, bedded down on a pallet in a corner of her room. The dim light of a single lamp suffused the room, and he was surprised to see Nynaeve, knitting in a rocking chair on the other side of the lone bed, its covers still in place. It was night outside.

Dark-eyed and slender, Nynaeve wore her hair in a fat braid, pulled over one shoulder and hanging almost to her waist. She had not given up on home. Her face was calm, and she seemed aware of nothing except her knitting as she rocked gently. The steady *click-click* of her knitting needles was the only sound. The rug silenced the rocking chair.

There had been nights of late when he had wished for a carpet on the cold stone floor of his room, but in Shienar men's rooms were always bare and stark. The walls here had two tapestries, mountain scenes with waterfalls, and flower-embroidered curtains alongside the arrowslits. Cut flowers, white morningstars, stood in a flat, round vase on the table by the bed, and more nodded in glazed white sconces on the walls. A tall mirror stood in a corner, and another hung over the washstand, with its blue-striped pitcher and bowl. He wondered why Egwene needed two mirrors; there was none in his room, and he did not miss it. There was only one lamp lit, but four more stood around the room, which was nearly as large as the one he shared with Mat and Perrin. Egwene had it alone.

Without looking up, Nynaeve said, "If you sleep in the afternoon, you can't expect to sleep at night."

He frowned, though she could not see it. At least, he thought she could not. She was only a few years older than he, but being Wisdom added fifty years of authority. "I needed a place to hide, and I was tired," he said, then quickly added, "I didn't just come here. Egwene invited me into the women's apartments."

Nynaeve lowered her knitting and gave him an amused smile. She was a pretty woman. That was something he would never have noticed back home; one just did not think of a Wisdom that way. "The Light help me, Rand, you are becoming more Shienaran every day. Invited into the women's apartments, indeed." She sniffed. "Any day now, you'll start talking about your honor, and asking peace to favor your sword." He colored, and hoped she did not notice in the dim light. She eyed his sword, its hilt sticking out of the long bundle beside him on the floor. He knew she did not approve of the sword, of any sword, but she said nothing about it for once. "Egwene told me why you need a place to hide. Don't worry. We will keep you hidden from the Amyrlin, or from any other Aes Sedai, if that is what you want."

She met his eyes and jerked hers away, but not before he saw her uneasiness. Her doubt. *That's right, I can channel the Power. A man wielding the One Power! You ought to be helping the Aes Sedai hunt me down and gentle me.*

Scowling, he straightened the leather jerkin Egwene had found for him and twisted around so he could lean back against the wall. "As soon as I can, I will hide in a cart, or sneak out. You won't have to hide me long." Nynaeve did not say anything; she fixed on her knitting, making an angry sound when she dropped a stitch. "Where is Egwene?"

She let the knitting fall onto her lap. "I don't know why I am even trying tonight. I can't keep track of my stitches for some reason. She has gone down to see Padan Fain. She thinks seeing faces he knows might help him."

"Mine certainly did not. She ought to stay away from him. He's dangerous."

"She wants to help him," Nynaeve said calmly. "Remember, she was training to be my assistant, and being a

Wisdom is not all predicting the weather. Healing is part of it, too. Egwene has the desire to heal, the need to. And if Padan Fain is so dangerous, Moiraine would have said something."

He barked a laugh. "You didn't ask her. Egwene admitted it, and I can just see you asking permission for anything." Her raised eyebrow wiped the laugh off his face. He refused to apologize, though. They were a long way from home, and he did not see how she could go on being Wisdom of Emond's Field if she was going to Tar Valon. "Have they started to search for me, yet? Egwene is not sure they will, but Lan says the Amyrlin Seat is here because of me, and I think I'll take his opinion over hers."

For a moment Nynaeve did not answer. Instead she fussed with her skeins of yarn. Finally she said, "I am not sure. One of the serving women came a little while ago. To turn down the bed, she said. As if Egwene would be going to sleep already, with the feast for the Amyrlin tonight. I sent her away; she didn't see you."

"Nobody turns your bed down for you in the men's quarters." She gave him a level look, one that would have set him stammering a year ago. He shook his head. "They wouldn't use the maids to look for me, Nynaeve."

"When I went to the buttery for a cup of milk earlier, there were too many women in the halls. Those who are attending the feast should have been getting dressed, and the others should either have been helping them or getting ready to serve, or to. . . ." She frowned worriedly. "There's more than enough work for everybody with the Amyrlin here. And they were not just here in the women's apartments. I saw the Lady Amalisa herself coming out of a storeroom near the buttery with her face all over dust."

"That's ridiculous. Why would she be part of a search? Or any of the women, for that matter. They'd be using Lord Agelmar's soldiers, and the Warders. And the Aes Sedai. They must just be doing something for the feast. Burn me if I know what a Shienaran feast takes."

"You are a woolhead, sometimes, Rand. The men I saw didn't know what the women were doing either. I heard some of them complaining about having to do all the work by themselves. I know it makes no sense that they were looking for you. None of the Aes Sedai seemed to be tak-

ing any interest. But Amalisa was not readying herself for
the feast by dirtying her dress in a storeroom. They were
looking for something, something important. Even if she
began right after I saw her, she would barely have time to
bathe and change. Speaking of which, if Egwene doesn't
come back soon, she'll have to choose between changing
and being late."

For the first time, he realized that Nynaeve was not wearing the Two Rivers woolens he was used to. Her dress was
pale blue silk, embroidered in snowdrop blossoms around
the neck and down the sleeves. Each blossom centered on a
small pearl, and her belt was tooled in silver, with a silver
buckle set with pearls. He had never seen her in anything
like that. Even feastday clothes back home might not match it.

"You're going to the feast?"

"Of course. Even if Moiraine had not said I should, I
would never let her think I was. . . ." Her eyes lit up fiercely
for a moment, and he knew what she meant. Nynaeve would
never let anyone think she was afraid, even if she was. Certainly not Moiraine, and especially not Lan. He hoped she
did not know he was aware of her feelings for the Warder.

After a moment her gaze softened as it fell on the sleeve
of her dress. "The Lady Amalisa gave me this," she said
so softly he wondered if she was speaking to herself. She
stroked the silk with her fingers, outlining the embroidered
flowers, smiling, lost in thought.

"It's very pretty on you, Nynaeve. You're pretty tonight."
He winced as soon as he said it. Any Wisdom was touchy
about her authority, but Nynaeve was touchier than most.
The Women's Circle back home had always looked over her
shoulder because she was young, and maybe because she
was pretty, and her fights with the Mayor and the Village
Council had been the stuff of stories.

She jerked her hand away from the embroidery and glared
at him, brows lowering. He spoke quickly to forestall her.

"They can't keep the gates barred forever. Once they are
opened, I will be gone, and the Aes Sedai will never find
me. Perrin says there are places in the Black Hills and the
Caralain Grass you can go for days without seeing a soul.
Maybe—maybe I can figure out what to do about. . . ." He
shrugged uncomfortably. There was no need to say it, not to
her. "And if I can't, there'll be no one to hurt."

Nynaeve was silent for a moment, then she said slowly, "I am not so sure, Rand. I can't say you look like more than another village boy to me, but Moiraine insists you are *ta'veren*, and I don't think she believes the Wheel is finished with you. The Dark One seems—"

"Shai'tan is dead," he said harshly, and abruptly the room seemed to lurch. He grabbed his head as waves of dizziness sloshed through him.

"You fool! You pure, blind, idiotic fool! Naming the Dark One, bringing his attention down on you! Don't you have enough trouble?"

"He's dead," Rand muttered, rubbing his head. He swallowed. The dizziness was already fading. "All right, all right. Ba'alzamon, if you want. But he's dead; I saw him die, saw him burn."

"And I wasn't watching you when the Dark One's eye fell on you just now? Don't tell me you felt nothing, or I'll box your ears; I saw your face."

"He's dead," Rand insisted. The unseen watcher flashed through his head, and the wind on the tower top. He shivered. "Strange things happen this close to the Blight."

"You *are* a fool, Rand al'Thor." She shook a fist at him. "I *would* box your ears for you if I thought it would knock any sense—"

The rest of her words were swallowed as bells crashed out ringing all over the keep.

He bounded to his feet. "That's an alarm! They're searching. . . ." *Name the Dark One, and his evil comes down on you.*

Nynaeve stood more slowly, shaking her head uneasily. "No, I don't think so. If they are searching for you, all the bells do is warn you. No, if it's an alarm, it is not for you."

"Then what?" He hurried to the nearest arrowslit and peered out.

Lights darted through the night-cloaked keep like fireflies, lamps and torches dashing here and there. Some went to the outer walls and towers, but most of those that he could see milled through the garden below and the one courtyard he could just glimpse part of. Whatever had caused the alarm was inside the keep. The bells fell silent, unmasking the shouts of men, but he could not make out what they were calling.

If it isn't for me. . . . "Egwene," he said suddenly. *If he's still alive, if there's any evil, it's supposed to come to me.*

Nynaeve turned from looking through another arrowslit. "What?"

"Egwene." He crossed the room in quick strides and snatched his sword and scabbard free of the bundle. *Light, it's supposed to hurt me, not her.* "She's in the dungeon with Fain. What if he's loose somehow?"

She caught him at the door, grabbing his arm. She was not as tall as his shoulder, but she held on like iron. "Don't be a worse goat-brained fool than you've already been, Rand al'Thor. Even if this doesn't have anything to do with you, the women are looking for something! Light, man, this is the women's apartments. There will be Aes Sedai out there in the halls, likely as not. Egwene will be all right. She was going to take Mat and Perrin with her. Even if she met trouble, they would look after her."

"What if she couldn't find them, Nynaeve? Egwene would never let that stop her. She would go alone, the same as you, and you know it. Light, I told her Fain is dangerous! Burn me, I told her!" Pulling free, he jerked open the door and dashed out. *Light burn me, it's supposed to hurt me!*

A woman screamed at the sight of him, in a laborer's coarse shirt and jerkin with a sword in his hand. Even invited, men did not go armed in the women's apartments unless the keep was under attack. Women filled the corridor, serving women in the black-and-gold, ladies of the keep in silks and laces, women in embroidered shawls with long fringes, all talking loudly at the same time, all demanding to know what was happening. Crying children clung to skirts everywhere. He plunged through them, dodging where he could, muttering apologies to those he shouldered aside, trying to ignore their startled stares.

One of the women in a shawl turned to go back into her room, and he saw the back of her shawl, saw the gleaming white teardrop in the middle of her back. Suddenly he recognized faces he had seen in the outer courtyard. Aes Sedai, staring at him in alarm, now.

"Who are you? What are you doing here?"

"Is the keep under attack? Answer me, man!"

"He's no soldier. Who is he? What's happening?"

"It's the young southland lord!"

"Someone stop him!"

Fear pushed his lips back, baring his teeth, but he kept moving, and tried to move faster.

Then a woman came out into the hall, face-to-face with him, and he stopped in spite of himself. He recognized that face above the rest; he thought he would remember it if he lived forever. The Amyrlin Seat. Her eyes widened at the sight of him, and she started back. Another Aes Sedai, the tall woman he had seen with the staff, put herself between him and the Amyrlin, shouting something at him that he could not make out over the increasing babble.

She knows. Light help me, she knows. Moiraine told her. Snarling, he ran on. *Light, just let me make sure Egwene's safe before they. . . .* He heard shouting behind him, but he did not listen.

There was enough turmoil around him out in the keep. Men running for the courtyards with swords in hand, never looking at him. Over the clamor of alarm bells, he could make out other noises, now. Shouts. Screams. Metal ringing on metal. He had just time to realize they were the sounds of battle—*Fighting? Inside Fal Dara?*—when three Trollocs came dashing around a corner in front of him.

Hairy snouts distorted otherwise human faces, and one of them had ram's horns. They bared teeth, raising scythe-like swords as they sped toward him.

The hallway that had been full of running men a moment before was empty now except for the three Trollocs and himself. Caught by surprise, he unsheathed his sword awk-wardly, tried Hummingbird Kisses the Honeyrose. Shaken at finding Trollocs in the heart of Fal Dara keep, he did the form so badly Lan would have stalked off in disgust. A bear-snouted Trolloc evaded it easily, bumping the other two off stride for just an instant.

Suddenly there were a dozen Shienarans rushing past him at the Trollocs, men half dressed in finery for the feast, but swords at the ready. The bear-snouted Trolloc snarled as it died, and its companions ran, pursued by shouting men waving steel. Shouts and screams filled the air from every-where.

Egwene!

Rand turned deeper into the keep, running down halls

empty of life, though now and again a dead Trolloc lay on the floor. Or a dead man.

Then he came to a crossing of corridors, and to his left was the tail end of a fight. Six top-knotted men lay bleeding and still, and a seventh was dying. The Myrddraal gave its sword an extra twist as it pulled the blade free of the man's belly, and the soldier screamed as he dropped his sword and fell. The Fade moved with viperous grace, the serpent illusion heightened by the armor of black, overlapping plates that covered its chest. It turned, and that pale, eyeless face studied Rand. It started toward him, smiling a bloodless smile, not hurrying. It had no need to hurry for one man alone.

He felt rooted where he stood; his tongue stuck to the roof of his mouth. *The look of the Eyeless is fear.* That was what they said along the Border. His hands shook as he raised his sword. He never even thought of assuming the void. *Light, it just killed seven armed soldiers together. Light, what am I going to do. Light!*

Abruptly the Myrddraal stopped, its smile gone.

"This one is mine, Rand." Rand gave a start as Ingtar stepped up beside him, dark and stocky in a yellow feastday coat, sword held in both hands. Ingtar's dark eyes never left the Fade's face; if the Shienaran felt the fear of that gaze, he gave no sign. "Try yourself on a Trolloc or two," he said softly, "before you face one of these."

"I was coming down to see if Egwene is safe. She was going to the dungeon to visit Fain, and—"

"Then go see to her."

Rand swallowed. "We'll take it together, Ingtar."

"You aren't ready for this. Go see to your girl. Go! You want Trollocs to find her unprotected?"

For a moment Rand hung there, undecided. The Fade had raised its sword, for Ingtar. A silent snarl twisted Ingtar's mouth, but Rand knew it was not fear. And Egwene could be alone in the dungeon with Fain, or worse. Still he felt ashamed as he ran for the stairs that led underground. He knew a Fade's look could make any man afraid, but Ingtar had conquered the dread. His stomach still felt knotted.

The corridors beneath the keep were silent, and feebly lit by flickering, far-spaced lamps on the walls. He slowed as he came closer to the dungeons, creeping as silently as he could on his toes. The grate of his boots on the bare stone seemed to fill his ears. The door to the dungeons stood cracked open a handbreadth. It should have been closed and bolted.

Staring at the door, he tried to swallow and could not. He opened his mouth to call out, then shut it again quickly. If Egwene was in there and in trouble, shouting would only warn whoever was endangering her. Or whatever. Taking a deep breath, he set himself.

In one motion he pushed the door wide open with the scabbard in his left hand and threw himself into the dungeon, tucking his shoulder under to roll through the straw covering the floor and come to his feet, spinning this way and that too quickly to get a clear picture of the room, looking desperately for anyone who might attack him, looking for Egwene. There was no one there.

His eyes fell on the table, and he stopped dead, breath and even thought freezing. On either side of the still-burning lamp, as if to make a centerpiece, sat the heads of the guards in two pools of blood. Their eyes stared at him, wide with fear, and their mouths gaped in a last scream no one could hear. Rand gagged and doubled over; his stomach heaved again and again as he vomited into the straw. Finally he managed to pull himself erect, scrubbing his mouth with his sleeve; his throat felt scraped raw.

Slowly he became aware of the rest of the room, only half seen and not taken in during his hasty search for an attacker. Bloody lumps of flesh lay scattered through the straw. There was nothing he could recognize as human except the two heads. Some of the pieces looked chewed. *So that's what happened to the rest of their bodies.* He was surprised at the calmness of his thoughts, almost as if he had achieved the void without trying. It was the shock, he knew vaguely.

He did not recognize either of the heads; the guards had been changed since he was there earlier. He was glad for that. Knowing who they were, even Changu, would have made it worse. Blood covered the walls, too, but in scrawled letters, single words and whole sentences splashed on every which way. Some were harsh and angular, in a language he did not know, though he recognized Trolloc script. Oth-

ers he could read, and wished he could not. Blasphemies
and obscenities bad enough to make a stablehand or a merchant's guard go pale.

"Egwene." Calmness vanished. Shoving his scabbard
through his belt, he snatched the lamp from the table,
hardly noticing when the heads toppled over. "Egwene!
Where are you?"

He started toward the inner door, took two steps, and
stopped, staring. The words on the door, dark and glistening wetly in the light of his lamp, were plain enough.

> WE WILL MEET AGAIN ON TOMAN HEAD.
> IT IS NEVER OVER, AL'THOR.

His sword dropped from a hand suddenly numb. Never
taking his eyes off the door, he bent to pick it up. Instead he
grabbed a handful of straw and began scrubbing furiously
at the words on the door. Panting, he scrubbed until it was
all one bloody smear, but he could not stop.

"What do you do?"

At the sharp voice behind him, he whirled, stooping to
seize his sword.

A woman stood in the outer doorway, back stiff with outrage. Her hair was like pale gold, in a dozen or more braids,
but her eyes were dark, and sharp on his face. She looked
not much older than he, and pretty in a sulky way, but there
was a tightness to her mouth he did not like. Then he saw
the shawl she had wrapped tightly around her, with its long,
red fringe.

Aes Sedai. And Light help me, she's Red Ajah. "I. . . . I
was just. . . . It's filthy stuff. Vile."

"Everything must be left exactly as it is for us to examine. Touch nothing." She took a step forward, peering at
him, and he took one back. "Yes. Yes, as I thought. One of
those with Moiraine. What do you have to do with this?"
Her gesture took in the heads on the table and the bloody
scrawl on the walls.

For a minute he goggled at her. "Me? Nothing! I came
down here to find. . . . Egwene!"

He turned to open the inner door, and the Aes Sedai
shouted, "No! You will answer me!"

Suddenly it was all he could do to stand up, to keep

holding the lamp and his sword. Icy cold squeezed at him
from all sides. His head felt caught in a frozen vise; he
could barely breathe for the pressure on his chest.

"Answer me, boy. Tell me your name."

Involuntarily he grunted, trying to answer against the
chill that seemed to be pressing his face back into his skull,
constricting his chest like frozen iron bands. He clenched
his jaws to keep the sound in. Painfully he rolled his eyes to
glare at her through a blur of tears. *The Light burn you, Aes
Sedai! I won't say a word, the Shadow take you!*

"Answer me, boy! Now!"

Frozen needles pierced his brain with agony, grated into
his bones. The void formed inside him before he even realized he had thought of it, but it could not hold out the pain.
Dimly he sensed light and warmth somewhere in the distance. It flickered queasily, but the light was warm, and he
was cold. Distant beyond knowing, but somehow just within
reach. *Light, so cold. I have to reach . . . what? She's killing me. I have to reach it, or she'll kill me.* Desperately he
stretched toward the light.

"What is going on here?"

Abruptly the cold and the pressure and the needles vanished. His knees sagged, but he forced them stiff. He would
not fall to his knees; he would not give her the satisfaction.
The void was gone, too, as suddenly as it had come. *She
was trying to kill me.* Panting, he raised his head. Moiraine
stood in the doorway.

"I asked what is going on here, Liandrin," she said.

"I found this boy here," the Red Aes Sedai replied
calmly. "The guards are murdered, and here he is. One of
yours. And what are you doing here, Moiraine? The battle
is above, not here."

"I could ask the same of you, Liandrin." Moiraine looked
around the room with only a slight tightening of her mouth
for the charnel. "Why *are* you here?"

Rand turned away from them, awkwardly shoved back
the bolts on the inner door and pulled it open. "Egwene
came down here," he announced for anyone who cared, and
went in, holding his lamp high. His knees kept wanting to
give way; he was not sure how he stayed on his feet, only
that he had to find Egwene. "Egwene!"

A hollow gurgle and a thrashing sound came from his

right, and he thrust the lamp that way. The prisoner in the fancy coat was sagging against the iron grille of his cell, his belt looped around the bars and then around his neck. As Rand looked, he gave one last kick, scraping across the straw-covered floor, and was still, tongue and eyes bulging out of a face gone almost black. His knees almost touched the floor; he could have stood anytime he wanted to.

Shivering, Rand peered into the next cell. The big man with the sunken knuckles huddled in the back of his cell, eyes as wide as they could open. At the sight of Rand, he screamed and twisted around, clawing frantically at the stone wall.

"I won't hurt you," Rand called. The man kept on screaming and digging. His hands were bloody, and his scrabblings streaked across dark, conjealed smears. This was not his first attempt to dig through the stone with his bare hands.

Rand turned away, relieved that his stomach was already empty. But there was nothing he could do for either of them. "Egwene!"

His light finally reached the end of the cells. The door to Fain's cell stood open, and the cell was empty, but it was the two shapes on the stone in front of the cell that made Rand leap forward and drop to his knees between them.

Egwene and Mat lay sprawled bonelessly, unconscious . . . or dead. With a flood of relief he saw their chests rise and fall. There did not seem to be a mark on either of them.

"Egwene? Mat?" Setting the sword down, he shook Egwene gently. "Egwene?" She did not open her eyes. "Moiraine! Egwene's hurt! And Mat!" Mat's breathing sounded labored, and his face was deathly pale. Rand felt almost like crying. *It was supposed to hurt me. I named the Dark One. Me!*

"Do not move them." Moiraine did not sound upset, or even surprised.

The chamber was suddenly flooded with light as the two Aes Sedai entered. Each balanced a glowing ball of cool light, floating in the air above her hand.

Liandrin marched straight down the middle of the wide hall, holding her skirts up out of the straw with her free hand, but Moiraine paused to look at the two prisoners before following. "There is nothing to do for the one," she said, "and the other can wait."

Liandrin reached Rand first and began to bend toward Egwene, but Moiraine darted in ahead of her and laid her free hand on Egwene's head. Liandrin straightened with a grimace.

"She is not badly hurt," Moiraine said after a moment. "She was struck here." She traced an area on the side of Egwene's head, covered by her hair; Rand could see nothing different about it. "That is the only injury she has taken. She will be all right."

Rand looked from one Aes Sedai to the other. "What about Mat?" Liandrin arched an eyebrow at him and turned to watch Moiraine with a wry expression.

"Be quiet," Moiraine said. Fingers still lying on the area where she said Egwene had been hit, she closed her eyes. Egwene murmured and stirred, then lay still.

"Is she . . . ?"

"She is sleeping, Rand. She will be well, but she must sleep." Moiraine shifted to Mat, but here she only touched him for a moment before drawing back. "This is more serious," she said softly. She fumbled at Mat's waist, pulling his coat open, and made an angry sound. "The dagger is gone."

"What dagger?" Liandrin asked.

Voices suddenly came from the outer room, men exclaiming in disgust and anger.

"In here," Moiraine called. "Bring two litters. Quickly." Someone in the outer room raised a cry for litters.

"Fain is gone," Rand said.

The two Aes Sedai looked at him. He could read nothing on their faces. Their eyes glittered in the light.

"So I see," Moiraine said in a flat voice.

"I told her not to come. I told her he was dangerous."

"When I came," Liandrin said in a cold voice, "he was destroying the writing in the outer chamber."

He shifted uneasily on his knees. The Aes Sedai's eyes seemed alike, now. Measuring and weighing him, cool and terrible.

"It—it was filth," he said. "Just filth." They still looked at him, not speaking. "You don't think I. . . . Moiraine, you can't think I had anything to do with—with what happened out there." *Light, did I? I named the Dark One.*

She did not answer, and he felt a chill that was not lessened by men rushing in with torches and lamps. Moiraine and Liandrin let their glowing balls wink out. The lamps and torches did not give as much light; shadows sprang up in the depths of the cells. Men with litters hurried to the figures lying on the floor. Ingtar led them. His topknot almost quivered with anger, and he looked eager to find something on which to use his sword.

"So the Darkfriend is gone, too," he growled. "Well, it's the least of what has happened this night."

"The least even here," Moiraine said sharply. She directed the men putting Egwene and Mat on the litters. "The girl is to be taken to her room. She needs a woman to watch in case she wakes in the night. She may be frightened, but more than anything else she needs sleep, now. The boy. . . ." She touched Mat as two men lifted his litter, and pulled her hand back quickly. "Take him to the Amyrlin Seat's chambers. Find the Amyrlin wherever she is, and tell her he is there. Tell her his name is Matrim Cauthon. I will join her as soon as I am able."

"The Amyrlin!" Liandrin exclaimed. "You think to have the Amyrlin as Healer for your—your pet? You are mad, Moiraine."

"The Amyrlin Seat," Moiraine said calmly, "does not share your Red Ajah prejudices, Liandrin. She will Heal a man without need of a special use for him. Go ahead," she told the litter bearers.

Liandrin watched them leave, Moiraine and the men carrying Mat and Egwene, then turned to stare at Rand. He tried to ignore her. He concentrated on scabbarding his sword and brushing off the straw that clung to his shirt and breeches. When he raised his head, though, she was still studying him, her face as blank as ice. Saying nothing, she turned to consider the other men thoughtfully. One held the body of the hanged man up while another worked to unfasten the belt. Ingtar and the others waited respectfully. With a last glance at Rand, she left, head held like a queen.

"A hard woman," Ingtar muttered, then seemed surprised that he had spoken. "What happened here, Rand al'Thor?"

Rand shook his head. "I don't know, except that Fain escaped somehow. And hurt Egwene and Mat doing it. I saw the guardroom"—he shuddered—"but in here. . . . Whatever it was, Ingtar, it scared that fellow bad enough that he hung himself. I think the other one's gone mad from seeing it."

"We are all going mad tonight."

"The Fade . . . you killed it?"

"No!" Ingtar slammed his sword into its sheath; the hilt stuck up above his right shoulder. He seemed angry and ashamed at the same time. "It's out of the keep by now, along with the rest of what we could not kill."

"At least you're alive, Ingtar. That Fade killed seven men!"

"Alive? Is that so important?" Suddenly Ingtar's face was no longer angry, but tired and full of pain. "We had it in our hands. In our hands! And we lost it, Rand. Lost it!" He sounded as if he could not believe what he was saying.

"Lost what?" Rand asked.

"The Horn! The Horn of Valere. It's gone, chest and all."

"But it was in the strongroom."

"The strongroom was looted," Ingtar said wearily. "They did not take much, except for the Horn. What they could stuff in their pockets. I wish they had taken everything else and left that. Ronan is dead, and the watchmen he had guarding the strongroom." His voice became quiet. "When I was a boy, Ronan held Jehaan Tower with twenty men against a thousand Trollocs. He did not go down easily, though. The old man had blood on his dagger. No man can ask more than that." He was silent for a moment. "They came in through the Dog Gate, and left the same way. We put an end to fifty or more, but too many escaped. Trollocs! We've never before had Trollocs inside the keep. Never!"

"How could they get in through the Dog Gate, Ingtar? One man could stop a hundred there. And all the gates were barred." He shifted uneasily, remembering why. "The guards would not have opened it to let anybody in."

"Their throats were cut," Ingtar said. "Both good men, and yet they were butchered like pigs. It was done from inside. Someone killed them, then opened the gate. Someone who could get close to them without suspicion. Someone they knew."

Rand looked at the empty cell where Padan Fain had been. "But that means. . . ."

"Yes. There are Darkfriends inside Fal Dara. Or were. We will soon know if that's the case. Kajin is checking now to see if anyone is missing. Peace! Treachery in Fal Dara keep!" Scowling, he looked around the dungeon, at the men waiting for him. They all had swords, worn over feastday clothes, and some had helmets. "We aren't doing any good here. Out! Everyone!" Rand joined the withdrawal. Ingtar tapped Rand's jerkin. "What is this? Have you decided to become a stableman?"

"It's a long story," Rand said. "Too long to tell here. Maybe some other time." *Maybe never, if I'm lucky. Maybe I can escape in all this confusion. No, I can't. Not until I know Egwene's all right. And Mat. Light, what will happen to him without the dagger?* "I suppose Lord Agelmar's doubled the guard on all the gates."

"Tripled," Ingtar said in tones of satisfaction. "No one will pass those gates, from inside or out. As soon as Lord Agelmar heard what had happened, he ordered that no one was to be allowed to leave the keep without his personal permission."

As soon as he heard . . . ? "Ingtar, what about before? What about the earlier order keeping everyone in?"

"Earlier order? What earlier order? Rand, the keep was not closed until Lord Agelmar heard of this. Someone told you wrong."

Rand shook his head slowly. Neither Ragan nor Tema would have made up something like that. And even if the Amyrlin Seat had given the order, Ingtar would have to know of it. *So who? And how?* He glanced sideways at Ingtar, wondering if the Shienaran was lying. *You really are going mad if you suspect Ingtar.*

They were in the dungeon guardroom, now. The severed heads and the pieces of the guards had been removed, though there were still red smears on the table and damp patches in the straw to show where they had been. Two Aes Sedai were there, placid-looking women with brown-fringed shawls, studying the words scrawled on the walls, careless of what their skirts dragged through in the straw. Each had an inkpot in a writing-case hung at her belt and was making notes in a small book with a pen. They never even glanced at the men trooping through.

"Look here, Verin," one of them said, pointing to a section of stone covered with lines of Trolloc script. "This looks interesting."

The other hurried over, picking up reddish stains on her skirt. "Yes, I see. A much better hand than the rest. Not a Trolloc. Very interesting." She began writing in her book, looking up every so often to read the angular letters on the wall.

Rand hurried out. Even if they had not been Aes Sedai, he would not have wanted to remain in the same room with anyone who thought reading Trolloc script written in human blood was "interesting."

Ingtar and his men stalked on ahead, intent on their duties. Rand dawdled, wondering where he could go now. Getting back into the women's apartments would not be easy without Egwene to help. *Light, let her be all right. Moiraine* said *she'd be all right.*

Lan found him before he reached the first stairs leading up. "You can go back to your room, if you want, sheepherder. Moiraine had your things fetched from Egwene's room and taken to yours."

"How did she know . . . ?"

"Moiraine knows a great many things, sheepherder. You should understand that by now. You had better watch yourself. The women are all talking about you running through the halls, waving a sword. Staring down the Amyrlin, so they say."

"Light! I am sorry they're angry, Lan, but I *was* invited in. And when I heard the alarm . . . burn me, Egwene was down here!"

Lan pursed his lips thoughtfully; it was the only expression on his face. "Oh, they're not angry, exactly. Though most of them think you need a strong hand to settle you down some. Fascinated is more like it. Even the Lady Amalisa can't stop asking questions about you. Some of them are starting to believe the servants' tales. They think you're a prince in disguise, sheepherder. Not a bad thing. There is an old saying here in the Borderlands: 'Better to have one woman on your side than ten men.' The way they are talking among themselves, they're trying to decide whose daughter is strong enough to handle you. If you don't watch your step, sheepherder, you will find yourself married into a Shienaran House before you realize what has happened." Suddenly he burst out laughing; it looked odd, like a rock laughing. "Running through the halls of the women's apartments in the middle of the night, wearing a laborer's jerkin and waving a sword. If they don't have you flogged, at the very least they'll talk about you for years. They have never seen a male as peculiar as you. Whatever wife they chose for you, she'd probably have you the head of your own House in ten years, and have you thinking you had done it yourself, besides. It is too bad you have to leave."

Rand had been gaping at the Warder, but now he growled, "I have been trying. The gates are guarded, and no one can leave. I tried while it was still daylight. I couldn't even take Red out of the stable."

"No matter, now. Moiraine sent me to tell you. You can leave anytime you want to. Even right now. Moiraine had Agelmar exempt you from the order."

"Why now, and not earlier? Why couldn't I leave before? Was she the one who had the gates barred then? Ingtar said he knew nothing about any order to keep people in before tonight."

Rand thought the Warder looked troubled, but all he said was, "When someone gives you a horse, sheepherder, don't complain that it isn't as fast as you'd like."

"What about Egwene? And Mat? Are they really all right? I can't leave until I know they're all right."

"The girl is fine. She'll wake in the morning, and probably not even remember what happened. Blows to the head are like that."

"What about Mat?"

"The choice is up to you, sheepherder. You can leave now, or tomorrow, or next week. It's up to you." He walked away, leaving Rand standing there in the corridor deep under Fal Dara keep.

CHAPTER
7

Blood Calls Blood

As the litter carrying Mat left the Amyrlin Seat's chambers, Moiraine carefully rewrapped the *angreal*—a small, age-darkened ivory carving of a woman in flowing robes—in a square of silk and put it back into her pouch. Working together with other Aes Sedai, merging their abilities, channeling the flow of the One Power to a single task, was tiring work under the best conditions, even with the aid of an *angreal,* and working through the night without sleep was not the best conditions. And the work they had done on the boy had not been easy.

Leane directed the litter bearers out with sharp gestures and a few crisp words. The two men kept ducking their heads, nervous at being around so many Aes Sedai at once, and one of them the Amyrlin herself, never mind that the Aes Sedai had been using the Power. They had waited in the corridor, squatting against the wall while the work was done, and they were anxious to be gone from the women's apartments. Mat lay with his eyes closed and his face pale, but his chest rose and fell in the even rhythm of a deep sleep.

How will this affect matters? Moiraine wondered. *He is not necessary with the Horn gone, and yet. . . .*

The door closed behind Leane and the litter bearers, and the Amyrlin drew an unsteady breath. "A nasty business that. Nasty." Her face was smooth, but she rubbed her hands together as if she wanted to wash them.

"But quite interesting," Verin said. She had been the fourth Aes Sedai the Amyrlin had chosen for the work. "It is too bad we do not have the dagger so the Healing could be complete. For all we did tonight, he will not live long. Months, perhaps, at best." The three Aes Sedai were alone in the Amyrlin's chambers. Beyond the arrowslits dawn pearled the sky.

"But he will have those months, now," Moiraine said sharply. "And if it can be retrieved, the link can still be broken." *If it can be retrieved. Yes, of course.*

"It can still be broken," Verin agreed. She was a plump, square-faced woman, and even with the Aes Sedai gift of agelessness, there was a touch of gray in her brown hair. That was her only sign of age, but for an Aes Sedai it meant she was very old indeed. Her voice held steady, though, matching her smooth cheeks. "He has been linked to the dagger a long time, however, as a thing like that must be reckoned. And he will be linked longer yet, whether it is found or not. He may already be changed beyond the reach of full Healing, even if no longer enough to contaminate others. Such a small thing, that dagger," she mused, "but it will corrupt whoever carries it long enough. He who carries it will in turn corrupt those who come in contact with him, and they will corrupt still others, and the hatred and suspicion that destroyed Shadar Logoth, every man and woman's hand turned against every other, will be loose in the world again. I wonder how many people it can taint in, say, a year. It should be possible to calculate a reasonable approximation."

Moiraine gave the Brown sister a wry look. *Another danger confronts us, and she sounds as if it is a puzzle in a book. Light, the Browns truly are* not *aware of the world at all.* "Then we must find the dagger, Sister. Agelmar is sending men to hunt those who took the Horn and slew his oathmen, the same who took the dagger. If one is found, the other will be."

Verin nodded, but frowned at the same time. "Yet, even if it is found, who can return it safely? Whoever touches it risks the taint if they handle it long. Perhaps in a chest, well wrapped and padded, but it would still be dangerous to those nearby for any great time. Without the dagger itself to study, we cannot be sure how much it must be shielded. But you saw it and more, Moiraine. You dealt with it, enough for that young man to survive carrying it and to stop him infecting others. You must have a good idea of how strong its influence is."

"There is one," Moiraine said, "who can retrieve the

dagger without being harmed by it. One whom we have shielded and buffered against that taint as much as anyone can be. Mat Cauthon."

The Amyrlin nodded. "Yes, of course. He can do it. If he lives long enough. The Light only knows how far it will be carried before Agelmar's men find it. If they do find it. And if the boy dies first . . . well, if the dagger is loose that long, we have another worry." She rubbed her eyes tiredly. "I think we must find this Padan Fain, too. Why is this Darkfriend important enough for them to risk what they did to rescue him? Much easier for them just to steal the Horn. Still risky as a winter gale in the Sea of Storms, coming into the very keep like that, but they compounded their risk to free this Darkfriend. If the Lurks think he is that important"—she paused, and Moiraine knew she was wondering if it truly was still only the Myrddraal giving commands—"then so must we."

"He must be found," Moiraine agreed, hoping that none of the urgency she felt showed, "but it is likely he will be found with the Horn."

"As you say, Daughter." The Amyrlin pressed fingers to her lips to stifle a yawn. "And now, Verin, if you will excuse me, I will just say a few words to Moiraine and then sleep a little. I suppose Agelmar will insist on feasting tonight since last night was spoiled. Your help was invaluable, Daughter. Please remember, say nothing of the nature of the boy's hurt to anyone. There are some of your sisters who would see the Shadow in him instead of a thing men made on their own."

There was no need to name the Red Ajah. And perhaps, Moiraine thought, the Reds were no longer the only ones of whom it was necessary to be wary.

"I will say nothing, of course, Mother." Verin bowed, but made no move toward the door. "I thought you might wish to see this, Mother." She pulled a small notebook, bound in soft, brown leather, from her belt. "What was written on the walls in the dungeon. There were few problems with translation. Most was the usual—blasphemy and boasting; Trollocs seem to know little else—but there was one part done in a better hand. An educated Darkfriend, or perhaps a Myrddraal. It could be only taunting, yet it has the form of poetry, or song, and the sound of prophecy. We know little of prophecies from the Shadow, Mother."

The Amyrlin hesitated only a moment before nodding. Prophecies from the Shadow, dark prophecies, had an unfortunate way of being fulfilled as well as prophecies from the Light. "Read it to me."

Verin ruffled through the pages, then cleared her throat and began in a calm, level voice.

Daughter of the Night, she walks again.
The ancient war, she yet fights.
Her new lover she seeks, who shall serve her and die,
    yet serve still.
Who shall stand against her coming?
The Shining Walls shall kneel.
Blood feeds blood.
Blood calls blood.
Blood is, and blood was, and blood shall ever be.

The man who channels stands alone.
He gives his friends for sacrifice.
Two roads before him, one to death beyond dying,
    one to life eternal.
Which will he choose? Which will he choose?
What hand shelters? What hand slays?
Blood feeds blood.
Blood calls blood.
Blood is, and blood was, and blood shall ever be.

Luc came to the Mountains of Dhoom.
Isam waited in the high passes.
The hunt is now begun. The Shadow's hounds
    now course, and kill.
One did live, and one did die, but both are.
The Time of Change has come.
Blood feeds blood.
Blood calls blood.
Blood is, and blood was, and blood shall ever be.

The Watchers wait on Toman's Head.
The seed of the Hammer burns the ancient tree.

Death shall sow, and summer burn,
   before the Great Lord comes.
Death shall reap, and bodies fail,
   before the Great Lord comes.
Again the seed slays ancient wrong,
   before the Great Lord comes.
Now the Great Lord comes.
Now the Great Lord comes.
Blood feeds blood.
Blood calls blood.
Blood is, and blood was, and blood shall ever be.
Now the Great Lord comes.

There was a long silence when she finished.

Finally the Amyrlin said, "Who else has seen this, Daughter? Who knows of it?"

"Only Serafelle, Mother. As soon as we had copied it down, I had men scrub the walls. They didn't question; they were eager to be rid of it."

The Amyrlin nodded. "Good. Too many in the Borderlands can puzzle out Trolloc script. No need to give them something else to worry over. They have enough."

"What do you make of it?" Moiraine asked Verin in a careful voice. "Is it prophecy, do you think?"

Verin tilted her head, peering at her notes in thought. "Possibly. It has the form of some of the few dark prophecies we know. And parts of it are clear enough. It could still be only a taunt, though." She rested a finger on one line. " 'Daughter of the Night, she walks again.' That can only mean Lanfear is loose again. Or someone wants us to think she is."

"That would be something to worry us, Daughter," the Amyrlin Seat said, "if it were true. But the Forsaken are still bound." She glanced at Moiraine, looking troubled for an instant before she schooled her features. "Even if the seals *are* weakening, the Forsaken are still bound."

Lanfear. In the Old Tongue, Daughter of the Night. Nowhere was her real name recorded, but that was the name she had taken for herself, unlike most of the Forsaken, who had been named by those they betrayed. Some said she had really been the most powerful of the Forsaken, next to Ishamael, the Betrayer of Hope, but had kept her powers hidden. Too little was left from that time for any scholar to say for certain.

"With all the false Dragons that are appearing, it is not surprising someone would try to bring Lanfear into it." Moiraine's voice was as unruffled as her face, but inside herself she roiled. Only one thing for certain was known of Lanfear beside the name: before she went over to the Shadow, before Lews Therin Telamon met Ilyena, Lanfear had been his lover. *A complication we do not need.*

The Amyrlin Seat frowned as if she had had the same thought, but Verin nodded as if it were all just words. "Other names are clear, too, Mother. Lord Luc, of course, was brother to Tigraine, then the Daughter-Heir of Andor, and he vanished in the Blight. Who Isam is, or what he has to do with Luc, I do not know, however."

"We will find out what we need to know in time," Moiraine said smoothly. "There is no proof as yet that this is prophecy." She knew the name. Isam had been the son of Breyan, wife of Lain Mandragoran, whose attempt to seize the throne of Malkier for her husband had brought the Trolloc hordes crashing down. Breyan and her infant son had both vanished when the Trollocs overran Malkier. And Isam had been blood kin to Lan. *Or is blood kin? I must keep this from him, until I know how he will react. Until we are away from the Blight. If he thought Isam were alive. . . .*

" 'The Watchers wait on Toman Head,' " Verin went on. "There are a few who still cling to the old belief that the armies Artur Hawkwing sent across the Aryth Ocean will return one day, though after all this time. . . ." She gave a disdainful sniff. "The Do Miere A'vron, the Watchers Over the Waves, still have a . . . community is the best word, I suppose . . . on Toman Head, at Falme. And one of the old names for Artur Hawkwing was Hammer of the Light."

"Are you suggesting, Daughter," the Amyrlin Seat said, "that Artur Hawkwing's armies, or rather their descendants, might actually return after a thousand years?"

"There are rumors of war on Almoth Plain and Toman Head," Moiraine said slowly. "And Hawkwing sent two of his sons, as well as armies. If they did survive in whatever lands they found, there could well be many descendants of Hawkwing. Or none."

The Amyrlin gave Moiraine a guarded look, obviously

wishing they were alone so she could demand to know what Moiraine was up to. Moiraine made a soothing gesture, and her old friend grimaced at her.

Verin, with her nose still buried in her notes, noticed none of it. "I don't know, Mother. I doubt it, though. We know nothing at all of those lands Artur Hawkwing set out to conquer. It's too bad the Sea Folk refuse to cross the Aryth Ocean. They say the Islands of the Dead lie on the other side. I wish I knew what they meant by that, but that accursed Sea Folk closemouthedness. . . ." She sighed, still not raising her head. "All we have is one reference to 'lands under the Shadow, beyond the setting sun, beyond the Aryth Ocean, where the Armies of Night reign.' Nothing there to tell us if the armies Hawkwing sent were enough by themselves to defeat these 'Armies of the Night,' or even to survive Hawkwing's death. Once the War of the Hundred Years started, everyone was too intent on carving out their own part of Hawkwing's empire to spare a thought for his armies across the sea. It seems to me, Mother, that if their descendants still lived, and if they ever intended to return, they would not have waited so long."

"Then you believe it is not prophecy, Daughter?"

"Now, 'the ancient tree,'" Verin said, immersed in her own thoughts. "There have always been rumors—no more than that—that while the nation of Almoth still lived, they had a branch of *Avendesora*, perhaps even a living sapling. And the banner of Almoth was 'blue for the sky above, black for the earth below, with the spreading Tree of Life to join them.' Of course, Taraboners call themselves the Tree of Man, and claim to be descended from rulers and nobles in the Age of Legends. And Domani claim descent from those who made the Tree of Life in the Age of Legends. There are other possibilities, but you will note, Mother, that at least three center around Almoth Plain and Toman Head."

The Amyrlin's voice became deceptively gentle. "Will you make up your mind, Daughter? If Artur Hawkwing's seed is *not* returning, then this is not prophecy and it doesn't matter a rotted fish head what ancient tree is meant."

"I can only give you what I know, Mother," Verin said, looking up from her notes, "and leave the decision in your hands. I believe the last of Artur Hawkwing's foreign armies died long ago, but because I believe it does not make it so. The Time of Change, of course, refers to the end of an Age, and the Great Lord—"

The Amyrlin slapped the tabletop like a thunderclap. "I know very well who the Great Lord is, Daughter. I think you had better go now." She took a deep breath, and took hold of herself visibly. "Go, Verin. I do not want to become angry with you. I do not want to forget who it was had the cooks leave sweetcakes out at night when I was a novice."

"Mother," Moiraine said, "there is nothing in this to suggest prophecy. Anyone with a little wit and a little knowledge could put together as much, and no one has ever said Myrddraal do not have a sly wit."

"And of course," Verin said calmly, "the man who channels must be one of the three young men traveling with you, Moiraine."

Moiraine stared in shock. *Not aware of the world? I am a fool.* Before she realized what she was doing, she had reached out to the pulsing glow she always felt there waiting, to the True Source. The One Power surged along her veins, charging her with energy, muting the sheen of Power from the Amyrlin Seat as she did the same. Moiraine had never before even thought of wielding the Power against another Aes Sedai. *We live in perilous times, and the world hangs in the balance, and what must be done, must be done. It must. Oh, Verin, why did you have to put your nose in where it does not belong?*

Verin closed her book and slipped it back behind her belt, then looked from one woman to the other. She could not but be aware of the nimbus surrounding each of them, the light that came from touching the True Source. Only someone trained in channeling herself could see the glow, but there was no chance of any Aes Sedai missing it in another woman.

A hint of satisfaction settled on Verin's face, but no sign that she realized she had hurled a lightning bolt. She only looked as if she had found another piece that fit in a puzzle. "Yes, I thought it must be so. Moiraine could not do this alone, and who better to help than her girlhood friend who used to sneak down with her to snitch sweetcakes." She blinked. "Forgive me, Mother. I should not have said that."

"Verin, Verin." The Amyrlin shook her head wonderingly.

"You accuse your sister—and me?—of. . . . I won't even
say it. And you are worried that you've spoken too famil-
iarly to the Amyrlin Seat? You bore a hole in the boat and
worry that it's raining. Think what you are suggesting,
Daughter."

It is too late for that, Siuan, Moiraine thought. *If we had
not panicked and reached for the Source, perhaps then. . . .
But she is sure, now.* "Why are you telling us this, Verin?"
she said aloud. "If you believe what you say, you should be
telling it to the other sisters, to the Reds in particular."

Verin's eyes widened in surprise. "Yes. Yes, I suppose
I should. I hadn't thought of that. But then, if I did, you
would be stilled, Moiraine, and you, Mother, and the man
gentled. No one has ever recorded the progression in a man
who wields the Power. When does the madness come, exactly, and how does it take him? How quickly does it grow?
Can he still function with his body rotting around him? For
how long? Unless he is gentled, what will happen to the
young man, whichever he is, will happen whether or not
I am there to put down the answers. If he is watched and
guided, we should be able to keep some record with reasonable safety, for a time, at least. And, too, there is *The
Karaethon Cycle.*" She calmly returned their startled looks.
"I assume, Mother, that he *is* the Dragon Reborn? I cannot
believe you would do this—leave walking free a man who
can channel—unless he was the Dragon."

She thinks only of the knowledge, Moiraine thought wonderingly. *The culmination of the direst prophecy the world
knows, perhaps the end of the world, and she cares only
about the knowledge. But she is still dangerous, for that.*

"Who else knows of this?" The Amyrlin's voice was faint,
but still sharp. "Serafelle, I suppose. Who else, Verin?"

"No one, Mother. Serafelle is not really interested in anything that someone hasn't already set down in a book, preferably as long ago as possible. She thinks there are enough
old books and manuscripts and fragments scattered about,
lost or forgotten, to equal ten times what we have gathered
in Tar Valon. She feels certain there is enough of the old
knowledge still there to be found for—"

"Enough, Sister," Moiraine said. She loosed her hold on
the True Source, and after a moment felt the Amyrlin do the
same. It was always a loss to feel the Power draining away,

like blood and life pouring from an open wound. A part of her wanted to hold on, but unlike some of her sisters, she made it a point of self-discipline not to grow too fond of the feeling. "Sit down, Verin, and tell us what you know and how you found it out. Leave out nothing."

As Verin took a chair—with a look to the Amyrlin for permission to sit in her presence—Moiraine watched her sadly.

"It is unlikely," Verin began, "that anyone who hasn't studied the old records thoroughly would notice anything except that you were behaving oddly. Forgive me, Mother. It was nearly twenty years ago, with Tar Valon besieged, that I had my first clue, and that was only. . . .

Light help me, Verin, how I loved you for those sweet-cakes, and for your bosom to weep on. But I will do what I must do. I will. I must.

Perrin peered around the corner at the retreating back of the Aes Sedai. She smelled of lavender soap, though most would not have scented it even close up. As soon as she turned out of sight, he hurried for the infirmary door. He had already tried to see Mat once, and that Aes Sedai—Leane, he had heard somebody call her—had nearly snapped his head off without even looking around to see who he was. He felt uneasy around Aes Sedai, especially if they started looking at his eyes.

Pausing at the door to listen—he could hear no footsteps down the corridor either way, and nothing on the other side of the door—he went in and closed it softly behind him.

The infirmary was a long room with white walls, and the entrances to archers' balconies at either end let in lots of light. Mat was in one of the narrow beds that lined the walls. After last night, Perrin had expected most of the beds to have men in them, but in a moment he realized the keep was full of Aes Sedai. The only thing an Aes Sedai could not cure by Healing was death. To him, the room smelled of sickness anyway.

Perrin grimaced when he thought of that. Mat lay still, eyes closed, hands unmoving atop his blankets. He looked exhausted. Not sick really, but as if he had worked three days in the fields and only now laid down to rest. He smelled . . . wrong, though. It was nothing Perrin could put a name to. Just wrong.

Perrin sat down carefully on the bed next to Mat's. He always did things carefully. He was bigger than most people, and had been bigger than the other boys as long as he could remember. He had had to be careful so he would not hurt someone accidentally, or break things. Now it was second nature to him. He liked to think things through, too, and sometimes talk them over with somebody. *With Rand thinking he's a lord, I can't talk to him, and Mat certainly isn't going to have much to say.*

He had gone into one of the gardens the night before, to think things through. The memory still made him a little ashamed. If he had not gone, he would have been in his room to go with Egwene and Mat, and maybe he could have kept them from being hurt. More likely, he knew, he would be in one of these beds, like Mat, or dead, but that did not change the way he felt. Still, he had gone to the garden, and it was nothing to do with the Trolloc attack that was worrying him now.

Serving women had found him sitting there in the dark, and one of the Lady Amalisa's attendants, the Lady Timora. As soon as they came upon him, Timora sent one of the others running, and he had heard her say, "Find Liandrin Sedai! Quickly!"

They had stood there watching him as if they had thought he might vanish in a puff of smoke like a gleeman. That had been when the first alarm bell rang, and everybody in the keep started running.

"Liandrin," he muttered now. "Red Ajah. About all they do is hunt for men who channel. You don't think she believes I'm one of those, do you?" Mat did not answer, of course. Perrin rubbed his nose ruefully. "Now I'm talking to myself. I don't need that on top of everything else."

Mat's eyelids fluttered. "Who . . . ? Perrin? What happened?" His eyes did not open all the way, and his voice sounded as if he were still mostly asleep.

"Don't you remember, Mat?"

"Remember?" Mat sleepily raised a hand toward his face, then let it fall again with a sigh. His eyes began to drift shut. "Remember Egwene. Asked me . . . go down . . . see Fain." He laughed, and it turned into a yawn. "She didn't ask. Told

me. . . . Don't know what happened after. . . ." He smacked
his lips, and resumed the deep, even breathing of sleep.

Perrin leaped to his feet as his ears caught the sound of
approaching footsteps, but there was nowhere to go. He was
still standing there beside Mat's bed when the door opened
and Leane came in. She stopped, put her fists on her hips,
and looked him slowly up and down. She was nearly as tall
as he was.

"Now you," she said, in tones quiet yet brisk, "are almost a pretty enough boy to make me wish I was a Green.
Almost. But if you've disturbed my patient . . . well, I dealt
with brothers almost as big as you before I went to the
Tower, so you needn't think those shoulders will help you any."

Perrin cleared his throat. Half the time he did not understand what women meant when they said things. *Not like
Rand. He always knows what to say to the girls.* He realized he was scowling and wiped it away. He did not want
to think about Rand, but he certainly did not want to upset an Aes Sedai, especially one who was beginning to tap
her foot impatiently. "Ah . . . I didn't disturb him. He's still
sleeping. See?"

"So he is. A good thing for you. Now, what are you doing in here? I remember chasing you out once; you needn't
think I don't."

"I only wanted to know how he is."

She hesitated. "He is sleeping is how he is. And in a few
hours, he will get out of that bed, and you'll think there was
never anything wrong with him."

The pause made his hackles rise. She was lying, somehow. Aes Sedai never lied, but they did not always tell
the truth, either. He was not certain what was going on—
Liandrin looking for him, Leane lying to him—but he
thought it was time he got away from Aes Sedai. There was
nothing he could do for Mat.

"Thank you," he said. "I'd better let him sleep, then. Excuse me."

He tried to slide around her to the door, but suddenly her
hands shot out and grabbed his face, tilting it down so she
could peer into his eyes. Something seemed to pass through
him, a warm ripple that started at the top of his head and
went to his feet, then came back again. He pulled his head
out of her hands.

"You're as healthy as a young wild animal," she said, pursing her lips. "But if you were born with those eyes, I am a Whitecloak."

"They're the only eyes I ever had," he growled. He felt a little abashed, speaking to an Aes Sedai in that tone, but he was as surprised as she when he took her gently by the arms and lifted her to one side, setting her down again out of his way. As they stared at each other, he wondered if his eyes were as wide with shock as hers. "Excuse me," he said again, and all but ran.

My eyes. My Light-cursed eyes! The morning sunlight caught his eyes, and they glinted like burnished gold.

Rand twisted on his bed, trying to find a comfortable position on the thin mattress. Sunlight streamed through the arrowslits, painting the bare stone walls. He had not slept during the remainder of the night, and tired as he was, he was sure he could not sleep now. The leather jerkin lay on the floor between his bed and the wall, but aside from that he was fully dressed, even to his new boots. His sword stood propped beside the bed, and his bow and quiver rested in a corner across the bundled cloaks.

He could not rid himself of the feeling that he should take the chance Moiraine had given him and leave immediately. The urge had been with him all night. Three times he had risen to go. Twice he had gone as far as opening the door. The halls had been empty except for a few servants doing late chores; the way had been clear. But he had to know.

Perrin came in, head down and yawning, and Rand sat up. "How is Egwene? And Mat?"

"She's asleep, so they tell me. They wouldn't let me into the women's apartments to see her. Mat is—" Suddenly Perrin scowled at the floor. "If you're so interested, why haven't you gone to see him yourself? I thought you were not interested in us anymore. You said you weren't." He pulled open his door of the wardrobe and began rummaging for a clean shirt.

"I did go to the infirmary, Perrin. There was an Aes Sedai there, that tall one who's always with the Amyrlin Seat. She said Mat was asleep, and I was in the way, and I could come back some other time. She sounded like Master

Thane ordering the men at the mill. You know how Master Thane is, all full of snap and do it right the first time, and do it right now."

Perrin did not answer. He just shucked off his coat and pulled his shirt off over his head.

Rand studied his friend's back for a moment, then dug up a laugh. "You want to hear something? You know what she said to me? The Aes Sedai in the infirmary, I mean. You saw how tall she is. As tall as most men. A hand taller, and she could almost look me in the eyes. Well, she stared me up and down, and then she muttered, 'Tall, aren't you? Where were you when I was sixteen? Or even thirty?' And then she laughed, as if it was all a joke. What do you think of that?"

Perrin finished tugging on a clean shirt and gave him a sidelong look. With his burly shoulders and thick curls, he made Rand think of a hurt bear. A bear that did not understand why had he been hurt.

"Perrin, I'm—"

"If you want to make jokes with Aes Sedai," Perrin broke in, "that's up to you. My Lord." He began stuffing his shirttail into his breeches. "I don't spend much time being— witty; is that the word?—witty with Aes Sedai. But then, I'm only a clumsy blacksmith, and I might be in somebody's way. My Lord." Snatching his coat from the floor, he started for the door.

"Burn me, Perrin, I'm sorry. I was afraid, and I thought I was in trouble—maybe I was; maybe I still am, I don't know—and I didn't want you and Mat to be in it with me. Light, all the women were looking for me last night. I think that's part of the trouble I'm in. I think so. And Liandrin. . . . She. . . ." He threw up his hands. "Perrin, believe me, you don't want any part of this."

Perrin had stopped, but he stood facing the door and only turned his head enough for Rand to see one golden eye. "Looking for you? Maybe they were looking for all of us."

"No, they were looking for me. I wish they hadn't been, but I know better."

Perrin shook his head. "Liandrin wanted me, anyway, I know. I heard."

Rand frowned. "Why would she . . . ? It doesn't change anything. Look, I opened my mouth and said what I shouldn't. I did not mean it, Perrin. Now, please, would you tell me about Mat?"

"He's asleep. Leane—that's the Aes Sedai—said he would be on his feet in a few hours." He shrugged uncomfortably. "I think she was lying. I know Aes Sedai never lie, not so you can catch them, but she was lying, or keeping something back." He paused, looking at Rand sideways. "You didn't mean all that? We will leave here together? You, and me, and Mat?"

"I can't, Perrin. I can't tell you why, but I really do have to go by myse— Perrin, wait!"

The door slammed behind his friend.

Rand fell back on the bed. "I can't tell you," he muttered. He pounded his fist on the side of the bed. "I can't." *But you can go now,* a voice said in the back of his head. *Egwene's going to be all right, and Mat will be up and around in an hour or two. You can go now. Before Moiraine changes her mind.*

He started to sit up when a pounding on the door made him leap to his feet. If it was Perrin come back, he would not knock. The pounding came again.

"Who is it?"

Lan strode in, pushing the door to behind him with his boot heel. As usual, he wore his sword over a plain coat of green that was nearly invisible in the woods. This time, though, he had a wide, golden cord tied high around his left arm, the fringed ends hanging almost to his elbow. On the knot was pinned a golden crane in flight, the symbol of Malkier.

"The Amyrlin Seat wants you, sheepherder. You can't go like that. Out of that shirt and brush your hair. You look like a haystack." He jerked open the wardrobe and began pawing through the clothes Rand meant to leave behind.

Rand stood stiff where he was; he felt as though he had been hit in the head with a hammer. He had expected it, of course, in a way, but he had been sure he would be gone before the summons came. *She knows. Light, I'm sure of it.* "What do you mean, she wants me? I'm leaving, Lan. You were right. I am going to the stable right now, get my horse, and leave."

"You should have done that last night." The Warder tossed a white silk shirt onto the bed. "No one refuses an audience with the Amyrlin Seat, sheepherder. Not the Lord Captain Commander of the Whitecloaks himself. Pedron Niall might spend the trip planning how to kill her, if he could do it and get away, but he would come." He turned around with one of the high-collared coats in his hands and held it up. "This one will do." Tangled, long-thorned briars climbed each red sleeve in a thick, gold-embroidered line, and ran around each cuff. Golden herons stood on the collars, which were edged with gold. "The color is right, too." He seemed to be amused at something, or satisfied. "Come on, sheepherder. Change your shirt. Move."

Reluctantly Rand pulled the coarse wool workman's shirt over his head. "I'll feel a fool," he muttered. "A silk shirt! I never wore a silk shirt in my life. And I never wore so fancy a coat, either, even on a feastday." *Light, if Perrin sees me in that. . . . Burn me, after all that fool talk about being a lord, if he sees me in that, he'll never listen to reason.*

"You can't go before the Amyrlin Seat dressed like a groom fresh out of the stables, sheepherder. Let me see your boots. They'll do. Well, get on with it, get on with it. You don't keep the Amyrlin waiting. Wear your sword."

"My sword!" The silk shirt over his head muffled Rand's yelp. He yanked it the rest of the way on. "In the women's apartments? Lan, if I go for an audience with the Amyrlin Seat—the Amyrlin Seat!—wearing a sword, she'll—"

"Do nothing," Lan cut him off dryly. "If the Amyrlin is afraid of you—and it's smarter for you to think she isn't, because I don't know anything that could frighten that woman—it won't be for a sword. Now remember, you kneel when you go before her. One knee only, mind," he added sharply. "You're not some merchant caught giving short weight. Maybe you had better practice it."

"I know how, I think. I saw how the Queen's Guards knelt to Queen Morgase."

The ghost of a smile touched the Warder's lips. "Yes, you do it just as they did. That will give them something to think about."

Rand frowned. "Why are you telling me this, Lan? You're a Warder. You're acting as if you are on my side."

"I am on your side, sheepherder. A little. Enough to help you a bit." The Warder's face was stone, and sympathetic words sounded strange in that rough voice. "What training you've had, I gave you, and I'll not have you groveling and sniveling. The Wheel weaves us all into the Pattern as it wills. You have less freedom about it than most, but by the Light, you can still face it on your feet. You remember who the Amyrlin Seat is, sheepherder, and you show her proper respect, but you do what I tell you, and you look her in the eye. Well, don't stand there gaping. Tuck in your shirt."

Rand shut his mouth and tucked in his shirt. *Remember who she is? Burn me, what I wouldn't give to forget who she is!*

Lan kept up a running flow of instructions while Rand shrugged into the red coat and buckled on his sword. What to say and to whom, and what not to say. What to do, and what not. How to move, even. He was not sure he could remember it all—most of it sounded odd, and easy to forget—and he was sure whatever he forgot would be just the thing to make the Aes Sedai angry with him. *If they aren't already. If Moiraine told the Amyrlin Seat, who else did she tell?*

"Lan, why can't I just leave the way I planned? By the time she knew I was not coming, I'd be a league outside the walls and galloping."

"And she'd have trackers after you before you had gone two. What the Amyrlin wants, sheepherder, she gets." He adjusted Rand's sword belt so the heavy buckle was centered. "What I do is the best I can for you. Believe it."

"But why all this? What does it mean? Why do I put my hand over my heart if the Amyrlin Seat stands up? Why refuse anything but water—not that I want to eat a meal with her—then dribble some on the floor and say 'The land thirsts'? And if she asks how old I am, why tell her how long it is since I was given the sword? I don't understand half of what you've told me."

"Three drops, sheepherder, don't pour it. You *sprinkle* three drops only. You can understand later so long as you remember now. Think of it as upholding custom. The Amyrlin will do with you as she must. If you believe you can avoid it, then you believe you can fly to the moon like Lenn. You can't escape, but maybe you can hold your own for a while, and perhaps you can keep your pride, at least. The Light burn me, I am probably wasting my time, but I've nothing better to do. Hold still." From his pocket the

Warder produced a long length of wide, fringed golden cord and tied it around Rand's left arm in a complicated knot. On the knot he fastened a red-enameled pin, an eagle with its wings spread. "I had that made to give you, and now is as good a time as any. That will make them think." There was no doubt about it, now. The Warder was smiling.

Rand looked down at the pin worriedly. *Caldazar.* The Red Eagle of Manetheren. "A thorn to the Dark One's foot," he murmured, "and a bramble to his hand." He looked at the Warder. "Manetheren's long dead and forgotten, Lan. It's just a name in a book, now. There is only the Two Rivers. Whatever else I am, I'm a shepherd and a farmer. That's all."

"Well, the sword that could not be broken was shattered in the end, sheepherder, but it fought the Shadow to the last. There is one rule, above all others, for being a man. Whatever comes, face it on your feet. Now, are you ready? The Amyrlin Seat waits."

With a cold knot in the pit of his belly, Rand followed the Warder into the hall.

CHAPTER 8

The Dragon Reborn

R and walked stiff-legged and nervous at first, beside the Warder. *Face it on your feet.* It was easy for Lan to say. He had not been summoned by the Amyrlin Seat. He was not wondering if he would be gentled before the day was done, or worse. Rand felt as if he had something caught in his throat; he could not swallow, and he wanted to, badly.

The corridors bustled with people, servants going about their morning chores, warriors wearing swords over lounging robes. A few young boys carrying small practice swords stayed near their elders, imitating the way they walked. No sign remained of the fighting, but an air of alertness clung even to the children. Grown men looked like cats waiting for a pack of rats.

Ingtar gave Rand and Lan a peculiar look, almost troubled, opening his mouth, then saying nothing as they passed him. Kajin, tall and lean and sallow, pumped his fists over his head and shouted, *"Tai'shar Malkier! Tai'shar Manetheren!"* True blood of Malkier. True blood of Manetheren.

Rand jumped. *Light, why did he say that? Don't be a fool,* he told himself. *They all know about Manetheren here. They know every old story, if it has fighting in it. Burn me, I have to take a rein on myself.*

Lan raised his fists in reply. *"Tai'shar Shienar!"*

If he made a run for it, could he lose himself in the crowd long enough to reach his horse? *If she sends trackers after me. . . .* With every step he grew more tense.

As they approached the women's apartments, Lan suddenly snapped, "Cat Crosses the Courtyard!"

Startled, Rand instinctively assumed the walking stance as he had been taught, back straight but every muscle loose, as if he hung from a wire at the top of his head. It was a relaxed, almost arrogant, saunter. Relaxed on the outside; he certainly did not feel it inside. He had no time to wonder what he was doing. They rounded the last corridor in step with each other.

The women at the entrance to the women's apartments looked up calmly as they came closer. Some sat behind slanted tables, checking large ledgers and sometimes making an entry. Others were knitting, or working with needle and embroidery hoop. Ladies in silks kept this watch, as well as women in livery. The arched doors stood open, unguarded except for the women. No more was needed. No Shienaran man would enter uninvited, but any Shienaran man stood ready to defend that door if needed, and he would be aghast at the need.

Rand's stomach churned, harsh and acid. *They'll take one look at our swords and turn us away. Well, that's what I want, isn't it? If they turn us back, maybe I can still get away. If they don't call the guards down on us.* He clung to the stance Lan had given him as he would have to a floating branch in a flood; holding it was the only thing that kept him from turning tail and running.

One of the Lady Amalisa's attendants, Nisura, a round-faced woman, put aside her embroidery and stood as they came to a stop. Her eyes flickered across their swords, and her mouth tightened, but she did not mention them. All the women stopped what they were doing to watch, silent and intent.

"Honor to you both," Nisura said, bowing her head slightly. She glanced at Rand, so quickly he was almost not sure he had seen it; it reminded him of what Perrin had said. "The Amyrlin Seat awaits you." She motioned, and two other ladies—not servants; they were being honored—stepped forward for escorts. The women bowed, a hair more than Nisura had, and motioned them through the archway. They both gave Rand a sidelong glance, then did not look at him again.

Were they looking for all of us, or just me? Why all of us?

Inside, they got the looks Rand expected—two men in the women's apartments where men were rare—and their swords caused more than one raised eyebrow, but none of the women spoke. The two men left knots of conversation in their path, soft murmurs too low for Rand to make out. Lan strode along as if he did not even notice. Rand kept pace behind their escorts and wished he could hear.

And then they reached the Amyrlin Seat's chambers, with three Aes Sedai in the hall outside the door. The tall Aes Sedai, Leane, held her golden-flamed staff. Rand did not know the other two, one of the White Ajah and one Yellow by their fringe. He remembered their faces, though, staring at him as he had run through these same halls. Smooth Aes Sedai faces, with knowing eyes. They studied him with arched eyebrows and pursed lips. The women who had brought Lan and Rand curtsied, handing them over to the Aes Sedai.

Leane looked Rand over with a slight smile. Despite the smile, her voice had a snap to it. "What have you brought the Amyrlin Seat today, Lan Gaidin? A young lion? Better you don't let any Greens see this one, or one of them will bond him before he can take a breath. Greens like to bond them young."

Rand wondered if it was really possible to sweat inside your skin. He felt as if he was. He wanted to look at Lan, but he remembered this part of the Warder's instructions. "I am Rand al'Thor, son of Tam al'Thor, of the Two Rivers, which once was Manetheren. As I have been summoned by the Amyrlin Seat, Leane Sedai, so do I come. I stand ready." He was surprised that his voice did not shake once.

Leane blinked, and her smile faded to a thoughtful look. "This is supposed to be a shepherd, Lan Gaidin? He was not so sure of himself this morning."

"He is a man, Leane Sedai," Lan said firmly, "no more, and no less. We are what we are."

The Aes Sedai shook her head. "The world grows stranger every day. I suppose the blacksmith will wear a crown and speak in High Chant. Wait here." She vanished inside to announce them.

She was only gone a few moments, but Rand was uncomfortably aware of the eyes of the remaining Aes Sedai. He tried to return their gaze levelly, the way Lan had told him to, and they put their heads together, whispering. *What are they saying? What do they know? Light, are they going to*

*gentle me? Was that what Lan meant about facing what-
ever comes?*

Leane returned, motioning Rand to go in. When Lan
started to follow, she thrust her staff across his chest, stopping him. "Not you, Lan Gaidin. Moiraine Sedai has a task
for you. Your lion cub will be safe enough by himself."

The door swung shut behind Rand, but not before he
heard Lan's voice, fierce and strong, but low for his ear
alone. *"Tai'shar Manetheren!"*

Moiraine sat to one side of the room, and one of the
Brown Aes Sedai he had seen in the dungeon sat to the
other, but it was the woman in the tall chair behind the wide
table who held his eyes. The curtains had been partially
drawn over the arrowslits, but the gaps let in enough light
behind her to make her face hard to see clearly. He still recognized her, though. The Amyrlin Seat.

Quickly he dropped to one knee, left hand on sword hilt,
right fist pressed to the patterned rug, and bowed his head.
"As you have summoned me, Mother, so have I come. I
stand ready." He lifted his head in time to see her eyebrows
rise.

"Do you now, boy?" She sounded almost amused. And
something else he could not make out. She certainly did not
look amused. "Stand up, boy, and let me have a look at you."

He straightened and tried to keep his face relaxed. It was
an effort not to clench his hands. *Three Aes Sedai. How
many does it take to gentle a man? They sent a dozen or
more after Logain. Would Moiraine do that to me?* He met
the Amyrlin Seat's look eye to eye. She did not blink.

"Sit, boy," she said finally, gesturing to a ladder-back
chair that had been pulled around squarely in front of the
table. "This will not be short, I fear."

"Thank you, Mother." He bowed his head, then, as Lan
had told him, glanced at the chair and touched his sword.
"By your leave, Mother, I will stand. The watch is not
done."

The Amyrlin Seat made an exasperated sound and looked
at Moiraine. "Have you let Lan at him, Daughter? This will
be difficult enough without him picking up Warder ways."

"Lan has been teaching all the boys, Mother," Moiraine
replied calmly. "He has spent a little more time with this
one than the others because he carries a sword."

The Brown Aes Sedai shifted on her chair. "The Gaidin are stiff-necked and proud, Mother, but useful. I would not be without Tomas, as you would not lose Alric. I have even heard a few Reds say they sometimes wish for a Warder. And the Greens, of course. . . ."

The three Aes Sedai were all ignoring him, now. "This sword," the Amyrlin Seat said. "It appears to be a heron-mark blade. How did he come by that, Moiraine?"

"Tam al'Thor left the Two Rivers as a boy, Mother. He joined the army of Illian, and served in the Whitecloak War and the last two wars with Tear. In time he rose to be a blademaster and the Second Captain of the Companions. After the Aiel War, Tam al'Thor returned to the Two Rivers with a wife from Caemlyn and an infant boy. It would have saved much, had I known this earlier, but I know it now."

Rand stared at Moiraine. He knew Tam had left the Two Rivers and come back with an outlander wife and the sword, but the rest. . . . *Where did you learn all that? Not in Emond's Field. Unless Nynaeve told you more than she's ever told me. An infant boy. She doesn't say his son. But I am.*

"Against Tear." The Amyrlin Seat frowned slightly. "Well, there was blame enough on both sides in those wars. Fool men who would rather fight than talk. Can you tell if the blade is authentic, Verin?"

"There are tests, Mother."

"Then take it and test it, Daughter."

The three women were not even looking at him. Rand stepped back, gripping the hilt hard. "My father gave this sword to me," he said angrily. "Nobody is taking it from me." It was only then that he realized Verin had not moved from her chair. He looked at them in confusion, trying to recover his equilibrium.

"So," the Amyrlin Seat said, "you have some fire in you besides whatever Lan put in. Good. You will need it."

"I am what I am, Mother," he managed smoothly enough. "I stand ready for what comes."

The Amyrlin Seat grimaced. "Lan *has* been at you. Listen to me, boy. In a few hours, Ingtar will leave to find the stolen Horn. Your friend, Mat, will go with him. I expect that your other friend—Perrin?—will go, also. Do you wish to accompany them?"

"Mat and Perrin are going? Why?" Belatedly he remembered to add a respectful, "Mother."

"You know of the dagger your friend carried?" A twist of her mouth showed what she thought of the dagger. "That was taken, too. Unless it is found, the link between him and the blade cannot be broken completely, and he will die. You can ride with them, if you want. Or you can stay here. No doubt Lord Agelmar will let you remain as a guest as long as you wish. I will be leaving today, as well. Moiraine Sedai will accompany me, and so will Egwene and Nynaeve, so you will stay alone, if you stay. The choice is yours."

Rand stared at her. *She is saying I can go as I want. Is that what she brought me here for? Mat is dying!* He glanced at Moiraine, sitting impassively with her hands folded in her lap. She looked as if nothing in the world could concern her less than where he went. *Which way are you trying to push me, Aes Sedai? Burn me, but I'll go another. But if Mat's dying. . . . I can't abandon him. Light, how are we going to find that dagger?*

"You do not have to make the choice now," the Amyrlin said. She did not seem to care, either. "But you will have to choose before Ingtar leaves."

"I will ride with Ingtar, Mother."

The Amyrlin Seat nodded absently. "Now that that is dealt with, we can move on to important matters. I know you can channel, boy. What do you know?"

Rand's mouth fell open. Caught up in worrying about Mat, her casual words hit him like a swinging barn door. All of Lan's advice and instructions went spinning. He stared at her, licking his lips. It was one thing to think she knew, entirely another to find out she really did. The sweat finally seeped out on his forehead.

She leaned forward in her seat, waiting for his answer, but he had the feeling she wanted to lean back. He remembered what Lan had said. *If she's afraid of you. . . .* He wanted to laugh. If *she* was afraid of *him*.

"No, I can't. I mean . . . I didn't do it on purpose. It just happened. I don't want to—to channel the Power. I won't ever do it again. I swear it."

"You don't want to," the Amyrlin Seat said. "Well, that's wise of you. And foolish, too. Some can be taught to channel; most cannot. A few, though, have the seed in them at

birth. Sooner or later, they wield the One Power whether
they want to or not, as surely as roe makes fish. You will
continue to channel, boy. You can't help it. And you had
better *learn* to channel, learn to control it, or you will not
live long enough to go mad. The One Power kills those who
cannot control its flow."

"How am I supposed to learn?" he demanded. Moiraine
and Verin just sat there, unruffled, watching him. *Like spiders.* "How? Moiraine claims she can't teach me anything,
and I don't know how to learn, or what. I don't want to,
anyway. I want to stop. Can't you understand that? To stop!"

"I told you the truth, Rand," Moiraine said. She sounded
as if they were having a pleasant conversation. "Those who
could teach you, the male Aes Sedai, are three thousand
years dead. No Aes Sedai living can teach you to touch
saidin any more than you could learn to touch *saidar.* A
bird cannot teach a fish to fly, nor a fish teach a bird to
swim."

"I have always thought that was a bad saying," Verin said
suddenly. "There are birds that dive and swim. And in the
Sea of Storms are fish that fly, with long fins that stretch out
as wide as your outstretched arms, and beaks like swords
that can pierce. . . ." Her words trailed off and she became
flustered. Moiraine and the Amyrlin Seat were staring at
her without expression.

Rand took the interruption to try to regain some control
of himself. As Tam had taught him long ago, he formed a
single flame in his mind and fed his fears into it, seeking
emptiness, the stillness of the void. The flame seemed to
grow until it enveloped everything, until it was too large
to contain or imagine any longer. With that it was gone,
leaving in its place a sense of peace. At its edges, emotions
still flickered, fear and anger like black blotches, but the
void held. Thought skimmed across its surface like pebbles
across ice. The Aes Sedai's attention was only off him for
a moment, but when they turned back his face was calm.

"Why are you talking to me like this, Mother?" he asked.
"You should be gentling me."

The Amyrlin Seat frowned and turned to Moiraine. "Did
Lan teach him this?"

"No, Mother. He had it from Tam al'Thor."

"Why?" Rand demanded again.

The Amyrlin Seat looked him straight in the eye and said, "Because you are the Dragon Reborn."

The void rocked. The world rocked. Everything seemed to spin around him. He concentrated on nothing, and the emptiness returned, the world steadied. "No, Mother. I can channel, the Light help me, but I am not Raolin Darksbane, nor Guaire Amalasan, nor Yurian Stonebow. You can gentle me, or kill me, or let me go, but I will not be a tame false Dragon on a Tar Valon leash."

He heard Verin gasp, and the Amyrlin's eyes widened, a gaze as hard as blue rock. It did not affect him; it slid off the void within.

"Where did you hear those names?" the Amyrlin demanded. "Who told you Tar Valon pulls the lines on *any* false Dragon?"

"A friend, Mother," he said. "A gleeman. His name was Thom Merrilin. He's dead, now." Moiraine made a sound, and he glanced at her. She claimed Thom was not dead, but she had never offered any proof, and he could not see how any man could survive grappling hand-to-hand with a Fade. The thought was extraneous, and it faded away. There was only the void and the oneness now.

"You are not a false Dragon," the Amyrlin said firmly. "You are the true Dragon Reborn."

"I am a shepherd from the Two Rivers, Mother."

"Daughter, tell him the story. A *true* story, boy. Listen well."

Moiraine began speaking. Rand kept his eyes on the Amyrlin's face, but he heard.

"Nearly twenty years ago the Aiel crossed the Spine of the World, the Dragonwall, the only time they have ever done so. They ravaged through Cairhien, destroyed every army sent against them, burned the city of Cairhien itself, and fought all the way to Tar Valon. It was winter and snowing, but cold or heat mean little to an Aiel. The final battle, the last that counted, was fought outside the Shining Walls, in the shadow of Dragonmount. In three days and three nights of fighting, the Aiel were turned back. Or rather they turned back, for they had done what they came to do, which was to kill King Laman of Cairhien, for his sin against the Tree. It is then that my story begins. And yours."

They came over the Dragonwall like a flood. All the way

to the Shining Walls. Rand waited for the memories to fade, but it was Tam's voice he heard, Tam sick and raving, pulling up secrets from his past. The voice clung outside the void, clamoring to get in.

"I was one of the Accepted, then," Moiraine said, "as was our Mother, the Amyrlin Seat. We were soon to be raised to sisterhood, and that night we stood attendance on the then Amyrlin. Her Keeper of the Chronicles, Gitara Moroso, was there. Every other full sister in Tar Valon was out Healing as many wounded as she could find, even the Reds. It was dawn. The fire on the hearth could not keep the cold out. The snow had finally stopped, and in the Amyrlin's chambers in the White Tower we could smell the smoke of outlying villages burned in the fighting."

Battles are always hot, even in the snow. Had to get away from the stink of death. Tam's delirious voice clawed at the empty calm inside Rand. The void trembled and shrank, steadied, then wavered again. The Amyrlin's eyes bored at him. He felt sweat on his face again. "It was all a feverdream," he said. "He was sick." He raised his voice. "My name is Rand al'Thor. I am a shepherd. My father is Tam al'Thor, and my mother was—"

Moiraine had paused for him, but now her unchanging voice cut him off, soft and relentless. "*The Karaethon Cycle,* the Prophecies of the Dragon, says that the Dragon will be reborn on the slopes of Dragonmount, where he died during the Breaking of the World. Gitara Sedai had the Foretelling sometimes. She was old, her hair as white as the snow outside, but when she had the Foretelling, it was strong. The morning light through the windows was strengthening as I handed her a cup of tea. The Amyrlin Seat asked me what news there was from the field of battle. And Gitara Sedai started up out of her chair, her arms and legs rigid, trembling, her face as if she looked into the Pit of Doom at Shayol Ghul, and she cried out, 'He is born again! I feel him! The Dragon takes his first breath on the slope of Dragonmount! He is coming! He is coming! Light help us! Light help the world! He lies in the snow and cries like the thunder! He burns like the sun!' And she fell forward into my arms, dead."

Slope of the mountain. Heard a baby cry. Gave birth there alone, before she died. Child blue with the cold. Rand tried to force Tam's voice away. The void grew smaller. "A fever-dream," he gasped. *I couldn't leave a child.* "I was born in the Two Rivers." *Always knew you wanted children, Kari.* He pulled his eyes away from the Amyrlin's gaze. He tried to force the void to hold. He knew that was not the way, but it was collapsing in him. *Yes, lass. Rand is a good name.* "I—am—Rand—al'Thor!" His legs trembled.

"And so we knew the Dragon was Reborn," Moiraine went on. "The Amyrlin swore us to secrecy, we two, for she knew not all the sisters would see the Rebirth as it must be seen. She set us to searching. There were many fatherless children after that battle. Too many. But we found a story, that one man had found an infant on the mountain. That was all. A man and an infant boy. So we searched on. For years we searched, finding other clues, poring over the Prophecies. 'He will be of the ancient blood, and raised by the old blood.' That was one; there were others. But there are many places where the old blood, descended from the Age of Legends, remains strong. Then, in the Two Rivers, where the old blood of Manetheren seethes still like a river in flood, in Emond's Field, I found three boys whose namedays were within weeks of the battle at Dragonmount. And one of them can channel. Did you think Trollocs came after you just because you are *ta'veren*? You are the Dragon Reborn."

Rand's knees gave way; he dropped to a squat, hands slapping the rug to catch himself from falling on his face. The void was gone, the stillness shattered. He raised his head, and they were looking at him, the three Aes Sedai. Their faces were serene, smooth as unruffled ponds, but their eyes did not blink. "My father is Tam al'Thor, and I was born. . . ." They stared at him, unmoving. *They're lying. I am not . . . what they say! Some way, somehow, they're lying, trying to use me.* "I will not be used by you."

"An anchor is not demeaned by being used to hold a boat," the Amyrlin said. "You were made for a purpose, Rand al'Thor. 'When the winds of Tarmon Gai'don scour the earth, he will face the Shadow and bring forth Light again in the world.' The Prophecies must be fulfilled, or the Dark One will break free and remake the world in his image. The Last Battle is coming, and you were born to unite mankind and lead them against the Dark One."

"Ba'alzamon is dead," Rand said hoarsely, and the Amyrlin snorted like a stablehand.

"If you believe that, you are as much a fool as the Domani. Many there believe he is dead, or say they do, but I notice they still won't risk naming him. The Dark One lives, and he is breaking free. You will face the Dark One. It is your destiny."

It is your destiny. He had heard that before, in a dream that had maybe not been entirely a dream. He wondered what the Amyrlin would say if she knew Ba'alzamon had spoken to him in dreams. *That's done with. Ba'alzamon is dead. I saw him die.*

Suddenly it came to him that he was crouching like a toad, huddling under their eyes. He tried to form the void again, but voices whirled through his head, sweeping away every effort. *It is your destiny. Babe lying in the snow. You are the Dragon Reborn. Ba'alzamon is dead. Rand is a good name, Kari. I will not be used!* Drawing on his own native stubbornness, he forced himself back upright. *Face it on your feet. You can keep your pride, at least.* The three Aes Sedai watched with no expression.

"What. . . ." With an effort he steadied his voice. "What are you going to do to me?"

"Nothing," the Amyrlin said, and he blinked. It was not the answer he had expected, the one he had feared. "You say you want to accompany your friend with Ingtar, and you may. I have not marked you out in any way. Some of the sisters may know you are *ta'veren*, but no more. Only we three know who you truly are. Your friend Perrin will be brought to me, as you were, and I will visit your other friend in the infirmary. You may go as you will, without fear that we will set the Red sisters on you."

Who you truly are. Anger flared up in him, hot and corrosive. He forced it to stay inside, hidden. "Why?"

"The Prophecies must be fulfilled. We let you walk free, knowing what you are, because otherwise the world we know will die, and the Dark One will cover the earth with fire and death. Mark me, not all Aes Sedai feel the same. There are some here in Fal Dara who would strike you down if they knew a tenth of what you are, and feel no more remorse than for gutting a fish. But then, there are men who've no doubt laughed with you who would do the same, if they knew. Have a care, Rand al'Thor, Dragon Reborn."

He looked at each of them in turn. *Your Prophecies are no part of me.* They returned his gaze so calmly it was hard to believe they were trying to convince him he was the most hated, the most feared man in the history of the world. He had gone right through fear and come out the other side in some place cold. Anger was all that kept him warm. They could gentle him, or burn him to a crisp where he stood, and he no longer cared.

A part of Lan's instructions came back to him. Left hand on the hilt, he twisted the sword behind him, catching the scabbard in his right, then bowed, arms straight. "By your leave, Mother, may I depart this place?"

"I give you leave to go, my son."

Straightening, he stood there a moment longer. "I will not be used," he told them. There was a long silence as he turned and left.

The silence stretched on in the room after Rand left until it was broken by a long breath from the Amyrlin. "I cannot make myself like what we just did," she said. "It was necessary, but. . . . Did it work, Daughters?"

Moiraine shook her head, just the slightest movement. "I do not know. But it *was* necessary, and is."

"Necessary," Verin agreed. She touched her forehead, then peered at the dampness on her fingers. "He is strong. And as stubborn as you said, Moiraine. Much stronger than I expected. We may have to gentle him after all before. . . ." Her eyes widened. "But we cannot, can we? The Prophecies. The Light forgive us for what we are loosing on the world."

"The Prophecies," Moiraine said, nodding. "Afterwards, we will do as we must. As we do now."

"As we must," the Amyrlin said. "Yes. But when he learns to channel, the Light help us all."

The silence returned.

There was a storm coming. Nynaeve felt it. A big storm, worse than she had ever seen. She could listen to the wind, and hear what the weather would be. All Wisdoms claimed to be able to do that, though many could not. Nynaeve had felt more comfortable with the ability before learning it was a manifestation of the Power. Any woman who could listen to the wind could channel, though most were probably as she had been, unaware of what she was doing, getting it only in fits and starts.

This time, though, something was wrong. Outside, the morning sun was a golden ball in a clear blue sky, and birds sang in the gardens, but that was not it. There would have been nothing to listening to the wind if she could not foretell the weather before the signs were visible. There was something wrong with the feeling this time, something not quite the way it usually was. The storm felt distant, too far off for her to feel at all. Yet it felt as if the sky above should have been pouring down rain, and snow, and hail, all at the same time, with winds howling to shake the stones of the keep. And she could feel the good weather, too, lasting for days yet, but that was muted under the other.

A bluefinch perched in an arrowslit like a mockery of her weather sense, peering into the hallway. When it saw her, it vanished in a flash of blue and white feathers.

She stared at the spot where the bird had been. *There is a storm, and there isn't. It means something. But what?*

Far down the hall full of women and small children she saw Rand striding away, his escort of women half running to keep up. Nynaeve nodded firmly. If there was a storm that was not a storm, he would be the center of it. Gathering her skirts, she hurried after him.

Women with whom she had grown friendly since coming to Fal Dara tried to speak to her; they knew Rand had come with her and that they were both from the Two Rivers, and they wanted to know why the Amyrlin had summoned him. *The Amyrlin Seat!* Ice in the pit of her belly, she broke into a run, but before she left the women's apartments, she had lost him around too many corners and beyond too many people.

"Which way did he go?" she asked Nisura. There was no need to say who. She heard Rand's name in the conversation of the other women clustered around the arched doors.

"I don't know, Nynaeve. He came out as fast as if he had Heartsbane himself at his heels. As well he might, coming here with a sword at his belt. The Dark One should be the least of his worries after that. What is the world coming to? And him presented to the Amyrlin in her chambers, no less. Tell me, Nynaeve, is he really a prince in your land?" The other women stopped talking and leaned closer to listen.

Nynaeve was not sure what she answered. Something that made them let her go on. She hurried away from the women's apartments, head swiveling at every crossing corridor to look for him, fists clenched. *Light, what have they done to him? I should have gotten him away from Moiraine somehow, the Light blind her. I'm his Wisdom.*

Are you, a small voice taunted. *You've abandoned Emond's Field to fend for itself. Can you still call yourself their Wisdom?*

I did not abandon them, she told herself fiercely. *I brought Mavra Mallen up from Deven Ride to look after matters till I get back. She can deal well enough with the Mayor and the Village Council, and she gets on well with the Women's Circle.*

Mavra will have to get back to her own village. No village can do without its Wisdom for long. Nynaeve cringed inside. She had been gone months from Emond's Field.

"I am the Wisdom of Emond's Field!" she said aloud.

A liveried servant carrying a bolt of cloth blinked at her, then bowed low before scurrying off. By his face he was eager to be anywhere else.

Blushing, Nynaeve looked around to see if anyone had noticed. There were only a few men in the hall, engrossed in their own conversations, and some women in black-and-gold going about their business, giving her a bow or curtsy as she passed. She had had that argument with herself a hundred times before, but this was the first time it had come to talking to herself out loud. She muttered under her breath, then pressed her lips firmly together when she realized what she was doing.

She was finally beginning to realize her search was futile when she came on Lan, his back to her, looking down on the outer courtyard through an arrowslit. The noise from the courtyard was all horses and men, neighing and shouting. So intent was Lan that he did not, for once, seem to hear her. She hated the fact that she could never sneak up on him, however softly she stepped. She had been accounted good at woodscraft back in Emond's Field, though it was not a skill in which many women took any interest.

She stopped in her tracks, pressing her hands to her stomach to quiet a flutter. *I ought to dose myself with rannel and sheepstongue root*, she thought sourly. It was the mixture she gave anyone who moped about and claimed they were sick, or behaved like a goose. Rannel and sheepstongue root would perk you up a little, and did no harm, but mainly it tasted horrible, and the taste lasted all day. It was a perfect cure for acting the fool.

Safe from his eyes, she studied the length of him, leaning against the stone and fingering his chin as he studied what was going on below. *He's too tall, for one thing, and old enough to be my father, for another. A man with a face like that would have to be cruel. No, he's not that. Never that.* And he was a king. His land was destroyed while he was a child, and he would not claim a crown, but he was a king, for that. *What would a king want with a village woman? He's a Warder, too. Bonded to Moiraine. She has his loyalty to death, and ties closer than any lover, and she has him. She has everything I want, the Light burn her!*

He turned from the arrowslit, and she whirled to go.

"Nynaeve." His voice caught and held her like a noose. "I wanted to speak to you alone. You always seem to be in the women's apartments, or in company."

It took an effort to face him, but she was sure her features were calm when she looked up at him. "I'm looking for Rand." She was not about to admit to avoiding him. "We said all we need to say long ago, you and I. I shamed myself—which I will not do again—and you told me to go away."

"I never said—" He took a deep breath. "I told you I had nothing to offer for brideprice but widow's clothes. Not a gift any man could give a woman. Not a man who can call himself a man."

"I understand," she said coolly. "In any case, a king does not give gifts to village women. And this village woman would not take them. Have you seen Rand? I need to talk to him. He was to see the Amyrlin. Do you know what she wanted with him?"

His eyes blazed like blue ice in the sun. She stiffened

her legs to keep from stepping back, and met him glare for
glare.

"The Dark One take Rand al'Thor and the Amyrlin Seat
both," he grated, pressing something into her hand. "I will
make you a gift and you will take it if I have to chain it
around your neck."

She pulled her eyes away from his. He had a stare like
a blue-eyed hawk when he was angry. In her hand was a
signet ring, heavy gold and worn with age, almost large
enough for both her thumbs to fit through. On it, a crane
flew above a lance and crown, all carefully wrought in detail. Her breath caught. The ring of Malkieri kings. Forgetting to glare, she lifted her face. "I cannot take this, Lan."

He shrugged in an offhand way. "It is nothing. Old, and
useless, now. But there are those who would know it when
they saw it. Show that, and you will have guestright, and
help if you need it, from any lord in the Borderlands. Show
it to a Warder, and he will give aid, or carry a message to
me. Send it to me, or a message marked with it, and I will
come to you, without delay and without fail. This I swear."

Her vision blurred at the edges. *If I cry now, I will kill
myself.* "I can't. . . . I do not want a gift from you, al'Lan
Mandragoran. Here, take it."

He fended off her attempts to give the ring back to him.
His hand enveloped hers, gentle but firm as a shackle. "Then
take it for my sake, as a favor to me. Or throw it away, if it
displeases you. I've no better use for it." He brushed her
cheek with a finger, and she gave a start. "I must go now,
Nynaeve *mashiara*. The Amyrlin wishes to leave before
midday, and there is much yet to be done. Perhaps we will
have time to talk on the journey to Tar Valon." He turned
and was gone, striding down the hall.

Nynaeve touched her cheek. She could still feel where
he had touched her. *Mashiara.* Beloved of heart and soul,
it meant, but a love lost too. Lost beyond regaining. *Fool
woman! Stop acting like a girl with her hair still not
braided. It's no use letting him make you feel. . . .*

Clutching the ring tightly, she turned around, and jumped
when she found herself face-to-face with Moiraine. "How
long have you been there?" she demanded.

"Not long enough to hear anything I should not have,"

the Aes Sedai replied smoothly. "We *will* be leaving soon. I heard that. You must see to your packing."

Leaving. It had not penetrated when Lan said it. "I will have to say goodbye to the boys," she muttered, then gave Moiraine a sharp look. "What have you done to Rand? He was taken to the Amyrlin. Why? Did you tell her about—about . . . ?" She could not say it. He was from her own village, and she was just enough older than he to have looked after him a time or two when he was little, but she could not even think about what he had become without her stomach twisting.

"The Amyrlin will be seeing all three, Nynaeve. *Ta'veren* are not so common that she would miss the chance to see three together in one place. Perhaps she will give them a few words of encouragement, since they are riding with Ingtar to hunt those who stole the Horn. They will be leaving about the time we do, so you had better hurry with any farewells."

Nynaeve dashed to the nearest arrowslit and peered down at the outer courtyard. Horses were everywhere, pack animals and saddle horses, and men hurrying about them, calling to each other. The only clear space was where the Amyrlin's palanquin stood, its paired horses waiting patiently without any attendants. Some of the Warders were out there, looking over their mounts, and on the other side of the courtyard, Ingtar stood with a knot of Shienarans around him in armor. Sometimes a Warder or one of Ingtar's men crossed the paving stones to exchange a word.

"I should have gotten the boys away from you," she said, still looking out. *Egwene, too, if I could do it without killing her. Light, why did she have to be born with this cursed ability?* "I should have taken them back home."

"They are more than old enough to be off apron strings," Moiraine said dryly. "And you know very well why you could never do that. For one of them, at least. Besides, it would mean leaving Egwene to go to Tar Valon alone. Or have you decided to forgo Tar Valon yourself? If your own use of the Power is not schooled, you will never be able to use it against me."

Nynaeve spun to face the Aes Sedai, her jaw dropping. She could not help it. "I don't know what you are talking about."

"Did you think I did not know, child? Well, as you wish it. I take it that you *are* coming to Tar Valon? Yes, I thought so."

Nynaeve wanted to hit her, to knock away the brief smile that flashed across the Aes Sedai's face. Aes Sedai had not been able to wield power openly since the Breaking, much less the One Power, but they plotted and manipulated, pulled strings like puppetmasters, used thrones and nations like stones on a stones board. *She wants to use me, too, somehow. If a king or a queen, why not a Wisdom? Just the way she's using Rand. I'm no child, Aes Sedai.*

"What are you doing with Rand, now? Have you not used him enough? I don't know why you have not had him gentled, now the Amyrlin's here with all those other Aes Sedai, but you must have a reason. It must be some plot you're hatching. If the Amyrlin knew what you were up to, I wager she'd—"

Moiraine cut her off. "What possible interest could the Amyrlin have in a shepherd? Of course, if he were brought to her attention in the wrong way, he might be gentled, or even killed. He is what he is, after all. And there is considerable anger about last night. Everyone is looking for whom to blame." The Aes Sedai fell silent, and let the silence stretch. Nynaeve stared at her, grinding her teeth.

"Yes," Moiraine said finally, "much better to let a sleeping lion sleep. Best you see to your packing, now." She moved off in the direction Lan had gone, seeming to glide across the floor.

Grimacing, Nynaeve swung her fist back against the wall; the ring dug at her palm. She opened her hand to look at it. The ring seemed to heat her anger, focus her hate. *I will learn. You think because you know, you can escape me. But I will learn better than you think, and I will pull you down for what you've done. For what you've done to Mat, and to Perrin. For Rand, the Light help him and the Creator shelter him. Especially for Rand.* Her hand closed around the heavy circlet of gold. *And for me.*

Egwene watched the liveried maid folding her dresses into a leather-covered travel chest, still a little uncomfortable, even after nearly a month's practice, with someone else doing what she could very well have done herself. They were such beautiful dresses, all gifts from the Lady Amalisa, just like the gray silk riding dress she wore, though that was plain except for a few white morningstar blossoms worked on the breast. Many of the dresses were much more elaborate. Any one of them would shine at Sunday, or at Bel Tine. She sighed, remembering that she would be in Tar Valon for the next Sunday, not Emond's Field. From the little Moiraine had told her of novice training—almost nothing, really—she expected she might not be home for Bel Tine, in the spring, or even the Sunday after that.

Nynaeve put her head into the room. "Are you ready?" She came the rest of the way in. "We must be down in the courtyard soon." She wore a riding dress, too, in blue silk with red loversknots on the bosom. Another gift from Amalisa.

"Nearly, Nynaeve. I am almost sorry to be going. I don't suppose we'll have many chances in Tar Valon to wear the nice dresses Amalisa gave us." She gave an abrupt laugh. "Still, Wisdom, I won't miss being able to bathe without looking over my shoulder the whole time."

"Much better to bathe alone," Nynaeve said briskly. Her face did not change, but after a moment her cheeks colored.

Egwene smiled. *She's thinking about Lan.* It was still odd to think of Nynaeve, the Wisdom, mooning after a man. She did not think it would be wise to put it to Nynaeve in quite that way, but of late, sometimes the Wisdom acted as strangely as any girl who had set her heart on a particular man. *And one who doesn't have enough sense to be worthy of her, at that. She loves him, and I can see he loves her, so why can't he have sense enough to speak up?*

"I don't think you should call me Wisdom any longer," Nynaeve said suddenly.

Egwene blinked. It was not required, exactly, and Nynaeve never insisted on it unless she was angry, or being formal, but this. . . . "Why ever not?"

"You are a woman, now." Nynaeve glanced at her unbraided hair, and Egwene resisted the urge to hurriedly twist it into a semblance of a braid. Aes Sedai wore their hair any way they wanted, but wearing hers loose had become a symbol of starting on a new life. "You are a woman," Nynaeve repeated firmly. "We are two women, a

long way from Emond's Field, and it will be longer still before we see home again. It will be better if you simply call
me Nynaeve."

"We will see home again, Nynaeve. We will."

"Don't try to comfort the Wisdom, girl," Nynaeve said
gruffly, but she smiled.

There was a knock at the door, but before Egwene
could open it, Nisura came in, agitation all over her face.
"Egwene, that young man of yours is trying to come into
the women's apartments." She sounded scandalized. "And
wearing a sword. Just because the Amyrlin let him enter
that way. . . . Lord Rand should know better. He is causing
an uproar. Egwene, you must speak to him."

"Lord Rand," Nynaeve snorted. "That young man is
growing too big for his breeches. When I get my hands on
him, I'll lord him."

Egwene put a hand on Nynaeve's arm. "Let me speak to
him, Nynaeve. Alone."

"Oh, very well. The best of men are not much better
than housebroken." Nynaeve paused, and added half to herself, "But then, the best of them are worth the trouble of
housebreaking."

Egwene shook her head as she followed Nisura into the
hall. Even half a year before, Nynaeve would never have
added the second part. *But she'll never housebreak Lan.*
Her thoughts turned to Rand. Causing an uproar, was he?
"Housebreak him?" she muttered. "If he hasn't learned
manners by this time, I'll skin him alive."

"Sometimes that is what it takes," Nisura said, walking quickly. "Men are never more than half-civilized until
they're wedded." She gave Egwene a sidelong glance. "Do
you intend to marry Lord Rand? I do not mean to pry, but
you are going to the White Tower, and Aes Sedai seldom
wed—none but some of the Green Ajah, that I've ever
heard, and not many of them—and. . . ."

Egwene could supply the rest. She had heard the talk in
the women's apartments about a suitable wife for Rand. At
first it had caused stabs of jealousy, and anger. He had been
all but promised to her since they were children. But she
was going to be an Aes Sedai, and he was what he was. A
man who could channel. She could marry him. And watch

him go mad, watch him die. The only way to stop it would be to have him gentled. *I can't do that to him. I can't!* "I do not know," she said sadly.

Nisura nodded. "No one will poach where you have a claim, but you are going to the Tower, and he will make a good husband. Once he has been trained. There he is."

The women gathered around the entrance to the women's apartments, both inside and out, were all watching three men in the hallway outside. Rand, with his sword buckled over his red coat, was being confronted by Agelmar and Kajin. Neither of them wore a sword; even after what had happened in the night, these were still the women's apartments. Egwene stopped at the back of the crowd.

"You understand why you cannot go in," Agelmar was saying. "I know that things are different in Andor, but you do understand?"

"I didn't try to go in." Rand sounded as if he had explained all this more than once already. "I told the Lady Nisura I wanted to see Egwene, and she said Egwene was busy, and I'd have to wait. All I did was shout for her from the door. I did not try to enter. You'd have thought I was naming the Dark One, the way they all started in on me."

"Women have their own ways," Kajin said. He was tall for a Shienaran, almost as tall as Rand, lanky and sallow. His topknot was black as pitch. "They set the rules for the women's apartments, and we abide by them even when they are foolish." A number of eyebrows were raised among the women, and he hastily cleared his throat. "You must send a message in if you wish to speak to one of the women, but it will be delivered when they choose, and until it is, you must wait. That is our custom."

"I have to see her," Rand said stubbornly. "We're leaving soon. Not soon enough for me, but I still have to see Egwene. We will get the Horn of Valere and the dagger back, and that will be the end of it. The end of it. But I want to see her before I go." Egwene frowned; he sounded odd.

"No need to be so fierce," Kajin said. "You and Ingtar will find the Horn, or not. And if not, then another will retrieve it. The Wheel weaves as the Wheel wills, and we are but threads in the Pattern."

"Do not let the Horn seize you, Rand," Agelmar said. "It can take hold of a man—I know how it can—and that is not the way. A man must seek duty, not glory. What will happen, will happen. If the Horn of Valere is meant to be sounded for the Light, then it will be."

"Here is your Egwene," Kajin said, spotting her.

Agelmar looked around, and nodded when he saw her with Nisura. "I will leave you in her hands, Rand al'Thor. Remember, here, her words are law, not yours. Lady Nisura, do not be too hard on him. He only wished to see his young woman, and he does not know our ways."

Egwene followed Nisura as the Shienaran woman threaded her way through the watching women. Nisura inclined her head briefly to Agelmar and Kajin; she pointedly did not include Rand. Her voice was tight. "Lord Agelmar. Lord Kajin. He should know this much of our ways by now, but he is too big to spank, so I will let Egwene deal with him."

Agelmar gave Rand a fatherly pat on the shoulder. "You see. You will speak with her, if not exactly in the way you wished. Come, Kajin. We have much to see to yet. The Amyrlin still insists on. . . ." His voice trailed away as he and the other man left. Rand stood there, looking at Egwene.

The women were still watching, Egwene realized. Watching her as well as Rand. Waiting to see what she would do. *So I'm supposed to deal with him, am I?* Yet she felt her heart going out to him. His hair needed brushing. His face showed anger, defiance, and weariness. "Walk with me," she told him. A murmur started up behind them as he walked down the hall beside her, away from the women's apartments. Rand seemed to be struggling with himself, hunting for what to say.

"I've heard about your . . . exploits," she said finally. "Running through the women's apartments last night with a sword. Wearing a sword to an audience with the Amyrlin Seat." He still said nothing, only walked along frowning at the floor. "She didn't . . . hurt you, did she?" She could not make herself ask if he had been gentled; he looked anything but gentle, but she had no idea what a man looked like afterwards.

He gave a jerk. "No. She didn't. . . . Egwene, the Amyrlin. . . ." He shook his head. "She didn't hurt me."

She had the feeling he had been going to say something

else entirely. Usually she could ferret out whatever he wanted to hide from her, but when he really wanted to be stubborn, she could more easily dig a brick out of a wall with her fingernails. By the set of his jaw, he was at his most stubborn right now.

"What did she want with you, Rand?"

"Nothing important. *Ta'veren*. She wanted to see *ta'veren*." His face softened as he looked down at her. "What about you, Egwene? Are you all right? Moiraine said you would be, but you were so still. I thought you were dead, at first."

"Well, I'm not." She laughed. She could not remember anything that had happened after she had asked Mat to go to the dungeons with her, not until waking in her own bed that morning. From what she had heard of the night, she was almost glad she could not remember. "Moiraine said she would have left me a headache for being foolish if she could have Healed the rest and not that, but she couldn't."

"I told you Fain was dangerous," he muttered. "I told you, but you wouldn't listen."

"If that's the way you are going to talk," she said firmly, "I will give you back to Nisura. She won't talk to you the way I am. The last man who tried to push his way into the women's apartments spent a month up to his elbows in soapy water, helping with the women's laundry, and he was only trying to find his betrothed and make up an argument. At least he knew enough not to wear his sword. The Light knows what they'd do to you."

"Everybody wants to do something to me," he growled. "Everybody wants to use me for something. Well, I won't be used. Once we find the Horn, and Mat's dagger, I'll never be used again."

With an exasperated grunt, she caught his shoulders and made him face her. She glared up at him. "If you don't start talking sense, Rand al'Thor, I swear I will box your ears."

"Now you sound like Nynaeve." He laughed. As he looked down at her, though, his laughter faded. "I suppose—I suppose I'll never see you again. I know you have to go to Tar Valon. I know that. And you'll become an Aes Sedai. I am done with Aes Sedai, Egwene. I won't be a puppet for them, not for Moiraine, or any of them."

He looked so lost she wanted to put his head on her

shoulder, and so stubborn she really did want to box his ears. "Listen to me, you great ox. I *am* going to be an Aes Sedai, and I'll find a way to help you. I will."

"The next time you see me, you will likely want to gentle me."

She looked around hastily; they were alone in their stretch of the hall. "If you don't watch your tongue, I will not be able to help you. Do you want everyone to know?"

"Too many know already," he said. "Egwene, I wish things were different, but they aren't. I wish. . . . Take care of yourself. And promise me you won't choose the Red Ajah."

Tears blurred her vision as she threw her arms around him. "You take care of yourself," she said fiercely into his chest. "If you don't, I'll—I'll. . . ." She thought she heard him murmur, "I love you," and then he was firmly unwrapping her arms, gently moving her away from him. He turned and strode away from her, almost running.

She jumped when Nisura touched her arm. "He looks as if you set him a task he won't enjoy. But you mustn't let him see you cry over it. That negates the purpose. Come. Nynaeve wants you."

Scrubbing her cheeks, Egwene followed the other woman. *Take care of yourself, you wool-headed lummox. Light, take care of him.*

CHAPTER
9

Leavetakings

The outer courtyard was in ordered turmoil when Rand finally reached it with his saddlebags and the bundle containing the harp and flute. The sun climbed toward midday. Men hurried around the horses, tugging at saddle girths and pack harness, voices raised. Others darted with last-minute additions to the packsaddles, or water for the men working, or dashed off to fetch something just remembered. But everyone seemed to know exactly what they were doing and where they were going. The guardwalks and archers' balconies were crowded again, and excitement crackled in the morning air. Hooves clattered on the paving stones. One of the packhorses began kicking, and stablemen ran to calm it. The smell of horses hung thick. Rand's cloak tried to flap in the breeze that rippled the swooping-hawk banners on the towers, but his bow, slung across his back, held it down.

From outside the open gates came the sounds of the Amyrlin's pikemen and archers forming up in the square. They had marched around from a side gate. One of the trumpeters tested his horn.

Some of the Warders glanced at Rand as he walked across the courtyard; a few raised eyebrows when they saw the heron-mark sword, but none spoke. Half wore the cloaks that were so queasy-making to look at. Mandarb, Lan's stallion, was there, tall, and black, and fierce-eyed, but the man himself was not, and none of the Aes Sedai, none of the women, were in evidence yet either. Moiraine's white mare, Aldieb, stepped daintily beside the stallion.

Rand's bay stallion was with the other group on the far

side of the courtyard, with Ingtar, and a bannerman holding Ingtar's Gray Owl banner, and twenty other armored
men with lances tipped with two feet of steel, all mounted
already. The bars of their helmets covered their faces, and
golden surcoats with the Black Hawk on the chest hid their
plate-and-mail. Only Ingtar's helmet had a crest, a crescent
moon above his brow, points up. Rand recognized some of
the men. Rough-tongued Uno, with a long scar down his
face and only one eye. Ragan and Masema. Others who
had exchanged a word, or played a game of stones. Ragan
waved to him, and Uno nodded, but Masema was not the
only one who gave him a cold stare and turned away. Their
packhorses stood placidly, tails swishing.

The big bay danced as Rand tied his saddlebags and bundle behind the high-cantled saddle. He put his foot in the
stirrup and murmured, "Easy, Red," as he swung into the
saddle, but he let the stallion frisk away some of his stable-
bound energy.

To Rand's surprise, Loial appeared from the direction
of the stables, riding to join them. The Ogier's hairy-
fetlocked mount was as big and heavy as a prime Dhurran
stallion. Beside it, all the other animals looked the size
of Bela, but with Loial in the saddle, the horse seemed
almost a pony.

Loial carried no weapon that Rand could see; he had
never heard of any Ogier using a weapon. Their *stedding*
were protection enough. And Loial had his own priorities,
his own ideas of what was needed for a journey. The pockets of his long coat had a telltale bulge, and his saddlebags
showed the square imprints of books.

The Ogier stopped his horse a little way off and looked at
Rand, his tufted ears twitching uncertainly.

"I didn't know you were coming," Rand said. "I'd think you
would have had enough of traveling with us. This time there's
no telling how long it will be, or where we will end up."

Loial's ears lifted a little. "There was no telling when I
first met you, either. Besides, what held then, holds now. I
can't let the chance pass to see history actually weave itself
around *ta'veren*. And to help find the Horn. . . ."

Mat and Perrin rode up behind Loial and paused. Mat
looked a little tired around the eyes, but his face wore a
bloom of health.

"Mat," Rand said, "I'm sorry for what I said. Perrin, I didn't mean it. I was being stupid."

Mat only glanced at him, then shook his head and mouthed something to Perrin that Rand could not hear. Mat had only his bow and quiver, but Perrin also wore his axe at his belt, with its big half-moon blade balanced by a thick spike.

"Mat? Perrin? Really, I didn't—" They rode on toward Ingtar.

"That is not a coat for traveling, Rand," Loial said.

Rand glanced down at the golden thorns climbing his crimson sleeve and grimaced. *Small wonder Mat and Perrin still think I'm putting on airs.* On returning to his room he had found everything already packed and sent on. All of the plain coats he had been given were on the packhorses, so the servants said; every coat left in the wardrobe was at least as ornate as the one he wore. His saddlebags held nothing in the way of clothes but a few shirts, some wool stockings, and a spare pair of breeches. At least he had removed the golden cord from his sleeve, though he had the red eagle pin in his pocket. Lan had meant it for a gift, after all.

"I'll change when we stop tonight," he muttered. He took a deep breath. "Loial, I said things to you I should not have, and I hope you'll forgive me. You have every right to hold them against me, but I hope you won't."

Loial grinned, and his ears stood up. He moved his horse closer. "I say things I should not all the time. The Elders always said I spoke an hour before I thought."

Suddenly Lan was at Rand's stirrup, in his gray-green scaled armor that would make him all but disappear in forest or darkness. "I need to talk to you, sheepherder." He looked at Loial. "Alone, if you please, Builder." Loial nodded and moved his big horse away.

"I don't know if I should listen to you," Rand told the Warder. "These fancy clothes, and all those things you told me, they didn't help much."

"When you can't win a big victory, sheepherder, learn to settle for the small ones. If you made them think of you as something more than a farmboy who'll be easy to handle, then you won a small victory. Now be quiet and listen. I've only time for one last lesson, the hardest. Sheathing the Sword."

"You've spent an hour every morning making me do nothing but draw this bloody sword and put it back in the scabbard. Standing, sitting, lying down. I think I can manage to get it back in the sheath without cutting myself."

"I said listen, sheepherder," the Warder growled. "There will come a time when you must achieve a goal at all costs. It may come in attack or in defense. And the only way will be to allow the sword to be sheathed in your own body."

"That's crazy," Rand said. "Why would I ever—?"

The Warder cut him off. "You will know when it comes, sheepherder, when the price is worth the gain, and there is no other choice left to you. That is called Sheathing the Sword. Remember it."

The Amyrlin appeared, striding across the crowded courtyard with Leane and her staff, and Lord Agelmar at her shoulder. Even in a green velvet coat, the Lord of Fal Dara did not look out of place among so many armored men. There was still no sign of the other Aes Sedai. As they went by, Rand caught part of their conversation.

"But, Mother," Agelmar was protesting, "you've had no time to rest from the journey here. Stay at least a few days more. I promise you a feast tonight such as you could hardly get in Tar Valon."

The Amyrlin shook her head without breaking stride. "I cannot, Agelmar. You know I would if I could. I had never planned to remain long, and matters urgently require my presence in the White Tower. I should be there now."

"Mother, it shames me that you come one day and leave the next. I swear to you, there will be no repetition of last night. I have tripled the guard on the city gates as well as the keep. I have tumblers in from the town, and a bard coming from Mos Shirare. Why, King Easar will be on his way from Fal Moran. I sent word as soon as. . . ."

Their voices faded as they crossed the courtyard, swallowed up by the din of preparation. The Amyrlin never as much as glanced in Rand's direction.

When Rand looked down, the Warder was gone, and nowhere to be seen. Loial brought his horse back to Rand's side. "That is a hard man to catch and hold, isn't he, Rand?

He's not here, then he's here, then he's gone, and you don't see him coming or going."

Sheathing the Sword. Rand shivered. *Warders must all be crazy.*

The Warder the Amyrlin was speaking to suddenly sprang into his saddle. He was at a dead gallop before he reached the wide-standing gates. She stood watching him go, and her stance seemed to urge him to go faster.

"Where is he headed in such a hurry?" Rand wondered aloud.

"I heard," Loial said, "that she was sending someone out today, all the way to Arad Doman. There is word of some sort of trouble on Almoth Plain, and the Amyrlin Seat wants to know exactly what. What I don't understand is, why now? From what I hear, the rumors of this trouble came from Tar Valon with the Aes Sedai."

Rand felt cold. Egwene's father had a big map back at home, a map Rand had pored over more than once, dreaming before he found out what the dreams were like when they came true. It was old, that map, showing some lands and nations the merchants from outside said no longer existed, but Almoth Plain was marked, butting against Toman Head. *We will meet again on Toman Head.* It was all the way across the world he knew, on the Aryth Ocean. "It has nothing to do with us," he whispered. "Nothing to do with me."

Loial appeared not to have heard. Rubbing the side of his nose with a finger like a sausage, the Ogier was still peering at the gate where the Warder had vanished. "If she wanted to know, why not send someone before she left Tar Valon? But you humans are always sudden and excitable, always jumping around and shouting." His ears stiffened with embarrassment. "I *am* sorry, Rand. You see what I mean about speaking before I think. I'm rash and excitable sometimes myself, as you know."

Rand laughed. It was a weak laugh, but it felt good to have something to laugh at. "Maybe if we lived as long as you Ogier, we'd be more settled." Loial was ninety years old; by Ogier standards, not old enough by ten years to be outside the *stedding* alone. That he had gone anyway was proof, he maintained, of his rashness. If Loial was an excitable Ogier, Rand thought most of them must be made of stone.

"Perhaps so," Loial mused, "but you humans do so much with your lives. We do nothing but huddle in our *stedding*. Planting the groves, and even the building, were all done before the Long Exile ended." It was the groves Loial held dear, not the cities men remembered the Ogier for building. It was the groves, planted to remind Ogier Builders of the *stedding*, that Loial had left his home to see. "Since we found our way back to the *stedding*, we. . . ." His words trailed off as the Amyrlin approached.

Ingtar and the other men shifted in their saddles, preparing to dismount and kneel, but she motioned them to stay as they were. Leane stood at her shoulder, and Agelmar a pace back. From his glum face, he appeared to have given up trying to convince her to remain longer.

The Amyrlin looked at them one by one before she spoke. Her gaze stayed on Rand no longer than on any other.

"Peace favor your sword, Lord Ingtar," she said finally. "Glory to the Builders, Loial Kiseran."

"You honor us, Mother. May peace favor Tar Valon." Ingtar bowed in his saddle, and the other Shienarans did, too.

"All honor to Tar Valon," Loial said, bowing.

Only Rand, and his two friends on the other side of the party, stayed upright. He wondered what she had said to them. Leane's frown took in all three of them, and Agelmar's eyes widened, but the Amyrlin took no notice.

"You ride to find the Horn of Valere," she said, "and the hope of the world rides with you. The Horn cannot be left in the wrong hands, especially in Darkfriend hands. Those who come to answer its call, will come whoever blows it, and they are bound to the Horn, not to the Light."

There was a stir among the listening men. Everyone believed that those heroes called back from the grave would fight for the Light. If they could fight for the Shadow, instead. . . .

The Amyrlin went on, but Rand was no longer listening. The watcher was back. The hair stirred on the back of his neck. He peered up at the packed archers' balconies overlooking the courtyard, at the rows of people jammed along the guardwalks atop the walls. Somewhere among them was the set of eyes that had followed him unseen. The gaze clung to him like dirty oil. *It can't be a Fade, not here. Then who? Or what?* He twisted in his saddle, pulling Red around, searching. The bay began to dance again.

Suddenly something flashed across in front of Rand's face. A man passing behind the Amyrlin cried out and fell, a black-fletched arrow jutting from his side. The Amyrlin stood calmly looking at a rent in her sleeve; blood slowly stained the gray silk.

A woman screamed, and abruptly the courtyard rang with cries and shouts. The people on the walls milled furiously, and every man in the courtyard had his sword out. Even Rand, he was surprised to realize.

Agelmar shook his blade at the sky. "Find him!" he roared. "Bring him to me!" His face went from red to white when he saw the blood on the Amyrlin's sleeve. He fell to his knees, head bowed. "Forgive, Mother. I have failed your safety. I am ashamed."

"Nonsense, Agelmar," the Amyrlin said. "Leane, stop fussing over me and see to that man. I've cut myself worse than this more than once cleaning fish, and he needs help now. Agelmar, stand up. Stand up, Lord of Fal Dara. You have not failed me, and you have no reason for shame. Last year in the White Tower, with my own guards at every gate and Warders all around me, a man with a knife came within five steps of me. A Whitecloak, no doubt, though I've no proof. Please stand up, or I will be shamed." As Agelmar slowly rose, she fingered her sliced sleeve. "A poor shot for a Whitecloak bowman, or even a Darkfriend." Her eyes flickered up to touch Rand's. "If it was at me he aimed." Her gaze was gone before he could read anything on her face, but he suddenly wanted to dismount and hide.

It wasn't aimed at her, and she knows it.

Leane straightened from where she had been kneeling. Someone had laid a cloak over the face of the man who had taken the arrow. "He is dead, Mother." She sounded tired. "He was dead when he struck the ground. Even if I had been at his side. . . ."

"You did what you could, Daughter. Death cannot be Healed."

Agelmar moved closer. "Mother, if there are Whitecloak killers about, or Darkfriends, you must allow me to send

men with you. As far as the river, at least. I could not live if
harm came to you in Shienar. Please, return to the women's
apartments. I will see them guarded with my life until you
are ready to travel."

"Be at ease," she told him. "This scratch will not delay
me a moment. Yes, yes, I will gladly accept your men as far
as the river, if you insist. But I will not let this delay Lord
Ingtar a moment, either. Every heartbeat counts until the
Horn is found again. Your leave, Lord Agelmar, to order
your oathmen?"

He bowed his head in assent. At that moment he would
have given her Fal Dara had she asked.

The Amyrlin turned back to Ingtar and the men gathered
behind him. She did not look at Rand again. He was surprised to see her smile suddenly.

"I wager Illian does not give its Great Hunt of the Horn
so rousing a send-off," she said. "But yours is the true Great
Hunt. You are few, so you may travel quickly, yet enough
to do what you must. I charge you, Lord Ingtar of House
Shinowa, I charge all of you, find the Horn of Valere, and
let nothing bar your way."

Ingtar whipped his sword from his back and kissed the
blade. "By my life and soul, by my House and honor, I
swear it, Mother."

"Then ride."

Ingtar swung his horse toward the gate.

Rand dug his heels into Red's flanks and galloped after
the column already disappearing through the gates.

Unaware of what had occurred within, the Amyrlin's
pikemen and archers stood walling a path from the gates to
the city proper, the Flame of Tar Valon on their chests. Her
drummers and trumpeters waited near the gates, ready to
fall in when she left. Behind the rows of armored men, people packed the square in front of the keep. Some cheered
Ingtar's banner, and others no doubt thought this was the
start of the Amyrlin Seat's departure. A swelling roar followed Rand across the square.

He caught up with Ingtar where low-eaved houses and
shops stood to either side, and more people thickly lined
the stone-paved street. Some of them cheered, too. Mat and
Perrin had been riding at the head of the column with Ingtar
and Loial, but the two of them fell back when Rand joined

them. *How am I ever going to apologize if they won't stay near me long enough for me to say anything? Burn me, he doesn't* look *like he's dying.*

"Changu and Nidao are gone," Ingtar said abruptly. He sounded cold and angry, but shaken, too. "We counted every head in the keep, alive or dead, last night and again this morning. They are the only ones not accounted for."

"Changu was on guard in the dungeon yesterday," Rand said slowly.

"And Nidao. They had the second watch. They always stayed together, even if they had to trade or do extra duty for it. They were not on guard when it happened, but. . . . They fought at Tarwin's Gap, a month gone, and saved Lord Agelmar when his horse went down with Trollocs all around him. Now this. Darkfriends." He drew a deep breath. "Everything is breaking apart."

A man on horseback forced his way through the throng lining the street and joined in behind Ingtar. He was a townsman, by his clothes, lean, with a lined face and graying hair cut long. A bundle and waterbottles were lashed behind his saddle, and a short-bladed sword and a notched sword-breaker hung at his belt, along with a cudgel.

Ingtar noticed Rand's glances. "This is Hurin, our sniffer. There was no need to let the Aes Sedai know about him. Not that what he does is wrong, you understand. The King keeps a sniffer in Fal Moran, and there's another in Ankor Dail. It's just that Aes Sedai seldom like what they do not understand, and with him being a man. . . . It's nothing to do with the Power, of course. Aaaah! You tell him, Hurin."

"Yes, Lord Ingtar," the man said. He bowed low to Rand from his saddle. "Honor to serve, my Lord."

"Call me Rand." Rand stuck out his hand, and after a moment Hurin grinned and took it.

"As you wish, my Lord Rand. Lord Ingtar and Lord Kajin don't mind a man's ways—and Lord Agelmar, of course—but they say in the town you're an outland prince from the south, and some outland lords are strict for every man in his place."

"I'm not a lord." *At least I'll get away from that, now.* "Just Rand."

Hurin blinked. "As you wish, my Lor—ah—Rand. I'm a sniffer, you see. Been one four years this Sunday. I never heard of such a thing before then, but I hear there's a few others like me. It started slow, catching bad smells where nobody else smelled anything, and it grew. Took a whole year before I realized what it was. I could smell violence, the killing and the hurting. Smell where it happened. Smell the trail of those who did it. Every trail's different, so there's no chance of mixing them up. Lord Ingtar heard of it, and took me in his service, to serve the King's justice."

"You can smell violence?" Rand said. He could not help looking at the man's nose. It was an ordinary nose, not large, not small. "You mean you can really follow somebody who, say, killed another man? By smell?"

"I can that, my Lor—ah—Rand. It fades with time, but the worse the violence, the longer it lasts. Aiie, I can smell a battlefield ten years old, though the trails of the men who were there are gone. Up near the Blight, the trails of the Trollocs almost never fade. Not much to a Trolloc but killing and hurting. A fight in a tavern, though, with maybe a broken arm . . . that smell's gone in hours."

"I can see where you wouldn't want Aes Sedai to find out."

"Ah, Lord Ingtar was right about the Aes Sedai, the Light illumine them—ah—Rand. There was one in Cairhien once—Brown Ajah, but I swear I thought she was Red before she let me go—she kept me a month trying to find out how I do it. She didn't like not knowing. She kept muttering, 'Is it old come again, or new?' and staring at me until you would have thought I *was* using the One Power. Almost had me doubting myself. But I haven't gone mad, and I don't *do* anything. I just smell it."

Rand could not help remembering Moiraine. *Old barriers weaken. There is something of dissolution and change about our time. Old things walk again, and new things are born. We may live to see the end of an Age.* He shivered. "So we'll track those who took the Horn with your nose."

Ingtar nodded. Hurin grinned proudly, and said, "We will that—ah—Rand. I followed a murderer to Cairhien, once, and another all the way to Maradon, to bring them back for the King's justice." His grin faded, and he looked troubled. "This is the worst ever, though. Murder smells bad, and the trail of a murderer stinks with it, but this. . . ." His nose wrinkled. "There were men in it last night. Darkfriends, must be, but you can't tell a Darkfriend by smell. What I'll follow is the Trollocs, and the Halfmen. And something even worse." He trailed off, frowning and muttering to himself, but Rand could hear it. "Something even worse, the Light help me."

They reached the city gates, and just beyond the walls Hurin lifted his face to the breeze. His nostrils flared, then he gave a snort of disgust. "That way, my Lord Ingtar." He pointed south.

Ingtar looked surprised. "Not toward the Blight?"

"No, Lord Ingtar. Faugh!" Hurin wiped his mouth on his sleeve. "I can almost taste them. South, they went."

"She was right, then, the Amyrlin Seat," Ingtar said slowly. "A great and wise woman, who deserves better than me to serve her. Take the trail, Hurin."

Rand turned and peered back through the gates, up the street to the keep. He hoped Egwene was all right. *Nynaeve will look after her. Maybe it's better this way, like a clean cut, too quick to hurt till after it's done.*

He rode after Ingtar and the Gray Owl banner, south. The wind was making up, and cold against his back despite the sun. He thought he heard laughter in it, faint and mocking.

The waxing moon lit the humid, night-dark streets of Illian, which still rang with celebration left over from daylight. In only a few more days, the Great Hunt of the Horn would be sent forth with pomp and ceremony that tradition claimed dated to the Age of Legends. The festivities for the Hunters had blended into the Feast of Teven, with its famed contests and prizes for gleemen. The greatest prize of all, as always, would go for the best telling of *The Great Hunt of the Horn*.

Tonight the gleemen entertained in the palaces and mansions of the city, where the great and mighty disported themselves, and the Hunters come from every nation to ride out and find, if not the Horn of Valere itself, at least immortality in song and story. They would have music and dancing, and fans and ices to dispel the year's first real heat, but carnival filled the streets, too, in the moon-bright muggy night. Every day was a carnival, until the Hunt departed, and every night.

People ran past Bayle Domon in masks and costumes bizarre and fanciful, many showing too much flesh. Shouting and singing they ran, a half dozen together, then scattered pairs giggling and clutching each other, then twenty in a raucous knot. Fireworks crackled in the sky, gold and silver bursts against the black. There were almost as many Illuminators in the city as there were gleemen.

Domon spared little thought for fireworks, or for the Hunt. He was on his way to meet men he thought might be trying to kill him.

He crossed the Bridge of Flowers, over one of the city's many canals, into the Perfumed Quarter, the port district of Illian. The canal smelled of too many chamber pots, with never a sign that there had ever been flowers near the bridge. The quarter smelled of hemp and pitch from the shipyards and docks, and sour harbor mud, all of it made fiercer by heated air that seemed nearly damp enough to drink. Domon breathed heavily; every time he returned from the northcountry he found himself surprised, for all he had been born there, at the early summer heat in Illian.

In one hand he carried a stout cudgel, and the other hand rested on the hilt of the short sword he had often used in defending the decks of his river trader from brigands. No few footpads stalked these nights of revelry, where the pickings were rich and most were deep in wine.

Yet he was a broad, muscular man, and none of those out for a catch of gold thought him rich enough, in his plain-cut coat, to risk his size and his cudgel. The few who caught a clear glimpse of him, when he passed through light spilling from a window, edged back till he was well past. Dark hair that hung to his shoulders and a long beard that left his upper lip bare framed a round face, but that face had never been soft, and now it was set as grimly as if he meant to batter his way through a wall. He had men to meet, and he was not happy about it.

More revelers ran past singing off-key, wine mangling their words. *"The Horn of Valere," my aged grandmother!* Domon thought glumly. *It be my ship I do want to hang on to. And my life, Fortune prick me.*

He pushed into an inn, under a sign of a big, white-striped badger dancing on its hind legs with a man carrying a silver

shovel. Easing the Badger, it was called, though not even
Nieda Sidoro, the innkeeper, knew what the name meant;
there had always been an inn of the name in Illian.

The common room, with sawdust on the floor and a musician softly strumming a twelve-stringed bittern in one of
the Sea Folk's sad songs, was well lighted and quiet. Nieda
allowed no commotion in her place, and her nephew, Bili,
was big enough to carry a man out with either hand. Sailors, dockworkers, and warehousemen came to the Badger
for a drink and maybe a little talk, for a game of stones or
darts. The room was half full now; even men who liked
quiet had been lured out by carnival. The talk was soft,
but Domon caught mentions of the Hunt, and of the false
Dragon the Murandians had taken, and of the one the Tairens were chasing through Haddon Mirk. There seemed to
be some question whether it would be preferable to see the
false Dragon die, or the Tairens.

Domon grimaced. *False Dragons! Fortune prick me,
there be no place safe these days.* But he had no real care
for false Dragons, any more than for the Hunt.

The stout proprietress, with her hair rolled at the back
of her head, was wiping a mug, keeping a sharp eye on her
establishment. She did not stop what she was doing, or even
look at him, really, but her left eyelid drooped, and her eyes
slanted toward three men at a table in the corner. They were
quiet even for the Badger, almost somber, and their bell-
shaped velvet caps and dark coats, embroidered across the
chest in bars of silver and scarlet and gold, stood out among
the plain dress of the other patrons.

Domon sighed and took a table in a corner by himself.
Cairhienin, this time. He took a mug of brown ale from
a serving girl and drew a long swallow. When he lowered
the mug, the three men in striped coats were standing beside his table. He made an unobtrusive gesture, to let Nieda
know that he did not need Bili.

"Captain Domon?" They were all three nondescript, but
there was an air about the speaker that made Domon take
him for their leader. They did not appear to be armed; despite their fine clothes, they looked as if they did not need
to be. There were hard eyes in those so very ordinary faces.
"Captain Bayle Domon, of the *Spray*?"

Domon gave a short nod, and the three sat down without

waiting for an invitation. The same man did the talking; the other two just watched, hardly blinking. *Guards*, Domon thought, *for all their fine clothes. Who do he be to have a pair of guards to look over him?*

"Captain Domon, we have a personage who must be brought from Mayene to Illian."

"*Spray* be a river craft," Domon cut him off. "Her draft be shallow, and she has no the keel for deep water." It was not exactly true, but close enough for landsmen. *At least it be a change from Tear. They be getting smarter.*

The man seemed unperturbed at the interruption. "We had heard you were giving up the river trade."

"Maybe I do, and maybe no. I have no decided." He had, though. He would not go back upriver, back to the Borderlands, for all the silk shipped in Tairen bottoms. Saldaean furs and ice peppers were not worth it, and it had nothing to do with the false Dragon he had heard of there. But he wondered again how anyone knew. He had not spoken of it to anyone, yet the others had known, too.

"You can coast to Mayene easily enough. Surely, Captain, you would be willing to sail along the shoreline for a thousand gold marks."

Despite himself, Domon goggled. It was four times the last offer, and that had been enough to make a man's jaw drop. "Who do you want me to fetch for that? The First of Mayene herself? Has Tear finally forced her all the way out, then?"

"You need no names, Captain." The man set a large leather pouch on the table, and a sealed parchment. The pouch clinked heavily as he pushed them across the table. The big red wax circle holding the folded parchment shut bore the many-rayed Rising Sun of Cairhien. "Two hundred on account. For a thousand marks, I think you need no names. Give that, seal unbroken, to the Port Captain of Mayene, and he will give you three hundred more, and your passenger. I will hand over the remainder when your passenger is delivered here. So long as you have made no effort to discover that personage's identity."

Domon drew a deep breath. *Fortune, it be worth the voyage if there be never another penny beyond what be in that sack.* And a thousand was more money than he would clear in three years. He suspected that if he probed a little more, there would be other hints, just hints, that the voyage involved hidden dealings between Illian's Council of Nine and the First of Mayene. The First's city-state was a province of Tear in all but name, and she would no doubt like Illian's aid. And there were many in Illian who said it was time for another war, that Tear was taking more than a fair share of the trade on the Sea of Storms. A likely net to snare him, if he had not seen three like it in the past month.

He reached to take the pouch, and the man who had done all the talking caught his wrist. Domon glared at him, but he looked back undisturbed.

"You must sail as soon as possible, Captain."

"At first light," Domon growled, and the man nodded and released his hold.

"At first light, then, Captain Domon. Remember, discretion keeps a man alive to spend his money."

Domon watched the three of them leave, then stared sourly at the pouch and the parchment on the table in front of him. Someone wanted him to go east. Tear or Mayene, it did not matter so long as he went east. He thought he knew who wanted it. *And then again, I have no a clue to them.* Who could know who was a Darkfriend? But he knew that Darkfriends had been after him since before he left Maradon to come back downriver. Darkfriends and Trollocs. Of that, he was sure. The real question, the one he had not even a glimmer of an answer for, was why?

"Trouble, Bayle?" Nieda asked. "You do look as if you had seen a Trolloc." She giggled, an improbable sound from a woman her size. Like most people who had never been to the Borderlands, Nieda did not believe in Trollocs. He had tried telling her the truth of it; she enjoyed his stories, and thought they were all lies. She did not believe in snow, either.

"No trouble, Nieda." He untied the pouch, dug a coin out without looking, and tossed it to her. "Drinks for everyone till that do run out, then I'll give you another."

Nieda looked at the coin in surprise. "A Tar Valon mark! Do you be trading with the witches now, Bayle?"

"No," he said hoarsely. "That I do not!"

She bit the coin, then quickly snugged it away behind her broad belt. "Well, it be gold for that. And I suspect the witches be no so bad as some make them out, anyway. I'd no say so much to many men. I know a money changer who do handle such. You'll no have to give me another, with as few as be here tonight. More ale for you, Bayle?"

He nodded numbly, though his mug was still almost full, and she trundled off. She was a friend, and would not speak of what she had seen. He sat staring at the leather pouch. Another mug was brought before he could make himself open it enough to look at the coins inside. He stirred them with a callused finger. Gold marks glittered up at him in the lamplight, every one of them bearing the damning Flame of Tar Valon. Hurriedly he tied the bag. Dangerous coins. One or two might pass, but so many would say to most people exactly what Nieda thought. There were Children of the Light in the city, and although there was no law in Illian against dealing with Aes Sedai, he would never make it to a magistrate if the Whitecloaks heard of this. These men had made sure he would not simply take the gold and stay in Illian.

While he was sitting there worrying, Yarin Maeldan, his brooding, stork-like second on *Spray*, came into the Badger with his brows pulled down to his long nose and stood over the captain's table. "Carn's dead, Captain."

Domon stared at him, frowning. Three others of his men had already been killed, one each time he refused a commission that would take him east. The magistrates had done nothing; the streets were dangerous at night, they said, and sailors a rough and quarrelsome lot. Magistrates seldom troubled themselves with what happened in the Perfumed Quarter, as long as no respectable citizens were injured.

"But this time I did accept them," he muttered.

"'Tisn't all, Captain," Yarin said. "They worked Carn with knives, like they wanted him to tell them something. And some more men tried to sneak aboard *Spray* not an hour gone. The dock watch ran them off. Third time in ten days, and I never knew wharf rats to be so persistent. They like to let an alarm die down before they try again. And somebody tossed my room at the Silver Dolphin last night. Took some silver, so I'd think it was thieves, but they left that belt buckle of mine, the one set with garnets and moonstones, lying right out in plain sight. What's going on, Captain? The men are afraid, and I'm a little nervous myself."

Domon reared to his feet. "Roust the crew, Yarin. Find

them and tell them *Spray* sails as soon as there do be men
enough aboard to handle her." Stuffing the parchment into
his coat pocket, he snatched up the bag of gold and pushed
his second out the door ahead of him. "Roust them, Yarin,
for I'll leave any man who no makes it, standing on the
quay as he is."

Domon gave Yarin a shove to start him running, then
stalked off toward the docks. Even footpads who heard the
clinking of the pouch he carried steered clear of him, for he
walked now like a man going to do murder.

There were already crewmen scrambling aboard *Spray*
when he arrived, and more running barefoot down the stone
quay. They did not know what he feared was pursuing him,
or even that anything did pursue him, but they knew he
made good profits, and after the Illianer way, he gave shares
to the crew.

Spray was eighty feet long, with two masts, and broad in
the beam, with room for deck cargo as well as in the holds.
Despite what Domon had told the Cairhienin—if they had
been Cairhienin—he thought she could stand the open
water. The Sea of Storms was quieter in the summer.

"She'll have to," he muttered, and strode below to his
cabin.

He tossed the sack of gold on his bed, built neatly against
the hull like everything else in the stern cabin, and dug out
the parchment. Lighting a lantern, hanging in its swivel
from the overhead, he studied the sealed document, turning
it as if he could read what was inside without opening it. A
rap on the door made him frown.

"Come."

Yarin stuck his head in. "They're all aboard but three
I couldn't find, Captain. But I've spread the word through
every tavern, hell, and crib in the quarter. They'll be aboard
before it's light enough to start upriver."

"*Spray* do sail now. To sea." Domon cut off Yarin's protests about light and tides, and *Spray* not being built for
the open sea. "Now! *Spray* can clear the bars at dead low
tide. You've no forgotten how to sail by the stars, have you?
Take her out, Yarin. Take her out now, and come back to me
when we be beyond the breakwater."

His second hesitated—Domon never let a tricky bit of

sailing pass without him on deck giving orders, and taking *Spray* out in the night would be all of that, shallow draft or no—then nodded and vanished. In moments the sounds of Yarin shouting orders and bare feet thumping on the decks overhead penetrated Domon's cabin. He ignored them, even when the ship lurched, catching the tide.

Finally he lifted the mantle of the lantern and stuck a knife into the flame. Smoke curled up as oil burned off the blade, but before the metal could turn red, he pushed charts out of the way and pressed the parchment flat on his desk, working the hot steel slowly under the sealing wax. The top fold lifted.

It was a simple document, without preamble or salutation, and it made sweat break out on his forehead.

The bearer of this is a Darkfriend wanted in Cairhien for murders and other foul crimes, least among them, theft from Our Person. We call upon you to seize this man and all things found in his keeping, to the smallest. Our representative will come to carry away what he has stolen from Us. Let all he possesses, save what We claim, go to you as reward for taking him. Let the vile miscreant himself be hanged immediately, that his Shadow-spawned villainy no longer taint the Light.

> *Sealed by Our Hand*
> *Galldrian su Riatin Rie*
> *King of Cairhien*
> *Defender of the Dragonwall*

In thin red wax below the signature were impressed the Rising Sun seal of Cairhien and the Five Stars of House Riatin.

"Defender of the Dragonwall, my aged grandmother," Domon croaked. "Fine right the man do have to call himself that any longer."

He examined the seals and signature minutely, holding the document close to the lamp, with his nose all but brushing the parchment, but he could find no flaw in the one, and for the other, he had no idea what Galldrian's hand looked like. If it was not the King himself who had signed it, he

suspected that whoever had had made a good imitation
of Galldrian's scrawl. In any case, it made no real difference. In Tear, the letter would be instantly damning in the
hands of an Illianer. Or in Mayene, with Tairen influence
so strong. There was no war now, and men from either port
came and went freely, but there was as little love for Illianers in Tear as the other way round. Especially with an excuse like this.

For a moment he thought of putting the parchment into
the lantern's flame—it was a dangerous thing to have, in
Tear or Illian or anywhere he could imagine—but finally he
tucked it carefully into a secret cubbyhole behind his desk,
concealed by a panel only he knew how to open.

"My possessions, eh?"

He collected old things, as much as he could living on
shipboard. What he could not buy, because it was too expensive or too large, he collected by seeing and remembering. All those remnants of times gone, those wonders
scattered around the world that had first pulled him aboard
a ship as boy. He had added four to his collection in Maradon this last trip, and it had been then that the Darkfriend
pursuit began. And Trollocs, too, for a time. He had heard
that Whitebridge had been burned to the ground right after
he sailed from there, and there had been rumors of Myrddraal as well as Trollocs. It was that, all of it together, that
had first convinced him he was not imagining things, that
had had him on guard when that first odd commission was
offered, too much money for a simple voyage to Tear, and a
thin tale for a reason.

Digging into his chest, he set out on the desk what he had
bought in Maradon. A lightstick, left from the Age of Legends, or so it was said. Certainly no one knew the making
of them any longer. Expensive, that, and rarer than an honest magistrate. It looked like a plain glass rod, thicker than
his thumb and not quite as long as his forearm, but when
held in the hand it glowed as brightly as a lantern. Lightsticks shattered like glass, too; he had nearly lost *Spray* in
the fire caused by the first he had owned. A small, age-dark
ivory carving of a man holding a sword. The fellow who
sold it claimed if you held it long enough you started to
feel warm. Domon never had, and neither had any of the
crew he let hold it, but it was old, and that was enough for

Domon. The skull of a cat as big as a lion, and so old it
was turned to stone. But no lion had ever had fangs, almost
tusks, a foot long. And a thick disk the size of a man's hand,
half white and half black, a sinuous line separating the colors. The shopkeeper in Maradon had said it was from the
Age of Legends, thinking he lied, but Domon had haggled
only a little before paying, because he recognized what the
shopkeeper did not: the ancient symbol of Aes Sedai from
before the Breaking of the World. Not a safe thing to have,
precisely, but neither a thing to be passed up by a man with
a fascination for the old.

And it was heartstone. The shopkeeper had never dared
add that to what he thought were lies. No riverfront shopkeeper in Maradon could afford even one piece of *cuendillar*.

The disk felt hard and smooth in his hand, and not at all
valuable except for its age, but he was afraid it was what
his pursuers were after. Lightsticks, and ivory carvings,
and even bones turned to stone, he had seen other times,
other places. Yet even knowing what they wanted—if he
did know—he still had no idea why, and he could no longer
be sure who his pursuers were. Tar Valon marks, and an
ancient Aes Sedai symbol. He scrubbed a hand across his
lips; the taste of fear lay bitter on his tongue.

A knock at the door. He set the disk down and pulled an
unrolled chart over what lay on his desk. "Come."

Yarin entered. "We're beyond the breakwater, Captain."

Domon felt a flash of surprise, then anger with himself.
He should never have gotten so engrossed that he failed to
feel *Spray* lifting on the swells. "Make west, Yarin. See to it."

"Ebou Dar, Captain?"

No far enough. No by five hundred leagues. "We'll put in
long enough for me to get charts and top the water barrels,
then we do sail west."

"West, Captain? Tremalking? The Sea Folk are tight
with any traders but their own."

"The Aryth Ocean, Yarin. Plenty of trade between Tarabon and Arad Doman, and hardly a Taraboner or Domani
bottom to worry about. They do no like the sea, I have
heard. And all those small towns on Toman Head, every
one holding itself free of any nation at all. We can even pick
up Saldaean furs and ice peppers brought down to Bandar
Eban."

Yarin shook his head slowly. He always looked at the dark side, but he was a good sailor. "Furs and peppers'll cost more there than running upriver for them, Captain. And I hear there's some kind of war. If Tarabon and Arad Doman are fighting, there may be no trade. I doubt we'll make much off the towns on Toman Head alone, even if they are safe. Falme's the largest, and it is not big."

"The Taraboners and the Domani have always squabbled over Almoth Plain and Toman Head. Even if it has come to blows this time, a careful man can always find trade. West, Yarin."

When Yarin had gone topside, Domon quickly added the black-and-white disk to the cubbyhole, and stowed the rest back in the bottom of his chest. *Darkfriends or Aes Sedai, I'll no run the way they want me. Fortune prick me, I'll no.*

Feeling safe for the first time in months, Domon went on deck as *Spray* heeled to catch the wind and put her bow west into the night-dark sea.

CHAPTER

10

The Hunt Begins

I ngtar set a fast pace for the beginning of a long journey, fast enough that Rand worried a little about the horses. The animals could keep up the trot for hours, but there was still most of the day ahead, and likely days more beyond that. The way Ingtar's face was set, though, Rand thought he might intend to catch those who had stolen the Horn in the first day, in the first hour. Remembering his voice when he swore his oath to the Amyrlin Seat, Rand would not have been surprised. He kept his mouth shut, though. It was Lord Ingtar's command; as friendly as he had been to Rand, he still would not appreciate a shepherd giving advice.

Hurin rode a pace behind Ingtar, but it was the sniffer who led them south, pointing the way for Ingtar. The land was rolling, forested hills, thick with fir and leatherleaf and oak, but the path Hurin set led almost straight as an arrow, never wavering except to go around a few of the taller hills, where the way was clearly quicker around than over. The Gray Owl banner rippled in the wind.

Rand tried to ride with Mat and Perrin, but when Rand let his horse drop back to them, Mat nudged Perrin, and Perrin reluctantly galloped to the head of the column with Mat. Telling himself there was no point riding at the back by himself, Rand rode back to the front. They fell to the rear again, Mat again urging Perrin.

Burn them. I only want to apologize. He felt alone. It did not help that he knew it was his own fault.

Atop one hill, Uno dismounted to examine ground churned by hooves. He poked at some horse droppings and grunted. "Bloody well moving fast, my Lord." He had a voice that sounded as if he were shouting when he was just speaking. "We've not made up an hour on them. Burn me, we may have lost a flaming hour. They'll kill their bloody horses, the way they're going." He fingered a hoofed track. "No horse, that. Bloody Trolloc. Some flaming goat feet over there."

"We will catch them," Ingtar said grimly.

"Our horses, my Lord. Does no good to ride them into the bloody ground before we do catch up, my Lord. Even if they do kill their horses, bloody Trollocs can keep going longer than horses."

"We will catch them. Mount, Uno."

Uno looked at Rand with his one eye, then shrugged and climbed into his saddle. Ingtar took them down the far slope at a run, half sliding all the way to the bottom, and galloped up the next.

Why did he look at me that way, Rand wondered. Uno was one of those who had never shown much friendliness toward him. It was not like Masema's open dislike; Uno was not friendly with anyone except a few veterans as grizzled as himself. *Surely* he *doesn't believe that tale about me being a lord.*

Uno spent his time studying the country ahead, but when he caught Rand looking at him, he gave back stare for stare, and never said a word. It did not mean much. He would stare Ingtar in the eye, too. That was Uno's way.

The path chosen by the Darkfriends— *And what else,* Rand wondered; Hurin kept muttering about "something worse"—who had stolen the Horn never came close to any village. Rand saw villages, from one hilltop to another, with a mile or more of up-and-down country between, but there was never one close enough to make out the people in the streets. Or close enough for those people to make out a party heading south. There were farms, too, with low-eaved houses and tall barns and smoking chimneys, on hilltops and on hillsides and in the bottoms, but never one close enough for the farmer to have seen their quarry.

Eventually even Ingtar had to realize that the horses could not keep on as they were going. Rand heard muttered curses, and Ingtar pounded his thigh with a gauntleted fist, but finally he ordered everyone to dismount. They trotted, leading their horses, uphill and down, for a mile, then mounted and rode again. Then it was down again and trot. Trot a mile, then ride a mile. Trot, then ride.

Rand was surprised to see Loial grinning when they were down on the ground, toiling up a hill. The Ogier had been uneasy about riding and horses when they first met, preferring to trust to his own feet, but Rand thought he had long gotten over that.

"Do you like to run, Rand?" Loial laughed. "I do. I was the fastest in Stedding Shangtai. I outran a horse, once."

Rand only shook his head. He did not want to waste breath on talk. He looked for Mat and Perrin, but they were still at the back, too many men between for Rand to make them out. He wondered how the Shienarans could manage this in their armor. Not a one of them slowed or voiced a complaint. Uno did not even look as if he were breaking a sweat, and the bannerman never let the Gray Owl waver.

It was a quick pace, but twilight began to close without any sight of those they hunted except their tracks. At last, reluctantly, Ingtar called a halt to make camp for the night in the forest. The Shienarans went about getting fires started and setting picket-lines for the horses with a smooth economy of effort born of long experience. Ingtar posted six guards, in pairs, for the first watch.

Rand's first order of business was finding his bundle in the wicker panniers from the packhorses. It was not hard—there were few personal bundles among the supplies—but when he had it open, he let out a shout that brought every man in the camp erect with sword in hand.

Ingtar came running. "What is it? Peace, did someone get through? I did not hear the guards."

"It's these coats," Rand growled, still staring at what he had unpacked. One coat was black, embroidered with silver thread, the other white worked in gold. Both had herons on the collars, and both were at least as ornate as the scarlet coat he was wearing. "The servants told me I had two good, serviceable coats in here. Look at them!"

Ingtar sheathed his sword over his shoulder. The other men began to settle back down. "Well, they are serviceable."

"I can't wear these. I can't go around dressed like this all the time."

"You can wear them. A coat's a coat. I understand Moiraine Sedai herself saw to your packing. Maybe Aes Sedai

do not exactly understand what a man wears in the field."
Ingtar grinned. "After we catch these Trollocs, perhaps
we'll have a feast. You will be dressed for it, at least, even
if the rest of us are not." He strolled back to where the cook
fires were already burning.

Rand had not moved since Ingtar mentioned Moiraine.
He stared at the coats. *What is she doing? Whatever it is, I
will not be used.* He bundled everything together again and
stuffed the bundle back into the pannier. *I can always go
naked,* he thought bitterly.

Shienarans took turns at the cooking when they were in
the field, and Masema was stirring the kettle when Rand
returned to the fires. The smell of a stew made from turnips, onions, and dried meat settled over the camp. Ingtar
was served first, and then Uno, but everyone else stood in
line however they happened to come. Masema slopped a big
ladle of stew on Rand's plate; Rand stepped back quickly to
keep from getting the overflow on his coat, and made room
for the next man while sucking a burned thumb. Masema
stared at him, with a fixed grin that never reached his eyes.
Until Uno stepped up and cuffed him.

"We didn't bloody bring enough for you to be spilling it
on the flaming ground." The one-eyed man looked at Rand
and left. Masema rubbed his ear, but his glare followed
Rand.

Rand went to join Ingtar and Loial, sitting on the ground
under a spreading oak. Ingtar had his helmet off, on the
ground beside him, but otherwise he was fully armored.
Mat and Perrin were already there, eating hungrily. Mat
gave a broad sneer at Rand's coat, but Perrin barely looked
up, golden eyes shining in the half-light from the fires, before bending back to his plate.

At least they didn't leave this time.

He sat cross-legged on the other side of Ingtar from them.
"I wish I knew why Uno keeps looking at me. It's probably
this bloody coat."

Ingtar paused thoughtfully around a mouthful of stew.
Finally he said, "Uno no doubt wonders if you are worthy
of a heron-mark blade." Mat snorted loudly, but Ingtar went
on unperturbed. "Do not let Uno upset you. He would treat
Lord Agelmar like a raw recruit if he could. Well, perhaps
not Agelmar, but anyone else. He has a tongue like a file,

but he gives good advice. He should; he's been campaigning since before I was born. Listen to his advice, don't mind his tongue, and you will do all right with Uno."

"I thought he was like Masema." Rand shoveled stew into his mouth. It was too hot, but he gulped it down. They had not eaten since leaving Fal Dara, and he had been too worried to eat that morning. His stomach rumbled, reminding him it was past time. He wondered if telling Masema he liked the food would help. "Masema acts like he hates me, and I don't understand it."

"Masema served three years in the Eastern Marches," Ingtar said. "At Ankor Dail, against the Aiel." He stirred his stew with his spoon, frowning. "I ask no questions, mind. If Lan Dai Shan and Moiraine Sedai want to say you are from Andor, from the Two Rivers, then you are. But Masema can't get the look of the Aiel out of his head, and when he sees you. . . ." He shrugged. "I ask no questions."

Rand dropped his spoon in the plate with a sigh. "Everybody thinks I'm somebody I am not. I am from the Two Rivers, Ingtar. I grew tabac with—with my father, and tended his sheep. That is what I am. A farmer and shepherd from the Two Rivers."

"He's from the Two Rivers," Mat said scornfully. "I grew up with him, though you'd never know it now. You put this Aiel nonsense in his head on top of what's already there, and the Light knows what we'll have. An Aiel lord, maybe."

"No," Loial said, "he has the look. You remember, Rand, I remarked on it once, though I thought it was just because I didn't know you humans well enough then. Remember? 'Till shade is gone, till water is gone, into the Shadow with teeth bared, screaming defiance with the last breath, to spit in Sightblinder's eye on the Last Day.' You remember, Rand."

Rand stared at his plate. *Wrap a shoufa around your head, and you would be the image of an Aielman.* That had been Gawyn, brother to Elayne, the Daughter-Heir of Andor. *Everybody thinks I'm somebody I'm not.*

"What was that?" Mat asked. "About spitting in the Dark One's eye."

"That's how long the Aiel say they'll fight," Ingtar said, "and I don't doubt they will. Except for peddlers and gleemen, Aiel divide the world in two. Aiel, and enemies. They changed that for Cairhien five hundred years ago, for some reason no one but an Aiel could understand, but I do not think they will ever do so again."

"I suppose not," Loial sighed. "But they do let the Tuatha'an, the Traveling People, cross the Waste. And they don't see Ogier as enemies, either, though I doubt any of us would want to go out into the Waste. Aiel come to Stedding Shangtai sometimes to trade for sung wood. A hard people, though."

Ingtar nodded. "I wish I had some as hard. Half as hard."

"Is that a joke?" Mat laughed. "If I ran a mile wearing all the iron you're wearing, I would fall down and sleep a week. You've done it mile after mile all day."

"Aiel are hard," Ingtar said. "Man and woman, hard. I've fought them, and I know. They will run fifty miles, and fight a battle at the end of it. They're death walking, with any weapon or none. Except a sword. They will not touch a sword, for some reason. Or ride a horse, not that they need to. If you have a sword, and the Aielman has his bare hands, it is an even fight. If you're good. They herd cattle and goats where you or I would die of thirst before the day was done. They dig their villages into huge rock spires out in the Waste. They've been there since the Breaking, near enough. Artur Hawkwing tried to dig them out and was bloodied, the only major defeats he ever suffered. By day the air in the Aiel Waste shimmers with heat, and by night it freezes. And an Aiel will give you that blue-eyed stare and tell you there is no place on earth he would rather be. He won't be lying, either. If they ever tried to come out, we would be hard-pressed to stop them. The Aiel War lasted three years, and that was only four out of thirteen clans."

"Gray eyes from his mother doesn't make him an Aiel," Mat said.

Ingtar shrugged. "As I said, I ask no questions."

When Rand finally settled down for the night, his head hummed with unwanted thoughts. *Image of an Aielman. Moiraine Sedai wants to say you're from the Two Rivers. Aiel ravaged all the way to Tar Valon. Born on the slopes of Dragonmount. The Dragon Reborn.*

"I will not be used," he muttered, but sleep was a long time coming.

Ingtar broke camp before the sun was up in the morn-

ing. They had breakfasted and were riding south while
the clouds in the east were still red with sunrise to come
and dew still hung on the leaves. This time Ingtar put out
scouts, and though the pace was hard, it was no longer
horse-killing. Rand thought maybe Ingtar had realized they
were not going to do it all in a day. The trail still led south,
Hurin said. Until, two hours after the sun rose, one of the
scouts came galloping back.

"Abandoned camp ahead, my Lord. Just on that hilltop
there. Must have been at least thirty or forty of them there
last night, my Lord."

Ingtar put spurs to horse as if he had been told the Darkfriends were still there, and Rand had to keep pace or be
trampled by the Shienarans who galloped up the hill behind
him.

There was not much to see. The cold ashes of campfires,
well hidden in the trees, with what looked like the remnants
of a meal tossed in them. A refuse heap too near the fires
and already buzzing with flies.

Ingtar kept the others back, and dismounted to walk
through the campsite with Uno, examining the ground.
Hurin rode the circumference of the site, sniffing. Rand sat
his stallion with the other men; he had no desire for any
closer look at a place where Trollocs and Darkfriends had
camped. And a Fade. *And something worse.*

Mat scrambled up the hill afoot and stalked into the
campsite. "Is this what a Darkfriend camp looks like?
Smells a bit, but I can't say it looks any different from anybody else's." He kicked at one of the ash heaps, knocking
out a piece of burned bone, and stooped to pick it up. "What
do Darkfriends eat? Doesn't look like a sheep bone, or
a cow."

"There was murder done here," Hurin said mournfully.
He scrubbed at his nose with a kerchief. "Worse than murder."

"There were Trollocs here," Ingtar said, looking straight
at Mat. "I suppose they got hungry, and the Darkfriends
were handy." Mat dropped the blackened bone; he looked as
if he were going to be sick.

"They are not going south any longer, my Lord," Hurin
said. That took everyone's attention. He pointed back, to the
northeast. "Maybe they've decided to break for the Blight

after all. Go around us. Maybe they were just trying to put us off by coming south." He did not sound as if he believed it. He sounded puzzled.

"Whatever they were trying," Ingtar snarled, "I'll have them now. Mount!"

Little more than an hour later, though, Hurin drew rein. "They changed again, my Lord. South again. And they killed someone else here."

There were no ashes there, in the gap between two hills, but a few minutes' search found the body. A man curled up and stuffed under some bushes. The back of his head was smashed in, and his eyes still bulged with the force of the blow. No one recognized him, though he was wearing Shienaran clothes.

"We'll waste no time burying Darkfriends," Ingtar growled. "We ride south." He suited his own words almost before they were out of his mouth.

The day was the same as the day before had been, though. Uno studied tracks and droppings, and said they had gained a little ground on their quarry. Twilight came with no sight of Trollocs or Darkfriends, and the next morning there was another abandoned camp—and another murder done, so Hurin said—and another change of direction, this time to the northwest. Less than two hours on that track found another body, a man with his skull split open by an axe, and another change of direction. South again. Again gaining ground, by Uno's reading of the tracks. Again seeing nothing but distant farms until nightfall. And the next day was the same, changes in direction, murders and all. And the next.

Every day brought them a little closer behind their prey, but Ingtar fumed. He suggested cutting straight across when the trail changed direction of a morning—surely they would come on the trail heading south again, and gain more time—and before anyone could speak, he said it was a bad idea, in case this once the men they hunted did not turn south. He urged everyone to greater speed, to start earlier and ride till full dark. He reminded them of the charge the Amyrlin Seat had given them, to recover the Horn of Valere, and let nothing bar their way. He spoke of the glory they would have, their names remembered in story and history, in gleemen's tales and bards' songs, the men who found the

Horn. He talked as if he could not stop, and he stared down the trail they followed as if his hope of the Light lay at the end of it. Even Uno began to look at him askance.

And so they came to the River Erinin.

It could not properly be called a village at all, to Rand's mind. He sat his horse among the trees, peering up at half a dozen small houses with wood-shingled roofs and eaves almost to the ground, on a hilltop overlooking the river beneath the morning sun. Few people passed this way. It was only a few hours since they had broken camp, but past time for them to have found the remains of the Darkfriends' resting place if the pattern held. They had seen nothing of the sort, however.

The river itself was not much like the mighty Erinin of story, here so far toward its source in the Spine of the World. Perhaps sixty paces of swift water to the far bank, lined with trees, and a barge-like ferry on a thick rope spanning the distance. The ferry sat snugged against the other side.

For once the trail had led straight to human habitation. Straight to the houses on the hill. No one moved on the single dirt street around which the dwellings clustered.

"Ambush, my Lord?" Uno said softly.

Ingtar gave the necessary orders, and the Shienarans unlimbered their lances, sweeping around to encircle the houses. At a hand signal from Ingtar they galloped between the houses from four directions, thundering in with eyes searching, lances ready, dust rising under their hooves. Nothing moved but them. They drew rein, and the dust began to settle.

Rand returned to his quiver the arrow he had nocked, and slung his bow on his back again. Mat and Perrin did the same. Loial and Hurin had just waited there where Ingtar had left them, watching uneasily.

Ingtar waved, and Rand and the others rode up to join the Shienarans.

"I don't like the smell of this place," Perrin muttered as they came among the houses. Hurin gave him a look, and he stared back until Hurin dropped his eyes. "It smells wrong."

"Bloody Darkfriends and Trollocs went straight through, my Lord," Uno said, pointing to a few tracks not chopped to pieces by the Shienarans. "Straight through to the goat-kissing ferry, which they bloody left on the other side. Blood and bloody ashes! We're flaming lucky they didn't cut it adrift."

"Where are the people?" Loial asked.

Doors stood open, curtains flapped at open windows, but no one had come out for all the thunder of hooves.

"Search the houses," Ingtar commanded. Men dismounted and ran to comply, but they came back shaking their heads.

"They're just gone, my Lord," Uno said. "Just bloody gone, burn me. Like they'd picked up and decided to flaming walk away in the middle of the bloody day." He stopped suddenly, pointing urgently to a house behind Ingtar. "There's a woman at that window. How I bloody missed her. . . ." He was running for the house before anyone else could move.

"Don't frighten her!" Ingtar shouted. "Uno, we need information. The Light blind you, Uno, don't frighten her!" The one-eyed man disappeared through the open door. Ingtar raised his voice again. "We will not harm you, good lady. We are Lord Agelmar's oathmen, from Fal Dara. Do not be afraid! We will not harm you."

A window at the top of the house flew up, and Uno stuck his head out, staring around wildly. With an oath he pulled back. Thumps and clatters marked his passage back, as if he were kicking things in frustration. Finally he appeared from the doorway.

"Gone, my Lord. But she was there. A woman in a white dress, at the window. I saw her. I even thought I saw her inside, for a moment, but then she was gone, and. . . ." He took a deep breath. "The house is empty, my Lord." It was a measure of his agitation that he did not curse.

"Curtains," Mat muttered. "He's jumping at bloody curtains." Uno gave him a sharp look, then returned to his horse.

"Where did they go?" Rand asked Loial. "Do you think they ran off when the Darkfriends came?" *And Trollocs, and a Myrddraal. And Hurin's something worse. Smart people, if they ran as hard as they could.*

"I fear the Darkfriends took them, Rand," Loial said slowly. He grimaced, almost a snarl with his broad nose like a snout. "For the Trollocs." Rand swallowed and wished he had not asked; it was never pleasant to think on how Trollocs fed.

"Whatever was done here," Ingtar said, "our Darkfriends did it. Hurin, was there violence here? Killing? Hurin!"

The sniffer gave a start in his saddle and looked around wildly. He had been staring across the river. "Violence, my Lord? Yes. Killing, no. Or not exactly." He glanced sideways at Perrin. "I've never smelled anything exactly like it before, my Lord. But there was hurting done."

"Is there any doubt they crossed over? Have they doubled back again?"

"They crossed, my Lord." Hurin looked uneasily at the far bank. "They crossed. What they did on the other side, though. . . ." He shrugged.

Ingtar nodded. "Uno, I want that ferry back on this side. And I want the other side scouted before we cross. Just because there was no ambush here doesn't mean there will not be one when we are split by the river. That ferry does not look big enough to carry us all in one trip. See to it."

Uno bowed, and in moments Ragan and Masema were helping each other out of their armor. Stripped down to breechclouts, with a dagger stuck behind in the small of the back, they trotted to the river on horsemen's bowed legs and waded in, beginning to work their way hand over hand along the thick rope along which the ferry ran. The cable sagged enough in the middle to put them in the river to their waists, and the current was strong, pulling them downstream, yet in less time than Rand expected they were hauling themselves over the slatted sides of the ferry. Drawing their daggers, they disappeared into the trees.

After what seemed like forever, the two men reappeared and began pulling the ferry slowly across. The barge butted against the bank below the village, and Masema tied it off while Ragan trotted up to where Ingtar waited. His face was pale, the arrow scar on his cheek sharp, and he sounded shaken.

"The far bank. . . . There is no ambush on the far bank, my Lord, but. . . ." He bowed deeply, still wet and shivering from his excursion. "My Lord, you must see for yourself. The big stoneoak, fifty paces south from the landing. I cannot say the words. You must see it yourself."

Ingtar frowned, looking from Ragan to the other bank. Finally, he said, "You have done well, Ragan. Both of you have." His voice became more brisk. "Find these men something to dry themselves on from the houses, Uno. And see if anybody left water on for tea. Put something hot into them, if you can. Then bring the second file and the pack animals over." He turned to Rand. "Well, are you ready to see the south bank of the Erinin?" He did not wait for an answer, but rode down to the ferry with Hurin and half the lancers.

Rand hesitated only a moment before following. Loial went with him. To his surprise, Perrin rode down ahead of them, looking grim. Some of the lancers, making gruff jokes, dismounted to haul on the rope and walk the ferry over.

Mat waited until the last minute, when one of the Shienarans was untying the ferry, before he kicked his horse and crowded aboard. "I have to come sooner or later, don't I?" he said, breathless, to no one in particular. "I have to find it."

Rand shook his head. With Mat looking as healthy as he ever had, he had almost forgotten why he was along. *To find the dagger. Let Ingtar have the Horn. I just want the dagger for Mat.* "We will find it, Mat."

Mat scowled at him—with a sneering glance for his fine red coat—and turned away. Rand sighed.

"It will all come right, Rand," Loial said quietly. "Somehow, it will."

The current took the ferry as it was hauled out from the bank, tugging it against the cable with a sharp creak. The lancers were odd ferrymen, walking the deck in helmets and armor, with swords on their backs, but they took the ferry out into the river well enough.

"This is how we left home," Perrin said suddenly. "At Taren Ferry. The ferrymen's boots clunking on the deck, and the water gurgling around the ferry. This is how we left. It will be worse, this time."

"How can it be worse?" Rand asked. Perrin did not answer. He searched the far bank, and his golden eyes almost seemed to shine, but not with eagerness.

After a minute, Mat asked, "How can it be worse?"

"It will be. I can smell it," was all Perrin would say. Hurin eyed him nervously, but then Hurin seemed to be eyeing everything nervously since they had left Fal Dara.

The ferry bumped against the south bank with a hollow thud of stout planks against hard clay, almost under overhanging trees, and the Shienarans who had been hauling on the rope mounted their horses, except for two Ingtar told to take the ferry back over for the others. The rest followed Ingtar up the bank.

"Fifty paces to a big stoneoak," Ingtar said as they rode into the trees. He sounded too matter-of-fact. If Ragan could not speak of it. . . . Some of the soldiers eased the swords on their backs, and held their lances ready.

At first Rand thought the figures hanging by their arms from the thick gray limbs of the stoneoak were scarecrows. Crimson scarecrows. Then he recognized the two faces. Changu, and the other man who had been on guard with him. Nidao. Eyes staring, teeth bared in a rictus of pain. They had lived a long time after it began.

Perrin made a sound in his throat, nearly a growl.

"As bad as ever I've seen, my Lord," Hurin said faintly. "As bad as ever I've smelled, excepting the dungeon at Fal Dara that night."

Frantically Rand sought the void. The flame seemed to get in the way, the queasy light fluttering in time with his convulsive swallows, but he pushed on until he had wrapped himself in emptiness. The queasiness pulsed in the void with him, though. Not outside, for once, but inside. *No wonder, looking at this.* The thought skittered across the void like a drop of water on a hot griddle. *What happened to them?*

"Skinned alive," he heard someone behind him say, and the sounds of somebody else retching. He thought it was Mat, but it was all far away from him, inside the void. But that nauseous flickering was in there, too. He thought he might throw up himself.

"Cut them down," Ingtar said harshly. He hesitated a moment, then added, "Bury them. We cannot be sure they were Darkfriends. They could have been taken prisoner. They could have been. Let them know the last embrace of the mother, at least." Men rode forward gingerly with knives; even for battle-hardened Shienarans it was no easy task, cutting down the flayed corpses of men they knew.

"Are you all right, Rand?" Ingtar said. "I am not used to this either."

"I . . . am all right, Ingtar." Rand let the void vanish. He felt less sick without it; his stomach still curdled, but it was better. Ingtar nodded and turned his horse so he could watch the men working.

The burial was simple. Two holes dug in the ground, and the bodies laid in as the rest of the Shienarans watched in silence. The grave diggers began shoveling earth into the graves with no more ado.

Rand was shocked, but Loial explained softly. "Shienarans believe we all came from earth, and must return to earth. They never use coffins or shrouds, and the bodies are never clothed. The earth must hold the body. The last embrace of the mother, they call it. And there are never any words except 'The Light shine on you, and the Creator shelter you. The last embrace of the mother welcome you home.' " Loial sighed and shook his huge head. "I do not think anyone will say them this time. No matter what Ingtar says, Rand, there cannot be much doubt that Changu and Nidao slew the guards at the Dog Gate and let the Darkfriends into the keep. It had to be they who were responsible for all of it."

"Then who shot the arrow at—at the Amyrlin?" Rand swallowed. *Who shot at me?* Loial said nothing.

Uno arrived with the rest of the men and the packhorses as the last earth was being shoveled onto the graves. Someone told him what they had found, and the one-eyed man spat. "Goat-kissing Trollocs do that along the Blight, sometimes. When they want to shake your bloody nerve, or flaming warn you not to follow. Burn me if it works here, either."

Before they rode away, Ingtar paused on his horse beside the unmarked graves, two mounds of bare earth that looked too small to hold men. After a moment he said, "The Light shine on you, and the Creator shelter you. The last embrace of the mother welcome you home." When he raised his head, he looked at each man in turn. There was no expression on any face, least of all on Ingtar's. "They saved Lord Agelmar at Tarwin's Gap," he said. Several of the lancers nodded. Ingtar turned his horse. "Which way, Hurin?"

"South, my Lord."

"Take the trail! We hunt!"

The forest soon gave way to gently rolling flatland, sometimes crossed by a shallow stream that had dug itself a high-banked channel, with never more than a low rise or a squat hill that barely deserved the name. Perfect country for the horses. Ingtar took advantage of it, setting a steady, ground-covering pace. Occasionally Rand saw what might have been a farmhouse in the distance, and once what he thought was a village, with smoke rising from chimneys a few miles off and something flashing white in the sun, but the land near them stayed empty of human life, long swathes of grass dotted with brush and occasional trees, with now and again a small thicket, never more than a hundred paces across.

Ingtar put out scouts, two men riding ahead, in sight only when they topped an occasional rise. He had a silver whistle hanging around his neck to call them back if Hurin said the trail had veered, but it did not. South. Always south.

"We will reach the field of Talidar in three or four days at this rate," Ingtar said as they rode. "Artur Hawkwing's greatest single victory, when the Halfmen led the Trollocs out of the Blight against him. Six days and nights, it lasted, and when it was done, the Trollocs fled back into the Blight and never dared challenge him again. He raised a monument there to his victory, a spire a hundred spans high. He would not let them put his own name on it, but rather the names of every man who fell, and a golden sun at the top, symbol that there the Light had triumphed over the Shadow."

"I would like to see that," Loial said. "I have never heard of this monument."

Ingtar was silent for a moment, and when he spoke his voice was quiet. "It is not there any longer, Builder. When Hawkwing died, the ones who fought over his empire could not bear to leave a monument to a victory of his, even if it did not mention his name. There's nothing left but the mound where it stood. In three or four days we can see that, at least." His tone did not allow much conversation afterwards.

With the sun hanging golden overhead, they passed a structure, square and made of plastered brick, less than a mile from their path. It was not tall, no more than two stories still standing anywhere he saw, but it covered a good hide of ground. An air of long abandonment hung about it, roofs gone except for a few stretches of dark tile clinging to

bits of rafter, most of the once-white plaster fallen to bare
the dark, weathered brick beneath, walls fallen to show
courtyards and decaying chambers inside. Brush, and even
trees, grew in the cracks of what had once been courtyards.

"A manor house," Ingtar explained. The little humor he
had regained seemed to fade as he looked at the structure.
"When Harad Dakar still stood, I expect the manorman
farmed this land for a league around. Orchards, maybe. The
Hardani loved their orchards."

"Harad Dakar?" Rand said, and Ingtar snorted.

"Does no one learn history any longer? Harad Dakar, the
capital city of Hardan, which nation this once was that we
are riding across."

"I've seen an old map," Rand replied in a tight voice. "I
know about the nations that aren't there anymore. Maredo,
and Goaban, and Caralain. But there wasn't any Hardan on it."

"There were once others that are gone now, too," Loial
said. "Mar Haddon, which is now Haddon Mirk, and Almoth.
Kintara. The War of the Hundred Years cut Artur Hawkwing's empire into many nations, large and small. The small
were gobbled up by the large, or else united, like Altara
and Murandy. Forced together would be a better word than
united, I suppose."

"So what happened to them?" Mat demanded. Rand had
not noticed Perrin and Mat ride up to join them. They had
been at the rear, as far from Rand al'Thor as they could get,
the last he had seen.

"They could not hold together," the Ogier replied. "Crops
failed, or trade failed. People failed. Something failed in
each case, and the nation dwindled. Often neighboring
countries absorbed the land, when the nations were gone,
but they never lasted, those annexations. In time, the land
truly was abandoned. Some villages hang on here and there,
but mostly they have all gone to wilderness. It is nearly
three hundred years since Harad Dakar was finally abandoned, but even before that it was a shell, with a king who
could not control what happened inside the city walls. Harad Dakar itself is completely gone now, I understand. All
the towns and cities of Hardan are gone, the stone carted
away by farmers and villagers for their own use. Most of
the farms and villages made with it are gone, too. So I read,
and I've seen nothing to change it."

"It was quite a quarry, Harad Dakar, for almost a hundred years," Ingtar said bitterly. "The people left, finally, and then the city was hauled away, stone by stone. All faded away, and what has not gone is fading. Everything, everywhere, fading. There is hardly a nation that truly controls the land it claims on a map, and there is hardly a land that claims today on a map what it did even a hundred years ago. When the War of the Hundred Years ended, a man rode from one nation into another without end from the Blight to the Sea of Storms. Now we can ride through wilderness claimed by no nation for almost the whole of the land. We in the Borderlands have our battle with the Blight to keep us strong, and whole. Perhaps they did not have what they needed to keep them strong. You say they failed, Builder? Yes, they failed, and what nation standing whole today will fail tomorrow? We are being swept away, humankind. Swept away like flotsam on a flood. How long until there is nothing left but the Borderlands? How long before we, too, go under, and there is nothing left but Trollocs and Myrddraal all the way to the Sea of Storms?"

There was a shocked silence. Not even Mat broke it. Ingtar rode lost in his own dark thoughts.

After a time the scouts came galloping back, straight in the saddles, lances erect against the sky. "A village ahead, my Lord. We were not seen, but it lies directly in our line of march."

Ingtar shook himself out of his brown study, but did not speak until they had reached the crest of a low ridge looking down on the village, and then it was only to command a halt while he dug a looking glass from his saddlebags and raised it to peer at the village.

Rand studied the village with interest. It was as big as Emond's Field, though that was not very big compared to some of the towns he had seen since leaving the Two Rivers, much less the cities. The houses were all low and plastered with white clay, and they appeared to have grass growing on sloping roofs. A dozen windmills, scattered through the village, turned lazily, their long, cloth-covered arms flashing white in the sun. A low wall encircled the village, grassy dirt and chest high, and outside that was a wide ditch with sharpened stakes thick in the bottom. There was no gate in the one opening he could see in the wall, but he supposed it could be blocked easily enough with a cart or wagon. He could not see any people.

"Not even a dog in sight," Ingtar said, returning the looking glass to his saddlebags. "Are you sure they did not see you?" he asked the scouts.

"Not unless they have the Dark One's own luck, my Lord," one of the men replied. "We never crested the rise. We didn't see anyone moving then either, my Lord."

Ingtar nodded. "The trail, Hurin?"

Hurin drew a deep breath. "Toward the village, my Lord. Straight to it, as near as I can tell from here."

"Watch sharp," Ingtar commanded, gathering his reins. "And do not believe that they're friendly just because they smile. If there is anyone there." He led them down toward the village at a slow walk, and reached up to loosen his sword in its scabbard.

Rand heard the sounds of others behind him doing the same. After a moment, he eased his, too. Trying to stay alive was not the same as trying to be a hero, he decided.

"You think these people would help Darkfriends?" Perrin asked Ingtar. The Shienaran was slow in answering.

"They have no great love for Shienarans," he said finally. "They think we should protect them. Us, or the Cairhienin. Cairhien did claim this land, once the last King of Hardan died. All the way to the Erinin, they claimed it. They could not hold it, though. They gave up the claim nearly a hundred years ago. The few people who still live here don't have to worry about Trollocs this far south, but there are plenty of human brigands. That's why they have the wall, and the ditch. All their villages do. Their fields will be hidden in hollows around here, but no one will live outside the wall. They would swear fealty to any king who would give them his protection, but we have all we can do against the Trollocs. They do not love us for it, though." As they reached the opening in the low wall, he added again, "Watch sharp!"

All the streets led toward a village square, but there was no one in the streets, no one peering from a window. Not even a dog moved, not so much as a chicken. Nothing living. Open doors swung, creaking in the wind, counterpoint to the rhythmic squeak of the windmills. The horses' hooves sounded loud on the packed dirt of the street.

"Like at the ferry," Hurin muttered, "but different." He

rode hunched in his saddle, head down as if he were trying to hide behind his own shoulders. "Violence done, but . . . I don't know. It was bad here. It smells bad."

"Uno," Ingtar said, "take one file and search the houses. If you find anyone, bring them to me in the square. Do not frighten them this time, though. I want answers, not people running for their lives." He led the other soldiers toward the center of the village as Uno got his ten dismounted.

Rand hesitated, looking around. The creaking doors, the squealing windmills, the horses' hooves, all made too much noise, as if there were not another sound in the world. He scanned the houses. The curtains in an open window beat against the outside of the house. They all seemed lifeless. With a sigh he got down and walked to the nearest house, then stopped, staring at the door.

It's just a door. What are you afraid of? He wished he did not feel as if there was something waiting on the other side. He pushed it open.

Inside was a tidy room. Or had been. The table was set for a meal, ladder-back chairs gathered around, some plates already served. A few flies buzzed above bowls of turnips and peas, and more crawled on a cold roast sitting in its own congealed grease. There was a slice half carved from the roast, the fork still standing stuck in the meat and the carving knife lying partway in the platter as if dropped. Rand stepped inside.

Blink.

A smiling, bald-headed man in rough clothes laid a slice of meat on a plate held by a woman with a worn face. She was smiling, too, though. She added peas and turnips to the plate and passed it to one of the children lining the table. There were half a dozen children, boys and girls, from nearly grown down to barely tall enough to look over the table. The woman said something, and the girl taking the plate from her laughed. The man started to cut another slice.

Suddenly another girl screamed, pointing at the door to the street. The man dropped the carving knife and whirled, then he screamed, too, face tight with horror, and snatched up a child. The woman grabbed another, and motioned desperately to the others, her mouth working frantically, silently. They all scrabbled toward a door in the back of the room.

That door burst open, and—

Blink.

Rand could not move. The flies buzzing over the table sounded louder. His breath made a cloud in front of his mouth.

Blink.

A smiling, bald-headed man in rough clothes laid a slice of meat on a plate held by a woman with a worn face. She was smiling, too, though. She added peas and turnips to the plate and passed it to one of the children lining the table. There were half a dozen children, boys and girls, from nearly grown down to barely tall enough to look over the table. The woman said something, and the girl taking the plate from her laughed. The man started to cut another slice.

Suddenly another girl screamed, pointing at the door to the street. The man dropped the carving knife and whirled, then he screamed, too, face tight with horror, and snatched up a child. The woman grabbed another, and motioned desperately to the others, her mouth working frantically, silently. They all scrabbled toward the door in the back of the room.

That door burst open, and—

Blink.

Rand struggled, but his muscles seemed frozen. The room was colder; he wanted to shiver, but he could not move even that much. Flies crawled all over the table. He groped for the void. The sour light was there, but he did not care. He had to—

Blink.

A smiling, bald-headed man in rough clothes laid a slice of meat on a plate held by a woman with a worn face. She was smiling, too, though. She added peas and turnips to the plate and passed it to one of the children lining the table. There were half a dozen children, boys and girls, from nearly grown down to barely tall enough to look over the table. The woman said something, and the girl taking the plate from her laughed. The man started to cut another slice.

Suddenly another girl screamed, pointing at the door to the street. The man dropped the carving knife and whirled, then he screamed, too, face tight with horror, and snatched up a child. The woman grabbed another, and motioned desperately to the others, her mouth working frantically, silently. They all scrabbled toward a door in the back of the room.

That door burst open, and—

Blink.

The room was freezing. *So cold.* Flies blackened the table; the walls were a shifting mass of flies, the floor, the ceiling, all black with them. They crawled on Rand, covering him, crawled over his face, his eyes, into his nose, his mouth. *Light, help me. Cold.* The flies buzzed like thunder. *Cold.* It penetrated the void, mocking the emptiness, encasing him in ice. Desperately he reached for the flickering light. His stomach twisted, but the light was warm. Warm. Hot. He was hot.

Suddenly he was tearing at . . . something. He did not know what, or how. Cobwebs made of steel. Moonbeams carved from stone. They crumbled at his touch, but he knew he had not touched anything. They shriveled and melted with the heat that surged through him, heat like a forge fire, heat like the world burning, heat like—

It was gone. Panting, he looked around with wide eyes. A few flies lay on the half-carved roast, in the platter. Dead flies. *Six flies. Only six.* There were more in the bowls, half a dozen tiny black specks among the cold vegetables. All dead. He staggered out into the street.

Mat was just coming out of a house across the street, shaking his head. "Nobody there," he told Perrin, still on his horse. "It looks like they just got up in the middle of supper and walked away."

A shout came from the square.

"They've found something," Perrin said, digging his heels into his horse's flanks. Mat scrambled into his saddle and galloped after him.

Rand mounted Red more slowly; the stallion shied as if feeling his unease. He glanced at the houses as he rode slowly toward the square, but he could not make himself look at them for long. *Mat went in one, and nothing happened to him.* He resolved not to set foot inside another house in that village no matter what. Booting Red, he quickened his pace.

Everyone was standing like statues in front of a large building with wide double doors. Rand did not think it could be an inn; there was no sign, for one thing. Perhaps a village meeting place. He joined the silent circle, and stared along with the rest.

There was a man spread-eagled across the doors with thick spikes through wrists and shoulders. More spikes had been driven into his eyes to hold his head up. Dark, dried blood made fans down his cheeks. Scuff marks on the wood behind his boots showed that he had been alive when it was done. When it began, anyway.

Rand's breath caught. Not a man. Those black clothes, blacker than black, had never been worn by any human. The wind flapped an end of the cloak caught behind the body—which it did not always, he knew too well; the wind did not always touch those clothes—but there had never been any eyes in that pale, bloodless face.

"Myrddraal," he breathed, and it was as if his speaking released all the others. They began to move again, and breathe.

"Who," Mat began, and had to stop to swallow. "Who could do this to a Fade?" His voice squeaked at the end.

"I don't know," Ingtar said. "I do not know." He looked around, examining faces, or perhaps counting to be sure everyone was there. "And I do not think we will learn anything here. We ride. Mount! Hurin, find the trail out of this place."

"Yes, my Lord. Yes. With pleasure. That way, my Lord. They're still heading south."

They rode away leaving the dead Myrddraal where it hung, the wind stirring its black cloak. Hurin was first beyond the wall, not waiting on Ingtar for a change, but Rand came close behind him.

CHAPTER
II

Glimmers of the Pattern

For once, Ingtar called a halt to the day's march with the sun still golden above the horizon. The toughened Shienarans were feeling the effects of what they had seen in the village. Ingtar had not stopped so early before, and the campsite he chose had the look of a place that could be defended. It was a deep hollow, almost round, and big enough to hold all the men and horses comfortably. A sparse thicket of scrub oak and leatherleaf covered the outer slopes. The rim itself stood more than high enough to hide anyone in the campsite even without the trees. The height nearly passed for a hill, in that country.

"All I'm bloody saying," he heard Uno tell Ragan as they dismounted, "is that I bloody saw her, burn you. Just before we found the goat-kissing Halfman. The same flaming woman as at the flaming ferry. She was there, and then she bloody wasn't. You say what you bloody want to, but you watch how you flaming say it, or I'll bloody skin you myself, and burn the goat-kissing hide, you sheep-gutted milk-drinker."

Rand paused with one foot on the ground and the other still in the stirrup. *The same woman? But there wasn't any woman at the ferry, just some curtains blowing in the wind. And she couldn't have gotten to that village ahead of us if there had been.* The village. . . .

He shied away from the thought. Even more than the Fade nailed to the door, he wanted to forget that room, and the flies, and the people who were there and not there. The Halfman had been real—everybody had seen that—but the room. . . . *Maybe I'm finally going mad.* He wished Moiraine was there to talk to. *Wishing for an Aes Sedai. You* are *a fool. You're well out of that, now stay out. But am I out? What happened there?*

"Packhorses and supplies in the middle," Ingtar commanded as the lancers went about setting up camp. "Rub the horses down, then saddle them again in case we must move quickly. Every man sleeps by his mount, and there'll be no fires tonight. Watch changes every two hours. Uno, I want scouts out, as far as they can ride and return before dark. I want to know what is out there."

He's feeling it, Rand thought. *It isn't just some Dark-friends and a few Trollocs and maybe a Fade anymore.* Just some Darkfriends and a few Trollocs, and maybe a Fade! Even a few days before there would not have been any "just" about it. Even in the Borderlands, even with the Blight less than a day's ride, Darkfriends and Trollocs and Myrddraal had been bad enough for a nightmare, then. Before he had seen a Myrddraal nailed to a door. *What in the Light could have done* that? *What* not *in the Light?* Before he had walked into a room where a family had had their supper and their laughter cut off. *I must have imagined it. I must have.* Even in his own head he did not sound very convincing. He had not imagined the wind on the tower top, or the Amyrlin saying—

"Rand?" He jumped as Ingtar spoke at his shoulder. "Are you going to stay all night with one foot in the stirrup?"

Rand put his other foot on the ground. "Ingtar, what happened back at that village?"

"Trollocs took them. The same as the people at the ferry. That is what happened. The Fade. . . ." Ingtar shrugged and stared down at a flat, canvas-wrapped bundle, large and square, in his arms; he stared at it as if he saw hidden secrets he would rather not know. "The Trollocs took them for food. They do it in villages and farms near the Blight, too, sometimes, if a raid gets past the border towers in the night. Sometimes we get the people back, and sometimes not. Sometimes we get them back and almost wish we hadn't. Trollocs don't always kill before they start butchering. And Halfmen like to have their . . . fun. That's worse than what the Trollocs do." His voice was as steady as if he were talking of every day, and perhaps he was, for a Shienaran soldier.

Rand took a deep breath to steady his stomach. "The Fade back there didn't have any fun, Ingtar. What could nail a Myrddraal to a door, alive?"

Ingtar hesitated, shaking his head, then pushed the big bundle at Rand. "Here. Moiraine Sedai told me to give you this at the first camp south of the Erinin. I don't know what is in it, but she said you would need it. She said to tell you to take care of it; your life may depend on it."

Rand took it reluctantly; his skin prickled at the touch of the canvas. There was something soft inside. Cloth, maybe. He held it gingerly. *He doesn't want to think about the Myrddraal either. What happened in that room?* He realized suddenly that for him, the Fade, or even that room, was preferable to thinking about what Moiraine might have sent him.

"I was told to tell you at the same time that if anything happens to me, the lances will follow you."

"Me!" Rand gasped, forgetting the bundle and everything else. Ingtar met his incredulous stare with a calm nod. "That's crazy! I've never led anything but a flock of sheep, Ingtar. They would not follow me anyway. Besides, Moiraine can't tell you who your second is. It's Uno."

"Uno and I were called to Lord Agelmar the morning we left. Moiraine Sedai was there, but it was Lord Agelmar who told me. You are second, Rand."

"But why, Ingtar? Why?" Moiraine's hand was bright and clear in it, hers and the Amyrlin's, pushing him along the path they had chosen, but he had to ask.

The Shienaran looked as if he did not understand it either, but he was a soldier, used to odd commands in the endless war along the Blight. "I heard rumors from the women's apartments that you were really a. . . ." He spread gauntleted hands. "No matter. I know you deny it. Just as you deny the look of your own face. Moiraine Sedai says you're a shepherd, but I never saw a shepherd with a heron-mark blade. No matter. I'll not claim I would have chosen you myself, but I think you have it in you to do what is needed. You will do your duty, if it comes to it."

Rand wanted to say it was no duty of his, but instead he said, "Uno knows about this. Who else, Ingtar?"

"All the lances. When we Shienarans ride, every man knows who is next in line if the man in command falls. A chain unbroken right down to the last man left, even if he's nothing but a horseholder. That way, you see, even if he *is* the last man, he is not just a straggler running and trying to stay alive. He has the command, and duty calls him to do what must be done. If I go to the last embrace of the mother, the duty is yours. You will find the Horn, and you will take it where it belongs. You will." There was a peculiar emphasis in Ingtar's last words.

The bundle in Rand's arms seemed to weigh ten stone. *Light, she could be a hundred leagues off, and she still reaches out and tugs the leash. This way, Rand. That way. You're the Dragon Reborn, Rand.* "I don't want the duty, Ingtar. I will not take it. Light, I'm just a shepherd! Why won't anybody believe that?"

"You will do your duty, Rand. When the man at the top of the chain fails, everything below him falls apart. Too much is falling apart. Too much already. Peace favor your sword, Rand al'Thor."

"Ingtar, I—" But Ingtar was walking away, calling to see if Uno had the scouts out yet.

Rand stared at the bundle in his arms and licked his lips. He was afraid he knew what was in it. He wanted to look, yet he wanted to throw it in a fire without opening it; he thought he might, if he could be sure it would burn without anyone seeing what was inside, if he could be sure what was inside would burn at all. But he could not look there, where other eyes than his might see.

He glanced around the camp. The Shienarans were unloading the pack animals, some already handing out a cold supper of dried meat and flatbread. Mat and Perrin tended their horses, and Loial sat on a stone reading a book, with his long-stemmed pipe clenched between his teeth and a wisp of smoke curling above his head. Gripping the bundle as if afraid he might drop it, Rand sneaked into the trees.

He knelt in a small clearing sheltered by thick-foliaged branches and set the bundle on the ground. For a time he just stared at it. *She wouldn't have. She couldn't.* A small voice answered, *Oh, yes, she could. She could and would.* Finally he set about untying the small knots in the cords that bound it. Neat knots, tied with a precision that spoke loudly of Moiraine's own hand; no servant had done this for her. She would not have dared let any servant see.

When he had the last cord unfastened, he opened out what was folded inside with hands that felt numb, then stared at it, his mouth full of dust. It was all of one piece, neither woven, nor dyed, nor painted. A banner, white as snow, big enough to be seen the length of a field of battle. And across it marched a rippling figure like a serpent scaled in gold and crimson, but a serpent with four scaled legs, each tipped with five golden claws, a serpent with eyes like the sun and a golden lion's mane. He had seen it once before, and Moiraine had told him what it was. The banner of Lews Therin Telamon, Lews Therin Kinslayer, in the War of the Shadow. The banner of the Dragon.

"Look at that! Look what he's got, now!" Mat burst into the clearing. Perrin came after him more slowly. "First fancy coats," Mat snarled, "and now a banner! We'll hear no end of lording it now, with—" Mat got close enough to see the banner clearly, and his jaw dropped. "Light!" He stumbled back a step. "Burn me!" He had been there, too, when Moiraine named the banner. So had Perrin.

Anger boiled up in Rand, anger at Moiraine and the Amyrlin Seat, pushing him, pulling him. He snatched up the banner in both hands and shook it at Mat, words boiling out uncontrollably. "That's right! The Dragon's banner!" Mat took another step back. "Moiraine wants me to be a puppet on Tar Valon strings, a false Dragon for the Aes Sedai. She's going to push it down my throat whatever I want. But—I—will—not—be—used!"

Mat had backed up against a tree trunk. "A false Dragon?" He swallowed. "You? That . . . that's crazy."

Perrin had not retreated. He squatted down with his thick arms on his knees and studied Rand with those bright golden eyes. In the evening shadows they seemed to shine. "If the Aes Sedai want you for a false Dragon. . . ." He paused, frowning, thinking things through. Finally, he said quietly, "Rand, can you channel?" Mat gave a strangled gasp.

Rand let the banner drop; he hesitated only a moment before nodding wearily. "I did not ask for it. I don't want it. But. . . . But I do not think I know how to stop it." The room with the flies came back unbidden to his mind. "I don't think they'll let me stop."

"Burn me!" Mat breathed. "Blood and bloody ashes!

They'll kill us, you know. All of us. Perrin and me as well as you. If Ingtar and the others find out, they will cut our bloody throats for Darkfriends. Light, they'll probably think we were part of stealing the Horn, and killing those people in Fal Dara."

"Shut up, Mat," Perrin said calmly.

"Don't tell me to shut up. If Ingtar doesn't kill us, Rand will go mad and do it for him. Burn me! Burn me!" Mat slid down the tree to sit on the ground. "Why didn't they gentle you? If the Aes Sedai know, why didn't they gentle you? I never heard of them letting a man who can wield the Power just walk away."

"They don't all know," Rand sighed. "The Amyrlin—"

"The Amyrlin Seat! *She* knows? Light, no wonder she looked at me so strange."

"—and Moiraine told me I'm the Dragon Reborn, and then they said I could go wherever I wanted. Don't you see, Mat? They are trying to use me."

"Doesn't change you being able to channel," Mat muttered. "If I were you, I'd be halfway to the Aryth Ocean by now. And I would not stop until I found someplace where there were no Aes Sedai, and never likely to be any. And no people. I mean . . . well. . . ."

"Shut up, Mat," Perrin said. "Why *are* you here, Rand? The longer you stay around people, the more likely it is somebody will find out and send for Aes Sedai. Aes Sedai who *won't* tell you to go on about your business." He paused, scratching his head over that. "And Mat's right about Ingtar. I don't doubt he would name you Darkfriend and kill you. Kill all of us, maybe. He seems to like you, but he'd still do it, I think. A false Dragon? So would the others. Masema wouldn't need that much excuse, for you. So why aren't you gone?"

Rand shrugged. "I was going, but first the Amyrlin came, and then the Horn was stolen, and the dagger, and Moiraine said Mat was dying, and. . . . Light, I thought I could stay with you until we found the dagger, at least; I thought I could help with that. Maybe I was wrong."

"You came because of the dagger?" Mat said quietly. He rubbed his nose and grimaced. "I never thought of that. I never thought you wanted to. . . . Aaaah! Are you feeling all right? I mean, you aren't going mad already, are you?"

Rand dug a pebble out of the ground and threw it at him.

"Ouch!" Mat rubbed his arm. "I was just asking. I mean, all those fancy clothes, and all that talk about being a lord. Well, that isn't exactly right in the head."

"I was trying to get rid of you, fool! I was afraid I'd go mad and hurt you." His eyes dropped to the banner, and his voice lowered. "I will, eventually, if I don't stop it. Light, I don't know how to stop it."

"That is what I'm afraid of," Mat said, standing. "No offense, Rand, but I think I will just sleep as far away from you as I can, if you don't mind. That's if you are staying. I heard about a fellow who could channel, once. A merchant's guard told me. Before the Red Ajah found him, he woke one morning, and his whole village was smashed flat. All the houses, all the people, everything but the bed he was sleeping in, like a mountain had rolled over them."

Perrin said, "In that case, Mat, you should sleep cheek by jowl with him."

"I may be a fool, but I intend to be a live fool." Mat hesitated, looking sideways at Rand. "Look, I know you came along to help me, and I am grateful. I really am. But you just are not the same anymore. You understand that, don't you?" He waited as if he expected an answer. None came. Finally he vanished into the trees, back toward the camp.

"What about you?" Rand asked.

Perrin shook his head, shaggy curls swinging. "I don't know, Rand. You are the same, but then again, you aren't. A man channeling; my mother used to frighten me with that, when I was little. I just do not know." He stretched out his hand and touched a corner of the banner. "I think I would burn this, or bury it, if I were you. Then I'd run so far, so fast, no Aes Sedai would ever find me. Mat was right about that." He stood up, squinting at the western sky, beginning to turn red with the sinking sun. "Time to get back to the camp. You think on what I said, Rand. I'd run. But maybe you can't run. Think of that, too." His yellow eyes seemed to look inward, and he sounded tired. "Sometimes you can't run." Then he was gone, too.

Rand knelt there, staring at the banner spread out on the ground. "Well, sometimes you *can* run," he muttered. "Only, maybe she gave me this to make me run. Maybe she has something waiting for me, if I run. I won't do what she

wants. I won't. I'll bury it right here. But she said my life
may depend on it, and Aes Sedai never lie so you can see
it. . . ." Suddenly his shoulders shook with silent laughter.
"Now I'm talking to myself. Maybe I *am* going mad already."

When he returned to the camp, he carried the banner
wrapped in the canvas once more, tied with knots less neat
than Moiraine's had been.

The light had begun to fail and the shadow of the rim
covered half the hollow. The soldiers were settling in, all
with their horses by their sides, lances propped to hand. Mat
and Perrin were bedding down alongside their horses. Rand
gave them a sad look, then fetched Red, standing where he
had been left with his reins dangling, and went to the other
side of the hollow, where Hurin had joined Loial. The Ogier
had given over reading and was examining the half-buried
stone on which he had been sitting, tracing something on
the stone with the long stem of his pipe.

Hurin stood and gave Rand something just short of
a bow. "Hope you don't mind me making my bed here,
Lord—uh—Rand. I was just listening to the Builder here."

"There you are, Rand," Loial said. "You know, I think
this stone was worked once. See, it's weathered, but it looks
as if it was a column of some kind. And there are markings,
also. I can't quite make them out, but they look familiar,
somehow."

"Maybe you'll be able to see them better in the morning," Rand said. He pulled the saddlebags from Red. "I'll
be glad of your company, Hurin." *I'm glad of anybody's
company who isn't afraid of me. How much longer can I
have it, though?*

He shifted everything into one side of the saddlebags—
spare shirts and breeches and woolen stockings, sewing kit,
tinder box, tin plate and cup, a greenwood box with knife
and fork and spoon, a packet of dried meat and flatbread for
emergency rations, and all the other traveler's necessaries—
then stuffed the canvas-wrapped banner into the empty
pocket. It bulged, the straps barely reaching the buckles,
but then, the other side bulged now, too. It would do.

Loial and Hurin seemed to sense his mood, leaving him
in silence while he stripped saddle and bridle from Red,
rubbed the big bay down with tufts of grass torn from the

ground, then resaddled him. Rand refused their offer of
food; he did not think he could have stomached the best
meal he had ever seen just then. All three of them made
their beds there beside the stone, a simple matter of a blanket folded for a pillow and cloak to cover.

The camp was silent now, but Rand lay awake past the
fall of full dark. His mind darted back and forth. The banner. *What is she trying to make me do?* The village. *What
could kill a Fade like that?* Worst of all, the house in the
village. *Did it really happen? Am I going mad already? Do
I run, or do I stay? I have to stay. I have to help Mat find
the dagger.*

An exhausted sleep finally came, and with sleep, unbidden, the void surrounded him, flickering with an uneasy
glow that disturbed his dreams.

Padan Fain stared northward out into the night, past the only
fire in his camp, smiling a fixed smile that never touched
his eyes. He still thought of himself as Padan Fain—Padan
Fain was the core of him—but he had been changed, and he
knew it. He knew many things, now, more than any of his
old masters could suspect. He had been a Darkfriend long
years before Ba'alzamon summoned him and set him on the
track of the three young men from Emond's Field, distilling
what he knew of them, distilling him, and feeding the essence back so that he could *feel* them, *smell* where they had
been, follow wherever they ran. Especially the one. A part
of him still cringed, remembering what Ba'alzamon had
done to him, but it was a small part, hidden, suppressed. He
was changed. Following the three had led him into Shadar
Logoth. He had not wanted to go, but he had had to obey.
Then. And in Shadar Logoth. . . .

Fain drew a deep breath and fingered the ruby-hilted
dagger at his belt. That had come from Shadar Logoth, too.
It was the only weapon he carried, the only one he needed;
it felt like a part of him. He was whole within himself, now.
That was all that mattered.

He cast a glance to either side of his fire. The twelve
Darkfriends who were left, their once-fine clothes now
rumpled and dirty, huddled in the darkness to one side,
staring not at the fire, but at him. On the other squatted his

Trollocs, twenty in number, the all-too-human eyes in those
animal-twisted men's faces following his every move like
mice watching a cat.

It had been a struggle at first, waking each morning to
find himself not completely whole, to find the Myrddraal
back in command, raging and demanding they go north, to
the Blight, to Shayol Ghul. But bit by bit those mornings of
weakness grew shorter, until. . . . He remembered the feel
of the hammer in his hand, driving the spikes in, and he
smiled; this time it did touch his eyes, with the joy of sweet
memory.

Weeping from the dark caught his ear, and his smile
faded. *I should never have let the Trollocs take so many.*
An entire village to slow them down. If those few houses at
the ferry had not been deserted, perhaps. . . . But Trollocs
were greedy by nature, and in the euphoria of watching the
Myrddraal die, he had not paid attention as he should.

He glanced at the Trollocs. Any one of them was nearly
twice as tall as he, strong enough to break him to flinders
with one hand, yet they edged back, still crouching. "Kill
them. All. You may feed, but then make a pile of everything that remains—for our friends to find. Put the heads
on top. Neatly, now." He laughed, and cut it off short. "Go!"

The Trollocs scrambled away, drawing scythe-like
swords and raising spiked axes. In moments shrieks and
bellows rose from where the villagers were bound. Pleas for
mercy and children's screams were cut off by solid thuds
and unpleasant squishing noises, like melons being broken.

Fain turned his back on the cacophony to look at his
Darkfriends. They were his, too, body and soul. Such souls
as they had left. Every one of them was mired as deeply as
he had been, before he found his way out. Every one with
nowhere to go except to follow him. Their eyes clung to
fearful, pleading. "You think they will grow hungry again
before we find another village or a farm? They may. You
think I will be letting them have some more of you? Well,
perhaps one or two. There aren't any more horses to spare."

"The others were only commoners," one woman managed in an unsteady voice. Dirt streaked her face above a
finely cut dress that marked her as a merchant, and wealthy.
Smears stained the good gray cloth, and a long tear marred

her skirt. "They were peasants. We have served—*I* have served—"

Fain cut her off, his easy tone making his words all the harder. "What are you, to me? Less than peasants. Herd cattle for the Trollocs, perhaps? If you want to live, cattle, you must be useful."

The woman's face broke. She sobbed, and suddenly all the rest were babbling, telling him how useful they were, men and women who had had influence and position before they were called to fulfill their oaths at Fal Dara. They spilled out the names of important, powerful people whom they knew in the Borderlands, in Cairhien, and other lands. They babbled of the knowledge they alone had of this land or that, of political situations, alliances, intrigues, all the things they could tell him if he let them serve him. The noise of them blended with the sounds of the Trollocs' slaughter and fit right in.

Fain ignored all of it—he had no fear of turning his back on them, not since they had seen the Fade dealt with—and went to his prize. Kneeling, he ran his hands over the ornate, golden chest, feeling the power locked inside. He had to have a Trolloc carry it—he did not trust the humans enough to load it on a horse and packsaddle; some dreams of power might be strong enough to overcome even fear of him, but Trollocs never dreamed of anything except killing—and he had not yet puzzled out how to open it. But that would come. Everything would come. Everything.

Unsheathing the dagger, he laid it atop the chest before settling himself down beside the fire. That blade was a better guard than Trolloc or human. They had all seen what happened when he used it, once; none would come within a span of that bared blade without his command, and then reluctantly.

Lying there in his blankets, he stared northward. He could not feel al'Thor, now; the distance between them was too great. Or perhaps al'Thor was doing his vanishing trick. Sometimes, in the keep, the boy had suddenly vanished from Fain's senses. He did not know how, but always al'Thor came back, just as suddenly as he had gone. He would come back this time, too.

"This time you come to me, Rand al'Thor. Before, I

followed you like a dog driven on the trail, but now you follow me." His laughter was a cackle that even he knew was mad, but he did not care. Madness was a part of him, too. "Come to me, al'Thor. The dance is not even begun yet. We'll dance on Toman Head, and I'll be free of you. I'll see you dead at last."

CHAPTER

12

Woven in the Pattern

E gwene hurried after Nynaeve toward the knot of
Aes Sedai around the Amyrlin Seat's horse-borne
palanquin, her desire to know what had caused the
turmoil in Fal Dara kept outweighing even her worry over
Rand. He was beyond her reach, for the moment. Bela,
her shaggy mare, was with the Aes Sedai's horses, and
Nynaeve's mount, too.

The Warders, hands on sword hilts and eyes searching
everywhere, made a steel circle around the Aes Sedai and
the palanquin. They were an island of relative calm in the
courtyard, where Shienaran soldiers still ran amid the keep's
horrified inhabitants. Egwene pushed in beside Nynaeve—
the two of them all but ignored after a single sharp glance
from the Warders; all knew they would be leaving with the
Amyrlin—and caught enough in the crowd's murmurs to
learn of an arrow that had flashed seemingly from nowhere
and a bowman yet uncaught.

Egwene stopped, wide-eyed, too shocked even to think
that she was surrounded by Aes Sedai. An attempt on the
life of the Amyrlin Seat. It went beyond thinking of.

The Amyrlin sat in her palanquin with the curtains drawn
back, the bloodstained rip in her sleeve drawing all eyes,
and faced down Lord Agelmar. "You will find the bowman
or you will not, my son. Either way, my business in Tar Valon
is as urgent as that of Ingtar on his quest. I leave now."

"But, Mother," Agelmar protested, "this attempt on your
life changes everything. We still do not know who sent the
man, or why. An hour more, and I will have the bowman
and the answers for you."

The Amyrlin barked a laugh with no amusement in it. "You'll need slyer bait or finer nets to catch this fish, my son. By the time you have the man, it will be too late in the day for leaving. There are too many who would cheer to see me dead for me to worry overmuch about this one. You may send me news of what you find, if you find anything at all." Her eyes traveled around the towers overlooking the courtyard, and the ramparts and archers' balconies, still jammed with people, though silent now. The arrow had to have come from one of those places. "I think this bowman is already fled from Fal Dara."

"But, Mother—"

The woman in the palanquin cut him off with a sharp gesture of finality. Not even the Lord of Fal Dara could press the Amyrlin Seat too far. Her eyes came to rest on Egwene and Nynaeve, piercing eyes that seemed to Egwene to be seeing everything about herself that she wanted to keep secret. Egwene took a step back, then caught herself and dropped a curtsy, wondering if that were proper; no one had ever explained to her the protocol of meeting the Amyrlin Seat. Nynaeve kept her back straight and returned the Amyrlin's stare, but she fumbled for Egwene's hand and gripped as hard as Egwene did.

"So these are your two, Moiraine," the Amyrlin said. Moiraine gave the barest nod, and the other Aes Sedai turned to stare at the two women from Emond's Field. Egwene swallowed. They all looked as if they *knew* things, things other people did not, and it was no help at all to know that they truly did. "Yes, I sense a fine spark in each of them. But what will kindle from it? That's the question, isn't it?"

Egwene's mouth felt dry as dust. She had seen Master Padwhin, the carpenter back home, look at his tools much the same way as the Amyrlin was looking at the two of them. This one for this purpose, that one for that.

The Amyrlin said abruptly, "It is time we were gone. To horse. Lord Agelmar and I can say what needs be said without you all gawking like novices on a freeday. To horse!"

At her command the Warders scattered to their mounts, still wary, and the Aes Sedai, all but Leane, glided away from the palanquin to their own horses. As Egwene and Nynaeve turned to obey, a servant appeared at Lord Agelmar's shoulder with a silver chalice. Agelmar took it with a dissatisfied twist to his mouth.

"With this cup from my hand, Mother, take my wish that you fare well on this day, and every. . . ."

Whatever else they said was lost to Egwene as she scrambled onto Bela. By the time she had given the shaggy mare a pat, and arranged her skirts, the palanquin was already moving toward the open gates, its horses stepping without rein or lead. Leane rode beside the palanquin, her staff propped at her stirrup. Egwene and Nynaeve brought their horses along behind with the rest of the Aes Sedai.

Roars and cheers from the crowds lining the town streets greeted the procession, all but drowning the thunder of the drummers and the blare of the trumpeters. Warders led the column, with the banner bearing the White Flame waving in ripples, and rode guard around the Aes Sedai, keeping the mass of people back; archers and pikemen, the Flame blazoned on their chests, followed behind in precise ranks. The trumpets fell silent as the column wound its way out of the town and turned southward, yet the sounds of cheering from within the town followed still. Egwene glanced back often, until trees and hills hid Fal Dara's walls and towers.

Nynaeve, riding alongside, shook her head. "Rand will be all right. He has Lord Ingtar and twenty lances with him. In any case, there is nothing you can do about it. Nothing either of us can do." She glanced toward Moiraine; the Aes Sedai's trim white mare and Lan's tall black stallion made an odd pair off to one side by themselves. "Not yet."

The column angled westward as it traveled, and it did not cover the ground quickly. Even footmen in half armor could not move fast through the Shienaran hills, not and maintain the pace for long. Still, they pushed as hard as they could.

Camps came late each night, the Amyrlin allowing no stop until barely enough light remained to pitch the tents, flattened white domes just tall enough to stand in. Each pair of Aes Sedai from the same Ajah had one, while the Amyrlin and the Keeper had tents to themselves. Moiraine shared the tent of her two sisters of the Blue. The soldiers slept on the ground in their own encampment, and the Warders wrapped themselves in their cloaks near the tents of the Aes Sedai to whom they were bonded. The tent shared by the Red sisters looked oddly lonely without any Warders, while that of the Greens seemed almost festive, the two Aes Sedai often sitting outside long past dark to talk with the four Warders they had brought between them.

Lan came once to the tent Egwene shared with Nynaeve, taking the Wisdom into the night a little distance away. Egwene peered around the tent flap to watch. She could not hear what they said, except that Nynaeve eventually erupted in anger and came stalking back to wrap herself in her blankets and refuse to talk at all. Egwene thought her cheeks were wet, though she hid her face with a corner of her blanket. Lan stood watching the tent from the darkness for a long time before he went away. After that he did not come again.

Moiraine did not come near them, giving them only a nod in passing. She seemed to spend her waking hours speaking with the other Aes Sedai, all but the Red sisters, drawing them aside one by one as they rode. The Amyrlin allowed few stops for rest, and those short.

"Maybe she doesn't have time for us anymore," Egwene observed sadly. Moiraine was the one Aes Sedai she knew. Perhaps—though she did not like to admit it—the only one she was sure she could trust. "She found us, and we are on our way to Tar Valon. I suppose she has other things to concern her, now."

Nynaeve snorted softly. "I'll believe she is done with us when she's dead—or we are. She is sly, that one."

Other Aes Sedai came to their tent. Egwene almost jumped out of her skin that first night out of Fal Dara, when the tent flap was pushed aside and a plump, square-faced Aes Sedai, with graying hair and a vaguely distracted look in her dark eyes, ducked into their tent. She glanced at the lantern hanging at the highest point of the tent, and the flame rose a little higher. Egwene thought she felt something, thought she almost saw something about the Aes Sedai when the flame grew brighter. Moiraine had told her that one day—when she had more training—she would be able to *see* when another woman channeled, and to tell a woman who could channel even if she did nothing.

"I am Verin Mathwin," the woman said with a smile. "And you are Egwene al'Vere and Nynaeve al'Maera. From the Two Rivers, which was once Manetheren. Strong blood, that. It sings."

Egwene exchanged glances with Nynaeve as they got to their feet.

"Is this a summons to the Amyrlin Seat?" Egwene asked.

Verin laughed. The Aes Sedai had a smudge of ink on her nose. "Oh, my, no. The Amyrlin has more important things to deal with than two young women who are not even novices yet. Although, you never can tell. You both have considerable potential, especially you, Nynaeve. One day. . . ." She paused, rubbing a finger thoughtfully right atop the ink smudge. "But this is not one day. I am here to give you a lesson, Egwene. You have been poking in ahead of yourself, I fear."

Nervously, Egwene looked at Nynaeve. "What have I done? Nothing that I'm aware of."

"Oh, nothing wrong. Not exactly. Somewhat dangerous, perhaps, but not exactly wrong." Verin lowered herself to the canvas floor, folding her legs under her. "Sit, both of you. Sit. I don't mean to crane my neck." She shifted around until she had a comfortable position. "Sit."

Egwene settled cross-legged across from the Aes Sedai and did her best not to look at Nynaeve. *No need to look guilty until I know if I am. And maybe not then.* "What is it I've done that's dangerous but not exactly wrong?"

"Why, you've been channeling the Power, child."

Egwene could only gape. Nynaeve burst out, "That is ridiculous. Why are we going to Tar Valon, if not for that?"

"Moiraine has . . . I mean, Moiraine Sedai has been giving me lessons," Egwene managed.

Verin held up her hands for quiet, and they fell silent. She might seem vague, but she was Aes Sedai, after all. "Child, do you think Aes Sedai immediately teach every girl who says she wants to be one of us how to channel? Well, I suppose you are not exactly every girl, but just the same. . . ." She shook her head gravely.

"Then why did she?" Nynaeve demanded. There had been no lessons for her, and Egwene was still not sure if it rankled Nynaeve or not.

"Because Egwene had already channeled," Verin said patiently.

"So. . . . So have I." Nynaeve did not sound happy about it.

"Your circumstances are different, child. That you are still alive shows you weathered the various crises, and did it on your own. I think you know how lucky you are. Of every four women forced to do what you did, only one survives. Of course, wilders—" Verin grimaced. "Forgive me, but I am afraid that *is* what we in the White Tower often call women who, without any training, have managed some rough control—random, and barely enough to be called control, usually, like you, but still control of a sort. Wilders have difficulties, it is true. Almost always they have built up walls to keep themselves from knowing what it was they were doing, and those walls interfere with conscious control. The longer those walls have to build, the harder it is to tear them down, but if they can be demolished—well, some of the most adept sisters ever have been wilders."

Nynaeve shifted irritably, and looked at the entrance as if thinking of leaving.

"I don't see what any of that has to do with me," Egwene said.

Verin blinked at her, almost as if wondering where she had come from. "With you? Why, nothing. Your problem is quite different. Most girls who want to become Aes Sedai—even most girls with the seed inside them, like you—are afraid of it, too. Even after they reach the Tower, even after they've learned what to do and how, for months they need to be led, step by step, by a sister, or by one of the Accepted. But not you. From what Moiraine tells me, you leaped into it as soon as you knew you could, fumbling your way through the dark with never a thought of whether there was a bottomless pit under your next step. Oh, there have been others like you; you are not unique. Moiraine was one herself. Once she knew what you had done, there was nothing for it but for her to begin teaching you. Did Moiraine never explain any of this to you?"

"Never." Egwene wished her voice was not so breathless. "She had . . . other matters to deal with." Nynaeve snorted softly.

"Well, Moiraine has never believed in telling anyone anything they did not need to know. Knowing serves no real purpose, but then, neither does not knowing. Myself, I always prefer knowing to not."

"Is there one? A pit, I mean?"

"Obviously not so far," Verin said, tilting her head. "But the next step?" She shrugged. "You see, child, the more you *try* to touch the True Source, the more you *try* to channel the One Power, the easier it becomes to actually do it. Yes, in the beginning, you stretch out to the Source and more often than not it is like grasping at air. Or you actually touch *saidar*, but even when you feel the One Power flowing through you, you find you can do nothing with it. Or you do something, and it isn't what you intended at all. That is the danger. Usually, with guidance and training—and the girl's own fear slowing her down—the ability to touch the Source and the ability to channel the Power come together with the ability to control what she is doing. But you began trying to channel without anyone there to teach you any control at all of what you do. I know you don't think you're very far along, and you are not, but you are like someone who has taught herself to run up hills—sometimes, at least— without ever learning how to run down the other side, or to walk. Sooner or later you are going to fall, if you don't learn the rest of it. Now, I am not talking about anything like what happens when one of those poor men begins channeling—you will not go mad; you won't die, not with sisters to teach and guide you—but what might you do entirely by accident, never meaning to?" For an instant the vagueness had dropped from Verin's eyes. For an instant, it seemed, the Aes Sedai's gaze had flicked from Egwene to Nynaeve as sharply as the Amyrlin's had. "Your innate abilities are strong, child, and they will grow stronger. You must learn to control them before you harm yourself, or someone else, or a great many people. That is what Moiraine was trying to teach you. That is what I will try to help you with tonight, and what a sister will help you with every night until we put you into Sheriam's most capable hands. She is Mistress of Novices."

Egwene thought, *Can she know about Rand? It isn't possible. She'd never have let him leave Fal Dara if she even suspected.* But she was sure she had not imagined what she saw. "Thank you, Verin Sedai. I will try."

Nynaeve rose smoothly to her feet. "I will go sit by the fire and leave you two alone."

"You should stay," Verin said. "You could profit by it. From what Moiraine has told me, it should take only a little training for you to be raised to the Accepted."

Nynaeve hesitated only a moment before shaking her

head firmly. "I thank you for the offer, but I can wait until we reach Tar Valon. Egwene, if you need me, I will be—"

"By any gauge," Verin cut in, "you are a woman grown, Nynaeve. Usually, the younger a novice, the better she does. Not with the training necessarily, but because a novice is expected to do as she is told, when she is told and without question. It is really only of use once the actual training has reached a certain point—a hesitation in the wrong place then, or a doubt of what you have been told to do, can have tragic consequences—but it is better to follow the discipline all the time. The Accepted, on the other hand, are expected to question things, as it is felt they know enough to know what questions to ask and when. Which do you think you would prefer?"

Nynaeve's hands tightened on her skirt, and she looked at the tent flap again, frowning. Finally she gave a short nod and settled back down on the floor. "I suppose I might as well," she said.

"Good," Verin said. "Now. You already know this part, Egwene, but for Nynaeve's sake I will take you through it step by step. In time, it will become second nature—you will do it all faster than you can think of it—but now it is best to go slowly. Close your eyes, please. It goes better in the beginning if you have no distractions at all." Egwene closed her eyes. There was a pause. "Nynaeve," Verin said, "please close your eyes. It will really go better." Another pause. "Thank you, child. Now, you must empty yourself. Empty your thoughts. There is only one thing in your mind. The bud of a flower. Only that. Only the bud. You can see it in every detail. You can smell it. You can feel it. Every vein of every leaf, every curve of every petal. You can feel the sap pulsing. Feel it. Know it. Be it. You and the bud are the same. You are one. You are the bud."

Her voice droned on hypnotically, but Egwene no longer really heard; she had done this exercise before, with Moiraine. It was slow, but Moiraine had said it would come more quickly with practice. Inside herself, she was a rosebud, red petals curled tightly. Yet suddenly there was something else. Light. Light pressing on the petals. Slowly the petals unfolded, turning toward the light, absorbing the light. The rose and the light were one. Egwene and the light were one. She could feel the merest trickle of it seeping through her. She stretched for more, strained for more. . . .

In an instant it was all gone, rose and light. Moiraine had also said it could not be forced. With a sigh, she opened her eyes. Nynaeve had a grim look on her face. Verin was as calm as ever.

"You cannot *make* it happen," the Aes Sedai was saying. "You must *let* it happen. You must surrender to the Power before you can control it."

"This is complete foolishness," Nynaeve muttered. "I don't feel like a flower. If anything, I feel like a blackthorn bush. I think I will wait by the fire after all."

"As you wish," Verin said. "Did I mention that novices do chores? They wash dishes, scrub floors, do laundry, serve at table, all sorts of things. I myself think the servants do a better job of it by far, but it is generally felt that such labor builds character. Oh, you are staying? Good. Well, child, remember that even a blackthorn bush has flowers sometimes, beautiful and white among the thorns. We will try it one at a time. Now, from the beginning, Egwene. Close your eyes."

Several times before Verin left, Egwene felt the flow of the Power through her, but it was never very strong, and the most she managed with it was to produce a stir in the air that made the tent flap stir slightly. She was sure a sneeze could have done as much. She had done better with Moiraine; sometimes, at least. She wished it was Moiraine doing the teaching.

Nynaeve never even felt a glimmer, or so she said. By the end her eyes were set and her mouth so tight that Egwene was afraid she was about to begin berating Verin as if the Aes Sedai were a village woman intruding on her privacy. But Verin simply told her to close her eyes once again, this time without Egwene.

Egwene was sitting, watching the other two between her yawns. The night had grown late, well past the time she would usually be asleep. Nynaeve wore a face like week-old death, her eyes clamped shut as if she never meant to open them and her hands white-knuckled fists in her lap. Egwene hoped the Wisdom's temper did not break loose, not after she had held it this long.

"Feel the flow through you," Verin was saying. Her voice did not change, but suddenly there was a gleam in her eyes. "Feel the flow. Flow of the Power. Flow like a breeze, a gentle stirring in the air." Egwene sat up straight. This was how Verin had guided her each time she had actually had the Power flowing through her. "A soft breeze, the slightest movement of air. Soft."

Abruptly the stacked blankets burst into flame like fatwood.

Nynaeve opened her eyes with a yell. Egwene was not sure if she screamed or not. All Egwene knew was that she was on her feet, trying to kick the burning blankets outside before they set the tent on fire. Before she managed a second kick, the flames vanished, leaving wispy smoke rising from a charred mass and the smell of burned wool.

"Well," Verin said. "Well. I did not expect to have to douse a fire. Don't faint on me, child. It's all right now. I took care of it."

"I—I was angry." Nynaeve spoke through trembling lips in a bloodless face. "I heard you talking about a breeze, telling me what to do, and fire just popped into my head. I—I didn't mean to burn anything. It was just a small fire, in—in my head." She shuddered.

"I suppose it was a small fire, at that." Verin barked a laugh that was gone with another look at Nynaeve's face. "Are you all right, child? If you feel ill, I can. . . ." Nynaeve shook her head, and Verin nodded. "Rest is what you need. Both of you. I've worked you too hard. You must rest. The Amyrlin will have us all up and away before first light." Standing, she toed the charred blankets. "I will have some more blankets brought to you. I hope this shows both of you how important control is. You must learn to do what you mean to do, and nothing more. Aside from harming someone else, if you draw more of the Power than you can safely handle—and you cannot handle much, yet; but it will grow—if you draw too much, you can destroy yourself. You can die. Or you can burn yourself out, destroy what ability you have." As if she had not told them they were walking a knife edge, she added a cheerful "Sleep well." With that, she was gone.

Egwene put her arms around Nynaeve and hugged her

tight. "It is all right, Nynaeve. There is no need to be frightened. Once you learn to control—"

Nynaeve gave a croaking laugh. "I am not frightened." She glanced sideways at the smoking blankets and twitched her eyes away. "It takes more than a little fire to frighten me." But she did not look at the blankets again, even when a Warder came to take them away and leave new.

Verin did not come again, as she had said she would not. Indeed, as they journeyed on, south and west, day by day, as fast as the footmen could move, Verin paid the two women from Emond's Field no more mind than Moiraine did, than did any of the Aes Sedai. They were not precisely unfriendly, the Aes Sedai, but rather distant and aloof, as if preoccupied. Their coolness heightened Egwene's unease, and brought back all the tales she had heard as a child.

Her mother had always told her the tales about Aes Sedai were a lot of fool men's nonsense, but neither her mother nor any other woman in Emond's Field had ever met an Aes Sedai before Moiraine came there. She herself had spent a good deal of time with Moiraine, and Moiraine was proof to her that not all Aes Sedai were like the tales. Cold manipulators and merciless destroyers. Breakers of the World. She knew now that *those*, at least—the Breakers of the World—had been male Aes Sedai, when there were such, in the Age of Legends, but it did not help a great deal. Not *all* Aes Sedai were like the tales, but how many, and which?

The Aes Sedai who came to the tent each night were so mixed that they did not help at all in clearing her thoughts. Alviarin was as cool and businesslike as a merchant come to buy wool and tabac, surprised that Nynaeve was part of the lesson but accepting, sharp in her criticisms but always ready to try again. Alanna Mosvani laughed and spent as much time talking about the world, and men, as she did teaching. Alanna showed too much interest in Rand and Perrin and Mat for Egwene's comfort, though. Especially Rand. Worst of all was Liandrin, the only one who wore her shawl; the others had all packed them away before leaving Fal Dara. Liandrin sat fingering her red fringe and taught little, and reluctantly at that. She questioned Egwene and Nynaeve as if they had been accused of a crime, and her questions were all about the three boys. She kept it up until Nynaeve threw her out—Egwene was not sure why Nynaeve did so—and then she left with a warning.

"Watch yourselves, my daughters. You are in your village no longer. Now you dabble your toes where there are things to bite you."

Finally the column reached the village of Medo, on the banks of the Mora, which ran along the border between Shienar and Arafel and so into the River Erinin.

Egwene was sure it was the Aes Sedai's questions about Rand that had made her start dreaming of him, that and worrying about him, about whether he and the others had had to follow the Horn of Valere into the Blight. The dreams were always bad, but at first they were just the ordinary sort of nightmare. By the night they reached Medo, the dreams had changed, though.

"Pardon, Aes Sedai," Egwene asked diffidently, "but have you seen Moiraine Sedai?" The slender Aes Sedai waved her away and hurried on down the crowded, torch-lit village street, calling for someone to be careful with her horse. The woman was of the Yellow Ajah, though not wearing her shawl now; Egwene knew no more of her than that, not even her name.

Medo was a small village—though Egwene was shocked to realize that what she now thought of as a "small village" was as big as Emond's Field—and it was overwhelmed now with many more outsiders than there were inhabitants. Horses and people filled the narrow streets, jostling to the docks past villagers who knelt whenever an unseeing Aes Sedai sped by. Harsh torchlight lit everything. The two docks jutted out into the River Mora like stone fingers, and each hosted a pair of small, two-masted ships. There, horses were being hoisted on board by booms and cables and canvas cradles under their bellies. More of the ships—high-sided and stout, with lanterns topping their masts—crowded the moon-streaked river, already loaded or waiting their turn. Rowboats ferried out archers and pikemen, the raised pikes making the boats look like gigantic prickle-backs swimming on the surface.

On the left-hand dock Egwene found Anaiya, watching the loading and chivying those who were not moving fast enough. Though she had never said more than two words to Egwene, Anaiya seemed different from the others, more

like a woman from home. Egwene could picture her baking in her kitchen; she could not see any of the others so.
"Anaiya Sedai, have you seen Moiraine Sedai? I need to
talk to her."

The Aes Sedai looked around with an absent frown.
"What? Oh, it's you, child. Moiraine is gone. And your
friend, Nynaeve, is already out on the *River Queen*. I had
to bundle her onto a boat myself, shouting that she would
not go without you. Light, what a scramble! You should be
aboard, yourself. Find a boat going out to the *River Queen*.
You two will be traveling with the Amyrlin Seat, so mind
yourself once you're on board. No scenes or tantrums."

"Which ship is Moiraine Sedai's?"

"Moiraine isn't on a ship, girl. She's gone, two days gone,
and the Amyrlin is in a taking over it." Anaiya grimaced
and shook her head, though most of her attention was still
on the workers. "First Moiraine vanishes with Lan, then Liandrin right on Moiraine's heels, and then Verin, none of
them with so much as a word for anyone. Verin did not even
take her Warder; Tomas is chewing nails with worry over
her." The Aes Sedai glanced at the sky. The waxing moon
shone without the hindrance of clouds. "We will have to
call the wind again, and the Amyrlin will not be pleased
with that, either. She says she wants us on our way to Tar
Valon within an hour, and she will brook no delays. I would
not want to be Moiraine, or Liandrin, or Verin, when she
sees them next. They'll wish they were novices again. Why,
child, what's the matter?"

Egwene drew a deep breath. *Moiraine gone? She can't
be! I have to tell somebody, somebody who won't laugh at
me.* She imagined Anaiya back in Emond's Field, listening to her daughter's problems; the woman fit the picture.
"Anaiya Sedai, Rand is in trouble."

Anaiya gave her a considering look. "That tall boy
from your village? Missing him already, are you? Well, I
shouldn't be surprised if he *is* in trouble. Young men his age
usually are. Though it was the other one—Mat?—who had
the look of trouble. Very well, child. I don't mean to mock
you or make light. What kind of trouble, and how do you
know? He and Lord Ingtar must have the Horn and be back
in Fal Dara by now. Or else they've had to follow it into the
Blight, and there's nothing to do about that."

"I—I don't think they're in the Blight, or back in Fal Dara. I had a dream." She said it half defiantly. It sounded silly when she said it, but it had seemed so real. A nightmare for true, but real. First there had been a man with a mask over his face, and fire in place of his eyes. Despite the mask, she had thought he was surprised to see her. His look had frightened her till she thought her bones would break from shivering, but suddenly he vanished, and she saw Rand sleeping on the ground, wrapped in a cloak. A woman had been standing over him, looking down. Her face was in shadow, but her eyes seemed to shine like the moon, and Egwene had known she was evil. Then there was a flash of light, and they were gone. Both of them. And behind it all, almost like another thing altogether, was the feel of danger, as if a trap was just beginning to snap shut on an unsuspecting lamb, a trap with many jaws. As though time had slowed, and she could watch the iron jaws creep closer together. The dream had not faded with waking, the way dreams did. And the danger felt so strong she still wanted to look over her shoulder—only somehow she knew that it was aimed at Rand, not at her.

She wondered if the woman had been Moiraine, and upbraided herself for the thought. Liandrin fit that part better. Or perhaps Alanna; she had been interested in Rand, too.

She could not bring herself to tell Anaiya. Formally, she said, "Anaiya Sedai, I know it sounds foolish, but he is in danger. Great danger. I know it. I could feel it. I still can."

Anaiya wore a thoughtful look. "Well, now," she said softly, "that's a possibility I'll wager no one has considered. You may be a Dreamer. It is a small chance, child, but. . . . We haven't had one of those in—oh—four or five hundred years. And Dreaming is close linked to Foretelling. If you really can Dream, it may be that you can Foretell, as well. *That* would be a finger in the Reds' eye. Of course, it could be just an ordinary nightmare, brought on by a late night, and cold food, and us traveling so hard since we left Fal Dara. And you missing your young man. Much more likely. Yes, yes, child, I know. You are worried about him. Did your dream indicate what kind of danger?"

Egwene shook her head. "He just vanished, and I felt danger. And evil. I felt it even before he vanished." She shivered and rubbed her hands together. "I can still feel it."

"Well, we will talk about it more on the *River Queen*. If you *are* a Dreamer, I will see you have the training Moiraine should be here to.... You there!" the Aes Sedai barked suddenly, and Egwene jumped. A tall man, who had just sat down on a cask of wine, jumped, too. Several others quickened their step. "That's for loading aboard, not resting on! We will talk on the boat, child. No, you fool! You can't carry it by yourself! Do you want to hurt yourself?" Anaiya went striding off down the dock, giving the unfortunate villagers a rougher side of her tongue than Egwene would have suspected she had.

Egwene peered into the dark, toward the south. He was out there, somewhere. Not in Fal Dara, not in the Blight. She was sure of it. *Hold on, you wool-headed idiot. If you get yourself killed before I can get you out of this, I will skin you alive.* It did not occur to her to ask how she was going to get him out of anything, going to Tar Valon as she was.

Snugging her cloak around her, she set out to find a boat to the *River Queen*.

CHAPTER
13

From Stone to Stone

The light of the rising sun woke Rand, and he wondered if he were dreaming. He sat up slowly, staring. Everything had changed, or almost everything. The sun and the sky were as he expected to see, if pallid and all but cloudless. Loial and Hurin still lay on either side of him, wrapped in their cloaks asleep, and their horses still stood hobbled a pace away, but everyone else was gone. Soldiers, horses, his friends, everyone and everything gone.

The hollow itself had changed, too, and they were in the middle of it now, no longer on the edge. At Rand's head rose a gray stone cylinder, every bit of three spans high and a full pace thick, covered with hundreds, perhaps thousands, of deeply incised diagrams and markings in some language he did not recognize. White stone paved the bottom of the hollow, as level as a floor, polished so smooth it almost glistened. Broad, high steps rose to the rim in concentric rings of different colored stone. And about the rim, the trees stood blackened and twisted as if a firestorm had roared through them. Everything seemed paler than it should be, just like the sun, more subdued, as if seen through mist. Only there was no mist. Just the three of them and the horses appeared truly solid. But when he touched the stone under him, it *felt* solid enough.

He reached out and shook Loial and Hurin. "Wake up! Wake up and tell me I'm dreaming. Please wake up!"

"Is it morning already?" Loial began, sitting up, then his mouth fell open, and his big, round eyes grew wider and wider.

Hurin woke with a start, then leaped to his feet, jumping

like a flea on a hot rock to look this way, then that. "Where are we? What's happened? Where is everybody? Where are we, Lord Rand?" He sank to his knees, wringing his hands, but his eyes still darted. "What's happened?"

"I don't know," Rand said slowly. "I was hoping it was a dream, but. . . . Maybe it is a dream." He had had experience of dreams that were not dreams, experience he wanted neither to repeat nor to remember. He stood up carefully. Everything stayed as it was.

"I do not think so," Loial said. He was studying the column, and he did not appear happy. His long eyebrows sagged across his cheeks, and his tufted ears seemed to have wilted. "I think this is the same stone we went to sleep beside last night. I think I know what it is, now." For once, he sounded miserable about knowing.

"That's. . . ." *No.* That being the same stone was no more crazy than what he could see around him, Mat and Perrin and the Shienarans gone, and everything changed. *I thought I'd escaped, but it's started again, and there's no such thing as crazy anymore. Unless I am.* He looked at Loial and Hurin. They were not acting as if he were mad; they saw it, too. Something about the steps caught his eye, the different colors, seven rising from blue to red. "One for each Ajah," he said.

"No, Lord Rand," Hurin moaned. "No. Aes Sedai would not do this to us. They wouldn't! I walk in the Light."

"We all do, Hurin," Rand said. "The Aes Sedai won't hurt you." *Unless you get in the way.* Could this be Moiraine's doing somehow? "Loial, you said you know what the stone is. What is it?"

"I said I think I know, Rand. There was a piece of an old book, just a few pages, but one of them had a drawing of this stone, this Stone"—there was a distinct difference in the way he said it that marked importance—"or one very like it. And underneath, it said, 'From Stone to Stone run the lines of "if," between the worlds that might be.'"

"What does that mean, Loial? It doesn't make any sense."

The Ogier shook his massive head sadly. "It was only a few pages. Part of it said Aes Sedai in the Age of Legends, some of those who could Travel, the most powerful of them, could use these Stones. It did not say how, but I think, from what I could puzzle out, that perhaps those Aes Sedai used the Stones somehow to journey to those worlds." He glanced up at the seared trees and pulled his eyes down again quickly, as he did not want to think about what lay beyond the rim. "Yet even if Aes Sedai can use them, or could, we had no Aes Sedai with us to channel the Power, so I don't see how it can be."

Rand's skin prickled. *Aes Sedai used them. In the Age of Legends, when there were male Aes Sedai.* He had a vague memory of the void closing round him as he fell asleep, filled with that uneasy glow. And he remembered the room in the village, and the light he had reached for to escape. *If that was the male half of True Source. . . . No, it can't be. But what if it is? Light, I was wondering whether to run or not, and all the time it's right inside my head. Maybe I brought us here.* He did not want to think about it. "Worlds that might be? I don't understand, Loial."

The Ogier shrugged massively, and uneasily. "Neither do I, Rand. Most of it sounded like this. 'If a woman go left, or right, does Time's flow divide? Does the Wheel then weave two Patterns? A thousand, for each of her turnings? As many as the stars? Is one real, the others merely shadows and reflections?' You see, it was not very clear. Mainly questions, most of which seemed to contradict each other. And there just wasn't much of it." He went back to staring at the column, but he looked as if he wished it would go away. "There are supposed to be a good many of these Stones, scattered all over the world, or there were, once, but I never heard of anyone finding one. I never heard of anyone finding anything like this at all."

"My Lord Rand?" Now on his feet, Hurin seemed calmer, but he clutched his coat at the waist with both hands, his face urgent. "My Lord Rand, you'll get us back, won't you? Back where we belong? I've a wife, my Lord, and children. Melia'd take it bad enough, me dying, but if she doesn't even have my body to give to the mother's embrace, she'll grieve to the end of her days. You understand, my Lord. I can't leave her not knowing. You'll get us back. And if I die, if you can't take her my body, you'll let her know, so she has that, at least." He was no longer questioning at the end. A note of confidence had crept into his voice.

Rand opened his mouth to say again he was not a lord, then shut it without speaking. That was hardly important enough to mention, now. *You got him into this.* He wanted to deny it, but he knew what he was, knew he could channel, even if it always seemed to happen all by itself. Loial said Aes Sedai used the Stones, and that meant the One Power. What Loial said he knew, you could be sure of—the Ogier never claimed to know if he did not—and there was no one else nearby who could wield the Power. *You got him into it, you have to get him out. You have to try.*

"I will do my best, Hurin." And because Hurin was Shienaran, he added, "By my House and honor. A shepherd's House and a shepherd's honor, but I'll make them do as well as a lord's."

Hurin loosed his hold on his coat. The confidence reached his eyes, too. He bowed deeply. "Honor to serve, my Lord."

Guilt rippled through Rand. *He thinks you'll see him home, now, because Shienaran lords always keep their word. What are you going to do, Lord Rand?* "None of that, Hurin. There'll be no bowing. I'm not—" Suddenly he knew he could not tell the man again that he was not a lord. All that was holding the sniffer together was his belief in a lord, and he could not take that away, not now. Not here. "No bowing," he finished awkwardly.

"As you say, Lord Rand." Hurin's grin was almost as wide as when Rand first met him.

Rand cleared his throat. "Yes. Well, that's what I say."

They were both watching him, Loial curious, Hurin confident, both waiting to see what he would do. *I brought them here. I must have. So I have to get them back. And that means. . . .*

Drawing a deep breath, he walked across the white paving stones to the symbol-covered cylinder. Small lines of some language he did not know surrounded each symbol, odd letters that flowed in curves and spirals, suddenly turned to jagged hooks and angles, then flowed on. At least it was not Trolloc script. Reluctantly, he put his hands on the column. It looked like any dry, polished stone, but it felt curiously slick, like oiled metal.

He closed his eyes and formed the flame. The void came slowly, hesitantly. He knew his own fear was holding it back, fear of what he was trying. As fast as he fed fear into the flame, more came. *I can't do it. Channel the Power. I don't want to. Light, there has to be another way.* Grimly he forced the thoughts to stillness. He could feel sweat beading on his face. Determinedly he kept on, pushing his fears into the consuming flame, making it grow, and grow. And the void was there.

The core of him floated in emptiness. He could see the light—*saidin*—even with his eyes closed, feel the warmth of it, surrounding him, surrounding everything, suffusing everything. It wavered like a candle flame seen through oiled paper. Rancid oil. Stinking oil.

He reached for it—he was not sure *how* he reached, but it was something, a movement, a stretching toward the light, toward *saidin*—and caught nothing, as if running his hands through water. It felt like a slimy pond, scum floating atop clean water below, but he could not scoop up any of the water. Time and again it trickled through his fingers, not even droplets of the water remaining, only the slick scum, making his skin crawl.

Desperately, he tried to form an image of the hollow as it had been, with Ingtar and the lances sleeping by their horses, with Mat and Perrin, and the Stone lying buried except for one end. Outside the void he formed it, clinging to the shell of emptiness that enclosed him. He tried to link the image with the light, tried to force them together. The hollow as it had been, and he and Loial and Hurin there together. His head hurt. Together, with Mat and Perrin and the Shienarans. Burning, in his head. Together!

The void shattered into a thousand razor shards, slicing his mind.

Shuddering, he staggered back, wide-eyed. His hands hurt from pressing the Stone, and his arms and shoulders quivered with aching; his stomach lurched from the feel of filth covering him, and his head. . . . He tried to steady his breathing. That had never happened before. When the void went, it went like a pricked bubble, just gone, in a twinkling. Never broken like glass. His head felt numb, as if the thousand slashes had happened so quickly the pain had not yet come. But every cut had felt as real as if done with a knife. He touched his temple, and was surprised not to see blood on his fingers.

Hurin still stood there watching him, still confident. If anything, the sniffer seemed more sure by the minute. Lord Rand was doing something. That was what lords were for.

They protected the land and the people with their bodies
and their lives, and when something was wrong, they set it
aright and saw fairness and justice done. As long as Rand
was doing something, anything, Hurin would have confidence that it would all come right in the end. That was what
lords did.

Loial had a different look, a slightly puzzled frown, but
his eyes were on Rand, too. Rand wondered what he was
thinking.

"It was worth a try," he told them. The rancid oil feel,
inside his head—*Light, it's inside me! I don't want it inside me!*—was fading slowly, but he still thought he might
vomit. "I will try again, in a few minutes."

He hoped he sounded confident. He had no idea how the
Stones worked, if what he was doing had any chance of success. *Maybe there are rules for working them. Maybe you
have to do something special. Light, maybe you can't use
the same Stone twice, or. . . .* He cut off that line of thought.
There was no good in thinking like that. He had to do it.
Looking at Loial and Hurin, he thought he knew what Lan
had meant about duty pressing down like a mountain.

"My Lord, I think. . . ." Hurin let his words trail off,
looking abashed for a moment. "My Lord, maybe, if we
find the Darkfriends, we can make one of them tell us how
to get back."

"I would ask a Darkfriend or the Dark One himself if I
thought I'd get a true answer back," Rand said. "But we are
all there is. Just us three." *Just me. I'm the one who has to
do it.*

"We could follow their trail, my Lord. If we catch
them. . . ."

Rand stared at the sniffer. "You can still smell them?"

"I can, my Lord." Hurin frowned. "It's faint, pale-like,
like everything else here, but I can smell the trail. Right
up there." He pointed to the rim of the hollow. "I don't understand it, my Lord, but— Last night, I could have sworn
the trail went right on by the hollow back—back where
we were. Well, it's in the same place now, only here, and
fainter, like I said. Not old, not faint like that, but. . . . I
don't know, Lord Rand, except that it's there."

Rand considered. If Fain and the Darkfriends were
here—wherever here was—they might know how to get

back. They had to, if they had reached here in the first
place. And they had the Horn, and the dagger. Mat had to
have that dagger. For that if for nothing else, he had to find
them. What finally decided him, he was ashamed to realize,
was that he was afraid to try again. Afraid to try channeling
the Power. He was less afraid of confronting Darkfriends
and Trollocs with only Hurin and Loial than he was of that.

"Then we will go after the Darkfriends." He tried to
sound sure, the way Lan would, or Ingtar. "The Horn must
be recovered. If we can't puzzle out a way to take it from
them, at least we will know where they are when we find
Ingtar again." *If only they don't ask how we're going to find
him again.* "Hurin, make sure it really is the trail we're after."

The sniffer leaped into his saddle, eager to be doing
something himself, perhaps eager to be away from the hollow, and scrambled his horse up the broad, colored steps.
The animal's hooves rang loudly on the stone, but they
made not a mark.

Rand stowed Red's hobbles in his saddlebags—the banner was still there; he would not have minded if that had
been left behind—then gathered his bow and quiver and
climbed to the stallion's back. The bundle of Thom Merrilin's
cloak made a mound behind his saddle.

Loial led his big mount over to him; with the Ogier
standing on the ground, Loial's head came almost to Rand's
shoulder, and him in his saddle. Loial still looked puzzled.

"You think we should stay here?" Rand said. "Try again
to use the Stone? If the Darkfriends are here, in place, we
have to find them. We can't leave the Horn of Valere in
Darkfriend hands; you heard the Amyrlin. And we have to
get that dagger back. Mat will die without it."

Loial nodded. "Yes, Rand, we do. But, Rand, the
Stones. . . ."

"We will find another. You said they were scattered all
over, and if they're all like this—all this stonework around
them—it should not be too hard to find one."

"Rand, that fragment said the Stones came from an older
Age than the Age of Legends, and even the Aes Sedai then
did not understand them, though they used them, some of
the truly powerful did. They used them with the One Power,
Rand. How did you think to use this Stone to take us back?
Or any other Stone we find?"

For a moment Rand could only stare at the Ogier, thinking faster than he ever had in his life. "If they are older than the Age of Legends, maybe the people who built them didn't use the Power. There must be another way. The Darkfriends got here, and they certainly couldn't use the Power. Whatever this other way is, I will find it out. I will get us back, Loial." He looked at the tall stone column with its odd markings, and felt a prickle of fear. *Light, if only I don't have to use the Power to do it.* "I will, Loial, I promise. One way or another."

The Ogier gave a doubtful nod. He swung up onto his huge horse and followed Rand up the steps to join Hurin among the blackened trees.

The land stretched out, low and rolling, sparsely forested here and there with grassland between, crossed by more than one stream. In the middle distance Rand thought he could see another burned patch. It was all pale, the colors washed. There was no sign of anything made by men except the stone circle behind them. The sky was empty, no chimney smoke, no birds, only a few clouds and the pale yellow sun.

Worst of all, though, the land seemed to twist the eye. What was close at hand looked all right, and what was seen straight ahead in the distance. But whenever Rand turned his head, things that appeared distant when seen from the corner of his eye seemed to rush toward him, to be nearer when he stared straight at them. It made for dizziness; even the horses whickered nervously and rolled their eyes. He tried moving his head slowly; the apparent movement of things that should have been fixed was still there, but it seemed to help a little.

"Did your piece of a book say anything about this?" Rand asked.

Loial shook his head, then swallowed hard as if he wished he had kept it still. "Nothing."

"I suppose there's nothing to do for it. Which way, Hurin?"

"South, Lord Rand." The sniffer kept his eyes on the ground.

"South, then." *There has to be a way back besides using the Power.* Rand heeled Red's flanks. He tried to make his voice lighthearted, as if he saw no difficulty at all in what they were about. "What was it Ingtar said? Three or four days to that monument to Artur Hawkwing? I wonder if that exists here, too, the way the Stones do. If this is a world that *could* be, maybe it's still standing. Wouldn't that be something to see, Loial?"

They rode south.

CHAPTER
14

Wolfbrother

G one?" Ingtar demanded of the air. "And my guards saw nothing. Nothing! They cannot just be gone!"

Listening, Perrin hunched his shoulders and looked at Mat, who stood a little way off frowning and muttering to himself. Arguing with himself was how Perrin saw it. The sun was peeking over the horizon, past time for them to have been riding. Shadows lay long across the hollow, stretched out and thinned, but still like the trees that made them. The packhorses, loaded and on their lead line, stamped impatiently, but everyone stood by his mount and waited.

Uno came striding up. "Not a goat-kissing track, my Lord." He sounded offended; failure touched on his skill. "Burn me, not so much as a flaming hoof scrape. They just bloody vanished."

"Three men and three horses do not just vanish," Ingtar growled. "Go over the ground again, Uno. If anyone can find where they went, it's you."

"Maybe they just ran away," Mat said. Uno stopped and glared at him. *Like he'd cursed an Aes Sedai*, Perrin thought wonderingly.

"Why would they run away?" Ingtar's voice was dangerously soft. "Rand, the Builder, my sniffer—my sniffer!—why would any of them run, much less all three?"

Mat shrugged. "I don't know. Rand was. . . ." Perrin wanted to throw something at him, hit him, anything to stop him, but Ingtar and Uno were watching. He felt a flood of relief when Mat hesitated, then spread his hands and muttered, "I don't know why. I just thought maybe they had."

Ingtar grimaced. "Ran away," he growled as if he did not

believe it for an instant. "The Builder can go as he will, but Hurin would not run away. And neither would Rand al'Thor. He would not; he knows his duty, now. Go on, Uno. Search the ground again." Uno gave a half bow and hurried away, sword hilt bobbing over his shoulder. Ingtar grumbled, "Why would Hurin leave like that, in the middle of the night, without a word? He knows what we're about. How am I to track this Shadow-spawned filth without him? I would give a thousand gold crowns for a pack of trail hounds. If I did not know better, I would say the Darkfriends managed this so they can slip east or west without me knowing. Peace, I don't know if I *do* know better." He stumped off after Uno.

Perrin shifted uneasily. The Darkfriends were doubtless getting further away with every minute. Getting further away, and with them the Horn of Valere—and the dagger from Shadar Logoth. He did not think that Rand, whatever he had become, whatever had happened to him, would abandon that chase. *But where* did *he go, and why?* Loial might go with Rand for friendship—but why Hurin?

"Maybe he did run away," he muttered, then looked around. No one appeared to have heard; even Mat was not paying him any mind. He scrubbed a hand through his hair. If Aes Sedai had been after him to be a false Dragon, he would have run, too. But worrying about Rand was doing nothing to help track the Darkfriends.

There was a way, perhaps, if he was willing to take it. He did not want to take it. He had been running away from it, but perhaps, now, he could no longer run. *Serves me right for what I told Rand. I wish I could run.* Even knowing what he could do to help—what he had to do—he hesitated.

No one was looking at him. No one would know what they were seeing even if they did look. Finally, reluctantly, he closed his eyes and let himself drift, let his thoughts drift, out, away from him.

He had tried denying it from the first, long before his eyes began to change from dark brown to burnished golden yellow. At that first meeting, that first instant of recognition, he had refused to believe, and he had run from the recognition ever since. He still wanted to run.

His thoughts drifted, feeling for what must be out there, what was always out there in country where men were few or far between, feeling for his brothers. He did not like to think of them that way, but they were.

In the beginning he had been afraid that what he did had some taint of the Dark One, or of the One Power—equally bad for a man who wanted nothing more than to be a blacksmith and live his life in the Light, and in peace. From that time, he knew something of how Rand felt, afraid of himself, feeling unclean. He was still not past that entirely. This thing he did was older than humans using the One Power, though, something from the birth of Time. Not the Power, Moiraine had told him. Something long vanished, now come again. Egwene knew, too, though he wished she did not. He wished no one did. He hoped she had not told anyone.

Contact. He felt them, felt other minds. Felt his brothers, the wolves.

Their thoughts came to him as a whirlpool blend of images and emotions. At first he had not been able to make out anything except the raw emotion, but now his mind put words to them. *Wolfbrother. Surprise. Two-legs that talks.* A faded image, dim with time, old beyond old, of men running with wolves, two packs hunting together. *We have heard this comes again. You are Long Tooth?*

It was a faint picture of a man dressed in clothes made of hides, with a long knife in his hand, but overlaid on the image, more central, was a shaggy wolf with one tooth longer than the rest, a steel tooth gleaming in the sunlight as the wolf led the pack in a desperate charge through deep snow toward the deer that would mean life instead of slow death by starvation, and the deer thrashing to run in powder to their bellies, and the sun glinting on the white until it hurt the eyes, and the wind howling down the passes, swirling the fine snow like mist, and. . . . Wolves' names were always complex images.

Perrin recognized the man. Elyas Machera, who had first introduced him to wolves. Sometimes he wished he had never met Elyas.

No, he thought, and tried to picture himself in his mind. *Yes. We have heard of you.*

It was not the image he had made, a young man with heavy shoulders and shaggy, brown curls, a young man with an axe at his belt, who others thought moved and thought

slowly. That man was there, somewhere in the mind picture that came from the wolves, but stronger by far was a
massive, wild bull with curved horns of shining metal, running through the night with the speed and exuberance of
youth, curly-haired coat gleaming in the moonlight, flinging himself in among Whitecloaks on their horses, with the
air crisp and cold and dark, and blood so red on the horns,
and. . . .

Young Bull.

For a moment Perrin lost the contact in his shock. He
had not dreamed they had given him a name. He wished he
could not remember how he had earned it. He touched the
axe at his belt, with its gleaming, half-moon blade. *Light
help me, I killed two men. They would have killed me even
quicker, and Egwene, but. . . .*

Pushing all that aside—it was done and behind him; he
had no wish to remember any of it—he gave the wolves the
smell of Rand, of Loial and Hurin, and asked if they had
scented the three. It was one of the things that had come to
him with the change in his eyes; he could identify people by
their smell even when he could not see them. He could see
more sharply, too, see in anything but pitch-darkness. He
was always careful to light lamps or candles, now, sometimes before anyone else thought they were needed.

From the wolves came a view of men on horses approaching the hollow in late day. That was the last they had
seen or smelled of Rand or the other two.

Perrin hesitated. The next step would be useless unless
he told Ingtar. *And Mat will die if we don't find that dagger.
Burn you, Rand, why did you take the sniffer?*

The one time he had gone to the dungeon, with Egwene,
the smell of Fain had made his hair stand on end; not even
Trollocs smelled so foul. He had wanted to rip through the
bars of the cell and tear the man apart, and finding that
inside himself had frightened him more than Fain did. To
mask Fain's smell in his own mind, he added the scent of
Trollocs before he howled aloud.

From the distance came the cries of a wolfpack, and in
the hollow horses stamped and whickered fearfully. Some
of the soldiers fingered their long-bladed lances and eyed
the rim of the hollow uneasily. Inside Perrin's head, it was
much worse. He felt the rage of the wolves, the hate. There

were only two things wolves hated. All else they merely endured, but fire and Trollocs they hated, and they would go through fire to kill Trollocs.

Even more than the Trollocs, Fain's scent had put them into a frenzy, as if they smelled something that made Trollocs seem natural and right.

Where?

The sky rolled in his head; the land spun. East and west, wolves did not know. They knew the movements of sun and moon, the shift of seasons, the contours of the land. Perrin puzzled it out. South. And something more. An eagerness to kill the Trollocs. The wolves would let Young Bull share in the killing. He could bring the two-legs with their hard skins if he wanted, but Young Bull, and Smoke, and Two Deer, and Winter Dawn, and all the rest of the pack would hunt down the Twisted Ones who had dared come into their land. The inedible flesh and bitter blood would burn the tongue, but they must be killed. Kill them. Kill the Twisted Ones.

Their fury infected him. His lips peeled back in a snarl, and he took a step, to join them, run with them in the hunt, in the killing.

With an effort he broke the contact except for a thin sense that the wolves were there. He could have pointed to them across the intervening distance. He felt cold inside. *I'm a man, not a wolf. Light help me, I am a man!*

"Are you well, Perrin?" Mat said, moving closer. He sounded the way he always did, flippant—and bitter under it, too, of late—but he looked worried. "That is all I need. Rand run off, and then you get sick. I don't know where I'll find a Wisdom to look after you out here. I think I have some willowbark in my saddlebags. I can make you some willowbark tea, if Ingtar lets us stay that long. Serve you right if I make it too strong."

"I . . . I'm all right, Mat." Shaking off his friend, he went to find Ingtar. The Shienaran lord was scanning the ground on the rim with Uno, and Ragan, and Masema. The others frowned at him as he drew Ingtar aside. He made sure Uno and the rest were too far away to hear before he spoke. "I don't know where Rand or the others went, Ingtar, but Padan Fain and the Trollocs—and I guess the rest of the Darkfriends—are still heading south."

"How do you know this?" Ingtar said.

Perrin drew a deep breath. "Wolves told me." He waited, for what he was not sure. Laughter, scorn, an accusation of being a Darkfriend, of being mad. Deliberately, he tucked his thumbs behind his belt, away from the axe. *I will not kill. Not again. If he tries to kill me for a Darkfriend, I'll run, but I won't kill anybody else.*

"I have heard of things like this," Ingtar said slowly, after a moment. "Rumors. There was a Warder, a man called Elyas Machera, who some said could talk to wolves. He disappeared years ago." He seemed to catch something in Perrin's eyes. "You know him?"

"I know him," Perrin said flatly. "He's the one. . . . I don't want to talk about it. I didn't ask for it." *That's what Rand said. Light, I wish I were home working Master Luhhan's forge.*

"These wolves," Ingtar said, "they will track the Darkfriends and Trollocs for us?" Perrin nodded. "Good. I will have the Horn, whatever it takes." The Shienaran glanced around at Uno and the others still searching for tracks. "Better not to tell anyone else, though. Wolves are considered good luck in the Borderlands. Trollocs fear them. But still, better to keep this between us for the time. Some of them might not understand."

"I would as soon nobody else ever found out," Perrin said.

"I will tell them you think you have Hurin's talent. They know about that; they're easy with it. Some of them saw you wrinkling your nose back in that village, and at the ferry. I've heard jokes about your delicate nose. Yes. You keep us on the trail today, Uno will see enough of their tracks to confirm it *is* the trail, and before nightfall every last man will be sure you are a sniffer. I *will* have the Horn." He glanced at the sky, and raised his voice. "Daylight is wasting! To horse!"

To Perrin's surprise, the Shienarans seemed to accept Ingtar's story. A few of them looked skeptical—Masema went so far as to spit—but Uno nodded thoughtfully, and that was enough for most. Mat was the hardest to convince.

"A sniffer! You? You're going to track murderers by smell? Perrin, you are as crazy as Rand. I am the only sane one left from Emond's Field, with Egwene and Nynaeve trotting off to Tar Valon to become—" He cut himself short with an uneasy glance for the Shienarans.

Perrin took Hurin's place beside Ingtar as the small column rode south. Mat kept up a string of disparaging remarks, until Uno found the first tracks left by Trollocs and by men on horses, but Perrin paid him little mind. It was all he could do to keep the wolves from dashing on ahead to kill the Trollocs. The wolves cared only about killing the Twisted Ones; to them, Darkfriends were no different from any other two-legs. Perrin could almost see the Darkfriends scattering in a dozen directions while the wolves slew Trollocs, running away with the Horn of Valere. Running away with the dagger. And once the Trollocs were dead, he did not think he could interest the wolves in tracking the humans even if he had any idea which of them to track. He had a running argument with them, and sweat covered his forehead long before he got the first flash of images that turned his stomach.

He drew rein, stopping his horse dead. The others did the same, looking at him, waiting. He stared straight ahead and cursed softly, bitterly.

Wolves would kill men, but men were not a preferred prey. Wolves remembered the old hunting together, for one thing, and two-legs tasted bad, for another. Wolves were more particular about their food than he would have believed. They would not eat carrion, unless they were starving, and few would kill more than they could eat. What Perrin felt from the wolves could best be described as disgust. And there were the images. He could see them much more clearly than he wished. Bodies, men and women and children, heaped and tumbled about. Blood-soaked earth churned by hooves and frenzied attempts to escape. Torn flesh. Heads severed. Vultures flapping, their white wings stained red; bloody, featherless heads tearing and gorging. He broke loose before his stomach emptied itself.

Above some trees in the far distance he could just make out black specks whirling low, dropping then rising again. Vultures fighting over their meal.

"There's something bad up there." He swallowed, meeting Ingtar's gaze. How could he fit telling them into the story of being a sniffer? *I don't want to get close enough to look at that. But they'll want to investigate once they can see the vultures. I have to tell them enough so they'll circle around.* "The people from that village. . . . I think the Trollocs killed them."

Uno began cursing quietly, and some of the other Shie-narans muttered to themselves. None of them seemed to take his announcement as odd, though. Lord Ingtar said he was a sniffer, and sniffers could smell killing.

"And there is someone following us," Ingtar said.

Mat turned his horse eagerly. "Maybe it's Rand. I knew he wouldn't run out on me."

Thin, scattered puffs of dust rose to the north; a horse was running across patches where the grass grew thin. The Shienarans spread out, lances ready, watching in all directions. It was no place to be casual about a stranger.

A speck appeared—a horse and rider; a woman, to Perrin's eyes, long before anyone else could discern the rider—and quickly drew closer. She slowed to a trot as she came up on them, fanning herself with one hand. A plump, graying woman, with her cloak tied behind her saddle, who blinked at them all vaguely.

"That's one of the Aes Sedai," Mat said disappointedly. "I recognize her. Verin."

"Verin Sedai," Ingtar said sharply, then bowed to her from his saddle.

"Moiraine Sedai sent me, Lord Ingtar," Verin announced with a satisfied smile. "She thought you might need me. Such a gallop I've had. I thought I might not catch you short of Cairhien. You saw that village, of course? Oh, that was very nasty, wasn't it? And that Myrddraal. There were ravens and crows all over the rooftops, but never a one went near it, dead as it was. I had to wave away the Dark One's own weight in flies, though, before I could make out what it was. A shame I did not have time to take it down. I've never had a chance to study a—" Suddenly her eyes narrowed, and the absent manner vanished like smoke. "Where is Rand al'Thor?"

Ingtar grimaced. "Gone, Verin Sedai. Vanished last night, without a trace. Him, the Ogier, and Hurin, one of my men."

"The Ogier, Lord Ingtar? And your sniffer went with him? What would those two have in common with . . . ?" Ingtar gaped at her, and she snorted. "Did you think you could keep something like that secret?" She snorted again. "Sniffers. Vanished, you say?"

"Yes, Verin Sedai." Ingtar sounded unsettled. It was never easy discovering Aes Sedai knew the secrets you were trying to keep from them; Perrin hoped Moiraine had not told anyone about him. "But I have—I have a new sniffer." The Shienaran Lord gestured to Perrin. "This man seems to have the ability, also. I will find the Horn of Valere, as I swore to, have no fear. Your company will be welcome, Aes Sedai, if you wish to ride with us." To Perrin's surprise, he did not sound as if he entirely meant it.

Verin glanced at Perrin, and he shifted uneasily. "A new sniffer, just when you lose your old one. How . . . providential. You found no tracks? No, of course not. You said no trace. Odd. Last night." She twisted in her saddle, looking back north, and for a moment Perrin almost thought she was going to ride back the way she had come.

Ingtar frowned at her. "You think their disappearance has something to do with the Horn, Aes Sedai?"

Verin settled back. "The Horn? No. No, I . . . think not. But it is odd. Very odd. I do not like odd things until I can understand them."

"I can have two men escort you back to where they disappeared, Verin Sedai. They will have no trouble taking you right to it."

"No. If you say they vanished without a trace. . . ." For a long moment she studied Ingtar, her face unreadable. "I will ride with you. Perhaps we will find them again, or they will find us. Talk to me as we ride, Lord Ingtar. Tell me everything you can about the young man. Everything he did, everything he said."

They started off in a jingle of harness and armor, Verin riding close beside Ingtar and questioning him closely, but too low to be overheard. She gave Perrin a look when he tried to maintain his place, and he fell back.

"It's Rand she's after," Mat murmured, "not the Horn."

Perrin nodded. *Wherever you've gotten to, Rand, stay there. It's safer than here.*

CHAPTER
15

Kinslayer

The way the strangely faded distant hills seemed to slide toward Rand when he looked straight at them made his head spin, unless he wrapped himself in the void. Sometimes the emptiness crept up on him unawares, but he avoided it like death. Better to be dizzy than share the void with that uneasy light. Better by far to stare at the faded land. Still, he tried not to look at anything too far away unless it lay right ahead of them.

Hurin wore a fixed look as he concentrated on sniffing the trail, as if he were trying to ignore the land the trail crossed. When the sniffer did notice what lay around them, he would give a start and wipe his hands on his coat, then push his nose forward like a hound, eyes glazing, excluding everything else. Loial rode slumped in his saddle and frowned as he glanced around, ears twitching uneasily, muttering to himself.

Again they crossed land blackened and burned, even the soil crunching under the horses' hooves as if it had been seared. The burned swathes, sometimes a mile wide, sometimes only a few hundred paces, all ran east and west as straight as an arrow's flight. Twice Rand saw the end of a burn, once as they rode over it, once as they passed nearby; they tapered to points at the ends. At least, the ends he saw were so, but he suspected they were all the same.

Once he had watched Whatley Eldin decorate a cart for Sunday, back home in Emond's Field, What painting the scenes in bright colors, and the intricate scrollwork that surrounded them. For the borders, What let the point of his brush touch the cart, making a thin line that grew thicker as he pressed harder, then thinner again as he eased up. That was how the land looked, as if someone had streaked it with a monstrous brush of fire.

Nothing grew where the burns were, though some burns, at least, had the feel of a thing long done. Not so much as a hint of char remained in the air there, not a whiff even when he leaned down to break off a black twig and smell it. Old, yet nothing had come in to reclaim the land. Black gave way to green, and green to black, along knife-edge lines.

In its own way, the rest of the land lay as dead as the burns, though grass covered the ground and leaves covered the trees. Everything had that faded look, like clothes too often washed and too long left in the sun. There were no birds or animals, not that Rand saw or heard. No hawk wheeling in the sky, no bark of a hunting fox, no bird singing. Nothing rustled in the grass or lit on a tree branch. No bees, or butterflies. Several times they crossed streams, the water shallow, though often it had dug itself a deep gulley with steep banks the horses had to scramble down and climb on the other side. The water ran clear except for the mud the horses' hooves stirred, but never a minnow or tadpole wriggled out of the roiling, not even a waterspider dancing across the surface, or a hovering lacewing.

The water was drinkable, which was just as well, since their waterbottles could not last forever. Rand tasted it first, and made Loial and Hurin wait to see if anything happened to him before he let them drink. He had gotten them into this; it was his responsibility. The water was cool and wet, but that was the best that could be said for it. It tasted flat, as if it had been boiled. Loial made a face, and the horses did not like it either, shaking their heads and drinking reluctantly.

There was one sign of life; at least, Rand thought it must be so. Twice he saw a wispy streak crawling across the sky like a line drawn with cloud. The lines were too straight to be natural, it seemed, but he could not imagine what might make them. He did not mention the lines to the others. Perhaps they did not see, Hurin intent on the trail as he was and Loial drawn in on himself. They said nothing of the lines, at any rate.

When they had ridden half the morning, Loial abruptly

swung down from his huge horse without a word and strode
to a stand of giantsbroom, their trunks splitting into many
thick branches, stiff and straight, not a pace above the
ground. At the top, all split again, into the leafy brush that
gave them their name.

Rand pulled Red up and started to ask what he was doing, but something about the Ogier's manner, as if he himself were uncertain, kept Rand silent. After staring at the
tree, Loial put his hands on a trunk and began to sing in a
deep, soft rumble.

Rand had heard Ogier Treesong, once, when Loial had
sung to a dying tree and brought it back to life, and he had
heard of sung wood, objects wrought from trees by the
Treesong. The Talent was fading, Loial said, he was one of
the few who had the ability, now; that was what made sung
wood even more sought after and treasured. When he had
heard Loial sing before, it had been as if the earth itself
sang, but now the Ogier murmured his song almost diffidently, and the land echoed it in a whisper.

It seemed pure song, music without words, at least none
that Rand could make out; if there were words, they faded
into the music just as water pours into a stream. Hurin
gasped and stared.

Rand was not sure what it was Loial did, or how; soft
as the song was, it caught him up hypnotically, filling his
mind almost the way the void did. Loial ran his big hands
along the trunk, singing, caressing with his voice as well as
his fingers. The trunk now seemed smoother, somehow, as
if his stroking were shaping it. Rand blinked. He was sure
the piece Loial worked on had had branches at its top just
like the others, but now it stopped in a rounded end right
above the Ogier's head. Rand opened his mouth, but the
song quieted him. It seemed so familiar, that song, as if he
should know it.

Abruptly Loial's voice rose to a climax—almost a hymn
of thanks, it sounded—and ended, fading as a breeze fades.

"Burn me," Hurin breathed. He looked stunned. "Burn
me, I never heard anything like. . . . Burn me."

In his hands Loial held a staff as tall as he was and as
thick as Rand's forearm, smooth and polished. Where the
trunk had been on the giantsbroom was a small stem of new
growth.

Rand took a deep breath. *Always something new, always something I didn't expect, and sometimes it isn't horrible.*

He watched Loial mount, resting the staff across his saddle in front of him, and wondered why the Ogier wanted a staff at all, since they were riding. Then he saw the thick rod, not as big as it was, but in relation to the Ogier, saw the way Loial handled it. "A quarterstaff," he said, surprised. "I didn't know Ogier carried weapons, Loial."

"Usually we do not," the Ogier replied almost curtly. "Usually. The price has always been too high." He hefted the huge quarterstaff and wrinkled his broad nose with distaste. "Elder Haman would surely say I am putting a long handle on my axe, but I am not just being hasty or rash, Rand. This place. . . ." He shivered, and his ears twitched.

"We'll find our way back soon," Rand said, trying to sound confident.

Loial spoke as if he had not heard. "Everything is . . . linked, Rand. Whether it lives or not, whether it thinks or not, everything that *is*, fits together. The tree does not think, but it is part of the whole, and the whole has a—a feeling. I can't explain any more than I can explain what being happy is, but. . . . Rand, this land was glad for a weapon to be made. Glad!"

"The Light shine on us," Hurin murmured nervously, "and the Creator's hand shelter us. Though we go to the last embrace of the mother, the Light illumine our way." He kept repeating the catechism as if it had a charm to protect him.

Rand resisted the impulse to look around. He definitely did not look up. All it would take to break them all was another of those smoky lines across the sky right at that moment. "There's nothing here to hurt us," he said firmly. "And we'll keep a good watch and make sure nothing does."

He wanted to laugh at himself, sounding so certain. He was not certain about anything. But watching the others— Loial with his tufted ears drooping, and Hurin trying not to look at anything—he knew one of them had to seem to be sure, at least, or fear and uncertainty would break them all apart. *The Wheel weaves as the Wheel wills.* He squeezed that thought out. *Nothing to do with the Wheel. Nothing to with ta'veren, or Aes Sedai, or the Dragon. It's just the way it is, that's all.*

"Loial, are you done here?" The Ogier nodded, regretfully rubbing the quarterstaff. Rand turned to Hurin. "Do you still have the trail?"

"I do, Lord Rand. I do that."

"Then let's keep on with it. Once we find Fain and the Darkfriends, why, we'll go home heroes, with the dagger for Mat, and the Horn of Valere. Lead out, Hurin." *Heroes? I'll settle for all of us getting out of here alive.*

"I do not like this place," the Ogier announced flatly. He held the quarterstaff as if he expected to have to use it soon.

"As well we don't mean to stay here, then, isn't it?" Rand said. Hurin barked a laugh as if he had made a joke, but Loial gave him a level look.

"As well we don't, Rand."

Yet as they rode on southward, he could see that his casual assumption that they would get home had picked them both up a little. Hurin sat a bit straighter in his saddle, and Loial's ears did not seem so wilted. It was no time or place to let them know he shared their fear, so he kept it to himself, and fought it by himself.

Hurin kept his humor through the morning, murmuring, "As well we don't mean to stay," then chuckling, until Rand felt like telling him to be quiet. Toward midday, the sniffer did fall silent, though, shaking his head and frowning, and Rand found he wished the man was still repeating his words and laughing.

"Is there something wrong with the trail, Hurin?" he asked.

The sniffer shrugged, looking troubled. "Yes, Lord Rand, and then again no, as you might say."

"It must be one or the other. Have you lost the trail? No shame if you have. You said it was weak to start. If we can't find the Darkfriends, we will find another Stone and get back that way." *Light, anything but that.* Rand kept his face smooth. "If Darkfriends can come here and leave, so can we."

"Oh, I haven't lost it, Lord Rand. I can still pick out the stink of them. It isn't that. It's just. . . . It's. . . ." With a grimace, Hurin burst out, "It's like I'm remembering it, Lord Rand, instead of smelling it. But I'm not. There's dozens of trails crossing it all the time, dozens and dozens, and all sorts of smells of violence, some of them fresh, almost, only washed out like everything else. This morning, right after we left the hollow, I could have sworn there were hundreds slaughtered right under my feet, just minutes before, but there weren't any bodies, and not a mark on the grass but our own hoofprints. A thing like that couldn't happen without the ground being torn up and bloodied, but there wasn't a mark. It's all like that, my Lord. But I am following the trail. I am. This place just has me all on edge. That's it. That must be it."

Rand glanced at Loial—the Ogier did come up with the oddest knowledge, at times—but he looked as puzzled as Hurin. Rand made his voice more confident than he felt. "I know you are doing your best, Hurin. We are all of us on edge. Just follow as best you can, and we'll find them."

"As you say, Lord Rand." Hurin booted his horse forward. "As you say."

But by nightfall, there was still no sign of the Darkfriends, and Hurin said the trail was fainter still. The sniffer kept muttering to himself about "remembering."

There had been no sign. Really no sign. Rand was not as good a tracker as Uno, but any boy in the Two Rivers was expected to track well enough to find a lost sheep, or a rabbit for dinner. He had seen nothing. It was as if no living thing had ever disturbed the land before they came. There should have been something if the Darkfriends were ahead of them. But Hurin kept following the trail he said he smelled.

As the sun touched the horizon they made camp in a stand of trees untouched by the burn, eating from their saddlebags. Flatbread and dried meat washed down with flat-tasting water; hardly a filling meal, tough and far from tasty. Rand thought they might have enough for a week. After that. . . . Hurin ate slowly, determinedly, but Loial gulped his down with a grimace and settled back with his pipe, the big quarterstaff close at hand. Rand kept their fire small and well hidden in the trees. Fain and his Darkfriends and Trollocs might be close enough to see a fire, for all of Hurin's worries about the oddness of their trail.

It seemed odd to him that he had begun to think of them as Fain's Darkfriends, Fain's Trollocs. Fain was just a madman. *Then why did they rescue him?* Fain had been part of the Dark One's scheme to find him. Perhaps it had something to do with that. *Then why is he running instead of chasing me? And what killed that Fade? What happened in that room full of flies? And those eyes, watching me in Fal Dara. And that wind, catching me like a beetle in pine sap. No. No, Ba'alzamon has to be dead.* The Aes Sedai did not believe it. Moiraine did not believe it, nor the Amyrlin. Stubbornly, he refused to think about it any longer. All he had to think about now was finding that dagger for Mat. Finding Fain, and the Horn.

It's never over, al'Thor.

The voice was like a thin breeze whispering in the back of his head, a thin, icy murmur working its way into the crevices of his mind. He almost sought the void to escape it, but remembering what waited for him there, he pushed down the desire.

In the half dark of twilight, he worked the forms with his sword, the way Lan had taught, though without the void. Parting the Silk. Hummingbird Kisses the Honeyrose. Heron Wading in the Rushes, for balance. Losing himself in the swift, sure movements, forgetting for a time where he was, he worked until sweat covered him. Yet when he was done, it all came back; nothing was changed. The weather was not cold, but he shivered and pulled his cloak around him as he hunched by the fire. The others caught his mood, and they finished eating quickly and in silence. No one complained when he kicked dirt over the last fitful flames.

Rand took the first watch himself, walking the edges of the copse with his bow, sometimes easing his sword in its scabbard. The chill moon was almost full, standing high in the blackness, and the night was as silent as the day had been, as empty. Empty was the right word. The land was as empty as a dusty milk crock. It was hard to believe there was anyone in the whole world, in this world, except for the three of them, hard to believe even the Darkfriends were there, somewhere ahead.

To keep himself company, he unwrapped Thom Merrilin's cloak, exposing the harp and flute in their hard leather cases atop the many-colored patches. He took the gold-and-silver flute from its case, remembering the gleeman teaching him as he fingered it, and played a few notes of "The

Wind That Shakes the Willow," softly so as not to wake the others. Even soft, the sad sound was too loud in that place, too real. With a sigh he replaced the flute and did up the bundle again.

He held the watch long into the night, letting the others sleep. He did not know how late it was when he suddenly realized a fog had risen. Close to the ground it lay, thick, making Hurin and Loial indistinct mounds seeming to hump out of clouds. Thinner higher up, it still shrouded the land around them, hiding everything except the nearest trees. The moon seemed viewed through watered silk. Anything at all could come right up to them unseen. He touched his sword.

"Swords do no good against me, Lews Therin. You should know that."

The fog swirled around Rand's feet as he spun, the sword coming into his hands, heron-mark blade upright before him. The void leaped up inside him; for the first time, he barely noticed the tainted light of *saidin*.

A shadowy figure drew nearer through the mist, walking with a tall staff. Behind it, as if the shadow's shadow were vast, the fog darkened till it was blacker than night. Rand's skin crawled. Closer the figure came, until it resolved into the shape of a man, clothed and gloved in black, with a black silk mask covering his face, and the shadow came with it. His staff was black, too, as if the wood had been charred, yet smooth and shining like water by moonlight. For an instant the eyeholes of the mask glowed, as if fires stood behind them rather than eyes, but Rand did not need that to know who it was.

"Ba'alzamon," he breathed. "This is a dream. It has to be. I fell asleep, and—"

Ba'alzamon laughed like the roar of an open furnace. "You always try to deny what is, Lews Therin. If I stretch out my hand, I can touch you, Kinslayer. I can always touch you. Always and everywhere."

"I am not the Dragon! My name is Rand al'—!" Rand clamped his teeth shut to stop himself.

"Oh, I know the name you use now, Lews Therin. I know every name you have used through Age after Age, long before you were even the Kinslayer." Ba'alzamon's voice began to rise in intensity; sometimes the fires of his eyes flared so high that Rand could see them through the openings in the silk mask, see them like endless seas of flame. "I know you, know your blood and your line back to the first spark of life that ever was, back to the First Moment. You can never hide from me. Never! We are tied together as surely as two sides of the same coin. Ordinary men may hide in the sweep of the Pattern, but *ta'veren* stand out like beacon fires on a hill, and you, *you* stand out as if ten thousand shining arrows stood in the sky to point you out! You are mine, and ever in reach of my hand!"

"Father of Lies!" Rand managed. Despite the void, his tongue wanted to cleave to the roof of his mouth. *Light, please let it be a dream.* The thought skittered outside the emptiness. *Even one of those dreams that isn't a dream. He can't really be standing in front of me. The Dark One is sealed in Shayol Ghul, sealed by the Creator at the moment of Creation. . . .* He knew too much of the truth for it to help. "You're well named! If you could just take me, why haven't you? Because you cannot. I walk in the Light, and you cannot touch me!"

Ba'alzamon leaned on his staff and looked at Rand a moment, then moved to stand over Loial and Hurin, peering down at them. The vast shadow moved with him. He did not disturb the fog, Rand saw—he moved, the staff swung with his steps, but the gray mist did not swirl and eddy around his feet as it did around Rand's. That gave him heart. Perhaps Ba'alzamon really was *not* there. Perhaps it *was* a dream.

"You find odd followers," Ba'alzamon mused. "You always did. These two. The girl who tries to watch over you. A poor guardian and weak, Kinslayer. If she had a lifetime to grow, she would never grow strong enough for you to hide behind."

Girl? Who? Moiraine is surely not a girl. "I don't know what you are talking about, Father of Lies. You lie, and lie, and even when you tell the truth, you twist it to a lie."

"Do I, Lews Therin? You know what you are, who you are. I have told you. And so have those women of Tar Valon." Rand shifted, and Ba'alzamon gave a laugh, like a small thunderclap. "They think themselves safe in their White Tower, but my followers number even some of their own.

The Aes Sedai called Moiraine told you who you are, did she not? Did she lie? Or is she one of mine? The White Tower means to use you like a hound on a leash. Do I lie? Do I lie when I say you seek the Horn of Valere?" He laughed again; calm of the void or no, it was all Rand could do not to cover his ears. "Sometimes old enemies fight so long that they become allies and never realize it. They think they strike at you, but they have become so closely linked it is as if you guided the blow yourself."

"You don't guide me," Rand said. "I deny you."

"I have a thousand strings tied to you, Kinslayer, each one finer than silk and stronger than steel. Time has tied a thousand cords between us. The battle we two have fought—do you remember any part of that? Do you have any glimmering that we have fought before, battles without number back to the beginning of Time? I know much that you do not! That battle will soon end. The Last Battle is coming. The last, Lews Therin. Do you really think you can avoid it? You poor, shivering worm. You will serve me or die! And this time the cycle will not begin anew with your death. The grave belongs to the Great Lord of the Dark. This time if you die, you will be destroyed utterly. This time the Wheel will be broken whatever you do, and the world remade to a new mold. Serve me! Serve Shai'tan, or be destroyed forever!"

With the utterance of that name, the air seemed to thicken. The darkness behind Ba'alzamon swelled and grew, threatening to swallow everything. Rand felt it engulfing him, colder than ice and hotter than coals both at the same time, blacker than death, sucking him into the depths of it, overwhelming the world.

He gripped his sword hilt till his knuckles hurt. "I deny you, and I deny your power. I walk in the Light. The Light preserves us, and we shelter in the palm of the Creator's hand." He blinked. Ba'alzamon still stood there, and the great darkness still hung behind him, but it was as if all the rest had been illusion.

"Do you want to see my face?" It was a whisper.

Rand swallowed. "No."

"You should." A gloved hand went to the black mask. "No!"

The mask came away. It was a man's face, horribly burned. Yet between the black-edged, red crevices crossing those features, the skin looked healthy and smooth. Dark eyes looked at Rand; cruel lips smiled with a flash of white teeth. "Look at me, Kinslayer, and see the hundredth part of your own fate." For a moment eyes and mouth became doorways into endless caverns of fire. "This is what the Power unchecked can do, even to me. But I heal, Lews Therin. I know the paths to greater power. It will burn you like a moth flying into a furnace."

"I will not touch it!" Rand felt the void around him, felt *saidin*. "I won't."

"You cannot stop yourself."

"Leave—me—ALONE!"

"Power." Ba'alzamon's voice became soft, insinuating. "You can have power again, Lews Therin. You are linked to it now, this moment. I know it. I can see it. Feel it, Lews Therin. Feel the glow inside you. Feel the power that could be yours. All you must do is reach out for it. But the Shadow is there between you and it. Madness and death. You need not die, Lews Therin, not ever again."

"No," Rand said, but the voice went on, burrowing into him.

"I can teach you to control that power so that it does not destroy you. No one else lives who can teach you that. The Great Lord of the Dark can shelter you from the madness. The power can be yours, and you can live forever. Forever! All you must do in return is serve. Only serve. Simple words—I am yours, Great Lord—and power will be yours. Power beyond anything those women of Tar Valon dream of, and life eternal, if you will only offer yourself up and serve."

Rand licked his lips. *Not to go mad. Not to die.* "Never! I walk in the Light," he grated hoarsely, "and you can never touch me!"

"Touch you, Lews Therin? Touch you? I can consume you! Taste it and know, as I knew!"

Those dark eyes became fire again, and that mouth, flame that blossomed and grew until it seemed brighter than a summer sun. Grew, and suddenly Rand's sword glowed as if just drawn from the forge. He cried out as the hilt burned his hands, screamed and dropped the sword. And the fog caught fire, fire that leaped, fire that burned everything.

Yelling, Rand beat at his clothes as they smoked and charred and fell in ashes, beat with hands that blackened and shriveled as naked flesh cracked and peeled away in the flames. He screamed. Pain beat at the void inside him, and he tried to crawl deeper into the emptiness. The glow was there, the tainted light just out of sight. Half mad, no longer caring what it was, he reached for *saidin*, tried to wrap it around him, tried to hide in it from the burning and the pain.

As suddenly as the fire began, it was gone. Rand stared wonderingly at his hand sticking out of the red sleeve of his coat. There was not so much as a singe on the wool. *I imagined it all.* Frantically, he looked around. Ba'alzamon was gone. Hurin shifted in his sleep; the sniffer and Loial were still only two mounds sticking up out of the low fog. *I did imagine it.*

Before relief had a chance to grow, pain stabbed his right hand, and he turned it up to look. There across the palm was branded a heron. The heron from the hilt of his sword, angry and red, as neatly done as though drawn with an artist's skill.

Fumbling a kerchief from his coat pocket, he wrapped it around his hand. The hand throbbed, now. The void would help with that—he was *aware* of pain in the void, but he did not *feel* it—but he put the thought out of his head. Twice now, unknowing—and once on purpose; he could not forget that—he had tried to channel the One Power while he was in the void. It was with that that Ba'alzamon wanted to tempt him. It was that that Moiraine and the Amyrlin Seat wanted him to do. He would not.

Chapter 16

In the Mirror of Darkness

You should not have done it, Lord Rand," Hurin said when Rand woke the others just at daybreak. The sun yet hid below the horizon, but there was light enough to see. The fog had melted away while dark still held, fading reluctantly. "If you use yourself up to spare us, my Lord, who will see to getting us home?"

"I needed to think," Rand said. Nothing showed the fog had ever been, or Ba'alzamon. He fingered the kerchief wrapped around his right hand. There was that to prove Ba'alzamon had been there. He wanted to be away from this place. "Time to be in the saddle if we are going to catch Fain's Darkfriends. Past time. We can eat flatbread while we ride."

Loial paused in the act of stretching, his arms reaching as high as Hurin could have standing on Rand's shoulders. "Your hand, Rand. What happened?"

"I hurt it. It's nothing."

"I have a salve in my saddlebags—"

"It is nothing!" Rand knew he sounded harsh, but one look at the brand would surely bring questions he did not want to answer. "Time's wasting. Let us be on our way." He set about saddling Red, awkwardly because of his injured hand, and Hurin jumped to his own horse.

"No need to be so touchy," Loial muttered.

A track, Rand decided as they set out, would be something natural in that world. There were too many unnatural things there. Even a single hoofprint would be welcome. Fain and the Darkfriends and the Trollocs had to leave some mark. He concentrated on the ground they passed over, trying to make out any trace that could have been made by another living thing.

There was nothing, not a turned stone, not a disturbed clod of earth. Once he looked at the ground behind them, just to reassure himself that the land did take hoofprints; scraped turf and bent grass marked their passage plainly, yet ahead the ground was undisturbed. But Hurin insisted he could smell the trail, faint and thin, but still heading south.

Once again the sniffer put all his attentions on the trail he followed, like a hound tracking deer, and once again Loial rode lost in his own thoughts, muttering to himself and rubbing the huge quarterstaff held across his saddle in front of him.

They had not been riding more than an hour when Rand saw the spire ahead. He was so busy watching for tracks that the tapering column already stood thick and tall above the trees in the middle distance when he first noticed it. "I wonder what that is." It lay directly in their path.

"I don't know what it can be, Rand," Loial said.

"If this—if this was our own world, Lord Rand. . . ." Hurin shifted uncomfortably in his saddle. "Well, that monument Lord Ingtar was talking about—the one to Artur Hawkwing's victory over the Trollocs—it was a great spire. But it was torn down a thousand years ago. There's nothing left but a big mound, like a hill. I saw it, when I went to Cairhien for Lord Agelmar."

"According to Ingtar," Loial said, "that is still three or four days ahead of us. If it is here at all. I don't know why it should be. I don't think there are any people here at all."

The sniffer put his eyes back on the ground. "That's just it, isn't it, Builder? No people, but there it is ahead of us. Maybe we ought to keep clear of it, my Lord Rand. No telling what it is, or who's there, in a place like this."

Rand drummed his fingers on the high pommel of his saddle for a moment, thinking. "We have to stick as close to the trail as we can," he said finally. "We don't seem to be getting any closer to Fain as it is, and I don't want to lose more time, if we can avoid it. If we see any people, or anything out of the ordinary, then we'll circle around until we pick it up again. But until then, we keep on."

"As you say, my Lord." The sniffer sounded odd, and he gave Rand a quick, sidelong look. "As you say."

Rand frowned for a moment before he understood, and then it was his turn to sigh. Lords did not explain to those who followed them, only to other lords. *I didn't ask him to take me for a bloody lord. But he did,* a small voice seemed to answer him, *and you let him. You made the choice; now the duty is yours.*

"Take the trail, Hurin," Rand said.

With a flash of relieved grin, the sniffer heeled his horse onward.

The weak sun climbed as they rode, and by the time it was overhead, they were only a mile or so from the spire. They had reached one of the streams, in a gully a pace deep, and the intervening trees were sparse. Rand could see the mound it was built on, like a round, flat-topped hill. The gray spire itself rose at least a hundred spans, and he could just make out now that the top was carved in the likeness of a bird with outstretched wings.

"A hawk," Rand said. "It *is* Hawkwing's monument. It must be. There were people here, whether there are now or not. They just built it in another place here, and never tore it down. Think of it, Hurin. When we get back, you'll be able to tell them what the monument really looked like. There will only be three of us in the whole world who have ever seen it."

Hurin nodded. "Yes, my Lord. My children would like to hear that tale, their father seeing Hawkwing's spire."

"Rand," Loial began worriedly.

"We can gallop the distance," Rand said. "Come on. A gallop will do us good. This place may be dead, but we're alive."

"Rand," Loial said, "I don't think that is a—"

Not waiting to hear, Rand dug his boots into Red's flanks, and the stallion sprang forward. He splashed across the shallow ribbon of water in two strides, then scrabbled up the far side. Hurin launched his horse right behind him. Rand heard Loial calling behind them, but he laughed, waved for the Ogier to follow, and galloped on. If he kept his eyes on one spot, the land did not seem to slip and slide so badly, and the wind felt good on his face.

The mound covered a good two hides, but the grassy slope rose at an easy slant. The gray spire reared into the sky, squared and broad enough despite its height to seem

massive, almost squat. Rand's laughter died, and he pulled
Red up, his face grim.

"Is that Hawkwing's monument, Lord Rand?" Hurin
asked uneasily. "It doesn't look right, somehow."

Rand recognized the harsh, angular script that covered
the face of the monument, and he recognized some of the
symbols chiseled on the breadth, chiseled as tall as a man.
The horned skull of the Dha'vol Trollocs. The iron fist of
the Dhai'mon. The trident of the Ko'bal, and the whirlwind
of the Ahf'frait. There was a hawk, too, carved near the
bottom. With a wingspan of ten paces, it lay on its back,
pierced by a lightning bolt, and ravens pecked at its eyes.
The huge wings atop the spire seemed to block the sun.

He heard Loial galloping up behind him.

"I tried to tell you, Rand," Loial said. "It is a raven, not a
hawk. I could see it clearly." Hurin turned his horse, refusing even to look at the spire any longer.

"But how?" Rand said. "Artur Hawkwing won a victory
over the Trollocs here. Ingtar said so."

"Not here," Loial said slowly. "Obviously not here. 'From
Stone to Stone run the lines of it, between the worlds that
might be.' I've been thinking on it, and I believe I know
what 'the worlds that might be' are. Maybe I do. Worlds our
world might have been if things had happened differently.
Maybe that's why it is all so . . . washed-out looking. Because it's an 'if,' a 'maybe.' Just a shadow of the real world.
In this world, I think, the Trollocs won. Maybe that's why
we have not seen any villages or people."

Rand's skin crawled. Where Trollocs won, they did not
leave humans alive except for food. If they had won across
an entire world. . . . "If the Trollocs had won, they would
be everywhere. We'd have seen a thousand of them by now.
We'd be dead since yesterday."

"I do not know, Rand. Perhaps, after they killed the people, they killed one another. Trollocs live to kill. That is all
they do; that is all they are. I just don't know."

"Lord Rand," Hurin said abruptly, "something moved
down there."

Rand whirled his horse, ready to see charging Trollocs,
but Hurin was pointing back the way they had come, at
nothing. "What did you see, Hurin? Where?"

The sniffer let his arm drop. "Right at the edge of that

clump of trees there, about a mile. I thought it was . . .
a woman . . . and something else I couldn't make out,
but. . . ." He shivered. "It's so hard to make out things that
aren't under your nose. Aaah, this place has my guts all
awhirl. I'm likely imagining things, my Lord. This is a
place for queer fancies." His shoulders hunched as if he felt
the spire pressing on them. "No doubt it was just the wind,
my Lord."

Loial said, "There's something else to consider, I'm
afraid." He sounded troubled again. He pointed southward.
"What do you see off there?"

Rand squinted against the way things far off seemed to
slide toward him. "Land like what we've been crossing.
Trees. Then some hills, and mountains. Nothing else. What
do you want me to see?"

"The mountains," Loial sighed. The tufts on his ears
drooped, and the ends of his eyebrows were down on his
cheeks. "That has to be Kinslayer's Dagger, Rand. There
aren't any other mountains they could be, unless this world
is completely different from ours. But Kinslayer's Dagger
lies more than a hundred leagues south of the Erinin. A
good bit more. Distances are hard to judge in this place,
but. . . . I think we will reach them before dark." He did not
have to say any more. They could not have covered over a
hundred leagues in less than three days.

Without thinking, Rand muttered, "Maybe this place is
like the Ways." He heard Hurin moan, and instantly regretted not keeping a rein on his tongue.

It was not a pleasant thought. Enter a Waygate—they
could be found just outside Ogier *stedding*, and in Ogier
groves—enter and walk for a day, and you could leave
by another Waygate a hundred leagues from where you
started. The Ways were dark, now, and foul, and to travel
them meant to risk death or madness. Even Fades feared to
travel the Ways.

"If it is, Rand," Loial said slowly, "can a misstep kill us
here, too? Are there things we have not yet seen that can do
worse than kill us?" Hurin moaned again.

They had been drinking the water, riding along as if
they had not a concern in the world. Unconcern would kill
quickly in the Ways. Rand swallowed, hoping his stomach
would settle.

"It is too late for worrying about what is past," he said. "From here on, though, we will watch our step." He glanced at Hurin. The sniffer's head had sunk between his shoulders, and his eyes darted as if he wondered what would leap at him, and from where. The man had run down murderers, but this was more than he had ever bargained for. "Hold on to yourself, Hurin. We are not dead, yet, and we won't be. We will just have to be careful from here on. That's all."

It was at that moment they heard the scream, thin with distance.

"A woman!" Hurin said. Even this much that was normal seemed to rouse him a little. "I knew I saw—"

Another scream came, more desperate than the first.

"Not unless she can fly," Rand said. "She's south of us." He kicked Red to a dead run in two strides.

"Be careful you said!" Loial shouted after him. "Light, Rand, remember! Be careful!"

Rand lay low on Red's back, letting the stallion run. The screams drew him on. It was easy to say be careful, but there was terror in that woman's voice. She did not sound as if she had time for him to be careful. On the edge of another stream, in a sheer-banked channel deeper than most, he drew rein; Red skidded in a shower of stones and dirt. The screams were coming. . . . *There!*

He took it all in at a glance. Perhaps two hundred paces away, the woman stood beside her horse in the stream, both of them backed against the far bank. With a broken length of branch, she was fending off a snarling . . . something. Rand swallowed, stunned for a moment. If a frog were as big as a bear, or if a bear had a frog's gray-green hide, it might look like that. A big bear.

Not letting himself think about the creature, he leaped to the ground, unlimbering his bow. If he took the time to ride closer, it might be too late. The woman was barely keeping the . . . thing . . . at the edge of the branch. It was a fair distance—he kept blinking as he tried to judge it; the distance seemed to change by spans every time the thing moved—yet a big target. His bandaged hand made drawing awkward, but he had an arrow loosed almost before his feet were set.

The shaft sank into the leathery hide for half its length, and the creature spun to face Rand. Rand took a step back despite the distance. That huge, wedge-shaped head had never been on any animal he could imagine, nor that wide, horny-lipped beak of a mouth, hooked for ripping flesh. And it had three eyes, small, and fierce, and ringed by hard-looking ridges. Gathering itself, the thing bounded toward him down the stream in great, splashing leaps. To Rand's eye, some of the leaps seemed to cover twice as much distance as others, though he was sure they were all the same.

"An eye," the woman called. She sounded surprisingly calm, considering her screams. "You must hit an eye to kill it."

He drew the fletching of another arrow back to his ear. Reluctantly, he sought the void; he did not want to, but it was for this that Tam had taught him, and he knew he could never make the shot without it. *My father*, he thought with a sense of loss, and emptiness filled him. The quavering light of *saidin* was there, but he shut it away. He was one with the bow, with the arrow, with the monstrous shape leaping toward him. One with the tiny eye. He did not even feel the arrow leave the bowstring.

The creature rose in another bound, and at the peak, the arrow struck its central eye. The thing landed, fountaining another huge splash of water and mud. Ripples spread out from it, but it did not move.

"Well shot, and bravely," the woman called. She was on her horse, riding to meet him. Rand felt vaguely surprised that she had not run once the thing's attention was diverted. She rode past the bulk, still surrounded by the ripples of its dying, without even a downward glance, scrambled her horse up the bank and dismounted. "Few men would stand to face the charge of a *grolm,* my Lord."

She was all in white, her dress divided for riding and belted in silver, and her boots, peeking out from under her hems, were tooled in silver, too. Even her saddle was white, and silver-mounted. Her snowy mare, with its arched neck and dainty step, was almost as tall as Rand's bay. But it was the woman herself—she was perhaps Nynaeve's age, he thought—who held his eyes. She was tall, for one thing; a hand taller and she could almost look him in the eyes. For another, she was beautiful, ivory-pale skin contrasting sharply with long, night-dark hair and black eyes. He had seen beautiful women. Moiraine was beautiful, if cool, and so was Nynaeve, when her temper did not get the better of her. Egwene, and Elayne, the Daughter-Heir of Andor, were each enough to take a man's breath. But this woman. . . . His tongue stuck to the roof of his mouth; he felt his heart start beating again.

"Your retainers, my Lord?"

Startled, he looked around. Hurin and Loial had joined them. Hurin was staring the way Rand knew he had been, and even the Ogier seemed fascinated. "My friends," he said. "Loial, and Hurin. My name is Rand. Rand al'Thor."

"I have never thought of it before," Loial said abruptly, sounding as if he were talking to himself; "but if there is such a thing as perfect human beauty, in face and form, then you—"

"Loial!" Rand shouted. The Ogier's ears stiffened in embarrassment. Rand's own ears were red; Loial's words had been too close to what he himself was thinking.

The woman laughed musically, but the next instant she was all regal formality, like a queen on her throne. "I am called Selene," she said. "You have risked your life, and saved mine. I am yours, Lord Rand al'Thor." And, to Rand's horror, she knelt before him.

Not looking at Hurin or Loial, he hastily pulled her to her feet. "A man who will not die to save a woman is no man." Immediately he disgraced himself by blushing. It was a Shienaran saying, and he knew it sounded pompous before it was out of his mouth, but her manner had infected him, and he could not stop it. "I mean. . . . That is, it was. . . ." *Fool, you can't tell a woman saving her life was nothing.* "It was my honor." That sounded vaguely Shienaran and formal. He hoped it would do; his mind was as blank of anything else to say as if he were still in the void.

Suddenly he became conscious of her eyes on him. Her expression had not changed, but her dark eyes made him feel as if he were naked. Unbidden, the thought came of Selene with no clothes. His face went red again. "Aaah! Ah, where are you from, Selene? We have not seen another human being since we came here. Is your town nearby?" She looked at him thoughtfully, and he stepped back. Her look made him too aware of how close to her he was.

"I'm not from this world, my Lord," she said. "There are no people here. Nothing living except the *grolm* and a few other creatures like them. I am from Cairhien. And as to how I came here, I don't know, exactly. I was out riding, and I stopped to nap, and when I woke, my horse and I were here. I can only hope, my Lord, that you can save me again, and help me go home."

"Selene, I am not a . . . that is, please call me Rand." His ears felt hot again. *Light, it won't hurt anything if she thinks I'm a lord. Burn me, it won't hurt anything.*

"If you wish it . . . Rand." Her smile made his throat tighten. "You will help me?"

"Of course, I will." *Burn me, but she's beautiful. And looking at me like I'm a hero in a story.* He shook his head to clear it of foolishness. "But first we have to find the men we are following. I'll try to keep you out of danger, but we must find them. Coming with us will be better than staying here alone."

For a moment she was silent, her face blank and smooth; Rand had no idea what she was thinking, except that she seemed to be studying him anew. "A man of duty," she said finally. A small smile touched her lips. "I like that. Yes. Who are these miscreants you follow?"

"Darkfriends and Trollocs, my Lady," Hurin burst out. He made an awkward bow to her from his saddle. "They did murder in Fal Dara keep and stole the Horn of Valere, my Lady, but Lord Rand will fetch it back."

Rand stared at the sniffer ruefully; Hurin gave a weak grin. *So much for secrecy.* It did not matter here, he supposed, but once back in their world. . . . "Selene, you must not say anything of the Horn to anyone. If it gets out, we'll have a hundred people on our heels trying to get the Horn for themselves."

"No, it would never do," Selene said, "for *that* to fall into the wrong hands. The Horn of Valere. I could not tell you how often I've dreamed of touching it, holding it in my hands. You must promise me, when you have it, you will let me touch it."

"Before I can do that, we have to find it. We had better be on our way." Rand offered his hand to help her mount; Hurin scrambled down to hold her stirrup. "Whatever that thing was I killed—a *grolm*?—there may be more of them around." Her hand was firm—there was surprising strength in her grip—and her skin was. . . . Silk? Something softer, smoother. Rand shivered.

"There always are," Selene said. The tall white mare frisked and bared her teeth once at Red, yet Selene's touch on the reins quieted her.

Rand slung his bow across his back and climbed onto Red. *Light, how could anyone's skin be so soft?* "Hurin, where's the trail? Hurin? Hurin!"

The sniffer gave a start, and left off staring at Selene. "Yes, Lord Rand. Ah . . . the trail. South, my Lord. Still south."

"Then let's ride." Rand gave an uneasy look at the gray-green bulk of the *grolm* lying in the stream. It had been better believing they were the only living things in that world. "Take the trail, Hurin."

Selene rode alongside Rand at first, talking of this and that, asking him questions and calling him lord. Half a dozen times he started to tell her he was no lord, only a shepherd, and every time, looking at her, he could not get the words out. A lady like her would not talk the same way with a shepherd, he was sure, even one who had saved her life.

"You will be a great man when you've found the Horn of Valere," she told him. "A man for the legends. The man who sounds the Horn will make his own legends."

"I don't want to sound it, and I don't want to be part of any legend." He did not know if she was wearing perfume, but there seemed to be a scent to her, something that filled his head with her. Spices, sharp and sweet, tickling his nose, making him swallow.

"Every man wants to be great. You could be the greatest man in all the Ages."

It sounded too close to what Moiraine had said. The Dragon Reborn would certainly stand out through the Ages. "Not me," he said fervently. "I'm just"—he thought of her scorn if he told her now that he was only a shepherd after letting her believe he was a lord, and changed what he had been going to say—"just trying to find it. And to help a friend."

She was silent a moment, then said, "You've hurt your hand."

"It is nothing." He started to put his injured hand inside his coat—it throbbed from holding the reins—but she reached out and took it.

He was so surprised he let her, and then there was nothing to do except either jerk away rudely or else let her unwrap the kerchief. Her touch felt cool and sure. His palm was angrily red and puffy, but the heron still stood out, plainly and clearly.

She touched the brand with a finger, but made no comment on it, not even to ask how he had come by it. "This could stiffen your hand if it's untended. I have an ointment that should help." From a pocket inside her cloak she produced a small stone vial, unstopped it, and began gently rubbing a white salve on the burn as they rode.

The ointment felt cold at first, then seemed to melt away warmly into his flesh. And it worked as well as Nynaeve's ointments sometimes did. He stared in amazement as the redness faded and the swelling went down under her stroking fingers.

"Some men," she said, not raising her eyes from his hand, "choose to seek greatness, while others are forced to it. It is always better to choose than to be forced. A man who's forced is never completely his own master. He must dance on the strings of those who forced him."

Rand pulled his hand free. The brand looked a week old or more, all but healed. "What do you mean?" he demanded.

She smiled at him, and he felt ashamed of his outburst. "Why, the Horn, of course," she said calmly, putting away her salve. Her mare, stepping along beside Red, was tall enough that her eyes were only a little below Rand's. "If you find the Horn of Valere, there will be no avoiding greatness. But will it be forced on you, or will you take it? That's the question."

He flexed his hand. She sounded so much like Moiraine. "Are you Aes Sedai?"

Selene's eyebrows lifted; her dark eyes glittered at him, but her voice was soft. "Aes Sedai? I? No."

"I didn't mean to offend you. I'm sorry."

"Offend me? I am not offended, but I'm no Aes Sedai." Her lip curled in a sneer; even that was beautiful. "They cower in what they think is safety when they could do so much. They serve when they could rule, let men fight wars when they could bring order to the world. No, never call me Aes Sedai." She smiled and laid her hand on his arm to show

she was not angry—her touch made him swallow—but he
was relieved when she let the mare drop back beside Loial.
Hurin bobbed his head at her like an old family retainer.

Rand was relieved, but he missed her presence, too. She
was only two spans away—he twisted in his saddle to stare
at her, riding by Loial's side; the Ogier was bent half double
in his saddle so he could talk with her—but that was not
the same as being right there beside him, close enough for
him to smell her heady scent, close enough to touch. He
settled back angrily. It was not that he wanted to touch her,
exactly—he reminded himself that he loved Egwene; he felt
guilty at the need for reminding—but she was beautiful,
and she thought he was a lord, and she said he could be a
great man. He argued sourly with himself inside his head.
*Moiraine says you can be great, too; the Dragon Reborn.
Selene is not Aes Sedai. That's right; she's a Cairhienin
noblewoman, and you're a shepherd. She doesn't know
that. How long do you let her believe a lie? It's only till we
get out of this place. If we get out. If.* On that note, his thoughts
subsided to sullen silence.

He tried to keep a watch on the country through which
they rode—if Selene said there were more of those things . . .
those *grolm* . . . about, he believed her, and Hurin was too
intent on smelling the trail to notice anything else; Loial was
too wrapped up in his talk with Selene to see anything until
it bit him on the heel—but it was hard to watch. Turning his
head too quickly made his eyes water; a hill or a stand of
trees could seem a mile off when seen from one angle and
only a few hundred spans when seen from another.

The mountains were growing closer, of that much he was
sure. Kinslayer's Dagger, looming against the sky now, a
sawtooth expanse of snow-capped peaks. The land around
them already rose in foothills heralding the coming of the
mountains. They would reach the edge of the mountains
proper well before dark, perhaps in only another hour or
so. *More than a hundred leagues in less than three days.
Worse than that. We spent most of a day south of the Erinin
in the real world. Over a hundred leagues in less than two
days, here.*

"She says you were right about this place, Rand."

Rand gave a start before he realized Loial had ridden up
beside him. He looked for Selene and found her riding with

Hurin; the sniffer was grinning and ducking his head and all but knuckling his forehead at everything she said. Rand glanced sideways at the Ogier. "I'm surprised you could let her go, the way you two had your heads together. What do you mean, I was right?"

"She is a fascinating woman, isn't she? Some of the Elders don't know as much as she does about history—especially the Age of Legends—and about—oh, yes. She says you were right about the Ways, Rand. The Aes Sedai, some of them, studied worlds like this, and that study was the basis of how they grew the Ways. She says there are worlds where it is time rather than distance that changes. Spend a day in one of those, and you might come back to find a year has passed in the real world, or twenty. Or it could be the other way round. Those worlds—this one, all the others—are reflections of the real world, she says. This one seems pale to us because it is a weak reflection, a world that had little chance of ever being. Others are almost as likely as ours. Those are as solid as our world, and have people. The same people, she says, Rand. Imagine it! You could go to one of them and meet yourself. The Pattern has infinite variation, she says, and every variation that can be, will be."

Rand shook his head, then wished he had not as the landscape flickered back and forth and his stomach lurched. He took a deep breath. "How does she know all that? You know about more things than anybody I ever met before, Loial, and all you knew about this world amounted to no more than a rumor."

"She's Cairhienin, Rand. The Royal Library in Cairhien is one of the greatest in the world, perhaps the greatest outside Tar Valon. The Aiel spared it deliberately, you know, when they burned Cairhien. They will not destroy a book. Did you know that they—"

"I don't care about Aielmen," Rand said hotly. "If Selene knows so much, I hope she read how to get us home from here. I wish Selene—"

"You wish Selene what?" The woman laughed as she joined them.

Rand stared at her as if she had been gone months; that was how he felt. "I wish Selene would come ride with me some more," he said. Loial chuckled, and Rand felt his face burn.

Selene smiled, and looked at Loial. "You will excuse us, *alantin*."

The Ogier bowed in his saddle and let his big horse fall back, the tufts on his ears drooping with reluctance.

For a time Rand rode in silence, enjoying Selene's presence. Now and again he looked at her out of the corner of his eye. He wished he could get his feelings about her straight. Could she be an Aes Sedai, despite her denial? Someone sent by Moiraine to push him along whatever path he was meant to follow in the Aes Sedai's plans? Moiraine could not have known he would be taken to this strange world, and no Aes Sedai would have tried to fend off that beast with a stick when she could strike it dead or send it running with the Power. Well. Since she took him for a lord and no one in Cairhien knew different, he might keep on letting her think it. She was surely the most beautiful woman he had ever seen, intelligent and learned, and she thought he was brave; what more could a man ask from a wife? *That's crazy, too. I'd marry Egwene if I could marry anyone, but I can't ask a woman to marry a man who's going to go mad, maybe hurt her.* But Selene was so beautiful.

She was studying his sword, he saw. He readied the words in his head. No, he was not a blademaster, but his father had given him the sword. *Tam. Light, why couldn't you really be my father?* He squashed the thought ruthlessly.

"That was a magnificent shot," Selene said.

"No, I'm not a—" Rand began, then blinked. "A shot?"

"Yes. A tiny target, that eye, moving, at a hundred paces. You've a wonderful hand with that bow."

Rand shifted awkwardly. "Ah . . . thank you. It's a trick my father taught me." He told her about the void, about how Tam had taught him how to use it with the bow. He even found himself telling her about Lan and his sword lessons.

"The Oneness," she said, sounding satisfied. She saw his questioning look and added, "That is what it is called . . . in some places. The Oneness. To learn the full use of it, it is best to wrap it around you continuously, to dwell in it at all times, or so I've heard."

He did not even have to think about what lay waiting for him in the void to know his answer to that, but what he said was, "I'll think about it."

"Wear this void of yours all the time, Rand al'Thor, and you'll learn uses for it you never suspected."

"I said I will think about it." She opened her mouth again, but he cut her off. "You know all these things. About the void—the Oneness, you call it. About this world. Loial reads books all the time; he's read more books than I've ever seen, and he's never seen anything but a fragment about the Stones."

Selene drew herself up straight in her saddle. Suddenly she reminded him of Moiraine, and of Queen Morgase, when they were angry.

"There was a book written about these worlds," she said tightly. "*Mirrors of the Wheel*. You see, the *alantin* has not seen *all* the books that are."

"What is this *alantin* you call him? I've never heard—"

"The Portal Stone beside which I woke is up there," Selene said, pointing into the mountains, off to the east of their path. Rand found himself wishing for her warmth again, and her smiles. "If you take me to it, you can return me to my home, as you promised. We can reach it in an hour."

Rand barely looked where she pointed. Using the Stone—Portal Stone, she called it—meant wielding the Power, if he were to take her back to the real world. "Hurin, how is the trail?"

"Fainter than ever, Lord Rand, but still there." The sniffer spared a quick grin and bob of his head for Selene. "I think it's starting to angle off to the west. There's some easier passes there, toward the tip of the Dagger, as I recall from when I went to Cairhien that time."

Rand sighed. *Fain, or one of his Darkfriends, has to know another way to use the Stones. A Darkfriend couldn't use the Power.* "I have to follow the Horn, Selene."

"How do you know your precious Horn is even in this world? Come with me, Rand. You'll find your legend, I promise you. Come with me."

"You can use the Stone, this Portal Stone, yourself," he said angrily. Before the words were out of his mouth he wanted them back. *Why does she have to keep talking about legends?* Stubbornly, he forced himself to go on. "The Portal Stone didn't bring you here by itself. You did it, Selene. If you made the Stone bring you here, you can make it take you back. I'll take you to it, but then I must go on after the Horn."

"I know nothing about using the Portal Stones, Rand. If I did anything, I don't know what it was."

Rand studied her. She sat her saddle, straight-backed and tall, just as regally as before, but somehow softer, too. Proud, yet vulnerable, and needing him. He had put Nynaeve's age to her—a handful of years older than himself—but he had been wrong, he realized. She was more his own age, and beautiful, and she needed him. The thought, just the thought, of the void flickered through his head, and of the light. *Saidin.* To use the Portal Stone, he must dip himself back into that taint.

"Stay with me, Selene," he said. "We'll find the Horn, and Mat's dagger, and we'll find a way back. I promise you. Just stay with me."

"You always. . . ." Selene drew a deep breath as if to calm herself. "You always are so stubborn. Well, I can admire stubbornness in a man. There is little to a man who's too easily biddable."

Rand colored; it was too much like the things Egwene sometimes said, and they had all but been promised in marriage since they were children. From Selene, the words, and the direct look that went with them, were a shock. He turned to tell Hurin to press on with the trail.

From behind them came a distant, coughing grunt. Before Rand could whirl Red to look, another bark sounded, and three more on its heels. At first he could make out nothing as the landscape seemed to waver in his eyes, but then he saw them through the widespread stands of trees, just topping a hill. Five shapes, it seemed, only half a mile distant, a bare thousand paces at most, and coming in thirty-foot bounds.

"*Grolm,*" Selene said calmly. "A small pack, but they have our scent, it seems."

CHAPTER
17

Choices

W e'll run for it," Rand said. "Hurin, can you gallop and still follow the trail?"

"Yes, Lord Rand."

"Then push on. We will—"

"It won't do any good," Selene said. Her white mare was the only one of their mounts not dancing at the gruff barks coming from the *grolm.* "They don't give up, not ever. Once they have your scent, *grolm* keep coming, day and night, until they run you down. You must kill them all, or find a way to go elsewhere. Rand, the Portal Stone can take us elsewhere."

"No! We *can* kill them. I can. I already killed one. There are only five. If I can just find. . . ." He cast around for the spot he needed, and found it. "Follow me!" Digging his heels in, he set Red to a gallop, confident before he heard their hooves that the others would come.

The place he had chosen was a low, round hill, bare of trees. Nothing could come close without him seeing. He swung down from his saddle and unlimbered his longbow. Loial and Hurin joined him on the ground, the Ogier hefting his huge quarterstaff, the sniffer with his short sword in his fist. Neither quarterstaff nor sword would be of much use if the *grolm* closed with them. *I won't let them get close.*

"This risk is not necessary," Selene said. She barely looked toward the *grolm,* bending from her saddle to concentrate on Rand. "We can easily reach the Portal Stone ahead of them."

"I will stop them." Hastily Rand counted the arrows remaining in his quiver. Eighteen, each as long as his arm, ten of them with points like chisels, designed to drive through Trolloc armor. They would do as well for *grolm* as for Trollocs. He stuck four of those upright in the ground in front of him; a fifth he nocked to the bow. "Loial, Hurin, you can do no good down here. Mount and be ready to take Selene to the Stone if any get through." He wondered whether he could kill one of the things with his sword, if it came to that. *You are mad! Even the Power is not as bad as this.*

Loial said something, but he did not hear; he was already seeking the void, as much to escape his own thoughts as for need. *You know what's waiting. But this way I don't have to touch it.* The glow was there, the light just out of sight. It seemed to flow toward him, but the emptiness was all. Thoughts darted across the surface of the void, visible in that tainted light. *Saidin. The Power. Madness. Death.* Extraneous thoughts. He was one with the bow, with the arrow, with the things topping the next rise.

The *grolm* came on, overreaching one another in their leaps, five great, leathery shapes, triple-eyed, with horny maws gaping. Their grunting calls rebounded from the void, barely heard.

Rand was not aware of raising his bow, or drawing the fletching against his cheek, to his ear. He was one with the beasts, one with the center eye of the first. Then the arrow was gone. The first *grolm* died; one of its companions leaped on it as it fell, beak of a mouth ripping gobbets of flesh. It snarled at the others, and they circled wide. But they came on, and as if compelled, it abandoned its meal and leaped after them, its horny maw already bloody.

Rand worked smoothly, unconsciously, nock and release. Nock and release.

The fifth arrow left his bow, and he lowered it, still deep in the void, as the fourth *grolm* fell like a huge puppet with its strings cut. Though the final arrow still flew, somehow he knew there was no need for another shot. The last beast collapsed as if its bones had melted, a feathered shaft jutting from its center eye. Always the center eye.

"Magnificent, Lord Rand," Hurin said. "I . . . I've never seen shooting like that."

The void held Rand. The light called to him, and he . . . reached . . . toward it. It surrounded him, filled him.

"Lord Rand?" Hurin touched his arm, and Rand gave a

start, the emptiness filling up with what was around him. "Are you all right, my Lord?"

Rand brushed his forehead with fingertips. It was dry; he felt as if it should have been covered with sweat. "I. . . . I'm fine, Hurin."

"It grows easier each time you do it, I've heard," Selene said. "The more you live in the Oneness, the easier."

Rand glanced at her. "Well, I won't need it again, not for a while." *What happened? I wanted to. . . .* He still wanted to, he realized with horror. He *wanted* to go back into the void, wanted to feel that light filling him again. It had seemed as if he were truly alive then, sickliness and all, and now was only an imitation. No, worse. He had been almost alive, knowing what "alive" would be like. All he had to do was reach out to *saidin*. . . .

"Not again," he muttered. He gazed off at the dead *grolm,* five monstrous shapes lying on the ground. Not dangerous anymore. "Now we can be on our—"

A coughing bark, all too familiar, sounded beyond the dead *grolm,* beyond the next hill, and others answered it. Still more came, from the east, from the west.

Rand half raised his bow.

"How many arrows do you have left?" Selene demanded. "Can you kill twenty *grolm*? Thirty? A hundred? We *must* go to the Portal Stone."

"She is right, Rand," Loial said slowly. "You do not have any choice now." Hurin was watching Rand anxiously. The *grolm* called, a score of barks overlapping.

"The Stone," Rand agreed reluctantly. Angrily he threw himself back into his saddle, slung the bow on his back. "Lead us to this Stone, Selene."

With a nod she turned her mare and heeled it to a trot. Rand and the others followed, they eagerly, he holding back. The barks of *grolm* pursued them, hundreds it seemed. It sounded as if the *grolm* were ranged in a semicircle around them, closing in from every direction but the front.

Swiftly and surely Selene led them through the hills. The land rose in the beginning of mountains, slopes steepening so the horses scrambled over washed-out-looking rocky outcrops and the sparse, faded-looking brush that clung to them. The way became harder, the land slanting more and more upward.

We're not going to make it, Rand thought, the fifth time Red slipped and slid backwards in a shower of stone. Loial threw his quarterstaff aside; it would be of no use against *grolm,* and it only slowed him. The Ogier had given up riding; he used one hand to haul himself up, and pulled his tall horse behind him with the other. The hairy-fetlocked animal made heavy going, but easier than with Loial on its back. *Grolm* barked behind them, closer now.

Then Selene drew rein and pointed to a hollow nestled below them in the granite. It was all there, the seven wide, colored stairs around a pale floor, and the tall stone column in the middle.

She dismounted and led her mare into the hollow, down the stairs to the column. It loomed over her. She turned to look back up at Rand and the others. The *grolm* gave their grunting barks, scores of them, loud. Near. "They will be on us soon," she said. "You must use the Stone, Rand. Or else find a way to kill all the *grolm.*"

With a sigh, Rand got down from his saddle and led Red into the hollow. Loial and Hurin followed hastily. He stared at the symbol-covered column, the Portal Stone, uneasily. *She must be able to channel, even if she doesn't know it, or it couldn't have brought her here. The Power doesn't harm women.* "If this brought you here," he began, but she interrupted him.

"I know what it is," she said firmly, "but I do not know how to use it. You must do what must be done." She traced one symbol, a little larger than the others, with a finger. A triangle standing on its point inside a circle. "This stands for the true world, our world. I believe it will help if you hold it in your mind while you. . . ." She spread her hands as if unsure exactly what it was he was supposed to do.

"Uh . . . my Lord?" Hurin said diffidently. "There isn't much time." He glanced over his shoulder at the rim of the hollow. The barking was louder. "Those things will be here in minutes, now." Loial nodded.

Drawing a deep breath, Rand put his hand on the symbol Selene had pointed out. He looked at her to see if he was doing it right, but she merely watched, not even the slightest frown of worry wrinkling her pale forehead. *She's confident you can save her. You have to.* The scent of her filled his nostrils.

"Uh . . . my Lord?"

Rand swallowed, and sought the void. It came easily, springing up around him without effort. Emptiness. Emptiness except for the light, wavering in a way that turned his stomach. Emptiness except for *saidin*. But even the queasiness was distant. He was one with the Portal Stone. The column felt smooth and slightly oily under his hand, but the triangle-and-circle seemed warm against the brand on his palm. *Have to get them to safety. Have to get them home.* The light drifted toward him, it seemed, surrounded him, and he . . . embraced . . . it.

Light filled him. Heat filled him. He could see the Stone, see the others watching him—Loial and Hurin anxiously, Selene showing no doubt that he could save her—but they might as well not have been there. The light was all. The heat and the light, suffusing his limbs like water sinking into dry sand, filling him. The symbol burned against his flesh. He tried to suck it all in, all the heat, all the light. All. The symbol. . . .

Suddenly, as if the sun had gone out for the blink of an eye, the world flickered. And again. The symbol was a live coal under his hand; he drank in the light. The world flickered. Flickered. It made him sick, that light; it was water to a man dying of thirst. Flicker. He sucked at it. It made him want to vomit; he wanted it all. Flicker. The triangle-and-circle seared him; he could feel it charring his hand. Flicker. He wanted it all! He screamed, howling with pain, howling with wanting.

Flicker . . . flicker . . . flickerflickerflicker. . . .

Hands pulled at him; he was only vaguely aware of them. He staggered back; the void was slipping away, the light, and the sickness that twisted at him. The light. He watched it go regretfully. *Light, that's crazy to want it. But I was so* full *of it! I was so. . . .* Dazed, he stared at Selene. It was she who held his shoulders, stared wonderingly into his eyes. He raised his hand in front of his face. The heron brand was there, but nothing else. No triangle-and-circle burned into his flesh.

"Remarkable," Selene said slowly. She glanced at Loial and Hurin. The Ogier looked stunned, his eyes as big as plates; the sniffer was squatting with one hand on the ground, as if unsure he could support himself else. "All of us here, and all of our horses. And you do not even know what you did. Remarkable."

"Are we . . . ?" Rand began hoarsely, and had to stop to swallow.

"Look around you," Selene said. "You've brought us home." She gave a sudden laugh. "You brought all of us home."

For the first time Rand became aware of his surroundings again. The hollow surrounded them without any stairs, though here and there lay a suspiciously smooth piece of stone, colored red, or blue. The column lay against the mountainside, half buried in the loose rock of a fall. The symbols were unclear, here; wind and water had worked long on them. And everything looked real. The colors were solid, the granite a strong gray, the brush green and brown. After that other place, it seemed almost too vivid.

"Home," Rand breathed, and then he was laughing, too. "We're home." Loial's laughter sounded like a bull bellowing. Hurin danced a caper.

"You did it," Selene said, leaning closer, until her face filled Rand's eyes. "I knew that you could."

Rand's laughter died. "I—I suppose I did." He glanced at the fallen Portal Stone and managed a weak laugh. "I wish I knew what it was I did, though."

Selene looked deep into his eyes. "Perhaps one day you will know," she said softly. "You are surely destined for great things."

Her eyes seemed as dark and deep as night, as soft as velvet. Her mouth. . . . *If I kissed her.* . . . He blinked and stepped back hurriedly, clearing his throat. "Selene, please don't tell anyone about this. About the Portal Stone, and me. I don't understand it, and neither will anybody else. You know how people are about things they don't understand."

Her face wore no expression at all. Suddenly he wished very much that Mat and Perrin were there. Perrin knew how to talk to girls, and Mat could lie with a straight face. He could manage neither very well.

Suddenly Selene smiled, and dropped a half-mocking curtsy. "I will keep your secret, my Lord Rand al'Thor."

Rand glanced at her, and cleared his throat again. *Is she angry with me? She'd certainly be angry if I had tried to kiss her. I think.* He wished she would not look at him as she was, as if she knew what he was thinking. "Hurin, is there any chance the Darkfriends used this Stone before us?"

The sniffer shook his head ruefully. "They were angling

to the west of here, Lord Rand. Unless these Portal Stone things are more common than I've seen, I'd say they're still in that other world. But it wouldn't take me an hour to check it. The land's the same here as there. I could find the place here where I lost the trail there, if you see what I mean, and see if they've already gone by."

Rand glanced at the sky. The sun—a wonderfully strong sun, not pale at all—sat low to the west, stretching their shadows out across the hollow. Another hour would bring full twilight. "In the morning," he said. "But I fear we've lost them." *We can't lose that dagger! We can't!* "Selene, if that's the case, in the morning we will take you on to your home. Is it in the city of Cairhien itself, or . . . ?"

"You may not have lost the Horn of Valere yet," Selene said slowly. "As you know, I do know a *few* things about those worlds."

"Mirrors of the Wheel," Loial said.

She gave him a look, then nodded. "Yes. Exactly. Those worlds truly are mirrors in a way, especially the ones where there are no people. Some of them reflect only great events in the true world, but some have a shadow of that reflection even before the event occurs. The passage of the Horn of Valere would certainly be a great event. Reflections of what will be are fainter than reflections of what is or what was, just as Hurin says the trail he followed was faint."

Hurin blinked incredulously. "You mean to say, my Lady, I've been smelling where those Darkfriends are *going* to be? The Light help me, I wouldn't like that. It's bad enough smelling where violence *has* been, without smelling where it *will* be, too. There can't be many spots where there won't be *some* kind of violence, *some* time. It would drive me crazy, like as not. That place we just left nearly did. I could smell it all the time, there, killing and hurting, and the vilest evil you could think of. I could even smell it on us. On all of us. Even on you, my Lady, if you'll forgive me for saying so. It was just that place, twisting me the way it twisted your eye." He gave himself a shake. "I'm glad we're out of there. I can't get it out of my nostrils yet, all the way."

Rand rubbed absently at the brand on his palm. "What do you think, Loial? Could we really be ahead of Fain's Darkfriends?"

The Ogier shrugged, frowning. "I don't know, Rand. I

don't know anything about any of this. I think we are back in our world. I think we are in Kinslayer's Dagger. Beyond that. . . ." He shrugged again.

"We should be seeing you home, Selene," Rand said. "Your people will be worried about you."

"A few days will see if I'm right," she said impatiently. "Hurin can find where he left the trail; he said so. We can watch over it. The Horn of Valere cannot be much longer reaching here. The Horn of Valere, Rand. Think of it. The man who sounds the Horn will live in legend forever."

"I don't want anything to do with legends," he said sharply. *But if the Darkfriends get by you. . . . What if Ingtar lost them? Then the Darkfriends have the Horn of Valere forever, and Mat dies.* "All right, a few days. At the worst, we will probably meet Ingtar and the others. I can't imagine they've stopped or turned back just because we . . . went away."

"A wise decision, Rand," Selene said, "and well thought out." She touched his arm and smiled, and he found himself again thinking of kissing her.

"Uh . . . we need to be closer to where they'll come. If they do come. Hurin, can you find us a camp before dark, somewhere we can watch the place where you lost the trail?" He glanced at the Portal Stone and thought about sleeping near it, thought of the way the void had crept up on him in sleep the last time, and the light in the void. "Somewhere well away from here."

"Leave it in my hands, Lord Rand." The sniffer scrambled to his saddle. "I vow, I'll never sleep again without first I see what kind of stone there is nearby."

As Rand rode Red up out of the hollow, he found himself watching Selene more than he did Hurin. She seemed so cool and self-possessed, no older than he, yet queenly, but when she smiled at him, as she did just then. . . . *Egwene wouldn't have said I was wise. Egwene would have called me a woolhead.* Irritably, he heeled Red's flanks.

CHAPTER 18

To the White Tower

Egwene balanced on the heeling deck as the *River Queen* sped down the wide Erinin under cloud-dark skies, sails full-bellied, White Flame banner whipping furiously at the mainmast. The wind had risen as soon as the last of them was aboard the ships, back in Medo, and it had not failed or flagged for an instant since, day or night. The river had begun to race in flood, as it still did, slapping the ships about while it drove them onward. Wind and river had not slowed, and neither had the ships, all clustered together. The *River Queen* led, only right for the vessel that carried the Amyrlin Seat.

The helmsman held his tiller grimly, feet planted and spread, and sailors padded barefoot at their work, intent on what they did; when they glanced at the sky or the river, they tore their eyes away with low mutters. A village was just fading from view behind, and a boy raced along the bank; he had kept up with the ships for a short distance, but now they were leaving him behind. When he vanished, Egwene made her way below.

In the small cabin they shared, Nynaeve glared up at her from her narrow bed. "They say we'll reach Tar Valon today. The Light help me, but I'll be glad to put foot on land again even if it is in Tar Valon." The ship lurched with wind and current, and Nynaeve swallowed. "I'll never step on a boat again," she said breathlessly.

Egwene shook the river spray out of her cloak and hung it on a peg by the door. It was not a big cabin—there were no big cabins on the ship, it seemed, not even the one the Amyrlin had taken over from the captain, though that was larger than the rest. With its two beds built into the walls, shelves beneath them and cabinets above, everything lay close to hand.

Except for keeping her balance, the movements of the ship did not bother her the way they did Nynaeve; she had given up offering Nynaeve food after the third time the Wisdom threw the bowl at her. "I'm worried about Rand," she said.

"I'm worried about all of them," Nynaeve replied dully. After a moment, she said, "Another dream last night? The way you've been staring at nothing since you got up. . . ."

Egwene nodded. She had never been very good at keeping things from Nynaeve, and she had not tried with the dreams. Nynaeve had tried to dose her at first, until she heard one of the Aes Sedai was interested; then she began to believe. "It was like the others. Different, but the same. Rand is in some kind of danger. I know it. And it is getting worse. He's done something, or he's going to do something, that puts him in. . . ." She dropped down on her bed and leaned toward the other woman. "I just wish I could make some sense of it."

"Channeling?" Nynaeve said softly.

Despite herself, Egwene looked around to see if anyone was there to hear. They were alone, with the door closed, but still she spoke just as softly. "I don't know. Maybe." There was no telling what Aes Sedai could do—she had seen enough already to make her believe every story of their powers—and she would not risk eavesdropping. *I won't risk Rand. If I did right, I'd tell them, but Moiraine knows, and she hasn't said anything. And it's Rand! I can't.* "I don't know what to do."

"Has Anaiya said anything more about these dreams?" Nynaeve seemed to make it a point never to add the honorific Sedai, even when the two of them were alone. Most of the Aes Sedai appeared not to care, but the habit had earned a few strange looks, and some hard ones; she was going to train in the White Tower, after all.

"'The Wheel weaves as the Wheel wills,'" Egwene quoted Anaiya. "'The boy is far away, child, and there's nothing we can do until we know more. I will see to testing you myself once we reach the White Tower, child.' Aaagh! She *knows* there is something in these dreams. I can tell she does. I like the woman, Nynaeve; I do. But she won't *tell* me what I want to know. And I can't tell her everything. Maybe if I could. . . ."

"The man in the mask again?"

Egwene nodded. Somehow, she was sure it was better not to tell Anaiya about him. She could not imagine why, but she was sure. Three times the man whose eyes were fire had been in her dreams each time when she dreamed a dream that convinced her Rand was in danger. He always wore a mask across his face; sometimes she could see his eyes, and sometimes she could only see fire where they should be. "He laughed at me. It was so . . . contemptuous. As though I were a puppy he was going to have to push out of his way with his foot. It frightens me. He frightens me."

"Are you sure it has anything to do with the other dreams, with Rand? Sometimes a dream is just a dream."

Egwene threw up her hands. "And sometimes, Nynaeve, you sound just like Anaiya Sedai!" She put a special emphasis on the title, and was pleased to see Nynaeve grimace.

"If I ever get out of this bed, Egwene—"

A knock at the door cut off whatever Nynaeve had been going to say. Before Egwene could speak or move, the Amyrlin herself came in and shut the door behind her. She was alone, for a wonder; she seldom left her cabin, and then always with Leane at her side, and maybe another of the Aes Sedai.

Egwene sprang to her feet. The room was a little crowded, with three of them in it.

"Both of you feeling well?" the Amyrlin said cheerily. She tilted her head at Nynaeve. "Eating well, too, I trust? In good temper?"

Nynaeve struggled to a sitting position, with her back against the wall. "My temper is just fine, thank you."

"We are honored, Mother," Egwene began, but the Amyrlin waved her to silence.

"It's good to be on the water again, but it grows boring as a mill pond after a while with nothing to do." The ship heeled, and she shifted her balance without seeming to notice. "I will give you your lesson today." She folded herself onto the end of Egwene's bed, feet tucked under her. "Sit, child."

Egwene sat, but Nynaeve began trying to push herself to her feet. "I think I will go on deck."

"I said, sit!" The Amyrlin's voice cracked like a whip, but Nynaeve kept rising, wavering. She still had both hands on the bed, but she was almost upright. Egwene held herself ready to catch her when she fell.

Closing her eyes, Nynaeve slowly lowered herself back to the bed. "Perhaps I will stay. It is no doubt windy up there."

The Amyrlin barked a laugh. "They told me you had a temper in you like a fisher-bird with a bone in its throat. Some of them, child, say you'd do well for some time as a novice, no matter how old you are. I say, if you have the ability I hear of, you deserve to be one of the Accepted." She gave another laugh. "I always believe in giving people what they deserve. Yes. I suspect you will learn a great deal once you reach the White Tower."

"I'd rather one of the Warders taught me how to use a sword," Nynaeve growled. She swallowed convulsively, and opened her eyes. "There is someone I'd like to use it on." Egwene looked at her sharply; did Nynaeve mean the Amyrlin—which was stupid, and dangerous besides—or Lan? She snapped at Egwene every time Lan was mentioned.

"A sword?" the Amyrlin said. "I never thought swords were much use—even if you have the skill, child, there are always men who have as much, and a deal more strength— but if you want a sword. . . ." She held up her hand— Egwene gasped, and even Nynaeve's eyes bulged—and there was a sword in it. With blade and hilt of an odd bluish white, it looked somehow . . . cold. "Made from the air, child, with Air. It's as good as most steel blades, better than most, but still not much use." The sword became a paring knife. There was no shrinking; it just was one thing, then the other. "This, now, is useful." The paring knife turned to mist, and the mist faded away. The Amyrlin put her empty hand back in her lap. "But either takes more effort than it is worth. Better, easier, simply to carry a good knife with you. You have to learn when to use your ability, as well as how, and when it's better to do things the way any other woman would. Let a blacksmith make knives for gutting fish. Use the One Power too often and too freely, and you can come to like it too much. That way lies danger. You begin to want more of it, and sooner or later you run the risk of drawing more than you've learned to handle. And that can burn you out like a guttered candle, or—"

"If I must learn all this," Nynaeve broke in stiffly, "I would as soon learn something useful. All this—this . . . 'Make the air stir, Nynaeve. Light the candle, Nynaeve. Now put it out. Light it again.' Paah!"

Egwene closed her eyes for a moment. *Please, Nynaeve. Please keep a check on your temper.* She bit her lip to keep from saying it out loud.

The Amyrlin was silent for a moment. "Useful," she said at last. "Something useful. You wanted a sword. Suppose a man came at me with a sword. What would I do? Something useful, you can be sure. This, I think."

For an instant, Egwene thought she saw a glow around the woman at the other end of her bed. Then the air seemed to thicken; nothing changed that Egwene could see, but she could surely feel it. She tried to lift her arm; it did not budge any more than if she were buried to her neck in thick jelly. Nothing could move except her head.

"Release me!" Nynaeve grated. Her eyes glared, and her head jerked from side to side, but the rest of her sat as rigidly as a statue. Egwene realized that she was not the only one held. "Let me go!"

"Useful, wouldn't you say? And it is nothing but Air." The Amyrlin spoke in a conversational tone, as if they were all chatting over tea. "Big man, with his muscles and his sword, and the sword does him as much good as the hair on his chest."

"Let me go, I say!"

"And if I don't like where he is, why, I can pick him up." Nynaeve squawked furiously as she slowly rose, still in a sitting position, until her head almost touched the ceiling. The Amyrlin smiled. "I've often wished I could use this to fly. The records say Aes Sedai *could* fly, in the Age of Legends, but they aren't clear on how, exactly. Not this way, though. It doesn't work like that. You might reach out with your hands and pick up a chest that weighs as much as you do; you look strong. But take hold of yourself however you will, you cannot pick yourself up."

Nynaeve's head jerked furiously, but not another muscle of her twitched. "The Light burn you, let me go!"

Egwene swallowed hard and hoped she was not also to be lifted.

"So," the Amyrlin continued, "big, hairy man, and so forth. He can do nothing to me, while I can do anything at all to him. Why, if I had a mind to"—she leaned forward, her eyes intent on Nynaeve; suddenly her smile did not seem very friendly—"I could turn him upside down and paddle his bottom. Just like—" Suddenly the Amyrlin flew backwards so hard her head rebounded from the wall, and there she stayed, as if something were pressing against her.

Egwene stared, her mouth dry. *This isn't happening. It isn't.*

"They were right," the Amyrlin said. Her voice sounded strained, as though she found it hard to breathe. "They said you learned quickly. And they said it took your temper burning to get to the heart of what you can do." She took a struggling breath. "Shall we release each other together, child?"

Nynaeve, floating in the air with her eyes ablaze, said, "You let me go right now, or I'll—" Abruptly a look of amazement came over her face, a look of loss. Her mouth worked silently.

The Amyrlin sat up, working her shoulders. "You don't know everything yet, do you, child? Not the hundredth part of everything. You did not suspect I could cut you off from the True Source. You can still feel it there, but you can't touch it any more than a fish can touch the moon. When you learn enough to be raised to full sisterhood, no one woman will be able to do that to you. The stronger you become, the more Aes Sedai it will take to shield you against your will. Do you think, now, you want to learn?" Nynaeve pressed her mouth shut in a thin line and stared her in the eye grimly. The Amyrlin sighed. "If you had a hair less potential than you do, child, I would send you to the Mistress of Novices and tell her to keep you the rest of your life. But you will get what you deserve."

Nynaeve's eyes widened, and she had just time to start a yell before she dropped, hitting her bed with a loud thud. Egwene winced; the mattresses were thin, and the wood beneath hard. Nynaeve's face stayed frozen as she shifted the way she sat, just a fraction.

"And now," the Amyrlin said firmly, "unless you would like further demonstration, we will get on with your lesson. Continue your lesson, we might say."

"Mother?" Egwene said faintly. She still could not twitch below her chin.

The Amyrlin looked at her questioningly, then smiled. "Oh. I am sorry, child. Your friend was occupying my attention, I'm afraid." Suddenly Egwene could move again; she raised her arms, just to convince herself that she could. "Are you both ready to learn?"

"Yes, Mother," Egwene said quickly.

The Amyrlin raised an eyebrow at Nynaeve.

After a moment, Nynaeve said in a tight voice, "Yes, Mother."

Egwene heaved a sigh of relief.

"Good. Now, then. Empty your thoughts of everything but a flower bud."

Egwene was sweating by the time the Amyrlin left. She had thought some of the other Aes Sedai had been hard teachers, but that smiling, plain-faced woman coaxed out every last drop of effort, drew it out, and when there was nothing left, she seemed to reach into you and pulled it out. It had gone well, though. As the door closed behind the Amyrlin, Egwene raised one hand; a tiny flame sprang to life, balanced a hairbreadth above the tip of her forefinger, then danced from fingertip to fingertip. She was not supposed to do this without a teacher—one of the Accepted, at the very least—to watch over her, but she was too excited at her progress to pay any mind to that.

Nynaeve bounded to her feet and threw her pillow at the closing door. "That—that vile, contemptible, miserable—hag! The Light burn her! I'd like to feed *her* to the fish. I'd like to dose her with things that would turn her green for the rest of her life! I don't care if she's old enough to be my mother, if I had her in Emond's Field, she wouldn't sit down comfortably for. . . ." Her teeth ground so loudly that Egwene jumped.

Letting the flame die, Egwene put her eyes firmly on her lap. She wished she could think of a way to sneak out of the room without catching Nynaeve's eye.

The lesson had not gone well for Nynaeve, because she had held her temper on a tight lead until the Amyrlin was gone. She never could do very much unless she was angry, and then it all burst out of her. After failure upon failure, the Amyrlin had done everything she could to rouse her again. Egwene wished Nynaeve could forget she had been there to see or hear any of it.

Nynaeve stalked stiffly to her bed and stood staring at the wall behind it, her fist clenched at her side. Egwene looked longingly at the door.

"It was not your fault," Nynaeve said, and Egwene gave a start.

"Nynaeve, I—"

Nynaeve turned to look down at her. "It was not your fault," she repeated, sounding unconvinced. "But if you ever breathe one word, I'll—I'll. . . ."

"Not a word," Egwene said quickly. "I don't even remember anything to breathe a word about."

Nynaeve stared at her a moment longer, then nodded. Abruptly she grimaced. "Light, I did not think *anything* tasted worse than raw sheepstongue root. I'll remember that, the next time you act the goose, so watch yourself."

Egwene winced. That had been the first thing the Amyrlin had done trying to rouse Nynaeve's anger. A dark glob of something that glistened like grease and smelled vile had suddenly appeared and, while the Amyrlin held Nynaeve with the Power, had been forced into the Wisdom's mouth. The Amyrlin had even held her nose to make her swallow. And Nynaeve remembered things, if she had seen them done once. Egwene did not think there was any way of stopping her if she took it into her mind to do it; for all her own success in making a flame dance, *she* could never have held the Amyrlin against a wall. "At least being on the ship isn't making you sick anymore."

Nynaeve grunted, then gave a short, sharp laugh. "I'm too angry to be sick." With another mirthless laugh, she shook her head. "I'm too miserable to be sick. Light, I feel as if I've been dragged through a knothole backwards. If that is what novice training is like, you will have incentive to learn quickly."

Egwene scowled at her knees. Compared to Nynaeve, the Amyrlin had only coaxed her, smiled at her successes, sympathized with her failures, then coaxed again. But all the Aes Sedai had said things would be different in the White Tower; harder, though they would not say how. If she had to go through what Nynaeve had, day after day, she did not think she could stand it.

Something changed in the motion of the ship. The rocking eased, and feet thumped on the deck above their heads. A man shouted something Egwene could not quite make out.

She looked up at Nynaeve. "Do you think. . . . Tar Valon?"

"There is only one way to find out," Nynaeve replied, and determinedly took her cloak from its peg.

When they reached the deck, sailors were running everywhere, heaving at lines, shortening sail, readying long sweeps. The wind had died to a breeze, and the clouds were scattering, now.

Egwene rushed to the rail. "It is! It is Tar Valon!" Nynaeve joined her with an expressionless face.

The island was so big it looked more as if the river split in two than contained a bit of land. Bridges that seemed to be made of lace arched from either bank to the island, crossing marshy ground as well as the river. The walls of the city, the Shining Walls of Tar Valon, glistened white as the sun broke through the clouds. And on the west bank, its broken top leaking a thin wisp of smoke, Dragonmount reared black against the sky, one mountain standing among flat lands and rolling hills. Dragonmount, where the Dragon had died. Dragonmount, made by the Dragon's dying.

Egwene wished she did not think of Rand when she looked at the mountain. *A man channeling. Light, help him.*

The *River Queen* passed through a wide opening in a tall, circular wall that thrust out into the river. Inside, one long wharf surrounded a round harbor. Sailors furled the last sails and used sweeps alone to move the ship stern-first to its docking. Around the long wharf, the other ships that had come downriver were now being snugged into their berths among the ships already there. The White Flame banner set workers scurrying along the already busy wharf.

The Amyrlin came on deck before the shore lines were tied off, but dockworkers ran a gangplank aboard as soon as she appeared. Leane walked at her side, flame-tipped staff in hand, and the other Aes Sedai on the ship followed them ashore. None of them so much as glanced at Egwene or Nynaeve. On the wharf a delegation greeted the Amyrlin— shawled Aes Sedai, bowing formally, kissing the Amyrlin's ring. The wharf bustled, between ships unloading and the Amyrlin Seat arriving; soldiers formed up on disembarking, men set booms for cargo; trumpet flourishes rang from the walls, competing with cheers from the onlookers.

Nynaeve gave a loud sniff. "It seems they've forgotten us. Come along. We'll see to ourselves."

Egwene was reluctant to leave her first sight of Tar Valon, but she followed Nynaeve below to gather their things. When they came back topside, bundles in their arms, soldiers and trumpets were gone—and Aes Sedai, too. Men were swinging back hatches along the deck and lowering cables into the holds.

On the deck, Nynaeve caught a dockman's arm, a burly fellow in a coarse brown shirt with no sleeves. "Our horses," she began.

"I'm busy," he growled, pulling free. "Horses'll all be took to the White Tower." He looked them up and down. "If you've business with the Tower, best you take yourselves on. Aes Sedai don't hold with newlings being tardy." Another man, wrestling with a bale being swung out of the hold on a cable, shouted to him, and he left the women without a backwards glance.

Egwene exchanged looks with Nynaeve. It seemed they really were on their own.

Nynaeve stalked off the ship with grim determination on her face, but Egwene made her way dejectedly down the gangplank and through the tarry smell that hung over the wharf. *All that talk about wanting us here, and now they don't seem to care.*

Broad stairs led up from the dock to a wide arch of dark redstone. On reaching it, Egwene and Nynaeve stopped to stare.

Every building seemed a palace, though most of those close to the arch seemed to contain inns or shops, from the signs over the doors. Fanciful stonework was everywhere, and the lines of one structure seemed designed to complement and set off the next, leading the eye along as if everything were part of one vast design. Some structures did not look like buildings at all, but like gigantic waves breaking, or huge shells, or fanciful, wind-sculpted cliffs. Right in front of the arch lay a broad square, with a fountain and trees, and Egwene could see another square further on. Above everything rose the towers, tall and graceful, some with sweeping bridges between them, high in the sky. And over all rose one tower, higher and wider than all the rest, as white as the Shining Walls themselves.

"Fair takes the breath at first sight," said a woman's voice behind them. "At tenth sight, for that. And at hundredth."

Egwene turned. The woman was Aes Sedai; Egwene was sure of it, though she wore no shawl. No one else had that ageless look; and she held herself with an assurance, a confidence that seemed to confirm it. A glance at her hand showed the golden ring, the serpent biting its own tail. The Aes Sedai was a little plump, with a warm smile, and one of the oddest-appearing women Egwene had ever seen. Her plumpness could not hide high cheekbones, her eyes had a tilt to them and were the clearest, palest green, and her hair was almost the color of fire. Egwene barely stopped herself from goggling at that hair, those slightly slanted eyes.

"Ogier built, of course," the Aes Sedai went on, "and their best work ever, some say. One of the first cities built after the Breaking. There weren't half a thousand people here altogether then—no more than twenty sisters—but they built for what would be needed."

"It is a lovely city," Nynaeve said. "We are supposed to go to the White Tower. We came here for training, but no one seems to care if we go or stay."

"They care," the woman said, smiling. "I came here to meet you, but I was delayed speaking with the Amyrlin. I am Sheriam, the Mistress of Novices."

"I am not to be a novice," Nynaeve said in a firm voice, but a little too quickly. "The Amyrlin herself said I was to be one of the Accepted."

"So I was told." Sheriam sounded amused. "I have never heard of it being done so before, but they say you are . . . exceptional. Remember, though, even one of the Accepted can be called to my study. It requires more breaking of the rules than for a novice, but it has been known to happen." She turned to Egwene as if she had not seen Nynaeve frown. "And you are our new novice. It is always good to see a novice come. We have too few, these days. You will make forty. Only forty. And no more than eight or nine of those will be raised to the Accepted. Though I don't think you will have to worry about that too much, if you work hard and apply yourself. The work is hard, and even for one with the potential they tell me you have, it will not be made any easier. If you cannot stick to it, no matter how hard it is, or if you will break under the strain, better we find it out now, and let you go on your way, than wait until you are a full sister and others are depending on you. An Aes Sedai's life is not easy. Here, we will prepare you for it, if you have in you what is required."

Egwene swallowed. *Break under the strain?* "I will try, Sheriam Sedai," she said faintly. *And I will not break.*

Nynaeve looked at her worriedly. "Sheriam. . . ." She stopped and took a deep breath. "Sheriam Sedai"—she seemed to force the honorific out—"does it have to be so hard on her? Flesh and blood can only take so much. I know . . . something . . . of what novices must go through. Surely there's no need to try to break her just to find out how strong she is."

"You mean what the Amyrlin did to you today?" Nynaeve's back stiffened; Sheriam looked as though she were trying to keep amusement from her face. "I told you I spoke with the Amyrlin. Rest your worries for your friend. Novice training is hard, but not that hard. That is for the first few weeks of being one of the Accepted." Nynaeve's mouth fell open; Egwene thought the Wisdom's eyes were going to come right out of her head. "To catch the few who might have slipped through novice training when they should not have. We cannot risk having one of our number—a full Aes Sedai—who will break under the stress of the world outside." The Aes Sedai gathered them both up, an arm around the shoulders of each. Nynaeve hardly seemed to realize where she was going. "Come," Sheriam said, "I will see you settled in your rooms. The White Tower awaits."

CHAPTER
19

Beneath the Dagger

Night on the edge of Kinslayer's Dagger was cold, as nights in the mountains are always cold. The wind whipped down from the high peaks carrying the iciness of the snowcaps. Rand shifted on the hard ground, tugging at his cloak and blanket, and only half asleep. His hand went to his sword, lying beside him. *One more day,* he thought drowsily. *Just one more, and then we go. If no one comes tomorrow, Ingtar or Darkfriends, either one, I'll take Selene to Cairhien.*

He had told himself that before. Every day they had been there on the mountainside, watching the place where Hurin said the trail had been, in that other world—where Selene said the Darkfriends would surely appear in this world—he told himself it was time to leave. And Selene talked of the Horn of Valere, and touched his arm, and looked into his eyes, and before he knew it he had agreed to yet another day before they went on.

He shrugged against the chill of the wind, thinking of Selene touching his arm and looking into his eyes. *If Egwene saw that, she'd shear me for a sheep, and Selene, too. Egwene could already be in Tar Valon by now, learning to be an Aes Sedai. The next time she sees me, she'll probably try to gentle me.*

As he shifted over, his hand slid past the sword and touched the bundle holding Thom Merrilin's harp and flute. Unconsciously, his fingers tightened on the gleeman's cloak. *I was happy then, I think, even running for my life. Playing the flute for my supper. I was too ignorant to know what was going on. There's no turning back.*

Shivering, he opened his eyes. The only light came from the waning moon, not far past full and low in the sky. A fire would give them away to those for whom they watched. Loial muttered in his sleep, a low rumble. One of the horses stamped a hoof. Hurin had the first watch, from a stone outcrop a little way up the mountain; he would be coming to wake Rand for his turn, soon.

Rand rolled over . . . and stopped. In the moonlight he could see the shape of Selene, bending over his saddlebags, her hands on the buckles. Her white dress gathered the faint light. "Do you need something?"

She gave a jump, and stared toward him. "You—you startled me."

He rolled to his feet, shedding the blanket and wrapping the cloak around himself, and went to her. He was sure he had left the saddlebags right by his side when he lay down; he always kept them close. He took them from her. All the buckles were fastened, even those on the side that held the damning banner. *How can my life depend on keeping it? If anybody sees it and knows what it is, I'll die for having it.* He peered at her suspiciously.

Selene stayed where she was, looking up at him. The moon glistened in her dark eyes. "It came to me," she said, "that I've been wearing this dress too long. I could brush it, at least, if I had something else to wear while I did. One of your shirts, perhaps."

Rand nodded, feeling a sudden relief. Her dress looked as clean to him as when he first saw her, but he knew that if a spot appeared on Egwene's dress, nothing would do but that she cleaned it immediately. "Of course." He opened the capacious pocket into which he had stuffed everything except the banner and pulled out one of the white silk shirts.

"Thank you." Her hands went behind her back. To the buttons, he realized.

Eyes wide, he spun away from her.

"If you could help me with these, it would be much easier."

Rand cleared his throat. "It would not be proper. It isn't as if we were promised, or. . . ." *Stop thinking about that! You can never marry anyone.* "It just wouldn't be proper."

Her soft laugh sent a shiver down his back, as if she had run a finger along his spine. He tried not to listen to the rustlings behind him. He said, "Ah . . . tomorrow . . . to-morrow, we'll leave for Cairhien."

"And what of the Horn of Valere?"

"Maybe we were wrong. Maybe they are not coming here at all. Hurin says there are a number of passes through Kinslayer's Dagger. If they went only a little further west, they do not have to come into the mountains at all."

"But the trail we followed came here. They will come here. The Horn will come here. You may turn around, now."

"You say that, but we don't know. . . ." He turned, and the words died in his mouth. Her dress lay across her arm, and she wore his shirt, hanging in baggy folds on her. It was a long-tailed shirt, made for his height, but she was tall for a woman. The bottom of it came little more than halfway down her thighs. It was not as if he had never seen a girl's legs before; girls in the Two Rivers always tied up their skirts to go wading in Waterwood ponds. But they stopped doing it well before they were old enough to braid their hair, and this was in the dark, besides. The moonlight seemed to make her skin glow.

"What is it you don't know, Rand?"

The sound of her voice unfroze his joints. With a loud cough, he whirled to face the other way. "Ah . . . I think . . . ah . . . I . . . ah. . . ."

"Think of the glory, Rand." Her hand touched his back, and he almost shamed himself with a squeak. "Think of the glory that will come to the one who finds the Horn of Valere. How proud I'll be to stand beside him who holds the Horn. You have no idea the heights we will scale together, you and I. With the Horn of Valere in your hand, you can be a king. You can be another Artur Hawkwing. You. . . ."

"Lord Rand!" Hurin panted into the campsite. "My Lord, they. . . ." He skidded to a halt, suddenly making a gurgling sound. His eyes dropped to the ground, and he stood wringing his hands. "Forgive me, my Lady. I didn't mean to. . . . I. . . . Forgive me."

Loial sat up, his blanket and cloak falling away. "What's happening? Is it my turn to watch already?" He looked toward Rand and Selene, and even in the moonlight the widening of his eyes was plain.

Rand heard Selene sigh behind him. He stepped away

from her, still not looking at her. *Her legs are so white, so smooth.* "What is it, Hurin?" He made his voice more moderate; was he angry with Hurin, himself, or Selene? *No reason to be angry with her.* "Did you see something, Hurin?"

The sniffer spoke without raising his eyes. "A fire, my Lord, down in the hills. I didn't see it at first. They made it small, and hid it, but they hid it from somebody following them, not somebody ahead, and up above. Two miles, Lord Rand. Less than three, for sure."

"Fain," Rand said. "Ingtar would not be afraid of anyone following him. It must be Fain." Suddenly he did not know what to do, now. They had been waiting for Fain, but now that the man was only a mile or so away, he was uncertain. "In the morning. . . . In the morning, we will follow. When Ingtar and the others catch up, we'll be able to point right to them."

"So," Selene said. "You will let this Ingtar take the Horn of Valere. And the glory."

"I don't want. . . ." Without thinking, he turned, and there she was, legs pale in the moonlight, and as unconcerned that they were bare as if she were alone. *As if we were alone,* the thought came. *She wants the man who finds the Horn.* "Three of us cannot take it away from them. Ingtar has twenty lances with him."

"You don't know you cannot take it. How many followers does this man have? You don't know that, either." Her voice was calm, but intent. "You don't even know if these men camped down there do have the Horn. The only way is to go down yourself and see. Take the *alantin;* his kind have sharp eyes, even by moonlight. And he has the strength to carry the Horn in its chest, if you make the right decision."

She's right. You do not know for sure if it's Fain. A fine thing it would be to have Hurin casting about for a trail that was not there, all of them out in the open if the real Darkfriends did finally come. "I will go alone," he said. "Hurin and Loial will stand guard for you."

Laughing, Selene came to him so gracefully it almost seemed she danced. Moonshadows veiled her face in mystery as she looked up at him, and mystery made her even more beautiful. "I am capable of guarding myself, until you return to protect me. Take the *alantin.*"

"She is right, Rand," Loial said, rising. "I can see better by moonlight than you. With my eyes, we may not need to go as close as you would alone."

"Very well." Rand strode over to his sword and buckled it at his waist. Bow and quiver he left where they lay; a bow was not of much use in the dark, and he intended to look, not fight. "Hurin, show me this fire."

The sniffer led him scrambling up the slope to the outcrop, like a huge stone thumb thrust out of the mountain. The fire was only a speck—he missed it the first time Hurin pointed. Whoever had made it did not mean for it to be seen. He fixed it in his head.

By the time they returned to the camp, Loial had saddled Red and his own horse. As Rand climbed to the bay's back, Selene caught his hand. "Remember the glory," she said softly. "Remember." The shirt seemed to fit her better than he recalled, molding itself to her form.

He drew a deep breath and took his hand back. "Guard her with your life, Hurin. Loial?" He heeled Red's flanks gently. The Ogier's big mount plodded along behind.

They did not try to move quickly. Night shrouded the mountainside, and moon-cast shadows made footing uncertain. Rand could not see the fire any longer—no doubt it was better hidden from eyes on the same level—but he had its location in his mind. For someone who had learned to hunt in the tangle of the Westwood, in the Two Rivers, finding the fire would be no great difficulty. *And what then?* Selene's face loomed before him. *How proud I'll be to stand beside him who holds the Horn.*

"Loial," he said suddenly, trying to clear his thoughts, "what's this *alantin* she calls you?"

"It's the Old Tongue, Rand." The Ogier's horse picked its way uncertainly, but he guided it almost as surely as if it were daylight. "It means Brother, and is short for *tia avende alantin*. Brother to the Trees. Treebrother. It is very formal, but then, I've heard the Cairhienin are formal. The noble Houses are, at least. The common people I saw there were not very formal at all."

Rand frowned. A shepherd would not be very acceptable to a formal Cairhienin noble House. *Light, Mat's right about you. You're crazy, and with a big head to boot. But if I could marry. . . .*

He wished he could stop thinking, and before he realized it, the void had formed within him, making thoughts distant things, as if part of someone else. *Saidin* shone at him, beckoned to him. He gritted his teeth and ignored it; it was like ignoring a burning coal inside his head, but at least he could hold it at bay. Barely. He almost left the void, but the Darkfriends were out there in the night, and closer, now. And the Trollocs. He needed the emptiness, needed even the uneasy calm of the void. *I don't have to touch it. I don't.*

After a time, he reined in Red. They stood at the base of a hill, the wide-scattered trees on its slopes black in the night. "I think we must be close by now," he said softly. "Best we go the rest of the way on foot." He slid from the saddle and tied the bay's reins to a branch.

"Are you all right?" Loial whispered, climbing down. "You sound odd."

"I'm fine." His voice sounded tight, he realized. Stretched. *Saidin* called to him. *No!* "Be careful. I can't be sure exactly how far it is, but that fire should be somewhere just ahead of us. On the hilltop, I think." The Ogier nodded.

Slowly Rand stole from tree to tree, placing each foot carefully, holding his sword tight so it did not clatter against a tree trunk. He was grateful for the lack of undergrowth. Loial followed like a big shadow; Rand could not see much more of him than that. Everything was moonshadows and darkness.

Suddenly some trick of the moonlight resolved the shadows ahead of him, and he froze, touching the rough bole of a leatherleaf. Dim mounds on the ground became men wrapped in blankets, and apart from them a group of larger mounds. Sleeping Trollocs. They had doused the fire. One moonbeam, moving through the branches, caught a shine of gold and silver on the ground, halfway between the two groups. The moonlight seemed to brighten; for an instant he could see clearly. The shape of a sleeping man lay close by to the gleam, but that was not what held his eye. *The chest. The Horn.* And something atop it, a point of red flashing in the moonbeam. *The dagger! Why would Fain put . . . ?*

Loial's huge hand settled over Rand's mouth, and a good part of his face besides. He twisted to look at the Ogier. Loial pointed off to his right, slowly, as if motion might attract attention.

At first Rand could not see anything, then a shadow moved, not ten paces away. A tall, bulky shadow, and snouted. Rand's breath caught. A Trolloc. It lifted its snout as if sniffing. Some of them hunted by scent.

For an instant the void wavered. Someone stirred in the Darkfriend camp, and the Trolloc turned to peer that way.

Rand froze, letting the calm of emptiness envelope him. His hand was on his sword, but he did not think of it. The void was all. Whatever happened, happened. He watched the Trolloc without blinking.

A moment longer the snouted shadow watched the Darkfriend camp, then, as if satisfied, folded itself down beside a tree. Almost immediately a low sound, like coarse cloth ripping, drifted from it.

Loial put his mouth close to Rand's ear. "It's asleep," he whispered incredulously.

Rand nodded. Tam had told him Trollocs were lazy, apt to give up any task but killing unless fear kept them to it. He turned back to the camp.

All was still and quiet there again. The moonbeam no longer shone on the chest, but he knew now which shadow it was. He could see it in his mind, floating beyond the void, glittering golden, chased with silver, in the glow of *saidin*. The Horn of Valere and the dagger Mat needed, both almost within reach of his hand. Selene's face drifted with the chest. They could follow Fain's party in the morning, and wait until Ingtar joined them. If Ingtar did come, if he still followed the trail without his sniffer. No, there would never be a better chance. All within reach of his hand. Selene was waiting on the mountain.

Motioning for Loial to follow, Rand dropped to his belly and crawled toward the chest. He heard the Ogier's muffled gasp, but his eyes were fixed on that one shadowed mound ahead.

Darkfriends and Trollocs lay to left and right of him, but once he had seen Tam stalk close enough to a deer to put his hand on its flank before the animal bounded off; he had tried to learn from Tam. *Madness!* The thought flew by dimly, almost out of reach. *This is madness! You—are—going—mad!* Dim thoughts; someone else's thoughts.

Slowly, silently, he slithered to that one special shadow, and put out a hand. Ornate traceries worked in gold met his touch. It *was* the chest that held the Horn of Valere. His hand touched something else, on the lid. The dagger, bare-bladed. In the dark, his eyes widened. Remembering what it had done to Mat, he jerked back, the void shifting with his agitation.

The man sleeping nearby—no more than two paces from the chest; no one else lay so close by spans—groaned in his sleep and thrashed at his blankets. Rand allowed the void to sweep thought and fear away. Murmuring uneasily in his sleep, the man stilled.

Rand let his hand go back to the dagger, not quite touching it. It had not harmed Mat in the beginning. Not much, at least; not quickly. In one swift motion he lifted the dagger, stuck it behind his belt, and pulled his hand away, as if it might help to minimize the time it touched his bare skin. Perhaps it would, and Mat would die without the dagger. He could feel it there, almost a weight pulling him down, pressing against him. But in the void sensation was as distant as thought, and the feel of the dagger faded quickly to something he was used to.

He wasted only a moment more staring at the shadow-wrapped chest—the Horn had to be inside, but he did not know how to open it and he could not lift it by himself—then he looked around for Loial. He found the Ogier crouched not far behind him, massive head swiveling as he peered back and forth from sleeping human Darkfriends to sleeping Trollocs. Even in the night it was plain Loial's eyes were as wide as they could go; they looked as big as saucers in the light of the moon. Rand reached out and took Loial's hand.

The Ogier gave a start and gasped. Rand put a finger across his lips, set Loial's hand on the chest, and mimed lifting. For a time—it seemed forever, in the night, with Darkfriends and Trollocs all around; it could not have been more than heartbeats—Loial stared. Then, slowly, he put his arms around the golden chest and stood. He made it seem effortless.

Ever so carefully, even more carefully than he had come in, Rand began to walk out of the camp, behind Loial and the chest. Both hands on his sword, he watched the sleeping Darkfriends, the still shapes of the Trollocs. All those shadowed figures began to be swallowed deeper in the darkness as they drew away. *Almost free. We've done it!*

The man who had been sleeping near the chest suddenly sat up with a strangled yell, then leaped to his feet. "It's gone! Wake, you filth! It's gooonnne!" Fain's voice; even in the void Rand recognized it. The others scrambled erect, Darkfriends and Trollocs, calling to know what was happening, growling and snarling. Fain's voice rose to a howl. "I know it is you, al'Thor! You're hiding from me, but I know you are out there! Find him! Find him! Al'Thoooor!" Men and Trollocs scattered in every direction.

Wrapped in emptiness, Rand kept moving. Almost forgotten in entering the camp, *saidin* pulsed at him.

"He cannot see us," Loial whispered low. "Once we reach the horses—"

A Trolloc leaped out of the dark at them, cruel eagle's beak in a man's face where mouth and nose should have been, scythe-like sword already whistling through the air.

Rand moved without thought. He was one with the blade. Cat Dances on the Wall. The Trolloc screamed as it fell, screamed again as it died.

"Run, Loial!" Rand commanded. *Saidin* called to him. "Run!"

He was dimly aware of Loial lumbering to an awkward gallop, but another Trolloc loomed from the night, boar-snouted and tusked, spiked axe raised. Smoothly Rand glided between Trolloc and Ogier; Loial must get the Horn away. Head and shoulders taller than Rand, half again as wide, the Trolloc came at him with a silent snarl. The Courtier Taps His Fan. No scream, this time. He walked backwards after Loial, watching the night. *Saidin* sang to him, such a sweet song. *The Power could burn them all, burn Fain and all the rest to cinders. No!*

Two more Trollocs, wolf and ram, gleaming teeth and curling horns. Lizard in the Thornbush. He rose smoothly from one knee as the second toppled, horns almost brushing his shoulder. The song of *saidin* caressed him with seduction, pulled him with a thousand silken strings. *Burn them all with the Power. No. No! Better dead than that. If I were dead, it would be done with.*

A knot of Trollocs came into sight, hunting uncertainly. Three of them, four. Suddenly one pointed to Rand and raised a howl the rest answered as they charged.

"Let it be done with!" Rand shouted, and leaped to meet them.

For an instant surprise slowed them, then they came on with guttural cries gleeful, bloodthirsty, swords and axes raised. He danced among them to the song of *saidin*. Hummingbird Kisses the Honeyrose. So cunning that song, filling him. Cat on Hot Sand. The sword seemed alive in his hands as it had never been before, and he fought as if a heron-mark blade could keep *saidin* from him. The Heron Spreads Its Wings.

Rand stared at the motionless shapes on the ground around him. "Better to be dead," he murmured. He raised his eyes, back up the hill toward where the camp lay. Fain was there, and Darkfriends, and more Trollocs. Too many to fight. Too many to face and live. He took a step that way. Another.

"Rand, come on!" Loial's urgent, whispered call drifted through the emptiness to him. "For life and the Light, Rand, come on!"

Carefully, Rand bent to wipe his blade on a Trolloc's coat. Then, as formally as if Lan were watching him train, he sheathed it.

"Rand!"

As though he knew of no urgency, Rand joined Loial by the horses. The Ogier was tying the golden chest atop his saddle with straps from his saddlebags. His cloak was stuffed underneath to help balance the chest on the rounded saddle seat.

Saidin sang no more. It was there, that stomach-turning glow, but it held back as if he truly had fought it off. Wonderingly, he let the void vanish. "I think I am going mad," he said. Suddenly realizing where they were, he peered back the way they had come. Shouts and howls came from half a dozen different directions; signs of search, but none of pursuit. Yet. He swung up onto Red's back.

"Sometimes I do not understand half of what you say," Loial said. "If you must go mad, could it at least wait until we are back with the Lady Selene and Hurin?"

"How are you going to ride with that in your saddle?"

"I will run!" The Ogier suited his words by breaking into a quick trot, pulling his horse behind him by the reins. Rand followed.

The pace Loial set was as fast as a horse could trot. Rand was sure the Ogier could not keep it for long, but Loial's feet did not flag. Rand decided that his boast of once out-running a horse might really be true. Now and again Loial looked behind them as he ran, but the shouts of Darkfriends and howls of Trollocs faded with distance.

Even when the ground began to slope upwards more sharply, Loial's pace barely slowed, and he trotted into their campsite on the mountainside with only a little hard breathing.

"You have it." Selene's voice was exultant as her gaze rested on the ornately worked chest on Loial's saddle. She was wearing her own dress again; it looked as white as new snow to Rand. "I knew you would make the right choice. May I . . . have a look at it?"

"Did any of them follow, my Lord?" Hurin asked anxiously. He stared at the chest with awe, but his eyes slid off into the night, down the mountain. "If they followed, we'll have to move quick."

"I do not think they did. Go to the outcrop and see if you can see anything." Rand climbed down from his saddle as Hurin hurried up the mountain. "Selene, I don't know how to open the chest. Loial, do you?" The Ogier shook his head.

"Let me try. . . ." Even for a woman of Selene's height, Loial's saddle was high above the ground. She reached up to touch the finely wrought patterns on the chest, ran her hands across them, pressed. There was a click, and she pushed the lid up, let it fall open.

As she stretched on tiptoe to put a hand inside, Rand reached over her shoulder and lifted out the Horn of Valere. He had seen it once before, but never touched it. Though beautifully made, it did not look a thing of great age, or power. A curled golden horn, gleaming in the faint light, with inlaid silver script flowing around the mouth of the bell. He touched the strange letters with a finger. They seemed to catch the moon.

"Tia mi aven Moridin isainde vadin," Selene said. " 'The grave is no bar to my call.' You *will* be greater than Artur Hawkwing ever was."

"I am taking it to Shienar, to Lord Agelmar." *It should go to Tar Valon*, he thought, *but I'm done with Aes Sedai. Let Agelmar or Ingtar take it to them.* He set the Horn back in the chest; it cast back the moonlight, pulled the eye.

"That is madness," Selene said.

Rand flinched at the word. "Mad or not, it is what I'm doing. I told you, Selene, I want no part of greatness. Back there, I thought I did. For a while, I thought I wanted things. . . ." *Light, she's so beautiful. Egwene. Selene. I'm not worthy of either of them.* "Something seemed to take hold of me." *Saidin came for me, but I fought it off with a sword. Or is that mad, too?* He breathed deeply. "Shienar is where the Horn of Valere belongs. Or if not there, Lord Agelmar will know what to do with it."

Hurin appeared from up the mountain. "The fire's there again, Lord Rand, and bigger than ever. And I thought I heard shouting. It was all down in the hills. I don't think they've come upon the mountain, yet."

"You misunderstand me, Rand," Selene said. "You cannot go back, now. You are committed. Those Friends of the Dark will not simply go away because you've taken the Horn from them. Far from it. Unless you know some way to kill them all, they will be hunting you now as you hunted them before."

"No!" Loial and Hurin looked surprised at Rand's vehemence. He softened his tone. "I don't know any way to kill them all. They can live forever for all of me."

Selene's long hair shifted in waves as she shook her head. "Then you cannot go back, only onward. You can reach the safety of Cairhien's walls long before you could return to Shienar. Does the thought of a few more days in my company seem so onerous?"

Rand stared at the chest. Selene's company was far from burdensome, but near her he could not help thinking things he should not. Still, trying to ride back north meant risking Fain and his followers. She was right in that. Fain would never give up. Ingtar would not give up, either. If Ingtar came on southward, and Rand knew of no reason for him to turn aside, he would arrive at Cairhien, soon or late.

"Cairhien," he agreed. "You will have to show me where you live, Selene. I've never been to Cairhien." He reached to close the chest.

"You took something else from the Friends of the Dark?" Selene said. "You spoke earlier of a dagger."

How could I forget? He left the chest as it was and pulled the dagger from his belt. The bare blade curved like a horn, and the quillons were golden serpents. Set in the hilt, a ruby as big as his thumbnail winked like an evil eye in the moonlight. Ornate as it was, tainted as he knew it was, it felt no different from any other knife.

"Be careful," Selene said. "Do not cut yourself."

Rand felt a shiver inside. If simply carrying it was dangerous, he did not want to know what a cut from it would do. "This is from Shadar Logoth," he told the others. "It will twist whoever carries it for long, taint them to the bone the way Shadar Logoth is tainted. Without Aes Sedai Healing, that taint will kill, eventually."

"So that is what ails Mat," Loial said softly. "I never suspected." Hurin stared at the dagger in Rand's hand and wiped his own hands on the front of his coat. The sniffer did not look happy.

"None of us must handle it any more than is necessary," Rand went on. "I will find some way to carry it—"

"It is dangerous." Selene frowned at the blade as if the snakes were real, and poisonous. "Throw it away. Leave it, or bury it if you wish to keep it from other hands, but be rid of it."

"Mat needs it," Rand said firmly.

"It is too dangerous. You said so yourself."

"He needs it. The Am . . . the Aes Sedai said he would die without it to use in Healing him." *They still have a string on him, but this blade will cut it. Until I'm rid of it, and the Horn, they have a string on me, but I'll not dance however much they pull.*

He set the dagger in the chest, inside the curl of the Horn—there was just room for it—and pulled the lid down. It locked with a sharp snap. "That should shield us from it." He hoped it would. Lan said the time to sound most sure was when you were least certain.

"The chest will surely shield us," Selene said in a tight voice. "And now I mean to finish what is left of my night's sleep."

Rand shook his head. "We are too close. Fain seems able to find me, sometimes."

"Seek the Oneness if you are afraid," Selene said.

"I want to be as far from those Darkfriends come morning as we can be. I will saddle your mare."

"Stubborn!" She sounded angry, and when he looked at

her, her mouth curved in a smile that never came close to her dark eyes. "A stubborn man is best, once. . . ." Her voice trailed off, and that worried him. Women often seemed to leave things unsaid, and in his limited experience it was what they did not say that proved the most trouble. She watched in silence as he slung her saddle onto the white mare's back and bent to fashion the girths.

"Gather them all in!" Fain snarled. The goat-snouted Trolloc backed away from him. The fire, piled high with wood now, lit the hilltop with flickering shadows. His human followers huddled near the blaze, fearful to be out in the dark with the rest of the Trollocs. "Gather them, every one that still lives, and if any think to run, let them know they'll get what that one got." He gestured to the first Trolloc that had brought him word al'Thor was not to be found. It still snapped at ground muddied with its own blood, hooves scraping trenches as they jerked. "Go," Fain whispered, and the goat-snouted Trolloc ran into the night.

Fain glanced contemptuously at the other humans—*They'll have their uses still*—then turned to stare into the night, toward Kinslayer's Dagger. Al'Thor was up there, somewhere, in the mountains. With the Horn. His teeth grated audibly at the thought. He did not know where, exactly, but something pulled him toward the mountains. Toward al'Thor. That much of the Dark One's . . . gift . . . remained to him. He had hardly thought of it, had tried not to think of it, until suddenly, after the Horn was gone—*Gone!*—al'Thor was there, drawing him as meat draws a starving dog.

"I am a dog no longer. A dog no longer!" He heard the others shifting uneasily around the fire, but he ignored them. "You will pay for what was done to me, al'Thor! The world will pay!" He cackled at the night with mad laughter. "The world will pay!"

CHAPTER

20

Saidin

Rand kept them moving through the night, allowing only a brief stop at dawn, to rest the horses. And to allow Loial rest. With the Horn of Valere in its gold-and-silver chest occupying his saddle, the Ogier walked or trotted ahead of his big horse, never complaining, never slowing them. Sometime during the night they had crossed the border of Cairhien.

"I want to see it again," Selene said as they halted. She dismounted and strode to Loial's horse. Their shadows, long and thin, pointed west from the sun just peeking over the horizon. "Bring it down for me, *alantin*." Loial began to undo the straps. "The Horn of Valere."

"No," Rand said, climbing down from Red's back. "Loial, no." The Ogier looked from Rand to Selene, his ears twitching doubtfully, but he took his hands away.

"I want to see the Horn," Selene demanded. Rand was sure she was no older than he, but at that moment she suddenly seemed as old and as cold as the mountains, and more regal than Queen Morgase at her haughtiest.

"I think we should keep the dagger shielded," Rand said. "For all I know, looking at it may be as bad as touching it. Let it stay where it is until I can put it in Mat's hands. He—he can take it to the Aes Sedai." *And what price will they demand for that Healing? But he hasn't any choice.* He felt a little guilty over feeling relief that he, at least, was through with Aes Sedai. *I am done with them. One way or another.*

"The dagger! All you seem to care about is that dagger. I told you to be rid of it. The Horn of Valere, Rand."

"No."

She came to him, a sway in her walk that made him feel as if he had something caught in his throat. "All I want is to see it in the light of day. I won't even touch it. You hold it. It would be something for me to remember, you holding the Horn of Valere in your hands." She took his hands as she said it; her touch made his skin tingle and his mouth go dry.

Something to remember—when she had gone. . . . He could close the dagger up again as soon as the Horn was out of the chest. It would be something to hold the Horn in his hands where he could see it in the light.

He wished he knew more of the Prophecies of the Dragon. The one time he heard a merchant's guard telling a part of it, back in Emond's Field, Nynaeve had broken a broom across the man's shoulders. None of the little he had heard mentioned the Horn of Valere.

Aes Sedai trying to make me do what they want. Selene was still gazing intently into his eyes, her face so young and beautiful that he wanted to kiss her despite what he was thinking. He had never seen an Aes Sedai act the way she did, and she looked young, not ageless. *A girl my age couldn't be Aes Sedai. But. . . .*

"Selene," he said softly, "*are* you an Aes Sedai?"

"Aes Sedai," she almost spat, flinging his hands away. "Aes Sedai! Always you hurl that at me!" She took a deep breath and smoothed her dress, as if gathering herself. "I am what and who I am. And I am no Aes Sedai!" And she wrapped herself in a silent coldness that made even the morning sun seem chill.

Loial and Hurin bore it all with as good a grace as they could manage, trying to make conversation and hiding their embarrassment when she froze them with a look. They rode on.

By the time they made camp that night beside a mountain stream that provided fish for their supper, Selene seemed to have regained some of her temper, chatting with the Ogier about books, speaking kindly to Hurin.

She barely spoke to Rand, though, unless he spoke first, either that evening or the following day as they rode through mountains that reared on either side of them like huge, jagged gray walls, ever climbing. But whenever he looked at her, she was watching him and smiling. Sometimes it was

the sort of smile that made him smile back, sometimes the
sort that made him clear his throat and blush at his own
thoughts, and sometimes the mysterious, knowing smile that
Egwene sometimes wore. It was a kind of smile that always
put his back up—but at least it was a smile.

She can't *be Aes Sedai.*

The way began to slope downwards, and with the promise
of twilight in the air, Kinslayer's Dagger at last gave way to
hills, rolling and round, with more brush than trees, more
thickets than forest. There was no road, just a dirt track,
such as might be used by a few carts now and again. Fields
carved some of the hills into terraces, fields full of crops
but empty of people at this hour. None of the scattered farm
buildings lay close enough to the path they rode for Rand to
make out more than that they were all made of stone.

When he saw the village ahead, lights already twinkled
in a few windows against the coming of night.

"We'll sleep in beds tonight," he said.

"That I will enjoy, Lord Rand." Hurin laughed. Loial
nodded agreement.

"A village inn," Selene sniffed. "Dirty, no doubt, and full
of unwashed men swilling ale. Why can't we sleep under
the stars again? I find I enjoy sleeping under the stars."

"You would not enjoy it if Fain caught up with us while
we slept," Rand said, "him and those Trollocs. He's coming
after me, Selene. After the Horn, too, but it is me he can
find. Why do you think I've kept such a close watch these
past nights?"

"If Fain catches us, you will deal with him." Her voice
was coolly confident. "And there could be Darkfriends in
the village, too."

"But even if they knew who we are, they can't do much
with the rest of the villagers around. Not unless you think
everyone in the village is a Darkfriend."

"And if they discover you carry the Horn? Whether you
want greatness or not, even farmers dream of it."

"She is right, Rand," Loial said. "I fear even farmers
might want to take it."

"Unroll your blanket, Loial, and throw it over the chest.
Keep it covered." Loial complied, and Rand nodded. It was
obvious there was a box or chest beneath the Ogier's striped
blanket, but nothing suggested it was more than a travel

chest. "My Lady's chest of clothes," Rand said with a grin and a bow.

Selene met his sally with silence and an unreadable look. After a moment, they started on again.

Almost immediately, off to Rand's left, a glitter from the setting sun reflected from something on the ground. Something large. Something very large, by the light it threw up. Curious, he turned his horse that way.

"My Lord?" Hurin said. "The village?"

"I just want to see this first," Rand said. *It's brighter than sunlight on water. What can it be?*

His eyes on the reflection, he was surprised when Red suddenly stopped. On the point of urging the bay on, he realized that they stood on the edge of a clay precipice, above a huge excavation. Most of the hill had been dug away to a depth of easily a hundred paces. Certainly more than one hill had vanished, and maybe some farmers' fields, for the hole was at least ten times as wide as it was deep. The far side appeared to have been packed hard to a ramp. There were men on the bottom, a dozen of them, getting a fire started; down there, night was already descending. Here and there among them armor turned the light, and swords swung at their sides. He hardly glanced at them.

Out of the clay at the bottom of the pit slanted a gigantic stone hand holding a crystal sphere, and it was this that shone with the last sunlight. Rand gaped at the size of it, a smooth ball—he was sure not so much as a scratch marred its surface—at least twenty paces through.

Some distance away from the hand, a stone face in proportion had been uncovered. A bearded man's face, it thrust out of the soil with the dignity of vast years; the broad features seemed to hold wisdom and knowledge.

Unsummoned, the void formed, whole and complete in an instant, *saidin* glowing, beckoning. So intent was he on the face and the hand that he did not even realize what had happened. He had once heard a ship captain speak of a giant hand holding a huge crystal sphere; Bayle Domon had claimed it stuck out of a hill on the island of Tremalking.

"This is dangerous," Selene said. "Come away, Rand."

"I believe I can find a way down there," he said absently. *Saidin* sang to him. The huge ball seemed to glow white with the light of the sinking sun. It seemed to him that in

the depths of the crystal, light swirled and danced in time
to the song of *saidin*. He wondered why the men below did
not appear to notice.

Selene rode close and took hold of his arm. "Please, Rand,
you must come away." He looked at her hand, puzzled, then
followed her arm up to her face. She seemed genuinely worried, perhaps even afraid. "If this bank doesn't give way beneath our horses and break our necks with the fall, those men
are guards, and no one puts guards on something they wish
every passerby to examine. What good will it do you to avoid
Fain, if some lord's guards arrest you? Come away."

Suddenly—a drifting, distant thought—he realized
that the void surrounded him. *Saidin* sang, and the sphere
pulsed—even without looking, he could *feel* it—and the
thought came that if he sang the song *saidin* sang, that huge
stone face would open its mouth and sing with him. With
him and with *saidin*. All one.

"Please, Rand," Selene said. "I will go to the village with
you. I won't mention the Horn again. Only come away!"

He released the void . . . and it did not go. *Saidin*
crooned, and the light in the sphere beat like a heart. Like
his heart. Loial, Hurin, Selene, they all stared at him, but
they seemed oblivious to the glorious blaze from the crystal. He tried to push the void away. It held like granite; he
floated in an emptiness as hard as stone. The song of *saidin,*
the song of the sphere, he could feel them quivering along
his bones. Grimly, he refused to give in, reached deep inside himself . . . *I will not.* . . .

"Rand." He did not know whose voice it was.

. . . reached for the core of who he was, the core of what
he was . . .

. . . *will not* . . .

"Rand." The song filled him, filled the emptiness.

. . . touched stone, hot from a pitiless sun, cold from a
merciless night. . . .

. . . *not* . . .

Light filled him, blinded him.

"Till shade is gone," he mumbled, "till water is gone . . ."
Power filled him. He was one with the sphere.

". . . into the Shadow with teeth bared . . ."
The power was his. The Power was his.

". . . to spit in Sightblinder's eye . . ."

Power to Break the World.

". . . on the last day!" It came out as a shout, and the void was gone. Red shied at his cry; clay crumbled under the stallion's hoof, spilling into the pit. The big bay went to his knees. Rand leaned forward, gathering the reins, and Red scrambled to safety, away from the edge.

They were all staring at him, he saw. Selene, Loial, Hurin, all of them. "What happened?" *The void. . . .* He touched his forehead. The void had not gone when he released it, and the glow of *saidin* had grown stronger, and. . . . He could not remember anything more. *Saidin.* He felt cold. "Did I . . . do something?" He frowned, trying to remember. "Did I say something?"

"You just sat there stiff as a statue," Loial said, "mumbling to yourself no matter what anyone said. I couldn't make out what you were saying, not until you shouted 'day!' loud enough to wake the dead and nearly put your horse over the edge. Are you ill? You're acting more and more oddly every day."

"I'm not sick," Rand said harshly, then softened it. "I am all right, Loial." Selene watched him warily.

From the pit came the sound of men calling, the words indistinguishable.

"Lord Rand," Hurin said, "I think those guards have finally noticed us. If they know a way up this side, they could be here any minute."

"Yes," Selene said. "Let us leave here quickly."

Rand glanced at the excavation, then away again, quickly. The great crystal held nothing but reflected light from the evening sun, but he did not want to look at it. He could almost remember . . . *something* about the sphere. "I don't see any reason to wait for them. We didn't do anything. Let's find an inn." He turned Red toward the village, and they soon left pit and shouting guards behind.

As many villages did, Tremonsien covered the top of a hill, but like the farms they had passed, this hill had been sculpted into terraces with stone retaining walls. Square stone houses sat on precise plots of land, with exact gardens behind, along a few straight streets that crossed each other at right angles. The necessity of a curve to streets going around the hill seemed begrudged.

Yet the people seemed open and friendly enough, pausing

to nod to each other as they hurried about their last chores before nightfall. They were a short folk—none taller than Rand's shoulder, and few as tall as Hurin—with dark eyes and pale, narrow faces, and dressed in dark clothes except for a few who wore slashes of color across the chest. Smells of cooking—oddly spiced, to Rand's nose—filled the air, though a handful of goodwives still hung over their doors to talk; the doors were split, so the top could stand open while the bottom was closed. The people eyed the newcomers curiously, with no sign of hostility. A few stared a moment longer at Loial, an Ogier walking alongside a horse as big as a Dhurran stallion, but never more than a moment longer.

The inn, at the very top of the hill, was stone like every other building in the town, and plainly marked by a painted sign hanging over the wide doors. The Nine Rings. Rand swung down with a smile and tied Red to one of the hitching posts out front. "The Nine Rings" had been one of his favorite adventure stories when he was a boy; he supposed it still was.

Selene still seemed uneasy when he helped her dismount. "Are you all right?" he asked. "I didn't frighten you back there, did I? Red would never fall over a cliff with me." He wondered what had really happened.

"You terrified me," she said in a tight voice, "and I do not frighten easily. You could have killed yourself, killed. . . ." She smoothed her dress. "Ride with me. Tonight. Now. Bring the Horn, and I will stay by your side forever. Think of it. Me by your side, and the Horn of Valere in your hands. And that will only be the beginning, I promise. What more could you ask for?"

Rand shook his head. "I can't, Selene. The Horn. . . ." He looked around. A man looked out his window across the way, then twitched the curtains closed; evening darkened the street, and there was no one else in sight now except Loial and Hurin. "The Horn is not mine. I told you that." She turned her back on him, her white cloak walling him off as effectively as bricks.

CHAPTER
21

The Nine Rings

Rand expected the common room to be empty, since it was nearly suppertime, but half a dozen men crowded one table, dicing among their jacks of ale, and another sat by himself over a meal. Though the dicers carried no weapons in sight and wore no armor, only plain coats and breeches of dark blue, something about the way they held themselves told Rand they were soldiers. His eyes went to the solitary man. An officer, with the tops of his high boots turned down, and his sword propped against the table beside his chair. A single slash of red and one of yellow crossed the chest of the officer's blue coat from shoulder to shoulder, and the front of his head was shaved, though his black hair hung long in the back. The soldiers' hair was clipped short, as if it all had been cut under the same bowl. All seven turned to look as Rand and the others came in.

The innkeeper was a lean woman with a long nose and graying hair, but her wrinkles seemed part of her ready smile more than anything else. She came bustling up, wiping her hands on a spotless white apron. "Good even to you"—her quick eyes took in Rand's gold-embroidered red coat, and Selene's fine white dress—"my Lord, my Lady. I am Maglin Madwen, my Lord. Be welcome to The Nine Rings. And an Ogier. Not many of your kind come this way, friend Ogier. Would you be up from Stedding Tsofu, then?"

Loial managed an awkward half bow under the weight of the chest. "No, good innkeeper. I come the other way, from the Borderlands."

"From the Borderlands, you say. Well. And you, my

Lord? Forgive me for asking, but you've not the look of the Borderlands, if you don't mind my saying it."

"I'm from the Two Rivers, Mistress Madwen, in Andor." He glanced at Selene—she did not seem to admit he existed; her level look barely admitted that the room existed, or anyone in it. "The Lady Selene is from Cairhien, from the capital, and I am from Andor."

"As you say, my Lord." Mistress Madwen's glance flickered to Rand's sword; the bronze herons were plain on scabbard and hilt. She frowned slightly, but her face was clear again in a blink. "You'll be wanting a meal for yourself and your beautiful Lady, and your followers. And rooms, I expect. I'll have your horses seen to. I've a good table for you, right this way, and pork with yellow peppers on the fire. Would you be hunting the Horn of Valere, then, my Lord, you and your Lady?"

In the act of following her, Rand almost stumbled. "No! Why would you think we were?"

"No offense, my Lord. We've had two through here already, all polished to look like heroes—not to suggest anything of the kind about you, my Lord—in the last month. Not many strangers come here, except traders up from the capital to buy oats and barley. I'd not suppose the Hunt has left Illian, yet, but maybe some don't think they really need the blessing, and they'll get a jump on the others by missing it."

"We are not hunting the Horn, mistress." Rand did not glance at the bundle in Loial's arms; the blanket with its colorful stripes hung bunched over the Ogier's thick arms and disguised the chest well. "We surely are not. We are on our way to the capital."

"As you say, my Lord. Forgive me for asking, but is your Lady well?"

Selene looked at her, and spoke for the first time. "I am quite well." Her voice left a chill in the air that stifled talk for a moment.

"You're not Cairhienin, Mistress Madwen," Hurin said suddenly. Burdened down with their saddlebags and Rand's bundle, he looked like a walking baggage cart. "Pardon, but you don't sound it."

Mistress Madwen's eyebrows rose, and she shot a glance at Rand, then grinned. "I should have known you'd let your man speak freely, but I've grown used to—" Her glance darted toward the officer, who had gone back to his own meal. "Light, no, I'm not Cairhienin, but for my sins, I married one. Twenty-three years I lived with him, and when he died on me—the Light shine on him—I was all ready to go back to Lugard, but he had the last laugh, he did. He left me the inn, and his brother the money, when I was sure it would be the other way round. Tricksome and scheming, Barin was, like every man I've ever known, Cairhienin most of all. Will you be seated, my Lord? My Lady?"

The innkeeper gave a surprised blink when Hurin sat at table with them—an Ogier, it seemed, was one thing, but Hurin was clearly a servant in her eyes. With another quick look at Rand, she bustled off to the kitchens, and soon serving girls came with their meal, giggling and staring at the lord and the lady, and the Ogier, till Mistress Madwen chased them back to their work.

At first, Rand stared at his food doubtfully. The pork was cut in small bits, mixed with long strips of yellow peppers, and peas, and a number of vegetables and things he did not recognize, all in some sort of clear, thick sauce. It smelled sweet and sharp, both at the same time. Selene only picked at hers, but Loial was eating with a will.

Hurin grinned at Rand over his fork. "They spice their food oddly, Cairhienin do, Lord Rand, but for all that, it's not bad."

"It won't bite you, Rand," Loial added.

Rand took a hesitant mouthful, and almost gasped. It tasted just as it smelled, sweet and sharp together, the pork crisp on the outside and tender inside, a dozen different flavors, spices, all blending and contrasting. It tasted like nothing he had ever put in his mouth before. It tasted wonderful. He cleaned his plate, and when Mistress Madwen returned with the serving girls to clear away, he nearly asked for more the way Loial did. Selene's was still half full, but she motioned curtly for one of the girls to take it.

"A pleasure, friend Ogier." The innkeeper smiled. "It takes a lot to fill up one of you. Catrine, bring another helping, and be quick." One of the girls darted away. Mistress Madwen turned her smile on Rand. "My Lord, I had a man here who played the bittern, but he married a girl off one of the farms, and she has him strumming reins behind a plow, now. I couldn't help noticing what looks like a flute case sticking out of your man's bundle. Since my musician's gone, would you let your man favor us with a little music?"

Hurin looked embarrassed.

"He doesn't play," Rand explained. "I do."

The woman blinked. It appeared lords did not play the flute, at least not in Cairhien. "I withdraw the request, my Lord. Light's own truth, I meant no offense, I assure you. I'd never ask one such as yourself to be playing in a common room."

Rand hesitated only a moment. It had been too long since he had practiced the flute rather than the sword, and the coins in his pouch would not last forever. Once he was rid of his fancy clothes—once he turned the Horn over to Ingtar and the dagger over to Mat—he would need the flute to earn his supper again while he searched for somewhere safe from Aes Sedai. *And safe from myself? Something* did *happen back there. What?*

"I don't mind," he said. "Hurin, hand me the case. Just slide it out." There was no need to show a gleeman's cloak; enough unspoken questions shone in Mistress Madwen's dark eyes as it was.

Worked gold chased with silver, the instrument looked the sort a lord might play, if lords anywhere played the flute. The heron branded on his right palm did not interfere with his fingering. Selene's salves had worked so well he hardly thought of the brand unless he saw it. Yet it was in his thoughts now, and unconsciously he began to play "Heron on the Wing."

Hurin bobbed his head to the tune, and Loial beat time on the table with a thick finger. Selene looked at Rand as if wondering what he was—*I'm not a lord, my Lady. I'm a shepherd, and I play the flute in common rooms*—but the soldiers turned from their talk to listen, and the officer closed the wooden cover of the book he had begun reading. Selene's steady gaze struck a stubborn spark inside Rand. Determinedly he avoided any song that might fit in a palace, or a lord's manor. He played "Only One Bucket of Water" and "The Old Two Rivers Leaf," "Old Jak's Up a Tree" and "Goodman Priket's Pipe."

With the last, the six soldiers began to sing in raucous tones, though not the words Rand knew.

We rode down to River Iralell
just to see the Tairen come.
We stood along the riverbank
with the rising of the sun.
Their horses blacked the summer plain,
their banners blacked the sky.
But we stood our ground on the banks of River Iralell.
Oh, we stood our ground.
Yes, we stood our ground.
Stood our ground along the river in the morning.

It was not the first time that Rand had discovered a tune
had different words and different names in different lands,
sometimes even in villages in the same land. He played
along with them until they let the words die away, slapping
each other's shoulders and making rude comments on one
another's singing.

When Rand lowered the flute, the officer rose and made a
sharp gesture. The soldiers fell silent in mid-laugh, scraped
back their chairs to bow to the officer with hand on breast—
and to Rand—and left without a backwards look.

The officer came to Rand's table and bowed, hand to
heart; the shaven front of his head looked as if he had
dusted it with white powder. "Grace favor you, my Lord.
I trust they did not bother you, singing as they did. They
are a common sort, but they meant no insult, I assure you.
I am Aldrin Caldevwin, my Lord. Captain in His Majesty's
Service, the Light illumine him." His eyes slid over Rand's
sword; Rand had the feeling Caldevwin had noticed the
herons as soon as he came in.

"They didn't insult me." The officer's accent reminded
him of Moiraine's, precise and every word pronounced to
its full. *Did she really let me go? I wonder if she's following
me. Or waiting for me.* "Sit down, Captain. Please." Caldevwin drew a chair from another table. "Tell me, Captain,
if you don't mind. Have you seen any other strangers recently? A lady, short and slender, and a fighting man with
blue eyes. He's tall, and sometimes he wears his sword on
his back."

"I have seen no strangers at all," he said, lowering himself stiffly to his seat. "Saving yourself and your Lady, my

Lord. Few of the nobility ever come here." His eyes flicked toward Loial with a minute frown; Hurin he ignored for a servant.

"It was only a thought."

"Under the Light, my Lord, I mean no disrespect, but may I hear your name? We have so few strangers here that I find I wish to know every one."

Rand gave it—he claimed no title, but the officer seemed not to notice—and said as he had to the innkeeper, "From the Two Rivers, in Andor."

"A wondrous place I have heard, Lord Rand—I may call you so?—and fine men, the Andormen. No Cairhienin has ever worn a blademaster's sword so young as you. I met some Andormen, once, the Captain-General of the Queen's Guards among them. I do not remember his name; an embarrassment. Perhaps you could favor me with it?"

Rand was conscious of the serving girls in the background, beginning to clean and sweep. Caldevwin seemed only to be making conversation, but there was a probing quality to his look. "Gareth Bryne."

"Of course. Young, to hold so much responsibility."

Rand kept his voice level. "Gareth Bryne has enough gray in his hair to be your father, Captain."

"Forgive me, my Lord Rand. I meant to say that he came to it young." Caldevwin turned to Selene, and for a moment he only stared. He shook himself, finally, as if coming out of a trance. "Forgive me for looking at you so, my Lady, and forgive me for speaking so, but Grace has surely favored you. Will you give me a name to put to such beauty?"

Just as Selene opened her mouth, one of the serving girls let out a cry and dropped a lamp she was taking down from a shelf. Oil splattered, and caught in a pool of flame on the floor. Rand leaped to his feet along with the others at the table, but before any of them could move, Mistress Madwen appeared, and she and the girl smothered the flames with their aprons.

"I have told you to be careful, Catrine," the innkeeper said, shaking her now-smutty apron under the girl's nose. "You'll be burning the inn down, and yourself in it."

The girl seemed on the point of tears. "I *was* being careful, Mistress, but I had such a twinge in my arm."

Mistress Madwen threw up her hands. "You always have

some excuse, and you still break more dishes than all the rest. Ah, it's all right. Clean it up, and don't burn yourself." The innkeeper turned to Rand and the others, all still standing around the table. "I hope none of you take this amiss. The girl really won't burn down the inn. She's hard on the dishes when she starts mooning over some young fellow, but she's never mishandled a lamp before."

"I would like to be shown to my room. I do not feel well after all." Selene spoke in careful tones, as though uncertain of her stomach, but despite that she looked and sounded as cool and calm as ever. "The journey, and the fire."

The innkeeper clucked like a mother hen. "Of course, my Lady. I have a fine room for you and your Lord. Shall I fetch Mother Caredwain? She has a fine hand with soothing herbs."

Selene's voice sharpened. "No. And I wish a room by myself."

Mistress Madwen glanced at Rand, but the next moment she was bowing Selene solicitously toward the stairs. "As you wish, my Lady. Lidan, fetch the Lady's things like a good girl, now." One of the serving girls ran to take Selene's saddlebags from Hurin, and the women disappeared upstairs, Selene stiff-backed and silent.

Caldevwin stared after them until they were gone, then shook himself again. He waited until Rand had seated himself before taking his chair again. "Forgive me, my Lord Rand, for staring so at your Lady, but Grace has surely favored you in her. I mean no insult."

"None taken," Rand said. He wondered if every man felt the way he did when they looked at Selene. "As I was riding to the village, Captain, I saw a huge sphere. Crystal, it seemed. What is it?"

The Cairhienin's eyes sharpened. "It is part of the statue, my Lord Rand," he said slowly. His gaze flickered toward Loial; for an instant he seemed to be considering something new.

"Statue? I saw a hand, and a face, too. It must be huge."

"It is, my Lord Rand. And old." Caldevwin paused. "From the Age of Legends, so I am told."

Rand felt a chill. The Age of Legends, when use of the One Power was everywhere, if the stories could be believed. *What happened there? I know there was something.*

"The Age of Legends," Loial said. "Yes, it must be. No one has done work so vast since. A great piece of work to dig that up, Captain." Hurin sat silently, as if he not only was not listening, but was not there at all.

Caldevwin nodded reluctantly. "I have five hundred laborers in camp beyond the diggings, and even so it will be past summer's end before we have it clear. They are men from the Foregate. Half my work is to keep them digging, and the other half to keep them out of this village. Foregaters have a fondness for drinking and carousing, you understand, and these people lead quiet lives." His tone said his sympathies were all with the villagers.

Rand nodded. He had no interest in Foregaters, whoever they were. "What will you do with it?" The captain hesitated, but Rand only looked back at him until he spoke.

"Galldrian himself has ordered that it be taken to the capital."

Loial blinked. "A very great piece of work, that. I am not sure how something that big could be moved so far."

"His Majesty has ordered it," Caldevwin said sharply. "It will be set up outside the city, a monument to the greatness of Cairhien and of House Riatin. Ogier are not the only ones who know how to move stone." Loial looked abashed, and the captain visibly calmed himself. "Your pardon, friend Ogier. I spoke in haste, and rudely." He still sounded a little gruff. "Will you be staying in Tremonsien long, my Lord Rand?"

"We leave in the morning," Rand said. "We are going to Cairhien."

"As it happens, I am sending some of my men back to the city tomorrow. I must rotate them; they grow stale after too long watching men swing picks and shovels. You will not mind if they ride in your company?" He put it as a question, but as if acceptance were a foregone conclusion. Mistress Madwen appeared on the stairs, and he rose. "If you will excuse me, my Lord Rand, I must be up early. Until the morning, then. Grace favor you." He bowed to Rand, nodded to Loial, and left.

As the doors closed behind the Cairhienin, the innkeeper came to the table.

"I have your Lady settled, my Lord. And I've good rooms prepared for you and your man, and you, friend Ogier." She paused, studying Rand. "Forgive me if I overstep myself, my Lord, but I think I can speak freely to a lord who lets his man speak up. If I'm wrong . . . well, I mean no insult. For twenty-three years Barin Madwen and I were arguing when we weren't kissing, so to speak. That's by way of saying I have some experience. Right now, you're thinking your Lady never wants to see you again, but it's my way of thinking that if you tap on her door tonight, she'll be taking you in. Smile and say it was your fault, whether it was or not."

Rand cleared his throat and hoped his face was not turning red. *Light, Egwene would kill me if she knew I'd even thought of it. And Selene would kill me if I did it. Or would she?* That did make his cheeks burn. "I . . . thank you for your suggestion, Mistress Madwen. The rooms. . . ." He avoided looking at the blanket-covered chest by Loial's chair; they did not dare leave it without someone awake and guarding it. "We three will all sleep in the same room."

The innkeeper looked startled, but she recovered quickly. "As you wish, my Lord. This way, if you please."

Rand followed her up the stairs. Loial carried the chest under its blanket—the stairs groaned under the weight of him and the chest together, but the innkeeper seemed to think it was just an Ogier's bulk—and Hurin still carried all the saddlebags and the bundled cloak with the harp and flute.

Mistress Madwen had a third bed brought in and hastily assembled and made up. One of the beds already there stretched nearly from wall to wall in length, and had obviously been meant for Loial from the start. There was barely room to walk between the beds. As soon as the innkeeper was gone, Rand turned to the others. Loial had pushed the still-covered chest under his bed and was trying the mattress. Hurin was setting out the saddlebags.

"Do either of you know why that captain was so suspicious of us? He was, I'm sure of it." He shook his head. "I almost think he thought we might steal that statue, the way he was talking."

"*Daes Dae'mar*, Lord Rand," Hurin said. "The Great Game. The Game of Houses, some call it. This Caldevwin thinks you must be doing something to your advantage or you wouldn't be here. And whatever you're doing might be to his disadvantage, so he has to be careful."

Rand shook his head. " 'The Great Game'? What game?"

"It isn't a game at all, Rand," Loial said from his bed. He had pulled a book from his pocket, but it lay unopened on his chest. "I don't know much about it—Ogier don't do such things—but I have heard of it. The nobles and the noble Houses maneuver for advantage. They do things they think will help them, or hurt an enemy, or both. Usually, it's all done in secrecy, or if not, they try to make it seem as if they're doing something other than what they are." He gave one tufted ear a puzzled scratch. "Even knowing what it is, I don't understand it. Elder Haman always said it would take a greater mind than his to understand the things humans do, and I don't know many as intelligent as Elder Haman. You humans are odd."

Hurin gave the Ogier a slanted look, but he said, "He has the right of *Daes Dae'mar*, Lord Rand. Cairhienin play it more than most, though all southerners do."

"These soldiers in the morning," Rand said. "Are they part of Caldevwin playing this Great Game? We can't afford to get mixed in anything like that." There was no need to mention the Horn. They were all too aware of its presence.

Loial shook his head. "I don't know, Rand. He's human, so it could mean anything."

"Hurin?"

"I don't know, either." Hurin sounded as worried as the Ogier looked. "He could be doing just what he said, or. . . . That's the way of the Game of Houses. You never know. I spent most of my time in Cairhien in the Foregate, Lord Rand, and I don't know much about Cairhienin nobles, but—well, *Daes Dae'mar* can be dangerous anywhere, but especially in Cairhien, I've heard." He brightened suddenly. "The Lady Selene, Lord Rand. She'll know better than me or the Builder. You can ask her in the morning."

But in the morning, Selene was gone. When Rand went down to the common room, Mistress Madwen handed him a sealed parchment. "If you'll forgive me, my Lord, you should have listened to me. You should have tapped on your Lady's door."

Rand waited until she went away before he broke the white wax seal. The wax had been impressed with a crescent moon and stars.

*I must leave you for a time. There are too many people
here, and I do not like Caldevwin. I will await you in
Cairhien. Never think that I am too far from you. You will
be in my thoughts always, as I know that I am in yours.*

It was not signed, but that elegant, flowing script had the
look of Selene.

He folded it carefully and put it in his pocket before going
outside, where Hurin had the horses waiting.

Captain Caldevwin was there, too, with another, younger
officer and fifty mounted soldiers crowding the street.
The two officers were bare-headed, but wore steel-backed
gauntlets, and gold-worked breastplates strapped over their
blue coats. A short staff was fastened to the harness on each
officer's back, bearing a small, stiff blue banner above his
head. Caldevwin's banner bore a single white star, while
the younger man's was crossed by two white bars. They
were a sharp contrast to the soldiers in their plain armor
and helmets that looked like bells with metal cut away to
expose their faces.

Caldevwin bowed as Rand came out of the inn. "Good
morning to you; my Lord Rand. This is Elricain Tavolin,
who will command your escort, if I may call it that." The
other officer bowed; his head was shaved as Caldevwin's
was. He did not speak.

"An escort will be welcome, Captain," Rand said, managing to sound at ease. Fain would not try anything against
fifty soldiers, but Rand wished he could be certain they
were only an escort.

The captain eyed Loial, on his way to his horse with the
blanket-covered chest. "A heavy burden, Ogier."

Loial almost missed a step. "I never like to be far from
my books, Captain." His wide mouth flashed teeth in a self-
conscious grin, and he hurried to strap the chest onto his
saddle.

Caldevwin looked around, frowning. "Your Lady is not
down yet. And her fine animal is not here."

"She left already," Rand told him. "She had to go on to
Cairhien quickly, during the night."

Caldevwin's eyebrows lifted. "During the night? But my
men. . . . Forgive me, my Lord Rand." He drew the younger
officer aside, whispering furiously.

"He had the inn watched, Lord Rand," Hurin whispered. "The Lady Selene must have gotten past them unseen somehow."

Rand climbed to Red's saddle with a grimace. If there had been any chance Caldevwin did not suspect them of something, it seemed Selene had finished it. "Too many people, she says," he muttered. "There'll be more people by far in Cairhien."

"You said something, my Lord?"

Rand looked up as Tavolin joined him, mounted on a tall, dust-colored gelding. Hurin was in his saddle, too, and Loial stood beside his big horse's head. The soldiers were formed up in ranks. Caldevwin was nowhere to be seen.

"Nothing is happening the way I expect," Rand said.

Tavolin gave him a brief smile, hardly more than a twitch of his lips. "Shall we ride, my Lord?"

The strange procession headed for the hard-packed road that led to the city of Cairhien.

CHAPTER
22

Watchers

N othing is happening as I expect," Moiraine muttered, not expecting an answer from Lan. The
long, polished table before her was littered with
books and papers, scrolls and manuscripts, many of them
dusty from long storage and tattered with age, some only
fragments. The room seemed almost made of books and
manuscripts, filling shelves except where there were doors
or windows or the fireplace. The chairs were high-backed
and well padded, but half of them, and most of the small
tables, held books, and some had books and scrolls tucked
under them. Only the clutter in front of Moiraine was hers,
though.

She rose and moved to the window, peered into the night
toward the lights of the village, not far off. No danger of
pursuit here. No one would expect her to come here. *Clear
my head, and begin again*, she thought. *That is all there is
to do.*

None of the villagers had any suspicion that the two el-
derly sisters living in this snug house were Aes Sedai. One
did not suspect such things in a small place like Tifan's
Well, a farming community deep in the grassy plains of
Arafel. The villagers came to the sisters for advice on their
problems and cures for their ills, and valued them as women
blessed by the Light, but no more. Adeleas and Vandene
had gone into voluntary retreat together so long ago that
few even in the White Tower remembered they still lived.

With the one equally aged Warder who remained to
them, they lived quietly, still intending to write the history
of the world since the Breaking, and as much as they could

include of before. One day. In the meantime, there was
so much information to gather, so many puzzles to solve.
Their house was the perfect place for Moiraine to find the
information she needed. Except that it was not there.

Movement caught her eye, and she turned. Lan was
lounging against the yellow brick fireplace, as imperturbable as a boulder. "Do you remember the first time we met,
Lan?"

She was watching for some sign, or she would not have
seen the quick twitch of his eyebrow. It was not often she
caught him by surprise. This was a subject neither of them
ever mentioned; nearly twenty years ago she had told him—
with all the stiff pride of one still young enough to be called
young, she recalled—that she would never speak of it again
and expected the same silence of him.

"I remember," was all he said.

"And still no apology, I suppose? You threw me into a
pond." She did not smile, though she could feel amusement
at it, now. "Every stitch I had was soaked, and in what you
Bordermen call new spring. I nearly froze."

"I recall I built a fire, too, and hung blankets so you could
warm yourself in privacy." He poked at the burning logs
and returned the firetool to its hook. Even summer nights
were cool in the Borderlands. "I also recall that while I slept
that night, you dumped half the pond on me. It would have
saved a great deal of shivering on both our parts if you had
simply told me you were Aes Sedai rather than demonstrat-
ing it. Rather than trying to separate me from my sword.
Not a good way to introduce yourself to a Borderman, even
for a young woman."

"I *was* young, and alone, and you were as large then as
you are now, and your fierceness more open. I did not want
you to know I was Aes Sedai. It seemed to me at the time
you might answer my questions more freely if you did not
know." She fell silent for a moment, thinking of the years
since that meeting. It had been good to find a companion to
join her in her quest. "In the weeks that followed, did you
suspect that I would ask you to bond to me? I decided you
were the one in the first day."

"I never guessed," he said dryly. "I was too busy wondering if I could escort you to Chachin and keep a whole skin.
A different surprise you had for me every night. The ants

I recall in particular. I don't think I had one good night's sleep that whole ride."

She permitted herself a small smile, remembering. "I was young," she repeated. "And does your bond chafe after all these years? You are not a man to wear a leash easily, even so light a one as mine." It was a stinging comment; she meant it to be so.

"No." His voice was cool, but he took up the firetool again and gave the blaze a fierce poking it did not need. Sparks cascaded up the chimney. "I chose freely, knowing what it entailed." The iron rod clattered back onto its hook, and he made a formal bow. "Honor to serve, Moiraine Aes Sedai. It has been and will be so, always."

Moiraine sniffed. "Your humility, Lan Gaidin, has always been more arrogance than most kings could manage with their armies at their backs. From the first day I met you, it has been so."

"Why all this talk of days past, Moiraine?"

For the hundredth time—or so it seemed to her—she considered the words to use. "Before we left Tar Valon I made arrangements, should anything happen to me, for your bond to pass to another." He stared at her, silent. "When you feel my death, you will find yourself compelled to seek her out immediately. I do not want you to be surprised by it."

"Compelled," he breathed softly, angrily. "Never once have you used my bond to compel me. I thought you more than disapproved of that."

"Had I left this thing undone, you would be free of the bond at my death, and not even my strongest command to you would hold. I will not allow you to die in a useless attempt to avenge me. And I will not allow you to return to your equally useless private war in the Blight. The war we fight is the same war, if you could only see it so, and I will see that you fight it to some purpose. Neither vengeance nor an unburied death in the Blight will do."

"And do you foresee your death coming soon?" His voice was quiet, his face expressionless, both like stone in a dead winter blizzard. It was a manner she had seen in him many times, usually when he was on the point of violence. "Have you planned something, without me, that will see you dead?"

"I am suddenly glad there is no pond in this room," she

murmured, then raised her hands when he stiffened, offended at her light tone. "I see my death in every day, as you do. How could I not, with the task we have followed these years? Now, with everything coming to a head, I must see it as even more possible."

For a moment he studied his hands, large and square. "I had never thought," he said slowly, "that I might not be the first of us to die. Somehow, even at the worst, it always seemed. . . ." Abruptly he scrubbed his hands against each other. "If there is a chance I might be given like a pet lapdog, I would at least like to know to whom I am being given."

"I have never seen you as a pet," Moiraine said sharply, "and neither does Myrelle."

"Myrelle." He grimaced. "Yes, she would have to be Green, or else some slip of a girl just raised to full sisterhood."

"If Myrelle can keep her three Gaidin in line, perhaps she has a chance to manage you. Though she would like to keep you, I know, she has promised to pass your bond to another when she finds one who suits you better."

"So. Not a pet but a parcel. Myrelle is to be a—a caretaker! Moiraine, not even the Greens treat their Warders so. No Aes Sedai has passed her Warder's bond to another in four hundred years, but you intend to do it to me not once, but twice!"

"It is done, and I will not undo it."

"The Light blind me, if I am to be passed from hand to hand, do you at least have some idea in whose hand I will end?"

"What I do is for your own good, and perhaps it may be for another's, as well. It may be that Myrelle will find a slip of a girl just raised to sisterhood—was that not what you said?—who needs a Warder hardened in battle and wise in the ways of the world, a slip of a girl who may need someone who will throw her into a pond. You have much to offer, Lan, and to see it wasted in an unmarked grave, or left to the ravens, when it could go to a woman who needs it would be worse than the sin of which the Whitecloaks prate. Yes, I think she will have need of you."

Lan's eyes widened slightly; for him it was the same as another man gasping in shocked surmise. She had seldom seen him so off balance. He opened his mouth twice before he spoke. "And who do you have in mind for this—"

She cut him off. "Are you sure the bond does not chafe, Lan Gaidin? Do you realize for the first time, only now, the strength of that bond, the depth of it? You could end with some budding White, all logic and no heart, or with a young Brown who sees you as nothing more than a pair of hands to carry her books and sketches. I can hand you where I will, like a parcel—or a lapdog—and you can do no more than go. Are you sure it does not chafe?"

"Is that what this has been for?" he grated. His eyes burned like blue fire, and his mouth twisted. Anger; for the first time ever that she had seen, open anger etched his face. "Has all this talk been a test—a test!—to see if you could make my bond rub? After all this time? From the day I pledged to you, I have ridden where you said ride, even when I thought it foolish, even when I had reason to ride another way. Never did you need my bond to force me. On your word I have watched you walk into danger and kept my hands at my sides when I wanted nothing more than to out sword and carve a path to safety for you. After this, you test me?"

"Not a test, Lan. I spoke plainly, not twisting, and I have done as I said. But at Fal Dara, I began to wonder if you were still wholly with me." A wariness entered his eyes. *Lan, forgive me. I would not have cracked the walls you hold so hard, but I must know.* "Why did you do as you did with Rand?" He blinked; it was obviously not what he expected. She knew what he had thought was coming, and she would not let up now that he was off balance. "You brought him to the Amyrlin speaking and acting as a Border lord and a soldier born. It fit, in a way, with what I planned for him, but you and I never spoke of teaching him any of that. Why, Lan?"

"It seemed . . . right. A young wolfhound must meet his first wolf someday, but if the wolf sees him as a puppy, if he acts the puppy, the wolf will surely kill him. The wolfhound must be a wolfhound in the wolf's eyes even more than in his own, if he is to survive."

"Is that how you see Aes Sedai? The Amyrlin? Me? Wolves out to pull down your young wolfhound?" Lan shook his head. "You know what he is, Lan. You know what he must become. Must. What I have worked for since the day you and I met, and before. Do you now doubt what I do?"

"No. No, but. . . ." He was recovering himself, building his walls again. But they were not rebuilt yet. "How many times have you said that *ta'veren* pull those around them like twigs in a whirlpool? Perhaps I was pulled, too. I only know that it felt right. Those farm folk needed someone on their side. Rand did, at least. Moiraine, I believe in what you do, even as now, when I know not half of it; believe as I believe in you. I have not asked to be released from my bond, nor will I. Whatever your plans for dying and seeing me safely—disposed of—I will take great pleasure in keeping you alive and seeing those plans, at least, go for nothing."

"Ta'veren," Moiraine sighed. "Perhaps it was that. Rather than guiding a chip floating down a stream, I am trying to guide a log through rapids. Every time I push at it, it pushes at me, and the log grows larger the farther we go. Yet I must see it through to the end." She gave a little laugh. "I will not be unhappy, my old friend, if you manage to put those plans awry. Now, please leave me. I need to be alone to think." He hesitated only a moment before turning for the door. At the last moment, though, she could not let him go without one more question. "Do you ever dream of something different, Lan?"

"All men dream. But I know dreams for dreams. This"—he touched his sword hilt—"is reality." The walls were back, as high and hard as ever.

For a time after he left, Moiraine leaned back in her chair, looking into the fire. She thought of Nynaeve and cracks in a wall. Without trying, without thinking what she was doing, that young woman had put cracks in Lan's walls and seeded the cracks with creepers. Lan thought he was secure, imprisoned in his fortress by fate and his own wishes, but slowly, patiently, the creepers were tearing down the walls to bare the man within. Already he was sharing some of Nynaeve's loyalties; in the beginning he had been indifferent to the Emond's Field folk, except as people in whom Moiraine had some interest. Nynaeve had changed that as she had changed Lan.

To her surprise, Moiraine felt a flash of jealousy. She had never felt that before, certainly not for any of the women who had thrown their hearts at his feet, or those who had shared his bed. Indeed, she had never thought of him as an object of jealousy, had never thought so of any man. She was married to her battle, as he was married to his. But they had been companions in those battles for so long. He had ridden a horse to death, then run himself nearly to death, carrying her in his arms at the last, to Anaiya for Healing. She had tended his wounds more than once, keeping with her arts a life he had been ready to throw away to save hers. He had always said he was wedded with death. Now a new bride had captured his eyes, though he was blind to it. He thought he still stood strong behind his walls, but Nynaeve had laced bridal flowers in his hair. Would he still find himself able to court death so blithely? Moiraine wondered when he would ask her to release him from his bond. And what she would do when he did.

With a grimace, she got to her feet. There were more important matters. Far more important. Her eyes ran over the open books and papers crowding the room. So many hints, but no answers.

Vandene came in with a teapot and cups on a tray. She was slender and graceful, with a straight back, and the hair gathered neatly at the nape of her neck was almost white. The agelessness of her smooth face was that of long, long years. "I would have had Jaem bring this, and not disturb you myself, but he's out in the barn practicing with his sword." She made a clucking sound as she pushed a battered manuscript aside to set the tray on the table. "Lan being here has him remembering he's more than a gardener and handyman. Gaidin are so stiff-necked. I thought Lan would still be here; that's why I brought an extra cup. Have you found what you were seeking?"

"I am not even sure what it is I am seeking." Moiraine frowned, studying the other woman. Vandene was of the Green Ajah, not Brown like her sister, yet the two of them had studied so long together that she knew as much of history as Adeleas.

"Whatever it is, you don't even seem to know where to look." Vandene shifted some of the books and manuscripts on the table, shaking her head. "So many subjects. The Trolloc Wars. The Watchers Over the Waves. The legend of the Return. Two treatises on the Horn of Valere. Three on dark prophecy, and— Light, here's Santhra's book on the Forsaken. Nasty, that. As nasty as this on Shadar Logoth. And the Prophecies of the Dragon, in three translations *and* the original. Moiraine, whatever *are* you after? The Prophecies, I can understand—we hear some news here, remote as we are. We hear some of what's happening in Illian. There's even a rumor in the village that someone has already found the Horn." She gestured with a manuscript on the Horn, and coughed in the dust that rose from it. "I discount that, of course. There would be rumors. But what—? No. You said you wanted privacy, and I'll give it to you."

"Stop a moment," Moiraine said, halting the other Aes Sedai short of the door. "Perhaps you can answer some questions for me."

"I will try." Vandene smiled suddenly. "Adeleas claims I should have chosen Brown. Ask." She poured two cups of tea and handed one to Moiraine, then took a chair by the fire.

Steam curled over the cups while Moiraine chose her questions carefully. *To find the answers, and not reveal too much.* "The Horn of Valere is not mentioned in the Prophecies, but is it linked to the Dragon anywhere?"

"No. Except for the fact that the Horn must be found before Tarmon Gai'don and that the Dragon Reborn is supposed to fight the Last Battle, there is no link between them at all." The white-haired woman sipped her tea and waited.

"Does anything link the Dragon with Toman Head?"

Vandene hesitated. "Yes, and no. This is a bone between Adeleas and me." Her voice took on a lecturing tone, and for a time she did sound like a Brown. "There is a verse in the original that translates literally as 'Five ride forth, and four return. Above the watchers shall he proclaim himself, bannered cross the sky in fire. . . .' Well, it goes on. The point is, the word *ma'vron*. I say it should be translated not simply as 'watchers,' which is *a'vron*. *Ma'vron* has more importance to it. I say it means the Watchers Over the Waves, though they call themselves *Do Miere A'vron*, of course, not *Ma'vron*. Adeleas tells me I am quibbling. But I believe it means the Dragon Reborn will appear somewhere above Toman Head, in Arad Doman, or Saldaea. Adeleas may think I'm foolish, but I listen to every scrap I hear coming from Saldaea these days. Mazrim Taim can channel, so I hear, and our sisters haven't managed to corner him yet. If the Dragon is Reborn, and the Horn of Valere found, then the Last Battle is coming soon. We may never finish our history." She gave a shiver, then abruptly laughed. "Odd thing to worry about. I suppose I *am* becoming more a Brown. Horrible thing to contemplate. Ask your next question."

"I do not think you need worry about Taim," Moiraine said absently. It was a link with Toman Head, however small and tenuous. "He will be dealt with as Logain was. What of Shadar Logoth?"

"Shadar Logoth!" Vandene snorted. "In brief, the city was destroyed by its own hate, every living thing except Mordeth, the councilor who began it all, using the tactics of the Darkfriends against the Darkfriends, and he now lies trapped there waiting for a soul to steal. It is not safe to enter, and nothing in the city is safe to touch. But every novice close to being Accepted knows as much as that. In full, you will have to stay here a month and listen to Adeleas lecture—she has the true knowledge of it—but even I can tell you there's nothing of the Dragon in it. That place was dead a hundred years before Yurian Stonebow rose from the ashes of the Trolloc Wars, and he lies closest to it in history of all the false Dragons."

Moiraine raised a hand. "I did not speak clearly, and I do not speak of the Dragon, now, Reborn or false. Can you think of any reason why a Fade would take something that had come from Shadar Logoth?"

"Not if it knew the thing for what it was. The hate that killed Shadar Logoth was hate they thought to use *against* the Dark One; it would destroy Shadowspawn as surely as it would those who walk in the Light. They rightly fear Shadar Logoth as much as we."

"And what can you tell me of the Forsaken?"

"You do leap from subject to subject. I can tell you little more than you learned as a novice. No one knows much more of the Nameless than that. Do you expect me to ramble on with what we both learned as girls?"

For an instant, Moiraine was silent. She did not want to say too much, but Vandene and Adeleas had more knowledge at their fingertips than existed anywhere else but the White Tower, and more complications awaited her there than she cared to deal with now. She let the name slip between her lips as if it were escaping. "Lanfear."

"For once," the other woman sighed, "I know not a whit more than I did as a novice. The Daughter of the Night remains as much a mystery as if she truly had cloaked herself in darkness." She paused, peering into her cup, and when she looked up, her eyes were sharp on Moiraine's face. "Lanfear was linked to the Dragon, to Lews Therin Telamon. Moiraine, do you have some clue as to where the Dragon will be Reborn? Or was Reborn? Has he come already?"

"If I did," Moiraine replied levelly, "would I be here, instead of in the White Tower? The Amyrlin knows as much as I, that I swear. Have you received a summons from her?"

"No, and I suppose we would. When the time comes that we must face the Dragon Reborn, the Amyrlin will need every sister, every Accepted, every novice who can light a candle unguided." Vandene's voice lowered, musing. "With such power as he will wield, we must overwhelm him before he has a chance to use it against us, before he can go mad and destroy the world. Yet first we must let him face the Dark One." She laughed mirthlessly at the look on Moiraine's face. "I am not a Red. I've studied the Prophecies enough to know we dare not gentle him first. If we *can* gentle him. I know as well as you, as well as any sister who cares to find out, that the seals holding the Dark One in Shayol Ghul are weakening. The Illianers call the Great Hunt of the Horn. False Dragons abound. And two of them, Logain and now this fellow in Saldaea, able to channel. When was the last time the Reds found two men channeling in less than a year? When did they last find one in five years? Not in my lifetime, and I am a good deal older than you. The signs are everywhere. Tarmon Gai'don is coming. The Dark One will break free. And the Dragon will be Reborn." Her cup rattled as she set it down. "I suppose that is why I feared you might have seen some sign of him."

"He will come," Moiraine said smoothly, "and we will do what must be done."

"If I thought it would do any good, I'd pull Adeleas's nose out of her book and set off for the White Tower. But I find I am glad to be here where I am instead. Perhaps we will have time to finish our history."

"I hope that you will, Sister."

Vandene rose to her feet. "Well, I have tasks to be about before bed. If you have no more questions, I will leave you to your studies." But she paused and revealed that however long she had spent with books, she was still of the Green Ajah. "You should do something about Lan, Moiraine. The man is rumbling inside worse than Dragonmount. Sooner or later, he will erupt. I've known enough men to see when one is troubled with a woman. You two have been together a long time. Perhaps he has finally come to see you are a woman as well as Aes Sedai."

"Lan sees me as what I am, Vandene. Aes Sedai. And still as a friend, I hope."

"You Blues. Always so ready to save the world that you lose yourselves."

After the white-haired Aes Sedai left, Moiraine gathered her cloak and, muttering to herself, went into the garden. There was something in what Vandene had said that tugged at her mind, but she could not remember what it was. An answer, or a hint to an answer, for a question she had not asked—but she could not bring the question to mind, either.

The garden was small, like the house, but neat even in moonlight aided by the yellow glow from the cottage windows, with sandy walks between careful beds of flowers. She settled her cloak loosely on her shoulders against the soft coolness of the night. *What was the answer, and what was the question?*

Sand crunched behind her, and she turned, thinking it was Lan.

A shadow loomed dimly only a few paces from her, a shadow that appeared to be a too-tall man wrapped in his cloak. But the face caught the moon, gaunt-cheeked, pale, with black eyes too big above a puckered, red-lipped mouth. The cloak opened, unfolding into great wings like a bat's.

Knowing it was too late, she opened herself to *saidar*, but the Draghkar began to croon, and its soft hum filled her, fragmenting her will. *Saidar* slipped away. She felt only a vague sadness as she stepped toward the creature; the deep crooning that drew her closer suppressed feeling. White, white hands—like a man's hands, but tipped with claws—reached for her, and lips the color of blood curved in a travesty of a smile, baring sharp teeth, but dimly, so dimly, she knew it would not bite or tear. Fear the Draghkar's kiss. Once those lips touched her, she would be as good as dead, to be drained of soul, then of life. Whoever found her, even if they came as the Draghkar let her fall, would find a corpse without a mark and cold as if dead two days. And if they came before she was dead, what they found would be worse, and not really her at all any longer. The croon pulled her within reach of those pale hands, and the Draghkar's head bent slowly toward her.

She felt only the smallest surprise when a sword blade flashed over her shoulder to pierce the Draghkar's breast, and little more when a second crossed her other shoulder to strike beside the first.

Dazed, swaying, she watched as if from a great distance as the creature was pushed back, away from her. Lan came into her view, then Jaem, the gray-haired Warder's bony arms holding his blade as straight and true as the younger man's. The Draghkar's pale hands bloodied as they tore at the sharp steel, wings buffeting the two men with thunderclaps. Suddenly, wounded and bleeding, it began to croon again. To the Warders.

With an effort, Moiraine gathered herself; she felt almost as drained as if the thing had managed its kiss. *No time to be weak.* In an instant she opened herself to *saidar* and, as the Power filled her, steeled herself to touch the Shadowspawn directly. The two men were too close; anything else would harm them, as well. Even using the One Power, she knew she would feel soiled by the Draghkar.

But even as she began, Lan cried out, "Embrace death!" Jaem echoed him firmly. "Embrace death!" And the two men stepped within reach of the Draghkar's touch, drove home their blades to the hilt.

Throwing back its head, the Draghkar bellowed, a shriek that seemed to pierce Moiraine's head with needles. Even wrapped in *saidar* she could feel it. Like a tree falling, the Draghkar toppled, one wing knocking Jaem to his knees. Lan sagged as if exhausted.

Lanterns hurried from the house, borne by Vandene and Adeleas.

"What was that noise?" Adeleas demanded. She was al-

most a mirror image of her sister. "Has Jaem gone and. . . ."
The lantern light fell on the Draghkar; her voice trailed off.

Vandene took Moiraine's hands. "It did not . . . ?" She
left the question unfinished as, to Moiraine's eyes, a nimbus
surrounded her. Feeling strength flowing into her from the
other woman, Moiraine wished, not for the first time, that
Aes Sedai could do as much for themselves as they could
for others.

"It did not," she said gratefully. "See to the Gaidin."

Lan looked at her, mouth tight. "If you had not made me
so angry I had to go work forms with Jaem, so angry I gave
it up to come back to the house. . . ."

"But I did," she said. "The Pattern takes everything into
the weaving." Jaem was muttering, but still allowing Vandene to see to his shoulder. He was all bone and tendon, yet
looked as hard as old roots.

"How," Adeleas demanded, "could any creature of the
Shadow come so close without us sensing it?"

"It was warded," Moiraine said.

"Impossible," Adeleas snapped. "Only a sister could—"
She stopped, and Vandene turned from Jaem to look at
Moiraine.

Moiraine said the words none of them wanted to hear.
"The Black Ajah." Shouts drifted from the village. "Best
you hide this"—she gestured to the Draghkar, sprawled
across a flower bed—"quickly. They will be coming to ask
if you need help, but seeing this will start talk you will not
like."

"Yes, of course," Adeleas said. "Jaem, go and meet them.
Tell them you don't know what made the noise, but all is
well here. Slow them down." The gray-haired Warder hurried into the night toward the sound of approaching villagers. Adeleas turned to study the Draghkar as if it were a
puzzling passage in one of her books. "Whether Aes Sedai
are involved or not, whatever could have brought it here?"
Vandene regarded Moiraine silently.

"I fear I must leave you," Moiraine said. "Lan, will you
ready the horses?" As he left, she said, "I will leave letters
with you to be sent on to the White Tower, if you will arrange it." Adeleas nodded absently, her attention still on the
thing on the ground.

"And will you find your answers where you are going?" Vandene asked.

"I may already have found one I did not know I sought. I only hope I am not too late. I will need pen and parchment." She drew Vandene toward the house, leaving Adeleas to deal with the Draghkar.

CHAPTER
23

The Testing

Nynaeve warily eyed the huge chamber, far beneath the White Tower, and eyed Sheriam, at her side, just as warily. The Mistress of Novices seemed expectant, perhaps even a little impatient. In her few days in Tar Valon, Nynaeve had seen only serenity in the Aes Sedai, and a smiling acceptance of events coming in their own time.

The domed room had been carved out of the bedrock of the island; the light of lamps on tall stands reflected from pale, smooth stone walls. Centered under the dome was a thing made of three rounded, silver arches, each just tall enough to walk under, sitting on a thick silver ring with their ends touching each other. Arches and ring were all of one piece. She could not see what lay inside; there the light flickered oddly, and made her stomach flutter with it if she looked too long. Where arch touched ring, an Aes Sedai sat cross-legged on the bare stone of the floor, staring at the silvery construction. Another stood nearby, beside a plain table on which sat three large silver chalices. Each, Nynaeve knew—or at least, she had been told—was filled with clear water. All four Aes Sedai wore their shawls, as Sheriam did; blue-fringed for Sheriam, red for the swarthy woman by the table, green, white, and gray for the three around the arches. Nynaeve still wore one of the dresses she had been given in Fal Dara, pale green embroidered with small white flowers.

"First you leave me to stare at my thumbs from morning to night," Nynaeve muttered, "and now it's all in a rush."

"The hour waits on no woman," Sheriam replied. "The

Wheel weaves as the Wheel wills, and *when* it wills. Patience is a virtue that must be learned, but we must all be ready for the change of an instant."

Nynaeve tried not to glare. The most irritating thing she had yet discovered about the flame-haired Aes Sedai was that she sometimes sounded as if she were quoting sayings even when she was not. "What is that thing?"

"A *ter'angreal*."

"Well, that tells me nothing. What does it do?"

"*Ter'angreal* do many things, child. Like *angreal* and *sa'angreal*, they are remnants of the Age of Legends that use the One Power, though they are not quite so rare as the other two. While some *ter'angreal* must be made to work by Aes Sedai, as this one must, others will do what they do simply with the presence of any woman who can channel. There are even supposed to be some that will function for anyone at all. Unlike *angreal* and *sa'angreal*, they were made to do specific things. One other we have in the Tower makes oaths binding. When you are raised to full sisterhood, you will take your final vows holding that *ter'angreal*. To speak no word that is not true. To make no weapon for one man to kill another. Never to use the One Power as a weapon except against Darkfriends or Shadowspawn, or in the last extreme of defending your own life, that of your Warder, or that of another sister."

Nynaeve shook her head. It sounded either like too much to swear or too little, and she said so.

"Once, Aes Sedai were not required to swear oaths. It was known what Aes Sedai were and what they stood for, and there was no need for more. Many of us wish it were so still. But the Wheel turns, and the times change. That we swear these oaths, that we are known to be bound, allows the nations to deal with us without fearing that we will throw up our own power, the One Power, against them. Between the Trolloc Wars and the War of the Hundred Years we made these choices, and because of them the White Tower still stands, and we can still do what we can against the Shadow." Sheriam drew a deep breath. "Light, child, I am trying to teach you what any other woman standing where you are would have learned over the course of years. It cannot be done. *Ter'angreal* are what must concern you, now. We don't know why they were made. We dare use only a handful of them, and the ways in which we do dare to use them may be nothing like the purposes the makers intended. Most, we have learned to our cost to avoid. Over the years, no few Aes Sedai have been killed or had their Talent burned out of them, learning that."

Nynaeve shivered. "And you want me to walk into this one?" The light inside the arches flickered less, now, but she could see what lay in it no better.

"We know what this one does. It will bring you face-to-face with your greatest fears." Sheriam smiled pleasantly. "No one will ask you what you have faced; you need tell no more than you wish. Every woman's fears are her own property."

Vaguely, Nynaeve thought about her nervousness concerning spiders, especially in the dark, but she did not think that was what Sheriam meant. "I just walk through one arch and out another? Three times through, and it's done?"

The Aes Sedai adjusted her shawl with an irritated hitch of her shoulder. "If you wish to boil it down that far, yes," she said dryly. "I told you on the way here what you must know about the ceremony, as much as anyone is allowed to know beforehand. If you were a novice come to this, you would know it by heart, but don't worry about making mistakes. I will remind you, if necessary. Are you sure you are ready to face it? If you want to stop now, I can still write your name in the novice book."

"No!"

"Very well, then. Two things I will tell you now that no woman hears until she is in this room. The first is this. Once you begin, you must continue to the end. Refuse to go on, and no matter your potential, you will be very kindly put out of the Tower with enough silver to support you for a year, and you will never be allowed back." Nynaeve opened her mouth to say she would not refuse, but Sheriam cut her off with a sharp gesture. "Listen, and speak when you know what to say. Second. To seek, to strive, is to know danger. You will know danger here. Some women have entered, and never come out. When the *ter'angreal* was allowed to grow quiet, they—were—not—there. And they were never seen again. If you will survive, you must be steadfast. Falter, fail, and. . . ." Her silence was more eloquent than any words. "This is your last chance, child. You may turn back now, right now, and I will put your name in the novice book, and you will have only one mark against you. Twice more you will be allowed to come here, and only at the third refusal will you be put out of the Tower. It is no shame to refuse. Many do. I myself could not do it, my first time here. Now you may speak."

Nynaeve gave the silver arches a sidelong look. The light in them no longer flickered; they were filled with a soft, white glow. To learn what she wanted to learn, she needed the freedom of the Accepted to question, to study on her own, with no more guidance than she asked for. *I must make Moiraine pay for what she has done to us. I must.* "I am ready."

Sheriam started slowly into the chamber. Nynaeve went beside her.

As if that were a signal, the Red sister spoke in loud, formal tones. "Whom do you bring with you, Sister?" The three Aes Sedai around the *ter'angreal* continued their attentions to it.

"One who comes as a candidate for Acceptance, Sister," Sheriam replied just as formally.

"Is she ready?"

"She is ready to leave behind what she was, and, passing through her fears, gain Acceptance."

"Does she know her fears?"

"She has never faced them, but now is willing."

"Then let her face what she fears."

Sheriam stopped, two spans from the arches, and Nynaeve stopped with her. "Your dress," Sheriam whispered, not looking at her.

Nynaeve's cheeks colored at forgetting already what Sheriam had told her on the way down from her room. Hastily she removed her clothes, her shoes and stockings. For a moment she could almost forget the arches in folding her garments and putting them neatly to one side. She tucked Lan's ring carefully under her dress; she did not want anyone staring at that. Then she was done, and the *ter'angreal* was still there, still waiting.

The stone felt cold under her bare feet, and she broke out all over in goose bumps, but she stood straight and breathed slowly. She would not let any of them see she was afraid.

"The first time," Sheriam said, "is for what was. The way back will come but once. Be steadfast."

Nynaeve hesitated. Then she stepped forward, through the arch and into the glow. It surrounded her, as if the air itself were shining, as if she were drowning in light. The light was everywhere. The light was everything.

Nynaeve gave a start when she realized she was naked, then stared in amazement. A stone wall stood to either side of her, twice as tall as she was and smooth, as if carved. Her toes wriggled on dusty, uneven stone paving. The sky above seemed flat and leaden, for all the lack of clouds, and the sun hung overhead swollen and red. In both directions were openings in the wall, gateways marked by short, square columns. The walls narrowed her field of view, but the ground sloped down from where she stood, both in front and behind. Through the gateways she could see more thick walls, and passages between. She was in a gigantic maze.

Where is this? How did I come here? Like a different voice, another thought came. *The way out will come but once.*

She shook her head. "If there's only one way out, I'll not find it standing here." At least the air was warm and dry. "I hope I find some clothes before I find people," she muttered.

Dimly, she remembered playing mazes on paper as a child; there had been a trick to finding your way out, but she could not bring it to mind. Everything in the past seemed vague, as if it had happened to someone else. Trailing a hand along the wall, she started out, dust rising in puffs beneath her bare feet.

At the first opening in the wall, she found herself peering down another passage that seemed indistinguishable from the one she was in already. Taking a deep breath, she went on straight, through more passages that all looked exactly alike. Presently she came to something different. The way forked. She took the left turning, and eventually it forked again. Once more she went left. At the third fork, left brought her to a blank wall.

Grimly she walked back to the last fork and went right. This time it took four turnings right to bring her to a dead end. For a moment, she stood glaring at it. "How did I get here?" she demanded loudly. "Where is this place?" *The way out will come but once.*

Once more she turned back. She was sure there had to be a trick to the maze. At the last fork, she went left, then right at the next. Determined, she kept on. Left, then right. Straight until she came to a fork. Left, then right.

It seemed to her to be working. At least, she had gone past a dozen forkings this time without finding an end. She came to another.

Out of the corner of her eye, she caught a flicker of motion. When she turned to look, there was only the dusty passage between smooth stone walls. She started to take the left fork . . . and spun around at another glimpse of movement. There was nothing there, but this time she was sure. There had been someone behind her. Was someone. She broke into a nervous trot in the opposite direction.

Again and again, now, just at the edge of vision down this side passage or that, she saw something move, too quick to make out, gone before she could turn her head to see it plainly. She broke into a run. Few boys had been able to outrun her when she was a girl in the Two Rivers. *The Two Rivers? What is that?*

A man stepped out from an opening ahead of her. His dark clothes had a musty, half-rotted look, and he was old. Older than old. Skin like crazed parchment covered his skull too tightly, as if there were no flesh beneath. Wispy tufts of brittle hair covered a scabbed scalp, and his eyes were so sunken they seemed to peer out of two caves.

She skidded to a stop, the uneven paving stones rough under her feet.

"I am Aginor," he said, smiling, "and I have come for you."

Her heart tried to leap out of her chest. One of the Forsaken. "No. No, it cannot be!"

"You are a pretty one, girl. I will enjoy you."

Suddenly Nynaeve remembered she wore not a stitch. With a yelp and a face red only partly from anger, she darted away down the nearest crossing passage. Cackling laughter pursued her, and the sound of a shuffling run that seemed to match her best speed, and breathy promises of what he would do when he caught her, promises that curdled her stomach even only half heard.

Desperately she searched for a way out, peering frantically as she ran with fists clenched. *The way out will come but once. Be steadfast.* There was nothing, only more of the endless maze. As hard as she could run, his filthy words came always right behind her. Slowly, fear turned completely to anger.

"Burn him!" she sobbed. "The Light burn him! He has no right!" Within her she felt a flowering, an opening up, an unfolding to light.

Teeth bared, she turned to face her pursuer just as Aginor appeared, laughing, in a lurching gallop.

"You have no right!" She flung her fist toward him, fingers opening as if she were throwing something. She was only half surprised to see a ball of fire leave her hand.

It exploded against Aginor's chest, knocking him to the ground. For only an instant he sprawled there, then rose, staggering. He seemed unaware of the smoldering front of his coat. "You dare? You dare!" He quivered, and spittle leaked down his chin.

Abruptly there were clouds in the sky, threatening billows of gray and black. Lightning leaped from the cloud, straight for Nynaeve's heart.

It seemed to her, just for a heartbeat, as if time had suddenly slowed, as though that heartbeat took forever. She felt the flow inside her—*saidar*, came a distant thought—felt the answering flow in the lightning. And she altered the direction of the flow. Time leaped forward.

With a crash, the bolt shattered stone above Aginor's head. The Forsaken's sunken eyes widened, and he tottered back. "You cannot! It cannot be!" He leaped away as lightning struck where he had stood, stone erupting in a fountain of shards.

Grimly Nynaeve started toward him. And Aginor fled.

Saidar was a torrent racing through her. She could feel the rocks around her, and the air, feel the tiny, flowing bits of the One Power that suffused them, and made them. And she could feel Aginor doing . . . something, as well. Dimly she felt it, and far distant, as if it were something she could never truly know, but around her she saw the effects and knew them for what they were.

The ground rumbled and heaved under her feet. Walls toppled in front of her, piles of stone to block her way. She scrambled over them, uncaring if sharp rock cut hands and feet, always keeping Aginor in sight. A wind rose, howling down the passages against her, raging till it flattened her cheeks and made her eyes water, trying to knock her down; she changed the flow, and Aginor tumbled along the passageway like an uprooted bush. She touched the flow in the ground, redirected it, and stone walls collapsed around Aginor, sealing him in. Lightning fell with her glare, striking around him, stone exploding ever closer and closer. She could feel him fighting to push it back at her, but foot by foot the dazzling bolts moved toward the Forsaken.

Something gleamed off to her right, something uncovered by the collapsing walls.

Nynaeve could feel Aginor weakening, feel his efforts to strike at her grow more feeble and more frantic. Yet somehow she knew he had not given up. If she let him go now, he would chase after her as strongly as before, convinced she was too weak to defeat him after all, too weak to stop him from doing with her as he wished.

A silver arch stood where stone had been, an arch filled with soft silver radiance. *The way back. . . .*

She knew when the Forsaken abandoned his attack, the moment when all his efforts were given over to staving her off. And his power was not enough, he could no longer deflect her blows. Now he had to fling himself away from the leaping gouts of stone thrown up by her lightning, the explosions flinging him down again.

The way back will come but once. Be steadfast.

The lightning no longer fell. Nynaeve turned from the scrabbling Aginor to look at the arch. She looked back at Aginor, just in time to see him crawl out of sight over the mounded stone and disappear. She hissed in frustration. Much of the maze still stood, and a hundred new places to hide in the rubble she and the Forsaken had made. It would take time to find him again, but she was sure if she did not find him first, he would find her. In his full strength, he would come on her when she least expected him.

The way back will come but once.

Frightened, she looked again and was relieved to see the arch still there. If she could find Aginor quickly. . . .

Be steadfast.

With a cry of thwarted anger, she climbed over the tumbled stone toward the arch. "Whoever's responsible for me being here," she muttered, "I'll make them wish they had gotten what Aginor got. I'll—" She stepped into the arch, and the light overwhelmed her.

"I'll—" Nynaeve stepped out of the arch and stopped to stare. It was all as she remembered—the silver *ter'angreal,* the Aes Sedai, the chamber—but remembering was like a blow, absent memories crashing back into her head. She had come out of the same arch by which she went in.

The Red sister raised one of the silver chalices high and poured a stream of cool, clear water over Nynaeve's head. "You are washed clean of what sin you may have done," the Aes Sedai intoned, "and of those done against you. You are washed clean of what crime you may have committed, and of those committed against you. You come to us washed clean and pure, in heart and soul."

Nynaeve shivered as the water ran down her body, dripping on the floor.

Sheriam took her arm with a relieved smile, but the Mistress of Novices' voice gave no hint of past worry. "You do well so far. Coming back is doing well. Remember what your purpose is, and you will continue to be well." The redhead began to lead her around the *ter'angreal* to another arch.

"It was so real," Nynaeve said in a whisper. She could remember everything, remember channeling the One Power as easily as lifting her hand. She could remember Aginor, and the things the Forsaken wanted to do to her. She shivered again. "Was it real?"

"No one knows," Sheriam replied. "It seems real in memory, and some have come out bearing the actual wounds of hurts taken inside. Others have been cut to the bone inside, and come back without a mark. It is all of it different every time for every woman who goes in. The ancients said there were many worlds. Perhaps this *ter'angreal* takes you to them. Yet if so, it does so under very stringent rules for something meant just to take you from one place to another. I believe it is not real. But remember, whether what happens is real or not, the *danger* is as real as a knife plunging into your heart."

"I channeled the Power. It was so easy."

Sheriam missed a step. "That isn't supposed to be possible. You should not even remember being able to channel." She studied Nynaeve. "And yet you are not harmed. I can still sense the ability in you, as strong as it ever was."

"You sound as if it were dangerous," Nynaeve said slowly, and Sheriam hesitated before answering.

"It isn't thought necessary to give a warning, since you shouldn't be able to remember it, but. . . . This *ter'angreal* was found during the Trolloc Wars. We have the records of its examination in the archives. The first sister to enter was warded as strongly as she could be, since no one knew what it would do. She kept her memories, and she channeled the One Power when she was threatened. And she came out with her abilities burned to nothing, unable to channel, unable even to sense the True Source. The second to go in was also warded, and she, too, was destroyed in the same way. The third went unprotected, remembered nothing once she was inside, and returned unharmed. That is one reason why we send you completely unprotected. Nynaeve, you must not channel inside the *ter'angreal* again. I know it is hard to remember anything, but try."

Nynaeve swallowed. She could remember everything, could remember not remembering. "I won't channel," she said. *If I can remember not to.* She wanted to laugh hysterically.

They had reached the next arch. The glow still filled them all. Sheriam gave Nynaeve a last warning look, and left her standing alone.

"The second time is for what is. The way back will come but once. Be steadfast."

Nynaeve stared at the shining silver arch. *What is in there this time?* The others were waiting, watching. She stepped firmly through into the light.

Nynaeve stared down at the plain brown dress she wore with surprise, then gave a start. Why was she staring at her own dress? *The way back will come but once.*

Looking around her, she smiled. She stood on the edge of the Green in Emond's Field, with thatch-roofed houses all around, and the Winespring Inn right in front of her. The Winespring itself rose in a gush from the stone outcrop thrusting up through the grass of the Green, and the Winespring Water rushed off east under the willows beside the inn. The streets were empty, but most people would be at their chores this time of the morning.

Looking at the inn, her smile faded. There was more than an air of neglect about it, whitewash faded, a shutter hanging loose, the rotted end of a rafter showing at a gap in the roof tiles. *What's gotten into Bran? Is he spending so much time being Mayor he's forgetting to take care of his inn?*

The inn door swung open, and Cenn Buie came out, stopping dead when he saw her. The old thatcher was as gnarled as an oak root, and the look he gave her was just as friendly. "So you've come back, have you? Well, you might as well be off again."

She frowned as he spat at her feet and hurried on past her; Cenn was never a pleasant man, but he was seldom openly rude. Never to her, at least. Never to her face. Following him with her eye, she saw signs of neglect all through the village, thatch that should have been mended, weeds filling yards. The door on Mistress al'Caar's house hung aslant on a broken hinge.

Shaking her head, Nynaeve pushed into the inn. *I'll have more than one word with Bran about this.*

The common room was empty except for a lone woman, her thick, graying braid pulled over her shoulder. She was wiping a table, but from the way she stared at the tabletop, Nynaeve did not think she was aware of what she doing. The room seemed dusty.

"Marin?"

Marin al'Vere jumped, one hand clutching her throat, and stared. She looked years older than Nynaeve remembered. Worn. "Nynaeve? Nynaeve! Oh, it is you. Egwene? Have you brought Egwene back? Say you have."

"I. . . ." Nynaeve put a hand to her head. *Where is Egwene?* It seemed she *should* be able to remember. "No. No, I haven't brought her back." *The way back will come but once.*

Mistress al'Vere sagged into one of the straight-backed chairs. "I was so hoping. Ever since Bran died. . . ."

"Bran is dead?" Nynaeve could not imagine it; that broad, smiling man had always seemed as if he would go on forever. "I should have been here."

The other woman jumped to her feet and hurried to peer anxiously through a window at the Green and the village. "If Malena knows you're here, there will be trouble. I just know Cenn went scurrying off to find her. He's the Mayor, now."

"Cenn? How did even those wool-headed men choose Cenn?"

"It was Malena. She had the whole Women's Circle after their husbands for him." Marin pressed her face almost against the window, trying to look every way at once. "Silly men don't talk about whose name they're putting in the box beforehand; I suppose every man who voted for Cenn thought he was the only one whose wife had badgered him into it. Thought one vote would make no difference. Well, they learned better. We all did."

"Who is this Malena who has the Women's Circle doing her bidding? I've never heard of her."

"She's from Watch Hill. She's the Wis. . . ." Marin turned from the window wringing her hands. "Malena Aylar's the Wisdom, Nynaeve. When you didn't come back. . . . Light, I hope she doesn't find out you're here."

Nynaeve shook her head in wonder. "Marin, you're afraid of her. You are shaking. What kind of woman is she? Why did the Women's Circle ever choose someone like her?"

Mistress al'Vere gave a bitter laugh. "We must have been mad. Malena came down to see Mavra Mallen the day before Mavra had to go back to Deven Ride, and that night some children took sick, and Malena stayed to look after them, and then the sheep started dying, and Malena took care of that, too. It just seemed natural to choose her, but. . . . She's a bully, Nynaeve. She browbeats you into doing what she wants. She keeps at you, and keeps at you, until you're too tired to say no anymore. And worse. She knocked Alsbet Luhhan down."

A picture flashed in Nynaeve's head of Alsbet Luhhan and her husband, Haral, the blacksmith. She was nearly as tall as him, and stoutly built, though handsome. "Alsbet's almost as strong as Haral. I can't believe. . . ."

"Malena's not a big woman, but she's—she's fierce,

Nynaeve. She beat Alsbet all around the Green with a stick, and none of us who saw had the nerve to try to stop it. When they found out, Bran and Haral said she had to go, even if they were interfering in Women's Circle business. I think some of the Circle might have listened, but Bran and Haral both took sick the same night, and died within a day of each other." Marin bit her lip and looked around the room as if she thought someone might be hiding there. Her voice lowered. "Malena mixed medicine for them. She said it was her duty even if they had spoken against her. I saw. . . . I saw gray fennel in what she took away with her."

Nynaeve gasped. "But. . . . Are you sure, Marin? Are you certain?" The other woman nodded, her face wrinkling on the point of tears. "Marin, if you even suspected this woman might have poisoned Bran, how could you not go to the Circle?"

"She said Bran and Haral didn't walk in the Light," Marin mumbled, "talking against the Wisdom the way they did. She said that was why they died; the Light abandoned them. She talks about sin all the time. She said Paet al'Caar sinned, talking against her after Bran and Haral died. All he said was she didn't have the way with Healing you did, but she drew the Dragon's Fang on his door, right out where everyone could see her with the charcoal in her hand. Both his boys were dead before the week was out—just dead when their mother went to wake them. Poor Nela. We found her wandering, laughing and crying all at the same time, screaming that Paet was the Dark One, and he'd killed her boys. Paet hung himself the next day." She shuddered, and her voice went so soft Nynaeve could barely hear it. "I have four daughters still living under my roof. Living, Nynaeve. Do you understand what I'm saying. They're still alive, and I want to keep them alive."

Nynaeve felt cold to her bones. "Marin, you can't allow this." *The way back will come but once. Be steadfast.* She pushed it away. "If the Women's Circle stands together, you can be rid of her."

"Stand together against Malena?" Marin's laugh was nearer a sob. "We're all afraid of her. But she's good with the children. There are always children sick these days, it seems, but Malena does the best she can. Almost no one ever died of sickness when you were Wisdom."

"Marin, listen to me. Don't you see why there are always children sick? If she can't make you afraid of her, she makes you think you need her for the children. She's doing it, Marin. Just as she did it to Bran."

"She couldn't," Marin breathed. "She wouldn't. Not the little ones."

"She is, Marin." *The way back*—Nynaeve suppressed the thought ruthlessly. "Is there anyone in the Circle who isn't afraid? Anyone who will listen?"

The other woman said, "No one who isn't afraid. But Corin Ayellin might listen. If she does, she might bring two or three more. Nynaeve, if enough of the Circle listens, will you be our Wisdom again? I think you may be the only one who won't back down to Malena, even if we all know. You don't know what she's like."

"I will." *The way back— No! These are my people!* "Get your cloak, and we'll go to Corin."

Marin was hesitant about leaving the inn, and once Nynaeve had her outside she slunk along from doorstep to doorstep, crouching and watching.

Before they were halfway to Corin Ayellin's house, Nynaeve saw a tall, scrawny woman striding down the other side of the Green toward the inn, slashing the heads off weeds with a thick willow switch. Bony as she was, she had a look of wiry strength, and a set, determined slash of a mouth. Cenn Buie scuttled along in her wake.

"Malena." Marin pulled Nynaeve into the space between two houses, and whispered as if afraid the woman might hear across the Green. "I knew Cenn would go to her."

Something made Nynaeve look over her shoulder. Behind her stood a silver arch, reaching from house to house, glowing whitely. *The way back will come but once. Be steadfast.*

Marin gave a soft scream. "She's seen us. Light help us, she's coming this way!"

The tall woman had turned across the Green, leaving Cenn standing uncertainly. There was no uncertainty on Malena's face. She walked slowly, as if there were no hope of escape, a cruel smile growing with every step.

Marin tugged at Nynaeve's sleeve. "We have to run. We have to hide. Nynaeve, come on. Cenn will have told her who you are. She hates anyone even to speak of you."

The silver arch pulled Nynaeve's eyes. *The way back. . . .* She shook her head, trying to remember. *It is not real.* She looked at Marin; stark terror twisted the woman's face. *You must be steadfast to survive.*

"Please, Nynaeve. She's seen me with you. She—has—seen—me! Please, Nynaeve!"

Malena came closer, implacable. *My people.* The arch shone. *The way back. It is not real.*

With a sob, Nynaeve tore her arm out of Marin's grasp and plunged toward the silvery glow.

Marin's shriek hounded her. "For the love of the Light, Nynaeve, help me! HELP ME!"

The glow enveloped her.

Staring, Nynaeve staggered out of the arch, barely aware of the chamber or the Aes Sedai. Marin's last cry still rang in her ears. She did not flinch when cold water was suddenly poured over her head.

"You are washed clean of false pride. You are washed clean of false ambition. You come to us washed clean, in heart and soul." As the Red Aes Sedai stepped back, Sheriam came to take Nynaeve's arm.

Nynaeve gave a start, then realized who it was. She seized the collar of Sheriam's dress in both hands. "Tell me it was not real. Tell me!"

"Bad?" Sheriam pried her hands loose as if she were used to this reaction. "It is always worse, and the third is the worst of all."

"I left my friend . . . I left my *people* . . . in the Pit of Doom to come back." *Please, Light, it was not real. I didn't really. . . . I* have *to make Moiraine pay. I* have *to!*

"There is always some reason not to return, something to prevent you, or distract you. This *ter'angreal* weaves traps for you from your own mind, weaves them tight and strong, harder than steel and more deadly than poison. That is why we use it as a test. You must want to be Aes Sedai more than anything else in the whole world, enough to face anything, fight free of anything, to achieve it. The White Tower cannot accept less. We demand it of you."

"You demand a great deal." Nynaeve stared at the third

arch as the red-haired Aes Sedai took her toward it. *The third is the worst.* "I'm afraid," she whispered. *What could be worse than what I just did?*

"Good," Sheriam said. "You seek to be Aes Sedai, to channel the One Power. No one should approach that without fear and awe. Fear will keep you cautious; caution will keep you alive." She turned Nynaeve to face the arch, but she did not step back immediately. "No one will force you to enter a third time, child."

Nynaeve licked her lips. "If I refuse, you'll put me out of the Tower and never let me come back." Sheriam nodded. "And this is the worst." Sheriam nodded again. Nynaeve drew breath. "I am ready."

"The third time," Sheriam intoned formally, "is for what will be. The way back will come but once. Be steadfast."

Nynaeve threw herself at the arch in a run.

Laughing, she ran through swirling clouds of butterflies rising from wildflowers that covered the hilltop meadow with a knee-deep blanket of color. Her gray mare danced nervously, reins dangling, at the edge of the meadow, and Nynaeve stopped running so as not to frighten the animal more. Some of the butterflies settled on her dress, on flowers of embroidery and seed pearls, or flittered around the sapphires and moonstones in her hair, hanging loose about her shoulders.

Below the hill, the necklace of the Thousand Lakes spread through the city of Malkier, reflecting the cloud-brushing Seven Towers, with Golden Crane banners flying at their heights in the mists. The city had a thousand gardens, but she preferred this wild garden on the hilltop. *The way back will come but once. Be steadfast.*

The sound of hooves made her turn.

Al'Lan Mandragoran, King of Malkier, leaped from the back of his charger and strolled toward her through the butterflies, laughing. His face had the look of a hard man, but the smiles he wore for her softened the stony planes.

She gaped at him, taken by surprise when he gathered her into his arms and kissed her. For a moment she clung to him, lost, kissing him back. Her feet dangled a foot in the air, and she did not care.

Suddenly she pushed at him, pulled her face back. "No." She pushed harder. "Let me go. Put me down." Puzzled, he lowered her until her feet touched ground; she backed away from him. "Not this," she said. "I cannot face this. Anything but this." *Please, let me face Aginor again.* Memory swirled. *Aginor?* She did not know where that thought had come from. Memory lurched and tilted, shifting fragments like broken ice on a flooding river. She clawed for the pieces, clawed for something to hang on to.

"Are you well, my love?" Lan asked worriedly.

"Do not call me that! I am not your love! I cannot marry you!"

He startled her by throwing back his head and roaring with laughter. "Your implication that we are not married might upset our children, wife. And how are you not my love? I have no other, and will have no other."

"I must go back." Desperately she looked for the arch, found only meadow and sky. *Harder than steel and more deadly than poison. Lan. Lan's babies. Light, help me!* "I must go back now."

"Go back? Where? To Emond's Field? If you wish it. I'll send letters to Morgase, and command an escort."

"Alone," she muttered, still searching. *Where is it? I have to go.* "I won't be tangled up in this. I couldn't bear it. Not this. I have to go *now!*"

"Tangled up in what, Nynaeve? What is it you couldn't bear? No, Nynaeve. You can ride alone here if you wish it, but if the Queen of the Malkieri came to Andor without a proper escort, Morgase would be scandalized, if not offended. You don't want to offend her, do you? I thought you two were friends."

Nynaeve felt as if she had been hit in the head, blow after dazing blow. "Queen?" she said hesitantly. "We have babies?"

"Are you certain you're well? I think I had better take you to Sharina Sedai."

"No." She backed away from him again. "No Aes Sedai." *It isn't real. I won't be pulled into it this time. I won't!*

"Very well," he said slowly. "As my wife, how could you not be Queen? We are Malkieri here, not southlanders. You were crowned in the Seven Towers at the same time we exchanged rings." Unconsciously he moved his left hand; a plain gold band encircled his forefinger. She glanced at her own hand, at the ring she knew would be there; she clasped her other hand over it, but whether to deny its presence by hiding it or to hold it, she could not have said. "Do you remember, now?" he went on. He stretched out a hand as if to brush her cheek, and she went back another six steps. He sighed. "As you wish, my love. We have three children, though only one can properly be called a baby. Maric is almost to your shoulder and can't decide if he likes horses or books better. Elnore has already begun practicing how to turn boys' heads, when she is not pestering Sharina about when she'll be old enough to go to the White Tower."

"Elnore was my mother's name," she said softly.

"So you said when you chose it. Nynaeve—"

"No. I will not be pulled into it this time. Not this. I won't!" Beyond him, among the trees beside the meadow, she saw the silver arch. The trees had hidden it before. *The way back will come but once.* She turned toward it. "I must go." He caught her hand, and it was as if her feet had become rooted in stone; she could not make herself pull away.

"I do not know what is troubling you, wife, but whatever it is, tell me and I will make it right. I know I am not the best of husbands. I was all hard edges when I found you, but you've smoothed some of them away, at least."

"You are the very best of husbands," she murmured. To her horror, she found herself remembering him as her husband, remembering laughter and tears, bitter arguments and sweet making up. They were dim memories, but she could feel them growing stronger, warmer. "I cannot." The arch stood there, only a few steps away. *The way back will come but once. Be steadfast.*

"I do not know what is happening, Nynaeve, but I feel as if I were losing you. I could not bear that." He put a hand in her hair; closing her eyes, she pressed her cheek against his fingers. "Stay with me, always."

"I want to stay," she said softly. "I want to stay with you." When she opened her eyes, the arch was gone . . . *come but once.* "No. No!"

Lan turned her to face him. "What troubles you? You must tell me if I'm to help."

"This is not real."

"Not real? Before I met you, I thought nothing except

the sword was real. Look around you, Nynaeve. It *is* real. Whatever you want to be real, we can make real together, you and I."

Wonderingly, she did look around. The meadow was still there. The Seven Towers still stood over the Thousand Lakes. The arch was gone, but nothing else had changed. *I could stay here. With Lan. Nothing has changed.* Her thoughts turned. *Nothing has changed. Egwene is alone in the White Tower. Rand will channel the Power and go mad. And what of Mat and Perrin? Can they take back any shred of their lives? And Moiraine, who tore all our lives apart, still walks free.*

"I must go back," she whispered. Unable to bear the pain on his face, she pulled free of him. Deliberately she formed a flower bud in her mind, a white bud on a blackthorn branch. She made the thorns sharp and cruel, wishing they could pierce her flesh, feeling as if she already hung in the blackthorn's branches. Sheriam Sedai's voice danced just out of hearing, telling her it was dangerous to attempt to channel the Power. The bud opened, and *saidar* filled her with light.

"Nynaeve, tell me what is the matter."

Lan's voice slid across her concentration; she refused to let herself hear it. There had to be a way back still. Staring at where the silver arch had been, she tried to find some trace of it. There was nothing.

"Nynaeve . . ."

She tried to picture the arch in her mind, to shape it and form it to the last detail, curve of gleaming metal filled with a glow like snowy fire. It seemed to waver there, in front of her, first there between her and the trees, then not, then there.

". . . I love you . . ."

She drew at *saidar*, drinking in the flow of the One Power till she thought she would burst. The radiance filling her, shining around her, hurt her own eyes. The heat seemed to consume her. The flickering arch firmed, steadied, stood whole before her. Fire and pain seemed to fill her; her bones felt as if they were burning; her skull seemed a roaring furnace.

". . . with all my heart."

She ran toward the silver curve, not letting herself look

back. She had been sure the bitterest thing she would ever hear was Marin al'Vere's cry for help as Nynaeve abandoned her, but that was honey beside the sound of Lan's anguished voice pursuing her. "Nynaeve, please don't leave me."

The white glow consumed her.

Naked, Nynaeve staggered through the arch and fell to her knees, slack-mouthed and sobbing, tears streaming down her cheeks. Sheriam knelt beside her. She glared at the red-haired Aes Sedai. "I hate you!" she managed fiercely, gulping. "I hate all Aes Sedai!"

Sheriam gave a small sigh, then pulled Nynaeve to her feet. "Child, almost every woman who does this says much the same thing. It is no small thing to be made to face your fears. What is this?" she said sharply, turning Nynaeve's palms up.

Nynaeve's hands quivered with a sudden pain she had not felt before. Driven through the palm of each hand, right in the center, was a long black thorn. Sheriam drew them out carefully; Nynaeve felt the cool Healing of the Aes Sedai's touch. When each thorn came free, it left only a small scar on front and back of the hand.

Sheriam frowned. "There shouldn't be any scarring. And how did you only get two, and both placed so precisely? If you tangled yourself in a blackthorn bush, you should be covered with scratches and thorns."

"I should," Nynaeve agreed bitterly. "Maybe I thought I had already paid enough."

"There is always a price," the Aes Sedai agreed. "Come, now. You have paid the first price. Take what you have paid for." She gave Nynaeve a slight push forward.

Nynaeve realized there were more Aes Sedai in the chamber. The Amyrlin in her striped stole was there, with a shawled sister from each Ajah ranged to either side of her, all of them watching Nynaeve. Remembering Sheriam's instruction, Nynaeve tottered forward and knelt before the Amyrlin. It was she who held the last chalice, and she tipped it slowly over Nynaeve's head.

"You are washed clean of Nynaeve al'Maera from Emond's Field. You are washed clean of all ties that bind you to the world. You come to us washed clean, in heart and soul. You are Nynaeve al'Maera, Accepted of the White Tower." Handing the chalice to one of the sisters, the Amyrlin drew Nynaeve to her feet. "You are sealed to us, now."

The Amyrlin's eyes seemed to hold a dark glow. Nynaeve's shiver had nothing to do with being naked and wet.

CHAPTER
24

New Friends and Old Enemies

Egwene followed the Accepted through the halls of
the White Tower. Tapestries and paintings covered
walls as white as the outside of the tower; patterned
tiles made the floor. The Accepted's white dress was exactly like hers, except for seven narrow bands of color at
hem and cuffs. Egwene frowned, looking at that dress.
Since yesterday Nynaeve had worn an Accepted's dress,
and she seemed to have no joy of it, nor of the golden ring,
a serpent eating its own tail, that marked her level. The few
times Egwene had been able to see the Wisdom, Nynaeve's
eyes had seemed shadowed, as if she had seen things she
wished with all her heart not to have seen.

"In here," the Accepted said curtly, gesturing to a door.
Named Pedra, she was a short, wiry woman, a little older
than Nynaeve, and with a briskness always in her voice.
"You're given this time because it is your first day, but I'll
expect you in the scullery when the gong sounds High, and
not one moment later."

Egwene curtsied, then stuck out her tongue at the Accepted's retreating back. It might have been only the evening
before that Sheriam had finally put her name in the novice book, but already she knew she did not like Pedra. She
pushed open the door and went in.

The room was plain and small, with white walls, and
there was a young woman, with reddish gold hair spilling
around her shoulders, sitting on one of two hard benches.
The floor was bare; novices did not get much use of rooms
with carpets. Egwene thought the girl was about her own
age, but there was a dignity and self-possession about her

that made her seem older. The plainly cut novice dress appeared somehow more, on her. Elegant. That was it.

"My name is Elayne," she said. She tilted her head, studying Egwene. "And you are Egwene. From Emond's Field, in the Two Rivers." She said it as if it had some significance, but went right on anyway. "Someone who has been here a little while is always assigned to a new novice for a few days, to help her find her way. Sit, please."

Egwene took the other bench, facing Elayne. "I thought the Aes Sedai would teach me, now that I'm finally a novice. But all that's happened so far is that Pedra woke me a good two hours before first light and put me to sweeping the halls. She says I have to help wash dishes after dinner, too."

Elayne grimaced. "I hate washing dishes. I never had to—well, that doesn't matter. You will have training. From now on, you will be at training at this hour every day, as a matter of fact. From breakfast until High, then again from dinner to Trine. If you are especially quick or especially slow, they may take you from supper to Full, as well, but that is usually for more chores." Elayne's blue eyes took on a thoughtful expression. "You were born with it, weren't you?" Egwene nodded. "Yes, I thought I felt it. So was I, born with it. Do not be disappointed if you did not know. You will learn to feel the ability in other women. I had the advantage of growing up around an Aes Sedai."

Egwene wanted to ask about that—*Who grows up with Aes Sedai?*—but Elayne went on.

"And also do not be disappointed if it takes you some time before you can achieve anything. With the One Power, I mean. Even the simplest thing takes a little time. Patience is a virtue that must be learned." Her nose wrinkled. "Sheriam Sedai always says that, and she does her best to make us all learn it, too. Try to run when she says walk, and she'll have you in her study before you can blink."

"I've had a few lessons already," Egwene said, trying to sound modest. She opened herself to *saidar*—that part of it was easier now—and felt the warmth suffuse her body. She decided to try the biggest thing she knew how to do. She stretched out her hand, and a glowing sphere formed over it, pure light. It wavered—she still could not manage to hold it steady—but it was there.

Calmly, Elayne held out her hand, and a ball of light appeared above her palm. Hers flickered, too.

After a moment, a faint light glowed all around Elayne. Egwene gasped, and her ball vanished.

Elayne giggled suddenly, and her light went out, both the sphere and the light around her. "You saw it around me?" she said excitedly. "I saw it around you. Sheriam Sedai said I would, eventually. This was the first time. For you, too?"

Egwene nodded, laughing along with the other girl. "I like you, Elayne. I think we're going to be friends."

"I think so, too, Egwene. You are from the Two Rivers, from Emond's Field. Do you know a boy named Rand al'Thor?"

"I know him." Abruptly Egwene found herself remembering a tale Rand had told, a tale she had not believed, about falling off a wall into a garden and meeting. . . . "You're the Daughter-Heir of Andor," she gasped.

"Yes," Elayne said simply. "If Sheriam Sedai as much as heard I'd mentioned it, I think she would have me into her study before I finished talking."

"Everyone talks about being called to Sheriam's study. Even the Accepted. Does she scold so fiercely? She seems kindly to me."

Elayne hesitated, and when she spoke it was slowly, not meeting Egwene's eye. "She keeps a willow switch on her desk. She says if you can't learn to follow the rules in a civilized way, she will teach you another way. There are so many rules for novices, it is very hard not to break some of them," she finished.

"But that's—that's horrible! I'm not a child, and neither are you. I won't be treated as one."

"But we are children. The Aes Sedai, the full sisters, are the grown women. The Accepted are the young women, old enough to be trusted without someone looking over their shoulders every moment. And novices are the children, to be protected and cared for, guided in the way they should go, and punished when they do what they should not. That is the way Sheriam Sedai explains it. No one is going to punish you over your lessons, not unless you try something you've been told not to. It is hard not to try, sometimes; you will find you want to channel as much as you want to breathe. But if you break too many dishes because you are daydreaming when you should be washing, if you're disrespectful to an Accepted, or leave the Tower without permission, or speak to an Aes Sedai before she speaks to you, or. . . . The only thing to do is the best you can. There isn't anything else *to* do."

"It sounds almost as if they're trying to make us want to leave," Egwene protested.

"They aren't, but then again, they are. Egwene, there are only forty novices in the Tower. Only forty, and no more than seven or eight will become Accepted. That is not enough, Sheriam Sedai says. She says there are not enough Aes Sedai now to do what needs to be done. But the Tower will not . . . cannot . . . lower its standards. The Aes Sedai cannot take a woman as a sister if she does not have the ability, and the strength, and the desire. They can't give the ring and the shawl to one who cannot channel the Power well enough, or who will allow herself to be intimidated, or who will turn back when the road turns rough. Training and testing take care of the channeling, and for strength and desire. . . . Well, if you want to go, they will let you. Once you know enough that you won't die of ignorance."

"I suppose," Egwene said slowly, "Sheriam told us some of that. I never thought about there not being enough Aes Sedai, though."

"She has a theory. She says we have culled humankind. You know about culling? Cutting out of the herd those animals that have traits you don't like?" Egwene nodded impatiently; no one could grow up around sheep without knowing about culling the flock. "Sheriam Sedai says that with the Red Ajah hunting down men who could channel for three thousand years, we are culling the ability to channel out of us all. I would not mention this around any Reds, if I were you. Sheriam Sedai has been in more than one shouting match over it, and we are only novices."

"I won't."

Elayne paused, and then said, "Is Rand well?"

Egwene felt a sudden stab of jealousy—Elayne was very pretty—but over it came a stronger stab of fear. She went over the little she knew of Rand's one meeting with the Daughter-Heir, reassuring herself: Elayne could not possibly know that Rand could channel.

"Egwene?"

"He is as well as he can be." *I hope he is, the wool-headed idiot.* "He was riding with some Shienaran soldiers the last I saw him."

"Shienarans! He told me he was a shepherd." She shook her head. "I find myself thinking of him at the oddest times. Elaida thinks he is important in some way. She didn't come right out and say so, but she ordered a search for him, and she was in a fury when she learned he had left Caemlyn."

"Elaida?"

"Elaida Sedai. My mother's councilor. She is Red Ajah, but Mother seems to like her despite that."

Egwene's mouth felt dry. *Red Ajah, and interested in Rand.* "I—I don't know where he is, now. He left Shienar, and I don't think he was going back."

Elayne gave her a level look. "I would not tell Elaida where to find him if I knew, Egwene. He has done no wrong that I know, and I fear she wants to use him in some manner. Anyway, I've not seen her since the day we arrived, with Whitecloaks dogging our trail. They are still camped on the Dragonmount side." Abruptly she bounded to her feet. "Let us talk of happier things. There are two others here who know Rand, and I would like you to meet one of them." She took Egwene's hand and pulled her out of the room.

"Two girls? Rand seems to meet a lot of girls."

"Ummm?" Still drawing Egwene down the corridor, Elayne studied her. "Yes. Well. One of them is a lazy chit named Else Grinwell. I don't think she will be here long. She shirks her chores, and she is always sneaking off to watch the Warders practice their swords. She says Rand came to her father's farm, with a friend of his. Mat. It seems they put notions of the world beyond the next village into her head, and she ran away to come be an Aes Sedai."

"Men," Egwene muttered. "I dance a few dances with a nice boy, and Rand goes around looking like a dog with a sore tooth, but he—" She cut off as a man stepped into the hall ahead of them. Beside her, Elayne stopped, too, and her hand tightened on Egwene's.

There was nothing alarming about him, aside from the suddenness of his appearance. He was tall and handsome, short of middle years, with long, dark curling hair, but his shoulders sagged, and there was sadness in his eyes.

He made no move toward Egwene and Elayne, only stood looking at them until one of the Accepted appeared at his shoulder.

"You should not be in here," she said to him, not unkindly.

"I wanted to walk." His voice was deep, and as sad as his eyes.

"You can walk out in the garden, where you are supposed to be. The sunshine will be good for you."

The man rumbled a bitter laugh. "With two or three of you watching my every move? You're just afraid I'll find a knife." At the look in the Accepted's eyes, he laughed again. "For myself, woman. For myself. Lead me to your garden, and your watching eyes."

The Accepted touched his arm lightly, and led him away.

"Logain," Elayne said when he was gone.

"The false Dragon!"

"He has been gentled, Egwene. He is no more dangerous than any other man, now. But I remember seeing him before, when it took six Aes Sedai to keep him from wielding the Power and destroying us all." She shivered.

Egwene did, too. That was what the Red Ajah would do to Rand.

"Do they always have to be gentled?" she asked. Elayne stared at her, mouth agape, and she quickly added, "It is just that I'd think the Aes Sedai would find some other way to deal with them. Anaiya and Moiraine both said the greatest feats of the Age of Legends required men and women working together with the Power. I just thought they'd try to find a way."

"Well, do not let any Red sister hear you thinking it aloud. Egwene, they did try. For three hundred years after the White Tower was built, they tried. They gave up because there was nothing to find. Come on. I want you to meet Min. Not in the garden where Logain is going, thank the Light."

The name sounded vaguely familiar to Egwene, and when she saw the young woman, she knew why. There was a narrow stream in the garden, with a low stone bridge over it, and Min sat cross-legged on the wall of the bridge. She wore a man's tight breeches and baggy shirt, and with her dark hair cut short she could almost pass for a boy, though an uncommonly pretty one. A gray coat lay beside her on the coping.

"I know you," Egwene said. "You worked at the inn in Baerlon." A light breeze riffled the water beneath the bridge, and graywings warbled in the trees of the garden.

Min smiled. "And you were one of those who brought the Darkfriends down on us to burn it down. No, don't worry. The messenger who came to fetch me brought enough gold that Master Fitch is building it back again twice as big. Good morning, Elayne. Not slaving over your lessons? Or over some pots?" It was said in a bantering tone, as between friends, as Elayne's answering grin proved.

"I see Sheriam has not yet managed to get you into a dress."

Min's laugh was wicked. "I'm no novice." She made her voice squeaky. "Yes, Aes Sedai. No, Aes Sedai. May I sweep another floor, Aes Sedai? I," she said, resuming her own low voice, "clothe myself the way I want." She turned to Egwene. "Is Rand well?"

Egwene's mouth tightened. *He should wear ram's horns like a Trolloc*, she thought angrily. "I was sorry when your inn caught fire, and I am glad Master Fitch was able to rebuild. Why have you come to Tar Valon? It's clear you do not mean to be an Aes Sedai." Min arched an eyebrow in what Egwene was sure was amusement.

"She likes him," Elayne explained.

"I know." Min glanced at Egwene, and for an instant Egwene thought she saw sadness—or regret?—in her eyes. "I am here," Min said carefully, "because I was sent for, and was given the choice between riding and coming tied in a sack."

"You always exaggerate it," Elayne said. "Sheriam Sedai saw the letter, and she says it was a request. Min sees things, Egwene. That's why she's here; so the Aes Sedai can study how she does it. It isn't the Power."

"Request," Min snorted. "When an Aes Sedai requests your presence, it's like a command from a queen with a hundred soldiers to back it up."

"Everybody sees things," Egwene said.

Elayne shook her head. "Not like Min. She sees— auras—around people. And images."

"Not all the time," Min put in. "Not around everybody."

"And she can read things about you from them, though I'm not sure she always tells the truth. She said I'd have to share my husband with two other women, and I'd never put up with that. She just laughs, and says it was never her idea of how to run things, either. But she said I would be a queen before she knew who I was; she said she saw a crown, and it was the Rose Crown of Andor."

Despite herself, Egwene asked, "What do you see when you look at me?"

Min glanced at her. "A white flame, and. . . . Oh, all sorts of things. I don't know what it means."

"She says that a great deal," Elayne said dryly. "One of the things she said she saw looking at me was a severed hand. Not mine, she says. She claims she does not know what it means, either."

"Because I don't," Min said. "I don't know what half of it means."

The crunch of boots on the walk brought them around to look at two young men with their shirts and coats across their arms, leaving sweaty chests bare, and scabbarded swords in their hands. Egwene found herself staring at the most handsome man she had ever seen. Tall and slim, but hard, he moved with a cat-like grace. She suddenly realized he was bowing over her hand—she had not even felt him take it in his—and fumbled in her mind for the name she had heard.

"Galad," she murmured. His dark eyes stared back into hers. He was older than she. Older than Rand. At the thought of Rand, she gave a start and came to herself.

"And I am Gawyn"—the other young man grinned—"since I don't think you heard the first time." Min was grinning, too, and only Elayne wore a frown.

Egwene abruptly remembered her hand, still held by Galad, and freed it.

"If your duties allow," Galad said, "I would like to see you again, Egwene. We could walk, or if you obtain permission to leave the Tower, we could picnic outside the city."

"That—that would be nice." She was uncomfortably aware of the others, Min and Gawyn still with their amused grins, Elayne still with her scowl. She tried to settle herself, to think of Rand. *He's so . . . beautiful.* She gave a jump, half afraid she had spoken aloud.

"Until then." Finally taking his eyes from hers, Galad bowed to Elayne. "Sister." Lithe as a blade, he strolled on across the bridge.

"That one," Min murmured, peering after him, "will always do what is right. No matter who it hurts."

"Sister?" Egwene said. Elayne's scowl had lessened only slightly. "I thought he was your. . . . I mean, the way you're frowning. . . ." She had thought Elayne was jealous, and she still was not sure.

"I am not his sister," Elayne said firmly. "I refuse to be."

"Our father was his father," Gawyn said dryly. "You cannot deny that, unless you want to call Mother a liar, and that, I think, would take more nerve than we have between us."

For the first time Egwene realized that he had the same reddish gold hair as Elayne, though darkened and curled by sweat.

"Min is right," Elayne said. "Galad has not the smallest part of humanity in him. He takes right above mercy, or pity, or. . . . He is no more human than a Trolloc."

Gawyn's grin came back. "I do not know about that. Not from the way he was looking at Egwene, here." He caught her look, and his sister's, and held up his hands as if to fend them off with his sheathed sword. "Besides, he has the best hand with a sword I've ever seen. The Warders only need show him something once, and he's learned it. They sweat me nearly to death to learn half what Galad does without trying."

"And being good with a sword is enough?" Elayne sniffed. "Men! Egwene, as you may have guessed, this disgracefully unclothed lummox is my brother. Gawyn, Egwene knows Rand al'Thor. She is from the same village."

"Is she? Was he really born in the Two Rivers, Egwene?"

Egwene made herself nod calmly. *What does he know?* "Of course, he was. I grew up with him."

"Of course," Gawyn said slowly. "Such a strange fellow. A shepherd, he said, though he never looked or acted like any shepherd I ever saw. Strange. I have met all sorts of people, and they've met Rand al'Thor. Some do not even know his name, but the description could not be anyone else, and he's shifted every one of their lives. There was an old farmer who came to Caemlyn just to see Logain, when

Logain was brought through on his way here; yet the farmer stayed to stand for Mother when the riots started. Because of a young man off to see the world, who made him think there was more to life than his farm. Rand al'Thor. You could almost think he was *ta'veren*. Elaida is certainly interested in him. I wonder if meeting him will shift our lives in the Pattern?"

Egwene looked at Elayne and Min. She was sure they could not have a clue that Rand really was *ta'veren*. She had never really thought about that part of it before; he was Rand, and he had been cursed with the ability to channel. But *ta'veren* did move people, whether they wanted to be moved or not. "I really do like you," she said abruptly, including both girls in her gesture. "I want to be your friend."

"And I want to be yours," Elayne said.

Impulsively, Egwene hugged her, and then Min jumped down, and the three of them stood there on the bridge hugging one another all together.

"We three *are* tied together," Min said, "and we cannot let any man get in the way of that. Not even him."

"Would one of you mind telling me what this is all about?" Gawyn inquired gently.

"You would not understand," his sister said, and the three girls all caught a fit of the giggles.

Gawyn scratched his head, then shook it. "Well, if it has anything to do with Rand al'Thor, be sure you don't let Elaida hear of it. She has been at me like a Whitecloak Questioner three times since we arrived. I do not think she means him any—" He gave a start; there was a woman crossing the garden, a woman in a red-fringed shawl. "'Name the Dark One,'" he quoted, "'and he appears.' I do not need another lecture about wearing my shirt when I'm out of the practice yards. Good morning to you all."

Elaida spared a glance for the departing Gawyn as she came up the bridge. She was a handsome woman rather than beautiful, Egwene thought, but that ageless look marked her as surely as her shawl; only the newest-made sisters lacked it. When her gaze swept over Egwene, pausing only a moment, Egwene suddenly saw a hardness in the Aes Sedai. She had always thought of Moiraine as strong, steel under silk, but Elaida dispensed with the silk.

"Elaida," Elayne said, "this is Egwene. She was born with the seed in her, too. And she has already had some lessons, so she is as far along as I am. Elaida?"

The Aes Sedai's face was blank and unreadable. "In Caemlyn, child, I am councilor to the Queen your mother, but this is the White Tower, and you, a novice." Min made as if to go, but Elaida stopped her with a sharp, "Stay, girl. I would speak with you."

"I've known you all my life, Elaida," Elayne said incredulously. "You watched me grow up, and made the gardens bloom in winter so I could play."

"Child, there you were the Daughter-Heir. Here you are a novice. You must learn that. You will be great one day, but you must learn!"

"Yes, Aes Sedai."

Egwene was astounded. If someone had snubbed her so before others, she would have been in a fury.

"Now, off with both of you." A gong began to toll, deep and sonorous, and Elaida tilted her head. The sun stood halfway to its pinnacle. "High," Elaida said. "You must hurry, if you do not want further admonishment. And Elayne? See the Mistress of Novices in her study after your chores. A novice does not speak to Aes Sedai unless bidden to. Run, both of you. You will be late. Run!"

They ran, holding their skirts up. Egwene looked at Elayne. Elayne had two spots of color in her cheeks and a determined look on her face.

"I will be Aes Sedai," Elayne said softly, but it sounded like a promise.

Behind them, Egwene heard the Aes Sedai begin, "I am given to understand, girl, that you were brought here by Moiraine Sedai."

She wanted to stay and listen, to hear if Elaida asked about Rand, but High rang through the White Tower, and she was summoned to chores. She ran as she had been commanded to run.

"I will be Aes Sedai," she growled. Elayne flashed a quick smile of understanding, and they ran faster.

Min's shirt clung to her when she finally left the bridge. Not sweat from the sun, but from the heat of Elaida's questions.

She looked over her shoulder to make sure the Aes Sedai was not following her, but Elaida was nowhere in sight.

How did Elaida know that Moiraine had summoned her? Min had been sure that was a secret known only to her, Moiraine, and Sheriam. And all those questions about Rand. It had not been easy keeping a smooth face and a steady eye while telling an Aes Sedai to her face that she had never heard of him and knew nothing of him. *What does* she *want with him? Light, what does Moiraine want with him? What is he? Light, I don't want to fall in love with a man I've only met once, and a farmboy at that.*

"Moiraine, the Light blind you," she muttered, "whatever you brought me here for, come out from wherever you're hiding and tell me so I can go!"

The only answer was the sweet song of the graywings. With a grimace she went in search of a place to cool off.

CHAPTER
25

Cairhien

The city of Cairhien lay across hills against the River
Alguenya, and Rand's first sight of it came from the
hills to the north, by the light of the midday sun. Elricain Tavolin and the fifty Cairhienin soldiers still seemed
like guards to him—the more since crossing the bridge at
the Gaelin; they became more stiff the further south they
rode—but Loial and Hurin did not appear to mind, so he
tried not to. He studied the city, as large as any he had seen.
Fat ships and broad barges filled the river, and tall granaries sprawled along the far bank, but Cairhien seemed to be
laid out in a precise grid behind its high, gray walls. Those
walls themselves made a perfect square, with one side hard
along the river. In just as exact a pattern, towers rose within
the walls, soaring as much as twenty times the height of the
wall, yet even from the hills Rand could see that each one
ended in a jagged top.

Outside the city walls, surrounding them from riverbank
to riverbank, lay a warren of streets, crisscrossing at all angles and teeming with people. Foregate, Rand knew it was
called, from Hurin; once there had been a market village
for every city gate, but over the years they had all grown
into one, a hodgepodge of streets and alleys growing up every which way.

As Rand and the others rode into those dirt streets, Tavolin put some of his soldiers to clearing a path through the
throng, shouting and urging their horses forward as if to
trample any who did not get out of the way quickly. People
moved aside with no more than a glance, as if it were an
everyday occurrence. Rand found himself smiling, though.

The Foregate people's clothes were shabby more often than not, yet much of it was colorful, and there was a raucous bustle of life to the place. Hawkers cried their wares, and shopkeepers called for people to examine the goods displayed on tables before their shops. Barbers, fruit-peddlers, knife-sharpeners, men and women offering a dozen services and a hundred things for sale, wandered through the crowds. Music drifted through the babble from more than one structure; at first Rand thought they were inns, but the signs out front all showed men playing flutes or harps, tumbling or juggling, and large as they were, they had no windows. Most of the buildings in Foregate seemed to be wood, however big they were, and a good many looked new, if poorly made. Rand gaped at several that stood seven stories or more; they swayed slightly, though the people hurrying in and out did not seem to notice.

"Peasants," Tavolin muttered, staring straight ahead in disgust. "Look at them, corrupted by outland ways. They should not be here."

"Where should they be?" Rand asked. The Cairhienin officer glared at him and spurred his horse forward, flogging at the crowd with his quirt.

Hurin touched Rand's arm. "It was the Aiel War, Lord Rand." He looked to make sure none of the soldiers were close enough to hear. "Many of the farmers were afraid to go back to their lands near the Spine of the World, and they all came here, near enough. That's why Galldrian has the river full of grain barges up from Andor and Tear. There's no crops coming from farms in the east because there aren't any farms anymore. Best not to mention it to a Cairhienin though, my Lord. They like to pretend the war never happened, or at least that they won it."

Despite Tavolin's quirt, they were forced to halt while a strange procession crossed their path. Half a dozen men, beating tambours and dancing, led the way for a string of huge puppets, each half again as tall as the men who worked them with long poles. Giant crowned figures of men and women in long, ornate robes bowed to the crowd amid the shapes of fanciful beasts. A lion with wings. A goat, walking on its hind legs, with two heads, both of which were apparently meant to be breathing fire, from the crimson streamers hanging from the two mouths. Something that seemed to be half cat and half eagle, and another with a bear's head on a man's body, which Rand took to be a Trolloc. The crowd cheered and laughed as they pranced by.

"Man who made that never saw a Trolloc," Hurin grumbled. "Head's too big, and it's too skinny. Likely didn't believe in them, either, my Lord, any more than in those other things. The only monsters these Foregate folk believe in are Aiel."

"Are they having a festival?" Rand asked. He did not see any sign of it other than the procession, but he thought that there must be a reason for that. Tavolin ordered his soldiers forward again.

"No more than every day, Rand," Loial said. Walking alongside his horse, the blanket-wrapped chest still strapped to his saddle, the Ogier drew as many looks as the puppets had. Some even laughed and clapped as they had for the puppets. "I fear Galldrian keeps his people quiet by entertaining them. He gives gleemen and musicians the King's Gift, a bounty in silver, to perform here in the Foregate, and he sponsors horse races down by the river every day. There are fireworks many nights, too." He sounded disgusted. "Elder Haman says Galldrian is a disgrace." He blinked, realizing what he had said, and looked around hurriedly to see if any of the soldiers had heard. None seemed to have.

"Fireworks," Hurin said, nodding. "The Illuminators have built a chapter house here, I've heard, the same as in Tanchico. I didn't half mind seeing the fireworks, when I was here before."

Rand shook his head. He had never seen fireworks elaborate enough to require even one Illuminator. He had heard they only left Tanchico to put on displays for rulers. It was a strange place he was coming to.

At the tall, square archway of the city gate, Tavolin ordered a halt and dismounted by a squat stone building just inside the walls. It had arrowslits instead of windows, and a heavy, iron-bound door.

"A moment, my Lord Rand," the officer said. Tossing his reins to one of the soldiers, he disappeared inside.

With a wary look at the soldiers—they sat their horses rigidly in two long files; Rand wondered what they would do if he and Loial and Hurin tried to leave—he took the opportunity to study the city that lay before him.

Cairhien proper was a sharp contrast to the chaotic bustle of the Foregate. Broad, paved streets, wide enough to make the people in them seem fewer than they were, crossed each other at right angles. Just as in Tremonsien, the hills had been carved and terraced to straight lines. Closed sedan chairs, some with small pennants bearing the sigil of a House, moved with deliberateness, and carriages rolled down the streets slowly. People went silently in dark clothes, with no bright colors except here and there slashes across the breast of coat or dress. The more slashes, the more proudly the wearer moved, but no one laughed, or even smiled. The buildings on their terraces were all of stone, and the ornamentation was straight-lined and sharp-angled. There were no hawkers or peddlers in the streets, and even the shops seemed subdued, with only small signs and no wares displayed outside.

He could see the great towers more clearly, now. Scaffolds of lashed poles surrounded them, and workmen swarmed on the scaffolding, laying new stones to push the towers higher still.

"The Topless Towers of Cairhien," Loial murmured sadly. "Well, they were tall enough to warrant the name, once. When the Aiel took Cairhien, about the time you were born, the towers burned, and cracked, and fell. I don't see any Ogier among the stonemasons. No Ogier could like working here—the Cairhienin want what they want, without embellishment—but there were Ogier when I was here before."

Tavolin came out, trailing another officer and two clerks, one carrying a large, wood-bound ledger and the other a tray with writing implements. The front of the officer's head was shaven like Tavolin's, though advancing baldness seemed to have taken more hair than the razor. Both officers looked from Rand to the chest hidden by Loial's striped blanket and back again. Neither asked what was under the blanket. Tavolin had looked at it often on the way from Tremonsien, but he had never asked, either. The balding man looked at Rand's sword, too, and pursed his lips for an instant.

Tavolin gave the other officer's name as Asan Sandair, and announced loudly, "Lord Rand of House al'Thor, in Andor, and his man, called Hurin, with Loial, an Ogier of Stedding Shangtai." The clerk with the ledger opened it across his two arms, and Sandair wrote the names in a round hand.

"You must return to this guardhouse by this same hour tomorrow, my Lord," Sandair said, leaving the sanding to the second clerk, "and give the name of the inn where you are staying."

Rand looked at the staid streets of Cairhien, then back at the liveliness of the Foregate. "Can you tell me the name of a good inn out there?" He nodded to the Foregate.

Hurin made a frantic *hsst* and leaned close. "It would not be proper, Lord Rand," he whispered. "If you stay in the Foregate, being a lord and all, they'll be sure you are up to something."

Rand could see the sniffer was right. Sandair's mouth had dropped open and Tavolin's brows had risen at his question, and they were both still watching him intently. He wanted to tell them he was not playing their Great Game, but instead he said, "We will take rooms in the city. We can go now?"

"Of course, my Lord Rand." Sandair made a bow. "But . . . the inn?"

"I will let you know when we find one." Rand turned Red, then paused. Selene's note crackled in his pocket. "I need to find a young woman from Cairhien. The Lady Selene. She is my age, and beautiful. I don't know her House."

Sandair and Tavolin exchanged looks, then Sandair said, "I will make inquiries, my Lord. Perhaps I will be able to tell you something when you come tomorrow."

Rand nodded and led Loial and Hurin into the city. They attracted little notice, though there were few riders. Even Loial attracted almost none. The people seemed nearly ostentatious about minding their own business.

"Will they take it the wrong way," Rand asked Hurin, "my asking after Selene?"

"Who can say with Cairhienin, Lord Rand? They seem to think everything has to do with *Daes Dae'mar*."

Rand shrugged. He felt as if people were looking at him. He could not wait to get a good, plain coat again, and stop pretending to be what he was not.

Hurin knew several inns in the city, though his time in Cairhien had been spent mainly in the Foregate. The sniffer led them to one called The Defender of the Dragonwall, the sign bearing a crowned man with his foot on another man's chest and his sword at the man's throat. The fellow on his back had red hair.

A hostler came to take their horses, darting quick looks at Rand and at Loial when he thought he was not observed. Rand told himself to stop having fancies; not everyone in the city could be playing this Game of theirs. And if they were, he was no part of it.

The common room was neat, with the tables laid out as strictly as the city, and only a few people at them. They glanced up at the newcomers, then back to their wine immediately; Rand had the feeling they were still watching, though, and listening. A small fire burned in the big fireplace, though the day was warming.

The innkeeper was a plump, unctuous man with a single stripe of green across his dark gray coat. He gave a start at his first sight of them, and Rand was not surprised. Loial, with the chest in his arms under its striped blanket, had to duck his head to make it in through the door, Hurin was burdened with all their saddlebags and bundles, and his own red coat was a sharp contrast to the somber colors the people at the tables wore.

The innkeeper took in Rand's coat and his sword, and his oily smile came back. He bowed, washing his smooth hands. "Forgive me, my Lord. It was just that for a moment I took you for—Forgive me. My brain is not what it was. You wish rooms, my Lord?" He added another, lesser bow for Loial. "I am called Cuale, my Lord."

He thought I was Aiel, Rand thought sourly. He wanted to be gone from Cairhien. But it was the one place Ingtar might find them. And Selene had said she would wait for him in Cairhien.

It took a little time for their rooms to be readied, Cuale explaining with too many smiles and bows that it was necessary to move a bed for Loial. Rand wanted them all to share a room again, but between the innkeeper's scandalized looks and Hurin's insistence—"We have to show these Cairhienin we know what's right as well as they do, Lord Rand"—they ended with two, one for him alone, with a connecting door.

The rooms were much the same except that theirs had

two beds, one sized for an Ogier, while his had only one bed, and that almost as big as the other two, with massive square posts that nearly reached the ceiling. His tall-backed, padded chair and the washstand were square and massive, too, and the wardrobe standing against his wall was carved in a heavy, rigid style that made the thing look ready enough to fall over on him. A pair of windows siding his bed looked out on the street, two floors below.

As soon as the innkeeper left, Rand opened the door and admitted Loial and Hurin into his room. "This place gnaws at me," he told them. "Everybody looks at you as if they think you're doing something. I'm going back to the Foregate, for an hour anyway. At least the people laugh, there. Which of you is willing to take the first watch on the Horn?"

"I will stay," Loial said quickly. "I'd like a chance to do a little reading. Just because I didn't see any Ogier does not mean there are no stonemasons down from Stedding Tsofu. It is not far from the city."

"I'd think you would want to meet them."

"Ah . . . no, Rand. They asked enough questions the last time about why I was outside alone as it was. If they've had word from Stedding Shangtai. . . . Well, I will just rest here and read, I think."

Rand shook his head. He often forgot that Loial had run away from home, in effect, to see the world. "What about you, Hurin? There's music in the Foregate, and people laughing. I'll wager no one is playing *Daes Dae'mar* there."

"I would not be so certain of that myself, Lord Rand. In any case, I thank you for the invitation, but I think not. There's so many fights—and killings, too—in Foregate, that it stinks, if you know what I mean. Not that they're likely to bother a lord, of course; the soldiers would be down on them if they did. But if it pleases you, I would like to have a drink in the common room."

"Hurin, you don't need my permission for anything. You know that."

"As you say, my Lord." The sniffer gave a suggestion of a bow.

Rand took a deep breath. If they did not leave Cairhien soon, Hurin would be bowing and scraping left and right. And if Mat and Perrin saw that, they would never let him forget it. "I hope nothing delays Ingtar. If he doesn't come quickly, we'll have to take the Horn back to Fal Dara ourselves." He touched Selene's note through his coat. "We will have to. Loial, I'll come back so you can see some of the city."

"I'd rather not risk it," Loial said.

Hurin accompanied Rand downstairs. As soon as they reached the common room, Cuale was bowing in front of Rand, pushing a tray at him. Three folded and sealed parchments lay on the tray. Rand took them, since that was what the innkeeper seemed to intend. They were a fine grade of parchment, soft and smooth to his touch. Expensive.

"What are these?" he asked.

Cuale bowed again. "Invitations, of course, my Lord. From three of the noble Houses." He bowed himself away.

"Who would send me invitations?" Rand turned them over in his hand. None of the men at the tables looked up, but he had the feeling they were watching just the same. He did not recognize the seals. None was the crescent moon and stars Selene had used. "Who would know I was here?"

"Everyone by now, Lord Rand," Hurin said quietly. He seemed to feel eyes watching, too. "The guards at the gate would not keep their mouths closed about an outland lord coming to Cairhien. The hostler, the innkeeper . . . everybody tells what they know where they think it will do them the most good, my Lord."

With a grimace, Rand took two steps and hurled the invitations into the fire. They caught immediately. "I am not playing *Daes Dae'mar*," he said, loudly enough for everyone to hear. Not even Cuale looked at him. "I've nothing to do with your Great Game. I am just here to wait for some friends."

Hurin caught his arm. "Please, Lord Rand." His voice was an urgent whisper. "Please don't do that again."

"Again? You really think I'll receive more?"

"I'm certain. Light, but you mind me of the time Teva got so mad at a hornet buzzing round his ears, he kicked the nest. You've likely just convinced everyone in the room you are in some deep part of the Game. It must be deep, as they'll see it, if you deny playing at all. *Every* lord and lady in Cairhien plays it." The sniffer glanced at the invitations, curling blackly in the fire, and winced. "And you have surely made enemies of three Houses. Not great Houses, or they'd not have moved so quickly, but still noble. You must answer any more invitations you receive, my Lord. Decline if you will—though they'll read things into whose invitations you do decline. And into whose you accept. Of course, if you decline them all, or accept them all—"

"I'll have no part of it," Rand said quietly. "We are leaving Cairhien as soon as we can." He thrust his fists into his coat pockets, and felt Selene's note crumple. Pulling it out, he smoothed it on his coat front. "As soon as we can," he muttered, putting it back in his pocket again. "Have your drink, Hurin."

He stalked out angrily, not sure whether he was angry with himself, or with Cairhien and its Great Game, or Selene for vanishing, or Moiraine. She had started it all, stealing his coats and giving him a lord's clothes instead. Even now that he called himself free of them, an Aes Sedai still managed to interfere in his life, and without even being there.

He went back through the same gate by which he had entered the city, since that was the way he knew. A man standing in front of the guardhouse took note of him—his bright coat marked him out, as well as his height among the Cairhienin—and hurried inside, but Rand did not notice. The laughter and music of the Foregate were pulling him on.

If his gold-embroidered red coat made him stand out inside the walls, it fit right into the Foregate. Many of the men milling through the crowded streets were dressed just as darkly as those in the city, but just as many wore coats of red, or blue, or green, or gold—some bright enough to be a Tinker's clothes—and even more of the women had embroidered dresses and colored scarves or shawls. Most of the finery was tattered and ill-fitting, as if made for someone else originally, but if some of those who wore it eyed his fine coat, none seemed to take it amiss.

Once he had to stop for another procession of giant puppets. While the drummers beat their tambours and capered, a pig-faced Trolloc with tusks fought a man in a crown. After a few desultory blows, the Trolloc collapsed to laughter and cheers from the onlookers.

Rand grunted. *They don't die so easily as that.*

He glanced into one of the large, windowless buildings, stopping to look through the door. To his surprise, it seemed to be one huge room, open to the sky in the middle and lined with balconies, with a large dais at one end. He had never seen or heard of anything like it. People jammed the balconies and the floor watching people perform on the dais. He peeked into others as he passed them, and saw jugglers, and musicians, any number of tumblers, and even a gleeman, with his cloak of patches, declaiming a story from *The Great Hunt of the Horn* in sonorous-voice High Chant.

That made him think of Thom Merrilin, and he hurried on. Memories of Thom were always sad. Thom had been a friend. A friend who had died for him. *While I ran away and let him die.*

In another of the big structures, a woman in voluminous white robes appeared to make things vanish from one basket and appear in another, then disappear from her hands in great puffs of smoke. The crowd watching her *oohed* and *aahed* loudly.

"Two coppers, my good Lord," a ratty little man in the doorway said. "Two coppers to see the Aes Sedai."

"I don't think so." Rand glanced back at the woman. A white dove had appeared in her hands. *Aes Sedai?* "No." He gave the ratty man a small bow and left.

He was making his way through the throng, wondering what to see next, when a deep voice, accompanied by the plucking of a harp, drifted out from a doorway with the sign of a juggler over it.

". . . cold blows the wind down Shara Pass; cold lies the grave unmarked. Yet every year at Sunday, upon those piled stones appears a single rose, one crystal teardrop like dew upon the petals, laid by the fair hand of Dunsinin, for she keeps fast to the bargain made by Rogosh Eagle-eye."

The voice drew Rand like a rope. He pushed through the doorway as applause rose within.

"Two coppers, my good Lord," said a rat-faced man who could have been twin to the other. "Two coppers to see—"

Rand dug out some coins and thrust them at the man. He walked on in a daze, staring at the man bowing on the dais to the clapping of his listeners, cradling his harp in one arm and with the other spreading his patch-covered cloak as if to trap all the sound they made. He was a tall man, lanky and not young, with long mustaches as white as the hair on his head. And when he straightened and saw Rand, the eyes that widened were sharp and blue.

"Thom." Rand's whisper was lost in the noise of the crowd.

Holding Rand's eye, Thom Merrilin nodded slightly toward a small door beside the dais. Then he was bowing again, smiling and basking in the applause.

Rand made his way to the door and through it. It was only a small hallway, with three steps leading up to the dais. In the other direction from the dais Rand could see a juggler practicing with colored balls, and six tumblers limbering themselves.

Thom appeared on the steps, limping as though his right leg did not bend as well as it had. He eyed the juggler and the tumblers, blew out his mustaches disdainfully, and turned to Rand. "All they want to hear is *The Great Hunt of the Horn*. You would think, with the news from Haddon Mirk and Saldaea, one of them would ask for *The Karaethon Cycle*. Well, maybe not that, but I'd pay myself to tell something else." He looked Rand up and down. "You look as if you're doing well, boy." He fingered Rand's collar and pursed his lips. "Very well."

Rand could not help laughing. "I left Whitebridge sure you were dead. Moiraine said you were still alive, but I. . . . Light, Thom, it's good to see you again! I should have gone back to help you."

"Bigger fool if you had, boy. That Fade"—he looked around; there was no one close enough to hear, but he lowered his voice anyway—"had no interest in me. It left me a little present of a stiff leg and ran off after you and Mat. All you could have done was die." He paused, looking thoughtful. "Moiraine said I was still alive, did she? Is she with you, then?"

Rand shook his head. To his surprise, Thom seemed disappointed.

"Too bad, in a way. She's a fine woman, even if she is. . . ." He left it unsaid. "So it was Mat or Perrin she was after. I won't ask which. They were good boys, and I don't want to know." Rand shifted uneasily, and gave a start when Thom fixed him with a bony finger. "What I do want to know is, do you still have my harp and flute? I want them back, boy. What I have now are not fit for a pig to play."

"I have them, Thom. I'll bring them to you, I promise. I can't believe you are alive. And I can't believe you aren't in Illian. The Great Hunt setting out. The prize for the best telling of *The Great Hunt of the Horn.* You were dying to go."

Thom snorted. "After Whitebridge? Likely I'd die if I did go. Even if I could have reached the boat before it sailed, Domon and his whole crew would be spreading the tale all over Illian about how I was being chased by Trollocs. If they saw the Fade, or heard of it, before Domon cut his lines. . . . Most Illianers think Trollocs and Fades are fables, but enough others might want to know why a man was pursued by them to make Illian somewhat more than uncomfortable."

"Thom, I have so much to tell you."

The gleeman cut him off. "Later, boy." He was exchanging glares down the length of the hall with the narrow-faced man from the door. "If I don't go back and tell another, he will no doubt send the juggler out, and that lot will tear the hall down around our heads. You come to The Bunch of Grapes, just beyond the Jangai Gate. I have a room there. Anyone can tell you where to find it. I'll be there in another hour or so. One more tale will have to satisfy them." He started back up the steps, flinging over his shoulder, "And bring my harp and my flute!"

CHAPTER
26

Discord

R and darted through the common room of The Defender of the Dragonwall and hurried upstairs, grinning at the startled look the innkeeper had given
him. Rand wanted to grin at everything. *Thom's alive!*

He flung open the door to his room and went straight to
the wardrobe.

Loial and Hurin put their heads in from the other room,
both in their shirtsleeves and with pipes in their teeth trailing thin streams of smoke.

"Has something happened, Lord Rand?" Hurin asked
anxiously.

Rand slung the bundle made from Thom's cloak on his
shoulder. "The best thing that could, next to Ingtar coming.
Thom Merrilin's alive. And he's here, in Cairhien."

"The gleeman you told me about?" Loial said. "That is
wonderful, Rand. I would like to meet him."

"Then come with me, if Hurin's willing to keep watch
awhile."

"It would be a pleasure, Lord Rand." Hurin took the pipe
out of his mouth. "That lot in the common room kept trying to pump me—without letting on what they were doing,
of course—about who you are, my Lord, and why we're in
Cairhien. I told them we were waiting here to meet friends,
but being Cairhienin, they figured I was hiding something
deeper."

"Let them think what they want. Come on, Loial."

"I think not." The Ogier sighed. "I really would rather
stay here." He raised a book with a thick finger marking his
place. "I can meet Thom Merrilin some other time."

"Loial, you can't stay cooped up in here forever. We do not even know how long we'll be in Cairhien. Anyway, we didn't see any Ogier. And if we do, they would not be hunting for you, would they?"

"Not hunting, precisely, but. . . . Rand, I may have been too hasty in leaving Stedding Shangtai the way I did. When I do go home, I may be in a great deal of trouble." His ears wilted. "Even if I wait until I'm as old as Elder Haman. Perhaps I could find an abandoned *stedding* to stay in until then."

"If Elder Haman won't let you come back, you can live in Emond's Field. It's a pretty place." *A beautiful place.*

"I am sure it is, Rand, but that would never work. You see—"

"We will talk about it when it comes to that, Loial. Now you are coming to see Thom."

The Ogier stood half again as tall as Rand, but Rand pushed him into his long tunic and cloak and down the stairs. When they came pounding through the common room, Rand winked at the innkeeper, then laughed at his startled look. *Let him think I'm off to play his bloody Great Game. Let him think what he wants. Thom's alive.*

Once through the Jangai Gate, in the east wall of the city, everyone seemed to know The Bunch of Grapes. Rand and Loial quickly found themselves there, on a street that was quiet for the Foregate, with the sun halfway down the afternoon sky.

It was an old three-story structure, wooden and rickety, but the common room was clean and full of people. Some men were playing at dice in one corner, and some women at darts in another. Half had the look of Cairhienin, slight and pale, but Rand heard Andoran accents as well as others he did not know. All wore the clothes of the Foregate, though, a blend of the styles of half a dozen countries. A few looked around when he and Loial came in, but they all turned back to what they had been doing.

The innkeeper was a woman with hair as white as Thom's, and sharp eyes that studied Loial as well as Rand. She was not Cairhienin, by her dark skin and her speech. "Thom Merrilin? Aye, he has a room. Top of the stairs, first door on the right. Likely Dena will let you wait for him there"—she eyed Rand's red coat, with its herons on the high collar and golden brambles embroidered up the sleeves, and his sword—"my Lord."

The stairs creaked under Rand's boots, let alone Loial's. Rand was not sure if the building would stand up much longer. He found the door and knocked, wondering who Dena was.

"Come in," a woman's voice called. "I cannot open it for you."

Rand opened the door hesitantly and put his head in. A big, rumpled bed was shoved against one wall, and the rest of the room was all but taken up by a pair of wardrobes, several brass-bound trunks and chests, a table and two wooden chairs. The slender woman sitting cross-legged on the bed with her skirts tucked under her was keeping six colored balls spinning in a wheel between her hands.

"Whatever it is," she said, looking at her juggling, "leave it on the table. Thom will pay you when he comes back."

"Are you Dena?" Rand asked.

She snatched the balls out of the air and turned to regard him. She was only a handful of years older than he, pretty, with fair Cairhienin skin and dark hair hanging loose to her shoulders. "I do not know you. This is my room, mine and Thom Merrilin's."

"The innkeeper said you might let us wait here for Thom," Rand said. "If you're Dena?"

"Us?" Rand moved into the room so Loial could duck inside, and the young woman's eyebrows lifted. "So the Ogier have come back. I am Dena. What do you want?" She looked at Rand's coat so deliberately that the failure to add "my Lord" had to be purposeful, though her brows went up again at the herons on his scabbard and sword hilt.

Rand hefted the bundle he carried. "I've brought Thom back his harp and his flute. And I want to visit with him," he added quickly; she seemed on the point of telling him to leave them. "I haven't seen him in a long time."

She eyed the bundle. "Thom always moans about losing the best flute and the best harp he ever had. You would think he was a court-bard, the way he carries on. Very well. You can wait, but I must practice. Thom says he will let me perform in the halls next week." She rose gracefully and took one of the two chairs, motioning Loial to sit on the bed. "Zera would make Thom pay for six chairs if you broke one of these, friend Ogier."

Rand gave their names as he sat in the other chair—it creaked alarmingly under even his weight—and asked doubtfully, "Are you Thom's apprentice?"

Dena gave a small smile. "You might say that." She had resumed her juggling, and her eyes were on the whirling balls.

"I have never heard of a woman gleeman," Loial said.

"I will be the first." The one big circle became two smaller, overlapping circles. "I will see the whole world before I am done. Thom says once we have enough money, we will go down to Tear." She switched to juggling three balls in each hand. "And then maybe out to the Sea Folk's islands. The Atha'an Miere pay gleemen well."

Rand eyed the room, with all the chests and trunks. It did not look like the room of someone intending to move on soon. There was even a flower growing in a pot on the windowsill. His gaze fell on the single big bed, where Loial was sitting. *This is my room, mine and Thom Merrilin's.* Dena gave him a challenging look through the large wheel she had resumed. Rand's face reddened.

He cleared his throat. "Maybe we ought to wait downstairs," he began when the door opened and Thom came in with his cloak flapping around his ankles, patches fluttering. Cased flute and harp hung on his back; the cases were reddish wood, polished by handling.

Dena made the balls disappear inside her dress and ran to throw her arms around Thom's neck, standing atiptoe to do it. "I missed you," she said, and kissed him.

The kiss went on for some time, so long that Rand was beginning to wonder if he and Loial should leave, but Dena let her heels drop to the floor with a sigh.

"Do you know what that lack-wit Seaghan's done now, girl?" Thom said, looking down at her. "He's taken on a pack of louts who call themselves 'players.' They walk around pretending to *be* Rogosh Eagle-eye, and Blaes, and Gaidal Cain, and. . . . Aaagh! They hang a scrap of painted canvas behind them, supposed to make the audience believe these fools are in Matuchin Hall, or the high passes of the Mountains of Dhoom. *I* make the listener see every banner, smell every battle, feel every emotion. I make them believe *they* are Gaidal Cain. Seaghan will have his hall torn down around his ears if he puts this lot on to follow me."

"Thom, we have visitors. Loial, son of Arent son of Halan. Oh, and a boy who calls himself Rand al'Thor."

Thom looked over her head at Rand, frowning. "Leave us for a while, Dena. Here." He pressed some silver coins into her hand. "Your knives are ready. Why don't you go pay Ivon for them?" He brushed her smooth cheek with a gnarled knuckle. "Go on. I'll make it up to you."

She gave him a dark look, but she tossed her cloak around her shoulders, muttering, "Ivon better have the balance right."

"She'll be a bard one day," Thom said with a note of pride after she was gone. "She listens to a tale once—once only, mind!—and she has it right, not just the words, but every nuance, every rhythm. She has a fine hand on the harp, and she played the flute better the first time she picked it up than you ever did." He set the wooden instrument cases atop one of the larger trunks, then dropped into the chair she had abandoned. "When I passed through Caemlyn on the way here, Basel Gill told me you'd left in company with an Ogier. Among others." He bowed toward Loial, even managing a flourish of his cloak despite the fact that he was sitting on it. "I am pleased to meet you, Loial, son of Arent son of Halan."

"And I to meet you, Thom Merrilin." Loial stood to make his bow in return; when he straightened, his head almost brushed the ceiling, and he quickly sat down again. "The young woman said she wants to be a gleeman."

Thom's head shake was disparaging. "That's no life for a woman. Not much of a life for a man, for that. Wandering from town to town, village to village, wondering how they'll try to cheat you this time, half the time wondering where your next meal is coming from. No, I'll talk her around. She'll be court-bard to a king or a queen before she's done. Aaaah! You didn't come here to talk about Dena. My instruments, boy. You've brought them?"

Rand pushed the bundle across the table. Thom undid it hurriedly—he blinked when he saw it was his old cloak, all covered with colorful patches like the one he wore—and opened the hard leather flute case, nodding at the sight of the gold-and-silver flute nestled inside.

"I earned my bed and meals with that after we parted," Rand said.

"I know," the gleeman replied dryly. "I stopped at some of the same inns, but I had to make do with juggling and a few simple stories since you had my— You didn't touch the harp?" He pulled open the other dark leather case and took out a gold-and-silver harp as ornate as the flute, cradling it in his hands like a baby. "Your clumsy sheepherder's fingers were never meant for the harp."

"I didn't touch it," Rand assured him.

Thom plucked two strings, wincing. "At least you weren't fool enough to try keeping it tuned," he muttered. "Could have ruined it."

Rand leaned across the table toward him. "Thom, you wanted to go to Illian, to see the Great Hunt set out, and be one of the first to make new stories about it, but you couldn't. What would you say if I told you you could still be a part of it? A big part?"

Loial stirred uneasily. "Rand, are you sure . . . ?" Rand waved him to silence, his eyes on Thom.

Thom glanced at the Ogier and frowned. "That would depend on what part, and how. If you've reason to believe one of the Hunters is coming this way. . . . I suppose they could have left Illian already, but he'd be weeks reaching here if he rode straight on, and why would he? Is this one of the fellows who never went to Illian? He'll never make it into the stories without the blessing, whatever he does."

"It doesn't matter if the Hunt has left Illian or not." Rand heard Loial's breath catch. "Thom, we have the Horn of Valere."

For a moment there was dead silence. Thom broke it with a great guffaw of laughter. "You two have the Horn? A shepherd and a beardless Ogier have the Horn of. . . ." He doubled over, pounding his knee. "The Horn of Valere!"

"But we do have it," Loial said seriously.

Thom drew a deep breath. Small aftershocks of laughter still seemed to catch him unaware. "I don't know what you found, but I can take you to ten taverns where a fellow will tell you that he knows a man who knows the man who's already found the Horn, and he will tell you how it was found, too—as long as you buy his ale. I can take you to three men who will *sell* you the Horn, and swear their souls under the Light it's the real one and true. There is even a lord in the city has what he claims is the Horn locked up inside his manor. He says it's a treasure handed down in his House since the Breaking. I don't know if the Hunters will ever find the Horn, but they will hunt down ten thousand lies along the way."

"Moiraine says it's the Horn," Rand said.

Thom's mirth was cut short. "She does, does she? I thought you said she was not with you."

"She isn't, Thom. I have not seen her since I left Fal Dara, in Shienar, and for a month before that she said no more than two words together to me." He could not keep the bitterness out of his voice. *And when she did talk, I wished she'd kept on ignoring me. I'll never dance to her tune again, the Light burn her and every other Aes Sedai. No. Not Egwene. Not Nynaeve.* He was conscious of Thom watching him closely. "She isn't here, Thom. I do not know where she is, and I do not care."

"Well, at least you have sense enough to keep it secret. If you hadn't, it would be all over the Foregate by now, and half of Cairhien would be lying in wait to take it away. Half the world."

"Oh, we've kept it secret, Thom. And I have to bring it back to Fal Dara without Darkfriends or anyone else taking it away. That's story enough for you right there, isn't it? I could use a friend who knows the world. You've been everywhere; you know things I can't even imagine. Loial and Hurin know more than I do, but we're all three floundering in deep water."

"Hurin . . . ? No, don't tell me how. I do not want to know." The gleeman pushed back his chair and went to stare out of the window. "The Horn of Valere. That means the Last Battle is coming. Who will notice? Did you see the people laughing in the streets out there? Let the grain barges stop a week, and they won't laugh. Galldrian will think they've all become Aiel. The nobles all play the Game of Houses, scheming to get close to the King, scheming to gain more power than the King, scheming to pull down

Galldrian and *be* the next King. Or Queen. They will think Tarmon Gai'don is only a ploy in the Game." He turned away from the window. "I don't suppose you are talking about simply riding to Shienar and handing the Horn to—who?—the King? Why Shienar? The legends all tie the Horn to Illian."

Rand looked at Loial. The Ogier's ears were sagging. "Shienar, because I know who to give it to, there. And there are Trollocs and Darkfriends after us."

"Why does that not surprise me? No. I may be an old fool, but I will be an old fool in my own way. You take the glory, boy."

"Thom—"

"No!"

There was a silence, broken only by the creaking of the bed as Loial shifted. Finally, Rand said, "Loial, would you mind leaving Thom and me alone for a bit? Please?"

Loial looked surprised—the tufts on his ears went almost to points—but he nodded and rose. "That dice game in the common room looked interesting. Perhaps they will let me play." Thom eyed Rand suspiciously as the door closed behind the Ogier.

Rand hesitated. There were things he needed to know, things he was sure Thom knew—the gleeman had once seemed to know a great deal about a surprising number of things—but he was not sure how to ask. "Thom," he said at last, "are there any books that have *The Karaethon Cycle* in them?" Easier to call it that than the Prophecies of the Dragon.

"In the great libraries," Thom said slowly. "Any number of translations, and even in the Old Tongue, here and there." Rand started to ask if there was any way for him to find one, but the gleeman went on. "The Old Tongue has music in it, but too many even of the nobles are impatient with listening to it these days. Nobles are all expected to know the Old Tongue, but many only learn enough to impress people who don't. Translations don't have the same sound, unless they're in High Chant, and sometimes that changes meanings even more than most translations. There is one verse in the Cycle—it doesn't scan well, translated word for word, but there's no meaning lost—that goes like this.

Twice and twice shall he be marked,
twice to live, and twice to die.
Once the heron, to set his path.
Twice the heron, to name him true.
Once the Dragon, for remembrance lost.
Twice the Dragon, for the price he must pay.

He reached out and touched the herons embroidered on
Rand's high collar.

For a moment, Rand could only gape at him, and when
he could speak, his voice was unsteady. "The sword makes
five. Hilt, scabbard, and blade." He turned his hand down
on the table, hiding the brand on his palm. For the first time
since Selene's salve had done its work, he could feel it. Not
hurting, but he knew it was there.

"So they do." Thom barked a laugh. "There's another
comes to mind.

Twice dawns the day when his blood is shed.
Once for mourning, once for birth.
Red on black, the Dragon's blood stains the rock of Shayol
Ghul.
In the Pit of Doom shall his blood free men from the
Shadow.

Rand shook his head, denying, but Thom seemed not to
notice. "I don't see how a day can dawn twice, but then a lot
of it doesn't really make much sense. The Stone of Tear will
never fall till *Callandor* is wielded by the Dragon Reborn,
but the Sword That Cannot Be Touched lies in the Heart of
the Stone, so how can he wield it first, eh? Well, be that as it
may. I suspect Aes Sedai would want to make events fit the
Prophecies as closely as they can. Dying somewhere in the
Blasted Lands would be a high price to pay for going along
with them."

It was an effort for Rand to make his voice calm, but he
did it. "No Aes Sedai are using me for anything. I told you,
the last I saw of Moiraine was in Shienar. She said I could
go where I wanted, and I left."

"And there's no Aes Sedai with you now? None at all?"

"None."

Thom knuckled his dangling white mustaches. He

seemed satisfied, and at the same time puzzled. "Then why ask about the Prophecies? Why send the Ogier out of the room?"

"I . . . didn't want to upset him. He's nervous enough about the Horn. That's what I wanted to ask. Is the Horn mentioned in the—the Prophecies?" He still could not make himself say it all the way out. "All these false Dragons, and now the Horn is found. Everybody thinks the Horn of Valere is supposed to summon dead heroes to fight the Dark One in the Last Battle, and the . . . the Dragon Reborn . . . is supposed to fight the Dark One in the Last Battle. It seemed natural enough to ask."

"I suppose it is. Not many know that about the Dragon Reborn fighting the Last Battle, or if they do, they think he'll fight alongside the Dark One. Not many read the Prophecies to find out. What was that you said about the Horn? 'Supposed to'?"

"I've learned a few things since we parted, Thom. They will come for whoever blows the Horn, even a Darkfriend."

Bushy eyebrows rose nearly to Thom's hairline. "Now that I didn't know. You have learned a few things."

"It doesn't mean I would let the White Tower use me for a false Dragon. I don't want anything to do with Aes Sedai, or false Dragons, or the Power, or. . . ." Rand bit his tongue. *Get mad and you start babbling. Fool!*

"For a time, boy, I thought you were the one Moiraine wanted, and I even thought I knew why. You know, no man chooses to channel the Power. It is something that happens to him, like a disease. You cannot blame a man for falling sick, even if it might kill you, too."

"Your nephew could channel, couldn't he? You told me that was why you helped us, because your nephew had had trouble with the White Tower and there was nobody to help him. There's only one kind of trouble men can have with Aes Sedai."

Thom studied the tabletop, pursing his lips. "I don't suppose there is any use in denying it. You understand, it is not the kind of thing a man talks about, having a male relative who could channel. Aaagh! The Red Ajah never gave Owyn a chance. They gentled him, and then he died. He just gave up wanting to live. . . ." He exhaled sadly.

Rand shivered. *Why didn't Moiraine do that to me?* "A

chance, Thom? Do you mean there was some way he could
have dealt with it? Not gone mad? Not died?"

"Owyn held it off almost three years. He never hurt anyone. He didn't use the Power unless he had to, and then only
to help his village. He. . . ." Thom threw up his hands. "I
suppose there was no choice. The people where he lived
told me he was acting strange that whole last year. They did
not much want to talk about it, and they nearly stoned me
when they found out I was his uncle. I suppose he *was* going mad. But he was my blood, boy. I can't love the Aes Sedai for what they did to him, even if they had to. If Moiraine's
let you go, then you are well out of it."

For a moment Rand was silent. *Fool! Of course there's
no way to deal with it. You're going to go mad and die
whatever you do. But Ba'alzamon said—* "No!" He colored
under Thom's scrutiny. "I mean . . . I am out of it, Thom.
But I still have the Horn of Valere. Think of it, Thom. The
Horn of Valere. Other gleemen might tell tales about it, but
you could say you had it in your hands." He realized he
sounded like Selene, but all that did was make him wonder where she was. "There's nobody I'd rather have with us
than you, Thom."

Thom frowned as if considering it, but in the end he
shook his head firmly. "Boy, I like you well enough, but
you know as well as I do that I only helped before because
there was an Aes Sedai mixed in it. Seaghan doesn't try
to cheat me more than I expect, and with the King's Gift
added in, I could never earn as much in the villages. To my
very great surprise, Dena seems to love me, and—as much
a surprise—I return the feeling. Now, why should I leave
that to go be chased by Trollocs and Darkfriends? The Horn
of Valere? Oh, it is a temptation, I'll admit, but no. No, I
will not get mixed up in it again."

He leaned over to pick up one of the wooden instrument
cases, long and narrow. When he opened it, a flute lay inside, plainly made but mounted with silver. He closed it
again and slid it across the table. "You might need to earn
your supper again someday, boy."

"I might at that," Rand said. "At least we can talk. I will
be in—"

The gleeman was shaking his head. "A clean break is
best, boy. If you're always coming around, even if you never

mention it, I won't be able to get the Horn out of my head. And I won't be tangled in it. I won't."

After Rand left, Thom threw his cloak on the bed and sat with his elbows on the table. *The Horn of Valere. How did that farmboy find. . . .* He shut off that line of thought. Think about the Horn too long, and he would find himself running off with Rand to carry it to Shienar. *That would make a story, carrying the Horn of Valere to the Borderlands with Trollocs and Darkfriends pursuing.* Scowling, he reminded himself of Dena. Even if she had not loved him, talent such as hers was not to be found every day. And she did love, even if he could not begin to imagine why.

"Old fool," he muttered.

"Aye, an old fool," Zera said from the door. He gave a start; he had been so absorbed in his thoughts that he had not heard the door open. He had known Zera for years, off and on in his wanderings, and she always took full advantage of the friendship to speak her mind. "An old fool who's playing the Game of Houses again. Unless my ears are failing, that young lord has the sound of Andor on his tongue. He's no Cairhienin, that's for certain sure. *Daes Dae'mar* is dangerous enough without letting an outland lord mix you in his schemes."

Thom blinked, then considered the way Rand had looked. That coat had surely been fine enough for a lord. He was growing old, letting things like that slip by him. Ruefully, he realized he was considering whether to tell Zera the truth or let her continue thinking as she did. *All it takes is to think about the Great Game, and I start playing it.* "The boy is a shepherd, Zera, from the Two Rivers."

She laughed scornfully. "And I'm the Queen of Ghealdan. I tell you, the Game has grown dangerous in Cairhien the last few years. Nothing like what you knew in Caemlyn. There are murders done, now. You'll have your throat cut for you, if you don't watch out."

"I tell you, I am not in the Great Game any longer. That's all twenty years in the past, near enough."

"Aye." She did not sound as if she believed it. "But be that as it may, and young outland lords aside, you've begun performing at the lords' manors."

"They pay well."

"And they'll pull you into their plots as soon as they see how. They see a man, and think how to use him, as naturally as breathing. This young lord of yours won't help you; they will eat him alive."

He gave up on trying to convince her he was out of it. "Is that what you came up to say, Zera?"

"Aye. Forget playing the Great Game, Thom. Marry Dena. She'll take you, the more fool her, bony and white-haired as you are. Marry her, and forget this young lord and *Daes Dae'mar.*"

"I thank you for the advice," he said dryly. *Marry her? Burden her with an old husband. She'll never be a bard with my past hanging around her neck.* "If you don't mind, Zera, I want to be alone for a while. I perform for Lady Arilyn and her guests tonight, and I need to prepare."

She gave him a snort and a shake of her head and banged the door shut behind her.

Thom drummed his fingers on the table. Coat or no coat, Rand was still only a shepherd. If he had been more, if he had been what Thom once suspected—a man who could channel—neither Moiraine nor any other Aes Sedai would ever have let him walk away ungentled. Horn or no Horn, the boy was only a shepherd.

"He is out of it," he said aloud, "and so am I."

CHAPTER
27

The Shadow in the Night

I do not understand it," Loial said. "I was winning, most of the time. And then Dena came in and joined the game, and she won it all right back. Every toss. She called it a little lesson. What did she mean by that?"

Rand and the Ogier were making their way through the Foregate, The Bunch of Grapes behind them. The sun sat low in the west, a red ball half below the horizon, throwing long shadows behind them. The street was empty save for one of the big puppets, a goat-horned Trolloc with a sword at its belt, coming toward them with five men working the poles, but sounds of merriment drifted still from other parts of the Foregate, where the halls of entertainment and the taverns stood. Here, doors were already barred and windows shuttered.

Rand stopped fingering the wooden flute case and slung it on his back. *I suppose I couldn't expect him to throw over everything and come with me, but at least he could talk to me. Light, I wish Ingtar would show up.* He stuffed his hands in his pockets and felt Selene's note.

"You don't suppose she. . . ." Loial paused uncomfortably. "You don't suppose she cheated, do you? Everybody was grinning as if she were doing something clever."

Rand shrugged at his cloak. *I have to take the Horn and go. If we wait for Ingtar, anything can happen. Fain will come sooner or later. I have to stay ahead of him.* The men with the puppet were almost to them.

"Rand," Loial said suddenly, "I don't think that's a—"

Abruptly the men let their poles clatter to the packed dirt

street; instead of collapsing, the Trolloc leaped for Rand with outstretched hands.

There was no time to think. Instinct brought the sword out of its sheath in a flashing arc. The Moon Rises Over the Lakes. The Trolloc staggered back with a bubbling cry, snarling even as it fell.

For an instant everyone stood frozen. Then the men—the Darkfriends, they had to be—looked from the Trolloc lying in the street to Rand, with the sword in his hands and Loial at his side. They turned and ran.

Rand was staring at the Trolloc, too. The void had surrounded him before his hand touched hilt; *saidin* shone in his mind, beckoning, sickening. With an effort, he made the void vanish, and licked his lips. Without the emptiness, fear crawled on his skin.

"Loial, we have to get back to the inn. Hurin's alone, and they—" He grunted as he was lifted into the air by a thick arm long enough to pin both of his to his chest. A hairy hand grabbed his throat. He caught sight of a tusked snout just over his head. A rank smell filled his nose, equal parts sour sweat and pigsty.

As quickly as it had seized him, the hand at his throat was torn away. Stunned, Rand stared at it, at the thick Ogier fingers clutching the Trolloc's wrist.

"Hold on, Rand." Loial's voice sounded strained. The Ogier's other hand came around and took hold of the arm still holding Rand above the ground. "Hold on."

Rand was shaken from side to side as Ogier and Trolloc struggled. Abruptly he fell free. Staggering, he took two steps to get clear and turned back with sword raised.

Standing behind the boar-snouted Trolloc, Loial had it by wrist and forearm, holding its arms spread wide, breathing hard with the effort. The Trolloc snarled gutturally in the harsh Trolloc tongue, throwing its head back in efforts to catch Loial with a tusk. Their boots scuffled across the dirt of the street.

Rand tried to find a place to put his blade in the Trolloc without hurting Loial, but Ogier and Trolloc spun in their rough dance so much that he could find no opening.

With a grunt, the Trolloc pulled its left arm free, but before it could loose itself completely, Loial snapped his own arm around its neck, hugging the creature close. The

Trolloc clawed at its sword; the scythe-like blade hung on the wrong side for left-handed use, but inch by inch the dark steel began sliding out of the scabbard. And still they thrashed about so that Rand could not strike without risking Loial.

The Power. That could do it. How, he did not know, but he knew nothing else to try. The Trolloc had its sword half unsheathed. When the curved blade was bare, it would kill Loial.

Reluctantly, Rand formed the void. *Saidin* shone at him, pulled at him. Dimly, he seemed to recall a time when it had sung to him, but now it only drew him, a flower's perfume drawing a bee, a midden's stench drawing a fly. He opened himself up, reached for it. There was nothing there. He could as well have been reaching for light in truth. The taint slid off onto him, soiling him, but there was no flow of light inside him. Driven by a distant desperation, he tried again and again. And again and again there was only the taint.

With a sudden heave, Loial threw the Trolloc aside, so hard that the thing cartwheeled against the side of a building. It struck, headfirst, with a loud crack, and slid down the wall to lie with its neck twisted at an impossible angle. Loial stood staring at it, his chest heaving.

Rand looked out of the emptiness for a moment before he realized what had happened. As soon as he did, though, he let void and tainted light go, and hurried to Loial's side.

"I never . . . killed before, Rand." Loial drew a shuddering breath.

"It would have killed you if you hadn't," Rand told him. Anxiously, he looked at the alleys and shuttered windows and barred doors. Where there were two Trollocs, there had to be more. "I'm sorry you had to do it, Loial, but it would have killed both of us, or worse."

"I know. But I cannot like it. Even a Trolloc." Pointing toward the setting sun, the Ogier seized Rand's arm. "There's another of them."

Against the sun, Rand could not make out details, but it appeared to be another group of men with a huge puppet, coming toward Loial and him. Except that now he knew what to look for, the "puppet" moved its legs too naturally, and the snouted head rose to sniff the air without anyone lifting a pole. He did not think the Trolloc and Darkfriends could see him among the evening shadows, or what lay in the street around him; they moved too slowly for that. Yet it was plain they were hunting, and coming closer.

"Fain knows I am out here somewhere," he said, hastily wiping his blade on a dead Trolloc's coat. "He's set them to find me. He is afraid of the Trollocs being seen, though, or he wouldn't have them disguised. If we can reach a street where there are people, we'll be safe. We have to get back to Hurin. If Fain finds him, alone with the Horn. . . ."

He pulled Loial along to the next corner and turned toward the nearest sounds of laughter and music, but long before they reached it, another group of men appeared ahead of them in the otherwise empty street with a puppet that was no puppet. Rand and Loial took the next turning. It led east.

Every time Rand tried to reach the music and laughter, there was a Trolloc in the way, often sniffing the air for a scent. Some Trollocs hunted by scent. Sometimes, here where there were no eyes to see, a Trolloc stalked alone. More than once he was sure it was one he had seen before. They were closing in, and making sure he and Loial did not leave the deserted streets with their shuttered windows. Slowly the two of them were forced east, away from the city and Hurin, away from other people, along narrow, slowly darkening streets that ran in all directions, uphill and down. Rand eyed the houses they passed, the tall buildings closed up tight for the night, with more than a little regret. Even if he pounded on a door until someone opened it, even if they took Loial and him in, none of the doors he saw would stop a Trolloc. All that would do would be to offer up more victims with Loial and himself.

"Rand," Loial said finally, "there is nowhere else to go."

They had reached the eastern edge of the Foregate; the tall buildings to either side of them were the last. Lights in windows on the upper stories mocked him, but the lower floors were all shut tight. Ahead lay the hills, cloaked in first twilight and bare of so much as a farmhouse. Not entirely empty, though. He could just make out pale walls surrounding one of the larger hills, perhaps a mile away, and buildings inside.

"Once they push us out there," Loial said, "they won't have to worry who sees them."

Rand gestured to the walls around the hill. "Those should stop a Trolloc. It must be a lord's manor. Maybe they'll let us in. An Ogier, and an outland lord? This coat has to be good for something sooner or later." He looked back down the street. No Trollocs in sight yet, but he drew Loial around the side of the building anyway.

"I think that is the Illuminators' chapter house, Rand. Illuminators guard their secrets tightly. I don't think they would let Galldrian himself inside there."

"What trouble have you gotten yourself into now?" said a familiar woman's voice. There was suddenly a spicy perfume in the air.

Rand stared: Selene stepped around the corner they had just rounded, her white dress bright in the dimness. "How did you get here? What are you doing here? You have to leave immediately. Run! There are Trollocs after us."

"So I saw." Her voice was dry, yet cool and composed. "I came to find you, and I find you allowing Trollocs to herd you like sheep. Can the man who possesses the Horn of Valere let himself be treated so?"

"I don't have it with me," he snapped, "and I don't know how it could help if I did. The dead heroes are not supposed to come back to save me from Trollocs. Selene, you have to get away. Now!" He peered around the corner.

Not more than a hundred paces away, a Trolloc was sticking its horned head cautiously into the street, smelling the night. A large shadow by its side had to be another Trolloc, and there were smaller shadows, too. Darkfriends.

"Too late," Rand muttered. He shifted the flute case to pull off his cloak and wrap it around her. It was long enough to hide her white dress entirely, and trail on the ground besides. "You'll have to hold that up to run," he told her. "Loial, if they won't let us in, we will have to find a way to sneak in."

"But, Rand—"

"Would you rather wait for the Trollocs?" He gave Loial a push to start him, and took Selene's hand to follow at a trot. "Find us a path that won't break our necks, Loial."

"You're letting yourself become flustered," Selene said. She seemed to have less trouble following Loial in the failing light than Rand did. "Seek the Oneness, and be calm. One who would be great must always be calm."

"The Trollocs might hear you," he told her. "I don't want greatness." He thought he heard an irritated grunt from her.

Stones sometimes turned underfoot, but the way across the hills was not hard despite the twilight shadows. Trees, and even brush, had long since been cleared from the hills for firewood. Nothing grew except knee-high grass that rustled softly around their legs. A night breeze came up softly. Rand worried that it might carry their scent to the Trollocs.

Loial stopped when they reached the wall; it stood twice as high as the Ogier, the stones covered with a whitish plaster. Rand peered back toward the Foregate. Bands of lighted windows reached out like spokes of a wheel from the city walls.

"Loial," he said softly, "can you see them? Are they following us?"

The Ogier looked in the direction of the Foregate, and nodded unhappily. "I only see some of the Trollocs, but they are coming this way. Running. Rand, I really don't think—"

Selene cut him off. "If he wants to go in, *alantin*, he needs a door. Such as that one." She pointed to a dark patch a little down the wall. Even with her telling him, Rand was not certain it *was* a door, but when she strode to it and pulled, it opened.

"Rand," Loial began.

Rand pushed him to the door. "Later, Loial. And softly. We're hiding, remember?" He got them inside and closed the door behind them. There were brackets for a bar, but no bar to be seen. It would not stop anyone, but maybe the Trollocs would hesitate to come inside the walls.

They were in an alleyway leading up the hill between two long, low windowless buildings. At first he thought they were stone, too, but then he realized the white plaster had been laid over wood. It was dark enough now for the moon reflecting from the walls to give a semblance of light.

"Better to be arrested by the Illuminators than taken by Trollocs," he murmured, starting up the hill.

"But that is what I was trying to tell you," Loial protested. "I've heard the Illuminators kill intruders. They keep their secrets hard and fast, Rand."

Rand stopped dead and stared back at the door. The Trollocs were still out there. At the worst, humans had to be better to deal with than Trollocs. He might be able to talk the Illuminators into letting them go; Trollocs did not listen before they killed. "I'm sorry I got you into this, Selene."

"Danger adds a certain something," she said softly. "And so far, you handle it well. Shall we see what we find?" She brushed past him up the alleyway. Rand followed, the spicy smell of her filling his nostrils.

Atop the hill, the alleyway opened onto a wide expanse of smoothly flattened clay, almost as pale as the plaster and nearly surrounded by more white, windowless buildings with the shadows of narrow alleys between, but to Rand's right stood one building with windows, light falling onto the pale clay. He pulled back into the shadows of the alley as a man and a woman appeared, walking slowly across the open space.

Their clothes were certainly not Cairhienin. The man wore breeches as baggy as his shirt sleeves, both in a soft yellow, with embroidery on the legs of his breeches and across the chest of his shirt. The woman's dress, worked elaborately across the breast, seemed a pale green, and her hair was done in a multitude of short braids.

"All is in readiness, you say?" the woman demanded. "You are certain, Tammuz? All?"

The man spread his hands. "Always you check behind me, Aludra. All is in readiness. The display, it could be given this very moment."

"The gates and doors, they are all barred? All of the . . . ?" Her voice faded as they moved on to the far end of the lighted building.

Rand studied the open area, recognizing almost nothing. In the middle of it, several dozen upright tubes, each nearly as tall as he and a foot or more across, sat on large wooden bases. From each tube, a dark, twisted cord ran across the ground and behind a low wall, perhaps three paces long, on the far side. All around the open space stood a welter of wooden racks with troughs and tubes and forked sticks and a score of other things.

All the fireworks he had ever seen could be held in one hand, and that was as much as he knew, except that they burst with a great roar, or whizzed along the ground in spirals of sparks, or sometimes shot into the air. They always came with warnings from the Illuminators that opening one could cause it to go off. In any case, fireworks were too expensive for the Village Council to have allowed anybody unskilled to open one. He could well remember the time when Mat had tried to do just that; it was nearly a week before anyone but Mat's own mother would speak to him. The only thing that Rand found familiar at all was the cords—the fuses. That, he knew, was where you set the fire.

With a glance back at the unbarred door, he motioned the others to follow and started around the tubes. If they were going to find a place to hide, he wanted to be as far from that door as he could.

It meant making their way between the racks, and Rand held his breath every time he brushed against one. The things in them shifted with the slightest touch, rattling. All of them seemed to be made of wood, without a piece of metal. He could imagine the racket if one were knocked over. He eyed the tall tubes warily, remembering the bang made by one the size of his finger. If those were fireworks, he did not want to be this close to them.

Loial muttered to himself continually, especially when he bumped one of the racks, then started back so fast that he bumped another. The Ogier crept along in a cloud of clatters and muttering.

Selene was no less unnerving. She strode as casually as if they were on a city street. She did not bump anything, did not make a sound, but she also made no effort to keep the cloak closed. The white of her dress seemed brighter than all the walls together. He peered at the lighted windows, waiting for someone to appear. All it would take was one; Selene could not fail to be seen, the alarm given.

The windows remained empty, though. Rand was just breathing a sigh of relief as they approached the low wall—and the alleys and buildings behind it—when Loial brushed against another rack, standing right beside the wall. It held ten soft-looking sticks, as long as Rand's arm, with thin streams of smoke rising from their tips. The rack made hardly a sound when it fell, the smoldering sticks sprawling across one of the fuses. With a crackling hiss, the fuse burst into flame, and the flame raced toward one of the tall tubes.

Rand goggled for an instant, then he tried to whisper a shout. "Behind the wall!"

Selene made an angry noise when he bore her to the ground behind the wall, but he did not care. He tried to spread himself over her protectively as Loial crowded beside them. Waiting for the tube to burst, he wondered if there would be anything left of the wall. There was a hollow thump that he felt through the ground as much as heard. Cautiously, he lifted himself off of Selene enough to peer around the edge of the wall. She fisted him in the ribs, hard, and wriggled out from under him with an oath in a language he did recognize, but he was beyond noticing.

A trickle of smoke was leaking from the top of one of the tubes. That was all. He shook his head wonderingly. *If that's all there is to it. . . .*

With a crash like thunder, a huge flower of red and white bloomed high in the now dark sky, then slowly began drifting away in sparkles.

As he goggled at it, the lighted building erupted with noise. Shouting men and women filled the windows, staring and pointing.

Rand longingly eyed the dark alleyway, only a dozen steps away. And the first step would be in full view of the people at the windows. Pounding feet poured from the building.

He pressed Loial and Selene back against the wall, hoping they looked like just another shadow. "Be still and be silent," he whispered. "It's our only hope."

"Sometimes," Selene said quietly, "if you are very still, no one can see you at all." She did not sound the least bit worried.

Boots thumped back and forth on the other side of the wall, and voices were raised in anger. Especially the one Rand recognized as Aludra.

"You great buffoon, Tammuz! You great pig, you! Your mother, she was a goat, Tammuz! One day you will kill us all."

"I am not to blame for this, Aludra," the man protested. "I have been sure to put everything where it belonged, and the punks, they were—"

"You will not speak to me, Tammuz! A great pig does not deserve to speak like a human!" Aludra's voice changed in answer to another man's question. "There is no time to prepare another. Galldrian, he must be satisfied with the rest for tonight. And one early. And you, Tammuz! You will set everything right, and tomorrow you will leave with the carts to buy the manure. Does anything else go wrong this night, I will not trust you again even with so much as the manure!"

Footsteps faded back toward the building to the accompaniment of Aludra's muttering. Tammuz remained, growling under his breath about the unfairness of it all.

Rand stopped breathing as the man came over to right the toppled stand. Pressed back in the shadows against the wall, he could see Tammuz's back and shoulder. All the man had to do was turn his head, and he could not miss seeing Rand and the others. Still complaining to himself, Tammuz arranged the smoldering sticks in the stand, then stalked off toward the building where everyone else had gone.

Letting his breath go, Rand took a quick look after the man, then pulled back into the shadows. A few people still stood at the windows. "We can't expect any more luck tonight," he whispered.

"It is said great men make their own luck," Selene said softly.

"Will you stop that," he told her wearily. He wished the smell of her did not fill his head so; it made it hard to think clearly. He could remember the feel of her body when he pushed her down—softness and firmness in a disturbing blend—and that did not help either.

"Rand?" Loial was peering around the end of the wall away from the lighted building. "I think we need some more luck, Rand."

Rand shifted to look over the Ogier's shoulder. Beyond open space, in the alleyway that led to the barless door, three Trollocs were peering cautiously out of the shadows toward the lighted windows. One woman was standing at a window; she did not seem to see the Trollocs.

"So," Selene said quietly. "It becomes a trap. These people may kill you if they take you. The Trollocs surely will. But perhaps you can slay the Trollocs too quickly for them to make any outcry. Perhaps you can stop the people from killing you to preserve their little secrets. You may not want greatness, but it will take a great man to do these things."

"You don't have to sound happy about it," Rand said. He tried to stop thinking about how she smelled, how she felt, and the void almost surrounded him. He shook it away.

The Trollocs did not seem to have located them, yet. He settled back, staring at the nearest dark alleyway. Once they made a move toward it, the Trollocs would surely see, and so would the woman at the window. It would be a race as to whether Trollocs or Illuminators reached them first.

"Your greatness will make me happy." Despite the words, Selene sounded angry. "Perhaps I should leave you to find your own way for a time. If you'll not take greatness when it is in your grasp, perhaps you deserve to die."

Rand refused to look at her. "Loial, can you see if there's another door down that alley?"

The Ogier shook his head. "There is too much light here and too much dark there. If I were in the alley, yes."

Rand fingered the hilt of his sword. "Take Selene. As soon as you see a door—*if* you do—call out, and I'll follow. If there isn't a door at the end, you will have to lift her so she can reach the top of the wall and climb over."

"All right, Rand." Loial sounded worried. "But when we move, those Trollocs will come after us, no matter who is watching. Even if there is a door, they will be on our heels."

"You let me worry about the Trollocs." *Three of them. I might do it, with the void.* The thought of *saidin* decided him. Too many strange things had happened when he let the male half of the True Source come close. "I will follow as soon as I can. Go." He turned to peer around the wall at the Trollocs.

From the corner of his eye, he had an impression of Loial's bulk moving, of Selene's white dress, half covered by his cloak. One of the Trollocs beyond the tubes pointed to them excitedly, but still the three hesitated, glancing up at the window where the woman still watched. *Three of them. There has to be a way. Not the void. Not* saidin.

"There is a door!" came Loial's soft call. One of the Trollocs took a step out of the shadows, and the others followed, gathering themselves. As from a distance, Rand heard the woman at the window cry out, and Loial shouted something.

Without thinking, Rand was on his feet. He had to stop the Trollocs somehow, or they would run him down, and Loial and Selene. He snatched one of the smoldering sticks and hurled himself at the nearest tube. It tilted, started to fall over, and he caught the square wooden base; the tube pointed straight at the Trollocs. They slowed uncertainly— the woman at the window screamed—and Rand touched the smoking end of the stick to the fuse right where it joined the tube.

The hollow thump came immediately, and the thick wooden base slammed against him, knocking him down. A roar like a thunderclap broke the night and a blinding burst of light tore away the dark.

Blinking, Rand staggered to his feet, coughing in thick, acrid smoke, ears ringing. He stared in amazement. Half the tubes and all of the racks lay on their sides, and one corner of the building beside which the Trollocs had stood was simply gone, flames licking at ends of planks and rafters. Of the Trollocs there was no sign.

Through the ringing in his ears, Rand heard shouts from the Illuminators in the building. He broke into a tottering run, lumbered into the alley. Halfway down it he stumbled over something and realized it was his cloak. He snatched it up without pausing. Behind him, the cries of the Illuminators filled the night.

Loial was bouncing impatiently on his feet beside the open door. And he was alone.

"Where is Selene?" Rand demanded.

"She went back, Rand. I tried to grab her, and she slipped right out of my hands."

Rand turned back toward the noise. Through the incessant sound in his ears, some of the shouts were barely distinguishable. There was light there, now, from the flames.

"The sand buckets! Fetch the sand buckets quickly!"

"This is disaster! Disaster!"

"Some of them went that way!"

Loial grabbed Rand's shoulder. "You cannot help her, Rand. Not by being taken yourself. We must go." Someone appeared at the end of the alley, a shadow outlined by the glow of flames behind, and pointed toward them. "Come on, Rand!"

Rand let himself be pulled out of the door into the darkness. The fire faded behind them until it was only a glow in the night, and the lights of the Foregate came closer. Rand almost wished more Trollocs would appear, something he could fight. But there was only the night breeze ruffling the grass.

"I tried to stop her," Loial said. There was a long silence. "We really couldn't have done anything. They would just have taken us, too."

Rand sighed. "I know, Loial. You did what you could." He walked backwards a few steps, staring at the glow. It seemed less; the Illuminators must be putting out the flames. "I have to help her somehow." *How?* Saidin? *The Power?* He shivered. "I have to."

They went through the Foregate by the lighted streets, wrapped in a silence that shut out the gaiety around them.

When they entered The Defender of the Dragonwall, the innkeeper held out his tray with a sealed parchment.

Rand took it, and stared at the white seal. A crescent moon and stars. "Who left this? When?"

"An old woman, my Lord. Not a quarter of an hour gone. A servant, though she did not say from what House." Cuale smiled as if inviting confidences.

"Thank you," Rand said, still staring at the seal. The innkeeper watched them go upstairs with a thoughtful look.

Hurin took his pipe out of his mouth when Rand and Loial entered the room. Hurin had his short sword and sword-breaker on the table, wiping them with an oily rag. "You were long with the gleeman, my Lord. Is he well?"

Rand gave a start. "What? Thom? Yes he's. . . ." He broke open the seal with his thumb and read.

When I think I know what you are going to do, you do something else. You are a dangerous man. Perhaps it will not be long before we are together again. Think of the Horn. Think of the glory. And think of me, for you are always mine.

Again, it bore no signature but the flowing hand itself.

"Are all women crazy?" Rand demanded of the ceiling. Hurin shrugged. Rand threw himself into the other chair, the one sized for an Ogier; his feet dangled above the floor, but he did not care. He stared at the blanket-covered chest under the edge of Loial's bed. *Think of the glory.* "I wish Ingtar would come."

CHAPTER
28

A New Thread in the Pattern

Perrin watched the mountains of Kinslayer's Dagger uncomfortably as he rode. The way still slanted upwards, and looked as if it would climb forever, though he thought the crest of the pass must not be too much further. To one side of the trail, the land sloped sharply down to a shallow mountain stream, dashing itself to froth over sharp rocks; to the other side the mountains reared in a series of jagged cliffs, like frozen stone waterfalls. The trail itself ran through fields of boulders, some the size of a man's head, and some as big as a cart. It would take no great skill to hide in that.

The wolves said there were people in the mountains. Perrin wondered if they were some of Fain's Darkfriends. The wolves did not know, or care. They only knew the Twisted Ones were somewhere ahead. Still far ahead, though Ingtar had pressed the column hard. Perrin noticed that Uno was watching the mountains around them much the way he himself was.

Mat, his bow slung across his back, rode with seeming unconcern, juggling three colored balls, yet he looked paler than he had. Verin examined him two and three times a day now, frowning, and Perrin was sure she had even tried Healing at least once, but it made no difference Perrin could see. In any case, she seemed to be more absorbed in something about which she did not speak.

Rand, Perrin thought, looking at the Aes Sedai's back. She always rode at the head of the column with Ingtar, and she always wanted them to move even faster than the Shienaran lord would allow. *Somehow, she knows about*

Rand. Images from the wolves flickered in his head—stone farmhouses and terraced villages, all beyond the mountain peaks; the wolves saw them no differently than they saw hills or meadows, except with a feeling that they were spoiled land. For a moment he found himself sharing that regret, remembering places the two-legs had long since abandoned, remembering the swift rush through the trees, and the ham-stringing snap of his jaws as the deer tried to flee, and. . . . With an effort he pushed the wolves out of his head. *These Aes Sedai are going to destroy all of us.*

Ingtar let his horse fall back beside Perrin's. Sometimes, to Perrin's eyes, the crescent crest on the Shienaran's helmet looked like a Trolloc's horns. Ingtar said softly, "Tell me again what the wolves said."

"I've told you ten times," Perrin muttered.

"Tell me again! Anything I may have missed, anything that will help me find the Horn. . . ." Ingtar drew a breath and let it out slowly. "I must find the Horn of Valere, Perrin. Tell me again."

There was no need for Perrin to order it in his mind, not after so many repetitions. He droned it out. "Someone—or something—attacked the Darkfriends in the night and killed those Trollocs we found." His stomach no longer lurched at that. Ravens and vultures were messy feeders. "The wolves call him—or it—Shadowkiller; I think it was a man, but they wouldn't go close enough to see clearly. They are not afraid of this Shadowkiller; awe is more like it. They say the Trollocs now follow Shadowkiller. And they say Fain is with them"—even after so long the remembered smell of Fain, the feel of the man, made his mouth twist—"so the rest of the Darkfriends must be, too."

"Shadowkiller," Ingtar murmured. "Something of the Dark One, like a Myrddraal? I have seen things in the Blight that might be called Shadowkillers, but. . . . Did they see nothing else?"

"They would not come close to him. It was not a Fade. I've told you, they will kill a Fade quicker than they will a Trolloc, even if they lose half the pack. Ingtar, the wolves who saw it passed this to others, then still others, before it reached me. I can only tell you what they passed on, and after so many tellings. . . ." He let the words die as Uno joined them.

"Aielman in the rocks," the one-eyed man said quietly.

"This far from the Waste?" Ingtar said incredulously. Uno somehow managed to look offended without changing his expression, and Ingtar added, "No, I don't doubt you. I am just surprised."

"He flaming wanted me to see him, or I likely wouldn't have." Uno sounded disgusted at admitting it. "And his bloody face wasn't veiled, so he's not out for killing. But when you see one bloody Aiel, there's always more you don't." Suddenly his eye widened. "Burn me if it doesn't look like he bloody wants more than to be seen." He pointed: a man had stepped into the way ahead of them.

Instantly Masema's lance dropped to a couch, and he dug his heels into his horse, leaping to a dead gallop in three strides. He was not the only one; four steel points hurtled toward the man on the ground.

"Hold!" Ingtar shouted. "Hold, I said! I'll have the ears of any man who doesn't stop where he stands!"

Masema pulled in his horse viciously, sawing the reins. The others also stopped, in a cloud of dust not ten paces from the man, their lances still held steady on the man's chest. He raised a hand to wave away the dust as it drifted toward him; it was the first move he had made.

He was a tall man, with skin dark from the sun and red hair cut short except for a tail in the back that hung to his shoulders. From his soft, laced knee-high boots to the cloth wrapped loosely around his neck, his clothes were all in shades of brown and gray that would blend into rock or earth. The end of a short horn bow peeked over his shoulder, and a quiver bristled with arrows at his belt at one side. A long knife hung at the other. In his left hand he gripped a round hide buckler and three short spears, no more than half as long as he was tall, with points fully as long as those of the Shienaran lances.

"I have no pipers to play the tune," the man announced with a smile, "but if you wish the dance. . . ." He did not change his stance, but Perrin caught a sudden air of readiness. "My name is Urien, of the Two Spires sept of the Reyn Aiel. I am a Red Shield. Remember me."

Ingtar dismounted and walked forward, removing his helmet. Perrin hesitated only a moment before climbing down to join him. He could not miss the chance to see an Aiel close up. Acting like a black-veiled Aiel. In story after story Aiel were as deadly and dangerous as Trollocs—some even said they were all Darkfriends—but Urien's smile somehow did not look dangerous despite the fact that he seemed poised to leap. His eyes were blue.

"He looks like Rand." Perrin looked around to see that Mat had joined them, too. "Maybe Ingtar's right," Mat added quietly. "Maybe Rand is an Aiel."

Perrin nodded. "But it doesn't change anything."

"No, it doesn't." Mat sounded as if he were talking about something beside what Perrin meant.

"We are both far from our homes," Ingtar said to the Aiel, "and we, at least, have come for other things than fighting." Perrin revised his opinion of Urien's smile; the man actually looked disappointed.

"As you wish it, Shienaran." Urien turned to Verin, just getting down off her horse, and made an odd bow, digging the points of his spears into the ground and extending his right hand, palm up. His voice became respectful. "Wise One, my water is yours."

Verin handed her reins to one of the soldiers. She studied the Aiel as she came closer. "Why do you call me that? Do you take me for an Aiel?"

"No, Wise One. But you have the look of those who have made the journey to Rhuidean and survived. The years do not touch the Wise Ones in the same way as other women, or as they touch men."

An excited look appeared on the Aes Sedai's face, but Ingtar spoke impatiently. "We are following Darkfriends and Trollocs, Urien. Have you seen any sign of them?"

"Trollocs? Here?" Urien's eyes brightened. "It is one of the signs the prophecies speak of. When the Trollocs come out of the Blight again, we will leave the Three-fold Land and take back our places of old." There was muttering from the mounted Shienarans. Urien eyed them with a pride that made him seem to be looking down from a height.

"The Three-fold Land?" Mat said.

Perrin thought he looked still paler; not sick, exactly, but as if he had been out of the sun too long.

"You call it the Waste," Urien said. "To us it is the Three-fold Land. A shaping stone, to make us; a testing ground, to prove our worth; and a punishment for the sin."

"What sin?" Mat asked. Perrin caught his breath, waiting for the spears in Urien's hand to flash.

The Aiel shrugged. "So long ago it was, that none remember. Except the Wise Ones and the clan chiefs, and they will not speak of it. It must have been a very great sin if they cannot bring themselves to tell us, but the Creator punishes us well."

"Trollocs," Ingtar persisted. "Have you seen Trollocs?"

Urien shook his head. "I would have killed them if I had, but I have seen nothing but the rocks and the sky."

Ingtar shook his head, losing interest, but Verin spoke, sharp concentration in her voice. "This Rhuidean. What is it? Where is it? How are the girls chosen to go?"

Urien's face went flat, his eyes hooded. "I cannot speak of it, Wise One."

In spite of himself Perrin's hand gripped his axe. There was that in Urien's voice. Ingtar had also set himself, ready to reach for his sword, and there was a stir among the mounted men. But Verin stepped up to the Aiel, until she was almost touching his chest, and looked up into his face.

"I am not a Wise One as you know them, Urien," she said insistently. "I am Aes Sedai. Tell me what you can say of Rhuidean."

The man who had been ready to face twenty men now looked as if he wished for an escape from this one plump woman with graying hair. "I . . . can tell you only what is known to all. Rhuidean lies in the lands of the Jenn Aiel, the thirteenth clan. I cannot speak of them except to name them. None may go there save women who wish to become Wise Ones, or men who wish to be clan chiefs. Perhaps the Jenn Aiel choose among them; I do not know. Many go; few return, and those are marked as what they are—Wise Ones, or clan chiefs. No more can I say, Aes Sedai. No more."

Verin continued to look up at him, pursing her lips.

Urien looked at the sky as though he was trying to remember it. "Will you slay me now, Aes Sedai?"

She blinked. "What?"

"Will you slay me now? One of the old prophecies says that if ever we fail the Aes Sedai again, they will slay us. I know your power is greater than that of the Wise Ones." The Aiel laughed suddenly, mirthlessly. There was a wild light in his eyes. "Bring your lightnings, Aes Sedai. I will dance with them."

The Aiel thought he was going to die, and he was not

afraid. Perrin realized his mouth was open and closed it with a snap.

"What would I not give," Verin murmured, gazing up at Urien, "to have you in the White Tower. Or just willing to talk. Oh, be still, man. I won't harm you. Unless you mean to harm me, with your talk of dancing."

Urien seemed astounded. He looked at the Shienarans, sitting their horses all around, as if he suspected some trick. "You are not a Maiden of the Spear," he said slowly. "How could I strike at a woman who has not wedded the spear? It is forbidden except to save life, and then I would take wounds to avoid it."

"Why are you here, so far from your own lands?" she asked. "Why did you come to us? You could have remained in the rocks, and we would never have known you were there." The Aiel hesitated, and she added, "Tell only what you are willing to say. I do not know what your Wise Ones do, but I'll not harm you, or try to force you."

"So the Wise Ones say," Urien said dryly, "yet even a clan chief must have a strong belly to avoid doing as they want." He seemed to be picking his words carefully. "I search for . . . someone. A man." His eye ran across Perrin, Mat, the Shienarans, dismissing them all. "He Who Comes With the Dawn. It is said there will be great signs and portents of his coming. I saw that you were from Shienar by your escort's armor, and you had the look of a Wise One, so I thought you might have word of great events, the events that might herald him."

"A man?" Verin's voice was soft, but her eyes were as sharp as daggers. "What are these signs?"

Urien shook his head. "It is said we will know them when we hear of them, as we will know him when we see him, for he will be marked. He will come from the west, beyond the Spine of the World, but be of our blood. He will go to Rhuidean, and lead us out of the Three-fold Land." He took a spear in his right hand. Leather and metal creaked as soldiers reached for their swords, and Perrin realized he had taken hold of his axe again, but Verin waved them all to stillness with an irritated look. In the dirt Urien scraped a circle with his spearpoint, then drew across it a sinuous line. "It is said that under this sign, he will conquer."

Ingtar frowned at the symbol, no recognition on his face,

but Mat muttered something coarsely under his breath, and
Perrin felt his mouth go dry. *The ancient symbol of the Aes
Sedai.*

Verin scraped the marking away with her foot. "I cannot
tell you where he is, Urien," she said, "and I have heard of
no signs or portents to guide you to him."

"Then I will continue my search." It was not a question,
yet Urien waited until she nodded before he eyed the Shienarans proudly, challengingly, then turned his back on
them. He walked away smoothly, and vanished into the
rocks without looking back.

Some of the soldiers began muttering. Uno said something about "crazy bloody Aiel," and Masema growled that
they should have left the Aiel for the ravens.

"We have wasted valuable time," Ingtar announced
loudly. "We will ride harder to make it up."

"Yes," Verin said, "we must ride harder."

Ingtar glanced at her, but the Aes Sedai was staring at the
smudged ground, where her foot had obliterated the symbol.
"Dismount," he ordered. "Armor on the packhorses. We're
inside Cairhien, now. We do not want the Cairhienin thinking we have come to fight them. Be quick about it!"

Mat leaned close to Perrin. "Do you . . . ? Do you think
he was talking about Rand? It's crazy, I know, but even
Ingtar thinks he's Aiel."

"I don't know," Perrin said. "Everything has been crazy
since we got mixed up with Aes Sedai."

Softly, as to herself, Verin spoke, still staring at the
ground. "It must be a part, and yet how? Does the Wheel
of Time weave threads into the Pattern of which we know
nothing? Or does the Dark One touch the Pattern again?"

Perrin felt a chill.

Verin looked up at the soldiers removing their armor.
"Hurry!" she commanded with more snap than Ingtar and
Uno combined. "We must hurry!"

CHAPTER
29

Seanchan

Geofram Bornhald ignored the smell of burning houses and the bodies that lay sprawled on the dirt of the street. Byar and a white-cloaked guard of a hundred rode into the village at his heels, half the men he had with him. His legion was too scattered for his liking, with Questioners having too many of the commands, but his orders had been explicit: Obey the Questioners.

There had been but slight resistance here; only half a dozen dwellings gave off columns of smoke. The inn was still standing, he saw, white-plastered stone like almost every structure on Almoth Plain.

Reining up before the inn, his eyes went past the prisoners his soldiers held near the village well to the long gibbet marring the village green. It was hastily made, only a long pole on uprights, but it held thirty bodies, their clothes ruffled by the breeze. There were small bodies hanging among their elders. Even Byar stared at that in disbelief.

"Muadh!" he roared. A grizzled man trotted away from those holding the prisoners. Muadh had fallen into the hands of Darkfriends, once; his scarred face took even the strongest aback. "Is this your work, Muadh, or the Seanchan?"

"Neither, my Lord Captain." Muadh's voice was a hoarse, whispered growl, another leaving of the Darkfriends. He said no more.

Bornhald frowned. "Surely that lot did not do it," he said, gesturing to the prisoners. The Children did not look so neat as when he had brought them across Tarabon, but they seemed ready to parade compared with the rabble that crouched under their watchful eyes. Men in rags and bits of armor, with sullen faces. Remnants of the army Tarabon had sent against the invaders on Toman Head.

Muadh hesitated, then said carefully, "The villagers say they wore Taraboner cloaks, my Lord Captain. There was a big man among them, with gray eyes and a long mustache, that sounds twin to Child Earwin, and a young lad, trying to hide a pretty face behind a yellow beard, who fought with his left hand. Sounds almost like Child Wuan, my Lord Captain."

"Questioners!" Bornhald spat. Earwin and Wuan were among those he had had to hand over to the Questioners' command. He had seen Questioner tactics before, but this was the first time he had ever been faced with children's bodies.

"If my Lord Captain says so." Muadh made it sound like fervent agreement.

"Cut them down," Bornhald said wearily. "Cut them down, and make sure the villagers know there will be no more killing." *Unless some fool decides to be brave because his woman is watching, and I have to make an example.* He dismounted, eyeing the prisoners again, as Muadh hurried off calling for ladders and knives. He had more to think about than Questioners' overzealousness; he wished he could stop thinking about Questioners altogether.

"They do not put up much fight, my Lord Captain," Byar said, "either these Taraboners or what is left of the Domani. They snap like cornered rats, but run as soon as anything snaps back."

"Let us see how we do against the invaders, Byar, before we look down on these men, yes?" The prisoners' faces bore a defeated look that had been there before his men came. "Have Muadh pick one out for me." Muadh's face was enough to soften most men's resolve by itself. "An officer, preferably. One who looks intelligent enough to tell what he has seen without embroidery, but young enough not to have yet grown a full backbone. Tell Muadh to be not too gentle about it, yes? Make the fellow believe that I mean to see worse happen to him than he ever dreamed of, unless he convinces me otherwise." He tossed his reins to one of the Children and strode into the inn.

The innkeeper was there, for a wonder, an obsequious,

sweating man, his dirty shirt straining over his belly until the embroidered red scrollwork seemed ready to pop off. Bornhald waved the man away; he was vaguely aware of a woman and some children huddling in a doorway, until the fat innkeeper shepherded them out.

Bornhald pulled off his gauntlets and sat at one of the tables. He knew too little about the invaders, the strangers. That was what almost everyone called them, those who did not just babble about Artur Hawkwing. He knew they called themselves the Seanchan, and *Hailene*. He had enough of the Old Tongue to know the latter meant Those Who Come Before, or the Forerunners. They also called themselves *Rhyagelle,* Those Who Come Home, and spoke of *Corenne,* the Return. It was almost enough to make him believe the tales of Artur Hawkwing's armies come back. No one knew where the Seanchan had come from, other than that they had landed in ships. Bornhald's requests for information from the Sea Folk had been met with silence. Amador did not hold the Atha'an Miere in good favor, and the attitude was returned with interest. All he knew of the Seanchan he had heard from men like those outside. Broken, beaten rabble who spoke, wide-eyed and sweating, of men who came into battle riding monsters as often as horses, who fought with monsters by their sides, and brought Aes Sedai to rend the earth under their enemies' feet.

A sound of boots in the doorway made him put on a wolfish grin, but Byar was not accompanied by Muadh. The Child of the Light who stood beside him, back braced and helmet in the crook of his arm, was Jeral, who Bornhald expected to be a hundred miles away. Over his armor, the young man wore a cloak of Domani cut, trimmed with blue, not the white cloak of the Children.

"Muadh is talking to a young fellow now, my Lord Captain," Byar said. "Child Jeral has just ridden in with a message."

Bornhald waved for Jeral to begin.

The young man did not unbend. "The compliments of Jaichim Carridin," he started, looking straight ahead, "who guides the Hand of the Light in—"

"I have no need of the Questioner's compliments," Bornhald growled, and saw the young man's startled look. Jeral was young, yet. For that matter, Byar looked uncomfortable, as well. "You will give me his message, yes? Not word for word, unless I ask it. Simply tell me what he wants."

The Child, set to recite, swallowed before he began. "My Lord Captain, he—he says you are moving too many men too close to Toman Head. He says the Darkfriends on Almoth Plain must be rooted out, and you are—forgive me, Lord Captain—you are to turn back at once and ride toward the heart of the plain." He stood stiffly, waiting.

Bornhald studied him. The dust of the plain stained Jeral's face as well as his cloak and his boots. "Go and get yourself something to eat," Bornhald told him. "There should be wash water in one of these houses, if you wish it. Return to me in an hour. I will have messages for you to carry." He waved the young man out.

"The Questioners may be right, my Lord Captain," Byar said when Jeral was gone. "There are many villages scattered on the plain, and the Darkfriends—"

Bornhald's hand slapping the table cut him off. "What Darkfriends? I have seen nothing in any village he has ordered taken except farmers and craftsmen worried that we will burn their livelihoods, and a few old women who tend the sick." Byar's face was a study in lack of expression; he was always readier than Bornhald to see Darkfriends. "And children, Byar? Do children here become Darkfriends?"

"The sins of the mother are visited to the fifth generation," Byar quoted, "and the sins of the father to the tenth." But he looked uneasy. Even Byar had never killed a child.

"Has it never occurred to you, Byar, to wonder why Carridin has taken away our banners, and the cloaks of the men the Questioners lead? Even the Questioners themselves have put off the white. This suggests something, yes?"

"He must have his reasons, Lord Captain," Byar said slowly. "The Questioners always have reasons, even when they do not tell the rest of us."

Bornhald reminded himself that Byar was a good soldier. "Children to the north wear Taraboner cloaks, Byar, and those to the south Domani. I do not like what this suggests to me. There are Darkfriends here, but they are in Falme, not on the plain. When Jeral rides, he will not ride alone. Messages will go to every group of the Children I know how to find. I mean to take the legion onto Toman Head, Byar, and see what the true Darkfriends, these Seanchan, are up to."

Byar looked troubled, but before he could speak, Muadh appeared with one of the prisoners. The sweating young man in a battered, ornate breastplate shot frightened looks at Muadh's hideous face.

Bornhald drew his dagger and began trimming his nails. He had never understood why that made some men nervous, but he used it just the same. Even his grandfatherly smile made the prisoner's dirty face pale. "Now, young man, you will tell me everything you know about these strangers, yes? If you need to think on what to say, I will send you back out with Child Muadh to consider it."

The prisoner darted a wide-eyed look at Muadh. Then words began to pour out of him.

The long swells of the Aryth Ocean made *Spray* roll, but Domon's spread feet balanced him as he held the long tube of the looking glass to his eye and studied the large vessel that pursued them. Pursued, and was slowly overtaking. The wind where *Spray* ran was not the best or the strongest, but where the other ship smashed the swells into mountains of foam with its bluff bow, it could not have blown better. The coastline of Toman Head loomed to the east, dark cliffs and narrow strips of sand. He had not cared to take *Spray* too far out, and now he feared he might pay for it.

"Strangers, Captain?" Yarin had the sound of sweat in his voice. "Is it a strangers' ship?"

Domon lowered the looking glass, but his eye still seemed filled by that tall, square-looking ship with its odd ribbed sails. "Seanchan," he said, and heard Yarin groan. He drummed his thick fingers on the rail, then told the helmsman, "Take her closer in. That ship will no dare enter the shallow waters *Spray* can sail."

Yarin shouted commands, and crewmen ran to haul in booms as the helmsman put the tiller over, pointing the bow more toward the shoreline. *Spray* moved more slowly, heading so far into the wind, but Domon was sure he could reach shoal waters before the other vessel came up on him. *Did her holds be full, she could still take shallower water than ever that great hull can.*

His ship rode a little higher in the water than she had on sailing from Tanchico. A third of the cargo of fireworks he had taken on there was gone, sold in the fishing villages on Toman Head, but with the silver that flowed for the fireworks had come disturbing reports. The people spoke of visits from the tall, boxy ships of the invaders. When Seanchan ships anchored off the coast, the villagers who drew up to defend their homes were rent by lightning from the sky while small boats were still ferrying the invaders ashore, and the earth erupted in fire under their feet. Domon had thought he was hearing nonsense until he was shown the blackened ground, and he had seen it in too many villages to doubt any longer. Monsters fought beside the Seanchan soldiers, not that there was ever much resistance left, the villagers said, and some even claimed that the Seanchan themselves were monsters, with heads like huge insects.

In Tanchico, no one had even known what they called themselves, and the Taraboners spoke confidently of their soldiers driving the invaders into the sea. But in every coastal town, it was different. The Seanchan told astonished people they must swear again oaths they had forsaken, though never deigning to explain when they had forsaken them, or what the oaths meant. The young women were taken away one by one to be examined, and some were carried aboard the ships and never seen again. A few older women had also vanished, some of the Guides and Healers. New mayors were chosen by the Seanchan, and new Councils, and any who protested the disappearances of the women or having no voice in the choosing might be hung, or burst suddenly into flame, or be brushed aside like yapping dogs. There was no way of telling which it would be until it was too late.

And when the people had been thoroughly cowed, when they had been made to kneel and swear, bewildered, to obey the Forerunners, await the Return, and serve Those Who Come Home with their lives, the Seanchan sailed away and usually never returned. Falme, it was said, was the only town they held fast.

In some of the villages they had left, men and women crept back toward their former lives, to the extent of talking about electing their Councils again, but most eyed the sea nervously and made pale-cheeked protests that they meant to hold to the oaths they had been made to swear even if they did not understand them.

Domon had no intention of meeting any Seanchan, if he could avoid it.

He was raising the glass to see what he could make out on the nearing Seanchan decks, when, with a roar, the surface of the sea broke into fountaining water and flame not a hundred paces from his larboard side. Before he had even begun to gape, another column of flame split the sea on the other side, and as he was spinning to stare at that, another burst up ahead. The eruptions died as quickly as they were born, spray from them blown across the deck. Where they had been, the sea bubbled and steamed as if boiling.

"We . . . we'll reach shallow water before they can close with us," Yarin said slowly. He seemed to be trying not to look at the water roiling under clouds of mist.

Domon shook his head. "Whatever they did, they can shatter us, even do I take her into the breakers." He shivered, thinking of the flame inside the fountains of water, and his holds full of fireworks. "Fortune prick me, we might no live to drown." He tugged at his beard and rubbed his bare upper lip, reluctant to give the order—the vessel and what it contained were all he had in the world—but finally he made himself speak. "Bring her into the wind, Yarin, and down sail. Quickly, man, quickly! Before they do think we still try to escape."

As crewmen ran to lower the triangular sails, Domon turned to watch the Seanchan ship approach. *Spray* lost headway and pitched in the swells. The other vessel stood taller above the water than Domon's ship, with wooden towers at bow and stern. Men were in the rigging, raising those strange sails, and armored figures stood atop the towers. A longboat was put over the side, and sped toward *Spray* under ten oars. It carried armored shapes, and—Domon frowned in surprise—two women crouched in the stern. The longboat thumped against *Spray*'s hull.

The first to climb up was one of the armored men, and Domon saw immediately why some of the villagers claimed the Seanchan themselves were monsters. The helmet looked very much like some monstrous insect's head, with thin red plumes like feelers; the wearer seemed to be peering out through mandibles. It was painted and gilded to increase the effect, and the rest of the man's armor was also worked with paint and gold. Overlapping plates in black and red outlined with gold covered his chest and ran down the outsides of his arms and the fronts of his thighs. Even the steel backs of his gauntlets were red and gold. Where he did not wear metal, his clothes were dark leather. The two-handed sword on his back, with its curved blade, was scabbarded and hilted in black-and-red leather.

Then the armored figure removed his helmet, and Domon stared. He was a woman. Her dark hair was cut short, and her face was hard, but there was no mistaking it. He had never heard of such a thing, except among the Aiel, and Aiel were well known to be crazed. Just as disconcerting was the fact that her face did not look as different as he had expected of a Seanchan. Her eyes were blue, it was true, and her skin exceedingly fair, but he had seen both before. If this woman wore a dress, no one would look at her twice. He eyed her and revised his opinion, that cold stare and those hard cheeks would make her remarked anywhere.

The other soldiers followed the woman onto the deck. Domon was relieved to see, when some of them removed their strange helmets, that they, at least, were men; men with black eyes, or brown, who could have gone unnoticed in Tanchico or Illian. He had begun to have visions of armies of blue-eyed women with swords. *Aes Sedai with swords*, he thought, remembering the sea erupting.

The Seanchan woman surveyed the ship arrogantly, then picked Domon out as captain—it had to be him or Yarin, by their clothes; the way Yarin had his eyes closed and was muttering prayers under his breath pointed to Domon—and fixed him with a stare like a spike.

"Are there any women among your crew or passengers?" She spoke with a soft slurring that made her hard to understand, but there was a snap in her voice that said she was used to getting answers. "Speak up, man, if you are the captain. If not, wake that other fool and tell him to speak."

"I do be captain, my Lady," Domon said cautiously. He had no idea how to address her, and he did not want to put a foot wrong. "I have no passengers, and there be no women in my crew." He thought of the girls and women who had been carried off, and, not for the first time, wondered what these folk wanted with them.

The two women dressed as women were coming up from the longboat, one drawing the other—Domon blinked—by a leash of silvery metal as she climbed aboard. The leash went from a bracelet worn by the first woman to a collar around the neck of the second. He could not tell whether it was woven or jointed—it seemed somehow to be both—but it was clearly of a piece with both bracelet and collar. The first woman gathered the leash in coils as the other came onto the deck. The collared woman wore plain dark gray and stood with her hands folded and her eyes on the planks under her feet. The other had red panels bearing forked, silver lightning bolts on the breast of her blue dress and on the sides of her skirts, which ended short of the ankles of her boots. Domon eyed the women uneasily.

"Speak slowly, man," the blue-eyed woman demanded in her slurred speech. She came across the deck to confront him, staring up at him and in some way seeming taller and larger than he. "You are even harder to understand than the rest in this Light-forsaken land. And I make no claim to be of the Blood. Not yet. After *Corenne.* . . . I am Captain Egeanin."

Domon repeated himself, trying to speak slowly, and added, "I do be a peaceful trader, Captain. I mean no harm to you, and I have no part in your war." He could not help eyeing the two women connected by the leash again.

"A peaceful trader?" Egeanin mused. "In that case, you will be free to go once you have sworn fealty again." She noticed his glances and turned to smile at the women with the pride of ownership. "You admire my *damane*? She cost me dear, but she was worth every coin. Few but nobles own a *damane*, and most are property of the throne. She is strong, trader. She could have broken your ship to splinters, had I wished it so."

Domon stared at the women and the silver leash. He had connected the one wearing the lightning with the fiery fountains in the sea, and assumed she was an Aes Sedai. Egeanin had just set his head whirling. *No one could do that to.* . . . "She is Aes Sedai?" he said disbelievingly.

He never saw the casual backhand blow coming. He staggered as her steel-backed gauntlet split his lip.

"That name is never spoken," Egeanin said with a dangerous softness. "There are only the *damane*, the Leashed Ones, and now they serve in truth as well as name." Her eyes made ice seem warm.

Domon swallowed blood and kept his hand clenched at his sides. If he had had a sword to hand, he would not have led his crew to slaughter against a dozen armored soldiers, but it was an effort to make his voice humble. "I meant no disrespect, Captain. I know nothing of you or your ways. If I do offend, it is ignorance, no intention."

She looked at him, then said, "You are all ignorant, Captain, but you will pay the debt of your forefathers. This land was ours, and it will be ours again. With the Return, it will be ours again." Domon did not know what to say—*Surely she can no mean that nattering about Artur Hawkwing be true?*—so he kept his mouth shut. "You will sail your vessel to Falme"—he tried to protest, but her glare silenced him—"where you and your ship will be examined. If you are no more than a peaceful trader, as you claim, you will be allowed to go your way when you have sworn the oaths."

"Oaths, Captain? What oaths?"

"To obey, to await, and to serve. Your ancestors should have remembered."

She gathered her people—except for a single man in plain armor, which marked him of low rank as much as the depth of his bow to Captain Egeanin—and their longboat pulled away toward the larger ship. The remaining Seanchan gave no orders, only sat cross-legged on the deck and began sharpening his sword while the crew put sail on and got under way. He seemed to have no fear at being alone, and Domon would have personally thrown overboard any crewman who raised a hand to him, for as *Spray* made her way along the coast, the Seanchan ship followed, out in deeper water. There was a mile between the two vessels, but Domon knew there was no hope of escape, and he meant to deliver the man back to Captain Egeanin as safely as if he had been cradled in his mother's arms.

It was a long passage to Falme, and Domon finally persuaded the Seanchan to talk, a little. A dark-eyed man in his middle years, with an old scar above his eyes and another nicking his chin, his name was Caban, and he had nothing but contempt for anyone this side of the Aryth Ocean. That gave Domon a moment's pause. *Maybe they truly do be. . . . No, that do be madness.* Caban's speech had the same slur as Egeanin's, but where hers was silk sliding across iron, his was leather rasping on rock, and mostly he wanted to talk about battles, drinking, and women he had known. Half the time, Domon was not certain if he were speaking of here and now, or of wherever he had come from. The man was certainly not forthcoming about anything Domon wanted to know.

Once Domon asked about the *damane*. Caban reached up from where he sat in front of the helmsman and put the point of his sword to Domon's throat. "Watch what your tongue touches, or you will lose it. That's the business of the Blood, not your kind. Or mine." He grinned while he said it, and as soon as he was done, he went back to sliding a stone along his heavy, curved blade.

Domon touched the point of blood welling above his collar and resolved not to ask that again, at least.

The closer the two vessels came to Falme, the more of the tall, square-looking Seanchan ships they passed, some under sail, but more anchored. Every one was bluff-bowed and towered, as big as anything Domon had ever seen, even among the Sea Folk. A few local craft, he saw, with their sharp bows and slanted sails, darted across the green swells. The sight gave him confidence that Egeanin had spoken the truth about letting him go free.

When *Spray* came up on the headland where Falme stood, Domon gaped at the numbers of the Seanchan ships anchored off the harbor. He tried counting them and gave up at a hundred, less than halfway done. He had seen as many ships in one place before—in Illian, and Tear, and even Tanchico—but those vessels had included many smaller craft. Muttering glumly to himself, he took *Spray* into the harbor, shepherded by her great Seanchan watchdog.

Falme stood on a spit of land at the very tip of Toman Head, with nothing further west of it except the Aryth Ocean. High cliffs ran to the harbor mouth on both sides, and atop one of those, where every ship running into the harbor had to pass under them, stood the towers of the Watchers Over the Waves. A cage hung over the side of one of the towers, with a man sitting in it despondently, legs dangling through the bars.

"Who is that?" Domon asked.

Caban had finally given over sharpening his sword, after Domon had begun to wonder if he meant to shave with it.

The Seanchan glanced up to where Domon pointed. "Oh.
That is the First Watcher. Not the one who sat in the chair
when we first came, of course. Every time he dies, they
choose another, and we put him in the cage."

"But why?" Domon demanded.

Caban's grin showed too many teeth. "They watched for
the wrong thing, and forgot when they should have been
remembering."

Domon tore his eyes away from the Seanchan. *Spray* slid
down the last real sea swell and into the quieter waters of
the harbor. *I do be a trader, and it is none of my business.*

Falme rose from stone docks up the slopes of the hollow
that made the harbor. Domon could not decide whether the
dark stone houses made up a goodly sized town or a small
city. Certainly he saw no building in it to rival the smallest
palace in Illian.

He guided *Spray* to a place at one of the docks, and wondered, while the crew tied the ship fast, if the Seanchan
might buy some of the fireworks in his hold. *None of my
business.*

To his surprise, Egeanin had herself rowed to the dock
with her *damane*. There was another woman wearing the
bracelet this time, with the red panels and forked lightning on her dress, but the *damane* was the same sad-faced
woman who never looked up unless the other spoke to her.
Egeanin had Domon and his crew herded off the ship to sit
on the dock under the eyes of a pair of her soldiers—she
seemed to think no more were needed, and Domon was not
about to argue with her—while others searched *Spray* under
her direction. The *damane* was part of the search.

Down the dock, a thing appeared. Domon could think
of no other way to describe it. A hulking creature with a
leathery, gray-green hide and a beak of a mouth in a wedge-
shaped head. And three eyes. It lumbered along beside a
man whose armor bore three painted eyes, just like those
of the creature. The local people, dockmen and sailors in
roughly embroidered shirts and long vests to their knees,
shied away as the pair passed, but no Seanchan gave them a
second glance. The man with the beast seemed to be directing it with hand signals.

Man and creature turned in among the buildings, leaving
Domon staring and his crew muttering to themselves. The

two Seanchan guards sneered at them silently. *No my business*, Domon reminded himself. His business was his ship.

The air had a familiar smell of salt water and pitch. He shifted uneasily on the stone, hot from the sun, and wondered what the Seanchan were searching for. What the *damane* was searching for. Wondered what that thing had been. Gulls cried, wheeling above the harbor. He thought of the sounds a caged man might make. *It is no my business.*

Eventually Egeanin led the others back onto the dock. The Seanchan captain had something wrapped in a piece of yellow silk, Domon noted warily. Something small enough to carry in one hand, but which she held carefully in both.

He got to his feet—slowly, for the soldiers' sake, though their eyes held the same contempt Caban's did. "You see, Captain? I do be only a peaceful trader. Perhaps your people would care to buy some fireworks?"

"Perhaps, trader." There was an air of suppressed excitement about her that made him uneasy, and her next words increased the feeling. "You will come with me."

She told two soldiers to come along, and one of them gave Domon a push to get him started. It was not a rough shove; Domon had seen farmers push a cow in the same way to make it move. Setting his teeth, he followed Egeanin.

The cobblestone street climbed the slope, leaving the smell of the harbor behind. The slate-roofed houses grew larger and taller as the street climbed. Surprisingly for a town held by invaders, the streets held more local people than Seanchan soldiers, and now and again a curtained palanquin was borne past by bare-chested men. The Falmen seemed to be going about their business as if the Seanchan were not there. Or almost not there. When palanquin or soldier passed, both poor folk, with only a curling line or two worked on their dirty clothes, and the richer, with shirts, vests, and dresses covered from shoulder to waist in intricately embroidered patterns, bowed and remained bent until the Seanchan were gone. They did the same for Domon and his guard. Neither Egeanin nor her soldiers so much as glanced at them.

Domon realized with a sudden shock that some of the local people they passed wore daggers at their belts, and in a few cases swords. He was so surprised that he spoke without thinking. "Some of them be on your side?"

Egeanin frowned over her shoulder at him, obviously puzzled. Without slowing, she looked at the people and nodded to herself. "You mean the swords. They are our people, now, trader; they have sworn the oaths." She stopped abruptly, pointing at a tall, heavy-shouldered man with a heavily embroidered vest and a sword swinging on a plain leather baldric. "You."

The man halted in mid-step, one foot in the air and a frightened look suddenly on his face. It was a hard face, but he looked as if he wanted to run. Instead, he turned to her and bowed, hands on knees, eyes fixed on her boots. "How may this one serve the captain?" he asked in a tight voice.

"You are a merchant?" Egeanin said. "You have sworn the oaths?"

"Yes, Captain. Yes." He did not take his eyes from her feet.

"What do you tell the people when you take your wagons inland?"

"That they must obey the Forerunners, Captain, await the Return, and serve Those Who Come Home."

"And do you never think to use that sword against us?"

The man's hands went white-knuckled gripping his knees, and there was suddenly sweat in his voice. "I have sworn the oaths, Captain. I obey, await, and serve."

"You see?" Egeanin said, turning to Domon. "There is no reason to forbid them weapons. There must be trade, and merchants must protect themselves from bandits. We allow the people to come and go as they will, so long as they obey, await, and serve. Their forefathers broke their oaths, but these have learned better." She started back up the hill, and the soldiers pushed Domon after her.

He looked back at the merchant. The man stayed bent as he was till Egeanin was ten paces up the street, then he straightened and hurried the other way, leaping down the sloping street.

Egeanin and his guards did not look around, either, when a mounted Seanchan troop passed them, climbing the street. The soldiers rode creatures that looked almost like cats the size of horses, but with lizards' scales rippling bronze beneath their saddles. Clawed feet grasped the cobblestones. A three-eyed head turned to regard Domon as the troop climbed by; aside from everything else, it seemed too—knowing—for Domon's peace of mind. He stumbled and almost fell. All along the street, the Falmen were pressing themselves back against the fronts of the buildings, some closing their eyes. The Seanchan paid them no heed.

Domon understood why the Seanchan could allow the people as much freedom as they did. He wondered if he would have had nerve enough to resist. *Damane.* Monsters. He wondered if there was anything to stop the Seanchan from marching all the way to the Spine of the World. *No my business*, he reminded himself roughly, and considered whether there was any way to avoid the Seanchan in his future trading.

They reached the top of the incline, where the town gave way to hills. There was no town wall. Ahead were the inns that served merchants who traded inland, and wagon yards and stables. Here, the houses would have made respectable manors for the minor lords in Illian. The largest of them had an honor guard of Seanchan soldiers out front, and a blue-edged banner bearing a golden, spread-winged hawk rippling above it. Egeanin surrendered her sword and dagger before taking Domon inside. Her two soldiers remained in the street. Domon began to sweat. He smelled a lord in this; it was never good to do business with a lord on the lord's own ground.

In the front hall Egeanin left Domon at the door and spoke to a servant. A local man, judging by the full sleeves of his shirt and the spirals embroidered across his chest; Domon believed he caught the words "High Lord." The servant hurried away, returning finally to lead them to what was surely the largest room in the house. Every stick of furniture had been cleared out of it, even the rugs, and the stone floor was polished to a bright gleam. Folding screens painted with strange birds hid walls and windows.

Egeanin stopped just inside the room. When Domon tried to ask where they were and why, she silenced him with a savage glare and a wordless growl. She did not move, but she seemed on the point of bouncing on her toes. She held whatever it was she had taken from his ship as if it were precious. He tried to imagine what it could be.

Suddenly a gong sounded softly, and the Seanchan

woman dropped to her knees, setting the silk-wrapped something carefully beside her. At a look from her, Domon got down as well. Lords had strange ways, and he suspected Seanchan lords might have stranger ones than he knew.

Two men appeared in the doorway at the far end of the room. One had the left side of his scalp shaved, his remaining pale golden hair braided and hanging down over his ear to his shoulder. His deep yellow robe was just long enough to let the toes of yellow slippers peek out when he walked. The other wore a blue silk robe, brocaded with birds and long enough to trail nearly a span on the floor behind him. His head was shaved bald, and his fingernails were at least an inch long, those on the first two fingers of each hand lacquered blue. Domon's mouth dropped open.

"You are in the presence of the High Lord Turak," the yellow-haired man intoned, "who leads Those Who Come Before, and succors the Return."

Egeanin prostrated herself with her hands at her sides. Domon imitated her with alacrity. *Even the High Lords of Tear would no demand this*, he thought. Out of the corner of his eye, he saw Egeanin kissing the floor. With a grimace, he decided there was a limit to imitation. *They can no see whether I do or no anyway.*

Egeanin suddenly stood. He started to rise as well, and made it as far as one knee before a growl in her throat and a scandalized look on the face of the man with the braid put him back down, face to the floor and muttering under his breath. *I would no do this for the King of Illian and the Council of Nine together.*

"Your name is Egeanin?" It had to be the voice of the man in the blue robe. His slurring speech had a rhythm almost like singing.

"I was so named on my sword-day, High Lord," she replied humbly.

"This is a fine specimen, Egeanin. Quite rare. Do you wish a payment?"

"That the High Lord is pleased is payment enough. I live to serve, High Lord."

"I will mention your name to the Empress, Egeanin. After the Return, new names will be called to the Blood.

Show yourself fit, and you may shed the name Egeanin for a higher."

"The High Lord honors me."

"Yes. You may leave me."

Domon could see nothing but her boots backing out of the room, pausing at intervals for bows. The door closed behind her. There was a long silence. He was watching sweat from his forehead drip onto the floor when Turak spoke again.

"You may rise, trader."

Domon got to his feet, and saw what Turak held in his long-nailed fingers. The *cuendillar* disk shaped into the ancient seal of the Aes Sedai. Remembering Egeanin's reaction when he mentioned Aes Sedai, Domon began to sweat in earnest. There was no animosity in the High Lord's dark eyes, only a slight curiosity, but Domon did not trust lords.

"Do you know what this is, trader?"

"No, High Lord." Domon's reply was as steady as a rock; no trader lasted long who could not lie with a straight face and an easy voice.

"And yet you kept it in a secret place."

"I do collect old things, High Lord, from times past. There do be those who would steal such, did they lay easy to hand."

Turak regarded the black-and-white disk for a moment. "This is *cuendillar*, trader—do you know that name?—and older than you perhaps know. Come with me."

Domon followed the man cautiously, feeling a little more sure of himself. With any lord of the lands he knew, if guards were going to be summoned, they already would have been. But the little he had seen of Seanchan told him they did not do things as other men did. He schooled his face to stillness.

He was led into another room. He thought the furniture here had to have been brought by Turak. It seemed to be made of curves, with no straight lines at all, and the wood was polished to bring out strange graining. There was one chair, on a silk carpet woven in birds and flowers, and one large cabinet made in a circle. Folding screens made new walls.

The man with the braid opened the doors of the cabinet to reveal shelves holding an odd assortment of figurines, cups, bowls, vases, fifty different things, no two alike in

size or shape. Domon's breath caught as Turak carefully set
the disk beside its exact twin.

"*Cuendillar,*" Turak said. "That is what I collect, trader.
Only the Empress herself has a finer collection."

Domon's eyes almost popped out of his head. If everything on those shelves was truly *cuendillar*, it was enough
to buy a kingdom, or at the least to found a great House.
Even a king might beggar himself to buy so much of it, if he
even knew where to find so much. He put on a smile.

"High Lord, please accept this piece as a gift." He did
not want to let it go, but that was better than angering this
Seanchan. *Maybe the Darkfriends will chase him now.* "I
do be but a simple trader. I want only to trade. Let me sail,
and I do promise that—"

Turak's expression never changed, but the man with the
braid cut Domon off with a snapped, "Unshaven dog! You
speak of giving the High Lord what Captain Egeanin has
already given. You bargain, as if the High Lord were a—a
merchant! You will be flayed alive over nine days, dog,
and—" The barest motion of Turak's finger silenced him.

"I cannot allow you to leave me, trader," the High Lord
said. "In this shadowed land of oath-breakers, I find none
who can converse with a man of sensibilities. But you are a
collector. Perhaps your conversation will be interesting." He
took the chair, lolling back in its curves to study Domon.

Domon put on what he hoped was an ingratiating smile.
"High Lord, I do be a simple trader, a simple man. I do no
have the way of talking with great Lords."

The man with the braid glared at him, but Turak seemed
not to hear. From behind one of the screens, a slim, pretty
young woman appeared on quick feet to kneel beside the
High Lord, offering a lacquered tray bearing a single cup,
thin and handleless, of some steaming black liquid. Her
dark, round face was vaguely reminiscent of the Sea Folk.
Turak took the cup carefully in his long-nailed fingers,
never looking at the young woman, and inhaled the fumes.
Domon took one look at the girl and pulled his eyes away
with a strangled gasp; her white silk robe was embroidered
with flowers, but so sheer he could see right through it, and
there was nothing beneath but her own slimness.

"The aroma of *kaf,*" Turak said, "is almost as enjoyable as
the flavor. Now, trader. I have learned that *cuendillar* is ever

more rare here than in Seanchan. Tell me how a simple trader came to possess a piece." He sipped his *kaf* and waited.

Domon took a deep breath and set about trying to lie his way out of Falme.

CHAPTER
30

Daes Dae'mar

In the room shared by Hurin and Loial, Rand peered through the window at the ordered lines and terraces of Cairhien, the stone buildings and slate roofs. He could not see the Illuminators' chapter house; even if huge towers and great lords' houses had not been in the way, the city walls would have prevented it. The Illuminators were on everyone's tongues in the city, even now, days after the night when they had lofted only one nightflower into the sky, and that early. A dozen different versions of the scandal were being told, discounting minor variations, but none close to the truth.

Rand turned away. He hoped no one had been hurt in the fire, but the Illuminators had not so far admitted there had been a fire. They were a close-mouthed lot about what went on inside their chapter house.

"I will take the next watch," he told Hurin, "as soon as I come back."

"There is no need, my Lord." Hurin bowed as deeply as any Cairhienin. "I can keep watch. Truly, my Lord need not trouble himself."

Rand drew a deep breath and exchanged looks with Loial. The Ogier only shrugged. The sniffer was growing more formal every day they remained in Cairhien; the Ogier simply commented that humans often acted oddly.

"Hurin," Rand said, "you used to call me Lord Rand, and you used not to bow every time I looked at you." *I want him to unbend and call me Lord Rand again*, he thought with amazement. *Lord Rand! Light, we have to get out of here before I start* wanting *him to bow.* "Will you please sit down? You make me tired, looking at you."

Hurin stood with his back stiff, yet appeared ready to leap to perform any task Rand might request. He neither sat down nor relaxed now. "It wouldn't be proper, my Lord. We have to show these Cairhienin we know how to be every bit as proper as—"

"Will you stop saying that!" Rand shouted.

"As you wish, my Lord."

It was an effort for Rand not to sigh again. "Hurin, I'm sorry. I should not have shouted at you."

"It's your right, my Lord," Hurin said simply. "If I don't do the way you want, it's your right to shout."

Rand stepped toward the sniffer with the intention of grabbing the man's collar and shaking him.

A knock on the connecting door to Rand's room froze them all, but Rand was pleased to see that Hurin did not wait to ask permission before picking up his sword. The heron-mark blade was at Rand's waist; going out, he touched its hilt. He waited for Loial to seat himself on his long bed, arranging his legs and the tails of his coat to further obscure the blanket-covered chest under the bed, then yanked open the door.

The innkeeper stood there, rocking with eagerness and pushing his tray at Rand. Two sealed parchments lay on the tray. "Forgive me, my Lord," Cuale said breathlessly. "I could not wait until you came down, and then you were not in your own room, and—and. . . . Forgive me, but. . . ." He jiggled the tray.

Rand snatched the invitations—there had been so many—without looking at them, took the innkeeper's arm, and turned him toward the door to the hall. "Thank you, Master Cuale, for taking the trouble. If you'll leave us alone, now, please. . . ."

"But, my Lord," Cuale protested, "these are from—"

"Thank you." Rand pushed the man into the hall and pulled the door shut firmly. He tossed the parchments onto the table. "He hasn't done that before. Loial, do you think he was listening at the door before he knocked?"

"You are starting to think like these Cairhienin." The Ogier laughed, but his ears twitched thoughtfully and he added, "Still, he is Cairhienin, so he may well have been. I don't think we said anything he should not have heard."

Rand tried to remember. None of them had mentioned the Horn of Valere, or Trollocs, or Darkfriends. When he found himself wondering what Cuale could make of what they actually had said, he gave himself a shake. "This place is getting to you, too," he muttered to himself.

"My Lord?" Hurin had picked up the sealed parchments and was gazing wide-eyed at the seals. "My Lord, these are from Lord Barthanes, High Seat of House Damodred, and from"—his voice dropped with awe—"the King."

Rand waved them away. "They still go in the fire like the rest. Un-opened."

"But, my Lord!"

"Hurin," Rand said patiently, "you and Loial between you have explained this Great Game to me. If I go wherever it is they've invited me, the Cairhienin will read something into it and think I am part of somebody's plot. If I don't go, they'll read something into that. If I send back an answer, they will dig for meaning in it, and the same if I don't answer. And since half of Cairhien apparently spies on the other half, everybody knows what I do. I burned the first two, and I will burn these, just like all the others." One day there had been twelve in the pile he tossed into the common-room fireplace, seals unbroken. "Whatever they make of it, at least it's the same for everybody. I am not for anyone in Cairhien, and I am not against anyone."

"I have tried to tell you," Loial said, "I don't think it works that way. Whatever you do, Cairhienin will see some sort of plot in it. At least, that is what Elder Haman always said."

Hurin held the sealed invitations out to Rand as if offering gold. "My Lord, this one bears the personal seal of Galldrian. His personal seal, my Lord. And this one the personal seal of Lord Barthanes, who is next to the King himself in power. My Lord, burn these, and you make enemies as powerful as you can find. Burning them's worked so far because the other Houses are all waiting to see what you're up to, and thinking you must have powerful allies to risk insulting them. But Lord Barthanes—and the King! Insult them, and they'll act for sure."

Rand scrubbed his hands through his hair. "What if I refuse them both?"

"It won't work, my Lord. Every last House has sent you an invitation, now. If you decline these—well, for sure at least one of the other Houses will figure, if you're not allied with the King or Lord Barthanes, then they can answer your insult of burning their invitation. My Lord, I hear the Houses in Cairhien use killers, now. A knife in the street. An arrow from a rooftop. Poison slipped in your wine."

"You could accept them both," Loial suggested. "I know you don't want to, Rand, but it might even be fun. An evening at a lord's manor, or even at the Royal Palace. Rand, the Shienarans believed in you."

Rand grimaced. He knew it had been chance that the Shienarans thought he was a lord; a chance likeness of names, a rumor among the servants, and Moiraine and the Amyrlin stirring it all. But Selene had believed it, too. *Maybe she'll be at one of these.*

Hurin was shaking his head violently, though. "Builder, you don't know *Daes Dae'mar* as well as you think you do. Not the way they play it in Cairhien, not now. With most Houses, it wouldn't matter. Even when they're plotting against each other to the knife, they act like they aren't, out where everybody can see. But not these two. House Damodred held the throne until Laman lost it, and they want it back. The King would crush them, if they weren't nearly as powerful as he is. You can't find bitterer rivals than House Riatin and House Damodred. If my Lord accepts both, both Houses will know it as soon as he sends his answers, and they'll both think he's part of some plot by the other against them. They'll use the knife and the poison as quick as look at you."

"And I suppose," Rand growled, "if I only accept one, the other will think I'm allied with that House." Hurin nodded. "And they will probably try to kill me to stop whatever I'm involved in." Hurin nodded again. "Then do you have any suggestion as to how I avoid *any* of them wanting to see me dead?" Hurin shook his head. "I wish I'd never burned those first two."

"Yes, my Lord. But it wouldn't have made much difference, I'm guessing. Whoever you accepted or rejected, these Cairhienin would see something in it."

Rand held out his hand, and Hurin laid the two folded parchments in it. The one was sealed, not with the Tree and

Crown of House Damodred, but with Barthanes's Charging Boar. The other bore Galldrian's Stag. Personal seals. Apparently he had managed to rouse interest in the highest quarters by doing nothing at all.

"These people are crazy," he said, trying to think of a way out of this.

"Yes, my Lord."

"I will let them see me in the common room with these," he said slowly. Whatever was seen in the common room at midday was known in ten Houses before nightfall, and in all of them by daybreak next. "I won't break the seals. That way, they will know I have not answered either one yet. As long as they are waiting to see which way I jump, maybe I can earn a few more days. Ingtar has to come soon. He has to."

"Now that is thinking like a Cairhienin, my Lord," Hurin said, grinning.

Rand gave him a sour look, then stuffed the parchments into his pocket on top of Selene's letters. "Let's go, Loial. Maybe Ingtar has arrived."

When he and Loial reached the common room, no man and woman in it looked at Rand. Cuale was polishing a silver tray as if his life depended on its gleam. The serving girls hurried between the tables as if Rand and the Ogier did not exist. Every last person at the tables stared into his or her mug as if the secrets of power lay in wine or ale. Not one of them said a word.

After a moment, he pulled the two invitations from his pocket and studied the seals, then stuck them back. Cuale gave a little jump as Rand started for the door. Before it closed behind him, he heard conversation spring up again.

Rand strode down the street so fast that Loial did not have to shorten his stride to stay beside him. "We have to find a way out of the city, Loial. This trick with the invitations can't work more than two or three days. If Ingtar doesn't come by then, we must leave anyway."

"Agreed," Loial said.

"But how?"

Loial began ticking off points on his thick fingers. "Fain is out there, or there would not have been Trollocs in the Foregate. If we ride out, they will be on us as soon as we are out of sight of the city. If we travel with a merchant train, they'll certainly attack it." No merchant would have

more than five or six guards, and they would probably run
as soon as they saw a Trolloc. "If only we knew how many
Trollocs Fain has, and how many Darkfriends. You have cut
his numbers down." He did not mention the Trolloc he had
killed, but from his frown, his long eyebrows hanging down
onto his cheeks, he was thinking of it.

"It doesn't matter how many he has," Rand said. "Ten are
as bad as a hundred. If ten Trollocs attack us, I don't think
we'll get away again." He avoided thinking of the way he
might, just might, deal with ten Trollocs. It had not worked
when he tried to help Loial, after all.

"I do not think we could, either. I don't think we have
money to take passage very far, but even so, if we tried
to reach the Foregate docks—well, Fain must have Darkfriends watching. If he thought we were taking ship, I don't
believe he would care who saw the Trollocs. Even if we
fought free of them somehow, we would have to explain
ourselves to the city guards, and they would certainly not
believe we cannot open the chest, so—"

"We are not letting any Cairhienin see that chest, Loial."

The Ogier nodded. "And the city docks are no good, either." The city docks were reserved for the grain barges and
the pleasure craft of the lords and ladies. No one came to
them without permission. One could look down on them
from the wall, but it was a drop that would break even
Loial's neck. Loial wiggled his thumb as if trying to think
of a point for that, too. "I suppose it is too bad we cannot reach Stedding Tsofu. Trollocs would never come into a
stedding. But I don't suppose they would let us get that far
without attacking."

Rand did not answer. They had reached the big guardhouse just inside the gate by which they had first entered
Cairhien. Outside, the Foregate teemed and milled, and a
pair of guards kept watch on them. Rand thought a man,
dressed in what had once been good Shienaran clothes,
ducked back into the crowd at the sight of him, but he could
not be sure. There were too many people in clothes from
too many lands, all of them hurrying. He went up the steps
into the guardhouse, past breastplated guards on either side
of the door.

The large anteroom had hard wooden benches for people
with business there, mainly folk waiting with a humble

patience, wearing the plain, dark garments that marked the poorer commoners. There were a few Foregaters among them, picked out by shabbiness and bright colors, no doubt hoping for permission to seek work inside the walls.

Rand went straight to the long table in the back of the room. There was only one man seated behind it, not a soldier, with one green bar across his coat. A plump fellow whose skin looked too tight, he adjusted documents on the table and shifted the position of his inkwell twice before looking up at Rand and Loial with a false smile.

"How may I help you, my Lord?"

"The same way I hoped you could help me yesterday," Rand said with more patience than he felt, "and the day before, and the day before that. Has Lord Ingtar come?"

"Lord Ingtar, my Lord?"

Rand took a deep breath and let it out slowly. "Lord Ingtar of House Shinowa, from Shienar. The same man I have asked after every day I've come here."

"No one of that name has entered the city, my Lord."

"Are you certain? Don't you need to look at your lists, at least?"

"My Lord, the lists of foreigners who have come to Cairhien are exchanged among the guardhouses at sunrise and at sunset, and I examine them as soon as they come before me. No Shienaran lord has entered Cairhien in some time."

"And the Lady Selene? Before you ask again, I do not know her House. But I've given you her name, and I have described her to you three times. Isn't that enough?"

The man spread his hands. "I am sorry, my Lord. Not knowing her House makes it very difficult." He had a bland look on his face. Rand wondered whether he would tell even if he knew.

A movement at one of the doors behind the desk caught Rand's eye—a man starting to step into the anteroom, then turning away hurriedly. "Perhaps Captain Caldevwin can help me," Rand told the clerk.

"Captain Caldevwin, my Lord?"

"I just saw him behind you."

"I am sorry, my Lord. If there was a Captain Caldevwin in the guardhouse, I would know."

Rand stared at him until Loial touched his shoulder. "Rand, I think we might as well go."

"Thank you for your help," Rand said in a tight voice. "I will return tomorrow."

"It is my pleasure to do what I may," the man said with his false smile.

Rand stalked out of the guardhouse so fast that Loial had to hurry to catch him up in the street. "He was lying, you know, Loial." He did not slow down, but rather hurried along as if he could burn away some of his frustration through physical exertion. "Caldevwin was there. He could be lying about all of it. Ingtar could already be here, looking for us. I'll bet he knows who Selene is, too."

"Perhaps, Rand. *Daes Dae'mar—*"

"Light, I'm tired of hearing about the Great Game. I don't want to play it. I do not want to be any part of it." Loial walked beside him, saying nothing. "I know," Rand said at last. "They think I'm a lord, and in Cairhien, even outland lords are part of the Game. I wish I'd never put on this coat." *Moiraine*, he thought bitterly. *She's still causing me trouble.* Almost immediately, though, if reluctantly, he admitted that she could hardly be blamed for this. There had always been some reason to pretend to be what he was not. First keeping Hurin's spirits up, and then trying to impress Selene. After Selene, there had not seemed to be any way out of it. His steps slowed until he came to a halt. "When Moiraine let me go, I thought things would be simple again. Even chasing after the Horn, even with—with everything, I thought it would be simple." *Even with* saidin *inside your head?* "Light, what I wouldn't give to have everything be simple again."

"*Ta'veren,*" Loial began.

"I do not want to hear about that, either." Rand started off again as fast as before. "All I want is to give the dagger to Mat, and the Horn to Ingtar." *Then what? Go mad? Die? If I die before I go mad, at least I won't hurt anybody else. But I don't want to die, either. Lan can talk about Sheathing the Sword, but I'm a shepherd, not a Warder.* "If I can just not touch it," he muttered, "maybe I can. . . . Owyn almost made it."

"What, Rand? I didn't hear that."

"It was nothing," Rand said wearily. "I wish Ingtar would get here. And Mat, and Perrin."

They walked along in silence for a time, with Rand lost in thought. Thom's nephew had lasted almost three years by channeling only when he thought he had to. If Owyn had managed to limit how often he channeled, it must be possible to not channel at all, no matter how seductive *saidin* was.

"Rand," Loial said, "there's a fire up ahead."

Rand got rid of his unwelcome thoughts and looked off into the city, frowning. A thick column of black smoke billowed up above the rooftops. He could not see what lay at the base of it, but it was too close to the inn.

"Darkfriends," he said, staring at the smoke. "Trollocs can't come inside the walls without being seen, but Darkfriends. . . . Hurin!" He broke into a run, Loial easily keeping pace beside him.

The closer they came, the more certain it was, until they rounded the last stone-terraced corner and there was The Defender of the Dragonwall, smoke pouring out of its upper windows and flames breaking through the roof. A crowd had gathered in front of the inn. Cuale, shouting and jumping about, was directing men carrying furnishings out into the street. A double line of men passed inside buckets filled with water from a well down the street and empty buckets back out. Most of the people only stood and watched; a new gout of flame burst through the slate roof, and they gave a loud *aaaah*.

Rand pushed through the crowd to the innkeeper. "Where is Hurin?"

"Careful with that table!" Cuale shouted. "Do not scrape it!" He looked at Rand and blinked. His face was smudged with smoke. "My Lord? Who? Your manservant? I do not remember seeing him, my Lord. No doubt he went out. Do not drop those candlesticks, fool! They are silver!" Cuale danced off to harangue the men lugging his belongings out of the inn.

"Hurin wouldn't have gone out," Loial said. "He would not have left the. . . ." He looked around and left it unsaid; some of the onlookers seemed to find an Ogier as interesting as the fire.

"I know," Rand said, and plunged into the inn.

The common room hardly seemed as if the building were on fire. The double line of men stretched up the stairs, passing their buckets, and others scrambled to carry out what furniture was left, but there was no more smoke down here than if something had been burning the kitchen. As Rand pressed upstairs, it began to thicken. Coughing, he ran up the steps.

The lines stopped short of the second landing, men halfway up the stairs hurling their water up into a smoke-filled hallway. Flames licking up the walls flickered red through the black smoke.

One of the men grabbed Rand's arm. "You cannot go up there, my Lord. It is all lost above here. Ogier, speak to him."

It was the first Rand realized that Loial had followed him. "Go back, Loial. I'll bring him out."

"You cannot carry Hurin and the chest both, Rand." The Ogier shrugged. "Besides, I won't leave my books to burn."

"Then keep low. Under the smoke." Rand dropped to his hands and knees on the stairs, and scrambled up the rest of the way. There was cleaner air down near the floor; still smoky enough to make him cough, but he could breathe it. Yet even the air seemed blistering hot. He could not get enough of it through his nose. He breathed through his mouth, and felt his tongue drying.

Some of the water the men threw landed on him, soaking him to the skin. The coolness was only a momentary relief; the heat came right back. He crawled on determinedly, aware of Loial behind him only from the Ogier's coughing.

One wall of the hallway was almost solid flame, and the floor near it had already begun to add thin tendrils to the cloud that hung over his head. He was glad he could not see what lay above the smoke. Ominous crackling told enough.

The door to Hurin's room had not caught yet, but it was hot enough that he had to try twice before he could manage to push it open. The first thing to meet his eye was Hurin, sprawled on the floor. Rand crawled to the sniffer and lifted him up. There was a lump on the side of his head the size of a plum.

Hurin opened unfocused eyes. "Lord Rand?" he murmured faintly. ". . . knock at the door . . . thought it was more invi. . . ." His eyes rolled back in his head. Rand felt for a heartbeat, and sagged with relief when he found it.

"Rand. . . ." Loial coughed. He was beside his bed, with the covers thrown up to reveal the bare boards underneath. The chest was gone.

Above the smoke, the ceiling creaked, and flaming pieces of wood fell to the floor.

Rand said, "Get your books. I will take Hurin. Hurry." He started to drape the limp sniffer over his shoulders, but Loial took Hurin from him.

"The books will have to burn, Rand. You can't carry him and crawl, and if you stand up, you will never reach the stairs." The Ogier pulled Hurin up onto his broad back, arms and legs hanging to either side. The ceiling gave a loud crack. "We must hurry, Rand."

"Go, Loial. Go, and I'll follow."

The Ogier crawled into the hall with his burden, and Rand started after him. Then he stopped, staring back at the connecting door to his room. The banner was still in there. The banner of the Dragon. *Let it burn*, he thought, and an answering thought came as if he had heard Moiraine say it. *Your life may depend on it. She's still trying to use me. Your life may depend on it. Aes Sedai never lie.*

With a groan, he rolled across the floor and kicked open the door to his room.

The other room was a mass of flame. The bed was a bonfire, red runners already crossed the floor. There would be no crawling across that. Getting to his feet, he ran crouching into the room, flinching from the heat, coughing, choking. Steam rose from his damp coat. One side of the wardrobe was already burning. He snatched open the door. His saddlebags lay inside, still protected from the fire, one side bulging with the banner of Lews Therin Telamon, the wooden flute case beside them. For an instant, he hesitated. *I could still let it burn.*

The ceiling above him groaned. He grabbed saddlebags and flute case and threw himself back through the door, landing on his knees as burning timbers crashed where he had stood. Dragging his burden, he crawled into the hall. The floor shook with more falling beams.

The men with the buckets were gone when he reached the stairs. He all but slid down the steps to the next landing, scrambled to his feet and ran through the now-empty building into the street. The onlookers stared at him, with his face blackened and his coat covered with smut, but he staggered to where Loial had propped Hurin against the wall of a house across the street. A woman from the crowd was wiping Hurin's face with a cloth, but his eyes were still closed, and his breath came in heaves.

"Is there a Wisdom nearby?" Rand demanded. "He needs help." The woman looked at him blankly, and he tried to remember the other names he had heard people call the women who would be Wisdoms in the Two Rivers. "A Wise Woman? A woman you call Mother somebody? A woman who knows herbs and healing?"

"I am a Reader, if that is what you mean," the woman said, "but all I know to do for this one is to make him comfortable. Something is broken inside his head, I fear."

"Rand! It *is* you!"

Rand stared. It was Mat, leading his horse through the crowd, with his bow strung across his back. A Mat whose face was pale and drawn, but still Mat, and grinning, if weakly. And behind him came Perrin, his yellow eyes shining in the fire and earning as many looks as the blaze. And Ingtar, dismounting in a high-collared coat instead of armor, but still with his sword hilt sticking up over his shoulder.

Rand felt a shiver run through him. "It's too late," he told them. "You came too late." And he sat down in the street and began to laugh.

CHAPTER

31

On the Scent

Rand did not know Verin was there until the Aes Sedai took his face in her hands. For a moment he could see worry in her face, perhaps even fear, and then suddenly he felt as if he had been doused with cold water, not the wet but the tingle. He gave one abrupt shudder and stopped laughing; she left him to crouch over Hurin. The Reader watched her carefully. So did Rand. *What is she doing here? As if I didn't know.*

"Where did you go?" Mat demanded hoarsely. "You all just disappeared, and now you're in Cairhien ahead of us. Loial?" The Ogier shrugged uncertainly and eyed the crowd, his ears twitching. Half the people had turned from the fire to watch the newcomers. A few edged closer trying to listen.

Rand let Perrin give him a hand up. "How did you find the inn?" He glanced at Verin, kneeling with her hands on the sniffer's head. "Her?"

"In a way," Perrin said. "The guards at the gate wanted our names, and a fellow coming out of the guardhouse gave a jump when he heard Ingtar's name. He said he didn't know it, but he had a smile that shouted 'lie' a mile off."

"I think I know the man you mean," Rand said. "He smiles that way all the time."

"Verin showed him her ring," Mat put in, "and whispered in his ear." He looked and sounded sick, his cheeks flushed and tight, but he managed a grin. Rand had never noticed his cheekbones before. "I couldn't hear what she said, but I didn't know whether his eyes were going to pop out of his head or he was going to swallow his tongue first. All of a

sudden, he couldn't do enough for us. He told us you were
waiting for us, and right where you were staying. Offered to
guide us himself, but he really looked relieved when Verin
told him no." He snorted. "Lord Rand of House al'Thor."

"It's too long a story to explain now," Rand said. "Where
are Uno and the rest? We will need them."

"In the Foregate." Mat frowned at him, and went on
slowly, "Uno said they'd rather stay there than inside the
walls. From what I can see, I'd rather be with them. Rand,
why will we need Uno? Have you found . . . *them*?"

It was the moment Rand realized suddenly he had been
avoiding. He took a deep breath and looked his friend in the
eye. "Mat, I had the dagger, and I lost it. The Darkfriends
took it back." He heard gasps from the Cairhienin listening,
but he did not care. They could play their Great Game if
they wanted, but Ingtar had come, and he was finished with
it at last. "They can't have gone far, though."

Ingtar had been silent, but now he stepped forward and
gripped Rand's arm. "You had it? And the"—he looked
around at the onlookers—"the other thing?"

"They took that back, too," Rand said quietly. Ingtar
pounded a fist into his palm and turned away; some of the
Cairhienin backed off from the look on his face.

Mat chewed his lip, then shook his head. "I didn't know
it was found, so it isn't as if I had lost it again. It is just still
lost." It was plain he was speaking of the dagger, not the
Horn of Valere. "We'll find it again. We have two sniffers,
now. Perrin is one, too. He followed the trail all the way
to the Foregate, after you vanished with Hurin and Loial.
I thought you might have just run off . . . well, you know
what I mean. Where *did* you go? I still don't understand
how you got so far ahead of us. That fellow said you have
been here days."

Rand glanced at Perrin—*He's a sniffer?*—and found
Perrin studying him in return. He thought Perrin muttered
something. *Shadowkiller? I must have heard him wrong.*
Perrin's yellow gaze held him for a moment, seeming to
hold secrets about him. Telling himself he was having
fancies—*I'm not mad. Not yet.*—he pulled his eyes away.

Verin was just helping a still-shaky Hurin to his feet. "I
feel right as goose feathers," he was saying. "Still a little
tired, but. . . ." He let the words trail off, seeming to see her

for the first time, to realize what had happened for the first time.

"The tiredness will last a few hours," she told him. "The body must strain to heal itself quickly."

The Cairhienin Reader rose. "Aes Sedai?" she said softly. Verin inclined her head, and the Reader made a full curtsy.

As quiet as they had been, the words "Aes Sedai" ran through the crowd in tones ranging from awe to fear to outrage. Everyone was watching now—not even Cuale gave any attention to his own burning inn—and Rand thought a little caution might not be amiss after all.

"Do you have rooms yet?" he asked. "We need to talk, and we can't do it here."

"A good idea," Verin said. "I have stayed here before at The Great Tree. We will go there."

Loial went to fetch the horses—the inn roof had now fallen in completely, but the stables had not been touched—and soon they were making their way through the streets, all riding except for Loial, who claimed he had grown used to walking again. Perrin held the lead line to one of the packhorses they had brought south.

"Hurin," Rand said, "how soon can you be ready to follow their trail again? Can you follow it? The men who hit you and started the fire left a trail, didn't they?"

"I can follow it now, my Lord. And I could smell them in the street. It won't last long, though. There weren't any Trollocs, and they didn't kill anybody. Just men, my Lord. Darkfriends, I suppose, but you can't always be sure of that by smell. A day, maybe, before it fades."

"I don't think they can open the chest either, Rand," Loial said, "or they would just have taken the Horn. It would be much easier to take that if they could, rather than the whole chest."

Rand nodded. "They must have put it in a cart, or on a horse. Once they get it beyond the Foregate, they'll join the Trollocs again, for sure. You will be able to follow that trail, Hurin."

"I will, my Lord."

"Then you rest until you're fit," Rand told him. The sniffer looked steadier, but he rode slumped, and his face was weary. "At best, they will only be a few hours ahead of us. If we ride hard. . . ." Suddenly he noticed that the others were looking at him, Verin and Ingtar, Mat and Perrin. He realized what he had been doing, and his face colored. "I am sorry, Ingtar. It's just that I've become used to being in charge, I suppose. I'm not trying to take your place."

Ingtar nodded slowly. "Moiraine chose well when she made Lord Agelmar name you my second. Perhaps it would have been better if the Amyrlin Seat had given you the charge." The Shienaran barked a laugh. "At least you have actually managed to touch the Horn."

After that they rode in silence.

The Great Tree could have been twin to The Defender of the Dragonwall, a tall stone cube of a building with a common room paneled in dark wood and decorated with silver, a large, polished clock on the mantel over the fireplace. The innkeeper could have been Cuale's sister. Mistress Tiedra had the same slightly plump look and the same unctuous manner—and the same sharp eyes, the same air of listening to what was behind the words you spoke. But Tiedra knew Verin, and her welcoming smile for the Aes Sedai was warm; she never mentioned Aes Sedai aloud, but Rand was sure she knew.

Tiedra and a swarm of servants saw to their horses and settled them in their rooms. Rand's room was as fine as the one that had burned, but he was more interested in the big copper bathtub two serving men wrestled through the door, and the steaming buckets of water scullery maids brought up from the kitchen. One look in the mirror above the washstand showed him a face that looked as if he had rubbed it with charcoal, and his coat had black smears across the red wool.

He stripped off and climbed into the tub, but he thought as much as washed. Verin was there. One of three Aes Sedai that he could trust not to try to gentle him themselves, or turn him over to those who would. Or so it seemed, at least. One of three who wanted him to believe he was the Dragon Reborn, to use him as a false Dragon. *She's Moiraine's eyes watching me, Moiraine's hand trying to pull my strings. But I have cut the strings.*

His saddlebags had been brought up, and a bundle from the packhorse containing fresh clothes. He toweled off and opened the bundle—and sighed. He had forgotten that both the other coats he had were as ornate as the one he had tossed on the back of a chair for a maid to clean. After a moment, he chose the black coat, to suit his mood. Silver herons stood on the high collar, and silver rapids ran down his sleeves, water battered to froth against jagged rocks.

Transferring things from his old coat to his new, he found the parchments. Absently, he stuffed the invitations in his pocket as he studied Selene's two letters. He wondered how he could have been such a fool. She was the beautiful young daughter of a noble House. He was a shepherd whom Aes Sedai were trying to use, a man doomed to go mad if he did not die first. Yet he could still feel the pull of her just looking at her writing, could almost smell the perfume of her.

"I am a shepherd," he told the letters, "not a great man, and if I could marry anyone, it would be Egwene, but she wants to be Aes Sedai, and how can I marry any woman, love any woman, when I'll go mad and maybe kill her?"

Words could not lessen his memory of Selene's beauty, though, or the way she made his blood go warm just by looking at him. It almost seemed to him that she was in the room with him, that he could smell her perfume, so much so that he looked around, and laughed to find himself alone.

"Having fancies like I'm addled already," he muttered.

Abruptly he tipped back the mantle of the lamp on the bedside table, lit it, and thrust the letters into the flame. Outside the inn, the wind picked up to a roar, leaking in through the shutters and fanning the flames to engulf the parchment. Hurriedly he tossed the burning letters into the cold hearth just before the fire reached his fingers. He waited until the last blackened curl went out before he buckled on his sword and left the room.

Verin had taken a private dining room, where shelves along the dark walls held even more silver than those in the common room. Mat was juggling three boiled eggs and trying to appear nonchalant. Ingtar peered into the unlit fireplace, frowning. Loial had a few books from Fal Dara still in his pockets, and was reading one beside a lamp.

Perrin slouched at the table, studying his hands clasped on the tabletop. To his nose, the room smelled of beeswax used to polish the paneling. *It was him*, he thought. *Rand is the Shadowkiller. Light, what's happening to all of us?* His hands tightened into fists, large and square. *These hands were meant for a smith's hammer, not an axe.*

He glanced up as Rand entered. Perrin thought he looked determined, set on some course of action. The Aes Sedai motioned Rand to a high-backed armchair across from her.

"How is Hurin?" Rand asked her, arranging his sword so he could sit. "Resting?"

"He insisted on going out," Ingtar answered. "I told him to follow the trail only until he smelled Trollocs. We can follow it from there tomorrow. Or do you want to go after them tonight?"

"Ingtar," Rand said uneasily, "I really wasn't trying to take command. I just didn't think." Yet not as nervously as he would have once, Perrin thought. *Shadowkiller. We're all of us changing.*

Ingtar did not answer, but only kept staring into the fireplace.

"There are some things that interest me greatly, Rand," Verin said quietly. "One is how you vanished from Ingtar's camp without a trace. Another is how you arrived in Cairhien a week before us. That clerk was very clear on that. You would have had to fly."

One of Mat's eggs hit the floor and cracked. He did not look at it, though. He was looking at Rand, and Ingtar had turned around. Loial pretended to be reading still, but he wore a worried look, and his ears were up in hairy points.

Perrin realized he was staring, too. "Well, he did not fly," he said. "I don't see any wings. Maybe he has more important things to tell us." Verin shifted her attention to him, just for a moment. He managed to meet her eyes, but he was the first to look away. *Aes Sedai. Light, why were we ever fools enough to follow an Aes Sedai?* Rand gave him a grateful look, too, and Perrin grinned at him. He was not the old Rand—he seemed to have grown into that fancy coat; it looked right on him, now—but he was still the boy Perrin had grown up with. *Shadowkiller. A man the wolves hold in awe. A man who can channel.*

"I don't mind," Rand said, and told his tale simply.

Perrin found himself gaping. Portal Stones. Other worlds, where the land seemed to shift. Hurin following the trail of where the Darkfriends *would* be. And a beautiful woman in distress, just like one in a gleeman's tale.

Mat gave a soft, wondering whistle. "And she brought you back? By one of these—these Stones?"

Rand hesitated for a second. "She must have," he said. "So you see, that's how we got so far ahead of you. When Fain came, Loial and I managed to steal back the Horn of Valere in the night, and we rode on to Cairhien because I didn't think we could make it past them once they were roused, and I knew Ingtar would keep coming south after them and reach Cairhien eventually."

Shadowkiller. Rand looked at him, eyes narrowing, and Perrin realized he had spoken the name aloud. Apparently not loud enough for anyone else to hear, though. No one else glanced at him. He found himself wanting to tell Rand about the wolves. *I know about you. It's only fair you know my secret, too.* But Verin was there. He could not say it in front of her.

"Interesting," the Aes Sedai said, a thoughtful expression on her face. "I would very much like to meet this girl. If she can use a Portal Stone. . . . Even that name is not very widely known." She gave herself a shake. "Well, that is for another time. A tall girl should not be difficult to find in the Cairhienin Houses. Aah, here is our meal."

Perrin smelled lamb even before Mistress Tiedra led in a procession bearing trays of food. His mouth watered more for that than for the peas and squash, the carrots and cabbage that came with it, or the hot crusty rolls. He still found vegetables tasty, but sometimes, of late, he dreamed of red meat. Not even cooked, usually. It was disconcerting to find himself thinking that the nicely pink slices of lamb that the innkeeper carved were too well done. He firmly took helpings of everything. And two of the lamb.

It was a quiet meal, with everyone concentrating on his own thoughts. Perrin found it painful to watch Mat eat. Mat's appetite was as healthy as ever, despite the feverish flush to his face, and the way he shoveled food into his mouth made it look like his last meal before dying. Perrin kept his eyes on his plate as much as possible, and wished they had never left Emond's Field.

After the maids cleared the table and left again, Verin insisted they remain together until Hurin returned. "He may bring word that will mean we must move at once."

Mat returned to his juggling, and Loial to his reading. Rand asked the innkeeper if there were any more books, and she brought him *The Travels of Jain Farstrider*. Perrin liked that one, too, with its stories of adventures among the Sea Folk and journeys to the lands beyond the Aiel Waste, where silk came from. He did not feel like reading, though, so he set up a stones board on the table with Ingtar. The Shienaran played with a slashing, daring style. Perrin had always played doggedly, giving ground reluctantly, but he found himself placing the stones with as much reckless-ness as Ingtar. Most of the games ended in a draw, but he managed to win as many as Ingtar did. The Shienaran was eyeing him with a new respect by early evening, when the sniffer returned.

Hurin's grin was at the same time triumphant and per-plexed. "I found them, Lord Ingtar. Lord Rand. I tracked them to their lair."

"Lair?" Ingtar said sharply. "You mean they're hiding somewhere close by?"

"Aye, Lord Ingtar. The ones who took the Horn, I fol-lowed straight there, and there was Trolloc scent all around the place, though sneaking as if they didn't dare be seen, even there. And no wonder." The sniffer took a deep breath. "It's the great manor Lord Barthanes just finished building."

"Lord Barthanes!" Ingtar exclaimed. "But he . . . he's . . . he's. . . ."

"There are Darkfriends among the high as well as the low," Verin said smoothly. "The mighty give their souls to the Shadow as often as the weak." Ingtar scowled as if he did not want to think of that.

"There's guards," Hurin went on. "We'll not get in with twenty men, not and get out again. A hundred could do it, but two would be better. That's what I think, my Lord."

"What about the King?" Mat demanded. "If this Bar-thanes is a Darkfriend, the King will help us."

"I am quite sure," Verin said dryly, "that Galldrian Ria-tin would move against Barthanes Damodred on the *ru-mor* that Barthanes is a Darkfriend, and glad of the excuse. I am also quite sure Galldrian would never let the Horn of Valere out of his grasp once he had it. He would bring it out on feastdays to show the people and tell them how great and mighty Cairhien is, and no one would ever see it else."

Perrin blinked with shock. "But the Horn of Valere has to be there when the Last Battle is fought. He couldn't just keep it."

"I know little of Cairhienin," Ingtar told him, "but I've heard enough of Galldrian. He would feast us and thank us for the glory we had brought to Cairhien. He would stuff our pockets with gold and heap honors on our heads. And if we tried to leave with the Horn, he'd cut our honored heads off without pausing to take a breath."

Perrin ran a hand through his hair. The more he found out about kings, the less he liked them.

"What about the dagger?" Mat asked diffidently. "He wouldn't want that, would he?" Ingtar glared at him, and he shifted uncomfortably. "I know the Horn is important, but I'm not going to be fighting in the Last Battle. That dagger. . . ."

Verin rested her hands on the arms of her chair. "Galldrian shall not have it, either. What we need is some way inside Barthanes's manor house. If we can only find the Horn, we may also find a way to take it back. Yes, Mat, and the dagger. Once it is known that an Aes Sedai is in the city—well, I usually avoid these things, but if I let slip to Tiedra that I would like to see Barthanes's new manor, I should have an invitation in a day or two. It should not be difficult to bring at least some of the rest of you. What is it, Hurin?"

The sniffer had been rocking anxiously on his heels from the moment she mentioned an invitation. "Lord Rand already has one. From Lord Barthanes."

Perrin stared at Rand, and he was not the only one.

Rand pulled two sealed parchments from his coat pocket and handed them to the Aes Sedai without a word.

Ingtar came to look wonderingly over her shoulder at the seals. "Barthanes, and. . . . And Galldrian! Rand, how did you come by these? What have you been doing?"

"Nothing," Rand said. "I haven't done anything. They just sent them to me." Ingtar let out a long breath. Mat's mouth was hanging open. "Well, they did just send them," Rand said quietly. There was a dignity to him that Perrin did not remember; Rand was looking at the Aes Sedai and the Shienaran lord as equals.

Perrin shook his head. *You are fitting that coat. We're all changing.*

"Lord Rand burned all the rest," Hurin said. "Every day they came, and every day he burned them. Until these, of course. Every day from mightier Houses." He sounded proud.

"The Wheel of Time weaves us all into the Pattern as it wills," Verin said, looking at the parchments, "but sometimes it provides what we need before we know we need it."

Casually she crumpled the King's invitation and tossed it into the fireplace, where it lay white on the cold logs. Breaking the other seal with her thumb, she read. "Yes. Yes, this will do very well."

"How can I go?" Rand asked her. "They will know I'm no lord. I am a shepherd, and a farmer." Ingtar looked skeptical. "I am, Ingtar. I told you I am." Ingtar shrugged; he still did not look convinced. Hurin stared at Rand with flat disbelief.

Burn me, Perrin thought, *if I didn't know him, I wouldn't believe it either.* Mat was watching Rand with his head tilted, frowning as if looking at something he had never seen before. *He sees it, too, now.* "You can do it, Rand," Perrin said. "You can."

"It will help," Verin said, "if you don't tell everyone what you are not. People see what they expect to see. Beyond that, look them in the eye and speak firmly. The way you have been talking to me," she added dryly, and Rand's cheeks colored, but he did not drop his eyes. "It doesn't matter what you say. They will attribute anything out of place to your being an outlander. It will also help if you remember the way you behaved before the Amyrlin. If you are that arrogant, they will believe you are a lord if you wear rags." Mat snickered.

Rand threw up his hands. "All right. I'll do it. But I still think they will know five minutes after I open my mouth. When?"

"Barthanes has asked you for five different dates, and one is tomorrow night."

"Tomorrow!" Ingtar exploded. "The Horn could be fifty miles downriver by tomorrow night, or—"

Verin cut him off. "Uno and your soldiers can watch the manor. If they try to take the Horn anywhere, we can easily follow, and perhaps retrieve it more easily than from inside Barthanes's walls."

"Perhaps so," Ingtar agreed grudgingly. "I just do not like to wait, now that the Horn is almost in my hands. I will have it. I must! I must!"

Hurin stared at him. "But, Lord Ingtar, that isn't the way. What happens, happens, and what is meant to be, will—" Ingtar's glare cut him off, though he still muttered under his breath, "It isn't the way, talking of 'must.' "

Ingtar turned back to Verin stiffly. "Verin Sedai, Cairhienin are very strict in their protocol. If Rand does not send a reply, Barthanes may be so insulted he will not let us in, even with that parchment in our hands. But if Rand does . . . well, Fain, at least, knows him. We could be warning them to set a trap."

"We will surprise them." Her brief smile was not pleasant. "But I think Barthanes will want to see Rand in any case. Darkfriend or not, I doubt he has given up plots against the throne. Rand, he says you took an interest in one of the King's projects, but he doesn't say what. What does he mean?"

"I don't know," Rand said slowly. "I haven't done anything at all since I arrived. Wait. Maybe he means the statue. We came through a village where they were digging up a huge statue. From the Age of Legends, they said. The King means to move it to Cairhien, though I don't know how he can move something that big. But all I did was ask what it was."

"We passed it in the day, and did not stop to ask questions." Verin let the invitation fall in her lap. "Not a wise thing for Galldrian to do, perhaps, unearthing that. Not that there is any real danger, but it is never wise for those who don't know what they are doing to meddle with things from the Age of Legends."

"What is it?" Rand asked.

"A *sa'angreal*." She sounded as if it were really not very important, but Perrin suddenly had the feeling the two of them had entered a private conversation, saying things no one else could hear. "One of a pair, the two largest ever made, that we know of. And an odd pair, as well. One, still buried on Tremalking, can only be used by a woman. This one can only be used by a man. They were made during the War of the Powers, to be a weapon, but if there is anything to be thankful for in the end of that Age or the Breaking of the World, it is that the end came before they could be used. Together, they might well be powerful enough to Break the World again, perhaps even worse than the first Breaking."

Perrin's hands tightened to knots. He avoided looking directly at Rand, but even from the corner of his eye he could see a whiteness around Rand's mouth. He thought Rand might be afraid, and he did not blame him a bit.

Ingtar looked shaken, as well he might. "That thing should be buried again, and as deeply as they can pile dirt and stone. What would have happened if Logain had found it? Or any wretched man who can channel, let alone one claiming he's the Dragon Reborn. Verin Sedai, you must warn Galldrian what he's doing."

"What? Oh, there is no need for that, I think. The two must be used in unison to handle enough of the One Power to Break the World—that was the way in the Age of Legends; a man and a woman working together were always ten times as strong as they were apart—and what Aes Sedai today would aid a man in channeling? One by itself is powerful enough, but I can think of few women strong enough to survive the flow through the one on Tremalking. The Amyrlin, of course. Moiraine, and Elaida. Perhaps one or two others. And three still in training. As for Logain, it would have taken all his strength simply to keep from being burned to a cinder, with nothing left for doing anything. No, Ingtar, I don't think you need worry. At least, not until the real Dragon Reborn proclaims himself, and then we will all have enough to worry about as it is. Let us worry now about what we shall do when we are inside Barthanes's manor."

She was talking to Rand. Perrin knew it, and from the queasy look in Mat's eye, he did, too. Even Loial shifted nervously in his chair. *Oh, Light, Rand,* Perrin thought. *Light, don't let her use you.*

Rand's hands were pressing the tabletop so hard that his knuckles were white, but his voice was steady. His eyes never left the Aes Sedai. "First we have to take back the Horn, and the dagger. And then it is done, Verin. Then it is done."

Watching Verin's smile, small and mysterious, Perrin felt a chill. He did not think Rand knew half what he thought he did. Not half.

CHAPTER

32

Dangerous Words

Lord Barthanes's manor crouched like a huge toad in the night, covering as much ground as a fortress, with all its walls and outbuildings. It was no fortress, though, with tall windows everywhere, and lights, and the sounds of music and laughter drifting out, yet Rand saw guards moving on the tower tops and along the roofwalks, and none of the windows were close to the ground. He got down from Red's back and smoothed his coat, adjusted his sword belt. The others dismounted around him, at the foot of broad, whitestone stairs leading up to the wide, heavily carved doors of the manor.

Ten Shienarans, under Uno, made an escort. The one-eyed man exchanged small nods with Ingtar before taking his men to join the other escorts, where ale had been provided and a whole ox was roasting on a spit by a big fire.

The other ten Shienarans had been left behind, along with Perrin. Every one of them had to be there for a purpose, Verin had said, and Perrin had no purpose to serve this night. An escort was necessary for dignity in Cairhienin eyes, but more than ten would seem suspicious. Rand was there because he had received the invitation. Ingtar had come to lend the prestige of his title, while Loial was there because Ogier were sought after in the upper reaches of the Cairhienin nobility. Hurin pretended to be Ingtar's bodyservant. His true purpose was to sniff out the Darkfriends and Trollocs if he could; the Horn of Valere should not be far from them. Mat, still grumbling about it, was pretending to be Rand's servant, since he could feel the dagger when it was close. If Hurin failed, perhaps he could find the Dark-friends.

When Rand had asked Verin why she was there, she had only smiled and said, "To keep the rest of you out of trouble."

As they mounted the stairs, Mat muttered, "I still don't see why I have to be a servant." He and Hurin followed behind the others. "Burn me, if Rand can be a lord, I can put on a fancy coat, too."

"A servant," Verin said without looking back at him, "can go many places another man cannot, and many nobles will not even see him. You and Hurin have your tasks."

"Be quiet now, Mat," Ingtar put in, "unless you want to give us away." They were approaching the doors, where half a dozen guards stood with the Tree and Crown of House Damodred on their chests, and an equal number of men in dark green livery with Tree and Crown on the sleeve.

Taking a deep breath, Rand proffered the invitation. "I am Lord Rand of House al'Thor," he said all in a rush, to get it over with. "And these are my guests. Verin Aes Sedai of the Brown Ajah. Lord Ingtar of House Shinowa, in Shienar. Loial, son of Arent son of Halan, from Stedding Shangtai." Loial had asked that his *stedding* be left out of it, but Verin insisted they needed every bit of formality they could offer.

The servant who had reached for the invitation with a perfunctory bow gave a little jerk at each additional name; his eyes popped at Verin's. In a strangled voice he said, "Be welcome in House Damodred, my lords. Be welcome, Aes Sedai. Be welcome, friend Ogier." He waved the other servants to open the doors wide, and bowed Rand and the others inside, where he hurriedly passed the invitation to another liveried man and whispered in his ear.

This man had the Tree and Crown large on the chest of his green coat. "Aes Sedai," he said, using his long staff to make a bow, almost bending his head to his knees, to each of them in turn. "My lords. Friend Ogier. I am called Ashin. Please to follow me."

The outer hall held only servants, but Ashin led them to a great room filled with nobles, with a juggler performing at one end and tumblers at the other. Voices and music coming from elsewhere said these were not the only guests, or the only entertainments. The nobles stood in twos, and threes and fours, sometimes men and women together, sometimes only one or the other, always with careful space between so no one could overhear what was said. The guests wore the dark Cairhienin colors, each with bright stripes at least halfway down his or her chest, and some had them all the way to their waists. The women had their hair piled high in elaborate towers of curls, every one different, and their dark skirts were so wide they would have had to turn sideways to pass through any doorway narrower than those of the manor. None of the men had the shaved heads of soldiers—they all wore dark velvet hats over long hair, some shaped like bells, others flat—and as with the women, lace ruffles like dark ivory almost hid their hands.

Ashin rapped his staff and announced them in a loud voice, Verin first.

They drew every eye. Verin wore her brown-fringed shawl, embroidered in grape vines; the announcement of an Aes Sedai sent a murmur through the lords and ladies, and made the juggler drop one of his hoops, though no one was watching him any longer. Loial received almost as many looks, even before Ashin spoke his name. Despite the silver embroidery on collar and sleeves, the otherwise unrelieved black of Rand's coat made him seem almost stark beside the Cairhienin, and his and Ingtar's swords drew many glances. None of the lords appeared to be armed. Rand heard the words "heron-mark blade" more than once. Some of the glances he was receiving looked like frowns; he suspected they came from men he had insulted by burning their invitations.

A slim, handsome man approached. He had long, graying hair, and multihued stripes crossed the front of his deep gray coat from his neck almost to the hem just above his knees. He was extremely tall for a Cairhienin, no more than half a head shorter than Rand, and he had a way of standing that made him seem even taller, with his chin up so he seemed to be looking down at everyone else. His eyes were black pebbles. He looked warily at Verin, though.

"Grace honors me with your presence, Aes Sedai." Barthanes Damodred's voice was deep and sure. His gaze swept across the others. "I did not expect so distinguished a company. Lord Ingtar. Friend Ogier." His bow to each was little more than a nod of the head; Barthanes knew exactly how powerful he was. "And you, my young Lord Rand. You excite much comment in the city, and in the Houses. Perhaps we will have a chance to talk this night." His tone said that he would not miss it if the chance never came, that he had not been excited to any comment, but his eyes slid a fraction before he caught them, to Ingtar and Loial, and to Verin. "Be welcome." He let himself be drawn away by a handsome woman who laid a beringed hand buried in lace on his arm, but his gaze drifted back to Rand as he walked away.

The murmur of conversation picked up once more, and the juggler spun his hoops again in a narrow loop that almost reached the worked plaster ceiling, a good four spans up. The tumblers had never stopped; a woman leaped into the air from the cupped hands of one of her compatriots, her oiled skin shining in the light of a hundred lamps as she spun, and landed on her feet on the hands of a man who was already standing atop another's shoulders. He lifted her up on outstretched arms as the man below raised him in the same way, and she spread her arms as if for applause. None of the Cairhienin seemed to notice.

Verin and Ingtar drifted into the crowd. The Shienaran received a few wary looks; some looked at the Aes Sedai with wide eyes, others with the worried frowns of those finding a rabid wolf within arm's reach. The latter came from men more often than women, and some of the women spoke to her.

Rand realized that Mat and Hurin had already disappeared to the kitchens, where all the servants who had come with the guests would be gathering until sent for. He hoped they would not have trouble sneaking away.

Loial bent down to speak for his ear alone. "Rand, there is a Waygate nearby. I can feel it."

"You mean this was an Ogier grove?" Rand said softly, and Loial nodded.

"Stedding Tsofu had not been found again when it was planted, or the Ogier who helped build Al'cair'rahienallen would not have needed a grove to remind them of the *stedding*. This was all forest when I came through Cairhien before, and belonged to the King."

"Barthanes probably took it away in some plot." Rand

looked around the room nervously. Everyone was still talking, but more than a few were watching the Ogier and him. He could not see Ingtar. Verin stood at the center of a knot of women. "I wish we could stay together."

"Verin says not, Rand. She says it would make them all suspicious and angry, thinking we were holding ourselves aloof. We have to allay suspicion until Mat and Hurin find whatever they find."

"I heard what she said as well as you, Loial. But I still say, if Barthanes is a Darkfriend, then he must know why we're here. Going off by ourselves is just asking to be knocked on the head."

"Verin says he won't do anything until he finds out whether he can make use of us. Just do what she told us, Rand. Aes Sedai know what they are about." Loial walked into the crowd, gathering a circle of lords and ladies before he had gone ten steps.

Others started toward Rand, now that he was alone, but he turned in the other direction and hurried away. *Aes Sedai may know what they're about, but I wish I did. I don't like this. Light, but I wish I knew if she was telling the truth. Aes Sedai never lie, but the truth you hear may not be the truth you think it is.*

He kept moving to avoid talking with the nobles. There were many other rooms, all filled with lords and ladies, all with entertainers: three different gleemen in their cloaks, more jugglers and tumblers, and musicians playing flutes, bitterns, dulcimers, and lutes, plus five different sizes of fiddle, six kinds of horn, straight or curved or curled, and ten sizes of drum from tambour to kettle. He gave some of the horn players a second look, those with curled horns, but the instruments were all plain brass.

They wouldn't have the Horn of Valere out here, fool, he thought. *Not unless Barthanes means to have dead heroes come as part of the entertainment.*

There was even a bard in silver-worked Tairen boots and a yellow coat, strolling through the rooms plucking his harp and sometimes stopping to declaim in High Chant. He glared contemptuously at the gleemen and did not linger in the rooms where they were, but Rand saw little difference between him and them except for their clothes.

Suddenly Barthanes was walking by Rand's side. A

liveried servant immediately offered his silver tray with a bow. Barthanes took a blown-glass goblet of wine. Walking backwards ahead of them still bowing, the servant held the tray toward Rand until Rand shook his head, then melted into the crowd.

"You seem restless," Barthanes said, sipping.

"I like to walk." Rand wondered how to follow Verin's advice, and remembering what she had said about his visit to the Amyrlin, he settled into Cat Crosses the Courtyard. He knew no more arrogant way to walk than that. Barthanes's mouth tightened, and Rand thought perhaps the lord found it too arrogant, but Verin's advice was all he had to go by, so he did not stop. To take some of the edge off, he said pleasantly, "This is a fine party. You have many friends, and I've never seen so many entertainers."

"Many friends," Barthanes agreed. "You can tell Galldrian how many, and who. Some of the names might surprise him."

"I have never met the King, Lord Barthanes, and I don't expect I ever will."

"Of course. You just happened to be in that flyspeck village. You were not checking on the progress of retrieving that statue. A great undertaking, that."

"Yes." He had begun thinking of Verin again, wishing she had given him some advice on how to talk with a man who assumed he was lying. He added without thinking, "It's dangerous to meddle with things from the Age of Legends if you don't know what you are doing."

Barthanes peered into his wine, musing as if Rand had just said something profound. "Are you saying you do not support Galldrian in this?" he asked finally.

"I told you, I've never met the King."

"Yes, of course. I did not know Andormen played at the Great Game so well. We do not see many here in Cairhien."

Rand took a deep breath to stop from telling the man angrily that he was not playing their Game. "There are many grain barges from Andor in the river."

"Merchants and traders. Who notices such as they? As well notice the beetles on the leaves." Barthanes's voice carried equal contempt for both beetles and merchants, but once again he frowned as if Rand had hinted at something. "Not many men travel in company with Aes Sedai. You seem too young to be a Warder. I suppose Lord Ingtar is Verin Sedai's Warder?"

"We are who we said we are," Rand said, and grimaced. *Except me.*

Barthanes was studying Rand's face almost openly. "Young. Young to carry a heron-mark blade."

"I am less than a year old," Rand said automatically, and immediately wished he had it back. It sounded foolish, to his ear, but Verin had said act as he had with the Amyrlin Seat, and that was the answer Lan had given him. A Borderman considered the day he was given his sword to be his nameday.

"So. An Andorman, and yet Borderland-trained. Or is it Warder-trained?" Barthanes's eyes narrowed, studying Rand. "I understand Morgase has only one son. Named Gawyn, I have heard. You must be much like him in age."

"I have met him," Rand said cautiously.

"Those eyes. That hair. I have heard the Andoran royal line has almost Aiel coloring in their hair and eyes."

Rand stumbled, though the floor was smooth marble. "I'm not Aiel, Lord Barthanes, and I'm not of the royal line, either."

"As you say. You have given me much to think on. I believe we may find common ground when we talk again." Barthanes nodded and raised his glass in a small salute, then turned to speak to a gray-haired man with many stripes of color down his coat.

Rand shook his head and moved on, away from more conversation. It had been bad enough talking to one Cairhienin lord; he did not want to risk two. Barthanes appeared to find deep meanings in the most trivial comments. Rand realized he had just now learned enough of *Daes Dae'mar* to know he had no idea at all how it was played. *Mat, Hurin, find something fast, so we can get out of here. These people are crazy.*

And then he entered another room, and the gleeman at the end of it, strumming his harp and reciting a tale from *The Great Hunt of the Horn*, was Thom Merrilin. Rand stopped dead. Thom did not seem to see him, though the gleeman's gaze passed over him twice. It seemed that Thom had meant what he said. A clean break.

Rand turned to go, but a woman stepped smoothly in

front of him and put a hand on his chest, the lace falling
back from a soft wrist. Her head did not quite come to his
shoulder, but her tall array of curls easily reached as high
as his eyes. The high neck of her gown put lace ruffles under her chin, and stripes covered the front of her dark blue
dress below her breasts. "I am Alaine Chuliandred, and you
are the famous Rand al'Thor. In Barthanes's own manor, I
suppose he has the right to speak to you first, but we are all
fascinated by what we hear of you. I even hear that you play
the flute. Can it be true?"

"I play the flute." *How did she . . . ? Caldevwin. Light,
everybody does hear everything in Cairhien.* "If you will
excuse—"

"I have heard that some outland lords play music, but I
never believed it. I would like very much to hear you play.
Perhaps you will talk with me, of this and that. Barthanes
seemed to find your conversation fascinating. My husband
spends his days sampling his own vineyards, and leaves me
quite alone. He is never there to talk with me."

"You must miss him," Rand said, trying to edge around
her and her wide skirts. She gave a tinkling laugh as if he
had said the funniest thing in the world.

Another woman sidled in beside the first, and another
hand was laid on his chest. She wore as many stripes as
Alaine, and they were of an age, a good ten years older than
he. "Do you think to keep him to yourself, Alaine?" The
two women smiled at each other while their eyes threw
daggers. The second turned her smile on Rand. "I am Belevaere Osiellin. Are all Andormen so tall? And so handsome?"

He cleared his throat. "Ah . . . some are as tall. Pardon
me, but if you will—"

"I saw you talking with Barthanes. They say you know
Galldrian, as well. You must come to see me, and talk. My
husband is visiting our estates in the south."

"You have the sublety of a tavern wench," Alaine hissed
at her, and immediately was smiling up at Rand. "She has
no polish. No man could like a woman with a manner so
rough. Bring your flute to my manor, and we will talk. Perhaps you will teach me to play?"

"What Alaine thinks of as subtlety," Belevaere said
sweetly, "is but lack of courage. A man who wears a heron-

mark sword must be brave. That truly is a heron-mark blade, is it not?"

Rand tried backing away from them. "If you will just excuse me, I—" They followed step for step until his back hit the wall; the width of their skirts together made another wall in front of him.

He jumped as a third woman crowded in beside the other two, her skirts joining theirs to the wall on that side. She was older than they, but just as pretty, with an amused smile that did not lessen the sharpness of her eyes. She wore half again as many stripes as Alaine and Belevaere; they made tiny curtsies and glared at her sullenly.

"Are these two spiders trying to toil you in their webs?" The older woman laughed. "Half the time they tangle themselves more firmly than anyone else. Come with me, my fine young Andoran, and I will tell you some of the troubles they would give you. For one thing, I have no husband to worry about. Husbands always make trouble."

Over Alaine's head he could see Thom, straightening from a bow to no applause or notice whatsoever. With a grimace the gleeman snatched a goblet from the tray of a startled servant.

"I see someone I must speak to," Rand told the women, and squeezed out of the box they had put him in just as the last woman reached for his arm. All three stared after him as he hurried to the gleeman.

Thom eyed him over the lip of the goblet, then took another long swallow.

"Thom, I know you said a clean break, but I had to get away from those women. All they wanted to talk about was their husbands being away, but they were already hinting at other things." Thom choked on his wine, and Rand slapped his back. "You drink too fast, and something always goes down the wrong way. Thom, they think I am plotting with Barthanes, or maybe Galldrian, and I don't think they will believe me when I say I'm not. I just needed an excuse to leave them."

Thom stroked his long mustaches with one knuckle and peered across the room at the three women. They were still standing together, watching Rand and him. "I recognize those three, boy. Breane Taborwin alone would give you an education such as every man should have at least once in his life, if he can live through it. Worried about their husbands. I like that, boy." Abruptly his eyes sharpened. "You told me you were clear of Aes Sedai. Half the talk here tonight is of the Andoran *lord* appearing with no warning, and an Aes Sedai at his side. Barthanes and Galldrian. You've let the White Tower put you in the cooking pot this time."

"She only came yesterday, Thom. And as soon as the Horn is safe, I'll be free of them again. I mean to see to it."

"You sound as if it isn't safe now," Thom said slowly. "You didn't sound that way before."

"Darkfriends stole it, Thom. They brought it here. Barthanes is one of them."

Thom seemed to study his wine, but his eyes darted to make sure no one was close enough to listen. More than the three women were watching them with sideways glances while pretending to talk among themselves, but every knot maintained its distance from every other. Still, Thom spoke softly. "A dangerous thing to say if it isn't true, and more dangerous if it is. An accusation like that, against the most powerful man in the kingdom. . . . You say he has the Horn? I suppose you're after my help again, now that you're tangled with the White Tower once more."

"No." He had decided Thom had been right, even if the gleeman did not know why. He could not involve anyone else in his troubles. "I just wanted to get away from those women."

The gleeman blew out his mustaches, taken aback. "Well. Yes. That is well. The last time I helped you, I got a limp out of it, and you seem to have let yourself be tied to Tar Valon strings again. You'll have to get yourself out of it this time." He sounded as if he were trying to convince himself.

"I will, Thom. I will." *Just as soon as the Horn is safe and Mat has that bloody dagger back. Mat, Hurin, where are you?*

As if the thought had been a summons, Hurin appeared in the room, eyes searching among the lords and ladies. They looked through him; servants did not exist unless needed. When he found Rand and Thom, he made his way between the small clusters of nobles and bowed to Rand. "My Lord, I was sent to tell you. Your manservant had a fall and twisted his knee. I don't know how bad, my Lord."

For a moment Rand stared before he understood. Conscious of all the eyes on him, he spoke loudly enough for the nobles closest to overhear. "Clumsy fool. What good is he to me if he can't walk? I suppose I'd better come see how badly he's hurt himself."

It seemed to be the right thing to say. Hurin sounded relieved when he bowed again and said, "As my Lord wishes. If my Lord will follow me?"

"You play very well at being a lord," Thom said softly. "But remember this. Cairhienin may play *Daes Dae'mar*, but it was the White Tower made the Great Game in the first place. Watch yourself, boy." With a glare at the nobles, he set his empty goblet on the tray of a passing servant and strolled away, plucking his harp. He began reciting *Goodwife Mili and the Silk Merchant*.

"Lead on, man," Rand told Hurin, feeling foolish. As he followed the sniffer out of the room, he could feel the eyes following him.

CHAPTER
33

A Message from the Dark

Have you found it?" Rand asked as he followed Hurin down a cramped flight of stairs. The kitchens lay on the lower levels, and the servants who had come attending the guests had all been sent there. "Or is Mat really hurt?"

"Oh, Mat's fine, Lord Rand." The sniffer frowned. "At least, he sounds all right, and he grumbles like a hale man. I didn't mean to worry you, but I needed a reason for you to come below. I found the trail easy enough. The men who set fire to the inn all entered a walled garden behind the manor. Trollocs joined them, went into the garden with them. Sometime yesterday, I think. Maybe even night before last." He hesitated. "Lord Rand, they didn't come out again. They must still be in there."

At the foot of the stairs the sounds of the servants enjoying themselves drifted down the hall, laughter and singing. Someone had a bittern, strumming a raucous tune to clapping and the thump of dancing. There was no worked plaster or fine tapestries here, only bare stone and plain wood. Light in the halls came from rush torches, smoking the ceiling and spread far enough apart that the light faded between them.

"I'm glad you are talking to me naturally again," Rand said. "The way you have been bowing and scraping, I was beginning to think you were more Cairhienin than the Cairhienin."

Hurin's face colored. "Well, as to that. . . ." He glanced down the hall toward the noise and looked as if he wanted to spit. "They all pretend to be so proper, but. . . . Lord

Rand, every one of them says he's loyal to his master or mistress, but they all hint they're willing to sell what they know, or have heard. And when they have a few drinks in them, they'll tell you, all whispering in your ear, things about the lords and ladies they serve that'd fair make your hair stand on end. I know they're Cairhienin, but I never heard of such goings on."

"We will be out of here soon, Hurin." Rand hoped it was true. "Where is this garden?" Hurin turned down a side hall leading toward the back of the manor. "Did you bring Ingtar and the others down already?"

The sniffer shook his head. "Lord Ingtar had let himself be cornered by six or seven of those who call themselves ladies. I couldn't get close enough to speak to him. And Verin Sedai was with Barthanes. She gave me such a look when I came near, I never even tried to tell her."

They rounded another corner just then, and there were Loial and Mat, the Ogier standing a little stooped for the lower ceiling.

Loial's grin almost split his face. "There you are. Rand, I was never so glad to get away from anyone as from those people upstairs. They kept asking me if the Ogier were coming back, and if Galldrian had agreed to pay what was owed. It seems the reason all the Ogier stonemasons left is because Galldrian stopped paying them, except with promises. I kept telling them I didn't know anything about it, but half of them seemed to think that I was lying, and the other half that I was hinting at something."

"We'll be out of here soon," Rand assured him. "Mat, are you all right?" His friend's face looked more hollow-cheeked than he remembered, even back at the inn, and his cheekbones more prominent.

"I feel fine," Mat said grumpily, "but I certainly didn't have any trouble leaving the *other* servants. The ones who weren't asking if you starved me thought I was sick and didn't want to come too close."

"Have you sensed the dagger?" Rand asked.

Mat shook his head glumly. "The only thing I've sensed is that somebody's watching me, most of the time. These people are as bad as Fades for sneaking around. Burn me, I nearly jumped out of my skin when Hurin told me he'd located the Darkfriends' trail. Rand, I can't feel it at all, and I've been through this bloody building from rafters to basement."

"That does not mean it isn't here, Mat. I put it in the chest with the Horn, remember. Maybe that keeps you from feeling it. I don't think Fain knows how to open it, else he'd not have gone to the trouble of carrying the weight when he fled Fal Dara. Even that much gold isn't important beside the Horn of Valere. When we find the Horn, we will find the dagger. You'll see."

"As long as I don't have to pretend to be your servant anymore," Mat muttered. "As long as you don't go mad and. . . ." He let the words die with a twist of his mouth.

"Rand is not mad, Mat," Loial said. "The Cairhienin would never have let him in here if he were not a lord. They are the ones who are mad."

"I'm not mad," Rand said harshly. "Not yet. Hurin, show me this garden."

"This way, Lord Rand."

They went out into the night by a small door that Rand had to duck to get through; Loial was forced to bend over and hunch his shoulders. There was enough light in yellow pools from the windows above for Rand to make out brick walks between square flower beds. The shadows of stables and other outbuildings bulked in the darkness to either side. Occasional fragments of music drifted out, from the servants below or from those entertaining their masters above.

Hurin led them along the walks until even the dim glow failed and they made their way by moonlight alone, their boots crunching softly on the brick. Bushes that would have been bright with flowers by daylight now made strange humps in the dark. Rand fingered his sword and did not let his eyes stay on any one spot too long. A hundred Trollocs could be hiding around them unseen. He knew Hurin would have smelled Trollocs if they were there, but that did not help a great deal. If Barthanes was a Darkfriend, then at least some of his servants and guards had to be, too, and Hurin could not always smell a Darkfriend. Darkfriends leaping out of the night would not be much better than Trollocs.

"There, Lord Rand," Hurin whispered, pointing.

Ahead, stone walls not much higher than Loial's head

enclosed a square perhaps fifty paces on a side. Rand could not be sure, in the shadows, but it looked as if the gardens stretched on beyond the walls. He wondered why Barthanes had built a walled enclosure in the middle of his garden. No roof showed above the wall. *Why would they go in there and stay?*

Loial bent to put his mouth close to Rand's ear. "I told you this was all an Ogier grove, once. Rand, the Waygate is within that wall. I can feel it."

Rand heard Mat sigh despairingly. "We can't give up, Mat," he said.

"I'm not giving up. I just have enough brains not to want to travel the Ways again."

"We may have to," Rand told him. "Go find Ingtar and Verin. Get them alone somehow—I don't care how—and tell them I think Fain has taken the Horn through a Waygate. Just don't let anyone else hear. And remember to limp; you are supposed to have had a fall." It was a wonder to him that even Fain would risk the Ways, but it seemed the only answer. *They wouldn't spend a day and a night just sitting in there, without a roof over their heads.*

Mat swept a low bow, and his voice was heavy with sarcasm. "At once, my Lord. As my Lord wishes. Shall I carry your banner, my Lord?" He started back for the manor, his grumbles fading away. "Now I have to limp. Next it'll be a broken neck, or. . . ."

"He's just worried about the dagger, Rand," Loial said.

"I know," Rand said. *But how long before he tells somebody what I am, not even meaning to?* He could not believe Mat would betray him on purpose; there was that much of their friendship left, at least. "Loial, boost me up where I can see over the wall."

"Rand, if the Darkfriends are still—"

"They aren't. Boost me up, Loial."

The three of them moved close to the wall, and Loial made a stirrup with his hands for Rand's foot. The Ogier straightened easily with the weight, lifting Rand's head just high enough to see over the top of the wall.

The thin, waning moon gave little light, and most of the area was in shadow, but there did not seem to be any flowers or shrubs inside the walled square. Only a lone bench

of pale marble, placed as if one man might sit on it to stare
at what stood in the middle of the space like a huge upright
stone slab.

Rand caught the top of the wall and pulled himself up.
Loial gave a low *hsst* and grabbed at his foot, but he jerked
free and rolled over the wall, dropping inside. There was
close-cropped grass under his feet; he thought vaguely that
Barthanes must let sheep in, at least. Staring at the shadowed stone slab, the Waygate, he was startled to hear boots
thump to the ground beside him.

Hurin climbed to his feet, dusting himself off. "You
should be careful doing that, Lord Rand. Could be anybody
hiding in here. Or anything." He peered into the darkness
within the walls, feeling at his belt as if for the short sword
and sword-breaker he had had to leave at the inn; servants
did not go armed in Cairhien. "Jump in a hole without looking, and there'll be a snake in it every time."

"You would smell them," Rand said.

"Maybe." The sniffer inhaled deeply. "But I can only
smell what they've done, not what they intend."

There was a scraping sound from over Rand's head, and
then Loial was letting himself down from the wall. The
Ogier did not even have to straighten his arms completely
before his boots touched the ground. "Rash," he muttered.
"You humans are always so rash and hasty. And now you
have me doing it. Elder Haman would speak to me severely,
and my mother. . . ." The darkness hid his face, but Rand
was sure his ears were twitching vigorously. "Rand, if you
don't start being a little careful, you are going to get me in
trouble."

Rand walked to the Waygate, walked all the way around
it. Even close up it looked like nothing more than a thick
square of stone, taller than he was. The back was smooth
and cool to the touch—he only brushed his hand against it
quickly—but the front had been carved by an artist's hands.
Vines, leaves, and flowers covered it, each so finely done
that in the dim moonlight they seemed almost real. He felt
the ground in front of it; the grass had been scraped partly
away in two arcs such as those gates would make in opening.

"Is that a Waygate?" Hurin asked uncertainly. "I've
heard tell of them, of course, but. . . ." He sniffed the air.
"The trail goes right to it and stops, Lord Rand. How are we

going to follow them, now? I've heard if you go through a Waygate, you come out mad, if you come out at all."

"It can be done, Hurin. I've done it, and Loial, and Mat and Perrin." Rand never took his eyes from the tangles of leaves on the stone. There was one unlike any other carved there, he knew. The trefoil leaf of fabled *Avendesora*, the Tree of Life. He put his hand on it. "I'll bet you can smell their trail along the Ways. We can follow anywhere they can run." It would not hurt to prove to himself that he could make himself step through a Waygate. "I'll prove it to you." He heard Hurin groan. The leaf was worked in the stone just as the others were, but it came away in his hand. Loial groaned, too.

In an instant the illusion of living plants seemed suddenly real. Stone leaves appeared to stir with a breeze, flowers appeared to have color even in the dark. Down the center of the mass a line appeared, and the two halves of the slab swung slowly toward Rand. He stepped back to let them open. He did not find himself looking at the other side of the walled square, but neither did he see the dull silver reflection he remembered. The space between the opening gates was a black so dark it seemed to make the night around it lighter. The pitch-blackness oozed out between the still-moving gates.

Rand leaped back with a shout, dropping the *Avendesora* leaf in his haste, and Loial cried out, "*Machin Shin*. The Black Wind."

The sound of wind filled their ears; the grass stirred in ripples toward the walls, and dirt swirled up, sucked into the air. And in the wind a thousand insane voices seemed to cry, ten thousand, overlapping, drowning each other. Rand could make out some of them, though he tried not to.

. . . *blood so sweet, so sweet to drink the blood, the blood that drips, drips, drops so red; pretty eyes, fine eyes, I have no eyes, pluck the eyes from out of your head; grind your bones, split your bones inside your flesh, suck your marrow while you scream; scream, scream, singing screams, sing your screams.* . . . And worst of all, a whispering thread through all the rest. *Al'Thor. Al'Thor. Al'Thor.*

Rand found the void around him and embraced it, never minding the tantalizing, sickening glow of *saidin* just out of his sight. Greatest of all the dangers along the Ways was the Black Wind that took the souls of those it killed, and drove mad those it let live, but *Machin Shin* was a part of the Ways; it could not leave them. Only it was flowing into the night, and the Black Wind called his name.

The Waygate was not yet fully open. If they could only put the *Avendesora* leaf back. . . . He saw Loial scrambling on his hands and knees, fumbling and searching the grass in the darkness.

Saidin filled him. He felt as if his bones were vibrating, felt the red-hot, ice-cold flow of the One Power, felt truly alive as he never was without it, felt the oil-slick taint. . . . *No!* And silently he screamed back at himself from beyond the emptiness, *It's coming for you! It'll kill all of us!* He hurled it all at the black bulge, standing out a full span from the Waygate, now. He did not know what it was that he hurled, or how, but in the heart of that darkness bloomed a coruscating fountain of light.

The Black Wind shrieked, ten thousand wordless howls of agony. Slowly, giving way inch by reluctant inch, the bulge lessened; slowly the oozing reversed, back into the still-open Waygate.

The Power raced through Rand in a torrent. He could feel the link between himself and *saidin*, like a river in flood, between himself and the pure fire blazing in the heart of the Black Wind, a raging cataract. The heat inside him went to white-heat, and beyond, to a shimmer that would have melted stone and vaporized steel and made the air burst into flame. The cold grew till the breath in his lungs should have frozen solid and hard as metal. He could feel it overwhelming him, feel life eroding like a soft clay riverbank, feel what was him wearing away.

Can't stop! If it gets out. . . . Have to kill it! I—can—not—stop! Desperately he clung to fragments of himself. The One Power roared through him; he rode it like a chip of wood in rapids. The void began to melt and flow; the emptiness steamed with freezing cold.

The motion of the Waygate halted, and reversed.

Rand stared, sure, in the dim thoughts floating outside the void, that he was only seeing what he wanted to see.

The gates drifted closer together, pushing back *Machin Shin* as if the Black Wind had solid substance. The inferno still roared in its breast.

With a vague, distant wondering, Rand saw Loial, still on hands and knees, backing away from the closing gates.

The gap narrowed, vanished. The leaves and vines merged into a solid wall, and were stone.

Rand felt the link between him and the fire snap, the flow of Power through him cease. A moment more, and it would have swept him away completely. Shaking, he dropped to his knees. It was still there inside. *Saidin*. No longer flowing, but there, in a pool. He was a pool of the One Power. He trembled with it. He could smell the grass, the dirt beneath, the stone of the walls. Even in the darkness he could see each blade of grass, separate and whole, all of them at once. He could feel each minute stirring of the air on his face. His tongue curdled with the taste of the taint; his stomach knotted and spasmed.

Frantically he clawed his way out of the void; still on his knees, not moving, he fought free. And then all that was left was the fading foulness on his tongue, and the cramping in his stomach, and the memory. *So—alive.*

"You saved us, Builder." Hurin had his back pressed against the wall, and his voice was hoarse. "That thing— that was the Black Wind?—it was worse than—was it going to hurl that fire at us? Lord Rand! Did it harm you? Did it touch you?" He came running as Rand got to his feet, helping him the last bit. Loial was getting up, too, dusting his hands and his knees.

"We'll never follow Fain through that." Rand touched Loial's arm. "Thank you. You *did* save us." *You saved me, at least. It was killing me. Killing me, and it felt— wonderful.* He swallowed; a faint trace of the taste still coated his mouth. "I want something to drink."

"I only found the leaf and put it back," Loial said, shrugging. "It seemed that if we could not get the Waygate closed, it would kill us. I am afraid I'm not a very good hero, Rand. I was so afraid I could hardly think."

"We were both afraid," Rand said. "We may be a poor pair of heroes, but we are what there is. It's a good thing Ingtar is with us."

"Lord Rand," Hurin said diffidently, "could we—leave, now?"

The sniffer made a fuss about Rand going over the wall first, with not knowing who was waiting outside, until Rand pointed out that he had the only weapon among them. Even then Hurin did not seem to like letting Loial lift Rand to catch the top of the wall and pull himself over.

Rand landed on his feet with a thud, listening and peering into the night. For a moment he thought he saw something move, heard a boot scrape on the brick walk, but neither was repeated, and he dismissed it as nervousness. He thought that he had a right to be nervous. He turned to help Hurin down.

"Lord Rand," the sniffer said as soon as his feet were solidly on the ground, "how are we going to follow them now? From what I've heard of those things, the whole lot of them could be halfway across the world by now, in any direction."

"Verin will know a way." Rand suddenly wanted to laugh; to find the Horn and the dagger—if they could be found, now—he had to go back to the Aes Sedai. They had let him loose, and now he had to go back. "I won't let Mat die without trying."

Loial joined them, and they went back toward the manor, to be met at the small door by Mat, who opened it just as Rand reached for the handle. "Verin says you're not to do anything. If Hurin's found where the Horn is kept, then she says that's all we can do, now. She says we'll leave as soon as you come back, and make a plan. And I say this is the last time I go running back and forth with messages. If you want to say something to somebody, you can talk to them yourself from now on." Mat peered past them into the darkness. "Is the Horn out there somewhere? In an outbuilding? Did you see the dagger?"

Rand turned him around and got him back inside. "It isn't in an outbuilding, Mat. I hope Verin has a good idea of what to do now; I don't have any."

Mat looked as if he wanted to ask questions, but he let himself be pushed along the dimly lit corridor. He even remembered to limp as they started upstairs.

When Rand and the others reentered the rooms filled with nobles, they received a number of looks. Rand wondered if they somehow knew something of what had happened outside, or if he should have sent Hurin and Mat to the front hall to wait, but then he realized the looks were no different from what they had been before, curious and calculating, wondering what the lord and the Ogier had been up to. Servants were invisible to these people. No one tried to approach them, since they were together. It seemed there were protocols to conspiracy in the Great Game; anyone might try to listen to a private conversation, but they would not intrude on it.

Verin and Ingtar were standing together, and thus also alone. Ingtar looked a little dazed. Verin gave Rand and the other three a brief glance, frowned at their expressions, then resettled her shawl and started for the entry hall.

As they reached it, Barthanes appeared as if someone had told him they were leaving. "You go so soon? Verin Sedai, can I not entreat you to stay longer?"

Verin shook her head. "We must go, Lord Barthanes. I've not been in Cairhien in some years. I was glad of your invitation to young Rand. It has been . . . interesting."

"Then Grace see you safely to your inn. The Great Tree, is it not? Perhaps you will favor me with your presence again? You would honor me, Verin Sedai, and you, Lord Rand, and you, Lord Ingtar, not to mention you, Loial, son of Arent son of Halan." His bow was a little deeper for the Aes Sedai than for the others, but still no more than a slight inclination.

Verin nodded in acknowledgment. "Perhaps. The Light illumine you, Lord Barthanes." She turned for the doors.

As Rand moved to follow the others, Barthanes caught his sleeve with two fingers, holding him back. Mat looked as if he might stay, too, until Hurin pulled him to join Verin and the rest.

"You wade even deeper in the Game than I thought," Barthanes said softly. "When I heard your name, I could not believe it, yet you came, and you fit the description, and. . . . I was given a message for you. I think I *will* deliver it after all."

Rand had felt a prickling along his backbone as Barthanes spoke, but at the last, he stared. "A message? From whom? Lady Selene?"

"A man. Not the sort for whom I would usually carry messages, but he has . . . certain . . . claims on me that I cannot ignore. He gave no name, but he was a Lugarder. Aaah! You know him."

"I know him." *Fain left a message?* Rand looked around

the wide hall. Mat and Verin and the others were waiting by the doors. Liveried servants stood stiffly along the walls, ready to leap at a command yet appearing neither to hear nor see. The sounds of the gathering floated from deeper in the manor. It did not look like a place where Darkfriends might attack. "What message?"

"He says he will wait for you on Toman Head. He has what you seek, and if you want it, you must follow. If you refuse to follow him, he says he will hound your blood, and your people, and those you love until you will face him. It sounds mad, of course, a man like that saying he will hound a lord, and yet, there was something about him. I think he *is* mad—he even denied you are a lord, as any eye can plainly see—but there is still something. What is it he carries with him, with Trollocs to guard it? What is it you seek?" Barthanes seemed shocked at the directness of his own questions.

"The Light illumine you, Lord Barthanes." Rand managed a bow, but his legs wobbled as he joined Verin and the others. *He* wants *me to follow? And he'll hurt Emond's Field, Tam, if I don't.* He had no doubt Fain could do it, would do it. *At least Egwene is safe, in the White Tower.* He had sickening images of Trollocs descending in hordes on Emond's Field, of eyeless Fades stalking Egwene. *But how can I follow him? How?*

Then he was out in the night, mounting Red. Verin and Ingtar and the others were all already on their horses, and the escort of Shienarans was closing round them.

"What did you find?" Verin demanded. "Where does he keep it?" Hurin cleared his throat loudly, and Loial shifted in his high saddle. The Aes Sedai peered at them.

"Fain has taken the Horn to Toman Head through a Way-gate," Rand said dully. "By this time, he's probably already waiting there for me."

"We will speak of this later," Verin said, so firmly that no one spoke at all on the ride back to the city, to The Great Tree.

Uno left them there, after a quiet word from Ingtar, taking the soldiers back to their inn in the Foregate. Hurin took one look at Verin's set face by the light of the common room, muttered something about ale, and scurried to a table in a corner, alone. The Aes Sedai brushed aside the innkeeper's solicitous hopes that she had enjoyed herself, and silently led Rand and the rest to the private dining room.

Perrin looked up from *The Travels of Jain Farstrider* when they walked in, and frowned when he saw their faces. "It didn't go well, did it?" he said, closing the leatherbound book. Lamps and beeswax candles around the room gave a good light; Mistress Tiedra charged heavily, but she did not stint.

Verin carefully folded her shawl and laid it across the back of a chair. "Tell me again. The Darkfriends took the Horn through a *Waygate*? At Barthanes's manor?"

"The ground under the manor used to be an Ogier grove," Loial explained. "When we built. . . ." His voice trailed off and his ears wilted under her look.

"Hurin followed them right to it." Rand wearily threw himself into a chair. *I have to follow more than ever, now. But how?* "I opened it to show him he could still follow the trail wherever they went, and the Black Wind was there. It tried to reach us, but Loial managed to close the gates before it could come all the way out." He colored a little at that, but Loial *had* closed the gates, and for all he knew *Machin Shin* might have made it out without that. "It was standing guard."

"The Black Wind," Mat breathed, frozen halfway into a chair. Perrin was staring at Rand, too. So were Verin and Ingtar. Mat dropped into the chair with a thump.

"You must be mistaken," Verin said at last. "*Machin Shin* could not be used as a guard. No one can constrain the Black Wind to do anything."

"It's a creature of the Dark One," Mat said numbly. "They're Darkfriends. Maybe they knew how to ask it for help, or make it help."

"No one knows exactly what *Machin Shin* is," Verin said, "unless, perhaps, it is the essence of madness and cruelty. It cannot be reasoned with, Mat, or bargained with, or talked to. It cannot even be forced, not by any Aes Sedai living today, and perhaps not by any who ever lived. Do you really think Padan Fain could do what ten Aes Sedai could not?" Mat shook his head.

There was an air of despair in the room, of hope and purpose lost. The goal they had sought had vanished, and even Verin's face wore a floundering expression.

"I'd never have thought Fain had the courage for the Ways." Ingtar sounded almost mild, but suddenly he banged his fist against the wall. "I do not care how, or even if, *Machin Shin* works on Fain's behalf. They have taken the Horn of Valere into the Ways, Aes Sedai. By now they could be in the Blight, or halfway to Tear or Tanchico, or the other side of the Aiel Waste. The Horn is lost. I am lost." His hands dropped to his sides, and his shoulders slumped. "I am lost."

"Fain is taking it to Toman Head," Rand said, and was immediately the object of all eyes again.

Verin studied him narrowly. "You said that before. How do you know?"

"He left a message with Barthanes," Rand said.

"A trick," Ingtar sneered. "He'd not tell us where to follow."

"I don't know what the rest of you are going to do," Rand said, "but I am going to Toman Head. I have to. I leave at first light."

"But, Rand," Loial said, "it will take us months to reach Toman Head. What makes you think Fain will wait there for us?"

"He will wait." *But how long before he decides I'm not coming? Why did he set that guard if he wants me to follow?* "Loial, I mean to ride as hard as I can, and if I ride Red to death, I'll buy another horse, or steal another, if I have to. Are you sure you want to come?"

"I've stayed with you this long, Rand. Why would I stop now?" Loial pulled out his pipe and pouch and began thumbing tabac into the big bowl. "You see, I like you. I would like you even if you weren't *ta'veren.* Maybe I like you despite it. You do seem to get me neck-deep in hot water. In any case, I am going with you." He sucked on the pipe-stem to test the draw, then took a splinter from the stone jar on the mantel and thrust it into a candle flame for a light. "And I don't think you can really stop me."

"Well, I'm going," Mat said. "Fain still has that dagger, so I'm going. But all that servant business ended tonight."

Perrin sighed, an introspective look in his yellow eyes. "I

suppose I'll come along, too." After a moment, he grinned. "Somebody has to keep Mat out of trouble."

"Not even a clever trick," Ingtar muttered. "Somehow, I'll get Barthanes alone, and I will learn the truth. I mean to have the Horn of Valere, not chase Jak o' the Wisps."

"It may not be a trick," Verin said carefully, seeming to study the floor under her toes. "There were certain things left in the dungeons at Fal Dara, writings that indicated a connection between what happened that night and"—she gave Rand a quick glance under lowered brows—"Toman Head. I still do not understand them completely, but I believe we must go to Toman Head. And I believe we will find the Horn there."

"Even if they are going to Toman Head," Ingtar said, "by the time we reach it, Fain or one of the other Darkfriends could have blown the Horn a hundred times, and the heroes returned from the grave will ride for the Shadow."

"Fain could have blown the Horn a hundred times since leaving Fal Dara," Verin told him. "And I think he would have, if he could open the chest. What we must worry about is that he might find someone who does know how to open it. We must follow him along the Ways."

Perrin's head came up sharply, and Mat shifted in his chair. Loial gave a low moan.

"Even if we could somehow sneak past Barthanes's guards," Rand said, "I think we'll find *Machin Shin* still there. We cannot use the Ways."

"How many of us could sneak onto Barthanes's grounds?" Verin said dismissively. "There are other Waygates. Stedding Tsofu lies not far from the city, south and east. It is a young *stedding*, rediscovered only perhaps six hundred years ago, but the Ogier Elders were still growing the Ways, then. Stedding Tsofu will have a Waygate. It is there and we will ride at first light."

Loial made a slightly louder sound, and Rand was not sure whether it referred to the Waygate or the *stedding*.

Ingtar still did not seem convinced, but Verin was as smooth and as implacable as snow sliding down a mountainside. "You will have your soldiers ready to ride, Ingtar. Send Hurin to tell Uno before he goes to bed. I think we should all go to bed as soon as possible. These Darkfriends have gained at least a day on us already, and I mean to make up as much of it as I can tomorrow." So firm was the plump Aes Sedai's manner that she was already herding Ingtar to the door before she finished speaking.

Rand followed the others out, but at the door he stopped beside the Aes Sedai and watched Mat heading down the candle-lit hall. "Why does he look like that?" he asked her. "I thought you Healed him, enough to give him some time, anyway."

She waited until Mat and the others had turned up the stairs before speaking. "Apparently, it did not work so well as we believed. The sickness takes an interesting course in him. His strength remains; he will keep that to the end, I think. But his body wastes away. Another few weeks, at most, I would say. You see, there is reason for haste."

"I do not need another spur, Aes Sedai," Rand said, making the title sound hard. *Mat. The Horn. Fain's threat. Light, Egwene! Burn me, I don't need another spur.*

"And what of you, Rand al'Thor? Do you feel well? Do you fight it still, or have you yet surrendered to the Wheel?"

"I ride with you to find the Horn," he told her. "Beyond that, there is nothing between me and any Aes Sedai. Do you understand me? Nothing!"

She did not speak, and he walked away from her, but when he turned to take the stairs she was still watching him, dark eyes sharp and considering.

CHAPTER
34

The Wheel Weaves

The first light of morning already pearled the sky by the time Thom Merrilin found himself trudging back to The Bunch of Grapes. Even where the halls and taverns lay thickest, there was a brief time when the Foregate lay quiet, gathering its breath. In his present mood, Thom would not have noticed if the empty street had been on fire.

Some of Barthanes's guests had insisted on keeping him long after most had gone, long after Barthanes had taken himself to bed. It had been his own fault for leaving *The Great Hunt of the Horn*, changing to the sort of tales he told and songs he sang in the villages, "Mara and the Three Foolish Kings" and *How Susa Tamed Jain Farstrider* and stories of Anla the Wise Councilor. He had meant the choices to be a private comment on their stupidity, never dreaming any of them might listen, much less be intrigued. Intrigued in a way. They had demanded more of the same, but they had laughed in the wrong places, at the wrong things. They had laughed at him, too, apparently thinking he would not notice, or else that a full purse stuffed in his pocket would heal any wounds. He had almost thrown it away twice already.

The heavy purse burning his pocket and pride was not the only reason for his mood, nor even the nobles' contempt. They had asked questions about Rand, not even bothering to be subtle with a mere gleeman. Why was Rand in Cairhien? Why had an Andoran lord taken him, a gleeman, aside? Too many questions. He was not sure his answers had been clever enough. His reflexes for the Great Game were rusty.

Before turning toward The Bunch of Grapes, he had gone to The Great Tree; it was not difficult to find where someone was staying in Cairhien, if you pressed a palm or two with silver. He was still not sure what he had intended to say. Rand was gone with his friends, and the Aes Sedai. It left a feeling of something not done. *The boy's on his own, now. Burn me, I'm out of it!*

He strode through the common room, empty as it seldom was, and took the steps two at a time. At least, he tried to; his right leg did not bend well, and he nearly fell. Muttering to himself, he climbed the rest of the way at a slower pace, and opened the door to his room softly, so as not to wake Dena.

Despite himself, he smiled when he saw her lying on the bed with her face turned to the wall, still in her dress. *Fell asleep waiting for me. Fool girl.* But it was a kindly thought; he was not sure there was anything she would do that he would not forgive or excuse. Deciding on the spur of the moment that tonight was the night he'd let her perform for the first time, he lowered his harp case to the floor and put a hand on her shoulder, to wake her and tell her.

She rolled limply onto her back, staring up at him, glazed eyes open wide above the gash across her throat. The side of the bed that had been hidden by her body was dark and sodden.

Thom's stomach heaved; if his throat had not been so tight he could not breathe, he would have vomited, or screamed, or both.

He had only the creaking of wardrobe doors for warning. He spun, knives coming out of his sleeves and leaving his hands in the same motion. The first blade took the throat of a fat, balding man with a dagger in his hand; the man stumbled back, blood bubbling around his clutching fingers as he tried to cry out.

Spinning on his bad leg threw Thom's other blade off, though; the knife stuck in the right shoulder of a heavily muscled man with scars on his face, who was climbing out of the other wardrobe. The big man's knife dropped from a hand that suddenly would not do what he wanted, and he lumbered for the door.

Before he could take a second step, Thom produced another knife and slashed him across the back of his leg. The big man yelled and stumbled, and Thom seized a handful of greasy hair, slamming his face against the wall beside the door; the man screamed again as the knife hilt sticking out of his shoulder hit the door.

Thom thrust the blade in his hand to within an inch of the man's dark eye. The scars on the big man's face gave him a hard look, but he stared at the point without blinking and did not move a muscle. The fat man, lying half in the wardrobe, kicked a last kick and was still.

"Before I kill you," Thom said, "tell me. Why?" His voice was quiet, numb; he felt numb inside.

"The Great Game," the man said quickly. His accent was of the streets, and his clothes as well, but they were a shade too fine, too unworn; he had more coin to spend than any Foregater should. "Nothing against you personal, you see? It is just the Game."

"The Game? I'm not mixed up in *Daes Dae'mar*! Who would want to kill me for the Great Game?" The man hesitated. Thom moved his blade closer. If the fellow blinked, his eyelashes would brush the point. "Who?"

"Barthanes," came the hoarse answer. "Lord Barthanes. We would not have killed you. Barthanes wants information. We just wanted to find out what you know. There can be gold in it for you. A nice, fat golden crown for what you know. Maybe two."

"Liar! I was in Barthanes's manor last night, as close to him as I am to you. If he wanted anything of me, I'd never have left alive."

"I tell you, we have been looking for you, or anyone who knows about this Andoran lord, for days. I never heard your name until last night, downstairs. Lord Barthanes is generous. It could be five crowns."

The man tried to pull his head away from the knife in Thom's hand, and Thom pushed him harder against the wall. "What Andoran lord?" But he knew. The Light help him, he knew.

"Rand. Of House al'Thor. Tall. Young. A blademaster, or at least he wears the sword. I know he came to see you. Him and an Ogier, and you talked. Tell me what you know. I might even throw in a crown or two, myself."

"You fool," Thom breathed. *Dena died for this? Oh, Light, she's dead.* He felt as if he wanted to cry. "The boy's a shepherd." *A shepherd in a fancy coat, with Aes Sedai around him like bees around honeyroses.* "Just a shepherd." He tightened his grip in the man's hair.

"Wait! Wait! You can make more than any five crowns, or even ten. A hundred, more like. Every House wants to know about this Rand al'Thor. Two or three have approached me. With what you know, and my knowing who wants to know it, we could both fill our pockets. And there has been a woman, a lady, I have seen more than once while asking after him. If we can find out who she is . . . why, we could sell that, too."

"You've made one real mistake in it all," Thom said.

"Mistake?" The man's far hand was beginning to slide down toward his belt. No doubt he had another dagger there. Thom ignored it.

"You should never have touched the girl."

The man's hand darted for his belt, then he gave one convulsive start as Thom's knife went home.

Thom let him fall over away from the door and stood a moment before bending tiredly to tug his blades free. The door banged open, and he whirled with a snarl on his face.

Zera jerked back, a hand to her throat, staring at him. "That fool Ella just told me," she said unsteadily, "that two of Barthanes's men were asking after you last night, and with what I've heard this morning. . . . I thought you said you didn't play in the Game anymore."

"They found me," he said wearily.

Her eyes dropped from his face and widened as they took in the bodies of the two men. Hastily she stepped into the room, shutting the door behind her. "This is bad, Thom. You'll have to leave Cairhien." Her gaze fell on the bed, and her breath caught. "Oh, no. Oh, no. Oh, Thom, I'm so sorry."

"I cannot leave yet, Zera." He hesitated, then tenderly drew a blanket over Dena, covering her face. "I have another man to kill, first."

The innkeeper gave herself a shake and pulled her eyes away from the bed. Her voice was more than a little breathy. "If you mean Barthanes, you're too late. Everybody's talking about it already. He is dead. His servants found him this morning, torn to pieces in his bedchamber. The only way they knew it was him was his head stuck on a spike over the fireplace." She laid a hand on his arm. "Thom, you can't hide that you were there last night, not from anybody who wants to know. Add these two in, and there's nobody in Cairhien who won't believe you were involved." There was a slight questioning note in her last words, as if she, too, were wondering.

"It doesn't matter, I suppose," he said dully. He could not stop looking down at the blanket-covered shape on the bed. "Perhaps I will go back to Andor. To Caemlyn."

She took his shoulders, turning him away from the bed. "You men," she sighed, "always thinking with either your muscles or your hearts, and never your heads. Caemlyn is as bad as Cairhien, for you. Either place, you'll end up dead, or in prison. Do you think she'd want that? If you want to honor her memory, stay alive."

"Will you take care of. . . ." He could not say it. *Growing old,* he thought. *Going soft.* He pulled the heavy purse from his pocket and folded her hands around it. "This should take care of . . . everything. And help when they start asking questions about me, too."

"I will see to everything," she said gently. "You must go, Thom. Now."

He nodded reluctantly, and slowly began stuffing a few things in a set of saddlebags. While he worked, Zera got her first close look at the fat man sprawled partway in the wardrobe, and she gave a loud gasp. He looked at her inquiringly; as long as he had known her, she had never been one to go faint over blood.

"These aren't Barthanes's men, Thom. At least, that one isn't." She nodded toward the fat man. "It's the worst kept secret in Cairhien that he works for House Riatin. For Galldrian."

"Galldrian," he said flatly. *What has that bloody shepherd gotten me into? What have the Aes Sedai gotten us both into? But it was Galldrian's men murdered her.*

There must have been something of his thoughts on his face. Zera said sharply, "Dena wants you alive, you fool! You try to kill the King, and you'll be dead before you get within a hundred spans of him, if you come that close!"

A roar came from the city walls, as if half of Cairhien

were shouting. Frowning, Thom peered from his window. Beyond the top of the gray walls above the rooftops of the Foregate, a thick column of smoke was rising into the sky. Far beyond the walls. Beside the first black pillar, a few gray tendrils quickly grew into another, and more wisps appeared further on. He estimated the distance and took a deep breath.

"Perhaps you had better think about leaving, too. It looks as if someone is firing the granaries."

"I have lived through riots before. Go now, Thom." With a last look at Dena's shrouded form, he gathered his things, but as he started to leave, Zera spoke again. "You have a dangerous look in your eyes, Thom Merrilin. Imagine Dena sitting here, alive and hale. Think what she would say. Would she let you go off and get yourself killed to no purpose?"

"I'm only an old gleeman," he said from the door. *And Rand al'Thor is only a shepherd, but we both do what we must.* "Who could I possibly be dangerous to?"

As he pulled the door to, hiding her, hiding Dena, a mirthless, wolfish grin came onto his face. His leg hurt, but he barely felt it as he hurried purposefully down the stairs and out of the inn.

Padan Fain reined in his horse atop a hill above Falme, in one of the few sparse thickets remaining on the hills outside the town. The packhorse bearing his precious burden bumped his leg, and he kicked it in the ribs without looking; the animal snorted and jerked back to the end of the lead he had tied to his saddle. The woman had not wanted to give up her horse, no more than any of the Darkfriends who had followed him had wanted to be left alone in the hills with the Trollocs, without Fain's protecting presence. He had solved both problems easily. Meat in a Trolloc cookpot had no need of a horse. The woman's companions had been shaken by the journey along the Ways, to a Waygate outside a long-abandoned *stedding* on Toman Head, and watching the Trollocs prepare their dinner had made the surviving Darkfriends extremely biddable.

From the edge of the trees, Fain studied the unwalled town and sneered. One short merchant train was rumbling in among the stables and horse lots and wagon yards that bordered the town, while another rumbled out, raising little dust from dirt packed by many years of such traffic. The men driving the wagons and the few riding beside them were all local men by their clothing, yet the mounted men, at least, had swords on baldrics, and even a few spears and bows. The soldiers he saw, and there were few, did not seem to be watching the armed men they had supposedly conquered.

He had learned something of these people, these Seanchan, in his day and a night on Toman Head. At least, as much as the defeated folk knew. It was never hard to find someone alone, and they always answered questions properly put. Men gathered more information on the invaders, as if they actually believed they would eventually do something with what they knew, but they sometimes tried to hold back. Women, by and large, seemed interested in going on with their lives whoever their rulers were, yet they noted details men did not, and they talked more quickly once they stopped screaming. Children talked the quickest of all, but they seldom said much that was worthwhile.

He had discarded three quarters of what he had heard as nonsense and rumors growing into fables, but he took some of those conclusions back, now. Anyone at all could enter Falme, it appeared. With a start, he saw the truth of a little more "nonsense" as twenty soldiers rode out of the town. He could not make out their mounts clearly, but they were certainly not horses. They ran with a fluid grace, and their dark skins seemed to have a glint in the morning sun, as of scales. He craned his neck to watch them disappear inland, then booted his horse toward the town.

The local folk among the stables and parked wagons and fenced horse lots gave him no more than a glance or two. He had no interest in them, either; he rode on into the town, onto its cobblestone streets sloping down to the harbor. He could see the harbor clearly, and the large, oddly shaped Seanchan ships anchored there. No one bothered him as he searched streets that were neither crowded nor empty. There were more Seanchan soldiers here. The people hurried about their business with eyes down, bowing whenever soldiers passed, but the Seanchan paid them no mind. It all seemed peaceful on the surface, despite the armored

Seanchan in the streets and the ships in the harbor, but Fain could sense the tension underneath. He always did well where men were tense and afraid.

He came to a large house with more than a dozen soldiers standing guard before it. Fain stopped and dismounted. Except for one obvious officer, most wore armor of unrelieved black, and their helmets made him think of locusts' heads. Two leathery-skinned beasts with three eyes and horny beaks instead of mouths flanked the front door, squatting like crouching frogs; the soldier standing by each of the creatures had three eyes painted on the breast of his armor. Fain eyed the blue-bordered banner flapping above the roof, the spread-winged hawk clutching lightning bolts, and chortled inside himself.

Women went in and out of a house across the street, women linked by silver leashes, but he ignored them. He knew about *damane* from the villagers. They might be of some use later, but not now.

The soldiers were looking at him, especially the officer, whose armor was all gold and red and green.

Forcing an ingratiating smile onto his face, Fain made himself bow deeply. "My lords, I have something here that will interest your Great Lord. I assure you, he will want to see it, and me, personally." He gestured to the squarish shape on his packhorse, still wrapped in the huge, striped blanket in which his people had found it.

The officer stared him up and down. "You sound a foreigner to this land. Have you taken the oaths?"

"I obey, await, and will serve," Fain replied smoothly. Everyone he had questioned spoke of the oaths, though none had understood what they meant. If these people wanted oaths, he was prepared to swear anything. He had long since lost count of the oaths he had taken.

The officer motioned two of his men to see what was under the blanket. Surprised grunts at the weight as they lifted it down from the packsaddle turned to gasps when they stripped the blanket away. The officer stared with no expression on his face at the silver-worked golden chest resting on the cobblestones, then looked at Fain. "A gift fit for the Empress herself. You will come with me."

One of the soldiers searched Fain roughly, but he endured it in silence, noting that the officer and the two soldiers who took up the chest surrendered their swords and daggers before going inside. Anything he could learn of these people, however small, might help, though he was confident of his plan already. He was always confident, but never more than where lords feared an assassin's knife from their own followers.

As they went through the door, the officer frowned at him, and for a moment Fain wondered why. *Of course. The beasts.* Whatever they were, they were certainly no worse than Trollocs, nothing at all beside a Myrddraal, and he had not given them a second look. It was too late to pretend to be afraid of them now. But the Seanchan said nothing, only led him deeper into the house.

And so Fain found himself on his face, in a room bare of furnishings except for folding screens that hid its walls, while the officer told the High Lord Turak of him and his offering. Servants brought a table on which to set the chest so the High Lord would have no need to stoop; all Fain saw of them were scurrying slippers. He bided his time impatiently. Eventually there would come a time when he was not the one to bow.

Then the soldiers were dismissed, and Fain told to rise. He did so slowly, studying both the High Lord, with his shaven head and his long fingernails and his blue silk robe brocaded with blossoms, and the man who stood beside him with the unshaven half of his pale hair in a long braid. Fain was sure the fellow in green was only a servant, however great, but servants could be useful, especially if they stood high in their master's sight.

"A marvelous gift." Turak's eyes lifted from the chest to Fain. A scent of roses wafted from the High Lord. "Yet the question asks itself; how did one like you come by a chest many lesser lords could not afford? Are you a thief?"

Fain tugged at his worn, none-too-clean coat. "It is sometimes necessary for a man to appear less than he is, High Lord. My present shabbiness allowed me to bring this to you unmolested. This chest is old, High Lord—as old as the Age of Legends—and within it lies a treasure such as few eyes have ever seen. Soon—very soon, High Lord—I will be able to open it, and give you that which will enable you to take this land as far as you wish, to the Spine of the World, the Aiel Waste, the lands beyond. Nothing will stand against you, High Lord, once I—" He cut off as Turak began running his long-nailed fingers over the chest.

"I have seen chests such as this, chests from the Age of Legends," the High Lord said, "though none so fine. They are meant to be opened only by those who know the pattern, but I—ah!" He pressed among the ornate whorls and bosses, there was a sharp click, and he lifted back the lid. A flicker of what might have been disappointment passed across his face.

Fain bit the inside of his mouth till blood came to keep from snarling. It lessened his bargaining position that he was not the one who had opened the chest. Still, all the rest could go as he had planned if he could only make himself be patient. But he had been patient so long.

"These are treasures from the Age of Legends?" Turak said, lifting out the curled Horn in one hand and the curved dagger with the ruby in its golden hilt in the other. Fain clutched his hands in fists at his sides so he would not grab the dagger. "The Age of Legends," Turak repeated softly, tracing the silver script inlaid around the golden bell of the Horn with the tip of the dagger's blade. His brows rose in startlement, the first open expression Fain had seen from him, but in the next instant Turak's face was as smooth as ever. "Do you have any idea what this is?"

"The Horn of Valere, High Lord," Fain said smoothly, pleased to see the mouth of the man with the braid drop open. Turak only nodded as if to himself.

The High Lord turned away. Fain blinked and opened his mouth, then, at a sharp gesture from the yellow-haired man, followed without speaking.

It was another room with all the original furnishings gone, replaced by folding screens and a single chair facing a tall round cabinet. Still holding the Horn and the dagger, Turak looked at the cabinet, then away. He said nothing, but the other Seanchan snapped quick orders, and in moments men in plain woolen robes appeared through a door behind the screens bearing another small table. A young woman with hair so pale it was almost white came behind them, her arms full of small stands of polished wood in various sizes and shapes. Her garment was white silk, and so thin that Fain could see her body clearly through it, but he had eyes only for the dagger. The Horn was a means to an end, but the dagger was a part of him.

Turak briefly touched one of the wooden stands the girl held, and she placed it on the center of the table. The men turned the chair to face it under the direction of the man with the braid. The lower servants' hair hung to their shoulders. They scurried out with bows that almost put their heads on their knees.

Placing the Horn on the stand so that it stood upright, Turak laid the dagger on the table in front of it and went to sit in the chair.

Fain could stand it no longer. He reached for the dagger.

The yellow-haired man caught his wrist in a crushing grip. "Unshaven dog! Know that the hand that touches the property of the High Lord unbidden is cut off."

"It is mine," Fain growled. *Patience! So long.*

Turak, lounging back in the chair, lifted one blue-lacquered fingernail, and Fain was pulled out of the way so the High Lord could view the Horn unobstructed.

"Yours?" Turak said. "Inside a chest you could not open? If you interest me sufficiently, I may give you the dagger. Even if it is from the Age of Legends, I have no interest in such as that. Before all else, you will answer me a question. Why have you brought the Horn of Valere to me?"

Fain eyed the dagger longingly a moment more, then jerked his wrist free and rubbed it as he bowed. "That you may sound it, High Lord. Then you may take all of this land, if you wish. All of the world. You may break the White Tower and grind the Aes Sedai to dust, for even their powers cannot stop heroes come back from the dead."

"*I* am to sound it." Turak's tone was flat. "And break the White Tower. Again, why? You claim to obey, await, and serve, but this is a land of oath-breakers. Why do you give your land to me? Do you have some private quarrel with these . . . women?"

Fain tried to make his voice convincing. *Patient, like a worm boring from within.* "High Lord, my family has passed down a tradition, generation upon generation. We served the High King, Artur Paendrag Tanreall, and when he was murdered by the witches of Tar Valon, we did not abandon our oaths. When others warred and tore apart what Artur Hawkwing had made, we held to our swearing, and suffered for it, but held to it still. This is our tradition, High Lord, handed father to son, and mother to daughter, down all the years since the High King was murdered. That we await the return of the armies Artur Hawkwing sent across the Aryth Ocean, that we await the return of Artur Hawkwing's blood to destroy the White Tower and take back what was the High King's. And when the Hawkwing's blood returns, we will serve and advise, as we did for the High King. High Lord, except for its border, the banner that flies over this roof is the banner of Luthair, the son Artur Paendrag Tanreall sent with his armies across the ocean." Fain dropped to his knees, giving a good imitation of being overwhelmed. "High Lord, I wish only to serve and advise the blood of the High King."

Turak was silent so long that Fain began to wonder if he needed further convincing; he was ready with more, as much as was required. Finally, though, the High Lord spoke. "You seem to know what none, neither the high nor the low, has spoken since sighting this land. The people here speak it as one rumor among ten, but you know. I can see it in your eyes, hear it in your voice. I could almost think you were sent to entangle me in a trap. But who, possessing the Horn of Valere, would use it so? None of those of the Blood who came with the *Hailene* could have had the Horn, for the legend says it was hidden in this land. And surely any lord of this land would use it against me rather than put it in my hands. How did you come to possess the Horn of Valere? Do you claim to be a hero, as in the legend? Have you done valorous deeds?"

"I am no hero, High Lord." Fain ventured a self-deprecating smile, but Turak's face did not alter, and he let it go. "The Horn was found by an ancestor of mine during the turmoil after the High King's death. He knew how to open the chest, but that secret died with him in the War of the Hundred Years, that rent Artur Hawkwing's empire, so that all we who followed him knew was that the Horn lay within and we must keep it safe until the High King's blood returned."

"Almost could I believe you."

"Believe, High Lord. Once you sound the Horn—"

"Do not ruin what convincing you have managed to do. I

shall not sound the Horn of Valere. When I return to Sean-chan, I shall present it to the Empress as the chiefest of my trophies. Perhaps the Empress will sound it herself."

"But, High Lord," Fain protested, "you must—" He found himself lying on his side, his head ringing. Only when his eyes cleared did he see the man with the pale braid rubbing his knuckles and realize what had happened.

"Some words," the fellow said softly, "are never used to the High Lord."

Fain decided how the man was going to die.

Turak looked from Fain to the Horn as placidly as if he had seen nothing. "Perhaps I will give you to the Empress along with the Horn of Valere. She might find you amus-ing, a man who claims his family held true where all others broke their oaths or forgot them."

Fain hid his sudden elation in the act of climbing back to his feet. He had not even known of the existence of an Empress until Turak mentioned her, but access to a ruler again . . . that opened new paths, new plans. Access to a ruler with the might of the Seanchan beneath her and the Horn of Valere in her hands. Much better than making this Turak a Great King. He could wait for some parts of his plan. *Softly. Mustn't let him know how much you want it. After so long, a little more patience will not hurt.* "As the High Lord wishes," he said, trying to sound like a man who only wanted to serve.

"You seem almost eager," Turak said, and Fain barely suppressed a wince. "I will tell you why I will not sound the Horn of Valere, or even keep it, and perhaps that will cure your eagerness. I do not wish a gift of mine to of-fend the Empress by his actions; if your eagerness cannot be cured, it will never be satisfied, for you will never leave these shores. Do you know that whoever blows the Horn of Valere is linked to it thereafter? That so long as he or she lives, it is no more than a horn to any other?" He did not sound as if he expected answers, and in any case, he did not pause for them. "I stand twelfth in line of succes-sion to the Crystal Throne. If I kept the Horn of Valere, all between myself and the throne would think I meant to be first hereafter, and while the Empress, of course, wishes that we contend with one another so that the strongest and most cunning will follow her, she currently favors her second daughter, and she would not look well on any threat to Tuon. If I sounded it, even if I then laid this land at her feet, and every woman in the White Tower leashed, the Empress, may she live forever, would surely believe I meant to be more than merely her heir."

Fain stopped himself short of suggesting how possible that would be with the aid of the Horn. Something in the High Lord's voice suggested—as hard as Fain found it to believe—that he actually meant his wish for her to live forever. *I must be patient. A worm in the root.*

"The Empress's Listeners may be anywhere," Turak continued. "They may be anyone. Huan was born and raised in the House of Aladon, and his family for eleven generations before him, yet even he could be a Listener." The man with the braid half made a protesting gesture, before jerking himself back to stillness. "Even a high lord or a high lady can find their deepest secrets known to Listeners, can wake to find themselves already handed over to the Seekers for Truth. Truth is always difficult to find, but the Seekers spare no pain in their search, and they will search as long as they think there is need. They make great efforts not to allow a high lord or high lady to die in their care, of course, for no man's hand may slay one in whose veins flows the blood of Artur Hawkwing. If the Empress must order such a death, the unfortunate one is placed alive in a silken bag, and that bag hung over the side of the Tower of the Ravens and left there until it rots away. No such care would be taken for one such as you. At the Court of the Nine Moons, in Seandar, one such as you could be given to the Seekers for a shift of your eye, for a misspoken word, for a whim. Are you still eager?"

Fain managed a tremble in his knees. "I wish only to serve and advise, High Lord. I know much that may be useful." This court of Seandar sounded a place where his plans and skills would find fertile soil.

"Until I sail back to Seanchan, you will amuse me with your tales of your family and its tradition. It is a relief to find a second man in this Light-forsaken land who can amuse me, even if you both tell lies, as I suspect. You may leave me." No other word was spoken, but the girl with the nearly white hair and the almost-transparent robe appeared on quick feet to kneel with downcast head beside the High Lord, offering a single steaming cup on a lacquered tray.

"High Lord," Fain said. The man with the braid, Huan, took hold of his arm, but he pulled loose. Huan's mouth tightened angrily as Fain made his deepest bow yet. *I will kill him slowly, yes.* "High Lord, there are those who follow me. They mean to take the Horn of Valere. Darkfriends and worse, High Lord, and they cannot be more than a day or two behind me."

Turak took a sip of black liquid from the thin cup balanced on long-nailed fingertips. "Few Darkfriends remain in Seanchan. Those who survive the Seekers for Truth meet the axe of the headsman. It might be amusing to meet a Darkfriend."

"High Lord, they are dangerous. They have Trollocs with them. They are led by one who calls himself Rand al'Thor. A young man, but vile in the Shadow beyond belief, with a lying, devious tongue. In many places he has claimed to be many things, but always the Trollocs come when he is there, High Lord. Always the Trollocs come . . . and kill."

"Trollocs," Turak mused. "There were no Trollocs in Seanchan. But the Armies of the Night had other allies. Other things. I have often wondered if a *grolm* could kill a Trolloc. I will have watch kept for your Trollocs and your Darkfriends, if they are not another lie. This land wearies me with boredom." He sighed and inhaled the fumes from his cup.

Fain let the grimacing Huan pull him out of the room, hardly even listening to the snarled lecture on what would happen if he ever again failed to leave Lord Turak's presence when given permission to do so. He barely noticed when he was pushed into the street with a coin and instructions to return on the morrow. Rand al'Thor was his, now. *I will see him dead at last. And then the world will pay for what was done to me.*

Giggling under his breath, he led his horses down into the town in search of an inn.

CHAPTER
35

Stedding Tsofu

The river hills on which the city of Cairhien stood gave way to flatter lands and forests when Rand and the others had ridden half a day, the Shienarans still with their armor on the packhorses. There were no roads where they went, only a scattering of cart tracks, and few farms or villages. Verin pressed for speed, and Ingtar—grumbling constantly that they were letting themselves be tricked, that Fain would never have told them where he was really going, yet grumbling at the same time about riding in the opposite direction from Toman Head, as if part of him believed and Toman Head were not months away except by the way they took—Ingtar obliged her. The Gray Owl banner flew on the wind of their passage.

Rand rode with grim determination, avoiding conversation with Verin. He had this thing to do—this duty, Ingtar would have called it—and then he could be free of Aes Sedai once and for all. Perrin seemed to share something of his mood, staring straight ahead at nothing as they rode. When they finally stopped for the night at the edge of a forest, with full dark almost on them, Perrin asked Loial questions about the *stedding*. Trollocs would not enter a *stedding*; would wolves? Loial replied shortly that it was only creatures of the Shadow that were reluctant to enter *stedding*. And Aes Sedai, of course, since they could not touch the True Source inside a *stedding*, or channel the One Power. The Ogier himself appeared the most reluctant of all to go to Stedding Tsofu. Mat was the only one who seemed eager, almost desperately so. His skin looked as if he had not seen the sun in a year, and his cheeks had begun to go hollow, though he said he felt ready to run a footrace. Verin put her hands on him for Healing before he rolled into his blankets, and again before they mounted their horses in the morning, but it made no difference in how he looked. Even Hurin frowned when he looked at Mat.

The sun stood high on the second day when Verin suddenly sat up straight in her saddle and looked around. Beside her, Ingtar gave a start.

Rand could not see anything different about the forest now surrounding them. The undergrowth was not too thick; they had found an easy way under the canopy of oak and hickory, blackgum and beech, pierced here and there by a tall pine or leatherleaf, or the white slash of a paperbark. But as he followed them, he suddenly felt a chill pass through him, as though he had leaped into a Waterwood pond in winter. It flashed through him and was gone, leaving behind a feeling of refreshment. And there was a dull and distant sense of loss, too, though he could not imagine of what.

Every rider, as he reached that point, gave a jerk or made some exclamation. Hurin's mouth dropped open, and Uno whispered, "Bloody, flaming. . . ." Then he shook his head as if he could not think of anything else to say. There was a look of recognition in Perrin's yellow eyes.

Loial took a deep, slow breath and let it out. "It feels . . . good . . . to be back in a *stedding*."

Frowning, Rand looked around. He had expected a *stedding* to be somehow different, but except for that one chill, the forest was the same as what they had been riding through all day. There was the sudden sense of being rested, of course. Then an Ogier stepped out from behind an oak.

She was shorter than Loial—which meant she stood head and shoulders taller than Rand—but with the same broad nose and big eyes, the same wide mouth and tufted ears. Her eyebrows were not so long as Loial's, though, and her features seemed delicate beside his, the tufts on her ears finer. She wore a long green dress and a green cloak embroidered with flowers, and carried a bunch of silverbell blossoms as if she had been gathering them. She looked at them calmly, waiting.

Loial scrambled down from his tall horse and bowed

hastily. Rand and the others did the same, if not so quickly as Loial; even Verin inclined her head. Loial gave their names formally, but he did not mention the name of his *stedding*.

For a moment the Ogier girl—Rand was sure she was no older than Loial—studied them, then smiled. "Be welcome to Stedding Tsofu." Her voice was a lighter version of Loial's, too; the softer rumble of a smaller bumblebee. "I am Erith, daughter of Iva daughter of Alar. Be welcome. We have had so few human visitors since the stonemasons left Cairhien, and now so many at once. Why, we even had some of the Traveling People, though, of course, they left when the. . . . Oh, I talk too much. I will take you to the Elders. Only. . . ." She searched among them for the one in charge, and settled finally on Verin. "Aes Sedai, you have so many men with you, and armed. Could you please leave some of them Outside? Forgive me, but it is always unsettling to have very many armed humans in the *stedding* at once."

"Of course, Erith," Verin said. "Ingtar, will you see to it?"

Ingtar gave orders to Uno, and so it was that he and Hurin were the only Shienarans to follow Erith deeper into the *stedding*.

Leading his horse like the others, Rand looked up as Loial came closer, with many glances at Erith up ahead with Verin and Ingtar. Hurin walked midway between, staring around in amazement, though Rand was not sure at what exactly. Loial bent to speak quietly. "Is she not beautiful, Rand? And her voice sings."

Mat snickered, but when Loial looked at him questioningly, he said, "Very pretty, Loial. A little tall for my taste, you understand, but very pretty, I'm sure."

Loial frowned uncertainly, but nodded. "Yes, she is." His expression lightened. "It does feel good to be back in a *stedding*. Not that the Longing was taking me, you understand."

"The Longing?" Perrin said. "I do not understand, Loial."

"We Ogier are bound to the *stedding*, Perrin. It is said that before the Breaking of the World, we could go where we wished for as long as we wished, like you humans, but that changed with the Breaking. Ogier were scattered like every other people, and they could not find any of the *sted-*

ding again. Everything was moved, everything changed. Mountains, rivers, even the seas."

"Everybody knows about the Breaking," Mat said impatiently. "What does it have to do with this—this Longing?"

"It was during the Exile, while we wandered lost, that the Longing first came on us. The desire to know the *stedding* once more, to know our homes again. Many died of it." Loial shook his head sadly. "More died than lived. When we finally began to find the *stedding* again, one at a time, in the years of the Covenant of the Ten Nations, it seemed we had defeated the Longing at last, but it had changed us, put seeds in us. Now, if an Ogier is Outside too long, the Longing comes again; he begins to weaken, and he dies if he does not return."

"Do you need to stay here awhile?" Rand asked anxiously. "There's no need to kill yourself to go with us."

"I will know it when it comes." Loial laughed. "It will be long before it is strong enough to cause harm to me. Why, Dalar spent ten years among the Sea Folk without ever seeing a *stedding,* and she came safely home."

An Ogier woman appeared out of the trees, pausing a moment to speak with Erith and Verin. She looked Ingtar up and down and seemed to dismiss him, which made him blink. Her eyes swept across Loial, flicked over Hurin and the Emond's Fielders, before she went off into the forest again; Loial seemed to be trying to hide behind his horse. "Besides," he said, peering cautiously across his saddle after her, "it is a dull life in the *stedding* compared to traveling with three *ta'veren.*"

"If you are going to start that again," Mat muttered, and Loial spoke up quickly. "Three friends, then. You are my friends, I hope."

"I am," Rand said simply, and Perrin nodded.

Mat laughed. "How could I not be friends with somebody who dices so badly?" He threw up his hands when Rand and Perrin looked at him. "Oh, all right. I like you, Loial. You're my friend. Just don't go on about. . . . Aaah! Sometimes you're as bad to be around as Rand." His voice sank to a mutter. "At least we're safe here in a *stedding.*"

Rand grimaced. He knew what Mat meant. *Here in a* stedding, *where I can't channel.*

Perrin punched Mat's shoulder, but looked sorry that he had when Mat grimaced at him with that gaunt face.

It was the music Rand became aware of first, unseen flutes and fiddles in a jolly tune that floated through the trees, and deep voices singing and laughing.

Clear the field, smooth it low.
Let no weed or stubble stand.
Here we labor, here we toil,
here the towering trees will grow.

Almost at the same moment he realized that the huge shape he was seeing through the trees was itself a tree, with a ridged, buttressed trunk that must have been twenty paces thick. Gaping, he followed it up with his eyes, up through the forest canopy, to branches spreading like the top of a gigantic mushroom a good hundred paces above the ground. And beyond it were taller still.

"Burn me," Mat breathed. "You could build ten houses from just one of those. Fifty houses."

"Cut down a Great Tree?" Loial sounded scandalized, and more than a little angry. His ears were stiff and still, his long eyebrows down on his cheeks. "We never cut down one of the Great Trees, not unless it dies, and they almost never do. Few survived the Breaking, but some of the largest were seedlings during the Age of Legends."

"I'm sorry," Mat said. "I was just saying how big they are. I won't hurt your trees." Loial nodded, seeming mollified.

More Ogier appeared now, walking among the trees. Most seemed intent on whatever they were about; though all looked at the newcomers, and even gave a friendly nod or a small bow, none stopped or spoke. They had a curious way of moving, in some manner blending a careful deliberateness with an almost childlike carefree joyfulness. They knew and liked who and what they were and where they were, and they seemed at peace with themselves and everything around them. Rand found himself envying them.

Few of the Ogier men were any taller than Loial, but it was easy to pick out the older men; one and all they wore mustaches as long as their dangling eyebrows and narrow beards under their chins. All of the younger were smooth-shaven, like Loial. Many of the men were in their shirt-sleeves, and carried shovels and mattocks or saws and buckets of pitch; the others wore plain coats that buttoned to the neck and flared about their knees like kilts. The women seemed to favor embroidered flowers, and many wore flowers in their hair, too. The embroidery was limited to the cloaks of the younger women; the older women's dresses were embroidered, as well, and some women with gray hair had flowers and vines from neck to hem. A handful of the Ogier, women and girls for the most part, did seem to take special notice of Loial; he walked staring straight ahead, ears twitching more wildly the further they went.

Rand was startled to see an Ogier apparently walking up out of the ground, out of one of the grassy, wildflower-covered mounds that lay scattered all among the trees here. Then he saw windows in the mounds, and an Ogier woman standing at one apparently rolling a piecrust, and realized he was looking at Ogier houses. The window frames were stone, but they not only seemed natural formations, they appeared to have been sculpted by wind and water over generations.

The Great Trees, with their massive trunks and spreading roots as thick as horses, needed a great deal of room between them, but several grew right in the town. Dirt ramps took the paths over the roots. In fact, aside from the pathways, the only way to tell town from forest at a glance was a large open space in the center of the town, around what could only be the stump of one of the Great Trees. Nearly a hundred paces across, its surface was polished as smooth as any floor, and there were steps built up to it at several places. Rand was imagining how tall that tree had been when Erith spoke loudly enough for them all to hear.

"Here come our other guests."

Three human women came walking around the side of the huge stump. The youngest was carrying a wooden bowl.

"Aiel," Ingtar said. "Maidens of the Spear. As well I *did* leave Masema with the others." Yet he stepped away from Verin and Erith, and reached over his shoulder to loosen his sword in its scabbard.

Rand studied the Aiel with an uneasy curiosity. They were what too many people had tried to tell him he was. Two of the women were mature, the other little more than a girl, but all three were tall for women. Their short-cut hair ranged from a reddish brown to almost golden, with a narrow, shoulder-length tail left long at the back. They wore loose breeches tucked into soft boots, and all their clothes were some shade of brown or gray or green; he thought the garments would fade into rock or woods almost as well as a Warder's cloak. Short bows poked over their shoulders, quivers and long knives hung at their belts, and each carried a small, round shield of hide and a cluster of spears with short shafts and long points. Even the youngest moved with a grace that suggested she knew how to use the weapons she carried.

Abruptly the women became aware of the other humans; they seemed as startled at being startled as they did at the sight of Rand and the others, but they moved like lightning. The youngest one shouted, "Shienarans!" and turned to set the bowl carefully behind her. The other two quickly lifted brown cloths from around their shoulders, wrapping them around their heads instead. The older women were raising black veils across their faces, hiding everything but their eyes, and the youngest straightened to imitate them. Crouching low, they advanced at a deliberate pace, shields held forward with their clusters of spears, except for the one each woman held ready in her other hand.

Ingtar's sword came out of its sheath. "Stand clear, Aes Sedai. Erith, stand clear." Hurin snatched out his sword-breaker, wavered between cudgel and sword for his other hand; after another glance at the Aiel's spears, he chose the sword.

"You must not," the Ogier girl protested. Wringing her hands, she turned from Ingtar to the Aiel and back. "You must not."

Rand realized the heron-mark blade was in his hands. Perrin had his axe half out of the loop at his belt and was hesitating, shaking his head.

"Are you two crazy?" Mat demanded. His bow still slanted across his back. "I don't care if they are Aiel, they're women."

"Stop this!" Verin demanded. "Stop this immediately!" The Aiel never broke stride, and the Aes Sedai clenched her fists in frustration.

Mat moved back to put a foot in his stirrup. "I'm leaving," he announced. "You hear me? I'm not staying to let them stick those things in me, and I am not going to shoot a woman!"

"The Pact!" Loial was shouting. "Remember the Pact!" It had no more effect than the continued pleas from Verin and Erith.

Rand noticed that both the Aes Sedai and the Ogier girl were keeping well out of the Aiel's way. He wondered if Mat had the right idea. He was not sure he could hurt a woman even if she *was* trying to kill him. What decided him was the thought that even if he did manage to reach Red's saddle, the Aiel were now no more than thirty paces away. He suspected those short spears could be thrown that far. As the women came closer, still crouching, spears ready, he stopped worrying about not hurting them and began worrying about how to stop them from hurting him.

Nervously, he sought the void, and it came. And the distant thought floated outside it that it was only the void. The glow of *saidin* was not there. The emptiness was more empty than he ever remembered, vaster, like a hunger great enough to consume him. A hunger for more; there was *supposed* to be something more.

Abruptly an Ogier strode in between the two groups, his narrow beard quivering. "What is the meaning of this? Put up your weapons." He sounded scandalized. "For you"— his glare took in Ingtar and Hurin, Rand and Perrin, and did not spare Mat for all his empty hands—"there is some excuse, but for you—" He rounded on the Aiel women, who had stopped their advance. "Have you forgotten the Pact?"

The women uncovered their heads and faces so hastily that it seemed they were trying to pretend they had never been covered. The girl's face was bright red, and the other women looked abashed. One of the older women, the one with the reddish hair, said, "Forgive us, Treebrother. We remember the Pact, and we would not have bared steel, but we are in the land of the Treekillers, where every hand is against us, and we saw armed men." Her eyes were gray, Rand saw, like his own.

"You are in a *stedding*, Rhian," the Ogier said gently. "Everyone is safe in the *stedding*, little sister. There is no fighting here, and no hand raised against another." She nodded, ashamed, and the Ogier looked at Ingtar and the others.

Ingtar sheathed his sword, and Rand did the same, though not so quickly as Hurin, who looked almost as embarrassed as the Aiel. Perrin had never gotten his axe all the way out. As he took hand from hilt, Rand let the void go, too, and shivered. The void went, but it left behind a slowly fading echo of the emptiness all through him, and a desire for something to fill it.

The Ogier turned to Verin and bowed. "Aes Sedai, I am Juin, son of Lacel son of Laud. I have come to take you to the Elders. They would know why an Aes Sedai comes among us, with armed men and one of our own youths." Loial hunched his shoulders as if trying to disappear.

Verin gave the Aiel a regretful look, as if she wanted to talk with them, then motioned Juin to lead, and he took her away without another word or even the first look at Loial.

For a few moments, Rand and the others stood facing the three Aiel women uneasily. At least, Rand knew he was uneasy. Ingtar seemed steady as a stone, with no more expression than one. The Aiel might have unveiled their faces, but they still had spears in their hands, and they studied the four men as though trying to see inside them. Rand in particular received increasingly angry looks. He heard the youngest woman mutter, "He is wearing a sword," in tones of mingled horror and contempt. Then the three were leaving, stopping to retrieve the wooden bowl and looking over their shoulders at Rand and the others until they vanished among the trees.

"Maidens of the Spear," Ingtar muttered. "I never thought they'd stop once they veiled their faces. Certainly not for a few words." He looked at Rand and his two friends. "You should see a charge by Red Shields, or Stone Dogs. As easy to stop as an avalanche."

"They would not break the Pact once it was recalled to them," Erith said, smiling. "They came for sung wood." A note of pride entered her voice. "We have two Treesingers in Stedding Tsofu. They are rare, now. I have heard that Stedding Shangtai has a young Treesinger who is very talented, but we have two." Loial blushed, but she did not appear to notice. "If you will come with me, I will show you where you may wait until the Elders have spoken."

As they followed her, Perrin murmured, "Sung wood, my

left foot. Those Aiel are searching for He Who Comes With the Dawn."

And Mat added dryly, "They're looking for you, Rand."

"For me! That is crazy. What makes you think—"

He cut off as Erith showed them down the steps of a wildflower-covered house apparently set aside for human guests. The rooms were twenty paces from stone wall to stone wall, with painted ceilings a good two spans above the floor, but the Ogier had done their best making something that would be comfortable for humans. Even so, the furniture was a little too large for comfort, the chairs tall enough to lift a man's heels off the floor, the table higher than Rand's waist. Hurin, at least, could have walked erect into the stone fireplace, which seemed to have been worn by water rather than made by hands. Erith eyed Loial doubtfully, but he waved away her concern and pulled one of the chairs into the corner least easily seen from the door.

As soon as the Ogier girl left, Rand got Mat and Perrin over to one side. "What do you mean they're looking for me? Why? For what reason? They looked right at me, and went away."

"They looked at you," Mat said with a grin, "like you hadn't bathed in a month, and had doused yourself with sheepdip besides." His grin faded. "But they could be looking for you. We met another Aiel."

Rand listened in growing amazement to their tale of the meeting in Kinslayer's Dagger. Mat told most of it, with Perrin putting in a correcting word now and again when he embellished too much. Mat made a great show of how dangerous the Aielman had been, and how close the meeting had come to a fight.

"And since you're the only Aiel we know," he finished, "well, it could be you. Ingtar says Aiel never live outside the Waste, so you must be the only one."

"I don't think that's funny, Mat," Rand growled. "I am not an Aiel." *The Amyrlin said you are. Ingtar thinks you are. Tam said. . . . He was sick, fevered.* They had severed the roots he had thought he had, the Aes Sedai and Tam between them, though Tam had been too sick to know what he was saying. They had cut him loose to tumble before the wind, then offered him something new to hold on to. False

Dragon. Aiel. He could not claim those for roots. He would
not. "Maybe I don't belong to anyone. But the Two Rivers is
the only home I know."

"I didn't mean anything," Mat protested. "It's just. . . .
Burn me, Ingtar says you are. Masema says you are. Urien
could have been your cousin, and if Rhian put on a dress
and said she was your aunt, you'd believe it yourself. Oh, all
right. Don't look at me like that, Perrin. If he wants to say
he isn't, all right. What difference does it make, anyway?"
Perrin shook his head.

Ogier girls brought water and towels for washing faces
and hands, and cheese and fruit and wine, with pewter goblets a little too large to be comfortable in the hand. Other
Ogier women came, too, their dresses all embroidered. One
by one they appeared, a dozen of them all told, to ask if the
humans were comfortable, if they needed anything. Each
turned her attentions to Loial just before she left. He gave
his answers respectfully but in as few words as Rand had
ever heard him use, standing with an Ogier-sized, wood-
bound book clutched to his chest like a shield, and when
they went, he huddled in his chair with the book held up in
front of his face. The books in the house were one thing not
sized for humans.

"Just smell this air, Lord Rand," Hurin said, filling his
lungs with a smile. His feet dangled from one of the chairs
at the table; he swung them like a boy. "I never thought
most places smelled bad, but this. . . . Lord Rand, I don't
think there's *ever* been any killing here. Not even any hurting,
except by accident."

"The *stedding* are supposed to be safe for everyone,"
Rand said. He was watching Loial. "That's what the stories
say, anyway." He swallowed a last bit of white cheese and
went over to the Ogier. Mat followed with a goblet in his
hand. "What's the matter, Loial?" Rand said. "You've been
as nervous as a cat in a dogyard ever since we came here."

"It is nothing," Loial said, giving the door an uneasy
glance from the corner of his eye.

"Are you afraid they'll find out you left Stedding Shangtai without permission from your Elders?"

Loial looked around wildly, the tufts on his ears vibrating. "Don't say that," he hissed. "Not where anyone can
hear. If they found out. . . ." With a heavy sigh, he slumped

back, looking from Rand to Mat. "I don't know how humans do it, but among Ogier. . . . If a girl sees a boy she likes, she goes to her mother. Or sometimes the mother sees someone she thinks is suitable. In any case, if they agree, the girl's mother goes to the boy's mother, and the next thing the boy knows, his marriage is all arranged."

"Doesn't the boy have any say in it?" Mat asked incredulously.

"None. The women always say we would spend our lives married to the trees if it was left to us." Loial shifted, grimacing. "Half of our marriages take place between *stedding;* groups of young Ogier visit from *stedding* to *stedding* so they can see, and be seen. If they discover I'm Outside without permission, the Elders will almost certainly decide I need a wife to settle me down. Before I know it, they'll have sent a message to Stedding Shangtai, to my mother, and she will come here and have me married before she washes off the dust of her journey. She's always said I am too hasty and need a wife. I think she was looking when I left. Whatever wife she chooses for me . . . well, any wife at all won't let me go back Outside until I have gray in my beard. Wives always say no man should be allowed Outside until he's settled enough to control his temper."

Mat gave a guffaw loud enough to draw every head, but at Loial's frantic gesture he spoke softly. "Among us, men do the choosing, and no wife can stop a man doing what he wants."

Rand frowned, remembering how Egwene had begun following him around when they were both little. It was then that Mistress al'Vere had begun taking a special interest in him, more than in any of the other boys. Later, some girls would dance with him on feastdays and some would not, and those who would were always Egwene's friends, while those who would not were girls Egwene did not like. He also seemed to remember Mistress al'Vere taking Tam aside—*And she was muttering about Tam not having a wife for her to talk to!*—and after that, Tam and everyone else had acted as if he and Egwene were promised, even though they had not knelt before the Women's Circle to say the words. He had never thought about it this way before; things between Egwene and him had always just seemed to be the way they were, and that was that.

"I think we do it the same way," he muttered, and when Mat laughed, he added, "Do you remember your father ever doing anything your mother really didn't want him to?" Mat opened his mouth with a grin, then frowned thoughtfully and closed it again.

Juin came down the steps from outside. "If you please, will all of you come with me? The Elders would see you." He did not look at Loial, but Loial still almost dropped the book.

"If the Elders try to make you stay," Rand said, "we'll say we need you to go with us."

"I'll bet it isn't about you at all," Mat said. "I'll bet they are just going to say we can use the Waygate." He shook himself, and his voice fell even lower. "We really have to do it, don't we." It was not a question.

"Stay and get married, or travel the Ways." Loial grimaced ruefully. "Life is very unsettling with *ta'veren* for friends."

CHAPTER
36

Among the Elders

As Juin took them through the Ogier town, Rand saw that Loial was growing more and more anxious. Loial's ears were as stiff as his back; his eyes grew bigger every time he saw another Ogier looking at him, especially the women and girls, and a large number of them did seem to take notice of him. He looked as if he expected his own execution.

The bearded Ogier gestured to wide steps leading down into a grassy mound that was bigger by far than any other; it was a hill, for all practical purposes, almost at the base of one of the Great Trees.

"Why don't you wait out here, Loial?" Rand said.

"The Elders—" Juin began.

"—Probably just want to see the rest of us," Rand finished for him.

"Why don't they leave him alone," Mat put in.

Loial nodded vigorously. "Yes. Yes, I think. . . ." A number of Ogier women were watching him, from white-haired grandmothers to daughters Erith's age, a knot of them talking among themselves but with all eyes on him. His ears jerked, but he looked at the broad door to which the stone steps led down, and nodded again. "Yes, I will sit out here, and I'll read. That is it. I will read." Fumbling in his coat pocket, he produced a book. He settled himself on the mound beside the steps, the book small in his hands, and fixed his eyes on the pages. "I will just sit here and read until you come out." His ears twitched as if he could feel the women's eyes.

Juin shook his head, then shrugged and motioned to the steps again. "If you please. The Elders are waiting."

The huge, windowless room inside the mound was scaled for Ogier, with a thick-beamed ceiling more than four spans up; it could have fit in any palace, for size at least. The seven Ogier seated on the dais directly in front of the door made it shrink a little by their size, but Rand still felt as if he were in a cavern. The somber floorstones were smooth, if large and irregular in shape, but the gray walls could have been the rough side of a cliff. The ceiling beams, rough-hewn as they were, looked like great roots.

Except for a high-backed chair where Verin sat facing the dais, the only furnishings were the heavy, vine-carved chairs of the Elders. The Ogier woman in the middle of the dais sat in a chair raised a little higher than those of the others, three bearded men to her left in long, flaring coats, three women to her right in dresses like her own, embroidered in vines and flowers from neckline to hem. All had aged faces and pure white hair, even to the tufts on their ears, and an air of massive dignity.

Hurin gaped at them openly, and Rand felt like staring himself. Not even Verin had the appearance of wisdom that was in the Elders' huge eyes, nor Morgase in her crown their authority, nor Moiraine their calm serenity. Ingtar was the first to bow, as formally as Rand had ever seen from him, while the others still stood rooted.

"I am Alar," the Ogier woman on the highest chair said when they had finally taken their places beside Verin, "Eldest of the Elders of Stedding Tsofu. Verin has told us that you have need to use the Waygate here. To recover the Horn of Valere from Darkfriends is a great need, indeed, but we have allowed none to travel the Ways in more than one hundred years. Neither us, nor the Elders of any other *stedding*."

"I will find the Horn," Ingtar said angrily. "I must. If you will not permit us to use the Waygate. . . ." He fell silent as Verin looked at him, but the scowl remained on his face.

Alar smiled. "Be not so hasty, Shienaran. You humans never take time for thought. Only decisions reached in calm can be sure." Her smile faded to seriousness, but her voice kept its own measured calm. "The dangers of the Ways are not to be faced with a sword in your hand, not charging Aiel or ravening Trollocs. I must tell you that to enter the Ways is to risk not only death and madness, but perhaps your very souls."

"We have seen *Machin Shin*," Rand said, and Mat and Perrin agreed. They could not manage to sound eager to do it again.

"I will follow the Horn to Shayol Ghul itself, if need be," Ingtar said firmly. Hurin only nodded as if including himself in Ingtar's words.

"Bring Trayal," Alar commanded, and Juin, who had remained by the door, bowed and left. "It is not enough," she told Verin, "to hear what can happen. You must see it, know it in your heart."

There was an uncomfortable silence until Juin returned, and it became more uncomfortable still as two Ogier women followed him, guiding a dark-bearded Ogier of middle years, who shambled between them as if he did not quite know how his legs worked. His face sagged, without any expression at all, and his big eyes were vacant and unblinking, not staring, not looking, not even seeming to see. One of the women gently wiped drool from the corner of his mouth. They took his arms to stop him; his foot went forward, hesitated, then fell back with a thump. He seemed as content to stand as to walk, or at least as uncaring.

"Trayal was one of the last among us to go along the Ways," Alar said softly. "He came out as you see him. Will you touch him, Verin?"

Verin gave her a long look, then rose and strode to Trayal. He did not move as she laid her hands on his wide chest, not even a flicker of an eye to acknowledge her touch. With a sharp hiss, she jerked back, staring up at him, then whirled to face the Elders. "He is . . . empty. This body lives, but there is nothing inside it. Nothing." Every Elder wore a look of unbearable sadness.

"Nothing," one of the Elders to Alar's right said softly. Her eyes seemed to hold all the pain Trayal's no longer could. "No mind. No soul. Nothing of Trayal remains but his body."

"He was a fine Treesinger," one of the men sighed.

Alar motioned, and the two women turned Trayal to lead him out; they had to move him before he began to walk.

"We know the risks," Verin said. "But whatever the risks, we must follow the Horn of Valere."

The Eldest nodded. "The Horn of Valere. I do not know whether it is worse news that it is in Darkfriend hands, or

that it has been found at all." She looked down the row of
Elders; each nodded in turn, one of the men tugging his
beard doubtfully first. "Very well. Verin tells me time is
urgent. I will show you to the Waygate myself." Rand was
feeling half relieved and half afraid, when she added, "You
have with you a young Ogier. Loial, son of Arent son of
Halan, from Stedding Shangtai. He is far from his home."

"We need him," Rand said quickly. His words slowed
under surprised stares from the Elders and Verin, but he
went on stubbornly. "We need him to go with us, and he
wants to."

"Loial's a friend," Perrin said, at the same time that Mat
said, "He doesn't get in the way, and he carries his own
weight." Neither of them appeared comfortable at having
the Elders' focus shift to them, but they did not back down.

"Is there some reason he cannot come with us?" Ingtar
asked. "As Mat says, he has held his own. I don't know that
we need him, but if he wants to come, why—?"

"We do need him," Verin broke in smoothly. "Few any
longer know the Ways, but Loial has studied them. He can
decipher the Guidings."

Alar eyed them each in turn, then settled to a study of
Rand. She looked as if she knew things; all the Elders did,
but she most of all. "Verin says you are *ta'veren*," she said
at last, "and I can feel it in you. That I can do so means that
you must be very strongly *ta'veren* indeed, for such Talents
ever run weakly in us, if at all. Have you drawn Loial, son
of Arent son of Halan, into *ta'maral'ailen,* the Web the
Pattern weaves around you?"

"I. . . . I just want to find the Horn and. . . ." Rand let the
rest of it die. Alar had not mentioned Mat's dagger. He did
not know whether Verin had told the Elders, or held it back
for some reason. "He is my friend, Eldest."

"Your friend," Alar said. "He is young by our way of
thinking. You are young, too, but *ta'veren*. You will look
after him, and when the weaving is done, you will see that
he comes safely home to Stedding Shangtai."

"I will," he told her. It had the feeling of a commitment,
the swearing of an oath.

"Then we will go to the Waygate."

Outside, Loial scrambled to his feet when they appeared, Alar and Verin leading. Ingtar sent Hurin off at

a run to fetch Uno and the other soldiers. Loial eyed the Eldest warily, then fell in with Rand at the rear of the procession. The Ogier women who had been watching him were all gone. "Did the Elders say anything about me? Did she . . . ?" He peered at Alar's broad back as she ordered Juin to have their horses brought. She started off with Verin while Juin was still bowing himself away, bending her head to talk quietly.

"She told Rand to take care of you," Mat told Loial solemnly as they followed, "and see you got home safely as a babe. I don't see why you can't stay here and get married."

"She said you could come with us." Rand glared at Mat, which made Mat chortle under his breath. It sounded odd, coming from that drawn face. Loial was twirling the stem of a trueheart blossom between his fingers. "Did you go picking flowers?" Rand asked.

"Erith gave it to me." Loial watched the yellow petals spin. "She really is very pretty, even if Mat does not see it."

"Does that mean you don't want to go with us after all?"

Loial gave a start. "What? Oh, no. I mean, yes. I do want to go. She only gave me a flower. Just a flower." He took a book out of his pocket, though, and pressed the blossom under the front cover. As he returned the book, he murmured to himself, barely loud enough for Rand to hear, "And she said I was handsome, too." Mat let out a wheeze and doubled over, staggering along clutching his sides, and Loial's cheeks colored. "Well . . . she said it. I didn't."

Perrin rapped Mat smartly on the top of his head with his knuckles. "Nobody ever said Mat was handsome. He's just jealous."

"That's not true," Mat said, straightening abruptly. "Marisa Ayellin thinks I'm handsome. She told me so more than once."

"Is Marisa pretty?" Loial asked.

"She has a face like a goat," Perrin said blandly. Mat choked, trying to get his protests out.

Rand grinned in spite of himself. Marisa was almost as pretty as Egwene. And this was almost like old times, almost like being back home, bantering back and forth, and nothing more important in the world than a laugh and twitting the other fellow.

As they made their way through the town, Ogier greeted

the Eldest, bowing or curtsying, eyeing the human visitors
with interest. Alar's set face kept anyone from stopping to
speak, though. The only thing that indicated when they left
the town was the absence of the mounds; there were still
Ogier about, examining trees, or sometimes working with
pitch and saw or axe where there were dead limbs or where
a tree needed more sunlight. They handled the tasks tenderly.

Juin joined them, leading their horses, and Hurin came
riding with Uno and the other soldiers, and the packhorses,
just before Alar pointed and said, "It is over there." The
banter died.

Rand felt a momentary surprise. The Waygate had to be
Outside the *stedding*—the Ways had been begun with the
One Power; they could not have been made inside—but
there was nothing to indicate they had crossed the boundary. Then he realized there was a difference; the sense of
something lost that he had felt since entering the *stedding*
was gone. That gave him another sort of chill. *Saidin* was
there again. Waiting.

Alar led them past a tall oak, and there in a small clearing stood the big slab of the Waygate, the front of it delicately worked in tightly woven vines and leaves from a
hundred different plants. Around the edge of the clearing
the Ogier had built a low stone coping that seemed as if it
had grown there, suggesting a circle of roots. The look of it
made Rand uncomfortable. It took him a moment to realize
that the roots suggested were those of bramble and briar,
burningleaf and itch oak. Not the sort of plants into which
anyone would want to stumble.

The Eldest stopped short of the coping. "The wall is
meant to warn away any who comes here. Not that many
of us do. I myself will not cross it. But you may." Juin did
not go as close as she did; he kept rubbing his hands on the
front of his coat, and would not look at the Waygate.

"Thank you," Verin told her. "The need is great, or I
would not have asked it."

Rand tensed as the Aes Sedai stepped over the coping
and approached the Waygate. Loial took a deep breath and
muttered to himself. Uno and the rest of the soldiers
shifted in their saddles and loosened swords in their scabbards. There was nothing along the Ways against which a

sword would be any use, but it was something to convince themselves they were ready. Only Ingtar and the Aes Sedai seemed calm; even Alar gripped her skirt with both hands.

Verin plucked the *Avendesora* leaf, and Rand leaned forward intently. He knew an urge to assume the void, to be where he could reach *saidin* if he needed to.

The greenery carved across the Waygate stirred in an unfelt breeze, leaves fluttering as a gap opened down the center of the mass and the two halves began to swing open.

Rand stared at the first crack. There was no dull, silvery reflection behind it, only blackness blacker than pitch. "Close it!" he shouted. "The Black Wind! Close it!"

Verin took one startled look and thrust the three-pointed leaf back in among all the varied leaves already there; it stayed when she took her hand away and backed toward the coping. As soon as the *Avendesora* leaf was back in its place, the Waygate immediately began to close. The crack disappeared, vines and leaves merging, hiding the blackness of *Machin Shin,* and the Waygate was only stone again, if stone carved in a nearer semblance of life than seemed possible.

Alar let out a shuddering breath. "*Machin Shin.* So close."

"It didn't try to come out," Rand said. Juin made a strangled sound.

"I have told you," Verin said, "the Black Wind is a creature of the Ways. It cannot leave them." She sounded calm, but she still wiped her hands on her skirt. Rand opened his mouth, then gave it up. "And yet," she went on, "I wonder at it being here. First in Cairhien, now here. I wonder." She gave Rand a sidelong glance that made him jump. The look was so quick that he did not think anyone else noticed it, but to Rand it seemed to connect him with the Black Wind.

"I have never heard of this," Alar said slowly, "*Machin Shin* waiting when a Waygate was opened. It always roamed the Ways. But it has been long, and perhaps the Black Wind hungers, and hopes to catch some unwary one entering a gate. Verin, assuredly you cannot use this Waygate. And however great your need, I cannot say I am sorry. The Ways belong to the Shadow, now."

Rand frowned at the Waygate. *Could it be following me?* There were too many questions. Had Fain somehow ordered the Black Wind? Verin said it could not be done.

And why would Fain demand that he follow, then try to stop him? He only knew that he believed the message. He had to go to Toman Head. If they found the Horn of Valere and Mat's dagger under a bush tomorrow, he still had to go.

Verin stood with eyes unfocused in thought. Mat was sitting on the coping with his head in his hands, and Perrin watched him worriedly. Loial seemed relieved that they could not use the Waygate, and ashamed at being relieved.

"We are done for here," Ingtar announced. "Verin Sedai, I followed you here against my better judgment, but I can no longer follow. I mean to return to Cairhien. Barthanes can tell me where the Darkfriends went, and somehow I will make him do it."

"Fain went to Toman Head," Rand said wearily. "And where he went, that's where the Horn is, and the dagger."

"I suppose. . . ." Perrin shrugged reluctantly. "I suppose we could try another Waygate. At another *stedding?*"

Loial stroked his chin and spoke quickly, as if to make up for his relief at the failure here. "Stedding Cantoine lies just above the River Iralell, and Stedding Taijing is east of it in the Spine of the World. But the Waygate in Caemlyn, where the grove was, is closer, and the gate in the grove at Tar Valon is closest of all."

"Whichever Waygate we try to use," Verin said absently, "I fear we will find *Machin Shin* waiting." Alar looked at her questioningly, but the Aes Sedai said no more that anyone could hear. She muttered to herself instead, shaking her head as if arguing with herself.

"What we need," Hurin said diffidently, "is one of those Portal Stones." He looked to Alar, then Verin, and when neither told him to stop, he went on, sounding increasingly confident. "The Lady Selene said those old Aes Sedai had studied those worlds, and that was how they knew how to make the Ways. And that place we were . . . well, it only took us two days—less—to travel a hundred leagues. If we could use a Portal Stone to go to that world, or one like it, why, it'd take no more than a week or two to reach the Aryth Ocean, and we could come back right on Toman Head. Maybe it isn't so quick as the Ways, but it's a long sight quicker than riding off west. What do you say, Lord Ingtar? Lord Rand?"

Verin answered him. "What you suggest might be possible, sniffer, but as well hope to open this Waygate again and find *Machin Shin* gone as hope to find a Portal Stone. I know none closer than the Aiel Waste. Though we could go back into Kinslayer's Dagger, if you, or Rand, or Loial think you could find that Stone again."

Rand looked at Mat. His friend had lifted his head hopefully at this talk of the Stones. A few weeks, Verin had said. If they simply rode west, Mat would never live to see Toman Head.

"I can find it," Rand said reluctantly. He felt ashamed. *Mat's going to die, Darkfriends have the Horn of Valere, Fain will hurt Emond's Field if you don't follow him, and you're afraid to channel the Power. Once to go and once to come back. Twice more won't drive you mad.* What really made him afraid, though, was the eagerness that leaped inside him at the thought of channeling again, of feeling the Power fill him, of feeling truly alive.

"I do not understand this," Alar said slowly. "The Portal Stones have not been used since the Age of Legends. I did not think there was anyone who still knew how to use them."

"The Brown Ajah knows many things," Verin said dryly, "and I know how the Stones may be used."

The Eldest nodded. "Truly there are wonders in the White Tower of which we do not dream. But if you can use a Portal Stone, there is no need for you to ride to Kinslayer's Dagger. There is a Stone not far from where we stand."

"The Wheel weaves as the Wheel wills, and the Pattern provides what is needful." The absent look dropped from Verin's face altogether. "Take us to it," she said briskly. "We have lost more than enough time already."

CHAPTER
37

What Might Be

Alar led them away from the Waygate at a dignified pace, though Juin seemed more than anxious to leave the Waygate behind. Mat, at least, looked ahead eagerly, and Hurin seemed confident, while Loial appeared concerned more that Alar might change her mind about his going than about anything else. Rand did not hurry as he pulled Red along by the reins. He did not think Verin meant to use the Stone herself.

The gray stone column stood upright near a beech almost a hundred feet tall and four paces thick; Rand would have thought it a big tree before he saw the Great Trees. There was no warning coping here, only a few wildflowers pushing through the leafy mulch of the forest floor. The Portal Stone itself was weathered, but the symbols covering it were still clear enough to make out.

The mounted Shienaran soldiers spread out in a loose circle around the Stone and those afoot.

"We stood it upright," Alar said, "when we found it many years ago, but we did not move it. It . . . seemed to . . . resist being moved." She went right up to it, and laid a big hand on the Stone. "I have always thought of it as a symbol of what has been lost, what has been forgotten. In the Age of Legends, it could be studied and somewhat understood. To us, it is only stone."

"More than that, I hope." Verin's voice grew brisker. "Eldest, I thank you for your help. Forgive us for our lack of ceremony in leaving you, but the Wheel waits for no woman. At least we will no longer disturb the peace of your *stedding*."

"We called the stonemasons back from Cairhien," Alar said, "but we still hear what happens in the world Outside. False Dragons. The Great Hunt of the Horn. We hear, and it passes us by. I do not think Tarmon Gai'don will pass us by, or leave us in peace. Fare you well, Verin Sedai. All of you, fare well, and may you shelter in the palm of the Creator's hand. Juin." She paused only for a glance at Loial and a last admonitory look at Rand, and then the Ogier were gone among the trees.

There was a creaking of saddles as the soldiers shifted. Ingtar looked around the circle they made. "Is this necessary, Verin Sedai? Even if it can be done. . . . We do not even know if the Darkfriends really have taken the Horn to Toman Head. I still believe I can make Barthanes—"

"If we cannot be sure," Verin said mildly, cutting him off, "then Toman Head is as good a place to look as any other. More than once I've heard you say you would ride to Shayol Ghul if need be to recover the Horn. Do you hold back now, at this?" She gestured to the Stone under the smooth-barked tree.

Ingtar's back stiffened. "I hold back at nothing. Take us to Toman Head or take us to Shayol Ghul. If the Horn of Valere lies at the end, I will follow you."

"That is well, Ingtar. Now, Rand, you have been transported by a Portal Stone more recently than I. Come." She motioned to him, and he led Red over to her at the Stone.

"You've used a Portal Stone?" He glanced over his shoulder to make sure no one else was close enough to hear. "Then you don't mean for me to." He gave a relieved shrug.

Verin looked at him blandly. "I have never used a Stone; that is why your use is more recent than mine. I am well aware of my limits. I would be destroyed before I came close to channeling enough Power to work a Portal Stone. But I know a little of them. Enough to help you, a bit."

"But I don't know *anything*." He led his horse around the Stone, looking it up and down. "The one thing I remember is the symbol for our world. Selene showed me, but I don't see it here."

"Of course not. Not on a Stone *in* our world; the symbols are aids in getting *to* a world." She shook her head. "What would I not give to talk with this girl of yours? Or better, to put my hands on her book. It is generally thought that no copy of *Mirrors of the Wheel* survived the Breaking whole. Serafelle always tells me there are more books that we believe lost than I could credit waiting to be found. Well, no use in worrying over what I don't know. I do know some things. The symbols on the top half of the Stone stand for worlds. Not all the Worlds That Might Be, of course. Apparently, not every Stone connects to every world, and the Aes Sedai of the Age of Legends believed that there were possible worlds no Stones at all touched. Do you see nothing that sparks a memory?"

"Nothing." If he found the right symbol, he could use it to find Fain and the Horn, to save Mat, to stop Fain hurting Emond's Field. If he found the symbol, he would have to touch *saidin*. He wanted to save Mat and stop Fain, but he did not want to touch *saidin*. He was afraid to channel, and he hungered for it like a starving man for food. "I don't remember anything."

Verin sighed. "The symbols at the bottom indicate Stones at other places. If you know the trick of it, you could take us, not to this same Stone in another world, but to one of those others there, or even to one of them here. It was something akin to Traveling, I think, but just as no one remembers how to Travel, no one remembers the trick. Without that knowledge, trying it might easily destroy us all." She pointed to two parallel wavy lines crossed by an odd squiggle, carved low on the column. "That indicates a Stone on Toman Head. It is one of three Stones for which I know the symbol; the only one of those three I've visited. And what I learned—after nearly being caught by the snows in the Mountains of Mist and freezing my way across Almoth Plain—was absolutely nothing. Do you play at dice, or cards, Rand al'Thor?"

"Mat's the gambler. Why?"

"Yes. Well, we'll leave him out of this, I think. These other symbols are also known to me."

With one finger she outlined a rectangle containing eight carvings that were much alike, a circle and an arrow, but in half the arrow was contained inside the circle, while in the others the point pierced the circle through. The arrows pointed left, right, up and down, and surrounding each circle was a different line of what Rand was sure was script, though in no language he knew, all curving lines that suddenly became jagged hooks, then flowed on again.

"At least," Verin went on, "I know this much about them. Each stands for a world, the study of which led eventually to the making of the Ways. These are not all of the worlds studied, but the only ones for which I know the symbols. This is where gambling comes in. I don't know what any of these worlds is like. It is believed there are worlds where a year is only a day here, and others where a day is a year here. There are supposed to be worlds where the very air would kill us at a breath, and worlds that barely have enough reality to hold together. I would not speculate on what might happen if we found ourselves in one of those. You must choose. As my father would have said, it's time to roll the dice."

Rand stared, shaking his head. "I could kill all of us, whatever I choose."

"Are you not willing to take that risk? For the Horn of Valere? For Mat?"

"Why are you so willing to take it? I don't even know if I can do it. It—it doesn't work every time I try." He knew no one had come any closer, but he looked anyway. All of them waited in a loose circle around the Stone, watching, but not close enough to eavesdrop. "Sometimes *saidin* is just there. I can feel it, but it might as well be on the moon as far as touching it. And even if it does work, what if I take us someplace we can't breathe? What good will that do Mat? Or the Horn?"

"You are the Dragon Reborn," she said quietly. "Oh, you can die, but I don't think the Pattern will let you die until it is done with you. Then again, the Shadow lies on the Pattern, now, and who can say how that affects the weaving? All you can do is follow your destiny."

"I am Rand al'Thor," he growled. "I am not the Dragon Reborn. I won't be a false Dragon."

"You are what you are. Will you choose, or will you stand here until your friend dies?"

Rand heard his teeth grinding and forced himself to unclench his jaw. The symbols could all have been exactly alike, for all they meant to him. The script could as well have been a chicken's scratchings. At last he settled on one, with an arrow pointing left because it pointed toward Toman Head, an arrow that pierced the circle because it had broken free, as he wanted to. He wanted to laugh. Such small things on which to gamble all their lives.

"Come closer," Verin ordered the others. "It will be best if you are near." They obeyed, with only a little hesitation. "It is time to begin," she said as they gathered round.

She threw back her cloak and put her hands on the column, but Rand saw her watching him from the corner of her eye. He was aware of nervous coughing and throat-clearing from the men around the Stone, a curse from Uno at someone hanging back, a weak joke from Mat, a loud gulp from Loial. He took the void.

It was so easy, now. The flame consumed fear and passion and was gone almost before he thought to form it. Gone, leaving only emptiness, and shining *saidin*, sickening, tantalizing, stomach-turning, seductive. He . . . reached for it . . . and it filled him, made him alive. He did not move a muscle, but he felt as if he were quivering with the rush of the One Power into him. The symbol formed itself, an arrow piercing a circle, floating just beyond the void, as hard as the stuff it was carved on. He let the One Power flow through him to the symbol.

The symbol shimmered, flickered.

"Something is happening," Verin said. "Something . . ."

The world flickered.

The iron lock spun across the farmhouse floor, and Rand dropped the hot teakettle as a huge figure with ram's horns on its head loomed in the doorway with the darkness of Winternight behind it.

"Run!" Tam shouted. His sword flashed, and the Trolloc toppled, but it grappled with Tam as it fell, pulling him down.

More crowded in at the door, black-mailed shapes with human faces distorted with muzzles and beaks and horns, oddly curved swords stabbing at Tam as he tried to struggle to his feet, spiked axes swinging, red blood on steel.

"Father!" Rand screamed. Clawing his belt knife from its sheath, he threw himself over the table to help his father, and screamed again as the first sword ran through his chest.

Blood bubbled up into his mouth, and a voice whispered inside his head, *I have won again, Lews Therin.*

Flicker.

Rand struggled to hold the symbol, dimly aware of Verin's voice. ". . . is not . . ."

The Power flooded.

Flicker.

Rand was happy after he married Egwene, and tried to not let the moods take him, the times when he thought there should have been something more, something different. News of the world outside came into the Two Rivers with peddlers, and merchants come to buy wool and tabac, always news of fresh troubles, of wars and false Dragons everywhere. There was a year when neither merchants nor peddlers came, and when they returned the next they brought word that Artur Hawkwing's armies had come back, or their descendants, at least. The old nations were broken, it was said, and the world's new masters, who used chained Aes Sedai in their battles, had torn down the White Tower and salted the ground where Tar Valon had stood. There were no more Aes Sedai.

It all made little difference in the Two Rivers. Crops still had to be planted, sheep sheared, lambs tended. Tam had grandsons and granddaughters to dandle on his knee before he was laid to rest beside his wife, and the old farmhouse grew new rooms. Egwene became Wisdom, and most thought she was even better than the old Wisdom, Nynaeve al'Maera, had been. It was as well she was, for her cures that worked so miraculously on others were only just able to keep Rand alive from the sickness that constantly seemed to threaten him. His moods grew worse, blacker, and he raged that this was not what was meant to be. Egwene grew frightened when the moods were on him, for strange things sometimes happened when he was at his bleakest—lightning storms she had not heard listening to

the wind, wildfires in the forest—but she loved him and
cared for him and kept him sane, though some muttered
that Rand al'Thor was crazy and dangerous.

When she died, he sat alone for long hours by her grave,
tears soaking his gray-flecked beard. His sickness came
back, and he wasted; he lost the last two fingers on his right
hand and one on his left, his ears looked like scars, and men
muttered that he smelled of decay. His blackness deepened.

Yet when the dire news came, none refused to accept him
at their side. Trollocs and Fades and things undreamed of
had burst out of the Blight, and the world's new masters
were being thrown back, for all the powers they wielded.
So Rand took up the bow he had just fingers enough left
to shoot and limped with those who marched north to the
River Taren, men from every village, farm, and corner of
the Two Rivers, with their bows, and axes, and boarspears,
and swords that had lain rusting in attics. Rand wore a
sword, too, with a heron on the blade, that he had found
after Tam died, though he knew nothing of how to use it.
Women came, too, shouldering what weapons they could
find, marching alongside the men. Some laughed, saying
that they had the strange feeling they had done this before.

And at the Taren the people of the Two Rivers met the
invaders, endless ranks of Trollocs led by nightmare Fades
beneath a dead black banner that seemed to eat the light.
Rand saw that banner and thought the madness had taken
him again, for it seemed that this was what he had been born
for, to fight that banner. He sent every arrow at it, straight as
his skill and the void would serve, never worrying about the
Trollocs forcing their way across the river, or the men and
women dying to either side of him. It was one of those Trollocs that ran him through, before it loped howling for blood
deeper into the Two Rivers. And as he lay on the bank of
the Taren, watching the sky seem to grow dark at noon,
breath coming ever slower, he heard a voice say, *I have won
again, Lews Therin.*

Flicker.

The arrow-and-circle contorted into parallel wavy lines,
and he fought it back again.

Verin's voice. ". . . right. Something . . ."

The Power raged.
Flicker.

Tam tried to console Rand when Egwene took sick and died just a week before their wedding. Nynaeve tried, too, but she was shaken herself, since for all her skill she had no idea what it was that had killed the girl. Rand had sat outside Egwene's house while she died, and there seemed to be nowhere in Emond's Field he could go that he did not still hear her screaming. He knew he could not stay. Tam gave him a sword with a heron-mark blade, and though he explained little of how a shepherd in the Two Rivers had come by such a thing, he taught Rand how to use it. On the day Rand left, Tam gave him a letter he said might get Rand taken into the army of Illian, and hugged him, and said, "I've never had another son, or wanted another. Come back with a wife like I did, if you can, boy, but come back in any case."

Rand had his money stolen in Baerlon, though, and his letter of introduction, and almost his sword, and he met a woman called Min who told him such crazy things about himself that he finally left the city to get away from her. Eventually his wanderings brought him to Caemlyn, and there his skill with the sword earned him a place in the Queen's Guards. Sometimes he found himself looking at the Daughter-Heir, Elayne, and at such times he was filled with odd thoughts that this was not the way things were supposed to be, that there should be something more to his life. Elayne did not look at him, of course; she married a Tairen prince, though she did not seem happy in it. Rand was just a soldier, once a shepherd from a small village so far toward the western border that only lines on a map any longer truly connected it to Andor. Besides, he had a dark reputation, as a man of violent moods.

Some said he was mad, and in ordinary times perhaps not even his skill with the sword would have kept him in the Guard, but these were not ordinary times. False Dragons sprang up like weeds. Every time one was taken down, two more proclaimed themselves, or three, till every nation was torn by war. And Rand's star rose, for he had learned the secret of his madness, a secret he knew he had to keep and did. He could channel. There were always places, times, in a battle when a little channeling, not big enough to be noticed in the confusion, could make luck. Sometimes it worked, this channeling, and sometimes not, but it worked often enough. He knew he was mad, and did not care. A wasting sickness came on him, and he did not care about that, either, and neither did anyone else, for word had come that Artur Hawkwing's armies had returned to reclaim the land.

Rand led a thousand men when the Queen's Guards crossed the Mountains of Mist—he never thought of turning aside to visit the Two Rivers; he seldom thought of the Two Rivers at all, anymore—and he commanded the Guard when the shattered remnants retreated back across the mountains. The length of Andor he fought and fell back, amid hordes of fleeing refugees, until at last he came to Caemlyn. Many of the people of Caemlyn had fled already, and many counseled the army to retreat further, but Elayne was Queen, now, and vowed she would not leave Caemlyn. She would not look at his ruined face, scarred by his sickness, but he could not leave her, and so what was left of the Queen's Guards prepared to defend the Queen while her people ran.

The Power came to him during the battle for Caemlyn, and he hurled lightning and fire among the invaders, and split the earth under their feet, yet the feeling came again, too, that he had been born for something else. For all he did, there were too many of the enemy to stop, and they also had those who could channel. At last, a lightning bolt hurled Rand from the Palace wall, broken, bleeding, and burned, and as his last breath rattled in his throat, he heard a voice whisper, *I have won again, Lews Therin.*
    Flicker.

Rand struggled to hold the void as it quivered under the hammer blows of the world flickering, to hold the one symbol as a thousand of them darted along the surface of the void. He struggled to hold on to any one symbol.

    ". . . is wrong!" Verin screamed.

    The Power was everything.

    Flicker. Flicker. Flicker. Flicker. Flicker. Flicker.

He was a soldier. He was a shepherd. He was a beggar, and a king. He was farmer, gleeman, sailor, carpenter. He was born, lived, and died an Aiel. He died mad, he died rotting, he died of sickness, accident, age. He was executed, and multitudes cheered his death. He proclaimed himself the Dragon Reborn and flung his banner across the sky; he ran from the Power and hid; he lived and died never knowing. He held off the madness and the sickness for years; he succumbed between two winters. Sometimes Moiraine came and took him away from the Two Rivers, alone or with those of his friends who had survived Winternight; sometimes she did not. Sometimes other Aes Sedai came for him. Sometimes the Red Ajah. Egwene married him; Egwene, stern-faced in the stole of the Amyrlin Seat, led the Aes Sedai who gentled him; Egwene, with tears in her eyes, plunged a dagger into his heart, and he thanked her as he died. He loved other women, married other women. Elayne, and Min, and a fair-haired farmer's daughter met on the road to Caemlyn, and women he had never seen before he lived those lives. A hundred lives. More. So many he could not count them. And at the end of every life, as he lay dying, as he drew his final breath, a voice whispered in his ear. *I have won again, Lews Therin. Flicker flicker.*

The void vanished, contact with *saidin* fled, and Rand fell with a thud that would have knocked the breath out of him if he had not already been half numb. He felt rough stone under his cheek, and his hands. It was cold.

He was aware of Verin, struggling from her back to hands and knees. He heard someone vomit roughly, and raised his head. Uno was kneeling on the ground, scrubbing the back of his hand across his mouth. Everyone was down, and the horses stood stiff-legged and quivering, eyes wild and rolling. Ingtar had his sword out, gripping the hilt so hard the blade shook, staring at nothing. Loial sat sprawled, wide-eyed and stunned. Mat was huddled in a ball with his arms wrapped around his head, and Perrin had his fingers dug into his face as if he wanted to rip away whatever he had seen, or perhaps rip out the eyes that had seen it. None of the soldiers were any better. Masema wept openly, tears streaming down his face, and Hurin was looking around as if for a place to run.

"What . . . ?" Rand stopped to swallow. He was lying on rough, weathered stone half buried in the dirt. "What happened?"

"A surge of the One Power." The Aes Sedai tottered to her feet and pulled her cloak tight with a shiver. "It was as if we were being forced . . . pushed. . . . It seemed to come out of nowhere. You must learn to control it. You must! That much of the Power could burn you to a cinder."

"Verin, I. . . . I lived. . . . I was. . . ." He realized the stone under him was rounded. The Portal Stone. Hastily, shakily, he pushed himself to his feet. "Verin, I lived and died, I don't know how many times. Every time it was different, but it was me. It was me."

"The Lines that join the Worlds That Might Be, laid by those who knew the Numbers of Chaos." Verin shuddered; she seemed to be talking to herself. "I've never heard it, but there is no reason we would not be born in those worlds, yet the lives we lived would be different lives. Of course. Different lives for the different ways things might have happened."

"Is that what happened? I . . . we . . . saw how our lives could have been?" *I have won again, Lews Therin. No! I am Rand al'Thor!*

Verin gave herself a shake and looked at him. "Does it surprise you that your life might go differently if you made different choices, or different things happened to you? Though I never thought I—Well. The important thing is, we are here. Though not as we hoped."

"Where is here?" he demanded. The woods of Stedding Tsofu were gone, replaced by rolling land. There seemed to be forest not far to the west, and a few hills. It had been high in the day when they gathered around the Stone in the *stedding* but here the sun stood low toward afternoon in a gray sky. The handful of trees nearby were bare branched, or else held a few leaves bright with color. A cold wind gusted from the east, sending leaves scurrying across the ground.

"Toman Head," Verin said. "This is the Stone I visited. You should not have tried to bring us directly here. I don't know what went wrong—I don't suppose I ever will—but from the trees, I would say it is well into late autumn. Rand, we haven't gained any time by it. We've lost time. I would say we have easily spent four months in coming here."

"But I didn't—"

"You must let me guide you in these things. I cannot teach you, it's true, but perhaps I can at least keep you from killing yourself—and the rest of us—by overreaching. Even if you do not kill yourself, if the Dragon Reborn burns himself out like a guttering candle, who will face the Dark One then?" She did not wait for him to renew his protests, but went to Ingtar instead.

The Shienaran gave a start when she touched his arm, and looked at her with frantic eyes. "I walk in the Light," he said hoarsely. "I will find the Horn of Valere and pull down Shayol Ghul's power. I will!"

"Of course you will," she said soothingly. She took his face in her hands, and he drew a sudden breath, abruptly recovering from whatever had held him. Except that memory still lay in his eyes. "There," she said. "That will do for you. I will see how I can help the rest. We may still recover the Horn, but our path has not grown smoother."

As she started around among the others, stopping briefly by each, Rand went to his friends. When he tried to straighten Mat, Mat jerked and stared at him, then grabbed Rand's coat with both hands. "Rand, I'd never tell anyone about—about you. I wouldn't betray you. You have to believe that!" He looked worse than ever, but Rand thought it was mostly fright.

"I do," Rand said. He wondered what lives Mat had lived, and what he had done. *He must have told someone, or he wouldn't be so anxious about it.* He could not hold it against him. Those had been other Mats, not this one. Besides, after some of the alternatives he had seen for himself. . . . "I believe you. Perrin?"

The curly-haired youth dropped his hands from his face with a sigh. Red marks scored his forehead and cheeks where his nails had dug in. His yellow eyes hid his thoughts. "We don't have many choices really, do we, Rand? Whatever happens, whatever we do, some things are almost always the same." He let out another long breath. "Where are we? Is this one of those worlds you and Hurin were talking about?"

"It's Toman Head," Rand told him. "In our world. Or so Verin says. And it is autumn."

Mat looked worried. "How could—? No, I don't want to know how it happened. But how are we going to find Fain and the dagger now? He could be anywhere by this time."

"He's here," Rand assured him. He hoped he was right. Fain had had time to take ship for anyplace he wanted to go. Time to ride to Emond's Field. Or Tar Valon. *Please, Light, he didn't get tired of waiting. If he's hurt Egwene, or anybody in Emond's Field, I'll. . . . Light burn me, I tried to come in time.*

"The larger towns on Toman Head are all west of here," Verin announced loudly enough for all to hear. Everyone was on their feet again, except for Rand and his two friends; she came and put her hands on Mat as she spoke. "Not that there are many villages large enough to call towns. If we are to find any trace of the Darkfriends, to the west is the place to begin. And I think we should not waste the daylight sitting here."

When Mat blinked and stood up—he still looked ill, but he moved spryly—she put her hands on Perrin. Rand backed away when she reached for him.

"Don't be foolish," she told him.

"I don't want your help," he said quietly. "Or any Aes Sedai help."

Her lips twitched. "As you wish."

They mounted immediately and rode west, leaving the Portal Stone behind. No one protested, Rand least of all. *Light, let me not be too late.*

CHAPTER
38

Practice

S itting cross-legged on her bed in her white dress, Egwene made three tiny balls of light weave patterns above her hands. She was not supposed to do this without at least one of the Accepted to supervise, but Nynaeve, glaring and striding up and down in front of the small fireplace, did after all wear the Serpent ring given to the Accepted, and her white dress had the colored rings encircling the hem, even if she was not allowed to try to teach anyone yet. And Egwene had found over these last thirteen weeks that she could not resist. She knew how easy it was to touch *saidar* now. She could always feel it there, waiting for her, like the smell of perfume or the feel of silk, drawing her, drawing her. And once she did touch it, she could rarely stop from channeling, or at least trying to. She failed almost as often as she succeeded, but that was only another spur to keep on.

It often frightened her. How much she wanted to channel frightened her, and how drab and dreary she felt when she was not channeling, compared to when she was. She wanted to drink it all in, despite the cautions about burning herself out, and that wanting frightened her most of all. Sometimes she wished she had never come to Tar Valon. But the fright could not make her stop for long, any more than the fear of being caught by an Aes Sedai or by any of the Accepted beside Nynaeve.

It was safe enough here, though, in her own room. Min was there, sitting on the three-legged stool watching her, but she knew Min well enough now to know Min would never report her. She thought she was lucky to have made two good friends since coming to Tar Valon.

It was a little, windowless room, as all novices' rooms were. Three short paces took Nynaeve from wall to white-plastered wall; Nynaeve's own room was much larger, but since she had made no friends among the other Accepted, she came to Egwene's room when she needed someone to talk to, even as now when she did not talk at all. The tiny fire on the narrow hearth handily kept the first chill of approaching autumn at bay, though Egwene was sure it would not serve so well when winter came. A small table for study completed the furnishings, and her belongings hung neatly on a row of pegs on the wall or sat on the short shelf above the table. Novices were usually kept too busy to spend time in their rooms, but today was a freeday, only the third since she and Nynaeve had come to the White Tower.

"Else was making calf's eyes at Galad today while he was working with the Warders," Min said, rocking the stool on two legs.

The small balls faltered for an instant above Egwene's hands. "She can look at whoever she wants," Egwene said casually. "I can't imagine why I would be interested."

"No reason, I suppose. He is awfully handsome, if you don't mind him being so rigid. Very nice to look at, especially with his shirt off."

The balls spun furiously. "I certainly have no desire to look at Galad, with or without his shirt."

"I shouldn't tease you," Min said contritely. "I'm sorry for that. But you do like to look at him—don't grimace at me like that—and so does nearly every woman in the White Tower who isn't a Red. I've seen Aes Sedai down at the practice yards when he's working forms, especially Greens. Checking on their Warders, they say, but I don't see so many when Galad isn't there. Even the cooks and maids come out to watch him."

The balls stopped dead, and for a moment Egwene stared at them. They vanished. Suddenly she giggled. "He *is* good-looking, isn't he? Even when he walks he looks as if he's dancing." The color in her cheeks deepened. "I know I shouldn't stare at him, but I can't help myself."

"I can't either," Min said, "and I can see what he is like."

"But if he is good—?"

"Egwene, Galad is so good he'd make you tear your hair out. He'd hurt a person because he had to serve a greater good. He wouldn't even notice who was hurt, because he'd be so intent on the other, but if he did, he would expect them to understand and think it was all well and right."

"I suppose you know," Egwene said. She had seen Min's ability to look at people and read all sorts of things about them; Min did not tell everything she saw, and she did not always see anything, but there had been enough for Egwene to believe. She glanced at Nynaeve—the other woman was still pacing, muttering to herself—then reached for *saidar* again and resumed her juggling in a desultory fashion.

Min shrugged. "I guess I might as well tell you. He didn't even notice what Else was doing. He asked her if she knew whether you might be walking the South Garden after supper, since today is a freeday. I felt sorry for her."

"Poor Else," Egwene murmured, and the balls of light became more lively above her hands. Min laughed.

The door banged open, caught by the wind. Egwene gave a yelp and let the balls vanish before she saw it was only Elayne.

The golden-haired Daughter-Heir of Andor pushed the door shut and hung up her cloak on a peg. "I just heard," she said. "The rumors are true. King Galldrian is dead. That makes it a war of succession."

Min snorted. "Civil war. War of succession. A lot of silly names for the same thing. Do you mind if we don't talk about it? That's all we hear. War in Cairhien. War on Toman Head. They may have caught the false Dragon in Saldaea, but there's still war in Tear. Most of it is rumors, anyway. Yesterday, I heard one of the cooks saying she'd heard Artur Hawkwing was marching on Tanchico. Artur Hawkwing!"

"I thought you did not want to talk about it," Egwene said.

"I saw Logain," Elayne said. "He was sitting on a bench in the Inner Court, crying. He ran when he saw me. I cannot help feeling sorry for him."

"Better he cries than the rest of us, Elayne," Min said.

"I know what he is," Elayne said calmly. "Or rather, what he was. He isn't anymore, and I can feel sorry for him."

Egwene slumped back against the wall. *Rand.* Logain

always made her think of Rand. She had not dreamed about him in months, now, not the kind of dreams she had had on the *River Queen.* Anaiya still made her write down everything she dreamed, and the Aes Sedai checked them for signs, or connections to events, but there was never anything about Rand except dreams that, Anaiya said, meant she missed him. Oddly, she felt almost as if he were not there any longer, as if he had ceased to exist, along with her dreams, a few weeks after reaching the White Tower. *And I sit thinking about how nicely Galad walks,* she thought bitterly. *Rand has to be all right. If he'd been caught and gentled, I'd have heard something.*

That sent a chill through her, as it never failed to do, the thought of Rand being gentled, Rand weeping and wanting to die as Logain did.

Elayne sat down beside her on the bed, tucking her feet up under her. "If you are mooning over Galad, Egwene, you will have no sympathy from me. I'll have Nynaeve dose you with one of those horrible concoctions she's always talking about." She frowned at Nynaeve, who had taken no notice of her entrance. "What is the matter with her? Don't tell me she has started sighing after Galad, too!"

"I wouldn't bother her." Min leaned toward the two of them and lowered her voice. "That skinny Accepted Irella told her she was as clumsy as a cow and had half the Talents, and Nynaeve clouted her ear." Elayne winced. "Exactly," Min murmured. "They had her up to Sheriam's study before you could blink, and she hasn't been fit to live with since."

Apparently Min had not dropped her voice enough, for there was a growl from Nynaeve. Suddenly the door whipped open once more, and a gale howled into the room. It did not ruffle the blankets on Egwene's bed, but Min and the stool toppled, to roll against the wall. Immediately the wind died, and Nynaeve stood with a stricken look on her face.

Egwene hurried to the door and peeked out. The noonday sun was burning off the last reminders of last night's rainstorm. The still-damp balcony around the Novices' Court was empty, the long row of doors to novices' rooms all shut. The novices who had taken advantage of the freeday to enjoy themselves in the gardens were no doubt catching up on their sleep. No one could have seen. She closed the door and took her place beside Elayne again as Nynaeve helped Min to her feet.

"I'm sorry, Min," Nynaeve said in a tight voice. "Sometimes my temper. . . . I can't ask you to forgive me, not for this." She took a deep breath. "If you want to report me to Sheriam, I will understand. I deserve it."

Egwene wished she had not heard that admission; Nynaeve could grow prickly over such things. Searching for something on which to focus, something Nynaeve could believe she had had her attention on, she found herself touching *saidar* once more, and began juggling the balls of light again. Elayne quickly joined her; Egwene saw the glow form around the Daughter-Heir even before three tiny balls appeared above her hands. They began to pass the little glowing spheres back and forth in increasingly intricate patterns. Sometimes one winked out as one girl or the other failed to maintain it as it came to her, then winked back a little altered in color or size.

The One Power filled Egwene with life. She smelled the faint rose aroma of soap from Elayne's morning bath. She could feel the rough plaster of the walls, the smooth stones of the floor, as well as she could the bed where she sat. She could hear Min and Nynaeve breathe, much less their quiet words.

"If it comes to forgiving," Min said, "maybe you should forgive me. You have a temper, and I have a big mouth. I will forgive you if you forgive me." With murmurs of "forgiven" that sounded meant on both sides, the two women hugged. "But if you do it again," Min said with a laugh, "I might clout *your* ear."

"Next time," Nynaeve replied, "I will throw something at you." She was laughing, too, but her laughter ceased abruptly as her eye fell on Egwene and Elayne. "You two stop that, or there *will* be someone going to the Mistress of Novices. Two someones."

"Nynaeve, you wouldn't!" Egwene protested. When she saw the look in Nynaeve's eyes, though, she hastily severed all contact with *saidar*. "Very well. I believe you. There's no need to prove it."

"We have to practice," Elayne said. "They ask more and

more of us. If we did not practice on our own, we would never keep up." Her face showed calm composure, but she had let go of *saidar* as hastily as Egwene herself had.

"And what happens when you draw too much," Nynaeve asked, "and there's no one there to stop you? I wish you were more afraid. I am. Don't you think I know what it is like for you? It's always there, and you want to fill yourself with it. Sometimes it is all I can do to make myself stop; I want all of it. I know it would burn me to a crisp, and I want it anyway." She shivered. "I just wish you were more afraid."

"I am afraid," Egwene said with a sigh. "I'm terrified. But it doesn't seem to help. What about you, Elayne?"

"The only thing that terrifies me," Elayne said airily, "is washing dishes. It seems as if I have to wash dishes every day." Egwene threw her pillow at her. Elayne pulled it off her head and threw it back, but then her shoulders slumped. "Oh, very well. I am so scared I don't know why my teeth are not chattering. Elaida told me I'd be so frightened that I would want to run away with the Traveling People, but I did not understand. A man who drove oxen as hard as they drive us would be shunned. I am tired all the time. I wake up tired and go to bed exhausted, and sometimes I'm so afraid that I will slip and channel more of the Power than I can handle that I. . . ." Peering into her lap, she let the words trail off.

Egwene knew what she had not spoken. Their rooms lay right next to each other, and as in many of the novice rooms, a small hole had long ago been bored through the wall between, too small to be seen unless you knew where to look, but useful for talk after the lamps were extinguished, when the girls could not leave their rooms. Egwene had heard Elayne crying herself to sleep more than once, and she had no doubt that Elayne had heard her own crying.

"The Traveling People are tempting," Nynaeve agreed, "but wherever you go, it will not change what you can do. You cannot run from *saidar*." She did not sound as if she liked what she was saying.

"What do you see, Min?" Elayne said. "Are we all going to be powerful Aes Sedai, or will we spend the rest of our lives washing dishes as novices, or. . . ." She shrugged uncomfortably as if she did not want to voice the third alternative that came to mind. Sent home. Put out of the Tower. Two novices had been put out since Egwene came, and everyone spoke of them in whispers, as if they were dead.

Min shifted on her stool. "I don't like reading friends," she muttered. "Friendship gets in the way of the reading. It makes me try to put the best face on what I see. That's why I don't do it for you three anymore. Anyway, nothing has changed about you that I can. . . ." She squinted at them, and suddenly frowned. "That's new," she breathed.

"What?" Nynaeve asked sharply.

Min hesitated before answering. "Danger. You are all in some kind of danger. Or you will be, very soon. I can't make it out, but it is danger."

"You see," Nynaeve said to the two girls sitting on the bed. "You must take care. We all must. You must both promise not to channel again without someone to guide you."

"I don't want to talk about it anymore," Egwene said.

Elayne nodded eagerly. "Yes. Let's talk about something else. Min, if you put on a dress, I'll wager Gawyn would ask you to go walking with him. You know he's been looking at you, but I think the breeches and the man's coat put him off."

"I dress the way I like, and I won't change for a lord, even if he is your brother." Min spoke absently, still squinting at them and frowning; it was a conversation they had had before. "Sometimes it is useful to pass as a boy."

"No one who looks twice believes you are a boy." Elayne smiled.

Egwene was uncomfortable. Elayne was forcing a semblance of gaiety, Min was hardly paying attention, and Nynaeve looked as if she wanted to warn them again.

When the door swung open once more, Egwene bounded to her feet to close it, grateful for something to do besides watch the others pretend. Before she reached it, though, a dark-eyed Aes Sedai with her blond hair done in a multitude of braids stepped into the room. Egwene blinked in surprise, as much at it being any Aes Sedai as at Liandrin. She had not heard that Liandrin had returned to the White Tower, but beyond that, novices were sent for if an Aes Sedai wanted them; it could mean no good, a sister coming herself.

The room was crowded with five women in it. Liandrin paused to adjust her red-fringed shawl, eyeing them. Min did not move, but Elayne rose, and the three standing curtsied, though Nynaeve barely flexed her knee. Egwene did not think Nynaeve would ever grow used to having others in authority over her.

Liandrin's eyes settled on Nynaeve. "And why are you here, in the novices' quarters, child?" Her tone was ice.

"I am visiting with friends," Nynaeve said in a tight voice. After a moment she added a belated, "Liandrin Sedai."

"The Accepted, they can have no friends among the novices. This you should have learned by this time, child. But it is as well that I find you here. You and you"—her finger stabbed at Elayne and Min—"will go."

"I will return later." Min rose casually, making a great show of being in no hurry to obey, and strolled by Liandrin with a grin, of which Liandrin took no notice at all. Elayne gave Egwene and Nynaeve a worried look before she dropped a curtsy and left.

After Elayne closed the door behind her, Liandrin stood studying Egwene and Nynaeve. Egwene began to fidget under the scrutiny, but Nynaeve held herself straight, with only a little heightening of her color.

"You two are from the same village as the boys who traveled with Moiraine. Is it not so?" Liandrin said suddenly.

"Do you have some word of Rand?" Egwene asked eagerly. Liandrin arched an eyebrow at her. "Forgive me, Aes Sedai. I forget myself."

"Have you word of them?" Nynaeve said, just short of a demand. The Accepted had no rule about not speaking to an Aes Sedai until spoken to.

"You have concern for them. That is good. They are in danger, and you might be able to help them."

"How do you know they're in trouble?" There was no doubt about the demand in Nynaeve's voice this time.

Liandrin's rosebud mouth tightened, but her tone did not change. "Though you are not aware of it, Moiraine has sent letters to the White Tower concerning you. Moiraine Sedai, she worries about you, and about your young . . . friends. These boys, they are in danger. Do you wish to help them, or leave them to their fate?"

"Yes," Egwene said, at the same time that Nynaeve said,

"What kind of trouble? Why do *you* care about helping them?" Nynaeve glanced at the red fringe on Liandrin's shawl. "And I thought you didn't like Moiraine."

"Do not presume too much, child," Liandrin said sharply. "To be Accepted is not to be a sister. Accepted and novices alike listen when a sister speaks, and do as they are told." She drew a breath and went on; her tone was coldy serene again, but angry white spots marred her cheeks. "Someday, I am sure, you will serve a cause, and you will learn then that to serve it you must work even with those whom you dislike. I tell you I have worked with many with whom I would not share a room if it were left to me alone. Would you not work alongside the one you hated worst, if it would save your friends?"

Nynaeve nodded reluctantly. "But you still haven't told us what kind of danger they're in, Liandrin Sedai."

"The danger comes from Shayol Ghul. They are hunted, as I understand they once before were. If you will come with me, some dangers, at least, may be eliminated. Do not ask how, for I cannot tell you, but I tell you flatly it is so."

"We will come, Liandrin Sedai," Egwene said.

"Come where?" Nynaeve said. Egwene shot her an exasperated look.

"Toman Head."

Egwene's mouth fell open, and Nynaeve muttered, "There's a war on Toman Head. Does this danger have something to do with Artur Hawkwing's armies?"

"You believe rumors, child? But even if they were true, is that enough to stop you? I thought you called these men friends." A twist to Liandrin's words said she would never do the same.

"We will come," Egwene said. Nynaeve opened her mouth again, but Egwene went right on. "We will go, Nynaeve. If Rand needs our help—and Mat, and Perrin—we have to give it."

"I know that," Nynaeve said, "but what I want to know is, why us? What can we do that Moiraine—or you, Liandrin—cannot?"

The white grew in Liandrin's cheeks—Egwene realized Nynaeve had forgotten the honorific in addressing her—but what she said was, "You two come from their village. In some way I do not entirely understand, you are connected to them. Beyond that, I cannot say. And no more of your foolish questions will I answer. Will you come with me for their sake?" She paused for their assent; a visible tension left her when they nodded. "Good. You will meet me at the northernmost edge of the Ogier grove one hour before sunset with your horses and whatever you will need for the journey. Tell no one of this."

"We are not supposed to leave the Tower grounds without permission," Nynaeve said slowly.

"You have my permission. Tell no one. No one at all. The Black Ajah walks the halls of the White Tower."

Egwene gasped, and heard an echoed gasp from Nynaeve, but Nynaeve recovered quickly. "I thought all Aes Sedai denied the existence of—of that."

Liandrin's mouth tightened into a sneer. "Many do, but Tarmon Gai'don approaches, and the time leaves when denials can be made. The Black Ajah, it is the opposite of everything for which the Tower stands, but it exists, child. It is everywhere, any woman could belong to it, and it serves the Dark One. If your friends are pursued by the Shadow, do you think the Black Ajah will leave you alive and free to help them? Tell no one—no one!—or you may not live to reach Toman Head. One hour before sunset. Do not fail me." With that, she was gone, the door closing firmly behind her.

Egwene collapsed onto her bed with her hands on her knees. "Nynaeve, she's Red Ajah. She can't know about Rand. If she did. . . ."

"She cannot know," Nynaeve agreed. "I wish I knew why a Red wanted to help. Or why she's willing to work with Moiraine. I'd have sworn neither of them would give the other water if she were dying of thirst."

"You think she's lying?"

"She is Aes Sedai," Nynaeve said dryly. "I'll wager my best silver pin against a blueberry that every word she said was true. But I wonder if we heard what we thought we did."

"The Black Ajah." Egwene shivered. "There was no mistaking what she said about that, the Light help us."

"No mistaking," Nynaeve said. "And she's forestalled us asking anyone for advice, because after that, who can we trust? The Light help us indeed."

Min and Elayne came bustling in, slamming the door behind them. "Are you really going?" Min asked, and Elayne gestured toward the tiny hole in the wall above Egwene's bed, saying, "We listened from my room. We heard everything."

Egwene exchanged glances with Nynaeve, wondering how much they had overheard, and saw the same concern on Nynaeve's face. *If they manage to cipher out about Rand. . . .*

"You have to keep this to yourselves," Nynaeve cautioned them. "I suppose Liandrin has arranged permission from Sheriam for us to go, but even if she hasn't, even if they start searching the Tower from top to bottom for us tomorrow, you mustn't say a word."

"Keep it to myself?" Min said. "No fear on that. I'm going with you. All I do all day is try to explain to one Brown sister or another something I don't understand myself. I can't even go for a walk without the Amyrlin herself popping out and asking me to read whoever we see. When that woman asks you to do something, there doesn't seem to be any way out of it. I must have read half the White Tower for her, but she always wants another demonstration. All I needed was an excuse to leave, and this is it." Her face wore a look of determination that allowed no argument.

Egwene wondered why Min was so determined to go with them rather than simply leaving on her own, but before she had time to do more than wonder, Elayne said, "I am going, too."

"Elayne," Nynaeve said gently, "Egwene and I are the boys' kith from Emond's Field. You are the Daughter-Heir of Andor. If you disappear from the White Tower, why, it—it could start a war."

"Mother wouldn't start a war with Tar Valon if they dried and salted me, which they may be trying to do. If you three can go off and have an adventure, you needn't think I am going to stay here and wash dishes, and scrub floors, and have some Accepted berating me because I didn't make the fire the exact shade of blue she wanted. Gawyn will die from envy when he finds out." Elayne grinned and reached over to tug playfully at Egwene's hair. "Besides, if you leave Rand lying about loose, I might have a chance to pick him up."

"I don't think either of us is going to have him," Egwene said sadly.

"Then we'll find whoever he does choose and make her life miserable. But he couldn't be fool enough to choose someone else when he could have one of us. Oh, please smile, Egwene. I know he's yours. I just feel"—she hesitated, searching for the word—"free. I've never had an adventure. I'll bet we won't either of us cry ourselves to sleep on an adventure. And if we do, we will make sure the gleemen leave that part out."

"This is foolishness," Nynaeve said. "We are going to Toman Head. You've heard the news, and the rumors. It will be dangerous. You must stay here."

"I heard what Liandrin Sedai said about the—the Black Ajah, too." Elayne's voice dropped almost to a whisper at that name. "How safe will I be here, if *they* are here? If Mother even suspected the Black Ajah really existed, she would pitch me into the middle of a battle to get me away from them."

"But, Elayne—"

"There is only one way for you to stop me coming. That is to tell the Mistress of Novices. We will make a pretty picture, all three of us lined up in her study. All four of us. I don't think Min would escape from something like this. So since you are not going to tell Sheriam Sedai, I am coming, too."

Nynaeve threw up her hands. "Perhaps you can say something to convince her," she told Min.

Min had been leaning against the door, squinting at Elayne, and now she shook her head. "I think she has to come as much as the rest of you. The rest of us. I can see the danger around all of you more clearly, now. Not clearly enough to make it out, but I think it has something to do with you deciding to go. That's why it is clearer; because it is more certain."

"That's no reason for her to come," Nynaeve said, but Min shook her head again.

"She is linked to—to those boys as much as you, or Egwene, or me. She's part of it, Nynaeve, whatever it is. Part of the Pattern, I suppose an Aes Sedai would say."

Elayne seemed taken aback, and interested, too. "I am? What part, Min?"

"I can't see it clearly." Min looked at the floor. "Sometimes I wish I couldn't read people at all. Most people aren't satisfied with what I see anyway."

"If we are all going," Nynaeve said, "then we had best be about making plans." However much she might argue beforehand, once a course of action had been decided, Nynaeve always went right to the practicalities: what they had to take with them, and how cold it would be by the time they reached Toman Head, and how they could get their horses from the stables without being stopped.

Listening to her, Egwene could not help wondering what the danger was that Min saw for them, and what danger threatened Rand. She knew of only one danger that could threaten him, and it made her cold to think of it. *Hold on, Rand. Hold on, you wool-headed idiot. I'll help you somehow.*

CHAPTER
39

Flight from the White Tower

Egwene and Elayne inclined their heads briefly to each group of women they passed as they made their way through the Tower. It was a good thing there were so many women from outside in the Tower today, Egwene thought, too many for each to have an Aes Sedai or an Accepted for escort. Alone or in small groups, garbed richly or poorly, in dress from half a dozen different lands, some still dusty from their journey to Tar Valon, they kept to themselves and waited their turn to ask their questions of the Aes Sedai, or present their petitions. Some women—ladies or merchants or merchants' wives—had female servants with them. Even a few men had come with petitions, standing by themselves, looking unsure about being in the White Tower, and eyeing everyone else uneasily.

In the lead, Nynaeve kept her eyes purposefully ahead, her cloak swirling behind her, walking as if she knew where they were going—which she did, as long as no one stopped them—and had a perfect right to go there—which was a different matter altogether, of course. Dressed now in the clothes they had brought to Tar Valon, they certainly did not look like residents of the Tower. Each had chosen her best dress that had a skirt divided for riding, and cloaks of fine wool rich with embroidery. As long as they kept away from all who might recognize them—they had already dodged several who knew their faces—Egwene thought they might make it.

"This would do better for a turn in some lord's park than a ride to Toman Head," Nynaeve had said dryly as Egwene helped her with the buttons of a gray silk with thread-of-gold work and pearled flowers across the bosom and down the sleeves, "but it may allow us to leave unnoticed."

Now Egwene shifted her cloak and smoothed her own gold-embroidered, green silk dress and glanced at Elayne, in blue slashed with cream, hoping Nynaeve had been right. So far, everyone had taken them for petitioners, nobles, or at least women of wealth, but it seemed that they should stand out. She was surprised to realize why; she felt uncomfortable in the fine dress after wearing a novice's plain white for the past few months.

A little cluster of village women in stout, dark woolens dropped curtsies as they passed. Egwene glanced back at Min as soon as they were beyond. Min had kept her breeches and baggy man's shirt under a boy's brown cloak and coat, with an old, wide-brimmed hat pulled down over her short hair. "One of us has to be the servant," she had said, laughing. "Women dressed the way you are always have at least one. You'll wish you had my breeches if we have to run." She was burdened with four sets of saddlebags bulging with warm clothes, for it would surely be winter before they returned. There were also packets of food pilfered from the kitchens, enough to last until they could buy more.

"Are you sure I can't carry some of those, Min?" Egwene asked softly.

"They're just awkward," Min said with a grin, "not heavy." She seemed to think it was all a game, or else was pretending to think so. "And people would be sure to wonder why a fine lady such as yourself was carrying her own saddlebags. You can carry yours—and mine, too, if you want—once we—" Her grin vanished, and she whispered fiercely, "Aes Sedai!"

Egwene whipped her eyes forward. An Aes Sedai with long, smooth black hair and aged-ivory skin was coming toward them down the corridor, listening to a woman wearing rough farm clothes and a patched cloak. The Aes Sedai had not seen them yet, but Egwene recognized her; Takima, of the Brown Ajah, who taught the history of the White Tower and Aes Sedai, and who could recognize one of her pupils at a hundred paces.

Nynaeve turned down a side hall without breaking stride, but there one of the Accepted, a lanky woman with a permanent frown, hurried past them hauling a red-faced novice by the ear.

Egwene had to swallow before she could speak. "That was Irella, and Else. Did they notice us?" She could not make herself look back to see.

"No," Min said after a moment. "All they saw was our clothes." Egwene let out a long, relieved breath, and heard one from Nynaeve, too.

"My heart may burst before we reach the stables," Elayne murmured. "Is this what an adventure is like all the time, Egwene? Your heart in your mouth, and your stomach in your feet?"

"I suppose it is," Egwene said slowly. She found it hard to think that there had been a time when she had been eager to have an adventure, to do something dangerous and exciting like the people in stories. Now she thought the exciting part was what you remembered when you looked back, and the stories left out a good deal of unpleasantness. She told Elayne as much.

"Still," the Daughter-Heir said firmly, "I have never had any real excitement before, and never likely to as long as Mother has any say in it, which she will until I take the throne myself."

"You two be quiet," Nynaeve said. They were alone in the hall for a change, with no one in sight in either direction. She pointed to a narrow flight of stairs going down. "That should be what we want. If I haven't gotten turned around completely, with all the twists and turns we've made."

She took the stairs as if she were certain anyway, and the others followed. Surely enough, the small door at the bottom let out into the dusty yard of the South Stable, where novices' horses were kept, for those who had them, until they had need of mounts again, which was generally not until they became Accepted or were sent home. The gleaming bulk of the Tower itself rose behind them; the Tower grounds spread over a good many hides of land, with its own walls higher than some city walls.

Nynaeve strode into the stable as if she owned it. It had a clean smell of hay and horse, and two long rows of stalls ran back into shadows barred with light from the vents above. For a wonder, shaggy Bela and Nynaeve's gray mare stood in stalls near the doors. Bela put her nose over the stall door and whickered softly to Egwene. There was only one groom in evidence, a pleasant-looking fellow with gray in his beard, chewing a straw.

"We will have our horses saddled," Nynaeve told him in her most commanding tone. "Those two. Min, find your horse and Elayne's." Min dropped the saddlebags and drew Elayne deeper into the stables.

The stableman frowned after them and slowly took the straw from his mouth. "There must be some mistake, my Lady. Those animals—"

"—are ours," Nynaeve said firmly, folding her arms so that the Serpent ring was obvious. "You will saddle them now."

Egwene held her breath; it was a last-ditch plan, that Nynaeve would try to pass as an Aes Sedai if they had difficulties with anyone who might actually accept her as one. No Aes Sedai or Accepted would, of course, and probably not even a novice, but a stableman. . . .

The man blinked at Nynaeve's ring, then at her. "I was told two," he said at last, sounding unimpressed. "One of the Accepted and a novice. Wasn't nothing said about four of you."

Egwene felt like laughing. Of course Liandrin would not have believed them able to get their horses by themselves.

Nynaeve looked disappointed, and her voice sharpened. "You trot those horses out and saddle them, or you'll have need of Liandrin's Healing, if she will give it to you."

The groom mouthed Liandrin's name, but one look at Nynaeve's face and he saw to the horses with no more than a mutter or two, not loud enough for any but himself to hear. Min and Elayne came back with their own mounts just as he finished tightening the second girth. Min's was a tall dust-colored gelding, Elayne's a bay mare with an arched neck.

When they were mounted, Nynaeve addressed herself to the stableman again. "No doubt you were told to keep this quiet, and that hasn't changed whether we are two or two hundred. If you think it has, think about what Liandrin will do if you talk what you were told to keep quiet."

As they were riding out, Elayne tossed him a coin and murmured, "For your trouble, goodman. You have done well." Outside, she caught Egwene's eye and smiled. "Mother says a stick and honey always work better than a stick alone."

"I hope we don't need either with the guards," Egwene said. "I hope Liandrin spoke to them, too."

At Tarlomen's Gate, though, piercing the tall south wall of the Tower grounds, there was no telling if anyone had spoken to the guards or not. They waved the four women through with no more than a glance and a cursory bow. Guards were meant to keep out those who were dangerous; apparently these had no orders about keeping anyone in.

A cool river breeze gave them an excuse to pull up the hoods of their cloaks as they rode slowly through the streets of the city. The ring of their horses' hooves on the paving stones was lost in the murmur of the crowds filling the streets and the music that came from some of the buildings they passed. People dressed in garments from every land, from the dark and somber mode of Cairhien to the bright, brilliant colors of the Traveling People, and every style in between, split around the horsewomen like a river around a rock, but they still could not move at more than a slow walk.

Egwene gave no attention to the fabulous towers with their sky-borne bridges or the buildings that looked more like breaking waves, or wind-sculpted cliffs, or fanciful shells, than anything made from stone. Aes Sedai often went into the city, and in that crowd they could come face-to-face with one before they knew it. After a time she realized the other women were keeping as close a watch as she, but she still felt more than a glimmer of relief when the Ogier grove came into view.

The Great Trees were now visible beyond the rooftops, their spreading tops a hundred spans and more in the air. Towering oaks and elms, leatherleafs and firs, were dwarfed beneath them. A wall of sorts encompassed the grove, which was a good two miles across, but it was only an endless series of spiraling stone arches, each five spans high and twice as wide. By the outer side of the wall, carriages, carts, and people bustled along a street, while inside lay a wilderness of sorts. The grove had neither the tame look of a park nor the complete haphazardness of the forest depths. Rather, it seemed to be the ideal of nature, as if this were the perfect woods, the most beautiful forest that could be. Some of the leaves had already begun to turn, and even the small swathes of orange and yellow and red among the green seemed to Egwene to be exactly the way autumn foliage should look.

A few people strolled just inside the open arches, and no one looked twice when the four women rode in under the trees. The city was quickly lost to view, even the sounds of it softened, then blocked, by the grove. In the space of ten strides they seemed to be miles from the nearest town.

"The north edge of the grove, she said," Nynaeve muttered, peering around. "There isn't any point of it further north than—" She cut off as two horses burst from a copse of black elder, a dark, glossy mare with a rider and a lightly laden packhorse.

The dark mare reared, pawing the air, as Liandrin reined her harshly. The Aes Sedai's face wore fury like a mask. "I told you not to tell anyone of this! Not anyone!" Egwene noticed pole-lanterns on the packhorse, and thought it odd.

"These are friends," Nynaeve began, her back stiffening, but Elayne broke in on her.

"Forgive us, Liandrin Sedai. They did not tell us; we overheard. We did not mean to listen to anything we should not have, but we did overhear. And we want to help Rand al'Thor, too. And the other boys, of course," she added quickly.

Liandrin peered at Elayne and Min. The late afternoon sunlight, slanting through the branches, shadowed their faces beneath the hoods of their cloaks. "So," she said finally, still watching those two. "I had made arrangements for you to be taken care of, but as you are here, you are here. Four can make this journey as well as two."

"Taken care of, Liandrin Sedai?" Elayne said. "I do not understand."

"Child, you and that other are known as friends of these two. Do you not think there are those who would question you when they are found to be gone? Do you believe the Black Ajah would be gentle with you just because you are heir to a throne? Had you remained in the White Tower, you might not have lived the night." That silenced them all for a moment, but Liandrin wheeled her horse and called, "Follow me!"

The Aes Sedai led them deeper into the grove, until they came to a tall fence of stout ironwork topped with a hedge of razor-sharp spikes. Curving slightly, as if it enclosed a large area, the fence ran out of sight among the trees to left and right. There was a gate in the fence, secured with a big lock. Liandrin unfastened this with a large key she produced from her cloak, motioned them through, then re-locked it behind them and rode on ahead immediately. A squirrel chittered at them from a branch overhead, and from somewhere came the sharp drumming of a woodpecker.

"Where are we going?" Nynaeve demanded. Liandrin did not answer, and Nynaeve looked angrily at the others. "Why are we just riding deeper into these woods? We have to cross a bridge, or else take ship, if we're going to leave Tar Valon, and there isn't any bridge or ship in—"

"There is this," Liandrin announced. "The fence, it keeps away those who might harm themselves, but we have a need this day." What she gestured to was a tall, thick slab of what seemed to be stone, standing on edge, one side carved intri-cately in vines and leaves.

Egwene's throat tightened; suddenly she knew why Liandrin had brought lanterns, and she did not like what she knew. She heard Nynaeve whisper, "A Waygate." They both remembered the Ways all too well.

"We did it once," she told herself as much as Nynaeve. "We can do it again." *If Rand and the others need us, we have to help them. That's all there is to it.*

"Is that really . . . ?" Min began in a choked voice and could not finish.

"A Waygate," Elayne breathed. "I did not think the Ways could be used any longer. At least, I did not think their use was allowed."

Liandrin had already dismounted and plucked the trefoil *Avendesora* leaf out of the carving; like two huge doors wo-ven of living vines, the gates were swinging open, revealing what appeared to be a dull, silvery mirror that gave their reflections back dimly.

"You do not have to come," Liandrin said. "You can wait here for me, safely enclosed by the fence until I come for you. Or perhaps the Black Ajah will find you before anyone else." Her smile was not pleasant. Behind her, the Waygate came open to its fullest and stopped.

"I did not say I wouldn't come," Elayne said, but she gave the shadowed woods a lingering look.

"If we are going to do this," Min said hoarsely, "then let's do it." She was staring at the Waygate, and Egwene thought she heard her mutter, "The Light burn you, Rand al'Thor."

"I must go last," Liandrin said. "All of you, in. I will follow." She was eyeing the woods now, too, as if she thought someone might be following them. "Quickly! Quickly!"

Egwene did not know what Liandrin expected to see, but if anyone at all came they would probably stop them from using the Waygate. *Rand, you wool-headed idiot,* she thought, *why can't you just once get yourself into some kind of trouble that doesn't force me to act like the heroine in a story?*

She dug her heels into Bela's flanks, and the shaggy mare, restive from too much time in a stable, leaped forward.

"Slowly!" Nynaeve shouted, but it was too late.

Egwene and Bela surged toward their own dull reflections; two shaggy horses touched noses, appeared to flow into each other. Then Egwene was merging into her own image with an icy shock. Time seemed to stretch out, as if the cold crept over her by the width of one hair at a time, and every hair took minutes.

Suddenly Bela was stumbling in pitch-blackness, moving so fast the mare almost pitched over on her head. She caught herself and stood trembling as Egwene dismounted hurriedly, feeling the mare's legs in the dark to see if she had been hurt. She was almost glad of the dark, to hide her crimson face. She knew that time as well as distance were different the other side of a Waygate; she had moved before thinking.

There was only the blackness around her in every direction, except for the rectangle of the open Waygate, like a window of smoked glass when seen from this side. It let no light in—the black seemed to press right up against it—but through it Egwene could see the others, moving by the slowest increments, like figures in a nightmare. Nynaeve was insisting on handing around the pole-lanterns and lighting them; Liandrin was acceding with a bad grace, apparently insisting on speed.

When Nynaeve came though the Waygate—leading her gray mare slowly, ever so slowly—Egwene almost ran to hug her, and at least half of her feeling was for the lantern Nynaeve carried. The lantern made a smaller pool of light than it should have—the darkness pressed against the light, trying to force it back into the lantern—but Egwene had begun to feel that darkness pressing against her, as if it had weight. Instead, she contented herself with saying, "Bela's all right, and I did not break my neck the way I deserved to."

Once there had been light along the Ways, before the taint on the Power with which they had first been made, the taint of the Dark One on *saidin,* had begun to corrupt them.

Nynaeve thrust the pole of the lantern into her hands and turned to pull another from under her saddle girth. "As long as you know you deserved to," she murmured, "then you didn't deserve to." Suddenly she chuckled. "Sometimes I think it was sayings like that more than anything else that created the title of Wisdom. Well, here's another. You break your neck, and I'll see it mended just so I can break it again."

It was said lightly, and Egwene found herself laughing, too—until she recalled where she was. Nynaeve's amusement did not last long either.

Min and Elayne came through the Waygate hesitantly, leading their horses and carrying lanterns, obviously expecting to find monsters waiting at the least. They looked relieved, at first, to find nothing but darkness, but the oppressiveness of it soon had them shifting nervously from foot to foot. Liandrin replaced the *Avendesora* leaf and rode through the closing Waygate leading the packhorse.

Liandrin did not wait for the gate to finish closing, but tossed the lead line of the packhorse to Min without a word and started along a white line, dimly made out by the light of her lantern, leading into the Ways. The floor seemed to be stone, eaten and pitted by acid. Egwene scrambled hurriedly onto Bela's back, but she was no quicker to follow the Aes Sedai than anyone else. There seemed to be nothing in the world except the rough floor under the horses' hooves.

Straight as an arrow the white line led through the dark to a large stone slab covered with Ogier script inlaid in silver. The same pocking that marked the floor also broke the script in places.

"A Guiding," Elayne murmured, twisting in her saddle to look around uneasily. "Elaida taught me a little about the Ways. She would not say much. Not enough," she added glumly. "Or maybe too much."

Calmly Liandrin compared the Guiding with a parchment, then stuffed it back into a pocket of her cloak before Egwene could get a look.

Their lanterns' light stopped abruptly rather than fading out at the edges, but it was enough for Egwene to see a thick stone balustrade, eaten away in places, as the Aes Sedai led them away from the Guiding. An Island, Elayne called it; the darkness made judging the Island's size difficult, but Egwene thought it might be a hundred paces across.

Stone bridges and ramps pierced the balustrade, each with a stone post beside it marked with a single line in Ogier script. The bridges seemed to arch out into nothing. The ramps led up or down. It was impossible to see more than the beginning of any of them, as they rode past.

Pausing only to eye the stone posts, Liandrin took a ramp that led down, and quickly there was nothing but the ramp and the darkness. A dampening silence hung over everything; Egwene had the feeling that even the clatter of the horses' hooves on the rough stone did not travel very far beyond the light.

Down and down the ramp ran, curving back on itself, until it reached another Island, with its broken balustrade between bridges and ramps, its Guiding that Liandrin compared with her parchment. The Island seemed like solid stone, just as the first one had. Egwene wished she was not sure that the first Island was directly over their heads.

Nynaeve spoke up suddenly, voicing Egwene's thoughts. Her voice sounded steady, but she paused to swallow in the middle of it.

"It—it might be," Elayne said faintly. Her eyes rolled upwards, and quickly dropped again. "Elaida says the rules of nature do not hold in the Ways. At least, not the way they do outside."

"Light!" Min muttered, then raised her voice. "How long do you mean us to stay in here?"

The Aes Sedai's honey-colored braids swung as she turned to regard them. "Until I take you out," she said flatly. "The more you bother me, the longer that will be." She bent back to studying the parchment and the Guiding.

Egwene and the others fell silent.

Liandrin pushed on from Guiding to Guiding, by ramps and bridges that seemed to run unsupported through the endless dark. The Aes Sedai paid very little heed to the rest of them, and Egwene found herself wondering whether Liandrin would turn back to search if one of them fell behind. The others perhaps had the same thought, for they all rode bunched tightly on the dark mare's heels.

Egwene was surprised to realize that she still felt the attraction of *saidar*, both the presence of the female half of the True Source and the desire to touch it, to channel its flow. Somehow, she had thought the Shadow's taint on the Ways would hide it from her. She could sense that taint, after a fashion. It was faint and had nothing to do with *saidar*, but she was sure that reaching for the True Source here would be like baring her arm to foul, greasy smoke in order to reach a clean cup. Whatever she did would be tainted. For the first time in weeks she had no trouble at all in resisting the attraction of *saidar*.

It was well into what would have been night in the world outside the Ways when, on an Island, Liandrin abruptly dismounted and announced that they would halt for supper and sleep, and that there was food on the packhorse.

"Parcel it out," she said, not bothering to assign the task. "It will take us the better part of two days to reach Toman Head. I would not have you arrive hungry if you were too foolish not to bring food yourselves." Briskly she unsaddled and hobbled her mare, but then she sat down on her saddle and waited for one of them to bring her something to eat.

Elayne took Liandrin her flatbread and cheese. The Aes Sedai made it obvious that she did not want their company, so the rest of them ate their bread and cheese a little apart from her, sitting on their saddles drawn close together. The darkness beyond their lanterns made a poor sauce.

After a time, Egwene said, "Liandrin Sedai, what if we encounter the Black Wind?" Min mouthed the word questioningly, but Elayne gave a squeak. "Moiraine Sedai said it could not be killed, or even hurt very much, and I can feel the taint on this place waiting to twist anything we do with the Power."

"You will not so much as think of the Source unless I tell you to," Liandrin said sharply. "Why, if one such as you tried to channel here, in the Ways, you might well go as mad as a man. You have not the training to deal with the taint of those men who made this. If the Black Wind appears, I will deal with it." She pursed her lips, studying a lump of white cheese. "Moiraine does not know so much as she thinks." She popped the cheese into her mouth with a smile.

"I do not like her," Egwene muttered, low enough to make sure the Aes Sedai could not hear.

"If Moiraine can work with her," Nynaeve said quietly, "so can we. Not that I like Moiraine any better than I do Liandrin, but if they're meddling with Rand and the others again. . . ." She fell silent, hitching her cloak up. The darkness was not cold, but it seemed as if it should be.

"What is this Black Wind?" Min asked. When Elayne had explained, with a great deal of what Elaida had said and what her mother had said, Min sighed. "The Pattern has a great deal to answer for. I don't know that any man is worth this."

"You did not have to come," Egwene reminded her. "You could have gone at any time. No one would have tried to stop you leaving the Tower."

"Oh, I could have wandered off," Min said wryly. "As easily as you, or Elayne. The Pattern doesn't much care what we want. Egwene, what if, after all you are going through for him, Rand doesn't marry you? What if he marries some woman you've never seen before, or Elayne, or me? What then?"

Elayne chortled. "Mother would never approve."

Egwene was silent for a time. Rand might not live to marry anyone. And if he did. . . . She could not imagine Rand hurting anyone. *Not even after he's gone mad?* There had to be some way to stop that, some way to change it; Aes Sedai knew so much, could do so much. *If they could stop it, why don't they?* The only answer was because they could not, and that was not the one she wanted.

She tried to put lightness in her voice. "I don't suppose I *will* marry him. Aes Sedai seldom do marry, you know. But I would not set my heart on him if were you. Or you, Elayne. I do not think. . . ." Her voice caught, and she coughed to cover it. "I do not think he will ever marry. But if he does, I wish well to whoever ends up with him, even one of you." She thought she sounded as if she meant it. "He is stubborn as a mule, and wrongheaded to a fault, but he *is* gentle." Her voice shook, but she managed to turn the quaver into a laugh.

"However much you say you do not care," Elayne said, "I think you'd approve less than Mother would. He *is* interesting, Egwene. More interesting than any man I've ever met, even if he is a shepherd. If you are silly enough to throw him away, you will have only yourself to blame if I decide to face down you and Mother both. It would not be the first time the Prince of Andor had no title before he wed. But you won't be that silly, so don't try to pretend you will. No doubt you will choose the Green Ajah, and make him one of your Warders. The only Greens I know with only one Warder are married to them."

Egwene made herself go along with it, saying if she did become a Green she would have ten Warders.

Min watched her, frowning, and Nynaeve watched Min thoughtfully. They all fell silent by the time they changed into more suitable clothes for traveling, from their saddlebags. It was not easy, keeping spirits up in that place.

Sleep came slowly to Egwene, fitfully, and it was filled with bad dreams. She did not dream of Rand, but of the man whose eyes were fire. His face was not masked this time, and it was horrible with almost healed burns. He only looked at her and laughed, but that was worse than the dreams that followed, the dreams of being lost in the Ways forever, the ones where the Black Wind was chasing her. She was grateful when the toe of Liandrin's riding boot dug into her ribs to waken her; she felt as if she had not slept at all.

Liandrin pushed them hard through the next day, or what passed for day, with only their lanterns for a sun, not letting them stop for sleep until they were swaying in their saddles. Stone made a hard bed, but Liandrin roused them ruthlessly after a few hours, hardly waiting for them to mount before riding on. Ramps and bridges, Islands and Guidings. Egwene saw so many of them in that pitch-dark that she lost count. She had long since lost any count of hours or of days. Liandrin allowed only brief halts to eat and rest the horses, and the darkness weighed down on their shoulders. They slumped in their saddles like sacks of grain, except for Liandrin. The Aes Sedai seemed unaffected by tiredness, or the dark. She was as fresh as she had been back in the White Tower, and as cold. She would not let anyone glimpse the parchment she compared to the Guidings, stuffing it away with a curt, "It is nothing you would understand," when Nynaeve asked.

And then, while Egwene blinked wearily, Liandrin was riding away from a Guiding, not toward another bridge or ramp, but down a pitted white line that led off into the darkness. Egwene stared at her friends, and then they all hurried to follow. Ahead, by the light of her lantern, the Aes Sedai was already removing the *Avendesora* leaf from the carvings on a Waygate.

"We are here," Liandrin said, smiling. "I have brought you at last to where you must go."

CHAPTER

40

Damane

Egwene dismounted as the Waygate opened, and when
Liandrin motioned them through, she led the shaggy
mare carefully out. Even so, she and Bela both stumbled in brush flattened by the opening Waygate as they
suddenly seemed to be moving even more slowly. A screen
of dense shrubs had surrounded and hidden the Waygate.
There were only a few trees close by, and a morning breeze
ruffled foliage with a little more color than the leaves had
had in Tar Valon.

Watching her friends emerge after her, she had been
standing there a good minute before she became aware that
others were already there, just out of sight on the other side
of the gates. When she did notice them she stared uncertainly; they were as odd a group as she had ever seen, and
she had heard too many rumors of the war on Toman Head.

Armored men, at least fifty of them, with overlapping
steel plates down their chests and dull black helmets shaped
like insects' heads, sat their saddles or stood beside their
horses, staring at her and the emerging women, staring at
the Waygate, muttering among themselves. The only bareheaded man among them, a tall, dark-faced, hook-nosed
fellow standing with a gilded-and-painted helmet on his
hip, looked astonished at what he was seeing. There were
women with the soldiers, too. Two wore plain, dark gray
dresses and wide silver collars, and stood staring intently
at those coming out of the Waygate, each with another
woman close behind her as if ready to speak into her ear.
Two other women, standing a little apart, wore wide, divided skirts that came well short of their ankles, and panels

embroidered with forked lightning bolts on their bosoms and skirts. Oddest of all was the last woman, reclining on a palanquin borne by eight muscular, bare-chested men in baggy black trousers. The sides of her scalp were shaved so that only a wide crest of black hair remained to fall down her back. A long, cream-colored robe worked in flowers and birds on blue ovals was carefully arranged to show her skirts of pleated white, and her fingernails were a good inch long, the first two on each hand lacquered blue.

"Liandrin Sedai," Egwene asked uneasily, "do you know who these people are?" Her friends fingered their reins as if wondering whether to mount and run, but Liandrin replaced the *Avendesora* leaf and stepped forward confidently as the Waygate began to close.

"The High Lady Suroth?" Liandrin said, making it halfway between a question and statement.

The women on the palanquin nodded fractionally. "You are Liandrin." Her speech was slurred, and it took Egwene a moment to understand. "Aes Sedai," Suroth added with a twist to her lips, and a murmur rose among the soldiers. "We must be done here quickly, Liandrin. There are patrols, and it would not do to be found. You would enjoy the attentions of the Seekers for Truth no more than I. I mean to be back in Falme before Turak knows I am gone."

"What are you talking about?" Nynaeve demanded. "What is she talking about, Liandrin?"

Liandrin laid a hand on Nynaeve's shoulder and one on Egwene's. "These are the two of whom you were told. And there is another." She nodded toward Elayne. "She is the Daughter-Heir of Andor."

The two women with the lightning on their dresses were approaching the party in front of the Waygate—they carried coils of some silvery metal in their hands, Egwene noticed—and the bareheaded soldier came with them. He did not put a hand near the sword hilt sticking up above his shoulder, and he wore a casual smile, but Egwene still watched him narrowly. Liandrin gave no sign of agitation; otherwise Egwene would have jumped onto Bela right then.

"Liandrin Sedai," she said urgently, "who are these people? Are they here to help Rand and the others, too?"

The hook-nosed man suddenly seized Min and Elayne by the scruffs of their necks, and in the next instant everything seemed to happen at once. The man yelled a curse, and a woman screamed, or perhaps more than one woman; Egwene could not be sure. Abruptly the breeze was a gale that whipped away Liandrin's angry shout in clouds of dirt and leaves and made the trees bend and groan. Horses reared and whinnied shrilly. And one of the women reached out and fastened something around Egwene's neck.

Cloak flapping like a sail, Egwene braced against the wind and tugged at what felt like a collar of smooth metal. It would not budge; under her frantic fingers, it felt all of one piece, though she knew it had to have some kind of clasp. The silvery coils the woman had carried now trailed over Egwene's shoulder, their other end joining a bright bracelet on the woman's left wrist. Balling her fist tightly, Egwene hit the woman as hard as she could, right in her eye—and staggered and fell to her knees herself, head ringing. It felt as if a large man had struck her in the face.

When she could see straight once more, the wind had died. A number of horses wandered loose, Bela and Elayne's mare among them, and some of the soldiers were cursing and picking themselves up off the ground. Liandrin was calmly brushing dust and leaves from her dress. Min knelt, supporting herself with her hands, groggily trying to rise further. The hook-nosed man stood over her, his hand dripping blood. Min's knife lay just out of her reach, the blade stained red along one side. Nynaeve and Elayne were nowhere to be seen, and Nynaeve's mare was gone, too. So were some of the soldiers, and one of the pairs of women. The other two were still there, and Egwene could see now that they were linked by a silver cord just like the one that still joined her to the woman standing over her.

That woman was rubbing her cheek as she squatted beside Egwene; there was a bruise already coming up around her left eye. With long, dark hair and big brown eyes, she was pretty, and perhaps as much as ten years older than Nynaeve. "Your first lesson," she said emphatically. There was no animosity in her voice, but what almost sounded like friendliness. "I will not punish you further this time, since I should have been on guard with a newly caught *damane*. Know this. You are a *damane*, a Leashed One, and I am a *sul'dam*, a Holder of the Leash. When *damane* and *sul'dam* are joined, whatever hurt the *sul'dam* feels, the *da*-

mane feels twice over. Even to death. So you must remember that you may never strike at a *sul'dam* in any way, and you must protect your *sul'dam* even more than yourself. I am Renna. How are you called?"

"I am not . . . what you said," Egwene muttered. She pulled at the collar again; it gave no more than before. She thought of knocking the woman down and trying to pry the bracelet from her wrist, but rejected it. Even if the soldiers did not try to stop her—and so far they seemed to be ignoring her and Renna altogether—she had the sinking feeling the woman was telling the truth. Touching her left eye brought a wince; it did not feel puffy, so perhaps she was not actually growing a bruise to match Renna's, but it still hurt. Her left eye, and Renna's left eye. She raised her voice. "Liandrin Sedai? Why are you letting them do this?" Liandrin dusted her hands together, never looking in her direction.

"The very first thing you must learn," Renna said, "is to do exactly as you are told, and without delay."

Egwene gasped. Suddenly her skin burned and prickled as if she had rolled in stinging nettles, from the soles of her feet to her scalp. She tossed her head as the burning sensation increased.

"Many *sul'dam*," Renna went on in that almost friendly tone, "do not believe *damane* should be allowed names, or at least only names they are given. But I am the one who took you, so I will be in charge of your training, and I will allow you to keep your own name. If you do not displease me too far. I am mildly upset with you now. Do you really wish to keep on until I am angry?"

Quivering, Egwene gritted her teeth. Her nails dug into her palms with the effort of not scratching wildly. *Idiot! It's only your name.* "Egwene," she managed to get out. "I am Egwene al'Vere." Instantly the burning itch was gone. She let out a long, unsteady breath.

"Egwene," Renna said. "That is a good name." And to Egwene's horror, Renna patted her on the head as she would a dog.

That, she realized, was what she had detected in the woman's voice—a certain good will for a dog in training, not quite the friendliness one might have toward another human being.

Renna chuckled. "Now you are even angrier. If you intend to strike at me again, remember to make it a small blow, for you will feel it twice as hard as I. Do not attempt to channel; that you will never do without my express command."

Egwene's eye throbbed. She pushed herself to her feet and tried to ignore Renna, as much as it was possible to ignore someone who held a leash fastened to a collar around your neck. Her cheeks burned when the other woman chuckled again. She wanted to go to Min, but the amount of leash Renna had let out would not reach that far. She called softly, "Min, are you all right?"

Sitting slowly back on her heels, Min nodded, then put a hand to her head as if she wished she had not moved it.

Jagged lightning crackled across the clear sky, then struck among the trees some distance off. Egwene jumped, and suddenly smiled. Nynaeve was still free, and Elayne. If anyone could free her and Min, Nynaeve could. Her smile faded into a glare for Liandrin. For whatever the reason the Aes Sedai had betrayed them, there would be a reckoning. *Someday. Somehow.* The glare did no good; Liandrin did not look away from the palanquin.

The bare-chested men knelt, lowering the palanquin to the ground, and Suroth stepped down, carefully arranging her robe, then picked her way to Liandrin on soft-slippered feet. The two women were much of a size. Brown eyes stared levelly into black.

"You were to bring me two," Suroth said. "Instead, I have only one, while two run loose, one of them more powerful by far than I had been led to believe. She will attract every patrol of ours within two leagues."

"I brought you three," Liandrin said calmly. "If you cannot manage to hold them, perhaps our master should find another among you to serve him. You take fright at trifles. If patrols come, kill them."

Lightning flashed again in the near distance, and moments later something roared like thunder not far from where it struck; a cloud of dust rose into the air. Neither Liandrin nor Suroth took any notice.

"I could still return to Falme with two new *damane,*" Suroth said. "It grieves me to allow an . . . Aes Sedai"—she twisted the words like a curse—"to walk free."

Liandrin's face did not change, but Egwene saw a nimbus abruptly glow around her.

"Beware, High Lady," Renna called. "She stands ready!"

There was a stir among the soldiers, a reaching for swords and lances, but Suroth only steepled her hands, smiling at Liandrin over her long nails. "You will make no move against me, Liandrin. Our master would disapprove, as I am surely needed here more than you, and you fear him more than you fear being made *damane*."

Liandrin smiled, though white spots marked her cheeks with anger. "And you, Suroth, fear him more than you fear me burning you to a cinder where you stand."

"Just so. We both fear him. Yet even our master's needs will change with time. All *marath'damane* will be leashed eventually. Perhaps I will be the one who places the collar around your lovely throat."

"As you say, Suroth. Our master's needs will change. I will remind you of it on the day when you kneel to me."

A tall leatherleaf perhaps a mile away suddenly became a roaring torch.

"This grows tiresome," Suroth said. "Elbar, recall them." The hook-nosed man produced a horn no bigger than his fist; it made a hoarse, piercing cry.

"You must find the woman Nynaeve," Liandrin said sharply. "Elayne is of no importance, but both the woman and this girl here must be taken with you on your ships when you sail."

"I know very well what has been commanded, *marath'damane*, though I would give much to know why."

"However much you were told, child," Liandrin sneered, "that is how much you are allowed to know. Remember that you serve and obey. These two must be removed to the other side of the Aryth Ocean and kept there."

Suroth sniffed. "I will not remain here to find this Nynaeve. My usefulness to our master will be at an end if Turak hands me over to the Seekers for Truth." Liandrin opened her mouth angrily, but Suroth refused to allow her a word. "The woman will not remain free for long. Neither of them will. When we sail again, we will take with us every woman on this miserable spit of land who can channel even slightly, leashed and collared. If you wish to remain and search for her, do so. Patrols will be here soon, thinking to engage the rabble that still hides in the countryside. Some patrols take *damane* with them, and they will not care what master you serve. Should you survive the encounter, the leash and collar will teach you a new life, and I do not believe our master will trouble to deliver one foolish enough to let herself be taken."

"If either is allowed to remain here," Liandrin said tightly, "our master will trouble himself with you, Suroth. Take them both, or pay the price." She strode to the Waygate, clutching the reins of her mare. Soon it was closing behind her.

The soldiers who had gone after Nynaeve and Elayne came galloping back with the two women linked by leash, collar, and bracelet, the *damane* and the *sul'dam* riding side by side. Three men led horses with bodies across the saddles. Egwene felt a surge of hope when she realized the bodies all wore armor. They had not caught Nynaeve or Elayne, either one.

Min started to rise to her feet, but the hook-nosed man planted a boot between her shoulder blades and drove her to the ground. Gasping for breath, she twitched there weakly. "I beg permission to speak, High Lady," he said. Suroth made a small motion with her hand, and he went on. "This peasant cut me, High Lady. If the High Lady has no use for her . . . ?" Suroth motioned slightly again, already turning away, and he reached over his shoulder for the hilt of his sword.

"No!" Egwene shouted. She heard Renna curse softly, and suddenly the burning itch covered her skin again, worse than before, but she did not stop. "Please! High Lady, please! She is my friend!" Pain such as she had never known wracked her through the burning. Every muscle knotted and cramped; she pitched on her face in the dirt, mewling, but she could still see Elbar's heavy, curved blade come free of its sheath, see him raise it with both hands. "Please! Oh, Min!"

Abruptly, the pain was gone as if it had never been; only the memory remained. Suroth's blue velvet slippers, dirt-stained now, appeared in front of her face, but it was at Elbar that she stared. He stood there with his sword over his head and all his weight on the foot on Min's back . . . and he did not move.

"This peasant is your friend?" Suroth said.

Egwene started to rise, but at a surprised arching of Suroth's eyebrow, she remained lying where she was and only raised her head. She had to save Min. *If it means groveling.* . . . She parted her lips and hoped her gritted teeth would pass for a smile. "Yes, High Lady."

"And if I spare her, if I allow her to visit you occasionally, you will work hard and learn as you are taught?"

"I will, High Lady." She would have promised much more to keep that sword from splitting Min's skull. *I'll even keep it*, she thought sourly, *as long as I have to.*

"Put the girl on her horse, Elbar," Suroth said. "Tie her on, if she cannot sit her saddle. If this *damane* proves a disappointment, perhaps then I will let you have the head of the girl." She was already moving toward her palanquin.

Renna pulled Egwene roughly to her feet and pushed her toward Bela, but Egwene had eyes only for Min. Elbar was no gentler with Min than Renna with her, but she thought Min was all right. At least Min shrugged off Elbar's attempt to tie her across her saddle and climbed onto her gelding with only a little help.

The odd party started off, westward, with Suroth leading and Elbar slightly to the rear of her palanquin, but close enough to heed any summons immediately. Renna and Egwene rode at the back with Min, and the other *sul'dam* and *damane*, behind the soldiers. The woman who had apparently meant to collar Nynaeve fondled the coiled silver leash she still carried and looked angry. Sparse forest covered the rolling land, and the smoke of the burning leatherleaf was soon only a smudge in the sky behind them.

"You were honored," Renna said after a time, "having the High Lady speak to you. Another time, I would let you wear a ribbon to mark the honor. But since you brought her attention on yourself. . . ."

Egwene cried out as a switch seemed to lash across her back, then another across her leg, her arm. From every direction they seemed to come; she knew there was nothing to block, but she could not help throwing her arms about as if to stop the blows. She bit her lip to stifle her moans, but tears still rolled down her cheeks. Bela whinnied and danced, but Renna's grip on the silver leash kept her from carrying Egwene away. None of the soldiers even looked back.

"What are you doing to her?" Min shouted. "Egwene? Stop it!"

"You live on sufferance . . . Min, is it?" Renna said mildly. "Let this be a lesson for you as well. So long as you try to interfere, it will not stop."

Min raised a fist, then let it fall. "I won't interfere. Only, please, stop it. Egwene, I'm sorry."

The unseen blows went on for a few moments more, as if to show Min her intervention had done nothing, then ceased, but Egwene could not stop shuddering. The pain did not go away this time. She pushed back the sleeve of her dress, thinking to see weals; her skin was unmarked, but the feel of them was still there. She swallowed. "It was not your fault, Min." Bela tossed her head, eyes rolling, and Egwene patted the mare's shaggy neck. "It wasn't yours, either."

"It was your fault, Egwene," Renna said. She sounded so patient, dealing so kindly with someone who was too dense to see the right, that Egwene wanted to scream. "When a *damane* is punished, it is always her fault, even if she does not know why. A *damane* must anticipate what her *sul'dam* wants. But this time, you do know why. *Damane* are like furniture, or tools, always there ready to be used, but never pushing themselves forward for attention. Especially not for the attention of one of the Blood."

Egwene bit her lip until she tasted blood. *This is a nightmare. It can't be real. Why did Liandrin do this? Why is this happening?* "May . . . may I ask a question?"

"Of me, you may." Renna smiled. "Many *sul'dam* will wear your bracelet over the years—there are always many more *sul'dam* than *damane*—and some would have your hide in strips if you took your eyes off the floor or opened your mouth without permission, but I see no reason not to let you speak, so long as you are careful in what you say." One of the other *sul'dam* snorted loudly; she was linked to a pretty, dark-haired woman in her middle years who kept her eyes on her hands.

"Liandrin"—Egwene would not give her the honorific, not ever again—"and the High Lady spoke of a master they both serve." The thought came into her head of a man with almost healed burns marring his face, and eyes and mouth that sometimes turned to fire, but even if he was only a figure in her dreams that seemed too horrible to contemplate. "Who is he? What does he want with me and—and Min?" She knew it was silly to avoid naming Nynaeve—she did not think any of these people would forget her just because her name was not mentioned, especially the blue-eyed *sul'dam* stroking her empty leash—but it was the only way she could think of fighting back at the moment.

"The affairs of the Blood," Renna said, "are not for me to take notice of, and certainly not for you. The High Lady will tell me what she wishes me to know, and I will tell you what I wish you to know. Anything else that you hear or see must be to you as if it never was said, as if it never happened. This way lies safety, most especially for a *damane*. *Damane* are too valuable to be killed out of hand, but you might find yourself not only soundly punished, but absent a tongue to speak or hands to write. *Damane* can do what they must without these things."

Egwene shivered, though the air was not very cold. Pulling her cloak up onto her shoulders, her hand brushed the leash, and she jerked at it fitfully. "This is a horrible thing. How can you do this to anyone? What diseased mind ever thought of it?"

The blue-eyed *sul'dam* with the empty leash growled, "This one could do without her tongue already, Renna."

Renna only smiled patiently. "How is it horrible? Could we allow anyone to run loose who can do what a *damane* can? Sometimes men are born who would be *marath'damane* if they were women—it is so here also, I have heard—and they must be killed, of course, but the women do not go mad. Better for them to become *damane* than make trouble contending for power. As for the mind that first thought of the *a'dam*, it was the mind of a woman who called herself Aes Sedai."

Egwene knew incredulity must be painting her face, because Renna laughed openly. "When Luthair Paendrag Mondwin, son of the Hawkwing, first faced the Armies of the Night, he found many among them who called themselves Aes Sedai. They contended for power among themselves and used the One Power on the field of battle. One such, a woman named Deain, who thought she could do better serving the Emperor—he was not Emperor then, of course—since he had no Aes Sedai in his armies, came to him with a device she had made, the first *a'dam*, fastened to the neck of one of her sisters. Though that woman did not want to serve Luthair, the *a'dam* required her to serve. Deain made more *a'dam*, the first *sul'dam* were found, and women captured who called themselves Aes Sedai discovered that they were in fact only *marath'damane*, Those Who Must Be Leashed. It is said that when she herself was leashed, Deain's screams shook the Towers of Midnight, but of course she, too, was a *marath'damane*, and *marath'damane* cannot be allowed to run free. Perhaps you will be one of those who has the ability to make *a'dam*. If so, you will be pampered, you may rest assured."

Egwene looked yearningly at the countryside through which they rode. The land was beginning to rise in low hills, and the thin forest had dwindled to scattered thickets, but she was sure she could lose herself in them. "Am I supposed to look forward to being pampered like a pet dog?" she said bitterly. "A lifetime of being chained to men and women who think I am some kind of animal?"

"Not men." Renna chuckled. "All *sul'dam* are women. If a man put on this bracelet, most of the time it would be no different than if it were hanging on a peg on the wall."

"And sometimes," the blue-eyed *sul'dam* put in harshly, "you and he would both die screaming." The woman had sharp features and a tight, thin-lipped mouth, and Egwene realized that anger was apparently her permanent expression. "From time to time the Empress plays with lords by linking them to a *damane*. It makes the lords sweat and entertains the Court of the Nine Moons. The lord never knows until it is done whether he will live or die, and neither does the *damane*." Her laugh was vicious.

"Only the Empress can afford to waste *damane* in such a way, Alwhin," Renna snapped, "and I do not mean to train this *damane* only to have her thrown away."

"I have not seen any training at all so far, Renna. Only a great deal of chatter, as if you and this *damane* were girlhood friends."

"Perhaps it is time to see what she can do," Renna said, studying Egwene. "Do you have enough control yet to channel at that distance?" She pointed to a tall oak standing alone on a hilltop.

Egwene frowned at the tree, perhaps half a mile from the line followed by the soldiers and Suroth's palanquin. She had never tried anything much beyond arm's reach, but she thought it might be possible. "I don't know," she said.

"Try," Renna told her. "Feel the tree. Feel the sap in the tree. I want you to make it all not only hot, but so hot that every drop of sap in every branch flashes to steam in an instant. Do it."

Egwene was shocked to discover an urge to do as Renna commanded. She had not channeled, or even touched *saidar*, in two days; the desire to fill herself with the One Power made her shiver. "I"—in half a heartbeat she discarded "will not"; the weals that were not there still burned too sharply for her to be quite that foolish—"cannot," she finished instead. "It is too far, and I've never done anything like that before."

One of the *sul'dam* laughed raucously, and Alwhin said, "She never even tried."

Renna shook her head almost sadly. "When one has been a *sul'dam* long enough," she told Egwene, "one learns to tell many things about *damane* even without the bracelet, but with the bracelet one can always tell whether a *damane* has tried to channel. You must never lie to me, or to any *sul'dam*, not even by a hair."

Suddenly the invisible switches were back, striking at her everywhere. Yelling, she tried to hit Renna, but the *sul'dam* casually knocked her fist away, and Egwene felt as if Renna had hit her arm with a stick. She dug her heels into Bela's flanks, but the *sul'dam*'s grip on the leash nearly pulled her out of her saddle. Frantically she reached for *saidar*, meaning to hurt Renna enough to make her stop, just the kind of hurt she herself had been given. The *sul'dam* shook her head wryly; Egwene howled as her own skin was suddenly scalded. Not until she fled from *saidar* completely did the burn begin to fade, and the unseen blows never ceased or slowed. She tried to shout that she would try, if only Renna would stop, but all she could manage was to scream and writhe.

Dimly, she was aware of Min shouting angrily and trying to ride to her side, of Alwhin tearing Min's reins from her hands, of another *sul'dam* speaking sharply to her *damane*, who looked at Min. And then Min was yelling, too, arms flapping as if trying to ward off blows or beat away stinging insects. In her own pain, Min's seemed distant.

Their cries together were enough to make some of the soldiers twist in their saddles. After one look, they laughed and turned back. How *sul'dam* dealt with *damane* was no affair of theirs.

To Egwene it seemed to go on forever, but at last there was an end. She lay sprawled weakly across the cantle of her saddle, cheeks wet with tears, sobbing into Bela's mane. The mare whickered uneasily.

"It is good that you have spirit," Renna said calmly. "The best *damane* are those who have spirit to be shaped and molded."

Egwene squeezed her eyes shut. She wished she could close her ears, too, to shut out Renna's voice. *I have to get away. I have to, but how? Nynaeve, help me. Light, somebody help me.*

"You will be one of the best," Renna said in tones of satisfaction. Her hand stroked Egwene's hair, a mistress soothing her dog.

Nynaeve leaned out of her saddle to peer around the screen of prickly leafed shrubs. Scattered trees met her eyes, some with leaves turning color. The expanses of grass and brush between seemed empty. Nothing moved that she could see except the thinning column of smoke, wavering in a breeze, from the leatherleaf.

That had been her work, the leatherleaf, and once the lightning called from a clear sky, and a few other things she had not thought to try until those two women tried them on her. She thought they must work together in some way, though she could not understand their relation to each other, apparently leashed as they were. One wore a collar, but the other was chained as surely as she. What Nynaeve was sure of was that one or both were Aes Sedai. She had never had a clear enough sight of them to see the glow of channeling, but it had to be.

I'll certainly take pleasure in telling Sheriam about them, she thought dryly. *Aes Sedai don't use the Power as a weapon, do they?*

She certainly had. She had at least knocked the two women down with that lightning strike, and she had seen one of the soldiers, or his body rather, burn from the ball of fire she made and hurled at them. But she had not seen any of the strangers at all in some time now.

Sweat beaded on her forehead, and it was not all from exertion. Her contact with *saidar* was gone, and she could not bring it back. In that first fury of knowing that Liandrin had betrayed them, *saidar* had been there almost before she knew it, the One Power flooding her. It had seemed she could do anything. And as long as they had chased her, rage at being hunted like an animal had fueled her. Now the chase had vanished. The longer she had gone without seeing an enemy at whom she could strike, the more she had begun to worry that they might be sneaking up on her somehow, and the more she had had time to worry about what was happening to Egwene, and Elayne, and Min. Now she was forced to admit that what she felt most was fear. Fear for them, fear for herself. It was anger she needed.

Something stirred behind a tree.

Her breath caught, and she fumbled for *saidar*, but all the exercises Sheriam and the others had taught her, all the blossoms unfolding in her mind, all the imagined streams that she held like riverbanks, did no good. She could feel it, sense the Source, but she could not touch it.

Elayne stepped from behind the tree in a wary crouch, and Nynaeve sagged with relief. The Daughter-Heir's dress was dirty and torn, her golden hair was a tangle of snarls and leaves, and her searching eyes were as wide as those of a frightened fawn, but she held her short-bladed dagger in a steady hand. Nynaeve picked up her reins and rode into the open.

Elayne gave a convulsive jump, then her hand went to her throat and she drew a deep breath. Nynaeve dismounted, and the two women hugged, taking comfort in having found each other.

"For a moment," Elayne said as they finally stepped apart, "I thought you were. . . . Do you know where they are? There were two men following me. Another few minutes and they would have caught me, but a horn sounded and they turned their horses and galloped off. They could see me, Nynaeve, and they just left."

"I heard it, too, and I haven't seen any of them since. Have you seen Egwene, or Min?"

Elayne shook her head, slumping to sit on the ground. "Not since. . . . That man hit Min, knocked her down. And one of those women was trying to put something around Egwene's neck. I saw that much before I ran. I don't think they got away, Nynaeve. I should have done something. Min cut the hand that was holding me, and Egwene. . . . I just ran, Nynaeve. I realized I was free, and I ran. Mother had better marry Gareth Bryne and have another daughter as soon as she can. I am not fit to take the throne."

"Don't be a goose," Nynaeve said sharply. "Remember, I have a packet of sheepstongue root among my herbs." Elayne had her head in her hands; the gibe did not even produce a murmur. "Listen to me, girl. Did you see me stay to fight twenty or thirty armed men, not to mention the Aes Sedai? If you had waited, the most likely thing by far is that you would be a prisoner, too. If they didn't just kill you. They seemed to be interested in Egwene and me for some reason. They might not have cared whether you remained alive or not." *Why* are *they interested in Egwene and me? Why us in particular? Why did Liandrin do this? Why?* She had no more answers now than she had had the first time she asked herself these questions.

"If I had died trying to help them—" Elayne began.

"—you'd be dead. And little good you'd be then, to yourself or them. Now get on your feet and brush off your dress." Nynaeve rummaged in her saddlebags for a hairbrush. "And fix your hair."

Elayne got up slowly, and took the brush with a small laugh. "You sound like Lini, my old nurse." She began to run the brush through her hair, wincing as tangles pulled. "But how are we going to help them, Nynaeve? You may be as strong as a full sister when you are angry, but they have women who can channel, too. I cannot think they're Aes Sedai, but they might as well be. We do not even know in which direction they took them."

"West," Nynaeve said. "That creature Suroth mentioned Falme, and that's as far west on Toman Head as you can go. We will go to Falme. I hope Liandrin is there. I will make her curse the day her mother laid eyes on her father. But first I think we had better find some clothes of the country. I've seen Taraboner and Domani women in the Tower, and what they wear is nothing like what we have on. We would stand out in Falme as strangers."

"I would not mind a Domani dress—though Mother would surely have a fit if she ever found out I'd worn one, and Lini would never let me hear the end of it—but even if we find a village, can we afford new dresses? I have no idea how much money you have, but I have only ten gold marks and perhaps twice that in silver. That will keep us two or three weeks, but I don't know what we will do after that."

"A few months as a novice in Tar Valon," Nynaeve said, laughing, "has not stopped you thinking like the heir to a throne. I don't have a tenth what you do, but altogether it will keep us two or three months, in comfort. Longer, if we are careful. I have no intention of buying us dresses, and they won't be new in any case. My gray silk dress will do us some good, with all those pearls and that gold thread. If I can't find a woman who will trade us each two or three sturdy changes for that, I will give you this ring, and I will be the novice." She swung up into her saddle and reached a hand down to pull Elayne up behind her.

"What are we going to do when we reach Falme?" Elayne asked as she settled on the mare's rump.

"I won't know that until we are there." Nynaeve paused, letting the horse stand. "Are you sure you want to do this? It will be dangerous."

"More dangerous than it is for Egwene and Min? They would come after us if our circumstances were reversed; I know they would. Are we going to stay here all day?" Elayne dug her heels in, and the mare started off.

Nynaeve turned the horse until the sun, still short of its noonday crest, shone at their backs. "We are going to have to be cautious. The Aes Sedai we know can recognize a woman who can channel just by being within arm's length of her. These Aes Sedai may be able to pick us out of a crowd if they are looking for us, and we had better assume they are." *They were certainly looking for Egwene and me. But why?*

"Yes, cautious. You were right before, too. We will not do them any good letting ourselves be caught as well."

Elayne was silent for a moment. "Do you think it was all lies, Nynaeve? What Liandrin told us about Rand being in danger? And the others? Aes Sedai do not lie."

It was Nynaeve's turn to be silent, remembering Sheriam telling her of the oaths a woman took on being raised to full sisterhood, oaths spoken holding a *ter'angreal* that bound her to keep them. *To speak no word that is not true.* That was one, but everyone knew that the truth an Aes Sedai said might not be the truth you thought you heard. "I expect Rand is warming his feet in front of Lord Agelmar's fire in Fal Dara this minute," she said. *I can't worry about him, now. I have to think about Egwene and Min.*

"I suppose he is," Elayne said with a sigh. She shifted behind the saddle. "If it is very far to Falme, Nynaeve, I expect to ride in the saddle half the time. This is not a very comfortable seat. We will never reach Falme at all if you let this horse set her own pace the whole way."

Nynaeve booted the mare to a quick trot, and Elayne yelped and caught at her cloak. Nynaeve told herself that she would take a turn riding behind and not complain if Elayne put the horse to a gallop, but for the most part she ignored the gasps of the woman bouncing behind her. She was too busy hoping that by the time they reached Falme, she could stop being afraid and start being angry.

The breeze freshened, cool and brisk with a hint of cold yet to come.

CHAPTER

41

Disagreements

T hunder rumbled across the slate-dark afternoon sky. Rand pulled the hood of his cloak further up, hoping to keep at least some of the cold rain off. Red stepped through muddy puddles doggedly. The hood hung sodden around Rand's head, as the rest of the cloak did around his shoulders, and his fine black coat was just as wet, and as cold. The temperature would not have far to drop before snow or sleet came down instead of rain. Snow would fall soon, again; the people in the village they had passed through said two snows had already come this year. Shivering, Rand almost wished it was snowing. Then, at least, he would not be soaked to the skin.

The column plodded along, keeping a wary eye on the rolling country. Ingtar's Gray Owl hung heavily even when the wind gusted. Hurin sometimes pulled his cowl back to sniff the air; he said neither rain nor cold had any effect on a trail, certainly not on the kind of trail he was seeking, but so far the sniffer had found nothing. Behind him, Rand heard Uno mutter a curse. Loial kept checking his saddlebags; he did not seem to mind getting wet himself, but he worried continually about his books. Everyone was miserable except for Verin, who appeared too lost in thought to even notice that her hood had slid back, exposing her face to the rain.

"Can't you do something about this?" Rand demanded of her. A small voice in the back of his head told him he could do it himself. All he need do was embrace *saidin*. So sweet, the call of *saidin*. To be filled with the One Power, to be one with the storm. Turn the skies to sunlight, or ride the storm as it raged, whip it to fury and scour Toman Head clean from the sea to the plain. Embrace *saidin*. He suppressed the longing ruthlessly.

The Aes Sedai gave a start. "What? Oh. I suppose. A little. I couldn't stop a storm this big, not by myself—it covers too much area—but I could lessen it some. Where we are, at least." She wiped rain from her face, seemed to realize for the first time that her hood had slipped, and pulled it back up absently.

"Then why don't you?" Mat said. The shivering face peering out from under his hood looked at death's door, but his voice was vigorous.

"Because if I used that much of the One Power, any Aes Sedai closer than ten miles would know someone had channeled. We don't want to bring these Seanchan down on us with some of their *damane*." Her mouth tightened angrily.

They had learned a little of the invaders in that village, called Atuan's Mill, though most of what they had heard hatched more questions than it answered. The people had babbled one moment and clamped their mouths shut the next, trembling and looking over their shoulders. They all shook with fear that the Seanchan would return with their monsters and their *damane*. That women who should have been Aes Sedai were instead leashed like animals frightened the villagers even more than the strange creatures the Seanchan commanded, things the folk of Atuan's Mill could only describe in whispers as coming from nightmares. And worst of all, the examples the Seanchan had made before leaving still chilled the people to their marrow. They had buried their dead, but they feared to clean away the large charred patch in the village square. None of them would say what had happened there, but Hurin had vomited as soon as they entered the village, and he would not go near the blackened ground.

Atuan's Mill had been half deserted. Some had fled to Falme, thinking the Seanchan would not be so harsh in a town they held fast, and others had gone east. More had said they were thinking of it. There was fighting on Almoth Plain, Taraboners battling Domani it was said, but such houses and barns as were burned there were kindled by torches in the hands of men. Even a war was easier to face than what the Seanchan had done, what they might do.

"Why did Fain bring the Horn here?" Perrin muttered.

The question had been asked by each of them at one time or another, and no one had an answer. "There's war, and these Seanchan, and their monsters. Why here?"

Ingtar turned in his saddle to look back at them. His face appeared almost as haggard as Mat's. "There are always men who see chances for their own advantage in the confusion of war. Fain is one like that. No doubt he thinks to steal the Horn again, from the Dark One this time, and use it for his own profit."

"The Father of Lies never lays simple plans," Verin said. "It may be that he wants Fain to bring the Horn here for some reason known only in Shayol Ghul."

"Monsters," Mat snorted. His cheeks were sunken, now, his eyes hollow. That he *sounded* healthy only made it worse. "They saw some Trollocs, or a Fade, if you ask me. Well, why not? If the Seanchan have Aes Sedai fighting for them, why not Fades and Trollocs?" He caught Verin staring at him and flinched. "Well, they are, on leashes or not. They can channel, and that makes them Aes Sedai." He glanced at Rand and gave a ragged laugh. "That makes you Aes Sedai, the Light help us all."

Masema came galloping from ahead, through the mud and the steady rain. "There is another village ahead, my Lord," he said as he pulled in beside Ingtar. His eyes only swept past Rand, but they tightened, and he did not look at Rand again. "It's empty, my Lord. No villagers, no Seanchan, nobody at all. The houses all look sound, though, except for two or three that . . . well, they aren't there anymore, my Lord."

Ingtar raised his hand and signaled for a trot.

The village Masema had found covered the slopes of a hill, with a paved square at the top around a circle of stone walls. The houses were of stone, all flat-roofed and few more than a single story. Three that had been larger, along one side of the square, were only heaps of blackened rubble; shattered chunks of stone and roof beams lay scattered across the square. A few shutters banged when the wind gusted.

Ingtar dismounted in front of the only large building still standing. The creaking sign above its door bore a woman juggling stars, but no name; rain came off the corners in two steady drizzles. Verin hurried inside while Ingtar spoke. "Uno, search every house. If there is anyone left, perhaps they can tell us what happened here, and maybe a little more about these Seanchan. And if there's any food, bring that, too. And blankets." Uno nodded and began telling off men. Ingtar turned to Hurin. "What do you smell? Did Fain come through here?"

Hurin, rubbing his nose, shook his head. "Not him, my Lord, and not the Trollocs, neither. Whoever did that left a stench, though." He pointed to the wreckage that had been houses. "It was killing, my Lord. There were people in there."

"Seanchan," Ingtar growled. "Let's get inside. Ragan, find some sort of stable for the horses."

Verin already had fires going in both of the big fireplaces, at either end of the common room, and was warming her hands at one, her sodden cloak spread out on one of the tables dotting the tiled floor. She had found a few candles, too, now burning on a table stuck in their own tallow. Emptiness and quiet, except for the occasional grumble of thunder, added to the flickering shadows to give the place a cavernous feel. Rand tossed his equally wet cloak and coat on a table and joined her. Only Loial seemed more interested in checking his books than in warming himself.

"We will never find the Horn of Valere this way," Ingtar said. "Three days since we . . . since we arrived here"—he shuddered and scrubbed a hand through his hair; Rand wondered what the Shienaran had seen in his other lives—"another two, at least, to Falme, and we have not found so much as a hair of Fain or Darkfriends. There are scores of villages along the coast. He could have gone to any of them and taken ship anywhere by now. If he was ever here."

"He is here," Verin said calmly, "and he went to Falme."

"And he's still here," Rand said. *Waiting for me. Please, Light, he's still waiting.*

"Hurin still hasn't caught a whiff of him," Ingtar said. The sniffer shrugged as if he felt himself at fault for the failure. "Why would he choose Falme? If those villagers are to be believed, Falme is held by these Seanchan. I would give my best hound to know who they are, and where they came from."

"Who they are is not important to us." Verin knelt and unfastened her saddlebags, pulling out dry clothes. "At least we have rooms in which to change our clothes, though it will do us little good unless the weather changes. Ingtar, it may well be that what the villagers told us is right, that they are the descendants of Artur Hawkwing's armies come back. What matters is that Padan Fain has gone to Falme. The writings in the dungeon at Fal Dara—"

"—never mentioned Fain. Forgive me, Aes Sedai, but that could have been a trick as easily as dark prophecy. I can't believe even Trollocs would be stupid enough to tell us everything they were going to do before they did it."

She twisted to look up at him. "And what do you mean to do, if you will not take my advice?"

"I mean to have the Horn of Valere," Ingtar said firmly. "Forgive me, but I have to trust my own senses before some words scrawled by a Trolloc . . ."

"A Myrddraal, surely," Verin murmured, but he did not even pause.

". . . or a Darkfriend seeming to betray himself out of his own mouth. I mean to quarter the ground until Hurin smells a trail or we find Fain in the flesh. I must have the Horn, Verin Sedai. I must!"

"That isn't the way," Hurin said softly. "Not 'must.' What happens, happens." No one paid him any mind.

"We all must," Verin murmured, peering into her saddle-bags, "yet some things may be even more important than that."

She did not say more, but Rand grimaced. He longed to get away from her and her prods and hints. *I am not the Dragon Reborn. Light, but I wish I could just get away from Aes Sedai completely.* "Ingtar, I think I'm riding on to Falme. Fain is there—I'm sure he is—and if I don't come soon, he—he will do something to hurt Emond's Field." He had not mentioned that part before.

They all stared at him, Mat and Perrin frowning, worried but considering; Verin as if she had just seen a new piece added to a puzzle. Loial looked astonished, and Hurin seemed confused. Ingtar was openly disbelieving.

"Why would he do that?" the Shienaran said.

"I don't know," Rand lied, "but that was part of the message he left with Barthanes."

"And did Barthanes say Fain was going to Falme?" Ingtar demanded. "No. It wouldn't matter if he had." He gave a bitter laugh. "Darkfriends lie as naturally as they breathe."

"Rand," Mat said, "if I knew how to stop Fain from hurting Emond's Field, I would. If I was sure he was going to. But I need that dagger, Rand, and Hurin has the best chance of finding it."

"I will go wherever you go, Rand," Loial said. He had finished making sure the books were dry and was taking off his sodden coat. "But I don't see where a few more days will change anything one way or another, now. Try being a little less hasty for once."

"It doesn't matter to me whether we go to Falme now, later, or never," Perrin said with a shrug, "but if Fain really is threatening Emond's Field . . . well, Mat's right. Hurin is the best way to find him."

"I can find him, Lord Rand," Hurin put in. "Let me get one sniff of him, and I'll take you right to him. There's never anything else left a trail like his."

"You must make your own choice, Rand," Verin said carefully, "but remember that Falme is held by invaders about whom we still know next to nothing. If you go to Falme alone, you may find yourself a prisoner, or worse, and that will serve nothing. I am sure whatever choice you make will be the right one."

"Ta'veren," Loial rumbled.

Rand threw up his hands.

Uno came in from the square, shaking rain off his cloak.

"Not a flaming soul to be found, my Lord. Looks to me like they ran like striped pigs. Livestock's all gone, and there isn't a bloody cart or wagon left, either. Half the houses are stripped to the flaming floors. I'll wager my next month's pay you could follow them by the bloody furniture they tossed on the side of the road when they realized it was only weighing down their flaming wagons."

"What about clothes?" Ingtar asked.

Uno blinked his one eye in surprise. "Just a few bits and pieces, my Lord. Mainly what they didn't think was bloody worth taking with them."

"They will have to do. Hurin, I mean to dress you and a few more as local people, as many as we can manage, so you won't stand out. I want you to swing wide, north and south, until you cross the trail." More soldiers were coming in, and they all gathered around Ingtar and Hurin to listen.

Rand leaned his hands on the mantel over the fireplace and stared into the flames. They made him think of Ba'alzamon's eyes. "There isn't much time," he said. "I feel . . . something . . . pulling me to Falme, and there isn't much time." He saw Verin watching him, and added harshly, "Not that. It's Fain I have to find. It has nothing to do with . . . that."

Verin nodded. "The Wheel weaves as the Wheel wills, and we are all woven into the Pattern. Fain has been here weeks before us, perhaps months. A few more days will make little difference in whatever is going to happen."

"I'm going to get some sleep," he muttered, picking up his saddlebags. "They can't have carried off all the beds."

Upstairs, he did find beds, but only a few still had mattresses, and those so lumpy he thought it might be more comfortable to sleep on the floor. Finally he chose a bed where the mattress simply sagged in the middle. There was nothing else in the room except one wooden chair and a table with a rickety leg.

He took off his wet things, putting on a dry shirt and breeches before lying down, since there were no sheets or blankets, and propped his sword beside the head of the bed. Wryly, he thought that the only thing dry he had for a coverlet was the Dragon's banner; he left it safely buckled inside the saddlebags.

Rain drummed on the roof, and thunder growled overhead, and now and again a lightning flash lit the windows. Shivering, he rolled this way and that on the mattress, seeking some comfortable way to lie, wondering if the banner would not do for a blanket after all, wondering if he should ride on to Falme.

He rolled to his other side, and Ba'alzamon was standing beside the chair with the pure white length of the Dragon's banner in his hands. The room seemed darker there, as if Ba'alzamon stood on the edge of a cloud of oily black smoke. Nearly healed burns crisscrossed his face, and as Rand looked, his pitch-dark eyes vanished for an instant, replaced by endless caverns of fire. Rand's saddlebags lay by his feet, buckles undone, flap thrown back where the banner had been hidden.

"The time comes closer, Lews Therin. A thousand

threads draw tight, and soon you will be tied and trapped, set to a course you cannot change. Madness. Death. Before you die, will you once more kill everything you love?"

Rand glanced at the door, but he made no move except to sit up on the side of the bed. What good to try running from the Dark One? His throat felt like sand. "I am not the Dragon, Father of Lies!" he said hoarsely.

The darkness behind Ba'alzamon roiled, and furnaces roared as Ba'alzamon laughed. "You honor me. And belittle yourself. I know you too well. I have faced you a thousand times. A thousand times a thousand. I know you to your miserable soul, Lews Therin Kinslayer." He laughed again; Rand put a hand in front of his face against the heat of that fiery mouth.

"What do you want? I will not serve you. I will not do anything that you want. I'll die first!"

"You *will* die, worm! How many times have you died across the span of the Ages, fool, and how much has death availed you? The grave is cold and lonely, save for the worms. The grave is mine. This time there will be no rebirth for you. This time the Wheel of Time will be broken and the world remade in the image of the Shadow. This time your death will be forever! Which will you choose? Death everlasting? Or life eternal—and power!"

Rand hardly realized that he was on his feet. The void had surrounded him, *saidin* was there, and the One Power flowed into him. That fact almost cracked the emptiness. Was this real? Was it a dream? Could he channel in a dream? But the torrent rushing into him swept away his doubts. He hurled it at Ba'alzamon, hurled the pure One Power, the force that turned the Wheel of Time, a force that could make seas burn and eat mountains.

Ba'alzamon took half a step back, holding the banner clutched before him. Flames leaped in his wide eyes and mouth, and the darkness seemed to cloak him in shadow. In the Shadow. The Power sank into that black mist and vanished, soaked up like water on parched sand.

Rand drew on *saidin*, pulled for more, and still more. His flesh seemed so cold it must shatter at a touch; it burned as if it must boil away. His bones felt on the point of crisping to cold crystal ash. He did not care; it was like drinking life itself.

"Fool!" Ba'alzamon roared. "You will destroy yourself!"

Mat. The thought floated somewhere beyond the consuming flood. *The dagger. The Horn. Fain. Emond's Field. I can't die yet.*

He was not sure how he did it, but suddenly the Power was gone, and *saidin,* and the void. Shuddering uncontrollably, he fell to his knees beside the bed, arms wrapped around himself in a vain effort to stop their twitching.

"That is better, Lews Therin." Ba'alzamon tossed the banner to the floor and put his hands on the chair back; wisps of smoke rose from between his fingers. The shadow no longer encompassed him. "There is your banner, Kinslayer. Much good will it do you. A thousand strings laid over a thousand years have drawn you here. Ten thousand woven throughout the Ages tie you like a sheep for slaughter. The Wheel itself holds you prisoner to your fate Age after Age. But I can set you free. You cowering cur, I alone in the entire world can teach you how to wield the Power. I alone can stop it killing you before you have a chance to go mad. I alone can stop the madness. You have served me before. Serve me again, Lews Therin, or be destroyed forever!"

"My name," Rand forced between chattering teeth, "is Rand al'Thor." His shivering forced him to squeeze his eyes shut, and when he opened them again, he was alone.

Ba'alzamon was gone. The shadow was gone. His saddlebags stood against the chair with the buckles done up and one side bulging with the bulk of the Dragon's banner, just as he had left it. But on the chair back, tendrils of smoke still rose from the charred impressions of fingers.

CHAPTER
42

Falme

Nynaeve pressed Elayne back into the narrow alleyway between a cloth merchant's shop and a potter's works as the pair of women linked by a silvery leash passed by, heading down the cobblestone street toward Falme harbor. They did not dare allow that pair to come too close. The people in the street made way for those two even more quickly than they did for Seanchan soldiers, or the occasional noble's palanquin, thickly curtained now that the days were cold. Even the street artists did not offer to draw them in chalks or pencils, although they pestered everyone else. Nynaeve's mouth tightened as her eyes followed the *sul'dam* and the *damane* through the crowd. Even after weeks in the town, the sight sickened her. Perhaps it sickened her more, now. She could not imagine doing that to any woman, not even Moiraine or Liandrin.

Well, maybe Liandrin, she admitted sourly. Sometimes, at night, in the small, smelly room the two of them had rented above a fishmonger, she thought of what she would like to do to Liandrin when she got her hands on her. Liandrin even more than Suroth. More than once she had been shocked at her own cruelty, even while she was delighted at her inventiveness.

Still trying to keep the pair in sight, her eyes fell on a bony man, well down the street, before the shifting throng hid him again. She had only a flash of a big nose in a narrow face. He wore a rich bronze velvet robe of Seanchan cut over his clothes, but she thought that he was no Seanchan, though the servant following him was, and a servant of high degree, with one temple shaved. The local people had not taken to Seanchan fashions, particularly that one. *That looked like Padan Fain,* she thought incredulously. *It couldn't be. Not here.*

"Nynaeve," Elayne said softly, "could we move on, now? That fellow selling apples is looking at his table as if he's thinking he had more a few moments ago, and I would not want him wondering what I have in my pockets."

They both wore long coats made of sheepskin, with the fleece turned in and bright red spirals embroidered across the breast. It was country garb, but it passed well enough in Falme, where many people had come in from the farms and villages. Among so many strangers the two of them had been able to sink in unnoticed. Nynaeve had combed out her braid, and her gold ring, the serpent eating its own tail, now nestled under her dress beside Lan's heavy ring on the leather cord around her neck.

The large pockets of Elayne's coat bulged suspiciously.

"You stole those apples?" Nynaeve hissed quietly, pulling Elayne out into the crowded street. "Elayne, we don't have to steal. Not yet, anyway."

"No? How much money do we have left? You have been 'not hungry' very often at mealtimes the last few days."

"Well, I am not hungry," Nynaeve snapped, trying to ignore the hollow in her middle. Everything cost considerably more than she had expected; she had heard local people complaining about how prices had risen since the Seanchan came. "Give me one of those." The apple Elayne dug out of her pocket was small and hard, but it crunched with a delicious sweetness when Nynaeve bit into it. She licked the juice from her lips. "How did you manage to—" She jerked Elayne to a halt and peered into her face. "Did you . . . ? Did you . . . ?" She could not think of a way to say it with so many streaming by, but Elayne understood.

"Only a little. I made that stack of old melons with the soft spots fall, and when he started putting them back. . . ." She did not even have the grace, as Nynaeve saw it, to blush or look embarrassed. Unconcernedly eating one of the apples, she shrugged. "There is no need to frown at me like that. I looked carefully to make sure there was no *damane* close." She sniffed. "If I were being held prisoner, I would not help my captors find other women to enslave. Although, the way these Falmen behave, you would think they were lifelong servants of those who should be their enemies to the death." She looked around, openly contemptuous, at the people hurrying by; it was possible to follow the path of any Seanchan, even common soldiers and even at a distance, by the ripples of bowing. "They should resist. They should fight back."

"How? Against . . . that."

They had to step to the side of the street along with everyone else as a Seanchan patrol neared, climbing from the direction of the harbor. Nynaeve managed the bow, hands on knees, with face schooled to a perfect smoothness; Elayne was slower, and made her bow with a distasteful twist of her mouth.

There were twenty armored men and women in the patrol, riding horses, for which Nynaeve was grateful. She could not become used to seeing people riding things that looked like bronze-scaled, tailless cats, and a rider on one of the flying beasts was always enough to make her feel dizzy; she was glad there were so few of them. Still, two leashed creatures trotted along with the patrol, like wingless birds with coarse leather skin, and sharp beaks higher above the cobblestones than the helmeted heads of the soldier. Their long, sinewy legs looked as if they could run faster than any horse.

She straightened slowly after the Seanchan were gone. Some of those who had bowed for the patrol came close to running; no one was comfortable at the sight of the Seanchan's beasts except the Seanchan themselves. "Elayne," she said softly as they resumed their climb, "if we are caught, I swear that before they kill us, or do whatever they do, I will beg them on bended knees to let me stripe you from top to bottom with the stoutest switch I can find! If you still can't learn to be careful, maybe it's time to think about sending you back to Tar Valon, or home to Caemlyn, or anywhere but here."

"I am careful. At least I looked to be sure there was no *damane* close by. What about you? I have seen you channel with one in plain sight."

"I made sure they weren't looking at me," Nynaeve muttered. She had had to ball up all her anger at women being chained like animals to manage it. "And I only did it once. And it was only a trickle."

"A trickle? We had to spend three days hiding in our room breathing fish while they searched the town for whoever had done it. Do you call that being careful?"

"I had to know if there was a way to unfasten those collars." She thought there was. She would have to test one more collar at least before she was certain, and she was not looking forward to it. She had thought, like Elayne, that the *damane* must all be prisoners eager to escape, but it had been the woman in the collar who raised the cry.

A man pushing a barrow that bumped over the cobblestones passed by them, crying his services to sharpen scissors and knives. "They should resist, somehow," Elayne growled. "They act as if they do not see anything that happens around them if there's a Seanchan in it."

Nynaeve only sighed. It did not help that she thought Elayne was at least partly right. At first she had thought some of the Falmen submission, at least, must be a pose, but she had found no evidence of any resistance at all. She had looked at first, hoping to find help in freeing Egwene and Min, but everyone took fright at the merest hint that they might oppose the Seanchan, and she stopped asking before she drew the wrong sort of attention. In truth, she could not imagine how the people *could* fight. *Monsters and Aes Sedai. How can you fight monsters and Aes Sedai?*

Ahead stood five tall stone houses, among the largest in the town, all together making up a block. One street short of them, Nynaeve found an alleyway beside a tailor shop, where they could keep an eye on some of the tall houses' entrances, at least. It was not possible to see every door at once—she did not want to risk letting Elayne go off on her own to watch more—but it was not wise to go any closer. Above the rooftops, on the next street, the golden hawk banner of the High Lord Turak flapped in the wind.

Only women went in or out of those houses, and most of those were *sul'dam,* alone or with *damane* in tow. The buildings had been taken over by the Seanchan to house the *damane.* Egwene had to be in there, and likely Min; they had found no sign of Min so far, though it was possible she was as hidden by the crowds as they. Nynaeve had heard many tales of women and girls being seized on the streets or brought in from the villages; they all went into those houses, and if they were seen again, they wore a collar.

Settling herself on a crate beside Elayne, she dug into the other woman's coat for a handful of the small apples. There were fewer local folk in the streets here. Everyone knew what the houses were, and everyone avoided them, just as they avoided the stables where the Seanchan kept their beasts. It was not difficult to keep an eye on the doors through spaces between the passersby. Just two women stopping for a bite; just two more people who could not afford to eat at an inn. Nothing to attract more than a passing glance.

Eating mechanically, Nynaeve tried once more to plan. Being able to open the collar—if she really could—did no good at all unless she could reach Egwene. The apples did not taste so sweet anymore.

From the narrow window of her tiny room under the eaves, one of a number roughly walled together from whatever had been there before, Egwene could see the garden where *damane* were being walked by their *sul'dam*. It had been several gardens before the Seanchan knocked down the walls that separated them and took the big houses to keep their *damane*. The trees were all but leafless, but the *damane* were still taken out for air, whether they wanted it or not. Egwene watched the garden because Renna was down there, talking with another *sul'dam*, and as long as she could see Renna, then Renna was not going to enter and surprise her.

Some other *sul'dam* might come—there were many more *sul'dam* than *damane*, and every *sul'dam* wanted her turn wearing a bracelet; they called it being complete—but Renna still had charge of her training, and it was Renna who wore her bracelet four times out of five. If anyone came, they would find no impediment to entering. There were no locks on the doors of *damane*'s rooms. Egwene's room held only a hard, narrow bed, a washstand with a chipped pitcher and bowl, one chair and a small table, but it had no room for more. *Damane* had no need of comfort, or privacy, or possessions. *Damane* were possessions. Min had a room just like this, in another house, but Min could come and go as she would, or almost as she would. Seanchan were great ones for rules; they had more, for everyone, than the White Tower did for novices.

Egwene stood far back from the window. She did not want any of the women below to look up and see the glow that she knew surrounded her as she channeled the One Power, probing delicately at the collar around her neck, searching futilely; she could not even tell whether the band was woven or made of links—sometimes it seemed one, sometimes the other—but it seemed all of a piece all the time. It was only a tiny trickle of the Power, the merest drip that she could imagine, but it still beaded sweat on her face and made her stomach clench. That was one of the properties of the *a'dam;* if a *damane* tried to channel without a *sul'dam* wearing her bracelet, she felt sick, and the more of the Power she channeled, the sicker she became. Lighting a candle beyond the reach of her arm would have made Egwene vomit. Once Renna had ordered her to juggle her tiny balls of light with the bracelet lying on the table. Remembering still made her shudder.

Now, the silver leash snaked across the bare floor and up the unpainted wooden wall to where the bracelet hung on a peg. The sight of it hanging there made her jaws clench with fury. A dog leashed so carelessly could have run away. If a *damane* moved her bracelet as much as a foot from where it had last been touched by a *sul'dam.* . . . Renna had made her do that, too—had made her carry her own bracelet across the room. Or try to. She was sure it had only been minutes before the *sul'dam* snapped the bracelet firmly on her own wrist, but to Egwene the screaming and the cramps that had had her writhing on the floor had seemed to go on for hours.

Someone tapped at the door, and Egwene jumped, before she realized it could not be a *sul'dam.* None of them would knock first. She let *saidar* go, anyway; she was beginning to feel decidedly ill. "Min?"

"Here I am for my weekly visit," Min announced as she slipped inside and shut the door. Her cheeriness sounded a little forced, but she always did what she could to keep Egwene's spirits up. "How do you like it?" She spun in a little circle, showing off her dark green wool dress of Seanchan cut. A heavy, matching cloak hung over her arm. There was even a green ribbon catching up her dark hair, though her hair was hardly long enough for it. Her knife was still in its sheath at her waist, though. Egwene had been surprised when Min first showed up wearing it, but it seemed the Seanchan trusted everyone. Until they broke a rule.

"It's pretty," Egwene said cautiously. "But, why?"

"I haven't gone over to the enemy, if that is what you are thinking. It was this, or else find someplace to stay out in the town, and maybe not be able to visit you again." She started to straddle the chair as she would have in breeches, gave a wry shake of her head, and turned it around to sit. "'Everyone has a place in the Pattern,'" she mimicked, "'and the place of everyone must be readily apparent.' That old hag Mulaen apparently got tired of not knowing what my place was on sight and decided I ranked with the serving girls. She gave me the choice. You should see some of the things Seanchan serving girls wear, the ones who serve the lords. It might be fun, but not unless I was betrothed, or, better yet, married. Well, there's no going back. Not yet, anyway. Mulaen burned my coat and breeches." Grimacing to show what she thought of that, she picked up a rock from a small pile on the table and bounced it from hand to hand. "It isn't so bad," she said with a laugh, "except that it has been so long since I wore skirts that I keep tripping over them."

Egwene had had to watch her clothes being burned, too, including that lovely green silk. It had made her glad she had not brought more of the clothes the Lady Amalisa had given her, though she might never see any of them, or the White Tower, again. What she had on now was the same dark gray all *damane* wore. Damane *have no possessions*, it had been explained to her. *The dress a* damane *wears, the food she eats, the bed she sleeps in, are all gifts from her* sul'dam. *If a* sul'dam *chooses that a* damane *sleep on the floor instead of in a bed, or in a stall in a stable, it is purely the choice of the* sul'dam. Mulaen, who had charge of the *damane* quarters, had a droning nasal voice, but she was sharp with any *damane* who did not remember every word of her boring lectures.

"I don't think there will be any going back for me ever," Egwene said, sighing, sinking down on her bed. She gestured to the rocks on the table. "Renna gave me a test, yesterday. I picked out the piece of iron ore, and the copper ore, blindfolded, every time she mixed them up. She left them all here to remind me of my success. She seemed to think it was some kind of reward to be reminded."

"It doesn't seem any worse than the rest—not nearly as bad as making things explode like fireworks—but couldn't you have lied? Told her you didn't know which was which?"

"You still do not know what this is like." Egwene tugged at the collar; pulling did no more good than channeling had. "When Renna is wearing that bracelet, she knows what I am doing with the Power, and what I am not. Sometimes she even seems to know when she isn't wearing it; she says *sul'dam* develop—an affinity, she calls it—after a while." She sighed. "No one even thought to test me on this earlier. Earth is one of the Five Powers that was strongest in men. When I picked out those rocks, she took me outside the town, and I was able to point right to an abandoned iron mine. It was all overgrown, and there wasn't any opening to be seen at all, but once I knew how, I could feel the iron ore still in the ground. There hasn't been enough to make it worth working in a hundred years, but I knew it was there. I couldn't lie to her, Min. She knew I had sensed the mine as soon as I did. She was so excited, she promised me a pudding with my supper." She felt her cheeks growing hot, in anger and embarrassment. "Apparently," she said bitterly, "I am now too valuable to be wasted making things explode. Any *damane* can do that; only a handful can find ores in the ground. Light, I hate making things explode, but I wish that was all I could do."

The color in her cheeks deepened. She did hate it, making trees tear themselves to splinters and the earth erupt; that was meant for battle, for killing, and she wanted no part of it. Yet anything the Seanchan let her do was another chance to touch *saidar*, to feel the Power flowing through her. She hated the things Renna and the other *sul'dam* made her do, but she was sure that she could handle much more of the Power now than she could before leaving Tar Valon. She certainly knew she could do things with it that no sister in the Tower had ever thought of doing; they never thought of tearing the earth apart to kill men.

"Perhaps you won't have to worry about any of it much longer," Min said, grinning. "I've found us a ship, Egwene.

The captain has been held here by the Seanchan, and he is about ready to sail with or without permission."

"If he will take you, Min, go with him," Egwene said wearily. "I told you I'm valuable, now. Renna says in a few days they're sending a ship back to Seanchan. Just to take me."

Min's grin vanished, and they stared at each other. Suddenly Min hurled her rock at the pile on the table, scattering them. "There has to be a way out of here. There has to be a way to take that bloody thing off your neck!"

Egwene leaned her head back against the wall. "You know the Seanchan have collected every woman they've been able to find who can channel even a speck. They come from all over, not just from here in Falme, but from the fishing villages, and from farming towns inland. Taraboner and Domani women, passengers off ships they've stopped. There are two Aes Sedai among them."

"Aes Sedai!" Min exclaimed. By habit she looked around to make sure no Seanchan had overheard her saying that name. "Egwene, if there are Aes Sedai here, they can help us. Let me talk to them, and—"

"They can't even help themselves, Min. I only talked to one—her name is Ryma; the *sul'dam* don't call her that, but that's her name; she wanted to make sure I knew it—and she told me there is another. She told me in between bouts of tears. She's Aes Sedai, and she was crying, Min! She has a collar on her neck, they make her answer to Pura, and she can't do anything more about it than I can. They captured her when Falme fell. She was crying because she's beginning to stop fighting against it, because she cannot take being punished anymore. She was crying because she wants to take her own life, and she cannot even do that without permission. Light, I know how she feels!"

Min shifted uneasily, smoothing her dress with suddenly nervous hands. "Egwene, you don't want to. . . . Egwene, you must not think of harming yourself. I will get you out somehow. I will!"

"I am not going to kill myself," Egwene said dryly. "Even if I could. Let me have your knife. Come on. I won't hurt myself. Just hand it to me."

Min hesitated before slowly taking her knife from its sheath at her waist. She held it out warily, obviously ready to leap if Egwene tried anything.

Egwene took a deep breath and reached for the hilt. A soft quiver ran through the muscles of her arm. As her hand came within a foot of the knife, a cramp suddenly contorted her fingers. Eyes fixed, she tried to force her hand closer. The cramp seized her whole arm, knotting muscles to her shoulder. With a groan, she sank back, rubbing her arm and concentrating her thoughts on *not* touching the knife. Slowly, the pain began to lessen.

Min stared at her incredulously. "What . . . ? I don't understand."

"*Damane* are not allowed to touch a weapon of any kind." She worked her arm, feeling the tightness go. "Even our meat is cut for us. I don't want to hurt myself, but I could not if I did want to. No *damane* is ever left alone where she might jump from a height—that window is nailed shut—or throw herself in a river."

"Well, that's a good thing. I mean. . . . Oh, I don't know what I mean. If you could jump in a river, you might escape."

Egwene went on dully, as if the other woman had not spoken. "They are training me, Min. The *sul'dam* and the *a'dam* are training me. I cannot touch anything I even think of as a weapon. A few weeks ago I considered hitting Renna over the head with that pitcher, and I could not pour wash water for three days. Once I'd thought of it that way, I not only had to stop thinking about hitting her with it, I had to convince myself I would never, under any circumstances, hit her with it before I could touch it again. She knew what had happened, told me what I had to do, and would not let me wash anywhere except with that pitcher and bowl. You are lucky it happened between your visiting days. Renna made sure I spent those days sweating from the time I woke to the time I fell asleep, exhausted. I am trying to fight them, but they are training me as surely as they're training Pura." She clapped a hand to her mouth, moaning through her teeth. "Her name is Ryma. I have to remember *her* name, not the name they've put on her. She is Ryma, and she's Yellow Ajah, and she has fought them as long and as hard as she could. It is no fault of hers that she hasn't the strength left to fight any longer. I wish I knew who the other sister is that Ryma mentioned. I wish I knew her name. Remember both of us, Min. Ryma, of the Yellow Ajah, and Egwene al'Vere. Not

Egwene the *damane;* Egwene al'Vere of Emond's Field. Will you do that?"

"Stop it!" Min snapped. "You stop it right this instant! If you get shipped off to Seanchan, I'll be right there with you. But I don't think you will. You know I've read you, Egwene. I don't understand most of it—I almost never do—but I see things I am sure link you to Rand, and Perrin, and Mat, and—yes, even Galad, the Light help you for a fool. How can any of that happen if the Seanchan take you off across the ocean?"

"Maybe they're going to conquer the whole world, Min. If they conquer the world, there's no reason Rand and Galad and the rest could not end up in Seanchan."

"You ninny-headed goose!"

"I am being practical," Egwene said sharply. "I don't intend to stop fighting, not as long as I can breathe, but I don't see any hope that I'll ever have the *a'dam* off me, either. Just as I don't see any hope that anyone is going to stop the Seanchan. Min, if this ship captain will take you, go with him. At least then one of us will be free."

The door swung open, and Renna stepped in.

Egwene jumped to her feet and bowed sharply, as did Min. The tiny room was crowded for bowing, but Seanchan insisted on protocol before comfort.

"Your visiting day, is it?" Renna said. "I had forgotten. Well, there is training to be done even on visiting days."

Egwene watched sharply as the *sul'dam* took down the bracelet, opened it, and fastened it again around her wrist. She could not see how it was done. If she could have probed with the One Power, she would have, but Renna would have known that immediately. As the bracelet closed around Renna's wrist a look came onto the *sul'dam*'s face that made Egwene's heart sink.

"You have been channeling." Renna's voice was deceptively mild; there was a spark of anger in her eyes. "You know that is forbidden except when we are complete." Egwene wet her lips. "Perhaps I have been too lenient with you. Perhaps you believe that because you are valuable now, you will be allowed license. I think I made a mistake letting you keep your old name. I had a kitten called Tuli when I was a child. From now on, your name is Tuli. You will go now, Min. Your visiting day with Tuli is ended."

Min hesitated only long enough for one anguished look at Egwene before leaving. Nothing Min could say or do would do anything except make matters worse, but Egwene could not help looking longingly at the door as it closed behind her friend.

Renna took the chair, frowning at Egwene. "I must punish you severely for this. We will both be called to the Court of the Nine Moons—you for what you can do; I as your *sul'dam* and trainer—and I will not allow you to disgrace me in the eyes of the Empress. I will stop when you tell me how much you love being *damane* and how obedient you will be after this. And, Tuli. Make me believe every word."

CHAPTER

43

A Plan

Outside in the low-ceilinged hallway, Min dug her nails into her palms at the first piercing cry from the room. She took a step toward the door before she could stop herself, and when she did stop, tears sprang up in her eyes. *Light help me, all I can do is make it worse. Egwene, I'm sorry. I'm sorry.*

Feeling worse than useless, she picked up her skirts and ran, and Egwene's screams pursued her. She could not make herself stay, and leaving made her feel a coward. Half blind with weeping, she found herself in the street before she knew it. She had intended to go back to her room, but now she could not do it. She could not stand the thought that Egwene was being hurt while she sat warm and safe under the next roof. Scrubbing the tears from her eyes, she swept her cloak around her shoulders and started down the street. Every time she cleared her eyes, new tears began trickling along her cheeks. She was not accustomed to weeping openly, but then she was not accustomed to feeling so helpless, so useless. She did not know where she was going, only that it had to be as far as she could reach from Egwene's cries.

"Min!"

The low-pitched shout brought her up short. At first, she could not make out who had called. Relatively few people walked the street this close to where the *damane* were housed. Aside from a lone man trying to interest two Seanchan soldiers in buying the picture he would draw of them with his colored chalks, everyone local tried to step along quickly without actually appearing to run. A pair

of *sul'dam* strolled by, *damane* trailing behind with eyes
down; the Seanchan women were talking about how many
more *marath'damane* they expected to find before they
sailed. Min's eyes passed right over the two women in long
fleece coats, then swung back in wonder as they came toward her. "Nynaeve? Elayne?"

"None other." Nynaeve's smile was strained; both
women had tight eyes, as if they fought worried frowns.
Min thought she had never seen anything as wonderful
as the sight of them. "That color becomes you," Nynaeve
continued. "You should have taken up dresses long since.
Though I've thought of breeches myself since I saw them
on you." Her voice sharpened as she drew close enough to
see Min's face. "What is the matter?"

"You've been crying," Elayne said. "Has something happened to Egwene?"

Min gave a start and looked back over her shoulder. A
sul'dam and *damane* came down the steps she had used and
turned the other way, toward the stables and horse yards.
Another woman with the lightning panels on her dress
stood at the top of the stairs talking with someone still inside. Min grabbed her friends by the arms and hurried them
down the street toward the harbor. "It's dangerous for you
two here. Light, it's dangerous for you to be in Falme. There
are *damane* everywhere, and if they find you. . . . You do
know what *damane* are? Oh, you don't know how good it is
to see you both."

"I imagine about as half as good as it is to see you,"
Nynaeve said. "Do you know where Egwene is? Is she in
one of those buildings? Is she all right?"

Min hesitated a fraction before saying, "She's as well as
can be expected." Min could see it all too well, if she told
them what was happening to Egwene right that moment.
Nynaeve was as likely as not to go storming back in an attempt to stop it. *Light, let it be over by now. Light, make her
bend her stubborn neck just once before they almost break
it first.* "I don't know how to get her out, though. I found a
ship captain who I think will take us if we can reach his
ship with her—he won't help unless we make it that far,
and I cannot say I blame him—but I have no idea how to do
even that much."

"A ship," Nynaeve said thoughtfully. "I had meant to

simply ride east, but I must say I've worried about it. As nearly as I can make out, we would have to be almost off Toman Head before we were clear of Seanchan patrols completely, and then there's supposed to be fighting of some sort on Almoth Plain. I never thought of a ship. We have horses, and we do not have money for passage. How much does this man want?"

Min shrugged. "I never got that far. We don't have any money, either. I thought I could put off paying until after we sail. Afterwards . . . well, I don't think he'll put into any port where there are Seanchan. Wherever he threw us off, it would have to be better than here. The problem is convincing him to sail at all. He wants to, but they patrol off the harbor, too, and there is no way of telling if there's a *damane* on one of their ships until it's too late. 'Give me a *damane* of my own on my deck,' he says, 'and I will sail this instant.' Then he starts talking about drafts and shoals and lee shores. I don't understand any of that, but as long as I smile and nod every now and then, he keeps talking, and I think if I can keep him talking long enough, he'll talk himself into sailing." She drew a shuddering breath; her eyes started stinging again. "Only, I don't think there's time to let him talk himself into it anymore. Nynaeve, they're going to send Egwene back to Seanchan, and soon."

Elayne gasped. "But, why?"

"She is able to find ore," Min said miserably. "A few days, she says, and I don't know if a few days is enough for this man to convince himself to sail. Even if it is, how do we take that Shadow-spawned collar off her? How do we get her out of the house?"

"I wish Rand were here." Elayne sighed, and when they both looked at her, she blushed and quickly added, "Well, he does have a sword. I wish we had somebody with a sword. Ten of them. A hundred."

"It isn't swords or brawn we need now," Nynaeve said, "but brains. Men usually think with the hair on their chests." She touched her chest absently, as if feeling something through her coat. "Most of them do."

"We would need an army," Min said. "A large army. The Seanchan were outnumbered when they faced the Taraboners, and the Domani, and they won every battle easily, from what I hear." She hurriedly pulled Nynaeve and Elayne to the opposite side of the street as a *damane* and *sul'dam* climbed past them on the other side. She was relieved there was no need for urging; the other two watched the linked women go as warily as she. "Since we don't have an army, the three of us will have to do it. I hope one of you can think of something I haven't; I've wracked my brains, and I always stumble when it comes to the *a'dam,* the leash and collar. *Sul'dam* don't like anyone watching too closely when they open them. I think I can get you inside, if that will help. One of you, anyway. They think of me as a servant, but servants may have visitors, as long as they keep to the servants' quarters."

Nynaeve wore a thoughtful frown, but her face cleared almost immediately, taking on a purposeful look. "Don't you worry, Min. I have a few ideas. I have not spent my time here idly. You take me to this man. If he is any harder to handle than the Village Council with their backs up, I will eat this coat."

Elayne nodded, grinning, and Min felt the first real hope she had had since arriving in Falme. For an instant Min found herself reading the auras of the other two women. There was danger, but that was to be expected—and new things, too, among the images she had seen before; it was like that, sometimes. A man's ring of heavy gold floated above Nynaeve's head, and above Elayne's, a red-hot iron and an axe. They meant trouble, she was sure, but it seemed distant, somewhere in the future. Only for a moment did the reading last, and then all she saw was Elayne and Nynaeve, watching her expectantly.

"It's down near the harbor," she said.

The sloping street became more crowded the further down they went. Street peddlers rubbed elbows with merchants who had brought wagons in from the inland villages and would not go out again until winter had come and gone, hawkers with their trays called to the passersby, Falmen in embroidered cloaks brushed past farm families in heavy fleece coats. Many people had fled here from villages further from the coast. Min saw no point to it—they had leaped from the possibility of a visit from the Seanchan to the certainty of Seanchan all around them—but she had heard what the Seanchan did when they first came to a village, and she could not blame the villagers too much for fearing another appearance. Everyone bowed when Sean-chan walked past or a curtained palanquin was carried by up the steep street.

Min was glad to see Nynaeve and Elayne knew about the bowing. Bare-chested bearers paid no more mind to the people who bent themselves than did arrogant, armored soldiers, but failure to bow would surely catch their eyes.

They talked a little as they moved down the street, and she was surprised at first to learn they had been in the town only a few days less than Egwene and herself. After a moment, though, she decided it was no wonder they had not met earlier, not with the crowds in the streets. She had been reluctant to spend time further from Egwene than was necessary; there was always the fear that she would go for her allowed visit and find Egwene gone. *And now she will be. Unless Nynaeve can think of something.*

The smell of salt and pitch grew heavy in the air, and gulls cried, wheeling overhead. Sailors appeared in the throng, many still barefoot despite the cold.

The inn had been hastily renamed The Three Plum Blossoms, but part of the word "Watcher" still showed through the slapdash paint work on the sign. Despite the crowds outside, the common room was little more than half full; prices were too high for many people to afford time sitting over ale. Roaring fires on hearths at either end of the room warmed it, and the fat innkeeper was in his shirtsleeves. He eyed the three women, frowning, and Min thought it was her Seanchan dress that stopped him from telling them to leave. Nynaeve and Elayne, in their farm women's coats, certainly did not look as if they had money to spend.

The man she was looking for was alone at a table in a corner, in his accustomed place, muttering into his wine. "Do you have time to talk, Captain Domon?" she said.

He looked up, brushing a hand across his beard when he saw she was not alone. She still thought his bare upper lip looked odd with the beard. "So you do bring friends to drink up my coin, do you? Well, that Seanchan lord bought my cargo, so coin I have. Sit." Elayne jumped as he suddenly bellowed, "Innkeeper! Mulled wine here!"

"It's all right," Min told her, taking a place on the end of one of the benches at the table. "He only looks and sounds like a bear." Elayne sat down on the other end, looking doubtful.

"A bear, do I be?" Domon laughed. "Maybe I do. But what of you, girl? Have you given over thought of leaving? That dress do look Seanchan to me."

"Never!" Min said fiercely, but the appearance of a serving girl with the steaming, spiced wine made her fall silent.

Domon was just as wary. He waited until the girl had gone with his coins before saying, "Fortune prick me, girl, I mean no offense. Most people only want to go on with their lives, whether their lords be Seanchan or any other."

Nynaeve leaned her forearms on the table. "We also want to go on with our lives, Captain, but without any Seanchan. I understand you intend to sail soon."

"I would sail today, if I could," Domon said glumly. "Every two or three days that Turak do send for me to tell him tales of the old things I have seen. Do I look a gleeman to you? I did think I could spin a tale or two and be on my way, but now I think when I no entertain him any longer, it be an even wager whether he do let me go or have my head cut off. The man do look soft, but he be as hard as iron, and as coldhearted."

"Can your ship avoid the Seanchan?" Nynaeve asked.

"Fortune prick me, could I make it out of the harbor without a *damane* rips *Spray* to splinters, I can. If I do no let a Seanchan ship with a *damane* come too close once I do make the sea. There be shoal waters all along this coast, and *Spray* do have a shallow draft. I can take her into waters those lumbering Seanchan hulks can no risk. They must be wary of the winds close inshore this time of year, and once I do have *Spray*—"

Nynaeve cut him off. "Then we will take passage with you, Captain. There will be four of us, and I will expect you to be ready to sail as soon as we are aboard."

Domon scrubbed a finger across his upper lip and peered into his wine. "Well, as to that, there still do be the matter of getting out of the harbor, you see. These *damane*—"

"What if I tell you you will sail with something better than *damane?*" Nynaeve said softly. Min's eyes widened as she realized what Nynaeve intended.

Almost under her breath, Elayne murmured, "And you tell me to be careful."

Domon had eyes only for Nynaeve, and they were wary eyes. "What do you mean?" he whispered.

Nynaeve opened her coat to fumble at the back of her neck, finally pulling out a leather cord that had been tucked inside her dress. Two gold rings hung on the cord. Min gasped when she saw one—it was the heavy man's ring she had seen when she read Nynaeve in the street—but she knew it was the other, slighter and made for a woman's slender finger, that made Domon's eyes bulge. A serpent biting its own tail.

"You know what this means," Nynaeve said, starting to slip the Serpent ring from the cord, but Domon closed his hand over it.

"Put it away." His eyes darted uneasily; no one was looking at them that Min could see, but he looked as if he thought everyone was staring. "That ring do be dangerous. If it be seen. . . ."

"As long as you know what it means," Nynaeve said with a calm that made Min envious. She pulled the cord from Domon's hand and retied it around her neck.

"I know," he said hoarsely. "I do know what it means. Maybe there do be a chance if you. . . . Four, you say? This girl who do like to listen to my tongue wag, she do be one of the four, I take it. And you, and. . . ." He frowned at Elayne. "Surely this child is no—no one like you."

Elayne straightened angrily, but Nynaeve put a hand on her arm and smiled soothingly at Domon. "She travels with me, Captain. You might be surprised by what we can do even before we earn the right to a ring. When we sail, you will have three on your ship who can fight *damane* if need be."

"Three," he breathed. "There do be a chance. Maybe. . . ." His face brightened for a moment, but as he looked at them, it grew serious again. "I should take you to *Spray* right now and cast off, but Fortune prick me if I can no tell you what you face here if you stay, and maybe even if you go with me. Listen to me, and mark what I do say." He took another cautious look around, and still lowered his voice and chose his words carefully. "I did see a—a woman who wore a ring like that taken by the Seanchan. A pretty, slender little woman she was, with a big War—a big man with her who did look as if he did know how to use his sword. One of them must have been careless, for the Seanchan did have

an ambush laid for them. The big man put six, seven soldiers on the ground before he did die himself. The—the
woman. . . . Six *damane* they did put around her, stepping
out of the alleys of a sudden. I did think she would . . . do
something—you know what I mean—but. . . . I know nothing of these things. One moment she did look as if she
would destroy them all, then a look of horror did come on
her face, and she did scream."

"They cut her off from the True Source." Elayne's face
was white.

"No matter," Nynaeve said calmly. "We will not allow
the same to be done to us."

"Aye, mayhap it will be as you say. But I will remember
it until I die. Ryma, help me. That is what she did scream.
And one of the *damane* did fall down crying, and they did
put one of those collars on the neck of the . . . woman, and
I . . . I did run." He shrugged, and rubbed his nose, and
peered into his wine. "I have seen three women taken, and I
have no stomach for it. I would leave my aged grandmother
standing on the dock to sail from here, but I did have to tell
you."

"Egwene said they have two prisoners," Min said slowly.
"Ryma, a Yellow, and she didn't know who the other is."
Nynaeve gave her a sharp look, and she fell silent, blushing.
From the look on Domon's face, it had not furthered their
cause any to tell him the Seanchan held two Aes Sedai, not
just one.

Yet abruptly he stared at Nynaeve and took a long gulp of
wine. "Do that be why you are here? To free . . . those two?
You did say there would be three of you."

"You know what you need to know," Nynaeve told him
briskly. "You must be ready to sail on the instant anytime
in the next two or three days. Will you do it, or will you
remain here to see if they will cut off your head after all?
There are other ships, Captain, and I mean to have passage
assured on one of them today."

Min held her breath; under the table, her fingers were
knotted.

Finally, Domon nodded. "I will be ready."

When they returned to the street, Min was surprised to
see Nynaeve sag against the front of the inn as soon as the
door closed. "Are you ill, Nynaeve?" she asked anxiously.

Nynaeve drew a long breath and stood up straight, tugging at her coat. "With some people," she said, "you have to be certain. If you show them one glimmer of doubt, they'll sweep you off in some direction you don't want to go. Light, but I was afraid he was going to say no. Come, we have plans yet to make. There are still one or two small problems to work out."

"I hope you don't mind fish, Min," Elayne said.

One or two small problems? Min thought as she followed them. She hoped very much that Nynaeve was not just being certain again.

CHAPTER
44

Five Will Ride Forth

Perrin eyed the villagers warily, self-consciously hitching at a too-short cloak, embroidered on the chest and with some holes in it not even patched, but none of them gave him a second glance despite his strange mix of clothes and the axe on his hip. Hurin had a coat with blue spirals across the chest under his cloak, and Mat wore a pair of baggy trousers that made bunches where they were stuffed into his boots. That had been all they had been able to find that would fit back in the abandoned village. Perrin wondered if this one would be abandoned soon. Half the stone houses were empty, and in front of the inn, up the dirt street from them, three ox carts, loaded too heavily in great mounds and everything covered with roped canvas, stood with families gathered around them.

As he watched them, huddling together and saying their goodbyes to those who were staying, at least for the time being, Perrin decided it was not lack of interest in strangers on the villagers' part; they were carefully avoiding looking at him and the others. These people had learned not to show curiosity about strangers, even strangers who were obviously not Seanchan. Strangers might be dangerous these days on Toman Head. They had encountered the same studious indifference in other villages. There were more towns here within a few leagues of the coast, every one holding itself independent. At any rate, they had until the Seanchan came.

"I say it's time to go get the horses," Mat said, "before they decide to start asking questions. There has to be a first time for it."

Hurin was staring at a big, blackened circle of ground that marred the brown grass of the village green. It had a weathered look, but no one had done anything to erase it. "Maybe six or eight months ago," he muttered, "and it still stinks. The whole Village Council and their families. Why would they do a thing like that?"

"Who knows why they do anything?" Mat muttered. "Seanchan don't seem to need a reason for killing people. None I can figure out, anyway."

Perrin tried not to look at the charred patch. "Hurin, are you sure about Fain? Hurin?" It had been hard to make the sniffer look at anything else since they entered the village. "Hurin!"

"What? Oh. Fain. Yes." Hurin's nostrils flared, and right away he wrinkled his nose. "There's no mistaking that, even old as it is. Makes a Myrddraal smell like roses. He passed through here all right, but I think he was alone. No Trollocs, anyway, and if he had any Darkfriends with him, they hadn't been up to much lately."

There was some sort of agitation up by the inn, people shouting and pointing. Not at Perrin and the other two, but at something Perrin could not see in the low hills east of the village.

"Can we get the horses now?" Mat said. "That could be Seanchan."

Perrin nodded, and they broke into a run for where they had tied their horses behind an abandoned house. As Mat and Hurin disappeared around the corner of the house, Perrin looked back toward the inn and stopped in astonishment. The Children of the Light were riding into town, a long column of them.

He leaped after the others. "Whitecloaks!"

They wasted only an instant staring at him in disbelief before they were scrambling into their saddles. Keeping houses between them and the main street of the village, the three galloped out of the village westward, watching over their shoulders for pursuit. Ingtar had told them to avoid anything that might slow them down, and Whitecloaks asking questions would certainly do that, even if they could manage answers that satisfied. Perrin kept an even closer watch than the other two; he had his own reasons for not wanting to meet Whitecloaks. *The axe in my hands. Light, what I wouldn't give to change that.*

The lightly wooded hills soon hid the village, and Perrin began to think maybe there was nothing chasing them after all. He reined in and motioned the other two to stop. When they did, eyeing him questioningly, he listened. His ears were sharper than they once had been, but he heard no sounds of hoofbeats.

Reluctantly, he reached out with his mind in search of wolves. Almost immediately he found them, a small pack lying up for the day in the hills above the village they had just left. There were moments of astonishment so strong he almost thought it was his own; these wolves had heard rumors, but they had not really believed there were two-legs who could talk to their kind. He sweated through the minutes it took to get past introducing himself—he gave the image of Young Bull in spite of himself, and added his own smell, according to the custom among wolves; wolves were great ones for formalities on first meetings—but finally he managed to get his question through. They really had no interest in any two-legs who could not talk to them, but at last they glided down to take a look, unseen by the dull eyes of the two-legs.

After a time, images came back to him, what the wolves saw. White-cloaked men on horses crowding around the village, riding among the houses, riding around it, but none leaving. Especially not westward. The wolves said all they smelled moving west was himself and two other two-legs with three of the hard-footed tall ones.

Perrin let go the contact with the wolves gratefully. He was aware of Hurin and Mat looking at him.

"They aren't following," he said.

"How can you be sure?" Mat demanded.

"I am!" he snapped, then more softly, "I just am."

Mat opened his mouth and closed it again, and finally said, "Well, if they aren't coming after us, I say we go back to Ingtar and get on Fain's trail. That dagger isn't coming any closer just standing here."

"We can't pick it up again this close to that village," Hurin said. "Not without risking running into Whitecloaks. I don't think Lord Ingtar would appreciate that, and not Verin Sedai, neither."

Perrin nodded. "We'll follow it on a few miles, anyway. But keep a close lookout. We can't be too far from Falme, now. It won't do any good to avoid the Whitecloaks and ride right into a Seanchan patrol."

As they started out again, he could not help wondering what Whitecloaks were doing there.

Geofram Bornhald peered down the village street, sitting his saddle while the legion spread through the small town and surrounded it. There had been something about the heavy-shouldered man who had dashed out of sight, something that tickled his memory. *Yes, of course. The lad who claimed to be a blacksmith. What was his name?*

Byar pulled up in front of him, hand on heart. "The village is secured, my Lord Captain."

Villagers in heavy sheepskin coats milled uneasily as white-cloaked soldiers herded them together near the overloaded carts in front of the inn. Crying children clung to their mothers' skirts, but no one looked defiant. Dull eyes stared out of the adult faces, waiting passively for whatever was going to happen. For that much, Bornhald was grateful. He had no real desire to make an example of any of these people, and no wish at all to waste time.

Dismounting, he tossed his reins to one of the Children. "See that the men are fed, Byar. Put the prisoners in the inn with as much food and water as they can carry, then nail all the doors and shutters closed. Make them think I am leaving some men to stand guard, yes?"

Byar touched his heart again and wheeled his horse to shout orders. The herding began anew, into the flat-roofed inn, while other Children ransacked houses searching for hammers and nails.

Watching the sullen faces that filed past him, Bornhald thought it should be two or three days before any of them found enough courage to break out of the inn and find there were no guards. Two or three days was all he needed, but he did not intend to risk alerting the Seanchan to his presence now.

Leaving enough men behind to make the Questioners believe his entire legion was still scattered across Almoth Plain, he had brought more than a thousand of the Children nearly the length of Toman Head without giving alarm, so far as he knew. Three skirmishes with Seanchan patrols had ended quickly. The Seanchan had grown used to facing already defeated rabble; the Children of the Light had been a deadly surprise. Yet the Seanchan knew how to fight like the Dark One's hordes, and he could not help remembering the one skirmish that had cost him better than fifty men. He was still not sure which of the two arrow-riddled women he had stared at afterwards had been the Aes Sedai.

"Byar!" One of Bornhald's men handed him water in a pottery cup from one of the carts; it was icy in his throat.

The gaunt-faced man swung down from his saddle. "Yes, my Lord Captain?"

"When I engage the enemy, Byar," Bornhald said slowly, "you will not take part. You will watch from a distance, and you will carry word to my son of what happens."

"But my Lord Captain—!"

"That is my order, Child Byar!" he snapped. "You will obey, yes?"

Byar's back stiffened, and he stared straight ahead. "As you command, my Lord Captain."

Bornhald studied him for a moment. The man would do as he was told, but it would be better to give him another reason than letting Dain know how his father had died. It was not as if he did not have knowledge that was urgently needed in Amador. Since that skirmish with the Aes Sedai—*Was it one of them, or both? Thirty Seanchan soldiers, good fighters, and two women cost me twice the casualties they did.*—since then, he no longer expected to live to leave Toman Head. In the small chance the Seanchan did not see to it, very likely the Questioners would.

"When you have found my son—he should be with Lord Captain Eamon Valda near Tar Valon—and told him, you will ride to Amador, and report to the Lord Captain Commander. To Pedron Niall personally, Child Byar. You will tell him what we have learned of the Seanchan; I will write it out for you. Be sure he understands that we can no longer count on the Tar Valon witches being content with manipulating events from the shadows. If they fight openly for the Seanchan, we will surely face them elsewhere." He hesitated. That last was the most important of all. They had to know under the Dome of Truth that for all their vaunted oaths, Aes

Sedai would march into battle. It gave him a sinking feeling, a world where Aes Sedai wielded the Power in battle; he was not sure that he would regret leaving it. But there was one more message he wanted carried to Amador. "And, Byar . . . tell Pedron Niall how we were used by the Questioners."

"As you command, my Lord Captain," Byar said, but Bornhald sighed at the expression on his face. The man did not understand. To Byar, orders were to be obeyed whether they came from the Lord Captain or the Questioners, whatever they were.

"I will write that out for you to hand to Pedron Niall as well," he said. He was not sure how much good it would do in any case. A thought came to him, and he frowned at the inn, where some of his men were loudly hammering nails through shutters and doors. "Perrin," he muttered. "That was his name. Perrin, from the Two Rivers."

"The Darkfriend, my Lord Captain?"

"Perhaps, Byar." He was not entirely certain, himself, but surely a man who seemed to have wolves fight for him could be nothing else. Certainly, this Perrin had killed two of the Children. "I thought I saw him when we rode in, but I do not remember anyone among the prisoners who looked like a blacksmith."

"Their blacksmith left a month ago, my Lord Captain. Some of them were complaining that they'd have been gone before we came if they had not had to mend their cartwheels themselves. Do you believe it was the man Perrin, my Lord Captain?"

"Whoever it was, he is not accounted for, no? And he may carry word of us to the Seanchan."

"A Darkfriend would surely do so, my Lord Captain."

Bornhald gulped the last of the water and tossed the cup aside. "There will be no meal for the men here, Byar. I will not let these Seanchan catch me napping, whether it is Perrin of the Two Rivers or someone else who warns them. Mount the legion, Child Byar!"

Far above their heads, a huge, winged shape circled, unnoticed.

In the clearing amid the hilltop thicket where they had made their camp, Rand worked the forms with his sword.

He wanted to keep from thinking. He had had his chances to search with Hurin for Fain's trail; they all had, in twos and threes so they would not attract attention, and they had all found nothing so far. Now they waited for Mat and Perrin to come back with the sniffer; they should have been back hours ago.

Loial was reading, of course, and there was no telling if his ear-twitching was over his book or the scouting party's lateness, but Uno and most of the Shienaran soldiers sat tensely, oiling their swords, or kept watch through the trees as if they expected Seanchan to appear any moment. Only Verin appeared unconcerned. The Aes Sedai sat on a log beside their small fire, murmuring to herself and writing in the dirt with a long stick; every so often she would shake her head and scrub it all out with her foot and start over again. All the horses were saddled and ready to go, the Shienarans' animals each tied to a lance driven into the ground.

"Heron Wading in the Rushes," Ingtar said. He sat with his back against a tree, sliding a sharpening stone along his sword and watching Rand. "You should not be bothering with that one. It leaves you completely open."

For an instant Rand balanced on the ball of one foot, sword held reversed in both hands over his head, then shifted smoothly to the other foot. "Lan says it's good for developing balance." It was not easy keeping his balance. In the void it often seemed he could maintain his equilibrium atop a rolling boulder, but he did not dare assume the void. He wanted to too much to trust himself.

"What you practice too often, you use without thinking. You will put your sword in the other man with that, if you're quick, but not before he has his through your ribs. You are practically inviting him. I don't think I could see a man face me so open and not put my sword in him, even knowing he might strike home at me if I did."

"It's only for balance, Ingtar." Rand wavered on one foot, and had to put the other down to keep from falling. He slammed the blade into its scabbard and picked up the gray cloak that had been his disguise. It was moth-eaten, and ragged around the bottom, but lined with thick fleece, and the wind was picking up, cold and out of the west. "I wish they'd come back."

As if his wish had been a signal, Uno spoke up with quiet urgency. "Bloody horsemen coming, my Lord." Scabbards rattled as men who did not already have their blades out bared them. Some leaped into their saddles, snatching up lances.

The tension faded as Hurin led the others into the clearing at a trot, and came again as he spoke. "We found the trail, Lord Ingtar."

"We followed it almost to Falme," Mat said as he dismounted. A flush in his pale cheeks seemed a mocking of health; the skin was tight over his skull. The Shienarans gathered around, as excited as he was. "It's just Fain, but there isn't anywhere else he could be going. He must have the dagger."

"We found Whitecloaks, too," Perrin said, swinging down from his saddle. "Hundreds of them."

"Whitecloaks?" Ingtar exclaimed, frowning. "Here? Well, if they do not trouble us, we will not trouble them. Perhaps if the Seanchan are occupied with them, it will help us reach the Horn." His eyes fell on Verin, still seated by the fire. "I suppose you will tell me I should have listened to you, Aes Sedai. The man did go to Falme."

"The Wheel weaves as the Wheel wills," Verin said placidly. "With *ta'veren*, what happens is what was meant to happen. It may be the Pattern demanded these extra days. The Pattern puts everything in its place precisely, and when we try to alter it, especially if *ta'veren* are involved, the weaving changes to put us back into the Pattern as we were meant to be." There was an uneasy silence that she did not seem to notice; she sketched on idly with the stick. "Now, however, I think perhaps we should make plans. The Pattern has brought us to Falme at last. The Horn of Valere has been taken to Falme."

Ingtar squatted across the fire from her. "When enough people say the same thing, I tend to believe it, and the local people say the Seanchan do not seem to care who comes or goes in Falme. I will take Hurin and a few others into the town. Once he follows Fain's trail to the Horn . . . well, then we shall see what we shall see."

With her foot, Verin scrubbed out a wheel she had drawn in the dirt. In its place she drew two short lines that touched at one end. "Ingtar and Hurin. And Mat, as he can sense the dagger if he comes close enough. You do want to go, don't you, Mat?"

Mat appeared torn, but he gave a jerky nod. "I have to, don't I? I have to find that dagger."

A third line made a bird track. Verin looked sideways at Rand.

"I'll go," he said. "That is why I came." An odd light appeared in the Aes Sedai's eyes, a knowing glimmer that made him uneasy. "To help Mat find the dagger," he said sharply, "and Ingtar find the Horn." *And Fain*, he added to himself. *I have to find Fain if it isn't already too late.*

Verin scratched a fourth line, turning the bird track to a lopsided star. "And who else?" she said softly. She held the stick poised.

"Me," Perrin said, a hair before Loial chimed in with, "I think I would like to go, too," and Uno and the other Shienarans all began clamoring to join.

"Perrin spoke first," Verin said, as if that settled it. She added a fifth line and drew a circle around all five. The hair on Rand's neck stirred; it was the same wheel she had rubbed out in the first place. "Five ride forth," she murmured.

"I really would like to see Falme," Loial said. "I've never seen the Aryth Ocean. Besides, I can carry the chest, if the Horn is still in it."

"You'd better include me at least, my Lord," Uno said. "You and Lord Rand will need another sword at your backs if those bloody Seanchan try to stop you." The rest of the soldiers rumbled the same sentiment.

"Do not be silly," Verin said sharply. Her stare silenced them all. "All of you cannot go. No matter how uncaring the Seanchan are about strangers, they will surely take notice of twenty soldiers, and you look like nothing else even without armor. And one or two of you will make no difference. Five is few enough to enter without attracting attention, and it is fitting that three of them should be the three *ta'veren* among us. No, Loial, you must stay behind, too. There are no Ogier on Toman Head. You would attract as many eyes as all the rest put together."

"What about you?" Rand asked.

Verin shook her head. "You forget the *damane*." Her mouth twisted around the word in distaste. "The only way

I could help you would be if I channeled the Power, and that would be no help at all if I brought those down on you. Even if they were not close enough to see, one might well feel a woman—or a man, for that matter—channeling, if care was not taken to keep the Power channeled small." She did not look at Rand; to him, she seemed ostentatious in not doing so, and Mat and Perrin were suddenly intent on their own feet.

"A man," Ingtar snorted. "Verin Sedai, why add problems? We have enough already without supposing men channeling. But it would be well if you were there. If we have need of you—"

"No, you five must go alone." Her foot scrubbed across the wheel drawn in the dirt, partially obliterating it. She studied each of them in turn, intent and frowning. "Five will ride forth."

For a moment it seemed that Ingtar would ask again, but meeting her level gaze, he shrugged and turned to Hurin. "How long to reach Falme?"

The sniffer scratched his head. "If we left now and rode through the night, we could be there by sunrise tomorrow morning."

"Then that is what we will do. I'll waste no more time. All of you saddle your horses. Uno, I want you to bring the others along behind us, but keep out of sight, and do not let anyone. . . ."

Rand peered at the sketched wheel as Ingtar went on with his instructions. It was a broken wheel, now, with only four spokes. For some reason that made him shiver. He realized Verin was watching him, dark eyes bright and intent like a bird's. It took an effort to pull his gaze away and begin getting his things together.

You're letting fancies take you, he told himself irritably. *She can't do anything if she isn't there.*

CHAPTER

45

Blademaster

The rising sun pushed its crimson edge above the horizon and sent long shadows down the cobblestone streets of Falme toward the harbor. A sea breeze bent the smoke of breakfast cook fires inland from the chimneys. Only the early risers were already out of doors, their breath making steam in the morning cold. Compared to the crowds that would fill the streets in another hour, the town seemed nearly empty.

Sitting on an upended barrel in front of a still-closed iron-monger's shop, Nynaeve warmed her hands under her arms and surveyed her army. Min sat on a doorstep across the way, swathed in her Seanchan cloak and eating a wrinkled plum, and Elayne in her fleece coat huddled at the edge of an alley just down the street from her. A large sack, pilfered from the docks, lay neatly folded beside Min. *My army,* Nynaeve thought grimly. *But there isn't anybody else.*

She caught sight of a *sul'dam* and a *damane* climbing the street, a yellow-haired woman wearing the bracelet and a dark woman the collar, both yawning sleepily. The few Falmen sharing the street with them averted their eyes and gave them a wide berth. As far as she could see down toward the harbor, there was not another Seanchan. She did not turn her head the other way. Instead, she stretched and shrugged as if working cold shoulders before settling back as she had been.

Min tossed her half-eaten plum aside, glanced casually up the street, and leaned back on the doorpost. The way was clear there, too, or she would have put her hands on her knees. Min had started rubbing her hands nervously, and

Nynaeve realized that Elayne was now bouncing eagerly on her toes.

If they give us away, I'll thump both their heads. But she knew if they were discovered, it would be the Seanchan who would say what happened to all three of them. She was all too aware that she had no real notion of whether what she planned would work or not. It could easily be her own failure that would give them away. Once again she resolved that if anything went wrong, she would somehow pull attention to herself while Min and Elayne escaped. She had told them to run if anything went wrong, and let them think she would run, too. What she would do then, she did not know. *Except I won't let them take me alive. Please, Light, not that.*

Sul'dam and *damane* came up the street until they were bracketed by the three waiting women. A dozen Falmen walked wide of the linked pair.

Nynaeve gathered all of her anger. Leashed Ones and Leash Holders. They had put their filthy collar on Egwene's neck, and they would put it on hers, and Elayne's, if they could. She had made Min tell her how *sul'dam* enforced their will. She was sure Min had kept some back, the worst, but what she told was enough to heat Nynaeve to white-hot fury. In an instant a white blossom on a black, thorny branch had opened to light, to *saidar*, and the One Power filled her. She knew there was a glow around her, for those who could see it. The pale-skinned *sul'dam* gave a start, and the dark *damane*'s mouth fell open, but Nynaeve gave them no chance. It was only a trickle of the Power that she channeled, but she cracked it, a whip snapping a dust mote out of the air.

The silver collar sprang open and clattered to the cobblestones. Nynaeve heaved a sigh of relief even as she leaped to her feet.

The *sul'dam* stared at the fallen collar as if at a poisonous snake. The *damane* put a shaking hand to her throat, but before the woman in the lightning-marked dress had time to move, the *damane* turned and punched her in the face; the *sul'dam*'s knees buckled, and she almost fell.

"Good for you!" Elayne shouted. She was already running forward, too, and so was Min.

Before any of them reached the two women, the *damane* took one startled look around, then ran as hard as she could.

"We won't hurt you!" Elayne called after her. "We are friends!"

"Be quiet!" Nynaeve hissed. She produced a handful of rags from her pocket and ruthlessly stuffed them into the gaping mouth of the still-staggering *sul'dam*. Min hastily shook out the sack in a cloud of dust and plunged it over the *sul'dam*'s head, shrouding the woman to the waist. "We are already attracting too much attention."

It was true, and yet not entirely true. The four of them stood in a rapidly emptying street, but the people who had decided to be elsewhere were avoiding looking at them. Nynaeve had been counting on that—people doing their best to ignore anything that had to do with Seanchan—to gain them a few moments. They would talk eventually, but in whispers; it might take hours for the Seanchan to learn anything had happened.

The hooded woman began to struggle, making rag-muffled shouts from the sack, but Nynaeve and Min threw their arms around her and wrestled her toward a nearby alley. The leash and collar trailed across the cobblestones behind them, clinking.

"Pick it up," Nynaeve snapped at Elayne. "It won't bite you!"

Elayne took a deep breath, then gathered the silver metal gingerly, as if she feared it very well might. Nynaeve felt some sympathy, but not much; everything rested on each of them doing as they had planned.

The *sul'dam* kicked and tried to throw herself free, but between them, Nynaeve and Min forced her along, down the alley into another, slightly wider passage behind houses, to yet another alley and at last into a rough wooden shed that had apparently once housed two horses, by the stalls. Few could afford to keep horses since the Seanchan came, and in a day of Nynaeve's watching, no one had gone near it. The interior had a musty dustiness that spoke of abandonment. As soon as they were inside, Elayne dropped the silver leash and wiped her hands on some straw.

Nynaeve channeled another trickle, and the bracelet fell to the dirt floor. The *sul'dam* squalled and hurled herself about.

"Ready?" Nynaeve asked. The other two nodded, and they yanked the sacking off their prisoner.

The *sul'dam* wheezed, blue eyes teary from dust, but her red face was red as much from anger as from the sack. She darted for the door, but they caught her in the first step. She was not weak, yet they were three, and when they were done the *sul'dam* was stripped to her shift and lying in one of the stalls, bound hand and foot with stout cord, with another piece of cord to keep her from forcing the gag out.

Soothing a puffy lip, Min eyed the lightning-paneled dress and soft boots they had laid out. "It might fit you, Nynaeve. It won't fit Elayne or me." Elayne was picking straw out of her hair.

"I can see that. You were never a choice anyway, not really. They know you too well." Nynaeve hurriedly removed her own clothes. She tossed them aside and donned the *sul'dam*'s dress. Min helped with the buttons.

Nynaeve wiggled her toes in the boots; they were a little tight. The dress was tight, too, across the bosom, and loose elsewhere. The hem hung almost to the ground, lower than *sul'dam* wore them, but the fit would have been even worse on any of the others. Snatching up the bracelet, she took a deep breath and closed it around her left wrist. The ends merged, and it seemed solid. It did not feel like anything except a bracelet. She had been afraid that it would.

"Get the dress, Elayne." They had dyed a pair of dresses—one of hers and one of Elayne's—to the gray *damane* were, or as close as they could manage, and hidden them here. Elayne did not move except to stare at the open collar and lick her lips. "Elayne, you have to wear it. Too many of them have seen Min for her to do it. I would have worn it, if this dress had fit you instead." She thought she would have gone mad if she had had to wear the collar; that was why she could not make her voice sharp with Elayne now.

"I know." Elayne sighed. "I just wish I knew more of what it does to you." She drew her red-gold hair out of the way. "Min, help me, please." Min began undoing the buttons down the back of her dress.

Nynaeve managed to pick up the silver collar without flinching. "There is one way to find out." With only a moment of hesitation, she bent and snapped it around the neck of the *sul'dam*. *She deserves it if anyone does*, she told herself firmly. "She might be able to tell us something useful,

anyway." The blue-eyed woman glanced at the leash trailing from her neck to Nynaeve's wrist, then glared up at her
contemptuously.

"It doesn't work that way," Min said, but Nynaeve barely
heard.

She was ... aware ... of the other woman, aware of
what she was feeling, cord digging into her ankles and into
her wrists behind her back, the rank fish taste of the rags in
her mouth, straw pricking her through the thin cloth of her
shift. It was not as if she, Nynaeve, felt these things, but in
her head was a lump of sensations that she knew belonged
to the *sul'dam*.

She swallowed, trying to ignore them—they would not
go away—and addressed the bound woman. "I won't hurt
you if you answer my questions truthfully. We aren't Seanchan. But if you lie to me. . . ." She lifted the leash threaten-
ingly.

The woman's shoulders shook, and her mouth curled
around the gag in a sneer. It took Nynaeve a moment to
realize the *sul'dam* was laughing.

Her mouth tightened, but then a thought came to her.
That bundle of sensation inside her head seemed to be everything physical that the other woman felt. Experimentally, she tried adding to it.

Eyes suddenly bulging out of her head, the *sul'dam* gave
a cry that the gag only partially stopped. Fanning her hands
behind her as if trying to ward off something, she humped
through the straw in a vain effort to escape.

Nynaeve gaped, and hastily rid herself of the extra feelings she had added. The *sul'dam* sagged, weeping.

"What. . . . What did you ... do to her?" Elayne asked
faintly. Min only stared, her mouth hanging open.

Nynaeve answered gruffly. "The same thing Sheriam did
to you when you threw a cup at Marith." *Light, but this is
a filthy thing.*

Elayne gulped loudly. "Oh."

"But an *a'dam* isn't supposed to work that way," Min
said. "They always claimed it won't work on any woman
who cannot channel."

"I do not care how it is supposed to work, so long as it
does." Nynaeve seized the silver metal leash right where it
joined the collar, and pulled the woman up enough to look

her in the eyes. Frightened eyes, she saw. "You listen to me, and listen well. I want answers, and if I don't get them, I'll make you think I have had the hide off you." Stark terror rolled across the woman's face, and Nynaeve's stomach heaved as she suddenly realized the *sul'dam* had taken her literally. *If she thinks I can, it's because she knows. That is what these leashes are for.* She took firm hold of herself to stop from clawing the bracelet off her wrist. Instead, she hardened her face. "Are you ready to answer me? Or do you need more convincing?"

The frantic head-shaking was answer enough. When Nynaeve removed the gag, the woman only paused to swallow once before babbling, "I will not report you. I swear it. Only take this from my neck. I have gold. Take it. I swear, I will never tell anyone."

"Be quiet," Nynaeve snapped, and the woman shut her mouth immediately. "What is your name?"

"Seta. Please. I will answer you, but please take—it—off! If anyone sees it on me. . . ." Seta's eyes rolled down to stare at the leash, then squeezed shut. "Please?" she whispered.

Nynaeve realized something. She could never make Elayne wear that collar.

"Best we get on with it," Elayne said firmly. She was down to her shift, too, now. "Give me a moment to put this other dress on, and—"

"Put your own clothes back on," Nynaeve said.

"Someone has to pretend to be a *damane*," Elayne said, "or we will never reach Egwene. That dress fits you, and it cannot be Min. That leaves me."

"I said put your clothes on. We have somebody to be our Leashed One." Nynaeve tugged at the leash that held Seta, and the *sul'dam* gasped.

"No! No, please! If anyone sees me—" She cut off at Nynaeve's cold stare.

"As far as I am concerned, you are worse than a murderer, worse than a Darkfriend. I can't think of anything worse than you. The fact that I have to wear this thing on my wrist, to be the same as you for even an hour, sickens me. So if you think there is anything I'll balk at doing to you, think again. You don't want to be seen? Good. Neither do we. No one really looks at a *damane*, though. As long as you keep your head down the way a Leashed One is supposed to, no one will even notice you. But you had better do the best you can to make sure the rest of us aren't noticed, either. If we are, you surely will be seen, and if that is not enough to hold you, I promise you I'll make you curse the first kiss your mother ever gave your father. Do we understand each other?"

"Yes," Seta said faintly. "I swear it."

Nynaeve had to remove the bracelet in order for them to slide Elayne's gray-dyed dress down the leash and over Seta's head. It did not fit the woman well, being loose at the bosom and tight across the hips, but Nynaeve's would have been as bad, and too short besides. Nynaeve hoped people really did not look at *damane*. She put the bracelet back on reluctantly.

Elayne gathered up Nynaeve's clothes, wrapped the other dyed dress around them, and made a bundle, a bundle for a woman in farm clothes to be carrying as she followed a *sul'dam* and a *damane*. "Gawyn will eat his heart out when he hears about this," she said, and laughed. It sounded forced.

Nynaeve looked at her closely, then at Min. It was time for the dangerous part. "Are you ready?"

Elayne's smile faded. "I am ready."

"Ready," Min said curtly.

"Where are you . . . we . . . going?" Seta said, quickly adding, "If I may ask?"

"Into the lions' den," Elayne told her.

"To dance with the Dark One," Min said.

Nynaeve sighed and shook her head. "What they are trying to say is, we are going where all the *damane* are kept, and we intend to free one of them."

Seta was still gaping in astonishment when they hustled her out of the shed.

Bayle Domon watched the rising sun from the deck of his ship. The docks were already beginning to bustle, though the streets leading up from the harbor stood largely empty. A gull perched on a piling stared at him; gulls had pitiless eyes.

"Are you sure about this, Captain?" Yarin asked. "If the Seanchan wonder what we're all doing aboard—"

"You just make certain there do be an axe near every

mooring line," Domon said curtly. "And, Yarin? Do any man try to cut a line before those women are aboard, I will split his skull."

"What if they don't come, Captain? What if it's Seanchan soldiers instead?"

"Settle your bowels, man! If soldiers come, I will make a run for the harbor mouth, and the Light have mercy on us all. But until soldiers do come, I mean to wait for those women. Now go look as if you are no doing anything."

Domon turned back to peering up into the town, toward where the *damane* were held. His fingers drummed a nervous tattoo on the railing.

The breeze from the sea brought the smell of breakfast cook fires to Rand's nose, and tried to flap at his moth-eaten cloak, but he held it closed with one hand as Red neared the town. There had not been a coat to fit him in the clothes they had found, and he thought it best to keep the fine silver embroidery on his sleeves and the herons on his collar hidden. The Seanchan attitude toward conquered people carrying weapons might not extend to those with heron-mark swords, either.

The first shadows of morning stretched out ahead of him. He could just see Hurin riding in among the wagon yards and horse lots. Only one or two men moved among the lines of merchant wagons, and they wore the long aprons of wheelwrights or blacksmiths. Ingtar, the first in, was already out of sight. Perrin and Mat followed behind Rand at spaced intervals. He did not look back to check on them. There was not supposed to be anything to connect them; five men coming into Falme at an early hour, but not together.

The horse lots surrounded him, horses already crowding the fences, waiting to be fed. Hurin put his head out from between two stables, their doors still closed and barred, saw Rand and motioned to him before ducking back. Rand turned the bay stallion that way.

Hurin stood holding his horse by the reins. He had on one of the long vests instead of his coat, and despite the heavy cloak that hid his short sword and sword-breaker, he shivered with the cold. "Lord Ingtar's back there," he said, nodding down the narrow passage. "He says we'll leave the horses here and go the rest of the way on foot." As Rand dismounted, the sniffer added, "Fain went right down that street, Lord Rand. I can almost smell it from here."

Rand led Red down the way to where Ingtar had already tied his own horse behind the stable. The Shienaran did not look very much a lord in a dirty fleece coat with holes worn through the leather in several places, and his sword looked odd belted over it. His eyes had a feverish intensity.

Tying Red alongside Ingtar's stallion, Rand hesitated over his saddlebags. He had not been able to leave the banner behind. He did not think any of the soldiers would have gone into the bags, but he could not say the same for Verin, nor predict what she would do if she found the banner. Still, it made him uneasy to have it with him. He decided to leave the saddlebags tied behind his saddle.

Mat joined them, and a few moments later Hurin came with Perrin. Mat wore baggy trousers stuffed into the tops of his boots, and Perrin his too-short cloak. Rand thought they all looked like villainous beggars, but they had all passed largely unnoticed in the villages.

"Now," Ingtar said. "Let us see what we see."

They strolled out to the dirt street as if they had no particular destination in mind, talking among themselves, and ambled past the wagon yards onto sloping cobblestone streets. Rand was not sure what he himself said, much less anyone else. Ingtar's plan had been for them to look like any other group of men walking together, but there were all too few people out-of-doors. Five men made a crowd on those cold morning streets.

They walked in a bunch, but it was Hurin who led them, sniffing the air and turning up this street and down that. The rest turned when he did, as if that was what they had intended all along. "He's crisscrossed this town," Hurin muttered, grimacing. "His smell is everywhere, and it stinks so, it's hard to tell old from new. At least I know he's still here. Some of it cannot be older than a day or two, I'm sure. I am sure," he added less doubtfully.

A few more people began to appear, here a fruit peddler setting his wares on tables, there a fellow hurrying along with a big roll of parchments under his arm and a sketch-board slung across his back, a knife-sharpener oiling the shaft of his grinding wheel on its barrow. Two women walked by, headed the other way, one with downcast eyes and a silver collar around her neck, the other, in a dress worked with lightning bolts, holding a coiled silver leash.

Rand's breath caught; it was an effort not to look back at them.

"Was that . . . ?" Mat's eyes were open wide, staring out of the hollows of his eye sockets. "Was that a *damane?*"

"That is the way they were described," Ingtar said curtly. "Hurin, are we going to walk every street in this Shadow-cursed town?"

"He's been everywhere, Lord Ingtar," Hurin said. "His stench is everywhere." They had come into an area where the stone houses were three and four stories high, as big as inns.

They rounded a corner, and Rand was taken aback by the sight of a score of Seanchan soldiers standing guard in front of a big house on one side of the street—and by the sight of two women in lightning-marked dresses talking on the doorsteps of another across from it. A banner flapped in the wind over the house the soldiers protected; a golden hawk clutching lightning bolts. Nothing marked out the house where the women talked except themselves. The officer's armor was resplendent in red and black and gold, his helmet gilded and painted to look like a spider's head. Then Rand saw the two big, leathery-skinned shapes crouched among the soldiers and missed a step.

Grolm. There was no mistaking those wedge-shaped heads with their three eyes. *They can't be.* Perhaps he was really asleep, and this was all a nightmare. *Maybe we haven't even left for Falme, yet.*

The others stared at the beasts as they walked past the guarded house.

"What in the name of the Light are they?" Mat asked.

Hurin's eyes seemed as big as his face. "Lord Rand, they're. . . . Those are. . . ."

"It doesn't matter," Rand said. After a moment, Hurin nodded.

"We are here for the Horn," Ingtar said, "not to stare at Seanchan monsters. Concentrate on finding Fain, Hurin."

The soldiers barely glanced at them. The street ran straight down to the round harbor. Rand could see ships anchored down there; tall, square-looking ships with high masts, small in that distance.

"He's been here a lot." Hurin scrubbed at his nose with the back of his hand. "The street stinks of layer on layer on layer of him. I think he might have been here as late as yesterday, Lord Ingtar. Maybe last night."

Mat suddenly clutched his coat with both hands. "It's in there," he whispered. He turned around and walked backwards, peering at the tall house with the banner. "The dagger is in there. I didn't even notice it before, because of those—those things, but I can feel it."

Perrin poked a finger in his ribs. "Well, stop that before they start wondering why you're goggling at them like a fool."

Rand glanced over his shoulder. The officer was looking after them.

Mat turned back around sullenly. "Are we just going to keep on walking? It's in there, I tell you."

"The Horn is what we are after," Ingtar growled. "I mean to find Fain and make him tell me where it is." He did not slow down.

Mat said nothing, but his entire face was a plea.

I have to find Fain, too, Rand thought. *I have to.* But when he looked at Mat's face, he said, "Ingtar, if the dagger is in that house, Fain likely is, too. I can't see him letting the dagger or the Horn, either one, far out of his sight."

Ingtar stopped. After a moment, he said, "It could be, but we will never know from out here."

"We could watch for him to come out," Rand said. "If he comes out at this time of the morning, then he spent the night there. And I'll wager where he sleeps is where the Horn is. If he does come out, we can be back to Verin by midday and have a plan made before nightfall."

"I do not mean to wait for Verin," Ingtar said, "and neither will I wait for night. I've waited too long already. I mean to have the Horn in my hands before the sun sets again."

"But we don't know, Ingtar."

"I know the dagger is in there," Mat said.

"And Hurin says Fain was here last night." Ingtar overrode Hurin's attempts to qualify that. "It is the first time you have been willing to say anything closer than a day or two. We are going to take back the Horn now. Now!"

"How?" Rand said. The officer was no longer watching them, but there were still at least twenty soldiers in front of the building. And a pair of *grolm*. *This is madness. There can't be* grolm *here.* Thinking it did not make the beasts disappear, though.

"There seem to be gardens behind all these houses," Ingtar said, looking around thoughtfully. "If one of those alleys runs by a garden wall. . . . Sometimes men are so busy guarding their front, they neglect their back. Come." He headed straight for the nearest narrow passage between two of the tall houses. Hurin and Mat trotted right after him.

Rand exchanged looks with Perrin—his curly-haired friend gave a resigned shrug—and they followed, too.

The alley was barely wider than their shoulders, but it ran between high garden walls until it crossed another alley big enough for a pushbarrow or small cart. That was cobblestoned, too, but only the backs of buildings looked down on it, shuttered windows and expanses of stone, and the high back walls of gardens overtopped by nearly leafless branches.

Ingtar led them along that alley until they were opposite the waving banner. Taking his steel-backed gauntlets from under his coat, he put them on and leaped up to catch the top of the wall, then pulled himself up enough to peek over. He reported in a low monotone. "Trees. Flower beds. Walks. There isn't a soul to be— Wait! A guard. One man. He isn't even wearing his helmet. Count to fifty, then follow me." He swung a boot to the top of the wall and rolled over inside, disappearing before Rand could say a word.

Mat began to count slowly. Rand held his breath. Perrin fingered his axe, and Hurin gripped the hilts of his weapons.

". . . fifty." Hurin scrambled up and over the wall before the word was well out of Mat's mouth. Perrin went right beside him.

Rand thought Mat might need some help—he looked so pale and drawn—but he gave no sign of it as he scrambled up. The stone wall provided plenty of handholds, and moments later Rand was crouched on the inside with Mat and Perrin and Hurin.

The garden was in the grip of deep autumn, flower beds empty except for a few evergreen shrubs, tree branches nearly bare. The wind that rippled the banner stirred dust across the flagstone walks. For a moment Rand could not find Ingtar. Then he saw the Shienaran, flat against the back wall of the house, motioning them on with sword in hand.

Rand ran in a crouch, more conscious of the windows blankly peering down from the house than of his friends running beside him. It was a relief to press himself against the house beside Ingtar.

Mat kept muttering to himself, "It's in there. I can feel it."

"Where is the guard?" Rand whispered.

"Dead," Ingtar said. "The man was overconfident. He never even tried to raise a cry. I hid his body under one of those bushes."

Rand stared at him. *The* Seanchan *was overconfident?* The only thing that kept him from going back right then was Mat's anguished murmurs.

"We are almost there." Ingtar sounded as if he were speaking to himself, too. "Almost there. Come."

Rand drew his sword as they started up the back steps. He was aware of Hurin unlimbering his short-bladed sword and notched sword-breaker, and Perrin reluctantly drawing his axe from the loop on his belt.

The hallway inside was narrow. A half-open door to their right smelled like a kitchen. Several people were moving about in that room; there was an indistinguishable sound of voices, and occasionally the soft clatter of a pot lid.

Ingtar motioned Mat to lead, and they crept by the door. Rand watched the narrowing opening until they were around the next corner.

A slender young woman with dark hair came out of a door ahead of them, carrying a tray with one cup. They all froze. She turned the other way without looking in their direction. Rand's eyes widened. Her long white robe was all but transparent. She vanished around another corner.

"Did you see that?" Mat said hoarsely. "You could see right through—"

Ingtar clapped a hand over Mat's mouth and whispered, "Keep your mind on why we are here. Now find it. Find the Horn for me."

Mat pointed to a narrow set of winding stairs. They climbed a flight, and he led them toward the front of the house. The furnishings in the hallways were sparse, and seemed all curves. Here and there a tapestry hung on a wall, or a folding screen stood against it, each painted with a few birds on branches, or a flower or two. A river flowed across one screen, but aside from rippling water and narrow strips of riverbank, the rest of it was blank.

All around them Rand could hear the sounds of people stirring, slippers scuffing on the floor, soft murmurs of speech. He did not see anyone, but he could imagine it all too well, someone stepping into the hall to see five slinking men with weapons in their hands, shouting an alarm. . . .

"In there," Mat whispered, pointing to a big pair of sliding doors ahead, carved handholds their only ornamentation. "At least, the dagger is."

Ingtar looked at Hurin; the sniffer slid the doors open, and Ingtar leaped through with his sword ready. There was no one there. Rand and the others hurried inside, and Hurin quickly closed the doors behind them.

Painted screens hid all the walls and any other doors, and veiled the light coming through windows that had to overlook the street. At one end of the big room stood a tall, circular cabinet. At the other was a small table, the lone chair on the carpet turned to face it. Rand heard Ingtar gasp, but he only felt like heaving a sigh of relief. The curling golden Horn of Valere sat on a stand on the table. Below it, the ruby in the hilt of the ornate dagger caught the light.

Mat darted to the table, snatching Horn and dagger. "We have it," he crowed, shaking the dagger in his fist. "We have both of them."

"Not so loud," Perrin said with a wince. "We don't have them out of here, yet." His hands were busy on the haft of his axe; they seemed to want to be holding something else.

"The Horn of Valere." There was sheer awe in Ingtar's voice. He touched the Horn hesitantly, tracing a finger along the silver script inlaid around the bell and mouthing the translation, then pulled his hand back with a shiver of excitement. "It is. By the Light, it is! I am saved."

Hurin was moving the screens that hid the windows. He shoved the last out of his way and peered into the street below. "Those soldiers are all still there, looking like they've took root." He shuddered. "Those . . . things, too."

Rand went to join him. The two beasts were *grolm;* there was no denying it. "How did they. . . ." As he lifted his eyes from the street, words died. He was looking over a wall into the garden of the big house across the street. He could see where further walls had been torn down, joining other gardens to it. Women sat on benches there, or strolled along the walks, always in pairs. Women linked, neck to wrist, by silver leashes. One of the women with a collar around her neck looked up. He was too far to make out her face clearly, but for an instant it seemed that their eyes met, and he knew. The blood drained from his face. "Egwene," he breathed.

"What are you talking about?" Mat said. "Egwene is safe in Tar Valon. I wish I were."

"She's here," Rand said. The two women were turning, walking toward one of the buildings on the far side of the joined gardens. "She is there, right across the street. Oh, Light, she's wearing one of those collars!"

"Are you sure?" Perrin said. He came to peer from the window. "I don't see her, Rand. And—and I could recognize her if I did, even at this distance."

"I am sure," Rand said. The two women disappeared into one of the houses that faced the next street over. His stomach was twisted into a knot. *She is supposed to be safe. She's supposed to be in the White Tower.* "I have to get her out. The rest of you—"

"So!" The slurring voice was as soft as the sound of the doors sliding in their tracks. "You are not who I expected."

For a brief moment, Rand stared. The tall man with the shaven head who had stepped into the room wore a long, trailing blue robe, and his fingernails were so long that Rand wondered if he could handle anything. The two men standing obsequiously behind him had only half their dark hair shaved, the rest hanging in a dark braid down each man's right cheek. One of them cradled a sheathed sword in his arms.

It was only a moment he had for staring, then screens toppled to reveal, at either end of the room, a doorway crowded with four or five Seanchan soldiers, bareheaded but armored, and swords in hand.

"You are in the presence of the High Lord Turak," the

man who carried the sword began, staring at Rand and the others angrily, but a brief motion of a finger with a blue-lacquered nail cut him short. The other servant stepped forward with a bow and began undoing Turak's robe.

"When one of my guards was found dead," the shaven-headed man said calmly, "I suspected the man who calls himself Fain. I have been suspicious of him since Huan died so mysteriously, and he has always wanted that dagger." He held out his arms for the servant to remove his robe. Despite his soft, almost-singing voice, hard muscles roped his arms and smooth chest, which was bare to a blue sash holding wide, white trousers that seemed made of hundreds of pleats. He sounded uninterested, and indifferent to the blades in their hands. "And now to find strangers with not only the dagger, but the Horn. It will please me to kill one or two of you for disturbing my morning. Those who survive will tell me of who you are and why you came." He stretched out a hand without looking—the man with the scabbarded sword laid the hilt in the hand—and drew the heavy, curved blade. "I would not have the Horn damaged."

Turak gave no other signal, but one of the soldiers stalked into the room and reached for the Horn. Rand did not know whether he should laugh, or not. The man wore armor, but his arrogant face seemed as oblivious to their weapons as Turak was.

Mat put an end to it. As the Seanchan reached out his hand, Mat slashed it with the ruby-hilted dagger. With a curse, the soldier leaped back, looking surprised. And then he screamed. It chilled the room, held everyone where they stood in astonishment. The trembling hand he held up in front of his face was turning black, darkness creeping outwards from the bleeding gash that crossed his palm. He opened his mouth wide and howled, clawing at his arm, then his shoulder. Kicking, jerking, he toppled to the floor, thrashing on the silken carpet, shrieking as his face grew black and his dark eyes bulged like overripe plums, until a dark, swollen tongue gagged him. He twitched, choking raggedly, heels drumming, and did not move again. Every bit of his exposed flesh was black as putrid pitch and looked ready to burst at a touch.

Mat licked his lips and swallowed; his grip shifted uneasily on the dagger. Even Turak stared, openmouthed.

"You see," Ingtar said softly, "we are no easy meat." Suddenly he leaped over the corpse, toward the soldiers still goggling at what was left of the man who had stood at their shoulders only moments before. "Shinowa!" he cried. "Follow me!" Hurin leaped after him, and the soldiers fell back before them, the sounds of steel on steel rising.

The Seanchan at the other end of the room started forward as Ingtar moved, but then they were falling back, too, before Mat's thrusting dagger even more than from the axe Perrin swung with wordless snarls.

In the space of heartbeats, Rand stood alone, facing Turak, who held his blade upright before him. His moment of shock was gone. His eyes were sharp on Rand's face; the black and swollen body of one of his soldiers might as well not have existed. It did not seem to exist for the two servants, either, any more than Rand and his sword existed, or the sounds of fighting, fading now from the rooms to either side out into the house. The servants had begun calmly folding Turak's robe as soon as the High Lord took his sword, and had not looked up even for the dead soldier's shrieks; now they knelt beside the door and watched with impassive eyes.

"I suspected it might come to you and me." Turak spun his blade easily, a full circle one way, then the other, his long-nailed fingers moving delicately on the hilt. His fingernails did not seem to hamper him at all. "You are young. Let us see what is required to earn the heron on this side of the ocean."

Suddenly Rand saw. Standing tall on Turak's blade was a heron. With the little training he had, he was face-to-face with a real blademaster. Hastily he tossed the fleece-lined cloak aside, ridding himself of weight and encumbrance. Turak waited.

Rand desperately wanted to seek the void. It was plain he would need every shred of ability he could muster, and even then his chances of leaving the room alive would be small. He had to leave alive. Egwene was almost close enough for him to shout to her, and he had to free her, somehow. But *saidin* waited in the void. The thought made his heart leap with eagerness at the same time that it turned his stomach. But just as close as Egwene were those other women. *Damane.* If he touched *saidin,* and if he could not stop himself channeling, they would know, Verin had told him. Know and wonder. So many, so close. He might survive Turak only to die facing *damane,* and he could not die before Egwene was free. Rand raised his blade.

Turak glided toward him on silent feet. Blade rang on blade like hammer on anvil.

From the first it was clear to Rand that the man was testing him, pushing only hard enough to see what he could do, then pushing a little harder, then just a little harder still. It was quick wrists and quick feet that kept Rand alive as much as skill. Without the void, he was always half a heartbeat behind. The tip of Turak's heavy sword made a stinging trench just under his left eye. A flap of coat sleeve hung away from his shoulder, the darker for being wet. Under a neat slash beneath his right arm, precise as a tailor's cut, he could feel warm dampness spreading down his ribs.

There was disappointment on the High Lord's face. He stepped back with a gesture of disgust. "Where did you find that blade, boy? Or do they here truly award the heron to those no more skilled than you? No matter. Make your peace. It is time to die." He came on again.

The void enveloped Rand. *Saidin* flowed toward him, glowing with the promise of the One Power, but he ignored it. It was no more difficult than ignoring a barbed thorn twisting in his flesh. He refused to be filled with the Power, refused to be one with the male half of the True Source. He was one with the sword in his hands, one with the floor beneath his feet, one with the walls. One with Turak.

He recognized the forms the High Lord used; they were a little different from what he had been taught, but not enough. The Swallow Takes Flight met Parting the Silk. Moon on the Water met The Wood Grouse Dances. Ribbon in the Air met Stones Falling From the Cliff. They moved about the room as in a dance, and their music was steel against steel.

Disappointment and disgust faded from Turak's dark eyes, replaced by surprise, then concentration. Sweat appeared on the High Lord's face as he pressed Rand harder. Lightning of Three Prongs met Leaf on the Breeze.

Rand's thoughts floated outside the void, apart from himself, hardly noticed. It was not enough. He faced a blademaster, and with the void and every ounce of his skill he was barely managing to hold his own. Barely. He had to end it before Turak finally did. *Saidin? No! Sometimes it is necessary to Sheathe the Sword in your own flesh.* But that would not help Egwene, either. He had to end it now. Now.

Turak's eyes widened as Rand glided forward. So far he had only defended; now he attacked, all out. The Boar Rushes Down the Mountain. Every movement of his blade was an attempt to reach the High Lord; now all Turak could do was retreat and defend, down the length of the room, almost to the door.

In an instant, while Turak still tried to face the Boar, Rand charged. The River Undercuts the Bank. He dropped to one knee, blade slashing across. He did not need Turak's gasp, or the feel of resistance to his cut to know. He heard two thumps and turned his head, knowing what he would see. He looked down the length of his blade, wet and red, to where the High Lord lay, sword tumbled from his limp hand, a dark dampness staining the birds woven in the carpet under his body. Turak's eyes were still open, but already filmed with death.

The void shook. He had faced Trollocs before, faced Shadowspawn. Never before had he confronted a human being with a sword except in practice or bluff. *I just killed a man.* The void shook, and *saidin* tried to fill him.

Desperately he clawed free, breathing hard as he looked around. He gave a start when he saw the two servants still kneeling beside the door. He had forgotten them, and now he did not know what to do about them. Neither man appeared armed, yet all they had to do was shout. . . .

They never looked at him, or at each other. Instead, they stared silently at the High Lord's body. They produced daggers from under their robes, and he tightened his grip on the sword, but each man placed the point to his own breast. "From birth to death," they intoned in unison, "I serve the Blood." And plunged the daggers into their own hearts. They folded forward almost peacefully, heads to the floor as if bowing deeply to their lord.

Rand stared at them in disbelief. *Mad*, he thought. *Maybe I will go mad, but they already were.*

He was getting to his feet shakily when Ingtar and the others came running back. They all bore nicks and cuts; the leather of Ingtar's coat was stained in more than one place.

Mat still had the Horn and his dagger, its blade darker than the ruby in its hilt. Perrin's axe was red, too, and he looked as if he might be sick at any moment.

"You dealt with them?" Ingtar said, looking at the bodies. "Then we're done, if no alarm is given. Those fools never cried for help, not once."

"I will see if the guards heard anything," Hurin said, and darted for the window.

Mat shook his head. "Rand, these people are crazy. I know I've said that before, but these people really are. Those servants. . . ." Rand held his breath, wondering if they had all killed themselves. Mat said, "Whenever they saw us fighting, they fell on their knees, put their faces to the floor, and wrapped their arms around their heads. They never moved, or cried out; never tried to help the soldiers, or give an alarm. They're still there, as far as I know."

"I would not count on them staying on their knees," Ingtar said dryly. "We are leaving now, as fast as we can run."

"You go," Rand said. "Egwene—"

"You fool!" Ingtar snapped. "We have what we came for. The Horn of Valere. The hope of salvation. What can one girl count, even if you love her, alongside the Horn, and what it stands for?"

"The Dark One can have the Horn for all I care! What does finding the Horn count if I abandon Egwene to this? If I did that, the Horn couldn't save me. The Creator couldn't save me. I would damn myself."

Ingtar stared at him, his face unreadable. "You mean that exactly, don't you?"

"Something's happening out here," Hurin said urgently. "A man just came running up, and they're all milling like fish in a bucket. Wait. The officer is coming inside!"

"Go!" Ingtar said. He tried to take the Horn, but Mat was already running. Rand hesitated, but Ingtar grabbed his arm and pulled him into the hall. The others were streaming after Mat; Perrin only gave Rand one pained look before he went. "You cannot save the girl if you stand here and die!"

He ran with them. Part of him hated himself for running, but another part whispered, *I'll come back. I'll free her somehow.*

By the time they reached the bottom of the narrow, winding staircase, he could hear a man's deep voice raised in the front part of the house, angrily demanding that someone stand up and speak. A serving girl in her nearly transparent robe knelt at the bottom of the stairs, and a gray-haired woman all in white wool, with a long floury apron, knelt by the kitchen door. They were both exactly as Mat had described, faces to the floor and arms wrapped around their heads, and they did not stir a hair as Rand and the others hurried by. He was relieved to see the motions of breathing.

They crossed the garden at a dead run, climbing over the back wall rapidly. Ingtar cursed when Mat tossed the Horn of Valere ahead of him, and tried again to take it when he dropped outside, but Mat snatched it up with a quick, "It isn't even scratched," and scampered up the alley.

More shouts rose from the house they had just left; a woman screamed, and someone began tolling a gong.

I will come back for her. Somehow. Rand sped after the others as fast as he could.

CHAPTER
46

To Come Out of the Shadow

Nynaeve and the others heard distant shouts as they approached the buildings where the *damane* were housed. The crowds were beginning to pick up, and there was a nervousness to the people in the street, an extra quickness to their step, an extra wariness in the way they glanced past Nynaeve, in her lightning-paneled dress, and the woman she held by a silver leash.

Shifting her bundle nervously, Elayne peered toward the noise of shouts, one street over, where the golden hawk clutching lightning rippled in the wind. "What is happening?"

"Nothing to do with us," Nynaeve said firmly.

"You hope," Min added. "And so do I." She increased her pace, hurrying up the steps ahead of the others, and disappeared inside the tall stone house.

Nynaeve shortened her grip on the leash. "Remember, Seta, you want us to make it through this safely as much as we do."

"I do," the Seanchan woman said fervently. She kept her chin on her chest, to hide her face. "I will cause you no trouble, I swear."

As they turned up the gray stone steps, a *sul'dam* and a *damane* appeared at the head of the stairs, coming down as they went up. After one glance to make sure the woman in the collar was not Egwene, Nynaeve did not look at them again. She used the *a'dam* to keep Seta close by her side, so if the *damane* sensed the ability to channel in one of them, she would think it was Seta. She felt sweat trickling down her spine, though, until she realized they were paying her no more attention than she gave them. All they saw was a dress with lightning panels and a gray dress, the women wearing them linked by the silver length of an *a'dam*. Just another Leash Holder with a Leashed One, and a local girl hurrying along behind with a bundle belonging to the *sul'dam*.

Nynaeve pushed open the door, and they went in.

Whatever the excitement beneath Turak's banner, it did not extend here, not yet. There were only women moving about in the entry hall, all easily placed by their dress. Three gray-dressed *damane,* with *sul'dam* wearing the bracelets. Two women in dresses paneled with forked lightning stood talking, and three crossed the hall alone. Four dressed like Min, in plain dark woolens, hurried on their way with trays.

Min stood waiting down the entry hall when they went in; she glanced at them once, then started deeper into the house. Nynaeve guided Seta down the hall after Min, with Elayne scurrying along in their wake. No one gave them a second glance, it seemed to Nynaeve, but she thought the trickle of sweat down her backbone might become a river soon. She kept Seta moving quickly so no one would have a chance for a good look—or worse, a question. With her eyes fixed on her toes, Seta needed so little urging that Nynaeve thought she would have been running if not for the physical restraint of the leash.

Near the back of the house, Min took a narrow stairs that spiraled upwards. Nynaeve pushed Seta up it ahead of her, all the way to the fourth floor. The ceilings were low, there, the halls empty and silent except for the soft sounds of weeping. Weeping seemed to fit the air of the chilly halls.

"This place . . ." Elayne began, then shook her head. "It feels. . . ."

"Yes, it does," Nynaeve said grimly. She glared at Seta, who kept her face down. A pallor of fear made the Seanchan woman's skin paler than it was normally.

Wordlessly, Min opened a door and went in, and they followed. The room beyond had been divided into smaller rooms by roughly made wooden walls, with a narrow hallway running to a window. Nynaeve crowded after Min as she hurried to the last door on the right and pushed in.

A slender, dark-haired girl in gray sat at a small table with her head resting on folded arms, but even before she looked up, Nynaeve knew it was Egwene. A ribbon of shining metal ran from the silver collar around Egwene's neck to a bracelet hanging on a peg on the wall. Her eyes widened at the sight of them, her mouth working silently. As Elayne closed the door, Egwene gave a sudden giggle, and pressed her hands to her mouth to stifle it. The tiny room was more than crowded with all of them in it.

"I know I'm not dreaming," she said in a quivering voice, "because if I was dreaming, you'd be Rand and Galad on tall stallions. I have been dreaming. I thought Rand was here. I couldn't see him, but I thought. . . ." Her voice trailed off.

"If you'd rather wait for them . . ." Min said dryly.

"Oh, no. No, you are all beautiful, the most beautiful thing I've ever seen. Where did you come from? How did you do it? That dress, Nynaeve, and the *a'dam*, and who is. . . ." She gave an abrupt squeak. "That's Seta. How . . . ?" Her voice hardened so that Nynaeve barely recognized it. "I'd like to put *her* in a pot of boiling water." Seta had her eyes squeezed shut, and her hands clutched her skirts; she was trembling.

"What have they done to you?" Elayne exclaimed. "What could they do to make you want something like that?"

Egwene never took her eyes off the Seanchan woman. "I'd like to make her feel it. That's what she did to me, made me feel like I was neck deep in. . . ." She shuddered. "You do not know what it is like wearing one of these, Elayne. You don't know what they can do to you. I can never decide whether Seta is worse than Renna, but they're all hateful."

"I think I know," Nynaeve said quietly. She could feel the sweat soaking Seta's skin, the cold tremors that shook her limbs. The yellow-haired Seanchan was terrified. It was all she could do not to make Seta's terrors come true then and there.

"Can you take this off of me?" Egwene asked, touching the collar. "You must be able to if you could put that one on—"

Nynaeve channeled, a pinpoint trickle. The collar on Egwene's neck provided anger enough, and if it had not, Seta's fear, the knowledge of how deserved it truly was, and her own knowledge of what she wanted to do to the woman, would have done it. The collar sprang open and fell away from Egwene's throat. With an expression of wonder, Egwene touched her neck.

"Put on my dress and coat," Nynaeve told her. Elayne was already unbundling the clothes on the bed. "We will walk out of here, and no one will even notice you." She considered holding her contact with *saidar*—she was certainly angry enough, and it felt so wonderful—but, reluctantly, she let it go. This was the one place in Falme where there was no chance of a *sul'dam* and *damane* coming to investigate if they sensed someone channeling, but they would certainly do so if a *damane* saw a woman she thought was a *sul'dam* with the glow of channeling around her. "I don't know why you aren't gone already. Alone here, even if you could not figure out how to get that thing off you, you could have just picked it up and run."

As Min and Elayne hurriedly helped her change into Nynaeve's old dress, Egwene explained about moving the bracelet from where a *sul'dam* left it, and how channeling made her sick unless a *sul'dam* wore the bracelet. Just that morning she had discovered how the collar could be opened without the Power—and found that touching the catch with the intention of opening it made her hand knot into uselessness. She could touch it as much as she wanted so long as she did not think of undoing the catch; the merest hint of that, though, and. . . .

Nynaeve felt sick herself. The bracelet on her wrist made her sick. It was too horrible. She wanted it off her wrist before she learned more about *a'dam*, before she perhaps learned something that would make her feel soiled forever for having worn it.

Unfastening the silver cuff, she pulled it loose, snapped it closed, and hung it on one of the pegs. "Don't think that means you can shout for help now." She shook a fist under Seta's nose. "I can still make you wish you were never born if you open your mouth, and I do not need that bloody . . . thing."

"You—you do not mean to leave me here with it," Seta said in a whisper. "You cannot. Tie me. Gag me so I cannot give an alarm. Please!"

Egwene gave a mirthless laugh. "Leave it on her. She

won't call for help even without a gag. You had better hope whoever finds you will remove the *a'dam* and keep your little secret, Seta. Your dirty secret, isn't it?"

"What are you talking about?" Elayne said.

"I have thought about it a great deal," Egwene said. "Thinking was all I could do when they left me alone up here. *Sul'dam* claim they develop an affinity after a few years. Most of them can tell when a woman is channeling whether they're leashed to her or not. I wasn't sure, but Seta proves it."

"Proves what?" Elayne demanded, and then her eyes widened in sudden realization, but Egwene went on.

"Nynaeve, *a'dam* only work on women who can channel. Don't you see? *Sul'dam* can channel the same as *damane*." Seta groaned through her teeth, shaking her head in violent denial. "A *sul'dam* would die before admitting she could channel, even if she knew, and they never train the ability, so they cannot do anything with it, but they can channel."

"I told you," Min said. "That collar shouldn't have worked on her." She was doing up the last buttons down Egwene's back. "Any woman who couldn't channel would be able to beat you silly while you tried to control her with it."

"How can that be?" Nynaeve said. "I thought the Seanchan put leashes on any woman who can channel."

"All of those they find," Egwene told her. "But those they can find are like you, and me, and Elayne. We were born with it, ready to channel whether anyone taught us or not. But what about Seanchan girls who aren't born with the ability, but who could be taught? Not just any woman can become a—a Leash Holder. Renna thought she was being friendly telling me about it. It is apparently a feastday in Seanchan villages when the *sul'dam* come to test the girls. They want to find any like you and me, and leash them, but they let all the others put on a bracelet to see if they can feel what the poor woman in the collar feels. Those who can are taken away to be trained as *sul'dam*. They are the women who could be taught."

Seta was moaning under her breath. "No. No. No." Over and over again.

"I know she is horrible," Elayne said, "but I feel as if I should help her somehow. She could be one of our sisters, only the Seanchan have twisted it all."

Nynaeve opened her mouth to say they had better worry about helping themselves, and the door opened.

"What is going on here?" Renna demanded, stepping into the room. "An audience?" She stared at Nynaeve, hands on hips. "I never gave permission for anyone else to link with my pet, Tuli. I do not even know who you—" Her eyes fell on Egwene—Egwene wearing Nynaeve's dress instead of *damane* gray. Egwene with no collar around her throat—and her eyes grew as big as saucers. She never had a chance to yell.

Before anyone else could move, Egwene snatched the pitcher from her washstand and smashed it into Renna's midriff. The pitcher shattered, and the *sul'dam* lost all her breath in a gurgling gasp and doubled over. As she fell, Egwene leaped on her with a snarl, shoving her flat, grabbing for the collar she had worn where it still lay on the floor, snapping it around the other woman's neck. With one jerk on the silver leash, Egwene pulled the bracelet from the peg and fitted it to her own wrist. Her lips were pulled back from her teeth, her eyes fixed on Renna's face with a terrible concentration. Kneeling on the *sul'dam*'s shoulders, she pressed both hands over the woman's mouth. Renna gave a tremendous convulsion, and her eyes bulged in her face; hoarse sounds came from her throat, screams held back by Egwene's hands; her heels drummed on the floor.

"Stop it, Egwene!" Nynaeve grabbed Egwene's shoulders, pulling her off of the other woman. "Egwene, stop it! That isn't what you want!" Renna lay gray-faced and panting, staring wildly at the ceiling.

Suddenly Egwene threw herself against Nynaeve, sobbing raggedly at her breast. "She hurt me, Nynaeve. She hurt me. They all did. They hurt me, and hurt me, until I did what they wanted. I hate them. I hate them for hurting me, and I hate them because I couldn't stop them from making me do what they wanted."

"I know," Nynaeve said gently. She smoothed Egwene's hair. "It is all right to hate them, Egwene. It is. They deserve it. But it isn't all right to let them make you like they are."

Seta's hands were pressed to her face. Renna touched the collar at her throat disbelievingly, with a shaking hand.

Egwene straightened, brushing her tears away quickly. "I'm not. I am not like them." She almost clawed the bracelet

off of her wrist and threw it down. "I'm not. But I wish I
could kill them."

"They deserve it." Min was staring grimly at the two
sul'dam.

"Rand would kill someone who did a thing like that,"
Elayne said. She seemed to be steeling herself. "I am sure
he would."

"Perhaps they do," Nynaeve said, "and perhaps he would.
But men often mistake revenge and killing for justice. They
seldom have the stomach for justice." She had often sat in
judgment with the Women's Circle. Sometimes men came
before them, thinking women might give them a better
hearing than the men of the Village Council, but men always thought they could sway the decision with eloquence,
or pleas for mercy. The Women's Circle gave mercy where
it was deserved, but justice always, and it was the Wisdom
who pronounced it. She picked up the bracelet Egwene had
discarded and closed it. "I would free every woman here,
if I could, and destroy every last one of these. But since I
cannot. . . ." She slipped the bracelet over the same peg that
held the other one, then addressed herself to the *sul'dam*.
Not Leash Holders any longer, she told herself. "Perhaps, if
you are very quiet, you will be left alone here long enough
to manage to remove the collars. The Wheel weaves as the
Wheel wills, and it may be that you've done enough good
to counterbalance the evil you have done, enough that you
will be allowed to remove them. If not, you will be found,
eventually. And I think whoever finds you will ask a great
many questions before they remove those collars. I think
perhaps you will learn at first hand the life you have given
to other women. That is justice," she added, to the others.

Renna wore a fixed stare of horror. Seta's shoulders
shook as she sobbed into her hands. Nynaeve hardened her
heart—*It is justice*, she told herself. *It is*—and herded the
others out of the room.

No one paid any more attention to them going out than
they had coming in. Nynaeve supposed she had the *sul'dam*
dress to thank for that, but she could not wait to change into
something else. Anything else. The dirtiest rag would feel
cleaner on her skin.

The girls were silent, walking close behind her, until
they were out on the cobblestone street again. She did not

know if it was what she had done or the fear that someone might stop them. She scowled. Would they have felt better if she had let them work themselves up to cutting the women's throats?

"Horses," Egwene said. "We will need horses. I know the stable where they took Bela, but I don't think we can get to her."

"We have to leave Bela here," Nynaeve told her. "We are leaving by ship."

"Where is everybody?" Min said, and suddenly Nynaeve realized the street was empty.

The crowds were gone, not a sign of them to be seen; every shop and window along the street were shuttered tight. But up the street from the harbor came a formation of Seanchan soldiers, a hundred or more in ordered ranks, with an officer at their head in his painted armor. They were still halfway down the street from the women, but they marched with a grim, implacable step, and it seemed to Nynaeve that every eye was fixed on her. *That's ridiculous. I can't see their eyes inside those helmets, and if anybody had given an alarm, it would be behind us.* She stopped anyway.

"There are more behind us," Min murmured. Nynaeve could hear those boots, now. "I don't know which will reach us first."

Nynaeve took a deep breath. "They are nothing to do with us." She looked beyond the approaching soldiers, to the harbor, filled with tall, boxy Seanchan ships. She could not make out *Spray;* she prayed it was still there, and ready. "We will walk right past them." *Light, I hope we can.*

"What if they want you to join them, Nynaeve?" Elayne asked. "You are wearing that dress. If they start asking questions. . . ."

"I will not go back," Egwene said grimly. "I'll die first. Let me show them what they've taught me." To Nynaeve's eye, a golden nimbus suddenly seemed to surround her.

"No!" she said, but it was too late.

With a roar like thunder, the street under the first ranks of Seanchan erupted, dirt and cobblestones and armored men thrown aside like spray from a fountain. Still glowing, Egwene spun to stare up the street, and the thunderous roar was repeated. Dirt rained down on the women. Shouting Seanchan soldiers scattered in good order to shelter in alleys and behind stoops. In moments they were all out of sight, except for those who lay around the two large holes marring the street. Some of those stirred feebly, and moans drifted along the street.

Nynaeve threw up her hands, trying to look in both directions at once. "You fool! We are trying *not* to attract attention!" There was no hope of that now. She only hoped they could manage to work their way around the soldiers to the harbor through the alleys. *The* damane *must know, too, now. They could not have missed that.*

"I won't go back to that collar," Egwene said fiercely. "I won't!"

"Look out!" Min shouted.

With a shrill whine, a fireball as big as a horse arched into the air over the rooftops and began to fall. Directly toward them.

"Run!" Nynaeve shouted, and threw herself into a dive toward the nearest alleyway, between two shuttered shops.

She landed awkwardly on her stomach with a grunt, losing half her breath, as the fireball struck. Hot wind washed over her down the narrow passage. Gulping air, she rolled onto her back and stared back into the street.

The cobblestones where they had been standing were chipped and cracked and blackened in a circle ten paces across. Elayne was crouched just inside another alley on the other side of the street. Of Min and Egwene, there was no sign. Nynaeve clapped a hand to her mouth in horror.

Elayne seemed to understand what she was thinking. The Daughter-Heir shook her head violently and pointed down the street. They had gone that way.

Nynaeve heaved a sigh of relief that immediately turned to a growl. *Fool girl! We could have gotten by them!* There was no time for recriminations, though. She scooted to the corner and peered cautiously around the edge of the building.

A head-sized fireball flashed down the street toward her. She leaped back just before it exploded against the corner where her own head had been, showering her with stone chips.

Anger had her awash in the One Power before she was aware of it. Lightning flashed out of the sky, striking somewhere up the street with a crash near the origin of the fireball. Another jagged bolt split the sky, and then she was running down the alley. Behind her, lightning lanced the mouth of the alley.

If Domon doesn't have that ship waiting, I'll. . . . Light, let us all reach it safely.

Bayle Domon jerked erect as lightning streaked across the slate-gray sky, striking somewhere in the town, then again. *There do no be enough clouds for that!*

Something rumbled loudly up in the town, and a ball of fire smashed into a rooftop just above the docks, throwing splintered slates in wide arcs. The docks had emptied themselves of people a while back, except for a few Seanchan; they ran wildly, now, drawing swords and shouting. A man appeared from one of the warehouses with a *grolm* at his side, running to keep up with the beast's long leaps as they vanished into one of the streets leading up from the water.

One of Domon's crewmen jumped for an axe and swung it high over a mooring cable.

In two strides, Domon seized the upraised axe with one hand and the man's throat with the other. "*Spray* do stay till *I* do say sail, Aedwin Cole!"

"They're going mad, Captain!" Yarin shouted. An explosion sent echoes rumbling across the harbor, sending the gulls into screaming circles, and lightning flickered again, crashing to earth inside Falme. "The *damane* will kill us all! Let us go while they're busy killing one another. They will never notice us till we are gone!"

"I did give my word," Domon said. He wrenched the axe from Cole's hand and threw it clattering onto the deck. "I did give my word." *Hurry, woman*, he thought, *Aes Sedai or whatever you be. Hurry!*

Geofram Bornhald eyed the lightning flashing over Falme and dismissed it from his mind. Some huge flying creature—one of the Seanchan monsters, no doubt—flew wildly to escape the bolts. If there was a storm, it would hinder the Seanchan as much as it did him. Nearly treeless hills, a few topped by sparse thickets, still hid the town from him, and him from it.

His thousand men lay spread out to either side of him, one long, mounted rank rippling along the hollows between hills. The cold wind tossed their white cloaks and flapped the banner at Bornhald's side, the wavy-rayed golden sun of the Children of the Light.

"Go now, Byar," he commanded. The gaunt-faced man hesitated, and Bornhald put a snap into his voice. "I said, go, Child Byar!"

Byar touched hand to heart and bowed. "As you command, my Lord Captain." He turned his horse away, every line of him shouting reluctance.

Bornhald put Byar out of his mind. He had done what he could, there. He raised his voice. "The legion will advance at a walk!"

With a creak of saddles the long line of white-cloaked men moved slowly toward Falme.

Rand peered around the corner at the approaching Seanchan, then ducked back into the narrow alley between two stables with a grimace. They would be there soon. There was blood crusted on his cheek. The cuts he had from Turak burned, but there was nothing to be done for them now. Lightning flashed across the sky again; he felt the rumble of its plummet through his boots. *What in the name of the Light is happening?*

"Close?" Ingtar said. "The Horn of Valere must be saved, Rand." Despite the Seanchan, despite the lightning and strange explosions down in the town proper, he seemed preoccupied with his own thoughts. Mat and Perrin and Hurin were down at the other end of the alley, watching another Seanchan patrol. The place where they had left the horses was close, now, if they could only reach it.

"She's in trouble," Rand muttered. Egwene. There was an odd feeling in his head, as if pieces of his life were in danger. Egwene was one piece, one thread of the cord that made his life, but there were others, and he could feel them threatened. Down there, in Falme. And if any of those threads was destroyed, his life would never be complete, the way it was meant to be. He did not understand it, but the feeling was sure and certain.

"One man could hold fifty here," Ingtar said. The two

stables stood close together, with barely room for the pair of them to stand side by side between them. "One man holding fifty at a narrow passage. Not a bad way to die. Songs have been made about less."

"There's no need for that," Rand said. "I hope." A rooftop in the town exploded. *How am I going to get back in here? I have to reach her. Reach them?* Shaking his head, he peeked around the corner again. The Seanchan were closer, still coming.

"I never knew what he was going to do," Ingtar said softly, as if talking to himself. He had his sword out, testing the edge with his thumb. "A pale little man you didn't seem to really notice even when you were looking at him. Take him inside Fal Dara, I was told, inside the fortress. I did not want to, but I had to do it. You understand? I had to. I never knew what he intended until he shot that arrow. I still don't know if it was meant for the Amyrlin, or for you."

Rand felt a chill. He stared at Ingtar. "What are you saying?" he whispered.

Studying his blade, Ingtar did not seem to hear. "Humankind is being swept away everywhere. Nations fail and vanish. Darkfriends are everywhere, and none of these southlanders seem to notice or care. We fight to hold the Borderlands, to keep them safe in their houses, and every year, despite all we can do, the Blight advances. And these southlanders think Trollocs are myths, and Myrddraal a gleeman's tale." He frowned and shook his head. "It seemed the only way. We would be destroyed for nothing, defending people who do not even know, or care. It seemed logical. Why should we be destroyed for them, when we could make our own peace? Better the Shadow, I thought, than useless oblivion, like Caralain, or Hardan, or. . . . It seemed so logical, then."

Rand grabbed Ingtar's lapels. "You aren't making any sense." *He can't mean what he's saying. He can't.* "Say it plain, whatever you mean. You are talking crazy!"

For the first time Ingtar looked at Rand. His eyes shone with unshed tears. "You are a better man than I. Shepherd or lord, a better man. The prophecy says, 'Let who sounds me think not of glory, but only salvation.' It was my salvation I was thinking of. I would sound the Horn, and lead the heroes of the Ages against Shayol Ghul. Surely that would have been enough to save me. No man can walk so long in the Shadow that he cannot come again to the Light. That is what they say. Surely that would have been enough to wash away what I have been, and done."

"Oh, Light, Ingtar." Rand released his hold on the other man and sagged back against the stable wall. "I think. . . . I think wanting to is enough. I think all you have to do is stop being . . . one of them." Ingtar flinched as if Rand had said it out loud. Darkfriend.

"Rand, when Verin brought us here with the Portal Stone, I—I lived other lives. Sometimes I held the Horn, but I never sounded it. I tried to escape what I'd become, but I never did. Always there was something else required of me, always something worse than the last, until I was. . . . You were ready to give it up to save a friend. Think not of glory. Oh, Light, help me."

Rand did not know what to say. It was as if Egwene had told him she had murdered children. Too horrible to be believed. Too horrible for anyone to admit unless it was true. Too horrible.

After a time, Ingtar spoke again, firmly. "There has to be a price, Rand. There is always a price. Perhaps I can pay it here."

"Ingtar, I—"

"It is every man's right, Rand, to choose when to Sheathe the Sword. Even one like me."

Before Rand could say anything, Hurin came running down the alley. "The patrol turned aside," he said hurriedly, "down into the town. They seem to be gathering down there. Mat and Perrin went on." He took a quick look down the street and pulled back. "We'd better do the same, Lord Ingtar, Lord Rand. Those bug-headed Seanchan are almost here."

"Go, Rand," Ingtar said. He turned to face the street and did not look at Rand or Hurin again. "Take the Horn where it belongs. I always knew the Amyrlin should have given you the charge. But all I ever wanted was to keep Shienar whole, to keep us from being swept away and forgotten."

"I know, Ingtar." Rand drew a deep breath. "The Light shine on you, Lord Ingtar of House Shinowa, and may you shelter in the palm of the Creator's hand." He touched Ingtar's shoulder. "The last embrace of the mother welcome you home." Hurin gasped.

"Thank you," Ingtar said softly. A tension seemed to go out of him. For the first time since the night of the Trolloc raid on Fal Dara, he stood as he had when Rand first saw him, confident and relaxed. Content.

Rand turned and found Hurin staring at him, staring at both of them. "It is time for us to go."

"But Lord Ingtar—"

"—does what he has to," Rand said sharply. "But we go." Hurin nodded, and Rand trotted after him. Rand could hear the steady tread of the Seanchan's boots, now. He did not look back.

CHAPTER
47

The Grave Is No Bar to My Call

Mat and Perrin were mounted by the time Rand and Hurin reached them. Far behind him, Rand heard Ingtar's voice rise. "The Light, and Shinowa!" The clash of steel joined the roar of other voices.

"Where's Ingtar?" Mat shouted. "What's going on?" He had the Horn of Valere lashed to the high pommel of his saddle as if it were just any horn, but the dagger was in his belt, the ruby-tipped hilt cupped protectively in a pale hand that seemed made of nothing but bone and sinew.

"He's dying," Rand said harshly as he swung onto Red's back.

"Then we have to help him," Perrin said. "Mat can take the Horn and the dagger on to—"

"He is doing it so we can all get away," Rand said. *For that, too.* "We will all take the Horn to Verin, and then you can help her take it wherever she says it belongs."

"What do you mean?" Perrin asked. Rand dug his heels into the bay's flanks, and Red leaped away toward the hills beyond the town.

"The Light, and Shinowa!" Ingtar's shout soared after him, sounding triumphant, and lightning crashed across the sky in answer.

Rand whipped Red with his reins, then lay against the stallion's neck as the bay laid out in a dead run, mane and tail streaming. He wished he did not feel as if he were running away from Ingtar's cry, running from what he was supposed to do. *Ingtar, a Darkfriend. I don't care. He was still my friend.* The bay's gallop could not take him away from his own thoughts. *Death is lighter than a feather, duty heavier than a mountain. So many duties. Egwene. The Horn. Fain. Mat and his dagger. Why can't there just be one at a time? I have to take care of all of them. Oh, Light, Egwene!*

He reined in so suddenly that Red slid to a halt, sitting back on his haunches. They were in a scanty copse of bare-branched trees atop one of the hills overlooking Falme. The others galloped up behind him.

"What do you mean?" Perrin demanded. "*We* can help Verin take the Horn where it's supposed to go? Where are *you* going to be?"

"Maybe he's going mad already," Mat said. "He wouldn't want to stay with us if he was going mad. Would you, Rand?"

"You three take the Horn to Verin," Rand said. *Egwene. So many threads, in so much danger. So many duties.* "You do not need me."

Mat caressed the dagger's hilt. "That's all very well, but what about you? Burn me, you can't be going mad yet. You can't!" Hurin gaped at them, not understanding half of it.

"I'm going back," Rand said. "I should never have left." Somehow, that did not sound exactly right in his own ears; it did not feel right inside his head. "I have to go back. Now." That sounded better. "Egwene is still there, remember. With one of those collars around her neck."

"Are you sure?" Mat said. "I never saw her. Aaaah! If you say she is there, then she's there. We'll all take the Horn to Verin, and then we will all go back for her. You don't think I would leave her there, do you?"

Rand shook his head. *Threads. Duties.* He felt as if he were about to explode like a firework. *Light, what's happening to me?* "Mat, Verin must take you and that dagger to Tar Valon, so you can finally be free of it. You don't have any time to waste."

"Saving Egwene isn't wasting time!" But Mat's hand had tightened on the dagger till it shook.

"We aren't any of us going back," Perrin said. "Not yet. Look." He pointed back toward Falme.

The wagon yards and horse lots were turning black with Seanchan soldiers, thousands of them rank on rank, with troops of cavalry riding scaled beasts as well as armored men on horses, colorful gonfanons marking the officers.

Grolm dotted the ranks, and other strange creatures, almost but not quite like monstrous birds and lizards, and great things like nothing he could describe, with gray, wrinkled skin and huge tusks. At intervals along the lines stood *sul'dam* and *damane* by the score. Rand wondered if Egwene were one of them. In the town behind the soldiers, a rooftop still exploded now and again, and lightning still streaked the sky. Two flying beasts, with leathery wings twenty spans tip to tip, soared high overhead, keeping well away from where the bright bolts danced.

"All that for us?" Mat said incredulously. "Who do they think we are?"

An answer came to Rand, but he shoved it away before it had a chance to form completely.

"We aren't going the other way either, Lord Rand," Hurin said. "Whitecloaks. Hundreds of them."

Rand wheeled his horse to look where the sniffer was pointing. A long, white-cloaked line rippled slowly toward them across the hills.

"Lord Rand," Hurin muttered, "if that lot lays an eye on the Horn of Valere, we'll never get it close to an Aes Sedai. We'll never get close to it again ourselves."

"Maybe that's why the Seanchan are gathering," Mat said hopefully. "Because of the Whitecloaks. Maybe it doesn't have anything to do with us at all."

"Whether it does or not," Perrin said dryly, "there is going to be a battle here in a few minutes."

"Either side could kill us," Hurin said, "even if they never see the Horn. If they do. . . ."

Rand could not manage to think about the Whitecloaks, or the Seanchan. *I have to go back. Have to.* He was staring at the Horn of Valere, he realized. They all were. The curled, golden Horn hung at Mat's pommel, the focus of every eye.

"It has to be there at the Last Battle," Mat said, licking his lips. "Nothing says it can't be used before then." He pulled the Horn free of its lashings and looked at them anxiously. "Nothing says it can't."

No one else said anything. Rand did not think he could speak; his own thoughts were too urgent to allow room for speech. *Have to go back. Have to go back.* The longer he looked at the Horn, the more urgent his thoughts became. *Have to. Have to.*

Mat's hand shook as he raised the Horn of Valere to his lips.

It was a clear note, golden as the Horn was golden. The trees around them seemed to resonate with it, and the ground under their feet, the sky overhead. That one long sound encompassed everything.

Out of nowhere, a fog began to rise. First thin wisps hanging in the air, then thicker billows, and thicker, until it blanketed the land like clouds.

Geofram Bornhald stiffened in his saddle as a sound filled the air, so sweet he wanted to laugh, so mournful he wanted to cry. It seemed to come from every direction at once. A mist began to rise, growing even as he watched.

The Seanchan. They are trying something. They know we are here.

It was too soon, the town too far, but he drew his sword—a clatter of scabbards ran down the rank of his half legion—and called, "The legion will advance at a trot."

The fog covered everything, now, but he knew Falme was still there, ahead. The pace of the horses picked up; he could not see them, but he could hear.

Abruptly the ground ahead flew up with a roar, showering him with dirt and pebbles. From the white blindness to his right he heard another roar, and men and horses screamed, then from his left, and again. Again. Thunder and screams, hidden by the fog.

"The legion will charge!" His horse leaped forward as he dug in his heels, and he heard the roar as the legion, as much of it as still lived, followed.

Thunder and screams, wrapped in whiteness.

His last thought was regret. Byar would not be able to tell his son Dain how he had died.

Rand could not see the trees around them any longer. Mat had lowered the Horn, eyes wide with awe, but the sound of it still rang in Rand's ears. The fog hid everything in rolling waves as white as the finest bleached wool, yet Rand could see. He could see, but it was mad. Falme floated somewhere beneath him, its landward border black with the Seanchan ranks, lightning ripping its streets. Falme hung over his head. There Whitecloaks charged and died as the earth opened in fire beneath their horses' hooves. There men ran about the decks of tall, square ships in the harbor, and on one ship, a familiar ship, fearful men waited. He could even recognize the face of the captain. Bayle Domon. He clutched his head with both hands. The trees were hidden, but he could still see each of the others clearly. Hurin anxious. Mat muttering, fearful. Perrin looking as if he knew this was meant to be. The fog roiled up all around them.

Hurin gasped. "Lord Rand!" There was no need for him to point.

Down the billowing fog, as if it were the side of a mountain, rode shapes on horses. At first the dense mists hid more than that, but slowly they came closer, and it was Rand's turn to gasp. He knew them. Men, not all in armor, and women. Their clothes and their weapons came from every Age, but he knew them all.

Rogosh Eagle-eye, a fatherly looking man with white hair and eyes so sharp as to make his name merely a hint. Gaidal Cain, a swarthy man with the hilts of his two swords sticking above his broad shoulders. Golden-haired Birgitte, with her gleaming silver bow and quiver bristling with silver arrows. More. He knew their faces, knew their names. But he heard a hundred names when he looked at each face, some so different he did not recognize them as names at all, though he knew they were. Michael instead of Mikel. Patrick instead of Paedrig. Oscar instead of Otarin.

He knew the man who rode at their head, too. Tall and hook-nosed, with dark, deep-set eyes, his great sword Justice at his side. Artur Hawkwing.

Mat gaped at them as they reined in before him and the others. "Is this . . . ? Is this all of you?" They were little more than a hundred, Rand saw, and realized that somehow he had known that they would be. Hurin's mouth hung open; his eyes bulged almost out of his head.

"It takes more than bravery to bind a man to the Horn." Artur Hawkwing's voice was deep and carrying, a voice used to giving commands.

"Or a woman," Birgitte said sharply.

"Or a woman," Hawkwing agreed. "Only a few are bound to the Wheel, spun out again and again to work the will of the Wheel in the Pattern of the Ages. You could tell him, Lews Therin, could you but remember when you wore flesh." He was looking at Rand.

Rand shook his head, but he would not waste time with denials. "Invaders have come, men who call themselves Seanchan, who use chained Aes Sedai in battle. They must be driven back into the sea. And—and there is a girl. Egwene al'Vere. A novice from the White Tower. The Seanchan have her prisoner. You must help me free her."

To his surprise, several of the small host behind Artur Hawkwing chuckled, and Birgitte, testing her bowstring, laughed. "You always choose women who cause you trouble, Lews Therin." It had a fond sound, as between old friends.

"My name is Rand al'Thor," he snapped. "You have to hurry. There isn't much time."

"Time?" Birgitte said, smiling. "We have all of time." Gaidal Cain dropped his reins and, guiding his horse with his knees, drew a sword in either hand. All along the small band of heroes there was an unsheathing of swords, an unlimbering of bows, a hefting of spears and axes.

Justice shone like a mirror in Artur Hawkwing's gauntleted fist. "I have fought by your side times beyond number, Lews Therin, and faced you as many more. The Wheel spins us out for its purposes, not ours, to serve the Pattern. I know you, if you do not know yourself. We will drive these invaders out for you." His warhorse pranced, and he looked around, frowning. "Something is wrong here. Something holds me." Suddenly he turned his sharp-eyed gaze on Rand. "You are here. Have you the banner?" A murmur ran through those behind him.

"Yes." Rand tore open the straps of his saddlebags and pulled out the Dragon's banner. It filled his hands and hung almost to his stallion's knees. The murmur among the heroes rose.

"The Pattern weaves itself around our necks like halters," Artur Hawkwing said. "You are here. The banner is here. The weave of this moment is set. We have come to the Horn, but we must follow the banner. And the Dragon." Hurin made a faint sound as if his throat had seized.

"Burn me," Mat breathed. "It's true. Burn me!"

Perrin hesitated only an instant before swinging down off his horse and striding into the mist. There came a chopping sound, and when he returned, he carried a straight length of sapling shorn of its branches. "Give it to me, Rand," he said gravely. "If they need it. . . . Give it to me."

Hastily, Rand helped him tie the banner to the pole. When Perrin remounted, pole in hand, a current of air seemed to ripple the pale length of the banner, so the serpentine Dragon appeared to move, alive. The wind did not touch the heavy fog, only the banner.

"You stay here," Rand told Hurin. "When it's over. . . . You will be safe, here."

Hurin drew his short sword, holding it as if it might actually be of some use from horseback. "Begging your pardon, Lord Rand, but I think not. I don't understand the tenth part of what I've heard . . . or what I'm seeing"—his voice dropped to a mutter before picking up again—"but I've come this far, and I think I'll go the rest of the way."

Artur Hawkwing clapped the sniffer on the shoulder. "Sometimes the Wheel adds to our number, friend. Perhaps you will find yourself among us, one day." Hurin sat up as if he had been offered a crown. Hawkwing bowed formally from his saddle to Rand. "With your permission . . . Lord Rand. Trumpeter, will you give us music on the Horn? Fitting that the Horn of Valere should sing us into battle. Bannerman, will you advance?"

Mat sounded the Horn again, long and high—the mists rang with it—and Perrin heeled his horse forward. Rand drew the heron-mark blade and rode between them.

He could see nothing but thick billows of white, but somehow he could still see what he had before, too. Falme, where someone used the Power in the streets, and the harbor, and the Seanchan host, and the dying Whitecloaks, all of it beneath him, all of him hanging above, all of it just as it had been. It seemed as if no time at all had passed since the Horn was first blown, as though time had paused while the heroes answered the call and now resumed counting.

The wild cries Mat wrung from the Horn echoed in the fog, and the drumming of hooves as the horses picked up speed. Rand charged into the mists, wondering if he knew where he was headed. The clouds thickened, hiding the far ends of the rank of heroes galloping to either side of him, obscuring more and more, till he could see only Mat and Perrin and Hurin clearly. Hurin crouched low in his saddle, wide-eyed, urging his horse on. Mat sounding the Horn, and laughing between. Perrin, his yellow eyes glowing, the Dragon's banner streaming behind him. Then they were gone, too, and Rand rode on alone, as it seemed.

In a way, he could still see them, but now it was the way he could see Falme, and the Seanchan. He could not tell where they were, or where he was. He tightened his grip on his sword, peered into the mists ahead. He charged alone through the fog, and somehow he knew that was how it was meant to be.

Suddenly Ba'alzamon was before him in the mists, throwing his arms wide.

Red reared wildly, hurling Rand from his saddle. Rand clung to his sword desperately as he soared. It was not a hard landing. In fact, he thought with a sense of wonder that it was very much like landing on . . . nothing at all. One instant he was sailing through the mists, and the next he was not.

When he climbed to his feet, his horse was gone, but Ba'alzamon was still there, striding toward him with a long, black-charred staff in his hands. They were alone, only they and the rolling fog. Behind Ba'alzamon was shadow. The mist was not dark behind him; this blackness excluded the white fog.

Rand was aware of the other things, too. Artur Hawkwing and the other heroes meeting the Seanchan in dense fog. Perrin, with the banner, swinging his axe more to fend off those who tried to reach him than harm them. Mat, still blowing wild notes on the Horn of Valere. Hurin down from his saddle, fighting with short sword and sword-breaker in the way he knew. It seemed as if the Seanchan numbers would overwhelm them in one rush, yet it was the dark-armored Seanchan who fell back.

Rand went forward to meet Ba'alzamon. Reluctantly, he assumed the void, reached for the True Source, was filled with the One Power. There was no other way. Perhaps he had no chance against the Dark One, but whatever chance he did have lay in the Power. It soaked into his limbs, seemed to suffuse everything about him, his clothes, his sword. He felt as if he should be glowing like the sun. It thrilled him; it made him want to vomit.

"Get out of my way," he grated. "I am not here for you!"

"The girl?" Ba'alzamon laughed. His mouth turned to flame. His burns were all but healed, leaving only a few pink scars that were already fading. He looked like a handsome man of middle years. Except for his mouth, and his eyes. "Which one, Lews Therin? You will not have anyone to help you this time. You are mine, or you are dead. In which case, you are mine anyway."

"Liar!" Rand snarled. He struck at Ba'alzamon, but the staff of charred wood turned his blade in a shower of sparks. "Father of Lies!"

"Fool! Did those other fools you summoned not tell you who you are?" The fires of Ba'alzamon's face roared with laughter.

Even floating in emptiness, Rand felt a chill. *Would they have lied? I don't* want *to be the Dragon Reborn.* He firmed his grip on his sword. Parting the Silk, but Ba'alzamon beat every cut aside; sparks flew as from a blacksmith's forge and hammer. "I have business in Falme, and none with you. Never with you," Rand said. *I have to hold his attention until they can free Egwene.* In that odd way, he could see the battle rage among the fog-shrouded wagon yards and horse lots.

"You pitiful wretch. You have sounded the Horn of Valere. You are linked to it, now. Do you think the worms of the White Tower will ever release you, now? They will put chains around your neck so heavy you will never cut them."

Rand was so surprised he felt it inside the void. *He doesn't know everything. He doesn't know!* He was sure it must show on his face. To cover it, he rushed at Ba'alzamon. Hummingbird Kisses the Honeyrose. The Moon on the Water. The Swallow Rides the Air. Lightning arched between sword and staff. Coruscating glitter showered the fog. Yet Ba'alzamon fell back, his eyes blazing in furious furnaces.

At the edge of his awareness, Rand saw the Seanchan falling back in the streets of Falme, fighting desperately. *Damane* tore the earth with the One Power, but it could not harm Artur Hawkwing, nor the other heroes of the Horn.

"Will you remain a slug beneath a rock?" Ba'alzamon

snarled. The darkness behind him boiled and stirred. "You kill yourself while we stand here. The Power rages in you. It burns you. It is killing you! I alone in all the world can teach you how to control it. Serve me, and live. Serve me, or die!"

"Never!" *Have to hold him long enough. Hurry, Hawkwing. Hurry!* He launched himself at Ba'alzamon again. The Dove Takes Flight. The Falling Leaf.

This time it was he who was driven back. Dimly, he saw the Seanchan fighting their way back in among the stables. He redoubled his efforts. The Kingfisher Takes a Silverback. The Seanchan gave way to a charge, Artur Hawkwing and Perrin side by side in the van. Bundling Straw. Ba'alzamon caught his blow in a fountain like crimson fireflies, and he had to leap away before the staff split his head; the wind of the blow ruffled his hair. The Seanchan surged forward. Striking the Spark. Sparks flew like hail, Ba'alzamon jumped from his stroke, and the Seanchan were driven back to the cobblestone streets.

Rand wanted to howl aloud. Suddenly he knew that the two battles were linked. When he advanced, the heroes called by the Horn drove the Seanchan back; when he fell back, the Seanchan rose up.

"They will not save you," Ba'alzamon said. "Those who might save you will be carried far across the Aryth Ocean. If ever you see them again, they will be collared slaves, and they will destroy you for their new masters."

Egwene. I can't let them do that to her.

Ba'alzamon's voice rode over his thoughts. "You have only one salvation, Rand al'Thor. Lews Therin Kinslayer. I am your only salvation. Serve me, and I will give you the world. Resist, and I will destroy you as I have so often before. But this time I will destroy you to your very soul, destroy you utterly and forever."

I have won again, Lews Therin. The thought was beyond the void, yet it took an effort to ignore it, not to think of all the lives where he had heard it. He shifted his sword, and Ba'alzamon readied his staff.

For the first time Rand realized that Ba'alzamon acted as if the heron-mark blade could harm him. *Steel can't hurt the Dark One.* But Ba'alzamon watched the sword warily. Rand was one with the sword. He could feel every particle of it, tiny bits a thousand times too small to be seen with the eye. And he could feel the Power that suffused him running into the sword, as well, threading through the intricate matrices wrought by Aes Sedai during the War of Power.

It was another voice he heard then. Lan's voice. *There will come a time when you want something more than you want life.* Ingtar's voice. *It is every man's right to choose when to Sheathe the Sword.* The picture formed of Egwene, collared, living her life as a *damane. Threads of my life in danger. Egwene. If Hawkwing gets into Falme, he can save her.* Before he knew it, he had taken the first position of Heron Wading in the Rushes, balanced on one foot, sword raised high, open and defenseless. *Death is lighter than a feather, duty heavier than a mountain.*

Ba'alzamon stared at him. "Why are you grinning like an idiot, fool? Do you not know I can destroy you utterly?"

Rand felt a calmness beyond that of the void. "I will never serve you, Father of Lies. In a thousand lives, I never have. I know that. I'm sure of it. Come. It is time to die."

Ba'alzamon's eyes widened; for an instant they were furnaces that put sweat on Rand's face. The blackness behind Ba'alzamon boiled up around him, and his face hardened. "Then die, worm!" He struck with the staff, as with a spear.

Rand screamed as he felt it pierce his side, burning like a white-hot poker. The void trembled, but he held on with the last of his strength, and drove the heron-mark blade into Ba'alzamon's heart. Ba'alzamon screamed, and the dark behind him screamed. The world exploded in fire.

CHAPTER
48

First Claiming

Min struggled up the cobblestone street, pushing through crowds that stood white-faced and staring, those who were not screaming hysterically. A few ran, seemingly without any idea of where they were running, but most moved like poorly handled puppets, more afraid to go than to stay. She searched the faces, hoping to find Egwene, or Elayne, or Nynaeve, but all she saw were Falmen. And there was something drawing her on, as surely as if she had a string tied to her.

Once she turned to look back. Seanchan ships burned in the harbor, and she could see more in flames off the harbor mouth. Many squarish vessels were already small against the setting sun, sailing west as fast as *damane* could make the winds drive them, and one small ship was beating away from the harbor, tilting to catch a wind to take it along the coast. *Spray*. She did not blame Bayle Domon for not waiting longer, not after what she had seen; she thought it a wonder he had remained so long.

There was one Seanchan vessel in the harbor not burning, though its towers were black from fires already extinguished. As the tall ship crept toward the harbor mouth, a figure on horseback suddenly appeared around the cliffs skirting the harbor. Riding across the water. Min's mouth fell open. Silver glittered as the figure raised a bow; a streak of silver lanced to the boxy ship, a gleaming line connecting bow and ship. With a roar she could hear even at that distance, fire engulfed the foretower anew, and sailors rushed about the deck.

Min blinked, and when she looked again, the mounted

figure was gone. The ship still slowly made way toward the ocean, the crew fighting the flames.

She gave herself a shake and started to climb the street again. She had seen too much that day for someone riding a horse across water to be more than a momentary distraction. *Even if it really was Birgitte and her bow. And Artur Hawkwing. I did see him. I did.*

In front of one of the tall stone buildings, she stopped uncertainly, ignoring the people who brushed past her as if stunned. It was in there, somewhere, that she had to go. She rushed up the stairs and pushed open the door.

No one tried to stop her. As far as she could tell, there was no one in the house. Most of Falme was out in the streets, trying to decide whether they had all gone mad together. She went on through the house, into the garden behind, and there he was.

Rand lay sprawled on his back under an oak, face pale and eyes closed, left hand gripping a hilt that ended in a foot of blade that appeared to have been melted at the end. His chest rose and fell too slowly, and not with the regular rhythm of someone breathing normally.

Taking a deep breath to calm herself, she went to see what she could do for him. First was to get rid of that stub of a blade; he could hurt himself, or her, if he started thrashing. She pried his hand open, and winced when the hilt stuck to his palm. She tossed it aside with a grimace. The heron on the hilt had branded itself into his hand. But it was obvious to her that that was not what had him lying there unconscious. *How did he come by that? Nynaeve can put a salve on it later.*

A hasty examination showed that most of his cuts and bruises were not new—at least, the blood had had time to dry in a crust, and the bruises had started to turn yellow at the edges—but there was a hole burned through his coat on the left side. Opening his coat, she pulled up his shirt. Breath whistled through her teeth. There was a wound burned into his side, but it had cauterized itself. What shook her was the feel of his flesh. It had a touch of ice in it; he made the air seem warm.

Grabbing his shoulders, she began to drag him toward the house. He hung limp, a dead weight. "Great lummox," she grunted. "You couldn't be short, and light, could you?

You have to have all that leg and shoulder. I ought to let you
lie out here."

But she struggled up the steps, careful not to bump him
any more than she could avoid, and pulled him inside.
Leaving him just within the door, she knuckled the small of
her back, muttering to herself about the Pattern, and made a
hasty search. There was a small bedroom in the back of the
house, perhaps a servant's room, with a bed piled high with
blankets, and logs already laid on the hearth. In moments,
she had the blankets thrown back and the fire lit, as well as
a lamp on the bedside table. Then she went back for Rand.

It was no small task getting him to the room, or up onto
the bed, but she managed it with only a little hard breathing, and covered him up. After a moment, she stuck a hand
under the blankets; she winced and shook her head. The
sheets were icy cold; he had no body warmth for the blankets to hold. With a put-upon sigh, she wriggled under the
covers beside him. Finally, she put his head on her arm. His
eyes were still closed, his breathing ragged, but she thought
he would be dead by the time she came back if she left to
find Nynaeve. *He needs an Aes Sedai,* she thought. *All I can
do is try to give him a little warmth.*

For a time she studied his face. It was only his face she
saw; she could never read anyone who was not conscious. "I
like older men," she told him. "I like men with education,
and wit. I have no interest in farms, or sheep, or shepherds.
Especially boy shepherds." With a sigh, she smoothed back
the hair from his face; he had silky hair. "But then, you
aren't a shepherd, are you? Not anymore. Light, why did the
Pattern have to catch me up with you? Why couldn't I have
something safe and simple, like being shipwrecked with no
food and a dozen hungry Aielmen?"

There was a sound in the hall, and she raised her head as
the door opened. Egwene stood there, staring at them by the
light of the fire and the lamp. "Oh," was all she said.

Min's cheeks colored. *Why am I behaving like I've done
something wrong? Fool!* "I . . . I'm keeping him warm. He
is unconscious, and he's as cold as ice."

Egwene did not come any further into the room. "I—I
felt him pulling at me. Needing me. Elayne felt it, too. I
thought it must be something to do with—with what he is,
but Nynaeve didn't feel anything." She drew a deep, un-

steady breath. "Elayne and Nynaeve are getting the horses. We found Bela. The Seanchan left most of their horses behind. Nynaeve says we should go as soon as we can, and— and. . . . Min, you know what he is, don't you, now?"

"I know." Min wanted to take her arm from under Rand's head, but she could not make herself move. "I think I do, anyway. Whatever he is, he is hurt. I can do nothing for him except keep him warm. Maybe Nynaeve can."

"Min, you know . . . you do know that he cannot marry. He isn't . . . safe . . . for any of us, Min."

"Speak for yourself," Min said. She pulled Rand's face against her breast. "It's like Elayne said. You tossed him aside for the White Tower. What should you care if I pick him up?"

Egwene looked at her for what seemed a long time. Not at Rand, not at all, only at her. She felt her face growing hotter and wanted to look away, but she could not.

"I will bring Nynaeve," Egwene said finally, and walked out of the room with her back straight and her head high.

Min wanted to call out, to go after her, but she lay there as if frozen. Frustrated tears stung her eyes. *It's what has to be. I know it. I read it in all of them. Light, I don't want to be part of this.* "It's all your fault," she told Rand's still shape. "No, it isn't. But you will pay for it, I think. We're all caught like flies in a spiderweb. What if I told her there's another woman yet to come, one she doesn't even know? For that matter, what would you think of that, my fine Lord Shepherd? You aren't bad-looking at all, but. . . . Light, I don't even know if I am the one you'll choose. I don't know if I want you to choose me. Or will you try to dandle all three of us on your knee? It may not be your fault, Rand al'Thor, but it isn't fair."

"Not Rand al'Thor," said a musical voice from the door. "Lews Therin Telamon. The Dragon Reborn."

Min stared. She was the most beautiful woman Min had ever seen, with pale, smooth skin, and long, black hair, and eyes as dark as night. Her dress was a white that would make snow seem dingy, belted in silver. All her jewelry was silver. Min felt herself bristle. "What do you mean? Who are you?"

The woman came to stand over the bed—her movements were so graceful, Min felt a stab of envy, though she had never before envied any woman anything—and smoothed

Rand's hair as if Min were not there. "He doesn't believe yet, I think. He knows, but he does not believe. I have guided his steps, pushed him, pulled him, enticed him. He was always stubborn, but this time I will shape him. Ishamael thinks he controls events, but I do." Her finger brushed Rand's forehead as if drawing a mark; Min thought uneasily that it looked like the Dragon's Fang. Rand stirred, murmuring, the first sound or movement he had made since she found him.

"Who are you?" Min demanded. The woman looked at her, only looked, but she found herself shrinking back into the pillows, clutching Rand to her fiercely.

"I am called Lanfear, girl."

Min's mouth was abruptly so dry she could not have spoken if her life depended on it. *One of the Forsaken! No! Light, no!* All she could do was shake her head. The denial made Lanfear smile.

"Lews Therin was and is mine, girl. Tend him well for me until I come for him." And she was gone.

Min gaped. One moment she was there, then she was gone. Min discovered she was hugging Rand's unconscious form tightly. She wished she did not feel as if she wanted him to protect her.

Gaunt face set with grim purpose, Byar galloped with the sinking sun behind him and never looked back. He had seen all he needed to, all he could with that accursed fog. The legion was dead, Lord Captain Geofram Bornhald was dead, and there was only one explanation for that; Darkfriends had betrayed them, Darkfriends like that Perrin of the Two Rivers. That word he had to carry to Dain Bornhald, the Lord Captain's son, with the Children of the Light watching Tar Valon. But he had worse to tell, and to none less than Pedron Niall himself. He had to tell what he had seen in the sky above Falme. He flogged his horse with his reins and never looked back.

CHAPTER
49

What Was Meant to Be

Rand opened his eyes and found himself staring up at sunlight slanting through the branches of a leatherleaf, its broad, tough leaves still green despite the time of year. The wind stirring the leaves carried a hint of snow, come nightfall. He lay on his back, and he could feel blankets covering him under his hands. His coat and shirt seemed to be gone, but something was binding his chest, and his left side hurt. He turned his head, and Min was sitting there on the ground, watching him. He almost did not know her, wearing skirts. She smiled uncertainly.

"Min. It is you. Where did you come from? Where are we?" His memory came in flashes and patches. Old things he could remember, but the last few days seemed like bits of broken mirror, spinning through his mind, showing glimpses that were gone before he could see them clearly.

"From Falme," she said. "We're five days east of there, now, and you've been asleep all that time."

"Falme." More memory. Mat had blown the Horn of Valere. "Egwene! Is she . . . ? Did they free her?" He held his breath.

"I don't know what 'they' you mean, but she's free. We freed her ourselves."

"We? I don't understand." *She's free. At least she is—*

"Nynaeve, and Elayne, and me."

"Nynaeve? Elayne? How? You were *all* in Falme?" He struggled to sit up, but she pushed him back down easily and stayed there, hands on his shoulders, eyes intent on his face. "Where is she?"

"Gone." Min's face colored. "They're all gone. Egwene,

and Nynaeve, and Mat, and Hurin, and Verin. Hurin didn't want to leave you, really. They're on their way to Tar Valon. Egwene and Nynaeve back to their training in the Tower, and Mat for whatever the Aes Sedai have to do about that dagger. They took the Horn of Valere with them. I can't believe I actually saw it."

"Gone," he muttered. "She didn't even wait till I woke up." The red in Min's cheeks deepened, and she sat back, staring at her lap.

He raised his hands to run them over his face, and stopped, staring at his palms in shock. There was a heron branded across his left palm, too, now, to match the one on his right, every line clean and true. *Once the heron to set his path; Twice the heron to name him true.* "No!"

"They are gone," she said. "Saying 'no' won't change it."

He shook his head. Something told him the pain in his side was important. He could not remember being injured, but it was important. He started to lift his blankets to look, but she slapped his hands away.

"You can't do any good with that. It isn't healed all the way, yet. Verin tried Healing, but she said it didn't work the way it should." She hesitated, nibbling her lip. "Moiraine says Nynaeve must have done something, or you wouldn't have lived till we carried you to Verin, but Nynaeve says she was too frightened to light a candle. There is . . . something wrong with your wound. You will have to wait for it to heal naturally." She seemed troubled.

"Moiraine is here?" He barked a bitter laugh. "When you said Verin was gone, I thought I was free of Aes Sedai again."

"I am here," Moiraine said. She appeared, all in blue and as serene as if she stood in the White Tower, strolling up to stand over him. Min was frowning at the Aes Sedai. Rand had the odd feeling that she meant to protect him from Moiraine.

"I wish you weren't here," he told the Aes Sedai. "As far as I am concerned, you can go back to wherever you've been hiding and stay there."

"I have not been hiding," Moiraine said calmly. "I have been doing what I could, here on Toman Head, and in Falme. It was little enough, though I learned much. I failed to rescue two of my sisters before the Seanchan herded them onto the ships with the Leashed Ones, but I did what I could."

"What you could. You sent Verin to shepherd me, but I'm no sheep, Moiraine. You said I could go where I wanted, and I mean to go where you are not."

"I did not send Verin." Moiraine frowned. "She did that on her own. You are of interest to a great many people, Rand. Did Fain find you, or you him?"

The sudden change of topic took him by surprise. "Fain? No. A fine hero I make. I tried to rescue Egwene, and Min did it before me. Fain said he would hurt Emond's Field if I didn't face him, and I never laid eyes on him. Did he go with the Seanchan, too?"

Moiraine shook her head. "I do not know. I wish I did. But it is as well you did not find him, not until you know what he is, at least."

"He's a Darkfriend."

"More than that. Worse than that. Padan Fain was the Dark One's creature to the depths of his soul, but I believe that in Shadar Logoth he fell afoul of Mordeth, who was as vile in fighting the Shadow as ever the Shadow itself was. Mordeth tried to consume Fain's soul, to have a human body again, but found a soul that had been touched directly by the Dark One, and what resulted. . . . What resulted was neither Padan Fain nor Mordeth, but something far more evil, a blend of the two. Fain—let us call him that—is more dangerous than you can believe. You might not have survived such a meeting, and if you had, you might have been worse than turned to the Shadow."

"If he is alive, if he did not go with the Seanchan, I have to—" He cut off as she produced his heron-mark sword from under her cloak. The blade ended abruptly a foot from the hilt, as if it had been melted. Memory came crashing back. "I killed him," he said softly. "This time I killed him."

Moiraine put the ruined sword aside like the useless thing it now was, and wiped her hands together. "The Dark One is not slain so easily. The mere fact that he appeared in the sky above Falme is more than merely troubling. He should not be able to do that, if he is bound as we believe. And if he is not, why has he not destroyed us all?" Min stirred uneasily.

"In the sky?" Rand said in wonder.

"Both of you," Moiraine said. "Your battle took place across the sky, in full view of every soul in Falme. Perhaps in other towns on Toman Head, too, if half what I hear is to be believed."

"We—we saw it all," Min said in a faint voice. She put a hand over one of Rand's comfortingly.

Moiraine reached under her cloak again and came out with a rolled parchment, one of the large sheets such as the street artists in Falme used. The chalks were a little smudged when she unfurled it, but the picture was still clear enough. A man whose face was a solid flame fought with a staff against another with a sword among clouds where lightning danced, and behind them rippled the Dragon banner. Rand's face was easily recognizable.

"How many have seen that?" he demanded. "Tear it up. Burn it."

The Aes Sedai let the parchment roll back up. "It would do no good, Rand. I bought that two days gone, in a village we passed through. There are hundreds of them, perhaps thousands, and the tale is being told everywhere of how the Dragon battled the Dark One in the skies above Falme."

Rand looked at Min. She nodded reluctantly, and squeezed his hand. She looked frightened, but she did not flinch away. *I wonder if that's why Egwene left. She was right to leave.*

"The Pattern weaves itself around you even more tightly," Moiraine said. "You need me now more than ever."

"I don't need you," he said harshly, "and I don't want you. I will not have anything to do with this." He remembered being called Lews Therin; not only by Ba'alzamon, but by Artur Hawkwing. "I won't. Light, the Dragon is supposed to Break the World again, to tear everything apart. I will not be the Dragon."

"You are what you are," Moiraine said. "Already you stir the world. The Black Ajah has revealed itself for the first time in two thousand years. Arad Doman and Tarabon were on the brink of war, and it will be worse when news of Falme reaches them. Cairhien is in civil war."

"I did nothing in Cairhien," he protested. "You can't blame that on me."

"Doing nothing was always a ploy in the Great Game," she said with a sigh, "and especially as they play it now.

You were the spark, and Cairhien exploded like an Illuminator's firework. What do you think will happen when word of Falme reaches Arad Doman and Tarabon? There have always been men willing to proclaim for any man who called himself the Dragon, but they have never before had such signs as this. There is more. Here." She tossed a pouch on his chest.

He hesitated a moment before opening it. Within lay shards of what seemed to be black-and-white glazed pottery. He had seen their like before. "Another seal on the Dark One's prison," he mumbled. Min gasped; her grip on his hand sought comfort, now, rather than offering it.

"Two," Moiraine said. "Three of the seven are broken now. The one I had, and two I found in the High Lord's dwelling in Falme. When all seven are broken, perhaps even before, the patch men put over the hole they drilled into the prison the Creator made will be torn asunder, and the Dark One will once more be able to put his hand through that hole and touch the world. And the only hope of the world is that the Dragon Reborn will be there to face him."

Min tried to stop Rand from throwing back the blankets, but he pushed her gently aside. "I need to walk." She helped him up, but with a great many sighs and grumbles about him making his wound worse. He discovered that his chest was wrapped round with bandages. Min draped one of the blankets about his shoulders like a cloak.

For a moment he stood staring down at the heron-mark sword, what was left of it, lying on the ground. *Tam's sword. My father's sword.* Reluctantly, more reluctantly than he had ever done anything in his life, he let go of the hope that he would discover Tam really was his father. It felt as if he were tearing his heart out. But it did not change the way he felt about Tam, and Emond's Field was the only home he had ever known. *Fain is the important thing. I have one duty left. Stopping him.*

The two women had to support him, one on either arm, down to where the campfires were already burning, not far from a road of hard-packed dirt. Loial was there, reading a book, *To Sail Beyond the Sunset,* and Perrin, staring into one of the fires. The Shienarans were making preparations for their evening meal. Lan sat under a tree sharpening his belt knife; the Warder gave Rand a careful look, then a nod.

There was something else, too. The Dragon banner rippled on the wind over the middle of the camp. Somewhere they had found a proper staff to replace Perrin's sapling.

Rand demanded, "What is that doing out where anybody who passes by can see it?"

"It is too late to hide, Rand," Moiraine said. "It was always too late for you to hide."

"You don't have to put up a sign saying 'here I am,' either. I'll never find Fain if somebody kills me because of that banner." He turned to Loial and Perrin. "I'm glad you stayed. I would have understood if you hadn't."

"Why would I not stay?" Loial said. "You are even more *ta'veren* than I believed, true, but you are still my friend. I hope you are still my friend." His ears twitched uncertainly.

"I am," Rand said. "For as long as it's safe for you to be around me, and even after, too." The Ogier's grin nearly split his face in two.

"I'm staying as well," Perrin said. There was a note of resignation, or acceptance, in his voice. "The Wheel weaves us tight in the Pattern, Rand. Who would have thought it, back in Emond's Field?"

The Shienarans were gathering around. To Rand's surprise, they all fell to their knees. Every one of them watched him.

"We would pledge ourselves to you," Uno said. The others kneeling with him nodded.

"Your oaths are to Ingtar, and Lord Agelmar," Rand protested. "Ingtar died well, Uno. He died so the rest of us could escape with the Horn." There was no need to tell them or anyone else the rest. He hoped that Ingtar had found the Light again. "Tell Lord Agelmar that when you return to Fal Dara."

"It is said," the one-eyed man said carefully, "that when the Dragon is Reborn, he will break all oaths, shatter all ties. Nothing holds us, now. We would give our oaths to you." He drew his sword and laid it before him, hilt toward Rand, and the rest of the Shienarans did the same.

"You battled the Dark One," Masema said. Masema, who hated him. Masema, who looked at him as if seeing a vision of the Light. "I saw you, Lord Dragon. I saw. I am your man, to the death." His dark eyes shone with fervor.

"You must choose, Rand," Moiraine said. "The world

will be broken whether you break it or not. Tarmon Gai'don will come, and that alone will tear the world apart. Will you still try to hide from what you are, and leave the world to face the Last Battle undefended? Choose."

They were all watching him, all waiting. *Death is lighter than a feather, duty heavier than a mountain.* He made his decision.

CHAPTER
50

After

By ship and horse the stories spread, by merchant wagon and man on foot, told and retold, changing yet always alike at the heart, to Arad Doman and Tarabon and beyond, of signs and portents in the sky above Falme. And men proclaimed themselves for the Dragon, and other men struck them down and were struck down in turn.

Other tales spread, of a column that rode from the sinking sun across Almoth Plain. A hundred Bordermen, it was said. No, a thousand. No, a thousand heroes come back from the grave to answer the call of the Horn of Valere. Ten thousand. They had destroyed a legion of the Children of the Light entire. They had thrown Artur Hawkwing's returned armies back into the sea. They were Artur Hawkwing's armies returned. Toward the mountains they rode, toward the dawn.

Yet one thing every tale had the same. At their head rode a man whose face had been seen in the sky above Falme, and they rode under the banner of the Dragon Reborn.

*And men cried out to the Creator, saying, O Light of
the Heavens, Light of the World, let the Promised One
be born of the mountain, according to the Prophecies, as he was in Ages past and will be in Ages to
come. Let the Prince of the Morning sing to the land
that green things will grow and the valleys give forth
lambs. Let the arm of the Lord of the Dawn shelter us
from the Dark, and the great sword of justice defend
us. Let the Dragon ride again on the winds of time.*

—*from* Charal Drianaan te Calamon,
The Cycle of the Dragon,
Author unknown, the Fourth Age

The End
of the Second Book of
The Wheel of Time

GLOSSARY

A Note on Dates in This Glossary. Three systems of recording dates have been in general use since the Breaking of the World. The first recorded years After the Breaking (AB). Since the years of the Breaking and immediately after were years of almost total chaos, and since this calendar was adopted a good hundred years after the end of the Breaking, its starting point was arbitrarily assigned. At the end of the Trolloc Wars many records had been lost, so much so that there was argument about the exact year under the old system. A new calendar was therefore established, dating from the end of the Wars and celebrating the supposed freedom of the world from the Trolloc threat. This second calendar recorded each year as Free Year (FY). After the disruption, death, and destruction caused by the War of the Hundred Years, a third calendar came into being. This calendar, of the New Era (NE), is currently in use.

a'dam (AYE-dam): A device, consisting of a collar and a bracelet linked by a silvery metal leash, that may be used to control, against her will, any woman who can channel. The collar is worn by the *damane*, the bracelet by the *sul'dam*. *See also* damane; sul'dam.

Aes Sedai (EYEZ seh-DEYE): Wielders of the One Power. Since the Time of Madness, all surviving Aes Sedai are women. Widely distrusted and feared, even hated, they are blamed by many for the Breaking of the World, and are thought to meddle in the affairs of nations. At the same time, few rulers will be without an Aes Sedai advisor, even in lands where the existence of such a connection must be kept secret. *See also* Ajah; Amyrlin Seat; Time of Madness.

Agelmar; Lord Agelmar of House Jagad (AGH-el-mar; JAH-gad): Lord of Fal Dara. His sign is three running red foxes.

Age of Legends: The Age ended by the War of the Shadow and the Breaking of the World. A time when Aes Sedai performed wonders now only dreamed of. *See also* Wheel of Time; Breaking of the World; War of the Shadow.

Aiel (eye-EEL): The people of the Aiel Waste. Fierce and hardy. Also called Aielmen. They veil their faces before they kill, giving rise to the saying "acting like a black-veiled Aiel" to describe someone who is being violent. Deadly warriors with weapons or with nothing but their bare hands, they will not touch a sword. Their pipers play them into battle with the music of dances, and Aielmen call battle "the Dance." *See also* Aiel warrior societies; Aiel Waste.

Aiel warrior societies: Aiel warriors are all members of one of the warrior societies, such as the Stone Dogs, the Red Shields, or the Maidens of the Spear. Each society has its own customs, and sometimes specific duties. For example, Red Shields act as police. Stone Dogs often vow not to retreat once battle has been joined, and will die to the last man if necessary to fulfill this vow. The clans of the Aiel frequently fight among themselves, but members of the same society will not fight one another even if their clans are doing so. In this way, there are always lines of contact between the clans even when they are in open warfare. *See also* Aiel; Aiel Waste; *Far Dareis Mai.*

Aiel Waste: The harsh, rugged, and all-but-waterless land east of the Spine of the World. Few outsiders venture there, not only because water is almost impossible to find for one not born there, but because the Aiel consider themselves at war with all other peoples and do not welcome strangers.

Ajah (AH-jah): Societies among the Aes Sedai to which all Aes Sedai except the Amyrlin Seat belong. They are designated by colors: Blue, Red, White, Green, Brown, Yellow, and Gray. Each follows a specific philosophy of the use of the One Power and the purposes of the Aes Sedai. For example, the Red Ajah bends all its energies to finding men who are attempting to wield the Power and to gentling them. The Brown Ajah, on the other hand, forsakes involvement with the mundane world and dedicates itself to seeking knowledge. There are rumors (hotly denied, and never safely mentioned in front of any Aes Sedai) of a Black Ajah, dedicated to serving the Dark One.

Alanna Mosvani (ah-LAN-nah mos-VANH-nie): An Aes Sedai of the Green Ajah.

alantin (ah-LANH-tin): In the Old Tongue, "Brother;" short for *tia avende alantin*, "Brother to the Trees;" "Treebrother."

Alar (AYE-lahr): Eldest of the Elders of Stedding Tsofu.

Aldieb (ahl-DEEB): In the Old Tongue, "West Wind," the wind that brings the spring rains.

al'Meara, Nynaeve (ahl-MEER-ah, NIGH-neev): A woman from Emond's Field, in the Two Rivers district of Andor (AN-door).

al'Thor, Rand (ahl-THOR, RAND): A young man from Emond's Field, once a shepherd.

al'Vere, Egwene (ahl-VEER, eh-GWAIN): A young woman from Emond's Field.

Amalisa, Lady (ah-mah-LEE-sah): Shienaran of House Jagad; Lord Agelmar's sister.

Amyrlin Seat (AHM-ehr-lin SEAT): (1) The title of the leader of the Aes Sedai. Elected for life by the Hall of the Tower, the highest council of the Aes Sedai, which consists of three representatives (called Sitters) from each of the seven Ajahs. The Amyrlin Seat has, theoretically at least, almost supreme authority among the Aes Sedai, and ranks socially as the equal of a king or queen. A slightly less formal usage is simply the Amyrlin. (2) The throne upon which the leader of the Aes Sedai sits.

Anaiya (ah-NYE-yah): An Aes Sedai of the Blue Ajah.

angreal (anh-gree-AHL): A very rare object that allows anyone capable of channeling the One Power to handle a greater amount of the Power than would be safely possible unaided. Remnants of the Age of Legends, the means of their making is no longer known. Few remain in existence. *See also sa'angreal; ter'angreal.*

Arad Doman (AH-rahd do-MAHN): A nation on the Aryth Ocean.

Arafel (AH-rah-fehl): One of the Borderlands.

Avendesora (AH-vehn-deh-SO-rah): In the Old Tongue, "the Tree of Life." Mentioned in many stories and legends.

Aybara, Perrin (ay-BAHR-ah, PEHR-rihn): A young man from Emond's Field, formerly a blacksmith's apprentice.

Ba'alzamon (bah-AHL-zah-mon): In the Trolloc tongue, "Heart of the Dark." Believed to be the Trolloc name for the Dark One. *See also* Dark One; Trollocs.

Barthanes, Lord, of House Damodred (bahr-THAN-nehs): Cairhienin lord, second only to the king in power. His personal sign is the Charging Boar. The sign of House Damodred is the Crown and Tree.

Bel Tine (BEHL TINE): Spring festival celebrating the end of winter, the first sprouting of crops, and the birth of the first lambs.

Betrayer of Hope: *See* Ishamael.

Birgitte (ber-GEET-teh): Golden-haired heroine of legend and a hundred gleemen's tales, she had a silver bow and silver arrows, with which she never missed.

bittern (BIHT-tehrn): A musical instrument that may have six, nine, or twelve strings, and is held flat on the knees and played by plucking or strumming.

Blasted Lands: Desolated lands surrounding Shayol Ghul, beyond the Great Blight.

Blight, the: *See* Great Blight, the.

Borderlands, the: The nations bordering the Great Blight. Saldaea, Arafel, Kandor, and Shienar.

Bornhald, Geofram (BOHRN-hahld, JEHF-rahm): A Lord Captain of the Children of the Light.

Breaking of the World, the: During the Time of Madness, male Aes Sedai who had gone insane, and who could wield the One Power to a degree now unknown, changed the face of the earth. They caused great earthquakes, leveled old mountain ranges and raised new mountains, lifted dry land where seas had been and made the ocean rush in where dry land had been. Many parts of the world were completely depopulated, and the survivors were scattered like dust on the wind. This destruction is remembered in stories, legends, and history as the Breaking of the World. *See also* Time of Madness.

Byar, Jaret (BY-ahr, JAH-ret): An officer of the Children of the Light.

Caemlyn (KAYM-lihn): The capital city of Andor.

Cairhien (KEYE-ree-EHN): Both a nation along the Spine of the World and the capital city of that nation. The city was burned and looted during the Aiel War (976–978 NE). The sign of Cairhien is a many-rayed golden sun rising from the bottom of a field of sky blue.

Caralain (KAH-rah-layn): One of the nations wrung from Artur Hawkwing's empire during the War of the Hundred Years. It weakened thereafter, and the last traces vanished about 500 NE.

Cauthon, Mat (CAW-thon, MAT): A young man from the Two Rivers. Full name: Matrim (MAT-rihm) Cauthon.

channel: (verb) To control the flow of the One Power. *See also* One Power.

Children of the Light: A society holding strict ascetic beliefs, dedicated to the defeat of the Dark One and the destruction of all Darkfriends. Founded during the War of the Hundred Years by Lothair Mantelar (LOH-thayr MAHN-tee-LAHR) to proselytize against the increasing numbers of Darkfriends, they evolved during the war into a completely military organization, extremely rigid in their beliefs, and completely certain that only they know the truth and the right. They hate Aes Sedai, considering them, and any who support or befriend them, Darkfriends. They are known disparagingly as Whitecloaks. Their sign is a golden sunburst on a field of white.

Chronicles, Keeper of the: Second in authority to the Amyrlin Seat among the Aes Sedai, she also acts as secretary to the Amyrlin. Chosen for life by the Hall of the Tower, and usually of the same Ajah as the Amyrlin. *See also* Amyrlin Seat; Ajah.

Corenne (koh-REEN-neh): In the Old Tongue, "Return," or "the Return."

Covenant of the Ten Nations: A union formed in the centuries after the Breaking of the World when nations were first recreated (circa 300 AB). Dedicated to the defeat of the Dark One. Broken apart by the Trolloc Wars. *See also* Trolloc Wars.

cuendillar (CWAIN-der-yar): Also known as heartstone. *See* heartstone.

Daes Dae'mar (DAH-ess day-MAR): The Great Game, also known as the Game of Houses. Name given the scheming, plots, and manipulations for advantage by the noble Houses. Great value is given to subtlety, to aiming at one thing while seeming to aim at another, and to achieving ends with the least visible effort.

Dai Shan (DYE SHAN): A title in the Borderlands meaning Diademed Battle Lord. *See also* Borderlands.

damane (dah-MAHN-ee): In the Old Tongue, "Leashed Ones." Women who can channel who are held prisoner by *a'dam* and used by the Seanchan for many purposes, chiefest of these being as weapons in battle. *See also* Seanchan; *a'dam; sul'dam.*

Damodred, Lord Galadedrid (DAHM-oh-drehd, gah-LAHD-eh-drihd): Half-brother to Elayne and Gawyn. His sign is a winged silver sword, point down.

Darkfriends: Those who follow the Dark One and believe they will gain great power and rewards, and even immortality, when he is freed from his prison.

Dark One: Most common name, used in every land, for Shai'tan. The source of evil, antithesis of the Creator. Imprisoned by the Creator at the moment of Creation in a prison at Shayol Ghul. An attempt to free him from that prison brought about the War of the Shadow, the tainting of *saidin*, the Breaking of the World, and the end of the Age of Legends.

Dark One, naming the: Saying the true name of the Dark One (Shai'tan) draws his attention, inevitably bringing ill fortune at best, disaster at worst. For that reason, many euphemisms are used, among them the Dark One, Father of Lies, Sightblinder, Lord of the Grave, Shepherd of the Night, Heartsbane, Heartfang, Grassburner, and Leafblighter. Someone who seems to be inviting ill fortune is often said to be "naming the Dark One."

Daughter-Heir: Title of the heir to the throne of Andor. The eldest daughter of the queen succeeds her mother on the throne. Without a surviving daughter, the throne goes to the nearest female blood relation of the queen.

Daughter of the Night: *See* Lanfear.

Dome of Truth: Great audience hall of the Children of the Light, located in Amador (AH-mah-door), the capital of Amadicia (AH-mah-DEE-cee-ah). There is a King of Amadicia, but the Children rule in all but name. *See also* Children of the Light.

Do Miere A'vron (DOH me-EHR a-VRAWN): *See* Watchers Over the Waves.

Domon, Bayle (DOH-mon, BAIL): The captain of the *Spray,* who collects old things.

Draghkar (DRAGH-kahr): A creature of the Dark One, made originally by twisting human stock. A Draghkar appears to be a large man with bat-like wings, whose skin is too pale and whose eyes are too large. The Draghkar's song can draw its prey to it, suppressing the victim's will. There is a saying: "The kiss of the Draghkar is death." It does not bite, but its kiss will consume first the soul of its victim, and then its life.

Dragon, false: Occasionally men claim to be the Dragon Reborn, and sometimes one of them gains following enough to require an army to put it down. Some have begun wars that involved many nations. Over the centuries most of these have been men unable to channel the One Power, but a few could do so. All, however, either disappeared or were captured or killed without fulfilling any of the Prophecies concerning the Rebirth of the Dragon. These men are called false Dragons. Among those who could channel, the most powerful were Raolin Darksbane (335–36AB), Yurian Stonebow (circa 1300–1308 AB), Davian (FY 351), Guaire Amalasan (FY 939–43), and Logain (997 NE). *See also* Dragon Reborn.

Dragon, Prophecies of the: Little known and seldom spoken of, the Prophecies, given in *The Karaethon Cycle,* foretell that the Dark One will be freed again to touch the world. And that Lews Therin Telamon, the Dragon, Breaker of the World, will be reborn to fight Tarmon Gai'don, the Last Battle against the Shadow. *See also* Dragon, the.

Dragon, the: The name by which Lews Therin Telamon was known during the War of the Shadow. In the madness that overtook all male Aes Sedai, Lews Therin killed every living person who carried any of his blood, as well as everyone he loved, thus earning the name Kinslayer. *See also* Dragon Reborn; Dragon, Prophecies of the.

Dragon Reborn: According to prophecy and legend the Dragon will be born again at mankind's greatest hour of need to save the world. This is not something people look forward to, both because the Prophecies say the Dragon Reborn will bring a new Breaking to the world and because Lews Therin Kinslayer, the Dragon, is a name to make men shudder, even more than three thousand years after his death. *See also* Dragon, the; Dragon, false; Dragon, Prophecies of the.

Dragon's Fang, the: A stylized mark in the shape of a teardrop balanced on its point. Scrawled on a door or a house, it is an accusation of evil against the people inside, or an attempt to bring the Dark One's attention, and thus harm, to them.

Dreadlords: Those men and women who, able to channel the One Power, went over to the Shadow during the Trolloc Wars, acting as commanders of the Trolloc forces.

Elaida (eh-LY-da): An Aes Sedai of the Red Ajah who advises Queen Morgase of Andor. She sometimes has the Foretelling. *See also* Foretelling.

Elayne (ee-LAIN): Queen Morgase's daughter, the Daughter-Heir to the Throne of Andor. Her sign is a golden lily.

Fain, Padan (FAIN, PAHD-ahn): A man imprisoned as a Darkfriend in Fal Dara keep.

Far Dareis Mai (FAHR DAH-rize MY): Literally "Maidens of the Spear." A warrior society of the Aiel, which, unlike any of the others, admits women and only women. A Maiden may not marry and remain in the society, nor may she fight while carrying a child. Any child born to a Maiden is given to another woman to raise, in such a way that no one knows who the child's mother was. ("You may belong to no man, nor may any man belong to you, nor any child. The spear is your lover, your child, and your life.") These children are treasured, for it is prophesied that a child born of a Maiden will unite the clans and return the Aiel to the greatness they knew during the Age of Legends. *See also* Aiel; Aiel warrior societies.

Five Powers, the: There are threads to the One Power, and each person who can channel can usually grasp some threads better than others. These threads are named according to the sorts of things that can be done using them—Earth, Air, Fire, Water, and Spirit—and are called the Five Powers. Any wielder of the Power will have a greater degree of strength with one, or possibly two, of these, and lesser strength in the others. Some few may have great strength with three, but since the Age of Legends no one has had great strength with all five. Even then this was extremely rare. The degree of strength can vary greatly between individuals, so that some who can channel are much stronger than others. Performing certain acts with the One Power requires ability in one or more of the Five Powers. For example, starting or controlling a fire requires Fire, and affecting the weather requires Air and Water, while Healing requires Water and Spirit. While Spirit was found equally in men and in women, great ability with Earth and/or Fire was found much more often among men; with Water and/or Air among women. There were exceptions, but it was so often so that Earth and Fire came to be regarded as male Powers, Air and Water as female. Generally, no ability is considered stronger than any other, though there is a saying among Aes Sedai: "There is no rock so strong that water and wind cannot wear it away, no fire so fierce that water cannot quench it or wind snuff it out." It should be noted this saying came into use long after the last male Aes Sedai was dead. Any equivalent saying among male Aes Sedai is long lost.

Flame of Tar Valon: The symbol of Tar Valon, the Amyrlin Seat, and the Aes Sedai. A stylized representation of a flame; a white teardrop with the point upward.

Forsaken, the: Name given to thirteen of the most powerful Aes Sedai ever known, who went over to the Dark One during the War of the Shadow in return for the promise of immortality. According to both legend and fragmentary records, they were imprisoned along with the Dark One when his prison was resealed. Their names are still used to frighten children.

Gaidin (GYE-deen): Literally, "Brother to Battles." A title used by Aes Sedai for the Warders. *See also* Warder.

Galad (gah-LAHD): *See* Damodred, Lord Galadedrid.

Galldrian su Riatin Rie (GAHL-dree-ahn soo REYE-ah-tin REE): Literally, Galldrian of House Riatin, King. King of Cairhien. *See also* Cairhien.

Game of Houses, the: *See Daes Dae'mar.*

Gawyn (GAH-wihn): Queen Morgase's son, and Elayne's brother. His sign is a white boar.

gentling: The act, performed by Aes Sedai, of shutting off a male who can channel from the One Power. This is necessary because any man who learns to channel will go insane from the taint on *saidin* and will almost certainly do horrible things with the Power in his madness. A man who has been gentled can still sense the True Source, but he cannot touch it. Whatever madness has come before gentling is arrested by the act of gentling, but not cured by it, and if it is done soon enough death can be averted. *See also* One Power, the; stilling.

gleeman: A traveling storyteller, musician, juggler, tumbler, and all-around entertainer. Known by their trademark cloaks of many-colored patches, they perform mainly in the villages and smaller towns.

Goaban (GO-ah-banh): One of the nations wrung from Artur Hawkwing's empire during the War of the Hundred Years. It weakened, and faded away approximately 500 NE. *See also* Artur Hawkwing; War of the Hundred Years.

Great Blight, the: A region in the far north, entirely corrupted by the Dark One. A haunt of Trollocs, Myrddraal, and other creatures of the Shadow.

Great Game, the: *See Daes Dae'mar.*

Great Hunt of the Horn, The: A cycle of stories concerning the legendary search for the Horn of Valere, in the years between the end of the Trolloc Wars and the beginning of the War of the Hundred Years. If told in its entirety, the cycle would take many days.

Great Lord of the Dark: The name by which Darkfriends refer to the Dark One, claiming that to use his true name would be blasphemous.

Great Serpent: *A* symbol for time and eternity, ancient before the Age of Legends began, consisting of a serpent eating its own tail. A ring in the shape of the Great Serpent is awarded to women who have been raised to the Accepted among the Aes Sedai.

Hailene (heye-LEE-neh): In the Old Tongue, "Those Who Come Before," or "Forerunners."

Halfman: *See* Myrddraal.

Hardan: One of the nations wrung from Artur Hawkwing's empire, now long forgotten. It lay between Cairhien and Shienar.

Hawkwing, Artur: A legendary king (ruled FY 943–994) who united all the lands west of the Spine of the World. He even sent armies across the Aryth Ocean (FY 992), but all contact with these was lost at his death, which set off the War of the Hundred Years. His sign was a golden hawk in flight. *See also* War of the Hundred Years.

heartstone: An indestructible substance created during the Age of Legends. Any force used in an attempt to break it is absorbed, making heartstone stronger. *See also cuendillar.*

hide: A unit of area for measuring land, equal to 100 paces by 100 paces.

Horn of Valere (vah-LEER): The legendary object of the Great Hunt of the Horn. The Horn supposedly can call back dead heroes from the grave to fight against the Shadow.

Hundred Companions, the: One hundred male Aes Sedai, among the most powerful of the Age of Legends, who, led by Lews Therin Telamon, launched the final stroke that ended the War of the Shadow by sealing the Dark One back into his prison. The Dark One's counterstroke tainted *saidin;* the Hundred Companions went mad and began the Breaking of the World. *See also* Time of Madness; Breaking of the World; True Source; One Power.

Hurin (HEW-rhin): A Shienaran who has the ability to smell where violence has been done, and to follow the scent of those who did it. Called a "sniffer," he serves the King's justice in Fal Dara, in Shienar.

Illian (IHL-lee-ahn): A great port on the Sea of Storms, capital city of the nation of the same name.

Ingtar, Lord, of House Shinowa (IHNG-tahr); (shih-NOH-wah): A Shienaran warrior. His sign is the Gray Owl.

Ishamael (ih-SHAH-may-EHL): In the Old Tongue, "Betrayer of Hope." One of the Forsaken. Name given to the leader of the Aes Sedai who went over to the Dark One in the War of the Shadow. It is said that even he forgot his true name. *See also* Forsaken.

Karaethon Cycle, The (ka-REE-ah-thon): *See* Dragon, Prophecies of the.

kith: Close friends and acquaintances.

Laman (LAY-mahn): A king of Cairhien, of House Damodred, who lost his throne and life in the Aiel War.

Lan; al'Lan Mandragoran (AHL-LAN man-DRAG-or-an): A Warder, bonded to Moiraine. Uncrowned King of Malkier, Dai Shan, and the last surviving Malkieri lord. *See also* Warder; Moiraine; Malkier; Dai Shan.

Lanfear (LAN-fear): In the Old Tongue, "Daughter of the Night." One of the Forsaken, perhaps the most powerful next to Ishamael. Unlike the other Forsaken, she chose this name herself. She is said to have been in love with Lews Therin Telamon. *See also* Forsaken; Dragon, the.

league: *See* Length, units of.

Leane (lee-AHN-eh): An Aes Sedai of the Blue Ajah, and Keeper of the Chronicles. *See also* Ajah; Chronicles, Keeper of the.

Leashed Ones: *See damane.*

Length, units of: 10 inches = 3 hands = 1 foot; 3 feet = 1 pace; 2 paces = 1 span; 1000 spans = 1 mile; 4 miles = 1 league.

Lews Therin Telamon; Lews Therin Kinslayer: *See* Dragon, the.

Liandrin (lee-AHN-drihn): An Aes Sedai of the Red Ajah, from Tarabon.

Logain (loh-GAYN): A false Dragon, gentled by the Aes Sedai.

Loial (LOY-ahl): An Ogier from Stedding Shangtai.

Luc; Lord Luc of House Mantear (LUKE; MAN-tee-ahr): Tigraine's brother. His disappearance in the Great Blight (971 NE) is believed to be connected to Tigraine's later disappearance. His sign was an acorn.

Luthair: See Mondwin, Luthair Paendrag.

Malkier (mahl-KEER): A nation, once one of the Borderlands, now consumed by the Blight. The sign of Malkier was a golden crane in flight.

Manetheren (mahn-EHTH-ehr-ehn): One of the Ten Nations that made the Second Covenant, and also the capital city of that nation. Both city and nation were utterly destroyed in the Trolloc Wars.

marath'damane (MAH-rahth'dah-MAHN-ee): In the Old Tongue, "Those Who Must Be Leashed." Term used by the Seanchan for women who can channel, but who have not yet been captured and collared. *See also damane; a'dam;* Seanchan.

Masema (mah-SEE-mah): A Shienaran soldier who hates Aiel.

mashiara (mah-shee-AH-rah): In the Old Tongue, "beloved," but meaning a love that is lost beyond redeeming.

Merrilin, Thom (MER-rih-lihn, TOM): A gleeman.

mile: *See* Length, units of.

Min (MIN): A young woman with the ability to read the auras she sometimes sees surrounding people.

Moiraine (mwah-RAIN): An Aes Sedai of the Blue Ajah.

Mondwin, Luthair Paendrag (LEW-thair PAY-ehn-DRAG MON-dwihn): Son of Artur Hawkwing, he commanded the armies Hawkwing sent across the Aryth Ocean. His banner was a golden, spread-winged hawk clutching lightning bolts. *See also* Hawkwing, Artur.

Mordeth (MOOR-death): Councilor who turned the city of Aridhol to use Darkfriends' ways against the Darkfriends, thus bringing its destruction and earning it a new name, Shadar Logoth ("Where the Shadow Waits"). Only one thing survives in Shadar Logoth beside the hate that killed it, and that is Mordeth himself, bound in the ruins for two thousand years, waiting for someone to come whose soul he can consume and so take on new flesh.

Morgase (moor-GAYZ): Queen of Andor, High Seat of House Trakand (TRAHK-ahnd).

Myrddraal (MUHRD-draal): Creatures of the Dark One, commanders of the Trollocs. Twisted offspring of Trollocs in which the human stock used to create the Trollocs has resurfaced, but tainted by the evil that made the Trollocs. Physically they are like men except they have no eyes, but can see like eagles in light or dark. They have

certain powers stemming from the Dark One, including the ability to cause paralyzing fear with a look and
the ability to vanish wherever there are shadows. One of
their few known weaknesses is that they are reluctant to
cross running water. In different lands they are known by
many names, among them Halfmen, the Eyeless, Shadowmen, Lurks, and Fades.

Niall, Pedron (NEYE-awl, PAY-drohn): Lord Captain
Commander of the Children of the Light. *See also* Children of the Light.

Nisura, Lady (nih-SOO-rah): A Shienaran noblewoman,
and one of the Lady Amalisa's attendants.

One Power, the: The power drawn from the True Source.
The vast majority of people are completely unable to
learn to channel the One Power. A very small number
can be taught to channel, and an even tinier number have
the ability inborn. For these few there is no need to be
taught; they will touch the True Source and channel the
Power whether they want to or not, perhaps without even
realizing what they are doing. This inborn ability usually manifests itself in late adolescence or early adulthood. If control is not taught, or self-learned (extremely
difficult, with a success rate of only one in four), death
is certain. Since the Time of Madness, no man has been
able to channel the Power without eventually going completely, horribly mad, and then, even if he has learned
some control, dying from a wasting sickness that causes
the sufferer to rot alive, a sickness caused, as is the madness, by the Dark One's taint on *saidin*. For a woman the
death that comes without control of the Power is less horrible, but it is death just the same. Aes Sedai search for
girls with the inborn ability as much to save their lives
as to increase Aes Sedai numbers, and for men with it in
order to stop the terrible things they inevitably do with
the Power in their madness. *See also* channel; Time of
Madness; True Source.

Pattern of an Age: The Wheel of Time weaves the threads
of human lives into the Pattern of an Age, often called

simply the Pattern, which forms the substance of reality for that Age. *See also ta'veren.*

Powers, the Five: *See* Five Powers.

Questioners, the: An order within the Children of the Light. Their avowed purposes are to discover the truth in disputations and to uncover Darkfriends. In the search for truth and the Light, their normal method of inquiry is by torture; their normal attitude that they know the truth already and must only make their victim confess to it. The Questioners refer to themselves as the Hand of the Light, the Hand that digs out truth, and at times act as if they were entirely separate from the Children and the Council of the Anointed, which commands the Children. The head of the Questioners is the High Inquisitor, who sits on the Council of the Anointed. Their sign is a blood-red shepherd's crook.

Ragan (rah-GAHN): A Shienaran warrior.

Red Shields: *See* Aiel warrior societies.

Renna (REEN-nah): A Seanchan woman; *a sul'dam. See also* Seanchan; *sul'dam.*

Rhyagelle (rheye-ah-GEHL): In the Old Tongue, "Those Who Come Home," or "Homecomers."

sa'angreal (SAH-ahn-GREE-ahl): Any one of a number of objects that allow an individual to channel much more of the One Power than would otherwise be possible or safe. *A sa'angreal* is like unto, but much more powerful than, an *angreal*. The amount of the Power that can be wielded with a *sa'angreal* compares to the amount of the Power that can be handled with an *angreal* as the Power wielded with the aid of an *angreal* does to the amount of the Power that can be handled unaided. Remnants of the Age of Legends, the means of making *sa'angreal* is no longer known. Only a handful remain, far fewer even than *angreal*.

saidar (sah-ih-DAHR): *saidin* (sah-ih-DEEN): *See* True Source.

Saldaea (sahl-DAY-ee-ah): One of the Borderlands.

Sanche, Siuan (SAHN-chay, swahn): An Aes Sedai formerly

of the Blue Ajah. Raised to the Amyrlin Seat 988 NE. The Amyrlin Seat is of all Ajahs, and of none.

Sea Folk: More properly, the Atha'an Miere (a-tha-AHN mee-AIR), the People of the Sea. Inhabitants of islands in the Aryth (AH-rihth) Ocean and the Sea of Storms, they spend little time on those islands, living most of their lives on their ships. Most seaborne trade is carried by the Sea Folk's ships.

Seanchan (SHAWN-CHAN): (1) Descendants of the armies Artur Hawkwing sent across the Aryth Ocean, who have returned to reclaim the lands of their forefathers. (2) The land from which the Seanchan come. *See also Hailene; Corenne; Rhyagelle.*

Seandar (shawn-DAHR): Capital city of Seanchan, where the Empress sits on the Crystal Throne in the Court of the Nine Moons.

Selene (seh-LEEN): A woman met on the journey to Cairhien.

Seta (SEE-tah): A Seanchan woman; a *sul'dam*. *See also* Seanchan; *sul'dam*.

Shadar Logoth (SHAH-dahr LOH-goth): A city abandoned and shunned since the Trolloc Wars. It is tainted ground, and not a pebble of it is safe. *See also* Mordeth.

Shai'tan (SHAY-ih-TAN): *See* Dark One.

Shayol Ghul (SHAY-ol GHOOL): A mountain in the Blasted Lands, the site of the Dark One's prison.

Sheriam (SHEER-ee-ahm): An Aes Sedai of the Blue Ajah. The Mistress of Novices in the White Tower.

Shienar (shy-NAHR): One of the Borderlands. The sign of Shienar is a stooping black hawk.

shoufa (SHOO-fah): A garment of the Aiel, a cloth, usually the color of sand or rock, that wraps around the head and neck, leaving only the face bare.

span: *See* Length, units of.

Spine of the World, the: A towering mountain range, with only a few passes, which separates the Aiel Waste from the lands to the west.

stedding (STEHD-ding): An Ogier (OH-geer) homeland. Many *stedding* have been abandoned since the Breaking of the World. They are shielded in some way, no longer understood, so that within them no Aes Sedai can channel the One Power, nor even sense that the True Source exists. Attempts to wield the One Power from outside a *stedding* have no effect inside a *stedding* boundary. No Trolloc will enter a *stedding* unless driven, and even a Myrddraal will do so only at the greatest need and then with the greatest reluctance and distaste. Even Darkfriends, if truly dedicated, feel uncomfortable within a *stedding*.

stilling: the act, performed by Aes Sedai, of shutting off a woman who can channel from the One Power. A woman who has been stilled can sense the True Source, but she cannot touch it. *See also* One Power, the; gentling.

Stone Dogs: *See* Aiel warrior societies.

sul'dam (SUHL-DAHM): A woman who has passed the tests to show that she can wear the bracelet of an *a'dam* and thus control a *damane. See also* a'dam; damane.

Sunday: A feastday and festival in midsummer, celebrated in many parts of the world.

sung wood: *See* Treesinger.

Suroth, High Lady (SUE-roth): A Seanchan noblewoman of high degree.

Tai'shar (TIE-SHAHR): In the Old Tongue, "True blood of."

ta'maral'ailen (tah-MAHR-ahl-EYE-lehn): In the Old Tongue, "Web of Destiny." A great change in the Pattern of an Age, centered around one or more people who are *ta'veren. See also* Pattern of an Age; *ta'veren*.

Tanreall, Artur Paendrag (tahn-REE-ahl, AHR-tuhr PAY-ehn-DRAG): *See* Hawkwing, Artur.

Tarmon Gai'don (TAHR-mohn GAY-dohn): The Last Battle. *See also* Dragon, Prophecies of the; Horn of Valere.

Tar Valon (TAHR VAH-lon): A city on an island in the River Erinin. The center of Aes Sedai power, and location of the White Tower.

ta'veren (tah-VEER-ehn): A person around whom the Wheel of Time weaves all surrounding life-threads, perhaps *all* life-threads, to form a Web of Destiny. *See also* Pattern of an Age.

Tear (TEER): A great seaport on the Sea of Storms.

Telamon, Lews Therin (TEHL-ah-mon, LOOZ THEH-rihn): *See* Dragon, the.

ter'angreal (TEER-ahn-GREE-ahl): Any one of a number of

remnants of the Age of Legends that use the One Power. Unlike *angreal* and *sa'angreal*, each *ter'angreal* was made to do a particular thing. For example, one makes oaths taken holding it binding. Some are used by Aes Sedai, but their original purposes are largely unknown. Some will kill or destroy the ability to channel of any woman who uses them. *See also angreal; sa'angreal.*

tia avende alantin (TEE-ah ah-VEN-day ah-LANH-tin): "Brother to the Trees."

Tia mi aven Moridin isainde vadin: In the Old Tongue, "The grave is no bar to my call." Inscription on the Horn of Valere. *See also* Horn of Valere.

Tigraine (tee-GRAIN): As Daughter-Heir of Andor, she married Taringail Damodred and bore his son Galad-edrid. Her disappearance in 972 NE, shortly after her brother Luc vanished in the Blight, led to the struggle in Andor called the Succession, and caused the events in Cairhien that eventually brought on the Aiel War. Her sign was a woman's hand gripping a thorny rose stem with a white blossom.

Time of Madness: The years after the Dark One's counterstroke tainted the male half of the True Source, when male Aes Sedai went mad and Broke the World. The exact duration of this period is unknown, but it is believed to have lasted nearly one hundred years. It ended completely only with the death of the last male Aes Sedai. *See also* Hundred Companions; True Source; One Power; Breaking of the World.

Tinkers: *See* Tuatha'an.

Traveling People: *See* Tuatha'an.

Tree, the: *See Avendesora.*

Treekillers: An Aiel name for the Cairhienin, always said in tones of horror and disgust.

Treesinger: An Ogier who has the ability to sing to trees (called "treesong"), either healing them, or helping them to grow and flower, or making things from the wood without damaging the tree. Objects made in this manner are called "sung wood" and are highly prized. Few Ogier remain who are Treesingers; the Talent seems to be dying out.

treesong: *See* Treesinger.

Trollocs (TRAHL-lohks): Creatures of the Dark One, created during the War of the Shadow. Huge in stature, they are a twisted blend of animal and human stock. Vicious by nature, they kill for the pure pleasure of killing. Deceitful in the extreme, they cannot be trusted unless coerced by fear. They are divided into tribe-like bands, among them the Dha'vol, the Ko'bal, and the Dhai'mon.

Trolloc Wars: A series of wars, beginning about 1000 AB and lasting more than three hundred years, during which Trolloc armies ravaged the world. Eventually the Trollocs were slain or driven back into the Great Blight, but some nations ceased to exist, while others were almost depopulated. All records of the time are fragmentary. *See also* Covenant of the Ten Nations.

True Source: The driving force of the universe, which turns the Wheel of Time. It is divided into a male half (*saidin*) and a female half (*saidar*), which work at the same time with and against each other. Only a man can draw on *saidin*, only a woman on *saidar*. Since the beginning of the Time of Madness, *saidin* has been tainted by the Dark One's touch. *See also* One Power.

Tuatha'an (too-AH-thah-AHN): A wandering folk, also known as the Tinkers and as the Traveling People, who live in brightly painted wagons and follow a totally pacifist philosophy called the Way of the Leaf. Things mended by Tinkers are often better than new. They are among the few who can cross the Aiel Waste unmolested, for the Aiel strictly avoid all contact with them.

Turak, High Lord of House Aladon (TOO-rak; AL-ah-dohn): A Seanchan of high degree, commander of the *Hailene*. *See also* Seanchan; *Hailene*.

Verin (VEHR-ihn): An Aes Sedai of the Brown Ajah.

Warder: A warrior bonded to an Aes Sedai. The bonding is a thing of the One Power, and by it he gains such gifts as quick healing, the ability to go long periods without food, water, or rest, and the ability to sense the taint of the Dark One at a distance. So long as a Warder lives, the Aes Sedai to whom he is bonded knows he is alive however far away he is, and when he dies she will know the moment and manner of his death. While most Ajahs believe an Aes Sedai may have one Warder bonded to her at a time, the Red Ajah refuses to bond any Warders at all, while the Green Ajah believe an Aes Sedai may bond as many Warders as she wishes. Ethically the Warder must accede to the bonding; but it has been known to be done involuntarily. What the Aes Sedai gain from the bonding is a closely held secret. *See also* Aes Sedai.

War of Power: *See* War of the Shadow.

War of the Hundred Years: A series of overlapping wars among constantly shifting alliances, precipitated by the death of Artur Hawkwing and the resulting struggle for his empire. It lasted from FY 994 to FY 1117. The war depopulated large parts of the lands between the Aryth Ocean and the Aiel Waste, from the Sea of Storms to the Great Blight. So great was the destruction that only fragmentary records of the time remain. The empire of Artur Hawkwing was pulled apart in the wars, and the nations of the present day were formed. *See also* Hawkwing, Artur.

War of the Shadow: Also known as the War of Power, it ended the Age of Legends. It began shortly after the attempt to free the Dark One, and soon involved the whole world. In a world where even the memory of war had been forgotten, every facet of war was rediscovered, often twisted by the Dark One's touch on the world, and the One Power was used as a weapon. The war was ended by the resealing of the Dark One into his prison. *See also* Hundred Companions, the; Dragon, the.

Watchers Over the Waves: A group who believe that the armies Artur Hawkwing sent across the Aryth Ocean will one day return, and so keep watch from the town of Falme (FAHL-may) on Toman Head.

Web of Destiny: *See* ta'maral'ailen.

Weight, units of: 10 ounces = 1 pound; 10 pounds = 1 stone; 10 stone = 1 hundredweight; 10 hundredweight = 1 ton.

Wheel of Time, the: Time is a wheel with seven spokes, each spoke an Age. As the Wheel turns, the Ages come and go, each leaving memories that fade to legend, then to myth, and are forgotten by the time that Age comes again. The Pattern of an Age is slightly different each time an Age comes, and each time it is subject to greater change, but each time it is the same Age.

Whitecloaks: *See* Children of the Light.

White Tower: The palace of the Amyrlin Seat in Tar Valon, and the place where Aes Sedai are trained.

Wisdom: In villages, a woman chosen by the Women's Circle for her knowledge of such things as healing, and foretelling the weather, as well as for common good sense. A position of great responsibility and authority, both actual and implied. She is generally considered the equal of the mayor, just as the Women's Circle is the equal of the Village Council. Unlike the mayor, the Wisdom is chosen for life, and it is very rare for a Wisdom to be removed from office before her death. Depending on the land, she may instead have another title, such as Guide, Healer, Wise Woman, or Reader.

PROLOGUE

A preview of
The Dragon Reborn

Book Three of
The Wheel of Time

Fortress of the Light

Pedron Niall's aged gaze wandered about his private
audience chamber, but dark eyes hazed with thought
saw nothing. Tattered wall hangings, once battle
banners of the enemies of his youth, faded into dark wood
paneling laid over stone walls, thick even here in the heart
of the Fortress of the Light. The single chair in the room—
heavy, high-backed, and almost a throne—was as invisible
to him as the few scattered tables that completed the furnishings. Even the white-cloaked man kneeling with barely
restrained eagerness on the great sunburst set in the wide
planks of the floor had vanished from Niall's mind for the
moment, though few would have dismissed him so lightly.

Jaret Byar had been given time to wash before being
brought to Niall, but both his helmet and his breastplate
were dulled from travel and battered from use. Dark, deep-
set eyes shone with a feverish, urgent light in a face that
seemed to have had every spare scrap of flesh boiled away.
He wore no sword—none was allowed in Niall's presence—
but he seemed poised on the edge of violence, like a hound
awaiting the loosing of the leash.

Twin fires on long hearths at either end of the room held
off the late winter cold. It was a plain, soldier's room, really,
everything well made but nothing extravagant—except for

the sunburst. Furnishings came to the audience chamber of the Lord Captain Commander of the Children of the Light with the man who rose to the office; the flaring sun of coin gold had been worn smooth by generations of petitioners, replaced and worn smooth again. Gold enough to buy any estate in Amadicia, and the patent of nobility to go with it. For ten years Niall had walked across that gold and never thought of it twice, any more than he thought of the sunburst embroidered across the chest of his white tunic. Gold held little interest for Pedron Niall.

Eventually his eyes went back to the table next to him, covered with maps and scattered letters and reports. Three loosely rolled drawings lay among the jumble. He took one up reluctantly. It did not matter which; all depicted the same scene, though by different hands.

Niall's skin was as thin as scraped parchment, drawn tight by age over a body that seemed all bone and sinew, but there was nothing of frailty about him. No man held Niall's office before his hair was white, nor did any man softer than the stones of the Dome of Truth. Still, he was suddenly aware of the tendon-ridged back of the hand holding the drawing, aware of the need for haste. Time was growing short. *His* time was growing short. It had to be enough. He had to make it enough.

He made himself unroll the thick parchment halfway, just enough to see the face that interested him. The chalks were a little smudged from travel in saddlebags, but the face was clear. A gray-eyed youth with reddish hair. He looked tall, but it was hard to say for certain. Aside from the hair and the eyes, he could have been set down in any town without exciting comment.

"This . . . this *boy* has proclaimed himself the Dragon Reborn?" Niall muttered.

The Dragon. The name made him feel the chills of winter and age. The name borne by Lews Therin Telamon when he doomed every man who could channel the One Power, then or ever after, to insanity and death, himself among them. It was more than three thousand years since Aes Sedai pride and the War of the Shadow had brought an end to the Age of Legends. Three thousand years, but prophecy and legend helped men remember—the heart of it, at least, if the details were gone. Lews Therin Kinslayer. The man who had begun the Breaking of the World, when madmen who could tap the power that drove the universe leveled mountains and sank ancient lands beneath the seas, when the whole face of the earth had been changed and all who survived fled like beasts before a wildfire. It had not ended until the last male Aes Sedai lay dead, and a scattered human race could begin trying to rebuild from the rubble—where even rubble remained. It was burned into memory by the stories mothers told children. And prophecy said the Dragon would be born again.

Niall had not really meant it for a question, but Byar took it for one. "Yes, my Lord Captain Commander, he has. It is a worse madness than any false Dragon I've ever heard of. Thousands have declared for him already. Tarabon and Arad Doman are in civil war, as well as at war with each other. There is fighting all across Almoth Plain and To-man Head, Taraboner against Domani against Darkfriends crying for the Dragon—or there was fighting until winter chilled most of it. I've never seen it spread so quickly, my Lord Captain Commander. Like throwing a lantern into a hay barn. The snow may have damped it down, but come spring, the flames will burst out hotter than before."

Niall cut him off with a raised finger. Twice already Niall had let him tell his story through, his voice burning with anger and hate. Parts of it Niall knew from other sources, and in some areas he knew more than Byar, but each time he heard it, it goaded him anew. "Geofram Bornhald and a thousand of the Children dead. And Aes Sedai did it. You have no doubts, Child Byar?"

"None, my Lord Captain Commander. After a skirmish on the way to Falme, I saw two of the Tar Valon witches. They cost us more than fifty dead before we stuck them full of arrows."

"You are *sure*—sure they were Aes Sedai?"

"The ground erupted under our feet." Byar's voice was firm and full of belief. He had little imagination, did Jaret Byar; death was part of a soldier's life, however it came. "Lightnings struck our ranks out of a clear sky. My Lord Captain Commander, what else could they have been?"

Niall nodded grimly. There had been no male Aes Sedai since the Breaking of the World, but the women who still claimed that title were bad enough. They prated of their Three Oaths: to speak no word that was not true, to make no weapon for one man to kill another, to use the One Power as a weapon only against Darkfriends or Shadowspawn. But now they had showed those oaths for the lies they were. He had always known no one could want the power they wielded except to challenge the Creator, and that meant to serve the Dark One.

"And you know nothing of those who took Falme and killed half of one of my legions?"

"Lord Captain Bornhald said they called themselves Seanchan, my Lord Captain Commander," Byar said stolidly. "He said they were Darkfriends. And his charge broke them, even if they killed him." His voice gained intensity. "There were many refugees from the city. Everyone I spoke to agreed the strangers had broken and fled. Lord Captain Bornhald did that."

Niall sighed softly. They were almost the same words Byar had used the first two times about the army that had seemingly come out of nowhere to take Falme. *A good soldier*, Niall thought, *so Geofram Bornhald always said, but not a man to think for himself.*

"My Lord Captain Commander," Byar said suddenly, "Lord Captain Bornhald *did* command me to stand aside from the battle. I was to watch, and report to you. And tell his son, Lord Dain, how he died."

"Yes, yes," Niall said impatiently. For a moment he studied Byar's hollow-cheeked face, then added, "No one doubts your honesty or courage. It is exactly the sort of thing Geofram Bornhald would do, facing a battle in which he feared his entire command might die." *And not the sort of thing you have imagination enough to think up.*

There was nothing more to learn from the man. "You have done well, Child Byar. You have my leave to carry word of Geofram Bornhald's death to his son. Dain Bornhald is with Eamon Valda—near Tar Valon at last report. You may join them."

"Thank you, my Lord Captain Commander. Thank you." Byar rose to his feet and bowed deeply. Yet as he straightened, he hesitated. "My Lord Captain Commander, we *were* betrayed." Hatred gave his voice a saw-toothed edge.

"By this one Darkfriend you spoke of, Child Byar?" He could not keep an edge out of his own voice. A year's planning lay in ruins amid the corpses of a thousand of the Children, and Byar wanted to talk only of this one man. "This young blacksmith you've only seen twice, this Perrin from the Two Rivers?"

"Yes, my Lord Captain Commander. I do not know how, but I know he is to blame. I know it."

"I will see what can be done about him, Child Byar." Byar opened his mouth again, but Niall raised a thin hand to forestall him. "You may leave me now." The gaunt-faced man had no choice but to bow again and leave.

As the door closed behind him, Niall lowered himself into his high-backed chair. What had brought on Byar's hatred of this Perrin? There were far too many Darkfriends to waste energy on hating any particular one. Too many Darkfriends, high and low, hiding behind glib tongues and open smiles, serving the Dark One. Still, one more name added to the lists would do no harm.

He shifted on the hard chair, trying to find comfort for his old bones. Not for the first time he thought vaguely that perhaps a cushion would not be too much luxury. And not for the first time, he pushed the thought away. The world tumbled toward chaos, and he had no time to give in to age.

He let all the signs that foretold disaster swirl through his mind. War gripped Tarabon and Arad Doman, civil war ripped at Cairhien, and war fever was rising in Tear and Illian, old enemies as they were. Perhaps these wars meant nothing in themselves—men fought wars—but they usually came one at a time. And aside from the false Dragon somewhere on Almoth Plain, another tore at Saldaea, and a third plagued Tear. Three at once. *They must all be false Dragons. They* must *be!*

A dozen small things besides, some perhaps only baseless rumors, but taken together with the rest. . . . Sightings of Aiel reported as far west as Murandy, and Kandor. Only two or three in one place, but one or a thousand, Aiel had come out of the Waste just once in all the years since the Breaking. Only in the Aiel War had they ever left that desolate wilderness. The Atha'an Miere, the Sea Folk, were said to be ignoring trade to seek signs and portents—of what, exactly, they did not say—sailing with ships half full or even empty. Illian had called the Great Hunt of the Horn for the first time in almost four hundred years, had sent out the

Hunters to seek the fabled Horn of Valere, which prophecy said would summon dead heroes from the grave to fight in Tarmon Gai'don, the Last Battle against the Shadow. Rumor said the Ogier, always so reclusive that most common people thought them only legend, had called meetings between their far-flung *stedding*.

Most telling of all, to Niall, the Aes Sedai had apparently come into the open. It was said they had sent some of their sisters to Saldaea to confront the false Dragon Mazrim Taim. Rare as it was in men, Taim could channel the One Power. That was a thing to fear and despise in itself, and few thought a man like that could be defeated except with the aid of Aes Sedai. Better to allow Aes Sedai help than to face the inevitable horrors when he went mad, as such men inevitably did. But Tar Valon had apparently sent other Aes Sedai to support the other false Dragon at Falme. Nothing else fit the facts.

The pattern chilled the marrow in his bones. Chaos multiplied; what was unheard of, happening again and again. The whole world seemed to be milling, stirring near the boil. It was clear to him. The Last Battle really was coming.

All his plans were destroyed, the plans that would have secured his name among the Children of the Light for a hundred generations. But turmoil meant opportunity, and he had new plans, with new objectives. If he could keep the strength and will to carry them out. *Light, let me hold on to life long enough.*

A deferential tap on the door brought him out of his dark thoughts. "Come!" he snapped.

A servant in coat and breeches of white-and-gold bowed his way in. Eyes to the floor, he announced that Jaichim Carridin, Anointed of the Light, Inquisitor of the Hand of the Light, came at the command of the Lord Captain Commander. Carridin appeared on the man's heels, not waiting for Niall to speak. Niall gestured the servant to leave.

Before the door was fully closed again, Carridin dropped to one knee with a flourish of his snowy cloak. Behind the sunburst on the cloak's breast lay the scarlet shepherd's crook of the Hand of the Light, called the Questioners by many, though seldom to their faces. "As you have commanded my presence, my Lord Captain Commander," he said in a strong voice, "so have I returned from Tarabon."

Niall examined him for a moment. Carridin was tall, well into his middle years, with a touch of gray in his hair, yet fit and hard. His dark, deep-set eyes had a knowing look about them, as always. And he did not blink under the silent study of the Lord Captain Commander. Few men had consciences so clear or nerves so steady. Carridin knelt there, waiting as calmly as if it were an everyday matter to be ordered curtly to leave his command and return to Amador without delay, no reasons given. But then, it was said Jaichim Carridin could outwait a stone.

"Rise, Child Carridin." As the other man straightened, Niall added, "I have had disturbing news from Falme."

Carridin straightened the folds of his cloak as he answered. His voice rode the edge of suitable respect, almost as if he spoke to an equal rather than to the man he had sworn to obey to the death. "My Lord Captain Commander refers to the news brought by Child Jaret Byar, late second to Lord Captain Bornhald."

The corner of Niall's left eye fluttered, an old presage of anger. Supposedly only three men knew Byar was in Amador, and none besides Niall knew from where he came. "Do not be too clever, Carridin. Your desire to know everything may one day lead you into the hands of your own Questioners."

Carridin showed no reaction beyond a slight tightening of his mouth at the name. "My Lord Captain Commander, the Hand seeks out truth everywhere, to serve the Light."

To serve the Light. Not to serve the Children of the Light. All the Children served the Light, but Pedron Niall often wondered if the Questioners really considered themselves part of the Children at all. "And what truth do you have for me about what occurred in Falme?"

"Darkfriends, my Lord Captain Commander."

"Darkfriends?" Niall's chuckle held no amusement. "A few weeks gone I was receiving reports from you that Geofram Bornhald was a servant of the Dark One because he moved soldiers onto Toman Head against your orders." His voice became dangerously soft. "Do you now mean me to believe that Bornhald, as a Darkfriend, led a thousand of the Children to their deaths fighting other Darkfriends?"

"Whether or not he was a Darkfriend will never be known," Carridin said blandly, "since he died before he could be put to the question. The Shadow's plots are murky, and often seem mad to those who walk in the Light. But that those who seized Falme were Darkfriends, I have no doubt. Darkfriends and Aes Sedai, in support of a false Dragon. It was the One Power that destroyed Bornhald and his men, of that I am sure, my Lord Captain Commander, just as it destroyed the armies that Tarabon and Arad Doman sent against the Darkfriends in Falme."

"And what of the stories that those who took Falme came from across the Aryth Ocean?"

Carridin shook his head. "My Lord Captain Commander, the people are full of rumors. Some claim they were the armies Artur Hawkwing sent across the ocean a thousand years ago, come back to claim the land. Why, some even claim to have seen Hawkwing himself in Falme. And half the heroes of legend besides. The west is boiling from Tarabon to Saldaea, and a hundred new rumors bubble to the surface every day, each more outrageous than the last. These so-called Seanchan were no more than another rabble of Darkfriends gathered to support a false Dragon, only this time with open Aes Sedai support."

"What proof have you?" Niall made his voice sound as if he doubted the point. "You have prisoners?"

"No, my Lord Captain Commander. As Child Byar no doubt told you, Bornhald managed to hurt them badly enough that they dispersed. And certainly no one we've questioned would admit to supporting a false Dragon. As for proof . . . it lies in two parts. If my Lord Captain Commander will permit me?"

Niall gestured impatiently.

"The first part is negative. Few ships have tried to cross the Aryth Ocean, and most never returned. Those that did, turned back before they ran out of food and water. Even the Sea Folk will not cross the Aryth, and they sail wherever there is trade, even to the lands beyond the Aiel Waste. My Lord Captain Commander, if there *are* any lands across the ocean, they are too far to reach, the ocean too wide. To carry an army across it would be as impossible as flying."

"Perhaps," Niall said slowly. "It is certainly indicative. What is your second part?"

"My Lord Captain Commander, many of those we questioned spoke of monsters fighting for the Darkfriends, and held to their claims even under the last degree of the question. What could they be but Trollocs and other Shadowspawn, in some way brought down from the Blight?" Carridin spread his hands as if that were conclusive. "Most people think Trollocs are only travelers' tales and lies, and most of the rest think they were all killed in the Trolloc Wars. What other name would they put to a Trolloc but monster?"

"Yes. Yes, you may be right, Child Carridin. May be, I say." He would not give Carridin the satisfaction of knowing he agreed. *Let him work awhile.* "But what of him?" He indicated the rolled drawings. If he knew Carridin, the Inquisitor had copies in his own chambers. "How dangerous is he? Can he channel the One Power?"

The Inquisitor merely shrugged. "Perhaps he can channel, perhaps not. Aes Sedai could no doubt make people believe a cat could channel, if they wanted to. As to how dangerous he is. . . . Any false Dragon is dangerous until he is put down, and one with Tar Valon openly behind him is ten times dangerous. But he is less dangerous now than he will be in half a year, unchecked. The captives I questioned had never seen him, had no idea where he is now. His forces are fragmented. I doubt there are more than two hundred gathered in any one place. The Taraboners or the Domani, either one, could sweep them away if they weren't so busy fighting each other."

"Even a false Dragon," Niall said dryly, "is not enough to make them forget four hundred years of squabbling over possession of Almoth Plain. As if either of them ever had the strength to hold it." Carridin's face did not change, and Niall wondered how he could keep so calm. *You will not be calm much longer, Questioner.*

"It is of no import, my Lord Captain Commander. Winter keeps them all in their camps, except for scattered skirmishes and raids. When the weather warms enough for troops to move. . . . Bornhald took only half his legion to their deaths on Toman Head. With the other half, I will hunt this false Dragon to his death. A corpse is not dangerous to anyone."

"And if you face what it seems Bornhald faced? Aes Sedai channeling the Power to kill?"

"Their witchery doesn't protect them from arrows, or a knife in the dark. They die as quickly as anyone else."

Carridin smiled. "I promise you, I will be successful before summer."

Niall nodded. The man was confident, now. Sure the dangerous questions would already have come, if they were coming. *You should have remembered, Carridin, I was accounted a fine tactician.* "Why," he said quietly, "did you not take your own forces to Falme? With Darkfriends on Toman Head, an army of them holding Falme, why did you try to stop Bornhald?"

Carridin blinked, but his voice remained steady. "At first they were only rumors, my Lord Captain Commander. Rumors so wild, no one could believe. By the time I learned the truth, Bornhald had joined battle. He was dead, and the Darkfriends scattered. Besides, my task was to bring the Light to Almoth Plain. I could not disobey my orders to chase after rumors."

"Your task?" Niall said, his voice rising as he stood. Carridin topped him by a head, but the Inquisitor stepped back. "Your task? Your task was to seize Almoth Plain! An empty bucket that no one holds except by words and claims, and all you had to do was fill it. The nation of Almoth would have lived again, ruled by the Children of the Light, with no need to pay lip service to a fool of a king. Amadicia and Almoth, a vise gripping Tarabon. In five years we would have held sway there as much as here in Amadicia. And you made a dog's dinner of it!"

The smile went at last. "My Lord Captain Commander," Carridin protested. "How could I foresee what happened? Yet another false Dragon. Tarabon and Arad Doman finally going to war after so long merely growling at each other. And Aes Sedai revealing their true selves after three thousand years of dissembling! Even with that, though, all is not lost. I can find and destroy this false Dragon before his followers unite. And once the Taraboners and Domani have weakened themselves, they can be cleared from the plain without—"

"No!" Niall snapped. "Your plans are done with, Carridin. Perhaps I should hand you over to your own Questioners right now. The High Inquisitor would not object. He is gnashing his teeth to find someone to blame for what happened. He would never put forward one of his own, but I doubt he'd quibble if I named you. A few days under the question, and you would confess to anything. Name yourself Darkfriend, even. You would go under the headsman's axe inside a week."

There was sweat beading on Carridin's forehead. "My Lord Captain Commander. . . ." He stopped to swallow. "My Lord Captain Commander seems to be saying there is another way. If he will but speak it, I am sworn to obey."

Now, Niall thought. *Now to toss the dice.* Prickles ran across his skin, as if he were in battle and had suddenly realized that every man for a hundred paces around him was an enemy. Lord Captain Commanders did not go to the headsman, but more than one had been known to die suddenly and unexpectedly, swiftly mourned and swiftly replaced by men with less dangerous ideas.

"Child Carridin," he said firmly, "you will make certain that this false Dragon does not die. And if any Aes Sedai come to oppose rather than support him, you will make use of your 'knives in the dark.'"

The Inquisitor's jaw dropped. Yet he recovered quickly, eyeing Niall in a speculative fashion. "To kill Aes Sedai is a duty, but. . . . To allow a false Dragon to roam free? That . . . that would be . . . treason. And blasphemy."

Niall drew a deep breath. He could sense the unseen knives waiting in the shadows. But he was committed, now. "It is no treason to do what must be done. And even blasphemy can be tolerated for a cause." Those two sentences alone were enough to kill him. "Do you know how to unite people behind you, Child Carridin? The quickest way? No? Loose a lion—a rabid lion—in the streets. And when panic grips the people, once it has turned their bowels to water, calmly tell them you will deal with it. Then you kill it, and order them to hang the carcass up where everyone can see. Before they have time to think, you give another order, and it will be obeyed. And if you continue to give orders, they will continue to obey, for you will be the one who saved them, and who better to lead?"

Carridin moved his head uncertainly. "Do you mean to . . . take it all, my Lord Captain Commander? Not just Almoth Plain, but Tarabon and Arad Doman as well?"

"What I mean is for me to know. It is for you to obey as you are sworn to do. I expect to hear of messengers on fast horses leaving for the plain by tonight. I am certain you know how to word the orders so no one suspects what they should not. If you must harry someone, let it be the Taraboners and Domani. It would not do to have them kill my lion. No, under the Light, we shall force peace between them."

"As my Lord Captain Commander commands," Carridin said smoothly. "I hear and obey." Too smoothly.

Niall smiled a cold smile. "In case your oath is not strong enough, know this. If this false Dragon dies before I command his death, or if he is taken by the Tar Valon witches, you will be found one morning with a dagger in your heart. And should any . . . accident . . . befall me—even if I should die of old age—you will not survive me the month."

"My Lord Captain Commander, I have sworn to obey—"

"So you have." Niall cut him off. "See that you remember it. Now, go!"

"As my Lord Captain Commander commands." This time Carridin's voice was not so steady.

The door closed behind the Inquisitor. Niall rubbed his hands together. He felt cold. The dice were spinning, with no way of telling what pips would show when they stopped. The Last Battle truly was coming. Not the Tarmon Gai'don of legend, with the Dark One breaking free to be faced by the Dragon Reborn. Not that, he was sure. The Aes Sedai of the Age of Legends might have made a hole in the Dark One's prison at Shayol Ghul, but Lews Therin Kinslayer and his Hundred Companions had sealed it up again. The counterstroke had tainted the male half of the True Source forever and driven them mad, and so begun the Breaking, but one of those ancient Aes Sedai could do what ten of the Tar Valon witches of today could not. The seals they had made would hold.

Pedron Niall was a man of cold logic, and he had reasoned out how Tarmon Gai'don would be. Bestial Trolloc hordes rolling south out of the Great Blight as they had in the Trolloc Wars, two thousand years before, with the Myrddraal—the Halfmen—leading, and perhaps even new human Dreadlords from among the Darkfriends. Humankind, split into nations squabbling among themselves, could not stand against that. But he, Pedron Niall, would unite humankind behind the banners of the Children of the Light. There would be new legends, to tell how Pedron Niall had fought Tarmon Gai'don, and won.

"First," he murmured, "loose a rabid lion in the streets."

"A rabid lion?"

Niall spun on his heel as a bony little man with a huge beak of a nose slipped from behind one of the hanging banners. There was just a glimpse of a panel swinging shut as the banner fell back against the wall.

"I showed you that passage, Ordeith," Niall snapped, "so you could come when I summoned you without half the fortress knowing, not so you could listen to my private conversation."

Ordeith made a smooth bow as he crossed the room. "Listen, Great Lord? I would never do such a thing. I only just arrived and could not avoid hearing your final words. No more than that." He wore a half-mocking smile, but it never left his face that Niall had ever seen, even when the fellow had no reason to know anyone was watching.

A month before, in the dead of winter, the gangly little man had arrived in Amadicia, ragged and half-frozen, and somehow managed to talk his way through all the layers of guards to Pedron Niall himself. He seemed to know things about events on Toman Head that were not in Carridin's voluminous if obscure reports, or in Byar's tale, or in any other report or rumor that had come to Niall. His name was a lie, of course. In the Old Tongue, Ordeith meant "wormwood." When Niall challenged him on it, though, all he said was, "Who we were is lost to all men, and life is bitter." But he was clever. It had been he who helped Niall see the pattern emerging in events.

Ordeith moved to the table and took up one of the drawings. As he unrolled it enough to reveal the young man's face, his smile deepened to nearly a grimace.

Niall was still irritated that the man had come unsummoned. "You find a false Dragon funny, Ordeith. Or does he frighten you?"

"A false Dragon?" Ordeith said softly. "Yes. Yes, of course, it must be. Who else could it be." And he barked a shrill laugh that grated on Niall's nerves. Sometimes Niall thought Ordeith was at least half-mad.

But he is clever, mad or not. "What do you mean, Ordeith? You sound as if you know him."

Ordeith gave a start, as though he had forgotten the Lord Captain Commander was there. "Know him? Oh, yes,

I know him. His name is Rand al'Thor. He comes from the Two Rivers, in the backcountry of Andor, and he is a Darkfriend so deep in the Shadow it would make your soul cringe to know the half."

"The Two Rivers," Niall mused. "Someone else mentioned another Darkfriend from there, another youth. Strange to think of Darkfriends coming from a place like that. But truly they are everywhere."

"Another, Great Lord?" Ordeith said. "From the Two Rivers? Would that be Matrim Cauthon or Perrin Aybara? They are of an age with him, and close behind in evil."

"His name was given as Perrin," Niall said, frowning. "Three of them, you say? Nothing comes out of the Two Rivers but wool and tabac. I doubt if there is another place men live that is more isolated from the rest of the world."

"In a city, Darkfriends must hide their nature to one extent or another. They must associate with others, with strangers come from other places and leaving to take word of what they have seen. But in quiet villages, cut off from the world, where few outsiders ever go. . . . What better places for all to be Darkfriends?"

"How is it you know the names of three Darkfriends, Ordeith? Three Darkfriends from the far end of forever. You keep too many secrets, Wormwood, and pull more surprises from your sleeve than a gleeman."

"How can any man tell *all* that he knows, Great Lord," the little man said smoothly. "It would be only prattle, until it becomes useful. I will tell you this, Great Lord. This Rand al'Thor, this Dragon, has deep roots in the Two Rivers."

"False Dragon!" Niall said sharply, and the other man bowed.

"Of course, Great Lord. I misspoke myself."

Suddenly Niall became aware of the drawing crumpled and torn in Ordeith's hands. Even while the man's face remained smooth except for that sardonic smile, his hands twitched convulsively around the parchment.

"Stop that!" Niall commanded. He snatched the drawing away from Ordeith and smoothed it as best he could. "I do not have so many likenesses of this man that I can allow them to be destroyed." Much of the drawing was only a smudge, and a rip ran across the young man's breast, but miraculously the face was untouched.

"Forgive me, Great Lord." Ordeith made a deep bow, his smile never slipping. "I hate Darkfriends."

Niall studied the face in chalks. *Rand al'Thor, of the Two Rivers.* "Perhaps I must make plans for the Two Rivers. When the snows clear. Perhaps."

"As the Great Lord wishes," Ordeith said blandly.

About the Author

Robert Jordan was born in 1948 in Charleston, South Carolina. He taught himself to read when he was four with the incidental aid of a twelve-years-older brother, and was tackling Mark Twain and Jules Verne by five. He was a graduate of the Citadel, the Military College of South Carolina, with a degree in physics. He served two tours in Vietnam with the U.S. Army; among his decorations are the Distinguished Flying Cross with bronze oak leaf cluster, the Bronze Star with "V" and bronze oak leaf cluster, and two Vietnamese Gallantry Crosses with Palm. A history buff, he also wrote dance and theater criticism. He enjoyed the outdoor sports of hunting, fishing, and sailing, and the indoor sports of poker, chess, pool, and pipe collecting. He began writing in 1977 and continued until his death on September 16, 2007.